MW01087981

CHILDREN OF DUNE

"A major event."
—Los Angeles Times

"Ranging from palace intrigue and desert chases to religious speculation and confrontations with the supreme intelligence of the universe, there is something here for all science fiction fans."
—Publishers Weekly

"Herbert adds enough new twists and turns to the ongoing saga that familiarity with the recurring elements brings pleasure."
—Challenging Destiny

GOD EMPEROR OF DUNE

"Rich fare. . . . Heady stuff."
—Los Angeles Times

"A fourth visit to distant Arrakis that is every bit as fascinating as the other three—every bit as timely."
—Time

"Book four of the Dune series has many of the same strengths as the previous three, and I was indeed kept up late at night."
—Challenging Destiny

HERETICS OF DUNE

"A monumental piece of imaginative architecture . . . indisputably magical."
—*Los Angeles Herald Examiner*

"Appealing and gripping. . . . Fascinating detail, yet cloaked in mystery and mysticism."
—*The Milwaukee Journal*

"Herbert works wonders with some new speculation and an entirely new batch of characters. He weaves together several fascinating story lines with almost the same mastery as informed *Dune*, and keeps the reader intent on the next revelation or twist."
—*Challenging Destiny*

CHAPTERHOUSE: DUNE

"Compelling . . . a worthy addition to this durable and deservedly popular series."
—*The New York Times*

"The vast and fascinating Dune saga sweeps on—as exciting and gripping as ever."
—*Kirkus Reviews*

BOOKS BY BRIAN HERBERT

DREAMER OF DUNE: THE BIOGRAPHY OF FRANK HERBERT

BOOKS EDITED BY BRIAN HERBERT

THE NOTEBOOKS OF FRANK HERBERT'S DUNE
SONGS OF MUAD'DIB

BOOKS BY BRIAN HERBERT AND KEVIN J. ANDERSON

DUNE: HOUSE ATREIDES
DUNE: HOUSE HARKONNEN
DUNE: HOUSE CORRINO
DUNE: THE BUTLERIAN JIHAD
DUNE: THE MACHINE CRUSADE
DUNE: THE BATTLE OF CORRIN

THE ROAD TO DUNE
(also by Frank Herbert; includes the novel *Spice Planet*)

HUNTERS OF DUNE
SANDWORMS OF DUNE
PAUL OF DUNE
THE WINDS OF DUNE
SISTERHOOD OF DUNE
MENTATS OF DUNE
NAVIGATORS OF DUNE
DUNE: THE DUKE OF CALADAN

DUNE
MESSIAH

BOOK TWO IN THE DUNE CHRONICLES

FRANK HERBERT

With an Introduction by
BRIAN HERBERT

ACE
NEW YORK

ACE

Published by Berkley

An imprint of Penguin Random House LLC

penguinrandomhouse.com

Copyright © 1969 by Herbert Properties LLC

"Introduction" by Brian Herbert copyright © 2008 by DreamStar, Inc.

A shorter version of this book appeared in *Galaxy* magazine
for July–September 1969. Copyright © 1969 by Galaxy Publishing Corporation.

ISBN: 9780593201732

The Library of Congress has cataloged the Ace hardcover edition
of this book as follows:

Herbert, Frank.
Dune messiah / Frank Herbert ; with a new introduction by Brian Herbert.
p. cm.—(Dune chronicles ; bk. 2)
ISBN 978-0-441-01561-0
1. Dune (Imaginary place)—Fiction.   I. Title.
PS3558.E63D86 2008
813'.54—dc22
2007040248

Berkley edition / September 1975
Ace mass-market edition / June 1987
Ace hardcover edition / February 2008
Ace premium edition / June 2019
Ace trade paperback edition / July 2020

Printed in the United States of America
6th Printing

Cover design and illustration by Jim Tierney
Interior art: Desert Cave © masher/Shutterstock Images
Book design by Kristin del Rosario

INTRODUCTION
by Brian Herbert

Dune Messiah is the most misunderstood of Frank Herbert's novels. The reasons for this are as fascinating and complex as the renowned author himself.

Just before this first sequel to *Dune* was published in 1969, it ran in installments in the science fiction magazine *Galaxy*. The serialized "Dune Messiah" was named "disappointment of the year" by the satirical magazine *National Lampoon*. The story had earlier been rejected by *Analog* editor John W. Campbell, who, like the Lampooners, loved the majestic, heroic aspects of *Dune* and hated the antithetical elements of the sequel. His readers wanted stories about heroes accomplishing great feats, he said, not stories of protagonists with "clay feet."

The detractors did not understand that *Dune Messiah* was a bridging work, connecting *Dune* with an as-yet-uncompleted third book in the trilogy. To get there, the second novel in the series flipped over the carefully crafted hero myth of Paul Muad'Dib and revealed the dark side of the messiah phenomenon that had appeared to be so glorious in *Dune*. Many readers didn't want that dose of reality; they couldn't stand the demotion of their beloved, charismatic champion, especially after the author had already killed off two of their favorite characters in *Dune*, the loyal Atreides swordmaster Duncan Idaho* and the idealistic planetologist Liet-Kynes.

---

* Frank Herbert was not entirely deaf to his readership. In *Dune Messiah*, he would resurrect Duncan Idaho in an altered form—a "ghola" named Hayt, who was cloned from the cells of the dead man, resulting in a creature who did not have the memories of the original.

But they overlooked important clues that Frank Herbert had left along the way. In *Dune*, when Liet-Kynes lay dying in the desert, he remembered these words of his father, Pardot, spoken years before and relegated to the back reaches of memory: "No more terrible disaster could befall your people than for them to fall into the hands of a Hero." Near the end of the novel, in a foreshadowing epigraph, Princess Irulan described the victorious Muad'Dib in multifaceted and sometimes conflicting terms as "warrior and mystic, ogre and saint, the fox and the innocent, chivalrous, ruthless, less than a god, more than a man." And in an appendix to *Dune*, Frank Herbert wrote that the desert planet "was afflicted by a Hero."

These sprinklings in *Dune* were markers pointing in the direction Frank Herbert had in mind, transforming a utopian civilization into a violent dystopia. In fact, the original working title for the second book in the series was *Fool Saint*, which he would change two more times before settling on *Dune Messiah*. But in the published novel, he wrote, concerning Muad'Dib:

> *He is the fool saint,*
> *The golden stranger living forever*
> *On the edge of reason.*
> *Let your guard fall and he is there!*

The author felt that heroic leaders often made mistakes . . . mistakes that were amplified by the number of followers who were held in thrall by charisma. As a political speechwriter in the 1950s, Dad had worked in Washington, D.C., and had seen the megalomania of leadership and the pitfalls of following magnetic, charming politicians. Planting yet another interesting seed in *Dune*, he wrote, "It is said in the desert that possession of water in great amount can inflict a man with fatal carelessness." This was an important reference to Greek hubris. Very few readers realized that the story of Paul Atreides was not only a Greek tragedy on an individual and familial scale. There was yet another layer, even larger, in which Frank Herbert was warning that entire societies could be led to ruination by heroes. In *Dune* and *Dune Messiah*, he was cautioning against pride and overconfidence, that form of narcissism described in Greek tragedies that invariably led to the great fall.

Among the dangerous leaders of human history, my father sometimes mentioned General George S. Patton because of his charismatic qualities—but more often his example was President John F. Kennedy. Around Kennedy, a myth of kingship had formed, and of Camelot. The handsome young president's followers did not question him and would have gone virtually anywhere he led them. This danger seems obvious to us now in the cases of such men as Adolf Hitler, whose powerful magnetism led his nation into ruination. It is less obvious, however, with men who are not deranged or evil in and of themselves—such as Kennedy, or the fictional Paul Muad'Dib, whose danger lay in the religious myth structure around him and what people did in his name.

Among my father's most important messages were that governments lie to protect themselves and they make incredibly stupid decisions. Years after the publication of *Dune*, Richard M. Nixon provided ample proof. Dad said that Nixon did the American people an immense favor in his attempt to cover up the Watergate misdeeds. By amplified example, albeit unwittingly, the thirty-seventh president of the United States taught people to question their leaders. In interviews and impassioned speeches on university campuses all across the country, Frank Herbert warned young people not to trust government, telling them that the American founding fathers had understood this and had attempted to establish safeguards in the Constitution.

In the transition from *Dune* to *Dune Messiah*, Dad accomplished something of a sleight of hand. In the sequel, while emphasizing the actions of the heroic Paul Muad'Dib, as he had done in *Dune*, the author was also orchestrating monumental background changes and dangers involving the machinations of the people surrounding that leader. Several people would vie for position to become closest to Paul; in the process they would secure for themselves as much power as possible, and some would misuse it, with dire consequences.

After the Dune series became wildly popular, many fans began to consider Frank Herbert in a light that he had not sought and which he did not appreciate. In one description of him, he was referred to as "a guru of science fiction." Others depicted him in heroic terms. To counter this, in remarks that were consistent with his Paul Atreides characterization, Frank Herbert told interviewers that he did not want to be considered a hero, and he sometimes said to them, with disarming humility, "I'm nobody."

Certainly my father was anything but that. In *Dreamer of Dune*, the biography I wrote about him, I described him as a legendary author. But in his lifetime, he sought to avoid such a mantle. As if whispering in his own ear, Frank Herbert constantly reminded himself that he was mortal. If he had been a politician, he would have undoubtedly been an honorable one, perhaps even one of our greatest U.S. presidents. He might have attained that high office, or reached any number of other lofty goals, had he decided to do so. But as a science fiction fan myself, I'm glad he took the course that he did. Because he was a great writer, his cautionary words will carry on through the ages and hopefully influence people in decision-making positions, causing them to set up safeguards that will protect against abuses of power, both by leaders and by their followers.

As you read *Dune Messiah*, enjoy the adventure story, the suspense, the marvelous characterizations and exotic settings. Then go back and read it again. You'll discover something new on each pass through the pages. And you'll get to know Frank Herbert better as a human being.

BRIAN HERBERT
SEATTLE, WASHINGTON
OCTOBER 16, 2007

EXCERPTS FROM THE
DEATH CELL INTERVIEW
WITH BRONSO OF IX—

Q: What led you to take your particular approach to a history of
Muad'Dib?

A: Why should I answer your questions?

Q: Because I will preserve your words.

A: Ahhh! The ultimate appeal to a historian!

Q: Will you cooperate then?

A: Why not? But you'll never understand what inspired my Analysis
of History. Never. You Priests have too much at stake to . . .

Q: Try me.

A: Try you? Well, again . . . why not? I was caught by the shallow-
ness of the common view of this planet which arises from its
popular name: Dune. Not Arrakis, notice, but Dune. History is
obsessed by Dune as desert, as birthplace of the Fremen. Such
history concentrates on the customs which grew out of water
scarcity and the fact that Fremen led semi-nomadic lives in stillsuits which recovered most of their body's moisture.

Q: Are these things not true, then?

A: They are surface truth. As well ignore what lies beneath that surface as . . . as try to understand my birthplanet, Ix, without exploring how we derived our name from the fact that we are the
ninth planet of our sun. No . . . no. It is not enough to see Dune

as a place of savage storms. It is not enough to talk about the threat posed by the gigantic sandworms.

Q: But such things are crucial to the Arrakeen character!

A: Crucial? Of course. But they produce a one-view planet in the same way that Dune is a one-crop planet because it is the sole and exclusive source of the spice, melange.

Q: Yes. Let us hear you expand on the sacred spice.

A: Sacred! As with all things sacred, it gives with one hand and takes with the other. It extends life and allows the adept to foresee his future, but it ties him to a cruel addiction and marks his eyes as yours are marked: total blue without any white. Your eyes, your organs of *sight*, become one thing without contrast, a single view.

Q: Such heresy brought you to this cell!

A: I was brought to this cell by your Priests. As with all priests, you learned early to call the truth heresy.

Q: You are here because you dared to say that Paul Atreides lost something essential to his humanity before he could become Muad'Dib.

A: Not to speak of his losing his father here in the Harkonnen war. Nor the death of Duncan Idaho, who sacrificed himself that Paul and the Lady Jessica could escape.

Q: Your cynicism is duly noted.

A: Cynicism! That, no doubt is a greater crime than heresy. But, you see, I'm not really a cynic. I'm just an observer and commentator. I saw true nobility in Paul as he fled into the desert with his pregnant mother. Of course, she was a great asset as well as a burden.

Q: The flaw in you historians is that you'll never leave well enough alone. You see true nobility in the Holy Muad'Dib, but you must append a cynical footnote. It's no wonder that the Bene Gesserit also denounce you.

A: You Priests do well to make common cause with the Bene Gesserit Sisterhood. They, too, survive by concealing what they do. But they cannot conceal the fact that the Lady Jessica was a Bene Gesserit–trained adept. You know she trained her son in the sisterhood's ways. My *crime* was to discuss this as a phenomenon, to expound upon their mental arts and their genetic program. You don't want attention called to the fact that Muad'Dib was the Sisterhood's hoped for captive messiah, that he was their *kwisatz haderach* before he was your prophet.

Q: If I had any doubts about your death sentence, you have dispelled them.

A: I can only die once.

Q: There are deaths and there are deaths.

A: Beware lest you make a martyr of *me*. I do not think Muad'Dib . . . Tell me, does Muad'Dib know what you do in these dungeons?

Q: We do not trouble the Holy Family with trivia.

A: (Laughter) And for this Paul Atreides fought his way to a niche among the Fremen! For this he learned to control and ride the sandworm! It was a mistake to answer your questions.

Q: But I will keep my promise to preserve your words.

A: Will you really? Then listen to me carefully, you Fremen degenerate, you Priest with no god except yourself! You have much to answer for. It was a Fremen ritual which gave Paul his first massive dose of melange, thereby opening him to visions of his futures. It was a Fremen ritual by which that same melange awakened the unborn Alia in the Lady Jessica's womb. Have you considered what it meant for Alia to be born into this universe fully cognitive, possessed of all her mother's memories and knowledge? No rape could be more terrifying.

Q: Without the sacred melange Muad'Dib would not have become leader of all Fremen. Without her holy experience Alia would not be Alia.

A: Without your blind Fremen cruelty you would not be a priest. Ahhh, I know you Fremen. You think Muad'Dib is yours because he mated with Chani, because he adopted Fremen customs. But he was an Atreides first and he was trained by a Bene Gesserit adept. He possessed disciplines totally unknown to you. You thought he brought you new organization and a new mission. He promised to transform your desert planet into a water-rich paradise. And while he dazzled you with such visions, he took your virginity!

Q: Such heresy does not change the fact that the Ecological Transformation of Dune proceeds apace.

A: And I committed the heresy of tracing the roots of that transformation, of exploring the consequences. That battle out there on the Plains of Arrakeen may have taught the universe that Fremen could defeat Imperial Sardaukar, but what else did it teach? When the stellar empire of the Corrino Family became a Fremen empire under Muad'Dib, what else did the Empire become? Your Jihad only took twelve years, but what a lesson it taught. Now, the Empire understands the sham of Muad'Dib's marriage to the Princess Irulan!

Q: You dare accuse Muad'Dib of sham!

A: Though you kill me for it, it's not heresy. The Princess became his consort, not his mate. Chani, his little Fremen darling—she's his mate. Everyone knows this. Irulan was the key to a throne, nothing more.

Q: It's easy to see why those who conspire against Muad'Dib use your Analysis of History as their rallying argument!

A: I'll not persuade you; I know that. But the argument of the conspiracy came before my Analysis. Twelve years of Muad'Dib's Jihad created the argument. That's what united the ancient power groups and ignited the conspiracy against Muad'Dib.

Such a rich store of myths enfolds Paul Muad'Dib, the Mentat Emperor, and his sister, Alia, it is difficult to see the real persons behind these veils. But there were, after all, a man born Paul Atreides and a woman born Alia. Their flesh was subject to space and time. And even though their oracular powers placed them beyond the usual limits of time and space, they came from human stock. They experienced real events which left real traces upon a real universe. To understand them, it must be seen that their catastrophe was the catastrophe of all mankind. This work is dedicated, then, not to Muad'Dib or his sister, but to their heirs—to all of us.

—DEDICATION IN THE MUAD'DIB CONCORDANCE
AS COPIED FROM THE TABLA MEMORIUM OF
THE MAHDI SPIRIT CULT

Muad'Dib's Imperial reign generated more historians than any other era in human history. Most of them argued a particular viewpoint, jealous and sectarian, but it says something about the peculiar impact of this man that he aroused such passions on so many diverse worlds.

Of course, he contained the ingredients of history, ideal and idealized. This man, born Paul Atreides in an ancient Great Family, received the deep *prana-bindu* training from the Lady Jessica, his Bene Gesserit mother, and had through this a superb control over muscles and nerves. But more than that, he was a *mentat*, an intellect whose capacities surpassed those of the religiously proscribed mechanical computers used by the ancients.

Above all else, Muad'Dib was the *kwisatz haderach* which the Sisterhood's breeding program had sought across thousands of generations.

The kwisatz haderach, then, the one who could be "many places at once," this prophet, this man through whom the Bene Gesserit hoped to control human destiny—this man became Emperor Muad'Dib and executed a marriage of convenience with a daughter of the Padishah Emperor he had defeated.

Think on the paradox, the failure implicit in this moment, for you surely have read other histories and know the surface facts. Muad'Dib's wild Fremen did, indeed, overwhelm the Padishah Shaddam IV. They toppled the Sardaukar legions, the allied forces of the Great Houses, the Harkonnen armies and the mercenaries bought with money voted in the Landsraad. He brought the Spacing Guild to its knees and placed his own sister, Alia, on the religious throne the Bene Gesserit had thought their own.

He did all these things and more.

Muad'Dib's Qizarate missionaries carried their religious war across space in a Jihad whose major impetus endured only twelve standard years, but in that time, religious colonialism brought all but a fraction of the human universe under one rule.

He did this because capture of Arrakis, that planet known more often as Dune, gave him a monopoly over the ultimate coin of the realm—the geriatric spice, melange, the poison that gave life.

Here was another ingredient of ideal history: a material whose psychic chemistry unraveled Time. Without melange, the Sisterhood's Reverend Mothers could not perform their feats of observation and human control. Without melange, the Guild's Steersmen could not navigate across space. Without melange, billions upon billions of Imperial citizens would die of addictive withdrawal.

Without melange, Paul-Muad'Dib could not prophesy.

We know this moment of supreme power contained failure. There can be only one answer, that completely accurate and total prediction is lethal.

Other histories say Muad'Dib was defeated by obvious plotters—the Guild, the Sisterhood and the scientific amoralists of the Bene Tleilax with their Face-Dancer disguises. Other histories point out the spies in Muad'Dib's household. They make much of the Dune Tarot which clouded Muad'Dib's powers of prophecy. Some show how Muad'Dib was made to accept the services of a *ghola*, the flesh brought back from the dead and trained to destroy him. But certainly they must know this ghola was Duncan Idaho, the Atreides lieutenant who perished saving the life of the young Paul.

Yet, they delineate the Qizarate cabal guided by Korba the Pane-gyrist. They take us step by step through Korba's plan to make a martyr of Muad'Dib and place the blame on Chani, the Fremen concubine.

How can any of this explain the facts as history has revealed them? They cannot. Only through the lethal nature of prophecy can we understand the failure of such enormous and far-seeing power.

Hopefully, other historians will learn something from this revelation.

—ANALYSIS OF HISTORY: MUAD'DIB
BY BRONSO OF IX

There exists no separation between gods and men; one
blends softly casual into the other.

—PROVERBS OF MUAD'DIB

Despite the murderous nature of the plot he hoped to devise, the
thoughts of Scytale, the Tleilaxu Face Dancer, returned again and
again to rueful compassion.

I shall regret causing death and misery to Muad'Dib, he told himself.

He kept this benignity carefully hidden from his fellow conspirators. Such feelings told him, though, that he found it easier to identify
with the victim than with the attackers—a thing characteristic of the
Tleilaxu.

Scytale stood in bemused silence somewhat apart from the others.
The argument about psychic poison had been going on for some time
now. It was energetic and vehement, but polite in that blindly compulsive way adepts of the Great Schools always adopted for matters
close to their dogma.

"When you think you have him skewered, right then you'll find
him unwounded!"

That was the old Reverend Mother of the Bene Gesserit, Gaius

Helen Mohiam, their hostess here on Wallach IX. She was a black-robed stick figure, a witch crone seated in a floater chair at Scytale's left. Her aba hood had been thrown back to expose a leathery face beneath silver hair. Deeply pocketed eyes stared out of skull-mask features.

They were using a *mirabhasa* language, honed phalange consonants and joined vowels. It was an instrument for conveying fine emotional subtleties. Edric, the Guild Steersman, replied to the Reverend Mother now with a vocal curtsy contained in a sneer—a lovely touch of disdainful politeness.

Scytale looked at the Guild envoy. Edric swam in a container of orange gas only a few paces away. His container sat in the center of the transparent dome which the Bene Gesserit had built for this meeting. The Guildsman was an elongated figure, vaguely humanoid with finned feet and hugely fanned membranous hands—a fish in a strange sea. His tank's vents emitted a pale orange cloud rich with the smell of the geriatric spice, melange.

"If we go on this way, we'll die of stupidity!"

That was the fourth person present—the *potential* member of the conspiracy—Princess Irulan, wife (*but not mate,* Scytale reminded himself) of their mutual foe. She stood at a corner of Edric's tank, a tall blond beauty, splendid in a robe of blue whale fur and matching hat. Gold buttons glittered at her ears. She carried herself with an aristocrat's hauteur, but something in the absorbed smoothness of her features betrayed the controls of her Bene Gesserit background.

Scytale's mind turned from nuances of language and faces to nuances of location. All around the dome lay hills mangy with melting snow which reflected mottled wet blueness from the small blue-white sun hanging at the meridian.

Why this particular place? Scytale wondered. The Bene Gesserit seldom did anything casually. Take the dome's open plan: a more conventional and confining space might've inflicted the Guildsman with claustrophobic nervousness. Inhibitions in his psyche were those of birth and life off-planet in open space.

To have built this place especially for Edric, though—what a sharp finger that pointed at his weakness.

What here, Scytale wondered, *was aimed at me?*

"Have you nothing to say for yourself, Scytale?" the Reverend Mother demanded.

"You wish to draw me into this fools' fight?" Scytale asked. "Very well. We're dealing with a potential messiah. You don't launch a frontal attack upon such a one. Martyrdom would defeat us."

They all stared at him.

"You think that's the only danger?" the Reverend Mother demanded, voice wheezing.

Scytale shrugged. He had chosen a bland, round-faced appearance for this meeting, jolly features and vapid full lips, the body of a bloated dumpling. It occurred to him now, as he studied his fellow conspirators, that he had made an ideal choice—out of instinct perhaps. He alone in this group could manipulate fleshly appearance across a wide spectrum of bodily shapes and features. He was the human chameleon, a Face Dancer, and the shape he wore now invited others to judge him too lightly.

"Well?" the Reverend Mother pressed.

"I was enjoying the silence," Scytale said. "Our hostilities are better left unvoiced."

The Reverend Mother drew back, and Scytale saw her reassessing him. They were all products of profound prana-bindu training, capable of muscle and nerve control that few humans ever achieved. But Scytale, a Face Dancer, had muscles and nerve linkages the others didn't even possess plus a special quality of *sympatico*, a mimic's insight with which he could put on the psyche of another as well as the other's appearance.

Scytale gave her enough time to complete the reassessment, said: "Poison!" He uttered the word with the atonals which said he alone understood its secret meaning.

The Guildsman stirred and his voice rolled from the glittering speaker globe which orbited a corner of his tank above Irulan. "We're discussing *psychic* poison, not a physical one."

Scytale laughed. Mirabhasa laughter could flay an opponent and he held nothing back now.

Irulan smiled in appreciation, but the corners of the Reverend Mother's eyes revealed a faint hint of anger.

"Stop that!" Mohiam rasped.

Scytale stopped, but he had their attention now, Edric in a silent rage, the Reverend Mother alert in her anger, Irulan amused but puzzled.

"Our friend Edric suggests," Scytale said, "that a pair of Bene Gesserit witches trained in all their subtle ways have not learned the true uses of deception."

Mohiam turned to stare out at the cold hills of her Bene Gesserit homeworld. She was beginning to see the vital thing here, Scytale realized. That was good. Irulan, though, was another matter.

"Are you one of us or not, Scytale?" Edric asked. He stared out of tiny rodent eyes.

"My allegiance is not the issue," Scytale said. He kept his attention on Irulan. "You are wondering, Princess, if this was why you came all those parsecs, risked so much?"

She nodded agreement.

"Was it to bandy platitudes with a humanoid fish or dispute with a fat Tleilaxu Face Dancer?" Scytale asked.

She stepped away from Edric's tank, shaking her head in annoyance at the thick odor of melange.

Edric took this moment to pop a melange pill into his mouth. He ate the spice and breathed it and, no doubt, drank it, Scytale noted. Understandable, because the spice heightened a Steersman's prescience, gave him the power to guide a Guild heighliner across space at translight speeds. With spice awareness he found that line of the ship's future which avoided peril. Edric smelled another kind of peril now, but his crutch of prescience might not find it.

"I think it was a mistake for me to come here," Irulan said.

The Reverend Mother turned, opened her eyes, closed them, a curiously reptilian gesture.

Scytale shifted his gaze from Irulan to the tank, inviting the Princess to share his viewpoint. She would, Scytale knew, see Edric as a repellent figure: the bold stare, those monstrous feet and hands moving softly in the gas, the smoky swirling of orange eddies around him. She would wonder about his sex habits, thinking how odd it would be to mate with such a one. Even the field-force generator which recreated for Edric the weightlessness of space would set him apart from her now.

"Princess," Scytale said, "because of Edric here, your husband's oracular sight cannot stumble upon certain incidents, including this one . . . presumably."

"Presumably," Irulan said.

Eyes closed, the Reverend Mother nodded. "The phenomenon of prescience is poorly understood even by its initiates," she said.

"I am a full Guild Navigator and have the Power," Edric said.

Again, the Reverend Mother opened her eyes. This time, she stared at the Face Dancer, eyes probing with that peculiar Bene Gesserit intensity. She was weighing minutiae.

"No, Reverend Mother," Scytale murmured, "I am not as simple as I appeared."

"We don't understand this Power of second sight," Irulan said. "There's a point. Edric says my husband cannot see, know or predict what happens within the sphere of a Navigator's influence. But how far does that influence extend?"

"There are people and things in our universe which I know only by their effects," Edric said, his fish mouth held in a thin line. "I know they have been here . . . there . . . somewhere. As water creatures stir up the currents in their passage, so the prescient stir up Time. I have seen where your husband has been; never have I seen him nor the people who truly share his aims and loyalties. This is the concealment which an adept gives to those who are his."

"Irulan is not yours," Scytale said. And he looked sideways at the Princess.

"We all know why the conspiracy must be conducted only in my presence," Edric said.

Using the voice mode for describing a machine, Irulan said: "You have your uses, apparently."

She sees him now for what he is, Scytale thought. *Good!*

"The future is a thing to be shaped," Scytale said. "Hold that thought, Princess."

Irulan glanced at the Face Dancer.

"People who share Paul's aims and loyalties," she said. "Certain of his Fremen legionaries, then, wear his cloak. I have seen him prophesy for them, heard their cries of adulation for their Mahdi, their Muad'Dib."

It has occurred to her, Scytale thought, *that she is on trial here, that a judgment remains to be made which could preserve her or destroy her. She sees the trap we set for her.*

Momentarily, Scytale's gaze locked with that of the Reverend Mother and he experienced the odd realization that they had shared this thought about Irulan. The Bene Gesserit, of course, had briefed their Princess, primed her with the *lie adroit*. But the moment always came when a Bene Gesserit must trust her own training and instincts.

"Princess, I know what it is you most desire from the Emperor," Edric said.

"Who does not know it?" Irulan asked.

"You wish to be the founding mother of the royal dynasty," Edric said, as though he had not heard her. "Unless you join us, that will never happen. Take my oracular word on it. The Emperor married you for political reasons, but you'll never share his bed."

"So the oracle is also a voyeur," Irulan sneered.

"The Emperor is more firmly wedded to his Fremen concubine than he is to you!" Edric snapped.

"And she gives him no heir," Irulan said.

"Reason is the first victim of strong emotion," Scytale murmured. He sensed the outpouring of Irulan's anger, saw his admonition take effect.

"She gives him no heir," Irulan said, her voice measuring out controlled calmness, "because I am secretly administering a contraceptive. Is that the sort of admission you wanted from me?"

"It'd not be a thing for the Emperor to discover," Edric said, smiling.

"I have lies ready for him," Irulan said. "He may have truthsense, but some lies are easier to believe than the truth."

"You must make the choice, Princess," Scytale said, "but understand what it is protects you."

"Paul is fair with me," she said. "I sit in his Council."

"In the twelve years you've been his Princess Consort," Edric asked, "has he shown you the slightest warmth?"

Irulan shook her head.

"He deposed your father with his infamous Fremen horde, married you to fix his claim to the throne, yet he has never crowned you Empress," Edric said.

"Edric tries to sway you with emotion, Princess," Scytale said. "Is that not interesting?"

She glanced at the Face Dancer, saw the bold smile on his features, answered it with raised eyebrows. She was fully aware now, Scytale saw, that if she left this conference under Edric's sway, part of their plot, these moments might be concealed from Paul's oracular vision. If she withheld commitment, though . . .

"Does it seem to you, Princess," Scytale asked, "that Edric holds undue sway in our conspiracy?"

"I've already agreed," Edric said, "that I'll defer to the best judgment offered in our councils."

"And who chooses the best judgment?" Scytale asked.

"Do you wish the Princess to leave here without joining us?" Edric asked.

"He wishes her commitment to be a real one," the Reverend Mother growled. "There should be no trickery between us."

Irulan, Scytale saw, had relaxed into a thinking posture, hands concealed in the sleeves of her robe. She would be thinking now of the bait Edric had offered: *to found a royal dynasty!* She would be wondering what scheme the conspirators had provided to protect themselves from her. She would be weighing many things.

"Scytale," Irulan said presently, "it is said that you Tleilaxu have an odd system of honor: your victims must always have a means of escape."

"If they can but find it," Scytale agreed.

"Am I a victim?" Irulan asked.

A burst of laughter escaped Scytale.

The Reverend Mother snorted.

"Princess," Edric said, his voice softly persuasive, "you already are one of us, have no fear of that. Do you not spy upon the Imperial Household for your Bene Gesserit superiors?"

"Paul knows I report to my teachers," she said.

"But don't you give them the material for strong propaganda against your Emperor?" Edric asked.

Not "our" Emperor, Scytale noted. "Your" Emperor. Irulan is too much the Bene Gesserit to miss that slip.

"The question is one of powers and how they may be used," Scytale said, moving closer to the Guildsman's tank. "We of the Tleilaxu believe that in all the universe there is only the insatiable appetite of matter, that energy is the only true *solid*. And energy learns. Hear me well, Princess: energy learns. This, we call power."

"You haven't convinced me we can defeat the Emperor," Irulan said.

"We haven't even convinced ourselves," Scytale said.

"Everywhere we turn," Irulan said, "his power confronts us. He's the kwisatz haderach, the one who can be many places at once. He's the Mahdi whose merest whim is absolute command to his Qizarate missionaries. He's the mentat whose computational mind surpasses the greatest ancient computers. He is Muad'Dib whose orders to the Fremen legions depopulate planets. He possesses oracular vision which sees into the future. He has that gene pattern which we Bene Gesserits covet for—"

"We know his attributes," the Reverend Mother interrupted. "And we know the abomination, his sister Alia, possesses this gene pattern. But they're also humans, both of them. Thus, they have weaknesses."

"And where are those human weaknesses?" the Face Dancer asked. "Shall we search for them in the religious arm of his Jihad? Can the Emperor's Qizara be turned against him? What about the civil authority of the Great Houses? Can the Landsraad Congress do more than raise a verbal clamor?"

"I suggest the Combine Honnete Ober Advancer Mercantiles," Edric said, turning in his tank. "CHOAM is business and business follows profits."

"Or perhaps the Emperor's mother," Scytale said. "The Lady Jessica, I understand, remains on Caladan, but is in frequent communication with her son."

"That traitorous bitch," Mohiam said, voice level. "Would I might disown my own hands which trained her."

"Our conspiracy requires a lever," Scytale said.

"We are more than conspirators," the Reverend Mother countered.

"Ah, yes," Scytale agreed. "We are energetic and we learn quickly. This makes us the one true hope, the certain salvation of humankind." He spoke in the speech mode for absolute conviction, which was perhaps the ultimate sneer coming, as it did, from a Tleilaxu.

Only the Reverend Mother appeared to understand the subtlety. "Why?" she asked, directing the question at Scytale.

Before the Face Dancer could answer, Edric cleared his throat, said: "Let us not bandy philosophical nonsense. Every question can be boiled down to the one: 'Why is there anything?' Every religious, business and governmental question has the single derivative: 'Who will exercise the power?' Alliances, combines, complexes, they all chase mirages unless they go for the power. All else is nonsense, as most thinking beings come to realize."

Scytale shrugged, a gesture designed solely for the Reverend Mother. Edric had answered her question for him. The pontificating fool was their major weakness. To make sure the Reverend Mother understood, Scytale said: "Listening carefully to the teacher, one acquires an education."

The Reverend Mother nodded slowly.

"Princess," Edric said, "make your choice. You have been chosen as an instrument of destiny, the very finest . . ."

"Save your praise for those who can be swayed by it," Irulan said. "Earlier, you mentioned a ghost, a revenant with which we may contaminate the Emperor. Explain this."

"The Atreides will defeat himself!" Edric crowed.

"Stop talking riddles!" Irulan snapped. "What is this ghost?"

"A very unusual ghost," Edric said. "It has a body and a name. The body—that's the flesh of a renowned swordmaster known as Duncan Idaho. The name . . ."

"Idaho's dead," Irulan said. "Paul has mourned the loss often in my presence. He saw Idaho killed by my father's Sardaukar."

"Even in defeat," Edric said, "your father's Sardaukar did not abandon wisdom. Let us suppose a wise Sardaukar commander recognized the swordmaster in a corpse his men had slain. What then? There exist uses for such flesh and training . . . if one acts swiftly."

"A Tleilaxu ghola," Irulan whispered, looking sideways at Scytale.

Scytale, observing her attention, exercised his Face Dancer powers—shape flowing into shape, flesh moving and readjusting. Presently, a slender man stood before her. The face remained somewhat round, but darker and with slightly flattened features. High cheekbones formed shelves for eyes with definite epicanthic folds. The hair was black and unruly.

"A ghola of this appearance," Edric said, pointing to Scytale.

"Or merely another Face Dancer?" Irulan asked.

"No Face Dancer," Edric said. "A Face Dancer risks exposure under prolonged surveillance. No; let us assume that our wise Sardaukar commander had Idaho's corpse preserved for the axolotl tanks. Why not? This corpse held the flesh and nerves of one of the finest swordsmen in history, an adviser to the Atreides, a military genius. What a waste to lose all that training and ability when it might be revived as an instructor for the Sardaukar."

"I heard not a whisper of this and I was one of my father's confidantes," Irulan said.

"Ahh, but your father was a defeated man and within a few hours you had been sold to the new Emperor," Edric said.

"Was it done?" she demanded.

With a maddening air of complacency, Edric said: "Let us presume that our wise Sardaukar commander, knowing the need for speed, immediately sent the preserved flesh of Idaho to the Bene Tleilax. Let us suppose further that the commander and his men died before conveying this information to your father—who couldn't have made much use of it anyway. There would remain then a physical fact, a bit of flesh which had been sent off to the Tleilaxu. There was only one way for it to be sent, of course, on a heighliner. We of the Guild naturally know every cargo we transport. Learning of this one, would we not think it additional wisdom to purchase the ghola as a gift befitting an Emperor?"

"You've done it then," Irulan said.

Scytale, who had resumed his roly-poly first appearance, said: "As our long-winded friend indicates, we've done it."

"How has Idaho been conditioned?" Irulan asked.

"Idaho?" Edric asked, looking at the Tleilaxu. "Do you know of an Idaho, Scytale?"

"We sold you a creature called Hayt," Scytale said.

"Ah, yes—Hayt," Edric said. "Why did you sell him to us?"

"Because we once bred a kwisatz haderach of our own," Scytale said.

With a quick movement of her old head, the Reverend Mother looked up at him. "You didn't tell us that!" she accused.

"You didn't ask," Scytale said.

"How did you overcome your kwisatz haderach?" Irulan asked.

"A creature who has spent his life creating one particular representation of his selfdom will die rather than become the antithesis of that representation," Scytale said.

"I do not understand," Edric ventured.

"He killed himself," the Reverend Mother growled.

"Follow me well, Reverend Mother," Scytale warned, using a voice mode which said: You are not a sex object, have never been a sex object, cannot be a sex object.

The Tleilaxu waited for the blatant emphasis to sink in. She must not mistake his intent. Realization must pass through anger into awareness that the Tleilaxu certainly could not make such an accusation, knowing as he must the breeding requirements of the Sisterhood. His words, though, contained a gutter insult, completely out of character for a Tleilaxu.

Swiftly, using the mirabhasa placative mode, Edric tried to smooth over the moment. "Scytale, you told us you sold Hayt because you shared our desire on how to use him."

"Edric, you will remain silent until I give you permission to speak," Scytale said. And as the Guildsman started to protest, the Reverend Mother snapped: "Shut up, Edric!"

The Guildsman drew back into his tank in flailing agitation.

"Our own transient emotions aren't pertinent to a solution of the mutual problem," Scytale said. "They cloud reasoning because the only relevant emotion is the basic fear which brought us to this meeting."

"We understand," Irulan said, glancing at the Reverend Mother.

"You must see the dangerous limitations of our shield," Scytale said. "The oracle cannot chance upon what it cannot understand."

"You are devious, Scytale," Irulan said.

How devious she must not guess, Scytale thought. *When this is done, we will possess a kwisatz haderach we can control. These others will possess nothing.*

"What was the origin of your kwisatz haderach?" the Reverend Mother asked.

"We've dabbled in various pure essences," Scytale said. "Pure good and pure evil. A pure villain who delights only in creating pain and terror can be quite educational."

"The old Baron Harkonnen, our Emperor's grandfather, was he a Tleilaxu creation?" Irulan asked.

"Not one of ours," Scytale said. "But then nature often produces creations as deadly as ours. We merely produce them under conditions where we can study them."

"I will not be passed by and treated this way!" Edric protested. "Who is it hides this meeting from—"

"You see?" Scytale asked. "Whose best judgment conceals us? What judgment?"

"I wish to discuss our mode of giving Hayt to the Emperor," Edric insisted. "It's my understanding that Hayt reflects the old morality that the Atreides learned on his birthworld. Hayt is supposed to make it easy for the Emperor to enlarge his moral nature, to delineate the positive-negative elements of life and religion."

Scytale smiled, passing a benign gaze over his companions. They were as he'd been led to expect. The old Reverend Mother wielded her emotions like a scythe. Irulan had been well trained for a task at which she had failed, a flawed Bene Gesserit creation. Edric was no more (and no less) than the magician's hand: he might conceal and distract. For now, Edric relapsed into sullen silence as the others ignored him.

"Do I understand that this Hayt is intended to poison Paul's psyche?" Irulan asked.

"More or less," Scytale said.

"And what of the Qizarate?" Irulan asked.

"It requires only the slightest shift in emphasis, a glissade of the emotions, to transform envy into enmity," Scytale said.

"And CHOAM?" Irulan asked.

"They will rally round profit," Scytale said.

"What of the other power groups?"

"One invokes the name of government," Scytale said. "We will annex the less powerful in the name of morality and progress. Our opposition will die of its own entanglements."

"Alia, too?"

"Hayt is a multi-purpose ghola," Scytale said. "The Emperor's sister is of an age when she can be distracted by a charming male designed for that purpose. She will be attracted by his maleness and by his abilities as a mentat."

Mohiam allowed her old eyes to go wide in surprise. "The ghola's a mentat? That's a dangerous move."

"To be accurate," Irulan said, "a mentat must have accurate data. What if Paul asks him to define the purpose behind our gift?"

"Hayt will tell the truth," Scytale said. "It makes no difference."

"So you leave an escape door open for Paul," Irulan said.

"A mentat!" Mohiam muttered.

Scytale glanced at the old Reverend Mother, seeing the ancient hates which colored her responses. From the days of the Butlerian Jihad when "thinking machines" had been wiped from most of the universe, computers had inspired distrust. Old emotions colored the human computer as well.

"I do not like the way you smile," Mohiam said abruptly, speaking in the truth mode as she glared up at Scytale.

In the same mode, Scytale said: "And I think less of what pleases you. But we must work together. We all see that." He glanced at the Guildsman. "Don't we, Edric?"

"You teach painful lessons," Edric said. "I presume you wished to make it plain that I must not assert myself against the combined judgments of my fellow conspirators."

"You see, he can be taught," Scytale said.

"I see other things as well," Edric growled. "The Atreides holds a monopoly on the spice. Without it I cannot probe the future. The Bene Gesserit lose their truthsense. We have stockpiles, but these are finite. Melange is a powerful coin."

"Our civilization has more than one coin," Scytale said. "Thus, the law of supply and demand fails."

"You think to steal the secret of it," Mohiam wheezed. "And him with a planet guarded by his mad Fremen!"

"The Fremen are civil, educated and ignorant," Scytale said. "They're not mad. They're trained to believe, not to know. Belief can be manipulated. Only knowledge is dangerous."

"But will I be left with something to father a royal dynasty?" Irulan asked.

They all heard the commitment in her voice, but only Edric smiled at it.

"Something," Scytale said. "Something."

"It means the end of this Atreides as a ruling force," Edric said.

"I should imagine that others less gifted as oracles have made that prediction," Scytale said. "For them, *mektub al mellah*, as the Fremen say."

"The thing was written with salt," Irulan translated.

As she spoke, Scytale recognized what the Bene Gesserit had arrayed here for him—a beautiful and intelligent female who could never be his. *Ah, well*, he thought, *perhaps I'll copy her for another.*

Every civilization must contend with an unconscious force which can block, betray or countermand almost any conscious intention of the collectivity.

—TLEILAXU THEOREM (UNPROVEN)

Paul sat on the edge of his bed and began stripping off his desert boots. They smelled rancid from the lubricant which eased the action of the heel-powered pumps that drove his stillsuit. It was late. He had prolonged his nighttime walk and caused worry for those who loved him. Admittedly, the walks were dangerous, but it was a kind of danger he could recognize and meet immediately. Something compelling and attractive surrounded walking anonymously at night in the streets of Arrakeen.

He tossed the boots into the corner beneath the room's lone glowglobe, attacked the seal strips of his stillsuit. Gods below, how tired he was! The tiredness stopped at his muscles, though, and left his mind seething. Watching the mundane activities of everyday life filled him with profound envy. Most of that nameless flowing life outside the walls of his Keep couldn't be shared by an Emperor—but . . . to walk down a public street without attracting attention: what a privilege! To pass by the clamoring of mendicant pilgrims, to hear a Fremen curse a shopkeeper: "You have damp hands!" . . .

Paul smiled at the memory, slipped out of his stillsuit.

He stood naked and oddly attuned to his world. Dune was a world of paradox now—a world under siege, yet the center of power. To come under siege, he decided, was the inevitable fate of power. He stared down at the green carpeting, feeling its rough texture against his soles.

The streets had been ankle deep in sand blown over the Shield Wall on the stratus wind. Foot traffic had churned it into choking dust which clogged stillsuit filters. He could smell the dust even now despite a blower cleaning at the portals of his Keep. It was an odor full of desert memories.

Other days . . . other dangers.

Compared to those other days, the peril in his lonely walks remained minor. But, putting on a stillsuit, he put on the desert. The suit with all its apparatus for reclaiming his body's moisture guided his thoughts in subtle ways, fixed his movements in a desert pattern. He became wild Fremen. More than a disguise, the suit made of him a stranger to his city self. In the stillsuit, he abandoned security and put on the old skills of violence. Pilgrims and townfolk passed him then with eyes downcast. They left the wild ones strictly alone out of prudence. If the desert had a face for city folk, it was a Fremen face concealed by a stillsuit's mouth-nose filters.

In truth, there existed now only the small danger that someone from the old *sietch* days might mark him by his walk, by his odor or by his eyes. Even then, the chances of meeting an enemy remained small.

A swish of door hangings and a wash of light broke his reverie.

Chani entered bearing his coffee service on a platinum tray. Two slaved glowglobes followed her, darting to their positions: one at the head of their bed, one hovering beside her to light her work.

Chani moved with an ageless air of fragile power—so self-contained, so vulnerable. Something about the way she bent over the coffee service reminded him then of their first days. Her features remained darkly elfin, seemingly unmarked by their years—unless one examined the outer corners of her whiteless eyes, noting the lines there: "sandtracks," the Fremen of the desert called them.

Steam wafted from the pot as she lifted the lid by its Hagar emerald knob. He could tell the coffee wasn't yet ready by the way she replaced the lid. The pot—fluting silver female shape, pregnant—had come to him as a *ghanima*, a spoil of battle won when he'd slain the former owner in single combat. Jamis, that'd been the man's name . . . Jamis. What an odd immortality death had earned for Jamis. Knowing death to be inevitable, had Jamis carried that particular one in his hand?

Chani put out cups: blue pottery squatting like attendants beneath the immense pot. There were three cups: one for each drinker and one for all the former owners.

"It'll only be a moment," she said.

She looked at him then, and Paul wondered how he appeared in her eyes. Was he yet the exotic offworlder, slim and wiry but water-fat when compared to Fremen? Had he remained the Usul of his tribal name who'd taken her in "Fremen *tau*" while they'd been fugitives in the desert?

Paul stared down at his own body: hard muscles, slender . . . a few more scars, but essentially the same despite twelve years as Emperor. Looking up, he glimpsed his face in a shelf mirror—blue-blue Fremen eyes, mark of spice addiction; a sharp Atreides nose. He looked the proper grandson for an Atreides who'd died in the bull ring creating a spectacle for his people.

Something the old man had said slipped then into Paul's mind: *"One who rules assumes irrevocable responsibility for the ruled. You are a husbandman. This demands, at times, a selfless act of love which may only be amusing to those you rule."*

People still remembered that old man with affection.

And what have I done for the Atreides name? Paul asked himself. *I've loosed the wolf among the sheep.*

For a moment, he contemplated all the death and violence going on in his name.

"Into bed now!" Chani said in a sharp tone of command that Paul knew would've shocked his Imperial subjects.

He obeyed, lay back with his hands behind his head, letting himself be lulled by the pleasant familiarity of Chani's movements.

The room around them struck him suddenly with amusement. It was not at all what the populace must imagine as the Emperor's bedchamber. The yellow light of restless glowglobes moved the shadows in an array of colored glass jars on a shelf behind Chani. Paul named their contents silently—the dry ingredients of the desert pharmacopoeia, unguents, incense, mementos . . . a pinch of sand from Sietch Tabr, a lock of hair from their firstborn . . . long dead . . . twelve years dead . . . an innocent bystander killed in the battle that had made Paul Emperor.

The rich odor of spice-coffee filled the room. Paul inhaled, his glance falling on a yellow bowl beside the tray where Chani was preparing the coffee. The bowl held ground nuts. The inevitable poison-snooper mounted beneath the table waved its insect arms over the food. The snooper angered him. They'd never needed snoopers in the desert days!

"Coffee's ready," Chani said. "Are you hungry?"

His angry denial was drowned in the whistling scream of a spice lighter hurling itself spaceward from the field outside Arrakeen.

Chani saw his anger, though, poured their coffee, put a cup near his hand. She sat down on the foot of the bed, exposed his legs, began rubbing them where the muscles were knotted from walking in the stillsuit. Softly, with a casual air which did not deceive him, she said: "Let us discuss Irulan's desire for a child."

Paul's eyes snapped wide open. He studied Chani carefully. "Irulan's been back from Wallach less than two days," he said. "Has she been at you already?"

"We've not discussed her frustrations," Chani said.

Paul forced his mind to mental alertness, examined Chani in the harsh light of observational minutiae, the Bene Gesserit Way his mother had taught him in violation of her vows. It was a thing he didn't like doing with Chani. Part of her hold on him lay in the fact he so seldom needed his tension-building powers with her. Chani mostly avoided indiscreet questions. She maintained a Fremen sense of good manners. Hers were more often practical questions. What interested Chani were facts which bore on the position of her man— his strength in Council, the loyalty of his legions, the abilities and talents of his allies. Her memory held catalogs of names and cross-indexed details. She could rattle off the major weakness of every known enemy, the potential dispositions of opposing forces, battle plans of their military leaders, the tooling and production capacities of basic industries.

Why now, Paul wondered, did she ask about Irulan?

"I've troubled your mind," Chani said. "That wasn't my intention."

"What was your intention?"

She smiled shyly, meeting his gaze. "If you're angered, love, please don't hide it."

Paul sank back against the headboard. "Shall I put her away?" he asked. "Her use is limited now and I don't like the things I sense about her trip home to the Sisterhood."

"You'll not put her away," Chani said. She went on massaging his legs, spoke matter-of-factly: "You've said many times she's your contact with our enemies, that you can read their plans through her actions."

"Then why ask about her desire for a child?"

"I think it'd disconcert our enemies and put Irulan in a vulnerable position should you make her pregnant."

He read by the movements of her hands on his legs what that statement had cost her. A lump rose in his throat. Softly, he said: "Chani, beloved, I swore an oath never to take her into my bed. A child would give her too much power. Would you have her displace you?"

"I have no place."

"Not so, Sihaya, my desert springtime. What is this sudden concern for Irulan?"

"It's concern for you, not for her! If she carried an Atreides child, her friends would question her loyalties. The less trust our enemies place in her, the less use she is to them."

"A child for her could mean your death," Paul said. "You know the plotting in this place." A movement of his arm encompassed the Keep.

"You must have an heir!" she husked.

"Ahhh," he said.

So that was it: Chani had not produced a child for him. Someone else, then, must do it. Why not Irulan? That was the way Chani's mind worked. And it must be done in an act of love because all the Empire avowed strong taboos against artificial ways. Chani had come to a Fremen decision.

Paul studied her face in this new light. It was a face he knew better in some ways than his own. He had seen this face soft with passion, in the sweetness of sleep, awash in fears and angers and griefs.

He closed his eyes, and Chani came into his memories as a girl once more—veiled in springtime, singing, waking from sleep beside him—so perfect that the very vision of her consumed him. In his memory, she smiled . . . shyly at first, then strained against the vision as though she longed to escape.

Paul's mouth went dry. For a moment, his nostrils tasted the smoke of a devastated future and the voice of another kind of vision commanding him to disengage . . . disengage . . . disengage. His prophetic visions had been eavesdropping on eternity for such a long while, catching snatches of foreign tongues, listening to stones and to flesh not his own. Since the day of his first encounter with terrible purpose, he had peered at the future, hoping to find peace.

There existed a way, of course. He knew it by heart without knowing the heart of it—a rote future, strict in its instructions to him: disengage, disengage, disengage . . .

Paul opened his eyes, looked at the decision in Chani's face. She had stopped massaging his legs, sat still now—purest Fremen. Her features remained familiar beneath the blue *nezhoni* scarf she often wore about her hair in the privacy of their chambers. But the mask of decision sat on her, an ancient and alien-to-him way of thinking. Fremen women had shared their men for thousands of years—not always in peace, but with a way of making the fact nondestructive. Something mysteriously Fremen in this fashion had happened in Chani.

"You'll give me the only heir I want," he said.

"You've seen this?" she asked, making it obvious by her emphasis that she referred to prescience.

As he had done many times, Paul wondered how he could explain the delicacy of the oracle, the Timelines without number which vision waved before him on an undulating fabric. He sighed, remembered water lifted from a river in the hollow of his hands—trembling, draining. Memory drenched his face in it. How could he drench himself in futures growing increasingly obscure from the pressures of too many oracles?

"You've not *seen* it, then," Chani said.

That vision-future scarce any longer accessible to him except at the expenditure of life-draining effort, what could it show them except grief? Paul asked himself. He felt that he occupied an inhospitable middle zone, a wasted place where his emotions drifted, swayed, swept outward in unchecked restlessness.

Chani covered his legs, said: "An heir to House Atreides, this is not something you leave to chance or one woman."

That was a thing his mother might've said, Paul thought. He wondered if the Lady Jessica had been in secret communication with Chani. His mother would think in terms of House Atreides. It was a pattern bred and conditioned into her by the Bene Gesserit, and would hold true even now when her powers were turned against the Sisterhood.

"You listened when Irulan came to me today," he accused.

"I listened." She spoke without looking at him.

Paul focused his memory on the encounter with Irulan. He'd let himself into the family salon, noted an unfinished robe on Chani's loom. There'd been an acrid wormsmell to the place, an evil odor which almost hid the underlying cinnamon bite of melange. Someone had spilled unchanged spice essence and left it to combine there with a spice-based rug. It had not been a felicitous combination. Spice essence had dissolved the rug. Oily marks lay congealed on the plastone floor where the rug had been. He'd thought to send for someone to clean away the mess, but Harah, Stilgar's wife and Chani's closest feminine friend, had slipped in to announce Irulan.

He'd been forced to conduct the interview in the presence of that evil smell, unable to escape a Fremen superstition that evil smells foretold disaster.

Harah withdrew as Irulan entered.

"Welcome," Paul said.

Irulan wore a robe of gray whale fur. She pulled it close, touched a hand to her hair. He could see her wondering at his mild tone. The angry words she'd obviously prepared for this meeting could be sensed leaving her mind in a welter of second thoughts.

"You came to report that the Sisterhood had lost its last vestige of morality," he said.

"Isn't it dangerous to be that ridiculous?" she asked.

"To be ridiculous and dangerous, a questionable alliance," he said. His renegade Bene Gesserit training detected her putting down an impulse to withdraw. The effort exposed a brief glimpse of underlying fear, and he saw she'd been assigned a task not to her liking.

"They expect a bit too much from a princess of the blood royal," he said.

Irulan grew very still and Paul became aware that she had locked herself into a viselike control. A heavy burden, indeed, he thought. And he wondered why prescient visions had given him no glimpse of this possible future.

Slowly, Irulan relaxed. There was no point in surrendering to fear, no point in retreat, she had decided.

"You've allowed the weather to fall into a very primitive pattern," she said, rubbing her arms through the robe. "It was dry and there was a sandstorm today. Are you never going to let it rain here?"

"You didn't come here to talk about the weather," Paul said. He felt that he had been submerged in double meanings. Was Irulan trying to tell him something which her training would not permit her to say openly? It seemed that way. He felt that he had been cast adrift suddenly and now must thrash his way back to some steady place.

"I must have a child," she said.

He shook his head from side to side.

"I must have my way!" she snapped. "If need be, I'll find another father for my child. I'll cuckold you and dare you to expose me."

"Cuckold me all you wish," he said, "but no child."

"How can you stop me?"

With a smile of utmost kindness, he said: "I'd have you garroted, if it came to that."

Shocked silence held her for a moment and Paul sensed Chani listening behind the heavy draperies into their private apartments.

"I am your wife," Irulan whispered.

"Let us not play these silly games," he said. "You play a part, no more. We both know who my wife is."

"And I am a convenience, nothing more," she said, voice heavy with bitterness.

"I have no wish to be cruel to you," he said.

"You chose me for this position."

"Not I," he said. "Fate chose you. Your father chose you. The Bene Gesserit chose you. The Guild chose you. And they have chosen you once more. For what have they chosen you, Irulan?"

"Why can't I have your child?"

"Because that's a role for which you weren't chosen."

"It's my right to bear the royal heir! My father was—"

"Your father was and is a beast. We both know he'd lost almost all touch with the humanity he was supposed to rule and protect."

"Was he hated less than you're hated?" she flared.

"A good question," he agreed, a sardonic smile touching the edges of his mouth.

"You say you've no wish to be cruel to me, yet . . ."

"And that's why I agree that you can take any lover you choose. But understand me well: take a lover, but bring no sour-fathered child into my household. I would deny such a child. I don't begrudge you any male alliance as long as you are discreet . . . and childless. I'd be silly to feel otherwise under the circumstances. But don't presume upon this license which I freely bestow. Where the throne is concerned, I control what blood is heir to it. The Bene Gesserit doesn't control this, nor does the Guild. This is one of the privileges I won when I smashed your father's Sardaukar legions out there on the Plain of Arrakeen."

"It's on your head, then," Irulan said. She whirled and swept out of the chamber.

Remembering the encounter now, Paul brought his awareness out of it and focused on Chani seated beside him on their bed. He could understand his ambivalent feelings about Irulan, understand Chani's Fremen decision. Under other circumstances Chani and Irulan might have been friends.

"What have you decided?" Chani asked.

"No child," he said.

Chani made the Fremen crysknife sign with the index finger and thumb of her right hand.

"It could come to that," he agreed.

"You don't think a child would solve anything with Irulan?" she asked.

"Only a fool would think that."

"I am not a fool, my love."

Anger possessed him. "I've never said you were! But this isn't some damned romantic novel we're discussing. That's a real princess down the hall. She was raised in all the nasty intrigues of an Imperial Court. Plotting is as natural to her as writing her stupid histories!"

"They are not stupid, love."

"Probably not." He brought his anger under control, took her hand in his. "Sorry. But that woman has many plots—plots within plots. Give in to one of her ambitions and you could advance another of them."

Her voice mild, Chani said: "Haven't I always said as much?"

"Yes, of course you have." He stared at her. "Then what are you really trying to say to me?"

She lay down beside him, placed her head against his neck. "They have come to a decision on how to fight you," she said. "Irulan reeks of secret decisions."

Paul stroked her hair.

Chani had peeled away the dross.

Terrible purpose brushed him. It was a *coriolis* wind in his soul. It whistled through the framework of his being. His body knew things then never learned in consciousness.

"Chani, beloved," he whispered, "do you know what I'd spend to end the Jihad—to separate myself from the damnable godhead the Qizarate forces onto me?"

She trembled. "You have but to command it," she said.

"Oh, no. Even if I died now, my name would still lead them. When I think of the Atreides name tied to this religious butchery . . ."

"But you're the Emperor! You've—"

"I'm a figurehead. When godhead's given, that's the one thing the so-called god no longer controls." A bitter laugh shook him. He sensed the future looking back at him out of dynasties not even dreamed. He felt his being cast out, crying, unchained from the rings of fate—only his name continued. "I was chosen," he said. "Perhaps at birth . . . certainly before I had much say in it. I was chosen."

"Then un-choose," she said.

His arm tightened around her shoulder. "In time, beloved. Give me yet a little time."

Unshed tears burned his eyes.

"We should return to Sietch Tabr," Chani said. "There's too much to contend with in this tent of stone."

He nodded, his chin moving against the smooth fabric of the scarf which covered her hair. The soothing spice smell of her filled his nostrils.

Sietch. The ancient Chakobsa word absorbed him: a place of retreat and safety in a time of peril. Chani's suggestion made him long for vistas of open sand, for clean distances where one could see an enemy coming from a long way off.

"The tribes expect Muad'Dib to return to them," she said. She lifted her head to look at him. "You belong to us."

"I belong to a vision," he whispered.

He thought then of the Jihad, of the gene mingling across parsecs and the vision which told him how he might end it. Should he pay the price? All the hatefulness would evaporate, dying as fires die—ember by ember. But . . . oh! The terrifying price!

I never wanted to be a god, he thought. *I wanted only to disappear*

like a jewel of trace dew caught by the morning. I wanted to escape the
angels and the damned . . . alone . . . as though by an oversight.

"Will we go back to the Sietch?" Chani pressed.

"Yes," he whispered. And he thought: *I must pay the price.*

Chani heaved a deep sigh, settled back against him.

I've loitered, he thought. And he saw how he'd been hemmed in
by boundaries of love and the Jihad. And what was one life, no matter
how beloved, against all the lives the Jihad was certain to take? Could
single misery be weighed against the agony of multitudes?

"Love?" Chani said, questioning.

He put a hand against her lips.

I'll yield up myself, he thought. *I'll rush out while I yet have the*
strength, fly through a space a bird might not find. It was a useless
thought, and he knew it. The Jihad would follow his ghost.

What could he answer? he wondered. How explain when people
taxed him with brutal foolishness? Who might understand?

I wanted only to look back and say: "There! There's an existence
which couldn't hold me. See! I vanish! No restraint or net of human
devising can trap me ever again. I renounce my religion! This glorious
instant is mine! I'm free!"

What empty words!

"A big worm was seen below the Shield Wall yesterday," Chani
said. "More than a hundred meters long, they say. Such big ones come
rarely into this region any more. The water repels them, I suppose.
They say this one came to summon Muad'Dib home to his desert."
She pinched his chest. "Don't laugh at me!"

"I'm not laughing."

Paul, caught by wonder at the persistent Fremen mythos, felt
a heart constriction, a thing inflicted upon his lifeline: *adab,* the
demanding memory. He recalled his childhood room on Caladan

then . . . dark night in the stone chamber . . . a vision! It'd been one of his earliest prescient moments. He felt his mind dive into the vision, saw through a veiled cloud-memory (vision-within-vision) a line of Fremen, their robes trimmed with dust. They paraded past a gap in tall rocks. They carried a long, cloth-wrapped burden.

And Paul heard himself say in the vision: "It was mostly sweet . . . but you were the sweetest of all . . ."

Adab released him.

"You're so quiet," Chani whispered. "What is it?"

Paul shuddered, sat up, face averted.

"You're angry because I've been to the desert's edge," Chani said.

He shook his head without speaking.

"I only went because I want a child," Chani said.

Paul was unable to speak. He felt himself consumed by the raw power of that early vision. Terrible purpose! In that moment, his whole life was a limb shaken by the departure of a bird . . . and the bird was *chance*. Free will.

I succumbed to the lure of the oracle, he thought.

And he sensed that succumbing to this lure might be to fix himself upon a single-track life. Could it be, he wondered, that the oracle didn't *tell* the future? Could it be that the oracle *made* the future? Had he exposed his life to some web of underlying threads, trapped himself there in that long-ago awakening, victim of a spider-future which even now advanced upon him with terrifying jaws?

A Bene Gesserit axiom slipped into his mind: *To use raw power is to make yourself infinitely vulnerable to greater powers.*

"I know it angers you," Chani said, touching his arm. "It's true that the tribes have revived the old rites and the blood sacrifices, but I took no part in those."

Paul inhaled a deep, trembling breath. The torrent of his vision dissipated, became a deep, still place whose currents moved with absorbing power beyond his reach.

"Please," Chani begged. "I want a child, our child. Is that a terrible thing?"

Paul caressed her arm where she touched him, pulled away. He climbed from the bed, extinguished the glowglobes, crossed to the balcony window, opened the draperies. The deep desert could not intrude here except by its odors. A windowless wall climbed to the night sky across from him. Moonlight slanted down into an enclosed garden, sentinel trees and broad leaves, wet foliage. He could see a fish pond reflecting stars among the leaves, pockets of white floral brilliance in the shadows. Momentarily, he saw the garden through Fremen eyes: alien, menacing, dangerous in its waste of water.

He thought of the Water Sellers, their way destroyed by the lavish dispensing from his hands. They hated him. He'd slain the past. And there were others, even those who'd fought for the sols to buy precious water, who hated him for changing the old ways. As the ecological pattern dictated by Muad'Dib remade the planet's landscape, human resistance increased. Was it not presumptuous, he wondered, to think he could make over an entire planet—everything growing where and how he told it to grow? Even if he succeeded, what of the universe waiting out there? Did it fear similar treatment?

Abruptly, he closed the draperies, sealed the ventilators. He turned toward Chani in the darkness, felt her waiting there. Her water rings tinkled like the almsbells of pilgrims. He groped his way to the sound, encountered her outstretched arms.

"Beloved," she whispered. "Have I troubled you?"

Her arms enclosed his future as they enclosed him.

"Not you," he said. "Oh . . . not you."

The advent of the Field Process shield and the lasgun with their explosive interaction, deadly to attacker and attacked, placed the current determinatives on weapons technology. We need not go into the special role of atomics. The fact that any Family in my Empire could so deploy its atomics as to destroy the planetary bases of fifty or more other Families causes some nervousness, true. But all of us possess precautionary plans for devastating retaliation. Guild and Landsraad contain the keys which hold this force in check. No, my concern goes to the development of humans as special weapons. Here is a virtually unlimited field which a few powers are developing.

—MUAD'DIB: LECTURE TO THE WAR COLLEGE
FROM THE STILGAR CHRONICLE

The old man stood in his doorway peering out with blue-in-blue eyes. The eyes were veiled by that native suspicion all desert folk held for strangers. Bitter lines tortured the edges of his mouth where it could be seen through a fringe of white beard. He wore no stillsuit and it said much that he ignored this fact in the full knowledge of the moisture pouring from his house through the open door.

Scytale bowed, gave the greeting signal of the conspiracy.

From somewhere behind the old man came the sound of a rebec wailing through the atonal dissonance of *semuta* music. The old man's manner carried no drug dullness, an indication that semuta was the weakness of another. It seemed strange to Scytale, though, to find that sophisticated vice in this place.

"Greetings from afar," Scytale said, smiling through the flat-featured face he had chosen for this encounter. It occurred to him, then, that this old man might recognize the chosen face. Some of the older Fremen here on Dune had known Duncan Idaho.

The choice of features, which he had thought amusing, might have been a mistake, Scytale decided. But he dared not change the face out here. He cast nervous glances up and down the street. Would the old man never invite him inside?

"Did you know my son?" the old man asked.

That, at least, was one of the countersigns. Scytale made the proper response, all the time keeping his eyes alert for any suspicious circumstance in his surroundings. He did not like his position here. The street was a cul-de-sac ending in this house. The houses all around had been built for veterans of the Jihad. They formed a suburb of Arrakeen which stretched into the Imperial Basin past Tiemag. The walls which hemmed in this street presented blank faces of dun plasmeld broken by dark shadows of sealed doorways and, here and there, scrawled obscenities. Beside this very door someone had chalked a pronouncement that one Beris had brought back to Arrakis a loathsome disease which deprived him of his manhood.

"Do you come in partnership?" the old man asked.

"Alone," Scytale said.

The old man cleared his throat, still hesitating in that maddening way.

Scytale cautioned himself to patience. Contact in this fashion carried its own dangers. Perhaps the old man knew some reason for carrying on this way. It was the proper hour, though. The pale sun stood almost directly overhead. People of this quarter remained sealed in their houses to sleep through the hot part of the day.

Was it the new neighbor who bothered the old man? Scytale wondered. The adjoining house, he knew, had been assigned to Otheym, once a member of Muad'Dib's dreaded Fedaykin death commandos. And Bijaz, the catalyst-dwarf, waited with Otheym.

Scytale returned his gaze to the old man, noted the empty sleeve dangling from the left shoulder and the lack of a stillsuit. An air of command hung about this old man. He'd been no foot slogger in the Jihad.

"May I know the visitor's name?" the old man asked.

Scytale suppressed a sigh of relief. He was to be accepted, after all. "I am Zaal," he said, giving the name assigned him for this mission.

"I am Farok," the old man said, "once Bashar of the Ninth Legion in the Jihad. Does this mean anything to you?"

Scytale read menace in the words, said: "You were born in Sietch Tabr with allegiance to Stilgar."

Farok relaxed, stepped aside. "You are welcome in my house."

Scytale slipped past him into a shadowy atrium—blue tile floor, glittering designs worked in crystal on the walls. Beyond the atrium was a covered courtyard. Light admitted by translucent filters spread an opalescence as silvery as the white-night of First Moon. The street door grated into its moisture seals behind him.

"We were a noble people," Farok said, leading the way toward the courtyard. "We were not of the cast-out. We lived in no *graben* village . . . such as this! We had a proper sietch in the Shield Wall above Habbanya Ridge. One worm could carry us into Kedem, the inner desert."

"Not like this," Scytale agreed, realizing now what had brought

Farok into the conspiracy. The Fremen longed for the old days and the old ways.

They entered the courtyard.

Farok struggled with an intense dislike for his visitor, Scytale realized. Fremen distrusted eyes that were not the total blue of the Ibad. Offworlders, Fremen said, had unfocused eyes which saw things they were not supposed to see.

The semuta music had stopped at their entrance. It was replaced now by the strum of a baliset, first a nine-scale chord, then the clear notes of a song which was popular on the Naraj worlds.

As his eyes adjusted to the light, Scytale saw a youth sitting cross-legged on a low divan beneath arches to his right. The youth's eyes were empty sockets. With that uncanny facility of the blind, he began singing the moment Scytale focused on him. The voice was high and sweet:

> *A wind has blown the land away*
> *And blown the sky away*
> *And all the men!*
> *Who is this wind?*
> *The trees stand unbent,*
> *Drinking where men drank.*
> *I've known too many worlds,*
> *Too many men,*
> *Too many trees,*
> *Too many winds.*

Those were not the original words of the song, Scytale noted. Farok led him away from the youth and under the arches on the opposite side, indicated cushions scattered over the tile floor. The tile was worked into designs of sea creatures.

"There is a cushion once occupied in sietch by Muad'Dib," Farok said, indicating a round, black mound: "It is yours now."

"I am in your debt," Scytale said, sinking to the black mound. He smiled. Farok displayed wisdom. A sage spoke of loyalty even while listening to songs of hidden meaning and words with secret messages. Who could deny the terrifying powers of the tyrant Emperor?

Inserting his words across the song without breaking the meter, Farok said: "Does my son's music disturb you?"

Scytale gestured to a cushion facing him, put his back against a cool pillar. "I enjoy music."

"My son lost his eyes in the conquest of Naraj," Farok said. "He was nursed there and should have stayed. No woman of the People will have him thus. I find it curious, though, to know I have grandchildren on Naraj that I may never see. Do you know the Naraj worlds, Zaal?"

"In my youth, I toured there with a troupe of my fellow Face Dancers," Scytale said.

"You are a Face Dancer, then," Farok said. "I had wondered at your features. They reminded me of a man I knew here once."

"Duncan Idaho?"

"That one, yes. A swordmaster in the Emperor's pay."

"He was killed, so it is said."

"So it is said," Farok agreed. "Are you truly a man, then? I've heard stories about Face Dancers that . . ." He shrugged.

"We are Jadacha hermaphrodites," Scytale said, "either sex at will. For the present, I am a man."

Farok pursed his lips in thought, then: "May I call for refreshments? Do you desire water? Iced fruit?"

"Talk will suffice," Scytale said.

"The guest's wish is a command," Farok said, settling to the cushion which faced Scytale.

"Blessed is Abu d' Dhur, Father of the Indefinite Roads of Time," Scytale said. And he thought: *There! I've told him straight out that I come from a Guild Steersman and wear the Steersman's concealment.*

"Thrice blessed," Farok said, folding his hands into his lap in the ritual clasp. They were old, heavily veined hands.

"An object seen from a distance betrays only its principle," Scytale said, revealing that he wished to discuss the Emperor's fortress Keep.

"That which is dark and evil may be seen for evil at any distance," Farok said, advising delay.

Why? Scytale wondered. But he said: "How did your son lose his eyes?"

"The Naraj defenders used a stone burner," Farok said. "My son was too close. Cursed atomics! Even the stone burner should be outlawed."

"It skirts the intent of the law," Scytale agreed. And he thought: *A stone burner on Naraj! We weren't told of that. Why does this old man speak of stone burners here?*

"I offered to buy Tleilaxu eyes for him from your masters," Farok said. "But there's a story in the legions that Tleilaxu eyes enslave their users. My son told me that such eyes are metal and he is flesh, that such a union must be sinful."

"The principle of an object must fit its original intent," Scytale said, trying to turn the conversation back to the information he sought.

Farok's lips went thin, but he nodded. "Speak openly of what you wish," he said. "We must put our trust in your Steersman."

"Have you ever entered the Imperial Keep?" Scytale asked.

"I was there for the feast celebrating the Molitor victory. It was cold in all that stone despite the best Ixian space heaters. We slept on the terrace of Alia's Fane the night before. He has trees in there, you know—trees from many worlds. We Bashars were dressed in our finest green robes and had our tables set apart. We ate and drank too much. I was disgusted with some of the things I saw. The walking wounded came, dragging themselves along on their crutches. I do not think our Muad'Dib knows how many men he has maimed."

"You objected to the feast?" Scytale asked, speaking from a knowledge of the Fremen orgies which were ignited by spice-beer.

"It was not like the mingling of our souls in the sietch," Farok said. "There was no tau. For entertainment, the troups had slave girls, and the men shared the stories of their battles and their wounds."

"So you were inside that great pile of stone," Scytale said.

"Muad'Dib came out to us on the terrace," Farok said. "'Good fortune to us all,' he said. The greeting drill of the desert in that place!"

"Do you know the location of his private apartments?" Scytale asked.

"Deep inside," Farok said. "Somewhere deep inside. I am told he and Chani live a nomadic life and that all within the walls of their Keep. Out to the Great Hall he comes for the public audiences. He has reception halls and formal meeting places, a whole wing for his personal guard, places for the ceremonies and an inner section for communications. There is a room far beneath his fortress, I am told, where he keeps a stunted worm surrounded by a water moat with which to poison it. Here is where he reads the future."

Myth all tangled up with facts, Scytale thought.

"The apparatus of government accompanies him everywhere," Farok grumbled. "Clerks and attendants and attendants for the attendants. He trusts only the ones such as Stilgar who were very close to him in the old days."

"Not you," Scytale said.

"I think he has forgotten my existence," Farok said.

"How does he come and go when he leaves that building?" Scytale asked.

"He has a tiny 'thopter landing which juts from an inner wall," Farok said. "I am told Muad'Dib will not permit another to handle the controls for a landing there. It requires an approach, so it is said, where the slightest miscalculation would plunge him down a sheer cliff of wall into one of his accursed gardens."

Scytale nodded. This, most likely, was true. Such an aerial entry to the Emperor's quarters would carry a certain measure of security. The Atreides were superb pilots all.

"He uses men to carry his *distrans* messages," Farok said. "It demeans men to implant wave translators in them. A man's voice should be his own to command. It should not carry another man's message hidden within its sounds."

Scytale shrugged. All great powers used the distrans in this age. One could never tell what obstacle might be placed between sender and addressee. The distrans defied political cryptology because it relied on subtle distortions of natural sound patterns which could be scrambled with enormous intricacy.

"Even his tax officials use this method," Farok complained. "In my day, the distrans was implanted only in the lower animals."

But revenue information must be kept secret, Scytale thought. *More than one government has fallen because people discovered the real extent of official wealth.*

"How do the Fremen cohorts feel now about Muad'Dib's Jihad?" Scytale asked. "Do they object to making a god out of their Emperor?"

"Most of them don't even consider this," Farok said. "They think of the Jihad the way I thought of it—most of them. It is a source of strange experiences, adventure, wealth. This graben hovel in which I live"—Farok gestured at the courtyard—"it cost sixty lidas of spice. Ninety kontars! There was a time when I could not even imagine such riches." He shook his head.

Across the courtyard, the blind youth took up the notes of a love ballad on his baliset.

Ninety kontars, Scytale thought. *How strange. Great riches, certainly. Farok's hovel would be a palace on many another world, but all things were relative—even the kontar. Did Farok, for example, know whence came his measure for this weight of spice? Did he ever think to himself that one and a half kontar once limited a camel load? Not likely. Farok might never even have heard of a camel or of the Golden Age of Earth.*

His words oddly in rhythm to the melody of his son's baliset, Farok said: "I owned a crysknife, water rings to ten liters, my own lance which had been my father's, a coffee service, a bottle made of red glass older than any memory in my sietch. I had my own share of our spice, but no money. I was rich and did not know it. Two wives I had: one plain and dear to me, the other stupid and obstinate, but with form and face of an angel. I was a Fremen Naib, a rider of worms, master of the leviathan and of the sand."

The youth across the courtyard picked up the beat of his melody.

"I knew many things without the need to think about them," Farok said. "I knew there was water far beneath our sand, held there in bondage by the Little Makers. I knew that my ancestors sacrificed virgins to Shai-hulud . . . before Liet-Kynes made us stop. It was wrong of us to stop. I had seen the jewels in the mouth of a worm. My soul had four gates and I knew them all."

He fell silent, musing.

"Then the Atreides came with his witch mother," Scytale said.

"The Atreides came," Farok agreed. "The one we named *Usul* in our sietch, his private name among us. Our Muad'Dib, our Mahdi! And when he called for the Jihad, I was one of those who asked: 'Why should I go to fight there? I have no relatives there.' But other men went—young men, friends, companions of my childhood. When they returned, they spoke of wizardry, of the power in this Atreides *savior*. He fought our enemy, the Harkonnen. Liet-Kynes, who had promised us a paradise upon our planet, blessed him. It was said this Atreides came to change our world and our universe, that he was the man to make the golden flower blossom in the night."

Farok held up his hands, examined the palms. "Men pointed to First Moon and said: 'His soul is there.' Thus, he was called Muad'Dib. I did not understand all this."

He lowered his hands, stared across the courtyard at his son. "I had no thoughts in my head. There were thoughts only in my heart and my belly and my loins."

Again, the tempo of the background music increased.

"Do you know why I enlisted in the Jihad?" The old eyes stared hard at Scytale. "I heard there was a thing called a sea. It is very hard to believe in a sea when you have lived only here among our dunes. We have no seas. Men of Dune had never known a sea. We had our windtraps. We collected water for the great change Liet-Kynes prom-ised us . . . this great change Muad'Dib is bringing with a wave of his hand. I could imagine a *qanat*, water flowing across the land in a canal. From this, my mind could picture a river. But a sea?"

Farok gazed at the translucent cover of his courtyard as though trying to probe into the universe beyond. "A sea," he said, voice low. "It was too much for my mind to picture. Yet, men I knew said they had seen this marvel. I thought they lied, but I had to know for my-self. It was for this reason that I enlisted."

The youth struck a loud final chord on the baliset, took up a new song with an oddly undulating rhythm.

"Did you find your sea?" Scytale asked.

Farok remained silent and Scytale thought the old man had not heard. The baliset music rose around them and fell like a tidal movement. Farok breathed to its rhythm.

"There was a sunset," Farok said presently. "One of the elder artists might have painted such a sunset. It had red in it the color of the glass in my bottle. There was gold . . . blue. It was on the world they call Enfeil, the one where I led my legion to victory. We came out of a mountain pass where the air was sick with water. I could scarcely breathe it. And there below me was the thing my friends had told me about: water as far as I could see and farther. We marched down to it. I waded out into it and drank. It was bitter and made me ill. But the wonder of it has never left me."

Scytale found himself sharing the old Fremen's awe.

"I immersed myself in that sea," Farok said, looking down at the water creatures worked into the tiles of his floor. "One man sank beneath that water . . . another man arose from it. I felt that I could remember a past which had never been. I stared around me with eyes which could accept anything . . . anything at all. I saw a body in the water—one of the defenders we had slain. There was a log nearby supported on that water, a piece of a great tree. I can close my eyes now and see that log. It was black on one end from a fire. And there was a piece of cloth in that water—no more than a yellow rag . . . torn, dirty. I looked at all these things and I understood why they had come to this place. It was for me to see them."

Farok turned slowly, stared into Scytale's eyes. "The universe is unfinished, you know," he said.

This one is garrulous, but deep, Scytale thought. And he said: "I can see it made a profound impression on you."

"You are a Tleilaxu," Farok said. "You have seen many seas. I have seen only this one, yet I know a thing about seas which you do not."

Scytale found himself in the grip of an odd feeling of disquiet.

"The Mother of Chaos was born in a sea," Farok said. "A Qizara Tafwid stood nearby when I came dripping from that water. He had not entered the sea. He stood on the sand . . . it was wet sand . . . with some of my men who shared his fear. He watched me with eyes that knew I had learned something which was denied to him. I had become a sea creature and I frightened him. The sea healed me of the Jihad and I think he saw this."

Scytale realized that somewhere in this recital the music had stopped. He found it disturbing that he could not place the instant when the baliset had fallen silent.

As though it were relevant to what he'd been recounting, Farok said: "Every gate is guarded. There's no way into the Emperor's fortress."

"That's its weakness," Scytale said.

Farok stretched his neck upward, peering.

"There's a way in," Scytale explained. "The fact that most men—including, we may hope, the Emperor—believe otherwise . . . that's to our advantage." He rubbed his lips, feeling the strangeness of the visage he'd chosen. The musician's silence bothered him. Did it mean Farok's son was through transmitting? That had been the way of it, naturally: The message condensed and transmitted within the music. It had been impressed upon Scytale's own neural system, there to be triggered at the proper moment by the distrans embedded in his adrenal cortex. If it was ended, he had become a container of unknown words. He was a vessel sloshing with data: every cell of the conspiracy here on Arrakis, every name, every contact phrase—all the vital information.

With this information, they could brave Arrakis, capture a sandworm, begin the culture of melange somewhere beyond Muad'Dib's writ. They could break the monopoly as they broke Muad'Dib. They could do many things with this information.

"We have the woman here," Farok said. "Do you wish to see her now?"

"I've seen her," Scytale said. "I've studied her with care. Where is she?"

Farok snapped his fingers.

The youth took up his rebec, drew the bow across it. Semuta music wailed from the strings. As though drawn by the sound, a young woman in a blue robe emerged from a doorway behind the musician. Narcotic dullness filled her eyes which were the total blue of the Ibad. She was a Fremen, addicted to the spice, and now caught by an off-world vice. Her awareness lay deep within the semuta, lost somewhere and riding the ecstasy of the music.

"Otheym's daughter," Farok said. "My son gave her the narcotic in the hope of winning a woman of the People for himself despite his blindness. As you can see, his victory is empty. Semuta has taken what he hoped to gain."

"Her father doesn't know?" Scytale asked.

"She doesn't even know," Farok said. "My son supplies false memories with which she accounts to herself for her visits. She thinks herself in love with him. This is what her family believes. They are outraged because he is not a complete man, but they won't interfere, of course."

The music trailed away to silence.

At a gesture from the musician, the young woman seated herself beside him, bent close to listen as he murmured to her.

"What will you do with her?" Farok asked.

Once more, Scytale studied the courtyard. "Who else is in this house?" he asked.

"We are all here now," Farok said. "You've not told me what you'll do with the woman. It is my son who wishes to know."

As though about to answer, Scytale extended his right arm. From the sleeve of his robe, a glistening needle darted, embedded itself in Farok's neck. There was no outcry, no change of posture. Farok would be dead in a minute, but he sat unmoving, frozen by the dart's poison.

Slowly, Scytale climbed to his feet, crossed to the blind musician. The youth was still murmuring to the young woman when the dart whipped into him.

Scytale took the young woman's arm, urged her gently to her feet, shifted his own appearance before she looked at him. She came erect, focused on him.

"What is it, Farok?" she asked.

"My son is tired and must rest," Scytale said. "Come. We'll go out the back way."

"We had such a nice talk," she said. "I think I've convinced him to get Tleilaxu eyes. It'd make a man of him again."

"Haven't I said it many times?" Scytale asked, urging her into a rear chamber.

His voice, he noted with pride, matched his features precisely. It unmistakably was the voice of the old Fremen, who certainly was dead by this time.

Scytale sighed. It had been done with sympathy, he told himself, and the victims certainly had known their peril. Now, the young woman would have to be given her chance.

Empires do not suffer emptiness of purpose at the time of their creation. It is when they have become established that aims are lost and replaced by vague ritual.

—WORDS OF MUAD'DIB
BY PRINCESS IRULAN

It was going to be a bad session, this meeting of the Imperial Council, Alia realized. She sensed contention gathering force, storing up energy—the way Irulan refused to look at Chani, Stilgar's nervous shuffling of papers, the scowls Paul directed at Korba the Qizara.

She seated herself at the end of the golden council table so she could look out the balcony windows at the dusty light of the afternoon.

Korba, interrupted by her entrance, went on with something he'd been saying to Paul. "What I mean, m'Lord, is that there aren't as many gods as once there were."

Alia laughed, throwing her head back. The movement dropped the black hood of her aba robe. Her features lay exposed—blue-in-blue "spice eyes," her mother's oval face beneath a cap of bronze hair, small nose, mouth wide and generous.

Korba's cheeks went almost the color of his orange robe. He glared at Alia, an angry gnome, bald and fuming.

"Do you know what's being said about your brother?" he demanded.

"I know what's being said about your Qizarate," Alia countered. "You're not divines, you're god's spies."

Korba glanced at Paul for support, said: "We are sent by the writ of Muad'Dib, that He shall know the truth of His people and they shall know the truth of Him."

"Spies," Alia said.

Korba pursed his lips in injured silence.

Paul looked at his sister, wondering why she provoked Korba. Abruptly, he saw that Alia had passed into womanhood, beautiful with the first blazing innocence of youth. He found himself surprised that he hadn't noticed it until this moment. She was fifteen—almost sixteen, a Reverend Mother without motherhood, virgin priestess, object of fearful veneration for the superstitious masses—Alia of the Knife.

"This is not the time or place for your sister's levity," Irulan said.

Paul ignored her, nodded to Korba. "The square's full of pilgrims. Go out and lead their prayer."

"But they expect *you*, m'Lord," Korba said.

"Put on your turban," Paul said. "They'll never know at this distance."

Irulan smothered irritation at being ignored, watched Korba arise to obey. She'd had the sudden disquieting thought that Edric might not hide her actions from Alia. *What do we really know of the sister?* she wondered.

Chani, hands tightly clasped in her lap, glanced across the table at Stilgar, her uncle, Paul's Minister of State. Did the old Fremen Naib ever long for the simpler life of his desert sietch? she wondered. Stilgar's black hair, she noted, had begun to gray at the edges, but his eyes beneath heavy brows remained far-seeing. It was the eagle stare of the wild, and his beard still carried the catchtube indentation of life in a stillsuit.

Made nervous by Chani's attention, Stilgar looked around the Council Chamber. His gaze fell on the balcony window and Korba standing outside. Korba raised outstretched arms for the benediction and a trick of the afternoon sun cast a red halo onto the window behind him. For a moment, Stilgar saw the Court Qizara as a figure crucified on a fiery wheel. Korba lowered his arms, destroyed the illusion, but Stilgar remained shaken by it. His thoughts went in angry frustration to the fawning supplicants waiting in the Audience Hall, and to the hateful pomp which surrounded Muad'Dib's throne.

Convening with the Emperor, one hoped for a fault in him, to find mistakes, Stilgar thought. He felt this might be sacrilege, but wanted it anyway.

Distant crowd murmuring entered the chamber as Korba returned. The balcony door thumped into its seals behind him, shutting off the sound.

Paul's gaze followed the Qizara. Korba took his seat at Paul's left, dark features composed, eyes glazed by fanaticism. He'd enjoyed that moment of religious power.

"The spirit presence has been invoked," he said.

"Thank the lord for that," Alia said.

Korba's lips went white.

Again, Paul studied his sister, wondered at her motives. Her innocence masked deception, he told himself. She'd come out of the same Bene Gesserit breeding program as he had. What had the kwisatz haderach genetics produced in her? There was always that mysterious difference: she'd been an embryo in the womb when her mother had survived the raw melange poison. Mother and unborn daughter had become Reverend Mothers simultaneously. But simultaneity didn't carry identity.

Of the experience, Alia said that in one terrifying instant she had awakened to consciousness, her memory absorbing the uncounted other-lives which her mother was assimilating.

"I became my mother and all the others," she said. "I was unformed, unborn, but I became an old woman then and there."

Sensing his thoughts on her, Alia smiled at Paul. His expression softened. *How could anyone react to Korba with other than cynical humor?* he asked himself. *What is more ridiculous than a Death Commando transformed into a priest?*

Stilgar tapped his papers. "If my liege permits," he said. "These are matters urgent and dire."

"The Tupile Treaty?" Paul asked.

"The Guild maintains that we must sign this treaty without knowing the precise location of the Tupile Entente," Stilgar said. "They've some support from Landsraad delegates."

"What pressures have you brought to bear?" Irulan asked.

"Those pressures which my Emperor has designated for this enterprise," Stilgar said. The stiff formality of his reply contained all his disapproval of the Princess Consort.

"My Lord and husband," Irulan said, turning to Paul, forcing him to acknowledge her.

Emphasizing the titular difference in front of Chani, Paul thought, *is a weakness.* In such moments, he shared Stilgar's dislike for Irulan, but sympathy tempered his emotions. What was Irulan but a Bene Gesserit pawn?

"Yes?" Paul said.

Irulan stared at him. "If you withheld their melange . . ."

Chani shook her head in dissent.

"We tread with caution," Paul said. "Tupile remains the place of sanctuary for defeated Great Houses. It symbolizes a last resort, a final place of safety for all our subjects. Exposing the sanctuary makes it vulnerable."

"If they can hide people they can hide other things," Stilgar rumbled. "An army, perhaps, or the beginnings of melange culture which—"

"You don't back people into a corner," Alia said. "Not if you want them to remain peaceful." Ruefully, she saw that she'd been drawn into the contention which she'd foreseen.

"So we've spent ten years of negotiation for nothing," Irulan said.

"None of my brother's actions is for nothing," Alia said.

Irulan picked up a scribe, gripped it with white-knuckled intensity. Paul saw her marshal emotional control in the Bene Gesserit way: the penetrating inward stare, deep breathing. He could almost hear her repeating the litany. Presently, she said: "What have we gained?"

"We've kept the Guild off balance," Chani said.

"We want to avoid a showdown confrontation with our enemies," Alia said. "We have no special desire to kill them. There's enough butchery going on under the Atreides banner."

She feels it, too, Paul thought. Strange, what a sense of compelling responsibility they both felt for that brawling, idolatrous universe with its ecstasies of tranquility and wild motion. *Must we protect them from themselves?* he wondered. *They play with nothingness every moment—empty lives, empty words. They ask too much of me.* His throat felt tight and full. How many moments would he lose? What sons? What dreams? Was it worth the price his vision had revealed? Who would ask the living of some far distant future, who would say to them: "But for Muad'Dib, you would not be here."

"Denying them their melange would solve nothing," Chani said. "So the Guild's navigators would lose their ability to see into timespace. Your Sisters of the Bene Gesserit would lose their truthsense. Some people might die before their time. Communication would break down. Who could be blamed?"

"They wouldn't let it come to that," Irulan said.

"Wouldn't they?" Chani asked. "Why not? Who could blame the Guild? They'd be helpless, demonstrably so."

"We'll sign the treaty as it stands," Paul said.

"M'Lord," Stilgar said, concentrating on his hands, "there is a question in our minds."

"Yes?" Paul gave the old Fremen his full attention.

"You have certain . . . powers," Stilgar said. "Can you not locate the Entente despite the Guild?"

Powers! Paul thought. Stilgar couldn't just say: *"You're prescient. Can't you trace a path in the future that leads to Tupile?"*

Paul looked at the golden surface of the table. Always the same problem: How could he express the limits of the inexpressible? Should he speak of fragmentation, the natural destiny of all power? How could someone who'd never experienced the spice change of prescience conceive an awareness containing no localized spacetime, no personal image-vector nor associated sensory captives?

He looked at Alia, found her attention on Irulan. Alia sensed his movement, glanced at him, nodded toward Irulan. Ahhh, yes: any answer they gave would find its way into one of Irulan's special reports to the Bene Gesserit. They never gave up seeking an answer to their kwisatz haderach.

Stilgar, though, deserved an answer of some kind. For that matter, so did Irulan.

"The uninitiated try to conceive of prescience as obeying a *Natu-*

ral Law," Paul said. He steepled his hands in front of him. "But it'd be just as correct to say it's heaven speaking to us, that being able to read the future is a harmonious act of man's being. In other words, prediction is a natural consequence in the wave of the present. It wears the guise of nature, you see. But such powers cannot be used from an attitude that prestates aims and purposes. Does a chip caught in the wave say where it's going? There's no cause and effect in the oracle. Causes become occasions of convections and confluences, places where the currents meet. Accepting prescience, you fill your being with concepts repugnant to the intellect. Your intellectual consciousness, therefore, rejects them. In rejecting, intellect becomes a part of the processes, and is subjugated."

"You cannot do it?" Stilgar asked.

"Were I to seek Tupile with prescience," Paul said, speaking directly to Irulan, "this might hide Tupile."

"Chaos!" Irulan protested. "It has no . . . no . . . consistency."

"I did say it obeys no Natural Law," Paul said.

"Then there are limits to what you can see or do with your powers?" Irulan asked.

Before Paul could answer, Alia said: "Dear Irulan, prescience has no limits. Not consistent? Consistency isn't a necessary aspect of the universe."

"But he said . . ."

"How can my brother give you explicit information about the limits of something which has no limits? The boundaries escape the intellect."

That was a nasty thing for Alia to do, Paul thought. It would alarm Irulan, who had such a careful consciousness, so dependent upon values derived from precise limits. His gaze went to Korba, who sat in a pose of religious reverie—*listening with the soul.* How could the

Qizarate use this exchange? More religious mystery? Something to evoke awe? No doubt.

"Then you'll sign the treaty in its present form?" Stilgar asked.

Paul smiled. The issue of the oracle, by Stilgar's judgment, had been closed. Stilgar aimed only at victory, not at discovering truth. Peace, justice and a sound coinage—these anchored Stilgar's universe. He wanted something visible and real—a signature on a treaty.

"I'll sign it," Paul said.

Stilgar took up a fresh folder. "The latest communication from our field commanders in Sector Ixian speaks of agitation for a constitution." The old Fremen glanced at Chani, who shrugged.

Irulan, who had closed her eyes and put both hands to her forehead in mnemonic impressment, opened her eyes, studied Paul intently.

"The Ixian Confederacy offers submission," Stilgar said, "but their negotiators question the amount of the Imperial Tax which they—"

"They want a legal limit to my Imperial will," Paul said. "Who would govern me, the Landsraad or CHOAM?"

Stilgar removed from the folder a note on *instroy* paper. "One of our agents sent this memorandum from a caucus of the CHOAM minority." He read the cipher in a flat voice: "The Throne must be stopped in its attempt at a power monopoly. We must tell the truth about the Atreides, how he maneuvers behind the triple sham of Landsraad legislation, religious sanction and bureaucratic efficiency." He pushed the note back into the folder.

"A constitution," Chani murmured.

Paul glanced at her, back to Stilgar. *Thus the Jihad falters,* Paul thought, *but not soon enough to save me.* The thought produced emotional tensions. He remembered his earliest visions of the Jihad-to-be, the terror and revulsion he'd experienced. Now, of course, he knew visions of greater terrors. He had lived with the real violence. He had seen his Fremen, charged with mystical strength, sweep all before them in the religious war. The Jihad gained a new perspective. It was finite, of course, a brief spasm when measured against eternity, but beyond lay horrors to overshadow anything in the past.

All in my name, Paul thought.

"Perhaps they could be given the *form* of a constitution," Chani suggested. "It needn't be actual."

"Deceit *is* a tool of statecraft," Irulan agreed.

"There are limits to power, as those who put their hopes in a constitution always discover," Paul said.

Korba straightened from his reverent pose. "M'Lord?"

"Yes?" And Paul thought, *Here now! Here's one who may harbor secret sympathies for an imagined rule of Law.*

"We could begin with a religious constitution," Korba said, "something for the faithful who—"

"No!" Paul snapped. "We will make this an Order in Council. Are you recording this, Irulan?"

"Yes, m'Lord," Irulan said, voice frigid with dislike for the menial role he forced upon her.

"Constitutions become the ultimate tyranny," Paul said. "They're organized power on such a scale as to be overwhelming. The constitution is social power mobilized and it has no conscience. It can crush the highest and the lowest, removing all dignity and individuality. It has an unstable balance point and no limitations. I, however, have limitations. In my desire to provide an ultimate protection for my people, I forbid a constitution. Order in Council, this date, etcetera, etcetera."

"What of the Ixian concern about the tax, m'Lord?" Stilgar asked.

Paul forced his attention away from the brooding, angry look on Korba's face, said: "You've a proposal, Stil?"

"We must have control of taxes, Sire."

"Our price to the Guild for my signature on the Tupile Treaty," Paul said, "is the submission of the Ixian Confederacy to our tax. The Confederacy cannot trade without Guild transport. They'll pay."

"Very good, m'Lord." Stilgar produced another folder, cleared his throat. "The Qizarate's report on Salusa Secundus. Irulan's father has been putting his legions through landing maneuvers."

Irulan found something of interest in the palm of her left hand. A pulse throbbed at her neck.

"Irulan," Paul asked, "do you persist in arguing that your father's one legion is nothing more than a toy?"

"What could he do with only one legion?" she asked. She stared at him out of slitted eyes.

"He could get himself killed," Chani said.

Paul nodded. "And I'd be blamed."

"I know a few commanders in the Jihad," Alia said, "who'd pounce if they learned of this."

"But it's only his police force!" Irulan protested.

"Then they have no need for landing maneuvers," Paul said. "I suggest that your next little note to your father contain a frank and direct discussion of my views about his delicate position."

She lowered her gaze. "Yes, m'Lord. I hope that will be the end of it. My father would make a good martyr."

"Mmmmmmm," Paul said. "My sister wouldn't send a message to those commanders she mentioned unless I ordered it."

"An attack on my father carries dangers other than the obvious military ones," Irulan said. "People are beginning to look back on his reign with a certain nostalgia."

"You'll go too far one day," Chani said in her deadly serious Fremen voice.

"Enough!" Paul ordered.

He weighed Irulan's revelation about public nostalgia—ah, now! that'd carried a note of truth. Once more, Irulan had proved her worth.

"The Bene Gesserit send a formal supplication," Stilgar said, presenting another folder. "They wish to consult you about the preservation of your bloodline."

Chani glanced sideways at the folder as though it contained a deadly device.

"Send the Sisterhood the usual excuses," Paul said.

"Must we?" Irulan demanded.

"Perhaps . . . this is the time to discuss it," Chani said.

Paul shook his head sharply. They couldn't know that this was part of the price he had not yet decided to pay.

But Chani wasn't to be stopped. "I have been to the prayer wall of Sietch Tabr where I was born," she said. "I have submitted to doctors. I have knelt in the desert and sent my thoughts into the depths where dwells Shai-hulud. Yet"—she shrugged—"nothing avails."

Science and superstition, all have failed her, Paul thought. *Do I fail her, too, by not telling her what bearing an heir to House Atreides will precipitate?* He looked up to find an expression of pity in Alia's eyes. The idea of pity from his sister repelled him. Had she, too, seen that terrifying future?

"My Lord must know the dangers to his realm when he has no heir," Irulan said, using her Bene Gesserit powers of voice with an oily persuasiveness. "These things are naturally difficult to discuss, but they must be brought into the open. An Emperor is more than a man. His figure leads the realm. Should he die without an heir, civil strife must follow. As you love your people, you cannot leave them thus?"

Paul pushed himself away from the table, strode to the balcony windows. A wind was flattening the smoke of the city's fires out there. The sky presented a darkening silver-blue softened by the evening fall of dust from the Shield Wall. He stared southward at the escarpment which protected his northern lands from the coriolis wind, and he wondered why his own peace of mind could find no such shield.

The Council sat silently waiting behind him, aware of how close to rage he was.

Paul sensed time rushing upon him. He tried to force himself into a tranquility of many balances where he might shape a new future.

Disengage . . . disengage . . . disengage, he thought. What would happen if he took Chani, just picked up and left with her, sought sanctuary on Tupile? His name would remain behind. The Jihad would find new and more terrible centers upon which to turn. He'd be blamed for that, too. He felt suddenly fearful that in reaching for any new thing he might let fall what was most precious, that even the slightest noise from him might send the universe crashing back, receding until he never could recapture any piece of it.

Below him, the square had become the setting for a band of pilgrims in the green and white of the hajj. They wended their way like a disjointed snake behind a striding Arrakeen guide. They reminded Paul that his reception hall would be packed with supplicants by now. Pilgrims! Their exercise in homelessness had become a disgusting source of wealth for his Imperium. The hajj filled the space-ways with religious tramps. They came and they came and they came.

How did I set this in motion? he asked himself.

It had, of course, set itself in motion. It was in the genes which might labor for centuries to achieve this brief spasm.

Driven by that deepest religious instinct, the people came, seeking their resurrection. The pilgrimage ended here—"Arrakis, the place of rebirth, the place to die."

Snide old Fremen said he wanted the pilgrims for their water.

What was it the pilgrims really sought? Paul wondered. They said they came to a holy place. But they must know the universe contained no Eden-source, no Tupile for the soul. They called Arrakis the place of the unknown where all mysteries were explained. This was a link between their universe and the next. And the frightening thing was that they appeared to go away satisfied.

What do they find here? Paul asked himself.

Often in their religious ecstasy, they filled the streets with screeching like some odd aviary. In fact, the Fremen called them "passage birds." And the few who died here were "winged souls."

With a sigh, Paul thought how each new planet his legions subjugated opened new sources of pilgrims. They came out of gratitude for "the peace of Muad'Dib."

Everywhere there is peace, Paul thought. *Everywhere . . . except in the heart of Muad'Dib.*

He felt that some element of himself lay immersed in frosty hoar-darkness without end. His prescient power had tampered with the image of the universe held by all mankind. He had shaken the safe cosmos and replaced security with his Jihad. He had out-fought and out-thought and out-predicted the universe of men, but a certainty filled him that this universe still eluded him.

This planet beneath him which he had commanded be remade from desert into a water-rich paradise, it was alive. It had a pulse as dynamic as that of any human. It fought him, resisted, slipped away from his commands . . .

A hand crept into Paul's. He looked down to see Chani peering up at him, concern in her eyes. Those eyes drank him, and she whispered: "Please, love, do not battle with your ruh-self." An outpouring of emotion swept upward from her hand, buoyed him.

"Sihaya," he whispered.

"We must go to the desert soon," she said in a low voice.

He squeezed her hand, released it, returned to the table where he remained standing.

Chani took her seat.

Irulan stared at the papers in front of Stilgar, her mouth a tight line.

"Irulan proposes herself as mother of the Imperial heir," Paul said. He glanced at Chani, back to Irulan, who refused to meet his gaze. "We all know she holds no love for me."

Irulan went very still.

"I know the political arguments," Paul said. "It's the human arguments which concern me. I think if the Princess Consort were not bound by the commands of the Bene Gesserit, if she did not seek this out of desires for personal power, my reaction might be very different. As matters stand, though, I reject this proposal."

Irulan took a deep, shaky breath.

Paul, resuming his seat, thought he had never seen her under such poor control. Leaning toward her, he said: "Irulan, I am truly sorry."

She lifted her chin, a look of pure fury in her eyes. "I don't want your pity!" she hissed. And turning to Stilgar: "Is there more that's urgent and dire?"

Holding his gaze firmly on Paul, Stilgar said: "One more matter, m'Lord. The Guild again proposes a formal embassy here on Arrakis."

"One of the deep-space kind?" Korba asked, his voice full of fanatic loathing.

"Presumably," Stilgar said.

"A matter to be considered with the utmost care, m'Lord," Korba warned. "The Council of Naibs would not like it, an actual Guilds-man here on Arrakis. They contaminate the very ground they touch."

"They live in tanks and don't touch the ground," Paul said, letting his voice reveal irritation.

"The Naibs might take matters into their own hands, m'Lord," Korba said.

Paul glared at him.

"They are Fremen, after all, m'Lord," Korba insisted. "We well remember how the Guild brought those who oppressed us. We have not forgotten the way they blackmailed a spice ransom from us to keep our secrets from our enemies. They drained us of every—"

"Enough!" Paul snapped. "Do you think *I* have forgotten?"

As though he had just awakened to the import of his own words, Korba stuttered unintelligibly, then: "M'lord, forgive me. I did not mean to imply you are not Fremen. I did not . . ."

"They'll send a Steersman," Paul said. "It isn't likely a Steersman would come here if he could see danger in it."

Her mouth dry with sudden fear, Irulan said: "You've . . . *seen* a Steersman come here?"

"Of course I haven't *seen* a Steersman," Paul said, mimicking her tone. "But I can see where one's been and where one's going. Let them send us a Steersman. Perhaps I have a use for such a one."

"So ordered," Stilgar said.

And Irulan, hiding a smile behind her hand, thought: *It's true then. Our Emperor cannot see a Steersman. They are mutually blind. The conspiracy is hidden.*

Once more the drama begins.

—THE EMPEROR PAUL MUAD'DIB
ON HIS ASCENSION TO THE LION THRONE

Alia peered down from her spy window into the great reception hall to watch the advance of the Guild entourage.

The sharply silver light of noon poured through clerestory windows onto a floor worked in green, blue and eggshell tiles to simulate a bayou with water plants and, here and there, a splash of exotic color to indicate bird or animal.

Guildsmen moved across the tile pattern like hunters stalking their prey in a strange jungle. They formed a moving design of gray robes, black robes, orange robes—all arrayed in a deceptively random way around the transparent tank where the Steersman-Ambassador swam in his orange gas. The tank slid on its supporting field, towed by two gray-robed attendants, like a rectangular ship being warped into its dock.

Directly beneath her, Paul sat on the Lion Throne on its raised dais. He wore the new formal crown with its fish and fist emblems. The jeweled golden robes of state covered his body. The shimmering of a personal shield surrounded him. Two wings of bodyguards fanned out on both sides along the dais and down the steps. Stilgar stood two steps below Paul's right hand in a white robe with a yellow rope for a belt.

Sibling empathy told her that Paul seethed with the same agitation she was experiencing, although she doubted another could detect it. His attention remained on an orange-robed attendant whose blindly staring metal eyes looked neither to right nor to left. This attendant walked at the right front corner of the Ambassador's troupe like a military outrider. A rather flat face beneath curly black hair, such of his figure as could be seen beneath the orange robe, every gesture shouted a familiar identity.

It was Duncan Idaho.

It could not be Duncan Idaho, yet it was.

Captive memories absorbed in the womb during the moment of her mother's spice change identified this man for Alia by a *rihani* decipherment which cut through all camouflage. Paul was seeing him, she knew, out of countless personal experiences, out of gratitudes and youthful sharing.

It was Duncan.

Alia shuddered. There could be only one answer: this was a Tleilaxu ghola, a being reconstructed from the dead flesh of the original. That original had perished saving Paul. This could only be a product of the axolotl tanks.

The ghola walked with the cock-footed alertness of a master swordsman. He came to a halt as the Ambassador's tank glided to a stop ten paces from the steps of the dais.

In the Bene Gesserit way she could not escape, Alia read Paul's disquiet. He no longer looked at the figure out of his past. Not looking, his whole being stared. Muscles strained against restrictions as he nodded to the Guild Ambassador, said: "I am told your name is

Edric. We welcome you to our Court in the hope this will bring new understanding between us."

The Steersman assumed a sybaritic reclining pose in his orange gas, popped a melange capsule into his mouth before meeting Paul's gaze. The tiny transducer orbiting a corner of the Guildsman's tank reproduced a coughing sound, then the rasping, uninvolved voice: "I abase myself before my Emperor and beg leave to present my credentials and offer a small gift."

An aide passed a scroll up to Stilgar, who studied it, scowling, then nodded to Paul. Both Stilgar and Paul turned then toward the ghola standing patiently below the dais.

"Indeed my Emperor has discerned the gift," Edric said.

"We are pleased to accept your credentials," Paul said. "Explain the gift."

Edric rolled in the tank, bringing his attention to bear on the ghola. "This is a man called Hayt," he said, spelling the name. "According to our investigators, he has a most curious history. He was killed here on Arrakis . . . a grievous head-wound which required many months of regrowth. The body was sold to the Bene Tleilax as that of a master swordsman, an adept of the Ginaz School. It came to our attention that this must be Duncan Idaho, the trusted retainer of your household. We bought him as a gift befitting an Emperor." Edric peered up at Paul. "Is it not Idaho, Sire?"

Restraint and caution gripped Paul's voice. "He has the aspect of Idaho."

Does Paul see something I don't? Alia wondered. *No! It's Duncan!*

The man called Hayt stood impassively, metal eyes fixed straight ahead, body relaxed. No sign escaped him to indicate he knew himself to be the object of discussion.

"According to our best knowledge, it's Idaho," Edric said.

"He's called Hayt now," Paul said. "A curious name."

"Sire, there's no divining how or why the Tleilaxu bestow names," Edric said. "But names can be changed. The Tleilaxu name is of little importance."

This is a Tleilaxu thing, Paul thought. *There's the problem.* The Bene Tleilax held little attachment to phenomenal nature. Good and evil carried strange meanings in their philosophy. What might they have incorporated in Idaho's flesh—out of design or whim?

Paul glanced at Stilgar, noted the Fremen's superstitious awe. It was an emotion echoed all through his Fremen guard. Stilgar's mind would be speculating about the loathsome habits of Guildsmen, of Tleilaxu and of gholas.

Turning toward the ghola, Paul said: "Hayt, is that your only name?"

A serene smile spread over the ghola's dark features. The metal eyes lifted, centered on Paul, but maintained their mechanical stare. "That is how I am called, my Lord: Hayt."

In her dark spy hole, Alia trembled. It was Idaho's voice, a quality of sound so precise she sensed its imprint upon her cells.

"May it please my Lord," the ghola added, "if I say his voice gives me pleasure. This is a sign, say the Bene Tleilax, that I have heard the voice . . . before."

"But you don't know this for sure," Paul said.

"I know nothing of my past for sure, my Lord. It was explained that I can have no memory of my former life. All that remains from before is the pattern set by the genes. There are, however, niches into which once-familiar things may fit. There are voices, places, foods, faces, sounds, actions—a sword in my hand, the controls of a 'thopter . . ."

Noting how intently the Guildsmen watched this exchange, Paul asked: "Do you understand that you're a gift?"

"It was explained to me, my Lord."

Paul sat back, hands resting on the arms of the throne.

What debt do I owe Duncan's flesh? he wondered. *The man died saving my life. But this is not Idaho, this is a ghola.* Yet, here were body and mind which had taught Paul to fly a 'thopter as though the wings grew from his own shoulders. Paul knew he could not pick up a sword without leaning on the harsh education Idaho had given him. A ghola. This was flesh full of false impressions, easily misread. Old associations would persist. *Duncan Idaho.* It wasn't so much a mask the ghola wore as it was a loose, concealing garment of personality which moved in a way different from whatever the Tleilaxu had hidden here.

"How might you serve us?" Paul asked.

"In any way my Lord's wishes and my capabilities agree."

Alia, watching from her vantage point, was touched by the ghola's air of diffidence. She detected nothing feigned. Something ultimately innocent shone from the new Duncan Idaho. The original had been worldly, devil-may-care. But this flesh had been cleansed of all that. It was a pure surface upon which the Tleilaxu had written . . . what?

She sensed the hidden perils in this gift then. This was a Tleilaxu thing. The Tleilaxu displayed a disturbing lack of inhibitions in what they created. Unbridled curiosity might guide their actions. They boasted they could make *anything* from the proper human raw material—devils or saints. They sold killer-mentats. They'd produced a killer medic, overcoming the Suk inhibitions against the taking of human life to do it. Their wares included willing menials, pliant sex toys for any whim, soldiers, generals, philosophers, even an occasional moralist.

Paul stirred, looked at Edric. "How has this *gift* been trained?" he asked.

"If it please my Lord," Edric said, "it amused the Tleilaxu to train this ghola as a mentat and philosopher of the Zensunni. Thus, they sought to increase his abilities with the sword."

"Did they succeed?"

"I do not know, my Lord."

Paul weighed the answer. Truthsense told him Edric sincerely believed the ghola to be Idaho. But there was more. The waters of Time through which this oracular Steersman moved suggested dangers without revealing them. *Hayt.* The Tleilaxu name spoke of peril. Paul felt himself tempted to reject the gift. Even as he felt the temptation, he knew he couldn't choose that way. This flesh made demands on House Atreides—a fact the enemy well knew.

"Zensunni philosopher," Paul mused, once more looking at the ghola. "You've examined your own role and motives?"

"I approach my service in an attitude of humility, Sire. I am a cleansed mind washed free of the imperatives from my human past."

"Would you prefer we called you Hayt or Duncan Idaho?"

"My Lord may call me what he wishes, for I am not a name."

"But do you *enjoy* the name Duncan Idaho?"

"I think that was my name, Sire. It fits within me. Yet . . . it stirs up curious responses. One's name, I think, must carry much that's unpleasant along with the pleasant."

"What gives you the most pleasure?" Paul asked.

Unexpectedly, the ghola laughed, said: "Looking for signs in others which reveal my former self."

"Do you see such signs here?"

"Oh, yes, my Lord. Your man Stilgar there is caught between suspicion and admiration. He was friend to my former self, but this ghola flesh repels him. You, my Lord, admired the man I was . . . and you trusted him."

"Cleansed mind," Paul said. "How can a cleansed mind put itself in bondage to us?"

"Bondage, my Lord? The cleansed mind makes decisions in the

presence of unknowns and without cause and effect. Is this bondage?"

Paul scowled. It was a Zensunni saying, cryptic, apt—immersed
in a creed which denied objective function in all mental activity.
Without cause and effect! Such thoughts shocked the mind. *Unknowns?* Unknowns lay in every decision, even in the oracular vision.

"You'd prefer we called you Duncan Idaho?" Paul asked.

"We live by differences, my Lord. Choose a name for me."

"Let your Tleilaxu name stand," Paul said. "Hayt—there's a name
inspires caution."

Hayt bowed, moved back one step.

And Alia wondered: *How did he know the interview was over? I
knew it because I know my brother. But there was no sign a stranger
could read. Did the Duncan Idaho in him know?*

Paul turned toward the Ambassador, said: "Quarters have been
set aside for your embassy. It is our desire to have a private consultation with you at the earliest opportunity. We will send for you. Let us
inform you further, before you hear it from an inaccurate source, that
a Reverend Mother of the Sisterhood, Gaius Helen Mohiam, has been
removed from the heighliner which brought you. It was done at our
command. Her presence on your ship will be an item in our talks."

A wave of Paul's left hand dismissed the envoy. "Hayt," Paul said,
"stay here."

The Ambassador's attendants backed away, towing the tank. Edric
became orange motion in orange gas—eyes, a mouth, gently waving
limbs.

Paul watched until the last Guildsman was gone, the great doors
swinging closed behind them.

I've done it now, Paul thought. *I've accepted the ghola.* The Tleilaxu creation was bait, no doubt of it. Very likely the old hag of a

Reverend Mother played the same role. But it was the time of the tarot which he'd forecast in an early vision. The damnable tarot! It muddied the waters of Time until the prescient strained to detect moments but an hour off. Many a fish took the bait and escaped, he reminded himself. And the tarot worked for him as well as against him. What he could not see, others might not detect as well.

The ghola stood, head cocked to one side, waiting.

Stilgar moved across the steps, hid the ghola from Paul's view. In Chakobsa, the hunting language of their sietch days, Stilgar said: "That creature in the tank gives me the shudders, Sire, but this *gift*! Send it away!"

In the same tongue, Paul said: "I cannot."

"Idaho's dead," Stilgar argued. "This isn't Idaho. Let me take its water for the tribe."

"The ghola is my problem, Stil. Your problem is our prisoner. I want the Reverend Mother guarded most carefully by the men I trained to resist the wiles of Voice."

"I like this not, Sire."

"I'll be cautious, Stil. See that you are, too."

"Very well, Sire." Stilgar stepped down to the floor of the hall, passed close to Hayt, sniffed him and strode out.

Evil can be detected by its smell, Paul thought. Stilgar had planted the green and white Atreides banner on a dozen worlds, but remained superstitious Fremen, proof against any sophistication.

Paul studied the gift.

"Duncan, Duncan," he whispered. "What have they done to you?"

"They gave me life, m'Lord," Hayt said.

"But why were you trained and given to us?" Paul asked.

Hayt pursed his lips, then: "They intend me to destroy you."

The statement's candor shook Paul. But then, how else could a

Zensunni-mentat respond? Even in a ghola, a mentat could speak no less than the truth, especially out of Zensunni inner calm. This was a human computer, mind and nervous system fitted to the tasks relegated long ago to hated mechanical devices. To condition him also as a Zensunni meant a double ration of honesty . . . unless the Tleilaxu had built something even more odd into this flesh.

Why, for example, the mechanical eyes? Tleilaxu boasted their metal eyes improved on the original. Strange, then, that more Tleilaxu didn't wear them out of choice.

Paul glanced up at Alia's spy hole, longed for her presence and advice, for counsel not clouded by feelings of responsibility and debt.

Once more, he looked at the ghola. This was no frivolous gift. It gave honest answers to dangerous questions.

It makes no difference that I know this is a weapon to be used against me, Paul thought.

"What should I do to protect myself from you?" Paul asked. It was direct speech, no royal "we," but a question as he might have put it to the old Duncan Idaho.

"Send me away, m'Lord."

Paul shook his head from side to side. "How are you to destroy me?"

Hayt looked at the guards, who'd moved closer to Paul after Stilgar's departure. He turned, cast his gaze around the hall, brought his metal eyes back to bear on Paul, nodded.

"This is a place where a man draws away from people," Hayt said. "It speaks of such power that one can contemplate it comfortably only in the remembrance that all things are finite. Did my Lord's oracular powers plot his course into this place?"

Paul drummed his fingers against the throne's arms. The mentat sought data, but the question disturbed him. "I came to this position by strong decisions . . . not always out of my other . . . abilities."

"Strong decisions," Hayt said. "These temper a man's life. One can take the temper from fine metal by heating it and allowing it to cool without quenching."

"Do you divert me with Zensunni prattle?" Paul asked.

"Zensunni has other avenues to explore, Sire, than diversion and display."

Paul wet his lips with his tongue, drew in a deep breath, set his own thoughts into the counterbalance poise of the mentat. Negative answers arose around him. It wasn't expected that he'd go haring after the ghola to the exclusion of other duties. No, that wasn't it. Why a *Zensunni*-mentat? Philosophy . . . words . . . contemplation . . . inward searching . . . He felt the weakness of his data.

"We need more data," he muttered.

"The facts needed by a mentat do not brush off onto one as you might gather pollen on your robe while passing through a field of flowers," Hayt said. "One chooses his pollen carefully, examines it under powerful amplification."

"You must teach me this Zensunni way with rhetoric," Paul said.

The metallic eyes glittered at him for a moment, then: "M'Lord, perhaps that's what was intended."

To blunt my will with words and ideas? Paul wondered.

"Ideas are most to be feared when they become actions," Paul said.

"Send me away, Sire," Hayt said, and it was Duncan Idaho's voice full of concern for "the young master."

Paul felt trapped by that voice. He couldn't send that voice away, even when it came from a ghola. "You will stay," he said, "and we'll both exercise caution."

Hayt bowed in submission.

Paul glanced up at the spy hole, eyes pleading for Alia to take this *gift* off his hands and ferret out its secrets. Gholas were ghosts to frighten children. He'd never thought to know one. To know this one, he had to set himself above all compassion . . . and he wasn't certain he could do it. *Duncan . . . Duncan . . .* Where was Idaho in this shaped-to-measure flesh? It wasn't flesh . . . it was a shroud in fleshly shape! Idaho lay dead forever on the floor of an Arrakeen cavern. His ghost stared out of metal eyes. Two beings stood side by side in this revenant flesh. One was a threat with its force and nature hidden behind unique veils.

Closing his eyes, Paul allowed old visions to sift through his awareness. He sensed the spirits of love and hate spouting there in a rolling sea from which no rock lifted above the chaos. No place at all from which to survey turmoil.

Why has no vision shown me this new Duncan Idaho? he asked himself. *What concealed Time from an oracle? Other oracles, obviously.*

Paul opened his eyes, asked: "Hayt, do you have the power of prescience?"

"No, m'Lord."

Sincerity spoke in that voice. It was possible the ghola didn't know he possessed this ability, of course. But that'd hamper his working as a mentat. What was the hidden design?

Old visions surged around Paul. Would he have to choose the terrible way? Distorted Time hinted at this ghola in that hideous future. Would that way close in upon him no matter what he did?

Disengage . . . disengage . . . disengage . . .

The thought tolled in his mind.

In her position above Paul, Alia sat with chin cupped in left hand, stared down at the ghola. A magnetic attraction about this Hayt reached up to her. Tleilaxu restoration had given him youth, an innocent intensity which called out to her. She'd understood Paul's unspoken plea. When oracles failed, one turned to real spies and physical powers. She wondered, though, at her own eagerness to accept this challenge. She felt a positive desire to be near this *new* man, perhaps to touch him.

He's a danger to both of us, she thought.

Truth suffers from too much analysis.

—ANCIENT FREMEN SAYING

"Reverend Mother, I shudder to see you in such circumstances," Irulan said.

She stood just inside the cell door, measuring the various capacities of the room in her Bene Gesserit way. It was a three-meter cube carved with cutterays from the veined brown rock beneath Paul's Keep. For furnishings, it contained one flimsy basket chair occupied now by the Reverend Mother Gaius Helen Mohiam, a pallet with a brown cover upon which had been spread a deck of the new Dune Tarot cards, a metered water tap above a reclamation basin, a Fremen privy with moisture seals. It was all sparse, primitive. Yellow light came from anchored and caged glowglobes at the four corners of the ceiling.

"You've sent word to the Lady Jessica?" the Reverend Mother asked.

"Yes, but I don't expect her to lift one finger against her firstborn," Irulan said. She glanced at the cards. They spoke of the powerful turning their backs on supplicants. The card of the Great Worm lay beneath Desolate Sand. Patience was counseled. *Did one require the tarot to see this?* she asked herself.

A guard stood outside watching them through a metaglass window in the door. Irulan knew there'd be other monitors on this encounter. She had put in much thought and planning before daring to come here. To have stayed away carried its own perils, though.

The Reverend Mother had been engaged in *prajna* meditation interspersed with examinations of the tarot. Despite a feeling that she would never leave Arrakis alive, she had achieved a measure of calm through this. One's oracular powers might be small, but muddy water was muddy water. And there was always the Litany Against Fear.

She had yet to assimilate the import of the actions which had precipitated her into this cell. Dark suspicions brooded in her mind (and the tarot hinted at confirmations). Was it possible the Guild had planned this?

A yellow-robed Qizara, head shaved for a turban, beady eyes of total blue in a bland round face, skin leathered by the wind and sun of Arrakis, had awaited her on the heighliner's reception bridge. He had looked up from a bulb of spice-coffee being served by an obsequious steward, studied her a moment, put down the coffee bulb.

"You are the Reverend Mother Gaius Helen Mohiam?"

To replay those words in her mind was to bring that moment alive in the memory. Her throat had constricted with an unmanageable spasm of fear. How had one of the Emperor's minions learned of her presence on the heighliner?

"It came to our attention that you were aboard," the Qizara said. "Have you forgotten that you are denied permission to set foot on the holy planet?"

"I am not on Arrakis," she said. "I'm a passenger on a Guild heighliner in free space."

"There is no such thing as free space, Madame."

She read hate mingled with profound suspicion in his tone.

"Muad'Dib rules everywhere," he said.

"Arrakis is not my destination," she insisted.

"Arrakis is the destination of everyone," he said. And she feared for a moment that he would launch into a recital of the mystical itinerary which pilgrims followed. (This very ship had carried thousands of them.)

But the Qizara had pulled a golden amulet from beneath his robe, kissed it, touched it to his forehead and placed it to his right ear, listened. Presently, he restored the amulet to its hidden place.

"You are ordered to gather your luggage and accompany me to Arrakis."

"But I have business elsewhere!"

In that moment, she suspected Guild perfidy . . . or exposure through some transcendant power of the Emperor or his sister. Perhaps the Steersman did not conceal the conspiracy, after all. The abomination, Alia, certainly possessed the abilities of a Bene Gesserit Reverend Mother. What happened when those powers were coupled with the forces which worked in her brother?

"At once!" the Qizara snapped.

Everything in her cried out against setting foot once more on that accursed desert planet. Here was where the Lady Jessica had turned against the Sisterhood. Here was where they'd lost Paul Atreides, the kwisatz haderach they'd sought through long generations of careful breeding.

"At once," she agreed.

"There's little time," the Qizara said. "When the Emperor commands, all his subjects obey."

So the order had come from Paul!

She thought of protesting to the heighliner's Navigator-

Commander, but the futility of such a gesture stopped her. What could the Guild do?

"The Emperor has said I must die if I set foot on Dune," she said, making a last desperate effort. "You spoke of this yourself. You are condemning me if you take me down there."

"Say no more," the Qizara ordered. "The thing is ordained."

That was how they always spoke of Imperial commands, she knew. *Ordained!* The holy ruler whose eyes could pierce the future had spoken. What must be must be. He had seen it, had He not?

With the sick feeling that she was caught in a web of her own spinning, she had turned to obey.

And the web had become a cell which Irulan could visit. She saw that Irulan had aged somewhat since their meeting on Wallach IX. New lines of worry spread from the corners of her eyes. Well . . . time to see if this Sister of the Bene Gesserit could obey her vows.

"I've had worse quarters," the Reverend Mother said. "Do you come from the Emperor?" And she allowed her fingers to move as though in agitation.

Irulan read the moving fingers and her own fingers flashed an answer as she spoke, saying: "No—I came as soon as I heard you were here."

"Won't the Emperor be angry?" the Reverend Mother asked. Again, her fingers moved: imperative, pressing, demanding.

"Let him be angry. You were my teacher in the Sisterhood, just as you were the teacher of his own mother. Does he think I will turn my back on you as she has done?" And Irulan's finger-talk made excuses, begged.

The Reverend Mother sighed. On the surface, it was the sigh of a prisoner bemoaning her fate, but inwardly she felt the response as a comment on Irulan. It was futile to hope the Atreides Emperor's precious gene pattern could be preserved through this instrument. No matter her beauty, this Princess was flawed. Under that veneer of sexual attraction lived a whining shrew more interested in words than in actions. Irulan was still a Bene Gesserit, though, and the Sisterhood reserved certain techniques to use on some of its weaker vessels as insurance that vital instructions would be carried out.

Beneath small talk about a softer pallet, better food, the Reverend Mother brought up her arsenal of persuasion and gave her orders: the brother-sister crossbreeding must be explored. (Irulan almost broke at receiving this command.)

"I must have my chance!" Irulan's fingers pleaded.

"You've had your chance," the Reverend Mother countered. And she was explicit in her instructions: Was the Emperor ever angry with his concubine? His unique powers must make him lonely. To whom could he speak in any hope of being understood? To the sister, obviously. She shared this loneliness. The depth of their communion must be exploited. Opportunities must be created to throw them together in privacy. Intimate encounters must be arranged. The possibility of eliminating the concubine must be explored. Grief dissolved traditional barriers.

Irulan protested. If Chani were killed, suspicion would fasten immediately upon the Princess-Consort. Besides, there were other problems. Chani had fastened upon an ancient Fremen diet supposed to promote fertility and the diet eliminated all opportunity for administering the contraceptive drugs. Lifting the suppressives would make Chani even more fertile.

The Reverend Mother was outraged and concealed it with difficulty while her fingers flashed their demands. Why had this information not been conveyed at the beginning of their conversation? How could Irulan be that stupid? If Chani conceived and bore a son, the Emperor would declare the child his heir!

Irulan protested that she understood the dangers, but the genes might not be totally lost.

Damn such stupidity! the Reverend Mother raged. Who knew what suppressions and genetic entanglements Chani might introduce from her wild Fremen strain? The Sisterhood must have only the pure line! And an heir would renew Paul's ambitions, spur him to new efforts in consolidating his Empire. The conspiracy could not afford such a setback.

Defensively, Irulan wanted to know how she could have prevented Chani from trying this diet?

But the Reverend Mother was in no mood for excuses. Irulan received explicit instructions now to meet this new threat. If Chani conceived, an abortifact must be introduced into her food or drink. Either that, or she must be killed. An heir to the throne from that source must be prevented at all costs.

An abortifact would be as dangerous as an open attack on the concubine, Irulan objected. She trembled at the thought of trying to kill Chani.

Was Irulan deterred by danger? The Reverend Mother wanted to know, her finger-talk conveying deep scorn.

Angered, Irulan signaled that she knew her value as an agent in the royal household. Did the conspiracy wish to waste such a valuable agent? Was she to be thrown away? In what other way could they keep this close a watch on the Emperor? Or had they introduced another agent into the household? Was that it? Was she to be used now, desperately, and for the last time?

In a war, all values acquired new relationships, the Reverend Mother countered. Their greatest peril was that House Atreides should secure itself with an Imperial line. The Sisterhood could not take such a risk. This went far beyond the danger to the Atreides genetic pattern. Let Paul anchor his family to the throne and the Sisterhood could look forward to centuries of disruption for its programs.

Irulan understood the argument, but she couldn't escape the thought that a decision had been made to spend the Princess-Consort for something of great value. Was there something she should know about the ghola? Irulan ventured.

The Reverend Mother wanted to know if Irulan thought the Sisterhood composed of fools. When had they ever failed to tell Irulan all she *should* know?

It was no answer, but an admission of concealment, Irulan saw. It said she would be told no more than she needed to know.

How could they be certain the ghola was capable of destroying the Emperor? Irulan asked.

She could just as well have asked if melange were capable of destruction, the Reverend Mother countered.

It was a rebuke with a subtle message, Irulan realized. The Bene Gesserit "whip that instructs" informed her that she should have understood long ago this similarity between the spice and the ghola. Melange was valuable, but it exacted a price—addiction. It added years to a life—decades for some—but it was still just another way to die.

The ghola was something of deadly value.

The obvious way to prevent an unwanted birth was to kill the prospective mother before conception, the Reverend Mother signaled, returning to the attack.

Of course, Irulan thought. *If you decide to spend a certain sum, get as much for it as you can.*

The Reverend Mother's eyes, dark with the blue brilliance of her melange addiction, stared up at Irulan, measuring, waiting, observing minutiae.

She reads me clearly, Irulan thought with dismay. *She trained me and observed me in that training. She knows I realize what decision has been taken here. She only observes now to see how I will take this knowledge. Well, I will take it as a Bene Gesserit and a princess.*

Irulan managed a smile, pulled herself erect, thought of the evocative opening passage of the Litany Against Fear:

"I must not fear. Fear is the mind-killer. Fear is the little-death that brings total obliteration. I will face my fear . . ."

When calmness had returned, she thought: *Let them spend me. I will show them what a princess is worth. Perhaps I'll buy them more than they expected.*

After a few more empty vocalizations to bind off the interview, Irulan departed.

When she had gone, the Reverend Mother returned to her tarot cards, laying them out in the fire-eddy pattern. Immediately, she got the Kwisatz Haderach of the Major Arcana and the card lay coupled with the Eight of Ships: the sibyl hoodwinked and betrayed. These were not cards of good omen: they spoke of concealed resources for her enemies.

She turned away from the cards, sat in agitation, wondering if Irulan might yet destroy them.

The Fremen see her as the Earth Figure, a demi-goddess whose special charge is to protect the tribes through her powers of violence. She is Reverend Mother to their Reverend Mothers. To pilgrims who seek her out with demands that she restore virility or make the barren fruitful, she is a form of antimentat. She feeds on that proof that the "analytic" has limits. She represents ultimate tension. She is the virgin-harlot—witty, vulgar, cruel, as destructive in her whims as a coriolis storm.

—ST. ALIA OF THE KNIFE
AS TAKEN FROM THE IRULAN REPORT

Alia stood like a black-robed sentinel figure on the south platform of her temple, the Fane of the Oracle which Paul's Fremen cohorts had built for her against a wall of his stronghold.

She hated this part of her life, but knew no way to evade the temple without bringing down destruction upon them all. The pilgrims (damn them!) grew more numerous every day. The temple's lower porch was crowded with them. Vendors moved among the pilgrims, and there were minor sorcerers, haruspices, diviners, all working their trade in pitiful imitation of Paul Muad'Dib and his sister.

Red and green packages containing the new Dune Tarot were prominent among the vendors' wares, Alia saw. She wondered about the tarot. Who was feeding this device into the Arrakeen market? Why had the tarot sprung to prominence at this particular time and place? Was it to muddy Time? Spice addiction always conveyed some sensitivity to prediction. Fremen were notoriously fey. Was it an accident that so many of them dabbled in portents and omens here and now? She decided to seek an answer at the first opportunity.

There was a wind from the southeast, a small leftover wind blunted by the scarp of the Shield Wall which loomed high in these northern reaches. The rim glowed orange through a thin dust haze underlighted by the late afternoon sun. It was a hot wind against her cheeks and it made her homesick for the sand, for the security of open spaces.

The last of the day's mob began descending the broad greenstone steps of the lower porch, singly and in groups, a few pausing to stare at the keepsakes and holy amulets on the street vendors' racks, some consulting one last minor sorcerer. Pilgrims, supplicants, townfolk, Fremen, vendors closing up for the day—they formed a straggling line that trailed off into the palm-lined avenue which led to the heart of the city.

Alia's eyes picked out the Fremen, marking the frozen looks of superstitious awe on their faces, the half-wild way they kept their distance from the others. They were her strength and her peril. They still captured giant worms for transport, for sport and for sacrifice. They resented the offworld pilgrims, barely tolerated the townfolk of graben and *pan*, hated the cynicism they saw in the street vendors. One did not jostle a wild Fremen, even in a mob such as the ones which swarmed to Alia's Fane. There were no knifings in the Sacred Precincts, but bodies had been found . . . later.

The departing swarm had stirred up dust. The flinty odor came to Alia's nostrils, ignited another pang of longing for the open *bled*. Her sense of the past, she realized, had been sharpened by the coming of the ghola. There'd been much pleasure in those untrammeled days before her brother had mounted the throne—time for joking, time for small things, time to enjoy a cool morning or a sunset, time . . . time . . . time . . . Even danger had been good in those days—clean danger from known sources. No need then to strain the limits of prescience, to peer through murky veils for frustrating glimpses of the future.

Wild Fremen said it well: "Four things cannot be hidden—love, smoke, a pillar of fire and a man striding across the open bled."

With an abrupt feeling of revulsion, Alia retreated from the platform into the shadows of the Fane, strode along the balcony which looked down into the glistening opalescence of her Hall of Oracles. Sand on the tiles rasped beneath her feet. *Supplicants always tracked sand into the Sacred Chambers!* She ignored attendants, guards, postulants, the Qizarate's omnipresent priest-sycophants, plunged into the spiral passage which twisted upward to her private quarters. There, amidst divans, deep rugs, tent hangings and mementos of the desert, she dismissed the Fremen amazons Stilgar had assigned as her personal guardians. *Watchdogs, more likely!* When they had gone, muttering and objecting, but more fearful of her than they were of Stilgar, she stripped off her robe, leaving only the sheathed crysknife on its thong around her neck, strewed garments behind as she made for the bath.

He was near, she knew—that shadow-figure of a man she could sense in her future, but could not see. It angered her that no power of prescience could put flesh on that figure. He could be sensed only at unexpected moments while she scanned the lives of others. Or she came upon a smoky outline in solitary darkness when innocence lay coupled with desire. He stood just beyond an unfixed horizon, and she felt that if she strained her talents to an unexpected intensity she might see him. He was *there*—a constant assault on her awareness: fierce, dangerous, immoral.

Moist warm air surrounded her in the tub. Here was a habit she had learned from the memory-entities of the uncounted Reverend Mothers who were strung out in her awareness like pearls on a glowing necklace. Water, warm water in a sunken tub, accepted her skin as she slid into it. Green tiles with figures of red fish worked into a sea pattern surrounded the water. Such an abundance of water occupied this space that a Fremen of old would have been outraged to see it used merely for washing human flesh.

He was near.

It was lust in tension with chastity, she thought. Her flesh desired a mate. Sex held no casual mystery for a Reverend Mother who had presided at the sietch orgies. The *tau* awareness of her *other-selves* could supply any detail her curiosity required. This feeling of nearness could be nothing other than flesh reaching for flesh.

Need for action fought lethargy in the warm water.

Abruptly, Alia climbed dripping from the bath, strode wet and naked into the training chamber which adjoined her bedroom. The chamber, oblong and skylighted, contained the gross and subtle instruments which toned a Bene Gesserit adept into ultimate physical and mental awareness/preparedness. There were mnemonic amplifiers, digit mills from Ix to strengthen and sensitize fingers and toes, odor synthesizers, tactility sensitizers, temperature gradient fields, pattern betrayers to prevent her falling into detectable habits, alpha-wave-response trainers, blink-synchronizers to tone abilities in light/dark/spectrum analysis . . .

In ten-centimeter letters along one wall, written by her own hand in mnemonic paint, stood the key reminder from the Bene Gesserit Creed:

"Before us, all methods of learning were tainted by instinct. We learned how to learn. Before us, instinct-ridden researchers possessed a limited attention span—often no longer than a single lifetime. Projects stretching across fifty or more lifetimes never occurred to them. The concept of total muscle/nerve training had not entered awareness."

As she moved into the training room, Alia caught her own reflection multiplied thousands of times in the crystal prisms of a fencing mirror swinging in the heart of a target dummy. She saw the long sword waiting on its brackets against the target, and she thought: *Yes! I'll work myself to exhaustion—drain the flesh and clear the mind.*

The sword felt right in her hand. She slipped the crysknife from its sheath at her neck, held it sinister, tapped the activating stud with the sword tip. Resistance came alive as the aura of the target shield built up, pushing her weapon slowly and firmly away.

Prisms glittered. The target slipped to her left.

Alia followed with the tip of the long blade, thinking as she often did that the thing could almost be alive. But it was only servomotors and complex reflector circuits designed to lure the eyes away from danger, to confuse and teach. It was an instrument geared to react as she reacted, an anti-self which moved as she moved, balancing light on its prisms, shifting its target, offering its counter-blade.

Many blades appeared to lunge at her from the prisms, but only one was real. She countered the real one, slipped the sword past shield resistance to tap the target. A marker light came alive: red and glistening among the prisms . . . more distraction.

Again the thing attacked, moving at one-marker speed now, just a bit faster than it had at the beginning.

She parried and, against all caution, moved into the danger zone, scored with the crysknife.

Two lights glowed from the prisms.

Again, the thing increased speed, moving out on its rollers, drawn like a magnet to the motions of her body and the tip of her sword.

Attack—parry—counter.

Attack—parry—counter . . .

She had four lights alive in there now, and the thing was becoming more dangerous, moving faster with each light, offering more areas of confusion.

Five lights.

Sweat glistened on her naked skin. She existed now in a universe whose dimensions were outlined by the threatening blade, the target, bare feet against the practice floor, senses/nerves/muscles—motion against motion.

Attack—parry—counter.

Six lights . . . seven . . .

Eight!

She had never before risked eight.

In a recess of her mind there grew a sense of urgency, a crying out against such wildness as this. The instrument of prisms and target could not think, feel caution or remorse. And it carried a real blade. To go against less defeated the purpose of such training. That attacking blade could maim and it could kill. But the finest swordsmen in the Imperium never went against more than seven lights.

Nine!

Alia experienced a sense of supreme exaltation. Attacking blade and target became blurs among blurs. She felt that the sword in her hand had come alive. She was an anti-target. She did not move the blade; it moved her.

Ten!

Eleven!

Something flashed past her shoulder, slowed at the shield aura around the target, slid through and tripped the deactivating stud. The lights darkened. Prisms and target twisted their way to stillness.

Alia whirled, angered by the intrusion, but her reaction was thrown into tension by awareness of the supreme ability which had hurled that knife. It had been a throw timed to exquisite nicety—just fast enough to get through the shield zone and not too fast to be deflected.

And it had touched a one-millimeter spot within an eleven-light target.

Alia found her own emotions and tensions running down in a manner not unlike that of the target dummy. She was not at all surprised to see who had thrown the knife.

Paul stood just inside the training room doorway, Stilgar three steps behind him. Her brother's eyes were squinted in anger.

Alia, growing conscious of her nudity, thought to cover herself, found the idea amusing. What the eyes had seen could not be erased. Slowly, she replaced the crysknife in its sheath at her neck.

"I might've known," she said.

"I presume you know how dangerous that was," Paul said. He took his time reading the reactions on her face and body: the flush of her exertions coloring her skin, the wet fullness of her lips. There was a disquieting femaleness about her that he had never considered in his sister. He found it odd that he could look at a person who was this close to him and no longer recognize her in the identity framework which had seemed so fixed and familiar.

"That was madness," Stilgar rasped, coming up to stand beside Paul.

The words were angry, but Alia heard awe in his voice, saw it in his eyes.

"Eleven lights," Paul said, shaking his head.

"I'd have made it twelve if you hadn't interfered," she said. She began to pale under his close regard, added: "And why do the damned things have that many lights if we're not supposed to try for them?"

"A Bene Gesserit should ask the reasoning behind an open-ended system?" Paul asked.

"I suppose you never tried for more than seven!" she said, anger returning. His attentive posture began to annoy her.

"Just once," Paul said. "Gurney Halleck caught me on ten. My punishment was sufficiently embarrassing that I won't tell you what he did. And speaking of embarrassment . . ."

"Next time, perhaps you'll have yourselves announced," she said. She brushed past Paul into the bedroom, found a loose gray robe, slipped into it, began brushing her hair before a wall mirror. She felt sweaty, sad, a post-coitum kind of sadness that left her with a desire to bathe once more . . . and to sleep. "Why're you here?" she asked.

"My Lord," Stilgar said. There was an odd inflection in his voice that brought Alia around to stare at him.

"We're here at Irulan's suggestion," Paul said, "as strange as that may seem. She believes, and information in Stil's possession appears to confirm it, that our enemies are about to make a major try for—"

"My Lord!" Stilgar said, his voice sharper.

As her brother turned, questioning, Alia continued to look at the old Fremen Naib. Something about him now made her intensely aware that he was one of the primitives. Stilgar believed in a super-natural world very near him. It spoke to him in a simple pagan tongue dispelling all doubts. The natural universe in which he stood was fierce, unstoppable, and it lacked the common morality of the Imperium.

"Yes, Stil," Paul said. "Do you want to tell her why we came?"

"This isn't the time to talk of why we came," Stilgar said.

"What's wrong, Stil?"

Stilgar continued to stare at Alia. "Sire, are you blind?"

Paul turned back to his sister, a feeling of unease beginning to fill him. Of all his aides, only Stilgar dared speak to him in that tone, but even Stilgar measured the occasion by its need.

"This one must have a mate!" Stilgar blurted. "There'll be trouble if she's not wed, and that soon."

Alia whirled away, her face suddenly hot. *How did he touch me?* she wondered. Bene Gesserit self-control had been powerless to prevent her reaction. How had Stilgar done that? He hadn't the power of the Voice. She felt dismayed and angry.

"Listen to the great Stilgar!" Alia said, keeping her back to them, aware of a shrewish quality in her voice and unable to hide it. "Advice to maidens from Stilgar, the Fremen!"

"As I love you both, I must speak," Stilgar said, a profound dignity in his tone. "I did not become a chieftain among the Fremen by being blind to what moves men and women together. One needs no mysterious powers for this."

Paul weighed Stilgar's meaning, reviewed what they had seen here and his own undeniable male reaction to his own sister. Yes—there'd been a ruttish air about Alia, something wildly wanton. What had made her enter the practice floor in the nude? And risking her life in that foolhardy way! Eleven lights in the fencing prisms! That brainless automaton loomed in his mind with all the aspects of an ancient horror creature. Its possession was the shibboleth of this age, but it carried also the taint of old immorality. Once, they'd been guided by an artificial intelligence, computer brains. The Butlerian Jihad had ended that, but it hadn't ended the aura of aristocratic vice which enclosed such things.

Stilgar was right, of course. They must find a mate for Alia.

"I will see to it," Paul said. "Alia and I will discuss this later—privately."

Alia turned around, focused on Paul. Knowing how his mind worked, she realized she'd been the subject of a mentat decision, uncounted bits falling together in that human-computer analysis. There was an inexorable quality to this realization—a movement like the movement of planets. It carried something of the order of the universe in it, inevitable and terrifying.

"Sire," Stilgar said, "perhaps we'd—"

"Not now!" Paul snapped. "We've other problems at the moment."

Aware that she dared not try to match logic with her brother, Alia put the past few moments aside, Bene Gesserit fashion, said: "Irulan sent you?" She found herself experiencing menace in that thought.

"Indirectly," Paul said. "The information she gives us confirms our suspicion that the Guild is about to try for a sandworm."

"They'll try to capture a small one and attempt to start the spice cycle on some other world," Stilgar said. "It means they've found a world they consider suitable."

"It means they have Fremen accomplices!" Alia argued. "No off-worlder could capture a worm!"

"That goes without saying," Stilgar said.

"No, it doesn't," Alia said. She was outraged by such obtuseness. "Paul, certainly you . . ."

"The rot is setting in," Paul said. "We've known that for quite some time. I've never *seen* this other world, though, and that bothers me. If they—"

"*That* bothers you?" Alia demanded. "It means only that they've clouded its location with Steersmen the way they hide their sanctuaries."

Stilgar opened his mouth, closed it without speaking. He had the overwhelming sensation that his idols had admitted blasphemous weakness.

Paul, sensing Stilgar's disquiet, said: "We've an immediate problem! I want your opinion, Alia. Stilgar suggests we expand our patrols in the open bled and reinforce the sietch watch. It's just possible we could spot a landing party and prevent the—"

"With a Steersman guiding them?" Alia asked.

"They *are* desperate, aren't they?" Paul agreed. "*That* is why I'm here."

"What've they *seen* that we haven't?" Alia asked.

"Precisely."

Alia nodded, remembering her thoughts about the new Dune Tarot. Quickly, she recounted her fears.

"Throwing a blanket over us," Paul said.

"With adequate patrols," Stilgar ventured, "we might prevent the—"

"We prevent nothing . . . forever," Alia said. She didn't like the *feel* of the way Stilgar's mind was working now. He had narrowed his scope, eliminated obvious essentials. This was not the Stilgar she remembered.

"We must count on their getting a worm," Paul said. "Whether they can start the melange cycle on another planet is a different question. They'll need more than a worm."

Stilgar looked from brother to sister. Out of ecological thinking that had been ground into him by sietch life, he grasped their meaning. A captive worm couldn't live except within a bit of Arrakis—sand plankton, Little Makers and all. The Guild's problem was large, but not impossible. His own growing uncertainty lay in a different area.

"Then your visions do not detect the Guild at its work?" he asked.

"Damnation!" Paul exploded.

Alia studied Stilgar, sensing the savage sideshow of ideas taking place in his mind. He was hung on a rack of enchantment. Magic! Magic! To glimpse the future was to steal terrifying fire from a sacred flame. It held the attraction of ultimate peril, souls ventured and lost. One brought back from the formless, dangerous distances something with form and power. But Stilgar was beginning to sense other forces, perhaps greater powers beyond that unknown horizon. His Queen Witch and Sorcerer Friend betrayed dangerous weaknesses.

"Stilgar," Alia said, fighting to hold him, "you stand in a valley between dunes. I stand on the crest. I see where you do not see. And, among other things, I see mountains which conceal the distances."

"There are things hidden from you," Stilgar said. "This you've always said."

"All power is limited," Alia said.

"And danger may come from behind the mountains," Stilgar said.

"It's *something* on that order," Alia said.

Stilgar nodded, his gaze fastened on Paul's face. "But whatever comes from behind the mountains must cross the dunes."

The most dangerous game in the universe is to govern from an oracular base. We do not consider ourselves wise enough or brave enough to play that game. The measures detailed here for regulation in lesser matters are as near as we dare venture to the brink of government. For our purposes, we borrow a definition from the Bene Gesserit and we consider the various worlds as gene pools, sources of teachings and teachers, sources of the possible. Our goal is not to rule, but to tap these gene pools, to learn, and to free ourselves from all restraints imposed by dependency and government.

—"THE ORGY AS A TOOL OF STATECRAFT," CHAPTER THREE OF THE STEERSMAN'S GUILD

"Is that where your father died?" Edric asked, sending a beam pointer from his tank to a jeweled marker on one of the relief maps adorning a wall of Paul's reception salon.

"That's the shrine of his skull," Paul said. "My father died a prisoner on a Harkonnen frigate in the sink below us."

"Oh, yes: I recall the story now," Edric said. "Something about killing the old Baron Harkonnen, his mortal enemy." Hoping he didn't betray too much of the terror which small enclosures such as this room imposed upon him, Edric rolled over in the orange gas, directed his gaze at Paul, who sat alone on a long divan of striped gray and black.

"My sister killed the Baron," Paul said, voice and manner dry, "just before the battle of Arrakeen."

And why, he wondered, did the Guild man-fish reopen old wounds in this place and at this time?

The Steersman appeared to be fighting a losing battle to contain his nervous energies. Gone were the languid fish motions of their earlier encounter. Edric's tiny eyes jerked here . . . there, questing and measuring. The one attendant who had accompanied him in here stood apart near the line of houseguards ranging the end wall at Paul's left. The attendant worried Paul—hulking, thick-necked, blunt and vacant face. The man had entered the salon, nudging Edric's tank along on its supporting field, walking with a stranger's gait, arms akimbo.

Scytale, Edric had called him. *Scytale, an aide.*

The aide's surface shouted stupidity, but the eyes betrayed him. They laughed at everything they saw.

"Your concubine appeared to enjoy the performance of the Face Dancers," Edric said. "It pleases me that I could provide that small entertainment. I particularly enjoyed her reaction to seeing her own features simultaneously repeated by the whole troupe."

"Isn't there a warning against Guildsmen bearing gifts?" Paul asked.

And he thought of the performance out there in the Great Hall. The dancers had entered in the costumes and guise of the Dune Tarot, flinging themselves about in seemingly random patterns that devolved into fire eddies and ancient prognostic designs. Then had come the rulers—a parade of kings and emperors like faces on coins, formal and stiff in outline, but curiously fluid. And the jokes: a copy of Paul's own face and body, Chani repeated across the floor of the Hall, even Stilgar, who had grunted and shuddered while others laughed.

"But our gifts have the kindest intent," Edric protested.

"How kindly can you be?" Paul asked. "The ghola you gave us believes he was designed to destroy us."

"Destroy you, Sire?" Edric asked, all bland attention. "Can one destroy a god?"

Stilgar, entering on the last words, stopped, glared at the guards. They were much farther from Paul than he liked. Angrily he motioned them closer.

"It's all right, Stil," Paul said, lifting a hand. "Just a friendly discussion. Why don't you move the Ambassador's tank over by the end of my divan?"

Stilgar, weighing the order, saw that it would put the Steersman's tank between Paul and the hulking aide, much too close to Paul, but . . .

"It's all right, Stil," Paul repeated, and he gave the private hand-signal which made the order an imperative.

Moving with obvious reluctance, Stilgar pushed the tank closer to Paul. He didn't like the feel of the container or the heavily perfumed smell of melange around it. He took up a position at the corner of the tank beneath the orbiting device through which the Steersman spoke.

"To kill a god," Paul said. "That's very interesting. But who says I'm a god?"

"Those who worship you," Edric said, glancing pointedly at Stilgar.

"Is this what you believe?" Paul asked.

"What I believe is of no moment, Sire," Edric said. "It seems to most observers, however, that you conspire to make a god of yourself. And one might ask if that is something any mortal can do . . . safely?"

Paul studied the Guildsman. Repellent creature, but perceptive. It was a question Paul had asked himself time and again. But he had seen enough alternate Timelines to know of worse possibilities than accepting godhead for himself. Much worse. These were not, however, the normal avenues for a Steersman to probe. Curious. Why had that question been asked? What could Edric hope to gain by such effrontery? Paul's thoughts went *flick* (the association of Tleilaxu would be behind this move)—*flick* (the Jihad's recent Sembou victory would bear on Edric's action)—*flick* (various Bene Gesserit credos showed themselves here)—*flick* . . .

A process involving thousands of information bits poured flickering through his computational awareness. It required perhaps three seconds.

"Does a Steersman question the guidelines of prescience?" Paul asked, putting Edric on the weakest ground.

This disturbed the Steersman, but he covered well, coming up with what sounded like a long aphorism: "No man of intelligence questions the fact of prescience, Sire. Oracular vision has been known to men since most ancient times. It has a way of entangling us when we least suspect. Luckily, there are other forces in our universe."

"Greater than prescience?" Paul asked, pressing him.

"If prescience alone existed and did everything, Sire, it would annihilate itself. Nothing but prescience? Where could it be applied except to its own degenerating movements?"

"There's always the human situation," Paul agreed.

"A precarious thing at best," Edric said, "without confusing it by hallucinations."

"Are my visions no more than hallucinations?" Paul asked, mock sadness in his voice. "Or do you imply that my worshippers hallucinate?"

Stilgar, sensing the mounting tensions, moved a step nearer Paul, fixed his attention on the Guildsman reclining in the tank.

"You twist my words, Sire," Edric protested. An odd sense of violence lay suspended in the words.

Violence here? Paul wondered. *They wouldn't dare! Unless* (and he glanced at his guards) *the forces which protected him were to be used in replacing him.*

"But you accuse me of conspiring to make a god of myself," Paul said, pitching his voice that only Edric and Stilgar might hear. "Conspire?"

"A poor choice of words, perhaps, my Lord," Edric said.

"But significant," Paul said. "It says you expect the worst of me."

Edric arched his neck, stared sideways at Stilgar with a look of apprehension. "People always expect the worst of the rich and powerful, Sire. It is said one can always tell an aristocrat: he reveals only those of his vices which will make him popular."

A tremor passed across Stilgar's face.

Paul looked up at the movement, sensing the thoughts and angers whispering in Stilgar's mind. How dared this Guildsman talk thus to Muad'Dib?

"You're not joking, of course," Paul said.

"Joking, Sire?"

Paul grew aware of dryness in his mouth. He felt that there were too many people in this room, that the air he breathed had passed through too many lungs. The taint of melange from Edric's tank felt threatening.

"Who might my accomplices be in such a conspiracy?" Paul asked presently. "Do you nominate the Qizarate?"

Edric's shrug stirred the orange gas around his head. He no longer appeared concerned by Stilgar, although the Fremen continued to glare at him.

"Are you suggesting that my missionaries of the Holy Orders, *all of them*, are preaching subtle falsehood?" Paul insisted.

"It could be a question of self-interest and sincerity," Edric said.

Stilgar put a hand to the crysknife beneath his robe.

Paul shook his head, said: "Then you accuse me of insincerity."

"I'm not sure that *accuse* is the proper word, Sire."

The boldness of this creature! Paul thought. And he said: "Accused or not, you're saying my bishops and I are no better than power-hungry brigands."

"Power-hungry, Sire?" Again, Edric looked at Stilgar. "Power tends to isolate those who hold too much of it. Eventually, they lose touch with reality . . . and fall."

"M'Lord," Stilgar growled, "you've had men executed for less!"

"Men, yes," Paul agreed. "But this is a Guild Ambassador."

"He accuses you of an unholy fraud!" Stilgar said.

"His thinking interests me, Stil," Paul said. "Contain your anger and remain alert."

"As Muad'Dib commands."

"Tell me, Steersman," Paul said, "how could we maintain this hypothetical fraud over such enormous distances of space and time without the means to watch every missionary, to examine every nuance in every Qizarate priory and temple?"

"What is time to you?" Edric asked.

Stilgar frowned in obvious puzzlement. And he thought: *Muad'Dib has often said he sees past the veils of time. What is the Guildsman really saying?*

"Wouldn't the structure of such a fraud begin to show holes?"

Paul asked. "Significant disagreements, schisms . . . doubts, confessions of guilt—surely fraud could not suppress all these."

"What religion and self-interest cannot hide, governments can," Edric said.

"Are you testing the limits of my tolerance?" Paul asked.

"Do my arguments lack all merit?" Edric countered.

Does he want us to kill him? Paul wondered. *Is Edric offering himself as a sacrifice?*

"I prefer the cynical view," Paul said, testing. "You obviously are trained in all the lying tricks of statecraft, the double meanings and the power words. Language is nothing more than a weapon to you and, thus, you test my armor."

"The cynical view," Edric said, a smile stretching his mouth. "And rulers are notoriously cynical where religions are concerned. Religion, too, is a weapon. What manner of weapon is religion when it becomes the government?"

Paul felt himself go inwardly still, a profound caution gripping him. To whom was Edric speaking? Damnable clever words, heavy with manipulation leverages—that undertone of comfortable humor, the unspoken air of shared secrets: his manner said he and Paul were two sophisticates, men of a wider universe who understood things not granted common folk. With a feeling of shock, Paul realized that he had not been the main target for all this rhetoric. This affliction visited upon the court had been speaking for the benefit of others—speaking to Stilgar, to the household guards . . . perhaps even to the hulking aide.

"Religious *mana* was thrust upon me," Paul said. "I did not seek it." And he thought: *There! Let this man-fish think himself victorious in our battle of words!*

"Then why have you not disavowed it, Sire?" Edric asked.

"Because of my sister Alia," Paul said, watching Edric carefully.

"She is a goddess. Let me urge caution where Alia is concerned lest she strike you dead with her glance."

A gloating smile began forming on Edric's mouth, was replaced by a look of shock.

"I am deadly serious," Paul said, watching the shock spread, seeing Stilgar nod.

In a bleak voice, Edric said: "You have mauled my confidence in you, Sire. And no doubt that was your intent."

"Do not be certain you know my intent," Paul said, and he signaled Stilgar that the audience was at an end.

To Stilgar's questioning gesture asking if Edric were to be assassinated, Paul gave a negative hand-sign, amplified it with an imperative lest Stilgar take matters into his own hands.

Scytale, Edric's aide, moved to the rear corner of the tank, nudged it toward the door. When he came opposite Paul, he stopped, turned that laughing gaze on Paul, said: "If my Lord permits?"

"Yes, what is it?" Paul asked, noting how Stilgar moved close in answer to the implied menace from this man.

"Some say," Scytale said, "that people cling to Imperial leadership because space is infinite. They feel lonely without a unifying symbol. For a lonely people, the Emperor is a definite place. They can turn toward him and say: 'See, there He is. He makes us one.' Perhaps religion serves the same purpose, m'Lord."

Scytale nodded pleasantly, gave Edric's tank another nudge. They moved out of the salon, Edric supine in his tank, eyes closed. The Steersman appeared spent, all his nervous energies exhausted.

Paul stared after the shambling figure of Scytale, wondering at the man's words. A peculiar fellow, that Scytale, he thought. While he was speaking, he had radiated a feeling of many people—as though his entire genetic inheritance lay exposed on his skin.

"That was odd," Stilgar said, speaking to no one in particular.

Paul arose from the divan as a guard closed the door behind Edric and the escort.

"Odd," Stilgar repeated. A vein throbbed at his temple.

Paul dimmed the salon's lights, moved to a window which opened onto an angled cliff of his Keep. Lights glittered far below—pigmy movement. A work gang moved down there bringing giant plasmeld blocks to repair a facade of Alia's temple which had been damaged by a freak twisting of a sandblast wind.

"That was a foolish thing, Usul, inviting that creature into these chambers," Stilgar said.

Usul, Paul thought. *My sietch name. Stilgar reminds me that he ruled over me once, that he saved me from the desert.*

"Why did you do it?" Stilgar asked, speaking from close behind Paul.

"Data," Paul said. "I need more data."

"Is it not dangerous to try meeting this threat *only* as a mentat?"

That was perceptive, Paul thought.

Mentat computation remained finite. You couldn't say something boundless within the boundaries of any language. Mentat abilities had their uses, though. He said as much now, daring Stilgar to refute his argument.

"There's always something outside," Stilgar said. "Some things best *kept* outside."

"Or inside," Paul said. And he accepted for a moment his own oracular/mentat summation. Outside, yes. And inside: here lay the true horror. How could he protect himself from himself? They certainly were setting him up to destroy himself, but this was a position hemmed in by even more terrifying possibilities.

His reverie was broken by the sound of rapid footsteps. The figure of Korba the Qizara surged through the doorway backlighted by the brilliant illumination in the hallways. He entered as though hurled by an unseen force and came to an almost immediate halt when he encountered the salon's gloom. His hands appeared to be full of shigawire reels. They glittered in the light from the hall, strange little round jewels that were extinguished as a guardsman's hand came into view, closed the door.

"Is that you, m'Lord?" Korba asked, peering into the shadows.

"What is it?" Stilgar asked.

"Stilgar?"

"We're both here. What is it?"

"I'm disturbed by this reception for the Guildsman."

"Disturbed?" Paul asked.

"The people say, m'Lord, that you honor our enemies."

"Is that all?" Paul said. "Are those the reels I asked you to bring earlier?" He indicated the shigawire orbs in Korba's hands.

"Reels . . . oh! Yes, m'Lord. These are the histories. Will you view them here?"

"I've viewed them. I want them for Stilgar here."

"For me?" Stilgar asked. He felt resentment grow at what he interpreted as caprice on Paul's part. Histories! Stilgar had sought out Paul earlier to discuss the logistics computations for the Zabulon conquest. The Guild Ambassador's presence had intervened. And now—Korba with histories!

"How much history do you know?" Paul mused aloud, studying the shadowy figure beside him.

"M'Lord, I can name every world our people touched in their migrations. I know the reaches of Imperial—"

"The Golden Age of Earth, have you ever studied that?"

"Earth? Golden Age?" Stilgar was irritated and puzzled. Why

would Paul wish to discuss myths from the dawn of time? Stilgar's mind still felt crammed with Zabulon data—computations from the staff mentats: two hundred and five attack frigates with thirty legions, support battalions, pacification cadres, Qizarate missionaries . . . the food requirements (he had the figures right here in his mind) and melange . . . weaponry, uniforms, medals . . . urns for the ashes of the dead . . . the number of specialists—men to produce raw materials of propaganda, clerks, accountants . . . spies . . . and spies upon the spies . . .

"I brought the pulse-synchronizer attachment, also, m'Lord," Korba ventured. He obviously sensed the tensions building between Paul and Stilgar and was disturbed by them.

Stilgar shook his head from side to side. *Pulse-synchronizer?* Why would Paul wish him to use a mnemonic flutter-system on a shigawire projector? Why scan for specific data in histories? This was mentat work! As usual, Stilgar found he couldn't escape a deep suspicion at the thought of using a projector and attachments. The thing always immersed him in disturbing sensations, an overwhelming shower of data which his mind sorted out later, surprising him with information he had not known he possessed.

"Sire, I came with the Zabulon computations," Stilgar said.

"Dehydrate the Zabulon computations!" Paul snapped, using the obscene Fremen term which meant that here was moisture no man could demean himself by touching.

"M'Lord!"

"Stilgar," Paul said, "you urgently need a sense of balance which can come only from an understanding of long-term effects. What little information we have about the old times, the pittance of data which the Butlerians left us, Korba has brought it for you. Start with the Genghis Khan."

"Ghengis . . . Khan? Was he of the Sardaukar, m'Lord?"

"Oh, long before that. He killed . . . perhaps four million."

"He must've had formidable weaponry to kill that many, Sire. Las-beams, perhaps, or . . ."

"He didn't kill them himself, Stil. He killed the way I kill, by sending out his legions. There's another emperor I want you to note in passing—a Hitler. He killed more than six million. Pretty good for those days."

"Killed . . . by his legions?" Stilgar asked.

"Yes."

"Not very impressive statistics, m'Lord."

"Very good, Stil." Paul glanced at the reels in Korba's hands. Korba stood with them as though he wished he could drop them and flee. "Statistics: at a conservative estimate, I've killed sixty-one billion, sterilized ninety planets, completely demoralized five hundred others. I've wiped out the followers of forty religions which had existed since—"

"Unbelievers!" Korba protested. "Unbelievers all!"

"No," Paul said. "Believers."

"My Liege makes a joke," Korba said, voice trembling. "The Jihad has brought ten thousand worlds into the shining light of—"

"Into the darkness," Paul said. "We'll be a hundred generations recovering from Muad'Dib's Jihad. I find it hard to imagine that anyone will ever surpass this." A barking laugh erupted from his throat.

"What amuses Muad'Dib?" Stilgar asked.

"I am not amused. I merely had a sudden vision of the Emperor Hitler saying something similar. No doubt he did."

"No other ruler ever had your powers," Korba argued. "Who would dare challenge you? Your legions control the known universe and all the—"

"The legions control," Paul said. "I wonder if they know this?"

"You control your legions, Sire," Stilgar interrupted, and it was obvious from the tone of his voice that he suddenly felt his own position in that chain of command, his own hand guiding all that power.

Having set Stilgar's thoughts in motion along the track he wanted, Paul turned his full attention to Korba, said: "Put the reels here on the divan." As Korba obeyed, Paul said: "How goes the reception, Korba? Does my sister have everything well in hand?"

"Yes, m'Lord." Korba's tone was wary. "And Chani watches from the spy hole. She suspects there may be Sardaukar in the Guild entourage."

"No doubt she's correct," Paul said. "The jackals gather."

"Bannerjee," Stilgar said, naming the chief of Paul's Security detail, "was worried earlier that some of them might try to penetrate the private areas of the Keep."

"Have they?"

"Not yet."

"But there was some confusion in the formal gardens," Korba said.

"What sort of confusion?" Stilgar demanded.

Paul nodded.

"Strangers coming and going," Korba said, "trampling the plants, whispered conversations—I heard reports of some disturbing remarks."

"Such as?" Paul asked.

"*Is this the way our taxes are spent?* I'm told the Ambassador himself asked that question."

"I don't find that surprising," Paul said. "Were there many strangers in the gardens?"

"Dozens, m'Lord."

"Bannerjee stationed picked troopers at the vulnerable doors, m'Lord," Stilgar said. He turned as he spoke, allowing the salon's single remaining light to illuminate half his face. The peculiar lighting, the face, all touched a node of memory in Paul's mind—something from the desert. Paul didn't bother bringing it to full recall, his attention being focused on how Stilgar had pulled back mentally. The Fremen had a tight-skinned forehead which mirrored almost every thought flickering across his mind. He was suspicious now, profoundly suspicious of his Emperor's odd behavior.

"I don't like the intrusion into the gardens," Paul said. "Courtesy to guests is one thing, and the formal necessities of greeting an envoy, but this . . ."

"I'll see to removing them," Korba said. "Immediately."

"Wait!" Paul ordered as Korba started to turn.

In the abrupt stillness of the moment, Stilgar edged himself into a position where he could study Paul's face. It was deftly done. Paul admired the way of it, an achievement devoid of any forwardness. It was a Fremen thing: slyness touched by respect for another's privacy, a movement of necessity.

"What time is it?" Paul asked.

"Almost midnight, Sire," Korba said.

"Korba, I think you may be my finest creation," Paul said.

"Sire!" There was injury in Korba's voice.

"Do you feel awe of me?" Paul asked.

"You are Paul-Muad'Dib who was Usul in our sietch," Korba said. "You know my devotion to—"

"Have you ever felt like an apostle?" Paul asked.

Korba obviously misunderstood the words, but correctly interpreted the tone. "My Emperor knows I have a clean conscience!"

"Shai-hulud save us," Paul murmured.

The questioning silence of the moment was broken by the sound of someone whistling as he walked down the outer hall. The whistling was stilled by a guardsman's barked command as it came opposite the door.

"Korba, I think you may survive all this," Paul said. And he read the growing light of understanding on Stilgar's face.

"The strangers in the gardens, Sire?" Stilgar asked.

"Ahh, yes," Paul said. "Have Bannerjee put them out, Stil. Korba will assist."

"Me, Sire?" Korba betrayed deep disquiet.

"Some of my friends have forgotten they once were Fremen," Paul said, speaking to Korba, but designing his words for Stilgar. "You will mark down the ones Chani identifies as Sardaukar and you will have them killed. Do it yourself. I want it done quietly and without undue disturbance. We must keep in mind that there's more to religion and government than approving treaties and sermons."

"I obey the orders of Muad'Dib," Korba whispered.

"The Zabulon computations?" Stilgar asked.

"Tomorrow," Paul said. "And when the strangers are removed from the gardens, announce that the reception is ended. The party's over, Stil."

"I understand, m'Lord."

"I'm sure you do," Paul said.

Here lies a toppled god—
His fall was not a small one.
We did but build his pedestal,
A narrow and a tall one.

—TLEILAXU EPIGRAM

Alia crouched, resting elbows on knees, chin on fists, stared at the body on the dune—a few bones and some tattered flesh that once had been a young woman. The hands, the head, most of the upper torso were gone—eaten by the coriolis wind. The sand all around bore the tracks of her brother's medics and questors. They were gone now, all excepting the mortuary attendants who stood to one side with Hayt, the ghola, waiting for her to finish her mysterious perusal of what had been written here.

A wheat-colored sky enfolded the scene in the glaucous light common to midafternoon for these latitudes.

The body had been discovered several hours earlier by a low-flying courier whose instruments had detected a faint water trace where none should be. His call had brought the experts. And they had learned—what? That this had been a woman of about twenty years,

Fremen, addicted to semuta . . . and she had died here in the crucible of the desert from the effects of a subtle poison of Tleilaxu origin.

To die in the desert was a common enough occurrence. But a Fremen addicted to semuta, this was such a rarity that Paul had sent her to examine the scene in the ways their mother had taught them.

Alia felt that she had accomplished nothing here except to cast her own aura of mystery about a scene that was already mysterious enough. She heard the ghola's feet stir the sand, looked at him. His attention rested momentarily upon the escort 'thopters circling overhead like a flock of ravens.

Beware of the Guild bearing gifts, Alia thought.

The mortuary 'thopter and her own craft stood on the sand near a rock outcropping behind the ghola. Focusing on the grounded 'thopters filled Alia with a craving to be airborne and away from here.

But Paul had thought she might see something here which others would miss. She squirmed in her stillsuit. It felt raspingly unfamiliar after all the suitless months of city life. She studied the ghola, wondering if he might know something important about this peculiar death. A lock of his black-goat hair, she saw, had escaped his stillsuit hood. She sensed her hand longing to tuck that hair back into place.

As though lured by this thought, his gleaming gray metal eyes turned toward her. The eyes set her trembling and she tore her gaze away from him.

A Fremen woman had died here from a poison called "the throat of hell."

A Fremen addicted to semuta.

She shared Paul's disquiet at this conjunction.

The mortuary attendants waited patiently. This corpse contained not enough water for them to salvage. They felt no need to hurry. And they'd believe that Alia, through some glyptic art, was reading a strange truth in these remains.

No strange truth came to her.

There was only a distant feeling of anger deep within her at the obvious thoughts in the attendants' minds. It was a product of the damned religious mystery. She and her brother could not be *people*. They had to be something more. The Bene Gesserit had seen to that by manipulating Atreides ancestry. Their mother had contributed to it by thrusting them onto the path of witchery.

And Paul perpetuated the difference.

The Reverend Mothers encapsulated in Alia's memories stirred restlessly, provoking adab flashes of thought: *"Peace, Little One! You are what you are. There are compensations."*

Compensations!

She summoned the ghola with a gesture.

He stopped beside her, attentive, patient.

"What do you see in this?" she asked.

"We may never learn who it was died here," he said. "The head, the teeth are gone. The hands ... Unlikely such a one had a genetic record somewhere to which her cells could be matched."

"Tleilaxu poison," she said. "What do you make of that?"

"Many people buy such poisons."

"True enough. And this flesh is too far gone to be regrown as was done with your body."

"Even if you could trust the Tleilaxu to do it," he said.

She nodded, stood. "You will fly me back to the city now."

When they were airborne and pointed north, she said: "You fly exactly as Duncan Idaho did."

He cast a speculative glance at her. "Others have told me this."

"What are you thinking now?" she asked.

"Many things."

"Stop dodging my question, damn you!"

"Which question?"

She glared at him.

He saw the glare, shrugged.

How like Duncan Idaho, that gesture, she thought. Accusingly, her voice thick and with a catch in it, she said: "I merely wanted your reactions voiced to play my own thoughts against them. That young woman's death bothers me."

"I was not thinking about that."

"What were you thinking about?"

"About the strange emotions I feel when people speak of the one I may have been."

"May have been?"

"The Tleilaxu are very clever."

"Not that clever. You were Duncan Idaho."

"Very likely. It's the prime computation."

"So you get emotional?"

"To a degree. I feel eagerness. I'm uneasy. There's a tendency to tremble and I must devote effort to controlling it. I get . . . flashes of imagery."

"What imagery?"

"It's too rapid to recognize. Flashes. Spasms . . . almost memories."

"Aren't you curious about such memories?"

"Of course. Curiosity urges me forward, but I move against a heavy reluctance. I think: 'What if I'm not the one they believe me to be?' I don't like that thought."

"And this is all you were thinking?"

"You know better than that, Alia."

How dare he use my given name? She felt anger rise and go down beneath the memory of the way he'd spoken: softly throbbing under-tones, casual male confidence. A muscle twitched along her jaw. She clenched her teeth.

"Isn't that El Kuds down there?" he asked, dipping a wing briefly, causing a sudden flurry in their escort.

She looked down at their shadows rippling across the promontory above Harg Pass, at the cliff and the rock pyramid containing the skull of her father. *El Kuds—the Holy Place.*

"That's the Holy Place," she said.

"I must visit that place one day," he said. "Nearness to your fa-ther's remains may bring memories I can capture."

She saw suddenly how strong must be this need to know who he'd been. It was a central compulsion with him. She looked back at the rocks, the cliff with its base sloping into a dry beach and a sea of sand—cinnamon rock lifting from the dunes like a ship breasting waves.

"Circle back," she said.

"The escort . . ."

"They'll follow. Swing under them."

He obeyed.

"Do you truly serve my brother?" she asked, when he was on the new course, the escort following.

"I serve the Atreides," he said, his tone formal.

And she saw his right hand lift, fall—almost the old salute of Caladan. A pensive look came over his face. She watched him peer down at the rock pyramid.

"What bothers you?" she asked.

His lips moved. A voice emerged, brittle, tight: "He was . . . he was . . ." A tear slid down his cheek.

Alia found herself stilled by Fremen awe. He gave water to the dead! Compulsively, she touched a finger to his cheek, felt the tear.

"Duncan," she whispered.

He appeared locked to the 'thopter's controls, gaze fastened to the tomb below.

She raised her voice: "Duncan!"

He swallowed, shook his head, looked at her, the metal eyes glistening. "I . . . felt . . . an arm . . . on my shoulders," he whispered. "I felt it! An arm." His throat worked. "It was . . . a friend. It was . . . my friend."

"Who?"

"I don't know. I think it was . . . I don't know."

The call light began flashing in front of Alia, their escort captain wanting to know why they returned to the desert. She took the microphone, explained that they had paid a brief homage to her father's tomb. The captain reminded her that it was late.

"We will go to Arrakeen now," she said, replacing the microphone.

Hayt took a deep breath, banked their 'thopter around to the north.

"It was my father's arm you felt, wasn't it?" she asked.

"Perhaps."

His voice was that of the mentat computing probabilities, and she saw he had regained his composure.

"Are you aware of how I know my father?" she asked.

"I have some idea."

"Let me make it clear," she said. Briefly, she explained how she had awakened to Reverend Mother awareness before birth, a terrified fetus with the knowledge of countless lives embedded in her nerve cells—and all this after the death of her father.

"I know my father as my mother knew him," she said. "In every last detail of every experience she shared with him. In a way, I am my mother. I have all her memories up to the moment when she drank the Water of Life and entered the trance of transmigration."

"Your brother explained something of this."

"He did? Why?"

"I asked."

"Why?"

"A mentat requires data."

"Oh." She looked down at the flat expanse of the Shield Wall—tortured rock, pits and crevices.

He saw the direction of her gaze, said: "A very exposed place, that down there."

"But an easy place to hide," she said. She looked at him. "It reminds me of a human mind . . . with all its concealments."

"Ahhh," he said.

"Ahhh? What does that mean—ahhh?" She was suddenly angry with him and the reason for it escaped her.

"You'd like to know what my mind conceals," he said. It was a statement, not a question.

"How do you know I haven't exposed you for what you are by my powers of prescience?" she demanded.

"Have you?" He seemed genuinely curious.

"No!"

"Sibyls have limits," he said.

He appeared to be amused and this reduced Alia's anger. "Amused? Have you no respect for my powers?" she asked. The question sounded weakly argumentative even to her own ears.

"I respect your omens and portents perhaps more than you think," he said. "I was in the audience for your Morning Ritual."

"And what does that signify?"

"You've great ability with symbols," he said, keeping his attention on the 'thopter's controls. "That's a Bene Gesserit thing, I'd say. But, as with many witches, you've become careless of your powers."

She felt a spasm of fear, blared: "How dare you?"

"I dare much more than my makers anticipated," he said. "Because of that rare fact, I remain with your brother."

Alia studied the steel balls which were his eyes: no human expression there. The stillsuit hood concealed the line of his jaw. His mouth remained firm, though. Great strength in it . . . and determination. His words had carried a reassuring intensity. ". . . dare much more . . ." That was a thing Duncan Idaho might have said. Had the Tleilaxu fashioned their ghola better than they knew—or was this mere sham, part of his conditioning?

"Explain yourself, ghola," she commanded.

"Know thyself, is that thy commandment?" he asked.

Again, she felt that he was amused. "Don't bandy words with me, you . . . you *thing*!" she said. She put a hand to the crysknife in its throat sheath. "Why were you given to my brother?"

"Your brother tells me that you watched the presentation," he said. "You've heard me answer that question for him."

"Answer it again . . . for me!"

"I am intended to destroy him."

"Is that the mentat speaking?"

"You know the answer to that without asking," he chided. "And you know, as well, that such a gift wasn't necessary. Your brother already was destroying himself quite adequately."

She weighed these words, her hand remaining on the haft of her knife. A tricky answer, but there was sincerity in the voice.

"Then why such a gift?" she probed.

"It may have amused the Tleilaxu. And, it is true, that the Guild asked for me as a gift."

"Why?"

"Same answer."

"How am I careless of my powers?"

"How are you employing them?" he countered.

His question slashed through to her own misgivings. She took her hand away from the knife, asked: "Why do you say my brother was destroying himself?"

"Oh, come now, child! Where are these vaunted powers? Have you no ability to reason?"

Controlling anger, she said: "Reason *for* me, mentat."

"Very well." He glanced around at their escort, returned his attention to their course. The plain of Arrakeen was beginning to show beyond the northern rim of the Shield Wall. The pattern of the pan and graben villages remained indistinct beneath a dust pall, but the distant gleam of Arrakeen could be discerned.

"Symptoms," he said. "Your brother keeps an official Panegyrist who—"

"Who was a gift of the Fremen Naibs!"

"An odd gift from friends," he said. "Why would they surround him with flattery and servility? Have you really listened to this Panegyrist? '*The people are illuminated by Muad'Dib. The Umma Regent, our Emperor, came out of darkness to shine resplendently upon all men. He is our Sire. He is precious water from an endless fountain. He spills joy for all the universe to drink,*' Pah!"

Speaking softly, Alia said: "If I but repeated your words for our Fremen escort, they'd hack you into bird feed."

"Then tell them."

"My brother rules by the natural law of heaven!"

"You don't believe that, so why say it?"

"How do you know what I believe?" She experienced trembling that no Bene Gesserit powers could control. This ghola was having an effect she hadn't anticipated.

"You commanded me to reason as a mentat," he reminded her.

"No mentat knows what I believe!" She took two deep, shuddering breaths. "How dare you judge us?"

"Judge you? I don't judge."

"You've no idea how we were taught!"

"Both of you were taught to govern," he said. "You were conditioned to an overweening thirst for power. You were imbued with a shrewd grasp of politics and a deep understanding for the uses of war and ritual. Natural law? What natural law? That myth haunts human history. Haunts! It's a ghost. It's insubstantial, unreal. Is your Jihad a natural law?"

"Mentat jabber," she sneered.

"I'm a servant of the Atreides and I speak with candor," he said.

"Servant? We've no servants; only disciples."

"And I am a disciple of awareness," he said. "Understand that, child, and you—"

"Don't call me child!" she snapped. She slipped her crysknife half out of its sheath.

"I stand corrected." He glanced at her, smiled, returned his attention to piloting the 'thopter. The cliffsided structure of the Atreides Keep could be made out now, dominating the northern suburbs of Arrakeen. "You are something ancient in flesh that is little more than a child," he said. "And the flesh is disturbed by its new womanhood."

"I don't know why I listen to you," she growled, but she let the crysknife fall back into its sheath, wiped her palm on her robe. The palm, wet with perspiration, disturbed her sense of Fremen frugality. Such a waste of the body's moisture!

"You listen because you know I'm devoted to your brother," he said. "My actions are clear and easily understood."

"Nothing about you is clear and easily understood. You're the most complex creature I've ever seen. How do I know what the Tleilaxu built into you?"

"By mistake or intent," he said, "they gave me freedom to mold myself."

"You retreat into Zensunni parables," she accused. "The wise man molds himself—the fool lives only to die." Her voice was heavy with mimicry. "Disciple of awareness!"

"Men cannot separate means and enlightenment," he said.

"You speak riddles!"

"I speak to the opening mind."

"I'm going to repeat all this to Paul."

"He's heard most of it already."

She found herself overwhelmed by curiosity. "How is it you're still alive . . . and free? What did he say?"

"He laughed. And he said, 'People don't want a bookkeeper for an Emperor; they want a master, someone who'll protect them from change.' But he agreed that destruction of his Empire arises from himself."

"Why would he say such things?"

"Because I convinced him I understand his problem and will help him."

"What could you possibly have said to do that?"

He remained silent, banking the 'thopter into the downwind leg for a landing at the guard complex on the roof of the Keep.

"I demand you tell me what you said!"

"I'm not sure you could take it."

"I'll be the judge of that! I command you to speak at once!"

"Permit me to land us first," he said. And not waiting for her permission, he turned onto the base leg, brought the wings into optimum lift, settled gently onto the bright orange pad atop the roof.

"Now," Alia said. "Speak."

"I told him that to endure oneself may be the hardest task in the universe."

She shook her head. "That's . . . that's . . ."

"A bitter pill," he said, watching the guards run toward them across the roof, taking up their escort positions.

"Bitter nonsense!"

"The greatest palatinate earl and the lowliest stipendiary serf share the same problem. You cannot hire a mentat or any other intellect to solve it for you. There's no writ of inquest or calling of witnesses to provide answers. No servant—or disciple—can dress the wound. You dress it yourself or continue bleeding for all to see."

She whirled away from him, realizing in the instant of action what this betrayed about her own feelings. Without wile of voice or witch-wrought trickery, he had reached into her psyche once more. How did he do this?

"What have you told him to do?" she whispered.

"I told him to judge, to impose order."

Alia stared out at the guard, marking how patiently they waited—how orderly. "To dispense justice," she murmured.

"Not that!" he snapped. "I suggested that he judge, no more, guided by one principle, perhaps . . ."

"And that?"

"To keep his friends and destroy his enemies."

"To judge unjustly, then."

"What is justice? Two forces collide. Each may have the right in his own sphere. And here's where an Emperor commands orderly solutions. Those collisions he cannot prevent—he solves."

"How?"

"In the simplest way: he decides."

"Keeping his friends and destroying his enemies."

"Isn't that stability? People want order, this kind or some other. They sit in the prison of their hungers and see that war has become the sport of the rich. That's a dangerous form of sophistication. It's disorderly."

"I will suggest to my brother that you are much too dangerous and must be destroyed," she said, turning to face him.

"A solution I've already suggested," he said.

"And that's why you are dangerous," she said, measuring out her words. "You've mastered your passions."

"That is *not* why I'm dangerous." Before she could move, he leaned across, gripped her chin in one hand, planted his lips on hers.

It was a gentle kiss, brief. He pulled away and she stared at him with a shock leavened by glimpses of spasmodic grins on the faces of her guardsmen still standing at orderly attention outside.

Alia put a finger to her lips. There'd been such a sense of familiarity about that kiss. His lips had been flesh of a future she'd seen in some prescient byway. Breast heaving, she said: "I should have you flayed."

"Because I'm dangerous?"

"Because you presume too much!"

"I presume nothing. I take nothing which is not first offered to me. Be glad I did not take all that was offered." He opened his door, slid out. "Come along. We've dallied too long on a fool's errand." He strode toward the entrance dome beyond the pad.

Alia leaped out, ran to match his stride. "I'll tell him everything you've said and everything you did," she said.

"Good." He held the door for her.

"He will order you executed," she said, slipping into the dome.

"Why? Because I took the kiss I wanted?" He followed her, his movement forcing her back. The door slid closed behind him.

"The kiss *you* wanted!" Outrage filled her.

"All right, Alia. The kiss you wanted, then." He started to move around her toward the drop field.

As though his movement had propelled her into heightened awareness, she realized his candor—the utter truthfulness of him. *The kiss I wanted,* she told herself. *True.*

"Your truthfulness, that's what's dangerous," she said, following him.

"You return to the ways of wisdom," he said, not breaking his stride. "A mentat could not've stated the matter more directly. Now: what is it you saw in the desert?"

She grabbed his arm, forcing him to a halt. He'd done it again: shocked her mind into sharpened awareness.

"I can't explain it," she said, "but I keep thinking of the Face Dancers. Why is that?"

"That is why your brother sent you to the desert," he said, nodding. "Tell him of this persistent thought."

"But why?" She shook her head. "Why Face Dancers?"

"There's a young woman dead out there," he said. "Perhaps no young woman is reported missing among the Fremen."

I think what a joy it is to be alive, and I wonder if I'll ever leap inward to the root of this flesh and know myself as once I was. The root is there. Whether any act of mine can find it, that remains tangled in the future. But all things a man can do are mine. Any act of mine may do it.

—THE GHOLA SPEAKS
ALIA'S COMMENTARY

As he lay immersed in the screaming odor of the spice, staring inward through the oracular trance, Paul saw the moon become an elongated sphere. It rolled and twisted, hissing—the terrible hissing of a star being quenched in an infinite sea—down . . . down . . . down . . . like a ball thrown by a child.

It was gone.

This moon had not set. Realization engulfed him. It was gone: no moon. The earth quaked like an animal shaking its skin. Terror swept over him.

Paul jerked upright on his pallet, eyes wide open, staring. Part of him looked outward, part inward. Outwardly, he saw the plasmeld grill-work which vented his private room, and he knew he lay beside a stone-like abyss of his Keep. Inwardly, he continued to see the moon fall.

Out! Out!

His grillwork of plasmeld looked onto the blazing light of noon across Arrakeen. Inward—there lay blackest night. A shower of sweet odors from a garden roof nibbled at his senses, but no floral perfume could roll back that fallen moon.

Paul swung his feet to the cold surface of the floor, peered through the grillwork. He could see directly across to the gentle arc of a foot-bridge constructed of crystal-stabilized gold and platinum. Fire jewels from far Cedon decorated the bridge. It led to the galleries of the inner city across a pool and fountain filled with waterflowers. If he stood, Paul knew, he could look down into petals as clean and red as fresh blood whirling, turning there—disks of ambient color tossed on an emerald freshet.

His eyes absorbed the scene without pulling him from spice thralldom.

That terrible vision of a lost moon.

The vision suggested a monstrous loss of individual security. Perhaps he'd seen his civilization fall, toppled by its own pretensions.

A moon . . . a moon . . . a falling moon.

It had taken a massive dose of the spice essence to penetrate the mud thrown up by the tarot. All it had shown him was a falling moon and the hateful way he'd known from the beginning. To buy an end for the Jihad, to silence the volcano of butchery, he must discredit himself.

Disengage . . . disengage . . . disengage . . .

Floral perfume from the garden roof reminded him of Chani. He longed for her arms now, for the clinging arms of love and forgetfulness. But even Chani could not exorcise this vision. What would Chani say if he went to her with the statement that he had a particular death in mind? Knowing it to be inevitable, why not choose an aristocrat's death, ending life on a secret flourish, squandering any years that might have been? To die before coming to the end of willpower, was that not an aristocrat's choice?

He stood, crossed to the lapped opening in the grillwork, went out onto a balcony which looked upward to flowers and vines trailing from the garden. His mouth held the dryness of a desert march.

Moon . . . moon—where is that moon?

He thought of Alia's description, the young woman's body found in the dunes. A Fremen addicted to semuta! Everything fitted the hateful pattern.

You do not take from this universe, he thought. *It grants what it will.*

The remains of a conch shell from the seas of Mother Earth lay on a low table beside the balcony rail. He took its lustrous smoothness into his hands, tried to feel backward in Time. The pearl surface reflected glittering moons of light. He tore his gaze from it, peered upward past the garden to a sky become a conflagration—trails of rainbow dust shining in the silver sun.

My Fremen call themselves "Children of the Moon," he thought.

He put down the conch, strode along the balcony. Did that terrifying moon hold out hope of escape? He probed for meaning in the region of mystic communion. He felt weak, shaken, still gripped by the spice.

At the north end of his plasmeld chasm, he came in sight of the lower buildings of the government warren. Foot traffic thronged the roof walks. He felt that the people moved there like a frieze against a background of doors, walls, tile designs. The people were tiles! When he blinked, he could hold them frozen in his mind. A frieze.

A moon falls and is gone.

A feeling came over him that the city out there had been translated into an odd symbol for his universe. The buildings he could see had been erected on the plain where his Fremen had obliterated the Sardaukar legions. Ground once trampled by battles rang now to the rushing clamor of business.

Keeping to the balcony's outer edge, Paul strode around the corner. Now, his vista was a suburb where city structures lost themselves in rocks and the blowing sand of the desert. Alia's temple dominated the foreground; green and black hangings along its two-thousand-meter sides displayed the moon symbol of Muad'Dib.

A falling moon.

Paul passed a hand across his forehead and eyes. The symbol-metropolis oppressed him. He despised his own thoughts. Such vacillation in another would have aroused his anger.

He loathed his city!

Rage rooted in boredom flickered and simmered deep within him, nurtured by decisions that couldn't be avoided. He knew which path his feet must follow. He'd seen it enough times, hadn't he? *Seen it!* Once . . . long ago, he'd thought of himself as an inventor of government. But the invention had fallen into old patterns. It was like some hideous contrivance with plastic memory. Shape it any way you wanted, but relax for a moment, and it snapped into the ancient forms. Forces at work beyond his reach in human breasts eluded and defied him.

Paul stared out across the rooftops. What treasures of untrammeled life lay beneath those roofs? He glimpsed leaf-green places, open plantings amidst the chalk-red and gold of the roofs. Green, the gift of Muad'Dib and his water. Orchards and groves lay within his view—open plantings to rival those of fabled Lebanon.

"Muad'Dib spends water like a madman," Fremen said.

Paul put his hands over his eyes.

The moon fell.

He dropped his hands, stared at his metropolis with clarified vision. Buildings took on an aura of monstrous imperial barbarity. They stood enormous and bright beneath the northern sun. Colossi! Every extravagance of architecture a demented history could produce lay within his view: terraces of mesa proportion, squares as large as some cities, parks, premises, bits of cultured wilderness.

Superb artistry abutted inexplicable prodigies of dismal tastlessness. Details impressed themselves upon him: a postern out of most ancient Baghdad . . . a dome dreamed in mythical Damascus . . . an arch from the low gravity of Atar . . . harmonious elevations and queer depths. All created an effect of unrivaled magnificence.

A moon! A moon! A moon!

Frustration tangled him. He felt the pressure of mass-unconscious, that burgeoning sweep of humankind across his universe. They rushed upon him with a force like a gigantic tidal bore. He sensed the vast migrations at work in human affairs: eddies, currents, gene flows. No dams of abstinence, no seizures of impotence nor maledictions could stop it.

Muad'Dib's Jihad was less than an eye-blink in this larger movement. The Bene Gesserit swimming in this tide, that corporate entity trading in genes, was trapped in the torrent as he was. Visions of a falling moon must be measured against other legends, other visions in a universe where even the seemingly eternal stars waned, flickered, died . . .

What mattered a single moon in such a universe?

Far within his fortress citadel, so deep within that the sound sometimes lost itself in the flow of city noises, a ten-string rebaba tinkled with a song of the Jihad, a lament for a woman left behind on Arrakis:

Her hips are dunes curved by the wind,
Her eyes shine like summer heat.
Two braids of hair hang down her back—
Rich with water rings, her hair!
My hands remember her skin,
Fragrant as amber, flower-scented.
Eyelids tremble with memories . . .
I am stricken by love's white flame!

The song sickened him. A tune for stupid creatures lost in sentimentality! As well sing to the dune-impregnated corpse Alia had seen.

A figure moved in shadows of the balcony's grillwork. Paul whirled.

The ghola emerged into the sun's full glare. His metal eyes glittered.

"Is it Duncan Idaho or the man called Hayt?" Paul asked.

The ghola came to a stop two paces from him. "Which would my Lord prefer?"

The voice carried a soft ring of caution.

"Play the Zensunni," Paul said bitterly. *Meanings within meanings!* What could a Zensunni philosopher say or do to change one jot of the reality unrolling before them at this instant?

"My Lord is troubled."

Paul turned away, stared at the Shield Wall's distant scarp, saw wind-carved arches and buttresses, terrible mimicry of his city. Nature playing a joke on him! *See what I can build!* He recognized a slash in the distant massif, a place where sand spilled from a crevasse, and thought: *There! Right there, we fought Sardaukar!*

"What troubles my lord?" the ghola asked.

"A vision," Paul whispered.

"Ahhhhh, when the Tleilaxu first awakened me, I had visions. I was restless, lonely . . . not really knowing I was lonely. Not then. My visions revealed nothing! The Tleilaxu told me it was an intrusion of the flesh which men and gholas all suffer, a sickness, no more."

Paul turned, studied the ghola's eyes, those pitted, steely balls without expression. What visions did those eyes see?

"Duncan . . . Duncan . . ." Paul whispered.

"I am called Hayt."

"I saw a moon fall," Paul said. "It was gone, destroyed. I heard a great hissing. The earth shook."

"You are drunk on too much time," the ghola said.

"I ask for the Zensunni and get the mentat!" Paul said. "Very well! Play my vision through your logic, mentat. Analyze it and reduce it to mere words laid out for burial."

"Burial, indeed," the ghola said. "You run from death. You strain at the next instant, refuse to live here and now. Augury! What a crutch for an Emperor!"

Paul found himself fascinated by a well-remembered mole on the ghola's chin.

"Trying to live in this future," the ghola said, "do you give substance to such a future? Do you make it real?"

"If I go the way of my vision-future, I'll be alive *then*," Paul muttered. "What makes you think I want to live there?"

The ghola shrugged. "You asked me for a substantial answer."

"Where is there substance in a universe composed of events?" Paul asked. "Is there a final answer? Doesn't each solution produce new questions?"

"You've digested so much time you have delusions of immortality," the ghola said. "Even *your* Empire, my lord, must live its time and die."

"Don't parade smoke-blackened altars before me," Paul growled. "I've heard enough sad histories of gods and messiahs. Why should I need special powers to forecast ruins of my own like all those others? The lowliest servant of my kitchens could do this." He shook his head. "The moon fell!"

"You've not brought your mind to rest at its beginning," the ghola said.

"Is that how you destroy me?" Paul demanded. "Prevent me from collecting my thoughts?"

"Can you collect chaos?" the ghola asked. "We Zensunni say: 'Not collecting, that is the ultimate gathering.' What can you gather without gathering yourself?"

"I'm deviled by a vision and you spew nonsense!" Paul raged. "What do you know of prescience?"

"I've seen the oracle at work," the ghola said. "I've seen those who seek signs and omens for their individual destiny. They fear what they seek."

"My falling moon is real," Paul whispered. He took a trembling breath. "It moves. It moves."

"Men always fear things which move by themselves," the ghola said. "You fear your own powers. Things fall into your head from nowhere. When they fall out, where do they go?"

"You comfort me with thorns," Paul growled.

An inner illumination came over the ghola's face. For a moment, he became pure Duncan Idaho. "I give you what comfort I can," he said.

Paul wondered at that momentary spasm. Had the ghola felt grief which his mind rejected? Had Hayt put down a vision of his own?

"My moon has a name," Paul whispered.

He let the vision flow over him then. Though his whole being shrieked, no sound escaped him. He was afraid to speak, fearful that his voice might betray him. The air of this terrifying future was thick with Chani's absence. Flesh that had cried in ecstasy, eyes that had burned him with their desire, the voice that had charmed him because it played no tricks of subtle control—all gone, back into the water and the sand.

Slowly, Paul turned away, looked out at the present and the plaza before Alia's temple. Three shaven-headed pilgrims entered from the processional avenue. They wore grimy yellow robes and hurried with their heads bent against the afternoon's wind. One walked with a limp, dragging his left foot. They beat their way against the wind, rounded a corner and were gone from his sight.

Just as his moon would go, they were gone. Still, his vision lay before him. Its terrible purpose gave him no choice.

The flesh surrenders itself, he thought. *Eternity takes back its own. Our bodies stirred these waters briefly, danced with a certain intoxication before the love of life and self, dealt with a few strange ideas, then submitted to the instruments of Time. What can we say of this? I occurred. I am not . . . yet, I occurred.*

You do not beg the sun for mercy.

—MUAD'DIB'S TRAVAIL
FROM THE STILGAR COMMENTARY

One moment of incompetence can be fatal, the Reverend Mother Gaius Helen Mohiam reminded herself.

She hobbled along, apparently unconcerned, within a ring of Fremen guards. One of those behind her, she knew, was a deaf-mute immune to any wiles of Voice. No doubt he'd been charged to kill her at the slightest provocation.

Why had Paul summoned her? she wondered. Was he about to pass sentence? She remembered the day long ago when she'd tested him . . . the child kwisatz haderach. He was a deep one.

Damn his mother for all eternity! It was her fault the Bene Gesserit had lost their hold on this gene line.

Silence surged along the vaulted passages ahead of her entourage. She sensed the word being passed. Paul would hear the silence. He'd know of her coming before it was announced. She didn't delude herself with ideas that her powers exceeded his.

Damn him!

She begrudged the burdens age had imposed on her: the aching joints, responses not as quick as once they'd been, muscles not as elastic as the whipcords of her youth. A long day lay behind her and a long life. She'd spent this day with the Dune Tarot in a fruitless search for some clue to her own fate. But the cards were sluggish.

The guards herded her around a corner into another of the seemingly endless vaulted passages. Triangular meta-glass windows on her left gave a view upward to trellised vines and indigo flowers in deep shadows cast by the afternoon sun. Tiles lay underfoot—figures of water creatures from exotic planets. Water reminders everywhere. Wealth . . . riches.

Robed figures passed across another hall in front of her, cast covert glances at the Reverend Mother. Recognition was obvious in their manner—and tension.

She kept her attention on the sharp hairline of the guard immediately in front: young flesh, pink creases at the uniform collar.

The immensity of this ighir citadel began to impress her. Passages . . . passages . . . They passed an open doorway from which emerged the sound of timbur and flute playing soft, elder music. A glance showed her blue-in-blue Fremen eyes staring from the room. She sensed in them the ferment of legendary revolts stirring in wild genes.

There lay the measure of her personal burden, she knew. A Bene Gesserit could not escape awareness of the genes and their possibilities. She was touched by a feeling of loss: that stubborn fool of an Atreides! How could he deny the jewels of posterity within his loins? A kwisatz haderach! Born out of this time, true, but real—as real as his abomination of a sister . . . and there lay a dangerous unknown. A wild Reverend Mother spawned without Bene Gesserit inhibitions, holding no loyalty to orderly development of the genes. She shared her brother's powers, no doubt—and more.

The size of the citadel began to oppress her. Would the passages never end? The place reeked of terrifying physical power. No planet, no civilization in all human history had ever before seen such man-made immensity. A dozen ancient cities could be hidden in its walls!

They passed oval doors with winking lights. She recognized them for Ixian handiwork: pneumatic transport orifices. Why was she being marched all this distance, then? The answer began to shape itself in her mind: to oppress her in preparation for this audience with the Emperor.

A small clue, but it joined other subtle indications—the relative suppression and selection of words by her escort, the traces of primitive shyness in their eyes when they called her *Reverend Mother*, the cold and bland, essentially odorless nature of these halls—all combined to reveal much that a Bene Gesserit could interpret.

Paul wanted something from her!

She concealed a feeling of elation. A bargaining lever existed. It remained only to find the nature of that lever and test its strength. Some levers had moved things greater than this citadel. A finger's touch had been known to topple civilizations.

The Reverend Mother reminded herself then of Scytale's assessment: *When a creature has developed into one thing, he will choose death rather than change into his opposite.*

The passages through which she was being escorted grew larger by subtle stages—tricks of arching, graduated amplification of pillared supports, displacement of the triangular windows by larger, oblong shapes. Ahead of her, finally, loomed double doors centered in the far wall of a tall antechamber. She sensed that the doors were *very* large, and was forced to suppress a gasp as her trained awareness measured out the true proportions. The doorway stood at least eighty meters high, half that in width.

As she approached with her escort, the doors swung inward—an immense and silent movement of hidden machinery. She recognized more Ixian handiwork. Through that towering doorway she marched with her guards into the Grand Reception Hall of the Emperor Paul Atreides—"Muad'Dib, before whom all people are dwarfed." Now, she saw the effect of that popular saying at work.

As she advanced toward Paul on the distant throne, the Reverend Mother found herself more impressed by the architectural subtleties of her surroundings than she was by the immensities. The space was large: it could've housed the entire citadel of any ruler in human history. The open sweep of the room said much about hidden structural forces balanced with nicety. Trusses and supporting beams behind these walls and the faraway domed ceiling must surpass anything ever before attempted. Everything spoke of engineering genius.

Without seeming to do so, the hall grew smaller at its far end, refusing to dwarf Paul on his throne centered on a dais. An untrained awareness, shocked by surrounding proportions, would see him at first as many times larger than his actual size. Colors played upon the unprotected psyche: Paul's green throne had been cut from a single Hagar emerald. It suggested growing things and, out of the Fremen mythos, reflected the mourning color. It whispered that here sat he who could make you mourn—life and death in one symbol, a clever stress of opposites. Behind the throne, draperies cascaded in burnt orange, curried gold of Dune earth, and cinnamon flecks of melange. To a trained eye, the symbolism was obvious, but it contained hammer blows to beat down the uninitiated.

Time played its role here.

The Reverend Mother measured the minutes required to approach the Imperial Presence at her hobbling pace. You had time to be cowed. Any tendency toward resentment would be squeezed out of you by the unbridled power which focused down upon your person. You might start the long march toward that throne as a human of dignity, but you ended the march as a gnat.

Aides and attendants stood around the Emperor in a curiously ordered sequence—attentive household guardsmen along the draped back wall; that abomination, Alia, two steps below Paul and on his left hand; Stilgar, the Imperial lackey, on the step directly below Alia; and on the right, one step up from the floor of the hall, a solitary figure: the fleshly revenant of Duncan Idaho, the ghola. She marked older Fremen among the guardsmen, bearded Naibs with stillsuit scars on their noses, sheathed crysknives at their waists, a few maula pistols, even some lasguns. Those must be trusted men, she thought, to carry lasguns in Paul's presence when he obviously wore a shield generator. She could see the shimmering of its field around him. One burst of a lasgun into that field and the entire citadel would be a hole in the ground.

Her guard stopped ten paces from the foot of the dais, parted to open an unobstructed view of the Emperor. She noted now the absence of Chani and Irulan, wondered at it. He held no important audience without them, so it was said.

Paul nodded to her, silent, measuring.

Immediately, she decided to take the offensive, said: "So, the great Paul Atreides deigns to see the one he banished."

Paul smiled wryly, thinking: *She knows I want something from her.* That knowledge had been inevitable, she being who she was. He recognized her powers. The Bene Gesserit didn't become Reverend Mothers by chance.

"Shall we dispense with fencing?" he asked.

Would it be this easy? she wondered. And she said: "Name the thing you want."

Stilgar stirred, cast a sharp glance at Paul. The Imperial lackey didn't like her tone.

"Stilgar wants me to send you away," Paul said.

"Not kill me?" she asked. "I would've expected something more direct from a Fremen Naib."

Stilgar scowled, said: "Often, I must speak otherwise than I think. That is called diplomacy."

"Then let us dispense with diplomacy as well," she said. "Was it necessary to have me walk all that distance? I am an old woman."

"You had to be shown how callous I can be," Paul said. "That way, you'll appreciate magnanimity."

"You dare such gaucheries with a Bene Gesserit?" she asked.

"Gross actions carry their own messages," Paul said.

She hesitated, weighed his words. So—he might yet dispense with her . . . grossly, obviously, if she . . . if she what?

"Say what it is you want from me," she muttered.

Alia glanced at her brother, nodded toward the draperies behind the throne. She knew Paul's reasoning in this, but disliked it all the same. Call it *wild prophecy*: She felt pregnant with reluctance to take part in this bargaining.

"You must be careful how you speak to me, old woman," Paul said.

He called me old woman when he was a stripling, the Reverend Mother thought. *Does he remind me now of my hand in his past? The decision I made then, must I remake it here?* She felt the weight of decision, a physical thing that set her knees to trembling. Muscles cried their fatigue.

"It was a long walk," Paul said, "and I can see that you're tired. We will retire to my private chamber behind the throne. You may sit there." He gave a hand-signal to Stilgar, arose.

Stilgar and the ghola converged on her, helped her up the steps, followed Paul through a passage concealed by the draperies. She realized then why he had greeted her in the hall: a dumb-show for the guards and Naibs. He feared them, then. And now—now, he displayed kindly benevolence, daring such wiles on a Bene Gesserit. Or was it daring? She sensed another presence behind, glanced back to see Alia following. The younger woman's eyes held a brooding, baleful cast. The Reverend Mother shuddered.

The private chamber at the end of the passage was a twenty-meter cube of plasmeld, yellow glowglobes for light, the deep orange hangings of a desert stilltent around the walls. It contained divans, soft cushions, a faint odor of melange, crystal water flagons on a low table. It felt cramped, tiny after the outer hall.

Paul seated her on a divan, stood over her, studying the ancient face—steely teeth, eyes that hid more than they revealed, deeply wrinkled skin. He indicated a water flagon. She shook her head, dislodging a wisp of gray hair.

In a low voice, Paul said: "I wish to bargain with you for the life of my beloved."

Stilgar cleared his throat.

Alia fingered the handle of the crysknife sheathed at her neck.

The ghola remained at the door, face impassive, metal eyes pointed at the air above the Reverend Mother's head.

"Have you had a vision of my hand in her death?" the Reverend Mother asked. She kept her attention on the ghola, oddly disturbed by him. Why should she feel threatened by the ghola? He was a tool of the conspiracy.

"I know what it is you want from me," Paul said, avoiding her question.

Then he only suspects, she thought. The Reverend Mother looked down at the tips of her shoes exposed by a fold of her robe. Black . . . black . . . shoes and robe showed marks of her confinement:

stains, wrinkles. She lifted her chin, met an angry glare in Paul's eyes. Elation surged through her, but she hid the emotion behind pursed lips, slitted eyelids.

"What coin do you offer?" she asked.

"You may have my seed, but not my person," Paul said. "Irulan banished and inseminated by artificial—"

"You dare!" the Reverend Mother flared, stiffening.

Stilgar took a half step forward.

Disconcertingly, the ghola smiled. And now Alia was studying him.

"We'll not discuss the things your Sisterhood forbids," Paul said. "I will listen to no talk of sins, abominations or the beliefs left over from past Jihads. You may have my seed for your plans, but no child of Irulan's will sit on my throne."

"Your throne," she sneered.

"*My* throne."

"Then who will bear the Imperial heir?"

"Chani."

"She is barren."

"She is with child."

An involuntary indrawn breath exposed her shock. "You lie!" she snapped.

Paul held up a restraining hand as Stilgar surged forward.

"We've known for two days that she carries my child."

"But Irulan . . ."

"By artificial means only. That's my offer."

The Reverend Mother closed her eyes to hide his face. Damnation! To cast the genetic dice in such a way! Loathing boiled in her breast. The teaching of the Bene Gesserit, the lessons of the Butlerian Jihad— all proscribed such an act. One did not demean the highest aspirations of humankind. No machine could function in the way of a human mind. No word or deed could imply that men might be bred on the level of animals.

"Your decision," Paul said.

She shook her head. The genes, the precious Atreides genes—only these were important. Need went deeper than proscription. For the Sisterhood, mating mingled more than sperm and ovum. One aimed to capture the psyche.

The Reverend Mother understood now the subtle depths of Paul's offer. He would make the Bene Gesserit party to an act which would bring down popular wrath . . . were it ever discovered. They could not admit such paternity if the Emperor denied it. This coin might save the Atreides genes for the Sisterhood, but it would never buy a throne.

She swept her gaze around the room, studying each face: Stilgar, passive and waiting now; the ghola frozen at some inward place; Alia watching the ghola . . . and Paul—wrath beneath a shallow veneer.

"This is your only offer?" she asked.

"My only offer."

She glanced at the ghola, caught by a brief movement of muscles across his cheeks. Emotion? "You, ghola," she said. "Should such an offer be made? Having been made, should it be accepted? Function as the mentat for us."

The metallic eyes turned to Paul.

"Answer as you will," Paul said.

The ghola returned his gleaming attention to the Reverend Mother, shocked her once more by smiling. "An offer is only as good as the real thing it buys," he said. "The exchange offered here is life-for-life, a high order of business."

Alia brushed a strand of coppery hair from her forehead, said: "And what else is hidden in this bargain?"

The Reverend Mother refused to look at Alia, but the words

burned in her mind. Yes, far deeper implications lay here. The sister was an abomination, true, but there could be no denying her status as a Reverend Mother with all the title implied. Gaius Helen Mohiam felt herself in this instant to be not one single person, but all the others who sat like tiny congeries in her memory. They were alert, every Reverend Mother she had absorbed in becoming a Priestess of the Sisterhood. Alia would be standing in the same situation here.

"What else?" the ghola asked. "One wonders why the witches of the Bene Gesserit have not used Tleilaxu methods."

Gaius Helen Mohiam and all the Reverend Mothers within her shuddered. Yes, the Tleilaxu did loathsome things. If one let down the barriers to artificial insemination, was the next step a Tleilaxu one—controlled mutation?

Paul, observing the play of emotion around him, felt abruptly that he no longer knew these people. He could see only strangers. Even Alia was a stranger.

Alia said: "If we set the Atreides genes adrift in a Bene Gesserit river, who knows what may result?"

Gaius Helen Mohiam's head snapped around, and she met Alia's gaze. For a flashing instant, they were two Reverend Mothers together, communing on a single thought: *What lay behind any Tleilaxu action? The ghola was a Tleilaxu thing. Had he put this plan into Paul's mind? Would Paul attempt to bargain directly with the Bene Tleilax?*

She broke her gaze from Alia's, feeling her own ambivalence and inadequacies. The pitfall of Bene Gesserit training, she reminded herself, lay in the powers granted: such powers predisposed one to vanity and pride. But power deluded those who used it. One tended to believe power could overcome any barrier . . . including one's own ignorance.

Only one thing stood paramount here for the Bene Gesserit, she told herself. That was the pyramid of generations which had reached an apex in Paul Atreides . . . and in his abomination of a sister. A wrong choice here and the pyramid would have to be rebuilt . . . starting generations back in the parallel lines and with breeding specimens lacking the choicest characteristics.

Controlled mutation, she thought. *Did the Tleilaxu really practice it? How tempting!* She shook her head, the better to rid it of such thoughts.

"You reject my proposal?" Paul asked.

"I'm thinking," she said.

And again, she looked at the sister. The optimum cross for this female Atreides had been lost . . . killed by Paul. Another possibility remained, however—one which would *cement* the desired characteristic into an offspring. Paul dared offer animal breeding to the Bene Gesserit! How much was he really prepared to pay for his Chani's life? Would he accept a cross with his own sister?

Sparring for time, the Reverend Mother said: "Tell me, oh flawless exemplar of all that's holy, has Irulan anything to say of your proposal?"

"Irulan will do what you tell her to do," Paul growled.

True enough, Mohiam thought. She firmed her jaw, offered a new gambit: "There are two Atreides."

Paul, sensing something of what lay in the old witch's mind, felt blood darken his face. "Careful what you suggest," he said.

"You'd just *use* Irulan to gain your own ends, eh?" she asked.

"Wasn't she trained to be used?" Paul asked.

And we trained her, that's what he's saying, Mohiam thought. *Well . . . Irulan's a divided coin. Was there another way to spend such a coin?*

"Will you put Chani's child on the throne?" the Reverend Mother asked.

"On *my* throne," Paul said. He glanced at Alia, wondering suddenly if she knew the divergent possibilities in this exchange. Alia stood with eyes closed, an odd stillness-of-person about her. With what inner force did she commune? Seeing his sister thus, Paul felt he'd been cast adrift. Alia stood on a shore that was receding from him.

The Reverend Mother made her decision, said: "This is too much for one person to decide. I must consult with my Council on Wallach. Will you permit a message?"

As though she needed my permission! Paul thought.

He said: "Agreed, then. But don't delay too long. I will not sit idly by while you debate."

"Will you bargain with the Bene Tleilax?" the ghola asked, his voice a sharp intrusion.

Alia's eyes popped open and she stared at the ghola as though she'd been wakened by a dangerous intruder.

"I've made no such decision," Paul said. "What I will do is go into the desert as soon as it can be arranged. Our child will be born in sietch."

"A wise decision," Stilgar intoned.

Alia refused to look at Stilgar. It was a wrong decision. She could feel this in every cell. Paul *must* know it. Why had he fixed himself upon such a path?

"Have the Bene Tleilax offered their services?" Alia asked. She saw Mohiam hanging on the answer.

Paul shook his head. "No." He glanced at Stilgar. "Stil, arrange for the message to be sent to Wallach."

"At once, m'Lord."

Paul turned away, waited while Stilgar summoned guards, left with the old witch. He sensed Alia debating whether to confront him with more questions. She turned, instead, to the ghola.

"Mentat," she said, "will the Tleilaxu bid for favor with my brother?"

The ghola shrugged.

Paul felt his attention wander. *The Tleilaxu? No . . . not in the way Alia meant.* Her question revealed, though, that she had not seen the alternatives here. Well . . . vision varied from sibyl to sibyl. Why not a variance from brother to sister? Wandering . . . wandering . . . He came back from each thought with a start to pick up shards of the nearby conversation.

". . . must know what the Tleilaxu . . ."

". . . the fullness of data is always . . ."

". . . healthy doubts where . . ."

Paul turned, looked at his sister, caught her attention. He knew she would see tears on his face and wonder at them. Let her wonder. Wondering was a kindness now. He glanced at the ghola, seeing only Duncan Idaho despite the metallic eyes. Sorrow and compassion warred in Paul. What might those metal eyes record?

There are many degrees of sight and many degrees of blindness, Paul thought. His mind turned to a paraphrase of the passage from the Orange Catholic Bible: *What senses do we lack that we cannot see another world all around us?*

Were those metal eyes another sense than sight?

Alia crossed to her brother, sensing his utter sadness. She touched a tear on his cheek with a Fremen gesture of awe, said: "We must not grieve for those dear to us before their passing."

"Before their passing," Paul whispered. "Tell me, little sister, what is *before*?"

I've had a bellyful of the god and priest business! You think I don't see my own mythos? Consult your data once more, Hayt. I've insinuated my rites into the most elementary human acts. The people eat in the name of Muad'Dib! They make love in my name, are born in my name—cross the street in my name. A roof beam cannot be raised in the lowliest hovel of far Gangishree without invoking the blessing of Muad'Dib!

—BOOK OF DIATRIBES
FROM THE HAYT CHRONICLE

"You risk much leaving your post and coming to me here at this time," Edric said, glaring through the walls of his tank at the Face Dancer.

"How weak and narrow is your thinking," Scytale said. "Who is it who comes to visit you?"

Edric hesitated, observing the hulk shape, heavy eyelids, blunt face. It was early in the day and Edric's metabolism had not yet cycled from night repose into full melange consumption.

"This is not the shape which walked the streets?" Edric asked.

"One would not look twice at some of the figures I have been today," Scytale said.

The chameleon thinks a change of shape will hide him from anything, Edric thought with rare insight. And he wondered if his presence in the conspiracy truly hid them from all oracular powers. The Emperor's sister, now . . .

Edric shook his head, stirring the orange gas of his tank, said: "Why are you here?"

"The gift must be prodded to swifter action," Scytale said.

"That cannot be done."

"A way must be found," Scytale insisted.

"Why?"

"Things are not to my liking. The Emperor is trying to split us. Already he has made his bid to the Bene Gesserit."

"Oh, *that.*"

"That! You must prod the ghola to . . ."

"You fashioned him, Tleilaxu," Edric said. "You know better than to ask this." He paused, moved closer to the transparent wall of his tank. "Or did you lie to us about this gift?"

"Lie?"

"You said the weapon was to be aimed and released, nothing more. Once the ghola was given we could not tamper."

"Any ghola can be disturbed," Scytale said. "You need do nothing more than question him about his original being."

"What will this do?"

"It will stir him to actions which will serve our purposes."

"He is a mentat with powers of logic and reason," Edric objected. "He may guess what I'm doing . . . or the sister. If her attention is focused upon—"

"Do you hide us from the sibyl or don't you?" Scytale asked.

"I'm not afraid of oracles," Edric said. "I'm concerned with logic, with real spies, with the physical powers of the Imperium, with the control of the spice, with—"

"One can contemplate the Emperor and his powers comfortably if one remembers that all things are finite," Scytale said.

Oddly, the Steersman recoiled in agitation, threshing his limbs like some weird newt. Scytale fought a sense of loathing at the sight. The Guild Navigator wore his usual dark leotard bulging at the belt with various containers. Yet . . . he gave the impression of nakedness when he moved. It was the swimming, reaching movements, Scytale decided, and he was struck once more by the delicate linkages of their conspiracy. They were not a compatible group. That was weakness.

Edric's agitation subsided. He stared out at Scytale, vision colored by the orange gas which sustained him. What plot did the Face Dancer hold in reserve to save himself? Edric wondered. The Tleilaxu was not acting in a predictable fashion. Evil omen.

Something in the Navigator's voice and actions told Scytale that the Guildsman feared the sister more than the Emperor. This was an abrupt thought flashed on the screen of awareness. Disturbing. Had they overlooked something important about Alia? Would the ghola be sufficient weapon to destroy both?

"You know what is said of Alia?" Scytale asked, probing.

"What do you mean?" Again, the fish-man was agitated.

"Never have philosophy and culture had such a patroness," Scytale said. "Pleasure and beauty unite in—"

"What is enduring about beauty and pleasure?" Edric demanded. "We will destroy both Atreides. Culture! They dispense culture the better to rule. Beauty! They promote the beauty which enslaves. They create a literate ignorance—easiest thing of all. They leave nothing to chance. Chains! Everything they do forges chains, enslaves. But slaves always revolt."

"The sister may wed and produce offspring," Scytale said.

"Why do you speak of the sister?" Edric asked.

"The Emperor may choose a mate for her," Scytale said.

"Let him choose. Already, it is too late."

"Even you cannot invent the next moment," Scytale warned. "You are not a creator . . . any more than are the Atreides." He nodded. "We must not presume too much."

"We aren't the ones to flap our tongues about creation," Edric protested. "We aren't the rabble trying to make a messiah out of Muad'Dib. What is this nonsense? Why are you raising such questions?"

"It's this planet," Scytale said. "*It* raises questions."

"Planets don't speak!"

"This one does."

"Oh?"

"It speaks of creation. Sand blowing in the night, that is creation."

"Sand blowing . . ."

"When you awaken, the first light shows you the new world—all fresh and ready for your tracks."

Untracked sand? Edric thought. *Creation?* He felt knotted with sudden anxiety. The confinement of his tank, the surrounding room, everything closed in upon him, constricted him.

Tracks in sand.

"You talk like a Fremen," Edric said.

"This is a Fremen thought and it's instructive," Scytale agreed. "They speak of Muad'Dib's Jihad as leaving tracks in the universe in the same way that a Fremen tracks new sand. They've marked out a trail in men's lives."

"So?"

"Another night comes," Scytale said. "Winds blow."

"Yes," Edric said, "the Jihad is finite. Muad'Dib has used his Jihad and—"

"He didn't use the Jihad," Scytale said. "The Jihad used him. I think he would've stopped it if he could."

"If he could? All he had to do was—"

"Oh, be still!" Scytale barked. "You can't stop a mental epidemic. It leaps from person to person across parsecs. It's overwhelmingly contagious. It strikes at the unprotected side, in the place where we lodge the fragments of other such plagues. Who can stop such a thing? Muad'Dib hasn't the antidote. The thing has roots in chaos. Can orders reach there?"

"Have you been infected, then?" Edric asked. He turned slowly in the orange gas, wondering why Scytale's words carried such a tone of fear. Had the Face Dancer broken from the conspiracy? There was no way to peer into the future and examine this now. The future had become a muddy stream, clogged with prophets.

"We're all contaminated," Scytale said, and he reminded himself that Edric's intelligence had severe limits. How could this point be made that the Guildsman would understand it?

"But when we destroy him," Edric said, "the contag—"

"I should leave you in this ignorance," Scytale said. "But my duties will not permit it. Besides, it's dangerous to all of us."

Edric recoiled, steadied himself with a kick of one webbed foot which sent the orange gas whipping around his legs. "You speak strangely," he said.

"This whole thing is explosive," Scytale said in a calmer voice. "It's ready to shatter. When it goes, it will send bits of itself out through the centuries. Don't you see this?"

"We've dealt with religions before," Edric protested. "If this new—"

"It is *not* just a religion!" Scytale said, wondering what the Reverend Mother would say to this harsh education of their fellow conspirator. "Religious government is something else. Muad'Dib has crowded his Qizarate in everywhere, displaced the old functions of government. But he has no permanent civil service, no interlocking embassies. He has bishoprics, islands of authority. At the center of each island is a man. Men learn how to gain and hold personal power. Men are jealous."

"When they're divided, we'll absorb them one by one," Edric said with a complacent smile. "Cut off the head and the body will fall to—"

"This body has two heads," Scytale said.

"The sister—who may wed."

"Who will certainly wed."

"I don't like your tone, Scytale."

"And I don't like your ignorance."

"What if she does wed? Will that shake our plans?"

"It will shake the universe."

"But they're not unique. I, myself, possess powers which—"

"You're an infant. You toddle where they stride."

"They are *not* unique!"

"You forget, Guildsman, that we once made a kwisatz haderach. This is a being filled by the spectacle of Time. It is a form of existence which cannot be threatened without enclosing yourself in the identical threat. Muad'Dib knows we would attack his Chani. We must move faster than we have. You must get to the ghola, prod him as I have instructed."

"And if I do not?"

"We will feel the thunderbolt."

Oh, worm of many teeth,

Canst thou deny what has no cure?

The flesh and breath which lure thee

To the ground of all beginnings

Feed on monsters twisting in a door of fire!

Thou hast no robe in all thy attire

To cover intoxications of divinity

Or hide the burnings of desire!

—WORMSONG
FROM THE DUNEBOOK

Paul had worked up a sweat on the practice floor using crysknife and short sword against the ghola. He stood now at a window looking down into the temple plaza, tried to imagine the scene with Chani at the clinic. She'd been taken ill at midmorning, the sixth week of her pregnancy. The medics were the best. They'd call when they had news.

Murky afternoon sandclouds darkened the sky over the plaza. Fremen called such weather "dirty air."

Would the medics never call? Each second struggled past, reluctant to enter his universe.

Waiting . . . waiting . . . The Bene Gesserit sent no word from Wallach. Deliberately delaying, of course.

Prescient vision had recorded these moments, but he shielded his awareness from the oracle, preferring the role here of a Timefish swimming not where he willed, but where the currents carried him. Destiny permitted no struggles now.

The ghola could be heard racking weapons, examining the equipment. Paul sighed, put a hand to his own belt, deactivated his shield. The tingling passage of its field ran down against his skin.

He'd face events when Chani came, Paul told himself. Time enough then to accept the fact that what he'd concealed from her had prolonged her life. Was it evil, he wondered, to prefer Chani to an heir? By what right did he make her choice for her? Foolish thoughts! Who could hesitate, given the alternatives—slave pits, torture, agonizing sorrow . . . and worse.

He heard the door open, Chani's footsteps.

Paul turned.

Murder sat on Chani's face. The wide Fremen belt which gathered the waist of her golden robe, the water rings worn as a necklace, one hand at her hip (never far from the knife), the trenchant stare which was her first inspection of any room—everything about her stood now only as a background for violence.

He opened his arms as she came to him, gathered her close.

"Someone," she rasped, speaking against his breast, "has been feeding me a contraceptive for a long time . . . before I began the new diet. There'll be problems with this birth because of it."

"But there are remedies?" he asked.

"Dangerous remedies. I know the source of that poison! I'll have her blood."

"My Sihaya," he whispered, holding her close to calm a sudden trembling. "You'll bear the heir we want. Isn't that enough?"

"My life burns faster," she said, pressing against him. "The birth now controls my life. The medics told me it goes at a terrible pace. I must eat and eat . . . and take more spice, as well . . . eat it, drink it. I'll kill her for this!"

Paul kissed her cheek. "No, my Sihaya. You'll kill no one." And he thought: *Irulan prolonged your life, beloved. For you, the time of birth is the time of death.*

He felt hidden grief drain his marrow then, empty his life into a black flask.

Chani pushed away from him. "She cannot be forgiven!"

"Who said anything about forgiving?"

"Then why shouldn't I kill her?"

It was such a flat, Fremen question that Paul felt himself almost overcome by a hysterical desire to laugh. He covered it by saying: "It wouldn't help."

"You've *seen* that?"

Paul felt his belly tighten with vision-memory.

"What I've seen . . . what I've seen . . ." he muttered. Every aspect of surrounding events fitted a present which paralyzed him. He felt chained to a future which, exposed too often, had locked onto him like a greedy succubus. Tight dryness clogged his throat. Had he followed the witchcall of his own oracle, he wondered, until it'd spilled him into a merciless present?

"Tell me what you've *seen*," Chani said.

"I can't."

"Why mustn't I kill her?"

"Because I ask it."

He watched her accept this. She did it the way sand accepted water: absorbing and concealing. Was there obedience beneath that hot, angry surface? he wondered. And he realized then that life in the royal Keep had left Chani unchanged. She'd merely stopped here for a time, inhabited a way station on a journey with her man. Nothing of the desert had been taken from her.

Chani stepped away from him then, glanced at the ghola who stood waiting near the diamond circle of the practice door.

"You've been crossing blades with him?" she asked.

"And I'm better for it."

Her gaze went to the circle on the floor, back to the ghola's metallic eyes.

"I don't like it," she said.

"He's not intended to do me violence," Paul said.

"You've seen *that*?"

"I've not *seen* it!"

"Then how do you know?"

"Because he's more than ghola; he's Duncan Idaho."

"The Bene Tleilax made him."

"They made more than they intended."

She shook her head. A corner of her nezhoni scarf rubbed the collar of her robe. "How can you change the fact that he is ghola?"

"Hayt," Paul said, "are you the tool of my undoing?"

"If the substance of here and now is changed, the future is changed," the ghola said.

"That is no answer!" Chani objected.

Paul raised his voice: "How will I die, Hayt?"

Light glinted from the artificial eyes. "It is said, m'Lord, that you will die of money and power."

Chani stiffened. "How dare he speak thus to you?"

"The mentat is truthful," Paul said.

"Was Duncan Idaho a real friend?" she asked.

"He gave his life for me."

"It is sad," Chani whispered, "that a ghola cannot be restored to his original being."

"Would you convert me?" the ghola asked, directing his gaze to Chani.

"What does he mean?" Chani asked.

"To be converted is to be turned around," Paul said. "But there's no going back."

"Every man carries his own past with him," Hayt said.

"And every ghola?" Paul asked.

"In a way, m'Lord."

"Then what of that past in your secret flesh?" Paul asked.

Chani saw how the question disturbed the ghola. His movements quickened, hands clenched into fists. She glanced at Paul, wondering why he probed thus. Was there a way to restore this creature to the man he'd been?

"Has a ghola ever remembered his real past?" Chani asked.

"Many attempts have been made," Hayt said, his gaze fixed on the floor near his feet. "No ghola has ever been restored to his former being."

"But you long for this to happen," Paul said.

The blank surfaces of the ghola's eyes came up to center on Paul with a pressing intensity. "Yes!"

Voice soft, Paul said: "If there's a way . . ."

"This flesh," Hayt said, touching left hand to forehead in a curious saluting movement, "is not the flesh of my original birth. It is . . . reborn. Only the shape is familiar. A Face Dancer might do as well."

"Not as well," Paul said. "And you're not a Face Dancer."

"That is true, m'Lord."

"Whence comes your shape?"

"The genetic imprint of the original cells."

"Somewhere," Paul said, "there's a plastic something which re-members the shape of Duncan Idaho. It's said the ancients probed this region before the Butlerian Jihad. What's the extent of this memory, Hayt? What did it learn from the original?"

The ghola shrugged.

"What if he wasn't Idaho?" Chani asked.

"He was."

"Can you be certain?" she asked.

"He is Duncan in every aspect. I cannot imagine a force strong enough to hold that shape thus without any relaxation or any deviation."

"M'Lord!" Hayt objected. "Because we cannot imagine a thing, that doesn't exclude it from reality. There are things I must do as a ghola that I would not do as a man."

Keeping his attention on Chani, Paul said: "You see?" She nodded.

Paul turned away, fighting deep sadness. He crossed to the balcony windows, drew the draperies. Lights came on in the sudden gloom. He pulled the sash of his robe tight, listened for sounds behind him.

Nothing.

He turned. Chani stood as though entranced, her gaze centered on the ghola.

Hayt, Paul saw, had retreated to some inner chamber of his being—had gone back to the ghola place.

Chani turned at the sound of Paul's return. She still felt the thralldom of the instant Paul had precipitated. For a brief moment, the ghola had been an intense, vital human being. For that moment, he had been someone she did not fear—indeed, someone she liked and admired. Now, she understood Paul's purpose in this probing. He had wanted her to see the *man* in the ghola flesh.

She stared at Paul. "That man, was that Duncan Idaho?"

"That was Duncan Idaho. He is still there."

"Would *he* have allowed Irulan to go on living?" Chani asked.

The water didn't sink too deep, Paul thought. And he said: "If I commanded it."

"I don't understand," she said. "Shouldn't you be angry?"

"I am angry."

"You don't sound . . . angry. You sound sorrowful."

He closed his eyes. "Yes. That, too."

"You're my man," she said. "I know this, but suddenly I don't understand you."

Abruptly, Paul felt that he walked down a long cavern. His flesh moved—one foot and then another—but his thoughts went elsewhere. "I don't understand myself," he whispered. When he opened his eyes, he found that he had moved away from Chani.

She spoke from somewhere behind him. "Beloved, I'll not ask again what you've *seen.* I only know I'm to give you the heir we want."

He nodded, then: "I've known that from the beginning." He turned, studied her. Chani seemed very far away.

She drew herself up, placed a hand on her abdomen. "I'm hungry. The medics tell me I must eat three or four times what I ate before. I'm frightened, beloved. It goes too fast."

Too fast, he agreed. *This fetus knows the necessity for speed.*

The audacious nature of Muad'Dib's actions may be seen in the fact that He knew from the beginning whither He was bound, yet not once did He step aside from that path. He put it clearly when He said: "I tell you that I come now to my time of testing when it will be shown that I am the Ultimate Servant." Thus He weaves all into One, that both friend and foe may worship Him. It is for this reason and this reason only that His Apostles prayed: "Lord, save us from the other paths which Muad'Dib covered with the Waters of His Life." Those "other paths" may be imagined only with the deepest revulsion.

—FROM THE YIAM-EL-DIN (BOOK OF JUDGMENT)

The messenger was a young woman—her face, name and family known to Chani—which was how she'd penetrated Imperial Security.

Chani had done no more than identify her for a Security Officer named Bannerjee, who then arranged the meeting with Muad'Dib. Bannerjee acted out of instinct and the assurance that the young woman's father had been a member of the Emperor's Death Commandos, the dreaded Fedaykin, in the days before the Jihad. Otherwise, he might have ignored her plea that her message was intended only for the ears of Muad'Dib.

She was, of course, screened and searched before the meeting in Paul's private office. Even so, Bannerjee accompanied her, hand on knife, other hand on her arm.

It was almost midday when they brought her into the room—an odd space, mixture of desert-Fremen and Family-Aristocrat. *Hiereg* hangings lined three walls: delicate tapestries adorned with figures out of Fremen mythology. A view screen covered the fourth wall, a silver-gray surface behind an oval desk whose top held only one object, a Fremen sandclock built into an *orrery*. The orrery, a suspensor mechanism from Ix, carried both moons of Arrakis in the classic Worm Trine aligned with the sun.

Paul, standing beside the desk, glanced at Bannerjee. The Security Officer was one of those who'd come up through the Fremen Constabulary, winning his place on brains and proven loyalty despite the smuggler ancestry attested by his name. He was a solid figure, almost fat. Wisps of black hair fell down over the dark, wet-appearing skin of his forehead like the crest of an exotic bird. His eyes were blue-blue and steady in a gaze which could look upon happiness or atrocity without change of expression. Both Chani and Stilgar trusted him. Paul knew that if he told Bannerjee to throttle the girl immediately, Bannerjee would do it.

"Sire, here is the messenger girl," Bannerjee said. "M'Lady Chani said she sent word to you."

"Yes." Paul nodded curtly.

Oddly, the girl didn't look at him. Her attention remained on the orrery. She was dark-skinned, of medium height, her figure concealed beneath a robe whose rich wine fabric and simple cut spoke of wealth. Her blue-black hair was held in a narrow band of material which matched the robe. The robe concealed her hands. Paul suspected that the hands were tightly clasped. It would be in character. Everything about her would be in character—including the robe: a last piece of finery saved for such a moment.

Paul motioned Bannerjee aside. He hesitated before obeying. Now, the girl moved—one step forward. When she moved there was grace. Still, her eyes avoided him.

Paul cleared his throat.

Now the girl lifted her gaze, the whiteless eyes widening with just the right shade of awe. She had an odd little face with delicate chin, a sense of reserve in the way she held her small mouth. The eyes appeared abnormally large above slanted cheeks. There was a cheerless air about her, something which said she seldom smiled. The corners of her eyes even held a faint yellow misting which could have been from dust irritation or the tracery of semuta.

Everything was in character.

"You asked to see me," Paul said.

The moment of supreme test for this girl-shape had come. Scytale had put on the shape, the mannerisms, the sex, the voice—everything his abilities could grasp and assume. But this was a female known to Muad'Dib in the sietch days. She'd been a child, then, but she and Muad'Dib shared common experiences. Certain areas of memory must be avoided delicately. It was the most exacting part Scytale had ever attempted.

"I am Otheym's Lichna of Berk al Dib."

The girl's voice came out small, but firm, giving name, father and pedigree.

Paul nodded. He saw how Chani had been fooled. The timbre of voice, everything reproduced with exactitude. Had it not been for his own Bene Gesserit training in voice and for the web of *dao* in which oracular vision enfolded him, this Face-Dancer disguise might have gulled even him.

Training exposed certain discrepancies: the girl was older than her known years; too much control tuned the vocal cords; set of neck and shoulders missed by a fraction the subtle hauteur of Fremen poise. But there were niceties, too: the rich robe had been patched to betray actual status . . . and the features were beautifully exact. They spoke a certain sympathy of this Face Dancer for the role being played.

"Rest in my home, daughter of Otheym," Paul said in formal Fremen greeting. "You are welcome as water after a dry crossing."

The faintest of relaxations exposed the confidence this apparent acceptance had conveyed.

"I bring a message," she said.

"A man's messenger is as himself," Paul said.

Scytale breathed softly. It went well, but now came the crucial task: the Atreides must be guided onto that special path. He must lose his Fremen concubine in circumstances where no other shared the blame. The failure must belong only to the *omnipotent* Muad'Dib. He had to be led into an ultimate realization of his failure and thence to acceptance of the Tleilaxu alternative.

"I am the smoke which banishes sleep in the night," Scytale said, employing a Fedaykin code phrase: *I bear bad tidings.*

Paul fought to maintain calmness. He felt naked, his soul abandoned in a groping-time concealed from every vision. Powerful oracles hid this Face Dancer. Only the edges of these moments were known to Paul. He knew only what he could *not* do. He could not slay this Face Dancer. That would precipitate the future which must be avoided at all cost. Somehow, a way must be found to reach into the darkness and change the terrifying pattern.

"Give me your message," Paul said.

Bannerjee moved to place himself where he could watch the girl's face. She seemed to notice him for the first time and her gaze went to the knife handle beneath the Security Officer's hand.

"The innocent do not believe in evil," she said, looking squarely at Bannerjee.

Ahhh, well done, Paul thought. It was what the real Lichna would've said. He felt a momentary pang for the real daughter of Otheym—dead now, a corpse in the sand. There was no time for such emotions, though. He scowled.

Bannerjee kept his attention on the girl.

"I was told to deliver my message in secret," she said.

"Why?" Bannerjee demanded, voice harsh, probing.

"Because it is my father's wish."

"This is my friend," Paul said. "Am I not a Fremen? Then my friend may hear anything I hear."

Scytale composed the girl-shape. Was this a true Fremen custom . . . or was it a test?

"The Emperor may make his own rules," Scytale said. "This is the message: My father wishes you to come to him, bringing Chani."

"Why must I bring Chani?"

"She is your woman and a Sayyadina. This is a Water matter, by the rules of our tribes. She must attest it that my father speaks according to the Fremen Way."

There truly are Fremen in the conspiracy, Paul thought. This moment fitted the shape of things to come for sure. And he had no alternative but to commit himself to this course.

"Of what will your father speak?" Paul asked.

"He will speak of a plot against you—a plot among the Fremen."

"Why doesn't he bring that message in person?" Bannerjee demanded.

She kept her gaze on Paul. "My father cannot come here. The plotters suspect him. He'd not survive the journey."

"Could he not divulge the plot to you?" Bannerjee asked. "How came he to risk his daughter on such a mission?"

"The details are locked in a distrans carrier that only Muad'Dib may open," she said. "This much I know."

"Why not send the distrans, then?" Paul asked.

"It is a human distrans," she said.

"I'll go, then," Paul said. "But I'll go alone."

"Chani must come with you!"

"Chani is with child."

"When has a Fremen woman refused to . . ."

"My enemies fed her a subtle poison," Paul said. "It will be a difficult birth. Her health will not permit her to accompany me now."

Before Scytale could still them, strange emotions passed over the girl-features: frustration, anger. Scytale was reminded that every victim must have a way of escape—even such a one as Muad'Dib. The conspiracy had not failed, though. This Atreides remained in the net. He was a creature who had developed firmly into one pattern. He'd destroy himself before changing into the opposite of that pattern. That had been the way with the Tleilaxu kwisatz haderach. It'd be the way with this one. And then . . . the ghola.

"Let me ask Chani to decide this," she said.

"I have decided it," Paul said. "You will accompany me in Chani's stead."

"It requires a Sayyadina of the Rite!"

"Are you not Chani's friend?"

Boxed! Scytale thought. *Does he suspect? No. He's being Fremen-cautious. And the contraceptive is a fact. Well—there are other ways.*

"My father told me I was not to return," Scytale said, "that I was to seek asylum with you. He said you'd not risk me."

Paul nodded. It was beautifully in character. He couldn't deny this asylum. She'd plead Fremen obedience to a father's command.

"I'll take Stilgar's wife, Harah," Paul said. "You'll tell us the way to your father."

"How do you know you can trust Stilgar's wife?"

"I know it."

"But I don't."

Paul pursed his lips, then: "Does your mother live?"

"My true mother has gone to Shai-hulud. My second mother still lives and cares for my father. Why?"

"She's of Sietch Tabr?"

"Yes."

"I remember her," Paul said. "She will serve in Chani's place." He motioned to Bannerjee. "Have attendants take Otheym's Lichna to suitable quarters."

Bannerjee nodded. *Attendants.* The key word meant that this messenger must be put under special guard. He took her arm. She resisted.

"How will you go to my father?" she pleaded.

"You'll describe the way to Bannerjee," Paul said. "He is my friend."

"No! My father has commanded it! I cannot!"

"Bannerjee?" Paul said.

Bannerjee paused. Paul saw the man searching that encyclopedic memory which had helped bring him to his position of trust. "I know a guide who can take you to Otheym," Bannerjee said.

"Then I'll go alone," Paul said.

"Sire, if you . . ."

"Otheym wants it this way," Paul said, barely concealing the irony which consumed him.

"Sire, it's too dangerous," Bannerjee protested.

"Even an Emperor must accept some risks," Paul said. "The decision is made. Do as I've commanded."

Reluctantly, Bannerjee led the Face Dancer from the room.

Paul turned toward the blank screen behind his desk. He felt that he waited for the arrival of a rock on its blind journey from some height.

Should he tell Bannerjee about the messenger's true nature? he wondered. No! Such an incident hadn't been written on the screen of his vision. Any deviation here carried precipitate violence. A moment of fulcrum had to be found, a place where he could will himself out of the vision.

If such a moment existed . . .

No matter how exotic human civilization becomes, no matter the developments of life and society nor the complexity of the machine/human interface, there always come interludes of lonely power when the course of humankind, the very future of humankind, depends upon the relatively simple actions of single individuals.

—FROM THE TLEILAXU GODBUK

As he crossed over on the high footbridge from his Keep to the Qizarate Office Building, Paul added a limp to his walk. It was almost sunset and he walked through long shadows that helped conceal him, but sharp eyes still might detect something in his carriage that identified him. He wore a shield, but it was not activated, his aides having decided that the shimmer of it might arouse suspicions.

Paul glanced left. Strings of sandclouds lay across the sunset like slatted shutters. The air was hiereg dry through his stillsuit filters.

He wasn't really alone out here, but the web of Security hadn't been this loose around him since he'd ceased walking the streets alone in the night. Ornithopters with night scanners drifted far overhead in seemingly random patterns, all of them tied to his movements through a transmitter concealed in his clothing. Picked men walked the streets below. Others had fanned out through the city after seeing the Emperor in his disguise—Fremen costume down to the stillsuit and *temag* desert boots, the darkened features. His cheeks had been distorted with plastene inserts. A catchtube ran down along his left jaw.

As he reached the opposite end of the bridge, Paul glanced back, noted a movement beside the stone lattice that concealed a balcony of his private quarters. Chani, no doubt. "Hunting for sand in the desert," she'd called this venture.

How little she understood the bitter choice. Selecting among agonies, he thought, made even lesser agonies near unbearable.

For a blurred, emotionally painful moment, he relived their parting. At the last instant, Chani had experienced a tau-glimpse of his feelings, but she had misinterpreted. She had thought his emotions were those experienced in the parting of loved ones when one entered the dangerous unknown.

Would that I did not know, he thought.

He had crossed the bridge now and entered the upper passageway through the office building. There were fixed glowglobes here and people hurrying on business. The Qizarate never slept. Paul found his attention caught by the signs above doorways, as though he were seeing them for the first time: *Speed Merchants. Wind Stills and Retorts. Prophetic Prospects. Tests of Faith. Religious Supply. Weaponry . . . Propagation of the Faith . . .*

A more honest label would've been *Propagation of the Bureaucracy,* he thought.

A type of religious civil servant had sprung up all through his universe. This new man of the Qizarate was more often a convert. He seldom displaced a Fremen in the key posts, but he was filling all the interstices. He used melange as much to show he could afford it as for the geriatric benefits. He stood apart from his rulers—Emperor,

Guild, Bene Gesserit, Landsraad, Family or Qizarate. His gods were Routine and Records. He was served by mentats and prodigious filing systems. Expediency was the first word in his catechism, although he gave proper lip-service to the precepts of the Butlerians. Machines could not be fashioned in the image of a man's mind, he said, but he betrayed by every action that he preferred machines to men, statistics to individuals, the faraway general view to the intimate personal touch requiring imagination and initiative.

As Paul emerged onto the ramp at the far side of the building, he heard the bells calling the Evening Rite at Alia's Fane.

There was an odd feeling of permanence about the bells.

The temple across the thronged square was new, its rituals of recent devising, but there was something about this setting in a desert sink at the edge of Arrakeen—something in the way wind-driven sand had begun to weather stones and plastene, something in the haphazard way buildings had gone up around the Fane. Everything conspired to produce the impression that this was a very old place full of traditions and mystery.

He was down into the press of people now—committed. The only guide his Security force could find had insisted it be done this way. Security hadn't liked Paul's ready agreement. Stilgar had liked it even less. And Chani had objected most of all.

The crowd around him, even while its members brushed against him, glanced his way unseeing and passed on, gave him a curious freedom of movement. It was the way they'd been conditioned to treat a Fremen, he knew. He carried himself like a man of the inner desert. Such men were quick to anger.

As he moved into the quickening flow to the temple steps, the crush of people became even greater. Those all around could not help but press against him now, but he found himself the target for ritual apologies: "Your pardon, noble sir. I cannot prevent this discourtesy." "Pardon, sir; this crush of people is the worst I've ever seen." "I abase myself, holy citizen. A lout shoved me."

Paul ignored the words after the first few. There was no feeling in them except a kind of ritual fear. He found himself, instead, thinking that he had come a long way from his boyhood days in Caladan Castle. Where had he put his foot on the path that led to this journey across a crowded square on a planet so far from Caladan? Had he really put his foot on a path? He could not say he had acted at any point in his life for one specific reason. The motives and impinging forces had been complex—more complex possibly than any other set of goads in human history. He had the heady feeling here that he might still avoid the fate he could see so clearly along this path. But the crowd pushed him forward and he experienced the dizzy sense that he had lost his way, lost personal direction over his life.

The crowd flowed with him up the steps now into the temple portico. Voices grew hushed. The smell of fear grew stronger—acrid, sweaty.

Acolytes had already begun the service within the temple. Their plain chant dominated the other sounds—whispers, rustle of garments, shuffling feet, coughs—telling the story of the Far Places visited by the Priestess in her holy trance.

> *She rides the sandworm of space!*
> *She guides through all storms*
> *Into the land of gentle winds.*
> *Though we sleep by the snake's den,*
> *She guards our dreaming souls.*
> *Shunning the desert heat,*
> *She hides us in a cool hollow.*

The gleaming of her white teeth
Guides us in the night.
By the braids of her hair
We are lifted up to heaven!
Sweet fragrance, flower-scented,
Surrounds us in her presence.

Balak! Paul thought, thinking in Fremen. *Look out! She can be filled with angry passion, too.*

The temple portico was lined with tall, slender glow-tubes simulating candle flame. They flickered. The flickering stirred ancestral memories in Paul even while he knew that was the intent. This setting was an atavism, subtly contrived, effective. He hated his own hand in it.

The crowd flowed with him through tall metal doors into the gigantic nave, a gloomy place with the flickering lights far away overhead, a brilliantly illuminated altar at the far end. Behind the altar, a deceptively simple affair of black wood encrusted with sand patterns from the Fremen mythology, hidden lights played on the field of a pru-door to create a rainbow borealis. The seven rows of chanting acolytes ranked below that spectral curtain took on an eerie quality: black robes, white faces, mouths moving in unison.

Paul studied the pilgrims around him, suddenly envious of their intentness, their air of listening to truths he could not hear. It seemed to him that they gained something here which was denied to him, something mysteriously healing.

He tried to inch his way closer to the altar, was stopped by a hand on his arm. Paul whipped his gaze around, met the probing stare of an ancient Fremen—blue-blue eyes beneath overhanging brows, recognition in them. A name flashed into Paul's mind: Rasir, a companion from the sietch days.

In the press of the crowd, Paul knew he was completely vulnerable if Rasir planned violence.

The old man pressed close, one hand beneath a sand-grimed robe—grasping the hilt of a crysknife, no doubt. Paul set himself as best he could to resist attack. The old man moved his head toward Paul's ear, whispered: "We will go with the others."

It was the signal to identify his guide. Paul nodded.

Rasir drew back, faced the altar.

"She comes from the east," the acolytes chanted. "The sun stands at her back. All things are exposed. In the full glare of light—her eyes miss no thing, neither light nor dark."

A wailing rebaba jarred across the voices, stilled them, receded into silence. With an electric abruptness, the crowd surged forward several meters. They were packed into a tight mass of flesh now, the air heavy with their breathing and the scent of spice.

"Shai-hulud writes on clean sand!" the acolytes shouted.

Paul felt his own breath catch in unison with those around him. A feminine chorus began singing faintly from the shadows behind the shimmering pru-door: "Alia . . . Alia . . . Alia . . ." It grew louder and louder, fell to a sudden silence.

Again—voices beginning vesper-soft:

She stills all storms—
Her eyes kill our enemies,
And torment the unbelievers.
From the spires of Tuono
Where dawnlight strikes
And clear water runs,
You see her shadow.
In the shining summer heat

She serves us bread and milk—
Cool, fragrant with spices.
Her eyes melt our enemies,
Torment our oppressors
And pierce all mysteries.
She is Alia . . . Alia . . . Alia . . .

Slowly, the voices trailed off.

Paul felt sickened. *What are we doing?* he asked himself. Alia was a child witch, but she was growing older. And he thought: *Growing older is to grow more wicked.*

The collective mental atmosphere of the temple ate at his psyche. He could sense that element of himself which was one with those all around him, but the differences formed a deadly contradiction. He stood immersed, isolated in a personal sin which he could never expiate. The immensity of the universe outside the temple flooded his awareness. How could one man, one ritual, hope to knit such immensity into a garment fitted to all men?

Paul shuddered.

The universe opposed him at every step. It eluded his grasp, conceived countless disguises to delude him. That universe would never agree with any shape he gave it.

A profound hush spread through the temple.

Alia emerged from the darkness behind the shimmering rainbows. She wore a yellow robe trimmed in Atreides green—yellow for sunlight, green for the death which produced life. Paul experienced the sudden surprising thought that Alia had emerged here just for him, for him alone. He stared across the mob in the temple at his sister. She *was* his sister. He knew her ritual and its roots, but he had never before stood out here with the pilgrims, watched her through their eyes. Here, performing the mystery of this place, he saw that she partook of the universe which opposed him.

Acolytes brought her a golden chalice.

Alia raised the chalice.

With part of his awareness, Paul knew that the chalice contained the unaltered melange, the subtle poison, her sacrament of the oracle.

Her gaze on the chalice, Alia spoke. Her voice caressed the ears, flower sound, flowing and musical:

"In the beginning, we were empty," she said.

"Ignorant of all things," the chorus sang.

"We did not know the Power that abides in every place," Alia said.

"And in every Time," the chorus sang.

"Here is the Power," Alia said, raising the chalice slightly.

"It brings us joy," sang the chorus.

And it brings us distress, Paul thought.

"It awakens the soul," Alia said.

"It dispels all doubts," the chorus sang.

"In worlds, we perish," Alia said.

"In the Power, we survive," sang the chorus.

Alia put the chalice to her lips, drank.

To his astonishment, Paul found he was holding his breath like the meanest pilgrim of this mob. Despite every shred of personal knowledge about the experience Alia was undergoing, he had been caught in the tao-web. He felt himself remembering how that fiery poison coursed into the body. Memory unfolded the time-stopping when awareness became a mote which changed the poison. He re-experienced the awakening into timelessness where all things were possible. He *knew* Alia's present experience, yet he saw now that he did not know it. Mystery blinded the eyes.

Alia trembled, sank to her knees.

Paul exhaled with the enraptured pilgrims. He nodded. Part of the veil began to lift from him. Absorbed in the bliss of a vision, he had forgotten that each vision belonged to all those who were still on-the-way, still to become. In the vision, one passed through a darkness, unable to distinguish reality from insubstantial accident. One hungered for absolutes which could never be.

Hungering, one lost the present.

Alia swayed with the rapture of spice change.

Paul felt that some transcendental presence spoke to him, saying: "Look! See there! See what you've ignored?" In that instant, he thought he looked through other eyes, that he saw an imagery and rhythm in this place which no artist or poet could reproduce. It was vital and beautiful, a glaring light that exposed all power-gluttony . . . even his own.

Alia spoke. Her amplified voice boomed across the nave.

"Luminous night," she cried.

A moan swept like a wave through the crush of pilgrims.

"Nothing hides in such a night!" Alia said. "What rare light is this darkness? You cannot fix your gaze upon it! Senses cannot record it. No words describe it." Her voice lowered. "The abyss remains. It is pregnant with all the things yet to be. Ahhhhh, what gentle violence!"

Paul felt that he waited for some private signal from his sister. It could be any action or word, something of wizardry and mystical processes, an outward streaming that would fit him like an arrow into a cosmic bow. This instant lay like quivering mercury in his awareness.

"There will be sadness," Alia intoned. "I remind you that all things are but a beginning, forever beginning. Worlds wait to be conquered. Some within the sound of my voice will attain exalted destinies. You will sneer at the past, forgetting what I tell you now: within all differences there is unity."

Paul suppressed a cry of disappointment as Alia lowered her head. She had not said the thing he waited to hear. His body felt like a dry shell, a husk abandoned by some desert insect.

Others must feel something similar, he thought. He sensed the restlessness about him. Abruptly, a woman in the mob, someone far down in the nave to Paul's left, cried out, a wordless noise of anguish.

Alia lifted her head and Paul had the giddy sensation that the distance between them collapsed, that he stared directly into her glazed eyes only inches away from her.

"Who summons me?" Alia asked.

"I do," the woman cried. "I do, Alia. Oh, Alia, help me. They say my son was killed on Muritan. Is he gone? Will I never see my son again . . . never?"

"You try to walk backward in the sand," Alia intoned. "Nothing is lost. Everything returns later, but you may not recognize the changed form that returns."

"Alia, I don't understand!" the woman wailed.

"You live in the air but you do not see it," Alia said, sharpness in her voice. "Are you a lizard? Your voice has the Fremen accent. Does a Fremen try to bring back the dead? What do we need from our dead except their water?"

Down in the center of the nave, a man in a rich red cloak lifted both hands, the sleeves falling to expose white-clad arms. "Alia," he shouted, "I have had a business proposal. Should I accept?"

"You come here like a beggar," Alia said. "You look for the golden bowl but you will find only a dagger."

"I have been asked to kill a man!" a voice shouted from off to the right—a deep voice with sietch tones. "Should I accept? Accepting, would I succeed?"

"Beginning and end are a single thing," Alia snapped. "Have I not told you this before? You didn't come here to ask that question. What is it you cannot believe that you must come here and cry out against it?"

"She's in a fierce mood tonight," a woman near Paul muttered. "Have you ever seen her this angry?"

She knows I'm out here, Paul thought. *Did she see something in the vision that angered her? Is she raging at me?*

"Alia," a man directly in front of Paul called. "Tell these business-men and faint-hearts how long your brother will rule!"

"I permit you to look around that corner by yourself," Alia snarled. "You carry your prejudice in your mouth! It is because my brother rides the worm of chaos that you have roof and water!"

With a fierce gesture, clutching her robe, Alia whirled away, strode through the shimmering ribbons of light, was lost in the darkness behind.

Immediately, the acolytes took up the closing chant, but their rhythm was off. Obviously, they'd been caught by the unexpected ending of the rite. An incoherent mumbling arose on all sides of the crowd. Paul felt the stirring around him—restless, dissatisfied.

"It was that fool with his stupid question about business," a woman near Paul muttered. "The hypocrite!"

What had Alia seen? What track through the future?

Something had happened here tonight, souring the rite of the oracle. Usually, the crowd clamored for Alia to answer their pitiful questions. They came as beggars to the oracle, yes. He had heard them thus many times as he'd watched, hidden in the darkness behind the altar. What had been different about this night?

The old Fremen tugged Paul's sleeve, nodded toward the exit. The crowd already was beginning to push in that direction. Paul allowed himself to be pressed along with them, the guide's hand upon his sleeve. There was the feeling in him then that his body had become the manifestation of some power he could no longer control. He had become a non-being, a stillness which moved itself. At the core of the non-being, there he existed, allowing himself to be led through the streets of his city, following a track so familiar to his visions that it froze his heart with grief.

I should know what Alia saw, he thought. *I have seen it enough times myself. And she didn't cry out against it . . . she saw the alternatives, too.*

Production growth and income growth must not get out of step in my Empire. That is the substance of my command. There are to be no balance-of-payment difficulties between the different spheres of influence. And the reason for this is simply because I command it. I want to emphasize my authority in this area. I am the supreme energy-eater of this domain, and will remain so, alive or dead. My Government is the economy.

—ORDER IN COUNCIL
THE EMPEROR PAUL MUAD'DIB

"I will leave you here," the old man said, taking his hand from Paul's sleeve. "It is on the right, second door from the far end. Go with Shai-hulud, Muad'Dib . . . and remember when you were Usul."

Paul's guide slipped away into the darkness.

There would be Security men somewhere out there waiting to grab the guide and take the man to a place of questioning, Paul knew. But Paul found himself hoping the old Fremen would escape.

There were stars overhead and the distant light of First Moon somewhere beyond the Shield Wall. But this place was not the open desert where a man could sight on a star to guide his course. The old man had brought him into one of the new suburbs; this much Paul recognized.

This street now was thick with sand blown in from encroaching dunes. A dim light glowed from a single public suspensor globe far down the street. It gave enough illumination to show that this was a dead-end street.

The air around him was thick with the smell of a reclamation still. The thing must be poorly capped for its fetid odors to escape, loosing a dangerously wasteful amount of moisture into the night air. How careless his people had grown, Paul thought. They were millionaires of water—forgetful of the days when a man on Arrakis could have been killed for just an eighth share of the water in his body.

Why am I hesitating? Paul wondered. *It is the second door from the far end. I knew that without being told. But this thing must be played out with precision. So . . . I hesitate.*

The noise of an argument arose suddenly from the corner house on Paul's left. A woman there berated someone: the new wing of their house leaked dust, she complained. Did he think water fell from heaven? If dust came in, moisture got out.

Some remember, Paul thought.

He moved down the street and the quarrel faded away behind.

Water from heaven! he thought.

Some Fremen had seen that wonder on other worlds. He had seen it himself, had ordered it for Arrakis, but the memory of it felt like something that had occurred to another person. Rain, it was called. Abruptly, he recalled a rainstorm on his birthworld—clouds thick and gray in the sky of Caladan, an electric storm presence, moist air, the big wet drops drumming on skylights. It ran in rivulets off the eaves. Storm drains took the water away to a river which ran muddy and turgid past the Family orchards . . . trees there with their barren branches glistening wetly.

Paul's foot caught in a low drift of sand across the street. For an instant, he felt mud clinging to the shoes of his childhood. Then he was back in the sand, in the dust-clotted, wind-muffled darkness with the Future hanging over him, taunting. He could feel the aridity of life around him like an accusation. *You did this!* They'd become a civilization of dry-eyed watchers and taletellers, people who solved all problems with power . . . and more power . . . and still more power—hating every erg of it.

Rough stones came underfoot. His vision remembered them. The dark rectangle of a doorway appeared on his right—black in black: Otheym's house, Fate's house, a place different from the ones around it only in the role Time had chosen for it. It was a strange place to be marked down in history.

The door opened to his knock. The gap revealed the dull green light of an atrium. A dwarf peered out, ancient face on a child's body, an apparition prescience had never seen.

"You've come then," the apparition said. The dwarf stepped aside, no awe in his manner, merely the gloating of a slow smile. "Come in! Come in!"

Paul hesitated. There'd been no dwarf in the vision, but all else remained identical. Visions could contain such disparities and still hold true to their original plunge into infinity. But the difference dared him to hope. He glanced back up the street at the creamy pearl glistening of his moon swimming out of jagged shadows. The moon haunted him. How did it fall?

"Come in," the dwarf insisted.

Paul entered, heard the door thud into its moisture seals behind. The dwarf passed him, led the way, enormous feet slapping the floor, opened the delicate lattice gate into the roofed central courtyard, gestured. "They await, Sire."

Sire, Paul thought. *He knows me, then.*

Before Paul could explore this discovery, the dwarf slipped away down a side passage. Hope was a dervish wind whirling, dancing in Paul. He headed across the courtyard. It was a dark and gloomy place, the smell of sickness and defeat in it. He felt daunted by the atmosphere. Was it defeat to choose a lesser evil? he wondered. How far down this track had he come?

Light poured from a narrow doorway in the far wall. He put down the feeling of watchers and evil smells, entered the doorway into a small room. It was a barren place by Fremen standards with hiereg hangings on only two walls. Opposite the door, a man sat on carmine cushions beneath the best hanging. A feminine figure hovered in shadows behind another doorway in a barren wall to the left.

Paul felt vision-trapped. This was the way it'd gone. Where was the dwarf? Where was the difference?

His senses absorbed the room in a single gestalten sweep. The place had received painstaking care despite its poor furnishings. Hooks and rods across the barren walls showed where hangings had been removed. Pilgrims paid enormous prices for authentic Fremen artifacts, Paul reminded himself. Rich pilgrims counted desert tapestries as treasures, true marks of a hajj.

Paul felt that the barren walls accused him with their fresh gypsum wash. The threadbare condition of the two remaining hangings amplified the sense of guilt.

A narrow shelf occupied the wall on his right. It held a row of portraits—mostly bearded Fremen, some in stillsuits with their catchtubes dangling, some in Imperial uniforms posed against exotic offworld backgrounds. The most common scene was a seascape.

The Fremen on cushions cleared his throat, forcing Paul to look at him. It was Otheym precisely as the vision had revealed him: neck grown scrawny, a bird thing which appeared too weak to support the large head. The face was a lopsided ruin—networks of crisscrossed scars on the left cheek below a drooping, wet eye, but clear skin on the other side and a straight, blue-in-blue Fremen gaze. A long kedge of a nose bisected the face.

Otheym's cushion sat in the center of a threadbare rug, brown with maroon and gold threads. The cushion fabric betrayed splotches of wear and patching, but every bit of metal around the seated figure shone from polishing—the portrait frames, shelf lip and brackets, the pedestal of a low table on the right.

Paul nodded to the clear half of Otheym's face, said: "Good luck to you and your dwelling place." It was the greeting of an old friend and sietch mate.

"So I see you once more, Usul."

The voice speaking his tribal name whined with an old man's quavering. The dull drooping eye on the ruined side of the face moved above the parchment skin and scars. Gray bristles stubbled that side and the jawline there hung with scabrous peelings. Otheym's mouth twisted as he spoke, the gap exposing silvery metal teeth.

"Muad'Dib always answers the call of a Fedaykin," Paul said.

The woman in the doorway shadows moved, said: "So Stilgar boasts."

She came forward into the light, an older version of the Lichna which the Face Dancer had copied. Paul recalled then that Otheym had married sisters. Her hair was gray, nose grown witch-sharp. Weavers' calluses ran along her forefingers and thumbs. A Fremen woman would've displayed such marks proudly in the sietch days, but she saw his attention on her hands, hid them under a fold of her pale blue robe.

Paul remembered her name then—Dhuri. The shock was he remembered her as a child, not as she'd been in his vision of these moments. It was the whine that edged her voice, Paul told himself. She'd whined even as a child.

"You see me here," Paul said. "Would I be here if Stilgar hadn't approved?" He turned toward Otheym. "I carry your water burden, Otheym. Command me."

This was the straight Fremen talk of sietch brothers.

Otheym produced a shaky nod, almost too much for that thin neck. He lifted a liver-marked left hand, pointed to the ruin of his face. "I caught the splitting disease on Tarahell, Usul," he wheezed. "Right after the victory when we'd all . . ." A fit of coughing stopped his voice.

"The tribe will collect his water soon," Dhuri said. She crossed to Otheym, propped pillows behind him, held his shoulder to steady him until the coughing passed. She wasn't really very old, Paul saw, but a look of lost hopes ringed her mouth, bitterness lay in her eyes.

"I'll summon doctors," Paul said.

Dhuri turned, hand on hip. "We've had medical men, as good as any you could summon." She sent an involuntary glance to the barren wall on her left.

And the medical men were costly, Paul thought.

He felt edgy, constrained by the vision but aware that minor differences had crept in. How could he exploit the differences? Time came out of its skein with subtle changes, but the background fabric held oppressive sameness. He knew with terrifying certainty that if he tried to break out of the enclosing pattern here, it'd become a thing of terrible violence. The power in this deceptively gentle flow of Time oppressed him.

"Say what you want of me," he growled.

"Couldn't it be that Otheym needed a friend to stand by him in

this time?" Dhuri asked. "Does a Fedaykin have to consign his flesh
to strangers?"

We shared Sietch Tabr, Paul reminded himself. *She has the right to
berate me for apparent callousness.*

"What I can do I will do," Paul said.

Another fit of coughing shook Otheym. When it had passed, he
gasped: "There's treachery, Usul. Fremen plot against you." His mouth
worked then without sound. Spittle escaped his lips. Dhuri wiped his
mouth with a corner of her robe, and Paul saw how her face betrayed
anger at such waste of moisture.

Frustrated rage threatened to overwhelm Paul then. *That Otheym
should be spent thus! A Fedaykin deserved better.* But no choice
remained—not for a Death Commando or his Emperor. They walked
occam's razor in this room. The slightest misstep multiplied horrors—
not just for themselves, but for all humankind, even for those who
would destroy them.

Paul squeezed calmness into his mind, looked at Dhuri. The expression of terrible longing with which she gazed at Otheym strengthened Paul. *Chani must never look at me that way,* he told himself.

"Lichna spoke of a message," Paul said.

"My dwarf," Otheym wheezed. "I bought him on . . . on . . . on a
world . . . I forget. He's a human distrans, a toy discarded by the Tleilaxu. He's recorded all the names . . . the traitors . . ."

Otheym fell silent, trembling.

"You speak of Lichna," Dhuri said. "When you arrived, we knew
she'd reached you safely. If you're thinking of this new burden
Otheym places upon you, Lichna is the sum of that burden. An even
exchange, Usul: take the dwarf and go."

Paul suppressed a shudder, closed his eyes. *Lichna!* The real daughter had perished in the desert, a semuta-wracked body abandoned to the sand and the wind.

Opening his eyes, Paul said: "You could've come to me at any time for . . ."

"Otheym stayed away that he might be numbered among those who hate you, Usul," Dhuri said. "The house to the south of us at the end of the street, that is a gathering place for your foes. It's why we took this hovel."

"Then summon the dwarf and we'll leave," Paul said.

"You've not listened well," Dhuri said.

"You must take the dwarf to a safe place," Otheym said, an odd strength in his voice. "He carries the only record of the traitors. No one suspects his talent. They think I keep him for amusement."

"We cannot leave," Dhuri said. "Only you and the dwarf. It's known . . . how poor we are. We've said we're selling the dwarf. They'll take you for the buyer. It's your only chance."

Paul consulted his memory of the vision: in it, he'd left here with the names of the traitors, but never seeing how those names were carried. The dwarf obviously moved under the protection of another oracle. It occurred to Paul then that all creatures must carry some kind of destiny stamped out by purposes of varying strengths, by the fixation of training and disposition. From the moment the Jihad had chosen him, he'd felt himself hemmed in by the forces of a multitude. Their fixed purposes demanded and controlled his course. Any delusions of Free Will he harbored now must be merely the prisoner rattling his cage. His curse lay in the fact that he *saw* the cage. He *saw* it!

He listened now to the emptiness of this house: only the four of them in it—Dhuri, Otheym, the dwarf and himself. He inhaled the fear and tension of his companions, sensed the watchers—his own force hovering in 'thopters far overhead . . . and those others . . . next door.

I was wrong to hope, Paul thought. But thinking of hope brought him a twisted *sense* of hope, and he felt that he might yet seize his moment.

"Summon the dwarf," he said.

"Bijaz!" Dhuri called.

"You call me?" The dwarf stepped into the room from the courtyard, an alert expression of worry on his face.

"You have a new master, Bijaz," Dhuri said. She stared at Paul. "You may call him . . . Usul."

"Usul, that's the base of the pillar," Bijaz said, translating. "How can Usul be base when I'm the basest thing living?"

"He always speaks thus," Otheym apologized.

"I don't speak," Bijaz said. "I operate a machine called language. It creaks and groans, but is mine own."

A Tleilaxu toy, learned and alert, Paul thought. *The Bene Tleilax never threw away something this valuable.* He turned, studied the dwarf. Round melange eyes returned his stare.

"What other talents have you, Bijaz?" Paul asked.

"I know when we should leave," Bijaz said. "It's a talent few men have. There's a time for endings—and that's a good beginning. Let us begin to go, Usul."

Paul examined his vision memory: no dwarf, but the little man's words fitted the occasion.

"At the door, you called me Sire," Paul said. "You know me, then?"

"You've sired, Sire," Bijaz said, grinning. "You are much more than the base Usul. You're the Atreides Emperor, Paul Muad'Dib. And you are my finger." He held up the index finger of his right hand.

"Bijaz!" Dhuri snapped. "You tempt fate."

"I tempt my finger," Bijaz protested, voice squeaking. He pointed at Usul. "I point at Usul. Is my finger not Usul himself? Or is it a reflection of something more base?" He brought the finger close to his eyes, examined it with a mocking grin, first one side then the other. "Ahhh, it's merely a finger, after all."

"He often rattles on thus," Dhuri said, worry in her voice. "I think it's why he was discarded by the Tleilaxu."

"I'll not be patronized," Bijaz said, "yet I have a new patron. How strange the workings of the finger." He peered at Dhuri and Otheym, eyes oddly bright. "A weak glue bound us, Otheym. A few tears and we part." The dwarf's big feet rasped on the floor as he whirled completely around, stopped facing Paul. "Ahhh, patron! I came the long way around to find you."

Paul nodded.

"You'll be kind, Usul?" Bijaz asked. "I'm a person, you know. Persons come in many shapes and sizes. This be but one of them. I'm weak of muscle, but strong of mouth; cheap to feed, but costly to fill. Empty me as you will, there's still more in me than men put there."

"We've no time for your stupid riddles," Dhuri growled. "You should be gone."

"I'm riddled with conundrums," Bijaz said, "but not all of them stupid. To be gone, Usul, is to be a bygone. Yes? Let us let bygones be bygones. Dhuri speaks truth, and I've the talent for hearing that, too."

"You've truthsense?" Paul asked, determined now to wait out the clockwork of his vision. Anything was better than shattering these moments and producing the new consequences. There remained things for Otheym to say lest Time be diverted into even more horrifying channels.

"I've *now*-sense," Bijaz said.

Paul noted that the dwarf had grown more nervous. Was the little man aware of things about to happen? Could Bijaz be his own oracle?

"Did you inquire of Lichna?" Otheym asked suddenly, peering up at Dhuri with his one good eye.

"Lichna is safe," Dhuri said.

Paul lowered his head, lest his expression betray the lie. *Safe!* Lichna was ashes in a secret grave.

"That's good then," Otheym said, taking Paul's lowered head for a nod of agreement. "One good thing among the evils, Usul. I don't like the world we're making, you know that? It was better when we were alone in the desert with only the Harkonnens for enemy."

"There's but a thin line between many an enemy and many a friend," Bijaz said. "Where that line stops, there's no beginning and no end. Let's end it, my friends." He moved to Paul's side, jittered from one foot to the other.

"What's *now*-sense?" Paul asked, dragging out these moments, goading the dwarf.

"Now!" Bijaz said, trembling. "Now! Now!" He tugged at Paul's robe. "Let us go now!"

"His mouth rattles, but there's no harm in him," Otheym said, affection in his voice, the one good eye staring at Bijaz.

"Even a rattle can signal departure," Bijaz said. "And so can tears. Let's be gone while there's time to begin."

"Bijaz, what do you fear?" Paul asked.

"I fear the spirit seeking me now," Bijaz muttered. Perspiration stood out on his forehead. His cheeks twitched. "I fear the one who thinks not and will have no body except mine—and that one gone back into itself! I fear the things I see and the things I do not see."

This dwarf does possess the power of prescience, Paul thought. Bijaz shared the terrifying oracle. Did he share the oracle's fate, as well?

How potent was the dwarf's power? Did he have the little prescience of those who dabbled in the Dune Tarot? Or was it something greater? How much had he seen?

"Best you go," Dhuri said. "Bijaz is right."

"Every minute we linger," Bijaz said, "prolongs . . . prolongs the present!"

Every minute I linger defers my guilt, Paul thought. A worm's poisonous breath, its teeth dripping dust, had washed over him. It had happened long ago, but he inhaled the memory of it now—spice and bitterness. He could sense his own worm waiting—"the urn of the desert."

"These are troubled times," he said, addressing himself to Otheym's judgment of their world.

"Fremen know what to do in time of trouble," Dhuri said.

Otheym contributed a shaky nod.

Paul glanced at Dhuri. He'd not expected gratitude, would have been burdened by it more than he could bear, but Otheym's bitterness and the passionate resentment he saw in Dhuri's eyes shook his resolve. Was *anything* worth this price?

"Delay serves no purpose," Dhuri said.

"Do what you must, Usul," Otheym wheezed.

Paul sighed. The words of the vision had been spoken. "There'll be an accounting," he said, to complete it. Turning, he strode from the room, heard Bijaz foot-slapping behind.

"Bygones, bygones," Bijaz muttered as they went. "Let bygones fall where they may. This has been a dirty day."

The convoluted wording of legalisms grew up around the necessity to hide from ourselves the violence we intend toward each other. Between depriving a man of one hour from his life and depriving him of his life there exists only a difference of degree. You have done violence to him, consumed his energy. Elaborate euphemisms may conceal your intent to kill, but behind any use of power over another the ultimate assumption remains: "I feed on your energy."

—ADDENDA TO ORDERS IN COUNCIL
THE EMPEROR PAUL MUAD'DIB

First Moon stood high over the city as Paul, his shield activated and shimmering around him, emerged from the cul-de-sac. A wind off the massif whirled sand and dust down the narrow street, causing Bijaz to blink and shield his eyes.

"We must hurry," the dwarf muttered. "Hurry! Hurry!"

"You sense danger?" Paul asked, probing.

"I *know* danger!"

An abrupt sense of peril very near was followed almost immediately by a figure joining them out of a doorway.

Bijaz crouched and whimpered.

It was only Stilgar moving like a war machine, head thrust forward, feet striking the street solidly.

Swiftly, Paul explained the value of the dwarf, handed Bijaz over to Stilgar. The pace of the vision moved here with great rapidity. Stilgar sped away with Bijaz. Security Guards enveloped Paul. Orders were given to send men down the street toward the house beyond Otheym's. The men hurried to obey, shadows among shadows.

More sacrifices, Paul thought.

"We want live prisoners," one of the guard officers hissed.

The sound was a vision-echo in Paul's ears. It went with solid precision here—vision/reality, tick for tick. Ornithopters drifted down across the moon.

The night was full of Imperial troopers attacking.

A soft hiss grew out of the other sounds, climbed to a roar while they still heard the sibilance. It picked up a terra-cotta glow that hid the stars, engulfed the moon.

Paul, knowing that sound and glow from the earliest nightmare glimpses of his vision, felt an odd sense of fulfillment. It went the way it must.

"Stone burner!" someone screamed.

"Stone burner!" The cry was all around him. "Stone burner . . . stone burner . . ."

Because it was required of him, Paul threw a protective arm across his face, dove for the low lip of a curb. It already was too late, of course.

Where Otheym's house had been there stood now a pillar of fire, a blinding jet roaring at the heavens. It gave off a dirty brilliance which threw into sharp relief every ballet movement of the fighting and fleeing men, the tipping retreat of ornithopters.

For every member of this frantic throng it was too late.

The ground grew hot beneath Paul. He heard the sound of running stop. Men threw themselves down all around him, every one of them aware that there was no point in running. The first damage had been done; and now they must wait out the extent of the stone burner's potency. The things's radiation, which no man could outrun, already had penetrated their flesh. The peculiar result of stone-burner radiation already was at work in them. What else this weapon might do now lay in the planning of the men who had used it, the men who had defied the Great Convention to use it.

"God's . . . a stone burner," someone whimpered. "I . . . don't . . . want . . . to . . . be . . . blind."

"Who does?" The harsh voice of a trooper far down the street.

"The Tleilaxu will sell many eyes here," someone near Paul growled. "Now, shut up and wait!"

They waited.

Paul remained silent, thinking what this weapon implied. Too much fuel in it and it'd cut its way into the planet's core. Dune's molten level lay deep, but the more dangerous for that. Such pressures released and out of control might split a planet, scattering lifeless bits and pieces through space.

"I think it's dying down a bit," someone said.

"It's just digging deeper," Paul cautioned. "Stay put, all of you. Stilgar will be sending help."

"Stilgar got away?"

"Stilgar got away."

"The ground's hot," someone complained.

"They dared use atomics!" a trooper near Paul protested.

"The sound's diminishing," someone down the street said.

Paul ignored the words, concentrated on his fingertips against the street. He could feel the rolling-rumbling of the thing—deep . . . deep . . .

"My eyes!" someone cried. "I can't see!"

Someone closer to it than I was, Paul thought. He still could see to the end of the cul-de-sac when he lifted his head, although there was a mistiness across the scene. A red-yellow glow filled the area where Otheym's house and its neighbor had been. Pieces of adjoining buildings made dark patterns as they crumbled into the glowing pit.

Paul climbed to his feet. He felt the stone burner die, silence beneath him. His body was wet with perspiration against the stillsuit's slickness—too much for the suit to accommodate. The air he drew into his lungs carried the heat and sulfur stench of the burner.

As he looked at the troopers beginning to stand up around him, the mist on Paul's eyes faded into darkness. He summoned up his oracular vision of these moments, then, turned and strode along the track that Time had carved for him, fitting himself into the vision so tightly that it could not escape. He felt himself grow aware of this place as a multitudinous possession, reality welded to prediction.

Moans and groans of his troopers arose all around him as the men realized their blindness.

"Hold fast!" Paul shouted. "Help is coming!" And, as the complaints persisted, he said: "This is Muad'Dib! I command you to hold fast! Help comes!"

Silence.

Then, true to his vision, a nearby guardsman said: "Is it truly the Emperor? Which of you can see? Tell me."

"None of us has eyes," Paul said. "They have taken my eyes, as well, but not my vision. I can *see* you standing there, a dirty wall within touching distance on your left. Now wait bravely. Stilgar comes with our friends."

The thwock-thwock of many 'thopters grew louder all around.

There was the sound of hurrying feet. Paul *watched* his friends come, matching their sounds to his oracular vision.

"Stilgar!" Paul shouted, waving an arm. "Over here!"

"Thanks to Shai-hulud," Stilgar cried, running up to Paul. "You're not . . ." In the sudden silence, Paul's vision showed him Stilgar staring with an expression of agony at the ruined eyes of his friend and Emperor. "Oh, m'Lord," Stilgar groaned. "Usul . . . Usul . . . Usul . . ."

"What of the stone burner?" one of the newcomers shouted.

"It's ended," Paul said, raising his voice. He gestured. "Get up there now and rescue the ones who were closest to it. Put up barriers. Lively now!" He turned back to Stilgar.

"Do you *see*, m'Lord?" Stilgar asked, wonder in his tone. "How can you see?"

For answer, Paul put a finger out to touch Stilgar's cheek above the stillsuit mouthcap, felt tears. "You need give no moisture to me, old friend," Paul said. "I am not dead."

"But your eyes!"

"They've blinded my body, but not my vision," Paul said. "Ah, Stil, I live in an apocalyptic dream. My steps fit into it so precisely that I fear most of all I will grow bored reliving the thing so exactly."

"Usul, I don't, I don't . . ."

"Don't try to understand it. Accept it. I am in the world beyond this world here. For me, they are the same. I need no hand to guide me. I see every movement all around me. I see every expression of your face. I have no eyes, yet I see."

Stilgar shook his head sharply. "Sire, we must conceal your affliction from—"

"We hide it from no man," Paul said.

"But the law . . ."

"We live by the Atreides Law now, Stil. The Fremen Law that the blind should be abandoned in the desert applies only to the blind. I am not blind. I live in the cycle of being where the war of good and evil has its arena. We are at a turning point in the succession of ages and we have our parts to play."

In a sudden stillness, Paul heard one of the wounded being led past him. "It was terrible," the man groaned, "a great fury of fire."

"None of these men shall be taken into the desert," Paul said. "You hear me, Stil?"

"I hear you, m'Lord."

"They are to be fitted with new eyes at my expense."

"It will be done, m'Lord."

Paul, hearing the awe grow in Stilgar's voice, said: "I will be at the Command 'thopter. Take charge here."

"Yes, m'Lord."

Paul stepped around Stilgar, strode down the street. His vision told him every movement, every irregularity beneath his feet, every face he encountered. He gave orders as he moved, pointing to men of his personal entourage, calling out names, summoning to himself the ones who represented the intimate apparatus of government. He could feel the terror grow behind him, the fearful whispers.

"His eyes!"

"But he looked right at you, called you by name!"

At the Command 'thopter, he deactivated his personal shield, reached into the machine and took the microphone from the hand of a startled communications officer, issued a swift string of orders, thrust the microphone back into the officer's hand. Turning, Paul summoned a weapons specialist, one of the eager and brilliant new breed who remembered sietch life only dimly.

"They used a stone burner," Paul said.

After the briefest pause, the man said: "So I was told, Sire."

"You know what that means, of course."

"The fuel could only have been atomic."

Paul nodded, thinking of how this man's mind must be racing. Atomics. The Great Convention prohibited such weapons. Discovery of the perpetrator would bring down the combined retributive assault of the Great Houses. Old feuds would be forgotten, discarded in the face of this threat and the ancient fears it aroused.

"It cannot have been manufactured without leaving some traces," Paul said. "You will assemble the proper equipment and search out the place where the stone burner was made."

"At once, Sire." With one last fearful glance, the man sped away.

"M'Lord," the communications officer ventured from behind him. "Your eyes . . ."

Paul turned, reached into the 'thopter, returned the command set to his personal band. "Call Chani," he ordered. "Tell her . . . tell her I am alive and will be with her soon."

Now the forces gather, Paul thought. And he noted how strong was the smell of fear in the perspiration all around.

He has gone from Alia,

The womb of heaven!

Holy, holy, holy!

Fire-sand leagues

Confront our Lord.

He can see

Without eyes!

A demon upon him!

Holy, holy, holy

Equation:

He solved for

Martyrdom!

—THE MOON FALLS DOWN
SONGS OF MUAD'DIB

After seven days of radiating fevered activity, the Keep took on an unnatural quiet. On this morning, there were people about, but they spoke in whispers, heads close together, and they walked softly. Some scurried with an oddly furtive gait. The sight of a guard detail coming in from the forecourt drew questioning looks and frowns at the noise which the newcomers brought with their tramping about and stacking of weapons. The newcomers caught the mood of the interior, though, and began moving in that furtive way.

Talk of the stone burner still floated around: "He said the fire had blue-green in it and a smell out of hell."

"Elpa is a fool! He says he'll commit suicide rather than take Tleilaxu eyes."

"I don't like talk of eyes."

"Muad'Dib passed me and called me by name!"

"How does *He* see without eyes?"

"People are leaving, had you heard? There's great fear. The Naibs say they'll go to Sietch Makab for a Grand Council."

"What've they done with the Panegyrist?"

"I saw them take him into the chamber where the Naibs are meeting. Imagine Korba a prisoner!"

Chani had arisen early, awakened by a stillness in the Keep. Awakening, she'd found Paul sitting beside her, his eyeless sockets aimed at some formless place beyond the far wall of their bedchamber. What the stone burner had done with its peculiar affinity for eye tissue, all that ruined flesh had been removed. Injections and unguents had saved the stronger flesh around the sockets, but she felt that the radiation had gone deeper.

Ravenous hunger seized her as she sat up. She fed on the food kept by the bedside—spicebread, a heavy cheese.

Paul gestured at the food. "Beloved, there was no way to spare you this. Believe me."

Chani stilled a fit of trembling when he aimed those empty sockets at her. She'd given up asking him to explain. He spoke so oddly: *"I was baptized in sand and it cost me the knack of believing. Who trades in faiths anymore? Who'll buy? Who'll sell?"*

What could he mean by such words?

He refused even to consider Tleilaxu eyes, although he bought them with a lavish hand for the men who'd shared his affliction.

Hunger satisfied, Chani slipped from bed, glanced back at Paul, noted his tiredness. Grim lines framed his mouth. The dark hair stood up, mussed from a sleep that hadn't healed. He appeared so saturnine and remote. The back and forth of waking and sleeping did nothing to change this. She forced herself to turn away, whispered: "My love . . . my love . . ."

He leaned over, pulled her back into the bed, kissed her cheeks. "Soon we'll go back to our desert," he whispered. "Only a few things remain to be done here."

She trembled at the finality in his voice.

He tightened his arms around her, murmured: "Don't fear me, my Sihaya. Forget mystery and accept love. There's no mystery about love. It comes from life. Can't you feel that?"

"Yes."

She put a palm against his chest, counting his heartbeats. His love cried out to the Fremen spirit in her—torrential, outpouring, savage. A magnetic power enveloped her.

"I promise you a thing, beloved," he said. "A child of ours will rule such an empire that mine will fade in comparison. Such achievements of living and art and sublime—"

"We're here now!" she protested, fighting a dry sob. "And . . . I feel we have so little . . . time."

"We have eternity, beloved."

"*You* may have eternity. I have only now."

"But this *is* eternity." He stroked her forehead.

She pressed against him, lips on his neck. The pressure agitated the life in her womb. She felt it stir.

Paul felt it, too. He put a hand on her abdomen, said: "Ahh, little ruler of the universe, wait your time. This moment is mine."

She wondered then why he always spoke of the life within her as singular. Hadn't the medics told him? She searched back in her own memory, curious that the subject had never arisen between them. Surely, he must know she carried twins. She hesitated on the point of raising this question. He *must* know. He knew everything. He knew all the things that were herself. His hands, his mouth—all of him knew her.

Presently, she said: "Yes, love. This is forever . . . this is real." And she closed her eyes tightly lest sight of his dark sockets stretch her soul from paradise to hell. No matter the rihani magic in which he'd enciphered their lives, his flesh remained real, his caresses could not be denied.

When they arose to dress for the day, she said: "If the people only knew your love . . ."

But his mood had changed. "You can't build politics on love," he said. "People aren't concerned with love; it's too disordered. They prefer despotism. Too much freedom breeds chaos. We can't have that, can we? And how do you make despotism lovable?"

"You're not a despot!" she protested, tying her scarf. "Your laws are just."

"Ahh, laws," he said. He crossed to the window, pulled back the draperies as though he could look out. "What's law? Control? Law filters chaos and what drips through? Serenity? Law—our highest ideal and our basest nature. Don't look too closely at the law. Do, and you'll find the rationalized interpretations, the legal casuistry, the precedents of convenience. You'll find the serenity, which is just another word for death."

Chani's mouth drew into a tight line. She couldn't deny his wisdom and sagacity, but these moods frightened her. He turned upon himself and she sensed internal wars. It was as though he took the Fremen maxim, *"Never to forgive—never to forget,"* and whipped his own flesh with it.

She crossed to his side, stared past him at an angle. The growing heat of the day had begun pulling the north wind out of these protected latitudes. The wind painted a false sky full of ochre plumes and sheets of crystal, strange designs in rushing gold and red. High and cold, the wind broke against the Shield Wall with fountains of dust.

Paul felt Chani's warmth beside him. Momentarily, he lowered a curtain of forgetfulness across his vision. He might just be standing here with his eyes closed. Time refused to stand still for him, though. He inhaled darkness—starless, tearless. His affliction dissolved substance until all that remained was astonishment at the way sounds condensed his universe. Everything around him leaned on his lonely sense of hearing, falling back only when he touched objects: the drapery, Chani's hand . . . He caught himself listening for Chani's breaths.

Where was the insecurity of things that were only probable? he asked himself. His mind carried such a burden of mutilated memories. For every instant of reality there existed countless projections, things fated never to be. An invisible self within him remembered the false pasts, their burden threatening at times to overwhelm the present.

Chani leaned against his arm.

He felt his body through her touch: dead flesh carried by time eddies. He reeked of memories that had glimpsed eternity. To see eternity was to be exposed to eternity's whims, oppressed by endless dimensions. The oracle's false immortality demanded retribution: Past and Future became simultaneous.

Once more, the vision arose from its black pit, locked onto him.

It was his eyes. It moved his muscles. It guided him into the next moment, the next hour, the next day . . . until he felt himself to be always
there!

"It's time we were going," Chani said. "The Council . . ."

"Alia will be there to stand in my place."

"Does she know what to do?"

"She knows."

Alia's day began with a guard squadron swarming into the parade
yard below her quarters. She stared down at a scene of frantic confusion, clamorous and intimidating babble. The scene became intelligible only when she recognized the prisoner they'd brought: Korba,
the Panegyrist.

She made her morning toilet, moving occasionally to the window,
keeping watch on the progress of impatience down there. Her gaze
kept straying to Korba. She tried to remember him as the rough and
bearded commander of the third wave in the battle of Arrakeen. It
was impossible. Korba had become an immaculate fop dressed now
in a Parato silk robe of exquisite cut. It lay open to the waist, revealing
a beautifully laundered ruff and embroidered undercoat set with
green gems. A purple belt gathered the waist. The sleeves poking
through the robe's armhole slits had been tailored into rivulet ridges
of dark green and black velvet.

A few Naibs had come out to observe the treatment accorded a
fellow Fremen. They'd brought on the clamor, exciting Korba to protest his innocence. Alia moved her gaze across the Fremen faces, trying to recapture memories of the original men. The present blotted
out the past. They'd all become hedonists, samplers of pleasures most
men couldn't even imagine.

Their uneasy glances, she saw, strayed often to the doorway
into the chamber where they would meet. They were thinking of

Muad'Dib's blind-sight, a new manifestation of mysterious powers. By their law, a blind man should be abandoned in the desert, his water given up to Shai-hulud. But eyeless Muad'Dib saw them. They disliked buildings, too, and felt vulnerable in space built above the ground. Give them a proper cave cut from rock, then they could relax—but not here, not with this new Muad'Dib waiting *inside*.

As she turned to go down to the meeting, she saw the letter where she'd left it on a table by the door: the latest message from their mother. Despite the special reverence held for Caladan as the place of Paul's birth, the Lady Jessica had emphasized her refusal to make her planet a stop on the hajj.

"No doubt my son is an epochal figure of history," she'd written, "but I cannot see this as an excuse for submitting to a rabble invasion."

Alia touched the letter, experienced an odd sensation of mutual contact. This paper had been in her mother's hands. Such an archaic device, the letter—but personal in a way no recording could achieve. Written in the Atreides battle tongue, it represented an almost invulnerable privacy of communication.

Thinking of her mother afflicted Alia with the usual inward blurring. The spice change that had mixed the psyches of mother and daughter forced her at times to think of Paul as a son to whom she had given birth. The capsule-complex of oneness could present her own father as a lover. Ghost shadows cavorted in her mind, people of possibility.

Alia reviewed the letter as she walked down the ramp to the antechamber where her guard amazons waited.

"You produce a deadly paradox," Jessica had written. "Government cannot be religious and self-assertive at the same time. Religious experience needs a spontaneity which laws inevitably suppress.

And you cannot govern without laws. Your laws eventually must replace morality, replace conscience, replace even the religion by which you think to govern. Sacred ritual must spring from praise and holy yearnings which hammer out a significant morality. Government, on the other hand, is a cultural organism particularly attractive to doubts, questions and contentions. I see the day coming when ceremony must take the place of faith and symbolism replaces morality."

The smell of spice-coffee greeted Alia in the antechamber. Four guard amazons in green watch-robes came to attention as she entered. They fell into step behind her, striding firmly in the bravado of their youth, eyes alert for trouble. They had zealot faces untouched by awe. They radiated that special Fremen quality of violence: they could kill casually with no sense of guilt.

In this, I am different, Alia thought. *The Atreides name has enough dirt on it without that.*

Word preceded her. A waiting page darted off as she entered the lower hall, running to summon the full guard detail. The hall stretched out windowless and gloomy, illuminated only by a few subdued glowglobes. Abruptly, the doors to the parade yard opened wide at the far end to admit a glaring shaft of daylight. The guard with Korba in their midst wavered into view from the outside with the light behind them.

"Where is Stilgar?" Alia demanded.

"Already inside," one of her amazons said.

Alia led the way into the chamber. It was one of the Keep's more pretentious meeting places. A high balcony with rows of soft seats occupied one side. Across from the balcony, orange draperies had been pulled back from tall windows. Bright sunlight poured through from an open space with a garden and a fountain. At the near end of the chamber on her right stood a dais with a single massive chair.

Moving to the chair, Alia glanced back and up, saw the gallery filled with Naibs.

Household guardsmen packed the open space beneath the gallery, Stilgar moving among them with a quiet word here, a command there. He gave no sign that he'd seen Alia enter.

Korba was brought in, seated at a low table with cushions beside it on the chamber floor below the dais. Despite his finery, the Panegyrist gave the appearance now of a surly, sleepy old man huddled up in his robes as against the outer cold. Two guardsmen took up positions behind him.

Stilgar approached the dais as Alia seated herself.

"Where is Muad'Dib?" he asked.

"My brother has delegated me to preside as Reverend Mother," Alia said.

Hearing this, the Naibs in the gallery began raising their voices in protest.

"Silence!" Alia commanded. In the abrupt quiet, she said: "Is it not Fremen law that a Reverend Mother presides when life and death are at issue?"

As the gravity of her statement penetrated, stillness came over the Naibs, but Alia marked angry stares across the rows of faces. She named them in her mind for discussion in Council—Hobars, Rajifiri, Tasmin, Saajid, Umbu, Legg . . . The names carried pieces of Dune in them: Umbu Sietch, Tasmin Sink, Hobars Gap . . .

She turned her attention to Korba.

Observing her attention, Korba lifted his chin, said: "I protest my innocence."

"Stilgar, read the charges," Alia said.

Stilgar produced a brown spicepaper scroll, stepped forward. He began reading, a solemn flourish in his voice as though to hidden rhythms. He gave the words an incisive quality, clear and full of probity:

"... that you did conspire with traitors to accomplish the destruction of our Lord and Emperor; that you did meet in vile secrecy with diverse enemies of the realm; that you ..."

Korba kept shaking his head with a look of pained anger.

Alia listened broodingly, chin planted on her left fist, head cocked to that side, the other arm extended along the chair arm. Bits of the formal procedure began dropping out of her awareness, screened by her own feelings of disquiet.

"... venerable tradition ... support of the legions and all Fremen everywhere ... violence met with violence according to the Law ... majesty of the Imperial Person ... forfeit all rights to ..."

It was nonsense, she thought. Nonsense! All of it—nonsense ... nonsense ... nonsense ...

Stilgar finished: "Thus the issue is brought to judgment."

In the immediate silence, Korba rocked forward, hands gripping his knees, veined neck stretched as though he were preparing to leap. His tongue flicked between his teeth as he spoke.

"Not by word or deed have I been traitor to my Fremen vows! I demand to confront my accuser!"

A simple enough protest, Alia thought.

And she saw that it had produced a considerable effect on the Naibs. They knew Korba. He was one of them. To become a Naib, he'd proved his Fremen courage and caution. Not brilliant, Korba, but reliable. Not one to lead a Jihad, perhaps, but a good choice as supply officer. Not a crusader, but one who cherished the old Fremen virtues: *The Tribe is paramount.*

Otheym's bitter words as Paul had recited them swept through Alia's mind. She scanned the gallery. Any of those men might see himself in Korba's place—some for good reason. But an innocent Naib was as dangerous as a guilty one here.

Korba felt it, too. "Who accuses me?" he demanded. "I have a Fremen right to confront my accuser."

"Perhaps you accuse yourself," Alia said.

Before he could mask it, mystical terror lay briefly on Korba's face. It was there for anyone to read: *With her powers, Alia had but to accuse him herself, saying she brought the evidence from the shadow region, the* alam al-mythal.

"Our enemies have Fremen allies," Alia pressed. "Water traps have been destroyed, qanats blasted, plantings poisoned and storage basins plundered . . ."

"And now—they've stolen a worm from the desert, taken it to another world!"

The voice of this intrusion was known to all of them—Muad'Dib. Paul came through the doorway from the hall, pressed through the guard ranks and crossed to Alia's side. Chani, accompanying him, remained on the sidelines.

"M'Lord," Stilgar said, refusing to look at Paul's face.

Paul aimed his empty sockets at the gallery, then down to Korba. "What, Korba—no words of praise?"

Muttering could be heard in the gallery. It grew louder, isolated words and phrases audible: ". . . law for the blind . . . Fremen way . . . in the desert . . . who breaks . . ."

"Who says I'm blind?" Paul demanded. He faced the gallery. "You, Rajifiri? I see you're wearing gold today, and that blue shirt beneath it which still has dust on it from the streets. You always were untidy."

Rajifiri made a warding gesture, three fingers against evil.

"Point those fingers at yourself!" Paul shouted. "We know where the evil is!" He turned back to Korba. "There's guilt on your face, Korba."

"Not my guilt! I may've associated with the guilty, but no . . ." He broke off, shot a frightened look at the gallery.

Taking her cue from Paul, Alia arose, stepped down to the floor of the chamber, advanced to the edge of Korba's table. From a range of less than a meter, she stared down at him, silent and intimidating.

Korba cowered under the burden of eyes. He fidgeted, shot anxious glances at the gallery.

"Whose eyes do you seek up there?" Paul asked.

"You cannot see!" Korba blurted.

Paul put down a momentary feeling of pity for Korba. The man lay trapped in the vision's snare as securely as any of those present. He played a part, no more.

"I don't need eyes to see you," Paul said. And he began describing Korba, every movement, every twitch, every alarmed and pleading look at the gallery.

Desperation grew in Korba.

Watching him, Alia saw he might break any second. Someone in the gallery must realize how near he was to breaking, she thought. Who? She studied the faces of the Naibs, noting small betrayals in the masked faces . . . angers, fears, uncertainties . . . guilts.

Paul fell silent.

Korba mustered a pitiful air of pomposity to plead: "Who accuses me?"

"Otheym accuses you," Alia said.

"But Otheym's dead!" Korba protested.

"How did you know that?" Paul asked. "Through your spy system? Oh, yes! We know about your spies and couriers. We know who brought the stone burner here from Tarahell."

"It was for the defense of the Qizarate!" Korba blurted.

"Is that how it got into traitorous hands?" Paul asked.

"It was stolen and we . . ." Korba fell silent, swallowed. His gaze darted left and right. "Everyone knows I've been the voice of love for Muad'Dib." He stared at the gallery. "How can a dead man accuse a Fremen?"

"Otheym's voice isn't dead," Alia said. She stopped as Paul touched her arm.

"Otheym sent us his voice," Paul said. "It gives the names, the acts of treachery, the meeting places and the times. Do you miss certain faces in the Council of Naibs, Korba? Where are Merkur and Fash? Keke the Lame isn't with us today. And Takim, where is he?"

Korba shook his head from side to side.

"They've fled Arrakis with the stolen worm," Paul said. "Even if I freed you now, Korba, Shai-hulud would have your water for your part in this. Why don't I free you, Korba? Think of all those men whose eyes were taken, the men who cannot see as I see. They have families and friends, Korba. Where could you hide from them?"

"It was an accident," Korba pleaded. "Anyway, they're getting Tleilaxu . . ." Again, he subsided.

"Who knows what bondage goes with metal eyes?" Paul asked.

The Naibs in their gallery began exchanging whispered comments, speaking behind raised hands. They gazed coldly at Korba now.

"Defense of the Qizarate," Paul murmured, returning to Korba's plea. "A device which either destroys a planet or produces J-rays to blind those too near it. Which effect, Korba, did you conceive as a defense? Does the Qizarate rely on stopping the eyes of all observers?"

"It was a curiosity, m'Lord," Korba pleaded. "We knew the Old Law said that only Families could possess atomics, but the Qizarate obeyed . . . obeyed . . ."

"Obeyed you," Paul said. "A curiosity, indeed."

"Even if it's only the voice of my accuser, you must face me with it!" Korba said. "A Fremen has rights."

"He speaks truth, Sire," Stilgar said.

Alia glanced sharply at Stilgar.

"The law is the law," Stilgar said, sensing Alia's protest. He began quoting Fremen Law, interspersing his own comments on how the Law pertained.

Alia experienced the odd sensation she was hearing Stilgar's words before he spoke them. How could he be this credulous? Stilgar had never appeared more official and conservative, more intent on adhering to the Dune Code. His chin was outthrust, aggressive. His mouth chopped. Was there really nothing in him but this outrageous pomposity?

"Korba is a Fremen and must be judged by Fremen Law," Stilgar concluded.

Alia turned away, looked out at the day shadows dropping down the wall across from the garden. She felt drained by frustration. They'd dragged this thing along well into midmorning. Now, what? Korba had relaxed. The Panegyrist's manner said he'd suffered an unjust attack, that everything he'd done had been for love of Muad'Dib. She glanced at Korba, surprised a look of sly self-importance sliding across his face.

He might almost have received a message, she thought. He acted the part of a man who'd heard friends shout: *"Hold fast! Help is on its way!"*

For an instant, they'd held this thing in their hands—the information out of the dwarf, the clues that others were in the plot, the names of informants. But the critical moment had flown. *Stilgar? Surely not Stilgar.* She turned, stared at the old Fremen.

Stilgar met her gaze without flinching.

"Thank you, Stil," Paul said, "for reminding us of the Law."

Stilgar inclined his head. He moved close, shaped silent words in a way he knew both Paul and Alia could read. *I'll wring him dry and then take care of the matter.*

Paul nodded, signaled the guardsmen behind Korba.

"Remove Korba to a maximum security cell," Paul said. "No visitors except counsel. As counsel, I appoint Stilgar."

"Let me choose my own counsel!" Korba shouted.

Paul whirled. "You deny the fairness and judgment of Stilgar?"

"Oh, no, m'Lord, but . . ."

"Take him away!" Paul barked.

The guardsmen lifted Korba off the cushions, herded him out.

With new mutterings, the Naibs began quitting their gallery. Attendants came from beneath the gallery, crossed to the windows and drew the orange draperies. Orange gloom took over the chamber.

"Paul," Alia said.

"When we precipitate violence," Paul said, "it'll be when we have full control of it. Thank you, Stil; you played your part well. Alia, I'm certain, has identified the Naibs who were with him. They couldn't help giving themselves away."

"You cooked this up between you?" Alia demanded.

"Had I ordered Korba slain out of hand, the Naibs would have understood," Paul said. "But this formal procedure without strict adherence to Fremen Law—they felt their own rights threatened. Which Naibs were with him, Alia?"

"Rajifiri for certain," she said, voice low. "And Saajid, but . . ."

"Give Stilgar the complete list," Paul said.

Alia swallowed in a dry throat, sharing the general fear of Paul in this moment. She knew how he moved among them without eyes, but the delicacy of it daunted her. To see their forms in the air of his vision! She sensed her person shimmering for him in a sidereal time whose accord with reality depended entirely on his words and actions. He held them all in the palm of his vision!

"It's past time for your morning audience, Sire," Stilgar said. "Many people—curious . . . afraid . . ."

"Are you afraid, Stil?"

It was barely a whisper: "Yes."

"You're my friend and have nothing to fear from me," Paul said.

Stilgar swallowed. "Yes, m'Lord."

"Alia, take the morning audience," Paul said. "Stilgar, give the signal."

Stilgar obeyed.

A flurry of movement erupted at the great doors. A crowd was pressed back from the shadowy room to permit entrance of officials. Many things began happening all at once: the household guard elbowing and shoving back the press of Supplicants, garishly robed Pleaders trying to break through, shouts, curses. Pleaders waved the papers of their calling. The Clerk of the Assemblage strode ahead of them through the opening cleared by the guard. He carried the List of Preferences, those who'd be permitted to approach the Throne. The Clerk, a wiry Fremen named Tecrube, carried himself with weary cynicism, flaunting his shaven head, clumped whiskers.

Alia moved to intercept him, giving Paul time to slip away with Chani through the private passage behind the dais. She experienced a momentary distrust of Tecrube at the prying curiosity in the stare he sent after Paul.

"I speak for my brother today," she said. "Have the Supplicants approach one at a time."

"Yes, m'Lady." He turned to arrange his throng.

"I can remember a time when you wouldn't have mistaken your brother's purpose here," Stilgar said.

"I was distracted," she said. "There's been a dramatic change in you, Stil. What is it?"

Stilgar drew himself up, shocked. One changed, of course. But dramatically? This was a particular view of himself that he'd never encountered. Drama was a questionable thing. Imported entertainers of dubious loyalty and more dubious virtue were dramatic. Enemies of the Empire employed drama in their attempts to sway the fickle populace. Korba had slipped away from Fremen virtues to employ drama for the Qizarate. And he'd die for that.

"You're being perverse," Stilgar said. "Do you distrust me?"

The distress in his voice softened her expression, but not her tone. "You *know* I don't distrust you. I've always agreed with my brother that once matters were in Stilgar's hands we could safely forget them."

"Then why do you say I've . . . changed?"

"You're preparing to disobey my brother," she said. "I can read it in you. I only hope it doesn't destroy you both."

The first of the Pleaders and Supplicants were approaching now. She turned away before Stilgar could respond. His face, though, was filled with the things she'd sensed in her mother's letter—the replacement of morality and conscience with law.

"You produce a deadly paradox."

Tibana was an apologist for Socratic Christianity, probably a native of IV Anbus who lived between the eighth and ninth centuries before Corrino, likely in the second reign of Dalamak. Of his writings, only a portion survives from which this fragment is taken: "The hearts of all men dwell in the same wilderness."

—FROM THE DUNEBUK OF IRULAN

"You are Bijaz," the ghola said, entering the small chamber where the dwarf was held under guard. "I am called Hayt."

A strong contingent of the household guard had come in with the ghola to take over the evening watch. Sand carried by the sunset wind had stung their cheeks while they crossed the outer yard, made them blink and hurry. They could be heard in the passage outside now exchanging the banter and ritual of their tasks.

"You are not Hayt," the dwarf said. "You are Duncan Idaho. I was there when they put your dead flesh into the tank and I was there when they removed it, alive and ready for training."

The ghola swallowed in a throat suddenly dry. The bright glow-globes of the chamber lost their yellowness in the room's green hangings. The light showed beads of perspiration on the dwarf's forehead. Bijaz seemed a creature of odd integrity, as though the purpose fashioned into him by the Tleilaxu were projected out through his skin. There was power beneath the dwarf's mask of cowardice and frivolity.

"Muad'Dib has charged me to question you to determine what it is the Tleilaxu intend you to do here," Hayt said.

"Tleilaxu, Tleilaxu," the dwarf sang. "I am the Tleilaxu, you dolt! For that matter, so are you."

Hayt stared at the dwarf. Bijaz radiated a charismatic alertness that made the observer think of ancient idols.

"You hear that guard outside?" Hayt asked. "If I gave them the order, they'd strangle you."

"Hai! Hai!" Bijaz cried. "What a callous lout you've become. And you said you came seeking truth."

Hayt found he didn't like the look of secret repose beneath the dwarf's expression. "Perhaps I only seek the future," he said.

"Well spoken," Bijaz said. "Now we know each other. When two thieves meet they need no introduction."

"So we're thieves," Hayt said. "What do we steal?"

"Not thieves, but dice," Bijaz said. "And you came here to read my spots. I, in turn, read yours. And lo! You have two faces!"

"Did you really see me go into the Tleilaxu tanks?" Hayt asked, fighting an odd reluctance to ask that question.

"Did I not say it?" Bijaz demanded. The dwarf bounced to his feet. "We had a terrific struggle with you. The flesh did not want to come back."

Hayt felt suddenly that he existed in a dream controlled by some other mind, and that he might momentarily forget this to become lost in the convolutions of that mind.

Bijaz tipped his head slyly to one side, walked all around the ghola, staring up at him. "Excitement kindles old patterns in you,"

Bijaz said. "You are the pursuer who doesn't want to find what he pursues."

"You're a weapon aimed at Muad'Dib," Hayt said, swiveling to follow the dwarf. "What is it you're to do?"

"Nothing!" Bijaz said, stopping. "I give you a common answer to a common question."

"Then you were aimed at Alia," Hayt said. "Is she your target?"

"They call her Hawt, the Fish Monster, on the out-worlds," Bijaz said. "How is it I hear your blood boiling when you speak of her?"

"So they call her Hawt," the ghola said, studying Bijaz for any clue to his purpose. The dwarf made such odd responses.

"She is the virgin-harlot," Bijaz said. "She is vulgar, witty, knowledgeable to a depth that terrifies, cruel when she is most kind, unthinking while she thinks, and when she seeks to build she is as destructive as a coriolis storm."

"So you came here to speak out against Alia," Hayt said.

"Against her?" Bijaz sank to a cushion against the wall. "I came here to be captured by the magnetism of her physical beauty." He grinned, a saurian expression in the big-featured face.

"To attack Alia is to attack her brother," Hayt said.

"That is so clear it is difficult to see," Bijaz said. "In truth, Emperor and sister are one person back to back, one being half male and half female."

"That is a thing we've heard said by the Fremen of the deep desert," Hayt said. "And those are the ones who've revived the blood sacrifice to Shai-hulud. How is it you repeat their nonsense?"

"You dare say nonsense?" Bijaz demanded. "You, who are both man and mask? Ahh, but the dice cannot read their own spots. I forget this. And you are doubly confused because you serve the Atreides double-being. Your senses are not as close to the answer as your mind is."

"Do you preach that false ritual about Muad'Dib to your guards?" Hayt asked, his voice low. He felt his mind being tangled by the dwarf's words.

"They preach to me!" Bijaz said. "And they pray. Why should they not? All of us should pray. Do we not live in the shadow of the most dangerous creation the universe has ever seen?"

"Dangerous creation . . ."

"Their own mother refuses to live on the same planet with them!"

"Why don't you answer me straight out?" Hayt demanded. "You know we have other ways of questioning you. We'll get our answers . . . one way or another."

"But I have answered you! Have I not said the myth is real? Am I the wind that carries death in its belly? No! I am words! Such words as the lightning which strikes from the sand in a dark sky. I have said: 'Blow out the lamp! Day is here!' And you keep saying: 'Give me a lamp so I can find the day.'"

"You play a dangerous game with me," Hayt said. "Did you think I could not understand these Zensunni ideas? You leave tracks as clear as those of a bird in mud."

Bijaz began to giggle.

"Why do you laugh?" Hayt demanded.

"Because I have teeth and wish I had not," Bijaz managed between giggles. "Having no teeth, I could not gnash them."

"And now I know your target," Hayt said. "You were aimed at me."

"And I've hit it right on!" Bijaz said. "You made such a big target, how could I miss?" He nodded as though to himself. "Now I will sing to you." He began to hum, a keening, whining monotonous theme, repeated over and over.

Hayt stiffened, experiencing odd pains that played up and down his spine. He stared at the face of the dwarf, seeing youthful eyes in an old face. The eyes were the center of a network of knobby white lines which ran to the hollows below his temples. Such a large head! Every feature focused on the pursed-up mouth from which that monotonous noise issued. The sound made Hayt think of ancient rituals, folk memories, old words and customs, half-forgotten meanings in lost mutterings. Something vital was happening here—a bloody play of ideas across Time. Elder ideas lay tangled in the dwarf's singing. It was like a blazing light in the distance, coming nearer and nearer, illuminating life across a span of centuries.

"What are you doing to me?" Hayt gasped.

"You are the instrument I was taught to play," Bijaz said. "I am playing you. Let me tell you the names of the other traitors among the Naibs. They are Bikouros and Cahueit. There is Djedida, who was secretary to Korba. There is Abumojandis, the aide to Bannerjee. Even now, one of them could be sinking a blade into your Muad'Dib."

Hayt shook his head from side to side. He found it too difficult to talk.

"We are like brothers," Bijaz said, interrupting his monotonous hum once more. "We grew in the same tank: I first and then you."

Hayt's metal eyes inflicted him with a sudden burning pain. Flickering red haze surrounded everything he saw. He felt he had been cut away from every immediate sense except the pain, and he experienced his surroundings through a thin separation like wind-blown gauze. All had become accident, the chance involvement of inanimate matter. His own will was no more than a subtle, shifting thing. It lived without breath and was intelligible only as an inward illumination.

With a clarity born of desperation, he broke through the gauze curtain with the lonely sense of sight. His attention focused like a blazing light under Bijaz. Hayt felt that his eyes cut through layers of the dwarf, seeing the little man as a hired intellect, and beneath that, a creature imprisoned by hungers and cravings which lay huddled in the eyes—layer after layer, until finally, there was only an entity-aspect being manipulated by symbols.

"We are upon a battleground," Bijaz said. "You may speak of it."

His voice freed by the command, Hayt said: "You cannot force me to slay Muad'Dib."

"I have heard the Bene Gesserit say," Bijaz said, "that there is nothing firm, nothing balanced, nothing durable in all the universe—that nothing remains in its state, that each day, sometimes each hour, brings change."

Hayt shook his head dumbly from side to side.

"You believed the silly Emperor was the prize we sought," Bijaz said. "How little you understand our masters, the Tleilaxu. The Guild and Bene Gesserit believe we produce artifacts. In reality, we produce tools and services. Anything can be a tool—poverty, war. War is useful because it is effective in so many areas. It stimulates the metabolism. It enforces government. It diffuses genetic strains. It possesses a vitality such as nothing else in the universe. Only those who recognize the value of war and exercise it have any degree of self-determination."

In an oddly placid voice, Hayt said: "Strange thoughts coming from you, almost enough to make me believe in a vengeful Providence. What restitution was exacted to create you? It would make a fascinating story, doubtless with an even more extraordinary epilogue."

"Magnificent!" Bijaz chortled. "You attack—therefore you have willpower and exercise self-determination."

"You're trying to awaken violence in me," Hayt said in a panting voice.

Bijaz denied this with a shake of the head. "Awaken, yes; violence, no. You are a disciple of awareness by training, so you have said. I have an awareness to awaken in you, Duncan Idaho."

"Hayt!"

"Duncan Idaho. Killer extraordinary. Lover of many women. Swordsman soldier. Atreides field-hand on the field of battle. Duncan Idaho."

"The past cannot be awakened."

"Cannot?"

"It has never been done!"

"True, but our masters defy the idea that something cannot be done. Always, they seek the proper tool, the right application of effort, the services of the proper—"

"You hide your real purpose! You throw up a screen of words and they mean nothing!"

"There is a Duncan Idaho in you," Bijaz said. "It will submit to emotion or to dispassionate examination, but submit it will. This awareness will rise through a screen of suppression and selection out of the dark past which dogs your footsteps. It goads you even now while it holds you back. There exists that being within you upon which awareness must focus and which you will obey."

"The Tleilaxu think I'm still their slave, but I—"

"Quiet, slave!" Bijaz said in that whining voice.

Hayt found himself frozen in silence.

"Now we are down to bedrock," Bijaz said. "I know you feel it.

And these are the power-words to manipulate you . . . I think they will have sufficient leverage."

Hayt felt the perspiration pouring down his cheeks, the trembling of his chest and arms, but he was powerless to move.

"One day," Bijaz said, "the Emperor will come to you. He will say: 'She is gone.' The grief mask will occupy his face. He will give water to the dead, as they call their tears hereabouts. And you will say, using my voice: 'Master! Oh, Master!'"

Hayt's jaw and throat ached with the locking of his muscles. He could only twist his head in a brief arc from side to side.

"You will say, 'I carry a message from Bijaz.'" The dwarf grimaced. "Poor Bijaz, who has no mind . . . poor Bijaz, a drum stuffed with messages, an essence for others to use . . . pound on Bijaz and he produces a noise . . ."

Again, he grimaced. "You think me a hypocrite, Duncan Idaho! I am not! I can grieve, too. But the time has come to substitute swords for words."

A hiccup shook Hayt.

Bijaz giggled, then: "Ah, thank you, Duncan, thank you. The demands of the body save us. As the Emperor carries the blood of the Harkonnens in his veins, he will do as we demand. He will turn into a spitting machine, a biter of words that ring with a lovely noise to our masters."

Hayt blinked, thinking how the dwarf appeared like an alert little animal, a thing of spite and rare intelligence. *Harkonnen blood in the Atreides?*

"You think of Beast Rabban, the vile Harkonnen, and you glare," Bijaz said. "You are like the Fremen in this. When words fail, the sword is always at hand, eh? You think of the torture inflicted upon your family by the Harkonnens. And, through his mother, your precious Paul is a Harkonnen! You would not find it difficult to slay a Harkonnen, now would you?"

Bitter frustration coursed through the ghola. Was it anger? Why should this cause anger?

"Ohhh," Bijaz said, and: "Ahhhh, hah! Click-click. There is more to the message. It is a trade the Tleilaxu offer your precious Paul Atreides. Our masters will restore his beloved. A sister to yourself—another ghola."

Hayt felt suddenly that he existed in a universe occupied only by his own heartbeats.

"A ghola," Bijaz said. "It will be the flesh of his beloved. She will bear his children. She will love only him. We can even improve on the original if he so desires. Did ever a man have greater opportunity to regain what he'd lost? It is a bargain he will leap to strike."

Bijaz nodded, eyes drooping as though tiring. Then: "He will be tempted . . . and in his distraction, you will move close. In the instant, you will strike! Two gholas, not one! That is what our masters demand!" The dwarf cleared his throat, nodded once more, said: "Speak."

"I will not do it," Hayt said.

"But Duncan Idaho would," Bijaz said. "It will be the moment of supreme vulnerability for this descendant of the Harkonnens. Do not forget this. You will suggest improvements to his beloved—perhaps a deathless heart, gentler emotions. You will offer asylum as you move close to him—a planet of his choice somewhere beyond the Imperium. Think of it! His beloved restored. No more need for tears, and a place of idyls to live out his years."

"A costly package," Hayt said, probing. "He'll ask the price."

"Tell him he must renounce his godhead and discredit the Qizarate. He must discredit himself, his sister."

"Nothing more?" Hayt asked, sneering.

"He must relinquish his CHOAM holdings, naturally."

"Naturally."

"And if you're not yet close enough to strike, speak of how much the Tleilaxu admire what he has taught them about the possibilities of religion. Tell him the Tleilaxu have a department of religious engineering, shaping religions to particular needs."

"How very clever," Hayt said.

"You think yourself free to sneer and disobey me," Bijaz said. He cocked his head slyly to one side. "Don't deny it . . ."

"They made you well, little animal," Hayt said.

"And you as well," the dwarf said. "You will tell him to hurry. Flesh decays and her flesh must be preserved in a cryological tank."

Hayt felt himself floundering, caught in a matrix of objects he could not recognize. The dwarf appeared so sure of himself! There had to be a flaw in the Tleilaxu logic. In making their ghola, they'd keyed him to the voice of Bijaz, but . . . But what? Logic/matrix/object . . . How easy it was to mistake clear reasoning for correct reasoning! Was Tleilaxu logic distorted?

Bijaz smiled, listened as though to a hidden voice. "Now, you will forget," he said. "When the moment comes, you will remember. He will say: 'She is gone.' Duncan Idaho will awaken then."

The dwarf clapped his hands together.

Hayt grunted, feeling that he had been interrupted in the middle of a thought . . . or perhaps in the middle of a sentence. What was it? Something about . . . targets?

"You think to confuse me and manipulate me," he said.

"How is that?" Bijaz asked.

"I am your target and you can't deny it," Hayt said.

"I would not think of denying it."

"What is it you'd try to do with me?"

"A kindness," Bijaz said. "A simple kindness."

The sequential nature of actual events is not illuminated with lengthy precision by the powers of prescience except under the most extraordinary circumstances. The oracle grasps incidents cut out of the historic chain. Eternity moves. It inflicts itself upon the oracle and the supplicant alike. Let Muad'Dib's subjects doubt his majesty and his oracular visions. Let them deny his powers. Let them never doubt Eternity.

—THE DUNE GOSPELS

Hayt watched Alia emerge from her temple and cross the plaza. Her guard was bunched close, fierce expressions on their faces to mask the lines molded by good living and complacency.

A heliograph of 'thopter wings flashed in the bright afternoon sun above the temple, part of the Royal Guard with Muad'Dib's fist-symbol on its fuselage.

Hayt returned his gaze to Alia. She looked out of place here in the city, he thought. Her proper setting was the desert—open, untrammeled space. An odd thing about her came back to him as he watched her approach: Alia appeared thoughtful only when she smiled. It was a trick of the eyes, he decided, recalling a cameo memory of her as she'd appeared at the reception for the Guild Ambassador: haughty against a background of music and brittle conversation among extravagant gowns and uniforms. And Alia had been wearing white, dazzling, a bright garment of chastity. He had looked down upon her from a window as she crossed an inner garden with its formal pond, its fluting fountains, fronds of pampas grass and a white belvedere.

Entirely wrong . . . all wrong. She belonged in the desert.

Hayt drew in a ragged breath. Alia had moved out of his view then as she did now. He waited, clenching and unclenching his fists. The interview with Bijaz had left him uneasy.

He heard Alia's entourage pass outside the room where he waited. She went into the Family quarters.

Now he tried to focus on the thing about her which troubled him. The way she'd walked across the plaza? Yes. She'd moved like a hunted creature fleeing some predator. He stepped out onto the connecting balcony, walked along it behind the plasmeld sunscreen, stopped while still in concealing shadows. Alia stood at the balustrade overlooking her temple.

He looked where she was looking—out over the city. He saw rectangles, blocks of color, creeping movements of life and sound. Structures gleamed, shimmered. Heat patterns spiraled off the rooftops. There was a boy across the way bouncing a ball in a cul-de-sac formed by a buttressed massif at a corner of the temple. Back and forth the ball went.

Alia, too, watched the ball. She felt a compelling identity with that ball—back and forth . . . back and forth. She sensed herself bouncing through corridors of Time.

The potion of melange she'd drained just before leaving the temple was the largest she'd ever attempted—a massive overdose. Even before beginning to take effect, it had terrified her.

Why did I do it? she asked herself.

One made a choice between dangers. Was that it? This was the way to penetrate the fog spread over the future by that damnable Dune Tarot. A barrier existed. It must be breached. She had acted out of a necessity to see where it was her brother walked with his eyeless stride.

The familiar melange fugue state began creeping into her awareness. She took a deep breath, experienced a brittle form of calm, poised and selfless.

Possession of second sight has a tendency to make one a dangerous fatalist, she thought. Unfortunately, there existed no abstract leverage, no calculus of prescience. Visions of the future could not be manipulated as formulas. One had to enter them, risking life and sanity.

A figure moved from the harsh shadows of the adjoining balcony. The ghola! In her heightened awareness, Alia saw him with intense clarity—the dark, lively features dominated by those glistening metal eyes. He was a union of terrifying opposites, something put together in a shocking linear way. He was shadow and blazing light, a product of the process which had revived his dead flesh . . . and of something intensely pure . . . innocent.

He was innocence under siege!

"Have you been there all along, Duncan?" she asked.

"So I'm to be Duncan," he said. "Why?"

"Don't question me," she said.

And she thought, looking at him, that the Tleilaxu had left no corner of their ghola unfinished.

"Only gods can safely risk perfection," she said. "It's a dangerous thing for a man."

"Duncan died," he said, wishing she would not call him that. "I am Hayt."

She studied his artificial eyes, wondering what they saw. Observed closely, they betrayed tiny black pockmarks, little wells of darkness in the glittering metal. Facets! The universe shimmered around her and lurched. She steadied herself with a hand on the sun-warmed surface of the balustrade. Ahhh, the melange moved swiftly.

"Are you ill?" Hayt asked. He moved closer, the steely eyes opened wide, staring.

Who spoke? she wondered. Was it Duncan Idaho? Was it the mentat-ghola or the Zensunni philosopher? Or was it a Tleilaxu pawn more dangerous than any Guild Steersman? Her brother knew.

Again, she looked at the ghola. There was something inactive about him now, a latent something. He was saturated with waiting and with powers beyond their common life.

"Out of my mother, I am like the Bene Gesserit," she said. "Do you know that?"

"I know it."

"I use their powers, think as they think. Part of me knows the sacred urgency of the breeding program . . . and its products."

She blinked, feeling part of her awareness begin to move freely in Time.

"It's said that the Bene Gesserit never let go," he said. And he watched her closely, noting how white her knuckles were where she gripped the edge of the balcony.

"Have I stumbled?" she asked.

He marked how deeply she breathed, with tension in every movement, the glazed appearance of her eyes.

"When you stumble," he said, "you may regain your balance by jumping beyond the thing that tripped you."

"The Bene Gesserit stumbled," she said. "Now they wish to regain their balance by leaping beyond my brother. They want Chani's baby . . . or mine."

"Are you with child?"

She struggled to fix herself in a timespace relationship to this question. With child? When? Where?

"I see . . . my child," she whispered.

She moved away from the balcony's edge, turned her head to look at the ghola. He had a face of salt, bitter eyes—two circles of glistening lead . . . and, as he turned away from the light to follow her movement, blue shadows.

"What . . . do you see with such eyes?" she whispered.

"What other eyes see," he said.

His words rang in her ears, stretching her awareness. She felt that she reached across the universe—such a stretching . . . out . . . out. She lay intertwined with all Time.

"You've taken the spice, a large dose," he said.

"Why can't I see him?" she muttered. The womb of all creation held her captive. "Tell me, Duncan, why I cannot see him."

"Who can't you see?"

"I cannot see the father of my children. I'm lost in a Tarot fog. Help me."

Mentat logic offered its prime computation, and he said: "The Bene Gesserit want a mating between you and your brother. It would lock the genetic . . ."

A wail escaped her. "The egg in the flesh," she gasped. A sensation of chill swept over her, followed by intense heat. The unseen mate of her darkest dreams! Flesh of her flesh that the oracle could not reveal—would it come to that?

"Have you risked a dangerous dose of the spice?" he asked. Something within him fought to express the utmost terror at the thought that an Atreides woman might die, that Paul might face him with the knowledge that a female of the royal family had . . . gone.

"You don't know what it's like to hunt the future," she said. "Sometimes I glimpse myself . . . but I get in my own way. I cannot see through myself." She lowered her head, shook it from side to side.

"How much of the spice did you take?" he asked.

"Nature abhors prescience," she said, raising her head. "Did you know that, Duncan?"

He spoke softly, reasonably, as to a small child: "Tell me how much of the spice you took." He took hold of her shoulder with his left hand.

"Words are such gross machinery, so primitive and ambiguous," she said. She pulled away from his hand.

"You must tell me," he said.

"Look at the Shield Wall," she commanded, pointing. She sent her gaze along her own outstretched hand, trembled as the landscape crumbled in an overwhelming vision—a sandcastle destroyed by invisible waves. She averted her eyes, was transfixed by the appearance of the ghola's face. His features crawled, became aged, then young . . . aged . . . young. He was life itself, assertive, endless . . . She turned to flee, but he grabbed her left wrist.

"I am going to summon a doctor," he said.

"No! You must let me have the vision! I have to know!"

"You are going inside now," he said.

She stared down at his hand. Where their flesh touched, she felt an electric presence that both lured and frightened her. She jerked free, gasped: "You can't hold the whirlwind!"

"You must have medical help!" he snapped.

"Don't you understand?" she demanded. "My vision's incomplete, just fragments. It flickers and jumps. I have to remember the future. Can't you see that?"

"What is the future if you die?" he asked, forcing her gently into the Family chambers.

"Words . . . words," she muttered. "I can't explain it. One thing is the occasion of another thing, but there's no cause . . . no effect. We can't leave the universe as it was. Try as we may, there's a gap."

"Stretch out here," he commanded.

He is so dense! she thought.

Cool shadows enveloped her. She felt her own muscles crawling like worms—a firm bed that she knew to be insubstantial. Only space was permanent. Nothing else had substance. The bed flowed with many bodies, all of them her own. Time became a multiple sensation, overloaded. It presented no single reaction for her to abstract. It was Time. It moved. The whole universe slipped backward, forward, sideways.

"It has no thing-aspect," she explained. "You can't get under it or around it. There's no place to get leverage."

There came a fluttering of people all around her. Many someones held her left hand. She looked at her own moving flesh, followed a twining arm out to a fluid mask of face: Duncan Idaho! His eyes were . . . wrong, but it was Duncan—child-man-adolescent-child-man-adolescent . . . Every line of his features betrayed concern for her.

"Duncan, don't be afraid," she whispered.

He squeezed her hand, nodded. "Be still," he said.

And he thought: *She must not die! She must not! No Atreides woman can die!* He shook his head sharply. Such thoughts defied mentat logic. Death was a necessity that life might continue.

The ghola loves me, Alia thought.

The thought became bedrock to which she might cling. He was a familiar face with a solid room behind him. She recognized one of the bedrooms in Paul's suite.

A fixed, immutable person did something with a tube in her throat. She fought against retching.

"We got her in time," a voice said, and she recognized the tones of a Family medic. "You should've called me sooner." There was suspicion in the medic's voice. She felt the tube slide out of her throat—a snake, a shimmering cord.

"The slapshot will make her sleep," the medic said. "I'll send one of her attendants to—"

"I will stay with her," the ghola said.

"That is not seemly!" the medic snapped.

"Stay . . . Duncan," Alia whispered.

He stroked her hand to tell her he'd heard.

"M'Lady," the medic said, "it'd be better if . . ."

"You do not tell me what is best," she rasped. Her throat ached with each syllable.

"M'Lady," the medic said, voice accusing, "*you* know the dangers of consuming too much melange. I can only assume someone gave it to you without—"

"You are a fool," she rasped. "Would you deny me my visions? I knew what I took and why." She put a hand to her throat. "Leave us. At once!"

The medic pulled out of her field of vision, said: "I will send word to your brother."

She felt him leave, turned her attention to the ghola. The vision lay clearly in her awareness now, a culture medium in which the present grew outward. She sensed the ghola move in that play of Time, no longer cryptic, fixed now against a recognizable background.

He is the crucible, she thought. *He is danger and salvation.*

And she shuddered, knowing she saw the vision her brother had seen. Unwanted tears burned her eyes. She shook her head sharply. No tears! They wasted moisture and, worse, distracted the harsh flow of vision. Paul must be stopped! Once, just once, she had bridged

Time to place her voice where he would pass. But stress and mutability would not permit that here. The web of Time passed through her brother now like rays of light through a lens. He stood at the focus and he knew it. He had gathered all the lines to himself and would not permit them to escape or change.

"Why?" she muttered. "Is it hate? Does he strike out at Time itself because it hurt him? Is that it . . . hate?"

Thinking he heard her speak his name, the ghola said: "M'Lady?"

"If I could only burn this thing out of me!" she cried. "I didn't want to be different."

"Please, Alia," he murmured. "Let yourself sleep."

"I wanted to be able to laugh," she whispered. Tears slid down her cheeks. "But I'm sister to an Emperor who's worshipped as a god. People fear me. I never wanted to be feared."

He wiped the tears from her face.

"I don't want to be part of history," she whispered. "I just want to be loved . . . and to love."

"You are loved," he said.

"Ahhh, loyal, loyal Duncan," she said.

"Please, don't call me that," he pleaded.

"But you are," she said. "And loyalty is a valued commodity. It can be sold . . . not bought, but sold."

"I don't like your cynicism," he said.

"Damn your logic! It's true!"

"Sleep," he said.

"Do you love me, Duncan?" she asked.

"Yes."

"Is that one of those lies," she asked, "one of the lies that are easier to believe than the truth? Why am I afraid to believe you?"

"You fear my differences as you fear your own."

"Be a man, not a mentat!" she snarled.

"I am a mentat and a man."

"Will you make me your woman, then?"

"I will do what love demands."

"And loyalty?"

"And loyalty."

"That's where you're dangerous," she said.

Her words disturbed him. No sign of the disturbance arose to his face, no muscle trembled—but she knew it. Vision-memory exposed the disturbance. She felt she had missed part of the vision, though, that she should remember something else from the future. There existed another perception which did not go precisely by the senses, a thing which fell into her head from nowhere the way prescience did. It lay in the Time shadows—infinitely painful.

Emotion! That was it—emotion! It had appeared in the vision, not directly, but as a product from which she could infer what lay behind. She had been possessed by emotion—a single constriction made up of fear, grief and love. They lay there in the vision, all collected into a single epidemic body, overpowering and primordial.

"Duncan, don't let me go," she whispered.

"Sleep," he said. "Don't fight it."

"I must . . . I must. He's the bait in his own trap. He's the servant of power and terror. Violence . . . deification is a prison enclosing him. He'll lose . . . everything. It'll tear him apart."

"You speak of Paul?"

"They drive him to destroy himself," she gasped, arching her back. "Too much weight, too much grief. They seduce him away from love." She sank back to the bed. "They're creating a universe where he won't permit himself to live."

"Who is doing this?"

"He is! Ohhh, you're so dense. He's part of the pattern. And it's too late . . . too late . . . too late . . ."

As she spoke, she felt her awareness descend, layer by layer. It came to rest directly behind her navel. Body and mind separated and merged in a storehouse of relic visions—moving, moving . . . She heard a fetal heartbeat, a child of the future. The melange still possessed her, then, setting her adrift in Time. She knew she had tasted the life of a child not yet conceived. One thing certain about this child—it would suffer the same awakening she had suffered. It would be an aware, thinking entity before birth.

There exists a limit to the force even the most powerful may apply without destroying themselves. Judging this limit is the true artistry of government. Misuse of power is the fatal sin. The law cannot be a tool of vengeance, never a hostage, nor a fortification against the martyrs it has created. You cannot threaten any individual and escape the consequences.

—MUAD'DIB ON LAW
FROM THE STILGAR COMMENTARY

Chani stared out at the morning desert framed in the fault cleft below Sietch Tabr. She wore no stillsuit, and this made her feel unprotected here in the desert. The sietch grotto's entrance lay hidden in the buttressed cliff above and behind her.

The desert . . . the desert . . . She felt that the desert had followed her wherever she had gone. Coming back to the desert was not so much a homecoming as a turning around to see what had always been there.

A painful constriction surged through her abdomen. The birth would be soon. She fought down the pain, wanting this moment alone with her desert.

Dawn stillness gripped the land. Shadows fled among the dunes and terraces of the Shield Wall all around. Daylight lunged over the high scarp and plunged her up to her eyes in a bleak landscape stretching beneath a washed blue sky. The scene matched the feeling of dreadful cynicism which had tormented her since the moment she'd learned of Paul's blindness.

Why are we here? she wondered.

It was not a hajra, a journey of seeking. Paul sought nothing here except, perhaps, a place for her to give birth. He had summoned odd companions for this journey, she thought—Bijaz, the Tleilaxu dwarf; the ghola, Hayt, who might be Duncan Idaho's revenant; Edric, the Guild Steersman-Ambassador; Gaius Helen Mohiam, the Bene Gesserit Reverend Mother he so obviously hated; Lichna, Otheym's strange daughter, who seemed unable to move beyond the watchful eyes of guards; Stilgar, her uncle of the Naibs, and his favorite wife, Harah . . . and Irulan . . . Alia . . .

The sound of wind through the rocks accompanied her thoughts. The desert day had become yellow on yellow, tan on tan, gray on gray.

Why such a strange mixture of companions?

"We have forgotten," Paul had said in response to her question, "that the word 'company' originally meant traveling companions. We are a company."

"But what value are they?"

"There!" he'd said, turning his frightful sockets toward her. "We've lost that clear, single-note of living. If it cannot be bottled, beaten, pointed or hoarded, we give it no value."

Hurt, she'd said: "That's not what I meant."

"Ahhh, dearest one," he'd said, soothing, "we are so money-rich and so life-poor. I am evil, obstinate, stupid . . ."

"You are not!"

"That, too, is true. But my hands are blue with time. I think . . . I think I tried to invent life, not realizing it'd already been invented."

And he'd touched her abdomen to feel the new life there.

Remembering, she placed both hands over her abdomen and trembled, sorry that she'd asked Paul to bring her here.

The desert wind had stirred up evil odors from the fringe plantings which anchored the dunes at the cliff base. Fremen superstition gripped her: *evil odors, evil times.* She faced into the wind, saw a worm appear outside the plantings. It arose like the prow of a demon ship out of the dunes, threshed sand, smelled the water deadly to its kind, and fled beneath a long, burrowing mound.

She hated the water then, inspired by the worm's fear. Water, once the spirit-soul of Arrakis, had become a poison. Water brought pestilence. Only the desert was clean.

Below her, a Fremen work gang appeared. They climbed to the sietch's middle entrance, and she saw that they had muddy feet.

Fremen with muddy feet!

The children of the sietch began singing to the morning above her, their voices piping from the upper entrance. The voices made her feel time fleeing from her like hawks before the wind. She shuddered.

What storms did Paul *see* with his eyeless vision?

She sensed a vicious madman in him, someone weary of songs and polemics.

The sky, she noted, had become crystal gray filled with alabaster rays, bizarre designs etched across the heavens by windborne sand. A line of gleaming white in the south caught her attention. Eyes suddenly alerted, she interpreted the sign: White sky in the south: Shai-hulud's mouth. A storm came, big wind. She felt the warning breeze, a crystal blowing of sand against her cheeks. The incense of death came on the wind: odors of water flowing in qanats, sweating sand, flint. The water—that was why Shai-hulud sent his coriolis wind.

Hawks appeared in the cleft where she stood, seeking safety from the wind. They were brown as the rocks and with scarlet in their wings. She felt her spirit go out to them: they had a place to hide; she had none.

"M'Lady, the wind comes!"

She turned, saw the ghola calling to her outside the upper entrance to the sietch. Fremen fears gripped her. Clean death and the body's water claimed for the tribe, these she understood. But . . . something brought back from death . . .

Windblown sand whipped at her, reddened her cheeks. She glanced over her shoulder at the frightful band of dust across the sky. The desert beneath the storm had taken on a tawny, restless appearance as though dune waves beat on a tempest shore the way Paul had once described a sea. She hesitated, caught by a feeling of the desert's transience. Measured against eternity, this was no more than a caldron. Dune surf thundered against cliffs.

The storm out there had become a universal thing for her—all the animals hiding from it . . . nothing left of the desert but its own private sounds: blown sand scraping along rock, a wind-surge whistling, the gallop of a boulder tumbled suddenly from its hill—then! somewhere out of sight, a capsized worm thumping its idiot way aright and slithering off to its dry depths.

It was only a moment as her life measured time, but in that moment she felt this planet being swept away—cosmic dust, part of other waves.

"We must hurry," the ghola said from right beside her.

She sensed fear in him then, concern for her safety.

"It'll shred the flesh from your bones," he said, as though he needed to explain such a storm to *her.*

Her fear of him dispelled by his obvious concern, Chani allowed the ghola to help her up the rock stairway to the sietch. They entered the twisting baffle which protected the entrance. Attendants opened the moisture seals, closed them behind.

Sietch odors assaulted her nostrils. The place was a ferment of nasal memories—the warren closeness of bodies, rank esters of the reclamation stills, familiar food aromas, the flinty burning of machines at work . . . and through it all, the omnipresent spice: melange everywhere.

She took a deep breath. "Home."

The ghola took his hand from her arm, stood aside, a patient figure now, almost as though turned off when not in use. Yet . . . he watched.

Chani hesitated in the entrance chamber, puzzled by something she could not name. This was truly her home. As a child, she'd hunted scorpions here by glowglobe light. Something was changed, though . . .

"Shouldn't you be going to your quarters, m'Lady?" the ghola asked.

As though ignited by his words, a rippling birth constriction seized her abdomen. She fought against revealing it.

"M'Lady?" the ghola said.

"Why is Paul afraid for me to bear our children?" she asked.

"It is a natural thing to fear for your safety," the ghola said.

She put a hand to her cheek where the sand had reddened it. "And he doesn't fear for the children?"

"M'Lady, he cannot think of a child without remembering that your firstborn was slain by the Sardaukar."

She studied the ghola—flat face, unreadable mechanical eyes. Was he truly Duncan Idaho, this creature? Was he friend to anyone? Had he spoken truthfully now?

"You should be with the medics," the ghola said.

Again, she heard the fear for her safety in his voice. She felt abruptly that her mind lay undefended, ready to be invaded by shocking perceptions.

"Hayt, I'm afraid," she whispered. "Where is my Usul?"

"Affairs of state detain him," the ghola said.

She nodded, thinking of the government apparatus which had accompanied them in a great flight of ornithopters. Abruptly, she realized what puzzled her about the sietch: outworld odors. The clerks and aides had brought their own perfumes into this environment, aromas of diet and clothing, of exotic toiletries. They were an undercurrent of odors here.

Chani shook herself, concealing an urge to bitter laughter. Even the smells changed in Muad'Dib's presence!

"There were pressing matters which he could not defer," the ghola said, misreading her hesitation.

"Yes . . . yes, I understand. I came with that swarm, too."

Recalling the flight from Arrakeen, she admitted to herself now that she had not expected to survive it. Paul had insisted on piloting his own 'thopter. Eyeless, he had guided the machine here. After that experience, she knew nothing he did could surprise her.

Another pain fanned out through her abdomen.

The ghola saw her indrawn breath, the tightening of her cheeks, said: "Is it your time?"

"I . . . yes, it is."

"You must not delay," he said. He grasped her arm, hurried her down the hall.

She sensed panic in him, said: "There's time."

He seemed not to hear. "The Zensunni approach to birth," he said, urging her even faster, "is to wait without purpose in the state of highest tension. Do not compete with what is happening. To compete is to prepare for failure. Do not be trapped by the need to achieve anything. This way, you achieve everything."

While he spoke, they reached the entrance to her quarters. He thrust her through the hangings, cried out: "Harah! Harah! It is Chani's time. Summon the medics!"

His call brought attendants running. There was a great bustling of people in which Chani felt herself an isolated island of calm . . . until the next pain came.

Hayt, dismissed to the outer passage, took time to wonder at his own actions. He felt fixated at some point of time where all truths were only temporary. Panic lay beneath his actions, he realized. Panic centered not on the possibility that Chani might die, but that Paul should come to him afterward . . . filled with grief . . . his loved one . . . gone . . . gone . . .

Something cannot emerge from nothing, the ghola told himself. *From what does this panic emerge?*

He felt that his mentat faculties had been dulled, let out a long, shuddering breath. A psychic shadow passed over him. In the emotional darkness of it, he felt himself waiting for some absolute sound—the snap of a branch in a jungle.

A sigh shook him. Danger had passed without striking.

Slowly, marshaling his powers, shedding bits of inhibition, he sank into mentat awareness. He forced it—not the best way—but somehow necessary. Ghost shadows moved within him in place of people. He was a trans-shipping station for every datum he had ever encountered. His being was inhabited by creatures of possibility. They passed in review to be compared, judged.

Perspiration broke out on his forehead.

Thoughts with fuzzy edges feathered away into darkness—unknown. Infinite systems! A mentat could not function without realizing he worked in infinite systems. Fixed knowledge could not surround the infinite. *Everywhere* could not be brought into finite perspective. Instead, he must *become* the infinite—momentarily.

In one gestalten spasm, he had it, seeing Bijaz seated before him blazing from some inner fire.

Bijaz!

The dwarf had done something to him!

Hayt felt himself teetering on the lip of a deadly pit. He projected the mentat computation line forward, seeing what could develop out of his own actions.

"A compulsion!" he gasped. "I've been rigged with a compulsion!"

A blue-robed courier, passing as Hayt spoke, hesitated. "Did you say something, sirra?"

Not looking at him, the ghola nodded. "I said everything."

There was a man so wise,

He jumped into

A sandy place

And burnt out both his eyes!

And when he knew his eyes were gone,

He offered no complaint.

He summoned up a vision

And made himself a saint.

—CHILDREN'S VERSE
FROM HISTORY OF MUAD'DIB

Paul stood in darkness outside the sietch. Oracular vision told him it was night, that moonlight silhouetted the shrine atop Chin Rock high on his left. This was a memory-saturated place, his first sietch, where he and Chani . . .

I must not think of Chani, he told himself.

The thinning cup of his vision told him of changes all around—a cluster of palms far down to the right, the black-silver line of a qanat carrying water through the dunes piled up by that morning's storm.

Water flowing in the desert! He recalled another kind of water flowing in a river of his birthworld, Caladan. He hadn't realized then the treasure of such a flow, even the murky slithering in a qanat across a desert basin. Treasure.

With a delicate cough, an aide came up from behind.

Paul held out his hands for a magnabord with a single sheet of metallic paper on it. He moved as sluggishly as the qanat's water. The vision flowed, but he found himself increasingly reluctant to move with it.

"Pardon, Sire," the aide said. "The Semboule Treaty—your signature?"

"I can read it!" Paul snapped. He scrawled "Atreides Imper." in the proper place, returned the board, thrusting it directly into the aide's outstretched hand, aware of the fear this inspired.

The man fled.

Paul turned away. *Ugly, barren land!* He imagined it sun-soaked and monstrous with heat, a place of sandslides and the drowned darkness of dust pools, blowdevils unreeling tiny dunes across the rocks, their narrow bellies full of ochre crystals. But it was a rich land, too: big, exploding out of narrow places with vistas of storm-trodden emptiness, rampart cliffs and tumbledown ridges.

All it required was water . . . and love.

Life changed those irascible wastes into shapes of grace and movement, he thought. That was the message of the desert. Contrast stunned him with realization. He wanted to turn to the aides massed in the sietch entrance, shout at them: If you need something to worship, then worship life—all life, every last crawling bit of it! We're all in this beauty together!

They wouldn't understand. In the desert, they were endlessly desert. Growing things performed no green ballet for them.

He clenched his fists at his sides, trying to halt the vision. He wanted to flee from his own mind. It was a beast come to devour him!

Awareness lay in him, sodden, heavy with all the living it had sponged up, saturated with too many experiences.

Desperately, Paul squeezed his thoughts outward.

Stars!

Awareness turned over at the thought of all those stars above him—an infinite volume. A man must be half mad to imagine he could rule even a teardrop of that volume. He couldn't begin to imagine the number of subjects his Imperium claimed.

Subjects? Worshippers and enemies, more likely. Did any among them see beyond rigid beliefs? Where was one man who'd escaped the narrow destiny of his prejudices? Not even an Emperor escaped. He'd lived a take-everything life, tried to create a universe in his own image. But the exultant universe was breaking across him at last with its silent waves.

I spit on Dune! he thought. *I give it my moisture!*

This myth he'd made out of intricate movements and imagination, out of moonlight and love, out of prayers older than Adam, and gray cliffs and crimson shadows, laments and rivers of martyrs— what had it come to at last? When the waves receded, the shores of Time would spread out there clean, empty, shining with infinite grains of memory and little else. Was this the golden genesis of man?

Sand scuffed against rocks told him that the ghola had joined him.

"You've been avoiding me today, Duncan," Paul said.

"It's dangerous for you to call me that," the ghola said.

"I know."

"I . . . came to warn you, m'Lord."

"I know."

The story of the compulsion Bijaz had put on him poured from the ghola then.

"Do you know the nature of the compulsion?" Paul asked.

"Violence."

Paul felt himself arriving at a place which had claimed him from the beginning. He stood suspended. The Jihad had seized him, fixed him onto a glidepath from which the terrible gravity of the Future would never release him.

"There'll be no violence from Duncan," Paul whispered.

"But, Sire . . ."

"Tell me what you see around us," Paul said.

"M'Lord?"

"The desert—how is it tonight?"

"Don't you *see* it?"

"I have no eyes, Duncan."

"But . . ."

"I've only my vision," Paul said, "and wish I didn't have it. I'm dying of prescience, did you know that, Duncan?"

"Perhaps . . . what you fear won't happen," the ghola said.

"What? Deny my own oracle? How can I when I've seen it fulfilled thousands of times? People call it a power, a gift. It's an affliction! It won't let me leave my life where I found it!"

"M'Lord," the ghola muttered, "I . . . it isn't . . . young master, you don't . . . I . . ." He fell silent.

Paul sensed the ghola's confusion, said: "What'd you call me, Duncan?"

"What? What I . . . for a moment . . ."

"You called me 'young master.'"

"I did, yes."

"That's what Duncan always called me." Paul reached out, touched the ghola's face. "Was that part of your Tleilaxu training?"

"No."

Paul lowered his hand. "What, then?"

"It came from . . . me."

"Do you serve two masters?"

"Perhaps."

"Free yourself from the ghola, Duncan."

"How?"

"You're human. Do a human thing."

"I'm a ghola!"

"But your flesh is human. Duncan's in there."

"*Something's* in there."

"I care not how you do it," Paul said, "but you'll do it."

"You've foreknowledge?"

"Foreknowledge be damned!" Paul turned away. His vision hurtled forward now, gaps in it, but it wasn't a thing to be stopped.

"M'Lord, if you've—"

"Quiet!" Paul held up a hand. "Did you hear that?"

"Hear what, m'Lord?"

Paul shook his head. Duncan hadn't heard it. Had he only imagined the sound? It'd been his tribal name called from the desert—far away and low: "Usul . . . Uuuussssuuuullll . . ."

"What is it, m'Lord?"

Paul shook his head. He felt watched. Something out there in the night shadows knew he was here. Something? No—some*one.*

"It was mostly sweet," he whispered, "and you were the sweetest of all."

"What'd you say, m'Lord?"

"It's the future," Paul said.

That amorphous human universe out there had undergone a spurt of motion, dancing to the tune of his vision. It had struck a powerful note then. The ghost-echoes might endure.

"I don't understand, m'Lord," the ghola said.

"A Fremen dies when he's too long from the desert," Paul said. "They call it the 'water sickness.' Isn't that odd?"

"That's very odd."

Paul strained at memories, tried to recall the sound of Chani breathing beside him in the night. *Where is there comfort?* he wondered. All he could remember was Chani at breakfast the day they'd left for the desert. She'd been restless, irritable.

"Why do you wear that old jacket?" she'd demanded, eyeing the black uniform coat with its red hawk crest beneath his Fremen robes. "You're an Emperor!"

"Even an Emperor has his favorite clothing," he'd said.

For no reason he could explain, this had brought real tears to Chani's eyes—the second time in her life when Fremen inhibitions had been shattered.

Now, in the darkness, Paul rubbed his own cheeks, felt moisture there. *Who gives moisture to the dead?* he wondered. It was his own face, yet not his. The wind chilled the wet skin. A frail dream formed, broke. What was this swelling in his breast? Was it something he'd eaten? How bitter and plaintive was this other self, giving moisture to the dead. The wind bristled with sand. The skin, dry now, was his own. But whose was the quivering which remained?

They heard the wailing then, far away in the sietch depths. It grew louder . . . louder . . .

The ghola whirled at a sudden glare of light, someone flinging wide the entrance seals. In the light, he saw a man with a raffish grin—no! Not a grin, but a grimace of grief! It was a Fedaykin lieutenant named Tandis. Behind him came a press of many people, all fallen silent now that they saw Muad'Dib.

"Chani . . ." Tandis said.

"Is dead," Paul whispered. "I heard her call."

He turned toward the sietch. He knew this place. It was a place where he could not hide. His onrushing vision illuminated the entire Fremen mob. He *saw* Tandis, felt the Fedaykin's grief, the fear and anger.

"She is gone," Paul said.

The ghola heard the words out of a blazing corona. They burned his chest, his backbone, the sockets of his metal eyes. He felt his right hand move toward the knife at his belt. His own thinking became strange, disjointed. He was a puppet held fast by strings reaching down from that awful corona. He moved to another's commands, to another's desires. The strings jerked his arms, his legs, his jaw. Sounds came squeezing out of his mouth, a terrifying repetitive noise—

"Hraak! Hraak! Hraak!"

The knife came up to strike. In that instant, he grabbed his own voice, shaped rasping words: "Run! Young master, run!"

"We will not run," Paul said. "We'll move with dignity. We'll do what must be done."

The ghola's muscles locked. He shuddered, swayed.

"... *what must be done!*" The words rolled in his mind like a great fish surfacing. "... *what must be done!*" Ahhh, that had sounded like the old Duke, Paul's grandfather. The young master had some of the old man in him. "... *what must be done!*"

The words began to unfold in the ghola's consciousness. A sensation of living two lives simultaneously spread out through his awareness: Hayt / Idaho / Hayt / Idaho ... He became a motionless chain of relative existence, singular, alone. Old memories flooded his mind. He marked them, adjusted them to new understandings, made a beginning at the integration of a new awareness. A new *persona* achieved a temporary form of internal tyranny. The masculating synthesis remained charged with potential disorder, but events pressed him to the temporary adjustment. The young master needed him.

It was done then. He knew himself as Duncan Idaho, remembering everything of Hayt as though it had been stored secretly in him and ignited by a flaming catalyst. The corona dissolved. He shed the Tleilaxu compulsions.

"Stay close to me, Duncan," Paul said. "I'll need to depend on you for many things." And, as Idaho continued to stand entranced: "Duncan!"

"Yes, I am Duncan."

"Of course you are! This was the moment when you came back. We'll go inside now."

Idaho fell into step beside Paul. It was like the old times, yet not like them. Now that he stood free of the Tleilaxu, he could appreciate what they had given him. Zensunni training permitted him to overcome the shock of events. The mentat accomplishment formed a counterbalance. He put off all fear, standing above the source. His entire consciousness looked outward from a position of infinite wonder: he had been dead; he was alive.

"Sire," the Fedaykin Tandis said as they approached him, "the woman, Lichna, says she must see you. I told her to wait."

"Thank you," Paul said. "The birth . . ."

"I spoke to the medics," Tandis said, falling into step. "They said you have two children, both of them alive and sound."

"Two?" Paul stumbled, caught himself on Idaho's arm.

"A boy and a girl," Tandis said. "I saw them. They're good Fremen babies."

"How . . . how did she die?" Paul whispered.

"M'Lord?" Tandis bent close.

"Chani?" Paul said.

"It was the birth, m'Lord," Tandis husked. "They said her body was drained by the speed of it. I don't understand, but that is what they said."

"Take me to her," Paul whispered.

"M'Lord?"

"Take me to her!"

"That's where we're going, m'Lord." Again, Tandis bent close to Paul. "Why does your ghola carry a bared knife?"

"Duncan, put away your knife," Paul said. "The time for violence is past."

As he spoke, Paul felt closer to the sound of his voice than to the mechanism which had created the sound. Two babies! The vision had contained but one. Yet, these moments went as the vision went. There was a person here who felt grief and anger. Someone. His own awareness lay in the grip of an awful treadmill, replaying his life from memory.

Two babies?

Again he stumbled. *Chani, Chani*, he thought. *There was no other way. Chani, beloved, believe me that this death was quicker for you . . . and kinder. They'd have held our children hostage, displayed you in a cage and slave pits, reviled you with the blame for my death. This way . . . this way we destroy them and save our children.*

Children?

Once more, he stumbled.

I permitted this, he thought. *I should feel guilty.*

The sound of noisy confusion filled the cavern ahead of them. It grew louder precisely as he remembered it growing louder. Yes, this was the pattern, the inexorable pattern, even with two children.

Chani is dead, he told himself.

At some faraway instant in a past which he had shared with others, this future had reached down to him. It had chivvied him and herded him into a chasm whose walls grew narrower and narrower. He could feel them closing in on him. This was the way the vision went.

Chani is dead. I should abandon myself to grief.

But that was *not* the way the vision went.

"Has Alia been summoned?" he asked.

"She is with Chani's friends," Tandis said.

Paul sensed the mob pressing back to give him passage. Their silence moved ahead of him like a wave. The noisy confusion began dying down. A sense of congested emotion filled the sietch. He wanted to remove the people from his vision, found it impossible. Every face turning to follow him carried its special imprint. They were pitiless with curiosity, those faces. They felt grief, yes, but he understood the cruelty which drenched them. They were watching the articulate become dumb, the wise become a fool. Didn't the clown always appeal to cruelty?

This was more than a deathwatch, less than a wake.

Paul felt his soul begging for respite, but still the vision moved him. *Just a little farther now,* he told himself. Black, visionless dark awaited him just ahead. There lay the place ripped out of the vision by grief and guilt, the place where the moon fell.

He stumbled into it, would've fallen had Idaho not taken his arm in a fierce grip, a solid presence knowing how to share his grief in silence.

"Here is the place," Tandis said.

"Watch your step, Sire," Idaho said, helping him over an entrance lip. Hangings brushed Paul's face. Idaho pulled him to a halt. Paul felt the room then, a reflection against his cheeks and ears. It was a rock-walled space with the rock hidden behind tapestries.

"Where is Chani?" Paul whispered.

Harah's voice answered him: "She is right here, Usul."

Paul heaved a trembling sigh. He had feared her body already had been removed to the stills where Fremen reclaimed the water of the tribe. Was that the way the vision went? He felt abandoned in his blindness.

"The children?" Paul asked.

"They are here, too, m'Lord," Idaho said.

"You have beautiful twins, Usul," Harah said, "a boy and a girl. See? We have them here in a creche."

Two children, Paul thought wonderingly. The vision had contained only a daughter. He cast himself adrift from Idaho's arm, moved toward the place where Harah had spoken, stumbled into a hard surface. His hands explored it: the metaglass outlines of a creche.

Someone took his left arm. "Usul?" It was Harah. She guided his hand into the creche. He felt soft-soft flesh. It was so warm! He felt ribs, breathing.

"That is your son," Harah whispered. She moved his hand. "And this is your daughter." Her hand tightened on his. "Usul, are you truly blind now?"

He knew what she was thinking. *The blind must be abandoned in the desert.* Fremen tribes carried no dead weight.

"Take me to Chani," Paul said, ignoring her question.

Harah turned him, guided him to the left.

Paul felt himself accepting now the fact that Chani was dead. He had taken his place in a universe he did not want, wearing flesh that did not fit. Every breath he drew bruised his emotions. *Two children!* He wondered if he had committed himself to a passage where his vision would never return. It seemed unimportant.

"Where is my brother?"

It was Alia's voice behind him. He heard the rush of her, the overwhelming presence as she took his arm from Harah.

"I must speak to you!" Alia hissed.

"In a moment," Paul said.

"Now! It's about Lichna."

"I know," Paul said. "In a moment."

"You don't have a moment!"

"I have many moments."

"But Chani doesn't!"

"Be still!" he ordered. "Chani is dead." He put a hand across her mouth as she started to protest. "I order you to be still!" He felt her subside and removed his hand. "Describe what you see," he said.

"Paul!" Frustration and tears battled in her voice.

"Never mind," he said. And he forced himself to inner stillness, opened the eyes of his vision to this moment. Yes—it was still here. Chani's body lay on a pallet within a ring of light. Someone had straightened her white robe, smoothed it trying to hide the blood from the birth. No matter; he could not turn his awareness from the vision of her face: such a mirror of eternity in the still features!

He turned away, but the vision moved with him. She was gone . . . never to return. The air, the universe, all vacant—everywhere vacant. Was this the essence of his penance? he wondered. He wanted tears, but they would not come. Had he lived too long a Fremen? This death demanded its moisture!

Nearby, a baby cried and was hushed. The sound pulled a curtain on his vision. Paul welcomed the darkness. *This is another world*, he thought. *Two children.*

The thought came out of some lost oracular trance. He tried to recapture the timeless mind-dilation of the melange, but awareness fell short. No burst of the future came into this new consciousness. He felt himself rejecting the future—any future.

"Goodbye, my Sihaya," he whispered.

Alia's voice, harsh and demanding, came from somewhere behind him. "I've brought Lichna!"

Paul turned. "That's not Lichna," he said. "That's a Face Dancer. Lichna's dead."

"But hear what she says," Alia said.

Slowly, Paul moved toward his sister's voice.

"I'm not surprised to find you alive, Atreides." The voice was like Lichna's, but with subtle differences, as though the speaker used Lichna's vocal cords, but no longer bothered to control them sufficiently. Paul found himself struck by an odd note of honesty in the voice.

"Not surprised?" Paul asked.

"I am Scytale, a Tleilaxu of the Face Dancers, and I would know a thing before we bargain. Is that a ghola I see behind you, or Duncan Idaho?"

"It's Duncan Idaho," Paul said. "And I will not bargain with you."

"I think you'll bargain," Scytale said.

"Duncan," Paul said, speaking over his shoulder, "will you kill this Tleilaxu if I ask it?"

"Yes, m'Lord." There was the suppressed rage of a berserker in Idaho's voice.

"Wait!" Alia said. "You don't know what you're rejecting."

"But I do know," Paul said.

"So it's truly Duncan Idaho of the Atreides," Scytale said. "We found the lever! A ghola *can* regain his past." Paul heard footsteps. Someone brushed past him on the left. Scytale's voice came from behind him now. "What do you remember of your past, Duncan?"

"Everything. From my childhood on. I even remember you at the tank when they removed me from it," Idaho said.

"Wonderful," Scytale breathed. "Wonderful."

Paul heard the voice moving. *I need a vision,* he thought. Darkness frustrated him. Bene Gesserit training warned him of terrifying menace in Scytale, yet the creature remained a voice, a shadow of movement—entirely beyond him.

"Are these the Atreides babies?" Scytale asked.

"Harah!" Paul cried. "Get her away from there!"

"Stay where you are!" Scytale shouted. "All of you! I warn you, a Face Dancer can move faster than you suspect. My knife can have both these lives before you touch me."

Paul felt someone touch his right arm, then move off to the right.

"That's far enough, Alia," Scytale said.

"Alia," Paul said. "Don't."

"It's my fault," Alia groaned. "My fault!"

"Atreides," Scytale said, "shall we bargain now?"

Behind him, Paul heard a single hoarse curse. His throat constricted at the suppressed violence in Idaho's voice. Idaho must not break! Scytale would kill the babies!

"To strike a bargain, one requires a thing to sell," Scytale said. "Not so, Atreides? Will you have your Chani back? We can restore her to you. A ghola, Atreides. A ghola *with full memory*! But we must hurry. Call your friends to bring a cryological tank to preserve the flesh."

To hear Chani's voice once more, Paul thought. *To feel her presence beside me. Ahhh, that's why they gave me Idaho as a ghola, to let me discover how much the re-creation is like the original. But now—full restoration . . . at their price. I'd be a Tleilaxu tool forevermore. And Chani . . . chained to the same fate by a threat to our children, exposed once more to the Qizarate's plotting . . .*

"What pressures would you use to restore Chani's memory to her?" Paul asked, fighting to keep his voice calm. "Would you condition her to . . . to kill one of her own children?"

"We use whatever pressures we need," Scytale said. "What say you, Atreides?"

"Alia," Paul said, "bargain with this *thing*. I cannot bargain with what I cannot see."

"A wise choice," Scytale gloated. "Well, Alia, what do you offer me as your brother's agent?"

Paul lowered his head, bringing himself to stillness within stillness. He'd glimpsed something just then—like a vision, but not a vision. It had been a knife close to him. There!

"Give me a moment to think," Alia said.

"My knife is patient," Scytale said, "but Chani's flesh is not. Take a *reasonable* amount of time."

Paul felt himself blinking. It could not be . . . but it was! He felt eyes! Their vantage point was odd and they moved in an erratic way. *There!* The knife swam into his view. With a breath-stilling shock, Paul recognized the viewpoint. It was that of one of his children! He was seeing Scytale's knife hand from within the creche! It glittered only inches from him. Yes—and he could see himself across the room, as well—head down, standing quietly, a figure of no menace, ignored by the others in this room.

"To begin, you might assign us all your CHOAM holdings," Scytale suggested.

"All of them?" Alia protested.

"All."

Watching himself through the eyes in the creche, Paul slipped his crysknife from its belt sheath. The movement produced a strange sensation of duality. He measured the distance, the angle. There'd be no second chance. He prepared his body then in the Bene Gesserit way, armed himself like a cocked spring for a single concentrated movement, a *prajna* thing requiring all his muscles balanced in one exquisite unity.

The crysknife leaped from his hand. The milky blur of it flashed into Scytale's right eye, jerked the Face Dancer's head back. Scytale threw both hands up and staggered backward against the wall. His knife clattered off the ceiling, to hit the floor. Scytale rebounded from the wall; he fell face forward, dead before he touched the floor.

Still through the eyes in the creche, Paul watched the faces in the room turn toward his eyeless figure, read the combined shock. Then Alia rushed to the creche, bent over it and hid the view from him.

"Oh, they're safe," Alia said. "They're safe."

"M'Lord," Idaho whispered, "was *that* part of your vision?"

"No." He waved a hand in Idaho's direction. "Let it be."

"Forgive me, Paul," Alia said. "But when that creature said they could . . . revive . . ."

"There are some prices an Atreides cannot pay," Paul said. "You know that."

"I know," she sighed. "But I was tempted . . ."

"Who was not tempted?" Paul asked.

He turned away from them, groped his way to a wall, leaned against it and tried to understand what he had done. *How? How? The eyes in the creche!* He felt poised on the brink of terrifying revelation.

"My eyes, father."

The word-shapings shimmered before his sightless vision.

"My son!" Paul whispered, too low for any to hear. "You're . . . aware."

"Yes, father. Look!"

Paul sagged against the wall in a spasm of dizziness. He felt that he'd been upended and drained. His own life whipped past him. He saw his father. He *was* his father. And the grandfather, and the grand-y2i5

2iyy2222iiiy222i

fathers before that. His awareness tumbled through a mind-shattering corridor of his whole male line.

"How?" he asked silently.

Faint word-shapings appeared, faded and were gone, as though the strain was too great. Paul wiped saliva from the corner of his mouth. He remembered the awakening of Alia in the Lady Jessica's womb. But there had been no Water of Life, no overdose of melange this time . . . or had there? Had Chani's hunger been for that? Or was this somehow the genetic product of his line, foreseen by the Reverend Mother Gaius Helen Mohiam?

Paul felt himself in the creche then, with Alia cooing over him. Her hands soothed him. Her face loomed, a giant thing directly over him. She turned him then and he saw his creche companion—a girl with that bony-ribbed look of strength which came from a desert heritage. She had a full head of tawny red hair. As he stared, she opened her eyes. Those eyes! Chani peered out of her eyes . . . and the Lady Jessica. A multitude peered out of those eyes.

"Look at that," Alia said. "They're staring at each other."

"Babies can't focus at this age," Harah said.

"I could," Alia said.

Slowly, Paul felt himself being disengaged from that endless awareness. He was back at his own wailing wall then, leaning against it. Idaho shook his shoulder gently.

"M'Lord?"

"Let my son be called Leto for my father," Paul said, straightening.

"At the time of naming," Harah said, "I will stand beside you as a friend of the mother and give that name."

"And my daughter," Paul said. "Let her be called Ghanima."

"Usul!" Harah objected. "Ghanima's an ill-omened name."

"It saved your life," Paul said. "What matter that Alia made fun of you with that name? My daughter is Ghanima, a spoil of war."

Paul heard wheels squeak behind him then—the pallet with Chani's body being moved. The chant of the Water Rite began.

"Hal yawm!" Harah said. "I must leave now if I am to be the observer of the holy truth and stand beside my friend for the last time. Her water belongs to the tribe."

"Her water belongs to the tribe," Paul murmured. He heard Harah leave. He groped outward and found Idaho's sleeve. "Take me to my quarters, Duncan."

Inside his quarters, he shook himself free gently. It was a time to be alone. But before Idaho could leave there was a disturbance at the door.

"Master!" It was Bijaz calling from the doorway.

"Duncan," Paul said, "let him come two paces forward. Kill him if he comes farther."

"Ayyah," Idaho said.

"Duncan is it?" Bijaz asked. "Is it *truly* Duncan Idaho?"

"It is," Idaho said. "I remember."

"Then Scytale's plan succeeded!"

"Scytale is dead," Paul said.

"But I am not and the plan is not," Bijaz said. "By the tank in which I grew! It can be done! I shall have my pasts—all of them. It needs only the right trigger."

"Trigger?" Paul asked.

"The compulsion to kill you," Idaho said, rage thick in his voice. "Mentat computation: They found that I thought of you as the son I never had. Rather than slay you, the true Duncan Idaho would take over the ghola body. But . . . it might have failed. Tell me, dwarf, if your plan had failed, if I'd killed him, what then?"

"Oh . . . then we'd have bargained with the sister to save her brother. But this way the bargaining is better."

Paul took a shuddering breath. He could hear the mourners moving down the last passage now toward the deep rooms and the water stills.

"It's not too late, m'Lord," Bijaz said. "Will you have your love back? We can restore her to you. A ghola, yes. But now—we hold out the full restoration. Shall we summon servants with a cryological tank, preserve the flesh of your beloved . . ."

It was harder now, Paul found. He had exhausted his powers in the first Tleilaxu temptation. And now all that was for nothing! To feel Chani's presence once more . . .

"Silence him," Paul told Idaho, speaking in Atreides battle tongue. He heard Idaho move toward the door.

"Master!" Bijaz squeaked.

"As you love me," Paul said, still in battle tongue, "do me this favor: Kill him before I succumb!"

"Noooooo . . ." Bijaz screamed.

The sound stopped abruptly with a frightened grunt.

"I did him the kindness," Idaho said.

Paul bent his head, listening. He no longer could hear the mourners. He thought of the ancient Fremen rite being performed now deep in the sietch, far down in the room of the death-still where the tribe recovered its water.

"There was no choice," Paul said. "You understand that, Duncan?"

"I understand."

"There are some things no one can bear. I meddled in all the possible futures I could create until, finally, they created me."

"M'Lord, you shouldn't . . ."

"There are problems in this universe for which there are no answers," Paul said. "Nothing. Nothing can be done."

As he spoke, Paul felt his link with the vision shatter. His mind cowered, overwhelmed by infinite possibilities. His lost vision became like the wind, blowing where it willed.

We say of Muad'Dib that he has gone on a journey into that land where we walk without footprints.

—PREAMBLE TO THE QIZARATE CREED

There was a dike of water against the sand, an outer limit for the plantings of the sietch holding. A rock bridge came next and then the open desert beneath Idaho's feet. The promontory of Sietch Tabr dominated the night sky behind him. The light of both moons frosted its high rim. An orchard had been brought right down to the water.

Idaho paused on the desert side and stared back at flowered branches over silent water—reflections and reality—four moons. The stillsuit felt greasy against his skin. Wet flint odors invaded his nostrils past the filters. There was a malignant simpering to the wind through the orchard. He listened for night sounds. Kangaroo mice inhabited the grass at the water verge; a hawk owl bounced its droning call into the cliff shadows; the wind-broken hiss of a sandfall came from the open bled.

Idaho turned toward the sound.

He could see no movement out there on the moonlit dunes.

It was Tandis who had brought Paul this far. Then the man had returned to tell his account. And Paul had walked out into the desert—like a Fremen.

"He was blind—truly blind," Tandis had said, as though that explained it. "Before that, he had the vision which he told to us . . . but . . ."

A shrug. Blind Fremen were abandoned in the desert. Muad'Dib might be Emperor, but he was also Fremen. Had he not made provision that Fremen guard and raise his children? He was Fremen.

It was a skeleton desert here, Idaho saw. Moon-silvered ribs of rock showed through the sand; then the dunes began.

I should not have left him alone, not even for a minute, Idaho thought. *I knew what was in his mind.*

"He told me the future no longer needed his physical presence," Tandis had reported. "When he left me, he called back. 'Now I am free' were his words."

Damn them! Idaho thought.

The Fremen had refused to send 'thopters or searchers of any kind. Rescue was against their ancient customs.

"There will be a worm for Muad'Dib," they said. And they began the chant for those committed to the desert, the ones whose water went to Shai-hulud: "Mother of sand, father of Time, beginning of Life, grant him passage."

Idaho seated himself on a flat rock and stared at the desert. The night out there was filled with camouflage patterns. There was no way to tell where Paul had gone.

"Now I am free."

Idaho spoke the words aloud, surprised by the sound of his own voice. For a time, he let his mind run, remembering a day when he'd taken the child Paul to the sea market on Caladan, the dazzling glare of a sun on water, the sea's riches brought up dead, there to be sold. Idaho remembered Gurney Halleck playing music of the baliset for them—pleasure, laughter. Rhythms pranced in his awareness, leading his mind like a thrall down channels of remembered delight.

Gurney Halleck. Gurney would blame him for this tragedy.

Memory music faded.

He recalled Paul's words: *"There are problems in this universe for which there are no answers."*

Idaho began to wonder how Paul would die out there in the desert. Quickly, killed by a worm? Slowly, in the sun? Some of the Fremen back there in the sietch had said Muad'Dib would never die, that he had entered the ruh-world where all possible futures existed, that he would be present henceforth in the *alam al-mythal*, wandering there endlessly even after his flesh had ceased to be.

He'll die and I'm powerless to prevent it, Idaho thought.

He began to realize that there might be a certain fastidious courtesy in dying without a trace—no remains, nothing, and an entire planet for a tomb.

Mentat, solve thyself, he thought.

Words intruded on his memory—the ritual words of the Fedaykin lieutenant, posting a guard over Muad'Dib's children: "It shall be the solemn duty of the officer in charge . . ."

The plodding, self-important language of government enraged him. It had seduced the Fremen. It had seduced everyone. A man, a great man, was dying out there, but language plodded on . . . and on . . . and on . . .

What had happened, he wondered, to all the clean meanings that screened out nonsense? Somewhere, in some lost *where* which the Imperium had created, they'd been walled off, sealed against chance rediscovery. His mind quested for solutions, mentat fashion. Patterns of knowledge glistened there. Lorelei hair might shimmer thus, beckoning . . . beckoning the enchanted seaman into emerald caverns . . .

With an abrupt start, Idaho drew back from catatonic forgetfulness.

So! he thought. *Rather than face my failure, I would disappear within myself!*

The instant of that almost-plunge remained in his memory. Examining it, he felt his life stretch out as long as the existence of the universe. Real flesh lay condensed, finite in its emerald cavern of awareness, but infinite life had shared his being.

Idaho stood up, feeling cleansed by the desert. Sand was beginning to chatter in the wind, pecking at the surfaces of leaves in the orchard behind him. There was the dry and abrasive smell of dust in the night air. His robe whipped to the pulse of a sudden gust.

Somewhere far out in the bled, Idaho realized, a mother storm raged, lifting vortices of winding dust in hissing violence—a giant worm of sand powerful enough to cut flesh from bones.

He will become one with the desert, Idaho thought. *The desert will fulfill him.*

It was a Zensunni thought washing through his mind like clear water. Paul would go on marching out there, he knew. An Atreides would not give himself up completely to destiny, not even in the full awareness of the inevitable.

A touch of prescience came over Idaho then, and he saw that people of the future would speak of Paul in terms of seas. Despite a life soaked in dust, water would follow him. "His flesh foundered," they would say, "but he swam on."

Behind Idaho, a man cleared his throat.

Idaho turned to discern the figure of Stilgar standing on the bridge over the qanat.

"He will not be found," Stilgar said. "Yet all men will find him."

"The desert takes him—and deifies him," Idaho said. "Yet he was an interloper here. He brought an alien chemistry to this planet—water."

"The desert imposes its own rhythms," Stilgar said. "We welcomed him, called him our Mahdi, our Muad'Dib, and gave him his secret name, Base of the Pillar: Usul."

"Still he was not born a Fremen."

"And that does not change the fact that we claimed him . . . and have claimed him finally." Stilgar put a hand on Idaho's shoulder. "All men are interlopers, old friend."

"You're a deep one, aren't you, Stil?"

"Deep enough. I can see how we clutter the universe with our migrations. Muad'Dib gave us something uncluttered. Men will remember his Jihad for that, at least."

"He won't give up to the desert," Idaho said. "He's blind, but he won't give up. He's a man of honor and principle. He was Atreides-trained."

"And his water will be poured on the sand," Stilgar said. "Come." He pulled gently at Idaho's arm. "Alia is back and is asking for you."

"She was with you at Sietch Makab?"

"Yes—she helped whip those soft Naibs into line. They take her orders now . . . as I do."

"What orders?"

"She commanded the execution of the traitors."

"Oh." Idaho suppressed a feeling of vertigo as he looked up at the promontory. "Which traitors?"

"The Guildsman, the Reverend Mother Mohiam, Korba . . . a few others."

"You slew a Reverend Mother?"

"I did. Muad'Dib left word that it should not be done." He shrugged. "But I disobeyed him, as Alia knew I would."

Idaho stared again into the desert, feeling himself become whole, one person capable of seeing the pattern of what Paul had created. *Judgment strategy*, the Atreides called it in their training manuals. *People are subordinate to government, but the ruled influence the rulers.* Did the ruled have any concept, he wondered, of what they had helped create here?

"Alia . . ." Stilgar said, clearing his throat. He sounded embarrassed. "She needs the comfort of your presence."

"And she is the government," Idaho murmured.

"A regency, no more."

"Fortune passes everywhere, as her father often said," Idaho muttered.

"We make our bargain with the future," Stilgar said. "Will you come now? We need you back there." Again, he sounded embarrassed. "She is . . . distraught. She cries out against her brother one moment, mourns him the next."

"Presently," Idaho promised. He heard Stilgar leave. He stood facing into the rising wind, letting the grains of sand rattle against the stillsuit.

Mentat awareness projected the outflowing patterns into the future. The possibilities dazzled him. Paul had set in motion a whirling vortex and nothing could stand in its path.

The Bene Tleilax and the Guild had overplayed their hands and had lost, were discredited. The Qizarate was shaken by the treason of Korba and others high within it. And Paul's final voluntary act, his ultimate acceptance of their customs, had ensured the loyalty of the Fremen to him and to his house. He was one of them forever now.

"Paul is gone!" Alia's voice was choked. She had come up almost silently to where Idaho stood and was now beside him. "He was a fool, Duncan!"

"Don't say that!" he snapped.

"The whole universe will say it before I'm through," she said.

"Why, for the love of heaven?"

"For the love of my brother, not of heaven."

Zensunni insight dilated his awareness. He could sense that there was no vision in her—had been none since Chani's death. "You practice an odd love," he said.

"Love? Duncan, he had but to step off the track! What matter that the rest of the universe would have come shattering down behind him? He'd have been safe . . . and Chani with him!"

"Then . . . why didn't he?"

"For the love of heaven," she whispered. Then, more loudly, she said: "Paul's entire life was a struggle to escape his Jihad and its deification. At least, he's free of it. He chose this!"

"Ah, yes—the oracle." Idaho shook his head in wonder. "Even Chani's death. His moon fell."

"He *was* a fool, wasn't he, Duncan?"

Idaho's throat tightened with suppressed grief.

"Such a fool!" Alia gasped, her control breaking. "He'll live forever while we must die!"

"Alia, don't . . ."

"It's just grief," she said, voice low. "Just grief. Do you know what I must do for him? I must save the life of the Princess Irulan. That one! You should hear *her* grief. Wailing, giving moisture to the dead; she swears she loved him and knew it not. She reviles her Sisterhood, says she'll spend her life teaching Paul's children."

"You trust her?"

"She reeks of trustworthiness!"

"Ahhh," Idaho murmured. The final pattern unreeled before his awareness like a design on fabric. The defection of the Princess Irulan was the last step. It left the Bene Gesserit with no remaining lever against the Atreides heirs.

Alia began to sob, leaned against him, face pressed into his chest. "Ohhh, Duncan, Duncan! He's gone!"

Idaho put his lips against her hair. "Please," he whispered. He felt her grief mingling with his like two streams entering the same pool.

"I need you, Duncan," she sobbed. "Love me!"

"I do," he whispered.

She lifted her head, peered at the moon-frosted outline of his face. "I know, Duncan. Love knows love."

Her words sent a shudder through him, a feeling of estrangement from his old self. He had come out here looking for one thing and had found another. It was as though he'd lurched into a room full of familiar people only to realize too late that he knew none of them.

She pushed away from him, took his hand. "Will you come with me, Duncan?"

"Wherever you lead," he said.

She led him back across the qanat into the darkness at the base of the massif and its Place of Safety.

EPILOGUE

No bitter stench of funeral-still for Muad'Dib.
No knell nor solemn rite to free the mind
From avaricious shadows.
He is the fool saint,
The golden stranger living forever
On the edge of reason.
Let your guard fall and he is there!
His crimson peace and sovereign pallor
Strike into our universe on prophetic webs
To the verge of a quiet glance—there!
Out of bristling star-jungles:
Mysterious, lethal, an oracle without eyes,
Catspaw of prophecy, whose voice never dies!
Shai-hulud, he awaits thee upon a strand
Where couples walk and fix, eye to eye,
The delicious ennui of love.
He strides through the long cavern of time,
Scattering the fool-self of his dream.

—THE GHOLA'S HYMN

FRANK HERBERT is the bestselling author of the Dune saga. He was born in Tacoma, Washington, and educated at the University of Washington, Seattle. He worked a wide variety of jobs—including TV cameraman, radio commentator, oyster diver, jungle survival instructor, lay analyst, creative writing teacher, reporter, and editor of several West Coast newspapers—before becoming a full-time writer.

In 1952, Herbert began publishing science fiction with "Looking for Something?" in *Startling Stories*. But his emergence as a writer of major stature did not occur until 1965, with the publication of *Dune*. This was followed by *Dune Messiah, Children of Dune, God Emperor of Dune, Heretics of Dune*, and *Chapterhouse: Dune* to complete the bestselling saga. Herbert is also the author of some twenty other books, including *The White Plague, The Dosadi Experiment*, and *Destination: Void*. He died in 1986.

THE DUNE CHRONICLES

BY FRANK HERBERT

AVAILABLE NOW FROM

CHILDREN OF DUNE

"A major event."   —*Los Angeles Times*

"Ranging from palace intrigue and desert chases to religious speculation and confrontations with the supreme intelligence of the universe,
there is something here for all science fiction fans."

—*Publishers Weekly*

"Herbert adds enough new twists and turns to the ongoing saga that
familiarity with the recurring elements brings pleasure."

—*Challenging Destiny*

GOD EMPEROR OF DUNE

"Rich fare. . . . Heady stuff."   —*Los Angeles Times*

"A fourth visit to distant Arrakis that is every bit as fascinating as the
other three—every bit as timely."   —*Time*

"Book four of the Dune series has many of the same strengths as the
previous three, and I was indeed kept up late at night."

—*Challenging Destiny*

HERETICS OF DUNE

"A monumental piece of imaginative architecture . . . indisputably magical."
—*Los Angeles Herald Examiner*

"Appealing and gripping. . . . Fascinating detail, yet cloaked in mystery and mysticism."
—*The Milwaukee Journal*

"Herbert works wonders with some new speculation and an entirely new batch of characters. He weaves together several fascinating story lines with almost the same mastery as informed *Dune*, and keeps the reader intent on the next revelation or twist."
—*Challenging Destiny*

CHAPTERHOUSE: DUNE

"Compelling . . . a worthy addition to this durable and deservedly popular series."
—*The New York Times*

"The vast and fascinating Dune saga sweeps on—as exciting and gripping as ever."
—*Kirkus Reviews*

THE DUNE CHRONICLES BY FRANK HERBERT

DUNE
DUNE MESSIAH
CHILDREN OF DUNE
GOD EMPEROR OF DUNE
HERETICS OF DUNE
CHAPTERHOUSE: DUNE

OTHER BOOKS BY FRANK HERBERT

THE BOOK OF FRANK HERBERT

DESTINATION: VOID
(revised edition)

DIRECT DESCENT

THE DOSADI EXPERIMENT

EYE

THE EYES OF HEISENBERG

THE GODMAKERS

THE GREEN BRAIN

THE MAKER OF DUNE

THE SANTAROGA BARRIER

SOUL CATCHER

WHIPPING STAR

THE WHITE PLAGUE

THE WORLDS OF FRANK HERBERT

MAN OF TWO WORLDS
(with Brian Herbert)

BOOKS BY FRANK HERBERT AND BILL RANSOM

THE JESUS INCIDENT
THE LAZARUS EFFECT
THE ASCENSION FACTOR

BOOKS BY BRIAN HERBERT

DREAMER OF DUNE: THE BIOGRAPHY OF FRANK HERBERT

BOOKS EDITED BY BRIAN HERBERT

THE NOTEBOOKS OF FRANK HERBERT'S DUNE

SONGS OF MUAD'DIB

BOOKS BY BRIAN HERBERT AND KEVIN J. ANDERSON

DUNE: HOUSE ATREIDES

DUNE: HOUSE HARKONNEN

DUNE: HOUSE CORRINO

DUNE: THE BUTLERIAN JIHAD

DUNE: THE MACHINE CRUSADE

DUNE: THE BATTLE OF CORRIN

THE ROAD TO DUNE
(also by Frank Herbert; includes the novel *Spice Planet*)

HUNTERS OF DUNE

SANDWORMS OF DUNE

PAUL OF DUNE

THE WINDS OF DUNE

SISTERHOOD OF DUNE

MENTATS OF DUNE

NAVIGATORS OF DUNE

CHILDREN OF
DUNE

BOOK THREE IN THE DUNE CHRONICLES

FRANK HERBERT

With an Introduction by
BRIAN HERBERT

ACE
NEW YORK

ACE
Published by Berkley
An imprint of Penguin Random House LLC
penguinrandomhouse.com

Copyright © 1976 by Herbert Properties LLC
"Introduction" by Brian Herbert copyright © 2008 by DreamStar, Inc.

ACE is a registered trademark and the A colophon is a trademark of
Penguin Random House LLC.

ISBN: 9780593201749

The Library of Congress has cataloged the Ace hardcover edition
of this book as follows:

Herbert, Frank.
Children of Dune / Frank Herbert; with a new introduction by Brian Herbert.
p. cm.—(The Dune chronicles; bk. 3)
ISBN 978-0-441-01590-0 (alk. paper)
1. Dune (Imaginary place)—Fiction.   I. Title.
PS3558.E63C49 2008
813'.54—dc22   2008009348

Berkley edition / February 1981
Ace mass-market edition / April 1987
Ace hardcover edition / June 2008
Ace premium edition / June 2019
Ace trade paperback edition / July 2020

Printed in the United States of America
6th Printing

Cover design and illustration by Jim Tierney
Interior art: Desert Cave © masher/Shutterstock Images
Book design by Kristin del Rosario

INTRODUCTION
by Brian Herbert

Frank Herbert had a remarkably inventive and original mind. In his first novel, *The Dragon in the Sea* (1956), he came up with the concept of containerized shipping, an idea that the Japanese later commercialized to enormous success. *Dune,* only his second novel, was published in 1965. A complex, revolutionary work, it featured layers of ecology, philosophy, history, religion, and politics beneath the epic tale of the heroic Paul Atreides.

By 1968, five more of Frank Herbert's novels had been published: *Destination: Void, The Eyes of Heisenberg, The Green Brain, The Heaven Makers,* and *The Santaroga Barrier.* All the while, the popularity of *Dune* was growing, particularly among university intellectuals who were impressed by the complex messages interwoven into the great adventure story. The novel became a textbook for many classes. The *Whole Earth Catalog* extolled it as an environmental handbook.

As his eldest son, I didn't even know what my father had created. In 1966, I was hitchhiking near Carmel, California, and a young hippie couple gave me a ride in their Volkswagen Beetle. I was sitting in the back of the small car as it puttered along, and we were chatting. I told them that my dad was a newspaperman for the *San Francisco Examiner* and that he had written a couple of books.

"Oh?" the young man said. "What did he write?"

"Uh, *Dune,*" I said.

"*Dune!*" He was so excited that he pulled the car off to the side of the road. "Your dad is Frank Herbert?"

Hesitantly I replied, "Yeah."

"*Dune!* I love that book! One of my friends at college turned me on to it. Wow! I can't believe it!"

I was dumbfounded. As I wrote in *Dreamer of Dune,* my biography of Frank Herbert, my bearded father and I did not get along well in those years. I was a rebellious teenager, and we had one shouting argument after another. The relationship seemed hopeless. But Dad had apparently written something remarkable. Even so, he was not making much money from his writing or from his newspaper job. As a family, we were on the poor side of average, and some of our relatives considered my father something of a black sheep. He was eccentric, they said, and went his own way. How little did they know. How little did *I* know. I hadn't even read the novel yet.

Dune Messiah, Frank Herbert's first sequel to *Dune,* was published in 1969. In that book, he flipped over what he called the "myth of the hero" and showed the dark side of Paul Atreides. Some readers didn't understand it. Why would the author do that to his great hero? In interviews, Dad spent years afterward explaining why, and his reasons were sound. He believed that charismatic leaders could be dangerous because they could lead their followers off the edge of a cliff.

His alternate way of looking at the universe fascinated many readers anyway, and they couldn't wait to see where he was going with the series. He was developing a core readership. In the early 1970s, Frank Herbert became involved with the environmental movement, just as the popularity of the novel *Dune* was skyrocketing. He spoke on college campuses all over the country. Readers wanted even more sequels, but Dad took his time with the third book, wanting the next novel in the series to be as skillfully written as possible. In conjunction with the first Earth Day, Dad wrote entries for and edited *New World or No World,* a book about the importance of protecting the environment. He followed that with two novels, *Soul Catcher* and *The Godmakers,* and then a third, *Hellstrom's Hive,* which had a movie tie-in. His book *Threshold: The Blue Angels Experience* was also published with a film connection.

By 1976, Frank Herbert had completed his long- awaited sequel, which he titled *Children of Dune.* A four-part *Analog* serialization of the novel early that year was a resounding success, causing issues to sell out at newsstands. Letters poured in from excited fans who loved the story.

For months, David Hartwell, Dad's astute editor at G. P. Putnam's Sons, had been trying to convince company management that they were not printing enough copies, that when *Children of Dune* was printed soon in hardcover, it was going to be a national best seller purchased by more than science fiction fans. Like *Dune*, it would be a genre buster, he said.

Dune itself had not made it onto very many best-seller lists since its popularity had been a gradual groundswell. Its sales since publication were impressive, though, and *Dune Messiah* had sold relatively well. But *Dune Messiah* hadn't been favorably received by the critics, and consensus held that its sales came on the coattails of *Dune*. Would *Children of Dune* be an even bigger critical disappointment than *Dune Messiah*?

There had never been a hardcover science fiction best seller, so Putnam management proceeded with extreme caution. Suddenly the *Analog* results provided David Hartwell with the necessary ammunition. Putnam increased the first print run to 75,000 copies, more than any science fiction hardcover printing in history. Publication was scheduled for later in the year, after completion of the magazine serialization.

When *Children of Dune* came out in hardback in 1976, it was an instant best seller. True to the prediction of David Hartwell and the gut feeling of my father, it became the top-selling hardback in science fiction history up to that time . . . more than 100,000 copies in a few months. When the novel came out in paperback the following year, Berkley Books initially printed 750,000 copies. That wasn't half enough, and they went back to press. Six months after the release of the paperback, Dad said paperback sales were approaching two million copies.

"It's a runaway best seller," he told me in a telephone conversation. Dad enjoyed this phrase, and I heard it often in the ensuing years regarding his numerous best sellers.

At the age of fifty-five, Dad went on his first book tour, and it was a big one—twenty-one cities in thirty days, including an appearance on *The Today Show* in New York City with fellow science fiction writers Frederik Pohl and Lester del Rey. The Literary Guild made arrangements to offer all three books of the Dune trilogy in a boxed hardbound set.

At the vanguard of an explosive growth of sales in science fiction, Frank Herbert blazed the trail for other writers in the genre. After the phenomenal success of the Dune series, Isaac Asimov, Arthur C. Clarke, Robert A. Heinlein, Ray Bradbury, and other science fiction writers had national hardcover best sellers.

Children of Dune is an exciting, vividly imagined novel. It is Frank Herbert at the top of his craft.

BRIAN HERBERT
SEATTLE, WASHINGTON
JANUARY 11, 2008

Muad'Dib's teachings have become the playground of scho-
lastics, of the superstitious and the corrupt. He taught a balanced way of life, a philosophy with which a human can meet
problems arising from an ever-changing universe. He said
humankind is still evolving, in a process which will never end.
He said this evolution moves on changing principles which
are known only to eternity. How can corrupted reasoning play
with such an essence?

—WORDS OF THE MENTAT DUNCAN IDAHO

A spot of light appeared on the deep red rug which covered the raw rock
of the cave floor. The light glowed without apparent source, having its
existence only on the red fabric surface woven of spice fiber. A questing
circle about two centimeters in diameter, it moved erratically—now
elongated, now an oval. Encountering the deep green side of a bed, it
leaped upward, folded itself across the bed's surface.

Beneath the green covering lay a child with rusty hair, face still
round with baby fat, a generous mouth—a figure lacking the lean
sparseness of Fremen tradition, but not as water-fat as an off-worlder.
As the light passed across closed eyelids, the small figure stirred. The
light winked out.

Now there was only the sound of even breathing and, faint behind
it, a reassuring drip-drip-drip of water collecting in a catch-basin from
the windstill far above the cave.

Again the light appeared in the chamber—slightly larger, a few lumens brighter. This time there was a suggestion of source and move-ment to it: a hooded figure filled the arched doorway at the chamber's edge and the light originated there. Once more the light flowed around the chamber, testing, questing. There was a sense of menace in it, a rest-less dissatisfaction. It avoided the sleeping child, paused on the gridded air inlet at an upper corner, probed a bulge in the green and gold wall hangings which softened the enclosing rock.

Presently the light winked out. The hooded figure moved with a betraying swish of fabric, took up a station at one side of the arched doorway. Anyone aware of the routine here in Sietch Tabr would have suspected at once that this must be Stilgar, Naib of the Sietch, guardian of the orphaned twins who would one day take up the mantle of their father, Paul Muad'Dib. Stilgar often made night inspections of the twins' quarters, always going first to the chamber where Ghanima slept and ending here in the adjoining room, where he could reassure himself that Leto was not threatened.

I'm an old fool, Stilgar thought.

He fingered the cold surface of the light projector before restoring it to the loop in his belt sash. The projector irritated him even while he depended upon it. The thing was a subtle instrument of the Imperium, a device to detect the presence of large living bodies. It had shown only the sleeping children in the royal bedchambers.

Stilgar knew his thoughts and emotions were like the light. He could not still a restless inner projection. Some greater power controlled *that* movement. It projected him into this moment where he sensed the ac-cumulated peril. Here lay the magnet for dreams of grandeur through-out the known universe. Here lay temporal riches, secular authority and that most powerful of all mystic talismans: the divine authenticity of Muad'Dib's religious bequest. In these twins—Leto and his sister Ghanima—an awesome power focused. While they lived, Muad'Dib, though dead, lived in them.

These were not merely nine-year-old children; they were a natural force, objects of veneration and fear. They were the children of Paul Atreides, who had become Muad'Dib, the Mahdi of all the Fremen.

Muad'Dib had ignited an explosion of humanity; Fremen had spread from this planet in a jihad, carrying their fervor across the human universe in a wave of religious government whose scope and ubiquitous authority had left its mark on every planet.

Yet these children of Muad'Dib are flesh and blood, Stilgar thought. *Two simple thrusts of my knife would still their hearts. Their water would return to the tribe.*

His wayward mind fell into turmoil at such a thought.

To kill Muad'Dib's children!

But the years had made him wise in introspection. Stilgar knew the origin of such a terrible thought. It came from the left hand of the damned, not from the right hand of the blessed. The *ayat* and *burhan* of Life held few mysteries for him. Once he'd been proud to think of himself as Fremen, to think of the desert as a friend, to name his planet Dune in his thoughts and not Arrakis, as it was marked on all of the Imperial star charts.

How simple things were when our Messiah was only a dream, he thought. *By finding our Mahdi we loosed upon the universe countless messianic dreams. Every people subjugated by the jihad now dreams of a leader to come.*

Stilgar glanced into the darkened bedchamber.

If my knife liberated all of those people, would they make a messiah of me?

Leto could be heard stirring restlessly in his bed.

Stilgar sighed. He had never known the Atreides grandfather whose name this child had taken. But many said the moral strength of Muad'Dib had come from that source. Would that terrifying quality of *rightness* skip a generation now? Stilgar found himself unable to answer this question.

He thought: *Sietch Tabr is mine. I rule here. I am a Naib of the Fremen. Without me there would have been no Muad'Dib. These twins, now . . . through Chani, their mother and my kinswoman, my blood flows in their veins. I am there with Muad'Dib and Chani and all the others. What have we done to our universe?*

Stilgar could not explain why such thoughts came to him in the night and why they made him feel so guilty. He crouched within his hooded robe. Reality was not at all like the dream. The Friendly Desert, which once had spread from pole to pole, was reduced to half its former size. The mythic paradise of spreading greenery filled him with dismay. It was not like the dream. And as his planet changed, he knew he had changed. He had become a far more subtle person than the one-time sietch chieftain. He was aware now of many things—of statecraft and profound consequences in the smallest decisions. Yet he felt this knowledge and subtlety as a thin veneer covering an iron core of simpler, more deterministic awareness. And that older core called out to him, pleaded with him for a return to cleaner values.

The morning sounds of the sietch began intruding upon his thoughts. People were beginning to move about in the cavern. He felt a breeze against his cheeks: people were going out through the doorseals into the predawn darkness. The breeze spoke of carelessness as it spoke of the time. Warren dwellers no longer maintained the tight water discipline of the old days. Why should they, when rain had been recorded on this planet, when clouds were seen, when eight Fremen had been inundated and killed by a flash flood in a wadi? Until that event, the word *drowned* had not existed in the language of Dune. But this was no longer Dune; this was Arrakis . . . and it was the morning of an eventful day.

He thought: *Jessica, mother of Muad'Dib and grandmother of these royal twins, returns to our planet today. Why does she end her self-imposed exile at this time? Why does she leave the softness and security of Caladan for the dangers of Arrakis?*

And there were other worries: Would she sense Stilgar's doubts? She was a Bene Gesserit witch, graduate of the Sisterhood's deepest training, and a Reverend Mother in her own right. Such females were acute and they were dangerous. Would she order him to fall upon his own knife as the Umma-Protector of Liet-Kynes had been ordered?

Would I obey her? he wondered.

He could not answer that question, but now he thought about Liet-

Kynes, the planetologist who had first dreamed of transforming the planetwide desert of Dune into the human-supportive green planet which it was becoming. Liet-Kynes had been Chani's father. Without him there would have been no dream, no Chani, no royal twins. The workings of this fragile chain dismayed Stilgar.

How have we met in this place? he asked himself. *How have we combined? For what purpose? Is it my duty to end it all, to shatter that great combination?*

Stilgar admitted the terrible urging within him now. He could make that choice, denying love and family to do what a Naib must do on occasion: make a deadly decision for the good of the tribe. By one view, such a murder represented ultimate betrayal and atrocity. *To kill mere children!* Yet they were not mere children. They had eaten melange, had shared in the sietch orgy, had probed the desert for sandtrout and played the other games of Fremen children. . . . And they sat in the Royal Council. Children of such tender years, yet wise enough to sit in the Council. They might be children in flesh, but they were ancient in experience, born with a totality of genetic memory, a terrifying awareness which set their Aunt Alia and themselves apart from all other living humans.

Many times in many nights had Stilgar found his mind circling this *difference* shared by the twins and their aunt; many times had he been awakened from sleep by these torments, coming here to the twins' bedchambers with his dreams unfinished. Now his doubts came to focus. Failure to make a decision was in itself a decision—he knew this. These twins and their aunt had awakened in the womb, knowing there all of the memories passed on to them by their ancestors. Spice addiction had done this, spice addiction of the mothers—the Lady Jessica and Chani. The Lady Jessica had borne a son, Muad'Dib, before her addiction. Alia had come after the addiction. That was clear in retrospect. The countless generations of selective breeding directed by the Bene Gesserits had achieved Muad'Dib, but nowhere in the Sisterhood's plans had they allowed for melange. Oh, they knew about this possibility, but they feared it and called it *Abomination*. That was the most dismaying fact.

Abomination. They must possess reasons for such a judgment. And if they said Alia was an Abomination, then that must apply equally to the twins, because Chani, too, had been addicted, her body saturated with spice, and her genes had somehow complemented those of Muad'Dib.

Stilgar's thoughts moved in ferment. There could be no doubt these twins went beyond their father. But in which direction? The boy spoke of an ability to *be* his father—and had proved it. Even as an infant, Leto had revealed memories which only Muad'Dib should have known. Were there other ancestors waiting in that vast spectrum of memories—ancestors whose beliefs and habits created unspeakable dangers for living humans?

Abominations, the holy witches of the Bene Gesserit said. Yet the Sisterhood coveted the genophase of these children. The witches wanted sperm and ovum without the disturbing flesh which carried them. Was that why the Lady Jessica returned at this time? She had broken with the Sisterhood to support her Ducal mate, but rumor said she had returned to the Bene Gesserit ways.

I could end all of these dreams, Stilgar thought. *How simple it would be.*

And yet again he wondered at himself that he could contemplate such a choice. Were Muad'Dib's twins responsible for the reality which obliterated the dreams of others? No. They were merely the lens through which light poured to reveal new shapes in the universe.

In torment, his mind reverted to primary Fremen beliefs, and he thought: *God's command comes; so seek not to hasten it. God's it is to show the way; and some do swerve from it.*

It was the religion of Muad'Dib which upset Stilgar most. Why did they make a god of Muad'Dib? Why deify a man known to be flesh? Muad'Dib's *Golden Elixir of Life* had created a bureaucratic monster which sat astride human affairs. Government and religion united, and breaking a law became sin. A smell of blasphemy arose like smoke around any questioning of governmental edicts. The guilt of rebellion invoked hellfire and self-righteous judgments.

Yet it was men who created these governmental edicts.

Stilgar shook his head sadly, not seeing the attendants who had moved into the Royal Antechamber for their morning duties.

He fingered the crysknife at his waist, thinking of the past it symbolized, thinking that more than once he had sympathized with rebels whose abortive uprisings had been crushed by his own orders. Confusion washed through his mind and he wished he knew how to obliterate it, returning to the simplicities represented by the knife. But the universe would not turn backward. It was a great engine projected upon the grey void of nonexistence. His knife, if it brought the deaths of the twins, would only reverberate against that void, weaving new complexities to echo through human history, creating new surges of chaos, inviting humankind to attempt other forms of order and disorder.

Stilgar sighed, growing aware of the movements around him. Yes, these attendants represented a kind of order which was bound around Muad'Dib's twins. They moved from one moment to the next, meeting whatever necessities occurred there. *Best to emulate them,* Stilgar told himself. *Best meet what comes when it comes.*

I am an attendant yet, he told himself. *And my master is God the Merciful, the Compassionate.* And he quoted to himself: *"Surely, We have put on their necks fetters up to the chin, so their heads are raised; and We have put before them a barrier and behind them a barrier; and We have covered them, so they do not see."*

Thus was it written in the old Fremen religion.

Stilgar nodded to himself.

To *see,* to anticipate the next moment as Muad'Dib had done with his awesome visions of the future, added a counterforce to human affairs. It created new places for decisions. To be unfettered, yes, that might well indicate a whim of God. Another complexity beyond ordinary human reach.

Stilgar removed his hand from the knife. His fingers tingled with remembrance of it. But the blade which once had glistened in a sandworm's gaping mouth remained in its sheath. Stilgar knew he would not draw this blade now to kill the twins. He had reached a decision. Better to retain that one old virtue which he still cherished: loyalty. Better the complexities one thought he knew than the complexities which defied understanding. Better the now than the future of a dream. The bitter taste in his mouth told Stilgar how empty and revolting some dreams could be.

No! No more dreams!

CHALLENGE: "Have you seen The Preacher?"

RESPONSE: "I have seen a sandworm."

CHALLENGE: "What about that sandworm?"

RESPONSE: "It gives us the air we breathe."

CHALLENGE: "Then why do we destroy its land?"

RESPONSE: "Because Shai-Hulud [*sandworm deified*] orders it."

—RIDDLES OF ARRAKIS
BY HARQ AL-ADA

As was the Fremen custom, the Atreides twins arose an hour before dawn. They yawned and stretched in secret unison in their adjoining chambers, feeling the activity of the cave-warren around them. They could hear attendants in the antechamber preparing breakfast, a simple gruel with dates and nuts blended in liquid skimmed from partially fermented spice. There were glowglobes in the antechamber and a soft yellow light entered through the open archways of the bedchambers. The twins dressed swiftly in the soft light, each hearing the other nearby. As they had agreed, they donned stillsuits against the desert's parching winds.

Presently the royal pair met in the antechamber, noting the sudden stillness of the attendants. Leto, it was observed, wore a black-edged tan cape over his stillsuit's grey slickness. His sister wore a green cape. The neck of each cape was held by a clasp in the form of an Atreides hawk—gold with red jewels for eyes.

Seeing this finery, Harah, who was one of Stilgar's wives, said: "I see you have dressed to honor your grandmother." Leto picked up his breakfast bowl before looking at Harah's dark and wind-creased face. He shook his head. Then: "How do you know it's not ourselves we honor?"

Harah met his taunting stare without flinching, said: "My eyes are just as blue as yours!"

Ghanima laughed aloud. Harah was always an adept at the Fremen challenge-game. In one sentence, she had said: "Don't taunt me, boy. You may be royalty, but we both bear the stigma of melange-addiction—eyes without whites. What Fremen needs more finery or more honor than that?"

Leto smiled, shook his head ruefully. "Harah, my love, if you were but younger and not already Stilgar's, I'd make you my own."

Harah accepted the small victory easily, signaling the other attendants to continue preparing the chambers for this day's important activities. "Eat your breakfasts," she said. "You'll need the energy today."

"Then you agree that we're not too fine for our grandmother?" Ghanima asked, speaking around a mouthful of gruel.

"Don't fear her, Ghani," Harah said.

Leto gulped a mouthful of gruel, sent a probing stare at Harah. The woman was infernally folk-wise, seeing through the game of finery so quickly. "Will she believe we fear her?" Leto asked.

"Like as not," Harah said. "She was our Reverend Mother, remember. I know her ways."

"How was Alia dressed?" Ghanima asked.

"I've not seen her." Harah spoke shortly, turning away.

Leto and Ghanima exchanged a look of shared secrets, bent quickly to their breakfast. Presently they went out into the great central passage.

Ghanima spoke in one of the ancient languages they shared in genetic memory: "So today we have a grandmother."

"It bothers Alia greatly," Leto said.

"Who likes to give up such authority?" Ghanima asked.

Leto laughed softly, an oddly adult sound from flesh so young. "It's more than that."

"Will her mother's eyes observe what we have observed?"

"And why not?" Leto asked.

"Yes. . . . That could be what Alia fears."

"Who knows Abomination better than Abomination?" Leto asked.

"We could be wrong, you know," Ghanima said.

"But we're not." And he quoted from the Bene Gesserit Azhar Book: "It is with reason and terrible experience that we call the pre-born *Abomination*. For who knows what lost and damned persona out of our evil past may take over the living flesh?"

"I know the history of it," Ghanima said. "But if that's true, why don't we suffer from this inner assault?"

"Perhaps our parents stand guard within us," Leto said.

"Then why not guardians for Alia as well?"

"I don't know. It could be because one of her parents remains among the living. It could be simply that we are still young and strong. Perhaps when we're older and more cynical . . ."

"We must take great care with this grandmother," Ghanima said.

"And not discuss this Preacher who wanders our planet speaking heresy?"

"You don't really think he's our father!"

"I make no judgment on it, but Alia fears him."

Ghanima shook her head sharply. "I don't believe this Abomination nonsense!"

"You've just as many memories as I have," Leto said. "You can believe what you want to believe."

"You think it's because we haven't dared the spice trance and Alia has," Ghanima said.

"That's exactly what I think."

They fell silent, moving out into the flow of people in the central passage. It was cool in Sietch Tabr, but the stillsuits were warm and the twins kept their condenser hoods thrown back from their red hair.

Their faces betrayed the stamp of shared genes: generous mouths, widely set eyes of spice addict blue-on-blue.

Leto was first to note the approach of their Aunt Alia.

"Here she comes now," he said, shifting to Atreides battle language as a warning.

Ghanima nodded to her aunt as Alia stopped in front of them, said: "*A spoil of war* greets her illustrious relative." Using the same Chakobsa language, Ghanima emphasized the meaning of her own name—*Spoil of War*.

"You see, Beloved Aunt," Leto said, "we prepare ourselves for today's encounter with your mother."

Alia, the one person in the teeming royal household who harbored not the faintest surprise at adult behavior from these children, glared from one to the other. Then: "Hold your tongues, both of you!"

Alia's bronze hair was pulled back into two golden water rings. Her oval face held a frown, the wide mouth with its downturned hint of self-indulgence was held in a tight line. Worry wrinkles fanned the corners of her blue-on-blue eyes.

"I've warned both of you how to behave today," Alia said. "You know the reasons as well as I."

"We know your reasons, but you may not know ours," Ghanima said.

"Ghani!" Alia growled.

Leto glared at his aunt, said: "Today of all days, we will not pretend to be simpering infants!"

"No one wants you to simper," Alia said. "But we think it unwise for you to provoke dangerous thoughts in my mother. Irulan agrees with me. Who knows what role the Lady Jessica will choose? She is, after all, Bene Gesserit."

Leto shook his head, wondering: *Why does Alia not see what we suspect? Is she too far gone?* And he made special note of the subtle gene-markers on Alia's face which betrayed the presence of her maternal grandfather. The Baron Vladimir Harkonnen had not been a pleasant person. At this observation, Leto felt the vague stirrings of his own disquiet, thinking: *My own ancestor, too.*

He said: "The Lady Jessica was trained to rule."

Ghanima nodded. "Why does she choose this time to come back?"

Alia scowled. Then: "Is it possible she merely wants to see her grand-children?"

Ghanima thought: *That's what you hope, my dear aunt. But it's damned well not likely.*

"She cannot rule here," Alia said. "She has Caladan. That should be enough."

Ghanima spoke placatingly: "When our father went into the desert to die, he left you as Regent. He . . ."

"Have you any complaint?" Alia demanded.

"It was a reasonable choice," Leto said, following his sister's lead. "You were the one person who knew what it was like to be born as we were born."

"It's rumored that my mother has returned to the Sisterhood," Alia said, "and you both know what the Bene Gesserit think about. . . ."

"Abomination," Leto said.

"Yes!" Alia bit the word off.

"Once a witch, always a witch—so it's said," Ghanima said.

Sister, you play a dangerous game, Leto thought, but he followed her lead, saying: "Our grandmother was a woman of greater simplicity than others of her kind. You share her memories, Alia; surely you must know what to expect."

"Simplicity!" Alia said, shaking her head, looking around her at the thronged passage, then back to the twins. "If my mother were less complex, neither of you would be here—nor I. I would have been her first-born and none of this. . . ." A shrug, half shudder, moved her shoulders. "I warn you two, be very careful what you do today." Alia looked up. "Here comes my guard."

"And you still don't think it safe for us to accompany you to the spaceport?" Leto asked.

"Wait here," Alia said. "I'll bring her back."

Leto exchanged a look with his sister, said: "You've told us many times that the memories we hold from those who've passed before us lack a certain usefulness until we've experienced enough with our own flesh to make them reality. My sister and I believe this. We anticipate dangerous changes with the arrival of our grandmother."

"Don't stop believing that," Alia said. She turned away to be enclosed by her guards and they moved swiftly down the passage toward the State Entrance where ornithopters awaited them.

Ghanima wiped a tear from her right eye.

"Water for the dead?" Leto whispered, taking his sister's arm.

Ghanima drew in a deep, sighing breath, thinking of how she had observed her aunt, using the way she knew best from her own accumulation of ancestral experiences. "Spice trance did it?" she asked, knowing what Leto would say.

"Do you have a better suggestion?"

"For the sake of argument, why didn't our father . . . or even our grandmother succumb?"

He studied her a moment. Then: "You know the answer as well as I do. They had secure personalities by the time they came to Arrakis. The spice trance—well . . ." He shrugged. "They weren't born into this world already possessed of their ancestors. Alia, though . . ."

"Why didn't she believe the Bene Gesserit warnings?" Ghanima chewed her lower lip. "Alia had the same information to draw upon that we do."

"They already were calling her Abomination," Leto said. "Don't you find it tempting to find out if you're stronger than all of those . . ."

"No, I don't!" Ghanima looked away from her brother's probing stare, shuddered. She had only to consult her genetic memories and the Sisterhood's warnings took on vivid shape. The pre-born observably tended to become adults of nasty habits. And the likely cause . . . Again she shuddered.

"Pity we don't have a few pre-born in our ancestry," Leto said.

"Perhaps we do."

"But we'd . . . Ahh, yes, the old unanswered question: Do we really have open access to every ancestor's total file of experiences?"

From his own inner turmoil, Leto knew how this conversation must be disturbing his sister. They'd considered this question many times, always without conclusion. He said: "We must delay and delay and delay every time she urges the trance upon us. Extreme caution with a spice overdose; that's our best course."

"An overdose would have to be pretty large," Ghanima said.

"Our tolerance is probably high," he agreed. "Look how much Alia requires."

"I pity her," Ghanima said. "The lure of it must've been subtle and insidious, creeping up on her until . . ."

"She's a victim, yes," Leto said. "Abomination."

"We could be wrong."

"True."

"I always wonder," Ghanima mused, "if the next ancestral memory I seek will be the one which . . ."

"The past is no farther away than your pillow," Leto said.

"We must make the opportunity to discuss this with our grandmother."

"So her memory within me urges," Leto said.

Ghanima met his gaze. Then: "Too much knowledge never makes for simple decisions."

The sietch at the desert's rim
Was Liet's, was Kynes's,
Was Stilgar's, was Muad'Dib's
And, once more, was Stilgar's.
The Naibs one by one sleep in the sand,
But the sietch endures.

—FROM A FREMEN SONG

Alia felt her heart pounding as she walked away from the twins. For a few pulsing seconds, she had felt herself near compulsion to stay with them and beg their help. What a foolish weakness! Memory of it sent a warning stillness through Alia. Would these twins dare practice prescience? The path which had engulfed their father must lure them—spice trance with its visions of the future wavering like gauze blown on a fickle wind.

Why cannot I see the future? Alia wondered. *Much as I try, why does it elude me?*

The twins must be made to try, she told herself. They could be lured into it. They had the curiosity of children and it was linked to memories which traversed millennia.

Just as I have, Alia thought.

Her guards opened the moisture seals at the State Entrance of the sietch, stood aside as she emerged onto the landing lip where the ornithopters waited. There was a wind from the desert blowing dust across the sky, but the day was bright. Emerging from the glowglobes of the sietch into the daylight sent her thoughts outward.

Why was the Lady Jessica returning at this moment? Had stories been carried to Caladan, stories of how the Regency was . . .

"We must hurry, My Lady," one of her guards said, raising his voice above the wind sounds.

Alia allowed herself to be helped into her ornithopter and secured the safety harness, but her thoughts went leaping ahead.

Why now?

As the ornithopter's wings dipped and the craft went skidding into the air, she felt the pomp and power of her position as physical things—but they were fragile, oh, how fragile!

Why now, when her plans were not completed?

The dust mists drifted, lifting, and she could see the bright sunlight upon the changing landscape of the planet: broad reaches of green vegetation where parched earth had once dominated.

Without a vision of the future, I could fail. Oh, what magic I could perform if only I could see as Paul saw! Not for me the bitterness which prescient visions brought.

A tormenting hunger shuddered through her and she wished she could put aside the power. Oh, to be as others were—blind in that safest of all blindnesses, living only the hypnoidal half-life into which birth-shock precipitated most humans. But no! She had been born an Atreides, victim of that eons-deep awareness inflicted by her mother's spice addiction.

Why does my mother return today?

Gurney Halleck would be with her—ever the devoted servant, the hired killer of ugly mien, loyal and straightforward, a musician who played murder with a sliptip, or entertained with equal ease upon his nine-string baliset. Some said he'd become her mother's lover. That would be a thing to ferret out; it might prove a most valuable leverage.

The wish to be as others were left her.

Leto must be lured into the spice trance.

She recalled asking the boy how he would deal with Gurney Halleck. And Leto, sensing undercurrents in her question, had said Halleck was loyal "to a fault," adding: "He adored . . . my father."

She'd noted the small hesitation. Leto had almost said "me" instead of "my father." Yes, it was hard at times to separate the genetic memory from the chord of living flesh. Gurney Halleck would not make that separation easier for Leto.

A harsh smile touched Alia's lips.

Gurney had chosen to return to Caladan with the Lady Jessica after Paul's death. His return would tangle many things. Coming back to Arrakis, he would add his own complexities to the existing lines. He had served Paul's father—and thus the succession went: Leto I to Paul to Leto II. And out of the Bene Gesserit breeding program: Jessica to Alia to Ghanima—a branching line. Gurney, adding to the confusion of identities, might prove valuable.

What would he do if he discovered we carry the blood of Harkonnens, the Harkonnens he hates so bitterly?

The smile on Alia's lips became introspective. The twins were, after all, children. They were like children with countless parents, whose memories belonged both to others and to self. They would stand at the lip of Sietch Tabr and watch the track of their grandmother's ship landing in the Arrakeen Basin. That burning mark of a ship's passage visible on the sky—would it make Jessica's arrival more real for her grandchildren?

My mother will ask me about their training, Alia thought. *Do I mix* prana-bindu *disciplines with a judicious hand? And I will tell her that they train themselves—just as I did. I will quote her grandson to her:* "Among the responsibilities of command is the necessity to punish . . . but only when the victim demands it."

It came to Alia then that if she could only focus the Lady Jessica's attention sharply enough onto the twins, others might escape a closer inspection.

Such a thing could be done. Leto was very much like Paul. And why not? He could be Paul whenever he chose. Even Ghanima possessed this shattering ability.

Just as I can be my mother or any of the others who've shared their lives with us.

She veered away from this thought, staring out at the passing landscape of the Shield Wall. Then: *How was it to leave the warm safety of water-rich Caladan and return to Arrakis, to this desert planet where her Duke was murdered and her son died a martyr?*

Why did the Lady Jessica come back at this time?

Alia found no answer—nothing certain. She could share another's ego-awareness, but when experiences went their separate ways, then motives diverged as well. The stuff of decisions lay in the private actions taken by individuals. For the pre-born, the *many-born* Atreides, this remained the paramount reality, in itself another kind of birth: it was the absolute separation of living, breathing flesh when that flesh left the womb which had afflicted it with multiple awareness.

Alia saw nothing strange in loving and hating her mother simultaneously. It was a necessity, a required balance without room for guilt or blame. Where could loving or hating stop? Was one to blame the Bene Gesserit because they set the Lady Jessica upon a certain course? Guilt and blame grew diffuse when memory covered millennia. The Sisterhood had only been seeking to breed a Kwisatz Haderach: the male counterpart of a fully developed Reverend Mother . . . and more—a human of superior sensitivity and awareness, the Kwisatz Haderach who could be many places simultaneously. And the Lady Jessica, merely a pawn in that breeding program, had the bad taste to fall in love with the breeding partner to whom she had been assigned. Responsive to her beloved Duke's wishes, she produced a son instead of the daughter which the Sisterhood had commanded as the firstborn.

Leaving me to be born after she became addicted to the spice! And now they don't want me. Now they fear me! With good reason . . .

They'd achieved Paul, their Kwisatz Haderach, one lifetime too early—a minor miscalculation in a plan that extended. And now they had another problem: the Abomination, who carried the precious genes they'd sought for so many generations.

Alia felt a shadow pass across her, glanced upward. Her escort was assuming the high guard position preparatory to landing. She shook her head in wonderment at her wandering thoughts. What good was served by calling up old lifetimes and rubbing their mistakes together? This was a new lifetime.

Duncan Idaho had put his mentat awareness to the question of why Jessica returned at this time, evaluating the problem in the human-computer fashion which was his gift. He said she returned to take over the twins for the Sisterhood. The twins, too, carried those precious genes. Duncan could well be right. That might be enough to take the Lady Jessica out of her self-imposed seclusion on Caladan. If the Sisterhood commanded . . . Well, why else would she come back to the scenes of so much that must be shatteringly painful to her?

"We shall see," Alia muttered.

She felt the ornithopter touch down on the roof of her Keep, a positive and jarring punctuation which filled her with grim anticipation.

The two big cats came over the rocky ridge in the dawn light, loping easily. They were not really into the passionate hunt as yet, merely looking over their territory. They were called Laza tigers, a special breed brought here to the planet Salusa Secundus almost eight thousand years past. Genetic manipulation of the ancient Terran stock had erased some of the original tiger features and refined other elements. The fangs remained long. Their faces were wide, eyes alert and intelligent. The paws were enlarged to give them support on uneven terrain and their sheathed claws could extend some ten centimeters, sharpened at the ends into razor tips by abrasive compression of the sheath. Their coats were a flat and even tan which made them almost invisible against sand.

They differed in another way from their ancestors: servo-stimulators had been implanted in their brains while they were cubs. The stimulators made them pawns of whoever possessed the transmitter.

It was cold and as the cats paused to scan the terrain, their breath made fog on the air. Around them lay a region of Salusa Secundus left sere and barren, a place which harbored a scant few sandtrout smuggled from Arrakis and kept precariously alive in the dream that the melange monopoly might be broken. Where the cats stood, the landscape was marked by tan rocks and a scattering of sparse bushes, silvery green in the long shadows of the morning sun.

With only the slightest movement the cats grew suddenly alert. Their eyes turned slowly left, then their heads turned. Far down in the scarred land two children struggled up a dry wash, hand in hand. The children appeared to be of an age, perhaps nine or ten standard years. They were red-haired and wore stillsuits partly covered by rich white bourkas which bore all around the hem and at the forehead the hawk crest of the House Atreides worked in flame-jewel threads. As they walked, the children chattered happily and their voices carried clearly to the hunting cats. The Laza tigers knew this game; they had played it before, but they remained quiescent, awaiting the triggering of the chase signal in their servo-stimulators.

Now a man appeared on the ridgetop behind the cats. He stopped and surveyed the scene: cats, children. The man wore a Sardaukar working uniform in grey and black with insignia of a Levenbrech, aide to a Bashar. A harness passed behind his neck and under his arms to carry the servo-transmitter in a thin package against his chest where the keys could be reached easily by either hand.

The cats did not turn at his approach. They knew this man by sound and smell. He scrambled down to stop two paces from the cats, mopped his forehead. The air was cold, but this was hot work. Again his pale eyes surveyed the scene: cats, children. He pushed a damp strand of blond hair back under his black working helmet, touched the implanted microphone in his throat.

"The cats have them in sight."

The answering voice came to him through receivers implanted behind each ear. "We see them."

"This time?" the Levenbrech asked.

"Will they do it without a chase command?" the voice countered.

"They're ready," the Levenbrech said.

"Very well. Let us see if four conditioning sessions will be enough."

"Tell me when you're ready."

"Any time."

"Now, then," the Levenbrech said.

He touched a red key on the right hand side of his servo-transmitter, first releasing a bar which shielded the key. Now the cats stood without any transmitted restraints. He held his hand over a black key below the red one, ready to stop the animals should they turn on him. But they took no notice of him, crouched, and began working their way down the ridge toward the children. Their great paws slid out in smooth gliding motions.

The Levenbrech squatted to observe, knowing that somewhere around him a hidden transeye carried this entire scene to a secret monitor within the Keep where his Prince lived.

Presently the cats began to lope, then to run.

The children, intent on climbing through the rocky terrain, still had not seen their peril. One of them laughed, a high and piping sound in the clear air. The other child stumbled and, recovering balance, turned and saw the cats. The child pointed. "Look!"

Both children stopped and stared at the interesting intrusion into their lives. They were still standing when the Laza tigers hit them, one cat to each child. The children died with a casual abruptness, necks broken swiftly. The cats began to feed.

"Shall I recall them?" the Levenbrech asked.

"Let them finish. They did well. I knew they would; this pair is superb."

"Best I've ever seen," the Levenbrech agreed.

"Very good, then. Transport is being sent for you. We will sign off now."

The Levenbrech stood and stretched. He refrained from looking directly off to the high ground on his left where a telltale glitter had revealed the location of the transeye, which had relayed his fine performance to his Bashar far away in the green lands of the Capitol. The Levenbrech smiled. There would be a promotion for this day's work.

Already he could feel a Bator's insignia at his neck—and someday, Burseg . . . Even, one day, Bashar. People who served well in the corps of Farad'n, grandson of the late Shaddam IV, earned rich promotions. One day, when the Prince was seated on his rightful throne, there would be even greater promotions. A Bashar's rank might not be the end of it. There were Baronies and Earldoms to be had on the many worlds of this realm . . . once the twin Atreides were removed.

The Fremen must return to his original faith, to his genius in forming human communities; he must return to the past, where that lesson of survival was learned in the struggle with Arrakis. The only business of the Fremen should be that of opening his soul to the inner teachings. The worlds of the Imperium, the Landsraad and the CHOAM Confederacy have no message to give him. They will only rob him of his soul.

—THE PREACHER AT ARRAKEEN

All around the Lady Jessica, reaching far out into the dun flatness of the landing plain upon which her transport rested, crackling and sighing after its dive from space, stood an ocean of humanity. She estimated half a million people were there and perhaps only a third of them pilgrims. They stood in awesome silence, attention fixed on the transport's exit platform, whose shadowy hatchway concealed her and her party.

It lacked two hours until noon, but already the air above that throng reflected a dusty shimmering in promise of the day's heat.

Jessica touched her silver-flecked copper hair where it framed her oval face beneath the aba hood of a Reverend Mother. She knew she did not look her best after the long trip, and the black of the aba was not her best color. But she had worn this garment here before. The significance of the aba robe would not be lost upon the Fremen. She sighed. Space travel did not agree with her, and there'd been that added burden of memories—the other trip from Caladan to Arrakis when her Duke had been forced into this fief against his better judgment.

Slowly, probing with her Bene Gesserit–trained ability to detect significant minutiae, she scanned the sea of people. There were stillsuit hoods of dull grey, garments of Fremen from the deep desert; there were white-robed pilgrims with penitence marks on their shoulders; there were scattered pockets of rich merchants, hoodless in light clothing to flaunt their disdain for water loss in Arrakeen's parching air . . . and there was the delegation from the Society of the Faithful, green robed and heavily hooded, standing aloof within the sanctity of their own group.

Only when she lifted her gaze from the crowd did the scene take on any similarity to that which had greeted her upon her arrival with her beloved Duke. How long ago had that been? *More than twenty years.* She did not like to think of those intervening heartbeats. Time lay within her like a dead weight, and it was as though her years away from this planet had never been.

Once more into the dragon's mouth, she thought.

Here, upon this plain, her son had wrested the Imperium from the late Shaddam IV. A convulsion of history had imprinted this place into men's minds and beliefs.

She heard the restless stirring of the entourage behind her and again she sighed. They must wait for Alia, who had been delayed. Alia's party could be seen now approaching from the far edge of the throng, creating a human wave as a wedge of Royal Guards opened a passage.

Jessica scanned the landscape once more. Many differences submitted to her searching stare. A prayer balcony had been added to the landing field's control tower. And visible far off to the left across the plain stood the awesome pile of plasteel which Paul had built as his fortress— his "sietch above the sand." It was the largest integrated single construction ever to rise from the hand of man. Entire cities could have been housed within its walls and room to spare. Now it housed the most powerful governing force in the Imperium, Alia's "Society of the Faithful," which she had built upon her brother's body.

That place must go, Jessica thought.

Alia's delegation had reached the foot of the exit ramp and stood there expectantly. Jessica recognized Stilgar's craggy features. And God forfend! There stood the Princess Irulan hiding her savagery in that seductive body with its cap of golden hair exposed by a vagrant breeze. Irulan seemed not to have aged a day; it was an affront. And there, at the point of the wedge, was Alia, her features impudently youthful, her eyes staring upward into the hatchway's shadows. Jessica's mouth drew into a straight line and she scanned her daughter's face. A leaden sensation pulsed through Jessica's body and she heard the surf of her own life within her ears. The rumors were true! Horrible! Horrible! Alia had fallen into the forbidden way. The evidence was there for the initiate to read. *Abomination!*

In the few moments it took her to recover, Jessica realized how much she had hoped to find the rumors false.

What of the twins? she asked herself. *Are they lost, too?*

Slowly, as befitted the mother of a god, Jessica moved out of the shadows and onto the lip of the ramp. Her entourage remained behind as instructed. These next few moments were the crucial ones. Jessica stood alone in full view of the throng. She heard Gurney Halleck cough nervously behind her. Gurney had objected: *"Not even a shield on you? Gods below, woman! You're insane!"*

But among Gurney's most valuable features was a core of obedience. He would say his piece and then he would obey. Now he obeyed.

The human sea emitted a sound like the hiss of a giant sandworm as Jessica emerged. She raised her arms in the benedictory to which the priesthood had conditioned the Imperium. With significant pockets of tardiness, but still like one giant organism, the people sank to their knees. Even the official party complied.

Jessica had marked out the places of delay, and she knew that other eyes behind her and among her agents in the throng had memorized a temporary map with which to seek out the tardy.

As Jessica remained with her arms upraised, Gurney and his men emerged. They moved swiftly past her down the ramp, ignoring the official party's startled looks, joining the agents who identified themselves by handsign. Quickly they fanned out through the human sea, leaping knots of kneeling figures, dashing through narrow lanes. A few of their targets saw the danger and tried to flee. They were the easiest: a thrown knife, a garrote loop and the runners went down. Others were herded out of the press, hands bound, feet hobbled.

Through it all, Jessica stood with arms outstretched, blessing by her presence, keeping the throng subservient. She read the signs of spreading rumors though, and knew the dominant one because it had been planted: *"The Reverend Mother returns to weed out the slackers. Bless the mother of our Lord!"*

When it was over—a few dead bodies sprawled on the sand, captives removed to holding pens beneath the landing tower—Jessica lowered her arms. Perhaps three minutes had elapsed. She knew there was little likelihood Gurney and his men had taken any of the ringleaders, the ones who posed the most potent threat. They would be the alert and sensitive ones. But the captives would contain some interesting fish as well as the usual culls and dullards.

Jessica lowered her arms and, cheering, the people surged to their feet.

As though nothing untoward had happened, Jessica walked alone down the ramp, avoiding her daughter, singling out Stilgar for concentrated attention. The black beard which fanned out across the neck of his stillsuit hood like a wild delta contained flecks of grey, but his eyes carried that same whiteless intensity they'd presented to her on their first encounter in the desert. Stilgar knew what had just occurred, and approved. Here stood a true Fremen Naib, a leader of men and capable of bloody decisions. His first words were completely in character.

"Welcome home, My Lady. It's always a pleasure to see direct and effective action."

Jessica allowed herself a tiny smile. "Close the port, Stil. No one leaves until we've questioned those we took."

"It's already done, My Lady," Stilgar said. "Gurney's man and I planned this together."

"Those were your men, then, the ones who helped."

"Some of them, My Lady."

She read the hidden reservations, nodded. "You studied me pretty well in those old days, Stil."

"As you once were at pains to tell me, My Lady, one observes the survivors and learns from them."

Alia stepped forward then and Stilgar stood aside while Jessica confronted her daughter.

Knowing there was no way to hide what she had learned, Jessica did not even try concealment. Alia could read the minutiae when she needed, could read as well as any adept of the Sisterhood. She would already know by Jessica's behavior what had been seen and interpreted. They were enemies for whom the word *mortal* touched only the surface.

Alia chose anger as the easiest and most proper reaction.

"How dare you plan an action such as this without consulting me?" she demanded, pushing her face close to Jessica's.

Jessica spoke mildly: "As you've just heard, Gurney didn't even let me in on the whole plan. It was thought . . ."

"And you, Stilgar!" Alia said, rounding on him. "To whom are *you* loyal?"

"My oath is to Muad'Dib's children," Stilgar said, speaking stiffly. "We have removed a threat to them."

"And why doesn't that fill you with joy . . . daughter?" Jessica asked.

Alia blinked, glanced once at her mother, suppressed the inner tempest, and even managed a straight-toothed smile. "I *am* filled with joy . . . mother," she said. And to her own surprise, Alia found that she *was* happy, experiencing a terrible delight that it was all out in the open at last between herself and her mother. The moment she had dreaded was past and the power balance had not really been changed. "We will discuss this in more detail at a more convenient time," Alia said, speaking both to her mother and Stilgar.

"But of course," Jessica said, turning with a movement of dismissal to face the Princess Irulan.

For a few brief heartbeats, Jessica and the Princess stood silently studying each other—two Bene Gesserits who had broken with the Sisterhood for the same reason: love . . . both of them for love of men who now were dead. This Princess had loved Paul in vain, becoming his wife but not his mate. And now she lived only for the children given to Paul by his Fremen concubine, Chani.

Jessica spoke first: "Where are my grandchildren?"

"At Sietch Tabr."

"Too dangerous for them here; I understand."

Irulan permitted herself a faint nod. She had observed the interchange between Jessica and Alia, but put upon it an interpretation for which Alia had prepared her. *"Jessica has returned to the Sisterhood and we both know they have plans for Paul's children."* Irulan had never been the most accomplished adept in the Bene Gesserit—valuable more for the fact that she was a daughter of Shaddam IV than for any other reason; often too proud to exert herself in extending her capabilities. Now she chose sides with an abruptness which did no credit to her training.

"Really, Jessica," Irulan said, "the Royal Council should have been consulted. It was wrong of you to work only through—"

"Am I to believe none of you trust Stilgar?" Jessica asked.

Irulan possessed the wit to realize there could be no answer to such a question. She was glad that the priestly delegates, unable to contain their impatience any longer, pressed forward. She exchanged a glance with Alia, thinking: *Jessica's as haughty and certain of herself as ever!* A Bene Gesserit axiom arose unbidden in her mind, though: *"The haughty do but build castle walls behind which they try to hide their doubts and fears."* Could that be true of Jessica? Surely not. Then it must be a pose. But for what purpose? The question disturbed Irulan.

The priests were noisy in their possession of Muad'Dib's mother. Some only touched her arms, but most bowed low and spoke greetings. At last the leaders of the delegation took their turn with the Most Holy Reverend Mother, accepting the ordained role—"The first shall be last"—with practiced smiles, telling her that the official Lustration ceremony awaited her at the Keep, Paul's old fortress-stronghold.

Jessica studied the pair, finding them repellent. One was called Javid, a young man of surly features and round cheeks, shadowed eyes which could not hide the suspicions lurking in their depths. The other was Zebataleph, second son of a Naib she'd known in her Fremen days, as he was quick to remind her. He was easily classified: jollity linked with ruthlessness, a thin face with blond beard, an air about him of secret excitements and powerful knowledge. Javid she judged far more dangerous of the two, a man of private counsel, simultaneously magnetic and—she could find no other word—*repellent*. She found his accents strange, full of old Fremen pronunciations, as though he'd come from some isolated pocket of his people.

"Tell me, Javid," she said, "whence come you?"

"I am but a simple Fremen of the desert," he said, every syllable giving the lie to the statement.

Zebataleph intruded with an offensive deference, almost mocking: "We have much to discuss of the old days, My Lady. I was one of the first, you know, to recognize the holy nature of your son's mission."

"But you weren't one of his Fedaykin," she said.

"No, My Lady. I possessed a more philosophic bent; I studied for the priesthood."

And insured the preservation of your skin, she thought.

Javid said: "They await us at the Keep, My Lady."

Again she found the strangeness of his accent an open question demanding an answer. "Who awaits us?" she asked.

"The Convocation of the Faith, all those who keep bright the name and the deeds of your holy son," Javid said.

Jessica glanced around her, saw Alia smiling at Javid, asked: "Is this man one of your appointees, daughter?"

Alia nodded. "A man destined for great deeds."

But Jessica saw that Javid had no pleasure in this attention, marked him for Gurney's special study. And there came Gurney with five trusted men, signaling that they had the suspicious laggards under interrogation. He walked with the rolling stride of a powerful man, glance flicking left, right, all around, every muscle flowing through the relaxed alertness she had taught him out of the Bene Gesserit *prana-bindu* manual. He was an ugly lump of trained reflexes, a killer, and altogether terrifying to some, but Jessica loved him and prized him above all other living men. The scar of an inkvine whip rippled along his jaw, giving him a sinister appearance, but a smile softened his face as he saw Stilgar.

"Well done, Stil," he said. And they gripped arms in the Fremen fashion.

"The Lustration," Javid said, touching Jessica's arm.

Jessica drew back, chose her words carefully in the controlled power of Voice, her tone and delivery calculated for a precise emotional effect upon Javid and Zebataleph: "I returned to Dune to see my grandchildren. Must we take time for this priestly nonsense?"

Zebataleph reacted with shock, his mouth dropping open, eyes alarmed, glancing about at those who had heard. The eyes marked each listener. *Priestly nonsense!* What effect would such words have, coming from the mother of their messiah?

Javid, however, confirmed Jessica's assessment. His mouth hardened, then smiled. The eyes did not smile, nor did they waver to mark the listeners. Javid already knew each member of this party. He had an earshot map of those who would be watched with special care from this point onward. Only seconds later, Javid stopped smiling with an abruptness which said he knew how he had betrayed himself. Javid had not failed to do his homework: he knew the observational powers possessed by the Lady Jessica. A short, jerking nod of his head acknowledged those powers.

In a lightning flash of mentation, Jessica weighed the necessities. A subtle hand signal to Gurney would bring Javid's death. It could be done here for effect, or in quiet later, and be made to appear an accident.

She thought: *When we try to conceal our innermost drives, the entire being screams betrayal.* Bene Gesserit training turned upon this revelation—raising the adepts above it and teaching them to read the open flesh of others. She saw Javid's intelligence as valuable, a temporary weight in the balance. If he could be won over, he could be the link she needed, the line into the Arrakeen priesthood. And he was Alia's man.

Jessica said: "My official party must remain small. We have room for one addition, however. Javid, you will join us. Zebataleph, I am sorry. And, Javid . . . I will attend this—this ceremony—if you insist."

Javid allowed himself a deep breath and a low-voiced "As Muad'Dib's mother commands." He glanced to Alia, to Zebataleph, back to Jessica. "It pains me to delay the reunion with your grandchildren, but there are, ahhh, reasons of state . . ."

Jessica thought: *Good. He's a businessman above all else. Once we've determined the proper coinage, we'll buy him.* And she found herself enjoying the fact that he insisted on his precious ceremony. This little victory would give him power with his fellows, and they both knew it. Accepting his Lustration could be a down payment on later services.

"I presume you've arranged transportation," she said.

I give you the desert chameleon, whose ability to blend itself
into the background tells you all you need to know about the
roots of ecology and the foundations of a personal identity.

—BOOK OF DIATRIBES
FROM THE HAYT CHRONICLE

Leto sat playing a small baliset which had been sent to him on his fifth
birthday by that consummate artist of the instrument, Gurney Halleck.
In four years of practice, Leto had achieved a certain fluency, although
the two bass side strings still gave him trouble. He had found the baliset
soothing, however, for particular feelings of upset—a fact which had
not escaped Ghanima. He sat now in twilight on a rock shelf at the
southernmost extremity of the craggy outcropping which sheltered Sietch Tabr. Softly he strummed the baliset.

Ghanima stood behind him, her small figure radiating protest. She
had not wanted to come here into the open after learning from Stilgar
that their grandmother was delayed in Arrakeen. She particularly objected to coming here with nightfall near. Attempting to hurry her
brother, she asked: "Well, what is it?"

For an answer, he began another tune.

For the first time since accepting the gift, Leto felt intensely aware that
this baliset had originated with a master craftsman on Caladan. He possessed inherited memories which could inflict him with profound nostalgia
for that beautiful planet where House Atreides had ruled. Leto had but to
relax his inner barriers in the presence of this music and he would hear

memories from those times when Gurney had employed the baliset to beguile his friend and charge, Paul Atreides. With the baliset sounding in his own hands, Leto felt himself more and more dominated by his father's psychical presence. Still he played, relating more strongly to the instrument with every second that passed. He sensed the absolute idealized summation within himself which *knew* how to play this baliset, though nine-year-old muscles had not yet been conditioned to that inner awareness.

Ghanima tapped her foot impatiently, unaware that she matched the rhythm of her brother's playing.

Setting his mouth in a grimace of concentration, Leto broke from the familiar music and tried a song more ancient than any even Gurney had played. It had been old when Fremen migrated to their fifth planet. The words echoed a Zensunni theme, and he heard them in his memory while his fingers elicited a faltering version of the tune.

> Nature's beauteous form
> Contains a lovely essence
> Called by some—decay.
> By this lovely presence
> New life finds its way.
> Tears shed silently
> Are but water of the soul:
> They bring new life
> To the pain of being—
> A separation from that seeing
> Which death makes whole.

Ghanima spoke behind him as he strummed the final note. "There's a mucky old song. Why that one?"

"Because it fits."

"Will you play it for Gurney?"

"Perhaps."

"He'll call it moody nonsense."

"I know."

Leto peered back over his shoulder at Ghanima. There was no surprise in him that she knew the song and its lyrics, but he felt a sudden onset of awe at the singleness of their twinned lives. One of them could die and yet remain alive in the other's consciousness, every shared memory intact; they were that close. He found himself frightened by the timeless web of that closeness, broke his gaze away from her. The web contained gaps, he knew. His fear arose from the newest of those gaps. He felt their lives beginning to separate and wondered: *How can I tell her of this thing which has happened only to me?*

He peered out over the desert, seeing the deep shadows behind the barachans—those high, crescent-shaped migratory dunes which moved like waves around Arrakis. This was *Kedem*, the inner desert, and its dunes were rarely marked these days by the irregularities of a giant worm's progress. Sunset drew bloody streaks over the dunes, imparting a fiery light to the shadow edges. A hawk falling from the crimson sky captured his awareness as it captured a rock partridge in flight.

Directly beneath him on the desert floor plants grew in a profusion of greens, watered by a qanat which flowed partly in the open, partly in covered tunnels. The water came from giant windtrap collectors behind him on the highest point of rock. The green flag of the Atreides flew openly there.

Water and green.

The new symbols of Arrakis: water and green.

A diamond-shaped oasis of planted dunes spread beneath his high perch, focusing his attention into sharp Fremen awareness. The bell call of a nightbird came from the cliff below him, and it amplified the sensation that he lived this moment out of a wild past.

Nous avons changé tout cela, he thought, falling easily into one of the ancient tongues which he and Ghanima employed in private. "We have altered all of that." He sighed. *Oublier je ne puis.* "I cannot forget."

Beyond the oasis, he could see in this failing light the land Fremen called "The Emptiness"—the land where nothing grows, the land never fertile. Water and the great ecological plan were changing that. There were places now on Arrakis where one could see the plush green velvet of forested hills. Forests on Arrakis! Some in the new generation found it difficult to imagine dunes beneath those undulant green hills. To such young eyes there was no shock value in seeing the flat foliage of rain trees. But Leto found himself thinking now in the Old Fremen manner, wary of change, fearful in the presence of the new.

He said: "The children tell me they seldom find sandtrout here near the surface anymore."

"What's that supposed to indicate?" Ghanima asked. There was petulance in her tone.

"Things are beginning to change very swiftly," he said.

Again the bird chimed in the cliff, and night fell upon the desert as the hawk had fallen upon the partridge. Night often subjected him to an assault of memories—all of those inner lives clamoring for their moment. Ghanima didn't object to this phenomenon in quite the way he did. She knew his disquiet, though, and he felt her hand touch his shoulder in sympathy.

He struck an angry chord from the baliset.

How could he tell her what was happening to him?

Within his head were wars, uncounted lives parceling out their ancient memories: violent accidents, love's languor, the colors of many places and many faces . . . the buried sorrows and leaping joys of multitudes. He heard elegies to springs on planets which no longer existed, green dances and firelight, wails and halloos, a harvest of conversations without number.

Their assault was hardest to bear at nightfall in the open.

"Shouldn't we be going in?" she asked.

He shook his head, and she felt the movement, realizing at last that his troubles went deeper than she had suspected.

Why do I so often greet the night out here? he asked himself. He did not feel Ghanima withdraw her hand.

"You know why you torment yourself this way," she said.

He heard the gentle chiding in her voice. Yes, he knew. The answer lay there in his awareness, obvious: *Because that great known-unknown within moves me like a wave.* He felt the cresting of his past as though he rode a surfboard. He had his father's time-spread memories of prescience superimposed upon everything else, yet he wanted all of those pasts. He wanted them. And they were so very dangerous. He knew that completely now with this new thing which he would have to tell Ghanima.

The desert was beginning to glow under the rising light of First Moon. He stared out at the false immobility of sand furls reaching into infinity. To his left, in the near distance, lay The Attendant, a rock outcropping which sandblast winds had reduced to a low, sinuous shape like a dark worm striking through the dunes. Someday the rock beneath him would be cut down to such a shape and Sietch Tabr would be no more, except in the memories of someone like himself. He did not doubt that there would be someone like himself.

"Why're you staring at The Attendant?" Ghanima asked.

He shrugged. In defiance of their guardians' orders, he and Ghanima often went to The Attendant. They had discovered a secret hiding place there, and Leto knew now why that place lured them.

Beneath him, its distance foreshortened by darkness, an open stretch of qanat gleamed in moonlight; its surface rippled with movements of predator fish which Fremen always planted in their stored water to keep out the sandtrout.

"I stand between fish and worm," he murmured.

"What?"

He repeated it louder.

She put a hand to her mouth, beginning to suspect the thing which moved him. Her father had acted thus; she had but to peer inward and compare.

Leto shuddered. Memories which fastened him to places his flesh had never known presented him with answers to questions he had not asked. He saw relationships and unfolding events against a gigantic inner screen. The sandworm of Dune would not cross water; water poisoned it. Yet water had been known here in prehistoric times. White gypsum pans attested to bygone lakes and seas. Wells, deep-drilled, found water which sandtrout sealed off. As clearly as if he'd witnessed

the events, he saw what had happened on this planet and it filled him
with foreboding for the cataclysmic changes which human intervention
was bringing.

His voice barely above a whisper, he said: "I know what happened,
Ghanima."

She bent close to him. "Yes?"

"The sandtrout . . ."

He fell silent and she wondered why he kept referring to the haploid
phase of the planet's giant sandworm, but she dared not prod him.

"The sandtrout," he repeated, "was introduced here from some other
place. This was a wet planet then. They proliferated beyond the capability
of existing ecosystems to deal with them. Sandtrout encysted the available free water, made this a desert planet . . . and they did it to survive. In
a planet sufficiently dry, they could move to their sandworm phase."

"The sandtrout?" She shook her head, not doubting him, but unwilling to search those depths where he gathered such information. And
she thought: *Sandtrout?* Many times in this flesh and others had she
played the childhood game, poling for sandtrout, teasing them into a
thin glove membrane before taking them to the deathstill for their water. It was difficult to think of this mindless little creature as a shaper of
enormous events.

Leto nodded to himself. Fremen had always known to plant predator fish in their water cisterns. The haploid sandtrout actively resisted
great accumulations of water near the planet's surface; predators swam
in that qanat below him. Their sandworm vector could handle small
amounts of water—the amounts held in cellular bondage by human
flesh, for example. But confronted by large bodies of water, their chemical factories went wild, exploded in the death-transformation which
produced the dangerous melange concentrate, the ultimate awareness
drug employed in a diluted fraction for the sietch orgy. That pure concentrate had taken Paul Muad'Dib through the walls of Time, deep into
the well of dissolution which no other male had ever dared.

Ghanima sensed her brother trembling where he sat in front of her.
"What have you done?" she demanded.

But he would not leave his own train of revelation. "Fewer sandtrout—the ecological transformation of the planet . . ."

"They resist it, of course," she said, and now she began to understand the fear in his voice, drawn into this thing against her will.

"When the sandtrout go, so do all the worms," he said. "The tribes must be warned."

"No more spice," she said.

Words merely touched high points of the system danger which they both saw hanging over human intrusion into Dune's ancient relationships.

"It's the thing Alia knows," he said. "It's why she gloats."

"How can you be sure of that?"

"I'm sure."

Now she knew for certain what disturbed him, and she felt the knowledge chill her.

"The tribes won't believe us if she denies it," he said.

His statement went to the primary problem of their existence: What Fremen expected wisdom from a nine-year-old? Alia, growing farther and farther from her own inner sharing each day, played upon this.

"We must convince Stilgar," Ghanima said.

As one, their heads turned and they stared out over the moonlit desert. It was a different place now, changed by just a few moments of awareness. Human interplay with that environment had never been more apparent to them. They felt themselves as integral parts of a dynamic system held in delicately balanced order. The new outlook involved a real change of consciousness which flooded them with observations. As Liet-Kynes had said, the universe was a place of constant conversation between animal populations. The haploid sandtrout had spoken to them as human animals.

"The tribes would understand a threat to water," Leto said.

"But it's a threat to more than water. It's a—" She fell silent, understanding the deeper meaning of his words. Water was the ultimate power symbol on Arrakis. At their roots Fremen remained special-application animals, desert survivors, governance experts under conditions of stress. And as water became plentiful, a strange symbol transfer came over them even while they understood the old necessities.

"You mean a threat to power," she corrected him.

"Of course."

"But will they believe us?"

"If they see it happening, if they see the imbalance."

"Balance," she said, and repeated her father's words from long ago: "It's what distinguishes a people from a mob."

Her words called up their father in him and he said: "Economics versus beauty—a story older than Sheba." He sighed, looked over his shoulder at her. "I'm beginning to have prescient dreams, Ghani."

A sharp gasp escaped her.

He said: "When Stilgar told us our grandmother was delayed—I already knew that moment. Now my other dreams are suspect."

"Leto . . ." She shook her head, eyes damp. "It came later for our father. Don't you think it might be—"

"I've dreamed myself enclosed in armor and racing across the dunes," he said. "And I've been to Jacurutu."

"Jacu . . ." She cleared her throat. "That old myth!"

"A real place, Ghani! I must find this man they call The Preacher. I must find him and question him."

"You think he's . . . our father?"

"Ask yourself that question."

"It'd be just like him," she agreed, "but . . ."

"I don't like the things I know I'll do," he said. "For the first time in my life I understand my father."

She felt excluded from his thoughts, said: "The Preacher's probably just an old mystic."

"I pray for that," he whispered. "Oh, how I pray for that!" He rocked forward, got to his feet. The baliset hummed in his hand as he moved. "Would that he were only Gabriel without a horn." He stared silently at the moonlit desert.

She turned to look where he looked, saw the foxfire glow of rotting vegetation at the edge of the sietch plantings, then the clean blending into lines of dunes. That was a living place out there. Even when the desert slept, something remained awake in it. She sensed that wakefulness, hearing animals below her drinking at the qanat. Leto's revelation had transformed the night: this was a living moment, a time to discover regularities within perpetual change, an instant in which to feel that long movement from their Terranic past, all of it encapsulated in her memories.

"Why Jacurutu?" she asked, and the flatness of her tone shattered the mood.

"Why . . . I don't know. When Stilgar first told us how they killed the people there and made the place tabu, I thought . . . what you thought. But danger comes from there now . . . and The Preacher."

She didn't respond, didn't demand that he share more of his prescient dreams with her, and she knew how much this told him of her terror. That way led to Abomination and they both knew it. The word hung unspoken between them as he turned and led the way back over the rocks to the sietch entrance. *Abomination.*

The Universe is God's. It is *one thing*, a wholeness against which all separations may be identified. Transient life, even that self-aware and reasoning life which we call sentient, holds only fragile trusteeship on any portion of the wholeness.

—COMMENTARIES FROM THE C.E.T.
(COMMISSION OF ECUMENICAL TRANSLATORS)

Halleck used hand signals to convey the actual message while speaking aloud of other matters. He didn't like the small anteroom the priests had assigned for this report, knowing it would be crawling with spy devices. Let them try to break the tiny hand signals, though. The Atreides had used this means of communication for centuries without anyone the wiser.

Night had fallen outside, but the room had no windows, depending upon glowglobes at the upper corners.

"Many of those we took were Alia's people," Halleck signaled, watching Jessica's face as he spoke aloud, telling her the interrogation still continued.

"It was as you anticipated then," Jessica replied, her fingers winking. She nodded and spoke an open reply: "I'll expect a full report when you're satisfied, Gurney."

"Of course, My Lady," he said, and his fingers continued: "There is another thing, quite disturbing. Under the deep drugs, some of our captives talked of Jacurutu and, as they spoke the name, they died."

"A conditioned heart-stopper?" Jessica's fingers asked. And she said: "Have you released any of the captives?"

"A few, My Lady—the more obvious culls." And his fingers darted: "We suspect a heart-compulsion but are not yet certain. The autopsies aren't completed. I thought you should know about this thing of Jacurutu, however, and came immediately."

"My Duke and I always thought Jacurutu an interesting legend probably based on fact," Jessica's fingers said, and she ignored the usual tug of sorrow as she spoke of her long-dead love.

"Do you have orders?" Halleck asked, speaking aloud.

Jessica answered in kind, telling him to return to the landing field and report when he had positive information, but her fingers conveyed another message: "Resume contact with your friends among the smugglers. If Jacurutu exists, they'll support themselves by selling spice. There'd be no other market for them except the smugglers."

Halleck bowed his head briefly while his fingers said: "I've already set this course in motion, My Lady." And because he could not ignore the training of a lifetime, added: "Be very careful in this place. Alia is your enemy and most of the priesthood belongs to her."

"Not Javid," Jessica's fingers responded. "He hates the Atreides. I doubt anyone but an adept could detect it, but I'm positive of it. He conspires and Alia doesn't know of it."

"I'm assigning additional guards to your person," Halleck said, speaking aloud, avoiding the light spark of displeasure which Jessica's eyes betrayed. "There are dangers, I'm certain. Will you spend the night here?"

"We'll go later to Sietch Tabr," she said and hesitated, on the point of telling him not to send more guards, but she held her silence. Gurney's instincts were to be trusted. More than one Atreides had learned this, both to his pleasure and his sorrow. "I have one more meeting—with the Master of Novitiates this time," she said. "That's the last one and I'll be happily shut of this place."

And I beheld another beast coming up out of the sand; and
he had two horns like a lamb, but his mouth was fanged and
fiery as the dragon and his body shimmered and burned with
great heat while it did hiss like the serpent.

—REVISED ORANGE CATHOLIC BIBLE

He called himself *The Preacher*, and there had come to be an awesome
fear among many on Arrakis that he might be Muad'Dib returned from
the desert, not dead at all. Muad'Dib could be alive; for who had seen
his body? For that matter, who saw any body that the desert took? But
still—Muad'Dib? Points of comparison could be made, although no
one from the old days came forward and said: "Yes, I see that this is
Muad'Dib. I know him."

Still . . . Like Muad'Dib, The Preacher was blind, his eye sockets
black and scarred in a way that could have been done by a stone burner.
And his voice conveyed that crackling penetration, that same compelling force which demanded a response from deep within you. Many
remarked this. He was lean, this Preacher, his leathery face seamed, his
hair grizzled. But the deep desert did that to many people. You had only
to look about you and see this proven. And there was another fact for
contention: The Preacher was led by a young Fremen, a lad without
known sietch who said, when questioned, that he worked for hire. It was
argued that Muad'Dib, knowing the future, had not needed such a
guide except at the very end, when his grief overcame him. But he'd
needed a guide then; everyone knew it.

The Preacher had appeared one winter morning in the streets of Arrakeen, a brown and ridge-veined hand on the shoulder of his young guide. The lad, who gave his name as Assan Tariq, moved through the flint-smelling dust of the early swarming, leading his charge with the practiced agility of the warren-born, never once losing contact.

It was observed that the blind man wore a traditional bourka over a stillsuit which bore the mark about it of those once made only in the sietch caves of the deepest desert. It wasn't like the shabby suits being turned out these days. The nose tube which captured moisture from his breath for the recycling layers beneath the bourka was wrapped in braid, and it was the black vine braid so seldom seen anymore. The suit's mask across the lower half of his face carried green patches etched by the blown sand. All in all, this Preacher was a figure from Dune's past.

Many among the early crowds of that winter day had noted his passage. After all, a blind Fremen remained a rarity. Fremen Law still consigned the blind to Shai-Hulud. The wording of the Law, although it was less honored in these modern, water-soft times, remained unchanged from the earliest days. The blind were a gift to Shai-Hulud. They were to be exposed in the open *bled* for the great worms to devour. When it was done—and there were stories which got back to the cities—it was always done out where the largest worms still ruled, those called Old Men of the Desert. A blind Fremen, then, was a curiosity, and people paused to watch the passing of this odd pair.

The lad appeared about fourteen standard, one of the new breed who wore modified stillsuits; it left the face open to the moisture-robbing air. He had slender features, the all-blue spice-tinted eyes, a nubbin nose, and that innocuous look of innocence which so often masks cynical knowledge in the young. In contrast, the blind man was a reminder of times almost forgotten—long in stride and with a wiriness that spoke of many years on the sand with only his feet or a captive worm to carry him. He held his head in that stiff-necked rigidity which some of the blind cannot put off. The hooded head moved only when he cocked an ear at an interesting sound.

Through the day's gathering crowds the strange pair came, arriving at last on the steps which led up like terraced hectares to the escarpment which was Alia's Temple, a fitting companion to Paul's Keep. Up the steps The Preacher went until he and his young guide came to the third landing, where pilgrims of the Hajj awaited the morning opening of those gigantic doors above them. They were doors large enough to have admitted an entire cathedral from one of the ancient religions. Passing through them was said to reduce a pilgrim's soul to *motedom*, sufficiently small that it could pass through the eye of a needle and enter heaven.

At the edge of the third landing The Preacher turned, and it was as though he looked about him, seeing with his empty eye sockets the foppish city dwellers, some of them Fremen, with garments which simulated stillsuits but were only decorative fabrics, *seeing* the eager pilgrims fresh off the Guild space transports and awaiting that first step on the devotion which would ensure them a place in paradise.

The landing was a noisy place: there were Mahdi Spirit Cultists in green robes and carrying live hawks trained to screech a "call to heaven." Food was being sold by shouting vendors. Many things were being offered for sale, the voices shouting in competitive stridence: there was the Dune Tarot with its booklets of commentaries imprinted on shigawire. One vendor had exotic bits of cloth "guaranteed to have been touched by Muad'Dib himself!" Another had vials of water "certified to have come from Sietch Tabr, where Muad'Dib lived." Through it all there were conversations in a hundred or more dialects of Galach interspersed with harsh gutturals and squeaks of *outrine* languages which were gathered under the Holy Imperium. Face dancers and little people from the suspected artisan planets of the Tleilaxu bounced and gyrated through the throng in bright clothing. There were lean faces and fat, water-rich faces. The susurration of nervous feet came from the gritty plasteel which formed the wide steps. And occasionally a keening voice would rise out of the cacophony in prayer—"Mua-a-a-ad'Dib! Mua-a-a-ad'Dib! Greet my soul's entreaty! You, who are God's anointed, greet my soul! Mua-a-a-ad'Dib!"

Nearby among the pilgrims, two mummers played for a few coins, reciting the lines of the currently popular "Disputation of Armistead and Leandgrah."

The Preacher cocked his head to listen.

The mummers were middle-aged city men with bored voices. At a word of command, the young guide described them for The Preacher. They were garbed in loose robes, not even deigning to simulate stillsuits on their water-rich bodies. Assan Tariq thought this amusing, but The Preacher reprimanded him.

The mummer who played the part of Leandgrah was just concluding his oration: "Bah! The universe can be grasped only by the sentient hand. That hand is what drives your precious brain, and it drives everything else that derives from the brain. You see what you have created, you *become* sentient, only after the hand has done its work!"

A scattering of applause greeted his performance.

The Preacher sniffed and his nostrils recorded the rich odors of this place: uncapped esters of poorly adjusted stillsuits, masking musks of diverse origin, the common flinty dust, exhalations of uncounted exotic diets and the aromas of rare incense which already had been ignited within Alia's Temple and now drifted down over the steps in cleverly directed currents. The Preacher's thoughts were mirrored on his face as he absorbed his surroundings: *We have come to this, we Fremen!*

A sudden diversion rippled through the crowd on the landing. Sand Dancers had come into the plaza at the foot of the steps, half a hundred of them tethered to each other by elacca ropes. They obviously had been dancing thus for days, seeking a state of ecstasy. Foam dribbled from their mouths as they jerked and stamped to their secret music. A full third of them dangled unconscious from the ropes, tugged back and forth by the others like dolls on strings. One of these dolls had come awake, though, and the crowd apparently knew what to expect.

"I have *see-ee-een!*" the newly awakened dancer shrieked. "I have *see-ee-een!*" He resisted the pull of the other dancers, darted his wild gaze right and left. "Where this city is, there will be only sand! I have *see-ee-een!*"

A great swelling laugh went up from the onlookers. Even the new pilgrims joined it.

This was too much for The Preacher. He raised both arms and roared in a voice which surely had commanded worm riders: *"Silence!"* The entire throng in the plaza went still at that battle cry.

The Preacher pointed a thin hand toward the dancers, and the illusion that he actually saw them was uncanny. "Did you not hear that man? Blasphemers and idolaters! All of you! The religion of Muad'Dib is not Muad'Dib. He spurns it as he spurns you! Sand will cover this place. Sand will cover you."

Saying this, he dropped his arms, put a hand on his young guide's shoulder, and commanded: "Take me from this place."

Perhaps it was The Preacher's choice of words: *He spurns it as he spurns you!* Perhaps it was his tone, certainly something more than human, a vocality trained surely in the arts of the Bene Gesserit Voice which commanded by mere nuances of subtle inflection. Perhaps it was only the inherent mysticism of this place where Muad'Dib had lived and walked and ruled. Someone called out from the landing, shouting at The Preacher's receding back in a voice which trembled with religious awe: "Is that Muad'Dib come back to us?"

The Preacher stopped, reached into the purse beneath his bourka, and removed an object which only those nearby recognized. It was a desert-mummified human hand, one of the planet's jokes on mortality which occasionally turned up in the sand and were universally regarded as communications from Shai-Hulud. The hand had been desiccated into a tight fist which ended in white bone scarred by sandblast winds.

"I bring the Hand of God, and that is all I bring!" The Preacher shouted. "I speak for the Hand of God. I am The Preacher."

Some took him to mean that the hand was Muad'Dib's, but others fastened on that commanding presence and the terrible voice—and that was how Arrakis came to know his name. But it was not the last time his voice was heard.

It is commonly reported, my dear Georad, that there exists great natural virtue in the melange experience. Perhaps this is true. There remain within me, however, profound doubts that every use of melange always brings virtue. Meseems that certain persons have corrupted the use of melange in defiance of God. In the words of the Ecumenon, they have disfigured the soul. They skim the surface of melange and believe thereby to attain grace. They deride their fellows, do great harm to godliness, and they distort the meaning of this abundant gift maliciously, surely a mutilation beyond the power of man to restore. To be truly at one with the virtue of the spice, uncorrupted in all ways, full of goodly honor, a man must permit his deeds and his words to agree. When your actions describe a system of evil consequences, you should be judged by those consequences and not by your explanations. It is thus that we should judge Muad'Dib.

—THE PEDANT HERESY

It was a small room tinged with the odor of ozone and reduced to a shadowy greyness by dimmed glowglobes and the metallic blue light of a single transeye monitoring screen. The screen was about a meter wide and only two-thirds of a meter in height. It revealed in remote detail a barren, rocky valley with two Laza tigers feeding on the bloody remnants of a recent kill. On the hillside above the tigers could be seen a slender man in Sardaukar working uniform, Levenbrech insignia at his collar. He wore a servo-control keyboard against his chest.

One veriform suspensor chair faced the screen, occupied by a fair-haired woman of indeterminate age. She had a heart-shaped face and slender hands which gripped the chair arms as she watched. The fullness of a white robe trimmed in gold concealed her figure. A pace to her right stood a blocky man dressed in the bronze and gold uniform of a Bashar Aide in the old Imperial Sardaukar. His greying hair had been closely cropped over square, emotionless features.

The woman coughed, said: "It went as you predicted, Tyekanik."

"Assuredly, Princess," the Bashar Aide said, his voice hoarse.

She smiled at the tension in his voice, asked: "Tell me, Tyekanik, how will my son like the sound of Emperor Farad'n I?"

"The title suits him, Princess."

"That was not my question."

"He might not approve some of the things done to gain him that, ahh, title."

"Then again . . ." She turned, peered up through the gloom at him. "You served my father well. It was not your fault that he lost the throne to the Atreides. But surely the sting of that loss must be felt as keenly by you as by any—"

"Does the Princess Wensicia have some special task for me?" Tyekanik asked. His voice remained hoarse, but there was a sharp edge to it now.

"You have a bad habit of interrupting me," she said.

Now he smiled, displaying thick teeth which glistened in the light from the screen. "At times you remind me of your father," he said. "Always these circumlocutions before a request for a delicate . . . ahh, assignment."

She jerked her gaze away from him to conceal anger, asked: "Do you really think those Lazas will put my son on the throne?"

"It's distinctly possible, Princess. You must admit that the bastard get of Paul Atreides would be no more than juicy morsels for those two. And with those twins gone . . ." He shrugged.

"The grandson of Shaddam IV becomes the logical successor," she said. "That is if we can remove the objections of the Fremen, the Landsraad and CHOAM, not to mention any surviving Atreides who might—"

"Javid assures me that his people can take care of Alia quite easily. I do not count the Lady Jessica as an Atreides. Who else remains?"

"Landsraad and CHOAM will go where the profit goes," she said, "but what of the Fremen?"

"We'll drown them in their Muad'Dib's religion!"

"Easier said than done, my dear Tyekanik."

"I see," he said. "We're back to that old argument."

"House Corrino has done worse things to gain power," she said.

"But to embrace this . . . this Mahdi's religion!"

"My son respects you," she said.

"Princess, I long for the day when House Corrino returns to its rightful seat of power. So does every remaining Sardaukar here on Salusa. But if you—"

"Tyekanik! This is the planet Salusa *Secundus*. Do not fall into the lazy ways which spread through our Imperium. Full name, complete title—attention to every detail. Those attributes will send the Atreides lifeblood into the sands of Arrakis. Every detail, Tyekanik!"

He knew what she was doing with this attack. It was part of the shifty trickiness she'd learned from her sister, Irulan. But he felt himself losing ground.

"Do you hear me, Tyekanik?"

"I hear, Princess."

"I want you to embrace this Muad'Dib religion," she said.

"Princess, I would walk into fire for you, but this . . ."

"That is an order, Tyekanik!"

He swallowed, stared into the screen. The Laza tigers had finished feeding and now lay on the sand completing their toilet, long tongues moving across their forepaws.

"An *order*, Tyekanik—do you understand me?"

"I hear and obey, Princess." His voice did not change tone.

She sighed. "Ohh, if my father were only alive . . ."

"Yes, Princess."

"Don't mock me, Tyekanik. I know how distasteful this is to you. But if you set the example . . ."

"He may not follow, Princess."

"He'll follow." She pointed at the screen. "It occurs to me that the Levenbrech out there could be a problem."

"A problem? How is that?"

"How many people know this thing of the tigers?"

"That Levenbrech who is their trainer . . . one transport pilot, you, and of course . . ." He tapped his own chest.

"What about the buyers?"

"They know nothing. What is it you fear, Princess?"

"My son is, well, sensitive."

"Sardaukar do not reveal secrets," he said.

"Neither do dead men." She reached forward and depressed a red key beneath the lighted screen.

Immediately the Laza tigers raised their heads. They got to their feet and looked up the hill at the Levenbrech. Moving as one, they turned and began a scrambling run up the hillside.

Appearing calm at first, the Levenbrech depressed a key on his console. His movements were assured but, as the cats continued their dash toward him, he became more frenzied, pressing the key harder and harder. A look of startled awareness came over his features and his hand jerked toward the working knife at his waist. The movement came too late. A raking claw hit his chest and sent him sprawling. As he fell, the other tiger took his neck in one great-fanged bite and shook him. His spine snapped.

"Attention to detail," the Princess said. She turned, stiffened as Tyekanik drew his knife. But he presented the blade to her, handle foremost.

"Perhaps you'd like to use my knife to attend to another detail," he said.

"Put that back in its sheath and don't act the fool!" she raged. "Sometimes, Tyekanik, you try me to the—"

"That was a good man out there, Princess. One of my best."

"One of *my* best," she corrected him.

He drew a deep, trembling breath, sheathed his knife. "And what of my transport pilot?"

"This will be ascribed to an accident," she said. "You will advise him to employ the utmost caution when he brings those tigers back to us. And of course, when he has delivered our pets to Javid's people on the transport . . ." She looked at his knife.

"Is that an order, Princess?"

"It is."

"Shall I, then, fall on my knife, or will you take care of that, ahhh, detail?"

She spoke with a false calm, her voice heavy: "Tyekanik, were I not absolutely convinced that you *would* fall on your knife at my command, you would not be standing here beside me—armed."

He swallowed, stared at the screen. The tigers once more were feeding.

She refused to look at the scene, continued to stare at Tyekanik as she said: "You will, as well, tell our buyers not to bring us any more matched pairs of children who fit the necessary description."

"As you command, Princess."

"Don't use that tone with me, Tyekanik."

"Yes, Princess."

Her lips drew into a straight line. Then: "How many more of those paired costumes do we have?"

"Six sets of the robes, complete with stillsuits and the sand shoes, all with the Atreides insignia worked into them."

"Fabrics as rich as the ones on that pair?" she nodded toward the screen.

"Fit for royalty, Princess."

"Attention to detail," she said. "The garments will be dispatched to Arrakis as gifts for our royal cousins. They will be gifts from my son, do you understand me, Tyekanik?"

"Completely, Princess."

"Have him inscribe a suitable note. It should say that he sends these few paltry garments as tokens of his devotion to House Atreides. Something on that order."

"And the occasion?"

"There must be a birthday or holy day or something, Tyekanik. I leave that to you. I trust you, my friend."

He stared at her silently.

Her face hardened. "Surely you must know that? Who else can I trust since the death of my husband?"

He shrugged, thinking how closely she emulated the spider. It would not do to get on intimate terms with her, as he now suspected his Levenbrech had done.

"And Tyekanik," she said, "one more detail."

"Yes, Princess."

"My son is being trained to rule. There will come a time when he must grasp the sword in his own hands. You will know when that moment arrives. I'll wish to be informed immediately."

"As you command, Princess."

She leaned back, peered knowingly at Tyekanik. "You do not approve of me, I know that. It is unimportant to me as long as you remember the lesson of the Levenbrech."

"He was very good with animals, but disposable; yes, Princess."

"That is not what I mean!"

"It isn't? Then . . . I don't understand."

"An army," she said, "is composed of disposable, completely replaceable parts. That is the lesson of the Levenbrech."

"Replaceable parts," he said. "Including the supreme command?"

"Without the supreme command there is seldom a reason for an army, Tyekanik. That is why you will immediately embrace this Mahdi religion and, at the same time, begin the campaign to convert my son."

"At once, Princess. I presume you don't want me to stint his education in the other martial arts at the expense of this, ahh, religion?"

She pushed herself out of the chair, strode around him, paused at the door, and spoke without looking back. "Someday you will try my patience once too often, Tyekanik." With that, she let herself out.

Either we abandon the long-honored Theory of Relativity, or we cease to believe that we can engage in continued accurate prediction of the future. Indeed, knowing the future raises a host of questions which cannot be answered under conventional assumptions unless one first projects an Observer outside of Time and, second, nullifies all movement. If you accept the Theory of Relativity, it can be shown that Time and the Observer must stand still in relationship to each or inaccuracies will intervene. This would seem to say that it is impossible to engage in accurate prediction of the future. How, then, do we explain the continued seeking after this visionary goal by respected scientists? How, then, do we explain Muad'Dib?

—LECTURES ON PRESCIENCE
BY HARQ AL-ADA

"I must tell you something," Jessica said, "even though I know my telling will remind you of many experiences from our mutual past, and that this will place you in jeopardy."

She paused to see how Ghanima was taking this.

They sat alone, just the two of them, occupying low cushions in a chamber of Sietch Tabr. It had required considerable skill to maneuver this meeting, and Jessica was not at all certain that she had been alone in the maneuvering. Ghanima had seemed to anticipate and augment every step.

It was almost two hours after daylight, and the excitements of greeting and all of the recognitions were past. Jessica forced her pulse back to a steady pace and focused her attention into this rock-walled room with its dark hangings and yellow cushions. To meet the accumulated tensions, she found herself for the first time in years recalling the Litany Against Fear from the Bene Gesserit rite.

"I must not fear. Fear is the mind-killer. Fear is the little-death that brings total obliteration. I will face my fear. I will permit it to pass over me and through me. And when it has gone past I will turn the inner eye to see its path. Where the fear has gone there will be nothing. Only I will remain."

She did this silently and took a deep, calming breath.

"It helps at times," Ghanima said. "The Litany, I mean."

Jessica closed her eyes to hide the shock of this insight. It had been a long time since anyone had been able to read her that intimately. The realization was disconcerting, especially when it was ignited by an intellect which hid behind a mask of childhood.

Having faced her fear, though, Jessica opened her eyes and knew the source of turmoil: *I fear for my grandchildren.* Neither of these children betrayed the stigmata of Abomination which Alia flaunted, although Leto showed every sign of some terrifying concealment. It was for that reason he'd been deftly excluded from this meeting.

On impulse, Jessica put aside her ingrained emotional masks, knowing them to be of little use here, barriers to communication. Not since those loving moments with her Duke had she lowered these barriers, and she found the action both relief and pain. There remained facts which no curse or prayer or litany could wash from existence. Flight would not leave such facts behind. They could not be ignored. Elements of Paul's vision had been rearranged and the times had caught up with his children. They were a magnet in the void; evil and all the sad misuses of power collected around them.

Ghanima, watching the play of emotions across her grandmother's face, marveled that Jessica had let down her controls.

With catching movements of their heads remarkably synchronized, both turned, eyes met, and they stared deeply, probingly at each other. Thoughts without spoken words passed between them.

Jessica: *I wish you to see my fear.*

Ghanima: *Now I know you love me.*

It was a swift moment of utter trust.

Jessica said: "When your father was but a boy, I brought a Reverend Mother to Caladan to test him."

Ghanima nodded. The memory of it was extremely vivid.

"We Bene Gesserits were already cautious to make sure that the children we raised were human and not animal. One cannot always tell by exterior appearances."

"It's the way you were trained," Ghanima said, and the memory flooded into her mind: that old Bene Gesserit, Gaius Helen Mohiam. She'd come to Castle Caladan with her poisoned gom jabbar and her box of burning pain. Paul's hand (Ghanima's own hand in the shared memory) screamed with the agony of that box while the old woman talked calmly of immediate death if the hand were withdrawn from the pain. And there had been no doubt of the death in that needle held ready against the child's neck while the aged voice droned its rationale:

"You've heard of animals chewing off a leg to escape a trap. There's an animal kind of trick. A human would remain in the trap, endure the pain, feigning death that he might kill the trapper and remove a threat to his kind."

Ghanima shook her head against the remembered pain. The burning! The burning! Paul had imagined his skin curling black on that agonized hand within the box, flesh crisping and dropping away until only charred bones remained. And it had been a trick—the hand unharmed. But sweat stood out on Ghanima's forehead at the memory.

"Of course you remember this in a way that I cannot," Jessica said.

For a moment, memory-driven, Ghanima saw her grandmother in a different light: what this woman might do out of the driving necessities of that early conditioning in the Bene Gesserit schools! It raised new questions about Jessica's return to Arrakis.

"It would be stupid to repeat such a test on you or your brother," Jessica said. "You already know the way it went. I must assume you are human, that you will not misuse your inherited powers."

"But you don't make that assumption at all," Ghanima said.

Jessica blinked, realized that the barriers had been creeping back in place, dropped them once more. She asked: "Will you believe my love for you?"

"Yes." Ghanima raised a hand as Jessica started to speak. "But that love wouldn't stop you from destroying us. Oh, I know the reasoning: 'Better the animal-human die than it re-create itself.' And that's especially true if the animal-human bears the name Atreides."

"You at least are human," Jessica blurted. "I trust my instinct on this."

Ghanima saw the truth in this, said: "But you're not sure of Leto."

"I'm not."

"Abomination?"

Jessica could only nod.

Ghanima said: "Not yet, at least. We both know the danger of it, though. We can see the way of it in Alia."

Jessica cupped her hands over her eyes, thought: *Even love can't protect us from unwanted facts.* And she knew then that she still loved her daughter, crying out silently against fate: *Alia! Oh, Alia! I am sorry for my part in your destruction.*

Ghanima cleared her throat loudly.

Jessica lowered her hands, thought: *I may mourn my poor daughter, but there are other necessities now.* She said: "So you've recognized what happened to Alia."

"Leto and I watched it happen. We were powerless to prevent it, although we discussed many possibilities."

"You're sure that your brother is free of this curse?"

"I'm sure."

The quiet assurance in that statement could not be denied. Jessica found herself accepting it. Then: "How is it you've escaped?"

Ghanima explained the theory upon which she and Leto had settled, that their avoiding of the spice trance while Alia entered it often made the difference. She went on to reveal his dreams and the plans they'd discussed—even Jacurutu.

Jessica nodded. "Alia is an Atreides, though, and that poses enormous problems."

Ghanima fell silent before the sudden realization that Jessica still mourned her Duke as though his death had been but yesterday, that she would guard his name and memory against all threats. Personal memories from the Duke's own lifetime fled through Ghanima's awareness to reinforce this assessment, to soften it with understanding.

"Now," Jessica said, voice brisk, "what about this Preacher? I heard some disquieting reports yesterday after that damnable Lustration."

Ghanima shrugged. "He could be—"

"Paul?"

"Yes, but we haven't seen him to examine."

"Javid laughs at the rumors," Jessica said.

Ghanima hesitated. Then: "Do you trust this Javid?"

A grim smile touched Jessica's lips. "No more than you do."

"Leto says Javid laughs at the wrong things," Ghanima said.

"So much for Javid's laughter," Jessica said. "But do you actually entertain the notion that my son is still alive, that he has returned in this guise?"

"We say it's possible. And Leto . . ." Ghanima found her mouth suddenly dry, remembered fears clutching her breast. She forced herself to overcome them, recounted Leto's other revelations of prescient dreams.

Jessica moved her head from side to side as though wounded.

Ghanima said: "Leto says he must find this Preacher and make sure."

"Yes . . . Of course. I should never have left here. It was cowardly of me."

"Why do you blame yourself? You had reached a limit. I know that. Leto knows it. Even Alia may know it."

Jessica put a hand to her own throat, rubbed it briefly. Then: "Yes, the problem of Alia."

"She works a strange attraction on Leto," Ghanima said. "That's why I helped you meet alone with me. He agrees that she is beyond hope, but still he finds ways to be with her and . . . study her. And . . . it's very disturbing. When I try to talk against this, he falls asleep. He—"

"Is she drugging him?"

"No-o-o." Ghanima shook her head. "But he has this odd empathy for her. And . . . in his sleep, he often mutters *Jacurutu*."

"That again!" And Jessica found herself recounting Gurney's report about the conspirators exposed at the landing field.

"I sometimes fear Alia wants Leto to seek out Jacurutu," Ghanima said. "And I always thought it only a legend. You know it, of course."

Jessica shuddered. "Terrible story. Terrible."

"What must we do?" Ghanima asked. "I fear to search all of my memories, all of my lives . . ."

"Ghani! I warn you against that. You mustn't risk—"

"It may happen even if I don't risk it. How do we know what really happened to Alia?"

"No! You could be spared that . . . that *possession*." She ground the word out. "Well . . . Jacurutu, is it? I've sent Gurney to find the place—if it exists."

"But how can he . . . Oh! Of course: the smugglers."

Jessica found herself silenced by this further example of how Ghanima's mind worked in concert with what must be an inner awareness of others. *Of me!* How truly strange it was, Jessica thought, that this young flesh could carry all of Paul's memories, at least until the moment of Paul's spermal separation from his own past. It was an invasion of privacy against which something primal in Jessica rebelled. Momentarily she felt herself sinking into the absolute and unswerving Bene Gesserit judgment: *Abomination!* But there was a sweetness about this child, a willingness to sacrifice for her brother, which could not be denied.

We are one life reaching out into a dark future, Jessica thought. *We are one blood.* And she girded herself to accept the events which she and Gurney Halleck had set in motion. Leto must be separated from his sister, must be trained as the Sisterhood insisted.

> I hear the wind blowing across the desert and I see the moons of a winter night rising like great ships in the void. To them I make my vow: I will be resolute and make an art of government; I will balance my inherited past and become a perfect storehouse of my relic memories. And I will be known for kindliness more than for knowledge. My face will shine down the corridors of time for as long as humans exist.
>
> —LETO'S VOW
> AFTER HARQ AL-ADA

When she had been quite young, Alia Atreides had practiced for hours in the *prana-bindu* trance, trying to strengthen her own private personality against the onslaught of *all those others*. She knew the problem—melange could not be escaped in a sietch warren. It infested everything: food, water, air, even the fabrics against which she cried at night. Very early she recognized the uses of the sietch orgy where the tribe drank the death-water of a worm. In the orgy, Fremen released the accumulated pressures of their own genetic memories, and they denied those memories. She saw her companions being temporarily possessed in the orgy.

For her, there was no such release, no denial. She had possessed full consciousness long before birth. With that consciousness came a cataclysmic awareness of her circumstances: womb-locked into intense, inescapable contact with the personas of all her ancestors and of those identities death-transmitted in spice-*tau* to the Lady Jessica. Before birth, Alia had contained every bit of the knowledge required in a

Bene Gesserit Reverend Mother—plus much, much more from *all those others.*

In that knowledge lay recognition of a terrible reality—Abomination. The totality of that knowledge weakened her. The pre-born did not escape. Still she'd fought against the more terrifying of her ancestors, winning for a time a Pyrrhic victory which had lasted through childhood. She'd known a private personality, but it had no immunity against casual intrusions from those who lived their reflected lives through her.

Thus will I be one day, she thought. This thought chilled her. To walk and dissemble through the life of a child from her own loins, intruding, grasping at consciousness to add a quantum of experience.

Fear stalked her childhood. It persisted into puberty. She had fought it, never asking for help. Who would understand the help she required? Not her mother, who could never quite drive away that specter of Bene Gesserit judgment: the pre-born were Abomination.

There had come that night when her brother walked alone into the desert seeking death, giving himself to Shai-Hulud as blind Fremen were supposed to do. Within the month, Alia had been married to Paul's swordmaster, Duncan Idaho, a mentat brought back from the dead by the arts of the Tleilaxu. Her mother fled back to Caladan. Paul's twins were Alia's legal charge.

And she controlled the Regency.

Pressures of responsibility had driven the old fears away and she had been wide open to the inner lives, demanding their advice, plunging into spice trance in search of guiding visions.

The crisis came on a day like many others in the spring month of Laab, a clear morning at Muad'Dib's Keep with a cold wind blowing down from the pole. Alia still wore the yellow for mourning, the color of the sterile sun. More and more these past few weeks she'd been denying the inner voice of her mother, who tended to sneer at preparation for the coming Holy Days to be centered on the Temple.

The inner-awareness of Jessica faded, faded . . . sinking away at last with a faceless demand that Alia would be better occupied working on

the Atreides Law. New lives began to clamor for their moment of consciousness. Alia felt that she had opened a bottomless pit, and faces
arose out of it like a swarm of locusts, until she came at last to focus on
one who was like a beast: the old Baron Harkonnen. In terrified outrage
she had screamed out against all of that inner clamor, winning a temporary silence.

On this morning, Alia took her pre-breakfast walk through the
Keep's roof garden. In a new attempt to win the inner battle, she tried
to hold her entire awareness within Choda's admonition to the
Zensunni:

"Leaving the ladder, one may fall upward!"

But morning's glow along the cliffs of the Shield Wall kept distracting
her. Plantings of resilient fuzz-grass filled the garden's pathways. When
she looked away from the Shield Wall she saw dew on the grass, the catch
of all the moisture which had passed here in the night. It reflected her
own passage as of a multitude.

That multitude made her giddy. Each reflection carried the imprint
of a face from the inner multitude.

She tried to focus her mind on what the grass implied. The presence
of plentiful dew told her how far the ecological transformation had progressed on Arrakis. The climate of these northern latitudes was growing warmer; atmospheric carbon dioxide was on the increase. She
reminded herself how many new hectares would be put under green
plants in the coming year—and it required thirty-seven thousand cubic
feet of water to irrigate just one hectare.

Despite every attempt at mundane thoughts, she could not drive
away the sharklike circling of all those others within her.

She put her hands to her forehead and pressed.

Her temple guards had brought her a prisoner to judge at sunset the
previous day: one Essas Paymon, a dark little man ostensibly in the pay
of a house minor, the Nebiros, who traded in holy artifacts and small
manufactured items for decoration. Actually Paymon was known to be
a CHOAM spy whose task was to assess the yearly spice crop. Alia had
been on the point of sending him into the dungeons when he'd pro-

tested loudly "the injustice of the Atreides." That could have brought him an immediate sentence of death on the hanging tripod, but Alia had been caught by his boldness. She'd spoken sternly from her Throne of Judgment, trying to frighten him into revealing more than he'd already told her inquisitors.

"Why are our spice crops of such interest to the Combine Honnete?" she demanded. "Tell us and we may spare you."

"I only collect something for which there is a market," Paymon said. "I know nothing of what is done with my harvest."

"And for this petty profit you interfere with our royal plans?" Alia demanded.

"Royalty never considers that we might have plans, too," he countered.

Alia, captivated by his desperate audacity, said: "Essas Paymon, will you work for me?"

At this a grin whitened his dark face, and he said: "You were about to obliterate me without a qualm. What is my new value that you should suddenly make a market for it?"

"You've a simple and practical value," she said. "You're bold and you're for hire to the highest bidder. I can bid higher than any other in the Empire."

At which, he named a remarkable sum which he required for his services, but Alia laughed and countered with a figure she considered more reasonable and undoubtedly far more than he'd ever before received. She added: "And, of course, I throw in the gift of your life upon which, I presume, you place an even more inordinate value."

"A bargain!" Paymon cried and, at a signal from Alia, was led away by her priestly Master of Appointments, Ziarenko Javid.

Less than an hour later, as Alia prepared to leave the Judgment Hall, Javid came hurrying to report that Paymon had been overheard to mutter the fateful lines from the Orange Catholic Bible: *"Maleficos non patieris vivere."*

"Thou shalt not suffer a witch to live," Alia translated. So that was his gratitude! He was one of those who plotted against her very life! In a flush of rage such as she'd never before experienced, she ordered Paymon's immediate execution, sending his body to the Temple deathstill where his water, at least, would be of some value in the priestly coffers.

And all night long Paymon's dark face haunted her.

She tried all of her tricks against this persistent, accusing image, reciting the *Bu Ji* from the Fremen Book of Kreos: "Nothing occurs! Nothing occurs!" But Paymon took her through a wearing night into this giddy new day, where she could see that his face had joined those in the jeweled reflections from the dew.

A female guard called her to breakfast from the roof door behind a low hedge of mimosa. Alia sighed. She felt small choice between hells: the outcry within her mind or the outcry from her attendants—all were pointless voices, but persistent in their demands, hourglass noises that she would like to silence with the edge of a knife.

Ignoring the guard, Alia stared across the roof garden toward the Shield Wall. A *bahada* had left its broad outwash like a detrital fan upon the sheltered floor of her domain. The delta of sand spread out before her gaze, outlined by the morning sun. It came to her that an uninitiated eye might see that broad fan as evidence of a river's flow, but it was no more than the place where her brother had shattered the Shield Wall with the Atreides Family atomics, opening a path from the desert for the sandworms which had carried his Fremen troops to shocking victory over his Imperial predecessor, Shaddam IV. Now a broad qanat flowed with water on the Shield Wall's far side to block off sandworm intrusions. Sandworms would not cross open water; it poisoned them.

Would that I had such a barrier within my mind, she thought.

The thought increased her giddy sensation of being separated from reality.

Sandworms! Sandworms!

Her memory presented a collection of sandworm images: mighty Shai-Hulud, the demiurge of the Fremen, deadly beast of the desert's depths whose outpourings included the priceless spice. How odd it was, this sandworm, to grow from a flat and leathery sandtrout, she thought. They were like the flocking multitude within her awareness. The sandtrout, when linked edge to edge against the planet's bedrock, formed living cisterns; they held back the water that their sandworm vector might live. Alia could feel the analogy: some of *those others* within her mind held back dangerous forces which could destroy her.

Again the guard called her to breakfast, a note of impatience apparent.

Angrily Alia turned, waved a dismissal signal.

The guard obeyed, but the roof door slammed.

At the sound of the slamming door, Alia felt herself caught by everything she had attempted to deny. The other lives welled up within her like a hideous tide. Each demanding life pressed its face against her vision centers—a cloud of faces. Some presented mange-spotted skin, other were callous and full of sooty shadows; there were mouths like moist lozenges. The pressure of the swarm washed over her in a current which demanded that she float free and plunge into them.

"No," she whispered. "No . . . no . . . no . . ."

She would have collapsed onto the path but for a bench beside her which accepted her sagging body. She tried to sit, could not, stretched out on the cold plasteel, still whispering denial.

The tide continued to rise within her.

She felt attuned to the slightest show of attention, aware of the risk, but alert for every exclamation from those guarded mouths which clamored within her. They were a cacophony of demand for her attention: *"Me! Me!" "No, me!"* And she knew that if she once gave her attention, gave it completely, she would be lost. To behold one face out of the multitude and follow the voice of that face would be to be held by the egocentrism which shared her existence.

"Prescience does this to you," a voice whispered.

She covered her ears with her hands, thinking: *I'm not prescient! The trance doesn't work for me!*

But the voice persisted: *"It might work, if you had help."*

"No . . . no," she whispered.

Other voices wove around her mind: "I, Agamemnon, your ancestor, demand audience!"

"No . . . no." She pressed her hands against her ears until the flesh answered her with pain.

An insane cackle within her head asked: "What has become of Ovid? Simple. He's John Bartlett's ibid!"

The names were meaningless in her extremity. She wanted to scream against them and against all the other voices but could not find her own voice.

Her guard, sent back to the roof by senior attendants, peered once more from the doorway behind the mimosa, saw Alia on the bench, spoke to a companion: "Ahhh, she is resting. You noted that she didn't sleep well last night. It is good for her to take the *zaha*, the morning siesta."

Alia did not hear her guard. Her awareness was caught by shrieks of singing: "Merry old birds are we, hurrah!" The voices echoed against the inside of her skull and she thought: *I'm going insane, I'm losing my mind.*

Her feet made feeble fleeing motions against the bench. She felt that if she could only command her body to run, she might escape. She had to escape lest any part of that inner tide sweep her into silence, forever contaminating her soul. But her body would not obey. The mightiest forces in the Imperial universe would obey her slightest whim, but her body would not.

An inner voice chuckled. Then: "From one viewpoint, child, each incident of creation represents a catastrophe." It was a basso voice which rumbled against her eyes, and again that chuckle as though deriding its own pontification. "My dear child, I will help you, but you must help me in return."

Against the swelling background clamor behind that basso voice, Alia spoke through chattering teeth: "Who . . . who . . ."

A face formed itself upon her awareness. It was a smiling face of such fatness that it could have been a baby's except for the glittering eagerness of the eyes. She tried to pull back, but achieved only a longer view which included the body attached to that face. The body was grossly, immensely fat, clothed in a robe which revealed by subtle bulges beneath it that this fat had required the support of portable suspensors.

"You see," the basso voice rumbled, "it is only your maternal grandfather. You know me. I was the Baron Vladimir Harkonnen."

"You're . . . you're dead!" she gasped.

"But, of course, my dear! *Most* of us within you are dead. But none of the others are really willing to help you. They don't understand you."

"Go away," she pleaded. "Oh, please go away."

"But you need help, granddaughter," the Baron's voice argued.

How remarkable he looks, she thought, watching the projection of the Baron against her closed eyelids.

"I'm willing to help you," the Baron wheedled. "The others in here would only fight to take over your entire consciousness. Any one of them would try to drive you out. But me . . . I want only a little corner of my own."

Again the other lives within her lifted their clamor. The tide once more threatened to engulf her and she heard her mother's voice screeching. And Alia thought: *She's not dead.*

"Shut up!" the Baron commanded.

Alia felt her own desires reinforcing that command, making it felt throughout her awareness.

Inner silence washed through her like a cool bath and she felt her hammering heart begin slowing to its normal pace. Soothingly the Baron's voice intruded: "You see? Together, we're invincible. You help me and I help you."

"What . . . what do you want?" she whispered.

A pensive look came over the fat face against her closed eyelids. "Ahhh, my darling granddaughter," he said, "I wish only a few simple pleasures. Give me but an occasional moment of contact with your senses. No one else need ever know. Let me feel but a small corner of your life when, for example, you are enfolded in the arms of your lover. Is that not a small price to ask?"

"Y-yes."

"Good, good," the Baron chortled. "In return, my darling granddaughter, I can serve you in many ways. I can advise you, help you with my counsel. You will be invincible within and without. You will sweep away all opposition. History will forget your brother and cherish you. The future will be yours."

"You . . . won't let . . . the . . . the others take over?"

"They cannot stand against us! Singly we can be overcome, but together we command. I will demonstrate. Listen."

And the Baron fell silent, withdrawing his image, his inner presence. Not one memory, face, or voice of the other lives intruded.

Alia allowed herself a trembling sigh.

Accompanying that sigh came a thought. It forced itself into her awareness as though it were her own, but she sensed silent voices behind it.

The old Baron was evil. He murdered your father. He would've killed you and Paul. He tried to and failed.

The Baron's voice came to her without a face: "Of course I would've killed you. Didn't you stand in my way? But that argument is ended. You've won it, child! You're the new truth."

She felt herself nodding and her cheek moved scratchingly against the harsh surface of the bench.

His words were reasonable, she thought. A Bene Gesserit precept reinforced the reasonable character of his words: *"The purpose of argument is to change the nature of truth."*

Yes . . . that was the way the Bene Gesserit would have it.

"Precisely!" the Baron said. "And I am dead while you are alive. I have only a fragile existence. I'm a mere memory-self within you. I am yours to command. And how little I ask in return for the profound advice which is mine to deliver."

"What do you advise me to do now?" she asked, testing.

"You're worried about the judgment you gave last night," he said. "You wonder if Paymon's words were reported truthfully. Perhaps Javid saw in this Paymon a threat to his position of trust. Is this not the doubt which assails you?"

"Y-yes."

"And your doubt is based on acute observation, is it not? Javid behaves with increasing intimacy toward your person. Even Duncan has noted it, hasn't he?"

"You know he has."

"Very well, then. Take Javid for your lover and—"

"No!"

"You worry about Duncan? But your husband is a mentat mystic. He cannot be touched or harmed by activities of the flesh. Have you not felt sometimes how distant he is from you?"

"B-but he . . ."

"Duncan's mentat part would understand should he ever have need to know the device you employed in destroying Javid."

"Destroy . . ."

"Certainly! Dangerous tools may be used, but they should be cast aside when they grow too dangerous."

"Then . . . why should . . . I mean . . ."

"Ahhh, you precious dunce! Because of the value contained in the lesson."

"I don't understand."

"Values, my dear grandchild, depend for their acceptance upon their success. Javid's obedience must be unconditional, his acceptance of your authority absolute, and his—"

"The morality of this *lesson* escapes—"

"Don't be dense, grandchild! Morality must always be based on practicality. Render unto Caesar and all that nonsense. A victory is useless unless it reflects your deepest wishes. Is it not true that you have admired Javid's manliness?"

Alia swallowed, hating the admission, but forced to it by her complete nakedness before the inner-watcher. "Ye-es."

"Good!" How jovial the word sounded within her head. "Now we begin to understand each other. When you have him helpless, then, in your bed, convinced that you are *his* thrall, you will ask him about Paymon. Do it jokingly: a rich laugh between you. And when he admits the deception, you will slip a crysknife between his ribs. Ahhh, the flow of blood can add so much to your satis—"

"No," she whispered, her mouth dry with horror. "No . . . no . . . no . . ."

"Then I will do it for you," the Baron argued. "It must be done; you admit that. If you but set up the conditions, I will assume temporary sway over . . ."

"No!"

"Your fear is so transparent, granddaughter. My sway of your senses cannot be else but temporary. There are others, now, who could mimic you to a perfection that . . . But you know this. With me, ahhh, people would spy out my presence immediately. You know the Fremen Law for those possessed. You'd be slain out of hand. Yes—even you. And you know I do not want *that* to happen. I'll take care of Javid for you and, once it's done, I'll step aside. You need only . . ."

"How is this good advice?"

"It rids you of a dangerous tool. And, child, it sets up the working relationship between us, a relationship which can only teach you well about future judgments which—"

"Teach me?"

"Naturally!"

Alia put her hands over her eyes, trying to think, knowing that any thought might be known to this presence within her, that a thought might originate with that presence and be taken as her own.

"You worry yourself needlessly," the Baron wheedled. "This Paymon fellow, now, was—"

"What I did was wrong! I was tired and acted hastily. I should've sought confirmation of—"

"You did right! Your judgments cannot be based on any such foolish abstract as that Atreides notion of equality. That's what kept you sleepless, not Paymon's death. You made a good decision! He was another dangerous tool. You acted to maintain order in your society. Now there's a good reason for judgments, not this *justice* nonsense! There's no such thing as equal justice anywhere. It's unsettling to a society when you try to achieve such a false balance."

Alia felt pleasure at this defense of her judgment against Paymon, but shocked at the amoral concept behind the argument. "Equal justice was an Atreides . . . was . . ." She took her hands from her eyes, but kept her eyes closed.

"All of your priestly judges should be admonished about this error," the Baron argued. "Decisions must be weighed only as to their merit in maintaining an orderly society. Past civilizations without number have foundered on the rocks of equal justice. Such foolishness destroys the natural hierarchies which are far more important. Any individual takes on significance only in his relationship to your total society. Unless that society be ordered in logical steps, no one can find a place in it—not the lowliest or the highest. Come, come, grandchild! You must be the stern mother of your people. It's your duty to maintain order."

"Everything Paul did was to . . ."

"Your brother's dead, a failure!"

"So are you!"

"True . . . but with me it was an accident beyond my designing. Come now, let us take care of this Javid as I have outlined for you."

She felt her body grow warm at the thought, spoke quickly: "I must think about it." And she thought: *If it's done, it'll be only to put Javid in his place. No need to kill him for that. And the fool might just give himself away . . . in my bed.*

"To whom do you talk, My Lady?" a voice asked.

For a confused moment, Alia thought this another intrusion by those clamorous multitudes within, but recognition of the voice opened her eyes. Ziarenka Valefor, chief of Alia's guardian amazons, stood beside the bench, a worried frown on her weathered Fremen features.

"I speak to my inner voices," Alia said, sitting up on the bench. She felt refreshed, buoyed up by the silencing of that distracting inner clamor.

"Your inner voices, My Lady. Yes." Ziarenka's eyes glistened at this information. Everyone knew the Holy Alia drew upon inner resources available to no other person.

"Bring Javid to my quarters," Alia said. "There's a serious matter I must discuss with him."

"To your quarters, My Lady?"

"Yes! To my private chamber."

"As My Lady commands." The guard turned to obey.

"One moment," Alia said. "Has Master Idaho already gone to Sietch Tabr?"

"Yes, My Lady. He left before dawn as you instructed. Do you wish me to send for . . ."

"No. I will manage this myself. And Zia, no one must know that Javid is being brought to me. Do it yourself. This is a very serious matter."

The guard touched the crysknife at her waist. "My Lady, is there a threat to—"

"Yes, there's a threat, and Javid may be at the heart of it."

"Ohhh, My Lady, perhaps I should not bring—"

"Zia! Do you think me incapable of handling such a one?"

A lupine smile touched the guard's mouth. "Forgive me, My Lady. I will bring him to your private chamber at once, but . . . with My Lady's permission, I will mount guard outside your door."

"You only," Alia said.

"Yes, My Lady. I go at once."

Alia nodded to herself, watching Ziarenka's retreating back. Javid was not loved among her guards, then. Another mark against him. But he was still valuable—very valuable. He was her key to Jacurutu and with that place, well . . .

"Perhaps you were right, Baron," she whispered.

"You see!" the voice within her chortled. "Ahhh, this will be a pleasant service to you, child, and it's only the beginning . . ."

These are illusions of popular history which a successful religion must promote: Evil men never prosper; only the brave deserve the fair; honesty is the best policy; actions speak louder than words; virtue always triumphs; a good deed is its own reward; any bad human can be reformed; religious talismans protect one from demon possession; only females understand the ancient mysteries; the rich are doomed to unhappiness . . .

—FROM THE INSTRUCTION MANUAL:
MISSIONARIA PROTECTIVA

"I am called Muriz," the leathery Fremen said.

He sat on cavern rock in the glow of a spice lamp whose fluttering light revealed damp walls and dark holes which were passages from this place. Sounds of dripping water could be heard down one of those passages and, although water sounds were essential to the Fremen paradise, the six bound men facing Muriz took no pleasure from the rhythmic dripping. There was the musty smell of a deathstill in the chamber.

A youth of perhaps fourteen standard years came out of the passage and stood at Muriz's left hand. An unsheathed crysknife reflected pale yellow from the spice lamp as the youth lifted the blade and pointed it briefly at each of the bound men.

With a gesture toward the youth, Muriz said: "This is my son, Assan Tariq, who is about to undergo his test of manhood."

Muriz cleared his throat, stared once at each of the six captives. They sat in a loose semicircle across from him, tightly restrained with spice-fiber ropes which held their legs crossed, their hands behind them. The bindings terminated in a tight noose at each man's throat. Their stillsuits had been cut away at the neck.

The bound men stared back at Muriz without flinching. Two of them wore loose off-world garments which marked them as wealthy residents of an Arrakeen city. These two had skin which was smoother, lighter than that of their companions, whose sere features and bony frames marked them as desert-born.

Muriz resembled the desert dwellers, but his eyes were more deeply sunken, whiteless pits which not even the glow of the spice lamp touched. His son appeared an unformed copy of the man, with a flatness of face which did not quite hide the turmoil boiling within him.

"Among the Cast Out we have a special test for manhood," Muriz said. "One day my son will be a judge in Shuloch. We must know that he can act as he must. Our judges cannot forget Jacurutu and our day of despair. Kralizec, the Typhoon Struggle, lives in our hearts." It was all spoken with the flat intonation of ritual.

One of the soft-featured city dwellers across from Muriz stirred, said: "You do wrong to threaten us and bind us captive. We came peacefully on *umma*."

Muriz nodded. "You came in search of a personal religious awakening? Good. You shall have that awakening."

The soft-featured man said: "If we—"

Beside him a darker desert Fremen snapped: "Be silent, fool! These are the water stealers. These are the ones we thought we'd wiped out."

"That old story," the soft-featured captive said.

"Jacurutu is more than a story," Muriz said. Once more he gestured to his son. "I have presented Assan Tariq. I am *arifa* in this place, your only judge. My son, too, will be trained to detect demons. The old ways are best."

"That's why we came into the deep desert," the soft-featured man protested. "We chose the old way, wandering in—"

"With paid guides," Muriz said, gesturing to the darker captives. "You would buy your way into heaven?" Muriz glanced up at his son. "Assan, are you prepared?"

"I have reflected long upon that night when men came and murdered our people," Assan said. His voice projected an uneasy straining. "They owe us water."

"Your father gives you six of them," Muriz said. "Their water is ours. Their shades are yours, your guardians forevermore. Their shades will warn you of demons. They will be your slaves when you cross over into the *alam al-mythal*. What do you say, my son?"

"I thank my father," Assan said. He took a short step forward. "I accept manhood among the Cast Out. This water is our water."

As he finished speaking, the youth crossed to the captives. Starting on the left, he gripped the man's hair and drove the crysknife up under the chin into the brain. It was skillfully done to spill the minimum blood. Only the one soft-featured city Fremen protested, squalling as the youth grabbed his hair. The others spat at Assan Tariq in the old way, saying by this: *"See how little I value my water when it is taken by animals!"*

When it was done, Muriz clapped his hands once. Attendants came and began removing the bodies, taking them to the deathstill where they could be rendered for their water.

Muriz arose, looked at his son who stood breathing deeply, watching the attendants remove the bodies. "Now you are a man," Muriz said. "The water of our enemies will feed slaves. And, my son . . ."

Assan Tariq turned an alert and pouncing look upon his father. The youth's lips were drawn back in a tight smile.

"The Preacher must not know of this," Muriz said.

"I understand, father."

"You did it well," Muriz said. "Those who stumble upon Shuloch must not survive."

"As you say, father."

"You are trusted with important duties," Muriz said. "I am proud of you."

A sophisticated human can become primitive. What this really means is that the human's way of life changes. Old values change, become linked to the landscape with its plants and animals. This new existence requires a working knowledge of those multiplex and cross-linked events usually referred to as *nature*. It requires a measure of respect for the inertial power within such *natural* systems. When a human gains this working knowledge and respect, that is called "being primitive." The converse, of course, is equally true: the primitive can become sophisticated, but not without accepting dreadful psychological damage.

—THE LETO COMMENTARY
AFTER HARQ AL-ADA

"How can we be sure?" Ghanima asked. "This is very dangerous."

"We've tested it before," Leto argued.

"It may not be the same this time. What if—"

"It's the only way open to us," Leto said. "You agree we can't go the way of the spice."

Ghanima sighed. She did not like this thrust and parry of words, but knew the necessity which pressed her brother. She also knew the fearful source of her own reluctance. They had but to look at Alia and know the perils of that inner world.

"Well?" Leto asked.

Again she sighed.

They sat cross-legged in one of their private places, a narrow opening from the cave to the cliff where often their mother and father had watched the sun set over the *bled.* It was two hours past the evening meal, a time when the twins were expected to exercise their bodies and their minds. They had chosen to flex their minds.

"I will try it alone if you refuse to help," Leto said.

Ghanima looked away from him toward the black hangings of the moisture seals which guarded this opening in the rock. Leto continued to stare out over the desert.

They had been speaking for some time in a language so ancient that even its name remained unknown in these times. The language gave their thoughts a privacy which no other human could penetrate. Even Alia, who avoided the intricacies of her inner world, lacked the mental linkages which would allow her to grasp any more than an occasional word.

Leto inhaled deeply, taking in the distinctive furry odor of a Fremen cavern-sietch which persisted in this windless alcove. The murmurous hubbub of the sietch and its damp heat were absent here, and both felt this as a relief.

"I agree we need guidance," Ghanima said. "But if we—"

"Ghani! We need more than guidance. We need protection."

"Perhaps there is no protection." She looked directly at her brother, met that gaze in his eyes like the waiting watchfulness of a predator. His eyes belied the placidity of his features.

"We must escape possession," Leto said. He used the special infinitive of the ancient language, a form strictly neutral in voice and tense but profoundly active in its implications.

Ghanima correctly interpreted his argument.

"Mohw'pwium d'mi hish pash moh'm ka," she intoned. *The capture of my soul is the capture of a thousand souls.*

"Much more than that," he countered.

"Knowing the dangers, you persist." She made it a statement, not a question.

"Wabun 'k wabunat!" he said. *Rising, thou risest!*

He felt his choice as an obvious necessity. Doing this thing, it were best done actively. They must wind the past into the present and allow it to unreel into their future.

"Muriyat," she conceded, her voice low. *It must be done lovingly.*

"Of course." He waved a hand to encompass total acceptance. "Then we will consult as our parents did."

Ghanima remained silent, tried to swallow past a lump in her throat. Instinctively she glanced south toward the great open *erg* which was showing a dim grey pattern of dunes in the last of the day's light. In that direction her father had gone on his last walk into the desert.

Leto stared downward over the cliff edge at the green of the sietch oasis. All was dusk down there, but he knew its shapes and colors: blossoms of copper, gold, red, yellow, rust, and russet spread right out to the rock markers which outlined the extent of the qanat-watered plantings. Beyond the rock markers stretched a stinking band of dead Arrakeen life, killed by foreign plants and too much water, now forming a barrier against the desert.

Presently Ghanima said: "I am ready. Let us begin."

"Yes, damn all!" He reached out, touched her arm to soften the exclamation, said, "Please, Ghani . . . Sing that song. It makes this easier for me."

Ghanima hitched herself closer to him, circled his waist with her left arm. She drew in two deep breaths, cleared her throat, and began singing in a clear piping voice the words her mother had so often sung for their father:

> *Here I redeem the pledge thou gavest;*
> *I pour sweet water upon thee.*
> *Life shall prevail in this windless place:*
> *My love, thou shalt live in a palace,*
> *Thy enemies shall fall to emptiness.*
> *We travel this path together*
> *Which love has traced for thee.*
> *Surely well do I show the way*
> *For my love is thy palace . . .*

Her voice fell into the desert silence which even a whisper might despoil, and Leto felt himself sinking, sinking—becoming the father whose memories spread like an overlayer in the genes of his immediate past.

For this brief space, I must be Paul, he told himself. *This is not Ghani beside me; it is my beloved Chani, whose wise counsel has saved us both many a time.*

For her part, Ghanima had slipped into the persona-memory of her mother with frightening ease, as she had known she would. How much easier this was for the female—and how much more dangerous.

In a voice turned suddenly husky, Ghanima said: "Look there, beloved!" First Moon had risen and, against its cold light, they saw an arc of orange fire falling upward into space. The transport which had brought the Lady Jessica, laden now with spice, was returning to its mother-cluster in orbit.

The keenest of remembrances ran through Leto then, bringing memories like bright bell-sounds. For a flickering instant he was another Leto—Jessica's Duke. Necessity pushed those memories aside, but not before he felt the piercing of the love and the pain.

I must be Paul, he reminded himself.

The transformation came over him with a frightening duality, as though Leto were a dark screen against which his father was projected. He felt both his own flesh and his father's, and the flickering differences threatened to overcome him.

"Help me, father," he whispered.

The flickering disturbance passed and now there was another imprint upon his awareness, while his own identity as Leto stood at one side as an observer.

"My last vision has not yet come to pass," he said, and the voice was Paul's. He turned to Ghanima. "You know what I saw."

She touched his cheek with her right hand. "Did you walk into the desert to die, beloved? Is that what you did?"

"It may be that I did, but that vision . . . Would that not be reason enough to stay alive?"

"But blind?" she asked.

"Even so."

"Where could you go?"

He took a deep, shuddering breath. "Jacurutu."

"Beloved!" Tears began flowing down her cheeks.

"Muad'Dib, the hero, must be destroyed utterly," he said. "Otherwise this child cannot bring us back from chaos."

"The Golden Path," she said. "It is not a good vision."

"It's the only possible vision."

"Alia has failed, then . . ."

"Utterly. You see the record of it."

"Your mother has returned too late." She nodded, and it was Chani's wise expression on the childish face of Ghanima. "Could there not be another vision? Perhaps if—"

"No, beloved. Not yet. This child cannot peer into the future yet and return safely."

Again a shuddering breath disturbed his body, and Leto-observer felt the deep longing of his father to live once more in vital flesh, to make living decisions and . . . How desperate the need to unmake past mistakes!

"Father!" Leto called, and it was as though he shouted echoingly within his own skull.

It was a profound act of will which Leto felt then: the slow, clinging withdrawal of his father's internal presence, the release of senses and muscles.

"Beloved," Chani's voice whispered beside him, and the withdrawal slowed. "What is happening?"

"Don't go yet," Leto said, and it was his own voice, rasping and uncertain, still his own. Then: "Chani, you must tell us: How do we avoid . . . what has happened to Alia?"

It was Paul-within who answered him, though, with words which fell upon his inner ear, halting and with long pauses: "There is no certainty. You . . . saw . . . what almost . . . happened . . . with . . . me."

"But Alia . . ."

"The damned Baron has her!"

Leto felt his throat burning with dryness. "Is he . . . have I . . ."

"He's in you . . . but . . . I . . . we cannot . . . sometimes we sense . . . each other, but you . . ."

"Can you not read my thoughts?" Leto asked. "Would you know then if . . . he . . ."

"Sometimes I can feel your thoughts . . . but I . . . we live only through . . . the . . . reflection of . . . your awareness. Your memory creates us. The danger . . . it is a precise memory. And . . . those of us . . . those of us who loved power . . . and gathered it at . . . any price . . . those can be . . . more precise."

"Stronger?" Leto whispered.

"Stronger."

"I know your vision," Leto said. "Rather than let him have me, I'll become you."

"Not that!"

Leto nodded to himself, sensing the enormous will-force his father had required to withdraw, recognizing the consequences of failure. *Any* possession reduced the possessed to Abomination. The recognition gave him a renewed sense of strength, and he felt his own body with abnormal acuteness and a deeply drawn awareness of past mistakes: his own and those of his ancestors. It was the uncertainties which weakened—he saw this now. For an instant, temptation warred with fear within him. This flesh possessed the ability to transform melange into a vision of the future. With the spice, he could breathe the future, shatter Time's veils. He found the temptation difficult to shed, clasped his hands and sank into the *prana-bindu* awareness. His flesh negated the temptation. His flesh wore the deep knowledge learned in blood by Paul. Those who sought the future hoped to gain the winning gamble on tomorrow's race. Instead they found themselves trapped into a lifetime whose every heartbeat and anguished wail was known. Paul's final vision had shown the precarious way out of that trap, and Leto knew now that he had no other choice but to follow that way.

"The joy of living, its beauty is all bound up in the fact that life can surprise you," he said.

A soft voice whispered in his ear: "I've always known that beauty."

Leto turned his head, stared into Ghanima's eyes which glistened in the bright moonlight. He saw Chani looking back at him. "Mother," he said, "you must withdraw."

"Ahhh, the temptation!" she said, and kissed him.

He pushed her away. "Would you take your daughter's life?" he demanded.

"It's so easy . . . so foolishly easy," she said.

Leto, feeling panic begin to grip him, remembered what an effort of will his father's persona-within had required to abandon the flesh. Was Ghanima lost in that observer-world where he had watched and listened, learning what he had required from his father?

"I will despise you, mother," he said.

"Others won't despise me," she said. "Be my beloved."

"If I do . . . you know what you both will become," he said. "My father will despise you."

"Never!"

"I will!"

The sound was jerked out of his throat without his volition and it carried all the old overtones of Voice which Paul had learned from his witch mother.

"Don't say it," she moaned.

"I will despise you!"

"Please . . . please don't say it."

Leto rubbed his throat, feeling the muscles become once more his own. "He will despise you. He will turn his back on you. He will go into the desert again."

"No . . . no . . ."

She shook her head from side to side.

"You must leave, mother," he said.

"No . . . no . . ." But the voice lacked its original force.

Leto watched his sister's face. How the muscles twitched! Emotions fled across the flesh at the turmoil within her.

"Leave," he whispered. "Leave."

"No-o-o-o . . ."

He gripped her arm, felt the tremors which pulsed through her muscles, the nerves twitching. She writhed, tried to pull away, but he held tightly to her arm, whispering: "Leave . . . leave . . ."

And all the time, Leto berated himself for talking Ghani into this *parent game* which once they'd played often, but she had lately resisted. It was true that the female had more weakness in that inner assault, he realized. There lay the origin of the Bene Gesserit fear.

Hours passed and still Ghanima's body trembled and twitched with the inner battle, but now his sister's voice joined the argument. He heard her talking to that imago within, the pleading.

"Mother . . . please—" And once: "You've seen Alia! Will you become another Alia?"

At last Ghanima leaned against him, whispered: "She has accepted it. She's gone."

He stroked her head. "Ghani, I'm sorry. I'm sorry. I'll never ask you to do that again. I was selfish. Forgive me."

"There's nothing to forgive," she said, and her voice came panting as though after great physical exertion. "We've learned much that we needed to know."

"She spoke to you of many things," he said. "We'll share it later when—"

"No! We'll do it now. You were right."

"My Golden Path?"

"Your damned Golden Path!"

"Logic's useless unless it's armed with essential data," he said. "But I—"

"Grandmother came back to guide our education and to see if we'd been . . . contaminated."

"That's what Duncan says. There's nothing new in—"

"Prime computation," she agreed, her voice strengthening. She pulled away from him, looked out at the desert which lay in a predawn hush. This battle . . . this knowledge, had cost them a night. The Royal Guard beyond the moisture seal must have had much to explain. Leto had charged that nothing disturb them.

"People often learn subtlety as they age," Leto said. "What is it we're learning with all of this agedness to draw upon?"

"The universe as we see it is never quite the exact physical universe," she said. "We mustn't perceive this grandmother just as a grandmother."

"That'd be dangerous," he agreed. "But my ques—"

"There's something beyond subtlety," she said. "We must have a place in our awareness to perceive what we can't preconceive. That's why . . . my mother spoke to me often of Jessica. At the last, when we were both reconciled to the inner exchange, she said many things." Ghanima sighed.

"We *know* she's our grandmother," he said. "You were with her for hours yesterday. Is that why—"

"If we allow it, our *knowing* will determine how we react to her," Ghanima said. "That's what my mother kept warning me. She quoted our grandmother once and—" Ghanima touched his arm. "—I heard the echo of it within me in our grandmother's voice."

"Warning you," Leto said. He found this thought disturbing. Was nothing in this world dependable?

"Most deadly errors arise from obsolete assumptions," Ghanima said. "That's what my mother kept quoting."

"That's pure Bene Gesserit."

"If . . . if Jessica has gone back to the Sisterhood completely . . ."

"That'd be very dangerous to us," he said, completing the thought. "We carry the blood of their Kwisatz Haderach—their male Bene Gesserit."

"They won't abandon that search," she said, "but they may abandon us. Our grandmother could be the instrument."

"There's another way," he said.

"Yes—the two of us . . . mated. But they know what recessives might complicate that pairing."

"It's a gamble they must've discussed."

"And with our grandmother, at that. I don't like that way."

"Nor I."

"Still, it's not the first time a royal line has tried to . . ."

"It repels me," he said, shuddering.

She felt the movement, fell silent.

"Power," he said.

And in that strange alchemy of their similarities she knew where his thoughts had been. "The power of the Kwisatz Haderach must fail," she agreed.

"Used in their way," he said.

In that instant, day came to the desert beyond their vantage point. They sensed the heat beginning. Colors leaped forth from the plantings beneath the cliff. Grey-green leaves sent spiked shadows along the ground. The low morning light of Dune's silvery sun revealed the verdant oasis full of golden and purple shadows in the well of the sheltering cliffs.

Leto stood, stretched.

"The Golden Path, then," Ghanima said, and she spoke as much to herself as to him, knowing how their father's last vision met and melted into Leto's dreams.

Something brushed against the moisture seals behind them and voices could be heard murmuring there.

Leto reverted to the ancient language they used for privacy: "L'ii ani howr samis sm'kwi owr samit sut."

That was where the decision lodged itself in their awareness. Literally: *We will accompany each other into deathliness, though only one may return to report it.*

Ghanima stood then and, together, they returned through the moisture seals to the sietch, where the guards roused themselves and fell in behind as the twins headed toward their own quarters. The throngs parted before them with a difference on this morning, exchanging glances with the guards. Spending the night alone above the desert was an old Fremen custom for the holy sages. All the Uma had practiced this form of vigil. Paul Muad'Dib had done it . . . and Alia. Now the royal twins had begun.

Leto noted the difference, mentioned it to Ghanima.

"They don't know what we've decided for them," she said. "They don't really know."

Still in the private language, he said: "It requires the most fortuitous beginning."

Ghanima hesitated a moment to form her thoughts. Then: "In that time, mourning for the sibling, it must be exactly real—even to the making of the tomb. The heart must follow the sleep lest there be no awakening."

In the ancient tongue it was an extremely convoluted statement, employing a pronominal object separated from the infinitive. It was a syntax which allowed each set of internal phrases to turn upon itself, becoming several different meanings, all definite and quite distinct but subtly interrelated. In part, what she had said was that they risked death with Leto's plan and, real or simulated, it made no difference. The resultant change would be like death, literally: "funeral murder." And there was an added meaning to the whole which pointed accusatively at whoever *survived* to report, that is: *act out the living part.* Any misstep there would negate the entire plan, and Leto's Golden Path would become a dead end.

"Extremely delicate," Leto agreed. He parted the hangings for them as they entered their own anteroom.

Activity among their attendants paused only for a heartbeat as the twins crossed to the arched passage which led into the quarters assigned to the Lady Jessica.

"You are not Osiris," Ghanima reminded him.

"Nor will I try to be."

Ghanima took his arm to stop him. "Alia darsatay haunus m'smow," she warned.

Leto stared into his sister's eyes. Indeed, Alia's actions did give off a foul smell which their grandmother must have noted. He smiled appreciatively at Ghanima. She had mixed the ancient tongue with Fremen superstition to call up a most basic tribal omen. *M'smow*, the foul odor of a summer night, was the harbinger of death at the hands of demons. And Isis had been the demon-goddess of death to the people whose tongue they now spoke.

"We Atreides have a reputation for audacity to maintain," he said.

"So we'll *take* what we need," she said.

"It's that or become petitioners before our own Regency," he said. "Alia would enjoy that."

"But our plan . . ." She let it trail off.

Our plan, he thought. She shared it completely now. He said: "I think of our plan as the toil of the shaduf."

Ghanima glanced back at the anteroom through which they'd passed, smelling the furry odors of morning with their sense of eternal beginning. She liked the way Leto had employed their private language. *Toil of the shaduf*. It was a pledge. He'd called their plan agricultural work of a very menial kind: fertilizing, irrigating, weeding, transplanting, pruning—yet with the Fremen implication that this labor occurred simultaneously in Another World where it symbolized cultivating the richness of the soul.

Ghanima studied her brother as they hesitated here in the rock passage. It had grown increasingly obvious to her that he was pleading on two levels: one, for the Golden Path of his vision and their father's, and two, that she allow him free reign to carry out the extremely dangerous myth-creation which the plan generated. This frightened her. Was there more to his private vision that he had not shared? Could he see himself as the potentially deified figure to lead humankind into a rebirth—like father, like son? The cult of Muad'Dib had turned sour, fermenting in Alia's mismanagement and the unbridled license of a military priesthood which rode the Fremen power. Leto wanted regeneration.

He's hiding something from me, she realized.

She reviewed what he had told her of his dream. It held such iridescent reality that he might walk around for hours afterward in a daze. The dream never varied, he said.

"I am on sand in bright yellow daylight, yet there is no sun. Then I

realize that I am the sun. My light shines out as a Golden Path. When I realize this, I move out of myself. I turn, expecting to see myself as the sun. But I am not the sun; I am a stick figure, a child's drawing with zig-zag lightning lines for eyes, stick legs and stick arms. There is a scepter in my left hand, and it's a real scepter—much more detailed in its reality than the stick figure which holds it. The scepter moves, and this terrifies me. As it moves, I feel myself awaken, yet I know I'm still dreaming. I realize then that my skin is encased in something—an armor which moves as my skin moves. I cannot see this armor, but I feel it. My terror leaves me then, for this armor gives me the strength of ten thousand men."

As Ghanima stared at him, Leto tried to pull away, to continue their course toward Jessica's quarters. Ghanima resisted.

"This Golden Path could be no better than any other path," she said.

Leto looked at the rock floor between them, feeling the strong return of Ghanima's doubts. "I must do it," he said.

"Alia is possessed," she said. "That could happen to us. It could already have happened and we might not know it."

"No." He shook his head, met her gaze. "Alia resisted. That gave the powers within her their strength. By her own strength she was overcome. We've dared to search within, to seek out the old languages and the old knowledge. We're already amalgams of those lives within us. We don't resist; we ride with them. This was what I learned from our father last night. It's what I had to learn."

"He said nothing of that within me."

"You listened to our mother. It's what we—"

"And I almost lost."

"Is she still strong within you?" Fear tightened his face.

"Yes . . . but now I think she guards me with her love. You were very good when you argued with her." And Ghanima thought about the reflected mother-within, said: "Our mother exists now for me in the *alam al-mythal* with the others, but she has tasted the fruit of hell. Now I can listen to her without fear. As to the others . . ."

"Yes," he said. "And I listened to my father, but I think I'm really following the counsel of the grandfather for whom I was named. Perhaps the name makes it easy."

"Are you counseled to speak to our grandmother of the Golden Path?"

Leto waited while an attendant pressed past them with a basket-tray carrying the Lady Jessica's breakfast. A strong smell of spice filled the air as the attendant passed.

"She lives in us and in her own flesh," Leto said. "Her counsel can be consulted twice."

"Not by me," Ghanima protested. "I'm not risking that again."

"Then by me."

"I thought we agreed that she's gone back to the Sisterhood."

"Indeed. Bene Gesserit at her beginning, her own creature in the middle, and Bene Gesserit at the end. But remember that she, too, carries Harkonnen blood and is closer to it than we are, that she has experienced a form of this inner sharing which we have."

"A very shallow form," Ghanima said. "And you haven't answered my question."

"I don't think I'll mention the Golden Path."

"I may."

"Ghani!"

"We don't need any more Atreides gods! We need a space for some humanity!"

"Have I ever denied it?"

"No." She took a deep breath and looked away from him. Attendants peered in at them from the anteroom, hearing the argument by its tone but unable to understand the ancient words.

"We have to do it," he said. "If we fail to act, we might just as well fall upon our knives." He used the Fremen form which carried the meaning of "spill our water into the tribal cistern."

Once more Ghanima looked at him. She was forced to agree. But she felt trapped within a construction of many walls. They both knew a day of reckoning lay across their path no matter what they did. Ghanima knew this with a certainty reinforced by the data garnered from those other memory-lives, but now she feared the strength which she gave those other psyches by using the data of their experiences. They lurked like harpies within her, shadow demons waiting in ambush.

Except for her mother, who had held the fleshly power and had renounced it. Ghanima still felt shaken by that inner struggle, knowing she would have lost but for Leto's persuasiveness.

Leto said his Golden Path led out of this trap. Except for the nagging realization that he withheld something from his vision, she could only accept his sincerity. He needed her fertile creativity to enrich the plan.

"We'll be tested," he said, knowing where her doubts led.

"Not in the spice."

"Perhaps even there. Surely, in the desert and in the Trial of Possession."

"You never mentioned the Trial of Possession!" she accused. "Is that part of your dream?"

He tried to swallow in a dry throat, cursed this betrayal. "Yes."

"Then we will be . . . possessed?"

"No."

She thought about the Trial—that ancient Fremen examination whose ending most often brought hideous death. Then this plan had other complexities. It would take them onto an edge where a plunge to either side might not be countenanced by the human mind and that mind remain sane.

Knowing where her thoughts meandered, Leto said: "Power attracts the psychotics. Always. That's what we have to avoid within ourselves."

"You're sure we won't be . . . possessed?"

"Not if we create the Golden Path."

Still doubtful, she said: "I'll not bear your children, Leto."

He shook his head, suppressing the inner betrayals, lapsed into the royal-formal form of the ancient tongue: "Sister mine, I love you more dearly than myself, but that is not the tender of my desires."

"Very well, then let us return to another argument before we join our grandmother. A knife slipped into Alia might settle most of our problems."

"If you believe that, you believe we can walk in mud and leave no tracks," he said. "Besides, when has Alia ever given anyone an opportunity?"

"There is talk about this Javid."

"Does Duncan show any signs of growing horns?"

Ghanima shrugged. "One poison, two poison." It was the common label applied to the royal habit of cataloguing companions by their threat to your person, a mark of rulers everywhere.

"We must do it my way," he said.

"The other way might be cleaner."

By her reply, he knew she had finally suppressed her doubts and come around to agreement with his plan. The realization brought him no happiness. He found himself looking at his own hands, wondering if the dirt would cling.

This was Muad'Dib's achievement: He saw the subliminal reservoir of each individual as an unconscious bank of memories going back to the primal cell of our common genesis. Each of us, he said, can measure out his distance from that common origin. Seeing this and telling of it, he made the audacious leap of decision. Muad'Dib set himself the task of integrating genetic memory into ongoing evaluation. Thus did he break through Time's veils, making a single thing of the future and the past. That was Muad'Dib's creation embodied in his son and his daughter.

—TESTAMENT OF ARRAKIS
BY HARQ AL-ADA

Farad'n strode through the garden compound of his grandfather's royal palace, watching his shadow grow shorter as the sun of Salusa Secundus climbed toward noon. He had to stretch himself a bit to keep step with the tall Bashar who accompanied him.

"I have doubts, Tyekanik," he said. "Oh, there's no denying the attractions of a throne, but—" He drew in a deep breath. "—I have so many interests."

Tyekanik, fresh from a savage argument with Farad'n's mother, glanced sidelong at the Prince, noting how the lad's flesh was firming as he approached his eighteenth birthday. There was less and less of Wensicia in him with each passing day and more and more of old Shaddam, who had preferred his private pursuits to the responsibilities of royalty. That was what had cost him the throne in the end, of course. He'd grown soft in the ways of command.

"You have to make a choice," Tyekanik said. "Oh, doubtless there'll be time for some of your interests, but . . ."

Farad'n chewed his lower lip. Duty held him here, but he felt frustrated. He would far rather have gone to the rock enclave where the sandtrout experiments were being conducted. Now *there* was a project with enormous potential: wrest the spice monopoly from the Atreides and anything might happen.

"You're sure these twins will be . . . eliminated?"

"Nothing absolutely certain, My Prince, but the prospects are good."

Farad'n shrugged. Assassination remained a fact of royal life. The language was filled with the subtle permutations of ways to eliminate important personages. By a single word, one could distinguish between poison in drink or poison in food. He presumed the elimination of the Atreides twins would be accomplished by a poison. It was not a pleasant thought. By all accounts the twins were a most interesting pair.

"Would we have to move to Arrakis?" Farad'n asked.

"It's the best choice, put us at the point of greatest pressure." Farad'n appeared to be avoiding some question and Tyekanik wondered what it might be.

"I'm troubled, Tyekanik," Farad'n said, speaking as they rounded a hedge corner and approached a fountain surrounded by giant black roses. Gardeners could be heard snipping beyond the hedges.

"Yes?" Tyekanik prompted.

"This, ah, religion which you've professed . . ."

"Nothing strange about that, My Prince," Tyekanik said and hoped his voice remained firm. "This religion speaks to the warrior in me. It's a fitting religion for a Sardaukar." That, at least, was true.

"Yesss . . . But my mother seems so pleased by it." *Damn Wensicia!* he thought. *She's made her son suspicious.*

"I care not what your mother thinks," Tyekanik said. "A man's religion is his own affair. Perhaps she sees something in this that may help to put you on the throne."

"That was my thought," Farad'n said.

Ahhh, this is a sharp lad! Tyekanik thought. He said: "Look into the religion for yourself; you'll see at once why I chose it."

"Still . . . Muad'Dib's preachings? He was an Atreides, after all."

"I can only say that the ways of God are mysterious," Tyekanik said.

"I see. Tell me, Tyek, why'd you ask me to walk with you just now? It's almost noon and usually you're off to someplace or other at my mother's command this time of day."

Tyekanik stopped at a stone bench which looked upon the fountain and the giant roses beyond. The splashing water soothed him and he kept his attention upon it as he spoke. "My Prince, I've done something which your mother may not like." And he thought: *If he believes that, her damnable scheme will work.* Tyekanik almost hoped Wensicia's scheme would fail. *Bringing that damnable Preacher here. She was insane. And the cost!*

As Tyekanik remained silent, waiting, Farad'n asked: "All right, Tyek, what've you done?"

"I've brought a practitioner of oneiromancy," Tyekanik said.

Farad'n shot a sharp glance at his companion. Some of the older Sardaukar played the dream-interpretation game, had done so increasingly since their defeat by that "Supreme Dreamer," Muad'Dib. Somewhere within their dreams, they reasoned, might lay a way back to power and glory. But Tyekanik had always eschewed this play.

"This doesn't sound like you, Tyek," Farad'n said.

"Then I can only speak from my new religion," he said, addressing the fountain. To speak of religion was, of course, why they'd risked bringing The Preacher here.

"Then speak from this religion," Farad'n said.

"As My Prince commands." He turned, looked at this youthful holder of all the dreams which now were distilled into the path which House Corrino would follow. "Church and state, My Prince, even scientific reason and faith, and even more: progress and tradition—all of these are reconciled in the teachings of Muad'Dib. He taught that there are no intransigent opposites except in the beliefs of men and, sometimes, in their dreams. One discovers the future in the past, and both are part of a whole."

In spite of doubts which he could not dispel, Farad'n found himself impressed by these words. He heard a note of reluctant sincerity in Tyekanik's voice, as though the man spoke against inner compulsions.

"And that's why you bring me this . . . this interpreter of dreams?"

"Yes, My Prince. Perhaps your dream penetrates Time. You win back your consciousness of your inner being when you recognize the universe as a coherent whole. Your dreams . . . well . . ."

"But I spoke idly of my dreams," Farad'n protested. "They are a curiosity, no more. I never once suspected that you . . ."

"My Prince, nothing you do can be unimportant."

"That's very flattering, Tyek. Do you really believe this fellow can see into the heart of great mysteries?"

"I do, My Prince."

"Then let my mother be displeased."

"You will see him?"

"Of course—since you've brought him to displease my mother."

Does he mock me? Tyekanik wondered. And he said: "I must warn you that the old man wears a mask. It is an Ixian device which enables the sightless to see with their skin."

"He is blind?"

"Yes, My Prince."

"Does he know who I am?"

"I told him, My Prince."

"Very well. Let us go to him."

"If My Prince will wait a moment here, I will bring the man to him."

Farad'n looked around the fountain garden, smiled. As good a place as any for this foolishness. "Have you told him what I dreamed?"

"Only in general terms, My Prince. He will ask you for a personal accounting."

"Oh, very well. I'll wait here. Bring the fellow."

Farad'n turned his back, heard Tyekanik retire in haste. A gardener could be seen working just beyond the hedge, the top of a brown-capped head, the flashing of shears poking above the greenery. The movement was hypnotic.

This dream business is nonsense, Farad'n thought. *It was wrong of Tyek to do this without consulting me. Strange that Tyek should get religion at his age. And now it's dreams.*

Presently he heard footsteps behind him. Tyekanik's familiar positive stride and a more dragging gait. Farad'n turned, stared at the approaching dream interpreter. The Ixian mask was a black, gauzy affair which concealed the face from the forehead to below the chin. There were no eye slits in the mask. If one were to believe the Ixian boasts, the entire mask was a single eye.

Tyekanik stopped two paces from Farad'n, but the masked old man approached to less than a pace.

"The interpreter of dreams," Tyekanik said.

Farad'n nodded.

The masked old man coughed in a remote grunting fashion, as though trying to bring something up from his stomach.

Farad'n was acutely conscious of a sour spice smell from the old man. It emanated from the long grey robe which covered his body.

"Is that mask truly a part of your flesh?" Farad'n asked, realizing he was trying to delay the subject of dreams.

"While I wear it," the old man said, and his voice carried a bitter twang and just a suggestion of Fremen accent. "Your dream," he said. "Tell me."

Farad'n shrugged. *Why not?* That was why Tyek had brought the old man. Or was it? Doubts gripped Farad'n and he asked: "Are you truly a practitioner of oneiromancy?"

"I have come to interpret your dream, Puissant Lord."

Again Farad'n shrugged. This masked figure made him nervous and he glanced at Tyekanik, who remained where he had stopped, arms folded, staring at the fountain.

"Your dream, then," the old man pressed.

Farad'n inhaled deeply, began to relate the dream. It became easier to talk as he got fully into it. He told about the water flowing upward in the well, about the worlds which were atoms dancing in his head, about the snake which transformed itself into a sandworm and exploded in a cloud of dust. Telling about the snake, he was surprised to discover, required more effort. A terrible reluctance inhibited him and this made him angry as he spoke.

The old man remained impassive as Farad'n at last fell silent. The black gauze mask moved slightly to his breathing. Farad'n waited. The silence continued.

Presently Farad'n asked: "Aren't you going to interpret my dream?"

"I have interpreted it," he said, his voice seeming to come from a long distance.

"Well?" Farad'n heard his own voice squeaking, telling him the tension his dream had produced.

Still the old man remained impassively silent.

"Tell me, then!" The anger was obvious in his tone.

"I said I'd interpret," the old man said. "I did not agree to tell you my interpretation."

Even Tyekanik was moved by this, dropping his arms into balled fists at his sides. "What?" he grated.

"I did not say I'd reveal my interpretation," the old man said.

"You wish more pay?" Farad'n asked.

"I did not ask pay when I was brought here." A certain cold pride in the response softened Farad'n's anger. This was a brave old man, at any rate. He must know death could follow disobedience.

"Allow me, My Prince," Tyekanik said as Farad'n started to speak. Then: "Will you tell us why you won't reveal your interpretation?"

"Yes, My Lords. The dream tells me there would be no purpose in explaining these things."

Farad'n could not contain himself. "Are you saying I already know the meaning of my dream?"

"Perhaps you do, My Lord, but that is not my gist."

Tyekanik moved up to stand beside Farad'n. Both glared at the old man. "Explain yourself," Tyekanik said.

"Indeed," Farad'n said.

"If I were to speak of this dream, to explore these matters of water and dust, snakes and worms, to analyze the atoms which dance in your head as they do in mine—ahh, Puissant Lord, my words would only confuse you and you would insist upon misunderstanding."

"Do you fear that your words might anger me?" Farad'n demanded.

"My Lord! You're already angry."

"Is it that you don't trust us?" Tyekanik asked.

"That is very close to the mark, My Lord. I do not trust either of you and for the simple reason that you do not trust yourselves."

"You walk dangerously close to the edge," Tyekanik said. "Men have been killed for behavior less abusive than yours."

Farad'n nodded, said: "Don't tempt us to anger."

"The fatal consequences of Corrino anger are well known, My Lord of Salusa Secundus," the old man said.

Tyekanik put a restraining hand on Farad'n's arm, asked: "Are you trying to goad us into killing you?"

Farad'n had not thought of that, felt a chill now as he considered what such behavior might mean. Was this old man who called himself Preacher . . . was he more than he appeared? What might be the consequences of his death? Martyrs could be dangerous creations.

"I doubt that you'll kill me no matter what I say," The Preacher said. "I think you know my value, Bashar, and your Prince now suspects it."

"You absolutely refuse to interpret his dream?" Tyekanik asked.

"I *have* interpreted it."

"And you will not reveal what you see in it?"

"Do you blame me, My Lord?"

"How can you be valuable to me?" Farad'n asked.

The Preacher held out his right hand. "If I but beckon with this hand, Duncan Idaho will come to me and he will obey me."

"What idle boast is this?" Farad'n asked.

But Tyekanik shook his head, recalling his argument with Wensicia.

He said: "My Prince, it could be true. This Preacher has many followers on Dune."

"Why didn't you tell me he was from that place?" Farad'n asked.

Before Tyekanik could answer, The Preacher addressed Farad'n: "My Lord, you must not feel guilty about Arrakis. You are but a product of your times. This is a special pleading which any man may make when his guilts assail him."

"Guilts!" Farad'n was outraged.

The Preacher only shrugged.

Oddly, this shifted Farad'n from outrage to amusement. He laughed, throwing his head back, drawing a startled glance from Tyekanik. Then: "I like you, Preacher."

"This gratifies me, Prince," the old man said.

Suppressing a chuckle, Farad'n said: "We'll find you an apartment here in the palace. You will be my official interpreter of dreams—even though you never give me a word of interpretation. And you can advise me about Dune. I have a great curiosity about that place."

"This I cannot do, Prince."

An edge of his anger returned. Farad'n glared at the black mask. "And why not, pray tell?"

"My Prince," Tyekanik said, again touching Farad'n's arm.

"What is it, Tyek?"

"We brought him here under bonded agreement with the Guild. He is to be returned to Dune."

"I am summoned back to Arrakis," The Preacher said.

"Who summons you?" Farad'n demanded.

"A power greater than thine, Prince."

Farad'n shot a questioning glance at Tyekanik. "Is he an Atreides spy?"

"Not likely, My Prince. Alia has put a price on his head."

"If it's not the Atreides, then who summons you?" Farad'n asked, returning his attention to The Preacher.

"A power greater than the Atreides."

A chuckle escaped Farad'n. This was only mystic nonsense. How could Tyek be fooled by such stuff? This Preacher had been *summoned*—most likely by a dream. Of what importance were dreams?

"This has been a waste of time, Tyek," Farad'n said. "Why did you subject me to this . . . this farce?"

"There is a double price here, My Prince," Tyekanik said. "This interpreter of dreams promised me to deliver Duncan Idaho as an agent of House Corrino. All he asked was to meet you and interpret your dream." And Tyekanik added to himself: *Or so he told Wensicia!* New doubts assailed the Bashar.

"Why is my dream so important to you, old man?" Farad'n asked.

"Your dream tells me that great events move toward a logical conclusion," The Preacher said. "I must hasten my return."

Mocking, Farad'n said: "And you will remain inscrutable, giving me no advice."

"Advice, Prince, is a dangerous commodity. But I will venture a few words which you may take as advice or in any other way which pleases you."

"By all means," Farad'n said.

The Preacher held his masked face rigidly confronting Farad'n. "Governments may rise and fall for reasons which appear insignificant, Prince. What small events! An argument between two women . . . which way the wind blows on a certain day . . . a sneeze, a cough, the length of a garment or the chance collision of a fleck of sand and a courtier's eye. It is not always the majestic concerns of Imperial ministers which dictate the course of history, nor is it necessarily the pontifications of priests which move the hands of God."

Farad'n found himself profoundly stirred by these words and could not explain his emotion.

Tyekanik, however, had focused on one phrase. Why did this Preacher speak of a garment? Tyekanik's mind focused on the Imperial costumes dispatched to the Atreides twins, the tigers trained to attack. Was this old man voicing a subtle warning? How much did he know?

"How is this advice?" Farad'n asked.

"If you would succeed," The Preacher said, "you must reduce your strategy to its point of application. Where does one apply strategy? At a particular place and with a particular people in mind. But even with the greatest concern for minutiae, some small detail with no significance attached to it will escape you. Can your strategy, Prince, be reduced to the ambitions of a regional governor's wife?"

His voice cold, Tyekanik interrupted: "Why do you harp upon strategy, Preacher? What is it you think My Prince will have?"

"He is being led to desire a throne," The Preacher said. "I wish him good luck, but he will need much more than luck."

"These are dangerous words," Farad'n said. "How is it you dare such words?"

"Ambitions tend to remain undisturbed by realities," The Preacher said. "I dare such words because you stand at a crossroad. You could become admirable. But now you are surrounded by those who do not seek moral justifications, by advisors who are strategy-oriented. You are young and strong and tough, but you lack a certain advanced training by which your character might evolve. This is sad because you have weaknesses whose dimensions I have described."

"What do you mean?" Tyekanik demanded.

"Have a care when you speak," Farad'n said. "What is this weakness?"

"You've given no thought to the kind of society you might prefer," The Preacher said. "You do not consider the hopes of your subjects. Even the form of the Imperium which you seek has little shape in your imaginings." He turned his masked face toward Tyekanik. "Your eye is upon the power, not upon its subtle uses and its perils. Your future is filled, thus, with manifest unknowns: with arguing women, with coughs and windy days. How can you create an epoch when you cannot see every detail? Your tough mind will not serve you. This is where you are weak."

Farad'n studied the old man for a long space, wondering at the deeper issues implied by such thoughts, at the persistence of such discredited concepts. Morality! Social goals! These were myths to put beside belief in an upward movement of evolution.

Tyekanik said: "We've had enough words. What of the price agreed upon, Preacher?"

"Duncan Idaho is yours," The Preacher said. "Have a care how you use him. He is a jewel beyond price."

"Oh, we've a suitable mission for him," Tyekanik said. He glanced at Farad'n. "By your leave, My Prince?"

"Send him packing before I change my mind," Farad'n said. Then, glaring at Tyekanik: "I don't like the way you've used me, Tyek!"

"Forgive him, Prince," The Preacher said. "Your faithful Bashar does God's will without even knowing it." Bowing, The Preacher departed, and Tyekanik hurried to see him away.

Farad'n watched the retreating backs, thought: *I must look into this religion which Tyek espouses.* And he smiled ruefully. *What a dream interpreter! But what matter? My dream was not an important thing.*

And he saw a vision of armor. The armor was not his own skin; it was stronger than plasteel. Nothing penetrated his armor—not knife or poison or sand, not the dust of the desert or its desiccating heat. In his right hand he carried the power to make the Coriolis storm, to shake the earth and erode it into nothing. His eyes were fixed upon the Golden Path and in his left hand he carried the scepter of absolute mastery. And beyond the Golden Path, his eyes looked into eternity which he knew to be the food of his soul and of his everlasting flesh.

—HEIGHIA, MY BROTHER'S DREAM
FROM THE BOOK OF GHANIMA

"It'd be better for me never to become Emperor," Leto said. "Oh, I don't imply that I've made my father's mistake and peered into the future with a glass of spice. I say this thing out of selfishness. My sister and I desperately need a time of freedom when we can learn how to live with what we are."

He fell silent, stared questioningly at the Lady Jessica. He'd spoken his piece as he and Ghanima had agreed. Now what would be their grandmother's response?

Jessica studied her grandson in the low light of glowglobes which illuminated her quarters in Sietch Tabr. It was still early morning of her second day here and she'd already had disturbing reports that the twins had spent a night of vigil outside the sietch. What were they doing? She had not slept well and she felt fatigue acids demanding that she come down from the hyper-level which had sustained her through all the demanding necessities since that crucial performance at the spaceport. This was the sietch of her nightmares—but outside, that was not the desert she remembered. *Where have all the flowers come from?* And the air around her felt too damp. Stillsuit discipline was lax among the young.

"What are you, child, that you need time to learn about yourself?" she asked.

He shook his head gently, knowing it to be a bizarre gesture of adulthood on a child's body, reminding himself that he must keep this woman off balance. "First, I am not a child. Oh . . ." He touched his chest. "This is a child's body; no doubt of that. But *I* am not a child."

Jessica chewed her upper lip, disregarding what this betrayed. Her Duke, so many years dead on this accursed planet, had laughed at her when she did this. *"Your one unbridled response,"* he'd called that chewing of the lip. *"It tells me that you're disturbed, and I must kiss those lips to still their fluttering."*

Now this grandson who bore the name of her Duke shocked her into heart-pounding stillness merely by smiling and saying: "You are disturbed; I see it by the fluttering of those lips."

It required the most profound discipline of her Bene Gesserit training to restore a semblance of calm. She managed: "Do you taunt me?"

"Taunt you? Never. But I must make it clear to you how much we differ. Let me remind you of that sietch orgy so long ago when the Old Reverend Mother gave you her lives and her memories. She tuned herself to you and gave you that . . . that long chain of sausages, each one a person. You have them yet. So you know something of what Ghanima and I experience."

"And Alia?" Jessica asked, testing him.

"Didn't you discuss that with Ghani?"

"I wish to discuss it with you."

"Very well. Alia denied what she was and became that which she most feared. The *past-within* cannot be relegated to the unconscious. That is a dangerous course for any human, but for us who are pre-born, it is worse than death. And that is all I will say about Alia."

"So you're not a child," Jessica said.

"I'm millions of years old. That requires adjustments which humans have never before been called upon to make."

Jessica nodded, calmer now, much more cautious than she'd been with Ghanima. And where was Ghanima? Why had Leto come here alone?

"Well, grandmother," he said, "are we Abominations or are we the hope of the Atreides?"

Jessica ignored the question. "Where is your sister?"

"She distracts Alia to keep us from being disturbed. It is necessary. But Ghani would say nothing more to you than I've said. Didn't you observe that yesterday?"

"What I observed yesterday is my affair. Why do you prattle about Abomination?"

"Prattle? Don't give me your Bene Gesserit cant, grandmother. I'll feed it back to you, word for word, right out of your own memories. I want more than the fluttering of your lips."

Jessica shook her head, feeling the coldness of this . . . *person* who carried her blood. The resources at his disposal daunted her. She tried to match his tone, asked: "What do you know of my intentions?"

He sniffed. "You needn't inquire whether I've made the mistake my father made. I've not looked outside our garden of time—at least not by seeking it out. Leave absolute knowledge of the future to those moments of *déjà vu* which any human may experience. I *know* the trap of pre-science. My father's life tells me what I need to know about it. No, grandmother: to know the future absolutely is to be trapped into that future absolutely. It collapses time. Present becomes future. I require more freedom than that."

Jessica felt her tongue twitch with unspoken words. How could she respond to him with something he didn't already know? This was monstrous! *He's me! He's my beloved Leto!* This thought shocked her. Momentarily she wondered if the childish mask might not lapse into those dear features and resurrect . . . *No!*

Leto lowered his head, looked upward to study her. Yes, she could be maneuvered after all. He said: "When you think of prescience, which I hope is rarely, you're probably no different from any other. Most people imagine how nice it would be to know tomorrow's quotation on the price of whale fur. Or whether a Harkonnen will once more govern their homeworld of Giedi Prime? But of course *we* know the Harkonnens without prescience, don't we, grandmother?"

She refused to rise to his baiting. Of course he would know about the cursed Harkonnen blood in his ancestry.

"Who is a Harkonnen?" he asked, goading. "Who is Beast Rabban? Any one of us, eh? But I digress. I speak the popular myth of prescience: to *know* the future absolutely! All of it! What fortunes could be made—and lost—on such absolute knowledge, eh? The rabble believes this. They believe that if a little bit is good, more must be better. How excellent! And if you handed one of them the complete scenario of his life, the unvarying dialogue up to his moment of death—what a hellish gift that'd be. What utter boredom! Every living instant he'd be replaying what he knew absolutely. No deviation. He could anticipate every response, every utterance—over and over and over and over and over and . . ."

Leto shook his head. "Ignorance has its advantages. A universe of surprises is what I pray for!"

It was a long speech and, as she listened, Jessica marveled at how his mannerisms, his intonations, echoed his father—her lost son. Even the ideas: these were things Paul might have said.

"You remind me of your father," she said.

"Is that hurtful to you?"

"In a way, but it's reassuring to know he lives on in you."

"How little you understand of how he lives on in me."

Jessica found his tone flat but dripping bitterness. She lifted her chin to look directly at him.

"Or how your Duke lives in me," Leto said. "Grandmother, Ghanima is *you*! She's you to such an extent that your life holds not a single secret from her up to the instant you bore our father. And me! What a catalogue of fleshly recordings am I. There are moments when it is too much to bear. You come here to judge us? You come here to judge Alia? Better that we judge you!"

Jessica demanded answers of herself and found none. What was he doing? Why this emphasis on his difference? Did he court rejection? Had he reached Alia's condition—Abomination?

"This disturbs you," he said.

"It disturbs me." She permitted herself a futile shrug. "Yes, it disturbs me—and for reasons you know full well. I'm sure you've reviewed my Bene Gesserit training. Ghanima admits it. I know Alia . . . did. You know the consequences of your *difference*."

He peered upward at her with disturbing intensity. "Almost, we did not take this tack with you," he said, and there was a sense of her own fatigue in his voice. "We know the fluttering of your lips as your lover knew them. Any bedchamber endearment your Duke whispered is ours to recall at will. You've accepted this intellectually, no doubt. But I warn you that intellectual acceptance is not enough. If any of us becomes Abomination—it could be you within us who creates it! Or my father . . . or mother! Your Duke! Any one of you could possess us—and the condition would be the same."

Jessica felt a burning in her chest, dampness in her eyes. "Leto . . ." she managed, allowing herself to use his name at last. She found the pain less than she'd imagined it would be, forced herself to continue. "What is it you want of me?"

"I would teach my grandmother."

"Teach me what?"

"Last night, Ghani and I played the mother-father roles almost to our destruction, but we learned much. There are things one can know, given an awareness of conditions. Actions can be predicted. Alia, now— it's well nigh certainty that she's plotting to abduct you."

Jessica blinked, shocked by the swift accusation. She knew this trick well, had employed it many times: set a person up along one line of reasoning, then introduce the shocker from another line. She recovered with a sharp intake of breath.

"I know what Alia has been doing . . . what she *is*, but . . ."

"Grandmother, pity her. Use your heart as well as your intelligence. You've done that before. You pose a threat, and Alia wants the Imperium for her own—at least, the thing she has become wants this."

"How do I know this isn't another Abomination speaking?"

He shrugged. "That's where your heart comes in. Ghani and I know how she fell. It isn't easy to adjust to the clamor of that inner multitude. Suppress their egos and they will come crowding back every time you invoke a memory. One day—" He swallowed in a dry throat. "—a strong one from that inner pack decides it's time to share the flesh."

"And there's nothing you can do?" She asked the question although she feared the answer.

"We believe there is something . . . yes. We cannot succumb to the spice; that's paramount. And we must not suppress the past entirely. We must use it, make an amalgam of it. Finally we will mix them all into ourselves. We will no longer be our original selves—*but we will not be possessed.*"

"You speak of a plot to abduct me."

"It's obvious. Wensicia is ambitious for her son. Alia is ambitious for herself, and . . ."

"Alia and Farad'n?"

"That's not indicated," he said. "But Alia and Wensicia run parallel courses right now. Wensicia has a sister in Alia's house. What simpler thing than a message to—"

"You know of such a message?"

"As though I'd seen it and read its every word."

"But you've not seen such a message?"

"No need. I have only to know that the Atreides are all here together on Arrakis. All of the water in one cistern." He gestured to encompass the planet.

"House Corrino wouldn't dare attack us here!"

"Alia would profit if they did." A sneer in his voice provoked her.

"I won't be patronized by my own grandson!" she said.

"Then dammit, woman, stop thinking of me as your grandson!

Think of me as your *Duke* Leto!" Tone and facial expression, even the abrupt hand gesture, were so exact that she fell silent in confusion.

In a dry, remote voice, Leto said: "I tried to prepare you. Give me that, at least."

"Why would Alia abduct me?"

"To blame it on House Corrino, of course."

"I don't believe it. Even for her, this would be . . . monstrous! Too dangerous! How could she do it without . . . I cannot believe this!"

"When it happens, you'll believe. Ahh, grandmother, Ghani and I have but to eavesdrop within ourselves and we *know*. It's simple self-preservation. How else can we even guess at the mistakes being made around us?"

"I do not for a minute accept that abduction is part of Alia's—"

"Gods below! How can you, a Bene Gesserit, be this dense? The whole Imperium suspects why you're here. Wensicia's propagandists are all prepared to discredit you. Alia can't wait for that to happen. If you go down, House Atreides could suffer a mortal blow."

"What does the whole Imperium suspect?"

She measured out the words as coldly as possible, knowing she could not sway this *unchild* with any wile of Voice.

"The Lady Jessica plans to breed those twins together!" he rasped. "That's what the Sisterhood wants. Incest!"

She blinked. "Idle rumor." She swallowed. "The Bene Gesserits will not let such a rumor run wild in the Imperium. We still have some influence. Remember that."

"Rumor? What rumor? You've certainly held your options open on interbreeding us." He shook his head as she started to speak. "Don't deny it. Let us pass puberty still living in the same household and *you* in that household, and your *influence* will be no more than a rag waved in the face of a sandworm."

"Do you believe us to be such utter fools?" Jessica asked.

"Indeed I do. Your Sisterhood is nothing but a bunch of damn fool old women who haven't thought beyond their precious breeding program! Ghani and I know the leverage they have. Do *you* think *us* fools?"

"Leverage?"

"They know you're a Harkonnen! It'll be in their breeding records: Jessica out of Tanidia Nerus by the Baron Vladimir Harkonnen. That record *accidentally* made public would pull your teeth to—"

"You think the Sisterhood would stoop to blackmail?"

"I *know* they would. Oh, they coated it sweetly. They told you to investigate the rumors about your daughter. They fed your curiosity and your fears. They invoked your sense of responsibility, made you feel guilty because you'd fled back to Caladan. And they offered you the prospect of *saving* your grandchildren."

Jessica could only stare at him in silence. It was as though he'd eavesdropped on the emotional meetings with her Proctors from the Sisterhood. She felt completely subdued by his words, and now began to accept the possibility that he spoke truth when he said Alia planned abduction.

"You see, grandmother, I have a difficult decision to make," he said. "Do I follow the Atreides mystique? Do I live for my subjects . . . and die for them? Or do I choose another course—one which would permit me to live thousands of years?"

Jessica recoiled involuntarily. These words spoken so easily touched on a subject the Bene Gesserits made almost unthinkable. Many Reverend Mothers could choose that course . . . or try it. The manipulation of internal chemistry was available to initiates of the Sisterhood. But if one did it, sooner or later all would try it. There could be no concealing such an accumulation of ageless women. They knew for a certainty that this course would lead them to destruction. Short-lived humanity would turn upon them. No—it was unthinkable.

"I don't like the trend of your thoughts," she said.

"You don't understand my thoughts," he said. "Ghani and I . . ." He shook his head. "Alia had it in her grasp and threw it away."

"Are you sure of that? I've already sent word to the Sisterhood that Alia practices the unthinkable. Look at her! She's not aged a day since last I . . ."

"Oh, that!" He dismissed Bene Gesserit body balance with a wave of his hand. "I'm speaking of something else—a perfection of being far beyond anything humans have ever before achieved."

Jessica remained silent, aghast at how easily he'd lifted her disclosure from her. He'd know surely that such a message represented a death sentence on Alia. And no matter how he changed the words, he could only be talking about committing the same offense. Didn't he know the peril of his words?

"You must explain," she said finally.

"How?" he asked. "Unless you understand that Time isn't what it appears, I can't even begin to explain. My father suspected it. He stood at the edge of realization, but fell back. Now it's up to Ghani and me."

"I insist that you explain," Jessica said and she fingered the poisoned needle she held beneath a fold of her robe. It was the gom jabbar, so deadly that the slightest prick of it killed within seconds. And she thought: *They warned me I might have to use it.* The thought sent the muscles of her arm trembling in waves and she was thankful for the concealing robe.

"Very well," he sighed. "First, as to Time: there is no difference between ten thousand years and one year; no difference between one hundred thousand years and a heartbeat. No difference. That is the first fact about Time. And the second fact: the entire universe with all of its Time is within me."

"What nonsense is this?" she demanded.

"You see? You don't understand. I will try to explain in another way, then." He raised his right hand to illustrate, moving it as he spoke. "We go forward, we come back."

"Those words explain nothing!"

"That is correct," he said. "There are things which words cannot explain. You must experience them without words. But you are not prepared for such a venture, just as when you look at me you do not see me."

"But . . . I'm looking directly at you. Of course I see you!" She glared at him. His words reflected knowledge of the Zensunni Codex as she'd been taught it in the Bene Gesserit schools: play of words to confuse one's understanding of philosophy.

"Some things occur beyond your control," he said.

"How does that explain this . . . this *perfection* which is so far beyond other human experiences?"

He nodded. "If one delays old age or death by the use of melange or by that learned adjustment of fleshly balance which you Bene Gesserits so rightly fear, such a delay invokes only an illusion of control. Whether one walks rapidly through the sietch or slowly, one traverses the sietch. And that passage of time is experienced internally."

"Why do you bandy words this way? I cut my wisdom teeth on such nonsense long before even your father was born."

"But only the teeth grew," he said.

"Words! Words!"

"Ahhh, you're very close!"

"Hah!"

"Grandmother?"

"Yes?"

He held his silence for a long space. Then: "You see? You can still respond as yourself." He smiled at her. "But you cannot see past the shadows. I am here." Again he smiled. "My father came very near to this. When he lived, he lived, but when he died, he failed to die."

"What're you saying?"

"Show me his body!"

"Do you think this Preacher . . ."

"Possible, but even so, that is not his body."

"You've explained nothing," she accused.

"Just as I warned you."

"Then why . . ."

"You asked. You had to be shown. Now let us return to Alia and her plan of abduction for—"

"Are you planning the unthinkable?" she demanded, holding the poisonous gom jabbar at the ready beneath her robe.

"Will you be her executioner?" he asked, his voice deceptively mild. He pointed a finger at the hand beneath her robe. "Do you think she'll permit you to use that? Or do you think I'd let you use it?"

Jessica found she could not swallow.

"In answer to your question," he said, "I do not plan the unthinkable. I am not that stupid. But I am shocked at you. You dare judge Alia. Of course she's broken the precious Bene Gesserit commandment! What'd you expect? You ran out on her, left her as queen here in all but name. All of that power! So you ran back to Caladan to nurse your wounds in Gurney's arms. Good enough. But who are you to judge Alia?"

"I tell you, I will not dis—"

"Oh, shut up!" He looked away from her in disgust. But his words had been uttered in that special Bene Gesserit way—the controlling *Voice.* It silenced her as though a hand had been clapped over her mouth. She thought: *Who'd know how to hit me with Voice better than this one?* It was a mitigating argument which eased her wounded feelings. As many times as she'd used Voice on others, she'd never expected to be susceptible to it . . . not ever again . . . not since the school days when . . .

He turned back to her. "I'm sorry. I just happen to know how blindly you can be expected to react when—"

"Blindly? Me?" She was more outraged by this than she'd been by his exquisite use of Voice against her.

"You," he said. "Blindly. If you've any honesty left in you at all, you'll recognize your own reactions. I call your name and you say, 'Yes?' I silence your tongue. I invoke all your Bene Gesserit myths. Look inward the way you were taught. That, at least, is something you can do for your—"

"How dare you! What do you know of . . ." Her voice trailed off. Of course he knew!

"Look inward, I say!" His voice was imperious.

Again, his voice enthralled her. She found her senses stilled, felt a quickening of breath. Just beyond awareness lurked a pounding heart, the panting of . . . Abruptly she realized that the quickened breath, the pounding heart, were not latent, not held at bay by her Bene Gesserit control. Eyes widening in shocked awareness, she felt her own flesh obeying other commands. Slowly she recovered her poise, but the realization remained. This *unchild* had been playing her like a fine instrument throughout their interview.

"Now you know how profoundly you were conditioned by your precious Bene Gesserits," he said.

She could only nod. Her belief in words lay shattered. Leto had forced her to look her physical universe squarely in the face, and she'd come away shaken, her mind running with a new awareness. "*Show me his body!*" He'd shown her her own body as though it were newborn. Not since her earliest schooling days on Wallach, not since those terrifying days before the Duke's buyers came for her, not since then had she felt such trembling uncertainty about her next moments.

"You will allow yourself to be abducted," Leto said.

"But—"

"I'm not asking for discussion on this point," he said. "You will allow it. Think of this as a command from your Duke. You'll see the purpose when it's done. You're going to confront a very interesting student."

Leto stood, nodded. He said: "Some actions have an end but no beginning; some begin but do not end. It all depends upon where the observer is standing." Turning, he left her chambers.

In the second anteroom, Leto met Ghanima hurrying into their private quarters. She stopped as she saw him, said: "Alia's busy with the Convocation of the Faith." She looked a question at the passage which led to Jessica's quarters.

"It worked," Leto said.

Atrocity is recognized as such by victim and perpetrator alike, by all who learn about it at whatever remove. Atrocity has no excuses, no mitigating argument. Atrocity never balances or rectifies the past. Atrocity merely arms the future for more atrocity. It is self-perpetuating upon itself—a barbarous form of incest. Whoever commits atrocity also commits those future atrocities thus bred.

—THE APOCRYPHA OF MUAD'DIB

Shortly after noon, when most of the pilgrims had wandered off to refresh themselves in whatever cooling shade and source of libation they could find, The Preacher entered the great square below Alia's Temple. He came on the arm of his surrogate eyes, young Assan Tariq. In a pocket beneath his flowing robe, The Preacher carried the black gauze mask he'd worn on Salusa Secundus. It amused him to think that the mask and the boy served the same purpose—disguise. While he needed surrogate eyes, doubts remained alive.

Let the myth grow, but keep doubts alive, he thought.

No one must discover that the mask was merely cloth, not an Ixian artifact at all. His hand must not slip from Assan Tariq's bony shoulder. Let The Preacher once walk as the sighted despite his eyeless sockets, and all doubts would dissolve. The small hope he nursed would be dead. Each day he prayed for a change, something different over which he might stumble, but even Salusa Secundus had been a pebble, every aspect known. Nothing changed; nothing could be changed . . . yet.

Many people marked his passage past the shops and arcades, noting the way he turned his head from side to side, holding it centered on a doorway or a person. The movements of his head were not always blind-natural, and this added to the growing myth.

Alia watched from a concealed slit in the towering battlement of her temple. She searched that scarred visage far below for some sign—a sure sign of identity. Every rumor was reported to her. Each new one came with its thrill of fear.

She'd thought her order to take The Preacher captive would remain secret, but that, too, came back to her now as a rumor. Even among her guards, someone could not remain silent. She hoped now that the guards would follow her new orders and not take this robed mystery captive in a public place where it could be seen and reported.

It was dusty hot in the square. The Preacher's young guide had pulled the veil of his robe up around his nose, leaving only the dark eyes and a thin patch of forehead exposed. The veil bulged with the outline of a stillsuit's catchtube. This told Alia that they'd come in from the desert. Where did they hide out there?

The Preacher wore no veil protection from the searing air. He had even dropped the catchtube flap of his stillsuit. His face lay open to the sunlight and the heat shiverings which lifted off the square's paving blocks in visible waves.

At the Temple steps there stood a group of nine pilgrims making their departure obeisance. The shadowed edge of the square held perhaps fifty more persons, mostly pilgrims devoting themselves to various penances imposed by the priesthood. Among the onlookers could be seen messengers and a few merchants who'd not yet made enough sales to close up for the worst of the day's heat.

WATCHING FROM THE OPEN SLIT, ALIA FELT THE DRENCHING HEAT and knew herself to be caught between thinking and sensation, the way she'd often seen her brother caught. The temptation to consult within herself rang like an ominous humming in her head. The Baron was there: dutiful, but always ready to play upon her terrors when rational judgment failed and the things around her lost their sense of past, present, and future.

What if that's Paul down there? she asked herself.

"Nonsense!" the voice within her said.

But the reports of The Preacher's words could not be doubted. *Heresy!* It terrified her to think that Paul himself might bring down the structure built on his name.

Why not?

She thought of what she'd said in Council just that morning, turning viciously upon Irulan, who'd urged acceptance of the gift of clothing from House Corrino.

"All gifts to the twins will be examined thoroughly, just as always," Irulan had argued.

"And when we find the gift harmless?" Alia had cried.

Somehow that had been the most frightening thing of all: to find that the gift carried no threat.

In the end they'd accepted the fine clothing and had gone on to the other issue: Was the Lady Jessica to be given a position on the Council? Alia had managed to delay a vote.

She thought of this as she stared down at The Preacher.

Things which happened to her Regency now were like the underside of that transformation they inflicted upon this planet. Dune had once symbolized the power of ultimate desert. That power dwindled physically, but the myth of its power grew apace. Only the ocean-desert remained, the great Mother Desert of the inner planet, with its rim of thorn bushes, which Fremen still called Queen of Night. Behind the thorn bushes arose soft green hills bending down to the sand. All the hills were man-made. Every last one of them had been planted by men who had labored like crawling insects. The green of those hills was almost overpowering to someone raised, as Alia had been, in the tradition of dun-shaded sand. In her mind, as in the minds of all Fremen, the ocean-desert still held Dune in a grip which would never relax. She had only to close her eyes and she would see that desert.

Open eyes at the desert edge saw now the verdant hills, marsh slime reaching out green pseudopods toward the sand—but the other desert remained as powerful as ever.

Alia shook her head, stared down at The Preacher.

He had mounted the first of the terraced steps below the Temple and turned to face the almost deserted square. Alia touched the button beside her window which would amplify voices from below. She felt a wave of self-pity, seeing herself held here in loneliness. Whom could she trust? She'd thought Stilgar remained reliable, but Stilgar had been infected by this blind man.

"You know how he counts?" Stilgar had asked her. "I heard him counting coins as he paid his guide. It's very strange to my Fremen ears, and that's a terrible thing. He counts 'shuc, ishcai, qimsa, chuascu, picha, sucta, and so on. I've not heard counting like that since the old days in the desert."

From this, Alia knew that Stilgar could not be sent to do the job which must be done. And she would have to be circumspect with her guards where the slightest emphasis from the Regency tended to be taken as absolute command.

What was he doing down there, this Preacher?

The surrounding marketplace beneath its protective balconies and arched arcade still presented a gaudy face: merchandise left on display with a few boys to watch over it. Some few merchants remained awake there sniffing for the spice-biscuit money of the back country or the jingle in a pilgrim's purse.

Alia studied The Preacher's back. He appeared poised for speech, but something withheld his voice.

Why do I stand here watching that ruin in ancient flesh? she asked herself. *That mortal wreckage down there cannot be the "vessel of magnificence" which once was my brother.*

Frustration bordering on anger filled her. How could she find out about The Preacher, find out for certain *without finding out*? She was trapped. She dared not reveal more than a passing curiosity about this heretic.

Irulan felt it. She'd lost her famous Bene Gesserit poise and screamed in Council: "We've lost the power to think well of ourselves!"

Even Stilgar had been shocked.

Javid had brought them back to their senses: "We don't have time for such nonsense!"

Javid was right. What did it matter how they thought of themselves? All that concerned them was holding onto the Imperial power.

But Irulan, recovering her poise, had been even more devastating: "We've lost something vital, I tell you. When we lost it, we lost the ability to make good decisions. We fall upon decisions these days the way we fall upon an enemy—or wait and wait, which is a form of giving up, and we allow the decisions of others to move us. Have we forgotten that we were the ones who set this current flowing?"

And all over the question of whether to accept a gift from House Corrino.

Irulan will have to be disposed of, Alia decided.

What was that old man down there waiting for? He called himself a preacher. Why didn't he preach?

Irulan was wrong about our decision-making, Alia told herself. *I can still make proper decisions!* The person with life-and-death decisions to make must make decisions or remain caught in the pendulum. Paul had always said that stasis was the most dangerous of those things which were not natural. The only permanence was fluid. Change was all that mattered.

I'll show them change! Alia thought.

The Preacher raised his arms in benediction.

A few of those remaining in the square moved closer to him, and Alia noted the slowness of that movement. Yes, the rumors were out that The Preacher had aroused Alia's displeasure. She bent closer to the Ixian speaker beside her spy hole. The speaker brought her the murmurings of the people in the square, the sound of wind, the scratching of feet on sand.

"I bring you four messages!" The Preacher said.

His voice blared from Alia's speaker, and she turned down the volume.

"Each message is for a certain person," The Preacher said. "The first message is for Alia, the suzerain of this place." He pointed behind him toward her spy hole. "I bring her a warning: You, who held the secret of duration in your loins, have sold your future for an empty purse!"

How dare he? Alia thought. But his words froze her.

"My second message," The Preacher said, "is for Stilgar, the Fremen Naib, who believes he can translate the power of the tribes into the power of the Imperium. My warning to you, Stilgar: The most dangerous of all creations is a rigid code of ethics. It will turn upon you and drive you into exile!"

He has gone too far! Alia thought. *I must send the guards for him no matter the consequences.* But her hands remained at her sides.

The Preacher turned to face the Temple, climbed to the second step and once more whirled to face the square, all the time keeping his left hand upon the shoulder of his guide. He called out now: "My third message is for the Princess Irulan. Princess! Humiliation is a thing which no person can forget. I warn you to flee!"

What's he saying? Alia asked herself. *We humiliated Irulan, but . . . Why does he warn her to flee? My decision was just made!* A thrill of fear shot through Alia. How did The Preacher know?

"My fourth message is for Duncan Idaho," he shouted. "Duncan! You were taught to believe that loyalty buys loyalty. Ohh, Duncan, do not believe in history, because history is impelled by whatever passes for money. Duncan! Take your horns and do what you know best how to do."

Alia chewed the back of her right hand. *Horns!* She wanted to reach out and press the button which would summon guards, but her hand refused to move.

"Now I will preach to you," The Preacher said. "This is a sermon of the desert. I direct it to the ears of Muad'Dib's priesthood, those who practice the ecumenism of the sword. Ohhh, you believers in manifest destiny! Know you not that manifest destiny has its demoniac side? You cry out that you find yourselves exalted merely to have lived in the blessed generations of Muad'Dib. I say to you that you have abandoned Muad'Dib. Holiness has replaced love in your religion! You court the vengeance of the desert!"

The Preacher lowered his head as though in prayer.

Alia felt herself shivering with awareness. Gods below! That voice! It had been cracked by years in the burning sands, but it could be the remnant of Paul's voice.

Once more The Preacher raised his head. His voice boomed out over the square where more people had begun to gather, attracted by this oddity out of the past.

"Thus it is written!" The Preacher shouted. "They who pray for dew at the desert's edge shall bring forth the deluge! They shall not escape their fate through powers of reason! Reason arises from pride that a man may not know in this way when he has done evil." He lowered his voice. "It was said of Muad'Dib that he died of prescience, that knowledge of the future killed him and he passed from the universe of reality into the *alam al-mythal*. I say to you that this is the illusion of Maya. Such thoughts have no independent reality. They cannot go out from you and do real things. Muad'Dib said of himself that he possessed no Rihani magic with which to encipher the universe. Do not doubt him."

Again The Preacher raised his arms, lifted his voice in a stentorian bellow: "I warn the priesthood of Muad'Dib! The fire on the cliff shall burn you! They who learn the lesson of self-deception too well shall perish by that deception. The blood of a brother cannot be cleansed away!"

He had lowered his arms, found his young guide, and was leaving the square before Alia could break herself from the trembling immobility which had overcome her. Such fearless heresy! It must be Paul. She had to warn her guards. They dared not move against this *Preacher* openly. The evidence in the square below her confirmed this.

Despite the heresy, no one moved to stop the departing Preacher. No Temple guard leaped to pursue him. No pilgrim tried to stop him. That charismatic blind man! Everyone who saw or heard him felt his power, the reflection of divine talent.

In spite of the day's heat, Alia felt suddenly cold. She felt the thin edge of her grip on the Imperium as a physical thing. She gripped the edge of her spy hole window as though to hold her power, thinking of its fragility. The balance of Landsraad, CHOAM, and Fremen arms held the core of power, while Spacing Guild and Bene Gesserit dealt silently in the shadows. The forbidden seepage of technological development which came from the edges of humankind's farthest migrations nibbled at the central power. Products permitted the Ixian and Tleilaxu factories could not relieve the pressure. And always in the wings there stood Farad'n of House Corrino, inheritor of Shaddam IV's titles and claims.

Without the Fremen, without House Atreides' monopoly on the geriatric spice, her grip would loosen. All the power would dissolve. She could feel it slipping from her right now. People heeded this Preacher. It would be dangerous to silence him; just as dangerous as it was to let him continue preaching such words as he'd shouted across her square today. She could see the first omens of her own defeat and the pattern of the problem stood out clearly in her mind. The Bene Gesserits had codified the problem:

"A large populace held in check by a small but powerful force is quite a common situation in our universe. And we know the major conditions wherein this large populace may turn upon its keepers—

"One: When they find a leader. This is the most volatile threat to the powerful; they must retain control of leaders.

"Two: When the populace recognizes its chains. Keep the populace blind and unquestioning.

"Three: When the populace perceives a hope of escape from bondage. They must never even believe that escape is possible!"

Alia shook her head, feeling her cheeks tremble with the force of movement. The signs were here in her populace. Every report she received from her spies throughout the Imperium reinforced her certain knowledge. Unceasing warfare of the Fremen Jihad left its mark everywhere. Wherever "the ecumenism of the sword" had touched, people retained the attitude of a subject population: defensive, concealing, evasive. All manifestations of authority—and this meant essentially *reli-*

gious authority—became subject to resentment. Oh, pilgrims still came in their thronging millions, and some among them were probably devout. But for the most part, pilgrimage had other motivations than devotion. Most often it was a canny surety for the future. It emphasized obedience and gained a real form of power which was easily translated into wealth. The Hajji who returned from Arrakis came home to new authority, new social status. The Hajji could make profitable economic decisions which the planet-bound of his homeworld dared not challenge.

Alia knew the popular riddle: "What do you see inside the empty purse brought home from Dune?" And the answer: "The eyes of Muad'Dib (fire diamonds)."

The traditional ways to counter growing unrest paraded themselves before Alia's awareness: people had to be taught that opposition was always punished and assistance to the ruler was always rewarded. Imperial forces must be shifted in random fashion. Major adjuncts to Imperial power had to be concealed. Every movement by which the Regency countered potential attack required delicate timing to keep the opposition off balance.

Have I lost my sense of timing? she wondered.

"What idle speculation is this?" a voice within her asked. She felt herself growing calmer. Yes, the Baron's plan was a good one. We eliminate the threat of the Lady Jessica and, at the same time, we discredit House Corrino. Yes.

The Preacher could be dealt with later. She understood his posture. The symbolism was clear. He was the ancient spirit of unbridled speculation, the spirit of heresy alive and functioning in her desert of orthodoxy. That was his strength. It didn't matter whether he was Paul . . . as long as that could be kept in doubt. But her Bene Gesserit knowledge told Alia that his strength would contain the key to his weakness.

The Preacher has a flaw which we will find. I will have him spied upon, watched every moment. And if the opportunity arises, he will be discredited.

I will not argue with the Fremen claims that they are divinely inspired to transmit a religious revelation. It is their concurrent claim to ideological revelation which inspires me to shower them with derision. Of course, they make the dual claim in the hope that it will strengthen their mandarinate and help them to endure in a universe which finds them increasingly oppressive. It is in the name of all those oppressed people that I warn the Fremen: short-term expediency always fails in the long term.

—THE PREACHER AT ARRAKEEN

Leto had come up in the night with Stilgar to the narrow ledge at the crest of the low rock outcropping which Sietch Tabr called The Attendant. Under the waning light of Second Moon, the ledge gave them a panoramic view—the Shield Wall with Mount Idaho to the north, the Great Flat to the south and rolling dunes eastward toward Habbanya Ridge. Winding dust, the aftermath of a storm, hid the southern horizon. Moonlight frosted the rim of the Shield Wall.

Stilgar had come against his will, joining the secretive venture finally because Leto aroused his curiosity. Why was it necessary to risk a sand crossing in the night? The lad had threatened to sneak away and make the journey alone if Stilgar refused. The way of it bothered him profoundly, though. Two such important targets alone in the night!

Leto squatted on the ledge facing south toward the flat. Occasionally he pounded his knee as though in frustration.

Stilgar waited. He was good at silent waiting, and stood two paces to one side of his charge, arms folded, his robe moving softly in the night breeze.

For Leto, the sand crossing represented a response to inner desperation, a need to seek a new alignment for his life in a silent conflict which Ghanima could no longer risk. He had maneuvered Stilgar into sharing the journey because there were things Stilgar had to know in preparation for the days ahead.

Again Leto pounded his knee. It was difficult to know a beginning! He felt, at times, like an extension of those countless other lives, all as real and immediate as his own. In the flow of those lives there was no ending, no accomplishment—only eternal beginning. They could be a mob, too, clamoring at him as though he were a single window through which each desired to peer. And there lay the peril which had destroyed Alia.

Leto stared outward at the moonlight silvering the storm remnants. Folds and overfolds of dunes spread across the flat: silica grit measured out by the winds, mounded into waves—pea sand, grit sand, pebbles. He felt himself caught in one of those poised moments just before dawn. Time pressed at him. It was already the month of Akkad and behind him lay the last of an interminable waiting time: long hot days and hot dry winds, nights like this one tormented by gusts and endless blowings from the furnace lands of the Hawkbled. He glanced over his shoulder toward the Shield Wall, a broken line in starlight. Beyond that wall in the Northern Sink lay the focus of his problems.

Once more he looked to the desert. As he stared into the hot darkness, day dawned, the sun rising out of dust scarves and placing a touch of lime into the storm's red streamers. He closed his eyes, willing himself to see how this day would appear from Arrakeen, and the city lay there in his consciousness, caught up like a scattering of boxes between the light and the new shadows. Desert . . . boxes . . . desert . . . boxes . . .

When he opened his eyes, the desert remained: a spreading curry expanse of wind-kicked sand. Oily shadows along the base of each dune reached out like rays of the night just past. They linked one time with the other. He thought of the night, squatting here with Stilgar restless beside him, the older man worried at the silence and the unexplained reasons for coming to this place. Stilgar must have many memories of passing this way with his beloved Muad'Dib. Even now Stilgar was moving, scanning all around, alert for dangers. Stilgar did not like the open in daylight. He was pure old Fremen in that.

Leto's mind was reluctant to leave the night and the clean exertions of a sand crossing. Once here in the rocks, the night had taken on its black stillness. He sympathized with Stilgar's daylight fears. Black was a single thing even when it contained boiling terrors. Light could be many things. Night held its fear smells and its things which came with slithering sounds. Dimensions separated in the night, everything amplified—thorns sharper, blades more cutting. But terrors of the day could be worse.

Stilgar cleared his throat.

Leto spoke without turning: "I have a very serious problem, Stil."

"So I surmised." The voice beside Leto came low and wary. The child had sounded disturbingly of the father. It was a thing of forbidden magic which touched a cord of revulsion in Stilgar. Fremen knew the terrors of *possession*. Those found possessed were rightfully killed and their water cast upon the sand lest it contaminate the tribal cistern. The dead should remain dead. It was correct to find one's immortality in children, but children had no right to assume too exact a shape from their past.

"My problem is that my father left so many things undone," Leto said. "Especially the focus of our lives. The Empire cannot go on this way, Stil, without a proper focus for human life. I am speaking of life, you understand? Life, not death."

"Once, when he was troubled by a vision, your father spoke in this vein to me," Stilgar said.

Leto found himself tempted to pass off that questioning fear beside him with a light response, perhaps a suggestion that they break their fast. He realized that he was very hungry. They had eaten the previous noon and Leto had insisted on fasting through the night. But another hunger drew him now.

The trouble with my life is the trouble with this place, Leto thought. *No preliminary creation. I just go back and back and back until distances fade away. I cannot see the horizon; I cannot see Habbanya Ridge. I can't find the original place of testing.*

"There's really no substitute for prescience," Leto said. "Perhaps I should risk the spice . . ."

"And be destroyed as your father was?"

"A dilemma," Leto said.

"Once your father confided in me that knowing the future too well was to be locked into that future to the exclusion of any freedom to change."

"The paradox which is our problem," Leto said. "It's a subtle and powerful thing, prescience. The future becomes now. To be sighted in the land of the blind carries its own perils. If you try to interpret what you see for the blind, you tend to forget that the blind possess an inherent movement conditioned by their blindness. They are like a monstrous machine moving along its own path. They have their own momentum, their own fixations. I fear the blind, Stil. I fear them. They can so easily crush anything in their path."

Stilgar stared at the desert. Lime dawn had become steel day. He said: "Why have we come to this place?"

"Because I wanted you to see the place where I may die."

Stilgar tensed. Then: "So you *have* had a vision!"

"Perhaps it was only a dream."

"Why do we come to such a dangerous place?" Stilgar glared down at his charge. "We will return at once."

"I won't die today, Stil."

"No? What was this vision?"

"I saw three paths," Leto said. His voice came out with the sleepy sound of remembrance. "One of those futures requires me to kill our grandmother."

Stilgar shot a sharp glance back toward Sietch Tabr, as though he feared the Lady Jessica could hear them across the sandy distance. "Why?"

"To keep from losing the spice monopoly."

"I don't understand."

"Nor do I. But that is the thought of my dream when I use the knife."

"Oh." Stilgar understood the use of a knife. He drew a deep breath. "What is the second path?"

"Ghani and I marry to seal the Atreides bloodline."

"Ghaaa!" Stilgar expelled his breath in a violent expression of distaste.

"It was usual in ancient times for kings and queens to do this," Leto said. "Ghani and I have decided we will not breed."

"I warn you to hold fast in that decision!" There was death in Stilgar's voice. By Fremen Law, incest was punishable by death on the hanging tripod. He cleared his throat, asked: "And the third path?"

"I am called to reduce my father to human stature."

"He was my friend, Muad'Dib," Stilgar muttered.

"He was your god! I must undeify him."

Stilgar turned his back on the desert, stared toward the oasis of his beloved Sietch Tabr. Such talk always disturbed him.

Leto sensed the sweaty smell of Stilgar's movement. It was such a temptation to avoid the purposeful things which had to be said here. They could talk half the day away, moving from the specific to the abstract as though drawn away from real decisions, from those immediate necessities which confronted them. And there was no doubt that House Corrino posed a real threat to real lives—his own and Ghani's. But everything he did now had to be weighed and tested against the secret necessities. Stilgar once had voted to have Farad'n assassinated, holding out for the subtle application of chaumurky: poison administered in a drink. Farad'n was known to be partial to certain sweet liquors. That could not be permitted.

"If I die here, Stil," Leto said, "you must beware of Alia. She is no longer your friend."

"What is this talk of death and your aunt?" Now Stilgar was truly outraged. *Kill the Lady Jessica! Beware of Alia! Die in this place!*

"Small men change their faces at her command," Leto said. "A ruler need not be a prophet, Stil. Nor even godlike. A ruler need only be sensitive. I brought you here with me to clarify what our Imperium requires. It requires good government. That does not depend upon laws or precedent, but upon the personal qualities of whoever governs."

"The Regency handles its Imperial duties quite well," Stilgar said. "When you come of age—"

"I *am* of age! I'm the oldest person here! You're a puling infant beside me. I can remember times more than fifty centuries past. Hah! I can even remember when we Fremen were on Thurgrod."

"Why do you play with such fancies?" Stilgar demanded, his tone peremptory.

Leto nodded to himself. Why indeed? Why recount his memories of those other centuries? Today's Fremen were his immediate problem, most of them still only half-tamed savages, prone to laugh at unlucky innocence.

"The crysknife dissolves at the death of its owner," Leto said. "Muad'Dib has dissolved. Why are the Fremen still alive?"

It was one of those abrupt thought changes which so confounded Stilgar. He found himself temporarily dumb. Such words contained meaning, but their intent eluded him.

"I am expected to be Emperor, but I must be the servant," Leto said. He glanced across his shoulder at Stilgar. "My grandfather for whom I was named added new words to his coat of arms when he came here to Dune: 'Here I am; here I remain.'"

"He had no choice," Stilgar said.

"Very good, Stil. Nor have I any choice. I should be the Emperor by birth, by the fitness of my understanding, by all that has gone into me. I even know what the Imperium requires: good government."

"Naib has an ancient meaning," Stilgar said. "It is 'servant of the Sietch.'"

"I remember your training, Stil," Leto said. "For proper government, the tribe must have ways to choose men whose lives reflect the way a government should behave."

From the depths of his Fremen soul, Stilgar said: "You'll assume the

Imperial Mantle if it's meet. First you must prove that you can behave in the fashion of a ruler!"

Unexpectedly, Leto laughed. Then: "Do you doubt my sincerity, Stil?"

"Of course not."

"My birthright?"

"You are who you are."

"And if I do what is expected of me, that is the measure of my sincerity, eh?"

"It is the Fremen practice."

"Then I cannot have inner feelings to guide my behavior?"

"I don't understand what—"

"If I always behave with propriety, no matter what it costs me to suppress my own desires, then that is the measure of me."

"Such is the essence of self-control, youngster."

"Youngster!" Leto shook his head. "Ahhh, Stil, you provide me with the key to a rational ethic of government. I must be constant, every action rooted in the traditions of the past."

"That is proper."

"But my past goes deeper than yours!"

"What difference—"

"I have no first person singular, Stil. I am a multiple person with memories of traditions more ancient than you could imagine. That's my burden, Stil. I'm past-directed. I'm abrim with innate knowledge which resists newness and change. Yet Muad'Dib changed all this." He gestured at the desert, his arm sweeping to encompass the Shield Wall behind him.

Stilgar turned to peer at the Shield Wall. A village had been built beneath the wall since Muad'Dib's time, houses to shelter a planetology crew helping spread plant life into the desert. Stilgar stared at the man-made intrusion into the landscape. Change? Yes: There was an alignment to the village, a trueness which offended him. He stood silently, ignoring the itching of grit particles under his stillsuit. That village was an offense against the thing this planet had been. Suddenly Stilgar wanted a circular howling of wind to leap over the dunes and obliterate that place. The sensation left him trembling.

Leto said: "Have you noticed, Stil, that the new stillsuits are of sloppy manufacture? Our water loss is too high."

Stilgar stopped himself on the point of asking: *Have I not said it?* Instead he said: "Our people grow increasingly dependent upon the pills."

Leto nodded. The pills shifted body temperature, reduced water loss. They were cheaper and easier than stillsuits. But they inflicted the user with other burdens, among them a tendency to slowed reaction time, occasional blurred vision.

"Is that why we came out here?" Stilgar asked. "To discuss stillsuit manufacture?"

"Why not?" Leto asked. "Since you will not face what I must talk about."

"Why must I beware of your aunt?" Anger edged his voice.

"Because she plays upon the old Fremen desire to resist change, yet would bring more terrible change than you can imagine."

"You make much out of little! She's a proper Fremen."

"Ahhh, then the proper Fremen holds to the ways of the past and I have an ancient past. Stil, were I to give free reign to this inclination, I would demand a closed society, completely dependent upon the sacred ways of the past. I would control migration, explaining that this fosters new ideas, and new ideas are a threat to the entire structure of life. Each little planetary polis would go its own way, becoming what it would. Finally the Empire would shatter under the weight of its differences."

Stilgar tried to swallow in a dry throat. These were words which Muad'Dib might have produced. They had his ring to them. They were paradox, frightening. But if one allowed any change . . . He shook his head.

"The past may show the right way to behave if you live in the past, Stil, but circumstances change."

Stilgar could only agree that circumstances did change. How must one behave then? He looked beyond Leto, seeing the desert and not seeing it. Muad'Dib had walked there. The flat was a place of golden shadows as the sun climbed, purple shadows, gritty rivulets crested in dust vapors. The dust fog which usually hung over Habbanya Ridge was visible in the far distance now, and the desert between presented his eyes with dunes diminishing, one curve into another. Through the smoky shimmer of heat he saw the plants which crept out from the desert edge. Muad'Dib had caused life to sprout in that desolate place. Copper, gold, red flowers, yellow flowers, rust and russet, grey-green leaves, spikes and harsh shadows beneath bushes. The motion of the day's heat set shadows quivering, vibrating in the air.

Presently Stilgar said: "I am only a leader of Fremen; you are the son of a Duke."

"Not knowing what you said, you said it," Leto said.

Stilgar scowled. Once, long ago, Muad'Dib had chided him thus.

"You remember it, don't you, Stil?" Leto asked. "We were under Habbanya Ridge and the Sardaukar captain—remember him: Aramsham? He killed his friend to save himself. And you warned several times that day about preserving the lives of Sardaukar who'd seen our secret ways. Finally you said they would surely reveal what they'd seen; they must be killed. And my father said: 'Not knowing what you said, you said it.' And you were hurt. You told him you were only a *simple* leader of Fremen. Dukes must know more important things."

Stilgar stared down at Leto. *We were under Habbanya Ridge! We!* This . . . this child, not even conceived on that day, knew what had taken place in exact detail, the kind of detail which could only be known to someone who had been there. It was only another proof that these Atreides children could not be judged by ordinary standards.

"Now you will listen to me," Leto said. "If I die or disappear in the desert, you are to flee from Sietch Tabr. I command it. You are to take Ghani and—"

"You are not yet my Duke! You're a . . . a child!"

"I'm an adult in a child's flesh," Leto said. He pointed down to a narrow crack in the rocks below them. "If I die here, it will be in that place. You will see the blood. You will know then. Take my sister and—"

"I'm doubling your guard," Stilgar said. "You're not coming out here again. We are leaving now and you—"

"Stil! You cannot hold me. Turn your mind once more to that time at Habbanya Ridge. Remember? The factory crawler was out there on the sand and a big Maker was coming. There was no way to save the crawler from the worm. And my father was annoyed that he couldn't save that crawler. But Gurney could think only of the men he'd lost in the sand. Remember what he said: 'Your father would've been more concerned for the men he couldn't save.' Stil, I charge you to save people. They're more important than things. And Ghani is the most precious of all because, without me, she is the only hope for the Atreides."

"I will hear no more," Stilgar said. He turned and began climbing down the rocks toward the oasis across the sand. He heard Leto following. Presently Leto passed him and, glancing back, said: "Have you noticed, Stil, how beautiful the young women are this year?"

The life of a single human, as the life of a family or an entire people, persists as memory. My people must come to see this as part of their maturing process. They are people as *organism*, and in this persistent memory they store more and more experiences in a subliminal reservoir. Humankind hopes to call upon this material if it is needed for a changing universe. But much that is stored can be lost in that chance play of accident which we call "fate." Much may not be integrated into evolutionary relationships, and thus may not be evaluated and keyed into activity by those ongoing environmental changes which inflict themselves upon flesh. The *species* can forget! This is the special value of the Kwisatz Haderach which the Bene Gesserits never suspected: the Kwisatz Haderach cannot forget.

—THE BOOK OF LETO
AFTER HARQ AL-ADA

Stilgar could not explain it, but he found Leto's casual observation profoundly disturbing. It ground through his awareness all the way back across the sand to Sietch Tabr, taking precedence over everything else Leto had said out there on The Attendant.

Indeed, the young women of Arrakis were very beautiful that year. And the young men, too. Their faces glowed serenely with water-richness. Their eyes looked outward and far. They exposed their features often without any pretense of stillsuit masks and the snaking lines of catchtubes. Frequently they did not even wear stillsuits in the open, preferring the new garments which, as they moved, offered flickering suggestions of the lithe young bodies beneath.

Such human beauty was set off against the new beauty of the landscape. By contrast with the old Arrakis, the eye could be spellbound by its collision with a tiny clump of green twigs growing among red-brown rocks. And the old sietch warrens of the cave-metropolis culture, complete with elaborate seals and moisture traps at every entrance, were giving way to open villages built often of mud bricks. Mud bricks!

Why did I want the village destroyed? Stilgar wondered, and he stumbled as he walked.

He knew himself to be of a dying breed. Old Fremen gasped in wonder at the prodigality of their planet—water wasted into the air for no more than its ability to mold building bricks. The water for a single one-family dwelling would keep an entire sietch alive for a year.

The new buildings even had transparent windows to let in the sun's heat and to desiccate the bodies within. Such windows opened outward.

New Fremen within their mud homes could look out upon their landscape. They no longer were enclosed and huddling in a sietch. Where the new vision moved, there also moved the imagination. Stilgar could feel this. The new vision joined Fremen to the rest of the Imperial universe, conditioned them to unbounded space. Once they'd been tied to water-poor Arrakis by their enslavement to its bitter necessities. They'd not shared that open-mindedness which conditioned inhabitants on most planets of the Imperium.

Stilgar could see the changes contrasting with his own doubts and fears. In the old days it had been a rare Fremen who even considered the possibility that he might leave Arrakis to begin a new life on one of the water-rich worlds. They'd not even been permitted the *dream* of escape.

He watched Leto's moving back as the youth walked ahead. Leto had spoken of prohibitions against movement off-planet. Well, that had always been a reality for most other-worlders, even where the dream was permitted as a safety valve. But planetary serfdom had reached its peak here on Arrakis. Fremen had turned inward, barricaded in their minds as they were barricaded in their cave warrens.

The very meaning of sietch—a place of sanctuary in times of trouble—had been perverted here into a monstrous confinement for an entire population.

Leto spoke the truth: Muad'Dib had changed all that.

Stilgar felt lost. He could feel his old beliefs crumbling. The new outward vision produced life which desired to move away from containment.

"How beautiful the young women are this year."

The old ways (*My ways!* he admitted) had forced his people to ignore all history except that which turned inward onto their own travail. The old Fremen had read history out of their own terrible migrations, their flights from persecution into persecution. The old planetary government had followed the stated policy of the old Imperium. They had suppressed creativity and all sense of progress, of evolution. Prosperity had been dangerous to the old Imperium and its holders of power.

With an abrupt shock, Stilgar realized that these things were equally dangerous to the course which Alia was setting.

Again Stilgar stumbled and fell farther behind Leto.

In the old ways and old religions, there'd been no future, only an endless *now*. Before Muad'Dib, Stilgar saw, the Fremen had been conditioned to believe in failure, never in the possibility of accomplishment. Well . . . they'd believed Liet-Kynes, but he'd set a forty-generation timescale. That was no accomplishment; that was a dream which, he saw now, had also turned inward.

Muad'Dib had changed that!

During the Jihad, Fremen had learned much about the old Padishah Emperor, Shaddam IV. The eighty-first Padishah of House Corrino to occupy the Golden Lion Throne and reign over this Imperium of uncounted worlds had used Arrakis as a testing place for those policies which he hoped to implement in the rest of his empire. His planetary governors on Arrakis had cultivated a persistent pessimism to bolster their power base. They'd made sure that everyone on Arrakis, even the free-roaming Fremen, became familiar with numerous cases of injustice and insoluble problems; they had been taught to think of themselves as a helpless people for whom there was no succor.

"How beautiful the young women are this year!"

As he watched Leto's retreating back, Stilgar began to wonder how the youth had set these thoughts flowing—and just by uttering a seemingly simple statement. Because of that statement, Stilgar found himself viewing Alia and his own role on the Council in an entirely different way.

Alia was fond of saying that old ways gave ground slowly. Stilgar admitted to himself that he'd always found this statement vaguely reassuring. Change was dangerous. Invention must be suppressed. Individual willpower must be denied. What other function did the priesthood serve than to deny individual will?

Alia kept saying that opportunities for open competition had to be reduced to manageable limits. But that meant the recurrent threat of technology could only be used to confine populations—just as it had served its ancient masters. Any permitted technology had to be rooted in ritual. Otherwise . . . otherwise . . .

Again Stilgar stumbled. He was at the qanat now and saw Leto waiting beneath the apricot orchard which grew along the flowing water. Stilgar heard his feet moving through uncut grass.

Uncut grass!

What can I believe? Stilgar asked himself.

It was proper for a Fremen of his generation to believe that individuals needed a profound sense of their own limitations. Traditions were surely the most controlling element in a secure society. People had to know the boundaries of their time, of their society, of their territory. What was wrong with the sietch as a model for all thinking? A sense of enclosure should pervade every individual choice—should fence in the family, the community, and every step taken by a proper government.

Stilgar came to a stop and stared across the orchard at Leto. The youth stood there, regarding him with a smile.

Does he know the turmoil in my head? Stilgar wondered.

And the old Fremen Naib tried to fall back on the traditional catechism of his people. Each aspect of life required a single form, its inherent circularity based on secret inner knowledge of what will work and
what will not work. The model for life, for the community, for every
element of the larger society right up to and beyond the peaks of
government—that model had to be the sietch and its counterpart in the
sand: Shai-Hulud. The giant sandworm was surely a most formidable
creature, but when threatened it hid in the impenetrable deeps.

Change is dangerous! Stilgar told himself. Sameness and stability
were the proper goals of government.

But the young men and women were beautiful.

And they remembered the words of Muad'Dib as he deposed Shaddam IV: "It's not long life to the Emperor that I seek; it's long life to the
Imperium."

Isn't that what I've been saying to myself? Stilgar wondered.

He resumed walking, headed toward the sietch entrance slightly to
Leto's right. The youth moved to intercept him.

Muad'Dib had said another thing, Stilgar reminded himself: *"Just
as individuals are born, mature, breed, and die, so do societies and civilizations and governments."*

Dangerous or not, there would be change. The beautiful young Fremen knew this. They could look outward and see it, prepare for it.

Stilgar was forced to stop. It was either that or walk right over Leto.

The youth peered up at him owlishly, said: "You see, Stil? Tradition
isn't the absolute guide you thought it was."

A Fremen dies when he is too long from the desert; this we call "the water sickness."

—STILGAR, THE COMMENTARIES

"It is difficult for me, asking you to do this," Alia said. "But . . . I must insure that there's an empire for Paul's children to inherit. There's no other reason for the Regency."

Alia turned from where she was seated at a mirror completing her morning toilet. She looked at her husband, measuring how he absorbed these words. Duncan Idaho deserved careful study in these moments; there was no doubt that he'd become something far more subtle and dangerous than the one-time swordmaster of House Atreides. The outer appearance remained similar—the black goat hair over sharp dark features—but in the long years since his awakening from the ghola state he had undergone an inner metamorphosis.

She wondered now, as she had wondered many times, what the ghola rebirth-after-death might have hidden in the secret loneliness of him. Before the Tleilaxu had worked their subtle science on him, Duncan's reactions had borne clear labels for the Atreides—loyalty, fanatic adherence to the moral code of his mercenary forebears, swift to anger and swift to recover. He had been implacable in his resolve for revenge against House Harkonnen. And he had died saving Paul. But the Tleilaxu had bought his body from the Sardaukar and, in their regeneration vats, they had grown a zombie-katrundo: the flesh of Duncan Idaho, but none of his conscious memories. He'd been trained as a mentat and sent as a gift, a human computer for Paul, a fine tool equipped with a hypnotic compulsion to slay his owner. The flesh of Duncan Idaho had resisted that compulsion and, in the intolerable stress, his cellular past had come back to him.

Alia had decided long ago that it was dangerous to think of him as Duncan in the privacy of her thoughts. Better to think of him by his ghola name, Hayt. Far better. And it was essential that he get not the slightest glimpse of the old Baron Harkonnen sitting there in her mind.

Duncan saw Alia studying him, turned away. Love could not hide the changes in her, nor conceal from him the transparency of her motives. The many-faceted metal eyes which the Tleilaxu had given him were cruel in their ability to penetrate deception. They limned her now as a gloating, almost masculine figure, and he could not stand to see her thus.

"Why do you turn away?" Alia asked.

"I must think about this thing," he said. "The Lady Jessica is . . . an Atreides."

"And your loyalty is to House Atreides, not to me," Alia pouted.

"Don't put such fickle interpretations into me," he said.

Alia pursed her lips. Had she moved too rapidly?

Duncan crossed to the chambered opening which looked down on a corner of the Temple plaza. He could see pilgrims beginning to gather there, the Arrakeen traders moving in to feed on the edges like a pack of predators upon a herd of beasts. He focused on a particular group of tradesmen, spice-fiber baskets over their arms, Fremen mercenaries a pace behind them. They moved with a stolid force through the gathering throng.

"They sell pieces of etched marble," he said, pointing. "Did you know that? They set the pieces out in the desert to be etched by storm-sands. Sometimes they find interesting patterns in the stone. They call it a new art form, very popular: genuine storm-etched marble from Dune. I bought a piece of it last week—a golden tree with five tassels, lovely but very fragile."

"Don't change the subject," Alia said.

"I haven't changed the subject," he said. "It's beautiful, but it's not art. Humans create art by their own violence, by their own volition." He put his right hand on the windowsill. "The twins detest this city and I'm afraid I see their point."

"I fail to see the association," Alia said. "The abduction of my mother is not a real abduction. She will be safe as your captive."

"This city was built by the blind," he said. "Did you know that Leto and Stilgar went out from Sietch Tabr into the desert last week? They were gone the whole night."

"It was reported to me," she said. "These baubles from the sand—would you have me prohibit their sale?"

"That'd be bad for business," he said, turning. "Do you know what Stilgar said when I asked why they went out on the sand that way? He said Leto wished to commune with the spirit of Muad'Dib."

Alia felt the sudden coldness of panic, looked in the mirror a moment to recover. Leto would not venture from the sietch at night for such nonsense. Was it a conspiracy?

Idaho put a hand over his eyes to blot out the sight of her, said: "Stilgar told me he went along with Leto because he still believes in Muad'Dib."

"Of course he does!"

Idaho chuckled, a hollow sound. "He said he still believes because Muad'Dib was always for the little people."

"What did you say to that?" Alia asked, her voice betraying her fear.

Idaho dropped his hand from his eyes. "I said, 'That must make you one of the little people.'"

"Duncan! That's a dangerous game. Bait *that* Fremen Naib and you could awaken a beast to destroy us all."

"He still believes in Muad'Dib," Idaho said. "That's our protection."

"What was his reply?"

"He said he knew his own mind."

"I see."

"No . . . I don't believe you do. Things that bite have longer teeth than Stilgar's."

"I don't understand you today, Duncan. I ask you to do a very important thing, a thing vital to . . . What is all of this rambling?"

How petulant she sounded. He turned back to the chambered window. "When I was trained as a mentat . . . It is very difficult, Alia, to learn how to work your own mind. You learn first that the mind must be allowed to work itself. That's very strange. You can work your own muscles, exercise them, strengthen them, but the mind acts of itself. Sometimes, when you have learned this about the mind, it shows you things you do not want to see."

"And that's why you tried to insult Stilgar?"

"Stilgar doesn't know his own mind; he doesn't let it run free."

"Except in the spice orgy."

"Not even there. That's what makes him a Naib. To be a leader of men, he controls and limits his reactions. He does what is expected of him. Once you know this, you know Stilgar and you can measure the length of his teeth."

"That's the Fremen way," she said. "Well, Duncan, will you do it, or won't you? She must be taken and it must be made to look like the work of House Corrino."

He remained silent, weighing her tone and arguments in his mentat way. This abduction plan spoke of a coldness and a cruelty whose dimensions, thus revealed, shocked him. Risk her own mother's life for the reasons thus far produced? Alia was lying. Perhaps the whisperings about Alia and Javid were true. This thought produced an icy hardness in his stomach.

"You're the only one I can trust for this," Alia said.

"I know that," he said.

She took this as acceptance, smiled at herself in the mirror.

"You know," Idaho said, "the mentat learns to look at every human as a series of relationships."

Alia did not respond. She sat, caught in a personal memory which drew a blank expression on her face. Idaho, glancing over his shoulder at her, saw the expression and shuddered. It was as though she communed with voices heard only by herself.

"Relationships," he whispered.

And he thought: *One must cast off old agonies as a snake casts off its skin—only to grow a new set and accept all of their limitations. It was the same with governments—even the Regency. Old governments can be traced like discarded molts. I must carry out this scheme, but not in the way Alia commands.*

Presently Alia shook her shoulders, said: "Leto should not be going out like that in these times. I will reprimand him."

"Not even with Stilgar?"

"Not even with him."

She arose from her mirror, crossed to where Idaho stood beside the window, put a hand on his arm.

He repressed a shiver, reduced this reaction to a mentat computation. Something in her revolted him.

Something in her.

He could not bring himself to look at her. He smelled the melange of her cosmetics, cleared his throat.

She said: "I will be busy today examining Farad'n's gifts."

"The clothing?"

"Yes. Nothing he does is what it seems. And we must remember that his Bashar, Tyekanik, is an adept of chaumurky, chaumas, and all the other subtleties of royal assassination."

"The price of power," he said, pulling away from her. "But we're still mobile and Farad'n is not."

She studied his chiseled profile. Sometimes the workings of his mind were difficult to fathom. Was he thinking only that freedom of action gave life to a military power? Well, life on Arrakis had been too secure for too long. Senses once whetted by omnipresent dangers could degenerate when not used.

"Yes," she said, "we still have the Fremen."

"Mobility," he repeated. "We cannot degenerate into infantry. That'd be foolish."

His tone annoyed her, and she said: "Farad'n will use any means to destroy us."

"Ahhh, that's it," he said. "That's a form of initiative, a mobility which we didn't have in the old days. We had a code, the code of House Atreides. We always paid our way and let the enemy be the pillagers. That restriction no longer holds, of course. We're equally mobile, House Atreides and House Corrino."

"We abduct my mother to save her from harm as much as for any other reason," Alia said. "We still live by the code!"

He looked down at her. She knew the dangers of inciting a mentat to compute. Didn't she realize what he had computed? Yet . . . he still loved her. He brushed a hand across his eyes. How youthful she looked. The Lady Jessica was correct: Alia gave the appearance of not having aged a day in their years together. She still possessed the soft features of her Bene Gesserit mother, but her eyes were Atreides—measuring, demanding, hawklike. And now something possessed of cruel calculation lurked behind those eyes.

Idaho had served House Atreides for too many years not to understand the family's strengths as well as their weaknesses. But this thing in Alia, this was new. The Atreides might play a devious game against enemies, but never against friends and allies, and not at all against Family. It was ground into the Atreides manner: support your own populace to the best of your ability; show them how much better they lived under the Atreides. Demonstrate your love for your friends by the candor of your behavior with them. What Alia asked now, though, was not Atreides. He felt this with all of his body's flesh and nerve structure. He was a unit, indivisible, feeling this alien attitude in Alia.

Abruptly his mentat sensorium clicked into full awareness and his mind leaped into the frozen trance where Time did not exist; only the computation existed. Alia would recognize what had happened to him, but that could not be helped. He gave himself up to the computation.

Computation: A *reflected* Lady Jessica lived out a pseudo-life in Alia's awareness. He saw this as he saw the reflected pre-ghola Duncan Idaho which remained a constant in his own awareness. Alia had this awareness by being one of the pre-born. He had it out of the Tleilaxu regeneration tanks. Yet Alia denied that reflection, risked her mother's life. Therefore Alia was not in contact with that pseudo-Jessica within. Therefore Alia was *completely* possessed by another pseudo-life to the exclusion of all others.

Possessed!

Alien!

Abomination!

Mentat fashion, he accepted this, turned to other facets of his problem. All of the Atreides were on this one planet. Would House Corrino risk attack from space? His mind flashed through the review of those conventions which had ended primitive forms of warfare:

One—All planets were vulnerable to attack from space; ergo: retaliation/revenge facilities were set up off-planet by every House Major. Farad'n would know that the Atreides had not omitted this elementary precaution.

Two—Force shields were a complete defense against projectiles and explosives of non-atomic type, the basic reason why hand-to-hand conflict had reentered human combat. But infantry had its limits. House Corrino might have brought their Sardaukar back to a pre-Arrakeen edge, but they still could be no match for the abandoned ferocity of Fremen.

Three—Planetary feudalism remained in constant danger from a large technical class, but the effects of the Butlerian Jihad continued as a damper on technological excesses. Ixians, Tleilaxu, and a few scattered outer planets were the only possible threat in this regard, and they were planet-vulnerable to the combined wrath of the rest of the Imperium. The Butlerian Jihad would not be undone. Mechanized warfare required a large technical class. The Atreides Imperium had channeled this force into other pursuits. No large technical class existed unwatched. And the Empire remained safely feudalist, naturally, since that was the best social form for spreading over widely dispersed wild frontiers—new planets.

Duncan felt his mentat awareness coruscate as it shot through memory data *of itself*, completely impervious to the passage of time. Arriving at the conviction that House Corrino would not risk an *illegal* atomic attack, he did this in flash-computation, the main decisional pathway, but he was perfectly aware of the elements which went into this conviction: The Imperium commanded as many nuclear and allied weapons as all the Great Houses combined. At least half the Great Houses would react without thinking if House Corrino broke the Convention. The Atreides off-planet retaliation system would be joined by overwhelming force, and no need to summon any of them. Fear would do the calling. Salusa Secundus and its allies would vanish in hot clouds. House Corrino would not risk such a holocaust. They were undoubtedly sincere in subscribing to the argument that nuclear weapons were a reserve held for one purpose: defense of humankind should a threatening "other intelligence" ever be encountered.

The computational thoughts had clean edges, sharp relief. There were no blurred between-places. Alia chose abduction and terror because she had become alien, non-Atreides. House Corrino was a threat, but not in the ways which Alia argued in Council. Alia wanted the Lady Jessica removed because that searing Bene Gesserit intelligence had seen what only now had become clear to him.

Idaho shook himself out of the mentat trance, saw Alia standing in front of him, a coldly measuring expression on her face.

"Wouldn't you rather the Lady Jessica were killed?" he asked.

The alien-flash of her joy lay exposed before his eyes for a brief instant before being covered by false outrage. "Duncan!"

Yes, this alien-Alia preferred matricide.

"You are afraid *of* your mother, not *for* her," he said.

She spoke without a change in her measuring stare. "Of course I am. She has reported about me to the Sisterhood."

"What do you mean?"

"Don't you know the greatest temptation for a Bene Gesserit?" She moved closer to him, seductive, looked upward at him through her lashes. "I thought only to keep myself strong and alert for the sake of the twins."

"You speak of temptation," he said, his voice mentat-flat.

"It's the thing which the Sisterhood hides most deeply, the thing they most fear. It's why they call me *Abomination*. They know their

CHILDREN OF DUNE 149

inhibitions won't hold me back. Temptation—they always speak with heavy emphasis: *Great Temptation.* You see, we who employ the Bene Gesserit teachings can influence such things as the internal adjustment of enzyme balance within our bodies. It can prolong youth—far longer than with melange. Do you see the consequences should many Bene Gesserits do this? It would be noticed. I'm sure you compute the accuracy of what I'm saying. Melange is what makes us the target for so many plots. We control a substance which prolongs life. What if it became known that Bene Gesserits controlled an even more potent secret? You see! Not one Reverend Mother would be safe. Abduction and torture of Bene Gesserits would become a most common activity."

"You've accomplished this enzyme balancing." It was a statement, not a question.

"I've defied the Sisterhood! My mother's reports to the Sisterhood will make the Bene Gesserits unswerving allies of House Corrino."

How very plausible, he thought.

He tested: "But surely your own mother would not turn against you!"

"She was Bene Gesserit long before she was my mother. Duncan, she permitted her own son, my brother, to undergo the test of the *gom jabbar*! She arranged it! And she knew he might not survive it! Bene Gesserits have always been short on faith and long on pragmatism. She'll act against me if she believes it's in the best interests of the Sisterhood."

He nodded. How convincing she was. It was a sad thought.

"We must hold the initiative," she said. "That's our sharpest weapon."

"There's the problem of Gurney Halleck," he said. "Do I have to kill my old friend?"

"Gurney's off on some spy errand in the desert," she said, knowing Idaho already was aware of this. "He's safely out of the way."

"Very odd," he said, "the Regent Governor of Caladan running errands here on Arrakis."

"Why not?" Alia demanded. "He's her lover—in his dreams if not in fact."

"Yes, of course." And he wondered that she did not hear the insincerity in his voice.

"When will you abduct her?" Alia asked.

"It's better that you don't know."

"Yes . . . yes, I see. Where'll you take her?"

"Where she cannot be found. Depend upon it; she won't be left here to threaten you."

The glee in Alia's eyes could not be mistaken. "But where will . . ."

"If you do not know, then you can answer before a Truthsayer, if necessary, that you do not know where she is."

"Ahhh, clever, Duncan."

Now she believes I will kill the Lady Jessica, he thought. And he said: "Goodbye, beloved."

She did not hear the finality in his voice, even kissed him lightly as he left.

And all the way down through the sietchlike maze of Temple corridors, Idaho brushed at his eyes. Tleilaxu eyes were not immune to tears.

You have loved Caladan
And lamented its lost host—
But pain discovers
New lovers cannot erase
Those forever ghost.

—REFRAIN FROM THE HABBANYA LAMENT

Stilgar quadrupled the sietch guard around the twins, but he knew it was useless. The lad was like his Atreides namesake, the grandfather Leto. Everyone who'd known the original Duke remarked on it. Leto had the measuring look about him, and caution, yes, but all of it had to be evaluated against that latent wildness, the susceptibility to dangerous decisions.

Ghanima was more like her mother. There was Chani's red hair, the set of Chani's eyes, and a calculating way about her when she adjusted to difficulties. She often said that she only did what she had to do, but where Leto led she would follow.

And Leto was going to lead them into danger.

Not once did Stilgar think of taking his problem to Alia. That ruled out Irulan, who ran to Alia with anything and everything. In coming to his decision, Stilgar realized he had accepted the possibility that Leto judged Alia correctly.

She uses people in a casual and callous way, he thought. *She even*

*uses Duncan that way. It isn't so much that she'd turn on me and kill me.
She'd discard me.*

Meanwhile the guard was strengthened and Stilgar stalked his sietch like a robed specter, prying everywhere. All the time, his mind
seethed with the doubts Leto had planted there. If one could not depend
upon tradition, then where was the rock upon which to anchor his life?

On the afternoon of the Convocation of Welcome for the Lady Jessica, Stilgar spied Ghanima standing with her grandmother at the entrance lip to the sietch's great assembly chamber. It was early and Alia
had not yet arrived, but people already were thronging into the chamber, casting surreptitious glances at the child and adult as they passed.

Stilgar paused in a shadowed alcove out of the crowd flow and
watched the pair of them, unable to hear their words above the murmuring throb of an assembling multitude. The people of many tribes
would be here today to welcome back their old Reverend Mother. But
he stared at Ghanima. Her eyes, the way they danced when she spoke!
The movement fascinated him. Those deep blue, steady, demanding,
measuring eyes. And that way of throwing her red-gold hair off her
shoulder with a twist of the head: that was Chani. It was a ghostly resurrection, an uncanny resemblance.

Slowly Stilgar drew closer and took up his station in another alcove.

He could not associate Ghanima's observing manner with any other
child of his experience—except her brother. Where was Leto? Stilgar
glanced back up the crowded passage. His guards would have spread an
alarm if anything were amiss. He shook his head. These twins assaulted
his sanity. They were a constant abrasion against his peace of mind. He
could almost hate them. Kin were not immune from one's hatred, but
blood (and its precious water) carried demands for one's countenance
which transcended most other concerns. These twins existed as his
greatest responsibility.

Dust-filtered brown light came from the cavernous assembly chamber beyond Ghanima and Jessica. It touched the child's shoulders and
the new white robe she wore, backlighting her hair as she turned to peer
into the passage at the people thronging past.

Why did Leto afflict me with these doubts? he wondered. There was no doubt that it had been done deliberately. *Perhaps Leto wanted me to have a small share of his own mental experience.* Stilgar *knew* why the twins were different, but had always found his reasoning processes unable to accept what he knew. He had never experienced the womb as prison to an awakened consciousness—a living awareness from the second month of gestation, so it was said.

Leto had once said that his memory was like "an internal holograph, expanding in size and in detail from that original shocked awakening, but never changing shape or outline."

For the first time, as he watched Ghanima and the Lady Jessica, Stilgar began to understand what it must be like to live in such a scrambled web of memories, unable to retreat or find a sealed room of the mind. Faced with such a condition, one had to integrate madness, to select and reject from a multitude of offerings in a system where answers changed as fast as the question.

There could be no fixed tradition. There could be no absolute answers to double-faced questions. What works? That which does not work. What does not work? That which works. He recognized this pattern. It was the old Fremen game of riddles. Question: "It brings death and life." Answer: "The Coriolis wind."

Why did Leto want me to understand this? Stilgar asked himself. From his cautious probings, Stilgar knew that the twins shared a common view of their difference: they thought of it as affliction. *The birth canal would be a draining place to such a one,* he thought. Ignorance reduces the shock of some experiences, but they would have no ignorance about birth. What would it be like to live a life where you knew all of the things that *could* go wrong? You would face a constant war with doubts. You would resent your difference from your fellows. It would be pleasant to inflict others with even a taste of that difference. "Why me?" would be your first unanswered question.

And what have I been asking myself? Stilgar thought. A wry smile touched his lips. *Why me?*

Seeing the twins in this new way, he understood the dangerous chances they took with their uncompleted bodies. Ghanima had put it to him succinctly once after he'd berated her for climbing the precipitous west face to the rim above Sietch Tabr.

"Why should I fear death? I've been there before—many times."

How can I presume to teach such children? Stilgar wondered. *How can anyone presume?*

ODDLY, JESSICA'S THOUGHTS WERE MOVING IN A SIMILAR VEIN AS she talked to her granddaughter. She'd been thinking how difficult it must be to carry mature minds in immature bodies. The body would have to learn what the mind already knew it could do—aligning responses and reflexes. The old Bene Gesserit *prana-bindu* regimen would be available to them, but even there the mind would run where the flesh could not. Gurney had a supremely difficult task carrying out her orders.

"Stilgar is watching us from an alcove back there," Ghanima said.

Jessica did not turn. But she found herself confounded by what she heard in Ghanima's voice. Ghanima loved the old Fremen as one would love a parent. Even while she spoke lightly of him and teased him, she loved him. The realization forced Jessica to see the old Naib in a new light, understanding in a gestalten revelation what the twins and Stilgar shared. This new Arrakis did not fit Stilgar well, Jessica realized. No more than this new universe fitted her grandchildren.

Unwanted and undemanded, a Bene Gesserit saying flowed through Jessica's mind: *"To suspect your own mortality is to know the beginning of terror; to learn irrefutably that you are mortal is to know the end of terror."*

Yes, death would not be a hard yoke to wear, but life was a slow fire to Stilgar and the twins. Each found an ill-fitting world and longed for other ways where variations might be known without threat. They were children of Abraham, learning more from a hawk stooping over the desert than from any book yet written.

Leto had confounded Jessica only that morning as they'd stood beside the qanat which flowed below the sietch. He'd said: "Water traps us, grandmother. We'd be better off living like dust because then the wind could carry us higher than the highest cliffs of the Shield Wall."

Although she was familiar with such devious maturity from the mouths of these children, Jessica had been caught by this utterance, but had managed: "Your father might've said that."

And Leto, throwing a handful of sand into the air to watch it fall: "Yes, he might've. But my father did not consider then how quickly water makes everything fall back to the ground from which it came."

Now, standing beside Ghanima in the sietch, Jessica felt the shock of those words anew. She turned, glanced back at the still-flowing throng, let her gaze wander across Stilgar's shadowy shape in the alcove. Stilgar was no tame Fremen, trained only to carry twigs to the nest. He was still a hawk. When he thought of the color red, he did not think of flowers but of blood.

"You're so quiet, suddenly," Ghanima said. "Is something wrong?"

Jessica shook her head. "It's something Leto said this morning, that's all."

"When you went out to the plantings? What'd he say?"

Jessica thought of the curious look of adult wisdom which had come over Leto's face out there in the morning. It was the same look which came over Ghanima's face right now. "He was recalling the time when Gurney came back from the smugglers to the Atreides banner," Jessica said.

"Then you were talking about Stilgar," Ghanima said.

Jessica did not question how this insight occurred. The twins appeared capable of reproducing each other's thought trains at will.

"Yes, we were," Jessica said. "Stilgar didn't like to hear Gurney calling . . . Paul his Duke, but Gurney's presence forced this upon all of the Fremen. Gurney kept saying 'My Duke.'"

"I see," Ghanima said. "And of course, Leto observed that *he* was not yet Stilgar's Duke."

"That's right."

"You know what he was doing to you, of course," Ghanima said.

"I'm not sure I do," Jessica admitted, and she found this admission particularly disturbing because it had not occurred to her that Leto was doing anything at all to her.

"He was trying to ignite your memories of our father," Ghanima said. "Leto's always hungry to know our father from the viewpoints of others who knew him."

"But . . . doesn't Leto have . . ."

"Oh, he can listen to the *inner life*. Certainly. But that's not the same. You spoke about him, of course. Our father, I mean. You spoke of him as your son."

"Yes." Jessica clipped it off. She did not like the feeling that these twins could turn her on and off at will, open her memories for observation, touch any emotion which attracted their interest. Ghanima might be doing that right now!

"Leto said something to disturb you," Ghanima said.

Jessica found herself shocked at the necessity to suppress anger. "Yes . . . he did."

"You don't like the fact that he knows our father as our mother knew him, and knows our mother as our father knew her," Ghanima said. "You don't like what that implies—what we may know about you."

"I'd never really thought about it that way before," Jessica said, finding her voice stiff.

"It's the knowledge of sensual things which usually disturbs," Ghanima said. "It's your conditioning. You find it extremely difficult to think of us as anything but children. But there's nothing our parents did together, in public or in private, that we would not know."

For a brief instant Jessica found herself returning to the reaction which had come over her out there beside the qanat, but now she focused that reaction upon Ghanima.

"He probably spoke of your Duke's 'rutting sensuality,'" Ghanima said. "Sometimes Leto needs a bridle on his mouth!"

Is there nothing these twins cannot profane? Jessica wondered, moving from shock to outrage to revulsion. How dared they speak of *her* Leto's sensuality? Of course a man and woman who loved each other would share the pleasure of their bodies! It was a private and beautiful thing, not to be paraded in casual conversation between a child and an adult.

Child and adult!

Abruptly Jessica realized that neither Leto nor Ghanima had done this casually.

As Jessica remained silent, Ghanima said: "We've shocked you. I apologize for both of us. Knowing Leto, I know he didn't consider apologizing. Sometimes when he's following a particular scent, he forgets how different we are . . . from you, for instance."

Jessica thought: *And that is why you both do this, of course. You are teaching me!* And she wondered then: *Who else are you teaching? Stilgar? Duncan?*

"Leto tries to see things as you see them," Ghanima said. "Memories are not enough. When you try the hardest, just then, you most often fail."

Jessica sighed.

Ghanima touched her grandmother's arm. "Your son left many things unsaid which yet must be said, even to you. Forgive us, but he loved you. Don't you know that?"

Jessica turned away to hide the tears glistening in her eyes.

"He knew your fears," Ghanima said. "Just as he knew Stilgar's fears. Dear Stil. Our father was his 'Doctor of Beasts' and Stil was no more than the green snail hidden in its shell." She hummed the tune from which she'd taken these words. The music hurled the lyrics against Jessica's awareness without compromise:

> *O Doctor of Beasts,*
> *To a green snail shell*
> *With its timid miracle*
> *Hidden, awaiting death,*
> *You come as a deity!*
> *Even snails know*
> *That gods obliterate,*

And cures bring pain,
That heaven is seen
Through a door of flame.
O Doctor of Beasts,
I am the man-snail
Who sees your single eye
Peering into my shell!
Why, Muad'Dib? Why?

Ghanima said: "Unfortunately, our father left many man-snails in our universe."

The assumption that humans exist within an essentially impermanent universe, taken as an operational precept, demands that the intellect become a totally aware balancing instrument. But the intellect cannot react thus without involving the entire organism. Such an organism may be recognized by its burning, driving behavior. And thus it is with a society treated as organism. But here we encounter an old inertia. Societies move to the goading of ancient, reactive impulses. They demand permanence. Any attempt to display the universe of impermanence arouses rejection patterns, fear, anger, and despair. Then how do we explain the acceptance of prescience? Simply: the giver of prescient visions, because he speaks of an absolute (permanent) realization, may be greeted with joy by humankind even while predicting the most dire events.

—THE BOOK OF LETO
AFTER HARQ AL-ADA

"It's like fighting in the dark," Alia said.

She paced the Council Chamber in angry strides, moving from the tall silvery draperies which softened the morning sun at the eastern windows to the divans grouped beneath decorated wall panels at the room's opposite end. Her sandals crossed spice-fiber rugs, parquet wood, tiles of giant garnet and, once more, rugs. At last she stood over Irulan and Idaho, who sat facing each other on divans of grey whale fur.

Idaho had resisted returning from Tabr, but she had sent peremptory orders. The abduction of Jessica was more important than ever now, but it had to wait. Idaho's mentat perceptions were required.

"These things are cut from the same pattern," Alia said. "They stink of a far-reaching plot."

"Perhaps not," Irulan ventured, but she glanced questioningly at Idaho.

Alia's face lapsed into an undisguised sneer. How could Irulan be that innocent? Unless . . . Alia bent a sharp and questioning stare onto the Princess. Irulan wore a simple black aba robe which matched the shadows in her spice-indigo eyes. Her blonde hair was tied in a tight coil at the nape of her neck, accenting a face thinned and toughened by years on Arrakis. She still retained the haughtiness she'd learned in the court of her father, Shaddam IV, and Alia often felt that this prideful attitude could mask the thoughts of a conspirator.

Idaho lounged in the black-and-green uniform of an Atreides House Guard, no insignia. It was an affectation which was secretly resented by many of Alia's actual guards, especially the amazons, who gloried in insignia of office. They did not like the plain presence of the ghola-swordmaster-mentat, the more so because he was the husband of their mistress.

"So the tribes want the Lady Jessica reinstated into the Regency Council," Idaho said. "How can that—"

"They make unanimous demand!" Alia said, pointing to an embossed sheet of spice-paper on the divan beside Irulan. "Farad'n is one thing, but this . . . this has the stink of other alignments!"

"What does Stilgar think?" Irulan asked.

"His signature's on that paper!" Alia said.

"But if he . . ."

"How could he deny the mother of his god?" Alia sneered.

Idaho looked up at her, thinking: *That's awfully close to the edge with Irulan!* Again he wondered why Alia had brought him back here when she knew that he was needed at Sietch Tabr if the abduction plot were to be carried off. Was it possible she'd heard about the message sent to him by The Preacher? This thought filled his breast with turmoil. How

could that mendicant mystic know the secret signal by which Paul Atreides had always summoned his swordmaster? Idaho longed to leave this
pointless meeting and return to the search for an answer to that question.

"There's no doubt that The Preacher has been off-planet," Alia said.
"The Guild wouldn't dare deceive us in such a thing. I will have him—"

"Careful!" Irulan said.

"Indeed, have a care," Idaho said. "Half the planet believe him to
be—" He shrugged. "—your brother." And Idaho hoped he had carried
this off with a properly casual attitude. How had the man known that
signal?

"But if he's a courier, or a spy of the—"

"He's made contact with no one from CHOAM or House Corrino,"
Irulan said. "We can be sure of—"

"We can be sure of nothing!" Alia did not try to hide her scorn. She
turned her back on Irulan, faced Idaho. He knew why he was here! Why
didn't he perform as expected? He was in Council because Irulan was
here. The history which had brought a Princess of House Corrino into
the Atreides fold could never be forgotten. Allegiance, once changed,
could change again. Duncan's mentat powers should be searching for
flaws, for subtle deviations in Irulan's behavior.

Idaho stirred, glanced at Irulan. There were times when he resented
the straight-line necessities imposed on mentat performance. He knew
what Alia was thinking. Irulan would know it as well. But this Princess-
wife to Paul Muad'Dib had overcome the decisions which had made her
less than the royal concubine, Chani. There could be no doubt of Irulan's devotion to the royal twins. She had renounced family and Bene
Gesserit in dedication to the Atreides.

"My mother is part of this plot!" Alia insisted. "For what other reason would the Sisterhood send her back here at a time such as this?"

"Hysteria isn't going to help us," Idaho said.

Alia whirled away from him, as he'd known she would. It helped
him that he did not have to look at that once-beloved face which was
now so twisted by alien possession.

"Well," Irulan said, "the Guild can't be completely trusted for—"

"The Guild!" Alia sneered.

"We can't rule out the enmity of the Guild or the Bene Gesserit," Idaho said. "But we must assign them special categories as essentially passive combatants. The Guild will live up to its basic rule: Never Govern. They're a parasitic growth, and they know it. They won't do anything to kill the organism which keeps them alive."

"Their idea of which organism keeps them alive may be different from ours," Irulan drawled. It was the closest she ever came to a sneer, that lazy tone of voice which said: "You missed a point, mentat."

Alia appeared puzzled. She had not expected Irulan to take this tack. It was not the kind of view which a conspirator would want examined.

"No doubt," Idaho said. "But the Guild won't come out overtly against House Atreides. The Sisterhood, on the other hand, might risk a certain kind of political break which—"

"If they do, it'll be through a front: someone or some group they can disavow," Irulan said. "The Bene Gesserit haven't existed all of these centuries without knowing the value of self-effacement. They prefer being behind the throne, not on it."

Self-effacement? Alia wondered. Was that Irulan's choice?

"Precisely the point I make about the Guild," Idaho said. He found the necessities of argument and explanation helpful. They kept his mind from other problems.

Alia strode back toward the sunlit windows. She knew Idaho's blind spot; every mentat had it. They had to make pronouncements. This brought about a tendency to depend upon absolutes, to see finite limits. They knew this about themselves. It was part of their training. Yet they continued to act beyond self-limiting parameters. *I should've left him at Sietch Tabr,* Alia thought. *It would've been better to just turn Irulan over to Javid for questioning.*

Within her skull, Alia heard a rumbling voice: "Exactly!"

Shut up! Shut up! Shut up! she thought. A dangerous mistake beckoned her in these moments and she could not recognize its outlines. All she could sense was the danger. Idaho had to help her out of this predicament. He was a mentat. Mentats were necessary. The human-computer replaced the mechanical devices destroyed by the Butlerian Jihad. *Thou shalt not make a machine in the likeness of a human mind!* But Alia longed now for a compliant machine. They could not have suffered from Idaho's limitations. You could never distrust a machine.

Alia heard Irulan's drawling voice.

"A feint within a feint within a feint within a feint," Irulan said. "We all know the accepted pattern of attack upon power. I don't blame Alia for her suspicions. Of course she suspects everyone—even us. Ignore that for the moment, though. What remains as the prime arena of motives, the most fertile source of danger to the Regency?"

"CHOAM," Idaho said, his voice mentat-flat.

Alia allowed herself a grim smile. The Combine Honnete Ober Advancer Mercantiles! But House Atreides dominated CHOAM with fifty-one percent of its shares. The Priesthood of Muad'Dib held another five percent, pragmatic acceptance by the Great Houses that Dune controlled the priceless melange. Not without reason was the spice often called "the secret coinage." Without melange, the Spacing Guild's heighliners could not move. Melange precipitated the "navigation trance" by which a translight pathway could be "seen" before it was traveled. Without melange and its amplification of the human immunogenic system, life expectancy for the very rich degenerated by a factor of at least four. Even the vast middle class of the Imperium ate diluted melange in small sprinklings with at least one meal a day.

But Alia had heard the mentat sincerity in Idaho's voice, a sound which she'd been awaiting with terrible expectancy.

CHOAM. The Combine Honnete was much more than House Atreides, much more than Dune, much more than the Priesthood or melange. It was inkvines, whale fur, shigawire, Ixian artifacts and entertainers, trade in people and places, the Hajj, those products which came from the borderline legality of Tleilaxu technology; it was addictive drugs and medical techniques; it was transportation (the Guild) and all of the supercomplex commerce of an empire which encompassed thousands of known planets plus some which fed secretly at the fringes, permitted there for services rendered. When Idaho said CHOAM, he spoke of a constant ferment, intrigue within intrigue, a play of powers where the shift of one duodecimal point in interest payments could change the ownership of an entire planet.

Alia returned to stand over the two seated on the divans. "Something specific about CHOAM bothers you?" she asked.

"There's always the heavy speculative stockpiling of spice by certain Houses," Irulan said.

Alia slapped her hands against her own thighs, then gestured at the embossed spice-paper beside Irulan. "That *demand* doesn't intrigue you, coming as it does—"

"All right!" Idaho barked. "Out with it. What're you withholding? You know better than to deny the data and still expect me to function as—"

"There has been a recent very significant increase in trade for people with four specific specialties," Alia said. And she wondered if this would be truly new information for this pair.

"Which specialties?" Irulan asked.

"Swordmasters, twisted mentats from Tleilax, conditioned medics from the Suk school, and fincap accountants, most especially the latter. Why would questionable bookkeeping be in demand right now?" She directed the question at Idaho.

Function as a mentat, he thought. Well, that was better than dwelling on what Alia had become. He focused on her words, replaying them in his mind mentat fashion. *Swordmasters?* That had been his own calling once. Swordmasters were, of course, more than personal fighters. They could repair force shields, plan military campaigns, design military support facilities, improvise weapons. *Twisted mentats?* The Tleilaxu persisted in this hoax, obviously. As a mentat himself, Idaho knew the fragile insecurity of Tleilaxu *twisting.* Great Houses which bought such mentats hoped to control them absolutely. Impossible! Even Piter de Vries, who'd served the Harkonnens in their assault on House Atreides, had maintained his own essential dignity, accepting death rather than surrender his inner core of selfdom at the end. *Suk doctors?* Their conditioning supposedly guaranteed them against disloyalty to their owner-patients. Suk doctors came very expensive. Increased purchase of Suks would involve substantial exchanges of funds.

Idaho weighed these facts against an increase in fincap accountants.

"Prime computation," he said, indicating a heavily weighted assurance that he spoke of inductive fact. "There's been a recent increase in wealth among Houses Minor. Some have to be moving quietly toward Great House status. Such wealth could only come from some specific shifts in political alignments."

"We come at last to the Landsraad," Alia said, voicing her own belief.

"The next Landsraad session is almost two standard years away," Irulan reminded her.

"But political bargaining never ceases," Alia said. "And I'll warrant some among those tribal signatories—" She gestured at the paper beside Irulan. "—are among the Houses Minor who've shifted their alignment."

"Perhaps," Irulan said.

"The Landsraad," Alia said. "What better front for the Bene Gesserits? And what better agent for the Sisterhood than my own mother?" Alia planted herself directly in front of Idaho. "Well, Duncan?"

Why not function as a mentat? Idaho asked himself. He saw the tenor of Alia's suspicions now. After all, Duncan Idaho had been personal house guard to the Lady Jessica for many years.

"Duncan?" Alia pressed.

"You should inquire closely after any advisory legislation which may be under preparation for the next session of the Landsraad," Idaho said. "They might take the legal position that a Regency can't veto certain kinds of legislation—specifically, adjustments of taxation and the policing of cartels. There are others, but . . ."

"Not a very good pragmatic bet on their part if they take that position," Irulan said.

"I agree," Alia said. "The Sardaukar have no teeth and we still have our Fremen legions."

"Careful, Alia," Idaho said. "Our enemies would like nothing better than to make us appear monstrous. No matter how many legions you command, power ultimately rides on popular sufferance in an empire as scattered as this one."

"Popular sufferance?" Irulan asked.

"You mean Great House sufferance," Alia said.

"And how many Great Houses will we face under this new alliance?" Idaho asked. "Money is collecting in strange places!"

"The fringes?" Irulan asked.

Idaho shrugged. It was an unanswerable question. All of them suspected that one day the Tleilaxu or technological tinkerers on the Imperial fringes would nullify the Holtzmann Effect. On that day, shields would be useless. The whole precarious balance which maintained planetary feudatories would collapse.

Alia refused to consider that possibility. "We'll ride with what we have," she said. "And what we have is a certain knowledge throughout the CHOAM directorate that *we* can destroy the spice if they force us to it. They won't risk that."

"Back to CHOAM again," Irulan said.

"Unless someone has managed to duplicate the sandtrout-sandworm cycle on another planet," Idaho said. He looked speculatively at Irulan, excited by this question. "Salusa Secundus?"

"My contacts there remain reliable," Irulan said. "Not Salusa."

"Then my answer stands," Alia said, staring at Idaho. "We ride with what we have."

My *move*, Idaho thought. He said: "Why'd you drag me away from *important work*? You could've worked this out yourself."

"Don't take that tone with me!" Alia snapped.

Idaho's eyes went wide. For an instant, he'd seen the alien on Alia's face, and it was a disconcerting sight. He turned his attention to Irulan, but she had not seen—or gave that appearance.

"I don't need an elementary education," Alia said, her voice still edged with alien anger.

Idaho managed a rueful smile, but his breast ached.

"We never get far from wealth and all of its masks when we deal with power," Irulan drawled. "Paul was a social mutation and, as such, we have to remember that he shifted the old balance of wealth."

"Such mutations are not irreversible," Alia said, turning away from them as though she'd not exposed her terrible difference. "Wherever there's wealth in this empire, they know this."

"They also know," Irulan said, "that there are three people who could perpetuate that mutation: the twins and . . ." She pointed at Alia.

Are they insane, this pair? Idaho wondered.

"They will try to assassinate me!" Alia rasped.

And Idaho sat in shocked silence, his mentat awareness whirling. Assassinate Alia? Why? They could discredit her too easily. They could cut her out of the Fremen pack and hunt her down at will. But the twins, now . . . He knew he was not in the proper mentat calm for such an assessment, but he had to try. He had to be as precise as possible. At the same time, he knew that precise thinking contained undigested absolutes. Nature was not precise. The universe was not precise when reduced to his scale; it was vague and fuzzy, full of unexpected movements and changes. Humankind as a whole had to be entered into this computation as a natural phenomenon. And the whole process of precise analysis represented a chopping off, a remove from the ongoing current of the universe. He had to get at that current, see it in motion.

"We were right to focus on CHOAM and the Landsraad," Irulan drawled. "And Duncan's suggestion offers a first line of inquiry for—"

"Money as a translation of energy can't be separated from the energy it expresses," Alia said. "We all know this. But we have to answer three specific questions: When? Using what weapons? Where?"

The twins . . . the twins, Idaho thought. *It's the twins who're in danger, not Alia.*

"You're not interested in who or how?" Irulan asked.

"If House Corrino or CHOAM or any other group employs human instruments on this planet," Alia said, "we stand a better than sixty percent chance of finding them before they act. Knowing when they'll act and where gives us a bigger leverage on those odds. How? That's just asking *what weapons?*"

Why can't they see it as I see it? Idaho wondered.

"All right," Irulan said. "When?"

"When attention is focused on someone else," Alia said.

"Attention was focused on your mother at the Convocation," Irulan said. "There was no attempt."

"Wrong place," Alia said.

What is she doing? Idaho wondered.

"Where, then?" Irulan asked.

"Right here in the Keep," Alia said. "It's the place where I'd feel most secure and least on my guard."

"What weapons?" Irulan asked.

"Conventional—something a Fremen might have on his person: poisoned crysknife, maula pistol, a—"

"They've not tried a hunter-seeker in a long while," Irulan said.

"Wouldn't work in a crowd," Alia said. "There'll have to be a crowd."

"Biological weapon?" Irulan asked.

"An infectious agent?" Alia asked, not masking her incredulity. How could Irulan think an infectious agent would succeed against the immunological barriers which protected an Atreides?

"I was thinking more in the line of some animal," Irulan said. "A small pet, say, trained to bite a specific victim, inflicting a poison with its bite."

"The House ferrets will prevent that," Alia said.

"One of *them*, then?" Irulan asked.

"Couldn't be done. The House ferrets would reject an outsider, kill it. You know that."

"I was just exploring possibilities in the hope that—"

"I'll alert my guards," Alia said.

As Alia said *guards*, Idaho put a hand over his Tleilaxu eyes, trying to prevent the demanding involvement which swept over him. It was Rhajia, the movement of Infinity as expressed by Life, the latent cup of total immersion in mentat awareness which lay in wait for every mentat. It threw his awareness onto the universe like a net, falling, defining the shapes within it. He saw the twins crouching in darkness while giant claws raked the air about them.

"No," he whispered.

"What?" Alia looked at him as though surprised to find him still there.

He took his hand from his eyes.

"The garments that House Corrino sent?" he asked. "Have they been sent on to the twins?"

"Of course," Irulan said. "They're perfectly safe."

"No one's going to try for the twins at Sietch Tabr," Alia said. "Not with all of those Stilgar-trained guards around."

Idaho stared at her. He had no particular datum to reinforce an argument based on mentat computation, but he knew. *He knew.* This thing he'd experienced came very close to the visionary power which Paul had known. Neither Irulan nor Alia would believe it, coming from him.

"I'd like to alert the port authorities against allowing the importation of any outside animals," he said.

"You're not taking Irulan's suggestion seriously," Alia protested.

"Why take any chances?" he asked.

"Tell that to the smugglers," Alia said. "I'll put my dependence on the House ferrets."

Idaho shook his head. What could House ferrets do against claws the size of those he envisioned? But Alia was right. Bribes in the right places, one acquiescent Guild navigator, and anyplace in the Empty Quarter became a landing port. The Guild would resist a front position in any attack on House Atreides, but if the price were high enough . . . Well, the Guild could only be thought of as something like a geological barrier which made attacks difficult, but not impossible. They could always protest that they were just "a transportation agency." How could they know to what use a particular cargo would be put?

Alia broke the silence with a purely Fremen gesture, a raised fist with thumb horizontal. She accompanied the gesture with a traditional expletive which meant, "I give Typhoon Conflict." She obviously saw herself as the only logical target for assassins, and the gesture protested a universe full of undigested threats. She was saying she would hurl the death wind at anyone who attacked her.

Idaho felt the hopelessness of any protest. He saw that she no longer suspected him. He was going back to Tabr and she expected a perfectly executed abduction of the Lady Jessica. He lifted himself from the divan in an adrenaline surge of anger, thinking: *If only Alia were the target! If only assassins could get to her!* For an instant, he rested his hand on his own knife, but it was not in him to do this. Far better, though, that she die a martyr than live to be discredited and hounded into a sandy grave.

"Yes," Alia said, misinterpreting his expression as concern for her. "You'd best hurry back to Tabr." And she thought: *How foolish of me to suspect Duncan! He's mine, not Jessica's!* It had been the demand from the tribes that'd upset her, Alia thought. She waved an airy goodbye to Idaho as he left.

Idaho left the Council Chamber feeling hopeless. Not only was Alia blind with her alien possession, but she became more insane with each crisis. She'd already passed her danger point and was doomed. But what could be done for the twins? Whom could he convince? Stilgar? And what could Stilgar do that he wasn't already doing?

The Lady Jessica, then?

Yes, he'd explore that possibility—but she, too, might be far gone in plotting with her Sisterhood. He carried few illusions about that Atreides concubine. She might do anything at the command of the Bene Gesserits—even turn against her own grandchildren.

Good government never depends upon laws, but upon the personal qualities of those who govern. The machinery of government is always subordinate to the will of those who administer that machinery. The most important element of government, therefore, is the method of choosing leaders.

—LAW AND GOVERNANCE
THE SPACING GUILD MANUAL

Why does Alia wish me to share the morning audience? Jessica wondered. *They've not voted me back into the Council.*

Jessica stood in the anteroom to the Keep's Great Hall. The anteroom itself would have been a great hall anywhere other than Arrakis. Following the Atreides lead, buildings in Arrakeen had become ever more gigantic as wealth and power concentrated, and this room epitomized her misgivings. She did not like this anteroom with its tiled floor depicting her son's victory over Shaddam IV.

She caught a reflection of her own face in the polished plasteel door which led into the Great Hall. Returning to Dune forced such comparisons upon her, and Jessica noted only the signs of aging in her own features: the oval face had developed tiny lines and the eyes were more brittle in their indigo reflection. She could remember when there had been white around the blue of her eyes. Only the careful ministrations of a professional dresser maintained the polished bronze of her hair. Her nose remained small, mouth generous, and her body was still slender, but even the Bene Gesserit–trained muscles had a tendency toward slow-

ing with the passage of time. Some might not note this and say: "You
haven't changed a bit!" But the Sisterhood's training was a two-edged
sword; small changes seldom escaped the notice of people thus trained.

And the lack of small changes in Alia had not escaped Jessica's notice.

Javid, the master of Alia's appointments, stood at the great door,
being very official this morning. He was a robed genie with a cynical
smile on his round face. Javid struck Jessica as a paradox: a well-fed
Fremen. Noting her attention upon him, Javid smiled knowingly,
shrugged. His attendance in Jessica's entourage had been short, as he'd
known it would be. He hated Atreides, but he was Alia's man in more
ways than one, if the rumors were to be believed.

Jessica saw the shrug, thought: *This is the age of the shrug. He knows
I've heard all the stories about him and he doesn't care. Our civilization
could well die of indifference within it before succumbing to external
attack.*

The guards Gurney had assigned her before leaving for the smugglers and the desert hadn't liked her coming here without their attendance. But Jessica felt oddly safe. Let someone make a martyr of her in
this place; Alia wouldn't survive it. Alia would know that.

When Jessica failed to respond to his shrug and smile, Javid
coughed, a belching disturbance of his larynx which could only have
been achieved with practice. It was like a secret language. It said: "We
understand the nonsense of all this pomp, My Lady. Isn't it wonderful
what humans can be made to believe!"

Wonderful! Jessica agreed, but her face gave no indication of the
thought.

The anteroom was quite full now, all of the morning's permitted
supplicants having received their right of entrance from Javid's people.
The outer doors had been closed. Supplicants and attendants kept a
polite distance from Jessica, but observed that she wore the formal
black aba of a Fremen Reverend Mother. This would raise many questions. No mark of Muad'Dib's priesthood could be seen on her person.
Conversations hummed as the people divided their attention between

Jessica and the small side door through which Alia would come to lead them into the Great Hall. It was obvious to Jessica that the old pattern which defined where the Regency's powers lay had been shaken.

I did that just by coming here, she thought. *But I came because Alia invited me.*

Reading the signs of disturbance, Jessica realized Alia was deliberately prolonging this moment, allowing the subtle currents to run their course here. Alia would be watching from a spy hole, of course. Few subtleties of Alia's behavior escaped Jessica, and she felt with each passing minute how right she'd been to accept the mission which the Sisterhood had pressed upon her.

"Matters cannot be allowed to continue in this way," the leader of the Bene Gesserit delegation had argued. "Surely the signs of decay have not escaped you—you of all people! We know why you left us, but we know also how you were trained. Nothing was stinted in your education. You are an adept of the Panoplia Prophetica and you must know when the souring of a powerful religion threatens us all."

Jessica had pursed her lips in thought while staring out a window at the soft signs of spring at Castle Caladan. She did not like to direct her thinking in such a logical fashion. One of the first lessons of the Sisterhood had been to reserve an attitude of questioning distrust for anything which came in the guise of logic. But the members of the delegation had known that, too.

How moist the air had been that morning, Jessica thought, looking around Alia's anteroom. How fresh and moist. Here there was a sweaty dampness to the air which evoked a sense of uneasiness in Jessica, and she thought: *I've reverted to Fremen ways.* The air was too moist in this sietch-above-ground. What was wrong with the Master of the Stills? Paul would never have permitted such laxness.

She noted that Javid, his shiny face alert and composed, appeared not to have noticed the fault of dampness in the anteroom's air. Bad training for one born on Arrakis.

The members of the Bene Gesserit delegation had wanted to know if she required proofs of their allegations. She'd given them an angry answer out of their own manuals: "All proofs inevitably lead to propositions which have no proof! All things are known because we want to believe in them."

"But we have submitted these questions to mentats," the delegation's leader had protested.

Jessica had stared at the woman, astonished. "I marvel that you have reached your present station and not yet learned the limits of mentats," Jessica had said.

At which the delegation had relaxed. Apparently it had all been a test, and she had passed. They'd feared, of course, that she had lost all touch with those balancing abilities which were at the core of Bene Gesserit training.

Now Jessica became softly alert as Javid left his door station and approached her. He bowed. "My Lady. It occurred to me that you might not've heard the latest exploit of The Preacher."

"I get daily reports on everything which occurs here," Jessica said. *Let him take that back to Alia!*

Javid smiled. "Then you know he rails against your family. Only last night, he preached in the south suburb and no one dared touch him. You know why, of course."

"Because they think he's my son come back to them," Jessica said, her voice bored.

"This question has not yet been put to the mentat Idaho," Javid said. "Perhaps that should be done and the thing settled."

Jessica thought: Here's one who truly doesn't know a mentat's limits, although he dares put horns on one—in his dreams if not in fact.

"Mentats share the fallibilities of those who use them," she said. "The human mind, as is the case with the mind of any animal, is a resonator. It responds to resonances in the environment. The mentat has learned to extend his awareness across many parallel loops of causality and to proceed along those loops for long chains of consequences." *Let him chew on that!*

"This Preacher doesn't disturb you, then?" Javid asked, his voice abruptly formal and portentous.

"I find him a healthy sign," she said. "I don't want him bothered."

Javid clearly had not expected that blunt a response. He tried to smile, failed. Then: "The ruling Council of the church which deifies thy son will, of course, bow to your wishes if you insist. But certainly some explanation—"

"Perhaps you'd rather I explained how *I* fit into your schemes," she said.

Javid stared at her narrowly. "Madame, I see no logical reason why thou refusest to denounce this Preacher. He cannot be thy son. I make a reasonable request: denounce him."

This is a set piece, Jessica thought. *Alia put him up to it.*

She said: "No."

"But he defiles the name of thy son! He preaches abominable things, cries out against thy holy daughter. He incites the populace against us. When asked, he said that even thou possessest the nature of evil and that thy—"

"Enough of this nonsense!" Jessica said. "Tell Alia that I refuse. I've heard nothing but tales of this Preacher since returning. He bores me."

"Does it bore thee, Madame, to learn that in his latest defilement he has said that thou wilt not turn against him? And here, clearly, thou—"

"Evil as I am, I still won't denounce him," she said.

"It is no joking matter, Madame!"

Jessica waved him away angrily. "Begone!" She spoke with sufficient carrying power that others heard, forcing him to obey.

His eyes glared with rage, but he managed a stiff bow and returned to his position at the door.

This argument fitted neatly into the observations Jessica already had made. When he spoke of Alia, Javid's voice carried the husky undertones of a lover; no mistaking it. The rumors no doubt were true. Alia had allowed her life to degenerate in a terrible way. Observing this, Jessica began to harbor the suspicion that Alia was a willing participant in Abomination. Was it a perverse will to self-destruction? Because surely Alia was working to destroy herself and the power base which fed on her brother's teachings.

Faint stirrings of unease began to grow apparent in the anteroom. The aficionados of this place would know when Alia delayed too long, and by now they'd all heard about Jessica's peremptory dismissal of Alia's favorite.

Jessica sighed. She felt that her body had walked into this place with her soul creeping behind. Movements among the courtiers were so transparent! The seeking out of important people was a dance like the wind through a field of cereal stalks. The cultivated inhabitants of this place furrowed their brows and gave pragmatic rating numbers to the importance of each of their fellows. Obviously her rebuff of Javid had hurt him; few spoke to him now. But the others! Her trained eye could read the rating numbers in the satellites attending the powerful.

They do not attend me because I am dangerous, she thought. *I have the stink of someone Alia fears.*

Jessica glanced around the room, seeing eyes turn away. They were such seriously futile people that she found herself wanting to cry out against their ready-made justifications for pointless lives. Oh, if only The Preacher could see this room as it looked now!

A fragment of a nearby conversation caught her attention. A tall, slender Priest was addressing his coterie, no doubt suppliants here under his auspices. "Often I must speak otherwise than I think," he said. "This is called diplomacy."

The resultant laughter was too loud, too quickly silenced. People in the group saw that Jessica had overheard.

My Duke would have transported such a one to the farthest available hellhole! Jessica thought. *I've returned none too soon.*

She knew now that she'd lived on faraway Caladan in an insulated capsule which had allowed only the most blatant of Alia's excesses to intrude. *I contributed to my own dream-existence,* she thought. Caladan had been something like that insulation provided by a really first-class frigate riding securely in the hold of a Guild heighliner. Only the most violent maneuvers could be felt, and those as mere softened movements.

How seductive it is to live in peace, she thought.

The more she saw of Alia's court, the more sympathy Jessica felt for the words reported as coming from this blind Preacher. Yes, Paul might have said such words on seeing what had become of his realm. And Jessica wondered what Gurney had found out among the smugglers.

Her first reaction to Arrakeen had been the right one, Jessica realized. On that first ride into the city with Javid, her attention had been caught by armored screens around dwellings, the heavily guarded pathways and alleys, the patient watchers at every turn, the tall walls and indications of deep underground places revealed by thick foundations. Arrakeen had become an ungenerous place, a contained place, unreasonable and self-righteous in its harsh outlines.

Abruptly the anteroom's small side door opened. A vanguard of priestess amazons spewed into the room with Alia shielded behind them, haughty and moving with a confined awareness of real and terrible power. Alia's face was composed; no emotion betrayed itself as her gaze caught and held her mother's. But both knew the battle had been joined.

At Javid's command, the giant doors into the Great Hall were opened, moving with a silent and inevitable sense of hidden energies.

Alia came to her mother's side as the guards enfolded them.

"Shall we go in now, mother?" Alia asked.

"It's high time," Jessica said. And she thought, seeing the sense of gloating in Alia's eyes: *She thinks she can destroy me and remain unscathed! She's mad!*

And Jessica wondered if that might not have been what Idaho had wanted. He'd sent a message, but she'd been unable to respond. Such an enigmatic message: *"Danger. Must see you."* It had been written in a variant of the old Chakobsa where the particular word chosen to denote danger signified a plot.

I'll see him immediately when I return to Tabr, she thought.

> This is the fallacy of power: ultimately it is effective only in an absolute, a limited universe. But the basic lesson of our relativistic universe is that things change. Any power must always meet a greater power. Paul Muad'Dib taught this lesson to the Sardaukar on the Plains of Arrakeen. His descendants have yet to learn the lesson for themselves.
>
> —THE PREACHER AT ARRAKEEN

The first supplicant for the morning audience was a Kadeshian troubadour, a pilgrim of the Hajj whose purse had been emptied by Arrakeen mercenaries. He stood on the water-green stone of the chamber floor with no air of begging about him.

Jessica admired his boldness from where she sat with Alia atop the seven-step platform. Identical thrones had been placed here for mother and daughter, and Jessica made particular note of the fact that Alia sat on the right, the *masculine* position.

As for the Kadeshian troubadour, it was obvious that Javid's people had passed him for just this quality he now displayed, his boldness. The troubadour was expected to provide some entertainment for the courtiers of the Great Hall; it was the payment he'd make in lieu of the money he no longer possessed.

From the report of the Priest-Advocate who now pled the troubadour's case, the Kadeshian had retained only the clothing on his back and the baliset slung over one shoulder on a leather cord.

"He says he was fed a dark drink," the Advocate said, barely hiding the smile which sought to twist his lips. "If it please your Holiness, the drink left him helpless but awake while his purse was cut."

Jessica studied the troubadour while the Advocate droned on and on with a false subservience, his voice full of mucky morals. The Kadeshian was tall, easily two meters. He had a roving eye which showed intelligent alertness and humor. His golden hair was worn to the shoulders in the style of his planet, and there was a sense of virile strength in the broad chest and neatly tapering body which a grey Hajj robe could not conceal. His name was given as Tagir Mohandis and he was descended from merchant engineers, proud of his ancestry and himself.

Alia finally cut off the pleading with a hand wave, spoke without turning: "The Lady Jessica will render first judgment in honor of her return to us."

"Thank you, daughter," Jessica said, stating the order of ascendancy to all who heard. *Daughter!* So this Tagir Mohandis was part of their plan. Or was he an innocent dupe? This judgment was designed to open attack on herself, Jessica realized. It was obvious in Alia's attitude.

"Do you play that instrument well?" Jessica asked, indicating the nine-string baliset on the troubadour's shoulder.

"As well as the Great Gurney Halleck himself!" Tagir Mohandis spoke loudly for all in the hall to hear, and his words evoked an interested stir among the courtiers.

"You seek the gift of transport money," Jessica said. "Where would that money take you?"

"To Salusa Secundus and Farad'n's court," Mohandis said. "I've heard he seeks troubadours and minstrels, that he supports the arts and builds a great renaissance of cultivated life around him."

Jessica refrained from glancing at Alia. They'd known, of course, what Mohandis would ask. She found herself enjoying this byplay. Did they think her unable to meet this thrust?

"Will you play for your passage?" Jessica asked. "My terms are Fremen terms. If I enjoy your music, I may keep you here to smooth away my cares; if your music offends me, I may send you to toil in the desert for your passage money. If I deem your playing just right for Farad'n, who is said to be an enemy of the Atreides, then I will send you to him with my blessing. Will you play on these terms, Tagir Mohandis?"

He threw his head back in a great roaring laugh. His blond hair danced as he unslung the baliset and tuned it deftly to indicate acceptance of her challenge.

The crowd in the chamber started to press closer, but were held back by courtiers and guards.

Presently Mohandis strummed a note, holding the bass hum of the side strings with a fine attention to their compelling vibration. Then, lifting his voice in a mellow tenor, he sang, obviously improvising, but his touch so deft that Jessica was enthralled before she focused on his lyrics:

> You say you long for Caladan seas,
> Where once you ruled, Atreides,
> Without surcease—
> But exiles dwell in stranger-lands!
>
> You say 'twere bitter, men so rude,
> To sell your dreams of Shai-Hulud,
> For tasteless food—
> And exiles, dwell in stranger-lands.
>
> You make Arrakis grow infirm,
> Silence the passage of the worm
> And end your term—
> As exiles, dwell in stranger-lands.
>
> Alia! They name you Coan-Teen,
> That spirit who is never seen
> Until—

"*Enough!*" Alia screamed. She pushed herself half out of her throne. "I'll have you—"

"Alia!" Jessica spoke just loud enough, voice pitched just right to avoid confrontation while gaining full attention. It was a masterful use of Voice and all who heard it recognized the trained powers in this demonstration. Alia sank back into her seat and Jessica noted that she showed not the slightest discomfiture.

This, too, was anticipated, Jessica thought. *How very interesting.*

"The judgment on this first one is mine," Jessica reminded her.

"Very well." Alia's words were barely audible.

"I find this one a fitting gift for Farad'n," Jessica said. "He has a tongue which cuts like a crysknife. Such bloodletting as that tongue can administer would be healthy for our own court, but I'd rather he ministered to House Corrino."

A light rippling of laughter spread through the hall.

Alia permitted herself a snorting exhalation. "Do you know what he called me?"

"He didn't call you anything, daughter. He but reported that which he or anyone else could hear in the streets. There they call you Coan-Teen. . . ."

"The female death-spirit who walks without feet," Alia snarled.

"If you put away those who report accurately, you'll keep only those who know what you want to hear," Jessica said, her voice sweet. "I can think of nothing more poisonous than to rot in the stink of your own reflections."

Audible gasps came from those immediately below the thrones.

Jessica focused on Mohandis, who remained silent, standing completely uncowed. He awaited whatever judgment was passed upon him as though it did not matter. Mohandis was exactly the kind of man her Duke would have chosen to have by his side in troubled times: one who acted with confidence of his own judgment, but accepted whatever befell, even death, without berating his fate. Then why had he chosen this course?

"Why did you sing those particular words?" Jessica asked him.

He lifted his head to speak clearly: "I'd heard that the Atreides were honorable and open-minded. I'd a thought to test it and perhaps to stay here in your service, thereby having the time to seek out those who robbed me and deal with them in my own fashion."

"He dares test *us*!" Alia muttered.

"Why not?" Jessica asked.

She smiled down at the troubadour to signal goodwill. He had come into this hall only because it offered him opportunity for another adventure, another passage through his universe. Jessica found herself tempted to bind him to her own entourage, but Alia's reaction boded evil for brave Mohandis. There were also those signs which said this was the course expected of the Lady Jessica—take a brave and handsome troubadour into her service as she'd taken brave Gurney Halleck. Best Mohandis were sent on his way, though it rankled to lose such a fine specimen to Farad'n.

"He shall go to Farad'n," Jessica said. "See that he gets his passage money. Let his tongue draw the blood of House Corrino and see how he survives it."

Alia glowered at the floor, then produced a belated smile. "The wisdom of the Lady Jessica prevails," she said, waving Mohandis away.

That did not go the way she wanted, Jessica thought, but there were indicators in Alia's manner that a more potent test remained.

Another supplicant was being brought forward.

Jessica, noting her daughter's reaction, felt the gnawing of doubts. The lesson learned from the twins was needed here. Let Alia be *Abomination*, still she was one of the pre-born. She could know her mother as she knew herself. It did not compute that Alia would misjudge her mother's reactions in the matter of the troubadour. *Why did Alia stage that confrontation? To distract me?*

There was no more time to reflect. The second supplicant had taken his place below the twin thrones, his Advocate at his side.

The supplicant was a Fremen this time, an old man with the sand marks of the desert-born on his face. He was not tall, but had a wiry body and the long *dishdasha* usually worn over a stillsuit gave him a stately appearance. The robe was in keeping with his narrow face and beaked nose, the glaring eyes of blue-on-blue. He wore no stillsuit and seemed uncomfortable without it. The gigantic space of the Audience Hall must seem to him like the dangerous open air which robbed his flesh of its priceless moisture. Under the hood, which had been thrown partly back, he wore the knotted *keffiya* headdress of a Naib.

"I am Ghadhean al-Fali," he said, placing one foot on the steps to the thrones to signify his status above that of the mob. "I was one of Muad'Dib's death commandos and I am here concerning a matter of the desert."

Alia stiffened only slightly, a small betrayal. Al-Fali's name had been on that demand to place Jessica on the Council.

A matter of the desert! Jessica thought.

Ghadhean al-Fali had spoken before his Advocate could open the pleading. With that formal Fremen phrase he had placed them on notice that he brought them something of concern to all of Dune—and that he spoke with the authority of a Fedaykin who had offered his life beside that of Paul Muad'Dib. Jessica doubted that this was what Ghadhean al-Fali had told Javid or the Advocate General in seeking audience here. Her guess was confirmed as an official of the Priesthood rushed forward from the rear of the chamber waving the black cloth of intercession.

"My Ladies!" the official called out. "Do not listen to this man! He comes under false—"

Jessica, watching the Priest run toward them, caught a movement out of the corners of her eyes, saw Alia's hand signaling in the old Atreides battle language: *"Now!"* Jessica could not determine where the signal was directed, but acted instinctively with a lurch to the left, taking throne and all. She rolled away from the crashing throne as she fell, came to her feet as she heard the sharp *spat* of a maula pistol . . . and again. But she was moving with the first sound, felt something tug at her right sleeve. She dove into the throng of supplicants and courtiers gathered below the dais. Alia, she noted, had not moved.

Surrounded by people, Jessica stopped.

Ghadhean al-Fali, she saw, had dodged to the other side of the dais, but the Advocate remained in his original position.

It had all happened with the rapidity of an ambush, but everyone in the Hall knew where trained reflexes should have taken anyone caught by surprise. Alia and the Advocate stood frozen in their exposure.

A disturbance toward the middle of the room caught Jessica's attention and she forced a way through the throng, saw four supplicants holding the Priest official. His black cloth of intercession lay near his feet, a maula pistol exposed in its folds.

Al-Fali thrust his way past Jessica, looked from the pistol to the Priest. The Fremen let out a cry of rage, came up from his belt with an *achag* blow, the fingers of his left hand rigid. They caught the Priest in the throat and he collapsed, strangling. Without a backward glance at the man he had killed, the old Naib turned an angry face toward the dais.

"Dalal-il 'an-nubuwwa!" al-Fali called, placing both palms against his forehead, then lowering them. "The Qadis as-Salaf will not let me be silenced! If I do not slay those who interfere, others will slay them!"

He thinks he was the target, Jessica realized. She looked down at her sleeve, put a finger in the neat hole left by the maula pellet. Poisoned, no doubt.

The supplicants had dropped the Priest. He lay writhing on the floor, dying with his larynx crushed. Jessica motioned to a pair of shocked courtiers standing at her left, said: "I want that man saved for questioning. If he dies, you die!" As they hesitated, peering toward the dais, she used Voice on them: "Move!"

The pair moved.

Jessica thrust herself to al-Fali's side, nudged him: "You are a fool, Naib! They were after me, not you."

Several people around them heard her. In the immediate shocked silence, al-Fali glanced at the dais with its one toppled throne and Alia still seated on the other. The look of realization which came over his face could've been read by a novice.

"Fedaykin," Jessica said, reminding him of his old service to her family, "we who have been scorched know how to stand back to back."

"Trust me, My Lady," he said, taking her meaning immediately.

A gasp behind Jessica brought her whirling, and she felt al-Fali move to stand with his back to her. A woman in the gaudy garb of a city Fremen was straightening from beside the Priest on the floor. The two courtiers were nowhere to be seen. The woman did not even glance at Jessica, but lifted her voice in the ancient keening of her people—the call for those who serviced the deathstills, the call for them to come and gather a body's water into the tribal cistern. It was a curiously incongruous noise coming from one dressed as this woman was. Jessica felt the persistence of the old ways even as she saw the falseness in this city woman. The creature in the gaudy dress obviously had killed the Priest to make sure he was silenced.

Why did she bother? Jessica wondered. *She had only to wait for the man to die of asphyxiation.* The act was a desperate one, a sign of deep fear.

Alia sat forward on the edge of her throne, her eyes aglitter with watchfulness. A slender woman wearing the braid knots of Alia's own guards strode past Jessica, bent over the Priest, straightened, and looked back at the dais. "He is dead."

"Have him removed," Alia called. She motioned to guards below the dais. "Straighten the Lady Jessica's chair."

So you'll try to brazen it out! Jessica thought. Did Alia think anyone had been fooled? Al-Fali had spoken of the Qadis as-Salaf, calling on the holy fathers of Fremen mythology as his protectors. But no supernatural agency had brought a maula pistol into this room where no weapons were permitted. A conspiracy involving Javid's people was the only answer, and Alia's unconcern about her own person told everyone she was a part of that conspiracy.

The old Naib spoke over his shoulder to Jessica: "Accept my apologies, My Lady. We of the desert come to you as our last desperate hope, and now we see that you still have need of us."

"Matricide does not sit well on my daughter," Jessica said.

"The tribes will hear of this," al-Fali promised.

"If you have such desperate need of me," Jessica asked, "why did you not approach me at the Convocation in Sietch Tabr?"

"Stilgar would not permit it."

Ahhh, Jessica thought, *the rule of the Naibs! In Tabr, Stilgar's word was law.*

The toppled throne had been straightened. Alia motioned for her mother to return, said: "All of you please note the death of that traitor-Priest. Those who threaten me die." She glanced at al-Fali. "My thanks to you, Naib."

"Thanks for a mistake," al-Fali muttered. He looked at Jessica. "You were right. My rage removed one who should've been questioned."

Jessica whispered: "Mark those two courtiers and the woman in the colorful dress, Fedaykin. I want them taken and questioned."

"It will be done," he said.

"If we get out of here alive," Jessica said. "Come, let us go back and play our parts."

"As you say, My Lady."

Together, they returned to the dais, Jessica mounting the steps and resuming her position beside Alia, al-Fali remaining in the supplicant's position below.

"Now," Alia said.

"One moment, daughter," Jessica said. She held up her sleeve, exposed the hole with a finger through it. "The attack was aimed at me. The pellet almost found me even as I was dodging. You will all note that the maula pistol is no longer down there." She pointed. "Who has it?"

There was no response.

"Perhaps it could be traced," Jessica said.

"What nonsense!" Alia said. "*I* was the—"

Jessica half turned toward her daughter, motioned with her left hand. "Someone down there has that pistol. Don't you have a fear that—"

"One of my guards has it!" Alia said.

"Then that guard will bring the weapon to me," Jessica said.

"She's already taken it away."

"How convenient," Jessica said.

"What are you saying?" Alia demanded.

Jessica allowed herself a grim smile. "I am saying that two of your people were charged with saving that *traitor-Priest*. I warned them that they would die if he died. They will die."

"I forbid it!"

Jessica merely shrugged.

"We have a brave Fedaykin here," Alia said, motioning toward al-Fali. "This argument can wait."

"It can wait forever," Jessica said, speaking in Chakobsa, her words double-barbed to tell Alia that no argument would stop the death command.

"We shall see!" Alia said. She turned to al-Fali. "Why are you here, Ghadhean al-Fali?"

"To see the mother of Muad'Dib," the Naib said. "What is left of the Fedaykin, that band of brothers who served her son, pooled their poor resources to buy my way in here past the avaricious guardians who shield the Atreides from the realities of Arrakis."

Alia said: "Anything the Fedaykin require, they have only—"

"He came to see me," Jessica interrupted. "What is your desperate need, Fedaykin?"

Alia said: "I speak for the Atreides here! What is—"

"Be silent, you murderous Abomination!" Jessica snapped. "You tried to have me killed, *daughter*! I say it for all here to know. You can't have everyone in this hall killed to silence them—as that Priest was silenced. Yes, the Naib's blow would've killed the man, but he could've been saved. He could've been questioned! You have no concern that he was silenced. Spray your protests upon us as you will, your guilt is written in your actions!"

Alia sat in frozen silence, face pale. And Jessica, watching the play of emotions across her daughter's face, saw a terrifyingly familiar movement of Alia's hands, an unconscious response which once had identified a deadly enemy of the Atreides. Alia's fingers moved in a tapping rhythm—little finger twice, index finger three times, ring finger twice, little finger once, ring finger twice . . . and back through the tapping in the same order.

The old Baron!

The focus of Jessica's eyes caught Alia's attention and she glanced down at her hand, held it still, looked back at her mother to see the terrible recognition. A gloating smile locked Alia's mouth.

"So you have your revenge upon us," Jessica whispered.

"Have you gone mad, mother?" Alia asked.

"I wish I had," Jessica said. And she thought: *She knows I will confirm this to the Sisterhood. She knows. She may even suspect I'll tell the Fremen and force her into a Trial of Possession. She cannot let me leave here alive.*

"Our brave Fedaykin waits while we argue," Alia said.

Jessica forced her attention back to the old Naib. She brought her responses under control, said: "You came to see me, Ghadhean."

"Yes, My Lady. We of the desert see terrible things happening. The Little Makers come out of the sand as was foretold in the oldest prophecies. Shai-Hulud no longer can be found except in the deeps of the Empty Quarter. We have abandoned our friend, the desert!"

Jessica glanced at Alia, who merely motioned for Jessica to continue. Jessica looked out over the throng in the Chamber, saw the shocked alertness on every face. The import of the fight between mother and daughter had not been lost on this throng, and they must wonder why the audience continued. She returned her attention to al-Fali.

"Ghadhean, what is this talk of Little Makers and the scarcity of sandworms?"

"Mother of Moisture," he said, using her old Fremen title, "we were warned of this in the Kitab al-Ibar. We beseech thee. Let it not be forgotten that on the day Muad'Dib died, Arrakis turned by itself! We cannot abandon the desert."

"Hah!" Alia sneered. "The superstitious riffraff of the Inner Desert fear the ecological transformation. They—"

"I hear you, Ghadhean," Jessica said. "If the worms go, the spice goes. If the spice goes, what coin do we have to buy our way?"

Sounds of surprise: gasps and startled whispers could be heard spreading across the Great Hall. The Chamber echoed to the sound.

Alia shrugged. "Superstitious nonsense!"

Al-Fali lifted his right hand to point at Alia. "I speak to the Mother of Moisture, not to the Coan-Teen!"

Alia's hands gripped the arms of her throne, but she remained seated.

Al-Fali looked at Jessica. "Once it was the land where nothing grew. Now there are plants. They spread like lice upon a wound. There have been clouds and rain along the belt of Dune! Rain, My Lady! Oh, precious mother of Muad'Dib, as sleep is death's brother, so is rain on the Belt of Dune. It is the death of us all."

"We do only what Liet-Kynes and Muad'Dib himself designed for us to do," Alia protested. "What is all of this superstitious gabble? We revere the words of Liet-Kynes, who told us: 'I wish to see this entire planet caught up in a net of green plants.' So it will be."

"And what of the worms and the spice?" Jessica asked.

"There'll always be *some* desert," Alia said. "The worms will survive."

She's lying, Jessica thought. *Why does she lie?*

"Help us, Mother of Moisture," al-Fali pleaded.

With an abrupt sensation of double vision, Jessica felt her awareness lurch, propelled by the old Naib's words. It was the unmistakable *adab,* the demanding memory which came upon one of itself. It came without qualifications and held her senses immobile while the lesson of the past was impressed upon her awareness. She was caught up in it completely, a fish in the net. Yet she felt the demand of it as a *human-most* moment, each small part a reminder of creation. Every element of the lesson-memory was real but insubstantial in its constant change, and she knew this was the closest she might ever come to experiencing the prescient dietgrasp which had inflicted itself upon her son.

Alia lied because she was possessed by one who would destroy the Atreides. She was, in herself, the first destruction. Then al-Fali spoke the truth: the sandworms are doomed unless the course of the ecological transformation is modified.

In the pressure of revelation, Jessica saw the people of the audience reduced to slow motion, their roles identified for her. She could pick the ones charged with seeing that she did not leave here alive! And the path through them lay there in her awareness as though outlined in bright light—confusion among them, one of them feinted to stumble into another, whole groups tangled. She saw, also, that she might leave this Great Hall only to fall into other hands. Alia did not care if she created a martyr. No—the *thing which possessed her* did not care.

Now, in this frozen time, Jessica chose a way to save the old Naib and send him as messenger. The way through the audience remained indelibly clear. How simple it was! They were buffoons with barricaded eyes, their shoulders held in positions of immovable defense. Each position upon the great floor could be seen as an atrophic collision from which dead flesh might slough away to reveal skeletons. Their bodies, their clothes, and their faces described individual hells—the insucked breast of concealed terrors, the glittering hook of a jewel become substitute armor; the mouths were judgments full of frightened absolutes, cathedral prisms of eyebrows showing lofty and religious sentiments which their loins denied.

Jessica sensed dissolution in the shaping forces loosed upon Arrakis. Al-Fali's voice had been like a distrans in her soul, awakening a beast from the deepest part of her.

In an eyeblink Jessica moved from the *adab* into the universe of movement, but it was a different universe from the one which had commanded her attention only a second before.

Alia was starting to speak, but Jessica said: "Silence!" Then: "There are those who fear that I have returned without reservation to the Sisterhood. But since that day in the desert when the Fremen gave the gift of life to me and to my son, I have been Fremen!" And she lapsed into the old tongue which only those in this room who could profit by it would understand: "Onsar akhaka zeliman aw maslumen!" *Support your brother in his time of need, whether he be just or unjust!*

Her words had the desired effect, a subtle shifting of positions within the Chamber.

But Jessica raged on: "This Ghadhean al-Fali, an honest Fremen, comes here to tell me what others should have revealed to me. Let no one deny this! The ecological transformation has become a tempest out of control!"

Wordless confirmations could be seen throughout the room.

"And my daughter delights in this!" Jessica said. "Mektub al-mellah! You carve wounds upon my flesh and write there in salt! Why did the Atreides find a home here? Because the *Mohalata* was natural to us. To the Atreides, government was always a protective partnership: *Mohalata*, as the Fremen have always known it. Now look at her!" Jessica pointed at Alia. "She laughs alone at night in contemplation of her own evil! Spice production will fall to nothing, or at best a fraction of its former level! And when word of *that* gets out—"

"We'll have a corner on the most priceless product in the universe!" Alia shouted.

"We'll have a corner on hell!" Jessica raged.

And Alia lapsed into the most ancient Chakobsa, the Atreides private language with its difficult glottal stops and clicks: "Now, you know, *mother*! Did you think a granddaughter of Baron Harkonnen would not appreciate all of the lifetimes you crushed into my awareness before I was even born? When I raged against what you'd done to me, I had only to ask myself what the Baron would've done. And he answered! Understand me, Atreides bitch! He answered *me*!"

Jessica heard the venom and the confirmation of her guess. *Abomination!* Alia had been overwhelmed within, possessed by that *cahueit* of evil, the Baron Vladimir Harkonnen. The Baron himself spoke from her mouth now, uncaring of what was revealed. He wanted her to see his revenge, wanted her to know that he could not be cast out.

I'm supposed to remain here helpless in my knowledge, Jessica thought. With the thought, she launched herself onto the path the *adab* had revealed, shouting: "Fedaykin, follow me!"

It turned out there were six Fedaykin in the room, and five of them won through behind her.

When I am weaker than you, I ask you for freedom because that is according to your principles; when I am stronger than you, I take away your freedom because that is according to my principles.

—WORDS OF AN ANCIENT PHILOSOPHER (ATTRIBUTED BY HARQ AL-ADA TO ONE LOUIS VEUILLOT)

Leto leaned out the covert exit from the sietch, saw the bight of the cliff towering above his limited view. Late afternoon sunlight cast long shadows in the cliff's vertical striations. A skeleton butterfly flew in and out of the shadows, its webbed wings a transparent lacery against the light. How delicate that butterfly was to exist here, he thought.

Directly ahead of him lay the apricot orchard, with children working there to gather the fallen fruit. Beyond the orchard was the qanat. He and Ghanima had given the slip to their guards by losing themselves in a sudden crush of incoming workers. It had been a relatively simple matter to worm their way down an air passage to its connection with the steps to the covert exit. Now they had only to mingle themselves with the children, work their way to the qanat and drop into the tunnel. There they could move beside the predator fish which kept sandtrout from encysting the tribe's irrigation water. No Fremen would yet think of a human risking accidental immersion in water.

He stepped out of the protective passages. The cliff stretched away on both sides of him, turned horizontal just by the act of his own movement.

Ghanima moved closely behind him. Both carried small fruit baskets woven of spice-fiber, but each basket carried a sealed package:
Fremkit, maula pistol, crysknife . . . and the new robes sent by Farad'n.

Ghanima followed her brother into the orchard, mingled with the
working children. Stillsuit masks concealed every face. They were just
two more workers here, but she felt the action drawing her life away
from protective boundaries and known ways. What a simple step it was,
that step from one danger into another!

In their baskets those new garments sent by Farad'n conveyed a
purpose well understood by both of them. Ghanima had accented this
knowledge by sewing their personal motto, *"We Share,"* in Chakobsa
above the hawk crest at each breast.

It would be twilight soon and, beyond the qanat which marked off
sietch cultivation, there would come a special quality of evening which
few places in the universe could match. It would be that softly lighted
desert world with its persistent solitude, its saturated sense that each
creature in it was alone in a new universe.

"We've been seen," Ghanima whispered, bending to work beside her
brother.

"Guards?"

"No—others."

"Good."

"We must move swiftly," she said.

Leto acknowledged this by moving away from the cliff through the
orchard. He thought with his father's thoughts: *Everything remains mobile in the desert or perishes.* Far out on the sand he could see The Attendant's outcropping, reminder of the need for mobility. The rocks lay
static and rigid in their watchful enigma, fading yearly before the onslaught of wind-driven sand. One day The Attendant would be sand.

As they neared the qanat they heard music from a high entrance of
the sietch. It was an old-style Fremen group—two-holed flutes, tambou-
rines, tympani made on spice-plastic drums with skins stretched taut
across one end. No one asked what animal on this planet provided that
much skin.

Stilgar will remember what I told him about that cleft in The Attendant, Leto thought. *He'll come in the dark when it's too late—and then he'll know.*

Presently they were at the qanat. They slipped into an open tube, climbed down the inspection ladder to the service ledge. It was dusky, damp, and cold in the qanat and they could hear the predator fish splashing. Any sandtrout trying to steal this water would find its water-softened inner surface attacked by the fish. Humans must be wary of them, too.

"Careful," Leto said, moving down the slippery ledge. He fastened his memory to times and places his flesh had never known. Ghanima followed.

At the end of the qanat they stripped to their stillsuits and put on the new robes. They left the old Fremen robes behind as they climbed out another inspection tube, wormed their way over a dune and down the far side. There they sat shielded from the sietch, strapped on maula pistols and crysknives, slipped the Fremkit packs onto their shoulders. They no longer could hear the music.

Leto arose, struck out through the valley between the dunes.

Ghanima fell into step behind him, moving with practiced unrhythmical quiet over the open sand.

Below the crest of each dune they bent low and crept across into the hidden lee, there to pause and peer backward seeking pursuit. No hunters had emerged upon the desert by the time they reached the first rocks.

In the shadows of the rocks they worked their way around The Attendant, climbed to a ledge looking out upon the desert. Colors blinked far out on the *bled*. The darkening air held the fragility of fine crystal. The landscape which met their gaze was beyond pity, nowhere did it pause—no hesitations in it at all. The gaze stayed upon no single place in its scanning movements across that immensity.

It is the horizon of eternity, Leto thought.

Ghanima crouched beside her brother, thinking: *The attack will come soon.* She listened for the slightest sound, her whole body transformed into a single sense of taut probing.

Leto sat equally alert. He knew now the culmination of all the training which had gone into the lives he shared so intimately. In this wilderness one developed a firm dependence upon the senses, *all* of the senses. Life became a hoard of stored perceptions, each one linked only to momentary survival.

Presently Ghanima climbed up the rocks and peered through a notch at the way they had come. The safety of the sietch seemed a lifetime away, a bulk of dumb cliffs rising out of the brown-purple distance, dust-blurred edges at the rim where the last of the sunlight cast its silver streaks. Still no pursuit could be seen in the intervening distance. She returned to Leto's side.

"It'll be a predatory animal," Leto said. "That's my tertiary computation."

"I think you stopped computing too soon," Ghanima said. "It'll be more than one animal. House Corrino has learned not to put all of its hopes into a single bag."

Leto nodded agreement.

His mind felt suddenly heavy with the multitude of lives which his *difference* provided him: all of those lives, his even before birth. He was saturated with living and wanted to flee from his own consciousness. The inner world was a heavy beast which could devour him.

Restlessly he arose, climbed to the notch Ghanima had used, peered at the cliffs of the sietch. Back there, beneath the cliff, he could see how the qanat drew a line between life and death. On the oasis edge he could see camel sage, onion grass, gobi feather grass, wild alfalfa. In the last of the light he could make out the black movements of birds pick-hopping in the alfalfa. The distant grain tassels were ruffled by a wind which drew shadows that moved right up to the orchard. The motion caught at his awareness, and he saw that the shadows hid within their fluid form a larger change, and that larger change gave ransom to the turning rainbows of a silver-dusted sky.

What will happen out here? he asked himself.

And he knew it would either be death or the play of death, himself the object. Ghanima would be the one to return, believing the reality of a death she had seen or reporting sincerely from a deep hypnotic compulsion that her brother was, indeed, slain.

The unknowns of this place haunted him. He thought how easy it would be to succumb to the demand for prescience, to risk launching his awareness into an unchanging, absolute future. The small vision of his dream was bad enough, though. He knew he dared not risk the larger vision.

Presently, he returned to Ghanima's side.

"No pursuit yet," he said.

"The beasts they send for us will be large," Ghanima said. "We may have time to see them coming."

"Not if they come in the night."

"It'll be dark very soon," she said.

"Yes. It's time we went down into *our* place." He indicated the rocks to their left and below them where windsand had eaten a tiny cleft in the basalt. It was large enough to admit them, but small enough to keep out large creatures. Leto felt himself reluctant to go there, but knew it must be done. That was the place he'd pointed out to Stilgar.

"They may really kill us," he said.

"This is the chance we have to take," she said. "We owe it to our father."

"I'm not arguing."

And he thought: *This is the correct path; we do the right thing.* But he knew how dangerous it was to be *right* in this universe. Their survival now demanded vigor and fitness and an understanding of the limitations in every moment. Fremen ways were their best armor, and the Bene Gesserit knowledge was a force held in reserve. They were both thinking now as Atreides-trained battle veterans with no other defenses than a Fremen toughness which was not even hinted at by their childish bodies and their formal attire.

Leto fingered the hilt of the poison-tipped crysknife at his waist. Unconsciously Ghanima duplicated the gesture.

"Shall we go down now?" Ghanima asked. As she spoke she saw the movement far below them, small movement made less threatening by distance. Her stillness alerted Leto before she could utter a warning.

"Tigers," he said.

"Laza tigers," she corrected him.

"They see us," he said.

"We'd better hurry," she said. "A maula would never stop those creatures. They will've been well trained for this."

"They'll have a human director somewhere around," he said, leading the way at a fast lope down the rocks to the left.

Ghanima agreed, but kept it to herself, saving her strength. There'd be a human around somewhere. Those tigers couldn't be allowed to run free until the proper moment.

The tigers moved fast in the last of the light, leaping from rock to rock. They were eye-minded creatures and soon it would be night, the time of the ear-minded. The bell-call of a nightbird came from The Attendant's rocks to emphasize the change. Creatures of the darkness already were hustling in the shadows of the etched crevasses.

Still the tigers remained visible to the running twins. The animals flowed with power, a rippling sense of golden sureness in every movement.

Leto felt that he had stumbled into this place to free himself from his soul. He ran with the sure knowledge that he and Ghanima could reach their narrow notch in time, but his gaze kept returning with fascination to the oncoming beasts.

One stumble and we're lost, he thought.

That thought reduced the sureness of his knowledge, and he ran faster.

You Bene Gesserit call your activity of the Panoplia Prophetica a "Science of Religion." Very well. I, a seeker after another
kind of *scientist*, find this an appropriate definition. You do,
indeed, build your own myths, but so do all societies. You I
must warn, however. You are behaving as so many other mis-
guided scientists have behaved. Your actions reveal that you
wish to take something out of [*away from*] life. It is time you
were reminded of that which you so often profess: One cannot have a single thing without its opposite.

—THE PREACHER AT ARRAKEEN:
A MESSAGE TO THE SISTERHOOD

In the hour before dawn, Jessica sat immobile on a worn rug of spice-
cloth. Around her were the bare rocks of an old and poor sietch, one of
the original settlements. It lay below the rim of Red Chasm, sheltered
from the westerlies of the desert. Al-Fali and his brothers had brought
her here; now they awaited word from Stilgar. The Fedaykin had moved
cautiously in the matter of communication, however. Stilgar was not to
know their location.

The Fedaykin already knew they were under a *procès-verbal,* an official report of crimes against the Imperium. Alia was taking the tack
that her mother had been suborned by enemies of the realm, although
the Sisterhood had not yet been named. The high-handed, tyrannical
nature of Alia's power was out in the open, however, and her belief that
because she controlled the Priesthood she controlled the Fremen was
about to be tested.

Jessica's message to Stilgar had been direct and simple: *"My daughter is possessed and must be put to the trial."*

Fears destroyed values, though, and it already was known that some Fremen would prefer not to believe this accusation. Their attempts to use the accusation as a passport had brought on two battles during the night, but the ornithopters al-Fali's people had stolen had brought the fugitives to this precarious safety: Red Chasm Sietch. Word was going out to the Fedaykin from here, but fewer than two hundred of them remained on Arrakis. The others held posts throughout the Empire.

Reflecting upon these facts, Jessica wondered if she had come to the place of her death. Some of the Fedaykin believed it, but the death commandos accepted this easily enough. Al-Fali had merely grinned at her when some of his young men voiced their fears.

"When God hath ordained a creature to die in a particular place, He causeth that creature's wants to direct him to that place," the old Naib had said.

The patched curtains at her doorway rustled; al-Fali entered. The old man's narrow, windburned face appeared drawn, his eyes feverish. Obviously he had not rested.

"Someone comes," he said.

"From Stilgar?"

"Perhaps." He lowered his eyes, glanced leftward in the manner of the old Fremen who brought bad news.

"What is it?" Jessica demanded.

"We have word from Tabr that your grandchildren are not there." He spoke without looking at her.

"Alia . . ."

"She has ordered that the twins be given over to her custody, but Sietch Tabr reports that the children are not there. That is all we know."

"Stilgar's sent them into the desert," Jessica said.

"Possibly, but it is known that he was searching for them all through the night. Perhaps it was a trick on his part. . . ."

"That's not Stilgar's way," she said, and thought: *Unless the twins put him up to it.* But that didn't feel right either. She wondered at herself: no

sensations of panic to suppress, and her fears for the twins were tempered by what Ghanima had revealed. She peered up at al-Fali, found him studying her with pity in his eyes. She said: "They've gone into the desert by themselves."

"Alone? Those two children!"

She did not bother to explain that "those two children" probably knew more about desert survival than most living Fremen. Her thoughts were fixed, instead, on Leto's odd behavior when he'd insisted that she allow herself to be abducted. She'd put the memory aside, but this moment demanded it. He'd said she would know the moment to obey him.

"The messenger should be in the sietch by now," al-Fali said. "I will bring him to you." He let himself out through the patched curtain.

Jessica stared at the curtain. It was red cloth of spice-fiber, but the patches were blue. The story was that this sietch had refused to profit from Muad'Dib's religion, earning the enmity of Alia's Priesthood. The people here reportedly had put their capital into a scheme to raise dogs as large as ponies, dogs bred for intelligence as guardians of children. The dogs had all died. Some said it was poison and the Priests were blamed.

She shook her head to drive out these reflections, recognizing them for what they were: *ghafla*, the gadfly distraction.

Where had those children gone? To Jacurutu? They had a plan. *They tried to enlighten me to the extent they thought I'd accept,* she remembered. And when they'd reached the limits as they saw them, Leto had commanded her to obey.

He'd commanded *her!*

Leto had recognized what Alia was doing; that much was obvious. Both twins had spoken of their aunt's "affliction," even when defending her. Alia was gambling on the *rightness* of her position in the Regency. Demanding custody of the twins confirmed that. Jessica found a harsh laugh shaking her own breast. The Reverend Mother Gaius Helen Mohiam had been fond of explaining this particular error to her student, Jessica. *"If you focus your awareness only upon your own rightness, then you invite the forces of opposition to overwhelm you. This is a common error. Even I, your teacher, have made it.*"

"And even I, your student, have made it," Jessica whispered to herself.

She heard fabrics whispering in the passage beyond the curtain. Two young Fremen entered, part of the entourage they'd picked up during the night. The two were obviously awed at being in the presence of Muad'Dib's mother. Jessica had read them completely: they were non-thinkers, attaching themselves to any fancied power for the identity which this gave them. Without a reflection from her they were empty. Thus, they were dangerous.

"We were sent ahead by al-Fali to prepare you," one of the young Fremen said.

Jessica felt an abrupt clenching tightness in her breast, but her voice remained calm. "Prepare me for what?"

"Stilgar has sent Duncan Idaho as his messenger."

Jessica pulled her aba hood up over her hair, an unconscious gesture. *Duncan?* But he was Alia's tool.

The Fremen who'd spoken took a half step forward. "Idaho says he has come to take you to safety, but al-Fali does not see how this can be."

"It seems passing strange, indeed," Jessica said. "But there are stranger things in our universe. Bring him."

They glanced at each other but obeyed, leaving together with such a rush that they tore another rent in the worn curtain.

Presently Idaho stepped through the curtain, followed by the two Fremen and al-Fali bringing up the rear, hand on his crysknife. Idaho appeared composed. He wore the dress casuals of an Atreides House Guard, a uniform which had changed little in more than fourteen centuries. Arrakis had replaced the old gold-handled plasteel blade with a crysknife, but that was minor.

"I'm told you wish to help me," Jessica said.

"As odd as that may seem," he said.

"But didn't Alia send you to abduct me?" she asked.

A slight raising of his black eyebrows was the only mark of surprise.

The many-faceted Tleilaxu eyes continued to stare at her with glittering intensity. "Those were her orders," he said.

Al-Fali's knuckles went white on his crysknife, but he did not draw.

"I've spent much of this night reviewing the mistakes I made with my daughter," she said.

"There were many," Idaho agreed, "and I shared in most of them."

She saw now that his jaw muscles were trembling.

"It was easy to listen to the arguments which led us astray," Jessica said. "I wanted to leave this place . . . You . . . you wanted a girl you saw as a younger version of me."

He accepted this silently.

"Where are my grandchildren?" she demanded, voice going harsh.

He blinked. Then: "Stilgar believes they have gone into the desert—hiding. Perhaps they saw this crisis coming."

Jessica glanced at al-Fali, who nodded his recognition that she had anticipated this.

"What is Alia doing?" Jessica asked.

"She risks civil war," he said.

"Do you believe it'll come to that?"

Idaho shrugged. "Probably not. These are softer times. There are more people willing to listen to pleasant arguments."

"I agree," she said. "Well and good, what of my grandchildren?"

"Stilgar will find them—if . . ."

"Yes, I see." It was really up to Gurney Halleck then. She turned to look at the rock wall on her left. "Alia grasps the power firmly now." She looked back at Idaho. "You understand? One uses power by grasping it lightly. To grasp too strongly is to be taken over by power, and thus to become its victim."

"As my Duke always told me," Idaho said.

Somehow Jessica knew he meant the older Leto, not Paul. She asked: "Where am I to be taken in this . . . abduction?"

Idaho peered down at her as though trying to see into the shadows created by the hood.

Al-Fali stepped forward: "My Lady, you are not seriously thinking . . ."

"Is it not my right to decide my own fate?" Jessica asked.

"But this . . ." Al-Fali's head nodded toward Idaho.

"This was my loyal guardian before Alia was born," Jessica said. "Before he died saving my son's life and mine. We Atreides always honor certain obligations."

"Then you will go with me?" Idaho asked.

"Where would you take her?" al-Fali asked.

"Best that you don't know," Jessica said.

Al-Fali scowled but remained silent. His face betrayed indecision, an understanding of the wisdom in her words but an unresolved doubt of Idaho's trustworthiness.

"What of the Fedaykin who helped me?" Jessica asked.

"They have Stilgar's countenance if they can get to Tabr," Idaho said. Jessica faced al-Fali: "I command you to go there, my friend. Stilgar can use Fedaykin in the search for my grandchildren."

The old Naib lowered his gaze. "As Muad'Dib's mother commands."
He's still obeying Paul, she thought.

"We should be out of here quickly," Idaho said. "The search is certain to include this place, and that early."

Jessica rocked forward and arose with that fluid grace which never quite left the Bene Gesserit, even when they felt the pangs of age. And she felt old now after her night of flight. Even as she moved, her mind remained on that peculiar interview with her grandson. What was he really doing? She shook her head, covered the motion by adjusting her hood. It was too easy to fall into the trap of underestimating Leto. Life with ordinary children conditioned one to a false view of the inheritance which the twins enjoyed.

Her attention was caught by Idaho's pose. He stood in the relaxed preparedness for violence, one foot ahead of the other, a stance which she herself had taught him. She shot a quick look at the two young Fremen, at al-Fali. Doubts still assailed the old Fremen Naib and the two young men felt this.

"I trust this man with my life," she said, addressing herself to al-Fali. "And it is not the first time."

"My Lady," al-Fali protested. "It's just . . ." He glared at Idaho. "He's the husband of the Coan-Teen!"

"And he was trained by my Duke and by me," she said.

"But he's a *ghola!*" The words were torn from al-Fali.

"My son's ghola," she reminded him.

It was too much for a former Fedaykin who'd once pledged himself to support Muad'Dib to the death. He sighed, stepped aside, and motioned the two young men to open the curtains.

Jessica stepped through, Idaho behind her. She turned, spoke to al-Fali in the doorway. "You are to go to Stilgar. He's to be trusted."

"Yes . . ." But she still heard doubts in the old man's voice.

Idaho touched her arm. "We should go at once. Is there anything you wish to take?"

"Only my common sense," she said.

"Why? Do you fear you're making a mistake?"

She glanced up at him. "You were always the best 'thopter pilot in our service, Duncan."

This did not amuse him. He stepped ahead of her, moving swiftly, retracing the way he'd come. Al-Fali fell into step beside Jessica. "How did you know he came by 'thopter?"

"He wears no stillsuit," Jessica said.

Al-Fali appeared abashed by this obvious perception. He would not be silenced, though. "Our messenger brought him here directly from Stilgar's. They could've been seen."

"Were you seen, Duncan?" Jessica asked Idaho's back.

"You know better than that," he said. "We flew lower than the dune-tops."

They turned into a side passage which led downward in spiral steps, debouching finally into an open chamber well-lighted by glowglobes high in the brown rock. A single ornithopter sat facing the far wall, crouched there like an insect waiting to spring. The wall would be false rock, then—a door opening onto the desert. As poor as this sietch was, it still maintained the instruments of secrecy and mobility.

Idaho opened the ornithopter's door for her, helped her into the right-hand seat. As she moved past him, she saw perspiration on his forehead where a lock of the black goat-hair lay tumbled. Unbidden, Jessica found herself recalling that head spouting blood in a noisy cavern. The steely marbles of the Tleilaxu eyes brought her out of that recollection. Nothing was as it seemed anymore. She busied herself fastening her seatbelt.

"It's been a long time since you've flown me, Duncan," she said.

"Long and far time," he said. He was already checking the controls.

Al-Fali and the two younger Fremen waited beside the controls to the false rock, prepared to open it.

"Do you think I harbor doubts about you?" Jessica asked, speaking softly to Idaho.

Idaho kept his attention on an engine instrument, ignited the impellers and watched a needle move. A smile touched his mouth, a quick and harsh gesture in his sharp features, gone as quickly as it had come.

"I am still Atreides," Jessica said. "Alia is not."

"Have no fear," he grated. "I still serve the Atreides."

"Alia is no longer Atreides," Jessica repeated.

"You needn't remind me!" he snarled. "Now shut up and let me fly this thing."

The desperation in his voice was quite unexpected, out of keeping with the Idaho she'd known. Putting down a renewed sense of fear, Jessica asked: "Where are we going, Duncan? You can tell me now."

But he nodded to al-Fali and the false rock opened outward into bright silvery sunlight. The ornithopter leaped outward and up, its wings throbbing with the effort, the jets roaring, and they mounted into an empty sky. Idaho set a southwesterly course toward Sahaya Ridge which could be seen as a dark line upon the sand.

Presently he said: "Do not think harshly of me, My Lady."

"I haven't thought harshly of you since that night you came into our Arrakeen great hall roaring drunk on spice-beer," she said. But his words renewed her doubts, and she fell into the relaxed preparedness of complete *prana-bindu* defense.

"I remember that night well," he said. "I was very young . . . inexperienced."

"But the best swordmaster in my Duke's retinue."

"Not quite, My Lady. Gurney could best me six times out of ten." He glanced at her. "Where is Gurney?"

"Doing my bidding."

He shook his head.

"Do you know where we're going?" she asked.

"Yes, My Lady."

"Then tell me."

"Very well. I promised that I would create a believable plot against House Atreides. Only one way, really, to do that." He pressed a button on the control wheel and cocoon restraints whipped from Jessica's seat, enfolded her in unbreakable softness, leaving only her head exposed. "I'm taking you to Salusa Secundus," he said. "To Farad'n."

In a rare, uncontrolled spasm, Jessica surged against the restraints, felt them tighten, easing only when she relaxed, but not before she felt the deadly shigawire concealed in the protective sheathing.

"The shigawire release has been disconnected," he said, not looking at her. "Oh yes, and don't try Voice on me. I've come a long way since the days when you could move me that way." He looked at her. "The Tleilaxu armored me against such wiles."

"You're obeying Alia," Jessica said, "and she—"

"Not Alia," he said. "We do The Preacher's bidding. He wants you to teach Farad'n as once you taught . . . Paul."

Jessica remained in frozen silence, remembering Leto's words, that she would find an interesting student. Presently she said: "This Preacher—is he my son?"

Idaho's voice seemed to come from a great distance: "I wish I knew."

The universe is just there; that's the only way a Fedaykin can view it and remain the master of his senses. The universe neither threatens nor promises. It holds things beyond our sway: the fall of a meteor, the eruption of a spiceblow, growing old and dying. These are the realities of this universe and they must be faced regardless of how you *feel* about them. You cannot fend off such realities with words. They will come at you in their own wordless way and then, then you will understand what is meant by "life and death." Understanding this, you will be filled with joy.

—MUAD'DIB TO HIS FEDAYKIN

"And those are the things we have set in motion," Wensicia said. "These things were done for *you*."

Farad'n remained motionless, seated across from his mother in her morning room. The sun's golden light came from behind him, casting his shadow on the white-carpeted floor. Light reflected from the wall behind his mother drew a nimbus around her hair. She wore her usual white robe trimmed in gold—reminders of royal days. Her heart-shaped face appeared composed, but he knew she was watching his every reaction. His stomach felt empty, although he'd just come from breakfast.

"You don't approve?" Wensicia asked.

"What is there to disapprove?" he asked.

"Well . . . that we kept this from you until now?"

"Oh, that." He studied his mother, tried to reflect upon his complex position in this matter. He could only think on a thing he had noticed recently, that Tyekanik no longer called her "My Princess." What did he call her? Queen Mother?

Why do I feel a sense of loss? he wondered. *What am I losing?* The answer was obvious: he was losing his carefree days, time for those pursuits of the mind which so attracted him. If this plot unfolded by his mother came off, those things would be gone forever. New responsibilities would demand his attention. He found that he resented this deeply. How dared they take such liberties with his time? And without even consulting him!

"Out with it," his mother said. "Something's wrong."

"What if this plan fails?" he asked, saying the first thing that came into his mind.

"How can it fail?"

"I don't know. . . . Any plan can fail. How're you using Idaho in all of this?"

"Idaho? What's this interest in . . . Oh, yes—that mystic fellow Tyek brought here without consulting me. That was wrong of him. The mystic spoke of Idaho, didn't he?"

It was a clumsy lie on her part, and Farad'n found himself staring at his mother in wonderment. She'd known about The Preacher all along!

"It's just that I've never seen a ghola," he said.

She accepted this, said: "We're saving Idaho for something important."

Farad'n chewed silently at his upper lip.

Wensicia found herself reminded of his dead father. Dalak had been like that at times, very inward and complex, difficult to read. Dalak, she reminded herself, had been related to Count Hasimir Fenring, and there'd been something of the dandy and the fanatic in both of them. Would Farad'n follow in that path? She began to regret having Tyek lead the lad into the Arrakeen religion. Who knew where that might take him?

"What does Tyek call you now?" Farad'n asked.

"What's that?" She was startled by this shift.

"I've noticed that he doesn't call you 'My Princess' anymore."

How observant he is, she thought, wondering why this filled her with disquiet. *Does he think I've taken Tyek as a lover? Nonsense, it wouldn't matter one way or the other. Then why this question?*

"He calls me 'My Lady,'" she said.

"Why?"

"Because that's the custom in all of the Great Houses."

Including the Atreides, he thought.

"It's less suggestive if overheard," she explained. "Some will think we've given up our legitimate aspirations."

"Who would be that stupid?" he asked.

She pursed her lips, decided to let it pass. A small thing, but great campaigns were made up of many small things.

"The Lady Jessica shouldn't have left Caladan," he said.

She shook her head sharply. What was this? His mind was darting around like a crazy thing! She said: "What do you mean?"

"She shouldn't have gone back to Arrakis," he said. "That's bad strategy. Makes one wonder. Would've been better to have her grandchildren visit her on Caladan."

He's right, she thought, dismayed that this had never occurred to her. Tyek would have to explore this immediately. Again she shook her head. *No!* What was Farad'n doing? He must know that the Priesthood would never risk both twins in space.

She said this.

"Is it the Priesthood or the Lady Alia?" he asked, noting that her thoughts had gone where he had wanted. He found exhilaration in his new importance, the mind-games available in political plotting. It had been a long time since his mother's mind had interested him. She was too easily maneuvered.

"You think Alia wants power for herself?" Wensicia asked.

He looked away from her. Of course Alia wanted the power for herself! All of the reports from that accursed planet agreed on this. His thoughts took off on a new course.

"I've been reading about their Planetologist," he said. "There has to be a clue to the sandworms and the haploids in there somewhere, if only . . ."

"Leave that to others now!" she said, beginning to lose patience with him. "Is this all you have to say about the things we've done for you?"

"You didn't do them for me," he said.

"Wha-a-at?"

"You did it for House Corrino," he said, "and you're House Corrino right now. I've not been invested."

"You have responsibilities!" she said. "What about all of the people who depend upon you?"

As if her words put the burden upon him, he felt the weight of all those hopes and dreams which followed House Corrino.

"Yes," he said, "I understand about them, but I find some of the things done in my *name* distasteful."

"Dis . . . How can you say such a thing? We do what any Great House would do in promoting its own fortunes!"

"Do you? I think you've been a bit gross. No! Don't interrupt me. If I'm to be an Emperor, then you'd better learn how to listen to me. Do you think I cannot read between the lines? How were those tigers trained?"

She remained speechless at this cutting demonstration of his perceptive abilities.

"I see," he said. "Well, I'll keep Tyek because I know you led him into this. He's a good officer under most circumstances, but he'll fight for his own principles only in a friendly arena."

"His . . . *principles*?"

"The difference between a good officer and a poor one is strength of character and about five heartbeats," he said. "He has to stick by his principles wherever they're challenged."

"The tigers were necessary," she said.

"I'll believe that if they succeed," he said. "But I will not condone what had to be done in training them. Don't protest. It's obvious. They were *conditioned*. You said it yourself."

"What're you going to do?" she asked.

"I'm going to wait and see," he said. "Perhaps I'll become Emperor."

She put a hand to her breast, sighed. For a few moments there he'd terrified her. She'd almost believed he would denounce her. Principles! But he was committed now; she could see that.

Farad'n got up, went to the door and rang for his mother's attendants. He looked back: "We are through, aren't we?"

"Yes." She raised a hand as he started to leave. "Where're you going?"

"To the library. I've become fascinated lately by Corrino history." He left her then, sensing how he carried his new commitment with him.

Damn her!

But he knew he was committed. And he recognized that there was a deep emotional difference between history as recorded on shigawire and read at leisure, a deep difference between that kind of history and the history which one lived. This new living history which he felt gathering around him possessed a sense of plunging into an irreversible future. Farad'n could feel himself driven now by the desires of all those whose fortunes rode with him. He found it strange that he could not pin down his own desires in this.

It is said of Muad'Dib that once when he saw a weed trying to grow between two rocks, he moved one of the rocks. Later, when the weed was seen to be flourishing, he covered it with the remaining rock. "That was its fate," he explained.

—THE COMMENTARIES

"Now!" Ghanima shouted.

Leto, two steps ahead of her in reaching the narrow cut in the rocks, did not hesitate. He dove into the slit, crawled forward until darkness enfolded him. He heard Ghanima drop behind him, a sudden stillness, and her voice, not hurrying or fearful:

"I'm stuck."

He stood up, knowing this would bring his head within reach of questing claws, reversed himself in the narrow passage, crept back until he felt Ghanima's outstretched hand.

"It's my robe," she said. "It's caught."

He heard rocks falling directly below them, pulled on her hand but felt only a small gain.

There was panting below them, a growl.

Leto tensed himself, wedging his hips against the rock, heaved on Ghanima's arm. Cloth ripped and he felt her jerk toward him. She hissed and he knew she felt pain, but he pulled once more, harder. She came farther into the hole, then all the way, dropping beside him. They were too close to the end of the cut, though. He turned, dropped to all fours, scrambled deeper. Ghanima pulled herself along behind him.

There was a panting intensity to her movements which told him she'd been hurt. He came to the end of the opening, rolled over and peered upward out the narrow gap of their sanctuary. The opening was about two meters above him, filled with stars. Something large obscured the stars.

A rumbling growl filled the air around the twins. It was deep, menacing, an ancient sound: hunter speaking to its prey.

"How badly are you hurt?" Leto asked, keeping his voice even.

She matched him, tone for tone: "One of them clawed me. Breached my stillsuit along the left leg. I'm bleeding."

"How bad?"

"Vein. I can stop it."

"Use pressure," he said. "Don't move. I'll take care of our friends."

"Careful," she said. "They're bigger than I expected."

Leto unsheathed his crysknife, reached up with it. He knew the tiger would be questing downward, claws raking the narrow passage where its body could not go.

Slowly, slowly, he extended the knife. Abruptly something struck the top of the blade. He felt the blow all along his arm, almost lost his grip on the knife. Blood gushed along his hand, spattered his face, and there came an immediate scream which deafened him. The stars became visible. Something threshed and flung itself down the rocks toward the sand in a violent caterwauling.

Once more, the stars were obscured and he heard the hunter's growl. The second tiger had moved into place, unmindful of its companion's fate.

"They're persistent," Leto said.

"You got one for sure," Ghanima said. "Listen!"

The screams and thrashing convulsions below them were growing fainter. The second tiger remained, though, a curtain against the stars.

Leto sheathed his blade, touched Ghanima's arm. "Give me your knife. I want a fresh tip to make sure of this one."

"Do you think they'll have a third one in reserve?" She asked.

"Not likely. Laza tigers hunt in pairs."

"Just as we do," she said.

"As we do," he agreed. He felt the handle of her crysknife slip into his palm, gripped it tightly. Once more he began that careful upward questing. The blade encountered only empty air, even when he reached into a level dangerous to his body. He withdrew, pondering this.

"Can't you find it?"

"It's not behaving the way the other one did."

"It's still there. Smell it?"

He swallowed in a dry throat. A fetid breath, moist with the musky smell of the cat, assaulted his nostrils. The stars were still blocked from view. Nothing could be heard of the first cat; the crysknife's poison had completed its work.

"I think I'm going to have to stand up," he said.

"No!"

"It has to be teased into reach of the knife."

"Yes, but we agreed that if one of us could avoid being wounded . . ."

"And you're wounded, so you're the one going back," he said.

"But if you're badly injured, I won't be able to leave you," she said.

"Do you have a better idea?"

"Give me back my knife."

"But your leg!"

"I can stand on the good one."

"That thing could take your head off with one sweep. Maybe the maula . . ."

"If there's anyone out there to hear, they'll know we came prepared for—"

"I don't like your taking this risk!" he said.

"Whoever's out there mustn't learn we have maulas—not yet." She touched his arm. "I'll be careful, keep my head down."

As he remained silent, she said: "You know I'm the one who has to do this. Give me back my knife."

Reluctantly he quested with his free hand, found her hand and returned the knife. It was the logical thing to do, but logic warred with every emotion in him.

He felt Ghanima pull away, heard the sandy rasping of her robe against the rock. She gasped, and he knew she must be standing. *Be very careful!* he thought. And he almost pulled her back to insist they use a maula pistol. But that could warn anyone out there that they had such weapons. Worse, it could drive the tiger out of reach, and they'd be trapped in here with a wounded tiger waiting for them in some unknown place out on those rocks.

Ghanima took a deep breath, braced her back against one wall of the cleft. *I must be quick,* she thought. She reached upward with the knife point. Her left leg throbbed where the claws had raked it. She felt the crusting of blood against her skin there and the warmth of a new flow. *Very quick!* She sank her senses into the calm preparation for crisis which the Bene Gesserit Way provided, put pain and all other distractions out of her awareness. The cat must reach down! Slowly she passed the blade along the opening. Where was the damned animal? Once more she raked the air. Nothing. The tiger would have to be lured into attack.

Carefully she probed with her sense of smell. Warm breath came from her left. She poised herself, drew in a deep breath, screamed: "Taqwa!" It was the old Fremen battlecry, its meaning found in the most ancient legends: *"The price of freedom!"* With the cry she tipped the blade and stabbed along the cleft's dark opening. Claws found her elbow before the knife touched flesh, and she had time only to tip her wrist toward the pain before agony raked her arm from elbow to wrist. Through the pain, she felt the poison tip sink into the tiger. The blade was wrenched from her numb fingers. But again the narrow gap of the cleft lay open to the stars and the wailing voice of a dying cat filled the night. They followed it by its death throes, a thrashing passage down the rocks. Presently the death-silence came.

"It got my arm," Ghanima said, trying to bind a loose fold of her robe around the wound.

"Badly?"

"I think so. I can't feel my hand."

"Let me get a light and—"

"Not until we get under cover!"

"I'll hurry."

She heard him twisting to reach his Fremkit, felt the dark slickness of a nightshield as it was slipped over her head, tucked in behind her. He didn't bother to make it moisture tight.

"My knife's on this side," she said. "I can feel the handle with my knee."

"Leave it for now."

He ignited a single small globe. The brilliance of it made her blink. Leto put the globe on the sandy floor at one side, gasped as he saw her arm. One claw had opened a long, gaping wound which twisted from the elbow along the back of her arm almost to the wrist. The wound described the way she had rotated her arm to present the knife tip to the tiger's paw.

Ghanima glanced once at the wound, closed her eyes and began reciting the Litany Against Fear.

Leto found himself sharing her need, but put aside the clamor of his own emotions while he set about binding up the wound. It had to be done carefully to stop the flow of blood while retaining the appearance of a clumsy job which Ghanima might have done by herself. He made her tie off the knot with her free hand, holding one end of the bandage in her teeth.

"Now let's look at the leg," he said.

She twisted around to present the other wound. It was not as bad: two shallow claw cuts along the calf. They had bled freely into the still-suit, however. He cleaned it up as best he could, bound the wound beneath the stillsuit. He sealed the suit over the bandage.

"I got sand in it," he said. "Have it treated as soon as you get back."

"Sand in our wounds," she said. "That's an old story for Fremen."

He managed a smile, sat back.

Ghanima took a deep breath. "We've pulled it off."

"Not yet."

She swallowed, fighting to recover from the aftermath of shock. Her face appeared pale in the light of the glowglobe. And she thought: *Yes, we must move fast now. Whoever controlled those tigers could be out there right now.*

Leto, staring at his sister, felt a sudden wrenching sense of loss. It was a deep pain which shot through his breast. He and Ghanima must separate now. For all of those years since birth they had been as one person. But their plan demanded now that they undergo a metamorphosis, going their separate ways into uniqueness where the sharing of daily experiences would never again unite them as they once had been united.

He retreated into the necessarily mundane. "Here's my Fremkit. I took the bandages from it. Someone may look."

"Yes." She exchanged kits with him.

"Someone out there has a transmitter for those cats," he said. "Most likely he'll be waiting near the qanat to make certain of us."

She touched her maula pistol where it sat atop the Fremkit, picked it up and thrust it into the sash beneath her robe. "My robe's torn."

"Yes."

"Searchers may get here soon," he said. "They may have a traitor among them. Best you slip back alone. Get Harah to hide you."

"I'll . . . I'll start the search for the traitor as soon as I get back," she said. She peered into her brother's face, sharing his painful knowledge that from this point on they would accumulate a store of differences. Never again would they be as one, sharing knowledge which no one else could understand.

"I'll go to Jacurutu," he said.

"Fondak," she said.

He nodded his agreement. Jacurutu/Fondak—they had to be the same place. It was the only way the legendary place could have been hidden. Smugglers had done it, of course. How easy for them to convert one label into another, acting under the cover of the unspoken convention by which they were allowed to exist. The ruling family of a planet must always have a back door for escape in extremis. And a small share in smuggling profits kept the channels open. In Fondak/Jacurutu, the smugglers had taken over a completely operative sietch untroubled by a resident population. And they had hidden Jacurutu right out in the open, secure in the taboo which kept Fremen from it.

"No Fremen will think to search for me in such a place," he said. "They'll inquire among the smugglers, of course, but . . ."

"We'll do as we agreed," she said. "It's just . . ."

"I know." Hearing his own voice, Leto realized they were drawing out these last moments of sameness. A wry grin touched his mouth, adding years to his appearance. Ghanima realized she was seeing him through a veil of time, looking at an older Leto. Tears burned her eyes.

"You needn't give water to the dead just yet," he said, brushing a finger against the dampness on her cheeks. "I'll go out far enough that no one will hear, and I'll call a worm." He indicated the collapsed Maker hooks strapped to the outside of his Fremkit. "I'll be at Jacurutu before dawn two days from now."

"Ride swiftly, my old friend," she whispered.

"I'll come back to you, my only friend," he said. "Remember to be careful at the qanat."

"Choose a good worm," she said, giving him the Fremen words of parting. Her left hand extinguished the glowglobe, and the nightseal rustled as she pulled it aside, folded it and tucked it into her kit. She felt him go, hearing only the softest of sounds quickly fading into silence as he crept down the rocks into the desert.

Ghanima steeled herself then for what she had to do. Leto must be dead to her. She had to make herself believe it. There could be no Jacurutu in her mind, no brother out there seeking a place lost in Fremen mythology. From this point onward she could not think of Leto as alive. She must condition herself to react out of a total belief that her brother was dead, killed here by Laza tigers. Not many humans could fool a Truthsayer, but she knew that she could do it . . . might have to do it. The multi-lives she and Leto shared had taught them the way: a hypnotic process old in Sheba's time, although she might be the only human alive who could recall Sheba as a reality. The deep compulsions had been designed with care and, for a long time after Leto had gone, Ghanima reworked her self-awareness, building the lonely sister, the surviving twin, until it was a believable totality. As she did this, she found the inner world becoming silent, blanked away from intrusion into her consciousness. It was a side effect she had not expected.

If only Leto could have lived to learn this, she thought, and she did not find the thought a paradox. Standing, she peered down at the desert where the tiger had taken Leto. There was a sound growing in the sand out there, a familiar sound to Fremen: the passage of a worm. Rare as they had become in these parts, a worm still came. Perhaps the first cat's death throes. . . . Yes, Leto had killed one cat before the other one got him. It was oddly symbolic that a worm should come. So deep was her compulsion that she saw three dark spots far down on the sand: the two tigers and Leto. Then the worm came and there was only sand with its surface broken into new waves by the passage of Shai-Hulud. It had not been a very large worm . . . but large enough. And her compulsion did not permit her to see a small figure riding on the ringed back.

Fighting her grief, Ghanima sealed her Fremkit, crept cautiously from her hiding place. Hand on her maula pistol, she scanned the area. No sign of a human with a transmitter. She worked her way up the rocks and across to the far side, creeping through moonshadows, waiting and waiting to be sure no assassin lurked in her path.

Across the open space she could see torches at Tabr, the wavering activity of a search. A dark patch moved across the sand toward The Attendant. She chose her path to run far to the north of the approaching party, went down to the sand and moved into the dune shadows. Careful to make her steps fall in a broken rhythm which would not attract a worm, she set out into the lonely distance which separated Tabr from the place where Leto had died. She would have to be careful at the qanat, she knew. Nothing must prevent her from telling how her brother had perished saving her from the tigers.

Governments, if they endure, always tend increasingly toward aristocratic forms. No government in history has been
known to evade this pattern. And as the aristocracy develops, government tends more and more to act exclusively in
the interests of the ruling class—whether that class be hereditary royalty, oligarchs of financial empires, or entrenched
bureaucracy.

—POLITICS AS REPEAT PHENOMENON:
BENE GESSERIT TRAINING MANUAL

"Why does he make us this offer?" Farad'n asked. "That's most essential."

He and the Bashar Tyekanik stood in the lounge of Farad'n's private quarters. Wensicia sat at one side on a low blue divan, almost as audience rather than participant. She knew her position and resented it, but Farad'n had undergone a terrifying change since that morning when she'd revealed their plots to him.

It was late afternoon at Corrino Castle and the low light accented the quiet comfort of this lounge—a room lined with actual books reproduced in plastino, with shelves revealing a horde of player spools, data blocks, shigawire reels, mnemonic amplifiers. There were signs all around that this room was much used—worn places on the books, bright metal on the amplifiers, frayed corners on the data blocks. There was only the one divan, but many chairs—all of them sensiform floaters designed for unobtrusive comfort.

Farad'n stood with his back to a window. He wore a plain Sardaukar uniform in grey and black with only the golden lion-claw symbols on the wings of his collar as decoration. He had chosen to receive the Bashar and his mother in this room, hoping to create an atmosphere of more relaxed communication than could be achieved in a more formal setting. But Tyekanik's constant "My Lord this" and "My Lady that" kept them at a distance.

"My Lord, I don't think he'd make this offer were he unable to deliver," Tyekanik said.

"Of course not!" Wensicia intruded.

Farad'n merely glanced at his mother to silence her, asked: "We've put no pressure on Idaho, made no attempt to seek delivery on The Preacher's promise?"

"None," Tyekanik said.

"Then why does Duncan Idaho, noted all of his life for his fanatic loyalty to the Atreides, offer now to deliver the Lady Jessica into our hands?"

"These rumors of trouble on Arrakis . . ." Wensicia ventured.

"Unconfirmed," Farad'n said. "Is it possible that The Preacher has precipitated this?"

"Possible," Tyekanik said, "but I fail to see a motive."

"He speaks of seeking asylum for her," Farad'n said. "That might follow if those rumors . . ."

"Precisely," his mother said.

"Or it could be a ruse of some sort," Tyekanik said.

"We can make several assumptions and explore them," Farad'n said. "What if Idaho has fallen into disfavor with his Lady Alia?"

"That might explain matters," Wensicia said, "but he—"

"No word yet from the smugglers?" Farad'n interrupted. "Why can't we—"

"Transmission is always slow in this season," Tyekanik said, "and the needs of security . . ."

"Yes, of course, but still . . ." Farad'n shook his head. "I don't like our assumption."

"Don't be too quick to abandon it," Wensicia said. "All of those stories about Alia and that Priest, whatever his name is . . ."

"Javid," Farad'n said. "But the man's obviously—"

"He's been a valuable source of information for us," Wensicia said.

"I was about to say that he's obviously a double agent," Farad'n said. "How could he indict himself in this? He's not to be trusted. There are too many signs . . ."

"I fail to see them," she said.

He was suddenly angry with her denseness. "Take my word for it, mother! The signs are there; I'll explain later."

"I'm afraid I must agree," Tyekanik said.

Wensicia lapsed into hurt silence. How dared they push her out of Council like this? As though she were some light-headed fancy woman with no—

"We mustn't forget that Idaho was once a ghola," Farad'n said. "The Tleilaxu . . ." He glanced sidelong at Tyekanik.

"That avenue will be explored," Tyekanik said. He found himself admiring the way Farad'n's mind worked: alert, questing, sharp. Yes, the Tleilaxu, in restoring life to Idaho, might have planted a powerful barb in him for their own use.

"But I fail to apprehend a Tleilaxu motive," Farad'n said.

"An investment in our fortunes," Tyekanik said. "A small insurance for future favors?"

"Large investment, I'd call it," Farad'n said.

"Dangerous," Wensicia said.

Farad'n had to agree with her. The Lady Jessica's capabilities were notorious in the Empire. After all, she'd been the one who'd trained Muad'Dib.

"If it became known that we hold her," Farad'n said.

"Yes, that'd be a two-edged sword," Tyekanik said. "But it need not be known."

"Let us assume," Farad'n said, "that we accept this offer. What's her value? Can we exchange her for something of greater importance?"

"Not openly," Wensicia said.

"Of course not!" He peered expectantly at Tyekanik.

"That remains to be seen," Tyekanik said.

Farad'n nodded. "Yes. I think if we accept, we should consider the Lady Jessica as money banked for indeterminate use. After all, wealth doesn't necessarily have to be spent on any particular thing. It's just . . . potentially useful."

"She'd be a very dangerous captive," Tyekanik said.

"There is that to consider, indeed," Farad'n said. "I'm told that her Bene Gesserit Ways permit her to manipulate a person just by the subtle employment of her voice."

"Or her body," Wensicia said. "Irulan once divulged to me some of the things she'd learned. She was showing off at the time, and I saw no demonstrations. Still the evidence is pretty conclusive that Bene Gesserits have their ways of achieving their ends."

"Were you suggesting," Farad'n asked, "that she might seduce me?" Wensicia merely shrugged.

"I'd say she's a little old for that, wouldn't you?" Farad'n asked.

"With a Bene Gesserit, nothing's certain," Tyekanik said.

Farad'n experienced a shiver of excitement tinged with fear. Playing this game to restore House of Corrino's high seat of power both attracted and repelled him. How attractive it remained, the urge to retire from this game into his preferred pursuits—historical research and learning the manifest duties for ruling here on Salusa Secundus. The restoration of his Sardaukar forces was a task in itself . . . and for that job, Tyek was still a good tool. One planet was, after all, an enormous responsibility. But the Empire was an even greater responsibility, far more attractive as an instrument of power. And the more he read about Muad'Dib/Paul Atreides, the more fascinated Farad'n became with the uses of power. As titular head of House Corrino, heir of Shaddam IV, what a great achievement it would be to restore his line to the Lion Throne. He wanted that! He wanted it. Farad'n had found that, by repeating this enticing litany to himself several times, he could overcome momentary doubts.

Tyekanik was speaking: ". . . and of course, the Bene Gesserit teach that peace encourages aggressions, thus igniting war. The paradox of—"

"How did we get on this subject?" Farad'n asked, bringing his attention back from the arena of speculation.

"Why," Wensicia said sweetly, having noted the wool-gathering expression on her son's face, "I merely asked if Tyek was familiar with the driving philosophy behind the Sisterhood."

"Philosophy should be approached with irreverence," Farad'n said, turning to face Tyekanik. "In regard to Idaho's offer, I think we should inquire further. When we think we know something, that's precisely the moment when we should look deeper into the thing."

"It will be done," Tyekanik said. He liked this cautious streak in Farad'n, but hoped it did not extend to those military decisions which required speed and precision.

With seeming irrelevancy, Farad'n asked: "Do you know what I find most interesting about the history of Arrakis? It was the custom in primitive times for Fremen to kill on sight anyone not clad in a stillsuit with its easily visible and characteristic hood."

"What is your fascination with the stillsuit?" Tyekanik asked.

"So you've noticed, eh?"

"How could we not notice?" Wensicia asked.

Farad'n sent an irritated glance at his mother. Why did she interrupt like that? He returned his attention to Tyekanik.

"The stillsuit is the key to that planet's character, Tyek. It's the hallmark of Dune. People tend to focus on the physical characteristics: the stillsuit conserves body moisture, recycles it, and makes it possible to exist on such a planet. You know, the Fremen custom was to have one stillsuit for each member of a family, *except* for food gatherers. They had spares. But please note, both of you—" He moved to include his mother in this. "—how garments which appear to be stillsuits, but really aren't, have become high fashion throughout the Empire. It's such a dominant characteristic for humans to copy the conqueror!"

"Do you really find such information valuable?" Tyekanik asked, his tone puzzled.

"Tyek, Tyek—without such information, one cannot govern. I said the stillsuit was the key to their character and it is! It's a conservative thing. The mistakes they make will be conservative mistakes."

Tyekanik glanced at Wensicia, who was staring at her son with a worried frown. This characteristic of Farad'n's both attracted and worried the Bashar. It was so unlike old Shaddam. Now, there had been an essential Sardaukar: a military killer with few inhibitions. But Shaddam had fallen to the Atreides under that damnable Paul. Indeed, what he read of Paul Atreides revealed just such characteristics as Farad'n now displayed. It was possible that Farad'n might hesitate less than the Atreides over brutal necessities, but that was his Sardaukar training.

"Many have governed without using this kind of information," Tyekanik said.

Farad'n merely stared at him for a moment. Then: "Governed and failed."

Tyekanik's mouth drew into a stiff line at this obvious allusion to Shaddam's failure. That had been a Sardaukar failure, too, and no Sardaukar could recall it easily.

Having made his point, Farad'n said: "You see, Tyek, the influence of a planet upon the mass unconscious of its inhabitants has never been fully appreciated. To defeat the Atreides, we must understand not only Caladan but Arrakis: one planet soft and the other a training ground for hard decisions. That was a unique event, that marriage of Atreides and Fremen. We must know how it worked or we won't be able to match it, let alone defeat it."

"What does this have to do with Idaho's offer?" Wensicia demanded.

Farad'n glanced pityingly down at his mother. "We begin their defeat by the kinds of stress we introduce into their society. That's a very powerful tool: stress. And the lack of it is important, too. Did you not mark how the Atreides helped things grow soft and easy here?"

Tyekanik allowed himself a curt nod of agreement. That was a good point. The Sardaukar could not be permitted to grow too soft. This offer from Idaho still bothered him, though. He said: "Perhaps it'd be best to reject the offer."

"Not yet," Wensicia said. "We've a spectrum of choices open to us. Our task is to identify as much of the spectrum as we can. My son is right: we need more information."

Farad'n stared at her, measuring her intent as well as the surface meaning of her words. "But will we know when we've passed the point of no alternate choice?" he asked.

A sour chuckle came from Tyekanik. "If you ask me, we're long past the point of no return."

Farad'n tipped his head back to laugh aloud. "But we still have alternate choices, Tyek! When we come to the end of our rope, that's an important place to recognize!"

In this age when the means of human transport include devices which can span the deeps of space in transtime, and other devices which can carry men swiftly over virtually impassable planetary surfaces, it seems odd to think of attempting long journeys afoot. Yet this remains a primary means of travel on Arrakis, a fact attributed partly to preference and partly to the brutal treatment which this planet reserves for anything mechanical. In the strictures of Arrakis, human flesh remains the most durable and reliable resource for the Hajj. Perhaps it is the implicit awareness of this fact which makes Arrakis the ultimate mirror of the soul.

—HANDBOOK OF THE HAJJ

Slowly, cautiously, Ghanima made her way back to Tabr, holding herself to the deepest shadows of the dunes, crouching in stillness as the search party passed to the south of her. Terrible awareness gripped her: the worm which had taken the tigers and Leto's body, the dangers ahead. He was gone; her twin was gone. She put aside all tears and nurtured her rage. In this, she was pure Fremen. And she knew this, reveling in it.

She understood what was said about Fremen. They were not supposed to have a conscience, having lost it in a burning for revenge against those who had driven them from planet to planet in the long wandering. That was foolishness, of course. Only the rawest primitive had no conscience. Fremen possessed a highly evolved conscience which centered on their own welfare as a people. It was only to outsiders that they seemed brutish—just as outsiders appeared brutish to Fremen.

Every Fremen knew very well that he could do a brutal thing and feel no guilt. Fremen did not feel guilt for the same things that aroused such feelings in others. Their rituals provided a freedom from guilts which might otherwise have destroyed them. They knew in their deepest awareness that any transgression could be ascribed, at least in part, to well recognized extenuating circumstances: "the failure of authority," or "a *natural* bad tendency" shared by all humans, or to "bad luck," which any sentient creature should be able to identify as a collision between mortal flesh and the outer chaos of the universe.

In this context Ghanima felt herself to be the pure Fremen, a carefully prepared extension of tribal brutality. She needed only a target—and that, obviously, was House Corrino. She longed to see Farad'n's blood spilled on the ground at her feet.

No enemy awaited her at the qanat. Even the search parties had gone elsewhere. She crossed the water on an earth bridge, crept through tall grass toward the covert exit of the sietch. Abruptly light flared ahead of her and Ghanima threw herself flat on the ground. She peered out through stalks of giant alfalfa. A woman had entered the covert passage from the outside, and someone had remembered to prepare that passage in the way any sietch entrance should be prepared. In troubled times, one greeted anyone entering the sietch with bright light, temporarily blinding the newcomer and giving guards time to decide. But such a greeting was never meant to be broadcast out over the desert. The light visible here meant the outer seals had been left aside.

Ghanima felt a tug of bitterness at this betrayal of sietch security: this flowing light. The ways of the lace-shirt Fremen were to be found everywhere!

The light continued to throw its fan over the ground at the cliff base. A young girl ran out of the orchard's darkness into the light, something fearful about her movements. Ghanima could see the bright circle of a glowglobe within the passage, a halo of insects around it. The light illuminated two dark shadows in the passage: a man and the girl. They were holding hands as they stared into each other's eyes.

Ghanima sensed something wrong about the man and woman

there. They were not just two lovers stealing a moment from the search. The light was suspended above and beyond them in the passage. The two talked against a glowing arch, throwing their shadows into the outer night where anyone could be a watcher of their movements. Now and again the man would free a hand. The hand would come gesturing into the light, a sharp and furtive movement which, once completed, returned to the shadows.

Lonely sounds of night creatures filled the darkness around Ghanima, but she screened out such distractions.

What was it about those two?

The man's motions were so static, so careful.

He turned. Reflection from the woman's robe illuminated him, exposing a raw red face with a large blotchy nose. Ghanima drew in a deep, silent breath of recognition. *Palimbasha!* He was a grandson of a Naib whose sons had fallen in Atreides service. The face—and another thing revealed by the open swinging of his robe as he turned—drew for Ghanima a complete picture. He wore a belt beneath the robe, and attached to the belt was a box which glistened with keys and dials. It was an instrument of the Tleilaxu or the Ixians for certain. And it had to be the transmitter which had released the tigers. Palimbasha. This meant that another Naibate family had gone over to House Corrino.

Who was the woman, then? No matter. She was someone being used by Palimbasha.

Unbidden, a Bene Gesserit thought came into Ghanima's mind: *Each planet has its own period, and each life likewise.*

She recalled Palimbasha well, watching him there with that woman, seeing the transmitter, the furtive movements. Palimbasha taught in the sietch school. Mathematics. The man was a mathematical boor. He had attempted to explain Muad'Dib through mathematics until censured by the Priesthood. He was a mind-slaver and his enslaving process could be understood with extreme simplicity: he transferred technical knowledge without a transfer of values.

I should've suspected him earlier, she thought. *The signs were all there.*

Then, with an acid tightening of her stomach: *He killed my brother!*

She forced herself to calmness. Palimbasha would kill her, too, if she tried to pass him there in the covert passage. Now she understood the reason for this un-Fremen display of light, this betrayal of the hidden entrance. They were watching by that light to see if either of their victims had escaped. It must be a terrible time of waiting for them, not knowing. And now that Ghanima had seen the transmitter, she could explain certain of the hand motions. Palimbasha was depressing one of the transmitter's keys frequently, an angry gesture.

The presence of this pair said much to Ghanima. Likely every way into the sietch carried a similar watcher in its depths.

She scratched her nose where dust tickled it. Her wounded leg still throbbed and the knife arm ached when it didn't burn. The fingers remained numb. Should it come to a knife, she would have to use the blade in her left hand.

Ghanima thought of using the maula pistol, but its characteristic sound would be sure to attract unwanted attention. Some other way would have to be found.

Palimbasha turned away from the entrance once more. He was a dark object against the light. The woman turned her attention to the outer night while she talked. There was a trained alertness about the woman, a sense that she knew how to look into the shadows, using the edges of her eyes. She was more than just a useful tool, then. She was part of the deeper conspiracy.

Ghanima recalled now that Palimbasha aspired to be a Kaymakam, a political governor under the Regency. He would be part of a larger plan, that was clear. There would be many others with him. Even here in Tabr. Ghanima examined the edges of the problem thus exposed, probed into it. If she could take one of these guardians alive, many others would be forfeit.

The *whiffle* of a small animal drinking at the qanat behind her caught Ghanima's awareness. Natural sounds and natural things. Her memory searched through a strange silent barrier in her mind, found a priestess of Jowf captured in Assyria by Sennacherib. The memories of that priestess told Ghanima what would have to be done here. Palimbasha and his woman there were mere children, wayward and dangerous. They knew nothing of Jowf, knew not even the name of the planet where Sennacherib and the priestess had faded into dust. The thing which was about to happen to the pair of conspirators, if it were explained to them, could only be explained in terms of beginning here.

And ending here.

Rolling onto her side, Ghanima freed her Fremkit, slipped the sandsnorkel from its bindings. She uncapped the sandsnorkel, removed the long filter within it. Now she had an open tube. She selected a needle from the repair pack, unsheathed her crysknife, and inserted the needle into the poison hollow at the knife's tip, that place where once a sandworm's nerve had fitted. Her injured arm made the work difficult. She moved carefully and slowly, handling the poisoned needle with caution while she took a wad of spice-fiber from its chamber in the kit. The needle's shank fitted tightly into the fiber wad, forming a missile which went tightly into the tube of the sandsnorkel.

Holding the weapon flat, Ghanima wormed her way closer to the light, moving slowly to cause minimal disturbance in the alfalfa. As she moved, she studied the insects around the light. Yes, there were piume flies in that fluttering mob. They were notorious biters of human flesh. The poisoned dart might go unnoticed, swatted aside as a biting fly. A decision remained: Which one of those two to take—the man or the woman!

Muriz. The name came unbidden into Ghanima's mind. That was the woman's name. It recalled things said about her. She was one of those who fluttered around Palimbasha as the insects fluttered around the light. She was easily swayed, a weak one.

Very well. Palimbasha had chosen the wrong companion for this night.

Ghanima put the tube to her mouth and, with the memory of the priestess of Jowf clearly in her awareness, she sighted carefully, expelled her breath in one strong surge.

Palimbasha batted at his cheek, drew away a hand with a speck of blood on it. The needle was nowhere to be seen, flicked away by the motion of his own hand.

The woman said something soothing and Palimbasha laughed. As he laughed, his legs began to give away beneath him. He sagged against the woman, who tried to support him. She was still staggering with the dead weight when Ghanima came up beside her and pressed the point of an unsheathed crysknife against her waist.

In a conversational tone, Ghanima said: "Make no sudden moves, Muriz. My knife is poisoned. You may let go of Palimbasha now. He is dead."

In all major socializing forces you will find an underlying movement to gain and maintain power through the use of words. From witch doctor to priest to bureaucrat it is all the same. A governed populace must be conditioned to accept power-words as actual things, to confuse the symbolized system with the tangible universe. In the maintenance of such a power structure, certain symbols are kept out of the reach of common understanding—symbols such as those dealing with economic manipulation or those which define the local interpretation of sanity. Symbol-secrecy of this form leads to the development of fragmented sub-languages, each being a signal that its users are accumulating some form of power. With this insight into a power process, our Imperial Security Force must be ever alert to the formation of sub-languages.

—LECTURE TO THE ARRAKEEN WAR COLLEGE
BY THE PRINCESS IRULAN

"It is perhaps unnecessary to tell you," Farad'n said, "but to avoid any errors I'll announce that a mute has been stationed with orders to kill you both should I show signs of succumbing to witchery."

He did not expect to see any effect from these words. Both the Lady Jessica and Idaho gratified his expectations.

Farad'n had chosen with care the setting for this first examination of the pair, Shaddam's old State Audience Chamber. What it lacked in grandeur it made up for with exotic appointments. Outside it was a winter afternoon, but the windowless chamber's lighting simulated a timeless summer day bathed in golden light from artfully scattered glowglobes of the purest Ixian crystal.

The news from Arrakis filled Farad'n with quiet elation. Leto, the male twin, was dead, killed by an assassin-tiger. Ghanima, the surviving sister, was in the custody of her aunt and reputedly was a hostage. The full report did much to explain the presence of Idaho and the Lady Jessica. Sanctuary was what they wanted. Corrino spies reported an uneasy truce on Arrakis. Alia had agreed to submit herself to a test called "the Trial of Possession," the purpose of which had not been fully explained. However, no date had been set for this trial and two Corrino spies believed it might never take place. This much was certain, though: there had been fighting between desert Fremen and the Imperial Military Fremen, an abortive civil war which had brought government to a temporary standstill. Stilgar's holdings were now neutral ground, designated after an exchange of hostages. Ghanima evidently had been considered one of these hostages, although the working of this remained unclear.

Jessica and Idaho had been brought to the audience securely bound in suspensor chairs. Both were held down by deadly thin strands of shigawire which would cut flesh at the slightest struggle. Two Sardaukar troopers had brought them, checked the bindings, and had gone away silently.

The warning had, indeed, been unnecessary. Jessica had seen the armed mute standing against a wall at her right, an old but efficient projectile weapon in his hand. She allowed her gaze to roam over the room's exotic inlays. The broad leaves of the rare iron bush had been set with eye pearls and interlaced to form the center crescent of the domed ceiling. The floor beneath her was alternate blocks of diamond wood and kabuzu shell arranged within rectangular borders of passaquet bones. These had been set on end, laser-cut and polished. Selected hard materials decorated the walls in stress-woven patterns which outlined the four positions of the Lion symbol claimed by descendants of the late Shaddam IV. The lions were executed in wild gold.

Farad'n had chosen to receive the captives while standing. He wore uniform shorts and a light golden jacket of elf-silk open at the throat. His only decoration was the princely starburst of his royal family worn at the left breast. He was attended by the Bashar Tyekanik wearing Sardaukar dress tans and heavy boots, an ornate lasegun carried in a front holster at the belt buckle. Tyekanik, whose heavy visage was known to Jessica from Bene Gesserit reports, stood three paces to the left and slightly behind Farad'n. A single throne of dark wood sat on the floor near the wall directly behind the two.

"Now," Farad'n said, addressing Jessica, "do you have anything to say?"

"I would inquire why we are bound thus?" Jessica said, indicating the shigawire.

"We have only just now received reports from Arrakis to explain your presence here," Farad'n said. "Perhaps I'll have you released presently." He smiled. "If you—" He broke off as his mother entered by the State doors behind the captives.

Wensicia hurried past Jessica and Idaho without a glance, presented a small message cube to Farad'n, actuated it. He studied the glowing face, glancing occasionally at Jessica, back to the cube. The glowing face went dark and he returned the cube to his mother, indicated that she should show it to Tyekanik. While she was doing this, he scowled at Jessica.

Presently Wensicia stationed herself at Farad'n's right hand, the darkened cube in her hand, partly concealed in a fold of her white gown.

Jessica glanced to her right at Idaho, but he refused to meet her gaze.

"The Bene Gesserit are displeased with me," Farad'n said. "They believe I was responsible for the death of your grandson."

Jessica held her face emotionless, thinking: *So Ghanima's story is to be trusted, unless* . . . She didn't like the suspected unknowns.

Idaho closed his eyes, opened them to glance at Jessica. She continued to stare at Farad'n. Idaho had told her about this Rhajia vision, but she'd seemed unworried. He didn't know how to catalogue her lack of emotion. She obviously knew something, though, that she wasn't revealing.

"This is the situation," Farad'n said, and he proceeded to explain everything he'd learned about events on Arrakis, leaving out nothing. He concluded: "Your granddaughter survives, but she's reportedly in the custody of the Lady Alia. This should gratify you."

"Did you kill my grandson?" Jessica asked.

Farad'n answered truthfully: "I did not. I recently learned of a plot, but it was not of my making."

Jessica looked at Wensicia, saw the gloating expression on that heart-shaped face, thought: *Her doing! The lioness schemes for her cub.* This was a game the lioness might live to regret.

Returning her attention to Farad'n, Jessica said: "But the Sisterhood believes you killed him."

Farad'n turned to his mother. "Show her the message."

As Wensicia hesitated, he spoke with an edge of anger which Jessica noted for future use. "I said show it to her!"

Face pale, Wensicia presented the message face of the cube to Jessica, activated it. Words flowed across the face, responding to Jessica's eye movements: *"Bene Gesserit Council on Wallach IX files formal protest against House Corrino in assassination of Leto Atreides II. Arguments and showing of evidence are assigned to Landsraad Internal Security Commission. Neutral ground will be chosen and names of judges will be submitted for approval by all parties. Your immediate response required. Sabit Rekush for the Landsraad."*

Wensicia returned to her son's side.

"How do you intend to respond?" Jessica asked.

Wensicia said: "Since my son has not yet been formally invested as head of House Corrino, I will—Where are you going?" This last was addressed to Farad'n who, as she spoke, turned and headed for a side door near the watchful mute.

Farad'n paused, half turned. "I'm going back to my books and the other pursuits which hold much more interest for me."

"How dare you?" Wensicia demanded. A dark flush spread from her neck up across her cheeks.

"I'll dare quite a few things in my own name," Farad'n said. "You have made decisions in my name, decisions which I find extremely distasteful. Either I will make the decisions in my own name from this point on or you can find yourself another heir for House Corrino!"

Jessica passed her gaze swiftly across the participants in this confrontation, seeing the real anger in Farad'n. The Bashar Aide stood stiffly at attention, trying to make it appear that he had heard nothing. Wensicia hesitated on the brink of screaming rage. Farad'n appeared perfectly willing to accept any outcome from his throw of the dice. Jessica rather admired his poise, seeing many things in this confrontation which could be of value to her. It seemed that the decision to send assassin tigers against her grandchildren had been made without Farad'n's knowledge. There could be little doubt of his truthfulness in saying he'd learned of the plot after its inception. There was no mistaking the real anger in his eyes as he stood there, ready to accept any decision.

Wensicia took a deep, trembling breath. Then: "Very well. The formal investiture will take place tomorrow. You may act in advance of it now." She looked at Tyekanik, who refused to meet her gaze.

There'll be a screaming fight once mother and son get out of here, Jessica thought. *But I do believe he has won.* She allowed her thoughts to return then to the message from the Landsraad. The Sisterhood had judged their messengers with a finesse which did credit to Bene Gesserit planning. Hidden in the formal notice of protest was a message for Jessica's eyes. The fact of the message said the Sisterhood's spies knew Jessica's situation and they'd gauged Farad'n with a superb nicety to guess he'd show it to his captive.

"I'd like an answer to my question," Jessica said, addressing herself to Farad'n as he returned to face her.

"I shall tell the Landsraad that I had nothing to do with this assassination," Farad'n said. "I will add that I share the Sisterhood's distaste for the manner of it, although I cannot be completely displeased at the outcome. My apologies for any grief this may have caused you. Fortune passes everywhere."

Fortune passes everywhere! Jessica thought. That'd been a favorite saying of her Duke, and there'd been something in Farad'n's manner which said he knew this. She forced herself to ignore the possibility that they'd really killed Leto. She had to assume that Ghanima's fears for Leto had motivated a complete revelation of the twins' plan. The smugglers would put Gurney in position to meet Leto then and the Sisterhood's devices would be carried out. Leto had to be tested. He had to be. Without the testing he was doomed as Alia was doomed. And Ghanima . . . Well, that could be faced later. There was no way to send the pre-born before the Reverend Mother Gaius Helen Mohiam.

Jessica allowed herself a deep sigh. "Sooner or later," she said, "it'll occur to someone that you and my granddaughter could unite our two Houses and heal old wounds."

"This has already been mentioned to me as a possibility," Farad'n said, glancing briefly at his mother. "My response was that I'd prefer to await the outcome of recent events on Arrakis. There's no need for a hasty decision."

"There's always the possibility that you've already played into my daughter's hands," Jessica said.

Farad'n stiffened. "Explain!"

"Matters on Arrakis are not as they may seem to you," Jessica said. "Alia plays her own game, Abomination's game. My granddaughter is in danger unless Alia can contrive a way to use her."

"You expect me to believe that you and your daughter oppose each other, that Atreides fights Atreides?"

Jessica looked at Wensicia, back to Farad'n. "Corrino fights Corrino."

A wry smile moved Farad'n's lips. "Well taken. How would I have played into your daughter's hands?"

"By becoming implicated in my grandson's death, by abducting me."

"Abduct . . ."

"Don't trust this witch," Wensicia cautioned.

"I'll choose whom to trust, mother," Farad'n said. "Forgive me, Lady Jessica, but I don't understand this matter of abduction. I'd understood that you and your faithful retainer—"

"Who is Alia's husband," Jessica said.

Farad'n turned a measuring stare on Idaho, looked to the Bashar. "What think you, Tyek?"

The Bashar apparently was having thoughts similar to those Jessica professed. He said: "I like her reasoning. Caution!"

"He's a ghola-mentat," Farad'n said. "We could test him to the death and not find a certain answer."

"But it's a safe working assumption that we may've been tricked," Tyekanik said.

Jessica knew the moment had come to make her move. Now if Idaho's grief only kept him locked in the part he'd chosen. She disliked using him this way, but there were larger considerations.

"To begin with," Jessica said, "I might announce publicly that I came here of my own free choice."

"Interesting," Farad'n said.

"You'd have to trust me and grant me the complete freedom of Salusa Secundus," Jessica said. "There could be no appearance that I spoke out of compulsion."

"No!" Wensicia protested.

Farad'n ignored her. "What reason would you give?"

"That I'm the Sisterhood's plenipotentiary sent here to take over your education."

"But the Sisterhood accuses—"

"That'd require a decisive action from you," Jessica said.

"Don't trust her!" Wensicia said.

With extreme politeness, Farad'n glanced at her, said: "If you interrupt me once more, I'll have Tyek remove you. He heard you consent to the formal investiture. That binds him to *me* now."

"She's a witch, I tell you!" Wensicia looked to the mute against the side wall.

Farad'n hesitated. Then: "Tyek, what think you? Have I been witched?"

"Not in my judgment. She—"

"You've both been witched!"

"Mother." His tone was flat and final.

Wensicia clenched her fists, tried to speak, whirled, and fled the room.

Addressing himself once more to Jessica, Farad'n asked: "Would the Bene Gesserit consent to this?"

"They would."

Farad'n absorbed the implications of this, smiled tightly. "What does the Sisterhood want in all of this?"

"Your marriage to my granddaughter."

Idaho shot a questioning look at Jessica, made as though to speak, but remained silent.

Jessica said: "You were going to say something, Duncan?"

"I was going to say that the Bene Gesserit want what they've always wanted: a universe which won't interfere with them."

"An obvious assumption," Farad'n said, "but I hardly see why you intrude with it."

Idaho's eyebrows managed the shrug which the shigawire would not permit his body. Disconcertingly, he smiled.

Farad'n saw the smile, whirled to confront Idaho. "I amuse you?"

"This whole situation amuses me. Someone in your family has compromised the Spacing Guild by using them to carry instruments of assassination to Arrakis, instruments whose intent could not be concealed. You've offended the Bene Gesserit by killing a male they wanted for their breeding pro—"

"You call me a liar, ghola?"

"No. I believe you didn't know about the plot. But I thought the situation needed bringing into focus."

"Don't forget that he's a mentat," Jessica cautioned.

"My very thought," Farad'n said. Once more he faced Jessica. "Let us say that I free you and you make your announcement. That still leaves the matter of your grandson's death. The mentat is correct."

"Was it your mother?" Jessica asked.

"My Lord!" Tyekanik warned.

"It's all right, Tyek." Farad'n waved a hand easily. "And if I say it was my mother?"

Risking everything in the test of this internal break among the Corrino, Jessica said: "You must denounce her and banish her."

"My Lord," Tyekanik said, "there could be trickery within trickery here."

Idaho said: "And the Lady Jessica and I are the ones who've been tricked."

Farad'n's jaw hardened.

And Jessica thought: *Don't interfere, Duncan! Not now!* But Idaho's words had sent her own Bene Gesserit abilities at logic into motion. He shocked her. She began to wonder if there were the possibility that she was being used in ways she didn't understand. Ghanima and Leto. . . . The pre-born could draw upon countless inner experiences, a storehouse of advice far more extensive than the living Bene Gesserit depended upon. And there was that other question: Had her own Sisterhood been completely candid with her? They still might not trust her. After all, she'd betrayed them once . . . to her Duke.

Farad'n looked at Idaho with a puzzled frown. "Mentat, I need to know what this Preacher is to you."

"He arranged the passage here. I. . . . We did not exchange ten words. Others acted for him. He could be. . . . He could be Paul Atreides, but I don't have enough data for certainty. All I know for certain is that it was time for me to leave and he had the means."

"You speak of being tricked," Farad'n reminded him.

"Alia expects you to kill us quietly and conceal the evidence of it," Idaho said. "Having rid her of the Lady Jessica, I'm no longer useful. And the Lady Jessica, having served her Sisterhood's purposes, is no longer useful to them. Alia will be calling the Bene Gesserit to account, but they will win."

Jessica closed her eyes in concentration. He was right! She could hear the mentat firmness in his voice, that deep sincerity of pronouncement. The pattern fell into place without a chink. She took two deep breaths and triggered the mnemonic trance, rolled the data through her mind, came out of the trance and opened her eyes. It was done while

Farad'n moved from in front of her to a position within half a step of Idaho—a space of no more than three steps.

"Say no more, Duncan," Jessica said, and she thought mournfully of how Leto had warned her against Bene Gesserit conditioning.

Idaho, about to speak, closed his mouth.

"I command here," Farad'n said. "Continue, mentat."

Idaho remained silent.

Farad'n half turned to study Jessica.

She stared at a point on the far wall, reviewing what Idaho and the trance had built. The Bene Gesserit hadn't abandoned the Atreides line, of course. But they wanted control of a Kwisatz Haderach and they'd invested too much in the long breeding program. They wanted the open clash between Atreides and Corrino, a situation where they could step in as arbiters. And Duncan was right. They'd emerge with control of both Ghanima and Farad'n. It was the only compromise possible. The wonder was that Alia hadn't seen it. Jessica swallowed past a tightness in her throat. Alia. . . . Abomination! Ghanima was right to pity her. But who was left to pity Ghanima?

"The Sisterhood has promised to put you on the throne with Ghanima as your mate," Jessica said.

Farad'n took a backward step. Did the witch read minds?

"They worked secretly and not through your mother," Jessica said. "They told you I was not privy to their plan."

Jessica read revelation in Farad'n's face. How open he was. But it was true, the whole structure. Idaho had demonstrated masterful abilities as a mentat in seeing through to the fabric on the limited data available to him.

"So they played a double game and told you," Farad'n said.

"They told me nothing of this," Jessica said. "Duncan was correct: they tricked me." She nodded to herself. It had been a classic delaying action in the Sisterhood's traditional pattern—a reasonable story, easily accepted because it squared with what one might believe of their motives. But they wanted Jessica out of the way—a flawed sister who'd failed them once.

Tyekanik moved to Farad'n's side. "My Lord, these two are too dangerous to—"

"Wait a bit, Tyek," Farad'n said. "There are wheels within wheels here." He faced Jessica. "We've had reasons to believe that Alia might offer herself as my bride."

Idaho gave an involuntary start, controlled himself. Blood began dripping from his left wrist where the shigawire had cut.

Jessica allowed herself a small, eye-widening response. She who'd known the original Leto as lover, father of her children, confidant and friend, saw his trait of cold reasoning filtered now through the twistings of an Abomination.

"Will you accept?" Idaho asked.

"It is being considered."

"Duncan, I told you to be silent," Jessica said. She addressed Farad'n. "Her price was two inconsequential deaths—the two of us."

"We suspected treachery," Farad'n said. "Wasn't it your son who said 'treachery breeds treachery?'"

"The Sisterhood is out to control both Atreides and Corrino," Jessica said. "Isn't that obvious?"

"We're toying now with the idea of accepting your offer, Lady Jessica, but Duncan Idaho should be sent back to his loving wife."

Pain is a function of nerves, Idaho reminded himself. *Pain comes as light comes to the eyes. Effort comes from the muscles, not from nerves.* It was an old mentat drill and he completed it in the space of one breath, flexed his right wrist and severed an artery against the shigawire.

Tyekanik leaped to the chair, hit its trip lock to release the bindings, shouted for medical aid. It was revealing that assistants came swarming at once through doors hidden in wall panels.

There was always a bit of foolishness in Duncan, Jessica thought.

Farad'n studied Jessica a moment while the medics ministered to Idaho. "I didn't say I was going to accept his Alia."

"That's not why he cut his wrist," Jessica said.

"Oh? I thought he was simply removing himself."

"You're not that stupid," Jessica said. "Stop pretending with me."

He smiled. "I'm well aware that Alia would destroy me. Not even the Bene Gesserit could expect me to accept her."

Jessica bent a weighted stare upon Farad'n. What was this young scion of House Corrino? He didn't play the fool well. Again, she recalled Leto's words that she'd encounter an interesting student. And The Preacher wanted this as well, Idaho said. She wished she'd met this Preacher.

"Will you banish Wensicia?" Jessica asked.

"It seems a reasonable bargain," Farad'n said.

Jessica glanced at Idaho. The medics had finished with him. Less dangerous restraints held him in the floater chair.

"Mentats should beware of absolutes," she said.

"I'm tired," Idaho said. "You've no idea how tired I am."

"When it's overexploited, even loyalty wears out finally," Farad'n said.

Again Jessica shot that measuring stare at him.

Farad'n, seeing this, thought: *In time she'll know me for certain and that could be valuable. A renegade Bene Gesserit of my own! It's the one thing her son had that I don't have. Let her get only a glimpse of me now. She can see the rest later.*

"A fair exchange," Farad'n said. "I accept your offer on your terms." He signaled the mute against the wall with a complex flickering of fingers. The mute nodded. Farad'n bent to the chair's controls, released Jessica.

Tyekanik asked: "My Lord, are you sure?"

"Isn't it what we discussed?" Farad'n asked.

"Yes, but . . ."

Farad'n chuckled, addressed Jessica. "Tyek suspects my sources. But one learns from books and reels only that certain things can be done. Actual learning requires that you do those things."

Jessica mused on this as she lifted herself from the chair. Her mind returned to Farad'n's hand signals. He had an Atreides-style battle language! It spoke of careful analysis. Someone here was consciously copying the Atreides.

"Of course," Jessica said, "you'll want me to teach you as the Bene Gesserit are taught."

Farad'n beamed at her. "The one offer I cannot resist," he said.

The password was given to me by a man who died in the dungeons of Arrakeen. You see, that is where I got this ring in the
shape of a tortoise. It was in the *suk* outside the city where I
was hidden by the rebels. The password? Oh, that has been
changed many times since then. It was "Persistence." And the
countersign was "Tortoise." It got me out of there alive. That's
why I bought this ring: a reminder.

—TAGIR MOHANDIS: CONVERSATIONS WITH A FRIEND

Leto was far out on the sand when he heard the worm behind him,
coming to his thumper there and the dusting of spice he'd spread
around the dead tigers. There was a good omen for this beginning of
their plan: worms were scarce enough in these parts most times. The
worm was not essential, but it helped. There would be no need for
Ghanima to explain a missing body.

By this time he knew that Ghanima had worked herself into the
belief that he was dead. Only a tiny, isolated capsule of awareness would
remain to her, a walled-off memory which could be recalled by words
uttered in the ancient language shared only by the two of them in all
of this universe. *Secher Nbiw.* If she heard those words: *Golden
Path* . . . only then would she remember him. Until then, he was dead.

Now Leto felt truly alone.

He moved with the random walk which made only those sounds
natural to the desert. Nothing in his passage would tell that worm back
there that human flesh moved here. It was a way of walking so deeply

conditioned in him that he didn't need to think about it. The feet moved of themselves, no measurable rhythm to their pacing. Any sound his feet made could be ascribed to the wind, to gravity. No human passed here.

When the worm had done its work behind him, Leto crouched behind a dune's slipface and peered back toward The Attendant. Yes, he was far enough. He planted a thumper and summoned his transportation. The worm came swiftly, giving him barely enough time to position himself before it engulfed the thumper. As it passed, he went up its side on the Maker hooks, opened the sensitive leading edge of a ring, and turned the mindless beast southeastward. It was a small worm, but strong. He could sense the strength in its twisting as it hissed across the dunes. There was a following breeze and he felt the heat of their passage, the friction which the worm converted to the beginnings of spice within itself.

As the worm moved, his mind moved. Stilgar had taken him up for his first worm journey. Leto had only to let his memory flow and he could hear Stilgar's voice: calm and precise, full of politeness from another age. Not for Stilgar the threatening staggers of a Fremen drunk on spice-liquor. Not for Stilgar the loud voice and bluster of these times. No—Stilgar had his duties. He was an instructor of royalty: "In the olden times, the birds were named for their songs. Each wind had its name. A six-klick wind was called a Pastaza, a twenty-klick wind was Cueshma, and a hundred-klick wind was Heinali—Heinali, the man-pusher. Then there was the wind of the demon in the open desert: Hulasikali Wala, the wind that eats flesh."

And Leto, who'd already known these things, had nodded his gratitude at the wisdom of such instruction.

But Stilgar's voice could be filled with many valuable things.

"There were in olden times certain tribes which were known to be water hunters. They were called Iduali, which meant 'water insects,' because those people wouldn't hesitate to steal the water of another Fremen. If they caught you alone in the desert they would not even leave you the water of your flesh. There was this place where they lived: Sietch Jacurutu. That's where the other tribes banded and wiped out the Iduali. That was a long time ago, before Kynes even—in my great-great-grandfather's days. And from that day to this, no Fremen has gone to Jacurutu. It is tabu."

Thus had Leto been reminded of knowledge which lay in his memory. It had been an important lesson about the working of memory. A memory was not enough, even for one whose past was as multiform as his, unless its use was known and its value revealed to judgment. Jacurutu would have water, a wind trap, all of the attributes of a Fremen sietch, plus the value without compare that no Fremen would venture there. Many of the young would not even know such a place as Jacurutu had ever existed. Oh, they would know about Fondak, of course, but that was a smuggler place.

It was a perfect place for the dead to hide—among the smugglers and the dead of another age.

Thank you, Stilgar.

The worm tired before dawn. Leto slid off its side and watched it dig itself into the dunes, moving slowly in the familiar pattern of the creatures. It would go deep and sulk.

I must wait out the day, he thought.

He stood atop a dune and scanned all around: emptiness, emptiness, emptiness. Only the wavering track of the vanished worm broke the pattern.

The slow cry of a nightbird challenged the first green line of light along the eastern horizon. Leto dug himself into the sand's concealment, inflated a stilltent around his body and sent the tip of a sand-snorkel questing for air.

For a long time before sleep came, he lay in the enforced darkness thinking about the decision he and Ghanima had made. It had not been an easy decision, especially for Ghanima. He had not told her all of his vision, nor all of the reasoning derived from it. It was a vision, not a dream, in his thinking now. But the peculiarity of this thing was that he saw it as a vision of a vision. If any argument existed to convince him that his father still lived, it lay in that vision-vision.

The life of the prophet locks us into his vision, Leto thought. *And a prophet could only break out of the vision by creating his death at vari-ance with that vision.* That was how it appeared in Leto's doubled vision, and he pondered this as it related to the choice he had made. *Poor Baptist John,* he thought. *If he'd only had the courage to die some other way. . . . But perhaps his choice had been the bravest one. How do I know what alternatives faced him? I know what alternatives faced my father, though.*

Leto sighed. To turn his back on his father was like betraying a god. But the Atreides Empire needed shaking up. It had fallen into the worst of Paul's vision. How casually it obliterated men. It was done without a second thought. The mainspring of a religious insanity had been wound tight and left ticking.

And we're locked in my father's vision.

A way out of that insanity lay along the Golden Path, Leto knew. His father had seen it. But humanity might come out of that Golden Path and look back down it at Muad'Dib's time, seeing that as a better age. Humankind had to experience the alternative to Muad'Dib, though, or never understand its own myths.

Security . . . peace . . . prosperity . . .

Given the choice, there was little doubt what most citizens of this Empire would select.

Though they hate me, he thought. *Though Ghani hate me.*

His right hand itched, and he thought of the terrible glove in his vision-vision. *It will be,* he thought. *Yes, it will be.*

Arrakis, give me strength, he prayed. His planet remained strong and alive beneath him and around him. Its sand pressed close against the stilltent. Dune was a giant counting its massed riches. It was a beguiling entity, both beautiful and grossly ugly. The only coin its merchants really knew was the bloodpulse of their own power, no matter how that power had been amassed. They possessed this planet the way a man might possess a captive mistress, or the way the Bene Gesserits possessed their Sisters.

No wonder Stilgar hated the merchant-priests.

Thank you, Stilgar.

Leto recalled then the beauties of the old sietch ways, the life lived before the coming of the Imperium's technocracy, and his mind flowed as he knew Stilgar's dreams flowed. Before the glowglobes and lasers, before the ornithopters and spice-crawlers, there'd been another kind of life: brown-skinned mothers with babies on their hips, lamps which burned spice-oil amidst a heavy fragrance of cinnamon, Naibs who persuaded their people while knowing none could be compelled. It had been a darkswarming of life in rocky burrows . . .

A terrible glove will restore the balance, Leto thought.

Presently, he slept.

I saw his blood and a piece of his robe which had been ripped by sharp claws. His sister reports vividly of the tigers, the sureness of their attack. We have questioned one of the plotters, and others are dead or in custody. Everything points to a Corrino plot. A Truthsayer has attested to this testimony.

—STILGAR'S REPORT TO THE LANDSRAAD COMMISSION

Farad'n studied Duncan Idaho through the spy circuit, seeking a clue to that strange man's behavior. It was shortly after noon and Idaho waited outside the quarters assigned to the Lady Jessica, seeking audience with her. Would she see him? She'd know they were spied upon, of course. But would she see him?

Around Farad'n lay the room where Tyekanik had guided the training of the Laza tigers—an illegal room, really, filled as it was with forbidden instruments from the hands of the Tleilaxu and Ixians. By the movement of switches at his right hand, Farad'n could look at Idaho from six different angles, or shift to the interior of the Lady Jessica's suite where the spying facilities were equally sophisticated.

Idaho's eyes bothered Farad'n. Those pitted metal orbs which the Tleilaxu had given their ghola in the regrowth tanks marked their possessor as profoundly different from other humans. Farad'n touched his own eyelids, feeling the hard surfaces of the permanent contact lenses which concealed the total blue of his spice addiction. Idaho's eyes must record a different universe. How could it be otherwise. It almost tempted Farad'n to seek out the Tleilaxu surgeons and answer that question himself.

Why did Idaho try to kill himself?

Was that really what he'd tried? He must've known we wouldn't permit it.

Idaho remained a dangerous question mark.

Tyekanik wanted to keep him on Salusa or kill him. Perhaps that would be best.

Farad'n shifted to a frontal view. Idaho sat on a hard bench outside the door to the Lady Jessica's suite. It was a windowless foyer with light wood walls decorated by lance pennants. Idaho had been on that bench more than an hour and appeared ready to wait there forever. Farad'n bent close to the screen. The loyal swordmaster of the Atreides, instructor of Paul Muad'Dib, had been treated kindly by his years on Arrakis. He'd arrived with a youthful spring in his step. A steady spice diet must have helped him, of course. And that marvelous metabolic balance which the Tleilaxu tanks always imparted. Did Idaho really remember his past before the tanks? No other whom the Tleilaxu had revived could claim this. What an enigma this Idaho was!

The reports of his death were in the library. The Sardaukar who'd slain him reported his prowess: nineteen of their number dispatched by Idaho before he'd fallen. Nineteen Sardaukar! His flesh had been well worth sending to the regrowth tanks. But the Tleilaxu had made a mentat out of him. What a strange creature lived in that regrown flesh. How did it feel to be a human computer in addition to all of his other talents?

Why did he try to kill himself?

Farad'n knew his own talents and held few illusions about them. He was a historian-archaeologist and judge of men. Necessity had forced him to become an expert on those who would serve him—necessity and a careful study of the Atreides. He saw it as the price always demanded of aristocracy. To rule required accurate and incisive judgments about those who wielded your power. More than one ruler had fallen through mistakes and excesses of his underlings.

Careful study of the Atreides revealed a superb talent in choosing servants. They'd known how to maintain loyalty, how to keep a fine edge on the ardor of their warriors.

Idaho was not acting in character.

Why?

Farad'n squinted his eyes, trying to see past the skin of this man. There was a sense of duration about Idaho, a feeling that he could not be worn down. He gave the impression of being self-contained, an organized and firmly integrated whole. The Tleilaxu tanks had set something more than human into motion. Farad'n sensed this. There was a self-renewing movement about the man, as though he acted in accordance with immutable laws, beginning anew at every ending. He moved in a fixed orbit with an endurance about him like that of a planet around a star. He would respond to pressure without breaking—merely shifting his orbit slightly but not really changing anything basic.

Why did he cut his wrist?

Whatever his motive, he had done it for the Atreides, for his ruling House. The Atreides were the star of his orbit.

Somehow he believes that my holding the Lady Jessica here strengthens the Atreides.

And Farad'n reminded himself: *A mentat thinks this.*

It gave the thought an added depth. Mentats made mistakes, but not often.

Having come to this conclusion, Farad'n almost summoned his aides to have them send the Lady Jessica away with Idaho. He poised himself on the point of acting, withdrew.

Both of those people—the ghola-mentat and the Bene Gesserit witch—remained counters of unknown denomination in this game of power. Idaho must be sent back because that would certainly stir up troubles on Arrakis. Jessica must be kept here, drained of her strange knowledge to benefit House Corrino.

Farad'n knew it was a subtle and deadly game he played. But he had prepared himself for this possibility over the years, ever since he'd realized that he was more intelligent, more sensitive than those around him. It had been a frightening discovery for a child, and he knew the library had been his refuge as well as his teacher.

Doubts ate at him now, though, and he wondered if he was quite up to this game. He'd alienated his mother, lost her counsel, but her decisions had always been dangerous to him. Tigers! Their training had been an atrocity and their use had been stupidity. How easy they were to trace! She should be thankful to suffer nothing more than banishment. The Lady Jessica's advice had fitted his needs with a lovely precision there. She must be made to divulge the way of that Atreides thinking.

His doubts began to fade away. He thought of his Sardaukar once more growing tough and resilient through the rigorous training and the denial of luxury which he commanded. His Sardaukar legions remained small, but once more they were a man-to-man match for the Fremen. That served little purpose as long as the limits imposed by the Treaty of Arrakeen governed the relative size of the forces. Fremen could overwhelm him by their numbers—unless they were tied up and weakened by civil war.

It was too soon for a battle of Sardaukar against Fremen. He needed time. He needed new allies from among the discontented Houses Major and the newly powerful from the Houses Minor. He needed access to CHOAM financing. He needed the time for his Sardaukar to grow stronger and the Fremen to grow weaker.

Again Farad'n looked at the screen which revealed the patient ghola. Why did Idaho want to see the Lady Jessica at this time? He would know they were spied upon, that every word, every gesture would be recorded and analyzed.

Why?

Farad'n glanced away from the screen to the ledge beside his control console. In the pale electronic light he could make out the spools which contained the latest reports from Arrakis. His spies were thorough; he had to give them credit. There was much to give him hope and pleasure in those reports. He closed his eyes, and the high points of those reports

passed through his mind in the oddly editorial form to which he'd reduced the spools for his own uses:

*As the planet is made fertile, Fremen are freed of land pressures and
their new communities lose the traditional sietch-stronghold character.
From infancy, in the old sietch culture, the Fremen was taught by the rota:
"Like the knowledge of your own being, the sietch forms a firm base from
which you move out into the world and into the universe."*

*The traditional Fremen says: "Look to the Massif," meaning that the
master science is the Law. But the new social structure is loosening those
old legal restrictions; discipline grows lax. The new Fremen leaders know
only their Low Catechism of ancestry plus the history which is camouflaged in the myth structure of their songs. People of the new communities
are more volatile, more open; they quarrel more often and are less responsive to authority. The old sietch folk are more disciplined, more inclined
to group actions and they tend to work harder; they are more careful of
their resources. The old folk still believe that the orderly society is the
fulfillment of the individual. The young grow away from this belief. Those
remnants of the older culture which remain look at the young and say:
"The death wind has etched away their past."*

Farad'n liked the pointedness of his own summary. The new diversity on Arrakis could only bring violence. He had the essential concepts
firmly etched into the spools:

*The religion of Muad'Dib is based firmly in the old Fremen sietch
cultural tradition while the new culture moves farther and farther from
those disciplines.*

Not for the first time, Farad'n asked himself why Tyekanik had embraced that religion. Tyekanik behaved oddly in his new morality. He
seemed utterly sincere, but carried along as though against his will.
Tyekanik was like one who had stepped into the whirlwind to test it and
had been caught up by forces beyond his control. Tyekanik's conversion
annoyed Farad'n by its characterless completeness. It was a reversion
to very old Sardaukar ways. He warned that the young Fremen might
yet revert in a similar way, that the inborn, ingrained traditions would
prevail.

Once more Farad'n thought about those report spools. They told of a disquieting thing: the persistence of a cultural remnant from the most ancient Fremen times—"The Water of Conception." The amniotic fluid of the newborn was saved at birth, distilled into the first water fed to that child. The traditional form required a godmother to serve the water, saying: "Here is the water of thy conception." Even the young Fremen still followed this tradition with their own newborn.

The water of thy conception.

Farad'n found himself revolted by the idea of drinking water distilled from the amniotic fluid which had borne him. And he thought about the surviving twin, Ghanima, her mother dead when she'd taken that strange water. Had she reflected later upon that odd link with her past? Probably not. She'd been raised Fremen. What was natural and acceptable to Fremen had been natural and acceptable to her.

Momentarily Farad'n regretted the death of Leto II. It would have been interesting to discuss this point with him. Perhaps an opportunity would come to discuss it with Ghanima.

Why did Idaho cut his wrists?

The question persisted every time he glanced at the spy screen. Again doubts assailed Farad'n. He longed for the ability to sink into the mysterious spice trance as Paul Muad'Dib had done, there to seek out the future and *know* the answers to his questions. No matter how much spice he ingested, though, his ordinary awareness persisted in its singular flow of *now*, reflecting a universe of uncertainties.

The spy screen showed a servant opening the Lady Jessica's door. The woman beckoned Idaho, who arose from the bench and went through the door. The servant would file a complete report later, but Farad'n, his curiosity once more fully aroused, touched another switch on his console, watched as Idaho entered the sitting room of the Lady Jessica's quarters.

How calm and contained the mentat appeared. And how fathomless were his ghola eyes.

Above all else, the mentat must be a generalist, not a specialist. It is wise to have decisions of great moment monitored by generalists. Experts and specialists lead you quickly into chaos. They are a source of useless nit-picking, the ferocious quibble over a comma. The mentat-generalist, on the other hand, should bring to decision-making a healthy common sense. He must not cut himself off from the broad sweep of what is happening in his universe. He must remain capable of saying: "There's no real mystery about this at the moment. This is what we want now. It may prove wrong later, but we'll correct that when we come to it." The mentat-generalist must understand that anything which we can identify as our universe is merely part of larger phenomena. But the expert looks backward; he looks into the narrow standards of his own specialty. The generalist looks outward; he looks for living principles, knowing full well that such principles change, that they develop. It is to the characteristics of change itself that the mentat-generalist must look. There can be no permanent catalogue of such change, no handbook or manual. You must look at it with as few preconceptions as possible, asking yourself: "Now what is this thing doing?"

—THE MENTAT HANDBOOK

It was the day of the Kwisatz Haderach, the first Holy Day of those who followed Muad'Dib. It recognized the deified Paul Atreides as that person who was everywhere simultaneously, the male Bene Gesserit who mingled both male and female ancestry in an inseparable power to become the One-with-All. The faithful called this day *Ayil*, the Sacrifice, to commemorate the death which made his presence "real in all places."

The Preacher chose the early morning of this day to appear once more in the plaza of Alia's temple, defying the order for his arrest which everyone knew had been issued. The delicate truce prevailed between Alia's Priesthood and those desert tribes which had rebelled, but the presence of this truce could be felt as a tangible thing which moved everyone in Arrakeen with uneasiness. The Preacher did not dispel that mood.

It was the twenty-eighth day of official mourning for Muad'Dib's son, six days following the memorial rite at Old Pass which had been delayed by the rebellion. Even the fighting had not stopped the Hajj, though. The Preacher knew the plaza would be heavily thronged on this day. Most pilgrims tried to time their stay on Arrakis to cross *Ayil*, "to feel then the Holy Presence of the Kwisatz Haderach on His day."

The Preacher entered the plaza at first light, finding the place already thronging with the faithful. He kept a hand lightly on the shoulder of his young guide, sensing the cynical pride in the lad's walk. Now, when the Preacher approached, people noticed every nuance of his behavior. Such attention was not entirely distasteful to the young guide. The Preacher merely accepted it as a necessity.

Taking his stance on the third of the Temple's steps, The Preacher waited for the hush to come. When silence had spread like a wave through the throng and the hurrying footsteps of others come to listen could be heard at the plaza's limits, he cleared his throat. It was still morning-cold around him and lights had not yet come down into the plaza from the building tops. He felt the grey hush of the great square as he began to speak.

"I have come to give homage and to preach in the memory of Leto Atreides II," he said, calling out in that strong voice so reminiscent of a wormsman from the desert. "I do it in compassion for all who suffer. I say to you what the dead Leto has learned, that tomorrow has not yet happened and may never happen. This moment here is the only observable time and place for us in our universe. I tell you to savor this moment and understand what it teaches. I tell you to learn that a government's growth and its death are apparent in the growth and death of its citizens."

A disturbed murmur passed through the plaza. Did he mock the death of Leto II? They wondered if Priest Guards would rush out now and arrest The Preacher.

Alia knew there would be no such interruption of The Preacher. It was her order that he be left unmolested on this day. She had disguised herself in a good stillsuit with a moisture mask to conceal her nose and mouth, and a common hooded robe to hide her hair. She stood in the second row beneath The Preacher, watching him carefully. Was this Paul? The years might have changed him thus. And he had always been superb with Voice, a fact which made it difficult to identify him by his speech. Still, this Preacher made his voice do what he wanted. Paul could not have done it better. She felt that she had to know his identity before she could act against him. How his words dazzled her!

She sensed no irony in The Preacher's statement. He was using the seductive attraction of definite sentences uttered with a driving sincerity. People might stumble only momentarily at his meanings, realizing that he had meant them to stumble, teaching them in this fashion. Indeed, he picked up the crowd's response, saying: "Irony often masks the inability to think beyond one's assumptions. I am not being ironic. Ghanima has said to you that the blood of her brother cannot be washed off. I concur.

"It will be said that Leto has gone where his father went, has done what his father did. Muad'Dib's Church says he chose in behalf of his own humanity a course which might appear absurd and foolhardy, but which history will validate. That history is being rewritten even now.

"I say to you that there is another lesson to be learned from these lives and their endings."

Alia, alert to every nuance, asked herself why The Preacher said *endings* instead of *deaths*. Was he saying that one or both were not truly dead? How could that be? A Truthsayer had confirmed Ghanima's story. What was this Preacher doing, then? Was he making a statement of myth or reality?

"Note this other lesson well!" The Preacher thundered, lifting his arms. "If you would possess your humanity, let go of the universe!"

He lowered his arms, pointed his empty sockets directly at Alia. He seemed to be speaking intimately to her, an action so obvious that several around her turned to peer inquiringly in her direction. Alia shivered at the power in him. This could be Paul. It could!

"But I realize that humans cannot bear very much reality," he said. "Most lives are a flight from selfhood. Most prefer the truths of the stable. You stick your heads into the stanchions and munch contentedly until you die. Others use you for their purposes. Not once do you live outside the stable to lift your head and be your own creature. Muad'Dib came to tell you about that. Without understanding his message, you cannot revere him!"

Someone in the throng, possibly a Priest in disguise, could stand no more. His hoarse male voice was lifted in a shout: "You don't live the life of Muad'Dib! How dare you to tell others how they must revere him!"

"Because he's dead!" The Preacher bellowed.

Alia turned to see who had challenged The Preacher. The man remained hidden from her, but his voice came over the intervening heads in another shout: "If you believe him truly dead, then you are alone from this time forward!"

Surely it was a Priest, Alia thought. But she failed to recognize the voice.

"I come only to ask a simple question," The Preacher said. "Is Muad'Dib's death to be followed by the moral suicide of all men? Is that the inevitable aftermath of a Messiah?"

"Then you admit him Messiah!" the voice from the crowd shouted.

"Why not, since I'm the prophet of his times?" The Preacher asked.

There was such calm assurance in his tone and manner that even his challenger fell silent. The crowd responded with a disturbed murmur, a low animal sound.

"Yes," The Preacher repeated, "I am the prophet of these times."

Alia, concentrating on him, detected the subtle inflections of Voice. He'd certainly controlled the crowd. Was he Bene Gesserit trained?

Was this another ploy of the Missionaria Protectiva? Not Paul at all, but just another part of the endless power game?

"I articulate the myth and the dream!" The Preacher shouted. "I am the physician who delivers the child and announces that the child is born. Yet I come to you at a time of death. Does that not disturb you? It should shake your souls!"

Even as she felt anger at his words, Alia understood the pointed way of his speech. With others, she found herself edging closer up the steps, crowding toward this tall man in desert garb. His young guide caught her attention: how bright-eyed and saucy the lad appeared! Would Muad'Dib employ such a cynical youth?

"I mean to disturb you!" The Preacher shouted. "It is my intention! I come here to combat the fraud and illusion of your conventional, in-stitutionalized religion. As with all such religions, your institution moves toward cowardice, it moves toward mediocrity, inertia, and self-satisfaction."

Angry murmurs began to arise in the center of the throng.

Alia felt the tensions and gloatingly wondered if there might not be a riot. Could The Preacher handle these tensions? If not, he could die right here!

"That Priest who challenged me!" The Preacher called, pointing into the crowd.

He knows! Alia thought. A thrill ran through her, almost sexual in its undertones. This Preacher played a dangerous game, but he played it consummately.

"You, Priest in your mufti," The Preacher called, "you are a chaplain to the self-satisfied. I come not to challenge Muad'Dib but to challenge you! Is your religion real when it costs you nothing and carries no risk? Is your religion real when you fatten upon it? Is your religion real when you commit atrocities in its name? Whence comes your downward de-generation from the original revelation? Answer me, Priest!"

But the challenger remained silent. And Alia noted that the crowd once more was listening with avid submission to The Preacher's every word. By attacking the Priesthood, he had their sympathy! And if her spies were correct, most of the pilgrims and Fremen on Arrakis believed this man was Muad'Dib.

"The son of Muad'Dib risked!" The Preacher shouted, and Alia heard tears in his voice. "Muad'Dib risked! They paid their price! And what did Muad'Dib achieve? A religion which is doing away with him!"

How different those words if they come from Paul himself, Alia thought. *I must find out!* She moved closer up the steps and others moved with her. She pressed through the throng until she could almost reach out and touch this mysterious prophet. She smelled the desert on him, a mixture of spice and flint. Both The Preacher and his young guide were dusty, as though they'd recently come from the *bled.* She could see where The Preacher's hands were deeply veined along the skin protruding from the wrist seals of his stillsuit. She could see that one finger of his left hand had worn a ring; the indentation remained. Paul had worn a ring on that finger: the Atreides Hawk which now reposed in Sietch Tabr. Leto would have worn it had he lived . . . or had she permitted him to ascend the throne.

Again The Preacher aimed his empty sockets at Alia, spoke intimately, but with a voice which carried across the throng.

"Muad'Dib showed you two things: a certain future and an uncertain future. With full awareness, he confronted the ultimate uncertainty of the larger universe. He stepped off *blindly* from his position on this world. He showed us that men must do this always, choosing the uncertain instead of the certain." His voice, Alia noted, took on a pleading tone at the end of this statement.

Alia glanced around, slipped a hand onto the hilt of her crysknife. *If I killed him right now, what would they do?* Again, she felt a thrill rush through her. *If I killed him and revealed myself, denouncing The Preacher as impostor and heretic!*

But what if they proved it was Paul?

Someone pushed Alia even closer to him. She felt herself enthralled by his presence even as she fought to still her anger. Was this Paul? Gods below! What could she do?

"Why has another Leto been taken from us?" The Preacher demanded. There was real pain in his voice. "Answer me if you can! Ahhhh, their message is clear: abandon certainty." He repeated it in a rolling stentorian shout: "Abandon certainty! That's life's deepest command. That's what life's all about. We're a probe into the unknown, into the uncertain. Why can't you hear Muad'Dib? If certainty is knowing absolutely an absolute future, then that's only death disguised! Such a future becomes *now*! He showed you this!"

With a terrifying directness The Preacher reached out, grabbed Alia's arm. It was done without any groping or hesitation. She tried to pull away, but he held her in a painful grip, speaking directly into her face as those around them edged back in confusion.

"What did Paul Atreides tell you, woman?" he demanded.

How does he know I'm a woman? she asked herself. She wanted to sink into her inner lives, ask their protection, but the world within remained frighteningly silent, mesmerized by this figure from their past.

"He told you that completion equals death!" The Preacher shouted. "Absolute prediction is completion . . . is death!"

She tried to pry his fingers away. She wanted to grab her knife and slash him away from her, but dared not. She had never felt this daunted in all of her life.

The Preacher lifted his chin to speak over her to the crowd, shouted: "I give you Muad'Dib's words! He said, 'I'm going to rub your faces in things you try to avoid. I don't find it strange that all you want to believe is only that which comforts you. How else do humans invent the traps which betray us into mediocrity? How else do we define cowardice?' That's what Muad'Dib told you!"

Abruptly he released Alia's arm, thrust her into the crowd. She would have fallen but for the press of people supporting her.

"To exist is to stand out, away from the background," The Preacher said. "You aren't thinking or really existing unless you're willing to risk even your own sanity in the judgment of your existence."

Stepping down, The Preacher once more took Alia's arm—no faltering or hesitation. He was gentler this time, though. Leaning close, he pitched his voice for her ears alone, said: "Stop trying to pull me once more into the background, sister."

Then, hand on his young guide's shoulder, he stepped into the throng. Way was made for the strange pair. Hands reached out to touch The Preacher, but people reached with an awesome tenderness, fearful of what they might find beneath that dusty Fremen robe.

Alia stood alone in her shock as the throng moved out behind The Preacher.

Certainty filled her. It was Paul. No doubt remained. It was her brother. She felt what the crowd felt. She had stood in the sacred presence and now her universe tumbled all about her. She wanted to run after him, pleading for him to save her from herself, but she could not move. While others pressed to follow The Preacher and his guide, she stood intoxicated with an absolute despair, a distress so deep that she could only tremble with it, unable to command her own muscles.

What will I do? What will I do? she asked herself.

Now she did not even have Duncan to lean upon, nor her mother. The inner lives remained silent. There was Ghanima, held securely under guard within the Keep, but Alia could not bring herself to take this distress to the surviving twin.

Everyone has turned against me. What can I do?

> The one-eyed view of our universe says you must not look far afield for problems. Such problems may never arrive. Instead, tend to the wolf within your fences. The packs ranging outside may not even exist.
>
> —THE AZHAR BOOK; SHAMRA 1:4

Jessica awaited Idaho at the window of her sitting room. It was a comfortable room with soft divans and old-fashioned chairs. There wasn't a suspensor in any of her rooms, and the glowglobes were crystal from another age. Her window overlooked a courtyard garden one story down.

She heard the servant open the door, then the sound of Idaho's footsteps on the wood floor, then on the carpet. She listened without turning, kept her gaze upon the dappled light of the courtyard's green floor. The silent, fearful warfare of her emotions must be suppressed now. She took the deep breaths of her *prana-bindu* training, felt the outflow of enforced calmness.

The high sun threw its searchlight along a dustbeam into the courtyard, highlighting the silver wheel of a spiderweb stretched in the branches of a linden tree which reached almost to her window. It was cool within her quarters, but outside the sealed window there was air which trembled with petrified heat. Castle Corrino sat in a stagnant place which belied the greens in her courtyard.

She heard Idaho stop directly behind her.

Without turning, she said: "The gift of words is the gift of deception and illusion, Duncan. Why do you wish words with me?"

"It may be that only one of us will survive," he said.

"And you wish me to make a good report of your efforts?" She turned, saw how calmly he stood there, watching her with those grey metal eyes which held no center of focus. How blank they were!

"Duncan, is it possible that you're jealous of your place in history?"

She spoke accusingly and remembered as she spoke that other time when she'd confronted this man. He'd been drunk then, set to spy upon her, and was torn by conflicting obligations. But that had been a pre-ghola Duncan. This was not the same man at all. This one was not divided in his actions, not torn.

He proved her summation by smiling. "History holds its own court and delivers its own judgments," he said. "I doubt that I'll be concerned when my judgment's handed down."

"Why are you here?" she asked.

"For the same reason you're here, My Lady."

No outward sign betrayed the shocking power of those simple words, but she reflected at a furious pace: *Does he really know why I'm here?* How could he? Only Ghanima knew. Then had he enough data for a mentat computation? That was possible. And what if he said something to give her away? Would he do that if he shared her reason for being here? He must know their every movement, every word was being spied upon by Farad'n or his servants.

"House Atreides has come to a bitter crossroads," she said. "Family turned against itself. You were among my Duke's most loyal men, Duncan. When the Baron Harkonnen—"

"Let us not speak of Harkonnens," he said. "That was another age and your Duke is dead." And he wondered: *Can't she guess that Paul revealed the Harkonnen blood in the Atreides?* What a risk that had been for Paul, but it had bound Duncan Idaho even more firmly to him. The trust in the revelation had been a coin almost too great to imagine. Paul had known what the Baron's people had done to Idaho.

"House Atreides is not dead," Jessica said.

"What is House Atreides?" he asked. "Are you House Atreides? Is it Alia? Ghanima? Is it the people who serve this House? I look at those people and they bear the stamp of a travail beyond words! How can they be Atreides? Your son said it rightly: 'Travail and persecution are the lot of all who follow me.' I would break myself away from that, My Lady."

"Have you really gone over to Farad'n?"

"Isn't that what you've done, My Lady? Didn't you come here to convince Farad'n that a marriage to Ghanima would solve all of our problems?"

Does he really think that? she wondered. *Or is he talking for the watchful spies?*

"House Atreides has always been essentially an idea," she said. "You know that, Duncan. We bought loyalty with loyalty."

"Service to the people," Idaho sneered. "Ahhh, many's the time I've heard your Duke say it. He must lie uneasy in his grave, My Lady."

"Do you really think us fallen that low?"

"My lady, did you not know that there are Fremen rebels—they call themselves 'Maquis of the Inner Desert'—who curse House Atreides and even Muad'Dib?"

"I heard Farad'n's report," she said, wondering where he was leading this conversation and to what point.

"More than that, My Lady. More than Farad'n's report. I've heard their curse myself. Here's the way of it: 'Burning be on you, Atreides! You shall have no souls, nor spirits, nor bodies, nor shades nor magic nor bones, nor hair nor utterances nor words. You shall have no grave, nor house nor hole nor tomb. You shall have no garden, nor tree nor bush. You shall have no water, nor bread nor light nor fire. You shall have no children, nor family nor heirs nor tribe. You shall have no head, nor arms nor legs nor gait nor seed. You shall have no seats on any planet. Your souls shall not be permitted to come up from the depths, and they shall never be among those permitted to live upon the earth. On no day shall you behold Shai-Hulud, but you shall be bound and fettered in the nethermost abomination and your souls shall never enter into the glorious light for ever and ever.' That's the way of the curse, My Lady. Can you imagine such hatred from Fremen? They consign all Atreides to the left hand of the damned, to the Woman-Sun which is full of burning."

Jessica allowed herself a shudder. Idaho undoubtedly had delivered those words with the same voice in which he'd heard the original curse. Why did he expose this to House Corrino? She could picture an outraged Fremen, terrible in his anger, standing before his tribe to vent that ancient curse. Why did Idaho want Farad'n to hear it?

"You make a strong argument for the marriage of Ghanima and Farad'n," she said.

"You always did have a single-minded approach to problems," he said. "Ghanima's Fremen. She can marry only one who pays no *fai*, no tax for protection. House Corrino gave up its entire CHOAM holdings to your son and his heirs. Farad'n exists on Atreides sufferance. And remember when your Duke planted the Hawk flag on Arrakis, remember what he said: 'Here I am; here I remain!' His bones are still there. And Farad'n would have to live on Arrakis, his Sardaukar with him."

Idaho shook his head at the very thought of such an alliance.

"There's an old saying that one peels a problem like an onion," she said, her voice cold. *How dare he patronize me? Unless he's performing for Farad'n's watchful eyes . . .*

"Somehow, I can't see Fremen and Sardaukar sharing a planet," Idaho said. "That's a layer which doesn't come off the onion."

She didn't like the thoughts which Idaho's words might arouse in Farad'n and his advisors, and spoke sharply: "House Atreides is still the law in this Empire!" And she thought: *Does Idaho want Farad'n to believe he can regain the throne without the Atreides?*

"Oh, yes," Idaho said. "I almost forgot. Atreides Law! As translated, of course, by the Priests of the Golden Elixir. I have but to close my eyes and I hear your Duke telling me that real estate is always gained and held by violence or the threat of it. Fortune passes everywhere, as Gurney used to sing it. The end justifies the means? Or do I have my proverbs mixed up? Well, it doesn't matter whether the mailed fist is brandished openly by Fremen legions or Sardaukar, or whether it's hidden in the Atreides Law—the fist is still there. And the onion layer won't come off, My Lady. You know, I wonder which fist Farad'n will demand?"

What is he doing? Jessica wondered. House Corrino would soak up this argument and gloat over it!

"So you think the Priests wouldn't let Ghanima marry Farad'n?" Jessica ventured, probing to see where Idaho's words might be leading.

"Let her? Gods below! The Priests will let Alia do whatever she decrees. She could marry Farad'n herself!"

Is that where he's fishing? Jessica wondered.

"No, My Lady," Idaho said. "That's not the issue. This Empire's people cannot distinguish between Atreides government and the government of Beast Rabban. Men die every day in Arrakeen's dungeons. I left because I could not give my sword arm another hour to the Atreides! Don't you understand what I'm saying, why I came here to you as the nearest Atreides representative? The Atreides Empire has betrayed your Duke and your son. I loved your daughter, but she went one way and I went another. If it comes down to it, I'll advise Farad'n to accept Ghanima's hand—or Alia's—only on his own terms!"

Ahhh, he sets the stage for a formal withdrawal with honor from Atreides service, she thought. But these other matters of which he spoke, could he possibly know how well they did her work for her? She scowled at him. "You know spies are listening to every word, don't you?"

"Spies?" He chuckled. "They listen as I would listen in their place. Don't you know how my loyalties move in a different way? Many's the night I've spent alone in the desert, and the Fremen are right about that place. In the desert, especially at night, you encounter the dangers of hard thinking."

"Is that where you heard Fremen curse us?"

"Yes. Among the al-Ourouba. At The Preacher's bidding I joined them, My Lady. We call ourselves the Zarr Sadus, those who refuse to submit to the Priests. I am here to make formal announcement to an Atreides that I've removed myself to enemy territory."

Jessica studied him, looking for betrayals of minutiae, but Idaho gave no indication that he spoke falsely or with hidden plans. Was it really possible that he'd gone over to Farad'n? She was reminded of her Sisterhood's maxim: *In human affairs, nothing remains enduring; all human affairs revolve in a helix, moving around and out.* If Idaho had really left the Atreides fold, that would explain his present behavior. He was moving around and out. She had to consider this as a possibility.

But why had he emphasized that he did The Preacher's bidding?

Jessica's mind raced and, having considered alternatives, she realized she might have to kill Idaho. The plan upon which she had staked her hopes remained so delicate that nothing could be allowed to interfere with it. Nothing. And Idaho's words hinted that he knew her plan. She gauged their relative positions in the room, moving and turning to place herself in position for a lethal blow.

"I've always considered the normalizing effect of the *faufreluches* to be a pillar of our strength," she said. Let him wonder why she shifted their conversation to the system of class distinction. "The Landsraad Council of the Great Houses, the regional Sysselraads, all deserve our—"

"You do not distract me," he said.

And Idaho wondered at how transparent her actions had become. Was it that she had grown lax in concealment, or had he finally breached the walls of her Bene Gesserit training? The latter, he decided, but some of it was in herself—a changing as she aged. It saddened him to see the small ways the new Fremen differed from the old. The passing of the desert was the passing of something precious to humans and he could not describe this thing, no more than he could describe what had happened to the Lady Jessica.

Jessica stared at Idaho in open astonishment, not trying to conceal her reaction. Could he read her that easily?

"You will not slay me," he said. He used the Fremen words of warning: "Don't throw your blood upon my knife." And he thought: *I've become very much the Fremen.* It gave him a wry sense of continuity to realize how deeply he had accepted the ways of the planet which had harbored his second life.

"I think you'd better leave," she said.

"Not until you accept my withdrawal from Atreides service."

"Accepted!" She bit it off. And only after she'd uttered the word did she realize how much pure reflex had gone into this exchange. She needed time to think and reconsider. How had Idaho known what she would do? She did not believe him capable of leaping Time in the spice way.

Idaho backed away from her until he felt the door behind him. He bowed. "Once more I call you My Lady, and then never again. My advice to Farad'n will be to send you back to Wallach, quietly and quickly, at the earliest practical moment. You are too dangerous a toy to keep around. Although I don't believe he thinks of you as a toy. You are working for the Sisterhood, not for the Atreides. I wonder now if you ever worked for the Atreides. You witches move too deeply and darkly for mere mortals ever to trust."

"A ghola considers himself a mere mortal," she jibed.

"Compared to you," he said.

"Leave!" she ordered.

"Such is my intention." He slipped out the door, passing the curious stare of the servant who'd obviously been listening.

It's done, he thought. *And they can read it in only one way.*

Only in the realm of mathematics can you understand Muad'Dib's precise view of the future. Thus: first, we postulate any number of point-dimensions in space. (This is the classic n-fold *extended aggregate of n* dimensions.) With this framework, *Time* as commonly understood becomes an aggregate of one-dimensional properties. Applying this to the Muad'Dib phenomenon, we find that we either are confronted by new properties of *Time* or (by reduction through the infinity calculus) we are dealing with separate systems which contain n body properties. For Muad'Dib, we assume the latter. As demonstrated by the reduction, the point dimensions of the n-fold can only have separate existence within different frameworks of *Time*. Separate dimensions of *Time* are thus demonstrated to coexist. This being the inescapable case, Muad'Dib's predictions required that he perceive the n-fold not as extended aggregate but as an operation within a single framework. In effect, he froze his universe into that one framework which was his view of *Time*.

—PALIMBASHA:
LECTURES AT SIETCH TABR

Leto lay at the crest of a dune, peering across open sand at a sinuous rock outcropping. The rock lay like an immense worm atop the sand, flat and threatening in the morning sunlight. Nothing stirred there. No bird circled overhead; no animal scampered among the rocks. He would see the slots of a windtrap almost at the center of the "worm's" back. There'd be water here. The rock-worm held the familiar appearance of a sietch shelter, except for the absence of living things. He lay quietly, blending with sand, watching.

One of Gurney Halleck's tunes kept flowing through his mind, monotonously persistent:

> Beneath the hill where the fox runs lightly,
> A dappled sun shines brightly
> Where my one love's still.
> Beneath the hill in the fennel brake
> I spy my love who cannot wake.
> He hides in a grave
> Beneath the hill.

Where was the entrance to that place? Leto wondered.

He felt the certainty that this must be Jacurutu/Fondak, but there was something wrong here beyond the lack of animal movement. Something flickered at the edges of conscious perception, warning him.

What hid beneath the hill?

Lack of animals was bothersome. It aroused his Fremen sense of caution: *The absence says more than the presence when it comes to desert survival.* But there was a windtrap. There would be water and humans to use it. This was the tabu place which hid behind Fondak's name, its other identity lost even to the memories of most Fremen. And no birds or animals could be seen there.

No humans—yet here the Golden Path began.

His father had once said: "There's unknown all around at every moment. That's where you seek knowledge."

Leto glanced out to his right along the dunecrests. There'd been a mother storm recently. Lake Azrak, the gypsum plain, had been exposed from beneath its sandy cover. Fremen superstition said that whoever saw the Biyan, the White Lands, was granted a two-edged wish, a wish which might destroy you. Leto saw only a gypsum plain which told him that open water had existed once here on Arrakis.

As it would exist once more.

He peered upward, swinging his gaze all around in the search for movement. The sky was porous after the storm. Light passing through it generated a sensation of milky presence, of a silver sun lost somewhere above the dust veil which persisted in the high altitudes.

Once more Leto brought his attention back to the sinuous rock. He slipped the binoculars from his Fremkit, focused their motile lenses and peered at the naked greyness, this outcropping where once the men of Jacurutu had lived. Amplification revealed a thorn bush, the one called Queen of Night. The bush nestled in shadows at a cleft which might be an entrance into the old sietch. He scanned the length of the outcropping. The silver sun turned reds into grey, casting a diffuse flatness over the long expanse of rock.

He rolled over, turning his back on Jacurutu, scanned the circle of his surroundings through the binoculars. Nothing in that wilderness preserved the marks of human passage. The wind already had obliterated his tracks, leaving only a vague roundness where he had dropped from his worm in the night.

Again he looked at Jacurutu. Except for the windtrap, there was no sign that men had ever passed this way. And without that sinuous length of rock, there was nothing here to subtract from the bleached sand, a wilderness from horizon to horizon.

Leto felt suddenly that he was in this place because he had refused to be confined in the system which his ancestors bequeathed him. He thought of how people looked at him, that universal mistake in every glance except Ghanima's.

Except for that ragged mob of other memories, this child was never a child.

I must accept responsibility for the decision we made, he thought.

Once more he scanned the length of rock. By all the descriptions this had to be Fondak, and no other place could be Jacurutu. He felt a strange resonant relationship with the tabu of this place. In the Bene Gesserit Way, he opened his mind to Jacurutu, seeking to know nothing about it. *Knowing* was a barrier which prevented learning. For a few moments he allowed himself merely to resonate, making no demands, asking no questions.

The problem lay within the lack of animal life, but it was a particular thing which alerted him. He perceived it then: there were no scavenger birds—no eagles, no vultures, no hawks. Even when other life hid, these remained. Every watering place in this desert held its chain of life. At the end of the chain were the omnipresent scavengers. Nothing had come to investigate his presence. How well he knew the "watchdogs of the sietch," that line of crouched birds on the cliff's edge at Tabr, primitive undertakers waiting for flesh. As the Fremen said: "Our competitors." But they said it with no sense of jealousy because questing birds often told when strangers approached.

What if this Fondak has been abandoned even by the smugglers?

Leto paused to drink from one of his catchtubes.

What if there's truly no water here?

He reviewed his position. He'd run two worms into the sand getting here, riding them with his flail through the night, leaving them half dead. This was the Inner Desert where the smugglers' haven was to be found. If life existed here, if it *could* exist, it would have to be in the presence of water.

What if there's no water? What if this isn't Fondak/ Jacurutu?

Once more he aimed his binoculars at the windtrap. Its outer edges were sand-etched, in need of maintenance, but enough of it remained. There should be water.

But what if there isn't?

An abandoned sietch might lose its water to the air, to any number of catastrophes. Why were there no scavenger birds? Killed for their water? By whom? How could all of them be eliminated? Poison?

Poisoned water.

The legend of Jacurutu contained no story of the cistern poisoned, but it might have been. If the original flocks were slain, would they not have been renewed by this time? The Iduali were wiped out generations ago and the stories never mentioned poison. Again he examined the rock with his binoculars. How could an entire sietch have been wiped out? Certainly some must have escaped. All of the inhabitants of a si-etch were seldom at home. Parties roamed the desert, trekked to the towns.

With a sigh of resignation Leto put away his binoculars. He slipped down the hidden face of the dune, took extra care to dig in his stilltent and conceal all sign of his intrusion as he prepared to spend the hot hours. The sluggish currents of fatigue stole along his limbs as he sealed himself in the darkness. Within the tent's sweaty confines he spent much of the day drowsing, imagining mistakes he could have made. His dreams were defensive, but there could be no self-defense in this trial he and Ghanima had chosen. Failure would scald their souls. He ate spice-biscuits and slept, awakened to eat once more, to drink and re-turn to sleep. It had been a long journey to this place, a severe test for the muscles of a child.

Toward evening he awoke refreshed, listened for signs of life. He crept out of his sandy shroud. There was dust high up in the sky blow-ing one way, but he could feel sand stinging his cheek from another direction—sure sign there would be a weather change. He sensed a storm coming.

Cautiously he crept to the crest of his dune, peered once more at those enigmatic rocks. The intervening air was yellow. The signs spoke of a Coriolis storm approaching, the wind that carried death in its belly. There'd be a great winding sheet of wind-driven sand that might stretch across four degrees of latitude. The desolate emptiness of the gypsum pan was a yellow surface now, reflecting the dust clouds. The false peace of evening enfolded him. Then the day collapsed and it was night, the quick night of the Inner Desert. The rocks were transformed into angu-lar peaks frosted by the light of First Moon. He felt sandthorns stinging his skin. A peal of dry thunder sounded like an echo from distant drums and, in the space between moonlight and darkness he saw sud-den movement: bats. He could hear the stirring of their wings, their tiny squeaks.

Bats.

By design or accident, this place conveyed a sense of abandoned desolation. It was where the half-legendary smuggler stronghold should be: Fondak. But what if it were not Fondak? What if the tabu still ruled and this were only the shell of ghostly Jacurutu?

Leto crouched in the lee of his dune and waited for the night to settle into its own rhythms. Patience and caution—caution and patience. For a time he amused himself by reviewing Chaucer's route from London to Canterbury, listing the places from Southwark: two miles to the watering-place of St. Thomas, five miles to Deptford, six miles to Greenwich, thirty miles to Rochester, forty miles to Sittingbourne, fifty-five miles to Boughton under Blean, fifty-eight miles to Harbledown, and sixty miles to Canterbury. It gave him a sense of timeless buoyancy to know that few in his universe would recall Chaucer or know any London except the village on Gansireed. St. Thomas was preserved in the Orange Catholic Bible and the Azhar Book, but Canterbury was gone from the memories of men, as was the planet which had known it. There lay the burden of his memories, of all those lives which threatened to engulf him. He had made that trip to Canterbury once.

His present trip was longer, though, and more dangerous.

Presently he crept over the dune's crest and made his way toward the moonlit rocks. He blended with shadows, slid across the crests, made no sounds that might signal his presence.

The dust had gone as it often did just before a storm, and the night was brilliant. The day had revealed no movement, but he heard small creatures hustling in the darkness as he neared the rocks.

In a valley between two dunes he came upon a family of jerboa which scampered away at his approach. He eased over the next crest, his emotions beset by salty anxieties. That cleft he had seen—did it lead up to an entrance? And there were other concerns: the old-time sietch had always been guarded by traps—poisoned barbs in pits, poisoned spines on plants. He felt himself caught up in the Fremen agrapha: *The ear-minded night*. And he listened for the slightest sound.

The grey rocks towered above him now, made giant by his nearness. As he listened, he heard birds invisible in that cliff, the soft calling of winged prey. They were the sounds of daybirds, but abroad by night. What had turned their world around? Human predation?

Abruptly Leto froze against the sand. There was fire on the cliff, a ballet of glittering and mysterious gems against the night's black gauze, the sort of signal a sietch might send to wanderers across the *bled*. Who were these occupants of this place? He crept forward into the deepest shadows at the cliff's base, felt along the rock with a hand, sliding his body behind the hand as he sought the fissure he'd seen by daylight. He located it on his eighth step, slipped the sandsnorkel from his kit and probed the darkness. As he moved, something tight and binding dropped over his shoulders and arms, immobilizing him.

Trapvine!

He resisted the urge to struggle; that only made the vine pull tighter. He dropped the snorkel, flexed the fingers of his right hand, trying for the knife at his waist. He felt like a bare innocent for not throwing something into that fissure from a distance, testing the darkness for its dangers. His mind had been too occupied by the fire on the cliff.

Each movement tightened the trapvine, but his fingers at last touched the knife hilt. Stealthily, he closed his hand around the hilt, began to slip it free.

Flaring light enveloped him, arresting all movement.

"Ahhh, a fine catch in our net." It was a heavy masculine voice from behind Leto, something vaguely familiar in the tone. Leto tried to turn his head, aware of the vine's dangerous propensity to crush a body which moved too freely.

A hand took his knife before he could see his captor. The hand moved expertly over his body, extracting the small devices he and Ghanima carried as a matter of survival. Nothing escaped the searcher, not even the shigawire garrote concealed in his hair.

Leto still had not seen the man.

Fingers did something with the trapvine and he found he could breathe easier, but the man said: "Do not struggle, Leto Atreides. I have your water in my cup."

By supreme effort Leto remained calm, said: "You know my name?"

"Of course! When one baits a trap, it's for a purpose. One aims for a specific quarry, not so?"

Leto remained silent, but his thoughts whirled.

"You feel betrayed!" the heavy voice said. Hands turned him around, gently but with an obvious show of strength. An adult male was telling the child what the odds were.

Leto stared up into the glare from twin floater flares, saw the black outline of a stillsuit-masked face, the hood. As his eyes adjusted he made out a dark strip of skin, the utterly shadowed eyes of melange addiction.

"You wonder why we went to all this trouble," the man said. His voice issued from the shielded lower part of his face with a curious muffled quality, as though he tried to conceal an accent.

"I long ago ceased to wonder at the numbers of people who want the Atreides twins dead," Leto said. "Their reasons are obvious."

As he spoke, Leto's mind flung itself against the unknown as against a cage, questing wildly for answers. A baited trap? But who had known except Ghanima? Impossible! Ghanima wouldn't betray her own brother. Then did someone know him well enough to predict his actions? Who? His grandmother? How could she?

"You could not be permitted to go on as you were," the man said. "Very bad. Before ascending the throne, you need to be educated." The whiteless eyes stared down at him. "You wonder how one could presume to educate such a person as yourself? You, with the knowledge of a multitude held there in your memories? That's just it, you see! You think yourself educated, but all you are is a repository of dead lives. You don't yet have a life of your own. You're just a walking surfeit of others, all with one goal—to seek death. Not good in a ruler, being a death seeker. You'd strew your surroundings with corpses. Your father, for example, never understood the—"

"You dare speak of him that way?"

"Many's the time I've dared it. He was only Paul Atreides, after all. Well, boy, welcome to your school."

The man brought a hand from beneath his robe, touched Leto's cheek. Leto felt the jolt of a slapshot and found himself winding downward into a darkness where a green flag waved. It was the green banner of the Atreides with its day and night symbols, its Dune staff which concealed a water tube. He heard the water gurgling as unconsciousness enfolded him. Or was it someone chuckling?

We can still remember the golden days before Heisenberg, who showed humans the walls enclosing our predestined arguments. The lives within me find this amusing. Knowledge, you see, has no uses without purpose, but purpose is what builds enclosing walls.

—LETO ATREIDES II
HIS VOICE

Alia found herself speaking harshly to the guards she confronted in the Temple foyer. There were nine of them in the dusty green uniforms of the suburban patrol, and they were still panting and sweating with their exertions. The light of late afternoon came in the door behind them. The area had been cleared of pilgrims.

"So my orders mean nothing to you?" she demanded.

And she wondered at her own anger, not trying to contain it but letting it run. Her body trembled with unleashed tensions. Idaho gone . . . the Lady Jessica . . . no reports . . . only rumors that they were on Salusa. Why hadn't Idaho sent a message? What had he done? Had he learned finally about Javid?

Alia wore the yellow of Arrakeen mourning, the color of the burning sun from Fremen history. In a few minutes she would be leading the second and final funeral procession to Old Gap, there to complete the stone marker for her lost nephew. The work would be completed in the night, fitting homage to one who'd been destined to lead Fremen.

The priestly guards appeared defiant in the face of her anger, not shamed at all. They stood in front of her, outlined by the waning light. The odor of their perspiration was easily detected through the light and inefficient stillsuits of city dwellers. Their leader, a tall blond Kaza with the bourka symbols of the Cadelam family, flung his stillsuit mask aside to speak more clearly. His voice was full of the prideful intonations to be expected from a scion of the family which once had ruled at Sietch Abbir.

"Certainly we tried to capture him!"

The man was obviously outraged at her attack. "He speaks blasphemy! We know your orders, but we heard him with our own ears!"

"And you failed to catch him," Alia said, her voice low and accusing.

One of the other guards, a short young woman, tried to defend them. "The crowds were thick there! I swear people interfered with us!"

"We'll keep after him," the Cadelam said. "We'll not always fail."

Alia scowled. "Why won't you understand and obey me?"

"My Lady, we—"

"What will you do, scion of the *Cade Lamb*, if you capture him and find him to be, in truth, my brother?"

He obviously did not hear her special emphasis on his name, although he could not be a priestly guard without some education and the wit to go with it. Did he want to sacrifice himself?

The guardsman swallowed, then: "We must kill him ourselves, for he breeds disorder."

The others stood aghast at this, but still defiant. They knew what they had heard.

"He calls upon the tribes to band against you," the Cadelam said.

Alia knew how to handle him now. She spoke in a quiet, matter-of-fact tone: "I see. Then if you must sacrifice yourself this way, taking him openly for all to see who you are and what you do, then I guess you must."

"Sacrifice my . . ." He broke off, glanced at his companions. As Kaza of this group, their appointed leader, he had the right to speak for them, but he showed signs that he wished he'd remained silent. The other guards stirred uncomfortably. In the heat of the chase they'd defied Alia. One could only reflect now upon such defiance of the "Womb of

Heaven." With obvious discomfort the guards opened a small space between themselves and their Kaza.

"For the good of the Church, our official reaction would have to be severe," Alia said. "You understand that, don't you?"

"But he—"

"I've heard him myself," she said. "But this is a special case."

"He cannot be Muad'Dib, My Lady!"

How little you know! she thought. She said: "We cannot risk taking him in the open, harming him where others could see it. If another opportunity presents itself, of course."

"He's always surrounded by crowds these days!"

"Then I fear you must be patient. Of course, if you insist on defying me. . . ." She left the consequences hanging in the air, unspoken, but well understood. The Cadelam was ambitious, a shining career before him.

"We didn't mean defiance, My Lady." The man had himself under control now. "We acted hastily; I can see that. Forgive us, but he—"

"Nothing has happened; nothing to forgive," she said, using the common Fremen formula. It was one of the many ways a tribe kept peace in its ranks, and this Cadelam was still Old Fremen enough to remember that. His family carried a long tradition of leadership. Guilt was the Naib's whip, to be used sparingly. Fremen served best when free of guilt or resentment.

He showed his realization of her judgment by bowing his head, saying: "For the good of the tribe; I understand."

"Go refresh yourselves," she said. "The procession begins in a few minutes."

"Yes, My Lady." They bustled away, every movement revealing their relief at this escape.

Within Alia's head a bass rumbled: "Ahhhhh, you handled that most adroitly. One or two of them still believe you desire The Preacher dead. They'll find a way."

"Shut up!" she hissed. "Shut up! I should never have listened to you! Look what you've done . . ."

"Set you on the road to immortality," the bass voice said.

She felt it echoing in her skull like a distant ache, thought: *Where can I hide? There's no place to go!*

"Ghanima's knife is sharp," the Baron said. "Remember that."

Alia blinked. Yes, that was something to remember. Ghanima's knife was sharp. That knife might yet cut them out of their present predicament.

If you believe certain words, you believe their hidden arguments. When you believe something is right or wrong, true or false, you believe the assumptions in the words which express the arguments. Such assumptions are often full of holes, but remain most precious to the convinced.

—THE OPEN-ENDED PROOF
FROM THE PANOPLIA PROPHETICA

Leto's mind floated in a stew of fierce odors. He recognized the heavy cinnamon of melange, the confined sweat of working bodies, the acridity of an uncapped deathstill, dust of many sorts with flint dominant. The odors formed a trail through dreamsand, created shapes of fog in a dead land. He knew these odors should tell him something, but part of him could not yet listen.

Thoughts like wraiths floated through his mind: *In this time I have no finished features; I am all of my ancestors. The sun setting into the sand is the sun setting into my soul. Once this multitude within me was great, but that's ended. I'm Fremen and I'll have a Fremen ending. The Golden Path is ended before it began. It's nothing but a windblown trail. We Fremen knew all the tricks to conceal ourselves: we left no feces, no water, no tracks. . . . Now, look at my trail vanish.*

A masculine voice spoke close to his ear: "I could kill you, Atreides. I could kill you, Atreides." It was repeated over and over until it lost meaning, became a wordless thing carried within Leto's dreaming, a litany of sorts: "I could kill you, Atreides."

Leto cleared his throat and felt the reality of this simple act shake his senses. His dry throat managed: "Who . . ."

The voice beside him said: "I'm an educated Fremen and I've killed my man. You took away our gods, Atreides. What do we care about your stinking Muad'Dib? Your god's dead!"

Was that a real Ouraba voice or another part of his dream? Leto opened his eyes, found himself unfettered on a hard couch. He looked upward at rock, dim glowglobes, an unmasked face staring down at him so close he could smell the breath with its familiar odors of a sietch diet. The face was Fremen; no mistaking the dark skin, those sharp features and water-wasted flesh. This was no fat city dweller. Here was a desert Fremen.

"I am Namri, father of Javid," the Fremen said. "Do you know me now, Atreides?"

"I know Javid," Leto husked.

"Yes, your family knows my son well. I am proud of him. You Atreides may know him even better soon."

"What . . ."

"I am one of your schoolmasters, Atreides. I have only one function: I am the one who could kill you. I'd do it gladly. In this school, to graduate is to live; to fail is to be given into my hands."

Leto heard implacable sincerity in that voice. It chilled him. This was a human gom jabbar, a high-handed enemy to test his right of entrance into the human concourse. Leto sensed his grandmother's hand in this and, behind her, the faceless masses of the Bene Gesserit. He writhed at this thought.

"Your education begins with me," Namri said. "That is just. It is fitting. Because it could end with me. Listen to me carefully now. My every word carries your life in it. Everything about me holds your death within it."

Leto shot his glance around the room: rock walls, barren—only this couch, the dim glowglobes, and a dark passage behind Namri.

"You will not get past me," Namri said. And Leto believed him.

"Why're you doing this?" Leto asked.

"That's already been explained. Think what plans are in your head! You are here and you cannot put a future into your present condition. The two don't go together: now and future. But if you really know your past, if you look backward and see where you've been, perhaps there'll be reason once more. If not, there will be your death."

Leto noted that Namri's tone was not unkind, but it was firm and no denying the death in it.

Namri rocked back on his heels, stared at the rock ceiling. "In olden times Fremen faced east at dawn. *Eos*, you know? That's dawn in one of the old tongues."

Bitter pride in his voice, Leto said: "I speak that tongue."

"You have not listened to me, then," Namri said, and there was a knife edge in his voice. "Night was the time of chaos. Day was the time of order. That's how it was in the time of that tongue you say you speak: darkness-disorder, light-order. We Fremen changed that. *Eos* was the light we distrusted. We preferred the light of a moon, or the stars. Light was too much order and that can be fatal. You see what you *Eos*-Atreides have done? Man is a creature of only that light which protects him. The sun was our enemy on Dune." Namri brought his gaze down to Leto's level. "What light do you prefer, Atreides?"

By Namri's poised attitude, Leto sensed that this question carried deep weight. Would the man kill him if he failed to answer correctly? He might. Leto saw Namri's hand resting quietly next to the polished hilt of a crysknife. A ring in the form of a magic tortoise glittered on the Fremen's knife hand.

Leto eased himself up onto his elbows, sent his mind questing into Fremen beliefs. They trusted the Law and loved to hear its lessons expounded in analogy, these old Fremen. The light of the moon?

"I prefer . . . the light of *Lisanu L'haqq*," Leto said, watching Namri for subtle revelations. The man seemed disappointed, but his hand moved away from his knife. "It is the light of truth, the light of the perfect man in which the influence of al-Mutakallim can clearly be seen," Leto continued. "What other light would a human prefer?"

"You speak as one who recites, not one who believes," Namri said.

And Leto thought: *I did recite.* But he began to sense the drift of Namri's thoughts, how his words were filtered through early training in the ancient riddle game. Thousands of these riddles went into Fremen training, and Leto had but to bend his attention upon this custom to find examples flooding his mind. *"Challenge: Silence? Answer: The friend of the hunted."*

Namri nodded to himself as though he shared this thought, said: "There is a cave which is the cave of life for Fremen. It is an actual cave which the desert has hidden. Shai-Hulud, the great-grandfather of all Fremen, sealed up that cave. My Uncle Ziamad told me about it and he never lied to me. There is such a cave."

Leto heard the challenging silence when Namri finished speaking. *Cave of life?* "My Uncle Stilgar also told me of that cave," Leto said. "It was sealed to keep cowards from hiding there."

The reflection of a glowglobe glittered in Namri's shadowed eyes. He asked: "Would you Atreides open that cave? You seek to control life through a ministry: your Central Ministry for Information, Auqaf and Hajj. The Maulana in charge is called Kausar. He has come a long way from his family's beginnings at the salt mines of Niazi. Tell me, Atreides, what is wrong with your ministry?"

Leto sat up, aware now that he was fully into the riddle game with Namri and that the forfeit was death. The man gave every indication that he'd use that crysknife at the first wrong answer.

Namri, recognizing this awareness in Leto, said: "Believe me, Atreides. I am the clod-crusher. I am the Iron Hammer."

Now Leto understood. Namri saw himself as Mirzabah, the Iron Hammer with which the dead are beaten who cannot reply satisfactorily to the questions they must answer before entry into paradise.

What was wrong with the central ministry which Alia and her priests had created?

Leto thought of why he'd come into the desert, and a small hope returned to him that the Golden Path might yet appear in his universe.

What this Namri implied by his question was no more than the motive which had driven Muad'Dib's own son into the desert.

"God's it is to show the way," Leto said.

Namri's chin jerked down and he stared sharply at Leto. "Can it be true that you believe this?" he demanded.

"It's why I am here," Leto said.

"To find the way?"

"To find it for myself." Leto put his feet over the edge of the cot. The rock floor was uncarpeted, cold. "The Priests created their ministry to hide the way."

"You speak like a true rebel," Namri said, and he rubbed the tortoise ring on his finger. "We shall see. Listen carefully once more. You know the high Shield Wall at Jalalud-Din? That Wall bears my family's marks carved there in the first days. Javid, my son, has seen those marks. Abedi Jalal, my nephew, has seen them. Mujahid Shafqat of the Other Ones, he too has seen our marks. In the season of the storms near Suk-kar, I came down with my friend Yakup Abad near that place. The winds were blistering hot like the whirlwinds from which we learned our dances. We did not take time to see the marks because a storm blocked the way. But when the storm passed we saw the vision of Thatta upon the blown sand. The face of Shakir Ali was there for a moment, looking down upon his city of tombs. The vision was gone in the in-stant, but we all saw it. Tell me, Atreides, where can I find that city of tombs?"

The whirlwinds from which we learned our dances, Leto thought. *The vision of Thatta and Shakir Ali.* These were the words of a Zensunni Wanderer, those who considered themselves to be the only true men of the desert.

And Fremen were forbidden to have tombs.

"The city of tombs is at the end of the path which all men follow," Leto said. And he dredged up the Zensunni beatifics. "It is in a garden one thousand paces square. There is a fine entry corridor two hundred and thirty-three paces long and one hundred paces wide all paved with marble from ancient Jaipur. Therein dwells ar-Razzaq, he who provides food for all who ask. And on the Day of Reckoning, all who stand up and seek the city of tombs shall not find it. For it is written: That which you know in one world, you shall not find in another."

"Again you recite without belief," Namri sneered. "But I'll accept it for now because I think you know why you're here." A cold smile touched his lips. "I give you a *provisional* future, Atreides."

Leto studied the man warily. Was this another question in disguise?

"Good!" Namri said. "Your awareness has been prepared. I've sunk home the barbs. One more thing, then. Have you heard that they use imitation stillsuits in the cities of far Kadrish?"

As Namri waited, Leto quested in his mind for a hidden meaning. *Imitation stillsuits? They were worn on many planets.* He said: "The foppish habits of Kadrish are an old story often repeated. The wise animal blends into its surroundings."

Namri nodded slowly. Then: "The one who trapped you and brought you here will see you presently. Do not try to leave this place. It would be your death." Arising as he spoke, Namri went out into the dark passage.

For a long time after he had gone, Leto stared into the passage. He could hear sounds out there, the quiet voices of men on guard duty. Namri's story of the mirage-vision stayed with Leto. It brought up the long desert crossing to this place. It no longer mattered whether this were Jacurutu/Fondak. Namri was not a smuggler. He was something much more potent. And the game Namri played smelled of the Lady Jessica; it stank of the Bene Gesserit. Leto sensed an enclosing peril in this realization. But that dark passage where Namri had gone was the only exit from this room. And outside lay a strange sietch—beyond that, the desert. The harsh severity of that desert, its ordered chaos with mirages and endless dunes, came over Leto as part of the trap in which he was caught. He could recross that sand, but where would flight take him? The thought was like stagnant water. It would not quench his thirst.

Because of the one-pointed Time awareness in which the conventional mind remains immersed, humans tend to think of everything in a sequential, word-oriented framework. This mental trap produces very short-term concepts of effectiveness and consequences, a condition of constant, unplanned response to crises.

—LIET-KYNES
THE ARRAKIS WORKBOOK

Words and movements simultaneous, Jessica reminded herself and she bent her thoughts to those necessary mental preparations for the coming encounter.

The hour was shortly after breakfast, the golden sun of Salusa Secundus just beginning to touch the far wall of the enclosed garden which she could see from her window. She had dressed herself carefully: the black hooded cloak of a Reverend Mother, but it carried the Atreides crest in gold worked into an embroidered ring around the hem and again at the cuff of each sleeve. Jessica arranged the drape of her garment carefully as she turned her back on the window, holding her left arm across her waist to present the Hawk motif of the crest.

Farad'n noted the Atreides symbols, commenting on them as he entered, but he betrayed no anger or surprise. She detected subtle humor in his voice and wondered at it. She saw that he had clad himself in the grey leotard which she had suggested. He sat on the low green divan to which she directed him, relaxing with his right arm along the back.

Why do I trust her? he wondered. *This is a Bene Gesserit witch!*

Jessica, reading the thought in the contrast between his relaxed body and the expression on his face, smiled and said: "You trust me because you know our bargain is a good one, and you want what I can teach you."

She saw the pinch of a scowl touch his brow, waved her left hand to calm him. "No, I don't read minds. I read the face, the body, the mannerisms, tone of voice, set of arms. Anyone can do this once they learn the Bene Gesserit Way."

"And you will teach me?"

"I'm sure you've studied the reports about us," she said. "Is there anywhere a report that we fail to deliver on a direct promise?"

"No reports, but . . ."

"We survive in part by the complete confidence which people can have in our truthfulness. That has not changed."

"I find this reasonable," he said. "I'm anxious to begin."

"I'm surprised you've never asked the Bene Gesserit for a teacher," she said. "They would've leaped at the opportunity to put you in their debt."

"My mother would never listen to me when I urged her to do this," he said. "But now. . . ." He shrugged, an eloquent comment on Wensicia's banishment. "Shall we start?"

"It would've been better to begin this when you were much younger," Jessica said. "It'll be harder for you now, and it'll take much longer. You'll have to begin by learning patience, extreme patience. I pray you'll not find it too high a price."

"Not for the reward you offer."

She heard the sincerity, the pressure of expectations, and the touch of awe in his voice. These formed a place to begin. She said: "The art of patience, then—starting with some elementary *prana-bindu* exercises for the legs and arms, for your breathing. We'll leave the hands and fingers for later. Are you ready?"

She seated herself on a stool facing him.

Farad'n nodded, holding an expectant expression on his face to conceal the sudden onset of fear. Tyekanik had warned him that there must be a trick in the Lady Jessica's offer, something brewed by the Sister-hood. "You cannot believe that she has abandoned them again or that they have abandoned her." Farad'n had stopped the argument with an angry outburst for which he'd been immediately sorry. His emotional reaction had made him agree more quickly with Tyekanik's precau-tions. Farad'n glanced at the corners of the room, the subtle gleam of *jems* in the coving. All that glittered was not *jems*: everything in this room would be recorded and good minds would review every nuance, every word, every movement.

Jessica smiled, noting the direction of his gaze, but not revealing that she knew where his attention had wandered. She said: "To learn patience in the Bene Gesserit Way, you must begin by recognizing the essential, raw instability of our universe. We call nature—meaning this totality in all of its manifestations—the Ultimate Non-Absolute. To free your vision and permit you to recognize this conditional nature's changing ways, you will hold your two hands at arm's length in front of you. Stare at your extended hands, first the palms and then the backs. Examine the fingers, front and back. Do it."

Farad'n complied, but he felt foolish. These were his own hands. He knew them.

"Imagine your hands aging," Jessica said. "They must grow very old in your eyes. Very, very old. Notice how dry the skin . . ."

"My hands don't change," he said. He already could feel the muscles of his upper arms trembling.

"Continue to stare at your hands. Make them old, as old as you can imagine. It may take time. But when you see them age, reverse the process. Make your hands young again—as young as you can make them. Strive to take them from infancy to great age at will, back and forth, back and forth."

"They don't change!" he protested. His shoulders ached.

"If you demand it of your senses, your hands will change," she said. "Concentrate upon visualizing the flow of time which you desire: in-fancy to age, age to infancy. It may take you hours, days, months. But it can be achieved. Reversing that change-flow will teach you to see every system as something spinning in relative stability . . . only relative."

"I thought I was learning patience." She heard anger in his voice, an edge of frustration.

"And relative stability," she said. "This is the perspective which you create with your own belief, and beliefs can be manipulated by imagination. You've learned only a limited way of looking at the universe. Now you must make the universe your own creation. This will permit you to harness any relative stability to your own uses, to whatever uses you are capable of imagining."

"How long did you say it takes?"

"Patience," she reminded him.

A spontaneous grin touched his lips. His eyes wavered toward her.

"Look at your hands!" she snapped.

The grin vanished. His gaze jerked back to a fixated concentration upon his extended hands.

"What do I do when my arms get tired?" he asked.

"Stop talking and concentrate," she said. "If you become too tired, stop. Return to it after a few minutes of relaxation and exercise. You must persist in this until you succeed. At your present stage, this is more important than you could possibly realize. Learn this lesson or the others will not come."

Farad'n inhaled a deep breath, chewed his lips, stared at his hands. He turned them slowly: front, back, front, back. . . . His shoulders trembled with fatigue. Front, back. . . . Nothing changed.

Jessica arose, crossed to the only door.

He spoke without removing his attention from his hands. "Where are you going?"

"You'll work better on this if you're alone. I'll return in about an hour. Patience."

"I know!"

She studied him a moment. How intent he looked. He reminded her with a heart-tugging abruptness of her own lost son. She permitted herself a sigh, said: "When I return I'll give you the exercise lessons to relieve your muscles. Give it time. You'll be astonished at what you can make your body and your senses do."

She let herself out.

The omnipresent guards took up station three paces behind her as she strode down the hall. Their awe and fear were obvious. They were Sardaukar, thrice-warned of her prowess, raised on the stories of their defeat by the Fremen of Arrakis. This witch was a Fremen Reverend Mother, a Bene Gesserit and an Atreides.

Jessica, glancing back, saw their stern faces as a mile-post in her design. She turned away as she came to the stairs, went down them and through a short passage into the garden below her windows.

Now if only Duncan and Gurney can do their parts, she thought as she felt the gravel of a pathway beneath her feet, saw the golden light filtered by greenery.

You will learn the integrated communication methods as you complete the next step in your mental education. This is a gestalten function which will overlay data paths in your awareness, resolving complexities and masses of input from the mentat index-catalogue techniques which you already have mastered. Your initial problem will be the breaking tensions arising from the divergent assembly of minutiae/data on specialized subjects. Be warned. Without mentat overlay integration, you can be immersed in the Babel Problem, which is the label we give to the omnipresent dangers of achieving wrong combinations from accurate information.

—THE MENTAT HANDBOOK

The sound of fabrics rubbing together sent sparks of awareness through Leto. He was surprised that he had tuned his sensitivity to the point where he automatically identified the fabrics from their sound: the combination came from a Fremen robe rubbing against the coarse hangings of a door curtain. He turned toward the sound. It came from the passage where Namri had gone minutes before. As Leto turned, he saw his captor enter. It was the same man who had taken him prisoner: the same dark strip of skin above the stillsuit mask, the identical searing eyes. The man lifted a hand to his mask, slipped the catchtube from his nostrils, lowered the mask and, in the same motion, flipped his hood back. Even before he focused on the scar of the inkvine whip along the man's jaw, Leto recognized him. The recognition was a totality in his awareness with the search for confirming details coming afterward. No mistake about it, this rolling lump of humanity, this warrior-troubadour, was Gurney Halleck!

Leto clenched his hands into fists, overcome momentarily by the shock of recognition. No Atreides retainer had ever been more loyal. None better at shield fighting. He'd been Paul's trusted confidant and teacher.

He was the Lady Jessica's servant.

These recognitions and more surged through Leto's mind. Gurney was his captor. Gurney and Namri were in this conspiracy together. And Jessica's hand was in it with them.

"I understand you've met our Namri," Halleck said. "Pray believe him, young sir. He has one function and one function only. He's the one capable of killing you should the need arise."

Leto responded automatically with his father's tones: "So you've joined my enemies, Gurney! I never thought the—"

"Try none of your devil tricks on me, lad," Halleck said. "I'm proof against them all. I follow your grandmother's orders. Your education has been planned to the last detail. It was she who approved my selection of Namri. What comes next, painful as it may seem, is at her command."

"And what does she command?"

Halleck lifted a hand from the folds of his robe, exposed a Fremen injector, primitive but efficient. Its transparent tube was charged with blue fluid.

Leto squirmed backward on the cot, was stopped by the rock wall. As he moved, Namri entered, stood beside Halleck with hand on crysknife. Together they blocked the only exit.

"I see you've recognized the spice essence," Halleck said. "You're to take the *worm trip*, lad. You must go through it. Otherwise, what your father dared and you dare not would hang over you for the rest of your days."

Leto shook his head wordlessly. This was the thing he and Ghanima knew could overwhelm them. Gurney was an ignorant fool! How could Jessica . . . Leto felt the father-presence in his memories. It surged into

his mind, trying to strip away his defenses. Leto wanted to shriek outrage, could not move his lips. But this was the wordless thing which his
pre-born awareness most feared. This was prescient trance, the reading
of immutable future with all of its fixity and its terrors. Surely Jessica
could not have ordered such an ordeal for her own grandson. But her
presence loomed in his mind, filling him with acceptance arguments.
Even the Litany Against Fear was pressed upon him with a repetitive
droning: "I must not fear. Fear is the mind-killer. Fear is the little-death
that brings total obliteration. I will face my fear. I will permit it to pass
over me and through me. And when it has gone past. . . ."

With an oath already ancient when Chaldea was young, Leto tried
to move, tried to leap at the two men standing over him, but his muscles
refused to obey. As though he already existed in the trance, Leto saw
Halleck's hand move, the injector approach. The light of a glowglobe
sparkled within the blue fluid. The injector touched Leto's left arm. Pain
lanced through him, shot upward to the muscles of his head.

Abruptly Leto saw a young woman sitting outside a crude hut in
dawnlight. She sat right there in front of him roasting coffee beans to a
rose brown, adding cardamom and melange. The voice of a rebeck
echoed from somewhere behind him. The music echoed and echoed
until it entered his head, still echoing. It suffused his body and he felt
himself to be large, very large, not a child at all. And his skin was not
his own. He knew that sensation! His skin was not his own. Warmth
spread through his body. As abruptly as his first vision, he found himself standing in darkness. It was night. Stars like a rain of embers fell in
gusts from a brilliant cosmos.

Part of him knew there was no escaping, but still he tried to fight it
until the father-presence intruded. "I will protect you in the trance. The
others within will not take you."

Wind tumbled Leto, rolled him, hissing, pouring dust and sand
over him, cutting his arms, his face, abrading his clothes, whipping the
loose-torn ends of now useless fabric. But he felt no pain and he saw the
cuts heal as rapidly as they appeared. Still he rolled with the wind. And
his skin was not his own.

It will happen! he thought.

But the thought was distant and came as though it were not his own, not really his own; no more than his skin.

The vision absorbed him. It evolved into a stereologic memory which separated past and present, future and present, future and past. Each separation mingled into a trinocular focus which he sensed as the multidimensional relief map of his own future existence.

He thought: *Time is a measure of space, just as a range-finder is a measure of space, but measuring locks us into the place we measure.*

He sensed the trance deepening. It came as an amplification of internal consciousness which his self-identity soaked up and through which he felt himself changing. It was living Time and he could not arrest an instant of it. Memory fragments, future and past, deluged him. But they existed as montage-in-motion. Their relationships underwent a constant dance. His memory was a lens, an illuminating searchlight which picked out fragments, isolating them, but forever failing to stop the ceaseless motion and modification which surged into his view.

That which he and Ghanima had planned came through the searchlight, dominating everything, but now it terrified him. Vision reality ached in him. The uncritical inevitability made his ego cringe.

And his skin was not his own! Past and present tumbled through him, surging across the barriers of his terror. He could not separate them. One moment he felt himself setting forth on the Butlerian Jihad, eager to destroy any machine which simulated human awareness. That had to be the past—over and done with. Yet his senses hurtled through the experience, absorbing the most minute details. He heard a minister-companion speaking from a pulpit: *"We must negate the machines-that-think. Humans must set their own guidelines. This is not something machines can do. Reasoning depends upon programming, not on hardware, and we are the ultimate program!"*

He heard the voice clearly, knew his surroundings—a vast wooden hall with dark windows. Light came from sputtering flames. And his minister-companion said: *"Our Jihad is a 'dump program.' We dump the things which destroy us as humans!"*

And it was in Leto's mind that the speaker had been a servant of computers, one who knew them and serviced them. But the scene vanished and Ghanima stood in front of him, saying: *"Gurney knows. He told me. They're Duncan's words and Duncan was speaking as a mentat. 'In doing good, avoid notoriety; in doing evil, avoid self-awareness.'"*

That had to be future—far future. But he felt the reality. It was as intense as any past from his multitude of lives. And he whispered: "Isn't that true, father?"

But the father-presence within spoke warningly: *"Don't invite disaster! You're learning stroboscopic awareness now. Without it you could overrun yourself, lose your place-mark in Time."*

And the bas-relief imagery persisted. Intrusions hammered at him. Past-present-now. There was no true separation. He knew he had to flow with this thing, but the flowing terrified him. How could he return to any recognizable place? Yet he felt himself being forced to cease every effort of resistance. He could not grasp his new universe in motionless, labeled bits. No bit would stand still. Things could not be forever ordered and formulated. He had to find the rhythm of change and see between the changes to the changing itself. Without knowing where it began he found himself moving within a gigantic *moment bienheureux*, able to see the past in the future, present in past, the *now* in both past and future. It was the accumulation of centuries experienced between one heartbeat and the next.

Leto's awareness floated free, no objective psyche to compensate for consciousness, no barriers. Namri's "provisional future" remained lightly in his memory, but it shared awareness with many futures. And in this shattering awareness, all of his past, every inner life became his own. With the help of the greatest within him, he dominated. They were *his*.

He thought: *When you study an object from a distance, only its principle may be seen.* He had achieved the distance and he could see his own life now: the multi-past and its memories were his burden, his joy, and his necessity. But the *worm trip* had added another dimension and his father no longer stood guard within him because the need no longer existed. Leto saw through the distances clearly—past and present. And the past presented him with an ultimate ancestor—one who was called Harum and without whom the distant future would not be. These clear distances provided new principles, new dimensions of sharing. Whichever life he now chose, he'd live it out in an autonomous sphere of mass experience, a trail of lives so convoluted that no single lifetime could count the generations of it. Aroused, this mass experience held the power to subdue his selfdom. It could make itself felt upon an individual, a nation, a society or an entire civilization. That, of course, was why Gurney had been taught to fear him; why Namri's knife waited. They could not be allowed to see this power within him. No one could ever see it in its fullness—not even Ghanima.

Presently Leto sat up, saw that only Namri remained, watching.

In an old voice, Leto said: "There's no single set of limits for all men. Universal prescience is an empty myth. Only the most powerful local currents of Time may be foretold. But in an infinite universe, *local* can be so gigantic that your mind shrinks from it."

Namri shook his head, not understanding.

"Where's Gurney?" Leto asked.

"He left lest he have to watch me slay you."

"Will you slay me, Namri?" It was almost a plea to have the man do it.

Namri took his hand from his knife. "Since you ask me to do it, I will not. If you were indifferent, though . . ."

"The malady of indifference is what destroys many things," Leto said. He nodded to himself. "Yes . . . even civilizations die of it. It's as though that were the price demanded for achieving new levels of complexity or consciousness." He looked up at Namri. "So they told you to look for indifference in me?" And he saw Namri was more than a killer—Namri was devious.

"As a sign of unbridled power," Namri said, but it was a lie.

"Indifferent power, yes." Leto sat up, sighed deeply. "There was no moral grandeur to my father's life, Namri; only a local trap which he built for himself."

O Paul, thou Muad'Dib,
Mahdi of all men,
Thy breath exhaled
Sent forth the huricen.

—SONGS OF MUAD'DIB

"Never!" Ghanima said. "I'd kill him on our wedding night." She spoke with a barbed stubbornness which thus far had resisted all blandishments. Alia and her advisors had been at it half the night, keeping the royal quarters in a state of unrest, sending out for new advisors, for food and drink. The entire Temple and its adjoining Keep seethed with the frustrations of unmade decisions.

Ghanima sat composedly on a green floater chair in her own quarters, a large room with rough tan walls to simulate sietch rock. The ceiling, however, was imbar crystal which flickered with blue light, and the floor was black tile. The furnishings were sparse: a small writing table, five floater chairs and a narrow cot set into an alcove, Fremen fashion. Ghanima wore a robe of yellow mourning.

"You are not a free person who can settle every aspect of her own life," Alia said for perhaps the hundredth time. *The little fool must come to realize this sooner or later! She must approve the betrothal to Farad'n. She must! Let her kill him later, but the betrothal requires open acknowledgment by the Fremen affianced.*

"He killed my brother," Ghanima said, holding to the single note which sustained her. "Everyone knows this. Fremen would spit at the mention of my name were I to consent to this betrothal."

And that is one of the reasons why you must consent, Alia thought. She said: "His mother did it. He has banished her for it. What more do you want of him?"

"His blood," Ghanima said. "He's a Corrino."

"He has denounced his own mother," Alia protested. "And why should you worry about the Fremen rabble? They'll accept whatever we tell them to accept. Ghani, the peace of the Empire demands that—"

"I will not consent," Ghanima said. "You cannot announce the betrothal without me."

Irulan, entering the room as Ghanima spoke, glanced inquiringly at Alia and the two female advisors who stood dejectedly beside her. Irulan saw Alia throw up her arms in disgust and drop into a chair facing Ghanima.

"You speak to her, Irulan," Alia said.

Irulan pulled a floater into place, sat down beside Alia.

"You're a Corrino, Irulan," Ghanima said. "Don't press your luck with me." Ghanima got up, crossed to her cot and sat on it cross-legged, glaring back at the women. Irulan, she saw, had dressed in a black aba to match Alia's, the hood thrown back to reveal her golden hair. It was mourning hair under the yellow glow of the floating globes which illuminated the room.

Irulan glanced at Alia, stood up and crossed to stand facing Ghanima. "Ghani, I'd kill him myself if that were the way to solve matters. And Farad'n's my own blood, as you so kindly emphasized. But you have duties far higher than your commitment to Fremen . . ."

"That doesn't sound any better coming from you than it does from my precious aunt," Ghanima said. "The blood of a brother cannot be washed off. That's more than some little Fremen aphorism."

Irulan pressed her lips together. Then: "Farad'n holds your grandmother captive. He holds Duncan and if we don't—"

"I'm not satisfied with your stories of how all this happened," Ghanima said, peering past Irulan at Alia. "Once Duncan died rather than let enemies take my father. Perhaps this new ghola-flesh is no longer the same as—"

"Duncan was charged with protecting your grandmother's life!" Alia said, whirling in her chair. "I'm confident he chose the only way to do that." And she thought: *Duncan! Duncan! You weren't supposed to do it this way.*

Ghanima, reading the overtones of contrivance in Alia's voice, stared across at her aunt. "You're lying, O Womb of Heaven. I've heard about your fight with my grandmother. What is it you fear to tell us about her and your precious Duncan?"

"You've heard it all," Alia said, but she felt a stab of fear at this bald accusation and what it implied. Fatigue had made her careless, she realized. She arose, said: "Everything I know, you know." Turning to Irulan: "You work on her. She must be made to—"

Ghanima interrupted with a coarse Fremen expletive which came shockingly from the immature lips. Into the quick silence she said: "You think me just a mere child, that you have years in which to work on me, that eventually I'll accept. Think again, O Heavenly Regent. You know better than anyone the years I have within me. I'll listen to them, not to you."

Alia barely suppressed an angry retort, stared hard at Ghanima. *Abomination?* Who was this child? A new fear of Ghanima began to rise in Alia. Had she accepted her own compromise with the lives which came to her pre-born? Alia said: "There's time yet for you to see reason."

"There may be time yet for me to see Farad'n's blood spurt around my knife," Ghanima said. "Depend on it. If I'm ever left alone with him, one of us will surely die."

"You think you loved your brother more than I?" Irulan demanded. "You play a fool's game! I was mother to him as I was to you. I was—"

"You never knew him," Ghanima said. "All of you, except at times my *beloved aunt*, persist in thinking us children. You're the fools! Alia knows! Look at her run away from . . ."

"I run from nothing," Alia said, but she turned her back on Irulan and Ghanima, and stared at the two amazons who were pretending not to hear this argument. They'd obviously given up on Ghanima. Perhaps they sympathized with her. Angrily, Alia sent them from the room. Relief was obvious on their faces as they obeyed.

"You run," Ghanima persisted.

"I've chosen a way of life which suits me," Alia said, turning back to stare at Ghanima sitting cross-legged on the cot. Was it possible she'd made that terrible inner compromise? Alia tried to see the signs of it in Ghanima, but was unable to read a single betrayal. Alia wondered then: *Has she seen it in me? But how could she?*

"You feared to be the window for a multitude," Ghanima accused. "But we're the pre-born and we know. You'll be their window, conscious or unconscious. You cannot deny them." And she thought: *Yes, I know you—Abomination. And perhaps I'll go as you have gone, but for now I can only pity you and despise you.*

Silence hung between Ghanima and Alia, an almost palpable thing which alerted the Bene Gesserit training in Irulan. She glanced from one to the other, then: "Why're you so quiet suddenly?"

"I've just had a thought which requires considerable reflection," Alia said.

"Reflect at your leisure, dear aunt," Ghanima sneered.

Alia, putting down fatigue-inflamed anger, said: "Enough for now! Leave her to think. Perhaps she'll come to her senses."

Irulan arose, said: "It's almost dawn anyway. Ghani, before we go, would you care to hear the latest message from Farad'n? He . . ."

"I would not," Ghanima said. "And hereafter, cease calling me by that ridiculous diminutive. Ghani! It merely supports the mistaken assumption that I'm a child you can . . ."

"Why'd you and Alia grow so suddenly quiet?" Irulan asked, reverting to her previous question, but casting it now in a delicate mode of Voice.

Ghanima threw her head back in laughter. "Irulan! You'd try Voice on me?"

"What?" Irulan was taken aback.

"You'd teach your grandmother to suck eggs," Ghanima said.

"I'd what?"

"The fact that I remember the expression and you've never even heard it before should give you pause," Ghanima said. "It was an old expression of scorn when you Bene Gesserit were young. But if that doesn't chasten you, ask yourself what your royal parents could've been thinking of when they named you Irulan? Or is it Ruinal?"

In spite of her training, Irulan flushed. "You're trying to goad me, Ghanima."

"And you tried to use Voice on me. On me! I remember the first human efforts in that direction. I remember *then*, Ruinous Irulan. Now, get out of here, all of you."

But Alia was intrigued now, caught by an inner suggestion which sluffed her fatigue aside. She said: "Perhaps I've a suggestion which could change your mind, Ghani."

"Still Ghani!" A brittle laugh escaped Ghanima, then: "Reflect but a moment: If I desire to kill Farad'n, I need but fall in with your plans. I presume you've thought of that. Beware of *Ghani* in a tractable mood. You see, I'm being utterly candid with you."

"That's what I hoped," Alia said. "If you . . ."

"The blood of a brother cannot be washed away," Ghanima said. "I'll not go before my Fremen loved ones a traitor to that. *Never to forgive, never to forget.* Isn't that our catechism? I warn you here, and I'll say it publicly: you cannot betroth me to Farad'n. Who, knowing me, would believe it? Farad'n himself could not believe it. Fremen, hearing of such a betrothal, would laugh into their sleeves and say, 'See! She lures him into a trap.' If you . . ."

"I understand that," Alia said, moving to Irulan's side. Irulan, she noted, was standing in shocked silence, aware already of where this conversation was headed.

"And so I would be luring him into a trap," Ghanima said. "If that's what you want, I'll agree, but he may not fall. If you wish this false betrothal as the empty coin with which to buy back my grandmother and your precious Duncan, so be it. But it's on your head. Buy them back. Farad'n, though, is mine. Him I'll kill."

Irulan whirled to face Alia before she could speak. "Alia! If we go back on our word . . ." She let it hang there a moment while Alia smilingly reflected on the potential wrath among the Great Houses in Faufreluches Assembled, the destructive consequences to believe in Atreides honor, the loss of religious trust, all of the great and small building blocs which would tumble.

"It'd rule against us," Irulan protested. "All belief in Paul's prophethood would be destroyed. It . . . the Empire . . ."

"Who could dare question our right to decide what is wrong and what is right?" Alia asked, voice mild. "We mediate between good and evil. I need but proclaim . . ."

"You can't do this!" Irulan protested. "Paul's memory . . ."

"Is just another tool of Church and State," Ghanima said. "Don't speak foolishness, Irulan." Ghanima touched the crysknife at her waist, looked up at Alia. "I've misjudged my clever aunt, Regent of all that's Holy in Muad'Dib's Empire. I have, indeed, misjudged you. Lure Farad'n into our parlor if you will."

"This is recklessness," Irulan pleaded.

"You agree to this betrothal, Ghanima?" Alia asked, ignoring Irulan.

"On my terms," Ghanima said, hand still on her crysknife.

"I wash my hands of this," Irulan said, actually wringing her hands. "I was willing to argue for a true betrothal to heal—"

"We'll give you a wound much more difficult to heal, Alia and I," Ghanima said. "Bring him quickly, if he'll come. And perhaps he will. Would he suspect a child of my tender years? Let us plan the formal ceremony of betrothal to require his presence. Let there be an opportunity for me to be alone with him . . . just a minute or two . . ."

Irulan shuddered at this evidence that Ghanima was, after all, Fremen entire, child no different from adult in this terrible bloodiness. After all, Fremen children were accustomed to slay the wounded on the battlefield, releasing women from this chore that they might collect the bodies and haul them away to the deathstills. And Ghanima, speaking with the voice of a Fremen child, piled horror upon horror by the studied maturity of her words, by the ancient sense of vendetta which hung like an aura around her.

"Done," Alia said, and she fought to keep voice and face from betraying her glee. "We'll prepare the formal charter of betrothal. We'll have the signatures witnessed by the proper assemblage from the Great Houses. Farad'n cannot possibly doubt—"

"He'll doubt, but he'll come," Ghanima said. "And he'll have guards. But will they think to guard him from me?"

"For the love of all that Paul tried to do," Irulan protested, "let us at least make Farad'n's death appear an accident, or the result of malice by outside—"

"I'll take joy in displaying my bloody knife to my brethren," Ghanima said.

"Alia, I beg you," Irulan said. "Abandon this rash insanity. Declare *kanly* against Farad'n, anything to—"

"We don't require formal declaration of vendetta against him," Ghanima said. "The whole Empire knows how we must feel." She pointed to the sleeve of her robe. "We wear the yellow of mourning. When I exchange it for the black of a Fremen betrothed, will that fool anyone?"

"Pray that it fools Farad'n," Alia said, "and the delegates of the Great Houses we invite to witness the—"

"Every one of those delegates will turn against you," Irulan said. "You know that!"

"Excellent point," Ghanima said. "Choose those delegates with care, Alia. They must be ones we won't mind eliminating later."

Irulan threw up her arms in despair, turned and fled.

"Have her put under close surveillance lest she try to warn her nephew," Ghanima said.

"Don't try to teach me how to conduct a plot," Alia said. She turned and followed Irulan, but at a slower pace. The guards outside and the waiting aides were sucked up in her wake like sand particles drawn into the vortex of a rising worm.

Ghanima shook her head sadly from side to side as the door closed, thought: *It's as poor Leto and I thought. Gods below! I wish it'd been me the tiger killed instead of him.*

Many forces sought control of the Atreides twins and, when the death of Leto was announced, this movement of plot and counterplot was amplified. Note the relative motivations: the Sisterhood feared Alia, an adult Abomination, but still wanted those genetic characteristics carried by the Atreides. The Church hierarchy of Auqaf and Hajj saw only the power implicit in control of Muad'Dib's heir. CHOAM wanted a doorway to the wealth of Dune. Farad'n and his Sardaukar sought a return to glory for House Corrino. The Spacing Guild feared the equation Arrakis = melange; without the spice they could not navigate. Jessica wished to repair what her disobedience to the Bene Gesserit had created. Few thought to ask the twins what their plans might be, until it was too late.

—THE BOOK OF KREOS

Shortly after the evening meal, Leto saw a man walking past the arched doorway to his chamber, and his mind went with the man. The passage had been left open and Leto had seen some activity out there—spice hampers being wheeled past, three women with the obvious off-world sophistication of dress which marked them as smugglers. This man who took Leto's mind walking might have been no different except that he moved like Stilgar, a much younger Stilgar.

It was a peculiar walk his mind took. Time filled Leto's awareness like a stellar globe. He could see infinite timespaces, but he had to press into his own future before knowing in which moment his flesh lay. His multifaceted memory-lives surged and receded, but they were his now.

They were like waves on a beach, but if they rose too high, he could command them and they would retreat, leaving the royal Harum behind.

Now and again he would listen to those memory-lives. One would rise like a prompter, poking its head up out of the stage and calling cues for his behavior. His father came during the mind-walk and said: "You are a child seeking to be a man. When you are a man, you will seek in vain for the child you were."

All the while, he felt his body being plagued by the fleas and lice of an old sietch poorly maintained. None of the attendants who brought his heavily spice-laced food appeared bothered by the creatures. Did these people have immunity from such things, or was it only that they had lived with them so long they could ignore discomfort?

Who were these people assembled around Gurney? How had they come to this place? Was this Jacurutu? His multi-memories produced answers he did not like. They were ugly people and Gurney was the ugliest. Perfection floated here, though, dormant and waiting beneath an ugly surface.

Part of him knew he remained spice-bound, held in bondage by the heavy dosages of melange in every meal. His child's body wanted to rebel while his persona raved with the immediate presence of memories carried over from thousands of eons.

His mind returned from its walk, and he wondered if his body had really stayed behind. Spice confused the senses. He felt the pressures of self-limitations piling up against him like the long barachan dunes of the *bled* slowly building themselves a ramp against a desert cliff. One day a few trickles of sand would flow over the cliff, then more and more and more . . . and only the sand would remain exposed to the sky.

But the cliff would still be there underneath.

I'm still within the trance, he thought.

He knew he would come soon to a branching of life and death. His captors kept sending him back into the spice thralldom, unsatisfied with his responses at every return. Always, treacherous Namri waited there with his knife. Leto knew countless pasts and futures, but he had yet to learn what would satisfy Namri . . . or Gurney Halleck. They wanted something outside of the visions. The life and death branching lured Leto. His life, he knew, would have to possess some inner meaning which carried it above the vision circumstances. Thinking of this demand, he felt that his inner awareness was his true being and his outer existence was the trance. This terrified him. He did not want to go back to the sietch with its fleas, its Namri, its Gurney Halleck.

I'm a coward, he thought.

But a coward, even a coward, might die bravely with nothing but a gesture. Where was that gesture which could make him whole once more? How could he awaken from trance and vision into the universe which Gurney demanded? Without that turning, without an awakening from aimless visions, he knew he could die in a prison of his own choosing. In this he had at last come to cooperate with his captors. Somewhere he had to find wisdom, an inner balance which would reflect upon the universe and return to him an image of calm strength. Only then might he seek his Golden Path and survive the skin which was not his own.

Someone was playing the baliset out there in the sietch. Leto felt that his body probably heard the music in the present. He sensed the cot beneath his back. He could hear music. It was Gurney at the baliset. No other fingers could quite compare with his mastery of that most difficult instrument. He played an old Fremen song, one called a *hadith* because of its internal narrative and the voice which invoked those patterns required for survival on Arrakis. The song told the story of human occupations within a sietch.

Leto felt the music move him through a marvelous ancient cavern. He saw women trampling spice residue for fuel, curding the spice for fermentation, forming spice-fabrics. Melange was everywhere in the sietch.

Those moments came when Leto could not distinguish between the music and the people of the cavern vision. The whine and slap of a power loom was the whine and slap of the baliset. But his inner eyes beheld fabrics of human hair, the long fur of mutated rats, threads of desert cotton, and strips curled from the skin of birds. He saw a sietch school. The eco-language of Dune raged through his mind on its wings of music. He saw the sun-powered kitchen, the long chamber where stillsuits were made and maintained. He saw weather forecasters reading the sticks they'd brought in from the sand.

Somewhere during this journey, someone brought him food and spooned it into his mouth, holding his head up with a strong arm. He knew this as a real-time sensation, but the marvelous play of motion continued within him.

As though it came in the next instant after the spice-laden food, he saw the hurtling of a sandstorm. Moving images within the sand breath became the golden reflections of a moth's eyes, and his own life was reduced to the viscous trail of a crawling insect.

Words from the Panoplia Prophetica raved through him: "It is said that there is nothing firm, nothing balanced, nothing durable in all the universe—that nothing remains in its state, that each day, some time each hour, brings change."

The old Missionaria Protectiva knew what they were doing, he thought. *They knew about Terrible Purposes. They knew how to manipulate people and religions. Even my father didn't escape them, not in the end.*

There lay the clue he'd been seeking. Leto studied it. He felt strength flowing back into his flesh. His entire multifaceted being turned over and looked out upon the universe. He sat up and found himself alone in the gloomy cell with only the light from the outer passage where the man had walked past and taken his mind an eon ago.

"Good fortune to us all!" he called in the traditional Fremen way.

Gurney Halleck appeared in the arched doorway, his head a black silhouette against the light from the outer passage.

"Bring light," Leto said.

"You wish to be tested further?"

Leto laughed. "No. It's my turn to test you."

"We shall see." Halleck turned away, returning in a moment with a bright blue glowglobe in the crook of his left elbow. He released it in the cell, allowing it to drift above their heads.

"Where's Namri?" Leto asked.

"Just outside where I can call him."

"Ahh, Old Father Eternity always waits patiently," Leto said. He felt curiously released, poised on the edge of discovery.

"You call Namri by the name reserved for Shai-Hulud?" Halleck asked.

"His knife's a worm's tooth," Leto said. "Thus, he's Old Father Eternity."

Halleck smiled grimly, but remained silent.

"You still wait to pass judgment on me," Leto said. "And there's no way to exchange information, I'll admit, without making judgments. You can't ask the universe to be exact, though."

A rustling sound behind Halleck alerted Leto to Namri's approach. He stopped half a pace to Halleck's left.

"Ahhh, the left hand of the damned," Leto said.

"It's not wise to joke about the Infinite and the Absolute," Namri growled. He glanced sideways at Halleck.

"Are you God, Namri, that you invoke absolutes?" Leto asked. But he kept his attention on Halleck. Judgment would come from there.

Both men merely stared at him without answering.

"Every judgment teeters on the brink of error," Leto explained. "To claim absolute knowledge is to become monstrous. Knowledge is an unending adventure at the edge of uncertainty."

"What word game is this you play?" Halleck demanded.

"Let him speak," Namri said.

"It's the game Namri initiated with me," Leto said, and saw the old Fremen's head nod agreement. He'd certainly recognized the riddle game. "Our senses always have at least two levels," Leto said.

"Trivia and message," Namri said.

"Excellent!" Leto said. "You gave me trivia; I give you message. I see, I hear, I detect odors, I touch; I feel changes in temperature, taste. I sense the passage of time. I may take emotive samples. Ahhhhh! I am happy. You see, Gurney? Namri? There's no mystery about a human life. It's not a problem to be solved, but a reality to be experienced."

"You try our patience, lad," Namri said. "Is this the place where you wish to die?"

But Halleck put out a restraining hand.

"First, I am not a lad," Leto said. He made the first sign at his right ear. "You'll not slay me; I've placed a water burden upon you."

Namri drew his crysknife half out of its sheath. "I owe you nothing!"

"But God created Arrakis to train the faithful," Leto said. "I've not only showed you my faith, I've made you conscious of your own existence. Life requires dispute. You've been made to *know*—by me!—that your reality differs from all others; thus, you know you're alive."

"Irreverence is a dangerous game to play with me," Namri said. He held his crysknife half drawn.

"Irreverence is a most necessary ingredient of religion," Leto said. "Not to speak of its importance in philosophy. Irreverence is the only way left to us for testing our universe."

"So you think you understand the universe?" Halleck asked, and he opened a space between himself and Namri.

"Ye-esss," Namri said, and there was death in his voice.

"The universe can be understood only by the wind," Leto said. "There's no mighty seat of reason which dwells within the brain. Creation is discovery. God discovered us in the Void because we moved against a background which He already knew. The wall was blank. Then there was movement."

"You play hide and seek with death," Halleck warned.

"But you are both my friends," Leto said. He faced Namri. "When you offer a candidate as Friend of your Sietch, do you not slay a hawk and an eagle as the offering? And is this not the response: 'God send each man at his end, such hawks, such eagles, and such friends'?"

Namri's hand slid from his knife. The blade slipped back into its sheath. He stared wide-eyed at Leto. Each sietch kept its friendship ritual secret, yet here was a selected part of the rite.

Halleck, though, asked: "Is this place your end?"

"I know what you need to hear from me, Gurney," Leto said, watching the play of hope and suspicion across the ugly face. Leto touched his own breast. "This child was never a child. My father lives within me, but he is not me. You loved him, and he was a gallant human whose affairs beat upon high shores. His intent was to close down the cycle of wars, but he reckoned without the movement of infinity as expressed by life. That's Rhajia! Namri knows. Its movement can be seen by any mortal. Beware paths which narrow future possibilities. Such paths divert you from infinity into lethal traps."

"What is it I need to hear from you?" Halleck asked.

"He's just word playing," Namri said, but his voice carried deep hesitation, doubts.

"I ally myself with Namri against my father," Leto said. "And my father within allies himself with us against what was made of him."

"Why?" Halleck demanded.

"Because it's the *amor fati* which I bring to humankind, the act of ultimate self-examination. In this universe, I choose to ally myself against any force which brings humiliation upon humankind. Gurney! Gurney! You were not born and raised in the desert. Your flesh doesn't know the truth of which I speak. But Namri knows. In the open land, one direction is as good as another."

"I still have not heard what I must hear," Halleck snarled.

"He speaks for war and against peace," Namri said.

"No," Leto said. "Nor did my father speak against war. But look what was made of him. Peace has only one meaning in this Imperium. It's the maintenance of a single way of life. You are commanded to be contented. Life must be uniform on all planets as it is in the Imperial Government. The major object of priestly study is to find the correct forms of human behavior. For this they go to the words of Muad'Dib! Tell me, Namri, are you content?"

"No." The word came out flat, spontaneous rejection.

"Then do you blaspheme?"

"Of course not!"

"But you aren't contented. You see, Gurney? Namri proves it to us. Every question, every problem doesn't have a single correct answer. One must permit diversity. A monolith is unstable. Then why do you demand a single correct statement from me? Is that to be the measure of your monstrous judgment?"

"Will you force me to have you slain?" Halleck asked, and there was agony in his voice.

"No, I'll have pity upon you," Leto said. "Send word to my grandmother that I'll cooperate. The Sisterhood may come to regret my cooperation, but an Atreides gives his word."

"A Truthsayer should test that," Namri said. "These Atreides . . ."

"He'll have his chance to say before his grandmother what must be said," Halleck said. He nodded with his head toward the passage.

Namri paused before leaving, glanced at Leto. "I pray we do the right thing in leaving him alive."

"Go, friends," Leto said. "Go and reflect."

As the two men departed, Leto threw himself onto his back, feeling the cold cot against his spine. Movement sent his head spinning over the edge of his spice-burdened consciousness. In that instant he saw the entire planet—every village, every town, every city, the desert places and the planted places. All of the shapes which smashed against his vision bore intimate relationships to a mixture of elements within themselves and without. He saw the structures of Imperial society reflected in physical structures of its planets and their communities. Like a gigantic unfolding within him, he saw this revelation for what it must be: a window into the society's invisible parts. Seeing this, Leto realized that every system had such a window. Even the system of himself and his universe. He began peering into windows, a cosmic voyeur.

This was what his grandmother and the Sisterhood sought! He knew it. His awareness flowed on a new, higher level. He felt the past carried in his cells, in his memories, in the archetypes which haunted his assumptions, in the myths which hemmed him, in his languages and their prehistoric detritus. It was all of the shapes out of his human and nonhuman past, all of the lives which he now commanded, all integrated in him at last. And he felt himself as a thing caught up in the ebb and flow of nucleotides. Against the backdrop of infinity he was a protozoan creature in which birth and death were virtually simultaneous, but he was both infinite and protozoan, a creature of molecular memories.

We humans are a form of colony organism! he thought.

They wanted his cooperation. Promising cooperation had won him another reprieve from Namri's knife. By summoning to cooperation, they sought to recognize a healer.

And he thought: *But I'll not bring them social order in the way they expect it!*

A grimace contorted Leto's mouth. He knew he'd not be as unconsciously malevolent as was his father—despotism at one terminal and slavery at the other—but this universe might pray for those "good old days."

His father-within spoke to him then, cautiously probing, unable to demand attention but pleading for audience.

And Leto answered: "No. We will give them complexities to occupy their minds. There are many modes of flight from danger. How will they know I'm dangerous unless they experience me for thousands of years? Yes, father-within, we'll give them question marks."

"It moves of itself!" Farad'n said, and his voice was barely a whisper.

He stood above the Lady Jessica's bed, a brace of guards close behind him. The Lady Jessica had propped herself up in the bed. She was clad in a parasilk gown of shimmering white with a matching band around her copper hair. Farad'n had come bursting in upon her moments before. He wore the grey leotard and his face was sweaty with excitement and the exertions of his dash through the palace corridors.

"What time is it?" Jessica asked.

"Time?" Farad'n appeared puzzled.

One of the guards spoke up: "It is the third hour past midnight, My Lady." The guard glanced fearfully at Farad'n. The young prince had come dashing through the night-lighted corridors, picking up startled guards in his wake.

"But it moves," Farad'n said. He held out his left hand, then his right. "I saw my own hands shrink into chubby fists, and I remembered! They were my hands when I was an infant. I remembered being an infant, but it was . . . a clearer memory. I was reorganizing my old memories!"

"Very good," Jessica said. His excitement was infectious. "And what happened when your hands became old?"

"My . . . mind was . . . sluggish," he said. "I felt an ache in my back. Right here." He touched a place over his left kidney.

"You've learned a most important lesson," Jessica said. "Do you know what that lesson is?"

He dropped his hands to his sides, stared at her. Then: "My mind controls my reality." His eyes glittered, and he repeated it, louder this time: "My mind controls my reality!"

"That is the beginning of *prana-bindu* balance," Jessica said. "It is only the beginning, though."

"What do I do next?" he asked.

"My Lady," the guard who had answered her question ventured now to interrupt. "The hour," he said.

Aren't their spy posts manned at this hour? Jessica wondered. She said: "Begone. We have work to do."

"But My Lady," the guard said, and he looked fearfully from Farad'n to Jessica and back.

"You think I'm going to seduce him?" Jessica asked.

The man stiffened.

Farad'n laughed, a joyous outburst. He waved a hand in dismissal. "You heard her. Begone."

The guards looked at each other, but they obeyed.

Farad'n sat on the edge of her bed. "What next?" He shook his head. "I wanted to believe you, yet I did not believe. Then . . . it was as though my mind melted. I was tired. My mind gave up its fighting against you. It happened. Just like that!" He snapped his fingers.

"It was not me that your mind fought against," Jessica said.

"Of course not," he admitted. "I was fighting against myself, all the nonsense I've learned. What next now?"

Jessica smiled. "I confess I didn't expect you to succeed this rapidly. It's been only eight days and . . ."

"I was patient," he said, grinning.

"And you've begun to learn patience, too," she said.

"Begun?"

"You've just crept over the lip of this learning," she said. "Now you're truly an infant. Before . . . you were only a potential, not even born."

The corners of his mouth drew down.

"Don't be so gloomy," she said. "You've done it. That's important. How many can say they were born anew?"

"What comes next?" he insisted.

"You will practice this thing you've learned," she said. "I want you able to do this at will, easily. Later you'll fill a new place in your awareness which this has opened. It will be filled by the ability to test any reality against your own demands."

"Is that all I do now . . . practice the—"

"No. Now you can begin the muscle training. Tell me, can you move the little toe on your left foot without moving any other muscle of your body?"

"My . . ." She saw a distant expression come over his face as he tried to move the toe. He looked down at his foot presently, staring at it. Sweat broke out on his forehead. A deep breath escaped him. "I can't do it."

"Yes you can," she said. "You will learn to do it. You will learn every muscle in your body. You will know these muscles the way you know your hands."

He swallowed hard at the magnitude of this prospect. Then: "What are you doing to me? What is your plan for me?"

"I intend to turn you loose upon the universe," she said. "You will become whatever it is you most deeply desire."

He mulled this for a moment. "Whatever I desire?"

"Yes."

"That's impossible!"

"Unless you learn to control your desires the way you control your reality," she said. And she thought: *There! Let his analysts examine that. They'll advise cautious approval, but Farad'n will move a step closer to realization of what I'm really doing.*

He proved his surmise by saying: "It's one thing to tell a person he'll realize his heart's desire. It's another thing to actually deliver that realization."

"You've come farther than I thought," Jessica said. "Very good. I promise you: if you complete this program of learning, you'll be your own man. Whatever you do, it'll be because that's what you want to do."

And let a Truthsayer try to pry that apart, she thought.

He stood up, but the expression he bent upon her was warm, a sense of camaraderie in it. "You know, I believe you. Damned if I know why, but I do. And I won't say a word about the other things I'm thinking."

Jessica watched his retreating back as he let himself out of her bedchamber. She turned off the glowglobes, lay back. This Farad'n was a deep one. He'd as much as told her that he was beginning to see her design, but he was joining her conspiracy of his own volition.

Wait until he begins to learn his own emotions, she thought. With that, she composed herself for the return to sleep. The morrow, she knew, would be plagued by casual encounters with palace personnel asking seemingly innocuous questions.

Humankind periodically goes through a speedup of its affairs, thereby experiencing the race between the renewable vitality of the living and the beckoning vitiation of decadence. In this periodic race, any pause becomes luxury. Only then can one reflect that all is permitted; all is possible.

—THE APOCRYPHA OF MUAD'DIB

The touch of sand is important, Leto told himself.

He could feel the grit beneath him where he sat beneath a brilliant sky. They had force-fed him another heavy dosage of melange, and Leto's mind turned upon itself like a whirlpool. An unanswered question lay deep within the funnel of the whirlpool: *Why do they insist that I say it?* Gurney was stubborn: no doubt of that. And he'd had his orders from his Lady Jessica.

They'd brought him out of the sietch into the daylight for this "lesson." He had the strange sensation that he'd let his body take the short trip from the sietch while his inner being mediated a battle between the Duke Leto I and the old Baron Harkonnen. They'd fought within him, through him, because he would not let them communicate directly. The fight had taught him what had happened to Alia. Poor Alia.

I was right to fear the spice trip, he thought.

A welling bitterness toward the Lady Jessica filled him. Her damned gom jabbar! Fight it and win, or die in the attempt. She couldn't put a poisoned needle against his neck, but she could send him into the valley of peril which had claimed her own daughter.

Snuffling sounds intruded upon his awareness. They wavered, growing louder, then softer, louder . . . softer. There was no way for him to determine whether they had current reality or came from the spice.

Leto's body sagged over his folded arms. He felt hot sand through his buttocks. There was a rug directly in front of him, but he sat on open sand. A shadow lay across the rug: Namri. Leto stared into the muddy pattern of the rug, feeling bubbles ripple there. His awareness drifted on its own current through a landscape which stretched out to a horizon of shock-headed greenery.

His skull thrummed with drums. He felt heat, fever. The fever was a pressure of burning which filled his senses, crowding out awareness of flesh until he could only feel the moving shadows of his peril. Namri and the knife. Pressure . . . pressure . . . Leto lay at last suspended between sky and sand, his mind lost to all but the fever. Now he waited for something to happen, sensing that any occurrence would be a first-and-only thing.

Hot-hot pounding sunshine crashed brilliantly around him, without tranquillity, without remedy. *Where is my Golden Path?* Everywhere bugs crawled. Everywhere. *My skin is not my own.* He sent messages along his nerves, waited out the dragging other-person responses.

Up head, he told his nerves.

A head which might have been his own crept upward, looked out at patches of blankness in the bright light.

Someone whispered: "He's deep into it now."

No answer.

Burn fire sun building heat on heat.

Slowly, outbending, the current of his awareness took him drifting through a last screen of green blankness and there, across low folding dunes, distant no more than a kilometer beyond the stretched out chalk line of a cliff, *there* lay the green burgeoning future, upflung, flowing into endless green, greenswelling, green-green moving outward endlessly.

In all of that green there was not one great worm.

Riches of wild growth, but nowhere Shai-Hulud.

Leto sensed that he had ventured across old boundaries into a new land which only the imagination had witnessed, and that he looked now directly through the very next veil which a yawning humankind called *Unknown*.

It was bloodthirsty reality.

He felt the red fruit of his life swaying on a limb, fluid slipping away from him, and the fluid was the spice essence flowing through his veins.

Without Shai-Hulud, no more spice.

He had seen a future without the great grey worm-serpent of Dune. He knew this, yet could not tear himself from the trance to rail against such a passage.

Abruptly his awareness plunged back—back, back, away from such a deadly future. His thoughts went into his bowels, becoming primitive, moved only by intense emotions. He found himself unable to focus on any particular aspect of his vision or his surroundings, but there was a voice within him. It spoke an ancient language and he understood it perfectly. The voice was musical and lilting, but its words bludgeoned him.

"It is not the present which influences the future, thou fool, but the future which forms the present. You have it all backward. Since the future is set, an unfolding of events which will assure that future is fixed and inevitable."

The words transfixed him. He felt terror rooted in the heavy matter of his body. By this he knew his body still existed, but the reckless nature and enormous power of his vision left him feeling contaminated, defenseless, unable to signal a muscle and gain its obedience. He knew he was submitting more and more to the onslaught of those collective lives whose memories once had made him believe he was real. Fear filled him. He thought that he might be losing the inner command, falling at last into Abomination.

Leto felt his body twisting in terror.

He had come to depend upon his victory and the newly won benevolent cooperation of those memories. They had turned against him, all of them—even royal Harum whom he'd trusted. He lay shimmering on a surface which had no roots, unable to give any expression to his own life. He tried to concentrate upon a mental picture of himself, was confronted by overlapping frames, each a different age: infant into doddering ancient. He recalled his father's early training: *Let the hands grow young, then old.* But his whole body was immersed now in this lost reality and the entire image progression melted into other faces, the features of those who had given him their memories.

A diamond thunderbolt shattered him.

Leto felt pieces of his awareness drifting apart, yet he retained a sense of himself somewhere between being and nonbeing. Hope quickening, he felt his body breathing. In . . . Out. He took in a deep breath: *yin.* He let it out: *yang.*

Somewhere just beyond his grasp lay a place of supreme independence, a victory over all of the confusions inherent in his multitude of lives—no false sense of command, but a true victory. He knew his previous mistake now: he had sought power in the reality of his trance, choosing that rather than face the fears which he and Ghanima had fed in each other.

Fear defeated Alia!

But the seeking after power spread another trap, diverting him into fantasy. He saw the illusion. The entire illusion process rotated half a turn and now he knew a center from which he could watch without purpose the flight of his visions, of his inner lives.

Elation flooded him. It made him want to laugh, but he denied himself this luxury, knowing it would bar the doors of memory.

Ahhhh, my memories, he thought. *I have seen your illusion. You no longer invent the next moment for me. You merely show me how to create new moments. I'll not lock myself on the old tracks.*

This thought passed through his awareness as though wiping a surface clean and in its wake he felt his entire body, an *einfalle* which reported in most minute detail on every cell, every nerve. He entered a state of intense quiet. In this quiet, he heard voices, knowing they came from a great distance, but he heard them clearly as though they echoed in a chasm.

One of the voices was Halleck's. "Perhaps we gave him too much of it."

Namri answered. "We gave him exactly what she told us to give him."

"Perhaps we should go back out there and have another look at him." Halleck.

"Sabiha is good at such things; she'll call us if anything starts to go wrong." Namri.

"I don't like this business of Sabiha." Halleck.

"She's a necessary ingredient." Namri.

Leto felt bright light outside himself and darkness within, but the darkness was secretive, protective, and warm. The light began to blaze up and he felt that it came from the darkness within, swirling outward like a brilliant cloud. His body became transparent, drawing him upward, yet he retained that *einfalle* contact with every cell and nerve. The multitude of inner lives fell into alignment, nothing tangled or mixed. They became very quiet in duplication of his own inner silence, each memory-life discrete, an entity incorporeal and undivided.

Leto spoke to them then: "I am your spirit. I am the only life you can realize. I am the house of your spirit in the land which is nowhere, the land which is your only remaining home. Without me, the intelligible universe reverts to chaos. Creative and abysmal are inextricably linked in me; only I can mediate between them. Without me, mankind will sink into the mire and vanity of *knowing*. Through me, you and they will find the only way out of chaos: *understanding by living.*"

With this he let go of himself and became himself, his own person compassing the entirety of his past. It was not victory, not defeat, but a new thing to be shared with any inner life he chose. Leto savored this newness, letting it possess every cell, every nerve, giving up what the *einfalle* had presented to him and recovering the totality in the same instant.

After a time, he awoke in white darkness. With a flash of awareness he knew where his flesh was: seated on sand about a kilometer from the cliff wall which marked the northern boundary of the sietch. He knew that sietch now: Jacurutu for certain . . . and Fondak. But it was far different from the myths and legends and the rumors which the smugglers allowed.

A young woman sat on a rug directly in front of him, a bright glow-globe anchored to her left sleeve and drifting just above her head. When Leto looked away from the glowglobe, there were stars. He knew this young woman; she was the one from his vision earlier, the roaster of coffee. She was Namri's niece, as ready with a knife as Namri was. There was the knife in her lap. She wore a simple green robe over a grey still-suit. *Sabiha*, that was her name. And Namri had his own plans for her.

Sabiha saw the awakening in his eyes, said: "It's almost dawn. You've spent the whole night here."

"And most of a day," he said. "You make good coffee."

This statement puzzled her, but she ignored it with a single-mindedness which spoke of harsh training and explicit instructions for her present behavior.

"It's the hour of assassins," Leto said. "But your knife is no longer needed." He glanced at the crysknife in her lap.

"Namri will be the judge of that," she said.

Not Halleck, then. She only confirmed his inner knowledge.

"Shai-Hulud is a great garbage collector and eraser of unwanted evidence," Leto said. "I've used him thus myself."

She rested her hand lightly on the knife handle.

"How much is revealed by where we sit and how we sit," he said. "You sit upon the rug and I upon the sand."

Her hand closed over the knife handle.

Leto yawned, a gaping and stretching which made his jaws ache. "I've had a vision which included you," he said.

Her shoulders relaxed slightly.

"We've been very one-sided about Arrakis," he said. "Barbaric of us. There's a certain momentum in what we've been doing, but now we must undo some of our work. The scales must be brought into better balance."

A puzzled frown touched Sabiha's face.

"My vision," he said. "Unless we restore the dance of life here on Dune, the dragon on the floor of the desert will be no more."

Because he'd used the Old Fremen name for the great worm, she was a moment understanding him. Then: "The worms?"

"We're in a dark passage," he said. "Without spice, the Empire falls apart. The Guild will not move. Planets will slowly lose their clear memories of each other. They'll turn inward upon themselves. Space will become a boundary when the Guild navigators lose their mastery. We'll cling to our dunetops and be ignorant of that which is above us and below us."

"You speak very strangely," she said. "How have you seen *me* in your vision?"

Trust Fremen superstition! he thought. He said: "I've become pasigraphic. I'm a living glyph to write out the changes which must come to pass. If I do not write them, you'll encounter such heartache as no human should experience."

"What words are these?" she asked, but her hand remained lightly on the knife.

Leto turned his head toward the cliffs of Jacurutu, seeing the beginning glow which would be Second Moon making its predawn passage behind the rocks. The death-scream of a desert hare shocked its way through him. He saw Sabiha shudder. There came the beating of wings—a predator bird, night creature here. He saw the ember glow of many eyes as they swept past above him, headed for crannies in the cliff.

"I must follow the dictates of my new heart," Leto said. "You look upon me as a mere child, Sabiha, but if—"

"They warned me about you," Sabiha said, and now her shoulders were stiff with readiness.

He heard the fear in her voice, said: "Don't fear me, Sabiha. You've lived eight more years than this flesh of mine. For that, I honor you. But I have untold thousands more years of other lives, far more than you have known. Don't look upon me as a child. I have bridged the many futures and, in one, saw us entwined in love. You and I, Sabiha."

"What are . . . This can't . . . ." She broke off in confusion.

"The idea could grow on you," he said. "Now help me back to the sietch, for I've been in far places and am weak with the weariness of my travels. Namri must hear where I have been."

He saw the indecision in her, said: "Am I not the Guest of the Cavern? Namri must learn what I have learned. We have many things to do lest our universe degenerate."

"I don't believe that . . . about the worms," she said.

"Nor about us entwined in love?"

She shook her head. But he could see the thoughts drifting through her mind like windblown feathers. His words both attracted and repelled her. To be consort of power, that certainly carried high allure. Yet there were her uncle's orders. But one day this son of Muad'Dib might rule here on Dune and in the farthest reaches of their universe. She encountered then an extremely Fremen, cavern-hiding aversion to such a future. The consort of Leto would be seen by everyone, would be an object of gossip and speculations. She could have wealth, though, and . . .

"I am the son of Muad'Dib, able to see the future," he said.

Slowly she replaced her knife in its sheath, lifted herself easily from the rug, crossed to his side and helped him to his feet. Leto found himself amused by her actions then: she folded the rug neatly and draped it across her right shoulder. He saw her measuring the difference in their sizes, reflecting upon his words: *Entwined in love?*

Size is another thing that changes, he thought.

She put a hand on his arm then to help him and control him. He stumbled and she spoke sharply: "We're too far from the sietch for *that!*" Meaning the unwanted sound which might attract a worm.

Leto felt that his body had become a dry shell like that abandoned by an insect. He knew this shell: it was one with the society which had been built upon the melange trade and its Religion of the Golden Elixir. It was emptied by its excesses. Muad'Dib's high aims had fallen into wizardry which was enforced by the military arm of Auqaf. Muad'Dib's religion had another name now; it was Shien-san-Shao, an Ixian label which designated the intensity and insanity of those who thought they could bring the universe to paradise at the point of a crysknife. But that too would change as Ix had changed. For they were merely the ninth planet of their sun, and had even forgotten the language which had given them their name.

"The Jihad was a kind of mass insanity," he muttered.

"What?" Sabiha had been concentrating on the problem of making him walk without rhythm, hiding their presence out here on open sand. She was a moment focusing on his words, then interpreted them as another product of his obvious fatigue. She felt the weakness of him, the way he'd been drained by the trance. It seemed pointless and cruel to her. If he were to be killed as Namri said, then it should be done quickly without all of this byplay. Leto had spoken of a marvelous revelation, though. Perhaps that was what Namri sought. Certainly that must be the motive behind the behavior of this child's own grandmother. Why else would Our Lady of Dune give her sanction to these perilous acts against a child?

Child?

Again she reflected upon his words. They were at the cliff base now and she stopped her charge, letting him relax a moment here where it was safer. Looking down at him in the dim starlight, she asked: "How could there be no more worms?"

"Only I can change that," he said. "Have no fear. I can change anything."

"But it's—"

"Some questions have no answers," he said. "I've seen that future, but the contradictions would only confuse you. This is a changing universe and we are the strangest change of all. We resonate to many influences. Our futures need constant updating. Now, there's a barrier which we must remove. This requires that we do brutal things, that we go against our most basic, our dearest wishes. . . . But it must be done."

"What must be done?"

"Have you ever killed a friend?" he asked and, turning, led the way into the gap which sloped upward to the sietch's hidden entrance. He moved as quickly as his trance-fatigue would permit, but she was right behind him, clutching his robe and pulling him to a stop.

"What's this of killing a friend?"

"He'll die anyway," Leto said. "I don't have to do it, but I could prevent it. If I don't prevent it, is that not killing him?"

"Who is this . . . who will die?"

"The alternative keeps me silent," he said. "I might have to give my sister to a monster."

Again he turned away from her, and this time when she pulled at his robe he resisted, refusing to answer her questions. *Best she not know until the time comes,* he thought.

Natural selection has been described as an environment selectively screening for those who will have progeny. Where humans are concerned, though, this is an extremely limiting viewpoint. Reproduction by sex tends toward experiment and innovation. It raises many questions, including the ancient one about whether environment is a selective agent after the variation occurs, or whether environment plays a pre-selective role in determining the variations which it screens. Dune did not really answer those questions: it merely raised new questions which Leto and the Sisterhood may attempt to answer over the next five hundred generations.

—THE DUNE CATASTROPHE
AFTER HARQ AL-ADA

The bare brown rocks of the Shield Wall loomed in the distance, visible to Ghanima as the embodiment of that apparition which threatened her future. She stood at the edge of the roof garden atop the Keep, the setting sun at her back. The sun held a deep orange glow from intervening dust clouds, a color as rich as the rim of a worm's mouth. She sighed, thinking: *Alia . . . Alia . . . Is your fate to be my fate?*

The inner lives had grown increasingly clamorous of late. There was something about female conditioning in a Fremen society—perhaps it was a real sexual difference, but whatever—the female was more susceptible to that inner tide. Her grandmother had warned about it as they'd schemed, drawing on the accumulated wisdom of the Bene Gesserit but awakening that wisdom's threats within Ghanima.

"Abomination," the Lady Jessica had said, "our term for the pre-born, has a long history of bitter experiences behind it. The way of it seems to be that the inner lives divide. They split into the benign and the malignant. The benign remain tractable, useful. The malignant appear to unite in one powerful psyche, trying to take over the living flesh and its consciousness. The process is known to take considerable time, but its signs are well known."

"Why did you abandon Alia?" Ghanima asked.

"I fled in terror of what I'd created," Jessica said, her voice low. "I gave up. And my burden now is that . . . perhaps I gave up too soon."

"What do you mean?"

"I cannot explain yet, but . . . maybe . . . no! I'll not give you false hopes. *Ghafla*, the abominable distraction, has a long history in human mythology. It was called many things, but chiefly it was called *possession*. That's what it seems to be. You lose your way in the malignancy and it takes possession of you."

"Leto . . . feared the spice," Ghanima said, finding that she could talk about him quietly. The terrible price demanded of them!

"And wisely," Jessica had said. She would say no more.

But Ghanima had risked an explosion of her inner memories, peering past an odd blurred veil and futilely expanding on the Bene Gesserit fears. To explain what had befallen Alia did not ease it one bit. The Bene Gesserit accumulation of experience had pointed to a possible way out of the trap, though, and when Ghanima ventured the inner sharing, she first called upon the *Mohalata*, a partnership of the benign which might protect her.

She recalled that sharing as she stood in the sunset glow at the edge of the Keep's roof garden. Immediately she felt the memory-presence of her mother. Chani stood there, an apparition between Ghanima and the distant cliffs.

"Enter here and you will eat the fruit of the Zaqquum, the food of hell!" Chani said. "Bar this door, my daughter: it is your only safety."

The inner clamor lifted itself around the vision and Ghanima fled, sinking her consciousness into the Sisterhood's Credo, reacting out of desperation more than trust. Quickly she recited the Credo, moving her lips, letting her voice rise to a whisper:

"Religion is the emulation of the adult by the child. Religion is the encystment of past beliefs: mythology, which is guesswork, the hidden assumptions of trust in the universe, those pronouncements which men have made in search of personal power, all of it mingled with shreds of enlightenment. And always the ultimate unspoken commandment is 'Thou shalt not question!' But we question. We break that commandment as a matter of course. The work to which we have set ourselves is the liberating of the imagination, the harnessing of imagination to mankind's deepest sense of creativity."

Slowly a sense of order returned to Ghanima's thoughts. She felt her body trembling, though, and knew how fragile was this peace she had attained—and that blurring veil remained in her mind.

"Leb Kamai," she whispered. "Heart of my enemy, you shall not be my heart."

And she called up a memory of Farad'n's features, the saturnine young face with its heavy brows and firm mouth.

Hate will make me strong, she thought. *In hate, I can resist Alia's fate.*

But the trembling fragility of her position remained, and all she could think about was how much Farad'n resembled his uncle, the late Shaddam IV.

"Here you are!"

It was Irulan coming up from Ghanima's right, striding along the parapet with movements reminiscent of a man. Turning, Ghanima thought: *And she's Shaddam's daughter.*

"Why will you persist in sneaking out alone?" Irulan demanded, stopping in front of Ghanima and towering over her with a scowling face.

Ghanima refrained from saying that she was not alone, that guards had seen her emerge onto the roof. Irulan's anger went to the fact that they were in the open here and that a distant weapon might find them.

"You're not wearing a stillsuit," Ghanima said. "Did you know that in the old days someone caught outside the sietch without a stillsuit was automatically killed? To waste water was to endanger the tribe."

"Water! Water!" Irulan snapped. "I want to know why you endanger yourself this way. Come back inside. You make trouble for all of us."

"What danger is there now?" Ghanima asked. "Stilgar has purged the traitors. Alia's guards are everywhere."

Irulan peered upward at the darkening sky. Stars were already visible against a grey-blue backdrop. She returned her attention to Ghanima. "I won't argue. I was sent to tell you we have word from Farad'n. He accepts, but for some reason he wishes to delay the ceremony."

"How long?"

"We don't know yet. It's being negotiated. But Duncan is being sent home."

"And my grandmother?"

"She chooses to stay on Salusa for the time being."

"Who can blame her?" Ghanima asked.

"That silly fight with Alia!"

"Don't try to gull me, Irulan! That was no silly fight. I've heard the stories."

"The Sisterhood's fears—"

"Are real," Ghanima said. "Well, you've delivered your message. Will you use this opportunity to have another try at dissuading me?"

"I've given up."

"You should know better than to try lying to me," Ghanima said.

"Very well! I'll keep trying to dissuade you. This course is madness." And Irulan wondered why she let Ghanima become so irritating. A Bene Gesserit didn't need to be irritated at anything. She said: "I'm concerned by the extreme danger to you. You know that. Ghani, Ghani . . . you're Paul's daughter. How can you—"

"Because I'm his daughter," Ghanima said. "We Atreides go back to Agamemnon and we know what's in our blood. Never forget that, childless wife of my father. We Atreides have a bloody history and we're not through with the blood."

Distracted, Irulan asked: "Who's Agamemnon?"

"How sparse your vaunted Bene Gesserit education proves itself," Ghanima said. "I keep forgetting that you foreshorten history. But my memories go back to . . ." She broke off; best not to arouse those shades from their fragile sleep.

"Whatever you remember," Irulan said, "you must know how dangerous this course is to—"

"I'll kill him," Ghanima said. "He owes me a life."

"And I'll prevent it if I can."

"We already know this. You won't get the opportunity. Alia is sending you south to one of the new towns until after it's done."

Irulan shook her head in dismay. "Ghani, I took my oath that I'd guard you against any danger. I'll do it with my own life if necessary. If you think I'm going to languish in some brickwalled djedida while you . . ."

"There's always the Huanui," Ghanima said, speaking softly. "We have the deathstill as an alternative. I'm sure you couldn't interfere from there."

Irulan paled, put a hand to her mouth, forgetting for a moment all of her training. It was a measure of how much care she had invested in Ghanima, this almost complete abandonment of everything except animal fear. She spoke out of that shattering emotion, allowing it to tremble on her lips. "Ghani, I don't fear for myself. I'd throw myself into the worm's mouth for you. Yes, I'm what you call me, the childless wife of your father, but you're the child I never had. I beg you . . ." Tears glistened at the corners of her eyes.

Ghanima fought down a tightness in her throat, said: "There is another difference between us. You were never Fremen. I'm nothing else. This is a chasm which divides us. Alia knows. Whatever else she may be, she knows this."

"You can't tell what Alia knows," Irulan said, speaking bitterly. "If I didn't know her for Atreides, I'd swear she has set herself to destroy her own Family."

And how do you know she's still Atreides? Ghanima thought, wondering at this blindness in Irulan. This was a Bene Gesserit, and who knew better than they the history of Abomination? She would not let herself even think about it, let alone believe it. Alia must have worked some witchery on this poor woman.

Ghanima said: "I owe you a water debt. For that, I'll guard your life. But your cousin's forfeit. Say no more of that."

Irulan stilled the trembling of her lips, wiped her eyes. "I did love your father," she whispered. "I didn't even know it until he was dead."

"Perhaps he isn't dead," Ghanima said. "This Preacher . . ."

"Ghani! Sometimes I don't understand you. Would Paul attack his own family?"

Ghanima shrugged, looked out at the darkening sky. "He might find amusement in such a—"

"How can you speak so lightly of this—"

"To keep away the dark depths," Ghanima said. "I don't taunt you. The gods know I don't. But I'm just my father's daughter. I'm every person who's contributed seed to the Atreides. You won't think of Abomination, but I can't think of anything else. I'm the pre-born. I know what's within me."

"That foolish old superstition about—"

"Don't!" Ghanima reached a hand toward Irulan's mouth. "I'm every Bene Gesserit of their damnable breeding program up to and including my grandmother. And I'm very much more." She tore at her left palm, drawing blood with a fingernail. "This is a young body, but its experiences . . . Oh, *gods*, Irulan! My experiences! No!" She put out her hand once more as Irulan moved closer. "I know all of those futures which my father explored. I've the wisdom of so many lifetimes, and all the ignorance, too . . . all the frailties. If you'd help me, Irulan, first learn who I am."

Instinctively Irulan bent and gathered Ghanima into her arms, holding her close, cheek against cheek.

Don't let me have to kill this woman, Ghanima thought. *Don't let that happen.*

As this thought swept through her, the whole desert passed into night.

One small bird has called thee
From a beak streaked crimson.
It cried once over Sietch Tabr
And thou went forth unto Funeral Plain.

—LAMENT FOR LETO II

Leto awoke to the tinkle of water rings in a woman's hair. He looked to the open doorway of his cell and saw Sabiha sitting there. In the half-immersed awareness of the spice he saw her outlined by all that his vision revealed about her. She was two years past the age when most Fremen women were wed or at least betrothed. Therefore her family was saving her for something . . . or someone. She was nubile . . . obviously. His vision-shrouded eyes saw her as a creature out of humankind's Terranic past: dark hair and pale skin, deep sockets which gave her blue-in-blue eyes a greenish cast. She possessed a small nose and a wide mouth above a sharp chin. And she was a living signal to him that the Bene Gesserit plan was known—or suspected—here in Jacurutu. So they hoped to revive Pharaonic Imperialism through him, did they? Then what was their design to force him into marrying his sister? Surely Sabiha could not prevent that.

His captors knew the plan, though. And how had they learned it? They'd not shared its vision. They'd not gone with him where life became a moving membrane in other dimensions. The reflexive and circular subjectivity of the visions which revealed Sabiha were his and his alone.

Again the water rings tinkled in Sabiha's hair and the sound stirred up his visions. He knew where he had been and what he had learned. Nothing could erase that. He was not riding a great Maker palanquin now, the tinkle of water rings among the passengers a rhythm for their passage songs. No. . . . He was here in the cell of Jacurutu, embarked on that most dangerous of all journeys: away from and back to the *Ahl as-sunna wal-jamas*, from the real world of the senses and back to that world.

What was she doing there with the water rings tinkling in her hair? Oh, yes. She was mixing more of the brew which they thought held him captive: food laced with spice essence to keep him half in and half out of the real universe until either he died or his grandmother's plan succeeded. And every time he thought he'd won, they sent him back. The Lady Jessica was right, of course—that old witch! But what a thing to do. The total recall of all those lives within him was of no use at all until he could organize the data and remember it at will. Those lives had been the raw stuff of anarchy. One or all of them could have overwhelmed him. The spice and its peculiar setting here in Jacurutu had been a desperate gamble.

Now Gurney waits for the sign and I refuse to give it to him. How long will his patience last?

He stared out at Sabiha. She'd thrown her hood back and revealed the tribal tattoos at her temples. Leto did not recognize the tattoos at first, then remembered where he was. Yes, Jacurutu still lived.

Leto did not know whether to be thankful toward his grandmother or hate her. She wanted him to have conscious-level instincts. But instincts were only racial memories of how to handle crises. His direct memories of those other lives told him far more than that. He had it all organized now, and could see the peril of revealing himself to Gurney. No way of keeping the revelation from Namri. And Namri was another problem.

Sabiha entered the cell with a bowl in her hands. He admired the way the light from outside made rainbow circles at the edges of her hair. Gently she raised his head and began feeding him from the bowl. It was only then he realized how weak he was. He allowed her to feed him while his mind went roving, recalling the session with Gurney and Namri. They believed him! Namri more than Gurney, but even Gurney could not deny what his senses had already reported to him about the planet.

Sabiha wiped his mouth with a hem of her robe.

Ahhh, Sabiha, he thought, recalling that other vision which filled his heart with pain. *Many nights have I dreamed beside the open water, hearing the winds pass overhead. Many nights my flesh lay beside the snake's den and I dreamed of Sabiha in the summer heat. I saw her storing spice-bread baked on red-hot sheets of plasteel. I saw the clear water in the qanat, gentle and shining, but a stormwind ran through my heart. She sips coffee and eats. Her teeth shine in the shadows. I see her braiding my water rings into her hair. The amber fragrance of her bosom strikes through to my innermost senses. She torments me and oppresses me by her very existence.*

The pressure of his multi-memories exploded the time-frozen englobement which he had tried to resist. He felt twining bodies, the sounds of sex, rhythms laced in every sensory impression: lips, breathing, moist breaths, tongues. Somewhere in his vision there were helix shapes, coal-colored, and he felt the beat of those shapes as they turned within him. A voice pleaded in his skull: "Please, please, please, please . . ." There was an adult beefswelling in his loins and he felt his mouth open, holding, clinging to the girder-shape of ecstasy. Then a sigh, a lingering groundswelling sweetness, a collapse.

Oh, how sweet to let that come into existence!

"Sabiha," he whispered. "Oh, my Sabiha."

When her charge had clearly gone deeply into the trance after his food, Sabiha took the bowl and left, pausing at the doorway to speak to Namri. "He called my name again."

"Go back and stay with him," Namri said. "I must find Halleck and discuss this with him."

Sabiha deposited the bowl beside the doorway and returned to the cell. She sat on the edge of the cot, staring at Leto's shadowed face.

Presently he opened his eyes and put a hand out, touching her cheek. He began to talk to her then, telling her about the vision in which she had lived.

She covered his hand with her own as he spoke. How sweet he was . . . how very swee—She sank onto the cot, cushioned by his hand, unconscious before he pulled the hand away. Leto sat up, feeling the depths of his weakness. The spice and its visions had drained him. He searched through his cells for every spare spark of energy, climbed from the cot without disturbing Sabiha. He had to go, but he knew he'd not get far. Slowly he sealed his stillsuit, drew the robe around him, slipped through the passage to the outer shaft. There were a few people about, busy at their own affairs. They knew him, but he was not their responsibility. Namri and Halleck would know what he was doing; Sabiha could not be far away.

He found the kind of side passage he needed and walked boldly down it.

Behind him Sabiha slept peacefully until Halleck roused her.

She sat up, rubbed her eyes, saw the empty cot, saw her uncle standing behind Halleck, the anger on their faces.

Namri answered the expression on her face: "Yes, he's gone."

"How could you let him escape?" Halleck raged. "How is this possible?"

"He was seen going toward the lower exit," Namri said, his voice oddly calm.

Sabiha cowered in front of them, remembering.

"How?" Halleck demanded.

"I don't know. I don't know."

"It's night and he's weak," Namri said. "He won't get far."

Halleck whirled on him. "You want the boy to die!"

"It wouldn't displease me."

Again Halleck confronted Sabiha. "Tell me what happened."

"He touched my cheek. He kept talking about his vision . . . us together." She looked down at the empty cot. "He made me sleep. He put some magic on me."

Halleck glanced at Namri. "Could he be hiding inside somewhere?"

"Nowhere inside. He'd be found, seen. He was headed for the exit. He's out there."

"Magic," Sabiha muttered.

"No magic," Namri said. "He hypnotized her. Almost did it to me, you remember? Said I was his friend."

"He's very weak," Halleck said.

"Only in his body," Namri said. "He won't go far, though. I disabled the heel pumps of his stillsuit. He'll die with no water if we don't find him."

Halleck almost turned and struck Namri, but held himself in rigid control. Jessica had warned him that Namri might have to kill the lad. Gods below! What a pass they'd come to, Atreides against Atreides. He said: "Is it possible he just wandered away in the spice trance?"

"What difference does it make?" Namri asked. "If he escapes us he must die."

"We'll start searching at first light," Halleck said. "Did he take a Fremkit?"

"There're always a few beside the doorseal," Namri said. "He'd've been a fool not to take one. Somehow he has never struck me as a fool."

"Then send a message to our friends," Halleck said. "Tell them what's happened."

"No messages this night," Namri said. "There's a storm coming. The tribes have been tracking it for three days now. It'll be here by midnight. Already communication's blanked out. The satellites signed off this sector two hours ago."

A deep sigh shook Halleck. The boy would die out there for sure if the sandblast storm caught him. It would eat the flesh from his bones and sliver the bones to fragments. The contrived false death would become real. He slapped a fist into an open palm. The storm could trap them in the sietch. They couldn't even mount a search. And storm static had already isolated the sietch.

"Distrans," he said, thinking they might imprint a message onto a bat's voice and dispatch it with the alarm.

Namri shook his head. "Bats won't fly in a storm. Come on, man. They're more sensitive than we are. They'll cower in the cliffs until it's past. Best to wait for the satellites to pick us up again. Then we can try to find his remains."

"Not if he took a Fremkit and hid in the sand," Sabiha said.

Cursing under his breath, Halleck whirled away from them, strode out into the sietch.

Peace demands solutions, but we never reach living solutions; we only work toward them. A fixed solution is, by definition, a dead solution. The trouble with peace is that it tends
to punish mistakes instead of rewarding brilliance.

—THE WORDS OF MY FATHER:
AN ACCOUNT OF MUAD'DIB
RECONSTRUCTED BY HARQ AL-ADA

"She's training him? She's training Farad'n?"

Alia glared at Duncan Idaho with a deliberate mix of anger and
incredulity. The Guild heighliner had swung into orbit around Arrakis
at noon local. An hour later the lighter had put Idaho down at Arrakeen, unannounced, but all casual and open. Within minutes a 'thopter
had deposited him atop the Keep. Warned of his impending arrival,
Alia had greeted him there, coldly formal before her guards, but now
they stood in her quarters beneath the north rim. He had just delivered
his report, truthfully, precisely, emphasizing each datum in mentat
fashion.

"She has taken leave of her senses," Alia said.

He treated the statement as a mentat problem. "All the indicators are
that she remains well balanced, sane. I should say her sanity index was—"

"Stop that!" Alia snapped. "What can she be thinking of?"

Idaho, who knew that his own emotional balance depended now
upon retreat into mentat coldness, said: "I compute she is thinking of
her granddaughter's betrothal." His features remained carefully bland,

a mask for the raging grief which threatened to engulf him. There was no Alia here. Alia was dead. For a time he'd maintained a myth-Alia before his senses, someone he'd manufactured out of his own needs, but a mentat could carry on such self-deception for only a limited time. This creature in human guise was possessed; a demon-psyche drove her. His steely eyes with their myriad facets available at will reproduced upon his vision centers a multiplicity of myth-Alias. But when he combined them into a single image, no Alia remained. Her features moved to other demands. She was a shell within which outrages had been committed.

"Where's Ghanima?" he asked.

She waved the question aside. "I've sent her with Irulan to stay in Stilgar's keeping."

Neutral territory, he thought. *There's been another negotiation with rebellious tribes. She's losing ground and doesn't know it . . . or does she? Is there another reason? Has Stilgar gone over to her?*

"The betrothal," Alia mused. "What are conditions in the Corrino House?"

"Salusa swarms with *outrine* relatives, all working upon Farad'n, hoping for a share in his return to power."

"And she's training him in the Bene Gesserit . . ."

"Is it not fitting for Ghanima's husband?"

Alia smiled to herself, thinking of Ghanima's adamant rage. Let Farad'n be trained. Jessica was training a corpse. It would all work out.

"I must consider this at length," she said. "You're very quiet, Duncan."

"I await your questions."

"I see. You know, I was very angry with you. Taking her to Farad'n!"

"You commanded me to make it real."

"I was forced to put out the report that you'd both been taken captive," she said.

"I obeyed your orders."

"You're so literal at times, Duncan. You almost frighten me. But if you hadn't, well . . ."

"The Lady Jessica's out of harm's way," he said. "And for Ghanima's sake we should be grateful that—"

"Exceedingly grateful," she agreed. And she thought: *He's no longer trustworthy. He has that damnable Atreides loyalty. I must make an excuse to send him away . . . and have him eliminated. An accident, of course.*

She touched his cheek.

Idaho forced himself to respond to the caress, taking her hand and kissing it.

"Duncan, Duncan, how sad it is," she said. "But I cannot keep you here with me. Too much is happening and I've so few I can completely trust."

He released her hand, waited.

"I was *forced* to send Ghanima to Tabr," she said. "Things are in deep unrest here. Raiders from the Broken Lands breached the qanats at Kagga Basin and spilled all of their waters into the sands. Arrakeen was on short rations. The Basin's alive with sandtrout yet, reaping the water harvest. They're being dealt with, of course, but we're spread very thin."

He'd already noted how few amazons of Alia's guard were to be seen in the Keep. And he thought: *The Maquis of the Inner Desert will keep on probing her defenses. Doesn't she know that?*

"Tabr is still neutral territory," she said. "Negotiations are continuing there right now. Javid's there with a delegation from the Priesthood. But I'd like you at Tabr to watch them, especially Irulan."

"She *is* Corrino," he agreed.

But he saw in her eyes that she was rejecting him. How transparent this Alia-creature had become!

She waved a hand. "Go now, Duncan, before I soften and keep you here beside me. I've missed you so . . ."

"And I've missed you," he said, allowing all of his grief to flow into his voice.

She stared at him, startled by the sadness. Then: "For my sake, Duncan." And she thought: *Too bad, Duncan.* She said: "Zia will take you to Tabr. We need the 'thopter back here."

Her pet amazon, he thought: *I must be careful of that one.*

"I understand," he said, once more taking her hand and kissing it. He stared at the dear flesh which once had been his Alia's. He could not bring himself to look at her face as he left. Someone else stared back at him from her eyes.

As he mounted to the Keep's roofpad, Idaho probed a growing sense of unanswered questions. The meeting with Alia had been extremely trying for the mentat part of him which kept reading data signs. He waited beside the 'thopter with one of the Keep's amazons, stared grimly southward. Imagination took his gaze beyond the Shield Wall to Sietch Tabr. *Why does Zia take me to Tabr? Returning a 'thopter is a menial task. What is the delay? Is Zia getting special instructions?*

Idaho glanced at the watchful guard, mounted to the pilot's position in the 'thopter. He leaned out, said: "Tell Alia I'll send the 'thopter back immediately with one of Stilgar's men."

Before the guard could protest he closed the door and started the 'thopter. He could see her standing there indecisively. Who could question Alia's consort? He had the 'thopter airborne before she could make up her mind what to do.

Now, alone in the 'thopter, he allowed his grief to spend itself in great wracking sobs. Alia was gone. They had parted forever. Tears flowed from his Tleilaxu eyes and he whispered: "Let all the waters of Dune flow into the sand. They will not match my tears."

This was a non-mentat excess, though, and he recognized it as such, forcing himself to sober assessment of present necessities. The 'thopter demanded his attention. The reactions of flying brought him some relief, and he had himself once more in hand.

Ghanima with Stilgar again. And Irulan.

Why had Zia been designated to accompany him? He made it a mentat problem and the answer chilled him. *I was to have a fatal accident.*

This rocky shrine to the skull of a ruler grants no prayers. It has become the grave of lamentations. Only the wind hears the voice of this place. The cries of night creatures and the passing wonder of two moons, all say his day has ended. No more supplicants come. The visitors have gone from the feast. How bare the pathway down this mountain.

—LINES AT THE SHRINE OF AN ATREIDES DUKE ANON.

The thing had the deceptive appearance of simplicity to Leto: avoiding the vision, do that which has not been seen. He knew the trap in his thought, how the casual threads of a locked future twisted themselves together until they held you fast, but he had a new grip on those threads. Nowhere had he seen himself running from Jacurutu. The thread to Sabiha must be cut first.

He crouched now in the last daylight at the eastern edge of the rock which protected Jacurutu. His Fremkit had produced energy tablets and food. He waited now for strength. To the west lay Lake Azrak, the gypsum plain where once there'd been open water in the days before the worm. Unseen to the east lay the Bene Sherk, a scattering of new settlements encroaching upon the open *bled*. To the south lay the Tanzerouft, the Land of Terror: thirty-eight hundred kilometers of wasteland broken only by patches of grass-locked dunes and windtraps to water them—the work of the ecological transformation remaking the landscape of Arrakis. They were serviced by airborne teams and no one stayed for long.

I will go south, he told himself. *Gurney will expect me to do that.* This was not the moment to do the completely unexpected.

It would be dark soon and he could leave this temporary hiding place. He stared at the southern skyline. There was a whistling of dun sky along that horizon, rolling there like smoke, a burning line of undulant dust—a storm. He watched the high center of the storm rising up out of the Great Flat like a questing worm. For a full minute he watched the center, saw that it did not move to the right or the left. The old Fremen saying leaped into his mind: *When the center does not move, you are in its path.*

That storm changed matters.

For a moment he stared back westward the direction of Tabr, feeling the deceptive grey-tan peace of the desert evening, seeing the white gypsum pan edged by wind-rounded pebbles, the desolate emptiness with its unreal surface of glaring white reflecting dust clouds. Nowhere in any vision had he seen himself surviving the grey serpent of a mother storm or buried too deeply in sand to survive. There was only that vision of rolling in wind . . . but that might come later.

And a storm was out there, winding across many degrees of latitude, whipping its world into submission. It could be risked. There were old stories, always heard from a friend of a friend, that one could lock an exhausted worm on the surface by propping a Maker hook beneath one of its wide rings and, having immobilized it, ride out a storm in the leeward shadow. There was a line between audacity and abandoned recklessness which tempted him. That storm would not come before midnight at the earliest. There was time. How many threads could be cut here? All, including the final one?

Gurney will expect me to go south, but not into a storm.

He stared down to the south, seeking a pathway, saw the fluent ebony brushstroke of a deep gorge curving through Jacurutu's rock. He saw sand curls in the bowels of the gorge, chimera sand. It uttered its haughty runnels onto the plain as though it were water. The gritty taste of thirst whispered in his mouth as he shouldered his Fremkit and let himself down onto the path which led into the canyon. It was still light enough that he might be seen, but he knew he was gambling with time.

As he reached the canyon's lip, the quick night of the central desert fell upon him. He was left with the parched glissando of moonglow to light his way toward the Tanzerouft. He felt his heartbeat quicken with all of the fears which his wealth of memories provided. He sensed that he might be going down into Huanui-naa, as Fremen fears labeled the greatest storms: the Earth's Deathstill. But whatever came, it would be visionless. Every step left farther behind him the spice-induced *dhyana*, that spreading awareness of his intuitive-creative nature with its unfolding to the motionless chain of causality. For every hundred steps he took now, there must be at least one step aside, beyond words and into communion with his newly grasped internal reality.

One way or another, father, I'm coming to you.

There were birds invisible in the rocks around him, making themselves known by small sounds. Fremen-wise, he listened for their echoes to guide his way where he could not see. Often as he passed crannies he marked the baleful green of eyes, creatures crouched in hiding because they knew a storm approached.

He emerged from the gorge onto the desert. Living sand moved and breathed beneath him, telling of deep actions and latent fumaroles. He looked back and up to the moon-touched lava caps on Jacurutu's buttes. The whole structure was metamorphic, mostly pressure-formed. Arrakis still had something to say in its own future. He planted his thumper to call a worm and, when it began beating against the sand, took his position to watch and listen. Unconsciously his right hand went to the Atreides hawk ring concealed in a knotted fold of his *dishdasha*. Gurney had found it, but had left it. What had he thought, seeing Paul's ring?

Father, expect me soon.

The worm came from the south. It angled in to avoid the rocks, not as large a worm as he'd hoped, but that could not be remedied. He gauged its passage, planted his hooks, and went up the scaled side with a quick scrambling as it swept over the thumper in a swishing dust spray. The worm turned easily under the pressure of his hooks. The wind of its passage began to whip his robe. He bent his gaze on the southern stars, dim through dust, and pointed the worm that way.

Right into the storm.

As First Moon rose, Leto gauged the storm height and put off his estimate of its arrival. Not before daylight. It was spreading out, gathering more energy for a great leap. There'd be plenty of work for the ecological transformation teams. It was as though the planet fought them with a conscious fury out here, the fury increasing as the transformation took in more land.

All night he pressed the worm southward, sensing the reserves of its energy in the movements transmitted through his feet. Occasionally he let the beast fall off to the west which it was forever trying to do, moved by the invisible boundaries of its territory or by a deep-seated awareness of the coming storm. Worms buried themselves to escape the sandblast winds, but this one would not sink beneath the desert while Maker hooks held any of its rings open.

At midnight the worm was showing many signs of exhaustion. He moved back along its great ridges and worked the flail, allowing it to slow down but continuing to drive it southward.

The storm arrived just after daybreak. First there was the beady stretched-out immobility of the desert dawn pressing dunes one into another. Next, the advancing dust caused him to seal his face flaps. In the thickening dust the desert became a dun picture without lines. Then sand needles began cutting his cheeks, stinging his lids. He felt the coarse grit on his tongue and knew the moment of decision had come. Should he risk the old stories by immobilizing the almost exhausted worm? He took only a heartbeat to discard this choice, worked his way back to the worm's tail, slacked off his hooks. Barely moving now, the worm began to burrow. But the excesses of the creature's heat-transfer system still churned up a cyclone oven behind him in the quickening storm. Fremen children learned the dangers of this position near the worm's tail with their earliest stories. Worms were oxygen factories; fire burned wildly in their passage, fed by the lavish exhalations from the chemical adaptations to friction within them.

Sand began to whip around his feet. Leto loosed his hooks and leaped wide to avoid the furnace at the tail. Everything depended now on getting beneath the sand where the worm had loosened it.

Grasping the static compaction tool in his left hand, he burrowed into a dune's slipface, knowing the worm was too tired to turn back and swallow him in its great white-orange mouth. As he burrowed with his left hand, his right hand worked the stilltent from his Fremkit and he readied it for inflation. It was all done in less than a minute: he had the tent into a hard-walled sand pocket on the lee face of a dune. He inflated the tent and crawled into it. Before sealing the sphincter, he reached out with the compaction tool, reversed its action. The slipface came sliding down over the tent. Only a few sand grains entered as he sealed the opening.

Now he had to work even more quickly. No sandsnorkel would reach up there to keep him supplied with breathing air. This was a great storm, the kind few survived. It would cover this place with tons of sand. Only the tender bubble of the stilltent with its compacted outer shell would protect him.

Leto stretched flat on his back, folded his hands over his breast and sent himself into a dormancy trance where his lungs would move only once an hour. In this he committed himself to the unknown. The storm would pass and, if it did not expose his fragile pocket, he might emerge . . . or he might enter the *Madinat assalam*, the Abode of Peace. Whatever happened, he knew he had to break the threads, one by one, leaving him at last only the Golden Path. It was that, or he could not return to the caliphate of his father's heirs. No more would he live the lie of that *Desposyni*, that terrible caliphate, chanting to the demiurge of his father. No more would he keep silent when a priest mouthed offensive nonsense: *"His crysknife will dissolve demons!"*

With this commitment, Leto's awareness slipped into the web of timeless *dao*.

There exist obvious higher-order influences in any planetary system. This is often demonstrated by introducing terraform life onto newly discovered planets. In all such cases, the life in similar zones develops striking similarities of adaptive form. This form signifies much more than shape; it connotes a survival organization and a relationship of such organizations. The human quest for this interdependent order and our niche within it represents a profound necessity. The quest can, however, be perverted into a conservative grip on sameness. This has always proved deadly for the entire system.

—THE DUNE CATASTROPHE
AFTER HARQ AL-ADA

"My son didn't really see *the future*; he saw the process of creation and its relationship to the myths in which men sleep," Jessica said. She spoke swiftly but without appearing to rush the matter. She knew the hidden observers would find a way to interrupt as soon as they recognized what she was doing.

Farad'n sat on the floor outlined in a shaft of afternoon sunlight which slanted through the window behind him. Jessica could just see the top of a tree in the courtyard garden when she glanced across from her position standing against the far wall. It was a new Farad'n she saw: more slender, more sinewy. The months of training had worked their inevitable magic on him. His eyes glittered when he stared at her.

"He saw the shapes which existing forces would create unless they were diverted," Jessica said. "Rather than turn against his fellow men, he turned against himself. He refused to accept only that which comforted him because that was moral cowardice."

Farad'n had learned to listen silently testing, probing, holding his questions until he had shaped them into a cutting edge. She had been talking about the Bene Gesserit view of molecular memory expressed as ritual and had, quite naturally, diverged to the Sisterhood's way of analyzing Paul Muad'Dib. Farad'n saw a shadow play in her words and actions, however, a projection of unconscious forms at variance with the surface intent of her statements.

"Of all our observations, this is the most crucial," she'd said. "Life is a mask through which the universe expresses itself. We assume that all of humankind and its supportive life forms represent a *natural* community and that the fate of all life is at stake in the fate of the individual. Thus, when it comes to that ultimate self-examination, the *amor fati*, we stop playing god and revert to teaching. In the crunch, we select individuals and we set them as free as we're able."

He saw now where she had to be going and knowing its effect upon those who watched through the spy eyes, refrained from casting an apprehensive glance at the door. Only a trained eye could have detected his momentary imbalance, but Jessica saw it and smiled. A smile, after all, could mean anything.

"This is a sort of graduation ceremony," she said. "I'm very pleased with you, Farad'n. Will you stand, please."

He obeyed, blocking off her view of the treetop through the window behind him.

Jessica held her arms stiffly at her sides, said: "I am charged to say this to you. 'I stand in the sacred human presence. As I do now, so should you stand someday. I pray to your presence that this be so. The future remains uncertain and so it should, for it is the canvas upon which we paint our desires. Thus always the human condition faces a beautifully empty canvas. We possess only this moment in which to dedicate ourselves continuously to the sacred presence which we share and create.'"

As Jessica finished speaking, Tyekanik came through the door on her left, moving with a false casualness which the scowl on his face belied. "My Lord," he said. But it already was too late. Jessica's words and all of the preparation which had gone before had done their work. Farad'n no longer was Corrino. He was now Bene Gesserit.

What you of the CHOAM directorate seem unable to understand is that you seldom find real loyalties in commerce. When did you last hear of a clerk giving his life for the company? Perhaps your deficiency rests in the false assumption that you can order men to think and cooperate. This has been a failure of everything from religions to general staffs throughout history. General staffs have a long record of destroying their own nations. As to religions, I recommend a rereading of Thomas Aquinas. As to you of CHOAM, what nonsense you believe! Men must want to do things out of their own innermost drives. People, not commercial organizations or chains of command, are what make great civilizations work. Every civilization depends upon the quality of the individuals it produces. If you over-organize humans, over-legalize them, suppress their urge to greatness—they cannot work and their civilization collapses.

—A LETTER TO CHOAM
ATTRIBUTED TO THE PREACHER

Leto came out of the trance with a softness of transition which did not define one condition as separate from another. One level of awareness simply moved into the other.

He knew where he was. A restoration of energy surged through him, but he sensed another message from the stale deadliness of the oxygen-depleted air within the stilltent. If he refused to move, he knew he would remain caught in the timeless web, the eternal *now* where all events coexisted. This prospect enticed him. He saw Time as a convention shaped by the collective mind of all sentience. Time and Space were categories imposed on the universe by his Mind. He had but to break free of the multiplicity where prescient visions lured him. Bold selection could change provisional futures.

What boldness did this moment require?

The trance state lured him. Leto felt that he had come from the *alam al-mythal* into the universe of reality only to find them identical. He wanted to maintain the Rihani magic of this revelation, but survival demanded decisions of him. His relentless taste for life sent its signals along his nerves.

Abruptly he reached out his right hand to where he had left the sand-compaction tool. He gripped it, rolled onto his stomach, and breached the tent's sphincter. A pool of sand drifted across his hand. Working in darkness, goaded by the stale air, he worked swiftly, tunneling upward at a steep angle. Six times his body length he went before he broke out into darkness and clean air. He slipped out onto the moonlight windface of a long curving dune, found himself about a third of the way from the dune's top.

It was Second Moon above him. It moved swiftly across him, departing beyond the dune, and the stars were laid out above him like bright rocks beside a path. Leto searched for the constellation of The Wanderer, found it, and let his gaze follow the outstretched arm to the brilliant glittering of Foum al-Hout, the polar star of the south.

There's your damned universe for you! he thought. Seen close up it was a hustling place like the sand all around him, a place of change, of uniqueness piled upon uniqueness. Seen from a distance, only the patterns lay revealed and those patterns tempted one to belief in absolutes.

In absolutes, we may lose our way. This made him think of the familiar warning from a Fremen ditty: *"Who loses his way in the Tanzerouft loses his life."* The patterns could guide and they could trap. One had to remember that patterns change.

He took a deep breath, stirred himself into action. Sliding back down his passage, he collapsed the tent, brought it out and repacked the Fremkit.

A wine glow began to develop along the eastern horizon. He shouldered the pack, climbed to the dunecrest and stood there in the chill predawn air until the rising sun felt warm on his right cheek. He stained his eyepits then to reduce reflection, knowing that he must woo this desert now rather than fight her. When he had put the stain back into the pack he sipped from one of his catchtubes, drew in a sputtering of drops and then air.

Dropping to the sand, he began going over his stillsuit, coming at last to the heel pumps. They had been cut cleverly with a needle knife. He slipped out of the suit and repaired it, but the damage had been done. At least half of his body's water was gone. Were it not for the stilltent's catch . . . He mused on this as he donned the suit, thinking how odd it was that he'd not anticipated this. Here was an obvious danger of visionless future.

Leto squatted on the dunetop then, pressed himself against the loneliness of this place. He let his gaze wander, fishing in the sand for a whistling vent, any irregularity of the dunes which might indicate spice or worm activity. But the storm had stamped its uniformity upon the land. Presently he removed a thumper from the kit, armed it, and sent it rotating to call Shai-Hulud from his depths. He then moved off to wait.

The worm was a long time coming. He heard it before he saw it, turned eastward where the earthshaking susurration made the air tremble, waited for the first glimpse of orange from the mouth rising out of the sand. The worm lifted itself from the depths in a gigantic hissing of dust which obscured its flanks. The curving grey wall swept past Leto and he planted his hooks, went up the side in easy steps. He turned the worm southward in a great curving track as he climbed.

Under his goading hooks, the worm picked up speed. Wind whipped his robe against him. He felt himself to be goaded as the worm was goaded, an intense current of creation in his loins. Each planet has its own period and each life likewise, he reminded himself.

The worm was a type Fremen called a "growler." It frequently dug in its foreplates while the tail was driving. This produced rumbling sounds and caused part of its body to rise clear of the sand in a moving hump. It was a fast worm, though, and when they picked up a following wind the furnace exhalation of his tail sent a hot breeze across him. It was filled with acrid odors carried on the freshet of oxygen.

As the worm sped southward, Leto allowed his mind to run free. He tried to think of this passage as a new ceremony for his life, one which kept him from considering the price he'd have to pay for his Golden Path. Like the Fremen of old, he knew he'd have to adopt many new ceremonies to keep his personality from dividing into its memory parts, to keep the ravening hunters of his soul forever at bay. Contradictory images, never to be unified, must now be encysted in a living tension, a polarizing force which drove him from within.

Always newness, he thought. *I must always find the new threads out of my vision.*

In the early afternoon his attention was caught by a protuberance ahead and slightly to the right of his course. Slowly the protuberance became a narrow butte, an upthrust rock precisely where he'd expected it.

Now Namri . . . Now Sabiha, let us see how your brethren take to my presence, he thought. This was a most delicate thread ahead of him, dangerous more for its lures than its open threats.

The butte was a long time changing dimensions. And it appeared for a while that it approached him instead of him approaching it.

The worm, tiring now, kept veering left. Leto slid down the immense slope to set his hooks anew and keep the giant on a straight course. A soft sharpness of melange came to his nostrils, the signal of a rich vein. They passed the leprous blotches of violet sand where a spiceblow had erupted and he held the worm firmly until they were well past the vein. The breeze, redolent with the gingery odor of cinnamon, pursued them for a time until Leto rolled the worm onto its new course, headed directly toward the rising butte.

Abruptly colors blinked far out on the southern *bled*: the unwary rainbow flashing of a man-made artifact in that immensity. He brought up his binoculars, focused the oil lenses, and saw in the distance the outbanking wings of a spice-scout glittering in the sunlight. Beneath it a big harvester was shedding its wings like a chrysalis before lumbering off. When Leto lowered the binoculars the harvester dwindled to a speck, and he felt himself overcome by the *hadhdhab*, the immense omnipresence of the desert. It told him how those spice-hunters would see him, a dark object between desert and sky, which was the Fremen symbol for *man*. They'd see him, of course, and they'd be cautious. They'd wait. Fremen were always suspicious of one another in the desert until they recognized the newcomer or saw for certain that he posed no threat. Even within the fine patina of Imperial civilization and its sophisticated rules they remained half-tamed savages, aware always that a crysknife dissolved at the death of its owner.

That's what can save us, Leto thought. *That wildness.*

In the distance the spice-scout banked right, then left, a signal to the ground. He imagined the occupants scanning the desert behind him for sign that he might be more than a single rider on a single worm.

Leto rolled the worm to the left, held it until it had reversed its course, dropped down the flank, and leaped clear. The worm, released from his goading, sulked on the surface for a few breaths, then sank its front third and lay there recuperating, a sure sign that it had been ridden too long.

He turned away from the worm; it would stay there now. The scout was circling its crawler, still giving wing signals. They were smuggler-paid renegades for certain, wary of electronic communications. The hunters would be on spice out there. That was the message of the crawler's presence.

The scout circled once more, dipped its wings, came out of the circle and headed directly toward him. He recognized it for a type of light 'thopter his grandfather had introduced on Arrakis. The craft circled once above him, went out along the dune where he stood, and banked to land against the breeze. It came down within ten meters of him, stirring up a scattering of dust. The door on his side cracked enough to emit a single figure in a heavy Fremen robe with a spear symbol at the right breast.

The Fremen approached slowly, giving each of them time to study the other. The man was tall with the total indigo of spice-eyes. The stillsuit mask concealed the lower half of his face and the hood had been drawn down to protect his brows. The movement of the robe revealed a hand beneath it holding a maula pistol.

The man stopped two paces from Leto, looked down at him with a puzzled crinkling around the eyes.

"Good fortune to us all," Leto said.

The man peered all around, scanning the emptiness, then returned his attention to Leto. "What do you here, child?" he demanded. His voice was muffled by the stillsuit mask. "Are you trying to be the cork in a wormhole?"

Again Leto used traditional Fremen formula: "The desert is my home."

"Wenn?" the man demanded. *Which way do you go?*

"I travel south from Jacurutu."

An abrupt laugh erupted from the man. "Well, Batigh! You are the strangest thing I've ever seen in the Tanzerouft."

"I'm not your Little Melon," Leto said, responding to *Batigh*. That was a label with dire overtones. The Little Melon on the desert's edge offered its water to any finder.

"We'll not drink you, Batigh," the man said. "I am Muriz. I am the arifa of this taif." He indicated with a head motion the distant spice-crawler.

Leto noted how the man called himself the Judge of his group and referred to the others as *taif*, a band or company. They were not *ichwan*, not a band of brothers. Paid renegades for sure. Here lay the thread he required.

When Leto remained silent, Muriz asked: "Do you have a name?"

"Batigh will do."

A chuckle shook Muriz. "You've not told me what you do here?"

"I seek the footprints of a worm," Leto said, using the religious phrase which said he was on hajj for his own *umma*, his personal revelation.

"One so young?" Muriz asked. He shook his head. "I don't know what to do with you. You have seen us."

"What have I seen?" Leto asked. "I speak of Jacurutu and you make no response."

"Riddle games," Muriz said. "What is that, then?" He nodded toward the distant butte.

Leto spoke from his vision: "Only Shuloch."

Muriz stiffened and Leto felt his own pulse quicken.

A long silence ensued and Leto could see the man debating and discarding various responses. *Shuloch!* In the quiet story time after a sietch meal, stories of the Shuloch caravanserie were often repeated. Listeners always assumed that Shuloch was a myth, a place for interesting things to happen and only for the sake of the story. Leto recalled a Shuloch story: A waif was found at the desert's edge and brought into the sietch. At first the waif refused to respond to his saviors, then when he spoke no one could understand his words. As days passed he continued unresponsive, refused to dress himself or cooperate in any way. Every time he was left alone he made odd motions with his hands. All the specialists in the sietch were called in to study this waif but arrived at no answer. Then a very old woman passed the doorway, saw the moving hands, and laughed. "He only imitates his father who rolls the spice-fibers into rope," she explained. "It's the way they still do it at Shuloch. He's just trying to feel less lonely." And the moral: *"In the old ways of Shuloch there is security and a sense of belonging to the golden thread of life."*

As Muriz remained silent, Leto said: "I'm the waif from Shuloch who knows only to move his hands."

In the quick movement of the man's head, Leto saw that Muriz knew the story. Muriz responded slowly, voice low and filled with menace. "Are you human?"

"Human as yourself," Leto said.

"You speak most strangely for a child. I remind you that I am a judge who can respond to the *taqwa*."

Ah, yes, Leto thought. In the mouth of such a judge, the *taqwa* carried immediate threat. *Taqwa* was the fear invoked by the presence of a demon, a very real belief among older Fremen. The arifa knew the ways to slay a demon and was always chosen "because he has the wisdom to be ruthless without being cruel, to know when kindness is in fact the way to greater cruelty."

But this thing had come to the point which Leto sought, and he said: "I can submit to the *Mashhad*."

"I'll be the judge of any Spiritual Test," Muriz said. "Do you accept this?"

"Bi-lal kaifa," Leto said. *Without qualification.*

A sly look came over Muriz's face. He said: "I don't know why I permit this. Best you were slain out of hand, but you're a small Batigh and I had a son who is dead. Come, we will go to Shuloch and I'll convene the Isnad for a decision about you."

Leto, noting how the man's every mannerism betrayed deadly decision, wondered how anyone could be fooled by this. He said: "I know Shuloch is the Ahl as-sunna wal-jamas."

"What does a child know of the real world?" Muriz asked, motioning for Leto to precede him to the 'thopter.

Leto obeyed, but listened carefully to the sound of the Fremen's footsteps. "The surest way to keep a secret is to make people believe they already know the answer," Leto said. "People don't ask questions then. It was clever of you who were cast out of Jacurutu. Who'd believe Shuloch, the story-myth place, is real? And how convenient for the smugglers or anyone else who desires access to Dune."

Muriz's footsteps stopped. Leto turned with his back against the 'thopter's side, the wing on his left.

Muriz stood half a pace away with his maula pistol drawn and pointed directly at Leto. "So you're not a child," Muriz said. "A cursed midget come to spy on us! I thought you spoke too wisely for a child, but you spoke too much too soon."

"Not enough," Leto said. "I'm Leto, the child of Paul Muad'Dib. If you slay me, you and your people will sink into the sand. If you spare me, I'll lead you to greatness."

"Don't play games with me, midget," Muriz snarled. "Leto is at the real Jacurutu from whence you say . . ." He broke off. The gun hand dropped slightly as a puzzled frown made his eyes squint.

It was the hesitation Leto had expected. He made every muscle indication of a move to the left which, deflecting his body no more than a millimeter, brought the Fremen's gun swinging wildly against the wing edge. The maula pistol flew from his hand and, before he could recover, Leto was beside him with Muriz's own crysknife pressed against the man's back.

"The tip's poisoned," Leto said. "Tell your friend in the 'thopter that he's to remain exactly where he is without moving at all. Otherwise I'll be forced to kill you."

Muriz, nursing his injured hand, shook his head at the figure in the 'thopter, said: "My companion Behaleth has heard you. He will be as unmoving as the rock."

Knowing he had very little time until the two worked out a plan of action or their friends came to investigate, Leto spoke swiftly: "You need me, Muriz. Without me, the worms and their spice will vanish from Dune." He felt the Fremen stiffen.

"But how do you know of Shuloch?" Muriz asked. "I know they said nothing at Jacurutu."

"So you admit I'm Leto Atreides?"

"Who else could you be? But how do you—"

"Because you are here," Leto said. "Shuloch exists, therefore the rest is utter simplicity. You are the Cast Out who escaped when Jacurutu was destroyed. I saw you signal with your wings, therefore you use no device which could be overheard at a distance. You collect spice, therefore you trade. You could only trade with the smugglers. You are a smuggler, yet you are Fremen. You must be of Shuloch."

"Why did you tempt me to slay you out of hand?"

"Because you would've slain me anyway when we'd returned to Shuloch."

A violent rigidity came over Muriz's body.

"Careful, Muriz," Leto cautioned. "I know about you. It was in your history that you took the water of unwary travelers. By now this would be common ritual with you. How else could you silence the ones who chanced upon you? How else keep your secret? Batigh! You'd seduce me with gentle epithets and kindly words. Why waste any of my water upon the sand? And if I were missed as were many of the others—well, the Tanzerouft got me."

Muriz made the *Horns-of-the-Worm* sign with his right hand to ward off the Rihani which Leto's words called up. And Leto, knowing how older Fremen distrusted mentats or anything which smacked of them by a show of extended logic, suppressed a smile.

"Manri spoke of us at Jacurutu," Muriz said. "I will have his water when—"

"You'll have nothing but empty sand if you continue playing the fool," Leto said. "What will you do, Muriz, when all of Dune has become green grass, trees, and open water?"

"It will never happen!"

"It is happening before your eyes."

Leto heard Muriz's teeth grinding in rage and frustration. Presently the man grated: "How would you prevent this?"

"I know the entire plan of the transformation," Leto said. "I know every weakness in it, every strength. Without me, Shai-Hulud will vanish forever."

A sly note returning to his voice, Muriz asked: "Well, why dispute it here? We're at a standoff. You have your knife. You could kill me, but Behaleth would shoot you."

"Not before I recovered your pistol," Leto said. "Then I'd have your 'thopter. Yes, I can fly it."

A scowl creased Muriz's forehead beneath the hood. "What if you're not who you say?"

"Will my father not identify me?" Leto asked.

"Ahhhh," Muriz said. "There's how you learned, eh? But . . ." He broke off, shook his head. "My own son guides him. He says you two have never . . . How could . . ."

"So you don't believe Muad'Dib reads the future," Leto said.

"Of course we believe! But he says of himself that . . ." Again Muriz broke off.

"And you thought him unaware of your distrust," Leto said. "I came to this exact place in this exact time to meet you, Muriz. I know all about you because I've *seen* you . . . and your son. I know how secure you believe yourselves, how you sneer at Muad'Dib, how you plot to save your little patch of desert. But your little patch of desert is doomed without me, Muriz. Lost forever. It has gone too far here on Dune. My father has almost run out of vision, and you can only turn to me."

"That blind . . ." Muriz stopped, swallowed.

"He'll return soon from Arrakeen," Leto said, "and then we shall see how blind he is. How far have you gone from the old Fremen ways, Muriz?"

"What?"

"He is *Wadquiyas* with you. Your people found him alone in the desert and brought him to Shuloch. What a rich discovery he was! Richer than a spice-vein. *Wadquiyas!* He has lived with you; his water mingled with your tribe's water. He's part of your Spirit River." Leto pressed the knife hard against Muriz's robe. "Careful, Muriz." Leto lifted his left hand, released the Fremen's face flap, dropped it.

Knowing what Leto planned, Muriz said: "Where would you go if you killed us both?"

"Back to Jacurutu."

Leto pressed the fleshy part of his own thumb against Muriz's mouth. "Bite and drink, Muriz. That or die."

Muriz hesitated, then bit viciously into Leto's flesh.

Leto watched the man's throat, saw the swallowing convulsion, withdrew the knife and returned it.

"*Wadquiyas*," Leto said. "I must offend the tribe before you can take my water."

Muriz nodded.

"Your pistol is over there." Leto gestured with his chin.

"You trust me now?" Muriz asked.

"How else can I live with the Cast Out?"

Again Leto saw the sly look in Muriz's eyes, but this time it was a measuring thing, a weighing of economics. The man turned away with an abruptness which told of secret decisions, recovered his maula pistol and returned to the wing step. "Come," he said. "We tarry too long in a worm's lair."

The future of prescience cannot always be locked into the rules of the past. The threads of existence tangle according to many unknown laws. Prescient future insists on its own rules. It will not conform to the ordering of the Zensunni nor to the ordering of science. Prescience builds a relative integrity. It demands the work of this instant, always warning that you cannot weave every thread into the fabric of the past.

—KALIMA: THE WORDS OF MUAD'DIB
THE SHULOCH COMMENTARY

Muriz brought the ornithopter in over Shuloch with a practiced ease. Leto, seated beside him, felt the armed presence of Behaleth behind them. Everything went on trust now and the narrow thread of his vision to which he clung. If that failed, *Allahu akbahr.* Sometimes one had to submit to a greater order.

The butte of Shuloch was impressive in this desert. Its unmarked presence here spoke of many bribes and many deaths, of many friends in high places. Leto could see at Shuloch's heart a cliff-walled pan with interfringing blind canyons leading down into it. A thick growth of shadescale and salt bushes lined the lower edges of these canyons with an inner ring of fan palms, indicating the water riches of this place. Crude buildings of greenbush and spice-fiber had been built out from the fan palms. The buildings were green buttons scattered on the sand. There would live the cast out of the Cast Out, those who could go no lower except into death.

Muriz landed in the pan near the base of one of the canyons. A single structure stood on the sand directly ahead of the 'thopter: a thatch of desert vines and bejato leaves, all lined with heat-fused spice-fabric. It was the living replica of the first crude stilltents and it spoke of degradation for some who lived in Shuloch. Leto knew the place would leak moisture and would be full of night-biters from the nearby growth. So this was how his father lived. And poor Sabiha. Here would be her punishment.

At Muriz's order Leto let himself out of the 'thopter, jumped down to the sand, and strode toward the hut. He could see many people working farther toward the canyon among the palms. They looked tattered, poor, and the fact that they barely glanced at him or at the 'thopter said much of the oppression here. Leto could see the rock lip of a qanat beyond the workers, and there was no mistaking the sense of moisture in this air: open water. Passing the hut, Leto saw it was as crude as he'd expected. He pressed on to the qanat, peered down and saw the swirl of predator fish in the dark flow. The workers, avoiding his eyes, went on with clearing sand away from the line of rock openings.

Muriz came up behind Leto, said: "You stand on the boundary between fish and worm. Each of these canyons has its worm. This qanat has been opened and we will remove the fish presently to attract sandtrout."

"Of course," Leto said. "Holding pens. You sell sandtrout and worms off-planet."

"It was Muad'Dib's suggestion!"

"I know. But none of your worms or sandtrout survive for long away from Dune."

"Not yet," Muriz said. "But someday . . ."

"Not in ten thousand years," Leto said. And he turned to watch the turmoil on Muriz's face. Questions flowed there like the water in the qanat. Could this son of Muad'Dib really read the future? Some still believed Muad'Dib had done it, but . . . How could a thing such as this be judged?

Presently Muriz turned away, led them back to the hut. He opened the crude doorseal, motioned for Leto to enter. There was a spice-oil lamp burning against the far wall and a small figure squatted beneath it, back to the door. The burning oil gave off a heavy fragrance of cinnamon.

"They've sent down a new captive to care for Muad'Dib's sietch," Muriz sneered. "If she serves well, she may keep her water for a time." He confronted Leto. "Some think it evil to take such water. Those lace-shirt Fremen now make rubbish heaps in their new towns! Rubbish heaps! When has Dune ever before seen rubbish heaps! When we get such as this one—" He gestured toward the figure by the lamp. "—they're usually half wild with fear, lost to their own kind and never accepted by true Fremen. Do you understand me, Leto-Batigh?"

"I understand you." The crouching figure had not moved.

"You speak of leading us," Muriz said. "Fremen are led by men who've been blooded. What could you lead us in?"

"Kralizec," Leto said, keeping his attention on the crouched figure.

Muriz glared at him, brows contracted over his indigo eyes. Kralizec? That wasn't merely war or revolution; that was the Typhoon Struggle. It was a word from the furthermost Fremen legends: the battle at the end of the universe. Kralizec?

The tall Fremen swallowed convulsively. This sprat was as unpredictable as a city dandy! Muriz turned to the squatting figure. "Woman! Liban wahid!" he commanded. *Bring us the spice-drink!*

She hesitated. "Do as he says, Sabiha," Leto said.

She jumped to her feet, whirling. She stared at him, unable to take her gaze from his face.

"You know this one?" Muriz asked.

"She is Namri's niece. She offended Jacurutu and they have sent her to you."

"Namri? But . . ."

"Liban wahid," Leto said.

She rushed past them, tore herself through the doorseal and they heard the sound of her running feet.

"She will not go far," Muriz said. He touched a finger to the side of his nose. "A kin of Namri, eh. Interesting. What did she do to offend?"

"She allowed me to escape." Leto turned then and followed Sabiha. He found her standing at the edge of the qanat. Leto moved up beside her and looked down at the water. There were birds in the nearby fan palms and he heard their calls, their wings. The workers made scraping sounds as they moved sand. Still he did as Sabiha did, looking down, deep into the water and its reflections. The corners of his eyes saw blue parakeets in the palm fronds. One flew across the qanat and he saw it reflected in a silver swirl of fish, all run together as though birds and predators swam in the same firmament.

Sabiha cleared her throat.

"You hate me," Leto said.

"You shamed me. You shamed me before my people. They held an Isnad and sent me here to lose my water. All because of you!"

Muriz laughed from close behind them. "And now you see, Leto-Batigh, that our Spirit River has many tributaries."

"But my water flows in your veins," Leto said, turning. "That is no tributary. Sabiha is the fate of my vision and I follow her. I fled across the desert to find my future here in Shuloch."

"You and . . ." He pointed at Sabiha, threw his head back in laughter.

"It will not be as either of you might believe," Leto said. "Remember this, Muriz. I have found the footprints of my worm." He felt tears swimming in his eyes then.

"He gives water to the dead," Sabiha whispered.

Even Muriz stared at him in awe. Fremen never cried unless it was the most profound gift of the soul. Almost embarrassed, Muriz closed his mouthseal, pulled his djellaba hood low over his brows.

Leto peered beyond the man, said: "Here in Shuloch they still pray for dew at the desert's edge. Go, Muriz, and pray for Kralizec. I promise you it will come."

Fremen speech implies great concision, a precise sense of expression. It is immersed in the illusion of absolutes. Its assumptions are a fertile ground for absolutist religions. Furthermore, Fremen are fond of moralizing. They confront the terrifying instability of all things with institutionalized statements. They say: "We know there is no *summa* of all attainable knowledge; that is the preserve of God. But whatever men can learn, men can contain." Out of this knife-edged approach to the universe they carve a fantastic belief in signs and omens and in their own destiny. This is an origin of their Kralizec legend: the war at the end of the universe.

—BENE GESSERIT PRIVATE REPORTS/FOLIO 800881

"They have him securely in a safe place," Namri said, smiling across the square stone room at Gurney Halleck. "You may report this to your friends."

"Where is this safe place?" Halleck asked. He didn't like Namri's tone, felt constrained by Jessica's orders. Damn the witch! Her explanations made no sense except the warning about what could happen if Leto failed to master his terrible memories.

"It's a safe place," Namri said. "That's all I'm permitted to tell you."

"How do you know this?"

"I've had a distrans. Sabiha is with him."

"Sabiha! She'll just let him—"

"Not this time."

"Are you going to kill him?"

"That's no longer up to me."

Halleck grimaced. *Distrans.* What was the range of those damned cave bats? He'd often seen them flitting across the desert with hidden messages imprinted upon their squeaking calls. But how far would they go on this hellhole planet?

"I must see him for myself," Halleck said.

"That's not permitted."

Halleck took a deep breath to quiet himself. He had spent two days and two nights waiting for search reports. Now it was another morning and he felt his role dissolving around him, leaving him naked. He had never liked command anyway. Command always waited while others did the interesting and dangerous things.

"Why isn't it permitted?" he asked. The smugglers who'd arranged this safe-sietch had left too many questions unanswered and he wanted no more of the same from Namri.

"Some believe you saw too much when you saw this sietch," Namri said.

Halleck heard the menace, relaxed into the easy stance of the trained fighter, hand near but not on his knife. He longed for a shield, but that had been ruled out by its effect on the worms, its short life in the presence of storm-generated static charges.

"This secrecy isn't part of our agreement," Halleck said.

"If I'd killed him, would that have been part of our agreement?"

Again Halleck felt the jockeying of unseen forces about which the Lady Jessica hadn't warned him. This damned plan of hers! Maybe it was right not to trust the Bene Gesserit. Immediately, he felt disloyal. She'd explained the problem, and he'd come into her plan with the expectation that it, like all plans, would need adjustments later. This wasn't *any* Bene Gesserit; this was Jessica of the Atreides who'd never been other than friend and supporter to him. Without her, he knew he'd have been adrift in a universe more dangerous than the one he now inhabited.

"You can't answer my question," Namri said.

"You were to kill him only if he showed himself to be . . . possessed," Halleck said. "Abomination."

Namri put his fist beside his right ear. "Your Lady knew we had tests for such. Wise of her to leave that judgment in my hands."

Halleck compressed his lips in frustration.

"You heard the Reverend Mother's words to me," Namri said. "We Fremen understand such women but you off-worlders never understand them. Fremen women often send their sons to death."

Halleck spoke past still lips. "Are you telling me you've killed him?"

"He lives. He is in a safe place. He'll continue to receive the spice."

"But I'm to escort him back to his grandmother if he survives," Halleck said.

Namri merely shrugged.

Halleck understood that this was all the answer he'd get. Damn! He couldn't go back to Jessica with such unanswered questions! He shook his head.

"Why question what you cannot change?" Namri asked. "You're being well paid."

Halleck scowled at the man. Fremen! They believed all foreigners were influenced primarily by money. But Namri was speaking more than Fremen prejudice. Other forces were at work here and that was obvious to one who'd been trained in observation by a Bene Gesserit. This whole thing had the smell of a feint within a feint within a feint . . .

Shifting to the insultingly familiar form, Halleck said: "The Lady Jessica will be wrathful. She could send cohorts against—"

"Zanadiq!" Namri cursed. "You office messenger! You stand outside the Mohalata! I take pleasure in possessing your water for the Noble People!"

Halleck rested a hand on his knife, readied his left sleeve where he'd prepared a small surprise for attackers. "I see no water spilled here," he said. "Perhaps you're blinded by your pride."

"You live because I wished you to learn before dying that your Lady Jessica will not send cohorts against anyone. You are not to be lured quietly into the Huanui, off-world scum. I am of the Noble People, and you—"

"And I'm just a servant of the Atreides," Halleck said, voice mild. "We're the scum who lifted the Harkonnen yoke from your smelly neck."

Namri showed white teeth in a grimace. "Your Lady is prisoner on Salusa Secundus. The notes you thought were from her came from her daughter!"

By extreme effort, Halleck managed to keep his voice even. "No matter. Alia will . . ."

Namri drew his crysknife. "What do you know of the Womb of Heaven? I am her servant, you male whore. I do her bidding when I take your water!" And he lunged across the room with foolhardy directness.

Halleck, not allowing himself to be tricked by such seeming clumsiness, flicked up the left arm of his robe, releasing the extra length of heavy fabric he'd had sewn there, letting that take Namri's knife. In the same movement, Halleck swept the folds of cloth over Namri's head, came in under and through the cloth with his own knife aimed directly for the face. He felt the point bite home as Namri's body hit him with a hard surface of metal armor beneath the robe. The Fremen emitted one outraged squeal, jerked backward, and fell. He lay there, blood gushing from his mouth as his eyes glared at Halleck then slowly dulled.

Halleck blew air through his lips. How could that fool Namri have expected anyone to miss the presence of armor beneath a robe? Halleck addressed the corpse as he recovered the trick sleeve, wiped his knife and sheathed it. "How did you think we Atreides *servants* were trained, fool?"

He took a deep breath thinking: *Well now. Whose feint am I?* There'd been the ring of truth in Namri's words. Jessica a prisoner of the Corrinos and Alia working her own devious schemes. Jessica herself had warned of many contingencies with Alia as enemy, but had not predicted herself as prisoner. He had his orders to obey, though. First there was the necessity of getting away from this place. Luckily one robed Fremen looked much like another. He rolled Namri's body into a corner, threw cushions over it, moved a rug to cover the blood. When it was done, Halleck adjusted the nose and mouth tubes of his stillsuit, brought up the mask as one would in preparing for the desert, pulled the hood of his robe forward and went out into the long passage.

The innocent move without care, he thought, setting his pace at an easy saunter. He felt curiously free, as though he'd moved out of danger, not into it.

I never did like her plan for the boy, he thought. *And I'll tell her so if I see her. If.* Because if Namri spoke the truth, the most dangerous alternate plan went into effect. Alia wouldn't let him live long if she caught him, but there was always Stilgar—a good Fremen with a good Fremen's superstitions.

Jessica had explained it: "There's a very thin layer of civilized behavior over Stilgar's original nature. And here's how you take that layer off him . . ."

The spirit of Muad'Dib is more than words, more than the letter of the Law which arises in his name. Muad'Dib must always be that inner outrage against the complacently powerful, against the charlatans and the dogmatic fanatics. It is that inner outrage which must have its say because Muad'Dib taught us one thing above all others: that humans can endure only in a fraternity of social justice.

—THE FEDAYKIN COMPACT

Leto sat with his back against the wall of the hut, his attention on Sabiha, watching the threads of his vision unroll. She had prepared the coffee and set it aside. Now she squatted across from him stirring his evening meal. It was a gruel redolent with melange. Her hands moved quickly with the ladle and liquid indigo stained the sides of his bowl. She bent her thin face over the bowl, blending in the concentrate. The crude membrane which made a stilltent of the hut had been patched with lighter material directly behind her, and this formed a grey halo against which her shadow danced in the flickering light of the cooking flame and the single lamp.

That lamp intrigued Leto. These people of Shuloch were profligate with spice-oil: a lamp, not a glowglobe. They kept slave outcasts within their walls in the fashion told by the most ancient Fremen traditions. Yet they employed ornithopters and the latest spice harvesters. They were a crude mixture of ancient and modern.

Sabiha pushed the bowl of gruel toward him, extinguished the cooking flame.

Leto ignored the bowl.

"I will be punished if you do not eat this," she said.

He stared at her, thinking: *If I kill her, that'll shatter one vision. If I tell her Muriz's plans, that'll shatter another vision. If I wait here for my father, this vision-thread will become a mighty rope.*

His mind sorted the threads. Some held a sweetness which haunted him. One future with Sabiha carried alluring reality within his prescient awareness. It threatened to block out all others until he followed it out to its ending agonies.

"Why do you stare at me that way?" she asked.

Still he did not answer.

She pushed the bowl closer to him.

Leto tried to swallow in a dry throat. The impulse to kill Sabiha welled in him. He found himself trembling with it. How easy it would be to shatter one vision and let the wildness run free!

"Muriz commands this," she said, touching the bowl.

Yes, Muriz commanded it. Superstition conquered everything. Muriz wanted a vision cast for him to read. He was an ancient savage asking the witch doctor to throw the ox bones and interpret their sprawl. Muriz had taken his captive's stillsuit "as a simple precaution." There'd been a sly jibe at Namri and Sabiha in that comment. *Only fools let a prisoner escape.*

Muriz had a deep emotional problem, though: the Spirit River. The captive's water flowed in Muriz's veins. Muriz sought a sign that would permit him to hold a threat of death over Leto.

Like father, like son, Leto thought.

"The spice will only give you visions," Sabiha said. The long silences made her uneasy. "I've had visions in the orgy many times. They don't mean anything."

That's it! he thought, his body locking itself into a stillness which left his skin cold and clammy. The Bene Gesserit training took over his consciousness, a pinpoint illumination which fanned out beyond him to throw the blazoning light of vision upon Sabiha and all of her Cast Out fellows. The ancient Bene Gesserit learning was explicit:

"Languages build up to reflect specializations in a way of life. Each specialization may be recognized by its words, by its assumptions and sentence structures. Look for stoppages. Specializations represent places where life is being stopped, where the movement is dammed up and frozen." He saw Sabiha then as a vision-maker in her own right, and every other human carried the same power. Yet she was disdainful of her spice-orgy visions. They caused disquiet and, therefore, must be put aside, forgotten deliberately. Her people prayed to Shai-Hulud because the worm dominated many of their visions. They prayed for dew at the desert's edge because moisture limited their lives. Yet they wallowed in spice wealth and lured sandtrout to open qanats. Sabiha fed him prescient visions with a casual callousness, yet within her words he saw the illuminated signals: she depended upon absolutes, sought finite limits, and all because she couldn't handle the rigors of terrible decisions which touched her own flesh. She clung to her one-eyed vision of the universe, englobing and time-freezing as it might be, because the alternatives terrified her.

In contrast, Leto felt the pure movement of himself. He was a membrane collecting infinite dimensions and, because he saw those dimensions, he could make the terrible decisions.

As my father did.

"You must eat this!" Sabiha said, her voice petulant.

Leto saw the whole pattern of the visions now and knew the thread he must follow. *My skin is not my own.* He stood, pulling his robe around him. It felt strange against his flesh with no stillsuit protecting his body. His feet were bare upon the fused spice-fabric of the floor, feeling the sand tracked in there.

"What're you doing?" Sabiha demanded.

"The air is bad in here. I'm going outside."

"You can't escape," she said. "Every canyon has its worm. If you go beyond the qanat, the worms will sense you by your moisture. These captive worms are very alert—not like the ones in the desert at all. Besides—" How gloating her voice became! "—you've no stillsuit."

"Then why do you worry?" he asked, wondering if he might yet provoke a real reaction from her.

"Because you've not eaten."

"And you'll be punished."

"Yes!"

"But I'm already saturated with spice," he said. "Every moment is a vision." He gestured with a bare foot at the bowl. "Pour that onto the sand. Who'll know?"

"They watch," she whispered.

He shook his head, shedding her from his visions, feeling new freedom envelop him. No need to kill this poor pawn. She danced to other music, not even knowing the steps, believing that she might yet share the power which lured the hungry pirates of Shuloch and Jacurutu. Leto went to the doorseal, put a hand upon it.

"When Muriz comes," she said, "he'll be very angry with—"

"Muriz is a merchant of emptiness," Leto said. "My aunt has drained him."

She got to her feet. "I'm going out with you."

And he thought: *She remembers how I escaped her. Now she feels the fragility of her hold upon me. Her visions stir within her.* But she would not listen to those visions. She had but to reflect: How could he outwit a captive worm in its narrow canyon? How could he live in the Tanzerouft without stillsuit or Fremkit?

"I must be alone to consult my visions," he said. "You'll remain here."

"Where will you go?"

"To the qanat."

"The sandtrout come out in swarms at night."

"They won't eat me."

"Sometimes the worm comes down to just beyond the water," she said. "If you cross the qanat . . ." She broke off, trying to edge her words with menace.

"How could I mount a worm without hooks?" he asked, wondering if she still could salvage some bit of her visions.

"Will you eat when you return?" she asked, squatting once more by the bowl, recovering the ladle and stirring the indigo broth.

"Everything in its own time," he said, knowing she'd be unable to detect his delicate use of Voice, the way he insinuated his own desires into her decision-making.

"Muriz will come and see if you've had a vision," she warned.

"I will deal with Muriz in my own way," he said, noting how heavy and slow her movements had become. The pattern of all Fremen lent itself naturally into the way he guided her now. Fremen were people of extraordinary energy at sunrise but a deep and lethargic melancholy often overcame them at nightfall. Already she wanted to sink into sleep and dreams.

Leto let himself out into the night alone.

The sky glittered with stars and he could make out the bulk of surrounding buttes against their pattern. He went up under the palms to the qanat.

For a long time Leto squatted at the qanat's edge, listening to the restless hiss of sand within the canyon beyond. A small worm by the sound of it; chosen for that reason, no doubt. A small worm would be easier to transport. He thought about the worm's capture: the hunters would dull it with a water mist, using the traditional Fremen method of taking a worm for the orgy/transformation rite. But this worm would not be killed by immersion. This one would go out on a Guild heighliner to some hopeful buyer whose desert probably would be too moist. Few off-worlders realized the basic desiccation which the sandtrout had maintained on Arrakis. *Had maintained.* Because even here in the Tanzerouft there would be many times more airborne moisture than any worm had ever before known short of its death in a Fremen cistern.

He heard Sabiha stirring in the hut behind him. She was restless, prodded by her own suppressed visions. He wondered how it would be to live outside a vision with her, sharing each moment just as it came, of itself. The thought attracted him far more strongly than had any spice vision. There was a certain cleanliness about facing an unknown future.

"A kiss in the sietch is worth two in the city."

The old Fremen maxim said it all. The traditional sietch had held a recognizable wildness mingled with shyness. There were traces of that shyness in the people of Jacurutu/Shuloch, but only traces. This saddened him by revealing what had been lost.

Slowly, so slowly that the knowledge was fully upon him before he recognized its beginnings, Leto grew aware of the soft rustling of many creatures all around him.

Sandtrout.

Soon it would be time to shift from one vision to another. He felt the movement of sandtrout as a movement within himself. Fremen had lived with the strange creatures for generations, knowing that if you risked a bit of water as bait, you could lure them into reach. Many a Fremen dying of thirst had risked his last few drops of water in this gamble, knowing that the sweet green syrup teased from a sandtrout might yield a small profit in energy. But the sandtrout were mostly the game of children who caught them for the Huanui. And for play.

Leto shuddered at the thought of what that *play* meant to him now.

He felt one of the creatures slither across his bare foot. It hesitated, then went on, attracted by the greater amount of water in the qanat.

For a moment, though, he'd felt the reality of his terrible decision. *The sandtrout glove.* It was the play of children. If one held a sandtrout in the hand, smoothing it over your skin, it formed a living glove. Traces of blood in the skin's capillaries could be sensed by the creatures, but something mingled with the blood's water repelled them. Sooner or later, the glove would slip off into the sand, there to be lifted into a spice-fiber basket. The spice soothed them until they were dumped into the deathstill.

He could hear sandtrout dropping into the qanat, the swirl of predators eating them. Water softened the sandtrout, made it pliable. Children learned this early. A bit of saliva teased out the sweet syrup. Leto listened to the splashing. This was a migration of sandtrout come up to the open water, but they could not contain a flowing qanat patrolled by predator fish.

Still they came; still they splashed.

Leto groped on the sand with his right hand until his fingers encountered the leathery skin of a sandtrout. It was the large one he had expected. The creature didn't try to evade him, but moved eagerly onto his flesh. He explored its outline with his free hand—roughly diamond-shaped. It had no head, no extremities, no eyes, yet it could find water unerringly. With its fellows it could join body to body, locking one on another by the coarse interlacings of extruded cilia until the whole became one large sack-organism enclosing the water, walling off the "poison" from the giant which the sandtrout would become: Shai-Hulud.

The sandtrout squirmed on his hand, elongating, stretching. As it moved, he felt a counterpart elongating and stretching of the vision he had chosen. *This thread, not that one.* He felt the sandtrout becoming thin, covering more and more of his hand. No sandtrout had ever before encountered a hand such as this one, every cell supersaturated with spice. No other human had ever before lived and reasoned in such a condition. Delicately Leto adjusted his enzyme balance, drawing on the illuminated sureness he'd gained in spice trance. The knowledge from those uncounted lifetimes which blended themselves within him provided the certainty through which he chose the precise adjustments, staving off the death from an overdose which would engulf him if he relaxed his watchfulness for only a heartbeat. And at the same time he blended himself with the sandtrout, feeding on it, feeding it, learning it. His trance vision provided the template and he followed it precisely.

Leto felt the sandtrout grow thin, spreading itself over more and more of his hand, reaching up his arm. He located another, placed it over the first one. Contact ignited a frenzied squirming in the creatures. Their cilia locked and they became a single membrane which enclosed him to the elbow. The sandtrout adjusted to the living glove of childhood play, but thinner and more sensitive as he lured it into the role of a skin symbiote. He reached down with the living glove, felt sand, each grain distinct to his senses. This was no longer sandtrout; it was tougher, stronger. And it would grow stronger and stronger . . . His groping hand encountered another sandtrout which whipped itself into union with the first two and adapted itself to the new role. Leathery softness insinuated itself up his arm to his shoulder.

With a terrible singleness of concentration he achieved the union of his new skin with his body, preventing rejection. No corner of his attention was left to dwell upon the terrifying consequences of what he did here. Only the necessities of his trance vision mattered. Only the Golden Path could come from this ordeal.

Leto shed his robe and lay naked upon the sand, his gloved arm outstretched into the path of migrating sandtrout. He remembered that once he and Ghanima had caught a sandtrout, abraded it against the sand until it contracted into the *child-worm*, a stiff tube, its interior pregnant with the green syrup. One bit gently upon the end and sucked swiftly before the wound was healed, gaining the few drops of sweetness.

They were all over his body now. He could feel the pulse of his blood against the living membrane. One tried to cover his face, but he moved it roughly until it elongated into a thin roll. The thing grew much longer than the child-worm, remaining flexible. Leto bit the end of it, tasted a thin stream of sweetness which continued far longer than any Fremen had ever before experienced. He could feel energy from the sweetness flow through him. A curious excitement suffused his body. He was kept busy for a time rolling the membrane away from his face until he'd built up a stiff ridge circling from jaw to forehead and leaving his ears exposed.

Now the vision must be tested.

He got to his feet, turned to run back toward the hut and, as he moved, found his feet moving too fast for him to balance. He plunged into the sand, rolled and leaped to his feet. The leap took him two meters off the sand and, when he fell back, trying to walk, he again moved too fast.

Stop! he commanded himself. He fell into the *prana-bindu* forced relaxation, gathering his senses into the pool of consciousness. This focused the inward ripples of the *constant-now* through which he experienced Time, and he allowed the vision-elation to warm him. The membrane worked precisely as the vision had predicted.

My skin is not my own.

But his muscles took some training to live with this amplified movement. When he walked, he fell, rolling. Presently he sat. In the quiet, the ridge below his jaw tried to become a membrane covering his mouth. He spat against it and bit, tasting the sweet syrup. It rolled downward to the pressure of his hand.

Enough time had passed to form the union with his body. Leto stretched flat and turned onto his face. He began to crawl, rasping the membrane against the sand. He could feel the sand distinctly, but nothing abraded his own flesh. With only a few swimming movements he traversed fifty meters of sand. The physical reaction was a friction-induced warming sensation.

The membrane no longer tried to cover his nose and mouth, but now he faced the second major step onto his Golden Path. His exertions had taken him beyond the qanat into the canyon where the trapped worm stayed. He heard it hissing toward him, attracted by his movements.

Leto leaped to his feet, intending to stand and wait, but the amplified movement sent him sprawling twenty meters farther into the canyon. Controlling his reactions with terrible effort, he sat back onto his haunches, straightened. Now the sand began to swell directly in front of him, rising up in a monstrous starlit curve. Sand opened only two body lengths from him. Crystal teeth flashed in the dim light. He saw the yawning mouth-cavern with, far back, the ambient movement of dim flame. The overpowering redolence of the spice swept over him. But the worm had stopped. It remained in front of him as First Moon lifted over the butte. The light reflected off the worm's teeth outlining the faery glow of chemical fires deep within the creature.

So deep was the inbred Fremen fear that Leto found himself torn by a desire to flee. But his vision held him motionless, fascinated by this prolonged moment. No one had ever before stood this close to the mouth of a living worm and survived. Gently Leto moved his right foot, met a sand ridge and, reacting too quickly, was propelled toward the worm's mouth. He came to a stop on his knees.

Still the worm did not move.

It sensed only the sandtrout and would not attack the deep-sand vector of its own kind. The worm would attack another worm in its territory and would come to exposed spice. Only a water barrier stopped it—and sandtrout, encapsulating water, were a water barrier.

Experimentally, Leto moved a hand toward that awesome mouth. The worm drew back a full meter.

Confidence restored, Leto turned away from the worm and began teaching his muscles to live with their new power. Cautiously he walked back toward the qanat. The worm remained motionless behind him. When Leto was beyond the water barrier he leaped with joy, went sailing ten meters across the sand, sprawled, rolled, laughed.

Light flared on the sand as the hut's doorseal was breached. Sabiha stood outlined in the yellow and purple glow of the lamp, staring out at him.

Laughing, Leto ran back across the qanat, stopped in front of the worm, turned and faced her with his arms outstretched.

"Look!" he called. "The worm does my bidding!"

As she stood in frozen shock, he whirled, went racing around the worm and into the canyon. Gaining experience with his new skin, he found he could run with only the lightest flexing of muscles. It was almost effortless. When he put effort into running, he raced over the sand with the wind burning the exposed circle of his face. At the canyon's dead end instead of stopping, he leaped up a full fifteen meters, clawed at the cliff, scrabbled, climbing like an insect, and came out on the crest above the Tanzerouft.

The desert stretched before him, a vast silvery undulance in the moonlight.

Leto's manic exhilaration receded.

He squatted, sensing how light his body felt. Exertion had produced a slick film of perspiration which a stillsuit would have absorbed and routed into the transfer tissue which removed the salts. Even as he re-laxed, the film disappeared now, absorbed by the membrane faster than a stillsuit could have done it. Thoughtfully Leto rolled a length of the membrane beneath his lips, pulled it into his mouth, and drank the sweetness.

His mouth was not masked, though. Fremen-wise, he sensed his body's moisture being wasted with every breath. Leto brought a section of the membrane over his mouth, rolled it back when it tried to seal his nostrils, kept at this until the rolled barrier remained in place. In the desert way, he fell into the automatic breathing pattern: in through his nose, out through his mouth. The membrane over his mouth protruded in a small bubble, but remained in place. No moisture collected on his lips and his nostrils remained open. The adaptation proceeded, then.

A 'thopter flew between Leto and the moon, banked, and came in for a spread-wing landing on the butte perhaps a hundred meters to his left. Leto glanced at it, turned, and looked back the way he had come up the canyon. Many lights could be seen down there beyond the qanat, a stirring of a multitude. He heard faint outcries, sensed hysteria in the sounds. Two men approached him from the 'thopter. Moonlight glinted on their weapons.

The Mashhad, Leto thought, and it was a sad thought. Here was the great leap onto the Golden Path. He had put on the living, self-repairing stillsuit of a sandtrout membrane, a thing of unmeasurable value on Arrakis . . . until you understood the price. *I am no longer human. The legends about this night will grow and magnify it beyond anything recognizable by the participants. But it will become truth, that legend.*

He peered down from the butte, estimated the desert floor lay two hundred meters below. The moon picked out ledges and cracks on the steep face but no connecting pathway. Leto stood, inhaled a deep breath, glanced back at the approaching men, then stepped to the cliff's edge and launched himself into space. Some thirty meters down his flexed legs encountered a narrow ledge. Amplified muscles absorbed the shock and rebounded in a leap sideways to another ledge, where he caught a narrow outcropping with his hands, dropped twenty meters, leaped to another handhold and once more went down, bouncing, leaping, grasping tiny ledges. He took the final forty meters in one jump, landing in a bent-knee roll which sent him plunging down the slipface of a dune in a shower of sand and dust. At the bottom he scrambled to his feet, launched himself to the next dunecrest in one jump. He could hear hoarse shouts from atop the cliff but ignored them to concentrate on the leaping strides from dunetop to dunetop.

As he grew more accustomed to amplified muscles he found a sensuous joy that he had not anticipated in this distance-gulping movement. It was a ballet on the desert, defiance of the Tanzerouft which no other had ever experienced.

When he judged that the ornithopter's occupants had overcome their shock enough to mount pursuit once more, he dove for the moon-shadowed face of a dune, burrowed into it. The sand was like heavy liquid to his new strength, but the temperature mounted dangerously when he moved too fast. He broke free on the far face of the dune, found that the membrane had covered his nostrils. He removed it, sensed the new skin pulsing over his body in its labor to absorb his perspiration.

Leto fashioned a tube at his mouth, drank the syrup while he peered upward at the starry sky. He estimated he had come fifteen kilometers from Shuloch. Presently a 'thopter drew its pattern across the stars, a great bird shape followed by another and another. He heard the soft swishing of their wings, the whisper of their muted jets.

Sipping at the living tube, he waited. First Moon passed through its track, then Second Moon.

An hour before dawn Leto crept out and up to the dunecrest, examined the sky. No hunters. Now he knew himself to be embarked upon a path of no return. Ahead lay the trap in Time and Space which had been prepared as an unforgettable lesson for himself and all of mankind.

Leto turned northeast and loped another fifty kilometers before burrowing into the sand for the day, leaving only a tiny hole to the surface which he kept open with a sandtrout tube. The membrane was learning how to live with him as he learned how to live with it. He tried not to think of the other things it was doing to his flesh.

Tomorrow I'll raid Gara Rulen, he thought. *I'll smash their qanat and loose its water into the sand. Then I'll go on to Windsack, Old Gap, and Harg. In a month the ecological transformation will have been set back a full generation. That'll give us space to develop the new timetable.*

And the wildness of the rebel tribes would be blamed, of course. Some would revive memories of Jacurutu. Alia would have her hands full. As for Ghanima . . . Silently to himself, Leto mouthed the words which would restore her memory. Time for that later . . . if they survived this terrible mixing of threads.

The Golden Path lured him out there on the desert, almost a physical thing which he could see with his open eyes. And he thought how it was: as animals must move across the land, their existence dependent upon that movement, the soul of humankind, blocked for eons, needed a track upon which it could move.

He thought of his father then, telling himself: *"Soon we'll dispute as man to man, and only one vision will emerge."*

Limits of survival are set by climate, those long drifts of change which a generation may fail to notice. And it is the extremes of climate which set the pattern. Lonely, finite humans may observe climatic provinces, fluctuations of annual weather and, occasionally may observe such things as "This is a colder year than I've ever known." Such things are sensible. But humans are seldom alerted to the shifting average through a great span of years. And it is precisely in this alerting that humans learn how to survive on any planet. They must learn climate.

—ARRAKIS, THE TRANSFORMATION
AFTER HARQ AL-ADA

Alia sat cross-legged on her bed, trying to compose herself by reciting the Litany Against Fear, but chuckling derision echoed in her skull to block every effort. She could hear the voice; it controlled her ears, her mind.

"What nonsense is this? What have you to fear?"

The muscles of her calves twitched as her feet tried to make running motions. There was nowhere to run.

She wore only a golden gown of the sheerest Palian silk and it revealed the plumpness which had begun to bulge her body. The Hour of Assassins had just passed; dawn was near. Reports covering the past three months lay before her on the red coverlet. She could hear the humming of the air conditioner and a small breeze stirred the labels on the shigawire spools.

Aides had awakened her fearfully two hours earlier, bringing news of the latest outrage, and Alia had called for the report spools, seeking an intelligible pattern.

She gave up on the Litany.

These attacks had to be the work of rebels. Obviously. More and more of them turned against Muad'Dib's religion.

"And what's wrong with that?" the derisive voice asked within her.

Alia shook her head savagely. Namri had failed her. She'd been a fool to trust such a dangerous double instrument. Her aides whispered that Stilgar was to blame, that he was a secret rebel. And what had become of Halleck? Gone to ground among his smuggler friends? Possibly.

She picked up one of the report spools. *And Muriz!* The man was hysterical. That was the only possible explanation. Otherwise she'd have to believe in miracles. No human, let alone a child (even a child such as Leto) could leap from the butte at Shuloch and survive to flee across the desert in leaps that took him from dunecrest to dunecrest.

Alia felt the coldness of the shigawire under her hand.

Where was Leto, then? Ghanima refused to believe him other than dead. A Truthsayer had confirmed her story: Leto slain by a Laza tiger. Then who was the child reported by Namri and Muriz?

She shuddered.

Forty qanats had been breached, their waters loosed into the sand. The loyal Fremen and even the rebels, superstitious louts, all! Her reports were flooded with stories of mysterious occurrences. Sandtrout leaped into qanats and shattered to become hosts of small replicas. Worms deliberately drowned themselves. Blood dripped from Second Moon and fell to Arrakis, where it stirred up great storms. And the storm frequency *was* increasing!

She thought of Duncan incommunicado at Tabr, fretting under the restraints she'd exacted from Stilgar. He and Irulan talked of little else than the *real* meaning behind these omens. Fools! Even her spies betrayed the influence of these outrageous stories!

Why did Ghanima insist on her story of the Laza tiger?

Alia sighed. Only one of the reports on the shigawire spools reassured her. Farad'n had sent a contingent of his household guard "to help you in troubles and to prepare the way for the Official Rite of Betrothal." Alia smiled to herself and shared the chuckle which rumbled in her skull. That plan, at least, remained intact. Logical explanations would be found to dispel all of this other superstitious nonsense.

Meanwhile she'd use Farad'n's men to help close down Shuloch and to arrest the known dissidents, especially among the Naibs. She debated moving against Stilgar, but the inner voice cautioned against this.

"Not yet."

"My mother and the Sisterhood still have some plan of their own," Alia whispered. "Why is she training Farad'n?"

"Perhaps he excites her," the Old Baron said.

"Not that cold one."

"You're not thinking of asking Farad'n to return her?"

"I know the dangers in that!"

"Good. Meanwhile, that young aide Zia recently brought in. I believe his name's Agarves—Buer Agarves. If you'd invite him here tonight . . ."

"No!"

"Alia . . ."

"It's almost dawn, you insatiable old fool! There's a Military Council meeting this morning, the Priests will have—"

"Don't trust them, darling Alia."

"Of course not!"

"Very well. Now, this Buer Agarves . . ."

"I said no!"

The Old Baron remained silent within her, but she began to feel a headache. A slow pain crept upward from her left cheek into her skull. Once he'd sent her raging down the corridors with this trick. Now, she resolved to resist him.

"If you persist, I'll take a sedative," she said.

He could see she meant it. The headache began to recede.

"Very well." Petulant. "Another time, then."

"Another time," she agreed.

It was the immutable prophecy, the threads become rope, a thing Leto
now seemed to have known all of his life. He looked out across the evening shadows on the Tanzerouft. One hundred and seventy kilometers
due north lay Old Gap, the deep and twisting crevasse through the
Shield Wall by which the first Fremen had migrated into the desert.

No doubts remained in Leto. He knew why he stood here alone in
the desert, yet filled with a sense that he owned this entire land, that it
must do his bidding. He felt the chord which connected him with all of
humankind and that profound need for a universe of experiences which
made logical sense, a universe of recognizable regularities within its
perpetual changes.

I know this universe.

The worm which had brought him here had come to the stamping
of his foot and, rising up in front of him, had stopped like an obedient
beast. He'd leaped atop it and, with only his membrane-amplified
hands, had exposed the leading lip of the worm's rings to keep it on the
surface. The worm had exhausted itself in the nightlong dash northward. Its silicon-sulfur internal "factory" had worked at capacity, ex-

haling lavish gusts of oxygen which a following wind had sent in enveloping eddies around Leto. At times the warm gusts had made him dizzy, filled his mind with strange perceptions. The reflexive and circular subjectivity of his visions had turned inward upon his ancestry, forcing him to relive portions of his Terranic past, then comparing those portions with his changing self.

Already he could feel how far he'd drifted from something recognizably human. Seduced by the spice which he gulped from every trace he found, the membrane which covered him no longer was sandtrout, just as he was no longer human. Cilia had crept into his flesh, forming a new creature which would seek its own metamorphosis in the eons ahead.

You saw this, father, and rejected it, he thought. *It was a thing too terrible to face.*

Leto knew what was believed of his father, and why.

Muad'Dib died of prescience.

But Paul Atreides had passed from the universe of reality into the *alam al-mythal* while still alive, fleeing from this thing which his son had dared.

Now there was only The Preacher.

Leto squatted on the sand and kept his attention northward. The worm would come from that direction, and on its back would ride two people: a young Fremen and a blind man.

A flight of pallid bats passed over Leto's head, bending their course southeast. They were random specks in the darkening sky, and a knowledgeable Fremen eye could mark their back-course to learn where shelter lay that way. The Preacher would avoid that shelter, though. His destination was Shuloch, where no wild bats were permitted lest they guide strangers to a secret place.

The worm appeared first as a dark movement between the desert and the northern sky. *Matar,* the rain of sand dropped from high altitudes by a dying stormwind, obscured the view for a few minutes, then it returned clearer and closer.

The cold-line at the base of the dune where Leto crouched began to produce its nightly moisture. He tasted the fragile dampness in his nostrils, adjusted the bubble cap of the membrane over his mouth. There no longer was any need for him to find soaks and sip-wells. From his mother's genes he had that longer, larger Fremen large intestine to take back water from everything which came its way. The living stillsuit grasped and retained every bit of moisture it encountered. And even while he sat here the membrane which touched sand extruded pseudopod-cilia to hunt for bits of energy which it could store.

Leto studied the approaching worm. He knew the youthful guide had seen him by this time, noting the spot atop the dune. The worm rider would discern no principle in this object seen from a distance, but that was a problem Fremen had learned how to handle. Any unknown object was dangerous. The young guide's reactions would be quite pre-dictable, even without the vision.

True to that prediction, the worm's course shifted slightly and aimed directly at Leto. Giant worms were a weapon which Fremen had employed many times. Worms had helped beat Shaddam at Arrakeen. This worm, however, failed to do its rider's bidding. It came to a halt ten meters away and no manner of goading would send it across another grain of sand.

Leto arose, feeling the cilia snap back into the membrane behind him. He freed his mouth and called out: "Achlan, wasachlan!" *Welcome, twice welcome!*

The blind man stood behind his guide atop the worm, one hand on the youth's shoulder. The man held his face high, nose pointed over Leto's head as though trying to sniff out this interruption. Sunset painted orange on his forehead.

"Who is that?" the blind man asked, shaking his guide's shoulder. "Why have we stopped?" His voice was nasal through the stillsuit plugs.

The youth stared fearfully down at Leto, said: "It is only someone alone in the desert. A child by his looks. I tried to send the worm over him, but the worm won't go."

"Why didn't you say?" the blind man demanded.

"I thought it was only someone alone in the desert!" the youth pro-tested. "But it's a demon."

"Spoken like a true son of Jacurutu," Leto said. "And you, sire, you are The Preacher."

"I am that one, yes." And there was fear in The Preacher's voice because, at last, he had met his own past.

"This is no garden," Leto said, "but you are welcome to share this place with me tonight."

"Who are you?" The Preacher demanded. "How have you stopped our worm?" There was an ominous tone of recognition in The Preacher's voice. Now he called up the memories of this alternate vision . . . knowing he could reach an end here.

"It's a demon!" the young guide protested. "We must flee this place or our souls—"

"Silence!" The Preacher roared.

"I am Leto Atreides," Leto said. "Your worm stopped because I commanded it."

The Preacher stood in frozen silence.

"Come, father," Leto said. "Alight and spend the night with me. I'll give you sweet syrup to sip. I see you've Fremkits with food and water jars. We'll share our riches here upon the sand."

"Leto's yet a child," The Preacher protested. "And they say he's dead of Corrino treachery. There's no childhood in your voice."

"You know me, sire," Leto said. "I'm small for my age as you were, but my experience is ancient and my voice has learned."

"What do you here in the Inner Desert?" The Preacher asked.

"Bu ji," Leto said. *Nothing from nothing.* It was the answer of a Zensunni wanderer, one who acted only from a position of rest, without effort and in harmony with his surroundings.

The Preacher shook his guide's shoulder. "Is it a child, truly a child?"

"Aiya," the youth said, keeping a fearful attention on Leto.

A great shuddering sigh shook The Preacher. "No," he said.

"It is a demon in child form," the guide said.

"You will spend the night here," Leto said.

"We will do as he says," The Preacher said. He released his grip on the guide, slipped off the worm's side and slid down a ring to the sand, leaping clear when his feet touched. Turning, he said: "Take the worm off and send it back into the sand. It is tired and will not bother us."

"The worm will not go!" the youth protested.

"It will go," Leto said. "But if you try to flee on it, I'll let it eat you." He moved to one side out of the worm's sensory range, pointed in the direction they had come. "Go that way."

The youth tapped a goad against the ring behind him, wiggled a hook where it held a ring open. Slowly the worm began to slide over the sand, turning as the youth shifted his hook down a side.

The Preacher, following the sound of Leto's voice, clambered up the duneslope and stood two paces away. It was done with a swift sureness which told Leto this would be no easy contest.

Here the visions parted.

Leto said: "Remove your suit mask, father."

The Preacher obeyed, dropping the fold of his hood and withdrawing the mouth cover.

Knowing his own appearance, Leto studied this face, seeing the lines of likeness as though they'd been outlined in light. The lines formed an indefinable reconciliation, a pathway of genes without sharp boundaries, and there was no mistaking them. Those lines came down to Leto from the humming days, from the water-dripping days, from the miracle seas of Caladan. But now they stood at a dividing point on Arrakis as night waited to fold itself into the dunes.

"So, father," Leto said, glancing to the left where he could see the youthful guide trudging back to them from where the worm had been abandoned.

"Mu zein!" The Preacher said, waving his right hand in a cutting gesture. *This is no good!*

"Koolish zein," Leto said, voice soft. *This is all the good we may ever have.* And he added, speaking in Chakobsa, the Atreides battle language: "Here I am; here I remain! We cannot forget that, father."

The Preacher's shoulders sagged. He put both hands to his empty sockets in a long-unused gesture.

"I gave you the sight of my eyes once and took your memories," Leto said. "I know your decisions and I've been to that place where you hid yourself."

"I know." The Preacher lowered his hands. "You will remain?"

"You named me for the man who put that on his coat of arms," Leto said. "J'y suis, j'y reste!"

The Preacher sighed deeply. "How far has it gone, this thing you've done to yourself?"

"My skin is not my own, father."

The Preacher shuddered. "Then I know how you found me here."

"Yes, I fastened my memory to a place my flesh had never known," Leto said. "I need an evening with my father."

"I'm not your father. I'm only a poor copy, a relic." He turned his head toward the sound of the approaching guide. "I no longer go to the visions for my future."

As he spoke, darkness covered the desert. Stars leaped out above them and Leto, too, turned toward the approaching guide. "Wubakh ul kuhar!" Leto called to the youth. *"Greetings!"*

Back came the response: "Subakh un nar!"

Speaking in a hoarse whisper, The Preacher said: "That young Assan Tariq is a dangerous one."

"All of the Cast Out are dangerous," Leto said. "But not to me." He spoke in a low, conversational tone.

"If that's your vision, I will not share it," The Preacher said.

"Perhaps you have no choice," Leto said. "You are the *fil-haquiqa*, The Reality. You are Abu Dhur, Father of the Indefinite Roads of Time."

"I'm no more than bait in a trap," The Preacher said, and his voice was bitter.

"And Alia already has eaten that bait," Leto said. "But I don't like its taste."

"You cannot do this!" The Preacher hissed.

"I've already done it. My skin is not my own."

"Perhaps it's not too late for you to—"

"It is too late." Leto bent his head to one side. He could hear Assan

Tariq trudging up the duneslope toward them, coming to the sound of their voices. "Greetings, Assan Tariq of Shuloch," Leto said.

The youth stopped just below Leto on the slope, a dark shadow there in the starlight. There was indecision in the set of his shoulders, the way he tipped his head.

"Yes," Leto said, "I'm the one who escaped from Shuloch."

"When I heard . . ." The Preacher began. And again: "You cannot do this!"

"I am doing it. What matter if you're made blind once more?"

"You think I fear that?" The Preacher asked. "Do you not see the fine guide they have provided for me?"

"I see him." Again Leto faced Tariq. "Didn't you hear me, Assan? I'm the one who escaped from Shuloch."

"You're a demon," the youth quavered.

"Your demon," Leto said. "But you are my demon." And Leto felt the tension grow between himself and his father. It was a shadow play all around them, a projection of unconscious forms. And Leto felt the memories of his father, a form of backward prophecy which sorted visions from the familiar reality of this moment.

Tariq sensed it, this battle of the visions. He slid several paces backward down the slope.

"You cannot control the future," The Preacher whispered, and the sound of his voice was filled with effort as though he lifted a great weight.

Leto felt the dissonance between them then. It was an element of the universe with which his entire life grappled. Either he or his father would be forced to act soon, making a decision by that act, choosing a vision. And his father was right: trying for some ultimate control of the universe, you only built weapons with which the universe eventually defeated you. To choose and manage a vision required you to balance on a single, thin thread—playing God on a high tightwire with cosmic solitude on both sides. Neither contestant could retreat into death-as-surcease-from-paradox. Each knew the visions and the rules. All of the old illusions were dying. And when one contestant moved, the other might countermove. The only real truth that mattered to them now was that which separated them from the vision background. There was no place of safety, only a transitory shifting of relationships, marked out within the limits which they now imposed and bound for inevitable changes. Each of them had only a desperate and lonely courage upon which to rely, but Leto possessed two advantages: he had committed himself upon a path from which there was no turning back, and he had accepted the terrible consequences to himself. His father still hoped there was a way back and had made no final commitment.

"You must not! You must not!" The Preacher rasped.

He sees my advantage, Leto thought.

Leto spoke in a conversational tone, masking his own tensions, the balancing effort this other-level contest required. "I have no passionate belief in truth, no faith other than what I create," he said. And he felt then a movement between himself and his father, something with granular characteristics which touched only Leto's own passionately subjective belief in himself. By such belief he knew that he posted the markers of the Golden Path. Someday such markers could tell others how to be human, a strange gift from a creature who no longer would be human on that day. But these markers were always set in place by gamblers. Leto felt them scattered throughout the landscape of his inner lives and, feeling this, poised himself for the ultimate gamble.

Softly he sniffed the air, seeking the signal which both he and his father knew must come. One question remained: Would his father warn the terrified young guide who waited below them?

Presently Leto sensed ozone in his nostrils, the betraying odor of a shield. True to his orders from the Cast Out, young Tariq was trying to kill both of these dangerous Atreides, not knowing the horrors which this would precipitate.

"Don't," The Preacher whispered.

But Leto knew the signal was a true one. He sensed ozone, but there was no tingling in the air around them. Tariq used a pseudo-shield in the desert, a weapon developed exclusively for Arrakis. The Holtzmann Effect would summon a worm while it maddened that worm. Nothing would stop such a worm—not water, not the presence of sand-trout . . . nothing. Yes, the youth had planted the device in the dune-slope and was beginning to edge away from the danger zone.

Leto launched himself off the dunetop, hearing his father scream in protest. But the awful impetus of Leto's amplified muscles threw his body like a missile. One outflung hand caught the neck of Tariq's stillsuit, the other slapped around to grip the doomed youth's robe at the waist. There came a single snap as the neck broke. Leto rolled, lifting his body like a finely balanced instrument which dove directly into the sand where the pseudo-shield had been hidden. Fingers found the thing and he had it out of the sand, throwing it in a looping arc far out to the south of them.

Presently there came a great hissing-thrashing din out on the desert where the pseudo-shield had gone. It subsided, and silence returned.

Leto looked up to the top of the dune where his father stood, still defiant, but defeated. That was Paul Muad'Dib up there, blind, angry, near despair as a consequence of his flight from the vision which Leto had accepted. Paul's mind would be reflecting now upon the Zensunni Long Koan: *"In the one act of predicting an accurate future, Muad'Dib introduced an element of development and growth into the very pre-science through which he saw human existence. By this, he brought un-certainty onto himself. Seeking the absolute of orderly prediction, he amplified disorder, distorted prediction."*

Returning to the dunetop in a single leap, Leto said: "Now I'm your guide."

"Never!"

"Would you go back to Shuloch? Even if they'd welcome you when you arrived without Tariq, where has Shuloch gone now? Do your *eyes* see it?"

Paul confronted his son then, aiming the eyeless sockets at Leto. "Do you really know the universe you have created here?"

Leto heard the particular emphasis. The vision which both of them knew had been set into terrible motion here had required an act of cre-ation at a certain *point* in time. For that moment, the entire sentient universe shared a linear view of time which possessed characteristics of orderly progression. They entered this time as they might step onto a moving vehicle, and they could only leave it the same way.

Against this, Leto held the multi-thread reins, balanced in his own vision-lighted view of time as multilinear and multilooped. He was the sighted man in the universe of the blind. Only he could scatter the orderly rationale because his father no longer held the reins. In Leto's view, a son had altered the past. And a thought as yet undreamed in the farthest future could reflect upon the *now* and move his hand.

Only *his* hand.

Paul knew this because he no longer could see how Leto might manipulate the reins, could only recognize the inhuman consequences which Leto had accepted. And he thought: *Here is the change for which I prayed. Why do I fear it? Because it's the Golden Path!*

"I'm here to give purpose to evolution and, therefore, to give purpose to our lives," Leto said.

"Do you *wish* to live those thousands of years, changing as you now know you will change?"

Leto recognized that his father was not speaking about physical changes. Both of them knew the physical consequences: Leto would adapt and adapt; the skin-which-was-not-his-own would adapt and adapt. The evolutionary thrust of each part would melt into the other and a single transformation would emerge. When metamorphosis came, *if* it came, a thinking creature of awesome dimensions would emerge upon the universe—and that universe would worship him.

No . . . Paul was referring to the inner changes, the thoughts and decisions which would inflict themselves upon the worshipers.

"Those who think you dead," Leto said, "you know what they say about your last words."

"Of course."

"*Now I do what all life must do in the service of life*," Leto said. "You never said that, but a Priest who thought you could never return and call him liar put those words into your mouth."

"I'd not call him liar." Paul took in a deep breath. "Those are good last words."

"Would you stay here or return to that hut in the basin of Shuloch?" Leto asked.

"This is your universe now," Paul said.

The words filled with defeat cut through Leto. Paul had tried to guide the last strands of a personal vision, a choice he'd made years before in Sietch Tabr. For that, he'd accepted his role as an instrument of revenge for the Cast Out, the remnants of Jacurutu. They had contaminated him, but he'd accepted this rather than his view of this universe which Leto had chosen.

The sadness in Leto was so great he could not speak for several minutes. When he could manage his voice, Leto said: "So you baited Alia, tempted her and confused her into inaction and the wrong decisions. And now she knows who you are."

"She knows . . . Yes, she knows."

Paul's voice was old then and filled with hidden protests. There was a reserve of defiance in him, though. He said: "I'll take the vision away from you if I can."

"Thousands of peaceful years," Leto said. "That's what I'll give them."

"Dormancy! Stagnation!"

"Of course. And those forms of violence which I permit. It'll be a lesson which humankind will never forget."

"I spit on your lesson!" Paul said. "You think I've not seen a thing similar to what you choose?"

"You saw it," Leto agreed.

"Is your vision any better than mine?"

"Not one whit better. Worse, perhaps," Leto said.

"Then what can I do but resist you?" Paul demanded.

"Kill me, perhaps?"

"I'm not that innocent. I know what you've set in motion. I know about the broken qanats and the unrest."

"And now Assan Tariq will never return to Shuloch. You must go back with me or not at all because this is my vision now."

"I choose not to go back."

How old his voice sounds, Leto thought, and the thought was a wrenching pain. He said: "I've the hawk ring of the Atreides concealed in my *dishdasha.* Do you wish me to return it to you?"

"If I'd only died," Paul whispered. "I truly wanted to die when I went into the desert that night, but I knew I could not leave this world. I had to come back and—"

"Restore the legend," Leto said. "I know. And the jackals of Jacurutu were waiting for you that night as you knew they would be. They wanted your visions! You knew that."

"I refused. I never gave them one vision."

"But they contaminated you. They fed you spice essence and plied you with women and dreams. And you *did* have visions."

"Sometimes." How sly his voice sounded.

"Will you take back your hawk ring?" Leto asked.

Paul sat down suddenly on the sand, a dark blotch in the starlight. "No!"

So he knows the futility of that path, Leto thought. This revealed much, but not enough. The contest of the visions had moved from its delicate plane of choices down to a gross discarding of alternates. Paul knew he could not win, but he hoped yet to nullify that single vision to which Leto clung.

Presently Paul said: "Yes, I was contaminated by the Jacurutu. But you contaminate yourself."

"That's true," Leto admitted. "I am your son."

"And are you a good Fremen?"

"Yes."

"Will you permit a blind man to go into the desert finally? Will you let me find peace on my own terms?" He pounded the sand beside him.

"No, I'll not permit that," Leto said. "But it's your right to fall upon your knife if you insist upon it."

"And you would have my body!"

"True."

"No!"

And so he knows that path, Leto thought. The enshrining of

Muad'Dib's body by his son could be contrived as a form of cement for Leto's vision.

"You never told them, did you, father?" Leto asked.

"I never told them."

"But I told them," Leto said. "I told Muriz. Kralizec, the Typhoon Struggle."

Paul's shoulders sagged. "You cannot," he whispered. "You cannot."

"I am a creature of this desert now, father," Leto said. "Would you speak thus to a Coriolis storm?"

"You think me coward for refusing that path," Paul said, his voice husky and trembling. "Oh, I understand you well, son. Augury and haruspication have always been their own torments. But I was never lost in the possible futures because this one is unspeakable!"

"Your Jihad will be a summer picnic on Caladan by comparison," Leto agreed. "I'll take you to Gurney Halleck now."

"Gurney! He serves the Sisterhood through my mother."

And now Leto understood the extent of his father's vision. "No, father. Gurney no longer serves anyone. I know the place to find him and I can take you there. It's time for the new legend to be created."

"I see that I cannot sway you. Let me touch you, then, for you are my son."

Leto held out his right hand to meet the groping fingers, felt their strength, matched it, and resisted every shift of Paul's arm. "Not even a poisoned knife will harm me now," Leto said. "I'm already a different chemistry."

Tears slipped from the sightless eyes and Paul released his grip, dropped his hand to his side. "If I'd chosen your way, I'd have become the *bicouros of shaitan*. What will you become?"

"For a time they'll call me the missionary of *shaitan*, too," Leto said. "Then they'll begin to wonder and, finally, they'll understand. You didn't take your vision far enough, father. Your hands did good things and evil."

"But the evil was known after the event!"

"Which is the way of many great evils," Leto said. "You crossed over only into a part of my vision. Was your strength not enough?"

"You know I couldn't stay there. I could never do an evil act which was known before the act. I'm not Jacurutu." He clambered to his feet. "Do you think me one of those who laughs alone at night?"

"It is sad that you were never really Fremen," Leto said. "We Fremen know how to commission the arifa. Our judges can choose between evils. It's always been that way for us."

"Fremen, is it? Slaves of the fate you helped to make?" Paul stepped toward Leto, reached out in an oddly shy movement, touched Leto's sheathed arm, explored up it to where the membrane exposed an ear, then the cheek and, finally, the mouth. "Ahhhh, that is your own flesh yet," he said. "Where will that flesh take you?" He dropped his hand.

"Into a place where humans may create their futures from instant to instant."

"So you say. An Abomination might say the same."

"I'm not Abomination, though I might've been," Leto said. "I saw how it goes with Alia. A demon lives in her, father. Ghani and I know that demon: it's the Baron, your grandfather."

Paul buried his face in his hands. His shoulders shook for a moment, then he lowered his hands and his mouth was set in a harsh line. "There is a curse upon our House. I prayed that you would throw that ring into the sand, that you'd deny me and run away to make . . . another life. It was there for you."

"At what price?"

After a long silence, Paul said: "The end adjusts the path behind it. Just once I failed to fight for my principles. Just once. I accepted the Mahdinate. I did it for Chani, but it made me a bad leader."

Leto found he couldn't answer this. The memory of that decision was there within him.

"I cannot lie to you any more than I could lie to myself," Paul said. "I know this. Every man should have such an auditor. I will only ask this one thing: is the Typhoon Struggle necessary?" •

"It's that or humans will be extinguished."

Paul heard the truth in Leto's words, spoke in a low voice which acknowledged the greater breadth of his son's vision. "I did not see that among the choices."

"I believe the Sisterhood suspects it," Leto said. "I cannot accept any other explanation of my grandmother's decision."

The night wind blew coldly around them then. It whipped Paul's robe around his legs. He trembled. Seeing this, Leto said: "You've a kit, father. I'll inflate the tent and we can spend this night in comfort."

But Paul could only shake his head, knowing he would have no comfort from this night or any other. Muad'Dib, The Hero, must be destroyed. He'd said it himself. Only The Preacher could go on now.

Fremen were the first humans to develop a conscious/unconscious symbology through which to experience the movements and relationships of their planetary system. They were the first people anywhere to express climate in terms of a semi-mathematic language whose written symbols embody (and internalize) the external relationships. The language itself was part of the system it described. Its written form carried the shape of what it described. The intimate local knowledge of what was available to support life was implicit in this development. One can measure the extent of this language/system interaction by the fact that Fremen accepted themselves as foraging and browsing animals.

—THE STORY OF LIET-KYNES
BY HARQ AL-ADA

"Kaveh wahid," Stilgar said. *Bring coffee.* He signaled with a raised hand to an aide who stood at one side near the single door to the austere rock-walled room where he had spent this wakeful night. This was the place where the old Fremen Naib usually took his spartan breakfast, and it was almost breakfast time, but after such a night he did not feel hungry. He stood, stretching his muscles.

Duncan Idaho sat on a low cushion near the door, trying to suppress a yawn. He had just realized that, while they talked, he and Stilgar had gone through an entire night.

"Forgive me, Stil," he said. "I've kept you up all night."

"To stay awake all night adds a day to your life," Stilgar said, accepting the tray with coffee as it was passed in the door. He pushed a low bench in front of Idaho, placed the tray on it and sat across from his guest.

Both men wore the yellow robes of mourning, but Idaho's was a borrowed garment worn because the people of Tabr had resented the Atreides green of his working uniform.

Stilgar poured the dark brew from the fat copper carafe, sipped first, and lifted his cup as a signal to Idaho—the ancient Fremen custom: *"It is safe; I have taken some of it."*

The coffee was Harah's work, done just as Stilgar preferred it: the beans roasted to a rose-brown, ground to a fine powder in a stone mortar while still hot, and boiled immediately; a pinch of melange added.

Idaho inhaled the spice-rich aroma, sipped carefully but noisily. He still did not know if he had convinced Stilgar. His mentat faculties had begun to work sluggishly in the early hours of the morning, all of his computations confronted at last by the inescapable datum supplied in the message from Gurney Halleck.

Alia had known about Leto! She'd known.

And Javid had to be a part of that knowing.

"I must be freed of your restraints," Idaho said at last, taking up the arguments once more.

Stilgar stood his ground. "The agreement of neutrality requires me to make hard judgments. Ghani is safe here. You and Irulan are safe here. But you may not send messages. Receive messages, yes, but you may not send them. I've given my word."

"This is not the treatment usually accorded a guest and an old friend who has shared your dangers," Idaho said, knowing he'd used this argument before.

Stilgar put down his cup, setting it carefully into its place on the tray and keeping his attention on it as he spoke. "We Fremen don't feel guilt for the same things that arouse such feelings in others," he said. He raised his attention to Idaho's face.

He must be made to take Ghani and flee this place, Idaho thought. He said: "It was not my intention to raise a storm of guilt."

"I understand that," Stilgar said. "I raise the question to impress upon you our Fremen attitude, because that is what we are dealing with: Fremen. Even Alia thinks Fremen."

"And the Priests?"

"They are another matter," Stilgar said. "They want the people to swallow the grey wind of sin, taking *that* into the everlasting. This is a great blotch by which they seek to know their own piety." He spoke in a level voice, but Idaho heard the bitterness and wondered why that bitterness could not sway Stilgar.

"It's an old, old trick of autocratic rule," Idaho said. "Alia knows it well. Good subjects must feel guilty. The guilt begins as a feeling of failure. The good autocrat provides many opportunities for failure in the populace."

"I've noticed." Stilgar spoke dryly. "But you must forgive me if I mention to you once more that this is your wife of whom you speak. It is the sister of Muad'Dib."

"She's possessed, I tell you!"

"Many say it. She will have to undergo the test one day. Meanwhile there are other considerations more important."

Idaho shook his head sadly. "Everything I've told you can be verified. The communication with Jacurutu was always through Alia's Temple. The plot against the twins had accomplices there. Money for the sale of worms off-planet goes there. All of the strings lead to Alia's office, to the Regency."

Stilgar shook his head, drew in a deep breath. "This is neutral territory. I've given my word."

"Things can't go on this way!" Idaho protested.

"I agree." Stilgar nodded. "Alia's caught inside the circle and every day the circle grows smaller. It's like our old custom of having many wives. This pinpoints male sterility." He bent a questioning gaze on Idaho. "You say she deceived you with other men—'using her sex as a weapon' is the way I believe you've expressed it. Then you have a perfectly legal avenue available to you. Javid's here in Tabr with messages from Alia. You have only to—"

"On your neutral territory?"

"No, but outside in the desert. . . ."

"And if I took that opportunity to escape?"

"You'll not be given such an opportunity."

"Still, I swear to you, Alia's possessed. What do I have to do to convince you of—"

"A difficult thing to prove," Stilgar said. It was the argument he'd used many times during the night.

Idaho recalled Jessica's words, said: "But you've ways of proving it."

"A way, yes," Stilgar said. Again he shook his head. "Painful, irrevocable. That is why I remind you about our attitude toward guilt. We can free ourselves from guilts which might destroy us in everything except the Trial of Possession. For that, the tribunal, which is all of the people, accepts complete responsibility."

"You've done it before, haven't you?"

"I'm sure the Reverend Mother didn't omit our history in her recital," Stilgar said. "You well know we've done it before."

Idaho responded to the irritation in Stilgar's voice. "I wasn't trying to trap you in a falsehood. It's just—"

"It's the long night and the questions without answers," Stilgar said. "And now it's morning."

"I must be allowed to send a message to Jessica," Idaho said.

"That would be a message to Salusa," Stilgar said. "I don't make evening promises. My word is meant to be kept; that is why Tabr's neutral territory. I will hold you in silence. I have pledged this for my entire household."

"Alia must be brought to your Trial!"

"Perhaps. First, we must find out if there are extenuating circumstances. A failure of authority, possibly. Or even bad luck. It could be a case of that natural bad tendency which all humans share, and not possession at all."

"You want to be sure I'm not just the husband wronged, seeking others to execute his revenge," Idaho said.

"The thought has occurred to others, not to me," Stilgar said. He smiled to take the sting out of his words. "We Fremen have our science of tradition, our *hadith*. When we fear a mentat or a Reverend Mother, we revert to the *hadith*. It is said that the only fear we cannot correct is the fear of our own mistakes."

"The Lady Jessica must be told," Idaho said. "Gurney says—"

"That message may not come from Gurney Halleck."

"It comes from no other. We Atreides have our ways of verifying messages. Stil, won't you at least explore some of—"

"Jacurutu is no more," Stilgar said. "It was destroyed many generations ago." He touched Idaho's sleeve. "In any event, I cannot spare the fighting men. These are troubled times, the threat to the qanat . . . you understand?" He sat back. "Now, when Alia—"

"There is no more Alia," Idaho said.

"So you say." Stilgar took another sip of coffee, replaced the cup. "Let it rest there, friend Idaho. Often there's no need to tear off an arm to remove a splinter."

"Then let's talk about Ghanima."

"There's no need. She has my countenance, my bond. No one can harm her here."

He cannot be that naïve, Idaho thought.

But Stilgar was rising to indicate that the interview was ended.

Idaho levered himself to his feet, feeling the stiffness in his knees. His calves felt numb. As Idaho stood, an aide entered and stood aside. Javid came into the room behind him. Idaho turned. Stilgar stood four paces away. Without hesitating, Idaho drew his knife in one swift motion and drove its point into the breast of the unsuspecting Javid. The man staggered backward, pulling himself off the knife. He turned, fell onto his face. His legs kicked and he was dead.

"That was to silence the gossip," Idaho said.

The aide stood with drawn knife, undecided how to react. Idaho had already sheathed his own knife, leaving a trace of blood on the edge of his yellow robe.

"You have defiled my honor!" Stilgar cried. "This is neutral—"

"Shut up!" Idaho glared at the shocked Naib. "You wear a collar, Stilgar!"

It was one of the three most deadly insults which could be directed at a Fremen. Stilgar's face went pale.

"You are a servant," Idaho said. "You've sold Fremen for their water."

This was the second most deadly insult, the one which had destroyed the original Jacurutu.

Stilgar ground his teeth, put a hand on his crysknife. The aide stepped back away from the body in the doorway.

Turning his back on the Naib, Idaho stepped into the door, taking the narrow opening beside Javid's body and speaking without turning, delivered the third insult. "You have no immortality, Stilgar. None of your descendants carry your blood!"

"Where do you go now, mentat?" Stilgar called as Idaho continued leaving the room. Stilgar's voice was as cold as a wind from the poles.

"To find Jacurutu," Idaho said, still not turning.

Stilgar drew his knife. "Perhaps I can help you."

Idaho was at the outer lip of the passage now. Without stopping, he said: "If you'd help me with your knife, water-thief, please do it in my back. That's the fitting way for one who wears the collar of a demon."

With two leaping strides Stilgar crossed the room, stepped on Javid's body and caught Idaho in the outer passage. One gnarled hand jerked Idaho around and to a stop. Stilgar confronted Idaho with bared teeth and a drawn knife. Such was his rage that Stilgar did not even see the curious smile on Idaho's face.

"Draw your knife, mentat scum!" Stilgar roared.

Idaho laughed. He cuffed Stilgar sharply—left hand, right hand—two stinging slaps to the head.

With an incoherent screech, Stilgar drove his knife into Idaho's abdomen, striking upward through the diaphragm into the heart.

Idaho sagged onto the blade, grinned up at Stilgar, whose rage dissolved into sudden icy shock.

"Two deaths for the Atreides," Idaho husked. "The second for no better reason than the first." He lurched sideways, collapsed to the stone floor on his face. Blood spread out from his wound.

Stilgar stared down past his dripping knife at the body of Idaho, took a deep, trembling breath. Javid lay dead behind him. And the consort of Alia, the Womb of Heaven, lay dead at Stilgar's own hands. It might be argued that a Naib had but protected the honor of his name, avenging the threat to his promised neutrality. But this dead man was Duncan Idaho. No matter the arguments available, no matter the "extenuating circumstances," nothing could erase such an act. Even were Alia to approve privately, she would be forced to respond publicly in revenge. She was, after all, Fremen. To rule Fremen, she could be nothing else, not even to the smallest degree.

Only then did it occur to Stilgar that this situation was precisely what Idaho had intended to buy with his "second death."

Stilgar looked up, saw the shocked face of Harah, his second wife, peering at him in an enclosing throng. Everywhere Stilgar turned there were faces with identical expressions: shock and an understanding of the consequences.

Slowly Stilgar drew himself erect, wiped the blade on his sleeve and sheathed it. Speaking to the faces, his tone casual, he said: "Those who'll go with me should pack at once. Send men to summon worms."

"Where will you go, Stilgar?" Harah asked.

"Into the desert."

"I will go with you," she said.

"Of course you'll go with me. All of my wives will go with me. And Ghanima. Get her, Harah. At once."

"Yes, Stilgar . . . at once." She hesitated. "And Irulan?"

"If she wishes."

"Yes, husband." Still she hesitated. "You take Ghani as hostage?"

"Hostage?" He was genuinely startled by the thought. "Woman . . ." He touched Idaho's body softly with a toe. "If this mentat was right, I'm Ghani's only hope." And he remembered then Leto's warning: *"Beware of Alia. You must take Ghani and flee."*

After the Fremen, all Planetologists see life as expressions of energy and look for the overriding relationships. In small pieces, bits and parcels which grow into general understanding, the Fremen racial wisdom is translated into a new certainty. The thing Fremen have as a people, any people can have. They need but develop a sense for energy relationships. They need but observe that energy soaks up the patterns of things and builds with those patterns.

—THE ARRAKEEN CATASTROPHE
AFTER HARQ AL-ADA

It was Tuek's Sietch on the inner lip of False Wall. Halleck stood in the shadow of the rock buttress which shielded the high entrance to the sietch, waiting for those inside to decide whether they would shelter him. He turned his gaze outward to the northern desert and then upward to the grey-blue morning sky. The smugglers here had been astonished to learn that he, an off-worlder, had captured a worm and ridden it. But Halleck had been equally astonished at their reaction. The thing was simple for an agile man who'd seen it done many times.

Halleck returned his attention to the desert, the silver desert of shining rocks and grey-green fields where water had worked its magic. All of this struck him suddenly as an enormously fragile containment of energy, of life—everything threatened by an abrupt shift in the pattern of change.

He knew the source of this reaction. It was the bustling scene on the desert floor below him. Containers of dead sandtrout were being trundled into the sietch for distillation and recovery of their water. There were thousands of the creatures. They had come to an outpouring of water. And it was this outpouring which had set Halleck's mind racing.

Halleck stared downward across the sietch fields and the qanat boundary which no longer flowed with precious water. He had seen the holes in the qanat's stone walls, the rending of the rock liner which had spilled water into the sand. What had made those holes? Some stretched along twenty meters of the qanat's most vulnerable sections, in places where soft sand led outward into water-absorbing depressions. It was those depressions which had swarmed with sandtrout. The children of the sietch were killing them and capturing them.

Repair teams worked on the shattered walls of the qanat. Others carried minims of irrigation water to the most needy plants. The water source in the gigantic cistern beneath Tuek's windtrap had been closed off, preventing the flow into the shattered qanat. The sun-powered pumps had been disconnected. The irrigation water came from dwindling pools at the bottom of the qanat and, laboriously, from the cistern within the sietch.

The metal frame of the doorseal behind Halleck crackled in the growing warmth of the day. As though the sound moved his eyes, Halleck found his gaze drawn to the farthest curve of the qanat, to the place where water had reached most impudently into the desert. The garden-hopeful planners of the sietch had planted a special tree there and it was doomed unless the water flow could be restored soon. Halleck stared at the silly, trailing plumage of a willow tree there shredded by sand and wind. For him, that tree symbolized the new reality for himself and for Arrakis.

Both of us are alien here.

They were taking a long time over their decision within the sietch, but they could use good fighting men. Smugglers always needed good men. Halleck had no illusions about them, though. The smugglers of this age were not the smugglers who'd sheltered him so many years ago when he'd fled the dissolution of his Duke's fief. No, these were a new breed, quick to seek profit.

Again he focused on the silly willow. It came to Halleck then that the stormwinds of his new reality might shred these smugglers and all of their friends. It might destroy Stilgar with his fragile neutrality and take with him all of the tribes who remained loyal to Alia. They'd all become colonial peoples. Halleck had seen it happen before, knowing the bitter taste of it on his own homeworld. He saw it clearly, recalling the mannerisms of the city Fremen, the pattern of the suburbs, and the unmistakable ways of the rural sietch which rubbed off even on this smugglers' hideaway. The rural districts were colonies of the urban centers. They'd learned how to wear a padded yoke, led into it by their greed if not their superstitions. Even here, especially here, the people had the attitude of a subject population, not the attitude of free men. They were defensive, concealing, evasive. Any manifestation of authority was subject to resentment—any authority: the Regency's, Stilgar's, their own Council . . .

I can't trust them, Halleck thought. He could only use them and nurture their distrust of others. It was sad. Gone was the old give and take of free men. The old ways had been reduced to ritual words, their origins lost to memory.

Alia had done her work well, punishing opposition and rewarding assistance, shifting the Imperial forces in random fashion, concealing the major elements of her Imperial power. The spies! Gods below, the spies she must have!

Halleck could almost see the deadly rhythm of movement and countermovement by which Alia hoped to keep her opposition off balance.

If the Fremen remain dormant, she'll win, he thought.

The doorseal behind him crackled as it was opened. A sietch attendant named Melides emerged. He was a short man with a gourd-like body which dwindled into spindly legs whose ugliness was only accented by a stillsuit.

"You have been accepted," Melides said.

And Halleck heard the sly dissimulation in the man's voice. What that voice revealed told Halleck there was sanctuary here for only a limited time.

Just until I can steal one of their 'thopters, he thought.

"My gratitude to your Council," he said. And he thought of Esmar Tuek, for whom this sietch had been named. Esmar, long dead of someone's treachery, would have slit the throat of this Melides on sight.

Any path which narrows future possibilities may become a lethal trap. Humans are not threading their way through a maze; they scan a vast horizon filled with unique opportunities. The narrowing viewpoint of the maze should appeal only to creatures with their noses buried in sand. Sexually produced uniqueness and differences are the life-protection of the species.

—THE SPACING GUILD HANDBOOK

"Why do I not feel grief?" Alia directed the question at the ceiling of her small audience chamber, a room she could cross in ten paces one way and fifteen the other. It had two tall and narrow windows which looked out across the Arrakeen rooftops at the Shield Wall.

It was almost noon. The sun burned down into the pan upon which the city had been built.

Alia lowered her gaze to Buer Agarves, the former Tabrite and now aide to Zia who directed the Temple guards. Agarves had brought the news that Javid and Idaho were dead. A mob of sycophants, aides and guards had come in with him and more crowded the areaway outside, revealing that they already knew Agarves's message.

Bad news traveled fast on Arrakis.

He was a small man, this Agarves, with a round face for a Fremen, almost infantile in its roundness. He was one of the new breed who had gone to water-fatness. Alia saw him as though he had been split into two images: one with a serious face and opaque indigo eyes, a worried expression around the mouth, the other image sensuous and vulnerable, excitingly vulnerable. She especially liked the thickness of his lips.

Although it was not yet noon, Alia felt something in the shocked silence around her that spoke of sunset.

Idaho should've died at sunset, she told herself.

"How is it, Buer, that you're the bearer of this news?" she asked, noting the watchful quickness which came into his expression.

Agarves tried to swallow, spoke in a hoarse voice hardly more than a whisper. "I went with Javid, you recall? And when . . . Stilgar sent me to you, he said for me to tell you that I carried his final obedience."

"Final obedience," she echoed. "What'd he mean by that?"

"I don't know, Lady Alia," he pleaded.

"Explain to me again what you saw," she ordered, and she wondered at how cold her skin felt.

"I saw . . ." He bobbed his head nervously, looked at the floor in front of Alia. "I saw the Holy Consort dead upon the floor of the central passage, and Javid lay dead nearby in a side passage. The women already were preparing them for Huanui."

"And Stilgar summoned you to this scene?"

"That is true, My Lady. Stilgar summoned me. He sent Modibo, the Bent One, his messenger in sietch. Modibo gave me no warning. He merely told me Stilgar wanted me."

"And you saw my husband's body there on the floor?"

He met her eyes with a darting glance, returned his attention once more to the floor in front of her before nodding. "Yes, My Lady. And Javid dead nearby. Stilgar told me . . . told me that the Holy Consort had slain Javid."

"And my husband, you say Stilgar—"

"He said it to me with his own mouth, My Lady. Stilgar said he had done this. He said the Holy Consort provoked him to rage."

"Rage," Alia repeated. "How was that done?"

"He didn't say. No one said. I asked and no one said."

"And that's when you were sent to me with this news?"

"Yes, My Lady."

"Was there nothing you could do?"

Agarves wet his lips with his tongue, then: "Stilgar commanded, My Lady. It was his sietch."

"I see. And you always obeyed Stilgar."

"I always did, My Lady, until he freed me from my bond."

"When you were sent to my service, you mean?"

"I obey only you now, My Lady."

"Is that right? Tell me, Buer, if I commanded you to slay Stilgar, your old Naib, would you do it?"

He met her gaze with a growing firmness. "If you commanded it, My Lady."

"I do command it. Have you any idea where he's gone?"

"Into the desert; that's all I know, My Lady."

"How many men did he take?"

"Perhaps half the effectives."

"And Ghanima and Irulan with him!"

"Yes, My Lady. Those who left are burdened with their women, their children and their baggage. Stilgar gave everyone a choice—go with him or be freed of their bond. Many chose to be freed. They will select a new Naib."

"I'll select their new Naib! And it'll be you, Buer Agarves, on the day you bring me Stilgar's head."

Agarves could accept selection by battle. It was a Fremen way. He said: "As you command, My Lady. What forces may I—"

"See Zia. I can't give you many 'thopters for the search. They're needed elsewhere. But you'll have enough fighting men. Stilgar has defamed his honor. Many will serve with you gladly."

"I'll get about it, then, My Lady."

"Wait!" She studied him a moment, reviewing whom she could send to watch over this vulnerable infant. He would need close watching until he'd proved himself. Zia would know whom to send.

"Am I not dismissed, My Lady?"

"You are not dismissed. I must consult you privately and at length on your plans to take Stilgar." She put a hand to her face. "I'll not grieve until you've exacted my revenge. Give me a few minutes to compose myself." She lowered her hand. "One of my attendants will show you the way." She gave a subtle hand signal to one of her attendants, whispered to Shalus, her new Dame of Chamber: "Have him washed and perfumed before you bring him. He smells of worm."

"Yes, mistress."

Alia turned then, feigning the grief she did not feel, and fled to her private chambers. There, in her bedroom, she slammed the door into its tracks, cursed and stamped her foot.

Damn that Duncan! Why? Why? Why?

She sensed a deliberate provocation from Idaho. He'd slain Javid and provoked Stilgar. It said he knew about Javid. The whole thing must be taken as a message from Duncan Idaho, a final gesture.

Again she stamped her foot and again, raging across the bedchamber.

Damn him! Damn him! Damn him!

Stilgar gone over to the rebels and Ghanima with him. Irulan, too.

Damn them all!

Her stamping foot encountered a painful obstacle, descending onto metal. Pain brought a cry from her and she peered down, finding that she'd bruised her foot on a metal buckle. She snatched it up, stood frozen at the sight of it in her hand. It was an old buckle, one of the silver-and-platinum originals from Caladan awarded originally by the Duke Leto Atreides I to his swordmaster, Duncan Idaho. She'd seen Duncan wear it many times. And he'd discarded it here.

Alia's fingers clutched convulsively on the buckle. Idaho had left it here when . . . when . . .

Tears sprang from her eyes, forced out against the great Fremen conditioning. Her mouth drew down into a frozen grimace and she sensed the old battle begin within her skull, reaching out to her fingertips, to her toes. She felt that she had become two people. One looked upon these fleshly contortions with astonishment. The other sought submission to an enormous pain spreading in her chest. The tears flowed freely from her eyes now, and the Astonished One within her demanded querulously: "Who cries? Who is it that cries? Who is crying now?"

But nothing stopped the tears, and she felt the painfulness which flamed through her breast as it moved her flesh and hurled her onto the bed.

Still something demanded out of that profound astonishment: "Who cries? Who is that . . ."

By these acts Leto II removed himself from the evolutionary succession. He did it with a deliberate cutting action, saying: "To be independent is to be removed." Both twins saw beyond the needs of memory as a measuring process, that is, a way of determining their distance from their human origins. But it was left to Leto II to do the audacious thing, recognizing that a real creation is independent of its creator. He refused to reenact the evolutionary sequence, saying, "That, too, takes me farther and farther from humanity." He saw the implications in this: that there can be no truly closed systems in life.

—THE HOLY METAMORPHOSIS
BY HARQ AL-ADA

There were birds thriving on the insect life which teemed in the damp sand beyond the broken qanat: parrots, magpies, jays. This had been a djedida, the last of the new towns, built on a foundation of exposed basalt. It was abandoned now. Ghanima, using the morning hours to study the area beyond the original plantings of the abandoned sietch, detected movement and saw a banded gecko lizard. There'd been a gila woodpecker earlier, nesting in a mud wall of the djedida.

She thought of it as a sietch, but it was really a collection of low walls made of stabilized mud brick surrounded by plantings to hold back the dunes. It lay within the Tanzerouft, six hundred kilometers south of Sihaya Ridge. Without human hands to maintain it, the sietch already was beginning to melt back into the desert, its walls eroded by sandblast winds, its plants dying, its plantation area cracked by the burning sun.

Yet the sand beyond the shattered qanat remained damp, attesting to the fact that the squat bulk of the windtrap still functioned.

In the months since their flight from Tabr the fugitives had sampled the protection of several such places made uninhabitable by the Desert Demon. Ghanima didn't believe in the Desert Demon, although there was no denying the visible evidence of the qanat's destruction.

Occasionally they had word from the northern settlements through encounters with rebel spice-hunters. A few 'thopters—some said no more than six—carried out search flights seeking Stilgar, but Arrakis was large and its desert was friendly to the fugitives. Reportedly there was a search-and-destroy force charged with finding Stilgar's band, but the force which was led by the former Tabrite Buer Agarves had other duties and often returned to Arrakeen.

The rebels said there was little fighting between their men and the troops of Alia. Random depredations of the Desert Demon made Home Guard duty the first concern of Alia and the Naibs. Even the smugglers had been hit, but they were said to be scouring the desert for Stilgar, wanting the price on his head.

Stilgar had brought his band into the djedida just before dark the previous day, following the unerring moisture sense of his old Fremen nose. He'd promised they would head south for the palmyries soon, but refused to put a date on the move. Although he carried a price on his head which once would have bought a planet, Stilgar seemed the happiest and most carefree of men.

"This is a good place for us," he'd said, pointing out that the windtrap still functioned. "Our friends have left us some water."

They were a small band now, sixty people in all. The old, the sick, and the very young had been filtered south into the palmyries, absorbed there by trusted families. Only the toughest remained, and they had many friends to the north and the south.

Ghanima wondered why Stilgar refused to discuss what was happening to the planet. Couldn't he see it? As qanats were shattered, Fremen pulled back to the northern and southern lines which once had marked the extent of their holdings. This movement could only signal what must be happening to the Empire. One condition was the mirror of the other.

Ghanima ran a hand under the collar of her stillsuit and resealed it. Despite her worries she felt remarkably free here. The inner lives no longer plagued her, although she sometimes felt their memories inserted into her consciousness. She knew from those memories what this desert had been once, before the work of the ecological transformation. It had been drier, for one thing. That unrepaired windtrap still functioned because it processed moist air.

Many creatures which once had shunned this desert ventured to live here now. Many in the band remarked how the daylight owls proliferated. Even now, Ghanima could see antbirds. They jigged and danced along the insect lines which swarmed in the damp sand at the end of the shattered qanat. Few badgers were to be seen out here, but there were kangaroo mice in uncounted numbers.

Superstitious fear ruled the new Fremen, and Stilgar was no better than the rest. This djedida had been given back to the desert after its qanat had been shattered a fifth time in eleven months. Four times they'd repaired the ravages of the Desert Demon, then they'd no longer had the surplus water to risk another loss.

It was the same all through the djedidas and in many of the old sietches. Eight out of nine new settlements had been abandoned. Many of the old sietch communities were more crowded than they had ever been before. And while the desert entered this new phase, Fremen reverted to their old ways. They saw omens in everything. Were worms increasingly scarce except in the Tanzerouft? It was the judgment of Shai-Hulud! And dead worms had been seen with nothing to say why they died. They went back to desert dust swiftly after death, but those crumbling hulks which Fremen chanced upon filled the observers with terror.

Stilgar's band had encountered such a hulk the previous month and it had taken four days for them to shake off the feeling of evil. The thing had reeked of sour and poisonous putrefaction. Its moldering hulk had been found sitting on top of a giant spiceblow, the spice mostly ruined.

Ghanima turned from observing the qanat and looked back at the djedida. Directly in front of her lay a broken wall which once had protected a *mushtamal*, a small garden annex. She'd explored the place with a firm dependence upon her own curiosity and had found a store of flat, unleavened spicebread in a stone box.

Stilgar had destroyed it, saying: "Fremen would never leave good food behind them."

Ghanima had suspected he was mistaken, but it hadn't been worth the argument or the risk. Fremen were changing. Once they'd moved freely across the *bled*, drawn by natural needs: water, spice, trade. Animal activities had been their alarm clocks. But animals moved to strange new rhythms now while most Fremen huddled close in their old cave-warrens within the shadow of the northern Shield Wall. Spice-hunters in the Tanzerouft were rare, and only Stilgar's band moved in the old ways.

She trusted Stilgar and his fear of Alia. Irulan reinforced his arguments now, reverting to odd Bene Gesserit musings. But on faraway Salusa, Farad'n still lived. Someday there would have to be a reckoning.

Ghanima looked up at the grey-silver morning sky, questing in her mind. Where was help to be found? Where was there someone to listen when she revealed what she saw happening all around them? The Lady Jessica stayed on Salusa, if the reports were to be believed. And Alia was a creature on a pedestal, involved only in being colossal while she drifted farther and farther from reality. Gurney Halleck was nowhere to be found, although he was reported seen everywhere. The Preacher had gone into hiding, his heretical rantings only a fading memory.

And Stilgar.

She looked across the broken wall to where Stilgar was helping repair the cistern. Stilgar reveled in his role as the will-o'-the-desert, the price upon his head growing monthly.

Nothing made sense anymore. Nothing.

Who was this Desert Demon, this creature able to destroy qanats as though they were false idols to be toppled into the sand? Was it a rogue worm? Was it a third force in rebellion—many people? No one believed it was a worm. The water would kill any worm venturing against a qanat. Many Fremen believed the Desert Demon was actually a revolutionary band bent on overthrowing Alia's Mahdinate and restoring Arrakis to its old ways. Those who believed this said it would be a good thing. Get rid of that greedy apostolic succession which did little else than uphold its own mediocrity. Get back to the true religion which Muad'Dib had espoused.

A deep sigh shook Ghanima. *Oh, Leto,* she thought. *I'm almost glad you didn't live to see these days. I'd join you myself, but I've a knife yet unblooded. Alia and Farad'n. Farad'n and Alia. The Old Baron's her demon, and that can't be permitted.*

Harah came out of the djedida, approaching Ghanima with a steady sand-swallowing pace. Harah stopped in front of Ghanima, demanded, "What do you alone out here?"

"This is a strange place, Harah. We should leave."

"Stilgar waits to meet someone here."

"Oh? He didn't tell me that."

"Why should he tell you everything? *Maku?*" Harah slapped the water pouch which bulged the front of Ghanima's robe. "Are you a grown woman to be pregnant?"

"I've been pregnant so many times there's no counting them," Ghanima said. "Don't play those adult-child games with me!"

Harah took a backward step at the venom in Ghanima's voice.

"You're a band of stupids," Ghanima said, waving her hand to encompass the djedida and the activities of Stilgar and his people. "I should never have come with you."

"You'd be dead by now if you hadn't."

"Perhaps. But you don't see what's right in front of your faces! Who is it that Stilgar waits to meet here?"

"Buer Agarves."

Ghanima stared at her.

"He is being brought here secretly by friends from Red Chasm Sietch," Harah explained.

"Alia's little plaything?"

"He is being brought under blindfold."

"Does Stilgar believe that?"

"Buer asked for the parley. He agreed to all of our terms."

"Why wasn't I told about this?"

"Stilgar knew you would argue against it."

"Argue against . . . This is madness!"

Harah scowled. "Don't forget that Buer is . . ."

"He's *Family*!" Ghanima snapped. "He's the grandson of Stilgar's cousin. I know. And the Farad'n whose blood I'll draw one day is as close a relative to me. Do you think that'll stay my knife?"

"We've had a distrans. No one follows his party."

Ghanima spoke in a low voice: "Nothing good will come of this, Harah. We should leave at once."

"Have you read an omen?" Harah asked. "That dead worm we saw! Was that—"

"Stuff that into your womb and give birth to it elsewhere!" Ghanima raged. "I don't like this meeting nor this place. Isn't that enough?"

"I'll tell Stilgar what you—"

"I'll tell him myself!" Ghanima strode past Harah, who made the sign of the worm horns at her back to ward off evil.

But Stilgar only laughed at Ghanima's fears and ordered her to look for sandtrout as though she were one of the children. She fled into one of the djedida's abandoned houses and crouched in a corner to nurse her anger. The emotion passed quickly, though; she felt the stirring of the inner lives and remembered someone saying: "If we can immobilize them, things will go as we plan."

What an odd thought.

But she couldn't recall who'd said those words.

Muad'Dib was disinherited and he spoke for the disinherited of all time. He cried out against that profound injustice which alienates the individual from that which he was taught to believe, from that which seemed to come to him as a right.

—THE MAHDINATE, AN ANALYSIS
BY HARQ AL-ADA

Gurney Halleck sat on the butte at Shuloch with his baliset beside him on a spice-fiber rug. Below him the enclosed basin swarmed with workers planting crops. The sand ramp up which the Cast Out had lured worms on a spice trail had been blocked off with a new qanat. Plantings moved down the slope to hold it.

It was almost time for the noon meal and Halleck had been on the butte for more than an hour, seeking privacy in which to think. Humans did the labor below him, but everything he saw was the work of melange. Leto's personal estimate was that spice production would fall soon to a stabilized one-tenth of its peak in the Harkonnen years. Stockpiles throughout the empire doubled in value at every new posting. Three hundred and twenty-one liters were said to have bought half of Novebruns Planet from the Metulli Family.

The Cast Out worked like men driven by a devil, and perhaps they were. Before every meal, they faced the Tanzerouft and prayed to Shai-Hulud personified. That was how they saw Leto and, through their eyes, Halleck saw a future where most of humankind shared that view. Halleck wasn't sure he liked the prospect.

Leto had set the pattern when he'd brought Halleck and The Preacher here in Halleck's stolen 'thopter. With his bare hands Leto had breached the Shuloch qanat, hurling large stones more than fifty meters. When the Cast Out had tried to intervene, Leto had decapitated the first to reach him, using no more than a blurred sweep of his arm. He'd hurled others back into their companions and had laughed at their weapons. In a demon-voice he'd roared at them: "Fire will not touch me! Your knives will not harm me! I wear the skin of Shai-Hulud!"

The Cast Out had recognized him then and recalled his escape, leaping from the butte "directly to the desert." They'd prostrated themselves before him and Leto had issued his orders. "I bring you two guests. You will guard them and honor them. You will rebuild your qanat and begin planting an oasis garden. One day I'll make my home here. You will prepare my home. You will sell no more spice, but you will store every bit you collect."

On and on he'd gone with his instructions, and the Cast Out had heard every word, seeing him through fear-glazed eyes, through a terrifying awe.

Here was Shai-Hulud come up from the sand at last!

There'd been no intimation of this metamorphosis when Leto had found Halleck with Ghadhean al-Fali in one of the small rebel sietches at Gare Ruden. With his blind companion, Leto had come up from the desert along the old spice route, traveling by worm through an area where worms were now a rarity. He'd spoken of several detours forced upon him by the presence of moisture in the sand, enough water to poison a worm. They'd arrived shortly after noon and had been brought into the stone-walled common room by guards.

The memory haunted Halleck now.

"So this is The Preacher," he'd said.

Striding around the blind man, studying him, Halleck recalled the stories about him. No stillsuit mask hid the old face in sietch, and the features were there for memory to make its comparisons. Yes, the man did look like the old Duke for whom Leto had been named. Was it a chance likeness?

"You know the stories about this one?" Halleck asked, speaking in an aside to Leto. "That he's your father come back from the desert?"

"I've heard the stories."

Halleck turned to examine the boy. Leto wore an odd stillsuit with rolled edges around his face and ears. A black robe covered it and sandboots sheathed his feet. There was much to be explained about his presence here—how he'd managed to escape once more.

"Why do you bring The Preacher here?" Halleck asked. "In Jacurutu they said he works for them."

"No more. I bring him because Alia wants him dead."

"So? You think this is a sanctuary?"

"You are his sanctuary."

All this time The Preacher stood near them, listening but giving no sign that he cared which turn their discussion took.

"He has served me well, Gurney," Leto said. "House Atreides has not lost all sense of obligation to those who serve us."

"House Atreides?"

"I am House Atreides."

"You fled Jacurutu before I could complete the testing which your grandmother ordered," Halleck said, his voice cold. "How can you assume—"

"This man's life is to be guarded as though it were your own." Leto spoke as though there were no argument and he met Halleck's stare without flinching.

Jessica had trained Halleck in many of the Bene Gesserit refinements of observation and he'd detected nothing in Leto which spoke of other than calm assurance. Jessica's orders remained, though. "Your grandmother charged me to complete your education and be sure you're not possessed."

"I'm not possessed." Just a flat statement.

"Why did you run away?"

"Namri had orders to kill me no matter what I did. His orders were from Alia."

"Are you a Truthsayer, then?"

"I am." Another flat statement filled with self-assurance.

"And Ghanima as well?"

"No."

The Preacher broke his silence then, turning his blind sockets toward Halleck but pointing at Leto. "You think *you* can test him?"

"Don't interfere when you know nothing of the problem or its consequences," Halleck ordered, not looking at the man.

"Oh, I know its consequences well enough," The Preacher said. "I was tested once by an old woman who thought she knew what she was doing. She didn't know, as it turned out."

Halleck looked at him then. "You're another Truthsayer?"

"Anyone can be a Truthsayer, even you," The Preacher said. "It's a matter of self-honesty about the nature of your own feelings. It requires that you have an inner agreement with truth which allows ready recognition."

"Why do you interfere?" Halleck asked, putting hand to crysknife. Who was this Preacher?

"I'm responsive to these events," The Preacher said. "My mother could put her own blood upon the altar, but I have other motives. And I do see your problem."

"Oh?" Halleck was actually curious now.

"The Lady Jessica ordered you to differentiate between the wolf and the dog, between *ze'eb* and *ke'leb*. By her definition a wolf is someone with power who misuses that power. However, between wolf and dog there is a dawn period when you cannot distinguish between them."

"That's close to the mark," Halleck said, noting how more and more people of the sietch had entered the common room to listen. "How do you know this?"

"Because I know this planet. You don't understand? Think how it is. Beneath the surface there are rocks, dirt, sediment, sand. That's the planet's memory, the picture of its history. It's the same with humans. The dog remembers the wolf. Each universe revolves around a core of *being*, and outward from that core go all of the memories, right out to the surface."

"Very interesting," Halleck said. "How does that help me carry out my orders?"

"Review the picture of your history which is within you. Communicate as animals would communicate."

Halleck shook his head. There was a compelling directness about this Preacher, a quality which he'd recognized many times in the Atreides, and there was more than a little hint that the man was employing the powers of Voice. Halleck felt his heart begin to hammer. Was it possible?

"Jessica wanted an ultimate test, a stress by which the underlying fabric of her grandson exposed itself," The Preacher said. "But the fabric's always there, open to your gaze."

Halleck turned to stare at Leto. The movement came of itself, compelled by irresistible forces.

The Preacher continued as though lecturing an obstinate pupil. "This young person confuses you because he's not a singular being. He's a community. As with any community under stress, any member of that community may assume command. This command isn't always benign, and we get our stories of Abomination. But you've already wounded this community enough, Gurney Halleck. Can't you see that the transformation already has taken place? This youth has achieved an inner cooperation which is enormously powerful, that cannot be subverted. Without eyes I see this. Once I opposed him, but now I do his bidding. He is the Healer."

"Who are you?" Halleck demanded.

"I'm no more than what you see. Don't look at me, look at this person you were ordered to teach and test. He has been formed by crisis. He survived a lethal environment. He is here."

"Who are you?" Halleck insisted.

"I tell you only to look at this Atreides youth! He is the ultimate feedback upon which our species depends. He'll reinsert into the system the results of its past performance. No other human could know that past performance as he knows it. And you consider destroying such a one!"

"I was ordered to test him and I've not—"

"But you have!"

"Is he Abomination?"

A weary laugh shook The Preacher. "You persist in Bene Gesserit nonsense. How they create the myths by which men sleep!"

"Are you Paul Atreides?" Halleck asked.

"Paul Atreides is no more. He tried to stand as a supreme moral symbol while he renounced all moral pretensions. He became a saint without a god, every word a blasphemy. How can you think—"

"Because you speak with his voice."

"Would you test *me*, now? Beware, Gurney Halleck."

Halleck swallowed, forced his attention back to the impassive Leto who still stood calmly observant. "Who's being tested?" The Preacher asked. "Is it, perhaps, that the Lady Jessica tests you, Gurney Halleck?"

Halleck found this thought deeply disturbing, wondering why he let this Preacher's words move him. But it was a deep thing in Atreides servants to obey that autocratic mystique. Jessica, explaining this, had made it even more mysterious. Halleck now felt something changing within himself, a *something* whose edges had only been touched by the Bene Gesserit training Jessica had pressed upon him. Inarticulate fury arose in him. He did not want to change!

"Which of you plays God and to what end?" The Preacher asked. "You cannot rely on reason alone to answer that question."

Slowly, deliberately, Halleck raised his attention from Leto to the blind man. Jessica kept saying he should achieve the balance of *kairits*—"thou shalt-thou shalt not." She called it a discipline without words and phrases, no rules or arguments. It was the sharpened edge of his own internal truth, all-engrossing. Something in the blind man's voice, his tone, his manner, ignited a fury which burned itself into blinding calmness within Halleck.

"Answer my question," The Preacher said.

Halleck felt the words deepen his concentration upon this place, this one moment and its demands. His position in the universe was defined only by his concentration. No doubt remained in him. This was Paul

Atreides, not dead, but returned. And this non-child, Leto. Halleck looked once more at Leto, really saw him. He saw the signs of stress around the eyes, the sense of balance in the stance, the passive mouth with its quirking sense of humor. Leto stood out from his background as though at the focus of a blinding light. He had achieved harmony simply by accepting it.

"Tell me, Paul," Halleck said. "Does your mother know?"

The Preacher sighed. "To the Sisterhood, all achieved harmony simply by accepting it.

"Tell me, Paul," Halleck said. "Does your mother know?"

The Preacher sighed. "To the Sisterhood, all of it, I am dead. Do not try to revive me."

Still not looking at him, Halleck asked: "But why does she—"

"She does what she must. She makes her own life, thinking she rules many lives. Thus we all play god."

"But you're alive," Halleck whispered, overcome now by his realization, turning at last to stare at this man, younger than himself, but so aged by the desert that he appeared to carry twice Halleck's years.

"What is that?" Paul demanded. "Alive?"

Halleck peered around them at the watching Fremen, their faces caught between doubt and awe.

"My mother never had to learn my lesson." It was Paul's voice! "To be a god can ultimately become boring and degrading. There'd be reason enough for the invention of free will! A god might wish to escape into sleep and be alive only in the unconscious projections of his dream-creatures."

"But you're alive!" Halleck spoke louder now.

Paul ignored the excitement in his old companion's voice, asked: "Would you really have pitted this lad against his sister in the test-Mashhad? What deadly nonsense! Each would have said: 'No! Kill me! Let the other live!' Where would such a test lead? What is it then to be alive, Gurney?"

"That was not the test," Halleck protested. He did not like the way the Fremen pressed closer around them, studying Paul, ignoring Leto.

But Leto intruded now. "Look at the fabric, father."

"Yes . . . yes . . ." Paul held his head high as though sniffing the air. "It's Farad'n, then!"

"How easy it is to follow our thoughts instead of our senses," Leto said.

Halleck had been unable to follow this thought and, about to ask, was interrupted by Leto's hand upon his arm. "Don't ask, Gurney. You might return to suspecting that I'm Abomination. No! Let it happen, Gurney. If you try to force it, you'll only destroy yourself."

But Halleck felt himself overcome by doubts. Jessica had warned him. *"They can be very beguiling, these pre-born. They have tricks you've never even dreamed."* Halleck shook his head slowly. And Paul! Gods below! Paul alive and in league with this question mark he'd fathered!

The Fremen around them could no longer be held back. They pressed between Halleck and Paul, between Leto and Paul, shoving the two to the background. The air was showered with hoarse questions. "Are you Muab'Dib? Are you truly Muad'Dib? Is it true, what he says? Tell us!"

"You must think of me only as The Preacher," Paul said, pushing against them. "I cannot be Paul Atreides or Muad'Dib, never again. I'm not Chani's mate or Emperor."

Halleck, fearing what might happen if these frustrated questions found no logical answer, was about to act when Leto moved ahead of him. It was there Halleck first saw an element of the terrible change which had been wrought in Leto. A bull voice roared, "Stand aside!"— and Leto moved forward, thrusting adult Fremen right and left, knocking them down, clubbing them with his hands, wrenching knives from their hands by grasping the blades.

In less than a minute those Fremen still standing were pressed back against the walls in silent consternation. Leto stood beside his father. "When Shai-Hulud speaks, you obey," Leto said.

And when a few of the Fremen had started to argue, Leto had torn a corner of rock from the passage wall beside the room's exit and crumbled it in his bare hands, smiling all the while.

"I will tear your sietch down around your faces," he said.

"The Desert Demon," someone whispered.

"And your qanats," Leto agreed. "I will rip them apart. We have not been here, do you hear me?"

Heads shook from side to side in terrified submission.

"No one here has seen us," Leto said. "One whisper from you and I will return to drive you into the desert without water."

Halleck saw hands being raised in the warding gesture, the sign of the worm.

"We will go now, my father and I, accompanied by our old friend," Leto said. "Make our 'thopter ready."

And Leto had guided them to Shuloch then, explaining en route that they must move swiftly because "Farad'n will be here on Arrakis very soon. And, as my father has said, then you'll see the real test, Gurney."

Looking down from the Shuloch butte, Halleck asked himself once more, as he asked every day: "What test? What does he mean?"

But Leto was no longer in Shuloch, and Paul refused to answer.

Church and State, scientific reason and faith, the individual and his community, even progress and tradition—all of these can be reconciled in the teachings of Muad'Dib. He taught us that there exist no intransigent opposites except in the beliefs of men. Anyone can rip aside the veil of Time. You can discover the future in the past or in your own imagination. Doing this, you win back your consciousness in your inner being. You know then that the universe is a coherent whole and you are indivisible from it.

—THE PREACHER AT ARRAKEEN
AFTER HARQ AL-ADA

Ghanima sat far back outside the circle of light from the spice lamps and watched this Buer Agarves. She didn't like his round face and agitated eyebrows, his way of moving his feet when he spoke, as though his words were a hidden music to which he danced.

He's not here to parley with Stil, Ghanima told herself, seeing this confirmed in every word and movement from this man. She moved farther back away from the Council circle.

Every sietch had a room such as this one, but the meeting hall of the abandoned djedida struck Ghanima as a cramped place because it was so low. Sixty people from Stilgar's band plus the nine who'd come with Agarves filled only one end of the hall. Spice-oil lamps reflected against low beams which supported the ceiling. The light cast wavering shadows which danced on the walls, and the pungent smoke filled the place with the smell of cinnamon.

The meeting had started at dusk after the moisture prayers and evening meal. It had been going on for more than an hour now, and Ghanima couldn't fathom the hidden currents in Agarves's performance. His words appeared clear enough, but his motions and eye movements didn't agree.

Agarves was speaking now, responding to a question from one of Stilgar's lieutenants, a niece of Harah's named Rajia. She was a darkly ascetic young woman whose mouth turned down at the corners, giving her an air of perpetual distrust. Ghanima found the expression satisfying in the circumstances.

"Certainly I believe Alia will grant a full and complete pardon to all of you," Agarves said. "I'd not be here with this message otherwise."

Stilgar intervened as Rajia made to speak once more. "I'm not so much worried about our trusting her as I am about whether she trusts you." Stilgar's voice carried growling undertones. He was uncomfortable with this suggestion that he return to his old status.

"It doesn't matter whether she trusts me," Agarves said. "To be candid about it, I don't believe she does. I've been too long searching for you without finding you. But I've always felt she didn't really want you captured. She was—"

"She was the wife of the man I slew," Stilgar said. "I grant you that he asked for it. Might just as well've fallen on his own knife. But this new attitude smells of—"

Agarves danced to his feet, anger plain on his face. "She forgives you! How many times must I say it? She had the Priests make a great show of asking divine guidance from—"

"You've only raised another issue." It was Irulan, leaning forward past Rajia, blonde head set off against Rajia's darkness. "She has convinced you, but she may have other plans."

"The Priesthood has—"

"But there are all of these stories," Irulan said. "That you're more than just a military advisor, that you're her—"

"Enough!" Agarves was beside himself with rage. His hand hovered near his knife. Warring emotions moved just below the surface of his skin, twisting his features. "Believe what you will, but I cannot go on with that woman! She fouls me! She dirties everything she touches! I am used. I am soiled. But I have not lifted my knife against my kin. Now—no more!"

Ghanima, observing this, thought: *That, at least, was truth coming out of him.*

Surprisingly, Stilgar broke into laughter. "Ahhhh, cousin," he said. "Forgive me, but there's truth in anger."

"Then you agree?"

"I've not said that." He raised a hand as Agarves threatened another outburst. "It's not for my sake, Buer, but there are these others." He gestured around him. "They are my responsibility. Let us consider for a moment what reparations Alia offers."

"Reparations? There's no word of reparations. Pardon, but no—"

"Then what does she offer as surety of her word?"

"Sietch Tabr and you as Naib, full autonomy as a neutral. She understands now how—"

"I'll not go back to her entourage or provide her with fighting men," Stilgar warned. "Is that understood?"

Ghanima could hear Stilgar beginning to weaken and thought: *No, Stil! No!*

"No need for that," Agarves said. "Alia wants only Ghanima returned to her and the carrying out of the betrothal promise which she—"

"So now it comes out!" Stilgar said, his brows drawing down. "Ghanima's the price of my pardon. Does she think me—"

"She thinks you sensible," Agarves argued, resuming his seat.

Gleefully, Ghanima thought: *He won't do it. Save your breath. He won't do it.*

As she thought this, Ghanima heard a soft rustling behind and to her left. She started to turn, felt powerful hands grab her. A heavy rag reeking of sleep-drugs covered her face before she could cry out. As consciousness faded, she felt herself being carried toward a door in the hall's darkest reaches. And she thought: *I should have guessed! I should've been prepared!* But the hands that held her were adult and strong. She could not squirm away from them.

Ghanima's last sensory impressions were of cold air, a glimpse of stars, and a hooded face which looked down at her, then asked: "She wasn't injured, was she?"

The answer was lost as the stars wheeled and streaked across her gaze, losing themselves in a blaze of light which was the inner core of her selfdom.

Muad'Dib gave us a particular kind of knowledge about prophetic insight, about the behavior which surrounds such insight and its influence upon events which are seen to be "on line." (That is, events which are set to occur in a related system which the prophet reveals and interprets.) As has been noted elsewhere, such insight operates as a peculiar trap for the prophet himself. He can become the victim of what he knows—which is a relatively common human failing. The danger is that those who predict real events may overlook the polarizing effect brought about by overindulgence in their own truth. They tend to forget that nothing in a polarized universe can exist without its opposite being present.

—THE PRESCIENT VISION
BY HARQ AL-ADA

Blowing sand hung like fog on the horizon, obscuring the rising sun. The sand was cold in the dune shadows. Leto stood outside the ring of the palmyrie looking into the desert. He smelled dust and the aroma of spiny plants, heard the morning sounds of people and animals. The Fremen maintained no qanat in this place. They had only a bare minimum of hand planting irrigated by the women, who carried water in skin bags. Their windtrap was a fragile thing, easily destroyed by the stormwinds but easily rebuilt. Hardship, the rigors of the spice trade, and adventure were a way of life here. These Fremen still believed heaven was the sound of running water, but they cherished an ancient concept of Freedom which Leto shared.

Freedom is a lonely state, he thought.

Leto adjusted the folds of the white robe which covered his living stillsuit. He could feel how the sandtrout membrane had changed him and, as always with this feeling, he was forced to overcome a deep sense of loss. He no longer was completely human. Odd things swam in his blood. Sandtrout cilia had penetrated every organ, adjusting, changing. The sandtrout itself was changing, adapting. But Leto, knowing this, felt himself torn by the old threads of his lost humanity, his life caught in primal anguish with its ancient continuity shattered. He knew the trap of indulging in such emotion, though. He knew it well.

Let the future happen of itself, he thought. *The only rule governing creativity is the act of creation itself.*

It was difficult to take his gaze away from the sands, the dunes—the great emptiness. Here at the edge of the sand lay a few rocks, but they led the imagination outward into the winds, the dust, the sparse and lonely plants and animals, dune merging into dune, desert into desert.

Behind him came the sound of a flute playing for the morning prayer, the chant for moisture which now was a subtly altered serenade to the new Shai-Hulud. This knowledge in Leto's mind gave the music a sense of eternal loneliness.

I could just walk away into that desert, he thought.

Everything would change then. One direction would be as good as another. He had already learned to live a life free of possessions. He had refined the Fremen mystique to a terrible edge: everything he took with him was necessary, and that was all he took. But he carried nothing except the robe on his back, the Atreides hawk ring hidden in its folds, and the skin-which-was-not-his-own.

It would be easy to walk away from here.

Movement high in the sky caught his attention: the splayed-gap wingtips identified a vulture. The sight filled his chest with aching. Like the wild Fremen, vultures lived in this land because this was where they were born. They knew nothing better. The desert made them what they were.

Another Fremen breed was coming up in the wake of Muad'Dib and Alia, though. They were the reason he could not let himself walk away

into the desert as his father had done. Leto recalled Idaho's words from
the early days: "These Fremen! They're magnificently alive. I've never
met a greedy Fremen."

There were plenty of greedy Fremen now.

A wave of sadness passed over Leto. He was committed to a course
which could change all of that, but at a terrible price. And the management of that course became increasingly difficult as they neared the
vortex.

Kralizec, the Typhoon Struggle, lay ahead . . . but Kralizec or worse
would be the price of a misstep.

Voices sounded behind Leto, then the clear piping sound of a child
speaking: "Here he is."

Leto turned.

The Preacher had come out of the palmyrie, led by a child.

Why do I still think of him as The Preacher? Leto wondered.

The answer lay there on the clean tablet of Leto's mind: *Because this
is no longer Muad'Dib, no longer Paul Atreides.* The desert had made
him what he was. The desert and the jackals of Jacurutu with their over-
doses of melange and their constant betrayals. The Preacher was old
before his time, old not despite the spice but because of it.

"They said you wanted to see me now," The Preacher said, speaking
as his child guide stopped.

Leto looked at the child of the palmyrie, a person almost as tall as
himself, with awe tempered by an avaricious curiosity. The young eyes
glinted darkly above the child-sized stillsuit mask.

Leto waved a hand. "Leave us."

For a moment there was rebellion in the child's shoulders, then the
awe and native Fremen respect for privacy took over. The child left them.

"You know Farad'n is here on Arrakis?" Leto asked.

"Gurney told me when he flew me down last night."

And The Preacher thought: *How coldly measured his words are. He's
like I was in the old days.*

"I face a difficult choice," Leto said.

"I thought you'd already made all the choices."

"We know *that* trap, father."

The Preacher cleared his throat. The tensions told him how near they were to the shattering crisis. Now Leto would not be relying on pure vision, but on vision management.

"You need my help?" The Preacher asked.

"Yes. I'm returning to Arrakeen and I wish to go as your guide."

"To what end?"

"Would you preach once more in Arrakeen?"

"Perhaps. There are things I've not said to them."

"You will not come back to the desert, father."

"If I go with you?"

"Yes."

"I'll do whatever you decide."

"Have you considered? With Farad'n there, your mother will be with him."

"Undoubtedly."

Once more, The Preacher cleared his throat. It was a betrayal of nervousness which Muad'Dib would never have permitted. This flesh had been too long away from the old regimen of self-discipline, his mind too often betrayed into madness by the Jacurutu. And The Preacher thought that perhaps it wouldn't be wise to return to Arrakeen.

"You don't have to go back there with me," Leto said. "But my sister is there and I must return. You could go with Gurney."

"And you'd go to Arrakeen alone?"

"Yes. I must meet Farad'n."

"I will go with you," The Preacher sighed.

And Leto sensed a touch of the old vision madness in The Preacher's manner, wondered: *Has he been playing the prescience game?* No. He'd never go that way again. He knew the trap of a partial commitment. The Preacher's every word confirmed that he had handed over the visions to his son, knowing that everything in this universe had been anticipated.

It was the old polarities which taunted The Preacher now. He had fled from paradox into paradox.

"We'll be leaving in a few minutes, then," Leto said. "Will you tell Gurney?"

"Gurney's not going with us?"

"I want Gurney to survive."

The Preacher opened himself to the tensions then. They were in the air around him, in the ground under his feet, a motile thing which focused onto the non-child who was his son. The blunt scream of his old visions waited in The Preacher's throat.

This cursed holiness!

The sandy juice of his fears could not be avoided. He knew what faced them in Arrakeen. They would play a game once more with terrifying and deadly forces which could never bring them peace.

The child who refuses to travel in the father's harness, this is the symbol of man's most unique capability. "I do not have to be what my father was. I do not have to obey my father's rules or even believe everything he believed. It is my strength as a human that I can make my own choices of what to believe and what not to believe, of what to be and what not to be."

—LETO ATREIDES II
THE HARQ AL-ADA BIOGRAPHY

Pilgrim women were dancing to drum and flute in the Temple plaza, no coverings on their heads, bangles at their necks, their dresses thin and revealing. Their long black hair was thrown straight out, then straggled across their faces as they whirled.

Alia looked down at the scene from her Temple aerie, both attracted and repelled. It was mid-morning, the hour when the aroma of spice-coffee began to waft across the plaza from the vendors beneath the shaded arches. Soon she would have to go out and greet Farad'n, present the formal gifts and supervise his first meeting with Ghanima.

It was all working out according to plan. Ghani would kill him and, in the shattering aftermath, only one person would be prepared to pick up the pieces. The puppets danced when the strings were pulled. Stilgar had killed Agarves just as she'd hoped. And Agarves had led the kidnappers to the djedida without knowing it, a secret signal transmitter hidden in the new boots she'd given him. Now Stilgar and Irulan waited in the Temple dungeons. Perhaps they would die, but there might be other uses for them. There was no harm in waiting.

She noted that two Fremen were watching the pilgrim dancers below her, their eyes intense and unwavering. A basic sexual equality had come out of the desert to persist in Fremen town and city, but social differences between male and female already were making themselves felt. That, too, went according to plan. Divide and weaken. Alia could sense the subtle change in the way the two Fremen watched those off-planet women and their exotic dance.

Let them watch. Let them fill their minds with ghafla.

The louvers of Alia's window had been opened and she could feel a sharp increase in the heat which began about sunrise in this season and would peak in mid-afternoon. The temperature on the stone floor of the plaza would be much higher. It would be uncomfortable for those dancers, but still they whirled and bent, swung their arms and their hair in the frenzy of their dedication. They had dedicated their dance to Alia, the Womb of Heaven. An aide had come to whisper this to Alia, sneering at the off-world women and their peculiar ways. The aide had explained that the women were from Ix, where remnants of the forbidden science and technology remained.

Alia sniffed. Those women were as ignorant, as superstitious and backward as the desert Fremen . . . just as that sneering aide had said, trying to curry favor by reporting the dedication of the dance. And neither the aide nor the Ixians even knew that Ix was merely a number in a forgotten language.

Laughing lightly to herself, Alia thought: *Let them dance.* The dancing wasted energy which might be put to more destructive uses. And the music was pleasant, a thin wailing played against flat tympani from gourd drums and clapped hands.

Abruptly the music was drowned beneath a roaring of many voices from the plaza's far side. The dancers missed a step, recovered in a brief confusion, but they had lost their sensuous singleness, and even their attention wandered to the far gate of the plaza, where a mob could be seen spreading onto the stones like water rushing through the opened valve of a qanat.

Alia stared at that oncoming wave.

She heard words now, and one above all others: "Preacher! Preacher!"

Then she saw him, striding with the first spread of the wave, one hand on the shoulder of his young guide.

The pilgrim dancers gave up their whirling, retired to the terraced steps below Alia. They were joined by their audience, and Alia sensed awe in the watchers. Her own emotion was fear.

How dare he!

She half turned to summon guards, but second thoughts stopped her. The mob already filled the plaza. They could turn ugly if thwarted in their obvious desire to hear the blind visionary.

Alia clenched her fists.

The Preacher! Why was Paul doing this? To half the population he was a "desert madman" and, therefore, sacred. Others whispered in the bazaars and shops that it must be Muad'Dib. Why else did the Mahdinate let him speak such angry heresy?

Alia could see refugees among the mob, remnants from the abandoned sietches, their robes in tatters. That would be a dangerous place down there, a place where mistakes could be made.

"Mistress?"

The voice came from behind Alia. She turned, saw Zia standing in the arched doorway to the outer chamber. Armed House Guards were close behind her.

"Yes, Zia?"

"My Lady, Farad'n is out here requesting audience."

"Here? In my chambers?"

"Yes, My Lady."

"Is he alone?"

"Two bodyguards and the Lady Jessica."

Alia put a hand to her throat, remembering her last encounter with her mother. Times had changed, though. New conditions ruled their relationship.

"How impetuous he is," Alia said. "What reason does he give?"

"He has heard about . . ." Zia pointed to the window over the plaza. "He says he was told you have the best vantage."

Alia frowned. "Do you believe this, Zia?"

"No, My Lady. I think he has heard the rumors. He wants to watch your reaction."

"My mother put him up to this!"

"Quite possibly, My Lady."

"Zia, my dear, I want you to carry out a specific set of very important orders for me. Come here."

Zia approached to within a pace. "My Lady?"

"Have Farad'n, his guards, *and* my mother admitted. Then prepare to bring Ghanima. She is to be accoutered as a Fremen bride in every detail—*complete*."

"With knife, My Lady?"

"With knife."

"My Lady, that's—"

"Ghanima poses no threat to me."

"My Lady, there's reason to believe she fled with Stilgar more to protect him than for any other—"

"Zia!"

"My Lady?"

"Ghanima already has made her plea for Stilgar's life and Stilgar remains alive."

"But she's the heir presumptive!"

"Just carry out my orders. Have Ghanima prepared. While you're seeing to that, send five attendants from the Temple Priesthood out into the plaza. They're to invite The Preacher up here. Have them wait their opportunity and speak to him, nothing more. They are to use no force. I want them to issue a polite invitation. Absolutely no force. And Zia . . ."

"My Lady?" How sullen she sounded.

"The Preacher and Ghanima are to be brought before me simultaneously. They are to enter together upon my signal. Do you understand?"

"I know the plan, My Lady, but—"

"Just do it! Together." And Alia nodded dismissal to the amazon aide. As Zia turned and left, Alia said: "On your way out, send in

Farad'n's party, but see that they're preceded by ten of your most trust-worthy people."

Zia glanced back but continued leaving the room. "It will be done as you command, My Lady."

Alia turned away to peer out the window. In just a few minutes the *plan* would bear its bloody fruit. And Paul would be here when his daughter delivered the *coup de grâce* to his holy pretensions. Alia heard Zia's guard detachment entering. It would be over soon. All over. She looked down with a swelling sense of triumph as The Preacher took his stance on the first step. His youthful guide squatted beside him. Alia saw the yellow robes of Temple Priests waiting on the left, held back by the press of the crowd. They were experienced with crowds, however. They'd find a way to approach their target. The Preacher's voice boomed out over the plaza, and the mob waited upon his words with rapt atten-tion. Let them listen! Soon his words would be made to mean things other than he intended. And there'd be no *Preacher* around to protest.

She heard Farad'n's party enter, Jessica's voice. "Alia?"

Without turning Alia said: "Welcome, Prince Farad'n, mother. Come and enjoy the show." She glanced back then, saw the big Sardau-kar, Tyekanik, scowling at her guards who were blocking the way. "But this isn't hospitable," Alia said. "Let them approach." Two of her guards, obviously acting on Zia's orders, came up to her and stood between her and the others. The other guards moved aside. Alia backed to the right side of the window, motioned to it. "This is truly the best vantage point."

Jessica, wearing her traditional black aba robe, glared at Alia, es-corted Farad'n to the window, but stood between him and Alia's guards.

"This is very kind of you, Lady Alia," Farad'n said. "I've heard so much about this Preacher."

"And there he is in the flesh," Alia said. She saw that Farad'n wore the dress grey of a Sardaukar commander without decorations. He moved with a lean grace which Alia admired. Perhaps there would be more than idle amusement in this Corrino Prince.

The Preacher's voice boomed into the room over the amplifier pickups beside the window. Alia felt the tremors of it in her bones, began to listen to his words with growing fascination.

"I found myself in the Desert of Zan," The Preacher shouted, "in that waste of howling wilderness. And God commanded me to make that place clean. For we were provoked in the desert, and grieved in the desert, and we were tempted in that wilderness to forsake our ways."

Desert of Zan, Alia thought. That was the name given to the place of the first trial of the Zensunni Wanderers from whom the Fremen sprang. But his words! Was he taking credit for the destruction wrought against the sietch strongholds of the loyal tribes?

"Wild beasts lie upon your lands," The Preacher said, his voice booming across the plaza. "Doleful creatures fill your houses. You who fled your homes no longer multiply your days upon the sand. Yea, you who have forsaken our ways, you will die in a fouled nest if you continue on this path. But if you heed my warning, the Lord shall lead you through a land of pits into the Mountains of God. Yea, Shai-Hulud shall lead you."

Soft moans arose from the crowd. The Preacher paused, swinging his eyeless sockets from side to side at the sound. Then he raised his arms, spreading them wide, called out: "O God, my flesh longeth for Thy way in a dry and thirsty land!"

An old woman in front of The Preacher, an obvious refugee by the patched and worn look of her garments, held up her hands to him, pleaded: "Help us, Muad'Dib. Help us!"

In a sudden fearful constriction of her breast, Alia asked herself if that old woman really knew the truth. Alia glanced at her mother, but Jessica remained unmoving, dividing her attention between Alia's guards, Farad'n and the view from the window. Farad'n stood rooted in fascinated attention.

Alia glanced out the window, trying to see her Temple Priests. They were not in view and she suspected they had worked their way around below her near the Temple doors, seeking a direct route down the steps.

The Preacher pointed his right hand over the old woman's head, shouted: "You are the only help remaining! You were rebellious. You brought the dry wind which does not cleanse, nor does it cool. You bear the burden of our desert, and the whirlwind cometh from that place, from that terrible land. I have been in that wilderness. Water runs upon the sand from shattered qanats. Streams cross the ground. Water has fallen from the sky in the Belt of Dune! O my friends, God has commanded me. Make straight in the desert a highway for our Lord, for I am the voice that cometh to thee from the wilderness."

He pointed to the steps beneath his feet, a stiff and quivering finger. "This is no lost djedida which is no more inhabited forever! Here have we eaten the bread of heaven. And here the noise of strangers drives us from our homes! They breed for us a desolation, a land wherein no man dwelleth, nor any man pass thereby."

The crowd stirred uncomfortably, refugees and town Fremen peering about, looking at the pilgrims of the Hajj who stood among them.

He could start a bloody riot! Alia thought. *Well, let him. My Priests can grab him in the confusion.*

She saw the five Priests then, a tight knot of yellow robes working down the steps behind The Preacher.

"The waters which we spread upon the desert have become blood," The Preacher said, waving his arms wide. "Blood upon our land! Behold our desert which could rejoice and blossom; it has lured the stranger and seduced him in our midst. They come for violence! Their faces are closed up as for the last wind of Kralizec! They gather the captivity of the sand. They suck up the abundance of the sand, the treasure hidden in the depths. Behold them as they go forth to their evil work. It is written: 'And I stood upon the sand, and I saw a beast rise up out of that sand, and upon the head of that beast was the name of God!'"

Angry mutterings arose from the crowd. Fists were raised, shaken.

"What is he doing?" Farad'n whispered.

"I wish I knew," Alia said. She put a hand to her breast, feeling the fearful excitement of this moment. The crowd would turn upon the pilgrims if he kept this up!

But The Preacher half turned, aimed his dead sockets toward the Temple and raised a hand to point at the high windows of Alia's aerie.

"One blasphemy remains!" he screamed. "Blasphemy! And the name of that blasphemy is Alia!"

Shocked silence gripped the plaza.

Alia stood in unmoving consternation. She knew the mob could not see her, but she felt overcome by a sense of exposure, of vulnerability. The echoes of calming words within her skull competed with the pounding of her heart. She could only stare down at that incredible tableau. The Preacher remained with a hand pointing at her windows.

His words had been too much for the Priests, though. They broke the silence with angry shouts, stormed down the steps, thrusting people aside. As they moved the crowd reacted, breaking like a wave upon the steps, sweeping over the first lines of onlookers, carrying The Preacher before them. He stumbled blindly, separated from his young guide. Then a yellow-clad arm arose from the press of people; a crysknife was brandished in its hand. She saw the knife strike downward, bury itself in The Preacher's chest.

The thunderous clang of the Temple's giant doors being closed broke Alia from her shock. Guards obviously had closed the doors against the mob. But people already were drawing back, making an open space around a crumpled figure on the steps. An eerie quiet fell over the plaza. Alia saw many bodies, but only this one lay by itself.

Then a voice screeched from the mob: "Muad'Dib! They've killed Muad'Dib!"

"Gods below," Alia quavered. "Gods below."

"A little late for that, don't you think?" Jessica asked.

Alia whirled, noting the sudden startled reaction of Farad'n as he saw the rage on her face. "That was Paul they killed!" Alia screamed. "That was your son! When they confirm it, do you know what'll happen?"

Jessica stood rooted for a long moment, thinking that she had just been told something already known to her. Farad'n's hand upon her arm shattered the moment. "My Lady," he said, and there was such compassion in his voice that Jessica thought she might die of it right there. She looked from the cold, glaring anger on Alia's face to the sympathetic misery on Farad'n's features, and thought: *Perhaps I did my job too well.*

There could be no doubting Alia's words. Jessica remembered every intonation of The Preacher's voice, hearing her own tricks in it, the long years of instruction she'd spent there upon a young man meant to be Emperor, but who now lay a shattered mound of bloody rags upon the Temple steps.

Ghafla blinded me, Jessica thought.

Alia gestured to one of her aides, called: "Bring Ghanima now."

Jessica forced herself into recognizing these words. *Ghanima? Why Ghanima now?*

The aide had turned toward the outer door, motioning for it to be unbarred, but before a word could be uttered the door bulged. Hinges popped. The bar snapped and the door, a thick plasteel construction meant to withstand terrible energies, toppled into the room. Guards leaped to avoid it, drawing their weapons.

Jessica and Farad'n's bodyguards closed in around the Corrino Prince.

But the opening revealed only two children: Ghanima on the left, clad in her black betrothal robe, and Leto on the right, the grey slickness of a stillsuit beneath a desert-stained white robe.

Alia stared from the fallen door to the children, found she was trembling uncontrollably.

"The family here to greet us," Leto said. "Grandmother." He nodded to Jessica, shifted his attention to the Corrino Prince. "And this must be Prince Farad'n. Welcome to Arrakis, Prince."

Ghanima's eyes appeared empty. She held her right hand on a ceremonial cryskvife at her waist, and she appeared to be trying to escape from Leto's grip on her arm. Leto shook her arm and her whole body shook with it.

"Behold me, family," Leto said. "I am Ari, the Lion of the Atreides. And here—" Again he shook Ghanima's arm with that powerful ease which set her whole body jerking. "—here is Aryeh, the Atreides Lioness. We come to set you onto Secher Nbiw, the Golden Path."

Ghanima, absorbing the trigger words, *Secher Nbiw*, felt the locked-away consciousness flow into her mind. It flowed with a linear nicety, the inner awareness of her mother hovering there behind it, a guardian at a gate. And Ghanima knew in that instant that she had conquered the clamorous past. She possessed a gate through which she could peer when she needed that past. The months of self-hypnotic suppression had built for her a safe place from which to manage her own flesh. She started to turn toward Leto with the need to explain this when she became aware of where she stood and with whom.

Leto released her arm.

"Did our plan work?" Ghanima whispered.

"Well enough," Leto said.

Recovering from her shock, Alia shouted at a clump of guards on her left: "Seize them!"

But Leto bent, took the fallen door with one hand, skidded it across the room into the guards. Two were pinned against the wall. The others fell back in terror. That door weighed half a metric ton and this child had thrown it.

Alia, growing aware that the corridor beyond the doorway contained fallen guards, realized that Leto must have dealt with them, that this child had shattered her impregnable door.

Jessica, too, had seen the bodies, seen the awesome power in Leto and had made similar assumptions, but Ghanima's words touched a core of Bene Gesserit discipline which forced Jessica to maintain her composure. This grandchild spoke of a plan.

"What plan?" Jessica asked.

"The Golden Path, our Imperial plan for our Imperium," Leto said. He nodded to Farad'n. "Don't think harshly of me, cousin. I act for you as well. Alia hoped to have Ghanima slay you. I'd rather you lived out your life in some degree of happiness."

Alia screamed at her guards cowering in the passage: "I command you to seize them!"

But the guards refused to enter the room.

"Wait for me here, sister," Leto said. "I have a disagreeable task to perform." He moved across the room toward Alia.

She backed away from him into a corner, crouched and drew her knife. The green jewels of its handle flashed in the light from the window.

Leto merely continued his advance, hands empty, but spread and ready.

Alia lunged with the knife.

Leto leaped almost to the ceiling, struck with his left foot. It caught Alia's head a glancing blow and sent her sprawling with a bloody mark on her forehead. She lost her grip on the knife and it skidded across the floor. Alia scrambled after the knife, but found Leto standing in front of her.

Alia hesitated, called up everything she knew of Bene Gesserit training. She came off the floor, body loose and poised.

Once more Leto advanced upon her.

Alia feinted to the left but her right shoulder came up and her right foot shot out in a toe-pointing kick which could disembowel a man if it struck precisely.

Leto caught the blow on his arm, grabbed the foot, and picked her up by it, swinging her around his head. The speed with which he swung her sent a flapping, hissing sound through the room as her robe beat against her body.

The others ducked away.

Alia screamed and screamed, but still she continued to swing around and around and around. Presently she fell silent.

Slowly Leto reduced the speed of her whirling, dropped her gently to the floor. She lay in a panting bundle.

Leto bent over her. "I could've thrown you through a wall," he said. "Perhaps that would've been best, but we're now at the center of the struggle. You deserve your chance."

Alia's eyes darted wildly from side to side.

"I have conquered those inner lives," Leto said. "Look at Ghani. She, too, can—"

Ghanima interrupted: "Alia, I can show you—"

"No!" The word was wrenched from Alia. Her chest heaved and voices began to pour from her mouth. They were disconnected, cursing, pleading. "You see! Why didn't you listen?" And again: "Why're you doing this? What's happening?" And another voice: "Stop them! Make them stop!"

Jessica covered her eyes, felt Farad'n's hand steady her.

Still Alia raved: "I'll kill you!" Hideous curses erupted from her. "I'll drink your blood!" The sounds of many languages began to pour from her, all jumbled and confused.

The huddled guards in the outer passage made the sign of the worm, then held clenched fists beside their ears. She was possessed!

Leto stood, shaking his head. He stepped to the window and with three swift blows shattered the supposedly unbreakable crystal-reinforced glass from its frame.

A sly look came over Alia's face. Jessica heard something like her own voice come from that twisting mouth, a parody of Bene Gesserit control. "All of you! Stay where you are!"

Jessica, lowering her hands, found them damp with tears.

Alia rolled to her knees, lurched to her feet.

"Don't you know who I am?" she demanded. It was her old voice, the sweet and lilting voice of the youthful Alia who was no more. "Why're you all looking at me that way?" She turned pleading eyes to Jessica. "Mother, make them stop it."

Jessica could only shake her head from side to side, consumed by ultimate horror. All of the old Bene Gesserit warnings were true. She looked at Leto and Ghani standing side by side near Alia. What did those warnings mean for these poor twins?

"Grandmother," Leto said, and there was pleading in his voice. "Must we have a Trial of Possession?"

"Who are you to speak of trial?" Alia asked, and her voice was that of a querulous man, an autocratic and sensual man far gone in self-indulgence.

Both Leto and Ghanima recognized the voice. The Old Baron Harkonnen. Ghanima heard the same voice begin to echo in her own head, but the inner gate closed and she sensed her mother standing there.

Jessica remained silent.

"Then the decision is mine," Leto said. "And the choice is yours, Alia. Trial of Possession, or . . ." He nodded toward the open window.

"Who're you to give me a choice?" Alia demanded, and it was still the voice of the Old Baron.

"Demon!" Ghanima screamed. "Let her make her own choice!"

"Mother," Alia pleaded in her little-girl tones. "Mother, what're they doing? What do you want me to do? Help me."

"Help yourself," Leto ordered and, for just an instant, he saw the shattered presence of his aunt in her eyes, a glaring hopelessness which peered out at him and was gone. But her body moved, a sticklike, thrusting walk. She wavered, stumbled, veered from her path but returned to it, nearer and nearer the open window.

Now the voice of the Old Baron raged from her lips: "Stop! Stop it, I say! I command you! Stop it! Feel this!" Alia clutched her head, stumbled closer to the window. She had the sill against her thighs then, but the voice still raved. "Don't do this! Stop it and I'll help you. I have a plan. Listen to me. Stop it, I say. Wait!" But Alia pulled her hands away from her head, clutched the broken casement. In one jerking motion, she pulled herself over the sill and was gone. Not even a screech came from her as she fell.

In the room they heard the crowd shout, the sodden thump as Alia struck the steps far below.

Leto looked at Jessica. "We told you to pity her."

Jessica turned and buried her face in Farad'n's tunic.

The assumption that a whole system can be made to work better through an assault on its conscious elements betrays a dangerous ignorance. This has often been the ignorant approach of those who call themselves scientists and technologists.

—THE BUTLERIAN JIHAD
BY HARQ AL-ADA

"He runs at night, cousin," Ghanima said. "He runs. Have you seen him run?"

"No," Farad'n said.

He waited with Ghanima outside the small audience hall of the Keep where Leto had called them to attend. Tyekanik stood at one side, uncomfortable with the Lady Jessica, who appeared withdrawn, as though her mind lived in another place. It was hardly an hour past the morning meal, but already many things had been set moving—a summons to the Guild, messages to CHOAM and the Landsraad.

Farad'n found it difficult to understand these Atreides. The Lady Jessica had warned him, but still the reality of them puzzled him. They still talked of the betrothal, although most political reasons for it seemed to have dissolved. Leto would assume the throne; there appeared little doubt of that. His odd *living skin* would have to be removed, of course . . . but, in time . . .

"He runs to tire himself," Ghanima said. "He's Kralizec embodied. No wind ever ran as he runs. He's a blur atop the dunes. I've seen him. He runs and runs. And when he has exhausted himself at last, he returns and rests his head in my lap. 'Ask our mother within to find a way for me to die,' he pleads."

Farad'n stared at her. In the week since the riot in the plaza, the Keep had moved to strange rhythms, mysterious comings and goings; stories of bitter fighting beyond the Shield Wall came to him through Tyekanik, whose military advice had been asked.

"I don't understand you," Farad'n said. "Find a way for him to die?"

"He asked me to prepare you," Ghanima said. Not for the first time, she was struck by the curious innocence of this Corrino Prince. Was that Jessica's doing, or something born in him?

"For what?"

"He's no longer human," Ghanima said. "Yesterday you asked when he was going to remove the *living skin*? Never. It's part of him now and he's part of it. Leto estimates he has perhaps four thousand years before metamorphosis destroys him."

Farad'n tried to swallow in a dry throat.

"You see why he runs?" Ghanima asked.

"But if he'll live so long and be so—"

"Because the memory of being human is so rich in him. Think of all those lives, cousin. No. You can't imagine what that is because you've no experience of it. But I know. I can imagine his pain. He gives more than anyone ever gave before. Our father walked into the desert trying to escape it. Alia became Abomination in fear of it. Our grandmother has only the blurred infancy of this condition, yet must use every Bene Gesserit wile to live with it—which is what Reverend Mother training amounts to anyway. But Leto! He's all alone, never to be duplicated."

Farad'n felt stunned by her words. Emperor for four thousand years?

"Jessica knows," Ghanima said, looking across at her grandmother. "He told her last night. He called himself the first truly long-range planner in human history."

"What . . . does he plan?"

"The Golden Path. He'll explain it to you later."

"And he has a role for me in this . . . plan?"

"As my mate," Ghanima said. "He's taking over the Sisterhood's breeding program. I'm sure my grandmother told you about the Bene Gesserit dream for a male Reverend with extraordinary powers. He's—"

"You mean we're just to be—"

"Not *just*." She took his arm, squeezed it with a warm familiarity. "He'll have many very responsible tasks for both of us. When we're not producing children, that is."

"Well, you're a little young yet," Farad'n said, disengaging his arm.

"Don't ever make that mistake again," she said. There was ice in her tone.

Jessica came up to them with Tyekanik.

"Tyek tells me the fighting has spread off-planet," Jessica said. "The Central Temple on Biarek is under siege."

Farad'n thought her oddly calm in this statement. He'd reviewed the reports with Tyekanik during the night. A wildfire of rebellion was spreading through the Empire. It would be put down, of course, but Leto would have a sorry Empire to restore.

"Here's Stilgar now," Ghanima said. "They've been waiting for him." And once more she took Farad'n's arm.

The old Fremen Naib had entered by the far door escorted by two former Death Commando companions from the desert days. All were dressed in formal black robes with white piping and yellow headbands for mourning. They approached with steady strides, but Stilgar kept his attention on Jessica. He stopped in front of her, nodded warily.

"You still worry about the death of Duncan Idaho," Jessica said. She didn't like this caution in her old friend.

"Reverend Mother," he said.

So it's going to be that way! Jessica thought. *All formal and according to the Fremen code, with blood difficult to expunge.*

She said: "By our view, you but played a part which Duncan assigned you. Not the first time a man has given his life for the Atreides. Why do they do it, Stil? You've been ready for it more than once. Why? Is it that you know how much the Atreides give in return?"

"I'm happy you seek no excuse for revenge," he said. "But there are matters I must discuss with your grandson. These matters may separate us from you forever."

"You mean Tabr will not pay him homage?" Ghanima asked.

"I mean I reserve my judgment." He looked coldly at Ghanima. "I don't like what my Fremen have become," he growled. "We will go back to the old ways. Without you if necessary."

"For a time, perhaps," Ghanima said. "But the desert is dying, Stil. What'll you do when there are no more worms, no more desert?"

"I don't believe it!"

"Within one hundred years," Ghanima said, "there'll be fewer than fifty worms, and those will be sick ones kept in a carefully managed reservation. Their spice will be for the Spacing Guild only, and the price . . ." She shook her head. "I've seen Leto's figures. He's been all over the planet. He knows."

"Is this another trick to keep the Fremen as your vassals?"

"When were you ever my vassal?" Ghanima asked.

Stilgar scowled. No matter what he said or did, these twins always made it his fault!

"Last night he told me about this Golden Path," Stilgar blurted. "I don't like it!"

"That's odd," Ghanima said, glancing at her grandmother. "Most of the Empire will welcome it."

"Destruction of us all," Stilgar muttered.

"But everyone longs for the Golden Age," Ghanima said. "Isn't that so, grandmother?"

"Everyone," Jessica agreed.

"They long for the Pharaonic Empire which Leto will give them," Ghanima said. "They long for a rich peace with abundant harvests, plentiful trade, a leveling of all except the Golden Ruler."

"It'll be the death of the Fremen!" Stilgar protested.

"How can you say that? Will we not need soldiers and brave men to remove the occasional dissatisfaction? Why, Stil, you and Tyek's brave companions will be hard pressed to do the job."

Stilgar looked at the Sardaukar officer and a strange light of understanding passed between them.

"And Leto will control the spice," Jessica reminded them.

"He'll control it absolutely," Ghanima said.

Farad'n, listening with the new awareness which Jessica had taught him, heard a set piece, a prepared performance between Ghanima and her grandmother.

"Peace will endure and endure and endure," Ghanima said. "Memory of war will all but vanish. Leto will lead humankind through that garden for at least four thousand years."

Tyekanik glanced questioningly at Farad'n, cleared his throat.

"Yes, Tyek?" Farad'n said.

"I'd speak privately with you, My Prince."

Farad'n smiled, knowing the question in Tyekanik's military mind, knowing that at least two others present also recognized this question. "I'll not sell the Sardaukar," Farad'n said.

"No need," Ghanima said.

"Do you listen to this child?" Tyekanik demanded. He was outraged. The old Naib there understood the problems being raised by all of this plotting, but nobody else knew a damned thing about the situation!

Ghanima smiled grimly, said: "Tell him, Farad'n."

Farad'n sighed. It was easy to forget the strangeness of this child who was not a child. He could imagine a lifetime married to her, the hidden reservations on every intimacy. It was not a totally pleasant prospect, but he was beginning to recognize its inevitability. Absolute control of dwindling spice supplies! Nothing would move in the universe without the spice.

"Later, Tyek," Farad'n said.

"But—"

"*Later, I said!*" For the first time, he used Voice on Tyekanik, saw the man blink with surprise and remain silent.

A tight smile touched Jessica's mouth.

"He talks of peace and death in the same breath," Stilgar muttered. "Golden Age!"

Ghanima said: "He'll lead humans through the cult of death into the free air of exuberant life! He speaks of death because that's necessary, Stil. It's a tension by which the living know they're alive. When his Empire falls . . . Oh, yes, it'll fall. You think this is Kralizec now, but Kralizec is yet to come. And when it comes, humans will have renewed their memory of what it's like to be alive. The memory will persist as long as there's a single human living. We'll go through the crucible once more, Stil. And we'll come out of it. We always arise from our own ashes. Always."

Farad'n, hearing her words, understood now what she'd meant in telling him about Leto running. *He'll not be human.*

Stilgar was not yet convinced. "No more worms," he growled.

"Oh, the worms will come back," Ghanima assured him. "All will be dead within two hundred years, but they'll come back."

"How . . ." Stilgar broke off.

Farad'n felt his mind awash in revelation. He knew what Ghanima would say before she spoke.

"The Guild will barely make it through the lean years, and only then because of its stockpiles and ours," Ghanima said. "But there'll be abundance after Kralizec. The worms will return after my brother goes into the sand."

As with so many other religions, Muad'Dib's Golden Elixir of Life degenerated into external wizardry. Its mystical signs became mere symbols for deeper psychological processes, and those processes, of course, ran wild. What they needed was a living god, and they didn't have one, a situation which Muad'Dib's son has corrected.

—SAYING ATTRIBUTED TO LU TUNG-PIN
(LU, THE GUEST OF THE CAVERN)

Leto sat on the Lion Throne to accept the homage of the tribes. Ghanima stood beside him, one step down. The ceremony in the Great Hall went on for hours. Tribe after Fremen tribe passed before him through their delegates and their Naibs. Each group bore gifts fitting for a god of terrifying powers, a god of vengeance who promised them peace.

He'd cowed them into submission the previous week, performing for the assembled arifa of all the tribes. The Judges had seen him walk through a pit of fire, emerging unscathed to demonstrate that his skin bore no marks by asking them to study him closely. He'd ordered them to strike him with knives, and the impenetrable skin had sealed his face while they struck at him to no avail. Acids ran off him with only the lightest mist of smoke. He'd eaten their poisons and laughed at them.

At the end he'd summoned a worm and stood facing them at its mouth. He'd moved from that to the landing field at Arrakeen, where he'd brazenly toppled a Guild frigate by lifting one of its landing fins.

The arifa had reported all of this with a fearful awe, and now the tribal delegates had come to seal their submission.

The vaulted space of the Great Hall with its acoustical dampening systems tended to absorb sharp noises, but a constant rustling of moving feet insinuated itself into the senses, riding on dust and the flint odors brought in from the open.

Jessica, who'd refused to attend, watched from a high spy hole behind the throne. Her attention was caught by Farad'n and the realization that both she and Farad'n had been outmaneuvered. Of course Leto and Ghanima had anticipated the Sisterhood! The twins could consult within themselves a host of Bene Gesserits greater than all now living in the Empire.

She was particularly bitter at the way the Sisterhood's mythology had trapped Alia. *Fear built on fear!* The habits of generations had imprinted the fate of Abomination upon her. Alia had known no hope. Of course she'd succumbed. Her fate made the accomplishment of Leto and Ghanima even more difficult to face. Not one way out of the trap, but two. Ghanima's victory over the inner lives and her insistence that Alia deserved only pity were the bitterest things of all. Hypnotic suppression under stress linked to the wooing of a benign ancestor had saved Ghanima. They might have saved Alia. But without hope, nothing had been attempted until it was too late. Alia's water had been poured upon the sand.

Jessica sighed, shifted her attention to Leto on the throne. A giant canopic jar containing the water of Muad'Dib occupied a place of honor at his right elbow. He'd boasted to Jessica that his father-within laughed at this gesture even while admiring it.

That jar and the boasting had firmed her resolve not to participate in this ritual. As long as she lived, she knew she could never accept Paul speaking through Leto's mouth. She rejoiced that House Atreides had survived, but the things-that-might-have-been were beyond bearing.

Farad'n sat cross-legged beside the jar of Muad'Dib's water. It was the position of the Royal Scribe, an honor newly conferred and newly accepted.

Farad'n felt that he was adjusting nicely to these new realities although Tyekanik still raged and promised dire consequences. Tyekanik and Stilgar had formed a partnership of distrust which seemed to amuse Leto.

In the hours of the homage ceremony, Farad'n had gone from awe to boredom to awe. They were an endless stream of humanity, these peerless fighting men. Their loyalty renewed to the Atreides on the throne could not be questioned. They stood in submissive terror before him, completely daunted by what the arifa had reported.

At last it drew to a close. The final Naib stood before Leto—Stilgar in the "rearguard position of honor." Instead of panniers heavy with spice, fire jewels, or any of the other costly gifts which lay in mounds around the throne, Stilgar bore a headband of braided spice-fiber. The Atreides Hawk had been worked in gold and green into its design.

Ghanima recognized it and shot a sidewise glance at Leto.

Stilgar placed the headband on the second step below the throne, bowed low. "I give you the headband worn by your sister when I took her into the desert to protect her," he said.

Leto suppressed a smile.

"I know you've fallen on hard times, Stilgar," Leto said. "Is there something here you would have in return?" He gestured at the piles of costly gifts.

"No, My Lord."

"I accept your gift then," Leto said. He rocked forward, brought up the hem of Ghanima's robe, ripped a thin strip from it. "In return, I give you this bit of Ghanima's robe, the robe she wore when she was stolen from your desert camp, forcing me to save her."

Stilgar accepted the cloth in a trembling hand. "Do you mock me, My Lord?"

"Mock you? By my name, Stilgar, never would I mock you. I have given you a gift without price. I command you to carry it always next to your heart as a reminder that all humans are prone to error and all leaders are human."

A thin chuckle escaped Stilgar. "What a Naib you would have made!"

"What a Naib I am! Naib of Naibs. Never forget that!"

"As you say, My Lord." Stilgar swallowed, remembering the report of his arifa. And he thought: *Once I thought of slaying him. Now it's too late.* His glance fell on the jar, a graceful opaque gold capped with green. "That is water of my tribe."

"And mine," Leto said. "I command you to read the inscription upon its side. Read it aloud that all may hear it."

Stilgar cast a questioning glance at Ghanima, but she returned it with a lift of her chin, a cold response which sent a chill through him. Were these Atreides imps bent on holding him to answer for his impetuosity and his mistakes?

"Read it," Leto said, pointing.

Slowly Stilgar mounted the steps, bent to look at the jar. Presently he read aloud: "This water is the ultimate essence, a source of outward streaming creativity. Though motionless, this water is the means of all movement."

"What does it mean, My Lord?" Stilgar whispered. He felt awed by the words, touched within himself in a place he could not understand.

"The body of Muad'Dib is a dry shell like that abandoned by an insect," Leto said. "He mastered the inner world while holding the outer in contempt, and this led to catastrophe. He mastered the outer world while excluding the inner world, and this delivered his descendants to the demons. The Golden Elixir will vanish from Dune, yet Muad'Dib's seed goes on, and his water moves our universe."

Stilgar bowed his head. Mystical things always left him in turmoil.

"The beginning and the end are one," Leto said. "You live in air but do not see it. A phase has closed. Out of that closing grows the beginning of its opposite. Thus, we will have Kralizec. Everything returns later in changed form. You have felt thoughts in your head; your descendants will feel thoughts in their bellies. Return to Sietch Tabr, Stilgar. Gurney Halleck will join you there as my advisor in your Council."

"Don't you trust me, My Lord?" Stilgar's voice was low.

"Completely, else I'd not send Gurney to you. He'll begin recruiting the new force we'll need soon. I accept your pledge of fealty, Stilgar. You are dismissed."

Stilgar bowed low, backed off the steps, turned and left the hall. The other Naibs fell into step behind him according to the Fremen principle that "the last shall be first." But some of their queries could be heard on the throne as they departed.

"What were you talking about up there, Stil? What does that mean, those words on Muad'Dib's water?"

Leto spoke to Farad'n. "Did you get all of that, Scribe?"

"Yes, My Lord."

"My grandmother tells me she trained you well in the mnemonic processes of the Bene Gesserit. That's good. I don't want you scribbling beside me."

"As you command, My Lord."

"Come and stand before me," Leto said.

Farad'n obeyed, more than ever thankful for Jessica's training. When you accepted the fact that Leto no longer was human, no longer could think as humans thought, the course of his Golden Path became ever more frightening.

Leto looked up at Farad'n. The guards stood well back out of earshot. Only the counselors of the Inner Presence remained on the floor of the Great Hall, and they stood in subservient groups well beyond the first step. Ghanima had moved closer to rest an arm on the back of the throne.

"You've not yet agreed to give me your Sardaukar," Leto said. "But you will."

"I owe you much, but not that," Farad'n said.

"You think they'd not mate well with my Fremen?"

"As well as those new friends, Stilgar and Tyekanik."

"Yet you refuse?"

"I await your offer."

"Then I must make the offer, knowing you will never repeat it. I pray my grandmother has done her part well, that you are prepared to understand."

"What must I understand?"

"There's always a prevailing mystique in any civilization," Leto said.

"It builds itself as a barrier against change, and that always leaves future generations unprepared for the universe's treachery. All mystiques are the same in building these barriers—the religious mystique, the hero-leader mystique, the messiah mystique, the mystique of science/technology, and the mystique of nature itself. We live in an Imperium which such a mystique has shaped, and now that Imperium is falling apart because most people don't distinguish between mystique and their universe. You see, the mystique is like demon possession; it tends to take over the consciousness, becoming all things to the observer."

"I recognize your grandmother's wisdom in these words," Farad'n said.

"Well and good, cousin. She asked me if I were Abomination. I answered in the negative. That was my first treachery. You see, Ghanima escaped this, but I did not. I was forced to balance the inner lives under the pressure of excessive melange. I had to seek the active cooperation of those aroused lives within me. Doing this, I avoided the most malignant and chose a dominant helper thrust upon me by the inner awareness which was my father. I am not, in truth, my father or this helper. Then again, I am not the Second Leto."

"Explain."

"You have an admirable directness," Leto said. "I'm a community dominated by one who was ancient and surpassingly powerful. He fathered a dynasty which endured for three thousand of our years. His name was Harum and, until his line trailed out in the congenital weaknesses and superstitions of a descendant, his subjects lived in a rhythmic sublimity. They moved unconsciously with the changes of the seasons. They bred individuals who tended to be short-lived, superstitious, and easily led by a god-king. Taken as a whole, they were a powerful people. Their survival as a species became habit."

"I don't like the sound of that," Farad'n said.

"Nor do I, really," Leto said. "But it's the universe I'll create."

"Why?"

"It's a lesson I learned on Dune. We kept the presence of death a dominant specter among the living here. By that presence, the dead changed the living. The people of such a society sink down into their bellies. But when the time comes for the opposite, when they arise, they are great and beautiful."

"That doesn't answer my question," Farad'n protested.

"You don't trust me, cousin."

"Nor does your own grandmother."

"And with good reason," Leto said. "But she acquiesces because she must. Bene Gesserits are pragmatists in the end. I share their view of our universe, you know. You wear the marks of that universe. You retain the habits of rule, cataloguing all around you in terms of their possible threat or value."

"I agreed to be your scribe."

"It amused you and flattered your real talent, which is that of historian. You've a definite genius for reading the present in terms of the past. You've anticipated me on several occasions."

"I don't like your veiled insinuations," Farad'n said.

"Good. You come from infinite ambition to your present lowered estate. Didn't my grandmother warn you about infinity? It attracts us like a floodlight in the night, blinding us to the excesses it can inflict upon the finite."

"Bene Gesserit aphorisms!" Farad'n protested.

"But much more precise," Leto said. "The Bene Gesserit believed they could predict the course of evolution. But they overlooked their own changes in the course of that evolution. They assumed they would stand still while their breeding plan evolved. I have no such reflexive blindness. Look carefully at me, Farad'n, for I am no longer human."

"So your sister assures me." Farad'n hesitated. Then: "Abomination?"

"By the Sisterhood's definition, perhaps. Harum is cruel and autocratic. I partake of his cruelty. Mark me well: I have the cruelty of the husbandman, and this human universe is my farm. Fremen once kept tame eagles as pets, but I'll keep a tame Farad'n."

Farad'n's face darkened. "Beware my claws, cousin. I well know my Sardaukar would fall in time before your Fremen. But we'd wound you sorely, and there are jackals waiting to pick off the weak."

"I will use you well, that I promise," Leto said. He leaned forward. "Did I not say I'm no longer human? Believe me, cousin. No children will spring from my loins, for I no longer have loins. And this forces my second treachery."

Farad'n waited in silence, seeing at last the direction of Leto's argument.

"I shall go against every Fremen precept," Leto said. "They will accept because they can do nothing else. I kept you here under the lure of a betrothal, but there will be no betrothal of you and Ghanima. My sister will marry me!"

"But you—"

"Marry, I said. Ghanima must continue the Atreides line. There's also the matter of the Bene Gesserit breeding program, which is now my breeding program."

"I refuse," Farad'n said.

"You refuse to father an Atreides dynasty?"

"What dynasty? You'll occupy the throne for thousands of years."

"And mold your descendants in my image. It will be the most intensive, the most inclusive training program in all of history. We'll be an ecosystem in miniature. You see, whatever system animals choose to survive by must be based on the pattern of interlocking communities, interdependence, working together in the common design which is the system. And this system will produce the most knowledgeable rulers ever seen."

"You put fancy words on a most distasteful—"

"Who will survive Kralizec?" Leto asked. "I promise you, Kralizec will come."

"You're a madman! You will shatter the Empire."

"Of course I will . . . and I'm not a man. But I'll create a new consciousness in all men. I tell you that below the desert of Dune there's a secret place with the greatest treasure of all time. I do not lie. When the last worm dies and the last melange is harvested upon our sands, these deep treasures will spring up throughout our universe. As the power of the spice monopoly fades and the hidden stockpiles make their mark, new powers will appear throughout our realm. It is time humans learned once more to live in their instincts."

Ghanima took her arm from the back of the throne, crossed to Farad'n's side, took his hand.

"As my mother was not wife, you will not be husband," Leto said. "But perhaps there will be love, and that will be enough."

"Each day, each moment brings its change," Ghanima said. "One learns by recognizing the moments."

Farad'n felt the warmth of Ghanima's tiny hand as an insistent presence. He recognized the ebb and flow of Leto's arguments, but not once had Voice been used. It was an appeal to the guts, not to the mind.

"Is this what you offer for my Sardaukar?" he asked.

"Much, much more, cousin. I offer your descendants the Imperium. I offer you peace."

"What will be the outcome of your peace?"

"Its opposite," Leto said, his voice calmly mocking.

Farad'n shook his head. "I find the price for my Sardaukar very high. Must I remain Scribe, the secret father of your royal line?"

"You must."

"Will you try to force me into your habit of peace?"

"I will."

"I'll resist you every day of my life."

"But that's the function I expect of you, cousin. It's why I chose you. I'll make it official. I will give you a new name. From this moment, you'll be called Breaking of the Habit, which in our tongue is Harq al-Ada. Come, cousin, don't be obtuse. My mother taught you well. Give me your Sardaukar."

"Give them," Ghanima echoed. "He'll have them one way or another."

Farad'n heard fear for himself in her voice. Love, then? Leto asked not for reason, but for an intuitive leap. "Take them," Farad'n said.

"Indeed," Leto said. He lifted himself from the throne, a curiously fluid motion as though he kept his terrible powers under most delicate control. Leto stepped down then to Ghanima's level, moved her gently until she faced away from him, turned and placed his back against hers. "Note this, cousin Harq al-Ada. This is the way it will always be with us. We'll stand thus when we are married. Back to back, each looking outward from the other to protect the one thing which we have always been." He turned, looked mockingly at Farad'n, lowered his voice: "Remember that, cousin, when you're face to face with my Ghanima. Remember that when you whisper of love and soft things, when you are most tempted by the habits of my peace and my contentment. Your back will remain exposed."

Turning from them, he strode down the steps into the waiting courtiers, picked them up in his wake like satellites, and left the hall.

Ghanima once more took Farad'n's hand, but her gaze looked beyond the far end of the hall long after Leto had left it. "One of us had to accept the agony," she said, "and he was always the stronger."

WHEN I WAS WRITING DUNE
by Frank Herbert

. . . there was no room in my mind for concerns about the book's success or failure. I was concerned only with the writing. Six years of research had preceded the day I sat down to put the story together, and the interweaving of the many plot layers I had planned required a degree of concentration I had never before experienced.

It was to be a story exploring the myth of the Messiah.

It was to produce another view of a human-occupied planet as an energy machine.

It was to penetrate the interlocked workings of politics and economics.

It was to be an examination of absolute prediction and its pitfalls.

It was to have an awareness drug in it and tell what could happen through dependence on such a substance.

Potable water was to be an analog for oil and for water itself, a substance whose supply diminishes each day.

It was to be an ecological novel, then, with many overtones, as well as a story about people and their human concerns with human values, and I had to monitor each of these levels at every stage in the book.

There wasn't room in my head to think about much else.

Following the first publication, reports from the publishers were slow and, as it turned out, inaccurate. The critics had panned it. More than twelve publishers had turned it down before publication. There was no advertising. Something was happening out there, though.

For two years, I was swamped with bookstore and reader complaints that they could not get the book. The *Whole Earth Catalog* praised it. I kept getting these telephone calls from people asking me if I were starting a cult.

The answer: "God no!"

What I'm describing is the slow realization of success. By the time the first three Dune books were completed, there was little doubt that this was a popular work—one of the most popular in history, I am told, with some ten million copies sold worldwide. Now the most common question people ask is: "What does this success mean to you?"

It surprises me. I didn't expect failure either. It was a work and I did it. Parts of *Dune Messiah* and *Children of Dune* were written before *Dune* was completed. They fleshed out more in the writing, but the essential story remained intact. I was a writer and I was writing. The success meant I could spend more time writing.

Looking back on it, I realize I did the right thing instinctively. You don't write for success. That takes part of your attention away from the writing. If you're really doing it, that's all you're doing: writing.

There's an unwritten compact between you and the reader. If someone enters a bookstore and sets down hard earned money (energy) for your book, you owe that person some entertainment and as much more as you can give.

That was really my intention all along.

Frank Herbert

Photo by Phil H. Webber

FRANK HERBERT is the bestselling author of the Dune saga. He was born in Tacoma, Washington, and educated at the University of Washington, Seattle. He worked a wide variety of jobs—including TV cameraman, radio commentator, oyster diver, jungle survival instructor, lay analyst, creative writing teacher, reporter, and editor of several West Coast newspapers—before becoming a full-time writer.

In 1952, Herbert began publishing science fiction with "Looking for Something?" in *Startling Stories*. But his emergence as a writer of major stature did not occur until 1965, with the publication of *Dune*. This was followed by *Dune Messiah, Children of Dune, God Emperor of Dune, Heretics of Dune*, and *Chapterhouse: Dune* to complete the bestselling saga. Herbert is also the author of some twenty other books, including *The White Plague, The Dosadi Experiment*, and *Destination: Void*. He died in 1986.

THE DUNE CHRONICLES

BY FRANK HERBERT

CHILDREN OF DUNE

"A major event." —*Los Angeles Times*

"Ranging from palace intrigue and desert chases to religious speculation and confrontations with the supreme intelligence of the universe, there is something here for all science fiction fans." —*Publishers Weekly*

"Herbert adds enough new twists and turns to the ongoing saga that familiarity with the recurring elements brings pleasure."
—*Challenging Destiny*

GOD EMPEROR OF DUNE

"Rich fare. . . . Heady stuff." —*Los Angeles Times*

"A fourth visit to distant Arrakis that is every bit as fascinating as the other three—every bit as timely." —*Time*

"Book four of the Dune series has many of the same strengths as the previous three, and I was indeed kept up late at night."
—*Challenging Destiny*

HERETICS OF DUNE

CHAPTERHOUSE: DUNE

THE DUNE CHRONICLES BY FRANK HERBERT

DUNE

DUNE MESSIAH

CHILDREN OF DUNE

GOD EMPEROR OF DUNE

HERETICS OF DUNE

CHAPTERHOUSE: DUNE

OTHER BOOKS BY FRANK HERBERT

THE BOOK OF FRANK HERBERT

DESTINATION: VOID
(revised edition)

DIRECT DESCENT

THE DOSADI EXPERIMENT

EYE

THE EYES OF HEISENBERG

THE GODMAKERS

THE GREEN BRAIN

THE MAKER OF DUNE

THE SANTAROGA BARRIER

SOUL CATCHER

WHIPPING STAR

THE WHITE PLAGUE

THE WORLDS OF FRANK HERBERT

MAN OF TWO WORLDS
(with Brian Herbert)

BOOKS BY FRANK HERBERT AND BILL RANSOM

THE JESUS INCIDENT

THE LAZARUS EFFECT

THE ASCENSION FACTOR

BOOKS BY BRIAN HERBERT

DREAMER OF DUNE: THE BIOGRAPHY OF FRANK HERBERT

BOOKS EDITED BY BRIAN HERBERT

THE NOTEBOOKS OF FRANK HERBERT'S DUNE

SONGS OF MUAD'DIB

BOOKS BY BRIAN HERBERT AND KEVIN J. ANDERSON

DUNE: HOUSE ATREIDES

DUNE: HOUSE HARKONNEN

DUNE: HOUSE CORRINO

DUNE: THE BUTLERIAN JIHAD

DUNE: THE MACHINE CRUSADE

DUNE: THE BATTLE OF CORRIN

THE ROAD TO DUNE
(also by Frank Herbert; includes the novel *Spice Planet*)

HUNTERS OF DUNE

SANDWORMS OF DUNE

PAUL OF DUNE

THE WINDS OF DUNE

SISTERHOOD OF DUNE

MENTATS OF DUNE

NAVIGATORS OF DUNE

HERETICS OF
DUNE

BOOK FIVE IN THE DUNE CHRONICLES

FRANK HERBERT

with an introduction by
BRIAN HERBERT

ACE
NEW YORK

ACE

Published by Berkley

An imprint of Penguin Random House LLC

penguinrandomhouse.com

Copyright © 1984 by Herbert Properties LLC
"Introduction" by Brian Herbert copyright © 2009 by DreamStar, Inc.
Penguin Random House supports copyright. Copyright fuels creativity, encourages
diverse voices, promotes free speech, and creates a vibrant culture. Thank you for buying
an authorized edition of this book and for complying with copyright laws by not
reproducing, scanning, or distributing any part of it in any form without permission.
You are supporting writers and allowing Penguin Random House to
continue to publish books for every reader.

ACE is a registered trademark and the A colophon is a trademark of
Penguin Random House LLC.

The excerpt from "The Vigil," copyright © 1953 by Theodore Roethke,
from *The Collected Poems of Theodore Roethke*, is reprinted by permission of
Doubleday & Company, Inc., and Faber and Faber Ltd.

ISBN: 9780593201763

The Library of Congress has cataloged the G. P. Putnam's Sons
hardcover edition of this book as follows:

Herbert, Frank.
Heretics of Dune.
I. Title.
PS3558.E63H4 1984 813'.54 83-16040
ISBN 0-399-12898-0
ISBN 0-399-12947-2 Limited edition

G. P. Putnam's Sons hardcover edition / April 1984
Berkley trade paperback edition / March 1985
Berkley mass-market edition / April 1986
Ace mass-market edition / August 1987
Ace hardcover edition / February 2009
Ace premium edition / June 2019
Ace trade paperback edition / July 2020

Printed in the United States of America
3   5   7   9   10   8   6   4

Cover art and design by Jim Tierney
Interior art: Desert Cave © masher/Shutterstock Images
Book design by Kristin del Rosario

INTRODUCTION
By Brian Herbert

Frank Herbert wrote much of the first draft of *Heretics of Dune* in Hawaii, a few miles outside the village of Hana on the eastern shore of Maui. He had not expected to be writing there, because the Pacific Northwest was his Tara, the place of his heart. But difficult circumstances led him to a distant, tropical isle.

When my father signed the contract for the novel in 1981, it was the largest science fiction book deal in history. World famous, he was at the top of his profession, having risen from poverty to success in a fashion that was reminiscent of the works of Horatio Alger, Jr. But Dad's remarkable achievement was bittersweet. The actual process of writing the fifth book in his classic Dune series would prove to be exceedingly arduous and much slower for him than usual, because of all the time he had to spend out of his study tending to the medical crises of my mother, Beverly Herbert.

She was seriously ill at the time, and for years had been battling valiantly for her life. The original diagnosis in 1974 had been terminal lung cancer from a lifetime of smoking cigarettes, sometimes as many as two packs a day. At the time of the discovery of the dread disease, the most optimistic prognosis had given her only a 5 percent chance of surviving beyond six months. Our family was devastated.

Under a rigorous program of chemotherapy and cobalt radiation treatments, my mother beat the cancer, but radiation seriously damaged her heart, which was inadequately shielded because of the limitations of medical technology in the 1970s. After these treatments, she suffered several life-threatening episodes, but Beverly Herbert was a fighter, and my father did everything possible to save her. He was her champion, and in true heroic fashion he sacrificed himself for her, just as she had done for him more than two decades earlier—when she gave up her own creative writing career in order to become the breadwinner for our family, thus enabling him to write. When she became gravely ill, he took time away from his writing to find the latest treatments for her and tended to her every need. He became her personal nurse, maid, and cook, preparing the low-salt meals required for her. Under his loving attention, she kept beating the odds, kept rising like Lazarus from ICU hospital beds and going on with her life. As soon as she was able, she continued to help Dad with his business operations, handling his accounting, scheduling, and management. But over the years, she had weakened physically and was slipping away from us, and from him.

Stretching their financial resources to the limit, in 1980 my parents purchased an incredible piece of property in a remote area of Maui and proceeded to have a wonderful home built there. Frank Herbert did this for my mother because she could breathe much easier in the warm air of Hawaii, far from the cold, damp Pacific Northwest, where she had been born and had lived more than thirty-five years of her life.

By late 1982, the home was still under construction but could be occupied. They arrived in October of that year. A swimming pool was being built for Mom on the property so that she could get some much-needed exercise, but work was progressing slowly, frustrating her and my father. Even so, she loved the eastern side of Maui, with its warmth, stunning beauty, and relaxed pace of life. It was a very spiritual, old-Hawaiian region, inhabited by a people reminiscent of a bygone, less-hectic time, and it was the perfect spot for her to recuperate.

Having researched old records, my mother had already found a map showing their property. It was five miles from Hana, in an area that used to be called "Kawaloa," which means "a nice long time" in the Hawaiian language. She said she hoped to spend a long time there herself and that it was a magical place, unlike anything she had ever seen. A five-acre piece of paradise, the land fronted an aquamarine sea with dancing whitecaps and a surf that pounded against the black lava shoreline. The property had palms, papayas, mangoes, bananas, breadfruit trees, and a graceful kamani tree overlooking the water. The flowers on the gentle slopes around the home were spectacular, with bougainvillaea, blue lilies, orchids, torch gingers, heliconias, bird-of-paradises, poinsettias, and huge hibiscus blossoms.

"It's warm here," my mother said to me over the telephone, "and there are flowers everywhere."

In Hawaii, Frank Herbert set to work on *Heretics of Dune*. I spoke with him by phone in early January 1983, and he told me he was putting in long hours on the new novel, pressing to complete it as soon as possible. Each morning he rose before dawn and worked out on a rowing machine and an Exercycle. Then he took a quick shower and made a light breakfast of toast and guava juice, which he carried to his loft study on the second floor of the house.

After writing for three hours, he would help Mom get ready for the day. He made her Cream of Wheat with sliced bananas on top, found books and knitting materials and art supplies and whatever else she needed, and sometimes adjusted the louvers in the walls to allow just the right amount of trade winds to enter, naturally ventilating the interior of the house. By nine thirty he was back at his desk upstairs, but he was always going to the interior railing and looking down into the living room to make sure she was comfortable. Under the circumstances, it was difficult for him to find the time or the energy to write, but he did the best that he possibly could. The novel, as important as it was, had to be secondary to Beverly Herbert, his loving wife and companion since 1946.

For the new book project, he was using a Compaq word processor since it was much faster than his customary electric typewriter. Each night he put the new machine away in a sealed "dry room" by the kitchen to prevent it from being damaged so quickly in the caustic, salty air that blew in from the ocean. By the middle of February, he told me he'd been having plot problems with the novel, but he was a little over halfway through the first draft. Only a few days later, he was interrupted by yet another of my mother's medical emergencies, one that forced them to return to a home they still owned in Port Townsend,

Washington. Choosing to stay there instead, a short distance from Seattle, they could more easily obtain the best medical treatment for her. It was the practical thing to do, though they would return to Hawaii later in the year.

By early June, they were still in Port Townsend, and Dad had the first draft completed—around 200,000 words, which would eventually be cut to 165,000. I remember visiting them at their home on the Olympic Peninsula and seeing my mother reading the manuscript. A slender brunette woman, she was seated on a dark yellow recliner in the sitting area adjacent to the kitchen, with manuscript pages spread out on the table beside her. She said the story was great, that she couldn't put it down. Mom felt that each book in the series was superior to the one before, with plots and characterizations that were even better than *Dune*.

The strong characterizations of women in the series—and particularly in *Heretics* and *Chapterhouse*—appealed greatly to my mother. In fact, Dad based the Lady Jessica on her, creating a memorable literary character who had my mother's beauty and grace. Remarkably, even though Beverly Herbert passed away years ago, she continues to live through the ages . . . a significant testimonial to the love that Frank Herbert felt for her.

It is interesting to note the progression of women in my father's Dune novels. Female characters get stronger and stronger as the series develops, and in *Heretics of Dune* and *Chapterhouse: Dune*, women are running most of the important planets in the Dune universe. By that time, the Bene Gesserit Sisterhood is the most important political power, although it is a more austere age, without the grandeur and pomposity of the Imperium back in the days of Shaddam Corrino IV, the Emperor Paul Muad'Dib, or the tyrannical God Emperor, Leto Atreides II. The glories of the desert planet Arrakis are long gone as well, and the sandworm species has been moved off world, where it may not survive.

Thousands of years before the events described in *Heretics of Dune*, the God Emperor set mankind on his "Golden Path" and scattered civilization across countless star systems, as if sprinkling human seeds in the wind. But now, in *Heretics of Dune*, evil, supremely powerful women have emerged from the Scattering and threaten the Sisterhood. They call themselves "Honored Matres," which is ironic because there is nothing honorable about them. Individually and collectively, they can outfight the Sisters, so that the Sisterhood—like the sandworms— seems in danger of being wiped out. The brutal Honored Matres appear to be unstoppable, and there are rumors about their origins. Could they possibly be descended from failed Reverend Mothers, making them the dark side of the Sisterhood? Or could something else be at play, something even more sinister that has been generated in the secret breeding laboratories of the fanatical Tleilaxu?

Heretics of Dune is a remarkable, cerebral excursion through the most fantastic universe in science fiction. In this novel, as in *God Emperor of Dune* before it and *Chapterhouse: Dune* afterward, the author explored layers that he originally interwove into the action of the first novel in the series, *Dune*—layers containing important messages about politics, religion, ecology, and a host of other interesting, timeless subjects. The last three novels he wrote in the series are intellectually stimulating, and sometimes the action almost seems secondary. Huge battles, and even one that is environmentally catastrophic, occur behind the scenes.

As I wrote in *Dreamer of Dune*, the biography of my father, *Heretics of Dune* was actually intended to be the first book of a new trilogy that would complete the epic story chronologically. It is set thousands of years in mankind's future, long after the events in *Dune*. Before his untimely death in 1986, Frank Herbert wrote the first two books of the trilogy (*Heretics* and *Chapterhouse*), but he left the third unwritten. Using my father's outline and notes, I eventually co-wrote the grand climax with Kevin J. Anderson, but it required two novels for us to do so—*Hunters of Dune* (2006) and *Sandworms of Dune* (2007).

Heretics of Dune is the beginning of that extraordinary, climactic adventure, a giant leap in time and space beyond the novels preceding it. In this novel, you will meet a diverse and complex cast of characters, inhabiting worlds that stretch the imagination. It is a journey into what my father liked to call one of humankind's "possible futures," showing where we might very well be headed, into a tableau that is at once terrifying and exhilarating. Even with its complexities, *Heretics* is a page-turner, a novel that will not disappoint the most critical of Dune fans. After reading the last page of the book, you will want to go back and read it again, revisiting old friends in a fantastic realm that never quite leaves your thoughts.

BRIAN HERBERT
SEATTLE, WASHINGTON
JUNE 24, 2008

Most discipline is hidden discipline, designed not to liberate but to limit. Do not ask *Why?* Be cautious with *How? Why?* leads inexorably to paradox. *How?* traps you in a universe of cause and effect. Both deny the infinite.

—THE APOCRYPHA OF ARRAKIS

"Taraza told you, did she not, that we have gone through eleven of these Duncan Idaho gholas? This one is the twelfth."

The old Reverend Mother Schwangyu spoke with deliberate bitterness as she looked down from the third-story parapet at the lone child playing on the enclosed lawn. The planet Gammu's bright midday sunlight bounced off the white courtyard walls filling the area beneath them with brilliance as though a spotlight had been directed onto the young ghola.

Gone through! the Reverend Mother Lucilla thought. She allowed herself a short nod, thinking how coldly impersonal were Schwangyu's manner and choice of words. *We have used up our supply; send us more!*

The child on the lawn appeared to be about twelve standard years of age, but appearance could be deceptive with a ghola not yet awakened to his original memories. The child took that moment to look up at the watchers above him. He was a sturdy figure with a direct gaze that focused intently from beneath a black cap of karakul hair. The yellow sunlight of early spring cast a small shadow at his feet. His skin was darkly tanned but a slight movement of his body shifted his blue singlesuit, revealing pale skin at the left shoulder.

"Not only are these gholas costly but they are supremely dangerous to us," Schwangyu said. Her voice came out flat and emotionless, all the more powerful because of that. It was the voice of a Reverend Mother Instructor speaking down to an acolyte and it emphasized for Lucilla that Schwangyu was one of those who protested openly against the ghola project.

Taraza had warned: "She will try to win you over."

"Eleven failures are enough," Schwangyu said.

Lucilla glanced at Schwangyu's wrinkled features, thinking suddenly: *Someday I may be old and wizened, too. And perhaps I will be a power in the Bene Gesserit as well.*

Schwangyu was a small woman with many age marks earned in the Sisterhood's affairs. Lucilla knew from her own assignment-studies that Schwangyu's conventional black robe concealed a skinny figure that few other than her acolyte dressers and the males bred to her had ever seen. Schwangyu's mouth was wide, the lower lip constricted by the age lines that fanned into a jutting chin. Her manner tended to a curt abruptness that the uninitiated often interpreted as anger. The commander of the Gammu Keep was one who kept herself to herself more than most Reverend Mothers.

Once more, Lucilla wished she knew the entire scope of the ghola project. Taraza had drawn the dividing line clearly enough, though: "Schwangyu is not to be trusted where the safety of the ghola is concerned."

"We think the Tleilaxu themselves killed most of the previous eleven," Schwangyu said. "That in itself should tell us something."

Matching Schwangyu's manner, Lucilla adopted a quiet attitude of almost emotionless waiting. Her manner said: "I may be much younger than you, Schwangyu, but I, too, am a full Reverend Mother." She could feel Schwangyu's gaze.

Schwangyu had seen the holos of this Lucilla but the woman in the flesh was more disconcerting. An Imprinter of the best training, no doubt of it. Blue-in-blue eyes uncorrected by any lens gave Lucilla a piercing expression that went with her long oval face. With the hood of her black aba robe thrown back as it was now, brown hair was revealed, drawn into a tight barette and then cascading down her back. Not even the stiffest robe could completely hide Lucilla's ample breasts. She was from a genetic line famous for its motherly nature and she already had borne three children for the Sisterhood, two by the same sire. Yes—a brown-haired charmer with full breasts and a motherly disposition.

"You say very little," Schwangyu said. "This tells me that Taraza has warned you against me."

"Do you have reason to believe assassins will try to kill this twelfth ghola?" Lucilla asked.

"They already have tried."

Strange how the word "heresy" came to mind when thinking of Schwangyu, Lucilla thought. Could there be heresy among the Reverend Mothers? The religious overtones of the word seemed out of place in a Bene Gesserit context. How could there be heretical movements among people who held a profoundly manipulative attitude toward all things religious?

Lucilla shifted her attention down to the ghola, who took this moment to perform a series of cartwheels that brought him around full circle until he once more stood looking up at the two observers on the parapet.

"How prettily he performs!" Schwangyu sneered. The old voice did not completely mask an underlying violence.

Lucilla glanced at Schwangyu. *Heresy.* "Dissidence" was not the proper word. "Opposition" did not cover what could be sensed in the older woman. This was something that could shatter the Bene Gesserit. Revolt against Taraza, against the Reverend Mother Superior? Unthinkable! Mother Superiors were cast in the mold of monarch. Once Taraza had accepted counsel and advice and *then* made her decision, the Sisters were committed to obedience.

"This is no time to be creating new problems!" Schwangyu said.

Her meaning was clear. People from the Scattering were coming back and the intent of some among those Lost Ones threatened the

Sisterhood. *Honored Matres!* How like "Reverend Mothers" the words sounded.

Lucilla ventured an exploratory sally: "So you think we should be concentrating on the problem of those Honored Matres from the Scattering?"

"Concentrating? Hah! They do not have our powers. They do not show good sense. And they do not have mastery of melange! That is what they want from us, our spice knowledge."

"Perhaps," Lucilla agreed. She was not willing to concede this on the scanty evidence.

"Mother Superior Taraza has taken leave of her senses to dally with this ghola thing now," Schwangyu said.

Lucilla remained silent. The ghola project definitely had touched an old nerve among the Sisters. The possibility, even remote, that they might arouse another Kwisatz Haderach sent shudders of angry fear through the ranks. To meddle with the worm-bound remnants of the Tyrant! That was dangerous in the extreme.

"We should never take that ghola to Rakis," Schwangyu muttered. "Let sleeping worms lie."

Lucilla gave her attention once more to the ghola-child. He had turned his back on the high parapet with its two Reverend Mothers, but something about his posture said he knew they discussed him and he awaited their response.

"You doubtless realize that you have been called in while he is yet too young," Schwangyu said.

"I have never heard of the deep imprinting on one that young," Lucilla agreed. She allowed something softly self-mocking in her tone, a thing she knew Schwangyu would hear and misinterpret. The management of procreation and all of its attendant necessities, that was the Bene Gesserit ultimate specialty. Use love but avoid it, Schwangyu would be thinking now. The Sisterhood's analysts knew the roots of love. They had examined this quite early in their development but had never dared breed it out of those they influenced. Tolerate love but guard against it, that was the rule. Know that it lay deep within the human genetic makeup, a safety net to insure continuation of the species. You used it where necessary, imprinting selected individuals (sometimes upon each other) for the Sisterhood's purposes, knowing then that such individuals would be linked by powerful bonding lines not readily available to the common awareness. Others might observe such links and plot the consequences but the linked ones would dance to unconscious music.

"I was not suggesting that it's a mistake to imprint him," Schwangyu said, misreading Lucilla's silence.

"We do what we are ordered to do," Lucilla chided. Let Schwangyu make of that what she would.

"Then you do not object to taking the ghola to Rakis," Schwangyu said. "I wonder if you would continue such unquestioning obedience if you knew the full story?"

Lucilla inhaled a deep breath. Was the entire design for the Duncan Idaho gholas to be shared with her now?

"There is a female child named Sheeana Brugh on Rakis," Schwangyu said. "She can control the giant worms."

Lucilla concealed her alertness. *Giant worms. Not Shai-hulud. Not Shaitan. Giant worms.* The sandrider predicted by the Tyrant had appeared at last!

"I do not make idle chatter," Schwangyu said when Lucilla continued silent.

Indeed not, Lucilla thought. *And you call a thing by its descriptive label, not by the name of its mystical import. Giant worms. And you're really thinking about the Tyrant, Leto II, whose endless dream is carried as a pearl of awareness in each of those worms. Or so we are led to believe.*

Schwangyu nodded toward the child on the lawn below them. "Do you think their ghola will be able to influence the girl who controls the worms?"

We're peeling away the skin at last, Lucilla thought. She said: "I have no need for the answer to such a question."

"You *are* a cautious one," Schwangyu said.

Lucilla arched her back and stretched. *Cautious? Yes, indeed!* Taraza had warned her: "Where Schwangyu is concerned, you must act with extreme caution but with speed. We have a very narrow window of time within which we can succeed."

Succeed at what? Lucilla wondered. She glanced sideways at Schwangyu. "I don't see how the Tleilaxu could succeed in killing eleven of these gholas. How could they get through our defenses?"

"We have the Bashar now," Schwangyu said. "Perhaps he can prevent disaster." Her tone said she did not believe this.

Mother Superior Taraza had said: "You are the Imprinter, Lucilla. When you get to Gammu you will recognize some of the pattern. But for your task you have no need for the full design."

"Think of the cost!" Schwangyu said, glaring down at the ghola, who now squatted, pulling at tufts of grass.

Cost had nothing to do with it, Lucilla knew. The open admission of failure was much more important. The Sisterhood could not reveal its fallibility. But the fact that an Imprinter had been summoned early—that was vital. Taraza had known the Imprinter would see this and recognize part of the pattern.

Schwangyu gestured with one bony hand at the child, who had returned to his solitary play, running and tumbling on the grass.

"Politics," Schwangyu said.

No doubt Sisterhood politics lay at the core of Schwangyu's *heresy*, Lucilla thought. The delicacy of the internal argument could be deduced from the fact that Schwangyu had been put in charge of the Keep here on Gammu. Those who opposed Taraza refused to sit on the sidelines.

Schwangyu turned and looked squarely at Lucilla. Enough had been said. Enough had been heard and screened through minds trained in Bene Gesserit awareness. The Chapter House had chosen this Lucilla with great care.

Lucilla felt the older woman's careful examination but refused to let this touch that innermost sense of purpose upon which every Reverend Mother could rely in times of stress. *Here. Let her look fully upon me.* Lucilla turned and set her mouth in a soft smile, passing her gaze across the rooftop opposite them.

A uniformed man armed with a heavy-duty lasgun appeared there, looked once at the two Reverend Mothers and then focused on the child below them.

"Who is that?" Lucilla asked.

"Patrin, the Bashar's most trusted aide. Says he's only the Bashar's batman but you'd have to be blind and a fool to believe that."

Lucilla examined the man across from them with care. So that was Patrin. A native of Gammu, Taraza had said. Chosen for this task by the Bashar himself. Thin and blond, much too old now to be soldiering, but then the Bashar had been called back from retirement and had insisted Patrin must share this duty.

Schwangyu noted the way Lucilla shifted her attention from Patrin to the ghola with real concern. Yes, if the Bashar had been called back to guard this Keep, then the ghola was in extreme peril.

Lucilla started in sudden surprise. "Why . . . he's . . ."

"Miles Teg's orders," Schwangyu said, naming the Bashar. "All of the ghola's play is training play. Muscles are to be prepared for the day when he is restored to his original self."

"But that's no simple exercise he's doing down there," Lucilla said. She felt her own muscles respond sympathetically to the remembered training.

"We hold back only the Sisterhood's arcana from this ghola," Schwangyu said. "Almost anything else in our storehouse of knowledge can be his." Her tone said she found this extremely objectionable.

"Surely, no one believes this ghola could become another Kwisatz Haderach," Lucilla objected.

Schwangyu merely shrugged.

Lucilla held herself quite still, thinking. Was it possible the ghola could be transformed into a male version of a Reverend Mother? Could this Duncan Idaho learn to look inward where no Reverend Mother dared?

Schwangyu began to speak, her voice almost a growling mutter:

"The design of this project . . . they have a dangerous plan. They could make the same mistake . . ." She broke off.

They, Lucilla thought. *Their ghola.*

"I would give anything to know for sure the position of Ix and the Fish Speakers in this," Lucilla said.

"Fish Speakers!" Schwangyu shook her head at the very thought of the remnant female army that had once served only the Tyrant. "They believe in truth and justice."

Lucilla overcame a sudden tightness in her throat. Schwangyu had all but declared open opposition. Yet, she commanded here. The political rule was a simple one: Those who opposed the project must monitor it that they might abort it at the first sign of trouble. But that was a genuine Duncan Idaho ghola down there on the lawn. Cell comparisons and Truthsayers had confirmed it.

Taraza had said: "You are to teach him love in all of its forms."

"He's so young," Lucilla said, keeping her attention on the ghola.

"Young, yes," Schwangyu said. "So, for now, I presume you will awaken his childish responses to maternal affection. Later . . ." Schwangyu shrugged.

Lucilla betrayed no emotional reaction. A Bene Gesserit obeyed. *I am an Imprinter. So . . .* Taraza's orders and the Imprinter's specialized training defined a particular course of events.

To Schwangyu, Lucilla said: "There is someone who looks like me and speaks with my voice. I am Imprinting for her. May I ask who that is?"

"No."

Lucilla held her silence. She had not expected revelation but it had been remarked more than once that she bore a striking resemblance to Senior Security Mother Darwi Odrade. "A *young Odrade.*" Lucilla had heard this on several occasions. Both Lucilla and Odrade were, of course, in the Atreides line with a strong backbreeding from Siona descendants. The Fish Speakers had no monopoly on *those* genes! But the *Other Memories* of a Reverend Mother, even with their linear selectivity and confinement to the female side, provided important clues to the broad shape of the ghola project. Lucilla, who had come to depend on her experiences of the Jessica persona buried some five thousand years back in the Sisterhood's genetic manipulations, felt a deep sense of dread from that source now. There was a familiar pattern here. It gave off such an intense feeling of doom that Lucilla fell automatically into the Litany Against Fear as she had been taught it in her first introduction to the Sisterhood's rites:

"I must not fear. Fear is the mind-killer. Fear is the little-death that brings total obliteration. I will face my fear. I will permit it to pass over me and through me. And when it has gone past I will turn the inner eye to see its path. Where the fear has gone there will be nothing. Only I will remain."

Calm returned to Lucilla.

Schwangyu, sensing some of this, allowed her guard to drop slightly. Lucilla was no dullard, no *special* Reverend Mother with an empty title and barely sufficient background to function without embarrassing the Sisterhood. Lucilla was the real thing and some reactions could not be hidden from her, not even reactions of another Reverend Mother. Very well, let her know the full extent of the opposition to this foolish, this *dangerous* project!

"I do not think their ghola will survive to see Rakis," Schwangyu said.

Lucilla let this pass. "Tell me about his friends," she said.

"He has no friends; only teachers."

"When will I meet them?" She kept her gaze on the opposite parapet where Patrin leaned idly against a low pillar, his heavy lasgun at the ready. Lucilla realized with an abrupt shock that Patrin was watching her. Patrin was a message from the Bashar! Schwangyu obviously saw and understood. *We guard him!*

"I presume it's Miles Teg you're so anxious to meet," Schwangyu said.

"Among others."

"Don't you want to make contact with the ghola first?"

"I've already made contact with him." Lucilla nodded toward the enclosed yard where the child once more stood almost motionless and looking up at her. "He's a thoughtful one."

"I've only the reports on the others," Schwangyu said, "but I suspect this is the most thoughtful one of the series."

Lucilla suppressed an involuntary shudder at the readiness for violent opposition in Schwangyu's words and attitude. There was not one hint that the child below them shared a common humanity.

While Lucilla was thinking this, clouds covered the sun as they often did here at this hour. A cold wind blew in over the Keep's walls, swirling around the courtyard. The child turned away and picked up the speed of his exercises, getting his warmth from increased activity.

"Where does he go to be alone?" Lucilla asked.

"Mostly to his room. He has tried a few dangerous escapades, but we have discouraged this."

"He must hate us very much."

"I'm sure of it."

"I will have to deal with that directly."

"Surely, an Imprinter has no doubts about her ability to overcome hate."

"I was thinking of Geasa." Lucilla sent a knowing look at Schwangyu. "I find it astonishing that you let Geasa make such a mistake."

"I don't interfere with the normal progress of the ghola's instructions. If one of his teachers develops a real affection for him, that is not my problem."

"An attractive child," Lucilla said.

They stood a bit longer watching the Duncan Idaho ghola at his training-play. Both Reverend Mothers thought briefly of Geasa, one of the first teachers brought here for the ghola project. Schwangyu's attitude was plain: *Geasa was a providential failure.* Lucilla thought only: *Schwangyu and Geasa complicated my task.* Neither woman gave even a passing moment to the way these thoughts reaffirmed their loyalties.

As she watched the child in the courtyard, Lucilla began to have a new appreciation of what the Tyrant God Emperor had actually achieved. Leto II had employed this ghola-type through uncounted lifetimes—some thirty-five hundred years of them, one after another. And the God Emperor Leto II had been no ordinary force of nature. He had been the biggest juggernaut in human history, rolling over everything: over social systems, over natural and unnatural hatreds, over governmental forms, over rituals (both taboo and mandatory), over religions casual and religions intense. The crushing weight of the Tyrant's passage had left nothing unmarked, not even the Bene Gesserit.

Leto II had called it "The Golden Path" and this Duncan Idaho–type ghola below her now had figured prominently in that awesome passage. Lucilla had studied the Bene Gesserit accounts, probably the best in the universe. Even today on most of the old Imperial Planets, newly married couples still scattered dollops of water east and west, mouthing the local version of "Let Thy blessings flow back to us from this offering, O God of Infinite Power and Infinite Mercy."

Once, it had been the task of Fish Speakers and their tame priesthood to enforce such obeisance. But the thing had developed its own momentum, becoming a pervasive compulsion. Even the most doubting of believers said: "Well, it can do no harm." It was an accomplishment that the finest religious engineers of the Bene Gesserit Missionaria Protectiva admired with frustrated awe. The Tyrant had surpassed the Bene Gesserit best. And fifteen hundred years since the Tyrant's death, the Sisterhood remained powerless to unlock the central knot of that fearsome accomplishment.

"Who has charge of the child's religious training?" Lucilla asked.

"No one," Schwangyu said. "Why bother? If he is reawakened to his original memories, he will have his own ideas. We will deal with those if we ever have to."

The child below them completed his allotted training time. Without another look up at the watchers on the parapet, he left the enclosed yard and entered a wide doorway on the left. Patrin, too, abandoned his guard position without glancing at the two Reverend Mothers.

"Don't be fooled by Teg's people," Schwangyu said. "They have eyes in the backs of their heads. Teg's birth-mother, you know, was one of us. He is teaching that ghola things better never shared!"

Explosions are also compressions of time. Observable changes in the natural universe all are explosive to some degree and from some point of view; otherwise you would not notice them. Smooth Continuity of change, if slowed sufficiently, goes without notice by observers whose time/attention span is too short. Thus, I tell you, I have seen changes you would never have marked.

—LETO II

The woman standing in Chapter House Planet's morning light across the table from the Reverend Mother Superior Alma Mavis Taraza was tall and supple. The long aba robe that encased her in shimmering black from shoulders to floor did not completely conceal the grace with which her body expressed every movement.

Taraza leaned forward in her chairdog and scanned the Records Relay projecting its condensed Bene Gesserit glyphs above the tabletop for her eyes only.

"Darwi Odrade," the display identified the standing woman, and then came the essential biography, which Taraza already knew in detail. The display served several purposes—it provided a secure reminder for the Mother Superior, it allowed an occasional delay for thought while she appeared to scan the records, and it was a final argument should something negative arise from this interview.

Odrade had borne nineteen children for the Bene Gesserit, Taraza observed as the information scrolled past her eyes. Each child by a different father. Not much unusual about that, but even the most searching gaze could see that this essential service to the Sisterhood had not grossened Odrade's flesh. Her features conveyed a natural hauteur in the long nose and the complementary angular cheeks. Every feature focused downward to a narrow chin. Her mouth, though, was full and promised a passion that she was careful to bridle.

We can always depend on the Atreides genes, Taraza thought.

A window curtain fluttered behind Odrade and she glanced back at it. They were in Taraza's morning room, a small and elegantly furnished space decorated in shades of green. Only the stark white of Taraza's chairdog separated her from the background. The room's bow windows looked eastward onto garden and lawn with faraway snowy mountains of Chapter House Planet as backdrop.

Without looking up, Taraza said: "I was glad when both you and Lucilla accepted the assignment. It makes my task much easier."

"I would like to have met this Lucilla," Odrade said, looking down at the top of Taraza's head. Odrade's voice came out a soft contralto.

Taraza cleared her throat. "No need. Lucilla is one of our finest Imprinters. Each of you, of course, received the identical liberal conditioning to prepare you for this."

There was something almost insulting in Taraza's casual tone and only the habits of long association put down Odrade's immediate resentment. It was partly that word "liberal," she realized. Atreides ancestors rose up in rebellion at the word. It was as though her accumulated female memories lashed out at the unconscious assumptions and unexamined prejudices behind the concept.

"Only liberals really think. Only liberals are intellectual. Only liberals understand the needs of their fellows."

How much viciousness lay concealed in that word! Odrade thought. How much secret ego demanding to feel superior.

Odrade reminded herself that Taraza, despite the casually insulting tone, had used the term only in its catholic sense: Lucilla's generalized education had been carefully matched to that of Odrade.

Taraza leaned back into a more comfortable position but still kept her attention on the display in front of her. The light from the eastern windows fell directly on her face, leaving shadows beneath nose and chin. A small woman just a bit older than Odrade, Taraza retained much of the beauty that had made her a most reliable breeder with difficult sires. Her face was a long oval with soft curved cheeks. She wore her black hair drawn back tightly from a high forehead with a pronounced peak. Taraza's mouth opened minimally when she spoke: superb control of movement. An observer's attention tended to focus on her eyes: that compelling blue-in-blue. The total effect was of a suave facial mask from which little escaped to betray her true emotions.

Odrade recognized this present pose in the Mother Superior. Taraza would mutter to herself presently. Indeed, right on cue, Taraza muttered to herself.

The Mother Superior was thinking while she followed the biographical display with great attention. Many matters occupied her attention.

This was a reassuring thought to Odrade. Taraza did not believe there was any such thing as a beneficent power guarding humankind. The Missionaria Protectiva and the intentions of the Sisterhood counted for everything in Taraza's universe. Whatever served those intentions, even the machinations of the long-dead Tyrant, could be judged good. All else was evil. Alien intrusions from the Scattering—especially those returning descendants who called themselves "Honored Matres"—were not to be trusted. Taraza's own people, even those Reverend Mothers who opposed her in Council, were the ultimate Bene Gesserit resource, the only thing that could be trusted.

Still without looking up, Taraza said: "Do you know that when you compare the millennia preceding the Tyrant with those after his death, the decrease in major conflicts is phenomenal. Since the Tyrant, the number of such conflicts has dropped to less than two percent of what it was before."

"As far as we know," Odrade said.

Taraza's gaze flicked upward and then down. "What?"

"We have no way of telling how many wars have been fought outside our ken. Have you statistics from the people of the Scattering?"

"Of course not!"

"Leto tamed us is what you're saying," Odrade said.

"If you care to put it that way." Taraza inserted a marker in something she saw on her display.

"Shouldn't some of the credit go to our beloved Bashar Miles Teg?" Odrade asked. "Or to his talented predecessors?"

"We chose those people," Taraza said.

"I don't see the pertinence of this martial discussion," Odrade said. "What does it have to do with our present problem?"

"There are some who think we may revert to the pre-Tyrant condition with a very nasty bang."

"Oh?" Odrade pursed her lips.

"Several groups among our returning Lost Ones are selling arms to anyone who wants to or *can* buy."

"Specifics?" Odrade asked.

"Sophisticated arms are flooding onto Gammu and there can be little doubt the Tleilaxu are stockpiling some of the nastier weapons."

Taraza leaned back and rubbed her temples. She spoke in a low, almost musing voice. "We think we make decisions of the greatest moment and out of the very highest principles."

Odrade had seen this before, too. She said: "Does the Mother Superior doubt the rightness of the Bene Gesserit?"

"Doubt? Oh, no. But I do experience frustration. We work all of our lives for these highly refined goals and in the end, what do we find? We find that many of the things to which we have dedicated our lives came from petty decisions. They can be traced to desires for personal comfort or convenience and had nothing at all to do with our high ideals. What really was at stake was some worldly working agreement that satisfied the needs of those who *could* make the decisions."

"I've heard you call that political necessity," Odrade said.

Taraza spoke with tight control while returning her attention to the display in front of her. "If we become institutionalized in our judgments, that's a sure way to extinguish the Bene Gesserit."

"You will not find petty decisions in my bio," Odrade said.

"I look for sources of weakness, for flaws."

"You won't find those, either."

Taraza concealed a smile. She recognized this egocentric remark: Odrade's way of needling the Mother Superior. Odrade was very good at seeming to be impatient while actually suspending herself in a timeless flow of patience.

When Taraza did not rise to the bait, Odrade resumed her calm waiting—easy breaths, the mind steady. Patience came without thinking of it. The Sisterhood had taught her long ago how to divide past and present into simultaneous flowings. While observing her immediate surroundings, she could pick up bits and pieces of her past and live through them as though they moved across a screen superimposed over the present.

Memory work, Odrade thought. Necessary things to haul out and lay to rest. Removing the barriers. When all else palled, there was still her tangled childhood.

There had been a time when Odrade lived as most children lived: in a house with a man and woman who, if not her parents, certainly acted in loco parentis. All of the other children she knew then lived in similar situations. They had *papas* and *mamas.* Sometimes only papa worked away from home. Sometimes only mama went out to her labors. In Odrade's case, the woman remained at home and no crèche nurse guarded the child in the working hours. Much later, Odrade learned that her birth-mother had given a large sum of money to provide this for the infant female hidden in plain sight that way.

"She hid you with us because she loved you," the woman explained when Odrade was old enough to understand. "That is why you must never reveal that we are not your real parents."

Love had nothing to do with it, Odrade learned later. Reverend

Mothers did not act from such mundane motives. And Odrade's birth-mother had been a Bene Gesserit Sister.

All of this was revealed to Odrade according to the original plan. Her name: Odrade. Darwi was what she had always been called when the caller was not being endearing or angry. Young friends naturally shortened it to Dar.

Everything, however, did not go according to the original plan. Odrade recalled a narrow bed in a room brightened by paintings of animals and fantasy landscapes on the pastel blue walls. White curtains fluttered at the window in the soft breezes of spring and summer. Odrade remembered jumping on the narrow bed—a marvelously happy game: up, down, up, down. Much laughter. Arms caught her in mid leap and hugged her close. They were a man's arms: a round face with a small mustache that tickled her into giggles. The bed thumped the wall when she jumped and the wall revealed indentations from this movement.

Odrade played over this memory now, reluctant to discard it into the well of rationality. Marks on a wall. Marks of laughter and joy. How small they were to represent so much.

Odd how she had been thinking more and more about papa recently. All of the memories were not happy. There had been times when he had been sad-angry, warning mama not to become "too involved." He had a face that reflected many frustrations. His voice barked when he was in his angry mood. Mama moved softly then, her eyes full of worry. Odrade sensed the worry and the fear and resented the man. The woman knew best how to deal with him. She kissed the nape of his neck, stroked his cheek and whispered into his ear.

These ancient "natural" emotions had engaged a Bene Gesserit analyst-proctor in much work with Odrade before they were exorcised. But even now there was residual detritus to pick up and discard. Even now, Odrade knew that all of it was not gone.

Seeing the way Taraza studied the biographical record with such care, Odrade wondered if that was the flaw the Mother Superior saw.

Surely they know by now that I can deal with the emotions of those early times.

It was all so long ago. Still, she had to admit that the memory of the man and woman lay within her, bonded with such force that it might never be erased completely. Especially mama.

The Reverend Mother in extremis who had borne Odrade had put her in that hiding place on Gammu for reasons Odrade now understood quite well. Odrade harbored no resentments. It had been necessary for the survival of them both. Problems arose from the fact that the foster mother gave Odrade that thing which most mothers give their children, that thing which the Sisterhood so distrusted—love.

When the Reverend Mothers came, the foster mother had not fought the removal of *her* child. Two Reverend Mothers came with a contingent of male and female proctors. Afterward Odrade was a long time understanding the significance of that wrenching moment. The woman had known in her heart that the day of parting would come. Only a matter of time. Still, as the days became years—almost six standards of years—the woman had dared to hope.

Then the Reverend Mothers came with their burly attendants. They had merely been waiting until it was safe, until they were sure no hunters knew this was a Bene Gesserit–planned Atreides scion.

Odrade saw a great deal of money passed to the foster mother. The woman threw the money on the floor. But no voice was raised in objection. The adults in the scene knew where the power lay.

Calling up those compressed emotions, Odrade could still see the woman take herself to a straight-backed chair beside the window onto the street, there to hug herself and rock back and forth, back and forth. Not a sound from her.

The Reverend Mothers used Voice and their considerable wiles plus the smoke of drugging herbs and their overpowering presence to lure Odrade into their waiting groundcar.

"It will be just for a little while. Your real mother sent us."

Odrade sensed the lies but curiosity compelled. *My real mother!*

Her last view of the woman who had been her only known female

parent was of that figure at the window rocking back and forth, a look
of misery on her face, arms wrapped around herself.

Later, when Odrade spoke of returning to the woman, that memory-
vision was incorporated into an essential Bene Gesserit lesson.

"Love leads to misery. Love is a very ancient force, which served its
purpose in its day but no longer is essential for the survival of the species. Remember that woman's mistake, the pain."

Until well into her teens, Odrade adjusted by daydreaming. She
would *really* return after she was a full Reverend Mother. She would
go back and find that loving woman, find her even though she had no
names except "mama" and "Sibia." Odrade recalled the laughter of
adult friends who had called the woman "Sibia."

Mama Sibia.

The Sisters, however, detected the daydreams and searched out
their source. That, too, was incorporated into a lesson.

"Daydreaming is the first awakening of what we call simulflow. It
is an essential tool of rational thought. With it you can clear the mind
for better thinking."

Simulflow.

Odrade focused on Taraza at the morning room table. Childhood
trauma must be placed carefully into a reconstructed memory-place.
All of that had been far away on Gammu, the planet that the people of
Dan had rebuilt after the Famine Times and the Scattering. The people
of Dan—Caladan in those days. Odrade took a firm grip on rational
thought, using the stance of the Other Memories that had flooded into
her awareness during the spice agony when she had really become a
full Reverend Mother.

Simulflow . . . the filter of consciousness . . . Other Memories.

What powerful tools the Sisterhood had given her. What dangerous tools. All of those other lives lay there just beyond the curtain of
awareness, tools of survival, not a way to satisfy casual curiosity.

Taraza spoke, translating from the material that scrolled past her
eyes: "You dig too much in your Other Memories. That drains away
energies better conserved."

The Mother Superior's blue-in-blue eyes sent a piercing stare upward at Odrade. "You sometimes go right to the edge of fleshly tolerance. That can lead to your premature death."

"I am careful with the spice, Mother."

"And well you should be! A body can take only so much melange, only so much prowling in its past!"

"Have you found my flaw?" Odrade asked.

"Gammu!" One word but an entire harangue.

Odrade knew. The unavoidable trauma of those lost years on Gammu. They were a distraction that had to be rooted out and made rationally acceptable.

"But I am sent to Rakis," Odrade said.

"And see that you remember the aphorisms of moderation. Remember who you are!"

Once more, Taraza bent to her display.

I am Odrade, Odrade thought.

In the Bene Gesserit schools where first names tended to slip away, roll call was by last name. Friends and acquaintances picked up the habit of using the roll-call name. They learned early that sharing secret or private names was an ancient device for ensnaring a person in affections.

Taraza, three classes ahead of Odrade, had been assigned to "bring the younger girl along," a deliberate association by watchful teachers.

"Bringing along" meant a certain amount of lording it over the younger but also incorporated essentials better taught by someone closer to peer relationship. Taraza, with access to the private records of her trainee, started calling the younger girl "Dar." Odrade responded by calling Taraza "Tar." The two names acquired a certain glue—Dar and Tar. Even after Reverend Mothers overheard and reprimanded them, they occasionally lapsed into error if only for the amusement.

Odrade, looking down at Taraza now, said: "Dar and Tar."

A smile twitched the edges of Taraza's mouth.

"What is it in my records that you don't already know several times over?" Odrade asked.

Taraza sat back and waited for the chairdog to adjust itself to the new position. She rested her clasped hands on the tabletop and looked up at the younger woman.

Not much younger, really, Taraza thought.

Since school, though, Taraza had thought of Odrade as completely removed into a younger age group, creating a gap no passage of years could close.

"Care at the beginning, Dar," Taraza said.

"This project is well past its beginning," Odrade said.

"But your part in it starts now. And we are launching ourselves into such a beginning as has never before been attempted."

"Am I now to learn the entire design for this ghola?"

"No."

That was it. All the evidence of high-level dispute and the "need to know" cast away with a single word. But Odrade understood. There was an organizational rubric laid down by the original Bene Gesserit Chapter House, which had endured with only minor changes for millennia. Bene Gesserit divisions were cut by hard vertical and horizontal barriers, divided into isolated groups that converged to a single command only here at the top. Duties (for which read "assigned roles") were conducted within separated cells. Active participants within a cell did not know their contemporaries within other parallel cells.

But I know that the Reverend Mother Lucilla is in a parallel cell, Odrade thought. *It's the logical answer.*

She recognized the necessity. It was an ancient design copied from secret revolutionary societies. The Bene Gesserit had always seen themselves as permanent revolutionaries. It was a revolution that had been dampened only in the time of the Tyrant, Leto II.

Dampened, but not diverted or stopped, Odrade reminded herself.

"In what you're about to do," Taraza said, "tell me if you sense any immediate threat to the Sisterhood."

It was one of Taraza's *peculiar* demands, which Odrade had learned to answer out of wordless instinct, which then could be formed into words. Quickly, she said: "If we fail to act, that is worse."

"We reasoned that there would be danger," Taraza said. She spoke in a dry, remote voice. Taraza did not like calling up this talent in Odrade. The younger woman possessed a prescient instinct for detecting threats to the Sisterhood. It came from the wild influence in her genetic line, of course—the Atreides with their dangerous talents. There was a special mark on Odrade's breeding file: "Careful examination of all offspring." Two of those offspring had been quietly put to death.

I should not have awakened Odrade's talent now, not even for a moment, Taraza thought. But sometimes temptation was very great.

Taraza sealed the projector into her tabletop and looked at the blank surface while speaking. "Even if you find a perfect sire, you are not to breed without our permission while you are away from us."

"The mistake of my natural mother," Odrade said.

"The mistake of your natural mother was to be recognized while she was breeding!"

Odrade had heard this before. There was that thing about the Atreides line that required the most careful monitoring by the breeding mistresses. The wild talent, of course. She knew about the wild talent, that genetic force which had produced the Kwisatz Haderach and the Tyrant. What did the breeding mistresses seek now, though? Was their approach mostly negative? No more dangerous births! She had never seen any of her babies after they were born, not necessarily a curious thing for the Sisterhood. And she never saw any of the records in her own genetic file. Here, too, the Sisterhood operated with careful separation of powers.

And those earlier prohibitions on my Other Memories!

She had found the blank spaces in her memories and opened them. It was probable that only Taraza and perhaps two other councillors (Bellonda, most likely, and one other older Reverend Mother) shared the more sensitive access to such breeding information.

Had Taraza and the other really sworn to die before revealing privileged information to an outsider? There was, after all, a precise ritual of succession should a key Reverend Mother die while away from her Sisters and with no chance to pass along her encapsulated lives. The ritual had been called into play many times during the reign of the Tyrant. A terrible period! Knowing that the revolutionary cells of the Sisterhood were transparent to him! Monster! She knew that her sisters had never deluded themselves that Leto II refrained from destroying the Bene Gesserit out of some deep-seated loyalty to his grandmother, the Lady Jessica.

Are you there, Jessica?

Odrade felt the stirring far within. The failure of one Reverend Mother: "She allowed herself to fall in love!" Such a small thing but how great the consequences. Thirty-five hundred years of tyranny!

The Golden Path. Infinite? What of the lost megatrillions gone into the Scattering? What threat was posed by those Lost Ones returning now?

As though she read Odrade's mind, which sometimes she appeared to do, Taraza said: "The Scattered ones are out there . . . just waiting to pounce."

Odrade had heard the arguments: Danger on the one hand and on the other, something magnetically attractive. So many magnificent unknowns. The Sisterhood with its talents honed by melange over the millennia—what might they not do with such untapped resources of humanity? Think of the uncounted genes out there! Think of the potential talents floating free in universes where they might be lost forever!

"It's the not knowing that conjures up the greatest terrors," Odrade said.

"And the greatest ambitions," Taraza said.

"Then do I go to Rakis?"

"In due course. I find you adequate to the task."

"Or you would not have assigned me."

It was an old exchange between them, going right back to their school days. Taraza realized, though, that she had not entered it consciously. Too many memories tangled the two of them: Dar and Tar. Have to watch that!

"Remember where your loyalties are," Taraza said.

The existence of no-ships raises the possibility of destroying entire planets without retaliation. A large object, asteroid or equivalent, may be sent against the planet. Or the people can be set against each other by sexual subversion, and then can be armed to destroy themselves. These Honored Matres appear to favor this latter technique.

—BENE GESSERIT ANALYSIS

From his position in the courtyard and even when not appearing to do so, Duncan Idaho kept his attention on the observers above him. There was Patrin, of course, but Patrin did not count. It was the Reverend Mothers across from Patrin who bore watching. Seeing Lucilla, he thought: *That's the new one.* This thought filled him with a surge of excitement, which he took out in renewed exercise.

He completed the first three patterns of the training-play Miles Teg had ordered, vaguely aware that Patrin would report on how well he did. Duncan liked Teg and old Patrin and sensed that the feeling was reciprocated. This new Reverend Mother, though—her presence suggested interesting changes. For one thing, she was younger than the others. Also, this new one did not try to hide the eyes that were a first clue to her membership in the Bene Gesserit. His first glimpse of Schwangyu had confronted him with eyes concealed behind contact lenses that simulated non-addict pupils and slightly bloodshot whites. He had heard one of the Keep's acolytes say Schwangyu's lenses also corrected for "an astigmatic weakness that has been accepted in her

genetic line as a reasonable exchange for the other qualities she trans-
mits to her offspring."

At the time, most of this remark was unintelligible to Duncan but
he had looked up the references in the Keep's library, references both
scarce and severely limited in content. Schwangyu herself parried all
of his questions on the subject, but the subsequent behavior of his
teachers told him she had been angry. Typically, she had taken out her
anger on others.

What really upset her, he suspected, was his demand to know
whether she was his mother.

For a long time now Duncan had known he was something special.
There were places in the elaborate compound of this Bene Gesserit
Keep where he was not permitted. He had found private ways to evade
such prohibitions and had stared out often through thick plaz and
open windows at guards and wide reaches of cleared ground that
could be enfiladed from strategically positioned pillboxes. Miles Teg
himself had taught the significance of enfilade positioning.

Gammu, the planet was called now. Once, it had been known as
Giedi Prime but someone named Gurney Halleck had changed that. It
was all ancient history. Dull stuff. There still remained a faint smell of
bitter oil in the planet's dirt from its pre-Danian days. Millennia of
special plantations were changing that, his teachers explained. He
could see part of this from the Keep. Forests of conifers and other trees
surrounded them here.

Still covertly watching the two Reverend Mothers, Duncan did a
series of cartwheels. He flexed his striking muscles as he moved, just
the way Teg had taught him.

Teg also instructed in planetary defenses. Gammu was ringed by
orbiting monitors whose crews could not have their families aboard.
The families remained down here on Gammu, hostage to the vigilance
of those guardian orbiters. Somewhere among the ships in space, there
were undetectable no-ships whose crews were composed entirely of
the Bashar's people and Bene Gesserit Sisters.

"I would not have taken this assignment without full charge of all defensive arrangements," Teg explained.

Duncan realized that *he* was "this assignment." The Keep was here to protect him. Teg's orbiting monitors, including the no-ships, protected the Keep.

It was all part of a military education whose elements Duncan found somehow familiar. Learning how to defend a seemingly vulnerable planet from attacks originating in space, he *knew* when those defenses were correctly placed. It was extremely complicated as a whole but the elements were identifiable and could be understood. There was, for instance, the constant monitoring of atmosphere and the blood serum of Gammu's inhabitants. Suk doctors in the pay of the Bene Gesserit were everywhere.

"Diseases are weapons," Teg said. "Our defense against diseases must be finely tuned."

Frequently, Teg railed against passive defenses. He called them "the product of a siege mentality long known to create deadly weaknesses."

When it came to military instructions from Teg, Duncan listened carefully. Patrin and the library records confirmed that the Mentat Bashar Miles Teg had been a famous military leader for the Bene Gesserit. Patrin often referred to their service together and always Teg was the hero.

"Mobility is the key to military success," Teg said. "If you're tied down in forts, even whole-planet forts, you are ultimately vulnerable."

Teg did not much care for Gammu.

"I see that you already know this place was called Giedi Prime once. The Harkonnens who ruled here taught us a few things. We have a better idea, thanks to them, of how terrifyingly brutal humans can become."

As he recalled this, Duncan observed that the two Reverend Mothers watching from the parapet obviously were discussing him.

Am I the new one's assignment?

Duncan did not like being watched and he hoped the new one would allow him some time to himself. She did not look like a tough one. Not like Schwangyu.

As he continued his exercises, Duncan timed them to a private litany: *Damn Schwangyu! Damn Schwangyu!*

He had hated Schwangyu from the age of nine—four years now. She did not know his hate, he thought. She had probably forgotten all about the incident where his hate had been ignited.

Barely nine and he had managed to slip through the inner guards out into a tunnel that led to one of the pillboxes. Smell of fungus in the tunnel. Dim lights. Dampness. He peered out through the box's weapons slits before being caught and hustled back into the core of the Keep.

This escapade occasioned a stern lecture from Schwangyu, a remote and threatening figure whose orders must be obeyed. That was how he still thought of her, although he had since learned about the Bene Gesserit Voice-of-Command, that vocal subtlety which could bend the will of an untrained listener.

She must be obeyed.

"You have occasioned the disciplining of an entire guard unit," Schwangyu said. "They will be severely punished."

That had been the most terrible part of her lecture. Duncan liked some of the guards and occasionally lured some of them into real play with laughter and tumbling. His prank, sneaking out to the pillbox, had hurt his friends.

Duncan knew what it was to be punished.

Damn Schwangyu! Damn Schwangyu! . . .

After Schwangyu's lecture, Duncan ran to his chief instructor of the moment, Reverend Mother Tamalane, another of the wizened old ones with a cool and aloof manner, snowy hair above a narrow face and a leather skin. He demanded of Tamalane to know about the punishment of his guards. Tamalane fell into a surprising pensive mood, her voice like sand rasping against wood.

"Punishments? Well, well."

They were in the small teaching room off the larger practice floor where Tamalane went each evening to prepare the next day's lessons. It was a place of bubble and spool readers and other sophisticated means for information storage and retrieval. Duncan far preferred it to the library but he was not allowed in the teaching room unattended. It was a bright room lighted by many suspensor-buoyed glowglobes. At his intrusion, Tamalane turned away from where she laid out his lessons.

"There's always something of a sacrificial banquet about our major punishments," she said. "The guards will, of course, receive major punishment."

"Banquet?" Duncan was puzzled.

Tamalane swung completely around in her swivel seat and looked directly into his eyes. Her steely teeth glittered in the bright lights. "History has seldom been good to those who must be punished," she said.

Duncan flinched at the word "history." It was one of Tamalane's signals. She was going to teach a lesson, another boring lesson.

"Bene Gesserit punishments cannot be forgotten."

Duncan focused on Tamalane's old mouth, sensing abruptly that she spoke out of painful personal experience. He was going to learn something interesting!

"Our punishments carry an inescapable lesson," Tamalane said. "It is much more than the pain."

Duncan sat on the floor at her feet. From this angle, Tamalane was a black-shrouded and ominous figure.

"We do not punish with the ultimate agony," she said. "That is reserved for a Reverend Mother's passage through the spice."

Duncan nodded. Library records referred to "spice agony," a mysterious trial that created a Reverend Mother.

"Major punishments are painful, nonetheless," she said. "They are also emotionally painful. Emotion evoked by punishment is always that emotion we judge to be the penitent's greatest weakness, and thus we strengthen the punished."

Her words filled Duncan with unfocused dread. What were they doing to his guards? He could not speak but there was no need. Tamalane was not finished.

"The punishment always ends with a dessert," she said and she clapped her hands against her knees.

Duncan frowned. Dessert? That was part of a banquet. How could a banquet be punishment?

"It is not really a banquet but the idea of a banquet," Tamalane said. One clawlike hand described a circle in the air. "The dessert comes, something totally unexpected. The penitent thinks: *Ahhh, I have been forgiven at last!* You understand?"

Duncan shook his head from side to side. No, he did not understand.

"It is the sweetness of the moment," she said. "You have been through every course of a painful banquet and come out at the end to something you can savor. But! As you savor it, *then* comes the most painful moment of all, the recognition, the *understanding* that this is not pleasure-at-the-end. No, indeed. This is the ultimate pain of the major punishment. It locks in the Bene Gesserit lesson."

"But what will she do to those guards?" The words were wrenched from Duncan.

"I cannot say what the specific elements of the individual punishments will be. I have no need to know. I can only tell you it will be different for each of them."

Tamalane would say no more. She returned to laying out the next day's lessons. "We will continue tomorrow," she said, "teaching you to identify the sources of the various accents of spoken Galach."

No one else, not even Teg or Patrin, would answer his questions about the punishments. Even the guards, when he saw them afterward, refused to speak of their ordeals. Some reacted curtly to his overtures and none would play with him anymore. There was no forgiveness among the punished. That much was clear.

Damn Schwangyu! Damn Schwangyu! . . .

That was where his deep hatred of her began. All of the old witches shared in his hatred. Would the new young one be the same as the old ones?

Damn Schwangyu!

When he demanded of Schwangyu: "Why did you have to punish them?" Schwangyu took some time before answering, then: "It is dangerous for you here on Gammu. There are people who wish you harm."

Duncan did not ask why. This was another area where his questions were never answered. Not even Teg would answer, although Teg's very presence emphasized the fact of that danger.

And Miles Teg was a Mentat who must know many answers. Duncan often saw the old man's eyes glisten while his thoughts went far away. But there was no Mentat response to such questions as:

"Why are we here on Gammu?"

"Who do you guard against? Who wants to harm me?"

"Who are my parents?"

Silence greeted such questions or sometimes Teg would growl: "I cannot answer you."

The library was useless. He had discovered this when he was only eight and his chief instructor was a failed Reverend Mother named Luran Geasa—not quite as ancient as Schwangyu but well along in years, more than a hundred, anyway.

At his demand, the library produced information about Gammu/Giedi Prime, about the Harkonnens and their fall, about various conflicts where Teg had commanded. None of those battles came through as very bloody; several commentators referred to Teg's "superb diplomacy." But, one datum leading to another, Duncan learned about the time of the God Emperor and the taming of his people. This period commanded Duncan's attention for weeks. He found an old map in the records and projected it on the focus wall. The commentator's superimpositions told him that this very Keep had been a Fish Speaker Command Center abandoned during the Scattering.

Fish Speakers!

Duncan wished then that he had lived during their time, serving as one of the rare male advisors in the female army that had worshiped the great God Emperor.

Oh, to have lived on Rakis in those days!

Teg was surprisingly forthcoming about the God Emperor, calling him always "the Tyrant." A library lock was opened and information about Rakis came pouring out for Duncan.

"Will I ever see Rakis?" he asked Geasa.

"You are being prepared to live there."

The answer astonished him. Everything they taught him about that faraway planet came into new focus.

"Why will I live there?"

"I cannot answer that."

With renewed interest, he returned to his studies of that mysterious planet and its miserable Church of Shai-hulud, the Divided God. *Worms.* The God Emperor had become those worms! The idea filled Duncan with awe. Perhaps here was something worthy of worship. The thought touched a chord in him. What had driven a man to accept that terrible metamorphosis?

Duncan knew what his guards and the others in the Keep thought about Rakis and the core of priesthood there. Sneering remarks and laughter told it all. Teg said: "We'll probably never know the whole truth of it, but I tell you, lad, that's no religion for a soldier."

Schwangyu capped it: "You are to learn about the Tyrant but you are not to believe in his religion. That is beneath you, contemptible."

In every spare study moment, Duncan pored over whatever the library produced for him: the Holy Book of the Divided God, the Guard Bible, the Orange Catholic Bible and even the Apocrypha. He learned about the long defunct Bureau of the Faith and "The Pearl that IS the Sun of Understanding."

The very idea of the worms fascinated him. Their size! A big one would stretch from one end of the Keep to the other. Men had ridden the pre-Tyrant worms but the Rakian priesthood forbade this now.

He found himself gripped by accounts from the archeological team that had found the Tyrant's primitive no-chamber on Rakis. Dar-es-

Balat, the place was called. The reports by Archeologist Hadi Benotto were marked "Suppressed by orders of the Rakian Priesthood." The file number on the accounts from Bene Gesserit Archives was a long one and what Benotto revealed was fascinating.

"A kernel of the God Emperor's awareness in each worm?" he asked Geasa.

"So it's said. And even if true, they are not conscious, not aware. The Tyrant himself said he would enter an endless dream."

Each study session occasioned a special lecture and Bene Gesserit explanations of religion until finally he encountered those accounts called "The Nine Daughters of Siona" and "The Thousand Sons of Idaho."

Confronting Geasa, he demanded: "My name is Duncan Idaho, too. What does that mean?"

Geasa always moved as though standing in the shadow of her failure, her long head bent forward and her watery eyes aimed at the ground. The confrontation occurred near evening in the long hall outside the practice floor. She paled at his question.

When she did not answer, he demanded: "Am I descended from Duncan Idaho?"

"You must ask Schwangyu." Geasa sounded as though the words pained her.

It was a familiar response and it angered him. She meant he would be told something to shut him up, little information in the telling. Schwangyu, however, was more open than expected.

"You carry the authentic blood of Duncan Idaho."

"Who are my parents?"

"They are long dead."

"How did they die?"

"I do not know. We received you as an orphan."

"Then why do people want to harm me?"

"They fear what you may do."

"What is it I may do?"

"Study your lessons. All will be made clear to you in time."

Shut up and study! Another familiar answer.

He obeyed because he had learned to recognize when the doors were closed on him. But now his questing intelligence met other accounts of the Famine Times and the Scattering, the no-chambers and no-ships that could not be traced, not even by the most powerful prescient minds in their universe. Here, he encountered the fact that descendants of Duncan Idaho and Siona, those ancients who had served the Tyrant God Emperor, also were invisible to prophets and prescients. Not even a Guild Steersman deep in melange trance could detect such people. Siona, the accounts told him, was a true-bred Atreides and Duncan Idaho was a ghola.

Ghola?

He probed the library for elaborations on this peculiar word. *Ghola.* The library produced for him no more than bare-boned accounts: *"Gholas: humans grown from a cadaver's cells in Tleilaxu axlotl tanks."*

Axlotl tanks?

"A Tleilaxu device for reproducing a living human being from the cells of a cadaver."

"Describe a ghola," he demanded.

"Innocent flesh devoid of its original memories. See Axlotl Tanks."

Duncan had learned to read the silences, the blank places in what the people of the Keep revealed to him. Revelation swept over him. He knew! Only ten and he knew!

I am a ghola.

Late afternoon in the library, all of the esoteric machinery around him faded into a sensory background, and a ten-year-old sat silently before a scanner hugging the knowledge to himself.

I am a ghola!

He could not remember the axlotl tanks where his cells had grown into an infant. His first memories were of Geasa picking him up from his cradle, the alert interest in those adult eyes that had so soon faded into wary lidding.

It was as though the information so grudgingly supplied him by the Keep's people and records had at last defined a central shape: himself.

"Tell me about the Bene Tleilax," he demanded of the library.

"They are a people self-divided into Face Dancers and Masters. Face Dancers are mules, sterile and submissive to the Masters."

Why did they do this to me?

The information machines of the library were suddenly alien and dangerous. He was afraid, not that his questions might meet more blank walls, but that he would receive answers.

Why am I so important to Schwangyu and the others?

He felt that they had wronged him, even Miles Teg and Patrin. Why was it right to take the cells of a human and produce a ghola?

He asked the next question with great hesitation. "Can a ghola ever remember who he was?"

"It can be done."

"How?"

"The psychological identity of ghola to original pre-sets certain responses, which can be ignited by trauma."

No answer at all!

"But how?"

Schwangyu intruded at this point, arriving at the library unannounced. So something about his questions had been set to alert her!

"All will be made clear to you in time," she said.

She talked down to him! He sensed the injustice in it, the lack of truthfulness. Something within him said he carried more human wisdom in his unawakened self than the ones who presumed themselves so superior. His hatred of Schwangyu reached a new intensity. She was the personification of all who tantalized him and frustrated his questions.

Now, though, his imagination was on fire. He would recapture his original memories! He felt the truth of this. He would remember his parents, his family, his friends . . . his enemies.

He demanded it of Schwangyu: "Did you produce me because of my enemies?"

"You have already learned silence, child," she said. "Rely on that knowledge."

Very well. That's how I will fight you, damned Schwangyu. I will be silent and I will learn. I won't show you how I really feel.

"You know," she said, "I think we're raising a stoic."

She patronized him! He would not be patronized. He would fight them all with silence and watchfulness. Duncan ran from the library and huddled in his room.

In the following months, many things confirmed that he was a ghola. Even a child knew when things around him were extraordinary. He saw other children occasionally beyond the walls, walking along the perimeter road, laughing and calling. He found accounts of children in the library. Adults did not come to those children and engage them in rigorous training of the sort imposed on him. Other children did not have a Reverend Mother Schwangyu to order every smallest aspect of their lives.

His discovery precipitated another change in Duncan's life. Luran Geasa was called away from him and did not return.

She was not supposed to let me know about gholas.

The truth was somewhat more complex, as Schwangyu explained to Lucilla on the observation parapet the day of Lucilla's arrival.

"We knew the inevitable moment would come. He would learn about gholas and ask the pointed questions."

"It was high time a Reverend Mother took over his everyday education. Geasa may have been a mistake."

"Are you questioning my judgment?" Schwangyu snapped.

"Is your judgment so perfect that it may never be questioned?" In Lucilla's soft contralto, the question had the impact of a slap.

Schwangyu remained silent for almost a minute. Presently, she said: "Geasa thought the ghola was an endearing child. She cried and said she would miss him."

"Wasn't she warned about that?"

"Geasa did not have our training."

"So you replaced her with Tamalane at that time. I do not know Tamalane but I presume she is quite old."

"Quite."

"What was his reaction to the removal of Geasa?"

"He asked where she had gone. We did not answer."

"How did Tamalane fare?"

"On his third day with her, he told her very calmly: 'I hate you. Is that what I'm supposed to do?'"

"So quickly!"

"Right now, he's watching you and thinking: I hate Schwangyu. Will I have to hate this new one? But he is also thinking that you are not like the other old witches. You're young. He will know that this must be important."

> Humans live best when each has his place to stand, when each knows where he belongs in the scheme of things and what he may achieve. Destroy the place and you destroy the person.
>
> —BENE GESSERIT TEACHING

Miles Teg had not wanted the Gammu assignment. Weapons master to a ghola-child? Even such a ghola-child as this one, with all of the history woven around him. It was an unwanted intrusion into Teg's well-ordered retirement.

But he had lived all of that life as a Military Mentat under the will of the Bene Gesserit and could not compute an act of disobedience.

Quis custodiet ipsos custodiet?

Who shall guard the guardians? Who shall see that the guardians commit no offenses?

This was a question that Teg had considered carefully on many occasions. It formed one of the basic tenets of his loyalty to the Bene Gesserit. Whatever else you might say about the Sisterhood, they displayed an admirable constancy of purpose.

Moral purpose, Teg labeled it.

The Bene Gesserit moral purpose agreed completely with Teg's principles. That those principles were Bene Gesserit–conditioned in him did not enter into the question. Rational thought, especially Mentat rationality, could make no other judgment.

Teg boiled it down to an essence: If only one person followed such guiding principles, this was a better universe. It was never a question of justice. Justice required resort to law and that could be a fickle mistress, subject always to the whims and prejudices of those who administered the laws. No, it was a question of fairness, a concept that went much deeper. The people upon whom judgment was passed must feel the fairness of it.

To Teg, statements such as "the letter of the law must be observed" were dangerous to his guiding principles. Being fair required agreement, predictable constancy and, above all else, loyalty upward and downward in the hierarchy. Leadership guided by such principles required no outside controls. You did your duty because it was right. And you did not obey because that was *predictably* correct. You did it because the rightness was a thing of this moment. Prediction and prescience had nothing whatsoever to do with it.

Teg knew the Atreides reputation for reliable prescience, but gnomic utterances had no place in his universe. You took the universe as you found it and applied your principles where you could. Absolute commands in the hierarchy were always obeyed. Not that Taraza had made it a question of absolute command, but the implications were there.

"You are the perfect person for this task."

He had lived a long life with many high points and he was retired with honor. Teg knew he was old, slow and with all the defects of age waiting just at the edges of his awareness, but the call to duty quickened him even while he was forced to put down the wish to say "No."

The assignment had come from Taraza personally. The powerful senior of all (including the Missionaria Protectiva) singled him out. Not just a Reverend Mother but *the* Reverend Mother Superior.

Taraza came to his retirement sanctuary on Lernaeus. It honored him for her to do this and he knew it. She appeared at his gate unannounced, accompanied only by two acolyte servers and a small guard force, some of whose faces he recognized. Teg had trained them himself. The time of her arrival was interesting. Morning, shortly after his breakfast. She knew the patterns of his life and certainly knew that he was most alert at this hour. So she wanted him awake and at his fullest capabilities.

Patrin, Teg's old batman, brought Taraza into the east wing sitting room, a small and elegant setting with only solid furniture in it. Teg's dislike of chairdogs and other living furniture was well known. Patrin had a sour look on his face as he ushered the black-robed Mother Superior into the room. Teg recognized the look immediately. Patrin's long, pale face with its many age wrinkles might appear an unmoved mask to others, but Teg was alert to the deepened wrinkles beside the man's mouth, the set stare in the old eyes. So Taraza had said something on the way in here that had disturbed Patrin.

Tall sliding doors of heavy plaz framed the room's eastward view down a long sloping lawn to trees beside the river. Taraza paused just inside the room to admire the view.

Without being told, Teg touched a button. Curtains slid across the view and glowglobes came alight. Teg's action told Taraza he had computed a need for privacy. He emphasized this by ordering Patrin: "Please see that we are not disturbed."

"The orders for the South Farm, sir," Patrin ventured.

"Please see to that yourself. You and Firus know what I want."

Patrin closed the door a little too sharply as he left, a tiny signal but it spoke much to Teg.

Taraza moved a pace into the room and examined it. "Lime green," she said. "One of my favorite colors. Your mother had a fine eye."

Teg warmed to the remark. He had a deep affection for this building and this land. His family had been here only three generations but their mark was on the place. His mother's touches had not really been changed in many rooms.

"It's safe to love land and places," Teg said.

"I particularly liked the burnt orange carpets in the hall and the stained glass fanlight over the entry door," Taraza said. "That fanlight is a real antique, I am sure."

"You did not come here to talk about interior decoration," Teg said.

Taraza chuckled.

She had a high-pitched voice, which the Sisterhood's training had taught her to use with devastating effectiveness. It was not a voice easy to ignore, even when she appeared most carefully casual as she did now. Teg had seen her in Bene Gesserit Council. Her manner there was powerful and persuasive, every word an indicator of the incisive mind that guided her decisions. He could sense an important decision beneath her demeanor now.

Teg indicated a green upholstered chair at his left. She glanced at it, swept her gaze once more around the room and suppressed a smile.

Not a chairdog in the house, she would wager. Teg was an antique surrounding himself with antiques. She seated herself and smoothed her robe while waiting for Teg to take a matching chair facing her.

"I regret the need to ask that you come out of retirement, Bashar," she said. "Unfortunately, circumstances give me little choice."

Teg rested his long arms casually on his chair's arms, a Mentat in repose, waiting. His attitude said: "Fill my mind with data."

Taraza was momentarily abashed. This was an imposition. Teg was still a regal figure, tall and with that large head topped by gray hair. He was, she knew, four SY short of three hundred. Granting that the Standard Year was some twenty hours less than the so-called primitive year, it was still an impressive age with experiences in Bene Gesserit service that demanded that she respect him. Teg wore, she noted, a light gray uniform with no insignia: carefully tailored trousers and jacket, white shirt open at the throat to reveal a deeply wrinkled neck. There was a glint of gold at his waist and she recognized the Bashar's sunburst he had received at retirement. How like the utilitarian Teg! He had made the golden bauble into a belt buckle. This reassured her. Teg would understand her problem.

"Could I have a drink of water?" Taraza asked. "It has been a long and tiresome journey. We came the last stage by one of our transports, which we should have replaced five hundred years ago."

Teg lifted himself from the chair, went to a wall panel and removed a chilled water bottle and glass from a cabinet behind the panel. He put these on a low table at Taraza's right hand. "I have melange," he said.

"No, thank you, Miles. I've my own supply."

Teg resumed his seat and she noted the signs of stiffness. He was still remarkably supple, however, considering his years.

Taraza poured herself a half glass of water and drank it in one swallow. She replaced the glass on the side table with elaborate care. How to approach this? Teg's manner did not fool her. He did not want to leave retirement. Her analysts had warned her about that. Since retirement, he had taken more than a casual interest in farming. His extensive acreage here on Lernaeus was essentially a research garden.

She lifted her gaze and studied him openly. Square shoulders accentuated Teg's narrow waist. He still kept himself active then. That long face with its sharp lines from the strong bones: typically Atreides. Teg returned her gaze as he always did, demanding attention but open to whatever the Mother Superior might say. His thin mouth was cocked into a slight smile, exposing bright and even teeth.

He knows I'm uncomfortable, she thought. *Damn it! He's just as much a servant of the Sisterhood as I am!*

Teg did not prompt her with questions. His manner remained impeccable, curiously withdrawn. She reminded herself that this was a common trait of Mentats and nothing else should be read into it.

Abruptly, Teg stood and strode to a sideboard at Taraza's left. He turned, folded his arms across his breast and leaned there looking down at her.

Taraza was forced to swivel her chair to face him. *Damn him!* Teg was not going to make this any easier for her. All of the Reverend Mother Examiners had remarked a difficulty in getting Teg to sit for conversation. He preferred to stand, his shoulders held with military stiffness, his gaze aimed downward. Few Reverend Mothers matched his height—more than two meters. This trait, the analysts agreed, was Teg's way (probably unconscious) of protesting the Sisterhood's authority over him. None of this, however, showed itself in his other behavior. Teg had always been the most reliable military commander the Sisterhood had ever employed.

In a multisociety universe whose major binding forces interacted with complexity despite the simplicity of labels, reliable military commanders were worth their weight in melange many times over. Religions and the common memory of imperial tyrannies always figured in the negotiations but it was economic forces that eventually carried the day and the military *coin* could be entered on anybody's adding machine. It was there in every negotiation and would be for as long as necessity drove the trading system—the need for particular things (such as spice or the technoproducts of Ix), the need for specialists (such as Mentats or Suk doctors), and all of the other mundane needs for which there were markets: for labor forces, for builders, for designers, for planiformed life, for artists, for exotic pleasures . . .

No legal system could bind such complexity into a whole and this fact quite obviously brought up another necessity—the constant need for arbiters with clout. Reverend Mothers had naturally fallen into this role within the economic web and Miles Teg knew this. He also knew that he was once more being brought out as a bargaining chip. Whether he enjoyed that role did not figure in the negotiations.

"It's not as though you had any family to hold you here," Taraza said.

Teg accepted this silently. Yes, his wife had been dead thirty-eight years now. His children were all grown and, with the exception of one daughter, gone from the nest. He had his many personal interests but no family obligations. True.

Taraza reminded him then of his long and faithful service to the Sisterhood, citing several memorable achievements. She knew the praise would have little effect on him but it provided her with a needed opening for what must follow.

"You have been apprised of your familial resemblance," she said.

Teg inclined his head no more than a millimeter.

"Your resemblance to the first Leto Atreides, grandfather of the Tyrant, is truly remarkable," she said.

Teg gave no sign that he heard or agreed. This was merely a datum, something already stored in his copious memory. He knew he bore Atreides genes. He had seen the likeness of Leto I at Chapter House. It had been oddly like looking into a mirror.

"You're a bit taller," Taraza said.

Teg continued to stare down at her.

"Damn it all, Bashar," Taraza said, "will you at least try to help me?"

"Is that an order, Mother Superior?"

"No, it's not an order!"

Teg smiled slowly. The fact that Taraza allowed herself such an explosion in front of him said many things. She would not do that with people she felt were untrustworthy. And she certainly would not permit herself such an emotional display with a person she considered *merely* an underling.

Taraza sat back in her chair and grinned up at him. "All right," she said. "You've had your fun. Patrin said you would be most upset with me if I called you back to duty. I assure you that you are crucial to our plans."

"What plans, Mother Superior?"

"We are raising a Duncan Idaho ghola on Gammu. He is almost six years old and ready for military education."

Teg allowed his eyes to widen slightly.

"It will be a taxing duty for you," Taraza said, "but I want you to take over his training and protection as soon as possible."

"My likeness to the Atreides Duke," Teg said. "You will use me to restore his original memories."

"In eight or ten years, yes."

"That long!" Teg shook his head. "Why Gammu?"

"His prana-bindu inheritance has been altered by the Bene Tleilax, at our orders. His reflexes will match in speed those of anyone born in our times. Gammu . . . the original Duncan Idaho was born and raised there. Because of the changes in his cellular inheritance we must keep all else as close to the original conditions as possible."

"Why are you doing this?" It was a Mentat's data-conscious tone.

"A female child with the ability to control the worms had been discovered on Rakis. We will have use for our ghola there."

"You will breed them?"

"I am not engaging you as a Mentat. It is your military abilities and your likeness to the original Leto that we need. You know how to re-store his original memories when the time comes."

"So you're really bringing me back as a Weapons Master."

"You think that's a comedown for the man who was Supreme Bashar of all our forces?"

"Mother Superior, you command and I obey. But I will not accept this post without full command of all of Gammu's defenses."

"That already has been arranged, Miles."

"You always did know how my mind works."

"And I've always been confident of your loyalty."

Teg pushed himself away from the sideboard and stood a moment in thought, then: "Who will brief me?"

"Bellonda from Records, the same as before. She will provide you with a cipher to secure the exchange of messages between us."

"I will give you a list of people," Teg said. "Old comrades and the children of some of them. I will want all of them waiting on Gammu when I arrive."

"You don't think any of them will refuse?"

His look said: *"Don't be silly!"*

Taraza chuckled and she thought: *There's a thing we learned well from the original Atreides—how to produce people who command the utmost devotion and loyalty.*

"Patrin will handle the recruiting," Teg said. "He won't accept rank, I know, but he's to get the full pay and courtesies of a colonel-aide."

"You will, of course, be restored to the rank of Supreme Bashar," she said. "We will . . ."

"No. You have Burzmali. We will not weaken him by bringing back his old Commander over him."

She studied him a moment, then: "We have not yet commissioned Burzmali as . . ."

"I am well aware of that. My old comrades keep me fully informed of Sisterhood politics. But you and I, Mother Superior, know it's only a matter of time. Burzmali is the best."

She could only accept this. It was more than a military Mentat's assessment. It was Teg's assessment. Another thought struck her.

"Then you already knew about our dispute in Council!" she accused. "And you let me . . ."

"Mother Superior, if I thought you would produce another monster on Rakis, I would have said so. You trust my decisions; I trust yours."

"Damn you, Miles, we've been apart too long." Taraza stood. "I feel calmer just knowing you'll be back in harness."

"Harness," he said. "Yes. Reinstate me as a Bashar on special assignment. That way, when word gets back to Burzmali, there'll be no silly questions."

Taraza produced a sheaf of ridulian papers from beneath her robe and passed them to Teg. "I've already signed these. Fill in your own reinstatement. The other authorizations are all there, transport vouchers and so on. I give you these orders personally. You are to obey me. You are *my* Bashar, do you understand?"

"Wasn't I always?" he asked.

"It's more important than ever now. Keep that ghola safe and train him well. He's your responsibility. And I will back you in that against anyone."

"I hear Schwangyu commands on Gammu."

"Against anyone, Miles. Don't trust Schwangyu."

"I see. Will you lunch with us? My daughter has . . ."

"Forgive me, Miles, but I must get back soonest. I will send Bellonda at once."

Teg saw her to the door, exchanged a few pleasantries with his old students in her party and watched as they left. They had an armored groundcar waiting in the drive, one of the new models that they obviously had brought with them. Sight of it gave Teg an uneasy feeling.

Urgency!

Taraza had come in person, the Mother Superior herself on a messenger's errand, knowing what that would reveal to him. Knowing so intimately how the Sisterhood performed, he saw the revelation in what had just happened. The dispute in the Bene Gesserit Council went far deeper than his informants had suggested.

"You are my Bashar."

Teg glanced through the sheaf of authorizations and vouchers Taraza had left with him. Already carrying her seal and signature. The trust this implied added to the other things he sensed and increased his disquiet.

"Don't trust Schwangyu."

He slipped the papers into his pocket and went in search of Patrin. Patrin would have to be briefed, and mollified. They would have to discuss whom to call in for this assignment. He began to list some of the names in his mind. Dangerous duty ahead. It called for only the best people. Damn! Everything on the estate here would have to be passed over to Firus and Dimela. So many details! He felt his pulse quicken as he strode through the house.

Passing a house guard, one of his old soldiers, Teg paused: "Martin, cancel all of my appointments for today. Find my daughter and tell her to meet me in my study."

Word spread through the house and, from there, across the estate. Servants and family, knowing that *The* Reverend Mother Superior had just conversed privately with him, automatically set up a protective screen to keep idle distractions away from Teg. His eldest daughter, Dimela, cut him short when he tried to list details necessary to carry on his experimental farm projects.

"Father, I am not an infant!"

They were in the small greenhouse attached to his study. Remains of Teg's lunch sat on the corner of a potting bench. Patrin's notebook was propped against the wall behind the luncheon tray.

Teg looked sharply at his daughter. Dimela favored him in appearance but not in height. Too angular to be a beauty but she had made a good marriage. They had three fine children, Dimela and Firus.

"Where is Firus?" Teg asked.

"He's out seeing to the replanting of the South Farm."

"Oh, yes. Patrin mentioned that."

Teg smiled. It had always pleased him that Dimela had refused the Sisterhood's bid, preferring to marry Firus, a native of Lernaeus, and remain in her father's entourage.

"All I know is that they're calling you back to duty," Dimela said. "Is it a dangerous assignment?"

"You know, you sound exactly like your mother," Teg said.

"So it is dangerous! Damn them, haven't you done enough for them?"

"Apparently not."

She turned away from him as Patrin entered the far end of the greenhouse. He heard her speak to Patrin as they passed.

"The older he gets the more he gets like a Reverend Mother himself!"

What else could she expect? Teg wondered. The son of a Reverend Mother, fathered by a minor functionary of the Combine Honnete Ober Advancer Mercantiles, he had matured in a household that moved to the Sisterhood's beat. It had been apparent to him at an early age that his father's allegiance to CHOAM's interplanetary trading network vanished when his mother objected.

This house had been his mother's house until her death less than a year after his father died. The imprint of her choices lay all around him.

Patrin stopped in front of him. "I came back for my notebook. Have you added any names?"

"A few. You'd better get right on it."

"Yes, sir!" Patrin did a smart about-face and strode back the way he had come, slapping the notebook against his leg.

He feels it, too, Teg thought.

Once more, Teg glanced around him. This house was still his mother's place. After all the years he had lived here, raised a family here! Still her place. Oh, he had built this greenhouse, but the study there had been her private room.

Janet Roxbrough of the Lernaeus Roxbroughs. The furnishings, the decor, still her place. Taraza had seen that. He and his wife had changed some of the surface objects, but the core remained Janet Roxbrough's.

No question about the Fish Speaker blood in that lineage. What a prize she had been for the Sisterhood! That she had wed Loschy Teg and lived out her life here, that was the oddity. An undigestible fact until you knew how the Sisterhood's breeding designs worked over the generations.

They've done it again, Teg thought. *They've had me waiting in the wings all these years just for this moment.*

Has not religion claimed a patent on creation for all of these millennia?

—THE TLEILAXU QUESTION,
FROM MUAD'DIB SPEAKS

The air of Tleilax was crystalline, gripped by a stillness that was part the morning chill and part a sense of fearful crouching, as though life waited out there in the city of Bandalong, life anticipating and ravenous, which would not stir until it received his personal signal. The Mahai, Tylwyth Waff, Master of the Masters, enjoyed this hour more than any other of the day. The city was his now as he looked out through his open window. Bandalong would come alive only at his command. This was what he told himself. The fear that he could sense out there was his hold on any reality that might arise from that incubating reservoir of life: the Tleilaxu civilization that had originated here and then spread its powers afar.

They had waited millennia for this time, his people. Waff savored the moment now. All through the bad times of the Prophet Leto II (not God Emperor but God's Messenger), all through the Famines and the Scattering, through every painful defeat at the hands of lesser creatures, through all of those agonies the Tleilaxu had built their patient forces for this moment.

We have come to our moment, O Prophet!

The city that lay beneath his high window he saw as a symbol, one strong mark on the page of Tleilaxu design. Other Tleilaxu planets, other great cities, interlinked, interdependent, and with central allegiance to his God and his city, awaited the signal that all of them knew must come soon. The twinned forces of Face Dancers and Masheikh had compressed their powers in preparation for the cosmic leap. The millennia of waiting were about to end.

Waff thought of it as "the long beginning."

Yes. He nodded to himself as he looked at the crouching city. From its inception, from that infinitesimal kernel of an idea, Bene Tleilax leaders had understood the perils of a plan so extended, so protracted, so convoluted and subtle. They had known they must surmount near disaster time and again, accept galling losses, submissions and humiliations. All of this and much more had gone into the construction of a particular Bene Tleilax image. By those millennia of pretense they had created a myth.

"The vile, detestable, dirty Tleilaxu! The stupid Tleilaxu! The predictable Tleilaxu! The impetuous Tleilaxu!"

Even the Prophet's minions had fallen prey to this myth. A captive Fish Speaker had stood in this very room and shouted at a Tleilaxu Master: "Long pretense creates a reality! You are truly vile!" So they had killed her and the Prophet did nothing.

How little all of those alien worlds and peoples understood Tleilaxu restraint. Impetuosity? Let them reconsider after the Bene Tleilax demonstrated how many millennia they were capable of waiting for their ascendancy.

"Spannungsbogen!"

Waff rolled the ancient word on his tongue: *The span of the bow!* How far back you draw the bow before releasing your arrow. This arrow would strike deep!

"The Masheikh have waited longer than any other," Waff whispered. He dared to utter the word to himself here in his tower fastness: "Masheikh."

The rooftops below him glittered as the sun lifted. He could hear the stirrings of the city's life. The sweet bitterness of Tleilaxu smells drifted on the air coming in his window. Waff inhaled deeply and closed his window.

He felt renewed by his moment of solitary observation. Turning away from the window, he donned the white khilat robe of honor to which all Domel were conditioned to bow. The robe completely covered his short body, giving him the distinct feeling that it actually was armor.

The armor of God!

"We are the people of the Yaghist," he had reminded his councillors only last night. "All else is frontier. We have fostered the myth of our weakness and evil practices for these millennia with only one purpose. Even the Bene Gesserit believe!"

Seated in the deep, windowless sagra with its no-chamber shield, his nine councillors had smiled in silent appreciation of his words. In the judgment of the ghufran, they knew. The stage upon which the Tleilaxu determined their own destiny had always been the kehl with its right of ghufran.

It was proper that even Waff, the most powerful of all Tleilaxu, could not leave his world and be readmitted without abasing himself in the ghufran, begging pardon for contact with the unimaginable sins of aliens. To go out among the powindah could soil even the mightiest. The khasadars who policed all Tleilaxu frontiers and guarded the selamliks of the women were right to suspect even Waff. He was of the people and the kehl, yes, but he must prove it each time he left the heartland and returned, and certainly every time he entered the selamlik for the distribution of his sperm.

Waff crossed to his long mirror and inspected himself and his robe. To the powindahs, he knew, he appeared an elfin figure barely a meter and a half tall. Eyes, hair, and skin were shades of gray, all a stage for the oval face with its tiny mouth and line of sharp teeth. A Face Dancer might mimic his features and pose, might dissemble at a Masheikh's command, but no Masheikh or khasadar would be fooled. Only the powindahs would be gulled.

Except for the Bene Gesserit!

This thought brought a scowl to his face. Well, the witches had yet to encounter one of the new Face Dancers.

No other people have mastered the genetic language as well as have the Bene Tleilax, he reassured himself. *We are right to call it "the language of God," for God Himself has given us this great power.*

Waff strode to his door and waited for the morning bell. There was no way, he thought, to describe the richness of emotion he felt now. Time unfolded for him. He did not ask why the Prophet's true message had been heard only by the Bene Tleilax. It had been God's doing and, in that, the Prophet had been the Arm of God, worthy of respect as God's Messenger.

You prepared them for us, O Prophet.

And the ghola on Gammu, this ghola at this time, was worth all of the waiting.

The morning bell sounded and Waff strode out into the hall, turned with other emerging white-robed figures and went onto the eastern balcony to greet the sun. As the Mahai and Abdl of his people, he now could identify himself with all Tleilaxu.

We are the legalists of the Shariat, the last of our kind in the universe.

Nowhere outside the sealed chambers of his malik-brothers could he reveal such a secret thought but he knew it was a thought shared in every mind around him now, and the workings of that thought were visible in Masheikh, Domel and Face Dancer alike. The paradox of kinship ties and a sense of social identity that permeated the khel from Masheikh down to the lowliest Domel was not a paradox to Waff.

We work for the same God.

A Face Dancer in the guise of Domel had bowed and opened the balcony doors. Waff, emerging into sunlight with his many companions close around, smiled at recognition of the Face Dancer. *A Domel yet!* It was a kin-joke but Face Dancers were not kin. They were constructs, tools, just as the ghola on Gammu was a tool, all designed with the language of God spoken only by Masheikhs.

With the others who pressed close around him Waff made obeisance

to the sun. He uttered the cry of the Abdl and heard it echoed by countless voices from the farthest reaches of the city.

"The sun is not God!" he shouted.

No, the sun was only a symbol of God's infinite powers and mercy—
another construct, another tool. Feeling cleansed by his passage through
the ghufran the previous night, renewed by the morning ritual, Waff
could think now about the trip outward to powindah places and the
return just completed, which had made ghufran necessary. Other worshipers made way for him as he went back to the inner corridors and
entered the slide passage that dropped him to the central garden where
he had asked his councillors to meet him.

It was a successful foray among the powindah, he thought.

Every time he left the inner worlds of the Bene Tleilax Waff felt himself to be on lashkar, a war party seeking that ultimate revenge which
his people named secretly as Bodal (always capitalized and always the
first thing reaffirmed in ghufran or khel). This most recent lashkar had
been exquisitely successful.

Waff emerged from the slide into a central garden filled with sunlight by prismatic reflectors on the surrounding rooftops. A small fountain played its visual fugue at the heart of a graveled circle. A low fence
of white palings at one side enclosed a closely cropped lawn, a space near
enough to the fountain that the air would be moist but not so close that
the splashing water would intrude on low-voiced conversation. Around
the grassy enclosure, ten narrow benches of an ancient plastic were
arranged—nine of them in a semicircle facing a tenth bench set slightly
apart.

Pausing at the edge of the grassy enclosure, Waff glanced around
him, wondering why he had never before felt quite this intense pleasure at sight of the place. The dark blue of the benches was intrinsic to
the material. Centuries of use had worn the benches into soft curves
along the arm rests and where countless bottoms had planted themselves, but the color was just as strong in the worn places as it was
elsewhere.

Waff sat down facing his nine councillors, marshaling the words he knew he must use. The document he had brought back from his latest lashkar, indeed, the very reason for that excursion, could not have been more exquisitely timed. The label on it and the words carried a mighty message for the Tleilaxu.

From an inner pocket Waff removed the thin sheaf of ridulian crystal. He noted the quickened interest of his councillors: nine faces similar to his own, Masheikhs of the innermost kehl. All reflected expectancy. They had read this document in kehl: "The Atreides Manifesto." They had spent a night of reflection on the manifesto's message. Now, the words must be confronted. Waff placed the document on his lap.

"I propose to spread these words far and wide," Waff said.

"Without change?" That was Mirlat, the councillor closest to gholatransformation among all of them. Mirlat no doubt aspired to Abdl and Mahai. Waff focused on the councillor's wide jaws where the cartilage had grown over the centuries as a visible mark of his current body's great age.

"Exactly as it has come into our hands," Waff said.

"Dangerous," Mirlat said.

Waff turned his head to the right, his childlike profile outlined against the fountain for his councillors to observe. *God's hand is on my right!* The sky above him was polished carnelian as though Bandalong, the most ancient city of the Tleilaxu, had been built under one of those gigantic artificial covers erected to protect pioneers on the harsher planets. When he returned his attention to his councillors, Waff's features remained bland.

"Not dangerous to us," he said.

"A matter of opinion," Mirlat said.

"Then let us consider opinions," Waff said. "Have we a need to fear Ix or the Fish Speakers? Indeed not. They are ours, although they do not know it."

Waff let this sink in; all of them knew that new Face Dancers sat in the highest councils of Ix and Fish Speakers, the exchange undetected.

"The Guild will not move against us or oppose us because we are their only secure source of melange," Waff said.

"Then what of these Honored Matres returned from the Scattering?" Mirlat demanded.

"We will deal with them when it is required of us," Waff said. "And we will be helped by the descendants of our own people who voluntarily went out into the Scattering."

"The time does appear opportune," one of the other councillors murmured.

It was Torg the Younger who had spoken, Waff observed. Good. There was a vote secured.

"The Bene Gesserit!" Mirlat snapped.

"I think the Honored Matres will remove the witches from our path," Waff said. "Already they growl against each other like animals in the fighting pit."

"What if the author of that manifesto is identified?" Mirlat demanded. "What then?"

Several heads nodded among the councillors. Waff marked them: people to be won over.

"It is dangerous to be called Atreides in this age," he said.

"Except perhaps on Gammu," Mirlat said. "And the name Atreides has been signed to that document!"

How odd, Waff thought. The CHOAM representative at the powindah conference that had taken Waff away from the inner planets of Tleilax had emphasized that very point. But most of CHOAM's people were secret atheists who looked on all religion as suspect, and certainly the Atreides had been a potent religious force. CHOAM worries had been almost palpable.

Waff recounted this CHOAM reaction now.

"This CHOAM hireling, damn his Godless soul, is right," Mirlat insisted. "The document's insidious."

Mirlat will have to be dealt with, Waff thought. He lifted the manifesto from his lap and read the first line aloud:

"In the beginning was the word and the word was God."

"Directly from the Orange Catholic Bible," Mirlat said. Once more, heads nodded in worried agreement.

Waff showed the points of his canines in a brief smile. "Do you suggest that there are those among the powindah who suspect the existence of the Shariat and the Masheikhs?"

It felt good to speak these words openly, reminding his listeners that only here among the innermost Tleilaxu were the old words and the old language preserved without change. Did Mirlat or any of the others fear that Atreides words could subvert the Shariat?

Waff posed this question, too, and saw the worried frowns.

"Is there one among you," Waff asked, "who believes that a single powindah knows how we use the language of God?"

There! Let them think on that! Every one of them here had been wakened time after time in ghola flesh. There was a fleshly continuity in this Council that no other people had ever achieved. Mirlat himself had seen the Prophet with his own eyes. Scytale had spoken to Muad'Dib! Learning how the flesh could be renewed and the memories restored, they had condensed this power into a single government whose potency was confined lest it be demanded everywhere. Only the witches had a similar storehouse of experience upon which to draw and they moved with fearful caution, terrified that they might produce another Kwisatz Haderach!

Waff said these things to his councillors, adding: "The time for action has come."

When no one spoke disagreement, Waff said: "This manifesto has a single author. Every analysis agrees. Mirlat?"

"Written by one person and that person a true Atreides, no doubt of it," Mirlat agreed.

"All at the powindah conference affirmed this," Waff said. "Even a third-stage Guild steersman agrees."

"But that one person has produced a thing that excites violent reactions among diverse peoples," Mirlat argued.

"Have we ever questioned the Atreides talent for disruption?" Waff asked. "When the powindah showed me this document I knew God had sent us a signal."

"Do the witches still deny authorship?" Torg the Younger asked.

How alertly apt he is, Waff thought.

"Every powindah religion is called into question by this manifesto," Waff said. "Every faith except ours is left hanging in limbo."

"Exactly the problem!" Mirlat pounced.

"But only we know this," Waff said. "Who else even suspects the existence of the Shariat?"

"The Guild," Mirlat said.

"They have never spoken of it and they never will. They know what our response would be."

Waff lifted the sheaf of papers from his lap and again read aloud:

"Forces that we cannot understand permeate our universe. We see the shadows of those forces when they are projected upon a screen available to our senses, but understand them we do not."

"The Atreides who wrote that knows of the Shariat," Mirlat muttered.

Waff continued reading as though there had been no interruption:

"Understanding requires words. Some things cannot be reduced to words. There are things that can only be experienced wordlessly."

As though he handled a holy relic, Waff returned the document to his lap. Softly, so that his listeners were required to bend toward him and some cupped a hand behind an ear, Waff said: "This says our universe is magical. It says all arbitrary forms are transient and subject to magical changes. Science has led us to this interpretation as though it placed us on a track from which we cannot deviate."

He allowed these words to fester for a moment, then: "No Rakian priest of the Divided God nor any other powindah charlatan can accept that. Only we know it because our God is a magical God whose language we speak."

"We will be accused of the authorship," Mirlat said. The moment he had spoken, Mirlat shook his head sharply from side to side. "No! I see it. I see what you mean."

Waff held his silence. He could see that all of them were reflecting on their Sufi origins, recalling the Great Belief and the Zensunni ecumenism that had spawned the Bene Tleilax. The people of this kehl knew the God-given facts of their origins but generations of secrecy assured that no powindah shared their knowledge.

Words flowed silently through Waff's mind: *"Assumptions based on understanding contain belief in an absolute ground out of which all things spring like plants growing from seeds."*

Knowing that his councillors also recalled this catechism of the Great Belief, Waff reminded them of the Zensunni admonition.

"Behind such assumptions lies a faith in words that the powindah do not question. Only the Shariat question and we do so silently."

His councillors nodded in unison.

Waff inclined his head slightly and continued: "The act of saying that things exist that cannot be described in words shakes a universe where words are the supreme belief."

"Powindah poison!" his councillors shouted.

He had them all now and Waff hammered home his victory by demanding: "What is the Sufi-Zensunni Credo?"

They could not speak it but all reflected on it: *To achieve s'tori no understanding is needed. S'tori exists without words, without even a name.*

In a moment, all of them looked up and exchanged knowing glances. Mirlat took it upon himself to recite the Tleilaxu pledge:

"I can say God, but that is not my God. That is only a noise and no more potent than any other noise."

"I now see," Waff said, "that you all sense the power that has fallen into our hands through this document. Millions upon millions of copies already are being circulated among the powindah."

"Who does this?" Mirlat asked.

"Who cares?" Waff countered. "Let the powindah chase after them, seeking their origin, trying to suppress them, preaching against them. With each such action, the powindah inject more power into these words."

"Should we not preach against these words, too?" Mirlat asked.

"Only if the occasion demands it," Waff said. "See you!" He slapped the papers against his knees. "The powindah have constricted their awareness to its tightest purpose and that is their weakness. We must insure that this manifesto gains as wide a circulation as possible."

"The magic of our God is our only bridge," the councillors intoned.

All of them, Waff observed, had been restored to the central security of their faith. It had been easily managed. No Masheikh shared the powindah stupidity that whined: "In thy infinite grace, God, why me?" In one sentence, the powindah invoked infinity and denied it, never once observing their own foolishness.

"Scytale," Waff said.

The youngest and most baby-faced of the councillors, seated at the far left as was fitting, leaned forward eagerly.

"Arm the faithful," Waff said.

"I marvel that an Atreides has given us this weapon," Mirlat said. "How can it be that the Atreides always fasten upon an ideal that enlists the billions who must follow?"

"It is not the Atreides, it is God," Waff said. He lifted his arms then and spoke the closing ritual: "The Masheikh have met in kehl and felt the presence of their God."

Waff closed his eyes and waited for the others to leave. *Masheikh!* How good it was to name themselves in kehl, speaking the language of Islamiyat, which no Tleilaxu spoke outside his own secret councils; not even to Face Dancers did they speak it. Nowhere in the Wekht of Jandola, not to the farthest reaches of the Tleilaxu Yaghist, was there a living powindah who knew this secret.

Yaghist, Waff thought, rising from his bench. *Yaghist, the land of the unruled.*

He thought he could feel the document vibrating in his hand. This Atreides Manifesto was the very kind of thing the masses of powindah would follow to their doom.

Some days it's melange; some days it's bitter dirt.

—RAKIAN APHORISM

In her third year with the priests of Rakis, the girl Sheeana lay full length atop a high curving dune. She peered into the morning distance where a great rumbling friction could be heard. The light was a ghostly silver that frosted the horizon with filmy haze. The night's chill still lay on the sand.

She knew the priests were watching her from the safety of their water-girded tower some two kilometers behind her, but this gave her little concern. The trembling of the sand beneath her body demanded full attention.

It's a big one, she thought. *Seventy meters at least. A beautiful big one.*

The gray stillsuit felt slick and smooth against her skin. It had none of the abrasive patches of the old hand-me-down she had worn before the priests took her into their care. She felt thankful for the fine stillsuit and the thick robe of white and purple that covered it, but most of all she felt the excitement of being here. Something rich and dangerous filled her at moments such as this.

The priests did not understand what happened here. She knew this. They were cowards. She glanced over her shoulder at the distant tower and saw sunglint on lenses.

A precocious child of eleven standard years, slender and dark-skinned with sun-streaked brown hair, she could visualize clearly what the priests saw through their spying lenses.

They see me doing what they do not dare. They see me in the path of Shaitan. I look very small on the sand and Shaitan looks very big. They can see him already.

From the rasping sound, she knew that she, too, would soon see the giant worm. Sheeana did not think of the approaching monster as Shai-hulud, God of the sands, a thing the priests chanted each morning in obeisance to the pearl of Leto II's awareness that lay encapsulated in each of the multi-ridged rulers of the desert. She thought of the worms mainly as "they who spared me," or as Shaitan.

They belonged to her now.

It was a relationship begun slightly more than three years ago during the month of her eighth birthday, the Month Igat by the old calendar. Her village had been a poor one, a pioneer venture built far beyond more secure barriers such as the qanats and ring canals of Keen. Only a moat of damp sand guarded such pioneer places. Shaitan avoided water but the sandtrout vector soon took away any dampness. Precious moisture captured in windtraps had to be expended each day to renew the barrier. Her village was a miserable cluster of shacks and hovels with two small windtraps, adequate for drinking water but with only a sporadic surplus that could be apportioned to the worm barrier.

That morning—much like this morning, the night's chill sharp in her nose and lungs, the horizon constricted by a ghostly haze—most of the village children had fanned out into the desert, there to seek bits and fragments of melange, which Shaitan sometimes left behind in his passage. Two big ones had been heard nearby in the night. Melange, even at modern deflated prices, could buy the glazed bricks to line a third windtrap.

Each searching child not only looked for the spice but also sought those signs which would reveal one of the old Fremen sietch strongholds. There were only remnants of such places now but the rock barriers provided a greater security against Shaitan. And some of the remnant sietch places were reputed to contain lost hoards of melange. Every villager dreamed of such a discovery.

Sheeana, wearing her patched stillsuit and flimsy robe, went alone to the northeast, toward the faraway smoky mound of air that told of the great city of Keen with its moisture richness lifting into the sun-warmed breezes.

Hunting scraps of melange in the sand was largely a matter of focusing attention into the nostrils. It was a form of concentration that left only bits of awareness attuned to the rasping sand that told of Shaitan's approach. Leg muscles moved automatically in the non-rhythmic walk that blended with the desert's natural sounds.

At first, Sheeana did not hear the screaming. It fitted intimately into the saltated friction of windblown sand across the barracans that concealed the village from her sight. Slowly the sound penetrated her consciousness and then it demanded her attention.

Many voices screaming!

Sheeana discarded the desert precaution of random strides. Moving swiftly as her childish muscles would carry her, she scrambled up the slipface of the barracan and stared along it toward that terrifying sound. She was in time to see that which cut off the last of the screams.

Wind and sandtrout had dried a wide arc of the barrier at the far side of her village. She could see the gap by the color difference. A wild worm had penetrated the opening. It circled close inside the remaining dampness. The gigantic flame-shadowed mouth scooped up people and hovels in a swiftly tightening circle.

Sheeana saw the last survivors huddled at the center of this destruction, a space already cleared of its rude hovels and tumbled with the remains of the windtraps. Even as she watched, some of the people tried to break away into the desert. Sheeana recognized her father among the frantic runners. None escaped. The great mouth engulfed all before turning to level the last of the village.

Smoking sand remained and nothing else of the puny village that had dared to claim a scrap of Shaitan's domain. The place where the village had been was as unmarked by human habitation as it had been before anyone walked there.

Sheeana took a gasping breath, inhaling through her nose to preserve the moisture of her body as any good child of the desert would do. She scanned the horizon for a sign of the other children but Shaitan's track had left great curves and loops all around the far side of the village. Not a single human remained in view. She shouted, the high-pitched cry that would carry far through the dry air. No response came back to her.

Alone.

She moved trancelike along the ridge of the dune toward where her village had been. As she neared the place a great wave of cinnamon odor filled her nostrils, carried on the wind that still dusted the tops of the dunes. She realized then what had happened. The village had been sited disastrously atop a pre-spice blow. As the great hoard far under the sand came to fruition, expanding in an explosion of melange, Shaitan had come. Every child knew Shaitan could not resist a spiceblow.

Rage and wild desperation began to fill Sheeana. Mindlessly, she raced down the dune toward Shaitan, coming up behind the worm as it turned back through the dry place where it had entered the village. Without thought, she dashed along beside the tail, scrambled onto it and ran forward along the great ridged back. At the hump behind its mouth, she crouched and beat her fists against the unyielding surface.

The worm stopped.

Her anger suddenly converted to terror, Sheeana broke off pounding on the worm. She realized only then that she had been screaming. A terrible sense of lonely exposure filled her. She did not know how she had come here. She knew only where she was and this gripped her with an agony of fear.

The worm continued quiescent on the sand.

Sheeana did not know what to do. At any moment, the worm could roll over and crush her. Or it could burrow beneath the sand, leaving her on the surface to be scooped up at leisure.

Abruptly, a long tremor worked its way down the worm's length from its tail to Sheeana's position behind the mouth. The worm began to move ahead. It turned in a wide arc and gathered speed on a course to the northeast.

Sheeana leaned forward and gripped the leading edge of a ring ridge on the worm's back. She feared that any second it would slide beneath the sand. What could she do then? But Shaitan did not burrow. As minutes passed without any deviation from that straight and swift passage across the dunes, Sheeana found her mind working once more. She knew about this ride. The priests of the Divided God forbade it but the histories, both written and oral, said Fremen rode thus in the ancient days. Fremen stood tall atop Shaitan's back supported by slender poles with hooked ends. The priests decreed that this had been done before Leto II shared His consciousness with the God of the desert. Now, nothing was permitted that might demean the scattered bits of Leto II.

With a speed that astonished her, the worm carried Sheeana toward the mist-dazzled shape of Keen. The great city lay like a mirage on the distorted horizon. Sheeana's threadbare robe whipped against the thin surface of her patched stillsuit. Her fingers ached where she gripped the leading edge of the giant ring. The cinnamon, burnt-rock and ozone of the worm's heat exchange swept over her on shifts in the wind.

Keen began to gain definition ahead of her.

The priests will see me and be angry, she thought.

She identified the low brick structures that marked the first line of qanats and, beyond them, the enclosed barrel-curve of a surface aqueduct. Above these structures rose the walls of terraced gardens and the high profiles of giant windtraps, then the temple complex within its own water barriers.

A day's march across open sand in little more than an hour!

Her parents and village neighbors had made this journey many times for trade and to join in the dancing but Sheeana had only accompanied them twice. She remembered mostly the dancing and the violence that followed. The size of Keen filled her with awe. So many buildings! So many people! Shaitan could not harm such a place as that.

But the worm plunged straight ahead as though it would ride over qanat and aqueduct. Sheeana stared at the city rising higher and higher in front of her. Fascination subdued her terror. Shaitan was not going to stop!

The worm ground to a halt.

The tubular surface vents of the qanat lay no more than fifty meters in front of its gaping mouth. She smelled the hot cinnamon exhalations, heard the deep rumblings of Shaitan's interior furnace.

It became apparent to her at last that the journey had ended. Slowly, Sheeana released her grip on the ring. She stood, expecting any moment the worm would renew its motion. Shaitan remained quiescent. Moving cautiously, she slid off her perch and dropped to the sand. She paused there. Would it move now? She held a vague idea of dashing for the qanat but this worm fascinated her. Slipping and sliding in the disturbed sand, Sheeana moved around to the front of the worm and stared into the fearsome mouth. Within the frame of crystal teeth flames rolled forward and backward. A searing exhalation of spice odors swept over her.

The madness of that first dash down off the dune and onto the worm came back to Sheeana. "Damn you, Shaitan!" she shouted, shaking a fist at the awful mouth. "What did we ever do to you?"

These were words she had heard her mother use at the destruction of a tuber garden. No part of Sheeana's awareness had ever questioned that name, Shaitan, nor her mother's fury. She was of the poorest dregs at the bottom of the Rakian heap and she knew it. Her people believed in Shaitan first and Shai-hulud second. Worms were worms and often much worse. There was no justice on the open sand. Only danger lurked there. Poverty and fear of priests might drive her people onto the perilous dunes but they moved even then with the same angry persistence that had driven the Fremen.

This time, however, Shaitan had won.

It entered Sheeana's awareness that she stood in the deadly path. Her thoughts, not yet fully formed, recognized only that she had done a crazy thing. Much later, as the Sisterhood's teachings rounded her consciousness, she would realize that she had been overcome by the terror of loneliness. She had wanted Shaitan to take her into the company of her dead.

A grating sound issued from beneath the worm.

Sheeana stifled a scream.

Slowly at first, then faster, the worm backed off several meters. It turned there and gathered speed beside the twin-mounded track it had created coming from the desert. The grating of its passage diminished in the distance. Sheeana grew aware of another sound. She lifted her gaze to the sky. The thwock-thwock of a priestly ornithopter swept over her, brushing her with its shadow. The craft glistened in the morning sunlight as it followed the worm into the desert.

Sheeana felt a more familiar fear then.

The priests!

She kept her gaze on the 'thopter. It hovered in the distance, then returned to settle gently onto a patch of worm-smoothed sand nearby. She could smell the lubricants and the sickly acridity of the 'thopter's fuel. The thing was a giant insect nestled on the sand, waiting to pounce upon her.

A hatch popped open.

Sheeana threw back her shoulders and stood her ground. Very well; they had caught her. She knew what to expect now. Nothing could be gained by flight. Only the priests used 'thopters. They could go anywhere and see anything.

Two richly robed priests, their garments all gold and white with purple trim, emerged and ran toward her across the sand. They knelt in front of Sheeana so close she could smell their perspiration and the musky melange incense which permeated their clothing. They were young but much like all the priests she could remember: soft of features, uncalloused hands, careless of their moisture losses. Neither of them wore a stillsuit under those robes.

The one on her left, his eyes on a level with Sheeana's, spoke.

"Child of Shai-hulud, we saw your Father bring you from His lands."

The words made no sense to Sheeana. Priests were men to be feared. Her parents and all the adults she had ever known had impressed this upon her by words and actions. Priests possessed ornithopters. Priests fed you to Shaitan for the slightest infraction or for no infraction at all, for only priestly whims. Her people knew many instances.

Sheeana backed away from the kneeling men and cast her glance around. Where could she run?

The one who had spoken raised an imploring hand. "Stay with us."

"You're bad!" Sheeana's voice cracked with emotion.

Both priests fell prostrate on the sand.

Far away on the city's towers, sunlight flashed off lenses. Sheeana saw them. She knew about such flashings. Priests were always watching you in the cities. When you saw the lenses flash that was the signal to be inconspicuous, to "be good."

Sheeana clasped her hands in front of her to still their trembling. She glanced left and right and then at the prostrate priests. Something was wrong here.

Heads on the sand, the two priests shuddered with fear and waited. Neither spoke.

Sheeana did not know how to respond. The crush of her immediate experiences could not be absorbed by an eight-year-old mind. She knew that her parents and all of her neighbors had been taken by Shaitan. Her own eyes had witnessed this. And Shaitan had brought her here, refusing to take her into his awful fires. She had been spared.

This was a word she understood. *Spared.* It had been explained to her when she learned the dancing song.

"*Shai-hulud spare us!*

"*Take Shaitan away . . .*"

Slowly, not wanting to arouse the prostrate priests, Sheeana began the shuffling, unrhythmic movements of the dance. As the remembered music grew within her, she unclasped her hands and swung her arms wide. Her feet lifted high in the stately movements. Her body turned, slowly at first and then more swiftly as the dance ecstasy increased. Her long brown hair whipped around her face.

The two priests dared to lift their heads. The strange child was performing The Dance! They recognized the movements: The Dance of Propitiation. She asked Shai-hulud to forgive His people. She asked God to forgive *them*!

They turned their heads to look at each other and, together, rocked back onto their knees. There, they began clapping in the time-honored effort to distract the dancer. Their hands clapped rhythmically as they chanted the ancient words:

"Our fathers ate manna in the desert,
"In the burning places where whirlwinds came!"

The priests excluded from their attention all except the child. She was a slender thing, they saw, with stringy muscles, thin arms and legs. Her robe and stillsuit were worn and patched like those of the poorest. Her cheekbones had high planes that drew shadows across her olive skin. Brown eyes, they noted. Reddish sun streaks drew their lines in her hair. There was a water-spare sharpness about her features—the narrow nose and chin, the wide forehead, the wide thin mouth, the long neck. She looked like the Fremen portraits in the holy of holies at Dar-es-Balat. Of course! The child of Shai-hulud would look thus.

She danced well, too. Not the slightest quickly repeatable rhythm entered her movements. There was rhythm but it was an admirably long beat, at least a hundred steps apart. She kept it up while the sun lifted higher and higher. It was almost noon before she fell exhausted to the sand.

The priests stood and looked out into the desert where Shai-hulud had gone. The stampings of the dance had not summoned Him back. They were forgiven.

That was how Sheeana's new life began.

Loudly in their own quarters and for many days, the senior priests engaged in arguments about her. At last, they brought their disputations and reports to the High Priest, Hedley Tuek. They met in the afternoon within the Hall of Small Convocations, Tuek and six priestly councillors. Murals of Leto II, a human face on the great wormshape, looked down upon them with benevolence.

Tuek seated himself on a stone bench that had been recovered from Windgap Sietch. Muad'Dib himself was reputed to have sat on this bench. One of the legs still bore the carvings of an Atreides hawk.

His councillors took lesser modern benches facing him.

The High Priest was an imposing figure; silky gray hair combed smoothly to his shoulders. It was a suitable frame for the square face with its wide, thick mouth and heavy chin. Tuek's eyes retained their original clear whites surrounding dark blue pupils. Bushy, untrimmed gray eyebrows shaded his eyes.

The councillors were a motley lot. Scions of old priestly families, each carried in his heart the belief that matters would move better if *he* were sitting on Tuek's bench.

The scrawny, pinch-faced Stiros put himself forward as opposition spokesman: "She is nothing but a poor desert waif and she rode Shai-hulud. That is forbidden and the punishment is mandatory."

Others spoke up immediately. "No! No, Stiros. You have it wrong! She did not stand on Shai-hulud's back as the Fremen did. She had no maker hooks or . . ."

Stiros tried to shout them down.

It was deadlocked, Tuek saw: three and three with Umphrud, a fat hedonist, as advocate for "cautious acceptance."

"She had no way to guide Shai-hulud's course," Umphrud argued. "We all saw how she came down to the sand unafraid and talked to Him."

Yes, they all had seen that, either at the moment or in the holo-photo that a thoughtful observer had recorded. Desert waif or not, she had confronted Shai-hulud and conversed with Him. And Shai-hulud had not engulfed her. No, indeed. The Worm-of-God had drawn back at the child's command and had returned to the desert.

"We will test her," Tuek said.

Early the following morning, an ornithopter flown by the two priests who had brought her from the desert conveyed Sheeana far out away from the sight of Keen's populace. The priests took her down to a dune top and planted a meticulous copy of a Fremen thumper in the sand. When the thumper's catch was released, a heavy beating trembled through the desert—the ancient summons to Shai-hulud. The priests fled to their 'thopter and waited high overhead while a terrified Sheeana, her worst fears realized, stood alone some twenty meters from the thumper.

Two worms came. They were not the largest the priests had ever seen, no more than thirty meters long. One of them scooped up the thumper and silenced it. Together, they rounded in parallel tracks and stopped side by side not six meters from Sheeana.

She stood submissive, fists clenched at her sides. This was what priests did. They fed you to Shaitan.

In their hovering 'thopter, the two priests watched with fascination. Their lenses transmitted the scene to equally fascinated observers in the High Priest's quarters at Keen. All of them had seen similar events before. It was a standard punishment, a handy way to remove obstructionists from the populace or priesthood, or to pave the way for acquisition of a new concubine. Never before, though, had they seen a lone child as victim. And such a child!

The Worms-of-God crept forward slowly after their first stop. They became motionless once more when only about three meters from Sheeana.

Resigned to her fate, Sheeana did not run. Soon, she thought, she would be with her parents and friends. As the worms remained motionless, anger replaced her terror. The bad priests had left her here! She could hear their 'thopter overhead. The hot spice smell from the worms filled the air around her. Abruptly, she raised her right hand and pointed up at the 'thopter.

"Go ahead and eat me! That's what they want!"

The priests overhead could not hear her words but the gesture was visible and they could see that she was talking to the two Worms-of-God. The finger pointing up at them did not bode well.

The worms did not move.

Sheeana lowered her hand. "You killed my mother and father and all my friends!" she accused. She took a step forward and shook a fist at them.

The worms retreated, keeping their distance.

"If you don't want me, go back where you came from!" She waved them away toward the desert.

Obediently, they backed farther and turned in unison.

The priests in the 'thopter tracked them until they slipped beneath the sand more than a kilometer away. Only then did the priests return, fear and trepidation in them. They plucked the child of Shai-hulud from the sand and returned her to Keen.

The Bene Gesserit embassy at Keen had a full report by nightfall. Word was on its way to the Chapter House by the following morning.

It had happened at last!

The trouble with some kinds of warfare (and be certain the Tyrant knew this, because it is implicit in his lesson) is that they destroy all moral decency in susceptible types. Warfare of these kinds will dump the destroyed survivors back into an innocent population that is incapable of even imagining what such returned soldiers might do.

—TEACHINGS OF THE GOLDEN PATH,
BENE GESSERIT ARCHIVES

One of Miles Teg's early memories was of sitting at dinner with his parents and his younger brother, Sabine. Teg had been only seven at the time, but the events lay indelibly in his memory: the dining room on Lernaeus colorful with freshly cut flowers, the low light of the yellow sun diffused by antique shades. Bright blue dinnerware and glistening silver graced the table. Acolyte servants stood ready at hand, because his mother might be permanently detached on special duty but her function as a Bene Gesserit teacher was not to be wasted.

Janet Roxbrough-Teg, a large-boned woman who appeared cast for the part of grande dame, looked down her nose from one end of the table, watching that the dinner service not be impaired by the slightest misplacement. Loschy Teg, Miles' father, always observed this with a faint air of amusement. He was a thin man with high forehead, a face so narrow his dark eyes appeared to bulge at the sides. His black hair was a perfect counterpoint for his wife's fairness.

Above the subdued sounds at the table and the rich smell of spiced edu soup, his mother instructed his father on how to deal with an importunate Free Trader. When she said "Tleilaxu," she had Miles' entire attention. His education had just recently touched on the Bene Tleilax.

Even Sabine, who succumbed many years later to a poisoner on Romo, listened with as much of his four-year-old awareness as he could muster. Sabine hero-worshiped his brother. Anything that caught the attention of Miles was of interest to Sabine. Both boys listened silently.

"The man is fronting for the Tleilaxu," Lady Janet said. "I can hear it in his voice."

"I do not doubt your ability to detect such things, my dear," Loschy Teg said. "But what am I to do? He has the proper tokens of credit and he wishes to buy the—"

"The order for the rice is unimportant at the moment. Never assume that what a Face Dancer appears to seek is actually what it seeks."

"I'm sure he's not a Face Dancer. He—"

"Loschy! I know you have learned this well at my instruction and can detect a Face Dancer. I agree that the Free Trader is not one of them. The Face Dancers remain on his ship. They know I am here."

"They know they could not fool you. Yes, but—"

"Tleilaxu strategy is always woven within a web of strategies, any one of which may be the real strategy. They learned that from us."

"My dear, if we are dealing with Tleilaxu, and I do not question your judgment, then it immediately becomes a question of melange."

Lady Janet nodded her head gently. Indeed, even Miles knew about the Tleilaxu connection with the spice. It was one of the things that fascinated him about the Tleilaxu. For every milligram of melange produced on Rakis, the Bene Tleilax tanks produced long tons. Use of melange had grown to fit the new supply and even the Spacing Guild bent its knee before this power.

"But the rice . . ." Loschy Teg ventured.

"My dear husband, the Bene Tleilax have no need of that much pongi rice in our sector. They require it for trade. We must find out who really needs the rice."

"You want me to delay," he said.

"Precisely. You are superb at what we now require. Don't give that Free Trader the chance to say yes or no. Someone trained by the Face Dancers will appreciate such subtlety."

"We lure the Face Dancers out of the ship while you initiate inquiries elsewhere."

Lady Janet smiled. "You are lovely when you leap ahead of me that way."

A look of understanding passed between them.

"He cannot go to another supplier in this sector," Loschy Teg said.

"He will wish to avoid a go, no-go confrontation," Lady Janet said, patting the table. "Delay, delay, and more delay. You must draw the Face Dancers out of the ship."

"They will realize, of course."

"Yes, my dear, and it is dangerous. You must always meet on your own ground and with our own guards nearby."

Miles Teg recalled that his father had, indeed, drawn the Face Dancers out of their ship. His mother had taken Miles to the viewer where he watched the copper-walled room in which his father drove the bargain that won CHOAM's highest commendation and a rich bonus.

The first Face Dancers Miles Teg ever saw: Two small men as alike as twins. Almost chinless round faces, pug noses, tiny mouths, black button eyes, and short-cropped white hair that stood up from their heads like the bristles on a brush. The two were dressed as the Free Trader had been—black tunics and trousers.

"Illusion, Miles," his mother said. "Illusion is their way. The fashioning of illusion to achieve real goals, that is how the Tleilaxu work."

"Like the magician at the Winter Show?" Miles asked, his gaze intent on the viewer and its toy-figure scene.

"Quite similar," his mother agreed. She too watched the viewer as she spoke but one arm went protectively around her son's shoulders.

"You are looking at evil, Miles. Study it carefully. The faces you see can be changed in an instant. They can grow taller, appear heavier.

They could mimic your father so that only I would recognize the substitution."

Miles Teg's mouth formed a soundless "O." He stared at the viewer, listening to his father explain that the price of CHOAM's pongi rice once more had gone up alarmingly.

"And the most terrible thing of all," his mother said. "Some of the newer Face Dancers can, by touching the flesh of a victim, absorb some of the victim's memories."

"They read minds?" Miles looked up at his mother.

"Not exactly. We think they take a print of the memories, almost a holophoto process. They do not yet know that we are aware of this."

Miles understood. He was not to speak of this to anyone, not even to his father or his mother. She had taught him the Bene Gesserit way of secrecy. He watched the figures in the screen with care.

At his father's words, the Face Dancers betrayed no emotion, but their eyes appeared to glitter more brightly.

"How did they get so evil?" Miles asked.

"They are communal beings, bred not to identify with any shape or face. The appearance they present now is for my benefit. They know I am watching. They have relaxed into their natural communal shape. Mark it closely."

Miles tipped his head to one side and studied the Face Dancers. They looked so bland and ineffectual.

"They have no sense of self," his mother said. "They have only the instinct to preserve their own lives unless ordered to die for their masters."

"Would they do that?"

"They have done it many times."

"Who are their masters?"

"Men who seldom leave the planets of the Bene Tleilax."

"Do they have children?"

"Not Face Dancers. They are mules, sterile. But their masters can breed. We have taken a few of them but the offspring are strange. Few female births and even then we cannot probe their Other Memories."

Miles frowned. He knew his mother was a Bene Gesserit. He knew the Reverend Mothers carried a marvelous reservoir of Other Memories going back through all the millennia of the Sisterhood. He even knew something of the Bene Gesserit breeding design. Reverend Mothers chose particular men and had children by those men.

"What are the Tleilaxu women like?" Miles asked.

It was a perceptive question that sent a surge of pride through the Lady Janet. Yes, it was almost a certainty that she had a potential Mentat here. The breeding mistresses had been right about the gene potential of Loschy Teg.

"No one outside of their planets has ever reported seeing a Tleilaxu female," the Lady Janet said.

"Do they exist or is it just the tanks?"

"They exist."

"Are any of the Face Dancers women?"

"At their own choice, they can be male or female. Observe them carefully. They know what your father is doing and it angers them."

"Will they try to hurt my father?"

"They don't dare. We have taken precautions and they know it. See how the one on the left works his jaws. That is one of their anger signs."

"You said they were com . . . communal beings."

"Like hive insects, Miles. They have no self-image. Without a sense of self, they go beyond amorality. Nothing they say or do can be trusted."

Miles shuddered.

"We have never been able to detect an ethical code in them," the Lady Janet said. "They are flesh made into automata. Without self, they have nothing to esteem or even doubt. They are bred only to obey their masters."

"And they were told to come here and buy the rice."

"Exactly. They were told to get it and there's no other place in this sector where they can do that."

"They must buy it from father?"

"He's their only source. At this very moment, son, they are paying in melange. You see?"

Miles saw the orange-brown spice markers change hands, a tall stack of them, which one of the Face Dancers removed from a case on the floor.

"The price is far, far higher than they ever anticipated," the Lady Janet said. "This will be an easy trail to follow."

"Why?"

"Someone will be bankrupted acquiring that shipment. We think we know who the buyer is. Whoever it is, we will learn of it. Then we will know what was really being traded here."

Lady Janet then began to point out the identifiable incongruities that betrayed a Face Dancer to trained eyes and ears. They were subtle signs but Miles picked up on them immediately. His mother told him then that she thought he might become a Mentat . . . perhaps even more.

Shortly before his thirteenth birthday, Miles Teg was sent away to advanced schooling at the Bene Gesserit stronghold on Lampadas, where his mother's assessment of him was confirmed. Word went back to her:

"You have given us the Warrior Mentat we had hoped for."

Teg did not see this note until sorting through his mother's effects after her death. The words inscribed on a small sheet of ridulian crystal with the Chapter House imprint below them filled him with an odd sense of displacement in time. His memory put him suddenly back on Lampadas where the love-awe he had felt for his mother was deftly transferred to the Sisterhood itself, as originally intended. He had come to understand this only during his later Mentat training but the understanding changed little. If anything, it bound him even more strongly to the Bene Gesserit. It confirmed that the Sisterhood must be one of his strengths. He already knew that the Bene Gesserit Sisterhood was one of the most powerful forces in his universe—equal at least to the Spacing Guild, superior to the Fish Speaker Council that had inherited the core of the old Atreides Empire, superior by far to CHOAM, and balanced somehow with the Fabricators of Ix and with the Bene Tleilax. A small measure of the Sisterhood's far-reaching authority could be deduced from the fact that they held this authority despite Tleilaxu tank-grown melange, which had broken the Rakian monopoly on the spice, just as Ixian navigation machines had broken the Guild monopoly on space travel.

Miles Teg knew his history well by then. Guild Navigators no longer were the only ones who could thread a ship through the folds of space—in this galaxy one instant, in a faraway galaxy the very next heartbeat.

The School Sisters held back little from him, revealing there for the first time the fact of his Atreides ancestry. That revelation was necessary because of the tests they gave him. They obviously were testing for prescience. Could he, like a Guild Navigator, detect fatal obstructions? He failed. They tried him next on no-chambers and no-ships. He was as blind to such devices as the rest of humankind. For this test, though, they fed him increased doses of the spice and he sensed the awakening of his True Self.

"The Mind at Its Beginning," a teaching Sister called it when he asked for an explanation of this odd sensation.

For a time, the universe was magical as he looked at it through this new awareness. His awareness was a circle, then a globe. Arbitrary forms became transient. He fell into trance state without warning until the Sisters taught him how to control this. They provided him with accounts of saints and mystics and forced him to draw a freehand circle with either hand, following the line with his awareness.

By the end of the term, his awareness resumed its touch with conventional labels, but the memory of the magic never left him. He found that memory a source of strength at the most difficult moments.

After accepting the assignment as Weapons Master to the ghola, Teg found his magical memory increasingly with him. It was especially useful during his first interview with Schwangyu at the Keep on Gammu. They met in the Reverend Mother's study, a place of shiny metal walls and numerous instruments, most of them with the stamp of Ix on them. Even the chair in which she sat, the morning sun coming through a window behind her and making her face difficult to see, even that chair was one of the Ixian self-molders. He was forced to sit in a chairdog, though he realized she must know he detested the use of any life form for such a demeaning task.

"You were chosen because you actually are a grandfatherly figure," Schwangyu said. The bright sunlight formed a corona around her hooded head. *Deliberate!* "Your wisdom will earn the child's love and respect."

"There's no way I could be a father figure."

"According to Taraza, you have the precise characteristics she requires. I know of your honorable scars and their value to us."

This only reconfirmed his previous Mentat summation: *They have been planning this for a long time. They have bred for it. I was bred for it. I am part of their larger plan.*

All he said was: "Taraza expects this child to become a redoubtable warrior when restored to his true self."

Schwangyu merely stared at him for a moment, then: "You must not answer any of his questions about gholas, should he encounter the subject. Do not even use the word until I give you permission. We will supply you with all of the ghola data your duties require."

Coldly parceling out his words for emphasis, Teg said: "Perhaps the Reverend Mother was not informed that I am well versed in the lore of Tleilaxu gholas. I have met Tleilaxu in battle."

"You think you know enough about the Idaho series?"

"The Idahos are reputed to have been brilliant military strategists," Teg said.

"Then perhaps the great Bashar was not informed about the other characteristics of our ghola."

No doubt of the mockery in her voice. Something else as well: jealousy and great anger poorly concealed. Teg's mother had taught him ways of reading through her own masks, a forbidden teaching, which he had always concealed. He feigned chagrin and shrugged.

It was obvious, though, that Schwangyu knew he was Taraza's Bashar. The lines had been drawn.

"At Bene Gesserit behest," Schwangyu said, "the Tleilaxu have made a significant alteration in the present Idaho series. His nerve-muscle system has been modernized."

"Without changing the original persona?" Teg fed the question to her blandly, wondering how far she would go in revelation.

"He is a ghola, not a clone!"

"I see."

"Do you really? He requires the most careful prana-bindu training at all stages."

"Taraza's orders exactly," Teg said. "And we will all obey those orders."

Schwangyu leaned forward, not concealing her anger. "You have been asked to train a ghola whose role in certain plans is most dangerous to us all. I don't think you even remotely understand what you will train!"

What you will train, Teg thought. Not *whom*. This ghola-child would never be a *whom* for Schwangyu or any of the others who opposed Taraza. Perhaps the ghola would not be a *whom* to anyone until restored to his original self, firmly seated in that original Duncan Idaho identity.

Teg saw clearly now that Schwangyu harbored more than hidden reservations about the ghola project. She was in active opposition just as Taraza had warned. Schwangyu was the enemy and Taraza's orders had been explicit.

"You will protect that child against any threat."

Ten thousand years since Leto II began his metamorphosis from human into the sandworm of Rakis and historians still argue over his motives. Was he driven by the desire for long life? He lived more than ten times the normal span of three hundred SY, but consider the price he paid. Was it the lure of power? He is called the Tyrant for good reason but what did power bring him that a human might want? Was he driven to save humankind from itself? We have only his own words about his Golden Path to answer this and I cannot accept the self-serving records of Dar-es-Balat. Might there have been other gratifications, which only his experiences would illuminate? Without better evidence the question is moot. We are reduced to saying only that "He did it!" The physical fact alone is undeniable.

—THE METAMORPHOSIS OF LETO II,
10,000TH ANNIVERSARY PERORATION BY GAUS ANDAUD

Once more, Waff knew he was on lashkar. This time the stakes were as high as they could go. An Honored Matre from the Scattering demanded his presence. A powindah of powindahs! Descendants of Tleilaxu from the Scattering had told him all they could about these terrible women.

"Far more terrible than Reverend Mothers of the Bene Gesserit," they said.

And more numerous, Waff reminded himself.

He did not fully trust the returned Tleilaxu descendants, either.

Their accents were strange, their manners even stranger and their observances of the rituals questionable. How could they be readmitted to the Great Kehl? What possible rite of ghufran could cleanse them after all these centuries? It was beyond belief that they had kept the Tleilaxu secret down the generations.

They were no longer malik-brothers and yet they were the only source of information the Tleilaxu possessed about these returning Lost Ones. And the revelations they had brought! Revelations that had been incorporated in the Duncan Idaho gholas—that was worth all of the risks of contamination by powindah evil.

The meeting place with the Honored Matres was the presumed neutrality of an Ixian no-ship that held a tight orbit around a mutually selected gas giant planet in a mined-out solar system of the old Imperium. The Prophet himself had drained the last of the wealth from this system. New Face Dancers walked as Ixians among the no-ship's crew but Waff still sweated the first encounter. If these Honored Matres were truly more terrible than the Bene Gesserit witches, would the exchange of Face Dancers for Ixian crewmen be detected?

Selection of this meeting place and the arrangements had put a strain on the Tleilaxu. Was it secure? He reassured himself that he carried two sealed weapons never before seen off the Tleilaxu core planets. The weapons were the painstaking result of long effort by his artificers: two minuscule dart throwers concealed in his sleeves. He had trained with them for years until the flipping of the sleeves and the discharge of the poisoned darts was almost an instinctive reflex.

The walls of the meeting room were properly copper-toned, evidence that they were shielded from Ixian spy devices. But what instruments might the people of the Scattering have developed beyond the Ixian ken?

Waff entered the room with a hesitant step. The Honored Matre already was there seated in a leather sling chair.

"You will call me what everyone else calls me," she greeted him. "Honored Matre."

He bowed as he had been warned to do. "Honored Matre."

No hint of hidden powers in her voice. A low contralto with over-tones that spoke of disdain for him. She looked like an aged athlete or acrobat, slowed and retired but still maintaining her muscle tone and some of her skills. Her face was tight skin over a skull with prominent cheekbones. The thin-lipped mouth produced a sense of arrogance when she spoke, as though every word were projected downward onto lesser folk.

"Well, come in and sit down!" she commanded, waving at a sling chair facing her.

Waff heard the hatch hiss closed behind him. He was alone with her! She was wearing a snooper. He could see the lead for it going into her left ear. His dart throwers had been sealed and "washed" against snoopers, then maintained at minus 340° Kelvin in a radiation bath for five SY to make them proof against snoopers. Had it been enough?

Gently, he lowered himself into the indicated chair.

Orange-tinted contact lenses covered the Honored Matre's eyes, giving them a feral appearance. She was altogether daunting. And her clothing! Red leotards beneath a dark blue cape. The surface of the cape had been decorated with some pearly material to produce strange ara-besques and dragon designs. She sat in the chair as though it were a throne, her clawlike hands resting easily on the arms.

Waff glanced around the room. His people had inspected this place in company with Ixian maintenance workers and representatives of the Honored Matre.

We have done our best, he thought, and he tried to relax.

The Honored Matre laughed.

Waff stared at her with as calm an expression as he could muster. "You are gauging me now," he accused. "You say to yourself that you have enormous resources to employ against me, subtle and gross in-struments to carry out your commands."

"Do not take that tone with me." The words were low and flat but carried such a weight of venom that Waff almost recoiled.

He stared at the stringy muscles of the woman's legs, that deep red leotard fabric which flowed over her skin as though it were organic to her.

Their meeting time had been adjusted to bring them together at a mutually personal mid-morning, their waking hours having been balanced en route. Waff felt dislocated, though, and at a disadvantage. What if the stories of his informants were true? She must have weapons here.

She smiled at him without humor.

"You are trying to intimidate me," Waff said.

"And succeeding." Anger surged through Waff. He kept this from his voice. "I have come at your invitation."

"I hope you did not come to engage in a confrontation that you would surely lose," she said.

"I came to forge a bond between us," he said. And he wondered: *What do they need from us? Surely they must need something.*

"What bond can there be between us?" she asked. "Would you build an edifice on a disintegrating raft? Hah! Agreements can be broken and often are."

"For what tokens do we bargain?" he asked.

"Bargain? I do not bargain. I am interested in this ghola you made for the witches." Her tone gave away nothing but Waff's heartbeat quickened at her question.

In one of his ghola lifetimes, Waff had trained under a renegade Mentat. The capabilities of a Mentat were beyond him and besides, reasoning required words. They had been forced to kill the powindah Mentat but there had been some things of value in the experience. Waff allowed himself a small moue of distaste at the memory but he recalled the things of value.

Attack and absorb the data that attack produces!

"You offer me nothing in exchange!" he said, his voice loud.

"Recompense is at my discretion," she said.

Waff produced a scornful gaze. "Do you play with me?"

She showed white teeth in a feral grin. "You would not survive my play, nor want to."

"So I must be dependent upon your good will!"

"Dependency!" The word curled from her mouth as though it

produced a distasteful sensation. "Why do you sell these gholas to the witches and then kill the gholas?"

Waff pressed his lips together and remained silent.

"You have somehow changed this ghola while still making it possible for him to regain his original memories," she said.

"You know so much!" Waff said. It was not quite a sneer and, he hoped, revealed nothing. *Spies!* She had spies among the witches! Was there also a traitor in the Tleilaxu heartlands?

"There is a girl-child on Rakis who figures in the plans of the witches," the Honored Matre said.

"How do you know this?"

"The witches do not make a move without our knowing! You think of spies but you cannot know how far our arms will reach!"

Waff was dismayed. Could she read his mind? Was it something born of the Scattering? A wild talent from out there where the original human seed could not observe?

"How have you changed this ghola?" she demanded.

Voice!

Waff, armed against such devices by his Mentat teacher, almost blurted an answer. This Honored Matre had some of the witches' powers! It had been so unexpected coming from her. You expected such things from a Reverend Mother and were prepared. He was a moment recovering his balance. Waff steepled his hands in front of his chin.

"You have interesting resources," she said.

A gamin expression came over Waff's features. He knew how disarmingly elflike he could look.

Attack!

"We know how much you have learned from the Bene Gesserit," he said.

A look of rage swept over her face and was gone. "They have taught us nothing!"

Waff pitched his voice at a humorously appealing level, cajoling. "Surely, this is not bargaining."

"Isn't it?" She actually appeared surprised.

Waff lowered his hands. "Come now, Honored Matre. You are interested in this ghola. You speak of things on Rakis. What do you take us for?"

"Very little. You become less valuable by the instant."

Waff sensed the coldest machine logic in her response. There was no smell of Mentat in it but something more chilling. *She is capable of killing me right here!*

Where were her weapons? Would she even require weapons? He did not like the look of those stringy muscles, the calluses on her hands, the hunter's gleam in her orange eyes. Could she possibly guess (or even know) about the dart throwers in his sleeves?

"We are confronted by a problem that cannot be resolved by logical means," she said.

Waff stared at her in shock. A Zensunni Master might have said that! He had said it himself on more than one occasion.

"You have probably never considered such a possibility," she said. It was as though her words dropped a mask away from her face. Waff suddenly saw through to the calculating person behind these postures. Did she take him for some padfooted seelie fit only for collecting slig shit?

Bringing as much hesitant puzzlement into his voice as possible, he asked: "How could such a problem be resolved?"

"The natural course of events will dispose of it," she said.

Waff continued to stare at her in simulated puzzlement. Her words did not smack of revelation. Still, the things implied! He said: "Your words leave me floundering."

"Humankind has become infinite," she said. "That is the true gift of the Scattering."

Waff fought to conceal the turmoil these words created. "Infinite universes, infinite time—anything may happen," he said.

"Ahhh, you are a bright little manikin," she said. "How does one allow for anything? It is not logical."

She sounded, Waff thought, like one of the ancient leaders of the Butlerian Jihad, which had tried to rid humankind of mechanical minds. This Honored Matre was strangely out of date.

"Our ancestors looked for an answer with computers," he ventured. *Let her try that!*

"You already know that computers lack infinite storage capacity," she said.

Again, her words disconcerted him. Could she actually read minds? Was this a form of mind-printing? What the Tleilaxu did with Face Dancers and gholas, others might do as well. He centered his awareness and concentrated on Ixians, on their evil machines. Powindah machines!

The Honored Matre swept her gaze around the room. "Are we wrong to trust the Ixians?" she asked.

Waff held his breath.

"I don't think you fully trust them," she said. "Come, come, little man. I offer you my good will."

Belatedly, Waff began to suspect that she was trying to be friendly and candid with him. She certainly had put aside her earlier pose of angry superiority. Waff's informants from the Lost Ones said the Honored Matres made sexual decisions much in the manner of the Bene Gesserit. Was she trying to be seductive? But she clearly *understood* and had exposed the weakness of logic.

It was very confusing!

"We are talking in circles," he said.

"Quite the contrary. Circles enclose. Circles limit. Humankind no longer is limited by the space in which to grow."

There she went again! He spoke past a dry tongue: "It is said that what you cannot control you must accept."

She leaned forward, the orange eyes intent on his face. "Do you accept the possibility of a final disaster for the Bene Tleilax?"

"If that were the case I would not be here."

"When logic fails, another tool must be used."

Waff grinned. "That sounds logical."

"Don't mock me! How dare you!"

Waff lifted his hands defensively and assumed a placating tone: "What tool would the Honored Matre suggest?"

"Energy!"

Her answer surprised him. "Energy? In what form and how much?"

"You demand logical answers," she said.

With a feeling of sadness, Waff realized that she was not, after all, Zensunni. The Honored Matre only played word games on the fringes of non-logic, circling it, but her tool was logic.

"Rot at the core spreads outward," he said.

It was as though she had not heard his testing statement. "There is untapped energy in the depths of any human we deign to touch," she said. She extended a skeletal finger to within a few millimeters of his nose.

Waff pulled back into his chair until she dropped her arm. He said: "Is that not what the Bene Gesserit said before producing their Kwisatz Haderach?"

"They lost control of themselves and of him," she sneered.

Again, Waff thought, she employed logic in thinking of the non-logical. How much she had told him in these little lapses. He could glimpse the probable history of these Honored Matres. One of the *natural* Reverend Mothers from the Fremen of Rakis had gone out in the Scattering. Diverse people had fled on the no-ships during and immediately after the Famine Times. A no-ship had seeded the wild witch and her concepts somewhere. That seed had returned in the form of this orange-eyed huntress.

Once more she hurled Voice at him, demanding: "What have you wrought with this ghola?"

This time, Waff was prepared and shrugged it off. This Honored Matre would have to be deflected or, if possible, slain. He had learned much from her but there was no way of telling how much she had learned from him with her unguessed talents.

They are sexual monsters, his informants had said. *They enslave men by the powers of sex.*

"How little you know the joys I could give you," she said. Her voice coiled like a whip around him. How tempting! How seductive!

Waff spoke defensively: "Tell me why you—"

"I need tell you nothing!"

"Then you did not come to bargain." He spoke sadly. The no-ships had, indeed, seeded those other universes with rot. Waff sensed the weight of necessity on his shoulders. What if he could not slay her?

"How dare you keep suggesting a bargain with an Honored Matre?" she demanded. "Know you that *we* set the price!"

"I do not know your ways, Honored Matre," Waff said. "But I sense in your words that I have offended."

"Apology accepted."

No apology intended! He stared at her blandly. Many things could be deduced from her performance. Out of his millennial experiences, Waff reviewed what he had learned here. This female from the Scattering came to him for an essential piece of information. Therefore, she had no other source. He sensed desperation in her. Well masked but definitely there. She needed confirmation or refutation of something she feared.

How like a predatory bird she was, sitting there with her claw hands so lightly on the arms of her chair! *Rot at the core spreads outward.* He had said it and she had not heard. Clearly, atomic humankind continued to explode on its Scatterings of Scatterings. The people represented by this Honored Matre had not found a way to trace the no-ships. That was it, of course. She hunted the no-ships just as the witches of the Bene Gesserit did.

"You seek the way to nullify a no-ship's invisibility," he said.

The statement obviously rocked her. She had not expected this from the elflike *manikin* seated in front of her. He saw fear, then anger, then resolution pass across her features before she resumed her predatory mask. She knew, though. She knew he had seen.

"So that is what you do with your ghola," she said.

"It is what the witches of the Bene Gesserit seek with him," Waff lied.

"I underestimated you," she said. "Did you make the same mistake with me?"

"I do not think so, Honored Matre. The breeding scheme that produced you is quite obviously formidable. I think you could kick out a foot and kill me before I blinked an eye. The witches are not in the same league with you."

A smile of pleasure softened her features. "Are the Tleilaxu to be our willing servants or compelled?"

He did not try to hide outrage. "You offer us slavery?"

"That is one of your options."

He had her now! Arrogance was her weakness. Submissively, he asked: "What would you command me to do?"

"You will take back as your guests two younger Honored Matres. They are to be bred with you and . . . teach you our ways of ecstasy."

Waff inhaled and exhaled two slow breaths.

"Are you sterile?" she asked.

"Only our Face Dancers are mules." She would already know that. It was common knowledge.

"You call yourself Master," she said, "yet you have not mastered yourself."

More than you, Honored Matre bitch! And I call myself Masheikh, a fact that may yet destroy you.

"The two Honored Matres I send with you will make an inspection of everything Tleilaxu and return to me with their report," she said.

He sighed as though in resignation. "Are the two younger women comely?"

"Honored Matres!" she corrected him.

"Is that the only name you use?"

"If they choose to give you names, that is their privilege, not yours." She leaned sideways and rapped a bony knuckle against the floor. Metal gleamed in her hand. She had a way of penetrating this room's shielding!

The hatch opened and two women dressed much like his Honored

Matre entered. Their dark capes carried less decoration and both women were younger. Waff stared at them. Were they both . . . He tried not to show elation but knew he failed. No matter. The older one would think he admired the beauty of these two. By signs known only to the Masters, he saw that one of the two newcomers was a new Face Dancer. A successful exchange had been made and these Scattered Ones could not detect it! The Tleilaxu had successfully passed a hurdle! Would the Bene Gesserit be as blind to these new gholas?

"You are being sensibly agreeable about this, for which you will be rewarded," the old Honored Matre said.

"I recognize your powers, Honored Matre," he said. That was true. He bowed his head to conceal the resolution that he knew he could not keep from his eyes.

She gestured to the newcomers. "These two will accompany you. Their slightest whim is your command. They will be treated with all honor and respect."

"Of course, Honored Matre." Keeping his head bowed, he lifted both arms as though in salutation and submission. A dart hissed from each sleeve. As he released the darts, Waff jerked himself sideways in his chair. The motion was not quite rapid enough. The old Honored Matre's right foot shot out, catching him in the left thigh and hurling him backward on his chair.

It was the old Honored Matre's last living act. The dart from his left sleeve caught her in the back of her throat, entering through her opened mouth, a mouth left gaping in surprise. Narcotic poison cut off any outcry. The other dart hit the non–Face Dancer of the newcomers in the right eye. His Face Dancer accomplice cut off any warning shout by a blurred chop to the throat.

Two bodies slumped in death.

Painfully, Waff disentangled himself from the chair and righted it as he got to his feet. His thigh throbbed. A fraction of a meter more and she would have broken his thigh! He realized that her reaction had not been mediated by her central nervous system. As with some insects, attack could be initiated by the required muscle system. That development would have to be investigated!

His Face Dancer accomplice was listening at the open hatch. She stepped aside to allow the entry of another Face Dancer in the guise of an Ixian guard.

Waff massaged his injured thigh while his Face Dancers disrobed the dead women. The one who copied the Ixian put her head to that of the dead old Honored Matre. Things moved swiftly after that. Presently, there was no Ixian guard, only a faithful copy of the old Honored Matre and a younger Honored Matre attendant. Another pseudo-Ixian entered and copied the younger Honored Matre. Soon, there were only ashes where dead flesh had been. A new Honored Matre scooped the ashes into a bag and concealed it beneath her robe.

Waff made a careful examination of the room. The consequences of discovery made him shudder. Such arrogance as he had seen here came from obviously awesome powers. Those powers must be probed. He detained the Face Dancer who had copied the old one.

"You have printed her?"

"Yes, Master. Her waking memories were still alive when I copied."

"Transfer to her." He gestured to the one who had been an Ixian guard. They touched foreheads for a few heartbeats then parted.

"It is done," said the older one.

"How many other copies of these Honored Matres have we made?"

"Four, Master."

"None of them detected?"

"None, Master."

"Those four must return to the heartland of these Honored Matres and learn all there is to know about them. One of those four must get back to us with what is learned."

"That is impossible, Master."

"Impossible?"

"They have cut themselves off from their source. This is their way, Master. They are a new cell and have established themselves on Gammu."

"But surely we could . . ."

"Your pardon, Master. The coordinates of their place in the Scattering were contained only in a no-ship's workings and have been erased."

"Their tracks are completely covered?" There was dismay in his voice.

"Completely, Master."

Disaster! He was forced to rein in his thoughts from a sudden frenzied darting. "They must not learn what we have done here," he muttered.

"They will not learn from us, Master."

"What talents have they developed? What powers? Quickly!"

"They are what you would expect from a Reverend Mother of the Bene Gesserit but without the melange memories."

"You're sure?"

"There is no hint of it. As you know, Master, we—"

"Yes, yes. I know." He waved her to silence. "But the old one was so arrogant, so . . ."

"Your pardon, Master, but time presses. These Honored Matres have perfected the pleasures of sex far beyond that developed by any others."

"So it's true what our informants said."

"They went back to the primitive Tantric and developed their own ways of sexual stimulation, Master. Through this, they accept the worship of their followers."

"Worship." He breathed the word. "Are they superior to the Breeding Mistresses of the Sisterhood?"

"The Honored Matres believe so, Master. Shall we demon—"

"No!" Waff dropped his elfin mask at this discovery and assumed the expression of a dominant Master. The Face Dancers nodded their heads in submission. A look of glee came over Waff's face. The returned Tleilaxu of the Scattering reported truthfully! By a simple mind-print he had confirmed this new weapon of his people!

"What are your orders, Master?" the old one asked.

Waff resumed his elfin mask. "We will explore these matters only when we have returned to the Tleilaxu core at Bandalong. Meanwhile, even a Master does not give orders to an Honored Matre. You are *my* masters until we are free of prying eyes."

"Of course, Master. Shall I now convey your orders to the others outside?"

"Yes, and these are my orders: This no-ship must never return to Gammu. It must vanish without a trace. No survivors."

"It will be done, Master."

Technology, in common with many other activities, tends toward avoidance of risks by investors. Uncertainty is ruled out if possible. Capital investment follows this rule, since people generally prefer the predictable. Few recognize how destructive this can be, how it imposes severe limits on variability and thus makes whole populations fatally vulnerable to the shocking ways our universe can throw the dice.

—ASSESSMENT OF IX,
BENE GESSERIT ARCHIVES

On the morning after that initial test in the desert, Sheeana awoke in the priestly complex to find her bed surrounded by white-robed people.

Priests and priestesses!

"She's awake," a priestess said.

Fear gripped Sheeana. She clutched the bed covers close to her chin while she stared out at those intent faces. Were they going to abandon her in the desert again? She had slept the sleep of exhaustion in the softest bed with the cleanest linen she had experienced in her eight years but she knew everything the priests did could have a double meaning. They were not to be trusted!

"Did you sleep well?" It was the priestess who had spoken first. She was a gray-haired older woman, her face framed in a white cowl with purple trim. The old eyes were watery but alert. Pale blue. The nose was an upturned stub above a narrow mouth and outjutting chin.

"Will you speak to us?" the woman persisted. "I am Cania, your night attendant. Remember? I helped you into your bed."

At least, the tone of voice was reassuring. Sheeana sat up and took a better look at these people. They were afraid! A desert child's nose could detect the telltale pheromones. To Sheeana, it was a simple, straightforward observation: *That smell equals fear.*

"You thought you would hurt me," she said. "Why did you do that?"

The people around her exchanged looks of consternation.

Sheeana's fear dissipated. She had sensed the new order of things and yesterday's trial in the desert meant more change. She recalled how subservient the older woman . . . Cania? She had been almost groveling the previous night. Sheeana would learn in time that any person who lived through the decision to die evolved a new emotional balance. Fears were transitory. This new condition was interesting.

Cania's voice trembled when she responded: "Truly, Child of God, we did not intend harm."

Sheeana straightened the bedcovers on her lap. "My name is Shee-ana." That was desert politeness. Cania already had produced a name. "Who are these others?"

"They will be sent away if you don't want them . . . Sheeana." Cania indicated a florid-faced woman at her left dressed in a robe similar to her own. "All except Alhosa, of course. She is your day attendant."

Alhosa curtsied at the introduction.

Sheeana stared up at a face puffy with waterfat, heavy features in a nimbus of fluffy blond hair. Shifting her attention abruptly, Sheeana looked at the men in the group. They watched her with heavy-lidded intentness, some with looks of trembling suspicion. The fear smell was strong.

Priests!

"Send them away." Sheeana waved a hand at the priests. "They are haram!" It was the gutter word, the lowest term of all for that which was most evil.

The priests recoiled in shock.

"Begone!" Cania commanded. There was no mistaking the look of malevolent glee on her face. Cania had not been included among the vile ones. But these priests clearly stood among those labeled as haram! They must have done something hideous for God to send a child-priestess to chastise them. Cania could believe it of priests. They had seldom treated her the way she deserved.

Like chastened bedogs, the priests bowed themselves backward and left Sheeana's chamber. Among those who went out into the hallway was a historian-locutor named Dromind, a dark man with a busy mind that tended to fasten onto ideas like the beak of a carrion bird onto a morsel of meat. When the chamber door closed behind them, Dromind told his trembling companions that the name Sheeana was a modern form of the ancient name, Siona.

"You all know Siona's place in the histories," he said. "She served Shai-hulud in His transformation from human shape into the Divided God."

Stiros, a wrinkled older priest with dark lips and pale, glistening eyes, looked wonderingly at Dromind. "That is extremely curious," Stiros said. "The Oral Histories claim that Siona was instrumental in His translation from the One into the Many. Sheeana. Do you think . . ."

"Let us not forget the Hadi Benotto translation of God's own holy words," another priest interrupted. "Shai-hulud referred many times to Siona."

"Not always with favor," Stiros reminded them. "Remember her full name: Siona Ibn Fuad al-Seyefa Atreides."

"Atreides," another priest whispered.

"We must study her with care," Dromind said.

A young acolyte-messenger hurried up the hallway to the group and sought among them until he spied Stiros. "Stiros," the messenger said, "you must clear this hallway immediately."

"Why?" It was an indignant voice from the press of the rejected priests.

"She is to be moved into the High Priest's quarters," the messenger said.

"By whose orders?" Stiros demanded.

"High Priest Tuek himself says this," the messenger said. "They have been listening." He waved a hand vaguely toward the direction from which he had come.

All of the group in the hall understood. Rooms could be shaped to send voices from them into other places. There were always listeners.

"What have they heard?" Stiros demanded. His old voice quavered.

"She asked if her quarters were the best. They are about to move her and she must not find any of you out here."

"But what are we to do?" Stiros asked.

"Study her," Dromind said.

The hall was cleared immediately and all of them began the process of studying Sheeana. The pattern born here would print itself on all of their lives over the subsequent years. The routine that took shape around Sheeana produced changes felt in the farthest reaches of the Divided God's influence. Two words ignited the change: "Study her."

How naive she was, the priests thought. How curiously naive. But she could read and she displayed an intense interest in the Holy Books she found in Tuek's quarters. Her quarters now.

All was propitiation from the highest to the lowest. Tuek moved into the quarters of his chief assistant and the bumping process moved downward. Fabricators waited upon Sheeana and measured her. The finest stillsuit was fashioned for her. She acquired new robes of priestly gold and white with purple trim.

People began avoiding historian-locutor Dromind. He took to buttonholing his fellows and expounding the history of the original Siona as though this said something important about the present bearer of the ancient name.

"Siona was the mate of the Holy Duncan Idaho," Dromind reminded anyone who would listen. "Their descendants are everywhere."

"Indeed? Pardon me for not listening further but I am really on an urgent errand."

At first, Tuek was more patient with Dromind. The history was interesting and its lessons obvious. "God has sent us a new Siona," Tuek said. "All should be clear."

Dromind went away and returned with more tidbits from the past. "The accounts from Dar-es-Balat take on a new meaning now," Dromind told his High Priest. "Should we not make further tests and comparisons of this child?"

Dromind had braced the High Priest immediately after breakfast. The remains of Tuek's meal still occupied the serving table on the balcony. Through the open window, they could hear stirrings overhead in Sheeana's quarters.

Tuek put a cautioning finger to his lips and spoke in a hushed voice. "The Holy Child goes of her own choice to the desert." He went to a wall map and pointed to an area southwest of Keen. "Apparently this is an area that interests her or . . . I should say, calls her."

"I am told she makes frequent use of dictionaries," Dromind said. "Surely, that cannot be a—"

"She is testing *us*," Tuek said. "Do not be fooled."

"But Lord Tuek, she asks the most childish questions of Cania and Alhosa."

"Do you question my judgment, Dromind?"

Belatedly, Dromind realized he had overstepped the proper bounds. He fell silent but his expression said many more words were compressed within him.

"God has sent her to weed out some evil that has crept into the ranks of the anointed," Tuek said. "Go! Pray and ask yourself if that evil has lodged itself within you."

When Dromind had gone, Tuek summoned a trusted aide. "Where is the Holy Child?"

"She has gone out into the desert, Lord, to commune with her Father."

"To the southwest?"

"Yes, Lord."

"Dromind must be taken far out to the east and left on the sand. Plant several thumpers to make sure he never returns."

"Dromind, Lord?"

"Dromind."

Even after Dromind was translated into the Mouth of God, the priests continued to follow his original injunction. They studied Sheeana.

Sheeana also studied.

Gradually, so gradually that she could not identify the point of transition, she recognized her great power over those around her. At first, it was a game, a continual Children's Day with adults jumping to obey each childish whim. But it appeared that no whim was too difficult.

Did she require a rare fruit for her table?

The fruit was served to her on a golden dish.

Did she glimpse a child far below on the teeming streets and require that child as a playmate?

That child was hustled up to Sheeana's temple quarters. When fear and shock passed, the child might even join in some game, which the priests and priestesses observed intently. Innocent skipping about on the rooftop garden, giggling whispers—all were subjected to intense analysis. Sheeana found the awe of such children a burden. She seldom called the same child back to her, preferring to learn new things from new playmates.

The priests achieved no consensus about the innocence of such encounters. The playmates were put through fearful interrogation until Sheeana discovered this and raged at her guardians.

Inevitably, word of Sheeana spread throughout Rakis and off-planet. The Sisterhood's reports accumulated. The years passed in a kind of sublimely autocratic routine—feeding Sheeana's curiosity. It was a curiosity that appeared to have no limits. None of those among the immediate attendants thought of this as education: Sheeana teaching the priests of Rakis and they teaching her. The Bene Gesserit, however, observed this aspect of Sheeana's life at once and watched it closely.

"She is in good hands. Leave her there until she is ready for us," Taraza ordered. "Keep a defense force on constant alert and see that I get regular reports."

Not once did Sheeana reveal her true origins nor what Shaitan had done to her family and neighbors. That was a private thing between Shaitan and herself. She thought of her silence as payment for having been spared.

Some things paled for Sheeana. She made fewer trips into the desert. Curiosity continued but it became obvious that an explanation of Shaitan's behavior toward her might not be found on the open sand. And although she knew there were embassies of other powers on Rakis, the Bene Gesserit spies among her attendants made sure that Sheeana did not express too much interest in the Sisterhood. Soothing answers to dampen such interest were provided and metered out to Sheeana as required.

The message from Taraza to her observers on Rakis was direct and pointed: "The generations of preparation have become the years of refinement. We will move only at the proper moment. There is no longer any doubt that this child is the one."

In my estimation, more misery has been created by reformers than by any other force in human history. Show me someone who says, "Something must be done!" and I will show you a head full of vicious intentions that have no other outlet. What we must strive for always! is to find the natural flow and go with it.

—THE REVEREND MOTHER TARAZA,
CONVERSATIONAL RECORD,
BG FILE GSXXMAT9

The overcast sky lifted as the sun of Gammu climbed, picking up the scents of grass and surrounding forest extracted and condensed by the morning dampness.

Duncan Idaho stood at a Forbidden Window inhaling the smells. This morning Patrin had told him: "You are fifteen years of age. You must consider yourself a young man. You no longer are a child."

"Is it my birthday?"

They were in Duncan's sleeping chamber where Patrin had just aroused him with a glass of citrus juice.

"I do not know your birthday."

"Do gholas have birthdays?"

Patrin remained silent. It was forbidden to speak of gholas with the ghola.

"Schwangyu says you can't answer that question," Duncan said.

Patrin spoke with obvious embarrassment. "The Bashar wishes me to tell you that your training class will be delayed this morning. He wishes you to do the leg and knee exercises until you are called."

"I did those yesterday!"

"I merely convey the Bashar's orders." Patrin took the empty glass and left Duncan alone.

Duncan dressed quickly. They would expect him for breakfast in the Commissary. *Damn them!* He did not need their breakfast. What was the Bashar doing? Why couldn't he start the classes on time? *Leg and knee exercises!* That was just make-work because Teg had some other unexpected duty. Angrily, Duncan took a Forbidden Route to a Forbidden Window. *Let the damned guards be punished!*

He found the odors coming through the open window evocative but could not place the memories that lurked at the edges of his awareness. He knew there were memories. Duncan found this frightening but magnetic—like walking along the edge of a cliff or openly confronting Schwangyu with his defiance. He had never walked along the edge of a cliff nor openly confronted Schwangyu with defiance, but he could imagine such things. Just seeing a filmbook holophoto of a cliff-edge path was enough to make his stomach tighten. As for Schwangyu, he often imagined angry disobedience and suffered the same physical reaction.

Someone else is in my mind, he thought.

Not just in his mind—*in his body.* He could sense other experiences as though he had just awakened, knowing he had dreamed but unable to recall the dream. This dream-stuff called up knowledge that he knew he could not possess.

Yet he did possess it.

He could name some of the trees he smelled out there but those names were not in the library's records.

This Forbidden Window was forbidden because it pierced an outer wall of the Keep and could be opened. It was often open, as now, for ventilation. The window was reached from his room by climbing over a balcony rail and slipping through a storeroom air shaft. He had learned to do this without the slightest disturbance of rail or storeroom or shaft. Quite early, it had been made clear to him that those trained by the Bene Gesserit could read extremely small signs. He could read some of those signs himself, thanks to the teachings of Teg and Lucilla.

Standing well back in the shadows of the upper hallway, Duncan focused on rolling slopes of forest climbing to rocky pinnacles. He found the forest compelling. The pinnacles beyond it possessed a magical quality. It was easy to imagine that no human had ever touched that land. How good it would be to lose himself there, to be only his own person without worrying that another person dwelled within him. A stranger there.

With a sigh, Duncan turned away and returned to his room along his secret route. Only when he was back in the safety of his room did he allow himself to say that he had done it once more. No one would be punished for this venture.

Punishments and pain, which hung like an aura around the places forbidden to him, only made Duncan exercise extreme caution when he broke the rules.

He did not like to think of the pain Schwangyu would cause him if she discovered him at a Forbidden Window. Even the worst pain, though, would not cause him to cry out, he told himself. He had never cried out even at her nastier tricks. He merely stared back at her, hating her but absorbing her lesson. To him, Schwangyu's lesson was direct: Refine his ability to move unobserved, unseen and unheard, leaving no spoor to betray his passage.

In his room, Duncan sat on the edge of his cot and contemplated the blank wall in front of him. Once, when he had stared at that wall, an image had formed there—a young woman with light amber hair and sweetly rounded features. She looked out of the wall at him and smiled. Her lips moved without sound. Duncan already had learned lip reading, though, and he read the words clearly.

"Duncan, my sweet Duncan."

Was that his mother? he wondered. His real mother?

Even gholas had real mothers somewhere back there. Lost in the time behind the axlotl tanks there had been a living woman who bore him and . . . and loved him. Yes, loved him because he was her child. If that face on the wall was his mother, how had her image found its way there? He could not identify the face but he wanted it to be his mother.

The experience frightened him but fear did not prevent him from wanting to repeat it. Whoever that young woman was, her fleeting presence tantalized him. The stranger within him knew that young woman. He felt sure of this. Sometimes, he wanted to be that stranger only for an instant—long enough to gather up all of those hidden memories—but he feared this desire. He would lose his real self, he thought, if the stranger entered his awareness.

Would that be like death? he wondered.

Duncan had seen death before he was six. His guards had repelled intruders and one of the guards was killed. Four intruders died as well. Duncan had watched the five bodies brought into the Keep—flaccid muscles, arms dragging. Some essential thing was gone from them. Nothing remained to call up memories—self-memories or stranger-memories.

The five were taken somewhere deep within the Keep. He heard a guard say later that the four intruders were loaded with "shere." That was his first encounter with the idea of an Ixian Probe.

"An Ixian Probe can raid the mind even of a dead person," Geasa explained. "Shere is a drug that protects you from the probe. Your cells will be totally dead before the drug effect is gone."

Adroit listening told Duncan the four intruders were being probed in other ways as well. These other ways were not explained to him but he suspected this must be something secret to the Bene Gesserit. He thought of it as another hellish trick of the Reverend Mothers. They must animate the dead and extract information from the unwilling flesh. Duncan visualized depersonalized muscles performing at the will of a diabolical observer.

The observer was always Schwangyu.

Such images filled Duncan's mind despite every effort by his teachers to dispel "foolishness invented by the ignorant." His teachers said these wild stories were valuable only to create fear of the Bene Gesserit among the *un*initiated. Duncan refused to believe that he was of the initiated. Looking at a Reverend Mother he always thought: *I'm not one of* them!

Lucilla was most persistent lately. "Religion is a source of energy," she said. "You must recognize this energy. It can be directed for your own purposes."

Their purposes, not mine, he thought.

He imagined his own purposes and projected his own images of himself triumphant over the Sisterhood, especially over Schwangyu. Duncan felt that his imaginative projections were a subterranean reality that worked on him from that place where the stranger dwelled. But he learned to nod and give the appearance that he, too, found such religious credulity amusing.

Lucilla recognized the dichotomy in him. She told Schwangyu: "He thinks mystical forces are to be feared and, if possible, avoided. As long as he persists in this belief he cannot learn to use our most essential knowledge."

They met for what Schwangyu called "a regular assessment session," just the two of them in Schwangyu's study. The time was shortly after their light supper. The sounds of the Keep around them were those of transition—night patrols beginning, off-duty personnel enjoying one of their brief free-time periods. Schwangyu's study had not been completely insulated from such things, a deliberate contrivance of the Sisterhood's renovators. The trained senses of a Reverend Mother could detect many things from the sounds around her.

Schwangyu felt more and more at a loss in these "assessment sessions." It was increasingly obvious that Lucilla could not be won over to those opposing Taraza. Lucilla also was immune to a Reverend Mother's manipulative subterfuges. Most damnable of all, Lucilla and Teg between them were imparting highly volatile abilities to the ghola. Dangerous in the extreme. Added to all of her other problems, Schwangyu nurtured a growing respect for Lucilla.

"He thinks we use occult powers to practice our arts," Lucilla said. "How did he arrive at such a peculiar idea?"

Schwangyu felt the disadvantage imposed by this question. Lucilla already knew this had been done to weaken the ghola. Lucilla was saying: *"Disobedience is a crime against our Sisterhood!"*

"If he wants our knowledge, he will surely get it from you," Schwangyu said. No matter how dangerous, in Schwangyu's view, this was certainly a truth.

"His desire for knowledge is my best lever," Lucilla said, "but we both know that is not enough." There was no reproof in Lucilla's tone but Schwangyu felt it nevertheless.

Damn her! She's trying to win me over! Schwangyu thought.

Several responses entered Schwangyu's mind: *"I have not disobeyed my orders."* Pah! A disgusting excuse! *"The ghola has been treated according to standard Bene Gesserit training practices."* Inadequate and untrue. And this ghola was not a standard object of education. There were depths in him that could only be matched by a potential Reverend Mother. And that was the problem!

"I have made mistakes," Schwangyu said.

There! That was a double-pronged answer that another Reverend Mother could appreciate.

"You made no mistake when you damaged him," Lucilla said.

"But I failed to anticipate that another Reverend Mother might expose the flaws in him," Schwangyu said.

"He wants our powers only to escape us," Lucilla said. "He's thinking: *Someday I'll know as much as they do and then I'll run away.*"

When Schwangyu did not respond, Lucilla said: "That was clever. If he runs, we will have to hunt him down and destroy him ourselves."

Schwangyu smiled.

"I will not make your mistake," Lucilla said. "I tell you openly what I know you would see anyway. I now understand why Taraza sent an Imprinter to one so young."

Schwangyu's smile vanished. "What are you doing?"

"I am bonding him to me the way we bond all of our acolytes to their teachers. I am treating him with candor and loyalty as one of our own."

"But he's male!"

"So the spice agony will be denied him, but nothing else. He is, I think, responding."

"And when the time comes for the ultimate stage of imprinting?" Schwangyu asked.

"Yes, that will be delicate. You think it will destroy him. That, of course, was your plan."

"Lucilla, the Sisterhood is not unanimous in following Taraza's designs for this ghola. Certainly, you know this."

It was Schwangyu's most powerful argument and the fact that it had been reserved for this moment said much. The fears that they might produce another Kwisatz Haderach were deep-seated and the dissension in the Bene Gesserit comparably powerful.

"He is primitive genetic stock and not bred to be a Kwisatz Haderach," Lucilla said.

"But the Tleilaxu have interfered with his genetic inheritance!"

"Yes; at our orders. They have sped up his nerve and muscle responses."

"Is that all they have done?" Schwangyu asked.

"You've seen the cell studies," Lucilla said.

"If we could do as much as the Tleilaxu we would not need them," Schwangyu said. "We would have our own axlotl tanks."

"You think they have hidden something from us," Lucilla said.

"They had him completely outside our observation for nine months!"

"I have heard all of these arguments," Lucilla said.

Schwangyu threw up her hands in a gesture of capitulation. "He's all yours, then, *Reverend Mother.* And the consequences are on your head. But you will not remove me from this post no matter what you report to Chapter House."

"Remove you? Certainly not. I don't want your faction sending someone unknown to us."

"There is a limit to the insults I will take from you," Schwangyu said.

"And there's a limit to how much treachery Taraza will accept," Lucilla said.

"If we get another Paul Atreides or, the Gods forbid, another Tyrant, it will be Taraza's doing," Schwangyu said. "Tell her I said so."

Lucilla stood. "You may as well know that Taraza left entirely at my discretion how much melange I feed this ghola. I have already begun increasing his intake of the spice."

Schwangyu pounded both fists on her desk. "Damn you all! You will destroy us yet!"

The Tleilaxu secret must be in their sperm. Our tests prove that their sperm does not carry forward in a straight genetic fashion. Gaps occur. Every Tleilaxu we have examined has hidden his inner self from us. They are naturally immune to an Ixian Probe! Secrecy at the deepest levels, that is their ultimate armor and their ultimate weapon.

—BENE GESSERIT ANALYSIS,
ARCHIVES CODE:
BTXX441WOR

On a morning of Sheeana's fourth year in priestly sanctuary, the reports of their spies brought a gleam of special interest to the Bene Gesserit watchers on Rakis.

"She was on the roof, you say?" the Mother Commander of the Rakian Keep asked.

Tamalane, the commander, had served previously on Gammu and knew more than most about what the Sisterhood hoped to conjoin here. The spies' report had interrupted Tamalane's breakfast of cifruit confit laced with melange. The messenger stood at ease beside the table while Tamalane resumed eating as she reread the report.

"On the roof, yes, Reverend Mother," the messenger said.

Tamalane glanced up at the messenger, Kipuna, a Rakian native acolyte being groomed for sensitive local duties. Swallowing a mouthful of her confit, Tamalane said: "*'Bring them back!'* Those were her exact words?"

Kipuna nodded curtly. She understood the question. Had Sheeana spoken with preemptory command?

Tamalane resumed scanning the report, looking for the sensitive signals. She was glad they had sent Kipuna herself. Tamalane respected the abilities of this Rakian woman. Kipuna had the soft round features and fuzzy hair common among much of the Rakian priestly class, but there was no fuzzy brain under that hair.

"Sheeana was displeased," Kipuna said. "The 'thopter passed nearby the rooftop and she saw the two manacled prisoners in it quite clearly. She knew they were being taken to death in the desert."

Tamalane put down the report and smiled. "So she ordered the prisoners brought back to her. I find her choice of words fascinating."

"Bring them back?" Kipuna asked. "That seems a simple enough order. How is it fascinating?"

Tamalane admired the directness of the acolyte's interest. Kipuna was not about to pass up a chance at learning how a real Reverend Mother's mind worked.

"It was not that part of her performance that interested me," Tamalane said. She bent to the report, reading aloud: "'You are servants unto Shaitan, not servants unto servants.'" Tamalane looked up at Kipuna. "You saw and heard all of this yourself?"

"Yes, Reverend Mother. It was judged important that I report to you personally should you have other questions."

"She still calls him Shaitan," Tamalane said. "How that must gall them! Of course, the Tyrant himself said it: 'They will call me Shaitan.'"

"I have seen the reports out of the hoard found at Dar-es-Balat," Kipuna said.

"There was no delay in bringing back the two prisoners?" Tamalane asked.

"As quickly as a message could be transmitted to the 'thopter, Reverend Mother. They were returned within minutes."

"So they are watching her and listening all the time. Good. Did Sheeana give any sign that she knew the two prisoners? Did any message pass between them?"

"I am sure they were strangers to her, Reverend Mother. Two ordinary people of the lower orders, rather dirty and poorly clothed. They smelled of the unwashed from the perimeter hovels."

"Sheeana ordered the manacles removed and then she spoke to this unwashed pair. Her exact words now: What did she say?"

"'You are my people.'"

"Lovely, lovely," Tamalane said. "Sheeana then ordered that these two be taken away, bathed and given new clothes before being released. Tell me in your own words what happened next."

"She summoned Tuek who came with three of his councillor-attendants. It was . . . almost an argument."

"Memory-trance, please," Tamalane said. "Replay the exchange for me."

Kipuna closed her eyes, breathed deeply and fell into memory-trance. Then: "Sheeana says, 'I do not like it when you feed my people to Shaitan.' Councillor Stiros says, 'They are sacrificed to Shai-hulud!' Sheeana says, 'To Shaitan!' Sheeana stamps her foot in anger. Tuek says, 'Enough, Stiros. I will not hear more of this dissension.' Sheeana says, 'When will you learn?' Stiros starts to speak but Tuek silences him with a glare and says, 'We have learned, Holy Child.' Sheeana says, 'I want—'"

"Enough," Tamalane said.

The acolyte opened her eyes and waited silently.

Presently, Tamalane said, "Return to your post, Kipuna. You have done very well, indeed."

"Thank you, Reverend Mother."

"There will be consternation among the priests," Tamalane said.

"Sheeana's wish is their command because Tuek believes in her. They will stop using the worms as instruments of punishment."

"The two prisoners," Kipuna said.

"Yes, very observant of you. The two prisoners will tell what happened to them. The story will be distorted. People will say that Sheeana protects them from the priests."

"Isn't that exactly what she's doing, Reverend Mother?"

"Ahhhh, but consider the options open to the priests. They will increase their alternative forms of punishment—whippings and certain deprivations. While fear of Shaitan eases because of Sheeana, fear of the priests will increase."

Within two months, Tamalane's reports to Chapter House contained confirmation of her own words.

"Short rations, especially short water rations, have become the dominant form of punishment," Tamalane reported. "Wild rumors have penetrated the farthest reaches of Rakis and soon will find lodging on many other planets as well."

Tamalane considered the implications of her report with care. Many eyes would see it, including some not in sympathy with Taraza. Any Reverend Mother would be able to call up an image of what must be happening on Rakis. Many on Rakis had seen Sheeana's arrival atop a wild worm from the desert. The priestly response of secrecy had been flawed from the beginning. Curiosity unsatisfied tended to create its own answers. Guesses were often more dangerous than facts.

Previous reports had told of the children brought to play with Sheeana. The much-garbled stories of such children were repeated with increasing distortions and those distortions had been dutifully sent on to Chapter House. The two prisoners, returned to the streets in their new finery, only compounded the growing mythology. The Sisterhood, artists in mythology, possessed on Rakis a ready-made energy to be subtly amplified and directed.

"We have fed a wish-fulfillment belief into the populace," Tamalane reported. She thought of the Bene Gesserit–originated phrases as she reread her latest report.

"Sheeana is the one we have long awaited."

It was a simple enough statement that its meaning could be spread without unacceptable distortion.

"The Child of Shai-hulud comes to chastise the priests!"

That one had been a bit more complicated. A few priests died in dark alleys as a result of popular fervency. This had fed a new alertness into the corps of priestly enforcers with predictable injustices inflicted upon the populace.

Tamalane thought of the priestly delegation that had waited upon Sheeana as a result of turmoil among Tuek's councillors. Seven of them led by Stiros had intruded upon Sheeana's luncheon with a child from the streets. Knowing that this would happen, Tamalane had been prepared and a secret recording of the incident had been brought to her, the words audible, every expression visible, the thoughts quite apparent to a Reverend Mother's trained eye.

"We were sacrificing to Shai-hulud!" Stiros protested.

"Tuek told you not to argue with me about that," Sheeana said.

How the priestesses smiled at the discomfiture of Stiros and the other priests!

"But Shai-hulud—" Stiros began.

"Shaitan!" Sheeana corrected him and her expression was easily read: *Did these stupid priests know nothing?*

"But we have always thought—"

"You were wrong!" Sheeana stamped a foot.

Stiros feigned the need for instruction. "Are we to believe that Shai-hulud, the Divided God, is also Shaitan?"

What a complete fool he was, Tamalane thought. Even a pubescent girl could confound him, as Sheeana proceeded to do.

"Any child of the streets knows this almost as soon as she can walk!" Sheeana ranted.

Stiros spoke slyly: "How do you know what is in the minds of street children?"

"You are evil to doubt me!" Sheeana accused. It was an answer she had learned to use often, knowing it would get back to Tuek and cause trouble.

Stiros knew this only too well. He waited with downcast eyes while Sheeana, speaking with heavy patience as one telling an old fable to a child, explained to him that either god or devil or both could inhabit the worm of the desert. Humans had only to accept this. It was not left to humans to decide such things.

Stiros had sent people into the desert for speaking such heresy. His expression (so carefully recorded for Bene Gesserit analysis) said such wild concepts were always springing up from the muck at the bottom of the Rakian heap. But now! He had to contend with Tuek's insistence that Sheeana spoke gospel truth!

As she looked at the recording, Tamalane thought the pot was boiling nicely. This she reported to Chapter House. Doubts flogged Stiros; doubts everywhere except among the populace in their devotion to Sheeana. Spies close to Tuek said he was even beginning to doubt the wisdom of his decision to translate the historian-locutor, Dromind.

"Was Dromind right to doubt her?" Tuek demanded of those around him.

"Impossible!" the sycophants said.

What else could they say? The High Priest could make no mistake in such decisions. God would not allow it. Sheeana clearly confounded him, though. She put the decisions of many previous High Priests into a terrible limbo. Reinterpretation was being demanded on all sides.

Stiros kept pounding at Tuek: "What do we really know about her?"

Tamalane had a full account of the most recent such confrontation. Stiros and Tuek alone, debating far into the night, just the two of them (they thought) in Tuek's quarters, comfortably ensconced in rare blue chairdogs, melange-laced confits close at hand. Tamalane's holophoto record of the meeting showed a single yellow glowglobe drifting on its suspensors close above the pair, the light dimmed to ease the strain on tired eyes.

"Perhaps that first time, leaving her in the desert with a thumper, was not a good test," Stiros said.

It was a sly statement. Tuek was noted for not having an excessively complicated mind. "Not a good test? Whatever do you mean?"

"God might wish us to perform other tests."

"You have seen her yourself! Many times in the desert talking to God!"

"Yes!" Stiros almost pounced. Clearly, it was the response he wanted. "If she can stand unharmed in the presence of God, perhaps she can teach others how this is accomplished."

"You know this angers her when we suggest it."

"Perhaps we have not approached the problem in quite the right way."

"Stiros! What if the child is right? We serve the *Divided* God. I have been thinking long and earnestly upon this. Why would God divide? Is this not God's ultimate test?"

The expression on Stiros' face said this was exactly the kind of mental gymnastics his faction feared. He tried to divert the High Priest but Tuek was not to be shifted from a single-track plunge into metaphysics.

"The ultimate test," Tuek insisted. "To see the good in evil and the evil in good."

Stiros' expression could only be described as consternation. Tuek was God's Supreme Anointed. No priest was allowed to doubt *that*! The thing that might now arise if Tuek went public with such a concept would shake the foundations of priestly authority! Clearly, Stiros was asking himself if the time had not come to *translate* his High Priest.

"I would never suggest that I might debate such profound ideas with my High Priest," Stiros said. "But perhaps I can offer a proposal that might resolve many doubts."

"Propose then," Tuek said.

"Subtle instruments could be introduced in her clothing. We might listen when she talks to—"

"Do you think God would not know what we did?"

"Such a thought never crossed my mind!"

"I will not order her taken into the desert," Tuek said.

"But if it is her own idea to go?" Stiros assumed his most ingratiating expression. "She has done this many times."

"But not recently. She appears to have lost her need to consult with God."

"Could we not offer suggestions to her?" Stiros asked.

"Such as?"

"Sheeana, when will you speak again with your Father? Do you not long to stand once more in His presence?"

"That has more the sound of prodding than suggestion."

"I am only proposing that—"

"This Holy Child is no simpleton! She talks to God, Stiros. God might punish us sorely for such presumption."

"Did God not put her here for us to study?" Stiros asked.

This was too close to the Dromind heresy for Tuek's liking. He sent a baleful stare at Stiros.

"What I mean," Stiros said, "is that surely God means us to learn from her."

Tuek himself had said this many times, never hearing in his own words a curious echo of Dromind's words.

"She is not to be prodded and tested," Tuek said.

"Heaven forbid!" Stiros said. "I will be the soul of holy caution. And everything I learn from the Holy Child will be reported to you immediately."

Tuek merely nodded. He had his own ways to be sure Stiros spoke the truth.

The subsequent sly proddings and testings were reported immediately to Chapter House by Tamalane and her subordinates.

"Sheeana has a thoughtful look," Tamalane reported.

Among the Reverend Mothers on Rakis and those to whom they reported, this thoughtful look had an obvious interpretation. Sheeana's antecedents had been deduced long ago. Stiros' intrusions were making the child homesick. Sheeana kept a wise silence but she clearly thought much about her life in a pioneer village. Despite all of the fears and perils, those obviously had been happy times for her. She would remember the laughter, poling the sand for its weather, hunting scorpions in the crannies of the village hovels, smelling out spice fragments in the dunes. From Sheeana's repeated trips to the area, the Sisterhood had made a reasonably accurate guess as to the location of the lost village and what had happened to it. Sheeana often stared at one of Tuek's old maps on the wall of her quarters.

As Tamalane expected, one morning Sheeana stabbed a finger at the place on the wall map where she had gone many times. "Take me there," Sheeana commanded her attendants.

A 'thopter was summoned.

While priests listened avidly in a 'thopter hovering far overhead, Sheeana once more confronted her nemesis in the sand. Tamalane and her advisors, tuned into the priestly circuits, observed just as avidly.

Nothing even remotely suggesting a village remained on the duneswept waste where Sheeana ordered herself deposited. She used a thumper this time, however. Another of Stiros' sly suggestions accompanied by careful instructions on use of the ancient means to summon the Divided God.

A worm came.

Tamalane watched on her own relay projector, thinking the worm only a middling monster. Its length she estimated at about fifty meters. Sheeana stood only about three meters in front of the gaping mouth. The huffing of the worm's interior fires was clearly audible to the observers.

"Will you tell me why you did it?" Sheeana demanded.

She did not flinch from the worm's hot breath. Sand crackled beneath the monster but she gave no sign that she heard.

"Answer me!" Sheeana commanded.

No voice came from the worm but Sheeana appeared to be listening, her head cocked to one side.

"Then go back where you came from," Sheeana said. She waved the worm away.

Obediently, the worm backed off and returned beneath the sands.

For days, while the Sisterhood spied upon them with glee, the priests debated that sparse encounter. Sheeana could not be questioned lest she learn that she had been overheard. As before, she refused to discuss anything about her visits to the desert.

Stiros continued his sly prodding. The result was precisely what the Sisterhood expected. Without any warning, Sheeana would awaken some days and say: "Today, I will go into the desert."

Sometimes she used a thumper, sometimes she danced her summons. Far out on the sands beyond the sight of Keen or any other inhabited place, the worms came to her. Sheeana alone in front of a worm talked to it while others listened. Tamalane found the accumulated recordings fascinating as they passed through her hands on their way to Chapter House.

"I should hate you!"

What a turmoil that caused among the priests! Tuek wanted an open debate: "Should all of us hate the Divided God at the same time we love Him?"

Stiros barely shut off this suggestion with the argument that God's wishes had not been made clear.

Sheeana asked one of her gigantic visitors: "Will you let me ride you again?"

When she approached, the worm retreated and would not let her mount.

On another occasion, she asked: "Must I stay with the priests?"

This particular worm proved to be the target of many questions, and among them:

"Where do people go when you eat them?"

"Why are people false to me?"

"Should I punish the bad priests?"

Tamalane laughed at that final question, thinking of the turmoil it would cause among Tuek's people. Her spies duly reported the dismay of the priests.

"How does He answer her?" Tuek asked. "Has anyone heard God respond?"

"Perhaps He speaks directly into her soul," a councillor ventured.

"That's it!" Tuek leaped at this offering. "We must ask her what God tells her to do."

Sheeana refused to be drawn into such discussions.

"She has a pretty fair assessment of her powers," Tamalane reported. "She's not going into the desert very much now despite Stiros' proddings. As we might expect, the attraction has waned. Fear and elation will carry her just so far before paling. She has, however, learned an effective command:

"Go away!"

The Sisterhood marked this as an important development. When even the Divided God obeyed, no priest or priestess was about to question her authority to issue such a command.

"The priests are building towers in the desert," Tamalane reported. "They want more secure places from which to observe Sheeana when she does go out there."

The Sisterhood had anticipated this development and had even done some of its own prodding to speed up the projects. Each tower had its own windtrap, its own maintenance staff, its own water barrier, gardens and other elements of civilization. Each was a small community spreading the established areas of Rakis farther and farther into the domain of the worms.

Pioneer villages no longer were necessary and Sheeana got the credit for this development.

"She is *our* priestess," the populace said.

Tuek and his councillors spun on the point of a pin: *Shaitan and Shai-hulud in one body?* Stiros lived in daily fear that Tuek would announce the fact. Stiros' advisors finally rejected the suggestion that Tuek be translated. Another suggestion that Priestess Sheeana have a fatal accident was greeted with horror by all, even Stiros finding it too great a venture.

"Even if we remove this thorn, God may visit us with an even more terrible intrusion," he said. And he warned: "The oldest books say that a little child shall lead us."

Stiros was only the most recent among those who looked upon Sheeana as something not quite mortal. It was observable that those around her, Cania included, had come to love Sheeana. She was so ingenuous, so bright and responsive.

Many observed that this growing affection for Sheeana extended even to Tuek.

For the people touched by this power, the Sisterhood had an immediate recognition. The Bene Gesserit knew a label for this ancient effect: *expanding worship.* Tamalane reported profound changes moving through Rakis as people everywhere on the planet began praying to Sheeana instead of to Shaitan or even to Shai-hulud.

"They see that Sheeana intercedes for the weakest people," Tamalane reported. "It is a familiar pattern. All goes as ordered. When do you send the ghola?"

The outer surface of a balloon is always larger than the center of the damned thing! That's the whole point of the Scattering!

—BENE GESSERIT RESPONSE TO AN IXIAN
SUGGESTION THAT NEW INVESTIGATIVE
PROBES BE SENT OUT AMONG THE LOST ONES

One of the Sisterhood's swifter lighters took Miles Teg up to the Guild Transport circling Gammu. He did not like leaving the Keep at this moment but the priorities were obvious. He also had a gut reaction about this venture. In his three centuries of experience, Teg had learned to trust his gut reactions. Matters were not going well on Gammu. Every patrol, every report of remote sensors, the accounts of Patrin's spies in the cities—everything fueled Teg's disquiet.

Mentat fashion, Teg felt the movement of forces around the Keep and within it. His ghola charge was threatened. The order for him to report aboard the Guild Transport prepared for violence, however, came from Taraza herself with an unmistakable crypto-identifier on it.

On the lighter taking him upward, Teg set himself for battle. Those preparations he could make had been made. Lucilla was warned. He felt confident about Lucilla. Schwangyu was another matter. He fully intended to discuss with Taraza a few essential changes in the Gammu Keep. First, though, he had another battle to win. Teg had not the slightest doubt that he was entering combat.

As his lighter moved in to dock, Teg looked out a port and saw the gigantic Ixian symbol within the Guild cartouche on the Transport's dark side. This was a ship the Guild had converted to Ixian mechanism, substituting machines for the traditional navigator. There would be Ixian technicians aboard to service the equipment. A genuine Guild navigator would be there, too. The Guild had never quite learned to trust a machine even while they paraded these converted Transports as a message to Tleilaxu and Rakians.

"You see: we do not absolutely require your melange!"

This was the announcement contained in that giant symbol of Ix on the spaceship's side.

Teg felt the slight lurch of the docking grapples and took a deep, quieting breath. He felt as he always did just before battle: Empty of all false dreams. This was a failure. The talking had failed and now came the contest of blood . . . unless he could prevail in some other way. Combat these days was seldom a massive thing but death was there nonetheless. That represented a more permanent kind of failure. *If we cannot adjust our differences peacefully we are less than human.*

An attendant with the unmistakable signs of Ix in his speech guided Teg to the room where Taraza waited. All along the corridors and in the pneumotubes carrying him to Taraza, Teg looked for signs to confirm the secret warning in the Mother Superior's message. All seemed serene and ordinary—the attendant properly deferential toward the Bashar. "I was a Tireg commander at Andioyu," the attendant said, naming one of the almost-battles where Teg had prevailed.

They came to an ordinary oval hatch in the wall of an ordinary corridor. The hatch opened and Teg entered a white-walled room of comfortable dimensions—sling chairs, low side tables, glowglobes tuned to yellow. The hatch slid into its seals behind him with a solid thump, leaving his guide behind him in the corridor.

A Bene Gesserit acolyte parted the gossamer hangings that concealed a passage on Teg's right. She nodded to him. He had been seen. Taraza would be notified.

Teg suppressed a trembling in his calf muscles.

Violence?

He had not misinterpreted Taraza's secret warning. Were his preparations adequate? There was a black sling chair at his left, a long table in front of it and another chair at the end of the table. Teg went to this side of the room and waited with his back to the wall. The brown dust of Gammu still clung to his boot toes, he noted.

Peculiar smell in the room. He sniffed. *Shere!* Had Taraza and her people armed themselves against an Ixian Probe? Teg had taken his usual shere capsule before embarking on the lighter. Too much knowledge in his head that might be useful to an enemy. The fact that Taraza left the smell of shere around her quarters had another implication: It was a statement to some observer whose presence she could not prevent.

Taraza entered through the gossamer hangings. She appeared tired, he thought. He found this remarkable because the Sisters were capable of concealing fatigue until almost ready to drop. Was she actually low in energy or was this another gesture for hidden observers?

Pausing just into the room, Taraza studied Teg. The Bashar appeared much older than when she had last seen him, Taraza thought. Duty on Gammu was having its effect, but she found this reassuring. Teg was doing his job.

"Your quick response is appreciated, Miles," she said.

Appreciated! Their agreed word for *"We are being watched secretly by a dangerous foe."*

Teg nodded while his gaze went to the hangings where Taraza had entered.

Taraza smiled and moved farther into the room. No signs of the melange cycle in Teg, she observed. Teg's advanced years always raised the suspicion that he might resort to the leavening effect of the spice. Nothing about him revealed even the faintest hint of the melange addiction that even the strongest sometimes turned to when they felt their end approaching. Teg wore his old uniform jacket of Supreme Bashar but without the gold starbursts at shoulder and collar. This was a signal she recognized. He said: "Remember how I earned this in your service. I have not failed you this time, either."

The eyes that studied her were level; no hint of judgment escaped them. His entire appearance spoke of quiet within, everything at variance with what she knew must be occurring in him at this moment. He awaited her signal.

"Our ghola must be awakened at the first opportunity," she said. She waved a hand to silence him as he started to respond. "I have seen Lucilla's reports and I know he is too young. But we are required to act."

She spoke for the watchers, he realized. Were her words to be believed?

"I now give you the order to awaken him," she said and she flexed her left wrist in the confirmation gesture of their secret language.

It was true! Teg glanced at the hangings that concealed the passage where Taraza had entered. Who was it listening there?

He put his Mentat talents to the problem. There were missing pieces but that did not stop him. A Mentat could work without certain pieces if he had enough to create a pattern. Sometimes, the sketchiest outline was enough. It supplied the hidden shape and then he could fit the missing pieces to complete a whole. Mentats seldom had all the data they might desire, but he was trained to sense patterns, to recognize systems and wholeness. Teg reminded himself now that he also had been trained in the ultimate military sense: You trained a recruit to *train* a weapon, *to aim the weapon correctly.*

Taraza was aiming him. His assessment of their situation had been confirmed.

"Desperate attempts will be made to kill or capture our ghola before you can awaken him," she said.

He recognized her tone: the coldly analytic offering of data to a Mentat. She saw that he was in Mentat mode, then.

The Mentat pattern-search rolled through his mind. First, there was the Sisterhood's design for the ghola, largely unknown to him, but ranging somehow around the presence of a young female on Rakis who (so they said) could command worms. Idaho gholas: charming persona and with something else that had made the Tyrant and the Tleilaxu repeat him countless times. Duncans by the shipload! What service did this ghola provide that the Tyrant had not let him remain among the dead? And the Tleilaxu: They had decanted Duncan Idaho gholas from their axlotl tanks for millennia, even after the death of the Tyrant. The Tleilaxu had sold this ghola to the Sisterhood twelve times and the Sisterhood had paid in the hardest currency: melange from their own precious stores. Why did the Tleilaxu accept in payment something they produced so copiously? Obvious: to deplete the Sisterhood's supplies. A special form of greed there. The Tleilaxu were buying supremacy—a *power game!*

Teg focused on the quietly waiting Mother Superior. "The Tleilaxu have been killing our gholas to control our timing," he said.

Taraza nodded but did not speak. So there was more. Once again, he fell into Mentat mode.

The Bene Gesserit were a valuable market for the Tleilaxu melange, not the only source because there was always the trickle from Rakis, but valuable, yes; very valuable. It was not reasonable that the Tleilaxu would alienate a valuable market unless they had a more valuable market standing ready.

Who else had an interest in Bene Gesserit activities? The Ixians without a doubt. But Ixians were not a good market for melange. The Ixian presence on this ship spoke of their independence. Since Ixians and Fish Speakers made common cause, the Fish Speakers could be set aside from this pattern quest.

What great power or assemblage of powers in this universe possessed . . .

Teg froze that thought as though he had applied the dive brakes in a 'thopter, letting his mind float free while he sorted other considerations.

Not in this universe.

The pattern took shape. *Wealth.* Gammu assumed a new role in his Mentat computations. Gammu had been gutted long ago by the Harkonnens, abandoned as a festering carcass, which the Danians had restored. There was a time, though, when even Gammu's hopes were gone.

Without hopes there had not even been dreams. Climbing from that cesspool, the population had employed only the basest pragmatism. *If it works, it is good.*

Wealth.

In his first survey of Gammu he had noted the numbers of banking houses. They were even marked, some of them, as Bene Gesserit–safe. Gammu served as the fulcrum for manipulation of enormous wealth. The bank he had visited to study its use as an emergency contact came back fully into his Mentat awareness. He had realized at once that the place did not confine itself to purely planetary business. It was a bankers' bank.

Not just wealth but WEALTH.

A Prime Pattern development did not come into Teg's mind but he had enough for a Testing Projection. Wealth not of this universe. People from the Scattering.

All of this Mentat sorting had taken only a few seconds. Having reached a testing point, Teg set himself loose-of-muscle and nerve, glanced once at Taraza and strode across to the concealed entry. He noted that Taraza gave no sign of alarm at his movements. Whipping aside the hangings, Teg confronted a man almost as tall as himself: military-style clothing with crossed spears at the collar tabs. The face was heavy, the jaws wide; green eyes. A look of surprised alertness, one hand poised above a pocket that bulged obviously with a weapon.

Teg smiled at the man, let the hangings fall and returned to Taraza.

"We are being observed by people from the Scattering," he said.

Taraza relaxed. Teg's performance had been memorable.

The hangings swished aside. The tall stranger entered and stopped about two paces from Teg. A glacial expression of anger gripped his features.

"I warned you not to tell him!" The voice was a grating baritone with an accent new to Teg.

"And I warned you about the powers of this Mentat Bashar," Taraza said. A look of loathing flashed across her features.

The man subsided and a subtle look of fear came over his face. "Honored Matre, I—"

"Don't you dare call me that!" Taraza's body tensed in a fighting posture that Teg had never before seen her display.

The man inclined his head slightly. "Dear lady, you do not control the situation here. I must remind you that my orders—"

Teg had heard enough. "Through me, she does control here," he said. "Before coming here I set certain protective measures in motion. This . . ." he glanced around him and returned his attention to the intruder, whose face now bore a wary expression ". . . is not a no-ship. Two of our no-ship monitors have you in their sights at this moment."

"You would not survive!" the man barked.

Teg smiled amiably. "No one on this ship would survive." He clenched his jaw to key the nerve signal and activate the tiny pulsetimer in his skull. It played its graphic signals against his visual centers. "And you don't have much time in which to make a decision."

"Tell him how you knew to do this," Taraza said.

"The Mother Superior and I have our own private means of communication," Teg said. "But further than that, there was no need for her to warn me. Her summons was enough. The Mother Superior on a Guild Transport at a time like this? Impossible!"

"Impasse," the man growled.

"Perhaps," Teg said. "But neither Guild nor Ix will risk a total and all-out attack by Bene Gesserit forces under the command of a leader trained by me. I refer to the Bashar Burzmali. Your support has just dissolved and vanished."

"I told him nothing of this," Taraza said. "You have just witnessed the performance of a Mentat Bashar, which I doubt could be equaled in your universe. Think of that if you consider going against Burzmali, a man trained by this Mentat."

The intruder looked from Taraza to Teg and back to Taraza.

"This is the way out of our seeming impasse," Teg said. "The Mother

Superior Taraza and her entourage leave with me. You must decide immediately. Time is running out."

"You're bluffing." There was no force in the words.

Teg faced Taraza and bowed. "It has been a great honor to serve you, Reverend Mother Superior. I bid you farewell."

"Perhaps death will not part us," Taraza said. It was the traditional farewell of a Reverend Mother to a Sister-equal.

"Go!" The heavy-featured man dashed to the corridor hatchway and flung it open, revealing two Ixian guards, looks of surprise on their faces. His voice hoarse, the man ordered: "Take them to their lighter."

Still relaxed and calm, Teg said: "Summon your people, Mother Superior." To the man standing at the hatchway, Teg said: "You value your own skin too much to be a good soldier. None of my people would have made such an error."

"There are true Honored Matres aboard this ship," the man grated. "I am sworn to protect them."

Teg grimaced and turned to where Taraza was leading her people from the adjoining room: two Reverend Mothers and four acolytes. Teg recognized one of the Reverend Mothers: Darwi Odrade. He had seen her before only at a distance but the oval face and lovely eyes were arresting: so like Lucilla.

"Do we have time for introductions?" Taraza asked.

"Of course, Mother Superior."

Teg nodded and grasped the hand of each woman as Taraza presented them.

As they left, Teg turned to the uniformed stranger. "One must always observe the niceties," Teg said. "Otherwise we are less than human."

Not until they were on the lighter, Taraza seated beside him and her entourage nearby, did Teg ask the overriding question.

"How did they take you?"

The lighter was plunging planetward. The screen in front of Teg showed that the Ix-branded Guildship obeyed his command to remain in orbit until his party was safely behind its planetary defenses.

Before Taraza could respond, Odrade leaned across the aisle separating them and said: "I have countermanded the Bashar's orders to destroy that Guildship, Mother."

Teg swiveled his head sharply and glared at Odrade. "But they took you captive and . . ." He scowled. "How did you know I—"

"Miles!"

Taraza's voice conveyed overwhelming reproof. He grinned ruefully. Yes, she knew him almost as well as he knew himself . . . better in some respects.

"They did not just capture us, Miles," Taraza said. "We allowed ourselves to be taken. Ostensibly, I was escorting Dar to Rakis. We left our no-ship at Junction and asked for the fastest Guild Transport. All of my Council, including Burzmali, agreed that these intruders from the Scattering would subvert the Transport and take us to you, aiming to pick up all the pieces of the ghola project."

Teg was aghast. *The risk!*

"We knew you would rescue us," Taraza said. "Burzmali was standing by in case you failed."

"That Guildship you've spared," Teg said, "will summon assistance and attack our—"

"They will not attack Gammu," Taraza said. "Too many diverse forces from the Scattering are assembled on Gammu. They would not dare alienate so many."

"I wish I were as certain of that as you appear to be," Teg said.

"Be certain, Miles. Besides, there are other reasons for not destroying the Guildship. Ix and the Guild have been caught taking sides. That's bad for business and they need all of the business they can get."

"Unless they have more important customers offering greater profits!"

"Ahhhhh, Miles." She spoke in a musing voice. "What we latter-day Bene Gesserit really do is try to let matters achieve a calmer tone, a balance. You know this."

Teg found this true but he locked on one phrase: ". . . latter-day . . ." The words conveyed a sense of summation-at-death. Before he could question this, Taraza continued:

"We like to settle the most passionate situations off the battlefield. I must admit we have the Tyrant to thank for that attitude. I don't suppose you've ever thought of yourself as a product of the Tyrant's conditioning, Miles, but you are."

Teg accepted this without comment. It was a factor in the entire spread of human society. No Mentat could avoid it as a datum.

"That quality in you, Miles, drew us to you in the first place," Taraza said. "You can be damnably frustrating at times but we wouldn't have you any other way."

By subtle revelations in tone and manner, Teg realized that Taraza was not speaking solely for his benefit, but was also directing her words at her entourage.

"Have you any idea, Miles, how maddening it is to hear you argue both sides of an issue with equal force? But your simpatico is a powerful weapon. How terrified some of our foes have been to find you confronting them where they had not the slightest suspicion you might appear!"

Teg allowed himself a tight smile. He glanced at the women seated across the aisle from them. Why was Taraza directing such words at this group? Darwi Odrade appeared to be resting, head back, eyes closed. Several of the others were chatting among themselves. None of this was conclusive to Teg. Even Bene Gesserit acolytes could follow several trains of thought simultaneously. He returned his attention to Taraza.

"You really feel things the way the enemy feels them," Taraza said. "That is what I mean. And, of course, when you're in that mental frame there is no enemy for you."

"Yes, there is!"

"Don't mistake my words, Miles. We have never doubted your loyalty. But it's uncanny how you make us see things we have no other way of seeing. There are times when you are our eyes."

Darwi Odrade, Teg saw, had opened her eyes and was looking at him. She was a lovely woman. Something disturbing about her appearance. As with Lucilla, she reminded him of someone in his past. Before Teg could follow this thought, Taraza spoke.

"Has the ghola this ability to balance between opposing forces?" she asked.

"He could be a Mentat," Teg said.

"He *was* a Mentat in one incarnation, Miles."

"Do you really want him awakened so young?"

"It is necessary, Miles. Deadly necessary."

The failure of CHOAM? Quite simple: They ignore the fact that larger commercial powers wait at the edges of their activities, powers that could swallow them the way a slig swallows garbage. This is the true threat of the Scattering—to them and to us all.

—BENE GESSERIT COUNCIL NOTES, ARCHIVES #SXX9OCH

Odrade spared only part of her awareness to the conversation between Teg and Taraza. Their lighter was a small one, its passenger quarters cramped. It would use atmospherics to dampen its descent, she knew, and she prepared herself for the buffeting. The pilot would be sparing of their suspensors on such a craft, saving energy.

She used these moments as she used all such time now to gird herself for the coming necessities. Time pressed; a special calendar drove her. She had looked at a calendar before leaving Chapter House, caught as often happened to her by the persistence of time and its language: seconds, minutes, hours, days, weeks, months, years . . . Standard Years, to be precise. Persistence was an inadequate word for the phenomenon. Inviolability was more like it. Tradition. Never disturb tradition. She held the comparisons firmly in mind, the ancient flow of time imposed on planets that did not tick to the primitive human clock. A week was seven days. Seven! How powerful that number remained. Mystical. It was enshrined in the Orange Catholic Bible. The Lord made a world in six days "and on the seventh day He rested."

Good for Him! Odrade thought. *We all should rest after great labors.*

Odrade turned her head slightly and looked across the aisle at Teg. He had no idea how many memories of him she possessed. She could mark how the years had treated that strong face. Teaching the ghola had drained his energies, she saw. That child in the Gammu Keep must be a sponge absorbing anything and everything around him.

Miles Teg, do you know how we use you? she wondered.

It was a thought that weakened her but she allowed it to persist in her awareness almost with a feeling of defiance. How easy it would be to love that old man! Not as a mate, of course . . . but love, nonetheless. She could feel the bond tugging at her and recognized it with the fine edge of her Bene Gesserit abilities. Love, damnable love, weakening love.

Odrade had felt this tugging with the first mate she had been sent to seduce. Curious sensation. Her years of Bene Gesserit conditioning had made her wary of it. None of her proctors had allowed her the luxury of that unquestioning warmth, and she had learned in time the reasons behind such isolating care. But there she was, sent by the breeding mistresses, ordered to get that close to a single individual, to let him enter her. All of the clinical data lay there in her awareness and she could read the sexual excitement in her partner even as she allowed it in herself. She had, after all, been carefully prepared for this role by men the Breeding Mistresses selected and conditioned with exquisite nicety for just such training.

Odrade sighed and looked away from Teg, closing her eyes in remembrance. Training Males never let their emotions reflect a bonding abandonment to their students. It was a necessary flaw in the sexual education.

That first seduction upon which she had been sent: She had been quite unprepared for the melting ecstasy of a simultaneous orgasm, a mutuality and sharing as old as humankind . . . older! And with powers capable of overwhelming the reason. The look on her male companion's face, the sweet kiss, his total abandonment of all self-protective reserves, unguarded and supremely vulnerable. No Training Male had ever done that! Desperately, she grasped for the Bene Gesserit lessons.

Through those lessons, she saw the essence of this man on his face, felt that essence in her deepest fibers. For just an instant, she permitted an equal response, experiencing a new height of ecstasy that none of her teachers had hinted might be attainable. For that instant, she understood what had happened to the Lady Jessica and the other Bene Gesserit *failures*.

This feeling was love!

Its power frightened her (as the Breeding Mistresses had known it would) and she fell back into the careful Bene Gesserit conditioning, allowing a mask of pleasure to take over the brief natural expression on her face, employing calculated caresses where natural caresses would have been easier (but less effective).

The male responded as expected, stupidly. It helped to think of him as stupid.

Her second seduction had been easier. She could still call up the features of that first one, though, doing it sometimes with a calloused sense of wonder. Sometimes, his face came to her of itself and for no reason she could identify immediately.

With the other males she had been sent to breed, the memory markers were different. She had to hunt her past for the look of them. The sensory recordings of those experiences did not go as deep. Not so with that first one!

Such was the dangerous power of love.

And look at the troubles this hidden force had caused the Bene Gesserit over the millennia. The Lady Jessica and her love for her Duke had been only one example among countless others. Love clouded reason. It diverted the Sisters from their duties. Love could be tolerated only where it caused no immediate and obvious disruptions or where it served the larger purposes of the Bene Gesserit. Otherwise it was to be avoided.

Always, though, it remained an object of disquieting watchfulness.

Odrade opened her eyes and glanced again at Teg and Taraza. The Mother Superior had taken up a new subject. How irritating Taraza's voice could be at times! Odrade closed her eyes and listened to the conversation, tied to those two voices by some link in her awareness that she could not avoid.

"Very few people realize how much of the infrastructure in a civilization is dependency infrastructure," Taraza said. "We have made quite a study of this."

Love is a dependency infrastructure, Odrade thought. Why had Taraza hit on this subject at this time? The Mother Superior seldom did anything without deep motives. "Dependency infrastructure is a term that includes all things necessary for a human population to survive at existing or increased numbers," Taraza said.

"Melange?" Teg asked.

"Of course, but most people look at the spice and say, 'How nice it is that we can have it and it can give us so much longer lives than were enjoyed by our ancestors.'"

"Providing they can afford it." Teg's voice had a bite in it, Odrade noted.

"As long as no single power controls all of the market, most people have enough," Taraza said.

"I learned economics at my mother's knee," Teg said. "Food, water, breathable air, living space not contaminated by poisons—there are many kinds of *money* and the value changes according to the dependency."

As she listened to him, Odrade almost nodded in agreement. His response was her own. *Don't belabor the obvious, Taraza! Get to your point.*

"I want you to remember your mother's teachings very clearly," Taraza said. *How mild her voice was suddenly!* Taraza's voice changed abruptly then and she snapped: "Hydraulic despotism!"

She does that shift of emphasis well, Odrade thought. Memory spewed up the data like a spigot suddenly opened full force. *Hydraulic despotism*: central control of an essential energy such as water, electricity, fuel, medicines, melange . . . Obey the central controlling power or the energy is shut off and you die!

Taraza was talking once more: "There's another useful concept that I'm sure your mother taught you—the key log."

Odrade was very curious now. Taraza was headed somewhere important with this conversation. *Key log*: a truly ancient concept from the days before suspensors when lumbermen sent their fallen timber rushing down rivers to central mill sites. Sometimes the logs jammed up in the river and an expert was brought in to find the one log, the key log, which would free the jam when removed. Teg, she knew, would have an intellectual understanding of the term but she and Taraza could call up actual witnesses from Other Memories, see the explosion of broken bits of wood and water as a jam was released.

"The Tyrant was a key log," Taraza said. "He created the jam and he released it."

The lighter began trembling sharply as it took its first bite of Gammu's atmosphere. Odrade felt the tightness of her restraining harness for a few seconds, then the craft's passage became steadier. Conversation stopped for this interval, then Taraza continued:

"Beyond the so-called natural dependencies are some religions that have been created psychologically. Even physical necessities can have such an underground component."

"A fact the Missionaria Protectiva understands quite well," Teg said. Again, Odrade heard that undercurrent of deep resentment in his voice. Taraza certainly must hear it, too. What was she doing? She could weaken Teg!

"Ahhh, yes," Taraza said. "Our Missionaria Protectiva. Humans have such a powerful need that their own belief structure be the 'true belief.' If it gives you pleasure or a sense of security *and* if it is incorporated into your belief structure, what a powerful dependency that creates!"

Again, Taraza fell silent while their lighter went through another atmospheric buffeting.

"I wish he would use his suspensors!" Taraza complained.

"It saves fuel," Teg said. "Less dependency."

Taraza chuckled. "Oh, yes, Miles. You know the lesson well. I see your mother's hand in it. Damn the dam when the child strikes out in a dangerous direction."

"You think of me as a child?" he asked.

"I think of you as someone who has just had his first direct encounter with the machinations of the so-called Honored Matres."

So that's it, Odrade thought. And with a feeling of shock, Odrade realized that Taraza was aiming her words at a broader target than just Teg.

She's talking to me!

"These Honored Matres, as they call themselves," Taraza said, "have combined sexual ecstasy and worship. I doubt that they have even guessed at the dangers."

Odrade opened her eyes and looked across the aisle at the Mother Superior. Taraza's gaze was fixed intently on Teg, an unreadable expression except for the eyes, which burned with the necessity for him to understand.

"Dangers," Taraza repeated. "The great mass of humankind possesses an unmistakable unit-identity. It can be one thing. It can act as a single organism."

"So the Tyrant said," Teg countered.

"So the Tyrant demonstrated! The Group Soul was his to manipulate. There are times, Miles, when survival demands that we commune with the soul. Souls, you know, are always seeking outlet."

"Hasn't communing with souls gone out of style in our time?" Teg asked. Odrade did not like the bantering tone in his voice and noted that it aroused a matching anger in Taraza.

"You think I talk about fashions in religion?" Taraza demanded, her high-pitched voice insistently harsh. "We both know religions can be created! I'm talking about these Honored Matres who ape some of our ways but have none of our deeper awareness. They dare place themselves at the center of worship!"

"A thing the Bene Gesserit always avoids," he said. "My mother said that worshipers and the worshiped are united by the faith."

"And they can be divided!"

Odrade saw Teg suddenly fall into Mentat mode, an unfocused stare in his eyes, his features placid. She saw now part of what Taraza was doing. *The Mentat rides Roman, one foot on each steed. Each foot is based on a different reality as the pattern-search hurtles him forward. He must ride different realities to a single goal.*

Teg spoke in a Mentat's musing, unaccented voice: "Divided forces will battle for supremacy."

Taraza gave a sigh of pleasure almost sensual in its natural venting.

"Dependency infrastructure," Taraza said. "These women from the Scattering would control dividing forces, all of those forces trying mightily to take the lead. That military officer on the Guildship, when he spoke of his Honored Matres, spoke with both awe and hatred. I'm sure you heard it in his voice, Miles. I know how well your mother taught you."

"I heard." Teg was once more focused on Taraza, hanging on her every word as was Odrade.

"Dependencies," Taraza said. "How simple they can be and how complex. Take, for example, tooth decay."

"Tooth decay?" Teg was shocked off his Mentat track and Odrade, observing this, saw that his reaction was precisely what Taraza wanted. Taraza was playing her Mentat Bashar with a fine hand.

And I am supposed to see this and learn from it, Odrade thought.

"Tooth decay," Taraza repeated. "A simple implant at birth prevents this bane for most of humankind. Still, we must brush the teeth and otherwise care for them. It is so natural to us that we seldom think about it. The devices we use are assumed to be wholly ordinary parts of our environment. Yet the devices, the materials in them, the instructors in tooth care and the Suk monitors, all have their interlocked relationships."

"A Mentat does not need interdependencies explained to him," Teg said. There was still curiosity in his voice but with a definite undertone of resentment.

"Quite," Taraza said. "That is the natural environment of a Mentat's thinking process."

"Then why do you belabor this?"

"Mentat, look at what you now know of these Honored Matres and tell me: What is their flaw?"

Teg spoke without hesitation: "They can only survive if they continue to increase the dependency of those who support them. It's an addict's dead-end street."

"Precisely. And the danger?"

"They could take much of humankind down with them."

"That was the Tyrant's problem, Miles. I'm sure he knew it. Now, pay attention to me with great care. And you, too, Dar." Taraza looked across the aisle and met Odrade's gaze. "Both of you listen to me. We of the Bene Gesserit are setting very powerful . . . *elements* adrift in the human current. They may jam up. They are sure to cause damage. And we . . ."

Once more, the lighter entered a period of severe buffeting. Conversation was impossible while they clung to their seats and listened to the roaring, creaking around them. When this interruption eased, Taraza raised her voice.

"If we survive this damnable machine and get down to Gammu, you must go aside with Dar there, Miles. You have seen the Atreides Manifesto. She will tell you about it and prepare you. That is all."

Teg turned and looked at Odrade. Once more, her features tugged at his memories: a remarkable likeness to Lucilla, but there was something else. He put this aside. *The Atreides Manifesto?* He had read it because it came to him from Taraza with instructions that he do so. *Prepare me? For what?*

Odrade saw the questioning look on Teg's face. Now, she understood Taraza's motive. The Mother Superior's orders took on a new meaning as did words from the Manifesto itself.

"Just as the universe is created by the participation of consciousness, the prescient human carries that creative faculty to its ultimate extreme.

This was the profoundly misunderstood power of the Atreides bastard, the power that he transmitted to his son, the Tyrant."

Odrade knew those words with an author's intimacy but they came back to her now as though she had never before encountered them.

Damn you, Tar! Odrade thought. *What if you're wrong?*

At the quantum level our universe can be seen as an indeterminate place, predictable in a statistical way only when you employ large enough numbers. Between that universe and a relatively predictable one where the passage of a single planet can be timed to a picosecond, other forces come into play. For the in-between universe where we find our daily lives, *that which you believe* is a dominant force. Your beliefs order the unfolding of daily events. If enough of us believe, a new thing can be made to exist. Belief structure creates a filter through which chaos is sifted into order.

—ANALYSIS OF THE TYRANT,
THE TARAZA FILE:
BG ARCHIVES

Teg's thoughts were in turmoil as he returned to Gammu from the Guildship. He stepped from the lighter at the black-charred edge of the Keep's private landing field and looked around him as though for the first time. Almost noon. So little time had passed and so much had changed.

To what extent would the Bene Gesserit go in imparting an essential lesson? he wondered. Taraza had dislodged him from his familiar Mentat processes. He felt that the whole incident on the Guildship had been staged just for him. He had been shaken from a predictable course. How strange Gammu appeared as he crossed the guarded strip to the entry pits.

Teg had seen many planets, learned their ways and how they

printed themselves on their inhabitants. Some planets had a big yellow sun that sat in close and kept living things warm, evolving, growing. Some planets had little shimmer-suns that hung far away in a dark sky, and their light touched very little. Variations existed within and even outside this range. Gammu was a yellow-green variation with a day of 31.27 standard hours and a 2.6 SY. Teg had thought he knew Gammu.

When the Harkonnens were forced to abandon it, colonists left behind by the Scattering came from the Danian group, calling it by the Halleck name given to it in the great remapping. The colonists had been known as Caladanian in those days but millennia tended to shorten some labels.

Teg paused at the entryway to the protective revetments that led from the field down beneath the Keep. Taraza and her party lagged behind him. He saw Taraza was talking intently to Odrade.

Atreides Manifesto, he thought.

Even on Gammu, few admitted to either Harkonnen or Atreides ancestry, although the genotypes were visible here—especially the dominant Atreides: those long, sharp noses, the high foreheads and sensual mouths. Often, the pieces were scattered—the mouth on one face, those piercing eyes on another and countless mixtures. Sometimes, though, one person carried it all and then you saw the pride, that inner knowledge:

"I am one of them!"

Gammu's natives recognized it and gave it walkway room but few labeled it.

Underlying all of this was what the Harkonnens had left behind—genetic lines tracing far away into the dawn times of Greek and Pathan and Mameluke, shadows of ancient history that few outside of professional historians or those trained by the Bene Gesserit could even name.

Taraza and her party caught up with Teg. He heard her say to Odrade: "You must tell Miles all of it."

Very well, she would tell him, he thought. He turned and led the way past the inner guards to the long passage under the pillboxes into the Keep proper.

Damn the Bene Gesserit! he thought. *What were they really doing here on Gammu?*

Plenty of Bene Gesserit signs could be seen on this planet: the back-breeding to fix selected traits, and here and there a visible emphasis on seductive eyes for women.

Teg returned a guard captain's salute without changing focus. *Seductive eyes, yes.* He had seen this soon after his arrival at the ghola's Keep and especially during his first inspection tour of the planet. He had seen himself in many faces, too, and recalled the thing old Patrin had mentioned so many times.

"You have the Gammu look, Bashar."

Seductive eyes! That guard captain back there had them. She and Odrade and Lucilla were alike in this. Few people paid much attention to the importance of eyes when it came to seduction, he thought. It took a Bene Gesserit upbringing to make that point. Big breasts in a woman and hard loins in a man (that tightly muscular look to the buttocks)—these were naturally important in sexual matchings. But without the eyes, the rest of it could go for nothing. Eyes were essential. You could drown in the right kind of eyes, he had learned, sink right into them and be unaware of what was being done to you until penis was firmly clasped in vagina.

He had noted Lucilla's eyes immediately after his arrival on Gammu and had walked cautiously. No doubts about how the Sisterhood used her talents!

There was Lucilla now, waiting at the central inspection and decontamination chamber. She gave him the flickering handsign that all was well with the ghola. Teg relaxed and watched as Lucilla and Odrade confronted each other. The two women had remarkably similar features despite the age difference. Their bodies were quite different, though, Lucilla more solid against Odrade's willowy form.

The guard captain of the seductive eyes came up beside Teg and leaned close to him. "Schwangyu has just learned who you brought back with you," she said, nodding toward Taraza. "Ahhh, there she is now."

Schwangyu stepped from a lift tube and crossed to Taraza, giving only an angry glare to Teg.

Taraza wanted to surprise you, he thought. *We all know why.*

"You don't appear happy to see me," Taraza said, addressing Schwangyu.

"I *am* surprised, Mother Superior," Schwangyu said. "I had no idea." She glanced once more at Teg, a look of venom in her eyes.

Odrade and Lucilla broke off their mutual examination. "I had heard about it, of course," Odrade said, "but it is a stopper to confront yourself in the face of another person."

"I warned you," Taraza said.

"What are your orders, Mother Superior?" Schwangyu asked. It was as close as she could come to asking the purpose of Taraza's visit.

"I would like a private word with Lucilla," Taraza said.

"I'll have quarters prepared for you," Schwangyu said.

"Don't bother," Taraza said. "I'm not staying. Miles has already arranged for my transport. Duty requires my presence at Chapter House. Lucilla and I will talk outside in the courtyard." Taraza put a finger to her cheek. "Oh, and I'd like to watch the ghola unobserved for a few minutes. I'm sure Lucilla can arrange it."

"He's taking the more intense training quite well," Lucilla said as the two moved off toward a lift tube.

Teg turned his attention to Odrade, noting as his gaze passed across Schwangyu's face the intensity of her anger. She was not trying to conceal it.

Was Lucilla a sister or a daughter of Odrade? Teg wondered. It occurred to him suddenly that there must be a Bene Gesserit purpose behind the resemblance. Yes, of course—Lucilla was an Imprinter!

Schwangyu overcame her anger. She looked with curiosity at Odrade. "I was just about to take lunch, Sister," Schwangyu said. "Would you care to join me?"

"I must have a word alone with the Bashar," Odrade said. "If it is all right, perhaps we could remain here for our talk? I must not be seen by the ghola."

Schwangyu scowled, not trying to hide her upset from Odrade. They knew at Chapter House where loyalties lay! But no one . . . no one! would remove her from this post of observational command. Opposition had its rights!

Her thoughts were clear even to Teg. He noted the stiffness of Schwangyu's back as she left them.

"It is bad when Sister is turned against Sister," Odrade said.

Teg gave a handsign to his guard captain, ordering her to clear the area. *Alone*, Odrade said. *Alone it would be.* To Odrade, he said: "This is one of my areas. No spies or other means of observing us here."

"I thought as much," Odrade said.

"We have a service room over there." Teg nodded to his left. "Furniture, even chairdogs if you prefer."

"I hate it when they try to cuddle me," she said. "Could we talk here?" She put a hand under Teg's arm. "Perhaps we could walk a bit. I got so stiff sitting in that lighter."

"What is it you're supposed to tell me?" he asked as they strolled.

"My memories are no longer selectively filtered," she said. "I have them all, only on the female side, naturally."

"So?" Teg pursed his lips. This was not the overture he had expected. Odrade appeared more like one who would take off on a direct approach.

"Taraza says you have read the Atreides Manifesto. Good. You know it will cause upset in many quarters."

"Schwangyu already has made it the subject of a diatribe against 'you Atreides.'"

Odrade stared at him solemnly. As the reports all said, Teg remained an imposing figure, but she had known that without the reports.

"We are both Atreides, you and I," Odrade said.

Teg came to full alert.

"Your mother explained that to you in detail," Odrade said, "when you took your first school leave back to Lernaeus."

Teg stopped and stared down at her. How could she know this? To his knowledge, he had never before met and conversed with this remote Darwi Odrade. Was he the subject of special discussions at Chapter House? He held his silence, forcing her to carry the conversation.

"I will recount a conversation between a man and my birth-mother," Odrade said. "They are in bed and the man says: 'I fathered a few children when I first escaped from the close bondage of the Bene Gesserit, back when I thought myself an independent agent, free to enlist and fight anywhere I chose.'"

Teg did not try to conceal his surprise. Those were his own words! Mentat memory told him Odrade had them down as accurately as a mechanical recorder. Even the tone!

"More?" she asked as he continued to stare at her. "Very well. The man says: 'That was before they sent me to Mentat training, of course. What an eye-opener that was! I had never been out of the Sisterhood's sight for an instant! I was never a free agent.'"

"Not even when I spoke *those* words," Teg said.

"True." She urged him by pressure on his arm as they continued their stroll across the chamber. "The children you fathered all be-longed to the Bene Gesserit. The Sisterhood takes no chances that our genotype will be sent into the wild gene pool."

"Let my body go to Shaitan, their precious genotype remains in Sisterhood care," he said.

"My care," Odrade said. "I am one of your daughters."

Again, he forced her to stop.

"I think you know who my mother was," she said. She held up a hand for silence as he started to respond. "Names are not necessary."

Teg studied Odrade's features, seeing the recognizable signs there. Mother and daughter were matched. But what of Lucilla?

As though she heard his question, Odrade said: "Lucilla is from a parallel breeding line. Quite remarkable, isn't it, what careful breed-matching can achieve?"

Teg cleared his throat. He felt no emotional attachment to this newly revealed daughter. Her words and other important signals of her performance demanded his primary attention.

"This is no casual conversation," he said. "Is this all of what you were to reveal to me? I thought the Mother Superior said . . ."

"There is more," Odrade agreed. "The Manifesto—I am its author. I wrote it at Taraza's orders and following her detailed instructions."

Teg glanced around the large chamber as though to make sure no one overheard. He spoke in a lowered voice: "The Tleilaxu are spreading it far and wide!"

"Just as we hoped."

"Why are you telling me this? Taraza said you were to prepare me for . . ."

"There will come a time when you must know our purpose. It is Taraza's wish that you make your own decisions then, that you really become a free agent."

Even as she spoke, Odrade saw the Mentat glaze in his eyes.

Teg breathed deeply. *Dependencies and key logs!* He felt the Mentat sense of an enormous pattern just beyond the reach of his accumulated data. He did not even consider for an instant that some form of filial devotion had prompted these revelations. There was a fundamentalist, dogmatic, and ritualistic essence apparent in all Bene Gesserit training despite every effort to prevent this. Odrade, this daughter out of his past, was a full Reverend Mother with extraordinary powers of muscle and nerve control—full memories on the female side! She was one of the special ones! She knew tricks of violence that few humans ever suspected. Still, that similarity, that essence remained and a Mentat always saw it.

What does she want?

Affirmation of his paternity? She already had all of the confirmation she could need.

Observing her now, the way she waited so patiently for his thoughts to resolve, Teg reflected that it often was said with truth that Reverend Mothers no longer were completely members of the human race. They moved somehow outside the main flow, perhaps parallel to it, perhaps diving into it occasionally for their own purposes, but always removed from humankind. They removed themselves. It was an identifying mark of the Reverend Mother, a sense of extra identity that made them closer to the long-dead Tyrant than to the human stock from which they sprang.

Manipulation. That was their mark. They manipulated everyone and everything.

"I am to be the Bene Gesserit eyes," Teg said. "Taraza wants me to make a *human* decision for all of you."

Obviously pleased, Odrade squeezed his arm. "What a father I have!"

"Do you really have a father?" he asked and he recounted for her what he had been thinking about the Bene Gesserit removing themselves from humanity.

"Outside humanity," she said. "What a curious idea. Are Guild navigators also outside their original humanity?"

He thought about this. Guild navigators diverged widely from humankind's more common shape. Born in space and living out their lives in tanks of melange gas, they distorted the original form, elongated and repositioned limbs and organs. But a young navigator in estrus and before entering the tank could breed with a norm. It had been demonstrated. They became non-human but not in the way of the Bene Gesserit.

"Navigators are not your mental kin," he said. "They think human. Guiding a ship through space, even with prescience to find the safe way, has a pattern a human can accept."

"You don't accept our pattern?"

"As far as I can, but somewhere in your development you shift outside the original pattern. I think you may perform a conscious act even to appear human. This way you hold my arm right now, as though you really were my daughter."

"I am your daughter but I'm surprised you think so little of us."

"Quite the contrary: I stand in awe of you."

"Of your own daughter?"

"Of any Reverend Mother."

"You think I exist only to manipulate lesser creatures?"

"I think you no longer really feel human. There's a gap in you, something missing, something you've removed. You no longer are one of us."

"Thank you," Odrade said. "Taraza told me you would not hesitate to answer truthfully, but I knew that for myself."

"For what have you prepared me?"

"You will know it when it occurs; that is all I can say . . . all I am permitted to say."

Manipulating again! he thought. *Damn them!*

Odrade cleared her throat. She appeared about to say something more but she remained silent as she guided Teg around and strolled with him back across the chamber.

Even though she had known what Teg must say, his words pained her. She wanted to tell him that she was one of those who still felt human, but his judgment of the Sisterhood could not be denied.

We are taught to reject love. We can simulate it but each of us is capable of cutting it off in an instant.

There were sounds behind them. They stopped and turned. Lucilla and Taraza emerged from a lift tube speaking idly about their observations of the ghola.

"You are absolutely right to treat him as one of us," Taraza said.

Teg heard but made no comment as they awaited the approach of the two women.

He knows, Odrade thought. *He will not ask me about my birth-mother. There was no bonding, no real imprint. Yes, he knows.*

Odrade closed her eyes and memory startled her by producing of itself an image of a painting. The thing occupied a space on the wall of Taraza's morning room. Ixian artifice had preserved the painting in the finest hermetically sealed frame behind a cover of invisible plaz. Odrade often stopped in front of the painting, feeling each time that her hand might reach out and actually touch the ancient canvas so cunningly preserved by the Ixians.

Cottages at Cordeville.

The artist's name for his work and his own name were preserved on a burnished plate beneath the painting: *Vincent Van Gogh.*

The thing dated from a time so ancient that only rare remnants such as this painting remained to send a physical impression down the ages. She had tried to imagine the journeys that painting had taken, the serial chance that had brought it intact to Taraza's room.

The Ixians had been at their best in the preservation and restoration. An observer could touch a dark spot on the lower left corner of the frame. Immediately, you were engulfed in the true genius, not only of the artist, but of the Ixian who had restored and preserved the work. His name was there on the frame: Martin Buro. When touched by the human finger, the dot became a sense projector, a benign spin-off of the technology that had produced the Ixian Probe. Buro had restored not only the painting but the painter—Van Gogh's feeling—accompaniment to each brush stroke. All had been captured in the brush strokes, recorded there by human movements.

Odrade had stood there engrossed through the whole performance so many times she felt she could re-create the painting independently.

Recalling this experience so near to Teg's accusation, she knew at once why her memory had reproduced the image for her, why that painting still fascinated her. For the brief space of that replay she always felt totally human, aware of the cottages as places where real people dwelled, aware in some complete way of the living chain that had paused there in the person of the mad Vincent Van Gogh, paused to record itself.

Taraza and Lucilla stopped about two paces from Teg and Odrade. There was a smell of garlic on Taraza's breath.

"We stopped for a small bite to eat," Taraza said. "Would you like anything?"

It was exactly the wrong question. Odrade freed her hand from Teg's arm. She turned quickly and wiped her eyes on her cuff. Looking up once more at Teg, she saw surprise on his face. *Yes,* she thought, *those were real tears!*

"I think we've done everything here that we can," Taraza said.

"It's time you were on your way to Rakis, Dar."

"Past time," Odrade said.

Life cannot find reasons to sustain it, cannot be a source of decent mutual regard, unless each of us resolves to breathe such qualities into it.

—CHENOEH: "CONVERSATIONS WITH LETO II"

Hedley Tuek, High Priest of the Divided God, had grown increasingly angry with Stiros. Although too old himself ever to hope for the High Priest's bench, Stiros had sons, grandsons, and numerous nephews. Stiros had transferred his personal ambitions to his family. A cynical man, Stiros. He represented a powerful faction in the priesthood, the so-called scientific community, whose influence was insidious and pervasive. They veered dangerously close to heresy.

Tuek reminded himself that more than one High Priest had been *lost* in the desert, regrettable accidents. Stiros and his faction were capable of creating such an accident.

It was afternoon in Keen and Stiros had just departed, obviously frustrated. Stiros wanted Tuek to go into the desert and personally observe Sheeana's next venture there. Suspicious of the invitation, Tuek declined.

A strange argument ensued, full of innuendo and vague references to Sheeana's behavior plus wordy attacks on the Bene Gesserit. Stiros, always suspicious of the Sisterhood, had taken an immediate dislike to the new commander of the Bene Gesserit Keep on Rakis, this . . . what was her name? Oh, yes, Odrade. Odd name but then the Sisters often took odd names. That was their privilege. God Himself had never spoken against the basic goodness of the Bene Gesserit. Against individual Sisters, yes, but the Sisterhood itself had shared God's Holy Vision.

Tuek did not like the way Stiros spoke of Sheeana. Cynical. Tuek had finally silenced Stiros with pronouncements delivered here in the Sanctus with its high altar and images of the Divided God. Prismatic beam-relays cast thin wedges of brilliance through drifting incense from burning melange onto the double line of tall pillars that led up to the altar. Tuek knew his words went directly to God from this setting.

"God works through our latter-day Siona," Tuek had told Stiros, noting the confusion on the old councillor's face. "Sheeana is the living reminder of Siona, that human instrument who translated Him into His present Divisions."

Stiros raged, saying things he would not dare repeat before the full Council. He presumed too much on his long association with Tuek.

"I tell you she is sitting here surrounded by adults intent upon justifying themselves to her and—"

"And to God!" Tuek could not let such words pass.

Leaning close to the High Priest, Stiros grated: "She is at the center of an educational system geared to anything her imagination demands. We deny her nothing!"

"Nor should we."

It was as though Tuek had not spoken. Stiros said, "Cania has provided her with recordings from Dar-es-Balat!"

"I am the Book of Fate," Tuek intoned, quoting God's own words from the hoard at Dar-es-Balat.

"Exactly! And she listens to every word!"

"Why does this disturb you?" Tuek asked in his calmest tone.

"We don't test *her* knowledge. She tests *ours!*"

"God must want it so."

No mistaking the bitter anger on Stiros' face. Tuek observed this and waited while the old councillor marshaled new arguments. Resources for such arguments were, of course, enormous. Tuek did not deny this. It was the interpretations that mattered. Which was why a High Priest must be the final interpreter. Despite (or perhaps because of) their way of viewing history, the priesthood knew a great deal of how God had come to reside on Rakis. They had Dar-es-Balat itself and all of its contents—the earliest known no-chamber in the universe. For millennia, while Shai-hulud translated the verdant planet of Arrakis into desert-Rakis, Dar-es-Balat waited under the sands. From that Holy Hoard, the priesthood possessed God's own voice, His printed words and even holophotos. Everything was explained and they knew that the desert surface of Rakis reproduced the original form of the planet, the way it looked in the beginning when it was the only known source of the Holy Spice.

"She asks about God's family," Stiros said. "Why should she have to ask about—"

"She tests us. Do we give Them Their proper places? The Reverend Mother Jessica to her son, Muad'Dib, to his son, Leto II—the Holy Triumvirate of Heaven."

"Leto III," Stiros muttered. "What of the other Leto who died at Sardaukar hands? What of him?"

"Careful, Stiros," Tuek intoned. "You know my great-grandfather pronounced upon that question from this very bench. Our Divided God was reincarnated with part of Him remaining in heaven to mediate the Ascendancy. That part of Him became nameless then, as the True Essence of God should always be!"

"Oh?"

Tuek heard the terrible cynicism in the old man's voice. Stiros' words seemed to tremble in the incense-laden air, inviting terrible retribution.

"Then why does she ask how our Leto was transformed into the Divided God?" Stiros demanded.

Did Stiros question the Holy Metamorphosis? Tuek was aghast. He said: "In time, she will enlighten us."

"Our feeble explanations must fill her with dismay," Stiros sneered.

"You go too far, Stiros!"

"Indeed? You do not think it enlightening that she asks how the sandtrout encapsulate most of Rakis' water and re-create the desert?"

Tuek tried to conceal his growing anger. Stiros *did* represent a powerful faction in the priesthood, but his tone and his words raised questions that had been answered by High Priests long ago. The Metamorphosis of Leto II had given birth to uncounted sandtrout, each carrying a Bit of Himself. Sandtrout to Divided God: The sequence was known and worshiped. To question this denied God.

"You sit here and do nothing!" Stiros accused. "We are pawns of—"

"Enough!" Tuek had heard all he wanted to hear of this old man's cynicism. Drawing his dignity around him, Tuek spoke the words of God:

"Your Lord knows very well what is in your heart. Your soul suffices this day as a reckoner against you. I need no witnesses. You do not listen to your soul, but listen instead to your anger and your rage."

Stiros retired in frustration.

After considerable thought, Tuek enrobed himself in his most suitable finery of white, gold, and purple. He went to visit Sheeana.

Sheeana was in the roof garden atop the central priestly complex, there with Cania and two others—a young priest named Baldik, who was in Tuek's private service, and an acolyte priestess named Kipuna, who behaved too much like a Reverend Mother for Tuek's liking. The Sisterhood had its spies here, of course, but Tuek did not like to be aware of it. Kipuna had taken over much of Sheeana's physical training and there had grown a rapport between child and acolyte priestess that aroused Cania's jealousy. Even Cania, however, could not stand in the way of Sheeana's commands.

The four of them stood beside a stone bench almost in the shadow of a ventilator tower. Kipuna held Sheeana's right hand, manipulating the child's fingers. Sheeana was growing tall, Tuek noted. Six years she had been his charge. He could see the first beginnings of breasts poking out her robe. There was not a breath of wind on the rooftop and the air felt heavy in Tuek's lungs.

Tuek glanced around the garden to assure himself that his security arrangements were not being ignored. One never knew from what quarter danger might appear. Four of Tuek's own personal guards, well armed but concealing it, shared the rooftop at a distance—one at each corner. The parapet enclosing the garden was a high one, just the guards' heads standing above the rim. The only building higher than this priestly tower was Keen's primary windtrap about a thousand meters to the west.

Despite the visible evidence that his security orders were being carried out, Tuek sensed danger. Was God warning him? Tuek still felt disturbed by Stiros' cynicism. Was it wrong to allow Stiros that much latitude?

Sheeana saw Tuek approaching and stopped the odd finger-flexing exercises she was performing at Kipuna's instructions. Giving every appearance of knowledgeable patience, the child stood silently with her gaze fixed on the High Priest, forcing her companions to turn and watch with her.

Sheeana did not find Tuek a fearsome figure. She rather liked the old man although some of his questions were so bumbling. And his answers! Quite by accident, she had discovered the question that most disturbed Tuek.

"Why?"

Some of the attendant priests interpreted her question aloud as: "Why do you believe this?" Sheeana immediately picked up on this and thereafter her probings of Tuek and the others took the unvarying form:

"Why do you believe this?"

Tuek stopped about two paces from Sheeana and bowed. "Good afternoon, Sheeana." He twisted his neck nervously against the collar of his robe. The sun felt hot on his shoulders and he wondered why the child chose to be out here so often.

Sheeana maintained her probing stare at Tuek. She knew this gaze disturbed him.

Tuek cleared his throat. When Sheeana looked at him that way, he always wondered: *Is it God looking at me through her eyes?*

Cania spoke. "Sheeana has been asking today about the Fish Speakers."

In his most unctuous tones, Tuek said: "God's own Holy Army."

"All of them women?" Sheeana asked. She spoke as though she could not believe it. To those at the base of Rakian society, Fish Speakers were a name from ancient history, people cast out in the Famine Times.

She is testing me, Tuek thought. Fish Speakers. The modern carriers of the name had only a small trading-spying delegation on Rakis, composed of both men and women. Their ancient origins no longer were significant to their current activities, mostly working as an arm of Ix.

"Men always served the Fish Speakers in an advisory capacity," Tuek said. He watched carefully to see how Sheeana would respond.

"Then there were always the Duncan Idahos," Cania said.

"Yes, yes, of course: the Duncans." Tuek tried not to scowl. That woman was always interrupting! Tuek did not like being reminded of this aspect to God's historical presence on Rakis. The recurrent ghola and his position in the Holy Army carried overtones of Bene Tleilax indulgence. But there was no avoiding the fact that Fish Speakers had guarded the Duncans from harm, acting of course at the behest of God. The Duncans were holy, no doubt of it, but in a special category. By God's own account, He had killed some of the Duncans himself, obviously *translating* them immediately into heaven.

"Kipuna had been telling me about the Bene Gesserit," Sheeana said.

How the child's mind darted around!

Tuek cleared his throat, recognizing his own ambivalent attitude toward the Reverend Mothers. Reverence was demanded for those who were "Beloved of God," such as the Saintly Chenoeh. And the first High Priest had constructed a logical account of how the Holy Hwi Noree, Bride of God, had been a secret Reverend Mother. Honoring these special circumstances, the priesthood felt an irritating responsibility toward the Bene Gesserit, which was carried out chiefly by selling melange to the Sisterhood at a price ridiculously below that charged by the Tleilaxu.

In her most ingenuous tones, Sheeana said: "Tell me about the Bene Gesserit, Hedley."

Tuek glanced sharply at the adults around Sheeana, trying to catch a smile on their faces. He did not know how to deal with Sheeana calling him by his first name that way. In one sense, it was demeaning. In another sense, she honored him by such intimacy.

God tests me sorely, he thought.

"Are the Reverend Mothers good people?" Sheeana asked.

Tuek sighed. The records all confirmed that God harbored reservations about the Sisterhood. God's words had been examined carefully and submitted finally to a High Priest's interpretation. God did not let the Sisterhood threaten his Golden Path. That much was clear.

"Many of them are good," Tuek said.

"Where is the nearest Reverend Mother?" Sheeana asked.

"At the Sisterhood's Embassy here in Keen," Tuek said.

"Do you know her?"

"There are many Reverend Mothers in the Bene Gesserit Keep," he said.

"What's a Keep?"

"That's what they call their home here."

"One Reverend Mother must be in charge. Do you know that one?"

"I knew her predecessor, Tamalane, but this one is new. She has only just arrived. Her name is Odrade."

"That's a funny name."

Tuek's own thought, but he said: "One of our historians tells me it is a form of the name Atreides."

Sheeana reflected upon this. *Atreides.* That was the family that had brought Shaitan into being. Before the Atreides there had been only the Fremen and Shai-hulud. The Oral History, which her people preserved against all priestly prohibition, chanted the begats of the most important people on Rakis. Sheeana had heard these names many nights in her village.

"Muad'Dib begat the Tyrant."

"The Tyrant begat Shaitan."

Sheeana did not feel like arguing truth with Tuek. Anyway, he looked tired today. She said merely: "Bring me this Reverend Mother Odrade."

Kipuna hid a gloating smile behind her hand.

Tuek stepped back, aghast. How could he comply with such a demand? Even the Rakian priesthood did not command the Bene Gesserit! What if the Sisterhood refused him? Could he offer a gift of melange in exchange? That might be a sign of weakness. The Reverend Mothers might bargain! No harder bargainers lived than the Sisterhood's cold-eyed Reverend Mothers. This new one, this Odrade, looked to be one of the worst.

All of these thoughts fled through Tuek's mind in an instant.

Cania intruded, giving Tuek the needed approach. "Perhaps Kipuna could convey Sheeana's invitation," Cania said.

Tuek darted a glance at the young acolyte priestess. Yes! Many suspected (Cania among them, obviously) that Kipuna spied for the Bene Gesserit. Of course, everyone on Rakis spied for someone. Tuek put on his most gracious smile as he nodded to Kipuna.

"Do you know any of the Reverend Mothers, Kipuna?"

"Some of them are known to me, My Lord High Priest," Kipuna said.

At least she still shows the proper deference!

"Excellent," Tuek said. "Would you be so kind as to start this gracious invitation from Sheeana moving up through the Sisterhood's embassy."

"I will do my poor best, My Lord High Priest."

"I'm sure you will!"

Kipuna began a prideful turn toward Sheeana, the knowledge of success growing within her. Sheeana's request had been ridiculously easy to ignite, given the techniques provided by the Sisterhood. Kipuna smiled and opened her mouth to speak. A movement at the parapet about forty meters behind Sheeana caught Kipuna's attention. Something glinted in the sunlight there. Something small and . . .

With a strangled cry, Kipuna grabbed up Sheeana, hurled her at the startled Tuek and shouted: "Run!" With that, Kipuna dashed toward the swiftly advancing brightness—a tiny seeker trailing a long length of shigawire.

In his younger days, Tuek had played batball. He caught Sheeana instinctively, hesitated for an instant and then recognized the danger. Whirling with the squirming, protesting girl in his arms, Tuek dashed through the open door of the stair tower. He heard the door slam behind him and Cania's rapid footsteps close on his heels.

"What is it? What is it?" Sheeana pounded her fists against Tuek's chest as she shouted.

"Hush, Sheeana! Hush!" Tuek paused on the first landing. Both a chute and suspensor-drop led from this landing into the building's core. Cania stopped beside Tuek, her panting loud in the narrow space.

"It killed Kipuna and two of your guards," Cania gasped. "Cut them up! I saw it. God preserve us!"

Tuek's mind was a maelstrom. Both the chute and the suspensor-drop system were enclosed wormholes through the tower. They could be sabotaged. The attack on the roof might be only one element in a far more complex plot.

"Put me down!" Sheeana insisted. "What's happening?"

Tuek eased her to the floor but kept one of her hands clutched in his hand. He bent over her, "Sheeana, dear, someone is trying to harm us."

Sheeana's mouth formed a silent "O," then: "They hurt Kipuna?"

Tuek looked up at the roof door. Was that an ornithopter he heard up there? *Stiros!* Conspirators could take three vulnerable people into the desert so easily!

Cania had regained her breath. "I hear a 'thopter," she said. "Shouldn't we be getting away from here?"

"We will go down by the stairs," Tuek said.

"But the—"

"Do as I say!"

Keeping a firm hold on Sheeana's hand, Tuek led the way down to the next landing. In addition to the chute and suspensor access, this landing had a door into a wide curving hall. Only a few short steps beyond the door lay the entrance to Sheeana's quarters, once Tuek's own quarters. Again, he hesitated.

"Something's happening on the roof," Cania whispered.

Tuek looked down at the fearfully silent child beside him. Her hand felt sweaty.

Yes, there was some sort of uproar on the roof—shouts, the hiss of burners, much running about. The roof door, now out of sight above them, crashed open. This decided Tuek. He flung open the door into the hallway and dashed out into the arms of a tightly grouped wedge of black-robed women. With an empty sense of defeat, Tuek recognized the woman at the point of the wedge: *Odrade!*

Someone plucked Sheeana away from him and hustled her back into the press of robed figures. Before Tuek or Cania could protest, hands were clapped over their mouths. Other hands pinioned them against a wall of the hallway. Some of the robed figures went through the doorway and up the stairs.

"The child is safe and that's all that's important for the moment," Odrade whispered. She looked into Tuek's eyes. "Make no outcry." The hand was removed from his mouth. Using Voice, she said: "Tell me about the roof!"

Tuek found himself complying without reservation. "A seeker towing a long shigawire. It came over the parapet. Kipuna saw it and—"

"Where is Kipuna?"

"Dead. Cania saw it." Tuek described Kipuna's brave dash toward the threat.

Kipuna dead! Odrade thought. She concealed a fiercely angry sense of loss. What a waste. There must be admiration for such a brave death, but the loss! The Sisterhood always needed such courage and devotion, but it also required the genetic wealth Kipuna had represented. *It was gone, taken by these stumbling fools!*

At a gesture from Odrade, the hand was removed from Cania's mouth. "Tell me what you saw," Odrade said.

"The seeker whipped the shigawire around Kipuna's neck and . . ." Cania shuddered.

The dull thump of an explosion reverberated above them, then silence. Odrade waved a hand. Robed women spread along the hallway, moving silently out of sight beyond the curve. Only Odrade and two others, both chill-eyed younger women with intense expressions, remained beside Tuek and Cania. Sheeana was nowhere to be seen.

"The Ixians are in this somewhere," Odrade said.

Tuek agreed. *That much shigawire . . .* "Where have you taken the child?" he asked.

"We are protecting her," Odrade said. "Be still." She tipped her head, listening.

A robed woman sped back around the curve of the hallway and whispered something in Odrade's ear. Odrade produced a tight smile.

"It is over," Odrade said. "We will go to Sheeana."

Sheeana occupied a softly cushioned blue chair in the main room of her quarters. Black-robed women stood in a protective arc behind her. The child appeared to Tuek quite recovered from the shock of the attack and escape but her eyes glittered with excitement and unasked questions. Sheeana's attention was directed at something off to Tuek's right. He stopped and looked there, gasping at what he saw.

A naked male body lay against the wall in an oddly crumpled position, the head twisted until the chin lay back over the left shoulder. Open eyes stared out with the emptiness of death.

Stiros!

The shredded rags of Stiros' robe, obviously torn from him violently, lay in an untidy heap near the body's feet.

Tuek looked at Odrade.

"He was in on it," she said. "There were Face Dancers with the Ixians."

Tuek tried to swallow in a dry throat.

Cania shuffled past him toward the body. Tuek could not see her face but Cania's presence reminded him that there had been something between Stiros and Cania in their younger days. Tuek moved instinctively to place himself between Cania and the seated child.

Cania stopped at the body and nudged it with a foot. She turned a gloating expression on Tuek. "I had to make sure he was really dead," she said.

Odrade glanced at a companion. "Get rid of the body." She looked at Sheeana. It was Odrade's first chance for a more careful study of the child since leading the assault force here to deal with the attack on the temple complex.

Tuek spoke behind Odrade. "Reverend Mother, could you explain please what—"

Odrade interrupted without turning. "Later."

Sheeana's expression quickened at Tuek's words. "I *thought* you were a Reverend Mother!"

Odrade merely nodded. What a fascinating child. Odrade experienced the sensations she felt while standing in front of the ancient painting in Taraza's quarters. Some of the fire that had gone into the work of art inspired Odrade now. Wild inspiration! That was the message from the mad Van Gogh. Chaos brought into magnificent order. Was that not part of the Sisterhood's coda?

This child is my canvas, Odrade thought. She felt her hand tingle to the feeling of that ancient brush. Her nostrils flared to the smells of oils and pigments.

"Leave me alone with Sheeana," Odrade ordered. "Everybody out."

Tuek started to protest but stopped when one of Odrade's robed companions gripped his arm. Odrade glared at him.

"The Bene Gesserit have served you before," she said. "This time, we saved your life."

The woman holding Tuek's arm tugged at him.

"Answer his questions," Odrade said. "But do it somewhere else."

Cania took a step toward Sheeana. "That child is my—"

"Leave!" Odrade barked, all the powers of Voice in the command. Cania froze.

"You almost lost her to a bumbling lot of conspirators!" Odrade said, glaring at Cania. "We will consider whether you get any further opportunity to associate with Sheeana."

Tears started in Cania's eyes but Odrade's condemnation could not be denied. Turning, Cania fled with the others.

Odrade returned her attention to the watchful child.

"We've been a long time waiting for you," Odrade said. "We will not give those fools another opportunity to lose you."

Law always chooses sides on the basis of enforcement power. Morality and legal niceties have little to do with it when the real question is: Who has the clout?

—BENE GESSERIT COUNCIL PROCEEDINGS: ARCHIVES #XOX232

Immediately after Taraza and her party left Gammu, Teg threw himself into his work. New in-Keep procedures had to be laid out, holding Schwangyu at arm's length from the ghola. Taraza's orders.

"She can observe all she wants. She can't touch."

In spite of the work pressures, Teg found himself staring into space at odd moments, prey to free-floating anxiety. The experience of rescuing Taraza's party from the Guildship and Odrade's odd revelations did not fit into any data classification he constructed.

Dependencies . . . key logs . . .

Teg found himself seated in his own workroom, an assignment schedule projected in front of him with shift changes to approve and, for a moment, he had no idea of the time or even the date. It took a moment to relocate himself.

Midmorning. Taraza and her party had been gone two days. He was alone. Yes, Patrin had taken over this day's training schedule with Duncan, freeing Teg for the command decisions.

The workroom around Teg felt alien. Yet, when he looked at each element in it, he found each thing familiar. Here was his own personal data console. His uniform jacket had been draped neatly across a chair-back beside him. He tried to fall into Mentat mode and found his own mind resisting. He had not encountered that phenomenon since training days.

Training days.

Taraza and Odrade between them had thrown him back into some form of training.

Self-training.

In a detached way, he felt his memory offering up a long-ago conversation with Taraza. How familiar it was. He was right there, caught in the moments of his own memory-snare.

Both he and Taraza had been quite tired after making the decisions and taking the actions to prevent a bloody confrontation—the Barandiko incident. Nothing but a hiccough in history now but at the time it had demanded all of their combined energies.

Taraza invited him into the small parlor of her quarters on her no-ship after the agreement was signed. She spoke casually, admiring his sagacity, the way he had seen through to the weaknesses that would force a compromise.

They had been awake and active for almost thirty hours and Teg was glad for the opportunity to sit while Taraza dialed her foodrink installation. It dutifully produced two tall glasses of creamy brown liquid.

Teg recognized the smell as she handed him his glass. It was a quick source of energy, a pick-me-up that the Bene Gesserit seldom shared with outsiders. But Taraza no longer considered him an outsider.

His head tipped back, Teg took a long swallow of the drink, his gaze on the ornate ceiling of Taraza's small parlor. This no-ship was an old-fashioned model, built in the days when more care had been taken with decoration—heavily incised cornices, baroque figures carved in every surface.

The taste of the drink pushed his memory back into childhood, the heavy infusion of melange . . .

"My mother made this for me whenever I was overly strenuous," he said, looking at the glass in his hand. He already could feel the calming energy flow through his body.

Taraza took her own drink to a chairdog opposite him, a fluffy white bit of animate furniture that fitted itself to her with the ease of long familiarity. For Teg, she had provided a traditional green upholstered chair, but she saw his glance flick across the chairdog and grinned at him.

"Tastes differ, Miles." She sipped her drink and sighed. "My, that was strenuous but it was good work. There were moments when it was right on the edge of getting very nasty."

Teg found himself touched by her relaxation. No pose, no readymade mask to set them apart and define their separate roles in the Bene Gesserit hierarchy. She was being obviously friendly and not even a hint of seductiveness. So this was just what it seemed to be—as much as that could be said about any encounter with a Reverend Mother.

With quick elation, Teg realized that he had become quite adept at reading Alma Mavis Taraza, even when she adopted one of her masks.

"Your mother taught you more than she was told to teach you," Taraza said. "A wise woman but another heretic. That's all we seem to be breeding nowadays."

"Heretic?" He was caught by resentment.

"That's a private joke in the Sisterhood," Taraza said. "We're supposed to follow a Mother Superior's orders with absolute devotion. And we do, except when we disagree."

Teg smiled and took a deep draught of his drink.

"It's odd," Taraza said, "but while we were in that tight little confrontation I found myself reacting to you as I would to one of my Sisters."

Teg felt the drink warming his stomach. It left a tingling in his nostrils. He placed the empty glass on a side table and spoke while looking at it. "My eldest daughter . . ."

"That would be Dimela. You should have let us have her, Miles."

"It was not my decision."

"But one word from you . . ." Taraza shrugged. "Well, that's past. What about Dimela?"

"She thinks I'm often too much like one of you."

"Too much?"

"She is fiercely loyal to me, Mother Superior. She doesn't really understand our relationship and—"

"What is our relationship?"

"You command and I obey."

Taraza looked at him over the lip of her glass. When she put down the glass, she said: "Yes, you've never really been a heretic, Miles. Perhaps . . . someday . . ."

He spoke quickly, wanting to divert Taraza from such ideas. "Dimela thinks the long use of melange makes many people become like you."

"Is that so? Isn't it odd, Miles, that a geriatric potion should have so many side effects?"

"I don't find that odd."

"No, of course you wouldn't." She drained her glass and put it aside. "I was addressing the way a significant life extension has produced in some people, you especially, a profound knowledge of human nature."

"We live longer and observe more," he said.

"I don't think it's quite that simple. Some people never observe anything. Life just happens to them. They get by on little more than a kind of dumb persistence, and they resist with anger and resentment anything that might lift them out of that false serenity."

"I've never been able to strike an acceptable balance sheet for the spice," he said, referring to a common Mentat process of data sorting.

Taraza nodded. Obviously, she found the same difficulty. "We of the Sisterhood tend to be more single-track than Mentats," she said. "We have routines to shake ourselves out of it but the condition persists."

"Our ancestors have had this problem for a long time," he said.

"It was different before the spice," she said.

"But they lived such short lives."

"Fifty, one hundred years; that doesn't seem very long to us, but still . . ."

"Did they compress more into the available time?"

"Oh, they were frenetic at times."

She was giving him observations from her Other Memories, he realized. Not the first time he had shared in such ancient lore. His mother had produced such memories on occasion, but always as a lesson. Was Taraza doing that now? Teaching him something?

"Melange is a many-handed monster," she said.

"Do you sometimes wish we had never found it?"

"The Bene Gesserit would not exist without it."

"Nor the Guild."

"But there would have been no Tyrant, no Muad'Dib. The spice gives with one hand and takes with all of its others."

"Which hand contains that which we desire?" he asked. "Isn't that always the question?"

"You're an oddity, you know that, Miles? Mentats so seldom dip into philosophy. I think it's one of your strengths. You are supremely able to doubt."

He shrugged. This turn in the conversation disturbed him.

"You are not amused," she said. "But cling to your doubts anyway. Doubt is necessary to a philosopher."

"So the Zensunni assure us."

"All mystics agree on it, Miles. Never underestimate the power of doubts. Very persuasive. S'tori holds up doubt and surety in a single hand."

Really quite surprised, he asked: "Do Reverend Mothers practice Zensunni rituals?" He had never even suspected this before.

"Just once," she said. "We achieve an exalted form of s'tori, total. It involves every cell."

"The spice agony," he said.

"I was sure your mother told you. Obviously, she never explained the affinity with the Zensunni."

Teg swallowed past a lump in his throat. Fascinating! She gave him a new insight into the Bene Gesserit. This changed his entire concept, including his image of his own mother. They were removed from him into an unattainable place where he could never follow. They might think of him as a comrade on occasion but he could never enter the intimate circle. He could simulate, no more. He would never be like Muad'Dib or the Tyrant.

"Prescience," Taraza said.

The word shifted his attention. She had changed the subject but not changed it.

"I *was* thinking about Muad'Dib," he said.

"You think he predicted the future," she said.

"That is the Mentat teaching."

"I hear the doubt in your voice, Miles. Did he predict or did he create? Prescience can be deadly. The people who demand that the oracle predict for them really want to know next year's price on whalefur or something equally mundane. None of them wants an instant-by-instant prediction of his personal life."

"No surprises," Teg said.

"Exactly. If you possessed such fore-knowledge, your life would become an unutterable bore."

"You think Muad'Dib's life was a bore?"

"And the Tyrant's, too. We think their entire lives were devoted to trying to break out of chains they themselves created."

"But they believed . . ."

"Remember your philosopher's doubts, Miles. Beware! The mind of the believer stagnates. It fails to grow outward into an unlimited, infinite universe."

Teg sat silently for a moment. He sensed the fatigue that had been driven beyond his immediate awareness by the drink, sensed also the way his thoughts were roiled by the intrusion of new concepts. These were things that he had been taught would weaken a Mentat, yet he felt strengthened by them.

She is teaching me, he thought. *There is a lesson here.*

As though projected into his mind and outlined there in fire, he found his entire Mentat-attention fixated on the Zensunni admonition that was taught to every beginning student in the Mentat School:

By your belief in granular singularities, you deny all movement— evolutionary or devolutionary. Belief fixes a granular universe and causes that universe to persist. Nothing can be allowed to change because that way your non-moving universe vanishes. But it moves of itself when you do not move. It evolves beyond you and is no longer accessible to you.

"The oddest thing of all," Taraza said, sinking into tune with this mood she had created, "is that the scientists of Ix cannot see how much their own beliefs dominate their universe."

Teg stared at her, silent and receptive.

"Ixian beliefs are perfectly submissive to the choices they make on how they will look at their universe," Taraza said. "Their universe does not act of itself but performs according to the kinds of experiments they choose."

With a start, Teg came out of the memories and awoke to find himself in the Gammu Keep. He still sat in the familiar chair in his workroom. A glance around the room showed nothing moved from where he had put it. Only a few minutes had passed but the room and its contents no longer were alien. He dipped into and out of Mentat mode. *Restored.*

The smell and taste of the drink Taraza had given him so long ago still tingled on his tongue and in his nostrils. A Mentat blink and he knew he could call up the scene entire once more—the low light of shaded glowglobes, the feeling of the chair beneath him, the sounds of their voices. It was all there for replay, frozen into a time-capsule of isolated memory.

Calling up that old memory created a magical universe where his abilities were amplified beyond his wildest expectations. No atoms existed in that magical universe, only waves and awesome movements all around. He was forced there to discard all barriers built of belief and understanding. This universe was transparent. He could see through it without any interfering screens upon which to project its forms. The magical universe reduced him to a core of active imagination where his own image-making abilities were the only screen upon which any projection might be sensed.

There, I am both the performer and the performed!

The workroom around Teg wavered into and out of his sensory reality. He felt his awareness constricted to its tightest purpose and yet that purpose filled his universe. He was open to infinity.

Taraza did this deliberately! he thought. *She has amplified me!*

A feeling of awe threatened him. He recognized how his daughter, Odrade, had drawn upon such powers to create the Atreides Manifesto for Taraza. His own Mentat powers were submerged in that greater pattern.

Taraza was demanding a fearful performance from him. The need for such a thing both challenged and terrified him. It could very well mean the end of the Sisterhood.

The basic rule is this: Never support weakness; always support strength.

—THE BENE GESSERIT CODA

"How is it that you can order the priests around?" Sheeana asked. "This is their place."

Odrade answered casually but picked her words to fit the knowledge she knew Sheeana already possessed: "The priests have Fremen roots. They've always had Reverend Mothers somewhere near. Besides, child, you order them around, too."

"That's different."

Odrade suppressed a smile.

Little more than three hours had passed since her assault force had broken the attack on the temple complex. In that time, Odrade had set up a command center in Sheeana's quarters, carried on the necessary business of assessment and preliminary retaliation, all the while prompting and observing Sheeana.

Simulflow.

Odrade glanced around the room she had chosen as command center. A scrap of Stiros' ripped garments still lay near the wall in front of her. *Casualties.* The room was an oddly shaped place. No two walls parallel. She sniffed. Still a residual smell of ozone from the snoopers with which her people had assured the privacy of these quarters.

Why the odd shape? The building was ancient, remodeled and

added to many times, but that did not explain this room. A pleasantly rough texture of creamy stucco on walls and ceiling. Elaborate spice-fiber hangings flanked the two doors. It was early evening and sunlight filtered by lattice shades stippled the wall opposite the windows. Silver-yellow glowglobes hovered near the ceiling, all tuned to match the sunlight. Muted street sounds came through the ventilators beneath the windows. The soft pattern of orange rugs and gray tiles on the floor spoke of wealth and security but Odrade suddenly did not feel secure.

A tall Reverend Mother came from the adjoining communications room. "Mother Commander," she said, "the messages have been sent to Guild, Ix, and Tleilaxu."

Odrade spoke absently. "Acknowledged."

The messenger returned to her duties.

"What are you doing?" Sheeana asked.

"Studying something."

Odrade pursed her lips in thought. Their guides through the temple complex had brought them along a maze of hallways and stairs, glimpses of courtyards through arches, then into a splendid Ixian suspensor-tube system, which carried them silently to another hallway, more stairs, another curved hallway . . . finally, into this room.

Once more, Odrade swept her gaze around the room.

"Why are you studying this room?" Sheeana asked.

"Hush, child!"

The room was an irregular polyhedron with the smaller side to the left. About thirty-five meters long, half that at the widest. Many low divans and chairs in various degrees of comfort. Sheeana sat in queenly splendor on a bright yellow chair with wide soft arms. Not a chairdog in the place. Much brown and blue and yellow fabric. Odrade stared at the white lattice of a ventilator above a painting of mountains on the wider end wall. A cool breeze came through the ventilators below the windows and wafted toward the ventilator above the painting.

"This was Hedley's room," Sheeana said.

"Why do you annoy him by using his first name, child?"

"Does that annoy him?"

"Don't play word games with me, child! You know it annoys him and that's why you do it."

"Then why did you ask?"

Odrade ignored this while continuing her careful study of the room. The wall opposite the painting stood at an oblique angle to the outer wall. She had it now. *Clever!* This room had been constructed so that even a whisper here could be heard by someone beyond the high ventilator. No doubt the painting concealed another airway to carry sounds from this room. No snooper, sniffer, or other instrument would detect such an arrangement. Nothing would "beep" at a spying eye or ear. Only the wary senses of someone trained in deception had winkled it out.

A hand signal summoned a waiting acolyte. Odrade's fingers flickered in silent communication: *"Find out who is listening beyond that ventilator."* She nodded toward the ventilator above the painting. *"Let them continue. We must know to whom they report."*

"How did you know to come and save me?" Sheeana asked.

The child had a lovely voice but it needed training, Odrade thought. There was a steadiness to it, though, that could be shaped into a powerful instrument.

"Answer me!" Sheeana ordered.

The imperious tone startled Odrade, arousing quick anger, which she was forced to suppress. Corrections would have to be made immediately!

"Calm yourself, child," Odrade said. She pitched the command in a precise tenor and saw it take effect.

Again, Sheeana startled her: "That's another kind of Voice. You're trying to calm me. Kipuna told me all about Voice."

Odrade turned squarely facing Sheeana and looked down at her. Sheeana's first grief had passed but there was still anger when she spoke of Kipuna.

"I am busy shaping our response to that attack," Odrade said. "Why do you distract me? I should think you would want them punished."

"What will you do to them? Tell me! What will you do?"

A surprisingly vindictive child, Odrade thought. That would have to be curbed. Hatred was as dangerous an emotion as love. The capacity for hatred was the capacity for its opposite.

Odrade said: "I have sent Guild, Ix, and Tleilaxu the message we always dispatch when we have been annoyed. Three words: 'You will pay.'"

"How will they pay?"

"A proper Bene Gesserit punishment is being fashioned. They will feel the consequences of their behavior."

"But *what* will you do?"

"In time, you may learn. You may even learn how we design our punishment. For now, there is no need that you know."

A sullen look came over Sheeana's face. She said: "You're not even angry. Annoyed. That's what you said."

"Curb your impatience, child! There are things you do not understand."

The Reverend Mother from the communications room returned, glanced once at Sheeana and spoke to Odrade. "Chapter House acknowledges receipt of your report. They approve your response."

When the Reverend Mother from communications remained standing there, Odrade said: "There is more?"

A flickering glance to Sheeana spoke of the woman's reservations. Odrade held up her right palm, the signal for silent communication.

The Reverend Mother responded, her fingers dancing with unleashed excitement: "*Taraza's message—The Tleilaxu are the pivotal element. Guild must be made to pay dearly for its melange. Shut down Rakian supply to them. Throw Guild and Ix together. They will overextend selves in face of crushing competition from the Scattering. Ignore Fish Speakers for now. They fall with Ix. Master of Masters responds to us from Tleilaxu. He goes to Rakis. Trap him.*"

Odrade smiled softly to acknowledge that she understood. She watched the other woman leave the room. Not only did Chapter House agree with actions taken on Rakis, a suitable Bene Gesserit punishment had been fashioned with fascinating speed. Obviously Taraza and her advisors had anticipated this moment.

Odrade allowed herself a sigh of relief. The message to Chapter House had been terse: an outline account of the attack, the list of the Sisterhood's casualties, identification of the attackers and a confirming note to Taraza that Odrade already had transmitted the required warning to the guilty: "You will pay."

Yes, those fool attackers now knew the hornet's nest had been aroused. That would create fear—an essential part of the punishment.

Sheeana squirmed in her chair. Her attitude said she would now try a new approach. "One of your people said there were Face Dancers." She gestured with her chin toward the roof.

What a vast reservoir of ignorance this child was, Odrade thought. That emptiness would have to be filled. *Face Dancers!* Odrade thought about the bodies they had examined. The Tleilaxu had finally sent their Face Dancers into action. It was a test of the Bene Gesserit, of course. These new ones were extremely difficult to detect. They still gave off the characteristic smell of their unique pheromones, though. Odrade had sent that datum in her message to Chapter House.

The problem now was to keep the Bene Gesserit knowledge secret. Odrade summoned an acolyte messenger. Indicating the ventilator with a flick of her eyes, Odrade spoke silently with her fingers: *"Kill those who listen!"*

"You are too interested in Voice, child," Odrade said, speaking down to Sheeana in the chair. "Silence is a most valuable tool for learning."

"But could I learn Voice? I want to learn it."

"I am telling you to be silent and to learn by your silence."

"I command you to teach me Voice!"

Odrade reflected on Kipuna's reports. Sheeana had established effective Voice control over most of those around her. The child had learned it on her own. An intermediate level Voice for a limited audience. She was a natural. Tuek and Cania and the others were frightened by Sheeana. Religious fantasies contributed to that fear, of course, but Sheeana's mastery of Voice pitch and tone displayed an admirable unconscious selectivity.

The indicated response to Sheeana was obvious, Odrade knew. Honesty. It was a most powerful lure and it served more than one purpose.

"I am here to teach you many things," Odrade said, "but I do not do this at your command."

"Everyone obeys me!" Sheeana said.

She's barely into puberty and already at Aristocrat level, Odrade thought. *Gods of our own making! What can she become?*

Sheeana slipped out of her chair and stood looking up at Odrade with a questioning expression. The child's eyes were on a level with Odrade's shoulders. Sheeana was going to be tall, a commanding presence. If she survived.

"You answer some of my questions but you won't answer others," Sheeana said. "You said you'd been waiting for me but you won't explain. Why won't you obey me?"

"A foolish question, child."

"Why do you keep calling me child?"

"Are you not a child?"

"I menstruate."

"But you're still a child."

"The priests obey me."

"They're afraid of you."

"You aren't?"

"No, I'm not."

"Good! It gets tiresome when people only fear you."

"The priests think you come from God."

"Don't you think that?"

"Why should I? We—" Odrade broke off as an acolyte messenger entered. The acolyte's fingers danced in silent communication: *"Four priests listened. They have been killed. All were minions of Tuek."*

Odrade waved the messenger away.

"She talks with her fingers," Sheeana said. "How does she do that?"

"You ask too many of the wrong questions, child. And you haven't told me why I should consider you an instrument of God."

"Shaitan spares me. I walk on the desert and when Shaitan comes, I talk to him."

"Why do you call him Shaitan instead of Shai- hulud?"

"Everybody asks that same stupid question!"

"Then give me your stupid answer."

The sullen expression returned to Sheeana's face. "It's because of how we met."

"And how did you meet?"

Sheeana tipped her head to one side and looked up at Odrade for a moment, then: "That's a secret."

"And you know how to keep secrets?"

Sheeana straightened and nodded but Odrade saw uncertainty in the movement. The child knew when she was being led into an impossible position!

"Excellent!" Odrade said. "The keeping of secrets is one of a Reverend Mother's most essential teachings. I'm glad we won't have to bother with that one."

"But I want to learn everything!"

Such petulance in her voice. Very poor emotional control.

"You must teach me everything!" Sheeana insisted.

Time for the whip, Odrade thought. Sheeana had spoken and postured sufficiently that even a fifth-grade acolyte could feel confident of controlling her now.

Using the full power of Voice, Odrade said: "Don't take that tone with me, child! Not if you wish to learn anything!"

Sheeana went rigid. She was more than a minute absorbing what had happened to her and then relaxing. Presently, she smiled, a warm and open expression. "Oh, I'm so glad you came! It's been so boring lately."

Nothing surpasses the complexity of the human mind.

—LETO II: DAR-ES-BALAT RECORDS

The Gammu night, often quickly foreboding in this latitude, was almost two hours away. Gathering clouds shadowed the Keep. At Lucilla's command, Duncan had returned to the courtyard for an intense session of self-directed practice.

Lucilla observed from the parapet where she had first watched him.

Duncan moved in the tumbling twists of the Bene Gesserit eight-fold combat, hurling his body across the grass, rolling, flipping himself from side to side, darting up and then down.

It was a fine display of random dodging, Lucilla thought. She could see no predictable pattern in his movements and the speed was dazzling. He was almost sixteen SY and already coming onto the platform potential of his prana-bindu endowment.

The carefully controlled movements of his training exercises revealed so much! He had responded quickly when she first ordered these evening sessions. The initial step of her instructions from Taraza had been accomplished. The ghola loved her. No doubt of it. She was mother-fixed to him. And it had been accomplished without seriously weakening him, although Teg's anxieties had been aroused.

My shadow is on this ghola but he is not a supplicant nor a dependent follower, she reassured herself. *Teg worries about it for no reason.*

Just that morning, she had told Teg, "Wherever his strengths dictate, he continues to express himself freely."

Teg should see him right now, she thought. These new practice movements were largely Duncan's own creation.

Lucilla suppressed a gasp of appreciation at a particularly nimble leap, which took Duncan almost to the center of the courtyard. The ghola was developing a nerve-muscle equilibrium that, given time, might be matched to a psychological equilibrium at least equal to Teg's. The cultural impact of such an achievement would be awesome. Look at all those who gave instinctive allegiance to Teg and, through Teg, to the Sisterhood.

We have the Tyrant to thank for much of that, she thought.

Before Leto II, no widespread system of cultural adjustments had ever endured long enough to approach the balance that the Bene Gesserit held as an ideal. It was this equilibrium—*"flowing along the blade of a sword"*—that fascinated Lucilla. It was why she lent herself so unreservedly to a project whose total design she did not know, but which demanded of her a performance that instinct labeled repugnant.

Duncan is so young!

What the Sisterhood required of her next had been spelled out explicitly by Taraza: *the Sexual Imprint.* Only that morning, Lucilla had posed naked before her mirror, forming the attitudes and motions of face and body that she knew she would use to obey Taraza's orders. In artificial repose, Lucilla had seen her own face appear like that of a prehistoric love goddess—opulent with flesh and the promise of softness into which an aroused male might hurl himself.

In her education, Lucilla had seen ancient statues from the First Times, little stone figures of human females with wide hips and sagging breasts that assured abundance for a suckling infant. At will, Lucilla could produce a youthful simulation of that ancient form.

In the courtyard below Lucilla, Duncan paused a moment and appeared to be thinking out his next movements. Presently, he nodded to himself, leaped high and twisted in the air, landing like a springbok on one leg, which kicked him sideways into gyrations more akin to dance than to combat.

Lucilla drew her mouth into a tight line of resolution.

Sexual Imprint.

The secret of sex was no secret at all, she thought. The roots were attached to life itself. This explained, of course, why her first command-seduction for the Sisterhood had planted a male face in her memory. The Breeding Mistress had told her to expect this and not be alarmed by it. But Lucilla had realized then that the Sexual Imprint was a two-edged sword. You might learn to flow along the edge of the blade but you could be cut by it. Sometimes, when that male face of her first command-seduction returned unbidden into her mind, Lucilla felt confounded by it. The memory came so frequently at the peak of an intimate moment, forcing her to great efforts of concealment.

"You are strengthened thus," the Breeding Mistresses reassured her.

Still, there were times when she felt that she had trivialized something better left a mystery.

A feeling of sourness at what she must do swept over Lucilla. These evenings when she observed Duncan's training sessions had been her favorite times each day. The lad's muscular development showed such definite progress—moving in the growth of sensitive muscle and nerve links—all of the prana-bindu marvels for which the Sisterhood was so famous. The next step was almost upon her, though, and she no longer could sink into watchful appreciation of her charge.

Miles Teg would come out presently, she knew. Duncan's training would move again into the practice room with its more deadly weapons.

Teg.

Once more, Lucilla wondered about him. She had felt herself more than once attracted to him in a particular way that she recognized immediately. An Imprinter enjoyed some latitude in selecting her own breeding partners, provided she had no prior commitments nor contrary orders. Teg was old but his records suggested he might still be virile. She would not be able to keep the child, of course, but she had learned to deal with that.

Why not? she had asked herself.

Her plan had been simple in the extreme. Complete the Imprint on the ghola and then, registering her intent with Taraza, conceive a child by the redoubtable Miles Teg. Practical introductory seduction had been indicated, but Teg had not succumbed. His Mentat cynicism stopped her one afternoon in the dressing chamber off the Weapons Room.

"My breeding days are over, Lucilla. The Sisterhood should be satisfied with what I already have given."

Teg, clad only in black exercise leotards, finished wiping his sweaty face with a towel and dropped the towel into a hamper. He spoke without looking at her: "Would you please leave me now?"

So he saw through her overtures!

She should have anticipated that, Teg being who he was. Lucilla knew she might still seduce him. No Reverend Mother of her training should fail, not even with a Mentat of Teg's obvious powers.

Lucilla stood there a moment undecided, her mind automatically planning how to circumvent this preliminary rejection. Something stopped her. Not anger at the rejection, not the remote possibility that he might indeed be proof against her wiles. Pride and its possible fall (there was always that possibility) had little to do with it.

Dignity.

There was a quiet dignity in Teg and she had the certain knowledge of what his courage and prowess had already given to the Sisterhood. Not quite sure of her motives, Lucilla turned away from him. Possibly it was the underlying gratitude that the Sisterhood felt toward him. To seduce Teg now would be demeaning, not only of him but of herself. She could not bring herself to such an action, not without a direct order from a superior.

As she stood on the parapet, some of these memories clouded her senses. There was movement in the shadows at the doorway from the

Weapons Wing. Teg could be glimpsed there. Lucilla took a firmer grip on her responses and focused on Duncan. The ghola had stopped his controlled tumbling across the lawn. He stood quietly, breathing deeply, his attention aimed upward at Lucilla. She saw perspiration on his face and in dark blotchings on his light blue singlesuit.

Leaning over the parapet, Lucilla called down to him: "That was very good, Duncan. Tomorrow, I will begin teaching you more of the foot-fist combinations."

The words came out of her without censoring and she knew their source at once. They were for Teg standing in the shadowed doorway down there, not for the ghola. She was saying to Teg: "See! You aren't the only one who teaches him deadly abilities."

Lucilla realized then that Teg had insinuated himself further into her psyche than she should permit. Grimly, she swung her gaze to the tall figure emerging from the doorway's shadows. Duncan already was running toward the Bashar.

As Lucilla focused on Teg, reaction flashed through her ignited by the most elemental Bene Gesserit responses. The steps of this reaction could be defined later: *Something wrong! Danger! Teg is not Teg!* In the reactive flash, however, none of this took separate form. She responded, hurling all the volume of Voice she could muster:

"Duncan! Down!"

Duncan dropped flat on the grass, his attention riveted to the Teg-figure emerging from the Weapons Wing. There was a field-model lasgun in the man's hands.

Face Dancer! Lucilla thought. Only hyperalertness revealed him to her. *One of the new ones!*

"Face Dancer!" Lucilla shouted.

Duncan kicked himself sideways and leaped up, twisting flat in the air at least a meter off the ground. The speed of his reaction shocked Lucilla. She had not known any human could move that fast! The lasgun's first bolt cut beneath Duncan as he seemed to float in the air.

Lucilla jumped to the parapet and dropped to a handhold on the window ledge of the next lower level. Before she was stopped, her right hand shot out and found the protruding rainspout that memory told her was there. Her body arched sideways and she dropped to a window ledge at the next level. Desperation drove her even though she knew she would be too late.

Something crackled on the wall above her. She saw a molten line cut toward her as she flung herself to the left, twisting and dropping onto the lawn. Her gaze captured the scene around her in a flashing deit-grasp as she landed.

Duncan moved toward the attacker, dodging and twisting in a terrifying replay of his practice session. The speed of his movements!

Lucilla saw indecision in the face of the false Teg.

She darted toward the Face Dancer, *feeling* the creature's thoughts: *Two of them after me!*

Failure was inevitable, though, and Lucilla knew it even as she ran. The Face Dancer had only to shift his weapon into full burn at close range. He could lace the air in front of him. Nothing could penetrate such a defense. As she cast about in her mind, desperately seeking some way to defeat the attacker, she saw red smoke appear on the false Teg's breast. A line of red darted upward at an oblique angle through the muscles of the arm holding the lasgun. The arm fell away like a piece dropping from a statue. The shoulder tipped away from the torso in a spout of blood. The figure toppled, dissolving into more red smoke and blood spray, crumbling into pieces on the steps, all dark tans and blue-tinged reds.

Lucilla smelled the distinctive Face Dancer pheromones as she stopped. Duncan came up beside her. He peered past the dead Face Dancer at movement in the hallway.

Another Teg emerged behind the dead one. Lucilla identified the reality: Teg himself.

"That's the Bashar," Duncan said.

Lucilla experienced a small surge of pleasure that Duncan had learned this identity-lesson so well: how to recognize your friends even if you only saw bits of them. She pointed to the dead Face Dancer. "Smell him."

Duncan inhaled. "Yes, I have it. But he wasn't a very good copy. I saw what he was as soon as you did."

Teg emerged into the courtyard carrying a heavy lasgun cradled across his left arm. His right hand held a firm grip on the stock and trigger. He swept his gaze around the courtyard, then focused on Duncan and finally on Lucilla.

"Bring Duncan inside," Teg said.

It was the order of a battlefield commander, depending only on superior knowledge of what should be done in the emergency. Lucilla obeyed without question.

Duncan did not speak as she led him by the hand past the bloody meat that had been the Face Dancer, then into the Weapons Wing. Once inside, he glanced back at the sodden heap and asked: "Who let him in?"

Not: "How did he get in?" she observed. Duncan already had seen past the inconsequentials to the heart of their problem.

Teg strode ahead of them toward his own quarters. He stopped at the door, glanced inside and motioned for Lucilla and Duncan to follow.

In Teg's bedroom there was the thick smell of burned flesh and wisps of smoke dominated by the charred barbecue odor that Lucilla so detested: cooked human meat! A figure in one of Teg's uniforms lay face down on the floor where it had fallen off his bed.

Teg rolled the figure over with one boot toe, exposing the face: staring eyes, a rictus grin. Lucilla recognized one of the perimeter guards, one of those who had come to the Keep with Schwangyu, so the Keep's records said.

"Their point man," Teg said. "Patrin took care of him and we put one of my uniforms on him. It was enough to fool the Face Dancers because we didn't let them see the face before we attacked. They didn't have time to make a memory print."

"You know about that?" Lucilla was startled.

"Bellonda briefed me thoroughly!"

Abruptly, Lucilla saw the further significance of what Teg said. She suppressed a swift flare of anger. "How did you let one of them get into the courtyard?"

His voice mild, Teg said: "There was rather urgent activity in here. I had to make a choice, which turned out to be the right one."

She did not try to hide her anger. "The choice to let Duncan fend for himself?"

"To leave him in your care or let other attackers get themselves firmly entrenched inside. Patrin and I had a bad time clearing this wing. We had our hands full." Teg glanced at Duncan. "He came through very well, thanks to our training."

"That . . . that *thing* almost got him!"

"Lucilla!" Teg shook his head. "I had it timed. You two could last at least a minute out there. I knew you would throw yourself in that *thing's* path and sacrifice yourself to save Duncan. Another twenty seconds."

At Teg's words, Duncan turned a shiny-eyed look on Lucilla. "Would you have done that?"

When Lucilla did not respond, Teg said: "She would have done that."

Lucilla did not deny it. She remembered now, though, the incredible speed with which Duncan had moved, the dazzling shifts of his attack.

"Battle decisions," Teg said, looking at Lucilla.

She accepted this. As usual, Teg had made the correct choice. She knew, though, that she would have to communicate with Taraza. The prana-bindu accelerations in this ghola went beyond anything she had expected. She stiffened as Teg straightened to full alert, his gaze on the doorway behind her. Lucilla whirled.

Schwangyu stood there, Patrin behind her, another heavy lasgun over his arm. Its muzzle, Lucilla noted, was aimed at Schwangyu.

"She insisted," Patrin said. There was an angry set to the old aide's face. The deep lines beside his mouth pointed downward.

"There's a trail of bodies clear out to the south pillbox," Schwangyu said. "Your people won't let me out there to inspect. I command you to countermand those orders immediately."

"Not until my clean-up crews are finished," Teg said.

"They're still killing people out there! I can hear it!" A venomous edge had entered Schwangyu's voice. She glared at Lucilla.

"We're also questioning people out there," Teg said.

Schwangyu shifted her glare to Teg. "If it's too dangerous here then we will take the . . . the child to my quarters. Now!"

"We will not do that," Teg said. His tone was low-key but positive.

Schwangyu stiffened with displeasure. Patrin's knuckles went white on the stock of his lasgun. Schwangyu swung her gaze past the gun and up to Lucilla's appraising stare. The two women looked into each other's eyes.

Teg allowed the moment to hold for a beat, then said: "Lucilla, take Duncan into my sitting room." He nodded toward a door behind him.

Lucilla obeyed, pointedly keeping her body between Schwangyu and Duncan the whole time.

Once behind the closed door, Duncan said: "She almost called me 'the ghola.' She's really upset."

"Schwangyu has let several things slip past her guard," Lucilla said.

She glanced around Teg's sitting room, her first view of this part of his quarters: the Bashar's inner sanctum. It reminded her of her own quarters—that same mixture of orderliness and casual disarray. Reading spools lay in a clutter on a small table beside an old-fashioned chair upholstered in soft gray. The spool reader had been swung aside as though its user had just stepped out for a moment, intending to return soon. A Bashar's black uniform jacket lay across a nearby hard chair with sewing material in a small open box atop it. The jacket's cuff showed a carefully patched hole.

So he does his own mending.

This was an aspect of the famous Miles Teg she had not expected. If she had thought about it, she would have said Patrin would absorb such chores.

"Schwangyu let the attackers in, didn't she?" Duncan asked.

"Her people did." Lucilla did not hide her anger. "She has gone too far. A pact with the Tleilaxu!"

"Will Patrin kill her?"

"I don't know nor do I care!"

Outside the door, Schwangyu spoke with anger, her voice loud and quite clear: "Are we just going to wait here, Bashar?"

"You can leave anytime you wish." That was Teg.

"But I can't enter the south tunnel!"

Schwangyu sounded petulant. Lucilla knew it for something the old woman did deliberately. What was she planning? Teg must be very cautious now. He had been clever out there, revealing for Lucilla the gaps in Schwangyu's control, but they had not plumbed Schwangyu's resources. Lucilla wondered if she should leave Duncan here and return to Teg's side.

Teg said: "You can go now but I advise you not to return to your quarters."

"And why not?" Schwangyu sounded surprised, really surprised and not covering it well.

"One moment," Teg said.

Lucilla became aware of shouting at a distance. A heavy thumping explosion sounded from nearby and then another one more distant. Dust sifted from the cornice above the door to Teg's sitting room.

"What was that?" Schwangyu again, her voice overly loud.

Lucilla moved to place herself between Duncan and the wall to the hallway.

Duncan stared at the door, his body poised for defense.

"That first blast was what I expected them to do." Teg again. "The second, I fear, was what *they* did not expect."

A whistle piped nearby loud enough to cover something Schwangyu said.

"That's it, Bashar!" Patrin.

"What is happening?" Schwangyu demanded.

"The first explosion, dear Reverend Mother, was your quarters being destroyed by our attackers. The second explosion was us destroying the attackers."

"I just got the signal, Bashar!" Patrin again. "We got them all. They came down by floater from the no-ship just as you expected."

"The ship?" Teg's voice was full of angry demand.

"Destroyed the instant it came through the space fold. No survivors."

"You fools!" Schwangyu screamed. "Do you know what you've done?"

"I carried out my orders to protect that boy from any attack," Teg said. "By the way, weren't you supposed to be in your quarters at this hour?"

"What?"

"They were after you when they blasted your quarters. The Tleilaxu are very dangerous, Reverend Mother."

"I don't believe you!"

"I suggest you go look. Patrin, let her pass."

As she listened, Lucilla heard the unspoken argument. The Mentat Bashar had been trusted here more than a Reverend Mother and Schwangyu knew it. She would be desperate. That was clever, suggesting her quarters had been destroyed. She might not believe it, though. Foremost in Schwangyu's mind now would be the realization that both Teg and Lucilla recognized her complicity in the attack. There was no telling how many others were aware of this. Patrin knew, of course.

Duncan stared at the closed door, his head tipped slightly to the right. There was a curious expression on his face, as though he saw through the door and actually watched the people out there.

Schwangyu spoke, the most careful control in her voice. "I don't believe my quarters were destroyed." She knew Lucilla was listening.

"There is only one way to make sure," Teg said.

Clever! Lucilla thought. Schwangyu could not make a decision until she was certain whether the Tleilaxu had acted treacherously.

"You will wait here for me, then! That's an order!" Lucilla heard the swish of Schwangyu's robes as the Reverend Mother departed.

Very bad emotional control, Lucilla thought. What this revealed about Teg, though, was equally disturbing. *He did it to her!* Teg had kept a Reverend Mother off balance.

The door in front of Duncan swung open. Teg stood there, one hand on the latch. "Quick!" Teg said. "We must be out of the Keep before she returns."

"Out of the Keep?" Lucilla did not hide her shock.

"Quick, I say! Patrin has prepared a way for us."

"But I must—"

"You must nothing! Come as you are. Follow me or we will be forced to take you."

"Do you really think you could take a . . ." Lucilla broke off. This was a new Teg in front of her and she knew he would not have made such a threat unless he was prepared to carry it out.

"Very well," she said. She took Duncan's hand and followed Teg out of his quarters.

Patrin stood in the hallway looking to his right. "She's gone," the old man said. He looked at Teg. "You know what to do, Bashar?"

"Pat!"

Lucilla had never before heard Teg use the batman's diminutive name.

Patrin grinned, a gleaming full-toothed smile. "Sorry, Bashar. The excitement, you know. I'll leave you to it, then. I have my part to play."

Teg waved Lucilla and Duncan down the hallway to the right. She obeyed and heard Teg close on her heels. Duncan's hand was sweaty in her hand. He pulled free and strode beside her without looking back.

The suspensor-drop at the end of the hallway was guarded by two of Teg's own people. He nodded to them. "Nobody follows."

They spoke in unison: "Right, Bashar."

Lucilla realized as she entered the drop with Duncan and Teg that she had chosen sides in a dispute whose workings she did not fully understand. She could feel the movements of the Sisterhood's politics like a swift current of water pouring all around her. Usually, the movement remained mostly a gentle wave washing the strand, but now she sensed a great destructive surge preparing to thunder its surf upon her.

Duncan spoke as they emerged into the sorting chamber for the south pillbox.

"We should all be armed," he said.

"We will be very soon," Teg said. "And I hope you're prepared to kill anyone who tries to stop us."

The significant fact is this: No Bene Tleilax female has ever been seen away from the protection of their core planets. (Face Dancer mules who simulate females do not count in this analysis. They cannot be breeders.) The Tleilaxu sequester their females to keep them from our hands. This is our primary deduction. It must also be in the eggs that the Tleilaxu Masters conceal their most essential secrets.

—BENE GESSERIT ANALYSIS,
ARCHIVES #XOXTM99 041

"So we meet at last," Taraza said.

She stared across the two meters of open space between their chairs at Tylwyth Waff. Her analysts assured her that this man was Tleilaxu Master of Masters. What an elfin little figure he was to hold so much power. The prejudices of appearance must be discarded here, she warned herself.

"Some would not believe this possible," Waff said.

He had a piping little voice, Taraza noted; something else to be measured by different standards.

They sat in the neutrality of a Guild no-ship with Bene Gesserit and Tleilaxu monitors clinging to the Guildship's hull like predatory birds on a carcass. (The Guild had been cravenly anxious to placate the Bene Gesserit. *"You will pay."* The Guild knew. Payment had been exacted from them before.) The small oval room in which they met was conventionally copper-walled and "spy-proof." Taraza did not believe this for an instant. She presumed also that the bonds between Guild and Tleilaxu, forged of melange, still existed in full force.

Waff did not try to delude himself about Taraza. This woman was far more dangerous than any Honored Matre. If he killed Taraza, she would be replaced immediately by someone just as dangerous, someone with every essential piece of information possessed by the present Mother Superior.

"We find your new Face Dancers very interesting," Taraza said.

Waff grimaced involuntarily. Yes, *far* more dangerous than the Honored Matres, who were not yet even blaming the Tleilaxu for the loss of an entire no-ship.

Taraza glanced at the small double-faced digital clock on the low side table at her right, a position where the clock could be read easily by either of them. The Waff-side face had been matched to his internal clock. She noted that the two internal-time readings stood within ten seconds of synchronization at an arbitrary midafternoon. It was one of the niceties of this confrontation where even the positioning and spacing between their chairs had been specified in the arrangements.

The two of them were alone in the room. The oval space around them was about six meters in its long dimension, half that in width. They occupied identical sling chairs of peg-fastened wood, which supported orange fabric; not a bit of metal or other foreign material in either of them. The only other furnishing of the room was the side table with its clock. The table was a thin black surface of plaz on three spindly wooden legs. Each of the principals in this meeting had been snooped with care. Each had three personal guards outside the room's one hatch. Taraza did not think the Tleilaxu would try a Face Dancer exchange, not under the present circumstances!

"You will pay."

The Tleilaxu, too, were extremely aware of their vulnerability, especially now that they knew a Reverend Mother could expose the new Face Dancers.

Waff cleared his throat. "I do not expect us to reach an agreement," he said.

"Then why did you come?"

"I seek an explanation of this odd message we have received from your Keep on Rakis. For what are we supposed to pay?"

"I beg of you, Ser Waff, drop these foolish pretenses in this room. There are facts known to both of us that cannot be avoided."

"Such as?"

"No female of the Bene Tleilax has ever been provided to us for breeding." And she thought: *Let him sweat that one!* It was damnably frustrating not to have a line of Tleilaxu Other Memories for Bene Gesserit investigation and Waff would know it.

Waff scowled. "Surely you don't think I would bargain with the life of—" He broke off and shook his head. "I cannot believe this is the payment you would ask."

When Taraza did not respond, Waff said: "The stupid attack on the Rakian temple was undertaken independently by people on the scene. They have been punished."

Expected gambit number three, Taraza thought.

She had participated in numerous analysis-briefings before this meeting, if one could call them briefings. Analyses there had been in excess. Very little was known about this Tleilaxu Master, this Tylwyth Waff. Some extremely important optional projections had been arrived at by inference (if these proved to be true). The trouble was that some of the most interesting data came from unreliable sources. One salient fact could be depended upon, however: The elfin figure seated across from her was deadly dangerous.

Waff's *gambit number three* engaged her attention. It was time to respond. Taraza produced a knowing smile.

"That is precisely the kind of lie we expected from you," she said.

"Do we begin with insults?" He spoke without heat.

"You set the pattern. Let me warn you that you will not be able to deal with us the way you dealt with those whores from the Scattering."

Waff's frozen stare invited Taraza to a daring gambit. The Sisterhood's deductions, based partly on the disappearance of an Ixian conference ship, were accurate! Maintaining her same smile, she now pursued the optional conjecture line as though it were known fact. "I think," she said, "the whores might like to learn that they have had Face Dancers among them."

Waff suppressed his anger. *These damnable witches! They knew! Somehow, they knew!* His councillors had been extremely doubtful about this meeting. A substantial minority had recommended against it. The witches were so . . . so devilish. And their retaliations!

Time to shift his attention to Gammu, Taraza thought. *Keep him off balance.* She said: "Even when you subvert one of us, as you did with Schwangyu on Gammu, you learn nothing of value!"

Waff flared: "She thought to . . . to *hire* us like a band of assassins! We only taught her a lesson!"

Ahhhh, his pride shows itself, Taraza thought. *Interesting. The implications of a moral structure behind such pride must be explored.*

"You've never really penetrated our ranks," Taraza said.

"And you have never penetrated the Tleilaxu!" Waff managed to produce this boast with passable calm. *He needed time to think! To plan!*

"Perhaps you would like to know the price of our silence," Taraza suggested. She took Waff's stony glare for agreement and added: "For one thing, you will share with us everything you learn about those Scattering-spawned whores who call themselves Honored Matres."

Waff shuddered. Much had been confirmed by killing the Honored Matres. The sexual intricacies! Only the strongest psyche could resist entanglement in such ecstasies. The potential of this tool was enormous! Must that be shared with these witches?

"*Everything* you learn from them," Taraza insisted.

"Why do you call them whores?"

"They try to copy us, yet they sell themselves for power and make a mockery of everything we represent. Honored Matres!"

"They outnumber you at least ten thousand to one! We have seen the evidence."

"One of us could defeat them all," Taraza said.

Waff sat in silence, studying her. Was that merely a boast? You could never be sure when it came to the Bene Gesserit witches. They *did* things. The dark side of the magic universe belonged to them. On more than one occasion the witches had blunted the Shariat. Was it God's will that the true believers pass through another trial?

Taraza allowed the silence to continue building its own tensions. She sensed Waff's turmoil. It reminded her of the Sisterhood's preliminary conference in preparation for this meeting with him. Bellonda had asked the question of deceptive simplicity:

"What do we *really* know about the Tleilaxu?"

Taraza had felt the answer surge into every mind around the Chapter House conference table: *We may know for sure only what they want us to know.*

None of her analysts could avoid the suspicion that the Tleilaxu had deliberately created a masking-image of themselves. Tleilaxu intelligence had to be measured against the fact that they alone controlled the secret of the axlotl tanks. Was that a lucky accident as some suggested? Then why had others been unable to duplicate this accomplishment in all of these millennia?

Gholas.

Were the Tleilaxu using the ghola process for their own kind of immortality? She could see suggestive hints in Waff's actions . . . nothing definite, but highly suspicious.

At the Chapter House conferences, Bellonda had returned repeatedly to their basic suspicions, hammering at them: "All of it . . . all of it, I say! Everything in our archives could be garbage fit only for slig fodder!"

This allusion had caused some of the more relaxed Reverend Mothers around the table to shudder.

Sligs!

Those slowly creeping crosses between giant slugs and pigs might provide meat for some of the most expensive meals in their universe but the creatures themselves embodied everything the Sisterhood held repugnant about the Tleilaxu. Sligs had been one of the earliest Bene Tleilax barter items, a product grown in their tanks and formed with the helical core from which all life took its shapes. That the Bene Tlei-lax made them added to the aura of obscenity around a creature whose multi-mouths ground incessantly on almost any garbage, passing that garbage swiftly into excrement that not only smelled of the sty but was slimy.

"The sweetest meat this side of heaven," Bellonda had quoted from a CHOAM promotion.

"And it comes from obscenity," Taraza had added.

Obscenity.

Taraza thought of this as she stared at Waff. For what possible rea-son might people build around themselves a mask of obscenity? Waff's flare of pride could not be fitted neatly into that image.

Waff coughed lightly into his hand. He felt the pressure of the seams where he had concealed two of his potent dart-throwers. The minority among his councillors had advised: "As with the Honored Matres, the winner in this encounter with the Bene Gesserit will be the one who emerges carrying the most secret information about the other. Death of the opponent guarantees success."

I might kill her but what then?

Three more full Reverend Mothers waited outside that hatch. Doubtless Taraza had a signal prepared for the instant the hatch was opened. Without that signal, violence and disaster were sure to ensue. He did not believe for an instant that even his new Face Dancers could overcome those Reverend Mothers out there. The witches would be on full alert. They would have recognized the nature of Waff's guards.

"We will share," Waff said. The admissions implicit in this hurt him but he knew he had no alternatives. Taraza's brag about relative abilities might be inaccurate because of its extreme claim, but he sensed truth in it nonetheless. He had no illusions, however, about what would ensue if the Honored Matres learned what had actually happened to their envoys. The missing no-ship could not yet be laid at the Tleilaxu door. Ships did vanish. Deliberate assassination was an-other matter altogether. The Honored Matres surely would try to ex-terminate such a brash opponent. If only as an example. Tleilaxu returned from the Scattering said as much. Having seen Honored Matres, Waff now believed those stories.

Taraza said: "My second agenda item for this meeting is our ghola."

Waff squirmed in the sling chair.

Taraza felt repelled by Waff's tiny eyes, the round face with its snub nose and too-sharp teeth.

"You have been killing our gholas to control the movement of a project in which you have no part other than to provide a single element," Taraza accused.

Waff once more wondered if he must kill her. Was nothing hidden from these damnable witches? The implication that the Bene Gesserit had a traitor in the Tleilaxu core could not be ignored. How else could they know?

He said: "I assure you, Reverend Mother Superior, that the ghola—"

"Assure me of nothing! We assure ourselves." A look of sadness on her face, Taraza shook her head slowly from side to side. "And you think we don't know that you sold us damaged goods."

Waff spoke quickly: "He meets every requirement imposed by your contract!"

Again, Taraza shook her head from side to side. This diminutive Tleilaxu Master had no idea what he was revealing here. "You have buried your own scheme in his psyche," Taraza said. "I warn you, Ser Waff, that if your *alterations* obstruct our design, we will wound you deeper than you think possible."

Waff passed a hand across his face, feeling the perspiration on his forehead. Damnable witches! But she did not know everything. The Tleilaxu returned from the Scattering and the Honored Matres she maligned so bitterly had provided the Tleilaxu with a sexually loaded weapon that would *not* be shared, no matter the promises made here!

Taraza digested Waff's reactions silently and decided on a bold lie. "When we captured your Ixian conference ship, your new Face Dancers did not die quite fast enough. We learned a great deal."

Waff poised himself on the edge of violence.

Bullseye! Taraza thought. The bold lie had opened an avenue of revelation into one of the more outrageous suggestions from her advisors. It did not seem outrageous now. *"The Tleilaxu ambition is to produce a complete prana-bindu mimic,"* her advisor had suggested.

"Complete?"

All of the Sisters at the conference had been astonished by the suggestion. It implied a form of mental copy going beyond the memory print about which they already knew.

The advisor, Sister Hesterion from Archives, had come armed with a tightly organized list of supporting material. *"We already know that what an Ixian Probe does mechanically, the Tleilaxu do with nerves and flesh. The next step is obvious."*

Seeing Waff's reaction to her bold lie, Taraza continued to watch him carefully. He was at his most dangerous right now.

A look of rage came over Waff's face. The things the witches knew were too dangerous! He did not doubt Taraza's claim in the slightest. *I must kill her no matter the consequences to me! We must kill them all. Abominations! It's their word and it describes them perfectly.*

Taraza correctly interpreted his expression. She spoke quickly: "You are in absolutely no danger from us as long as you do not injure our designs. Your religion, your way of life, those are your business."

Waff hesitated, not so much from what Taraza said as from the reminder of her powers. What else did they know? To continue in a subservient position, though! After rejecting such an alliance with the Honored Matres. And with ascendancy so near after all of those millennia. Dismay filled him. The minority among his councillors had been right after all: *"There can be no bond between our peoples. Any accord with powindah forces is a union based upon evil."*

Taraza still sensed the potential violence in him. Had she pushed him too far? She held herself in defensive readiness. An involuntary jerking of his arms alerted her. *Weapons in his sleeves!* Tleilaxu resources were not to be underestimated. Her snoopers had detected nothing.

"We know about the weapons you carry," she said. Another bold lie suggested itself. "If you make a mistake now, the whores will also learn how you use those weapons."

Waff took three shallow breaths. When he spoke, he had himself under control: "We will not be Bene Gesserit satellites!"

Taraza responded in an even-toned, soothing voice: "I have not by word or action suggested such a role for you."

She waited. There was no change in Waff's expression, no slightest shift in the unfocused glare he directed at her.

"You threaten us," he muttered. "You demand that we share everything we—"

"Share!" she snapped. "One does not *share* with unequal partners."

"And what would you share with us?" he demanded.

She spoke with the chiding tone she would use to a child: "Ser Waff, ask yourself why you, a ruling member of your oligarchy, came to this meeting?"

His voice still firmly controlled, Waff countered: "And why did you, Mother Superior of the Bene Gesserit, come here?"

She spoke mildly: "To strengthen us."

"You did not say what you would share," he accused. "You still hope for advantage."

Taraza continued to watch him carefully. She had seldom sensed such suppressed rage in a human. "Ask me openly what you want," she said.

"And you will give it out of your great generosity!"

"I will negotiate."

"Where was the negotiation when you ordered me . . . ORDERED ME! to—"

"You came here firmly resolved to break any agreement we made," she said. "Not once have you tried to negotiate! You sit in front of someone willing to bargain with you and you can only—"

"Bargain?" Waff's memory was hurled back to the Honored Matre's anger at that word.

"I said it," Taraza said. "Bargain."

Something like a smile twitched the corners of Waff's mouth. "You think I have authority to *bargain* with you?"

"Have a care, Ser Waff," she said. "You have the ultimate authority. It resides in that final ability to destroy an opponent utterly. I have not threatened that, but you have." She glanced at his sleeves.

Waff sighed. What a quandary. She was powindah! How could one bargain with a powindah?

"We have a problem that cannot be resolved by rational means," Taraza said.

Waff hid his surprise. Those were the very words the Honored Matre had used! He cringed inwardly at what that might signify. Could Bene Gesserit and Honored Matres make common cause? Taraza's bitterness argued otherwise, but when were the witches to be trusted?

Once more, Waff wondered if he dared sacrifice himself to eliminate this witch. What would it serve? Others among them surely knew what she knew. It would only precipitate the disaster. There was that internal dispute among the witches, but, again, that might just be another ruse.

"You ask us to share something," Taraza said. "What if I were to offer you some of our prize human bloodlines?"

There was no mistaking how Waff's interest quickened.

He said: "Why should we come to you for such things? We have our tanks and we can pick up genetic examples almost anywhere."

"Examples of what?" she asked.

Waff sighed. You could never escape that Bene Gesserit incisiveness. It was like a sword thrust. He guessed that he had revealed things to her that led naturally to this subject. The damage already had been done. She correctly deduced (or spies had told her!) that the wild pool of human genes held little interest for the Tleilaxu with their more sophisticated knowledge of life's innermost language. It never paid to underestimate either the Bene Gesserit or the products of their breeding programs. God Himself knew they had produced Muad'Dib and the Prophet!

"What more would you demand in exchange for this?" he asked.

"Bargaining at last!" Taraza said. "We both know, of course, that I am offering breeding mothers of the Atreides line." And she thought: *"Let him hope for that! They will look like Atreides but they will not be Atreides!"*

Waff felt his pulse quicken. Was this possible? Did she have the slightest idea what the Tleilaxu might learn from an examination of such source material?

"We would want first selection of their offspring," Taraza said.

"No!"

"Alternate first selection, then?"

"Perhaps."

"What do you mean, perhaps?" She leaned forward. Waff's intensity told her she was on a hot trail.

"What else would you ask of us?"

"Our breeding mothers must have unfettered access to your genetic laboratories."

"Are you mad?" Waff shook his head in exasperation. Did she think the Tleilaxu would give away their strongest weapon just like that?

"Then we will accept a fully operational axlotl tank."

Waff merely stared at her.

Taraza shrugged. "I had to try."

"I suppose you did."

Taraza sat back and reviewed what she had learned here. Waff's reaction to that Zensunni probe had been interesting. *"A problem that cannot be resolved by rational means."* The words had produced a subtle effect on him. He had seemed to rise out of some place within himself, a questioning look in his eyes. *Gods preserve us all! Is Waff a secret Zensunni?*

No matter the dangers, this had to be explored. Odrade must be armed with every possible advantage on Rakis.

"Perhaps we have done all we can for now," Taraza said. "There is time to complete our bargain. God alone in His infinite mercy has given us infinite universes where anything may happen."

Waff clapped his hands once without thinking. "The gift of surprises is the greatest gift of all!" he said.

Not just Zensunni, Taraza thought. *Sufi also. Sufi!* She began to readjust her perspective on the Tleilaxu. *How long have they been holding this close to their breasts?*

"Time does not count itself," Taraza said, probing. "One has only to look at any circle."

"Suns are circles," Waff said. "Each universe is a circle." He held his breath waiting for her response.

"Circles are enclosures," Taraza said, picking the proper response out of her Other Memories. "Whatever encloses and limits must expose itself to the infinite."

Waff raised his hands to show her his palms then dropped his arms into his lap. His shoulders lost some of their tense upward thrust. "Why did you not say these things at the beginning?" he asked.

I must exercise great care, Taraza cautioned herself. The admissions in Waff's words and manner required careful review.

"What has passed between us reveals nothing unless we speak more openly," she said. "Even then, we would only be using words."

Waff studied her face, trying to read in that Bene Gesserit mask some confirmation of the things implied by her words and manner. She was powindah, he reminded himself. The powindah could never be trusted . . . but if she shared the Great Belief . . .

"Did God not send His Prophet to Rakis, there to test us and teach us?" he asked.

Taraza delved deep into her Other Memories. *A Prophet on Rakis? Muad'Dib? No . . . that did not square with either Sufi or Zensunni beliefs in . . .*

The Tyrant! She closed her mouth into a grim line. "What one cannot control one must accept," she said.

"For surely that is God's doing," Waff replied.

Taraza had seen and heard enough. The Missionaria Protectiva had immersed her in every known religion. Other Memories reinforced this knowledge and filled it out. She felt a great need to get herself safely away from this room. Odrade must be alerted!

"May I make a suggestion?" Taraza asked.

Waff nodded politely.

"Perhaps there is here the substance of a greater bond between us than we imagined," she said. "I offer you the hospitality of our Keep on Rakis and the services of our commander there."

"An Atreides?" he asked.

"No," Taraza lied. "But I will, of course, alert our Breeding Mistresses to your needs."

"And I will assemble the things you require in payment," he said. "Why will the bargain be completed on Rakis?"

"Is that not the proper place?" she asked. "Who could be false in the home of the Prophet?"

Waff sat back in his chair, his arms relaxed in his lap. Taraza certainly knew the proper responses. It was a revelation he had never expected.

Taraza stood. "Each of us listens to God personally," she said.

And together in the kehl, he thought. He looked up at her, reminding himself that she was powindah. None of them could be trusted. *Caution!* This woman was, after all, a Bene Gesserit witch. They were known to create religions for their own ends. *Powindah!*

Taraza went to the hatch, opened it and gave her security signal. She turned once more toward Waff who still sat in his chair. *He has not penetrated our true design*, she thought. *The ones we send to him must be chosen with extreme care. He must never suspect that he is part of our bait.*

His elfin features composed, Waff stared back at her.

How bland he looked, Taraza thought. But he could be trapped! An alliance between Sisterhood and Tleilaxu offered new attractions. *But on our terms!*

"Until Rakis," she said.

What social inheritances went outward with the Scattering? We know those times intimately. We know both the mental and physical settings. The Lost Ones took with them a consciousness confined mostly to manpower and hardware. There was a desperate need for room to expand driven by the myth of Freedom. Most had not learned the deeper lesson of the Tyrant, that violence builds its own limits. The Scattering was wild and random movement interpreted as growth (expansion). It was goaded by a profound fear (often unconscious) of stagnation and death.

—THE SCATTERING: BENE GESSERIT ANALYSIS (ARCHIVES)

Odrade lay full length on her side along the ledge of the bow window, her cheek lightly touching the warm plaz through which she could see the Great Square of Keen. Her back was supported by a red cushion, which smelled of melange as did many things here on Rakis. Behind her lay three rooms, small but efficient and well removed from both Temple and Bene Gesserit Keep. This removal had been a requirement of the Sisterhood's agreement with the priests.

"Sheeana must be guarded more securely," Odrade had insisted.

"She cannot become the ward of only the Sisterhood!" Tuek had objected.

"Nor of the priests," Odrade countered.

Six stories below Odrade's bow window vantage, an enormous

bazaar spread out in loosely organized confusion, almost filling the Great Square. The silvered yellow light of a lowering sun washed the scene with brilliance, picking out the bright colors of canopies, drawing long shadows across the uneven ground. There was a dusty radiance about the light where scattered clumps of people milled about patched umbrellas and the jumbled alignments of wares.

The Great Square was not actually square. It stretched out around the bazaar a full kilometer across from Odrade's window and easily twice that distance to the left and right—a giant rectangle of packed earth and old stones, which had been churned into bitter dust by daytime shoppers braving the heat in hopes of gaining a bargain then.

As evening advanced, a different sense of activity unfolded beneath Odrade—more people arriving, a quickening and more frenetic pulse to the movement.

Odrade tipped her head to peer down sharply at the ground near her building. Some of the merchants directly beneath her window had wandered off to their nearby quarters. They would return soon, after a meal and short siesta, ready to make full use of those more valuable hours when people in the open could breathe air that did not burn their throats.

Sheeana was overdue, Odrade noted. The priests dared not delay much longer. They would be working frantically now, firing questions at Sheeana, admonishing her to remember that she was God's own emissary to His Church. Reminding Sheeana of many contrived allegiances that Odrade would have to ferret out and make humorous before dispatching such trivia into proper perspective.

Odrade arched her back and went through a silent minute of tiny exercises to relieve tensions. She admitted to a certain sympathy for Sheeana. The girl's thoughts would be chaos right now. Sheeana knew little or nothing about what to expect once she came fully under a Reverend Mother's tutelage. There was little doubt that the young mind was cluttered with myths and other misinformation.

As my mind was, Odrade thought.

She could not avoid remembrance at a moment such as this. Her immediate task was clear: exorcism, not only for Sheeana but for herself.

She thought the haunting thoughts of a Reverend Mother in her memories: *Odrade, age five, the comfortable house on Gammu. The road outside the house is lined with what pass for middle-echelon mansions in the planet's seacoast cities—low one-story buildings on wide avenues. The houses reach far down to an outcurving sea frontage where they are much wider than along the avenues. Only on the sea side do they become more expansive and less jealous of every square meter.*

Odrade's Bene Gesserit–honed memory rolled through that faraway house, its occupants, the avenue, the playmates. She felt the tightness in her breast that told her such memories were attached to later events.

The Bene Gesserit crèche on Al Dhanab's artificial world, one of the original Sisterhood safe planets. (Later, she learned that the Bene Gesserit once considered making the entire planet into a no-chamber. Energy requirements defeated this plan.)

The crèche was a cascade of variety to a child from Gammu's comforts and friendships. Bene Gesserit education included intense physical training. There were regular admonishments that she could not hope to become a Reverend Mother without passage through much pain and frequent periods of seemingly hopeless muscular exercises.

Some of her companions failed at this stage. They left to become nurses, servants, laborers, casual breeders. They filled niches of necessity wherever the Sisterhood required them. There were times when Odrade felt longingly that this *failure* might not be a bad life—fewer responsibilities, lesser goals. That had been before she emerged from Primary Training.

I thought of it as emerging, coming through victorious. I came out the other side.

Only to find herself immersed in new and harsher demands.

Odrade sat up on her Rakian window ledge and pushed her cushion aside. She turned her back on the bazaar. It was becoming noisier out there. Damned priests! They were stretching delay to its absolute limits!

I must think about my own childhood because that will help me with Sheeana, she thought. Immediately, she sneered at her own weakness. *Another excuse!*

It took some postulants at least fifty years to become Reverend Mothers. This was ground into them during Secondary Training: a lesson of patience. Odrade showed an early penchant for deep study. There was consideration that she might become one of the Bene Gesserit Mentats and probably an Archivist. This idea was dropped on the discovery that her talents lay in a more profitable direction. She was aimed at more sensitive duties in Chapter House.

Security.

That wild talent among the Atreides often had this employment. Care with details, that was Odrade's hallmark. She knew her sisters could predict some of her actions simply from their deep knowledge of her. Taraza did it regularly. Odrade had overheard the explanation from Taraza's own lips:

"Odrade's persona is exquisitely reflected in her performance of duties."

There was a joke in Chapter House: "Where does Odrade go when she's off duty? She goes to work."

Chapter House imposed little need to adopt the covering masks that a Reverend Mother used automatically on the Outside. She might show emotions momentarily, deal openly with mistakes of her own and of others, feel sad or bitter or even, sometimes, happy. Men were available— not for breeding, but for occasional solace. All such Bene Gesserit Chapter House males were quite charming and a few were even sincere in their charm. These few, of course, were much in demand.

Emotions.

Recognition twisted through Odrade's mind.

So I come to it as I always do.

Odrade felt the warm evening sunlight of Rakis on her back. She knew where her body sat, but her mind opened itself to the coming encounter with Sheeana.

Love!

It would be so easy and so dangerous.

In this moment, she envied the Station Mothers, the ones allowed to live out a lifetime with a mated breeding partner. Miles Teg came from such a union. Other Memories told her how it had been for the Lady Jessica and her Duke. Even Muad'Dib had chosen that form of mating.

It is not for me.

Odrade admitted to a bitter jealousy that she had not been permitted such a life. What were the compensations of the life into which she had been guided?

"A life without love can be devoted more intensely to the Sisterhood. We provide our own forms of support to the initiated. Do not worry about sexual enjoyment. That is available whenever you feel the need."

With charming men!

Since the days of the Lady Jessica, through the Tyrant's times and beyond, many things had changed . . . including the Bene Gesserit. Every Reverend Mother knew it.

A deep sigh shuddered through Odrade. She glanced back over her shoulder at the bazaar. Still no sign of Sheeana.

I must not love this child!

It was done. Odrade knew she had played out the mnemonic game in its required Bene Gesserit form. She swiveled her body and sat cross-legged on the ledge. It was a commanding view of the bazaar and over the rooftops of the city and its basin. Those few remnant hills out there south of here were, she knew, the last of what had been the Shield Wall of Dune, the high ramparts of basement rock breached by Muad'Dib and his sandworm-mounted legions.

Heat danced from the ground beyond the qanat and canal that protected Keen from intrusions by the new worms. Odrade smiled softly. The priests found nothing strange in moating their communities to keep their Divided God from intruding upon them.

We will worship you, God, but don't bother us. This is our religion, our city. You see, we no longer call this place Arrakeen. Now, it's Keen.

The planet no longer is Dune or Arrakis. Now, it's Rakis. Keep your distance, God. You are the past and the past is an embarrassment.

Odrade stared at those distant hills dancing in the heat shimmer. Other Memories could superimpose the ancient landscape. She knew that past.

If the priests delay bringing Sheeana much longer I will punish them.

Heat still filled the bazaar below her, held there by storage in the ground and the thick walls surrounding the Great Square. Temperature diffusion was amplified by the smoke of many small fires lighted in the surrounding buildings and among the tent-sheltered congeries of life scattered through the bazaar. It had been a hot day, well above thirty-eight degrees. This building, though, had been a Fish Speaker Center in the old days and was cooled by Ixian machinery with evaporation pools on the roof.

We will be comfortable here.

And they would be as secure as Bene Gesserit protective measures could make them. Reverend Mothers walked those halls out there. The priests had their representatives in the building but none of those would intrude where Odrade did not want them. Sheeana would meet with them here on occasion but the occasions would be only as Odrade permitted.

It is happening, Odrade thought. *Taraza's plan moves ahead.*

Fresh in Odrade's mind was the latest communication from Chapter House. What that revealed about the Tleilaxu filled Odrade with excitement that she carefully dampened. This Waff, this Tleilaxu Master, would be a fascinating study.

Zensunni! And Sufi!

"A ritual pattern frozen for millennia," Taraza said.

Unspoken in Taraza's report was another message. *Taraza is placing her complete confidence in me.* Odrade felt strength flow into her from this awareness.

Sheeana is the fulcrum. We are the lever. Our strength will come from many sources.

Odrade relaxed. She knew that Sheeana would not permit the

priests to delay much longer. Odrade's own patience had suffered the assaults of anticipation. It would be worse for Sheeana.

They had become conspirators, Odrade and Sheeana. The first step. It was a marvelous game to Sheeana. She had been born and bred to distrust priests. What fun to have an ally at last!

Some form of activity stirred the people directly below Odrade's window. She peered downward, curious. Five naked men there had linked arms in a circle. Their robes and stillsuits lay in a pile at one side watched over by a dark-skinned young girl in a long brown dress of spice fiber. Her hair was bound by a red rag.

Dancers!

Odrade had seen many reports of this phenomenon but this was her first personal view of it since arriving. The onlookers included a trio of tall Priest Guardians in yellow helmets with high crests. The Guardians wore short robes that freed their legs for action, and each carried a metal-clad staff.

As the dancers circled, the watchful crowd grew predictably restive. Odrade knew the pattern. Soon, there would be a chanting outcry and a great melee. Heads would be cracked. Blood would flow. People would scream and run about. Eventually, it would all subside without official intervention. Some would go away weeping. Some would depart laughing. And the Priest Guardians would not interfere.

The pointless insanity of this dance and its consequences had fascinated the Bene Gesserit for centuries. Now it held Odrade's rapt attention. The devolution of this ritual had been followed by the Missionaria Protectiva. Rakians called it "Dance Diversion." They had other names for it, as well, and the most significant was "Siaynoq." This dance was what had become of the Tyrant's greatest ritual, his moment of sharing with his Fish Speakers.

Odrade recognized and respected the energy in this phenomenon. No Reverend Mother could fail to see that. The waste of it, however, disturbed her. Such things should be channeled and focused. This ritual needed some useful employment. All it did now was drain away forces that might prove destructive to the priests if left untapped.

A sweet fruit odor wafted into Odrade's nostrils. She sniffed and looked at the vents beside her window; heat from the mob and the warmed earth created an updraft. This carried odors from below through the Ixian vents. She pressed her forehead and nose against the plaz to peer directly downward. Ahhh, the dancers or the mob had tipped over a merchant's stall. The dancers were stomping in the fruit. Yellow pulp spurted up to their thighs.

Odrade recognized the fruit merchant among the onlookers, a familiar wizened face she had seen several times at his stall beside her building's entrance. He appeared unconcerned by his loss. Like all the others around him, he concentrated his attention on the dancers. The five naked men moved with a disjointed high lift of their feet, an unrhythmic and seemingly uncoordinated display, which came around periodically to a repeated pattern—three of the dancers with both feet on the ground and the other two held aloft by their partners.

Odrade recognized it. This was related to the ancient Fremen way of sandwalking. This curious dance was a fossil with roots in the need to move without signaling your presence to a worm.

People began to crowd nearer the dancers out of the bazaar's great rectangle, hopping upward like children's toys to raise their eyes above the throng for a glimpse of the five naked men.

Odrade saw Sheeana's escort then, movement far off to the right where a wide avenue entered the square. Animal-track symbols on a building there said the wide avenue was God's Way. Historical awareness said the avenue had been Leto II's route into the city from his high-walled Sareer far off to the south. With a care for details, one could still discern some of the forms and patterns that had been the Tyrant's city of Onn, the festival center built around the more ancient city of Arrakeen. Onn had obliterated many marks of Arrakeen but some avenues persisted: some buildings were too useful to replace. Buildings inevitably defined streets.

Sheeana's escort came to a stop where the avenue debouched into the bazaar. Yellow-helmeted Guardians probed ahead, clearing a path with their staves. The guards were tall: When grounded, the thick, two-meter staff would come only to the shoulders of the shortest among them. Even in the most disordered crowd you could not miss a Priest Guardian, but Sheeana's protectors were the tallest of the tall.

They were in motion once more leading their party toward Odrade. Their robes swung open at each stride revealing the slick gray of the best stillsuits. They walked straight ahead, fifteen of them in a shallow vee which skirted the thicker clusters of stalls.

A loose band of priestesses with Sheeana at their center marched behind the guards. Odrade caught glimpses of Sheeana's distinctive figure, that sun-streaked hair and proudly upthrust face, within her escort. It was the yellow-helmeted Priest Guardians, though, who attracted Odrade's attention. They moved with an arrogance conditioned into them from infancy. These guards knew they were better than the ordinary folk. And the ordinary folk reacted predictably by opening a way for Sheeana's party.

It was all done so naturally that Odrade could see the ancient pattern of it as though she watched another ritual dance, which had not changed in millennia.

As she had often done, Odrade thought of herself now as an archeologist, not one who sifted the dusty detritus of the ages but rather a person who focused where the Sisterhood frequently concentrated its awareness: on the ways people carried their past within them. The Tyrant's own design was apparent here. Sheeana's approach was a thing laid down by the God Emperor himself.

Beneath Odrade's window the five naked men continued to dance. Among the onlookers, however, Odrade saw a new awareness. Without any concerted turning of heads toward the approaching phalanx of Priest Guardians, the watchers below Odrade *knew.*

Animals always know when the herders arrive.

Now, the crowd's restiveness produced a quicker pulse. They would not be denied their chaos! A clod of dirt flew from the throng's outskirts and struck the ground near the dancers. The five men did not miss a step in their extended pattern but their speed increased. The length of the series between repetitions spoke of remarkable memories.

Another clod of dirt flew from the crowd and struck a dancer's shoulder. None of the five men faltered.

The crowd began to scream and chant. Some shouted curses. The chanting became a hand-clapping intrusion onto the dancers' movements.

Still, the pattern did not change.

The mob's chanting became a harsh rhythm, repeated shouts that echoed against the Great Square's walls. They were trying to break the dancers' pattern. Odrade sensed a profound importance in the scene below her.

Sheeana's party had come more than halfway across the bazaar. They moved through the wider lanes between stalls and turned now directly toward Odrade. The crowd was at its densest about fifty meters ahead of the Priest Guardians. The Guardians moved at a steady pace, disdainful of those who scurried aside. Under the yellow helmets, eyes were fixed straight ahead, staring over the mob. Not one of the advancing Guardians gave any outward sign that he saw mob or dancers or any other barrier that might impede him.

The mob stopped its chanting abruptly as though an invisible conductor had waved his hand for silence. The five men continued to dance. The silence below Odrade was charged with a power that made her neck hairs stand up. Directly below Odrade, the three Priest Guardians among the onlookers turned as one man and moved out of view into her building.

Deep within the crowd, a woman shouted a curse.

The dancers gave no sign that they heard.

The mob crowded forward, diminishing the space around the dancers by at least half. The girl who guarded the dancers' stillsuits and robes no longer was visible.

Onward, Sheeana's phalanx marched, the priestesses and their young charge directly behind.

Violence erupted off to Odrade's right. People there began striking each other. More missiles arced toward the five dancing men. The mob resumed its chant in a quicker beat.

At the same time, the rear of the crowd parted for the Guardians. Watchers there did not take their attention from the dancers, did not pause in their contributions to the growing chaos, but a way was opened through them.

Absolutely captivated, Odrade stared downward. Many things occurred simultaneously: the melee, the people cursing and striking each other, the continuing chant, the implacable advance of the Guardians.

Within the shield of priestesses, Sheeana could be seen darting her gaze from side to side, trying to see the excitement around her.

Some within the crowd produced clubs and struck out at the people around them, but nobody threatened the Guardians or any other member of Sheeana's party.

The dancers continued to prance within a tightening circle of watchers. Everyone crowded close against Odrade's building, forcing her to press her head against the plaz and peer at a sharp angle downward.

The Guardians leading Sheeana's party advanced through a widening lane amidst this chaos. The priestesses looked neither left nor right. Yellow-helmeted Guardians stared straight ahead.

Disdain was too feeble a word for this performance, Odrade decided. And it was not correct to say that the swirling mob ignored the incoming party. Each was aware of the other but they existed in separate worlds, observing the strict rules of that separation. Only Sheeana ignored the secret protocol, hopping upward to try for a glimpse past the bodies shielding her.

Directly beneath Odrade, the mob surged forward. The dancers were overwhelmed by the crush, swept aside like ships caught in a gigantic wave. Odrade saw spots of naked flesh being pummeled and thrust from hand to hand through the screaming chaos. Only by the most intense concentration could Odrade separate the sounds being carried up to her.

It was madness!

None of the dancers resisted. Were they being killed? Was it a sacrifice? The Sisterhood's analyses did not even begin to touch this actuality.

Yellow helmets moved aside beneath Odrade, opening a way for Sheeana and her priestesses to pass into the building, then the Guardians closed ranks. They turned and formed a protective arc around the building's entrance. They held their staves horizontally and overlapped at waist height.

The chaos beyond them began to subside. None of the dancers was visible but there were casualties, people sprawled on the ground, others staggering. Bloody heads could be seen.

Sheeana and the priestesses were out of Odrade's view in the building. Odrade sat back and tried to sort out what she had just witnessed.

Incredible.

Absolutely none of the Sisterhood's accounts or holophoto records captured this thing! Part of it was the smells—dust, sweat, an intense concentration of human pheromones. Odrade took a deep breath. She felt herself trembling inside. The mob had become individuals who moved out into the bazaar. She saw weepers. Some cursed. Some laughed.

The door behind Odrade burst open. Sheeana entered laughing. Odrade whirled and glimpsed her own guards and some of the priestesses in the hallway before Sheeana closed the door.

The girl's dark brown eyes glittered with excitement. Her narrow face, already beginning to soften with the curves she would display as an adult, was tense with suppressed emotion. The tension dissolved as she focused on Odrade.

Very good, Odrade thought, as she observed this. *Lesson one of the bonding already has begun.*

"You saw the dancers?" Sheeana demanded, whirling and skipping across the floor to stop in front of Odrade. "Weren't they beautiful? I think they're so beautiful! Cania didn't want me to look. She says it's dangerous for me to take part in Siaynoq. But I don't care! Shaitan would never eat those dancers!"

With a sudden outflowing awareness, which she had experienced before only during the spice agony, Odrade saw through to the total pattern of what she had just witnessed in the Great Square. It had needed only Sheeana's words and presence to make the thing clear.

A language!

Deep within the collective awareness of these people they carried, all unconsciously, a language that could say things to them they did not want to hear. The dancers spoke it. Sheeana spoke it. The thing was composed of voice tones and movements and pheromones, a complex and subtle combination that had evolved the way all languages evolved.

Out of necessity.

Odrade grinned at the happy girl standing in front of her. Now, Odrade knew how to trap the Tleilaxu. Now, she knew more of Taraza's design.

I must accompany Sheeana into the desert at the first opportunity. We will wait only for the arrival of this Tleilaxu Master, this Waff. We will take him with us!

Liberty and Freedom are complex concepts. They go back to religious ideas of Free Will and are related to the Ruler Mystique implicit in absolute monarchs. Without absolute monarchs patterned after the Old Gods and ruling by the grace of a belief in religious indulgence, Liberty and Freedom would never have gained their present meaning. These ideals owe their very existence to past examples of oppression. And the forces that maintain such ideas will erode unless renewed by dramatic teaching or new oppressions. This is the most basic key to my life.

—LETO II, GOD EMPEROR OF DUNE:
DAR-ES-BALAT RECORDS

Some thirty kilometers into the thick forest northeast of the Gammu Keep, Teg kept them waiting under the cover of a life-shield blanket until the sun dipped behind the high ground to the west.

"Tonight, we go a new direction," he said.

For three nights now, he had led them through tree-enclosed darkness with a masterful demonstration of Mentat Memory, each step directed precisely along the track that Patrin had laid out for him.

"I'm stiff from too much sitting," Lucilla complained. "And it's going to be another cold night."

Teg folded the life-shield blanket and put it in the top of his pack. "You two can start moving around a bit," he said. "But we won't leave here until full dark."

Teg sat up with his back against the bole of a thickly branched conifer, looking out from the deeper shadows as Lucilla and Duncan moved into the glade. The two of them stood there a moment, shivering as the last of the day's warmth fled into the night's chill. Yes, it would be cold again tonight, Teg thought, but they would have little chance to think about that.

The unexpected.

Schwangyu would never expect them still to be this close to the Keep and on foot.

Taraza should have been more emphatic in her warnings about Schwangyu, Teg thought. Schwangyu's violent and open disobedience of a Mother Superior defied tradition. Mentat logic would not accept the situation without more data.

His memory brought up a saying from school days, one of those warning aphorisms by which a Mentat was supposed to rein in his logic.

"Given a trail of logic, occam's razor laid out with impeccable detail, the Mentat may follow such logic to personal disaster."

So logic was known to fail.

He thought back to Taraza's behavior on the Guildship and immediately afterward. *She wanted me to know I would be completely on my own. I must see the problem in my own way, not in her way.*

So the threat from Schwangyu had to be a real threat that he discovered and faced and solved on his own.

Taraza had not known what would happen to Patrin because of all this.

Taraza did not really care what happened to Patrin. Or to me. Or to Lucilla.

But what about the ghola?

Taraza must care!

It was not logical that she would ... Teg dumped this line of reasoning. Taraza did not want him to act logically. She wanted him to do exactly what he was doing, what he had always done in the tight spots.

The unexpected.

So there was a species of logic to all of this but it kicked the performers out of the nest into chaos.

From which we must make our own order.

Grief welled up in his consciousness. *Patrin! Damn you, Patrin! You knew and I didn't! What will I do without you?*

Teg could almost hear the old aide's response, that stiffly formal voice Patrin always used when he was chiding his commander.

"You will do your best, Bashar."

The most coldly progressive reasoning said Teg would never again see Patrin in the flesh nor hear the old man's actual voice. Still . . . the voice remained. The person persisted in memory.

"Shouldn't we be going?"

It was Lucilla, standing close in front of his position beneath the tree. Duncan waited beside her. Both of them had shouldered their packs.

While he sat thinking, night had fallen. Rich starlight created vague shadows in the glade. Teg lifted himself to his feet, took his pack and, bending to avoid the low branches, emerged into the glade. Duncan helped Teg shoulder his pack.

"Schwangyu will consider this eventually," Lucilla said. "Her searchers will come after us here. You know it."

"Not until they have followed out the false trail and found the end of it," Teg said. "Come."

He led the way westward through an opening in the trees.

Three nights he had led them along what he called "Patrin's memory-path." As he walked on this fourth night, Teg berated himself for not projecting the logical consequences of Patrin's behavior.

I understood the depths of his loyalty but I did not project that loyalty into a most obvious result. We were together so many years I thought I knew his mind as I knew my own. Patrin, damn you! There was no need for you to die!

Teg admitted to himself then that there *had* been a need. Patrin had seen it. The Mentat had not permitted himself to see it. Logic could move just as blindly as any other faculty.

As the Bene Gesserit often said *and demonstrated.*

So we walk. Schwangyu does not expect this.

Teg was forced to admit that walking the wild places of Gammu created a whole new perspective for him. This entire region had been allowed to overgrow with plant life during the Famine Times and the Scattering. It had been replanted later but mostly as a random wilderness. Secret trails and private landmarks guided today's access. Teg imagined Patrin as a youth learning this region—that rocky butte visible in starlight through a gap in the trees, that spiked promontory, these lanes through giant trees.

"*They will expect us to make a run for a no-ship,*" he and Patrin had agreed, fleshing out their plan. "*The decoy must take the searchers in that direction.*"

Patrin had not said that *he* would be the decoy.

Teg swallowed past a lump in his throat.

Duncan could not be protected in the Keep, he justified himself.

That was true.

Lucilla had jittered through their first day under the life-shield that protected them from discovery by the instruments of aerial searchers.

"We must get word to Taraza!"

"When we can."

"What if something happens to you? I must know all of your escape plan."

"If something happens to me, you will not be able to follow Patrin's path. There isn't time to put it in your memory."

Duncan took little part in the conversation that day. He watched them silently or dozed, awakening fitful and with an angry look in his eyes.

On the second day under the shielding blanket, Duncan suddenly demanded of Teg: "Why do they want to kill me?"

"To frustrate the Sisterhood's plan for you," Teg said.

Duncan glared at Lucilla. "What is that plan?"

When Lucilla did not answer, Duncan said: "She knows. She knows because I'm supposed to depend on her. I'm supposed to love her!"

Teg thought Lucilla concealed her dismay quite well. Obviously, her plans for the ghola had fallen into disarray, all of the sequencing thrown out of joint by this flight.

Duncan's behavior revealed another possibility: Was the ghola a latent Truthsayer? What additional powers had been bred into this ghola by the sly Tleilaxu?

At their second nightfall in the wilderness, Lucilla was full of accusations. "Taraza ordered you to restore his original memories! How can you do that out here?"

"When we reach sanctuary."

A silent and acutely alert Duncan accompanied them that night. There was a new vitality in him. He had heard!

Nothing must harm Teg, Duncan thought. Wherever and whatever sanctuary might be, Teg must reach it safely. *Then, I will know!*

Duncan was not sure *what* he would know but now he fully accepted the prize in it. This wilderness must lead to that goal. He recalled staring out at the wild places from the Keep and how he had thought to be free here. That sense of untouched freedom had vanished. The wilderness was only a path to something more important.

Lucilla, bringing up the rear of this march, forced herself to remain calm, alert, and to accept what she could not change. Part of her awareness held firmly to Taraza's orders:

"Stay close to the ghola and, when the moment comes, complete your assignment."

One pace at a time, Teg's body measured out the kilometers. This was the fourth night. Patrin had estimated four nights to reach their goal.

And what a goal!

The emergency escape plan centered on a discovery Patrin had made here as a teenager of one of Gammu's many mysteries. Patrin's words came back to Teg: "On the excuse of a personal reconnaissance, I returned to the place two days ago. It is untouched. I am still the only person who has ever been there."

"How can you be sure?"

"I took my own precautions when I left Gammu years ago, little things that would be disturbed by another person. Nothing has been moved."

"A Harkonnen no-globe?"

"Very ancient but the chambers are still intact and functioning."

"What about food, water . . ."

"Everything you could want or need is there, laid down in the nullentropy bins at the core."

Teg and Patrin made their plans, hoping they would never have to use this emergency bolt hole, holding the secret of it close while Patrin replayed for Teg the hidden way to this childhood discovery.

Behind Teg, Lucilla let out a small gasp as she tripped over a root.

I should have warned her, Teg thought. Duncan obviously was following Teg's lead by sound. Lucilla, just as obviously, had much of her attention on her own private thoughts.

Her facial resemblance to Darwi Odrade was remarkable, Teg told himself. Back there at the Keep, the two women side by side, he had marked the differences dictated by their differing ages. Lucilla's youth showed itself in more subcutaneous fat, a rounding of the facial flesh. But the voices! Timbre, accent, tricks of atonal inflection, the common stamp of Bene Gesserit speech mannerisms. They would be almost impossible to tell apart in the dark.

Knowing the Bene Gesserit as he did, Teg knew this was no accident. Given the Sisterhood's propensity for doubling and redoubling its prized genetic lines to protect the investment, there had to be a common ancestral source.

Atreides, all of us, he thought.

Taraza had not revealed her design for the ghola, but just being within that design gave Teg access to the growing shape of it. No complete pattern, but he could already sense a wholeness there.

Generation after generation, the Sisterhood dealing with the Tleilaxu, buying Idaho gholas, training them here on Gammu, only to have them assassinated. All of that time waiting for the right moment. It was like a terrible game, which had come into frenetic prominence because a girl capable of commanding the worms had appeared on Rakis.

Gammu itself had to be part of the design. Caladanian marks all over the place. Danian subtleties piled atop the more brutal ancient ways. Something other than population had come out of the Danian Sanctuary where the Tyrant's grandmother, the Lady Jessica, had lived out her days.

Teg had seen the overt and covert marks when he made his first reconnaissance tour of Gammu.

Wealth!

The signs were here to be read. It flowed around their universe, moving amoebalike to insinuate itself into any place where it could lodge. There was wealth from the Scattering on Gammu, Teg knew. Wealth so great that few suspected (or could imagine) its size and power.

He stopped walking abruptly. Physical patterns in the immediate landscape demanded his full attention. Ahead of them lay an exposed ledge of barren rock, its identifying markers planted in his memory by Patrin. This passage would be one of the more dangerous.

"No caves or heavy growth to conceal you. Have the blanket ready."

Teg removed the life-shield from his pack and carried it over his arm. Once more he indicated that they should continue. The dark weave of the shield fabric hissed against his body as he moved.

Lucilla was becoming less of a cipher, he thought. She aspired to a *Lady* in front of her name. *The Lady Lucilla.* No doubt that had a pleasing sound to her. A few such titled Reverend Mothers were appearing now that Major Houses were emerging from the long obscurity imposed by the Tyrant's Golden Path.

Lucilla, the Seductress-Imprinter.

All such women of the Sisterhood were sexual adepts. Teg's own mother had educated him in the workings of that system, sending him to well-selected local women when he was quite young, sensitizing him to the signs he must observe within himself as well as in the women. It was a forbidden training outside of Chapter House surveillance, but Teg's mother had been one of the Sisterhood's *heretics.*

"You will have a need for this, Miles."

No doubt there had been some prescience in her. She had armed him against the Imprinters who were trained in orgasmic amplification—to fix the unconscious ties—male to female.

Lucilla and Duncan. An imprint on her would be an imprint on Odrade.

Teg almost heard the pieces go *snick* as they locked together in his mind. Then what of the young woman on Rakis? Would Lucilla teach the techniques of seduction to her imprinted pupil, arm him to ensnare the one who commanded worms?

Not enough data yet for a Prime Computation.

Teg paused at the end of the dangerous open rock passage. He put away the blanket and sealed his pack while Duncan and Lucilla waited close behind. Teg heaved a sigh. The blanket always worried him. It did not have the deflective powers of a full battle shield but if a lasgun's beam hit the thing the consequent quick-fire could be fatal.

Dangerous toys!

This was how Teg always classified such weapons and mechanical devices. Better to rely on your wits, your own flesh, and the Five Attitudes of the Bene Gesserit Way as his mother had taught him.

Use the instruments only when they are absolutely required to amplify the flesh: that was the Bene Gesserit teaching.

"Why are we stopping?" Lucilla whispered.

"I am listening to the night," Teg said.

Duncan, his face a ghostly blur in the tree-filtered starlight, stared at Teg. Teg's features reassured him. They were lodged somewhere in an unavailable memory, Duncan thought. *I can trust this man.*

Lucilla suspected that they were stopping here because Teg's old body demanded respite but she could not bring herself to say this. Teg said his escape plan included a way of getting Duncan to Rakis. Very well. That was all that mattered for the moment.

She already had figured out that this sanctuary somewhere ahead of them must involve a no-ship or a no-chamber. Nothing else would suffice. Somehow, Patrin had been the key to it. Teg's few hints had revealed that Patrin was the source of their escape route.

Lucilla had been the first to realize how Patrin would have to pay for their escape. Patrin was the weakest link. He remained behind where Schwangyu could capture him. Capture of the decoy was inevitable. Only a fool would suppose that a Reverend Mother of Schwangyu's powers would be incapable of wresting secrets from a mere male. Schwangyu would not even require the heavy persuasion. The subtleties of Voice and those painful forms of interrogation that remained a Sisterhood monopoly—the agony box and nerve-node pressures—those were all she would require.

The form Patrin's loyalty would take had been clear to Lucilla then. How could Teg have been so blind?

Love!

That long, trusting bond between the two men. Schwangyu would act swiftly and brutally. Patrin knew it. Teg had not examined his own certain knowledge.

Duncan's voice shocked her from these thoughts.

" 'Thopter! Behind us!"

"Quick!" Teg whipped the blanket from his pack and threw it over them. They huddled in earth-smelling darkness, listening to the ornithopter pass above them. It did not pause or return.

When they felt certain they had not been detected, Teg once more led them up Patrin's *memory-track*.

"That was a searcher," Lucilla said. "They are beginning to suspect . . . or Patrin . . ."

"Save your energy for walking," Teg snapped.

She did not press him. They both knew Patrin was dead. Argument over this had been exhausted.

This Mentat goes deep, Lucilla told herself.

Teg was the child of a Reverend Mother and that mother had trained him beyond the permitted limits before the Sisterhood took him into their manipulative hands. The ghola was not the only one here with unknown resources.

Their trail turned back and forth upon itself, a game track climbing a steep hill through thick forest. Starlight did not penetrate the trees. Only the Mentat's marvelous memory kept them on the path.

Lucilla felt duff underfoot. She listened to Teg's movements, reading them to guide her feet.

How silent Duncan is, she thought. *How closed in upon himself.* He obeyed orders. He followed where Teg led them. She sensed the quality of Duncan's obedience. He kept his own counsel. Duncan obeyed because it suited him to do so—for now. Schwangyu's rebellion had planted something wildly independent in the ghola. And what things of their own had the Tleilaxu planted in him?

Teg stopped at a level spot beneath tall trees to regain his wind. Lucilla could hear him breathing deeply. This reminded her once more that the Mentat was a very old man, far too old for these exertions. She spoke quietly:

"Are you all right, Miles?"

"I'll tell you when I'm not."

"How much farther?" Duncan asked.

"Only a short way now."

Presently, he resumed his course through the night. "We must hurry," he said. "This saddle-back ridge is the last bit."

Now that he had accepted the fact of Patrin's death, Teg's thoughts swung like a compass needle to Schwangyu and what she must be experiencing. Schwangyu would feel her world falling in around her. The fugitives had been gone four nights! People who could elude a Reverend Mother this way might do anything! Of course, the fugitives probably were off-planet by now. A no-ship. But what if . . .

Schwangyu's thoughts would be full of what-ifs.

Patrin had been the fragile link but Patrin had been well trained in the removal of fragile links, trained by a master—Miles Teg.

Teg dashed dampness from his eyes with a quick shake of his head. Immediate necessity required that core of internal honesty which he could not avoid. Teg had never been a good liar, not even to himself. Quite early in his training, he had realized that his mother and the others involved in his upbringing had conditioned him to a deep sense of personal honesty.

Adherence to a code of honor.

The code itself, as he recognized its shape in him, attracted Teg's fascinated attention. It began with recognition that humans were not created equal, that they possessed different inherited abilities and experienced different events in their lives. This produced people of different accomplishments and different worth.

To obey this code, Teg realized early that he must place himself accurately into the flow of observable hierarchies accepting that a moment might come when he could evolve no further.

The code's conditioning went deep. He could never find its ultimate roots. It obviously was attached to something intrinsic to his humanity. It dictated with enormous power the limits of behavior permitted to those above as well as to those below him in the hierarchical pyramid.

The key token of exchange: loyalty.

Loyalty went upward and downward, lodging wherever it found a deserving attachment. Such loyalties, Teg knew, were securely locked into him. He felt no doubts that Taraza would support him in everything except a situation demanding that he be sacrificed to the survival of the Sisterhood. And that was right in itself. That was where the loyalties of all of them eventually lodged.

I am Taraza's Bashar. That is what the code says.

And this was the code that had killed Patrin.

I hope you suffered no pain, old friend.

Once more, Teg paused under the trees. Taking his fighting knife from its boot sheath, he scratched a small mark in a tree beside him.

"What are you doing?" Lucilla demanded.

"This is a secret mark," Teg said. "Only the people I have trained know about it. And Taraza, of course."

"But why are you . . ."

"I will explain later."

Teg moved forward, stopping at another tree where he made the tiny mark, a thing which an animal might make with a claw, something to blend into the natural forms of this wilderness.

As he worked his way ahead, Teg realized he had come to a decision about Lucilla. Her plans for Duncan must be deflected. Every Mentat projection Teg could make about Duncan's safety and sanity required this. The awakening of Duncan's pre-ghola memories must come ahead of any Imprint by Lucilla. It would not be easy to block her, Teg knew. It required a better liar than he had ever been to dissemble for a Reverend Mother.

It must be made to appear accidental, the normal outcome of the circumstances. Lucilla must never suspect opposition. Teg held few illusions about succeeding against an aroused Reverend Mother in close quarters. Better to kill her. That, he thought he could do. But the consequences! Taraza could never be made to see such a bloody act as obedience to her orders.

No, he would have to bide his time, wait and watch and listen.

They emerged into a small open area with a high barrier of volcanic rock close ahead of them. Scrubby bushes and low thorn trees grew close against the rock, visible as dark blotches in the starlight.

Teg saw the blacker outline of a crawl space under the bushes.

"It's belly crawling from here in," Teg said.

"I smell ashes," Lucilla said. "Something's been burned here."

"This is where the decoy came," Teg said. "He left a charred area just down to our left—simulating the marks of a no-ship's take-off burn."

Lucilla's quickly indrawn breath was audible. *The audacity!* Should Schwangyu dare bring in a prescient searcher to follow Duncan's tracks (because Duncan alone among them had no Siona blood in his ancestry to shield him) all of the marks would agree that they had come this way and fled off-planet in a no-ship . . . provided . . .

"But where are you taking us?" she asked.

"It's a Harkonnen no-globe," Teg said. "It has been here for millennia and now it's ours."

Quite naturally, holders of power wish to suppress wild research. Unrestricted questing after knowledge has a long history of producing unwanted competition. The powerful want a "safe line of investigations," which will develop only those products and ideas that can be controlled and, most important, that will allow the larger part of the benefits to be captured by inside investors. Unfortunately, a random universe full of relative variables does not insure such a "safe line of investigations."

—ASSESSMENT OF IX, BENE GESSERIT ARCHIVES

Hedley Tuek, High Priest and titular ruler of Rakis, felt himself inadequate to the demands just imposed upon him.

Dust-fogged night enveloped the city of Keen, but here in his private audience chamber the brilliance of many glowglobes dispelled shadows. Even here, in the heart of the Temple, though, the wind could be heard, a distant moan, this planet's periodic torment.

The audience chamber was an irregular room seven meters long and four meters at its widest end. The opposite end was almost imperceptibly narrower. The ceiling, too, made a gentle slope in that direction. Spice fiber hangings and clever shadings in light yellows and grays concealed these irregularities. One of the hangings covered a focusing horn that carried even the smallest sounds to listeners outside the room.

Only Darwi Odrade, the new commander of the Bene Gesserit Keep on Rakis, sat with Tuek in the audience chamber. The two of them faced each other across a narrow space defined by their soft green cushions.

Tuek tried to conceal a grimace. The effort twisted his normally imposing features into a revealing mask. He had taken great care in preparing himself for this night's confrontations. Dressers had smoothed his robe over his tall, rather stout figure. Golden sandals covered his long feet. The stillsuit under his robe was only for display: no pumps or catchpockets, no uncomfortable and time-consuming adjustments required. His silky gray hair was combed long to his shoulders, a suitable frame for his square face with its wide thick mouth and heavy chin. His eyes fell abruptly into a look of benevolence, an expression he had copied from his grandfather. This was how he had looked on entering the audience chamber to meet Odrade. He had felt himself altogether imposing, but, now, he suddenly felt naked and disheveled.

He's really a rather empty-headed fellow, Odrade thought.

Tuek was thinking: *I cannot discuss that terrible Manifesto with her! Not with a Tleilaxu Master and those Face Dancers listening in the other room. What ever possessed me to allow that?*

"It is heresy, pure and simple," Tuek said.

"But you are only one religion among many," Odrade countered. "And with people returning from the Scattering, the proliferation of schisms and variant beliefs . . ."

"We are the only true belief!" Tuek said.

Odrade hid a smile. *He said it right on cue. And Waff surely heard him.* Tuek was remarkably easy to lead. If the Sisterhood was right about Waff, Tuek's words would enrage the Tleilaxu Master.

In a deep and portentous tone, Odrade said: "The Manifesto raises questions that all must address, believers and non-believers alike."

"What has all this to do with the Holy Child?" Tuek demanded. "You told me we must meet on matters concerning—"

"Indeed! Don't try to deny that you know there are many people who are beginning to worship Sheeana. The Manifesto implicates—"

"Manifesto! Manifesto! It is a heretical document, which will be obliterated. As for Sheeana, she must be returned to our exclusive care!"

"No." Odrade spoke softly.

How agitated Tuek was, she thought. His stiff neck moved minimally as he turned his head from side to side. The movements pointed to a wall hanging on Odrade's right, defining the place as though Tuek's head carried an illuminating beam to reveal that particular hanging. What a transparent man, this High Priest. He might just as well announce that Waff listened to them somewhere behind that hanging.

"Next, you will spirit her away from Rakis," Tuek said.

"She stays here," Odrade said. "Just as we promised you."

"But why can't she . . ."

"Come now! Sheeana has made her wishes clear and I'm sure her words have been reported to you. She wishes to be a Reverend Mother."

"She already is the—"

"M'Lord Tuek! Don't try to dissemble with me. She has stated her wishes and we are happy to comply. Why should you object? Reverend Mothers served the Divided God in the Fremen times. Why not now?"

"You Bene Gesserit have ways of making people say things they do not want to say," Tuek accused. "We should not be discussing this privately. My councillors—"

"Your councillors would only muddy our discussion. The implications of the Atreides Manifesto—"

"I will discuss only Sheeana!" Tuek drew himself up in what he thought of as his posture of adamant High Priest.

"We *are* discussing her," Odrade said.

"Then let me make it clear that we require more of our people in her entourage. She must be guarded at all—"

"The way she was guarded on that rooftop?" Odrade asked.

"Reverend Mother Odrade, this is Holy Rakis! You have no rights here that we do not grant!"

"Rights? Sheeana has become the target, yes the target! of many ambitions and you wish to discuss rights?"

"My duties as High Priest are clear. The Holy Church of the Divided God will—"

"M'Lord Tuek! I am trying very hard to maintain the necessary

courtesies. What I do is for your benefit as well as our own. The actions
we have taken—"

"Actions? What actions?" The words were pressed from Tuek with a
hoarse grunting. These terrible Bene Gesserit witches! Tleilaxu behind
him and a Reverend Mother in front! Tuek felt like a ball in a fearsome
game, bounced back and forth between terrifying energies. Peaceful
Rakis, the secure place of his daily routines, had vanished and he had
been projected into an arena whose rules he did not fully understand.

"I have sent for the Bashar Miles Teg," Odrade said. "That is all.
His advance party should arrive soon. We are going to reinforce your
planetary defenses."

"You dare to take over—"

"We take over nothing. At your own father's request, Teg's people
redesigned your defenses. The agreement under which this was done
contains, at your father's insistence, a clause requiring our periodic
review."

Tuek sat in dazed silence. Waff, that ominous little Tleilaxu, had
heard all of this. There would be conflict! The Tleilaxu wanted a secret
agreement setting melange prices. They would not permit Bene Gesserit interference.

Odrade had spoken of Tuek's father and now Tuek wished only
that his long-dead father sat here. A hard man. He would have known
how to deal with these opposing forces. *He* had always handled the
Tleilaxu quite well. Tuek recalled listening (just as Waff listened now!)
to a Tleilaxu envoy named Wose . . . and another one named Pook.
Ledden Pook. What odd names they had.

Tuek's confused thoughts abruptly offered up another name.
Odrade had just mentioned it: *Teg!* Was that old monster still active?

Odrade was speaking once more. Tuek tried to swallow in a dry
throat as he leaned forward, forcing himself to pay attention.

"Teg will also look into your on-planet defenses. After that rooftop
fiasco—"

"I officially forbid this interference with our internal affairs," Tuek
said. "There is no need. Our Priest Guardians are adequate to—"

"Adequate?" Odrade shook her head sadly. "What an inadequate word, given the new circumstances on Rakis."

"What new circumstances?" There was terror in Tuek's voice.

Odrade merely sat there staring at him.

Tuek tried to force some order into his thoughts. Could she know about the Tleilaxu listening back there? Impossible! He inhaled a trembling breath. What was this about the defenses of Rakis? The defenses were excellent, he reassured himself. They had the best Ixian monitors and no-ships. More than that, it was to the advantage of all independent powers that Rakis remain equally independent as another source of the spice.

To the advantage of everyone except the Tleilaxu with the damnable melange overproduction from their axlotl tanks!

This was a shattering thought. A Tleilaxu Master had heard every word spoken in this audience chamber!

Tuek called on Shai-hulud, the Divided God, to protect him. That terrible little man back there said he spoke also for Ixians and Fish Speakers. He produced documents. Was that the "new circumstances" of which Odrade spoke? Nothing remained long hidden from the witches!

The High Priest could not repress a shudder at the thought of Waff: that round little head, those glittering eyes; that pug nose and those sharp teeth in that brittle smile. Waff looked like a slightly enlarged child until you met those eyes and heard him speak in his squeaky voice. Tuek recalled that his own father had complained of those voices: "The Tleilaxu say such terrible things in their childish voices!"

Odrade shifted on her cushions. She thought of Waff listening out there. Had he heard enough? Her own secret listeners certainly would be asking themselves that question now. Reverend Mothers always replayed these verbal contests, seeking improvements and new advantages for the Sisterhood.

Waff has heard enough, Odrade told herself. *Time to shift the play.*

In her most matter-of-fact tones, Odrade said: "M'Lord Tuek, someone important is listening to what we say here. Is it polite that such a person listen secretly?"

Tuek closed his eyes. *She knows!*

He opened his eyes and met Odrade's unrevealing stare. She looked like someone who might wait through eternity for his response.

"Polite? I . . . I . . ."

"Invite the secret listener to come sit with us," Odrade said.

Tuek passed a hand across his damp forehead. His father and grandfather, High Priests before him, had laid down ritual responses for most occasions, but nothing for a moment such as this. Invite the Tleilaxu to sit here? In this chamber with . . . Tuek was reminded suddenly that he did not like the smell of Tleilaxu Masters. His father had complained of that: "They smell of disgusting food!"

Odrade got to her feet. "I would much rather look upon those who hear my words," she said. "Shall I go myself and invite the hidden listener to—"

"Please!" Tuek remained seated but lifted a hand to stop her. "I had little choice. He comes with documents from Fish Speakers and Ixians. He said he would help us to return Sheeana to our—"

"Help you?" Odrade looked down at the sweating priest with something akin to pity. This one thought he ruled Rakis?

"He is of the Bene Tleilax," Tuek said. "He is called Waff and—"

"I know what he is called and I know why he is here, M'Lord Tuek. What astonishes me is that you would allow him to spy on—"

"It is not spying! We were negotiating. I mean, there are new forces to which we must adjust our—"

"New forces? Oh, yes: the whores from the Scattering. Does this Waff bring some of them with him?"

Before Tuek could respond, the audience chamber's side door opened. Waff entered right on cue, two Face Dancers behind him.

He was told not to bring Face Dancers! Odrade thought.

"Just you!" Odrade said, pointing. "Those others were not invited, were they, M'Lord Tuek?"

Tuek lifted himself heavily to his feet, noting the nearness of Odrade, remembering all of the terrible stories about the Reverend

Mothers' physical prowess. The presence of Face Dancers added to his confusion. They always filled him with such terrible misgivings.

Turning toward the door and trying to compose his features into a look of invitation, Tuek said: "Only . . . only Ambassador Waff, please."

Speech hurt Tuek's throat. This was worse than terrible! He felt naked before these people.

Odrade gestured to a cushion near her. "Waff is it? Please come and sit down."

Waff nodded to her as though he had never seen her before. *How polite!* With a gesture to his Face Dancers that they remain outside, he crossed to the indicated cushion but stood waiting beside it.

Odrade saw a flux of tensions move through the little Tleilaxu. Something like a snarl flickered across his lips. He still had those weapons in his sleeves. Was he about to break their agreement?

It was time, Odrade knew, for Waff's suspicions to regain all of their original strength and more. He would be feeling trapped by Taraza's maneuverings. Waff wanted his breeding mothers! The reek of his pheromones announced his deepest fears. He carried in his mind, then, his part of their agreement—or at least a *form* of that sharing. Taraza did not expect Waff really to share all of the knowledge he had gained from the Honored Matres.

"M'Lord Tuek tells me you have been . . . ahhh, negotiating," Odrade said. *Let him remember that word!* Waff knew where the real negotiation must be concluded. As she spoke, Odrade sank to her knees, then back onto her cushion, but her feet remained positioned to throw her out of any line of attack from Waff.

Waff glanced down at her and at the cushion she had indicated for him. Slowly, he sank onto his cushion but his arms remained on his knees, the sleeves directed at Tuek.

What is he doing? Odrade wondered. Waff's movements said he was embarked on a plan of his own.

Odrade said: "I have been trying to impress upon the High Priest the importance of the Atreides Manifesto to our mutual—"

"Atreides!" Tuek blurted. He almost collapsed onto his cushion. "It cannot be Atreides."

"A very persuasive manifesto," Waff said, reinforcing Tuek's obvious fears.

At least *that* was according to plan, Odrade thought. She said: "The promise of s'tori cannot be ignored. Many people equate s'tori with the presence of their god."

Waff sent a surprised and angry stare at her.

Tuek said: "Ambassador Waff tells me that Ixians and Fish Speakers are alarmed by that document, but I have reassured him that—"

"I think we may ignore the Fish Speakers," Odrade said. "They hear the noise of god everywhere."

Waff recognized the cant in her words. Was she jibing at him? She was right about the Fish Speakers, of course. They had been so far weaned from their old devotions that they influenced very little and whatever they *did* influence could be guided by the new Face Dancers who now led them.

Tuek tried to smile at Waff. "You spoke of helping us to . . ."

"Time for that later," Odrade interrupted. She had to keep Tuek's attention on the document that disturbed him so much. She paraphrased from the Manifesto: "Your will and your faith—your belief system—dominate your universe."

Tuek recognized the words. He had read the terrible document. This *Manifesto* said God and all of His works were no more than human creations. He wondered how he should respond. No High Priest could let such a thing go unchallenged.

Before Tuek could find words, Waff locked eyes with Odrade and responded in a way he knew she would interpret correctly. Odrade could do no less, being who she was.

"The error of prescience," Waff said. "Isn't that what this document calls it? Isn't that where it says the mind of the believer stagnates?"

"Exactly!" Tuek said. He felt thankful for the Tleilaxu intervention. That was precisely the core of this dangerous heresy!

Waff did not look at him, but continued to stare at Odrade. Did the

Bene Gesserit think their design inscrutable? Let her meet a greater power. She thought herself so strong! But the Bene Gesserit could not really know how the Almighty guarded the future of the Shariat!

Tuek was not to be stopped. "It assaults everything we hold sacred! And it's being spread everywhere!"

"By the Tleilaxu," Odrade said.

Waff lifted his sleeves, directing his weapons at Tuek. He hesitated only because he saw that Odrade had recognized part of his intentions.

Tuek stared from one to the other. Was Odrade's accusation true? Or was that just another Bene Gesserit trick?

Odrade saw Waff's hesitation and guessed its reason. She cast through her mind, seeking an answer to his motivations. What advantage could the Tleilaxu gain by killing Tuek? Obviously, Waff aimed to substitute one of his Face Dancers for the High Priest. But what would that gain him?

Sparring for time, Odrade said: "You should be very cautious, *Ambassador* Waff."

"When has caution ever governed great necessities?" Waff asked.

Tuek lifted himself to his feet and moved heavily to one side, wringing his hands. "Please! These are holy precincts. It is wrong to discuss heresies here unless we plan to destroy them." He looked down on Waff. "It's not true, is it? You are not the authors of that terrible document?"

"It is not ours," Waff agreed. *Damn that fop of a priest!* Tuek had moved well to one side and once more presented a moving target.

"I knew it!" Tuek said, striding around behind Waff and Odrade.

Odrade kept her gaze on Waff. He planned murder! She was sure of it.

Tuek spoke from behind her. "You do not know how you wrong us, Reverend Mother. Ser Waff has asked that we form a melange cartel. I explained that our price to you must remain unchanged because one of you was the grandmother of God."

Waff bowed his head, waiting. The priest would come back into range. God would not permit a failure.

Tuek stood behind Odrade looking down at Waff. A shudder passed through the priest. Tleilaxu were so . . . so repellent and amoral. They could not be trusted. How could Waff's denial be accepted?

Not wavering from her contemplation of Waff, Odrade said: "But, M'Lord Tuek, was not the prospect of increased income attractive to you?" She saw Waff's right arm come around slightly, almost aimed at her. His intentions became clear.

"M'Lord Tuek," Odrade said, "this Tleilaxu intends to murder us both."

At her words, Waff jerked both arms up, trying to aim at the two separated and difficult targets. Before his muscles responded, Odrade was under his guard. She heard the faint hiss of dart throwers but felt no sting. Her left arm came up in a slashing blow to break Waff's right arm. Her right foot broke his left arm.

Waff screamed.

He had never suspected such speed in the Bene Gesserit. It was almost a match for what he had seen in the Honored Matre on the Ixian conference ship. Even through his pain he realized that he must report this. Reverend Mothers command synaptic bypasses under duress!

The door behind Odrade burst open. Waff's Face Dancers rushed into the chamber. But Odrade already was behind Waff, both hands on his throat. "Stop or he dies!" she shouted.

The two froze.

Waff squirmed under her hands.

"Be still!" she commanded. Odrade glanced at Tuek sprawled on the floor to her right. One dart had hit its target.

"Waff has killed the High Priest," Odrade said, speaking for her own secret listeners.

The two Face Dancers continued to stare at her. Their indecision was easy to see. None of them, she saw, had realized how this played into Bene Gesserit hands. Trap the Tleilaxu indeed!

Odrade spoke to the Face Dancers. "Remove yourselves and that body to the corridor and close the door. Your Master has done a foolish thing. He will have need of you later." To Waff, she said: "For the moment, you need me more than you need your Face Dancers. Send them away."

"Go," Waff squeaked.

When the Face Dancers continued to stare at her, Odrade said: "If you do not leave immediately, I will kill him and then I will dispatch both of you."

"Do it!" Waff screamed.

The Face Dancers took this as the command to obey their Master. Odrade heard something else in Waff's voice. He obviously would have to be talked out of suicidal hysteria.

Once she was alone with him, Odrade removed the exhausted weapons from his sleeves and pocketed them. They could be examined in detail later. There was little she could do for his broken bones except render him briefly unconscious and set them. She improvised splints from cushions and torn strips of green fabric from the High Priest's furnishings.

Waff reawakened quickly. He groaned when he looked at Odrade.

"You and I are now allies," Odrade said. "The things that have transpired in this chamber have been heard by some of my people and by representatives from a faction that wants to replace Tuek with one of their own number."

It was too fast for Waff. He was a moment grasping what she had said. His mind fastened, though, on the most important thing.

"Allies?"

"I imagine Tuek was difficult to deal with," she said. "Offer him obvious benefits and he invariably waffled. You have done some of the priests a favor by killing him."

"They are listening now?" Waff squeaked.

"Of course. Let us discuss your proposed spice monopoly. The late lamented High Priest said you mentioned this. Let me see if I can deduce the extent of your offer."

"My arms," Waff moaned.

"You're still alive," she said. "Be thankful for my wisdom. I could have killed you."

He turned his head away from her. "That would have been better."

"Not for the Bene Tleilax and certainly not for my Sisterhood," she said. "Let me see. Yes, you promised to provide Rakis with many new spice harvesters, the new airborne ones, which only touch the desert with their sweeper heads."

"You listened!" Waff accused.

"Not at all. A very attractive proposal, since I'm sure the Ixians are providing them free for their own reasons. Shall I continue?"

"You said we are allies."

"A monopoly would force the Guild to buy more Ixian navigation machines," she said. "You would have the Guild in the jaws of your crusher."

Waff lifted his head to glare at her. The movement sent agony through his broken arms and he groaned. Despite the pain, he studied Odrade through almost lidded eyes. Did the witches really believe that was the extent of the Tleilaxu plan? He hardly dared hope the Bene Gesserit were so misled.

"Of course that was not your basic plan," Odrade said.

Waff's eyes snapped wide open. She was reading his mind! "I am dishonored," he said. "When you saved my life you saved a useless thing." He sank back.

Odrade inhaled a deep breath. *Time to use the results of the Chapter House analyses.* She leaned close to Waff and whispered in his ear: "The Shariat needs you yet."

Waff gasped.

Odrade sat back. That gasp said it all. Analysis confirmed.

"You thought you had better allies in the people from the Scattering," she said. "Those Honored Matres and other hetairas of that ilk. I ask you: does the slig make alliance with its garbage?"

Waff had heard that question uttered only in khel. His face pale, he breathed in shallow gasps. The implications in her words! He forced himself to ignore the pain in his arms. *Allies*, she said. She knew about the Shariat! How could she possibly know?

"How can either of us be unmindful of the many advantages in an alliance between Bene Tleilax and Bene Gesserit?" Odrade asked.

Alliance with the powindah witches? Waff's mind was filled with turmoil. The agony of his arms was held so tentatively at bay. This moment felt so fragile! He tasted acid bile on the back of his tongue.

"Ahhhh," Odrade said. "Do you hear that? The priest, Krutansik, and his faction have arrived outside our door. They will propose that one of your Face Dancers assume the guise of the late Hedley Tuek. Any other course would cause too much turmoil. Krutansik is a fairly wise man who has held himself in the background until now. His Uncle Stiros groomed him well."

"What does your Sisterhood gain from alliance with us?" Waff managed.

Odrade smiled. Now she could speak the truth. That was always much easier and often the most powerful argument.

"Our survival in the face of the storm that is brewing among the Scattered Ones," she said. "Tleilaxu survival, too. The farthest thing from our desires is an end to those who preserve the *Great Belief.*"

Waff cringed. She spoke it openly! Then he understood. What matter if others heard? They could not see through to the secrets beneath her words.

"Our breeding mothers are ready for you," Odrade said. She stared hard into his eyes and made the handsign of a Zensunni priest.

Waff felt a tight band release itself from his breast. The unexpected, the unthinkable, the *unbelievable* thing was true! The Bene Gesserit were not powindah! All the universe would yet follow the Bene Tleilax into the True Faith! God would not permit otherwise. Especially not here on the planet of the Prophet!

> Bureaucracy destroys initiative. There is little that bureau-
> crats hate more than innovation, especially innovation that
> produces better results than the old routines. Improve-
> ments always make those at the top of the heap look inept.
> Who enjoys appearing inept?
>
> —A GUIDE TO TRIAL AND ERROR IN GOVERNMENT,
> BENE GESSERIT ARCHIVES

The reports, the summations and scattered tidbits lay in rows across the long table where Taraza sat. Except for the night watch and essential services, Chapter House Core slumbered around her. Only the familiar sounds of maintenance activities penetrated her private chambers. Two glowglobes hovered over her table, bathing the dark wood surface and rows of ridulian paper in yellow light. The window beyond her table was a dark mirror reflecting the room.

Archives!

The holoprojector flickered with its continuing production above the tabletop—more bits and pieces that she had summoned.

Taraza rather distrusted Archivists, which she knew was an ambivalent attitude because she recognized the underlying necessity for data. But Chapter House Records could only be viewed as a jungle of abbreviations, special notations, coded insertions, and footnotes. Such material often required a Mentat for translation or, what was worse, in times of extreme fatigue demanded that she delve into Other Memories. All Archivists were Mentats, of course, but this did not reassure

Taraza. You could never consult Archival Records in a straightforward manner. Much of the interpretation that emerged from that source had to be accepted on the word of the ones who brought it or (hateful!) you had to rely on the mechanical search by the holosystem. This, in its turn, required a dependency on those who maintained the system. It gave functionaries more power than Taraza cared to delegate.

Dependencies!

Taraza hated dependency. This was a rueful admission, reminding her that few developing situations were ever precisely what you imagined they would be. Even the best of Mentat projections accumulated errors . . . given enough time.

Still, every move the Sisterhood made required the consultation of Archives and seemingly endless analyses. Even ordinary commerce demanded it. She found this a frequent irritation. Should they form this group? Sign that agreement?

There always came the moment during a conference when she was forced to introduce a note of decision:

"Analysis by Archivist Hesterion accepted."

Or, as was often the case: "Archivists' report rejected; not pertinent."

Taraza leaned forward to study the holoprojection: "Possible breeding plan for Subject Waff."

She scanned the numbers, gene plans from the cell sample forwarded by Odrade. Fingernail scrapings seldom produced enough material for a secure analysis but Odrade had done quite well under the cover of setting the man's broken bones. Taraza shook her head at the data. Offspring would surely be like all the previous ones the Bene Gesserit had attempted with Tleilaxu: The females would be immune to memory probing: males, of course, would be an impenetrable and repellent chaos.

Taraza sat back and sighed. When it came to breeding records, the monumental cross-referencing assumed staggering proportions. Officially, it was the "College of Ancestral Pertinence," CAP to the Archivists. Among the Sisters at large, it was known as the "Stud Record," which, although accurate, failed to convey the sense of detail listed under the proper Archival headings. She had asked for Waff's projections to be carried out into three hundred generations, an easy and rather rapid task, sufficient for all practical purposes. Three-hundred-Gen mainlines (such as Teg, his collaterals and siblings) had proved themselves dependable for millennia. Instinct told her it would be bootless to waste more time on the Waff projections.

Fatigue welled up in Taraza. She put her head in her hands and rested them for a moment on the table, feeling the coolness of the wood.

What if I am wrong about Rakis?

Opposition arguments could not be shuffled away into Archival dust. *Damn this dependency on computers!* The Sisterhood had carried its main lines in computers even back in the Forbidden Days after the Butlerian Jihad's wild smashing of "the thinking machines." In these "more enlightened" days, one tended not to question the unconscious motives behind that ancient orgy of destruction.

Sometimes, we make very responsible decisions for unconscious reasons. A conscious search of Archives or Other Memories carries no guarantees.

Taraza released one of her hands and slapped it against the table-top. She did not like dealing with the Archivists who came trotting in with *answers* to her questions. A disdainful lot they were, full of secret jokes. She had heard them comparing their CAP work to stock breeding, to Farm Forms and Animal Racing Authority. Damn their jokes! The right decision now was far more important than they could possibly imagine. Those serving sisters who only obeyed orders did not have Taraza's responsibilities.

She lifted her head and looked across the room at the niche with its bust of Sister Chenoeh, the ancient one who had met and conversed with the Tyrant.

You knew, Taraza thought. *You were never a Reverend Mother but still you knew. Your reports show it. How did you know to make the right decision?*

Odrade's request for military assistance required an immediate answer. The time limits were too tight. But with Teg, Lucilla, and the ghola missing, the contingency plan had to be brought into play.

Damn Teg!

More of his unexpected behavior. He could not leave the ghola in jeopardy, of course. Schwangyu's actions had been predictable.

What had Teg done? Had he gone to ground in Ysai or one of the other major cities on Gammu? No. If that were the case, Teg would have reported by now through one of the secret contacts they had prepared. He possessed a complete list of those contacts and had investigated some of them personally.

Obviously, Teg did not place full trust in the contacts. He had seen something during his inspection tour that he had not passed along through Bellonda.

Burzmali would have to be called in and briefed, of course. Burzmali was the best, trained by Teg himself; prime candidate for Supreme Bashar. Burzmali must be sent to Gammu.

I'm playing a hunch, Taraza thought.

But if Teg had gone to ground, the trail started on Gammu. The trail could have ended there as well. Yes, Burzmali to Gammu. Rakis must wait. There were certain obvious attractions in this move. It would not alert the Guild. The Tleilaxu and the ones from the Scattering, however, would certainly rise to the bait. If Odrade failed to trap the Tleilaxu . . . no, Odrade would not fail. That one had become almost a certainty.

The unexpected.

You see, Miles? I have learned from you.

None of this deflected the opposition within the Sisterhood, though.

Taraza put both palms flat on her table and pressed hard, as though trying to sense the people out there in Chapter House, the ones who shared Schwangyu's opinions. Vocal opposition had subsided but that always meant the violence was being readied.

What shall I do?

The Mother Superior was supposed to be immune to indecision in a crisis. But the Tleilaxu connection had unbalanced their data. Some of the recommendations for Odrade appeared obvious and already had been transmitted. That much of the plan was plausible and simple.

Take Waff into the desert far beyond unwanted eyes. Contrive a situation-in-extremis and the consequent religious experience in the old and reliable pattern dictated by the Missionaria Protectiva. Test whether the Tleilaxu were using the ghola process for their own kind of immortality. Odrade was perfectly capable of carrying out that much of the revised plan. It depended heavily on this young woman, Sheeana, though.

The worm itself is the unknown.

Taraza reminded herself that today's worm was not the original worm of Rakis. Despite Sheeana's demonstrated command over them, they were unpredictable. As Archives would say, they had no track record. Taraza held little doubt that Odrade had made an accurate deduction about the Rakians and their dances. That was a plus.

A language.

But we do not yet speak it. That was a negative.

I must make a decision tonight!

Taraza sent her surface awareness roaming backward along that unbroken line of Mothers Superior, all of those female memories encapsulated within the fragile awareness of herself and two others— Bellonda and Hesterion. It was a tortuous track through Other Memories, which she felt too tired to follow. Right at the edge of the track would be observations of Muad'Dib, the Atreides bastard who had shaken the universe twice—once by dominating the Imperium with his Fremen hordes, and then by spawning the Tyrant.

If we are defeated this time it could be the end of us, she thought. *We could be swallowed whole by these hell-spawned females from the Scattering.*

Alternatives presented themselves: The female child on Rakis could be passed into the Sisterhood's core to live out her life somewhere at the end of a no-ship's flight. An ignominious retreat.

So much depended on Teg. Had he failed the Sisterhood at last or had he found an unexpected way to conceal the ghola?

I must find a way to delay, Taraza thought. *We must give Teg time to communicate with us. Odrade will have to drag out the plan on Rakis.*

It was dangerous but it had to be done.

Stiffly, Taraza lifted herself from her chairdog and went to the darkened window across from her. Chapter House Planet lay in star-shadowed darkness. A refuge: Chapter House Planet. Such planets were not even recipients of names anymore; only numbers somewhere in Archives. This planet had seen fourteen hundred years of Bene Gesserit occupancy but even that must be considered temporary. She thought of the guardian no-ships orbiting overhead: Teg's own defense system in depth. Still, Chapter House remained vulnerable.

The problem had a name: "accidental discovery."

It was an eternal flaw. Out there in the Scattering, humankind expanded exponentially, swarming across unlimited space. The Tyrant's Golden Path secure at last. Or was it? Surely, the Atreides worm had planned more than the simple survival of the species.

He did something to us that we have not yet unearthed—even after all of these millennia. I think I know what he did. My opposition says otherwise.

It was never easy for a Reverend Mother to contemplate the bondage they had suffered under Leto II as he whipped his Imperium for thirty-five hundred years along his Golden Path.

We stumble when we review those times.

Seeing her own reflection in the window's dark plaz, Taraza glared at herself. It was a grim face and the fatigue easily visible.

I have every right to be tired and grim!

She knew that her training had channeled her deliberately into negative patterns. These were her defenses and her strengths. She remained distant in all human relationships, even in the seductions she had performed for the Breeding Mistresses. Taraza was the perpetual devil's advocate and this had become a dominant force in the entire

Sisterhood, a natural consequence of her elevation to Mother Superior. Opposition developed easily in that environment.

As the Sufis said: *Rot at the core always spreads outward.*

What they did not say was that some rots were noble and valuable.

She reassured herself now with her more dependable data: The Scattering took the Tyrant's lessons outward in the human migrations, changed in unknown ways but ultimately submissive to recognition. And in time, a way would be found to nullify a no-ship's invisibility. Taraza did not think the people of the Scattering had found this—at least not the ones skulking back into the places that had spawned them.

There was absolutely no safe course through the conflicting forces, but she thought the Sisterhood had armed itself as well as it could. The problem was akin to that of a Guild navigator threading his ship through the folds of space in a way that avoided collisions and entrapments.

Entrapments, they were the key, and there was Odrade springing the Sisterhood's traps on the Tleilaxu.

When Taraza thought about Odrade, which was often in these crisis times, their long association reasserted itself. It was as though she looked at a faded tapestry in which some figures remained bright. Brightest of all, assuring Odrade's position close to the seats of Sisterhood command, was her capacity for cutting across details and getting at the surprising meat of a conflict. It was a form of that dangerous Atreides prescience working secretly within her. Using this hidden talent was the one thing that had aroused the most opposition, and it was the one argument that Taraza admitted had the most validity. That thing working far below the surface, its hidden movements indicated only by occasional turbulence, *that* was the problem!

"Use her but stand ready to eliminate her," Taraza had argued. "We will still have most of her offspring."

Taraza knew she could depend on Lucilla . . . provided Lucilla had found sanctuary somewhere with Teg and the ghola. Alternate assassins existed at the Keep on Rakis, of course. That weapon might have to be armed soon.

Taraza experienced a sudden turmoil within herself. Other Memories advised caution in the utmost. Never again lose control of the breeding lines! Yes, if Odrade escaped an elimination attempt, she would be alienated forever. Odrade was a full Reverend Mother and some of those must still remain out there in the Scattering—not among the Honored Matres the Sisterhood had observed . . . but still . . .

Never Again! That was the operational motto. Never another Kwisatz Haderach or another Tyrant.

Control the breeders: Control their offspring.

Reverend Mothers did not die when their flesh died. They sank farther and farther into the Bene Gesserit living core until their casual instructions and even their unconscious observations became a part of the continuing Sisterhood.

Make no mistakes about Odrade!

The response to Odrade required specific tailoring and exquisite care. Odrade, who allowed certain limited affections, "a mild warmth," she called them, argued that emotions provided valuable insights if you did not let them govern you. Taraza saw this *mild warmth* as a way into the heart of Odrade, a vulnerable opening.

I know what you think of me, Dar, with your mild warmth toward an old companion from school days. You think I am a potential danger to the Sisterhood but that I can be saved from myself by watchful "friends."

Taraza knew that some of her advisors shared Odrade's opinion, listened quietly and reserved judgment. Most of them still followed the Mother Superior's lead but many knew of Odrade's wild talent and had recognized Odrade's doubts. Only one thing kept most of the Sisters in line and Taraza did not try to delude herself about it.

Every Mother Superior acted out of a profound loyalty to her Sisterhood. Nothing must endanger Bene Gesserit continuity, not even herself. In her precise and harshly self-judgmental way, Taraza examined her relationship to the Sisterhood's continuing life.

Obviously, there was no immediate necessity to eliminate Odrade. Yet, Odrade was now so close to the center of the ghola design that little occurring there could escape her sensitive observation. Much that had not been revealed to her would become known. The Atreides Manifesto had been almost a gamble. Odrade, the obvious person to produce the Manifesto, could only achieve a deeper insight as she wrote the document, but the words themselves were the ultimate barrier to revelation.

Waff would appreciate that, Taraza knew.

Turning from the dark window, Taraza went back to her chairdog. The moment of crucial decision—go or no-go—could be delayed but intermediate steps must be taken. She composed a sample message in her mind and examined it while sending a summons to Burzmali. The Bashar's favorite student would have to be sent into action but not as Odrade wanted.

The message to Odrade was essentially simple:

"Help is on the way. You are on the scene, Dar. Where safety of girl Sheeana is concerned, use own judgment. In all other matters that do not conflict with my orders, carry out the plan."

There. That was it. Odrade had her instructions, the essentials that she would accept as "the plan" even while she would recognize an incomplete pattern. Odrade would obey. The "Dar" was a nice touch, Taraza thought. Dar and Tar. That opening into Odrade's *mild warmth* would not be well shielded from the Dar-and-Tar direction.

The long table on the right is set for a banquet of roast desert hare in sauce cepeda. The other dishes, clockwise to the
right from the far end of the table, are aplomage sirian,
chukka under glass, coffee with melange (note the hawk
crest of the Atreides on the urn), pot-a-oie and, in the Balut
crystal bottle, sparkling Caladan wine. Note the ancient poison detector concealed in the chandelier.

—DAR-ES-BALAT, DESCRIPTION AT A MUSEUM DISPLAY

Teg found Duncan in the tiny dining alcove off the no-globe's gleaming kitchen. Pausing in the passage to the alcove, Teg studied Duncan
carefully: eight days here and the lad appeared finally to have recovered from the peculiar rage that had seized him as they entered the
globe's access tube.

They had come through a shallow cave musky with the odors of a
native bear. The rocks at the back of the lair were not rocks, although
they would have deceived even the most sophisticated examination. A
slight protrusion in the *rocks* would shift if you knew or stumbled
upon the secret code. That circular and twisting movement opened the
entire rear wall of the cave.

The access tube, brilliantly lighted automatically once they sealed
the portal behind them, was decorated with Harkonnen griffins on
walls and ceiling. Teg was struck by the image of a young Patrin stumbling into this place for the first time (*The shock! The awe! The elation!*)

and he failed to observe Duncan's reaction until a low growl swelled in the enclosed space.

Duncan stood growling (almost a moan), fists clenched, gaze fixed on a Harkonnen griffin along the right-hand wall. Rage and confusion warred for supremacy on his face. He lifted both fists and crashed them against the raised figure, drawing blood from his hands.

"Damn them to the deepest pits of hell!" he shouted.

It was an oddly mature curse issuing from the youthful mouth.

The instant the words were out Duncan relapsed into uncontrolled shudders. Lucilla put an arm around him and stroked his neck in a soothing, almost sensual way, until the shuddering subsided.

"Why did I do that?" Duncan whispered.

"You will know when your original memories are restored," she said.

"Harkonnens," Duncan whispered and blood suffused his face. He looked up at Lucilla. "Why do I hate them so much?"

"Words cannot explain it," she said. "You will have to wait for the memories."

"I don't want the memories!" Duncan shot a startled look at Teg. "Yes! Yes, I do want them."

Later as he looked up at Teg in the no-globe's dining alcove, Duncan's memory obviously returned to that moment.

"When, Bashar?"

"Soon."

Teg glanced around the area. Duncan sat alone at the auto-scrubbed table, a cup of brown liquid in front of him. Teg recognized the smell: one of the many melange-laced items from the nullentropy bins. The bins were a treasure house of exotic foods, clothing, weapons, and other artifacts—a museum whose value could not be calculated. There was a thin layer of dust all through the globe but no deterioration of the things stored here. Every bit of the food was laced with melange, not at an addict level unless you were a glutton, but always noticeable. Even the preserved fruit had been dusted with the spice.

The brown liquid in Duncan's cup was one of the things Lucilla had tasted and pronounced capable of sustaining life. Teg did not know precisely how Reverend Mothers did this, but his own mother had been capable of it. One taste and they knew the contents of food or drink.

A glance at the ornate clock set into the wall at the closed end of the alcove told Teg it was later than he thought, well into the third hour of their arbitrary afternoon. Duncan should still be up on the elaborate practice floor but they both had seen Lucilla take off into the globe's upper reaches and Teg saw this as a chance for them to talk unobserved.

Pulling up a chair, Teg seated himself on the opposite side of the table.

Duncan said, "I hate those clocks!"

"You hate everything here," Teg said, but he took a second look at the clock. It was another antique, a round face with two analog hands and a digital second counter. The two hands were priapean—naked human figures: a large male with enormous phallus and a smaller female with legs spread wide. Each time the two clock hands met, the male appeared to enter the female.

"Gross," Teg agreed. He pointed to Duncan's drink: "You like that?"

"It's all right, sir. Lucilla says I should have it after exercise."

"My mother used to make me a similar drink for after heavy exertions," Teg said. He leaned forward and inhaled, remembering the aftertaste, the cloying melange in his nostrils.

"Sir, how long must we stay here?" Duncan asked.

"Until we are found by the right people or until we're sure we will not be found."

"But . . . cut off in here, how will we know?"

"When I judge it's time, I'll take the life-shield blanket and start keeping watch outside."

"I *hate* this place!"

"Obviously. But have you learned nothing about patience?"

Duncan grimaced. "Sir, why are you keeping me from being alone with Lucilla?"

Teg, exhaling as Duncan spoke, locked on the partial exhalation

and then resumed breathing. He knew, though, that the lad had observed. If Duncan knew, then Lucilla must know!

"I don't think Lucilla knows what you're doing, sir," Duncan said,
"but it's getting pretty obvious." He glanced around him. "If this place
didn't take so much of her attention . . . Where does she dash off to
like that?"

"I think she's up in the library."

"Library!"

"I agree it's primitive but it's also fascinating." Teg lifted his gaze to
the scrollwork on the nearby kitchen ceiling. The moment of decision
had arrived. Lucilla could not be depended upon to remain distracted
much longer. Teg shared her fascination, though. It was easy to lose
yourself in these marvels. The whole no-globe complex, some two
hundred meters in diameter, was a fossil preserved intact from the
time of the Tyrant.

When she spoke about it, Lucilla's voice took on a husky, whispering quality. "Surely, the Tyrant must have known about this place."

Teg's Mentat awareness had been immersed immediately in this
suggestion. *Why did the Tyrant permit Family Harkonnen to squander
so much of their last remaining wealth on such an enterprise?*

Perhaps for that very reason—to drain them.

The cost in bribes and Guild shipping from the Ixian factories
must have been astronomical.

"Did the Tyrant know that one day we would need this place?"
Lucilla asked.

No avoiding the prescient powers that Leto II had so often demonstrated, Teg agreed.

Looking at Duncan seated across from him, Teg felt his neck hairs
rising. There was something eerie about this Harkonnen hideaway, as
though the Tyrant himself might have been here. What had happened
to the Harkonnens who built it? Teg and Lucilla had found absolutely
no clues to why the globe had been abandoned.

Neither of them could wander through the no-globe without experiencing an acute sense of history. Teg was constantly confounded by unanswered questions.

Lucilla, too, commented on this.

"Where did they go? There's nothing in my Other Memories to give the slightest clue."

"Did the Tyrant lure them out and kill them?"

"I'm going back to the library. Perhaps today I'll find something."

For the first two days of their occupation, the globe had received a careful examination by Lucilla and Teg. A silent and sullen Duncan tagged along as though he feared to be left alone. Each new discovery awed them or shocked them.

Twenty-one skeletons preserved in transparent plaz along a wall near the core! Macabre observers of everyone who passed through there to the machinery chambers and the nullentropy bins.

Patrin had warned Teg about the skeletons. On one of his first youthful examinations of the globe, Patrin had found records that said the dead ones were the artisans who had built the place, all slain by the Harkonnens to preserve the secret.

Altogether, the globe was a remarkable achievement, an enclosure cut out of Time, sealed away from everything external. After all of these millennia, its frictionless machinery still created a mimetic projection that even the most modern instruments could not distinguish from the background of dirt and rock.

"The Sisterhood must acquire this place intact!" Lucilla kept saying. "It's a treasure house! They even kept their family's breeding records!"

That wasn't all the Harkonnens had preserved here. Teg kept finding himself repelled by subtle and gross touches on almost everything in the globe. Like that clock! Clothing, instruments for maintaining the environment, for education and pleasure—everything had been marked by that Harkonnen compulsion to flaunt their uncaring sense of superiority to all other people and all other standards.

Once more, Teg thought of Patrin as a youth in this place, probably no older than the ghola. What had prompted Patrin to keep it a secret even from his wife of so many years? Patrin had never touched on the reasons for secrecy, but Teg made his own deductions. An unhappy childhood. The need for his own secret place. Friends who were not friends but only people waiting to sneer at him. None of those companions could be permitted to share such a wonder. It was his! This was more than a place of lonely security. It had been Patrin's private token of victory.

"I spent many happy hours there, Bashar. Everything still works. The records are ancient but excellent once you grasp the dialect. There is much knowledge in the place. But you will understand when you get there. You will understand many things I have never told you."

The antique practice floor showed signs of Patrin's frequent usage. He had changed the weapons coding on some of the automata in a way Teg recognized. The time-counters told of muscle-torturing hours at the complicated exercises. This globe explained those abilities which Teg had always found so remarkable in Patrin. Natural talents had been honed here.

The automata of the no-globe were another matter.

Most of them represented defiance of the ancient proscriptions against such devices. More than that, some had been designed for pleasure functions that confirmed the more revolting stories Teg had heard about the Harkonnens. Pain as pleasure! In its own way, these things explained the primly unbending morality that Patrin had taken away from Gammu.

Revulsion created its own patterns.

Duncan took a deep swallow of his drink and looked at Teg over the lip of the cup.

"Why did you come down here alone when I asked you to complete that last round of exercises?" Teg asked.

"The exercises made no sense." Duncan put down his cup.

Well, Taraza, you were wrong, Teg thought. *He has struck out for complete independence sooner than you predicted.*

Also, Duncan had stopped addressing his Bashar as "sir."

"You disobey me?"

"Not exactly."

"Then *exactly* what is it you're doing?"

"I have to *know*!"

"You won't like me very much when you do know."

Duncan looked startled. "Sir?"

Ahhhh, the "sir" is back!

"I have been preparing you for certain kinds of very intense pain," Teg said. "It is necessary before we can restore your original memories."

"Pain, sir?"

"We know of no other way to bring back the original Duncan Idaho—the one who died."

"Sir, if you can do that, I will be nothing but grateful."

"So you say. But you may very well see me then as just one more whip in the hands of those who have recalled you to life."

"Isn't it better to know, sir?"

Teg passed the back of a hand across his mouth. "If you hate me . . . can't say I'd blame you."

"Sir, if you were in my place, is that how you would feel?" Duncan's posture, tone of voice, facial expression—all showed trembling confusion.

So far so good, Teg thought. The procedural steps were laid out with a precision that demanded that every response from the ghola be interpreted with care. Duncan was now filled with uncertainty. He wanted something and he feared that thing.

"I'm only your teacher, not your father!" Teg said.

Duncan recoiled at the harsh tone. "Aren't you my friend?"

"That's a two-way street. The original Duncan Idaho will have to answer that for himself."

A veiled look entered Duncan's eyes. "Will I remember this place, the Keep, Schwangyu and . . ."

"Everything. You'll undergo a kind of double-vision memory for a time, but you'll remember it all."

A cynical look came over the young face and, when he spoke, it was with bitterness. "So you and I will become comrades."

All of a Bashar's command and presence in his voice, Teg followed the reawakening instructions precisely.

"I'm not particularly interested in becoming your comrade." He fixed a searching glare on Duncan's face. "You might make Bashar someday. I think it possible you have the right stuff. But I'll be long dead by then."

"You're only comrades with Bashars?"

"Patrin was my comrade and he never rose above squad leader."

Duncan looked into his empty cup and then at Teg. "Why didn't you order something to drink? You worked hard up there, too."

Perceptive question. It did not do to underestimate this youth. He knew that food sharing was one of the most ancient rituals of association.

"The smell of yours was enough," Teg said. "Old memories. I don't need them right now."

"Then why did you come down here?"

There it was, revealed in the young voice—hope and fear. He wanted Teg to say a particular thing.

"I wanted to take a careful measurement of how far those exercises have carried you," Teg said. "I needed to come down here and look at you."

"Why so careful?"

Hope and fear! It was time for the precise shift of focus.

"I've never trained a ghola before."

Ghola. The word lay suspended between them, hanging on the cooking smells that the globe's filters had not scrubbed from the air. *Ghola!* It was laced with spice pungency from Duncan's empty cup.

Duncan leaned forward without speaking, his expression eager. Lucilla's observation came into Teg's mind: *"He knows how to use silence."*

When it became obvious that Teg would not expand on that simple statement, Duncan sank back with a disappointed look. The left corner of his mouth turned downward, a sullen, festering expression. Everything focused inward the way it had to be.

"You did not come down here to be alone," Teg said. "You came here to hide. You're still hiding in there and you think no one will ever find you."

Duncan put a hand in front of his mouth. It was a signal gesture for which Teg had been waiting. The instructions for this moment were clear: *"The ghola wants the original memories wakened and fears this utterly. That is the major barrier you must sunder."*

"Take your hand away from your mouth!" Teg ordered.

Duncan dropped his hand as though it had been burned. He stared at Teg like a trapped animal.

"Speak the truth," Teg's instructions warned. *"At this moment, every sense afire, the ghola will see into your heart."*

"I want you to know," Teg said, "that what the Sisterhood has ordered me to do to you, that this is distasteful to me."

Duncan appeared to crouch into himself. "What did they order you to do?"

"The skills I was ordered to give you are flawed."

"F-flawed?"

"Part of it was comprehensive training, the intellectual part. In that respect, you have been brought to the level of regimental commander."

"Better than Patrin?"

"Why must you be better than Patrin?"

"Wasn't he your comrade?"

"Yes."

"You said he never rose above squad leader!"

"Patrin was fully capable of taking over command of an entire multi-planet force. He was a tactical magician whose wisdom I employed on many occasions."

"But you said he never—"

"It was his choice. The low rank gave him the common touch that we both found useful many times."

"Regimental commander?" Duncan's voice was little more than a whisper. He stared at the tabletop.

"You have an intellectual grasp of the functions, a bit impetuous but experience usually smooths that out. Your weapons skills are superior for your age."

Still not looking at Teg, Duncan asked: "What is my age . . . sir?"

Just as the instructions cautioned: *"The ghola will dance all around the central issue. 'What is my age?' How old is a ghola?"*

His voice coldly accusing, Teg said: "If you want to know your ghola-age, why don't you ask that?"

"Wha . . . what is that age, sir?"

There was such a weight of misery in the youthful voice that Teg felt tears start in the corners of his eyes. He had been warned about this, too. *"Do not reveal too much compassion!"* Teg covered the moment by clearing his throat. He said: "That's a question only you can answer."

The instructions were explicit: *"Turn it back on him! Keep him focused inward. Emotional pain is as important to this process as the physical pain."*

A deep sigh shuddered through Duncan. He closed his eyes tightly. When Teg had first seated himself at the table, Duncan had thought: *Is this the moment? Will he do it now?* But Teg's accusing tone, the verbal attacks, were completely unexpected. And now Teg sounded patronizing.

He's patronizing me!

Cynical anger surged into Duncan. Did Teg think him such a fool that he could be taken in by the most common ploy of a commander? *Tone of voice and attitude alone can subjugate another's will.* Duncan sensed something else in the patronizing, though: a core of plasteel that would not be penetrated. Integrity . . . purpose. And Duncan had seen the tears start, the covering gesture.

Opening his eyes and looking directly at Teg, Duncan said: "I don't mean to be disrespectful or ungrateful or rude, sir. But I can't go on without answers."

Teg's instructions were clear: *"You will know when the ghola reaches the point of desperation. No ghola will try to hide this. It is intrinsic to their psyche. You will recognize it in voice and posture."*

Duncan had almost reached the critical point. Silence was mandatory for Teg now. Force Duncan to ask his questions, to take his own course.

Duncan said: "Did you know that I once thought of killing Schwangyu?"

Teg opened his mouth and closed it without a sound. *Silence!* But the lad was serious!

"I was afraid of her," Duncan said. "I don't like being afraid." He lowered his gaze. "You once told me that we only hate what's really dangerous to us."

"He will approach it and retreat, approach and retreat. Wait until he plunges."

"I don't hate you," Duncan said, looking once more at Teg. "I resented it when you said *ghola* to my face. But Lucilla's right: We should never resent the truth even when it hurts."

Teg rubbed his own lips. The desire to speak filled him but it was not yet plunge time.

"Doesn't it surprise you that I considered killing Schwangyu?" Duncan asked.

Teg held himself rigid. Even the shaking of his head would be taken as a response.

"I thought of slipping something into her drink," Duncan said. "But that's a coward's way and I'm not a coward. Whatever else, I'm not that."

Teg remained silently immobile.

"I think you really care what happens to me, Bashar," Duncan said. "But you're right: we will never be comrades. If I survive, I will surpass you. Then . . . it will be too late for us to be comrades. You spoke the truth."

Teg was unable to prevent himself from inhaling a deep breath of Mentat realization: no avoiding the signs of strength in the ghola. Somewhere recently, perhaps in this very alcove just now, the youth had ceased being a youth and had become a man. The realization saddened Teg. It went so fast! No normal growing-up in between.

"Lucilla does not really care what happens to me the way you do," Duncan said. "She's just following her orders from that Mother Superior, Taraza."

Not yet! Teg cautioned himself. He wet his lips with his tongue.

"You have been obstructing Lucilla's orders," Duncan said. "What is it she's supposed to do to me?"

The moment had come. "What do you think she's supposed to do?" Teg demanded.

"I don't know!"

"The original Duncan Idaho would know."

"You know! Why won't you tell me?"

"I'm only supposed to help restore your original memories."

"Then do it!"

"Only you can really do it."

"I don't know how!"

Teg sat forward on the edge of his chair, but did not speak. *Plunge point?* He sensed something lacking in Duncan's desperation.

"You know I can read lips, sir," Duncan said. "Once I went up to the tower observatory. I saw Lucilla and Schwangyu down below talking. Schwangyu said: 'Never mind that he's so young! You've had your orders.'"

Once more cautiously silent, Teg stared back at Duncan. It was like Duncan to move around secretly in the Keep, spying, seeking knowledge. And he had seated himself in that memory-mode now, not realizing that he still was spying and seeking . . . but in a different way.

"I didn't think she was supposed to kill me," Duncan said. "But you know what she was supposed to do because you've been obstructing her." Duncan pounded a fist on the table. "Answer me, damn you!"

Ahhhh, full desperation!

"I can only tell you that what she intends conflicts with my orders. I was commanded by Taraza herself to strengthen you and guard you from harm."

"But you said my training was . . . was flawed!"

"Necessary. It was done to prepare you for your original memories."

"What am I supposed to do?"

"You already know."

"I don't, I tell you! Please teach me!"

"You do many things without having been taught them. Did we teach you disobedience?"

"Please help me!" It was a desperate wail.

Teg forced himself to chilly remoteness. "What in the nether hell do you think I'm doing?"

Duncan clenched both fists and pounded them on the table, making his cup dance. He glared at Teg. Abruptly, an odd expression came over Duncan's face—something grasping in his eyes.

"Who are you?" Duncan whispered.

The key question!

Teg's voice was a lash striking out at a suddenly defenseless victim: "Who do you think I am?"

A look of utter desperation twisted Duncan's features. He managed only a gasping stutter: "You're . . . you're . . ."

"Duncan! Stop this nonsense!" Teg jumped to his feet and stared down with assumed rage.

"You're . . ."

Teg's right hand shot out in a swift arc. The open palm cracked against Duncan's cheek. "How dare you disobey me?" Left hand out, another rocking slap. "How *dare* you?"

Duncan reacted so swiftly that Teg experienced an electric instant of absolute shock. *Such speed!* Although there were separate elements in Duncan's attack, it occurred in one fluid blur: a leap upward, both feet on the chair, rocking the chair, using that motion to slash the right arm down at Teg's vulnerable shoulder nerves.

Responding out of trained instincts, Teg dodged sideways and flailed his left leg over the table into Duncan's groin. Teg still did not completely escape. The heel of Duncan's hand continued downward to strike beside the knee of Teg's flailing leg. It numbed the whole leg.

Duncan sprawled across the tabletop, trying to slide backward in spite of the disabling kick. Teg supported himself, left hand on table, and chopped with the other hand to the base of Duncan's spine, into the nexus deliberately weakened by the exercises of the past few days.

Duncan groaned as paralyzing agony shot through his body. Another person would have been immobilized, screaming, but Duncan merely groaned as he clawed toward Teg, continuing the attack.

Relentless in the necessities of the moment, Teg proceeded to create greater pain in his victim, making sure each time that Duncan saw the attacker's face at the instant of greatest agony.

"Watch his eyes!" the instructions warned. And Bellonda, reinforcing the procedure, had cautioned: *"His eyes will seem to look through you but he will call you Leto."*

Much later. Teg found difficulty in recalling each detail of his obedience to the reawakening procedure. He knew that he continued to function as commanded but his memory went elsewhere, leaving the flesh free to carry out his orders. Oddly, his trick memory fastened onto another act of disobedience: the Cerbol Revolt, himself at middle age but already a Bashar with a formidable reputation. He had donned his best uniform without its medals (a subtle touch, that) and had presented himself in the scorching noon heat of Cerbol's battle-plowed fields. Completely unarmed in the path of the advancing rebels!

Many among the attackers owed him their lives. Most of them had once given him their deepest allegiance. Now, they were in violent disobedience. And Teg's presence in their path said to those advancing soldiers:

"I will not wear the medals that tell what I did for you when we were comrades. I will not be anything that says I am one of you. I wear only the uniform that announces that I am still the Bashar. Kill me if that is how far you will carry your disobedience."

When most of the attacking force threw down their arms and

came forward, some of their commanders bent the knee to their old Bashar and he remonstrated: "You never needed to bow to me or get on your knees! Your new leaders have taught you bad habits."

Later, he told the rebels he shared some of their grievances. Cerbol had been badly misused. But he also warned them:

"One of the most dangerous things in the universe is an ignorant people with real grievances. That is nowhere near as dangerous, however, as an informed and intelligent society with grievances. The damage that vengeful intelligence can wreak, you cannot even imagine. The Tyrant would seem a benevolent father figure by comparison with what you were about to create!"

It was all true, of course, but in a Bene Gesserit context, and it helped little with what he was commanded to do to the Duncan Idaho ghola—creating mental and physical agony in an almost helpless victim.

Easiest to recall was the look in Duncan's eyes. They did not change focus, but glared directly up into Teg's face, even at the instant of the final screaming shout:

"Damn you, Leto! What are you doing?"

He called me Leto.

Teg limped backward two steps. His left leg tingled and ached where Duncan had struck it. Teg realized that he was panting and at the end of his reserves. He was much too old for such exertions and the things he had just done made him feel dirty. The reawakening procedure was thoroughly fixed in his awareness, though. He knew that gholas once had been awakened by conditioning them unconsciously to attempt murder on someone they loved. The ghola psyche, shattered and forced to reassemble, was always psychologically scarred. This new technique left the scars in the one who managed the process.

Slowly, moving against the outcry of muscles and nerves that had been stunned by agony, Duncan slid backward off the table and stood leaning against his chair, trembling and glaring at Teg.

Teg's instructions said: *"You must stand very quietly. Do not move. Let him look at you as he will."*

Teg stood unmoving as he had been instructed. Memory of the Cerbol Revolt left his mind: He knew what he had done then and now. In a way, the two times were similar. He had told the rebels no ultimate truths (if such existed); only enough to lure them back into the fold. Pain and its predictable consequences. *"This is for your own good."*

Was it really good, what they did to this Duncan Idaho ghola?

Teg wondered what was occurring in Duncan's consciousness. Teg had been told as much as was known about these moments, but he could see that the words were inadequate. Duncan's eyes and face gave abundant evidence of internal turmoil—a hideous twisting of mouth and cheeks, the gaze darting this way and that.

Slowly, exquisite in its slowness, Duncan's face relaxed. His body continued to tremble. He felt the throbbing of his body as a distant thing, aches and darting pains that had happened to someone else. He was here, though, in this immediate moment—whatever and wherever this was. His memories would not mesh. He felt suddenly out of place in flesh too young, not fitted to his pre-ghola existence. The darting and twisting of awareness was all internal now.

Teg's instructors had said: *"He will have ghola-imposed filters on his pre-ghola memories. Some of the original memories will come flooding back. Other recollections will return more slowly. There will be no meshing, though, until he recalls that original moment of death."* Bellonda had then given Teg the known details of that fatal moment.

"Sardaukar," Duncan whispered. He looked around him at the Harkonnen symbols that permeated the no-globe. "The Emperor's crack troops wearing Harkonnen uniforms!" A wolfish grin twisted his mouth. "How they must have hated that!"

Teg remained silently watchful.

"They killed me," Duncan said. It was a flatly unemotional statement, all the more chilling for its positive delivery. A violent shudder passed through him and the trembling subsided. "At least a dozen of them in that little room." He looked directly at Teg. "One of them got through at me like a meat cleaver right down on my head." He hesitated, his throat working convulsively. His gaze remained on Teg. "Did I buy Paul enough time to escape?"

"Answer all of his questions truthfully."

"He escaped."

Now, they came to a testing moment. Where had the Tleilaxu acquired the Idaho cells? The Sisterhood's tests said they were original, but suspicions remained. The Tleilaxu had done something of their own to this ghola. His memories could be a valuable clue to that thing.

"But the Harkonnens . . ." Duncan said. His memories from the Keep meshed. "Oh, yes. Oh, *yes!*" A fierce laugh shook him. He sent a roaring victory shout at the long-dead Baron Vladimir Harkonnen: "I paid you back, Baron! Oh, I did it to you for all of the ones you destroyed!"

"You remember the Keep and the things we taught you?" Teg asked.

A puzzled frown drew deep crease lines across Duncan's forehead. Emotional pain warred with his physical pains. He nodded in response to Teg's question. There were two lives, one that had been walled off behind the axlotl tanks and another . . . another . . . Duncan felt incomplete. Something remained suppressed within him. The reawakening was not finished. He stared angrily at Teg. Was there more? Teg had been brutal. Necessary brutality? Was this how you had to restore a ghola?

"I . . ." Duncan shook his head from side to side like a great wounded animal in front of the hunter.

"Do you have all of your memories?" Teg insisted.

"All? Oh, yes. I remember Gammu when it was Giedi Prime—the oil-soaked, blood-soaked hell hole of the Imperium! Yes, indeed, Bashar. I was your dutiful student. Regimental commander!" Again, he laughed, throwing his head back in an oddly adult gesture for that young body.

Teg experienced the sudden release of a deep satisfaction, far deeper than relief. It had worked as they said it would.

"Do you hate me?" he asked.

"Hate you? Didn't I tell you I would be grateful?"

Abruptly, Duncan lifted his hands and peered at them. He shifted his gaze downward at his youthful body. "What a temptation!" he muttered. He dropped his hands and focused on Teg's face, tracing the lines of identity. "Atreides," he said. "You're all so damned alike!"

"Not all," Teg said.

"I'm not talking about appearance, Bashar." His eyes went out of focus. "I asked my age." There was a long silence, then: "Gods of the deep! So much time has passed!"

Teg said what he had been instructed to say: "The Sisterhood has need of you."

"In this immature body? What am I supposed to do?"

"Truly, I don't know, Duncan. The body will mature and I presume a Reverend Mother will explain matters to you."

"Lucilla?"

Abruptly, Duncan looked up at the ornate ceiling, then at the alcove and its baroque clock. He remembered coming here with Teg and Lucilla. This place was the same but it was different. "Harkonnens," he whispered. He sent a glowering look at Teg. "Do you know how many of my family the Harkonnens tortured and killed?"

"One of Taraza's Archivists gave me a report."

"A report? You think words can tell it?"

"No. But that was the only answer I had to your question."

"Damn you, Bashar! Why do you Atreides always have to be so truthful and honorable?"

"I think it's bred into us."

"That's quite right." The voice was Lucilla's and came from behind Teg.

Teg did not turn. How much had she heard? How long had she been there?

Lucilla came up to stand beside Teg but her attention was on Duncan. "I see that you've done it, Miles."

"Taraza's orders to the letter," Teg said.

"You have been very clever, Miles," she said. "Much more clever than I suspected you could be. That mother of yours should have been severely punished for what she taught you."

"Ahhhh, Lucilla the seductress," Duncan said. He glanced at Teg and returned his attention to Lucilla. "Yes, now I can answer my other question—what she's supposed to do."

"They're called Imprinters," Teg said.

"Miles," Lucilla said, "if you have complicated my task in ways that prevent me from carrying out my orders, I will have you roasted on a skewer."

The emotionless quality of her voice sent a shudder through Teg. He knew her threat was a metaphor, but the implications in the threat were real.

"A punishment banquet!" Duncan said. "How nice."

Teg addressed himself to Duncan: "There's nothing romantic about what we've done to you, Duncan. I've assisted the Bene Gesserit in more than one assignment that left me feeling dirty, but never dirtier than this one."

"Silence!" Lucilla ordered. The full force of Voice was in the command.

Teg let it flow through him and past him as his mother had taught, then: "Those of us who give our true loyalty to the Sisterhood have only one concern: survival of the Bene Gesserit. Not survival of any individual but of the Sisterhood itself. Deceptions, dishonesties— those are empty words when the question is the Sisterhood's survival."

"Damn that mother of yours, Miles!" Lucilla paid him the compliment of not hiding her rage.

Duncan stared at Lucilla. Who was she? Lucilla? He felt his memories stirring of themselves. Lucilla was not the same person . . . not the same at all, and yet . . . bits and pieces were the same. Her voice. Her features. Abruptly, he saw again the face of the woman he had glimpsed on the wall of his room at the Keep.

"*Duncan, my sweet Duncan.*"

Tears fell from Duncan's eyes. His own mother—another Harkonnen victim. Tortured . . . who knew what else? Never seen again by her "sweet Duncan."

"Gods, I wish I had one of them to kill right now," Duncan moaned.

Once more, he focused on Lucilla. Tears blurred her features and made the comparisons easier. Lucilla's face blended with that of the Lady Jessica, beloved of Leto Atreides. Duncan glanced at Teg, back to Lucilla, shaking the tears from his eyes as he moved. The memory faces dissolved into that of the real Lucilla standing in front of him. Similarities . . . but never the same. Never again the same.

Imprinter.

He could guess the meaning. A pure Duncan Idaho wildness arose in him. "Is it my child you want in your womb, Imprinter? I know you're not called mothers for nothing."

Her voice cold, Lucilla said: "We'll discuss it another time."

"Let us discuss it in a congenial place," Duncan said, "Perhaps I'll sing you a song. Not as good as old Gurney Halleck would do it but good enough to prepare for a little bedsport."

"You find this amusing?" she asked.

"Amusing? No, but I *am* reminded of Gurney. Tell me, Bashar, have you brought him back from the dead, too?"

"Not to my knowledge," Teg said.

"Ahhhh, there was a singing man!" Duncan said. "He could be killing you while he sang and never miss a note."

Her manner still icy, Lucilla said: "We of the Bene Gesserit have learned to avoid music. It evokes too many confusing emotions. Memory-emotions, of course."

It was meant to awe him with a reminder of all those Other Memories and the Bene Gesserit powers these implied but Duncan only laughed louder.

"What a shame that is," he said. "You miss so much of life." And he began humming an old Halleck refrain:

"Review friends, troops long past review . . ."

But his mind whirled elsewhere with the rich new flavor of these reborn moments and once more he felt the eager touch of something powerful that remained buried within him. Whatever it was, it was violent and it concerned Lucilla, the Imprinter. In imagination, he saw her dead and her body awash in blood.

People always want something more than immediate joy or that deeper sense called happiness. This is one of the secrets by which we shape the fulfillment of our designs. The something more assumes amplified power with people who cannot give it a name or who (most often the case) do not even suspect its existence. Most people only react unconsciously to such hidden forces. Thus, we have only to call a calculated *something more* into existence, define it and give it shape, then people will follow.

—LEADERSHIP SECRETS OF THE BENE GESSERIT

With a silent Waff about twenty paces ahead of them, Odrade and Sheeana walked down a weed-fringed road beside a spice-storage yard. All of them wore new desert robes and glistening stillsuits. The gray nulplaz fence that defined the yard beside them held bits of grass and cottony seedpods in its meshes. Looking at the seedpods, Odrade thought of them as life trying to break through a human intervention.

Behind them, the blocky buildings that had arisen around Dar-es-Balat baked in the sunlight of early afternoon. Hot dry air burned her throat when she inhaled too quickly. Odrade felt dizzy and at war within herself. Thirst nagged at her. She walked as though balanced on the edge of a precipice. The situation she had created at Taraza's command might explode momentarily.

How fragile it is!

Three forces balanced, not really supporting each other but joined by motives that could shift in an instant and topple the whole alliance. The military people sent by Taraza did not reassure Odrade. Where was Teg? Where was Burzmali? For that matter, where was the ghola? He should be here by now. Why had she been ordered to delay matters?

Today's venture would certainly delay matters! Although it had Taraza's blessing, Odrade thought this excursion into the desert of the worms might be a permanent delay. And there was Waff. If he survived, would there be any pieces for him to pick up?

Despite the healing applications of the Sisterhood's best quicknit amplifiers, Waff said his arms still ached where Odrade had broken them. He was not complaining, merely providing information. He appeared to accept their fragile alliance, even the modifications that incorporated the Rakian priestly cabal. No doubt he was reassured that one of his own Face Dancers occupied the High Priest's bench in the guise of Tuek. Waff spoke forcefully when he demanded his "breeding mothers" from the Bene Gesserit and, consequently, withheld his part of their bargain.

"Only a small delay while the Sisterhood reviews the new agreement," Odrade explained. "Meanwhile . . ."

Today was "meanwhile."

Odrade put aside her misgivings and began to enter the mood of this venture. Waff's behavior fascinated her, especially his reaction on meeting Sheeana: quite plainly fearful and more than a little in awe.

The minion of his Prophet.

Odrade glanced sideways at the girl walking dutifully beside her. There was the real leverage for shaping these events into the Bene Gesserit design.

The Sisterhood's breakthrough into the reality behind Tleilaxu behavior excited Odrade. Waff's fanatic "true faith" gained shape with each new response from him. She felt fortunate just to be here studying a Tleilaxu Master in a religious setting. The very grit under Waff's feet ignited behavior that she had been trained to identify.

We should have guessed, Odrade thought. *The manipulations of our own Missionaria Protectiva should have told us how the Tleilaxu did it:*

keeping themselves to themselves, blocking off every intrusion for all of those plodding millennia.

They did not appear to have copied the Bene Gesserit structure. And what other force could do such a thing? It was a religion. The Great Belief!

Unless the Tleilaxu are using their ghola system as a kind of immortality.

Taraza could be right. Reincarnated Tleilaxu Masters would not be like Reverend Mothers—no Other Memories, only personal memories. But prolonged!

Fascinating!

Odrade looked ahead at Waff's back. *Plodding.* It appeared to come naturally to him. She recalled that he called Sheeana "Alyama." Another confirming linguistic insight into Waff's Great Belief. It meant "Blessed One." The Tleilaxu had kept an ancient language not only alive but unchanged.

Did Waff not know that only powerful forces such as religions did that?

We have the roots of your obsession in our grasp, Waff! It is not unlike some that we have created. We know how to manipulate such things for our own purposes.

Taraza's communication burned in Odrade's awareness: "The Tleilaxu plan is transparent: Ascendancy. The human universe must be made into a Tleilaxu universe. They could not hope to achieve such a goal without help from the Scattering. Ergo."

The Mother Superior's reasoning could not be denied. Even the opposition within that deep schism that threatened to shatter the Sisterhood agreed. But the thought of those human masses in the Scattering, their numbers exploding exponentially, produced a lonely sense of desperation in Odrade.

We are so few compared to them.

Sheeana stooped and picked up a pebble. She looked at it a moment and then threw it at the fence beside them. The pebble sailed through the meshes without touching them.

Odrade took a firmer grip on herself. The sounds of their footsteps on the blown sand that drifted across this little-used roadway seemed suddenly over-loud. The spindly causeway leading out over the Dar-es-Balat ring-qanat and moat lay no more than two hundred paces ahead at the end of this narrow road.

Sheeana spoke: "I am doing this because you ordered it, Mother. But I still don't know why."

Because this is the crucible where we test Waff and, through him, reshape the Tleilaxu!

"It is a demonstration," Odrade said.

That was true. It was not the whole truth, but it served.

Sheeana walked head down, gaze intent on where she placed each step. Was this how she always approached her Shaitan? Odrade wondered. Thoughtful and remote?

Odrade heard a faint *thwocking* sound high up behind her. The watchful ornithopters were arriving. They would keep their distance, but many eyes would observe this *demonstration*.

"I will dance," Sheeana said. "That usually calls a big one."

Odrade felt her heartbeat quicken. Would the "big one" continue to obey Sheeana despite the presence of two companions?

This is suicidal madness!

But it had to be done: Taraza's orders.

Odrade glanced at the fenced spice yard beside them. The place appeared oddly familiar. More than déjà vu. Inner certainty informed by Other Memories told her this place remained virtually unchanged from ancient times. The design of the spice silos in the yard was as old as Rakis: oval tanks on tall legs, metal and plaz insects waiting stilt-legged to leap upon their prey. She suspected an unconscious message from the original designers: *Melange is both boon and bane.*

Beneath the silos, a sandy wasteland where no growth was permitted spread out beside mud-walled buildings, an amoeba arm of Dar-es-Balat reaching almost to the qanat edge. The Tyrant's long-hidden no-globe had produced a teeming religious community that hid most of its activities behind windowless walls and underground.

The secret working of our unconscious desires!

Once more, Sheeana spoke: "Tuek is different."

Odrade saw Waff's head lift sharply. He had heard. He would be thinking: *Can we conceal things from the Prophet's messenger?*

Too many people already knew that a Face Dancer masqueraded as Tuek, Odrade thought. The priestly cabal, of course, believed they were giving the Tleilaxu enough netting in which to snare not only the Bene Tleilax but the Sisterhood as well.

Odrade smelled the biting odors of chemicals that had been used to kill wild growth in the spice storage yard. The odors forced her attention back to necessities. She did not dare indulge in mental wanderings out here! It would be so easy for the Sisterhood to become caught in its own trap.

Sheeana stumbled and emitted a small cry, more irritation than pain. Waff turned his head sharply and looked at Sheeana before returning his attention to the roadway. The child had merely stumbled on a break in the road surface, he saw. Drifted sand concealed places where the roadway had been cracked. The faery structure of the causeway ahead of him appeared sound, however. Not substantial enough to support one of the Prophet's descendants, but more than enough for a supplicant human to cross it into the desert.

Waff thought of himself chiefly as a supplicant.

I come as a beggar into the land of thy messenger, God.

He had his suspicions about Odrade. The Reverend Mother had brought him here to drain him of his knowledge before killing him. *With God's help, I may surprise her yet.* He knew his body was proof against an Ixian Probe, although she obviously did not have such a cumbersome device on her person. But it was the strength of his own will and confidence in God's grace that reassured Waff.

And what if the hand they hold out to us is held out in sincerity?

That, too, would be God's doing.

Alliance with the Bene Gesserit, firm control of Rakis: What a dream that was! The Shariat ascendant at last and the Bene Gesserit as missionaries.

When Sheeana again missed her footing and uttered another small sound of complaint, Odrade said: "Don't favor yourself, child!"

Odrade saw Waff's shoulders stiffen. He did not like that peremptory manner with his "Blessed One." There was backbone in the little man. Odrade recognized it as the strength of fanaticism. Even if the worm came to kill him, Waff would not flee. Faith in God's will would carry him directly into his own death—unless he were shaken out of his religious security.

Odrade suppressed a smile. She could follow his thinking process: *God will soon reveal His Purpose.*

But Waff was thinking about his cells growing in the slow renewal at Bandalong. No matter what happened here, his cells would carry on for the Bene Tleilax . . . and for God—a serial-Waff always serving the Great Belief.

"I can smell Shaitan, you know," Sheeana said.

"Right now?" Odrade looked up at the causeway ahead of them. Waff already was a few steps onto that arching surface.

"No, only when he comes," Sheeana said.

"Of course you can, child. Anyone could."

"I can smell him a long way off."

Odrade inhaled deeply through her nose, sorting the smells from the background of burnt flint: faint whiffs of melange . . . ozone, something distinctly acid. She motioned for Sheeana to precede her single-file onto the causeway. Waff was holding his steady twenty paces ahead. The causeway dipped down to the desert some sixty meters ahead of him.

I will taste the sand at the first opportunity, Odrade thought. *That will tell me many things.*

As she mounted the causeway over the water moat, she looked off to the southwest at a low barrier along the horizon. Abruptly, Odrade was confronted by a compelling Other Memory. There was none of the crispness in it of actual vision, but she recognized it—a mingling of images from the deepest sources within her.

Damn! she thought. *Not now!*

There was no escape. Such intrusions came with purpose, an unavoidable demand upon her awareness.

Warning!

She squinted at the horizon, allowing the Other Memory to superimpose itself: a long-ago high barrier far away out there . . . people moving along the top of it. There was a faery bridge in that memory-distance, insubstantial and beautiful. It linked one part of that vanished barrier to another part and she knew without seeing it that a river ran beneath that long-gone bridge. The Idaho River! Now, the superimposed image provided movement: objects falling from the bridge. They were too far away to identify but she had the labels for this image projection now. With a sense of horror and elation, she identified that scene.

The faery bridge was collapsing! Tumbling into the river below it.

This vision was not some random destruction. This was classical violence carried in many memories, which had come down to her in the moments of spice agony. Odrade could classify the finely tuned components of the image: Thousands of her ancestors had watched that scene in imaginative reconstruction. Not a real visual memory but an assemblage of accurate reports.

That is where it happened!

Odrade stopped and let the image projections have their way with her awareness. *Warning!* Something dangerous had been identified. She did not try to dig out the warning's substance. If she did that, she knew it could fall apart in skeins, any one of which might be relevant, but the original certainty would vanish.

This thing out there was fixed in the Atreides history. Leto II, the Tyrant, had fallen to his dissolution from that faery bridge. The great worm of Rakis, the Tyrant God Emperor himself, had been tumbled from that bridge on his wedding peregrination.

There! Right there in the Idaho River beneath his destroyed bridge, the Tyrant had been submerged in his own agony. Right there, the transubstantiation from which the Divided God was born—it all began there.

Why is that a warning?

Bridge and river had vanished from this land. The high wall that had enclosed the Tyrant's dryland Sareer was eroded into a broken line on a heat-shimmering horizon.

If a worm came now with its encapsulated pearl of the Tyrant's forever-dreaming memory, would that memory be dangerous? So Taraza's opposition in the Sisterhood argued.

"He will awaken!"

Taraza and her advisors denied even the possibility.

Still, this claxon from Odrade's Other Memories could not be shunted aside.

"Reverend Mother, why have we stopped?"

Odrade felt her awareness lurch back into an immediate present that demanded her attention. Out there in that warning vision was where the Tyrant's endless dream began but other dreams intruded. Sheeana stood in front of her with a puzzled expression.

"I was looking out there." Odrade pointed. "That was where Shai-hulud began, Sheeana."

Waff stopped at the end of the causeway, one step short of the encroaching sand and now about forty paces ahead of Odrade and Sheeana. Odrade's voice brought him to stiff alertness but he did not turn. Odrade could feel the displeasure in his posture. Waff would not like even a hint of cynicism directed at his Prophet. He always suspected cynicism from Reverend Mothers. Especially where religious matters were concerned. Waff was not yet ready to accept that the long-detested and feared Bene Gesserit might share his Great Belief. That ground would have to be filled in with care—as was always the way with the Missionaria Protectiva.

"They say there was a big river," Sheeana said.

Odrade heard the lilting note of derision in Sheeana's voice. The child learned quickly!

Waff turned and scowled at them. He heard it, too. What was he thinking about Sheeana now?

Odrade held Sheeana's shoulder with one hand and pointed with the other. "There was a bridge right there. The great wall of the Sareer was left open there to permit the passage of the Idaho River. The bridge spanned that break."

Sheeana sighed. "A real river," she whispered.

"Not a qanat and too big for a canal," Odrade said.

"I've never seen a river," Sheeana said.

"That was where they dumped Shai-hulud into the river," Odrade said. She gestured to her left. "Over on this side, many kilometers in that direction, he built his palace."

"There's nothing over there but sand," Sheeana said.

"The palace was torn down in the Famine Times," Odrade said. "People thought there was a hoard of spice in it. They were wrong, of course. He was much too clever for that."

Sheeana leaned close to Odrade and whispered: "There is a great treasure of the spice, though. The chantings tell about it. I've heard it many times. My . . . they say it's in a cave."

Odrade smiled. Sheeana referred to the Oral History, of course. And she had almost said: "My father . . ." meaning her real father who had died in this desert. Odrade already had lured that story from the girl.

Still whispering close to Odrade's ear, Sheeana said: "Why is that little man with us? I don't like him."

"It is necessary for the demonstration," Odrade said.

Waff took that moment to step off the causeway onto the first soft slope of open sand. He moved with care but no visible hesitation. Once on the sand, he turned, his eyes glistening in the hot sunlight, and stared first at Sheeana and then at Odrade.

Still that awe in him when he looks at Sheeana, Odrade thought. *What great things he believes he will discover here. He will be restored. And the prestige!*

Sheeana sheltered her eyes with one hand and studied the desert.

"Shaitan likes the heat," Sheeana said. "People hide inside when it's hot but that's when Shaitan comes."

Not Shai-hulud, Odrade thought. *Shaitan! You predicted it well, Tyrant. What else did you know about our times?*

Was it really the Tyrant out there dormant in all of his worm descendants?

None of the analyses Odrade had studied gave a sure explanation of what had driven one human being to make himself into a symbiote with that original worm of Arrakis. What went through his mind in the millennia of that awful transformation? Was any of that, even the smallest fragment, preserved in today's Rakian worms?

"He is near, Mother," Sheeana said. "Do you smell him?"

Waff peered apprehensively at Sheeana.

Odrade inhaled deeply: a rich swelling of cinnamon on the bitter flint undertones. Fire, brimstone—the crystal-banked inferno of the great worm. She stooped and brought up a pinch of blown sand to her tongue. All of the background was there: the Dune of Other Memory and the Rakis of this day.

Sheeana pointed at an angle to her left, directly into the light breeze from the desert. "Out there. We must hurry."

Without waiting for permission from Odrade, Sheeana ran lightly down the causeway, past Waff and out onto the first dune. She stopped there until Odrade and Waff caught up with her. Off the dune face she led them, up another with sand clogging their passage, out along a great curving barracan with wisps of dusty saltation blowing from its crest. Soon, they had put almost a kilometer between themselves and the water-girded security of Dar-es-Balat.

Again, Sheeana stopped.

Waff came to a panting halt behind her. Perspiration glistened where his stillsuit hood crossed his brow.

Odrade stopped a pace behind Waff. She took deep, calming breaths while she peered past Waff to where Sheeana's attention was fixed.

A furious tide of sand had poured across the desert beyond the dune where they stood, driven by a storm wind. Bedrock lay exposed in a long narrow avenue of giant boulders, which lay scattered and upturned like the broken building blocks of a mad promethean. Through this wild maze, the sand had poured like a river, leaving its

signature in deep scratches and gouges, then plunging off a low escarpment to lose itself in more dunes.

"Down there," Sheeana said, pointing at the avenue of bedrock. Off
their dune she went, sliding and scrambling in spilled sand. At the
bottom, she stopped beside a boulder at least twice her height.

Waff and Odrade paused just behind her.

The slipface of another giant barracan, sinuous as the back of a
sporting whale, lifted into the silver-blue sky beside them.

Odrade used the pause to recompose her oxygen balance. That mad
run had made great demands on flesh. Waff, she noted, was red-faced
and breathing deeply. The flinty cinnamon smell was oppressive in the
confined passage. Waff sniffed and rubbed at his nose with the back of
a hand. Sheeana lifted herself on one toe, pivoted and darted ten paces
across the rocky avenue. She put one foot up on the sandy incline of the
outer dune and lifted both arms to the sky. Slowly at first and then with
increasing tempo, she began to dance, moving up onto the sand.

The 'thopter sounds grew louder overhead.

"Listen!" Sheeana called, not pausing in her dance.

It was not to the 'thopters that she called their attention. Odrade
turned her head to present both ears to a new sound intruding on their
rock-tumbled maze.

A sibilant hiss, subterranean and muted by sand—it became louder
with shocking swiftness. There was heat in it, a noticeable warming of
the breeze that twisted down their rocky avenue. The hissing swelled
to a crescendo roar. Abruptly, the crystal-ringed gaping of a gigantic
mouth lifted over the dune directly above Sheeana.

"Shaitan!" Sheeana screamed, not breaking the rhythm of her
dance. "Here I am, Shaitan!"

As it crested the dune, the worm dipped its mouth downward toward Sheeana. Sand cascaded around her feet, forcing her to stop her
dance. The smell of cinnamon filled the rocky defile. The worm
stopped above them.

"Messenger of God," Waff breathed.

Heat dried the perspiration on Odrade's exposed face and made the automatic insulation of her stillsuit puff outward perceptibly. She inhaled deeply, sorting the components behind that cinnamon assault. The air around them was sharp with ozone and swiftly oxygen rich. Her senses at full alert, Odrade stored impressions.

If I survive, she thought.

Yes, this was valuable data. The day might come when others would use it.

Sheeana backed out of the spilled sand onto the exposed rock. She resumed her dance, moving more wildly, flinging her head at each turn. Hair whipped across her face and each time she whirled to confront the worm, she screamed "Shaitan!"

Daintily, like a child on unfamiliar ground, the worm once more moved forward. It slid across the dune crest, curled itself down onto the exposed rock and presented its burning mouth slightly above and about two paces from Sheeana.

As it stopped, Odrade became conscious of the deep furnace rumbling of the worm. She could not tear her gaze away from the reflections of lambent orange flames within the creature. It was a cave of mysterious fire.

Sheeana stopped her dance. She clenched both fists at her sides and stared back at the monster she had summoned.

Odrade took timed breaths, the controlled pacing of a Reverend Mother gathering all of her powers. If this was the end—well, she had obeyed Taraza's orders. Let the Mother Superior learn what she would from the watchers overhead.

"Hello, Shaitan," Sheeana said. "I have brought a Reverend Mother and a man of the Tleilaxu with me."

Waff slumped to his knees and bowed.

Odrade slipped past him to stand beside Sheeana.

Sheeana breathed deeply. Her face was flushed.

Odrade heard the click-ticking of their overworked stillsuits. The hot, cinnamon-drenched air around them was charged with the sounds of this meeting, all dominated by the murmurous burning within the quiescent worm.

Waff came up beside Odrade, his trancelike gaze fixed on the worm.

"I am here," he whispered.

Odrade silently cursed him. Any unwarranted noise could attract this beast onto them. She knew what Waff was thinking, though: No other Tleilaxu had ever stood this close to a descendant of his Prophet. Not even the Rakian priests had ever done this!

With her right hand, Sheeana made a sudden downward gesture. "Down to us, Shaitan!" she said.

The worm lowered its gaping mouth until the internal firepit filled the rocky defile in front of them.

Her voice little more than a whisper, Sheeana said: "See how Shaitan obeys me, Mother?"

Odrade could feel Sheeana's control over the worm, a pulse of hidden language between child and monster. It was uncanny.

Her voice rising in impudent arrogance, Sheeana said: "I will ask Shaitan to let us ride him!" She scrambled up the slipface of the dune beside the worm.

Immediately, the great mouth lifted to follow her movements. "Stay there!" Sheeana shouted. The worm stopped.

It's not her words that command it, Odrade thought. *Something else . . . something else . . .*

"Mother, come with me," Sheeana called.

Thrusting Waff ahead of her, Odrade obeyed. They scrambled up the sandy slope behind Sheeana. Dislodged sand spilled down beside the waiting worm, piling up in the defile. Ahead of them, the worm's tapering tail curved along the dune crest. Sheeana led them at a sand-clotted trot to the very tip of the thing. There, she gripped the leading edge of a ring in the corrugated surface and scrambled up onto her desert beast.

More slowly, Odrade and Waff followed. The worm's warm surface felt non-organic to Odrade, as though it were some Ixian artifact.

Sheeana skipped forward along the back and squatted just behind its mouth where the rings bulged thick and wide.

"Like this," Sheeana said. She leaned forward and clutched beneath the leading edge of a ring, lifting it slightly to expose pink softness underneath.

Waff obeyed her immediately but Odrade moved with more caution, storing impressions. The ring surface was as hard as plascrete and covered with tiny encrustations. Odrade's fingers probed the softness under the leading edge. It pulsed faintly. The surface around them lifted and fell with an almost imperceptible rhythm. Odrade heard a tiny rasping with each movement.

Sheeana kicked the worm surface behind her.

"Shaitan, go!" she said.

The worm did not respond.

"Please, Shaitan," Sheeana pleaded.

Odrade heard the desperation in Sheeana's voice. The child was so confident of her Shaitan but Odrade knew that the girl had been allowed to ride only that first time. Odrade had the full story from death-wish to priestly confusion but none of it told her what would happen next.

Abruptly, the worm lurched into motion. It lifted sharply, twisted to the left and made a tight curve out of the rocky defile, then moved directly away from Dar-es-Balat into the open desert.

"We go with God!" Waff shouted.

The sound of his voice shocked Odrade. Such wildness! She sensed the power in his faith. The thwock-thwock of following ornithopters came from overhead. The wind of their passage whipped past Odrade full of ozone and the hot furnace odors stirred up by the friction of the rushing behemoth.

Odrade glanced over her shoulders at the 'thopters, thinking how easy it would be for enemies to rid this planet of a troublesome child, an equally troublesome Reverend Mother and a despised Tleilaxu—all in one violently vulnerable moment on the open desert. The priestly cabal might attempt it, she knew, hoping that Odrade's own watchers up there would be too late to prevent it.

Would curiosity and fear hold them back?

Odrade admitted to a mighty curiosity herself.

Where is this thing taking us?

Certainly, it was not headed toward Keen. She lifted her head and peered past Sheeana. On the horizon directly ahead lay that telltale indentation of fallen stones, that place where the Tyrant had been spilled from the surface of his faery bridge.

The place of Other Memory warning.

Abrupt revelation locked Odrade's mind. She understood the warning. The Tyrant had died at a place of his own choosing. Many deaths had left their imprint on that place but his the greatest. The Tyrant chose his peregrination route with purpose. Sheeana had not told her worm to go there. It moved that way of its own volition. The magnet of the Tyrant's endless dream drew it back to the place where the dream began.

There was this drylander who was asked which was more important, a literjon of water or a vast pool of water? The drylander thought a moment and then said: "The literjon is more important. No single person could own a great pool of water. But a literjon you could hide under your cloak and run away with it. No one would know."

—THE JOKES OF ANCIENT DUNE,
BENE GESSERIT ARCHIVES

It was a long session in the no-globe's practice hall, Duncan in a mobile cage driving the exercise, adamant that this particular training series would continue until his new body had adapted to the seven central attitudes of combat response against attack from eight directions. His green singlesuit was dark with perspiration. Twenty days they had been at this one lesson!

Teg knew the ancient lore that Duncan revived here but knew it by different names and sequencing. Before they had been into it five days, Teg doubted the superiority of modern methods. Now, he was convinced that Duncan did something completely new—mixing the old with what he had learned in the Keep.

Teg sat at his own control console, as much an observer as a participant. The consoles that guided the dangerous shadow forces in this practice had required mental adjustment by Teg, but he felt familiar with them now and moved the attack with facility and frequent inspiration.

A simmering Lucilla glanced into the hall occasionally. She watched and then left without comment. Teg did not know what Duncan was doing about the Imprinter but there was a feeling that the reawakened ghola played a delaying game with his *seductress*. She would not allow that to continue long, Teg knew, but it was out of his hands. Duncan no longer was "too young" for the Imprinter. That young body carried a mature male mind with experiences from which to make his own decisions.

Duncan and Teg had been on the floor with only one break all morning. Hunger pangs gnawed at Teg but he felt reluctant to halt the session. Duncan's abilities had climbed to a new level today and he was still improving.

Teg, seated in a fixed console's cage seat, twisted the attack forces into a complex maneuver, striking from left, right, and above.

The Harkonnen armory had produced an abundance of these exotic weapons and training instruments, some of which Teg had known only from historical accounts. Duncan knew them all, apparently, and with an intimacy that Teg admired. Hunter-seekers geared to penetrate a force shield were part of the shadow system they used now.

"They automatically slow down to go through the shield," Duncan explained in his young-old voice. "Too fast a strike, of course, and the shield repels."

"Shields of that type have almost gone out of fashion," Teg said. "A few societies maintain them as a kind of sport but otherwise . . ."

Duncan executed a riposte of blurred speed that dropped three hunter-seekers to the floor damaged enough to require the no-globe's maintenance services. He removed the cage and damped the system but left it idling while he came over to Teg, breathing deeply but easily. Looking past Teg, Duncan smiled and nodded. Teg whirled but there was only the flick of Lucilla's gown as she left them.

"It's like a duel," Duncan said. "She tries to thrust through my guard and I counterattack."

"Have a care," Teg said. "That's a full Reverend Mother."

"I've known a few of them in my time, Bashar."

Once more, Teg found himself confounded. He had been warned that he would have to readjust to this different Duncan Idaho but he had not fully anticipated the constant mental demands of that readjustment. The look in Duncan's eyes right now was disconcerting.

"Our roles are changed a bit, Bashar," Duncan said. He picked up a towel from the floor and mopped his face.

"I'm no longer sure of what I can teach you," Teg admitted. He wished, though, that Duncan would take his warning about Lucilla. Did Duncan imagine that the Reverend Mothers of those ancient days were identical with the women of today? Teg thought that highly unlikely. In the way of all other life, the Sisterhood evolved and changed.

It was obvious to Teg that Duncan had come to a decision about his place in Taraza's machinations. Duncan was not merely biding his time. He was training his body to a personally chosen peak and he had made a judgment about the Bene Gesserit.

He has made that judgment on insufficient data, Teg thought.

Duncan dropped the towel and looked at it for a moment. "Let me be the judge of what you can teach me, Bashar." He turned and stared narrowly at Teg seated in the cage.

Teg inhaled deeply. He smelled the faint ozone from all of this durable Harkonnen equipment ticking away in readiness for Duncan's return to action. The ghola's perspiration carried a bitter dominant.

Duncan sneezed.

Teg sniffed, recognizing the omnipresent dust of their activities. It could be more tasted than smelled at times. Alkaline. Over it all was the fragrance of the air scrubbers and oxy regenerators. There was a distinct floral aroma built into the system but Teg could not identify the flower. In the month of their occupation, the globe also had taken on human odors, slowly insinuated into the original composite— perspiration, cooking smells, the never-quite-suppressed acridity of waste reclamation. To Teg, these reminders of their presence were oddly offensive. And he found himself sniffing and listening for sounds of intrusion—something more than the echoing passage of their own footsteps and the subdued metallic clashings from the kitchen area.

Duncan's voice intruded: "You're an odd man, Bashar."

"What do you mean?"

"There's your resemblance to the Duke Leto. The facial identity is weird. He was a bit shorter than you but the identity . . ." He shook his head, thinking of the Bene Gesserit designs behind those genetic markers in Teg's face—that hawk look, the crease lines and that inner thing, that certainty of moral superiority.

How moral and how superior?

According to the records he had seen at the Keep (and Duncan was sure they had been placed there especially for him to discover) Teg's reputation was an almost universal thing throughout human society of this age. At the Battle of Markon, it had been enough for the enemy to know that Teg was there opposite them in person. They sued for terms. Was that true?

Duncan looked at Teg in the console cage and put this question to him.

"Reputation can be a beautiful weapon," Teg said. "It often spills less blood."

"At Arbelough, why did you go to the front with your troops?" Duncan asked.

Teg showed surprise. "Where did you learn that?"

"At the Keep. You might have been killed. What would that have served?"

Teg reminded himself that this young flesh standing over him held unknown knowledge, which must guide Duncan's quest for information. It was in that unknown area, Teg suspected, that Duncan was most valuable to the Sisterhood.

"We took severe losses at Arbelough on the preceding two days," Teg said. "I failed to make a correct assessment of the enemy's fear and fanaticism."

"But the risk of . . ."

"My presence at the front said to my own people: 'I share your risks.'"

"The Keep's records said Arbelough had been perverted by Face Dancers. Patrin told me you vetoed your aides when they urged you to sweep the planet clean, sterilize it and—"

"You were not there, Duncan."

"I am trying to be. So you spared your enemy against all advice."

"Except for the Face Dancers."

"But then you walked unarmed through the enemy ranks and before they had laid down their weapons."

"To assure them they would not be mistreated."

"That was very dangerous."

"Was it? Many of them came over to us for the final assault on Kroinin where we broke the anti-Sisterhood forces."

Duncan stared hard at Teg. Not only did this old Bashar resemble Duke Leto in appearance, but he also had that same Atreides charisma: a legendary figure even among his former enemies. Teg had said he was descended from Ghanima of the Atreides, but there had to be more in it than that. The ways of the Bene Gesserit breeding mastery awed him.

"We will go back to the practice now," Duncan said.

"Don't damage yourself."

"You forget, Bashar. I remember a body as young as this one and right here on Giedi Prime."

"Gammu!"

"It was properly renamed but my body still recalls the original. That is why they sent me here. I know it."

Of course he would know it, Teg thought.

Restored by the brief respite, Teg introduced a new element in the attack and sent a sudden burn-line against Duncan's left side.

How easily Duncan parried the attack!

He was using an oddly mixed variation on the five attitudes, each response seemingly invented before it was required.

"Each attack is a feather floating on the infinite road," Duncan said. His voice gave no hint of exertion. "As the feather approaches, it is diverted and removed."

As he spoke, he parried the shifting attack and countered.

Teg's Mentat logic followed the movements into what he recognized as dangerous places. *Dependencies and key logs!*

Duncan shifted over to attack, moving ahead of it, pacing his movements rather than responding. Teg was forced to his utmost abilities as the shadow forces burned and flickered across the floor. Duncan's weaving figure in its mobile cage danced along the space between them. Not one of Teg's hunter-seekers or burn-line counters touched the moving figure. Duncan was over them, under them, seeming totally unafraid of the real pain that this equipment could bring him.

Once more, Duncan increased the speed of his attack.

A bolt of pain shot up Teg's left arm from his hand on the controls to his shoulder.

With a sharp exclamation, Duncan shut down the equipment. "Sorry, Bashar. That was superb defense on your part but I'm afraid age defeated you."

Once more, Duncan crossed the floor and stood over Teg.

"A little pain to remind me of the pain I caused you," Teg said. He rubbed his tingling arm.

"Blame the heat of the moment," Duncan said. "We have done enough for now."

"Not quite," Teg said. "It is not enough to strengthen only your muscles."

At Teg's words, Duncan felt an alerting sensation throughout his body. He sensed the disorganized touch of that uncompleted thing that the reawakening had failed to arouse. Something crouched within him, Duncan thought. It was like a coiled spring waiting for release.

"What more would you do?" Duncan asked. His voice sounded hoarse.

"Your survival is in the balance here," Teg said. "All of this is being done to save you and get you to Rakis."

"For Bene Gesserit reasons, which you say you do not know!"

"I don't know them, Duncan."

"But you're a Mentat."

"Mentats require data to make projections."

"Do you think Lucilla knows?"

"I'm not sure but let me warn you again about her. She has orders to get you to Rakis *prepared* for what you must do there."

"Must?" Duncan shook his head from side to side. "Am I not my own person with rights to make my own choices? What do you think you've reawakened here, a damned Face Dancer capable only of obeying orders?"

"Are you telling me you will not go to Rakis?"

"I'm telling you I will make my own decisions when I know what it is I'm to do. I'm not a hired assassin."

"You think I am, Duncan?"

"I think you're an honorable man, someone to be admired. Give me credit for having my own standards of duty and honor."

"You've been given another chance at life and—"

"But you are not my father and Lucilla is not my mother. Imprinter? For what does she hope to *prepare* me?"

"It may be that she does not know, Duncan. Like me, she may have only part of the design. Knowing how the Sisterhood works, that is highly likely."

"So the two of you just train me and deliver me to Arrakis. Here's the package you ordered!"

"This is a far different universe than the one where you were originally born," Teg said. "As it was in your day, we still have a Great Convention against atomics and the pseudo-atomics of lasgunshield interaction. We still say that sneak attacks are forbidden. There are pieces of paper scattered around to which we have put our names and we—"

"But the no-ships have changed the basis for all of those treaties," Duncan said. "I think I learned my history fairly well at the Keep. Tell me, Bashar, why did Paul's son have the Tleilaxu provide him with my ghola-self, hundreds of me! for all those thousands of years?"

"Paul's son?"

"The Keep's records call him the God Emperor. You name him Tyrant."

"Oh. I don't think we know why he did it. Perhaps he was lonely for someone from—"

"You brought me back to confront the worm!" Duncan said.

Is that what we're doing? Teg wondered. He had considered this possibility more than once, but it was only a possibility, not a projection. Even so, there had to be something more in Taraza's design. Teg sensed this with every fiber of his Mentat training. Did Lucilla know? Teg did not delude himself that he could pry revelation from a full Reverend Mother. No . . . he would have to bide his time, wait and watch and listen. In his own way, this obviously was what Duncan had decided. It was a dangerous course if he thwarted Lucilla!

Teg shook his head. "Truly, Duncan, I do not know."

"But you follow orders."

"By my oath to the Sisterhood."

"Deceptions, dishonesties—those are empty words when the question is the Sisterhood's survival," Duncan quoted him.

"Yes, I said that," Teg agreed.

"I trust you now *because* you said it," Duncan said. "But I do not trust Lucilla."

Teg dropped his chin to his breast. *Dangerous . . . dangerous . . .*

Much more slowly than once he had done, Teg brought his attention out of such thoughts and went through the mental cleansing process, concentrating on the necessities laid upon him by Taraza.

"You are my Bashar."

Duncan studied the Bashar for a moment. Fatigue lines were obvious on the old man's face. Duncan was reminded suddenly of Teg's great age, wondering if it ever tempted men such as Teg to seek out the Tleilaxu and become gholas. Probably not. They knew they might become Tleilaxu puppets.

This thought flooded Duncan's awareness, holding him immobile so plainly that Teg, lifting his gaze, saw it at once.

"Is something wrong?"

"The Tleilaxu have done something to me, something that has not yet been exposed," Duncan husked.

"Exactly what we feared!" It was Lucilla speaking from the doorway behind Teg. She advanced to within two paces of Duncan. "I have been listening. You two are very informative."

Teg spoke quickly, hoping to blunt the anger he sensed in her. "He has mastered the seven attitudes today."

"He strikes like fire," Lucilla said, "but remember that we of the Sisterhood flow like water and fill in every place." She glanced down at Teg. "Do you not see that our ghola has gone beyond the attitudes?"

"No fixed position, no attitude," Duncan said.

Teg looked up sharply at Duncan, who stood with his head erect, his forehead smooth, his eyes clear as he returned Teg's gaze. Duncan had grown surprisingly in the short time since being awakened to his original memories.

"Damn you, Miles!" Lucilla muttered.

But Teg kept his attention on Duncan. The youth's entire body seemed wired to a new kind of vigor. There was a poise about him that had not been there before.

Duncan shifted his attention to Lucilla. "You think you will fail in your assignment?"

"Surely not," she said. "You're still a male."

And she thought: *Yes, that young body must flow hot with the juices of procreation. Indeed, the hormonal igniters are all intact and susceptible to arousing.* His present stance, though, and the way he looked at her, forced her to raise her awareness to new, energy-demanding levels.

"What have the Tleilaxu done to you?" she demanded.

Duncan spoke with a flippancy that he did not feel: "O Great Imprinter, if I knew I would tell you."

"You think it's a game we play?" she demanded.

"I do not know *what* it is we play at!"

"By now, many people know we are not on Rakis where we would have been expected to flee," she said.

"And Gammu swarms with people returned from the Scattering," Teg said. "They have the numbers to explore many possibilities here."

"Who would suspect the existence of a lost no-globe from the Harkonnen days?" Duncan asked.

"Anyone who made the association between Rakis and Dar-es-Balat," Teg said.

"If you think this is a game, consider the urgencies of the play," Lucilla said. She pivoted on one foot to concentrate on Teg. "And *you* have disobeyed Taraza!"

"You are wrong! I have done exactly what she ordered me to do. I am her Bashar and you forget how well she knows me."

With an abruptness that shocked her to silence, the subtleties of Taraza's maneuverings impressed themselves upon Lucilla . . .

We are pawns!

What a delicate touch Taraza always demonstrated in the way she moved her pawns about. Lucilla did not feel diminished by the realization that she was a pawn. That was knowledge bred and trained into every Reverend Mother of the Sisterhood. Even Teg knew it. *Not diminished, no.* The thing around them had escalated in Lucilla's awareness. She felt awed by Teg's words. How shallow had been her previous view of the forces within which they were enmeshed. It was as though she had seen only the surface of a turbulent river and, from that, had glimpsed the currents beneath. Now, however, she felt the flow all around her and a dismaying realization.

Pawns are expendable.

By your belief in singularities, in granular absolutes, you deny movement, even the movement of evolution! While you cause a granular universe to persist in your awareness, you are blind to movement. When things change, your absolute universe vanishes, no longer accessible to your self-limiting perceptions. The universe has moved beyond you.

—FIRST DRAFT, ATREIDES MANIFESTO,
BENE GESSERIT ARCHIVES

Taraza put her hands beside her temples, palms flat in front of her ears, and pressed inward. Even her fingers could feel the tiredness in there: right between the hands—fatigue. A brief flicker of eyelids and she fell into the relaxation trance. Hands against head were the sole focal points of fleshly awareness.

One hundred heartbeats.

She had practiced this regularly since learning it as a child, one of her first Bene Gesserit skills. Exactly one hundred heartbeats. After all of those years of practice, her body could pace them automatically by an unconscious metronome.

When she opened her eyes at the count of one hundred, her head felt better. She hoped she would have at least two more hours in which to work before fatigue overcame her once more. Those one hundred heartbeats had given her extra years of wakefulness in her lifetime.

Tonight, though, thinking of that old trick sent her memories spiraling backward. She found herself caught in her own childhood, the dormitory with the Sister Proctor pacing the aisle at night to make sure they all remained properly asleep in their beds.

Sister Baram, the Night Proctor.

Taraza had not thought of that name in years. Sister Baram had been short and fat, a failed Reverend Mother. Not for any immediately visible reason, but the Medical Sisters and their Suk doctors had found something. Baram had never been permitted to try the spice agony. She had been quite forthcoming about what she knew of her defect. It had been discovered while she was still in her teens: periodic nerve tremors, which manifested when she began to sink into sleep. A symptom of something deeper that had caused her to be sterilized. The tremors made Baram wakeful in the night. Aisle patrol was a logical assignment.

Baram had other weaknesses not detected by her superiors. A wakeful child toddling to the washroom could lure Baram into low-voiced conversation. Naive questions elicited mostly naive answers, but sometimes Baram imparted useful knowledge. She had taught Taraza the relaxation trick.

One of the older girls had found Sister Baram dead in the washroom one morning. The Night Proctor's tremors had been the symptom of a fatal defect, a fact important mostly to the Breeding Mistresses and their endless records.

Because the Bene Gesserit did not usually schedule the full "solo death education" until well into the acolyte stage, Sister Baram was the first dead person Taraza had seen. Sister Baram's body had been found partly beneath a washbasin, the right cheek pressed to the tile floor, her left hand caught in the plumbing under a sink. She had tried to pull her failing body upright and death had caught her in the attempt, exposing that last motion like an insect caught in amber.

When they rolled Sister Baram over to carry her away, Taraza saw the red mark where a cheek had been pressed to the floor. The Day Proctor explained this mark with a scientific practicality. Any experience could be turned into data for these potential Reverend Mothers to incorporate later into their acolyte "Conversations With Death."

Post Mortem lividity.

Seated at her Chapter House table, all of those years removed from the event, Taraza was forced to use her carefully focused powers of concentration to dispel that memory, leaving her free to deal with the work spread before her. So many lessons. So fearfully full, her memory. So many lifetimes stored there. It reaffirmed her sense of being alive to see the work in front of her. Things to do. She was needed. Eagerly, Taraza bent to her labors.

Damn the necessity to train the ghola on Gammu!

But this ghola required it. Familiarity with dirt underfoot preceded the required restoration of that original persona.

It had been wise to send Burzmali into the Gammu arena. If Miles had really found a hideaway ... if he were to emerge now, he would need all the help he could get. Once more, she considered whether it was time to play the prescient game. So dangerous! And the Tleilaxu had been alerted that their replacement ghola might be required.

"Ready him for delivery."

Her mind swung to the Rakis problem. That fool Tuek should have been monitored more carefully. How long could a Face Dancer safely impersonate him? There was no faulting Odrade's on-scene decision, though. She had put the Tleilaxu into an untenable position. The impersonator could be exposed, plunging the Bene Tleilaxu into a sink of hatred.

The game within the Bene Gesserit design had become very delicate. For generations now, they had held out to the Rakian priesthood the bait of a Bene Gesserit alliance. But now! The Tleilaxu must consider that *they* had been chosen instead of the priests. Odrade's three-cornered alliance, let the priests think every Reverend Mother would take the Oath of Subservience to the Divided God. The Priestly Council would stutter with excitement at the prospect. The Tleilaxu, of course, saw the chance to monopolize melange, controlling at last the one source independent of them.

A rap at Taraza's door told her the acolyte had arrived with tea. It was a standing order when the Mother Superior worked late. Taraza glanced at the table chrono, an Ixian device so accurate it would gain or lose only one second in a century: 1:23:11 A.M.

She called to admit the acolyte. The girl, a pale blond with coldly observant eyes, entered and bent to arrange the contents of her tray beside Taraza.

Taraza ignored the girl and stared at the work remaining on the table. So much to do. Work was more important than sleep. But her head ached and she felt the telltale dazed sensation akin to a stunned brain that told her the tea would provide little relief. She had worked herself into mental starvation and it would have to be put right before she could even stand. Her shoulders and back throbbed.

The acolyte started to leave but Taraza motioned for her to wait. "Rub my back please, Sister."

The acolyte's educated hands slowly worked out the constrictions in Taraza's back. *Good girl.* Taraza smiled at this thought. Of course she was good. No lesser creature could be assigned to the Mother Superior.

When the girl had gone, Taraza sat silently in deep thought. *So little time.* She begrudged every minute of sleep. There was no escaping it, though. Eventually, the body made its unavoidable demands. She had pressed herself beyond easy recuperation for days now. Ignoring the tea laid out beside her, Taraza arose and went down the hall to her tiny sleeping cell. There, she left a call with the Night Guard for 11:00 A.M. and composed herself fully robed on the hard cot.

Quietly, she regulated her breathing, insulated her senses from distraction and fell into the between-state.

Sleep did not come.

She went through her full repertoire and still sleep evaded her.

Taraza lay there for a long time, recognizing at last the futility of willing herself to sleep with any of the techniques at her disposal. The between-state would have to do its slow mending first. Meanwhile, her mind continued to churn.

The Rakian priesthood she had never considered to be a central problem. Already caught up in religion, the priests could be manipulated by religion. They saw the Bene Gesserit chiefly as a power that could enforce their dogma. Let them continue to think this. It was bait that would blind them.

Damn that Miles Teg! Three months of silence, and no favorable report from Burzmali, either. Charred ground, signs of a no-ship's lift-off. Where could Teg have gone? The ghola might be dead. Teg had never before done such a thing. Old Reliability. That was why she had chosen him. That and his military skills and his likeness to the old Duke Leto—all of the things they had prepared in him.

Teg and Lucilla. A perfect team.

If not dead, was the ghola beyond their reach? Did the Tleilaxu have him? Attackers from the Scattering? Many things were possible. Old Reliability. Silent. Was his silence a message? If so, what was he trying to say?

With both Schwangyu and Patrin dead, there was the smell of con-spiracy around the Gammu events. Could Teg be someone planted long ago by the Sisterhood's enemies? Impossible! His own family was proof against such doubts. Teg's daughter at the family home was as mystified as anyone.

Three months now and not a word.

Caution. She had warned Teg to exercise the utmost caution in protecting the ghola. Teg had seen the great danger on Gammu. Schwangyu's last reports made that clear.

Where could Teg and Lucilla have taken the ghola?

Where had they acquired a no-ship? Conspiracy?

Taraza's mind kept circling around her deep suspicions. Was it Odrade's doing? Then who conspired with Odrade? Lucilla? Odrade and Lucilla had never met before that brief encounter on Gammu. Or had they? Who bent close to Odrade and breathed a mutual air weighted with whispers? Odrade gave no sign, but what proof was that? Lucilla's loyalty had never been doubted. They both functioned perfectly as assigned. But so would conspirators.

Facts! Taraza hungered for facts. The bed rustled beneath her and her sense-insulation collapsed, shattered by worries as much as by the

sound of her own movements. Resignedly, Taraza once more composed herself for relaxation.

Relaxation and *then* sleep.

Ships from the Scattering flitted through Taraza's fatigue-fogged
imagination. Lost Ones returned in their uncounted no-ships. Was that
where Teg found a ship? This possibility was being explored as quietly
as they could on Gammu and elsewhere. She tried counting imaginary
ships but they refused to proceed in the orderly fashion required for
sleep induction. Taraza came alert without moving on her cot.

Her deepest mind was trying to reveal something. Fatigue had
blocked that path of communication but now—she sat up fully awake.

The Tleilaxu had been dealing with people returned from the Scattering. With these whorish Honored Matres and with returned Bene
Tleilax as well. Taraza sensed a single design behind events. The Lost
Ones did not return out of simple curiosity about their roots. The gregarious desire to reunite all of humankind was not enough in itself to
bring them back. The Honored Matres clearly came with dreams of
conquest.

But what if the Tleilaxu sent out in the Scattering had not carried
with them the secret of the axlotl tanks? What then? Melange. The
orange-eyed whores obviously used an inadequate substitute. The
people of the Scattering might not have solved the mystery of the Tleilaxu tanks. They *would* know about axlotl tanks and try to re-create
them. But if they failed—melange!

She began to explore this projection.

The Lost Ones ran out of the true melange their ancestors took into
the Scattering. What sources did they have then? The worms of Rakis
and the original Bene Tleilax. The whores would not dare reveal their
true interest. Their ancestors believed that the worms could not be
transplanted. Was it possible the Lost Ones had found a suitable planet
for the worms? Of course it was possible. They might begin bargaining
with the Tleilaxu as a diversion. Rakis would be their real target. Or
the reverse could be true.

Transportable wealth.

She had seen Teg's reports on the wealth being accumulated on Gammu. Some among the ones returning had coinages and other negotiable chips. That much was plain from the banking activities.

What greater currency was there, though, than the spice?

Wealth. That was it, of course. And whatever the chips, the bargaining had begun.

Taraza grew aware of voices outside her door. The acolyte Sleep-Guard was arguing with someone. The voices were low but Taraza heard enough to bring her into full alert.

"She left a wake-up for late morning," the Sleep-Guard protested.

Someone else whispered: "She said she was to be told the moment I returned."

"I tell you she is very tired. She needs—"

"She needs to be obeyed! Tell her I'm back!"

Taraza sat up and swung her legs over the edge of the cot. Her feet found the floor. Gods! How her knees ached. It pained her, too, that she could not place the intruding whisper, the person arguing with her guard.

Whose return did I . . . Burzmali!

"I'm awake," Taraza called.

Her door opened and the Sleep-Guard leaned in. "Mother Superior, Burzmali has returned from Gammu."

"Send him in at once!" Taraza activated a single glowglobe at the head of her cot. Its yellow light washed away the room's darkness.

Burzmali entered and closed the door behind him. Without being told, he touched the sound-insulation switch on the door and all outside noises vanished.

Privacy? It was bad news then.

She looked up at Burzmali. He was a short, slender fellow with a sharply triangular face narrowing to a thin chin. Blond hair swept over a high forehead. His widely spaced green eyes were alert and watchful. He looked far too young for the responsibilities of a Bashar, but then Teg had looked even younger at Arbelough. *We are getting old, damn it.* She forced herself to relax and place her trust in the fact that Teg had trained this man and expressed full confidence in him.

"Tell me the bad news," Taraza said.

Burzmali cleared his throat. "Still no sign of the Bashar and his party on Gammu, Mother Superior." He had a heavy, masculine voice.

And that's not the worst of it, Taraza thought. She saw the clear signs of Burzmali's nervousness.

"Let's have it all," she ordered. "Obviously, you have completed your examination of the Keep's ruins."

"No survivors," he said. "The attackers were thorough."

"Tleilaxu?"

"Possible."

"You have doubts?"

"The attackers used that new Ixian explosive, 12-Uri. I . . . I think it may have been used to mislead us. There were mechanical brain-probe holes in Schwangyu's skull, too."

"What of Patrin?"

"Exactly as Schwangyu reported. He blew himself up in that decoy ship. They identified him from bits of two fingers and one intact eye. There was nothing left big enough to probe."

"But you have doubts! Get to them!"

"Schwangyu left a message that only we might read."

"In the wear marks on furniture?"

"Yes, Mother Superior, and—"

"Then she knew she would be attacked and had time to leave a message. I saw your earlier report on the devastation of the attack."

"It was quick and totally overpowering. The attackers did not try to take captives."

"What did she say?"

"Whores."

Taraza tried to contain her shock, although she had been expecting that word. The effort to remain calm almost drained her energies. This was very bad. Taraza permitted herself a deep sigh. Schwangyu's opposition had persisted to the end. But then, seeing disaster, she had made a proper decision. Knowing she would die without the opportunity to transfer her Memory Lives to another Reverend Mother, she had acted from the most basic loyalty. If you can do nothing else, arm your Sisters and frustrate the enemy.

So the Honored Matres have acted!

"Tell me about your search for the ghola," Taraza ordered.

"We were not the first searchers over that ground, Mother Superior. There was much additional burning of trees and rocks and underbrush."

"But it was a no-ship?"

"The *marks* of a no-ship."

Taraza nodded to herself. A silent message from Old Reliability?

"How closely did you examine the area?"

"I flew over it but on a routine trip from one place to another."

Taraza motioned Burzmali to a chair near the foot of her cot. "Sit down and relax. I want you to do some guessing for me."

Burzmali lowered himself carefully onto the chair. "Guessing?"

"You were his favorite student. I want you to imagine that you are Miles Teg. You know you must get the ghola out of the Keep. You do not place your full trust in anyone around you, not even in Lucilla. What will you do?"

"An unexpected thing, of course."

"Of course."

Burzmali rubbed his narrow chin. Presently, he said: "I trust Patrin. I trust him fully."

"All right, you and Patrin. What do you do?"

"Patrin is a native of Gammu."

"I have been wondering about that myself," she said.

Burzmali looked at the floor in front of him. "Patrin and I will make an emergency plan long before it is needed. I always prepare secondary ways of dealing with problems."

"Very good. Now—the plan. What do you do?"

"Why did Patrin kill himself?" Burzmali asked.

"You're sure that's what he did."

"You saw the reports. Schwangyu and several others were sure of it. I accept it. Patrin was loyal enough to do that for his Bashar."

"For you! You are Miles Teg now. What plan have you and Patrin concocted?"

"I would not deliberately send Patrin to certain death."

"Unless?"

"Patrin did that on his own. He might if the plan originated with him and not with . . . me. He might do it to protect me, to make sure no one discovered the plan."

"How could Patrin summon a no-ship without our learning of it?"

"Patrin was a Gammu native. His family goes back to the Giedi Prime days."

Taraza closed her eyes and turned her head away from Burzmali. So Burzmali followed the same suggestive tracks that she had been probing in her mind. *We knew Patrin's origins.* What was the significance of that Gammu association? Her mind refused to speculate. This was what came of allowing herself to become too tired! She looked once more at Burzmali.

"Did Patrin find a way to make secret contact with family and old friends?"

"We've explored every contact we could find."

"Depend on it; you haven't traced them all."

Burzmali shrugged. "Of course not. I have not acted on that assumption."

Taraza took a deep breath. "Go back to Gammu. Take with you as much help as our Security can spare. Tell Bellonda those are my orders. You must insinuate agents into every walk of life. Find out who Patrin knew. What of his surviving family? Friends? Winkle them out."

"That will cause a stir no matter how careful we are. Others will know."

"That cannot be helped. And Burzmali!"

He was on his feet. "Yes, Mother Superior?"

"The other searchers: You must stay ahead of them."

"May I use a Guild navigator?"

"No!"

"Then how—"

"Burzmali, what if Miles and Lucilla and our ghola are still on Gammu?"

"I've already told you that I do not accept the idea of their leaving in a no-ship!"

For a long silent period, Taraza studied the man standing at the foot of her cot. Trained by Miles Teg. The old Bashar's favorite student. What was Burzmali's trained instinct suggesting.

In a low voice, she prompted: "Yes?"

"Gammu was Giedi Prime, a Harkonnen place."

"What does that suggest to you?"

"They were rich, Mother Superior. Very rich."

"So?"

"Rich enough to accomplish the secret installation of a no-room . . . even of a large no-globe."

"There are no records! Ix has never even vaguely suggested such a thing. They have not probed on Gammu for . . ."

"Bribes, third-party purchases, many transshipments," Burzmali said. "The Famine Times were very disruptive and before that there were all those millennia of the Tyrant."

"When the Harkonnens kept their heads down or lost them. Still, I will admit the possibility."

"Records could have been lost," Burzmali said.

"Not by us or the other governments that survived. What prompts this line of speculation?"

"Patrin."

"Ahhhhh."

He spoke quickly: "If such a thing were discovered, a Gammu native might know about it."

"How many of them would know? Do you think they could have kept such a secret for . . . Yes! I see what you mean. If it were a secret of Patrin's family . . ."

"I have not dared question any of them about it."

"Of course not! But where would you look . . . without alerting . . ."

"That place on the mountain where the no-ship marks were left."

"It would require you to go there in person!"

"Very hard to conceal from spies," he agreed. "Unless I went with a very small force and seemingly on another purpose."

"What other purpose?"

"To place a funeral marker in memory of my old Bashar."

"Suggesting that we know he is dead? Yes!"

"You've already asked the Tleilaxu to replace our ghola."

"That was a simple precaution and does not bear on . . . Burzmali, this is extremely dangerous. I doubt we can mislead the kinds of people who will observe you on Gammu."

"The mourning of myself and the people I take with me will be dramatic and believable."

"The believable does not necessarily convince a wary observer."

"Do you not trust my loyalty and the loyalty of the people I will take with me?"

Taraza pursed her lips in thought. She reminded herself that fixed loyalty was a thing they had learned to improve upon from the Atreides pattern. How to produce people who command the utmost devotion. Burzmali and Teg both were fine examples.

"It might work," Taraza agreed. She stared speculatively at Burzmali. Teg's favorite student could be right!

"Then I'll go," Burzmali said. He turned to leave.

"One moment," Taraza said.

Burzmali turned. "You will saturate yourselves with shere, all of you. And if you're captured by Face Dancers—these new ones!—you must burn your own heads or shatter them completely. Take the necessary precautions."

The suddenly sobered expression on Burzmali's face reassured Taraza. He had been proud of himself for a moment there. Better to dampen his pride. No need for him to be reckless.

We have long known that the objects of our palpable sense experiences can be influenced by choice—both conscious choice and unconscious. This is a demonstrated fact that does not require that we believe some force within us reaches out and touches the universe. I address a pragmatic relationship between belief and what we identify as "real." All of our judgments carry a heavy burden of ancestral beliefs to which we of the Bene Gesserit tend to be more susceptible than most. It is not enough that we are aware of this and guard against it. Alternative interpretations must always receive our attention.

—MOTHER SUPERIOR TARAZA: ARGUMENT IN COUNCIL

"God will judge us here," Waff gloated.

He had been doing that at unpredictable moments all during this long ride across the desert. Sheeana appeared not to notice but Waff's voice and comments had begun to wear on Odrade.

The Rakian sun had moved far down to the west but the worm that carried them appeared untiring in its drive across the ancient Sareer toward the remnant mounds of the Tyrant's barrier wall.

Why this direction? Odrade wondered.

No answer satisfied. The fanaticism and renewed danger from Waff, though, demanded immediate response. She called up the cant of the Shariat that she knew drove him.

"Let God do the judging and not men."

Waff scowled at the taunting note in her voice. He looked at the horizon ahead and then up at the 'thopters, which kept pace with them.

"Men must do God's work," he muttered.

Odrade did not answer. Waff had been deflected into his doubts and now would be asking himself: Did these Bene Gesserit witches really share the Great Belief?

Her thoughts dove back into the unanswered questions, tumbling through all she knew about the worms of Rakis. Personal memories and Other Memories wove a mad montage. She could visualize robed Fremen atop a worm even larger than this one, each rider leaning back against a long hooked pole that dug into a worm's rings as her hands now gripped this one. She felt the wind against her cheeks, the robe whipping against her shanks. This ride and others merged into a long familiarity.

It has been a long time since an Atreides rode this way.

Was there a clue to their destination back in Dar-es-Balat? How could there be? But it had been so hot and her mind had been questing forward to what might happen on this venture into the desert. She had not been as alert as she might have been.

In common with every other community on Rakis, Dar-es-Balat pulled inward from its edges during the heat of the early afternoon. Odrade recalled the chafing of her new stillsuit while she waited in a building's shadows near the western limits of Dar-es-Balat. She waited for the separate escorts to bring Sheeana and Waff from the safe houses where Odrade had installed them.

What a tempting target she had made. But they had to be certain of Rakian compliance. The Bene Gesserit escorts delayed deliberately.

"Shaitan likes the heat," Sheeana had said.

Rakians hid from the heat but the worms came out then. Was that a significant fact, revealing the reason for this worm to take them in a particular direction?

My mind is bouncing around like a child's ball!

What did it signify that Rakians hid from the sun while a little Tleilaxu, a Reverend Mother, and a wild young girl went coursing across the desert atop a worm? It was an ancient pattern on Rakis. Nothing surprising about it at all. The ancient Fremen had been mostly nocturnal, though. Their modern descendants depended more on shade to protect them from the hottest sunlight.

How safe the priests felt behind their guardian moats!

Every resident of a Rakian urban center knew the qanat was out there, water running slick in shadowed darkness, trickles diverted to feed the narrow canals whose evaporation was recaptured in the windtraps.

"Our prayers protect us," they said, but they knew very well what really protected them.

"His holy presence is seen in the desert."

The Holy Worm.

The Divided God.

Odrade looked down at the worm rings in front of her. *And here he is!*

She thought of the priests among the watchers in the 'thopters overhead. How they loved to spy on others! She had felt them watching her back in Dar-es-Balat while she awaited the arrival of Sheeana and Waff. Eyes behind the high grills of hidden balconies. Eyes peering through slits in thick walls. Eyes concealed behind mirror-plaz or staring out from shadowed places.

Odrade had forced herself to ignore the dangers while she marked the passage of time by the movement of the shadow line on a wall above her: a sure clock in this land where few kept other than suntime.

Tensions had built, amplified by the need to appear unconcerned. Would they attack? Would they dare, knowing that she had taken her own precautions? How angry were the priests at being forced to join the Tleilaxu in this secret triumvirate? Her Reverend Mother advisors from the Keep had not liked this dangerous baiting of the priests.

"Let one of *us* be the bait!"

Odrade had been adamant: "They would not believe it. Suspicions would keep them away. Besides, they are sure to send Albertus."

So Odrade had waited in the Dar-es-Balat courtyard, green-shadowed in the depths where she stood looking upward at the sunline six stories overhead—past lacy balustrades at each balconied level: green plants, brilliant red, orange, and blue flowers, a rectangle of silvery sky above the tiers.

And the hidden eyes.

Motion at the wide street door to her right! A single figure in priestly gold, purple, and white let himself into the courtyard. She studied him, looking for signs that the Tleilaxu might have extended their sway by another Face Dancer mimic. But this was a man, a priest she recognized: Albertus, the senior of Dar-es-Balat.

Just as we expected.

Albertus moved through the wide atrium and across the courtyard toward her, walking with careful dignity. Were there dangerous portents in him? Would he signal his assassins? She glanced upward at the tiered balconies: little flickering motions at the higher levels. The approaching priest was not alone.

But neither am I!

Albertus came to a stop two paces from Odrade and looked up at her from where he had kept his attention—on the intricate gold and purple designs of the courtyard's tiled floor.

He has weak bones, Odrade thought.

She gave no sign of recognition. Albertus was one of those who knew that his High Priest had been replaced by a Face Dancer mimic.

Albertus cleared his throat and took a trembling breath.

Weak bones! Weak flesh!

While the thought amused Odrade, it did not reduce her wariness. Reverend Mothers always noted that sort of thing. You looked for the marks of the breeding. Such selectivity as existed in the ancestry of Albertus carried flaws, elementals that the Sisterhood would try to correct in his descendants if it ever appeared worthwhile to breed him. This would be considered, of course. Albertus had risen to a position of power, doing it quietly but definitely, and it must be determined whether that implied valuable genetic material. Albertus had been poorly educated, though. A first-year acolyte could have handled him.

Conditioning among the Rakian priesthood had degenerated badly since the old Fish Speaker days.

"Why are you here?" Odrade demanded, making it as much an accusation as a question.

Albertus trembled. "I bring a message from your people, Reverend Mother."

"Then say it!"

"There has been a slight delay, something about the route here being known by too many."

That, at least, was the story they had agreed to tell the priests. But the other things on the face of Albertus were easy to read. Secrets shared with him were dangerously close to exposure.

"I almost wish I had ordered you killed," Odrade said.

Albertus recoiled two full paces. His eyes went vacant, as though he had died right there in front of her. She recognized the reaction. Albertus had entered that fully revelatory phase where fear gripped his scrotum. He knew that this terrible Reverend Mother Odrade might pass a death sentence upon him quite casually or kill him with her own hands. Nothing he said or did would escape her awful scrutiny.

"You have been considering whether to kill *me* and destroy our Keep at Keen," Odrade accused.

Albertus trembled violently. "Why do you say such things, Reverend Mother?" There was a revealing whine in his voice.

"Don't try to deny it," she said. "I wonder how many have found you as easy to read as I do? You are supposed to be a keeper of secrets. You are not supposed to be walking around with all of our secrets written on your face!"

Albertus fell to his knees. She thought he would grovel.

"But your own people sent me!"

"And you were only too happy to come and decide whether it might be possible to kill me."

"Why would we—"

"Silence! You do not like it that we control Sheeana. You are fearful of the Tleilaxu. Matters have been taken from your *priestly* hands and things have been set in motion that terrify you."

"Reverend Mother! What are we to do? What are we to do?"

"You will obey us! More than that, you will obey Sheeana! You fear what we venture this day? You have greater things to fear!"

She shook her head in mock dismay, knowing the effect all of this was having on poor Albertus. He cringed beneath the weight of her anger.

"On your feet!" she ordered. "And remember that you are a priest and the truth is demanded of you!"

Albertus stumbled to his feet and kept his head bowed. She could see his body responding to the decision that he abandon subterfuge. What a trial that must be for him! Dutiful to the Reverend Mother who so obviously read his heart, now he must be dutiful to his religion. He must confront the ultimate paradox of all religions:

God knows!

"You hide nothing from me, nothing from Sheeana, and nothing from God," Odrade said.

"Forgive me, Reverend Mother."

"Forgive you? It is not in my power to forgive you nor should you ask it of me. You are a priest!"

He lifted his gaze to Odrade's angry face.

The paradox was upon him completely now. God was surely here! But God was usually a long way away and confrontations could be put off. Tomorrow was another day of life. Surely it was. And it was acceptable if you permitted yourself a few small sins, perhaps a lie or two. For the time being only. And maybe a big sin if temptations were great. Gods were supposed to be more understanding of great sinners. There would be time to make amends.

Odrade stared at Albertus with the analyzing eye of the Missionaria Protectiva.

Ahhh, Albertus, she thought. *But now you stand in the presence of a fellow human who knows all of the things you believed were secrets between you and your god.*

For Albertus, his present situation could be little different from death and that ultimate submission to the final judgment of his god. That surely described the unconscious setting for the way Albertus let his will power crumble now. All of his religious fears had been called up and were focused on a *Reverend* Mother.

In her driest tones, not even compelling him with Voice, Odrade said: "I want this farce ended immediately."

Albertus tried to swallow. He knew he could not lie. He might know a remote capability of lying but that was useless. Submissively, he looked up at Odrade's forehead where the line of her stillsuit cap had been drawn tightly across her brow. He spoke in little more than a whisper:

"Reverend Mother, it is only that we feel deprived. You and the Tleilaxu go into the desert with *our* Sheeana. Both of you will learn from her and . . ." His shoulders sagged. "Why do you take the Tleilaxu?"

"Sheeana wishes it," Odrade lied.

Albertus opened his mouth and closed it without speaking. She could see acceptance flood through him.

"You will return to your fellows with my warning," Odrade said. "The survival of Rakis and of your priesthood depend utterly on how well you obey me. You will not hinder us in the slightest! And as to these puerile plots against us—Sheeana reveals to us your every evil thought!"

Albertus surprised her then. He shook his head and emitted a dry chuckle. Odrade already had noted that many of these priests enjoyed discomfiture but had not suspected that they might find amusement in their own failures.

"I find your laughter shallow," she said.

Albertus shrugged and restored some of his facial mask. Odrade had seen several such masks on him. Facades! He wore them in layers. And far down under all of that defensiveness lay the someone who cared, the one she had exposed here so briefly. These priests had a dangerous way of falling into florid explanations, though, when taxed too heavily with questions.

I must restore the one who cares, Odrade thought. She cut him off as he started to speak.

"No more! You will wait upon me when I return from the desert. For now, you are *my* messenger. Carry my message accurately and you will win a greater reward than you have ever imagined. Fail and you will suffer the agonies of Shaitan!"

Odrade watched Albertus scurry out of the courtyard, shoulders hunched, his head thrust forward as though he could not get his mouth within speaking distance of his peers soon enough.

On the whole, she thought, it had gone well. A calculated risk and very dangerous to her personally. She was sure there had been assassins on the balconies above her waiting for a signal from Albertus. And now, the fear he carried back with him was a thing the Bene Gesserit understood intimately through millennia of manipulations. As contagiously virulent as any plague. The teaching Sisters called it "a directed hysteria." It had been *directed* (aimed was more accurate) at the heart of the Rakian priesthood. It could be relied upon, especially with the reinforcement that now would be set in motion. The priests would submit. Only the few immune heretics were to be feared now.

This is the awe-inspiring universe of magic: There are no atoms, only waves and motions all around. Here, you discard all belief in barriers to understanding. You put aside understanding itself. This universe cannot be seen, cannot be heard, cannot be detected in any way by fixed perceptions. It is the ultimate void where no preordained screens occur upon which forms may be projected. You have only one awareness here—the screen of the magi: Imagination! Here, you learn what it is to be human. You are a creator of order, of beautiful shapes and systems, an organizer of chaos.

—THE ATREIDES MANIFESTO, BENE GESSERIT ARCHIVES

"What you are doing is too dangerous," Teg said. "My orders are to protect you and strengthen you. I cannot permit this to continue."

Teg and Duncan stood in the long, wood-paneled hallway just outside the no-globe's practice floor. It was late afternoon by the clock of their arbitrary routine and Lucilla had just swept away in anger after a vituperative confrontation.

Every meeting between Duncan and Lucilla lately had taken on the nature of a battle. Just now, she had stood in the doorway to the practice hall, a solid figure saved from being stolid by her softening curves, the seductive movements obvious to both males.

"Stop it, Lucilla!" Duncan had ordered.

Only her voice betrayed her anger: "How long do you think I will wait to carry out my orders?"

"Until you or someone else tells me that I—"

"Taraza requires things of you that none of us here knows!" Lucilla said.

Teg tried to soothe the mounting angers: "Please. Isn't it enough that Duncan continues to improve his performance? In a few days, I will start keeping regular watch outside. We can—"

"You can stop interfering with me, damn you!" Lucilla snapped. She whirled and stalked away.

As he saw the hard resolution on Duncan's face now, something furious began to work in Teg. He felt impelled by the necessities of their isolated situation. His intellect, that marvelously honed Mentat instrument, was shielded here from the mental uproar to which it adjusted on the outside. He thought that if he could only silence his mind, bring everything to stillness, all things would become clear to him.

"Why are you holding your breath, Bashar?"

Duncan's voice impaled Teg. It required a supreme act of will to resume normal breathing. He felt the emotions of his two companions in the no-globe as an ebb and flow temporarily removed from other forces.

Other forces.

Mentat awareness could be an idiot in the presence of other forces that swept through the universe. There might exist in the universe people whose lives were infused with powers he could not imagine. Before such forces he would be chaff moved on the froth of wild currents.

Who could plunge into such an uproar and emerge intact?

"What can Lucilla possibly do if I continue to resist her?" Duncan asked.

"Has she used Voice on you?" Teg asked. His own voice sounded remote to him.

"Once."

"You resisted?" Remote surprise lurked somewhere within Teg.

"I learned the way of that from Paul Muad'Dib himself."

"She is capable of paralyzing you and—"

"I think her orders prohibit violence."

"What is violence, Duncan?"

"I'm going to the showers, Bashar. Are you coming?"

"In a few minutes." Teg took a deep breath, sensing how close he was to exhaustion. This afternoon on the practice floor and afterward had drained him. He watched Duncan leave. Where was Lucilla? What was she planning? How long could she wait? That was the central question and it put the no-globe's peculiar emphasis on their isolation from Time.

Again, he sensed that ebb and flow which their three lives influenced. *I must talk to Lucilla! Where has she gone? The library? No! There is something else I must do first.*

Lucilla sat in the room she had chosen for her personal quarters. It was a small space with an ornate bed filling an inset into one wall. Gross and subtle signs around her said this had been the room of a favorite Harkonnen hetaira. Pastel blues with darker blue accents shaded the fabrics. Despite the baroque carvings on bed, alcove, ceiling, and every functioning appurtenance, the room itself could be swept out of her consciousness once she relaxed here. She lay back on the bed and closed her eyes against the sexually gross figures on the alcove ceiling.

Teg will have to be dealt with.

It would have to be done in such a way that it did not offend Taraza or weaken the ghola. Teg presented a special problem in many ways, especially in the way his mental processes could dip into and out of deeper sources akin to those of the Bene Gesserit.

The Reverend Mother who bore him, of course!

Something passed from such a mother to such a child. It began in the womb and probably did not end even when they were finally separated. He had never undergone the all-ravening transmutation that produced Abominations . . . no, not that. But he had subtle and real powers. Those born of Reverend Mothers learned things impossible to others.

Teg knew precisely how Lucilla viewed love in all of its manifestations. She had seen it on his face that once in his quarters at the Keep.

"Calculating witch!"

He might as well have spoken it aloud.

She recalled the way she had favored him with her benign smile and dominating expression. That had been a mistake, demeaning to both of them. She sensed in such thoughts a latent sympathy for Teg. Somewhere within her, despite all of the careful Bene Gesserit training, there were chinks in her armor. Her teachers had warned her about that many times.

"To be capable of inducing real love, you must feel it, but only temporarily. And once is enough!"

Teg's reactions to the Duncan Idaho ghola said much. Teg was both drawn to and repelled by their young charge.

As I am.

Perhaps it had been a mistake not to seduce Teg.

In her sex education, where she had been taught to gain strength from intercourse rather than lose herself in it, her teachers had emphasized analysis and historical comparisons, of which there were many in a Reverend Mother's Other Memories.

Lucilla focused her thoughts on Teg's male presence. Doing this, she could feel a female response, her flesh wanting Teg close to her and aroused to sexual peak—ready for the moment of mystery.

Faint amusement crept into Lucilla's awareness. Not orgasm. No scientific labels! It was purest Bene Gesserit cant: *moment of mystery,* the Imprinter's ultimate specialty. Immersion in the long Bene Gesserit continuity required this concept. She had been taught to believe deeply in a duality: the scientific knowledge by which the Breeding Mistresses guided them *but,* at the same time, the moment of mystery that confounded all knowledge. Bene Gesserit history and science said the procreative drive must remain irretrievably buried in the psyche. It could not be removed without destroying the species.

The safety net.

Lucilla gathered her sexual forces around her now as only a Bene Gesserit Imprinter could. She began to focus her thoughts on Duncan. By now, he would be in the showers and thinking about this evening's training session with his Reverend Mother–teacher.

I will go to my student presently, she thought. *The important lesson must be taught or he will not be fully prepared for Rakis.*

Those were Taraza's instructions.

Lucilla swung the focus of her thoughts fully onto Duncan. It was almost as though she saw him standing naked under the shower.

How little he understood of what there might be to learn!

Duncan sat alone in the dressing cubicle off the showers which adjoined the practice hall. He was immersed in a deep sadness. This brought remembered pains to old wounds that this young flesh had never experienced.

Some things never changed! The Sisterhood was at its old-old games again.

He looked up and around this dark-paneled Harkonnen place. Arabesques were carved into walls and ceiling, strange designs in the tesserae of the floor. Monsters and lovely human bodies intermingled across the same defining lines. Only a flicker of attention separated one from the other.

Duncan looked down at this body that the Tleilaxu and their axlotl tanks had produced for him. It still felt strange at moments. He had been a man of many adult experiences in the last instant he remembered from his pre-ghola life—fighting off a swarm of Sardaukar warriors, giving his young Duke a chance to escape.

His Duke! Paul had been no older than this flesh then. Conditioned, though, the way the Atreides always were: Loyalty and honor above all else.

The way they conditioned me after they saved me from the Harkonnens.

Something within him could not evade that ancient debt. He knew its source. He could outline the process by which it had been embedded in him.

There it remained.

Duncan glanced at the tiled floor. Words had been worked in the tile along the cubicle's splashboard. It was a script that one part of him identified as an ancient thing from the old Harkonnen times but that another part of him found to be an all-too-familiar Galach.

"CLEAN SWEET CLEAN BRIGHT CLEAN PURE CLEAN"

The ancient script repeated itself around the room's perimeter as though the words themselves might create something that Duncan knew was alien to the Harkonnens of his memories.

Over the door to the showers, more script:

"CONFESS THY HEART AND FIND PURITY"

A religious admonition in a Harkonnen stronghold? Had the Harkonnens changed in the centuries after his death? Duncan found this hard to believe. These words were things that the builders probably had thought appropriate.

He felt rather than heard Lucilla enter the room behind him. Duncan stood and fastened the clips of the tunic he had appropriated from the nullentropy bins (but only after removing all Harkonnen insignia!).

Without turning, he said: "What now, Lucilla?"

She stroked the fabric of the tunic along his left arm. "The Harkonnens had rich tastes."

Duncan spoke quietly: "Lucilla, if you touch me again without my permission, I will *try* to kill you. I will try so hard that you very likely will have to kill me."

She recoiled.

He stared into her eyes. "I am not some damned stud for the witches!"

"Is that what you think we want of you?"

"Nobody has said what you want of me but your actions are obvious!"

He stood poised on the balls of his feet. The unawakened thing within him stirred and sent his pulse racing.

Lucilla studied him carefully. *Damn that Miles Teg!* She had not expected resistance to take this form. There was no doubting Duncan's sincerity. Words by themselves no longer would serve. He was immune to Voice.

Truth.

It was the only weapon left to her.

"Duncan, I do not know precisely what it is Taraza expects you to do on Rakis. I can guess but my guess may be wrong."

"Guess, then."

"There is a young girl on Rakis, barely into her teens. Her name is Sheeana. The worms of Rakis obey her. Somehow, the Sisterhood must gather this talent into its own store of abilities."

"What could I possibly . . ."

"If I knew, I certainly would tell you now."

He heard her sincerity unmasked by her desperation.

"What does your *talent* have to do with this?" he demanded.

"Only Taraza and her councillors know."

"They want some hold on me, something from which I cannot escape!"

Lucilla already had arrived at this deduction but she had not expected him to see it that quickly. Duncan's youthful face concealed a mind that worked in ways she had not yet fathomed. Lucilla's thoughts raced.

"Control the worms and you could revive the old religion." It was Teg's voice from the doorway behind Lucilla.

I did not hear him arrive!

She whirled. Teg stood there with one of the antique Harkonnen lasguns held casually across his left arm, its muzzle directed at her.

"This is to insure that you listen to me," he said.

"How long have you been there listening?"

Her angry glare did not change his expression.

"From the moment you admitted you don't know what Taraza expects of Duncan," Teg said. "Nor do I. But I can make a few Mentat projections—nothing firm yet but all of them suggestive. Tell me if I am wrong."

"About what?"

He glanced at Duncan. "One of the things you were told to do was to make him irresistible to most women."

Lucilla tried to conceal her dismay. Taraza had warned her to conceal this from Teg as long as possible. She saw that concealment no longer was possible. Teg had read her reaction with those damnable abilities imparted to him by his damnable mother!

"A great deal of energy is being gathered and aimed at Rakis," Teg said. He looked steadily at Duncan. "No matter what the Tleilaxu have buried in him, he has the stamp of ancient humankind in his genes. Is that what the Breeding Mistresses need?"

"A damned Bene Gesserit stud!" Duncan said.

"What do you intend to do with that weapon?" Lucilla asked. She nodded at the antique lasgun in Teg's hands.

"This? I didn't even put a charge cartridge in it." He lowered the lasgun and leaned it into a corner beside him.

"Miles Teg, you will be punished!" Lucilla grated.

"That will have to wait," he said. "It's almost night outside. I've been out there under the life-shield. Burzmali has been here. He has left his sign to tell me he read the message I scratched with those animal marks on the trees."

A glittering alertness came into Duncan's eyes.

"What will you do?" Lucilla asked.

"I have left new marks arranging a rendezvous. Right now, we are all going up to the library. We are going to study the maps. We will commit them to memory. At the very least, we should know where we are when we run."

She gave him the benefit of a curt nod.

Duncan noted her movement with only part of his awareness. His mind already had leaped ahead to the ancient equipment in the Harkonnen library. He had been the one to show both Lucilla and Teg how to use it correctly, calling up an ancient map of Giedi Prime dating from the time when the no-globe had been built.

With Duncan's pre-ghola memory as guide and his own more modern knowledge of the planet, Teg had tried to bring the map up to date.

"Forest Guard Station" became "Bene Gesserit Keep."

"Part of it was a Harkonnen hunting lodge," Duncan had said. "They hunted human game raised and conditioned specifically for that purpose."

Towns vanished under Teg's updating. Some cities remained but received new labels. "Ysai," the nearest metropolis, had been marked "Barony" on the original map.

Duncan's eyes went hard in memory. "That's where they tortured me."

When Teg exhausted his memory of the planet, much was marked *unknown* but there were frequent curly-ended Bene Gesserit symbols to identify the places where Taraza's people had told Teg he might find temporary sanctuary.

Those were the places Teg wanted committed to memory.

As he turned to lead them up to the library, Teg said: "I will erase the map when we have learned it. There's no telling who might find this place and study it."

Lucilla swept past him. "It's on your head, Miles!" she said.

Teg called after her retreating back: "A Mentat tells you that I did what was required of me."

She spoke without turning: "How logical!"

This room reconstructs a bit of the desert of Dune. The sandcrawler directly in front of you dates from the Atreides times. Grouped around it, moving clockwise from your left, are a small harvester, a carryall, a primitive spice factory and the other support equipment. All are explained at each station. Note the illuminated quotation above the display: "FOR THEY SHALL SUCK OF THE ABUNDANCE OF THE SEAS AND OF THE TREASURE IN THE SAND." This ancient religious quotation was oft repeated by the famous Gurney Halleck.

—GUIDE ANNOUNCEMENT, MUSEUM OF DAR-ES-BALAT

The worm did not slow its relentless progress until just before dusk. By then, Odrade had played out her questions and still had no answers. How did Sheeana control the worms? Sheeana said she was not steering her *Shaitan* in this direction. What was this hidden language to which the desert monster responded? Odrade knew that her Sister-guardians up there in the 'thopters that paced them would be exhausting the same questions plus one more.

Why did Odrade let this ride continue?

They might even hazard a few guesses: *She does not call us in because that might disturb the beast. She does not trust us to pluck her party from its back.*

The truth was far simpler: curiosity.

The hissing passage of the worm could have been a surging vessel breasting seas. The dry flinty odors of overheated sand, swept across them by a following wind, said otherwise. Only open desert stretched around them now, kilometer after kilometer of whaleback dunes as regular in their spacing as ocean waves.

Waff had been silent for a long period. He crouched in a miniature reproduction of Odrade's position, his attention directed ahead, a blank expression on his face. His most recent statement:

"God guard the faithful in the hour of our trial!"

Odrade thought of him as living proof that a strong enough fanaticism could endure for ages. Zensunni and the old Sufi survived in the Tleilaxu. It was like a deadly microbe that had lain dormant all of those millennia, waiting for the right host to feed its virulence.

What will happen to the thing I planted in the Rakian priesthood? she wondered. Saint Sheeana was a certainty.

Sheeana sat on a ring of her Shaitan, her robe pulled up to expose her thin shanks. She gripped the ring with both hands between her legs.

She had said that her first worm ride went directly to the city of Keen. Why there? Had the worm simply been taking her to her own kind?

This one beneath them now certainly had a different goal. Sheeana no longer questioned but then Odrade had ordered her to remain silent and practice the low trance. That, at least, would assure that every last detail of this experience could be recalled easily from her memory. If there were a hidden language between Sheeana and worm, they would find it later.

Odrade peered at the horizon. The remnant base of the ancient wall around the Sareer was only a few kilometers ahead. Long shadows from it lay across the dunes, telling Odrade that the remnant was higher than she had originally suspected. It was a shattered and broken outline now, with great boulders strewn along its base. The notch where the Tyrant had tumbled from his bridge into the Idaho River lay well to their right, at least three kilometers off their path. No river flowed there now.

Waff stirred beside her. "I heed Thy call, God," he said. "It is Waff of the Entio who prays in Thy Holy Place."

Odrade swiveled her gaze toward him without moving her head. *Entio?* Her Other Memories knew an Entio, a tribal leader in the great Zensunni Wandering, long before Dune. What was this? What ancient memories did these Tleilaxu keep alive?

Sheeana broke her silence. "Shaitan is slowing."

The remains of the ancient wall blocked their way. It loomed at least fifty meters over the highest dunes. The worm turned slightly to the right and moved between two giant boulders that towered above them. It came to a stop. The long ridged back lay parallel to a mostly intact section of the wall's base.

Sheeana stood and looked at the barrier.

"What is this place?" Waff asked. He raised his voice above the sound of the 'thopters circling overhead.

Odrade released her tiring grip and flexed her fingers. She continued to kneel while she studied their surroundings. Shadows from the tumbled boulders drew hard lines on sand spills and smaller rocks. Seen close up, not twenty meters away, the wall revealed cracks and fissures, dark openings into the ancient foundation.

Waff stood and massaged his hands.

"Why have we been brought here?" he asked. His voice was faintly plaintive.

The worm twitched.

"Shaitan wants us to get off," Sheeana said.

How does she know? Odrade wondered. The worm's movement had not been enough to make any of them stumble. It could have been some private reflex after the long journey.

But Sheeana faced the ancient wall's foundation, sat down on the curve of the worm and slid off. She dropped in a crouch on soft sand.

Odrade and Waff moved forward and watched with fascination as Sheeana slogged through the sand to the front of the creature. There, Sheeana placed both hands on her hips and faced the gaping mouth. Hidden flames played orange light across the young face.

"Shaitan, why are we here?" Sheeana demanded.

Again, the worm twitched.

"He wants all of you off him," Sheeana called.

Waff looked at Odrade. "If God wishes thee to die, He causes thy steps to lead thee to the place of thy death."

Odrade gave him back a paraphrase from the cant of the Shariat: "Obey God's messenger in all things."

Waff sighed. Doubt was plain on his face. But he turned and was first off the worm, dropping just ahead of Odrade. They followed Sheeana's example, moving to the front of the creature. Odrade, every sense alert, fixed her gaze on Sheeana.

It was much hotter in front of the gaping mouth. The familiar bite of melange filled the air around them.

"We are here, God," Waff said.

Odrade, getting more than a little tired of his religious awe, spared a glance for their surroundings—the shattered rocks, the eroded barrier reaching into the dusky sky, sand sloping against the time-scarred stones, and the slow scorching huff-huff of the worm's internal fires.

But where is here? Odrade wondered. *What is special about this place to make it the worm's destination?*

Four of the watching 'thopters passed in line overhead. The sound of their wing fans and the hissing jets momentarily drowned out the worm's background rumblings.

Shall I call them down? Odrade wondered. It would take only a hand signal. Instead, she lifted two hands in the signal for the watchers to remain aloft.

Evening's chill was on the sand now. Odrade shivered and adjusted her metabolism to the new demands. She felt confident that the worm would not engulf them with Sheeana beside them.

Sheeana turned her back on the worm. "He wants us to be here," she said.

As though her words were a command, the worm twisted its head away from them and slid off through the tall scattering of giant boulders. They could hear it speeding away back into the desert.

Odrade faced the base of the ancient wall. Darkness would be upon them soon but enough light remained in the high desert's long dusk that they might yet see some explanation of why the creature had brought them here. A tall fissure in the rock wall to her right seemed as good a place to investigate as any. Keeping part of her attention on the sounds from Waff, Odrade climbed a sandy incline toward the dark opening. Sheeana kept pace with her.

"Why are we here, Mother?"

Odrade shook her head. She heard Waff following.

The fissure directly in front of her was a shadowy hole into darkness. Odrade stopped and held Sheeana beside her. She judged the opening to be about a meter wide and some four times that in height. The rocky sides were curiously smooth, as though polished by human hands. Sand had drifted into the opening. Light from the setting sun reflected off the sand to bathe one side of the opening in a wash of gold.

Waff spoke from behind them: "What is this place?"

"There are many old caves," Sheeana said. "Fremen hid their spice in caves." She inhaled deeply through her nose. "Do you smell it, Mother?"

There was a definite melange odor to the place, Odrade agreed.

Waff moved past Odrade and into the fissure. He turned there, looking up at the walls where they met in a sharp angle above him. Facing Odrade and Sheeana, he backed farther into the opening, his attention on the walls. Odrade and Sheeana stepped closer to him. With an abrupt hissing of spilled sand, Waff vanished from their sight. In the same instant, the sand all around Odrade and Sheeana slipped forward into the fissure, dragging both of them with it. Odrade grabbed Sheeana's hand.

"Mother!" Sheeana cried.

The sound echoed from invisible rock walls as they slid down a long slope of spilling sand into concealing darkness. The sand drifted them to a stop in a final wash of gentle movement. Odrade, in sand up to her knees, extricated herself and pulled Sheeana with her onto a hard surface.

Sheeana started to speak but Odrade said: "Hush! Listen!"

There was a grating disturbance off to the left.

"Waff?"

"I'm in it up to my waist." There was terror in his voice.

Odrade spoke dryly. "God must want it that way. Pull yourself out gently. It feels like rock under our feet. Gently now! We don't need another avalanche."

As her eyes adjusted, Odrade looked up the sand slope down which they had tumbled. The opening where they had entered this place was a distant slit of dusky gold far away above them.

"Mother," Sheeana whispered. "I'm scared."

"Say the Litany Against Fear," Odrade ordered. "And be still. Our friends know we are here. They will help us get out."

"God has brought us to this place," Waff said.

Odrade did not respond. In the silence, she pursed her lips and gave a high-pitched whistle, listening for the echoes. Her ears told her they were in a large space with some sort of low obstruction behind them. She turned her back on the narrow fissure and gave another whistle.

The low barrier lay about a hundred meters away.

Odrade freed her hand from Sheeana's. "Stay right here, please. Waff?"

"I hear the 'thopters," he said.

"We all hear them," Odrade said. "They are landing. We will have help presently. Meanwhile, please stay where you are and remain silent. I need the silence."

Whistling and listening for the echoes, placing each foot carefully, Odrade worked her way deeper into the darkness. An outstretched hand encountered a rough rock surface. She felt along it. Only about waist high. She could feel nothing beyond it. The echoes of her whistles said it was a smaller space there and partly enclosed.

A voice called from high behind her. "Reverend Mother! Are you there?"

Odrade turned, cupped her hands around her mouth and shouted: "Stay back! We've been spilled into a deep cave. Bring a light and a long rope."

A tiny dark figure moved back out of the distant opening. The light up there was growing dimmer. She lowered her cupped hands and spoke into the darkness.

"Sheeana? Waff? Come toward me about ten paces and wait there."

"Where are we, Mother?" Sheeana asked.

"Patience, child."

A low, muttering sound came from Waff. Odrade recognized the ancient words of the Islamiyat. He was praying. Waff had dropped all attempts to conceal his origins from her. Good. The believer was a receptacle for her to feed with the sweets of the Missionaria Protectiva.

Meanwhile, the possibilities of this place where the worm had brought them excited Odrade. Guided by one hand on the rock barrier, she explored along it to her left. The top was quite smooth in places. All of it sloped inward away from her. Other Memories offered a sudden projection:

Catchbasin!

This was a Fremen water storage basin. Odrade inhaled deeply, testing for moisture. The air was flint dry.

A bright light from the fissure stabbed downward, driving away the darkness. A voice called from the opening and Odrade recognized it as one of her Sisters.

"We can see you!"

Odrade stepped back from the low barrier and turned, peering all around. Waff and Sheeana stood about sixty meters away staring at their surroundings. The chamber was roughly circular, some two hundred meters in diameter. A rock dome arched high overhead. She examined the low barrier beside her: yes, a Fremen catchbasin. She could discern the small rock island in its center where a captive worm could be kept ready to spill into the water. Other Memories replayed that agonized, twisting death which produced the spice poison to ignite a Fremen orgy.

A low arch framed more darkness on the far side of the basin. She could see the spillway there where water had been brought down from a windtrap. There would be more catchbasins back there, an entire complex of them designed to hold a wealth of moisture for an ancient tribe. She knew the name of this place now.

"Sietch Tabr," Odrade whispered.

The words ignited a flood of useful memories. This had been Stilgar's place in the time of Muad'Dib. *Why did that worm bring us to Sietch Tabr?*

A worm took Sheeana to the City of Keen. That others might know of her? Then what was there to know here? Were there people back there in that darkness? Odrade sensed no indications of life in that direction.

Her Sister at the opening interrupted these thoughts. "We've had to ask for the rope to be brought from Dar-es-Balat! The people at the museum say this is probably Sietch Tabr! They thought it had been destroyed!"

"Send down a light so I can explore it," Odrade called.

"The priests ask that we leave it undisturbed!"

"Send me a light!" Odrade insisted.

Presently, a dark object tumbled down the sandslope in a small spill of sand. Odrade sent Sheeana scampering for it. A touch on the switch and a bright beam went lancing at the dark archway beyond the catchbasin. *Yes, more basins there.* And beside this basin, a narrow stairway cut into the rock. The steps led upward, turning and removing themselves from her view.

Odrade bent and whispered in Sheeana's ear. "Watch Waff carefully. If he moves after us, call out."

"Yes, Mother. Where are we going?"

"I must look at this place. I am the one who has been brought here for a purpose." She raised her voice and addressed Waff: "Waff, please wait there for the rope."

"What have you been whispering?" he demanded. "Why must I wait? What are you doing?"

"I have been praying," Odrade said. "Now, I must continue this pilgrimage alone."

"Why alone?"

In the old language of the Islamiyat, she said: "It is written."

That stopped him!

Odrade led the way at a fast walk toward the rock stairs.

Sheeana, hurrying along beside Odrade, said: "We must tell people about this place. The old Fremen caves are safe from Shaitan."

"Be still, child," Odrade said. She aimed the light up into the stairway. It curved through the rock, angling sharply to the right up there. Odrade hesitated. The warning sense of danger she had felt at the beginning of this venture came back intensified. It was an almost palpable thing within her.

What is up there?

"Wait here, Sheeana," Odrade said. "Don't let Waff follow me."

"How can I stop him?" Sheeana glanced fearfully back across the chamber where Waff stood.

"Tell him it is God's will that he remain. Say it this way . . ." Odrade bent close to Sheeana and repeated the words in Waff's ancient language, then: "Say nothing else. Stand in his way and repeat it if he tries to pass."

Sheeana mouthed the new words quietly. She had them, Odrade saw. The girl was quick.

"He's afraid of you," Odrade said. "He won't try to harm you."

"Yes, Mother." Sheeana turned, folded her arms across her breast and looked across the chamber at Waff.

Aiming the light ahead of her, Odrade went up the rock stairs. *Sietch Tabr! What surprise have you left for us here, old worm?*

In a long low hallway at the top of the stairs, Odrade came on the first desert-mummified bodies. There were five of them, two men and three women, no identifying marks or clothing on them. They had been completely stripped and left for the desert's dryness to preserve. Dehydration had pulled skin and flesh tightly around the bones. The bodies were propped in a row, their feet extended across the passage. Odrade was forced to step over each of these macabre obstructions.

She passed her handlight across each body as she went. They had been stabbed almost identically. A slashing blade had been thrust upward just below the arch of the sternum.

Ritual killings?

Dryly puckered flesh had been withdrawn from the wounds, leaving a dark spot to mark them. These bodies were not from Fremen times, Odrade knew. Fremen death stills made ashes of all flesh to recover a body's water.

Odrade probed ahead with her light and paused to consider her position. Discovery of the bodies intensified her sense of peril. *I should have brought a weapon.* But that would have aroused Waff's suspicions.

The persistence of that inner warning could not be evaded. This relic of Sietch Tabr was perilous.

The beam of her light revealed another stairway at the end of this hall. Cautiously, Odrade moved forward. At the first step, she sent the beam of her light probing upward. Shallow steps. Only a little way up, more rock—a wider space up there. Odrade turned and sent the light stabbing around this hallway. Chips and burn marks scarred the rock walls. Once more, she looked up the stairway.

What is up there?

The sense of danger was intense.

One slow step at a time, pausing often, Odrade climbed. She emerged into a larger passage hewn through the native rock. More bodies greeted her. These had been abandoned in the disarray of their final moments. Again, she saw only mummified flesh stripped of clothing. They lay scattered along this wider passage—twenty of them. She wove her way around them. Some had been stabbed in the same way as the five on the lower level. Some had been slashed and hacked and burned by lasgun beams. One had been beheaded and the skin-masked skull lay against a wall of the passage like a ball abandoned from some terrible game.

This new passage led straight ahead past openings into small chambers on both sides. She saw nothing of value in the small chambers where she sent her probing light: a few scattered strands of spice fiber, small spills of melted rock, melt bubbles occasionally on floors, walls, and ceilings.

What violence was this?

Suggestive stains could be seen on some of the chamber floors. Spilled blood? One chamber had a tiny mound of brown cloth in a corner. Scraps of torn fabric scattered under Odrade's foot.

There was dust. Dust everywhere. Her feet stirred it up in passing.

The passage ended at an archway that gave onto a deep ledge. She sent her light beyond the ledge: an enormous chamber, far larger than the one down below. Its curved ceiling went so high she knew it must extend into the rock base of the great wall. Wide, shallow steps led down from the ledge onto the chamber floor. Hesitantly, Odrade went down the steps and out onto the floor. She sent her light sweeping all around. Other passages led out of the great chamber. Some, she saw, had been blocked by stone and the stones torn away to be left scattered on the ledge and on this great floor.

Odrade sniffed the air. Carried on the dust stirred up by her feet there was a definite smell of melange. The smell wove through her sense of peril. She wanted to leave, hurry back to the others. But the danger was a beacon. She had to learn where that beacon led.

She knew where she was now, though. This was the great gathering chamber of Sietch Tabr, site of countless Fremen spice orgies and tribal convocations. Here, the Naib Stilgar had presided. Gurney Halleck had been here. The Lady Jessica. Paul Muad'Dib. Chani, mother of Ghanima. Here, Muad'Dib trained his fighters. The original Duncan Idaho was here . . . and the first Idaho ghola!

Why have we been brought here? What is the danger?

It was here, right here! She could feel it.

In this place, the Tyrant had concealed a spice hoard. Bene Gesserit records said the hoard had filled this entire chamber to the ceiling and into many of the surrounding passages as well.

Odrade pivoted, her gaze following the path of her light. Over there was the ledge of the Naibs. And there, the deeper Royal Ledge Muad'Dib had commissioned.

And there is the archway where I entered.

She sent her light along the floor, noting places where searchers had chipped and burned the rock seeking more of the Tyrant's fabulous hoard. Fish Speakers had taken most of that melange, its hiding place revealed by the Idaho ghola who had been consort of the famed Siona. The records said subsequent searchers had found more caches hidden behind false walls and floors. There were many authenticated accounts and the verifications of Other Memories. The Famine Times had seen violence here when desperate searchers won through to this place. That might explain the bodies. Many had fought just for the chance to search Sietch Tabr.

As she had been taught, Odrade tried to use her sense of danger as a guide. Did the miasma of past violence cling to these stones after all of those millennia? That was not her warning. Her warning was something immediate. Odrade's left foot encountered an uneven place on the floor. Her light picked out a dark line in the dust. She scattered the dust with a foot, revealing a letter and then an entire word burned in a flowing script.

Odrade read the word silently and then aloud.

"Arafel."

She knew this word. Reverend Mothers of the Tyrant's time had impressed it into the Bene Gesserit consciousness, tracing its roots out to the most ancient sources.

"Arafel: the cloud darkness at the end of the universe."

Odrade felt the gasping accumulation of her warning sense. It focused on that single word.

"The Tyrant's holy judgment," the priests called that word. "The cloud darkness of holy judgment!"

She moved out along the word, staring down at it, noting the curling at the end that trailed off into a small arrow. She looked where the arrow pointed. Someone else had seen the arrow and had cut into the ledge where it pointed. Odrade crossed to where the searcher's burner had left a darker pool of melted rock on the chamber floor. Streams of melted stone ran out in fingers away from the ledge, each finger trailing from a deep hole burned into the rock of the ledge.

Bending, Odrade peered into each hole with her light: Nothing. She sensed the treasure hunter's excitement riding on her warning-fear. The extent of the wealth this chamber had once held staggered imagination. In the worst of the old times, a hand-carried luggage case could hold enough spice to buy a planet. And the Fish Speakers had squandered this hoard, losing it in squabbles and shattering misjudgments and ordinary foolishness too picayune for history to record. They had been glad to accept Ixian alliance when the Tleilaxu broke the melange monopoly.

Did the searchers find it all? The Tyrant was superbly clever.

Arafel.

At the end of the universe.

Had he sent a message down the eons to the Bene Gesserit of today?

She cast the beam of her light once more around the chamber and then upward.

The ceiling described an almost perfect half globe overhead. It had been intended, she knew, as a model of the night sky seen from the entrance to Sietch Tabr. But even by the time of Liet Kynes, the first planetologist here, the original stars painted on that ceiling had been gone, lost in the tiny rock chippings of small quakes and the everyday abrasions of life.

Odrade's breath quickened. The sense of peril had never been greater. The danger beacon shone within her! Quickly, she trotted directly across to the steps where she had descended to this floor. Turning there, she cast backward in her mind for Other Memories to limn this place. They came slowly, forcing past that heart-pounding sense of doom. Pointing the beam of her light upward and peering along it, Odrade placed those ancient memories over the scene in front of her.

Bits of reflected brilliance!

Other Memories positioned them: indicators of the stars in a long-gone sky and right there! The silvery-yellow half circle of the Arrakeen sun. She knew it for a sunset sign.

The Fremen day starts at night.

Arafel!

Keeping her light on that sunset marker, she mounted the steps backward and went around the chamber on the ledge to the exact position she had seen in Other Memories.

Nothing remained of that ancient sun arc.

Searchers had chipped at the wall where it had been. Stone bubbles glistened where a burner had been passed along the wall. No breaks entered the original rock.

By the tightness in her chest, Odrade knew she teetered on the edge of a dangerous discovery. The beacon had led her here!

Arafel . . . at the edge of the universe. Beyond the setting sun!

She swept her light right and left. Another passage entrance opened on her left. Stones that had blocked it lay scattered on the ledge. Her heart pounding, Odrade slipped through the opening and found a short hall plugged with melted stone at the end. On her right, directly behind where the sunset marker had been, she found a small room thick with the smell of melange. Odrade entered the room and saw more signs of chipping and burning on walls and ceiling. The danger sense was oppressive here. She chanted the Litany Against Fear silently while she swept the beam of her light over the room. The place was almost square, about two meters on a side. The ceiling was less than half a meter above her head. Cinnamon pulsed in her nostrils. She sneezed and, blinking, saw a tiny discoloration on the floor beside the threshold.

More marks of that ancient search?

Bending close with her light held at a sharp angle on one side, she saw that she had glimpsed only the shadow of something etched deeply into the rock. Dust concealed most of it. She knelt and brushed the dust aside. Very thin etching and very deep. Whatever this was, it had been meant to endure. The last message of a lost Reverend Mother?

This was a known Bene Gesserit artifice. She pressed sensitive finger-tips against the etching and reconstructed its tracery in her mind.

Recognition leaped into her awareness: one word—inscribed in ancient Chakobsa, "Here."

This was no ordinary "here" to mark an ordinary place but the ac-cented and emphatic "here" that said: "You have found me!" Her ham-mering heart emphasized it.

Odrade rested her handlight on the floor near her right knee and let her fingers explore the threshold beside that ancient summons. The stonework appeared unbroken to the eye but her fingers detected a tiny discontinuity. She pressed the discontinuity, twisted, turned, changed the angle of pressure several times and repeated her effort.

Nothing.

Sitting back on her heels, Odrade studied the situation.

"Here."

The warning sense had grown even more acute. She could feel it as a pressure on her breathing.

Withdrawing slightly, she pulled her light back and lay full length on the floor to stare narrowly along the base of the threshold. *Here!* Could she place a tool there beside that word and lever the threshold? No . . . a tool was not indicated. This thing had the smell of the Tyrant, not of a Reverend Mother. She tried to push the threshold sideways. Nothing moved.

Feeling the tensions and danger sense accentuated by frustration, Odrade stood and kicked at the threshold beside the etched word. It moved! Something grated roughly against sand over her head.

Odrade dodged backward as sand cascaded onto the floor in front of her. A deep rumbling sound filled the tiny chamber. The stones shook under her feet. The floor tipped downward in front of her toward the doorway, opening a space under the door and its wall.

Once more, Odrade found herself precipitated forward and down into an unknown. Her light tumbled with her, its beam rolling over and over. She saw mounds of dark reddish brown in front of her. Cin-namon filled her nostrils.

She fell beside her light onto a soft mounding of melange. The opening through which she had fallen lay out of reach some five meters overhead. She grabbed up her light. Its beam picked out wide stone steps cut into the rock beside the opening. Something written on the risers but she saw only that there was a way out. Her first panic subsided, but the sense of danger left her almost breathless, forcing the movements of her chest muscles.

Left and right she sent the beam of her light into this place where she had fallen. It was a long room directly beneath the passage she had taken from the great chamber. The entire length of it was piled with melange!

Odrade probed upward with her light and saw why no searcher tapping on that passage floor overhead had detected this chamber. Criss-crossed rock bracings transferred all strain deep into the stone walls. Anyone tapping overhead would get back the sounds of solid rock.

Once more, Odrade looked at the melange around her. Even at today's tank-deflated prices, she knew she was standing on a treasure. This hoard would measure many long tons.

Is that the danger?

The warning sense within her remained just as acute as ever. The Tyrant's melange was not what she should fear. The triumvirate would make an equitable distribution of this lot and that would be the end of it. A bonus in the ghola project.

Another danger remained. She could not avoid the warning.

Again, she sent the light beam along the mounded melange. Her attention was drawn to the strip of wall above the spice. More words! Still in Chakobsa, written with a cutter in a fine flowing script, there was another message:

"A REVEREND MOTHER WILL READ MY WORDS!"

Something cold settled in Odrade's guts. She moved to her right with the light, plowing through an empire's ransom in melange. There was more to the message:

"I BEQUEATH TO YOU MY FEAR AND LONELINESS. TO

YOU I GIVE THE CERTAINTY THAT THE BODY AND SOUL OF
THE BENE GESSERIT WILL MEET THE SAME FATE AS ALL
OTHER BODIES AND ALL OTHER SOULS."

Another paragraph of the message backoned to the right of this
one. She plowed through the cloying melange and stopped to read.

"WHAT IS SURVIVAL IF YOU DO NOT SURVIVE WHOLE?
ASK THE BENE TLEILAX THAT! WHAT IF YOU NO LONGER
HEAR THE MUSIC OF LIFE? MEMORIES ARE NOT ENOUGH
UNLESS THEY CALL YOU TO NOBLE PURPOSE!"

There was more of it on the narrow end wall of the long chamber.
Odrade stumbled through the melange and knelt to read:

"WHY DID YOUR SISTERHOOD NOT BUILD THE GOLDEN
PATH? YOU KNEW THE NECESSITY. YOUR FAILURE CON-
DEMNED ME, THE GOD EMPEROR, TO MILLENNIA OF PER-
SONAL DESPAIR."

The words "God Emperor" were not in Chakobsa but in the language
of the Islamiyat, where they conveyed an explicit second meaning to
any speaker of that tongue:

"Your God and Your Emperor because you made me so."

Odrade smiled grimly. *That* would drive Waff into a religious
frenzy! The higher he went, the easier to shatter his security.

She did not doubt the accuracy of the Tyrant's accusation, nor the
potential in his prediction that the Sisterhood could end. The sense of
danger had led her to this place unerringly. Something more had been
at work, too. The worms of Rakis still moved to the Tyrant's ancient
beat. He might slumber in his endless dream but monstrous life, a pearl
in each worm to remind it, carried on as the Tyrant had predicted.

What was it he had told the Sisterhood in his own time? She recalled his words:

"When I am gone, they must call me Shaitan, Emperor of Gehenna. The wheel must turn and turn along the Golden Path."

Yes—that was what Taraza had meant. *"But don't you see? The common people of Rakis have been calling him Shaitan for more than a
thousand years!"*

So Taraza had known this thing. Without ever seeing these words, she had known.

I see your design, Taraza. And now I know the burden of fear you have carried all these years. I can feel it every bit as deeply as you do.

Odrade knew then that this warning sense would not leave until she ended, or the Sisterhood vanished from existence, or the peril was resolved.

Odrade lifted her light, got to her feet and slogged through the melange to the wide steps out of this place. At the steps, she recoiled. More of the Tyrant's words had been cut into each riser. Trembling, she read them as they moved upward to the opening.

"MY WORDS ARE YOUR PAST,

"MY QUESTIONS ARE SIMPLE:

"WITH WHOM DO YOU ALLY?

"WITH THE SELF-IDOLATORS OF TLEILAX?

"WITH MY FISH SPEAKER BUREAUCRACY?

"WITH THE COSMOS-WANDERING GUILD?

"WITH HARKONNEN BLOOD SACRIFICERS?

"WITH A DOGMATIC SINK OF YOUR OWN CREATION?

"HOW WILL YOU MEET YOUR END?

"AS NO MORE THAN A SECRET SOCIETY?"

Odrade climbed past the questions, reading them a second time as she went. *Noble purpose?* What a fragile thing that always was. And how easily distorted. But the power was there immersed in constant peril. It was all spelled out on the walls and stairs of that chamber. Taraza knew without having it explained. The Tyrant's meaning was clear:

"Join me!"

As she emerged into the small room, finding a narrow ledge along which she could swing herself to the door, Odrade looked down at the treasure she had found. She shook her head in wonder at Taraza's wisdom. So that was how the Sisterhood might end. Taraza's design was clear, all the pieces in place. Nothing certain. Wealth and power, it was all the same in the end. The noble design had been started and it must be completed even if that meant the death of the Sisterhood.

What poor tools we have chosen!

That girl waiting back there in the deep chamber below the desert, that girl and the ghola being prepared on Rakis.

I speak your language now, old worm. It has no words but I know the heart of it.

Our fathers ate manna in the desert,
In the burning place where whirlwinds came.
Lord, save us from that horrible land!
Save us, oh-h-h-h-h save us
From that dry and thirsty land.

—SONGS OF GURNEY HALLECK, MUSEUM OF DAR-ES-BALAT

Teg and Duncan, both heavily armed, emerged from the no-globe with Lucilla into the coldest part of the night. The stars were like needlepoints overhead, the air absolutely still until they disturbed it.

The dominant smell in Teg's nostrils was the brittle mustiness of snow. The odor infused every breath and when they exhaled, fat clouds of vapor puffed around their faces.

Tears of cold started in Duncan's eyes. He had been thinking much of old Gurney as they prepared to leave the no-globe, Gurney with his cheek scarred by a Harkonnen inkvine whip. Trusted companions would be needed now, Duncan thought. He did not trust Lucilla much and Teg was old, old. Duncan could see Teg's eyes glinting in the starlight.

Slinging a heavy antique lasgun over his left shoulder, Duncan thrust his hands deep into his pockets for warmth. He had forgotten how cold this planet could get. Lucilla seemed impervious to it, obviously drawing warmth from one of her Bene Gesserit tricks.

Looking at her, Duncan realized he had never trusted the witches much, not even the Lady Jessica. It was easy to think of them as traitors, devoid of any loyalty except to their own Sisterhood. They had so damned *many* secret tricks! Lucilla had given up her seductive ways, though. She knew he meant what he had said. He could feel her anger simmering. *Let her simmer!*

Teg stood quite still, his attention focused outward, listening. Was it right to trust the single plan he and Burzmali had worked out? They had no backup. Was it only eight days ago they had settled on it? It felt longer despite the press of preparations. He glanced at Duncan and Lucilla. Duncan carried a heavy old Harkonnen lasgun, the long field model. Even the extra charge cartridges were heavy. Lucilla had refused to carry more than a single tiny lasgun in her bodice. One small burst was all it held. An assassin's toy.

"We of the Sisterhood are noted for going into battle with only our skills as weapons," she said. "It diminishes us to change that pattern."

She had knives in her leg sheaths, though. Teg had seen them. Poison on them, too, he suspected.

Teg hefted the long weapon in his own hands: a modern field-style lasgun he had brought from the Keep. Over his shoulder, a mate to Duncan's weapon hung from its sling.

I must rely on Burzmali, Teg told himself. *I trained him; I know his qualities. If he says we trust these new allies, we trust them.*

Burzmali had been obviously overjoyed to find his old commander alive and safe.

But it had snowed since their last encounter and the snow lay all around them, a tabula rasa upon which all tracks would be written. They had not counted on snow. Were there traitors in Weather Management?

Teg shivered. The air was cold. It felt like the chill of off-planet space, empty and giving starlight free access to the forest glade around them. The thin light reflected cleanly off the snow-covered ground and the white dusting on the rocks. Dark outlines of conifers and the leafless branches of deciduous trees displayed only their whitely diffused edges. All else was deepest shadow.

Lucilla blew on her fingers and leaned close to Teg to whisper "Shouldn't he be here by now?"

He knew that was not her real question. *"Can Burzmali be trusted?"*

That was her question. She had been asking it one way and another ever since Teg had explained the plan to her eight days ago.

All he could say was: "I have staked my life on it."

"Our lives, too!"

Teg too disliked the accumulated uncertainties, but all plans relied ultimately on the skills of those who executed them.

"You're the one who insisted we must get out of there and go on to Rakis," he reminded her. He hoped she could see his smile, a gesture to take the sting out of his words.

Lucilla was not placated. Teg had never seen a Reverend Mother this obviously nervous. She would be even more nervous if she knew of their new allies! Of course, there was the fact that she had failed to carry out her full assignment from Taraza. How that must gall her!

"We took an oath to protect the ghola," she reminded him.

"Burzmali has taken that same oath."

Teg glanced at Duncan standing silently between them. Duncan gave no sign that he heard the argument or shared the nervousness. An ancient composure held his features motionless. He was listening to the night, Teg realized, doing what all three of them should be doing just now. There was an odd look of ageless maturity on his young features.

If ever I needed trusted companions, it's now! Duncan thought. His mind had gone questing backward into the Giedi Prime days of his pre-ghola roots. This was what they had called "a Harkonnen night." Safe within the warm shielding of their suspensor-buoyed armor, the Harkonnens had enjoyed hunting their subjects on such nights. A wounded fugitive could die of the cold. *The Harkonnens knew! Damn their souls!*

Predictably, Lucilla caught Duncan's attention with a look that said: *"We have unfinished business, you and I."*

Duncan turned his face up into the starlight, making sure she could see his smile, an offensive and knowing look that caused Lucilla to stiffen inwardly. He slipped the heavy lasgun from his shoulder and checked it. She noted the ornate scrollwork on its stock and along the barrel. It was an antique but still it gave off a deadly sense of purpose.

Duncan rested it over his left arm, right hand on the grip, finger on the trigger, exactly as Teg was carrying his own modern weapon.

Lucilla turned her back on her companions and sent her senses probing onto the hillside above them and below. Even as she moved, sound erupted all around. Globs of sound filled their night—a great burst of rumblings off to the right, then silence. Another burst from downslope. Silence. From upslope! On all sides!

At the first sound, all three of them crouched into the shelter of the rocks outside the no-globe's cave entrance.

The sounds filling their night carried little definition: intrusive racketing, partly mechanical, partly squeaks and wails and hisses. Intermittently, a subterranean drumming made the ground vibrate.

Teg knew these sounds. There was a battle going on out there. He could hear the background hissing of burners and, in the distant sky, the lancing beams of armored lasguns.

Something flashed overhead trailing blue and red sparks. Another and another! The earth trembled. Teg inhaled through his nose: burned acid and a suggestion of garlic.

No-ships! Many of them!

They were landing in the valley below the ancient no-globe.

"Back inside!" Teg ordered.

As he spoke, he saw it was too late. People were moving in from all around them. Teg lifted his long lasgun and aimed it downslope toward the loudest of the intrusive noises and the nearest detectable movement. Many people could be heard shouting down there. Free glowglobes moved among the screening trees, set loose by whoever came from there. The dancing lights drifted upslope on a cold breeze. Dark figures moved in the shifting illumination.

"Face Dancers!" Teg grunted, recognizing the attackers. Those drifting lights would be clear of the trees within seconds and on his position in less than a minute!

"We've been betrayed!" Lucilla said.

A great shout roared from the hill above them: "Bashar!" Many voices!

Burzmali? Teg asked himself. He glanced back in that direction and then down at the steadily advancing Face Dancers. No time to pick and choose. He leaned toward Lucilla. "That's Burzmali above us. Take Duncan and run!"

"But what if—"

"It's your only chance!"

"You fool!" she accused, even as she turned to obey.

Teg's "Yes!" did nothing to ease her fears. This was what came of depending on the plans of others!

Duncan had other thoughts. He understood what Teg was about to do—sacrifice himself that two might escape. Duncan hesitated, looking at the advancing attackers below them.

Seeing the hesitation, Teg blared at him: "This is a battle order! I am your commander!"

It was the closest thing to Voice Lucilla had ever heard from a man. She gaped at Teg.

Duncan saw only the face of the Old Duke telling him to obey. It was too much. He grabbed Lucilla's arm, but before hustling her up the slope, he said: "We'll lay down a covering fire once we're clear!"

Teg did not respond. He crouched against a snow-dusted rock as Lucilla and Duncan scrambled away. He knew he must sell himself dearly now. And there must be something else: *the unexpected.* A final signature from the old Bashar.

The advancing attackers were coming up faster, exchanging excited shouts.

Setting his lasgun on maxibeam, Teg pressed the trigger. A fiery arc swept across the slope below him. Trees burst into flame and crashed. People screamed. The weapon would not perform long at this discharge level but while it did the carnage produced its desired effect.

In the abrupt silence after that first sweep, Teg shifted his position to another screening rock on his left and again sent a flaming lance down the dark slope. Only a few of the drifting glowglobes had survived that first slashing violence with its falling trees and dismembered bodies.

More screams greeted his second counterattack. He turned and scrambled across the rocks to the other side of the no-globe's access cave. There, he sent sweeping fire down the opposite slope. More screams. More flames and crashing trees.

No answering fire came back.

They want us alive!

The Tleilaxu were prepared to spend whatever number of Face Dancer lives it required to run his lasgun out of its charges!

Teg shifted the sling of the old Harkonnen weapon to a better position on his shoulder, getting it ready to swing into action. He discarded the almost empty charge in his modern lasgun, recharged it and rested the weapon across the rocks. Teg doubted he would get the chance to recharge the second weapon. Let them think down there that he had run out of charge cartridges. But there were two Harkonnen handguns in his belt as a last resort. They would be potent at close range. Some of the Tleilaxu Masters, the ones who ordered such carnage, let *them* come closer!

Cautiously, Teg lifted his long lasgun from the rock and moved backward, drifting up into the higher rocks, slipping left and then right. He paused twice to sweep the slopes below him with short bursts as though conserving the gun's charge. There was no sense in trying to conceal his movements. They would have a life-tracer on him by now and, besides, there were the tracks in the snow.

The unexpected! Could he suck them in close?

Well above the no-globe's access cave he found a deeper pocket in the rocks, its bottom filled with snow. Teg dropped into this position, admiring the fine field of fire this new vantage provided. He studied it briefly: protected behind him by higher crags and open downslope on three sides. He lifted his head cautiously and tried to see around the screening rocks upslope.

Only silence there.

Had that shout come from Burzmali's people? Even so, there was no guarantee that Duncan and Lucilla could escape in these circumstances. It depended on Burzmali now.

Is he as resourceful as I always thought?

There was no time to consider the possibilities or change a single element of the situation. Battle had been joined. He was committed. Teg drew a deep breath and peered downslope over the rocks.

Yes, they had recovered and were resuming the advance. Without telltale glowglobes this time and silently now. No more shouts of encouragement. Teg rested the long lasgun on a rock in front of him and swept a burning arc from left to right in one long burst, letting it fade out at the end in an obvious loss of charge.

Unslinging the old Harkonnen weapon, he readied it, waiting in silence. They would expect him to flee up the hill. He crouched behind the screening rocks, hoping there was enough movement above him to confuse the life-tracers. He still heard people below him on that fire-wracked slope. Teg counted silently to himself, spacing out the distance, knowing from long experience how much time the attackers would require to come within deadly range. And he listened carefully for another sound he knew from previous encounters with the Tleilaxu: the sharp barking of commands in high-pitched voices.

There they were!

The Masters were spread out farther downslope than he had anticipated. Fearful creatures! Teg set the old lasgun on maxibeam and lifted himself suddenly from his protective cradle in the rocks.

He saw the arc of advancing Face Dancers in the light of burning trees and brush. The high-pitched voices of command came from behind the advance, well out of the dancing orange light.

Aiming over the heads of the nearest attackers, Teg sighted beyond the jumble of flames and pressed the trigger: two long bursts, back and forth. He was momentarily surprised by the extent of the destructive energy in the antique weapon. The thing obviously was the product of superb craftsmanship but there had been no way to test it in the no-globe.

This time, the screams carried a different pitch: high and frantic!

Teg lowered his aim and cleared the immediate slope of Face Dancers, letting them feel the full force of the beam, revealing that he carried more than one weapon. Back and forth he swept the deadly arc, giving the attackers plenty of time to see the charge ebb into a final sputter.

Now! They had been sucked in once and would be more cautious. There just might be a chance to join Duncan and Lucilla. This thought full in his mind, Teg turned and scrambled out of his shelter across the upslope rocks. At his fifth step, he thought he had run into a hot wall. There was time for his mind to recognize what had happened: the shocking blast of a stunner full into his face and chest! It came from directly upslope where he had sent Duncan and Lucilla. Chagrin filled Teg as he fell into darkness.

Others could do the unexpected, too!

All organized religions face a common problem, a tender spot through which we may enter and shift them to our designs: How do they distinguish hubris from revelation?

—MISSIONARIA PROTECTIVA, THE INNER TEACHINGS

Odrade kept her gaze carefully away from the cool green of the quadrangle below her where Sheeana sat with one of the teaching Sisters. The teaching Sister was the best, precisely fitted to this next phase in Sheeana's education. Taraza had chosen them all with care.

We proceed with your plan, Odrade thought. *But did you anticipate, Mother Superior, how we might be marked by a chance discovery here on Rakis?*

Or was it chance?

Odrade sent her gaze over the lower rooftops to the spread of the Sisterhood's central stronghold on Rakis. Rainbow tiles baked out there in glaring noon light.

All of this ours.

This was, she knew, quite the largest embassy the priests permitted in their holy city of Keen. And her presence in this Bene Gesserit stronghold defied the agreement she had made with Tuek. But that had been before the discoveries at Sietch Tabr. Besides, Tuek no longer really existed. The Tuek who marched the priestly precincts was a Face Dancer living out a precarious charade.

Odrade brought her thoughts back to Waff, who stood with two guardian Sisters, behind her, waiting near the door of this penthouse sanctuary with its fine view through armor-plaz windows and its impressive black furnishings into which a robed Reverend Mother might blend with only the lighter shades of her face visible to a visitor.

Had she gauged Waff correctly? Everything had been done precisely according to Missionaria Protectiva teachings. Had she opened the crack in his psychic armor sufficiently? He should be goaded to speak soon. Then she would know.

Waff stood back there calmly enough. She could see his reflection in the plaz. He gave no sign of understanding that the two tall, dark-haired Sisters flanking him were there to prevent his possible violence. But he certainly knew.

My guardians, not his.

He stood with his head bent to conceal his features from her but she knew he was uncertain. That part was sure. Doubts could be like a starving animal and she had fed those hungry doubts well. He had been so sure that their venture into the desert would be the occasion for his death. His Zensunni and Sufi beliefs were telling him now that God's will preserved him there.

Surely, though, Waff was reviewing now his agreement with the Bene Gesserit, seeing at last the ways he had compromised his people, how he had put his precious Tleilaxu civilization in terrible jeopardy. Yes, his composure was wearing thin, but only Bene Gesserit eyes detected this. It would be time soon to begin rebuilding his awareness into a pattern more amenable to the Sisterhood's needs. Let him stew a bit longer.

Odrade returned her attention to the view, loading the suspense of this delay. The Bene Gesserit had chosen this embassy location because of the extensive rebuilding that had changed the entire northeastern quarter of the old city. They could build and remodel here in their own way and for their own purposes. Ancient structures designed for easy access by people on foot, wide lanes for official groundcars and occasional squares in which ornithopters might land—all of that had been changed.

Keeping up with the times.

These new buildings stood much closer to the green-planted ave-nues whose tall and exotic trees flaunted their enormous water con-sumption. 'Thopters were relegated to rooftop landing pads on selected buildings. Pedestrian lanes clung to narrow elevations attached to the buildings. Coin-operated, key-operated and palm-identification lift-slots had been inset into the new buildings, their glowing energy fields masked by dark brown, vaguely transparent covers. The liftslots were spines of darker color in the flat gray of plascrete and plaz. Humans dimly seen in the tubes gave the effect of impurities moving up and down in otherwise pure mechanical sausages.

All in the name of modernization.

Waff stirred behind her and cleared his throat.

Odrade did not turn. The two guardian Sisters knew what she was doing and gave no sign. Waff's mounting nervousness was merely con-firmation that all went well.

Odrade did not feel that all was going truly well.

She interpreted the view out her window as just another disquiet-ing symptom of this disquieting planet. Tuek, she recalled, had not liked this modernization of his city. He had complained that some way must be found to stop it and preserve the old landmarks. His Face Dancer replacement continued that argument.

How like Tuek himself this new Face Dancer was. Did such Face Dancers think for themselves or just play out their parts in accordance with a Master's orders? Were they still mules, these new ones? How much different were these Face Dancers from the fully human?

Things about the deception worried Odrade.

The false Tuek's councillors, the ones fully involved in what they thought of as "the Tleilaxu plot," spoke of public support for moderni-zation and openly gloated that they had their way at last. Albertus regularly reported everything to Odrade. Each new report worried her more. Even the obvious subservience of Albertus bothered her.

"Of course, the councillors do not mean *public* public support," Albertus said.

She could only agree. The behavior of the councillors signaled that they had powerful backing among the middle echelons of the priest-hood, among the climbers who dared joke about their Divided God at weekend parties . . . among those being soothed by the hoard Odrade had found at Sietch Tabr.

Ninety thousand long tons! Half a year's harvest from the deserts of Rakis. Even a third of it represented a significant bargaining chip in the new balances.

I wish I had never met you, Albertus.

She had wanted to restore in him *the one who cares*. What she had actually done was easily recognized by one trained in the Missionaria Protectiva's ways.

A groveling sycophant!

It made no difference now that his subservience was driven by an absolute belief in her holy association with Sheeana. Odrade had never before focused on how easily the Missionaria Protectiva's teachings destroyed human independence. That was always the goal, of course: *Make them followers, obedient to our needs.*

The Tyrant's words in that secret chamber had done more than ignite her fears for the Sisterhood's future.

"I bequeath to you my fear and loneliness."

From that millennial distance, he had planted doubts in her as surely as she had planted them in Waff.

She saw the Tyrant's questions as though they had been limned with glowing light on her inner eye.

"WITH WHOM DO YOU ALLY?"

Are we no more than a secret society? How will we meet our end? In a dogmatic stink of our own creation?

The Tyrant's words had been burned into her consciousness. Where was the "noble purpose" in what the Sisterhood did? Odrade could almost hear Taraza's sneering response to such a question.

"Survival, Dar! That's all the noble purpose we need. Survival! Even the Tyrant knew that!"

Perhaps even Tuek had known it. And what had that bought him in the end?

Odrade felt a haunting sympathy for the late High Priest. Tuek had been a superb example of what a tightly knit family could produce. Even his name was a clue: unchanged from Atreides days on this planet. The founding ancestor had been a smuggler, confidant of the first Leto. Tuek had come from a family that held firmly to its roots, saying: "There is something worth preserving in our past." The example this set for descendants was not lost on a Reverend Mother.

But you failed, Tuek.

These blocks of modernization visible out her window were a sign of that failure—sops to the rising power elements in Rakian society, those elements that the Sisterhood had worked so long to foster and strengthen. Tuek had seen this as a harbinger of the day when he would be too weak politically to prevent the things implied by such modernization:

A shorter and more upbeat ritual.

New songs, more in the modern manner.

Changes in the dancing. ("Traditional dances take so long!")

Above all, fewer ventures into the dangerous desert for the young postulants from the powerful families.

Odrade sighed and glanced back at Waff. The little Tleilaxu chewed his lower lip. Good!

Damn you, Albertus! I would welcome your rebellion!

Behind the closed doors of the Temple, the transition of the High Priesthood already was being debated. The new Rakians spoke of the need "to keep up with the times." They meant: "Give us more power!"

It has always been this way, Odrade thought. *Even in the Bene Gesserit.*

Still, she could not escape the thought: *Poor Tuek.*

Albertus reported that Tuek, just before his death and replacement by the Face Dancer, had warned his kin they might not retain familial control of the High Priesthood when he died. Tuek had been more subtle and resourceful than his enemies expected. His family already was calling in its debts, gathering its resources to retain a power base.

And the Face Dancer in Tuek's place revealed much by his mimic performance. The Tuek family had not yet learned of the substitution and one might almost believe the original High Priest had not been replaced, so good was this Face Dancer. Observing that Face Dancer in action betrayed much to the watchful Reverend Mothers. That, of course, was one of the things that had Waff squirming now.

Odrade turned abruptly on one heel and strode across to the Tleilaxu Master. *Time to have at him!*

She stopped two paces from Waff and glared down at him. Waff met her gaze with defiance.

"You've had enough time to consider your position," she accused. "Why do you remain silent?"

"My position? You think you give us a choice?"

"Man is but a pebble dropped in a pool," she quoted at him from his own beliefs.

Waff took a trembling breath. She spoke the proper words, but what lay behind such words? They no longer sounded right coming from the mouth of a powindah woman.

When Waff did not respond, Odrade continued her quotation: "And if man is but a pebble, then all his works can be no more."

An involuntary shudder swept through Odrade, causing a look of carefully masked surprise in the watchful guardian Sisters. That shudder was not part of the required performance.

Why do I think of the Tyrant's words at this moment? Odrade wondered.

"THE BODY AND SOUL OF THE BENE GESSERIT WILL MEET THE SAME FATE AS ALL OTHER BODIES AND ALL OTHER SOULS."

His barb had gone deep into her.

How was I made so vulnerable? The answer leaped into her awareness: *The Atreides Manifesto!*

Composing those words under Taraza's watchful guidance opened a flaw within me.

Could that have been Taraza's purpose: to make Odrade vulnerable? How could Taraza have known what would be found here on Rakis? The Mother Superior not only displayed no prescient abilities, she tended to avoid this talent in others. On the rare occasions when Taraza had demanded such a performance of Odrade herself, the reluctance had been obvious to the trained eye of a Sister.

Yet she made me vulnerable.

Had it been an accident?

Odrade sank into a swift recital of the Litany Against Fear, only a few eyeblinks but in that time Waff visibly came to a decision.

"You would force it upon us," he said. "But you do not know what powers we have reserved for such a moment." He lifted his sleeves to show where the dart throwers had been. "These were but paltry toys by comparison with our real weapons."

"The Sisterhood has never doubted this," Odrade said.

"Is it to be violent conflict between us?" he asked.

"It is your choice to make," she said.

"Why do you court violence?"

"There are those who would love to see Bene Gesserit and Bene Tleilax at each other's throats," Odrade said. "Our enemies would enjoy stepping in to pick up the pieces after we had weakened ourselves sufficiently."

"You state the argument for agreement but you give my people no room to negotiate! Perhaps your Mother Superior gave you no authority to negotiate!"

How tempting it was to pass it all back into Taraza's hands, just as Taraza wanted. Odrade glanced at the guardian Sisters. The two faces were masks betraying nothing. What did they really know? Would they realize if she went against Taraza's orders?

"Do you have such authority?" Waff persisted.

Noble purpose, Odrade thought. *Surely, the Tyrant's Golden Path demonstrated at least one quality of such purpose.*

Odrade decided on a creative truth. "I have such authority," she said. Her own words made it true. Having taken the authority, she made it impossible for Taraza to deny it. Odrade knew, though, that her own words committed her to a course sharply divergent from the sequential steps of Taraza's design.

Independent action. The very thing *she* had desired of Albertus.

But I am on the scene and know what is needed.

Odrade glanced at the guardian Sisters. "Remain here, please, and see that we are not disturbed." To Waff, she said: "We might as well be comfortable." She indicated two chairdogs set at right angles to each other across the room.

Odrade waited until they were seated before resuming the conversation. "We require a degree of candor between us that diplomacy seldom allows. Too much hangs in the balance for us to engage in shallow evasions."

Waff looked at her strangely. He said: "We know there is dissension in your highest councils. Subtle overtures have been made to us. Is this part of . . ."

"I am loyal to the Sisterhood," she said. "Even those who approached you had no other loyalty."

"Is this another trick of—"

"No tricks!"

"With the Bene Gesserit there are always tricks," he accused.

"What is it you fear from us? Name it."

"Perhaps I have learned too much from you for you to allow me to go on living."

"Could I not say the same of you?" she asked. "Who else knows of our secret affinity? This is no *powindah* female talking to you here!"

She had ventured the word with some trepidation, but the effect could not have been more revealing. Waff was visibly shaken. He was a long minute recovering. Doubts remained, though, because she had planted them in him.

"What do words prove?" he asked. "You might still take the things you have learned from me and leave my people nothing. You still hold the whip over us."

"I carry no weapons in *my* sleeves," Odrade said.

"But in your mind is knowledge that could ruin us!" He glanced back at the guardian Sisters.

"They are part of my arsenal," Odrade agreed. "Shall I send them away?"

"And in their minds everything they have heard here," he said. He returned his wary gaze to Odrade. "Better if you all sent your memories away!"

Odrade pitched her voice in its most reasonable tones. "What would we gain by exposing your missionary zeal before you are ready to move? Would it serve us to blacken your reputation by revealing where you have placed your new Face Dancers? Oh, yes, we know about Ix and the Fish Speakers. Once we had studied your new ones, we went searching for them."

"You see!" His voice was dangerously edged.

"I see no other way to prove our affinity than to reveal something equally damaging about ourselves," Odrade said.

Waff was speechless.

"We would plant the worms of the Prophet on uncounted planets of the Scattering," she said. "What would the Rakian priesthood say and do if you revealed that?"

The guardian Sisters looked at her with thinly masked amusement. They thought she was lying.

"I have no guards with *me*," Waff said. "When only one person knows a dangerous thing, how easy it is to gain that person's eternal silence."

She lifted her empty sleeves.

He looked at the guardian Sisters.

"Very well," Odrade said. She glanced at the Sisters and gave a subtle handsign to reassure them. "Wait outside, please, Sisters."

When the door closed behind them, Waff returned to his doubts. "My people have not searched these rooms. What do I know of the things that could be hidden here to record our words?"

Odrade shifted into the language of the Islamiyat. "Then perhaps we should speak another tongue, one known only to us."

Waff's eyes glittered. In the same tongue, he said: "Very well! I will gamble on it. And I ask you to tell me the real cause of dissension among the . . . the Bene Gesserit."

Odrade allowed herself a smile. With the change of language, Waff's entire personality, his whole manner, changed. He was performing exactly as expected. None of his doubts had been reinforced in *this* tongue!

She responded with an equal confidence: "Fools fear that we may bring back another Kwisatz Haderach! That is what a few of my Sisters argue."

"There is no more need of such a one," Waff said. "The one who could be many places simultaneously has been and he has gone. He came only to bring the Prophet."

"God would not send such a message twice," she said.

It was the very sort of thing Waff had heard often in this tongue. He no longer thought it strange that a woman could utter such words. The language and the familiar words were enough.

"Has Schwangyu's death restored unity among your Sisters?" he asked.

"We have a common enemy," Odrade said.

"The Honored Matres!"

"You were wise to kill them and learn from them."

Waff leaned forward, completely caught up in his familiar tongue and the flow of their conversation. "They rule with sex!" he exulted. "Remarkable techniques of orgasmic amplification! We—" Belatedly, he became aware of who was sitting in front of him hearing all of this.

"We already know such techniques," Odrade reassured him. "It will be interesting to compare, but there are obvious reasons why we have never tried to ride to power on such a dangerous conveyance. Those whores are just stupid enough to make that mistake!"

"Mistake?" He was clearly puzzled.

"They are holding the reins in their own hands!" she said. "As the power grows, their control of it must grow. The thing will shatter of its own momentum!"

"Power, always power," Waff muttered. Another thought struck him. "Are you saying this was how the Prophet fell?"

"He knew what he was doing," she said. "Millennia of enforced peace followed by the Famine Times and the Scattering. A message of direct results. Remember! He did not destroy the Bene Tleilax or the Bene Gesserit."

"For what do you hope from an alliance between our two peoples?" Waff asked.

"Hope is one thing, survival another," she said.

"Always pragmatism," Waff said. "And some among you fear that you may restore the Prophet on Rakis with all of his powers intact?"

"Did I not say it?" The language of the Islamiyat was particularly potent in this questioning form. It placed the burden of proof on Waff.

"So they doubt God's hand in the creation of your Kwisatz Haderach," he said. "Do they also doubt the Prophet?"

"Very well, let us have it all out in the open," Odrade said, and launched herself on the chosen course of deception: "Schwangyu and those who supported her broke away from the Great Belief. We harbor no anger toward any Bene Tleilax for having killed them. They saved us the trouble."

Waff accepted this utterly. Given the circumstances, it was precisely what could be expected. He knew he had revealed much here that might better have been held in reserve but there were still things the Bene Gesserit did not know. And the things he had learned!

Odrade shocked him totally then by saying: "Waff, if you think your descendants from the Scattering have returned to you unchanged, then foolishness has become your way of life."

He held himself silent.

"You have all of the pieces in your hands," she said. "Your descendants belong to the whores of the Scattering. And if you think any of *them* will abide by an agreement, then your stupidity goes beyond description!"

Waff's reactions told her she had him. The pieces were clicking into place. She had told him truth where it was required. His doubts were refocused where they belonged: against the people of the Scattering. And it had been done in his own tongue.

He tried to speak past a constriction in his throat and was forced to massage his throat before speech returned. "What can we do?"

"It's obvious. The Lost Ones have their eyes on us as just one more conquest. They think of it as cleaning up behind them. Common prudence."

"But they are so many!"

"Unless we unite in a common plan to defeat them, they will chew us up the way a slig chews up its dinner."

"We cannot submit to powindah filth! God will not permit it!"

"Submit? Who suggests that we submit?"

"But the Bene Gesserit always use that ancient excuse: 'If you can't beat them, join them.'"

Odrade smiled grimly. "God will not permit you to submit! Do you suggest He would permit it of us?"

"Then what is your plan? What would you do against such numbers?"

"Exactly what you plan to do: convert them. When you say the word, the Sisterhood will openly espouse the true faith."

Waff sat in stunned silence. So she knew the heart of the Tleilaxu plan. Did she know also how the Tleilaxu would enforce it?

Odrade stared at him, openly speculative. *Grasp the beast by the balls if you must,* she thought. But what if the projection by the Sisterhood's analysts was wrong? This whole *negotiation* would be a joke in that case. And there was that look in the back of Waff's eyes, that suggestion of older wisdom . . . much older than his flesh. She spoke with more confidence than she felt:

"What you have achieved with gholas from your tanks and kept secretly for yourselves alone, others will pay a great price to achieve."

Her words were sufficiently cryptic (Were others listening?) but Waff did not doubt for an instant that the Bene Gesserit knew even this thing.

"Will you demand a share in that as well?" he asked. The words rasped in his dry throat.

"Everything! We will share everything."

"What will you bring to this great sharing?"

"Ask."

"All of your breeding records."

"They are yours."

"Breeding mothers of our choice."

"Name them."

Waff gasped. This was far more than the Mother Superior had offered. It was like a blossom opening in his awareness. She was right about the Honored Matres, naturally—and about the Tleilaxu descendants from the Scattering. He had never completely trusted them. Never!

"You will want an unrestricted source of melange, of course," he said.

"Of course."

He stared at her, hardly believing the extent of his good fortune. The axlotl tanks would offer immortality only to those who espoused the Great Belief. No one would dare attack and attempt to seize a thing they knew the Tleilaxu would destroy rather than lose. And now! He had gained the services of the most powerful and enduring missionary force known. Surely, the hand of God was visible here. Waff was first awed and then inspired. He spoke softly to Odrade.

"And you, Reverend Mother, how do you name our accord?"

"Noble purpose," she said. "You already know the Prophet's words from Sietch Tabr. Do you doubt him?"

"Never! But . . . but there is one thing: What do you propose with that ghola of Duncan Idaho and the girl, Sheeana?"

"We will breed them, of course. And their descendants will speak for us to all of those descendants of the Prophet."

"On all of those planets where you would take them!"

"On all of those planets," she agreed.

Waff sat back. *I have you, Reverend Mother!* he thought. *We will rule this alliance, not you. The ghola is not yours; he is ours!*

Odrade saw the shadow of his reservations in Waff's eyes but knew she had ventured as much as she dared. More would reawaken doubts. Whatever happened, she had committed the Sisterhood to this course. Taraza could not escape this alliance now.

Waff squared his shoulders, a curiously juvenile gesture belied by the ancient intelligence peering from his eyes. "Ahhhh, one thing more," he said, every bit the Master of Masters speaking his own language and commanding all of those who heard him. "Will you also help spread this . . . this Atreides Manifesto?"

"Why not? I wrote it."

Waff jerked forward. "You?"

"Did you think someone of lesser abilities could have done it?"

He nodded, convinced without further argument. This was fuel for a thought that had entered his own mind, a final point in their alliance: The powerful minds of Reverend Mothers would advise the Tleilaxu at every turn! What did it matter that they were outnumbered by those whores of the Scattering? Who could match such combined wisdom and insurmountable weapons?

"The title of the Manifesto is valid, too," Odrade said. "I am a true descendant of the Atreides."

"Would you be one of our breeders?" he ventured.

"I am almost past the age of breeding, but I am yours to command."

I remember friends from wars all but we forgot.
All of them distilled into each wound we caught.
Those wounds are all the painful places where we fought.
Battles better left behind, ones we never sought.
What is it that we spent and what was it we bought?

—SONGS OF THE SCATTERING

Burzmali based his planning on the best of what he had learned from his Bashar, keeping his own counsel about multiple options and fallback positions. That was a commander's prerogative! Necessarily, he learned everything he could about the terrain.

In the time of the Old Empire and even under the reign of Muad'Dib, the region around the Gammu Keep had been a forest reserve, high ground rising well above the oily residue that tended to cover Harkonnen land. On this ground, the Harkonnens had grown some of the finest pilingitam, a wood of steady currency, always valued by the supremely rich. From the most ancient times, the knowledgeable had preferred to surround themselves with fine woods rather than with the mass-produced artificial materials known then as polastine, polaz, and pormabat (latterly: tine, laz, and bat). As far back as the Old Empire there had been a pejorative label for the small rich and Families Minor arising from the knowledge of a rare wood's value.

"He's a three P-O," they said, meaning that such a person surrounded himself with cheap copies made from déclassé substances. Even when the supremely rich were forced to employ one of the distressful three

P-Os, they disguised it where possible behind O-P (the Only P), pilingitam.

Burzmali knew all of this and more as he set his people to searching for a strategically situated pilingitam near the no-globe. The wood of the tree had many qualities that endeared it to master artisans: Newly cut, it worked like a softwood; dried and aged, it endured as a hardwood. It absorbed many pigments and the finish could be made to appear as though it occurred naturally within the grain. More important, pilingitam was anti-fungal and no known insect had ever considered it a suitable dinner. Lastly, it was fire-resistant, and aged specimens of the living tree grew outward from an enlarged and empty tube at the core.

"We will do the unexpected," Burzmali told his searchers.

He had noted the distinctive lime green of pilingitam leaves during his first overflight of the region. The forests of this planet had been raided and otherwise logged off during the Famine Times but venerable O-Ps were still nurtured among the evergreens and hardwoods replanted at the Sisterhood's orders.

Burzmali's searchers found one such O-P dominating a ridge above the no-globe site. It spread its leaves over almost three hectares. On the afternoon of the critical day, Burzmali placed decoys at a distance from this position and opened a tunnel from a shallow swale into the pilingitam's roomy core. There, he set up his command post and the backup necessities for escape.

"The tree is a life form," he explained to his people. "It will mask us from tracers."

The unexpected.

Nowhere in his planning did Burzmali assume that all of his actions would go undetected. He could only spread his vulnerability.

When the attack came, he saw that it appeared to follow a predicted pattern. He had anticipated that attackers would rely on no-ships and great numbers as they had in the assault on the Gammu Keep. The Sisterhood's analysts assured him that the major threat was from forces out of the Scattering—descendants of the Tleilaxu deployed by wildly brutal women calling themselves Honored Matres. He saw this as over-confidence and not audacity. A real audacity was in the arsenal of every student taught by the Bashar Miles Teg. It also helped that Teg could be relied upon to improvise within the limits of a plan.

Through his relays, Burzmali followed the scrambling escape of Duncan and Lucilla. Troopers with com-helmets and night lenses created a great display of activity at the decoy positions while Burzmali and his select reserves kept watch on the attackers, never betraying their position. Teg's movements were easily followed by his violent response to the attackers.

Burzmali noted with approval that Lucilla did not pause when she heard the battle sounds intensify. Duncan, however, tried to stop and almost ruined the plan. Lucilla saved the moment by jabbing Duncan in a sensitive nerve and barking: "You can't help him!"

Hearing her voice clearly through his helmet amplifiers, Burzmali cursed under his breath. Others would hear her, too! No doubt they already were tracking her, though.

Burzmali issued a subvocal command through the microphone implanted in his neck and prepared to abandon his post. He kept most of his attention on the approach of Lucilla and Duncan. If all went as planned, his people would bring down the pair of them while two helmetless and suitably garbed troopers continued the flight toward the decoy positions.

In the interim, Teg was creating an admirable path of destruction through which a groundcar might escape.

An aide intruded on Burzmali: "Two attackers are closing in behind the Bashar!"

Burzmali waved the man aside. He could give little thought to Teg's chances. Everything had to be focused on saving the ghola. Burzmali's thoughts were intense as he watched:

Come on! Run! Run, damn you!

Lucilla held a similar thought as she urged Duncan forward, keeping herself close behind him to shield him from the rear. Everything about her was marshaled for ultimate resistance. Everything in her breeding and training came to the fore in these moments. *Never give up!* To give up was to pass her consciousness into the Memory Lives of a Sister or into oblivion. Even Schwangyu had redeemed herself in the end by reverting to total resistance and had died admirably in the Bene Gesserit tradition, resisting to the last. Burzmali had reported it through Teg. Lucilla, assembling her uncounted lives, thought: *I can do no less!*

She followed Duncan down into a shallow swale beside the bole of a giant pilingitam and, when people arose out of the darkness to drag them down, she almost responded in berserker mode but a voice speaking Chakobsa in her ear said: "Friends!" This delayed her response for a heartbeat while she saw the decoys continue the flight out of the swale. That more than anything else revealed the plan and the identity of the people holding them against the rich leafy smells of the earth. When the people slid Duncan ahead of her into a tunnel aimed at the giant tree and (still in Chakobsa) cautioned speed, Lucilla knew she was caught in a typical Teg-style audacity.

Duncan saw it, too. At the stygian outlet of the tunnel, he identified her by smell and tapped out a message against her arm in the old Atreides silent battle language.

"Let them lead."

The form of the message startled her momentarily until she realized that the ghola of course would know this communication method.

Without speaking, the people around them removed Duncan's bulky antique lasgun and hustled the fugitives into the hatch of a vehicle that she did not identify. A brief red light flared in the darkness.

Burzmali spoke subvocally to his people: "There they go!"

Twenty-eight groundcars and eleven flitter-thopters scrambled from the decoy positions. *A proper diversion,* Burzmali thought.

Pressure in Lucilla's ears told her a hatch had been sealed. Again the red light flared and went dark.

Explosives shattered the great tree around them and their vehicle, now identifiable as an armored groundcar, surged up and out on suspensors and jets. Lucilla could follow their course only by flashes of fire and the twisting patterns of stars visible through frames of oval plaz. The enclosing suspensor field made the motions eerie, sensed only by the eyes. They sat cradled in plasteel seats while their car rocketed downslope directly across Teg's holdout position, shifting and darting in violent changes of direction. None of this wild motion transmitted itself to the flesh of the occupants. There were only the dancing blurs of trees and brush, some of them burning, and then the stars.

They were hugging the tops of the forest wreckage left by Teg's lasguns! Only then did she dare to hope that they might win free. Abruptly, their vehicle trembled into slow flight. The visible stars, framed by the tiny ovals of plaz, tipped and were obscured by a dark obstruction. Gravity returned and there was dim light. Lucilla saw Burzmali fling open a hatch on her left.

"Out!" he snapped. "Not a second to spare!"

Duncan ahead of her, Lucilla scrambled out of the hatch onto damp earth. Burzmali thumped her back, grabbed Duncan's arm and hustled them away from the car. "Quick! This way!" They crashed through tall bushes onto a narrow paved roadway. Burzmali, a hand on each of them now, rushed them across the road and pushed them flat in a ditch. He whipped a life-shield blanket over them and lifted his head to look back in the direction from which they had come.

Lucilla peered past him and saw starlight on a snowy slope. She felt Duncan stir beside her.

Far up the slope, a speeding groundcar, its jet-pod modifications visible against the stars, lifted on a plume of red, climbing, climbing . . . climbing. Suddenly, it darted off to the right.

"Ours?" Duncan whispered.

"Yes."

"How did it get up there without showing a . . ."

"An abandoned aqueduct tunnel," Burzmali whispered. "The car was programed to go on automatic." He continued to stare at the distant red plume. Abruptly, a gigantic burst of blue light rolled outward from the faraway red tracery. The light was followed immediately by a dull thump.

"Ahhhhh," Burzmali breathed.

Duncan, his voice low, said: "They are supposed to think you over-loaded your drive."

Burzmali shot a startled look at the young face, ghostly gray in starlight.

"Duncan Idaho was one of the finest pilots in Atreides service," Lucilla said. It was an esoteric bit of knowledge and it served its purpose. Burzmali saw immediately that he was not just guardian of two fugitives. His charges possessed abilities that could be used if needed.

Blue and red sparks flashed across the sky where the modified groundcar had exploded. The no-ships were sniffing that distant globe of hot gases. What would the sniffers decide? The blue and red sparks slipped down behind the starlit bulges of the hills.

Burzmali whirled at the sound of footsteps on the roadway. Duncan had a handgun out so swiftly that Lucilla gasped. She put a restraining hand on his arm but he shook it off. Didn't he see that Burzmali had accepted this intrusion?

A voice called softly from the roadway above them: "Follow me. Hurry."

The speaker, a moving blot of darkness, jumped down beside them and went crashing through a gap in the bushes lining the road. Dark spots on the snowy slope beyond the screening bushes resolved themselves into at least a dozen armed figures. Five of this party grouped themselves around Duncan and Lucilla and urged them silently along a snow-covered trail beside the bushes. The rest of the armed party ran openly down across the snowslope into a dark line of trees.

Within a hundred paces, the five silent figures formed their party into single file, two of their number ahead, three behind, the fugitives sheltered between them with Burzmali leading and Lucilla close behind Duncan. They came presently to a cleft in dark rocks and under a ledge where they waited, listening to more modified groundcars thunder into the air behind them.

"Decoys upon decoys," Burzmali whispered. "We overload them with decoys. They *know* we must flee in panic as fast as possible. Now, we will wait nearby in concealment. Later, we will proceed slowly . . . on foot."

"The unexpected," Lucilla whispered.

"Teg?" It was Duncan, his voice little more than a breath.

Burzmali leaned close to Duncan's left ear: "I think they got him." Burzmali's whisper carried a deep tone of sadness.

One of their dark companions said: "Quickly now. Down here."

They were herded through the narrow cleft. Something emitted a creaking sound nearby. Hands hustled them into an enclosed passage. The creaking sounded from behind them.

"Get that door fixed," someone said.

Light flared around them.

Duncan and Lucilla stared around at a large, richly furnished room apparently cut into rock. Soft carpets covered the floor—dark reds and golds with a figured pattern like repetitive battlements worked in pale green. A bundle of clothing lay in a jumble on a table near Burzmali, who was in low-voiced conversation with one of their escort: a fair-haired man with high forehead and piercing green eyes.

Lucilla listened carefully. The words were understandable, relating how guards had been posted, but the green-eyed man's accent was one she had never before heard, a tumble of gutturals and consonants clicked off with surprising abruptness.

"Is this a no-chamber?" she asked.

"No." The answer was supplied by a man behind her speaking in that same accent. "The algae protect us."

She did not turn toward the speaker but looked up instead at the light yellow-green algae thick on the ceiling and walls. Only a few patches of dark rock were visible near the floors.

Burzmali broke off his conversation. "We are safe here. The algae is grown especially for this. Life scanners report only the presence of plant life and nothing else that the algae shields."

Lucilla pivoted on one heel, sorting the room's details: that Harkonnen griffin worked into a crystal table, the exotic fabrics on chairs and couches. A weapons rack against one wall held two rows of long field-style lasguns of a design she had never before seen. Each was bell-mouthed and with a curling gold guard over the trigger.

Burzmali had returned to his conversation with the green-eyed man. It was an argument over how they would be disguised. She listened with part of her mind while she studied the two members of their escort remaining in the room. The other three from the escort had filed out through a passage near the weapons cabinet, an opening covered by a thick hanging of shimmering silvery threads. Duncan, she saw, was watching her responses with care, his hand on the small lasgun in his belt.

People of the Scattering? Lucilla wondered. *What are their loyalties?*

Casually, she crossed to Duncan's side and, using the finger-touch language on his arm, relayed her suspicions. Both of them looked at Burzmali. *Treachery?*

Lucilla went back to her study of the room. Were they being watched by unseen eyes?

Nine glowglobes lighted the space, creating their own peculiar islands of intense illumination. It reached outward into a common concentration near where Burzmali still talked to the green-eyed man. Part of the light came directly from the drifting globes, all of them tuned into rich gold, and part of it was reflected more softly off the algae. The result was a lack of dark shadows, even under the furnishings.

The shimmering silver threads of the inner doorway parted. An old woman entered the room. Lucilla stared at her. The woman had a seamed face as dark as old rosewood. Her features were sharply defined in a narrow frame of straggling gray hair that fell almost to her shoulders. She wore a long black robe worked with golden threads in a pattern of mythological dragons. The woman stopped behind a settee and placed her deeply veined hands on the back.

Burzmali and his companion broke off their conversation.

Lucilla looked from the old woman down to her own robe. Except for the golden dragons, the garments were similar in design, the hoods draped back onto the shoulders. Only in the side cut and the way it opened down the front was the design of the dragon robe different.

When the woman did not speak, Lucilla looked to Burzmali for explanation. Burzmali stared back at her with a look of intense concentration. The old woman continued to study Lucilla silently.

The intensity of attention filled Lucilla with disquiet. Duncan felt it, too, she saw. He kept his hand on the small lasgun. The long silence while eyes examined her amplified her unease. There was something almost Bene Gesserit about the way the old woman just stood there looking.

Duncan broke the silence, demanding of Burzmali: "Who is she?"

"I'm the one who'll save your skins," the old woman said. She had a thin voice that crackled weakly, but that same strange accent.

Lucilla's Other Memories brought up a suggestive comparison for the old woman's garment: *Similar to that worn by ancient playfems.*

Lucilla almost shook her head. Surely this woman was too old for such a role. And the shape of the mythic dragons worked into the fabric differed from those supplied by memory. Lucilla returned her attention to the old face: eyes humid with the illnesses of age. A dry crust had settled into the creases where each eyelid touched the channels beside her nose. Far too old for a playfem.

The old woman spoke to Burzmali. "I think she can wear it well enough." She began divesting herself of her dragon robe. To Lucilla she said: "This is for you. Wear it with respect. We killed to get it for you."

"Who did you kill?" Lucilla demanded.

"A postulant of the Honored Matres!" There was pride in the old woman's husky tone.

"Why should I wear that robe?" Lucilla demanded.

"You will trade garments with me," the old woman said.

"Not without explanation." Lucilla refused to accept the robe being extended to her.

Burzmali took one step forward. "You can trust her."

"I am a friend of your friends," the old woman said. She shook the robe in front of Lucilla. "Here, take it."

Lucilla addressed Burzmali. "I must know your plan."

"We both must know it," Duncan said. "On whose authority are we asked to trust these people?"

"Teg's," Burzmali said. "And mine." He looked at the old woman. "You can tell them, Sirafa. We have time."

"You will wear this robe while you accompany Burzmali into Ysai," Sirafa said.

Sirafa, Lucilla thought. The name had almost the sound of a Bene Gesserit Lineal Variant.

Sirafa studied Duncan. "Yes, he is small enough yet. He will be disguised and conveyed separately."

"No!" Lucilla said. "I am commanded to guard him!"

"You are being foolish," Sirafa said. "They will be looking for a woman of your appearance accompanied by someone of this young man's appearance. They will not be looking for a playfem of the Honored Matres with her companion of the night . . . nor for a Tleilaxu Master and his entourage."

Lucilla wet her lips with her tongue. Sirafa spoke with the confident assurance of a House Proctor.

Sirafa draped the dragon robe over the back of the settee. She stood revealed in a clinging black leotard that concealed nothing of a body still lithe and supple, even well rounded. The body looked much younger than the face. As Lucilla looked at her, Sirafa passed her palms across her forehead and cheeks, smoothing them backward. Age lines grew shallow and a younger face was revealed.

A Face Dancer?

Lucilla stared hard at the woman. There were none of the other Face Dancer stigmata. Still . . .

"Get your robe off!" Sirafa ordered. Now her voice was younger and even more commanding.

"You must do it," Burzmali pleaded. "Sirafa will take your place as another decoy. It's the only way we'll get through."

"Get through to what?" Duncan asked.

"To a no-ship," Burzmali said.

"And where will that take us?" Lucilla demanded.

"To safety," Burzmali said. "We will be loaded with shere but I cannot say more. Even shere wears off in time."

"How will I be disguised as a Tleilaxu?" Duncan asked.

"Trust us that it will be done," Burzmali said. He kept his attention on Lucilla. "Reverend Mother?"

"You give me no choice," Lucilla said. She undid the quick fasteners and dropped her robe. She removed the small handgun from her bodice and tossed it onto the settee. Her own leotard was light gray and she saw Sirafa making note of this and of the knives in their leg sheaths.

"We sometimes wear black undergarments," Lucilla said as she slipped into the dragon robe. The fabric looked heavy but felt light. She pivoted in it, sensing the way it flared and fitted itself to her body almost as though it had been made just for her. There was a rough spot at the neck. She reached up and ran a finger along it.

"That is where the dart struck her," Sirafa said. "We moved fast but the acid scarred the fabric slightly. It is not visible to the eye."

"Is the appearance correct?" Burzmali asked Sirafa.

"Very good. But I will have to instruct her. She must make no mistakes or they will have both of you like that!" Sirafa clapped her hands for emphasis.

Where have I seen that gesture? Lucilla asked herself.

Duncan touched the back of Lucilla's right arm, his fingers secretly quick-talking: *"That hand clap! A mannerism of Giedi Prime."*

Other Memories confirmed this for Lucilla. Was this woman part of an isolated community preserving archaic ways?

"The lad should go now," Sirafa said. She gestured to the two remaining members of the escort. "Take him to the place."

"I don't like this," Lucilla said.

"We have no choice!" Burzmali barked.

Lucilla could only agree. She was relying on Burzmali's oath of loyalty to the Sisterhood, she knew. And Duncan was not a child, she reminded herself. His prana-bindu reactions had been conditioned by the old Bashar and herself. There were abilities in the ghola that few people outside of the Bene Gesserit could match. She watched silently as Duncan and the two men left through the shimmering curtain.

When they were gone, Sirafa came around the settee and stood in front of Lucilla, hands on hips. Their gazes met at a level.

Burzmali cleared his throat and fingered the rough pile of clothing on the table beside him.

Sirafa's face, especially the eyes, held a remarkably compelling quality. The eyes were light green with clear whites. No lens or other artifice masked them.

"You have the right look about you," Sirafa said. "Remember that you are a special kind of playfem and Burzmali is your customer. No ordinary person would interfere with that."

Lucilla heard a veiled hint in this. "But there are those who might interfere?"

"Embassies from great religions are on Gammu now," Sirafa said. "Some you have never encountered. They are from what you call the Scattering."

"And what do you call it?"

"The Seeking." Sirafa raised a placating hand. "Do not fear! We have a common enemy."

"The Honored Matres?"

Sirafa turned her head to the left and spat on the floor. "Look at me, Bene Gesserit! I was trained only to kill them! That is my only function and purpose!"

Lucilla spoke carefully: "From what we know, you must be very good."

"In some things, perhaps I am better than you. Now listen! You are a sexual adept. Do you understand?"

"Why would priests interfere?"

"You call them priests? Well . . . yes. They would not interfere for any reason you might imagine. Sex for pleasure, the enemy of religion, eh?"

"Accept no substitutes for holy joy," Lucilla said.

"Tantrus protect you, woman! There are different *priests* from the Seeking, ones who do not mind offering immediate ecstasy instead of a promised hereafter."

Lucilla almost smiled. Did this self-styled killer of Honored Matres think she could advise a Reverend Mother on religions?

"There are people here who go about disguised as *priests*," Sirafa said. "Very dangerous. The most dangerous of all are those who follow Tantrus and claim that sex is the exclusive worship of their god."

"How will I know them?" Lucilla heard sincerity in Sirafa's voice and a sense of foreboding.

"That is not a concern. You must never act as though you recognize such distinctions. Your first concern is to make sure of your pay. You, I think, should ask fifty solari."

"You have not told me why they would interfere." Lucilla glanced back at Burzmali. He had laid out the rough clothing and was taking off his battle fatigues. She returned her attention to Sirafa.

"Some follow an ancient convention that grants them the right to disrupt your arrangement with Burzmali. In actuality, some will be testing you."

"Listen carefully," Burzmali said. "This is important."

Sirafa said: "Burzmali will be dressed as a field worker. Nothing else could disguise his weapon's calluses. You will address him as Skar, a common name here."

"But how do I deal with a priest's interruption?"

Sirafa produced a small pouch from her bodice and passed it to Lucilla, who hefted it in one hand. "That contains two hundred and eighty-three solari. If someone identifying himself as a divine . . . You remember that? Divine?"

"How could I forget it?" Lucilla's voice was almost a sneer but Sirafa paid no heed.

"If such a one interferes, you will return fifty solari to Burzmali with your regrets. Also, in that pouch is your playfem card in the name of Pira. Let me hear you say your name."

"Pira."

"No! Accent much harder on the 'a'!"

"Pira!"

"That is passable. Now listen to me with extreme care. You and Burzmali will be on the streets late. It will be expected that you have had previous customers. There must be evidence. Therefore, you will . . . ahhh, entertain Burzmali before leaving here. You understand?"

"Such delicacy!" Lucilla said.

Sirafa took it as a compliment and smiled, but it was a tightly controlled expression. Her reactions were so alien!

"One thing," Lucilla said. "If I must *entertain* a divine, how will I find Burzmali afterward?"

"Skar!"

"Yes. How will I find Skar?"

"He will wait nearby wherever you go. Skar will find you when you emerge."

"Very well. If a *divine* interrupts, I return one hundred solari to Skar and—"

"Fifty!"

"I think not, Sirafa." Lucilla shook her head slowly from side to side. "After being *entertained* by me, the divine will know that fifty solari is too small a sum."

Sirafa pursed her lips and glanced past Lucilla at Burzmali. "You warned me about her kind but I did not suppose that . . ."

Using only a touch of Voice, Lucilla said: "You suppose *nothing* unless you hear it from me!"

Sirafa scowled. She was obviously startled by Voice, but her tone was just as arrogant when she resumed. "Do I presume that you need no explanation of sexual variations?"

"A safe assumption," Lucilla said.

"And I do not need to tell you that your robe identifies you as a fifth-stage adept in the Order of Hormu?"

It was Lucilla's turn to scowl. "What if I show abilities beyond this fifth stage?"

"Ahhhhh," Sirafa said. "You will continue to heed my words, then?"

Lucilla nodded curtly.

"Very good," Sirafa said. "May I presume you can administer vaginal pulsing?"

"I can."

"From any position?"

"I can control any muscle in my body!"

Sirafa glanced past Lucilla at Burzmali. "True?"

Burzmali spoke from close behind Lucilla: "Or she would not claim it."

Sirafa looked thoughtful, her focus on Lucilla's chin. "This is a complication, I think."

"Lest you get the wrong idea," Lucilla said, "the abilities I was taught are not usually marketed. They have another purpose."

"Oh, I'm sure they do," Sirafa said. "But sexual agility is a—"

"Agility!" Lucilla allowed her tone to convey the full weight of a Reverend Mother's outrage. No matter that this might be what Sirafa hoped to achieve, she had to be put in her place! "Agility, you say? I can control genital temperature. I know and can arouse the fifty-one excitation points. I—"

"Fifty-one? But there are only—"

"Fifty-one!" Lucilla snapped. "And the sequencing plus the combinations number two thousand and eight. Furthermore, in combination with the two hundred and five sexual positions—"

"Two hundred and five?" Sirafa was clearly startled. "Surely, you don't mean—"

"More, actually, if you count minor variations. I am an Imprinter, which means I have mastered the three hundred steps of orgasmic amplification!"

Sirafa cleared her throat and wet her lips with her tongue. "I must warn you then to restrain yourself. Keep your full abilities unexpressed or . . ." Once more, she looked at Burzmali. "Why didn't you warn me?"

"I did."

Lucilla clearly heard amusement in his voice but did not look back to confirm it.

Sirafa inhaled and expelled two hard breaths. "If any questions are asked, you will say you are about to undergo testing for advancement. That may quiet suspicion."

"And if I'm asked about the test."

"Oh, that is easy. You smile mysteriously and remain silent."

"What if I'm asked about this Order of Hormu?"

"Threaten to report the questioner to your superiors. The questions should stop."

"And if they don't?"

Sirafa shrugged. "Make up any story you like. Even a Truth-sayer would be amused by your evasions."

Lucilla held her face in repose while she thought about her situation. She heard Burzmali—Skar!—stirring directly behind her. She saw no serious difficulties in carrying out this deception. It might even provide an amusing interlude she could recount later at Chapter House. Sirafa, she noted, was grinning at Burz—Skar! Lucilla turned and looked at her *customer.*

Burzmali stood there naked, his battle garb and helmet neatly stacked beside the small mound of rough clothing.

"I can see that Skar does not object to your preparations for this venture," Sirafa said. She waved a hand at his stiffly upcocked penis. "I will leave you, then."

Lucilla heard Sirafa depart through the shimmering curtain. Filling Lucilla's thoughts was an angry realization:

"This should be the ghola here now!"

"In the name of our Order and its unbroken Sisterhood, this account has been judged reliable and worthy of entry into the Chronicles of Chapter House."

Taraza stared at the words on her display projection with an expression of distaste. Morning light painted a fuzz of yellow reflections in the projection, making the words there appear dimly mysterious.

With an angry motion, Taraza pushed herself back from the projection table, arose and went to a south window. The day was young yet and the shadows long in her courtyard.

Shall I go in person?

Reluctance filled her at this thought. These quarters felt so . . . so secure. But that was foolishness and she knew it in every fiber. The Bene Gesserit had been here more than fourteen hundred years and still Chapter House Planet must be considered only temporary.

She rested her left hand on the smooth frame of the window. Each of her windows had been positioned to focus the attention on a splendid view. The room—its proportions, furnishing, colors—all reflected architects and builders who had worked single-mindedly to create a sense of support for the occupants.

Taraza tried to immerse herself in that supportive feeling and failed.

The arguments she had just experienced left a bitterness in this room even though the words had been voiced in the mildest tones. Her councillors had been stubborn and (she agreed without reservation) for understandable reasons.

Make ourselves into missionaries? And for the Tleilaxu?

She touched a control plate beside the window and opened it. A warm breeze perfumed by spring blossoms from the apple orchards wafted into the room. The Sisterhood was proud of the fruit they grew here at the power center of all their strongholds. No finer orchards existed at any of the Keeps and Dependent Chapters that wove the Bene Gesserit web through most of the planets humans had occupied under the Old Imperium.

"By their fruits, ye shall know them," she thought. *Some of the old religions can still produce wisdom.*

From her high vantage, Taraza could see the entire southern sprawl of Chapter House buildings. The shadow of a nearby watchtower drew a long uneven line across rooftops and courtyards.

When she thought about it, she knew this was a surprisingly small establishment to contain so much power. Beyond the ring of orchards and gardens lay a careful checkerboard of private residences, each with its surrounding plantation. Retired Sisters and selected loyal families occupied these privileged estates. Sawtoothed mountains, their tops often brilliant with snow, drew the western limits. The spacefield lay twenty kilometers eastward. All around this core of Chapter House were open plains where grazed a peculiar breed of cattle, a cattle so susceptible to alien odors they would stampede in raucous bellowing at the slightest intrusion of people not marked by the local smell. The innermost homes with their pain-fenced plantings had been sited by an early Bashar in such a way that no one could move through the twisting ground-level channels day or night without being observed.

It all appeared so haphazard and casual, yet there was harsh order in it. And that, Taraza knew, personified the Sisterhood.

The clearing of a throat behind her reminded Taraza that one of those who had argued most vehemently in Council remained waiting patiently in the open doorway.

Waiting for my decision.

The Reverend Mother Bellonda wanted Odrade "killed out of hand." No decision had been reached.

You've really done it this time, Dar. I expected your wild independence. I even wanted it. But this!

Bellonda, old, fat and florid, cold-eyed and valued for her natural viciousness, wanted Odrade condemned as a traitor.

"The Tyrant would have crushed her immediately!" Bellonda argued.

Is that all we learned from him? Taraza wondered.

Bellonda argued that Odrade was not only an Atreides but also a Corrino. There were emperors and vice-regents and powerful administrators to a very large number in her ancestry.

With all of the power hunger this implies.

"Her ancestors survived Salusa Secundus!" Bellonda kept repeating. "Have we learned nothing from our breeding experiences?"

We learned how to create Odrades, Taraza thought.

After surviving the spice agony, Odrade had been sent to Al Dhanab, an equivalent of Salusa Secundus, there to be conditioned deliberately on a planet of constant testing: high cliffs and dry gorges, hot winds and frigid winds, little moisture and too much. It was judged a suitable proving ground for someone whose destiny might take her to Rakis. Tough survivors emerged from such conditioning. The tall, supple, and muscular Odrade was one of the toughest.

How can I salvage this situation?

Odrade's most recent message said that any peace, even the Tyrant's millennia of suppression, radiated a false aura that could be fatal to those who trusted it too much. That was both the strength and flaw in Bellonda's argument.

Taraza lifted her gaze to Bellonda waiting in the doorway. *She is too fat! She flaunts that before us!*

"We can no more eliminate Odrade than we can eliminate the ghola," Taraza said.

Bellonda's voice came low and level: "Both are now too dangerous to us. Look how Odrade weakens you with her account of those words at Sietch Tabr!"

"Has the Tyrant's message weakened me, Bell?"

"You know what I mean. The Bene Tleilax have no morals."

"Quit changing the subject, Bell. Your thoughts are darting around like an insect among the blossoms. What is it you really smell here?"

"The Tleilaxu! They made that ghola for their own purposes. And now Odrade wants us to—"

"You're repeating yourself, Bell."

"The Tleilaxu take shortcuts. Their view of genetics is not our view. It is not a *human* view. They make monsters."

"Is that what they do?"

Bellonda came into the room, walked around the table and stood close to Taraza, blocking the Mother Superior's view of the niche and its statuette of Chenoeh.

"Alliance with the priests of Rakis, yes, but not with the Tleilaxu." Bellonda's robes rustled as she gestured with a clenched fist.

"Bell! The High Priest is now a mimic Face Dancer. Ally with him, you mean?"

Bellonda shook her head angrily. "Believers in Shai-hulud are legion! You find them everywhere. What will be their reaction to us if our part in the deception is ever exposed?"

"No you don't, Bell! We have seen to it that only the Tleilaxu are vulnerable there. In that, Odrade's right."

"Wrong! If we ally with them we are both vulnerable. We will be forced to serve the Tleilaxu design. It will be worse than our long subservience to the Tyrant."

Taraza saw the vicious glinting of Bellonda's eyes. Her reaction was understandable. No Reverend Mother could contemplate the special bondage they had endured under the God Emperor without at least some chilling remembrances. Whipped along against their will, never sure of Bene Gesserit survival from one day to the next.

"You think we assure our spice supply by such a stupid alliance?" Bellonda demanded.

It was the same old argument, Taraza saw. Without melange and the agony of its transformation, there could be no Reverend Mothers. The whores from the Scattering surely had melange as one of their targets— the spice and the Bene Gesserit mastery of it.

Taraza returned to her table and sank into her chairdog, leaning back while it molded itself to her contours. It was a problem. A peculiar Bene Gesserit problem. Although they searched and experimented constantly, the Sisterhood had never found a substitute for the spice. The Spacing Guild might want melange to trance-form its navigators, but *they* could substitute Ixian machinery. Ix and its subsidiaries competed in the Guild's markets. *They* had alternatives.

We have none.

Bellonda crossed to the other side of Taraza's table, put both fists on the smooth surface and leaned forward to look down at the Mother Superior.

"And we still don't know what the Tleilaxu did to our ghola!"

"Odrade will find out."

"Not reason enough to forgive her treachery!"

Taraza spoke in a low voice: "We waited for this moment through generation after generation and you would abort the project just like that." She slapped a palm lightly against the table.

"The precious Rakian project is no longer our project," Bellonda said. "It may never have been."

All of her considerable mental powers in hard focus, Taraza reexamined the implications of this familiar argument. It was a thing spoken frequently in the wrangling session they had concluded earlier.

Was the ghola scheme something set in motion by the Tyrant? If so, what could they do about it now? What *should* they do about it?

During the long dispute, the Minority Report had been in all of their minds. Schwangyu might be dead but her faction survived and it looked now as though Bellonda had joined them. Was the Sisterhood blinding itself to a fatal possibility? Odrade's report of that hidden message on Rakis could be interpreted as an ominous warning. Odrade emphasized this by reporting how she had been alerted by her inner sense of alarm. No Reverend Mother could treat such an event lightly.

Bellonda straightened and folded her arms across her breast. "We never completely escape the teachers of our childhood nor any of the patterns that formed us, do we?"

That was an argument peculiar to Bene Gesserit disputes. It reminded them of their own particular susceptibility.

We are the secret aristocrats and it is our offspring who inherit the power. Yes, we are susceptible to that and Miles Teg is a superb example.

Bellonda found a straight chair and sat down, bringing her eyes level with Taraza's. "At the height of the Scattering," she said, "we lost some twenty percent of our failures."

"It is not failures who are coming back to us."

"But the Tyrant surely knew this would happen!"

"The Scattering was his goal, Bell. That was his Golden Path, humankind's survival!"

"But we know how he felt about the Tleilaxu and yet he did not exterminate them. He could have and he did not!"

"He wanted diversity."

Bellonda pounded a fist on the table. "He certainly got that!"

"We've been through all of these arguments over and over, Bell, and I still see no way to escape what Odrade has done."

"Subservience!"

"Not at all. Were we ever totally subservient to one of the pre-Tyrant emperors? Not even to Muad'Dib!"

"We're still in the Tyrant's trap," Bellonda accused. "Tell me, why have the Tleilaxu continued to produce his favorite ghola? Millennia, and still that ghola keeps coming out of their tanks like a dancing doll."

"You think the Tleilaxu still follow a secret order from the Tyrant?

If so, then you argue for Odrade. She has created admirable conditions for us to examine this."

"He ordered nothing of the kind! He merely made that particular ghola deliciously attractive to the Bene Tleilax."

"And not to us?"

"Mother Superior, we must get ourselves out of the Tyrant's trap now! And by the most direct method."

"The decision is mine, Bell. I still lean toward a cautious alliance."

"Then at the very least let us kill the ghola. Sheeana can have children. We could—"

"This is not now and never was purely a breeding project!"

"But it could be. What if you're wrong about the power behind the Atreides prescience?"

"All of your proposals lead to alienation from Rakis and from the Tleilaxu, Bell."

"The Sisterhood could weather fifty generations on our present stockpiles of melange. More with rationing."

"You think fifty generations is a long time, Bell? Don't you see that this very attitude is why you are not sitting in my chair?"

Bellonda pushed herself back from the table, her chair scraping harshly against the floor. Taraza could see that she was not convinced. Bellonda no longer could be trusted. She might be the one who would have to die. And where was the noble purpose in that?

"This gets us nowhere," Taraza said. "Leave me."

When she was alone, Taraza once more considered Odrade's message. Ominous. It was easy to see why Bellonda and others reacted violently. But that showed a dangerous lack of control.

It is not yet time to write the Sisterhood's final will and testament.

In an odd way, Odrade and Bellonda shared the same fear but came to different decisions because of that fear. Odrade's interpretation of that message in the stones of Rakis conveyed an old warning:

This, too, shall pass away.

Are we to end now, crushed by ravenous hordes from the Scattering?

But the secret of the axlotl tanks was almost within the Sisterhood's grasp.

If we gain that, nothing can stop us!

Taraza swung her gaze around the details of her room. The Bene Gesserit power was still here. Chapter House remained concealed behind a moat of no-ships, its location unrecorded except in the minds of her own people. Invisibility.

Temporary invisibility! Accidents occurred.

Taraza squared her shoulders. *Take precautions but don't live in their shadows, constantly furtive.* The Litany Against Fear served a useful purpose when avoiding shadows.

From anyone but Odrade, the warning message with its disturbing implications that the Tyrant still guided his Golden Path would have been far less fearsome.

That damnable Atreides talent!

"No more than a secret society?"

Taraza gritted her teeth in frustration.

"Memories are not enough unless they call you to noble purpose!"

And what if it was true that the Sisterhood no longer heard the music of life?

Damn him! The Tyrant could still touch them.

What is he trying to tell us? His Golden Path could not be in peril. The Scattering had seen to that. Humans had spread their kind outward on uncounted courses like the spines of a hedgehog.

Had he seen a vision of the Scattered Ones returning? Could he possibly have anticipated this bramble patch at the foot of his Golden Path?

He knew we would suspect his powers. He knew it!

Taraza thought about the mounting reports of the Lost Ones who were returning to their roots. A remarkable diversity of people and artifacts accompanied by a remarkable degree of secrecy and wide evidence of conspiracy. No-ships of a peculiar design, weapons and artifacts of breathtaking sophistication. Diverse peoples and diverse ways.

Some, astonishingly primitive. At least on the surface.

And they wanted much more than melange. Taraza recognized the peculiar form of mysticism that drove the Scattered Ones back: *"We want your elder secrets!"*

The message of the Honored Matres was clear enough, too: "We will take what we want."

Odrade has it all right in her hands, Taraza thought. She had Sheeana. Soon, if Burzmali succeeded, she would have the ghola. She had the Tleilaxu Master of Masters. She could have Rakis itself!

If only she were not an Atreides.

Taraza glanced at the projected words still dancing above her tabletop: a comparison of this newest Duncan Idaho with all of the slain ones. Each new ghola had been slightly different from its predecessors. That was clear enough. The Tleilaxu were perfecting something. But what? Was the clue hidden in these new Face Dancers? The Tleilaxu obviously sought an undetectable Face Dancer, mimics whose mimicry reached perfection, shape-copiers who copied not only the surface memories of their victims but the deepest thoughts and identity as well. It was a form of immortality even more enticing than the one the Tleilaxu Masters used at present. That obviously was why they followed this course.

Her own analysis agreed with the majority of her advisors: Such a mimic would *become* the copied person. Odrade's reports on the Face Dancer–Tuek were highly suggestive. Even the Tleilaxu Masters might not be able to shake such a Face Dancer out of its mimic shape and behavior.

And its beliefs.

Damn Odrade! She had painted her Sisters into a corner. They had no choice except to follow Odrade's lead and Odrade knew it!

How did she know it? Was it that wild talent again?

I cannot act blindly. I must know.

Taraza went through the well-remembered regimen to restore a sense of calm. She dared not make momentous decisions in a frustrated mood. A long look at the statuette of Chenoeh helped. Lifting herself from the chairdog, Taraza returned to her favorite window.

It often soothed her to stare out at this landscape, observing how the distances changed with the daily movement of sunlight and shifts in the planet's well-managed weather.

Hunger prodded her.

I will eat with the acolytes and lay Sisters today.

It helped at times to gather the young around her and remember the persistence of the eating rituals, the daily timing—morning, noon, and evening. That formed a reliable cement. She enjoyed watching her people. They were like a tide speaking of deeper things, of unseen forces and greater powers that persisted because the Bene Gesserit had found the ways of flowing with that persistence.

These thoughts renewed Taraza's balance. Nagging questions could be placed temporarily at a distance. She could look at them without passion.

Odrade and the Tyrant were right: *Without noble purpose we are nothing.*

One could not escape, though, the fact that critical decisions were being made on Rakis by a person who suffered from those recurring Atreides flaws. Odrade had always displayed typical Atreides weakness. She had been positively benevolent to erring acolytes. Affections developed out of such behavior!

Dangerous and mind-clouding affections.

This weakened others, who then were required to compensate for such laxity. More competent Sisters were called upon to take erring acolytes in hand and correct the weaknesses. Of course, Odrade's behavior had exposed these flaws in acolytes. One must admit this. Perhaps Odrade reasoned thus.

When she thought this way, something subtle and powerful shifted in Taraza's perceptions. She was forced to put down a deep sense of loneliness. It rankled. Melancholy could be quite as mind-clouding as affection . . . or even love. Taraza and her watchful Memory Sisters ascribed such emotional responses to awareness of mortality. She was forced to confront the fact that one day she would be no more than a set of memories in someone else's living flesh.

Memories and accidental discoveries, she saw, had made her vulnerable. And just when she needed every available faculty!

But I am not yet dead.

Taraza knew how to restore herself. And she knew the consequences. Always after these bouts of melancholy she regained an even firmer grip on her life and its purposes. Odrade's flawed behavior was a source of her Mother Superior's strength.

Odrade knew it. Taraza smiled grimly at this awareness. The Mother Superior's authority over her Sisters always became stronger when she returned from melancholy. Others had observed this but only Odrade knew about the rage.

There!

Taraza realized that she had confronted the distressful seeds of her frustration.

Odrade had clearly recognized on several occasions what sat at the core of the Mother Superior's behavior. A giant howl of rage against the uses others had made of her life. The power of that suppressed rage was daunting even though it could never be expressed in a way that vented it. That rage must never be allowed to heal. How it hurt! Odrade's awareness made the pain even more intense.

Such things did what they were supposed to do, of course. Bene Gesserit impositions developed certain mental muscles. They built up layers of callousness that could never be revealed to outsiders. Love was one of the most dangerous forces in the universe. They had to protect themselves against it. A Reverend Mother could never become intimately personal, not even in the services of the Bene Gesserit.

Simulation: We play the necessary role that saves us. The Bene Gesserit will persist!

How long would they be subservient this time? Another thirty-five hundred years? Well, damn them all! It would still be only a temporary thing.

Taraza turned her back on the window and its restorative view. She *did* feel restored. New strength flowed into her. There was strength enough to overcome that gnawing reluctance which had kept her from making the essential decision.

I will go to Rakis.

She no longer could evade the source of her own reluctance.

I may have to do what Bellonda wants.

Survival of self, of species, and of environment, these are what drive humans. You can observe how the order of importance changes in a lifetime. What are the things of immediate concern at a given age? Weather? The state of the digestion? Does she (or he) really care? All of those various hungers that flesh can sense and hope to satisfy. What else could possibly matter?

—LETO II TO HWI NOREE, HIS VOICE: DAR-ES-BALAT

Miles Teg awoke in darkness to find himself being carried on a litter sling supported by suspensors. By their faint energy glow, he could see the tiny suspensor bulbs in an updangling row around him.

There was a gag in his mouth. His hands were securely tied behind his back. His eyes remained uncovered.

So they don't care what I see.

Who *they* were he could not tell. The bobbing motions of the dark shapes around him suggested they were descending uneven terrain. A trail? The litter sling rode smoothly on its suspensors. He could sense the faint humming from the suspensors when his party stopped to negotiate the turn of a difficult passage.

Now and then through some intervening obstruction, he saw the flickering of a light ahead. They entered the lighted area presently and stopped. He saw a single glowglobe about three meters off the ground, tethered on a pole and moving gently in a cold breeze. By its yellow glow he discerned a shack in the center of a muddy clearing, many tracks in trampled snow. He saw bushes and a few sparse trees around the clearing. Someone passed a brighter handlight across his face. Nothing was said but Teg saw a hand gesture toward the shack. He had seldom seen such a dilapidated structure. It looked ready to collapse at the slightest touch. He bet himself that the roof leaked.

Once more, his party lurched into motion, swinging him toward the shack. He studied his escort in the dim light—faces muffled to the eyes in a cover that obscured mouths and chins. Hoods hid their hair. The clothing was bulky and concealed body details except for the general articulation of arms and legs.

The pole-tethered glowglobe went dark.

A door opened in the shack, sending a brilliant glare across the clearing. His escort hustled him inside and left him there. He heard the door close behind them.

It was almost blindingly bright inside after the darkness. Teg blinked until his eyes adapted to the change. With an odd sense of displacement, he looked around him. He had expected the shack's interior to match its exterior but here was a neat room almost bare of furnishings—only three chairs, a small table and . . . he drew in a sharp breath: an Ixian Probe! Couldn't they smell the shere on his breath?

If they were that unaware, let them use the probe. It would be agony for him but they would get nothing from his mind.

Something clicked behind him and he heard motion. Three people came into his field of vision and ranged themselves around the foot of the litter. They stared at him silently. Teg moved his attention across the three. The one on his left wore a dark singlesuit with open lapels. Male. He had the squarish face Teg had seen on some Gammu natives—small, beady eyes that stared straight through Teg. It was the face of an inquisitor, one who would not be moved by your agony. The Harkonnens had imported a lot of those in their day. Single-purpose types who could create pain without the slightest change of expression.

The one directly at Teg's feet wore bulky clothing of black and gray similar to that of the escort but the hood was thrown back to reveal a bland face under closely cropped gray hair. The face gave nothing away and the clothing revealed little. No telling if this one was male or female. Teg recorded the face: wide forehead, square chin, large green eyes above a knife-ridged nose; a tiny mouth pursed around a moue of distaste.

The third member of this group held Teg's attention longest: tall, a tailored black singlesuit with a severe black jacket over it. Perfectly fitted. Expensive. No decorations or insignia. Male definitely. The man affected boredom and this gave Teg a tag for him. Narrow, supercilious face, brown eyes, thin-lipped mouth. Bored, bored, bored! All of this in here was an unwarranted demand on his very important time. He had vital business elsewhere and these other two, these *underlings,* must be made to realize that.

That one, Teg thought, *is the official observer.*

The bored one had been sent by the masters of this place to watch and report what he saw. Where was his datacase? Ahhhh, yes: There it was, propped against a wall behind him. Those cases were like a badge for such functionaries. On his inspection tour, Teg had seen these people walking the streets of Ysai and other Gammu cities. Small, thin cases. The more important the functionary, the smaller the case. This one's case would barely contain a few dataspools and a tiny comeye. He would never be without an 'eye to link him with his superiors. Thin case: This was an important functionary.

Teg found himself wondering what the observer would say if Teg asked: "What will you tell them about my composure?"

The answer was already there on that bored face. He would not even answer. He was not here to answer. When this one leaves, Teg thought, he will walk with long strides. His attention will be on distances where only he knows what powers await him. He will slap that case against his leg to remind himself of his importance and to call the attention of these others to his badge of authority.

The bulky figure at Teg's feet spoke, a compelling voice and definitely female in those vibrant tones.

"See how he holds himself and watches us? Silence will not break him. I told you that before we entered. You are wasting our time and we do not have all that much time for such nonsense."

Teg stared at her. Something vaguely familiar in the voice. It had some of that compelling quality found in a Reverend Mother. Was that possible?

The heavy-faced Gammu type nodded. "You are right, Materly. But I do not give the orders here."

Materly? Teg wondered. *Name or title?*

Both of them looked at the functionary. That one turned and bent to his datacase. He removed a small comeye from it and stood with the screen concealed from his companions and Teg. The 'eye came alight with a green glow, which cast a sickly illumination over the observer's features. His self-important smile vanished. He moved his lips silently, words formed only for someone on that 'eye to see.

Teg hid his ability to read lips. Anyone trained by the Bene Gesserit could read lips from almost any angle where they were visible. This man spoke a version of Old Galach.

"It is the Bashar Teg for sure," he said. "I have made identification."

The green light danced on the functionary's face while he stared into the 'eye. Whoever communicated with him was in agitated movement if that light meant anything.

Again, the functionary's lips moved soundlessly: "None of us doubts that he has been conditioned against pain and I can smell shere on him. He will . . ."

He fell silent as the green light once more danced on his face.

"I do not make excuses." His lips shaped the Old Galach words with care. "You know we will do our best but I recommend that we pursue with vigor all other means of intercepting the ghola."

The green light winked off.

The functionary clipped the 'eye to his waist, turned toward his companions and nodded once.

"The T-probe," the woman said.

They swung the probe over Teg's head.

She called it a T-probe, Teg thought. He looked up at the hood as they brought it over him. There was no Ixian stamp on the thing.

Teg experienced an odd sense of déjà vu. He had the feeling that his own captivity here had occurred many times before. No single-incident déjà vu, it was a deeply familiar recognition: the captive and the interrogators—these three . . . the probe. He felt emptied. How could he know this moment? He had never personally employed a probe but he had studied their use thoroughly. The Bene Gesserit often used pain but relied mostly on Truthsayers. Even more than that, the Sisterhood believed that some equipment could put them too much under Ixian influence. It was an admission of weakness, a sign that they could not do without such despicable devices. Teg had even suspected there was something in this attitude of a hangover from the Butlerian Jihad, rebellion against machines that could copy out the essence of a human's thoughts and memories.

Déjà vu!

Mentat logic demanded of him: *How do I know this moment?* He *knew* that he had never before been a captive. It was such a ridiculous switch of roles. The great Bashar Teg a captive? He could almost smile. But that deep sense of familiarity persisted.

His captors positioned the hood directly over his head and began releasing the medusa contacts one at a time, fixing them to his scalp. The functionary watched his companions work, producing small signs of impatience on an otherwise emotionless face.

Teg moved his attention across the three faces. Which one of these would act the part of "friend"? Ahhhh, yes: the one called Materly. Fascinating. Was it a form of Honored Matre? But neither of the others deferred to her as one would expect from what Teg had heard of those returning Lost Ones.

These were people from the Scattering, though—except possibly for the square-faced male in the brown singlesuit. Teg studied the woman with care: the mat of gray hair, the quiet composure in those widely spaced green eyes, the slightly protruding chin with its sense of solidity and reliability. She had been chosen well for "friend." Materly's face was a map of respectability, someone you could trust. Teg saw a withdrawn quality in her, though. She was one who would also observe carefully to catch the moment when she must become involved. Surely, she was Bene Gesserit–trained at the very least.

Or trained by the Honored Matres.

They finished attaching the contacts to his head. The Gammu type swung the probe's console into position where all three could watch the display. The probe's screen was concealed from Teg.

The woman removed Teg's gag, confirming his judgment. She would be the source of comfort. He moved his tongue around in his mouth, restoring sensation. His face and chest still felt a bit numb from the stunner that had brought him down. How long ago had that been? But if he was to believe the silent words of the functionary, Duncan had escaped.

The Gammu type looked to the observer.

"You may begin, Yar," the functionary said.

Yar? Teg wondered. *Curious name.* Almost had a Tleilaxu sound. But Yar was not a Face Dancer . . . or a Tleilaxu Master. Too big for one and no stigmata of the other. As one trained by the Sisterhood, Teg felt confident of this.

Yar touched a control on the probe's console.

Teg heard himself grunt with pain. Nothing had prepared him for that much pain. They must have turned their devil's machine to maximum for the first thrust. No question about it! They knew he was a Mentat. A Mentat could remove himself from some demands of flesh. But this was excruciating! He could not escape it. Agony shivered through his entire body, threatening to blank out his consciousness. Could shere shield him from this?

The pain diminished gradually and went away, leaving only quivering memories.

Again!

He thought suddenly that the spice agony must be like this for a Reverend Mother. Surely, there could be no greater pain. He fought to remain silent but heard himself grunting, moaning. Every ability he had ever learned, Mentat and Bene Gesserit, was called into play, keeping him from forming words, from begging for surcease, from promising to tell them anything if they would only stop.

Once more the agony receded and then surged back.

"Enough!" That was the woman. Teg groped for her name. *Materly?*

Yar spoke in a sullen voice: "He's loaded with shere, enough to last him a year at least." He gestured at his console. "Blank."

Teg breathed in shallow gasps. The agony! It continued to increase despite Materly's demand.

"I said enough!" Materly snapped.

Such sincerity, Teg thought. He felt the pain recede, withdrawing as though every nerve were being removed from his body, pulled out like threads of the remembered agony.

"It is wrong what we're doing," Materly said. "This man is—"

"He is like any other man," Yar said. "Shall I attach the special contact to his penis?"

"Not while I'm here!" Materly said.

Teg felt himself almost taken in by her sincerity. The last of the agony threads left his flesh and he lay there with a feeling that he had been suspended off the surface that supported him. The sense of déjà vu remained. He was here and not here. He had been here and he had not.

"They will not like it if we fail," Yar said. "Are you prepared to face them with another failure?"

Materly shook her head sharply. She bent over to bring her face into Teg's line of vision through the medusa tangle of probe contacts. "Bashar, I am sorry for what we do. Believe me. This is not of my making. Please, I find all of this disgusting. Tell us what we need to know and let me make you comfortable."

Teg formed a smile for her. She was good! He shifted his gaze to the watchful functionary. "Tell your masters for me. She is very good at this."

Blood darkened the functionary's face. He scowled. "Give him the maximum, Yar." His voice was a clipped tenor without any of the deep training apparent in Materly's voice.

"Please!" Materly said. She straightened but kept her attention on Teg's eyes.

Teg's Bene Gesserit teachers had taught him that: "Watch the eyes! Observe how they change focus. As the focus moves outward, the awareness moves inward."

He focused deliberately on her nose. It was not an ugly face. Rather distinctive. He wondered what the figure might be under those bulky clothes.

"Yar!" That was the functionary.

Yar adjusted something on his console and pressed a switch.

The agony that surged through Teg now told him the previous level had, indeed, been lower. With the new pain came an odd clarity. Teg found himself almost capable of removing his awareness from this intrusion. All of that pain was happening to someone else. He had found a haven where little touched him. There was pain. Agony even. He accepted reports about these sensations. That was partly the shere's doing, of course. He knew that and was thankful.

Materly's voice intruded: "I think we're losing him. Better ease off."

Another voice responded but the sound faded into stillness before Teg could identify the words. He realized abruptly that he had no anchor point for his awareness. Stillness! He thought he heard his heart beating rapidly in fear but he was not sure. All was stillness, profound quiet with nothing behind it.

Am I still alive?

He found a heartbeat then, but no certainty that it was his own. *Thump-thump! Thump-thump!* It was a sensation of movement and no sound. He could not fix the source.

What is happening to me?

Words blazoned in brilliant white against a black background played across his visual centers:

"I'm back to one-third."

"Leave it at that. See if we can read him through his physical reactions."

"Can he still hear us?"

"Not consciously."

None of Teg's instructions had told him a probe could do its evil work in the presence of shere. But they called this a T-probe. Could bodily reactions provide a clue to suppressed thoughts? Were there revelations to be explored by physical means?

Again, words played against Teg's visual centers: "Is he still isolated?"

"Completely."

"Make sure. Take him a little deeper."

Teg tried to lift his awareness above his fears.

I must remain in control!

What might his body reveal if he had no contact with it? He could imagine what they were doing and his mind registered panic but his flesh could not feel it.

Isolate the subject. Give him nowhere to seat his identity.

Who had said that? Someone. The sense of déjà vu returned in full force.

I am a Mentat, he reminded himself. *My mind and its workings are my center.* He possessed experiences and memories upon which a center could rely.

Pain returned. Sounds. Loud! Much too loud!

"He's hearing again." That was Yar.

"How can that be?" The functionary's tenor.

"Perhaps you've set it too low." Materly.

Teg tried to open his eyes. The lids would not obey. He remembered then. They had called it a T-probe. This was no Ixian device. This was something from the Scattering. He could identify where it took over his muscles and senses. It was like another person sharing his flesh, preempting his own reactive patterns. He allowed himself to follow the workings of this machine's intrusions. It was a hellish device! It could order him to blink, fart, gasp, shit, piss—anything. It could command his body as though he had no thinking part in his own behavior. He was relegated to the role of observer.

Odors assailed him—disgusting odors. He would not command himself to frown but he thought of frowning. That was sufficient. These odors had been elicited by the probe. It was playing his senses, learning them.

"Do you have enough to read him?" The functionary's tenor.

"He's still hearing us!" Yar.

"Damn all Mentats!" Materly.

"Dit, Dat, and Dot," Teg said, naming the puppets of the Winter Show from his childhood on long-ago Lernaeus.

"He's talking!" The functionary.

Teg felt his awareness being blocked off by the machine. Yar was doing something at the console. Still, Teg knew his own Mentat logic had told him something vital: These three were puppets. Only the puppet masters were important. How the puppets moved—that told you what the puppet masters were doing.

The probe continued to intrude. Despite the force being applied, Teg felt his awareness matching the thing. It was learning him but he was also learning it.

He understood now. The whole spectrum of his senses could be copied into this T-probe and identified, tagged for Yar to call up when needed. An organic chain of responses existed within Teg. The machine could trace those out as though it made a duplicate of him. The shere and his Mentat resistance shunted the searchers away from his memories but everything else could be copied.

It will not think like me, he reassured himself.

The machine would not be the same as his nerves and flesh. It would not have Teg-memories or Teg-experiences. It had not been born of woman. It had never traveled down a birth canal and emerged into this astonishing universe.

Part of Teg's awareness applied a memory marker, telling him that this observation revealed something about the ghola.

Duncan was decanted from an axlotl tank.

The observation came to Teg with a sudden sharp biting of acid on his tongue.

The T-probe again!

Teg allowed himself to flow through a multiple simultaneous awareness. He followed the T-probe's workings and continued to explore this observation about the ghola, all the while listening for Dit, Dat, and

Dot. The three puppets were oddly silent. Yes, waiting for their T-probe to complete its task.

The ghola: Duncan was an extension of cells that *had* been born of a woman impregnated by a man.

Machine and ghola!

Observation: *The machine cannot share that birth experience except in a remotely vicarious way sure to miss important personal nuances.*

Just as it was missing other things in him right now.

The T-probe was replaying smells. With each induced odor, memories revealed their presence in Teg's mind. He felt the great speed of the T-probe but his own awareness lived outside of that headlong rushing search, able to entangle him for as long as he desired in the memories being called up here.

There!

That was the hot wax he had spilled on his left hand when only fourteen and a student in the Bene Gesserit school. He recalled school and laboratory as though his only existence were there at this moment. *The school is attached to Chapter House.* By being admitted here, Teg knew he had the blood of Siona in his veins. No prescient could track him here.

He saw the lab and smelled the wax—a compound of artificial esters and the natural product of bees kept by failed Sisters and their helpers. He turned his memory to a moment when he watched bees and people at their labors in the apple orchards.

The workings of the Bene Gesserit social structure appeared so complicated until you saw through to the necessities: food, clothing, warmth, communication, learning, protection from enemies (a subset of the survival drive). Bene Gesserit survival took some adjustments before it could be understood. They did not procreate for the sake of humankind in general. No unmonitored racial involvement! They procreated to extend their own powers, to continue the Bene Gesserit, deeming that a sufficient service to humankind. Perhaps it was. Procreative motivation went deep and the Sisterhood was so thorough.

A new smell assailed him.

He recognized the wet wool of his clothing as he came into the command pod after the Battle of Ponciard. The smell filled his nostrils and elicited the ozone of the pod's instruments, the sweat of the other occupants. *Wool!* The Sisterhood had always thought it a bit odd of him, the way he preferred natural fabrics and shunned the synthetics turned out in captive factories.

No more did he care for chairdogs.

I don't like the smells of oppression in any form.

Did these puppets—Dit, Dat, and Dot—know how oppressed they were?

Mentat logic sneered at him. Were not wool fabrics also a product of captive factories?

It was different.

Part of him argued otherwise. Synthetics could be stored almost indefinitely. Look how long they had endured in the nullentropy bins of the Harkonnen no-globe.

"I still prefer woolens and cottons!"

So be it!

"But how did I come by such a preference?"

It is an Atreides prejudice. You inherited it.

Teg shunted the smells aside and concentrated on the total movement of the intrusive probe. He found presently that he could anticipate the thing. It was a new muscle. He allowed himself to flex it while he continued to examine the induced memories for valuable insights.

I sit outside my mother's door on Lernaeus.

Teg removed part of his awareness and watched the scene: age eleven. He is talking to a small Bene Gesserit acolyte who came as part of the escort for Somebody Important. The acolyte is a tiny thing with red-blond hair and a doll's face. Upturned nose, green-gray eyes. The SI is a black-robed Reverend Mother of truly ancient appearance. She has gone behind that nearby door with Teg's mother. The acolyte, who is named Carlana, is trying her fledgling skills on the young son of the house.

Before Carlana utters twenty words, Miles Teg recognizes the pattern.

She is trying to pry information out of him! This was one of the first lessons in delicate dissembling taught by his mother. There were, after all, people who might question a young boy about a Reverend Mother's household, hoping thereby to gain salable information. There is always a market for data about Reverend Mothers.

His mother explained: "You judge the questioner and fit your responses according to the susceptibilities." None of this would have served against a full Reverend Mother, but against an acolyte, especially this one!

For Carlana, he produces an appearance of coy reluctance. Carlana has an inflated view of her own attractions. He allows her to overcome his reluctance after a suitable marshaling of her forces. What she gets is a handful of lies, which, if she ever repeats them to the SI behind that closed door, are sure to win Carlana a severe censuring if not something more painful.

Words from Dit, Dat, and Dot: "I think we have him now."

Teg recognized Yar's voice yanking him out of old memories. *"Fit your responses according to the susceptibilities."* Teg heard the words in his mother's voice.

Puppets.

Puppet masters.

The functionary speaks: "Ask the simulation where they have taken the ghola."

Silence and then a faint humming.

"I'm not getting anything." Yar.

Teg hears their voices with painful sensitivity. He forces his eyes to open against the opposing commands of the probe.

"Look!" Yar says.

Three sets of eyes stare back at Teg. How slowly they move. Dit, Dat, and Dot: the eyes go blink . . . blink . . . at least a minute between blinks. Yar is reaching for something on his console. His fingers will take a week to reach their destination.

Teg explores the bindings on his hands and arms. Ordinary rope! Taking his time, he squirms his fingers into contact with the knots.

They loosen, slowly at first, and then flying apart. He moves on to the straps holding him to the sling litter. These are easier: simple slip locks. Yar's hand is not even a fourth of the way to the console.

Blink . . . blink . . . blink . . .

The three sets of eyes show faint surprise.

Teg releases himself from the medusa tangle of probe contacts. *Pop-pop-pop!* The grippers fly away from him. He is surprised to notice a slow start of bleeding on the back of his right hand where it has brushed the probe contacts aside.

Mentat projection: *I am moving with dangerous speed.*

But now he is off the litter. Functionary is reaching a slow-slow hand toward a bulge in a side pocket. Teg's hand crushes the functionary's throat. Functionary will never again touch that little lasgun he always carries. Yar's outstretched hand is still not a third of the way to the probe console. There is definite surprise in his eyes, though. Teg doubts that the man even sees the hand that breaks his neck. Materly is moving a bit faster. Her left foot is coming toward where Teg had been just the flick of an instant previously. Still too slow! Materly's head is thrown back, the throat exposed for Teg's down-chopping hand.

How slowly they fall to the floor!

Teg became aware of perspiration pouring from him but he could not spare time to worry about this.

I knew every move they would make before they made it! What has happened to me?

Mentat projection: *The probe agony has lifted me to a new level of ability.*

Intense hunger pangs made him aware of the energy drain. He pushed the sensation aside, feeling himself return to a normal time-beat. Three dull sounds: bodies falling to the floor.

Teg examined the probe console. Definitely not Ixian. Similar controls, though. He shorted out the data storage system, erasing it.

Room lights?

Controls beside the door from the outside. He extinguished the lights, took three deep breaths. A whirling blur of motion erupted into the night.

The ones who had brought him here, clad in their bulky clothing against the winter chill, barely had time to turn toward the odd sound before the whirling blur struck them down.

Teg returned to normal time-beat more quickly. Starlight showed him a trail leading downslope through thick brush. He slipped and slid on the snow-churned mud for a space and then found the way to balance himself, anticipating the terrain. Each step went where he knew it must go. He found himself presently in an open space that looked out across a valley.

The lights of a city and a great black rectangle of building near the center. He knew this place: Ysai. The puppet masters were there.

I am free!

There was a man who sat each day looking out through a narrow vertical opening where a single board had been removed from a tall wooden fence. Each day a wild ass of the desert passed outside the fence and across the narrow opening—first the nose, then the head, the forelegs, the long brown back, the hindlegs, and lastly the tail. One day, the man leaped to his feet with the light of discovery in his eyes and he shouted for all who could hear him: "It is obvious! The nose causes the tail!"

—STORIES OF THE HIDDEN WISDOM,
FROM THE ORAL HISTORY OF RAKIS

Several times since coming to Rakis, Odrade had found herself caught in the memory of that ancient painting which occupied such a prominent place on the wall of Taraza's Chapter House quarters. When the memory came, she felt her hands tingle to the touch of the brush. Her nostrils swelled to the induced smells of oils and pigments. Her emotions assaulted the canvas. Each time, Odrade emerged from the memory with new doubts that Sheeana was her canvas.

Which of us paints the other?

It had happened again this morning. Still dark outside the Rakian Keep's penthouse where she quartered with Sheeana: An acolyte entered softly to waken Odrade and tell her that Taraza would arrive shortly. Odrade looked up at the softly illuminated face of the dark-haired acolyte and immediately that memory-painting flashed into her awareness.

Which of us truly creates another?

"Let Sheeana sleep a bit longer," Odrade said before dismissing the acolyte.

"Will you breakfast before the Mother Superior's arrival?" the acolyte asked.

"We will wait upon Taraza's pleasure."

Arising, Odrade went through a swift toilet and donned her best black robe. She strode then to the east window of the penthouse common room and looked out in the direction of the spacefield. Many moving lights cast a glow on the dusty sky there. She activated all of the room's glowglobes to soften the exterior view. The globes became reflected golden starbursts on the thick armor-plaz of the windows. The dusky surface also reflected a dim outline of her own features, showing the fatigue lines clearly.

I knew she would come, Odrade thought.

Even as she thought this, the Rakian sun came over the dust-blurred horizon like a child's orange ball thrust into view. Immediately, there was the heat-bounce that so many observers of Rakis had mentioned. Odrade turned away from the view and saw the hall door open.

Taraza entered with a rustle of robes. A hand closed the door behind her, leaving the two of them alone. The Mother Superior advanced on Odrade, black hood up and the cowl framing her face. It was not a reassuring sight.

Recognizing the disturbance in Odrade, Taraza played on it. "Well, Dar, I think we finally meet as strangers."

The effect of Taraza's words startled Odrade. She correctly interpreted the threat but fear left her, spilling out as though it were water poured from a jug. For the first time in her life, Odrade recognized the precise moment of crossing a dividing line. This was a line whose existence she thought few of her Sisters suspected. As she crossed it, she realized that she had always known it was there: a place where she could enter the void and float free. She no longer was vulnerable. She could be killed but she could not be defeated.

"So it's not Dar and Tar anymore," Odrade said.

Taraza heard the clear, uninhibited tone of Odrade's voice and interpreted this as confidence. "Perhaps it never was Dar and Tar," she said, her voice icy. "I see that you think you have been extremely clever."

The battle has been joined, Odrade thought. *But I do not stand in the path of her attack.*

Odrade said: "The alternatives to alliance with the Tleilaxu could not be accepted. Especially when I recognized what it was you truly sought for us."

Taraza felt suddenly weary. It had been a long trip despite the space-folding leaps of her no-ship. The flesh always knew when it had been twisted out of its familiar rhythms. She chose a soft divan and sat down, sighing in the luxurious comfort.

Odrade recognized the Mother Superior's fatigue and felt immediate sympathy. They were suddenly two Reverend Mothers with common problems.

Taraza obviously sensed this. She patted the cushion beside her and waited for Odrade to be seated.

"We must preserve the Sisterhood," Taraza said. "That is the only important thing."

"Of course."

Taraza fixed her gaze searchingly on Odrade's familiar features. *Yes, Odrade, too, is weary.* "You have been here, intimately touching the people and the problem," Taraza said. "I want . . . no, Dar, I *need* your views."

"The Tleilaxu give the appearance of full cooperation," Odrade said, "but there is dissembling in this. I have begun to ask myself some extremely disturbing questions."

"Such as?"

"What if the axlotl tanks are not . . . tanks?"

"What do you mean?"

"Waff reveals the kinds of behavior you see when a family tries to conceal a deformed child or a mad uncle. I swear to you, he is embarrassed when we begin to touch on the tanks."

"But what could they possibly . . ."

"Surrogate mothers."

"But they would have to be . . ." Taraza fell silent, shocked by the possibilities this question opened.

"Who has ever seen a Tleilaxu female?" Odrade asked.

Taraza's mind was filled with objections: "But the precise chemical control, the need to limit variables . . ." She threw her hood back and shook her hair free. "You are correct: we must question everything. This, though . . . this is monstrous."

"He is still not telling the full truth about our ghola."

"What does he say?"

"No more than what I have already reported: a variation on the original Duncan Idaho and meeting all of the prana-bindu requirements we specified."

"That does not explain why they killed or tried to kill our previous purchases."

"He swears the holy oath of the Great Belief that they acted out of shame because the eleven previous gholas did not live up to expectations."

"How could they know? Does he suggest they have spies among . . ."

"He swears not. I taxed him with this and he said that a successful ghola would be sure to create a visible disturbance among us."

"What visible disturbance? What is he . . ."

"He will not say. He returns each time to the claim that they have met their contractual obligations. Where is the ghola, Tar?"

"What . . . oh. On Gammu."

"I hear rumors of . . ."

"Burzmali has the situation well in hand." Taraza closed her mouth tightly, hoping that was the truth. The most recent report did not fill her with confidence.

"You obviously are debating whether to have the ghola killed," Odrade said.

"Not just the ghola!"

Odrade smiled. "Then it's true that Bellonda wants me permanently eliminated."

"How did you . . ."

"Friendships can be a very valuable asset at times, Tar."

"You tread on dangerous ground, Reverend Mother Odrade."

"But I am not stumbling, Mother Superior Taraza. I am thinking long hard thoughts about the things Waff has revealed about those Honored Matres."

"Tell me some of your thoughts." There was implacable determination in Taraza's voice.

"Let us make no mistakes about this," Odrade said. "They have surpassed the sexual skills of our Imprinters."

"Whores!"

"Yes, they employ their skills in a way ultimately fatal to themselves and others. They have been blinded by their own power."

"Is that the extent of your long hard thoughts?"

"Tell me, Tar, why did they attack and obliterate our Keep on Gammu?"

"Obviously they were after our Idaho ghola, to capture him or kill him."

"Why would that be so important to them?"

"What are you trying to say?" Taraza demanded.

"Could the *whores* have been acting upon information revealed to them by the Tleilaxu? Tar, what if this secret thing Waff's people have introduced into our ghola is something that would make the ghola a male equivalent of the Honored Matres?"

Taraza put a hand to her mouth and dropped it quickly when she saw how much the gesture revealed. It was too late. No matter. They were still two Reverend Mothers together.

Odrade said: "And we have ordered Lucilla to make him irresistible to most women."

"How long have the Tleilaxu been dealing with those whores?" Taraza demanded.

Odrade shrugged. "A better question is this: How long have they been dealing with their own Lost Ones returned from the Scattering? Tleilaxu speak to Tleilaxu and many secrets could be revealed."

"A brilliant projection on your part," Taraza said. "What probability value do you attach to it?"

"You know that as well as I do. It would explain many things."

Taraza spoke bitterly. "What do you think of your alliance with the Tleilaxu now?"

"More necessary than ever. We must be on the inside. We must be where we can influence those who contend."

"Abomination!" Taraza snapped.

"What?"

"This ghola is like a recording device in human shape. They have planted him in our midst. If the Tleilaxu get their hands on him they will know many things about us."

"That would be clumsy."

"And typical of them!"

"I agree that there are other implications in our situation," Odrade said. "But such arguments only tell me that we dare not kill the ghola until we have examined him ourselves."

"That might be too late! Damn your alliance, Dar! You gave them a hold on us . . . and us a hold on them—and neither of us dares let go."

"Is that not the perfect alliance?"

Taraza sighed. "How soon must we give them access to our breeding records?"

"Soon. Waff is pressing the matter."

"Then, will we see their axlotl . . . tanks?"

"That is, of course, the lever I am using. He has given his reluctant agreement."

"Deeper and deeper into each other's pockets," Taraza growled.

Her tone all innocence, Odrade said: "A perfect alliance, just as I said."

"Damn, damn, damn," Taraza muttered. "And Teg has reawakened the ghola's original memories!"

"But has Lucilla . . ."

"I don't know!" Taraza turned a grim expression on Odrade and recounted the most recent reports from Gammu: Teg and his party located, the briefest of accounts about them and nothing from Lucilla; plans made to bring them out.

Her own words produced an unsettling picture in Taraza's mind. What was this ghola? They had always known the Duncan Idahos were not ordinary gholas. But now, with augmented nerve and muscle capabilities plus this unknown thing the Tleilaxu had introduced—it was like holding a burning club. You knew you might have to use the club for your own survival but the flames approached at a terrifying speed.

Odrade spoke in a musing tone: "Have you ever tried to imagine what it must be like for a ghola suddenly to awaken in renewed flesh?"

"What? What are you . . ."

"Realizing that your flesh was grown from the cells of a cadaver," Odrade said. "He remembers his own death."

"The Idahos were never ordinary people," Taraza said.

"The same may be said for these Tleilaxu Masters."

"What are you trying to say?"

Odrade rubbed her own forehead, taking a moment to review her thoughts. This was so difficult with someone who rejected affection, with someone who thrust outward from a core of rage. Taraza had no . . . no *simpatico.* She could not assume the flesh and senses of another except as an exercise in logic.

"A ghola's awakening must be a shattering experience," Odrade said, lowering her hand. "Only the ones with enormous mental resilience would survive."

"We assume that the Tleilaxu Masters are more than they appear to be."

"And the Duncan Idahos?"

"Of course. Why else would the Tyrant keep buying them from the Tleilaxu?"

Odrade saw that the argument was pointless. She said: "The Idahos were notoriously loyal to the Atreides and we must remember that I am Atreides."

"You think loyalty will bind this one to you?"

"Especially after Lucilla—"

"That may be too dangerous!"

Odrade sat back into a corner of the divan. Taraza wanted certainty. And the lives of the serial gholas were like melange, presenting a different taste in different surroundings. How could they be sure of their ghola?

"The Tleilaxu meddle with the forces that produced our Kwisatz Haderach," Taraza muttered.

"You think that's why they want our breeding records?"

"I don't know! Damn you, Dar! Don't you see what you've done?"

"I think I had no choice," Odrade said.

Taraza produced a cold smile. Odrade's performance remained superb but she needed to be put in her place.

"You think I would have done the same?" Taraza asked.

She still does not see what has happened to me, Odrade thought. Taraza had expected her pliant Dar to act with independence but the extent of that independence had shaken the High Council. Taraza refused to see her own hand in this.

"Customary practice," Odrade said.

The words struck Taraza like a slap in the face. Only the hard training of a Bene Gesserit lifetime prevented her from striking out violently at Odrade.

Customary practice!

How many times had Taraza herself revealed this as a source of irritation, a constant goad to her carefully capped rage? Odrade had heard it often.

Odrade quoted the Mother Superior now: "Immovable custom is dangerous. Enemies can find a pattern and use it against you."

The words were forced from Taraza: "That is a weakness, yes."

"Our enemies thought they knew our way," Odrade said. "Even you, *Mother Superior,* thought you knew the limits within which I would perform. I was like Bellonda. Before she even spoke, you knew what Bellonda would say."

"Have we made a mistake, not elevating you above me?" Taraza asked. She spoke from her deepest allegiance.

"No, Mother Superior. We walk a delicate path but both of us can see where we must go."

"Where is Waff now?" Taraza asked.

"Asleep and well guarded."

"Summon Sheeana. We must decide whether to abort that part of the project."

"And take our lumps?"

"As you say, Dar."

Sheeana was still sleepy and rubbing her eyes when she appeared in the common room but she obviously had taken the time to splash water on her face and dress in a clean white robe. Her hair was still damp.

Taraza and Odrade stood near an eastern window with their backs to the light.

"This is Sheeana, Mother Superior," Odrade said.

Sheeana came fully alert with an abrupt stiffening of her back. She had heard of this powerful woman, this Taraza, who ruled the Sisterhood from a distant citadel called Chapter House. Sunlight was bright in the window behind the two women, shining full into Sheeana's face, dazzling her. It left the faces of the two Reverend Mothers partly obscured, the black outlines of their figures fuzzy in the brilliance.

Acolyte instructors had prepared her against this encounter: "You stand at attention before the Mother Superior and speak respectfully. Respond only when she speaks to you."

Sheeana stood at rigid attention the way she had been told.

"I am informed that you may become one of us," Taraza said.

Both women could see the effect of this on the girl. By now, Sheeana was more fully aware of a Reverend Mother's accomplishments. The powerful beam of truth had been focused on her. She had begun to grasp at the enormous body of knowledge the Sisterhood had accumulated over the millennia. She had been told about selective memory transmission, about the workings of Other Memories, about the spice agony. And here before her stood the most powerful of all Reverend Mothers, one from whom nothing was hidden.

When Sheeana did not respond, Taraza said: "Have you nothing to say, child?"

"What is there to say, Mother Superior? You have said it all."

Taraza sent a searching glance at Odrade. "Have you any other little surprises for me, Dar?"

"I told you she was superior," Odrade said.

Taraza returned her attention to Sheeana. "Are you proud of that opinion, child?"

"It frightens me, Mother Superior."

Still holding her face as immobile as she could, Sheeana breathed more easily. *Say only the deepest truth you can sense,* she reminded herself. Those warning words from a teacher carried more meaning now. She kept her eyes slightly unfocused and aimed at the floor directly in front of the two women, avoiding the worst of the brilliant sunlight. She still felt her heart beating too rapidly and knew the Reverend Mothers would detect this. Odrade had demonstrated it many times.

"Well it should frighten you," Taraza said.

Odrade asked: "Do you understand what is being said to you, Sheeana?"

"The Mother Superior wishes to know if I am fully committed to the Sisterhood," Sheeana said.

Odrade looked at Taraza and shrugged. There was no need for more discussion of this between them. That was the way of it when you were part of one family as they were in the Bene Gesserit.

Taraza continued her silent study of Sheeana. It was a heavy gaze, energy-draining for Sheeana, who knew she must remain silent and permit that scorching examination.

Odrade put down feelings of sympathy. Sheeana was like herself as a young girl, in so many ways. She had that globular intellect which expanded on all surfaces the way a balloon expanded when filled. Odrade recalled how her own teachers had been admiring of this, but wary, just the way Taraza was now wary. Odrade had recognized this wariness while even younger than Sheeana and held no doubts that Sheeana saw it here. Intellect had its uses.

"Mmmmmm," Taraza said.

Odrade heard the humming sound of the Mother Superior's internal reflections as part of a simulflow. Odrade's own memory had surged backward. The Sisters who had brought Odrade her food when she studied late had always loitered to observe her in their special way, just as Sheeana was watched and monitored at all times. Odrade had known about those special ways of observing from an early age. That was, after all, one of the great lures of the Bene Gesserit. You wanted to be capable of such esoteric abilities. Sheeana certainly possessed this desire. It was the dream of every postulant.

That such things might be possible for me!

Taraza spoke finally: "What is it you think you want from us, child?"

"The same things you thought you wanted when you were my age, Mother Superior."

Odrade suppressed a smile. Sheeana's wild sense of independence had skated close to insolence there and Taraza certainly recognized this.

"You think that is a proper use for the gift of life?" Taraza asked.

"It is the only use I know, Mother Superior."

"Your candor is appreciated but I warn you to be careful in your use of it," Taraza said.

"Yes, Mother Superior."

"You already owe us much and you will owe us more," Taraza said. "Remember that. Our gifts do not come cheaply."

Sheeana has not the vaguest appreciation of what she will pay for our gifts, Odrade thought.

The Sisterhood never let its initiates forget what they owed and must repay. You did not repay with love. Love was dangerous and Sheeana already was learning this. *The gift of life?* A shudder began to course through Odrade and she cleared her throat to compensate.

Am I alive? Perhaps when they took me away from Mama Sibia I died. I was alive there in that house but did I live after the Sisters removed me?

Taraza said: "You may leave us now, Sheeana."

Sheeana turned on one heel and left the room but not before Odrade saw the tight smile on the young face. Sheeana knew she had passed the Mother Superior's examination.

When the door closed behind Sheeana, Taraza said: "You mentioned her natural ability with Voice. I heard it, of course. Remarkable."

"She kept it well bridled," Odrade said. "She has learned not to try it on us."

"What do we have there, Dar?"

"Perhaps someday a Mother Superior of extraordinary abilities."

"Not too extraordinary?"

"We will have to see."

"Do you think she is capable of killing for us?"

Odrade was startled and showed it. "Now?"

"Yes, of course."

"The ghola?"

"Teg would not do it," Taraza said. "I even have doubts about Lucilla. Their reports make it clear that he is capable of forging powerful bonds of . . . of affinity."

"Even as I?"

"Schwangyu herself was not completely immune."

"Where is the noble purpose in such an act?" Odrade asked. "Isn't this what the Tyrant's warning has—"

"Him? He killed many times!"

"And paid for it."

"We pay for everything we take, Dar."

"Even for a life?"

"Never forget for one instant, Dar, that a Mother Superior is capable of making any necessary decision for the Sisterhood's survival!"

"So be it," Odrade said. "Take what you want and pay for it."

It was the proper reply but it reinforced the new strength Odrade felt, this freedom to respond in her own way within a new universe. Where had such toughness originated? Was it something out of her cruel Bene Gesserit conditioning? Was it from her Atreides ancestry? She did not try to fool herself that this came from a decision never again to follow another's moral guidance rather than her own. This inner stability upon which she now stationed herself was not a pure morality. Not bravado, either. Those were never enough.

"You are very like your father," Taraza said. "Usually, it's the dam who provides most of the courage but this time I think it was the father."

"Miles Teg is admirably courageous but I think you oversimplify," Odrade said.

"Perhaps I do. But I have been right about you at every turn, Dar, even back there when we were student postulants."

She knows! Odrade thought.

"We don't need to explain it," Odrade said. And she thought: *It comes from being born who I am, trained and shaped the way I was . . . the way we both were: Dar and Tar.*

"It's something in the Atreides line that we have not fully analyzed," Taraza said.

"No genetic accidents?"

"I sometimes wonder if we've suffered any real accidents since the Tyrant," Taraza said.

"Did he stretch out back there in his citadel and look across the millennia to this very moment?"

"How far back would you reach for the roots?" Taraza asked.

Odrade said: "What really happens when a Mother Superior commands the Breeding Mistresses: 'Have that one go breed with that one'?"

Taraza produced a cold smile.

Odrade felt herself suddenly at the crest of a wave, awareness pushing all of her over into this new realm. *Taraza wants my rebellion! She wants me as her opponent!*

"Will you see Waff now?" Odrade asked.

"First, I want your assessment of him."

"He sees us as the ultimate tool to create the 'Tleilaxu Ascendancy.' We are God's gift to his people."

"They have been waiting a long time for this," Taraza said. "To dissemble so carefully, all of them for all of those eons!"

"They have our view of time," Odrade agreed. "That was the final thing to convince them we share their Great Belief."

"But why the clumsiness?" Taraza asked. "They are not stupid."

"It diverted our attention from how they were really using their ghola process," Odrade said. "Who could believe stupid people would do such a thing?"

"And what have they created?" Taraza asked. "Only the *image* of evil stupidity?"

"Act stupid long enough and you become stupid," Odrade said. "Perfect the mimicry of your Face Dancers and . . ."

"Whatever happens, we must punish them," Taraza said. "I see that clearly. Have him brought up here."

After Odrade had given the order and while they waited, Taraza said: "The sequencing of the ghola's education became a shambles even before they escaped from the Gammu Keep. He leaped ahead of his teachers to grasp things that were only implied and he did this at an alarmingly accelerated rate. Who knows what he has become by now?"

Historians exercise great power and some of them know it. They re-create the past, changing it to fit their own interpretations. Thus, they change the future as well.

—LETO II, HIS VOICE, FROM DAR-ES-BALAT

Duncan followed his guide through the dawn light at a punishing clip. The man might look old but he was as springy as a gazelle and seemed incapable of tiring.

Only a few minutes ago they had put aside their night goggles. Duncan was glad to be rid of them. Everything outside the reach of the glasses had been black in the dim starlight filtering through heavy branches. There had been no world ahead of him beyond the range of the glasses. The view at both sides jerked and flowed—now a clump of yellow bushes, now two silver-bark trees, now a stone wall with a plas-teel gate cut into it and guarded by the flickering blue of a burn-shield, then an arched bridge of native rock, all green and black underfoot. After that, an arched entry of polished white stone. The structures all appeared very old and expensive, maintained by costly handwork.

Duncan had no idea where he was. None of this terrain recalled his memories of the long-lost Giedi Prime days.

Dawn revealed that they were following a tree-shielded animal track up a hillside. The climb became steep. Occasional glimpses through trees on their left revealed a valley. A hanging mist stood guard over the sky, hiding the distances, enclosing them as they climbed. Their world became progressively a smaller place as it lost its connection with a larger universe.

At one brief pause, not for rest but for listening to the forest around them, Duncan studied his mist-capped surroundings. He felt dislodged, removed from a universe that possessed sky and the open features that linked it to other planets.

His disguise was simple: Tleilaxu cold-weather garments and cheek pads to make his face appear rounder. His curly black hair had been straightened by some chemical applied with heat. The hair was then bleached to a sandy blond and hidden under a dark watchcap. All of his genital hair had been shaved away. He hardly recognized himself in the mirror they held up for him.

A dirty Tleilaxu!

The artisan who created this transformation was an old woman with glittering gray-green eyes. "You are now a Tleilaxu Master," she said. "Your name is Wose. A guide will take you to the next place. You will treat him like a Face Dancer if you meet strangers. Otherwise, do as he commands."

They led him out of the cave complex along a twisting passage, its walls and ceiling thick with the musky green algae. In starlighted darkness, they thrust him from the passage into a chilly night and the hands of an unseen man—a bulky figure in padded clothing.

A voice behind Duncan whispered: "Here he is, Ambitorm. Get him through."

The guide spoke in an accent of gutturals: "Follow me." He clipped a lead cord to Duncan's belt, adjusted the night goggles and turned away. Duncan felt the cord tug once and they were off.

Duncan recognized the use of the cord. It was not something to keep him close behind. He could see this Ambitorm clearly enough with the night goggles. No, the cord was to spill him quickly if they met danger. No need for a command.

For a long time during the night they crisscrossed small ice-lined watercourses on a flatland. The light of Gammu's early moons penetrated

the covering growth only occasionally. They emerged finally onto a low
hill with a view of bushy wasteland all silvery with snow cover in the
moonlight. Down into this they went. The bushes, about twice the height
of the guide, arched over muddy animal passages little larger than the
tunnels where they had begun this journey. It was warmer here, the
warmth of a compost heap. Almost no light penetrated to a ground
spongy with rotted vegetation. Duncan inhaled the fungal odors of de-
composing plant life. The night goggles showed him a seemingly endless repetition of thick growth on both sides. The cord linking him to
Ambitorm was a tenuous grip on an alien world.

Ambitorm discouraged conversation. He said "Yes," when Duncan
asked confirmation of the man's name, then: "Don't talk."

The whole night was a disquieting traverse for Duncan. He did not
like being thrown back into his own thoughts. Giedi Prime memories
persisted. This place was like nothing he remembered from his pre-
ghola youth. He wondered how Ambitorm had learned the way
through here and how he remembered it. One animal tunnel appeared
much like another.

In the steady, jogging pace there was time for Duncan's thoughts
to roam.

Must I permit the Sisterhood to use me? What do I owe them?

And he thought of Teg, that last gallant stand to permit two of
them to escape.

I did the same for Paul and Jessica.

It was a bond with Teg and it touched Duncan with grief. Teg was
loyal to the Sisterhood. *Did he buy my loyalty with that last brave act?*

Damn the Atreides!

The night's exertions increased Duncan's familiarity with his new
flesh. How young this body was! A small lurch of recollection and he
could see that last pre-ghola memory; he could feel the Sardaukar
blade strike his head—a blinding explosion of pain and light. Knowledge of his certain death and then . . . nothing until that moment with
Teg in the Harkonnen no-globe.

The gift of another life. Was it more than a gift or something less? The Atreides were demanding another payment from him.

For a time just before dawn, Ambitorm led him at a sloshing run along a narrow stream whose icy chill penetrated the waterproof insulated boots of Duncan's Tleilaxu garments. The watercourse reflected bush-shadowed silver from the light of the planet's pre-dawn moon setting ahead of them.

Daylight saw them come out into the larger, tree-shielded animal track and up the steep hill. This passage emerged onto a narrow rocky ledge below a ridgetop of sawtoothed boulders. Ambitorm led him behind a screen of dead brown bushes, their tops dirty with wind-blown snow. He released the cord from Duncan's belt. Directly in front of them was a shallow declivity in the rocks, not quite a cave, but Duncan saw that it would offer some protection unless they got a hard wind over the bushes behind them. There was no snow on the floor of the place.

Ambitorm went to the back of the declivity and carefully removed a layer of icy dirt and several flat rocks, which concealed a small pit. He lifted a round black object from the pit and busied himself over it.

Duncan squatted under the overhang and studied his guide. Ambitorm had a dished-in face with skin like dark brown leather. Yes, those could be the features of a Face Dancer. Deep creases cut into the skin at the edges of the man's brown eyes. Creases radiated from the sides of the thin mouth and lined the wide brow. They spread out beside the flat nose and deepened the cleft of a narrow chin. Creases of time all over his face.

Appetizing odors began to arise from the black object in front of Ambitorm.

"We will eat here and wait a bit before we continue," Ambitorm said.

He spoke Old Galach but with that guttural accent which Duncan had never heard before, an odd stress on adjacent vowels. Was Ambitorm from the Scattering or a Gammu native? There obviously had been many linguistic drifts since the Dune days of Muad'Dib. For that matter, Duncan recognized that all of the people in the Gammu Keep, including Teg and Lucilla, spoke a Galach that had shifted from the one he had learned as a pre-ghola child.

"Ambitorm," Duncan said. "Is that a Gammu name?"

"You will call me Tormsa," the guide said.

"Is that a nickname?"

"It is what you will call me."

"Why did those people back there call you Ambitorm?"

"That was the name I gave them."

"But why would you . . ."

"You lived under the Harkonnens and you did not learn how to change your identity?"

Duncan fell silent. Was that it? Another disguise. Ambi . . . Tormsa had not changed his appearance. Tormsa. Was it a Tleilaxu name?

The guide extended a steaming cup toward Duncan. "A drink to restore you, *Wose*. Drink it fast. It will keep you warm."

Duncan closed both hands around the cup. *Wose. Wose and Tormsa. Tleilaxu Master and his Face Dancer companion.*

Duncan lifted the cup toward Tormsa in the ancient gesture of Atreides battle comrades, then put it to his lips. Hot! But it warmed him as it went down. The drink had a faintly sweet flavor over some vegetable tang. He blew on it and drank it down as he saw Tormsa was doing.

Odd that I should not suspect poison or some drug, Duncan thought. But this Tormsa and the others last night had something of the Bashar about them. The gesture to a battle comrade had come naturally.

"Why are you risking your life this way?" Duncan asked.

"You know the Bashar and you have to ask?"

Duncan fell silent, abashed.

Tormsa leaned forward and recovered Duncan's cup. Soon, all evidence of their breakfast lay hidden under the concealing rocks and dirt.

That food spoke of careful planning, Duncan thought. He turned and squatted on the cold ground. The mist was still out there beyond the screening bushes. Leafless limbs cut the view into odd bits and pieces. As he watched, the mist began to lift, revealing the blurred outlines of a city at the far edge of the valley.

Tormsa squatted beside him. "Very old city," he said. "Harkonnen place. Look." He passed a small monoscope to Duncan. "That is where we go tonight."

Duncan put the monoscope to his left eye and tried to focus the oil lens. The controls felt unfamiliar, not at all like those he had learned as a pre-ghola youth or had been taught at the Keep. He removed it from his eye and examined it.

"Ixian?" he asked.

"No. We made it." Tormsa reached over and pointed out two tiny buttons raised above the black tube. "Slow, fast. Push left to cycle out, right to cycle back."

Again, Duncan lifted the scope to his eye.

Who were the *we* who had made this thing?

A touch of the fast button and the view leaped into his gaze. Tiny dots moved in the city. People! He increased the amplification. The people became small dolls. With them to give him scale, Duncan realized that the city at the valley's edge was immense . . . and farther away than he had thought. A single rectangular structure stood in the center of the city, its top lost in the clouds. Gigantic.

Duncan knew this place now. The surroundings had changed but that central structure lay fixed in his memory.

How many of us vanished into that black hellhole and never returned?

"Nine hundred and fifty stories," Tormsa said, seeing where Duncan's gaze was directed. "Forty-five kilometers long, thirty kilometers wide. Plasteel and armor-plaz, all of it."

"I know." Duncan lowered the scope and returned it to Tormsa. "It was called Barony."

"Ysai," Tormsa said.

"That's what they call it now," Duncan said. "I have some different names for it."

Duncan took a deep breath to put down the old hatreds. Those people were all dead. Only the building remained. And the memories. He scanned the city around that enormous structure. The place was a sprawling mass of warrens. Green spaces lay scattered throughout, each of them behind high walls. Single residences with private parks, Teg had said. The monoscope had revealed guards walking the wall tops.

Tormsa spat on the ground in front of him. "Harkonnen place."

"They built to make people feel small," Duncan said.

Tormsa nodded. "Small, no power in you."

The guide had become almost loquacious, Duncan thought.

Occasionally during the night, Duncan had defied the order for silence and tried to make conversation.

"What animals made these passages?"

It had seemed a logical question for people trotting along an obvious animal track, even the musty smell of beasts in it.

"Do not talk!" Tormsa snapped.

Later, Duncan asked why they could not get a vehicle of some sort and escape in that. Even a groundcar would be preferable to this painful march across country where one route felt much like another.

Tormsa stopped them in a patch of moonlight and looked at Duncan as though he suspected his charge had suddenly become bereft of sense.

"Vehicles can follow!"

"No one can follow us when we're on foot?"

"Followers also must be on foot. Here, they will be killed. They know."

What a weird place! What a primitive place.

In the shelter of the Bene Gesserit Keep, Duncan had not realized the nature of the planet around him. Later, in the no-globe, he had been removed from contact with the outside. He had pre-ghola and ghola memories, but how inadequate those were! When he thought about it now, he realized there had been clues. It was obvious that Gammu possessed rudimentary weather control. And Teg had said that the orbiting monitors that guarded the planet from attack were of the best.

Everything for protection, damned little for comfort! It was like Arrakis in that respect.

Rakis, he corrected himself.

Teg. Did the old man survive? A captive? What did it mean to be captured here in this age? It had meant brutal slavery in the old Harkonnen days. Burzmali and Lucilla . . . He glanced at Tormsa.

"Will we find Burzmali and Lucilla in the city?"

"If they get through."

Duncan glanced down at his clothing. Was it a sufficient disguise? A Tleilaxu Master and companion? People would think the companion a Face Dancer, of course. Face Dancers were dangerous.

The baggy trousers were of some material Duncan had never before seen. It felt like wool to the hand, but he sensed that it was artificial. When he spat on it, spittle did not adhere and the smell was not of wool. His fingers detected a uniformity of texture that no natural material could present. The long soft boots and watchcap were of the same fabric. The garments were loose and puffy except at the ankles. Not quilted, though. Insulated by some trick of manufacture that trapped dead air between the layers. The color was a mottled green and gray—excellent camouflage here.

Tormsa was dressed in similar garments.

"How long do we wait here?" Duncan asked.

Tormsa shook his head for silence. The guide was seated now, knees up, arms wrapped around his legs, head cradled against his knees, eyes looking outward over the valley.

During the night's trip, Duncan had found the clothing remarkably comfortable. Except for that once in the water, his feet stayed warm but not too warm. There was plenty of room in trousers, shirt, and jacket for his body to move easily. Nothing abraded his flesh.

"Who makes clothing such as this?" Duncan asked.

"We made it," Tormsa growled. "Be silent."

This was no different than the pre-awakening days at the Sisterhood's Keep, Duncan thought. Tormsa was saying: "No need for you to know."

Presently, Tormsa stretched out his legs and straightened. He appeared to relax. He glanced at Duncan. "Friends in the city signal that there are searchers overhead."

"'Thopters?"

"Yes."

"Then what do we do?"

"You must do what I do and nothing else."

"You're just sitting there."

"For now. We will go down into the valley soon."

"But how—"

"When you traverse such country as this you become one of the animals that live here. Look at the tracks and see how they walk and how they lie down for a rest."

"But can't the searchers tell the difference between . . ."

"If the animals browse, you make the motions of browsing. If searchers come, you continue to do what it was you were doing, what any animal would do. Searchers will be high in the air. That is lucky for us. They cannot tell animal from human unless they come down."

"But won't they—"

"They trust their machines and the motions they see. They are lazy. They fly high. That way, the search goes faster. They trust their own intelligence to read their instruments and tell which is animal and which is human."

"So they'll just go by us if they think we're wild animals."

"If they doubt, they will scan us a second time. We must not change the pattern of movements after being scanned."

It was a long speech for the usually taciturn Tormsa. He studied Duncan carefully now. "You understand?"

"How will I know when we're being scanned?"

"Your gut will tingle. You will feel in your stomach the fizz of a drink that no man should swallow."

Duncan nodded. "Ixian scanners."

"Let it not alarm you," Tormsa said. "Animals here are accustomed to it. Sometimes, they may pause, but only for an instant and then they go on as if nothing has happened. Which, for them, is true. It is only for us that something evil may happen."

Presently, Tormsa stood. "We will go down into the valley now. Follow closely. Do exactly what I do and nothing else."

Duncan fell into step behind his guide. Soon, they were under the covering trees. Sometime during the night's passage, Duncan realized, he had begun to accept his place in the schemes of others. A new patience was taking over his awareness. And there was excitement goaded by curiosity.

What kind of a universe had come out of the Atreides times? *Gammu.* What a strange place Giedi Prime had become.

Slowly but distinctly, things were being revealed and each new thing opened a view to more that could be learned. He could feel patterns taking shape. One day, he thought, there would be a single pattern and then he would know why they had brought him back from the dead.

Yes, it was a matter of opening doors, he thought. You opened one door and that let you into a place where there were other doors. You chose a door in this new place and examined what that revealed to you. There might be times when you were forced to try all of the doors but the more doors you opened, the more certain you became of which door to open next. Finally, a door would open into a place you recognized. Then you could say: "Ahhhh, this explains everything."

"Searchers come," Tormsa said. "We are browsing animals now." He reached up to a screening bush and tore down a small limb.

Duncan did the same.

> I must rule with eye and claw—as the hawk among lesser birds.
>
> —ATREIDES ASSERTION (REF: BG ARCHIVES)

At daybreak, Teg emerged from the concealing windbreaks beside a main road. The road was a wide, flat thoroughfare—beam-hardened and kept bare of plant life. Ten lanes, Teg estimated, suitable for both vehicle and foot traffic. There was mostly foot traffic on it at this hour.

He had brushed most of the dust off his clothing and made sure there were no signs of rank on it. His gray hair was not as neat as he usually preferred but he had only his fingers for a comb.

Traffic on the road was headed toward the city of Ysai many kilometers across the valley. The morning was cloudless with a light breeze in his face moving toward the sea somewhere far behind him.

During the night he had come to a delicate balance with his new awareness. Things flickered in his second vision: knowledge of things around him before those things occurred, awareness of where he must put his foot in the next step. Behind this lay the reactive trigger that he knew could snap him into the blurring responses that flesh should not be able to accommodate. Reason could not explain the thing. He felt that he walked precariously along the cutting edge of a knife.

Try as he might, he could not resolve what had happened to him under the T-probe. Was it akin to what a Reverend Mother experienced in the spice agony? But he sensed no accumulation of

Other Memories out of his past. He did not think the Sisters could do what he did. The doubled vision that told him what to anticipate from every movement within the range of his senses seemed a new kind of truth.

Teg's Mentat teachers had always assured him there was a form of living-truth not susceptible to proof by the marshaling of ordinary facts. It was carried sometimes in fables and poetry and often went contrary to desires, so he had been told.

"The most difficult experience for a Mentat to accept," they said.

Teg had always reserved judgment on this pronouncement but now he was forced to accept it. The T-probe had thrust him over a threshold into a new reality.

He did not know why he chose this particular moment to emerge from hiding, except that it fitted him into an acceptable flow of human movement.

Most of that movement on the road was composed of market gardeners towing panniers of vegetables and fruit. The panniers were supported behind them on cheap suspensors. Awareness of that food sent sharp hunger pains through him but he forced himself to ignore them. With experience of more primitive planets in his long service to the Bene Gesserit, he saw this human activity as little different from that of farmers leading loaded animals. The foot traffic struck him as an odd mixture of ancient and modern—farmers afoot, their produce floating behind them on perfectly ordinary technological devices. Except for the suspensors this scene was very like a similar day in humankind's most ancient past. A draft animal was a draft animal, even if it came off an assembly line in an Ixian factory.

Using his new second vision, Teg chose one of the farmers, a squat, dark-skinned man with heavy features and thickly calloused hands. The man walked with a defiant sense of independence. He towed eight large panniers piled with rough-skinned melons. The smell of them was a mouth-watering agony to Teg as he matched his stride to that of the farmer. Teg strode for a few minutes in silence, then ventured: "Is this the best road to Ysai?"

"It is a long way," the man said. He had a guttural voice, something cautious in it.

Teg glanced back at the loaded panniers.

The farmer looked sidelong at Teg. "We go to a market center. Others take our produce from there to Ysai."

As they talked, Teg realized the farmer had guided (almost herded) him close to the edge of the road. The man glanced back and jerked his head slightly, nodding forward. Three more farmers came up beside them and closed in around Teg and his companion until tall panniers concealed them from the rest of the traffic.

Teg tensed. What were they planning? He sensed no menace, though. His doubled vision detected nothing violent in his immediate vicinity.

A heavy vehicle sped past them and on ahead. Teg knew of its passage only by the smell of burned fuel, the wind that shook the panniers, the thrumming of a powerful engine and sudden tension in his companions. The high panniers completely hid the passing vehicle.

"We have been looking for you to protect you, Bashar," the farmer beside him said. "There are many who hunt you but none of them with us along here."

Teg shot a startled glance at the man.

"We served with you at Renditai," the farmer said.

Teg swallowed. *Renditai?* He was a moment recalling it—only a minor skirmish in his long history of conflicts and negotiations.

"I am sorry but I do not know your name," Teg said.

"Be glad that you do not know our names. It is better that way."

"But I'm grateful."

"This is a small repayment, which we are glad to make, Bashar."

"I must get to Ysai," Teg said.

"It is dangerous there."

"It is dangerous everywhere."

"We guessed you would go to Ysai. Someone will come soon and you will ride in concealment. Ahhhh, here he comes. We have not seen you here, Bashar. You have not been here."

One of the other farmers took over the towing of his companion's load, pulling two strings of panniers while the farmer Teg had chosen hustled Teg under a tow rope and into a dark vehicle. Teg glimpsed shiny plasteel and plaz as the vehicle slowed only briefly for the pickup. The door closed sharply behind him and he found himself on a soft upholstered seat, alone in the back of a groundcar. The car picked up speed and soon was beyond the marching farmers. The windows around Teg had been darkened, giving him a dusky view of the passing scene. The driver was a shaded silhouette.

This first chance to relax in warm comfort since his capture almost lured Teg into sleep. He sensed no threats. His body still ached from the demands he had made on it and from the agonies of the T-probe.

He told himself, though, that he must stay awake and alert.

The driver leaned sideways and spoke over his shoulder without turning: "They have been hunting for you for two days, Bashar. Some think you already off-planet."

Two days?

The stunner and whatever else they had done to him had left him unconscious for a long time. This only added to his hunger. He tried to make the flesh-embedded chrono play against his vision centers and it only flickered as it had done each time he consulted it since the T-probe. His time sense and all references to it were changed.

So some thought he had left Gammu.

Teg did not ask who hunted him. Tleilaxu and people from the Scattering had been in that attack and the subsequent torture.

Teg glanced around his conveyance. It was one of those beautiful old pre-Scattering groundcars, the marks of the finest Ixian manufacture on it. He had never before ridden in one but he knew about them. Restorers picked them up to renew, rebuild—whatever they did that brought back the ancient sense of quality. Teg had been told that such vehicles often were found abandoned in strange places—in old broken-down buildings, in culverts, locked away in machinery warehouses, in farm fields.

Again, his driver leaned slightly sideways and spoke over one shoulder: "Do you have an address where you wish to be taken in Ysai, Bashar?"

Teg called up his memory of the contact points he had identified on his first tour of Gammu and gave one of these to the man. "Do you know that place?"

"It is mostly a meeting and drinking establishment, Bashar. I hear they serve good food, too, but anyone can enter if he has the price."

Not knowing why he had made that particular choice, Teg said: "We will chance it." He did not think it necessary to tell the driver that there were private dining rooms at the address.

The mention of food brought back sharp hunger cramps. Teg's arms began to tremble and he was several minutes restoring calmness. Last night's activities had almost drained him, he realized. He sent a searching gaze around the car's interior, wondering if there might be food or drink concealed here. The car's restoration had been accomplished with loving care but he saw no hidden compartments.

Such cars were not all that rare in some quarters, he knew, but all of them spoke of wealth. Who owned this one? Not the driver, certainly. That one had all the signs of a hired professional. But if a message had been sent to bring this car then others knew of Teg's location.

"Will we be stopped and searched?" Teg asked.

"Not this car, Bashar. The Planetary Bank of Gammu owns it."

Teg absorbed this silently. That bank had been one of his contact points. He had studied key branches carefully on his inspection tour. This memory drew him back into his responsibilities as guardian of the ghola.

"My companions," Teg ventured. "Are they . . ."

"Others have that in hand, Bashar. I cannot say."

"Can word be taken to . . ."

"When it is safe, Bashar."

"Of course."

Teg sank back into the cushions and studied his surroundings. These groundcars had been built with much plaz and almost indestructible plasteel. It was other things that went sour with age—upholstery, headliners, the electronics, the suspensor installations, the ablative liners of the turbofan ducts. And the adhesives deteriorated no matter what you did to preserve them. The restorers had made this one look as though it had just been cranked out of the factory—all subdued glowing in the metals, upholstery that molded itself to him with a faint sound of crinkling. And the smell: that indefinable aroma of newness, a mixture of polish and fine fabrics with just a hint of ozone bite underneath from the smoothly working electronics. Nowhere in it, though, was there the smell of food.

"How long to Ysai?" Teg asked.

"Another half hour, Bashar. Is there a problem that requires more speed? I don't want to attract . . ."

"I am very hungry."

The driver glanced left and right. There were no more farmers around them here. The roadway was almost empty except for two heavy transport pods with their tractors holding to the right verge and a large lorry hauling a towering automatic fruit picker.

"It is dangerous to delay for long," the driver said. "But I know a place where I think I can at least get you a quick bowl of soup."

"Anything would be welcome. I have not eaten for two days and there has been much activity."

They came to a crossroads and the driver turned left onto a narrow track through tall, evenly spaced conifers. Presently, he turned onto a one-lane drive through the trees. The low building at the end of this track was built of dark stones and had a blackplaz roof. The windows were narrow and glistened with protective burner nozzles.

The driver said: "Just a minute, sir." He got out and Teg had his first look at the man's face: extremely thin with a long nose and tiny mouth. The visible tracery of surgical reconstruction laced his cheeks. The eyes glowed silver, obviously artificial. He turned away and went into the house. When he returned, he opened Teg's door. "Please be quick, sir. The one inside is heating soup for you. I have said you are a banker. No need to pay."

The ground was icy crisp underfoot. Teg had to stoop slightly for the doorway. He entered a dark hallway, wood-paneled and with a well-lighted room at the end. The smell of food there drew him like a magnet. His arms were trembling once more. A small table had been set beside a window with a view of an enclosed and covered garden. Bushes heavy with red flowers almost concealed the stone wall that defined the garden. Yellow hotplaz gleamed over the space, bathing it in a summery artificial light. Teg sank gratefully into the single chair at the table. White linen, he saw, with an embossed edge. A single soup spoon.

A door creaked at his right and a squat figure entered carrying a bowl from which steam arose. The man hesitated when he saw Teg, then brought the bowl to the table and placed it in front of Teg. Alerted by that hesitation, Teg forced himself to ignore the tempting aroma drifting to his nostrils and concentrated instead on his companion.

"It is good soup, sir. I made it myself."

An artificial voice. Teg saw the scars at the sides of the jaw. There was the look of an ancient mechanical about this man—an almost neckless head attached to thick shoulders, arms that seemed oddly jointed at both shoulders and elbows, legs that appeared to swing only from the hips. He stood motionless now but he had entered here with a slightly jerking sway that said he was mostly replacement artificials. The look of suffering in his eyes could not be avoided.

"I know I'm not pretty, sir," the man rasped. "I was ruined in the Alajory explosion."

Teg had no idea what the Alajory explosion might have been but it obviously was presumed he knew. "Ruined," however, was an interesting accusation against Fate.

"I was wondering if I knew you," Teg said.

"No one here knows anyone else," the man said. "Eat your soup." He pointed upward at the coiled tip of quiescent snooper, the glow of its lights revealing that it read its surroundings and found no poison. "The food is safe here."

Teg looked at the dark brown liquid in his bowl. Lumps of solid meat were visible in it. He reached for the spoon. His trembling hand made two attempts before grasping the spoon and even then he sloshed most of the liquid out of the spoon before he could lift it a millimeter.

A steadying hand gripped Teg's wrist and the artificial voice spoke softly in Teg's ear: "I do not know what they did to you, Bashar, but no one will harm you here without crossing my dead body."

"You know me?"

"Many would die for you, Bashar. My son lives because of you."

Teg allowed himself to be helped. It was all he could do to swallow the first spoonful. The liquid was rich, hot and soothing. His hand steadied presently and he nodded to the man to release the wrist.

"More, sir?"

Teg realized then that he had emptied the bowl. It was tempting to say "yes" but the driver had said to make haste.

"Thank you, but I must go."

"You have not been here," the man said.

When they were once more back on the main road, Teg sat back against the groundcar's cushions and reflected on the curious echoing quality of what the *ruined* man had said. The same words the farmer had used: "You have not been here." It had the feeling of a common response and it said something about changes in Gammu since Teg had surveyed the place.

They entered the outskirts of Ysai presently and Teg wondered if he should attempt a disguise. The *ruined* man had recognized him quickly.

"Where do the Honored Matres hunt for me now?" Teg asked.

"Everywhere, Bashar. We cannot guarantee your safety but steps are being taken. I will make it known where I have delivered you."

"Do they say why they hunt me?"

"They never explain, Bashar."

"How long have they been on Gammu?"

"Too long, sir. Since I was a child and I was a baltern at Renditai."

A hundred years at least, Teg thought. *Time to gather many forces into their hands . . . if Taraza's fears were to be credited.*

Teg credited them.

"Trust no one those whores can influence," Taraza had said.

Teg sensed no threat to him in his present position, though. He could only absorb the secrecy that obviously enclosed him now. He did not press for more details.

They were well into Ysai and he glimpsed the black bulk of the ancient Harkonnen seat of Barony through occasional gaps between the walls that enclosed the great private residences. The car turned onto a street of small commercial establishments: cheap buildings constructed for the most part of salvaged materials that displayed their origins in poor fits and unmatched colors. Gaudy signs advised that the wares inside were the finest, the repair services better than those elsewhere.

It was not that Ysai had deteriorated or even gone to seed, Teg thought. Growth here had been diverted into something worse than ugly. Someone had chosen to make this place repellent. That was the key to most of what he saw in the city.

Time had not stopped here, it had retreated. This was no modern city full of bright transport pods and insulated usiform buildings. This was random jumbles, ancient structures joined to ancient structures, some built to individual tastes and some obviously designed with some long-gone necessity in mind. Everything about Ysai was joined in a proximity whose disarray just managed to avoid chaos. What saved it, Teg knew, was the old pattern of thoroughfares along which this hodgepodge had been assembled. Chaos was held at bay, although what pattern there was in the streets conformed to no master plan. Streets met and crossed at odd angles, seldom squared. Seen from the air, the place was a crazy quilt with only the giant black rectangle of ancient Barony to speak of an organizing plan. The rest of it was architectural rebellion.

Teg saw suddenly that this place was a lie plastered over with other lies, based on previous lies, and such a mad mixup that they might never dig through to a usable truth. All of Gammu was that way. Where could such insanity have had its beginnings? Was it the Harkonnens' doing?

"We are here, sir."

The driver drew up to the curb in front of a windowless building face, all flat black plasteel and with a single ground-level door. No salvaged material in this construction. Teg recognized the place: the bolt hole he had chosen. Unidentified things flickered in Teg's second vision but he sensed no immediate menace. The driver opened Teg's door and stood to one side.

"Not much activity here at this hour, sir. I would get inside quickly."

Without a backward glance, Teg darted across the narrow walk and into the building—a small brightly lighted foyer of polished white plaz and only banks of comeyes to greet him. He ducked into a lift tube and punched the remembered coordinates. This tube, he knew, angled upward through the building to the fifty-seventh floor rear where there were some windows. He remembered a private dining room of dark reds and heavy brown furnishings, a hard-eyed female with the obvious signs of Bene Gesserit training, but no Reverend Mother.

The tube disgorged him into the remembered room but there was no one to receive him. Teg glanced around at the solid brown furnishings. Four windows along the far wall were concealed behind thick maroon draperies.

Teg knew he had been seen. He waited patiently, using his newly learned doubling-vision to anticipate trouble. There was no indication of attack. He took up a position to one side of the tube outlet and glanced around him once more.

Teg had a theory about the relationship between rooms and their windows—the number of windows, their placement, their size, height from the floor, relationship of room size to window size, the elevation of the room, windows curtained or draped, and all of this Mentat-interpreted against knowledge of the uses to which a room was put. Rooms could be fitted to a kind of pecking order defined with extreme sophistication. Emergency uses might throw such distinctions out the window but they otherwise were quite reliable.

Lack of windows in an aboveground room conveyed a particular message. If humans occupied such a room, it did not necessarily mean secrecy was the main goal. He had seen unmistakable signs in scholastic settings that windowless schoolrooms were both a retreat from the exterior world and a strong statement of dislike for children.

This room, however, presented something different: conditional secrecy plus the need to keep occasional watch on that exterior world. *Protective secrecy when required.* His opinion was reinforced when he crossed the room and twitched one of the draperies aside. The windows were tripled armor-plaz. So! Keeping watch on that world outside might draw attack. That was the opinion of whoever had ordered the room protected this way.

Once more, Teg twitched the drapery aside. He glanced at the corner glazing. Prismatic reflectors there amplified the view along the adjacent wall to both sides and from roof to ground.

Well!

His previous visit had not given him time for this closer examination but now he made a more positive assessment. A very interesting room. Teg dropped the drapery and turned just in time to see a tall man enter from the tube slot.

Teg's doubled vision provided a firm prediction on the stranger. This man brought concealed danger. The newcomer was plainly military—the way he carried himself, the quick eye for details that only a trained and experienced officer would observe. And there was something else in his manner that made Teg stiffen. This was a betrayer! A mercenary available to the highest bidder.

"Damned nasty the way they treated you," the man greeted Teg. The voice was a deep baritone with an unconscious assumption of personal power in it. The accent was one Teg had never before heard. This was someone from the Scattering! A Bashar or equivalent, Teg estimated.

Still, there was no indication of immediate attack.

When Teg did not answer, the man said: "Oh, sorry: I'm Muzzafar. Jafa Muzzafar, regional commander for the forces of Dur."

Teg had never heard of the forces of Dur.

Questions crowded Teg's mind but he kept them to himself. Anything he said here might betray weakness.

Where were the people who had met him here before? *Why did I choose this place?* The decision had been made with such inner assurance.

"Please be comfortable," Muzzafar said, indicating a small divan with a low serving table in front of it. "I assure you that none of what has happened to you was of my doing. Tried to put a stop to it when I heard but you'd already . . . left the scene."

Teg heard the other thing in this Muzzafar's voice now: caution bordering on fear. So this man had either heard about or seen the shack and the clearing.

"Damned clever of you," Muzzafar said. "Having your attack force wait until your captors were concentrating on trying to get information out of you. Did they learn anything?"

Teg shook his head silently from side to side. He felt on the edge of being ignited in a blurred response to attack, yet he sensed no immediate violence here. What were these Lost Ones doing? But Muzzafar and his people had made a wrong assessment of what had happened in the room of the T-probe. That was clear.

"Please, be seated," Muzzafar said.

Teg took the proffered seat on the divan.

Muzzafar sat in a deep chair facing Teg at a slight angle on the other side of the serving table. There was a crouching sense of alertness in Muzzafar. He was prepared for violence.

Teg studied the man with interest. Muzzafar had revealed no real rank—only commander. Tall fellow with a wide, ruddy face and a big nose. The eyes were gray-green and had the trick of focusing just behind Teg's right shoulder when either of them spoke. Teg had known a spy once who did that.

"Well, well," Muzzafar said. "I've read and heard a great deal about you since coming here."

Teg continued to study him silently. Muzzafar's hair had been cropped close and there was a purple scar about three millimeters long across the scalp line above the left eye. He wore an open bush jacket of light green and matching trousers—not quite a uniform but there was a neatness about him that spoke of customary spit and polish. The shoes attested to this. Teg thought he probably could see his own reflection in their light brown surfaces if he bent close.

"Never expected to meet you personally, of course," Muzzafar said. "Consider it a great honor."

"I know very little about you except that you command a force from the Scattering," Teg said.

"Mmmmmph! Not much to know, really."

Once more, hunger pangs gripped Teg. His gaze went to the button beside the tube slot, which, he remembered, would summon a waiter. This was a place where humans did the work usually assigned to automata, an excuse for keeping a large force assembled at the ready.

Misinterpreting Teg's interest in the tube slot, Muzzafar said: "Please don't think of leaving. Having my own medic come in to take a look at you. Shouldn't be but a moment. Appreciate it if you'd wait quietly until he arrives."

"I was merely thinking of placing an order for some food," Teg said.

"Advise you to wait until the doctor's had his look-see. Stunners leave some nasty aftereffects."

"So you know about that."

"Know about the whole damned fiasco. You and your man Burzmali are a force to be reckoned with."

Before Teg could respond, the tube slot disgorged a tall man in a jacketed red singlesuit, a man so bone-skinny that his clothing gaped and flapped about him. The diamond tattoo of a Suk doctor had been burned into his high forehead but the mark was orange and not the customary black. The doctor's eyes were concealed by a glistening orange cover that hid their true color.

An addict of some kind? Teg wondered. There was no smell of the familiar narcotics around him, not even melange. There was a tart smell, though, almost like some fruit.

"There you are, Solitz!" Muzzafar said. He gestured at Teg. "Give him a good scan. Stunner hit him day before yesterday."

Solitz produced a recognizable Suk scanner, compact and fitting into one hand. Its probe field produced a low hum.

"So you're a Suk doctor," Teg said, looking pointedly at the orange brand on the forehead.

"Yes, Bashar. My training and conditioning are the finest in our ancient tradition."

"I've never seen the identifying mark in that color," Teg said.

The doctor passed his scanner around Teg's head. "The color of the tattoo makes no difference, Bashar. What is behind it is all that matters." He lowered the scanner to Teg's shoulders, then down across the body.

Teg waited for the humming to stop.

The doctor stood back and addressed Muzzafar: "He is quite fit, Field Marshal. Remarkably fit, considering his age, but he desperately needs sustenance."

"Yes . . . well, that's fine then, Solitz. Take care of that. The Bashar is our guest."

"I will order a meal suited to his needs," Solitz said. "Eat it slowly, Bashar." Solitz did a smart about-face that set his jacket and trousers flapping. The tube slot swallowed him.

"Field Marshal?" Teg asked.

"A revival of ancient titles in the Dur," Muzzafar said.

"The Dur?" Teg ventured.

"Stupid of me!" Muzzafar produced a small case from a side pocket of his jacket and extracted a thin folder. Teg recognized a holostat similar to one he had carried himself during his long service—pictures of home and family. Muzzafar placed the holostat on the table between them and tapped the control button.

The full-color image of a bushy green expanse of jungle came alive in miniature above the tabletop.

"Home," Muzzafar said. "Frame bush in the center there." A finger indicated a place in the projection. "First one that ever obeyed me. People laughed at me for choosing the first one that way and sticking with it."

Teg stared at the projection, aware of a deep sadness in Muzzafar's voice. The indicated bush was a spindly grouping of thin limbs with bright blue bulbs dangling from the tips.

Frame bush?

"Rather thin thing, I know," Muzzafar said, removing his pointing finger from the projection. "Not secure at all. Had to defend myself a few times in the first months with it. Grew rather fond of it, though. They respond to that, you know. It's the best home in all the deep valleys now, by the Eternal Rock of Dur!"

Muzzafar stared at Teg's puzzled expression. "Damn! You don't have frame bushes, of course. You must forgive my crashing ignorance. We've a great deal to teach each other, I think."

"You called that home," Teg said.

"Oh, yes. With proper direction, once they learn to obey, of course, a frame bush will grow itself into a magnificent residence. It only takes four or five standards."

Standards, Teg thought. So the Lost Ones still used the Standard Year.

The tube slot hissed and a young woman in a blue serving gown backed into the room towing a suspensor-buoyed hotpod, which she positioned near the table in front of Teg. Her clothing was of the type Teg had seen during his original inspection but the pleasantly round face she turned to him was unfamiliar. Her scalp had been depilated, leaving an expanse of prominent veins. Her eyes were watery blue and there was something cowed in her posture. She opened the hotpod and the spicy odors of the food wafted across Teg's nostrils.

Teg was alerted but he sensed no immediate threat. He could see himself eating the food without ill effect.

The young woman put a row of dishes on to the table in front of him and arranged the eating implements neatly at one side.

"I've no snooper, but I'll taste the foods if you wish," Muzzafar said.

"Not necessary," Teg said. He knew this would raise questions but felt they would suspect him of being a Truthsayer. Teg's gaze locked onto the food. Without any conscious decision, he leaned forward and began eating. Familiar with Mentat-hunger, he was surprised at his own reactions. Using the brain in Mentat mode consumed calories at an alarming rate, but this was a new necessity driving him. He felt his own survival controlling his actions. This hunger went beyond anything of previous experience. The soup he had eaten with some caution at the house of the *ruined* man had not aroused such a demanding reaction.

The Suk doctor chose correctly, Teg thought. This food had been selected directly out of the scanner's summation.

The young woman kept bringing more dishes from hotpods ordered via the tube slot.

Teg had to get up in the middle of the meal and relieve himself in an adjoining washroom, conscious there of the hidden comeyes that were keeping him under surveillance. He knew by his physical reactions that his digestive system had speeded up to a new level of bodily necessity. When he returned to the table, he felt just as hungry as though he had not eaten.

The serving woman began to show signs of surprise and then alarm. Still, she kept bringing more food at his demand.

Muzzafar watched with growing amazement but said nothing.

Teg felt the supportive replacement of the food, the precise caloric adjustment that the Suk doctor had ordered. They obviously had not thought about quantity, though. The girl obeyed his demands in a kind of walking shock.

Muzzafar spoke finally. "Must say I've never before seen anyone eat that much at one sitting. Can't see how you do it. Nor why."

Teg sat back, satisfied at last, knowing he had aroused questions that could not be answered truthfully.

"A Mentat thing," Teg lied. "I've been through a very strenuous time."

"Amazing," Muzzafar said. He arose.

When Teg started to stand, Muzzafar gestured for him to remain. "No need. We've prepared quarters for you right next door. Safer not to move you yet."

The young woman departed with the empty hotpods.

Teg studied Muzzafar. Something had changed during the meal. Muzzafar watched him with a coldly measuring stare.

"You've an implanted communicator," Teg said. "You have received new orders."

"It would not be advisable for your friends to attack this place," Muzzafar said.

"You think that's my plan?"

"What is your plan, Bashar?"

Teg smiled.

"Very well." Muzzafar's gaze went out of focus as he listened to his communicator. When he once more concentrated on Teg, his gaze had the look of a predator. Teg felt himself buffeted by that gaze, recognizing that someone else was coming to this room. The Field Marshal thought of this new development as something extremely dangerous to his dinner guest but Teg saw nothing that could defeat his new abilities.

"You think I am your prisoner," Teg said.

"By the Eternal Rock, Bashar! You are not what I expected!"

"The Honored Matre who is coming, what does she expect?" Teg asked.

"Bashar, I warn you: Do not take that tone with her. You have not the slightest concept of what is about to happen to you."

"An Honored Matre is about to happen to me," Teg said.

"And I wish you well of her!"

Muzzafar pivoted and left via the tube slot.

Teg stared after him. He could see the flickering of second vision like a light blinking around the tube slot. The Honored Matre was near but not yet ready to enter this room. First, she would consult with Muzzafar. The Field Marshal would not be able to tell this dangerous female anything really important.

Memory never recaptures reality. Memory reconstructs. All reconstructions change the original, becoming external frames of reference that inevitably fall short.

—MENTAT HANDBOOK

Lucilla and Burzmali entered Ysai from the south into a lower-class quarter with widely spaced streetlights. It lacked only an hour of midnight and yet people thronged the streets in this quarter. Some walked quietly, some chatted with drug-enhanced vigor, some only watched expectantly. They wadded up at the corners and held Lucilla's fascinated attention as she passed.

Burzmali urged her to walk faster, an eager customer anxious to get her alone. Lucilla kept her covert attention on the people.

What did they do here? Those men waiting in the doorway: For what did they wait? Workers in heavy aprons emerged from a wide passage as Lucilla and Burzmali passed. There was a thick smell of rank sewage and perspiration about them. The workers, almost equally divided between male and female, were tall, heavy-bodied and with thick arms. Lucilla could not imagine what their occupation might be but they were of a single type and they made her realize how little she knew of Gammu.

The workers hawked and spat into the gutter as they emerged into the night. *Ridding themselves of some contaminant?*

Burzmali put his mouth close to Lucilla's ear and whispered: "Those workers are the Bordanos."

She risked a glance back at them where they walked toward a side street. *Bordanos?* Ahhh, yes: people trained and bred to work the compression machinery that harnessed sewer gases. They had been bred to remove the sense of smell and the musculature of shoulders and arms had been increased. Burzmali guided her around a corner and out of sight of the Bordanos.

Five children emerged from a dark doorway beside them and wheeled into line following Lucilla and Burzmali. Lucilla noted their hands clutching small objects. They followed with a strange intensity. Abruptly, Burzmali stopped and turned. The children also stopped and stared at him. It was clear to Lucilla that the children were prepared for some violence.

Burzmali clasped both hands in front of him and bowed to the children. He said: "Guldur!"

When Burzmali resumed guiding her down the street, the children no longer followed.

"They would have stoned us," he said.

"Why?"

"They are children of a sect that follows Guldur—the local name for the Tyrant."

Lucilla looked back but the children were no longer in sight. They had set off in search of another victim.

Burzmali guided her around another corner. Now, they were in a street crowded with small merchants selling their wares from wheeled stands—food, clothing, small tools, and knives. A singsong of shouts filled the air as the merchants tried to attract buyers. Their voices had that end of the workday lift—a false brilliance composed of the hope that old dreams would be fulfilled, yet colored by the knowledge that life would not change for them. It occurred to Lucilla that the people of these streets pursued a fleeting dream, that the fulfillment they sought was not the thing itself but a myth they had been conditioned to seek the way racing animals were trained to chase after the whirling bait on the endless oval of the racetrack.

In the street directly ahead of them a burly figure in a thickly padded coat was engaged in loud-voiced argument with a merchant who offered a string bag filled with the dark red bulbs of a sweetly acid fruit. The fruit smell was thick all around them. The merchant complained: "You would steal the food from the mouths of my children!"

The bulky figure spoke in a piping voice, the accent chillingly familiar to Lucilla: "I, too, have children!"

Lucilla controlled herself with an effort.

When they were clear of the market street, she whispered to Burzmali: "That man in the heavy coat back there—a Tleilaxu Master!"

"Couldn't be," Burzmali protested. "Too tall."

"Two of them, one on the shoulders of the other."

"You're sure?"

"I'm sure."

"I've seen others like that since we arrived, but I didn't suspect."

"Many searchers are in these streets," she said.

Lucilla found that she did not much care for the everyday life of the gutter inhabitants on this gutter planet. She no longer trusted the explanation for bringing the ghola here. Of all those planets on which the precious ghola could have been raised, why had the Sisterhood chosen this one? Or was the ghola truly precious? Could it be that he was merely bait?

Almost blocking the narrow mouth of an alley beside them was a man plying a tall device of whirling lights.

"Live!" he shouted. "Live!"

Lucilla slowed her pace to watch a passerby step into the alleyway and pass a coin to the proprietor, then lean into a concave basin made brilliant by the lights. The proprietor stared back at Lucilla. She saw a man with a narrow dark face, the face of a Caladanian primitive on a body only slightly taller than that of a Tleilaxu Master. There had been a look of contempt on his brooding face as he took the customer's money.

The customer lifted his face from the basin with a shudder and then left the alley, staggering slightly, his eyes glazed.

Lucilla recognized the device. Users called it a hypnobong and it was outlawed on all of the more civilized worlds.

Burzmali hurried her out of the view of the brooding hypnobong proprietor.

They came to a wider side street with a corner doorway set into the building across from them. Foot traffic all around; not a vehicle in sight. A tall man sat on the first step in the corner doorway, his knees drawn up close to his chin. His long arms were wrapped around his knees, the thin-fingered hands clasped tightly together. He wore a wide-brimmed black hat that shaded his face from the streetlights, but twin gleams from the shadows under that brim told Lucilla that this was no kind of human she had ever before encountered. This was something about which the Bene Gesserit had only speculated.

Burzmali waited until they were well away from the seated figure before satisfying her curiosity.

"Futar," he whispered. "That's what they call themselves. They've only recently been seen here on Gammu."

"A Tleilaxu experiment," Lucilla guessed. And she thought: *A mistake that has returned from the Scattering.* "What are they doing here?" she asked.

"Trading colony, so the natives here tell us."

"Don't you believe it. Those are hunting animals that have been crossed with humans."

"Ahhh, here we are," Burzmali said.

He guided Lucilla through a narrow doorway into a dimly lighted eating establishment. This was part of their disguise, Lucilla knew: Do what others in this quarter did, but she did not relish eating in this place, not with what she could interpret from the smells.

The place had been crowded but it was emptying as they entered.

"This commerciel was recommended highly," Burzmali said as they seated themselves in a mechaslot and waited for the menu to be projected.

Lucilla watched the departing customers. Night workers from nearby factories and offices, she guessed. They appeared anxious in their hurry, perhaps fearful of what might be done to them if they were tardy.

How insulated she had been at the Keep, she thought. She did not like what she was learning of Gammu. What a scruffy place this commerciel was! The stools at the counter to her right had been scarred and chipped. The tabletop in front of her had been scored and rubbed with gritty cleaners until it no longer could be kept clean by the vacusweep whose nozzle she could see near her left elbow. There was no sign of even the cheapest sonic to maintain cleanliness. Food and other evidence of deterioration had accumulated in the table's scratches. Lucilla shuddered. She could not avoid the feeling that it had been a mistake to separate from the ghola.

The menu had been projected, she saw, and Burzmali already was scanning it.

"I will order for you," he said.

Burzmali's way of saying he did not want her to make a mistake by ordering something a woman of the Hormu might avoid.

It galled her to feel dependent. She was a Reverend Mother! She was trained to take command in any situation, mistress of her own destiny. How tiring all of this was. She gestured at the dirty window on her left where people could be seen passing on the narrow street.

"I am losing business while we dally, Skar."

There! That was in character.

Burzmali almost sighed. *At last!* he thought. She had begun to function once more as a Reverend Mother. He could not understand her abstracted attitude, the way she looked at the city and its people.

Two milky drinks slid from the slot onto the table. Burzmali drank his in one swallow. Lucilla tested her drink on the tip of her tongue, sorting the contents. An imitation caffiate diluted with a nut-flavored juice.

Burzmali gestured upward with his chin for her to drink it quickly. She obeyed, concealing a grimace at the chemical flavors. Burzmali's attention was on something over her right shoulder but she dared not turn. That would be out of character.

"Come." He placed a coin on the table and hurried her out into the street. He smiled the smile of an eager customer but there was wariness in his eyes.

The tempo of the streets had changed. There were fewer people. The shadowy doors conveyed a deeper sense of menace. Lucilla reminded herself that she was supposed to represent a powerful guild whose members were immune to the common violence of the gutter. The few people on the street *did* make way for her, eyeing the dragons of her robe with every appearance of awe.

Burzmali stopped at a doorway.

It was like the others along this street, set back slightly from the walkway, so tall that it appeared narrower than it actually was. An old-fashioned security beam guarded the entrance. None of the newer systems had penetrated to the slum, apparently. The streets themselves were testimony to that: designed for groundcars. She doubted that there was a roofpad in the entire area. No sign of flitters or 'thopters could be heard or seen. There was music, though—a faint susurration reminiscent of semuta. Something new in semuta addiction? This would certainly be an area where addicts would go to ground.

Lucilla looked up at the face of the building as Burzmali moved ahead of her and made their presence known by breaking the doorway beam.

There were no windows in the building's face. Only the faint glitterings of surface 'eyes here and there in the dull sheen of ancient plasteel. They were old-fashioned comeyes, she noted, much bigger than modern ones.

A door deep in the shadows swung inward on silent hinges.

"This way." Burzmali reached back and urged her forward with a hand on her elbow.

They entered a dimly lighted hallway that smelled of exotic foods and bitter essences. She was a moment identifying some of the things that assailed her nostrils. Melange. She caught the unmistakable cinnamon ripeness. And yes, semuta. She identified burned rice, higet salts. Someone was masking another kind of *cooking*. There were explosives being made here. She thought of warning Burzmali but reconsidered. It was not necessary for him to know and there might be ears in this confined space to hear whatever she said.

Burzmali led the way up a shadowy flight of stairs with a dim glowstrip along the slanting baseboard. At the top he found a hidden switch concealed behind a patch in the patched and repatched wall. There was no sound when he pushed the switch but Lucilla felt a change in the movement all around them. Silence. It was a new kind of silence in her experience, a crouching preparation for flight or violence.

It was cold in the stairwell and she shivered, but not from the chill. Footsteps sounded beyond the doorway beside the patch-masked switch.

A gray-haired hag in a yellow smock opened the door and peered up at them past her straggling eyebrows.

"It's you," she said, her voice wavering. She stood aside for them to enter.

Lucilla glanced swiftly around the room as she heard the door close behind them. It was a room the unobservant might think shabby, but that was superficial. Underneath, it was quality. The shabbiness was another mask, partly a matter of this place having been fitted to a particularly demanding person: This goes here and nowhere else! That goes over there and it stays there! The furnishings and bric-a-brac looked a little worn but someone here did not object to that. The room felt better this way. It was that kind of room.

Who possessed this room? The old woman? She was making her painful way toward a door on their left.

"We are not to be disturbed until dawn," Burzmali said.

The old woman stopped and turned.

Lucilla studied her. Was this another who shammed advanced age? No. The age was real. Every motion was diffused by unsteadiness—a trembling of the neck, a failure of the body that betrayed her in ways she could not prevent.

"Even if it's somebody important?" the old woman asked in her wavering voice.

The eyes twitched when she spoke. Her mouth moved only minimally to emit the necessary sounds, spacing out her words as though she drew them from somewhere deep within. Her shoulders, curved from years of bending at some fixed work, would not straighten enough for her to look Burzmali in the eyes. She peered upward past her brows instead, an oddly furtive posture.

"What important person are you expecting?" Burzmali asked.

The old woman shuddered and appeared to take a long time understanding.

"Impor-r-rtant people come here," she said.

Lucilla recognized the body signals and blurted it because Burzmali must know:

"She's from Rakis!"

The old woman's curious upward gaze locked on Lucilla. The ancient voice said: "I was a priestess, Hormu Lady."

"Of course she's from Rakis," Burzmali said. His tone warned her not to question.

"I would not harm you," the hag whined.

"Do you still serve the Divided God?"

Again, there was that long delay for the old woman to respond.

"Many serve the Great Guldur," she said.

Lucilla pursed her lips and once more scanned the room. The old woman had been reduced greatly in importance. "I am glad I do not have to kill you," Lucilla said.

The old woman's jaw drooped open in a parody of surprise while spittle dripped from her lips.

This was a descendant of Fremen? Lucilla let her revulsion come out in a long shudder. This mendicant bit of flotsam had been shaped from a people who walked tall and proud, a people who died bravely. This one would die whining.

"Please trust me," the hag whined and fled the room.

"Why did you do that?" Burzmali demanded. "These are the ones who will get us to Rakis!"

She merely looked at him, recognizing the fear in his question. It was fear *for* her.

But I did not imprint him back there, she thought.

With a sense of shock she realized that Burzmali had recognized hate in her. *I hate them!* she thought. *I hate the people of this planet!*

That was a dangerous emotion for a Reverend Mother. Still it burned in her. This planet had changed her in a way she did not want. She did not want the realization that such things could be. Intellectual understanding was one thing; experience was another.

Damn them!

But they already were damned.

Her chest pained her. Frustration! There was no escaping this new awareness. What had happened to these people?

People?

The shells were here but they no longer could be called fully alive. Dangerous, though. Supremely dangerous.

"We must rest while we can," Burzmali said.

"I do not have to earn my money?" she demanded.

Burzmali paled. "What we did was necessary! We were lucky and were not stopped but it could have happened!"

"And this place is safe?"

"As safe as I can make it. Everyone here has been screened by me or by my people."

Lucilla found a long couch that smelled of old perfumes and composed herself there to scour her emotions of the dangerous hate. Where hate entered, love might follow! She heard Burzmali stretching out to rest on cushions against a nearby wall. Soon, he was breathing deeply, but sleep evaded Lucilla. She kept sensing crowds of memories, things thrust forward by the Others who shared her inner storerooms of thinking. Abruptly, inner vision gave her a glimpse of a street and faces, people moving in bright sunlight. It took a moment for her to realize that she saw all of this from a peculiar angle—that she was being cradled in someone's arms. She knew then that this was one of her own personal memories. She could place the one who held her, feel the warm heartbeat next to a warm cheek.

Lucilla tasted the salt of her own tears.

She realized then that Gammu had touched her more deeply than any experience since her first days in the Bene Gesserit schools.

Concealed behind strong barriers the heart becomes ice.

—DARWI ODRADE, ARGUMENT IN COUNCIL

It was a group filled with fierce tensions: Taraza (wearing secret mail under her robe and mindful of the other precautions she had taken), Odrade (certain that there could be violence and consequently wary), Sheeana (thoroughly briefed on the probabilities here and shielded behind three Security Mothers who moved with her like fleshly armor), Waff (worried that his reason might have been clouded by some mysterious Bene Gesserit artifice), the false Tuek (giving every evidence that he was about to erupt in rage), and nine of Tuek's Rakian counselors (each angrily engaged in seeking ascendancy for self or family).

In addition, five guardian acolytes, bred and trained by the Sisterhood for physical violence, stayed close to Taraza. Waff moved with an equal number of new Face Dancers.

They had convened in the penthouse atop the Dar-es-Balat Museum. It was a long room with a wall of plaz facing west across a roof garden of lacy greenery. The interior was furnished with soft divans and was decorated with artful displays from the Tyrant's no-room.

Odrade had argued against including Sheeana but Taraza remained adamant. The girl's effect on Waff and some of the priesthood represented an overwhelming advantage for the Bene Gesserit.

There were dolban screens over the long wall of windows to keep out the worst glare of a westering sun. That the room faced west said something to Odrade. The windows looked into the land of gloaming where Shai-hulud took his repose. It was a room focused on the past, on death.

She admired the dolbans in front of her. They were flat black slats ten molecules wide and rotating in a transparent liquid medium. Set automatically, the best Ixian dolbans admitted a predetermined level of light without much diminishing the view. Artists and antique dealers preferred them to polarizing systems, Odrade knew, because they admitted a full spectrum of available light. Their installation spoke of the uses to which this room was put—a display case for the best of the God Emperor's hoard. Yes—there was a gown that had been worn by his intended bride.

The priestly counselors were arguing fiercely among themselves at one end of the room, ignoring the false Tuek. Taraza stood nearby listening. Her expression said she thought the priests fools.

Waff stood with his Face Dancer entourage near the wide entrance door. His attention shifted from Sheeana to Odrade to Taraza and only occasionally to the arguing priests. Every movement Waff made betrayed his uncertainties. Would the Bene Gesserit really support him? Could they together override Rakian opposition by peaceful means?

Sheeana and her shielding escort came to stand beside Odrade. The girl still showed stringy muscles, Odrade observed, but she was filling out and the muscles had taken on a recognizable Bene Gesserit definition. The high planes of her cheekbones had grown softer under that olive skin, the brown eyes more liquid, but there were still red sunstreaks in her brown hair. The attention she spared for the arguing priests said she was assessing what had been revealed to her in the briefing.

"Will they really fight?" she whispered.

"Listen to them," Odrade said.

"What will the Mother Superior do?"

"Watch her carefully."

Both of them looked at Taraza standing in her group of muscular acolytes. Taraza now looked amused as she continued to observe the priests.

The Rakian group had started their argument out in the roof garden. They had brought it inside as the shadows lengthened. They breathed angrily, muttering sometimes and then raising their voices. Did they not see how the mimic Tuek watched them?

Odrade returned her attention to the horizon visible beyond the roof garden: not another sign of life out there in the desert. Any direction you looked outward from Dar-es-Balat showed empty sand. People born and raised here had a different view of life and their planet than most of those priestly counselors. This was not the Rakis of green belts and watered oases, which abounded in the higher latitudes like flowered fingers pointing into the long desert tracks. Out from Dar-es-Balat was the meridian desert that stretched like a cummerbund around the entire planet.

"I have heard enough of this nonsense!" the false Tuek exploded. He pushed one of the counselors roughly aside and strode into the middle of the arguing group, pivoting to stare into each face. "Are you all mad?"

One of the priests (It was old Albertus, by the gods!) looked across the room at Waff and called out: "Ser Waff! Will you please control your Face Dancer?"

Waff hesitated and then moved toward the disputants, his entourage close behind.

The false Tuek whirled and pointed a finger at Waff: "You! Stay where you are! I will brook no Tleilaxu interference! Your conspiracy is quite clear to me!"

Odrade had been watching Waff as the mimic Tuek spoke. Surprise! The Bene Tleilax Master had never before been addressed thus by one of his minions. What a shock! Rage convulsed his features. Humming sounds like the noises of angry insects came from his mouth, a modulated thing that clearly was some kind of language. The Face Dancers of his entourage froze but the false Tuek merely returned attention to his counselors.

Waff stopped humming. Consternation! His Face Dancer Tuek would not come to heel! He lurched into motion toward the priests.

The false Tuek saw it and once more leveled a hand at him, the finger quivering.

"I told you to stay out of this! You might be able to do away with me but you'll not saddle me with your Tleilaxu filth!"

That did it. Waff stopped. Realization came over him. He shot a glance at Taraza, seeing her amused recognition of his predicament. Now, he had a new target for his rage.

"You knew!"

"I suspected."

"You . . . you . . ."

"You fashioned too well," Taraza said. "It's your own doing."

The priests were oblivious to this exchange. They shouted at the false Tuek, ordering him to shut up and remove himself, calling him a "damned Face Dancer!"

Odrade studied the object of this attack with care. How deep did the print go? Had he really convinced himself that he was Tuek?

In a sudden lull, the mimic drew himself up with dignity and sent a scornful glance at his accusers. "You all know me," he said. "You all know my years of service to the Divided God Who is One God. I will go to Him now if your conspiracy extends to that but remember this: He knows what is in your hearts!"

The priests looked as one man to Waff. None of them had seen a Face Dancer replace their High Priest. There had been no body to see. Every bit of evidence was the evidence of human voices saying things that might be lies. Belatedly, several looked at Odrade. Her voice was one of those that had convinced them.

Waff, too, was looking at Odrade.

She smiled and addressed herself to the Tleilaxu Master. "It suits our purposes that the High Priesthood not pass into other hands at this time," she said.

Waff immediately saw the advantage to himself. This was a wedge between priests and Bene Gesserit. This removed one of the most dangerous holds the Sisterhood had on the Tleilaxu.

"It suits my purposes, too," he said.

As the priests once more lifted their voices in anger, Taraza came in right on cue: "Which of you will break our accord?" she demanded.

Tuek thrust two of his counselors aside and strode across the room to the Mother Superior. He stopped only a pace from her.

"What game is this?" he asked.

"We support you against those who would replace you," she said. "The Bene Tleilaxu join us in this. It is our way of demonstrating that we, too, have a vote in selecting the High Priest."

Several priestly voices were raised in unison: "Is he or is he not a Face Dancer?"

Taraza looked benignly at the man in front of her: "Are you a Face Dancer?"

"Of course not!"

Taraza looked at Odrade, who said: "There seems to have been a mistake."

Odrade singled out Albertus among the priests and locked eyes with him. "Sheeana," Odrade said, "what should the Church of the Divided God do now?"

As she had been briefed to do, Sheeana stepped out of her guardian enclosure and spoke with all of the hauteur she had been taught: "They shall continue to serve God!"

"The business of this meeting appears to have been concluded," Taraza said. "If you need protection, High Priest Tuek, a squad of our guardians awaits in the hall. They are yours to command."

They could see acceptance and understanding in him. He had become a creature of the Bene Gesserit. He remembered nothing of his Face Dancer origins.

When the priests and Tuek had gone, Waff sent a single word at Taraza, speaking in the language of the Islamiyat: "Explain!"

Taraza stepped away from her guards, appearing to make herself vulnerable. It was a calculated move they had debated in front of Sheeana. In the same language, Taraza said: "We release our grip on the Bene Tleilax."

They waited while he weighed her words. Taraza reminded herself that the Tleilaxu name for themselves could be translated as "the un-nameable." That was a label often reserved for gods.

This *god* obviously had not extended the discovery in here to what might be happening with his mimics among Ixians and Fish Speakers. Waff had more shocks coming. He appeared quite puzzled, though.

Waff confronted many unanswered questions. He was not satisfied with his reports from Gammu. It was a dangerous double game he played now. Did the Sisterhood play a similar game? But the Tleilaxu Lost Ones could not be shunted aside without inviting attack by the Honored Matres. Taraza herself had warned of this. Did the old Bashar on Gammu still represent a force worthy of consideration?

He voiced this question.

Taraza countered with her own question: "How did you change our ghola? What did you hope to gain?" She felt certain she already knew. But the pose of ignorance was necessary.

Waff wanted to say: "The death of all Bene Gesserit!" They were too dangerous. Yet their value was incalculable. He sank into a sulking silence, looking at the Reverend Mothers with a brooding expression that made his elfin features even more childlike.

A petulant child, Taraza thought. She warned herself then that it was dangerous to underestimate Waff. You broke the Tleilaxu egg only to find another egg inside—ad infinitum! Everything circled back to Odrade's suspicions about the contentions that might still lead them to bloody violence in this room. Had the Tleilaxu really revealed what they had learned from the whores and the other Lost Ones? Was the ghola only a potential Tleilaxu weapon?

Taraza decided to prod him once more, using the approach of her Council's "Analysis Nine." Still in the language of the Islamiyat, she said: "Would you dishonor yourself in the land of the Prophet? You have not shared openly as you said you would."

"We told you the sexual—"

"You do not share all!" she interrupted. "It's because of the ghola and we know this."

She could see his reactions. He was a cornered animal. Such

animals were dangerous in the extreme. She had once seen a mongrel hound, a feral and tail-tucked survivor of ancient pets from Dan, cornered by a pack of youths. The animal turned on its pursuers, slashing its way to freedom in totally unexpected savagery. Two youths crippled for life and only one without injuries! Waff was like that animal right now. She could see his hands longing for a weapon, but Tleilaxu and Bene Gesserit had searched one another with exquisite care before coming here. She felt sure he had no weapon. Still . . .

Waff spoke, baited suspense in his manner. "You think me unaware of how you hope to rule us!"

"And *there* is the rot that the people of the Scattering took with them," she said. "Rot at the core."

Waff's manner changed. It did not do to ignore the deeper implications of Bene Gesserit thought. But was she sowing discord?

"The Prophet set a locator ticking in the minds of every human, Scattered or not," Taraza said. "He has brought them back to us with all of the rot intact."

Waff ground his teeth. What was she doing? He entertained the mad thought that the Sisterhood had clogged his mind with some secret drug in the air. They *knew* things denied to others! He stared from Taraza to Odrade and back to Taraza. He knew he was old with serial ghola resurrections but not old in the way of the Bene Gesserit. These people were old! They seldom looked old but they were old, old beyond anything he dared imagine.

Taraza was having similar thoughts. She had seen the flash of deeper awareness in Waff's eyes. Necessity opened new doors of reason. How deep did the Tleilaxu go? His eyes were so old! She had the feeling that whatever had been a brain in these Tleilaxu Masters was now something else—a holo-recording from which all weakening emotions had been erased. She shared the distrust of emotions that she suspected in him. Was that a bond to unite them?

The tropism of common thoughts.

"You say you release your grip on us," Waff growled, "but I feel your fingers around my throat."

"Then here is a grip on our throat," she said. "Some of your Lost Ones have returned to you. Never has a Reverend Mother come back to us from the Scattering."

"But you said you knew all of the—"

"We have other ways of gaining knowledge. What do you suppose happened to the Reverend Mothers we sent out into the Scattering?"

"A common disaster?" He shook his head. This was absolutely new information. None of the returned Tleilaxu had said anything at all about this. The discrepancy fed his suspicions. Whom was he to believe?

"They were subverted," Taraza said.

Odrade, hearing the general suspicion voiced for the first time by the Mother Superior, sensed the enormous power implicit in Taraza's simple statement. Odrade was cowed by it. She knew the resources, the contingency plans, the improvised ways a Reverend Mother might use to surmount barriers. Something Out There could stop *that*?

When Waff did not respond, Taraza said: "You come to us with dirty hands."

"You dare say this?" Waff asked. "You who continue to deplete our resources in the ways taught you by the Bashar's mother?"

"We knew you could afford the losses if you had resources from the Scattering," Taraza said.

Waff inhaled a trembling breath. So the Bene Gesserit knew even this. He saw in part how they had learned it. Well, a way would have to be found to bring the false Tuek back under control. Rakis was the prize the Scattered Ones really sought and it might yet be demanded of the Tleilaxu.

Taraza moved even closer to Waff, alone and vulnerable. She saw her guards grow tense. Sheeana took a small step toward the Mother Superior and was pulled back by Odrade.

Odrade kept her attention on the Mother Superior and not on potential attackers. Were the Tleilaxu truly convinced that the Bene Gesserit would serve them? Taraza had tested the limits of it, no doubt of that. And in the language of the Islamiyat. But she looked very alone out there away from her guards and so near Waff and his people. Where would Waff's obvious suspicions lead him now?

Taraza shivered.

Odrade saw it. Taraza had been abnormally thin as a child and had never put on an excess ounce of fat. This made her exquisitely sensitive to temperature changes, intolerant of cold, but Odrade sensed no such change in the room. Taraza had made a dangerous decision then, so dangerous that her body betrayed her. Not dangerous to herself, of course, but dangerous to the Sisterhood. *There* was the most awful Bene Gesserit crime: disloyalty to their own order.

"We will serve you in all ways except one," Taraza said. "We will never become receptacles for gholas!"

Waff paled.

Taraza continued: "None of us is now nor will ever become . . ." she paused ". . . an axlotl tank."

Waff raised his right hand in the start of a gesture every Reverend Mother knew: the signal for his Face Dancers to attack.

Taraza pointed at his upraised hand. "If you complete that gesture, the Tleilaxu will lose everything. The messenger of God—" Taraza nodded over a shoulder toward Sheeana "—will turn her back upon you and the words of the Prophet will be dust in your mouths."

In the language of the Islamiyat, such words were too much for Waff. He lowered his hand but he continued to glower at Taraza.

"My ambassador said we would share everything we know," Taraza said. "You said you, too, would share. The messenger of God listens with the ears of the Prophet! What pours forth from the Abdl of the Tleilaxu?"

Waff's shoulders sagged.

Taraza turned her back on him. It was an artful move but both she and the other Reverend Mothers present knew she did it now in perfect safety. Looking across the room at Odrade, Taraza allowed herself a smile that she knew Odrade would interpret correctly. Time for a bit of Bene Gesserit punishment!

"The Tleilaxu desire an Atreides for breeding," Taraza said. "I give you Darwi Odrade. More will be supplied."

Waff came to a decision. "You may know much about the Honored Matres," he said, "but you—"

"Whores!" Taraza whirled on him.

"As you will. But there is a thing from them that your words reveal you do not know. I seal our bargain by telling you this. They can magnify the sensations of the orgasmic platform, transmitting this throughout a male body. They elicit the total sensual involvement of the male. Multiple orgasmic waves are created and may be continued by the . . . the female for an extended period."

"Total involvement?" Taraza did not try to hide her astonishment.

Odrade, too, listened with a sense of shock that she saw was shared by her Sisters present, even the acolytes. Only Sheeana seemed not to understand.

"I tell you, Mother Superior Taraza," Waff said, a gloating smile on his face, "that we have duplicated this with our own people. Myself even! In my anger, I caused the Face Dancer who played the . . . female part to destroy itself. No one . . . I say, no one! may have such a hold on me!"

"What hold?"

"If it had been one of these . . . these whores, as you call them, I would have obeyed her without question in anything." He shuddered. "I barely had the will to . . . to destroy . . ." He shook his head in bewilderment at the memory. "Anger saved me."

Taraza tried to swallow in a dry throat. "How . . ."

"How is it done? Very well! But before I share this knowledge I warn you: If one of you ever tries to use this power over one of us, bloody slaughter will follow! We have prepared our Domel and all of our people to respond by killing all Reverend Mothers they can find at the slightest sign that you seek this power over us!"

"None of us would do that, but not because of your threat. We are restrained by the knowledge that this would destroy us. Your bloody slaughter would not be necessary."

"Oh? Then why does it not destroy these . . . these whores?"

"It does! And it destroys everyone they touch!"

"It has not destroyed me!"

"God protects you, my Abdl," Taraza said. "As He protects all of the faithful."

Convinced, Waff glanced around the room and back to Taraza. "Let all know that I fulfill my bond in the land of the Prophet. This is the way of it, then . . ." He waved a hand to two of his Face Dancer guards. "We will demonstrate."

Much later, alone in the penthouse room, Odrade wondered if it had been wise to let Sheeana see the whole performance. Well, why not? Sheeana already was committed to the Sisterhood. And it would have aroused Waff's suspicions to send Sheeana away.

There had been obvious sensual arousal in Sheeana as she watched the Face Dancer performance. The Training Proctors would have to call in their male assistants earlier than usual for Sheeana. What would Sheeana do then? Would she try this new knowledge on the men? Inhibitions must be raised in Sheeana to prevent that! She must be taught the dangers to herself.

The Sisters and acolytes present had controlled themselves well, storing what they learned firmly in memory. Sheeana's education must be built on that observation. Others mastered such internal forces.

The Face Dancer observers had remained inscrutable, but there had been things to see in Waff. He said he would destroy the two demonstrators but what would he do first? Would he succumb to temptation? What thoughts went through his mind as he watched the Face Dancer male squirm in mind-blanking ecstasy?

In a way, the demonstration reminded Odrade of the Rakian dance she had seen in the Great Square of Keen. In the short term, the dance had been deliberately unrhythmic but the progression created a long-term rhythm that repeated itself in some two hundred . . . steps. The dancers had stretched out their rhythm to a remarkable degree.

As had the Face Dancer demonstrators.

Siaynoq become a sexual grip on uncounted billions in the Scattering!

Odrade thought about the dance, the long rhythm followed by cha-otic violence. Siaynoq's glorious focusing of religious energies had de-volved into a different kind of exchange. She thought about Sheeana's excited response to her glimpses of that dance in the Great Square. Odrade remembered asking Sheeana: "What did they share down there?"

"The dancers, silly!"

That response had not been permissible. "I've warned you about that tone, Sheeana. Do you wish to learn immediately what a Reverend Mother can do to punish you?"

The words played themselves like ghost messages in Odrade's mind as she looked at the gathering darkness outside the Dar-es-Balat pent-house. A great loneliness welled up in her. All the others had gone from this room.

Only the punished one remains!

How bright-eyed Sheeana had been in that room above the Great Square, her mind so full of questions. "Why do you always talk about hurting and punishment?"

"You must learn discipline. How can you control others when you cannot control yourself?"

"I don't like that lesson."

"None of us does very much . . . until later when we've learned the value of it by experience."

As intended, that response had festered long in Sheeana's aware-ness. In the end, she had revealed all she knew about the dance.

"Some of the dancers escape. Others go directly to Shaitan. The priests say they go to Shai-hulud."

"What of the ones who survive?"

"When they recover, they must join a great dance in the desert. If Shaitan comes there, they die. If Shaitan does not come, they are re-warded."

Odrade had seen the pattern. Sheeana's explanatory words had not been necessary beyond that point, even though the recital had been allowed to continue. How bitter Sheeana's voice had been!

"They get money, space in a bazaar, that kind of reward. The priests say they have proved that they are human."

"Are the ones who fail not human?"

Sheeana had remained silent for a long time in deep thought. The track was clear to Odrade, though: the Sisterhood's test of humanity! Her own passage into the acceptable humanity of the Sisterhood had already been duplicated by Sheeana. How soft that passage seemed in comparison to the other pains!

In the dim light of the museum penthouse, Odrade held up her right hand, looking at it, remembering the agony box, and the gom jabbar poised at her neck ready to kill her if she flinched or cried out.

Sheeana had not cried out, either. But she had known the answer to Odrade's question even before the agony box.

"They are human but different."

Odrade spoke aloud in the empty room with its displays from the Tyrant's no-chamber hoard.

"What did you do to us, Leto? Are you only Shaitan talking to us? What would you force us to share now?"

Was the fossil dance to become fossil sex?

"Who are you talking to, Mother?"

It was Sheeana's voice from the open doorway across the room. Her gray postulant's robe was only a faint shape there, growing larger as she approached.

"Mother Superior sent me for you," Sheeana said as she came to a stop near Odrade.

"I was talking to myself," Odrade said. She looked at the strangely quiet girl, remembering the gut-wrenching excitement of that moment when the Fulcrum Question had been asked of Sheeana.

"Do you wish to be a Reverend Mother?"

"Why are you talking to yourself, Mother?" There was a load of concern in Sheeana's voice. The Teaching Proctors would have their hands full removing those emotions.

"I was remembering when I asked you if you wished to be a Reverend Mother," Odrade said. "It prompted other thoughts."

"You said I must give myself to your direction in all things, holding back nothing, disobeying you in nothing."

"And you said: 'Is that all?'"

"I didn't know very much, did I? I still don't know very much."

"None of us does, child. Except that we're all in the dance together. And Shaitan will certainly come if the least of us fails."

When strangers meet, great allowance should be made for differences of custom and training.

—THE LADY JESSICA, FROM "WISDOM OF ARRAKIS"

The last greenish line of light fell out of the horizon before Burzmali gave the signal for them to move. It was dark by the time they reached the far side of Ysai and the perimeter road that was to lead them to Duncan. Clouds covered the sky, reflecting the city's lights downward onto the shapes of the urban hovels through which their guides directed them.

These guides bothered Lucilla. They appeared out of side streets and from suddenly opened doorways to whisper new directions.

Too many people knew about the fugitive pair and their intended rendezvous!

She had come to grips with her hatred but the residue was a profound distrust of every person they saw. Hiding this behind the mechanical attitudes of a playfem with her customer had become increasingly difficult.

There was slush on the pedestrian way beside the road, most of it scattered there by the passage of groundcars. Lucilla's feet were cold before they had gone half a kilometer and she was forced to expend energy compensating for the added bloodflow in her extremities.

Burzmali walked silently, his head down, apparently lost in his own worries. Lucilla was not fooled. He heard every sound around them, saw every approaching vehicle. He hustled them off the pathway each time a groundcar approached. The cars went swishing past on their suspensors, the dirty slush flying from under their fanskirts and peppering the bushes along the road. Burzmali held her down beside him in the snow until he was sure the cars were out of sight and sound. Not that anyone riding in them could hear much except their own whirling passage.

They had been walking for two hours before Burzmali stopped and took stock of the way ahead. Their destination was a perimeter community that had been described to them as "completely safe." Lucilla knew better. No place on Gammu was completely safe.

Yellow lights cast an undershot glow on the clouds ahead of them, marking the location of the community. Their slushy progress took them through a tunnel under the perimeter road and up a low hill planted to some sort of orchard. The limbs were stark in the dim light.

Lucilla glanced upward. The clouds were thinning. Gammu had many small moons—fortress no-ships. Some of them had been placed by Teg but she glimpsed lines of new ones sharing the guardian role. They appeared to be about four times the size of the brightest stars and they often traveled together, which made their reflected light useful but erratic because they moved fast—up across the sky and below the horizon in only a few hours. She glimpsed a string of six such moons through a break in the clouds, wondering if they were part of Teg's defense system.

Momentarily, she reflected on the inherent weakness of the siege mentality that such defenses represented. Teg had been right about them. Mobility was the key to military success but she doubted that he had meant mobility on foot.

There were no easy hiding places on the snow-whitened slope and Lucilla felt Burzmali's nervousness. What could they do here if someone came? A snow-covered depression led down from their position to the left, angling toward the community. It was not a road but she thought it might be a path.

"Down this way," Burzmali said, leading them into the depression. The snow came up to their calves.

"I hope these people are trustworthy," she said.

"They hate the Honored Matres," he said. "That's enough for me."

"The ghola had better be there!" She held back an even more angry response but could not keep herself from adding: "Their hatred isn't enough for me."

It was better to expect the worst, she thought.

She had come to a reassuring thought about Burzmali, though. He was like Teg. Neither of them pursued a course that would lead them into a dead end—not if they could help it. She suspected there were support forces concealed in the bushes around them even now.

The snow-covered trail ended in a paved pathway, gently curved inward from the edges and kept free of snow by a melt system. There was a trickle of dampness in the center. Lucilla was several steps onto this path before she recognized what it must be—a magchute. It was an ancient magnetic transport base that once had carried goods or raw materials to a pre-Scattering factory.

"It gets steeper here," Burzmali warned her. "They've carved steps in it but watch it. They're not very deep."

They came presently to the end of the magchute. It stopped at a decrepit wall—local brick atop a plasteel foundation. The faint light of stars in a clearing sky revealed crude workmanship in the bricks—typical Famine-Times construction. The wall was a mass of vines and mottled fungus. The growth did little to conceal the cracked courses of the bricks and the crude efforts to fill chinks with mortar. A single row of narrow windows looked down onto the place where the magchute debouched into a mass of bushes and weeds. Three of the windows glowed electric blue with some inner activity that was accompanied by faint crackling sounds.

"This was a factory in the old days," Burzmali said.

"I have eyes and a memory," Lucilla snapped. Did this grunting male think her completely devoid of intelligence?

Something creaked dismally off to their left. A patch of sod and weeds lifted atop a cellar door accompanied by an upward glow of brilliant yellow light.

"Quick!" Burzmali led her at a swift run across thick vegetation and down a flight of steps exposed by the lifting door. The door creaked closed behind them in a grumbling of machinery.

Lucilla found herself in a large space with a low ceiling. Light came from long lines of modern glowglobes strung along massive plasteel girders overhead. The floor was swept clean but showed scratches and indentations of activity, the locations no doubt of bygone machinery. She glimpsed movement far off across the open space. A young woman in a version of Lucilla's dragon robe trotted toward them.

Lucilla sniffed. There was a stink of acid in the room and undertones of something foul.

"This was a Harkonnen factory," Burzmali said. "I wonder what they made here?"

The young woman stopped in front of Lucilla. She had a willowy figure, elegant in shape and motion under the clinging robe. A subcutaneous glow came from her face. It spoke of exercise and good health. The green eyes, though, were hard and chilling in the way they measured everything they saw.

"So they sent more than one of us to watch this place," she said.

Lucilla put out a restraining hand as Burzmali started to respond. This woman was not what she seemed. *No more than I am!* Lucilla chose her words carefully. "We always know each other, it seems."

The young woman smiled. "I watched your approach. I could not believe my eyes." She swept a sneering glance across Burzmali. "This was supposed to be a customer?"

"And guide," Lucilla said. She noted the puzzlement on Burzmali's face and prayed he would not ask the wrong question. This young woman was danger!

"Weren't we expected?" Burzmali asked.

"Ahhhh, it speaks," the young woman said, laughing. Her laugh was as cold as her eyes.

"I prefer that you do not refer to me as 'it,'" Burzmali said.

"I call Gammu scum anything I wish," the young woman said. "Don't speak to me of your preferences!"

"What did you call me?" Burzmali was tired and his anger came boiling up at this unexpected attack.

"I call you anything I choose, scum!"

Burzmali had suffered enough. Before Lucilla could stop him, he uttered a low growl and aimed a heavy slap at the young woman.

The blow did not land.

Lucilla watched in fascination as the woman dropped under the attack, caught Burzmali's sleeve as one might catch a bit of fabric blowing in the wind and, in a blindingly fast pirouette whose speed almost hid its delicacy, sent Burzmali skidding across the floor. The woman dropped to a half crouch on one foot, the other prepared to kick.

"I shall kill him now," she said.

Lucilla, not knowing what might happen next, folded her body sideways, barely avoiding the woman's suddenly outthrust foot, and countered with a standard Bene Gesserit sabard that dumped the young woman on her back doubled up where the blow had caught her in the abdomen.

"A suggestion that you kill my guide is uncalled for, whatever your name is," Lucilla said.

The young woman gasped for breath, then, panting between words: "I am called Murbella, Great Honored Matre. You shame me by defeating me with such a slow attack. Why do you do that?"

"You needed a lesson," Lucilla said.

"I am only newly robed, Great Honored Matre. Please forgive me. I thank you for the splendid lesson and will thank you every time I employ your response, which I now commit to memory." She bowed her head, then leaped lightly to her feet, an impish grin on her face.

In her coldest voice, Lucilla asked: "Do you know who I am?" Out of the corners of her eyes, she saw Burzmali regain his feet with painful slowness. He remained at one side, watching the women, but anger burned his face.

"From your ability to teach me that lesson, I see that you are who you are, Great Honored Matre. Am I forgiven?" The impish grin had vanished from Murbella's face. She stood with head bowed.

"You are forgiven. Is there a no-ship coming?"

"So they say here. We are prepared for it." Murbella glanced at Burzmali.

"He is still useful to me and it is required that he accompany me," Lucilla said.

"Very good, Great Honored Matre. Does your forgiveness include your name?"

"No!"

Murbella sighed. "We have captured the ghola," she said. "He came as a Tleilaxu from the south. I was just about to bed him when you arrived."

Burzmali hobbled toward them. Lucilla saw that he had recognized the danger. This "completely safe" place had been infested by enemies! But the enemies still knew very little.

"The ghola was not injured?" Burzmali asked.

"It still speaks," Murbella said. "How odd."

"You will not bed the ghola," Lucilla said. "That one is my special charge!"

"Fair game, Great Honored Matre. And I marked him first. He is already partly subdued."

She laughed once more, with a callous abandonment that shocked Lucilla. "This way. There is a place where you can watch."

Duncan tried to remember where he was. He knew Tormsa was dead. Blood had spurted from Tormsa's eyes. Yes, he remembered that clearly. They had entered a dark building and light had flared abruptly all around them. Duncan felt an ache in the back of his head. A blow? He tried to move and his muscles refused to obey.

He remembered sitting at the edge of a wide lawn. There was some kind of bowling game in progress—eccentric balls that bounced and darted with no apparent design. The players were young men in a common costume of . . . Giedi Prime!

"They are practicing to be old men," he said. He remembered saying that.

His companion, a young woman, looked at him blankly.

"Only old men should play these outdoor games," he said.

"Oh?"

It was an unanswerable question. She put him down with only the simplest of verbal gestures.

And betrayed me the next instant to the Harkonnens!

So that was a pre-ghola memory.

Ghola!

He remembered the Bene Gesserit Keep on Gammu. The library: holophotos and triphotos of the Atreides Duke, Leto I. Teg's resemblance was not an accident: a bit taller but otherwise it was all there—that long, thin face with its high-bridged nose, the renowned Atreides charisma . . .

Teg!

He remembered the old Bashar's last gallant stand in the Gammu night.

Where am I?

Tormsa had brought him here. They had been moving along an overgrown track on the outskirts of Ysai. *Barony.* It started to snow before they were two hundred meters up the track. Wet snow that clung to them. Cold, miserable snow that set their teeth chattering within a minute. They paused to bring up their hoods and close the insulated jackets. That was better. But it would be night soon. Much colder.

"There is a shelter of sorts up ahead," Tormsa said. "We will wait there for the night."

When Duncan did not speak, Tormsa said: "It won't be warm but it will be dry."

Duncan saw the gray outline of the place in about three hundred paces. It stood out against the dirty snow some two stories tall. He recognized it immediately: a Harkonnen counting outpost. Observers here had counted (and sometimes killed) the people who passed. It was built of native dirt turned into one giant brick by the simple expedient of preforming it in mud bricks and then superheating it with a wide-bore burner, the kind the Harkonnens had used to control mobs.

As they came up to it, Duncan saw the remains of a full-field defensive screen with fire-lance gaps aimed at the approaches. Someone had smashed the system a long time ago. Twisted holes in the field net were partly overgrown with bushes. But the fire-lance gaps remained open. Oh, yes—to allow people inside a view of the approaches.

Tormsa paused and listened, studying their surroundings with care.

Duncan looked at the counting station. He remembered them well. What confronted him was a thing that had sprouted like a deformed growth from an original tubular seed. The surface had been baked to a glassine finish. Warts and protrusions betrayed where it had been superheated. The erosion of eons had left fine scratches in it but the original shape remained. He looked upward and identified part of the old suspensor lift system. Someone had jury-rigged a block and tackle to the outbar.

So the opening through the full-field screen was of recent making. Tormsa disappeared into this opening.

As though a switch had been thrown, Duncan's memory vision changed. He was in the no-globe's library with Teg. The projector was producing a series of views through modern Ysai. The idea of *modern* took on an odd overtone for him. Barony had been a modern city, if you thought of modern as meaning technologically uniform up to the norms of its time. It had relied exclusively on suspensor guide-beams for transport of people and material—all of them high up. No ground-level openings. He was explaining this to Teg.

The plan translated physically into a city that used every possible square meter of vertical and horizontal space for things other than movement of goods and humans. The guide-beam openings required only enough head room and elbow room for the universal transport pods.

Teg spoke: "The ideal shape would be tubular with a flat top for the 'thopters."

"The Harkonnens preferred squares and rectangles."

That was true.

Duncan remembered Barony with a clearness that made him shiver. Suspensor tracks shot through it like worm holes—straight, curved, flipping off at oblique angles . . . up, down, sideways. Except for the rectangular absolute imposed by Harkonnen whim, Barony was built to a particular population-design criterion: maximum stuffing with minimum expenditure of materials.

"The flat top was the only human-oriented space in the damned thing!" He remembered telling that to Teg and Lucilla both.

Up there on top were penthouses, guard stations at all the edges, at the 'thopter pads, at all the entries from below, around all of the parks. People living on the top could forget about the mass of flesh squirming in close proximity just below them. No smell or noise from that jumble was allowed on top. Servants were forced to bathe and change into sanitary clothing before emerging.

Teg had a question: "Why did that massed humanity permit itself to live in such a crush?"

The answer was obvious and he explained it. The outside was a dangerous place. The city's managers made it appear even more dangerous than it actually was. Besides, few in there knew anything about a better life Outside. The only better life they knew about was on top. And the only way up there was through an absolutely abasing servility.

"It will happen and there's nothing you can do about it!"

That was another voice echoing in Duncan's skull. He heard it clearly.

Paul!

How odd it was, Duncan thought. There was an arrogance in the prescient like the arrogance of the Mentat seated in his most brittle logic.

I never before thought of Paul as arrogant.

Duncan stared at his own face in a mirror. He realized with part of his mind that this was a pre-ghola memory. Abruptly, it was another mirror, his own face but different. That darkly rounded face had begun to shape into the harsher lines it could have if it matured. He looked into his own eyes. Yes, those were his eyes. He had heard someone describe his eyes once as "cave sitters." They were deeply inset under the brows and riding atop high cheeks. He had been told it was difficult to determine if his eyes were dark blue or dark green unless the light were just right.

A woman said that. He could not remember the woman.

He tried to reach up and touch his hair but his hands would not obey. He remembered then that his hair had been bleached. Who did that? An old woman. His hair was no longer a cap of dark ringlets.

There was the Duke Leto staring at him in the doorway to the dining room on Caladan.

"We will eat now," the Duke said. It was a royal command saved from arrogance by a faint grin that said: "Somebody had to say it."

What is happening to my mind?

He remembered following Tormsa to the place where Tormsa said the no-ship would meet them.

It was a large building bulking in the night. There were several smaller outbuildings below the larger structure. They appeared to be occupied. Voices and machine sounds could be heard in them. No faces showed at the narrow windows. No door opened. Duncan smelled cooking as they passed the larger of the outbuildings. This reminded him that they had only eaten dry strips of leathery stuff that Tormsa called "travel food" that day.

They entered the dark building.

Light flared.

Tormsa's eyes exploded in blood.

Darkness.

Duncan looked at a woman's face. He had seen a face like this one before: a single *tride* taken from a longer holo sequence. Where was that? Where had he seen that? It was an almost oval face with just a small widening at the brow to mar its curved perfection.

She spoke: "My name is Murbella. You will not remember that but I share it now as I mark you. I have selected you."

I do remember you, Murbella.

Green eyes set wide under arched brows gave her features a focal region that left chin and small mouth for later examination. The mouth was full-lipped and he knew it could become pouting in repose.

The green eyes stared into his eyes. How cold that look. The power in it.

Something touched his cheek.

He opened his eyes. This was no memory! This was happening to him. It was happening now!

Murbella! She had been here and she had left him. Now she was back. He remembered awakening naked on a soft surface . . . a sleeping pad. His hands recognized it. Murbella unclothed just above him, green eyes staring at him with a terrible intensity. She touched him simultaneously in many places. A soft humming issued from between her lips.

He felt the swift erection, painful in its rigidity.

No power of resistance remained in him. Her hands moved over his body. Her tongue. The humming! All around him, her mouth touching him. The nipples of her breasts grazed his cheeks, his chest. When he saw her eyes, he saw conscious design.

Murbella had returned and she was doing it once more!

Over her right shoulder, he glimpsed a wide plaz window—Lucilla and Burzmali behind that barrier. *A dream?* Burzmali pressed his palms against the plaz. Lucilla stood with folded arms, a look of mingled rage and curiosity on her face.

Murbella murmured in his right ear: "My hands are fire."

Her body hid the faces behind the plaz. He felt the fire wherever she touched him.

Abruptly, the flame engulfed his mind. Hidden places within him came alive. He saw red capsules like a string of gleaming sausages passing before his eyes. He felt feverish. He was an engorged capsule, excitement flaring throughout his awareness. Those capsules! He knew them! They were himself . . . they were . . .

All of the Duncan Idahos, original and the serial gholas flowed into his mind. They were like bursting seedpods denying all other existence except themselves. He saw himself crushed beneath a great worm with a human face.

"Damn you, Leto!"

Crushed and crushed and crushed . . . time and again.

"Damn you! Damn you! Damn you! . . ."

He died under a Sardaukar sword. Pain exploded into a bright glare swallowed by darkness.

He died in a 'thopter crash. He died under the knife of a Fish Speaker assassin. He died and died and died.

And he lived.

The memories flooded him until he wondered how he could hold them all. The sweetness of a newborn daughter held in his arms. The musky odors of a passionate mate. The cascade of flavors from a fine Danian wine. The panting exertions of the practice floor.

The axlotl tanks!

He remembered emerging time after time: bright lights and padded mechanical hands. The hands rotated him and, in the unfocused blurs of the newborn, he saw a great mound of female flesh—monstrous in her almost immobile grossness . . . a maze of dark tubes linked her body to giant metal containers.

Axlotl tank?

He gasped in the grip of the serial memories that cascaded into him. *All of those lives! All of those lives!*

Now, he remembered what the Tleilaxu had planted in him, the submerged awareness that awaited only this moment of seduction by a Bene Gesserit Imprinter.

But this was Murbella and she was not Bene Gesserit.

She was here, though, ready at hand and the Tleilaxu pattern took over his reactions.

Duncan hummed softly and touched her, moving with an agility that shocked Murbella. *He should not be this responsive! Not this way!* His right hand fluttered against the lips of her vagina while his left hand caressed the base of her spine. At the same time, his mouth moved gently over her nose, down to her lips, down to the crease of her left armpit.

And all the time he hummed softly in a rhythm that pulsed through her body, lulling . . . weakening . . .

She tried to push away from him as he increased the pace of her responses.

How did he know to touch me there at just that instant? And there! And there! Oh, Holy Rock of Dur, how does he know this?

Duncan marked the swelling of her breasts and saw the congestion in her nose. He saw the way her nipples stood out stiffly, the areolae darkening around them. She moaned and spread her legs wide.

Great Matre, help me!

But the only Great Matre she could think of was locked securely away from this room, restrained by a bolted door and a plaz barrier.

Desperate energy flowed into Murbella. She responded in the only way she knew: touching, caressing—using all of the techniques she had learned so carefully in the long years of her apprenticeship.

To each thing she did, Duncan produced a wildly stimulating countermove.

Murbella found that she no longer could control all of her own responses. She was reacting automatically from some well of knowledge deeper than her training. She felt her vaginal muscles tighten. She felt the swift release of lubricant fluid. When Duncan entered her she heard herself groan. Her arms, her hands, her legs, her entire body moved with both of the response systems—well-trained automation and the deeper, deeper plunging awareness of other demands.

How did he do this to me?

Waves of ecstatic contractions began in the smooth muscles of her pelvis. She sensed his simultaneous response and felt the hard slap of his ejaculation. This heightened her own response. Ecstatic pulsations drove outward from the contractions in her vagina . . . outward . . . outward. The ecstasy engulfed her entire sensorium. She saw a spreading blaze of whiteness against her eyelids. Every muscle quivered with an ecstasy she had not imagined possible for herself.

Again, the waves spread outward.

Again and again . . .

She lost count of the repetitions.

When Duncan moaned, she moaned and the waves swept outward once more.

And again . . .

There was no sensation of time or surroundings, only this immersion in a continuing ecstasy.

She wanted it to go on forever and she wanted it to stop. This should not be happening to a female! An Honored Matre must not experience this. These were the sensations by which men were governed.

Duncan emerged from the response pattern that had been implanted in him. There was something else he was supposed to do. He could not remember what it was.

Lucilla?

He imagined her dead in front of him. But this woman was not Lucilla; this was . . . this was Murbella.

There was very little strength in him. He lifted himself off Murbella and managed to sink back onto his knees. Her hands were fluttering in an agitation he could not understand.

Murbella tried to push Duncan away from her and he was not there. Her eyes snapped open.

Duncan knelt above her. She had no idea how much time had passed. She tried to find the energy to sit up and failed. Slowly, reason returned.

She stared into Duncan's eyes, knowing now who this man must be. Man? He was only a youth. But he had done things . . . things . . . All of the Honored Matres had been warned. There was a ghola armed with forbidden knowledge by the Tleilaxu. That ghola must be killed!

A small burst of energy surged into her muscles. She raised herself on her elbows. Gasping for breath, she tried to roll away from him and fell back to the soft surface.

By the Holy Rock of Dur! This male could not be permitted to live! He was a ghola and he could do things permitted only to Honored Matres. She wanted to strike out at him and, at the same time, she wanted to pull him back onto her body. *The ecstasy!* She knew that whatever he asked of her at this moment she would do. She would do it for him.

No! I must kill him!

Once more, she raised herself onto her elbows and, from there, managed to sit up. Her weakened gaze crossed the window where she had confined the Great Honored Matre and the guide. They still stood there looking at her. The man's face was flushed. The face of the Great Honored Matre was as unmoving as the Rock of Dur itself.

How can she just stand there after what she has seen here? The Great Honored Matre must kill this ghola!

Murbella beckoned to the woman behind the plaz and rolled toward the locked door beside the sleeping pad. She barely managed to unbolt and open the door before falling back. Her eyes looked up at the kneeling youth. Sweat glistened on his body. His lovely body . . .

No!

Desperation drove her off onto the floor. She was on her knees there and then, mostly by will power, she stood. Energy was returning but her legs trembled as she staggered around the foot of the sleeping pad.

I will do it myself without thinking. I must do it.

Her body swayed from side to side. She tried to steady herself and aimed a blow at his neck. She knew this blow from long hours of practice. It would crush the larynx. The victim would die of asphyxiation.

Duncan dodged the blow easily, but he was slow . . . slow.

Murbella almost fell beside him but the hands of the Great Honored Matre saved her.

"Kill him," Murbella gasped. "He's the one we were warned about. He's the one!"

Murbella felt hands on her neck, the fingers pressing fiercely at the nerve bundles beneath the ears.

The last thing Murbella heard before unconsciousness was the Great Honored Matre saying: "We will kill no one. This ghola goes to Rakis."

The worst potential competition for any organism can come from its own kind. The species consumes necessities. Growth is limited by that necessity which is present in the least amount. The least favorable condition controls the rate of growth. (Law of the Minimum)

—FROM "LESSONS OF ARRAKIS"

The building stood back from a wide avenue behind a screen of trees and carefully tended flowering hedges. The hedges had been staggered in a maze pattern with man-high white posts to define the planted areas. No vehicle entering or leaving could do so at any speed above a slow crawl. Teg's military awareness took all of this in as the armored groundcar carried him up to the door. Field Marshal Muzzafar, the only other occupant in the rear of the car, recognized Teg's assessment and said:

"We're protected from above by a beam enfilading system."

A soldier in camouflage uniform with a long lasgun on a sling over one shoulder opened the door and snapped to attention as Muzzafar emerged.

Teg followed. He recognized this place. It was one of the "safe" addresses Bene Gesserit Security had provided for him. Obviously, the Sisterhood's information was out of date. Recently out of date, though, because Muzzafar gave no indication that Teg might know this place.

As they crossed to the door, Teg noted that another protective system he had seen on his first tour of Ysai remained intact. It was a barely noticeable difference in the posts along the trees-and-hedges barriers. Those posts were scanlyzers operated from a room somewhere in the building. Their diamond-shaped connectors "read" the area between them and the building. At the gentle push of a button in the watchers' room, the scanlyzers would make small chunks of meat out of any living flesh crossing their fields.

At the door, Muzzafar paused and looked at Teg. "The Honored Matre you are about to meet is the most powerful of all who have come here. She does not tolerate anything but complete obedience."

"I take it that you are warning me."

"I thought you would understand. Call her Honored Matre. Nothing else. In we go. I've taken the liberty of having a new uniform made for you."

The room where Muzzafar ushered him was one Teg had not seen on his previous visit. Small and crammed with ticking black-paneled boxes, it left little room for the two of them. A single yellow glowglobe at the ceiling illuminated the place. Muzzafar crowded himself into a corner while Teg got out of the grimed and wrinkled singlesuit he had worn since the no-globe.

"Sorry I can't offer you a bath as well," Muzzafar said. "But we must not delay. She gets impatient."

A different personality came over Teg with the uniform. It was a familiar black garment, even to the starbursts at the collar. So he was to appear before this Honored Matre as the Sisterhood's Bashar. Interesting. He was once more completely the Bashar, not that this powerful sense of identity had ever left him. The uniform completed it and announced it, though. In this garment there was no need to emphasize in any other way precisely who he was.

"That's better," Muzzafar said as he led Teg out into the entry hallway and through a door Teg remembered. Yes, this was where he had met the "safe" contacts. He had recognized the room's function then and nothing appeared to have changed it. Rows of microscopic comeyes lined the intersection of ceiling and walls, disguised as silver guide strips for the hovering glowglobes.

The one who is watched does not see, Teg thought. *And the Watchers have a billion eyes.*

His doubled vision told him there was danger here but nothing immediately violent.

This room, about five meters long and four wide, was a place for doing very high-level business. The merchandise would never be an actual exposure of money. People here would see only portable equivalents of whatever passed for currency—melange, perhaps, or milky soostones about the size of an eyeball, perfectly round, at once glossy and soft in appearance but radiant with rainbow changes directed by whatever light fell on them or whatever flesh they touched. This was a place where a danikin of melange or a small fold-pouch of soostones would be accepted as a natural occurrence. The price of a planet could be exchanged here with only a nod, an eyeblink or a low-voiced murmur. No wallets of currency would ever be produced here. The closest thing might be a thin case of translux out of whose poison-guarded interior would come thinner sheets of ridulian crystal with very large numbers inscribed on them by unforgeable dataprint.

"This is a bank," Teg said.

"What?" Muzzafar had been staring at the closed door in the opposite wall. "Oh, yes. She'll be along presently."

"She is watching us now, of course."

Muzzafar did not answer but he looked gloomy.

Teg glanced around him. Had anything been changed since his previous visit? He saw no significant alterations. He wondered if shrines such as this one had undergone much change at all over the eons. There was a dewcarpet on the floor as soft as brantdown and as white as the underbelly of a fur whale. It shimmered with a false sense of wetness that only the eye detected. A bare foot (not that this place had ever seen a bare foot) would feel caressing dryness.

There was a narrow table about two meters long almost in the center of the room. The top was at least twenty millimeters thick. Teg guessed it was Danian jacaranda. The deep brown surface had been polished to a sheen that drank the vision and revealed far underneath veins like river currents. There were only four admiral's chairs around the table, chairs crafted by a master artisan from the same wood as the table, cushioned on seat and back with lyrleather of the exact tone of the polished wood.

Only four chairs. More would have been an overstatement. He had not tried one of the chairs before and he did not seat himself now, but he knew what his flesh would find there—comfort almost up to the level of a despised chairdog. Not quite at that degree of softness and conformity to bodily shape, of course. Too much comfort could lure the sitter into relaxation. This room and its furnishings said: "Be comfortable here but remain alert."

You not only had to have your wits about you in this place but also a great power of violence behind you, Teg thought. He had summed it up that way before and his opinion had not changed.

There were no windows but the ones he had seen from the outside had danced with lines of light—energy barriers to repel intruders and prevent escape. Such barriers brought their own dangers, Teg knew, but the implications were important. Just keeping the energy flow in them would feed a large city for the lifetime of its longest-lived inhabitant.

There was nothing casual about this display of wealth.

The door that Muzzafar watched opened with a gentle click.

Danger!

A woman in a shimmering golden robe swept into the room. Lines of red-orange danced in the fabric.

She is old!

Teg had not expected her to be this ancient. Her face was a wrinkled mask. The eyes were deeply set green ice. Her nose was an elongated beak whose shadow touched thin lips and repeated the sharp angle of the chin. A black skullcap almost covered her gray hair.

Muzzafar bowed.

"Leave us," she said.

He left without a word, going out through the door by which she had entered. When the door closed behind him, Teg said, "Honored Matre."

"So you recognize this as a bank." Her voice carried only a slight trembling.

"Of course."

"There are always means of transferring large sums or selling power," she said. "I do not speak of the power that runs factories but of the power that runs people."

"And that usually passes under the strange names of government or society or civilization," Teg said.

"I suspected you would be very intelligent," she said. She pulled out a chair and sat but did not indicate that Teg should seat himself. "I think of myself as a banker. That saves a lot of muddy and distressful circumlocutions."

Teg did not respond. There seemed no need. He continued to study her.

"Why are you looking at me like that?" she demanded.

"I did not expect you to be this old," he said.

"Heh, heh, heh. We have many surprises for you, Bashar. Later, a younger Honored Matre may murmur her name to mark you. Praise Dur if that happens."

He nodded, not understanding much of what she said.

"This is also a very old building," she said. "I watched you when you came in. Does that surprise you, too?"

"No."

"This building has remained essentially unchanged for several thousand years. It is built of materials that will last much longer still."

He glanced at the table.

"Oh, not the wood. But underneath, it's polastine, polaz, and pormabat. The three P-Os are never sneered at where necessity calls for them."

Teg remained silent.

"Necessity," she said. "Do you object to any of the necessary things that have been done to you?"

"My objections don't matter," he said. What was she getting at? Studying him, of course. As he studied her.

"Do you think others have ever objected to what you did to them?"

"Undoubtedly."

"You're a natural commander, Bashar. I think you'll be very valuable to us."

"I've always thought I was most valuable to myself."

"Bashar! Look at my eyes!"

He obeyed, seeing little flecks of orange drifting in across the whites. The sense of peril was acute.

"If you ever see my eyes fully orange, beware!" she said. "You will have offended me beyond my ability to tolerate."

He nodded.

"I like it that you can command but you cannot command me! You command the muck and that is the only function we have for such as you."

"The muck?"

She waved a hand, a negligent motion. "Out there. You know them. Their curiosity is narrow gauge. No great issues ever enter their awareness."

"I thought that was what you meant."

"We work to keep it that way," she said. "Everything goes to them through a tight filter, which excludes all but that which has immediate survival value."

"No great issues," he said.

"You are offended but it doesn't matter," she said. "To those out there, a great issue is: 'Will I eat today?' 'Do I have shelter tonight that will not be invaded by attackers or vermin?' Luxury? Luxury is the possession of a drug or a member of the opposite sex who can, for a time, keep the beast at bay."

And you are the beast, he thought.

"I am taking some time with you, Bashar, because I see that you could be more valuable to us even than Muzzafar. And he is extremely valuable indeed. Even now, we are repaying him for bringing you to us in a receptive condition."

When Teg still remained silent, she chuckled. "You do not think you are receptive?"

Teg held himself quiet. Had they given him some drug in his food? He saw the flickering of doubled vision but the movements of violence had receded as the orange flecks left the Honored Matre's eyes. Her feet were to be avoided, though. They were deadly weapons.

"It's just that you think of the muck in the wrong way," she said. "Luckily, they are most self-limiting. They know this somewhere in the damps of their deepest consciousness but cannot spare the time to deal with that or anything else except the immediate scramble for survival."

"They cannot be improved?" he asked.

"They must not be improved! Oh, we see to it that self-improvement remains a great fad among them. Nothing real about it, of course."

"Another luxury they must be denied," he said.

"Not a luxury! Nonexistent! It must be occluded at all times behind a barrier that we like to call protective ignorance."

"What you don't know cannot hurt you."

"I don't like your tone, Bashar."

Again, the orange flecks danced in her eyes. The sense of violence diminished, however, as she once more chuckled. "The thing you be- ware of is the opposite of *what-you-don't-know*. We teach that new knowledge can be dangerous. You see the obvious extension: All new knowledge is non-survival!"

The door behind the Honored Matre opened and Muzzafar re- turned. It was a changed Muzzafar, his face flushed, his eyes bright. He stopped behind the Honored Matre's chair.

"One day, I will be able to permit you behind me this way," she said. "It is in my power to do this."

What had they done to Muzzafar? Teg wondered. The man looked almost drugged.

"You do see that I have power?" she asked.

He cleared his throat. "That's obvious."

"I am a banker, remember? We have just made a deposit with our loyal Muzzafar. Do you thank us, Muzzafar?"

"I do, Honored Matre." His voice was hoarse.

"I'm sure you understand this kind of power generally, Bashar," she said. "The Bene Gesserit trained you well. They are quite talented but not, I fear, as talented as we are."

"And I am told you are quite numerous," he said.

"Our numbers are not the key, Bashar. Power such as ours has a way of becoming channeled so that it can be controlled by small numbers."

She was like a Reverend Mother, he thought, in the way she could appear to answer without revealing much.

"In essence," she said, "power such as ours is allowed to become the substance of survival for many people. *Then,* the threat of withdrawal is all that's required for us to rule." She glanced over her shoulder. "Would you wish us to withdraw our favor from you, Muzzafar?"

"No, Honored Matre." He was actually trembling!

"You have found a new drug," Teg said.

Her laughter was spontaneous and loud, almost raucous. "No, Bashar! We have an old one."

"And you would make an addict of me?"

"Like all the others we control, Bashar, you have a choice: death or obedience."

"That is a rather old choice," he agreed. What was her immediate threat? He could sense no violence. Quite the contrary. His doubled vision showed him broken glimpses of extremely sensuous overtones. Did they think they could imprint him?

She smiled at him, a knowing expression with something frigid under it.

"Will he serve us well, Muzzafar?"

"I believe so, Honored Matre."

Teg frowned in thought. There was something deeply evil about this pair. They went against every morality by which he modeled his behavior. It was well to remember that neither of them knew this strange thing that had speeded his reactions.

They seemed to be enjoying his puzzled discomfiture.

Teg took some reassurance from the realization that neither of these two really enjoyed life. He could see that in them clearly with eyes the Sisterhood had educated. The Honored Matre and Muzzafar had forgotten or, most likely, abandoned everything that supported the survival of joyous humans. He thought they probably no longer were capable of finding a real wellspring of joy in their own flesh. Theirs would have to be mostly a voyeur's existence, the eternal observer, always remembering what it had been like before they had taken the turning into whatever it was they had become. Even when they wallowed in the performance of something that once had meant gratification, they would have to reach for new extremes each time just to touch the edges of their own memories.

The Honored Matre's grin widened, showing a line of gleaming white teeth. "Look at him, Muzzafar. He has not the slightest conception of what we can do."

Teg heard this but he also saw with eyes trained by the Bene Gesserit. Not a milligram of naivete remained in either of these two. Nothing was expected to surprise them. Nothing could be truly new for them. Still, they plotted and devised, hoping that *this* extreme would produce the remembered thrill. They knew it would not, of course, and they expected to carry away from the experience only more burning rage out of which to fashion another attempt at the unreachable. That was how their thinking went.

Teg designed a smile for them, using all of the skills he had learned at Bene Gesserit hands. It was a smile full of compassion, of understanding and real pleasure in his own existence. He knew it for the most deadly insult he could hurl at them and he saw it hit. Muzzafar glowered at him. The Honored Matre went from orange-eyed rage to an abrupt surprise and then, quite slowly, to dawning pleasure. She had not expected this! It was something new!

"Muzzafar," she said, the orange receding from her eyes, "bring the Honored Matre who has been chosen to mark our Bashar."

Teg, his doubled vision showing the immediate peril, understood at last. He could feel awareness of his own future spreading outward like waves as the power grew in him. The wild change in him was continuing! He felt the energy expand. With it came understanding and choices. He saw himself as the whirlwind rampaging through this building—bodies scattered behind him (Muzzafar and the Honored Matre among them) and the whole complex looking like an abattoir when he departed.

Must I do that? he wondered.

For each one he killed, more would have to be killed. He saw the necessity of it, though, as he saw at last the Tyrant's design. The pain he could see for himself almost made him cry out but he held it back.

"Yes, bring this Honored Matre to me," he said, knowing that this would be one less for him to seek out and destroy elsewhere in the building. The room of the scanlyzer controls must be taken out first.

O you who know what we suffer here, do not forget us in your prayers.

—SIGN OVER ARRAKEEN LANDING FIELD
(HISTORICAL RECORDS: DAR-ES-BALAT)

Taraza watched a snow-flutter of falling blossoms against the silvery sky of a Rakian morning. There was an opalescent sheen to the sky that, despite all of her preparatory briefings, she had not anticipated. Rakis held many surprises. The smell of mock orange was powerful here at the edge of the Dar-es-Balat roof garden, overriding all other odors.

Never believe that you have plumbed the depths of any place . . . or of any human, she reminded herself.

Conversation was ended out here but not the echoes of the spoken thoughts they had exchanged only minutes ago. All agreed, though, that it was time for action. Soon, Sheeana would "dance a worm" for them and once more demonstrate her mastery.

Waff and a new priestly representative would share this "holy event" but Taraza was sure neither of them knew the real nature of what they were about to witness. Waff bore watching, of course. He still carried that air of irritated disbelief in everything he saw or heard. It was a strange mixture with his underlying awe at being on Rakis. The catalyst was obviously his rage over the fact that fools ruled here.

Odrade returned from the meeting room and stopped beside Taraza.

"I am extremely disquieted by the reports from Gammu," Taraza said. "Do you bring something new?"

"No. Things are obviously still chaotic there."

"Tell me, Dar, what do you think we should do?"

"I keep remembering the Tyrant's words to Chenoeh: 'The Bene Gesserit are so close to what they should be, yet so far.'"

Taraza pointed at the open desert beyond the museum city's qanat. "He's still out there, Dar. I'm sure of it." Taraza turned to face Odrade. "And Sheeana speaks to him."

"He told so many lies," Odrade said.

"But he didn't lie about his own incarnation. Remember what he said. 'Every descendant part of me will carry some of my awareness locked away within it, lost and helpless—pearls of me moving blindly in the sand, caught in an endless dream.'"

"You bank a great deal on your belief in the power of that dream," Odrade said.

"We must recover the Tyrant's design! All of it!"

Odrade sighed but did not speak.

"Never underestimate the power of an idea," Taraza said. "The Atreides were ever philosophers in their governance. Philosophy is always dangerous because it promotes the creation of new ideas."

Still, Odrade did not respond.

"The worm carries it all within him, Dar! All of the forces he set in motion are still in him."

"Are you trying to convince me or yourself, Tar?"

"I am punishing you, Dar. Just as the Tyrant is still punishing us."

"For not being what we should be? Ahh, here come Sheeana and the others."

"The worm's language, Dar. That is the important thing."

"If you say so, Mother Superior."

Taraza sent an angry stare at Odrade, who moved forward to greet the newcomers. There was a disturbing gloom in Odrade.

The presence of Sheeana, though, restored Taraza's sense of purpose. An alert little thing, Sheeana. Very good material. Sheeana had demonstrated her dance the previous night, performing in the great museum room against a tapestry background, an exotic dance against an exotic spice-fiber hanging with its image of desert and worms. She appeared to be almost a part of the hanging, a figure projected forward from the stylized dunes and their elaborately detailed coursing worms. Taraza recalled how Sheeana's brown hair had been thrown outward by the whirling movements of the dance, swinging in a fuzzy arc. Side-lighting accented the reddish glints in her hair. Her eyes had been closed but it was not a face in repose. Excitement betrayed itself in the passionate set of her wide mouth, the flaring of her nostrils, the forward thrust of her chin. Her motions had conveyed an inner sophistication that belied her youth.

The dance is her language, Taraza thought. *Odrade is correct. Seeing it, we will learn it.*

Waff had something of a withdrawn look this morning. It was difficult to determine if his eyes were looking outward or inward.

With Waff was Tulushan, a darkly handsome Rakian, the priesthood's chosen representative at today's "holy event." Taraza, meeting him at the demonstration dance, had found it extraordinary how Tulushan never needed to say "but," and yet the word was always there in everything he uttered. A perfect bureaucrat. He rightly expected to go far but those expectations would soon encounter their ultimate surprise. She felt no pity for him at this knowledge. Tulushan was a soft-faced youth of too few standards for such a position of trust. There was more to him than met the eye, of course. And less.

Waff moved to one side in the garden, leaving Odrade and Sheeana with Tulushan.

The young priest was expendable, naturally. That explained much about why he had been chosen for this venture. It told her that she had achieved the proper level of potential violence. Taraza did not think, though, that any of the priestly factions would dare harm Sheeana.

We will stay close to Sheeana.

They had spent a busy week since the demonstration of the whores' sexual accomplishments. A very disturbing week, when it came to that. Odrade had been kept busy with Sheeana. Taraza would have preferred Lucilla for this educational chore but you made do with what was available and Odrade obviously was the best available on Rakis for such teaching.

Taraza looked back toward the desert. They were waiting for the 'thopters from Keen with their cargoes of Very Important Observers. The VIOs were not yet late but crowding it as such people always did.

Sheeana seemed to be taking the sexual education well, although Taraza's estimation of the Sisterhood's available teaching males on Rakis was not high. Her first night here, Taraza had called in one of the servant males. Afterward, she had judged it too much trouble for the little joy and forgetfulness it provided. Besides, what was there to forget? To forget was to allow a weakness.

Never forget!

That's what the whores did, though. They traded in forgetfulness. And they had not the least awareness of the Tyrant's continuing vise-like hold on human destiny nor of the need to break that hold.

Taraza had listened secretly to the previous day's session between Sheeana and Odrade.

What was I listening for?

Young girl and teacher had been out here in the roof garden, facing each other on two benches, a portable Ixian damper hiding their words from anyone who did not have the coded translator. The suspensor-buoyed damper hovered over the two like a strange umbrella, a black disc projecting distortions that hid the precise movements of lips and the sounds of voices.

To Taraza, standing within the long meeting room, the tiny translator in her left ear, the lesson had occurred like an equally distorted memory.

When I was taught these things, we had not seen what the whores of the Scattering could do.

"Why do we say it's the complexity of sex?" Sheeana asked. "The man you sent last night kept saying that."

"Many believe they understand it, Sheeana. Perhaps no one has ever understood it, because such words require more of the mind than they do of the flesh."

"Why must I not use any of the things we saw the Face Dancers do?"

"Sheeana, complexity hides within complexity. Great deeds and foul ones have been done at the goading of sexual forces. We speak of 'sexual strength' and 'sexual energies' and such things as 'the over-mounting urge of desire.' I don't deny that such things are observable. But what we are looking at here is a force so powerful that it can destroy you and everything you hold worthwhile."

"That's what I'm trying to understand. What is it the whores are doing wrong?"

"They ignore the species at its work, Sheeana. I think you can already sense this. The Tyrant certainly knew about it. What was his Golden Path but a vision of sexual forces at work recreating humankind endlessly?"

"And the whores don't create?"

"They mostly try to control their worlds with this force."

"They seem to be doing that."

"Ahhh, but what counterforces do they call forth?"

"I don't understand."

"You know about Voice and how it can control some people?"

"But not control everybody."

"Exactly. A civilization subjected to Voice over a long period develops ways of adapting to this force, preventing manipulation by those who use Voice."

"So there are people who know how to resist the whores?"

"We see unmistakable signs of it. And that is one of the reasons we are here on Rakis."

"Will the whores come here?"

"I'm afraid so. They want to control the core of the Old Empire because they see us as an easy conquest."

"Aren't you afraid they'll win?"

"They won't win, Sheeana. Depend on it. But they are good for us."

"How is that?"

Sheeana's tone echoed Taraza's own shock at hearing such words from Odrade. How much did Odrade suspect? In the next instant, Taraza understood and she wondered if the lesson was equally understandable to the young girl.

"The core is static, Sheeana. We have been almost at a standstill for thousands of years. Life and movement are 'out there' with the people of the Scattering who resist the whores. Whatever we do, we must make that resistance even stronger."

The sound of approaching 'thopters broke Taraza from her reverie of remembrance. The VIOs were arriving from Keen. Still at some distance, but the sound carried far in the clear air.

Odrade's teaching method was a good one, Taraza had to admit as she scanned the sky for a first glimpse of the 'thopters. Apparently they were coming in low and from the other side of the building. That was the wrong direction but perhaps they had taken the VIOs on a short excursion over the remains of the Tyrant's wall. Many people were curious about the place where Odrade had found the spice hoard.

Sheeana, Odrade, Waff, and Tulushan went back into the long meeting room. They had heard the 'thopters, too. Sheeana was anxious to show her power over the worms. Taraza hesitated. There was a laboring sound in the approaching 'thopters. Were they overloaded? How many observers had they brought?

The first 'thopter lifted over the penthouse roof and Taraza saw the armored cockpit. She recognized treachery even before the first beam arced out of the machine, slicing through her legs below the knees. She fell heavily against a potted tree, her legs completely severed. Another beam slashed out at her, slicing at an angle across her hip. The 'thopter swept over her in an abrupt roar of booster jets and banked away to the left.

Taraza clung to the tree, shunting the agony aside. She managed to cut off most of the bloodflow from her wounds but the pain was great. Not as great as the spice agony, though, she reminded herself. That helped but she knew she was doomed. She heard shouts and the multiple sounds of violence all around the museum now.

I have won! Taraza thought.

Odrade darted from the penthouse and bent over Taraza. They said nothing but Odrade showed that she understood by putting her forehead to Taraza's temple. It was the ages-old cue of the Bene Gesserit. Taraza began pouring her life into Odrade—Other Memories, hopes, fears . . . everything.

One of them might yet escape.

Sheeana watched from the penthouse, staying where she had been ordered to wait. She knew what was happening out there in the roof garden. This was the ultimate mystery of the Bene Gesserit and every postulant was aware of it.

Waff and Tulushan, already out of the room when the attack came, did not return.

Sheeana shuddered with apprehension.

Abruptly, Odrade stood and ran back into the penthouse. There was a wild look in her eyes but she moved with purpose. Leaping up, she gathered glowglobes, grabbing them in bundles by their toggle cords. She thrust several bundles into Sheeana's hands and Sheeana felt her body grow lighter with the lift of the globes' suspensor fields. Trailing more clusters of the globes beyond their field range, Odrade hurried across to the narrow end of the room where a grill in the wall indicated what she sought. With Sheeana's help, she lifted the grill out of its slots, revealing a deep airshaft. The light of the clustered glowglobes showed rough walls inside.

"Hold the globes close to get the maximum field effect," Odrade said. "Push them away to lower yourself. In you go."

Sheeana clutched the toggle cords in a sweaty hand and hopped over the sill. She let herself fall, then fearfully clutched the globes close. Light from above told her Odrade was following.

At the bottom, they emerged into a pump room, the susurrations of many fans a background for the sounds of violence from outside.

"We must get to the no-room and then to the desert," Odrade said. "All of these machinery systems are interconnected. There will be a passage."

"Is she dead?" Sheeana whispered.

"Yes."

"Poor Mother Superior."

"I am the Mother Superior now, Sheeana. At least temporarily." She pointed upward. "Those were the whores attacking us. We must hurry."

The world is for the living. Who are they?
We dared the dark to reach the white and warm.
She was the wind when the wind was in my way.
Alive at noon, I perished in her form.
Who rise from the flesh to spirit know the fall:
The word outleaps the world and light is all.

—THEODORE ROETHKE
(HISTORICAL QUOTATIONS: DAR-ES-BALAT)

It required little conscious volition for Teg to become the whirlwind. He had recognized at last the nature of the threat from the Honored Matres. Recognition fitted itself into the blurred requirements made upon him by the new Mentat awareness that went with his magnified speed.

Monstrous threat required monstrous countermeasures. Blood spattered him as he drove himself through the headquarters building, slaughtering everyone he met.

As he had learned from his Bene Gesserit teachers, the great problem of the human universe lay in how you managed procreation. He could hear the voice of his first teacher as he carried destruction through the building.

"You may think of this only as sexuality but we prefer the more basic term: procreation. It has many facets and offshoots and it has apparently unlimited energy. The emotion called 'love' is only one small aspect."

Teg crushed the throat of a man standing rigidly in his path and, at last, found the control room for the building's defenses. Only one man was seated in it, his right hand almost touching a red key on the console in front of him.

With a slashing left hand, Teg almost decapitated the man. The body tipped backward in slow motion, blood welling from the gaping neck.

The Sisterhood is right to call them whores!

You could drag humankind almost anywhere by manipulating the enormous energies of procreation. You could goad humans into actions they would never have believed possible. One of his teachers had said it directly:

"This energy must have an outlet. Bottle it up and it becomes monstrously dangerous. Redirect it and it will sweep over anything in its path. This is an ultimate secret of all religions."

Teg was conscious of leaving more than fifty bodies behind him as he left the building. The last fatality was a soldier in camouflage uniform standing in the open doorway, apparently about to enter.

As he ran past apparently unmoving people and vehicles, Teg's revved-up mind had time to reflect on what he had left behind him. Was there any consolation, he wondered, in the fact that the old Honored Matre's last living expression was one of real surprise? Could he congratulate himself that Muzzafar would never again see his frame bush home?

The necessity for what he had accomplished in a few heartbeats was very clear, though, to one trained by the Bene Gesserit. Teg knew his history. There were many paradise planets in the Old Empire, probably many more among the people of the Scattering. Humans always seemed capable of trying that foolish experiment. People in such places mostly lazed along. A quick-smart analysis said this was because of the easy climates on such planets. He knew this for stupidity. It was because sexual energy was easily released in such places. Let the Missionaries of the Divided God or some denominational construct enter one of these paradises and you got outrageous violence.

"We of the Sisterhood know," one of Teg's teachers had said. "We have put a flame to that fuse more than once with our Missionaria Protectiva."

Teg did not stop running until he was in an alley at least five kilometers from the abattoir that had been the headquarters for the old Honored Matre. He knew that very little time had passed but there was something much more important upon which he had to focus. He had not killed every occupant of that building. There were eyes back there belonging to people who knew now what he could do. They had seen him kill Honored Matres. They had seen Muzzafar topple dead at his hands. The evidence of the bodies left behind and the slowed replay of recordings would tell it all.

Teg leaned against a wall. Skin was torn from his left palm. He let himself return to normal time as he watched blood oozing from the wound. The blood was almost black.

More oxygen in my blood?

He was panting but not as much as these exertions would seem to require.

What has happened to me?

It was something from his Atreides ancestry, he knew. Crisis had tipped him over into another dimension of human possibilities. Whatever the transformation, it was profound. He could see outward now into many necessities. And the people he had passed on his run to this alley had seemed like statues.

Will I ever think of them as muck?

It could only happen if he let it happen, he knew. But the temptation was there and he allowed himself a brief commiseration for the Honored Matres. Great Temptation had toppled them into their own muck.

What to do now?

The main line lay open to him. There was a man here in Ysai, one man who would be sure to know everyone Teg required. Teg looked around the alley. Yes, that man was near.

The fragrance of flowers and herbs wafted to Teg from somewhere down this alley. He moved toward this fragrance, aware that it led him where he needed to go and that no violent attack awaited him here. This was, temporarily, a quiet backwater.

He came to the fragrant source quickly. It was an inset doorway marked by a blue awning with two words on it in modern Galach: "Personal Service."

Teg entered and saw immediately what he had found. They were to be seen at many places in the Old Empire: eating establishments harking back to ancient times, eschewing automata from kitchen to table. Most of them were "in" establishments. You told friends about your latest "discovery" with an admonition to them not to spread the word.

"Don't want to spoil it with crowding."

This idea had always amused Teg. You spread the word about such places but you did it under the guise of keeping a secret.

Mouth-watering odors of cooking emerged from the kitchen at the rear. A waiter passed bearing a tray from which steam lifted, carrying the promise of good things.

A young woman in a short black dress with a white apron came up to him. "This way, sir. We have a table open in the corner."

She held a chair for him to be seated with his back to the wall. "Someone will be with you in a moment, sir." She passed him a stiff sheet of cheap double-thickness paper. "Our menu is printed. I hope you won't mind."

He watched her leave. The waiter he had seen passed going the other way toward the kitchen. The tray was empty.

Teg's feet had led him here as though he had been running on a fixed track. And there was the man he required, dining nearby.

The waiter had stopped to talk to the man Teg knew held the answer to the next moves required here. The two were laughing together. Teg scanned the rest of the room: only three other tables occupied. An older woman sat at a table in the far corner nibbling at some frosty confection. She was dressed in what Teg thought must be the peak of current fashion, a clinging short red gown cut low at the neck. Her shoes matched. A young couple sat at a table off to his right. They saw no one except each other. An older man in a tightly fitted old-fashioned brown tunic ate sparingly of a green vegetable dish near the door. He had eyes only for his food.

The man talking to the waiter laughed loudly.

Teg stared at the back of the waiter's head. Tufts of blond hair sprang from the nape of the waiter's neck like broken bunches of dead grass. The man's collar was frayed beneath the tufted hair. Teg lowered his gaze. The waiter's shoes were run over at the heels. The hem of his black jacket had been darned. Was it thrift in this place? Thrift or some other form of economic pressure? The odors from the kitchen did not suggest any stinting there. The tableware was shining and clean. No cracked dishes. But the striped red and white cloth on the table had been darned in several places, care taken to match the original fabric.

Once more, Teg studied the other customers. They looked substantial. None of the starving poor in this place. Teg had it registered then. Not only was this an "in" place, somebody had designed it for just that effect. There was a clever mind behind such an establishment. This was the kind of restaurant that rising young executives revealed to make points with prospective customers or to please a superior. The food would be superb and the portions generous. Teg realized that his instincts had led him here correctly. He bent his attention to the menu then, allowing hunger to enter his consciousness at last. The hunger was at least as fierce as that which had astonished the late Field Marshal Muzzafar.

The waiter appeared beside him with a tray on which were placed a small open box and a jar from which wafted the pungent odor of newskin ointment.

"I see you have injured your hand, Bashar," the man said. He placed the tray on the table. "Allow me to dress the injury before you order."

Teg lifted the injured hand and watched the swift competence of the treatment.

"You know me?" Teg asked.

"Yes, sir. And after what I've been hearing, it seems strange to see you in full uniform. There." He finished the dressing.

"What have you been hearing?" Teg spoke in a low voice.

"That the Honored Matres hunt you."

"I've just killed some of them and many of their . . . What should we call them?"

The man paled but he spoke firmly. "Slaves would be a good word, sir."

"You were at Renditai, weren't you," Teg said.

"Yes, sir. Many of us settled here afterward."

"I need food but I cannot pay you," Teg said.

"No one from Renditai has need of your money, Bashar. Do they know you came this way?"

"I don't believe they do."

"The people here now are regulars. None of them would betray you. I will try to warn you if someone dangerous comes. What did you wish to eat?"

"A great deal of food. I will leave the choice to you. About twice as much carbohydrate as protein. No stimulants."

"What do you mean by a great deal, sir?"

"Keep bringing it until I tell you to stop . . . or until you feel I have overstepped your generosity."

"In spite of appearances, sir, this is not a poor establishment. The extras here have made me a rich man."

Score one for his assessment, Teg thought. The thrift here was a calculated pose.

The waiter left and again spoke to the man at the central table. Teg studied the man openly after the waiter went on into the kitchen. Yes, that was the man. The diner concentrated on a plate heaped with some green-garnished pasta.

There was very little sign in this man of a woman's care, Teg thought. His collar had been closed awry, the clingstraps tangled. Spots of the greenish sauce soiled his left cuff. He was naturally right-handed but ate while his left hand remained in the path of spillage. Frayed cuffs on his trousers. One trouser hem, partly released from its threaded bondage, dragged at the heel. Stockings mismatched—one blue and one pale yellow. None of this appeared to bother him. No mother or other woman had ever dragged this one back from a doorway with orders to make himself presentable. His basic attitude was announced in his whole appearance:

"What you see is as presentable as it gets."

The man looked up suddenly, a jerking motion as though he had been goosed. He sent a brown-eyed gaze around the room, pausing at each face in turn as though he looked for a particular visage. This done, he returned his attention to his plate.

The waiter returned with a clear soup in which shreds of egg and some green vegetables could be seen.

"While the rest of your meal is being prepared, sir," he said.

"Did you come here directly after Renditai?" Teg asked.

"Yes, sir. But I served with you also at Acline."

"The sixty-seventh Gammu," Teg said.

"Yes, sir!"

"We saved a good many lives that time," Teg said. "Theirs and ours."

When Teg still did not begin eating, the waiter spoke in a rather cold voice, "Would you require a snooper, sir?"

"Not while you're serving me," Teg said. He meant what he said but he felt a bit of a fraud because doubled vision told him the food was safe.

The waiter started to turn away, pleased.

"One moment," Teg said.

"Sir?"

"The man at that central table. He is one of your regulars?"

"Professor Delnay? Oh, yes, sir."

"Delnay. Yes, I thought so."

"Professor of martial arts, sir. And the history of same."

"I know. When it comes time to serve my dessert, please ask Professor Delnay if he would join me."

"Shall I tell him who you are, sir?"

"Don't you think he already knows?"

"That would seem likely, sir, but still . . ."

"Caution where caution belongs," Teg said. "Bring on the food."

Delnay's interest was fully aroused long before the waiter relayed Teg's invitation. The professor's first words as he seated himself across from Teg were: "That was the most remarkable gastronomic performance I have ever seen. Are you sure you can eat a dessert?"

"Two or three of them at least," Teg said.

"Astonishing!"

Teg sampled a spoonful of a honey-sweetened confection. He swallowed it, then: "This place is a jewel."

"I have kept it a careful secret," Delnay said. "Except for a few close friends, of course. To what do I owe the honor of your invitation?"

"Have you ever been . . . ah, *marked* by an Honored Matre?"

"Lords of perdition, no! I'm not important enough for that."

"I was hoping to ask you to risk your life, Delnay."

"In what way?" No hesitation. That was reassuring.

"There is a place in Ysai where my old soldiers meet. I want to go there and see as many of them as possible."

"Through the streets in full regalia the way you are now?"

"In any way you can arrange it."

Delnay put a finger to his lower lip and leaned back to stare at Teg. "You're not an easy figure to disguise, you know. However, there may be a way." He nodded thoughtfully. "Yes." He smiled. "You won't like it, I'm afraid."

"What do you have in mind?"

"Some padding and other alterations. We will pass you off as a Bordano overseer. You'll smell of the sewer, of course. And you'll have to carry it off that you don't notice."

"Why do you think that will succeed?" Teg asked.

"Oh, there's going to be a storm tonight. Regular thing this time of year. Laying down the moisture for next year's open crops. And filling the reservoirs for the heated fields, you know."

"I don't understand your reasoning, but when I've finished another of these confections, we'll go," Teg said.

"You'll like the place where we take refuge from the storm," Delnay said. "I'm mad, you know, to do this. But the proprietor here said I was to help you or never come here again."

It was an hour after dark when Delnay led him to the rendezvous point. Teg, dressed in leathers and affecting a limp, was forced to use much of his mental power to ignore his own odors. Delnay's friends had plastered Teg with sewage and then hosed him off. The forced-air drying brought back most of the effluent aromas.

A remote-reading weather station at the door of the meeting place told Teg it had dropped fifteen degrees outside in the preceding hour. Delnay preceded him and hurried away into a crowded room where there was much noise and the sound of clinking glassware. Teg paused to study the doorside station. The wind was gusting to thirty klicks, he saw. Barometric pressure down. He looked at the sign above the station:

"A service to our customers."

Presumably, a service to the bar as well. Departing customers might well take one look at these readings and return to the warmth and camaraderie behind them.

In a large fireplace with inglenook at the far end of the bar there was a real fire burning. Aromatic wood.

Delnay returned, wrinkled his nose at Teg's smell and led him around the edge of the crowd into a back room, then through this into a private bathroom. Teg's uniform—cleaned and pressed—was laid out over a chair there.

"I'll be in the inglenook when you come out," Delnay said.

"In full regalia, eh?" Teg asked.

"It's only dangerous out in the streets," Delnay said. He went back the way they had come.

Teg emerged presently and found his way to the inglenook through groups that turned suddenly silent as people recognized him. Murmurous comments swept through the room. "The old Bashar himself." "Oh, yes, it's Teg. Served with him, I did. Know that face and figure anywhere."

Customers had crowded into the atavistic warmth of the fireside. There was a rich smell of wet clothing and drink-fogged breaths there.

So the storm had driven this crowd into the bar? Teg looked at the battle-hardened military faces all around him, thinking that this was not a usual gathering, no matter what Delnay said. The people here knew one another, though, and had expected to meet one another here at this time.

Delnay was sitting on one of the benches in the inglenook, a glass containing an amber drink in his hand.

"You put out the word to meet us here," Teg said.

"Isn't that what you wanted, Bashar?"

"Who are you, Delnay?"

"I own a winter farm a few klicks south of here and I have some banker friends who will occasionally loan me a groundcar. If you want me to be more specific, I'm like the rest of the people in this room—someone who wants the Honored Matres off our necks."

A man behind Teg asked: "Is it true that you killed a hundred of them today, Bashar?"

Teg spoke dryly without turning. "The number is greatly exaggerated. Could I have a drink, please?"

From his greater height, Teg scanned the room while someone was getting him a glass. When it was thrust into his hand, it was, as he expected, the deep blue of Danian Marinete. These old soldiers knew his preferences.

The drinking activity in the room continued but at a more subdued pace. They were waiting for him to state his purpose.

Gregarious human nature got a natural boost on such a stormy night, Teg thought. Band together behind the fire in the mouth of the cave, fellow tribesmen! Nothing dangerous will get past us, especially when the beasts see our fire. How many other similar gatherings were there around Gammu on such a night? he wondered, sipping his drink. Bad weather could mask movements that the gathered companions did not want observed. The weather might also keep certain people inside who were otherwise not supposed to remain inside.

He recognized a few faces from his past—officers and ordinary soldiers—a mixed bag. For some of them, he had good memories: reliable people. Some of them would die tonight.

The noise level began to increase as people relaxed in his presence. No one pressed him for an explanation. They knew that about him, too. Teg set his own timetable.

The sounds of conversation and laughter were of a kind he knew must have accompanied such gatherings since the dawn times when humans clustered for mutual protection. Clinking of glassware, sudden bursts of laughter, a few quiet chuckles. Those would be the ones more conscious of their personal power. Quiet chuckles said you could be amused but you did not have to make a guffawing fool of yourself. Delnay was a quiet chuckler.

Teg glanced up and saw that the beamed ceiling had been built conventionally low. It made the enclosed space seem at once more extended and yet more intimate. Careful attention to human psychology here. It was a thing he had observed many places on this planet. It was a care to keep a damper on unwanted awareness. Make them feel comfortable and secure. They were not, of course, but don't let that get through to them.

For a few moments longer, Teg watched the drinks being distributed by the skilled waiting staff: dark local beers and some expensive imports. Scattered along the bar and on the softly illuminated tables were bowls containing crisp-fried local vegetables, heavily salted. Such an obvious move to heighten thirst apparently offended no one. It was merely expected in this trade. The beers would be heavily salted, too, of course. They always were. Brewers knew how to kick off the thirst response.

Some of the groups were getting louder. The drinks had begun to work their ancient magic. Bacchus was here! Teg knew that if this gathering were allowed to run its natural course, the room would reach a crescendo later in the night and then gradually, very gradually, the noise level would subside. Someone would go look at the doorside weather station. Depending on what that one saw, the place might wind down immediately or continue at the more subdued pace for some time. He realized then that somewhere behind the bar there would be a way to distort the weather station's readouts. This bar would not overlook such a way of extending its trade.

Get 'em inside and keep 'em here by any means they don't find objectionable.

The people behind this institution would fall in with the Honored Matres and not blink an eye.

Teg put his drink aside and called out: "May I have your attention, please?"

Silence.

Even the waiting staff stopped in what they were doing.

"Some of you guard the doors," Teg said. "No one goes in or out until I give the order. Those back doors, too, if you please."

When this had been sorted out, he stared carefully around the room, picking the ones his doubled vision and old military experience told him could be most trusted. What he had to do now had become quite plain to him. Burzmali, Lucilla, and Duncan were out there at the edge of his new vision, their needs easily seen.

"I presume you can get your hands on weapons rather quickly," he said.

"We came prepared, Bashar!" Someone out in the room shouted. Teg heard the drink in that voice but also the old adrenaline pumping that would be so dear to these people.

"We are going to capture a no-ship," Teg said.

That grabbed them. No other artifact of civilization was as closely guarded. These ships came to the landing fields and other places and they left. Their armored surfaces bristled with weapons. Crews were on constant alert in vulnerable locations. Trickery might succeed; open assault stood little chance. But here in this room Teg had reached a new awareness, driven by necessity and the wild genes in his Atreides ancestry. The positions of the no-ships on and around Gammu were visible to him. Bright dots occupied his inner vision and, like threads leading from one bauble to another, his doubled vision saw the way through this maze.

Oh, but I do not want to go, he thought.

The thing driving him would not be denied.

"Specifically, we are going to capture a no-ship from the Scattering," he said. "They have some of the best. You, you and you and you." He pointed, singling out individuals. "You will stay here and see that no one leaves or communicates with anyone outside of this establishment. I think you will be attacked. Hold out as long as you can. The rest of you, get your weapons and let's go."

> Justice? Who asks for justice. We make our own justice. We make it here on Arrakis—win or die. Let us not rail about justice as long as we have arms and the freedom to use them.
>
> —LETO I: BENE GESSERIT ARCHIVES

The no-ship came in low over the Rakian sands. Its passage stirred up dusty whirlwinds that drifted around it as it settled in a crunching disturbance of the dunes. The silvered yellow sun was sinking into a horizon disturbed by the heat devils of a long hot day. The no-ship sat there creaking, a glistening steely ball whose presence could be detected by the eyes and ears but not by any prescient or long-range instrument. Teg's doubled vision made him confident that no unwanted eyes saw his arrival.

"I want the armored 'thopters and cars out there in no more than ten minutes," he said.

People stirred into action behind him.

"Are you certain they're here, Bashar?" The voice was that of a drinking companion from the Gammu bar, a trusted officer from Renditai whose mood no longer was that of someone recapturing the thrills of his youth. This one had seen old friends die in the battle on Gammu. As with most of the others who survived to come here, he had left a family whose fate he did not know. There was a touch of bitterness in his voice, as though he were trying to convince himself that he had been tricked into this venture.

"They will be here soon," Teg said. "They will arrive riding on the back of a worm."

"How do you know that?"

"It was all arranged."

Teg closed his eyes. He did not need eyes to see the activity all around him. This was like so many command posts he had occupied: an oval room of instruments and people who operated them, officers waiting to obey.

"What is this place?" someone asked.

"Those rocks to the north of us," Teg said. "See them? They were a high cliff once. It was called Wind Trap. There was a Fremen sietch there, little more than a cave now. A few Rakian pioneers live in it."

"Fremen," someone whispered. "Gods! I want to see that worm coming. I never thought I'd ever see such a thing."

"Another one of your unexpected arrangements, eh?" asked the officer of the growing bitterness.

What would he say if I revealed my new abilities? Teg wondered. *He might think I concealed purposes that would not bear close examination. And he would be right. That man is on the edge of a revelation. Would he remain loyal if his eyes were opened?* Teg shook his head. The officer would have little choice. None of them had much choice except to fight and die.

It was true, Teg thought then, that the process of arranging conflicts involved the hoodwinking of large masses. How easy it was to fall into the attitude of the Honored Matres.

Muck!

The hoodwinking was not as difficult as some supposed. Most people wanted to be led. That officer back there had wanted it. There were deep tribal instincts (powerful unconscious motivations) to account for this. The natural reaction when you began to recognize how easily you were led was to look for scapegoats. That officer back there wanted a scapegoat now.

"Burzmali wants to see you," someone off to Teg's left said.

"Not now," Teg said.

Burzmali could wait. He would have his day of command soon enough. Meanwhile, he was a distraction. There would be time later for him to skirt dangerously near the role of scapegoat.

How easy it was to produce scapegoats and how readily they were accepted! This was especially true when the alternative was to find yourself either guilty or stupid or both. Teg wanted to say for all of those around him:

"Look to the hoodwinking! Then you'll know our true intentions!"

The communications officer on Teg's left said: "That Reverend Mother is with Burzmali now. She insists they be allowed in to see you."

"Tell Burzmali I want him to go back and stay with Duncan," Teg said. "And have him look in on Murbella, make sure she's secured. Lucilla can come in."

It had to be, Teg thought.

Lucilla was increasingly suspicious about the changes in him. Trust a Reverend Mother to see the difference.

Lucilla swept in, her robes swishing to accent her vehemence. She was angry but concealing it well.

"I demand an explanation, Miles!"

That was a good opening line, he thought. "Of what?" he said.

"Why didn't we just go in at the—"

"Because the Honored Matres and their Tleilaxu companions from the Scattering hold most of the Rakian centers."

"How . . . how do you . . ."

"They've killed Taraza, you know," he said.

That stopped her, but not for long. "Miles, I insist that you tell me—"

"We don't have much time," he said. "The next satellite passage will show us on the surface here."

"But the defenses of Rakis—"

"Are as vulnerable as any other defenses when they become static," he said. "The families of the defenders are down here. Take the families and you have effective control of the defenders."

"But why are we out here in—"

"To pick up Odrade and that girl with her. Oh, and their worm, too."

"What will we do with a—"

"Odrade will know what to do with the worm. She's your Mother Superior now, you know."

"So you're going to whisk us off into—"

"You'll whisk yourselves! My people and I will remain to create a diversion."

That brought a shocked silence throughout the command station.

Diversion, Teg thought. *What an inadequate word.*

The resistance he had in mind would create hysteria among the Honored Matres, especially when they were made to believe the ghola was here. Not only would they counterattack, they eventually would resort to sterilization procedures. Most of Rakis would become a charred ruin. There was little likelihood that any humans, worms, or sandtrout would survive.

"The Honored Matres have been trying to locate and capture a worm without success," he said. "I really don't understand how they could be so blind in their concept of how you transplant one of them."

"Transplant?" Lucilla was floundering. Teg had seldom seen a Reverend Mother at such a loss. She was trying to assemble the things he had said. The Sisterhood had some of the Mentats' capabilities, he had observed. A Mentat could come to a qualified conviction without sufficient data. He thought that he would be long out of her reach (or the reach of any other Reverend Mother) before she assembled this data. Then there would be a scrambling for his offspring! They would pick up Dimela for their Breeding Mistresses, of course. And Odrade. She would not escape.

They had the key to the Tleilaxu axlotl tanks, too. It would be only a matter of time now until the Bene Gesserit overcame its scruples and mastered that source of the spice. A human body produced it!

"We're in danger here, then," Lucilla said.

"Some danger, yes. The trouble with the Honored Matres is that they're too wealthy. They make the mistakes of the wealthy."

"Depraved whores!" she said.

"I suggest you get to the entry port," he said. "Odrade will be here soon."

She left him without another word.

"Armor is all out and deployed," the communications officer said.

"Alert Burzmali to be ready for command here," Teg said. "The rest of us will be going out soon."

"You expect all of us to join you?" That was the one who looked for a scapegoat.

"I am going out," Teg said. "I will go alone if necessary. Only those who wish need join me."

After that, all of them would come, he thought. Peer pressure was little understood by anyone except those trained by the Bene Gesserit.

It grew silent in the command station except for the faint hummings and clicks of instruments. Teg fell to thinking about the "depraved whores."

It was not correct to call them depraved, he thought. Sometimes, the supremely rich did become depraved. That came from believing that money (power) could buy anything and everything. And why shouldn't they believe this? They saw it happening every day. It was easy to believe in absolutes.

Hope springs eternal and all of that gornaw!

It was like another faith. Money would buy the impossible.

Then came depravity.

It was not the same for the Honored Matres. They were, somehow, beyond depravity. They had come through it; he could see that. But now they were into something else so far beyond depravity that Teg wondered if he really wanted to know about it.

The knowledge was there, though, inescapable in his new awareness. Not one of those people would hesitate an instant before consigning an entire planet to torture if that meant personal gain. Or if the payoff were some imagined pleasure. Or if the torture produced even a few more days or hours of living.

What pleased them? What gratified? They were like semuta addicts. Whatever simulated pleasure for them, they required more of it every time.

And they know this!

How they must rage inside! Caught in such a trap! They had seen it all and none of it was enough—not good enough nor evil enough. They had entirely lost the knack of moderation.

They were dangerous, though. And perhaps he was wrong about one thing: Perhaps they no longer remembered what it had been like before the awful transformation of that strange tart-smelling stimulant that painted orange in their eyes. Memories of memories could become distorted. Every Mentat was sensitized to this flaw in himself.

"There's the worm!"

It was the communications officer.

Teg swiveled in his chair and looked at the projection, a miniature holo of the exterior to the southwest. The worm with its two tiny dots of human passengers was a distant sliver of wriggling movement.

"Bring Odrade in here alone when they arrive," he said. "Sheeana—that's the young girl—will remain behind to help herd that worm into the hold. It will obey her. Be sure Burzmali is standing ready nearby. We won't have much time for the transfer of command."

When Odrade entered the command station she was still breathing hard and exuding the smells of the desert, a compound of melange, flint, and human perspiration. Teg sat in his chair apparently resting. His eyes remained closed.

Odrade thought she had caught the Bashar in an uncharacteristic attitude of repose, almost pensive. He opened his eyes then and she saw the change about which Lucilla had only been able to blurt a small warning—along with a few hasty words about the ghola's transformation. What was it that had happened to Teg? He was almost posing for her, daring her to see it in him. The chin was firm and held slightly upthrust in his normal attitude of observation. The narrow face with its webwork of age lines had lost none of its alertness. The long, thin nose so characteristic of the Corrinos and Atreides in his ancestry had grown a bit longer with advancing years. But the gray hair remained thick and that small peak at the forehead centered the observing gaze . . .

On his eyes!

"How did you know to meet us here?" Odrade demanded. "We had no idea where the worm was taking us."

"There are very few inhabited places here in the meridian desert," he said. "Gambler's choice. This seemed likely."

Gambler's choice? She knew the Mentat phrase but had never understood it.

Teg lifted himself from his chair. "Take this ship and go to the place you know best," he said.

Chapter House? She almost said it but thought of the others around her, these military strangers Teg had assembled. Who were they? Lucilla's brief explanation did not satisfy.

"We change Taraza's design somewhat," Teg said. "The ghola does not stay. He must go with you."

She understood. They would need Duncan Idaho's new talents to counter the whores. He was no longer merely bait for the destruction of Rakis.

"He will not be able to leave the no-ship's concealment, of course," Teg said.

She nodded. Duncan was not shielded from prescient searchers . . . such as the Guild navigators.

"Bashar!" It was the communications officer. "We've been bleeped by a satellite!"

"All right, you ground hogs!" Teg shouted. "Everybody outside! Get Burzmali in here."

A hatch at the rear of the station flew open. Burzmali lunged through. "Bashar, what are we—"

"No time! Take over!" Teg lifted himself from his command chair and waved for Burzmali to take it. "Odrade here will tell you where to go." On an impulse that he knew was partly vindictive, Teg grasped

Odrade's left arm, leaned close, and kissed her cheek. "Do what you must, daughter," he whispered. "That worm in the hold may soon be the only one in the universe."

Odrade saw it then: Teg knew Taraza's complete design and intended to carry out his Mother Superior's orders to the very end.

"Do what you must." That said it all.

We are not looking at a new state of matter but at a newly recognized relationship between consciousness and matter, which provides a more penetrating insight into the workings of prescience. The oracle shapes a projected inner universe to produce new external probabilities out of forces that are not understood. There is no need to understand these forces before using them to shape the physical universe. Ancient metal workers had no need to understand the molecular and submolecular complexities of their steel, bronze, copper, gold, and tin. They invented mystical powers to describe the unknown while they continued to operate their forges and wield their hammers.

—MOTHER SUPERIOR TARAZA, ARGUMENT IN COUNCIL

The ancient structure in which the Sisterhood secreted its Chapter House, its Archives, and the offices of its most sacrosanct leadership did not just make sounds in the night. The noises were more like signals. Odrade had learned to read those signals over her many years here. That particular sound there, that strained creaking, was a wooden beam in the floor not replaced in some eight hundred years. It contracted in the night to produce those sounds.

She had Taraza's memories to expand on such signals. The memories were not fully integrated; there had been very little time. Here at night in Taraza's old working room, Odrade used a few available moments to continue the integration.

Dar and Tar, one at last.

That was a quite identifiable Taraza comment.

To haunt the Other Memories was to exist on several planes simultaneously, some of them very deep, but Taraza remained near the surface. Odrade allowed herself to sink farther into the multiple existences. Presently, she recognized a self who was currently breathing but remote while others demanded that she plunge into the all-enfolding visions, everything complete with smells, touches, emotions—all of the originals held intact within her own awareness.

It is unsettling to dream another's dreams.

Taraza again.

Taraza who had played such a dangerous game with the future of the entire Sisterhood hanging in the balance! How carefully she had timed the leaking of word to the whores that the Tleilaxu had built dangerous abilities into the ghola. And the attack on the Gammu Keep confirmed that the information had reached its source. The brutal nature of that attack, though, had warned Taraza that she had little time. The whores would be sure to assemble forces for the total destruction of Gammu—just to kill that one ghola.

So much had depended on Teg.

She saw the Bashar there in her own assemblage of Other Memories: the father she had never really known.

I didn't know him at the end, either.

It could be weakening to dig into those memories, but she could not escape the demands of that luring reservoir.

Odrade thought of the Tyrant's words: "The terrible field of my past! Answers leap up like a frightened flock blackening the sky of my inescapable memories."

Odrade held herself like a swimmer balanced just below the water's surface.

I most likely will be replaced, Odrade thought. *I may even be reviled.* Bellonda certainly was not giving easy agreement to the new state of command. No matter. Survival of the Sisterhood was all that should concern any of them.

Odrade floated up out of the Other Memories and lifted her gaze to look across the room into the shadowy niche where the bust of a woman could be discerned in the low light of the room's glowglobes. The bust remained a vague shape in its shadows but Odrade knew that face well: Chenoeh, guardian symbol of Chapter House.

"There but for the grace of God . . ."

Every sister who came through the spice agony (as Chenoeh had not) said or thought that same thing, but what did it really mean? Careful breeding and careful training produced the successful ones in sufficient numbers. Where was the hand of God in that? God certainly was not the worm they had brought from Rakis. Was the presence of God felt only in the successes of the Sisterhood?

I fall prey to the pretensions of my own Missionaria Protectiva!

She knew that these were similar to thoughts and questions that had been heard in this room on countless occasions. Bootless! Still, she could not bring herself to remove that guardian bust from the niche where it had reposed for so long.

I am not superstitious, she told herself. *I am not a compulsive person. This is a matter of tradition. Such things have a value well known to us.*

Certainly, no bust of me will ever be so honored.

She thought of Waff and his Face Dancers dead with Miles Teg in the terrible destruction of Rakis. It did not do to dwell on the bloody attrition being suffered in the Old Empire. Better to think about the muscles of retribution being created by the blundering violence of the Honored Matres.

Teg knew!

The recently concluded Council session had subsided in fatigue without firm conclusions. Odrade counted herself lucky to have diverted attention into a few immediate concerns dear to them all.

The punishments: Those had occupied them for a time. Historical precedents fleshed out the Archival analyses to a satisfying form. Those assemblages of humans who allied themselves with the Honored Matres were in for some shocks.

Ix would certainly overextend itself. They had not the slightest appreciation of how competition from the Scattering would crush them.

The Guild would be shunted aside and made to pay dearly for its melange and its machinery. Guild and Ix, thrown together, would fall together.

The Fish Speakers could be mostly ignored. Satellites of Ix, they were already fading into a past that humans would abandon.

And the Bene Tleilax. Ah, yes, the Tleilaxu. Waff had succumbed to the Honored Matres. He had never admitted it but the truth was plain. *"Just once and with one of my own Face Dancers."*

Odrade smiled grimly, remembering her father's bitter kiss.

I will have another niche made, she thought. *I will commission another bust: Miles Teg, the Great Heretic!*

Lucilla's suspicions about Teg were disquieting, though. Had he been prescient at last and able to see the no-ships? Well, the Breeding Mistresses could explore those suspicions.

"We have laagered up!" Bellonda accused.

They all knew the meaning of that word: they had retreated into a fortress position for the long night of the whores.

Odrade realized she did not much care for Bellonda, the way she laughed occasionally to expose those wide, blunt teeth.

They had discussed the cell samples from Sheeana for a long time. The "proof of Siona" was there. She had the ancestry that shielded her from prescience and could leave the no-ship.

Duncan was an unknown.

Odrade turned her thoughts to the ghola out there in the grounded no-ship. Lifting herself from the chair, she crossed to the dark window and looked in the direction of the distant landing field.

Did they dare risk releasing Duncan from the shielding of that ship? The cell studies said he was a mixture of many Idaho gholas—some descendant of Siona. But what of the taint from the original?

No. He must remain confined.

And what of Murbella?—*pregnant* Murbella? An Honored Matre dishonored.

"The Tleilaxu intended for me to kill the Imprinter," Duncan said.

"Will you try to kill the whore?" That was Lucilla's question.

"She is not an Imprinter," Duncan said.

The Council had discussed at length the possible nature of the bonding between Duncan and Murbella. Lucilla maintained there was no bonding at all, that the two remained wary opponents.

"Best not to risk putting them together."

The sexual prowess of the whores would have to be studied at length, though. Perhaps a meeting between Duncan and Murbella in the no-ship could be risked. With careful protective measures, of course.

Lastly, she thought about the worm in the no-ship's hold—a worm nearing the moment of its metamorphosis. A small earth-dammed basin filled with melange awaited that worm. When the moment came, it would be lured out by Sheeana into the bath of melange and water. The resulting sandtrout could then begin their long transformation.

You were right, father. It was so simple when you looked at it clearly.

No need to seek a desert planet for the worms. The sandtrout would create their own habitat for Shai-hulud. It was not pleasant to think of Chapter House Planet transformed into vast areas of wasteland but it had to be done.

The "Last Will and Testament of Miles Teg," which he had planted in the no-ship's submolecular storage systems, could not be discredited. Even Bellonda agreed to that.

Chapter House required a complete revision of all its historical records. A new look had been demanded of them by what Teg had seen of the Lost Ones—the whores from the Scattering.

"You seldom learn the names of the truly wealthy and powerful. You see only their spokesmen. The political arena makes a few exceptions to this but does not reveal the full power structure."

The Mentat philosopher had chewed deep into everything they accepted and what he disgorged did not agree with Archival dependence upon "our inviolate summations."

We knew it, Miles, we just never faced up to it. We're all going to be digging in our Other Memories for the next few generations.

Fixed data storage systems could not be trusted.

"If you destroy most copies, time will take care of the rest."

How Archives had raged at that telling pronouncement by the Bashar!

"The writing of history is largely a process of diversion. Most historical accounts divert attention from the secret influences around the recorded events."

That was the one that had brought down Bellonda. She had taken it up on her own, admitting: "The few histories that escape this restrictive process vanish into obscurity through obvious processes."

Teg had listed some of the processes: "Destruction of as many copies as possible, burying the too revealing accounts in ridicule, ignoring them in the centers of education, insuring that they are not quoted elsewhere and, in some cases, elimination of the authors."

Not to mention the scapegoat process that brought death to more than one messenger bearing unwelcome news, Odrade thought. She recalled an ancient ruler who kept a pikestaff handy with which to kill messengers who brought bad news.

"We have a good base of information upon which to build a better understanding of our past," Odrade had argued. "We've always known that what was at stake in conflicts was the determination of who would control the wealth or its equivalent."

Maybe it was not a real "noble purpose" but it would do for the time being.

I am avoiding the central issue, she thought.

Something would have to be done about Duncan Idaho and they all knew it.

With a sigh, Odrade summoned a 'thopter and prepared herself for the short trip to the no-ship.

Duncan's prison was at least comfortable, Odrade thought when she entered it. This had been the ship commander's quarters lately occupied by Miles Teg. There were still signs of his presence here—a small holostat projector revealing a scene of his home on Lernaeus; the stately old house, the long lawn, the river. Teg had left a sewing kit behind on a bedside table.

The ghola sat in a sling chair staring at the projection. He looked up listlessly when Odrade entered.

"You just left him back there to die, didn't you?" Duncan asked.

"We do what we must," she said. "And I obeyed his orders."

"I know why you're here," Duncan said. "And you're not going to change my mind. I'm not a damned stud for the witches. You understand me?"

Odrade smoothed her robe and sat on the edge of the bed facing Duncan. "Have you examined the record my father left for us?" she asked.

"Your father?"

"Miles Teg was my father. I commend his last words to you. He was our eyes there at the end. He had to *see* the death on Rakis. The 'mind at its beginning' understood dependencies and key logs."

When Duncan looked puzzled, she explained: "We were trapped too long in the Tyrant's oracular maze."

She saw how he sat up more alertly, the feline movements that spoke of muscles well conditioned to attack.

"There is no way you can escape alive from this ship," she said. "You know why."

"Siona."

"You are a danger to us but we would prefer that you lived a useful life."

"I'm still not going to breed for you, especially not with that little twit from Rakis."

Odrade smiled, wondering how Sheeana would respond to that description.

"You think it's funny?" Duncan demanded.

"Not really. But we'll still have Murbella's child, of course. I guess that will have to satisfy us."

"I've been talking to Murbella on the com," Duncan said. "She thinks she's going to be a Reverend Mother, that you're going to accept her into the Bene Gesserit."

"Why not? Her cells pass the proof of Siona. I think she will make a superb Sister."

"Has she really taken you in?"

"You mean, have we failed to observe that she thinks she will go along with us until she learns our secrets and then she will escape? Oh, we know that, Duncan."

"You don't think she can get away from you?"

"Once we get them, Duncan, we never really lose them."

"You don't think you lost the Lady Jessica?"

"She came back to us in the end."

"Why did you really come out here to see me?"

"I thought you deserved an explanation of the Mother Superior's design. It was aimed at the destruction of Rakis, you see. What she really wanted was the elimination of almost all of the worms."

"Great Gods below! Why?"

"They were an oracular force holding us in bondage. Those pearls of the Tyrant's awareness magnified that hold. He didn't predict events, he created them."

Duncan pointed toward the rear of the ship. "But what about . . ."

"That one? It's just one now. By the time it reaches sufficient numbers to be an influence once more, humankind will have gone its own way beyond him. We'll be too numerous by then, doing too many different things on our own. No single force will rule all of our futures completely, never again."

She stood.

When he did not respond, she said: "Within the imposed limits, which I know you appreciate, please think about the kind of life you want to lead. I promise to help you in any way I can."

"Why would you do that?"

"Because my ancestors loved you. Because my father loved you."

"Love? You witches can't feel love!"

She stared down at him for almost a minute. The bleached hair was growing out dark at the roots and curling once more into ringlets, especially at his neck, she saw.

"I feel what I feel," she said. "And your water is ours, Duncan Idaho."

She saw the Fremen admonition have its effect on him and then turned away and was passed out of the room by the guards.

Before leaving the ship, she went back to the hold and stared down at the quiescent worm on its bed of Rakian sand. Her viewport looked down from some two hundred meters onto the captive. As she looked, she shared a silent laugh with the increasingly integrated Taraza.

We were right and Schwangyu and her people were wrong. We knew he wanted out. He had to want that after what he did.

She spoke aloud in a soft whisper, as much for herself as for the nearby observers stationed there to watch for the moment when metamorphosis began in that worm.

"We have your language now," she said.

There were no words in the language, only a moving, dancing adaptation to a moving, dancing universe. You could only *speak* the language, not translate it. To know the meaning you had to go through the experience and even then the meaning changed before your eyes. "Noble purpose" was, after all, an untranslatable experience. But when she looked down at the rough, heat-immune hide of that worm from the Rakian desert, Odrade knew what she saw: the visible evidence of noble purpose.

Softly, she called down to him: "Hey! Old worm! Was this your design?"

There was no answer but then she had not really expected an answer.

FRANK HERBERT is the bestselling author of the Dune saga. He was born in Tacoma, Washington, and educated at the University of Washington, Seattle. He worked a wide variety of jobs—including TV cameraman, radio commentator, oyster diver, jungle survival instructor, lay analyst, creative writing teacher, reporter, and editor of several West Coast newspapers—before becoming a full-time writer.

In 1952, Herbert began publishing science fiction with "Looking for Something?" in *Startling Stories*. But his emergence as a writer of major stature did not occur until 1965, with the publication of *Dune*. This was followed by *Dune Messiah*, *Children of Dune*, *God Emperor of Dune*, *Heretics of Dune*, and *Chapterhouse: Dune* to complete the bestselling saga. Herbert is also the author of some twenty other books, including *The White Plague*, *The Dosadi Experiment*, and *Destination: Void*. He died in 1986.

CHILDREN OF DUNE

"A major event."

—Los Angeles Times

"Ranging from palace intrigue and desert chases to religious speculation and confrontations with the supreme intelligence of the universe,
there is something here for all science fiction fans."

—Publishers Weekly

"Herbert adds enough new twists and turns to the ongoing saga that
familiarity with the recurring elements brings pleasure."

—Challenging Destiny

GOD EMPEROR OF DUNE

"Rich fare. . . . Heady stuff."

—Los Angeles Times

"A fourth visit to distant Arrakis that is every bit as fascinating as the
other three—every bit as timely."

—Time

"Book four of the Dune series has many of the same strengths as the
previous three, and I was indeed kept up late at night."

—Challenging Destiny

HERETICS OF DUNE

"A monumental piece of imaginative architecture . . . indisputably magical."
—*Los Angeles Herald Examiner*

"Appealing and gripping. . . . Fascinating detail, yet cloaked in mystery and mysticism."
—*The Milwaukee Journal*

"Herbert works wonders with some new speculation and an entirely new batch of characters. He weaves together several fascinating story lines with almost the same mastery as informed *Dune*, and keeps the reader intent on the next revelation or twist."
—*Challenging Destiny*

CHAPTERHOUSE: DUNE

"Compelling . . . a worthy addition to this durable and deservedly popular series."
—*The New York Times*

"The vast and fascinating Dune saga sweeps on—as exciting and gripping as ever."
—*Kirkus Reviews*

THE DUNE CHRONICLES BY FRANK HERBERT

DUNE

DUNE MESSIAH

CHILDREN OF DUNE

GOD EMPEROR OF DUNE

HERETICS OF DUNE

CHAPTERHOUSE: DUNE

OTHER BOOKS BY FRANK HERBERT

THE BOOK OF FRANK HERBERT

DESTINATION: VOID
(revised edition)

DIRECT DESCENT

THE DOSADI EXPERIMENT

EYE

THE EYES OF HEISENBERG

THE GODMAKERS

THE GREEN BRAIN

THE MAKER OF DUNE

THE SANTAROGA BARRIER

SOUL CATCHER

WHIPPING STAR

THE WHITE PLAGUE

THE WORLDS OF FRANK HERBERT

MAN OF TWO WORLDS
(with Brian Herbert)

BOOKS BY FRANK HERBERT AND BILL RANSOM

THE JESUS INCIDENT

THE LAZARUS EFFECT

THE ASCENSION FACTOR

GOD EMPEROR OF
DUNE

BOOK FOUR IN THE DUNE CHRONICLES

FRANK HERBERT

With an Introduction by
BRIAN HERBERT

ACE
NEW YORK

ACE

Published by Berkley

An imprint of Penguin Random House LLC

penguinrandomhouse.com

Copyright © 1981 by Herbert Properties LLC

"Introduction" by Brian Herbert copyright © 2008 by DreamStar, Inc.

Portions of this novel appeared in *Playboy* magazine.

ISBN: 9780593201756

The Library of Congress has cataloged the Ace hardcover edition
of this book as follows:

Herbert, Frank.
God Emperor of Dune / Frank Herbert ; with a new introduction by Brian Herbert.
p. cm.—(The Dune chronicles ; bk. 4)
ISBN 9780441016310
1. Dune (Imaginary place)—Fiction.   I. Title.
PS3558.E63G6 2008
813'.54—dc22
2008025629

G. P. Putnam's Sons Edition / May 1981
Berkley trade paperback edition / April 1982
Berkley edition / May 1983
Ace mass-market edition / June 1987
Ace hardcover edition / September 2008
Ace premium edition / June 2019
Ace trade paperback edition / July 2020

Printed in the United States of America
6th Printing

Cover design and illustration by Jim Tierney
Interior art: Desert Cave © masher/Shutterstock Images
Book design by Kristin del Rosario

To Peggy Rowntree
with love and admiration
and deep appreciation

INTRODUCTION
by Brian Herbert

In the summer of 1980, I was visiting my mother and father at their home in Port Townsend, Washington. On a small table beside my mother's favorite chair, I noticed a draft of *God Emperor of Dune*. She had the manuscript open to page 516, near the conclusion of the novel. When I asked Dad how it was going, he said it was a totally new kind of love story, unlike anything ever written before. When I finally got the opportunity to read the story, I found it was that, and a great deal more.

To understand this complex novel, it is important to realize that *Dune, Dune Messiah,* and *Children of Dune* form a trilogy. The fourth entry in the series, *God Emperor of Dune*, is a bridging work leading to a new trilogy. Before Frank Herbert died in 1986, he wrote the first two books in that trilogy, *Heretics of Dune* and *Chapterhouse: Dune*, and made notes for the third volume, to which he gave the working title *Dune 7*. (In collaboration with Kevin J. Anderson, I later wrote *Dune 7* as two novels: *Hunters of Dune* and *Sandworms of Dune*.)

God Emperor of Dune also marks a change in writing style for the series. The first three novels are filled with action and layers of important messages about politics, philosophy, religion, ecology, women's issues, history, and the very nature of humanity. While *God Emperor* begins with action, and ends with it, there are many pages of dialogue in between. In those pages, there is a great deal of conversation about important, interesting subjects—much of it spewing from the God Emperor, Leto Atreides II. The thoughts are so brilliant, springing as they do from the mind of Frank Herbert, that I scarcely notice the difference in writing style when I'm reading. I like the book very much, and it was my mother's favorite in the series. But it is different, and it marks a change in style that the author carried forward to the next two books in the series, *Heretics of Dune* and *Chapterhouse: Dune*.

Think of the style of *Dune*, with its adventure story following the classical hero's journey of Paul Atreides, and so many important messages layered beneath. The presentation is accomplished so expertly on the pages, so seamlessly, that when you get to the end, you hardly realize you've just learned a great deal about ecology and things that matter to this planet and to all of humankind. You only know that you want to read the book again, spending even more time with Paul Atreides, Duncan Idaho, the Lady Jessica, and the other characters in the incredible Dune universe. Bits and pieces of the story cling to you afterward, luring you back into it. So you return again to page one and continue on. This time you might focus on other aspects, other layers, things you didn't notice before.

God Emperor of Dune is different. When you finish it, you realize that you've just absorbed a large amount of data from a great mind, so much that you need to go back and study the material to see what the author intended. Realize, though, that in this novel Frank Herbert was exploring some of the layers of *Dune*, *Dune Messiah*, and *Children of Dune* that he had already established, taking the dangers of government and organized religion to new levels, merging them, and extrapolating to an extreme, providing a scenario of what it might be like if a holy tyrant led humanity and if that despot could not die. The stakes could not be any higher. And what a fantastic concept, combining human flesh with supernatural elements of nature to create a godhead. A frightening notion—and even more terrifying than the dangers of following a charismatic leader that Frank Herbert wrote about so eloquently in the second and third books of the series.

It is also interesting to note that Frank Herbert often wrote about beings with godlike powers, entities that took on differing forms. In his own *Destination: Void* and its sequel *The Jesus Incident* (cowritten with Bill Ransom), the entity is a supercomputer. In *Whipping Star*, it is a celestial body, a star. In *The Godmakers* and *Dune*, the gods are in human form. In *God Emperor of Dune*, the entity is part mysterious sandworm, part human, a creature that contains a vast storehouse of knowledge.

The God Emperor, Leto Atreides II, is one of the most unusual characters in the annals of science fiction. He has lived for more than 3,500 years and possesses a wisdom that spans time and space. He seems capable of living forever, of leading humankind into the eternal future. For millennia after the events in the novel *Dune*, Leto has enforced a peace—a "Golden Path"—under which he has ensured the continued existence of the human species. As Leto puts it, "The Golden Path . . . is the survival of humankind, nothing more nor less."

But Frank Herbert, who saw the dark side of the hero, also saw the dark side of the perfect civilization. He called this way of thinking "myth-busting" or seeing the "dystopia in the utopia." As a newspaper reporter for many years, he often turned over stones to see what would scurry out. At the University of Washington in Seattle, he taught a political science class about shattering the myth structures under which we live. A modern-day Socrates, he tore into what he called "unexamined linguistic and cultural assumptions."

My father knew how to do his research. Back in the 1950s, he was a speechwriter for a U.S. senator and worked in Washington, D.C. With C-9 security clearance, Frank Herbert had special access to the Legislative Reference Service of the Library of Congress, through which he could use virtually any document or book in the vast library. He just got on the telephone, ordered what he wanted, and presently it arrived in a cart, with blue bookmarks designating the pages that were of interest to him. Notes were included on material available at other government facilities, including the National Archives and the Army Corps of Engineers. If he wanted any of the additional materials, he simply ordered them through the Library of Congress and soon they were in front of him.

A man of boundless energy and enthusiasm, Frank Herbert possessed a mind that went in fifty directions at once. He was always thinking, always reading at every opportunity, always researching something. For each novel he wrote, he first pored over as many books as he could get his hands on about particular subjects, then spoke with scientists, doctors, and other experts. Time was critical to him, and he didn't like to waste a moment of it. Physically and mentally, he went from point A to point B quickly. Sometimes he learned what he needed with a phone call. To see how easy it might be for an unbalanced, dangerous person to obtain the ingredients and materials necessary for recombinant DNA research (for the novel *The White Plague*), Dad acted as if he were a doctor and telephoned medical suppliers.

Frank Herbert was a man full of intriguing ideas, the most interesting person in any room. His personality, like the characters he created in his stories, was larger than life. He had a full, fantastic beard, and with his twinkling eyes, you never quite knew what he would say next. A reviewer for the *New York Times* once quipped that Frank Herbert's head was so overloaded with ideas that it was likely to fall off. In *God Emperor of Dune*, my father described Leto II, who, through genetic processes, had acquired all human information. In "Pack Rat Planet" and *Direct Descent*, he wrote of a vast Galactic Library, a storehouse containing the written wisdom of humankind. Frank Herbert, like Leto II and the Galactic Library, was a repository of incredible, wondrous information. His words captivated millions of people all over the world.

My father respected his readers. He challenged them by using words they might have to look up in the dictionary, and kept them turning the pages with surprising twists and turns of plot and characterization. Who could have predicted that he would turn the hero myth of Paul Atreides upside down in the space of the first two novels in the Dune series, and show a dark path that humanity might find itself on if it followed a charismatic leader? This is a significant message, an urgent social warning that governments and leaders lie.

It is just one of many thought-provoking messages that Frank Herbert layered into his novels beneath the ongoing adventures, causing his readers to think about deep issues. But in his hands, the material never seems oppressive or boring, because he accomplished his art so cleverly, by deftly intertwining the messages with the unfolding action of the series. He was not pedantic, did not preach to his readers. He sought to entertain first, while teaching along the way.

I wrote a comprehensive biography of my father, *Dreamer of Dune*, a book that succeeded in capturing the essence of Frank Herbert. But he was more than any words could possibly describe, even those of a son who loved him. As much as I struggled to understand this complex, great man—and I made significant strides on that journey—I came to realize that he was always a step beyond any attempt to describe him, to capture him on the page. Even in death, he was still moving ahead, eluding discovery. I think about him every day, and about my incredible mother, Beverly Herbert. She understood him better than anyone, and I learned about him through her, as well as through my own observations and conversations I had with him. But often, thinking back, I find myself realizing something new and intriguing about Frank Herbert, something I had not previously noticed or considered. Concerning the spice melange, he wrote in his magnum opus, "It's like life—it presents a different face each time you take it." He was like that himself, different each time you looked at him.

My father's Dune novels are like that as well, revealing something new about the author on each pass through the pages. I like that. In life, Frank Herbert had such tremendous energy that he never walked beside me in the customary fashion of two people; he was always a half step ahead, leading the way. Dan Lodholm, his best friend from childhood, told me something similar. He remembered hikes they took together on the Olympic Peninsula of Washington State in the 1930s, and how he was always looking at the back of Frank Herbert's head, following him on the trail.

Now in *God Emperor of Dune*, we are treated to an intriguing look *inside* the head of Frank Herbert—through his character Leto Atreides II. This is a remarkable novel and another fantastic journey through the unparalleled Dune universe.

BRIAN HERBERT
SEATTLE, WASHINGTON
MAY 8, 2008

Excerpt from the speech by Hadi Benotto announcing the discoveries at Dar-es-Balat on the planet of Rakis:

It not only is my pleasure to announce to you this morning our discovery of this marvelous storehouse containing, among other things, a monumental collection of manuscripts inscribed on ridulian crystal paper, but I also take pride in giving you our arguments for the authenticity of our discoveries, to tell you why we believe we have uncovered the original journals of Leto II, the God Emperor.

First, let me recall to you the historical treasure which we all know by the name of *The Stolen Journals*, those volumes of known antiquity which over the centuries have been so valuable in helping us to understand our ancestors. As you all know, *The Stolen Journals* were deciphered by the Spacing Guild, and the method of the Guild Key was employed to translate these newly discovered volumes. No one denies the antiquity of the Guild Key and it, *and it alone*, translates these volumes.

Second, these volumes were printed by an Ixian dictatel of truly ancient make. *The Stolen Journals* leave no doubt that this was in fact the method employed by Leto II to record his historical observations.

Third, and we believe that this is equal in portent to the actual discovery, there is the storehouse itself. The repository for these *journals* is an undoubted Ixian artifact of such primitive and yet marvelous construction that it is sure to throw new light on the historical epoch known as "The Scattering." As was to be expected, the storehouse was invisible. It was buried far deeper than myth and the Oral History had led us to expect and it emitted radiation and absorbed radiation to simulate the natural character of its surroundings, a mechanical mimesis which is not surprising of itself. What has surprised our engineers, however, is the way this was done with the most rudimentary and truly primitive mechanical skills.

I can see that some of you are as excited by this as we were. We believe we are looking at the first Ixian Globe, the no-room from which all such devices evolved. If it is not actually the first, we believe it must be *one* of the first and embodying the same principles as the first.

Let me address your obvious curiosity by assuring you that we will take you on a brief tour of the storehouse presently. We will ask only that you maintain silence while within the storehouse because our engineers and other specialists are still at work there unraveling the mysteries.

Which brings me to my fourth point, and this may well be the capstone of our discoveries. It is with emotions difficult to describe that I reveal to you now another discovery at this site—namely, actual oral recordings which are labeled as having been made by Leto II in the voice of his father, Paul Muad'Dib. Since authenticated recordings of the God Emperor are lodged in the Bene Gesserit Archives, we have sent a sampling of our recordings, all of which were made on an ancient microbubble system, to the Sisterhood with a formal request that they conduct a comparison test. We have little doubt that the recordings will be authenticated.

Now, please turn your attention to the translated excerpts which were handed to you as you entered. Let me take this opportunity to apologize for their weight. I have heard some of you joking about that. We used ordinary paper for a practical reason—economy. The original volumes are inscribed in symbols so small that they must be magnified substantially before they can be read. In fact, it requires more than forty ordinary volumes of the type you now hold just to reprint the contents of one of the ridulian crystal originals.

If the projector—yes. We are now projecting part of an original page onto the screen at your left. This is from the first page of the first volume. Our translation is on the screens to the right. I call your attention to the internal evidence, the poetic vanity of the words as well as the meaning derived from the translation. The style conveys a personality which is identifiable and consistent. We believe that this could only have been written by someone who had the direct experience of ancestral memories, by someone laboring to share that extraordinary experience of previous lives in a way that could be understood by those not so gifted.

Look now at the actual meaning content. All of the references accord with everything history has told us about the one person whom we believe is the only person who could have written such an account.

We have another surprise for you now. I have taken the liberty of inviting the well-known poet, Rebeth Vreeb, to share the platform with us this morning and to read from this first page a short passage of our translation. It is our observation that, even in translation, these words take on a different character when read aloud. We want to share with you a truly extraordinary quality which we have discovered in these volumes.

Ladies and gentlemen, please welcome Rebeth Vreeb.

From the reading by Rebeth Vreeb:

I assure you that I am the book of fate.

Questions are my enemies. For my questions explode! Answers leap up like a frightened flock, blackening the sky of my inescapable memories. Not one answer, not one suffices.

What prisms flash when I enter the terrible field of my past. I am a chip of shattered flint enclosed in a box. The box gyrates and quakes. I am tossed about in a storm of mysteries. And when the box opens, I return to this presence like a stranger in a primitive land.

Slowly (slowly, I say) I relearn my name.

But that is not to know myself!

This person of my name, this Leto who is the second of that calling, finds other voices in his mind, other names and other places. Oh, I promise you (as I have been promised) that I answer to but a single name. If you say, "Leto," I respond. Sufferance makes this true, sufferance and one thing more:

I hold the threads!

All of them are mine. Let me but imagine a topic—say . . . *men who have died by the sword*—and I have them in all of their gore, every image intact, every moan, every grimace.

Joys of motherhood, I think, and the birthing beds are mine. Serial baby smiles and the sweet cooings of new generations. The first walkings of the toddlers and the first victories of youths brought forth for me to share. They tumble one upon another until I can see little else but sameness and repetition.

"Keep it all intact," I warn myself.

Who can deny the value of such experiences, the worth of learning through which I view each new instant?

Ahhh, but it's the past.

Don't you understand?

It's only the past!

This morning I was born in a yurt at the edge of a horse-plain in a land of a planet which no longer exists. Tomorrow I will be born someone else in another place. I have not yet chosen. This morning, though—ahhh, this life! When my eyes had learned to focus, I looked out at sunshine on trampled grass and I saw vigorous people going about the sweet activities of their lives. Where . . . oh where has all of that vigor gone?

—THE STOLEN JOURNALS

The three people running northward through moon shadows in the Forbidden Forest were strung out along almost half a kilometer. The last runner in the line ran less than a hundred meters ahead of the pursuing D-wolves. The animals could be heard yelping and panting in their eagerness, the way they do when they have the prey in sight.

With First Moon almost directly overhead, it was quite light in the forest and, although these were the higher latitudes of Arrakis, it was still warm from the heat of a summer day. The nightly drift of air from the Last Desert of the Sareer carried resin smells and the damp exhalations of the duff underfoot. Now and again, a breeze from the Kynes Sea beyond the Sareer drifted across the runners' tracks with hints of salt and fishes.

By a quirk of fate, the last runner was called Ulot, which in the Fremen tongue means *"Beloved Straggler."* Ulot was short in stature and with a tendency to fat which had placed an extra dieting burden on him in training for this venture. Even when slimmed down for their desperate run, his face remained round, the large brown eyes vulnerable in that suggestion of too much flesh.

To Ulot it was obvious that he could not run much farther. He panted and wheezed. Occasionally, he staggered. But he did not call out to his companions. He knew they could not help him. All of them had taken the same oath, knowing they had no defenses except the old virtues and Fremen loyalties. This remained true even though everything that once had been Fremen had now a museum quality—rote recitals learned from Museum Fremen.

It was Fremen loyalty that kept Ulot silent in the full awareness of his doom. A fine display of the ancient qualities, and rather pitiful when none of the runners had any but book knowledge and the legends of the Oral History about the virtues they aped.

The D-wolves ran close behind Ulot, giant gray figures almost man-height at the shoulders. They leaped and whined in their eagerness, heads lifted, eyes focused on the moon-betrayed figure of their quarry.

A root caught Ulot's left foot and he almost fell. This gave him renewed energy. He put on a burst of speed, gaining perhaps a wolf-length on his pursuers. His arms pumped. He breathed noisily through his open mouth.

The D-wolves did not change pace. They were silver shadows which went flick-flick through the loud green smells of their forest. They knew they had won. It was a familiar experience.

Again, Ulot stumbled. He caught his balance against a sapling and continued his panting flight, gasping, his legs trembling in rebellion against these demands. No energy remained for another burst of speed.

One of the D-wolves, a large female, moved out on Ulot's left flank. She swerved inward and leaped across his path. Giant fangs ripped Ulot's shoulder and staggered him but he did not fall. The pungency of blood was added to the forest smells. A smaller male caught his right hip and at last Ulot fell, screaming. The pack pounced and his screams were cut off in abrupt finality.

Not stopping to feed, the D-wolves again took up the chase. Their noses probed the forest floor and the vagrant eddies in the air, scenting the warm tracery of two more running humans.

The next runner in the line was named Kwuteg, an old and honorable name on Arrakis, a name from the Dune times. An ancestor had served Sietch Tabr as Master of the Deathstills, but that was more than three thousand years lost in a past which many no longer believed. Kwuteg ran with the long strides of a tall and slender body which seemed perfectly fitted to such exertion. Long black hair streamed back from his aquiline features. As with his companions, he wore a black running suit of tightly knitted cotton. It revealed the workings of his buttocks and stringy thighs, the deep and steady rhythm of his breathing. Only his pace, which was markedly slow for Kwuteg, betrayed the fact that he had injured his right knee coming down from the manmade precipices which girdled the God Emperor's Citadel fortress in the Sareer.

Kwuteg heard Ulot's screams, the abrupt and potent silence, then the renewed chase-yelps of the D-wolves. He tried not to let his mind create the image of another friend being slain by Leto's monster guardians but imagination worked its sorcery on him. Kwuteg thought a curse against the tyrant but wasted no breath to voice it. There remained a chance that he could reach the sanctuary of the Idaho River. Kwuteg knew what his friends thought about him—even Siona. He had always been known as a conservative. Even as a child he had saved his energy until it counted most, parceling out his reserves like a miser.

In spite of the injured knee, Kwuteg increased his pace. He knew the river was near. His injury had gone beyond agony into a steady flame which filled his entire leg and side with its burning. He knew the limits of his endurance. He knew also that Siona should be almost at the water. The fastest runner of them all, she carried the sealed packet and, in it, the things they had stolen from the fortress in the Sareer. Kwuteg focused his thoughts on that packet as he ran.

Save it, Siona! Use it to destroy him!

The eager whining of the D-wolves penetrated Kwuteg's consciousness. They were too close. He knew then that he would not escape.

But Siona must escape!

He risked a backward glance and saw one of the wolves move to flank him. The pattern of their attack plan imprinted itself on his awareness. As the flanking wolf leaped Kwuteg also leaped. Placing a tree between himself and the pack, he ducked beneath the flanking wolf, grasped one of its hind legs in both hands and, without stopping, whirled the captive wolf as a flail which scattered the others. Finding the creature not as heavy as he had expected, almost welcoming the change of action, he flailed his living bludgeon at the attackers in a dervish whirl which brought two of them down in a crash of skulls. But he could not guard every side. A lean male caught him in the back, hurling him against a tree and he lost his bludgeon.

"Go!" he screamed.

The pack bored in and Kwuteg caught the throat of the lean male in his teeth. He bit down with every gram of his final desperation. Wolf blood spurted over his face, blinding him. Rolling without any knowledge of where he went, Kwuteg grappled another wolf. Part of the pack dissolved into a yelping, whirling mob, some turning against their own injured. Most of the pack remained intent on the quarry, though. Teeth ripped Kwuteg's throat from both sides.

Siona, too, had heard Ulot scream, then the unmistakable silence followed by the yelping of the pack as the wolves resumed the chase. Such anger filled her that she felt she might explode with it. Ulot had been included in this venture because of his analytical ability, his way of seeing a whole from only a few parts. It had been Ulot who, taking the inevitable magnifier from his kit, had examined the two strange volumes they had found in with the Citadel's plans.

"I think it's a cipher," Ulot had said.

And Radi, poor Radi who had been the first of their team to die. . . . Radi had said, "We can't afford the extra weight. Throw them away."

Ulot had objected: "Unimportant things aren't concealed this way."

Kwuteg had joined Radi. "We came for the Citadel plans and we have them. Those things are too heavy."

But Siona had agreed with Ulot. "I will carry them."

That had ended the argument.

Poor Ulot.

They had all known him as the worst runner in the team. Ulot was slow in most things, but the clarity of his mind could not be denied.

He is trustworthy.

Ulot *had been* trustworthy.

Siona mastered her anger and used its energy to increase her pace. Trees whipped past her in the moonlight. She had entered that timeless void of the running when there was nothing else but her own movements, her own body doing what it had been conditioned to do.

Men thought her beautiful when she ran. Siona knew this. Her long dark hair was tied tightly to keep it from whipping in the wind of her passage. She had accused Kwuteg of foolishness when he had refused to copy her style.

Where is Kwuteg?

Her hair was not like Kwuteg's. It was that deep brown which is sometimes confused with black, but is not truly black, not like Kwuteg's at all.

In the way genes occasionally do, her features copied those of a long dead ancestor: gently oval and with a generous mouth, eyes of alert awareness above a small nose. Her body had grown lanky from years of running, but it sent strong sexual signals to the males around her.

Where is Kwuteg?

The wolf pack had fallen silent and this filled her with alarm. They had done that before bringing down Radi. It had been the same when they got Setuse.

She told herself the silence could mean other things. Kwuteg, too, was silent . . . and strong. The injury had not appeared to bother him too much.

Siona began to feel pain in her chest, the gasping-to-come which she knew well from the long kilometers of training. Perspiration still poured down her body under the thin, black running garment. The kit, with its precious contents sealed against the river passage ahead, rode high on her back. She thought about the Citadel charts folded there.

Where does Leto hide his hoard of spice?

It had to be somewhere within the Citadel. It had to be. Somewhere in the charts there would be a clue. The melange-spice for which the Bene Gesserit, the Guild and all the others hungered . . . that was a prize worth this risk.

And those two cryptic volumes. Kwuteg had been right in one thing. Ridulian crystal paper was heavy. But she shared Ulot's excitement. Something important was concealed in those lines of cipher.

Once more the eager chase-yelps of the wolves sounded in the forest behind her.

Run, Kwuteg! Run!

Now, just ahead of her through the trees, she could see the wide cleared strip which bordered the Idaho River. She glimpsed moon brightness on water beyond the clearing.

Run, Kwuteg!

She longed for a sound from Kwuteg, any sound. Only the two of them remained now from the eleven who had started the run. Nine had paid for this venture with their lives: *Radi, Aline, Ulot, Setuse, Inineg, Onemao, Hutye, Memar and Oala.*

Siona thought their names and with each sent a silent prayer to the old gods, not to the tyrant Leto. Especially, she prayed to Shai-Hulud.

I pray to Shai-Hulud, who lives in the sand.

Abruptly, she was out of the forest and onto the moon-bright stretch of mowed ground along the river. Straight ahead beyond a narrow shingle of beach, the water beckoned to her. The beach was silver against the oily flow.

A loud yell from back in the trees almost made her falter. She recognized Kwuteg's voice above the wild wolf sounds. Kwuteg called out to her without name, an unmistakable cry with one word containing countless conversations—a message of death and life.

"Go!"

The pack sounds took on a terrible commotion of frenzied yelps, but nothing more from Kwuteg. She knew then how Kwuteg was spending the last energies of his life.

Delaying them to help me escape.

Obeying Kwuteg's cry, she dashed to the river's edge and plunged headfirst into the water. The river was a freezing shock after the heat of the run. It stunned her for a moment and she floundered outward, struggling to swim and regain her breath. The precious kit floated and bumped against the back of her head.

The Idaho River was not wide here, no more than fifty meters, a gently sweeping curve with sandy indentations fringed by roots and shelving banks of lush reeds and grass where the water refused to stay in the straight lines Leto's engineers had designed. Siona was strengthened by the knowledge that the D-wolves had been conditioned to stop at the water. Their territorial boundaries had been drawn, the river on this side and the desert wall on the other side. Still, she swam the last few meters underwater and surfaced in the shadows of a cutbank before turning and looking back.

The wolf pack stood ranged along the bank, all except one which had come down to the river's edge. It leaned forward with its forefeet almost into the flow. She heard it whine.

Siona knew the wolf saw her. No doubt of that. D-wolves were noted for their keen eyesight. There were Gaze Hounds in the ancestry of Leto's forest guardians and he bred the wolves for their eyesight. She wondered if this once the wolves might break through their conditioning. They were mostly sight-hunters. If that one wolf at the river's edge should enter the water, all might follow. Siona held her breath. She felt the dragging of exhaustion. They had come almost thirty kilometers, the last half of it with the D-wolves close behind.

The wolf at the river's edge whined once more, then leaped back up to its companions. At some silent signal, they turned and loped back into the forest.

Siona knew where they would go. D-wolves were allowed to eat anything they brought down in the Forbidden Forest. Everyone knew this. It was why the wolves roamed the forest—the guardians of the Sareer.

"You'll pay for this, Leto," she whispered. It was a low sound, her voice, very close to the quiet rustling of the water against the reeds just behind her. "You'll pay for Ulot, for Kwuteg and for all the others. You'll pay."

She pushed outward gently and drifted with the current until her feet met the first shelving of a narrow beach. Slowly, her body dragged down by fatigue, she climbed from the water and paused to check that the sealed contents of her kit had remained dry. The seal was unbroken. She stared at it a moment in the moonlight, then lifted her gaze to the forest wall across the river.

The price we paid. Ten dear friends.

Tears glimmered in her eyes, but she had the stuff of the ancient Fremen and her tears were few. The venture across the river, directly through the forest while the wolves patrolled the northern boundaries, then across the Last Desert of the Sareer and over the Citadel's ramparts—all of this already was assuming dream proportions in her mind . . . even the flight from the wolves which she had anticipated because it was a certainty that the guardian pack would cross the track of the invaders and be waiting . . . all a dream. It was the past.

I escaped.

She restored the kit with its sealed packet and fastened it once more against her back.

I have broken through your defenses, Leto.

Siona thought then about the cryptic volumes. She felt certain that something hidden in those lines of cipher would open the way for her revenge.

I will destroy you, Leto!

Not *We will destroy you!* That was not Siona's way. She would do it herself.

She turned and strode toward the orchards beyond the river's mowed border. As she walked she repeated her oath, adding to it aloud the old Fremen formula which terminated in her full name:

"Siona Ibn Fuad al-Seyefa Atreides it is who curses you, Leto. You will pay in full!"

The following is from the Hadi Benotto translation of the volumes discovered at Dar-es-Balat:

I was born Leto Atreides II more than three thousand standard years ago, measuring from the moment when I cause these words to be printed. My father was Paul Muad'Dib. My mother was his Fremen consort, Chani. My maternal grandmother was Faroula, a noted herbalist among the Fremen. My paternal grandmother was Jessica, a product of the Bene Gesserit breeding scheme in their search for a male who could share the powers of the Sisterhood's Reverend Mothers. My maternal grandfather was Liet-Kynes, the planetologist who organized the ecological transformation of Arrakis. My paternal grandfather was *The* Atreides, descendant of the House of Atreus and tracing his ancestry directly back to the Greek original.

Enough of these begats!

My paternal grandfather died as many good Greeks did, attempting to kill his mortal enemy, the old Baron Vladimir Harkonnen. Both of them rest uncomfortably now in my ancestral memories. Even my father is not content. I have done what he feared to do and now his shade must share in the consequences.

The Golden Path demands it. And what is the Golden Path? you ask. It is the survival of humankind, nothing more nor less. We who have prescience, we who know the pitfalls in our human futures, this has always been our responsibility.

Survival.

How you feel about this—your petty woes and joys, even your agonies and raptures—seldom concerns us. My father had this power. I have it stronger. We can peer now and again through the veils of Time.

This planet of Arrakis from which I direct my multigalactic Empire is no longer what it was in the days when it was known as Dune. In those days, the entire planet was a desert. Now, there is just this little remnant, my Sareer. No longer does the giant sandworm roam free, producing the spice melange. The spice! Dune was noteworthy only as the source of melange, *the only source*. What an extraordinary substance. No laboratory has ever been able to duplicate it. And it is the most valuable substance humankind has ever found.

Without melange to ignite the linear prescience of Guild Navigators, people cross the parsecs of space only at a snail's crawl. Without melange, the Bene Gesserit cannot endow Truthsayers or Reverend Mothers. Without the geriatric properties of melange, people live and die according to the ancient measure—no more than a hundred years or so. Now, the only spice is held in Guild and Bene Gesserit storehouses, a few small hoards among the remnants of the Great Houses, and my gigantic hoard which they all covet. How they would like to raid me! But they don't dare. They know I would destroy it all before surrendering it.

No. They come hat in hand and petition me for melange. I dole it out as a reward and hold it back as punishment. How they hate that.

It is my power, I tell them. It is my gift.

With it, I create Peace. They have had more than three thousand years of Leto's Peace. It is an enforced tranquility which humankind knew only for the briefest periods before my ascendancy. Lest you have forgotten, study Leto's Peace once more in these, my journals.

I began this account in the first year of my stewardship, in the first throes of my metamorphosis when I was still mostly human, even visibly so. The sandtrout skin which I accepted (and my father refused) and which gave me greatly amplified strength plus virtual immunity from conventional attack and aging—that skin still covered a form recognizably human: two legs, two arms, a human face framed in the scrolled folds of the sandtrout.

Ahhh, that face! I still have it—the only human skin I expose to the universe. All the rest of my flesh has remained covered by the linked bodies of those tiny deep sand vectors which one day can become giant sandworms.

As they will ... someday.

I often think about my final metamorphosis, that *likeness of death.* I know the way it must come but I do not know the moment or the other players. This is the one thing I cannot know. I only know whether the Golden Path continues or ends. As I cause these words to be recorded, the Golden Path continues and for that, at least, I am content.

I no longer feel the sandtrout cilia probing my flesh, encapsulating the water of my body within their placental barriers. We are virtually one body now, they my skin and I the force which moves the whole ... most of the time.

At this writing, the *whole* could be considered rather gross. I am what could be called a pre-worm. My body is about seven meters long and somewhat more than two meters in diameter, ribbed for most of its length, with my Atreides face positioned man-height at one end, the arms and hands (still quite recognizable as human) just below. My legs and feet? Well, they are mostly atrophied. Just flippers, really, and they have wandered back along my body. The whole of me weighs approximately five old tons. These items I append because I know they will have historical interest.

How do I carry this weight around? Mostly on my Royal Cart, which is of Ixian manufacture. You are shocked? People invariably hated and feared the Ixians even more than they hated and feared me. Better the devil you know. And who knows what the Ixians might manufacture or invent? Who knows?

I certainly don't. Not all of it.

But I have a certain sympathy for the Ixians. They believe so strongly in their technology, their science, their machines. Because we believe (no matter the content) we understand each other, the Ixians and I. They make many devices for me and think they earn my gratitude thus. These very words you are reading were printed by an Ixian device, a dictatel it is called. If I cast my thoughts in a particular mode, the dictatel is activated. I merely think in this mode and the words are printed for me on ridulian crystal sheets only one molecule thick. Sometimes I order copies printed on material of lesser permanence. It was two of these latter types that were stolen from me by Siona.

Isn't she fascinating, my Siona? As you come to understand her importance to me, you may even question whether I really would have let her die there in the forest. Have no doubt about it. Death is a very personal thing. I will seldom interfere with it. Never in the case of someone who must be tested as Siona requires. I could let her die at any stage. After all, I could bring up a new candidate in very little time as I measure time.

She fascinates even me, though. I watched her there in the forest. Through my Ixian devices I watched her, wondering why I had not anticipated this venture. But Siona is . . . Siona. That is why I made no move to stop the wolves. It would have been wrong to do that. The D-wolves are but an extension of my purpose and my purpose is to be the greatest predator ever known.

—THE JOURNALS OF LETO II

The following brief dialogue is credited to a manuscript source called "The Welbeck Fragment." The reputed author is Siona Atreides. The participants are Siona herself and her father, Moneo, who was (as all the histories tell us) a majordomo and chief aide to Leto II. It is dated at a time when Siona was still in her teens and was being visited by her father at her quarters in the Fish Speakers' School at the Festival City of Onn, a major population center on the planet now known as Rakis. According to the manuscript identification papers, Moneo had visited his daughter secretly to warn her that she risked destruction.

SIONA: How have you survived with him for so long a time, father? He kills those who are close to him. Everyone knows that.

MONEO: No! You are wrong. He kills no one.

SIONA: You needn't lie about him.

MONEO: I mean it. He kills no one.

SIONA: Then how do you account for the known deaths?

MONEO: It is the Worm that kills. The Worm is God. Leto lives in the bosom of God, but he kills no one.

SIONA: Then how do you survive?

MONEO: I can recognize the Worm. I can see it in his face and in his movements. I know when Shai-Hulud approaches.

SIONA: He is not Shai-Hulud!

MONEO: Well, that's what they called the Worm in the Fremen days.

SIONA: I've read about that. But he is not the God of the desert.

MONEO: Be quiet, you foolish girl! You know nothing of such things.

SIONA: I know that you are a coward.

MONEO: How little you know. You have never stood where I have stood and seen it in his eyes, in the movements of his hands.

SIONA: What do you do when the Worm approaches?

MONEO: I leave.

SIONA: That's prudent. He has killed nine Duncan Idahos that we know about for sure.

MONEO: I tell you he kills no one!

SIONA: What's the difference? Leto or Worm, they are one body now.

MONEO: But they are two separate beings—Leto the Emperor and *The Worm Who Is God.*

SIONA: You're mad!

MONEO: Perhaps. But I do serve God.

I am the most ardent people-watcher who ever lived. I watch them inside me and outside. Past and present can mingle with odd impositions in me. And as the metamorphosis continues in my flesh wonderful things happen to my senses. It's as though I sensed everything in close-up. I have extremely acute hearing and vision, plus a sense of smell extraordinarily discriminating. I can detect and identify pheromones at three parts per million. I know. I have tested it. You cannot hide very much from my senses. I think it would horrify you what I can detect by smell alone. Your pheromones tell me what you are doing or are prepared to do. And gesture and posture! I stared for half a day once at an old man sitting on a bench in Arrakeen. He was a fifth-generation descendant of Stilgar the Naib and did not even know it. I studied the angle of his neck, the skin flaps below his chin, the cracked lips and moistness about his nostrils, the pores behind his ears, the wisps of gray hair which crept from beneath the hood of his antique stillsuit. Not once did he detect that he was being watched. Hah! Stilgar would have known it in a second or two. But this old man was just waiting for someone who never came. He got up finally and tottered off. He was very stiff after all of that sitting. I knew I would never see him in the flesh again. He was that near death and his water was sure to be wasted. Well, that no longer mattered.

—THE STOLEN JOURNALS

Leto thought it the most interesting place in the universe, this place where he awaited the arrival of his current Duncan Idaho. By most human standards, it was a gigantic space, the core of an elaborate series of catacombs beneath his Citadel. Radiating chambers thirty meters high and twenty meters wide ran like spokes from the hub where he waited. His cart had been positioned at the center of the hub in a domed and circular chamber four hundred meters in diameter and one hundred meters high at its tallest point above him.

He found these dimensions reassuring.

It was early afternoon at the Citadel, but the only light in his chamber came from the random drifting of a few suspensor-borne glowglobes tuned into low orange. The light did not penetrate far into the spokes, but Leto's memories told him the exact position of everything there—the water, the bones, the dust of his ancestors and of the Atreides who had lived and died since the Dune times. All of them were here, plus a few containers of melange to create the illusion that this was all of his hoard should it ever come to such an extreme.

Leto knew why the Duncan was coming. Idaho had learned that the Tleilaxu were making another Duncan, another ghola created to the specifications demanded by the God Emperor. This Duncan feared that he was being replaced after almost sixty years of service. It was always something of that nature which began the subversion of the Duncans. A Guild envoy had waited upon Leto earlier to warn that the Ixians had delivered a lasgun to this Duncan.

Leto chuckled. The Guild remained extremely sensitive to anything which might threaten their slender supply of spice. They were terrified at the thought that Leto was the last link with the sandworms which had produced the original stockpiles of melange.

If I die away from water, there will be no more spice—not ever.

That was the Guild's fear. And their historian-accountants assured them Leto sat on the largest store of melange in the universe. This knowledge made the Guild almost reliable as allies.

While he waited, Leto did the hand and finger exercises of his Bene Gesserit inheritance. The hands were his pride. Beneath a gray membrane of sandtrout skin, their long digits and opposable thumbs could be used much as any human hands. The almost useless flippers which once had been his feet and legs were more inconvenience than shame.

He could crawl, roll and toss his body with astonishing speed, but he sometimes fell on the flippers and there was pain.

What was delaying the Duncan?

Leto imagined the man vacillating, staring out a window across the fluid horizon of the Sareer. The air was alive with heat today. Before descending to the crypt, Leto had seen a mirage in the southwest. The heat-mirror tipped and flashed an image across the sand, showing him a band of Museum Fremen trudging past a Display Sietch for the edification of tourists.

It was cool in the crypt, always cool, the illumination always low. Tunnel spokes were dark holes sloping upward and downward in gentle gradients to accommodate the Royal Cart. Some tunnels extended beyond false walls for many kilometers, passages Leto had created for himself with Ixian tools—feeding tunnels and secret ways.

As he contemplated the coming interview, a sense of nervousness began to grow in Leto. He found this an interesting emotion, one he had been known to enjoy. Leto knew that he had grown reasonably fond of the current Duncan. There was a reservoir of hope in Leto that the man would survive the coming interview. Sometimes they did. There was little likelihood the Duncan posed a mortal threat, although this had to be left to such chance as existed. Leto had tried to explain this to one of the earlier Duncans . . . right here in this room.

"You will think it strange that I, with my powers, can speak of luck and chance," Leto had said.

The Duncan had been angry. "You leave nothing to chance! I know you!"

"How naive. Chance is the nature of our universe."

"Not chance! Mischief. And you're the author of mischief!"

"Excellent, Duncan! Mischief is a most profound pleasure. It's in the ways we deal with mischief that we sharpen creativity."

"You're not even human anymore!" Oh, how angry the Duncan had been.

Leto had found his accusation irritating, like a grain of sand in an eye. He held onto the remnants of his once-human self with a grimness which could not be denied, although irritation was the closest he could come to anger.

"Your life is becoming a cliché," Leto had accused.

Whereupon the Duncan had produced a small explosive from the folds of his uniform robe. What a surprise!

Leto loved surprises, even nasty ones.

It is something I did not predict! And he said as much to Duncan, who had stood there oddly undecided now that decision was absolutely demanded of him.

"This could kill you," the Duncan said.

"I'm sorry, Duncan. It will do a small amount of injury, no more."

"But you said you didn't predict this!" The Duncan's voice had grown shrill.

"Duncan, Duncan, it is absolute prediction which equals death to me. How unutterably boring death is."

At the last instant, the Duncan had tried to throw the explosive to one side, but the material in it had been unstable and it had gone off too soon. The Duncan had died. Ahh, well—the Tleilaxu always had another in their axlotl tanks.

One of the drifting glowglobes above Leto began to blink. Excitement gripped him. Moneo's signal! Faithful Moneo had alerted his God Emperor that the Duncan was descending to the crypt.

The door to the human lift between two spoked passages in the northwest arc of the hub swung open. The Duncan strode forth, a small figure at that distance, but Leto's eyes discerned even tiny details—a wrinkle on the uniform elbow which said the man had been leaning somewhere, chin in hand. Yes, there were still the marks of his hand on the chin. The Duncan's odor preceded him: the man was high on his own adrenalin.

Leto remained silent while the Duncan approached, observing details. The Duncan still walked with the spring of youth despite all of his long service. He could thank a minimal ingestion of melange for that. The man wore the old Atreides uniform, black with a golden hawk at the left breast. An interesting statement, that: "I serve the honor of the *old* Atreides!" His hair was still the black cap of *karakul,* the features fixed in stony sharpness with high cheekbones.

The Tleilaxu make their gholas well, Leto thought.

The Duncan carried a thin briefcase woven of dark brown fibers, one he had carried for many years. It usually contained the material upon which he based his reports, but today it bulged with some heavier weight.

The Ixian lasgun.

Idaho kept his attention on Leto's face as he walked. The face remained disconcertingly Atreides, lean features with eyes of total blue which the nervous felt as a physical intrusion. It lurked deep within a gray cowl of sandtrout skin which, Idaho knew, could roll forward protectively in a flickering reflex—a faceblink rather than an eyeblink. The skin was pink within its gray frame. It was difficult avoiding the thought that Leto's face was an obscenity, a lost bit of humanity trapped in something alien.

Stopping only six paces from the Royal Cart, Idaho did not attempt to conceal his angry determination. He did not even think about whether Leto knew of the lasgun. This Imperium had wandered too far from the old Atreides morality, had become an impersonal juggernaut which crushed the innocent in its path. It had to be ended!

"I have come to talk to you about Siona and other matters," Idaho said. He brought the case into position where he could withdraw the lasgun easily.

"Very well." Leto's voice was full of boredom.

"Siona was the only one who escaped, but she still has a base of rebel companions."

"You think I don't know this!"

"I know your dangerous tolerance for rebels! What I don't know is the contents of that package she stole."

"Oh, that. She has the complete plans for the Citadel."

For just a moment, Idaho was Leto's Guard Commander, deeply shocked at such a breach of security.

"You let her escape with that?"

"No, you did."

Idaho recoiled from this accusation. Slowly, the newly resolved assassin in him regained ascendancy.

"Is that all she got?" Idaho asked.

"I had two volumes, copies of my journal, in with the charts. She stole the copies."

Idaho studied Leto's immobile face. "What is in these journals? Sometimes you say it's a diary, sometimes a history."

"A bit of both. You might even call it a textbook."

"Does it bother you that she took these volumes?"

Leto allowed himself a soft smile which Idaho accepted as a negative answer. A momentary tension rippled through Leto's body then as Idaho reached into the slim case. Would it be the weapon or the reports? Although the core of his body possessed a powerful resistance to heat, Leto knew that some of his flesh was vulnerable to lasguns, especially the face.

Idaho brought a report from his case and, even before he began reading from it, the signals were obvious to Leto. Idaho was seeking answers, not providing information. Idaho wanted justification for a course of action already chosen.

"We have discovered a Cult of Alia on Giedi Prime," Idaho said.

Leto remained silent while Idaho recounted the details. *How boring*. Leto let his thoughts wander. The worshippers of his father's long-dead sister served these days only to provide occasional amusement. The Duncans predictably saw such activity as a kind of underground threat.

Idaho finished reading. His agents were thorough, no denying it. Boringly thorough.

"This is nothing more than a revival of Isis," Leto said. "My priests and priestesses will have some sport suppressing this cult and its followers."

Idaho shook his head as though responding to a voice within it.

"The Bene Gesserit knew about the cult," he said.

Now *that* interested Leto.

"The Sisterhood has never forgiven me for taking their breeding program away from them," he said.

"This has nothing to do with breeding."

Leto concealed mild amusement. The Duncans were always so sensitive on the subject of breeding, although some of them occasionally stood at stud.

"I see," Leto said. "Well, the Bene Gesserit are all more than a little insane, but madness represents a chaotic reservoir of surprises. Some surprises can be valuable."

"I fail to see any value in this."

"Do you think the Sisterhood was behind this cult?" Leto asked.

"I do."

"Explain."

"They had a shrine. They called it 'The Shrine of the Crysknife.'"

"Did they now?"

"And their chief priestess was called 'The Keeper of Jessica's Light.' Does that suggest anything?"

"It's lovely!" Leto did not try to conceal his amusement.

"What is lovely about it?"

"They unite my grandmother and my aunt into a single goddess."

Idaho shook his head slowly from side to side, not understanding.

Leto permitted himself a small internal pause, less than a blink. The grandmother-within did not particularly care for this Giedi Prime cult. He was required to wall off her memories and her identity.

"What do you suppose was the purpose of this cult?" Leto asked.

"Obvious. A competing religion to undermine your authority."

"That's too simple. Whatever else they may be, the Bene Gesserit are not simpletons."

Idaho waited for an explanation.

"They want more spice!" Leto said. "More Reverend Mothers."

"So they annoy you until you buy them off?"

"I am disappointed in you, Duncan."

Idaho merely stared up at Leto, who contrived a sigh, a complicated gesture no longer intrinsic to his new form. The Duncans usually were brighter, but Leto supposed that this one's plot had clouded his alertness.

"They chose Giedi Prime as their home," Leto said. "What does that suggest?"

"It was a Harkonnen stronghold, but that's ancient history."

"Your sister died there, a victim of the Harkonnens. It is right that the Harkonnens and Giedi Prime be united in your thoughts. Why did you not mention this earlier?"

"I didn't think it was important."

Leto drew his mouth into a tight line. The reference to his sister had troubled the Duncan. The man knew *intellectually* that he was only the latest in a long line of fleshly revivals, all products of the Tleilaxu axlotl tanks and taken from the original cells at that. The Duncan could not escape his revived memories. He knew that the Atreides had rescued him from Harkonnen bondage.

And whatever else I may be, Leto thought, *I am still Atreides.*

"What're you trying to say?" Idaho demanded.

Leto decided that a shout was required. He let it be a loud one: "The Harkonnens were spice hoarders!"

Idaho recoiled a full step.

Leto continued in a lower voice: "There's an undiscovered melange hoard on Giedi Prime. The Sisterhood was trying to winkle it out with their religious tricks as a cover."

Idaho was abashed. Once it was spoken, the answer appeared obvious.

And I missed it, he thought.

Leto's shout had shaken him back into his role as Commander of the Royal Guard. Idaho knew about the economics of the Empire, simplified in the extreme: no interest charges permitted; cash on the barrelhead. The only coinage bore a likeness of Leto's cowled face: the God Emperor. But it was all based on the spice, a substance whose value, though enormous, kept increasing. A man could carry the price of an entire planet in his hand luggage.

"Control the coinage and the courts. Let the rabble have the rest,"

Leto thought. Old Jacob Broom said it and Leto could hear the old man chortling within. *"Things haven't changed all that much, Jacob."*

Idaho took a deep breath. "The Bureau of the Faith should be notified immediately."

Leto remained silent.

Taking this as a cue to continue, Idaho went on with his reports, but Leto listened with only a fraction of his awareness. It was like a monitoring circuit which only recorded Idaho's words and actions with but an occasional intensification for an internal comment:

And *now* he wants to talk about the Tleilaxu.

That is dangerous ground for you, Duncan.

But this opened up a new avenue for Leto's reflection.

The wily Tleilaxu still produce my Duncans from the original cells. They do a religiously forbidden thing and we both know it. I do not permit the artificial manipulation of human genetics. But the Tleilaxu have learned how I treasure the Duncans as the Commanders of my Guard. I do not think they suspect the amusement value in this. It amuses me that a river now bears the Idaho name where once it was a mountain. That mountain no longer exists. We brought it down to get material for the high walls which girdle my Sareer.

Of course, the Tleilaxu know that I occasionally breed the Duncans back into my own program. The Duncans represent mongrel strength . . . and much more. Every fire must have its damper.

It was my intent to breed this one with Siona, but that may not be possible now.

Hah! He says he wants me to "crack down" on the Tleilaxu. Why will he not ask it straight out? "Are you preparing to replace me?"

I am tempted to tell him.

Once more, Idaho's hand went into the slender pouch. Leto's introspective monitoring did not miss a beat.

The lasgun or more reports? It is more reports.

The Duncan remains wary. He wants not only the assurance that I am ignorant of his intent but more "proofs" that I am unworthy of his loyalty. He hesitates in a prolonged fashion. He always has. I have told him enough times that I will not use my prescience to predict the moment of my exit from this ancient form. But he doubts. He always was a doubter.

This cavernous chamber drinks up his voice and, were it not for my sensitivity, the dankness here would mask the chemical evidence of his fears. I fade his voice out of immediate awareness. What a bore this Duncan has become. He is recounting the history, the history of Siona's rebellion, no doubt leading up to personal admonitions about her latest escapade.

"It's not an ordinary rebellion," *he says.*

That brings me back! Fool. All rebellions are ordinary and an ultimate bore. They are copied out of the same pattern, one much like another. The driving force is adrenalin addiction and the desire to gain personal power. All rebels are closet aristocrats. That's why I can convert them so easily.

Why do the Duncans never really hear me when I tell them about this? I have had the argument with this very Duncan. It was one of our earliest confrontations and right here in the crypt.

"The art of government requires that you never give up the initiative to radical elements," *he said.*

How pedantic. Radicals crop up in every generation and you must not try to prevent this. That's what he means by "give up the initiative." *He wants to crush them, suppress them, control them, prevent them. He is living proof that there is little difference between the police mind and the military mind.*

I told him, "Radicals are only to be feared when you try to suppress them. You must demonstrate that you will use the best of what they offer."

"They are dangerous. They are dangerous!" *He thinks that by repeating he creates some kind of truth.*

Slowly, step by step, I lead him through my method and he even gives the appearance of listening.

"This is their weakness, Duncan. Radicals always see matters in terms which are too simple—black and white, good and evil, them and us. By addressing complex matters in that way, they rip open a passage for chaos. The art of government as you call it, is the mastery of chaos."

"No one can deal with every surprise."

"Surprise? Who's talking about surprise? Chaos is no surprise. It has predictable characteristics. For one thing, it carries away order and strengthens the forces at the extremes."

"Isn't that what radicals are trying to do? Aren't they trying to shake things up so they can grab control?"

"That's what they think they're doing. Actually, they're creating new extremists, new radicals and they are continuing the old process."

"What about a radical who sees the complexities and comes at you that way?"

"That's no radical. That's a rival for leadership."

"But what do you do?"

"You co-opt them or kill them. That's how the struggle for leadership originated, at the grunt level."

"Yes, but what about messiahs?"

"Like my father?"

The Duncan does not like this question. He knows that in a very special way I am my father. He knows I can speak with my father's voice and persona, that the memories are precise, never edited and inescapable.

Reluctantly, he says: "Well . . . if you want."

"Duncan, I am all of them and I know. There has never been a truly selfless rebel, just hypocrites—conscious hypocrites or unconscious hypocrites, it's all the same."

That stirs up a small hornet's nest among my ancestral memories. Some of them have never given up the belief that they and they alone held the key to all of humankind's problems. Well, in that, they are like me. I can sympathize even while I tell them that failure is its own demonstration.

I am forced to block them off, though. There's no sense dwelling on them. They now are little more than poignant reminders . . . as is this Duncan who stands in front of me with his lasgun. . . .

Great Gods below! He has caught me napping. He has the lasgun in his hand and it is pointed at my face.

"You, Duncan? Have you betrayed me, too?"

Et tu, Brute?

Every fiber of Leto's awareness came to full alert. He could feel his body twitching. The worm-flesh had a will of its own.

Idaho spoke with derision: "Tell me, Leto: How many times must I pay the debt of loyalty?"

Leto recognized the inner question: *"How many of me have there been?"* The Duncans always wanted to know this. Every Duncan asked it and no answer satisfied. They doubted.

In his saddest Muad'Dib voice, Leto asked: "Do you take no pride in my admiration, Duncan? Haven't you ever wondered what it is about you that makes me desire you as my constant companion through the centuries?"

"You know me to be the ultimate fool!"

"Duncan!"

The voice of an angry Muad'Dib could always be counted on to shatter Idaho. Despite the fact that Idaho knew no Bene Gesserit had ever mastered the powers of Voice as Leto had mastered them, it was predictable that he would dance to this one voice. The lasgun wavered in his hand.

That was enough. Leto was off the cart in a hurtling roll. Idaho had never seen him leave the cart this way, had not even suspected it could happen. For Leto, there were only two requirements—a real threat which the worm-body could sense and the release of that body. The rest was automatic and the speed of it always astonished even Leto.

The lasgun was his major concern. It could scratch him badly, but few understood the abilities of the pre-worm body to deal with heat.

Leto struck Idaho while rolling and the lasgun was deflected as it was fired. One of the useless flippers which had been Leto's legs and feet sent a shocking burst of sensations crashing into his awareness. For an instant, there was only pain. But the worm-body was free to act and reflexes ignited a violent paroxysm of flopping. Leto heard bones cracking. The lasgun was thrown far across the floor of the crypt by a spasmodic jerk of Idaho's hand.

Rolling off of Idaho, Leto poised himself for a renewed attack but there was no need. The injured flipper still sent pain signals and he sensed that the tip of the flipper had been burned away. The sandtrout skin already had sealed the wound. The pain had eased to an ugly throbbing.

Idaho stirred. There could be little doubt that he had been mortally injured. His chest was visibly crushed. There was obvious agony when he tried to breathe, but he opened his eyes and stared up at Leto.

The persistence of these mortal possessions! Leto thought.

"Siona," Idaho gasped.

Leto saw the life leave him then.

Interesting, Leto thought. *Is it possible that this Duncan and Siona . . . No! This Duncan always displayed a true sneering disdain for Siona's foolishness.*

Leto climbed back onto the Royal Cart. That had been a close one. There could be little doubt that the Duncan had been aiming for the *brain.* Leto was always aware that his hands and feet were vulnerable, but he had allowed no one to learn that what had once been his brain was no longer directly associated with his face. It was not even a brain of human dimensions anymore, but had spread in nodal congeries throughout his body. He had told this to no one but his journals.

Oh, the landscapes I have seen! And the people! The far wanderings of the Fremen and all the rest of it. Even back through the myths to Terra. Oh, the lessons in astronomy and intrigue, the migrations, the disheveled flights, the leg-aching and lung-aching runs through so many nights on all of those cosmic specks where we have defended our transient possession. I tell you we are a marvel and my memories leave no doubt of this.

—THE STOLEN JOURNALS

The woman working at the small wall desk was too big for the narrow chair on which she perched. Outside, it was midmorning, but in this windowless room deep beneath the city of Onn there was but a single glowglobe high in a corner. It had been tuned to warm yellow but the light failed to dispel the gray utility of the small room. Walls and ceiling were covered by identical rectangular panels of dull gray metal.

There was only one other piece of furniture, a narrow cot with a thin pallet covered by a featureless gray blanket. It was obvious that neither piece of furniture had been designed for the occupant.

She wore a one-piece pajama suit of dark blue which stretched tightly across her wide shoulders as she hunched over the desk. The glowglobe illuminated closely cropped blonde hair and the right side of her face, emphasizing the square block of jaw. The jaw moved with silent words as her thick fingers carefully depressed the keys of a thin keyboard on the desk. She handled the machine with a deference which had originated as awe and moved reluctantly into fearsome excitement. Long familiarity with the machine had eliminated neither emotion.

As she wrote, words appeared on a screen concealed within the wall rectangle exposed by the downward folding of the desk.

"Siona continues actions which predict violent attack on Your Holy Person," she wrote. "Siona remains unswerving in her avowed purpose. She told me today that she will give copies of the stolen books to groups whose loyalty to You cannot be trusted. The named recipients are the Bene Gesserit, the Guild and the Ixians. She says the books contain Your enciphered words and, by this gift, she seeks help in translating Your Holy Words.

"Lord, I do not know what great revelations may be concealed on those pages but if they contain anything of threat to Your Holy Person, I beg You to relieve me from my vow of obedience to Siona. I do not understand why You made me take this vow, but I fear it.

"I remain Your worshipful servant, Nayla."

The chair creaked as Nayla sat back and thought about her words. The room fell into the almost soundless withdrawal of thick insulation. There was only Nayla's faint breathing and a distant throbbing of machinery felt more in the floor than in the air.

Nayla stared at her message on the screen. Destined only for the eyes of the God Emperor, it required more than holy truthfulness. It demanded a deep candor which she found draining. Presently, she nodded and pressed the key which would encode the words and prepare them for transmission. Bowing her head, she prayed silently before concealing the desk within the wall. These actions, she knew, transmitted the message. God himself had implanted a physical device within her head, swearing her to secrecy and warning her that there might come a time when he would speak to her through the thing within her skull. He had never done this. She suspected that Ixians had fashioned the device. It had possessed some of their *look*. But God Himself had done this thing and she could ignore the suspicion that there might be a *computer* in it, that it might be prohibited by the Great Convention.

"Make no device in the likeness of the mind!"

Nayla shuddered. She stood then and moved her chair to its regular position beside the cot. Her heavy, muscular body strained against the thin blue garment. There was a steady deliberation about her, the actions of someone constantly adjusting to great physical strength. She turned at the cot and studied the place where the desk had been. There was only a rectangular gray panel like all the others. No bit of lint, no strand of hair, nothing caught there to reveal the panel's secret.

Nayla took a deep, restorative breath and let herself out of the room's only door into a gray passage dimly lighted by widely spaced white glowglobes. The machinery sounds were louder here. She turned left and a few minutes later was with Siona in a somewhat larger room, a table at its center upon which things stolen from the Citadel had been arranged. Two silvery glowglobes illuminated the scene—Siona seated at the table, with an assistant named Topri standing beside her.

Nayla nurtured grudging admiration for Siona, but Topri, there was a man worthy of nothing except active dislike. He was a nervous fat man with bulging green eyes, a pug nose and thin lips above a dimpled chin. Topri squeaked when he spoke.

"Look here, Nayla! Look what Siona has found pressed between the pages of these two books."

Nayla closed and locked the room's single door.

"You talk too much, Topri," Nayla said. "You're a blurter. How could you know if I was alone in the passage?"

Topri paled. An angry scowl settled onto his face.

"I'm afraid she's right," Siona said. "What made you think I wanted Nayla to know about my discovery?"

"You trust her with everything!"

Siona turned her attention to Nayla. "Do you know why I trust you, Nayla?" The question was asked in a flat, unemotional voice.

Nayla put down a sudden surge of fear. Had Siona discovered her secret?

Have I failed my Lord?

"Have you no response to my question?" Siona asked.

"Have I ever given you cause to do otherwise?" Nayla asked.

"That's not a sufficient cause for trust," Siona said. "There's no such thing as perfection—not in human or machine."

"Then why *do* you trust me?"

"Your words and your actions always agree. It's a marvelous quality. For instance, you don't like Topri and you never try to conceal your dislike."

Nayla glanced at Topri, who cleared his throat.

"I don't trust him," Nayla said.

The words popped into her mind and out of her mouth without reflection. Only after she had spoken did Nayla realize the true core of her dislike: Topri would betray anyone for personal gain.

Has he found me out?

Still scowling, Topri said, "I am not going to stand here and accept your abuse." He started to leave but Siona held up a restraining hand. Topri hesitated.

"Although we speak the old Fremen words and swear our loyalty to each other, that is not what holds us together," Siona said. "Everything is based on performance. That is all I measure. Do you understand, both of you?"

Topri nodded automatically, but Nayla shook her head from side to side.

Siona smiled up at her. "You don't always agree with my decisions, do you, Nayla?"

"No." The word was forced from her.

"And you have never tried to conceal your disagreement, yet you always obey me. Why?"

"That is what I have sworn to do."

"But I have said this is not enough."

Nayla knew she was perspiring, knew this was revealing, but she could not move. *What am I to do? I swore to God that I would obey Siona but I cannot tell her this.*

"You must answer my question," Siona said. "I command it."

Nayla caught her breath. This was the dilemma she had most feared. There was no way out. She said a silent prayer and spoke in a low voice.

"I have sworn to God that I will obey you."

Siona clapped her hands in glee and laughed.

"I knew it!"

Topri chuckled.

"Shut up, Topri," Siona said. "I am trying to teach *you* a lesson. You don't believe in anything, not even in yourself."

"But I . . ."

"Be still, I say! Nayla believes. I believe. This is what holds us together. Belief."

Topri was astonished. "Belief? You believe in . . ."

"Not in the God Emperor, you fool! We believe that a higher power will settle with the tyrant worm. We are that higher power."

Nayla took a trembling breath.

"It's all right, Nayla," Siona said. "I don't care where you draw your strength, just as long as you believe."

Nayla managed a smile, then grinned. She had never been more profoundly stirred by the wisdom of her Lord. *I may speak the truth and it works only for my God!*

"Let me show you what I've found in these books," Siona said. She gestured at some sheets of ordinary paper on the table. "Pressed between the pages."

Nayla stepped around the table and looked down at it.

"First, there's this." Siona held up an object which Nayla had not noticed. It was a thin strand of something . . . and what appeared to be a . . .

"A flower?" Nayla asked.

"This was between two pages of paper. On the paper was written this."

Siona leaned over the table and read: "A strand of Ghanima's hair with a starflower blossom which she once brought me."

Looking up at Nayla, Siona said: "Our God Emperor is revealed as a sentimentalist. That is a weakness I had not expected."

"Ghanima?" Nayla asked.

"His sister! Remember your Oral History."

"Oh . . . oh, yes. The Prayer to Ghanima."

"Now, listen to this." Siona took up another sheet of paper and read from it.

> "*The sand beach as gray as a dead cheek,*
> *A green tideflow reflects cloud ripples;*
> *I stand on the dark wet edge.*
> *Cold foam cleanses my toes.*
> *I smell driftwood smoke.*"

Again, Siona looked up at Nayla. "This is identified as 'Words I wrote when told of Ghani's death.' What do you think of that?"

"He . . . he loved his sister."

"Yes! He is *capable* of love. Oh, yes! We have him now."

Sometimes I indulge myself in safaris which no other being may take. I strike inward along the axis of my memories. Like a schoolchild reporting on a vacation trip, I take up my subject. Let it be . . . female intellectuals! I course backward into the ocean which is my ancestors. I am a great winged fish in the depths. The mouth of my awareness opens and I scoop them up! Sometimes . . . sometimes I hunt out specific persons recorded in our histories. What a private joy to relive the life of such a one while I mock the academic pretensions which supposedly formed a biography.

—THE STOLEN JOURNALS

Moneo descended to the crypt with sad resignation. There was no escaping the duties required of him now. The God Emperor required a small passage of time to grieve the loss of another Duncan . . . but then life went on . . . and on . . . and on. . . .

The lift slid silently downward with its superb Ixian dependability. Once, just once, the God Emperor had cried out to his majordomo: "Moneo! Sometimes I think *you* were made by the Ixians!"

Moneo felt the lift stop. The door opened and he looked out across the crypt at the shadowy bulk on the Royal Cart. There was no indication that Leto had noticed the arrival. Moneo sighed and began the long walk through the echoing gloom. There was a body on the floor near the cart. No need for *déjà vu*. This was merely familiar.

Once, in Moneo's early days of service, Leto had said: "You don't like this place, Moneo. I can see that."

"No, Lord."

With just a little prodding of memory, Moneo could hear his own voice in that naive past. And the voice of the God Emperor responding: "You don't think of a mausoleum as a comforting place, Moneo. I find it a source of infinite strength."

Moneo remembered that he had been anxious to get off this topic. "Yes, Lord."

Leto had persisted: "There are only a few of my ancestors here. The water of Muad'Dib is here. Ghani and Harq al-Ada are here, of course, but they're not *my* ancestors. No, if there's any true crypt of *my* ancestors, *I* am that crypt. This is mostly the Duncans and the products of my breeding program. You'll be here someday."

Moneo found that these memories had slowed his pace. He sighed and moved a bit faster. Leto could be violently impatient on occasion but there was still no sign from him. Moneo did not take this to mean that his approach went unobserved.

Leto lay with his eyes closed and only his other senses to record Moneo's progress across the crypt. Thoughts of Siona had been occupying Leto's attention.

Siona is my ardent enemy, he thought. *I do not need Nayla's words to confirm this. Siona is a woman of action. She lives on the surface of enormous energies which fill me with fantasies of delight. I cannot contemplate those living energies without a feeling of ecstasy. They are my reason for being, the justification for everything I have ever done . . . even for the corpse of this foolish Duncan in front of me now.*

Leto's ears told him that Moneo had not yet crossed half the distance to the Royal Cart. The man moved slower and slower, then picked up his pace.

What a gift Moneo has given me in this daughter, Leto thought. *Siona is fresh and precious. She is the new while I am a collection of the obsolete, a relic of the damned, of the lost and strayed. I am the waylaid pieces of history which sank out of sight in all of our pasts. Such an accumulation of riffraff has never before been imagined.*

Leto paraded the past within him then to let them observe what had happened in the crypt.

The minutiae are mine!

Siona, though . . . Siona was like a clean slate upon which great things might yet be written.

I guard that slate with infinite care. I am preparing it, cleansing it.

What did the Duncan mean when he called out her name?

Moneo approached the cart diffidently yet consummately aware. Surely Leto did not sleep.

Leto opened his eyes and looked down as Moneo came to a stop near the corpse. At this moment, Leto found the majordomo a delight to observe. Moneo wore a white Atreides uniform with no insignia, a subtle comment. His face, almost as well known as Leto's, was all the insignia he needed. Moneo waited patiently. There was no change of expression on his flat, even features. His thick, sandy hair lay in a neat, equally divided part. Deep within his gray eyes there was that look of directness which went with knowledge of great personal power. It was a look which he modified only in the God Emperor's presence, and sometimes not even there. Not once did he glance toward the body on the crypt's floor.

When Leto continued silent, Moneo cleared his throat, then: "I am saddened, Lord."

Exquisite! Leto thought. *He knows I feel true remorse about the Duncans. Moneo has seen their records and has seen enough of them dead. He knows that only nineteen Duncans died what people usually refer to as natural deaths.*

"He had an Ixian lasgun," Leto said.

Moneo's gaze went directly to the gun on the floor of the crypt off to his left, demonstrating that he already had seen it. He returned his attention to Leto, sweeping a glance down the length of the great body.

"You are injured, Lord?"

"Inconsequential."

"But he hurt you."

"Those flippers are useless to me. They will be entirely gone within another two hundred years."

"I will dispose of the Duncan's body personally, Lord," Moneo said.

"Is there . . ."

"The piece of me he burned away is entirely ash. We will let it blow away. This is a fitting place for ashes."

"As my Lord says."

"Before you dispose of the body, disable the lasgun and keep it where I can present it to the Ixian ambassador. As for the Guildsman who warned us about it, present him *personally* with ten grams of spice. Oh—and our priestesses on Giedi Prime should be alerted to a hidden store of melange there, probably old Harkonnen contraband."

"What do you wish done with it when it's found, Lord?"

"Use a bit of it to pay the Tleilaxu for the new ghola. The rest of it can go into our stores here in the crypt."

"Lord." Moneo acknowledged the orders with a nod, a gesture which was not quite a bow. His gaze met Leto's.

Leto smiled. He thought: *We both know that Moneo will not leave without addressing directly the matter which most concerns us.*

"I have seen the report on Siona," Moneo said.

Leto's smile widened. Moneo was such a pleasure in these moments. His words conveyed many things which did not require open discussion between them. His words and actions were in precise alignment, carried on the mutual awareness that he, of course, spied on everything. Now, there was a natural concern for his daughter, but he wished it understood that his concern for the God Emperor remained paramount. From his own traverse through a similar evolution, Moneo knew with precision the delicate nature of Siona's present fortunes.

"Have I not created her, Moneo?" Leto asked. "Have I not controlled the conditions of her ancestry and her upbringing?"

"She is my only daughter, my only child, Lord."

"In a way, she reminds me of Harq al-Ada," Leto said. "There doesn't appear to be much of Ghani in her, although that has to be there. Perhaps she harks back to our ancestors in the Sisterhood's breeding program."

"Why do you say that, Lord?"

Leto reflected. Was there need for Moneo to know this peculiar thing about his daughter? Siona could fade from the prescient view at times. The Golden Path remained, but Siona faded. Yet . . . she was not prescient. She was a unique phenomenon . . . and if she survived . . . Leto decided he would not cloud Moneo's efficiency with unnecessary information.

"Remember your own past," Leto said.

"Indeed, Lord! And she has such a potential, so much more than I ever had. But that makes her dangerous, too."

"And she will not listen to you," Leto said.

"No, but I have an agent in her rebellion."

That will be Topri, Leto thought.

It required no prescience to know that Moneo would have an agent in place. Ever since the death of Siona's mother, Leto had known with increasing sureness the course of Moneo's actions. Nayla's suspicions pinpointed Topri. And now, Moneo paraded his fears and actions, offering them as the price of his daughter's continued safety.

How unfortunate he fathered only the one child on that mother.

"Recall how I treated you in similar circumstances," Leto said. "You know the demands of the Golden Path as well as I do."

"But I was young and foolish, Lord."

"Young and brash, never foolish."

Moneo managed a tight smile at this compliment, his thoughts leaning more and more toward the belief that he now understood Leto's intentions. *The dangers, though!*

Feeding his belief, Leto said: "You know how much I enjoy surprises."

That is true, Leto thought. *Moneo does know it. But even while Siona surprises me, she reminds me of what I fear most—the sameness and boredom which could break the Golden Path. Look at how boredom put*

*me temporarily in the Duncan's power! Siona is the contrast by which I
know my deepest fears. Moneo's concern for me is well grounded.*

"My agent will continue to watch her new companions, Lord," Moneo said. "I do not like them."

"Her companions? I myself had such companions once long ago."

"Rebellious, Lord? You?" Moneo was genuinely surprised.

"Have I not proved a friend of rebellion?"

"But, Lord . . ."

"The aberrations of our past are more numerous than you may think!"

"Yes, Lord." Moneo was abashed, yet still curious. And he knew that the God Emperor sometimes waxed loquacious after the death of a Duncan. "You must have seen many rebellions, Lord."

Involuntarily, Leto's thoughts sank into the memories aroused by these words.

"Ahhh, Moneo," he muttered. "My travels in the ancestral mazes have memorized uncounted places and events which I never desire to see repeated."

"I can imagine your inward travels, Lord."

"No, you cannot. I have seen peoples and planets in such numbers that they lose meaning even in imagination. Ohhh, the landscapes I have passed. The calligraphy of alien roads glimpsed from space and imprinted upon my innermost sight. The eroded sculpture of canyons and cliffs and galaxies has imprinted upon me the certain knowledge that I am a mote."

"Not you, Lord. Certainly not you."

"Less than a mote! I have seen people and their fruitless societies in such repetitive posturings that their nonsense fills me with boredom, do you hear?"

"I did not mean to anger my Lord." Moneo spoke meekly.

"You don't anger me. Sometimes you irritate me, that is the extent of it. You cannot imagine what I have seen—caliphs and mjeeds, rakahs, rajas and bashars, kings and emperors, primitos and presidents—I've seen them all. Feudal chieftains, every one. Every one a little pharaoh."

"Forgive my presumption, Lord."

"Damn the Romans!" Leto cried.

He spoke it inwardly to his ancestors: *"Damn the Romans!"*

Their laughter drove him from the inward arena.

"I don't understand, Lord," Moneo ventured.

"That's true. You don't understand. The Romans broadcast the pharaonic disease like grain farmers scattering the seeds of next season's harvest—Caesars, kaisers, tsars, imperators, caseris . . . palatos . . . damned pharaohs!"

"My knowledge does not encompass all of those titles, Lord."

"I may be the last of the lot, Moneo. Pray that this is so."

"Whatever my Lord commands."

Leto stared down at the man. "We are myth-killers, you and I, Moneo. That's the dream we share. I assure you from a God's Olympian perch that government is a shared myth. When the myth dies, the government dies."

"Thus you have taught me, Lord."

"That man-machine, the Army, created our present dream, my friend."

Moneo cleared his throat.

Leto recognized the small signs of the majordomo's impatience.

Moneo understands about armies. He knows it was a fool's dream that armies were the basic instrument of governance.

As Leto continued silent, Moneo crossed to the lasgun and retrieved it from the crypt's cold floor. He began disabling it.

Leto watched him, thinking how this tiny scene encapsulated the essence of the Army myth. The Army fostered technology because the power of machines appeared so obvious to the shortsighted.

That lasgun is no more than a machine. But all machines fail or are superceded. Still, the Army worships at the shrine of such things—both fascinated and fearful. Look at how people fear the Ixians! In its guts, the Army knows it is the Sorcerer's Apprentice. It unleashes technology and never again can the magic be stuffed back into the bottle.

I teach them another magic.

Leto spoke to the hordes within then:

"You see? Moneo has disabled the deadly instrument. A connection broken here, a small capsule crushed there."

Leto sniffed. He smelled the esters of a preservative oil riding on the stink of Moneo's perspiration.

Still speaking inwardly, Leto said: *"But the genie is not dead. Technology breeds anarchy. It distributes these tools at random. And with them goes the provocation for violence. The ability to make and use savage destroyers falls inevitably into the hands of smaller and smaller groups until at last the group is a single individual."*

Moneo returned to a point below Leto, holding the disabled lasgun casually in his right hand. "There is talk on Parella and the planets of Dan about another jihad against such things as this."

Moneo lifted the lasgun and smiled, signaling that he knew the paradox in such empty dreams.

Leto closed his eyes. The hordes within wanted to argue, but he shut them off, thinking: *Jihads create armies. The Butlerian Jihad tried to rid our universe of machines which simulate the mind of man. The Butlerians left armies in their wake and the Ixians still make questionable devices . . . for which I thank them. What is anathema? The motivation to ravage, no matter the instruments.*

"It happened," he muttered.

"Lord?"

Leto opened his eyes. "I will go to my tower," he said. "I must have more time to mourn my Duncan."

"The new one is already on his way here," Moneo said.

You, the first person to encounter my chronicles for at least four thousand years, beware. Do not feel honored by your primacy in reading the revelations of my Ixian storehouse. You will find much pain in it. Other than the few glimpses required to assure me that the Golden Path continued, I never wanted to peer beyond those four millennia. Therefore, I am not sure what the events in my journals may signify to your times. I only know that my journals have suffered oblivion and that the events which I recount have undoubtedly been submitted to historical distortion for eons. I assure you that the ability to view our futures can become a bore. Even to be thought of as a god, as I certainly was, can become ultimately boring. It has occurred to me more than once that holy boredom is good and sufficient reason for the invention of free will.

—INSCRIPTION ON THE STOREHOUSE AT DAR-ES-BALAT

I am Duncan Idaho.

That was about all he wanted to know for sure. He did not like the Tleilaxu explanations, their *stories*. But then the Tleilaxu had always been feared. Disbelieved and feared.

They had brought him down to the planet on a small Guild shuttle, arriving at the dusk line with a green glimmer of sun corona along the horizon as they dipped into the shadow. The spaceport had not looked at all like anything he remembered. It was larger and with a ring of strange buildings.

"Are you sure this is Dune?" he had asked.

"Arrakis," his Tleilaxu escort had corrected him.

They had sped him in a sealed groundcar to this building somewhere within a city they called Onn, giving the *"n"* sound a strange rising nasal inflection. The room in which they left him was about three meters square, a cube really. There was no sign of glowglobes, but the place was filled with warm yellow light.

I am a ghola, he told himself.

That had been a shock, but he had to believe it. To find himself living when he knew he had died, that was proof enough. The Tleilaxu had taken cells from his dead flesh and they had grown a bud in one of their axlotl tanks. That bud had become this body in a process which had made him feel at first an alien in his own flesh.

He looked down at the body. It was clothed in dark brown trousers and jacket of a coarse weave which irritated his skin. Sandals protected his feet. Except for the body, that was all they had given him, a parsimony which said something about the real Tleilaxu character.

There was no furniture in the room. They had let him in through a single door which had no handle on the inside. He looked up at the ceiling and around at the walls, at the door. Despite the featureless character of the place, he felt that he was being watched.

"Women of the Imperial Guard will come for you," they had said. Then they had gone away, smiling slyly among themselves.

Women *of the Imperial Guard?*

The Tleilaxu escort had taken sadistic delight in exposing their shape-changing abilities. He had not known from one minute to the next what new form the plastic flow of their flesh would present.

Damned Face Dancers!

They had known all about him, of course, had known how much the Shape Changers disgusted him.

What could he trust if it came from Face Dancers? Very little. Could anything they said be believed?

My name. I know my name.

And he had his memories. They had shocked the identity back into him. Gholas were supposed to be incapable of recovering the original identity. But the Tleilaxu had done it and he was forced to believe because he understood how it had been done.

In the beginning, he knew, there had been the fully formed ghola, adult flesh without name or memories—a palimpsest upon which the Tleilaxu could write almost anything they wished.

"You are Ghola," they had said. That had been his only name for a long time. Ghola had been taken like a malleable infant and conditioned to kill a particular man—a man so like the original Paul Muad'Dib he had served and adored that Idaho now suspected it might have been another ghola. But if that were true, where had they obtained the original cells?

Something in the Idaho cells had rebelled at killing an Atreides. He had found himself standing with a knife in one hand, the bound form of the pseudo-Paul staring up at him in angry terror.

Memories had gushered into his awareness. He remembered Ghola and he remembered Duncan Idaho.

I am Duncan Idaho, swordmaster of the Atreides.

He clung to this memory as he stood in the yellow room.

I died defending Paul and his mother in a cave-sietch beneath the sands of Dune. I have been returned to that planet, but Dune is no more. Now it is only Arrakis.

He had read the truncated history which the Tleilaxu provided, but he did not believe it. *More than thirty-five hundred years?* Who could believe his flesh existed after such a time? Except . . . with the Tleilaxu it was possible. He had to believe his own senses.

"There have been many of you," his instructors had said.

"How many?"

"The Lord Leto will provide that information."

The Lord Leto?

The Tleilaxu history said this Lord Leto was Leto II, grandson of the Leto whom Idaho had served with fanatical devotion. But this second Leto (so the history said) had become something . . . something so strange that Idaho despaired of understanding the transformation.

How could a human slowly turn into a sandworm? How could any thinking creature live more than three thousand years? Not even the wildest projections of geriatric spice allowed such a lifespan.

Leto II, the God Emperor?

The Tleilaxu history was not to be believed!

Idaho remembered a strange child—twins, really: Leto and Ghanima, Paul's children, the children of Chani, who had died delivering them. The Tleilaxu history said Ghanima had died after a relatively normal life, but the God Emperor Leto lived on and on and on. . . .

"He is a tyrant," Idaho's instructors had said. "He has ordered us to produce you from our axlotl tanks and to send you into his service. We do not know what has happened to your predecessor."

And here I am.

Once more, Idaho let his gaze wander around the featureless walls and ceiling.

The faint sound of voices intruded upon his awareness. He looked at the door. The voices were muted, but at least one of them sounded female.

Women of the Imperial Guard?

The door swung inward on noiseless hinges. Two women entered. The first thing to catch his attention was the fact that one of the women wore a mask, a cibus hood of shapeless, light-drinking black. She would see him clearly through the hood, he knew, but her features would never reveal themselves, not even to the most subtle instruments of penetration. The hood said that the Ixians or their inheritors were still at work in the Imperium. Both women wore one-piece uniforms of rich blue with the Atreides hawk in red braid at the left breast.

Idaho studied them as they closed the door and faced him.

The masked woman had a blocky, powerful body. She moved with the deceptive care of a professional muscle fanatic. The other woman was graceful and slender with almond eyes in sharp, high-boned features. Idaho had the feeling that he had seen her somewhere, but he could not fix the memory. Both women carried needle knives in hip sheaths. Something about their movements told Idaho these women would be extremely competent with such weapons.

The slender one spoke first.

"My name is Luli. Let me be the first to address you as Commander. My companion must remain anonymous. Our Lord Leto has commanded it. You may address her as Friend."

"Commander?" he asked.

"It is the Lord Leto's wish that you command his Royal Guard," Luli said.

"That so? Let's go talk to him about it."

"Oh, no!" Luli was visibly shocked. "The Lord Leto will summon you when it is time. For now, he wishes us to make you comfortable and happy."

"And I must obey?"

Luli merely shook her head in puzzlement.

"Am I a slave?"

Luli relaxed and smiled. "By no means. It's just that the Lord Leto has many great concerns which require his personal attention. He must make time for you. He sent us because he was concerned about his Duncan Idaho. You have been a long time in the hands of the dirty Tleilaxu."

Dirty Tleilaxu, Idaho thought.

That, at least, had not changed.

He was concerned, though, by a particular reference in Luli's explanation.

"*His* Duncan Idaho?"

"Are you not an Atreides warrior?" Luli asked.

She had him there. Idaho nodded, turning his head slightly to stare at the enigmatic masked woman.

"Why are you masked?"

"It must not be known that I serve the Lord Leto," she said. Her voice was a pleasant contralto, but Idaho suspected that this, too, was masked by the cibus hood.

"Then why are you here?"

"The Lord Leto trusts me to determine if you have been tampered with by the dirty Tleilaxu."

Idaho tried to swallow in a suddenly dry throat. This thought had occurred to him several times aboard the Guild transport. If the Tleilaxu could condition a ghola to attempt the murder of a dear friend, what else might they plant in the psyche of the regrown flesh?

"I see that you have thought about this," the masked woman said.

"Are you a mentat?" Idaho asked.

"Oh, no!" Luli interrupted. "The Lord Leto does not permit the training of mentats."

Idaho glanced at Luli, then returned his attention to the masked woman. *No mentats.* The Tleilaxu history had not mentioned that interesting fact. Why would Leto prohibit mentats? Surely, the human mind trained in the super abilities of computation still had its uses. The Tleilaxu had assured him that the Great Convention remained in force and that mechanical computers were still anathema. Surely, these women would know that the Atreides themselves had used mentats.

"What is your opinion?" the masked woman asked. "Have the dirty Tleilaxu tampered with your psyche?"

"I don't . . . think so."

"But you are not certain?"

"No."

"Do not fear, Commander Idaho," she said. "We have ways of making sure and ways of dealing with such problems should they arise. The dirty Tleilaxu have tried it only once and they paid dearly for their mistake."

"That's reassuring. Did the Lord Leto send me any messages?"

Luli spoke up: "He told us to assure you that he still loves you as the Atreides have always loved you." She was obviously awed by her own words.

Idaho relaxed slightly. As an old Atreides hand, superbly trained by them, he had found it easy to determine several things from this encounter. These two had been heavily conditioned to a fanatic obedience. If a cibus mask could hide the identity of that woman, there had to be many more whose bodies were very similar. All of this spoke of dangers around Leto which still required the old and subtle services of spies and an imaginative arsenal of weapons.

Luli looked at her companion. "What say you, Friend?"

"He may be brought to the Citadel," the masked woman said. "This is not a good place. Tleilaxu have been here."

"A warm bath and change of clothing would be pleasant," Idaho said.

Luli continued to look at her Friend. "You are certain?"

"The wisdom of the Lord cannot be questioned," the masked woman said.

Idaho did not like the sound of fanaticism in this *Friend's* voice, but he felt secure in the integrity of the Atreides. They could appear cynical and cruel to outsiders and enemies, but to their own people they were just and they were loyal. Above all else, the Atreides were loyal to their own.

And I am one of theirs, Idaho thought. *But what happened to the* me *that I am replacing?* He felt strongly that these two would not answer this question.

But Leto will.

"Shall we go?" he asked. "I'm anxious to wash the stink of the dirty Tleilaxu off me."

Luli grinned at him.

"Come. I shall bathe you myself."

Enemies strengthen you.

Allies weaken.

I tell you this in the hope that it will help you understand why I act as I do in the full knowledge that great forces accumulate in my Empire with but one wish—the wish to destroy me. You who read these words may know full well what actually happened, but I doubt that you understand it.

—THE STOLEN JOURNALS

The ceremony of "Showing" by which the rebels began their meetings dragged on interminably for Siona. She sat in the front row and looked everywhere but at Topri, who was conducting the ceremony only a few paces away. This room in the service burrows beneath Onn was one they had never used before but it was so like all of their other meeting places that it could have been used as a standard model.

Rebel Meeting Room—Class B, she thought.

It was officially designated as a storage chamber and the fixed glowglobes could not be tuned away from their blank white glaring. The room was about thirty paces long and slightly less in width. It could be reached only through a labyrinthine series of similar chambers, one of which was conveniently stocked with a supply of stiff folding chairs intended for the small sleeping chambers of the service personnel. Nineteen of Siona's fellow rebels now occupied these chairs around her, with a few empty for any latecomers who might still make the meeting.

The time had been set between the midnight and morning shifts to mask the flow of extra people in the service warrens. Most of the rebels wore energy-worker disguises—thin gray disposable trousers and jackets. Some few, including Siona, were garbed in the green of machinery inspectors.

Topri's voice was an insistent monotone in the room. He did not squeak at all while conducting the ceremony. In fact, Siona had to admit he was rather good at it, especially with new recruits. Since Nayla's flat statement that she did not trust the man, though, Siona had looked at Topri in a different way. Nayla could speak with a cutting naiveté which pulled away masks. And there were things that Siona had learned about Topri since that confrontation.

Siona turned at last and looked at the man. The cold silvery light did not help Topri's pale skin. He used a copy of a crysknife in the ceremony, a contraband copy bought from the Museum Fremen. Siona recalled the transaction as she looked at the blade in Topri's hands. It had been Topri's idea, and she had thought it a good one at the time. He had led her to the rendezvous in a hovel on the city's outskirts, leaving Onn just at dusk. They had waited well into the night until darkness could mask the Museum Fremen's coming. Fremen were not supposed to leave their sietch quarters without a special dispensation from the God Emperor.

She had almost given up on him when the Fremen arrived, slipping in out of the night, his escort left behind to guard the door. Topri and Siona had been waiting on a crude bench against a dank wall of the absolutely plain room. The only light had come from a dim yellow torch supported on a stick driven into the crumbling mud wall.

The Fremen's first words had filled Siona with misgivings.

"Have you brought the money?"

Both Topri and Siona had risen at his entry. Topri did not appear bothered by the question. He tapped the pouch beneath his robe, making it jingle.

"I have the money right here."

The Fremen was a wizened figure, crabbed and bent, wearing a copy of the old Fremen robes and some glistening garment underneath, probably their version of a stillsuit. His hood was drawn forward, shading his features. The torchlight sent shadows dancing across his face.

He peered first at Topri, then at Siona before removing an object wrapped in cloth from beneath his robe.

"It is a true copy, but it is made of plastic," he said. "It will not cut cold grease."

He pulled the blade from its wrappings then and held it up.

Siona, who had seen crysknives only in museums and in the rare old visual recordings of her family's archives, had found herself oddly gripped by the sight of the blade in this setting. She felt something atavistic working on her and imagined this poor Museum Fremen with his plastic crysknife as a real Fremen of the old days. The thing he held was suddenly a silver-bladed crysknife shimmering in the yellow shadows.

"I guarantee the authenticity of the blade from which we copied it," the Fremen said. He spoke in a low voice, somehow made menacing by its lack of emphasis.

Siona heard it then, the way he carried his venom in a sleeve of soft vowels and she was suddenly alerted.

"Try treachery and we will hunt you down like vermin," she said.

Topri shot a startled glance at her.

The Museum Fremen appeared to shrivel, drawing in upon himself. The blade trembled in his hand, but his gnome fingers still curled inward around it as though clasping a throat.

"Treachery, Lady? Oh, no. But it occurred to us that we asked too little for this copy. Poor as it is, making it and selling it this way puts us in dreadful peril."

Siona glared at him, thinking of the old Fremen words from the Oral History: *"Once you acquire a marketplace soul, the* suk *is the totality of existence."*

"How much do you want?" she demanded.

He named a sum twice his original figure.

Topri gasped.

Siona looked at Topri. "Do you have that much?"

"Not quite, but we agreed on . . ."

"Give him what you have, all of it," Siona said.

"All of it?"

"Isn't that what I said? Every coin in that bag." She faced the Museum Fremen. "You will accept this payment." It was not a question and the old man heard her correctly. He wrapped the blade in its cloth and passed it to her.

Topri handed over the pouch of coins, muttering under his breath.

Siona addressed herself to the Museum Fremen. "We know your name. You are Teishar, aide to Garun of Tuono. You have a *suk* mentality and you make me shudder at what Fremen have become."

"Lady, we all have to live," he protested.

"You are not alive," she said. "Be gone!"

Teishar had turned and scurried away, clutching the money pouch close to his chest.

Memory of that night did not sit well in Siona's mind as she watched Topri wave the crysknife copy in their rebel ceremony. *We're no better than Teishar*, she thought. *A copy is worse than nothing.* Topri brandished the stupid blade over his head as he neared the ceremony's conclusion.

Siona looked away from him and stared at Nayla seated off to her left. Nayla was looking first one direction and now another. She paid special attention to the new cadre of recruits at the back of the room. Nayla did not give her trust easily. Siona wrinkled her nose as a stirring of the air brought the smell of lubricants. The depths of Onn always smelled dangerously *mechanical*! She sniffed. And this room! She did not like their meeting place. It could easily be a trap. Guards could seal off the outer corridors and send in armed searchers. This could be too easily the place where their rebellion ended. Siona was made doubly uneasy by the fact that this room had been Topri's choice.

One of Ulot's few mistakes, she thought. Poor dead Ulot had approved Topri's admission to the rebellion.

"He is a minor functionary in city services," Ulot had explained. "Topri can find us many useful places to meet and arm ourselves."

Topri had reached almost the end of his ceremony. He placed the knife in an ornate case and put the case on the floor beside him.

"My face is my pledge," he said. He turned his profile to the room, first one side and then the other. "I show my face that you may know me anywhere and know that I am one of you."

Stupid ceremony, Siona thought.

But she dared not break the pattern of it. And when Topri pulled a black gauze mask from a pocket and placed it over his head, she took out her own mask and donned it. Everyone in the room did the same thing. There was a stirring around the room now. Most of the people here had been alerted that Topri had brought a special visitor. Siona secured her mask's tie behind her neck. She was anxious to see this visitor.

Topri moved to the room's one door. There was a clattering bustle as everyone stood and the chairs were folded and stacked against the wall opposite the door. At a signal from Siona, Topri tapped three times on the door panel, waited for a two-count, then tapped four times.

The door opened and a tall man in a dark brown official singlet slipped into the room. He wore no mask, his face open for all of them to see—thin and imperious with a narrow mouth, a skinny blade of a nose, dark brown eyes deeply set under bushy brows. It was a face recognized by most of the room's occupants.

"My friends," Topri said, "I present Iyo Kobat, Ambassador from Ix."

"Ex-Ambassador," Kobat said. His voice was guttural and tightly controlled. He took a position with his back to the wall facing the masked people in the room. "I have this day received orders from our God Emperor to leave Arrakis in disgrace."

"Why?"

Siona snapped the question at him without formality.

Kobat jerked his head around, a quick movement which fixed his gaze on her masked face. "There has been an attempt on the God Emperor's life. He traced the weapon to me."

Siona's companions opened a space between her and the ex-Ambassador, clearly signaling that they deferred to her.

"Then why didn't he kill you?" she demanded.

"I think he is telling me that I am not worth killing. There is also the fact that he uses me now to carry a message to Ix."

"What message?" Siona moved through the cleared space to stop within two paces of Kobat. She recognized the sexual alertness in him as he studied her body.

"You are Moneo's daughter," he said.

Soundless tension exploded across the room. Why did he reveal that he recognized her? Who else did he recognize here? Kobat did not appear the fool. Why had he done this?

"Your body, your voice and your manner are well known here in Onn," he said. "That mask is a foolishness."

She ripped the mask from her head and smiled at him. "I agree. Now answer my question."

She heard Nayla move up close on her left; two more aides chosen by Nayla came up beside her.

Siona saw the moment of realization come over Kobat—his death if he failed to satisfy her demands. His voice did not lose its tight control but he spoke slower, choosing his words more carefully.

"The God Emperor has told me that he knows about an agreement between Ix and the Guild. We are attempting to make a mechanical amplifier of . . . those Guild navigational talents which presently rely on melange."

"In this room we call him the Worm," Siona said. "What would your Ixian machine do?"

"You are aware that Guild Navigators require the spice before they can *see* the safe path to traverse?"

"You would replace the navigators with a machine?"

"It may be possible."

"What message do you carry to your people concerning this machine?"

"I am to tell my people that they may continue the project only if they send him daily reports on their progress."

She shook her head. "He needs no such reports! That's a stupid message."

Kobat swallowed, no longer concealing nervousness.

"The Guild and the Sisterhood are excited by our project," he said. "They are participating."

Siona nodded once. "And they pay for their participation by sharing spice with Ix."

Kobat glared at her. "It's expensive work and we need the spice for comparative testing by Guild Navigators."

"It is a lie and a cheat," she said. "Your device will never work and the Worm knows it."

"How dare you accuse us of . . ."

"Be still! I have just told you the real message. The Worm is telling you Ixians to continue cheating the Guild and the Bene Gesserit. It amuses him."

"It could work!" Kobat insisted.

She merely smiled at him. "Who tried to kill the Worm?"

"Duncan Idaho."

Nayla gasped. There were other small signs of surprise around the room, a frown, an indrawn breath.

"Is Idaho dead?" Siona asked.

"I presume so, but the . . . ahhh, Worm refuses to confirm it."

"Why do you presume him dead?"

"The Tleilaxu have sent another Idaho ghola."

"I see."

Siona turned and signaled to Nayla, who went to the side of the room and returned with a slim package wrapped in pink Suk paper, the kind of paper shopkeepers used to enclose small purchases. Nayla handed the package to Siona.

"This is the price of our silence," Siona said, extending the package to Kobat. "This is why Topri was permitted to bring you here tonight."

Kobat took the package without removing his attention from her face.

"Silence?" he asked.

"We undertake not to inform the Guild and Sisterhood that you are cheating them."

"We are not cheat . . ."

"Don't be a fool!"

Kobat tried to swallow in a dry throat. Her meaning had become plain to him: true or not, if the rebellion spread such a story it would be believed. It was "common sense" as Topri was fond of saying.

Siona glanced at Topri who stood just behind Kobat. No one joined this rebellion for reasons of "common sense." Did Topri not realize that his "common sense" might betray him? She returned her attention to Kobat.

"What's in this package?" he asked.

Something in the way he asked it told Siona he already knew.

"That is something I am sending to Ix. You will take it there for me. That is copies of two volumes we removed from the Worm's fortress."

Kobat stared down at the package in his hands. It was obvious that he wanted to drop the thing, that his venture into rebellion had loaded him with a burden more deadly than he had expected. He shot a scowling glance at Topri which said as though he had spoken it: *Why didn't you warn me?*

"What . . ." He brought his gaze back to Siona, cleared his throat. "What's in these . . . volumes?"

"Your people may tell us that. We think they are the Worm's own words, written in a cipher which we cannot read."

"What makes you think we . . ."

"You Ixians are clever at such things."

"And if we fail?"

She shrugged. "We will not blame you for that. However, should you use those volumes for any other purpose or fail to report a success fully . . ."

"How can anyone be sure we . . ."

"We will not depend only on you. Others will get copies. I think the Sisterhood and the Guild will not hesitate to try deciphering those volumes."

Kobat slipped the package under his arm and pressed it against his body.

"What makes you think the . . . the Worm doesn't know about your intentions . . . even about this meeting?"

"I think he knows many such things, that he may even know who took those volumes. My father believes he is truly prescient."

"Your father believes the Oral History!"

"Everyone in this room believes it. The Oral History does not disagree with the Formal History on important matters."

"Then why doesn't the Worm act against you?"

She pointed to the package under Kobat's arm. "Perhaps the answer is in there."

"Or you and these cryptic volumes are no real threat to him!" Kobat was not concealing his anger. He did not like being forced into decisions.

"Perhaps. Tell me why you mentioned the Oral History."

Once more, Kobat heard the menace.

"It says the Worm is incapable of human emotions."

"That is not the reason," she said. "You will get one more chance to tell me the reason."

Nayla moved two steps closer to Kobat.

"I . . . I was told to review the Oral History before coming here, that your people . . ." He shrugged.

"That we chant it?"

"Yes."

"Who told you this?"

Kobat swallowed, cast a fearful glance at Topri, then back to Siona.

"Topri?" Siona asked.

"I thought it would help him to understand us," Topri said.

"And you told him the name of your leader," Siona said.

"He already knew!" Topri's voice had found its squeak.

"What particular parts of the Oral History were you told to review?" Siona asked.

"The . . . uhhh, the Atreides line."

"And now you think you know why people join me in rebellion."

"The Oral History tells exactly how he treats everyone in the Atreides line!" Kobat said.

"He gives us a little rope and then he hauls us in?" Siona asked. Her voice was deceptively flat.

"That's what he did with your own father," Kobat said.

"And now he's letting *me* play at rebellion?"

"I'm just a messenger," Kobat said. "If you kill me, who will carry your message?"

"Or the message of the Worm," Siona said.

Kobat remained silent.

"I do not think you understand the Oral History," Siona said. "I think also you do not know the Worm very well, nor do you understand his messages."

Kobat's face flushed with anger. "What's to prevent you from becoming like all the rest of the Atreides, a nice obedient part of . . ." Kobat broke off, aware suddenly of what anger had made him say.

"Just another recruit for the Worm's inner circle," Siona said. "Just like the Duncan Idahos?"

She turned and looked at Nayla. The two aides, Anouk and Taw, became suddenly alert, but Nayla remained impassive.

Siona nodded once to Nayla.

As they were sworn to do, Anouk and Taw moved to positions blocking the door. Nayla went around to stand at Topri's shoulder.

"What's . . . what's happening?" Topri asked.

"We wish to know everything of importance that the ex-Ambassador can share with us," Siona said. "We want the entire message."

Topri began to tremble. Perspiration started from Kobat's forehead. He glanced once at Topri, then returned his attention to Siona. That one glance was like a veil pulled aside for Siona to peer into the relationship between these two.

She smiled. This merely confirmed what she had already learned.

Kobat became very still.

"You may begin," Siona said.

"I . . . what do you . . ."

"The Worm gave you a private message for your masters. I will hear it."

"He . . . he wants an extension for his cart."

"Then he expects to grow longer. What else?"

"We are to send him a large supply of ridulian crystal paper."

"For what purpose?"

"He never explains his demands."

"This smacks of things he forbids to others," she said.

Kobat spoke bitterly. "He never forbids himself anything!"

"Have you made forbidden toys for him?"

"I do not know."

He's lying, she thought, but she chose not to pursue this. It was enough to know the existence of another chink in the Worm's armor.

"Who will replace you?" Siona asked.

"They are sending a niece of Malky," Kobat said. "You may remember that he . . ."

"We remember Malky," she said. "Why does a niece of Malky become the new Ambassador?"

"I don't know. But it was ordered even before the Go . . . the Worm dismissed me."

"Her name?"

"Hwi Noree."

"We will cultivate Hwi Noree," Siona said. "You were not worth cultivating. This Hwi Noree may be something else. When do you return to Ix?"

"Immediately after the Festival, the first Guild ship."

"What will you tell your masters?"

"About what?"

"My message!"

"They will do as you ask."

"I know. You may go, ex-Ambassador Kobat."

Kobat almost collided with the door guards in his haste to leave. Topri made to follow him, but Nayla caught Topri's arm and held him. Topri swept a fearful glance across Nayla's muscular body, then looked at Siona, who waited for the door to shut behind Kobat before speaking.

"The message was not merely to the Ixians, but to us as well," she said. "The Worm challenges us and tells us the rules of the combat."

Topri tried to wrest his arm from Nayla's grip. "What do you . . ."

"Topri!" Siona said. "I, too, can send a message. Tell my father to inform the Worm that we accept."

Nayla released his arm. Topri rubbed the place where she had gripped him. "Surely you don't . . ."

"Leave while you can and never come back," Siona said.

"You can't possibly mean that you sus . . ."

"I told you to leave! You are clumsy, Topri. I have been in the Fish Speaker schools for most of my life. They taught me to recognize clumsiness."

"Kobat is leaving. What harm was there in . . ."

"He not only knew me, he knew what I had stolen from the Citadel! But he did *not* know that I would send that package to Ix with him. Your actions have told me that the Worm wants me to send those volumes to Ix!"

Topri backed away from Siona toward the door. Anouk and Taw opened a passage for him, swung the door wide. Siona followed him with her voice.

"Do not argue that it was the Worm who spoke of me and my package to Kobat! The Worm does not send clumsy messages. Tell him I said that!"

Some say I have no conscience. How false they are, even to themselves. I am the only conscience which has ever existed. As wine retains the perfume of its cask, I retain the essence of my most ancient genesis, and that is the seed of conscience. That is what makes me holy. I am God because I am the only one who really knows his heredity!

—THE STOLEN JOURNALS

The Inquisitors of Ix having assembled in the Grand Palais with the candidate for Ambassador to the Court of the Lord Leto, the following questions and answers were recorded:

INQUISITOR: You indicate that you wish to speak to us of the Lord Leto's motives. Speak.

HWI NOREE: Your Formal Analyses do not satisfy the questions I would raise.

INQUISITOR: What questions?

HWI NOREE: I ask myself what would motivate the Lord Leto to accept this hideous transformation, this worm-body, this loss of his humanity? You suggest merely that he did it for power and for long life.

INQUISITOR: Are those not enough?

HWI NOREE: Ask yourselves if one of you would make such payment for so paltry a return.

INQUISITOR: From your infinite wisdom then, tell us why the Lord Leto chose to become a worm.

HWI NOREE: Does anyone here doubt his ability to predict the future?

INQUISITOR: Now then! Is that not payment enough for his transformation?

HWI NOREE: But he already had the prescient ability as did his father before him. No! I propose that he made this desperate choice because he saw in our future something that only such a sacrifice would prevent.

INQUISITOR: What was this peculiar thing which only he saw in our future?

HWI NOREE: I do not know, but I propose to discover it.

INQUISITOR: You make the tyrant appear a selfless servant of the people!

HWI NOREE: Was that not a prominent characteristic of his Atreides Family?

INQUISITOR: So the official histories would have us believe.

HWI NOREE: The Oral History affirms it.

INQUISITOR: What other good character would you give to the tyrant Worm?

HWI NOREE: *Good* character, sirra?

INQUISITOR: Character, then?

HWI NOREE: My Uncle Malky often said that the Lord Leto was given to moods of great tolerance for selected companions.

INQUISITOR: Other companions he executes for no apparent reason.

HWI NOREE: I think there are reasons and my Uncle Malky deduced some of those reasons.

INQUISITOR: Give us one such deduction.

HWI NOREE: Clumsy threats to his person.

INQUISITOR: *Clumsy* threats now!

HWI NOREE: And he does not tolerate pretensions. Recall the execution of the historians and the destruction of their works.

INQUISITOR: He does not want the truth known!

HWI NOREE: He told my Uncle Malky that they lied about the past. And mark you! Who would know this better than he? We all know the subject of his introversion.

INQUISITOR: What proof have we that all of his ancestors live in him?

HWI NOREE: I will not enter that bootless argument. I will merely say that I believe it on the evidence of my Uncle Malky's belief, and his reasons for that belief.

INQUISITOR: We have read your uncle's reports and interpret them otherwise. Malky was overly fond of the Worm.

HWI NOREE: My uncle accounted him the most supremely artful diplomat in the Empire, a master conversationalist and expert in any subject you could name.

INQUISITOR: Did your uncle not speak of the Worm's brutality?

HWI NOREE: My uncle judged him ultimately civilized.

INQUISITOR: I asked about brutality.

HWI NOREE: Capable of brutality, yes.

INQUISITOR: Your uncle feared him.

HWI NOREE: The Lord Leto lacks all innocence and naiveté. He is to be feared only when he pretends these traits. *That* was what my uncle said.

INQUISITOR: Those were his words, yes.

HWI NOREE: More than that! Malky said, "The Lord Leto delights in the surprising genius and diversity of humankind. He is my favorite companion."

INQUISITOR: Giving us the benefit of your supreme wisdom, how do you interpret these words of your uncle?

HWI NOREE: Do not mock me!

INQUISITOR: We do not mock. We seek enlightenment.

HWI NOREE: These words of Malky, and many other things that he wrote directly to me, suggest that the Lord Leto is always seeking after newness and originality but that he is wary of the destructive potential in such things. So my uncle believed.

INQUISITOR: Is there more which you wish to add to these beliefs which you share with your uncle?

HWI NOREE: I see no point in adding to what I've already said. I am sorry to have wasted the Inquisitors' time.

INQUISITOR: But you have not wasted our time. You are confirmed as Ambassador to the Court of Lord Leto, the God Emperor of the known universe.

You must remember that I have at my internal demand every expertise known to our history. This is the fund of energy I draw upon when I address the mentality of war. If you have not heard the moaning cries of the wounded and the dying, you do not know about war. I have heard those cries in such numbers that they haunt me. I have cried out myself in the aftermath of battle. I have suffered wounds in every epoch— wounds from fist and club and rock, from shell-studded limb and bronze sword, from the mace and the cannon, from arrows and lasguns and the silent smothering of atomic dust, from biological invasions which blacken the tongue and drown the lungs, from the swift gush of flame and the silent working of slow poisons . . . and more I will not recount! I have seen and felt them all. To those who dare ask why I behave as I do, I say: With my memories, I can do nothing else. I am not a coward and once I was human.

—THE STOLEN JOURNALS

In the warm season when the satellite weather controllers were forced to contend with winds across the great seas, evening often saw rainfall at the edges of the Sareer. Moneo, coming in from one of his periodic inspections of the Citadel's perimeter, was caught in a sudden shower. Night fell before he reached shelter. A Fish Speaker guard helped him out of his damp cloak at the south portal. She was a heavyset, blocky woman with a square face, a type Leto favored for his guardians.

"Those damned weather controllers should be made to shape up," she said as she handed him his damp cloak.

Moneo gave her a curt nod before beginning the climb to his quarters. All of the Fish Speaker guards knew the God Emperor's aversion to moisture, but none of them made Moneo's distinction.

It is the Worm who hates water, Moneo thought. *Shai-Hulud hungers for Dune.*

In his quarters, Moneo dried himself and changed to dry clothing before descending to the crypt. There was no point in inviting the Worm's antagonism. Uninterrupted conversation with Leto was required now, plain talk about the impending peregrination to the Festival City of Onn.

Leaning against a wall of the descending lift, Moneo closed his eyes. Immediately, fatigue swept over him. He knew he had not slept enough in days and there was no letup in sight. He envied Leto's apparent freedom from the need for sleep. A few hours of semirepose a month appeared to be sufficient for the God Emperor.

The smell of the crypt and the stopping of the lift jarred Moneo from his catnap. He opened his eyes and looked out at the God Emperor on his cart in the center of the great chamber. Moneo composed himself and strode out for the familiar long walk into the terrible presence. As expected, Leto appeared alert. That, at least, was a good sign.

Leto had heard the lift approaching and saw Moneo awaken. The man looked tired and that was understandable. The peregrination to Onn was at hand with all of the tiresome business of off-planet visitors, the ritual with the Fish Speakers, the new ambassadors, the changing of the Imperial Guard, the retirements and the appointments, and now a new Duncan Idaho ghola to fit into the smooth working of the Imperial apparatus. Moneo was occupied with mounting details and he was beginning to show his age.

Let me see, Leto thought. *Moneo will be one hundred and eighteen years old in the week after our return from Onn.*

The man could live many times that long if he would take the spice, but he refused. Leto had no doubt of the reason. Moneo had entered that peculiar human state where he longed for death. He lingered now only to see Siona installed in the Royal Service, the next director of the Imperial Society of Fish Speakers.

My houris, as Malky used to call them.

And Moneo knew it was Leto's intention to breed Siona with a Duncan. It was time.

Moneo stopped two paces from the cart and looked up at Leto. Something in his eyes reminded Leto of the look on the face of a pagan priest in the Terran times, a crafty supplication at the familiar shrine.

"Lord, you have spent many hours observing the new Duncan," Moneo said. "Have the Tleilaxu tampered with his cells or his psyche?"

"He is untainted."

A deep sigh shook Moneo. There was no pleasure in it.

"You object to his use as a stud?" Leto asked.

"I find it peculiar to think of him as both an ancestor and the father of my descendants."

"But he gives me access to a first-generation cross between an older human form and the current products of my breeding program. Siona is twenty-one generations removed from such a cross."

"I fail to see the purpose. The Duncans are slower and less alert than anyone in your Guard."

"I am not looking for good segregant offspring, Moneo. Did you think me unaware of the progression geometrics dictated by the laws which govern my breeding program?"

"I have seen your stock book, Lord."

"Then you know that I keep track of the recessives and weed them out. The key genetic dominants are my concern."

"And the mutations, Lord?" There was a sly note in Moneo's voice which caused Leto to study the man intently.

"We will not discuss that subject, Moneo."

Leto watched Moneo pull back into his cautious shell.

How extremely sensitive he is to my moods, Leto thought. *I do believe he has some of my abilities there, although they operate at an unconscious level. His question suggests that he may even suspect what we have achieved in Siona.*

Testing this, Leto said, "It is clear to me that you do not yet understand what I hope to achieve in my breeding program."

Moneo brightened. "My Lord knows I try to fathom the rules of it."

"Laws tend to be temporary over the long haul, Moneo. There is no such thing as rule-governed creativity."

"But, Lord, you yourself speak of laws which govern your breeding program."

"What have I just said to you, Moneo? Trying to find rules for creation is like trying to separate mind from body."

"But something is evolving, Lord. I know it in myself!"

He knows it in himself! Dear Moneo. He is so close.

"Why do you always seek after absolutely derivative translations, Moneo?"

"I have heard you speak of *transformational evolution,* Lord. That is the label on your stock book. But what of surprise . . ."

"Moneo! Rules change with each surprise."

"Lord, have you no improvement of the human stock in mind?"

Leto glared down at him, thinking: *If I use the key word now, will he understand? Perhaps . . .*

"I am a predator, Moneo."

"Pred . . ." Moneo broke off and shook his head. He knew the meaning of the word, he thought, but the word itself shocked him. Was the God Emperor joking?

"Predator, Lord?"

"The predator improves the stock."

"How can this be, Lord? You do not hate us."

"You disappoint me, Moneo. The predator does not hate its prey."

"Predators kill, Lord."

"I kill, but I do not hate. Prey assuages hunger. Prey is good."

Moneo peered up at Leto's face in its gray cowl.

Have I missed the approach of the Worm? Moneo wondered.

Fearfully, Moneo looked for the signs. There were no tremors in the giant body, no glazing of the eyes, no twisting of the useless flippers.

"For what do you hunger, Lord?" Moneo ventured.

"For a humankind which can make truly long-term decisions. Do you know the key to that ability, Moneo?"

"You have said it many times, Lord. It is the ability to change your mind."

"Change, yes. And do you know what I mean by long-term?"

"For you, it must be measured in millennia, Lord."

"Moneo, even my thousands of years are but a puny blip against Infinity."

"But your perspective must be different from mine, Lord."

"In the view of Infinity, any defined long term is short-term."

"Then are there no rules at all, Lord?" Moneo's voice conveyed a faint hint of hysteria.

Leto smiled to ease the man's tensions. "Perhaps one. Short-term decisions tend to fail in the long term."

Moneo shook his head in frustration. "But, Lord, your perspective is . . ."

"Time runs out for any finite observer. There are no closed systems. Even I only stretch the finite matrix."

Moneo jerked his attention from Leto's face and peered into the distances of the mausoleum corridors. *I will be here someday. The Golden Path may continue, but I will end.* That was not important, of course. Only the Golden Path which he could sense in unbroken continuity, only *that* mattered. He returned his attention to Leto, but not to the all-blue eyes. Was there truly a predator lurking in that gross body?

"You do not understand the function of a predator," Leto said.

The words shocked Moneo because they smacked of mind-reading. He lifted his gaze to Leto's eyes.

"You know *intellectually* that even I will suffer a kind of death someday," Leto said. "But you do not believe it."

"How can I believe what I will never see?"

Moneo had never felt more lonely and fearful. What was the God Emperor doing? *I came down here to discuss the problems of the peregrination . . . and to find out about his intentions toward Siona. Does he toy with me?*

"Let us talk about Siona," Leto said.

Mind-reading again!

"When will you test her, Lord?" The question had been waiting in the front of his awareness all this time, but now that he had spoken it, Moneo feared it.

"Soon."

"Forgive me, Lord, but surely you know how much I fear for the well-being of my only child."

"Others have survived the test, Moneo. You did."

Moneo gulped, remembering how he had been sensitized to the Golden Path.

"My mother prepared me. Siona has no mother."

"She has the Fish Speakers. She has you."

"Accidents happen, Lord."

Tears sprang into Moneo's eyes.

Leto looked away from him, thinking: *He is torn by his loyalty to me and his love of Siona. How poignant it is, this concern for an offspring. Can he not see that all of humankind is my only child?*

Returning his attention to Moneo, Leto said, "You are right to observe that accidents happen even in my universe. Does this teach you nothing?"

"Lord, just this once couldn't you . . ."

"Moneo! Surely you do not ask me to delegate authority to a weak administrator."

Moneo recoiled one step. "No, Lord. Of course not."

"Then trust Siona's strength."

Moneo squared his shoulders. "I will do what I must."

"Siona must be awakened to her duties as an Atreides."

"Yes, of course, Lord."

"Is that not our commitment, Moneo?"

"I do not deny it, Lord. When will you introduce her to the new Duncan?"

"The test comes first."

Moneo looked down at the cold floor of the crypt.

He stares at the floor so often, Leto thought. *What can he possibly see there? Is it the millennial tracks of my cart? Ahhh, no—it is into the depths that he peers, into the realm of treasure and mystery which he expects to enter soon.*

Once more, Moneo lifted his gaze to Leto's face. "I hope she will like the Duncan's company, Lord."

"Be assured of it. The Tleilaxu have brought him to me in the undistorted image."

"That is reassuring, Lord."

"No doubt you have noted that his genotype is remarkably attractive to females."

"That has been my observation, Lord."

"There's something about those gently observant eyes, those strong features and that black-goat hair which positively melts the female psyche."

"As you say, Lord."

"You know he's with the Fish Speakers right now?"

"I was informed, Lord."

Leto smiled. Of course Moneo was informed. "They will bring him to me soon for his first view of the God Emperor."

"I have inspected the viewing room personally, Lord. Everything is in readiness."

"Sometimes I think you wish to weaken me, Moneo. Leave some of these details for me."

Moneo tried to conceal a constriction of fear. He bowed and backed away. "Yes, Lord, but there are some things which I must do."

Turning, he hurried away. It was not until he was ascending in the lift that Moneo realized he had left without being dismissed.

He must know how tired I am. He will forgive.

Your Lord knows very well what is in your heart. Your soul suffices this day as a reckoner against you. I need no witnesses. You do not listen to your soul, but listen instead to your anger and your rage.

—LORD LETO TO A PENITENT,
FROM THE ORAL HISTORY

The following assessment of the state of the Empire in the year 3508 of the reign of the Lord Leto is taken from The Welbeck Abridgment. The original is in the Chapter House Archives of the Bene Gesserit Order. A comparison reveals that the deletions do not subtract from the essential accuracy of this account.

In the name of our Sacred Order and its unbroken Sisterhood, this accounting has been judged reliable and worthy of entry into the Chronicles of the Chapter House.

Sisters Chenoeh and Tawsuoko have returned safely from Arrakis to report confirmation of the long-suspected execution of the nine historians who disappeared into his Citadel in the year 2116 of Lord Leto's reign. The Sisters report that the nine were rendered unconscious, then burned on pyres of their own published works. This conforms exactly with the stories which spread across the Empire at the time. The accounts of that time were judged to have originated with Lord Leto himself.

Sisters Chenoeh and Tawsuoko bring the handwritten records of an eyewitness account which says that when Lord Leto was petitioned by other historians seeking word of their fellows, Lord Leto said:

"They were destroyed because they lied pretentiously. Have no fear that my wrath will fall upon you because of your innocent mistakes. I am not overly fond of creating martyrs. Martyrs tend to set dramatic events adrift in human affairs. Drama is one of the targets of my predation. Tremble only if you build false accounts and stand pridefully upon them. Go now and do not speak of this."

Internal evidence of the handwritten account identifies its author as Ikonicre, Lord Leto's majordomo in the year 2116.

Attention is called to Lord Leto's use of the word *predation*. This is highly suggestive in view of theories advanced by Reverend Mother Syaksa that the God Emperor views himself as a predator in the *natural* sense.

Sister Chenoeh was invited to accompany the Fish Speakers in an entourage which accompanied one of Lord Leto's infrequent peregrinations. At one point, she was invited to trot beside the Royal Cart and converse with the Lord Leto himself. She reports the exchange as follows:

The Lord Leto said: "Here on the Royal Road, I sometimes feel that I stand on battlements protecting myself against invaders."

Sister Chenoeh said: "No one attacks you here, Lord."

The Lord Leto said: "You Bene Gesserit assail me on all sides. Even now, you seek to suborn my Fish Speakers."

Sister Chenoeh says that she steeled herself for death, but the God Emperor merely stopped his cart and looked across her at his entourage. She says the others stopped and waited on the road in well-trained passivity, all of them at a respectful distance.

The Lord Leto said, "There is my little multitude and they tell me everything. Do not deny my accusation."

Sister Chenoeh said, "I do not deny it."

The Lord Leto looked at her then and said, "Have no fear for your person. It is my wish that you report my words in your Chapter House."

Sister Chenoeh says she could see then that the Lord Leto knew all about her, about her mission, her special training as an oral recorder, everything. "He was like a Reverend Mother," she said. "I could hide nothing from him."

The Lord Leto then commanded her, "Look toward my Festival City and tell me what you see."

Sister Chenoeh looked toward Onn and said, "I see the City in the distance. It is beautiful in this morning light. There is your forest on the right. It has so many greens in it I could spend all day describing them. On the left and all around the City there are the houses and the gardens of your servitors. Some of them look very rich and some look very poor."

The Lord Leto said, "We have cluttered this landscape! Trees are a clutter. Houses, gardens . . . You cannot exult at new mysteries in such a landscape."

Sister Chenoeh, emboldened by Lord Leto's assurances, asked, "Does the Lord truly want mysteries?"

The Lord Leto said, "There is no outward spiritual freedom in such a landscape. Do you not see it? You have no open universe here with which to share. Everything is closures—doors, latches, locks!"

Sister Chenoeh asked, "Has mankind no longer any need for privacy and protection?"

The Lord Leto said, "When you return, tell your Sisters that I will restore the outward view. Such a landscape as this one turns you inward in search for whatever freedom your spirits can find within. Most humans are not strong enough to find freedom within."

Sister Chenoeh said, "I will report your words accurately, Lord."

The Lord Leto said, "See that you do. Tell your Sisters also that the Bene Gesserit of all people should know the dangers of breeding for a particular characteristic, of seeking a defined genetic goal."

Sister Chenoeh says this was an obvious reference to the Lord Leto's father, Paul Atreides. Let it be noted that our breeding program achieved the Kwisatz Haderach one generation early. In becoming Muad'Dib, the leader of the Fremen, Paul Atreides escaped from our control. There is no doubt that he was a male with the powers of a Reverend Mother and other powers for which humankind still is paying a heavy price. As the Lord Leto said:

"You got the unexpected. You got me, the wild card. And I have achieved Siona."

The Lord Leto refused to elaborate on this reference to the daughter of his majordomo, Moneo. The matter is being investigated.

In other matters of concern to the Chapter House, our investigators have supplied information on:

THE FISH SPEAKERS

The Lord Leto's female legions have elected their representatives to attend the Decennial Festival on Arrakis. Three representatives will attend from each planetary garrison. *(See attached list of those chosen.)* As usual, no adult males will attend, not even consorts of Fish Speaker officers. The consort list has changed very little in this reporting period. We have appended the new names with genealogical information where available. Note that only two of the names can be starred as descendants of the Duncan Idaho gholas. We can add nothing new to our speculations about his use of the gholas in his breeding program.

None of our efforts to form an alliance between Fish Speakers and Bene Gesserit succeeded during this period. Lord Leto continues to increase certain garrison sizes. He also continues to emphasize the alternative missions of the Fish Speakers, deemphasizing their military missions. This has had the expected result of increasing local admiration and respect *and gratitude* for the presence of the Fish Speaker garrisons. *(See attached list for garrisons which were increased in size. Editor's note: The only pertinent garrisons were those on the home planets of the Bene Gesserit, Ixians and Tleilaxu. Spacing Guild monitors were not increased.)*

PRIESTHOOD

Except for the few natural deaths and replacements which are listed in attachments, there have been no significant changes. Those consorts and officers delegated to perform the ritual duties remain few, their powers abridged by continuing requirement for consultation with Arrakis before taking any important action. It is the opinion of the Reverend Mother Syaksa and some others that the religious character of the Fish Speakers is slowly being devolved.

BREEDING PROGRAM

Other than the unexplained reference to Siona and to our failure with his father, we have nothing significant to add to our continued monitoring of the Lord Leto's breeding program. There is evidence of a certain randomness in his plan which is reinforced by the Lord Leto's statement about *genetic goals*, but we cannot be certain that he was truthful with Sister Chenoeh. We call your attention to the many instances where he has either lied or changed directions dramatically and without warning.

The Lord Leto continues to prohibit our participation in his breeding program. His monitors from our Fish Speaker garrison remain adamant in "weeding out" our births to which they object. Only by the most stringent controls were we able to maintain the level of Reverend Mothers during this reporting period. Our protests are not answered. In response to a direct question from Sister Chenoeh, the Lord Leto said:

"Be thankful for what you have."

This warning is duly noted here. We have transmitted a gracious letter of thankfulness to the Lord Leto.

ECONOMICS

The Chapter House continues to maintain its solvency, but the measures of conservation cannot be eased. In fact, as a precaution, certain new measures will be instituted in the next reporting period. These include a reduction in the ritual uses of melange and an increase in the rates charged for our usual services. We expect to double the fees for the schooling of Great House females across the next four reporting periods. You are hereby charged to begin preparing your arguments in defense of this action.

The Lord Leto has denied our petition for an increase in our melange allotment. No reason was given.

Our relationship with the Combine Honnete Ober Advancer Mercantiles remains on a sound footing. CHOAM has accomplished in the preceding period a regional cartel in Star Jewels, a project whereby we gained a substantial return through our advisory and bargaining functions. The ongoing profits from this arrangement should more than offset our losses on Giedi Prime. The Giedi Prime investment has been written off.

GREAT HOUSES

Thirty-one former Great Houses suffered economic disaster in this reporting period. Only six managed to maintain House Minor status. *(See attached list.)* This continues the general trend noted over the past thousand years where the once Great Houses melt gradually into the background. It is to be noted that the six who averted total disaster were all heavy investors in CHOAM and that five of these six were deeply involved in the Star Jewel project. The lone exception held a diversified portfolio, including a substantial investment in antique whale fur from Caladan.

(Our ponji rice reserves were increased almost twofold in this period at the expense of our whale fur holdings. The reasons for this decision will be reviewed in the next period.)

FAMILY LIFE

As has been observed by our investigators over the preceding two thousand years, the homogenization of family life continues unabated. The exceptions are those you would expect: the Guild, the Fish Speakers, the Royal Courtiers, the shape-changing Face Dancers of the Tleilaxu (who are still mules despite all efforts to change that condition), and our own situation, of course.

It is to be noted that familial conditions grow more and more similar no matter the planet of residence, a circumstance which cannot be attributed to accident. We are seeing here the emergence of a portion of the Lord Leto's grand design. Even the poorest families are well fed, yes, but the circumstances of daily life grow increasingly static.

We remind you of a statement from the Lord Leto which was reported here almost eight generations ago:

"I am the only spectacle remaining in the Empire."

Reverend Mother Syaksa has proposed a theoretical explanation for this trend, a theory which many of us are beginning to share. RM Syaksa attributes to Lord Leto a motive based on the concept of hydraulic despotism. As you know, hydraulic despotism is possible only when a substance or condition upon which life in general absolutely depends can be controlled by a relatively small and centralized force. The concept of hydraulic despotism originated when the flow of irrigation water increased local human populations to a demand level of absolute dependence. When the water was shut off, people died in large numbers.

This phenomenon has been repeated many times in human history, not only with water and the products of arable land, but with hydrocarbon fuels such as petroleum and coal which were controlled through pipelines and other distribution networks. At one time, when distribution of electricity was only through complicated mazes of lines strung across the landscape, even this energy resource fell into the role of a hydraulic-despotism substance.

RM Syaksa proposes that the Lord Leto is building the Empire toward an even greater dependence upon melange. It is worth noting that the aging process can be called a disease for which melange is the specific treatment, although not a cure. RM Syaksa proposes that the Lord Leto may even go so far as introducing a new disease which can only be suppressed by melange. Although this may appear farfetched, it should not be discarded out of hand. Stranger things have happened, and we should not overlook the role of syphilis in early human history.

TRANSPORT/GUILD

The three-mode transportation system once peculiar to Arrakis (that is, on foot with heavy loads relegated to suspensor-borne pallets; in the air via ornithopter; or off-planet by Guild transport) is coming to dominate more and more planets of the Empire. Ix is the primary exception.

We attribute this in part to planetary devolution into sedentary and static lifestyles. And partly it is the attempt to copy the pattern of Arrakis. The generalized aversion to things Ixian plays no small part in this trend. There is also the fact that the Fish Speakers promote this pattern to reduce their work in maintaining order.

Over the Guild's part in this trend hangs the absolute dependence of the Guild Navigators upon melange. We are, therefore, keeping a close watch upon the joint effort of Guild and Ix to develop a mechanical substitute for the Navigators' predictive talents. Without melange or some other means of projecting a heighliner's course, every translight Guild voyage risks disaster. Although we are not very sanguine about this Guild-Ixian project, there is always the possibility and we shall report on this as conditions warrant.

THE GOD EMPEROR

Other than some small increments of growth, we note little change in the bodily characteristics of the Lord Leto. A rumored aversion to water has not been confirmed, although the use of water as a barrier against the original sandworms of Dune is well documented in our records, as is the *water-death* by which Fremen killed a small worm to produce the spice-essence employed in their orgies.

There is considerable evidence for the belief that the Lord Leto has increased his surveillance of Ix, possibly because of the Guild-Ixian project. Certainly, success in that project would reduce his hold upon the Empire.

He continues to do business with Ix, ordering replacement parts for his Royal Cart.

A new ghola Duncan Idaho has been sent to the Lord Leto by the Tleilaxu. This makes it certain that the previous ghola is dead, although the manner of his death is not known. We call your attention to previous indications that the Lord Leto himself has killed some of his gholas.

There is increasing evidence that the Lord Leto employs computers. If he is, in fact, defying his own prohibitions and the proscriptions of the Butlerian Jihad, the possession of proof by us could increase our influence over him, possibly even to the extent of certain joint ventures which we have long contemplated. Sovereign control of our breeding program is still a primary concern. We will continue our investigation with, however, the following *caveat*:

As with every report preceding this one, we must address the Lord Leto's prescience. There is no doubt that his ability to predict future events, an oracular ability much more powerful than that of any ancestor, is still the mainstay of his political control.

We do not defy it!

It is our belief that he knows every important action we take far in advance of the event. We guide ourselves, therefore, by the rule that we will not knowingly threaten either his person or such of his grand plan as we can discern. Our address to him will continue to be:

"Tell us if we threaten you that we may desist."

And:

"Tell us of your grand plan that we may help."

He has provided no new answers to either question during this period.

THE IXIANS

Other than the Guild-Ix project, there is little of significance to report. Ix is sending a new Ambassador to the Court of the Lord Leto, one Hwi Noree, a niece of the Malky who once was reputed to be such a boon companion of the God Emperor. The reason for the choice of replacement is not known, although there is a small body of evidence that this Hwi Noree was bred for a specific purpose, possibly as the Ixian representative at the Court. We have reason to believe that Malky also was genetically designed with that official context in mind.

We will continue to investigate.

The Museum Fremen

These degenerate relics of the once-proud warriors continue to function as our major source of reliable information about affairs on Arrakis. They represent a major budget item for our next reporting period because their demands for payment are increasing and we dare not antagonize them.

It is interesting to note that although their lives bear little resemblance to that of their ancestors, their performance of Fremen rituals and their ability to ape Fremen ways remain flawless. We attribute this to Fish Speaker influence upon Fremen training.

The Tleilaxu

We do not expect the new ghola of Duncan Idaho to provide any surprises. The Tleilaxu continue to be much chastened by the Lord Leto's reaction to their one attempt at changing the cellular nature and the psyche of the original.

A recent envoy from the Tleilaxu renewed their attempts to entice us into a joint venture, the avowed purpose being the production of a totally female society without the need for males. For all of the obvious reasons, including our distrust of everything Tleilaxu, we responded with our usual polite negative. Our Embassy to the Lord Leto's Decennial Festival will make a full report of this to him.

Respectfully submitted:

The Reverend Mothers Syaksa, Yitob, Mamulut, Eknekosk and Akeli.

Odd as it may seem, great struggles such as the one you can see emerging from my journals are not always visible to the participants. Much depends on what people dream in the secrecy of their hearts. I have always been as concerned with the shaping of dreams as with the shaping of actions. Between the lines of my journals is the struggle with humankind's view of itself—a sweaty contest on a field where motives from our darkest past can well up out of an unconscious reservoir and become events with which we not only must live but contend. It is the hydra-headed monster which always attacks from your blind side. I pray, therefore, that when you have traversed my portion of the Golden Path you no longer will be innocent children dancing to music you cannot hear.

—THE STOLEN JOURNALS

Nayla moved in a steady, plodding pace as she climbed the circular stairs to the God Emperor's audience chamber atop the Citadel's south tower. Each time she traversed the southwest arc of the tower, the narrow slitted windows drew dust-defined golden lines across her path. She knew that the central wall beside her confined a lift of Ixian make large enough to carry her Lord's bulk to the upper chamber, certainly large enough to hold her relatively smaller body, but she did not resent the fact that she was required to use the stairs.

The breeze through the open slits brought her the burnt-flint smell of blown sand. The low-lying sun ignited the light of red mineral flakes in the inner wall, ruby matches glowing there. Now and then she cast a glance through a slitted window at the dunes. Never once did she pause to admire the things to be seen around her.

"You have heroic patience, Nayla," the Lord had once told her.

Remembrance of those words warmed Nayla now.

Within the tower, Leto followed Nayla's progress up the long circular stairs that spiraled around the Ixian tube. Her progress was transmitted to him by an Ixian device which projected her approaching image quarter-size onto a region of three-dimensional focus directly in front of his eyes.

How precisely she moves, he thought.

The precision, he knew, came from a passionate simplicity.

She wore her Fish Speaker blues and a cape-robe without the hawk at the breast. Once past the guard station at the foot of the tower, she had thrown back the cibus mask he required her to wear on these personal visits. Her blocky, muscular body was like that of many others among his guardians, but her face was like no other in all of his memory—almost square with a mouth so wide it seemed to extend around the cheeks, an illusion caused by deep creases at the corners. Her eyes were pale green, the closely cropped hair like old ivory. Her forehead added to the square effect, almost flat with pale eyebrows which often went unnoticed because of the compelling eyes. The nose was a straight, shallow line which terminated close to the thin-lipped mouth.

When Nayla spoke, her great jaws opened and closed like those of some primordial animal. Her strength, known to few outside the corps of Fish Speakers, was legendary there. Leto had seen her lift a one-hundred-kilo man with one hand. Her presence on Arrakis had been arranged originally without Moneo's intervention, although the major-domo knew Leto employed his Fish Speakers as secret agents.

Leto turned his head away from the plodding image and looked out the wide opening beside him at the desert to the south. The colors of the distant rocks danced in his awareness—brown, gold, a deep amber. There was a line of pink on a faraway cliff the exact hue of an egret's feathers. Egrets did not exist anymore except in Leto's memory, but he could place that pale pastel ribbon of stone against an inner eye and it was as though the extinct bird flew past him.

The climb, he knew, should be starting to tire even Nayla. She paused at last to rest, stopping at a point two steps past the three-quarter mark, precisely the place where she rested every time. It was part of her precision, one of the reasons he had brought her back from the distant garrison on Seprek.

A Dune hawk floated past the opening beside Leto only a few wing lengths from the tower wall. Its attention was held on the shadows at the base of the Citadel. Small animals sometimes emerged there, Leto knew. Dimly on the horizon beyond the hawk's path he could see a line of clouds.

What a strange thing those were to the Old Fremen in him: clouds on Arrakis and rain and open water.

Leto reminded the inner voices: *Except for this last desert, my Sareer, the remodeling of Dune into verdant Arrakis has gone on remorselessly since the first days of my rule.*

The influence of geography on history went mostly unrecognized, Leto thought. Humans tended to look more at the influence of history on geography.

Who owns this river passage? This verdant valley? This peninsula? This planet?

None of us.

Nayla was climbing once more, her gaze fixed upward on the stairs she must traverse. Leto's thoughts locked on her.

In many ways, she is the most useful assistant I have ever had. I am her God. She worships me quite unquestioningly. Even when I playfully attack her faith, she takes this merely as testing. She knows herself superior to any test.

When he had sent her to the rebellion and had told her to obey Siona in all things, she did not question. When Nayla doubted, even when she framed her doubts in words, her own thoughts were enough to restore faith . . . or had been enough. Recent messages, however, made it clear that Nayla required the Holy Presence to rebuild her inner strength.

Leto recalled the first conversation with Nayla, the woman trembling in her eagerness to please.

"Even if Siona sends you to kill me, you must obey. She must never learn that you serve me."

"No one can kill you, Lord."

"But you must obey Siona."

"Of course, Lord. That is your command."

"You must obey her in all things."

"I will do it, Lord."

Another test. Nayla does not question my tests. She treats them as flea bites. Her Lord commands? Nayla obeys. I must not let anything change that relationship.

She would have made a superb Shadout in the old days, Leto thought. It was one of the reasons he had given Nayla a crysknife, a real one preserved from Sietch Tabr. It had belonged to one of Stilgar's wives. Nayla wore it in a concealed sheath beneath her robes, more a talisman than a weapon. He had given it to her in the original ritual, a ceremony which had surprised him by evoking emotions he had thought forever buried.

"This is the tooth of Shai-Hulud."

He had extended the blade to her on his silvery-skinned hands.

"Take it and you become part of both past and future. Soil it and the past will give you no future."

Nayla had accepted the blade, then the sheath.

"Draw the blood of a finger," Leto had commanded.

Nayla had obeyed.

"Sheath the blade. Never remove it without drawing blood."

Again, Nayla had obeyed.

As Leto watched the three-dimensional image of Nayla's approach, his reflections on that old ceremony were touched by sadness. Unless fixed in the Old Fremen way, the blade would grow increasingly brittle and useless. It would keep its crysknife shape throughout Nayla's life, but little longer.

I have thrown away a bit of the past.

How sad it was that the Shadout of old had become today's Fish Speaker. And a true cryskaife had been used to bind a servant more strongly to her master. He knew that some thought his Fish Speakers were really priestesses—Leto's answer to the Bene Gesserit.

"He creates another religion," the Bene Gesserit said.

Nonsense! I have not created a religion. I am the religion!

Nayla entered the tower sanctuary and stood three paces from Leto's cart, her gaze lowered in proper subservience.

Still in his memories, Leto said: "Look at me, woman!"

She obeyed.

"I have created a holy obscenity!" he said. "This religion built around my person disgusts me!"

"Yes, Lord."

Nayla's green eyes on the gilded cushions of her cheeks stared out at him without questioning, without comprehension, without the need of either response.

If I sent her out to collect the stars, she would go and she would attempt it. She thinks I am testing her again. I do believe she could anger me.

"This damnable religion should end with me!" Leto shouted. "Why should I want to loose a religion upon my people? Religions wreck from within—Empires and individuals alike! It's all the same."

"Yes, Lord."

"Religions create radicals and fanatics like you!"

"Thank You, Lord."

The short-lived pseudo-rage sank back out of sight into the depths of his memories. Nothing dented the hard surface of Nayla's faith.

"Topri has reported to me through Moneo," Leto said. "Tell me about this Topri."

"Topri is a worm."

"Isn't that what you call *me* when you're among the rebels?"

"I obey my Lord in everything."

Touché!

"Topri is not worth cultivating then?" Leto asked.

"Siona assessed him correctly. He is clumsy. He says things which others will repeat, thus exposing his hand in the matter. Within seconds after Kobat began to speak, she had confirmation that Topri was a spy."

Everyone agrees, even Moneo, Leto thought. *Topri is not a good spy.*

The agreement amused Leto. The petty machinations muddied water which remained completely transparent to him. The performers, however, still suited his designs.

"Siona does not suspect you?" Leto asked.

"I am not clumsy."

"Do you know why I summoned you?"

"To test my faith."

Ahhh, Nayla. How little you know of testing.

"I want your assessment of Siona. I want to see it on your face and see it in your movements and hear it in your voice," Leto said. "Is she ready?"

"The Fish Speakers need that one, Lord. Why do You risk losing her?"

"Forcing the issue is the surest way of losing what I treasure most in her," Leto said. "She must come to me with all of her strengths intact."

Nayla lowered her gaze. "As my Lord commands."

Leto recognized the response. It was a Nayla reaction to whatever she failed to understand.

"Will she survive the test, Nayla?"

"As my Lord describes the test . . ." Nayla lifted her gaze to Leto's face, shrugged. "I do not know, Lord. Certainly, she is strong. She was the only one to survive the wolves. But she is ruled by hate."

"Quite naturally. Tell me, Nayla, what will she do with the things she stole from me?"

"Did Topri not inform you about the books which they say contain Your Sacred Words?"

Odd how she can capitalize words only with her voice, Leto thought. He spoke curtly.

"Yes, yes. The Ixians have a copy and soon the Guild and Sisterhood as well will be hard at work on them."

"What are those books, Lord?"

"They are my words for my people. I want them to be read. What I want to know is what Siona has said about the Citadel charts she took."

"She says there is a great hoard of melange beneath Your Citadel, Lord, and the charts will reveal it."

"The charts will not reveal it. Will she tunnel?"

"She seeks Ixian tools for that."

"Ix will not provide them."

"Is there such a hoard of spice, Lord?"

"Yes."

"There is a story about how Your hoard is defended, Lord. That Arrakis itself would be destroyed if anyone tried to steal Your melange. Is it true?"

"Yes. And that would shatter the Empire. Nothing would survive— not Guild or Sisterhood, not Ix or Tleilaxu, not even the Fish Speakers."

She shuddered, then: "I will not let Siona try to get Your spice."

"Nayla! I commanded you to obey Siona in everything. Is this how you serve me?"

"Lord?" She stood in fear of his anger, closer to a loss of faith than he had ever seen her. It was the crisis he had created, knowing how it must end. Slowly, Nayla relaxed. He could see the shape of her thought as though she had laid it out for him in illuminated words.

The ultimate test!

"You will return to Siona and guard her life with your own," Leto said. "That is the task I set for you and that you accepted. It is why you were chosen. It is why you carry a blade from Stilgar's household."

Her right hand went to the cryknife concealed beneath her robe.

How sure it is, Leto thought, *that a weapon can lock a person into a predictable pattern of behavior.*

He stared with fascination at Nayla's rigid body. Her eyes were empty of everything except adoration.

The ultimate rhetorical despotism . . . and I despise it!

"Go then!" he barked.

Nayla turned and fled the Holy Presence.

Is it worth this? Leto wondered.

But Nayla had told him what he needed to know. Nayla had re-newed her faith and revealed with accuracy the thing which Leto could not find in Siona's fading image. Nayla's instincts were to be trusted.

Siona has reached that explosive moment which I require.

The Duncans always think it odd that I choose women for combat forces, but my Fish Speakers are a temporary army in every sense. While they can be violent and vicious, women are profoundly different from men in their dedication to battle. The cradle of genesis ultimately predisposes them to behavior more protective of life. They have proved to be the best keepers of the Golden Path. I reinforce this in my design for their training. They are set aside for a time from ordinary routines. I give them special sharings which they can look back upon with pleasure for the rest of their lives. They come of age in the company of their sisters in preparation for events more profound. What you share in such companionship always prepares you for greater things. The haze of nostalgia covers their days among their sisters, making those days into something different than they were. That's the way today changes history. All contemporaries do not inhabit the same time. The past is always changing, but few realize it.

—THE STOLEN JOURNALS

After sending word to the Fish Speakers, Leto descended to the crypt in the late evening. He had found it best to begin the first interview with a new Duncan Idaho in a darkened room where the ghola could hear Leto describe himself before actually seeing the pre-worm body. There was a small side room carved in black stone off the central rotunda of the crypt which suited this requirement. The chamber was large enough to accommodate Leto on his cart, but the ceiling was low.

Illumination came from hidden glowglobes which he controlled. There was only the one door, but it was in two segments—one swinging wide to admit the Royal Cart, the other a small portal in human dimensions.

Leto rolled his Royal Cart into the chamber, sealed the large portal and opened the smaller one. He composed himself then for the ordeal.

Boredom was an increasing problem. The pattern of the Tleilaxu gholas had become boringly repetitive. Once, Leto had sent word warning the Tleilaxu to send no more Duncans, but they had known they could disobey him in this thing.

Sometimes I think they do it just to keep disobedience alive!

The Tleilaxu relied on an important thing which they knew protected them in other matters.

The presence of a Duncan pleases the Paul Atreides in me.

As Leto had explained it to Moneo in the majordomo's first days at the Citadel:

"The Duncans must come to me with much more than Tleilaxu preparation. You must see to it that my houris gentle the Duncans and that the women answer *some* of his questions."

"Which questions may they answer, Lord?"

"They know."

Moneo had, of course, learned all about this procedure over the years.

Leto heard Moneo's voice outside the darkened room, then the sound of the Fish Speaker escort and the hesitantly distinctive footsteps of the new ghola.

"Through that door," Moneo said. "It will be dark inside and we will close the door behind you. Stop just inside and wait for the Lord Leto to speak."

"Why will it be dark?" The Duncan's voice was full of aggressive misgivings.

"He will explain."

Idaho was thrust into the room and the door was sealed behind him.

Leto knew what the ghola saw—only shadows among shadows and

blackness where not even the source of a voice could be fixed. As usual, Leto brought the Paul Muad'Dib voice into play.

"It pleases me to see you again, Duncan."

"I can't see you!"

Idaho was a warrior, and the warrior attacks. This reassured Leto that the ghola was a fully restored original. The morality play by which the Tleilaxu reawakened a ghola's pre-death memories always left some uncertainties in the gholas' minds. Some of the Duncans believed they had threatened a real Paul Muad'Dib. This one carried such illusions.

"I hear Paul's voice but I can't see him," Idaho said. He didn't try to conceal the frustrations, let them all come out in his voice.

Why was an Atreides playing this stupid game? Paul was truly dead in some long-ago and this was Leto, the carrier of Paul's resurrected memories . . . and the memories of many others!—if the Tleilaxu stories were to be believed.

"You have been told that you are only the latest in a long line of duplicates," Leto said.

"I have none of those memories."

Leto recognized hysteria in the Duncan, barely covered by the warrior bravado. The cursed Tleilaxu post-tank restoration tactics had produced the usual mental chaos. This Duncan had arrived in a state of near shock, strongly suspecting he was insane. Leto knew that the most subtle powers of reassurance would be required now to soothe the poor fellow. This would be emotionally draining for both of them.

"There have been many changes, Duncan," Leto said. "One thing, though, does not change. I am still Atreides."

"They said your body is . . ."

"Yes, that has changed."

"The damned Tleilaxu! They tried to make me kill someone I . . . well, he looked like you. I suddenly remembered who I was and there was this . . . Could that have been a Muad'Dib ghola?"

"A Face Dancer mimic, I assure you."

"He looked and talked so much like . . . Are you sure?"

"An actor, no more. Did he survive?"

"Of course! That's how they wakened my memories. They explained the whole damned thing. Is it true?"

"It's true, Duncan. I detest it, but I permit it for the pleasure of your company."

The potential victims always survive, Leto thought. *At least for the Duncans I see. There have been slips, the fake Paul slain and the Duncans wasted. But there are always more cells carefully preserved from the original.*

"What about your body?" Idaho demanded.

Muad'Dib could be retired now; Leto resumed his usual voice. "I accepted the sandtrout as my skin. They have been changing me ever since."

"Why?"

"I will explain that in due course."

"The Tleilaxu said you look like a sandworm."

"What did my Fish Speakers say?"

"They said you're God. Why do you call them Fish Speakers?"

"An old conceit. The first priestesses spoke to fish in their dreams. They learned valuable things that way."

"How do you know?"

"I *am* those women . . . and everything that came before and after them."

Leto heard the dry swallowing in Idaho's throat, then: "I see why the darkness. You're giving me time to adjust."

"You always were quick, Duncan."

Except when you were slow.

"How long have you been changing?"

"More than thirty-five hundred years."

"Then what the Tleilaxu told me is true."

"They seldom dare to lie anymore."

"That's a long time."

"Very long."

"The Tleilaxu have . . . copied me many times?"

"Many."

It's time you asked how many, Duncan.

"How many of me?"

"I will let you see the records for yourself."

And so it starts, Leto thought.

This exchange always appeared to satisfy the Duncans, but there was no escaping the nature of the question:

"How many of me?"

The Duncans made no distinctions of the flesh even though no mutual memories passed between gholas of the same stock.

"I remember my death," Idaho said. "Harkonnen blades, lots of them trying to get at you and Jessica."

Leto restored the Muad'Dib voice for momentary play: "I was there, Duncan."

"I'm a replacement, is that right?" Idaho asked.

"That's right," Leto said.

"How did the other . . . me . . . I mean, how did he die?"

"All flesh wears out, Duncan. It's in the records."

Leto waited patiently, wondering how long it would be until the tamed history failed to satisfy this Duncan.

"What do you really look like?" Idaho asked. "What's this sandworm body the Tleilaxu described?"

"It will make sandworms of sorts someday. It's already far down the road of metamorphosis."

"What do you mean *of sorts*?"

"It will have more ganglia. It will be aware."

"Can't we have some light? I'd like to see you."

Leto commanded the floodlights. Brilliant illumination filled the room. The black walls and the lighting had been arranged to focus the illumination on Leto, every visible detail revealed.

Idaho swept his gaze along the faceted silvery-gray body, noted the beginnings of a sandworm's ribbed sections, the sinuous flexings . . . the small protuberances which had once been feet and legs, one of them somewhat shorter than the other. He brought his attention back to the well-defined arms and hands and finally lifted his attention to the cowled face with its pink skin almost lost in the immensity, a ridiculous extrusion on such a body.

"Well, Duncan," Leto said. "You were warned."

Idaho gestured mutely toward the pre-worm body.

Leto asked it for him: "Why?"

Idaho nodded.

"I'm still Atreides, Duncan, and I assure you with all the honor of that name, there were compelling reasons."

"What could possibly . . ."

"You will learn in time."

Idaho merely shook his head from side to side.

"It's not a pleasant revelation," Leto said. "It requires that you learn other things first. Trust the word of an Atreides."

Over the centuries, Leto had found that this invocation of Idaho's profound loyalties to all things Atreides dampened the immediate wellspring of personal questions. Once more, the formula worked.

"So I'm to serve the Atreides again," Idaho said. "That sounds familiar. Is it?"

"In many ways, old friend."

"Old to you, maybe, but not to me. How will I serve?"

"Didn't my Fish Speakers tell you?"

"They said I would command your elite Guard, a force chosen from among them. I don't understand that. An army of *women*?"

"I need a trusted companion who can command my Guard. You object?"

"Why women?"

"There are behavioral differences between the sexes which make women extremely valuable in this role."

"You're not answering my question."

"You think them inadequate?"

"Some of them looked pretty tough, but . . ."

"Others were, ahhh, *soft* with you?"

Idaho blushed.

Leto found this a charming reaction. The Duncans were among the few humans of these times who could do this. It was understandable, a product of the Duncans' early training, their sense of personal honor—very chivalrous.

"I don't see why you trust women to protect you," Idaho said. The blood slowly receded from his cheeks. He glared at Leto.

"But I have always trusted them as I trust you—with my life."

"What do we protect you from?"

"Moneo and my Fish Speakers will bring you up to date."

Idaho shifted from one foot to the other, his body swaying in a heartbeat rhythm. He stared around the small room, his eyes not focusing. With the abruptness of sudden decision, he returned his attention to Leto.

"What do I call you?"

It was the sign of acceptance for which Leto had been waiting. "Will Lord Leto do?"

"Yes . . . m'Lord." Idaho stared directly into Leto's Fremen-blue eyes. "Is it true what your Fish Speakers say—you have . . . memories of . . ."

"We're all here, Duncan." Leto spoke it in the voice of his paternal grandfather, then:

"Even the women are here, Duncan." It was the voice of Jessica, Leto's paternal grandmother.

"You knew them well," Leto said. "And they know you."

Idaho inhaled a slow, trembling breath. "That will take a little getting used to."

"My own initial reaction exactly," Leto said.

An explosion of laughter shook Idaho, and Leto thought it more than the weak jest deserved, but he remained silent.

Presently, Idaho said: "Your Fish Speakers were *supposed* to put me in a good mood, weren't they?"

"Did they succeed?"

Idaho studied Leto's face, recognizing the distinctive Atreides features.

"You Atreides always did know me too well," Idaho said.

"That's better," Leto said. "You're beginning to accept that I'm not just one Atreides. I'm all of them."

"Paul said that once."

"So I did!" As much as the original personality could be conveyed by tone and accent, it was Muad'Dib speaking.

Idaho gulped, looked away at the room's door.

"You've taken something away from us," he said. "I can feel it. Those women . . . Moneo . . ."

Us against you, Leto thought. *The Duncans always choose the human side.*

Idaho returned his attention to Leto's face. "What have you given us in exchange?"

"Throughout the Empire, Leto's Peace!"

"And I can see that everyone's delightfully happy! That's why you need a personal guard."

Leto smiled. "My peace is actually enforced tranquility. Humans have a long history of reacting against tranquility."

"So you give us the Fish Speakers."

"And a hierarchy you can identify without any mistakes."

"A female army," Idaho muttered.

"The ultimate male-enticing force," Leto said. "Sex always was a way of subduing the aggressive male."

"Is that what they do?"

"They prevent or ameliorate excesses which could lead to more painful violence."

"And you let them believe you're a god. I don't think I like this."

"The curse of holiness is as offensive to me as it is to you!"

Idaho frowned. It was not the response he had expected.

"What kind of game are you playing, *Lord* Leto?"

"A very old one but with new rules."

"Your rules!"

"Would you rather I turned it all back to CHOAM and Landsraad and the Great Houses?"

"The Tleilaxu say there is no more Landsraad. You don't allow any real self-rule."

"Well then, I could step aside for the Bene Gesserit. Or maybe the Ixians or the Tleilaxu? Would you like me to find another Baron Harkonnen to assume power over the Empire? Say the word, Duncan, and I'll abdicate!"

Under this avalanche of meanings, Idaho again shook his head from side to side.

"In the wrong hands," Leto said, "monolithic centralized power is a dangerous and volatile instrument."

"And your hands are the right ones?"

"I'm not certain about my hands, but I will tell you, Duncan, I'm certain about the hands of those who've gone before me. I *know* them."

Idaho turned his back on Leto.

What a fascinating, ultimately human gesture, Leto thought. *Rejection coupled to acceptance of his vulnerability.*

Leto spoke to Idaho's back.

"You object quite rightly that I use people without their full knowledge and consent."

Idaho turned his profile to Leto, then turned his head to look up at the cowled face, cocking his head forward a bit to peer into the all-blue eyes.

He is studying me, Leto thought, *but he has only the face to measure me by.*

The Atreides had taught their people to know the subtle signals of face and body, and Idaho was good at it, but the realization could be seen coming over him: he was beyond his depth here.

Idaho cleared his throat. "What's the worst thing you would ask of me?"

How like a Duncan! Leto thought. This one was a classic. Idaho would give his loyalty to an Atreides, to the guardian of his oath, but he sent a signal that he would not go beyond the personal limits of his own morality.

"You will be asked to guard me by whatever means necessary, and you will be asked to guard my secret."

"What secret?"

"That I am vulnerable."

"That you're not God?"

"Not in that ultimate sense."

"Your Fish Speakers talk about rebels."

"They exist."

"Why?"

"They are young and I have not convinced them that my way is better. It's very difficult convincing the young of anything. They're born knowing so much."

"I never before heard an Atreides sneer at the young that way."

"Perhaps it's because I'm so much older—old compounded by old. And my task gets more difficult with each passing generation."

"What is your task?"

"You will come to understand it as we go along."

"What happens if I fail you? Do your women eliminate me?"

"I try not to burden the Fish Speakers with guilt."

"But you would burden me?"

"If you accept it."

"If I find that you're worse than the Harkonnens, I'll turn against you."

How like a Duncan. They measure all evil against the Harkonnens. How little they know of evil.

Leto said: "The Baron ate whole planets, Duncan. What could be worse than that?"

"Eating the Empire."

"I am pregnant with my Empire. I'll die giving birth to it."

"If I could believe that . . ."

"Will you command my Guard?"

"Why me?"

"You're the best."

"Dangerous work, I'd imagine. Is that how my predecessors died, doing your dangerous work?"

"Some of them."

"I wish I had the memories of those others!"

"You couldn't have and still be the original."

"I want to learn about them, though."

"You will."

"So the Atreides still need a sharp knife?"

"We have jobs that only a Duncan Idaho can do."

"You say . . . we . . ." Idaho swallowed, looked at the door, then at Leto's face.

Leto spoke to him as Muad'Dib would have, but still in the Leto-voice.

"When we climbed to Sietch Tabr for the last time together, you had my loyalty then and I had yours. Nothing of that has really changed."

"That was your father."

"That was me!" Paul Muad'Dib's voice of command coming from Leto's bulk always shocked the gholas.

Idaho whispered: "All of you . . . in that one . . . body . . ." He broke off.

Leto remained silent. This was the decision moment.

Presently, Idaho permitted himself that devil-may-care grin for which he had been so well known. "Then I will speak to the first Leto and to Paul, the ones who know me best. Use me well, for I did love you."

Leto closed his eyes. Such words always distressed him. He knew it was love to which he was most vulnerable.

Moneo, who had been listening, came to the rescue. He entered and said: "Lord, shall I take Duncan Idaho to the guards he will command?"

"Yes." The one word was all that Leto could manage.

Moneo took Idaho's arm and led him away.

Good Moneo, Leto thought. *So good. He knows me so well, but I despair of his ever understanding me.*

I know the evil of my ancestors because I am those people. The balance is delicate in the extreme. I know that few of you who read my words have ever thought about your ancestors this way. It has not occurred to you that your ancestors were survivors and that the survival itself sometimes involved savage decisions, a kind of wanton brutality which civilized humankind works very hard to suppress. What price will you pay for that suppression? Will you accept your own extinction?

—THE STOLEN JOURNALS

As he dressed for his first morning of Fish Speaker command, Idaho tried to shake off a nightmare. It had awakened him twice and both times he had gone out on the balcony to stare up at the stars, the dream still roaring in his head.

Women . . . weaponless women in black armor . . . rushing at him with the hoarse, mindless shouting of a mob . . . waving hands moist with red blood . . . and as they swarmed over him, their mouths opened to display terrible fangs!

In that moment, he awoke.

Morning light did little to dispel the effects of the nightmare.

They had provided him with a room in the north tower. The balcony looked out over a vista of dunes to a distant cliff with what appeared to be a mud-hut village at its base.

Idaho buttoned his tunic as he stared at the scene.

Why does Leto choose only women for his army?

Several comely Fish Speakers had offered to spend the night with their new commander, but Idaho had rejected them.

It was not like the Atreides to use sex as a persuader!

He looked down at his clothing: a black uniform with golden piping, a red hawk at the left breast. That, at least, was familiar. No insignia of rank.

"They know your face," Moneo had said.

Strange little man, Moneo.

This thought brought Idaho up short. Reflection told him that Moneo was not little. *Very controlled, yes, but no shorter than I am.* Moneo appeared drawn into himself, though . . . collected.

Idaho glanced around his room—sybaritic in its attention to comfort—soft cushions, appliances concealed behind panels of brown polished wood. The bath was an ornate display of pastel blue tiles with a combination bath and shower in which at least six people could bathe at the same time. The whole place invited self-indulgence. These were quarters where you could let your senses indulge in remembered pleasures.

"Clever," Idaho whispered.

A gentle tapping on his door was followed by a female voice saying: "Commander? Moneo is here."

Idaho glanced out at the sunburnt colors on the distant cliff.

"Commander?" The voice was a bit louder.

"Come in," Idaho called.

Moneo entered, closing the door behind him. He wore tunic and trousers of chalk-white which forced the eyes to concentrate on his face. Moneo glanced once around the room.

"So this is where they put you. Those damned women! I suppose they thought they were being kind, but they ought to know better."

"How do you know what I like?" Idaho demanded. Even as he asked it, he realized it was a foolish question.

I'm not the first Duncan Idaho that Moneo has seen.

Moneo merely smiled and shrugged.

"I did not mean to offend you, Commander. Will you keep these quarters, then?"

"I like the view."

"But not the furnishings." It was a statement.

"Those can be changed," Idaho said.

"I will see to it."

"I suppose you're here to explain my duties."

"As much as I can. I know how strange everything must appear to you at first. This civilization is profoundly different from the one you knew."

"I can see that. How did my . . . predecessor die?"

Moneo shrugged. It appeared to be his standard gesture, but there was nothing self-effacing about it.

"He was not fast enough to escape the consequences of a decision he had made," Moneo said.

"Be specific."

Moneo sighed. The Duncans were always like this—so demanding.

"The rebellion killed him. Do you wish the details?"

"Would they be useful to me?"

"No."

"I'll want a complete briefing on this rebellion today, but first: why are there no men in Leto's army?"

"He has you."

"You know what I mean."

"He has a curious theory about armies. I have discussed it with him on many occasions. But do you not want to breakfast before I explain?"

"Can't we have both at the same time?"

Moneo turned toward the door and called out a single word: "Now!"

The effect was immediate and fascinating to Idaho. A troop of young Fish Speakers swarmed into the room. Two of them took a folding table and chairs from behind a panel and placed them on the balcony. Others set the table for two people. More brought food—fresh fruit, hot rolls and a steaming drink which smelled faintly of spice and caffeine. It was all done with a swift and silent efficiency which spoke of long practice. They left as they had come, without a word.

Idaho found himself seated across from Moneo at the table within a minute after the start of this curious performance.

"Every morning like that?" Idaho asked.

"Only if you wish it."

Idaho sampled the drink: melange-coffee. He recognized the fruit, the soft Caladan melon called *paradan*.

My favorite.

"You know me pretty well," Idaho said.

Moneo smiled. "We've had some practice. Now, about your question."

"And Leto's curious theory."

"Yes. He says that the all-male army was too dangerous to its civilian support base."

"That's crazy! Without the army, there would've been no . . ."

"I know the argument. But he says that the male army was a survival of the screening function delegated to the nonbreeding males in the prehistoric pack. He says it was a curiously consistent fact that it was always the older males who sent the younger males into battle."

"What does that mean, *screening function*?"

"The ones who were always out on the dangerous perimeter protecting the core of breeding males, females and the young. The ones who first encountered the predator."

"How is that dangerous to the . . . civilians?"

Idaho took a bite of the melon, found it ripened perfectly.

"The Lord Leto says that when it was denied an external enemy, the all-male army always turned against its own population. Always."

"Contending for the females?"

"Perhaps. He obviously does not believe, however, that it was *that* simple."

"I don't find this a curious theory."

"You have not heard all of it."

"There's more?"

"Oh, yes. He says that the all-male army has a strong tendency toward homosexual activities."

Idaho glared across the table at Moneo. "I never . . ."

"Of course not. He is speaking about sublimation, about deflected energies and all the rest of it."

"The rest of what?" Idaho was prickly with anger at what he saw as an attack on his male self-image.

"Adolescent attitudes, just boys together, jokes designed purely to cause pain, loyalty only to your pack-mates . . . things of that nature."

Idaho spoke coldly. "What's your opinion?"

"I remind myself"—Moneo turned and spoke while looking out at the view—"of something which he has said and which I am sure is true. He is every soldier in human history. He offered to parade for me a series of examples—famous military figures who were frozen in adolescence. I declined the offer. I have read my history with care and have recognized this characteristic for myself."

Moneo turned and looked directly into Idaho's eyes.

"Think about it, Commander."

Idaho prided himself on self-honesty and this hit him. Cults of youth and adolescence preserved in the military? It had the ring of truth. There were examples in his own experience . . .

Moneo nodded. "The homosexual, latent or otherwise, who maintains that condition for reasons which could be called purely psychological, tends to indulge in pain-causing behavior—seeking it for himself and inflicting it upon others. Lord Leto says this goes back to the testing behavior in the prehistoric pack."

"You believe him?"

"I do."

Idaho took a bite of the melon. It had lost its sweet savor. He swallowed and put down his spoon.

"I will have to think about this," Idaho said.

"Of course."

"You're not eating," Idaho said.

"I was up before dawn and ate then." Moneo gestured at his plate. "The women continually try to tempt me."

"Do they ever succeed?"

"Occasionally."

"You're right. I find his theory curious. Is there more to it?"

"Ohhh, he says that when it breaks out of the adolescent-homosexual restraints, the male army is essentially rapist. Rape is often murderous and that's not survival behavior."

Idaho scowled.

A tight smile flitted across Moneo's mouth. "Lord Leto says that only Atreides discipline and moral restraints prevented some of the worst excesses in your times."

A deep sigh shook Idaho.

Moneo sat back, thinking of a thing the God Emperor had once said: *"No matter how much we ask after the truth, self-awareness is often unpleasant. We do not feel kindly toward the Truthsayer."*

"Those damned Atreides!" Idaho said.

"I am Atreides," Moneo said.

"What?" Idaho was shocked.

"His breeding program," Moneo said. "I'm sure the Tleilaxu mentioned it. I am directly descended from the mating of his sister and Harq al-Ada."

Idaho leaned toward him. "Then tell me, Atreides, how are women better soldiers than men?"

"They find it easier to mature."

Idaho shook his head in bewilderment.

"They have a compelling physical way of moving from adolescence into maturity," Moneo said. "As Lord Leto says, 'Carry a baby in you for nine months and that changes you.' "

Idaho sat back. "What does he know about it?"

Moneo merely stared at him until Idaho recalled the multitude in Leto—both male and female. The realization plunged over Idaho. Moneo saw it, recalling a comment of the God Emperor's: *"Your words brand him with the look you want him to have."*

As the silence continued, Moneo cleared his throat. Presently, he said: "The immensity of the Lord Leto's memories has been known to stop my tongue, too."

"Is he being honest with us?" Idaho asked.

"I believe him."

"But he does so many . . . I mean, take this breeding program. How long has that been going on?"

"From the very first. From the day he took it away from the Bene Gesserit."

"What does he want from it?"

"I wish I knew."

"But you're . . ."

"An Atreides and his chief aide, yes."

"You haven't convinced me that a female army is best."

"They continue the species."

At last, Idaho's frustration and anger had an object. "Is that what I was doing with them that first night—breeding?"

"Possibly. The Fish Speakers take no precautions against pregnancy."

"Damn him! I'm not some animal he can move from stall to stall like a . . . like a . . ."

"Like a stud?"

"Yes!"

"But the Lord Leto refuses to follow the Tleilaxu pattern of gene surgery and artificial insemination."

"What have the Tleilaxu got to . . ."

"They are the object lesson. Even I can see that. Their Face Dancers are mules, closer to a colony organism than to human."

"Those others of . . . me . . . were any of them his studs?"

"Some. You have descendants."

"Who?"

"I am one."

Idaho stared into Moneo's eyes, lost suddenly in a tangle of relationships. Idaho found the relationships impossible to understand. Moneo obviously was so much older than . . . *But I am* . . . Which of them was truly the older? Which the ancestor and which the descendant?

"I sometimes have trouble with this myself," Moneo said. "If it helps, the Lord Leto assures me that you are not my descendant, not in any ordinary sense. However, you may well father some of my descendants."

Idaho shook his head from side to side.

"Sometimes I think only the God Emperor himself can understand these things," Moneo said.

"That's another thing!" Idaho said. "This god business."

"The Lord Leto says he has created a holy obscenity."

This was not the response Idaho had expected. *What did I expect?*
A defense of the Lord Leto?

"Holy obscenity," Moneo repeated. The words rolled from his
tongue with a strange sense of gloating in them.

Idaho focused a probing stare on Moneo. *He hates his God Em-*
peror! No . . . he fears him. But don't we always hate what we fear?

"Why do you believe in him?" Idaho demanded.

"You ask if I share in the popular religion?"

"No! Does he?"

"I think so."

"Why? Why do you think so?"

"Because he says he wishes to create no more Face Dancers. He
insists that his human stock, once it has been paired, breeds in the way
it has always bred."

"What the hell does that have to do with it?"

"You asked me what he believes in. I think he believes in chance. I
think that's his god."

"That's superstition!"

"Considering the circumstances of the Empire, a very daring superstition."

Idaho glared at Moneo. "You damned Atreides," he muttered.
"You'll dare anything!"

Moneo noted that there was dislike mixed with admiration in Idaho's voice.

The Duncans always begin that way.

What is the most profound difference between us, between you and me? You already know it. It's these ancestral memories. Mine come at me in the full glare of awareness. Yours work from your blind side. Some call it instinct or fate. The memories apply their leverages to each of us—on what we think and what we do. You think you are immune to such influences? I am Galileo. I stand here and tell you: "Yet it moves." That which moves can exert its force in ways no mortal power ever before dared stem. I am here to dare this.

—THE STOLEN JOURNALS

"When she was a child, she watched me, remember? When she thought I was not aware, Siona watched me like the desert hawk which circles above the lair of its prey. You yourself mentioned it."

Leto rolled his body a quarter turn on his cart while speaking. This brought his cowled face close to that of Moneo, who trotted beside the cart.

It was barely dawn on the desert road which followed the high artificial ridge from the Citadel in the Sareer to the Festival City. The road from the desert ran laser-beam straight until it reached this point where it curved widely and dipped into terraced canyons before crossing the Idaho River. The air was full of thick mists from the river tumbling in its distant clamor, but Leto had opened the bubble cover which sealed the front of his cart. The moisture made his worm-self tingle with vague distress, but there was the smell of sweet desert growth in the mist and his human nostrils savored it. He ordered the cortege to stop.

"Why are we stopping, Lord?" Moneo asked.

Leto did not answer. The cart creaked as he heaved his bulk into an arching curve which lifted his head and allowed him to look across the Forbidden Forest to the Kynes Sea glistening silver far off to the right. He turned left and there were the remains of the Shield Wall, a sinuous low shadow in the morning light. The ridge here had been raised almost two thousand meters to enclose the Sareer and limit airborne moisture there. From his vantage, Leto could see the distant notch where he had caused the Festival City of Onn to be built.

"It is a whim which stops me," Leto said.

"Shouldn't we cross the bridge before resting?" Moneo asked.

"I am not resting."

Leto stared ahead. After a series of switchbacks which were visible from here only as a twisting shadow, the high road crossed the river on a faery bridge, climbed to a buffer ridge and then sloped down to the city which presented a vista of glittering spires at this distance.

"The Duncan acts subdued," Leto said. "Have you had your long conversation with him?"

"Precisely as you required, Lord."

"Well, it's only been four days," Leto said. "They often take longer to recover."

"He has been busy with your Guard, Lord. They were out until late again last night."

"The Duncans do not like to walk in the open. They think about the things which could be used to attack us."

"I know, Lord."

Leto turned and looked squarely at Moneo. The majordomo wore a green cloak over his white uniform. He stood beside the open bubble cover, exactly in the place where duty required that he station himself on these excursions.

"You are very dutiful, Moneo," Leto said.

"Thank you, Lord."

Guards and courtiers kept themselves at a respectful distance well behind the cart. Most of them were trying to avoid even the appearance of eavesdropping on Leto and Moneo. Not so Idaho. He had positioned some of the Fish Speaker guards at both sides of the Royal Road, spreading them out. Now, he stood staring at the cart. Idaho wore a black uniform with white piping, a gift of the Fish Speakers, Moneo had said.

"They like this one very much. He is good at what he does."

"What does he do, Moneo?"

"Why, guard your person, Lord."

The women of the Guard all wore skintight green uniforms, each with a red Atreides hawk at the left breast.

"They watch him very closely," Leto said.

"Yes. He is teaching them hand signals. He says it's the Atreides way."

"That is certainly correct. I wonder why the previous one didn't do that?"

"Lord, if you don't know . . ."

"I jest, Moneo. The previous Duncan did not feel threatened until it was too late. Has this one accepted our explanations?"

"So I'm told, Lord. He is well started in your service."

"Why is he carrying only that knife in the belt sheath?"

"The women have convinced him that only the specially trained among them should have lasguns."

"Your caution is groundless, Moneo. Tell the women that it's much too early for us to begin fearing this one."

"As my Lord commands."

It was obvious to Leto that his new Guard Commander did not enjoy the presence of the courtiers. He stood well away from them. Most of the courtiers, he had been told, were civil functionaries. They were decked out in their brightest and finest for this day when they could parade themselves in their full power and in the presence of the God Emperor. Leto could see how foolish the courtiers must appear to Idaho. But Leto could remember far more foolish finery and he thought that this day's display might be an improvement.

"Have you introduced him to Siona?" Leto asked.

At the mention of Siona, Moneo's brows congealed into a scowl.

"Calm yourself," Leto said. "Even when she spied on me, I cherished her."

"I sense danger in her, Lord. I think sometimes she sees into my most secret thoughts."

"The wise child knows her father."

"I do not joke, Lord."

"Yes, I can see that. Have you noticed that the Duncan grows impatient?"

"They scouted the road almost to the bridge," Moneo said.

"What did they find?"

"The same thing I found—a new Museum Fremen."

"Another petition?"

"Do not be angry, Lord."

Once more, Leto peered ahead. This necessary exposure to the open air, the long and stately journey with all of its ritual requirements to reassure the Fish Speakers, all of it troubled Leto. And now, another petition!

Idaho strode forward to stop directly behind Moneo.

There was a sense of menace about Idaho's movements. *Surely not this soon,* Leto thought.

"Why are we stopping, m'Lord?" Idaho asked.

"I often stop here," Leto said.

It was true. He turned and looked beyond the faery bridge. The way twisted downward out of the canyon heights into the Forbidden Forest and thence through fields beside the river. Leto had often stopped here to watch the sunrise. There was something about this morning, though, the sun striking across the familiar vista . . . something which stirred old memories.

The fields of the Royal Plantations reached outward beyond the forest and, when the sun lifted over the far curve of land, it beamed glowing gold across grain rippling in the fields. The grain reminded Leto of sand, of sweeping dunes which once had marched across this very ground.

And will march once more.

The grain was not quite the bright silica amber of his remembered desert. Leto looked back at the cliff-enclosed distances of his Sareer, his sanctuary of the past. The colors were distinctly different. All the same, when he looked once more toward the Festival City, he felt an ache where his many hearts once more were reforming in their slow transformation toward something profoundly alien.

What is it about this morning that makes me think about my lost humanity? Leto wondered.

Of all the Royal party looking at that familiar scene of grain fields and forest, Leto knew that only he still thought of the lush landscape as the *bahr bela ma*, the ocean without water.

"Duncan," Leto said. "You see that out there toward the city? That was the Tanzerouft."

"The Land of Terror?" Idaho revealed his surprise in the quick look toward Onn and the sudden return of his gaze to Leto.

"The *bahr bela ma*," Leto said. "It has been concealed under a carpet of plants for more than three thousand years. Of all who live on Arrakis today, only the two of us ever saw the desert original."

Idaho looked toward Onn. "Where is the Shield Wall?" he asked.

"Muad'Dib's Gap is right there, right where we built the City."

"That line of little hills, that was the Shield Wall? What happened to it?"

"You are standing on it."

Idaho looked up at Leto, then down to the roadway and all around.

"Lord, shall we proceed?" Moneo asked.

Moneo, with that clock ticking in his breast, is the goad to duty, Leto thought. There were important visitors to see and other vital matters. Time pressed him. And he did not like it when his God Emperor talked about old times with the Duncans.

Leto was suddenly aware that he had paused here far longer than ever before. The courtiers and guards were cold after their run in the morning air. Some had chosen their clothing more for show than protection.

Then again, Leto thought, *perhaps show is a form of protection.*

"There were dunes," Idaho said.

"Stretching for thousands of kilometers," Leto agreed.

Moneo's thoughts churned. He was familiar with the God Emperor's reflexive mood, but there was a sense of sadness in it this day. Perhaps the recent death of a Duncan. Leto sometimes let important information drop when he was sad. You never questioned the God Emperor's moods or his whims, but sometimes they could be employed.

Siona will have to be warned, Moneo thought. *If the young fool will listen to me!*

She was far more of a rebel than he had been. Far more. Leto had tamed his Moneo, sensitized him to the Golden Path and the rightful duties for which he had been bred, but methods used on a Moneo would not work with Siona. In his observation of this, Moneo had learned things about his own training which he had never before suspected.

"I don't see any identifiable landmarks," Idaho was saying.

"Right over there," Leto said, pointing. "Where the forest ends. That was the way to Splintered Rock."

Moneo shut out their voices. *It was ultimate fascination with the God Emperor which finally brought me to heel.* Leto never ceased to surprise and amaze. He could not be reliably predicted. Moneo glanced at the God Emperor's profile. *What has he become?*

As part of his early duties, Moneo had studied the Citadel's private records, the historical accounts of Leto's transformation. But symbiosis with sandtrout remained a mystery which even Leto's own words could not dispel. If the accounts were to be believed, the sandtrout skin made his body almost invulnerable to time and violence. The great body's ribbed core could even absorb lasgun bursts!

First the sandtrout, then the worm—all part of the great cycle which had produced melange. That cycle lay within the God Emperor . . . marking time.

"Let us proceed," Leto said.

Moneo realized that he had missed something. He came out of his reverie and looked at a smiling Duncan Idaho.

"We used to call that woolgathering," Leto said.

"I'm sorry, Lord," Moneo said. "I was . . ."

"You were woolgathering, but it's all right."

His mood's improved, Moneo thought. *I can thank the Duncan for that, I think.*

Leto adjusted his position on the cart, closed part of the bubble cover and left only his head free. The cart crunched over small rocks on the roadbed as Leto activated it.

Idaho took up position at Moneo's shoulder and trotted along beside him.

"There are floater bulbs under that cart, but he uses the wheels," Idaho said. "Why is that?"

"It pleases the Lord Leto to use wheels instead of antigravity."

"What makes the thing go? How does he steer it?"

"Have you asked him?"

"I haven't had the opportunity."

"The Royal Cart is of Ixian manufacture."

"What does that mean?"

"It is said that the Lord Leto activates his cart and steers it just by thinking in a particular way."

"Don't you know?"

"Questions such as this do not please him."

Even to his intimates, Moneo thought, *the God Emperor remains a mystery.*

"Moneo!" Leto called.

"You had better return to your guards," Moneo said, gesturing for Idaho to fall back.

"I'd rather be out in front with them," Idaho said.

"The Lord Leto does not want that! Now go back."

Moneo hurried to place himself close beside Leto's face, noting that Idaho was falling back through the courtiers to the rear ring of guards.

Leto looked down at Moneo. "I thought you handled that very well, Moneo."

"Thank you, Lord."

"Do you know why the Duncan wants to be out in front?"

"Certainly, Lord. It's where your Guard should be."

"And this one senses danger."

"I don't understand you, Lord. I cannot understand why you do these things."

"That's true, Moneo."

The female sense of sharing originated as familial sharing—
care of the young, the gathering and preparation of food,
sharing joys, love and sorrows. Funeral lamentation originated with women. Religion began as a female monopoly,
wrested from them only after its social power became too
dominant. Women were the first medical researchers and
practitioners. There has never been any clear balance between the sexes because power goes with certain roles as it
certainly goes with knowledge.

—THE STOLEN JOURNALS

For the Reverend Mother Tertius Eileen Anteac, this had been a disas-
trous morning. She had arrived on Arrakis with her fellow Truthsayer,
Marcus Claire Luyseyal, both of them coming down with their official
party less than three hours ago aboard the first shuttle from the Guild
heighliner hanging in stationary orbit. First, they had been assigned
rooms at the absolute edge of the Festival City's Embassy Quarter. The
rooms were small and not quite clean.

"Any farther out and we'd be camping in the slums," Luyseyal had
said.

Next they had been denied communications facilities. All of the
screens remained blank no matter how many switches were toggled
and palm-dials turned.

Anteac had addressed herself sharply to the heavyset officer commanding the Fish Speaker escort, a glowering woman with low brows and the muscles of a manual laborer.

"I wish to complain to your commander!"

"No complaints allowed at Festival Time," the amazon had rasped.

Anteac had glared at the officer, a look which in Anteac's old and seamed face had been known to make even her fellow Reverend Mothers hesitate.

The amazon had merely smiled and said: "I have a message. I am to tell you that your audience with the God Emperor has been moved to the last position."

Most of the Bene Gesserit party had heard this and even the lowliest attendant-postulate had recognized the significance. All of the spice allotments would be fixed or *(The Gods protect us!)* even gone by that time.

"We were to have been third," Anteac had said, her voice remarkably mild in the circumstances.

"It is the God Emperor's command!"

Anteac knew that tone in a Fish Speaker. To defy it risked violence. *A morning of disasters and now this!*

Anteac occupied a low stool against one wall of a tiny, almost empty room near the center of their inadequate quarters. Beside her there was a low pallet, no more than you would assign to an acolyte! The walls were a pale, scabrous green and there was but one aging glowglobe so defective it could not be tuned out of the yellow. The room gave signs of having been a storage chamber. It smelled musty. Dents and scratches marred the black plastic of the floor.

Smoothing her black aba robe across her knees, Anteac leaned close to the postulate messenger who knelt, head bowed, directly in front of the Reverend Mother. The messenger was a doe-eyed blonde creature with the perspiration of fear and excitement on her face and neck. She wore a dusty tan robe with the dirt of the streets along its hem.

"You are certain, absolutely certain?" Anteac spoke softly to soothe the poor girl, who still trembled with the gravity of her message.

"Yes, Reverend Mother." She kept her gaze lowered.

"Go through it once more," Anteac said, and she thought: *I'm sparring for time. I heard her correctly.*

The messenger lifted her gaze to Anteac and looked directly into the totally blue eyes as all the postulates and acolytes were taught to do.

"As I was commanded, I made contact with the Ixians at their Embassy and presented your greetings. I then inquired if they had any messages for me to bring back."

"Yes, yes, girl! I know. Get to the heart of it."

The messenger gulped. "The spokesman identified himself as Othwi Yake, temporary superior in the Embassy and assistant to the former Ambassador."

"You're sure he was not a Face Dancer substitute?"

"None of the signs were there, Reverend Mother."

"Very well. We know this Yake. You may continue."

"Yake said they were awaiting the arrival of the new . . ."

"Hwi Noree, the new Ambassador, yes. She's due here today."

The messenger wet her lips with her tongue.

Anteac made a mental note to return this poor creature to a more elementary training schedule. Messengers should have better self-control, although some allowance had to be made for the seriousness of this message.

"He then asked me to wait," the messenger said. "He left the room and returned shortly with a Tleilaxu, a Face Dancer, I'm sure of it. There were the certain signs of the . . ."

"I'm sure you're correct, girl," Anteac said. "Now, get to the . . ." Anteac broke off as Luyseyal entered.

"What's this I hear about messages from the Ixians and Tleilaxu?" Luyseyal asked.

"The girl's repeating it now," Anteac said.

"Why wasn't I summoned?" Anteac looked up at her fellow Truthsayer, thinking that Luyseyal might be one of the finest practitioners of the *art* but she remained too conscious of rank. Luyseyal was young, however, with the sensuous oval features of the Jessica-type, and those genes tended to carry a headstrong nature.

Anteac spoke softly: "Your acolyte said you were meditating."

Luyseyal nodded, sat down on the pallet and spoke to the messenger. "Continue."

"The Face Dancer said he had a message for the Reverend Mothers. He used the plural," the messenger said.

"He knew there were two of us this time," Anteac said.

"Everyone knows it," Luyseyal said.

Anteac returned her full attention to the messenger. "Would you enter memory-trance now, girl, and give us the Face Dancer's words verbatim?"

The messenger nodded, sat back onto her heels and clasped her hands in her lap. She took three deep breaths, closed her eyes and let her shoulders sag. When she spoke, her voice had a high-pitched, nasal twang.

"Tell the Reverend Mothers that by tonight the Empire will be rid of its God Emperor. We will strike him today before he reaches Onn. We cannot fail."

A deep breath shook the messenger. Her eyes opened and she looked up at Anteac.

"The Ixian, Yake, told me to hurry back with this message. He then touched the back of my left hand in that particular way, further convincing me that he was not . . ."

"Yake is one of ours," Anteac said. "Tell Luyseyal the message of the fingers."

The messenger looked at Luyseyal. "We have been invaded by Face Dancers and cannot move."

As Luyseyal started and began to rise from the pallet, Anteac said: "I already have taken the appropriate steps to guard our doors." Anteac looked at the messenger. "You may go now, girl. You have been adequate to your task."

"Yes, Reverend Mother." The messenger lifted her lithe body with a certain amount of grace, but there was no doubt in her movements that she knew the import of Anteac's words. *Adequate* was not *well done*.

When the messenger had gone, Luyseyal said: "She should've made some excuse to study the Embassy and find out how many of the Ixians have been replaced."

"I think not," Anteac said. "In that respect, she performed well. No, but it would have been better had she found a way to get a more detailed report from Yake. I fear we have lost him."

"The reason the Tleilaxu sent us that message is obvious, of course," Luyseyal said.

"They are really going to attack him," Anteac said.

"Naturally. It's what the *fools* would do. But I address myself to why they sent the message to us."

Anteac nodded. "They think we now have no choice except to join them."

"And if we try to warn the Lord Leto, the Tleilaxu will learn our messengers and their contacts."

"What if the Tleilaxu succeed?" Anteac asked.

"Not likely."

"We do not know their actual plan, only its general timing."

"What if this girl, this Siona, has a part in it?" Luyseyal asked.

"I have asked myself that same question. Have you heard the full report from the Guild?"

"Only the summary. Is that enough?"

"Yes, with high probability."

"You should be careful with terms such as *high probability*," Luyseyal said. "We don't want anyone thinking you're a Mentat."

Anteac's tone was dry. "I presume you will not give me away."

"Do you think the Guild is right about this Siona?" Luyseyal asked.

"I do not have enough information. If they are right, she is something extraordinary."

"As the Lord Leto's father was extraordinary?"

"A Guild navigator could conceal himself from the oracular eye of the Lord Leto's father."

"But not from the Lord Leto."

"I have read the full Guild report with care. She does not so much conceal herself and the actions around her as, well . . ."

"She fades," Luyseyal said. "She fades from their *sight*."

"She alone," Anteac said.

"And from the *sight* of the Lord Leto as well?"

"They do not know."

"Do we dare make contact with her?"

"Do we dare not?" Anteac asked.

"This all may be moot if the Tleilaxu . . . Anteac, we should at least make the attempt to warn him."

"We have no communications devices and there now are Fish Speaker guards at the door. They permit our people to enter, but not to leave."

"Should we speak to one of them?"

"I have thought about that. We can always say we feared they were Face Dancer substitutes."

"Guards at the door," Luyseyal muttered. "Is it possible that he knows?"

"Anything is possible."

"With the Lord Leto that's the only thing you can say for sure," Luyseyal said.

Anteac permitted herself a small sigh as she lifted herself from the stool. "How I long for the old days when we had all of the spice we could ever need."

"*Ever* was just another illusion," Luyseyal said. "I hope we have learned our lesson well, no matter how the Tleilaxu make out today."

"They will do it clumsily whatever the outcome," Anteac grumbled. "Gods! There are no good assassins to be found anymore."

"There are always the ghola Idahos," Luyseyal said.

"What did you say?" Anteac stared at her companion.

"There are always . . ."

"Yes!"

"The gholas are too slow in the body," Luyseyal said.

"But not in the head."

"What're you thinking?"

"Is it possible that the Tleilaxu . . . No, not even they could be that . . ."

"An Idaho Face Dancer?" Luyseyal whispered.

Anteac nodded mutely.

"Put it out of your mind," Luyseyal said. "They could not be that stupid."

"That's a dangerous judgment to make about Tleilaxu," Anteac said. "We must prepare ourselves for the worst. Get one of those Fish Speaker guards in here!"

Unceasing warfare gives rise to its own social conditions which have been similar in all epochs. People enter a permanent state of alertness to ward off attacks. You see the absolute rule of the autocrat. All new things become dangerous frontier districts—new planets, new economic areas to exploit, new ideas or new devices, visitors—everything suspect. Feudalism takes firm hold, sometimes disguised as a politbureau or similar structure, but always present. Hereditary succession follows the lines of power. The blood of the powerful dominates. The vice regents of heaven or their equivalent apportion the wealth. And they know they must control inheritance or slowly let the power melt away. Now, do you understand Leto's Peace?

—THE STOLEN JOURNALS

"Have the Bene Gesserit been informed of the new schedule?" Leto asked.

His entourage had entered the first shallow cut which would wind into switchbacks at the approach to the bridge across the Idaho River. The sun stood at the morning's first quarter and a few courtiers were shedding cloaks. Idaho walked with a small troop of Fish Speakers at the left flank, his uniform beginning to show traces of dust and perspiration. Walking and trotting at the speed of a Royal peregrination was hard work.

Moneo stumbled and caught himself. "They have been informed, Lord." The change of schedule had not been easy, but Moneo had learned to expect erratic shifts of direction at Festival time. He kept contingency plans at the ready.

"Are they still petitioning for a permanent Embassy on Arrakis?" Leto asked.

"Yes, Lord. I gave them the usual answer."

"A simple *'no'* should suffice," Leto said. "They no longer need to be reminded that I abhor their religious pretensions."

"Yes, Lord." Moneo held himself to just within the prescribed distance beside Leto's cart. The Worm was very much present this morning—the bodily signs quite apparent to Moneo's eyes. No doubt it was the moisture in the air. That always seemed to bring out the Worm.

"Religion always leads to rhetorical despotism," Leto said. "Before the Bene Gesserit, the Jesuits were the best at it."

"Jesuits, Lord?"

"Surely you've met them in your histories?"

"I'm not certain, Lord. When were they?"

"No matter. You learn enough about rhetorical despotism from a study of the Bene Gesserit. Of course, they do not begin by deluding themselves with it."

The Reverend Mothers are in for a bad time, Moneo told himself. *He's going to preach at them. They detest that. This could cause serious trouble.*

"What was their reaction?" Leto asked.

"I'm told they were disappointed but did not press the matter."

And Moneo thought: *I'd best prepare them for more disappointment. And they'll have to be kept away from the delegations of Ix and Tleilaxu.*

Moneo shook his head. This could lead to some very nasty plotting. The Duncan had better be warned.

"It leads to self-fulfilling prophecy and justifications for all manner of obscenities," Leto said.

"This . . . rhetorical despotism, Lord?"

"Yes! It shields evil behind walls of self-righteousness which are proof against all arguments against the evil."

Moneo kept a wary eye on Leto's body, noting the way the hands twisted, almost a random movement, the twitching of the great ribbed segments. *What will I do if the Worm comes out of him here?* Perspiration broke out on Moneo's forehead.

"It feeds on deliberately twisted meanings to discredit opposition," Leto said.

"All of that, Lord?"

"The Jesuits called that 'securing your power base.' It leads directly to hypocrisy which is always betrayed by the gap between actions and explanations. They never agree."

"I must study this more carefully, Lord."

"Ultimately, it rules by guilt because hypocrisy brings on the witch hunt and the demand for scapegoats."

"Shocking, Lord."

The cortege rounded a corner where the rock had been opened for a glimpse of the bridge in the distance.

"Moneo, are you paying close attention to me?"

"Yes, Lord. Indeed."

"I'm describing a tool of the religious power base."

"I recognize that, Lord."

"Then why are you so afraid?"

"Talk of religious power always makes me uneasy, Lord."

"Because you and the Fish Speakers wield it in my name?"

"Of course, Lord."

"Power bases are very dangerous because they attract people who are truly insane, people who seek power only for the sake of power. Do you understand?"

"Yes, Lord. That is why you so seldom grant petitions for appointments in your government."

"Excellent, Moneo!"

"Thank you, Lord."

"In the shadow of every religion lurks a Torquemada," Leto said. "You have never encountered that name. I know because I caused it to be expunged from all the records."

"Why was that, Lord?"

"He was an obscenity. He made living torches out of people who disagreed with him."

Moneo pitched his voice low. "Like the historians who angered you, Lord?"

"Do you question my actions, Moneo?"

"No, Lord!"

"Good. The historians died peacefully. Not a one felt the flames. Torquemada, however, delighted in commending to his god the agonized screams of his burning victims."

"How horrible, Lord."

The cortege turned another corner with a view of the bridge. The span appeared to be no closer.

Once more, Moneo studied his God Emperor. The Worm appeared no closer. Still too close, though. Moneo could feel the menace of that unpredictable presence, the Holy Presence which could kill without warning.

Moneo shuddered.

What had been the meaning of that strange . . . sermon? Moneo knew that few had ever heard the God Emperor speak thus. It was a privilege and a burden. It was part of the price paid for Leto's Peace. Generation after generation marched in their ordered way under the dictates of that peace. Only the Citadel's inner circle knew all of the infrequent breaks in that peace—the *incidents* when Fish Speakers were sent out in anticipation of violence.

Anticipation!

Moneo glanced at the now-silent Leto. The God Emperor's eyes were closed and a look of brooding had come over his face. That was another of the Worm signs—a bad one. Moneo trembled.

Did Leto anticipate even his own moments of wild violence? It was the anticipation of violence which sent tremors of awe and fear throughout the Empire. Leto knew where guards must be posted to put down a transitory uprising. He knew it before the event.

Even thinking about such matters dried Moneo's mouth. There

were times, Moneo believed, when the God Emperor could read any mind. Oh, Leto employed spies. An occasional shrouded figure passed by the Fish Speakers for the climb to Leto's tower aerie or descended to the crypt. Spies, no doubt of it, but Moneo suspected they were used merely to confirm what Leto already knew.

As though to confirm the fears in Moneo's mind, Leto said: "Do not try to force an understanding of my ways, Moneo. Let understanding come of itself."

"I will try, Lord."

"No, do *not* try. Tell me, instead, if you have announced yet that there will be no changes in the spice allotments."

"Not yet, Lord."

"Delay the announcement. I am changing my mind. You know, of course, that there will be new offers of bribes."

Moneo sighed. The amounts offered him in bribes had reached ridiculous heights. Leto, however, had appeared amused by the escalation.

"Draw them out," he had said earlier. "See how high they will go. Make it appear that you can be bribed at last."

Now, as they turned another corner with a view of the bridge, Leto asked: "Has House Corrino offered you a bribe?"

"Yes, Lord."

"Do you know the myth which says that someday House Corrino will be restored to its ancient powers?"

"I have heard it, Lord."

"Have the Corrino killed. It is a task for the Duncan. We will test him."

"So soon, Lord?"

"It is still known that melange can extend human life. Let it also be known that the spice can shorten life."

"As you command, Lord."

Moneo knew this response in himself. It was the way he spoke when he could not voice a deep objection which he felt. He also knew that the Lord Leto understood this and was amused by it. The amusement rankled.

"Try not to be impatient with me, Moneo," Leto said.

Moneo suppressed his feeling of bitterness. Bitterness brought peril. Rebels were bitter. The Duncans grew bitter before they died.

"Time has a different meaning for you than it has for me, Lord," Moneo said. "I wish I could know that meaning."

"You could but you will not."

Moneo heard rebuke in the words and fell silent, turning his thoughts instead to the melange problems. It was not often that the Lord Leto spoke of the spice, and then it usually was to set allotments or withdraw them, to apportion rewards or send the Fish Speakers after some newly revealed hoard. The greatest remaining store of spice, Moneo knew, lay in some place known only to the God Emperor. In his first days of Royal Service, Moneo had been covered in a hood and led by the Lord Leto himself to that secret place along twisting passages which Moneo had sensed were underground.

When I removed the hood, we were underground.

The place had filled Moneo with awe. Great bins of melange lay all around in a gigantic room cut from native rock and illuminated by glowglobes of an ancient design with arabesques of metal scrollwork upon them. The spice had glowed radiant blue in the dim silver light. And the smell—bitter cinnamon, unmistakable. There had been water dripping nearby. Their voices had echoed against the stone.

"One day all of this will be gone," the Lord Leto had said.

Shocked, Moneo had asked: "What will the Guild and Bene Gesserit do then?"

"What they are doing now, but more violently."

Staring around the gigantic room with its enormous store of melange, Moneo could only think of things he knew were happening in the Empire at that moment—bloody assassinations, piratical raids, spying and intrigue. The God Emperor kept a lid on the worst of it, but what remained was bad enough.

"The temptation," Moneo whispered.

"The temptation, indeed."

"Will there be no more melange, ever, Lord?"

"Someday, I will go back into the sand. I will be the source of spice then."

"You, Lord?"

"And I will produce something just as wonderful—more sandtrout—a hybrid and a prolific breeder."

Trembling at this revelation, Moneo stared at the shadowy figure of the God Emperor who spoke of such marvels.

"The sandtrout," Lord Leto said, "will link themselves into large living bubbles to enclose this planet's water deep underground. Just as it was in the Dune times."

"All of the water, Lord?"

"Most of it. Within three hundred years, the sandworm once more will reign here. It will be a new kind of sandworm, I promise you."

"How is that, Lord?"

"It will have animal awareness and a new cunning. The spice will be more dangerous to seek and far more perilous to keep."

Moneo had looked up at the cavern's rocky ceiling, his imagination probing through the rock to the surface.

"Everything desert again, Lord?"

"Watercourses will fill with sand. Crops will be choked and killed. Trees will be covered by great moving dunes. The sand-death will spread until . . . until a subtle signal is heard in the barren lands."

"What signal, Lord?"

"The signal for the next cycle, the coming of the Maker, the coming of Shai-Hulud."

"Will that be you, Lord?"

"Yes! The great sandworm of Dune will rise once more from the deeps. This land will be again the domain of spice and worm."

"But what of the people, Lord? All of the people?"

"Many will die. Food plants and the abundant growth of this land will be parched. Without nourishment, meat animals will die."

"Will everyone go hungry, Lord?"

"Undernourishment and the old diseases will stalk the land, while only the hardiest survive . . . the hardiest and most brutal."

"Must that be, Lord?"

"The alternatives are worse."

"Teach me about those alternatives, Lord."

"In time, you will know them."

As he marched beside the God Emperor in the morning light of their peregrination to Onn, Moneo could only admit that he had, indeed, learned of alternative evils.

To most of the Empire's docile citizens, Moneo knew, the firm knowledge which he held in his own head lay concealed in the Oral History, in the myths and wild stories told by infrequent mad prophets who cropped up on one planet or another to gather a short-lived following.

But I know what the Fish Speakers do.

And he knew also about evil men who sat at table, gorging themselves on rare delicacies while they watched the torture of fellow humans.

Until the Fish Speakers came, and gore erased such scenes.

"I enjoyed the way your daughter watched me," Leto said. "She was so unaware that I knew."

"Lord, I fear for her! She is my blood, my . . ."

"Mine, too, Moneo. Am I not Atreides? You would be better employed fearing for yourself."

Moneo cast a fearful glance along the God Emperor's body. The signs of the Worm remained too near. Moneo glanced at the cortege following, then along the road ahead. They now were into the steep descent, the switchbacks short and cut into high walls in the man-piled rocks of the cliff barrier which girdled the Sareer.

"Siona does not offend me, Moneo."

"But she . . ."

"Moneo! Here, in its mysterious capsule is one of life's great secrets. To be *surprised,* to have a new thing occur, *that* is what I desire most."

"Lord, I . . ."

"New! Isn't that a radiant, a *wonderful* word?"

"If you say it, Lord."

Leto was forced to remind himself then: *Moneo is my creature. I created him.*

"Your child is worth almost any price to me, Moneo. You decry her companions, but there may be one among them that she will love."

Moneo cast an involuntary glance back at Duncan Idaho marching with the guards. Idaho was glaring ahead as though trying to probe each turn in the road before they reached it. He did not like this place with its high walls all around from which attack might come. Idaho had sent scouts up there in the night and Moneo knew that some of them still lurked on the heights, but there also were ravines ahead before the marchers reached the river. And there had not been enough guards to station them everywhere.

"We will depend upon the Fremen," Moneo had reassured him.

"Fremen?" Idaho did not like what he heard about the Museum Fremen.

"At least they can sound an alarm against intruders," Moneo had said.

"You saw them and asked them to do that?"

"Of course."

Moneo had not dared to broach the subject of Siona to Idaho. Time enough for that later, but now the God Emperor had said a disturbing thing. Had there been a change in plans?

Moneo returned his attention to the God Emperor and lowered his voice.

"Love a companion, Lord? But you said the Duncan . . ."

"I said *love*, not *breed with!*"

Moneo trembled, thinking of how his own mating had been arranged, the wrenching away from . . .

No! Best not follow those memories!

There had been affection, even a real love . . . later, but in the first days . . .

"You are woolgathering again, Moneo."

"Forgive me, Lord, but when you speak of love . . ."

"You think I have no tender thoughts?"

"It's not that, Lord, but . . ."

"You think I have no memories of love and breeding, then?" The cart swerved toward Moneo, forcing him to dodge away, frightened by the glowering look on the Lord Leto's face.

"Lord, I beg your . . ."

"This *body* may never have known such tenderness, but *all* of the memories are mine!"

Moneo could see the signs of the Worm growing more dominant in the God Emperor's body and there was no escaping recognition of this mood.

I am in grave danger. We all are.

Moneo grew aware of every sound around him, the creaking of the Royal Cart, the coughs and low conversation from the entourage, the feet on the roadway. There was an exhalation of cinnamon from the God Emperor. The air here between the enclosing rock walls still held its morning chill and there was dampness from the river.

Was it the moisture bringing out the Worm?

"Listen to me, Moneo, as though your life depended on it."

"Yes, Lord," Moneo whispered, and he knew his life did depend on the care he took now, not only in listening but in observing.

"Part of me dwells forever underground without thought," Leto said. "That part reacts. It does things without a care for knowing or logic."

Moneo nodded, his attention glued on the God Emperor's face. Were the eyes about to glaze?

"I am forced to stand off and watch such things, nothing more," Leto said. "Such a reaction could cause your death. The choice is not mine. Do you hear?"

"I hear you, Lord," Moneo whispered.

"There is no such thing as *choice* in such an event! You accept it, merely accept it. You will never understand it or know it. What do you say to that?"

"I fear the unknown, Lord."

"But I don't fear it. Tell me why!"

Moneo had been expecting a crisis such as this and, now that it had come, he almost welcomed it. He knew that his life depended on his answer. He stared at his God Emperor, mind racing.

"It is because of all your memories, Lord."

"Yes?"

An incomplete answer, then. Moneo grasped at words. "You see everything that we know . . . all of it as it once was—unknown! A surprise to you . . . a surprise must be merely something new for you to know?" As he spoke, Moneo realized he had put a defensive question mark on something that should have been a bold statement, but the God Emperor only smiled.

"For such wisdom I grant you a boon, Moneo. What is your wish?"

Sudden relief only opened a path for other fears to emerge. "Could I bring Siona back to the Citadel?"

"That will cause me to test her sooner."

"She must be separated from her companions, Lord."

"Very well."

"My Lord is gracious."

"I am selfish."

The God Emperor turned away from Moneo then and fell silent.

Looking along the segmented body, Moneo observed that the Worm signs had subsided somewhat. This had turned out well after all. He thought then of the Fremen with their petition and fear returned.

That was a mistake. They will only arouse Him again. Why did I say they could present their petition?

The Fremen would be waiting up ahead, marshalled on this side of the river with their foolish papers waving in their hands.

Moneo marched in silence, his apprehension increasing with each step.

Over here sand blows; over there sand blows.
Over there a rich man waits; over here I wait.

—THE VOICE OF SHAI-HULUD,
FROM THE ORAL HISTORY

Sister Chenoeh's account, found among her papers after her death:

I obey both my tenets as a Bene Gesserit and the commands of the God
Emperor by withholding these words from my report while secreting
them that they may be found when I am gone. For the Lord Leto said to
me: "You will return to your Superiors with my message, but these words
keep secret for now. I will visit my rage upon your Sisterhood if you fail."

As the Reverend Mother Syaksa warned me before I left: "You must
do nothing which will bring down his wrath upon us."

While I ran beside the Lord Leto on that short peregrination of
which I had spoken, I thought to ask him about his likeness to a Reverend Mother. I said:

"Lord, I know how it is that a Reverend Mother acquires the memories of her ancestors and of others. How was it with you?"

"It was a design of our genetic history and the working of the spice.
My twin sister, Ghanima, and I were awakened in the womb, aroused
before birth into the presence of our ancestral memories."

"Lord . . . my Sisterhood calls that Abomination."

"And rightly so," the Lord Leto said. "The ancestral numbers can be overwhelming. And who knows before the event which force will command such a horde—good or evil?"

"Lord, how did you overcome such a force?"

"I did not overcome it," the Lord Leto said. "But the persistence of the pharaonic model saved both Ghani and me. Do you know that model, Sister Chenoeh?"

"We of the Sisterhood are well coached in history, Lord."

"Yes, but you do not think of this as I do," the Lord Leto said. "I speak of a disease of government which was caught by the Greeks who spread it to the Romans who distributed it so far and wide that it never has completely died out."

"Does my Lord speak riddles?"

"No riddles. I hate this thing, but it saved us. Ghani and I formed powerful internal alliances with ancestors who followed the pharaonic model. They helped us form a mingled identity within that long-dormant mob."

"I find this disturbing, Lord."

"And well you should."

"Why are you telling me this now, Lord? You have never answered one of us before in this manner, not that I know of."

"Because you listen well, Sister Chenoeh; because you will obey me and because I will never see you again."

The Lord Leto spoke those strange words to me and then he asked:

"Why have you not inquired about what your Sisterhood calls my *insane tyranny*?"

Emboldened by his manner, I ventured to say: "Lord, we know about some of your bloody executions. They trouble us."

The Lord Leto then did a strange thing. He closed his eyes as we went, and he said:

"Because I know you have been trained to record accurately whatever words you hear, I will speak to you now, Sister Chenoeh, as though you were a page in one of my journals. Preserve these words well, for I do not want them lost."

I assure my Sisterhood now that what follows, exactly as he spoke them, are the words uttered then by the Lord Leto:

"To my certain knowledge, when I am no longer consciously present here among you, when I am here only as a fearsome creature of the desert, many people will look back upon me as a tyrant.

"Fair enough. I have been tyrannical.

"A tyrant—not fully human, not insane, merely a tyrant. But even ordinary tyrants have motives and feelings beyond those usually assigned them by facile historians, and they will think of me as a *great* tyrant. Thus, my feelings and motives are a legacy I would preserve lest history distort them too much. History has a way of magnifying some characteristics while it discards others.

"People will try to understand me and to frame me in their words. They will seek truth. But the truth always carries the ambiguity of the words used to express it.

"You will not understand me. The harder you try the more remote I will become until finally I vanish into eternal myth—a Living God at last!

"That's it, you see. I am not a leader nor even a guide. A god. Remember that. I am quite different from leaders and guides. Gods need take no responsibility for anything except genesis. Gods accept everything and thus accept nothing. Gods must be identifiable yet remain anonymous. Gods do not need a spirit world. My spirits dwell within me, answerable to my slightest summons. I share with you, because it pleases me to do so, what I have learned about them and through them. They are *my* truth.

"Beware of *the* truth, gentle Sister. Although much sought after, truth can be dangerous to the seeker. Myths and reassuring lies are much easier to find and believe. If you find a truth, even a temporary one, it can demand that you make painful changes. Conceal your truths within words. Natural ambiguity will protect you then. Words are much easier to absorb than are the sharp Delphic stabs of wordless portent. With words, you can cry out in the chorus:

"'Why didn't someone warn me?'

"'But I did warn you. I warned you by example, not with words.'

"There are inevitably more than enough words. You record them in your marvelous memory even now. And someday, my journals will be discovered—more words. I warn you that you read my words at your peril. The wordless movement of terrible events lies just below their surface. Be deaf! You do not need to hear or, hearing, you do not need to remember. How soothing it is to forget. And how dangerous!

"Words such as mine have long been recognized for their mysterious power. There is a secret knowledge here which can be used to rule the forgetful. My truths are the substance of myths and lies which tyrants have always counted on to maneuver the masses for selfish design.

"You see? I share it all with you, even the greatest mystery of all time, the mystery by which I compose my life. I reveal it to you in words:

"The only past which endures lies wordlessly within you."

The God Emperor fell silent then. I dared to ask: "Are those all of the words that my Lord wishes me to preserve?"

"Those are the words," the God Emperor said, and I thought he sounded tired, discouraged. He had the sound of someone uttering a last testament. I recalled that he had said he would never see me again, and I was fearful but I praise my teachers because the fear did not emerge in my voice.

"Lord Leto," I said, "these journals of which you speak, for whom are they written?"

"For posterity after the span of millennia. I personalize those distant readers, Sister Chenoeh. I think of them as distant cousins filled with family curiosities. They are intent on unraveling the dramas which only I can recount. They want to make the personal connections to their own lives. They want the meanings, the *truth!*"

"But you warn us against truth, Lord," I said.

"Indeed! All of history is a malleable instrument in my hands. Ohhh, I have accumulated all of these pasts and I possess every *fact*—

yet the facts are mine to use as I will and, even using them truthfully, I change them. What am I speaking to you now? What is a diary, a journal? Words."

Again, the Lord Leto fell silent. I weighed the portent of what he had said, weighed it against the admonition of Reverend Mother Syaksa, and against the things that the God Emperor had uttered to me earlier. He said I was his messenger and thus I felt that I was under his protection and might dare more than any other. Thus it was that I said:

"Lord Leto, you have said that you will not see me again. Does that mean you are about to die?"

I swear it here in my record of this event, the Lord Leto laughed! Then he said:

"No, gentle Sister, it is you who will die. You will not live to be a Reverend Mother. Do not be saddened by this for by your presence here today, by carrying my message back to the Sisterhood, by preserving my secret words as well, you will achieve a far greater status. You become here an integral part of my myth. Our distant cousins will pray to you for intercession with me!"

Again, the Lord Leto laughed, but it was gentle laughter and he smiled upon me warmly. I find it difficult to record here with that accuracy which I am enjoined to employ in every accounting such as this one, yet in the moment that the Lord Leto spoke these terrible words to me, I felt a profound bond of friendship with him, as though some physical thing had leaped between us, tying us together in a way that words cannot fully describe. It was not until the instant of this experience that I understood what he had meant by the *wordless truth*. It happened, yet I cannot describe it.

ARCHIVISTS' NOTE:

Because of intervening events, the discovery of this private record is now little more than a footnote to history, interesting because it contains one of the earliest references to the God Emperor's secret journals. For those wishing to explore further into this account, reference may be made to Archive Records, subheadings: *Chenoeh, Holy Sister Quintinius Violet: Chenoeh Report, The,* and *Melange Rejection, Medical Aspects of.*

(Footnote: Sister Quintinius Violet Chenoeh died in the fifty-third year of her Sisterhood, the cause being ascribed to melange incompatibility during her attempt to achieve the status of Reverend Mother.)

Our ancestor, Assur-nasir-apli, who was known as the cruelest of the cruel, seized the throne by slaying his own father and starting the reign of the sword. His conquests included the Urumia Lake region, which led him to Commagene and Khabur. His son received tribute from the Shuites, from Tyre, Sidon, Gebel and even from Jehu, son of Omri, whose very name struck terror into thousands. The conquests which began with Assur-nasir-apli carried arms into Media and later into Israel, Damascus, Edom, Arpad, Babylon and Umlias. Does anyone remember these names and places now? I have given you enough clues: Try to name the planet.

—THE STOLEN JOURNALS

The air was stagnant deep within the carved cut of the Royal Road leading down to the flat approach to the bridge across the Idaho River. The road turned to the right out of the man-made immensity of rock and earth. Moneo, walking beside the Royal Cart, saw the paved ribbon leading across a narrow ridgetop to the lacery of plasteel which was the bridge almost a kilometer distant.

The river, still deep in a chasm, turned inward toward him on the right and then ran straight through multi-stage cascades toward the far side of the Forbidden Forest where the confining walls dropped down almost to the level of the water. There at the outskirts of Onn lay the orchards and gardens which helped to feed the city.

Moneo, looking at the distant stretch of river visible from where he walked, saw that the canyon top was bathed in light, while the water still flowed in shadows broken only by the faint silvery shimmering of the cascades.

Straight ahead of him, the road to the bridge was brilliant in sunlight, the dark shadows of erosion gullies on both sides set off like arrows to indicate the correct path. The rising sun already had made the roadway hot. The air trembled above it, a warning of the day to come.

We'll be safely into the City before the worst of the heat, Moneo thought.

He trotted along in the weary patience which always overcame him at this point, his gaze fixed forward in expectation of the petitioning Museum Fremen. They would come up out of one of the erosion gullies, he knew. Somewhere on this side of the bridge. That was the agreement he had made with them. No way to stop them now. And the God Emperor still showed signs of the Worm.

Leto heard the Fremen before any of his party either saw or heard them.

"Listen!" he called.

Moneo came to full alert.

Leto rolled his body on the cart, arched the front upward out of the bubble shield and peered ahead.

Moneo knew this kind of thing well. The God Emperor's senses, so much more acute than any of those around him, had detected a disturbance ahead. The Fremen were beginning to move up to the road. Moneo let himself fall back one pace and moved out to the limit of his dutiful position. He heard it himself then.

There was the sound of gravel spilling.

The first Fremen appeared, coming up out of gullies on both sides of the road no more than a hundred meters ahead of the Royal party.

Duncan Idaho dashed forward and slowed himself to a trot beside Moneo.

"Are those the Fremen?" Idaho asked.

"Yes." Moneo spoke with his attention on the God Emperor, who had lowered his bulk back onto the cart.

The Museum Fremen assembled on the road, dropped their outer robes to reveal inner robes of red and purple. Moneo gasped. The Fremen were togged out as pilgrims with some kind of black garment under the colorful robes. The ones in the foreground waved rolls of paper as the entire group began singing and dancing toward the royal entourage.

"A petition, Lord," the leaders cried. "Hear our petition!"

"Duncan!" Leto cried. "Clear them out!"

Fish Speakers surged forward through the courtiers as their Lord shouted. Idaho waved them forward and began running toward the approaching mob. The guards formed a phalanx, Idaho at the apex.

Leto slammed closed the bubble cover of his cart, increased its speed and called out in an amplified roar: "Clear away! Clear away!"

The Museum Fremen, seeing the guards run forward, the cart picking up speed as Leto shouted, made as though to open a path up the center of the road. Moneo, forced to run to keep up with the cart, his attention momentarily on the running footsteps of the courtiers behind him, saw the first unexpected change of program by the Fremen.

As one person, the chanting throng threw off the pilgrim cloaks to reveal black uniforms identical to those worn by Idaho.

What are they doing? Moneo wondered.

Even while he was asking himself this question, Moneo saw the flesh of the approaching faces melt away in Face Dancer mockery, every face resolving into a likeness of Duncan Idaho.

"Face Dancers!" someone screamed.

Leto, too, had been distracted by the confusion of events, the sounds of many feet running on the road, the barked orders as Fish Speakers formed their phalanx. He had applied more speed to his cart, closing the distance between himself and the guards, beginning then to ring a warning bell and sound the cart's distortion klaxon. White noise blared across the scene, disorienting even some of the Fish Speakers who were conditioned to it.

At that instant, the petitioners discarded their pilgrim cloaks and began the transformation maneuver, their faces flickering into likenesses of Duncan Idaho. Leto heard the scream: "Face Dancers!" He identified its source, a consort clerk in Royal Accounting.

Leto's initial reaction was amusement.

Guards and Face Dancers collided. Screams and shouts replaced the petitioners' chanting. Leto recognized Tleilaxu battle-commands. A thick knot of Fish Speakers formed around the black-clad figure of his Duncan. The guards were obeying Leto's oft-repeated instruction to protect their ghola-commander.

But how will they tell him from the others?

Leto brought his cart almost to a stop. He could see Fish Speakers on the left swinging their stunclubs. Sunlight flashed from knives. Then came the buzzing hum of lasguns, a sound Leto's grandmother had once described as "the most terrible in our universe." More hoarse shouts and screams erupted from the vanguard.

Leto reacted with the first sound of lasguns. He swerved the Royal Cart off the road to his right, shifted from wheels to suspensors and drove the vehicle back like a battering ram into a clot of Face Dancers trying to enter the fray from his side. Turning in a tight arc, he hit more of them on the other side, feeling the crushing impact of flesh against plasteel, a red spray of blood, then he was down off the road into an erosion gully. The brown serrated sides of the gully flashed past him. He swept upward and swooped across the river canyon to a high, rock-girt viewpoint beside the Royal Road. There, he stopped and turned, well beyond the range of handheld lasguns.

What a surprise!

Laughter shook his great body with grunting, trembling convulsions. Slowly, the amusement subsided.

From his vantage, Leto could see the bridge and the area of the attack. Bodies lay in tangled disarray all across the scene and into the flanking gullies. He recognized courtier finery, Fish Speaker uniforms, the bloodied black of the Face Dancer disguises. Surviving courtiers huddled in the background while Fish Speakers sped among the fallen making sure the attackers were dead with a swift knife stroke into each body.

Leto swept his gaze across the scene searching for the black uniform of his Duncan. There was not one such uniform standing. Not one! Leto put down a surge of frustration, then saw a clutch of Fish Speaker guards among the courtiers and . . . and a naked figure there.

Naked!

It was Duncan! *Naked! Of course!* The Duncan Idaho *without* a uniform was not a Face Dancer.

Again, laughter shook him. Surprises on both sides. What a shock that must have been to the attackers. Obviously, they had not prepared themselves for such a response.

Leto eased his cart out onto the roadway, dropped the wheels into position and rolled down to the bridge. He crossed the bridge with a sense of *déjà vu,* aware of the countless bridges in his memories, the crossings to view the aftermaths of battles. As he cleared the bridge, Idaho broke from the knot of guards and ran toward him, skipping and dodging the bodies. Leto stopped his cart and stared at the naked runner. The Duncan was like a Greek warrior-messenger dashing toward his commander to report the outcome of battle. The condensation of history stunned Leto's memories.

Idaho skidded to a stop beside the cart. Leto opened the bubble cover.

"Face Dancers, every damned one!" Idaho panted.

Not trying to conceal his amusement, Leto asked: "Whose idea was it to strip off your uniform?"

"Mine! But they wouldn't let me fight!"

Moneo came running up then with a group of guards. One of the Fish Speakers tossed a guard's blue cloak to Idaho, calling out: "We're trying to salvage a complete uniform from the bodies."

"I ripped mine off," Idaho explained.

"Did any of the Face Dancers escape?" Moneo asked.

"Not a one," Idaho said. "I admit your women are good fighters, but why wouldn't they let me get into . . ."

"Because they have instructions to protect you," Leto said. "They always protect the most valuable . . ."

"Four of them died getting me out of there!" Idaho said.

"We lost more than thirty people altogether, Lord," Moneo said. "We're still counting."

"How many Face Dancers?" Leto asked.

"It looks like there were an even fifty of them, Lord," Moneo said. He spoke softly, a stricken look on his face.

Leto began to chuckle.

"Why are you laughing?" Idaho demanded. "More than thirty of our people . . ."

"But the Tleilaxu were so inept," Leto said. "Do you not realize that only about five hundred years ago they would've been far more efficient, far more dangerous? Imagine them daring that foolish masquerade! And not anticipating your brilliant response!"

"They had lasguns," Idaho said.

Leto twisted his bulky forward segments around and pointed at a hole burned in his canopy almost at the cart's midpoint. A melted and fused starburst surrounded the hole.

"They hit several other places underneath," Leto said. "Fortunately, they did not damage any suspensors or wheels."

Idaho stared at the hole in the canopy, noted that it lined up with Leto's body.

"Didn't it hit you?" he asked.

"Oh, yes," Leto said.

"Are you injured?"

"I am immune to lasguns," Leto lied. "When we get time, I will demonstrate."

"Well, I'm not immune," Idaho said. "And neither are your guards. Every one of us should have a shield belt."

"Shields are banned throughout the Empire," Leto said. "It is a capital offense to have a shield."

"The question of shields," Moneo ventured.

Idaho thought Moneo was asking for an explanation of shields and said: "The belts develop a force field which will repel any object trying to enter at a dangerous speed. They have one major drawback. If you intersect the force field with a lasgun beam, the resultant explosion rivals that of a very large fusion bomb. Attacker and attacked go together."

Moneo only stared at Idaho, who nodded.

"I see why they were banned," Idaho said. "I presume the Great Convention against atomics is still in force and working well?"

"Working even better since we searched out all of the Family atomics and removed them to a safe place," Leto said. "But we do not have time to discuss such matters here."

"We can discuss one thing," Idaho said. "Walking out here in the open is too dangerous. We should . . ."

"It is the tradition and we will continue it," Leto said.

Moneo leaned close to Idaho's ear. "You are disturbing the Lord Leto," he said.

"But . . ."

"Have you not considered how much easier it is to control a *walking* population?" Moneo asked.

Idaho jerked around to stare into Moneo's eyes with sudden comprehension.

Leto took the opportunity to begin issuing orders. "Moneo, see that there is no sign of the attack left here, not one spot of blood or a torn rag of clothing—nothing."

"Yes, Lord."

Idaho turned at the sound of people pressing close around them, saw that all of the survivors, even the wounded wearing emergency bandages, had come up to listen.

"All of you," Leto said, addressing the throng around the cart. "Not a word of this. Let the Tleilaxu worry." He looked at Idaho.

"Duncan, how did those Face Dancers get into a region where only my Museum Fremen should roam free?"

Idaho glanced involuntarily at Moneo.

"Lord, it is my fault," Moneo said. "I was the one who arranged for the Fremen to present their petition here. I even reassured Duncan Idaho about them."

"I recall your mentioning the petition," Leto said.

"I thought it might amuse you, Lord."

"Petitions do not amuse me, they annoy me. I am especially annoyed by petitions from people whose one purpose in my scheme of things is to preserve the ancient forms."

"Lord, it was just that you have spoken so many times about the boredom of these peregrinations into . . ."

"But I am not here to ease the boredom of others!"

"Lord?"

"The Museum Fremen understand nothing about the old ways. They are only good at going through the motions. This naturally bores them and their petitions always seek to introduce changes. *That's* what annoys me. I will not permit changes. Now, where did you learn of the supposed petition?"

"From the Fremen themselves," Moneo said. "A dele . . ." He broke off, scowling.

"Were the members of the delegation known to you?"

"Of course, Lord. Otherwise I'd . . ."

"They're dead," Idaho said.

Moneo looked at him, uncomprehending.

"The people you knew were killed and replaced by Face Dancer mimics," Idaho said.

"I have been remiss," Leto said. "I should've taught all of you how to detect Face Dancers. It will be corrected now that they grow foolishly bold."

"Why are they so bold?" Idaho asked.

"Perhaps to distract us from something else," Moneo said.

Leto smiled at Moneo. Under the stress of personal threat, the majordomo's mind worked well. He had failed his Lord by mistaking Face Dancer mimics for known Fremen. Now, Moneo felt that his continued service might depend upon those abilities for which the God Emperor had originally chosen him.

"And now we have time to prepare ourselves," Leto said.

"Distract us from what?" Idaho demanded.

"From another plot in which they participate," Leto said. "They think I will punish them severely for this, but the Tleilaxu core remains safe because of you, Duncan."

"They didn't intend to fail here," Idaho said.

"But it was a contingency for which they were prepared," Moneo said.

"They believe I will not destroy them because they hold the original cells of my Duncan Idaho," Leto said. "Do you understand, Duncan?"

"Are they right?" Idaho demanded.

"They approach being wrong," Leto said. He returned his attention to Moneo. "No sign of this event must go with us to Onn. Fresh uniforms, new guards to replace the dead and wounded . . . everything just as it was."

"There are dead among your courtiers, Lord," Moneo said.

"Replace them!"

Moneo bowed. "Yes, Lord."

"And send for a new canopy to my cart!"

"As my Lord commands."

Leto backed his cart a few paces away, turned it and headed for the bridge, calling back to Idaho. "Duncan, you will accompany me."

Slowly at first, reluctance heavy in every movement, Idaho left Moneo and the others, then, increasing his pace, came up beside the cart's open bubble and walked there while staring in at Leto.

"What troubles you, Duncan?" Leto asked.

"Do you really think of me as *your* Duncan?"

"Of course, just as you think of me as *your* Leto."

"Why didn't you *know* this attack was coming?"

"Through my vaunted prescience?"

"Yes!"

"The Face Dancers have not attracted my attention for a long time," Leto said.

"I presume that is changed now?"

"Not to any great degree."

"Why not?"

"Because Moneo was correct. I will not let myself be distracted."

"Could they really have killed you there?"

"A distinct possibility. You know, Duncan, few understand what a disaster my end will be."

"What're the Tleilaxu plotting?"

"A snare, I think. A lovely snare. They have sent me a signal, Duncan."

"What signal?"

"There is a new escalation in the desperate motives which drive some of my subjects."

They left the bridge and began the climb to Leto's viewpoint. Idaho walked in a fermenting silence.

At the top, Leto lifted his gaze over the far cliffs and looked at the barrens of the Sareer.

The lamentations of those in his entourage who had lost loved ones continued at the attack scene beyond the bridge. With his acute hearing, Leto could separate Moneo's voice warning them that the time of mourning was necessarily short. They had other loved ones at the Citadel and they well knew the God Emperor's wrath.

Their tears will be gone and smiles will be pasted on their faces by the time we reach Onn, Leto thought. *They think I spurn them! What does that really matter? This is a flickering nuisance among the short-lived and the short-thoughted.*

The view of the desert soothed him. He could not see the river in its canyon from this point without turning completely around and looking toward the Festival City. The Duncan remained mercifully silent beside the cart. Turning his gaze slightly to the left, Leto could see an edge of the Forbidden Forest. Against that glimpse of verdant landscape, his memory suddenly compressed the Sareer into a tiny, weak remnant of the planet-wide desert which once had been so mighty that all men feared it, even the wild Fremen who had roamed it.

It is the river, Leto thought. *If I turn, I will see the thing that I have done.*

The man-made chasm through which the Idaho River tumbled was only an extension of the Gap which Paul Muad'Dib had blasted through the towering Shield Wall for the passage of his worm-mounted legions. Where water flowed now, Muad'Dib had led his Fremen out of a Coriolis storm's dust into history . . . *and into this.*

Leto heard Moneo's familiar footsteps, the sounds of the major-domo laboring up to the viewpoint. Moneo came up to stand beside Idaho and paused a moment to catch his breath.

"How long until we can go on?" Idaho asked.

Moneo waved him to silence and addressed Leto. "Lord, we have had a message from Onn. The Bene Gesserit send word that the Tleilaxu will attack before you reach the bridge."

Idaho snorted. "Aren't they a little late?"

"It is not their fault," Moneo said. "The captain of the Fish Speaker Guard would not believe them."

Other members of Leto's entourage began trickling onto the viewpoint level. Some of them appeared drugged, still in shock. The Fish Speakers moved briskly among them, commanding a show of good spirits.

"Remove the Guard from the Bene Gesserit Embassy," Leto said. "Send them a message. Tell them that their audience will still be the last one, but they are not to fear this. Tell them that the last will be first. They will know the allusion."

"What about the Tleilaxu?" Idaho asked.

Leto kept his attention on Moneo. "Yes, the Tleilaxu. We will send them a signal."

"Yes, Lord?"

"When I order it, and not until then, you will have the Tleilaxu Ambassador publicly flogged and expelled."

"Lord!"

"You disagree?"

"If we are to keep this secret"—Moneo glanced over his shoulder—"how will you explain the flogging?"

"We will not explain."

"We will give no reason at all?"

"No reason."

"But, Lord, the rumors and the stories that will . . ."

"I am reacting, Moneo! Let them sense the underground part of me which does things without my knowing because it has not the where-withal of knowing."

"This will cause great fear, Lord."

A gruff burst of laughter escaped Idaho. He stepped between Moneo and the cart. "He does a kindness to this Ambassador! There've been rulers who would've killed the fool over a slow fire."

Moneo tried to speak to Leto around Idaho's shoulder. "But, Lord, this action will confirm for the Tleilaxu that you were attacked."

"They already know that," Leto said. "But they will not talk about it."

"And when none of the attackers return . . ." Idaho said.

"Do you understand, Moneo?" Leto asked. "When we march into Onn apparently unscathed, the Tleilaxu will believe they have suffered utter failure."

Moneo glanced around at the Fish Speakers and courtiers listening spellbound to this conversation. Seldom had any of them heard such a revealing exchange between the God Emperor and his most immediate aides.

"When will my Lord signal punishment of the Ambassador?" Moneo asked.

"During the audience."

Leto heard 'thopters coming, saw the glint of sunlight on their wings and rotors and, when he focused intently, made out the fresh canopy for his cart slung beneath one of them.

"Have this damaged canopy returned to the Citadel and restored," Leto said, still peering at the approaching 'thopters. "If questions are asked, tell the artisans to say that it's just routine, another canopy scratched by blown sand."

Moneo sighed. "Yes, Lord. It will be done as you say."

"Come, Moneo, cheer up," Leto said. "Walk beside me as we continue." Turning to Idaho, Leto said, "Take some of the guards and scout ahead."

"Do you think there'll be another attack?" Idaho asked.

"No, but it'll give the guards something to do. And get a fresh uniform. I don't want you wearing something that has been contaminated by the dirty Tleilaxu."

Idaho moved off in obedience.

Leto signaled Moneo to come closer, closer. When Moneo was bending into the cart, face less than a meter from Leto's, Leto pitched his voice low and said:

"There is a special lesson here for you, Moneo."

"Lord, I know I should have suspected the Face . . ."

"Not the Face Dancers! It is a lesson for your daughter."

"Siona? What could she . . ."

"Tell her this: In a fragile way, she is like that force within me which acts without knowing. Because of her, I remember what it was to be human . . . and to love."

Moneo stared at Leto without comprehension.

"Simply give her the message," Leto said. "You needn't try to understand it. Merely tell her my words."

Moneo withdrew. "As my Lord commands."

Leto closed the bubble canopy, making a single unit of the entire cover for the approaching crews on the 'thopters to replace.

Moneo turned and glanced around at the people waiting on the flat area of the viewpoint. He noted then a thing he had not observed earlier, a thing revealed by the disarray which some of the people had not yet repaired. Some of the courtiers had fitted themselves with delicate devices to assist their hearing. They had been eavesdropping. And such devices could only come from Ix.

I will warn the Duncan and the Guard, Moneo thought.

Somehow, he thought of this discovery as a symptom of rot. How could they prohibit such things when most of the courtiers and the Fish Speakers either knew or suspected that the God Emperor traded with Ix for forbidden machines?

I am beginning to hate water. The sandtrout skin which impels my metamorphosis has learned the sensitivities of the worm. Moneo and many of my guards know my aversion. Only Moneo suspects the truth, that this marks an important waypoint. I can feel my ending in it, not soon as Moneo measures time, but soon enough as I endure it. Sandtrout swarmed to water in the Dune days, a problem during the early stages of our symbiosis. The enforcement of my willpower controlled the urge then, and until we reached a time of balance. Now, I must avoid water because there are no other sandtrout, only the half-dormant creatures of my skin. Without sandtrout to bring this world back to desert, Shai-Hulud will not emerge; the sandworm cannot evolve until the land is parched. I am their only hope.

—THE STOLEN JOURNALS

It was midafternoon before the Royal Entourage came down the final slope into the precincts of the Festival City. Throngs lined the streets to greet them, held back by tight lines of ursine Fish Speakers in uniforms of Atreides green, their stunclubs crossed and linked.

As the Royal party approached, a bedlam of shouts erupted from the crowd. Then the Fish Speaker guardians began to chant:

"Siaynoq! Siaynoq! Siaynoq!"

As it echoed back and forth between the high buildings, the chanted word had a strange effect on the crowd which was not initiated into the meanings of it. A wave of silence swept up the thronged avenues while the guardians continued to chant. People stared in awe at the women armed with stunclubs who guarded the Royal passage, the women who chanted while they fixed their gaze on the face of their passing Lord.

Idaho, marching with the Fish Speaker guards behind the Royal Cart, heard the chant for the first time and felt the hair on the back of his neck rise.

Moneo marched beside the cart, not looking left or right. He had once asked Leto the meaning of the word.

"I give the Fish Speakers only one ritual," Leto had said. They had been in the God Emperor's audience chamber beneath Onn's central plaza at the time, with Moneo fatigued after a long day of directing the flow of dignitaries who crowded the city for Decennial festivities.

"What has the chanting of that word to do with it, Lord?"

"The ritual is called Siaynoq—the Feast of Leto. It is the adoration of my person in my presence."

"An ancient ritual, Lord?"

"It was with the Fremen before they were Fremen. But the keys to the Festival secrets died with the old ones. Only I remember them now. I recreate the Festival in my own likeness and for my own ends."

"Then the Museum Fremen do not use this ritual?"

"Never. It is mine and mine alone. I claim eternal right to it because I *am* that ritual."

"It is a strange word, Lord. I have never heard its like."

"It has many meanings, Moneo. If I tell them to you, will you hold them secret?"

"My Lord commands!"

"Never share this with another nor reveal to the Fish Speakers what I tell you now."

"I swear it, Lord."

"Very well. Siaynoq means giving honor to one who speaks with sincerity. It signifies the remembrance of things which are spoken with sincerity."

"But, Lord, doesn't sincerity really mean that the speaker *believes* . . . has faith in what is said?"

"Yes, but Siaynoq also contains the idea of light as that which reveals reality. You continue to shine light on what you see."

"Reality . . . that is a very ambiguous word, Lord."

"Indeed! But Siaynoq also stands for fermentation because reality—or the belief that you know a reality, which is the same thing—always sets up a ferment in the universe."

"All of that in a single word, Lord?"

"And more! Siaynoq also contains the summoning to prayer *and* the name of the Recording Angel, Sihaya, who interrogates the newly dead."

"A great burden for one word, Lord."

"Words can carry any burden we wish. All that's required is agreement and a tradition upon which to build."

"Why must I not speak of this to the Fish Speakers, Lord?"

"Because this is a word reserved for them. They resent my sharing it with a male."

Moneo's lips pressed into a thin line of remembrance as he marched beside the Royal Cart into the Festival City. He had heard the Fish Speakers chant the God Emperor into their presence many times since that first explanation and had even added his own meanings to the strange word.

It means mystery and prestige. It means power. It invokes a license to act in the name of God.

"Siaynoq! Siaynoq! Siaynoq!"

The word had a sour sound in Moneo's ears.

They were well into the city, almost to the central plaza. Afternoon sunlight came down the Royal Road behind the procession to illuminate the way. It gave brilliance to the citizenry's colorful costumes. It shone on the upturned faces of the Fish Speakers lining the way.

Marching beside the cart with the guards, Idaho put down a first alarm as the chant continued. He asked one of the Fish Speakers beside him about it.

"It is not a word for men," she said. "But sometimes the Lord shares Siaynoq with a Duncan."

A *Duncan*! He had asked Leto about it earlier and disliked the mysterious evasions.

"You will learn about it soon enough."

Idaho relegated the chant to the background while he looked around him with a tourist's curiosity. In preparation for his duties as Guard Commander, Idaho had inquired after the history of Onn, finding that he shared Leto's wry amusement in the fact that it was the Idaho River flowing nearby.

They had been in one of the large open rooms of the Citadel at the time, an airy place full of morning light and with wide tables upon which Fish Speaker archivists had spread charts of the Sareer and of Onn. Leto had wheeled his cart onto a ramp which allowed him to look down on the charts. Idaho stood across a chart-littered table from him studying the plan of the Festival City.

"Peculiar design for a city," Idaho mused.

"It has one primary purpose—public viewing of the God Emperor."

Idaho looked up at the segmented body on the cart, brought his gaze to the cowled face. He wondered if he would ever find it easy to look on that bizarre figure.

"But that's only once every ten years," Idaho said.

"At the Great Sharing, yes."

"And you just close it down between times?"

"The embassies are there, the offices of the trading factors, the Fish Speaker schools, the service and maintenance cadres, the museums and libraries."

"What space do they take?" Idaho rapped the chart with his knuckles. "A tenth of the City at most?"

"Less than that."

Idaho let his gaze wander pensively over the chart.

"Are there other purposes in this design, m'Lord?"

"It is dominated by the need for public viewing of my person."

"There must be clerks, government workers, even common laborers. Where do they live?"

"Mostly in the suburbs."

Idaho pointed at the chart. "These tiers of apartments?"

"Note the balconies, Duncan."

"All around the plaza." He leaned close to peer down at the chart. "That plaza is two kilometers across!"

"Note how the balconies are set back in steps right up to the ring of spires. The elite are lodged in the spires."

"And they can all look down on you in the plaza?"

"You do not like that?"

"There's not even an energy barrier to protect you!"

"What an inviting target I make."

"Why do you do it?"

"There is a delightful myth about the design of Onn. I foster and promote the myth. It is said that once there lived a people whose ruler was required to walk among them once a year in total darkness, without weapons or armor. The mythical ruler wore a luminescent suit while he made his walk through the night-shrouded throng of his subjects. And his subjects—they wore black for the occasion and were never searched for weapons."

"What's that have to do with Onn . . . and you?"

"Well, obviously, if the ruler survived his walk, he was a good ruler."

"You don't search for weapons?"

"Not openly."

"You think people see you in this myth." It was not a question.

"Many do."

Idaho stared up at Leto's face deep in its gray cowl. The blue-on-blue eyes stared back at him without expression.

Melange eyes, Idaho thought. But Leto said he no longer consumed any spice. His body supplied what spice his addiction demanded.

"You don't like my holy obscenity, my enforced tranquility," Leto said.

"I don't like you playing god!"

"But a god can conduct the Empire as a musical conductor guides a symphony through its movements. My performance is limited only by my restriction to Arrakis. I must direct the symphony from here."

Idaho shook his head and looked once more at the city plan. "What're these apartments behind the spires?"

"Lesser accommodations for our visitors."

"They can't see the plaza."

"But they can. Ixian devices project my image into those rooms."

"And the inner ring looks directly down on you. How do you enter the plaza?"

"A presentation stage rises from the center to display me to my people."

"Do they cheer?" Idaho looked directly into Leto's eyes.

"They are permitted to cheer."

"You Atreides always did see yourselves as part of history."

"How astute of you to understand a cheer's meaning."

Idaho returned his attention to the city map. "And the Fish Speaker schools are here?"

"Under your left hand, yes. That's the academy where Siona was sent to be educated. She was ten at the time."

"Siona . . . I must learn more about her," Idaho mused.

"I assure you that nothing will get in the way of your desire."

As he marched along in the Royal peregrination, Idaho was lifted from his reverie by awareness that the Fish Speaker chant was diminishing. Ahead of him, the Royal Cart had begun its descent into the chambers beneath the plaza, rolling down a long ramp. Idaho, still in sunlight, looked up and around at the glistening spires—this reality for which the charts had not prepared him. People crowded the balconies of the great tiered ring around the plaza, silent people who stared down at the procession.

No cheering from the privileged, Idaho thought. The silence of the people on the balconies filled Idaho with foreboding.

He entered the ramp-tunnel and its lip hid the plaza. The Fish Speaker chant faded away as he descended into the depths. The sound of marching feet all around him was curiously amplified.

Curiosity replaced the sense of oppressive foreboding. Idaho stared around him. The flat-floored tube was artifically illuminated and wide, very wide. Idaho estimated that seventy people could march abreast into the bowels of the plaza. There were no mobs of greeters here, only a widely spaced line of Fish Speakers who did not chant, contenting themselves to stare at the passage of their God.

Memory of the charts told Idaho the layout of this gigantic complex beneath the plaza—a private city within the City, a place where only the God Emperor, the courtiers and the Fish Speakers could go without escort. But the charts had told nothing of the thick pillars, the sense of massive, guarded spaces, the eerie quiet broken by the tramping of feet and the creaking of Leto's cart.

Idaho looked suddenly at the Fish Speakers lining the way and realized that their mouths were moving in unison, a silent word on their lips. He recognized the word:

"Siaynoq."

"Another Festival so soon?" the Lord Leto asked.

"It has been ten years," the majordomo said.

Do you think by this exchange that the Lord Leto betrays an ignorance of time's passage?

—THE ORAL HISTORY

During the private audience period preceding the Festival proper, many commented that the God Emperor spent more than the allotted time with the new Ixian Ambassador, a young woman named Hwi Noree.

She was brought down at midmorning by two Fish Speakers who were still full of first-day excitement. The private audience chamber beneath the plaza was brilliantly illuminated. The light revealed a room about fifty meters long by thirty-five wide. Antique Fremen rugs decorated the walls, their bright patterns worked in jewels and precious metals, all combined in weavings of priceless spice-fibers. The dull reds of which the Old Fremen had been so fond predominated. The chamber's floor was mostly transparent, a setting for exotic fishes worked in radiant crystal. Beneath the floor flowed a stream of clear blue water, all of its moisture sealed away from the audience chamber, but excitingly near Leto, who rested on a padded elevation at the end of the room opposite the door.

His first view of Hwi Noree revealed a remarkable likeness to her Uncle Malky, but her grave movements and the calmness of her stride

were equally remarkable in their difference from Malky. She did have
that dark skin, though, the oval face with its regular features. Placid
brown eyes stared back at Leto. And where Malky's hair had been gray,
hers was a luminous brown.

Hwi Noree radiated an inner peace which Leto sensed spreading its
influence around her as she approached. She stopped ten paces away, below
him. There was a classical balance about her, something not accidental.

With growing excitement, Leto realized a betrayal of Ixian machinations in the new Ambassador. They were well along in their own
program to breed selected types for specific functions. Hwi Noree's
function was distressingly obvious—to charm the God Emperor, to
find a chink in his armor.

Despite this, as the meeting progressed, Leto found himself truly
enjoying her company. Hwi Noree stood in a puddle of daylight which
was guided into the chamber by a system of Ixian prisms. The light
filled Leto's end of the chamber with glowing gold which centered on
the Ambassador, dimming behind the God Emperor where stood a
short line of Fish Speaker guards—twelve women chosen for their inability to hear or speak.

Hwi Noree wore a simple gown of purple ambiel decorated only by
a silver necklace pendant stamped with the symbol of IX. Soft sandals
the color of her gown peeked from beneath her hem.

"Are you aware," Leto asked her, "that I killed one of your ancestors?"

She smiled softly. "My Uncle Malky included that information in
my early training, Lord."

As she spoke, Leto realized that part of her education had been
conducted by the Bene Gesserit. She had their way of controlling her
responses, of sensing the undertones in a conversation. He could see,
however, that the Bene Gesserit overlay had been a delicate thing, never
penetrating the basic sweetness of her nature.

"You were told that I would introduce this subject," he said.

"Yes, Lord. I know that my ancestor had the temerity to bring a
weapon here in the attempt to harm you."

"As did your immediate predecessor. Were you told that, as well?"

"I did not learn it until my arrival, Lord. They were fools! Why did you spare my predecessor?"

"When I did not spare your ancestor?"

"Yes, Lord."

"Kobat, your predecessor, was more valuable to me as a messenger."

"Then they told me the truth," she said. Again, she smiled. "One cannot always depend on hearing truth from one's associates and superiors."

The response was so utterly open that Leto could not suppress a chuckle. Even as he laughed, he realized that this young woman still possessed the Mind of First Awakening, the elemental mind which came in the first shock of birth-awareness. She was alive!

"Then you do not hold it against me that I killed your ancestor?" he asked.

"He tried to assassinate you! I am told you crushed him, Lord, with your own body."

"True."

"And next you turned his weapon against your own Holy Self to demonstrate that the weapon was ineffectual . . . and it was the best lasgun we Ixians could make."

"The witnesses reported correctly," Leto said.

And he thought: *Which shows how much you can depend on witnesses!* As a matter of historical accuracy, he knew that he had turned the lasgun only against his ribbed body, not against hands, face or flippers. The pre-worm body possessed a remarkable capacity for absorbing heat. The chemical factory within him converted heat to oxygen.

"I never doubted the story," she said.

"Why has Ix repeated this foolish gesture?" Leto asked.

"They have not told me, Lord. Perhaps Kobat took it onto himself to behave this way."

"I think not. It has occurred to me that your people desired only the death of their chosen assassin."

"The death of Kobat?"

"No, the death of the one they chose to use the weapon."

"Who was that, Lord? I've not been told."

"It's unimportant. Do you recall what I said at the time of your ancestor's foolishness?"

"You threatened terrible punishment should such violence ever again enter our thoughts." She lowered her gaze, but not before Leto glimpsed a deep determination in her eyes. She would use the best of her abilities to blunt his wrath.

"I promised that none of you would escape my anger," Leto said.

She jerked her attention up to his face. "Yes, Lord." And now her manner revealed personal fear.

"None can escape me, not even the futile colony you've recently planted at . . ." And Leto reeled off for her the standard chart coordinates of a new colony the Ixians had planted secretly far beyond what they thought were the reaches of his Empire.

She betrayed no surprise. "Lord, I think it was because I warned them you would know of this that I was chosen as Ambassador."

Leto studied her more carefully. *What have we here?* he wondered. Her observation had been subtle and penetrating. The Ixians, he knew, had thought distance and enormously magnified transportation costs would insulate the new colony. Hwi Noree thought not and had said so. But she believed her masters had chosen her as Ambassador because of this—a comment on the Ixian caution. They thought they had a friend at court here, but one who also would be seen as Leto's friend. He nodded as the pattern took shape. Quite early in his ascendancy he had revealed to the Ixians the exact location of the supposedly secret Ixian Core, the heartland of the technological federation which they governed. It had been a secret the Ixians thought safe because they paid gigantic bribes for it to the Spacing Guild. Leto had winkled them out by prescient observation and deduction—and by consulting his memories, where there were more than a few Ixians.

At the time, Leto had warned the Ixians that he would punish them if they acted against him. They had responded with consternation and accused the Guild of betraying them. This had amused Leto and he had responded with such a burst of laughter that the Ixians were abashed. He had then informed them in a cold and accusatory tone that he had no need of spies or traitors or other ordinary trappings of government.

Did they not believe he was a god?

For a time thereafter, the Ixians were responsive to his requests. Leto had not abused the relationship. His demands were modest—a machine for this, a device for that. He would state his needs and presently the Ixians would deliver the required technological toy. Only once had they tried to deliver a violent instrument into one of his machines. He had slain the entire Ixian delegation before they could even unwrap the thing.

Hwi Noree waited patiently while Leto mused. Not the slightest sign of impatience surfaced.

Beautiful, he thought.

In view of his long association with the Ixians, this new stance sent the juices coursing through Leto's body. Ordinarily, the passions, crises and necessities which had produced and impelled him burned low. He often felt that he had outlived his times. But the presence of Hwi Noree said he was needed. This pleased him. Leto felt that it might even be possible that the Ixians had achieved a partial success with their machine to amplify the linear prescience of a Guild navigator. A small *blip* in the flow of great events might have escaped him. Could they really make such a machine? What a marvel that would be! Purposefully, he refused to use his powers for even the smallest search through this possibility.

I wish to be surprised!

Leto smiled benignly at Hwi. "How have they prepared you to woo me?" he asked.

She did not blink. "I was provided with a set of memorized responses for particular exigencies," she said. "I learned them as I was required, but I do not intend to use them."

Which is exactly what they want, Leto thought.

"Tell your masters," he said, "that you are precisely the right kind of bait to dangle in front of me."

She bowed her head. "If it pleases my Lord."

"Yes, you do."

He indulged himself then in a small temporal probe to examine Hwi's immediate future, tracing the threads of her past through this. Hwi appeared in a fluid future, a current whose movements were susceptible to many deflections. She would know Siona in only a casual way unless . . . Questions flowed through Leto's mind. A Guild steersman was advising the Ixians and he obviously had detected Siona's disturbance in the temporal fabric. Did the steersman really believe he could provide security against the God Emperor's detection?

The temporal probe took several minutes, but Hwi did not fidget. Leto looked at her carefully. She seemed timeless—*outside* of time in a deeply peaceful way. He had never before encountered a common mortal able to wait thus in front of him without some nervousness.

"Where were you born, Hwi?" he asked.

"On Ix itself, Lord."

"I mean specifically—the building, its location, your parents, the people around you, friends and family, your schooling—all of it."

"I never knew my parents, Lord. I was told they died while I was still an infant."

"Did you believe this?"

"At first . . . of course. Later, I built fantasies. I even imagined that Malky was my father . . . but . . ." She shook her head.

"You did not like your Uncle Malky?"

"No, I didn't. Oh, I admired him."

"My reaction precisely," Leto said. "But what of your friends and your schooling?"

"My teachers were specialists, even some Bene Gesserit were brought in to train me in emotional control and observation. Malky said I was being prepared for great things."

"And your friends?"

"I don't think I ever had any real friends—only people who were brought in contact with me for specific purposes in my education."

"And these great things for which you were trained, did anyone ever speak of those?"

"Malky said I was being prepared to charm you, Lord."

"How old are you, Hwi?"

"I don't know my exact age. I guess I'm about twenty-six. I've never celebrated a birthday. I only learned about birthdays by accident, one of my teachers giving an excuse for her absence. I never saw that teacher again."

Leto found himself fascinated by this response. His observations provided him with certainty that there had been no Tleilaxu interventions into her Ixian flesh. She had not come from a Tleilaxu axlotl tank. Why the secrecy, then?

"Does your Uncle Malky know your age?"

"Perhaps. But I haven't seen him for many years."

"Didn't *anyone* ever tell you how old you were?"

"No."

"Why do you suppose that is?"

"Maybe they thought I'd ask if I were interested."

"Were you interested?"

"Yes."

"Then why didn't you ask?"

"I thought at first there might be a record somewhere. I looked. There was nothing. I reasoned then that they would not answer my question."

"For what it tells me about you, Hwi, that answer pleases me *very* much. I, too, am ignorant of your background, but I can make an enlightened guess at your birthplace."

Her eyes focused on his face with a charged intensity which had no pretense in it.

"You were born within this machine your masters are trying to perfect for the Guild," Leto said. "You were conceived there, as well. It may even be that Malky was your father. That is not important. Do you know about this machine, Hwi?"

"I'm not supposed to know about it, Lord, but . . ."

"Another indiscretion by one of your teachers?"

"By my uncle himself."

A burst of laughter erupted from Leto. "What a rogue!" he said. "What a charming rogue!"

"Lord?"

"This is his revenge on your masters. He did not like being removed from my court. He told me at the time that his replacement was less than a fool."

Hwi shrugged. "A complex man, my uncle."

"Listen to me carefully, Hwi. Some of your associations here on Arrakis could be dangerous to you. I will protect you as I can. Do you understand?"

"I think so, Lord." She stared up at him solemnly.

"Now, a message for your masters. It is clear to me that they have been listening to a Guild steersman *and* they have joined themselves to the Tleilaxu in a perilous fashion. Tell them for me that their purposes are quite transparent."

"Lord, I have no knowledge of . . ."

"I am aware of how they use you, Hwi. For this reason you may tell your masters also that you are to be the permanent Ambassador to my court. I will not welcome another Ixian. And should your masters ignore my warnings, trying further interference with my wishes, I shall crush them."

Tears welled from her eyes and ran down her cheeks, but Leto was grateful that she did not indulge in any other display such as falling to her knees.

"I already have warned them," she said. "Truly I did. I told them they must obey you."

Leto could see that this was true.

What a marvelous creature, this Hwi Noree, he thought. She appeared the epitome of goodness, obviously bred and conditioned for this quality by her Ixian masters with their careful calculation of the effect this would have on the God Emperor.

Out of his thronging ancestral memories, Leto could see her as an idealized nun, kindly and self-sacrificing, all sincerity. It was her most basic nature, the place where she lived. She found it easiest to be truthful and open, capable of shading this only to prevent pain for others. He saw this latter trait as the deepest change the Bene Gesserit had been able to effect in her. Hwi's real manner remained outgoing, sensitive and naturally sweet. Leto could find little sense of manipulative calculation in her. She appeared immediately responsive and wholesome, excellent at listening (another Bene Gesserit attribute). There was nothing openly seductive about her, yet this very fact made her profoundly seductive to Leto.

As he had remarked to one of the earlier Duncans on a similar occasion: "You must understand this about me, a thing which some obviously suspect—sometimes it's unavoidable that I have delusionary sensations, the feeling that somewhere inside this changeling form of mine there exists an adult human body with all of the necessary functions."

"*All* of them, Lord?" the Duncan had asked.

"All! I feel the vanished parts of myself. I can feel my legs, quite unremarkable and so real to my senses. I can feel the pumping of my human glands, some of which no longer exist. I can even feel genitalia which I know, intellectually, vanished centuries ago."

"But surely if you know . . ."

"Knowledge does not suppress such feelings. The vanished parts of myself are still there in my personal memories and in the multiple identity of all my ancestors."

As Leto looked at Hwi standing in front of him, it helped not one whit to know he had no skull and that what once had been his brain was now a massive web of ganglia spread through his pre-worm flesh. Nothing helped. He could still feel his *brain* aching where it once had reposed; he could still feel his *skull* throbbing.

By just standing there in front of him, Hwi cried out to his lost humanity. It was too much for him and he moaned in despair:

"Why do your masters torture me?"

"Lord?"

"By sending you!"

"I would not hurt you, Lord."

"Just by existing you hurt me!"

"I did not know." Tears fell unrestrained from her eyes. "They never told me what they were really doing."

He calmed himself and spoke softly: "Leave me now, Hwi. Go about your business, but return quickly if I summon you!"

She left quietly, but Leto could see that Hwi, too, was tortured. There was no mistaking the deep sadness in her for the humanity Leto had sacrificed. She knew what Leto knew: they would have been friends, lovers, companions in an ultimate sharing between the sexes. Her masters had planned for her to know.

The Ixians are cruel! he thought. *They knew what our pain would be.*

Hwi's departure ignited memories of her Uncle Malky. Malky was cruel, but Leto had rather enjoyed his company. Malky had possessed all of the industrious virtues of his people and enough of their vices to make him thoroughly human. Malky had reveled in the company of Leto's Fish Speakers. "Your *houris*," he had called them, and Leto could seldom think of the Fish Speakers thereafter without recalling Malky's label.

Why do I think of Malky now? It's not just because of Hwi. I shall ask her what charge her masters gave her when they sent her to me.

Leto hesitated on the verge of calling her back.

She'll tell me if I ask.

Ixian ambassadors had always been told to find out why the God Emperor tolerated Ix. They knew they could not hide from him. This stupid attempt to plant a colony beyond his vision! Were they testing his limits? The Ixians suspected that Leto did not really need their industries.

I've never concealed my opinion of them. I said it to Malky:

"Technological innovators? No! You are the criminals of science in my Empire!"

Malky had laughed.

Irritated, Leto had accused: "Why try to hide secret laboratories and factories beyond the Empire's rim? You cannot escape me."

"Yes, Lord." Laughing.

"I know your intent: leak a bit of this and some of that back into my Imperial domains. Disrupt! Cause doubts and questioning!"

"Lord, you yourself are one of our best customers!"

"That's not what I mean and you know it, you terrible man!"

"You like me *because* I'm a terrible man. I tell you stories about what we do out there."

"I know it without your stories!"

"But some stories are believed and some are doubted. I dispel your doubts."

"I have no doubts!"

Which had only ignited more of Malky's laughter.

And I must continue tolerating them, Leto thought. The Ixians operated in the terra incognita of creative invention which had been outlawed by the Butlerian Jihad. They made their devices in the image of the mind—the very thing which had ignited the Jihad's destruction and slaughter. That was what they did on Ix and Leto could only let them continue.

I buy from them! I could not even write my journals without their dictatels to respond to my unspoken thought. Without Ix, I could not have hidden my journals and the printers.

But they must be reminded of the dangers in what they do!

And the Guild could not be allowed to forget. That was easier. Even while Guildsmen cooperated with Ix, they distrusted the Ixians mightily.

If this new Ixian machine works, the Guild has lost its monopoly on space travel!

From that welter of memories which I can tap at will, patterns emerge. They are like another language which I see so clearly. The social-alarm signals which put societies into the postures of defense/attack are like shouted words to me. As a people, you react against threats to innocence and the peril of the helpless young. Unexplained sounds, visions and smells raise the hackles you have forgotten you possess. When alarmed, you cling to your native language because all the other patterned sounds are strange. You demand acceptable dress because a strange costume is threatening. This is system-feedback at its most primitive level. Your cells remember.

—THE STOLEN JOURNALS

The acolyte Fish Speakers who served as pages at the portal of Leto's audience chamber brought in Duro Nunepi, the Tleilaxu Ambassador. It was early for an audience and Nunepi was being taken out of his announced order, but he moved calmly with only the faintest hint of resigned acceptance.

Leto waited silently, stretched out along his cart on the raised platform at the end of the chamber. As he watched Nunepi approach, Leto's memories produced a comparison: the swimming-cobra of a periscope brushing its almost invisible wake upon water. The memory brought a smile to Leto's lips. That was Nunepi—a proud, flinty-faced man who had come up through the ranks of Tleilaxu management. Not a Face Dancer himself, he considered the Dancers his personal servants; they were the *water* through which he moved. One had to be truly adept to see his wake. Nunepi was a nasty piece of business who had left his traces in the attack along the Royal Road.

Despite the early hour, the man wore his full ambassadorial regalia—billowing black trousers and black sandals trimmed in gold, a flowery red jacket open at the breast to reveal a bushy chest behind his Tleilaxu crest worked in gold and jewels.

At the required ten paces distance, Nunepi stopped and swept his gaze along the rank of armed Fish Speaker guards in an arc around and behind Leto. Nunepi's gray eyes were bright with some secret amusement when he brought his attention to his Emperor and bowed slightly.

Duncan Idaho entered then, a lasgun holstered at his hip, and took up his position beside the God Emperor's cowled face.

Idaho's appearance required a careful study by Nunepi, a study which did not please the Ambassador.

"I find Shape Changers particularly obnoxious," Leto said.

"I am not a Shape Changer, Lord," Nunepi said. His voice was low and cultured, with only a trace of hesitancy in it.

"But you represent them and that makes you an item of annoyance," Leto said.

Nunepi had expected an open statement of hostility, but this was not the language of diplomacy, and it shocked him into a bold reference to what he believed to be Tleilaxu strength.

"Lord, by preserving the flesh of the original Duncan Idaho and providing you with restored gholas in his image and identity, we have always assumed . . ."

"Duncan!" Leto glanced at Idaho. "If I command it, Duncan, will you lead an expedition to exterminate the Tleilaxu?"

"With pleasure, m'Lord."

"Even if it means the loss of your *original cells* and all of the axlotl tanks?"

"I do not find the tanks a pleasant memory, m'lord, and those cells are not me."

"Lord, how have we offended you?" Nunepi asked.

Leto scowled. Did this inept fool really expect the God Emperor to speak openly of the recent Face Dancer attack?

"It has come to my attention," Leto said, "that you and your people have been spreading lies about what you call my 'disgusting sexual habits.' "

Nunepi gaped. The accusation was a bold lie, completely unexpected. But Nunepi realized that if he denied it, no one would believe him. The God Emperor had said it. This was an attack of unknown dimensions. Nunepi started to speak while looking at Idaho.

"Lord, if we . . ."

"Look at me!" Leto commanded.

Nunepi jerked his gaze up to Leto's face.

"I will inform you only this once," Leto said. "I have no sexual habits whatsoever. None."

Perspiration rolled off Nunepi's face. He stared at Leto with the fixed intensity of a trapped animal. When Nunepi found his voice, it no longer was the low, controlled instrument of a diplomat, but a trembling and fearful thing.

"Lord, I . . . there must be a mistake of . . ."

"Be still, you Tleilaxu sneak!" Leto roared. Then: "I am a metamorphic vector of the holy sandworm—Shai-Hulud! I am your God!"

"Forgive us, Lord," Nunepi whispered.

"Forgive you?" Leto's voice was full of sweet reason. "Of course I forgive you. That is your God's function. Your crime is forgiven. However, your stupidity requires a response."

"Lord, if I could but . . ."

"Be still! The spice allotment passes over the Tleilaxu for this decade. You get nothing. As for you personally, my Fish Speakers will now take you into the plaza."

Two burly guardswomen moved in and held Nunepi's arms. They looked up to Leto for instructions.

"In the plaza," Leto said, "his clothing is to be stripped from him. He is to be publicly flogged—fifty lashes."

Nunepi struggled against the grip of his guards, consternation on his face mingled with rage.

"Lord, I remind you that I am the Ambassador of . . ."

"You are a common criminal and will be treated as such." Leto nodded to the guards, who began dragging Nunepi away.

"I wish they'd killed you!" Nunepi raged. "I wish . . ."

"Who?" Leto called. "You wish who had killed me? Don't you know I cannot be killed?"

The guards dragged Nunepi out of the chamber as he still raged: "I am innocent! I am innocent!" The protest faded away.

Idaho leaned close to Leto.

"Yes, Duncan?" Leto asked.

"M'Lord, all the envoys will feel fear at this."

"Yes. I teach a lesson in responsibility."

"M'Lord?"

"Membership in a conspiracy, as in an army, frees people from the sense of personal responsibility."

"But this will cause trouble, m'Lord. I'd best post extra guards."

"Not one additional guard!"

"But you invite . . ."

"I invite a bit of military nonsense."

"That's what I . . ."

"Duncan, I am a teacher. Remember that. By repetition, I impress the lesson."

"What lesson?"

"The ultimately suicidal nature of military foolishness."

"M'Lord, I don't . . ."

"Duncan, consider the inept Nunepi. He is the essence of this lesson."

"Forgive my denseness, m'Lord, but I do not understand this thing about military . . ."

"They believe that by risking death they pay the price of any violent behavior against enemies of their own choosing. They have the invader mentality. Nunepi does not believe himself responsible for anything done against *aliens*."

Idaho looked at the portal where the guards had taken Nunepi. "He tried and he lost, m'Lord."

"But he cut himself loose from the restraints of the past and he objects to paying the price."

"To his people, he's a patriot."

"And how does he see himself, Duncan? As an instrument of history."

Idaho lowered his voice and leaned closer to Leto.

"How are you different, m'Lord?"

Leto chuckled. "Ahhh, Duncan, how I love your perceptiveness. You have observed that I am the ultimate alien. Do you not wonder if I also can be a loser?"

"The thought has crossed my mind."

"Even losers can shroud themselves in the proud mantle of 'the past,' old friend."

"Are you and Nunepi alike in that?"

"Militant missionary religions can share this illusion of the 'proud past,' but few understand the ultimate peril to humankind—that false sense of freedom from responsibility for your own actions."

"These are strange words, m'Lord. How do I take their meaning?"

"Their meaning is whatever speaks to you. Are you incapable of listening?"

"I have ears, m'Lord!"

"Do you now? I cannot see them."

"Here, m'lord. Here and here!" Idaho pointed at his own ears as he spoke.

"But they do not hear. Therefore you have no ears, neither here nor hear."

"You make a joke of me, m'Lord?"

"To hear is to hear. That which exists cannot be made into itself for it already exists. To be is to be."

"Your strange words . . ."

"Are but words. I spoke them. They are gone. No one heard them, therefore they no longer exist. If they no longer exist, perhaps they can be made to exist again and then perhaps someone will hear them."

"Why do you poke fun at me, m'Lord?"

"I poke nothing at you except words. I do it without fear of offending because I have learned that you have no ears."

"I don't understand you, m'Lord."

"That is the beginning of knowledge—the discovery of something we do not understand."

Before Idaho could respond, Leto gave a hand signal to a nearby guard who waved a hand in front of a crystalline control panel on the wall behind the God Emperor's dais. A three-dimensional view of Nunepi's punishment appeared in the center of the chamber.

Idaho stepped down to the floor of the chamber and peered closely at the scene. It was shown from a slight elevation looking down on the plaza, and was complete with sounds of the swelling throng who had run to the scene at the first signs of excitement.

Nunepi was bound to two legs of a tripod, his feet spread wide, his arms tied together above him almost at the apex of the tripod. His clothing had been ripped from his body and lay around him in rags. A bulky, masked Fish Speaker stood nearby holding an improvised whip fashioned of elacca rope which had been frayed at the end into wirelike fine strands. Idaho thought he recognized the masked woman as the *Friend* of his first interview.

At a signal from a Guard officer, the masked Fish Speaker stepped forward and brought the elacca whip down in a slashing arc onto Nunepi's exposed back.

Idaho winced. The crowd gasped.

Welts appeared where the whip had struck, but Nunepi remained silent.

Again, the whip descended. Blood betrayed the lines of this second stroke.

Once more, the whip flayed Nunepi's back. More blood appeared.

Leto felt remote sadness. *Nayla is too ardent,* he thought. *She will kill him and that will cause problems.*

"Duncan!" Leto called.

Idaho turned from his fascinated examination of the projected scene just as a shout lifted from the crowd—response to a particularly bloody stroke.

"Send someone to stop the flogging after twenty lashes," Leto said. "Have it announced that the magnanimity of the God Emperor has reduced the punishment."

Idaho raised a hand to one of the guards, who nodded and ran from the chamber.

"Come here, Duncan," Leto said.

Still smarting under what he believed was Leto's poking fun at him, Idaho returned to Leto's side.

"Whatever I do," Leto said, "it is to teach a lesson."

Idaho rigidly willed himself not to look back at the scene of Nunepi's punishment. Was that the sound of Nunepi groaning? The shouts of the crowd pierced Idaho. He stared up into Leto's eyes.

"There is a question in your mind," Leto said.

"Many questions, m'Lord."

"Speak them."

"What is the lesson in that fool's punishment? What do we say when asked?"

"We say that no one is permitted to blaspheme against the God Emperor."

"A *bloody* lesson, m'Lord."

"Not as bloody as some I've taught."

Idaho shook his head from side to side in obvious dismay. "Nothing good's going to come of this!"

"Precisely!"

Safaris through ancestral memories teach me many things. The patterns, ahhh, the patterns. Liberal bigots are the ones who trouble me most. I distrust the extremes. Scratch a conservative and you find someone who prefers the past over any future. Scratch a liberal and find a closet aristocrat. It's true! Liberal governments always develop into aristocracies. The bureaucracies betray the true intent of people who form such governments. Right from the first, the *little people* who formed the governments which promised to equalize the social burdens found themselves suddenly in the hands of bureaucratic aristocracies. Of course, all bureaucracies follow this pattern, but what a hypocrisy to find this even under a communized banner. Ahhh, well, if patterns teach me anything it's that patterns are repeated. My oppressions, by and large, are no worse than any of the others and, at least, I teach a new lesson.

—THE STOLEN JOURNALS

It was well into the darkness of Audience Day before Leto could meet with the Bene Gesserit delegation. Moneo had prepared the Reverend Mothers for the delay, repeating the God Emperor's reassurances.

Reporting back to his Emperor, Moneo had said: "They expect a rich reward."

"We shall see," Leto had said. "We shall see. Now, tell me what it was the Duncan demanded of you as you entered."

"He wished to know if you had ever before had someone flogged."

"And you replied?"

"That there was no record of, nor had I ever before witnessed, such a punishment."

"His response?"

"This is not Atreides."

"Does he think I'm insane?"

"He did not say that."

"There was more to your encounter. What else troubles our new Duncan?"

"He has met the Ixian Ambassador, Lord. He finds Hwi Noree attractive. He inquired of . . ."

"That must be prevented, Moneo! I trust you to raise barriers against any liaison between the Duncan and Hwi."

"My Lord commands."

"Indeed I do! Go now and prepare for our meeting with the women of the Bene Gesserit. I will receive them at False Sietch."

"Lord, is there significance in this choice of a meeting place?"

"A whim. On your way out, tell the Duncan he may take out a troop of guards and scour the City for trouble."

Waiting for the Bene Gesserit delegation at False Sietch, Leto reviewed this exchange, finding some amusement in it. He could imagine the reactions through the Festival City at the approach of a disturbed Duncan Idaho in command of a Fish Speaker troop.

Like the quick silence of frogs when a predator comes.

Now that he was in False Sietch, Leto found himself pleased by the choice. A free-form building of irregular domes at the edge of Onn, False Sietch was almost a kilometer across. It had been the first abode of the Museum Fremen and now was their school, its corridors and chambers patrolled by alert Fish Speakers.

The reception hall where Leto waited, an oval about two hundred meters in its long dimension, was illuminated by giant glowglobes which floated in blue-green isolation some thirty meters above the floor. The light muted the dull browns and tans of the imitation stone from which the entire structure had been fashioned. Leto waited on a low ledge at one end of the chamber, looking outward through a half-circle window longer than his body. The opening, four stories above the ground, framed a view which included a remnant of the ancient Shield Wall preserved for its cliffside caves where Atreides troops had once been slaughtered by Harkonnen attackers. The frosty light of First Moon silvered the cliff's outlines. Fires dotted the cliffside, the flames exposed where no Fremen would have dared betray his presence. The fires winked at Leto as people passed in front of them—Museum Fremen exercising their right to occupy the sacred precincts.

Museum Fremen! Leto thought.

They were such narrow thinkers with near horizons.

But why should I object? They are what I made them.

Leto heard the Bene Gesserit delegation then. They chanted as they approached, a heavy sound all a-jostle with vowels.

Moneo preceded them with a guard detail which took up position on Leto's ledge. Moneo stood on the chamber floor just below Leto's face, glanced at Leto, turned to the open hall.

The women entered in a double file, ten of them led by two Reverend Mothers in traditional black robes.

"That is Anteac on the left, Luyseyal on the right," Moneo said.

The names recalled for Leto the earlier words about the Reverend Mothers brought in by Moneo, agitated and distrustful. Moneo did not like the *witches*.

"They're both Truthsayers," Moneo had said. "Anteac is much older than Luyseyal, but the latter is reputed to be the best Truthsayer the Bene Gesserit have. You may note that Anteac has a scar on her forehead whose origin we have been unable to discover. Luyseyal has red hair and appears remarkably young for one of her reputation."

As he watched the Reverend Mothers approach with their entourage, Leto felt the quick surge of his memories. The women wore their hoods forward, shrouding their faces. The attendants and acolytes walked at a respectful distance behind . . . it was all of a piece. Some patterns did not change. These women might have been entering a real sietch with real Fremen here to honor them.

Their heads know what their bodies deny, he thought.

Leto's penetrating vision saw the subservient caution in their eyes, but they strode up the long chamber like people confident of their religious power.

It pleased Leto to think that the Bene Gesserit possessed only such powers as he permitted. The reasons for this indulgence were clear to him. Of all the people in his Empire, Reverend Mothers were most like him—limited to the memories of only their female ancestors and the collateral female identities of their inheritance ritual—still, each of them did exist as somewhat of an integrated mob.

The Reverend Mothers came to a stop at the required ten paces from Leto's ledge. The entourage spread out on each side.

It amused Leto to greet such delegations in the voice and persona of his grandmother, Jessica. The Bene Gesserit had come to expect this and he did not disappoint them.

"Welcome, Sisters," he said. The voice was a smooth contralto, definitely Jessica's controlled feminine tones with just a hint of mockery—a voice recorded and often studied in the Sisterhood's Chapter House.

As he spoke, Leto sensed menace. Reverend Mothers were never pleased when he greeted them this way, but the reaction here carried different undertones. Moneo, too, sensed it. He raised a finger and the guards moved closer to Leto.

Anteac spoke first: "Lord, we watched that display in the plaza this morning. What do you gain by such antics?"

So that's the tone we wish to set, he thought.

Speaking in his own voice, he said: "You are temporarily in my good graces. Would you change that?"

"Lord," Anteac said, "we are shocked that you could thus punish an Ambassador. We do not understand what you gain by this."

"I gain nothing. I am diminished."

Luyseyal spoke up: "This can only reinforce thoughts of oppression."

"I wonder why so few ever thought of the Bene Gesserit as oppressors?" Leto asked.

Anteac spoke to her companion: "If it pleases the God Emperor to inform us, he will do so. Let us get to the purposes of our Embassy."

Leto smiled. "The two of you can come closer. Leave your attendants and approach."

Moneo stepped two paces to his right as the Reverend Mothers moved in characteristic silent gliding to within three paces of the ledge.

"It's almost as though they had no feet!" Moneo had once complained.

Recalling this, Leto observed how carefully Moneo watched the two women. They were menacing, but Moneo dared not object to their nearness. The God Emperor had ordered it; thus it would be.

Leto lifted his attention to the attendants waiting where the Bene Gesserit entourage had first stopped. The acolytes wore hoodless black gowns. He saw tiny clues to forbidden rituals about them—an amulet, a small trinket, a colorful corner of a kerchief so arranged that more color might be flashed carefully. Leto knew that the Reverend Mothers allowed this because they no longer could share the spice as once they had.

Ritual substitutes.

There were significant changes across the past ten years. A new parsimony had entered the Sisterhood's thinking.

They are coming out, Leto told himself. *The old, old mysteries are still here.*

The ancient patterns had lain dormant in the Bene Gesserit memories for all of those millennia.

Now, they emerge. I must warn my Fish Speakers.

He returned his attention to the Reverend Mothers.

"You have requests?"

"What is it like to be you?" Luyseyal asked.

Leto blinked. That was an interesting attack. They had not tried it in more than a generation. Well . . . why not?

"Sometimes my dreams are blocked off and redirected into strange places," he said. "If my cosmic memories are a web, as you two certainly know, then think about the dimensions of *my* web and where such memories and dreams might lead."

"You speak of our certain knowledge," Anteac said. "Why can't we join forces at last? We are more alike than we are different."

"I would sooner link myself to those degenerate Great Houses bewailing their lost spice riches!"

Anteac held herself still, but Luyseyal pointed a finger at Leto. "We offer community!"

"And I insist on conflict?"

Anteac stirred, then: "It is said that there is a principle of conflict which originated with the single cell and has never deteriorated."

"Some things remain incompatible," Leto agreed.

"Then how does our Sisterhood maintain its community?" Luyseyal demanded.

Leto hardened his voice. "As you well know, the secret of community lies in suppression of the incompatible."

"There can be enormous value in cooperation," Anteac said.

"To you, not to me."

Anteac contrived a sigh. "Then, Lord, will you tell us about the physical changes in your person?"

"Someone besides yourself should know about and record such things," Luyseyal said.

"In case something dreadful should happen to me?" Leto asked.

"Lord!" Anteac protested. "We do not . . ."

"You dissect me with words when you would prefer sharper instruments," Leto said. "Hypocrisy offends me."

"We protest, Lord," Anteac said.

"Indeed you do. I hear you."

Luyseyal crept a few millimeters closer to the ledge, bringing a sharp stare from Moneo, who glanced up at Leto then. Moneo's expression demanded action, but Leto ignored him, curious now about Luyseyal's intentions. The sense of menace was centered in the red-haired one.

What is she? Leto wondered. *Could she be a Face Dancer, after all?*

No. None of the telltale signs were there. No. Luyseyal presented an elaborately relaxed appearance, not even a little twist of her features to test the God Emperor's powers of observation.

"Will you not tell us about your physical changes, Lord?" Anteac asked.

Diversion! Leto thought.

"My brain grows enormous," he said. "Most of the human skull has dissolved away. There are no severe limits to the growth of my cortex and its attendant nervous system."

Moneo darted a startled glance at Leto. Why was the God Emperor giving away such vital information? These two would trade it.

But both women were obviously fascinated by this revelation, hesitating in whatever plan they had evolved.

"Does your brain have a center?" Luyseyal asked.

"I am the center," Leto said.

"A location?" Anteac asked. She gestured vaguely at him. Luyseyal glided a few millimeters closer to the ledge.

"What value do you place on the things I reveal to you?" Leto asked.

The two women betrayed no change of expression, which was betrayal enough by itself. A smile flitted across Leto's lips.

"The marketplace has captured you," he said. "Even the Bene Gesserit has been infected by the *suk* mentality."

"We do not deserve that accusation," Anteac said.

"But you do. The *suk* mentality dominates my Empire. The uses of the market have only been sharpened and amplified by the demands of our times. We have all become traders."

"Even you, Lord?" Luyseyal asked.

"You tempt my wrath," he said. "You're a specialist in that, aren't you?"

"Lord?" Luyseyal's voice was calm, but overly controlled.

"Specialists are not to be trusted," Leto said. "Specialists are masters of exclusion, experts in the narrow."

"We hope to be architects of a better future," Anteac said.

"Better than what?" Leto asked.

Luyseyal eased herself a fractional pace closer to Leto.

"We hope to set our standards by your judgment, Lord," Anteac said.

"But you would be architects. Would you build higher walls? Never forget, Sisters, that I know you. You are efficient purveyors of blinders."

"Life continues, Lord," Anteac said.

"Indeed! And so does the universe."

Luyseyal eased herself a bit closer, ignoring the fixity of Moneo's attention.

Leto smelled it then and almost laughed aloud.

Spice-essence!

They had brought some spice-essence. They knew the old stories about sandworms and spice-essence, of course. Luyseyal carried it. She thought of it as a specific poison for sandworms. That was obvious. Bene Gesserit records and the Oral History agreed on this. The essence shattered the worm, precipitating its dissolution and resulting (eventually) in sandtrout which would produce more sandworms—etcetera, etcetera, etcetera . . .

"There is another change in me that you should know about," Leto said. "I am not yet sandworm, not fully. Think of me as something closer to a colony creature with sensory alterations."

Luyseyal's left hand moved almost imperceptibly toward a fold in her gown. Moneo saw it and looked to Leto for instructions, but Leto only returned the hooded glare of Luyseyal's eyes.

"There have been fads in smells," Leto said.

Luyseyal's hand hesitated.

"Perfumes and essences," he said. "I remember them all, even the cults of the non-smells are mine. People have used underarm sprays and crotch sprays to mask their natural odors. Did you know that? Of course you knew it!"

Anteac's gaze moved toward Luyseyal.

Neither woman dared speak.

"People knew instinctively that their pheromones betrayed them," Leto said.

The women stood immobile. They heard him. Of all his people, Reverend Mothers were best equipped to understand his hidden message.

"You'd like to mine me for my riches of memory," Leto said, his voice accusing.

"We are jealous, Lord," Luyseyal confessed.

"You have misread the history of spice-essence," Leto said. "Sand-trout sense it only as water."

"It was a test, Lord," Anteac said. "That is all."

"You would test me?"

"Blame our curiosity, Lord," Anteac said.

"I, too, am curious. Put your spice-essence on the ledge beside Moneo. I will keep it."

Slowly, demonstrating by the steadiness of her movements that she intended no attack, Luyseyal reached beneath her gown and removed a small vial which glistened with an inner blue radiance. She placed the vial gently on the ledge. Not by any sign did she indicate that she might try something desperate.

"Truthsayer, indeed," Leto said.

She favored him with a faint grimace which might have been a smile, then withdrew to Anteac's side.

"Where did you get the spice-essence?" Leto asked.

"We bought it from smugglers," Anteac said.

"There've been no smugglers for almost twenty-five hundred years."

"Waste not, want not," Anteac said.

"I see. And now you must reevaluate what you think of as your own patience, is that not so?"

"We have been watching the evolution of your body, Lord," Anteac said. "We thought . . ." She permitted herself a small shrug, the level of gesture warranted for use with a Sister and not given lightly.

Leto pursed his lips in response. "I cannot shrug," he said.

"Will you punish us?" Luyseyal asked.

"For amusing me?"

Luyseyal glanced at the vial on the ledge.

"I swore to reward you," Leto said. "I shall."

"We would prefer to protect you in our community, Lord," Anteac said.

"Do not seek too great a reward," he said.

Anteac nodded. "You deal with the Ixians, Lord. We have reason to believe they may venture against you."

"I fear them no more than I fear you."

"Surely you've heard what the Ixians are doing," Luyseyal said.

"Moneo brings me an occasional copy of a message between persons or groups in my Empire. I hear many stories."

"We speak of a new Abomination, Lord!" Anteac said.

"You think the Ixians can produce an artificial intelligence?" he asked. "Conscious the way you are conscious?"

"We fear it, Lord," Anteac said.

"You would have me believe that the Butlerian Jihad survives among the Sisterhood?"

"We do not trust the unknown which can arise from imaginative technology," Anteac said.

Luyseyal leaned toward him. "The Ixians boast that their machine will transcend Time in the way that you do it, Lord."

"And the Guild says there's Time-chaos around the Ixians," Leto mocked. "Are we to fear all creation, then?"

Anteac drew herself up stiffly.

"I speak truth with you two," Leto said. "I recognize your abilities. Will you not recognize mine?"

Luyseyal gave him a curt nod. "Tleilax and Ix make alliance with the Guild and seek our full cooperation."

"And you fear Ix the most?"

"We fear anything we do not control," Anteac said.

"And you do not control me."

"Without you, people would need us!" Anteac said.

"Truth at last!" Leto said. "You come to me as your Oracle and you ask me to put your fears to rest."

Anteac's voice was frigidly controlled. "Will Ix make a mechanical brain?"

"A brain? Of course not!"

Luyseyal appeared to relax, but Anteac remained unmoving. She was not satisfied with the Oracle.

Why is it that foolishness repeats itself with such monotonous precision? Leto wondered. His memories offered up countless scenes to match this one—caverns, priests and priestesses caught up in holy ecstasy, portentous voices delivering dangerous prophecies through the smoke of holy narcotics.

He glanced down at the iridescent vial on the ledge beside Moneo. What was the current value of that thing? Enormous. It was the *essence*. Concentrated wealth concentrated.

"You have already paid the Oracle," he said. "It amuses me to give you full value."

How alert the women became!

"Hear me!" he said. "What you fear is not what you fear."

Leto liked the sound of that. Sufficiently portentous for any Oracle. Anteac and Luyseyal stared up at him, dutiful supplicants. Behind them, an acolyte cleared her throat.

That one will be identified and reprimanded later, Leto thought.

Anteac had now had sufficient time to ruminate on Leto's words. She said: "An obscure truth is not the truth."

"But I have directed your attention correctly," Leto said.

"Are you telling us not to fear the machine?" Luyseyal asked.

"You have the power of reason," he said. "Why come begging to me?"

"But we do not have *your* powers," Anteac said.

"You complain then that you do not sense the gossamer waves of Time. You do not sense my continuum. And you fear a mere machine!"

"Then you will not answer us," Anteac said.

"Do not make the mistake of thinking me ignorant about your Sisterhood's ways," he said. "You are alive. Your senses are exquisitely tuned. I do not stop this, nor should you."

"But the Ixians play with automation!" Anteac protested.

"Discrete pieces, finite bits linked one to another," he agreed. "Once set in motion, what is to stop it?"

Luyseyal discarded all pretense of Bene Gesserit self-control, a fine comment on her recognition of Leto's powers. Her voice almost screeched: "Do you know what the Ixians boast? That their machine will predict *your* actions!"

"Why should I fear that? The closer they come to me, the more they must be my allies. They cannot conquer me, but I can conquer them."

Anteac made to speak but stopped when Luyseyal touched her arm.

"Are you already allied with Ix?" Luyseyal asked. "We hear that you conferred overlong with their new Ambassador, this Hwi Noree."

"I have no allies," he said. "Only servants, students and enemies."

"And you do not fear the Ixians' machine?" Anteac insisted.

"Is automation synonymous with conscious intelligence?" he asked.

Anteac's eyes went wide and filmy as she withdrew into her memories. Leto found himself caught by fascination with what she must be encountering there within her own internal mob.

We share some of those memories, he thought.

Leto felt then the seductive attraction of community with Reverend Mothers. It would be so familiar, so supportive . . . and so deadly. Anteac was trying to lure him once more.

She spoke: "The machine cannot anticipate every problem of importance to humans. It is the difference between serial bits and an unbroken continuum. We have the one; machines are confined to the other."

"You still have the power of reason," he said.

"Share!" Luyseyal said. It was a command to Anteac and it revealed with sharp abruptness who really dominated this pair—the younger over the older.

Exquisite, Leto thought.

"Intelligence adapts," Anteac said.

Parsimonious with her words, too, Leto thought, hiding his amusement.

"Intelligence creates," Leto said. "That means you must deal with responses never before imagined. You must confront the *new*."

"Such as the possibility of the Ixian Machine," Anteac said. It was not a question.

"Isn't it interesting," Leto asked, "that being a superb Reverend Mother is not enough?"

His acute senses detected the sudden fearful tightening in both of the women. Truthsayers, indeed!

"You are right to fear me," he said. Raising his voice, he demanded: "How do you know you're even alive?"

As Moneo had done so many times, they heard in his voice the deadly consequences of failure to answer him correctly. It fascinated Leto that both women glanced at Moneo before either responded.

"I am the mirror of myself," Luyseyal said, a pat Bene Gesserit answer which Leto found offensive.

"I don't need preset tools to deal with my human problems," Anteac said. "Your question is sophomoric!"

"Hah, hah!" Leto laughed. "How would you like to quit the Bene Gesserit and join me?"

He could see her consider and then reject the invitation, but she did not hide her amusement.

Leto looked at the puzzled Luyseyal. "If it falls outside your yardsticks, then you are engaged with intelligence, not with automation," he said. And he thought: *That Luyseyal will never again dominate old Anteac.*

Luyseyal was angry now and not bothering to conceal it. She said: "The Ixians are rumored to have provided you with machines that simulate human thinking. If you have such a low opinion of them, why . . ."

"She should not be let out of the Chapter House without a guardian," Leto said, addressing Anteac. "Is she afraid to address her own memories?"

Luyseyal paled, but remained silent.

Leto studied her coldly. "Our ancestors' long unconscious relationship with machines has taught us something, don't you think?"

Luyseyal merely glared at him, not ready yet to risk death through open defiance of the God Emperor.

"Would you say we at least know the attraction of machines?" Leto asked.

Luyseyal nodded.

"A well-maintained machine can be more reliable than a human servant," Leto said. "We can trust machines not to indulge in emotional distractions."

Luyseyal found her voice. "Does this mean you intend to remove the Butlerian prohibition against abominable machines?"

"I swear to you," Leto said, speaking in his icy voice of disdain, "that if you display further such stupidity, I will have you publicly executed. I am *not* your Oracle!"

Luyseyal opened her mouth and closed it without speaking.

Anteac touched her companion's arm, sending a quick tremor through Luyseyal's body. Anteac spoke softly in an exquisite demonstration of Voice: "Our God Emperor will never openly defy the proscriptions of the Butlerian Jihad."

Leto smiled at her, a gentle commendation. It was such a pleasure to see a professional performing at her best.

"That should be obvious to any conscious intelligence," he said. "There are limits of my own choosing, places where I will not interfere."

He could see both women absorbing the multi-pronged thrust of his words, weighing the possible meanings and intents. Was the God Emperor distracting them, focusing their attention on the Ixians while he maneuvered elsewhere? Was he telling the Bene Gesserit that the time had come to choose sides against the Ixians? Was it possible his words had no more than their surface motivations? Whatever his reasons, they could not be ignored. He was undoubtedly the most devious creature the universe had ever spawned.

Leto scowled at Luyseyal, knowing he could only add to their confusion. "I point out to you, Marcus Claire Luyseyal, a lesson from past over-machined societies which you appear *not* to have learned. The devices themselves condition the users to employ each other the way they employ machines."

He turned his attention to Moneo. "Moneo?"

"I see him, Lord."

Moneo craned his neck to peer over the Bene Gesserit entourage. Duncan Idaho had entered the far portal, and strode across the open floor of the chamber toward Leto. Moneo did not relax his wariness, his distrust of the Bene Gesserit, but he recognized the nature of Leto's lecture. *He is testing, always testing.*

Anteac cleared her throat. "Lord, what of our reward?"

"You are brave," Leto said. "No doubt that's why you were chosen for this Embassy. Very well, for the next decade I will continue your spice allotment at its present level. As for the rest, I will ignore what you really intended with the spice-essence. Am I not generous?"

"Most generous, Lord," Anteac said, and there was not the slightest hint of bitterness in her voice.

Duncan Idaho brushed past the women then and stopped beside Moneo to peer up at Leto. "M'Lord, there's . . ." He broke off and glanced at the two Reverend Mothers.

"Speak openly," Leto commanded.

"Yes, m'Lord." There was reluctance in him, but he obeyed. "We were attacked at the southeast edge of the City, a distraction I believe because there now are reports of more violence in the City and in the Forbidden Forest—many scattered raiding parties."

"They are hunting my wolves," Leto said. "In the forest and in the City, they are hunting my wolves."

Idaho's brows contracted into a puzzled frown. "Wolves in the City, m'Lord?"

"Predators," Leto said. "Wolves—to me there is no essential difference."

Moneo gasped.

Leto smiled at him, thinking how beautiful it was to observe a moment of realization—a veil pulled away from the eyes, the mind opened.

"I have brought a large force of guards to protect this place," Idaho said. "They are posted through the . . ."

"I knew you would," Leto said. "Now pay close attention while I tell you where to send the rest of your forces."

As the Reverend Mothers watched in awe, Leto laid out for Idaho the exact points for ambushes, detailing the size of each force and even some of the specific personnel, the timing, the necessary weapons, the precise deployments at each place. Idaho's capacious memory catalogued each instruction. He was too caught up in the recital to question it until Leto fell silent, but a look of puzzled fear came over Idaho then.

For Leto, it was as though he peered directly into Idaho's most essential awareness to read the thoughts there. *I was a trusted soldier of the original Lord Leto*, Idaho was thinking. *That Leto, the grandfather of this one, saved me and took me into his household like a son. But even though that Leto still has some kind of existence in this one . . . this is not him.*

"M'Lord, why do you need *me*?" Idaho asked.

"For your strength and loyalty."

Idaho shook his head. "But . . ."

"You obey," Leto said, and he noted the way these words were being absorbed by the Reverend Mothers. *Truth, only truth, for they are Truthsayers.*

"Because I owe a debt to the Atreides," Idaho said.

"That is where we place our trust," Leto said. "And, Duncan?"

"M'Lord?" Idaho's voice said he had found ground where he could stand.

"Leave at least one survivor at each place," Leto said. "Otherwise, our efforts are wasted."

Idaho nodded once, curtly, and left, striding back across the hall the way he had come. And Leto thought it would take an extremely sensitive eye indeed to see that it was a different Idaho leaving, far different from the one who had entered.

Anteac said: "This comes of flogging that Ambassador."

"Exactly," Leto agreed. "Recount this carefully to your Superior, the admirable Reverend Mother Syaksa. Tell her for me that I prefer the company of predators above that of the prey." He glanced at Moneo, who drew himself to attention. "Moneo, the wolves are gone from my forest. They must be replaced by human wolves. See to it."

The trance-state of prophecy is like no other visionary experience. It is not a retreat from the raw exposure of the senses (as are many trance-states) but an immersion in a multitude of new movements. Things move. It is an ultimate pragmatism in the midst of Infinity, a demanding consciousness where you come at last into the unbroken awareness that the universe moves of itself, that it changes, that its rules change, that nothing remains permanent or absolute throughout all such movement, that mechanical explanations for anything can work only within precise confinements and, once the walls are broken down, the old explanations shatter and dissolve, blown away by new movements. The things you see in this trance are sobering, often shattering. They demand your utmost effort to remain whole and, even so, you emerge from that state profoundly changed.

—THE STOLEN JOURNALS

That night of Audience Day, while others slept and fought and dreamed and died, Leto took his repose in the isolation of his audience chamber, only a few trusted Fish Speaker guards at the portals.

He did not sleep. His mind whirled with necessities and disappointments.

Hwi! Hwi!

He knew why Hwi Noree had been sent to him now. How well he knew!

My most secret secret is exposed.

They had discovered his secret. Hwi was the evidence of it.

He thought desperate thoughts. Could this terrible metamorphosis be reversed? Could he return to a human state?

Not possible.

Even if it were possible, the process would take him just as long as it had taken to reach this point. Where would Hwi be in more than three thousand years? Dry dust and bones in the crypt.

I could breed something like her and prepare that one for me . . . but that would not be my gentle Hwi.

And what of the Golden Path while he indulged in such selfish goals?

To hell with the Golden Path! Have these folly-bound idiots ever thought once of me? Not once!

But that was not true. Hwi thought of him. She shared his torture.

These were thoughts of madness and he tried to put them away while his senses reported the soft movement of the guards and the flow of water beneath his chamber.

When I made this choice, what were my expectations?

How the mob within laughed at that question! Did he not have a task to complete? Was that not the very essence of the agreement which kept the mob in check?

"You have a task to complete," they said. "You have but one purpose."

Single purpose is the mark of the fanatic and I am not a fanatic!

"You must be cynical and cruel. You cannot break the trust."

Why not?

"Who took that oath? You did. You chose this course."

Expectations!

"The expectations which history creates for one generation are often shattered in the next generation. Who knows that better than you?"

Yes . . . and shattered expectations can alienate whole populations. I alone am a whole population!

"Remember your oath!"

Indeed. I am the disruptive force unleashed across the centuries. I limit expectations . . . including my own. I dampen the pendulum.

"And then release it. Never forget that."

I am tired. Oh, how tired I am. If only I could sleep . . . really sleep.

"You're full of self-pity, too."

Why not? What am I? The ultimate loner forced to look at what might have been. Every day I look at it . . . and now. Hwi!

"Your original unselfish choice fills you now with selfishness."

There is danger all around. I must wear my selfishness like a suit of armor.

"There's danger for everyone who touches you. Isn't that your very nature?"

Danger even for Hwi. Dear, delectable, dear Hwi.

"Did you build high walls around you only to sit within them and indulge in self-pity?"

The walls were built because great forces have been unleashed in my Empire.

"You unleashed them. Will you now compromise with them?"

It's Hwi's doing. These feelings have never before been this powerful in me. It's the damnable Ixians!

"How interesting that they should assault you with flesh rather than with a machine."

Because they have discovered my secret.

"You know the antidote."

Leto's great body trembled through its entire length at this thought. He well knew the antidote which had always worked before: lose himself for a time in his own past. Not even the Bene Gesserit Sisters could take such safaris, striking inward along the axis of memories—back, back to the very limits of cellular awareness, or stopping by a wayside to revel in a sophisticated sensory delight. Once, after the death of a particularly superb Duncan, he had toured great musical performances preserved in his memories. Mozart had tired him quickly. *Pretentious! But Bach . . . ahhh, Bach.*

Leto remembered the joy of it.

I sat at the organ and let the music drench me.

Only three times in all memory had there been an equal to Bach. But even Licallo was not better, as good, but not better.

Would female intellectuals be the proper choice for this night? Grandmother Jessica had been one of the best. Experience told him that someone as close to him as Jessica would not be the proper antidote for his present tensions. The search would have to venture much farther.

He imagined then describing such a safari to some awestruck visitor, a totally imaginary visitor because none would dare question him about such a *holy* matter.

"I course backward down the flight of ancestors, hunting along the tributaries, darting into nooks and crannies. You would not recognize many of their names. Who has ever heard of Norma Cenva? I have lived her!"

"Lived her?" his imaginary visitor asked.

"Of course. Why else would one keep one's ancestors around? You think a man designed the first Guild ship? Your history books told you it was Aurelius Venport? They lied. It was his mistress, Norma. She gave him the design, along with five children. He thought his ego would take no less. In the end, the knowledge that he had not really fulfilled his own image, that was what destroyed him."

"You have lived him, too?"

"Naturally. And I have traversed the far wanderings of the Fremen. Through my father's line and the others, I have gone right back to the House of Atreus."

"Such an illustrious line!"

"With its fair share of fools."

Distraction is what I need, he thought.

Would it be a tour through sexual dalliances and exploits, then?

"You have no idea what internal orgies are available to me! I am the ultimate voyeur—participant(s) and observer(s). Ignorance and misunderstandings about sexuality have caused so much distress. How abysmally narrow we have been—how miserly."

Leto knew he could not make that choice, not this night, not with Hwi out there in his City.

Would he choose a review of warfare, then?

"Which Napoleon was the greater coward?" he asked his imaginary visitor. "I will not reveal it, but I know. Oh, yes, I know."

Where can I go? With all of the past open to me, where can I go?

The brothels, the atrocities, the tyrants, the acrobats, nudists, surgeons, male whores, musicians, magicians, ungenciers, priests, artisans, priestesses . . .

"Are you aware," he asked his imaginary visitor, "that the hula preserves an ancient sign language which once belonged only to males? You've never heard of the hula? Of course. Who dances it anymore? Dancers have preserved many things, though. The translations have been lost, but I know them.

"One whole night I was a series of caliphs moving eastward and westward with Islam—a traverse of centuries. I will not bore you with the details. Be gone now, visitor!"

How seductive it is, he thought, *this call of the siren which would have me live only in the past.*

And how useless that past now, thanks to the damnable Ixians. How boring the past when Hwi is here. She would come to me right now if I summoned her. But I cannot call for her . . . not now . . . not tonight.

The past continued to beckon.

I could make a pilgrimage into my past. It does not have to be a safari. I could go alone. Pilgrimage purifies. Safaris make me into a tourist. That's the difference. I could go alone into my inner world.

And never return.

Leto felt the inevitability of it, that the dream-state would eventually trap him.

I create a special dream-state throughout my Empire. Within this dream, new myths form, new directions appear and new movements. New . . . new . . . new . . . The things emerge from my own dreams, out of my myths. Who more susceptible to them than I? The hunter is caught in his own net.

Leto knew then that he had encountered a condition for which no antidote existed—past, present or future. His great body trembled and shivered in the gloom of his audience chamber.

At the portal, one Fish Speaker guard whispered to another: "Is God troubled?"

And her companion replied: "The sins of this universe would trouble anyone."

Leto heard them and wept silently.

When I set out to lead humankind along my Golden Path, I promised them a lesson their bones would remember. I know a profound pattern which humans deny with their words even while their actions affirm it. They say they seek security and quiet, the condition they call peace. Even as they speak, they create the seeds of turmoil and violence. If they find their quiet security, they squirm in it. How boring they find it. Look at them now. Look at what they do while I record these words. Hah! I give them enduring eons of enforced tranquility which plods on and on despite their every effort to escape into chaos. Believe me, the memory of Leto's Peace shall abide with them forever. They will seek their quiet security thereafter only with extreme caution and steadfast preparation.

—THE STOLEN JOURNALS

Much against his will, Idaho found himself at dawn with Siona beside him being taken to "a safe place" in an Imperial ornithopter. It raced eastward toward the golden arc of sunlight which lifted over a landscape carved into rectangular green plantations.

The 'thopter was a big one, large enough to carry a small squad of Fish Speakers with their two *guests*. The pilot captain of the squad, a brawny woman with a face Idaho could believe had never smiled, had given her name as Inmeir. She sat in the pilot's seat directly ahead of Idaho, two muscular Fish Speaker guards on either side of her. Five more guards sat behind Idaho and Siona.

"God has ordered me to take you away from the City," Inmeir had said, coming up to him in the command post beneath the central plaza. "It is for your own safety. We will return by tomorrow morning for Siaynoq."

Idaho, fatigued by a night of alarms, had sensed the futility of arguing against the orders of "God Himself." Inmeir appeared quite capable of trundling him off under one of her thick arms. She had led him from the command post into a chilly night canopied with stars like stone-edged facets of shattered brilliants. It was only when they reached the 'thopter and Idaho recognized Siona waiting there that he had begun to question the purpose of this outing.

During the night, Idaho had come to realize that not all of the violence in Onn had originated with the organized rebels. When he had inquired after Siona, Moneo had sent word that "my daughter is safely out of the way," adding at the end of the message: "I commend her to your care."

In the 'thopter, Siona had not responded to Idaho's questions. Even now, she sat in sullen silence beside him. She reminded him of himself in those first bitter days when he had vowed vengeance against the Harkonnens. He wondered at her bitterness. What drove her?

Without knowing why, Idaho found himself comparing Siona with Hwi Noree. It had not been easy to encounter Hwi, but he had managed it in spite of the importunate demands of Fish Speakers that he attend to duties elsewhere.

Gentle, that was the word for Hwi. She acted from a core of unchanging gentleness which was, in its own way, a thing of enormous power. He found this intensely attractive.

I must see more of her.

For now, though, he had to contend with the sullen silence of Siona seated beside him. Well . . . silence could be met with silence.

Idaho peered down at the passing landscape. Here and there he could see the clustered lights of villages winking out as the sunlight approached. The desert of the Sareer lay far behind and this was land that, by its appearance, might never have been parched.

Some things do not change very much, he thought. *They are merely taken from one place and re-formed in another place.*

This landscape reminded him of Caladan's lush gardens and made him wonder what had become of the verdant planet where the Atreides had lived for so many generations before coming to Dune. He could identify narrow roads, market roads with a scattered traffic of vehicles drawn by six-legged animals which he guessed were thorses. Moneo had said that thorses tailored to the needs of such a landscape were the main work beasts not only here but throughout the Empire.

"A population which walks is easier to control."

Moneo's words rang in Idaho's memory as he peered downward. Pastureland appeared ahead of the 'thopter, softly rolling green hills cut into irregular patterns by black stone walls. Idaho recognized sheep and several kinds of large cattle. The 'thopter passed over a narrow valley still in gloom and with only a hint of the water coursing down its depths. A single light and a blue plume of smoke lifting out of the valley's shadows spoke of human occupation.

Siona suddenly stirred and tapped their pilot on the shoulder, pointing off to the right ahead of them.

"Isn't that Goygoa over there?" Siona asked.

"Yes." Inmeir spoke without turning, her voice clipped and touched by some emotion which Idaho could not identify.

"Is that not a safe place?" Siona asked.

"It is safe."

Siona looked at Idaho. "Order her to take us to Goygoa."

Without knowing why he complied, Idaho said: "Take us to that place."

Inmeir turned then and her features, which Idaho had thought a square block of non-emotion during the night, revealed the clear evidence of some deep feeling. Her mouth was drawn down into a scowl. A nerve twitched at the corner of her right eye.

"Not Goygoa, Commander," Inmeir said. "There are better . . ."

"Did the God Emperor tell you to take us to a specific place?" Siona demanded.

Inmeir glared her anger at this interruption, but did not look directly at Siona. "No, but He . . ."

"Then take us to this Goygoa," Idaho said.

Inmeir jerked her attention back to the 'thopter's controls and Idaho was thrown against Siona as the craft banked sharply and flew toward a round pocket nestled in the green hills.

Idaho peered over Inmeir's shoulder to look at their destination. At the very center of the pocket lay a village built of the same black stones as the surrounding fences. Idaho saw orchards on some of the slopes above the village, terraced gardens rising in steps toward a small saddle where hawks could be seen gliding on the day's first updrafts.

Looking at Siona, Idaho asked: "What is this Goygoa?"

"You will see."

Inmeir set the 'thopter into a shallow glide which brought them to a gentle landing on a flat stretch of grass at the edge of the village. One of the Fish Speakers opened the door on the village side. Idaho's nostrils were immediately assaulted by a heady mixture of aromas—crushed grass, animal droppings, the acridity of cooking fires. He slipped out of the 'thopter and looked up a village street where people were emerging from their houses to stare at the visitors. Idaho saw an older woman in a long green dress bend over and whisper something to a child who immediately turned and went dashing away up the street.

"Do you like this place?" Siona asked. She dropped down beside him.

"It appears pleasant."

Siona looked at Inmeir as the pilot and the other Fish Speakers joined them on the grass. "When do we go back to Onn?"

"You do not go back," Inmeir said. "My orders are to take you to the Citadel. The Commander goes back."

"I see." Siona nodded. "When will we leave?"

"At dawn tomorrow. I will see the village leader about quarters." Inmeir strode off into the village.

"Goygoa," Idaho said. "That's a strange name. I wonder what this place was in the Dune days?"

"I happen to know," Siona said. "It is on the old charts as Shuloch, which means '*haunted place.*' The Oral History says great crimes were committed here before all of the inhabitants were wiped out."

"Jacurutu," Idaho whispered, recalling the old legends of the water stealers. He glanced around, looking for the evidence of dunes and ridges; there was nothing—only two older men with placid faces returning with Inmeir. The men wore faded blue trousers and ragged shirts. Their feet were bare.

"Did you know this place?" Siona asked.

"Only as a name in a legend."

"Some say there are ghosts," she said, "but I do not believe it."

Inmeir stopped in front of Idaho and motioned the two barefooted men to wait behind her. "The quarters are poor but adequate," she said, "unless you would care to stay in one of the private residences." She turned and looked at Siona as she said this.

"We will decide later," Siona said. She took Idaho's arm. "The Commander and I wish to stroll through Goygoa and admire the sights."

Inmeir shaped her mouth to speak, but remained silent.

Idaho allowed Siona to lead him past the peering faces of the two local men.

"I will send two guards with you," Inmeir called out.

Siona stopped and turned. "Is it not safe in Goygoa?"

"It is very peaceful here," one of the men said.

"Then we will not need guards," Siona said. "Have them guard the 'thopter."

Again, she led Idaho toward the village.

"All right," Idaho said, disengaging his arm from Siona's grasp. "What is this place?"

"It is very likely that you will find this a very restful place," Siona said. "It is not like the old Shuloch at all. Very peaceful."

"You're up to something," Idaho said, striding beside her. "What is it?"

"I've always heard that gholas were full of questions," Siona said. "I, too, have questions."

"Oh?"

"What was he like in your day, the man Leto?"

"Which one?"

"Yes, I forget there were two—the grandfather and our Leto. I mean our Leto, of course."

"He was just a child, that's all I know."

"The Oral History says one of his early brides came from this village."

"Brides? I thought . . ."

"When he still had a manly shape. It was after the death of his sister but before he began to change into the Worm. The Oral History says the brides of Leto vanished into the maze of the Imperial Citadel, never to be seen again except as faces and voices transmitted by holo. He has not had a bride for thousands of years."

They had arrived at a small square at the center of the village, a space about fifty meters on a side and with a low-walled pool of clear water in its center. Siona crossed to the pool's wall and sat on the rock ledge, patting beside her for Idaho to join her there. Idaho looked around at the village first, noting how people peered out at him from behind curtained windows, how the children pointed and whispered. He turned and stood looking down at Siona.

"What is this place?"

"I've told you. Tell me what Muad'Dib was like."

"He was the best friend a man could ever have."

"So the Oral History is true, but it calls the caliphate of his heirs *The Desposyni*, and that has an evil sound."

She's baiting me, Idaho thought.

He allowed himself a tight smile, wondering at Siona's motives. She appeared to be waiting for some important event, anxious . . . even dreading . . . but with an undertone of something like elation. It was all there. Nothing she said now could be accounted as more than small talk, a way of occupying the moments until . . . until what?

The light sound of running feet intruded on his reverie. Idaho turned and saw a child of perhaps eight years racing toward him out of a side street. The child's bare feet kicked up little dust geysers as he ran and there was the sound of a woman shouting, a despairing sound somewhere up the street. The runner stopped about ten paces away and stared up at Idaho with a hungering look, an intensity which Idaho found disturbing. The child appeared vaguely familiar—a boy, a stalwart figure with dark curly hair, an unfinished face but with hints of the man to be—rather high cheekbones, a flat line across the brows. He wore a faded blue singlesuit which betrayed the effects of much laundering but obviously had begun as a garment of excellent material. It had the look of punji cotton woven in a cordlock that did not permit even the frayed edges to unravel.

"You're not my father," the child said. Whirling away, he raced back up the street and vanished around a corner.

Idaho turned and scowled at Siona, almost afraid to ask the question: *Was that a child of my predecessor?* He knew the answer without asking—that familiar face, the genotype carried true. *Myself as a child.* Realization left him with an empty feeling, a sense of frustration. *What is my responsibility?*

Siona put both hands over her face and hunched her shoulders. It had not happened at all the way she had imagined it might. She felt betrayed by her own desires for revenge. Idaho was not simply a *ghola*, something alien and unworthy of consideration. She had felt him thrown against her in the 'thopter, had seen the obvious emotions on his face. And that child . . .

"What happened to my predecessor?" Idaho asked. His voice came out flat and accusatory.

She lowered her hands. There was suppressed rage in his face.

"We are not certain," she said, "but he entered the Citadel one day and never emerged."

"That was his child?"

She nodded.

"You're sure you did not kill my predecessor?"

"I . . ." She shook her head, shocked by the doubts, the latent accusation in him.

"That child, that is the reason we came here?"

She swallowed. "Yes."

"What am I supposed to do about him?"

She shrugged, feeling soiled and guilty because of her own actions.

"What about his mother?" Idaho asked.

"She and the others live up that street." Siona nodded in the direction the boy had gone.

"Others?"

"There is an older son . . . a daughter. Will you . . . I mean, I could arrange . . ."

"No! The boy was right. I'm not his father."

"I'm sorry," Siona whispered. "I should not have done this."

"Why did *he* choose this place?" Idaho asked.

"The father . . . your . . ."

"My *predecessor!*"

"Because this was Irti's home and she would not leave. That is what people said."

"Irti . . . the mother?"

"Wife, by the old rite, the one from the Oral History."

Idaho looked around at the stone fronts of the buildings which enclosed the square, the curtained windows, the narrow doors. "So he lived here?"

"When he could."

"How did he die, Siona?"

"Truly, I do not know . . . but the Worm has killed others. We know that for sure!"

"How do you know it?" He centered a probing stare on her face. The intensity of it forced her to look away.

"I do not doubt the stories of my ancestors," she said. "They are told in bits and pieces, a note here, a whispered account there, but I believe them. My father believes them, too!"

"Moneo has said nothing to me of this."

"One thing you can say about the Atreides," she said. "We're loyal and that's a fact. We keep our word."

Idaho opened his mouth to speak, closed it without making a

sound. *Of course! Siona, too, was Atreides.* The thought shook him. He had known it, but he had not accepted it. Siona was some kind of a rebel, a rebel whose actions were almost sanctioned by Leto. The limits of his permission were unclear, but Idaho sensed them.

"You must not harm her," Leto had said. "She is to be tested."

Idaho turned his back on Siona.

"You don't know anything for sure," he said. "Bits and pieces, rumors!"

Siona did not respond.

"He's an Atreides!" Idaho said.

"He's the Worm!" Siona said and the venom in her voice was almost palpable.

"Your damned Oral History is nothing but a bunch of ancient gossip!" Idaho accused. "Only a fool would believe it."

"You still trust him," she said. "That will change."

Idaho whirled and glared at her.

"You've never talked to him!"

"I have. When I was a child."

"You're still a child. He's all of the Atreides who were, all of them. It's a terrible thing, but I knew those people. They were my friends."

Siona only shook her head.

Again, Idaho turned away. He felt that he had been wrung dry of emotion. He was spiritually boneless. Without willing it, he began walking across the square and up the street where the boy had gone. Siona came running after him and fell into step, but he ignored her.

The street was narrow, enclosed by the one-story stone walls, the doors set back within arched frames, all of the doors closed. The windows were small versions of the doors. Curtains twitched as he passed.

At the first cross-street, Idaho stopped and looked to the right where the boy had gone. Two gray-haired women in long black skirts and dark green blouses stood a few paces away down the street, gossiping with their heads close together. They fell silent when they saw Idaho and stared at him with open curiosity. He returned their stare, then looked down the side-street. It was empty.

Idaho turned toward the women, passed them within a pace. They drew closer together and turned to watch him. They looked only once at Siona, then returned their attention to Idaho. Siona moved quietly beside him, an odd expression on her face.

Sadness? he wondered. *Regret? Curiosity?*

It was difficult to say. He was more curious about the doorways and windows they were passing.

"Have you ever been to Goygoa before?" Idaho asked.

"No." Siona spoke in a subdued voice, as though afraid of it.

Why am I walking down this street? Idaho wondered. Even as he asked himself the question, he knew the answer. *This woman, this Irti: What kind of a woman would bring me to Goygoa?*

The corner of a curtain on his right lifted and Idaho saw a face—the boy from the square. The curtain dropped then was flung aside to reveal a woman standing there. Idaho stared speechlessly at her face, stopped in a completed step. It was the face of a woman known only to his deepest fantasies—a soft oval with penetrating dark eyes, a full and sensuous mouth . . .

"Jessica," he whispered.

"What did you say?" Siona asked.

Idaho could not answer. It was the face of Jessica resurrected out of a past he had believed gone forever, a genetic prank—Muad'Dib's mother recreated in new flesh.

The woman closed the curtain, leaving the memory of her features in Idaho's mind, an after-image which he knew he could never remove. She had been older than the Jessica who had shared their dangers on Dune—age lines beside the mouth and eyes, the body a bit more full . . .

More motherly, Idaho told himself. Then: *Did I ever tell her . . . who she resembled?*

Siona tugged at his sleeve. "Do you wish to go in, to meet her?"

"No. This was a mistake."

Idaho started to turn back the way they had come, but the door of Irti's house was flung open. A young man emerged and closed the door behind him, turning then to confront Idaho.

Idaho guessed the youth's age at sixteen and there was no denying the parentage—that *karakul* hair, the strong features.

"You are the new one," the youth said. His voice had already deepened into manhood.

"Yes." Idaho found if difficult to speak.

"Why have you come?" the youth asked.

"It was not my idea," Idaho said. He found this easier to say, the words driven by resentment against Siona.

The youth looked at Siona. "We have had word that my father is dead."

Siona nodded.

The youth returned his attention to Idaho. "Please go away and do not return. You cause pain for my mother."

"Of course," Idaho said. "Please apologize to the Lady Irti for this intrusion. I was brought here against my will."

"Who brought you?"

"The Fish Speakers," Idaho said.

The youth nodded once, a curt movement of the head. He looked once more at Siona. "I always thought that you Fish Speakers were taught to treat your own more kindly." With that, he turned and reentered the house, closing the door firmly behind him.

Idaho turned back the way they had come, grabbing Siona's arm as he strode away. She stumbled, then fell into step, disengaging his grasp.

"He thought I was a Fish Speaker," she said.

"Of course. You have the look." He glanced at her. "Why didn't you tell me that Irti was a Fish Speaker?"

"It didn't seem important."

"Oh."

"That's how they met."

They came to the intersection with the street from the square. Idaho turned away from the square, striding briskly up to the end where the village merged into gardens and orchards. He felt insulated by shock, his awareness recoiling from too much that could not be assimilated.

A low wall blocked his path. He climbed over it, heard Siona follow. Trees around them were in bloom, white flowers with orange centers where dark brown insects worked. The air was full of insect buzzing and a floral scent which reminded Idaho of jungle flowers from Caladan.

He stopped when he reached the crest of a hill where he could turn and look back down at Goygoa's rectangular neatness. The roofs were flat and black.

Siona sat down on the thick grass of the hilltop and embraced her knees.

"That was not what you intended, was it?" Idaho asked.

She shook her head and he saw that she was close to tears.

"Why do you hate him so much?" he asked.

"We have no lives of our own!"

Idaho looked down at the village. "Are there many villages like this one?"

"This is the shape of the Worm's Empire!"

"What's wrong with it?"

"Nothing—if that's all you want."

"You're saying that this is all he allows?"

"This, a few market cities . . . Onn. I'm told that even planetary capitals are just big villages."

"And I repeat: What's wrong with that?"

"It's a prison!"

"Then leave it."

"Where? How? You think we can just get on a Guild ship and go anywhere else, anywhere we want?" She pointed down toward Goygoa where the 'thopter could be seen off to one side, the Fish Speakers seated on the grass nearby. "Our jailers won't let us leave!"

"They leave," Idaho said. "They go anywhere they want."

"Anywhere the Worm sends them!"

She pressed her face against her knees and spoke, her voice muffled. "What was it like in the old days?"

"It was different, often very dangerous." He looked around at the walls which set off pastureland, gardens and orchards. "Here on Dune, there were no imaginary lines to show the limits of ownership on the land. It was all the Dukedom of the Atreides."

"Except for the Fremen."

"Yes. But they knew where they belonged—on this side of a particular escarpment . . . or beyond where the pan turns white against the sand."

"They could go wherever they wanted!"

"With some limits."

"Some of us long for the desert," she said.

"You have the Sareer."

She lifted her head to glare at him. "That little thing!"

"Fifteen hundred kilometers by five hundred—not so little."

Siona got to her feet. "Have you asked the Worm why he confines us this way?"

"Leto's Peace, the Golden Path to insure our survival. That's what he *says*."

"Do you know what he told my father? I spied on them when I was a child. I heard him."

"What did he say?"

"He said he denies us most crises, to limit our forming forces. He said: 'People can be sustained by affliction, but I am the affliction now. Gods can become afflictions.' Those were his words, Duncan. The Worm is a sickness!"

Idaho did not doubt the accuracy of her recital, but the words failed to stir him. He thought instead of the Corrino he had been ordered to kill. *Affliction*. The Corrino, descendant of a Family which once had ruled this Empire, had been revealed as a softly fat middle-aged man who hungered after power and conspired for spice. Idaho had ordered a Fish Speaker to kill him, an act which had aroused Moneo to a fit of intense questioning.

"Why didn't you kill him yourself?"

"I wanted to see how the Fish Speakers performed."

"And your judgment of their performance?"

"Efficient."

But the death of the Corrino had inflicted Idaho with a sense of unreality. A fat little man lying in a pool of his own blood, an undistinguished shadow among the night shadows of a plastone street. It was unreal. Idaho could remember Muad'Dib saying: *"The mind imposes this framework which it calls 'reality.' That arbitrary framework has a tendency to be quite independent of what your senses report."* What *reality* moved the Lord Leto?

Idaho looked at Siona standing against the orchard background and the green hills of Goygoa. "Let's go down to the village and find our quarters. I'd like to be alone."

"The Fish Speakers will put us in the same quarters."

"With them?"

"No, just the two of us together. The reason's simple enough. The Worm wants me to breed with the great Duncan Idaho."

"I pick my own partners," Idaho growled.

"I'm sure one of our Fish Speakers would be delighted," Siona said. She whirled away from him and set off down the hill.

Idaho watched her for a moment, the lithe young body swaying like the limbs of the orchard trees in the wind.

"I'm not his stud," Idaho muttered. "That's one thing he'll have to understand."

As each day passes, you become increasingly unreal, more alien and remote from what I find myself to be on that new day. I am the only reality and, as you differ from me, you lose reality. The more curious I become, the less curious are those who worship me. Religion suppresses curiosity. What I do subtracts from the worshipper. Thus it is that eventually I will do nothing, giving it all back to frightened people who will find themselves on that day alone and forced to act for themselves.

—THE STOLEN JOURNALS

It was a sound like no other, the sound of a waiting mob, and it came down the long tunnel to where Idaho marched ahead of the Royal Cart—nervous whispers magnified into an ultimate whisper, the shuffling of one gigantic foot, the stirring of an enormous garment. And the smell—sweet perspiration mixed with the milky breath of sexual excitement.

Inmeir and the others of his Fish Speaker escort had brought Idaho here in the first hour after dawn, coming down to the plaza of Onn while it lay in cold green shadows. They had lifted off immediately after turning him over to other Fish Speakers, Inmeir obviously unhappy because she was required to take Siona to the Citadel and thus would miss the ritual of Siaynoq.

The new escort, vibrant with repressed emotion, had taken him into a region deep beneath the plaza, a place not on any of the city charts Idaho had studied. It was a maze—first one direction and then another through corridors wide enough and high enough to accommodate the Royal Cart. Idaho lost track of directions and fell to reflecting on the preceding night.

The sleeping quarters in Goygoa, although Spartan and small, had been comfortable—two cots to a room, each room a box with whitewashed walls, a single window and a single door. The rooms were strung along a corridor in a building designated as Goygoa's "Guest House."

And Siona had been right. Without asking if it suited him, Idaho had been quartered with her, Inmeir acting as though this were an accepted thing.

When the door closed on them, Siona said: "If you touch me, I will try to kill you."

It was uttered with such dry sincerity that Idaho almost laughed. "I would prefer privacy," he said. "Consider yourself alone."

He had slept with a light wariness, remembering dangerous nights in the Atreides service, the readiness for combat. The room was seldom truly dark—moonlight coming through the curtained window, even starlight reflecting from the chalk-white walls. He had found himself nervously sensitive to Siona, to the smell of her, the stirrings, her breathing. Several times he had come fully awake to listen, aware on two of those occasions that she, too, was listening.

Morning and the flight to Onn had come as a relief. They had broken their fast with a drink of cold fruit juice, Idaho glad to enter the predawn darkness for a brisk walk to the 'thopter. He did not speak directly to Siona and he found himself resenting the curious glances of the Fish Speakers.

Siona spoke to him only once, leaning out of the 'thopter as he left it in the plaza.

"It would not offend me to be your friend," she said.

Such a curious way of putting it. He had felt vaguely embarrassed. "Yes . . . well, certainly."

The new escort had led him away then, coming at last to a terminal in the maze. Leto awaited him there on the Royal Cart. The meeting place was a wide spot in a corridor which stretched off into the converging distance on Idaho's right. The walls were dark brown streaked with golden lines which glittered in the yellow light of glowglobes. The escort took up positions behind the cart, moving smartly and leaving Idaho to stand confronting Leto's cowled face.

"Duncan, you will precede me when we go to Siaynoq," Leto said.

Idaho stared into the dark blue wells of the God Emperor's eyes, angered by the mystery and secrecy, the obvious air of private excitement in this place. He felt that everything he had been told about Siaynoq only deepened the mystery.

"Am I truly the Commander of your Guard, m'Lord?" Idaho asked, resentment heavy in his voice.

"Indeed! And I bestow a signal honor upon you now. Few adult males ever share Siaynoq."

"What happened in the city last night?"

"Bloody violence in some places. It is quite calm this morning, however."

"Casualties?"

"Not worth mentioning."

Idaho nodded. Leto's prescient powers had warned of some peril to *his* Duncan. Thus, the flight into the rural safety of Goygoa.

"You have been to Goygoa," Leto said. "Were you tempted to stay?"

"No!"

"Do not be angry with me," Leto said. "I did not send you to Goygoa."

Idaho sighed. "What was the danger which required that you send me away?"

"It was not to you," Leto said. "But you excite my guards to excessive displays of their abilities. Last night's activities did not require this."

"Oh?" This thought shocked Idaho. He had never thought of himself as one to inspire particular heroism unless he personally demanded it. One *whipped up* the troops. Leaders such as the original Leto, this one's grandfather, had inspired by their presence.

"You are extremely precious to me, Duncan," Leto said.

"Yes . . . well, I'm still not your stud!"

"Your wishes will be honored, of course. We will discuss it another time."

Idaho glanced at the Fish Speaker escort, all of them wide-eyed and attentive.

"Is there always violence when you come to Onn?" Idaho asked.

"It goes in cycles. The malcontents are quite subdued now. It will be more peaceful for a time."

Idaho looked back at Leto's inscrutable face. "What happened to my predecessor?"

"Haven't my Fish Speakers told you?"

"They say he died in defense of his God."

"And you have heard a contrary rumor."

"What happened?"

"He died because he was too close to me. I did not remove him to a safe place in time."

"A place like Goygoa."

"I would have preferred him to live out his days there in peace, but you well know, Duncan, that you are not a seeker after peace."

Idaho swallowed, encountering an odd lump in his throat. "I would still like the particulars of his death. He has a family . . ."

"You will get the particulars and do not fear for his family. They are my wards. I will keep them safely at a distance. You know how violence seeks me out. That is one of my functions. It is unfortunate that those I admire and love must suffer because of this."

Idaho pursed his lips, not satisfied with what he heard.

"Set your mind at ease, Duncan," Leto said. "Your predecessor died because he was too close to me."

The Fish Speaker escort stirred restively. Idaho glanced at them, then looked to the right up the tunnel.

"Yes, it is time," Leto said. "We must not keep the women waiting. March close ahead of me, Duncan, and I will answer your questions about Siaynoq."

Obedient because he could think of no suitable alternative, Idaho turned on his heel and led off the procession. He heard the cart creak into motion behind him, the faint footsteps of the escort following.

The cart fell silent with an abruptness which jerked Idaho's attention around. The reason was immediately apparent.

"You're on the suspensors," he said, returning his attention to the front.

"I have retracted the wheels because the women will press close around me," Leto said. "We can't crush their feet."

"What is Siaynoq? What is it really?" Idaho asked.

"I have told you. It is the Great Sharing."

"Do I smell spice?"

"Your nostrils are sensitive. There is a small amount of melange in the wafers."

Idaho shook his head.

Trying to understand this event, Idaho had asked Leto directly at the first opportunity after their arrival in Onn, "What is the Feast of Siaynoq?"

"We share a wafer, no more. Even I partake."

"Is it like the Orange Catholic ritual?"

"Oh, no! It is not my flesh. It is the sharing. They are reminded that they are only female, as you are only male, but I am *all*. They share with the *all*."

Idaho had not liked the tone of this. "*Only* male?"

"Do you know who they lampoon at the Feast, Duncan?"

"Who?"

"Men who have offended them. Listen to them when they talk softly among themselves."

Idaho had taken this as a warning: *Don't offend the Fish Speakers. You incur their wrath at your mortal peril!*

Now, as he marched ahead of Leto in the tunnel, Idaho felt that he had heard the words correctly but learned nothing from them. He spoke over his shoulder.

"I don't understand the Sharing."

"We are together in the ritual. You will see it. You will feel it. My Fish Speakers are the repository of a special knowledge, an unbroken line which only they share. Now, you will partake of it and they will love you for it. Listen to them carefully. They are open to ideas of affinity. Their terms of endearment for each other have no reservations."

More words, Idaho thought. *More mystery.*

He could discern a gradual widening in the tunnel; the ceiling sloped higher. There were more glowglobes, tuned now into the deep orange. He could see the high arch of an opening about three hundred meters away, rich red light there in which he could make out glistening faces which swayed gently left and right. Their bodies below the faces presented a dark wall of clothing. The perspiration of excitement was thick here.

As he neared the waiting women, Idaho saw a passage through them and a ramp slanting up to a low ledge on his right. A great arched ceiling curved away above the women, a gigantic space illuminated by glowglobes tuned high into the red.

"Go up the ramp on your right," Leto said. "Stop just beyond the center of the ledge and turn to face the women."

Idaho lifted his right hand in acknowledgment. He was emerging into the open space now and the dimensions of this enclosed place awed him. He set his trained eyes the task of estimating the dimensions as he mounted to the ledge and guessed the hall to be at least eleven hundred meters on a side—a square with rounded corners. It was packed with women, and Idaho reminded himself that these were only the chosen representatives of the far scattered Fish Speaker regiments—three women from each planet. They stood now, their bodies pressed so closely together that Idaho doubted one of them could fall. They had left only a space about fifty meters wide along the ledge where Idaho now stopped and surveyed the scene. The faces looked up at him—faces, faces.

Leto stopped his cart just behind Idaho and lifted one of his silver-skinned arms.

Immediately, a roaring cry of "Siaynoq! Siaynoq!" filled the great hall.

Idaho was deafened by it. *Surely that sound must be heard throughout the City,* he thought. *Unless we are too far underground.*

"My brides," Leto said. "I welcome you to Siaynoq."

Idaho glanced up at Leto, saw the dark eyes glistening, the radiant expression. Leto had said: "This cursed holiness!" But he basked in it.

Has Moneo ever seen this gathering? Idaho wondered. It was an odd thought, but Idaho knew its origin. There had to be some other mortal human with whom this could be discussed. The escort had said Moneo was dispatched on "affairs of state" whose details they did not know. Hearing this, Idaho had felt himself sense another element in Leto's government. The lines of power extended directly from Leto out into the populace, but the lines did not often cross. That required many things, including trusted servants who would accept responsibility for carrying out orders without question.

"Few see the God Emperor do hurtful things," Siona had said. "Is that like the Atreides you knew?"

Idaho looked out over the massed Fish Speakers as these thoughts flitted through his mind. The adulation in their eyes! The awe! How had Leto done this? Why?

"My beloveds," Leto said. His voice boomed out over the upturned faces, carried to the farthest corners by subtle Ixian amplifiers concealed in the Royal Cart.

The steaming images of the women's faces filled Idaho with memory of Leto's warning. *Incur their wrath at your mortal peril!*

It was easy to believe that warning in this place. One word from Leto and these women would tear an offender to pieces. They would not question. They would act. Idaho began to feel a new appreciation of these women as an army. Personal peril would not stop them. They served God!

The Royal Cart creaked slightly as Leto arched his front segments upward, lifting his head.

"You are the keepers of the faith!" Leto said.

They replied as one voice: "Lord, we obey!"

"In me you live without end!" Leto said.

"We are the Infinite!" they shouted.

"I love you as I love no others!" Leto said.

"Love!" they screamed.

Idaho shuddered.

"I give you my beloved Duncan!" Leto said.

"Love!" they screamed.

Idaho felt his whole body trembling. He felt that he might collapse from the weight of this adulation. He wanted to run away and he wanted to stay and accept this. There was power in this room. Power!

In a lower voice, Leto said: "Change the Guard."

The women bowed their heads, a single movement, unhesitating. From off to Idaho's right a line of women in white gowns appeared. They marched into the open space below the ledge and Idaho noted that some of them carried babies and small children, none more than a year or two old.

From the outline explanation provided him earlier, Idaho recognized these women as the ones leaving the immediate service of the Fish Speakers. Some would become priestesses and some would spend full time as mothers . . . but none would truly leave Leto's service.

As he looked down on the children, Idaho thought how the buried memory of this experience must be impressed on any of the male children. They would carry the mystery of it throughout their lives, a memory lost to consciousness but always present, shading responses from this moment onward.

The last of the newcomers came to a stop below Leto and looked up at him. The other women in the hall now lifted their faces and focused on Leto.

Idaho glanced left and right. The whiteclad women filled the space below the ledge for at least five hundred meters in both directions. Some of them lifted their children toward Leto. The awe and submission was something absolute. If Leto ordered it, Idaho sensed, these women would smash their babies to death against the ledge. They would do anything!

Leto lowered his front segments onto the cart, a gentle rippling motion. He peered down benignly and his voice came as a soft caress. "I give you the reward which your faith and service have earned. Ask and it shall be given."

The entire hall reverberated to the response: "It shall be given!"

"What is mine is thine," Leto said.

"What is mine is thine," the women shouted.

"Share with me now," Leto said, "the silent prayer for my intercession in all things—that humankind may never end."

As one, every head in the hall bowed. The whiteclad women cradled their children close, looking down at them. Idaho felt the silent unity, a force which sought to enter him and take him over. He opened his mouth wide and breathed deeply, fighting against something which he sensed as a physical invasion. His mind searched frantically for something to which he could cling, something to shield him.

These women were an army whose force and union Idaho had not suspected. He knew he did not understand this force. He could only observe it, recognize that it existed.

This was what Leto had created.

Leto's words from a meeting at the Citadel came back to Idaho: "Loyalty in a male army fastens onto the army itself rather than onto the civilization which fosters the army. Loyalty in a female army fastens onto the leader."

Idaho stared out across the visible evidence of Leto's creation, seeing the penetrating accuracy of those words, fearing that accuracy.

He offers me a share in this, Idaho thought.

His own response to Leto's words struck Idaho now as puerile.

"I don't see the reason," Idaho had said.

"Most people are not creatures of reason."

"No army, male or female, guarantees peace! Your Empire isn't peaceful! You only . . ."

"My Fish Speakers have provided you with our histories?"

"Yes, but I've also walked about in your city and I've watched your people. Your people are aggressive!"

"You see, Duncan? Peace encourages aggression."

"And you say that your Golden Path . . ."

"Is not precisely peace. It is tranquility, a fertile ground for the growth of rigid classes and many other forms of aggression."

"You talk riddles!"

"I talk accumulated observations which tell me that the peaceful posture is the posture of the defeated. It is the posture of the victim. Victims invite aggression."

"Your damned enforced tranquility! What good does it do?"

"If there is no enemy, one must be invented. The military force which is denied an external target always turns against its own people."

"What's your game?"

"I modify the human desire for war."

"People don't want war!"

"They want chaos. War is the most readily available form of chaos."

"I don't believe any of this! You're playing some dangerous game of your own."

"Very dangerous. I address ancient wellsprings of human behavior to redirect them. The danger is that I could suppress the forces of human survival. But I assure you that my Golden Path endures."

"You haven't suppressed antagonism!"

"I dissipate energies in one place and point them toward another place. What you cannot control, you harness."

"What's to keep your female army from taking over?"

"I am their leader."

As he looked out over the massed women in the great hall, Idaho could not deny the focus of leadership. He saw also that part of this adulation was directed at his own person. The temptation in this held him fixated—anything he wanted from them . . . anything! The latent power in this great hall was explosive. This realization forced him into a deeper questioning of Leto's earlier words.

Leto had said something about exploding violence. Even as he watched the women at their silent prayer, Idaho recalled what Leto had said: "Men are susceptible to class fixations. They create layered societies. The layered society is an ultimate invitation to violence. It does not fall apart. It explodes."

"Women never do this?"

"Not unless they are almost completely male dominated or locked into a male-role model."

"The sexes can't be that different!"

"But they are. Women make common cause based on their sex, a cause which transcends class and caste. That is why I let my women hold the reins."

Idaho was forced to admit that these praying women held the reins. *What part of that power would he pass into my hands?*

The temptation was monstrous! Idaho found himself trembling with it. With chilling abruptness, he realized that this must be Leto's intention—*to tempt me!*

On the floor of the great hall, the women finished their prayer and lifted their gaze to Leto. Idaho felt that he had never before seen such rapture in human faces—not in the ecstasy of sex, not in glorious victory-at-arms—nowhere had he seen anything to approach this intense adulation.

"Duncan Idaho stands beside me today," Leto said. "Duncan is here to declare his loyalty that all may hear it. Duncan?"

Idaho felt a physical chill shoot through his intestines. Leto gave him a simple choice: *Declare your loyalty to the God Emperor or die!*

If I sneer, vacillate or object in any way, the women will kill me with their own hands.

A deep anger suffused Idaho. He swallowed, cleared his throat, then: "Let no one question my loyalty. I am loyal to the Atreides."

He heard his own voice booming out over the room, amplified by Leto's Ixian device.

The effect startled Idaho.

"We share!" the women screamed. "We share! We share!"

"We share," Leto said.

Young Fish Speaker trainees, identifiable by their short green robes, swarmed into the hall from all sides, little knots of movement which eddied throughout the pattern of the adoring faces. Each trainee carried a tray piled high with tiny brown wafers. As the trays moved through the throng, hands reached out in waves of graceful grasping, an undulant dancing of the arms. Each hand took a wafer and held it aloft. When a tray bearer came to the ledge and lifted her burden toward Idaho, Leto said:

"Take two and pass one into my hand."

Idaho knelt and took two wafers. The things felt crisp and fragile. He stood and passed one gently to Leto.

In a stentorian voice, Leto asked: "Has the new Guard been chosen?"

"Yes, Lord!" the women shouted.

"Do you keep my faith?"

"Yes, Lord!"

"Do you walk the Golden Path?"

"Yes, Lord!"

The vibration of the women's shouts sent shock waves through Idaho, stunning him.

"Do we share?" Leto asked.

"Yes, Lord!"

As the women responded, Leto popped his wafer into his mouth. Each mother below the ledge took a bite from her wafer and offered the rest to her child. The massed Fish Speakers behind the whiteclad women lowered their arms and ate their wafers.

"Duncan, eat your wafer," Leto said.

Idaho slipped the thing into his mouth. His ghola body had not been conditioned to the spice but memory spoke to his senses. The wafer tasted faintly bitter with a soft undertone of melange. The taste swept old memories through Idaho's awareness—meals in sietch, banquets at the Atreides Residency . . . the way spice flavors permeated everything in the old days.

As he swallowed the wafer, Idaho grew conscious of the stillness in the hall, a breath-held quiet into which came a loud *click* from Leto's cart. Idaho turned and sought the source of the sound. Leto had opened a compartment in the bed of his cart and was removing a crystal box from it. The box glowed with a blue-gray inner light. Leto placed the box on the bed of his cart, opened the glowing lid and removed a crysknife. Idaho recognized the blade immediately—the hawk engraved on the handle's butt, the green jewels at the hilt.

The crysknife of Paul Muad'Dib!

Idaho found himself deeply moved at the sight of this blade. He stared at it as though the image in his eyes might reproduce the original owner.

Leto lifted the blade and held it high, revealing the elegant curve and milky iridescence.

"The talisman of our lives," Leto said.

The women remained silent, raptly attentive.

"The knife of Muad'Dib," Leto said. "The tooth of Shai-Hulud. Will Shai-Hulud come again?"

The response was a subdued murmur made deeply powerful by contrast with the previous shouting.

"Yes, Lord."

Idaho returned his attention to the enraptured faces of the Fish Speakers.

"Who is Shai-Hulud?" Leto asked.

Again, that deep murmur: "You, Lord."

Idaho nodded to himself. Here was undeniable evidence that Leto had tapped into a monstrous reservoir of power never before unleashed in quite this way. Leto had said it but the words were a meaningless noise compared to the thing seen and felt in this great hall. Leto's words came back to Idaho, though, as if they had waited for this moment to cloak themselves in their true meaning. Idaho recalled that they had been in the crypt, that dank and shadowy place which Leto seemed to find so attractive but which Idaho found so repellent—the dust of centuries there and the odors of ancient decay.

"I have been forming this human society, shaping it for more than three thousand years, opening a door out of adolescence for the entire species," Leto had said.

"Nothing you say explains a female army!" Idaho had protested.

"Rape is foreign to women, Duncan. You ask for a sex-rooted behavioral difference? There's one."

"Stop changing the subject!"

"I do not change it. Rape was always the pay-off in male military conquest. Males did not have to abandon any of their adolescent fantasies while engaging in rape."

Idaho recalled the glowering anger which had come over him at this thrust.

"My *houris* tame the males," Leto said. "It is domestication, a thing that females know from eons of necessity."

Idaho stared wordlessly at Leto's cowled face.

"To tame," Leto said. "To fit into some orderly survival pattern. Women learned it at the hands of men; now men learn it at the hands of women."

"But you said . . ."

"My *houris* often submit to a form of rape at first only to convert this into a deep and binding mutual dependence."

"Dammit! You're . . ."

"Binding, Duncan! Binding."

"I don't feel bound to . . ."

"Education takes time. You are the ancient norm against which the new can be measured."

Leto's words momentarily flushed Idaho of all emotion except a deep sense of loss.

"My *houris* teach maturation," Leto said. "They know that they must supervise the maturation of males. Through this they find their own maturation. Eventually, *houris* merge into wives and mothers and we wean the violent drives away from their adolescent fixations."

"I'll have to see it to believe it!"

"You will see it at the Great Sharing."

As he stood beside Leto in the hall of Siaynoq, Idaho admitted to himself that he had seen something of enormous power, something which *might* create the kind of human universe Leto's words projected.

Leto was restoring the crysknife to its box, returning the box to its compartment in the bed of the Royal Cart. The women watched in silence, even the small children quiet—everyone subdued by the force which could be felt in this great hall.

Idaho looked down at the children, knowing from Leto's explanation that these children would be rewarded with positions of power—male or female, each in a puissant niche. The male children would be female-dominated throughout their lives, making (in Leto's words) "an easy transition from adolescence into breeding males."

Fish Speakers and their progeny lived lives "possessed of a certain excitement not available to most others."

What will happen to Irti's children? Idaho wondered. *Did my predecessor stand here and watch his whiteclad wife share in Leto's ritual?*

What does Leto offer me here?

With that female army, an ambitious commander could take over Leto's Empire. Or could he? No . . . not while Leto lived. Leto said the women were not militarily aggressive "by nature."

He said: "I do not foster that in them. They know a cyclical pattern with a Royal Festival every ten years, a changing of the Guard, a blessing for the new generation, a silent thought for fallen sisters and loved ones gone forever. Siaynoq after Siaynoq marches onward in predictable measure. The change itself becomes non-change."

Idaho lifted his gaze from the women in white and their children. He looked across the mass of silent faces, telling himself that this was only a small core of that enormous female force which spread its feminine web across the Empire. He could believe Leto's words:

"The power does not weaken. It grows stronger every decade."

To what end? Idaho asked himself.

He glanced at Leto who was lifting his hands in benediction over the hall of his *houris.*

"We will move among you now," Leto said.

The women below the ledge opened a path, pressing backward. The path opened deeper into the throng like a fissure spreading through the earth after some tremendous natural upheaval.

"Duncan, you will precede me," Leto said.

Idaho swallowed in a dry throat. He put a palm on the lip of the ledge and dropped down into the open space, moving out into the *fissure* because he knew only that could end this trial.

A quick glance backward showed him Leto's cart drifting majestically down on its suspensors.

Idaho turned and quickened his pace.

The women narrowed the path through their ranks. It was done in an odd stillness, with fixity of attention—first on Idaho and then on that gross pre-worm body riding behind Idaho on the Ixian cart.

As Idaho marched stoically ahead, women reached from all sides to touch him, to touch Leto, or merely to touch the Royal Cart. Idaho felt the restrained passion in their touch and knew the deepest fear in his experience.

The problem of leadership is inevitably: Who will play God?

—MUAD'DIB,
FROM THE ORAL HISTORY

Hwi Noree followed a young Fish Speaker guide down a wide ramp which spiraled into the depths of Onn. The summons from the Lord Leto had come in late evening of the Festival's third day, interrupting a development which had taxed her ability to maintain emotional balance.

Her first assistant, Othwi Yake, was not a pleasant man—a sandy-haired creature with a long, narrow face and eyes which never looked long at anything and never *ever* looked directly into the eyes of someone he addressed. Yake had presented her with a single sheet of mem-erase paper containing what he described as "a summation of recently reported violence in the Festival City."

Standing close to the desk at which she was seated, he had stared down somewhere to her left and said: "Fish Speakers are slaughtering Face Dancers throughout the City." He did not appear particularly moved by this.

"Why?" she demanded.

"It is said that the Bene Tleilax made an attempt on the God Emperor's life."

A thrill of fear shot through her. She sat back and glanced around the ambassadorial office—a round room with a single half-circle desk which concealed the controls for many Ixian devices beneath its highly polished surface. The room was a darkly important-appearing place with brown wood panels covering instruments which shielded it from spying. There were no windows.

Trying not to show her upset, Hwi looked up at Yake. "And the Lord Leto is . . ."

"The attempt on his life appears to have been totally without effect. But it might explain that flogging."

"Then you think there *was* such an attempt?"

"Yes."

The Fish Speaker from the Lord Leto entered at that moment, hard on the announcement of her presence in the outer office. She was followed by a Bene Gesserit crone, a person she introduced as "The Reverend Mother Anteac." Anteac stared intently at Yake while the Fish Speaker, a young woman with smooth, almost childlike features, delivered her message:

"He told me to remind you: 'Return quickly if I summon you.' He summons you."

Yake began fidgeting as the Fish Speaker spoke. He darted his attention all around the room as though looking for something which was not there. Hwi paused only to pull a dark blue robe over her gown, instructing Yake to remain in the office until she returned.

In orange evening light outside the Embassy, on a street oddly empty of other traffic, Anteac looked at the Fish Speaker and said simply: "Yes." Anteac left them then and the Fish Speaker had brought Hwi through empty streets to a tall, windowless building whose depths contained this down-plunging spiral ramp.

The tight curves of the ramp made Hwi dizzy. Brilliant tiny white glowglobes drifted in the central well, illuminating a purple-green vine with elephantine leaves. The vine was suspended on shimmering golden wires.

The soft black surface of the ramp swallowed the sounds of their feet, making Hwi extremely conscious of the faint abrasive swishing caused by the movements of her robe.

"Where are you taking me?" Hwi asked.

"To the Lord Leto."

"I know, but where is he?"

"In his private room."

"It's awfully far down."

"Yes, the Lord often prefers the depths."

"It makes me dizzy walking around and around like this."

"It helps if you do not look at the vine."

"What is that plant?"

"It is called a Tunyon Vine and is supposed to have absolutely no smell."

"I've never heard of it. Where does it come from?"

"Only the Lord Leto knows."

They walked on in silence, Hwi trying to understand her own feelings. The God Emperor filled her with sadness. She could sense the man in him, the man who might have been. Why had such a man chosen this course for his life? Did anyone know? Did Moneo know?

Perhaps Duncan Idaho knew.

Her thoughts gravitated to Idaho—such a physically attractive man. So intense! She could feel herself drawn to him. If only Leto had the body and appearance of Idaho. Moneo, though—that was another matter. She looked at the back of her Fish Speaker escort.

"Can you tell me about Moneo?" Hwi asked.

The Fish Speaker glanced back over her shoulder, an odd expression in her pale blue eyes—apprehension or some bizarre form of awe.

"Is something wrong?" Hwi asked.

The Fish Speaker returned her attention to the downward spiral of the ramp.

"The Lord said you would ask about Moneo," she said.

"Then tell me about him."

"What is there to say? He is the Lord's closest confidant."

"Closer even than Duncan Idaho?"

"Oh, yes. Moneo is an Atreides."

"Moneo came to me yesterday," Hwi said. "He said I should know something about the God Emperor. Moneo said the God Emperor is capable of doing *anything*, anything at all if it is thought to be instructive."

"Many believe this," the Fish Speaker said.

"You do not believe it?"

Hwi asked the question as the ramp rounded a final turn and opened into a small anteroom with an arched entrance only a few steps away.

"The Lord Leto will receive you immediately," the Fish Speaker said. She turned back up the ramp then without speaking of her own belief.

Hwi stepped through the arch and found herself in a low-ceilinged room. It was much smaller than the audience chamber. The air felt crisp and dry. Pale yellow light came from a concealed source at the upper corners. She allowed her eyes to adjust to the lowered illumination, noting carpets and soft cushions scattered around a low mound of . . . She put a hand to her mouth as the mound moved, realizing then that it was the Lord Leto on his cart, but the cart lay in a sunken area. She knew immediately why the room provided this feature. It made him less imposing to human guests, less overpowering by his physical elevation. Nothing could be done, however, about his length and the inescapable mass of his body except to keep them in shadows, throwing most of the light onto his face and hands.

"Come in and sit down," Leto said. He spoke in a low voice, pleasantly conversational.

Hwi crossed to a red cushion only a few meters in front of Leto's face and sat on it.

Leto watched her movements with obvious pleasure. She wore a dark golden gown and her hair was tied back in braids which made her face appear fresh and innocent.

"I have sent your message to Ix," she said. "And I have told them that you wish to know my age."

"Perhaps they will answer," he said. "Their answer may even be truthful."

"I would like to know when I was born, all of the circumstances," she said, "but I don't know why this interests you."

"Everything about you interests me."

"They will not like it that you make me the permanent Ambassador."

"Your masters are a curious mixture of punctilio and laxity," he said. "I do not suffer fools gladly."

"You think me a fool, Lord?"

"Malky was not a fool; neither are you, my dear."

"I have not heard from my uncle in years. Sometimes I wonder if he still lives."

"Perhaps we will learn that as well. Did Malky ever discuss with you my practice of *Taquiyya*?"

She thought about this a moment, then: "It was called *Ketman* among the ancient Fremen?"

"Yes. It is the practice of concealing the identity when revealing it might be harmful."

"I recall it now. He told me you wrote pseudonymous histories, some of them quite famous."

"That was the occasion when we discussed *Taquiyya*."

"Why do you speak of this, Lord?"

"To avoid other subjects. Did you know that I wrote the books of Noah Arkwright?"

She could not suppress a chuckle. "How amusing, Lord. I was required to read about his *life*."

"I wrote that account, too. What secrets were you asked to wrest from me?"

She did not even blink at his strategic change of subject.

"They are curious about the inner workings of the religion of the Lord Leto."

"Are they now?"

"They wish to know how you took religious control away from the Bene Gesserit."

"No doubt hoping to repeat my performance for themselves?"

"I'm sure that's in their minds, Lord."

"Hwi, you are a terrible representative of the Ixians."

"I am your servant, Lord."

"Have you no curiosities of your own?"

"I fear that my curiosities might disturb you," she said.

He stared at her a moment, then: "I see. Yes, you are right. We should avoid more intimate conversation for now. Would you like me to talk about the Sisterhood?"

"Yes, that would be good. Do you know that I met one of the Bene Gesserit delegation today?"

"That would be Anteac."

"I found her frightening," she said.

"You have nothing to fear from Anteac. She went to your Embassy at my command. Were you aware that you had been invaded by Face Dancers?"

Hwi gasped, then held herself still while a cold sensation filled her breast. "Othwi Yake?" she asked.

"You suspected?"

"It's just that I did not like him, and I had been told that . . ." She shrugged, then, as realization swept over her: "What has happened to him?"

"The original? He is dead. That's the usual Face Dancer practice in such circumstances. My Fish Speakers have explicit orders to leave no Face Dancer alive in your Embassy."

Hwi remained silent, but tears trickled down her cheeks. *This explained the empty streets, Anteac's enigmatic "Yes." It explained many things.*

"I will provide Fish Speaker assistance for you until you can make other arrangements," Leto said. "My Fish Speakers will guard you well."

Hwi shook the tears from her face. The Inquisitors of Ix would react with rage against Tleilax. Would Ix believe her report? Everyone in her Embassy taken over by Face Dancers! It was difficult to believe.

"Everyone?" she asked.

"The Face Dancers had no reason to leave any of your original people alive. You would have been next."

She shuddered.

"They delayed," he said, "because they knew they would have to copy you with a precision to defy my senses. They are not sure about my abilities."

"Then Anteac . . ."

"The Sisterhood and I share an ability to detect Face Dancers. And Anteac . . . well, she is very good at what she does."

"No one trusts the Tleilaxu," she said. "Why haven't they been wiped out long ago?"

"Specialists have their uses as well as their limitations. You surprise me, Hwi. I had not suspected you could be that bloody-minded."

"The Tleilaxu . . . they are too cruel to be human. They aren't human!"

"I assure you that humans can be just as cruel. I myself have been cruel on occasion."

"I know, Lord."

"With provocation," he said. "But the only people I have considered eliminating are the Bene Gesserit."

Her shock was too great for words.

"They are so close to what they should be and yet so far," he said.

She found her voice. "But the Oral History says . . ."

"The religion of the Reverend Mothers, yes. Once they designed specific religions for specific societies. They called it *engineering*. How does that strike you?"

"Callous."

"Indeed. The results fit the mistake. Even after all the grand attempts at ecumenism there were countless gods, minor deities and would-be prophets throughout the Empire."

"You changed that, Lord."

"Somewhat. But gods die hard, Hwi. My monotheism dominates, but the original pantheon remains; it has gone underground in various disguises."

"Lord, I sense in your words . . . a . . ." She shook her head.

"Am I as coldly calculating as the Sisterhood?"

She nodded.

"It was the Fremen who deified my father, the great Muad'Dib. Although he doesn't really care to be called great."

"But were the Fremen . . ."

"Were they right? My dearest Hwi, they were sensitive to the uses of power and they were greedy to maintain their ascendancy."

"I find this . . . disturbing, Lord."

"I can see that. You don't like the idea that becoming a god could be that simple, as though anyone could do it."

"It sounds much too casual, Lord." Her voice had a remote and testing quality.

"I assure you that *anyone* could *not* do it."

"But you imply that you inherited your godhood from . . ."

"Never suggest that to a Fish Speaker," he said. "They react violently against heresy."

She tried to swallow in a dry throat.

"I say this only to protect you," he said.

Her voice was faint: "Thank you, Lord."

"My godhood began when I told my Fremen I no longer could give the death-water to the tribes. You know about the death-water?"

"In the Dune days, the water recovered from the bodies of the dead," she said.

"Ahhh, you have read Noah Arkwright."

She managed a faint smile.

"I told my Fremen the water would be consecrated to a Supreme Deity, left nameless. Fremen were still allowed to control this water through my largesse."

"Water must have been very precious in those days."

"Very! And I, as delegate of this nameless deity, held loose control of that precious water for almost three hundred years."

She chewed at her lower lip.

"It still sounds calculating?" he asked.

She nodded.

"It was. When it came time to consecrate my sister's water, I performed a miracle. The voices of all the Atreides spoke from Ghani's urn. Thus, my Fremen discovered that I was their Supreme Deity."

Hwi spoke fearfully, her voice full of puzzled uncertainties at this revelation. "Lord, are you telling me that you are not really a god?"

"I am telling you that I do not play hide-and-seek with death."

She stared at him for several minutes before responding in a way which assured him that she understood his deeper meaning. It was a reaction which only intensified her endearment to him.

"Your death will not be like other deaths," she said.

"Precious Hwi," he murmured.

"I wonder that you do not fear the judgment of a true Supreme Deity," she said.

"Do you judge me, Hwi?"

"No, but I fear for you."

"Think on the price I pay," he said. "Every descendant part of me will carry some of my awareness locked away within it, lost and helpless."

She put both hands over her mouth and stared at him.

"This is the horror which my father could not face and which he tried to prevent: the infinite division and subdivision of a blind identity."

She lowered her hands and whispered: "You will be conscious?"

"In a way . . . but mute. A little pearl of my awareness will go with every sandworm and every sandtrout—knowing yet unable to move a single cell, aware in an endless dream."

She shuddered.

Leto watched her try to understand such an existence. Could she imagine the final *clamor* when the subdivided bits of his identity grappled for a fading control of the Ixian machine which recorded his journals? Could she sense the wrenching silence which would follow that awful fragmentation?

"Lord, they would use this knowledge against you were I to reveal it."

"Will you tell?"

"Of course not!" She shook her head slowly from side to side. Why had he accepted this terrible transformation? Was there no escape?

Presently, she said: "The machine which writes your thoughts, could it not be attuned to . . ."

"To a million of me? To a billion? To more? My dear Hwi, none of those knowing-pearls will be truly me."

Her eyes filmed with tears. She blinked and inhaled a deep breath.

Leto recognized the Bene Gesserit training in this, the way she accepted a flow of calmness.

"Lord, you have made me terribly afraid."

"And you do not understand why I have done this."

"Is it possible for me to understand?"

"Oh, yes. Many could understand it. What people do with understanding is another matter."

"Will you teach me what to do?"

"You already know."

She absorbed this silently, then: "It has something to do with your religion. I can feel it."

Leto smiled. "I can forgive your Ixian masters almost anything for the precious gift of you. Ask and you shall receive."

She leaned toward him, rocking forward on her pillow. "Tell me about the inner workings of your religion."

"You will know all of me soon enough, Hwi. I promise it. Just remember that sun worship among our primitive ancestors was not far off the mark."

"Sun . . . worship?" She rocked backward.

"That sun which controls all of the movement but which cannot be touched—that sun is death."

"Your . . . death?"

"Any religion circles like a planet around a sun which it must use for its energy, upon which it depends for its very existence."

Her voice came barely above a whisper: "What do you see in *your* sun, Lord?"

"A universe of many windows through which I may peer. Whatever the window frames, that is what I see."

"The future?"

"The universe is timeless at its roots and contains therefore all times and all futures."

"It's true then," she said. "You saw a thing which this"—she gestured at his long, ribbed body—"prevents."

"Do you find it in you to believe that this may be, in some small way, holy?" he asked.

She could only nod her head.

"If you share it all with me," he said, "I warn you that it will be a terrible burden."

"Will it make your burden lighter, Lord?"

"Not lighter, but easier to accept."

"Then I will share. Tell me, Lord."

"Not yet, Hwi. You must be patient a while longer."

She swallowed her disappointment, sighing.

"It's only that my Duncan Idaho grows impatient," Leto said. "I must deal with him."

She glanced backward, but the small room remained empty.

"Do you wish me to leave now?"

"I wish you would never leave me."

She stared at him, noting the intensity of his regard, a hungry emptiness in his expression which filled her with sadness. "Lord, why do you tell *me* your secrets?"

"I would not ask you to be the bride of a god."

Her eyes went wide with shock.

"Do not answer," he said.

Barely moving her head, she sent her gaze along the shadowy length of his body.

"Do not search for parts of me which no longer exist," he said. "Some forms of physical intimacy are no longer possible for me."

She returned her attention to his cowled face, noting the pink skin of his cheeks, the intensely human effect of his features in that alien frame.

"If you require children," he said, "I would ask only that you let me choose the father. But I have not yet asked you anything."

Her voice was faint. "Lord, I do not know what to . . ."

"I will return to the Citadel soon," he said. "You will come to me there and we will talk. I will tell you then about the thing which I prevent."

"I am frightened, Lord, more frightened than I ever imagined I could be."

"Do not fear me. I can be nothing but gentle with my gentle Hwi. As for other dangers, my Fish Speakers will shield you with their own bodies. They dare not let harm come to you!"

Hwi lifted herself to her feet and stood trembling.

Leto saw how deeply his words had affected her and he felt the pain of it. Hwi's eyes glistened with tears. She clasped her hands tightly to still the trembling. He knew she would come to him willingly at the Citadel. No matter what he asked, her response would be the response of his Fish Speakers:

"Yes, Lord."

It came to Leto that if she could change places with him, take up his burden, she would offer herself. The fact that she could not do this added to her pain. She was intelligence built on profound sensitivity, without any of Malky's hedonistic weaknesses. She was frightening in her perfection. Everything about her reaffirmed his awareness that she was *precisely* the kind of woman who, if he had grown to normal manhood, he would have wanted (*No! Demanded!*) as his mate.

And the Ixians knew it.

"Leave me now," he whispered.

I am both father and mother to my people. I have known the ecstasy of birth and the ecstasy of death and I know the patterns that you must learn. Have I not wandered intoxicated through the universe of shapes? Yes! I have seen you outlined in light. That universe which you say you see and feel, that universe is my dream. My energies focus upon it and I am in any realm and every realm. Thus, you are born.

—THE STOLEN JOURNALS

"My Fish Speakers tell me that you went to the Citadel immediately after Siaynoq," Leto said.

He stared accusingly at Idaho, who stood near where Hwi had sat only an hour ago. Such a small passage of time—yet Leto felt the emptiness as centuries.

"I needed time to think," Idaho said. He looked into the shadowy pit where Leto's cart rested.

"And to talk to Siona?"

"Yes." Idaho lifted his gaze to Leto's face.

"But you asked for Moneo," Leto said.

"Do they report on every movement I make?" Idaho demanded.

"Not *every* movement."

"Sometimes people need to be alone."

"Of course. But do not blame the Fish Speakers for being concerned about you."

"Siona says she is to be tested!"

"Was that why you asked for Moneo?"

"What is this test?"

"Moneo knows. I presumed that was why you wanted to see him."

"You presume nothing! You *know*."

"Siaynoq has upset you, Duncan. I am sorry."

"Do you have any idea what it's like to be me . . . here?"

"The ghola's lot is not easy," Leto said. "Some lives are harder than others."

"I don't need any juvenile philosophy!"

"What do you need, Duncan?"

"I need to know some things."

"Such as?"

"I don't understand *any* of these people around you! Without showing any surprise about it, Moneo tells me that Siona was part of a rebellion against you. His own daughter!"

"In his day, Moneo too was a rebel."

"See what I mean? Did you test him, too?"

"Yes."

"Will you test me?"

"I am testing you."

Idaho glared at him, then: "I don't understand your government, your Empire, anything. The more I find out, the more I realize that I don't know what's going on."

"How fortunate that you have discovered the way of wisdom," Leto said.

"What?" Idaho's baffled outrage raised his voice to a battlefield roar which filled the small room.

Leto smiled. "Duncan, have I not told you that when you think you know something, that is a most perfect barrier against learning?"

"Then tell me what's going on."

"My friend Duncan Idaho is acquiring a new habit. He is learning always to look beyond what he thinks he knows."

"All right, all right." Idaho nodded his head slowly in time to the words. "Then what's *beyond* letting me take part in that Siaynoq thing?"

"I am binding the Fish Speakers to the Commander of my Guard."

"And I have to fight them off! The escort that took me out to the Citadel wanted to stop for an orgy. And the ones who brought me back here when you . . ."

"They know how much it pleases me to see children of Duncan Idaho."

"Damn you! I'm not your stud!"

"No need to shout, Duncan."

Idaho took several deep breaths, then: "When I tell them 'no,' they act hurt at first and then they treat me like some damned"—he shook his head—"holy man or something."

"Don't they obey you?"

"They don't question anything . . . unless it's contrary to your orders. I didn't want to come back here."

"Yet they brought you."

"You know damned well they won't disobey *you*!"

"I'm glad you came, Duncan."

"Oh, I can see that!"

"The Fish Speakers know how special you are, how fond I am of you, how much I owe you. It's never a question of obedience and disobedience where you and I are concerned."

"Then what is it a question of?"

"Loyalty."

Idaho fell into pensive silence.

"You felt the power of Siaynoq?" Leto asked.

"Mumbo jumbo."

"Then why are you disturbed by it?"

"Your Fish Speakers aren't an army, they're a police force."

"By my name, I assure you that's not so. Police are inevitably corrupted."

"You tempted me with power," Idaho accused.

"That's the test, Duncan."

"You don't trust me?"

"I trust your loyalty to the Atreides implicitly, without question."

"Then what's this talk of corruption and testing?"

"You were the one who accused me of having a police force. Police always observe that criminals prosper. It takes a pretty dull policeman to miss the fact that the position of authority is the most prosperous criminal position available."

Idaho wet his lips with his tongue and stared at Leto with obvious puzzlement. "But the moral training of . . . I mean, the legal . . . the prisons to . . ."

"What good are laws and prisons when the breaking of a law is not a sin?"

Idaho cocked his head slightly to the right. "Are you trying to tell me that your damned religion is . . ."

"Punishment of sins can be quite extravagant."

Idaho hooked a thumb over his shoulder toward the world outside the door. "All this talk about death penalties . . . that flogging and . . ."

"I try to dispense with casual laws and prisons wherever possible."

"You have to have *some* prisons!"

"Do I? Prisons are needed only to provide the illusion that courts and police are effective. They're a kind of job insurance."

Idaho turned slightly and thrust a pointing finger toward the door through which he had entered the small room. "You've got whole planets that are nothing but prisons!"

"I guess you could think of anywhere as a prison if that's the way your illusions go."

"Illusions!" Idaho dropped his hand to his side and stood dumbfounded.

"Yes. You talk of prisons and police and legalities, the perfect illusions behind which a prosperous power structure can operate while observing, quite accurately, that it is above its own laws."

"And you think crimes can be dealt with by . . ."

"Not crimes, Duncan, sins."

"So you think your religion can . . ."

"Have you noted the primary sins?"

"What?"

"Attempting to corrupt a member of my government, and corruption by a member of my government."

"And what is this corruption?"

"Essentially, it's the failure to observe and worship the holiness of the God Leto."

"You?"

"Me."

"But you told me right at the beginning that . . ."

"You think I don't believe in my own godhead? Be careful, Duncan."

Idaho's voice came with angry flatness. "You told me that one of my jobs was to help keep your secret, that you . . ."

"You don't know my secret."

"That you're a tyrant? That's no . . ."

"Gods have more power than tyrants, Duncan."

"I don't like what I'm hearing."

"When has an Atreides ever asked you to *like* your job?"

"You ask me to command your Fish Speakers who are judge, jury and executioner . . ." Idaho broke off.

"And what?"

Idaho remained silent.

Leto stared across the chill distance between them, so short a space yet so far.

It's like playing a fish on a line, Leto thought. *You must calculate the breaking point of every element in the contest.*

The problem with Idaho was that bringing him to the net always hastened his end. And it was happening too rapidly this time. Leto felt sadness.

"I won't worship you," Idaho said.

"The Fish Speakers recognize that you have a special dispensation," Leto said.

"Like Moneo and Siona?"

"Much different."

"So rebels are a special case."

Leto grinned. "All of my most trusted administrators were rebels at one time."

"I wasn't a . . ."

"You were a brilliant rebel! You helped the Atreides wrest an Empire from a reigning monarch."

Idaho's eyes went out of focus with introspection. "So I did." He shook his head sharply as though tossing something out of his hair. "And look what you've done with that Empire!"

"I have set up a pattern in it, a pattern of patterns."

"So you say."

"Information is frozen in patterns, Duncan. We can use one pattern to solve another pattern. Flow patterns are the hardest to recognize and understand."

"More mumbo jumbo."

"You made that mistake once before."

"Why do you let the Tleilaxu keep bringing me back to life—one ghola after another? Where's the *pattern* in that?"

"Because of the qualities which you possess in abundance. I will let my father say it."

Idaho's mouth drew into a grim line.

Leto spoke in Muad'Dib's voice, and even the cowled face fell into a semblance of the paternal features. "You were my truest friend, Duncan, better even than Gurney Halleck. But I am the past."

Idaho swallowed hard. "The things you're doing!"

"They cut against the Atreides grain?"

"You're damned right!"

Leto resumed his ordinary tones. "Yet I'm still Atreides."

"Are you really?"

"What else could I be?"

"I wish I knew!"

"You think I play tricks with words and voices?"

"What in all the seven hells are you really doing?"

"I preserve life while setting the stage for the next cycle."

"You preserve it by killing?"

"Death has often been useful to life."

"That's not Atreides!"

"But it is. We often saw the value of death. The Ixians, however, have never seen that value."

"What've the Ixians got to do with . . ."

"Everything. They would make a machine to conceal their other machinations."

Idaho spoke in a musing tone. "Is that why the Ixian Ambassador was here?"

"You've seen Hwi Noree," Leto said.

Idaho pointed upward. "She was leaving as I arrived."

"You spoke to her?"

"I asked her what she was doing here. She said she was choosing sides."

A burst of laughter erupted from Leto. "Oh, my," he said. "She is so good. Did she reveal her choice?"

"She said she serves the God Emperor now. I didn't believe her, of course."

"But you should believe her."

"Why?"

"Ahhh, yes; I forgot that you once doubted even my grandmother, the Lady Jessica."

"I had good reason!"

"Do you also doubt Siona?"

"I'm beginning to doubt everyone!"

"And you say you don't know your value to me," Leto accused.

"What about Siona?" Idaho demanded. "She says you want us . . . I mean, dammit . . ."

"The thing you must always trust about Siona is her creativity. She can create the new and beautiful. One always trusts the truly creative."

"Even the machinations of the Ixians?"

"That is not creative. You always know the creative because it is revealed openly. Concealment betrays the existence of another force entirely."

"Then you don't trust this Hwi Noree, but you . . ."

"I *do* trust her, and precisely for the reasons I have just given you."

Idaho scowled, then relaxed and sighed. "I had better cultivate her acquaintance. If she is someone you . . ."

"No! You will stay away from Hwi Noree. I have something special in mind for her."

I have isolated the city-experience within me and have examined it closely. The idea of a city fascinates me. The formation of a biological community without a functioning, supportive social community leads to havoc. Whole worlds have become single biological communities without an interrelated social structure and this has always led to ruin. It becomes dramatically instructive under overcrowded conditions. The ghetto is lethal. Psychic stresses of overcrowding create pressures which will erupt. The city is an attempt to manage these forces. The social forms by which cities make the attempt are worth study. Remember that there exists a certain malevolence about the formation of any social order. It is the struggle for existence by an artificial entity. Despotism and slavery hover at the edges. Many injuries occur and, thus, the need for laws. The law develops its own power structure, creating more wounds and new injustices. Such trauma can be healed by cooperation, not by confrontation. The summons to cooperate identifies the healer.

—THE STOLEN JOURNALS

Moneo entered Leto's small chamber with evident agitation. He actually preferred this meeting place because the God Emperor's cart lay in a depression from which a deadly attack by the Worm would be more difficult, and there was the undeniable fact that Leto allowed his majordomo to descend in an Ixian tube-lift rather than via that intermi-

nable ramp. But Moneo felt that the news he brought this morning was
guaranteed to arouse *The Worm Who Is God.*

How to present it?

Dawn lay only an hour past, the fourth Festival Day, a fact Moneo
could greet with equanimity only because it brought him that much
nearer the end of these tribulations.

Leto stirred as Moneo entered the small chamber. Illumination
came on at his signal, focusing only on his face.

"Good morning, Moneo," he said. "My guard tells me you insisted
on entering immediately. Why?"

The danger, Moneo knew from experience, lay in the temptation to
reveal too much too soon.

"I have spent some time with the Reverend Mother Anteac," he
said. "Although she keeps it well hidden, I'm sure she is a Mentat."

"Yes. The Bene Gesserit were bound to disobey me sometime. This
form of disobedience amuses me."

"Then you will not punish them?"

"Moneo, I am ultimately the only parent my people have. A parent
must be generous as well as severe."

He's in a good mood, Moneo thought. A small sigh escaped Moneo,
at which Leto smiled.

"Anteac objected when I told her you had ordered an amnesty for a
selected few Face Dancers among our captives."

"I have a Festive use for them," Leto said.

"Lord?"

"I will tell you later. Let's get to the news which brings you bursting
in upon me at this hour."

"I . . . ahhh . . ." Moneo chewed at his upper lip. "The Tleilaxu have
been quite garrulous in the attempt to ingratiate themselves with me."

"Of course they have. And what have they revealed?"

"They . . . ahhh, provided the Ixians with sufficient advice and
equipment to make a . . . uhhh, not exactly a ghola, and not even a
clone. Perhaps we should use the Tleilaxu term: *a cellular restructuring.*
The . . . ahhh, *experiment* was conducted within some sort of shielding

device which the Guildsmen assured them your powers could not penetrate."

"And the result?" Leto felt that he was asking the question in a cold vacuum.

"They are not certain. Tleilaxu were not permitted to witness. However, they did observe that Malky entered this . . . ahhh, chamber and that he emerged later with an infant."

"Yes! I know!"

"You do?" Moneo was puzzled.

"By inference. And all of this happened some twenty-six years ago?"

"That is correct, Lord."

"They identify the infant as Hwi Noree?"

"They are not certain, Lord, but . . ." Moneo shrugged.

"Of course. And what do you deduce from this, Moneo?"

"There is a deep purpose built into the new Ixian Ambassador."

"Certainly there is. Moneo, has it not struck you as odd how much Hwi, the gentle Hwi, represents a mirror of the redoubtable Malky? His opposite in everything, including sex."

"I had not thought of that, Lord."

"I have."

"I will have her sent back to Ix immediately," Moneo said.

"You will do nothing of the kind!"

"But, Lord, if they . . ."

"Moneo, I have observed that you seldom turn your back on danger. Others often do, but you—seldom. Why would you have me engage in such an obvious stupidity?"

Moneo swallowed.

"Good. I like it when you recognize the error of your ways," Leto said.

"Thank you, Lord."

"I also like it when you express your gratitude sincerely, as you have just done. Now, Anteac was with you when you heard these revelations?"

"As you ordered, Lord."

"Excellent. That will stir things up a bit. You will leave now and go to the Lady Hwi. You will tell her that I desire to see her immediately. This will disturb her. She is thinking that we will not meet again until I summon her to the Citadel. I want you to quiet her fears."

"In what way, Lord?"

Leto spoke sadly: "Moneo, why do you ask advice on something at which you are an expert? Calm her and bring her here reassured of my kindly intentions toward her."

"Yes, Lord." Moneo bowed and backed away a step.

"One moment, Moneo!"

Moneo stiffened, his gaze fixed on Leto's face.

"You are puzzled, Moneo," Leto said. "Sometimes you do not know what to think of me. Am I all-powerful and all-prescient? You bring me these little dibs and dabs and you wonder: *Does he already know this? If he does, why do I bother?* But I have ordered you to report such things, Moneo. Is your obedience not instructive?"

Moneo started to shrug and thought better of it. His lips trembled.

"Time can also be a place, Moneo," Leto said. "Everything depends upon where you are standing, on where you look or what you hear. The measure of it is found in consciousness itself."

After a long silence, Moneo ventured: "Is that all, Lord?"

"No, it is *not* all. Siona will receive today a package delivered to her by a Guild courier. Nothing is to interfere with delivery of that package. Do you understand?"

"What is . . . what is in the package, Lord?"

"Some translations, reading matter which I wish her to see. You will do nothing to interfere. There is no melange in the package."

"How . . . how did you know what I feared was in the . . ."

"Because you fear the spice. It could extend your life, but you avoid it."

"I fear its *other* effects, Lord."

"A bountiful nature has decreed that melange will unveil for some of us unexpected depths of the psyche, yet you fear this?"

"I am *Atreides*, Lord!"

"Ahhh, yes, and for the Atreides, melange may roll the mystery of Time through a peculiar process of internal revelation."

"I have only to remember the way you tested me, Lord."

"Do you not see the necessity for you to sense the Golden Path?"

"That is not what I fear, Lord."

"You fear the other astonishment, the thing which made me make *my* choice."

"I have only to look at you, Lord, and know that fear. We Atreides . . ." He broke off, his mouth dry.

"You do not want all of these memories of ancestors and the others who flock within me!"

"Sometimes . . . sometimes, Lord, I think the spice is the Atreides curse!"

"Do you wish that *I* had never occurred?"

Moneo remained silent.

"But melange has its values, Moneo. The Guild navigators need it. And without it, the Bene Gesserit would degenerate into a helpless band of whining females!"

"We must live with it or without it, Lord. I know that."

"Very perceptive, Moneo. But you choose to live without it."

"Do I not have that choice, Lord?"

"For now."

"Lord, what do you . . ."

"There are twenty-eight different words for melange in common Galach. They describe it by its intended use, by its dilution, by its age, by whether it came through honest purchase, through theft or conquest, whether it was the dower gift for a male or for a female, and in many other ways is it named. What do you make of this, Moneo?"

"We are offered many choices, Lord."

"Only where the spice is concerned?"

Moneo's brow wrinkled in thought, then: "No."

"You so seldom say '*no*' in my presence," Leto said. "I enjoy watching your lips form around the word."

Moneo's mouth twitched in an attempted smile.

Leto spoke briskly: "Well! You must go now to the Lady Hwi. I will give you one parting piece of advice which may help."

Moneo paid studious attention to Leto's face.

"Drug knowledge originated mostly with males because they tend to be more venturesome—an outgrowth of male aggression. You've read your Orange Catholic Bible, thus you know the story of Eve and the apple. Here's an interesting fact about that story: Eve was not the first to pluck and sample the apple. Adam was first and he learned by this to put the blame on Eve. My story tells you something about how our societies find a structural necessity for sub-groups."

Moneo tipped his head slightly to the left. "Lord, how does this help me?"

"It will help you with the Lady Hwi!"

> The singular multiplicity of this universe draws my deepest
> attention. It is a thing of ultimate beauty.
>
> —THE STOLEN JOURNALS

Leto heard Moneo in the antechamber just before Hwi entered the small audience room. She wore voluminous pale green pantaloons tightly tied at the ankles with darker green bows to match her sandals. A loose blouse of the same dark green could be seen under her black cloak.

She appeared calm as she approached Leto and sat without being invited, choosing a golden cushion rather than the red one she had occupied earlier. It had taken less than an hour for Moneo to bring her. Leto's acute hearing detected Moneo fidgeting in the anteroom and Leto sent a signal which sealed the arched doorway there.

"Something has disturbed Moneo," Hwi said. "He tried very hard not to reveal this to me, but the more he tried to soothe me the more he aroused my curiosity."

"He did not frighten you?"

"Oh, no. He did say something very interesting, though. He said that I must remember it at all times, that the God Leto is a different person to each of us."

"How is this interesting?" Leto asked.

"The interesting thing is the question for which this was the pref-

ace. He said he often wonders what part we play in creating that difference in you."

"That *is* interesting."

"I think it is a truthful insight," Hwi said. "Why have you summoned me?"

"At one time, your masters on Ix . . ."

"They are no longer my masters, Lord."

"Forgive me. I will refer to them hereafter as the Ixians."

She nodded gravely, prompting: "At one time . . ."

"The Ixians contemplated making a weapon—a type of hunter-
seeker, self-propelled death with a machine mind. It was to be designed
as a self-improving thing which would seek out life and reduce that life
to its inorganic matter."

"I have not heard of this thing, Lord."

"I know that. The Ixians do not recognize that machine-makers
always run the risk of becoming totally machine. This is ultimate sterility. Machines always fail . . . given time. And when these machines
failed there would be nothing left, no life at all."

"Sometimes I think they are mad," she said.

"Anteac's opinion. That is the immediate problem. The Ixians are
now engaged in an endeavor which they are concealing."

"Even from you?"

"Even from me. I am sending the Reverend Mother Anteac to investigate for me. To help her, I want you to tell her everything you can
about the place where you spent your childhood. Omit no detail, no
matter how small. Anteac will help you remember. We want every
sound, every smell, the shapes and names of visitors, the colors and
even the tinglings of your skin. The slightest thing may be vital."

"You think it is the place of concealment?"

"I know it is."

"And you think they are making this weapon in . . ."

"No, but this will be our excuse for investigating the place where
you were born."

She opened her mouth and gradually formed a smile, then: "My

Lord is devious. I will speak to the Reverend Mother immediately."
Hwi started to rise, but he stopped her with a gesture.

"We must not give the appearance of haste," he said.

She sank back onto the cushion.

"Each of us is different in the way of Moneo's observation," he said.
"Genesis does not stop. Your god continues creating you."

"What will Anteac find? You know, don't you?"

"Let us say that I have a strong conviction. Now, you have not once
mentioned the subject which I broached earlier. Have you no questions?"

"You will provide the answers as I require them." It was a statement
full of such trust that it stopped Leto's voice. He could only look at her,
realizing how extraordinary was this accomplishment of the Ixians—
this *human*. Hwi remained precisely true to the dictates of her personally
chosen morality. She was comely, warm and honest and possessed
of an emphatic sense which forced her to share every anguish in those
with whom she identified. He could imagine the dismay of her Bene
Gesserit teachers when confronted by this immovable core of self-
honesty. The teachers obviously had been reduced to adding a touch
here, an ability there, everything strengthening that power which prevented her from becoming a Bene Gesserit. How that must have rankled!

"Lord," she said, "I would know the motives which forced you to
choose your life."

"First, you must understand what it is like to see our future."

"With your help, I will try."

"Nothing is ever separated from its source," he said. "Seeing futures
is a vision of a *continuum* in which all things take shape like bubbles
forming beneath a waterfall. You see them and then they vanish into
the stream. If the *stream* ends, it is as though the bubbles never were.
That stream is my Golden Path and I saw it end."

"Your choice"—she gestured at his body—"changed that?"

"It is changing. The change comes not only from the manner of my
life but from the manner of my death."

"You know how you will die?"

"Not *how*. I know only the Golden Path in which it will occur."

"Lord, I do not . . ."

"It is difficult to understand, I know. I will die four deaths—the death of the flesh, the death of the soul, the death of the myth and the death of reason. And all of these deaths contain the seed of resurrection."

"You will return from . . ."

"The seeds will return."

"When you are gone, what will happen to your religion?"

"All religions are a single communion. The spectrum remains unbroken within the Golden Path. It is only that humans see first one part and then another. Delusions can be called accidents of the senses."

"People will still worship you," she said.

"Yes."

"But when *forever* ends, there will be anger," she said. "There will be denial. Some will say you were just an ordinary tyrant."

"Delusion," he agreed.

A lump in her throat prevented her from speaking for a moment, then: "How does your life and your death change the . . ." She shook her head.

"Life will continue."

"I believe that, Lord, but how?"

"Each cycle is a reaction to the preceding cycle. If you think about the shape of my Empire, then you know the shape of the next cycle."

She looked away from him. "Everything I learned about your Family told me that you would do this"—she gestured blindly in his direction without looking at him—"only with a selfless motive. I do not think I truly know the *shape* of your Empire, though."

"Leto's Golden Peace?"

"There is less peace than some would have us believe," she said, looking back at him.

The honesty of her! he thought. *Nothing deterred it.*

"This is the time of the stomach," he said. "This is the time when we expand as a single cell expands."

"But something is missing," she said.

She is like the Duncans, he thought. *Something is missing and they sense it immediately.*

"The flesh grows, but the psyche does not grow," he said.

"The psyche?"

"That reflexive awareness which tells us how *very* alive we can become. You know it well, Hwi. It is that sense which tells you how to be true to yourself."

"Your religion is not enough," she said.

"No religion can ever be enough. It is a matter of choice—a single, lonely choice. Do you understand now why your friendship and your company mean so much to me?"

She blinked back tears, nodding, then: "Why don't people know this?"

"Because the conditions don't permit it."

"The conditions which you dictate?"

"Precisely. Look throughout my Empire. Do you see the shape?"

She closed her eyes, thinking.

"One wishes to sit by a river and fish every day?" he asked. "Excellent. That is this life. You desire to sail a small boat across an island sea and visit strangers? Superb! What else is there to do?"

"Travel in space?" she asked and there was a defiant note in her voice. She opened her eyes.

"You have observed that the Guild and I do not allow this."

"*You* do not allow it."

"True. If the Guild disobeys me, it gets no spice."

"And holding people planetbound keeps them out of mischief."

"It does something more important than that. It fills them with a longing to travel. It creates a *need* to make far voyages and see strange things. Eventually, travel comes to mean freedom."

"But the spice dwindles," she said.

"And freedom becomes more precious every day."

"This can only lead to desperation and violence," she said.

"A wise man in my ancestry—I was actually that person, you know? Do you understand that there are no strangers in my past?"

She nodded, awed.

"This wise man observed that wealth is a tool of freedom. But the pursuit of wealth is the way to slavery."

"The Guild and the Sisterhood enslave themselves!"

"And the Ixians and the Tleilaxu and all the others. Oh, they ferret out a bit of hidden melange from time to time and that keeps the attention fixed. A very interesting game, don't you think?"

"But when the violence comes . . ."

"There will be famines and hard thoughts."

"Here on Arrakis, too?"

"Here, there, everywhere. People will look back on my tyranny as *the good old days*. I will be the mirror of their future."

"But it will be terrible!" she objected.

She could have no other reaction, he thought.

He said: "As the land refuses to support the people, the survivors will crowd into smaller and smaller refuges. A terrible selection process will be repeated on many worlds—explosive birthrates and dwindling food."

"But couldn't the Guild . . ."

"The Guild will be largely helpless without sufficient melange to operate available transports."

"Won't the rich escape?"

"Some of them."

"Then you haven't really changed anything. We will just go on struggling and dying."

"Until the sandworm reigns once more on Arrakis. We will have tested ourselves by then with a profound experience shared by all. We will have learned that a thing which can happen on one planet can happen on any planet."

"So much pain and death," she whispered.

"Don't you understand about death?" he asked. "You must understand. The species must understand. All life must understand."

"Help me, Lord," she whispered.

"It is the most profound experience of any creature," he said. "Short of death come the things which risk and mirror it—life-threatening diseases, injuries and accidents . . . childbirth for a woman . . . and once it was combat for the males."

"But your Fish Speakers are . . ."

"They teach about survival," he said.

Her eyes went wide with understanding. "The survivors. Of course!"

"How precious you are," he said. "How rare and precious. Bless the Ixians!"

"And curse them?"

"That, too."

"I did not think I could ever understand about your Fish Speakers," she said.

"Not even Moneo sees it," he said. "And I despair of the Duncans."

"You have to appreciate life before you want to preserve it," she said.

"And it's the survivors who maintain the most light and poignant hold upon the beauties of living. Women know this more often than men because birth is the reflection of death."

"My Uncle Malky always said you had good reasons for denying combat and casual violence to men. What a bitter lesson!"

"Without readily available violence, men have few ways of testing how they will meet that final experience," he said. "Something is missing. The psyche does not grow. What is it people say about Leto's Peace?"

"That you make us wallow in pointless decadence like pigs in our own filth."

"Always recognize the accuracy of folk wisdom," he said. "Decadence."

"Most men have no principles," she said. "The women of Ix complain about it constantly."

"When I need to identify rebels, I look for men with principles," he said.

She stared at him silently, and he thought how that simple reaction spoke so deeply of her intelligence.

"Where do you think I find my best administrators?" he asked.

A small gasp escaped her.

"Principles," he said, "are what you fight for. Most men go through a lifetime unchallenged, except at the final moment. They have so few unfriendly arenas in which to test themselves."

"They have you," she said.

"But I am so powerful," he said. "I am the equivalent of suicide. Who would seek certain death?"

"Madmen . . . or desperate ones. Rebels?"

"I am their equivalent of war," he said. "The ultimate predator. I am the cohesive force which shatters them."

"I've never thought of myself as a rebel," she said.

"You are something far better."

"And you would use me in some way?"

"I would."

"Not as an administrator," she said.

"I already have good administrators—uncorruptible, sagacious, philosophical and open about their errors, quick to see decisions."

"They were rebels?"

"Most of them."

"How are they chosen?"

"I could say they chose themselves."

"By surviving?"

"That, too. But there's more. The difference between a good administrator and a bad one is about five heartbeats. Good administrators make immediate choices."

"Acceptable choices?"

"They usually can be made to work. A bad administrator, on the other hand, hesitates, diddles around, asks for committees, for research and reports. Eventually, he acts in ways which create serious problems."

"But don't they sometimes need more information to make . . ."

"A bad administrator is more concerned with reports than with decisions. He wants the hard record which he can display as an excuse for his errors."

"And good administrators?"

"Oh, they depend on verbal orders. They never lie about what they've done if their verbal orders cause problems, and they surround themselves with people able to act wisely on the basis of verbal orders. Often, the most important piece of information is that something has gone wrong. Bad administrators hide their mistakes until it's too late to make corrections."

Leto watched her as she thought about the people who served him—especially about Moneo.

"Men of decision," she said.

"One of the hardest things for a tyrant to find," he said, "is people who actually make decisions."

"Doesn't your intimate knowledge of the past give you some . . ."

"It gives me some amusement. Most bureaucracies before mine sought out and promoted people who avoided decisions."

"I see. How would you use me, Lord?"

"Will you wed me?"

A faint smile touched her lips. "Women, too, can make decisions. I will wed you."

"Then go and instruct the Reverend Mother. Make sure she knows what she's looking for."

"For my genesis," she said. "You and I already know my purpose."

"Which is not separated from its source," he said.

She arose, then: "Lord, could you be wrong about your Golden Path? Does the possibility of failure . . ."

"Anything and anyone can fail," he said, "but brave good friends help."

Groups tend to condition their surroundings for group survival. When they deviate from this it may be taken as a sign
of group sickness. There are many telltale symptoms. I watch
the sharing of food. This is a form of communication, an inescapable sign of mutual aid which also contains a deadly
signal of dependency. It is interesting that men are the ones
who usually tend the landscape today. They are *husband-
men*. Once, that was the sole province of women.

—THE STOLEN JOURNALS

"You must forgive the inadequacies of this report," the Reverend
Mother Anteac wrote. "Ascribe it to the necessity for haste. I leave on
the morrow for Ix, my purpose being the same one I reported in greater
detail earlier. The God Emperor's intense and sincere interest in Ix cannot be denied, but what I must recount here is the strange visit I have
just had from the Ixian Ambassador, Hwi Noree."

Anteac sat back on the inadequate stool which was the best
she could manage in these Spartan quarters. She sat alone in her tiny
bedchamber, the space-within-a-space which the Lord Leto had
refused to change even after the Bene Gesserit warning of Tleilaxu
treachery.

On Anteac's lap lay a small square of inky black about ten millimeters on a side and no more than three millimeters thick. She wrote
upon this square with a glittering needle—one word upon another, all
of them absorbed into the square. The completed message would be

impressed upon the nerve receptors of an acolyte-messenger's eyes, latent there until they could be replayed at the Chapter House.

Hwi Noree posed such a dilemma!

Anteac knew the accounts of Bene Gesserit teachers sent to instruct Hwi on Ix. But those accounts left out more than they told. They raised greater questions.

What adventures have you experienced, child?

What were the hardships of your youth?

Anteac sniffed and glanced down at the waiting square of black. Such thoughts reminded her of the Fremen belief that the land of your birth made you what you were.

"Are there strange animals on your planet?" the Fremen would ask.

Hwi had come with an impressive Fish Speaker escort, more than a hundred brawny women, all of them heavily armed. Anteac had seldom seen such a display of weapons—lasguns, long knives, silver-blades, stungrenades . . .

It had been at midmorning. Hwi had swept in, leaving the Fish Speakers to invest the Bene Gesserit quarters, all except this Spartan inner room.

Anteac swept her gaze around her quarters. The Lord Leto was telling her something by keeping her here.

"This is how you measure your worth to the God Emperor!"

Except . . . now he sent a Reverend Mother to Ix and the avowed purpose of this journey suggested many things about the Lord Leto. Perhaps times were about to change, new honors and more melange for the Sisterhood.

Everything depends upon how well I perform.

Hwi had entered this room alone and had sat demurely on Anteac's pallet, her head lower than that of the Reverend Mother's. A nice touch, and no accident. The Fish Speakers obviously could have placed the two of them anywhere in any relationship Hwi commanded. Hwi's shocking first words left little doubt of that.

"You must know at the outset that I will wed the Lord Leto."

It had required the deep control to keep from gaping. Anteac's truthsense told her the sincerity of Hwi's words, but the full portent could not be assessed.

"The Lord Leto commands that you say nothing of this to anyone," Hwi added.

Such a dilemma! Anteac thought. *Can I even report this to my Sisters at the Chapter House?*

"Everyone will know in time," Hwi said. "This is not the time. I tell you because it helps impress upon you the gravity of the Lord Leto's trust."

"His trust in you?"

"In both of us."

This had sent a barely concealed, shuddering thrill through Anteac. The power inherent in such trust!

"Do you know why Ix chose you as Ambassador?" Anteac asked.

"Yes. They intended me to beguile him."

"You appear to have succeeded. Does this mean that the Ixians believe those Tleilaxu stories about the Lord Leto's gross habits?"

"Even the Tleilaxu don't believe them."

"I take it that you confirm the falsehood of such stories?"

Hwi had spoken in an odd flatness which even Anteac's truthsense and abilities as a Mentat found hard to decipher.

"You have talked to him and observed him. Answer that question for yourself."

Anteac put down a small surge of irritation. Despite her youth, this Hwi was not an acolyte . . . and would never make a good Bene Gesserit. Such a pity!

"Have you reported this to your government on Ix?" Anteac asked.

"No."

"Why?"

"They will learn soon enough. Premature revelation could harm the Lord Leto."

She is truthful, Anteac reminded herself.

"Isn't your first loyalty to Ix?" Anteac asked.

"Truth is my first loyalty." She smiled then. "Ix contrived better than it thought."

"Does Ix think of you as a threat to the God Emperor?"

"I think their primary concern is knowledge. I discussed this with Ampre before leaving."

"The Director of Ix's Outfederation Affairs? That Ampre?"

"Yes. Ampre is convinced that the Lord Leto permits threats to his person only up to certain limits."

"Ampre said that?"

"Ampre does not believe the future can be hidden from the Lord Leto."

"But my mission to Ix has about it the suggestion that . . ." Anteac broke off and shook her head, then: "Why does Ix provide the Lord with machines and weapons?"

"Ampre believes that Ix has no choice. Overwhelming force destroys people who pose too great a threat."

"And if Ix refused, that would pass the Lord Leto's limits. No middle point. Have you thought about the consequences of wedding the Lord Leto?"

"You mean the doubts such an act will raise about his godhead?"

"Some will believe the Tleilaxu stories."

Hwi only smiled.

Damnation! Anteac thought. *How did we lose this girl?*

"He is changing the design of his religion," Anteac accused. "That's it, of course."

"Do not make the mistake of judging all others by yourselves," Hwi said. And, as Anteac started to bridle, Hwi added: "But I did not come here to argue with you about the Lord."

"No. Of course not."

"The Lord Leto has commanded me," Hwi said, "to tell you every detail in my memory about the place where I was born and raised."

As she reflected on Hwi's words, Anteac stared down at the cryptic square of black in her lap. Hwi had proceeded to recount the details which her Lord (and now bridegroom!) had commanded, details which would have been boring at times were it not for Anteac's Mentat abilities at data absorption.

Anteac shook her head as she considered what must be reported to her Sisters at the Chapter House. They already would be studying the import of her previous message. A machine which could shield itself and contents from the penetrating prescience of even the God Emperor? Was that possible? Or was this a different kind of test, a test of Bene Gesserit candor with their Lord Leto? But now! If he did *not* already know the genesis of this enigmatic Hwi Noree . . .

This new development reinforced Anteac's Mentat summation of why she had been chosen for the mission to Ix. The God Emperor did not trust this knowledge to his Fish Speakers. He did not want Fish Speakers suspecting a weakness in their Lord!

Or was that as obvious as it appeared? Wheels within wheels—that was the way of the Lord Leto.

Again, Anteac shook her head. She bent then and resumed her account for the Chapter House, leaving out the revelation that the God Emperor had chosen a bride.

They would learn it soon enough. Meanwhile, Anteac herself would consider the implications.

If you know all of your ancestors, you were a personal witness to the events which created the myths and religions of our past. Recognizing this, you must think of me as a mythmaker.

—THE STOLEN JOURNALS

The first explosion came just as darkness enfolded the City of Onn. The blast caught a few venturesome revelers outside the Ixian Embassy, passing on their way to a party where (it was promised) Face Dancers would perform an ancient drama about a king who slew his children. After the violent events of the first four Festival Days, it had taken some courage for the revelers to emerge from the relative safety of their quarters. Stories of death and injury to innocent bystanders circulated all through the City—and here it was again—more fuel for the cautious.

None of the victims and survivors would have appreciated Leto's observation that innocent bystanders were in relatively short supply.

Leto's acute senses detected the explosion and located it. With an instant fury which he was later to regret, he shouted for his Fish Speakers and commanded them to "wipe out the Face Dancers," even the ones he had spared earlier.

On immediate reflection, the sensation of fury itself fascinated Leto. It had been so long since he had felt even mild anger. Frustration, irritation—these had been his limits. But now, at a threat to Hwi Noree, fury!

Reflection caused him to modify his initial command, but not before some Fish Speakers had raced from the Royal Presence, their most violent desires released by what they had seen in their Lord.

"God is furious!" some of them shouted.

The second blast caught some of the Fish Speakers emerging into the plaza, limiting the spread of Leto's modified command and igniting more violence. The third explosion, located near the first one, sent Leto himself into action. He propelled his cart like a berserk juggernaut out of his resting chamber into the Ixian lift and surged to the surface.

Leto emerged at the edge of the plaza to find a scene of chaos lighted by thousands of free-floating glowglobes released by his Fish Speakers. The central stage of the plaza had been shattered, leaving only the plasteel base intact beneath the paved surface. Broken pieces of masonry lay all around, mixed with dead and wounded.

In the direction of the Ixian Embassy, directly across the plaza from him, there was a wild surging of combat.

"Where is my Duncan?" Leto bellowed.

A guard bashar came racing across the plaza to his side where she reported through panting breaths: "We have taken him to the Citadel, Lord!"

"What is happening over there?" Leto demanded, pointing at the battle outside the Ixian Embassy.

"The rebels and the Tleilaxu are attacking the Ixian Embassy, Lord. They have explosives."

Even as she spoke, another blast erupted in front of the Embassy's shattered facade. He saw bodies twisting in the air, arching outward and falling at the perimeter of a bright flash which left an orange afterimage, studded with black dots.

With no thought of consequences, Leto shifted his cart onto suspensors and sent it bulleting across the plaza—a hurtling behemoth which sucked glowglobes into its wake. At the battle's edge, he arched over his own defenders and plunged into the attackers' flank, aware only then of lasguns which sent livid blue arcs leaping toward him. He felt his cart thudding into flesh, scattering bodies all around.

The cart spilled him directly in front of the Embassy, rolling him off onto a hard surface as it struck the rubble there. He felt lasgun beams tickle his ribbed body, then the inner surge of heat followed by a venting belch of oxygen at his tail. Instinct tucked his face deep into its cowl and folded his arms into the protective depths of his front segment. The worm-body took over, arching and flailing, rolling like an insane wheel, lashing out on all sides.

Blood lubricated the street. Blood was buffered water to his body, but death released the water. His flailing body slipped and slithered in it, the water igniting blue smoke from every flexion place where it slipped through the sandtrout skin. This filled him with water-agony which ignited more violence in the great flailing body.

At Leto's first lashing out, the Fish Speaker perimeter fell back. An alert bashar saw the opportunity now presented. She shouted above the battle noise:

"Pick off the stragglers!"

The ranks of guardian women rushed forward.

It was bloody play among the Fish Speakers for a few minutes, blades thrusting in the merciless light of the glowglobes, the dancing of lasgun arcs, even hands chopping and toes digging into vulnerable flesh. The Fish Speakers left no survivors.

Leto rolled beyond the bloody mush in front of the Embassy, barely able to think through the waves of water-agony. The air was heavy with oxygen all around him and this helped his human senses. He summoned his cart and it drifted toward him, tipping perilously on damaged suspensors. Slowly, he wriggled onto the tipping cart and gave it the mental command to return to his quarters beneath the plaza.

Long ago, he had prepared himself against water-damage—a room where blasts of superheated dry air would cleanse and restore him. Sand would serve but there was no place in the confines of Onn for the necessary expanse of sand in which he might heat and rasp his surface to its normal purity.

In the lift, he thought of Hwi and sent a message to have her brought down to him immediately.

If she survived.

He had no time now to make a prescient search; he could only hope while his body, both pre-worm and human, longed for the cleansing heat.

Once into the cleansing room, he thought to reaffirm his modified command—"Save some of the Face Dancers!" But by then the maddened Fish Speakers were spreading out through the City and he had not the strength to make a prescient sweep which would send his messengers to the proper meeting points.

A Guard captain brought him word as he was emerging from the cleansing room that Hwi Noree, although slightly wounded, was safe and would be brought to him as soon as the local commander thought it prudent.

Leto promoted the Guard captain to sub-bashar on the spot. She was a heavyset Nayla-type but without Nayla's square face—features more rounded and closer to the older norms. She trembled in the warmth of her Lord's approval and, when he told her to return and "make doubly certain" no more harm came to Hwi, she whirled and dashed from his presence.

I didn't even ask her name, Leto thought, as he rolled himself onto the new cart in the depression of his small audience room. It took a few moments of reflection to recall the new sub-bashar's name—Kieuemo. The promotion would have to be reaffirmed. He lodged a mental reminder to do this personally. The Fish Speakers, all of them, would have to learn immediately how much he valued Hwi Noree. Not that there could be much doubt after tonight.

He made his prescient scan then and dispatched messengers to his rampaging Fish Speakers. By then the damage had been done—corpses all over Onn, some Face Dancers and some only-suspected Face Dancers.

And many have seen me kill, he thought.

While he waited for Hwi's arrival, he reviewed what had just happened. This had not been a typical Tleilaxu attack, but the previous attack on the road to Onn fitted into a new pattern, all of it pointing at a single mind with lethal purpose.

I could have died out there, he thought.

That began to explain why he had not anticipated this attack, but there was a deeper reason. Leto could see that reason rising into his awareness, a summation of all the clues. What human knew the God Emperor best? What human possessed a secret place from which to conspire?

Malky!

Leto summoned a guard and told her to ask if the Reverend Mother Anteac had yet left Arrakis. The guard returned in a moment to report.

"Anteac is still in her quarters. The Commander of the Fish Speaker Guard there says they have not come under attack."

"Send word to Anteac," Leto said. "Ask if she now understands why I put her delegation in quarters at a distance from me. Then tell her that while she is on Ix she must locate Malky. She is to report that location to our local garrison on Ix."

"Malky, the former Ixian Ambassador?"

"The same. He is not to remain alive and free. You will inform our garrison commander on Ix that she is to make close liaison with Anteac, providing every necessary assistance. Malky is to be brought here to me or executed, whichever our commander finds necessary."

The guard-messenger nodded, shadows lurching across her features where she stood in the ring of light around Leto's face. She did not ask for a repetition of the orders. Each of his close guards had been trained as a human-recorder. They could repeat Leto's words exactly, even the intonations, and would never forget what they had heard him say.

When the messenger had gone, Leto sent a private signal of inquiry and, within seconds, had a response from Nayla. The Ixian device within his cart reproduced a nonidentifiable version of her voice, a flatly metallic recital for his ears alone.

Yes, Siona was at the Citadel. No, Siona had not contacted her rebel companions. *"No, she does not yet know that I am here observing her."* The attack on the Embassy? That had been by a splinter group called "The Tleilaxu-Contact Element."

Leto allowed himself a mental sigh. Rebels always gave their groups such pretentious labels.

"Any survivors?" he asked.

"No known survivors."

Leto found it amusing that, while the metallic voice provided no emotional tones, his memory supplied them.

"You will make contact with Siona," he said. "Reveal that you are a Fish Speaker. Tell her you did not reveal this earlier because you knew she would not trust you and because you feared exposure since you are quite alone among Fish Speakers in your allegiance to Siona. Reaffirm your oath to her. Tell her that you swear *by all that you hold holy* to obey Siona in anything. If she commands it, you will do it. All of this is truth, as you well know."

"Yes, Lord."

Memory supplied the fanatic emphasis in Nayla's response. She would obey.

"If possible, provide opportunities for Siona and Duncan Idaho to be alone together," he said.

"Yes, Lord."

Let propinquity take its usual course, he thought.

He broke contact with Nayla, thought for a moment, then sent for the commander of his plaza forces. The bashar arrived presently, her dark uniform stained and dusty, evidence of gore still on her boots. She was a tall, bone-thin woman with age lines which gave her aquiline features an air of powerful dignity. Leto recalled her troop-name, Iylyo, which meant "*Dependable*" in Old Fremen. He called her, however, by her matronymic, Nyshae, "*Daughter of Shae*," which set a tone of subtle intimacy for this meeting.

"Rest yourself on a cushion, Nyshae," he said. "You have been working hard."

"Thank you, Lord."

She sank onto the red cushion which Hwi had used. Leto noted the fatigue lines around Nyshae's mouth, but her eyes remained alert. She stared up at him, eager to hear his words.

"Matters are once more tranquil in my City." He made it not quite a question, leaving the interpretation to Nyshae.

"Tranquil but not good, Lord."

He glanced at the gore on her boots.

"The street in front of the Ixian Embassy?"

"It is being cleansed, Lord. Repairs already are under way."

"The plaza?"

"By morning, it will appear as it has always appeared."

Her gaze remained steady on his face. Both of them knew he had not yet reached the nubbin of this interview. But Leto now identified a thing lurking within Nyshae's expression.

Pride in her Lord!

For the first time, she had seen the God Emperor kill. The seeds of a terrible dependency had been planted. *If disaster threatens, my Lord will come.* That was how it appeared in her eyes. She would no longer act with complete independence, taking her power from the God Emperor and being personally responsible for the use of that power. There was something possessive in her expression. A terrible death-machine waited in the wings, available at her summons.

Leto did not like what he saw, but the damage had been done. Any remedies would require slow and subtle pressures.

"Where did the attackers get lasguns?" he asked.

"From our own stores, Lord. The Arsenal Guard has been replaced."

Replaced. It was a euphemism with a certain nicety. Errant Fish Speakers were isolated and reserved until Leto found a problem which required Death Commandos. They would die gladly, of course, believing that thus they expiated their sin. And even the rumor that such berserkers had been dispatched could quiet a trouble spot.

"The arsenal was breached by explosives?" he asked.

"*Stealth* and explosives, Lord. The Arsenal Guard was careless."

"The source of the explosives?"

Some of Nyshae's fatigue was visible in her shrug.

Leto could only agree. He knew he could search out and identify those sources, but it would serve little purpose. Resourceful people could always find the ingredients for homemade explosives—common things such as sugar and bleaches, quite ordinary oils and innocent fertilizers, plastics and solvents and extracts from the dirt beneath a manure pile. The list was virtually endless, growing with each addition to human experience and knowledge. Even a society such as the one he had created, one which tried to limit the admixture of technology and new ideas, had no real hope of totally eliminating dangerously violent small weapons. The whole idea of controlling such things was chimera, a dangerous and distracting myth. The key was to limit the *desire* for violence. In that respect, this night had been a disaster.

So much new injustice, he thought.

As though she read his thought, Nyshae sighed.

Of course. Fish Speakers were trained from childhood to avoid injustice wherever possible.

"We must see to the survivors in the populace," he said. "See to it that their needs are met. They must be brought to the realization that the Tleilaxu were to blame."

Nyshae nodded. She had not reached bashar rank while remaining ignorant of the drill. By now, she believed it. Merely by hearing Leto say it, she believed in the Tleilaxu guilt. And there was a certain practicality in her understanding. She knew why they did not slay *all* of the Tleilaxu.

You do not eliminate every scapegoat.

"And we must provide a distraction," Leto said. "Luckily, there may be one ready at hand. I will send word to you after conferring with the Lady Hwi Noree."

"The Ixian Ambassador, Lord? Is she not implicated in . . ."

"She is entirely guiltless," he said.

He saw belief settle into Nyshae's features, a ready-made plastic underlayment which could lock her jaw and glaze her eyes. *Even Nyshae.* He knew the reasons because he had created those reasons, but sometimes he felt a bit awed by his creation.

"I hear the Lady Hwi arriving in my anteroom," he said. "Send her in as you leave. And, Nyshae . . ."

She already was on her feet, but she stood expectantly silent.

"Tonight, I have elevated Kieuemo to sub-bashar," he said. "See that it is made official. As for yourself, I am pleased. Ask and you shall receive."

He saw the formula send a wave of pleasure through Nyshae, but she tempered it immediately, proving once more her worth to him.

"I shall test Kieuemo, Lord," she said. "If she suits, I may take a holiday. I have not seen my family on Salusa Secundus for many years."

"At a time of your own choosing," he said.

And he thought: *Salusa Secundus. Of course!*

That one reference to her origins reminded him of who she resembled: *Harq al-Ada. She has Corrino blood. We are closer relatives than I had thought.*

"My Lord is generous," she said.

She left him then, a new spring in her stride. He heard her voice in the anteroom: "Lady Hwi, our Lord will see you now."

Hwi entered, backlighted and framed in the archway for a moment, hesitancy in her step until her eyes adjusted to the inner chamber. She came like a moth to the brightness around Leto's face, looking away only to seek along his shadowy length for signs of injury. He knew that no such sign was visible, but there were still aches and interior tremblings.

His eyes detected a slight limp, Hwi favoring her right leg, but a long gown of jade green concealed the injury. She stopped at the edge of the declivity which held his cart, looking directly into his eyes.

"They said you were wounded, Hwi. Are you in pain?"

"A cut on my leg below the knee, Lord. A small piece of masonry from the explosion. Your Fish Speakers treated it with a salve which removed the pain. Lord, I feared for you."

"And I feared for you, gentle Hwi."

"Except for that first explosion, I was not in danger, Lord. They rushed me into a room deep beneath the Embassy."

So she did not see my performance, he thought. *I can be thankful for that.*

"I sent for you to ask your forgiveness," he said.

She sank onto a golden cushion. "What is there to forgive, Lord? You are not the reason for . . ."

"I am being tested, Hwi."

"You?"

"There are those who wish to know the depths of my concern for the safety of Hwi Noree."

She pointed upward. "That . . . was because of me?"

"Because of us."

"Oh. But who . . ."

"You have agreed to wed me, Hwi, and I . . ." He raised a hand to silence her as she started to speak. "Anteac has told us what you revealed to her, but this did not originate with Anteac."

"Then who is . . ."

"The *who* is not important. It is important that you reconsider. I must give you this opportunity to change your mind."

She lowered her gaze.

How sweet her features are, he thought.

It was possible for him to create only in his imagination an entire *human* lifetime with Hwi. Enough examples lay in the welter of his memories upon which to build a fantasy of wedded life. It gathered nuances in his fancy—small details of mutual experience, a touch, a kiss, all of the sweet sharings upon which arose something of painful beauty. He ached with it, a pain far deeper than the physical reminders of his violence at the Embassy.

Hwi lifted her chin and looked into his eyes. He saw there a compassionate longing to help him.

"But how else may I serve you, Lord?"

He reminded himself that she was a primate, while he no longer was fully primate. The differences grew deeper by the minute.

The ache remained within him.

Hwi was an inescapable reality, something so basic that no word could ever fully express it. The ache within him was almost more than he could bear.

"I love you, Hwi. I love you as a man loves a woman . . . but it cannot be. That will never be."

Tears flowed from her eyes. "Should I leave? Should I return to Ix?"

"They would only hurt you, trying to find out what went wrong with their plan."

She has seen my pain, he thought. *She knows the futility and frustration. What will she do? She will not lie. She will not say she returns my love as a woman to a man. She recognizes the futility. And she knows her own feelings for me—compassion, awe, a questioning which ignores fear.*

"Then I will stay," she said. "We will take such pleasure as we can from being together. I think it is best that we do this. If it means we should wed, so be it."

"Then I must share knowledge with you which I have shared with no other person," he said. "It will give you a power over me which . . ."

"Do not do this, Lord! What if someone forced me to . . ."

"You will never again leave my household. My quarters here, the Citadel, the safe places of the Sareer—these will be your home."

"As you will."

How gentle and open her quiet acceptance, he thought.

The aching pulse within him had to be calmed. In itself, it was a danger to him and to the Golden Path.

Those clever Ixians!

Malky had seen how the all-powerful were forced to contend with a constant siren song—the will to self-delight.

Constant awareness of the power in your slightest whim.

Hwi took his silence to be uncertainty. "Will we wed, Lord?"

"Yes."

"Should anything be done about the Tleilaxu stories which . . ."

"Nothing."

She stared at him, remembering their earlier conversation. *The seeds of dissolution were being planted.*

"It is my fear, Lord, that I will weaken you," she said.

"Then you must find ways to strengthen me."

"Can it strengthen you if we diminish belief in the God Leto?"

He heard a hint of Malky in her voice, that measured weighing which had made him so revoltingly charming. *We never completely escape the teachers of our childhood.*

"Your question begs the answer," he said. "Many will continue to worship according to my design. Others will believe the lies."

"Lord . . . would you ask *me* to lie for you?"

"Of course not. But I will ask you to remain silent when you might wish to speak."

"But if they revile . . ."

"You will not protest."

Once more, tears flowed down her cheeks. Leto longed to touch them, but they were water . . . painful water.

"It must be done this way," he said.

"Will you explain it to me, Lord?"

"When I am gone, they must call me *Shaitan*, the Emperor of Gehenna. The wheel must turn and turn and turn along the Golden Path."

"Lord, could the anger not be directed at me alone? I would not . . ."

"No! The Ixians made you much more perfectly than they thought. I truly love you. I cannot help it."

"I do not wish to cause you pain!" The words were wrenched from her.

"What's done is done. Do not mourn it."

"Help me to understand."

"The hate which will blossom after I am gone, that, too, will fade into the inevitable past. A long time will pass. Then, on a far-distant day, my journals will be found."

"Journals?" She was shaken by the seeming shift of subject.

"My chronicle of my time. My arguments, the apologia. Copies exist and scattered fragments will survive, some in distorted form, but the original journals will wait and wait and wait. I have hidden them well."

"And when they are discovered?"

"People will learn that I was something quite different from what they supposed."

Her voice came in a trembling hush. "I already know what they will learn."

"Yes, my darling Hwi, I think you do."

"You are neither devil nor god, but something never seen before and never to be seen again because your presence removes the need."

She brushed tears from her cheeks.

"Hwi, do you realize how dangerous you are?"

Alarm showed in her expression, the tensing of her arms.

"You have the makings of a saint," he said. "Do you understand how painful it can be to find a saint in the wrong place and the wrong time?"

She shook her head.

"People have to be prepared for saints," he said. "Otherwise, they simply become followers, supplicants, beggars and weakened sycophants forever in the shadow of the saint. People are destroyed by this because it nurtures only weakness."

After a moment of thought, she nodded, then: "Will there be saints when you are gone?"

"That's the purpose of my Golden Path."

"Moneo's daughter, Siona, will she . . ."

"For now she is only a rebel. As to sainthood, we will let her decide. Perhaps she will only do what she was bred to do."

"What is that, Lord?"

"Stop calling me *Lord*," he said. "We will be Worm and wife. Call me Leto if you wish. *Lord* interferes."

"Yes, L . . . Leto. But what is . . ."

"Siona was bred to rule. There is danger in such breeding. When you rule, you gain knowledge of power. This can lead into impetuous irresponsibility, into painful excesses, and that can lead to the terrible destroyer—wild hedonism."

"Siona would . . ."

"All we know about Siona is that she can remain dedicated to a particular performance, to the pattern which fills her senses. She is necessarily an aristocrat, but aristocracy looks mostly to the past. That's a failure. You don't see much of any path unless you are Janus, looking simultaneously backward and forward."

"Janus? Oh, yes, the god with the two opposed faces." She wet her lips with her tongue. "Are you Janus, Leto?"

"I am Janus magnified a billionfold. And I am also something less. I have been, for example, what my administrators admire most—the decision-maker whose every decision can be made to work."

"But if you fail them . . ."

"They will turn against me, yes."

"Will Siona replace you if . . ."

"Ahhh, what an enormous if! You observe that Siona threatens my person. However, she does not threaten the Golden Path. There is also the fact that my Fish Speakers have a certain *attachment* to the Duncan."

"Siona seems . . . so young."

"And I am her favorite *poseur*, the sham who holds power under false pretenses, never consulting the needs of his people."

"Could I not talk to her and . . ."

"No! You must never try to persuade Siona of anything. Promise me, Hwi."

"If you ask it, of course, but I . . ."

"All gods have this problem, Hwi. In the perception of deeper needs, I must often ignore immediate ones. Not addressing immediate needs is an offense to the young."

"Could you not reason with her and . . ."

"Never attempt to reason with people who know they are right!"

"But when you know they are wrong . . ."

"Do you believe in me?"

"Yes."

"And if someone tried to convince you that I am the greatest evil of all time . . ."

"I would become very angry. I would . . ." She broke off.

"Reason is valuable," he said, "only when it performs against the wordless physical background of the universe."

Her brows drew together in thought. It fascinated Leto to sense the arousal of her awareness. "Ahhhh." She breathed the word.

"No reasoning creature will ever again be able to deny the Leto experience," he said. "I see your understanding begin. Beginnings! They are what life is all about!"

She nodded.

No arguments, he thought. *When she sees the tracks, she follows them to find where they will lead.*

"As long as there is life, every ending is a beginning," he said. "And I would save humankind, even from itself."

Again, she nodded. The tracks still led onward.

"This is why no death in the perpetuation of humankind can be a complete failure," he said. "This is why a birth touches us so deeply. This is why the most tragic death is the death of a youth."

"Does Ix still threaten your Golden Path? I've always known they conspired in something evil."

They conspire. *Hwi does not hear the inner message of her own words. She has no need to hear it.*

He stared at her, full of the marvel that was Hwi. She possessed a form of honesty which some would call naive, but which Leto recognized as merely non-self-conscious. The honesty was not her core, it was Hwi herself.

"Then I will arrange a performance in the plaza tomorrow," Leto said. "It will be a performance of the surviving Face Dancers. Afterward, our betrothal will be announced."

Let there be no doubt that I am the assemblage of our ancestors, the arena in which they exercise my moments. They are my cells and I am their body. This is the *favrashi* of which I speak, the soul, the collective unconscious, the source of archetypes, the repository of all trauma and joy. I am the choice of their awakening. My *samhadi* is their *samhadi*. Their experiences are mine! Their knowledge distilled is my inheritance. Those billions are my one.

—THE STOLEN JOURNALS

The Face Dancer performance occupied almost two hours of the morning, and afterward came the announcement which sent shock waves through the Festival City.

"It has been centuries since he took a bride!"

"More than a thousand years, my dear."

The trooping of the Fish Speakers had been brief. They cheered him loudly, but they were disturbed.

"You are my only brides," he had said. Was that not the meaning of Siaynoq?

Leto thought the Face Dancers performed well despite their obvious terror. Garments had been found in the depths of a Fremen museum—hooded black robes with white cord belts, spread-winged green hawks appliquéd across the shoulders at the back—uniforms of Muad'Dib's itinerant priests. The Face Dancers had put on dark, seamed faces with these robes and performed a dance which told how Muad'Dib's legions had spread *their* religion through the Empire.

Hwi, wearing a brilliant silver dress with a green jade necklace, sat beside Leto on the Royal Cart throughout the ritual. Once, she leaned close to his face and asked: "Is that not a parody?"

"To me, perhaps."

"Do the Face Dancers know?"

"They suspect."

"Then they are not as frightened as they appear."

"Oh, yes, they are frightened. It's just that they are braver than most people expect them to be."

"Bravery can be so foolish," she whispered.

"And vice-versa."

She had favored him with a measuring stare before returning her attention to the performance. Almost two hundred Face Dancers had survived unscathed. All of them had been pressed into the dance. The intricate weavings and posturings could fascinate the eye. It was possible to watch them and, for a time, forget the bloody preliminaries to this day.

Leto remembered this as he lay alone in his small reception room shortly before noon when Moneo arrived. Moneo had seen the Reverend Mother Anteac onto a Guild lighter, had conferred with the Fish Speaker Command about the previous night's violence, had made a quick flight to the Citadel and back to make sure Siona was under a secure watch and that she had not been implicated in the Embassy attack. He had returned to Onn just after the betrothal announcement, having had no previous warning.

Moneo was furious. Leto had never seen him this angry. He stormed into the room and stopped only two meters from Leto's face.

"Now the Tleilaxu lies will be believed!" he said.

Leto responded in a reasoned tone. "How persistent it is, this demand that our gods be perfect. The Greeks were much more reasonable about such things."

"Where is she?" Moneo demanded. "Where is this . . ."

"Hwi is resting. It was a difficult night and a long morning. I want her well rested when we return to the Citadel this evening."

"How did she work this?" Moneo demanded.

"Really, Moneo! Have you lost all sense of caution?"

"I am concerned about you! Have you any idea what they're saying in the City?"

"I'm fully aware of the stories."

"What *are* you doing?"

"You know, Moneo, I think that only the old pantheists had the right idea about deities: mortal foibles in immortal guise."

Moneo raised both arms to the heavens. "I saw the looks on their faces!" He lowered his arms. "It'll be all over the Empire within two weeks."

"Surely it'll take longer than that."

"If your enemies needed one thing to bring them all together . . ."

"The defiling of the god is an ancient human tradition, Moneo. Why should I be an exception?"

Moneo tried to speak, found he could not utter a word. He stamped down along the edge of the pit which held Leto's cart, stamped back and resumed his former position glaring into Leto's face.

"If I am to help you, I need an explanation," Moneo said. "Why are you doing this?"

"Emotions."

Moneo's mouth formed the word without speaking it.

"They have come over me just when I thought them gone forever," Leto said. "How sweet these last few sips of humanity are."

"With Hwi? But you surely cannot . . ."

"Memories of emotions are never enough, Moneo."

"Are you telling me that you are indulging yourself in a . . ."

"Indulgence? Certainly not! But the tripod upon which Eternity swings is composed of flesh and thought and emotion. I felt that I had been reduced to flesh and thought."

"She has worked some kind of witchery," Moneo accused.

"Of course she has. And how grateful I am for it. If we deny the need for thought, Moneo, as some do, we lose the powers of reflection; we cannot define what our senses report. If we deny the flesh, we unwheel the vehicle which bears us. But if we deny emotion, we lose all touch with our internal universe. It was emotions which I missed the most."

"I insist, Lord, that you . . ."

"You are making me angry, Moneo. That *is* an emotion."

Leto saw Moneo's frustrated fury cool, quenched like a hot iron plunged into icy water. There was still some steam in him, though.

"I care not for myself, Lord. My concern is mostly for you, and you know this."

Leto spoke softly. "It is your *emotion*, Moneo, and I hold it dear."

Moneo inhaled a deep, trembling breath. He had never before seen the God Emperor in this mood, reflecting this *emotion*. Leto appeared both elated and resigned, if Moneo were reading it correctly. One could not be certain.

"That which makes life sweet for the living," Leto said, "that which makes life warm and filled with beauty, that is what I would preserve even though it were denied to me."

"Then this Hwi Noree . . ."

"She makes me recall the Butlerian Jihad in a poignant way. She is the antithesis of all that's mechanical and non-human. How odd it is, Moneo, that the Ixians, of all people, should produce this one person who so perfectly embodies those qualities which I hold most dear."

"I do not understand your reference to the Butlerian Jihad, Lord. Machines that think have no place in . . ."

"The target of the Jihad was a machine-attitude as much as the machines," Leto said. "Humans had set those machines to usurp our sense of beauty, our necessary selfdom out of which we make living judgments. Naturally, the machines were destroyed."

"Lord, I still resent the fact that you welcome this . . ."

"Moneo! Hwi reassures me merely by her presence. For the first time in centuries, I am not lonely unless she is away from my side. If I had no other proof of the emotion, this would serve."

Moneo fell silent, obviously touched by Leto's evocation of loneliness. Surely, Moneo could understand the absence of the intimate shar-ing in love. His expression betrayed as much.

For the first time in a long while, Leto noted how much Moneo had aged.

It happens so suddenly to them, Leto thought.

It made Leto deeply aware of how much he cared for Moneo.

I should not let attachments happen to me, but I cannot help it . . . especially now that Hwi is here.

"They will laugh at you and make obscene jests," Moneo said.

"That is a good thing."

"How can it be good?"

"This is something new. Our task has always been to bring the new into balance and, with it, modify behavior while not suppressing sur-vival."

"Even so, how can you welcome this?"

"The making of obscenities?" Leto asked. "What is the opposite of obscenity?"

Moneo's eyes went wide with a sudden questioning awareness. He had seen the action of many polarities—the thing made known by its opposite.

The thing stands out against a background which defines it, Leto thought. *Surely Moneo will see this.*

"It's too dangerous," Moneo said.

The ultimate verdict of conservatism!

Moneo was not convinced. A deep sigh wracked him.

I must remember not to take away their doubts, Leto thought. *That's how I failed my Fish Speakers in the plaza. The Ixians are holding on to the ragged end of human doubts. Hwi is the evidence of that.*

A disturbance sounded in the anteroom. Leto sealed the portal against impetuous intrusions.

"My Duncan has come," he said.

"He's probably heard about your wedding plans—"

"Probably."

Leto watched Moneo wrestle with doubts, his thoughts utterly transparent. In that moment, Moneo fit so precisely into his human niche that Leto wanted to hug him.

He has the full spectrum: doubt-to-trust, love-to-hate . . . everything! All of those dear qualities which come to fruition in the warmth of emotion, in the willingness to spend yourself on Life.

"Why is Hwi accepting this?" Moneo asked.

Leto smiled. *Moneo cannot doubt me; he must doubt others.*

"I admit it is not a conventional union. She is a primate and I no longer am fully primate."

Again, Moneo wrestled with things he could only feel and not express.

Watching Moneo, Leto felt the flow of an observational-awareness, a thought process which occurred so rarely but with such vivid amplification when it did occur, that Leto did not stir lest he cause a ripple in the flow.

The primate thinks and, by thinking, survives. Beneath his thinking is a thing which came with his cells. It is the current of human concerns for the species. Sometimes, they cover it up, wall it off and hide it behind thick barriers, but I have deliberately sensitized Moneo to these workings of his innermost self. He follows me because he believes I hold the best course for human survival. He knows there is a cellular awareness. It is what I find when I scan the Golden Path. This is humanity and both of us agree: it must endure!

"Where, when and how will the wedding ceremony be conducted?" Moneo asked.

Not why? Leto noted. Moneo no longer sought to understand the *why.* He had returned to safe ground. He was the majordomo, the director of the God Emperor's household, the First Minister.

He has names and verbs and modifiers with which he can perform. The words will work for him in their usual ways. Moneo may never glimpse the transcendental potential of his words, but he well understands their everyday, mundane uses.

"What of my question?" Moneo pressed.

Leto blinked at him, thinking: *I, on the other hand, feel that words*

are mostly useful if they open for me a glimpse of attractive and undis-
covered places. But the use of words is so little understood by a civiliza-
tion which still believes unquestioningly in a mechanical universe of
absolute cause and effect—obviously reducible to one single root-cause
and one primary seminal-effect.

"How like a limpet the Ixian-Tleilaxu fallacy clings to human affairs," Leto said.

"Lord, it disturbs me deeply when you don't pay attention."

"But I do pay attention, Moneo."

"Not to me."

"Even to you."

"Your attention wanders, Lord. You do not have to conceal that
from me. I would betray myself before I would betray you."

"You think I'm woolgathering?"

"Whatgathering, Lord?" Moneo had never questioned this word
earlier, but now . . .

Leto explained the allusion, thinking: *How ancient!* The looms
and shuttles clicked in Leto's memory. *Animal fur to human gar-*
ments . . . huntsman to herdsman . . . the long steps up the ladder of
awareness . . . and now they must make another long step, longer even
than the ancient ones.

"You indulge in idle thoughts," Moneo accused.

"I have time for idle thoughts. That's one of the most interesting
things about my existence as a singular multitude."

"But, Lord, there are matters which demand our . . ."

"You'd be surprised what comes of idle thinking, Moneo. I've never
minded spending an entire day on things a human would not bother
with for one minute. Why not? With my life expectancy of some four
thousand years, what's one day more or less? How much time does one
human life count? A million minutes? I've already experienced almost
that many days."

Moneo stood frozen in silence, diminished by this comparison. He
felt his own lifetime reduced to a mote in Leto's eye. The source of the
allusion did not escape him.

Words . . . words . . . words, Moneo thought.

"Words are often almost useless in sentient affairs," Leto said.

Moneo held his breathing to a shallow minimum. *The Lord can read thoughts!*

"Throughout our history," Leto said, "the most potent use of words has been to round out some transcendental event, giving that event a place in the accepted chronicles, *explaining* the event in such a way that ever afterward we can use those words and say: "This is what it meant."

Moneo felt beaten down by these words, terrified by unspoken things they might make him think.

"That's how events get lost in history," Leto said.

After a long silence, Moneo ventured: "You have not answered my question, Lord. The wedding?"

How tired he sounds, Leto thought. *How utterly defeated.*

Leto spoke briskly: "I have never needed your good offices more. The wedding must be managed with utmost care. It must have the precision of which only you are capable."

"Where, Lord?"

A bit more life in his voice.

"At Tabur Village in the Sareer."

"When?"

"I leave the date to you. Announce it when all things are arranged."

"And the ceremony itself?"

"I will conduct it."

"Will you need assistants, Lord? Artifacts of any kind?"

"The trappings of ritual?"

"Any particular thing which I may not . . ."

"We will not need much for our little charade."

"Lord! I beg of you! Please . . ."

"You will stand beside the bride and give her in marriage," Leto said. "We will use the Old Fremen ritual."

"We will need water rings then," Moneo said.

"Yes! I will use Ghani's water rings."

"And who will attend, Lord?"

"Only a Fish Speaker guard and the aristocracy."

Moneo stared at Leto's face. "What . . . what does my Lord mean by 'aristocracy'?"

"You, your family, the household entourage, the courtiers of the Citadel."

"My fam . . ." Moneo swallowed. "Do you include Siona?"

"If she survives the test."

"But . . ."

"Is she not family?"

"Of course, Lord. She is Atreides and . . ."

"Then by all means include Siona!"

Moneo brought a tiny memocorder from his pocket, a dull black Ixian artifact whose existence crowded the proscriptions of the Butlerian Jihad. A soft smile touched Leto's lips. Moneo knew his duties and would now perform them.

The clamor of Duncan Idaho outside the portal grew more strident, but Moneo ignored the sound.

Moneo knows the price of his privileges, Leto thought. *It is another kind of marriage—the marriage of privilege and duty. It is the aristocrat's explanation and his excuse.*

Moneo finished his note taking.

"A few details, Lord," Moneo said. "Will there be some special garb for Hwi?"

"The stillsuit and robe of a Fremen bride, real ones."

"Jewelry or other baubles?"

Leto's gaze locked on Moneo's fingers scrabbling over the tiny recorder, seeing there a dissolution.

Leadership, courage, a sense of knowledge and order—Moneo has these in abundance. They surround him like a holy aura, but they conceal from all eyes except mine the rot which eats from within. It is inevitable. Were I gone, it would be visible to everyone.

"Lord?" Moneo pressed. "Are you woolgathering?"

Ahhh! He likes that word!

"That is all," Leto said. "Only the robe, the stillsuit and the water rings."

Moneo bowed and turned away.

He is looking ahead now, Leto thought, *but even this new thing will pass. He will turn toward the past once more. And I had such high hopes for him once. Well . . . perhaps Siona . . .*

"Make no heroes," my father said.

—THE VOICE OF GHANIMA,
FROM THE ORAL HISTORY

Just by the way Idaho strode across the small chamber, his loud demands for audience now gratified, Leto could see an important transformation in the ghola. It was a thing repeated so many times that it had become deeply familiar to Leto. The Duncan had not even exchanged words of greeting with the departing Moneo. It all fitted into the pattern. How boring that pattern had become!

Leto had a name for this transformation of the Duncans. He called it "The Since Syndrome."

The gholas often nurtured suspicions about the *secret things* which might have been developed across the centuries of oblivion *since* they last knew awareness. What had people been doing all that time? *Why could they possibly want me, this relic from their past?* No ego could overcome such doubts forever—especially in a doubting man.

One of the gholas had accused Leto: "You've put things in my body, things I know nothing about! These things in my body tell you everything I'm doing! You spy on me everywhere!"

Another had charged him with possessing a "manipulative machine which makes us want to do whatever you want."

Once it started, the Since Syndrome could never be entirely eliminated. It could be checked, even diverted, but the dormant seed might sprout at the slightest provocation.

Idaho stopped where Moneo had stood and there was a veiled look of nonspecific suspicions in his eyes, in the set of his shoulders. Leto allowed the situation to simmer, bringing the condition to a head. Idaho locked gazes with him, then broke away to dart his glances around the room. Leto recognized the manner behind the gaze.

The Duncans never forget!

As he studied the room, using the sightful ways he had been taught centuries before by the Lady Jessica and the Mentat Thufir Hawat, Idaho began to feel a giddy sense of dislocation. He thought the room rejected him, each thing—the soft cushions: big bulbous things in gold, green and a red that was almost purple; the Fremen rugs, each a museum piece, lapping over each other in thick piles around Leto's pit; the false sunlight of Ixian glowglobes, light which enveloped the Emperor's face in dry warmth, making the shadows around it deeper and more mysterious; the smell of spice-tea somewhere nearby; and that rich melange odor which radiated from the worm-body.

Idaho felt that too much had happened to him too fast since the Tleilaxu had abandoned him to the mercies of Luli and Friend in that featureless prison-cell room.

Too much . . . too much . . .

Am I really here? he wondered. *Is this me? What are these thoughts that I think?*

He stared at Leto's quiescent body, the shadowy and enormous mass which lay so silently there on its cart within the pit. The very quietness of that fleshly mass only suggested mysterious energies, terrible energies which might be unleashed in ways nobody could anticipate.

Idaho had heard the stories about the fight at the Ixian Embassy, but the Fish Speaker accounts had an aura of *miraculous visitation* about them which obscured the physical data.

"He flew down from above them and executed a terrible slaughter among the sinners."

"How did he do that?" Idaho had asked.

"He was an *angry* God," his informant had said.

Angry, Idaho thought. *Was it because of the threat to Hwi?* The stories he had heard! None were believable. Hwi wedded to this gross . . . It was not possible! Not the lovely Hwi, the Hwi of gentle delicacy. *He is playing some terrible game, testing us . . . testing us . . .* There was no honest reality in these times, no peace except in the presence of Hwi. All else was insanity.

As he returned his attention to Leto's face—that silently waiting Atreides face—the sense of dislocation grew stronger in Idaho. He began to wonder if, by a slight increase in mental effort along some strange new pathway, he might break through ghostly barriers to remember all of the experiences of the other Ghola Idahos.

What did they think when they entered this room? Did they feel this dislocation, this rejection?

Just a little extra effort.

He felt dizzy and wondered if he was going to faint.

"Is something wrong, Duncan?" It was Leto's most reasonable and calming tone.

"It's not real," Idaho said. "I don't belong here."

Leto chose to misunderstand. "But my guard tells me you came here of your own accord, that you flew back from the Citadel and demanded an immediate audience."

"I mean *here*, now! In this time!"

"But I need you."

"For what?"

"Look around you, Duncan. The ways you can help me are so numerous that you could not do them all."

"But your women won't let me fight! Every time I want to go where . . ."

"Do you question that you're more valuable alive than dead?" Leto made a clucking sound, then: "Use your wits, Duncan! That's what I value."

"And my sperm. You value that."

"Your sperm is your own to put where you wish."

"I will not leave a widow and orphans behind me the way . . ."

"Duncan! I've said the choice is yours."

Idaho swallowed, then: "You've committed a crime against us, Leto, against all of us—the gholas you resurrect without ever asking us if that's what we want."

This was a new turn in Duncan-thinking. Leto peered at Idaho with renewed interest.

"What crime?"

"Oh, I've heard you spouting your deep thoughts," Idaho accused. He hooked a thumb over his shoulder, pointing at the room's entrance. "Did you know you can be heard out there in the anteroom?"

"When I wish to be heard, yes." *But only my journals hear it all!* "I would like to know the nature of my crime, though."

"There's a time, Leto, a time when you're alive. A time when you're supposed to be alive. It can have a magic, that time, while you're living it. You know you're never going to see a time like that again."

Leto blinked, touched by the Duncan's distress. The words were evocative.

Idaho raised both hands, palms up, to chest-height, a beggar asking for something he knew he could not receive.

"Then . . . one day you wake up and you remember dying . . . and you remember the axlotl tank . . . and the Tleilaxu nastiness which awakened you . . . and it's supposed to start all over again. But it doesn't. It never does, Leto. That's a crime!"

"I have taken away the magic?"

"Yes!"

Idaho dropped his hands to his sides and clenched them into fists. He felt that he stood alone in the path of a millrace tide which would overwhelm him at his slightest relaxation.

And what of my time? Leto thought. *This, too, will never happen again. But the Duncan would not understand the difference.*

"What brought you rushing back from the Citadel?" Leto asked.

Idaho took a deep breath, then: "Is it true? You're to be married?"

"That's correct."

"To this Hwi Noree, the Ixian Ambassador?"

"True."

Idaho darted a quick glance along Leto's supine length.

They always look for genitalia, Leto thought. *Perhaps I should have something made, a gross protuberance to shock them.* He choked back the small burst of amusement which threatened to erupt from his throat. *Another emotion amplified. Thank you, Hwi. Thank you, Ixians.*

Idaho shook his head. "But you . . ."

"There are strong elements to a marriage other than sex," Leto said. "Will we have children of our flesh? No. But the effects of this union will be profound."

"I listened while you were talking to Moneo," Idaho said. "I thought it must be some kind of joke, a . . ."

"Careful, Duncan!"

"Do you *love* her?"

"More deeply than any man ever loved a woman."

"Well, what about her? Does she . . ."

"She feels . . . a compelling compassion, a need to share with me, to give whatever she can give. It is her nature."

Idaho suppressed a feeling of revulsion.

"Moneo's right. They'll believe the Tleilaxu stories."

"That is one of the profound effects."

"And you still want me to . . . to mate with Siona!"

"You know my wishes. I leave the choice to you."

"Who's that Nayla woman?"

"You've met Nayla! Good."

"She and Siona act like sisters. That big hunk! What's going on there, Leto?"

"What would you want to go on? And what does it matter?"

"I've never met such a brute! She reminds me of Beast Rabban. You'd never know she was female if she didn't . . ."

"You have met her before," Leto said. "You knew her as Friend."

Idaho stared at him in quick silence, the silence of a burrowing creature who senses the hawk.

"Then you trust her," Idaho said.

"Trust? What is trust?"

The moment arrives, Leto thought. He could see it shaping in Idaho's thoughts.

"Trust is what goes with a pledge of loyalty," Idaho said.

"Such as the trust between you and me?" Leto asked.

A bitter smile touched Idaho's lips. "So that's what you're doing with Hwi Noree? A marriage, a pledge . . ."

"Hwi and I already have trust for each other."

"Do you trust me, Leto?"

"If I cannot trust Duncan Idaho, I cannot trust anyone."

"And if I can't trust you?"

"Then I pity you."

Idaho took this as almost a physical shock. His eyes were wide with unspoken demands. He *wanted* to trust. He *wanted* the magic which would never come again.

Idaho indicated his thoughts were taking off in an odd tangent then.

"Can they hear us out in the anteroom?" he asked.

"No." *But my journals hear!*

"Moneo was furious. Anyone could see it. But he went away like a docile lamb."

"Moneo is an aristocrat. He is married to duty, to responsibilities. When he is reminded of these things, his anger vanishes."

"So that's how you control him," Idaho said.

"He controls himself," Leto said, remembering how Moneo had glanced up from the notetaking, not for reassurances, but to prompt his sense of duty.

"No," Idaho said. "He doesn't control himself. You do it."

"Moneo has locked *himself* into his past. I did not do that."

"But he's an aristocrat . . . an Atreides."

Leto recalled Moneo's aging features, thinking how inevitable it was that the aristocrat would refuse his final duty—which was to step aside and vanish into history. He would have to be driven aside.

And he would be. No aristocrat had ever overcome the demands of change.

Idaho was not through. "Are you an aristocrat, Leto?"

Leto smiled. "The ultimate aristocrat dies within me." And he thought: *Privilege becomes arrogance. Arrogance promotes injustice. The seeds of ruin blossom.*

"Maybe I will not attend your wedding," Idaho said. "I never thought of myself as an aristocrat."

"But you were. You were *the* aristocrat of the sword."

"Paul was better," Idaho said.

Leto spoke in the voice of Muad'Dib: "Because you taught me!" He resumed his normal tones: "The aristocrat's unspoken duty—to teach, and sometimes by horrible example."

And he thought: *Pride of birth trails out into penury and the weaknesses of interbreeding. The way is opened for pride of wealth and accomplishment. Enter the* nouveaux riches, *riding to power as the Harkonnens did, on the backs of the* ancient régime.

The cycle repeated itself with such persistence that Leto felt anyone should have seen how it must be built into long forgotten survival patterns which the species had outgrown, but never lost.

But no, we still carry the detritus which I must weed out.

"Is there some frontier?" Idaho asked. "Is there some frontier where I could go and never again be a part of this?"

"If there is to be any frontier, you must help me create it," Leto said. "There is now no place to go where others of us cannot follow and find you."

"Then you won't let me go."

"Go if you wish. Others of you have tried it. I tell you there is no frontier, no place to hide. Right now, as it has been for a long, long time, humankind is like a single-celled creature, bound together by a dangerous glue."

"No new planets? No strange . . ."

"Oh, we grow, but we do not separate."

"Because *you* hold us together!" he accused.

"I do not know if you can understand this, Duncan, but if there is a frontier, any kind of frontier, then what lies behind you cannot be more important than what lies ahead."

"You're the past!"

"No, Moneo is the past. He is quick to raise the traditional aristocratic barriers against all frontiers. You must understand the power of those barriers. They not only enclose planets and land on those planets, they enclose ideas. They repress change."

"*You* repress change!"

He will not deviate, Leto thought. *One more try.*

"The surest sign that an aristocracy exists is the discovery of barriers against change, curtains of iron or steel or stone or of any substance which excludes the new, the different."

"I know there must be a frontier somewhere," Idaho said. "You're hiding it."

"I hide nothing of frontiers. I want frontiers! I want surprises!"

They come right up against it, Leto thought. *Then they refuse to enter.*

True to this prediction, Idaho's thoughts darted off on a new tack. "Did you really have Face Dancers perform at your betrothal?"

Leto felt a surge of anger, followed immediately by a wry enjoyment of the fact that he could experience the emotion in such depth. He wanted to let it shout at Duncan . . . but that would solve nothing.

"The Face Dancers performed," he said.

"Why?"

"I want everyone to share in my happiness."

Idaho stared at him as though just discovering a repellent insect in his drink. In a flat voice, Idaho said: "That is the most cynical thing I have ever heard an Atreides say."

"But an Atreides said it."

"You're deliberately trying to put me off! You're avoiding my question."

Once more into the fray, Leto thought. He said: "The Face Dancers of the Bene Tleilax are a colony organism. Individually, they are mules. This is a choice they made for and *by* themselves."

Leto waited, thinking: *I must be patient. They have to discover it for themselves. If I say it, they will not believe. Think, Duncan. Think!*

After a long silence, Idaho said: "I have given you my oath. That is important to me. It is still important. I don't know what you're doing or why. I can only say I don't like what's happening. There! I've said it."

"Is that why you returned from the Citadel?"

"Yes!"

"Will you go back to the Citadel now?"

"What other *frontier* is there?"

"*Very* good, Duncan! Your anger knows even when your reason does not. Hwi goes to the Citadel tonight. I will join her there tomorrow."

"I want to get to know her better," Idaho said.

"You will avoid her," Leto said. "That is an order. Hwi is not for you."

"I've always known there were witches," Idaho said. "Your grandmother was one."

He turned on his heel and, not asking leave, strode back the way he had come.

How like a little boy he is, Leto thought, watching the stiffness in Idaho's back. *The oldest man in our universe and the youngest—both in one flesh.*

The prophet is not diverted by illusions of past, present and future. The fixity of language determines such linear distinctions. Prophets hold a key to the lock in a language. The mechanical image remains only an image to them. This is not a mechanical universe. The linear progression of events is imposed by the observer. Cause and effect? That's not it at all. The prophet utters fateful words. You glimpse a thing "destined to occur." But the prophetic instant releases something of infinite portent and power. The universe undergoes a ghostly shift. Thus, the wise prophet conceals actuality behind shimmering labels. The uninitiated then believe the prophetic language is ambiguous. The listener distrusts the prophetic messenger. Instinct tells you how the utterance blunts the power of such words. The best prophets lead you up to the curtain and let you peer through for yourself.

—THE STOLEN JOURNALS

Leto addressed Moneo in the coldest voice he had ever used: "The Duncan disobeys me."

They were in the airy room of golden stone atop the Citadel's south tower, Leto's third full day back from the Decennial Festival in Onn. An open portal beside him looked out over the harsh noonday of the Sareer. The wind made a deep humming sound through the opening. It stirred up dust and sand which made Moneo squint. Leto seemed not to notice the irritation. He stared out across the Sareer, where the air was alive with heat movements. The distant flow of dunes suggested a mobility in the landscape which only his eyes observed.

Moneo stood immersed in the sour odors of his own fear, knowing that the wind conveyed the message of these odors to Leto's senses. The arrangements for the wedding, the upset among the Fish Speakers— everything was paradox. It reminded Moneo of something the God Emperor had said in the first days of their association.

"Paradox is a pointer telling you to look beyond it. If paradoxes bother you, that betrays your deep desire for absolutes. The relativist treats a paradox merely as interesting, perhaps amusing or even, dreadful thought, educational."

"You do not respond," Leto said. He turned from his examination of the Sareer and focused the weight of his attention on Moneo.

Moneo could only shrug. *How near is the Worm?* he wondered. Moneo had noticed that the return to the Citadel from Onn sometimes aroused the Worm. No sign of that awful shift in the God Emperor's presence had yet betrayed itself, but Moneo sensed it. Could the Worm come without warning?

"Accelerate arrangements for the wedding," Leto said. "Make it as soon as possible."

"Before you test Siona?"

Leto was silent for a moment, then: "No. What will you do about the Duncan?"

"What would you have me do, Lord?"

"I told him not to see Noree, to avoid her. I told him it was an order."

"She has sympathy for him, Lord. Nothing more."

"Why would she have sympathy for him?"

"He is a ghola. He has no connection to our times, no roots."

"He has roots as deep as mine!"

"But he does not know this, Lord."

"Are you arguing with me, Moneo?"

Moneo backed away a half step, knowing that this did not remove him from danger. "Oh, no, Lord. But I always try to tell you truly what I believe is happening."

"I will tell *you* what is happening. He is courting her."

"But she initiates their meetings, Lord."

"Then you knew about this!"

"I did not know you had absolutely prohibited it, Lord."

Leto spoke in a musing voice: "He is clever with women, Moneo, exceedingly clever. He sees into their souls and makes them do what he wants. It has always been that way with the Duncans."

"I did not know you had prohibited all meetings between them, Lord!" Moneo's voice was almost strident.

"He is more dangerous than any of the others," Leto said. "It is the fault of our times."

"Lord, the Tleilaxu do not have a successor for him ready to deliver."

"And we need this one?"

"You said it yourself, Lord. It is a paradox which I do not understand, but you did say it."

"How long until there could be a replacement?"

"At least a year, Lord. Shall I inquire as to a specific date?"

"Do it today."

"He may hear about it, Lord. The previous one did."

"I do not want it to happen this way, Moneo!"

"I know, Lord."

"And I dare not speak of this to Noree," Leto said. "The Duncan is not for her. Yet, I cannot hurt her!" This last was almost a wail.

Moneo stood in awed silence.

"Can't you see this?" Leto demanded. "Moneo, help me."

"I see that it is different with Noree," Moneo said. "But I do not know what to do."

"What is different?" Leto's voice had a penetrating quality which cut right through Moneo.

"I mean your attitude toward her, Lord. It is different from anything I have ever seen in you."

Moneo noted then the first signs—twitching in the God Emperor's hands, the beginning glaze in the eyes. *Gods! The Worm is coming!*

Moneo felt totally exposed. A simple flick of the great body would crush Moneo against a wall. *I must appeal to the human in him.*

"Lord," Moneo said, "I have read the accounts and heard your own words about your marriage to your sister, Ghanima."

"If only she were with me now," Leto said.

"She was never your mate, Lord."

"What're you suggesting?" Leto demanded.

The twitching of Leto's hands had become a spasmodic vibration.

"She was . . . I mean, Lord, that Ghanima was Harq al-Ada's mate."

"Of course she was! All of you Atreides are descended from them!"

"Is there something you have not told me, Lord? Is it possible . . . that is, with Hwi Noree . . . could you mate?"

Leto's hands shook so strongly Moneo wondered that their owner did not know it. The glazing of the great blue eyes deepened.

Moneo backed another step toward the door to the stairs leading down from this deadly place.

"Do not question me about possibilities," Leto said, and his voice was hideously distant, gone somewhere into the layers of his past.

"Never again, Lord," Moneo said. He bowed himself back to only a single pace from the door. "I will speak to Noree, Lord . . . and to the Duncan."

"Do what you can." Leto's voice was far away in those interior chambers which only he could enter.

Softly, Moneo let himself out of the door. He closed it behind him and placed his back against it, trembling. *Ahhh, that was the closest ever.*

And the paradox remained. Where did it point? What was the meaning of the God Emperor's odd and painful decisions? What had brought *The Worm Who Is God?*

A thumping sounded from within Leto's aerie, a heavy beating against stone. Moneo dared not open the door to investigate. He pushed himself away from the surface which reflected that dreadful thumping and went down the stairs, moving cautiously, not drawing an easy breath until he reached ground level and the Fish Speaker guard there.

"Is he disturbed?" she asked, looking up the stairs.

Moneo nodded. They both could hear the thumping quite plainly.

"What disturbs him?" the guard asked.

"He is God and we are mortal," Moneo said. This was an answer which usually satisfied Fish Speakers, but new forces were at work now.

She looked directly at him and Moneo saw the killer training close to the surface of her soft features. She was a relatively young woman with auburn hair and a face usually dominated by a turned-up nose and full lips, but now her eyes were hard and demanding. Only a fool would turn his back on those eyes.

"I did not disturb him," Moneo said.

"Of course not," she agreed. Her look softened slightly. "But I would like to know *who* or what did."

"I think he is impatient for his marriage," Moneo said. "I think that's all it is."

"Then hurry the day!" she said.

"That's what I'm about," Moneo said. He turned and hurried away down the long hall to his own area of the Citadel. Gods! The Fish Speakers were becoming as dangerous as the God Emperor.

That stupid Duncan! He puts us all in peril. And Hwi Noree! What's to be done about her?

The pattern of monarchies and similar systems has a message of value for all political forms. My memories assure me that governments of any kind could profit from this message. Governments can be useful to the governed only so long as inherent tendencies toward tyranny are restrained. Monarchies have some good features beyond their star qualities. They can reduce the size and parasitic nature of the management bureaucracy. They can make speedy decisions when necessary. They fit an ancient human demand for a parental (tribal/feudal) hierarchy where every person knows his place. It is valuable to know your place, even if that place is temporary. It is galling to be held in place against your will. This is why I teach about tyranny in the best possible way— by example. Even though you read these words after a passage of eons, my tyranny will not be forgotten. My Golden Path assures this. Knowing my message, I expect you to be exceedingly careful about the powers you delegate to any government.

—THE STOLEN JOURNALS

Leto prepared with patient care for his first private meeting with Siona since her childhood banishment to the Fish Speaker schools in the Festival City. He told Moneo that he would see her at the Little Citadel, a vantage tower he had built in the central Sareer. The site had been chosen to provide views of old and new and places between. There were no roads to the Little Citadel. Visitors arrived by 'thopter. Leto went there as though by magic.

With his own hands, in the early days of his ascendancy, Leto had used an Ixian machine to dig a secret tunnel under the Sareer to his tower, doing all of the work himself. In those days, a few wild sandworms still roamed the desert. He had lined his tunnel with massive walls of fused silica and had imbedded countless bubbles of worm-repelling water in the outer layers. The tunnel anticipated his maximum growth and the requirements of a Royal Cart which, at that time, had been only a figment of his visions.

In the early predawn hours of the day assigned to Siona, Leto descended to the crypt and gave orders to his guard that he was not to be disturbed by anyone. His cart sped him down one of the crypt's dark spokes where he opened a hidden portal, emerging in less than an hour at the Little Citadel.

One of his delights was to go out alone onto the sand. No cart. Only his pre-worm body to carry him. The sand felt luxuriously sensuous against him. The heat of his passage through the dunes in the day's first light sent up a wake of steam which required him to keep moving. He brought himself to a stop only when he found a relatively dry pocket about five kilometers out. He lay there at the center of an uncomfortable dampness from the trace-dew, his body just outside the long shadow of the tower which stretched eastward from him across the dunes.

From a distance, the three thousand meters of the tower could be seen as an impossible needle stabbing the sky. Only the inspired blend of Leto's commands and Ixian imagination made the structure conceivable. One hundred and fifty meters in diameter, the tower sat on a foundation which plunged as deeply under the sand as it climbed above. The magic of plasteel and superlight alloys kept it supple in the wind and resistant to sandblast abrasions.

Leto enjoyed the place so much that he rationed his visits, making up a long list of personal rules which had to be met. The rules added up to "Great Necessity."

For a few moments while he lay there, he could shed the loads of the Golden Path. Moneo, good and reliable Moneo, would see that Siona arrived promptly, just at nightfall. Leto had a full day in which to relax and think, to play and pretend that he possessed no cares, to drink up the raw sustenance of the earth in a feeding frenzy which he could never indulge in at Onn or at the Citadel. In those places, he was required to confine himself to furtive burrowings through narrow passages where only prescient caution kept him from encountering water-pockets. Here, though, he could race through the sand and across it, feed and grow strong.

Sand crunched beneath him as he rolled, flexing his body in pure animal enjoyment. He could feel his worm-self being restored, an electric sensation which sent messages of health all through him.

The sun was well above the horizon now, painting a golden line up the side of the tower. There was the smell of bitter dust in the air and an odor of distant spiny plants which had responded to the morning's trace-dew. Gently at first, then more rapidly, he moved out in a wide circle around the tower, thinking about Siona as he went.

There could be no more delays. She had to be tested. Moneo knew this as well as Leto did.

Just that morning, Moneo had said: "Lord, there is terrible violence in her."

"She has the beginnings of adrenalin addiction," Leto had said. "It's cold-turkey time."

"Cold what, Lord?"

"It's an ancient expression. It means she must be subjected to a complete withdrawal. She must go through a necessity-shock."

"Oh . . . I see."

For once, Leto realized, Moneo did *see*. Moneo had gone through his own cold-turkey time.

"The young generally are incapable of making hard decisions unless those decisions are associated with immediate violence and the consequent sharp flow of adrenalin," Leto had explained.

Moneo had held himself in reflexive silence, remembering, then: "It is a great peril."

"That's the violence you see in Siona. Even old people can cling to it, but the young wallow in it."

As he circled his tower in the growing light of the day, enjoying the feel of the sand even more as it dried, Leto thought about the conversation. He slowed his passage over the sand. A wind from behind him carried the vented oxygen and a burnt-flint smell over his human nostrils. He inhaled deeply, lifting his magnified awareness to a new level.

This preliminary day contained a multiple purpose. He thought of the coming encounter much as an ancient bullfighter had thought about the first examination of a horned adversary. Siona possessed her own version of horns, although Moneo would make certain that she brought no physical weapons to this encounter. Leto had to be sure, though, that he knew Siona's every strength and every weakness. And he would have to create special susceptibilities in her wherever possible. She had to be prepared for the test, her psychic muscles blunted by well-planted barbs.

Shortly after noon, his worm-self satiated, Leto returned to the tower, crawled back onto his cart and lifted on suspensors to the very tip of a portal there which opened only at his command. Throughout the rest of the day, he lay there in the aerie, thinking, plotting.

The fluttering wings of an ornithopter whispered on the air just at nightfall to signal Moneo's arrival.

Faithful Moneo.

Leto caused a landing-lip to extrude from his aerie. The 'thopter glided in, its wings cupped. It settled gently onto the lip. Leto stared out through the gathering darkness. Siona emerged and darted in toward him, fearful of the unprotected height. She wore a white robe over a black uniform without insignia. She stole one look backward when she stopped just inside the tower, then she turned her attention to Leto's bulk waiting on the cart almost at the center of the aerie. The 'thopter lifted away and jetted off into the darkness. Leto left the lip extruded, the portal open.

"There is a balcony on the other side of the tower," he said. "We will go there."

"Why?"

Siona's voice carried almost pure suspicion.

"I'm told it's a cool place," Leto said. "And there is indeed a faint sensation of cold on my cheeks when I expose them to the breeze there."

Curiosity brought her closer to him.

Leto closed the portal behind her.

"The night view from the balcony is magnificent," Leto said.

"Why are we here?"

"Because here we will not be overheard."

Leto turned his cart and moved it silently out to the balcony. The faintest of hidden illumination within the aerie showed her his movement. He heard her follow.

The balcony was a half-ring on the southeast arc of the tower, a lacy railing at chest-height around the perimeter. Siona moved to the rail and swept her gaze around the open land.

Leto sensed the waiting receptivity. Something was to be spoken here for her ears alone. Whatever it was, she would listen and respond from the well of her own motives. Leto looked across her toward the edge of the Sareer where the man-made boundary wall was a low flat line just barely visible in the light of First Moon lifting above the horizon. His amplified vision identified the distant movement of a convoy from Onn, a dull glow of lights from the beast-drawn vehicles pacing along the high road toward Tabur Village.

He could call up a memory-image of the village nestled among the plants which grew in the moist area along the inner base of the wall. His Museum Fremen tended date palms, tall grasses and even truck gardens there. It was not like the old days when any inhabited place, even a tiny basin with a few low plants fed by a single cistern and windtrap, could appear lush by comparison with the open sand. Tabur Village was a water-rich paradise when compared with Sietch Tabr. Everyone in today's village knew that just beyond the Sareer's boundary wall the Idaho River slid southward in a long straight line which would be silver now in the moonlight. Museum Fremen could not climb the wall's sheer inner face, but they knew the water was there. The earth knew, too. If a Tabur inhabitant put an ear against the ground, the earth spoke with the sound of distant rapids.

There would be nightbirds along the bankment now, Leto thought, creatures which would live in sunlight on another world. Dune had worked its evolutionary magic on them and they still lived at the mercies of the Sareer. Leto had seen the birds draw dumb shadows across the water and, when they dipped to drink, there were ripples which the river took away.

Even at this distance, Leto sensed a power in that faraway water, something forceful out of his past which moved away from him like the current slipping southward into the reaches of farm and forest. The water searched through rolling hills, along the margins of an abundant plantlife which had replaced all of Dune's desert except for this one last place, this Sareer, this sanctuary of the past.

Leto recalled the growling thrust of Ixian machines which had inflicted that watercourse upon the landscape. It seemed such a short time ago, little more than three thousand years.

Siona stirred and looked back at him, but Leto remained silent, his attention fixed beyond her. A pale amber light shone above the horizon, reflection of a town on faraway clouds. From its direction and distance, Leto knew it to be the town of Wallport transplanted far into a warmer clime of the south from its once-austere location in the cold, low-slanted light of the north. The glow of the town was like a window into his past. He felt the beam of it striking through to his breast, straight through the thick and scaled membrane which had replaced his human skin.

I am vulnerable, he thought.

Yet, he knew himself to be the master of this place. And the planet was the master of him.

I am part of it.

He devoured the soil directly, rejecting only the water. His human mouth and lungs had been relegated to breathing just enough to sustain a remnant humanity . . . and talking.

Leto spoke to Siona's back: "I like to talk and I dread the day when I no longer will be able to engage in conversations."

With a certain diffidence, she turned and stared at him in the moonlight, quite obvious distaste in her expression.

"I agree that I am a monster in many human eyes," he said.

"Why am I here?"

Directly to the point! She would not deviate. Most of the Atreides had been that way, he thought. It was a characteristic which he hoped to maintain in the breeding of them. It spoke of a strong inner sense of identity.

"I need to find out what Time has done to you," he said.

"Why do you need that?"

A little fear in her voice there, he thought. *She thinks I will probe after her puny rebellion and the names of her surviving associates.*

When he remained silent, she said: "Do you intend to kill me the way you killed my friends?"

So she has heard about the fight at the Embassy. And she assumes I know all about her past rebellious activities. Moneo has been lecturing her, damn him! Well . . . I might have done the same in his circumstances.

"Are you really a god?" she demanded. "I don't understand why my father believes that."

She has some doubts, he thought. *I still have room to maneuver.*

"Definitions vary," he said. "To Moneo, I am a god . . . and that is a truth."

"You were human once."

He began to enjoy the leaps of her intellect. She had that sure, hunting curiosity which was the hallmark of the Atreides.

"You are curious about me," he said. "It is the same with me. I am curious about you."

"What makes you think I'm curious?"

"You used to watch me very carefully when you were a child. I see that same look in your eyes tonight."

"Yes, I have wondered what it's like to be you."

He studied her for a moment. The moonlight drew shadows under her eyes, concealing them. He could let himself imagine that her eyes were the total blue of his own eyes, the blue of spice addiction. With that imaginative addition, Siona bore a curious resemblance to his long-dead Ghani. It was in the outline of her face and the placement of the eyes. He almost told Siona this, then thought better of it.

"Do you eat human food?" Siona asked.

"For a long time after I put on the sandtrout skin, I felt stomach hunger," he said. "Occasionally, I would attempt food. My stomach mostly rejected it. The cilia of the sandtrout spread almost everywhere in my human flesh. Eating became a bothersome thing. These days, I only ingest dry substances which sometimes contain a bit of the spice."

"You . . . eat melange?"

"Sometimes."

"But you no longer have human hungers?"

"I didn't say that."

She stared at him, waiting.

Leto admired the way she let unspoken questions work for her. She was bright and she had learned much during her short life.

"The stomach hunger was a black feeling, a pain I could not relieve," he said. "I would run then, run like an insane creature across the dunes."

"You . . . ran?"

"My legs were longer in proportion to my body in those days. I could move myself about quite easily. But the hungry pain has never left me. I think it's hunger for my lost humanity."

He saw the beginnings of reluctant sympathy in her, the questioning.

"You still have this . . . pain?"

"It's only a soft burning now. That's one of the signs of my final metamorphosis. In a few hundred years, I'll be back under the sand."

He saw her clench her fists at her sides. "Why?" she demanded. "Why did you do this?"

"This change isn't all bad. Today, for example, has been very pleasant. I feel quite mellow."

"There are changes we cannot see," she said. "I know there must be." She relaxed her hands.

"My sight and hearing have become extremely acute, but not my sense of touch. Except for my face, I don't feel things the way I could once. I miss that."

Again, he noted the reluctant sympathy, the striving toward an empathic understanding. She wanted to *know*!

"When you live so long," she said, "how does the passage of Time feel? Does it move more rapidly as the years go by?"

"That's a strange thing, Siona. Sometimes, Time rushes by me; sometimes, it creeps."

Gradually, as they spoke, Leto had been dimming the concealed lights of his aerie, moving his cart closer and closer to Siona. Now, he shut off the lights, leaving only the moon. The front of his cart protruded onto the balcony, his face only about two meters from Siona.

"My father tells me," she said, "that the older you get, the slower your time goes. Is that what you told him?"

Testing my veracity, he thought. *She's not a Truthsayer, then.*

"All things are relative, but compared to the human time-sense, this is true."

"Why?"

"It is involved in what I will become. At the end, Time will stop for me and I will be frozen like a pearl caught in ice. My new bodies will scatter, each with a pearl hidden within it."

She turned and looked away from him, peering out at the desert, speaking without looking at him.

"When I talk to you like this here in the darkness I can almost forget what you are."

"That's why I chose this hour for our meeting."

"But why this place?"

"Because it is the last place where I can feel at home."

Siona turned against the rail, leaning on it and looking at him. "I want to see you."

He turned on all of the aerie's lights, including the harsh white globes along the roof of the balcony's outer edge. As the light came on, an Ixian-made transparent mask slid out of wall recesses and sealed off the balcony behind Siona. She felt it move behind her and was startled, but nodded as though she understood. She thought it was a defense against attack. It was not. The wall merely kept out the damp insects of the night.

Siona stared at Leto, sweeping her gaze along his body, pausing at the stubs which once had been his legs, bringing her attention then to his arms and hands, then to his face.

"Your approved histories tell us that all Atreides are descended from you and your sister, Ghanima," she said. "The Oral History disagrees."

"The Oral History is correct. Your ancestor was Harq al-Ada. Ghani and I were married only in name, a move to consolidate the power."

"Like your marriage to this Ixian woman?"

"That is different."

"You will have children?"

"I have never been capable of having children. I chose the metamorphosis before that was possible."

"You were a child and then you were"—she pointed—"this?"

"Nothing between."

"How does a child know what to choose?"

"I was one of the oldest children this universe has ever seen. Ghani was the other."

"That story about your ancestral memories!"

"A true story. We're all here. Doesn't the Oral History agree?"

She whirled away and held her back stiffly presented to him. Once more, Leto found himself fascinated by this *human* gesture: rejection coupled to vulnerability. Presently, she turned around and concentrated on his features within the hooded folds.

"You have the Atreides look," she said.

"I come by it just as honestly as you do."

"You're so old . . . why aren't you wrinkled?"

"Nothing about the human part of me ages in a normal way."

"Is that why you did this to yourself?"

"To enjoy long life? No."

"I don't see how anyone could make such a choice," she muttered. Then louder: "Never to know love . . ."

"You're playing the fool!" he said. "You don't mean love, you mean sex."

She shrugged.

"You think the most terrible thing I gave up was sex? No, the greatest loss was something far different."

"What?" She asked it reluctantly, betraying how deeply he touched her.

"I cannot walk among my fellows without their special notice. I am no longer one of you. I am alone. Love? Many people love me, but my shape keeps us apart. We are separated, Siona, by a gulf that no other human dares to bridge."

"Not even your Ixian woman?"

"Yes, she would if she could, but she cannot. She's not an Atreides."

"You mean that I . . . could?" She touched her breast with a finger.

"If there were enough sandtrout around. Unfortunately, all of them enclose my flesh. However, if I were to die . . ."

She shook her head in dumb horror at the thought.

"The Oral History tells it accurately," he said. "And we must never forget that you believe the Oral History."

She continued to shake her head from side to side.

"There's no secret about it," he said. "The first moments of the transformation are the critical ones. Your awareness must drive inward and outward simultaneously, one with Infinity. I could provide you with enough melange to accomplish this. Given enough spice, you can live through those first awful moments . . . and all the other moments."

She shuddered uncontrollably, her gaze fixed on his eyes.

"You know I'm telling you the truth, don't you?"

She nodded, inhaled a deep trembling breath, then: "Why did you do it?"

"The alternative was far more horrible."

"What alternative?"

"In time, you may understand it. Moneo did."

"Your damned Golden Path!"

"Not damned at all. Quite holy."

"You think I'm a fool who can't . . ."

"I think you're inexperienced, but possessed of great capability whose potential you do not even suspect."

She took three deep breaths and regained some of her composure, then: "If you can't mate with the Ixian, what . . ."

"Child, why do you persist in misunderstanding? It's not sex. Before Hwi, I could not *pair*. I had no other like me. In all of the cosmic void, I was the only one."

"She's like . . . you?"

"Deliberately so. The Ixians made her that way."

"Made her . . ."

"Don't be a complete fool!" he snapped. "She is the essential god-trap. Even the victim cannot reject her."

"Why do you tell me these things?" she whispered.

"You stole two copies of my journals," he said. "You've read the Guild translations and you already know what could catch me."

"You knew?"

He saw boldness return to her stance, a sense of her own power. "Of course you knew," she said, answering her own question.

"It *was* my secret," he said. "You cannot imagine how many times I have loved a companion and seen that companion slip away . . . as your father is slipping away now."

"You love . . . him?"

"And I loved your mother. Sometimes they go quickly; sometimes with agonizing slowness. Each time I am wracked. I can play callous and I can make the necessary decisions, even decisions which kill, but I cannot escape the suffering. For a long, long time—those journals you stole tell it truly—that was the only emotion I knew."

He saw the moistness in her eyes, but the line of her jaw still spoke of angry resolution.

"None of this gives you the right to govern," she said.

Leto suppressed a smile. At last they were down to the root of Siona's rebellion.

By what right? Where is justice in my rule? By imposing my rules upon them with the weight of Fish Speaker arms, am I being fair to the evolutionary thrust of humankind? I know all of the revolutionary cant, the catch-prattle and the resounding phrases.

"Nowhere do you see your own rebellious hand in the power I wield," he said.

Her youth still demanded its moment.

"I never chose you to govern," she said.

"But you strengthen me."

"How?"

"By opposing me. I sharpen my claws on the likes of you."

She shot a sudden glance at his hands.

"A figure of speech," he said.

"So I've offended you at last," she said, hearing only the cutting anger in his words and tone.

"You've not offended me. We're related and can speak bluntly to each other within the family. The fact is, I have much more to fear from you than you from me."

This took her aback, but only momentarily. He saw belief stiffen her shoulders, then doubt. Her chin lowered and she peered upward at him.

"What could the great God Leto fear from me?"

"Your ignorant violence."

"Are you saying that you're *physically* vulnerable?"

"I will not warn you again, Siona. There are limits to the word games I will play. You and the Ixians both know that it's the ones I love who are physically vulnerable. Soon, most of the Empire will know it. This is the kind of information which travels fast."

"And they'll *all* ask what right you have to rule!"

There was glee in her voice. It aroused an abrupt anger in Leto. He found it difficult to suppress. This was a side of human emotions he detested. *Gloating!* It was some time before he dared answer, then he chose to slash through her defenses at the vulnerability he already had seen.

"I rule by the right of loneliness, Siona. My loneliness is part-freedom and part-slavery. It says I cannot be bought by any human group. My slavery to you says that I will serve all of you to the best of my lordly abilities."

"But the Ixians have caught you!" she said.

"No. They have given me a gift which strengthens me."

"It weakens you!"

"That, too," he admitted. "But very powerful forces still obey me."

"Ohhh, yes." She nodded. "I understand *that*."

"You don't understand it."

"Then I'm sure you'll explain it to me," she taunted.

He spoke so softly that she had to lean toward him to hear: "There are no others of any kind anywhere who can call upon me for anything—not for sharing, not for compromise, not even for the slightest beginning of another government. I am the only one."

"Not even this Ixian woman can . . ."

"She is so much like me that she would not weaken me in that way."

"But when the Ixian Embassy was attacked . . ."

"I can still be irritated by stupidity," he said.

She scowled at him.

Leto thought it a pretty gesture in that light, quite unconscious. He knew he had made her think. He was sure she had never before considered that any rights might adhere to uniqueness.

He addressed her silent scowl: "There has never before been a government exactly like mine. Not in all of our history. I am responsible only to myself, exacting payment in full for what I have sacrificed."

"Sacrificed!" she sneered, but he heard the doubts. "Every despot says something like that. You're responsible only to yourself!"

"Which makes every living thing my responsibility. I watch over you through these times."

"Through what times?"

"The times that might have been and then no more."

He saw the indecision in her. She did not trust her *instincts*, her untrained abilities at prediction. She might leap occasionally as she had done when she took his journals, but the motivation for the leap was lost in the revelation which followed.

"My father says you can be very tricky with words," she said.

"And he ought to know. But there is knowledge you can only gain by participating in it. There's no way to learn it by standing off and looking and talking."

"That's the kind of thing he means," she said.

"You're quite right," he agreed. "It's not logical. But it is a light, an eye which can see, but does not see itself."

"I'm tired of talking," she said.

"As am I." And he thought: *I have seen enough, done enough. She is wide open to her doubts. How vulnerable they are in their ignorance!*

"You haven't convinced me of anything," she said.

"That was not the purpose of this meeting."

"What was the purpose?"

"To see if you are ready to be tested."

"Test . . ." She tipped her head a bit to the right and stared at him.

"Don't play the innocent with me," he said. "Moneo has told you. And I tell you that you are ready!"

She tried to swallow, then: "What are . . ."

"I have sent for Moneo to return you to the Citadel," he said. "When we meet again, we will really learn what you are made of."

You know the myth of the Great Spice Hoard? Yes, I know about that story, too. A majordomo brought it to me one day to amuse me. The story says there is a hoard of melange, a gigantic hoard, big as a great mountain. The hoard is concealed in the depths of a distant planet. It is not Arrakis, that planet. It is not Dune. The spice was hidden there long ago, even before the First Empire and the Spacing Guild. The story says Paul Muad'Dib went there and lives yet beside the hoard, kept alive by it, waiting. The majordomo did not understand why the story disturbed me.

—THE STOLEN JOURNALS

Idaho trembled with anger as he strode along the gray plastone halls toward his quarters in the Citadel. At each guard post he passed, the woman there snapped to attention. He did not respond. Idaho knew he was causing disturbance among them. Nobody could mistake the Commander's mood. But he did not abate his purposeful stride. The heavy thumping of his boots echoed along the walls.

He could still taste the noon meal—oddly familiar Atreides chopstick-fare of mixed grains herb-seasoned and baked around a pungent morsel of pseudomeat, all of it washed down with a drink of clear *cidrit* juice. Moneo had found him at table in the Guard Mess, alone in a corner with a regional operations schedule propped up beside his plate.

Without invitation, Moneo had seated himself opposite Idaho and had pushed aside the operations schedule.

"I bring a message from the God Emperor," Moneo said.

The tightly controlled tone warned Idaho that this was no casual encounter. Others sensed it. Listening silence settled over the women at nearby tables, spreading out through the room.

Idaho put down his chopsticks. "Yes?"

"These were the words of the God Emperor," Moneo said. " 'It is my bad luck that Duncan Idaho should become enamored of Hwi Noree. This mischance must not continue.' "

Anger thinned Idaho's lips, but he remained silent.

"Such foolishness endangers us all," Moneo said. "Noree is the God Emperor's intended."

Idaho tried to control his anger, but the words were a betrayal: "He can't marry her!"

"Why not?"

"What game is he playing, Moneo?"

"I am a messenger with a single message, no more," Moneo said.

Idaho's voice was low and threatening. "But he confides in you."

"The God Emperor sympathizes with you," Moneo lied.

"Sympathizes!" Idaho shouted the word, creating a new depth to the room's silence.

"Noree is a woman of obvious attractions," Moneo said. "But she is not for you."

"The God Emperor has spoken," Idaho sneered, "and there is no appeal."

"I see that you understand the message," Moneo said.

Idaho started to push himself away from the table.

"Where are you going?" Moneo demanded.

"I'm going to have this out with him right now!"

"That is certain suicide," Moneo said.

Idaho glared at him, aware suddenly of the listening intensity in the women at the tables around them. An expression which Muad'Dib would have recognized immediately came over Idaho's face: *"Playing to the Devil's Gallery,"* Muad'Dib had called it.

"D'you know what the original Atreides Dukes always said?" Idaho asked. There was a mocking tone in his voice.

"Is it pertinent?"

"They said your liberties all vanish when you look up to any absolute ruler."

Rigid with fear, Moneo leaned toward Idaho. Moneo's lips barely moved. His voice was little more than a whisper. "Don't say such things."

"Because one of these women will report it?"

Moneo shook his head in disbelief. "You are more reckless than any of the others."

"Really?"

"Please! It is perilous in the extreme to take this attitude."

Idaho heard the nervous stirring that swept through the room.

"He can only kill us," Idaho said.

Moneo spoke in a tight whisper: "You fool! The Worm can dominate him at the slightest provocation!"

"The Worm, you say?" Idaho's voice was unnecessarily loud.

"You must trust him," Moneo said.

Idaho glanced left and right. "Yes, I think they heard that."

"He is billions upon billions of people united in that one body," Moneo said.

"So I've been told."

"He is God and we are mortal," Moneo said.

"How is it a god can do evil things?" Idaho asked.

Moneo thrust his chair backward and leaped to his feet. "I wash my hands of you!" Whirling away, he dashed from the room.

Idaho looked out into the room, finding himself the center of attention for all of the guards' faces.

"Moneo doesn't judge, but I do," Idaho said.

It surprised him then to glimpse a few wry smiles among the women. They all returned to their eating.

As he strode down the hall of the Citadel, Idaho replayed the conversation, seeking out the oddities in Moneo's behavior. The terror could be recognized and even understood, but it had seemed far more than fear of death . . . far, far more.

The Worm can dominate him.

Idaho felt that this had slipped out of Moneo, an inadvertent betrayal. What could it mean?

More reckless than any of the others.

It galled Idaho that he should have to bear comparisons to himself-as-an-unknown. How careful had *the others* been?

Idaho came to his own door, put a hand on the palm-lock and hesitated. He felt like a hunted animal retreating to his den. The guards in the mess surely would have reported that conversation to Leto by now. What would the *God* Emperor do? Idaho's hand moved across the lock. The door swung inward. He entered the anteroom of his apartment and sealed the door, looking at it.

Will he send his Fish Speakers for me?

Idaho glanced around the entry area. It was a conventional space—racks for clothing and shoes, a full-length mirror, a weapons cupboard. He looked at the closed door of the cupboard. Not one of the weapons behind that door offered any real threat to the God Emperor. There wasn't even a lasgun . . . although even lasguns were ineffectual against *the Worm*, according to all the accounts.

He knows I will defy him.

Idaho sighed and looked toward the arched portal which led into the sitting area. Moneo had replaced the soft furniture with heavier, stiffer pieces, some of them recognizably Fremen—culled from the coffers of the Museum Fremen.

Museum Fremen!

Idaho spat and strode through the portal. Two steps into the room he stopped, shocked. The soft light from the north windows revealed Hwi Noree seated on the low sling-divan. She wore a shimmering blue gown which draped itself revealingly around her figure. Hwi looked up at his entrance.

"Thank the gods you've not been harmed," she said.

Idaho glanced back at his entry, at the palm-locked door. He returned a speculative look at Hwi. No one but a few selected guards should be able to open that door.

She smiled at his confusion. "We Ixians manufactured those locks," she said.

He found himself filled with fear for her. "What are you doing here?"

"We must talk."

"About what?"

"Duncan . . ." She shook her head. "About us."

"They warned you," he said.

"I've been told to reject you."

"Moneo sent you!"

"Two guardswomen who overheard you in the mess—they brought me. They think you are in terrible danger."

"Is that why you're here?"

She stood, one graceful motion which reminded him of the way Leto's grandmother, Jessica, had moved—the same fluid control of muscles, every movement beautiful.

Realization came as a shock. "You're Bene Gesserit . . ."

"No! They were among my teachers, but I am not Bene Gesserit."

Suspicions clouded his mind. What allegiances were really at work in Leto's Empire? What does a ghola know about such things?

The changes since last I lived . . .

"I suppose you're still just a simple Ixian," he said.

"Please don't sneer at me, Duncan."

"What are you?"

"I am the intended bride of the God Emperor."

"And you'll serve him faithfully!"

"I will."

"Then there's nothing for us to talk about."

"Except this thing between us."

He cleared his throat. "What thing?"

"This attraction." She raised a hand as he started to speak. "I want to hurl myself into your arms, to find the love and shelter I know is there. You want it, too."

He held himself rigid. "The God Emperor forbids!"

"But I am here." She took two steps toward him, the gown rippling across her body.

"Hwi . . ." He tried to swallow in a dry throat. "It's best you leave."

"Prudent, but not best," she said.

"If he finds that you've been here . . ."

"It is not my way to leave you like this." Again, she stopped his response with a lifted hand. "I was bred and trained for just one purpose."

Her words filled him with icy caution. "What purpose?"

"To woo the God Emperor. Oh, he knows this. He would not change a thing about me."

"Nor would I."

She moved a step closer. He smelled the milky warmth of her breath.

"They made me too well," she said. "I was designed to please an Atreides. Leto says his Duncan is more an Atreides than many born to the name."

"Leto?"

"How else should I address the one I'll wed?"

Even as she spoke, Hwi leaned toward Idaho. As though a magnet had found its point of critical attraction, they moved together. Hwi pressed her cheek against his tunic, her arms around him feeling the hard muscles. Idaho rested his chin in her hair, the musk filling his senses.

"This is insane," he whispered.

"Yes."

He lifted her chin and kissed her.

She pressed herself against him.

Neither of them doubted where this must lead. She did not resist when he lifted her off her feet and carried her into the bedroom.

Only once did Idaho speak. "You're not a virgin."

"Nor are you, Love."

"Love," he whispered. "Love, love, love . . ."

"Yes . . . yes!"

In the post-coital peace, Hwi put both hands behind her head and stretched, twisting on the rumpled bed. Idaho sat with his back to her looking out the window.

"Who were your other lovers?" he asked.

She lifted herself on one elbow. "I've had no other lovers."

"But . . ." He turned and looked down at her.

"In my teens," she said, "there was a young man who needed me very much." She smiled. "Afterward, I was very ashamed. How trusting I was! I thought I had failed the people who depended on me. But they found out and they were elated. You know, I think I was being tested."

Idaho scowled. "Is that how it was with me? I needed you?"

"No, Duncan." Her features were grave. "We gave joy to each other because that's how it is with love."

"Love!" he said, and it was a bitter sound.

She said: "My Uncle Malky used to say that love was a bad bargain because you get no guarantees."

"Your Uncle Malky was a wise man."

"He was stupid! Love *needs* no guarantees."

A smile twitched at the corners of Idaho's mouth.

She grinned up at him. "You know it's love when you want to give joy and damn the consequences."

He nodded. "I think only of the danger to you."

"We are what we are," she said.

"What will we do?"

"We'll cherish this for as long as we live."

"You sound . . . so final."

"I am."

"But we'll see each other every . . ."

"Never again like this."

"Hwi!" He hurled himself across the bed and buried his face in her breast.

She stroked his hair.

His voice muffled against her, he said: "What if I've impreg . . ."

"Shush! If there's to be a child, there will be a child."

Idaho lifted his head and looked at her. "But he'll know for sure!"

"He'll know anyway."

"You think he really knows everything?"

"Not everything, but he'll know this."

"How?"

"I will tell him."

Idaho pushed himself away from her and sat up on the bed. Anger warred with confusion in his expression.

"I must," she said.

"If he turns against you . . . Hwi, there are stories. You could be in terrible danger!"

"No. I have needs, too. He knows this. He will not harm either of us."

"But he . . ."

"He will not destroy *me*. He will know that if he harms you that would destroy me."

"How can you marry him?"

"Dear Duncan, have you not seen that he needs me more than you do?"

"But he cannot . . . I mean, you can't possibly . . ."

"The joy that you and I have in each other, I'll not have that with Leto. It's impossible for him. He has confessed this to me."

"Then why can't . . . If he loves you . . ."

"He has larger plans and larger needs." She reached out and took Idaho's right hand in both of hers. "I've known that since I first began to study about him. Needs larger than either of us have."

"What plans? What needs?"

"Ask him."

"Do *you* know?"

"Yes."

"You mean you believe those stories about . . ."

"There is honesty and goodness in him. I know it by my own

responses to him. What my Ixian masters made in me was, I think, a reagent which reveals more than they wanted me to know."

"Then you believe him!" Idaho accused. He tried to pull his hand away from her.

"If you go to him, Duncan, and . . ."

"He'll never see me again!"

"He will."

She pulled his hand to her mouth and kissed his fingers.

"I'm a hostage," he said. "You've made me fearful . . . the two of you together . . ."

"I never thought it would be easy to serve God," she said. "I just didn't think it would be this hard."

Memory has a curious meaning to me, a meaning I have hoped others might share. It continually astonishes me how people hide from their ancestral memories, shielding themselves behind a thick barrier of mythos. Ohhh, I do not expect them to seek the terrible immediacy of every living moment which I must experience. I can understand that they might not want to be submerged in a mush of petty ancestral details. You have reason to fear that your living moments might be taken over by others. Yet, the meaning is there within those memories. We carry all of our ancestry forward like a living wave, all of the hopes and joys and griefs, the agonies and the exultations of our past. Nothing within those memories remains completely without meaning or influence, not as long as there is a humankind somewhere. We have that bright Infinity all around us, that Golden Path of forever to which we can continually pledge our puny but inspired allegiance.

—THE STOLEN JOURNALS

"I have summoned you, Moneo, because of what my guards tell me," Leto said.

They stood in the darkness of the crypt where, Moneo reminded himself, some of the God Emperor's most painful decisions originated. Moneo, too, had heard reports. He had been expecting the summons all afternoon and, when it came shortly after the evening meal, a moment of terror had engulfed him.

"Is it about . . . about the Duncan, Lord?"

"Of course it's about the Duncan!"

"I'm told, Lord . . . his behavior . . ."

"Terminal behavior, Moneo?"

Moneo bowed his head. "If you say it, Lord."

"How long until the Tleilaxu could supply us with another one?"

"They say they have had problems, Lord. It might be as much as two years."

"Do you know what my guards tell me, Moneo?"

Moneo held his breath. If the God Emperor had learned about this latest . . . No! Even the Fish Speakers were terrified by the affront. Had it been anyone but a Duncan, the women would have taken it upon themselves to eliminate him.

"Well, Moneo?"

"I am told, Lord, that he called out a levy of guards and questioned them about their origins. On what worlds were they born? What of their parentage, their childhood?"

"And the answers did not please him."

"He frightened them, Lord. He kept insisting."

"As though repetition could elicit the truth, yes."

Moneo allowed himself to hope that this might be the whole of his Lord's concern. "Why do the Duncans always do this, Lord?"

"It was their early training, the Atreides training."

"But how did that differ from . . ."

"The Atreides lived in the service of the people they governed. The measure of their government was found in the lives of the governed. Thus, the Duncans always want to know how the people live."

"He has spent a night in one village, Lord. He has been to some of the towns. He has seen . . ."

"It's all in how you interpret the results, Moneo. Evidence is nothing without judgments."

"I have observed that he judges, Lord."

"We all do, but the Duncans tend to believe that this universe is hostage to my will. And they know that you cannot do wrong in the name of right."

"Is that what he says you . . ."

"It is what *I* say, what all of the Atreides in me say. This universe will not permit it. The things you attempt will not endure if you . . ."

"But, Lord! You do no wrong!"

"Poor Moneo. You cannot see that I have created a vehicle of injustice."

Moneo could not speak. He realized that he had been diverted by a seeming return to mildness in the God Emperor. But now, Moneo sensed changes moving in that great body, and at this proximity . . . Moneo glanced around the crypt's central chamber, reminding himself of the many deaths which had occurred here and which were enshrined here.

Is it my time?

Leto spoke in a musing tone. "You cannot succeed by taking hostages. That is a form of enslavement. One kind of human cannot own another kind of human. This universe will not permit it."

The words lay there, simmering in Moneo's awareness, a terrifying contrast to the rumblings of transformation which he sensed in his Lord.

The Worm comes!

Again, Moneo glanced around the crypt chamber. This place was far worse than the aerie! Sanctuary was too remote.

"Well, Moneo, do you have any response?" Leto asked.

Moneo ventured a whisper: "The Lord's words enlighten me."

"Enlighten? You are not enlightened!"

Moneo spoke out of desperation. "But I serve my Lord!"

"You claim service to God?"

"Yes, Lord."

"Who created your religion, Moneo?"

"You did, Lord."

"That's a sensible answer."

"Thank you, Lord."

"Don't thank me! Tell me what religious institutions perpetuate!"

Moneo backed away four steps.

"Stand where you are!" Leto ordered.

Trembling all through his body, Moneo shook his head dumbly. At last, he had encountered the question without answer. Failure to answer would precipitate his death. He waited for it, head bowed.

"Then I will tell you, poor servant," Leto said.

Moneo dared to hope. He lifted his gaze to the God Emperor's face, noting that the eyes were not glazed . . . and the hands were not trembling. Perhaps the Worm did not come.

"Religious institutions perpetuate a mortal master-servant relationship," Leto said. "They create an arena which attracts prideful human power-seekers with all of their nearsighted prejudices!"

Moneo could only nod. Was that a trembling in the God Emperor's hands? Was the terrible face withdrawing slightly into its cowl?

"The secret revelations of infamy, that is what the Duncans ask after," Leto said. "The Duncans have too much compassion for their fellows and too sharp a limit on fellowship."

Moneo had studied holos of Dune's ancient sandworms, the gigantic mouths full of crysknife teeth around consuming fire. He noted the tumescence of the latent rings on Leto's tubular surface. Were they more prominent? Would a new mouth open below that cowled face?

"The Duncans know in their hearts," Leto said, "that I have deliberately ignored the admonition of Mohammed and Moses. Even you know it, Moneo!"

It was an accusation. Moneo started to nod, then shook his head from side to side. He wondered if he dared renew his retreat. Moneo knew from experience that lectures in this tenor did not long continue without the coming of the Worm.

"What might that admonition be?" Leto asked. There was a mocking lightness in his voice.

Moneo allowed himself a faint shrug.

Abruptly, Leto's voice filled the chamber with a rumbling baritone, an ancient voice which spoke across the centuries: "You are servants unto *God*, not servants unto servants!"

Moneo wrung his hands and cried out: "I *serve* you, Lord!"

"Moneo, Moneo," Leto said, his voice low and resonant, "a million wrongs cannot give rise to one right. The right is known because it endures."

Moneo could only stand in trembling silence.

"I had intended Hwi to mate with *you*, Moneo," Leto said. "Now, it is too late."

The words took a moment penetrating Moneo's consciousness. He felt that their meaning was out of any known context. *Hwi? Who was Hwi? Oh, yes—the God Emperor's Ixian bride-to-be. Mate . . . with me?*

Moneo shook his head.

Leto spoke with infinite sadness: "You, too, shall pass away. Will all your works be as dust forgotten?"

Without any warning, even as he spoke, Leto's body convulsed in a thrashing roll which heaved him from the cart. The speed of it, the monstrous violence, threw him within centimeters of Moneo, who screamed and fled across the crypt.

"Moneo!"

Leto's call stopped the majordomo at the entrance to the lift.

"The test, Moneo! I will test Siona tomorrow!"

The realization of what I am occurs in the timeless awareness which does not stimulate nor delude. I create a field without self or center, a field where even death becomes only analogy. I desire no results. I merely permit this field which has no goals nor desires, no perfections nor even visions of achievements. In that field, omnipresent primal awareness is all. It is the light which pours through the windows of my universe.

—THE STOLEN JOURNALS

The sun came up, sending its harsh glare across the dunes. Leto felt the sand beneath him as a soft caress. Only his human ears, hearing the abrasive rasp of his heavy body, reported otherwise. It was a sensory conflict which he had learned to accept.

He heard Siona walking behind him, a lightness in her tread, a gentle spilling of sand as she climbed to his level atop a dune.

The longer I endure, the more vulnerable I become, he thought.

This thought often occurred to him these days when he went into his desert. He peered upward. The sky was cloudless with a blue density which the old days of Dune had never seen.

What was a desert without a cloudless sky? Too bad it could not have Dune's silvery hue.

Ixian satellites controlled this sky, not always to the perfection he might desire. Such perfection was a machine-fantasy which faltered under human management. Still, the satellites held a sufficiently steady grip to give him this morning of desert stillness. He gave his human lungs a deep breath of it and listened for Siona's approach. She had stopped. He knew she was admiring the view.

Leto felt his imagination like a conjurer calling up everything which had produced the physical setting for this moment. He *felt* the satellites. Fine instruments which played the music for the dance of warming and cooling air masses, perpetually monitoring and adjusting the powerful vertical and horizontal currents. It amused him to recall that the Ixians had thought he would use this exquisite machinery in a new kind of hydraulic despotism—withholding moisture from those who defied their ruler, punishing others with terrible storms. How surprised they had been to find themselves mistaken!

My controls are more subtle.

Slowly, gently, he began to move, swimming on the sand surface, gliding down off the dune, never once looking back at the thin spire of his tower, knowing that it would vanish presently into the haze of daytime heat.

Siona followed him with an uncharacteristic docility. Doubt had done its work. She had read the stolen journals. She had listened to the admonitions of her father. Now, she did not know what to think.

"What is this test?" she had asked Moneo. "What will he do?"

"It is never the same."

"How did he test you?"

"It will be different with you. I would only confuse you if I told you my experience."

Leto had listened secretly while Moneo prepared his daughter, dressing her in an authentic Fremen stillsuit with a dark robe over it, fitting the boot-pumps correctly. Moneo had not forgotten.

Moneo had looked up from where he bent to adjust her boots. "The Worm will come. That is all I can tell you. You must find a way to live in the presence of the Worm."

He had stood then, explaining about the stillsuit, how it recycled her body's own waters. He made her pull the tube from a catchpocket and suck on it, then reseal the tube.

"You will be alone with him on the desert," Moneo had said. "Shai-Hulud is never far away when you're on the desert."

"What if I refuse to go?" she asked.

"You will go . . . but you may not return."

This conversation had occurred in the ground-level chamber of the Little Citadel while Leto waited in the aerie. He had come down when he knew Siona was ready, drifting down in the predawn darkness on his cart's suspensors. The cart had gone into the ground-level room after Moneo and Siona emerged. While Moneo marched across the flat ground to his 'thopter and left in a whispering of wings, Leto had required Siona to test the sealed portal of the ground-level chamber, then look upward at the tower's impossible heights.

"The only way out is across the Sareer," he said.

He led her away from the tower then, not even commanding her to follow, depending on her good sense, her curiosity and her doubts.

Leto's swimming progress took him down the dune's slip-face and onto an exposed section of the rocky basement complex, then up another sandy face at a shallow angle, creating a path for Siona to follow. Fremen had called such compression tracks *God's gift to the weary.* He moved slowly, giving Siona plenty of time in which to recognize that this was his domain, his natural habitat.

He came out atop another dune and turned to watch her progress. She held to the track he had provided and stopped only when she reached the top. Her glance went once to his face, then she turned a full circle to examine the horizon. He heard the sharp intake of her breath. Heat haze hid the spire's top. The base might have been a distant outcropping.

"This is how it was," he said.

There was something about the desert which spoke to the eternal soul of people who possessed Fremen blood, he knew. He had chosen this place for its desert impact—a dune slightly higher than the others.

"Take a good look at it," he said, and he slipped down the dune's other side to remove his bulk from her view.

Siona took one more slow turn, looking outward.

Leto knew the innermost sensation of what she saw. Except for that insignificant, blurred *blip* of his tower's base, there was not the slightest lift of horizon—flat, everywhere flat. No plants, no living movement. From her vantage, there was a limit of approximately eight kilometers to the line where the planet's curvature hid everything beyond.

Leto spoke from where he had stopped, just below the dune's crest. "This is the real Sareer. You only know it when you're down here afoot. This is all that's left of the *bahr bela ma.*"

"The ocean without water," she whispered.

Again, she turned and examined the entire horizon.

There was no wind and, Leto knew, without wind, the silence ate at the human soul. Siona was feeling the loss of all familiar reference points. She was abandoned in dangerous space.

Leto glanced at the next dune. In that direction, they would come presently to a low line of hills which originally had been mountains but now were broken into remnant slag and rubble. He continued to rest quietly, letting the silence do its work for him. It was even pleasant to imagine that these dunes went on, as they once had, without end completely around the planet. But even these few dunes were degenerating. Without the original Coriolis storms of Dune, the Sareer saw nothing stronger than a stiff breeze and occasional heat vortices which had no more than local effect.

One of these tiny "wind devils" danced across the middle distance to the south. Siona's gaze followed its track. She spoke abruptly: "Do you have a personal religion?"

Leto took a moment composing his reply. It always astonished him how a desert provoked thoughts of religion.

"You dare ask me if I have a personal religion?" he demanded.

Betraying no surface sign of the fears he knew she felt, Siona turned and stared down at him. Audacity was always an Atreides hallmark, he reminded himself.

When she didn't answer, he said: "You are an Atreides for sure."

"Is that your answer?" she asked.

"What is it you really want to know, Siona?"

"What *you* believe!"

"Ho! You ask after my faith. Well, now—I believe that something cannot emerge from nothing without divine intervention."

His answer puzzled her. "How is that an . . ."

"Natura non facit saltus," he said.

She shook her head, not understanding the ancient allusion which had sprung to his lips. Leto translated:

"Nature makes no leaps."

"What language was that?" she asked.

"A language no longer spoken anywhere else in my universe."

"Why did you use it then?"

"To prod your ancient memories."

"I don't have any! I just need to know why you brought me here."

"To give you a taste of your past. Come down here and climb onto my back."

She hesitated at first, then seeing the futility of defiance, slid down the dune and clambered onto his back.

Leto waited until she was kneeling atop him. It was not the same as the old times he knew. She had no Maker hooks and could not stand on his back. He lifted his front segments slightly off the surface.

"Why am I doing this?" she asked. Her tone said she felt silly up there.

"I want you to taste the way our people once moved proudly across this land, high atop the back of a giant sandworm."

He began to glide along the dune just below the crest. Siona had seen holos. She knew this experience intellectually, but the pulse of reality had a different beat and he knew she would resonate to it.

Ahhh, Siona, he thought, *you do not even begin to suspect how I will test you.*

Leto steeled himself then. *I must have no pity. If she dies, she dies. If any of them dies, that is a required event, no more.*

And he had to remind himself that this applied even to Hwi Noree. It was just that *all* of them could not die.

He sensed it when Siona began to enjoy the sensation of riding on his back. He felt a faint shift in her weight as she eased back onto her legs to lift her head.

He drove outward then along a curving *barracan*, joining Siona in enjoyment of the old sensations. Leto could just glimpse the remnant hills at the horizon ahead of him. They were like a seed from the past waiting there, a reminder of the self-sustaining and expanding force which operated in a desert. He could forget for a moment that on this planet where only a small fraction of the surface remained desert, the Sareer's dynamism existed in a precarious environment.

The illusion of the past was here, though. He felt it as he moved. Fantasy, of course, he told himself, a vanishing fantasy as long as his enforced tranquility continued. Even the sweeping *barracan* which he traversed now was not as great as the ones of the past. None of the dunes were that great.

This whole *maintained* desert struck him suddenly as ridiculous. He almost stopped on a pebbled surface between the dunes, continuing but more slowly as he tried to conjure up the necessities which kept the whole system working. He imagined the planet's rotation setting up great air currents which shifted cold and heated air to new regions in enormous volume—everything monitored and ruled by those tiny satellites with their Ixian instruments and heat-focusing dishes. If the high monitors *saw* anything, they saw the Sareer partly as a "relief desert" with both physical and cold-air walls girdling it. This tended to create ice at the edges and required even more climatic adjustments.

It was not easy and Leto forgave the occasional mistakes for that reason.

As he moved once more out onto dunes, he lost that sense of delicate balance, put aside memories of the pebbly wastelands outside the central sands, and gave himself up to enjoyment of his "petrified ocean" with its frozen and apparently immovable waves. He turned southward, parallel to the remnant hills.

He knew that most people were offended by his infatuation with desert. They were uneasy and turned away. Siona, however, could not turn away. Everywhere she looked, the desert demanded recognition.

She rode silently on his back, but he knew her eyes were full. And the old-old memories were beginning to churn.

He came within three hours to a region of cylindrical whaleback dunes, some of them more than one hundred and fifty kilometers long at an angle to the prevailing wind. Beyond them lay a rocky corridor between dunes and into a region of star dunes almost four hundred meters high. Finally, they entered the braided dunes of the central erg where the general high pressure and electrically charged air gave his spirits a lift. He knew the same magic would be working on Siona.

"Here is where the songs of the Long Trek originated," he said. "They are perfectly preserved in the Oral History."

She did not answer, but he knew she heard.

Leto slowed his pace and began to speak to Siona, telling her about their Fremen past. He sensed the quickening of her interest. She even asked questions occasionally, but he could also feel her fears building. Even the base of his Little Citadel was no longer visible here. She could recognize nothing man-made. And she would think he engaged now in small talk, unimportant things to put off something portentous.

"Equality between our men and women originated here," he said.

"Your Fish Speakers deny that men and women are equal," she said.

Her voice, full of questioning disbelief, was a better locator than the sensation of her crouched on his back. Leto stopped at the intersection of two braided dunes and let the venting of his heat-generated oxygen subside.

"Things are not the same today," he said. "But men and women do have different evolutionary demands upon them. With the Fremen, though, there was an interdependence. That fostered equality out here where questions of survival can become immediate."

"Why did you bring me here?" she demanded.

"Look behind us," he said.

He felt her turn. Presently, she said: "What am I supposed to see?"

"Have we left any tracks? Can you tell where we've been?"

"There's a little wind now."

"It has covered our tracks?"

"I guess so . . . yes."

"This desert made us what we were and are," he said. "It's the real museum of all our traditions. Not one of those traditions has really been lost."

Leto saw a small sandstorm, a *ghibli*, moving across the southern horizon. He noted the narrow ribbons of dust and sand moving out ahead of it. Surely, Siona had seen it.

"Why won't you tell me why you brought me here?" she asked. Fear was obvious in her voice.

"But I have told you."

"You have not!"

"How far have we come, Siona?"

She thought about this. "Thirty kilometers? Twenty?"

"Farther," he said. "I can move very fast in my own land. Didn't you feel the wind on your face?"

"Yes." Sullen. "So why ask *me* how far?"

"Come down and stand where I can see you."

"Why?"

Good, he thought. *She believes I will abandon her here and speed off faster than she can follow.*

"Come down and I'll explain," he said.

She slid off his back and came around to where she could look into his face.

"Time passes swiftly when your senses are full," he said. "We have been out almost four hours. We have come about sixty kilometers."

"Why is *that* important?"

"Moneo put dried food in the pouch of your robe," he said. "Eat a little and I will tell you."

She found a dried cube of protomor in the pouch and chewed on it while she watched him. It was the authentic old Fremen food even to the slight addition of melange.

"You have felt your past," he said. "Now, you must be sensitized to your future, to the Golden Path."

She swallowed. "I don't believe in your Golden Path."

"If you are to live, you will believe in it."

"Is *that* your test? Have faith in the Great God Leto or die?"

"You need no faith in me whatsoever. I want you to have faith in yourself."

"Then why is it important how far we've come?"

"So you'll understand how far you still have to go."

She put a hand to her cheek. "I don't . . ."

"Right where you stand," he said, "you are in the unmistakable midst of Infinity. Look around you at the meaning of Infinity."

She glanced left and right at the unbroken desert.

"We are going to walk out of my desert together," he said. "Just the two of us."

"You don't walk," she sneered.

"A figure of speech. But *you* will walk. I assure you of that."

She looked in the direction they had come. "So that's why you asked me about tracks."

"Even if there were tracks, you could not go back. There is nothing at my Little Citadel that you could get to and use for survival."

"No water?"

"Nothing."

She found the catchpocket tube at her shoulder, sucked at it and restored it. He noted the care with which she sealed the end, but she did not pull the face flap across her mouth, although Leto had heard her father warning her about this. She wanted her mouth free for talking!

"You're telling me I can't run away from you," she said.

"Run away if you want."

She turned a full circle, examining the wasteland.

"There is a saying about the open land," he said, "that one direction is as good as another. In some ways, that's still true, but I would not depend on it."

"But I'm really free to leave you if I want?"

"Freedom can be a very lonely estate," he said.

She pointed to the steep side of the dune on which they had stopped. "But I could just go down there and . . ."

"Were I you, Siona, I would not go down where you are pointing."

She glared at him. "Why?"

"On the dune's steep side, unless you follow the natural curves, the sand may slide down upon you and bury you."

She looked down the slope, absorbing this.

"See how beautiful words can be?" he asked.

She returned her attention to his face. "Should we be going?"

"You learn to value leisure out here. And courtesy. There's no hurry."

"But we have no water except the . . ."

"Used wisely, that stillsuit will keep you alive."

"But how long will it take us to . . ."

"Your impatience alarms me."

"But we have only this dried food in my pouch. What will we eat when . . ."

"Siona! Have you noticed that you are expressing our situation as mutual. What will *we* eat? *We* have no water. Should *we* be going? How long will it take *us*?"

He sensed the dryness of her mouth as she tried to swallow.

"Could it be that we're interdependent?" he asked.

She spoke reluctantly. "I don't know how to survive out here."

"But I do?"

She nodded.

"Why should I share such precious knowledge with you?" he asked.

She shrugged, a pitiful gesture which touched him. How quickly the desert cut away previous attitudes.

"I will share my knowledge with you," he said. "And you must find something valuable that you can share with me."

Her gaze traversed his length, paused a moment at the flippers which once were his legs and feet, then came back to his face.

"Agreement bought with threats is no agreement," she said.

"I offer you no violence."

"There are many kinds of violence," she said.

"And I brought you out here where you may die?"

"Did I have a choice in it?"

"It is difficult to be born an Atreides," he said. "Believe me, I know."

"You don't have to do it this way," she said.

"And there you are wrong."

He turned away from her and set off in a sinusoidal track down the dune. He heard her slipping and stumbling as she followed. Leto stopped well into the dune shadow.

"We'll wait out the day here," he said. "It uses less water to travel by night."

One of the most terrible words in any language is *Soldier*. The synonyms parade through our history: yogahnee, trooper, hussar, kareebo, cossack, deranzeef, legionnaire, sardaukar, fish speaker...I know them all. They stand there in the ranks of my memory to remind me: *Always make sure you have the army with you.*

—THE STOLEN JOURNALS

Idaho found Moneo at last in the long underground corridor which connected the Citadel's eastern and western complexes. Since daybreak two hours before, Idaho had been prowling the Citadel seeking the majordomo and there he was, far off down the corridor, talking to someone concealed in a doorway, but Moneo was recognizable even at this distance by his stance and that inevitable white uniform.

The corridor's plastone walls were amber here fifty meters below the surface and lighted by glowstrips keyed to the daylight hours. Cool breezes were drawn into these depths by a simple arrangement of free-swinging wings which stood like gigantic robed figures on perimeter towers at the surface. Now that the sun had warmed the sands, all of the wings pointed northward for the cool air pouring into the Sareer. Idaho smelled the flinty breeze as he walked.

He knew what this corridor was supposed to represent. It *did* have some characteristics of an ancient Fremen sietch. The corridor was wide, big enough to take Leto on his cart. The arched ceiling *looked* like rock. But the twin glowstrips were discord. Idaho had never seen glowstrips before coming to the Citadel; they had been considered impractical in *his day*, requiring too much energy, too costly to maintain. Glowglobes were simpler and easily replaced. He had come to realize, however, that Leto considered few things impractical.

What Leto wants, someone provides.

The thought had an ominous feeling as Idaho marched down the corridor toward Moneo.

Small rooms lined the corridor sietch-fashion, no doors, only thin hangings of russet fabric which swayed in the breeze. Idaho knew that this area was mostly quarters for the younger Fish Speakers. He had recognized an assembly chamber with attendant rooms for weapons storage, kitchen, a dining hall, maintenance shops. He had also seen other things behind the inadequate privacy of the hangings, things which fed his rage.

Moneo turned at Idaho's approach. The woman to whom Moneo had been talking retreated and let the hanging drop, but not before Idaho glimpsed an older face with an air of command about it. Idaho did not recognize that particular commander.

Moneo nodded as Idaho stopped two paces away.

"The guards say you've been looking for me," Moneo said.

"Where is he, Moneo?"

"Where is who?"

Moneo swept his gaze up and down Idaho's figure, noting the old-fashioned Atreides uniform, black with a red hawk at the breast, the high boots glistening with polish. There was a *ritual* look about the man.

Idaho took a shallow breath and spoke through clenched teeth: "Don't you start that game with me!"

Moneo took his attention away from the sheathed knife at Idaho's waist. It looked like a museum piece with its jeweled handle. Where had Idaho found it?

"If you mean the God Emperor . . ." Moneo said.

"Where?"

Moneo kept his voice mild. "Why are you so anxious to die?"

"They said you were with him."

"That was earlier."

"I'll find him, Moneo!"

"Not right now."

Idaho put a hand on his knife. "Do I have to use force to make you talk?"

"I would not advise that."

"Where . . . is . . . he?"

"Since you insist, he is out in the desert with Siona."

"With your daughter?"

"Is there another Siona?"

"What're they doing?"

"She is being tested."

"When will they return?"

Moneo shrugged, then: "Why this unseemly anger, Duncan?"

"What's this test of your . . ."

"I don't know. Now, why are you so upset?"

"I'm sick of this place! Fish Speakers!" He turned his head and spat.

Moneo glanced down the corridor behind Idaho, recalling the man's approach. Knowing the Duncans, it was easy to recognize what had fed his current rage.

"Duncan," Moneo said, "it's perfectly normal for adolescent females as well as males to have feelings of physical attraction toward members of their own sex. Most of them will grow out of it."

"It should be stamped out!"

"But it's part of our heritage."

"Stamped out! And that's not . . ."

"Oh, be still. If you try to suppress it, you only increase its power."

Idaho glared at him. "And you say you don't know what's going on up there with your own daughter!"

"Siona is being tested, I told you."

"And what's *that* supposed to mean?"

Moneo put a hand over his eyes and sighed. He lowered the hand, wondering why he put up with this foolish, dangerous, *antique* human.

"It means that she may die out there."

Idaho was taken aback, some of his anger cooling. "How can you allow ..."

"Allow? You think I have a choice?"

"Every man has a choice!"

A bitter smile flitted across Moneo's lips. "How is it that you are so much more foolish than the other Duncans?"

"Other Duncans!" Idaho said. "How did those others die, Moneo?"

"The way we all die. They ran out of time."

"You lie." Idaho spoke past gritted teeth, his knuckles white on the knife handle.

Still speaking mildly, Moneo said: "Have a care. There are limits even to what I will take, especially just now."

"This place is rotten!" Idaho said. He gestured with his free hand at the corridor behind him. "There are some things I'll never accept!"

Moneo stared down the empty corridor without seeing. "You *must* mature, Duncan. You must."

Idaho's hand tensed on the knife. "What does *that* mean?"

"These are sensitive times. Anything unsettling to him, *anything* ... must be prevented."

Idaho held himself on the edge of violence, his anger restrained only by something puzzling in Moneo's manner. Words had been spoken, though, which could not be ignored.

"I'm not some damned immature child you can ..."

"Duncan!" It was the loudest sound Idaho had ever heard from the mild-mannered Moneo. Surprise stayed Idaho's hand while Moneo continued: "If the demands of your flesh are for maturity, but something holds you in adolescence, quite nasty behavior develops. Let go."

"Are ... you ... accusing ... me ... of ..."

"No!" Moneo gestured at the corridor. "Oh, I know what you must've seen back there, but it ..."

"Two women in a passionate kiss! You think that's not ..."

"It's not important. Youth explores its potential in many ways."

Idaho balanced himself on the edge of an explosion, rocking forward on his toes. "I'm glad to learn about you, Moneo."

"Yes, well, I've learned about you, *several* times."

Moneo watched the effect of these words as they twisted through Idaho, tangling him. The gholas could never avoid a fascination with *the others* who had preceded them.

Idaho spoke in a hoarse whisper: "What have you learned?"

"You have taught me valuable things," Moneo said. "All of us try to evolve, but if something blocks us, we can transfer our potential into pain—seeking it or giving it. Adolescents are particularly vulnerable."

Idaho leaned close to Moneo. "I'm talking about sex!"

"Of course you are."

"Are you accusing me of adolescent . . ."

"That's right."

"I should cut your . . ."

"Oh, shut up!"

Moneo's response did not have the training nuances of Bene Gesserit Voice control, but it had a lifetime of command behind it. Something in Idaho could only obey.

"I'm sorry," Moneo said. "But I'm distracted by the fact that my only daughter . . ." He broke off and shrugged.

Idaho inhaled two deep breaths. "You're crazy, all of you! You say your daughter may be dying and yet you . . ."

"You fool!" Moneo snapped. "Have you any idea how your petty concerns appear to me? Your stupid questions and your selfish . . ." He broke off, shaking his head.

"I make allowances because you have personal problems," Idaho said. "But if you . . ."

"Allowances? *You* make allowances?" Moneo took a trembling breath. It was too much!

Idaho spoke stiffly: "I can forgive you for . . ."

"You! You prattle about sex and forgiving and pain and . . . you think you and Hwi Noree . . ."

"Leave her out of this!"

"Oh, yes. Leave her out. Leave out *that* pain! You share sex with her and you *never* think about parting. Tell me, fool, how do you give of yourself in the face of *that*?"

Abashed, Idaho inhaled deeply. He had not suspected such passion smoldering in the quiet Moneo, but this attack, this could not be . . .

"You think I'm cruel?" Moneo demanded. "I make you think about things you'd rather avoid. Hah! Crueler things have been done to the Lord Leto for no better reason than the cruelty!"

"You defend him? You . . ."

"I know him best!"

"He uses you!"

"To what ends?"

"You tell me!"

"He's our best hope to perpetuate . . ."

"Perverts don't perpetuate!"

Moneo spoke in a soothing tone, but his words shook Idaho. "I will tell you this only once. Homosexuals have been among the best warriors in our history, the berserkers of last resort. They were among our best priests and priestesses. Celibacy was no accident in religions. It is also no accident that adolescents make the best soldiers."

"That's perversion!"

"Quite right. Military commanders have known about the perverted displacement of sex into pain for thousands upon thousands of centuries."

"Is *that* what the Great Lord Leto's doing?"

Still mild, Moneo said: "Violence requires that you inflict pain and suffer it. How much more manageable a military force driven to this by its deepest urgings."

"He's made a monster out of you, too!"

"You suggested that he uses me," Moneo said. "I permit this because I know that the price he pays is much greater than what he demands of me."

"Even your daughter?"

"*He* holds back nothing. Why should I? Ohhh, I think you

understand this about the Atreides. The Duncans are always good at *that*."

"The Duncans! Damn you, I won't be . . ."

"You just haven't the guts to pay the price he's asking," Moneo said.

In one blurred motion, Idaho whipped his knife from its sheath and lunged at Moneo. As fast as he moved, Moneo moved faster— sidestepping, tripping Idaho and propelling him facedown onto the floor. Idaho scrambled forward, rolled and started to leap to his feet, then hesitated, realizing that he had actually tried to attack an Atreides. Moneo was Atreides. Shock held Idaho immobile.

Moneo stood unmoving, looking down at him. There was an odd look of sadness on the majordomo's face.

"If you're going to kill me, Duncan, you'd best do it in the back by stealth," Moneo said. "You might succeed that way."

Idaho levered himself to one knee, put a foot flat on the floor, but remained there still clutching his knife. Moneo had moved so quickly and with such grace—so . . . so casually! Idaho cleared his throat. "How did you . . ."

"He has been breeding us for a long time, Duncan, strengthening many things in us. He has bred us for speed, for intelligence, for self-restraint, for sensitivity. You're . . . you're just an older model."

Do you know what guerrillas often say? They claim that their rebellions are invulnerable to economic warfare because they have no economy, that they are parasitic on those they would overthrow. The fools merely fail to assess the coin in which they must inevitably pay. The pattern is inexorable in its degenerative failures. You see it repeated in the systems of slavery, of welfare states, of caste-ridden religions, of socializing bureaucracies—in any system which creates and maintains dependencies. Too long a parasite and you cannot exist without a host.

—THE STOLEN JOURNALS

Leto and Siona lay all day in the duneshadows, moving only as the sun moved. He taught her how to protect herself under a blanket of sand in the noontime heat; it never grew too warm at the rock-level between the dunes.

In the afternoon, Siona crept close to Leto for warmth, a warmth he knew he had in excess these days.

They talked sporadically. He told her about the Fremen graces which once had dominated this landscape. She probed for secret knowledge of him.

Once, he said: "You may find it odd, but out here is where I can be most human."

His words failed to make her fully conscious of her human vulnerability and the fact that she might die out here. Even when she was not talking, she did not restore the face flap of her stillsuit.

Leto recognized the unconscious motivation behind this failure, but knew the futility of addressing that directly.

In the late afternoon, night's chill already starting to creep over the land, he began regaling her with songs of the Long Trek which had not been saved in the Oral History. He enjoyed the fact that she liked one of his favorites, "Liet's March."

"The tune is really ancient," he said, "a pre-space thing of Old Terra."

"Would you sing it again?"

He chose one of his best baritones, a long-dead artist who had filled many a concert hall.

> *"The wall of past-beyond-recall*
> *Hides me from an ancient fall*
> *Where all the waters tumble!*
> *And plays of sprays*
> *Carve caves in clays*
> *Beneath a torrent's rumble."*

When he had finished, she was silent for a moment, then: "That's an odd song for marching."

"They liked it because they could dissect it," he said.

"Dissect?"

"Before our Fremen ancestors came to this planet, night was the time for storytelling, songs and poetry. In the Dune days, though, that was reserved for the false dark, the daytime gloom of the sietch. The night was when they could emerge and move about . . . just as we do now."

"But you said *dissect*."

"What does that song mean?" he asked.

"Oh. It's . . . it's just a song."

"Siona!"

She heard anger in his voice and remained silent.

"This planet is the child of the worm," he warned her, "and *I* am that worm."

She responded with a surprising insouciance: "Then tell me what it means."

"The insect has no more freedom from its hive than we have freedom from our past," he said. "The caves are there and all of the messages written in the sprays of the torrents."

"I prefer dancing songs," she said.

It was a flippant answer, but Leto chose to take it as a change of subject. He told her about the marriage dance of Fremen women, tracing the steps back to the whirling of dust devils. Leto prided himself on telling a good story. It was clear from her rapt attention that she could see the women whirling before her inner eye, long black hair thrown in the ancient movements, straggling across long-dead faces.

Darkness was almost upon them when he finished.

"Come," he said. "Morning and evening are still the times of silhouettes. Let us see if anyone shares our desert."

Siona followed him up to a dunecrest and they stared all around at the darkening desert. There was only one bird high overhead, attracted by their movements. From the splayed-gap tips on its wings and the shape, he knew it was a vulture. He pointed this out to Siona.

"But what do they eat?" she asked.

"Anything that's dead or nearly so."

This hit her and she stared up at the last of the sunlight gilding the lone bird's flight feathers.

Leto pressed it: "A few people still venture into my Sareer. Sometimes, a Museum Fremen wanders off and gets lost. They're really only good at the rituals. And then there are the desert's edges and the remains of whatever my wolves leave."

At this, she whirled away from him, but not before he saw the passion still consuming her. Siona was being sorely tested.

"There's little daytime graciousness about a desert," he said. "That's another reason we travel by night. To a Fremen, the image of the day was that of windblown sand filling your tracks."

Her eyes glistened with unshed tears when she turned back to him, but her features were composed.

"What lives here now?" she asked.

"The vultures, a few night creatures, an occasional remnant of plant life out of the old days, burrowing things."

"Is that all?"

"Yes."

"Why?"

"Because this is where they were born and I permit them to know nothing better."

It was almost dark with that sudden glowing light his desert acquired in these moments. He studied her in that luminous moment, recognizing that she had not yet understood his other message. He knew that message would sit there, though, and fester in her.

"Silhouettes," she said, reminding him. "What did you expect to find when we came up here?"

"Perhaps people at a distance. You're never certain."

"What people?"

"I've already told you."

"What would you've done if you'd seen anyone?"

"It was the Fremen custom to treat distant people as hostile until they threw sand into the air."

As he spoke, darkness fell over them like a curtain.

Siona became ghostly movement in the sudden starlight. "Sand?" she asked.

"Thrown sand is a profound gesture. It says: 'We share the same burden. Sand is our only enemy. This is what we drink. The hand that holds sand holds no weapon.' Do you understand this?"

"No!" She taunted him with a defiant falsehood.

"You will," he said.

Without a word, she set out along the arc of their dune, striding away from him with an angry excess of energy. Leto allowed himself to fall far behind her, interested that she had instinctively chosen the right direction. Fremen memories could be felt churning in her.

Where the dune dipped to cross another, she waited for him. He saw that the face flap of her stillsuit remained open, hanging loose. It was not yet time to chide her about this. Some unconscious things had to run their natural course.

As he came up to her, she said: "Is this as good a direction as any other?"

"If you keep to it," he said.

She glanced up at the stars and he saw her identify the Pointers, those Fremen Arrows which had led her ancestors across this land. He could see, though, that her recognition was mostly intellectual. She had not yet come to accept the other things working within her.

Leto lifted his front segments to peer ahead in the starlight. They were moving a little west of north on a track that once had led across Habbanya Ridge and Cave of Birds into the erg below False Wall West and the way to Wind Pass. None of those landmarks remained. He sniffed a cool breeze with flint smells in it and more moisture than he found pleasant.

Once more, Siona set off—slower this time, holding her course by occasional glances at the stars. She had trusted Leto to confirm the way, but now she guided herself. He sensed the turmoil beneath her wary thoughts, and he knew the things which were emerging. She had the beginnings of that intense loyalty to traveling companions which desert folk always trusted.

We know, he thought. *If you are separated from your companions, you are lost among dunes and rocks. The lone traveler in the desert is dead. Only the worm lives alone out here.*

He let her get well ahead of him where the grating sand of his passage would not be too prominent. She had to think of his human-self. He counted on loyalty to work for him. Siona was brittle, though, filled with suppressed rage—more of a rebel than any other he had ever tested.

Leto glided along behind her, reviewing the breeding program, shaping the necessary decisions for a replacement should she fail.

As the night progressed, Siona moved slower and slower. First

Moon was high overhead and Second Moon well above the horizon before she stopped to rest and eat.

Leto was glad of the pause. Friction had set up a worm-dominance, the air around him full of the chemical exhalations from his temperature adjustments. The thing he thought of as his *oxygen supercharger* vented steadily, making him intensely aware of the protein factories and amino acid resources his worm-self had acquired to accommodate the placental relationship with his human cells. Desert quickened the movement toward his final metamorphosis.

Siona had stopped near the crest of a star dune. "Is it true that you eat the sand?" she asked as he came up to her.

"It's true."

She stared all around the moon-frosted horizon. "Why didn't we bring a signal device?"

"I wanted you to learn about possessions."

She turned toward him. He sensed her breath close to his face. She was losing too much moisture into the dry air. Still, she did not remember Moneo's admonition. It would be a bitter lesson, no doubt of that.

"I don't understand you at all," she said.

"Yet, you are committed to doing just that."

"Am I?"

"How else can you give me something of value in exchange for what I give you?"

"What do you give me?" All of the bitterness was there and a hint of the spice from her dried food.

"I give you this opportunity to be alone with me, to share with me, and you spend this time without concern. You waste it."

"What about possessions?" she demanded.

He heard fatigue in her voice, the water message beginning to scream within her.

"They were magnificently alive in the old days, those Fremen," he said. "And their eye for beauty was limited to that which was useful. I never met a greedy Fremen."

"What's that supposed to mean?"

"In the old days, everything you took into the desert was a necessity and that was all you took. Your life is no longer free of possessions, Siona, or you would not have asked about a signal device."

"Why isn't a signal device necessary?"

"It would teach you nothing."

He moved out around her along the track indicated by the Pointers. "Come. Let us use this night to our profit."

She came hurrying up to walk beside his cowled face. "What happens if I don't learn your damned lesson?"

"You'll probably die," he said.

That silenced her for a time. She trudged along beside him with only an occasional sideward glance, ignoring the worm-body, concentrating on the visible remnants of his humanity. After a time, she said: "The Fish Speakers told me that you ordered the mating from which I was born."

"That's true."

"They say you keep records and that you order these Atreides matings for your own purposes."

"That also is true."

"Then the Oral History is correct."

"I thought you believed the Oral History without question?"

She was on a single track, though: "What if one of us objects when you order a mating?"

"I allow a wide latitude just as long as there are the children I have ordered."

"Ordered?" She was outraged.

"That's what I do."

"You can't creep into every bedroom or follow every one of us every minute of our lives! How do you know your *orders* are obeyed?"

"I know."

"Then you know I'm not going to obey you!"

"Are you thirsty, Siona?"

She was startled. "What?"

"Thirsty people speak of water, not of sex."

Still, she did not seal her mouth flap, and he thought: *Atreides passions always did run strong, even at the expense of reason.*

Within two hours, they came down out of the dunes onto a wind-scoured flat of pebbles. Leto moved onto it, Siona close to his side. She looked frequently at the Pointers. Both moons were low on the horizon now and their light cast long shadows behind every boulder.

In some ways, Leto found such places more comfortable to traverse than the sand. Solid rock was a better heat conductor than sand. He could flatten himself against the rock and ease the working of his chemical factories. Pebbles and even sizable rocks did not impede him.

Siona had more trouble here, though, and almost turned an ankle several times.

The flatland could be a very trying place for humans unaccustomed to it, he thought. If they stayed close to the ground, they saw only the great emptiness, an eerie place especially in moonlight—dunes at a distance, a distance which seemed not to change as the traveler moved—nothing anywhere except the seemingly eternal wind, a few rocks and, when they looked upward, stars without mercy. This was the desert of the desert.

"Here's where Fremen music acquired its eternal loneliness," he said, "not up on the dunes. Here's where you really learn to think that heaven must be the sound of running water and relief—any relief—from that endless wind."

Even this did not remind her of that face flap. Leto began to despair.

Morning found them far out on the flat.

Leto stopped beside three large boulders, all piled against each other, one of them taller even than his back. Siona leaned against him for a moment, a gesture which restored Leto's hopes somewhat. She pushed herself away presently and clambered up onto the highest boulder. He watched her turn up there, examining the landscape.

Without even looking at it Leto knew what she saw: blowing sand like fog on the horizon obscured the rising sun. For the rest, there was only the flat and the wind.

The rock was cold beneath him with the chill of a desert morning. The cold made the air much drier and he found it more pleasant. Without Siona, he would have moved on, but she was visibly exhausted. She leaned against him once more when she came down from the rock and it was almost a minute before he realized that she was listening.

"What do you hear?" he asked.

She spoke sleepily. "You rumble inside."

"The fire never goes completely out."

This interested her. She pushed herself away from his side and came around to look into his face. "Fire?"

"Every living thing has a fire within it, some slow, some very fast. Mine is hotter than most."

She hugged herself against the chill. "Then you're not cold here?"

"No, but I can see that you are." He pulled his face partly into its cowl and created a depression at the bottom arc of his first segment. "It's almost like a hammock," he said, looking down. "If you curl up there, you will be warm."

Without hesitating, she accepted his invitation.

Even though he had prepared her for it, he found the trusting response touching. He had to fight against a feeling of pity far stronger than any he had experienced before knowing Hwi. There could be no room for pity out here, though, he told himself. Siona was betraying clear signs that she would more than likely die here. He had to prepare himself for disappointment.

Siona shielded her face with an arm, closed her eyes and went to sleep.

Nobody has ever had as many yesterdays as I have had, he reminded himself.

From the popular human viewpoint, he knew that the things he did here could only appear cruel and callous. He was forced now to strengthen himself by retreating into his memories, deliberately selecting *mistakes of our common past*. Firsthand access to human mistakes was his greatest strength now. Knowledge of mistakes taught him long-term corrections. He had to be constantly aware of consequences. If consequences were lost or concealed, lessons were lost.

But the closer he came to being a sandworm, the harder he found it to make decisions which others would call inhuman. Once, he had done it with ease. As his humanity slipped away, though, he found himself filled with more and more human concerns.

In the cradle of our past, I lay upon my back in a cave so shallow I could penetrate it only by squirming, not by crawling. There, by the dancing light of a resin torch, I drew upon walls and ceiling the creatures of the hunt and the souls of my people. How illuminating it is to peer backward through a perfect circle at that ancient struggle for the visible moment of the soul. All time vibrates to that call: "Here I am!" With a mind informed by artist-giants who came afterward, I peer at handprints and flowing muscles drawn upon the rock with charcoal and vegetable dyes. How much more we are than mere mechanical events! And my anticivil self demands: "Why is it that they do not want to leave the cave?"

—THE STOLEN JOURNALS

The invitation to attend Moneo in his workroom came to Idaho late in the afternoon. All day, Idaho had sat upon the sling couch of his quarters, thinking. Every thought radiated outward from the ease with which Moneo had spilled him onto the corridor floor that morning.

"You're just an older model."

With every thought, Idaho felt himself diminished. He sensed the will to live as it faded, leaving ashes where his anger had burned itself out.

I am the conveyance of some useful sperm and nothing more, he thought.

It was a thought which invited either death or hedonism. He felt himself impaled on a thorn of chance with irritating forces pecking at him from all sides.

The young messenger in her neat blue uniform was merely another irritation. She entered at his low-voiced response to her knock and she stopped under the arched portal from his anteroom, hesitating until she had assessed his mood.

How quickly the word travels, he thought.

He saw her there, framed in the portal, a projection of Fish Speaker essence—more voluptuous than some, but no more blatantly sexual. The blue uniform did not conceal graceful hips, firm breasts. He looked up at her puckish face under a brush of blonde hair—acolyte cut.

"Moneo sends me to inquire after you," she said. "He asks that you attend him in his workroom."

Idaho had seen that workroom several times, but still remembered it best from his first view of it. He had known on entering the room that it was where Moneo spent most of his time. There was a table of dark brown wood streaked by fine golden graining, a table about two meters by one meter and set low on stubby legs in the midst of gray cushions. The table had struck Idaho as something rare and expensive, chosen for a single accent. It and the cushions—which were the same gray as floor, walls and ceiling—were the only furnishings.

Considering the power of its occupant, the room was small, no more than five meters by four, but with a high ceiling. Light came from two slender glazed windows opposite each other on the narrower walls. The windows looked out from a considerable height, one onto the northwest fringes of the Sareer and the bordering green of the Forbidden Forest, the other providing a southwest view over rolling dunes.

Contrast.

The table had put an interesting accent on this initial thought. The surface had appeared as an arrangement demonstrating the idea of *clutter*. Thin sheets of crystal paper lay scattered across the surface, leaving only glimpses of the wood grain underneath. Fine printing covered some of the paper. Idaho recognized words in Galach and four other languages, including the rare transite tongue of Perth. Several sheets of the paper revealed plan drawings and some were scrawled with black strokes of brush-script in the bold style of the Bene Gesserit.

Most interesting of all had been four rolled white tubes about a meter long—tri-D printouts from an illegal computer. He had suspected the terminal lay concealed behind a panel in one of the walls.

The young messenger from Moneo cleared her throat to awaken Idaho from his reverie. "What response shall I return to Moneo?" she asked.

Idaho focused on her face. "Would you like me to impregnate you?" he asked.

"Commander!" She was obviously shocked not so much by his suggestion as by its non sequitur intrusion.

"Ahhh, yes," Idaho said. "Moneo. What shall we tell Moneo?"

"He awaits your reply, Commander."

"Is there really any point in my responding?" Idaho asked.

"Moneo told me to inform you that he wishes to confer with both you and the Lady Hwi together."

Idaho sensed a vague arousal of interest. "Hwi is with him?"

"She has been summoned, Commander." The messenger cleared her throat once more. "Would the Commander wish me to visit him here later tonight?"

"No. Thank you, anyway. I've changed my mind."

He thought she concealed her disappointment well, but her voice came out stiffly formal: "Shall I say that you will attend Moneo?"

"Do that." He waved her away.

After she had gone, he considered just ignoring the summons. Curiosity grew in him, though. Moneo wanted to talk to him with Hwi present? Why? Did he think this would bring Idaho running? Idaho swallowed. When he thought of Hwi, the emptiness in his breast became full. The message of that could not be ignored. Something of terrible power bound him to Hwi.

He stood up, his muscles stiff after their long inaction. Curiosity and this binding force impelled him. He went out into the corridor, ignored the curious glances of guards he passed, and followed that compelling inner force up to Moneo's workroom.

Hwi was already there when Idaho entered the room. She was

across the cluttered table from Moneo, her feet in red slippers tucked back beside the gray cushion on which she sat. Idaho saw only that she wore a long brown gown with a braided green belt, then she turned and he could look at nothing except her face. Her mouth formed his name without speaking it.

Even she has heard, he thought.

Oddly, this thought strengthened him. The thoughts of this day began to form new shapes in his mind.

"Please sit down, Duncan," Moneo said. He gestured to a cushion beside Hwi. His voice conveyed a curious, halting tone, a manner that few people other than Leto had ever observed in him. He kept his gaze directed downward at the cluttered surface of his table. The late afternoon sunlight cast a spidery shadow across the jumble from a golden paperweight in the shape of a fanciful tree with jeweled fruit, all mounted on a flame-crystal mountain.

Idaho took the indicated cushion, watching Hwi's gaze follow him until he was seated. She looked at Moneo then and he thought he saw anger in her expression. Moneo's usual plain-white uniform was open at the throat, revealing a wrinkled neck and a bit of dewlap. Idaho stared into the man's eyes, prepared to wait, forcing Moneo to open the conversation.

Moneo returned the stare, noting that Idaho still wore the black uniform of their morning encounter. There was even a small trace of grime down the front, memento of the corridor floor where Moneo had spilled him. But Idaho no longer wore the antique Atreides knife. That bothered Moneo.

"What I did this morning was unforgivable," Moneo said. "Therefore, I do not ask you to forgive me. I merely ask that you try to understand."

Hwi did not appear surprised by this opening, Idaho noted. It revealed much about what the two of them had been discussing before Idaho's arrival.

When Idaho did not respond, Moneo said: "I had no right to make you feel inadequate."

Idaho found himself undergoing a curious response to Moneo's words and manner. There was still the feeling of being outmaneuvered and outclassed, too far from his time, but he no longer suspected that Moneo might be toying with him. Something had reduced the major-domo to a gritty substratum of honesty. The realization put Leto's universe, the deadly eroticism of the Fish Speakers, Hwi's undeniable candor—*everything*—into a new relationship, a form which Idaho felt that he understood. It was as though the three of them in this room were the last true humans in the entire universe. He spoke from a sense of wry self-deprecation:

"You had every right to protect yourself when I attacked you. It pleases me that you were so capable."

Idaho turned toward Hwi, but before he could speak, Moneo said: "You needn't plead for me. I think her displeasure toward me is quite adamant."

Idaho shook his head. "Does everyone here know what I'm going to say before I say it, what I'm going to feel before I feel it?"

"One of your admirable qualities," Moneo said. "You do not conceal your feelings. We"—he shrugged—"are necessarily more circumspect."

Idaho looked at Hwi. "Does he speak for you?"

She put her hand in Idaho's. "I speak for myself."

Moneo craned to peer at the clasped hands, sank back on his cushion. He sighed. "You must not."

Idaho clasped her hand more tightly, felt her equal response.

"Before either of you asks," Moneo said, "my daughter and the God Emperor have not yet returned from the testing."

Idaho sensed the effort Moneo had required to speak calmly. Hwi heard it, too.

"Is it true what the Fish Speakers say?" she asked. "Siona dies if she fails?"

Moneo remained silent, but his face was a rock.

"Is it like the Bene Gesserit test?" Idaho asked. "Muad'Dib said the Sisterhood tests to try to find out if you are human."

Hwi's hand began to tremble. Idaho felt it and looked at her. "Did they test you?"

"No," Hwi said, "but I heard the young ones talking about it. They said you must pass through agony without losing your sense of self."

Idaho returned his attention to Moneo, noting the start of a tic beside the majordomo's left eye.

"Moneo," Idaho breathed, overcome by sudden realization. "He tested you!"

"I do not wish to discuss tests," Moneo said. "We are here to decide what must be done about you two."

"Isn't that up to us?" Idaho asked. He felt Hwi's hand in his grow slippery with perspiration.

"It is up to the God Emperor," Moneo said.

"Even if Siona fails?" Idaho asked.

"Especially then!"

"How did he test you?" Idaho asked.

"He showed me a small glimpse of what it's like to be the God Emperor."

"And?"

"I saw as much as I'm capable of seeing."

Hwi's hand tightened convulsively in Idaho's.

"Then it's true that you were a rebel once," Idaho said.

"I began with love and prayer," Moneo said. "I changed to anger and rebellion. I was transformed into what you see before you. I recognize my duty and I do it."

"What did he do to you?" Idaho demanded.

"He quoted to me the prayer of my childhood: 'I give my life in dedication to the greater glory of God.'" Moneo spoke in a musing voice.

Idaho noted Hwi's stillness, her stare fixed on Moneo's face. What was she thinking?

"I admitted that this had been my prayer," Moneo said. "And the God Emperor asked me what I would give up if my life were not enough. He shouted at me: 'What is your life when you hold back the greater gift?'"

Hwi nodded, but Idaho felt only confusion.

"I could hear the truth in his voice," Moneo said.

"Are you a Truthsayer?" Hwi asked.

"In the power of desperation, yes," Moneo said. "But only then. I swear to you he spoke truth to me."

"Some of the Atreides had the power of Voice," Idaho muttered.

Moneo shook his head. "No, it was truth. He said to me: 'I look at you now and if I could shed tears, I would. Consider the wish to be the act!'"

Hwi rocked forward, almost touching the table. "He cannot cry?"

"Sandworms," Idaho whispered.

"What?" Hwi turned toward him.

"Fremen killed sandworms with water," Idaho said. "From the drowning they produced the spice-essence for their religious orgies."

"But the Lord Leto is not yet a sandworm entire," Moneo said.

Hwi rocked back onto her cushion and looked at Moneo.

Idaho pursed his lips in thought. Did Leto have the Fremen prohibition against tears, then? How awed the Fremen had always been about such a waste of moisture! *Giving water to the dead.*

Moneo addressed himself to Idaho: "I had hoped you could be brought to an understanding. The Lord Leto has spoken. You and Hwi must separate and never see each other again."

Hwi removed her hand from Idaho's. "We know."

Idaho spoke with resigned bitterness: "We know his power."

"But you do not understand him," Moneo said.

"I want nothing more than that," Hwi said. She put a hand on Idaho's arm to silence him. "No, Duncan. Our private desires have no place here."

"Maybe you should *pray* to him," Idaho said.

She whirled and looked at him, staring and staring until Idaho lowered his gaze. When she spoke, her voice carried a lilting quality that Idaho had never heard there before. "My Uncle Malky always said the Lord Leto never responded to prayer. He said the Lord Leto looked on prayer as attempted coercion, a form of violence against the chosen god, telling the immortal what to do: *Give me a miracle, God, or I won't believe in you!*"

"Prayer as *hubris*," Moneo said. "Intercession on demand."

"How can he be a god?" Idaho demanded. "By his own admission, he's not immortal."

"I will quote the Lord Leto on that," Moneo said. " 'I am all of God that need be seen. I am the word become a miracle. I am all of my ancestors. Is that not miracle enough? What more could you possibly want? Ask yourself: Where is there a greater miracle?' "

"Empty words," Idaho sneered.

"I sneered at him, too," Moneo said. "I threw his own words from the Oral History back at him: 'Give to the greater glory of God!' "

Hwi gasped.

"He laughed at me," Moneo said. "He laughed and asked how I could give what already belonged to God?"

"You were angry?" Hwi asked.

"Oh, yes. He saw this and said he would tell me how to give to that glory. He said: 'You may observe that you are every bit as great a miracle as I am.' " Moneo turned and looked out the window on his left. "I'm afraid my anger made me deaf and I was totally unprepared."

"Ohhh, he is clever," Idaho said.

"Clever?" Moneo looked at him. "I don't think so, not in the way you mean. I think the Lord Leto may be no more clever than I am in that way."

"Unprepared for what?" Hwi asked.

"The risk," Moneo said.

"But you risked much in your anger," she said.

"Not as much as he. I see in your eyes, Hwi, that you understand this. Does his body revolt you?"

"No more," she said.

Idaho ground his teeth in frustration. "He disgusts me!"

"Love, you must not say such things," Hwi said.

"And you must not call him Love," Moneo said.

"You'd rather she learned to love someone more gross and evil than any Baron Harkonnen ever dreamed of being," Idaho said.

Moneo worked his lips in and out, then: "The Lord Leto has told me about that evil old man of your time, Duncan. I don't think you understood your enemy."

"He was a fat, monstrous . . ."

"He was a seeker after sensations," Moneo said. "The fat was a side-effect, then perhaps something to experience for itself because it offended people and he enjoyed offending."

"The Baron only consumed a few planets," Idaho said. "Leto consumes the universe."

"Love, please!" Hwi protested.

"Let him rant," Moneo said. "When I was young and ignorant, even as my Siona and this poor fool, I said similar things."

"Is that why you let your daughter go out to die?" Idaho demanded.

"Love, that's cruel," Hwi said.

"Duncan, it has always been one of your flaws to seek hysteria," Moneo said. "I warn you that ignorance thrives on hysteria. Your genes provide vigor and you may inspire some among the Fish Speakers, but you are a poor leader."

"Don't try to anger me," Idaho said. "I know better than to attack you, but don't push me too far."

Hwi tried to take Idaho's hand, but he pulled away.

"I know my place," Idaho said. "I'm a useful follower. I can carry the Atreides banner. The green and black is on my back!"

"The undeserving maintain power by promoting hysteria," Moneo said. "The Atreides art is the art of ruling without hysteria, the art of being responsible for the uses of power."

Idaho pushed back and heaved himself to his feet. "When has your damned God Emperor ever been responsible for anything?"

Moneo looked down at his cluttered table and spoke without looking up. "He is responsible for what he has done to himself." Moneo looked up then, his eyes frosty. "You haven't the guts, Duncan, to learn why he did that to himself!"

"And you have?" Idaho asked.

"When I was most angry," Moneo said, "and he saw himself through my eyes, he said: 'How dare you be offended by me?' It was then"—

Moneo swallowed—"that he made me look into the horror . . . that he had seen." Tears welled from Moneo's eyes and ran down his cheeks. "And I was only glad that I did not have to make his decision . . . that I could content myself with being a follower."

"I have touched him," Hwi whispered.

"Then you know?" Moneo asked her.

"Without seeing it, I know," she said.

In a low voice, Moneo said: "I almost died of it. I . . ." He shuddered, then looked up at Idaho. "You must not . . ."

"Damn you all!" Idaho snarled. He turned and dashed from the room.

Hwi stared after him, her face a mask of anguish. "Ohhh, Duncan," she whispered.

"You see?" Moneo asked. "You were wrong. Neither you nor the Fish Speakers have gentled him. But you, Hwi, you have only contributed to his destruction."

Hwi turned her anguish toward Moneo. "I will not see him again," she said.

For Idaho, the passage down to his quarters became one of the most difficult times in his memory. He tried to imagine that his face was a plasteel mask held immobile to hide the turmoil within. None of the guards he passed could be permitted to see his pain. He did not know that most of them made accurate guesses about his emotion and shared a compassion for him. All of them had sat through briefings on the Duncans and had learned to read them well.

In the corridor near his quarters, Idaho encountered Nayla walking slowly toward him. Something in her face, a look of indecision and loss, stopped him briefly and almost brought him out of his internal concentration.

"Friend?" he said, speaking when he was only a few paces from her.

She looked at him, abrupt recognition obvious on her square face.

What an odd-looking woman, he thought.

"I am no longer Friend," she said and passed by him down the corridor.

Idaho turned on one heel and stared at her retreating back—those heavy shoulders, that plodding sense of terrible muscles.

What was she bred for? he wondered.

It was only a passing thought. His own concerns returned more strongly than before. He strode the few paces to his door and into his quarters.

Once inside, Idaho stood a moment with clenched fists at his sides.

I have no more ties to any *time*, he thought. And how odd that this was not a liberating thought. He knew, though, that he had done the thing which would begin freeing Hwi from her love for him. He was diminished. She would think of him soon as a small, petulant fool, a subject only of his own emotions. He could feel himself fading from her immediate concerns.

And that poor Moneo!

Idaho sensed the shape of the things which had formed the pliant majordomo. *Duty and responsibility.* What a safe haven those were in a time of difficult decisions.

I was like that once, Idaho thought. *But that was in another life, another time.*

The Duncans sometimes ask if I understand the exotic ideas of our past. And if I understand them, why can't I explain them? Knowledge, the Duncans believe, resides only in particulars. I try to tell them that all words are plastic. Word images begin to distort in the instant of utterance. Ideas imbedded in a language require that particular language for expression. This is the very essence of the meaning within the word *exotic*. See how it begins to distort? Translation squirms in the presence of the exotic. The Galach which I speak here imposes itself. It is an outside frame of reference, a particular system. Dangers lurk in all systems. Systems incorporate the unexamined beliefs of their creators. Adopt a system, accept its beliefs, and you help strengthen the resistance to change. Does it serve any purpose for me to tell the Duncans that there are no languages for some things? Ahhh! But the Duncans believe that all languages are mine.

—THE STOLEN JOURNALS

For two full turns of days and nights, Siona failed to seal her face mask, losing precious water with every breath. It had taken the Fremen admonition to children before Siona remembered her father's words. Leto had spoken to her finally on the cold third morning of their traverse when they stopped within a rock shadow on the windswept flat of the erg.

"Guard every breath for it carries the warmth and moisture of your life," he said.

He had known they would be three more days on the erg and three more nights beyond that before they reached water. Now, it was the fifth morning from the Little Citadel's tower. They had entered shallow drifts of sand during the night—not dunes, but dunes could be glimpsed ahead of them and even the remnants of Habbanya Ridge were a thin, broken line in the distance if you knew where to look. Now, Siona took down the mouth flap of her stillsuit only to speak clearly. And she spoke through black and bleeding lips.

She has the thirst of desperation, he thought, as he let his senses probe their surroundings. *She will reach the moments of crisis soon.* His senses told him that they were still alone here at the edge of the flat. Dawn lay only minutes behind them. The low light created barriers of dust reflection which twisted and lifted and dipped in the unceasing wind. His senses filtered out the wind that he might hear other things— Siona's heaving breaths, the tumble of a small sandspill from the rocks beside them, his own gross body grating in the thin sand cover.

Siona peeled her face mask aside but held it in her hand for quick restoration.

"How much longer until we find water?" she asked.

"Three nights."

"Is there a better direction to go?"

"No."

She had come to appreciate the Fremen economy with important information. She sipped greedily at a few drops in her catchpocket.

Leto recognized the message of her movements—familiar gestures for Fremen *in extremis*. Siona was now fully aware of a common experience among her ancestors—*patiyeh*, the thirst at the edge of death.

The few drops in her catchpocket were gone. He heard her sucking air. She restored the mask and spoke in a muffled voice.

"I won't make it, will I?"

Leto looked into her eyes, seeing there the clarity of thought brought on by the nearness of death, a penetrating awareness seldom otherwise achieved. It amplified only that which was required for survival. Yes, she was well into the *tedah riagrimi*, the agony which opens the mind. Soon, she would have to make that ultimate decision which she yet believed she had already made. Leto knew by the signs that he was required to treat Siona now with extreme courtesy. He would have to answer every question with candor for in every question lurked a judgment.

"Will I?" she insisted.

There was still a trace of hope in her desperation.

"Nothing is certain," he said.

This dropped her into despair.

That had not been Leto's intention, but he knew that it often happened—an accurate, though ambiguous, answer was taken as confirmation of one's deepest fears.

She sighed.

Her mask-muffled voice probed at him once more. "You had some special intention for me in your breeding program."

It was not a question.

"All people have intentions," he told her.

"But you wanted my full agreement."

"That is true."

"How could you expect agreement when you know I hate everything about you? Be honest with me!"

"The three legs of the agreement-tripod are desire, data and doubt. Accuracy and honesty have little to do with it."

"Please don't argue with me. You know I'm dying."

"I respect you too much to argue with you."

He lifted his front segments slightly then, probing the wind. It already was beginning to bring the day's heat but there was too much moisture in it for his comfort. He was reminded that the more he ordered the weather controlled, the more there was that required control. Absolutes only brought him closer to vagaries.

"You say you're not arguing, but . . ."

"Argument closes off the doors of the senses," he said, lowering himself back to the surface. "It always masks violence. Continued too long, argument always leads to violence. I have no violent intentions toward you."

"What do you mean—desire, data and doubt?"

"Desire brings the participants together. Data set the limits of their dialogue. Doubt frames the questions."

She moved closer to stare directly into his face from less than a meter away.

How odd, he thought, that hatred could be mingled so completely with hope and fear and awe.

"Could you save me?"

"There is a way."

She nodded and he knew she had leaped to the wrong conclusion.

"You want to trade *that* for my agreement!" she accused.

"No."

"If I pass your test . . ."

"It is not my test."

"Whose?"

"It derives from our common ancestors."

Siona sank to a sitting position on the cold rock and remained silent, not yet ready to ask for a resting place within the lip of his warm front segment. Leto thought he could hear the soft scream waiting in her throat. Now, her doubts were at work. She was beginning to wonder if he really could be fitted into her image of Ultimate Tyrant. She looked up at him with that terrible clarity he had identified in her.

"What makes you do what you do?"

The question was well framed. He said: "My need to save the people."

"What people?"

"My definition is much broader than that of anyone else—even of the Bene Gesserit, who think they have defined what it is to be human. I refer to the eternal thread of all humankind by whatever definition."

"You're trying to tell me . . ." Her mouth became too dry for speaking. She tried to accumulate saliva. He saw the movements within her face mask. Her question was obvious, though, and he did not wait.

"Without me there would have been by now no people anywhere, none whatsoever. And the path to that extinction was more hideous than your wildest imaginings."

"Your *supposed* prescience," she sneered.

"The Golden Path still stands open," he said.

"I don't trust you!"

"Because we are not equals?"

"Yes!"

"But we're interdependent."

"What need have you for me?"

Ahhh, the cry of youth unsure of its niche. He felt the strength within the secret bonds of dependency and forced himself to be hard. *Dependency fosters weakness!*

"You are the Golden Path," he said.

"Me?" It was barely a whisper.

"You've read those journals you stole from me," he said. "I am in them, but where are you? Look at what I have created, Siona. And you, you can create nothing except yourself."

"Words, more tricky words!"

"I do not suffer from being worshipped, Siona. I suffer from never being appreciated. Perhaps . . . No, I dare not hope for you."

"What's the purpose of those journals?"

"An Ixian machine records them. They are to be found on a faraway day. They will make people think."

"An Ixian machine? You defy the Jihad!"

"There's a lesson in that, too. What do such machines really do? They increase the number of things we can do without thinking. Things we do without thinking—there's the real danger. Look at how long you walked across this desert without thinking about your face mask."

"You could have warned me!"

"And increased your dependency."

She stared at him a moment, then: "Why would you want me to command your Fish Speakers?"

"You are an Atreides woman, resourceful and capable of independent thought. You can be truthful just for the sake of truth as you see it. You were bred and trained for command—which means freedom from dependence."

The wind whirled dust and sand around them while she weighed his words. "And if I agree, you'll save me?"

"No."

She had been so sure of the opposite answer that it was several heartbeats before she translated that single word. In that time, the wind fell slightly, exposing a vista across the dune-scape to the remnants of Habbanya Ridge. The air was suddenly chilled with that cold which did as much to rob the flesh of moisture as did the hottest sunlight. Part of Leto's awareness detected an oscillation in weather control.

"No?" She was both puzzled and outraged.

"I do not make bloody bargains with people I must trust."

She shook her head slowly from side to side, but her gaze remained fixed on his face. "What will make you save me?"

"Nothing will make me do it. Why do you think you could do to me what I will not do to you? That is not the way of interdependence."

Her shoulders slumped. "If I cannot bargain with you or force you . . ."

"Then you must choose another path."

What a marvelous thing to observe the explosive growth of aware-ness, he thought. Siona's expressive features hid nothing of it from him. She focused on his eyes and glared at him as though seeking to move completely into his thoughts. New strength entered her muffled voice.

"You would have me know everything about you—even every weakness?"

"Would you steal what I would give openly?"

The morning light was harsh on her face. "I promise you nothing!"

"Nor do I require that."

"But you will give me . . . water if I ask?"

"It is not just water."

She nodded. "And I am Atreides."

The Fish Speakers had not withheld the lesson of that special sus-ceptibility in the Atreides genes. She knew where the spice originated and what it might do to her. The teachers in the Fish Speaker schools never failed him. And the gentle additions of melange in Siona's dried food had done their work, too.

"These little curled flaps beside my face," he said. "Tease one of them gently with a finger and it will give up drops of moisture heavily laced with spice-essence."

He saw the recognition in her eyes. Memories which she did not know as memories were speaking to her. And she was the result of many generations in which the Atreides sensitivity had been increased.

Even the urgency of her thirst would not yet move her.

To ease her through the crisis, he told her about Fremen children poling for sandtrout at an oasis edge, teasing the moisture out of them for quick vitalization.

"But I am Atreides," she said.

"The Oral History tells it truthfully," he said.

"Then I could die of it."

"That's the test."

"You would make a real Fremen out of me!"

"How else can you teach your descendants to survive here after I am gone?"

She pulled away her mask and moved her face to within a handsbreadth of his. A finger came up and touched one of the curled flaps of his cowl.

"Stroke it gently," he said.

Her hand obeyed not his voice but something from within her. The finger movements were precise, eliciting his own memories, a thing passed from child to child to child . . . the way so much information and misinformation survived. He turned his face to its limit and looked sideways at her face so close to his. Pale blue drops began to form at the flap's edge. Rich cinnamon smells enveloped them. She leaned toward the drops. He saw the pores beside her nose, the way her tongue moved as she drank.

Presently, she retreated—not completely satisfied, but driven by caution and suspicion much the way Moneo had been. *Like father, like daughter.*

"How long before it begins to work?" she asked.

"It is already working."

"I mean . . ."

"A minute or so."

"I owe you nothing for this!"

"I will demand no payment."

She sealed her face mask.

He saw the milky distances enter her eyes. Without asking permission, she tapped his front segment, demanding that he prepare the warm *hammock* of his flesh. He obeyed. She fitted herself to the gentle curve. By peering sharply downward, he could see her. Siona's eyes remained opened, but they no longer saw this place. She jerked abruptly and began to tremble like a small creature dying. He knew this experience, but could not change the smallest part of it. No ancestral presences would remain in her consciousness, but she would carry with her forever afterward the clear sights and sounds and smells. The seeking machines would be there, the smell of blood and entrails, the cowering humans in their burrows aware only that they could not escape . . . while all the time the mechanical movement approached, nearer and nearer and nearer . . . louder . . . louder!

Everywhere she searched, it would be the same. No escape anywhere.

He felt her life ebbing. *Fight the darkness, Siona!* That was one thing the Atreides did. They fought for life. And now she was fighting for lives other than her own. He felt the dimming, though . . . the terrible outflow of vitality. She went deeper and deeper into the darkness, far deeper than any other had ever gone. He began to rock her gently, a cradle movement of his front segment. That or the thin hot thread of determination, perhaps both together, prevailed. By early afternoon, her flesh had trembled its way into something approaching real sleep. Only an occasional gasp betrayed the vision's echoes. He rocked her gently, rolling from side to side.

Could she possibly come back from those depths? He felt the vital responses reassuring him. The strength in her!

She awakened in the late afternoon, a stillness coming over her abruptly, the breathing rhythm changed. Her eyes snapped open. She peered up at him, then rolled out of the *hammock* to stand with her back to him for almost an hour of silent thinking.

Moneo had done that same thing. It was a new pattern in these Atreides. Some of the preceding ones had ranted at him. Others had backed away from him, stumbling and staring, forcing him to follow, squirming and grating over the pebbles. Some of them had squatted and stared at the ground. None of them had turned their backs on him. Leto took this new development as a hopeful sign.

"You are beginning to have some concept of how far my family extends," he said.

She turned, her mouth a prim line, but did not meet his gaze. He could see her accepting it, though, the realization which few humans could share as she had shared it: His singular multitude made all of humankind his family.

"You could have saved my friends in the forest," she accused.

"You, too, could have saved them."

She clenched her fists and pressed them against her temples while she glared at him. "But you know *everything*!"

"Siona!"

"Did I have to learn it that way?" she whispered.

He remained silent, forcing her to answer the question for herself. She had to be made to recognize that his primary consciousness worked in a Fremen way and that, like the terrible machines of that apocalyptic vision, the predator could follow any creature who left tracks.

"The Golden Path," she whispered. "I can *feel* it." Then, glaring at him. "It's so cruel!"

"Survival has always been cruel."

"They couldn't hide," she whispered. Then loud: "What have you done to me?"

"You tried to be a Fremen rebel," he said. "Fremen had an almost incredible ability to read signs on the desert. They could even read the faint tracery of windblown tracks in sand."

He saw the beginnings of remorse in her, memories of her dead companions floating in her awareness. He spoke quickly, knowing that guilt would follow quickly and then anger against him. "Would you have believed me if I had merely brought you in and told you?"

Remorse threatened to overwhelm her. She opened her mouth behind the mask and gasped with it.

"You have not yet survived the desert," he told her.

Slowly, her trembling subsided. The Fremen instincts he had set to work in her did their usual tempering.

"I will survive," she said. She met his gaze. "You read us by our emotions, don't you?"

"The igniters of thought," he said. "I can recognize the slightest behavioral nuance for its emotional origins."

He saw her accept her own nakedness the way Moneo had accepted it, with fear and hate. It was of little matter. He probed the time ahead of them. Yes, she *would* survive his desert because her tracks were in the sand beside him . . . but he saw no sign of her flesh in those tracks. Just beyond her tracks, though, he saw a sudden opening where things had been concealed. Anteac's death-shout echoed through his prescient awareness . . . and the swarming of Fish Speakers attacking!

Malky is coming, he thought. *We will meet again, Malky and I.*

Leto opened his outer eyes and saw Siona still there glaring at him.

"I still hate you!" she said.

"You hate the predator's necessary cruelty."

She spoke with venomous elation: "But I saw another thing! You can't follow my tracks!"

"Which is why you must breed and preserve this."

Even as he spoke, it began to rain. The sudden cloud darkness and the downpour came upon them simultaneously. In spite of the fact that he had sensed weather control's oscillations, Leto was shocked by the onslaught. He knew it rained sometimes in the Sareer, a rain quickly dispersed as the water ran off and vanished. The few pools would evaporate as the sun returned. Most times, the downpour never touched the ground; it was ghost rain, vaporized when it hit the superheated air layer just above the desert's surface, then dispersing on the wind. But this rainfall drenched him.

Siona pulled back her face flap and lifted her face greedily to the falling water, not even noticing the effect on Leto.

As the first drenching swept in from behind the sandtrout overlappings, he stiffened and curled into a ball of agony. Separate drives of sandtrout and sandworm produced a new meaning for the word *pain*. He felt that he was being ripped apart. Sandtrout wanted to rush to the water and encapsulate it. Sandworm felt the drenching wash of death. Curls of blue smoke spurted from every place the rain touched him. The inner workings of his body began to manufacture the true spice-essence. Blue smoke lifted around him from where he lay in puddles of water. He writhed and groaned.

The clouds passed and it was a few moments before Siona sensed his disturbance.

"What's wrong with you?"

He was unable to answer. The rain was gone but water remained on the rocks and in puddles all around and beneath him. There was no escape.

Siona saw the blue smoke rising from every place the water touched him.

"It's the water!"

There was a slightly higher bulge of land off to the right where the water did not stay. Painfully, he made his way toward it, groaning at each new puddle. The bulge was almost dry when he reached it. The agony subsided slowly and he grew aware that Siona stood directly in front of him. She probed at him with words of false concern.

"Why does water hurt you?"

Hurt? What an inadequate word! There was no evading her questions, though. She knew enough now to go searching for the answer. That answer could be found. Haltingly, he explained the relationship of sandtrout and sandworm to water. She heard him out in silence.

"But the moisture you gave me . . ."

"Is buffered and masked by the spice."

"Then why do you risk it out here without your cart?"

"You can't be a Fremen in the Citadel or on a cart."

She nodded.

He saw the flame of rebellion return to her eyes. She did not have to feel guilty or dependent. She no longer could avoid belief in his Golden Path, but what difference did that make? His cruelties could not be forgiven! She could reject him, deny him a place in her family. He was not a human, not like her at all. And she possessed the secret of his undoing! Ring him with water, destroy his desert, immobilize him within a moat of agony! Did she think she hid her thoughts from him by turning away?

And what can I do about it? he wondered. *She must live now while I must demonstrate nonviolence.*

Now that he knew something of Siona's nature, how easy it would be to surrender, to sink blindly into his own thoughts. It was seductive, this temptation to live only within his memories, but his *children* still required another lesson-by-example if they were to escape the last threat to the Golden Path.

What a painful decision! He experienced a new sympathy for the Bene Gesserit. His quandary was akin to the one they had experienced when they had confronted the fact of Muad'Dib. *The ultimate goal of their breeding program—my father—they could not contain him, either.*

Once more into the breach, dear friends, he thought, and he suppressed a wry smile at his own histrionics.

Given enough time for the generations to evolve, the predator produces particular survival adaptations in its prey which, through the circular operation of feedback, produce changes in the predator which again change the prey—etcetera, etcetera, etcetera. . . . Many powerful forces do the same thing. You can count religions among such forces.

—THE STOLEN JOURNALS

"The Lord has commanded me to tell you that your daughter lives."

Nayla delivered the message to Moneo in a singsong voice, looking down across the workroom table at his figure seated there amidst a chaos of notes and papers and communications instruments.

Moneo pressed his palms together firmly and looked down at the elongated shadow drawn on his table by late afternoon sunlight across the jeweled tree of his paperweight.

Without looking up at Nayla's stocky figure standing at proper attention in front of him, he asked: "Both of them have returned to the Citadel?"

"Yes."

Moneo looked out the window to his left, not really seeing the flinty borderline of darkness hanging on the Sareer's horizon nor the greedy wind collecting sand grains from every dunetop.

"That matter which we discussed earlier?" he asked.

"It has been arranged."

"Very well." He waved to dismiss her, but Nayla remained standing in front of him. Surprised, Moneo actually focused on her for the first time since she had entered.

"Is it required that I personally attend this"—she swallowed—"wedding?"

"The Lord Leto has commanded it. You will be the only one there armed with a lasgun. It is an honor."

She remained in position, her gaze fixed somewhere over Moneo's head.

"Yes?" he prompted.

Nayla's great lantern jaw worked convulsively, then: "He is God and I am mortal." She turned on one heel and left the workroom.

Moneo wondered vaguely what was bothering that hulking Fish Speaker, but his thoughts turned like a compass arrow to Siona.

She has survived as I did. Siona now had an inner sense which told her that the Golden Path remained unbroken. *As I have.* He found no sense of sharing in this, nothing to make him feel closer to his daughter. It was a burden and it would inevitably curb her rebellious nature. No Atreides could go against the Golden Path. Leto had seen to that!

Moneo remembered his own rebel days. Every night a new bed and the constant urge to run. The cobwebs of his past clung to his mind, sticking there no matter how hard he tried to shake away troublesome memories.

Siona has been caged. As I was caged. As poor Leto was caged.

The tolling of the nightfall bell intruded on his thoughts and activated his workroom's lights. He looked down at the work still undone in preparation for the God Emperor's wedding to Hwi Noree. So much work! Presently, he pressed a call-button and asked the Fish Speaker acolyte who appeared at the summons to bring him a tumbler of water and then call Duncan Idaho to the workroom.

She returned quickly with the water and placed the tumbler near his left hand on the table. He noted the long fingers, a lute-player's fingers, but did not look up at her face.

"I have sent someone for Idaho," she said.

He nodded and went on with his work. He heard her leave and only then did he look up to drink the water.

Some live lives like summer moths, he thought. *But I have burdens without end.*

The water tasted flat. It weighed down his senses, making his body feel torpid. He looked out at the sunset colors on the Sareer as they shaded away into darkness, thinking that he should recognize beauty in that familiar sense, but all he could think was that the light changed in its own patterns. *It is not moved by me at all.*

With the full darkness, the light level of his workroom increased automatically, bringing a clarity of thought with it. He felt himself quite prepared for Idaho. This one had to be taught the necessities, and quickly.

Moneo's door opened, the acolyte again. "Will you eat now?"

"Later." He raised a hand as she started to leave. "I would like the door left open."

She frowned.

"You may practice your music," he said. "I want to listen."

She had a smooth, round, almost childlike face which became radiant when she smiled. The smile still on her lips, she turned away.

Presently, he heard the sounds of a *biwa* lute in the outer office. Yes, that young acolyte had a talent. The bass strings were like rain drumming on a rooftop, a whisper of middle strings underneath. Perhaps she could move up to the baliset someday. He recognized the song: a deeply humming memory of autumn wind from some faraway planet where they had never known a desert. Sad music, pitiful music, yet marvelous.

It is the cry of the caged, he thought. *The memory of freedom.* This thought struck him as odd. Was it always the case that freedom required rebellion?

The lute fell silent. There came the sound of low voices. Idaho entered the workroom. Moneo watched him enter. A trick of light gave Idaho a face like a grimacing mask with pitted eyes. Without invitation, he sat down across from Moneo and the trickery was gone. *Just another Duncan.* He had changed into a plain black uniform without insignia.

"I have been asking myself a peculiar question," Idaho said. "I'm glad you summoned me. I want to ask this question of you. What is it, Moneo, that my predecessor did *not* learn?"

Stiff with surprise, Moneo sat up straight. What an un-Duncan question! Could there be a peculiar Tleilaxu difference in this one after all?

"What prompts this question?" Moneo asked.

"I've been thinking like a Fremen."

"You weren't a Fremen."

"Closer to it than you think. Stilgar the Naib once said I was probably born Fremen without knowing it until I came to Dune."

"What happens when you think like a Fremen?"

"You remember that you should never be in company that you wouldn't want to die with."

Moneo put his hands palms down on the surface of his table. A wolfish smile came over Idaho's face.

"Then what are you doing here?" Moneo asked.

"I suspect that you may be good company, Moneo. And I ask myself why Leto would choose you as his closest companion."

"I passed the test."

"The same one your daughter passed?"

So he has heard they are back. It meant some of the Fish Speakers were reporting things to him . . . unless the God Emperor had summoned the Duncan. . . . *No, I would have heard.*

"The tests are never identical," Moneo said. "I was made to go alone into a cavern maze with nothing but a bag of food and a vial of spice-essence."

"Which did you choose?"

"What? Oh . . . if you are tested, you will learn."

"There's a Leto I don't know," Idaho said.

"Have I not told you this?"

"And there's a Leto you don't know," Idaho said.

"Because he's the loneliest person this universe has ever seen," Moneo said.

"Don't play mood games trying to arouse my sympathy," Idaho said.

"Mood games, yes. That's very good," Moneo nodded. "The God Emperor's moods are like a river—smooth where nothing obstructs him, foaming and violent at the least suggestion of a barrier. He is not to be obstructed."

Idaho looked around at the brightly lighted workroom, turned his gaze to the outside darkness and thought about the tamed course of the *Idaho* River somewhere out there. Bringing his attention back to Moneo, he asked: "What do you know of rivers?"

"In my youth, I traveled for him. I have even trusted my life to a floating shell of a vessel on a river and then on a sea whose shores were lost in the crossing."

As he spoke, Moneo felt that he had brushed against a clue to some deep truth in the Lord Leto. The sensation dropped Moneo into reverie, thinking of that far planet where he had crossed a sea from one shore to another. There had been a storm on the first evening of that passage and, somewhere deep within the ship, an irritating non-directional "*sug-sug-sug-sug-sug*" of laboring engines. He had stood on deck with the captain. His mind had kept focusing on the engine sound, retreating and coming back to it like the oversurging of the watery green-black mountains which passed and came, repeating and repeating. Each down crash of the keel opened the sea's flesh like a fist smashing. It was insane motion, a sodden shaking, up . . . up, down! His lungs had ached with repressed fear. The lunging of the ship and the sea trying to put them down—wild explosions of solid water, hour after hour, white blisters of water spilling off the decks, then another sea and another . . .

All of this was a clue to the God Emperor.

He is both the storm and the ship.

Moneo focused on Idaho seated across the table from him in the workroom's cold light. Not a tremor in the man, but a hungering was there.

"So you will not help me learn what the other Duncan Idahos did not learn," Idaho said.

"But I will help you."

"Then what have I always failed to learn?"

"How to trust."

Idaho pushed himself back from the table and glared at Moneo. When Idaho's voice came, it was harsh and rasping: "I'd say I trusted too much."

Moneo was implacable. "But how do you trust?"

"What do you mean?"

Moneo put his hands in his lap. "You choose male companions for their ability to fight and die on the side of right as you see it. You choose females who can complement this masculine view of yourself. You allow for no differences which can come from goodwill."

Something moved in the doorway to Moneo's workroom. He looked up in time to see Siona enter. She stopped, one hand on her hip.

"Well, father, up to your old tricks, I see."

Idaho jerked around to stare at the speaker.

Moneo studied her, looking for signs of the change. She had bathed and put on a fresh uniform, the black and gold of Fish Speaker command, but her face and hands still betrayed the evidence of her desert ordeal. She had lost weight and her cheekbones stood out. Unguent did little to conceal cracks in her lips. Veins stood out on her hands. Her eyes looked ancient and her expression was that of someone who had tasted bitter dregs.

"I've been listening to you two," she said. She dropped her hand from her hip and moved farther into the room. "How dare you speak of goodwill, father?"

Idaho had noted the uniform. He pursed his lips in thought. *Fish Speaker Command? Siona?*

"I understand your bitterness," Moneo said. "I had similar feelings once."

"Did you really?" She came closer, stopping just beside Idaho, who continued to regard her with a look of speculation.

"I am filled with joy to see you alive," Moneo said.

"How gratifying for you to see me safely into the God Emperor's Service," she said. "You waited so long to have a child and look! See how successful I am." She turned slowly to display her uniform. "Commander of the Fish Speakers. A commander with a troop of one, but nonetheless a commander."

Moneo forced his voice to be cold and professional. "Sit down."

"I prefer to stand." She looked down at Idaho's upturned face. "Ahhh, Duncan Idaho, my intended mate. Don't you find this interesting, Duncan? The Lord Leto tells me I will be *fitted into* the command structure of the Fish Speakers in time. Meanwhile, I have one attendant. Do you know the one called Nayla, Duncan?"

Idaho nodded.

"Really? I think perhaps I *don't* know her." Siona looked at Moneo. "Do I know her, father?"

Moneo shrugged.

"But you speak of trust, father," Siona said. "Who does the powerful minister, Moneo, trust?"

Idaho turned to see the effect of these words on the majordomo. The man's face appeared brittle with repressed emotion. *Anger? No . . . something else.*

"I trust the God Emperor," Moneo said. "And, in the hope that it will teach both of you something, I am here to convey his wishes to you."

"His *wishes!*" Siona taunted. "Hear that, Duncan? The God Emperor's commands are now *wishes*."

"Speak your piece," Idaho said. "I know we have little choice in whatever it is."

"You always have a choice," Moneo said.

"Don't listen to him," Siona said. "He's full of tricks. They expect us to fall into each other's arms and breed more like my father. Your descendant, my father!"

Moneo's face went pale. He gripped the edge of his worktable with both hands and leaned forward. "You are both fools! But I will try to save you. In spite of yourselves, I will try to save you."

Idaho saw Moneo's cheeks tremble, the intensity of the man's stare, and felt oddly moved by this. "I'm not his stud, but I'll listen to you."

"Always a mistake," Siona said.

"Be still, woman," Idaho said.

She glared at the top of Idaho's head. "Don't address me that way or I'll wrap your neck around your ankles!"

Idaho stiffened and started to turn.

Moneo grimaced and waved a hand for Idaho to remain seated. "I caution you, Duncan, that she could probably do it. I am no match for her and you do recall your attempt at violence against me?"

Idaho inhaled a deep, quick breath, let it out slowly, then: "Say what you have to say."

Siona moved to perch at the end of Moneo's table and looked down at both of them. "Much better," she said. "Let him have his say, but don't listen."

Idaho pressed his lips tightly together.

Moneo released his grip on the edge of his desk. He sat back and looked from Idaho to Siona. "I have almost completed the arrangements for the God Emperor's wedding to Hwi Noree. During those festivities, I want you both out of the way."

Siona turned a questioning look on Moneo. "Your idea or his?"

"Mine!" Moneo returned his daughter's glare. "Have you no sense of honor and duty? Have you learned nothing from being with him?"

"Oh, I learned what you learned, father. And I gave my word, which I will keep."

"Then you'll command the Fish Speakers?"

"Whenever he *trusts* me with command. You know, father, he's ever so much more devious than you are."

"Where are you sending us?" Idaho asked.

"Provided we agree to go," Siona said.

"There is a small village of Museum Fremen at the edge of the Sareer," Moneo said. "It is called Tuono. The village is relatively pleasant. It's in the shadow of the Wall with the river just beyond the Wall. There is a well and the food is good."

Tuono? Idaho wondered. The name sounded familiar. "There was a Tuono Basin on the way to Sietch Tabr," he said.

"And the nights are long and there's no entertainment," Siona said.

Idaho shot a sharp glance at her. She returned it. "He wants us breeding and the Worm satisfied," she said. "He wants babies in my belly, new lives to warp and twist. I'll see him dead before I'll give him that!"

Idaho looked back at Moneo with a bemused expression. "And if we refuse to go?"

"I think you'll go," Moneo said.

Siona's lips twitched. "Duncan, have you even seen one of these little desert villages? No comforts, no . . ."

"I have seen Tabur Village," Idaho said.

"I'm sure that is a metropolis beside Tuono. Our God Emperor would not celebrate his nuptials in any cluster of mud hovels! Oh, no. Tuono will be mud hovels and no amenities, as close to the original Fremen as possible."

Idaho kept his attention on Moneo while speaking: "Fremen did not live in mud huts."

"Who cares where they conducted their cultish games?" she sneered.

Still looking at Moneo, Idaho said: "Real Fremen had only one cult, the cult of personal honesty. I worry more about honesty than about comfort."

"Don't expect comfort from me!" Siona snapped.

"I don't expect anything from you," Idaho said. "When would we leave for this Tuono, Moneo?"

"You're going?" she asked.

"I am considering an acceptance of your father's kindness," Idaho said.

"Kindness!" She looked from Idaho to Moneo.

"You would leave immediately," Moneo said. "I have detailed a detachment of Fish Speakers under Nayla to escort you and provide for you at Tuono."

"Nayla?" Siona asked. "Really? Will she stay with us there?"

"Until the day of the wedding."

Siona nodded slowly. "Then we accept."

"Accept for yourself!" Idaho snapped.

Siona smiled. "Sorry. May I formally request that the great Duncan

Idaho join me at this primitive garrison where he will keep his hands off my person?"

Idaho peered up at her from under his brows. "Have no fears about where I will put my hands." He looked at Moneo. "Are you being kind, Moneo? Is that why you're sending me away?"

"It's a question of trust," Siona said. "Who does he trust?"

"Will I be forced to go with your daughter?" Idaho insisted.

Siona stood. "We either accept or the troopers will bind us and carry us out in a most uncomfortable fashion. You can see it in his face."

"So I really have no choice," Idaho said.

"You have the choice anyone has," Siona said. "Die now or later."

Still, Idaho stared at Moneo. "Your real intentions, Moneo? Won't you satisfy my curiosity?"

"Curiosity has kept many people alive when all else failed," Moneo said. "I am trying to keep you alive, Duncan. I have never done that before."

It required almost a thousand years before the dust of Dune's old planet-wide desert left the atmosphere to be bound up in soil and water. The wind called *sandblaster* has not been seen on Arrakis for some twenty-five hundred years. Twenty billion tons of dust could be carried suspended in the wind of just one of those storms. The sky often had a silvery look to it then. Fremen said: "The desert is a surgeon cutting away the skin to expose what's underneath." The planet and the people had layers. You could see them. My Sareer is but a weak echo of what was. I must be the *sandblaster* today.

—THE STOLEN JOURNALS

"You sent them to Tuono without consulting me? How surprising of you, Moneo! You've not done such an independent thing in a long while."

Moneo stood about ten paces from Leto in the gloomy center of the crypt, head bowed, using every artifice he knew to keep from trembling, aware that even this could be seen and interpreted by the God Emperor. It was almost midnight. Leto had kept his majordomo waiting and waiting.

"I pray I have not offended my Lord," Moneo said.

"You have amused me, but take no heart from that. Lately, I cannot separate the comic from the sad."

"Forgive me, Lord," Moneo whispered.

"What is this forgiveness you ask? Must you always require judgment? Can't your universe merely *be*?"

Moneo lifted his gaze to that awful cowled face. *He is both ship and storm. The sunset exists in itself.* Moneo felt that he stood on the brink of terrifying revelations. The God Emperor's eyes bored into him, burning, probing. "Lord, what would you have of me?"

"That you have faith in yourself."

Feeling that something might explode in him, Moneo said: "Then the fact that I did not consult you before . . ."

"How enlightened of you, Moneo! Small souls who seek power over others first destroy the faith those others might have in themselves."

The words were shattering to Moneo. He sensed accusation in them, confession. He felt his hold on a fearsome but infinitely desirable thing weakening. He tried to find words to call it back, but his mind remained blank. Perhaps if he asked the God Emperor . . .

"Lord, if you would but tell me your thoughts on . . ."

"My thoughts vanish on contact!"

Leto stared down at Moneo. How strange were the majordomo's eyes perched there above that hawkish Atreides nose—free-verse eyes in a metronome face. Did Moneo hear that rhythmic pulsebeat? *Malky is coming! Malky is coming! Malky is coming!*

Moneo wanted to cry out in anguish. The thing he had felt—all gone! He put both his hands over his mouth.

"Your universe is a two-dimensional hourglass," Leto accused. "Why do you try to hold back the sand?"

Moneo lowered his hands and sighed. "Do you wish to hear about the wedding arrangements, Lord?"

"Don't be tiresome! Where is Hwi?"

"The Fish Speakers are preparing her for . . ."

"Have you consulted her about the arrangements?"

"Yes, Lord."

"She approved?"

"Yes, Lord, but she accused me of living for the quantity of activity and not for the quality."

"Isn't she marvelous, Moneo? Does she see the unrest among the Fish Speakers?"

"I think so, Lord."

"The idea of my marriage disturbs them."

"It's why I sent the Duncan away, Lord."

"Of course it is, and Siona with him to . . ."

"Lord, I know you have tested her and she . . ."

"She senses the Golden Path as deeply as you do, Moneo."

"Then why do I fear her, Lord?"

"Because you raise reason above all else."

"But I do not know the reason for my fear!"

Leto smiled. This was like playing bubble dice in an infinite bowl. Moneo's emotions were a marvelous play performed only on this stage. How near the edge he walked without ever seeing it!

"Moneo, why do you insist on taking pieces out of the continuum?" Leto asked. "When you see a spectrum, do you desire one color there above all the others?"

"Lord, I don't understand you!"

Leto closed his eyes, remembering the countless times he had heard this cry. The faces were an unseparated blend. He opened his eyes to erase them.

"As long as one human remains alive to see them, the colors will not suffer a linear *mortis* even if you die, Moneo."

"What is this thing of colors, Lord?"

"The continuum, the neverending, the Golden Path."

"But you see things which we do not, Lord!"

"Because you refuse!"

Moneo sank his chin to his chest. "Lord, I know you have evolved beyond the rest of us. That is why we worship you and . . ."

"Damn you, Moneo!"

Moneo jerked his head up and stared at Leto in terror.

"Civilizations collapse when their powers outrun their religions!" Leto said. "Why can't you see this? Hwi does."

"She is Ixian, Lord. Perhaps she . . ."

"She's a Fish Speaker! She has been from birth, born to serve me. No!" Leto raised one of his tiny hands as Moneo tried to speak. "The Fish Speakers are disturbed because I called them my brides, and now they see a stranger not trained in Siaynoq who knows it better than they."

"How can that be, Lord, when your Fish . . ."

"What are you saying? Each of us comes into being knowing who he is and what he is supposed to do."

Moneo opened his mouth but closed it without speaking.

"Small children know," Leto said. "It's only after adults have confused them that children hide this knowledge even from themselves. Moneo! Uncover yourself!"

"Lord, I cannot!" The words were torn from Moneo. He trembled with anguish. "I do not have your powers, your knowledge of . . ."

"Enough!"

Moneo fell silent. His body shook.

Leto spoke soothingly to him. "It's all right, Moneo. I asked too much of you and I can see your fatigue."

Slowly, Moneo's trembling subsided. He drew in deep, gulping breaths.

Leto said: "There will be some change in my Fremen wedding. We will not use the water rings of my sister, Ghanima. We will use, instead, the rings of my mother."

"The Lady Chani, Lord? But where are her rings?"

Leto twisted his bulk on the cart and pointed to the intersection of two cavernous spokes on his left where the dim light revealed the earliest burial niches of the Atreides on Arrakis. "In her tomb, the first niche. You will remove those rings, Moneo, and bring them to the ceremony."

Moneo stared across the gloomy distance of the crypt. "Lord . . . is it not a desecration to . . ."

"You forget, Moneo, who lives in me." He spoke then in Chani's voice: "I can do what I want with my water rings!"

Moneo cowered. "Yes, Lord. I will bring them with me to Tabur Village when . . ."

"Tabur Village?" Leto asked in his usual voice. "But I have changed my mind. We will be wed at Tuono Village!"

Most civilization is based on cowardice. It's so easy to civilize by teaching cowardice. You water down the standards which would lead to bravery. You restrain the will. You regulate the appetites. You fence in the horizons. You make a law for every movement. You deny the existence of chaos. You teach even the children to breathe slowly. You tame.

—THE STOLEN JOURNALS

Idaho stood aghast at his first close glimpse of Tuono Village. *That* was the home of Fremen?

The Fish Speaker troop had taken them from the Citadel at daybreak, Idaho and Siona bundled into a large ornithopter, accompanied by two smaller guard ships. And the flight had been slow, almost three hours. They had landed at a flat, round plastone hangar almost a kilometer from the village, separated from it by old dunes locked in shape with plantings of poverty grasses and a few scrubby bushes. As they came down, the wall directly behind the village had seemed to grow taller and taller, the village shrinking beneath such immensity.

"The Museum Fremen are kept generally uncontaminated by off-planet technology," Nayla had explained as the escort sealed the 'thopters into the low hangar. One of the troop already had been sent trotting off toward Tuono with the announcement of their arrival.

Siona had remained mostly silent all during the flight, but she had studied Nayla with covert intensity.

For a time during the march across the morning-lighted dunes,

Idaho had tried to imagine that he was back in the old days. Sand was visible in the plantings and, in the valleys between dunes, there was parched ground, yellow grass, the sticklike shrubs. Three vultures, their gap-tipped wings spread wide, circled in the vault of sky—*"the soaring search,"* Fremen had called it. Idaho had tried to explain this to Siona walking beside him. You worried about the carrion-eaters only when they began to descend.

"I have been told about vultures," she said, her voice cold.

Idaho had noted the perspiration on her upper lip. There was a spicy smell of sweat in the troop pressed close around them.

His imagination was not equal to the task of defocusing the differences between the past and this time. The issue stillsuits they wore were more for show than for efficient collection of the body's water. No true Fremen would have trusted his life to one of them, not even here, where the air smelled of nearby water. And the Fish Speakers of Nayla's troop did not walk in Fremen silence. They chattered among themselves like children.

Siona trudged beside him in sullen withdrawal, her attention frequently on the broad muscular back of Nayla, who strode along a few paces ahead of the troop.

What was between those two women? Idaho wondered. Nayla appeared devoted to Siona, hanging on Siona's every word, obeying every whim Siona uttered . . . except that Nayla would not deviate from the orders which brought them to Tuono Village. Still, Nayla deferred to Siona and called her "Commander." There was something deep between those two, something which aroused awe and fear in Nayla.

They came at last to a slope which dropped down to the village and the wall behind it. From the air, Tuono had been a cluster of glittering rectangles just outside the shadow of the wall. From this close vantage, though, it had been reduced to a cluster of decaying huts made even more pitiful by attempts to decorate the place. Bits of shiny minerals and scraps of metal picked out scroll designs on the building walls. A tattered green banner fluttered from a metal pole atop the largest structure. A fitful breeze brought the smell of garbage and uncovered cesspools to Idaho's nostrils. The central street of the village extended out across the sparsely planted sand toward the troop, ending in a ragged edge of broken paving.

A robed delegation waited near the building of the green flag, standing there expectantly with the Fish Speaker messenger Nayla had sent on ahead. Idaho counted eight in the delegation, all men in what appeared to be authentic Fremen robes of dark brown. A green head-band could be glimpsed beneath the hood on one of the delegation—the Naib, no doubt. Children waited to one side with flowers. Black-hooded women could be seen peering from side-streets in the background. Idaho found the whole scene distressing.

"Let's get it over with," Siona said.

Nayla nodded and led the way down the slope onto the street. Siona and Idaho stayed a few paces behind her. The rest of the troop straggled along after them, silent now and peering around with undisguised curiosity.

As Nayla neared the delegation, the one with the green headband stepped forward and bowed. He moved like an old man but Idaho saw that he was not old, barely into his middle years, the cheeks smooth and unwrinkled, a stubby nose with no scars from breath-filter tubes, and the eyes! The eyes revealed definite pupils, not the all-blue of spice addiction. They were brown eyes. Brown eyes in a Fremen!

"I am Garun," the man said as Nayla stopped in front of him. "I am Naib of this place. I give you a Fremen welcome to Tuono."

Nayla gestured over her shoulder at Siona and Idaho, who had stopped just behind her. "Are quarters prepared for your guests?"

"We Fremen are noted for our hospitality," Garun said. "All is ready."

Idaho sniffed at the sour smells and sounds of this place. He glanced through open windows of the flag-topped building on his right. The Atreides banner flying over that? The window opened into an auditorium with a low ceiling, a bandshell at the far end enclosing a small platform. He saw rows of seats, maroon carpeting on the floor. It had all the look of a stage setting, a place to entertain tourists.

The sound of shuffling feet brought Idaho's attention back to Garun. Children were pressing forward around the delegation, extending clumps of garish red flowers in their grimy hands. The flowers were wilted.

Garun addressed himself to Siona, correctly identifying the gold piping of Fish Speaker Command in her uniform.

"Will you wish a performance of our Fremen rituals?" he asked. "The music, perhaps? The dance?"

Nayla accepted a bunch of flowers from one of the children, sniffed them and sneezed.

Another urchin extended flowers toward Siona, lifting a wide-eyed stare toward her. She accepted the flowers without looking at the child. Idaho merely waved the children aside as they approached him. They hesitated, staring up at him, then scurried around him toward the rest of the troop.

Garun spoke to Idaho. "If you give them a few coins, they will not bother you."

Idaho shuddered. Was this the training for Fremen children?

Garun returned his attention to Siona. With Nayla listening, Garun began explaining the layout of his village.

Idaho moved away from them down the street, noting how glances flicked toward him and then avoided his gaze. He felt deeply offended by the surface decorations on the buildings, none of it disguising the evidence of decay. He stared in an open doorway at the auditorium. There was a harshness in Tuono, a struggling *something* behind the wilting flowers and the servile tone of Garun's voice. In another time and on another planet, this would have been a donkey-in-the-street village—rope-belted peasants pressing forward with petitions. He could hear the whine of supplication in Garun's voice. These were not Fremen! These poor creatures lived on the margins, trying to retain parts of an ancient wholeness. And all the while, that lost reality slipped farther and farther from their grasp. What had Leto created here? These *Museum* Fremen were lost to everything except a bare existence and the rote mouthing of old words which they did not understand and which they did not even pronounce correctly!

Returning to Siona, Idaho bent to study the cut of Garun's brown robe, seeing a tightness in it dictated by a need to conserve fabric. The gray slick of a stillsuit could be seen underneath, exposed to sunlight which no real Fremen would ever have let touch his stillsuit that way. Idaho looked at the rest of the delegation, noting an identical parsimonious treatment of fabric. It betrayed their emotional bent. Such garments allowed no expansive gestures, no freedom of movement. The robes were tight and confining in the way of these entire people!

Disgust propelling him, Idaho strode forward abruptly and parted Garun's robe to look at the stillsuit. Just as he suspected! The suit was another sham—no arms to it, no boot-pumps!

Garun pulled back, putting a hand to the knife hilt Idaho had exposed at the man's belt. "Here! What're you doing?" Garun demanded, his voice querulous. "You don't touch a Fremen thus!"

"You, a Fremen?" Idaho demanded. "I lived with Fremen! I fought by their sides against Harkonnens! I died with Fremen! You? You're a sham!"

Garun's knuckles went white on the knife haft. He addressed himself to Siona. "Who is this man?"

Nayla spoke up: "This is Duncan Idaho."

"The ghola?" Garun turned to look at Idaho's face. "We have never seen your like here before."

Idaho felt himself almost overcome with desire to cleanse this place even if it cost him his life, this diminished life which could be repeated endlessly by people who had no real concerns for him. *An older model, yes!* But this was no Fremen.

"Draw that knife or take your hand off it," Idaho said.

Garun jerked his hand away from the knife. "It is not a real knife," he said. "Only for decoration." His voice became eager. "But we have real knives, even crysknives! They are kept locked in the display cases to preserve them."

Idaho could not help himself. He threw his head back in laughter. Siona smiled, but Nayla looked thoughtful and the rest of the Fish Speaker troop drew into a close, watchful circle around them.

The laughter had an odd effect on Garun. He lowered his head and clasped his hands tightly together, but not before Idaho saw them trembling. When Garun peered upward once more, it was to look at Idaho from beneath heavy brows. Idaho felt abruptly sobered. It was as though some terrible boot had crushed Garun's ego into fearful subservience. There was watchful waiting in the man's eyes. And for no reason he could explain, Idaho remembered a passage from the Orange Catholic Bible. He asked himself: *Are these the meek who will outwait us all and inherit the universe?*

Garun cleared his throat, then: "Perhaps the ghola Duncan Idaho will witness our ways and our ritual and judge them?"

Idaho felt shamed by the plaintive request. He spoke without thinking: "I will teach you anything Fremen that I know." He looked up to see Nayla scowling at him. "It will help to pass the time," he said. "And who knows? It may return something of the true Fremen to this land."

Siona said: "We've no need to play old cultish games! Take us to our quarters."

Nayla lowered her head in embarrassment and spoke without looking at Siona. "Commander, there is a thing I have not ventured to tell you."

"That you must make sure we stay in this filthy place," Siona said.

"Oh, no!" Nayla looked up at Siona's face. "Where could you go? The Wall cannot be climbed and there is only the river beyond it, anyway. And in the other direction, it is the Sareer. Oh, no . . . it is something else." Nayla shook her head.

"Out with it!" Siona snapped.

"I am under the strictest orders, Commander, which I dare not disobey." Nayla glanced at the other members of the troop, then back to Siona. "You and the . . . Duncan Idaho are to be quartered together."

"My father's orders?"

"Lady Commander, they are said to be the orders of the God Emperor himself and we dare not disobey."

Siona looked full at Idaho. "You will remember my warning, Duncan, when last we spoke at the Citadel?"

"My hands are mine to do with as I wish," Idaho snarled. "I don't think you have any doubts about my wishes!"

She turned away from him after a curt nod and looked at Garun. "What does it matter where we bed in this disgusting place? Take us to our quarters."

Idaho found Garun's response fascinating—a turning of the head toward the ghola, shielding the face behind the Fremen hood, then a secret conspiratorial wink. Only then did Garun lead them away down the dirty street.

What is the most immediate danger to my stewardship? I will tell you. It is a true visionary, a person who has stood in the presence of God with the full knowledge of where he stands. Visionary ecstasy releases energies which are like the energies of sex—uncaring for anything except creation. One act of creation can be much like another. Everything depends upon the vision.

—THE STOLEN JOURNALS

Leto lay without his cart on the high, sheltered balcony of his Little Citadel tower, subduing a fretfulness which he knew came from the necessary delays putting off the date of his wedding to Hwi Noree. He stared toward the southwest. Somewhere off there beyond the darkening horizon, the Duncan, Siona and their companions had been six days in Tuono Village.

The delays are my own fault, Leto thought. *I am the one who changed the place for the wedding, making it necessary for poor Moneo to revise all of his preparations.*

And now, of course, there was the matter of Malky.

None of these necessities could be explained to Moneo, who could be heard stirring about within the central chamber of the aerie, worrying about his absence from the command post where he directed the *festive* preparations. Moneo was such a worrier!

Leto looked toward the setting sun. It floated low to the horizon, faded a dim orange by a recent storm. Rain crouched low in the clouds to the south beyond the Sareer now. In a prolonged silence, Leto had watched the rain there for a time which had stretched out with no beginning or end. The clouds had grown out of a hard gray sky, rain walking in visible lines. He had felt himself clothed in memories that came unbidden. The mood was hard to shake off and, without even thinking, he muttered the remembered lines of an ancient verse.

"Did you speak, Lord?" Moneo's voice came from close beside Leto. By merely turning his eyes, Leto could see the faithful majordomo standing attentively waiting.

Leto translated into Galach as he quoted: "The nightingale nests in the plum tree, but what will she do with the wind?"

"Is that a question, Lord?"

"An old question. The answer is simple. Let the nightingale keep to her flowers."

"I don't understand, Lord."

"Stop mouthing the obvious, Moneo. It disturbs me when you do that."

"Forgive me, Lord."

"What else can I do?" Leto studied Moneo's downcast features. "You and I, Moneo, whatever else we do, we provide good theater."

Moneo peered at Leto's face. "Lord?"

"The rites of the religious festival of Bacchus were the seeds of Greek theater, Moneo. Religion often leads to theater. They will have fine theater out of us." Once more, Leto turned and looked at the southwest horizon.

There was a wind there now piling up the clouds. Leto thought he could hear driven sand blustering along the dunes, but there was only resonant quiet in the tower aerie, a quiet with the faintest of wind hiss behind it.

"The clouds," he whispered. "I would take a cup of moonlight once more, an ancient sea barge at my feet, thin clouds clinging to my darkling sky, the blue-gray cloak around my shoulders and horses neighing nearby."

"My Lord is troubled," Moneo said. The compassion in his voice wrenched at Leto.

"The bright shadows of my pasts," Leto said. "They never leave me in peace. I listened for a soothing sound, the bell of a country town at nightfall, and it told me only that I am the sound and soul of this place."

As he spoke, darkness enclosed the tower. Automatic lights came on around them. Leto kept his attention directed outward where a thin melon slice of First Moon drifted above the clouds with orange planet-light revealing the satellite's full circle.

"Lord, why have we come out here?" Moneo asked. "Why won't you tell me?"

"I wanted the benefit of your surprise," Leto said. "A Guild lighter will land beside us out here soon. My Fish Speakers bring Malky to me."

Moneo inhaled a quick breath and held it a moment before exhaling. "Hwi's . . . uncle? That Malky?"

"You are surprised that you had no warning of this," Leto said.

Moneo felt a chill all through his body. "Lord, when you wish to keep things secret from . . ."

"Moneo?" Leto spoke in a softly persuasive tone. "I know that Malky offered you greater temptations than any other . . ."

"Lord! I never . . ."

"I know that, Moneo." Still in that soft tone. "But surprise has shocked your memories alive. You are armed for anything I may require of you."

"What . . . what does my Lord . . ."

"Perhaps we will have to dispose of Malky. He is a problem."

"Me? You want me to . . ."

"Perhaps."

Moneo swallowed, then: "The Reverend Mother . . ."

"Anteac is dead. She served me well, but she is dead. There was extreme violence when my Fish Speakers attacked the . . . *place* where Malky lay hidden."

"We are better off without Anteac," Moneo said.

"I appreciate your distrust of the Bene Gesserit, but I would that Anteac had left us in another way. She was faithful to us, Moneo."

"A Reverend Mother was . . ."

"Both the Bene Tleilax and the Guild wanted Malky's secret," Leto said. "When they saw us move against the Ixians, they struck ahead of my Fish Speakers. Anteac . . . well, she could only delay them a bit, but it was enough. My Fish Speakers invested the place . . ."

"Malky's *secret,* Lord?"

"When a thing vanishes," Leto said, "that is as much of a message as when a thing suddenly appears. The empty spaces are always worthy of our study."

"What does my Lord mean, *empty* . . ."

"Malky did not die! Certainly I would have known that. Where did he go when he vanished?"

"Vanished . . . from you, Lord? Do you mean that the Ixians . . ."

"They have improved upon a device they gave me long ago. They improved it slowly and subtly, hidden shells within hidden shells, but I noted the shadows. I was surprised. I was pleased."

Moneo thought about this. *A device which concealed . . . Ahhhh!* The God Emperor had mentioned a thing on several occasions, a way of concealing the thoughts he recorded. Moneo spoke:

"And Malky brings the secret of . . ."

"Oh, yes! But that is not Malky's real secret. He holds another thing in his bosom which he does not think that I suspect."

"Another . . . but, Lord, if they can hide even from you . . ."

"Many can do that now, Moneo. They scattered when my Fish Speakers attacked. The secret of the Ixian device is spread far and wide."

Moneo's eyes went wide with alarm. "Lord, if anyone . . ."

"If they learn to be clever, they will leave no tracks," Leto said. "Tell me, Moneo, what does Nayla say about the Duncan? Does she resent reporting directly to you?"

"Whatever my Lord commands . . ." Moneo cleared his throat. He could not fathom why his God Emperor spoke of hidden tracks, the Duncan and Nayla in the same breath.

"Yes, of course," Leto said. "Whatever I command, Nayla obeys. And what does she say of the Duncan?"

"He has not tried to breed with Siona, if that is my Lord's . . ."

"But what does he do with my puppet Naib, Garun, and the other Museum Fremen?"

"He speaks to them of the old ways, of the wars against the Harkonnens, of the first Atreides here on Arrakis."

"On Dune!"

"Dune, yes."

"It's because there's no more Dune that there are no more Fremen," Leto said. "Have you conveyed my message to Nayla?"

"Lord, why do you add to your peril?"

"Did you convey my message?"

"The messenger has been sent to Tuono, but I could still call her back."

"You will *not* call her back!"

"But, Lord . . ."

"What will she say to Nayla?"

"That . . . that it is your command for Nayla to continue in absolute and unquestioning obedience of my daughter except insofar . . . Lord! This is dangerous!"

"Dangerous? Nayla is a Fish Speaker. She will obey me."

"But Siona . . . Lord, I fear that my daughter does not serve you with all of her heart. And Nayla is . . ."

"Nayla must not deviate."

"Lord, let us hold your wedding in some other place."

"No!"

"Lord, I know that your vision has revealed . . ."

"The Golden Path endures, Moneo. You know that as well as I."

Moneo sighed. "Infinity is yours, Lord. I do not question the . . ." He broke off as a monstrous shuddering roar shook the tower, louder and louder.

Both of them turned toward the sound—a descending plume of blue-orange light filled with swirling shockwaves came down to the desert less than a kilometer away to the south.

"Ahhh, my guest arrives," Leto said. "I will send you down on my cart, Moneo. Bring only Malky back with you. Tell the Guildsmen this has earned my forgiveness, then send them away."

"Your for . . . yes, Lord. But if they have the secret of . . ."

"They serve my purpose, Moneo. You must do the same. Bring Malky to me."

Obediently, Moneo went to the cart which lay in shadows at the far side of the aerie chamber. He clambered on it, watched a mouth of night appear in the Wall. A landing-lip extruded into that night. The cart drifted outward, feather-light, and floated at an angle to the sand beside a Guild lighter which stood upright like a distorted miniature of the Little Citadel's tower.

Leto watched from the balcony, his front segments lifted slightly to provide him a better viewing angle. His acute eyesight identified the white movement of Moneo standing on the cart in the moonlight. Long-legged Guild servitors came out with a litter which they slid onto the cart, standing there a moment in conversation with Moneo. When they left, Leto closed the cart's bubble cover and saw moonlight reflected from it. At his beckoning thought, the cart and its burden returned to the landing-lip. The Guild lighter lifted in its noisy rumbling while Leto was bringing the cart into the chamber's lights, closing the entrance behind it. Leto opened the bubble cover. Sand grated beneath him as he rolled to the litter and lifted his front segments to peer in at Malky who lay as though sleeping, lashed into the litter by broad gray elastic bindings. The man's face was ashen under dark gray hair.

How he has aged, Leto thought.

Moneo stepped down off the cart and looked back at the litter's occupant. "He is injured, Lord. They want to send a medical . . ."

"They wanted to send a spy."

Leto studied Malky—the dark wrinkled skin, the sunken cheeks, that sharp nose at such contrast with the rounded oval of his face. The heavy eyebrows had turned almost white. There but for a lifetime of testosterone . . . yes.

Malky's eyes opened. Such a shock to find evil in those doe-like brown eyes! A smile twitched Malky's mouth.

"Lord Leto." Malky's voice was little more than a husky whisper. His eyes turned right, focusing on the majordomo. "And Moneo. Forgive me for not rising to the occasion."

"Are you in pain?" Leto asked.

"Sometimes." Malky's eyes moved to study his surroundings. "Where are the *houris*?"

"I'm afraid I must deny you that pleasure, Malky."

"Just as well," Malky husked. "I don't really feel up to their demands. Those were not *houris* you sent after me, Leto."

"They were professional in their obedience to me," Leto said.

"They were bloody hunters!"

"Anteac was the hunter. My Fish Speakers were merely the clean-up crew."

Moneo shifted his attention from one speaker to the other, back and forth. There were disturbing undertones in this conversation. Despite the huskiness, Malky sounded almost flippant . . . but then he had always been that way. A dangerous man!

Leto said: "Just before your arrival, Moneo and I were discussing Infinity."

"Poor Moneo," Malky said.

Leto smiled. "Do you remember, Malky? You once asked me to demonstrate Infinity."

"You said no Infinity exists to be demonstrated." Malky swept his gaze toward Moneo. "Leto likes to play with paradox. He knows all the tricks of language that have ever been discovered."

Moneo put down a surge of anger. He felt excluded from this conversation, an object of amusement by two superior beings. Malky and the God Emperor were almost like two old friends reliving the pleasures of a mutual past.

"Moneo accuses me of being the sole possessor of Infinity," Leto said. "He refuses to believe that he has just as much of Infinity as I have."

Malky stared up at Leto. "You see, Moneo? You see how tricky he is with words?"

"Tell me about your niece, Hwi Noree," Leto said.

"Is it true, Leto, what they say? That you are going to wed the gentle Hwi?"

"It is true."

Malky chuckled, then grimaced with pain. "They did terrible damage to me, Leto," he whispered, then: "Tell me, old worm . . ."

Moneo gasped.

Malky took a moment to recover from pain, then: "Tell me, old worm, is there a monster penis hidden in that monster body of yours? What a shock for the gentle Hwi!"

"I told you the truth about that long ago," Leto said.

"Nobody tells the truth," Malky husked.

"You often told me the truth," Leto said. "Even when you didn't know it."

"That's because you're cleverer than the rest of us."

"Will you tell me about Hwi?"

"I think you already know it."

"I want to hear it from you," Leto said. "Did you get help from the Tleilaxu?"

"They gave us knowledge, nothing more. Everything else we did for ourselves."

"I thought it was not the Tleilaxu's doing."

Moneo could no longer contain his curiosity. "Lord, what is this of Hwi and Tleilaxu? Why do you . . ."

"Here there, old friend Moneo," Malky said, rolling his gaze toward the majordomo. "Don't you know what he . . ."

"I was never your friend!" Moneo snapped.

"Companion among the *houris* then," Malky said.

"Lord," Moneo said, turning toward Leto, "why do you speak of . . ."

"Shhh, Moneo," Leto said. "We are tiring your old companion and I have things to learn from him yet."

"Did you ever wonder, Leto," Malky asked, "why Moneo never tried to take the whole shebang away from you?"

"The *what*?" Moneo demanded.

"Another of Leto's old words," Malky said. "She and bang—shebang.

It's perfect. Why don't you rename your Empire, Leto? The Grand Shebang!"

Leto raised a hand to silence Moneo. "Will you tell me, Malky? About Hwi?"

"Just a few tiny cells from my body," Malky said. "Then the carefully nurtured growth and education—everything an exact opposite to your old friend Malky. We did it all in the no-room where you cannot see!"

"But I notice when something vanishes," Leto said.

"No-room?" Moneo asked, then as the import of Malky's words sank home: "You? You and Hwi . . ."

"That is the shape I saw in the shadows," Leto said.

Moneo looked full at Leto's face. "Lord, I will call off the wedding. I will say . . ."

"You will do nothing of the kind!"

"But Lord, if she and Malky are . . ."

"Moneo," Malky husked. "Your Lord commands and you must obey!"

That mocking tone! Moneo glared at Malky.

"The exact opposite of Malky," Leto said. "Didn't you hear him?"

"What could be better?" Malky asked.

"But surely, Lord, if you now know . . ."

"Moneo," Leto said, "you are beginning to disturb me."

Moneo fell into abashed silence.

Leto said: "That's better. You know, Moneo, once tens of thousands of years ago when I was another person, I made a mistake."

"You, a mistake?" Malky mocked.

Leto merely smiled. "My mistake was compounded by the beautiful way in which I expressed it."

"Tricks with words," Malky taunted.

"Indeed! This is what I said: 'The present is distraction; the future a dream; only memory can unlock the meaning of life.' Aren't those beautiful words, Malky?"

"Exquisite, old worm."

Moneo put a hand over his mouth.

425 GOD EMPEROR OF DUNE 425

"But my words were a foolish lie," Leto said. "I knew it at the time, but I was infatuated with the *beautiful* words. No—memory unlocks no meanings. Without anguish of the spirit, which is a wordless experience, there are no meanings anywhere."

"I fail to see the meaning of the anguish caused me by your bloody Fish Speakers," Malky said.

"You're suffering no anguish," Leto said.

"If you were in this body, you'd . . ."

"That's just physical pain," Leto said. "It will end soon."

"Then when will I know the anguish?" Malky asked.

"Perhaps later."

Leto flexed his front segments away from Malky to face Moneo. "Do you really serve the Golden Path, Moneo?"

"Ahhh, the Golden Path," Malky taunted.

"You know I do, Lord," Moneo said.

"Then you must promise me," Leto said, "that what you have learned here must never pass your lips. Not by word or sign can you reveal it."

"I promise, Lord."

"He promises, Lord," Malky sneered.

One of Leto's tiny hands gestured at Malky, who lay staring up at the blunt profile of a face within its gray cowl. "For reasons of old admiration and . . . many other reasons, I cannot kill Malky. I cannot even ask it of you . . . yet he must be eliminated."

"Ohhh, how clever you are!" Malky said.

"Lord, if you will wait at the other end of the chamber," Moneo said. "Perhaps when you return Malky no longer will be a problem."

"He's going to do it," Malky husked. "Gods below! He's going to do it."

Leto squirmed away and went to the shadowed limit of the chamber, keeping his attention on the faint arc of a line which would become an opening into the night if he merely converted the wish into a thought-of-command. What a long drop that would be out there—just roll off the landing-lip. He doubted that even his body would survive it. But there was no water in the sand beneath his tower and he could feel the Golden Path winking in and out of existence merely because he allowed himself to think of such an end.

"Leto!" Malky called from behind him.

Leto heard the litter grating on the wind-scattered sand which peppered the floor of his aerie.

Once more, Malky called: "Leto, you are the best! There's no evil in this universe which can surpass . . ."

A sodden thump shut off Malky's voice. *A blow to the throat,* Leto thought. *Yes, Moneo knows that one.* There came the sound of the balcony's transparent shield sliding open, the rasping of the litter on the rail, then silence.

Moneo will have to bury the body in the sand, Leto thought. *There is as yet no worm to come and devour the evidence.* Leto turned then and looked across the chamber. Moneo stood leaning over the railing, peering down . . . down . . . down . . .

I cannot pray for you, Malky, nor for you, Moneo, Leto thought. *I may be the only religious consciousness in the Empire because I am truly alone . . . so I cannot pray.*

You cannot understand history unless you understand its flowings, its currents and the ways leaders move within such forces. A leader tries to perpetuate the conditions which demand his leadership. Thus, the leader requires the *outsider*. I caution you to examine my career with care. I am both leader *and* outsider. Do not make the mistake of assuming that I only created the Church which was the State. That was my function as leader and I had many historical models to use as pattern. For a clue to my role as outsider, look at the arts of my time. The arts are barbaric. The favorite poetry? The Epic. The popular dramatic ideal? Heroism. Dances? Wildly abandoned. From Moneo's viewpoint, he is correct in describing this as dangerous. It stimulates the imagination. It makes people feel the lack of that which I have taken from them. What did I take from them? The right to participate in history.

—THE STOLEN JOURNALS

Idaho, stretched out on his cot with his eyes closed, heard a weight drop onto the other cot. He sat up into the midafternoon light which slanted through the room's single window at a sharp angle, reflecting off the white-tiled floor onto the light yellow walls. Siona, he saw, had come in and stretched herself on her cot. She already was reading one of the books she carried around with her in a green fabric pack.

Why books? he wondered.

He swung his feet to the floor and glanced around the room. How could this high-ceilinged, spacious *box* be considered even remotely Fremen? A wide table/desk of some dark brown local plastic separated the two cots. There were two doors. One led directly outside across a garden. The other admitted them to a luxurious bath whose pale blue tiles glistened under a broad skylight. The bath contained, among its many functional services, a sunken tub and a shower, each at least two meters square. The door to this sybaritic space remained open and Idaho could hear water running out of the tub. Siona appeared oddly fond of bathing in an excess of water.

Stilgar, Idaho's Naib of the ancient days on Dune, would have looked on that room with scorn. "Shameful!" he would have said. "Decadent! Weak!" Stilgar would have used many scornful words about this entire village which dared to compare itself with a true Fremen sietch.

Paper rustled as Siona turned a page. She lay with her head propped on two pillows, a thin white robe covering her body. The robe still revealed clinging wetness from her bath.

Idaho shook his head. What was it on those pages which held her interest this way? She had been reading and rereading since their arrival at Tuono. The volumes were thin but numerous, bearing only numbers on their black bindings. Idaho had seen a number *nine*.

Swinging his feet to the floor, he stood and went to the window. There was an old man out there at a distance, digging in flowers. The garden was protected by buildings on three sides. The flowers bore large blossoms—red on the outside but, when they unfolded, white in the center. The old man's uncovered gray hair was a kind of blossom waving among the floral white and jeweled buds. Idaho smelled moldering leaves and freshly turned dirt against a background of pungent floral perfume.

A Fremen tending flowers in the open!

Siona volunteered nothing about her strange reading matter. *She's taunting me*, Idaho thought. *She wants me to ask.*

He tried not to think about Hwi. Rage threatened to engulf him when he did. He remembered the Fremen word for that intense emotion: *kanawa*, the iron ring of jealousy. *Where is Hwi? What is she doing at this moment?*

The door from the garden opened without a knock and Teishar, an aide to Garun, entered. Teishar had a dead colored face full of dark wrinkles. His eyes were sunken with pale yellow around the pupils. Teishar wore a brown robe. He had hair like old grass that had been left out to rot. He seemed unnecessarily ugly, like a dark and elemental spirit. Teishar closed the door and stood there looking at them.

Siona's voice came from behind Idaho. "Well, what is it?"

Idaho noticed then that Teishar seemed strangely excited, vibrating with it.

"The God Emperor . . ." Teishar cleared his throat and began again. "The God Emperor will come to Tuono!"

Siona sat upright on the bed, folding her white robe over her knees. Idaho glanced back at her, then once more to Teishar.

"He will be wed here, here in Tuono!" Teishar said. "It will be done in the ancient Fremen way! The God Emperor and his bride will be guests of Tuono!"

Full in the grip of *kanawa*, Idaho glared at him, fists clenched. Teishar bobbed his head briefly, turned and let himself out, shutting the door hard.

"Let me read you something, Duncan," Siona said.

Idaho was a moment understanding her words. Fists still clenched at his sides, he turned and looked at her. Siona sat on the edge of her cot, a book in her lap. She took his attention as agreement.

"Some believe," she read, "that you must compromise integrity with a certain amount of dirty work before you can put genius to work. They say the compromise begins when you come out of the *sanctus* intending to realize your ideals. Moneo says my solution is to stay within the *sanctus*, sending others to do my dirty work."

She looked up at Idaho. "The God Emperor—his own words."

Slowly, Idaho relaxed his fists. He knew he needed this distraction. And it interested him that Siona had emerged from her silence.

"What is that book?" he asked.

Briefly, she told him how she and her companions had stolen the Citadel charts and the copies of Leto's journals.

"Of course you knew about that," she said. "My father has made it plain that spies betrayed our raid."

He saw the tears latent in her eyes. "Nine of you killed by the wolves?"

She nodded.

"You're a lousy Commander!" he said.

She bristled but before she could speak, he asked: "Who translated them for you?"

"This is from Ix. They say the Guild found the Key."

"We already knew our God Emperor indulged in expedience," Idaho said. "Is that all he has to say?"

"Read it for yourself." She rummaged in her pack beside the cot and came up with the first volume of the translation, which she tossed across to his cot. As Idaho returned to the cot, she demanded: "What do you mean I'm a lousy Commander?"

"Wasting nine of your friends that way."

"You fool!" She shook her head. "You obviously never saw those wolves!"

He picked up the book and found it heavy, realizing then that it had been printed on crystal paper. "You should have armed yourselves against the wolves," he said, opening the volume.

"What arms? Any arms we could get would've been useless!"

"Lasguns?" he asked, turning a page.

"Touch a lasgun on Arrakis and the Worm knows it!"

He turned another page. "Your friends got lasguns eventually."

"And look what it got them!"

Idaho read a line, then: "Poisons were available."

She swallowed convulsively.

Idaho looked at her. "You did poison the wolves after all, didn't you?"

Her voice was almost a whisper: "Yes."

"Then why didn't you do that in advance?" he asked.

"We . . . didn't . . . know . . . we . . . could."

"But you didn't test it," Idaho said. He turned back to the open volume. "A lousy Commander."

"He's so devious!" Siona said.

Idaho read a passage in the volume before returning his attention to Siona. "That hardly describes him. Have you read all of this?"

"Every word! Some of them several times."

Idaho looked at the open page and read aloud: "I have created what I intended—a powerful spiritual tension throughout my Empire. Few sense the strength of it. With what energies did I create this condition? I am not that strong. The only power I possess is the control of individual prosperity. That is the sum of all the things I do. Then why do people seek my presence for other reasons? What could lead them to certain death in the futile attempt to reach my presence? Do they want to be saints? Do they think that *thus* they gain the vision of God?"

"He's the ultimate cynic," Siona said, tears apparent in her voice.

"How did he test you?" Idaho asked.

"He showed me a . . . he showed me his Golden Path."

"That's convenient . . ."

"It's real enough, Duncan." She looked up at him, her eyes glistening with unshed tears. "But if it was *ever* a reason for our *God* Emperor, it is not reason for what he has become!"

Idaho inhaled deeply, then: "The Atreides come to this!"

"The Worm must go!" Siona said.

"I wonder when he's arriving," Idaho said.

"Garun's little rat friend didn't say."

"We must ask," Idaho said.

"We have no weapons," Siona said.

"Nayla has a lasgun," he said. "We have knives . . . rope. I saw rope in one of Garun's storage rooms."

"Against the Worm?" she asked. "Even if we could get Nayla's lasgun, you know it won't touch him."

"But is his cart proof against it?" Idaho asked.

"I don't trust Nayla," Siona said.

"Doesn't she obey you?"

"Yes, but . . ."

"We will proceed one step at a time," Idaho said. "Ask Nayla if she would use her lasgun against the Worm's cart."

"And if she refuses?"

"Kill her."

Siona stood, tossing her book aside.

"How will the Worm come to Tuono?" Idaho asked. "He's too big and heavy for an ordinary 'thopter."

"Garun will tell us," she said. "But I think he will come as he usually travels." She looked up at the ceiling which concealed the Sareer's perimeter Wall. "I think he will come on peregrination with his entire crew. He will come along the Royal Road and drop down to here on suspensors." She looked at Idaho. "What of Garun?"

"A strange man," Idaho said. "He wants most desperately to be a real Fremen. He knows he is not anything like what they were in my day."

"What were they like in your day, Duncan?"

"They had a saying which describes it," Idaho said.

"You should never be in the company of anyone with whom you would not want to die."

"Did you say this to Garun?" she asked.

"Yes."

"And his response?"

"He said I was the only such person he had ever met."

"Garun may be wiser than any of us," she said.

You think power may be the most unstable of all human achievements? Then what of the apparent exceptions to this inherent instability? Some families endure. Very powerful religious bureaucracies have been known to endure. Consider the relationship between faith and power. Are they mutually exclusive when each depends upon the other? The Bene Gesserit have been reasonably secure within the loyal walls of faith for thousands of years. But where has their power gone?

—THE STOLEN JOURNALS

Moneo spoke in a petulant tone: "Lord, I wish you had given me more time."

He stood outside the Citadel in the short shadows of noon. Leto lay directly in front of him on the Imperial Cart, its bubble hood retracted. He had been touring the environs with Hwi Noree, who occupied a newly installed seat within the bubble cover's perimeter and just beside Leto's face. Hwi appeared merely curious about all the bustle which was beginning to increase around them.

How calm she is, Moneo thought. He repressed an involuntary shudder at what he had learned of her from Malky. The God Emperor was right. Hwi was exactly what she appeared to be—an ultimately sweet and sensible human being. *Would she really have mated with me?* Moneo wondered.

Distractions drew his attention away from her. While Leto had toured Hwi around the Citadel on the suspensor-borne cart, a great troop of courtiers and Fish Speakers had been assembled here, all the courtiers in celebration finery, brilliant reds and golds dominant. The Fish Speakers wore their best dark blues, distinguished only by the different colors in the piping and hawks. A baggage caravan on suspensor sleds had been drawn up at the rear with Fish Speakers to pull it. The air was full of dust and the sounds and smells of excitement. Most of the courtiers had reacted with dismay when told their destination. Some had immediately purchased their own tents and pavilions. These had been sent on ahead with the other impediments piled now on the sand just outside Tuono's view. The Fish Speakers in the entourage were not taking this in a festive mood. They had complained loudly when told they could not carry lasguns.

"Just a *little* more time, Lord," Moneo was saying. "I still don't know how we will . . ."

"There's no substitute for time in solving many problems," Leto said. "However, you can place too much reliance on it. I can accept no more delays."

"We will be three days just getting there," Moneo complained.

Leto thought about that time—the swift walk-trot-walk of a peregrination . . . one hundred and eighty kilometers. Yes, three days.

"I'm sure you've made good arrangements for the way-stops," Leto said. "Plenty of hot water for the muscle cramps?"

"We'll be comfortable enough," Moneo said, "but I don't like leaving the Citadel in these times! And you know why!"

"We have communications devices, loyal assistants. The Guild is suitably chastened. Calm yourself, Moneo."

"We could hold the ceremony in the Citadel!"

For answer, Leto closed the bubble cover around him, isolating Hwi with him.

"Is there danger, Leto?" she asked.

"There's always danger."

Moneo sighed, turned and trotted toward where the Royal Road began its long climb eastward before turning south around the Sareer.

Leto set his cart in motion behind the majordomo, heard his motley troop fall into step behind them.

"Are we all moving?" Leto asked.

Hwi glanced backward around him. "Yes." She turned toward his face. "Why was Moneo being so difficult?"

"Moneo has discovered that the instant which has just left him is forever beyond his reach."

"He has been very moody and distracted since you returned from the Little Citadel. He's not the same at all."

"He is an Atreides, my love, and you were designed to please an Atreides."

"It's not that. I would know if it were that."

"Yes . . . well, I think Moneo has also discovered the reality of death."

"What's it like at the Little Citadel when you're there with Moneo?" she asked.

"It's the loneliest place in my Empire."

"I think you avoid my questions," she said.

"No, Love. I share your concern for Moneo, but no explanation of mine will help him now. Moneo is trapped. He has learned that it is difficult to live in the present, pointless to live in the future and impossible to live in the past."

"I think it's you who have trapped him, Leto."

"But he must free himself."

"Why can't you free him?"

"Because he thinks my memories are his key to freedom. He thinks I am building our future out of our past."

"Isn't that always the way of it, Leto?"

"No, dear Hwi."

"Then how is it?"

"Most believe that a satisfactory future requires a return to an idealized past, a past which never in fact existed."

"And you with all of your memories know otherwise."

Leto turned his face within its cowl to stare at her, probing . . .

remembering. Out of the multitudes within him, he could form a composite, a genetic suggestion of Hwi, but the suggestion fell far short of the living flesh. That was it, of course. The past became row-on-row of eyes staring outward like the eyes of gasping fish, but Hwi was vibrant life. Her mouth was set in Grecian curves designed for a Delphic chant, but she hummed no prophetic syllables. She was content to live, an opening person like a flower perpetually unfolding into fragrant blossom.

"Why are you looking at me like that?" she asked.

"I was basking in the love of you."

"Love, yes." She smiled. "I think that since we cannot share the love of the flesh, we must share the love of the soul. Would you share that with me, Leto?"

He was taken aback. "You ask about my soul?"

"Surely others have asked."

He spoke shortly: "My soul digests its experiences, nothing more."

"Have I asked too much of you?" she asked.

"I think that you cannot ask too much of me."

"Then I presume upon our love to disagree with you. My Uncle Malky talked about your soul."

He found that he could not respond. She took his silence as an invitation to continue. "He said that you were the ultimate artist at probing the soul, your own soul first."

"But your Uncle Malky denied that he had a soul of his own!"

She heard the harshness in his voice, but was not deterred. "Still, I think he was right. You are the genius of the soul, the brilliant one."

"You need only the plodding perseverance of duration," he said. "No brilliance."

They were well onto the long climb to the top of the Sareer's perimeter Wall now. He lowered his cart's wheels and deactivated the suspensors.

Hwi spoke softly, her voice barely audible above the grating sound of the cart's wheels and the running feet all around them. "May I call you Love, anyway?"

He spoke around a remembered tightness in a throat which was no longer completely human. "Yes."

"I was born an Ixian, Love," she said. "Why don't I share their mechanical view of our universe? Do you know my view, Leto, my love?"

He could only stare at her.

"I sense the supernatural at every turning," she said.

Leto's voice rasped, sounding angry even to him: "Each person creates his own supernatural."

"Don't be angry with me, Love."

Again, that awful rasping: "It is impossible for me to be angry with you."

"But something happened between you and Malky once," she said. "He would never tell me what it was, but he said he often wondered why you spared him."

"Because of what he taught me."

"What happened between you two, Love?"

"I would rather not talk about Malky."

"Please, Love. I feel that it's important for me to know."

"I suggested to Malky that there might be some things men should not invent."

"And that's all?"

"No." He spoke reluctantly. "My words angered him. He said: 'You think that in a world without birds, men would not invent aircraft! What a fool you are! Men can invent anything!' "

"He called you a fool?" There was shock in Hwi's voice.

"He was right. And although he denied it, he spoke the truth. He taught me that there was a reason for running away from inventions."

"Then you fear the Ixians?"

"Of course I do! They can invent catastrophe."

"Then what could you do?"

"Run faster. History is a constant race between invention and catastrophe. Education helps but it's never enough. You also must run."

"You are sharing your soul with me, Love. Do you know that?"

Leto looked away from her and focused on Moneo's back, the motions of the majordomo, the tucked-in pretenses of secrecy so apparent there. The procession had come off the first gentle incline. It turned now to begin the climb onto Ringwall West. Moneo moved as he had always moved, one foot ahead of another, aware of the ground where he would place each step, but there was something new in the major-domo. Leto could feel the man drawing away, no longer content to march beside his Lord's cowled face, no longer trying to match himself to his master's destiny. Off to the east, the Sareer waited. Off to the west, there was the river, the plantations. Moneo looked neither left nor right. He had seen another destination.

"You do not answer me," Hwi said.

"You already know the answer."

"Yes. I am beginning to understand something of you," she said. "I can sense some of your fears. And I think I already know where it is that you live."

He turned a startled glance on her and found himself locked in her gaze. It was astonishing. He could not move his eyes away from her. A profound fear coursed through and he felt his hands begin to twitch.

"You live where the fear of being and the love of being are com-bined, all in one person," she said.

He could not blink.

"You are a mystic," she said, "gentle to yourself only because you are in the middle of that universe looking outward, looking in ways that others cannot. You fear to share this, yet you want to share it more than anything else."

"What have you seen?" he whispered.

"I have no inner eye, no inner voices," she said. "But I have seen my Lord Leto, whose soul I love, and I *know* the only thing that you truly understand."

He broke from her gaze, fearful of what she might say. The trem-bling of his hands could be felt all through his front segment.

"Love, that is what you understand," she said. "Love, and that is all of it."

His hands stopped trembling. A tear rolled down each of his cheeks.

When the tears touched his cowl, wisps of blue smoke erupted. He sensed the burning and was thankful for the pain.

"You have faith in life," Hwi said. "I know that the courage of love can reside only in this faith."

She reached out with her left hand and brushed the tears from his cheeks. It surprised him that the cowl did not react with its ordinary reflex to prevent the touch.

"Do you know," he asked, "that since I have become thus, you are the first person to touch my cheeks?"

"But I know what you are and what you were," she said.

"What I was . . . ahhh, Hwi. What I was has become only this face, and all the rest is lost in the shadows of memory . . . hidden . . . gone."

"Not hidden from me, Love."

He looked directly at her, no longer afraid to lock gazes. "Is it possible that the Ixians know what they have created in you?"

"I assure you, Leto, love of my soul, that they do not know. You are the first person, the only person to whom I have ever completely revealed myself."

"Then I will not mourn for what might have been," he said. "Yes, my love, I will share my soul with you."

Think of it as plastic memory, this force within you which trends you and your fellows toward tribal forms. This plastic memory seeks to return to its ancient shape, the tribal society. It is all around you—the feudatory, the diocese, the corporation, the platoon, the sports club, the dance troupes, the rebel cell, the planning council, the prayer group ... each with its master and servants, its host and parasites. And the swarms of alienating devices (including these very words!) tend eventually to be enlisted in the argument for a return to "those better times." I despair of teaching you other ways. You have square thoughts which resist circles.

—THE STOLEN JOURNALS

Idaho found he could manage the climb without thinking about it. This body grown by the Tleilaxu remembered things the Tleilaxu did not even suspect. His original youth might be lost in the eons, but his muscles were Tleilaxu-young and he could bury his childhood in forgetfulness while he climbed. In that childhood, he had learned survival by flight into the high rocks of his home planet. It did not matter that these rocks in front of him now had been brought here by men, they also had been shaped by ages of weather.

The morning sun was hot on Idaho's back. He could hear Siona's efforts to reach the relatively simple support position of a narrow ledge far below him. The position was virtually useless to Idaho, but it had been the argument which had brought Siona finally into agreement that they should attempt this climb.

They.

She had objected that he might try it alone.

Nayla, three of her Fish Speaker aides, Garun and three chosen from his Museum Fremen waited on the sand at the foot of the barrier Wall which enclosed the Sareer.

Idaho did not think about the Wall's height. He thought only about where he would next put a hand or a foot. He thought about the coil of light rope around his shoulders. That rope was the *tallness* of this Wall. He had measured it out on the ground, triangulating across the sand, not counting his steps. When the rope was long enough it was long enough. The Wall was as high as the rope was long. Any other way of thinking could only dull his mind.

Feeling for handholds which he could not see, Idaho groped his way up the sheer face . . . well, not quite sheer. Wind and sand and even some rain, the forces of cold and heat, had been at their erosive work here for more than three thousand years. For one full day, Idaho had sat on the sand below the Wall and he had studied what had been accomplished by Time. He had fixed certain patterns in his mind—a slanting shadow, a thin line, a crumbling bulge, a tiny lip of rock here and another over there.

His fingers wriggled upward into a sharp crack. He tested his weight gently on the support. Yes. Briefly, he rested, pressing his face against warm rock, not looking up or down. He was simply *here*. Everything was a matter of the pacing. His shoulders must not be allowed to tire too soon. Weight must be adjusted between feet and arms. Fingers took inevitable damage, but while bone and tendons held, the skin could be ignored.

Once more, he crept upward. A bit of rock broke away from his hand; dust and shards fell across his right cheek, but he did not even feel it. Every bit of his awareness concentrated on the groping hand, the balance of his feet on the tiniest of protrusions. He was a mote, a particle which defied gravity . . . a fingerhold here, a toehold there, clinging to the rock surface at times by the sheer power of his will.

Nine makeshift pitons bulged one of his pockets, but he resisted using them. The equally makeshift hammer dangled from his belt on a short cord whose knot his fingers had memorized.

Nayla had been difficult. She would not give up her lasgun. She had, however, obeyed Siona's direct order to accompany them. A strange woman . . . strangely obedient.

"Have you not sworn to obey me?" Siona had demanded.

Nayla's reluctance had vanished.

Later, Siona had said: "She always obeys my direct orders."

"Then we may not have to kill her," Idaho had said.

"I would rather not attempt it. I don't think you have even the faintest idea of her strength and quickness."

Garun, the Museum Fremen who dreamed of becoming a "true Naib in the old fashion," had set the stage for this climb by answering Idaho's question: "How will the God Emperor come to Tuono?"

"In the same way he chose for a visit during my great-grandfather's time."

"And that was?" Siona had prompted him.

They had been sitting in the dusty shadows outside the guest house, sheltering from the afternoon sun on the day of the announcement that the Lord Leto would be wed in Tuono. A semicircle of Garun's aides squatted around the doorstep where Siona and Idaho sat with Garun. Two Fish Speakers lounged nearby, listening. Nayla was due to arrive momentarily.

Garun pointed to the high Wall behind the village, its rim glistening distant gold in the sunlight. "The Royal Road runs there and the God Emperor has a device which lowers him gently from the heights."

"It's built into his cart," Idaho said.

"Suspensors," Siona agreed. "I've seen them."

"My great-grandfather said they came along the Royal Road, a great troop of them. The God Emperor glided down to our village square on his device. The others came down on ropes."

Idaho spoke thoughtfully: "Ropes."

"Why did they come?" Siona asked.

"To affirm that the God Emperor had not forgotten his Fremen, so my great-grandfather said. It was a great honor, but not as great as this wedding."

Idaho arose while Garun was still talking. There was a clear view of the high Wall from nearby—straight down the central street, a view from the base in the sand to the top in the sunlight. Idaho strode to the corner of the guest house out into the central street. He stopped there, turned and looked at the Wall. The first look told why everyone said it was not possible to climb that face. Even then, he resisted thinking about a measurement of the height. It could be five hundred meters or five thousand. The important thing lay in what a more careful study revealed—tiny transverse cracks, broken places, even a narrow ledge about twenty meters above the drifting sand at the bottom . . . and another ledge about two-thirds of the way up the face.

He knew that an unconscious part of him, an ancient and dependable part, was making the necessary measurements, scaling them to his own body—so many Duncan-lengths to that place, a handgrip here, another there. His own hands. He could already feel himself climbing.

Siona's voice came from near his right shoulder as he stood in that first examination. "What're you doing?" She had come up soundlessly, looking now where he looked.

"I can climb that Wall," Idaho said. "If I carried a light rope, I could pull up a heavier rope. The rest of you could climb it easily then."

Garun joined them in time to hear this. "Why would you climb the Wall, Duncan Idaho?"

Siona answered for him, smiling at Garun. "To provide a suitable greeting for the God Emperor."

This had been before her doubts, before her own eyes and the ignorance of such a climb, had begun to erode that first confidence.

With that first elation, Idaho asked: "How wide is the Royal Road up there?"

"I have never seen it," Garun said. "But I am told it is very wide. A great troop can march abreast along it, so they say. And there are bridges, places to view the river and . . . and . . . oh, it is a marvel."

"Why have you never gone up there to see it yourself?" Idaho asked.

Garun merely shrugged and pointed at the Wall.

Nayla arrived then and the argument about the climb had begun. Idaho thought about that argument as he climbed. How strange, the relationship between Nayla and Siona! They were like two conspirators . . . yet not conspirators. Siona commanded and Nayla obeyed. But Nayla was a Fish Speaker, the *Friend* who was trusted by Leto to make a first examination of the new ghola. She admitted that she had been in the Royal Constabulary since childhood. Such strength in her! Given that strength, there was something awesome about the way she bowed to Siona's will. It was as though Nayla listened for secret voices which told her what to do. *Then* she obeyed.

Idaho groped upward for another handhold. His fingers wriggled along the rock, up and outward to the right, finding at last an unseen crack where they might enter. His memory provided the natural line of ascent, but only his body could learn the way by following that line. His left foot found a toehold . . . up . . . up . . . slowly, testing. Left hand up now . . . no crack but a ledge. His eyes, then his chin lifted over the high ledge he had seen from below. He elbowed his way onto it, rolled over and rested, looking only outward, not up or down. It was a sand horizon out there, a breeze with dust in it limiting the view. He had seen many such horizons in the Dune days.

Presently, he turned to face the Wall, lifted himself onto his knees, hands groping upward, and he resumed the climb. The picture of the Wall remained in his mind as he had seen it from below. He had only to close his eyes and the pattern lay there, fixed the way he had learned to do it as a child hiding from Harkonnen slave raiders. Fingertips found a crack where they could be wedged. He clawed his way upward.

Watching from below, Nayla experienced a growing affinity for the climber. Idaho had been reduced by distance to such a small and lonely shape upon the Wall. He must know what it was like to be alone with momentous decisions.

I would like to have his child, she thought. *A child from both of us would be strong and resourceful. What is it that God wants from a child of Siona and this man?*

Nayla had awakened before dawn and had walked out to the top of a low dune at the village edge to think about this thing that Idaho proposed. It had been a lime dawn with a familiar winding cloth of dust in the distance, then steel day and the baleful immensity of the Sareer. She knew then that these matters certainly had been anticipated by God. What could be hidden from God? Nothing could be hidden, not even the remote figure of Duncan Idaho groping for a pathway up to the edge of heaven.

As she watched Idaho climb, Nayla's mind played a trick on her, tipping the wall to the horizontal. Idaho became a child crawling across a broken surface. How small he looked . . . and growing smaller.

An aide offered Nayla water which she drank. The water brought the Wall back into its true perspective.

Siona crouched on the first ledge, leaning out to peer upward. "If you fall, I will try it," Siona had promised Idaho. Nayla had thought it a strange promise. Why would both of them want to try the impossible?

Idaho had failed to dissuade Siona from the impossible promise.

It is fate, Nayla thought. *It is God's will.*

They were the same thing.

A bit of rock fell from where Idaho clutched at it. That had happened several times. Nayla watched the falling rock. It took a long time coming down, bounding and rebounding from the Wall's face, demonstrating that the eye did not report truthfully when it said the Wall was sheer.

He will succeed or he will not, Nayla thought. *Whatever happens, it is God's will.*

She could feel her heart hammering, though. Idaho's venture was like sex, she thought. It was not passively erotic, but akin to rare magic in the way it seized her. She had to keep reminding herself that Idaho was not for her.

He is for Siona. If he survives.

And if he failed, then Siona would try. Siona would succeed or she would not. Nayla wondered, though, if she might experience an orgasm should Idaho reach the top. He was so close to it now.

Idaho took several deep breaths after dislodging the rock. It was a bad moment and he took the time to recover, clinging to a three-point hold on the Wall. Almost of its own accord, his free hand groped upward once more, wriggling past the rotten place into another slender crack. Slowly, he shifted his weight onto that hand. Slowly . . . slowly. His left knee felt the place where a toehold could be achieved. He lifted his foot to that place, tested it. Memory told him the top was near, but he pushed the memory aside. There was only the climb and the knowledge that Leto would arrive tomorrow.

Leto and Hwi.

He could not think about that, either. But it would not go away. *The top . . . Hwi . . . Leto . . . tomorrow . . .*

Every thought fed his desperation, forced him into the immediate remembrance of the climbs of his childhood. The more he remembered consciously, the more his abilities were blocked. He was forced to pause, breathing deeply in the attempt to center himself, to go back to the *natural* ways of his past.

But were those ways *natural*?

There was a blockage in his mind. He could sense intrusions, a finality . . . the *fatality* of what might have been and now would never be.

Leto would arrive up there tomorrow.

Idaho felt perspiration run down his face around the place where he pressed a cheek against the rock.

Leto.

I will defeat you, Leto. I will defeat you for myself, not for Hwi, but only for myself.

A sensation of cleansing began to spread through him. It was like the thing which had happened in the night while he prepared himself mentally for this climb. Siona had sensed his sleeplessness. She had begun to talk to him, telling him the smallest details of her desperate run through the Forbidden Forest and her oath at the edge of the river.

"Now I have given an oath to command his Fish Speakers," she said. "I will honor that oath, but I hope it will not happen in the way he wants."

"What does he want?" Idaho asked.

"He has many motives and I cannot see them all. Who could possibly understand *him*? I only know that I will never forgive him."

This memory brought Idaho back to the sensation of the Wall's rock against his cheek. His perspiration had dried in the light breeze and he felt chilled. But he had found his center.

Never forgive.

Idaho felt the ghosts of all his other selves, the gholas who had died in Leto's service. Could he believe Siona's suspicions? Yes. Leto was capable of killing with his own body, his own hands. The rumor which Siona recounted had a feeling of truth in it. And Siona, too, was Atreides. Leto had become something else . . . no longer Atreides, not even human. He had become not so much a living creature as a brute fact of nature, opaque and impenetrable, all of his experiences sealed off within him. And Siona opposed him. The real Atreides turned away from him.

As I do.

A brute fact of nature, nothing more. Just like this Wall.

Idaho's right hand groped upward and found a sharp ledge. He could feel nothing above the ledge and tried to remember a wide crack at this place in the pattern. He could not dare to allow himself into the belief that he had reached the top . . . not yet. The sharp edge cut into his fingers as he put his weight on it. He brought his left hand up to that level, found a purchase and pulled himself slowly upward. His eyes reached the level of his hands. He stared across a flat space which reached outward . . . outward into blue sky. The surface where his hands clutched showed ancient weather cracks. He crawled his fingers across that surface, one hand at a time, seeking out the cracks, dragging his chest up . . . his waist . . . his hips. He rolled then, twisting and crawling until the Wall was far behind him. Only then did he stand and tell himself what his senses reported.

The top. And he had not required pitons or hammer.

A faint sound reached him. Cheering?

He walked back to the edge and looked down, waving to them. Yes, they were cheering. Turning back, he strode to the center of the roadway, letting elation still the trembling of his muscles, soothe the aching of his shoulders. Slowly, he turned full circle, examining the top while he let his memories at last estimate the height of that climb.

Nine hundred meters . . . at least that.

The Royal Roadway interested him. It was not like what he had seen on the way to Onn. It was wide, wide . . . at least five hundred meters. The roadbed was a smooth, unbroken gray with its edge some one hundred meters from each lip of the Wall. Rock pillars at man height marked the road's edge, stretching away like sentinels along the path Leto would use.

Idaho walked to the far side of the Wall opposite the Sareer and peered down. Far away in the depths, a hurtling green flow of river battered itself into foam against buttress rocks. He looked to the right. Leto would come from there. Road and Wall curved gently to the right, the curve beginning about three hundred meters from the place where Idaho stood. Idaho returned to the road and walked along its edge, following the curve until it made a returning "S" and narrowed, sloping gently downward. He stopped and looked at what was revealed for him, seeing the new pattern take shape.

About three kilometers away down the gentle slope, the roadway narrowed and crossed the river gorge on a bridge whose faery trusses appeared insubstantial and toylike at this distance. Idaho remembered a similar bridge on the road to Onn, the substantial feel of it beneath his feet. He trusted his memory, thinking about bridges as a military leader was forced to think about them—passages or traps.

Moving out to his left, he looked down and outward to another high Wall at the far anchor of the faery bridge. The road continued there, turning gently until it was a line running straight northward. There were two Walls along there and the river between them. The river glided in a man-made chasm, its moisture confined and channeled into a northward wind-drift while the water itself flowed southward.

Idaho ignored the river then. It was there and it would be there tomorrow. He fixed his attention on the bridge, letting his military training examine it. He nodded once to himself before turning back the way he had come, lifting the light rope from his shoulders as he walked.

It was only when she saw the rope come snaking down that Nayla had her orgasm.

What am I eliminating? The bourgeois infatuation with peaceful conservation of the past. This is a binding force, a thing which holds humankind into one vulnerable unit in spite of illusionary separations across parsecs of space. If I can find the scattered bits, others can find them. When you are together, you can share a common catastrophe. You can be exterminated together. Thus, I demonstrate the terrible danger of a gliding, passionless mediocrity, a movement without ambitions or aims. I show you that entire civilizations can do this thing. I give you eons of life which slips gently toward death without fuss or stirring, without even asking "Why?" I show you the false happiness and the shadow-catastrophe called Leto, the God Emperor. Now, will you learn the real happiness?

—THE STOLEN JOURNALS

Having spent the night with only one brief catnap, Leto was awake when Moneo emerged from the guest house at dawn. The Royal Cart had been parked almost in the center of a three-sided courtyard. The cart's cover had been set on one-way opaque, concealing its occupant, and was tightly sealed against moisture. Leto could hear the faint stirring of the fans which pulsed his air through a drying cycle.

Moneo's feet scratched on the courtyard's cobbles as he approached the cart. Dawnlight edged the guest house roof with orange above the majordomo.

Leto opened the cart's cover as Moneo stopped in front of him.

There was a yeasting dirt smell to the air and the accumulation of moisture in the breeze was painful.

"We should arrive at Tuono about noon," Moneo said. "I wish you'd let me bring in 'thopters to guard the sky."

"I do not want 'thopters," Leto said. "We can go down to Tuono on suspensors and ropes."

Leto marveled at the plastic images in this brief exchange. Moneo had never liked peregrinations. His youth as a rebel had left him with suspicions of everything he could not see or label. He remained a mass of latent judgments.

"You know I don't want 'thopters for transport," Moneo said. "I want them to guard . . ."

"Yes, Moneo."

Moneo looked past Leto at the open end of the courtyard which overlooked the river canyon. Dawnlight was frosting the mist which arose from the depths. He thought of how far down that canyon dropped . . . a body twisting, twisting as it fell. Moneo had found himself unable to go to the canyon's lip last night and peer down into it. The drop was such a . . . such a temptation.

With that insightful power which filled Moneo with such awe, Leto said: "There's a lesson in every temptation, Moneo."

Speechless, Moneo turned to stare directly into Leto's eyes.

"See the lesson in my life, Moneo."

"Lord?" It was only a whisper.

"They tempt me first with evil, then with good. Each temptation is fashioned with exquisite attention to my susceptibilities. Tell me, Moneo, if I choose the good, does that make me good?"

"Of course it does, Lord."

"Perhaps you will never lose the habit of judgment," Leto said.

Moneo looked away from him once more and stared at the chasm's edge. Leto rolled his body to look where Moneo looked. Dwarf pines had been cultured along the lip of the canyon. There were hanging dewdrops on the damp needles, each of them sending a promise of pain to Leto. He longed to close the cart's cover, but there was an immediacy in those jewels which attracted his memories even while they repelled his body. The opposed synchrony threatened to fill him with turmoil.

"I just don't like going around on foot," Moneo said.

"It was the Fremen way," Leto said.

Moneo sighed. "The others will be ready in a few minutes. Hwi was breakfasting when I came out."

Leto did not respond. His thoughts were lost in memories of night—the one just past and the millennial others which crowded his pasts—clouds and stars, the rains and the open blackness pocked with glittering flakes from a shredded cosmos, a universe of nights, extravagant with them as he had been with his heartbeats.

Moneo suddenly demanded: "Where are your guards?"

"I sent them to eat."

"I don't like them leaving you unguarded!"

The crystal sound of Moneo's voice rang in Leto's memories, speaking things not cast in words. Moneo feared a universe where there was no God Emperor. He would rather die than see such a universe.

"What will happen today?" Moneo demanded.

It was a question directed not to the God Emperor but to the prophet.

"A seed blown on the wind could be tomorrow's willow tree," Leto said.

"You know our future! Why won't you share it?" Moneo was close to hysteria . . . refusing anything his immediate senses did not report.

Leto turned to glare at the majordomo, a gaze so obviously filled with pent-up emotions that Moneo recoiled from it.

"Take charge of your own existence, Moneo!"

Moneo took a deep, trembling breath. "Lord, I meant no offense. I sought only . . ."

"Look upward, Moneo!"

Involuntarily, Moneo obeyed, peering into the cloudless sky where morning light was increasing. "What is it, Lord?"

"There's no reassuring ceiling over you, Moneo. Only an open sky full of changes. Welcome it. Every sense you possess is an instrument for reacting to change. Does that tell you nothing?"

"Lord, I only came out to inquire when you would be ready to proceed."

"Moneo, I beg you to be truthful with me."

"I am truthful, Lord!"

"But if you live in bad faith, lies will appear to you like the truth."

"Lord, if I lie . . . then I do not know it."

"That has the ring of truth. But I know what you dread and will not speak."

Moneo began to tremble. The God Emperor was in the most terrible of moods, a deep threat in every word.

"You dread the imperialism of consciousness," Leto said, "and you are right to fear it. Send Hwi out here immediately!"

Moneo whirled and fled back into the guest house. It was as though his entrance stirred up an insect colony. Within seconds, Fish Speakers emerged and spread around the Royal Cart. Courtiers peered from the guest house windows or came out and stood under deep eaves, afraid to approach him. In contrast to this excitement, Hwi emerged presently from the wide central doorway and strode out of the shadows, moving slowly toward Leto, her chin up, her gaze seeking his face.

Leto felt himself becoming calm as he looked at her. She wore a golden gown he had not seen before. It had been piped with silver and jade at the neck and the cuffs of its long sleeves. The hem, almost dragging on the ground, had heavy green braid to outline deep red crenelations.

Hwi smiled as she stopped in front of him.

"Good morning, Love." She spoke softly. "What have you done to get poor Moneo so upset?"

Soothed by her presence and her voice, he smiled. "I did what I always hope to do. I produced an effect."

"You certainly did. He told the Fish Speakers you were in an angry and terrifying mood. Are you terrifying, Love?"

"Only to those who refuse to live by their own strengths."

"Ahhh, yes." She pirouetted for him then, displaying her new gown. "Do you like it? Your Fish Speakers gave it to me. They decorated it themselves."

"My love," he said, a warning note in his voice, "decoration! That is how you prepare the sacrifice."

She came up to the edge of the cart and leaned on it just below his face, a mock solemn expression on her lips. "Will they sacrifice me, then?"

"Some of them would like to."

"But you will not permit it."

"Our fates are joined," he said.

"Then I shall not fear." She reached up and touched one of his silver-skinned hands, but jerked away as his fingers began to tremble.

"Forgive me, Love. I forget that we are joined in soul and not in flesh," she said.

The sandtrout skin still shuddered from Hwi's touch. "Moisture in the air makes me overly sensitive," he said. Slowly, the shuddering subsided.

"I refuse to regret what cannot be," she whispered.

"Be strong, Hwi, for your soul is mine."

She turned at a sound from the guest house. "Moneo returns," she said. "Please, Love, do not frighten him."

"Is Moneo your friend, too?"

"We are friends of the stomach. We both like yogurt."

Leto was still chuckling when Moneo stopped beside Hwi. Moneo ventured a smile, casting a puzzled glance at Hwi. There was gratitude in the majordomo's manner and some of the subservience he was accustomed to show to Leto he now directed at Hwi. "Is it well with you, Lady Hwi?"

"It is well with me."

Leto said: "In the time of the stomach, friendships of the stomach are to be nurtured and cultivated. Let us be on our way, Moneo. Tuono awaits."

Moneo turned and shouted orders to the Fish Speakers and courtiers.

Leto grinned at Hwi. "Do I not play the impatient bridegroom with a certain style?"

She leaped lightly up to the bed of his cart, her skirt gathered in one hand. He unfolded her seat. Only when she was seated, her eyes level with Leto's, did she respond, and then it was in a voice pitched for his ears alone.

"Love of my soul, I have captured another of your secrets."

"Release it from your lips," he said, joking in this new intimacy between them.

"You seldom need words," she said. "You speak directly to the senses with your own life."

A shudder flexed its way through the length of his body. It was a moment before he could speak and then it was in a voice she had to strain to hear above the hubbub of the assembling cortege.

"Between the superhuman and the inhuman," he said, "I have had little space in which to be human. I thank you, gentle and lovely Hwi, for this little space."

In all of my universe I have seen no *law of nature,* unchanging and inexorable. This universe presents only changing relationships which are sometimes seen as laws by short-lived awareness. These fleshly sensoria which we call *self* are ephemera withering in the blaze of infinity, fleetingly aware of temporary conditions which confine our activities and change as our activities change. If you must label the *absolute*, use its proper name: *Temporary.*

—THE STOLEN JOURNALS

Nayla was the first to glimpse the approaching cortege. Perspiring heavily in the midday heat, she stood near one of the rock pillars which marked the edges of the Royal Road. A sudden flash of distant reflection caught her attention. She peered in that direction, squinting, realizing with a thrill of awareness that she saw sun-dazzle on the cover of the God Emperor's cart.

"They come!" she called.

She felt hunger then. In their excitement and singleness of purpose, none of them had brought food. Only the Fremen had brought water and that because "Fremen always carry water when they leave sietch." They did it by rote.

Nayla touched one finger to the butt of the lasgun holstered at her hip. The bridge lay no more than twenty meters ahead of her, its faery structure arching across the chasm like an alien fantasy joining one barren surface to another.

This is madness, she thought.

But the God Emperor had reinforced his command. He required his Nayla to obey Siona in all things.

Siona's orders were explicit, leaving no way for evasions. And Nayla had no way here to query her God Emperor. Siona had said: "When his cart is in the middle of the bridge—then!"

"But why?"

They had been standing well away from the others in the chill dawn atop the barrier Wall, Nayla feeling precariously isolated here, remote and vulnerable.

Siona's grim features, her low, intense voice, could not be denied. "Do you think you can harm God?"

"I . . ." Nayla could only shrug.

"You *must* obey me!"

"I must," Nayla agreed.

Nayla studied the approach of the distant cortege, noting the colors of the courtiers, the thick masses of blue marking her sisters of the Fish Speakers . . . the shiny surface of her Lord's cart.

It was another test, she decided. The God Emperor would know. He would know the devotion in His Nayla's heart. It was a test. The God Emperor's commands must be obeyed in all things. That was the earliest lesson of her Fish Speaker childhood. The God Emperor had said that Nayla must obey Siona. It was a test. What else could it be?

She looked toward the four Fremen. They had been positioned by Duncan Idaho directly in the roadway and blocking part of the exit from this end of the bridge. They sat with their backs to her and looked out across the bridge, four brown-robed mounds. Nayla had heard Idaho's words to them.

"Do not leave this place. You must greet him from here. Stand when he nears you and bow low."

Greet, yes.

Nayla nodded to herself.

The three other Fish Speakers who had climbed the Barrier Wall with her had been sent to the center of the bridge. All they knew was what Siona had told them in Nayla's presence. They were to wait until the Royal Cart was only a few paces from them, then they were to turn and dance away from the cart, leading it and the procession toward the vantage point above Tuono.

If I cut the bridge with my lasgun, those three will die, Nayla thought. *And all the others who come with our Lord.*

Nayla craned her neck to peer down into the gorge. She could not see the river from here, but she could hear its distant rumblings, a movement of rocks.

They would all die!

Unless He performs a Miracle.

That had to be it. Siona had set the stage for a Holy Miracle. What else could Siona intend now that she had been tested, now that she wore the uniform of Fish Speaker Command? Siona had given her oath to the God Emperor. She had been tested by God, the two of them alone in the Sareer.

Nayla turned only her eyes to the right, peering at the architects of this greeting. Siona and Idaho stood shoulder-to-shoulder in the roadway about twenty meters to Nayla's right. They were deep in conversation, looking at each other occasionally, nodding.

Presently, Idaho touched Siona's arm—an oddly possessive gesture. He nodded once and strode off toward the bridge, stopping at the buttress corner directly in front of Nayla. He peered down, then crossed to the other near corner of the bridge. Again, he peered downward, standing there for several minutes before returning to Siona.

What a strange creature, that ghola, Nayla thought. After that awesome climb, she no longer thought of him as quite human. He was something else, a demiurge who stood next to God. But he could breed.

A distant shout caught Nayla's attention. She turned and looked across the bridge. The cortege had been in the familiar trot of a royal peregrination. Now, they were slowing to a sedate walk only a few minutes away from the bridge. Nayla recognized Moneo marching in the van, his uniform brilliant white, the even, undeviating stride with his gaze straight ahead. The cover of the Emperor's cart had been sealed. It glittered in mirror-opacity as it rolled behind Moneo on its wheels.

The mystery of it all filled Nayla.

A miracle was about to happen!

Nayla glanced to the right at Siona. Siona returned her gaze and nodded once. Nayla drew the lasgun from its holster and rested it against the rock pillar as she sighted along it. The cable on the left first, then the cable on the right, then the faery trellis of plasteel on the left. The lasgun felt cold and alien against Nayla's hand. She took a trembling breath to restore calm.

I must obey. It is a test.

She saw Moneo lift his gaze from the roadway and, not changing stride, turn to shout something at the cart or the ones behind it. Nayla could not make out the words. Moneo faced front once more. Nayla steadied herself, a part of the rock pillar which concealed most of her body.

A test.

Moneo had seen the people on the bridge and at the far end. He identified Fish Speaker uniforms and his first thought was to wonder who had ordered these greeters. He turned and shouted a question at Leto, but the God Emperor's cart cover remained opaque, hiding Hwi and Leto within it.

Moneo was onto the bridge, the cart rasping in blown sand behind him, before he recognized Siona and Idaho standing well back from the far end. He identified four Museum Fremen seated on the roadway. Doubts began squirming through Moneo's mind, but he could not change the pattern. He ventured a glance down at the river—a platinum world there caught in the noonday light. The sound of the cart was loud behind him. The flow of the river, the flow of the cortege, the sweeping importance of these things in which he played a role—all of it caught up his mind in a dizzying sensation of the inevitable.

We are not people passing this way, he thought. *We are primal elements linking one piece of Time to another. And when we have passed, everything behind us will drop off into no-sound, a place like the no-room of the Ixians, yet never again the same as it was before we came.*

A bit from one of the lute-player's songs wafted through Moneo's memory and his eyes went out of focus in the remembrance. He knew that song for its wishfulness, a wish that all of this were ended, all past, all doubts banished, tranquility returned. The plaintive song drifted through his awareness like smoke, twisting and compelling:

"Insect cries in roots of pampas grass."

Moneo hummed the song to himself:

"Insect cries mark the end.
Autumn and my song are the color
Of the last leaves
In roots of pampas grass."

Moneo nodded his head to the refrain:

"Day is ended,
Visitors gone.
Day is ended.
In our Sietch,
Day is ended.
Storm wind sounds.
Day is ended.
Visitors gone."

Moneo decided that the lute-player's song had to be a really old one, an Old Fremen song, no doubt of it. And it told him something about himself. He wished the visitors truly gone, the excitements ended, peace once more. Peace was so near . . . yet he could not leave his duties. He thought of all that impedimenta piled out there on the sand just beyond visibility range from Tuono. They would see it all soon—tents, food, tables, golden plates and jeweled knives, glowglobes fashioned in the arabesque shapes of ancient lamps . . . everything rich and full of expectations from completely different lives.

They will never be the same in Tuono.

Moneo had spent two nights in Tuono once on an inspection tour. He remembered the smells of their cooking fires—aromatic bushes kindled and flaming in the dark. They would not use sunstoves because "that is not the most ancient way."

Most ancient!

There was little smell of melange in Tuono. A sweet acridity and the musky oils of oasis shrubs, these dominated the odors. Yes . . . and the cesspools and the stink of rotting garbage. He recalled the God Emperor's comment when Moneo had finished reporting on that tour.

"These *Fremen* do not know what is lost from their lives. They think they keep the essence of the old ways. This is a failure of all museums. Something fades; it dries out of the exhibits and is gone. The people who administer the museum and the people who come to bend over the cases and stare—few of them sense this missing thing. It drove the engine of life in earlier times. When the life is gone, it is gone."

Moneo focused on the three Fish Speakers who stood just ahead of him on the bridge. They lifted their arms high and began to dance, whirling and skipping away from him only a few paces distant.

How odd, he thought. *I've seen the other people dance in the open, but never Fish Speakers. They only dance in the privacy of their quarters, in the intimacy of their own company.*

This thought was still in his mind when he heard the first awful humming of the lasgun and felt the bridge lurch beneath him.

This is not happening, his mind told him.

He heard the Royal Cart scrape sideways across the roadbed, then the *snap-slap* of the cart's cover slamming open. A bedlam of screams and cries arose from behind him, but he could not turn. The bridge's roadbed had tipped steeply to Moneo's right, spilling him onto his face while he went sliding toward the abyss. He clutched a severed strand of cable to stop himself. The cable went with him, everything grating in the spilling film of sand which had covered the roadbed. He clutched the cable with both hands, turning with it. He saw the Royal Cart then. It skewed sideways toward the edge of the bridge, its cover open. Hwi stood there, one hand steadying her on the folding seat while she stared past Moneo.

A horrible screaming of metal filled the air as the roadbed tipped even farther. He saw people from the cortege falling, their mouths open, arms waving. Something had caught Moneo's cable. His arms were stretched out over his head as he turned once more, twisting. He felt his hands, greased by the perspiration of fear, slipping along the cable.

Once more, his gaze came around to the Royal Cart. It lay jammed against the stubs of broken girders. Even as Moneo looked, the God Emperor's futile hands groped for Hwi Noree, but failed to reach her. She fell from the cart's open end, silently, the golden gown whipping upward to reveal her body stretched out as straight as an arrow.

A deep, rumbling groan came from the God Emperor.

Why doesn't he activate the suspensors? Moneo wondered. *The suspensors will support him.*

But the lasgun was still humming and, as Moneo's hands slipped from the cable's severed end, he saw lancing flame strike the cart's suspensor bubbles, piercing one after another in eruptions of golden smoke. Moneo stretched his hands over his head as he fell.

The smoke! The golden smoke!

His robe whipped upward, turning him until his face was directed downward into the abyss. With his gaze on the depths, he recognized a maelstrom of boiling rapids there, the mirror of his life—precipitous currents and plunges, all movement gathering up all substance. Leto's words wound through his mind on a path of golden smoke: *"Caution is the path to mediocrity. Gliding, passionless mediocrity is all that most people think they can achieve."* Moneo fell freely then in the ecstasy of awareness. The universe opened for him like clear glass, everything flowing in a no-Time.

The golden smoke!

"Leto!" he screamed. "Siaynoq! I believe!"

The robe tore away from his shoulders then. He turned in the wind of the canyon—one last glimpse of the Royal Cart tipping . . . tipping from the shattered roadbed. The God Emperor slid out of the open end.

Something solid smashed into Moneo's back—his last sensation.

Leto felt himself sliding from the cart. His awareness held only the image of Hwi striking the river—the distant pearly fountain which marked her plunge into the myths and dreams of termination. Her last words, calm and steady, rolled through all of his memories: "I shall go on ahead, Love."

As he slipped from the cart, he saw the scimitar arc of the river, a silver-edged thing which shimmered in its mottled shadows, a vicious blade of a river honed through Eternity and ready now to receive him into its agony.

I cannot cry, nor even shout, he thought. *Tears are no longer possible. They're water. I'll have water enough in a moment. I can only moan in my grief. I am alone, more alone than ever before.*

His great ridged body flexed as it fell, twisting him about until his amplified vision revealed Siona standing at the broken brink of the bridge.

Now, you will learn! he thought.

The body continued to turn. He watched the river approach. The water was a dream inhabited by glimpses of fish which ignited an ancient memory of a banquet beside a granite pool—pink flesh dazzling his hungers.

I join you, Hwi, in the banquet of the gods!

A bursting flash of bubbles enclosed him in agony. Water, vicious currents of it, buffeted him all around. He felt the gnashing of rocks as he struggled upward to broach in a torrential cascade, his body flexing in a paroxysm of involuntary, writhing splashes. The canyon Wall, wet and black, sped past his frantic gaze. Shattered spangles of what had been his skin exploded away from him, a rain of silver all around him darting away into the river, a ring of dazzling movement, brittle sequins—the scale-glitter of sandtrout leaving him to begin their own colony lives.

The agony continued. Leto marveled that he could remain conscious, that he had a body to feel.

Instinct drove him. He clutched at a rock around which the torrent spilled him, felt a clutching finger torn from his hand before he could release his grip. The sensation of it was only a minor accent in the symphony of pain.

The river's course swept to the left around a chasm buttress and, as though saying it had enough of him, it sent him rolling onto the sloping edge of a sandbar. He lay there a moment, the blue dye of spice-essence drifting away from him in the current. The agony moved him, the worm body moving of itself, retreating from the water. All the covering sandtrout were gone and he felt every touch more immediate, a lost sense restored when all it could bring him was pain. He could not see his body, but he felt the thing that would have been a worm as it made its writhing, crawling progress out of the water. He peered upward through eyes that saw everything in sheets of flame from which shapes coalesced of their own accord. At last, he recognized this place. The river had swept him to the turn where it left the Sareer forever. Behind him lay Tuono and, just a ways down the barrier Wall, was all that remained of Sietch Tabr—Stilgar's realm, the place where all of Leto's spice had been concealed.

Exuding blue fumes, his agonized body writhed its way noisily along a shingle of beach, dragged its blue-dyed way across broken boulders and into a damp hole which might have been part of the original sietch. It was only a shallow cave now, blocked at its inner end by a rock fall. His nostrils reported the wet dirt smell and clean spice-essence.

Sounds intruded on his agony. He turned in the confinement of the cave and saw a rope dangling at the entrance. A figure slid down the rope. He recognized Nayla. She dropped to the rocks and crouched there, staring into the shadows at him. The flame which was Leto's vision parted to reveal another figure dropping from the rope: Siona. She and Nayla scrambled toward him in a rattle of rocks and stopped, peering in at him. A third figure dropped off the rope: Idaho. He moved with frantic rage, hurling himself at Nayla, screaming:

"Why did you kill her! You weren't supposed to kill Hwi!"

Nayla sent him sprawling with a casual, almost indifferent sweep of her left arm. She scrambled closer up the rocks and stopped on all fours to peer in at Leto.

"Lord? You live?"

Idaho was right behind her, snatching the lasgun from her holster. Nayla turned, astonished, as he leveled the weapon and pulled its trigger. The burning started at the top of Nayla's head. It split her, the pieces slumping apart. A shining crysknife spilled from her burning uniform and shattered on the rocks. Idaho did not see it. A grimace of rage on his face, he kept burning and burning the pieces of Nayla until the weapon's charge was gone. The blazing arc vanished. Only wet and smoking bits of meat and cloth lay scattered among the glowing rocks.

It was the moment for which Siona had waited. She scrambled up to him and pulled the useless lasgun from Idaho's hands. He whirled toward her and she poised herself to subdue him, but all the rage was gone.

"Why?" he whispered.

"It's done," she said.

They turned and looked into the cave shadows at Leto.

Leto could not even imagine what they saw. The sandtrout skin was gone, he knew. There would be some kind of surface pocked with cilia holes from the departed skin. As for the rest, he could only look back at the two figures from a universe furrowed by sorrow. Through the vision flames he saw Siona as a female demon. The demon name came unbidden to his minds and he spoke it aloud, amplified by the cave and much louder than he had expected:

"Hanmya!"

"What?" She moved a step closer to him.

Idaho put both hands over his face.

"Look at what you've done to poor Duncan," Leto said.

"He'll find other loves." How callous she sounded, an echo of his own angry youth.

"You don't know what it is to love," he said. "What have you ever given?" He could only wring his hands then, those travesties which once had been his hands. "Gods below! What I've given!"

She scrambled closer and reached toward him, then drew back.

"I am reality, Siona. Look upon me. I exist. You can touch me if you dare. Reach out your hand. Do it!"

Slowly, she reached toward what had been his front segment, the place where she had slept in the Sareer. Her hand was touched with blue when she withdrew it.

"You have touched me and felt my body," he said. "Is that not strange beyond any other thing in this universe?"

She started to turn away.

"No! Don't turn away from me! Look at what you have wrought, Siona. How is it that you can touch me but you cannot touch yourself?"

She whirled away from him.

"*There* is the difference between us," he said. "You are God embodied. You walk around within the greatest miracle of this universe, yet you refuse to touch or see or feel or believe in it."

Leto's awareness went wandering then into a night-encircled place, a place where he thought he could hear the metal insect song of his hidden printers clacking away in their lightless room. There was a complete absence of radiation in this place, an Ixian no-thing which made it a place of anxiety and spiritual alienation because it had no connection with the rest of the universe.

But it will have a connection.

He sensed then that his Ixian printers had been set in motion, that they were recording his thoughts without any special command.

Remember what I did! Remember me! I will be innocent again!

The flame of his vision parted to reveal Idaho standing where Siona had stood. There was gesturing motion somewhere out of focus behind Idaho . . . ah, yes: Siona waving instructions to someone atop the barrier Wall.

"Are you still alive?" Idaho asked.

Leto's voice came in wheezing gasps: "Let them scatter, Duncan. Let them run and hide anywhere they want in any universe they choose."

"Damn you! What're you saying? I'd have sooner let her live with you!"

"Let? I did not *let* anything."

"Why did you let Hwi die?" Idaho moaned. "We didn't know she was in there with you."

Idaho's head sagged forward.

"You will be recompensed," Leto husked. "My Fish Speakers will choose you over Siona. Be kind to her, Duncan. She is more than Atreides and she carries the seed of your survival."

Leto sank back into his memories. They were delicate myths now, held fleetingly in his awareness. He sensed that he might have fallen into a time which, by its very being, had changed the past. There were sounds, though, and he struggled to interpret them. *Someone scrambling on rocks?* The flames parted to reveal Siona standing beside Idaho. They stood hand-in-hand like two children reassuring each other before venturing into an unknown place.

"How can he live like that?" Siona whispered.

Leto waited for the strength to respond. "Hwi helps me," he said. "We had something few experience. We were joined in our strengths rather than in our weaknesses."

"And look what it got you!" Siona sneered.

"Yes, and pray that you get the same," he husked. "Perhaps the spice will give you time."

"Where is your spice?" she demanded.

"Deep in Sietch Tabr," he said. "Duncan will find it. You know the place, Duncan. They call it Tabur now. The outlines are still there."

"Why did you do it?" Idaho whispered.

"My gift," Leto said. "Nobody will find the descendants of Siona. The Oracle cannot see her."

"What?" They spoke in unison, leaning close to hear his fading voice.

"I give you a new kind of time without parallels," he said. "It will always diverge. There will be no concurrent points on its curves. I give you the Golden Path. That is my gift. Never again will you have the kinds of concurrence that once you had."

Flames covered his vision. The agony was fading, but he could still sense odors and hear sounds with a terrible acuity. Both Idaho and

Siona were breathing in quick, shallow gasps. Odd kinesthetic sensations began to weave their way through Leto—echoes of bones and joints which he knew he no longer possessed.

"Look!" Siona said.

"He's disintegrating." That was Idaho.

"No." Siona. "The outside is falling away. Look! The Worm!"

Leto felt parts of himself settling into warm softness. The agony removed itself.

"What're those holes in him?" Siona.

"I think they were the sandtrout. See the shapes?"

"I am here to prove one of my ancestors wrong," Leto said (or thought he said, which was the same thing as far as his journals were concerned). "I was born a man but I do not die a man."

"I can't look!" Siona said.

Leto heard her turn away, a rattle of rocks.

"Are you still there, Duncan?"

"Yes."

So I still have a voice.

"Look at me," Leto said. "I was a bloody bit of pulp in a human womb, a bit no larger than a cherry. Look at me, I say!"

"I'm looking." Idaho's voice was faint.

"You expected a giant and you found a gnome," Leto said. "Now, you're beginning to know the responsibilities which come as a result of actions. What will you do with your new power, Duncan?"

There was a long silence, then Siona's voice: "Don't listen to him! He was mad!"

"Of course," Leto said. "Madness in method, that is genius."

"Siona, do you understand this?" Idaho asked. How plaintive, the ghola voice.

"She understands," Leto said. "It is human to have your soul brought to a crisis you did not anticipate. That's the way it always is with humans. Moneo understood at last."

"I wish he'd hurry up and die!" Siona said.

"I am the divided god and you would make me whole," Leto said. "Duncan? I think of all my Duncans I approve of you the most."

"Approve?" Some of the rage returned to Idaho's voice.

"There's magic in my approval," Leto said. "Anything's possible in a magic universe. *Your* life has been dominated by the Oracle's fatality, not mine. Now, you see the mysterious caprices and you would ask me to dispel this? I wished only to increase it."

The *others* within Leto began to reassert themselves. Without the solidarity of the colonial group to support his identity, he began to lose his place among them. They started speaking the language of the constant "IF." "If you had only . . . If we had but . . ." He wanted to shout them into silence.

"Only fools prefer the past!"

Leto did not know if he truly shouted or only thought it. The response was a momentary inner silence matched to an outer silence and he felt some of the threads of his old identity still intact. He tried to speak and knew the reality of it because Idaho said, "Listen, he's trying to say something."

"Do not fear the Ixians," he said, and he heard his own voice as a fading whisper. "They can make the machines, but they no longer can make *arafel*. I know. I was there."

He fell silent, gathering his strength, but he felt the energy flowing from him even as he tried to hold it. Once more, the clamor arose within him—voices pleading and shouting.

"Stop that foolishness!" he cried, or thought he cried.

Idaho and Siona heard only a gasping hiss.

Presently, Siona said: "I think he's dead."

"And everyone thought he was immortal," Idaho said.

"Do you know what the Oral History says?" Siona asked. "If you want immortality, then deny form. Whatever has form has mortality. Beyond form is the formless, the immortal."

"That sounds like *him*," Idaho accused.

"I think it was," she said.

"What did he mean about your descendants . . . hiding, not finding them?" Idaho asked.

"He created a new kind of mimesis," she said, "a new biological imitation. He knew he had succeeded. He could not see me in his futures."

"What are you?" Idaho demanded.

"I'm the new Atreides."

"Atreides!" It was a curse in Idaho's voice.

Siona stared down at the disintegrating hulk which once had been Leto Atreides II . . . and something else. The *something* else was sloughing away in faint wisps of blue smoke where the smell of melange was strongest. Puddles of blue liquid formed in the rocks beneath his melting bulk. Only faint vague shapes which might once have been human remained—a collapsed foaming pinkness, a bit of red-streaked bone which could have held the forms of cheeks and brow . . .

Siona said: "I am different, but still I am what he was."

Idaho spoke in a hushed whisper: "The ancestors, all of . . ."

"The multitude is there but I walk silently among them and no one sees me. The old images are gone and only the essence remains to light his Golden Path."

She turned and took Idaho's cold hand in hers. Carefully, she led him out of the cave into the light where the rope dangled invitingly from the barrier Wall's top, from the place where the frightened Museum Fremen waited.

Poor material with which to shape a new universe, she thought, but they would have to serve. Idaho would require gentle seduction, a care within which love *might* appear.

When she looked down the river to where the flow emerged from its man-made chasm to spread across the green lands, she saw a wind from the south driving dark clouds toward her.

Idaho withdrew his hand from hers, but he appeared calmer. "Weather control is increasingly unstable," he said. "Moneo thought it was the Guild's doing."

"My father was seldom mistaken about such things," she said. "You will have to look into that."

Idaho experienced a sudden memory of the silvery shapes of sand-trout darting away from Leto's body in the river.

"I heard the Worm," Siona said. "The Fish Speakers will follow you, not me."

Again, Idaho sensed the temptation from the ritual of Siaynoq. "We will see," he said. He turned and looked at Siona. "What did he mean when he said the Ixians cannot create *arafel*?"

"You haven't read all the journals," she said. "I'll show you when we return to Tuono."

"But what does it mean—*arafel*?"

"That's the cloud-darkness of holy judgment. It's from an old story. You'll find it all in my journals."

Excerpt from the Hadi Benotto secret summation on the discoveries at Dar-es-Balat:

Herewith the minority report. We will, of course, comply with the majority decision to apply a careful screening, editing and censorship to the journals from Dar-es-Balat, but our arguments must be heard. We recognize the interest of Holy Church in these matters and the political dangers have not escaped our notice. We share a desire with the Church that Rakis and the Holy Reservation of the Divided God not become "an attraction for gawking tourists."

However, now that all of the journals are in our hands, authenticated and translated, the clear shape of the Atreides Design emerges. As a woman trained by the Bene Gesserit to understand the ways of our ancestors, I have a natural desire to share the pattern we have exposed—which is so much more than Dune to Arrakis to Dune, thence to Rakis.

The interests of history and science must be served. The journals throw a valuable new light onto that accumulation of personal recollections and biographies from the Duncan Days, the Guard Bible. We cannot be unmindful of those familiar oaths: *"By the Thousand Sons of Idaho!"* and *"By the Nine Daughters of Siona!"* The persistent Cult of Sister Chenoeh assumes new significance because of the journals' disclosures. Certainly, the Church's characterization of Judas/Nayla deserves careful reevaluation.

We of the Minority must remind the political censors that the poor sandworms in their Rakian Reservation cannot provide us with an alternative to Ixian Navigation Machines, nor are the tiny amounts of Church-controlled melange any real commercial threat to the products of the Tleilaxu vats. No! We argue that the myths, the Oral History, the Guard Bible, and even the Holy Books of the Divided God must be compared with the journals from Dar-es-Balat. Every historical reference to the Scattering and the Famine Times has to be taken out and reexamined! What have we to fear? No Ixian machine can do what we, the descendants of Duncan Idaho and Siona, have done. How many universes have we populated? None can guess. No one person will ever know. Does the Church fear the occasional prophet? We know that the visionaries cannot *see* us nor predict our decisions. No death can find all of humankind. Must we of the Minority join our fellows of the Scattering before we can be heard? Must we leave the original core of humankind ignorant and uninformed? If the Majority drives us out, you know we never again can be found!

We do not want to leave. We are held here by those *pearls* in the sand. We are fascinated by the Church's use of the pearl as "the sun of understanding." Surely, no reasoning human can escape the journals' revelations in this regard. The admittedly fugitive but vital uses of archeology must have their day! Just as the primitive machine with which Leto II concealed his journals can only teach us about the evolution of our machines, just so, that ancient awareness must be allowed to speak to us. It would be a crime against both historical accuracy and science for us to abandon our attempts at communication with those "pearls of awareness" which the journals have located. Is Leto II lost in his endless dream or could he be reawakened to our times, brought to full consciousness as a storehouse of historical accuracy? How can Holy Church fear this truth?

For the Minority, we have no doubt that historians must listen to that voice from our beginnings. If it is only the journals, we must listen. We must listen across at least as many years into our future as those journals lay hidden in our past. We will not try to predict the discoveries yet to be made within those pages. We say only that they must be made. How can we turn our backs on our most important inheritance? As the poet, Lon Bramlis, has said: "We are the fountain of surprises!"

Photo by Phil H. Webber

FRANK HERBERT is the bestselling author of the Dune saga. He was born in Tacoma, Washington, and educated at the University of Washington, Seattle. He worked a wide variety of jobs—including TV cameraman, radio commentator, oyster diver, jungle survival instructor, lay analyst, creative writing teacher, reporter, and editor of several West Coast newspapers—before becoming a full-time writer.

In 1952, Herbert began publishing science fiction with "Looking for Something?" in *Startling Stories*. But his emergence as a writer of major stature did not occur until 1965, with the publication of *Dune*. This was followed by *Dune Messiah, Children of Dune, God Emperor of Dune, Heretics of Dune*, and *Chapterhouse: Dune* to complete the bestselling saga. Herbert is also the author of some twenty other books, including *The White Plague, The Dosadi Experiment*, and *Destination: Void*. He died in 1986.

THE DUNE CHRONICLES

BY FRANK HERBERT

DUNE

THE DUNE CHRONICLES BY FRANK HERBERT

DUNE

DUNE MESSIAH

CHILDREN OF DUNE

GOD EMPEROR OF DUNE

HERETICS OF DUNE

CHAPTERHOUSE: DUNE

OTHER BOOKS BY FRANK HERBERT

THE BOOK OF FRANK HERBERT

DESTINATION: VOID
(revised edition)

DIRECT DESCENT

THE DOSADI EXPERIMENT

EYE

THE EYES OF HEISENBERG

THE GODMAKERS

THE GREEN BRAIN

THE MAKER OF DUNE

THE SANTAROGA BARRIER

SOUL CATCHER

WHIPPING STAR

THE WHITE PLAGUE

THE WORLDS OF FRANK HERBERT

MAN OF TWO WORLDS
(with Brian Herbert)

BOOKS BY FRANK HERBERT AND BILL RANSOM

THE JESUS INCIDENT

THE LAZARUS EFFECT

THE ASCENSION FACTOR

BOOKS BY BRIAN HERBERT

DREAMER OF DUNE: THE BIOGRAPHY OF FRANK HERBERT

BOOKS EDITED BY BRIAN HERBERT

THE NOTEBOOKS OF FRANK HERBERT'S DUNE
SONGS OF MUAD'DIB

BOOKS BY BRIAN HERBERT AND KEVIN J. ANDERSON

DUNE: HOUSE ATREIDES
DUNE: HOUSE HARKONNEN
DUNE: HOUSE CORRINO
DUNE: THE BUTLERIAN JIHAD
DUNE: THE MACHINE CRUSADE
DUNE: THE BATTLE OF CORRIN
THE ROAD TO DUNE
(also by Frank Herbert; includes the novel *Spice Planet*)
HUNTERS OF DUNE
SANDWORMS OF DUNE
PAUL OF DUNE
THE WINDS OF DUNE
SISTERHOOD OF DUNE
MENTATS OF DUNE
NAVIGATORS OF DUNE

DUNE

FRANK HERBERT

ACE
NEW YORK

ACE

Published by Berkley

An imprint of Penguin Random House LLC

375 Hudson Street, New York, New York 10014

Copyright © 1965 by Herbert Properties LLC

"Afterword" by Brian Herbert copyright © 2005 by DreamStar, Inc.

ACE is a registered trademark and the A colophon is a trademark of
Penguin Random House LLC.

Ace trade paperback ISBN: 9780441013593

The Library of Congress has cataloged the G. P. Putnam's Sons
hardcover edition as follows:

Herbert, Frank
Dune.
1. Title
PS3558.E63D8 1984 813.54   83-16030
ISBN 0-399-12896-4

G. P. Putnam's Sons hardcover edition / 1984
Ace hardcover edition / October 1999
Ace trade paperback edition / August 2005

Printed in the United States of America

49th Printing

Cover illustration and design by Jim Tierney
Interior art: Desert Cave © masher/Shutterstock Images
Book design by Kristin del Rosario

*To the people whose labors go beyond ideas
into the realm of "real materials"—
to the dry-land ecologists, wherever they may be, in
whatever time they work,
this effort at prediction is dedicated
in humility and admiration.*

CONTENTS

DUNE

A beginning is the time for taking the most delicate care that the balances are correct. This every sister of the Bene Gesserit knows. To begin your study of the life of Muad'Dib, then, take care that you first place him in his time: born in the 57th year of the Padishah Emperor, Shaddam IV. And take the most special care that you locate Muad'Dib in his place: the planet Arrakis. Do not be deceived by the fact that he was born on Caladan and lived his first fifteen years there. Arrakis, the planet known as Dune, is forever his place.

—FROM "MANUAL OF MUAD'DIB"
BY THE PRINCESS IRULAN

In the week before their departure to Arrakis, when all the final scurrying about had reached a nearly unbearable frenzy, an old crone came to visit the mother of the boy, Paul.

It was a warm night at Castle Caladan, and the ancient pile of stone that had served the Atreides family as home for twenty-six generations bore that cooled-sweat feeling it acquired before a change in the weather.

The old woman was let in by the side door down the vaulted passage by Paul's room and she was allowed a moment to peer in at him where he lay in his bed.

By the half-light of a suspensor lamp, dimmed and hanging near the floor, the awakened boy could see a bulky female shape at his door, standing one step ahead of his mother. The old woman was a witch shadow—hair like matted spiderwebs, hooded 'round darkness of features, eyes like glittering jewels.

"Is he not small for his age, Jessica?" the old woman asked. Her voice wheezed and twanged like an untuned baliset.

Paul's mother answered in her soft contralto: "The Atreides are known to start late getting their growth, Your Reverence."

"So I've heard, so I've heard," wheezed the old woman. "Yet he's already fifteen."

"Yes, Your Reverence."

"He's awake and listening to us," said the old woman. "Sly little rascal." She chuckled. "But royalty has need of slyness. And if he's really the Kwisatz Haderach . . . well. . . ."

Within the shadows of his bed, Paul held his eyes open to mere slits. Two bird-bright ovals—the eyes of the old woman—seemed to expand and glow as they stared into his.

"Sleep well, you sly little rascal," said the old woman. "Tomorrow you'll need all your faculties to meet my gom jabbar."

And she was gone, pushing his mother out, closing the door with a solid thump.

Paul lay awake wondering: *What's a gom jabbar?*

In all the upset during this time of change, the old woman was the strangest thing he had seen.

Your Reverence.

And the way she called his mother Jessica like a common serving wench instead of what she was—a Bene Gesserit Lady, a duke's concubine and mother of the ducal heir.

Is a gom jabbar something of Arrakis I must know before we go there? he wondered.

He mouthed her strange words: *Gom jabbar . . . Kwisatz Haderach.*

There had been so many things to learn. Arrakis would be a place so different from Caladan that Paul's mind whirled with the new knowledge. *Arrakis—Dune—Desert Planet.*

Thufir Hawat, his father's Master of Assassins, had explained it: their mortal enemies, the Harkonnens, had been on Arrakis eighty years, holding the planet in quasi-fief under a CHOAM Company contract to mine the geriatric spice, melange. Now the Harkonnens were leaving to be replaced by the House of Atreides in fief-complete—an apparent victory for the Duke Leto. Yet, Hawat had said, this appearance contained the deadliest peril, for the Duke Leto was popular among the Great Houses of the Landsraad.

"A popular man arouses the jealousy of the powerful," Hawat had said.

Arrakis—Dune—Desert Planet.

Paul fell asleep to dream of an Arrakeen cavern, silent people all around him moving in the dim light of glowglobes. It was solemn there and like a cathedral as he listened to a faint sound—the drip-drip-drip of water. Even while he remained in the dream, Paul knew he would remember it upon awakening. He always remembered the dreams that were predictions.

The dream faded.

Paul awoke to feel himself in the warmth of his bed—thinking . . . thinking. This world of Castle Caladan, without play or companions his own age, perhaps did not deserve sadness in farewell. Dr. Yueh, his teacher, had hinted that the faufreluches class system was not rigidly guarded on Arrakis. The planet sheltered people who lived at the desert edge without caid or bashar to command them: will-o'-the-sand people called Fremen, marked down on no census of the Imperial Regate.

Arrakis—Dune—Desert Planet.

Paul sensed his own tensions, decided to practice one of the mind-body lessons his mother had taught him. Three quick breaths triggered the responses: he fell into the floating awareness . . . focusing the consciousness . . . aortal dilation . . . avoiding the unfocused mechanism of consciousness . . . to be conscious by choice . . . blood enriched and swift-flooding the overload regions . . . *one does not obtain food-safety-freedom by instinct alone* . . . animal consciousness does not extend beyond the given moment nor into the idea that its victims may become extinct . . . the animal destroys and does not produce . . . animal pleasures remain close to sensation levels and avoid the perceptual . . . the human requires a background grid through which to see his universe . . . focused consciousness by choice, this forms your grid . . . bodily integrity follows nerve-blood flow according to the deepest awareness of cell needs . . . all things/cells/beings are impermanent . . . strive for flow-permanence within. . . .

Over and over and over within Paul's floating awareness the lesson rolled.

When dawn touched Paul's window sill with yellow light, he sensed it through closed eyelids, opened them, hearing then the renewed bustle and hurry in the castle, seeing the familiar patterned beams of his bedroom ceiling.

The hall door opened and his mother peered in, hair like shaded bronze held with black ribbon at the crown, her oval face emotionless and green eyes staring solemnly.

"You're awake," she said. "Did you sleep well?"

"Yes."

He studied the tallness of her, saw the hint of tension in her shoulders as she chose clothing for him from the closet racks. Another might have missed the tension, but she had trained him in the Bene Gesserit Way—in the minutiae of observation. She turned, holding a semiformal jacket for him. It carried the red Atreides hawk crest above the breast pocket.

"Hurry and dress," she said. "Reverend Mother is waiting."

"I dreamed of her once," Paul said. "Who is she?"

"She was my teacher at the Bene Gesserit school. Now, she's the Emperor's Truthsayer. And Paul. . . ." She hesitated. "You must tell her about your dreams."

"I will. Is she the reason we got Arrakis?"

"We did not *get* Arrakis." Jessica flicked dust from a pair of trousers, hung them with the jacket on the dressing stand beside his bed. "Don't keep Reverend Mother waiting."

Paul sat up, hugged his knees. "What's a gom jabbar?"

Again, the training she had given him exposed her almost invisible hesitation, a nervous betrayal he felt as fear.

Jessica crossed to the window, flung wide the draperies, stared across the river orchards toward Mount Syubi. "You'll learn about . . . the gom jabbar soon enough," she said.

He heard the fear in her voice and wondered at it.

Jessica spoke without turning. "Reverend Mother is waiting in my morning room. Please hurry."

THE REVEREND MOTHER GAIUS HELEN MOHIAM SAT IN A TAPESTRIED chair watching mother and son approach. Windows on each side of her overlooked the curving southern bend of the river and the green farmlands of the Atreides family holding, but the Reverend Mother ignored the view. She was feeling her age this morning, more than a little petulant. She blamed it on space travel and association with that abominable Spacing Guild and its secretive ways. But here was a mission that required personal attention from a Bene Gesserit-with-the-Sight. Even the Padishah Emperor's Truthsayer couldn't evade that responsibility when the duty call came.

Damn that Jessica! the Reverend Mother thought. *If only she'd borne us a girl as she was ordered to do!*

Jessica stopped three paces from the chair, dropped a small curtsy, a gentle flick of left hand along the line of her skirt. Paul gave the short bow his dancing master had taught—the one used "when in doubt of another's station."

The nuances of Paul's greeting were not lost on the Reverend Mother. She said: "He's a cautious one, Jessica."

Jessica's hand went to Paul's shoulder, tightened there. For a heartbeat, fear pulsed through her palm. Then she had herself under control. "Thus he has been taught, Your Reverence."

What does she fear? Paul wondered.

The old woman studied Paul in one gestalten flicker: face oval like Jessica's, but strong bones . . . hair: the Duke's black-black but with browline of the maternal grandfather who cannot be named, and that thin, disdainful nose; shape of directly staring green eyes: like the old Duke, the paternal grandfather who is dead.

Now, there was a man who appreciated the power of bravura—even in death, the Reverend Mother thought.

"Teaching is one thing," she said, "the basic ingredient is another. We shall see." The old eyes darted a hard glance at Jessica. "Leave us. I enjoin you to practice the meditation of peace."

Jessica took her hand from Paul's shoulder. "Your Reverence, I—"

"Jessica, you know it must be done."

Paul looked up at his mother, puzzled.

Jessica straightened. "Yes . . . of course."

Paul looked back at the Reverend Mother. Politeness and his mother's obvious awe of this old woman argued caution. Yet he felt an angry apprehension at the fear he sensed radiating from his mother.

"Paul. . . ." Jessica took a deep breath. ". . . this test you're about to receive . . . it's important to me."

"Test?" He looked up at her.

"Remember that you're a duke's son," Jessica said. She whirled and strode from the room in a dry swishing of skirt. The door closed solidly behind her.

Paul faced the old woman, holding anger in check. "Does one dismiss the Lady Jessica as though she were a serving wench?"

A smile flicked the corners of the wrinkled old mouth. "The Lady Jessica *was* my serving wench, lad, for fourteen years at school." She nodded. "And a good one, too. Now, *you* come here!"

The command whipped out at him. Paul found himself obeying before he could think about it. *Using the Voice on me*, he thought. He stopped at her gesture, standing beside her knees.

"See this?" she asked. From the folds of her gown, she lifted a green metal cube about fifteen centimeters on a side. She turned it and Paul saw that one side was open—black and oddly frightening. No light penetrated that open blackness.

"Put your right hand in the box," she said.

Fear shot through Paul. He started to back away, but the old woman said: "Is this how you obey your mother?"

He looked up into bird-bright eyes.

Slowly, feeling the compulsions and unable to inhibit them, Paul put his hand into the box. He felt first a sense of cold as the blackness closed around his hand, then slick metal against his fingers and a prickling as though his hand were asleep.

A predatory look filled the old woman's features. She lifted her right hand away from the box and poised the hand close to the side of Paul's neck. He saw a glint of metal there and started to turn toward it.

"Stop!" she snapped.

Using the Voice again! He swung his attention back to her face.

"I hold at your neck the gom jabbar," she said. "The gom jabbar, the high-handed enemy. It's a needle with a drop of poison on its tip. Ah-ah! Don't pull away or you'll feel that poison."

Paul tried to swallow in a dry throat. He could not take his attention from the seamed old face, the glistening eyes, the pale gums around silvery metal teeth that flashed as she spoke.

"A duke's son *must* know about poisons," she said. "It's the way of our times, eh? Musky, to be poisoned in your drink. Aumas, to be poisoned in your food. The quick ones and the slow ones and the ones in between. Here's a new one for you: the gom jabbar. It kills only animals."

Pride overcame Paul's fear. "You dare suggest a duke's son is an animal?" he demanded.

"Let us say I suggest you may be human," she said. "Steady! I warn you not to try jerking away. I am old, but my hand can drive this needle into your neck before you escape me."

"Who are you?" he whispered. "How did you trick my mother into leaving me alone with you? Are you from the Harkonnens?"

"The Harkonnens? Bless us, no! Now, be silent." A dry finger touched his neck and he stilled the involuntary urge to leap away.

"Good," she said. "You pass the first test. Now, here's the way of the rest of it: If you withdraw your hand from the box you die. This is the only rule. Keep your hand in the box and live. Withdraw it and die."

Paul took a deep breath to still his trembling. "If I call out there'll be servants on you in seconds and *you'll* die."

"Servants will not pass your mother who stands guard outside that door. Depend on it. Your mother survived this test. Now it's your turn. Be honored. We seldom administer this to men-children."

Curiosity reduced Paul's fear to a manageable level. He heard truth in the old woman's voice, no denying it. If his mother stood guard out there . . . if this were truly a test. . . . And whatever it was, he knew himself caught in it, trapped by that hand at his neck: the gom jabbar. He recalled the response from the Litany against Fear as his mother had taught him out of the Bene Gesserit rite.

"I must not fear. Fear is the mind-killer. Fear is the little-death that brings total obliteration. I will face my fear. I will permit it to pass over me and through me. And when it has gone past I will turn the inner eye to see its path. Where the fear has gone there will be nothing. Only I will remain."

He felt calmness return, said: "Get on with it, old woman."

"Old woman!" she snapped. "You've courage, and that can't be denied. Well, we shall see, sirra." She bent close, lowered her voice almost to a whisper. "You will feel pain in this hand within the box. Pain. But! Withdraw the hand and I'll touch your neck with my gom jabbar—the death so swift it's like the fall of the headsman's axe. Withdraw your hand and the gom jabbar takes you. Understand?"

"What's in the box?"

"Pain."

He felt increased tingling in his hand, pressed his lips tightly together. *How could this be a test?* he wondered. The tingling became an itch.

The old woman said: "You've heard of animals chewing off a leg to escape a trap? There's an animal kind of trick. A human would remain in the trap, endure the pain, feigning death that he might kill the trapper and remove a threat to his kind."

The itch became the faintest burning. "Why are you doing this?" he demanded.

"To determine if you're human. Be silent."

Paul clenched his left hand into a fist as the burning sensation increased in the other hand. It mounted slowly: heat upon heat upon heat . . . upon heat. He felt the fingernails of his free hand biting the palm. He tried to flex the fingers of the burning hand, but couldn't move them.

"It burns," he whispered.

"Silence!"

Pain throbbed up his arm. Sweat stood out on his forehead. Every fiber cried out to withdraw the hand from that burning pit . . . but . . . the gom jabbar. Without turning his head, he tried to move his eyes to see that terrible needle poised beside his neck. He sensed that he was breathing in gasps, tried to slow his breaths and couldn't.

Pain!

His world emptied of everything except that hand immersed in agony, the ancient face inches away staring at him.

His lips were so dry he had difficulty separating them.

The burning! The burning!

He thought he could feel skin curling black on that agonized hand, the flesh crisping and dropping away until only charred bones remained.

It stopped!

As though a switch had been turned off, the pain stopped.

Paul felt his right arm trembling, felt sweat bathing his body.

"Enough," the old woman muttered. "Kull wahad! No woman-child ever withstood that much. I must've wanted you to fail." She leaned back, withdrawing the gom jabbar from the side of his neck. "Take your hand from the box, young human, and look at it."

He fought down an aching shiver, stared at the lightless void where his hand seemed to remain of its own volition. Memory of pain inhibited every movement. Reason told him he would withdraw a blackened stump from that box.

"Do it!" she snapped.

He jerked his hand from the box, stared at it astonished. Not a mark. No sign of agony on the flesh. He held up the hand, turned it, flexed the fingers.

"Pain by nerve induction," she said. "Can't go around maiming potential humans. There're those who'd give a pretty for the secret of this box, though." She slipped it into the folds of her gown.

"But the pain—" he said.

"Pain," she sniffed. "A human can override any nerve in the body."

Paul felt his left hand aching, uncurled the clenched fingers, looked at four bloody marks where fingernails had bitten his palm. He dropped the hand to his side, looked at the old woman. "You did that to my mother once?"

"Ever sift sand through a screen?" she asked.

The tangential slash of her question shocked his mind into a higher awareness: *Sand through a screen.* He nodded.

"We Bene Gesserit sift people to find the humans."

He lifted his right hand, willing the memory of the pain. "And that's all there is to it—pain?"

"I observed you in pain, lad. Pain's merely the axis of the test. Your mother's told you about our ways of observing. I see the signs of her teaching in you. Our test is crisis and observation."

He heard the confirmation in her voice, said: "It's truth!"

She stared at him. *He senses truth! Could he be the one? Could he truly be the one?* She extinguished the excitement, reminding herself: *"Hope clouds observation."*

"You know when people believe what they say," she said.

"I know it."

The harmonics of ability confirmed by repeated test were in his voice. She heard them, said: "Perhaps you are the Kwisatz Haderach. Sit down, little brother, here at my feet."

"I prefer to stand."

"Your mother sat at my feet once."

"I'm not my mother."

"You hate us a little, eh?" She looked toward the door, called out: "Jessica!"

The door flew open and Jessica stood there staring hard-eyed into the room. Hardness melted from her as she saw Paul. She managed a faint smile.

"Jessica, have you ever stopped hating me?" the old woman asked.

"I both love and hate you," Jessica said. "The hate—that's from pains I must never forget. The love—that's. . . ."

"Just the basic fact," the old woman said, but her voice was gentle. "You may come in now, but remain silent. Close that door and mind it that no one interrupts us."

Jessica stepped into the room, closed the door and stood with her back to it. *My son lives*, she thought. *My son lives and is . . . human. I knew he was . . . but . . . he lives. Now, I can go on living.* The door felt hard and real against her back. Everything in the room was immediate and pressing against her senses.

My son lives.

Paul looked at his mother. *She told the truth.* He wanted to get away alone and think this experience through, but knew he could not leave until he was dismissed. The old woman had gained a power over him. *They spoke truth.* His mother had undergone this test. There must be terrible purpose in it . . . the pain and fear had been terrible. He understood terrible purposes. They drove against all odds. They were their own necessity. Paul felt that he had been infected with terrible purpose. He did not know yet what the terrible purpose was.

"Someday, lad," the old woman said, "you, too, may have to stand outside a door like that. It takes a measure of doing."

Paul looked down at the hand that had known pain, then up to the Reverend Mother. The sound of her voice had contained a difference then from any other voice in his experience. The words were outlined in brilliance. There was an edge to them. He felt that any question he might ask her would bring an answer that could lift him out of his flesh-world into something greater.

"Why do you test for humans?" he asked.

"To set you free."

"Free?"

"Once, men turned their thinking over to machines in the hope that this would set them free. But that only permitted other men with machines to enslave them."

"'Thou shalt not make a machine in the likeness of a man's mind,'" Paul quoted.

"Right out of the Butlerian Jihad and the Orange Catholic Bible," she said. "But what the O.C. Bible should've said is: 'Thou shalt not make a machine to counterfeit a *human* mind.' Have you studied the Mentat in your service?"

"I've studied *with* Thufir Hawat."

"The Great Revolt took away a crutch," she said. "It forced *human* minds to develop. Schools were started to train *human* talents."

"Bene Gesserit schools?"

She nodded. "We have two chief survivors of those ancient schools: the Bene Gesserit and the Spacing Guild. The Guild, so we think, emphasizes almost pure mathematics. Bene Gesserit performs another function."

"Politics," he said.

"Kull wahad!" the old woman said. She sent a hard glance at Jessica.

"I've not told him, Your Reverence," Jessica said.

The Reverend Mother returned her attention to Paul. "You did that on remarkably few clues," she said. "Politics indeed. The original Bene Gesserit school was directed by those who saw the need of a thread of continuity in human affairs. They saw there could be no such continuity without separating human stock from animal stock—for breeding purposes."

The old woman's words abruptly lost their special sharpness for Paul. He felt an offense against what his mother called his *instinct for rightness.* It wasn't that Reverend Mother lied to him. She obviously believed what she said. It was something deeper, something tied to his terrible purpose.

He said: "But my mother tells me many Bene Gesserit of the schools don't know their ancestry."

"The genetic lines are always in our records," she said. "Your mother knows that either she's of Bene Gesserit descent or her stock was acceptable in itself."

"Then why couldn't she know who her parents are?"

"Some do. . . . Many don't. We might, for example, have wanted to breed her to a close relative to set up a dominant in some genetic trait. We have many reasons."

Again, Paul felt the offense against rightness. He said: "You take a lot on yourselves."

The Reverend Mother stared at him, wondering: *Did I hear criticism in his voice?* "We carry a heavy burden," she said.

Paul felt himself coming more and more out of the shock of the test. He leveled a measuring stare at her, said: "You say maybe I'm the . . . Kwisatz Haderach. What's that, a human gom jabbar?"

"Paul," Jessica said. "You mustn't take that tone with—"

"I'll handle this, Jessica," the old woman said. "Now, lad, do you know about the Truthsayer drug?"

"You take it to improve your ability to detect falsehood," he said. "My mother's told me."

"Have you ever seen truthtrance?"

He shook his head. "No."

"The drug's dangerous," she said, "but it gives insight. When a Truthsayer's gifted by the drug, she can look many places in her memory—in her body's memory. We look down so many avenues of the past . . . but only feminine avenues." Her voice took on a note of sadness. "Yet, there's a place where no Truthsayer can see. We are repelled by it, terrorized. It is said a man will come one day and find in the gift of the drug his inward eye. He will look where we cannot—into both feminine and masculine pasts."

"Your Kwisatz Haderach?"

"Yes, the one who can be many places at once: the Kwisatz Hader-

ach. Many men have tried the drug . . . so many, but none has succeeded."

"They tried and failed, all of them?"

"Oh, no." She shook her head. "They tried and died."

To attempt an understanding of Muad'Dib without understanding his mortal enemies, the Harkonnens, is to attempt seeing Truth without knowing Falsehood. It is the attempt to see the Light without knowing Darkness. It cannot be.

—FROM "MANUAL OF MUAD'DIB"
BY THE PRINCESS IRULAN

It was a relief globe of a world, partly in shadows, spinning under the impetus of a fat hand that glittered with rings. The globe sat on a free-form stand at one wall of a windowless room whose other walls presented a patchwork of multicolored scrolls, filmbooks, tapes and reels. Light glowed in the room from golden balls hanging in mobile suspensor fields.

An ellipsoid desk with a top of jade-pink petrified elacca wood stood at the center of the room. Veriform suspensor chairs ringed it, two of them occupied. In one sat a dark-haired youth of about sixteen years, round of face and with sullen eyes. The other held a slender, short man with an effeminate face.

Both youth and man stared at the globe and the man half-hidden in shadows spinning it.

A chuckle sounded beside the globe. A basso voice rumbled out of the chuckle: "There it is, Piter—the biggest mantrap in all history. And the Duke's headed into its jaws. Is it not a magnificent thing that I, the Baron Vladimir Harkonnen, do?"

"Assuredly, Baron," said the man. His voice came out tenor with a sweet, musical quality.

The fat hand descended onto the globe, stopped the spinning. Now, all eyes in the room could focus on the motionless surface and see that it was the kind of globe made for wealthy collectors or planetary governors of the Empire. It had the stamp of Imperial handicraft about it. Latitude and longitude lines were laid in with hair-fine platinum wire. The polar caps were insets of finest cloudmilk diamonds.

The fat hand moved, tracing details on the surface. "I invite you to observe," the basso voice rumbled. "Observe closely, Piter, and you, too, Feyd-Rautha, my darling: from sixty degrees north to seventy degrees south—these exquisite ripples. Their coloring: does it not remind you of sweet caramels? And nowhere do you see blue of lakes or rivers or seas. And these lovely polar caps—so small. Could anyone mistake this place? Arrakis! Truly unique. A superb setting for a unique victory."

A smile touched Piter's lips. "And to think, Baron: the Padishah Emperor believes he's given the Duke your spice planet. How poignant."

"That's a nonsensical statement," the Baron rumbled. "You say this to confuse young Feyd-Rautha, but it is not necessary to confuse my nephew."

The sullen-faced youth stirred in his chair, smoothed a wrinkle in the black leotards he wore. He sat upright as a discreet tapping sounded at the door in the wall behind him.

Piter unfolded from his chair, crossed to the door, cracked it wide enough to accept a message cylinder. He closed the door, unrolled the cylinder and scanned it. A chuckle sounded from him. Another.

"Well?" the Baron demanded.

"The fool answered us, Baron!"

"Whenever did an Atreides refuse the opportunity for a gesture?" the Baron asked. "Well, what does he say?"

"He's most uncouth, Baron. Addresses you as 'Harkonnen'—no 'Sire et Cher Cousin,' no title, nothing."

"It's a good name," the Baron growled, and his voice betrayed his impatience. "What does dear Leto say?"

"He says: 'Your offer of a meeting is refused. I have ofttimes met your treachery and this all men know.'"

"And?" the Baron asked.

"He says: 'The art of kanly still has admirers in the Empire.' He signs it: 'Duke Leto of Arrakis.'" Piter began to laugh. "Of Arrakis! Oh, my! This is almost too rich!"

"Be silent, Piter," the Baron said, and the laughter stopped as though shut off with a switch. "Kanly, is it?" the Baron asked. "Vendetta, heh? And he uses the nice old word so rich in tradition to be sure I know he means it."

"You made the peace gesture," Piter said. "The forms have been obeyed."

"For a Mentat, you talk too much, Piter," the Baron said. And he thought: *I must do away with that one soon. He has almost outlived his usefulness.* The Baron stared across the room at his Mentat assassin, seeing the feature about him that most people noticed first: the eyes, the shaded slits of blue within blue, the eyes without any white in them at all.

A grin flashed across Piter's face. It was like a mask grimace beneath those eyes like holes. "But, Baron! Never has revenge been more beautiful. It is to see a plan of the most exquisite treachery: to *make* Leto exchange Caladan for Dune—and without alternative because the Emperor orders it. How waggish of you!"

In a cold voice, the Baron said: "You have a flux of the mouth, Piter."

"But I am happy, my Baron. Whereas you . . . you are touched by jealousy."

"Piter!"

"Ah-ah, Baron! Is it not regrettable you were unable to devise this delicious scheme by yourself?"

"Someday I will have you strangled, Piter."

"Of a certainty, Baron. Enfin! But a kind act is never lost, eh?"

"Have you been chewing verite or semuta, Piter?"

"Truth without fear surprises the Baron," Piter said. His face drew down into a caricature of a frowning mask. "Ah, hah! But you see, Baron, I know as a Mentat when you will send the executioner. You will hold back just so long as I am useful. To move sooner would be wasteful and I'm yet of much use. I know what it is you learned from that lovely Dune planet—waste not. True, Baron?"

The Baron continued to stare at Piter.

Feyd-Rautha squirmed in his chair. *These wrangling fools!* he thought. *My uncle cannot talk to his Mentat without arguing. Do they think I've nothing to do except listen to their arguments?*

"Feyd," the Baron said. "I told you to listen and learn when I invited you in here. Are you learning?"

"Yes, Uncle." The voice was carefully subservient.

"Sometimes I wonder about Piter," the Baron said. "I cause pain out of necessity, but he . . . I swear he takes a positive delight in it. For myself, I can feel pity toward the poor Duke Leto. Dr. Yueh will move against him soon, and that'll be the end of all the Atreides. But surely Leto will know whose hand directed the pliant doctor . . . and knowing that will be a terrible thing."

"Then why haven't you directed the doctor to slip a kindjal between his ribs quietly and efficiently?" Piter asked. "You talk of pity, but—"

"The Duke *must* know when I encompass his doom," the Baron said. "And the other Great Houses must learn of it. The knowledge will give them pause. I'll gain a bit more room to maneuver. The necessity is obvious, but I don't have to like it."

"Room to maneuver," Piter sneered. "Already you have the Emperor's eyes on you, Baron. You move too boldly. One day the Emperor will send a legion or two of his Sardaukar down here onto Giedi Prime and that'll be an end to the Baron Vladimir Harkonnen."

"You'd like to see that, wouldn't you, Piter?" the Baron asked. "You'd enjoy seeing the Corps of Sardaukar pillage through my cities and sack this castle. You'd truly enjoy that."

"Does the Baron need to ask?" Piter whispered.

"You should've been a Bashar of the Corps," the Baron said. "You're too interested in blood and pain. Perhaps I was too quick with my promise of the spoils of Arrakis."

Piter took five curiously mincing steps into the room, stopped directly behind Feyd-Rautha. There was a tight air of tension in the room, and the youth looked up at Piter with a worried frown.

"Do not toy with Piter, Baron," Piter said. "You promised me the Lady Jessica. You promised her to me."

"For what, Piter?" the Baron asked. "For pain?"

Piter stared at him, dragging out the silence.

Feyd-Rautha moved his suspensor chair to one side, said: "Uncle, do I have to stay? You said you'd—"

"My darling Feyd-Rautha grows impatient," the Baron said. He moved within the shadows beside the globe. "Patience, Feyd." And he turned his attention back to the Mentat. "What of the Dukeling, the child Paul, my dear Piter?"

"The trap will bring him to you, Baron," Piter muttered.

"That's not my question," the Baron said. "You'll recall that you predicted the Bene Gesserit witch would bear a daughter to the Duke. You were wrong, eh, Mentat?"

"I'm not often wrong, Baron," Piter said, and for the first time there was fear in his voice. "Give me that: I'm not often wrong. And you know yourself these Bene Gesserit bear mostly daughters. Even the Emperor's consort had produced only females."

"Uncle," said Feyd-Rautha, "you said there'd be something important here for me to—"

"Listen to my nephew," the Baron said. "He aspires to rule my Barony, yet he cannot rule himself." The Baron stirred beside the globe, a shadow among shadows. "Well then, Feyd-Rautha Harkonnen, I summoned you here hoping to teach you a bit of wisdom. Have you observed our good Mentat? You should've learned something from this exchange."

"But, Uncle—"

"A most efficient Mentat, Piter, wouldn't you say, Feyd?"

"Yes, but—"

"Ah! Indeed *but*! But he consumes too much spice, eats it like candy.

Look at his eyes! He might've come directly from the Arrakeen labor pool. Efficient, Piter, *but* he's still emotional and prone to passionate outbursts. Efficient, Piter, *but* he still can err."

Piter spoke in a low, sullen tone: "Did you call me in here to impair my efficiency with criticism, Baron?"

"Impair your efficiency? You know me better, Piter. I wish only for my nephew to understand the limitations of a Mentat."

"Are you already training my replacement?" Piter demanded.

"Replace *you*? Why, Piter, where could I find another Mentat with your cunning and venom?"

"The same place you found me, Baron."

"Perhaps I should at that," the Baron mused. "You do seem a bit unstable lately. And the spice you eat!"

"Are my pleasures too expensive, Baron? Do you object to them?"

"My dear Piter, your pleasures are what tie you to me. How could I object to that? I merely wish my nephew to observe this about you."

"Then I'm on display," Piter said. "Shall I dance? Shall I perform my various functions for the eminent Feyd-Rau—"

"Precisely," the Baron said. "You are on display. Now, be silent." He glanced at Feyd-Rautha, noting his nephew's lips, the full and pouting look of them, the Harkonnen genetic marker, now twisted slightly in amusement. "This is a Mentat, Feyd. It has been trained and conditioned to perform certain duties. The fact that it's encased in a human body, however, must not be overlooked. A serious drawback, that. I sometimes think the ancients with their thinking machines had the right idea."

"They were toys compared to me," Piter snarled. "You yourself, Baron, could outperform those *machines*."

"Perhaps," the Baron said. "Ah, well. . . ." He took a deep breath, belched. "Now, Piter, outline for my nephew the salient features of our campaign against the House of Atreides. Function as a Mentat for us, if you please."

"Baron, I've warned you not to trust one so young with this information. My observations of—"

"I'll be the judge of this," the Baron said. "I give you an order, Mentat. Perform one of your various functions."

"So be it," Piter said. He straightened, assuming an odd attitude of dignity—as though it were another mask, but this time clothing his entire body. "In a few days Standard, the entire household of the Duke Leto will embark on a Spacing Guild liner for Arrakis. The Guild will deposit them at the city of Arrakeen rather than at our city of Carthag. The Duke's Mentat, Thufir Hawat, will have concluded rightly that Arrakeen is easier to defend."

"Listen carefully, Feyd," the Baron said. "Observe the plans within plans within plans."

Feyd-Rautha nodded, thinking: *This is more like it. The old monster is letting me in on secret things at last. He must really mean for me to be his heir.*

"There are several tangential possibilities," Piter said. "I indicate that House Atreides will go to Arrakis. We must not, however, ignore the possibility the Duke has contracted with the Guild to remove him to a place of safety outside the System. Others in like circumstances have become renegade Houses, taking family atomics and shields and fleeing beyond the Imperium."

"The Duke's too proud a man for that," the Baron said.

"It is a possibility," Piter said. "The ultimate effect for us would be the same, however."

"No, it would not!" the Baron growled. "I must have him dead and his line ended."

"That's the high probability," Piter said. "There are certain preparations that indicate when a House is going renegade. The Duke appears to be doing none of these things."

"So," the Baron sighed. "Get on with it, Piter."

"At Arrakeen," Piter said, "the Duke and his family will occupy the Residency, lately the home of Count and Lady Fenring."

"The Ambassador to the Smugglers," the Baron chuckled.

"Ambassador to what?" Feyd-Rautha asked.

"Your uncle makes a joke," Piter said. "He calls Count Fenring Ambassador to the Smugglers, indicating the Emperor's interest in smuggling operations on Arrakis."

Feyd-Rautha turned a puzzled stare on his uncle. "Why?"

"Don't be dense, Feyd," the Baron snapped. "As long as the Guild remains effectively outside Imperial control, how could it be otherwise? How else could spies and assassins move about?"

Feyd-Rautha's mouth made a soundless "Oh-h-h-h."

"We've arranged diversions at the Residency," Piter said. "There'll be an attempt on the life of the Atreides heir—an attempt which could succeed."

"Piter," the Baron rumbled, "you indicated—"

"I indicated accidents can happen," Piter said. "And the attempt must appear valid."

"Ah, but the lad has such a sweet young body," the Baron said. "Of course, he's potentially more dangerous than the father . . . with that witch mother training him. Accursed woman! Ah, well, please continue, Piter."

"Hawat will have divined that we have an agent planted on him," Piter said. "The obvious suspect is Dr. Yueh, who is indeed our agent. But Hawat has investigated and found that our doctor is a Suk School graduate with Imperial Conditioning—supposedly safe enough to minister even to the Emperor. Great store is set on Imperial Conditioning. It's assumed that ultimate conditioning cannot be removed without killing the subject. However, as someone once observed, given the right lever you can move a planet. We found the lever that moved the doctor."

"How?" Feyd-Rautha asked. He found this a fascinating subject. *Everyone* knew you couldn't subvert Imperial Conditioning!

"Another time," the Baron said. "Continue, Piter."

"In place of Yueh," Piter said, "we'll drag a most interesting suspect across Hawat's path. The very audacity of this suspect will recommend her to Hawat's attention."

"Her?" Feyd-Rautha asked.

"The Lady Jessica herself," the Baron said.

"Is it not sublime?" Piter asked. "Hawat's mind will be so filled with this prospect it'll impair his function as a Mentat. He may even try to kill her." Piter frowned, then: "But I don't think he'll be able to carry it off."

"You don't want him to, eh?" the Baron asked.

"Don't distract me," Piter said. "While Hawat's occupied with the Lady Jessica, we'll divert him further with uprisings in a few garrison towns and the like. These will be put down. The Duke must believe he's gaining a measure of security. Then, when the moment is ripe, we'll signal Yueh and move in with our major force . . . ah. . . ."

"Go ahead, tell him all of it," the Baron said.

"We'll move in strengthened by two legions of Sardaukar disguised in Harkonnen livery."

"Sardaukar!" Feyd-Rautha breathed. His mind focused on the dread Imperial troops, the killers without mercy, the soldier-fanatics of the Padishah Emperor.

"You see how I trust you, Feyd," the Baron said. "No hint of this must ever reach another Great House, else the Landsraad might unite against the Imperial House and there'd be chaos."

"The main point," Piter said, "is this: since House Harkonnen is being used to do the Imperial dirty work, we've gained a true advantage. It's a dangerous advantage, to be sure, but if used cautiously, will bring House Harkonnen greater wealth than that of any other House in the Imperium."

"You have no idea how much wealth is involved, Feyd," the Baron said. "Not in your wildest imaginings. To begin, we'll have an irrevocable directorship in the CHOAM Company."

Feyd-Rautha nodded. Wealth was the thing. CHOAM was the key to wealth, each noble House dipping from the company's coffers whatever it could under the power of the directorships. Those CHOAM directorships—they were the real evidence of political power in the Imperium, passing with the shifts of voting strength within the Landsraad as it balanced itself against the Emperor and *his* supporters.

"The Duke Leto," Piter said, "may attempt to flee to the new Fremen scum along the desert's edge. Or he may try to send his family into that imagined security. But that path is blocked by one of His Majesty's agents—the planetary ecologist. You may remember him—Kynes."

"Feyd remembers him," the Baron said. "Get on with it."

"You do not drool very prettily, Baron," Piter said.

"Get on with it, I command you!" the Baron roared.

Piter shrugged. "If matters go as planned," he said, "House Harkonnen will have a subfief on Arrakis within a Standard year. Your uncle will have dispensation of that fief. His own *personal* agent will rule on Arrakis."

"More profits," Feyd-Rautha said.

"Indeed," the Baron said. And he thought: *It's only just. We're the ones who tamed Arrakis . . . except for the few mongrel Fremen hiding in the skirts of the desert . . . and some tame smugglers bound to the planet almost as tightly as the native labor pool.*

"And the Great Houses will know that the Baron has destroyed the Atreides," Piter said. "They will know."

"They will know," the Baron breathed.

"Loveliest of all," Piter said, "is that the Duke will know, too. He knows now. He can already feel the trap."

"It's true the Duke knows," the Baron said, and his voice held a note of sadness. "He could not help but know . . . more's the pity."

The Baron moved out and away from the globe of Arrakis. As he emerged from the shadows, his figure took on dimension—grossly and immensely fat. And with subtle bulges beneath folds of his dark robes to reveal that all this fat was sustained partly by portable suspensors harnessed to his flesh. He might weigh two hundred Standard kilos in actuality, but his feet would carry no more than fifty of them.

"I am hungry," the Baron rumbled, and he rubbed his protruding lips with a beringed hand, stared down at Feyd-Rautha through fat-enfolded eyes. "Send for food, my darling. We will eat before we retire."

Thus spoke St. Alia-of-the-Knife: "The Reverend Mother must combine the seductive wiles of a courtesan with the untouchable majesty of a virgin goddess, holding these attributes in tension so long as the powers of her youth endure. For when youth and beauty have gone, she will find that the *place-between,* once occupied by tension, has become a wellspring of cunning and resourcefulness."

—FROM "MUAD'DIB, FAMILY COMMENTARIES" BY THE PRINCESS IRULAN

"Well, Jessica, what have you to say for yourself?" asked the Reverend Mother.

It was near sunset at Castle Caladan on the day of Paul's ordeal. The two women were alone in Jessica's morning room while Paul waited in the adjoining soundproofed Meditation Chamber.

Jessica stood facing the south windows. She saw and yet did not see the evening's banked colors across meadow and river. She heard and yet did not hear the Reverend Mother's question.

There had been another ordeal once—so many years ago. A skinny girl with hair the color of bronze, her body tortured by the winds of puberty, had entered the study of the Reverend Mother Gaius Helen Mohiam, Proctor Superior of the Bene Gesserit school on Wallach IX. Jessica looked down at her right hand, flexed the fingers, remembering the pain, the terror, the anger.

"Poor Paul," she whispered.

"I asked you a question, Jessica!" The old woman's voice was snappish, demanding.

"What? Oh. . . ." Jessica tore her attention away from the past, faced the Reverend Mother, who sat with back to the stone wall between the two west windows. "What do you want me to say?"

"What do I want you to say? What do I want you to say?" The old voice carried a tone of cruel mimicry.

"So I had a son!" Jessica flared. And she knew she was being goaded into this anger deliberately.

"You were told to bear only daughters to the Atreides."

"It meant so much to him," Jessica pleaded.

"And you in your pride thought you could produce the Kwisatz Haderach!"

Jessica lifted her chin. "I sensed the possibility."

"You thought only of your Duke's desire for a son," the old woman snapped. "And his desires don't figure in this. An Atreides daughter could've been wed to a Harkonnen heir and sealed the breach. You've hopelessly complicated matters. We may lose both bloodlines now."

"You're not infallible," Jessica said. She braved the steady stare from the old eyes.

Presently, the old woman muttered: "What's done is done."

"I vowed never to regret my decision," Jessica said.

"How noble," the Reverend Mother sneered. "No regrets. We shall see when you're a fugitive with a price on your head and every man's hand turned against you to seek your life and the life of your son."

Jessica paled. "Is there no alternative?"

"Alternative? A Bene Gesserit should ask that?"

"I ask only what you see in the future with your superior abilities."

"I see in the future what I've seen in the past. You well know the pattern of our affairs, Jessica. The race knows its own mortality and fears stagnation of its heredity. It's in the bloodstream—the urge to mingle genetic strains without plan. The Imperium, the CHOAM Company, all the Great Houses, they are but bits of flotsam in the path of the flood."

"CHOAM," Jessica muttered. "I suppose it's already decided how they'll redivide the spoils of Arrakis."

"What is CHOAM but the weather vane of our times," the old woman said. "The Emperor and his friends now command fifty-nine point six-five per cent of the CHOAM directorship's votes. Certainly they smell profits, and likely as others smell those same profits his voting strength will increase. This is the pattern of history, girl."

"That's certainly what I need right now," Jessica said. "A review of history."

"Don't be facetious, girl! You know as well as I do what forces surround us. We've a three-point civilization: the Imperial Household balanced against the Federated Great Houses of the Landsraad, and between them, the Guild with its damnable monopoly on interstellar transport. In politics, the tripod is the most unstable of all structures. It'd be bad enough without the complication of a feudal trade culture which turns its back on most science."

Jessica spoke bitterly: "Chips in the path of the flood—and this chip here, this is the Duke Leto, and this one's his son, and this one's—"

"Oh, shut up, girl. You entered this with full knowledge of the delicate edge you walked."

"'I am Bene Gesserit: I exist only to serve,'" Jessica quoted.

"Truth," the old woman said. "And all we can hope for now is to prevent this from erupting into general conflagration, to salvage what we can of the key bloodlines."

Jessica closed her eyes, feeling tears press out beneath the lids. She fought down the inner trembling, the outer trembling, the uneven breathing, the ragged pulse, the sweating of the palms. Presently, she said, "I'll pay for my own mistake."

"And your son will pay with you."

"I'll shield him as well as I'm able."

"Shield!" the old woman snapped. "You well know the weakness there! Shield your son too much, Jessica, and he'll not grow strong enough to fulfill *any* destiny."

Jessica turned away, looked out the window at the gathering darkness. "Is it really that terrible, this planet of Arrakis?"

"Bad enough, but not all bad. The Missionaria Protectiva has been in there and softened it up somewhat." The Reverend Mother heaved herself to her feet, straightened a fold in her gown. "Call the boy in here. I must be leaving soon."

"Must you?"

The old woman's voice softened. "Jessica, girl, I wish I could stand in your place and take your sufferings. But each of us must make her own path."

"I know."

"You're as dear to me as any of my own daughters, but I cannot let that interfere with duty."

"I understand . . . the necessity."

"What you did, Jessica, and why you did it—we both know. But kindness forces me to tell you there's little chance your lad will be the Bene Gesserit Totality. You mustn't let yourself hope too much."

Jessica shook tears from the corners of her eyes. It was an angry gesture. "You make me feel like a little girl again—reciting my first lesson." She forced the words out: "'Humans must never submit to animals.'" A dry sob shook her. In a low voice, she said: "I've been so lonely."

"It should be one of the tests," the old woman said. "Humans are almost always lonely. Now summon the boy. He's had a long, frightening day. But he's had time to think and remember, and I must ask the other questions about these dreams of his."

Jessica nodded, went to the door of the Meditation Chamber, opened it. "Paul, come in now, please."

Paul emerged with a stubborn slowness. He stared at his mother as though she were a stranger. Wariness veiled his eyes when he glanced at the Reverend Mother, but this time he nodded to her, the nod one gives an equal. He heard his mother close the door behind him.

"Young man," the old woman said, "let's return to this dream business."

"What do you want?"

"Do you dream every night?"

"Not dreams worth remembering. I can remember every dream, but some are worth remembering and some aren't."

"How do you know the difference?"

"I just know it."

The old woman glanced at Jessica, back to Paul. "What did you dream last night? Was it worth remembering?"

"Yes." Paul closed his eyes. "I dreamed a cavern . . . and water . . . and a girl there—very skinny with big eyes. Her eyes are all blue, no whites in them. I talk to her and tell her about you, about seeing the Reverend Mother on Caladan." Paul opened his eyes.

"And the thing you tell this strange girl about seeing me, did it happen today?"

Paul thought about this, then: "Yes. I tell the girl you came and put a stamp of strangeness on me."

"Stamp of strangeness," the old woman breathed, and again she shot a glance at Jessica, returned her attention to Paul. "Tell me truly now, Paul, do you often have dreams of things that happen afterward exactly as you dreamed them?"

"Yes. And I've dreamed about that girl before."

"Oh? You know her?"

"I will know her."

"Tell me about her."

Again, Paul closed his eyes. "We're in a little place in some rocks where it's sheltered. It's almost night, but it's hot and I can see patches of sand out of an opening in the rocks. We're . . . waiting for something . . . for me to go meet some people. And she's frightened but trying to hide it from me, and I'm excited. And she says: 'Tell me about the waters of your homeworld, Usul.'" Paul opened his eyes. "Isn't that strange? My homeworld's Caladan. I've never even heard of a planet called Usul."

"Is there more to this dream?" Jessica prompted.

"Yes. But maybe she was calling *me* Usul," Paul said. "I just thought of that." Again, he closed his eyes. "She asks me to tell her about the waters. And I take her hand. And I say I'll tell her a poem. And I tell her the poem, but I have to explain some of the words—like beach and surf and seaweed and seagulls."

"What poem?" the Reverend Mother asked.

Paul opened his eyes. "It's just one of Gurney Halleck's tone poems for sad times."

Behind Paul, Jessica began to recite:

> *"I remember salt smoke from a beach fire*
> *And shadows under the pines—*
> *Solid, clean . . . fixed—*
> *Seagulls perched at the tip of land,*
> *White upon green . . .*
> *And a wind comes through the pines*
> *To sway the shadows;*
> *The seagulls spread their wings,*
> *Lift*
> *And fill the sky with screeches.*
> *And I hear the wind*
> *Blowing across our beach,*
> *And the surf,*
> *And I see that our fire*
> *Has scorched the seaweed."*

"That's the one," Paul said.

The old woman stared at Paul, then: "Young man, as a Proctor of the Bene Gesserit, I seek the Kwisatz Haderach, the male who truly can become one of us. Your mother sees this possibility in you, but she sees with the eyes of a mother. Possibility I see, too, but no more."

She fell silent and Paul saw that she wanted him to speak. He waited her out.

Presently, she said: "As you will, then. You've depths in you; that I'll grant."

"May I go now?" he asked.

"Don't you want to hear what the Reverend Mother can tell you about the Kwisatz Haderach?" Jessica asked.

"She said those who tried for it died."

"But I can help you with a few hints at why they failed," the Reverend Mother said.

She talks of hints, Paul thought. *She doesn't really know anything.* And he said: "Hint then."

"And be damned to me?" She smiled wryly, a crisscross of wrinkles in the old face. "Very well: 'That which submits rules.'"

He felt astonishment: she was talking about such elementary things as tension within meaning. Did she think his mother had taught him nothing at all?

"That's a hint?" he asked.

"We're not here to bandy words or quibble over their meaning," the old woman said. "The willow submits to the wind and prospers until one day it is many willows—a wall against the wind. This is the willow's purpose."

Paul stared at her. She said *purpose* and he felt the word buffet him, reinfecting him with terrible purpose. He experienced a sudden anger at her: fatuous old witch with her mouth full of platitudes.

"You think I could be this Kwisatz Haderach," he said. "You talk about me, but you haven't said one thing about what we can do to help my father. I've heard you talking to my mother. You talk as though my father were dead. Well, he isn't!"

"If there were a thing to be done for him, we'd have done it," the old woman growled. "We may be able to salvage you. Doubtful, but possible. But for your father, nothing. When you've learned to accept that as a fact, you've learned a *real* Bene Gesserit lesson."

Paul saw how the words shook his mother. He glared at the old woman. How could she say such a thing about his father? What made her so sure? His mind seethed with resentment.

The Reverend Mother looked at Jessica. "You've been training him in the Way—I've seen the signs of it. I'd have done the same in your shoes and devil take the Rules."

Jessica nodded.

"Now, I caution you," said the old woman, "to ignore the regular order of training. His own safety requires the Voice. He already has a good start in it, but we both know how much more he needs . . . and that desperately." She stepped close to Paul, stared down at him. "Goodbye, young human. I hope you make it. But if you don't—well, we shall yet succeed."

Once more she looked at Jessica. A flicker sign of understanding passed between them. Then the old woman swept from the room, her robes hissing, with not another backward glance. The room and its occupants already were shut from her thoughts.

But Jessica had caught one glimpse of the Reverend Mother's face as she turned away. There had been tears on the seamed cheeks. The tears were more unnerving than any other word or sign that had passed between them this day.

You have read that Muad'Dib had no playmates his own age on Caladan. The dangers were too great. But Muad'Dib did have wonderful companion-teachers. There was Gurney Halleck, the troubadour-warrior. You will sing some of Gurney's songs as you read along in this book. There was Thufir Hawat, the old Mentat Master of Assassins, who struck fear even into the heart of the Padishah Emperor. There were Duncan Idaho, the Swordmaster of the Ginaz; Dr. Wellington Yueh, a name black in treachery but bright in knowledge; the Lady Jessica, who guided her son in the Bene Gesserit Way, and—of course—the Duke Leto, whose qualities as a father have long been overlooked.

—FROM "A CHILD'S HISTORY OF MUAD'DIB"
BY THE PRINCESS IRULAN

Thufir Hawat slipped into the training room of Castle Caladan, closed the door softly. He stood there a moment, feeling old and tired and storm-leathered. His left leg ached where it had been slashed once in the service of the Old Duke.

Three generations of them now, he thought.

He stared across the big room bright with the light of noon pouring through the skylights, saw the boy seated with back to the door, intent on papers and charts spread across an ell table.

How many times must I tell that lad never to settle himself with his back to a door? Hawat cleared his throat.

Paul remained bent over his studies.

A cloud shadow passed over the skylights. Again, Hawat cleared his throat.

Paul straightened, spoke without turning: "I know. I'm sitting with my back to a door."

Hawat suppressed a smile, strode across the room.

Paul looked up at the grizzled old man who stopped at a corner of the table. Hawat's eyes were two pools of alertness in a dark and deeply seamed face.

"I heard you coming down the hall," Paul said. "And I heard you open the door."

"The sounds I make could be imitated."

"I'd know the difference."

He might at that, Hawat thought. *That witch mother of his is giving him the deep training, certainly. I wonder what her precious school thinks of that? Maybe that's why they sent the old Proctor here—to whip our dear Lady Jessica into line.*

Hawat pulled up a chair across from Paul, sat down facing the door. He did it pointedly, leaned back and studied the room. It struck him as an odd place suddenly, a stranger-place with most of its hardware already gone off to Arrakis. A training table remained, and a fencing mirror with its crystal prisms quiescent, the target dummy beside it patched and padded, looking like an ancient foot soldier maimed and battered in the wars.

There stand I, Hawat thought.

"Thufir, what're you thinking?" Paul asked.

Hawat looked at the boy. "I was thinking we'll all be out of here soon and likely never see the place again."

"Does that make you sad?"

"Sad? Nonsense! Parting with friends is a sadness. A place is only a place." He glanced at the charts on the table. "And Arrakis is just another place."

"Did my father send you up to test me?"

Hawat scowled—the boy had such observing ways about him. He nodded. "You're thinking it'd have been nicer if he'd come up himself, but you must know how busy he is. He'll be along later."

"I've been studying about the storms on Arrakis."

"The storms. I see."

"They sound pretty bad."

"That's too cautious a word: *bad.* Those storms build up across six or seven thousand kilometers of flatlands, feed on anything that can give them a push—coriolis force, other storms, anything that has an ounce of energy in it. They can blow up to seven hundred kilometers an hour, loaded with everything loose that's in their way—sand, dust, everything. They can eat flesh off bones and etch the bones to slivers."

"Why don't they have weather control?"

"Arrakis has special problems, costs are higher, and there'd be maintenance and the like. The Guild wants a dreadful high price for satellite control and your father's House isn't one of the big rich ones, lad. You know that."

"Have you ever seen the Fremen?"

The lad's mind is darting all over today, Hawat thought.

"Like as not I have seen them," he said. "There's little to tell them from the folk of the graben and sink. They all wear those great flowing robes. And they stink to heaven in any closed space. It's from those suits they wear—call them 'stillsuits'—that reclaim the body's own water."

Paul swallowed, suddenly aware of the moisture in his mouth, remembering a dream of thirst. That people could want so for water they had to recycle their body moisture struck him with a feeling of desolation. "Water's precious there," he said.

Hawat nodded, thinking: *Perhaps I'm doing it, getting across to him the importance of this planet as an enemy. It's madness to go in there without that caution in our minds.*

Paul looked up at the skylight, aware that it had begun to rain. He saw the spreading wetness on the gray meta-glass. "Water," he said.

"You'll learn a great concern for water," Hawat said. "As the Duke's son you'll never want for it, but you'll see the pressures of thirst all around you."

Paul wet his lips with his tongue, thinking back to the day a week ago and the ordeal with the Reverend Mother. She, too, had said something about water starvation.

"You'll learn about the funeral plains," she'd said, "about the wilderness that is empty, the wasteland where nothing lives except the spice and the sandworms. You'll stain your eyepits to reduce the sun glare. Shelter will mean a hollow out of the wind and hidden from view. You'll ride upon your own two feet without 'thopter or ground car or mount."

And Paul had been caught more by her tone—singsong and wavering—than by her words.

"When you live upon Arrakis," she had said, "khala, the land is empty. The moons will be your friends, the sun your enemy."

Paul had sensed his mother come up beside him away from her post guarding the door. She had looked at the Reverend Mother and asked: "Do you see no hope, Your Reverence?"

"Not for the father." And the old woman had waved Jessica to silence, looked down at Paul. "Grave this on your memory, lad: A world is supported by four things. . . ." She held up four big-knuckled fingers. ". . . the learning of the wise, the justice of the great, the prayers of the righteous and the valor of the brave. But all of these are as nothing. . . ." She closed her fingers into a fist. ". . . without a ruler who knows the art of ruling. Make *that* the science of your tradition!"

A week had passed since that day with the Reverend Mother. Her words were only now beginning to come into full register. Now, sitting in the training room with Thufir Hawat, Paul felt a sharp pang of fear. He looked across at the Mentat's puzzled frown.

"Where were you woolgathering that time?" Hawat asked.

"Did you meet the Reverend Mother?"

"That Truthsayer witch from the Imperium?" Hawat's eyes quickened with interest. "I met her."

"She. . . ." Paul hesitated, found that he couldn't tell Hawat about the ordeal. The inhibitions went deep.

"Yes? What did she?"

Paul took two deep breaths. "She said a thing." He closed his eyes, calling up the words, and when he spoke his voice unconsciously took on some of the old woman's tone: "'You, Paul Atreides, descendant of kings, son of a Duke, you must learn to rule. It's something none of your ancestors learned.'" Paul opened his eyes, said: "That made me angry and I said my father rules an entire planet. And she said, 'He's losing it.' And I said my father was getting a richer planet. And she said, 'He'll lose that one, too.' And I wanted to run and warn my father, but she said he'd already been warned—by you, by Mother, by many people."

"True enough," Hawat muttered.

"Then why're we going?" Paul demanded.

"Because the Emperor ordered it. And because there's hope in spite of what that witch-spy said. What else spouted from this ancient fountain of wisdom?"

Paul looked down at his right hand clenched into a fist beneath the table. Slowly, he willed the muscles to relax. *She put some kind of hold on me*, he thought. *How?*

"She asked me to tell her what it is to rule," Paul said. "And I said that one commands. And she said I had some unlearning to do."

She hit a mark there right enough, Hawat thought. He nodded for Paul to continue.

"She said a ruler must learn to persuade and not to compel. She said he must lay the best coffee hearth to attract the finest men."

"How'd she figure your father attracted men like Duncan and Gurney?" Hawat asked.

Paul shrugged. "Then she said a good ruler has to learn his world's language, that it's different for every world. And I thought she meant they didn't speak Galach on Arrakis, but she said that wasn't it at all. She said she meant the language of the rocks and growing things, the language you don't hear just with your ears. And I said that's what Dr. Yueh calls the Mystery of Life."

Hawat chuckled. "How'd that sit with her?"

"I think she got mad. She said the mystery of life isn't a problem to solve, but a reality to experience. So I quoted the First Law of Mentat at her: 'A process cannot be understood by stopping it. Understanding must move with the flow of the process, must join it and flow with it.' That seemed to satisfy her."

He seems to be getting over it, Hawat thought, *but that old witch frightened him. Why did she do it?*

"Thufir," Paul said, "will Arrakis be as bad as she said?"

"Nothing could be that bad," Hawat said and forced a smile. "Take those Fremen, for example, the renegade people of the desert. By first-approximation analysis, I can tell you there're many, many more of them than the Imperium suspects. People live there, lad: a great many people, and. . . ." Hawat put a sinewy finger beside his eye. ". . . they hate Harkonnens with a bloody passion. You must not breathe a word of this, lad. I tell you only as your father's helper."

"My father has told me of Salusa Secundus," Paul said. "Do you know, Thufir, it sounds much like Arrakis . . . perhaps not quite as bad, but much like it."

"We do not really know of Salusa Secundus today," Hawat said. "Only what it was like long ago . . . mostly. But what is known—you're right on that score."

"Will the Fremen help us?"

"It's a possibility." Hawat stood up. "I leave today for Arrakis. Meanwhile, you take care of yourself for an old man who's fond of you, heh? Come around here like the good lad and sit facing the door. It's not that I think there's any danger in the castle; it's just a habit I want you to form."

Paul got to his feet, moved around the table. "You're going today?"

"Today it is, and you'll be following tomorrow. Next time we meet it'll be on the soil of your new world." He gripped Paul's right arm at the bicep. "Keep your knife arm free, heh? And your shield at full charge." He released the arm, patted Paul's shoulder, whirled and strode quickly to the door.

"Thufir!" Paul called.

Hawat turned, standing in the open doorway.

"Don't sit with your back to any doors," Paul said.

A grin spread across the seamed old face. "That I won't, lad. Depend on it." And he was gone, shutting the door softly behind.

Paul sat down where Hawat had been, straightened the papers. *One more day here,* he thought. He looked around the room. *We're leaving.* The idea of departure was suddenly more real to him than it had ever been before. He recalled another thing the old woman had said about a world being the sum of many things—the people, the dirt, the growing things, the moons, the tides, the suns—the unknown sum called *nature*, a vague summation without any sense of the *now*. And he wondered: *What is the now?*

The door across from Paul banged open and an ugly lump of a man lurched through it preceded by a handful of weapons.

"Well, Gurney Halleck," Paul called, "are you the new weapons master?"

Halleck kicked the door shut with one heel. "You'd rather I came to play games, I know," he said. He glanced around the room, noting that Hawat's men already had been over it, checking, making it safe for a duke's heir. The subtle code signs were all around.

Paul watched the rolling, ugly man set himself back in motion, veer toward the training table with the load of weapons, saw the nine-string baliset slung over Gurney's shoulder with the multipick woven through the strings near the head of the fingerboard.

Halleck dropped the weapons on the exercise table, lined them up— the rapiers, the bodkins, the kindjals, the slow-pellet stunners, the shield belts. The inkvine scar along his jawline writhed as he turned, casting a smile across the room.

"So you don't even have a good morning for me, you young imp," Halleck said. "And what barb did you sink in old Hawat? He passed me in the hall like a man running to his enemy's funeral."

Paul grinned. Of all his father's men, he liked Gurney Halleck best, knew the man's moods and deviltry, his *humors*, and thought of him more as a friend than as a hired sword.

Halleck swung the baliset off his shoulder, began tuning it. "If y' won't talk, y' won't," he said.

Paul stood, advanced across the room, calling out: "Well, Gurney, do we come prepared for music when it's fighting time?"

"So it's sass for our elders today," Halleck said. He tried a chord on the instrument, nodded.

"Where's Duncan Idaho?" Paul asked. "Isn't he supposed to be teaching me weaponry?"

"Duncan's gone to lead the second wave onto Arrakis," Halleck said. "All you have left is poor Gurney who's fresh out of fight and spoiling for music." He struck another chord, listened to it, smiled. "And it was decided in council that you being such a poor fighter we'd best teach you the music trade so's you won't waste your life entire."

"Maybe you'd better sing me a lay then," Paul said. "I want to be sure how *not* to do it."

"Ah-h-h, hah!" Gurney laughed, and he swung into "Galacian Girls," his multipick a blur over the strings as he sang:

> "Oh-h-h, the Galacian girls
> Will do it for pearls,
> And the Arrakeen for water!
> But if you desire dames
> Like consuming flames,
> Try a Caladanin daughter!"

"Not bad for such a poor hand with the pick," Paul said, "but if my mother heard you singing a bawdy like that in the castle, she'd have your ears on the outer wall for decoration."

Gurney pulled at his left ear. "Poor decoration, too, they having been bruised so much listening at keyholes while a young lad I know practiced some strange ditties on his baliset."

"So you've forgotten what it's like to find sand in your bed," Paul said. He pulled a shield belt from the table, buckled it fast around his waist. "Then, let's fight!"

Halleck's eyes went wide in mock surprise. "So! It was your wicked hand did that deed! Guard yourself today, young Master—guard yourself." He grabbed up a rapier, laced the air with it. "I'm a hellfiend out for revenge!"

Paul lifted the companion rapier, bent it in his hands, stood in the *aguile*, one foot forward. He let his manner go solemn in a comic imitation of Dr. Yueh.

"What a dolt my father sends me for weaponry," Paul intoned. "This doltish Gurney Halleck has forgotten the first lesson for a fighting man armed and shielded." Paul snapped the force button at his waist, felt the crinkled-skin tingling of the defensive field at his forehead and down his back, heard external sounds take on characteristic shield-filtered flatness. "In shield fighting, one moves fast on defense, slow on attack," Paul said. "Attack has the sole purpose of tricking the opponent into a misstep, setting him up for the attack sinister. The shield turns the fast blow, admits the slow kindjal!" Paul snapped up the rapier, feinted fast and whipped it back for a slow thrust timed to enter a shield's mindless defenses.

Halleck watched the action, turned at the last minute to let the blunted blade pass his chest. "Speed, excellent," he said. "But you were wide open for an underhanded counter with a slip-tip."

Paul stepped back, chagrined.

"I should whap your backside for such carelessness," Halleck said. He lifted a naked kindjal from the table and held it up. "This in the hand of an enemy can let out your life's blood! You're an apt pupil, none better, but I've warned you that not even in play do you let a man inside your guard with death in his hand."

"I guess I'm not in the mood for it today," Paul said.

"Mood?" Halleck's voice betrayed his outrage even through the shield's filtering. "What has *mood* to do with it? You fight when the necessity arises—no matter the mood! Mood's a thing for cattle or making love or playing the baliset. It's not for fighting."

"I'm sorry, Gurney."

"You're not sorry enough!"

Halleck activated his own shield, crouched with kindjal outthrust in left hand, the rapier poised high in his right. "Now I say guard yourself for true!" He leaped high to one side, then forward, pressing a furious attack.

Paul fell back, parrying. He felt the field crackling as shield edges touched and repelled each other, sensed the electric tingling of the contact along his skin. *What's gotten into Gurney?* he asked himself. *He's not faking this!* Paul moved his left hand, dropped his bodkin into his palm from its wrist sheath.

"You see a need for an extra blade, eh?" Halleck grunted.

Is this betrayal? Paul wondered. *Surely not Gurney!*

Around the room they fought—thrust and parry, feint and counterfeint. The air within their shield bubbles grew stale from the demands on it that the slow interchange along barrier edges could not replenish. With each new shield contact, the smell of ozone grew stronger.

Paul continued to back, but now he directed his retreat toward the exercise table. *If I can turn him beside the table, I'll show him a trick,* Paul thought. *One more step, Gurney.*

Halleck took the step.

Paul directed a parry downward, turned, saw Halleck's rapier catch against the table's edge. Paul flung himself aside, thrust high with rapier and came in across Halleck's neckline with the bodkin. He stopped the blade an inch from the jugular.

"Is this what you seek?" Paul whispered.

"Look down, lad," Gurney panted.

Paul obeyed, saw Halleck's kindjal thrust under the table's edge, the tip almost touching Paul's groin.

"We'd have joined each other in death," Halleck said. "But I'll admit you fought some better when pressed to it. You seemed to get the *mood*." And he grinned wolfishly, the inkvine scar rippling along his jaw.

"The way you came at me," Paul said. "Would you really have drawn my blood?"

Halleck withdrew the kindjal, straightened. "If you'd fought one whit beneath your abilities, I'd have scratched you a good one, a scar you'd remember. I'll not have my favorite pupil fall to the first Harkonnen tramp who happens along."

Paul deactivated his shield, leaned on the table to catch his breath. "I deserved that, Gurney. But it would've angered my father if you'd hurt me. I'll not have you punished for my failing."

"As to that," Halleck said, "it was my failing, too. And you needn't worry about a training scar or two. You're lucky you have so few. As to your father—the Duke'd punish me only if I failed to make a first-class fighting man out of you. And I'd have been failing there if I hadn't explained the fallacy in this *mood* thing you've suddenly developed."

Paul straightened, slipped his bodkin back into its wrist sheath.

"It's not exactly play we do here," Halleck said.

Paul nodded. He felt a sense of wonder at the uncharacteristic seriousness in Halleck's manner, the sobering intensity. He looked at the beet-colored inkvine scar on the man's jaw, remembering the story of how it had been put there by Beast Rabban in a Harkonnen slave pit on Giedi Prime. And Paul felt a sudden shame that he had doubted Halleck even for an instant. It occurred to Paul, then, that the making of Halleck's scar had been accompanied by pain—a pain as intense, perhaps, as that inflicted by a Reverend Mother. He thrust this thought aside; it chilled their world.

"I guess I did hope for some play today," Paul said. "Things are so serious around here lately."

Halleck turned away to hide his emotions. Something burned in his eyes. There was pain in him—like a blister, all that was left of some lost yesterday that Time had pruned off him.

How soon this child must assume his manhood, Halleck thought. *How soon he must read that form within his mind, that contract of brutal caution, to enter the necessary fact on the necessary line: "Please list your next of kin."*

Halleck spoke without turning: "I sensed the play in you, lad, and I'd like nothing better than to join in it. But this no longer can be play. Tomorrow we go to Arrakis. Arrakis is real. The Harkonnens are real."

Paul touched his forehead with his rapier blade held vertical.

Halleck turned, saw the salute and acknowledged it with a nod. He gestured to the practice dummy. "Now, we'll work on your timing. Let me see you catch that thing sinister. I'll control it from over here where I can have a full view of the action. And I warn you I'll be trying new counters today. There's a warning you'd not get from a real enemy."

Paul stretched up on his toes to relieve his muscles. He felt solemn with the sudden realization that his life had become filled with swift changes. He crossed to the dummy, slapped the switch on its chest with his rapier tip and felt the defensive field forcing his blade away.

"En garde!" Halleck called, and the dummy pressed the attack.

Paul activated his shield, parried and countered.

Halleck watched as he manipulated the controls. His mind seemed to be in two parts: one alert to the needs of the training fight, and the other wandering in fly-buzz.

I'm the well-trained fruit tree, he thought. *Full of well-trained feelings and abilities and all of them grafted onto me—all bearing for someone else to pick.*

For some reason, he recalled his younger sister, her elfin face so clear in his mind. But she was dead now—in a pleasure house for Harkonnen troops. She had loved pansies . . . or was it daisies? He couldn't remember. It bothered him that he couldn't remember.

Paul countered a slow swing of the dummy, brought up his left hand *entretisser*.

The clever little devil! Halleck thought, intent now on Paul's interweaving hand motions. *He's been practicing and studying on his own. That's not Duncan style, and it's certainly nothing I've taught him.*

This thought only added to Halleck's sadness. *I'm infected by mood*, he thought. And he began to wonder about Paul, if the boy ever listened fearfully to his pillow throbbing in the night.

"If wishes were fishes we'd all cast nets," he murmured.

It was his mother's expression and he always used it when he felt the blackness of tomorrow on him. Then he thought what an odd expression that was to be taking to a planet that had never known seas or fishes.

YUEH (yü´ē), Wellington (weling-tun), Stdrd 10,082–10,191; medical doctor of the Suk School (grd Stdrd 10,112); md: Wanna Marcus, B. G. (Stdrd 10,092–10,186?); chiefly noted as betrayer of Duke Leto Atreides. (Cf: Bibliography, Appendix VII Imperial Conditioning and Betrayal, The.)

—FROM "DICTIONARY OF MUAD'DIB"
BY THE PRINCESS IRULAN

Although he heard Dr. Yueh enter the training room, noting the stiff deliberation of the man's pace, Paul remained stretched out face down on the exercise table where the masseuse had left him. He felt deliciously relaxed after the workout with Gurney Halleck.

"You do look comfortable," said Yueh in his calm, high-pitched voice.

Paul raised his head, saw the man's stick figure standing several paces away, took in at a glance the wrinkled black clothing, the square block of a head with purple lips and drooping mustache, the diamond tattoo of Imperial Conditioning on his forehead, the long black hair caught in the Suk School's silver ring at the left shoulder.

"You'll be happy to hear we haven't time for regular lessons today," Yueh said. "Your father will be along presently."

Paul sat up.

"However, I've arranged for you to have a filmbook viewer and several lessons during the crossing to Arrakis."

"Oh."

Paul began pulling on his clothes. He felt excitement that his father would be coming. They had spent so little time together since the Emperor's command to take over the fief of Arrakis.

Yueh crossed to the ell table, thinking: *How the boy has filled out these past few months. Such a waste! Oh, such a sad waste.* And he reminded himself: *I must not falter. What I do is done to be certain my Wanna no longer can be hurt by the Harkonnen beasts.*

Paul joined him at the table, buttoning his jacket. "What'll I be studying on the way across?"

"Ah-h-h, the terranic life forms of Arrakis. The planet seems to have opened its arms to certain terranic life forms. It's not clear how. I must seek out the planetary ecologist when we arrive—a Dr. Kynes—and offer my help in the investigation."

And Yueh thought: *What am I saying? I play the hypocrite even with myself.*

"Will there be something on the Fremen?" Paul asked.

"The Fremen?" Yueh drummed his fingers on the table, caught Paul staring at the nervous motion, withdrew his hand.

"Maybe you have something on the whole Arrakeen population," Paul said.

"Yes, to be sure," Yueh said. "There are two general separations of the people—Fremen, they are one group, and the others are the people of the graben, the sink, and the pan. There's some intermarriage, I'm told. The women of pan and sink villages prefer Fremen husbands; their men prefer Fremen wives. They have a saying: 'Polish comes from the cities; wisdom from the desert.'"

"Do you have pictures of them?"

"I'll see what I can get you. The most interesting feature, of course, is their eyes—totally blue, no whites in them."

"Mutation?"

"No; it's linked to saturation of the blood with melange."

"The Fremen must be brave to live at the edge of that desert."

"By all accounts," Yueh said. "They compose poems to their knives. Their women are as fierce as the men. Even Fremen children are violent and dangerous. You'll not be permitted to mingle with them, I daresay."

Paul stared at Yueh, finding in these few glimpses of the Fremen a power of words that caught his entire attention. *What a people to win as allies!*

"And the worms?" Paul asked.

"What?"

"I'd like to study more about the sandworms."

"Ah-h-h, to be sure. I've a filmbook on a small specimen, only one hundred and ten meters long and twenty-two meters in diameter. It was taken in the northern latitudes. Worms of more than four hundred meters in length have been recorded by reliable witnesses, and there's reason to believe even larger ones exist."

Paul glanced down at a conical projection chart of the northern Arrakeen latitudes spread on the table. "The desert belt and south polar regions are marked uninhabitable. Is it the worms?"

"And the storms."

"But any place can be made habitable."

"If it's economically feasible," Yueh said. "Arrakis has many costly perils." He smoothed his drooping mustache. "Your father will be here soon. Before I go, I've a gift for you, something I came across in packing." He put an object on the table between them—black, oblong, no larger than the end of Paul's thumb.

Paul looked at it. Yueh noted how the boy did not reach for it, and thought: *How cautious he is.*

"It's a very old Orange Catholic Bible made for space travelers. Not a filmbook, but actually printed on filament paper. It has its own magnifier and electrostatic charge system." He picked it up, demonstrated. "The book is held closed by the charge, which forces against spring-locked covers. You press the edge—thus, and the pages you've selected repel each other and the book opens."

"It's so small."

"But it has eighteen hundred pages. You press the edge—thus, and so . . . and the charge moves ahead one page at a time as you read. Never touch the actual pages with your fingers. The filament tissue is too delicate." He closed the book, handed it to Paul. "Try it."

Yueh watched Paul work the page adjustment, thought: *I salve my own conscience. I give him the surcease of religion before betraying him. Thus may I say to myself that he has gone where I cannot go.*

"This must've been made before filmbooks," Paul said.

"It's quite old. Let it be our secret, eh? Your parents might think it too valuable for one so young."

And Yueh thought: *His mother would surely wonder at my motives.*

"Well. . . ." Paul closed the book, held it in his hand. "If it's so valuable. . . ."

"Indulge an old man's whim," Yueh said. "It was given to me when I was very young." And he thought: *I must catch his mind as well as his cupidity.* "Open it to four-sixty-seven Kalima—where it says: 'From water does all life begin.' There's a slight notch on the edge of the cover to mark the place."

Paul felt the cover, detected two notches, one shallower than the other. He pressed the shallower one and the book spread open on his palm, its magnifier sliding into place.

"Read it aloud," Yueh said.

Paul wet his lips with his tongue, read: "'Think you of the fact that a deaf person cannot hear. Then, what deafness may we not all possess? What senses do we lack that we cannot see and cannot hear another world all around us? What is there around us that we cannot—'"

"Stop it!" Yueh barked.

Paul broke off, stared at him.

Yueh closed his eyes, fought to regain composure. *What perversity caused the book to open at my Wanna's favorite passage?* He opened his eyes, saw Paul staring at him.

"Is something wrong?" Paul asked.

"I'm sorry," Yueh said. "That was . . . my . . . dead wife's favorite passage. It's not the one I intended you to read. It brings up memories that are . . . painful."

"There are two notches," Paul said.

Of course, Yueh thought. *Wanna marked her passage. His fingers are more sensitive than mine and found her mark. It was an accident, no more.*

"You may find the book interesting," Yueh said. "It has much historical truth in it as well as good ethical philosophy."

Paul looked down at the tiny book in his palm—such a small thing. Yet, it contained a mystery . . . something had happened while he read from it. He had felt something stir his terrible purpose.

"Your father will be here any minute," Yueh said. "Put the book away and read it at your leisure."

Paul touched the edge of it as Yueh had shown him. The book sealed itself. He slipped it into his tunic. For a moment there when Yueh had barked at him, Paul had feared the man would demand the book's return.

"I thank you for the gift, Dr. Yueh," Paul said, speaking formally. "It will be our secret. If there is a gift of favor you wish from me, please do not hesitate to ask."

"I . . . need for nothing," Yueh said.

And he thought: *Why do I stand here torturing myself? And torturing this poor lad . . . though he does not know it. Oeyh! Damn those Harkonnen beasts! Why did they choose me for their abomination?*

How do we approach the study of Muad'Dib's father? A man of surpassing warmth and surprising coldness was the Duke Leto Atreides. Yet, many facts open the way to this Duke: his abiding love for his Bene Gesserit lady; the dreams he held for his son; the devotion with which men served him. You see him there—a man snared by Destiny, a lonely figure with his light dimmed behind the glory of his son. Still, one must ask: What is the son but an extension of the father?

—FROM "MUAD'DIB, FAMILY COMMENTARIES"
BY THE PRINCESS IRULAN

Paul watched his father enter the training room, saw the guards take up stations outside. One of them closed the door. As always, Paul experienced a sense of *presence* in his father, someone totally *here*.

The Duke was tall, olive-skinned. His thin face held harsh angles warmed only by deep gray eyes. He wore a black working uniform with red armorial hawk crest at the breast. A silvered shield belt with the patina of much use girded his narrow waist.

The Duke said: "Hard at work, Son?"

He crossed to the ell table, glanced at the papers on it, swept his gaze around the room and back to Paul. He felt tired, filled with the ache of not showing his fatigue. *I must use every opportunity to rest during the crossing to Arrakis*, he thought. *There'll be no rest on Arrakis.*

"Not very hard," Paul said. "Everything's so. . . ." He shrugged.

"Yes. Well, tomorrow we leave. It'll be good to get settled in our new home, put all this upset behind."

Paul nodded, suddenly overcome by memory of the Reverend Mother's words: ". . . *for the father, nothing.*"

"Father," Paul said, "will Arrakis be as dangerous as everyone says?"

The Duke forced himself to the casual gesture, sat down on a corner of the table, smiled. A whole pattern of conversation welled up in his mind—the kind of thing he might use to dispel the vapors in his men before a battle. The pattern froze before it could be vocalized, confronted by the single thought:

This is my son.

"It'll be dangerous," he admitted.

"Hawat tells me we have a plan for the Fremen," Paul said. And he wondered: *Why don't I tell him what that old woman said? How did she seal my tongue?*

The Duke noted his son's distress, said: "As always, Hawat sees the main chance. But there's much more. I see also the Combine Honnete Ober Advancer Mercantiles—the CHOAM Company. By giving me Arrakis, His Majesty is forced to give us a CHOAM directorship . . . a subtle gain."

"CHOAM controls the spice," Paul said.

"And Arrakis with its spice is our avenue into CHOAM," the Duke said. "There's more to CHOAM than melange."

"Did the Reverend Mother warn you?" Paul blurted. He clenched his fists, feeling his palms slippery with perspiration. The *effort* it had taken to ask that question.

"Hawat tells me she frightened you with warnings about Arrakis," the Duke said. "Don't let a woman's fears cloud your mind. No woman wants her loved ones endangered. The hand behind those warnings was your mother's. Take this as a sign of her love for us."

"Does she know about the Fremen?"

"Yes, and about much more."

"What?"

And the Duke thought: *The truth could be worse than he imagines, but even dangerous facts are valuable if you've been trained to deal with them. And there's one place where nothing has been spared for my son—dealing with dangerous facts. This must be leavened, though; he is young.*

"Few products escape the CHOAM touch," the Duke said. "Logs, donkeys, horses, cows, lumber, dung, sharks, whale fur—the most prosaic and the most exotic . . . even our poor pundi rice from Caladan. Anything the Guild will transport, the art forms of Ecaz, the machines of Richesse and Ix. But all fades before melange. A handful of spice will buy a home on Tupile. It cannot be manufactured, it must be mined on Arrakis. It is unique and it has true geriatric properties."

"And now we control it?"

"To a certain degree. But the important thing is to consider all the Houses that depend on CHOAM profits. And think of the enormous proportion of those profits dependent upon a single product—the spice. Imagine what would happen if something should reduce spice production."

"Whoever had stockpiled melange could make a killing," Paul said. "Others would be out in the cold."

The Duke permitted himself a moment of grim satisfaction, looking at his son and thinking how penetrating, how truly *educated* that observation had been. He nodded. "The Harkonnens have been stockpiling for more than twenty years."

"They mean spice production to fail and you to be blamed."

"They wish the Atreides name to become unpopular," the Duke said. "Think of the Landsraad Houses that look to me for a certain amount of leadership—their unofficial spokesman. Think how they'd react if I were responsible for a serious reduction in their income. After all, one's own profits come first. The Great Convention be damned! You can't let someone pauperize you!" A harsh smile twisted the Duke's mouth. "They'd look the other way no matter *what* was done to me."

"Even if we were attacked with atomics?"

"Nothing that flagrant. No *open* defiance of the Convention. But almost anything else short of that . . . perhaps even dusting and a bit of soil poisoning."

"Then why are we walking into this?"

"Paul!" The Duke frowned at his son. "Knowing where the trap is— that's the first step in evading it. This is like single combat, Son, only on a larger scale—a feint within a feint within a feint . . . seemingly without end. The task is to unravel it. Knowing that the Harkonnens stockpile melange, we ask another question: Who else is stockpiling? That's the list of our enemies."

"Who?"

"Certain Houses we knew were unfriendly and some we'd thought friendly. We need not consider them for the moment because there is one other much more important: our beloved Padishah Emperor."

Paul tried to swallow in a throat suddenly dry. "Couldn't you convene the Landsraad, expose—"

"Make our enemy aware we know which hand holds the knife? Ah, now, Paul—we *see* the knife, now. Who knows where it might be shifted next? If we put this before the Landsraad it'd only create a great cloud of confusion. The Emperor would deny it. Who could gainsay him? All we'd gain is a little time while risking chaos. And where would the next attack come from?"

"All the Houses might start stockpiling spice."

"Our enemies have a head start—too much of a lead to overcome."

"The Emperor," Paul said. "That means the Sardaukar."

"Disguised in Harkonnen livery, no doubt," the Duke said. "But the soldier fanatics nonetheless."

"How can Fremen help us against Sardaukar?"

"Did Hawat talk to you about Salusa Secundus?"

"The Emperor's prison planet? No."

"What if it were more than a prison planet, Paul? There's a question you never hear asked about the Imperial Corps of Sardaukar: Where do they come from?"

"From the prison planet?"

"They come from somewhere."

"But the supporting levies the Emperor demands from—"

"That's what we're led to believe: they're just the Emperor's levies trained young and superbly. You hear an occasional muttering about the Emperor's training cadres, but the balance of our civilization remains the same: the military forces of the Landsraad Great Houses on one side, the Sardaukar and their supporting levies on the other. *And* their supporting levies, Paul. The Sardaukar remain the Sardaukar."

"But every report on Salusa Secundus says S.S. is a hell world!"

"Undoubtedly. But if you were going to raise tough, strong, ferocious men, what environmental conditions would you impose on them?"

"How could you win the loyalty of such men?"

"There are proven ways: play on the certain knowledge of their superiority, the mystique of secret covenant, the esprit of shared suffering. It can be done. It has been done on many worlds in many times."

Paul nodded, holding his attention on his father's face. He felt some revelation impending.

"Consider Arrakis," the Duke said. "When you get outside the towns and garrison villages, it's every bit as terrible a place as Salusa Secundus."

Paul's eyes went wide. "The Fremen!"

"We have there the potential of a corps as strong and deadly as the Sardaukar. It'll require patience to exploit them secretly and wealth to equip them properly. But the Fremen are there . . . and the spice wealth is there. You see now why we walk into Arrakis, knowing the trap is there."

"Don't the Harkonnens know about the Fremen?"

"The Harkonnens sneered at the Fremen, hunted them for sport, never even bothered trying to count them. We know the Harkonnen policy with planetary populations—spend as little as possible to maintain them."

The metallic threads in the hawk symbol above his father's breast glistened as the Duke shifted his position. "You see?"

"We're negotiating with the Fremen right now," Paul said.

"I sent a mission headed by Duncan Idaho," the Duke said. "A proud and ruthless man, Duncan, but fond of the truth. I think the Fremen will admire him. If we're lucky, they may judge us by him: Duncan, the moral."

"Duncan, the moral," Paul said, "and Gurney the valorous."

"You name them well," the Duke said.

And Paul thought: *Gurney's one of those the Reverend Mother meant, a supporter of worlds—". . . the valor of the brave."*

"Gurney tells me you did well in weapons today," the Duke said.

"That isn't what he told me."

The Duke laughed aloud. "I figured Gurney to be sparse with his praise. He says you have a nicety of awareness—in his own words—of the difference between a blade's edge and its tip."

"Gurney says there's no artistry in killing with the tip, that it should be done with the edge."

"Gurney's a romantic," the Duke growled. This talk of killing suddenly disturbed him, coming from his son. "I'd sooner you never had to kill . . . but if the need arises, you do it however you can—tip or edge." He looked up at the skylight, on which the rain was drumming.

Seeing the direction of his father's stare, Paul thought of the wet skies out there—a thing never to be seen on Arrakis from all accounts—and this thought of skies put him in mind of the space beyond. "Are the Guild ships really big?" he asked.

The Duke looked at him. "This *will* be your first time off planet," he said. "Yes, they're big. We'll be riding a Heighliner because it's a long trip. A Heighliner is truly big. Its hold will tuck all our frigates and transports into a little corner—we'll be just a small part of the ship's manifest."

"And we won't be able to leave our frigates?"

"That's part of the price you pay for Guild Security. There could be Harkonnen ships right alongside us and we'd have nothing to fear from them. The Harkonnens know better than to endanger their shipping privileges."

"I'm going to watch our screens and try to see a Guildsman."

"You won't. Not even their agents ever see a Guildsman. The Guild's as jealous of its privacy as it is of its monopoly. Don't do anything to endanger our shipping privileges, Paul."

"Do you think they hide because they've mutated and don't look . . . *human* anymore?"

"Who knows?" The Duke shrugged. "It's a mystery we're not likely to solve. We've more immediate problems—among them: you."

"Me?"

"Your mother wanted me to be the one to tell you, Son. You see, you may have Mentat capabilities."

Paul stared at his father, unable to speak for a moment, then: "A Mentat? Me? But I. . . ."

"Hawat agrees, Son. It's true."

"But I thought Mentat training had to start during infancy and the subject couldn't be told because it might inhibit the early. . . ." He broke off, all his past circumstances coming to focus in one flashing computation. "I see," he said.

"A day comes," the Duke said, "when the potential Mentat must learn what's being done. It may no longer be done *to* him. The Mentat has to share in the choice of whether to continue or abandon the training. Some can continue; some are incapable of it. Only the potential Mentat can tell this for sure about himself."

Paul rubbed his chin. All the special training from Hawat and his mother—the mnemonics, the focusing of awareness, the muscle control and sharpening of sensitivities, the study of languages and nuances of voices—all of it clicked into a new kind of understanding in his mind.

"You'll be the Duke someday, Son," his father said. "A Mentat Duke would be formidable indeed. Can you decide now . . . or do you need more time?"

There was no hesitation in his answer. "I'll go on with the training."

"Formidable indeed," the Duke murmured, and Paul saw the proud smile on his father's face. The smile shocked Paul: it had a skull look on the Duke's narrow features. Paul closed his eyes, feeling the terrible purpose reawaken within him. *Perhaps being a Mentat is terrible purpose*, he thought.

But even as he focused on this thought, his new awareness denied it.

With the Lady Jessica and Arrakis, the Bene Gesserit system of sowing implant-legends through the Missionaria Protectiva came to its full fruition. The wisdom of seeding the known universe with a prophecy pattern for the protection of B.G. personnel has long been appreciated, but never have we seen a condition-ut-extremis with more ideal mating of person and preparation. The prophetic legends had taken on Arrakis even to the extent of adopted labels (including Reverend Mother, canto and respondu, and most of the Shari-a panoplia propheticus). And it is generally accepted now that the Lady Jessica's latent abilities were grossly underestimated.

—FROM "ANALYSIS: THE ARRAKEEN CRISIS"
BY THE PRINCESS IRULAN
(PRIVATE CIRCULATION: B.G. FILE NUMBER AR-81088587)

All around the Lady Jessica—piled in corners of the Arrakeen Great Hall, mounded in the open spaces—stood the packaged freight of their lives: boxes, trunks, cartons, cases—some partly unpacked. She could hear the cargo handlers from the Guild shuttle depositing another load in the entry.

Jessica stood in the center of the hall. She moved in a slow turn, looking up and around at shadowed carvings, crannies and deeply recessed windows. This giant anachronism of a room reminded her of the Sisters' Hall at her Bene Gesserit school. But at the school the effect had been of warmth. Here, all was bleak stone.

Some architect had reached far back into history for these but-tressed walls and dark hangings, she thought. The arched ceiling stood two stories above her with great crossbeams she felt sure had been shipped here to Arrakis across space at monstrous cost. No planet of this system grew trees to make such beams—unless the beams were imitation wood.

She thought not.

This had been the government mansion in the days of the Old Em-pire. Costs had been of less importance then. It had been before the Harkonnens and their new megalopolis of Carthag—a cheap and brassy place some two hundred kilometers northeast across the Broken Land. Leto had been wise to choose this place for his seat of government. The name, Arrakeen, had a good sound, filled with tradition. And this was a smaller city, easier to sterilize and defend.

Again there came the clatter of boxes being unloaded in the entry. Jessica sighed.

Against a carton to her right stood the painting of the Duke's father. Wrapping twine hung from it like a frayed decoration. A piece of the twine was still clutched in Jessica's left hand. Beside the painting lay a black bull's head mounted on a polished board. The head was a dark island in a sea of wadded paper. Its plaque lay flat on the floor, and the bull's shiny muzzle pointed at the ceiling as though the beast were ready to bellow a challenge into this echoing room.

Jessica wondered what compulsion had brought her to uncover those two things first—the head and the painting. She knew there was something symbolic in the action. Not since the day when the Duke's buyers had taken her from the school had she felt this frightened and unsure of herself.

The head and the picture.

They heightened her feelings of confusion. She shuddered, glanced at the slit windows high overhead. It was still early afternoon here, and in these latitudes the sky looked black and cold—so much darker than the warm blue of Caladan. A pang of homesickness throbbed through her.

So far away, Caladan.

"Here we are!"

The voice was Duke Leto's.

She whirled, saw him striding from the arched passage to the dining hall. His black working uniform with red armorial hawk crest at the breast looked dusty and rumpled.

"I thought you might have lost yourself in this hideous place," he said.

"It is a cold house," she said. She looked at his tallness, at the dark skin that made her think of olive groves and golden sun on blue waters. There was woodsmoke in the gray of his eyes, but the face was predatory: thin, full of sharp angles and planes.

A sudden fear of him tightened her breast. He had become such a savage, driving person since the decision to bow to the Emperor's command.

"The whole city feels cold," she said.

"It's a dirty, dusty little garrison town," he agreed. "But we'll change that." He looked around the hall. "These are public rooms for state occasions. I've just glanced at some of the family apartments in the south wing. They're much nicer." He stepped closer, touched her arm, admiring her stateliness.

And again, he wondered at her unknown ancestry—a renegade House, perhaps? Some black-barred royalty? She looked more regal than the Emperor's own blood.

Under the pressure of his stare, she turned half away, exposing her profile. And he realized there was no single and precise thing that brought her beauty to focus. The face was oval under a cap of hair the color of polished bronze. Her eyes were set wide, as green and clear as the morning skies of Caladan. The nose was small, the mouth wide and generous. Her figure was good but scant: tall and with its curves gone to slimness.

He remembered that the lay sisters at the school had called her skinny, so his buyers had told him. But that description oversimplified. She had brought a regal beauty back into the Atreides line. He was glad that Paul favored her.

"Where's Paul?" he asked.

"Someplace around the house taking his lessons with Yueh."

"Probably in the south wing," he said. "I thought I heard Yueh's voice, but I couldn't take time to look." He glanced down at her, hesitating. "I came here only to hang the key of Caladan Castle in the dining hall."

She caught her breath, stopped the impulse to reach out to him. Hanging the key—there was finality in that action. But this was not the time or place for comforting. "I saw our banner over the house as we came in," she said.

He glanced at the painting of his father. "Where were you going to hang that?"

"Somewhere in here."

"No." The word rang flat and final, telling her she could use trickery to persuade, but open argument was useless. Still, she had to try, even if the gesture served only to remind herself that she would not trick him.

"My Lord," she said, "if you'd only. . . ."

"The answer remains no. I indulge you shamefully in most things, not in this. I've just come from the dining hall where there are—"

"My Lord! Please."

"The choice is between your digestion and my ancestral dignity, my dear," he said. "They will hang in the dining hall."

She sighed. "Yes, my Lord."

"You may resume your custom of dining in your rooms whenever possible. I shall expect you at your proper position only on formal occasions."

"Thank you, my Lord."

"And don't go all cold and formal on me! Be thankful that I never married you, my dear. Then it'd be your *duty* to join me at table for every meal."

She held her face immobile, nodded.

"Hawat already has our own poison snooper over the dining table," he said. "There's a portable in your room."

"You anticipated this . . . disagreement," she said.

"My dear, I think also of your comfort. I've engaged servants. They're locals, but Hawat has cleared them—they're Fremen all. They'll do until our own people can be released from their other duties."

"Can anyone from this place be truly safe?"

"Anyone who hates Harkonnens. You may even want to keep the head housekeeper: the Shadout Mapes."

"Shadout," Jessica said. "A Fremen title?"

"I'm told it means 'well-dipper,' a meaning with rather important overtones here. She may not strike you as a servant type, although Hawat speaks highly of her on the basis of Duncan's report. They're convinced she wants to serve—specifically that she wants to serve you."

"Me?"

"The Fremen have learned that you're Bene Gesserit," he said. "There are legends here about the Bene Gesserit."

The Missionaria Protectiva, Jessica thought. *No place escapes them.*

"Does this mean Duncan was successful?" she asked. "Will the Fremen be our allies?"

"There's nothing definite," he said. "They wish to observe us for a while, Duncan believes. They did, however, promise to stop raiding our outlying villages during a truce period. That's a more important gain than it might seem. Hawat tells me the Fremen were a deep thorn in the Harkonnen side, that the extent of their ravages was a carefully guarded secret. It wouldn't have helped for the Emperor to learn the ineffectiveness of the Harkonnen military."

"A Fremen housekeeper," Jessica mused, returning to the subject of the Shadout Mapes. "She'll have the all-blue eyes."

"Don't let the appearance of these people deceive you," he said. "There's a deep strength and healthy vitality in them. I think they'll be everything we need."

"It's a dangerous gamble," she said.

"Let's not go into that again," he said.

She forced a smile. "We *are* committed, no doubt of that." She went through the quick regimen of calmness—the two deep breaths, the ritual thought, then: "When I assign rooms, is there anything special I should reserve for you?"

"You must teach me someday how you do that," he said, "the way you thrust your worries aside and turn to practical matters. It must be a Bene Gesserit thing."

"It's a female thing," she said.

He smiled. "Well, assignment of rooms: make certain I have large office space next to my sleeping quarters. There'll be more paper work here than on Caladan. A guard room, of course. That should cover it. Don't worry about security of the house. Hawat's men have been over it in depth."

"I'm sure they have."

He glanced at his wristwatch. "And you might see that all our time-pieces are adjusted for Arrakeen local. I've assigned a tech to take care of it. He'll be along presently." He brushed a strand of her hair back from her forehead. "I must return to the landing field now. The second shuttle's due any minute with my staff reserves."

"Couldn't Hawat meet them, my Lord? You look so tired."

"The good Thufir is even busier than I am. You know this planet's infested with Harkonnen intrigues. Besides, I must try persuading some of the trained spice hunters against leaving. They have the option, you know, with the change of fief—and this planetologist the Emperor and the Landsraad installed as Judge of the Change cannot be bought. He's allowing the opt. About eight hundred trained hands expect to go out on the spice shuttle and there's a Guild cargo ship standing by."

"My Lord. . . ." She broke off, hesitating.

"Yes?"

He will not be persuaded against trying to make this planet secure for us, she thought. *And I cannot use my tricks on him.*

"At what time will you be expecting dinner?" she asked.

That's not what she was going to say, he thought. *Ah-h-h-h, my Jessica, would that we were somewhere else, anywhere away from this terrible place—alone, the two of us, without a care.*

"I'll eat in the officers' mess at the field," he said. "Don't expect me until very late. And . . . ah, I'll be sending a guardcar for Paul. I want him to attend our strategy conference."

He cleared his throat as though to say something else, then, without warning, turned and strode out, headed for the entry where she could hear more boxes being deposited. His voice sounded once from there, commanding and disdainful, the way he always spoke to servants when he was in a hurry: "The Lady Jessica's in the Great Hall. Join her there immediately."

The outer door slammed.

Jessica turned away, faced the painting of Leto's father. It had been done by the famed artist, Albe, during the Old Duke's middle years. He was portrayed in matador costume with a magenta cape flung over his left arm. The face looked young, hardly older than Leto's now, and with the same hawk features, the same gray stare. She clenched her fists at her sides, glared at the painting.

"Damn you! Damn you! Damn you!" she whispered.

"What are your orders, Noble Born?"

It was a woman's voice, thin and stringy.

Jessica whirled, stared down at a knobby, gray-haired woman in a shapeless sack dress of bondsman brown. The woman looked as wrinkled and desiccated as any member of the mob that had greeted them along the way from the landing field that morning. Every native she had seen on this planet, Jessica thought, looked prune dry and undernourished. Yet, Leto had said they were strong and vital. And there were the eyes, of course—that wash of deepest, darkest blue without any white—secretive, mysterious. Jessica forced herself not to stare.

The woman gave a stiff-necked nod, said: "I am called the Shadout Mapes, Noble Born. What are your orders?"

"You may refer to me as 'my Lady,'" Jessica said. "I'm not noble born. I'm the bound concubine of the Duke Leto."

Again that strange nod, and the woman peered upward at Jessica with a sly questioning. "There's a wife, then?"

"There is not, nor has there ever been. I am the Duke's only . . . companion, the mother of his heir-designate."

Even as she spoke, Jessica laughed inwardly at the pride behind her words. *What was it St. Augustine said?* she asked herself. *"The mind commands the body and it obeys. The mind orders itself and meets resistance." Yes—I am meeting more resistance lately. I could use a quiet retreat by myself.*

A weird cry sounded from the road outside the house. It was repeated: "Soo-soo Sook! Soo-soo Sook!" Then: "Ikhut-eigh! Ikhut-eigh!" And again: "Soo-soo Sook!"

"What *is* that?" Jessica asked. "I heard it several times as we drove through the streets this morning."

"Only a water-seller, my Lady. But you've no need to interest yourself in such as they. The cistern here holds fifty thousand liters and it's always kept full." She glanced down at her dress. "Why, you know, my Lady, I don't even have to wear my stillsuit here?" She cackled. "And me not even dead!"

Jessica hesitated, wanting to question this Fremen woman, needing data to guide her. But bringing order of the confusion in the castle was more imperative. Still, she found the thought unsettling that water was a major mark of wealth here.

"My husband told me of your title, Shadout," Jessica said. "I recognized the word. It's a very ancient word."

"You know the ancient tongues then?" Mapes asked, and she waited with an odd intensity.

"Tongues are the Bene Gesserit's first learning," Jessica said. "I know the Bhotani Jib and the Chakobsa, all the hunting languages."

Mapes nodded. "Just as the legend says."

And Jessica wondered: *Why do I play out this sham?* But the Bene Gesserit ways were devious and compelling.

"I know the Dark Things and the ways of the Great Mother," Jessica said. She read the more obvious signs in Mapes' actions and appearance, the petit betrayals. "Miseces prejia," she said in the Chakobsa tongue. "Andral t're pera! Trada cik buscakri miseces perakri—"

Mapes took a backward step, appeared poised to flee.

"I know many things," Jessica said. "I know that you have borne children, that you have lost loved ones, that you have hidden in fear and that you have done violence and will yet do more violence. I know many things."

In a low voice, Mapes said: "I meant no offense, my Lady."

"You speak of the legend and seek answers," Jessica said. "Beware the answers you may find. I know you came prepared for violence with a weapon in your bodice."

"My Lady, I. . . ."

"There's a remote possibility you could draw my life's blood," Jessica said, "but in so doing you'd bring down more ruin than your wildest fears could imagine. There are worse things than dying, you know—even for an entire people."

"My Lady!" Mapes pleaded. She appeared about to fall to her knees. "The weapon was sent as a gift to *you* should you prove to be the One."

"And as the means of my death should I prove otherwise," Jessica said. She waited in the seeming relaxation that made the Bene Gesserit-trained so terrifying in combat.

Now we see which way the decision tips, she thought.

Slowly, Mapes reached into the neck of her dress, brought out a dark sheath. A black handle with deep finger ridges protruded from it. She took sheath in one hand and handle in the other, withdrew a milk-white blade, held it up. The blade seemed to shine and glitter with a light of its own. It was double-edged like a kindjal and the blade was perhaps twenty centimeters long.

"Do you know this, my Lady?" Mapes asked.

It could only be one thing, Jessica knew, the fabled crysknife of Arrakis, the blade that had never been taken off the planet, and was known only by rumor and wild gossip.

"It's a crysknife," she said.

"Say it not lightly," Mapes said. "Do you know its meaning?"

And Jessica thought: *There was an edge to that question. Here's the reason this Fremen has taken service with me, to ask that one question. My answer could precipitate violence or . . . what? She seeks an answer from me: the meaning of a knife. She's called the Shadout in the Cha kobsa tongue. Knife, that's "Death Maker" in Chakobsa. She's getting restive. I must answer now. Delay is as dangerous as the wrong answer.*

Jessica said: "It's a maker—"

"Eighe-e-e-e-e!" Mapes wailed. It was a sound of both grief and elation. She trembled so hard the knife blade sent glittering shards of reflection shooting around the room.

Jessica waited, poised. She had intended to say the knife was a *maker of death* and then add the ancient word, but every sense warned her now, all the deep training of alertness that exposed meaning in the most casual muscle twitch.

The key word was . . . *maker.*

Maker? Maker.

Still, Mapes held the knife as though ready to use it.

Jessica said: "Did you think that I, knowing the mysteries of the Great Mother, would not know the Maker?"

Mapes lowered the knife. "My Lady, when one has lived with prophecy for so long, the moment of revelation is a shock."

Jessica thought about the prophecy—the Shari-a and all the panoplia propheticus, a Bene Gesserit of the Missionaria Protectiva dropped here long centuries ago—long dead, no doubt, but her purpose accomplished: the protective legends implanted in these people against the day of a Bene Gesserit's need.

Well, that day had come.

Mapes returned knife to sheath, said: "This is an unfixed blade, my Lady. Keep it near you. More than a week away from flesh and it begins to disintegrate. It's yours, a tooth of shai-hulud, for as long as you live."

Jessica reached out her right hand, risked a gamble: "Mapes, you've sheathed that blade unblooded."

With a gasp, Mapes dropped the sheathed knife into Jessica's hand, tore open the brown bodice, wailing: "Take the water of my life!"

Jessica withdrew the blade from its sheath. How it glittered! She directed the point toward Mapes, saw a fear greater than death-panic come over the woman. *Poison in the point?* Jessica wondered. She tipped up the point, drew a delicate scratch with the blade's edge above Mapes' left breast. There was a thick welling of blood that stopped almost immediately. *Ultrafast coagulation*, Jessica thought. *A moisture-conserving mutation?*

She sheathed the blade, said: "Button your dress, Mapes."

Mapes obeyed, trembling. The eyes without whites stared at Jessica. "You are ours," she muttered. "You are the One."

There came another sound of unloading in the entry. Swiftly, Mapes grabbed the sheathed knife, concealed it in Jessica's bodice. "Who sees that knife must be cleansed or slain!" she snarled. "You *know* that, my Lady!"

I know it now, Jessica thought.

The cargo handlers left without intruding on the Great Hall.

Mapes composed herself, said: "The uncleansed who have seen a crysknife may not leave Arrakis alive. Never forget that, my Lady. You've been entrusted with a crysknife." She took a deep breath. "Now the thing must take its course. It cannot be hurried." She glanced at the stacked boxes and piled goods around them. "And there's work aplenty to while the time for us here."

Jessica hesitated. "*The thing must take its course.*" That was a specific catchphrase from the Missionaria Protectiva's stock of incantations— *The coming of the Reverend Mother to free you.*

But I'm not a Reverend Mother, Jessica thought. And then: *Great Mother! They planted that one here! This must be a hideous place!*

In matter-of-fact tones, Mapes said: "What'll you be wanting me to do first, my Lady?"

Instinct warned Jessica to match that casual tone. She said: "The painting of the Old Duke over there, it must be hung on one side of the dining hall. The bull's head must go on the wall opposite the painting."

Mapes crossed to the bull's head. "What a great beast it must have been to carry such a head," she said. She stooped. "I'll have to be cleaning this first, won't I, my Lady?"

"No."

"But there's dirt caked on its horns."

"That's not dirt, Mapes. That's the blood of our Duke's father. Those horns were sprayed with a transparent fixative within hours after this beast killed the Old Duke."

Mapes stood up. "Ah, now!" she said.

"It's just blood," Jessica said. "Old blood at that. Get some help hanging these now. The beastly things are heavy."

"Did you think the blood bothered me?" Mapes asked. "I'm of the desert and I've seen blood aplenty."

"I . . . see that you have," Jessica said.

"And some of it my own," Mapes said. "More'n you drew with your puny scratch."

"You'd rather I'd cut deeper?"

"Ah, no! The body's water is scant enough 'thout gushing a wasteful lot of it into the air. You did the thing right."

And Jessica, noting the words and manner, caught the deeper implications in the phrase, "the body's water." Again she felt a sense of oppression at the importance of water on Arrakis.

"On which side of the dining hall shall I hang which one of these pretties, my Lady?" Mapes asked.

Ever the practical one, this Mapes, Jessica thought. She said: "Use your own judgment, Mapes. It makes no real difference."

"As you say, my Lady." Mapes stooped, began clearing wrappings and twine from the head. "Killed an old duke, did you?" she crooned.

"Shall I summon a handler to help you?" Jessica asked.

"I'll manage, my Lady."

Yes, she'll manage, Jessica thought. *There's that about this Fremen creature: the drive to manage.*

Jessica felt the cold sheath of the crysknife beneath her bodice, thought of the long chain of Bene Gesserit scheming that had forged another link here. Because of that scheming, she had survived a deadly crisis. "It cannot be hurried," Mapes had said. Yet there was a tempo of headlong rushing to this place that filled Jessica with foreboding. And not all the preparations of the Missionaria Protectiva nor Hawat's suspicious inspection of this castellated pile of rocks could dispel the feeling.

"When you've finished hanging those, start unpacking the boxes," Jessica said. "One of the cargo men at the entry has all the keys and knows where things should go. Get the keys and the list from him. If there are any questions I'll be in the south wing."

"As you will, my Lady," Mapes said.

Jessica turned away, thinking: *Hawat may have passed this residency as safe, but there's something wrong about the place. I can feel it.*

An urgent need to see her son gripped Jessica. She began walking toward the arched doorway that led into the passage to the dining hall and the family wings. Faster and faster she walked until she was almost running.

Behind her, Mapes paused in clearing the wrappings from the bull's head, looked at the retreating back. "She's the One all right," she muttered. "Poor thing."

> "Yueh! Yueh! Yueh!" goes the refrain. "A million deaths were not enough for Yueh!"
>
> —FROM "A CHILD'S HISTORY OF MUAD'DIB" BY THE PRINCESS IRULAN

The door stood ajar, and Jessica stepped through it into a room with yellow walls. To her left stretched a low settee of black hide and two empty bookcases, a hanging waterflask with dust on its bulging sides. To her right, bracketing another door, stood more empty bookcases, a desk from Caladan and three chairs. At the windows directly ahead of her stood Dr. Yueh, his back to her, his attention fixed upon the outside world.

Jessica took another silent step into the room.

She saw that Yueh's coat was wrinkled, a white smudge near the left elbow as though he had leaned against chalk. He looked, from behind, like a fleshless stick figure in overlarge black clothing, a caricature poised for stringy movement at the direction of a puppet master. Only the squarish block of head with long ebony hair caught in its silver Suk School ring at the shoulder seemed alive—turning slightly to follow some movement outside.

Again, she glanced around the room, seeing no sign of her son, but the closed door on her right, she knew, let into a small bedroom for which Paul had expressed a liking.

"Good afternoon, Dr. Yueh," she said. "Where's Paul?"

He nodded as though to something out the window, spoke in an absent manner without turning: "Your son grew tired, Jessica. I sent him into the next room to rest."

Abruptly, he stiffened, whirled with mustache flopping over his purpled lips. "Forgive me, my Lady! My thoughts were far away . . . I . . . did not mean to be familiar."

She smiled, held out her right hand. For a moment, she was afraid he might kneel. "Wellington, please."

"To use your name like that . . . I. . . ."

"We've known each other six years," she said. "It's long past time formalities should've been dropped between us—in private."

Yueh ventured a thin smile, thinking: *I believe it has worked. Now, she'll think anything unusual in my manner is due to embarrassment. She'll not look for deeper reasons when she believes she already knows the answer.*

"I'm afraid I was woolgathering," he said. "Whenever I . . . feel especially sorry for you, I'm afraid I think of you as . . . well, Jessica."

"Sorry for me? Whatever for?"

Yueh shrugged. Long ago, he had realized Jessica was not gifted with the full Truthsay as his Wanna had been. Still, he always used the truth with Jessica whenever possible. It was safest.

"You've seen this place, my . . . Jessica." He stumbled over the name, plunged ahead: "So barren after Caladan. And the people! Those townswomen we passed on the way here wailing beneath their veils. The way they looked at us."

She folded her arms across her breast, hugging herself, feeling the crysknife there, a blade ground from a sandworm's tooth, if the reports were right. "It's just that we're strange to them—different people, different customs. They've known only the Harkonnens." She looked past him out the windows. "What were you staring at out there?"

He turned back to the window. "The people."

Jessica crossed to his side, looked to the left toward the front of the house where Yueh's attention was focused. A line of twenty palm trees grew there, the ground beneath them swept clean, barren. A screen fence separated them from the road upon which robed people were passing. Jessica detected a faint shimmering in the air between her and the people—a house shield—and went on to study the passing throng, wondering why Yueh found them so absorbing.

The pattern emerged and she put a hand to her cheek. The way the passing people looked at the palm trees! She saw envy, some hate . . . even a sense of hope. Each person raked those trees with a fixity of expression.

"Do you know what they're thinking?" Yueh asked.

"You profess to read minds?" she asked.

"Those minds," he said. "They look at those trees and they think: 'There are one hundred of us.' That's what they think."

She turned a puzzled frown on him. "Why?"

"Those are date palms," he said. "One date palm requires forty liters of water a day. A man requires but eight liters. A palm, then, equals five men. There are twenty palms out there—one hundred men."

"But some of those people look at the trees hopefully."

"They but hope some dates will fall, except it's the wrong season."

"We look at this place with too critical an eye," she said. "There's hope as well as danger here. The spice *could* make us rich. With a fat treasury, we can make this world into whatever we wish."

And she laughed silently at herself: *Who am I trying to convince?* The laugh broke through her restraints, emerging brittle, without humor. "But you can't buy security," she said.

Yueh turned away to hide his face from her. *If only it were possible to hate these people instead of love them!* In her manner, in many ways, Jessica was like his Wanna. Yet that thought carried its own rigors, hardening him to his purpose. The ways of the Harkonnen cruelty were devious. Wanna might not be dead. He had to be certain.

"Do not worry for us, Wellington," Jessica said. "The problem's ours, not yours."

She thinks I worry for her! He blinked back tears. *And I do, of course. But I must stand before that black Baron with his deed accomplished, and take my one chance to strike him where he is weakest—in his gloating moment!*

He sighed.

"Would it disturb Paul if I looked in on him?" she asked.

"Not at all. I gave him a sedative."

"He's taking the change well?" she asked.

"Except for getting a bit overtired. He's excited, but what fifteen-year-old wouldn't be under these circumstances?" He crossed to the door, opened it. "He's in here."

Jessica followed, peered into a shadowy room.

Paul lay on a narrow cot, one arm beneath a light cover, the other thrown back over his head. Slatted blinds at a window beside the bed wove a loom of shadows across face and blanket.

Jessica stared at her son, seeing the oval shape of face so like her own. But the hair was the Duke's—coal-colored and tousled. Long lashes concealed the lime-toned eyes. Jessica smiled, feeling her fears retreat. She was suddenly caught by the idea of genetic traces in her son's features—her lines in eyes and facial outline, but sharp touches of the father peering through that outline like maturity emerging from childhood.

She thought of the boy's features as an exquisite distillation out of random patterns—endless queues of happenstance meeting at this nexus. The thought made her want to kneel beside the bed and take her son in her arms, but she was inhibited by Yueh's presence. She stepped back, closed the door softly.

Yueh had returned to the window, unable to bear watching the way Jessica stared at her son. *Why did Wanna never give me children?* he asked himself. *I know as a doctor there was no physical reason against it. Was there some Bene Gesserit reason? Was she, perhaps, instructed to serve a different purpose? What could it have been? She loved me, certainly.*

For the first time, he was caught up in the thought that he might be part of a pattern more involuted and complicated than his mind could grasp.

Jessica stopped beside him, said: "What delicious abandon in the sleep of a child."

He spoke mechanically: "If only adults could relax like that."

"Yes."

"Where do we lose it?" he murmured.

She glanced at him, catching the odd tone, but her mind was still on Paul, thinking of the new rigors in his training here, thinking of the differences in his life now—so very different from the life they once had planned for him.

"We do, indeed, lose something," she said.

She glanced out to the right at a slope humped with a wind-troubled gray-green of bushes—dusty leaves and dry claw branches. The too-dark sky hung over the slope like a blot, and the milky light of the Arrakeen sun gave the scene a silver cast—light like the crysknife concealed in her bodice.

"The sky's so dark," she said.

"That's partly the lack of moisture," he said.

"Water!" she snapped. "Everywhere you turn here, you're involved with the lack of water!"

"It's the precious mystery of Arrakis," he said.

"Why is there so little of it? There's volcanic rock here. There're a dozen power sources I could name. There's polar ice. They say you can't drill in the desert—storms and sandtides destroy equipment faster than it can be installed, if the worms don't get you first. They've never found water traces there, anyway. But the mystery, Wellington, the real mystery is the wells that've been drilled up here in the sinks and basins. Have you read about those?"

"First a trickle, then nothing," he said.

"But, Wellington, that's the mystery. The water was there. It dries up. And never again is there water. Yet another hole nearby produces the same result: a trickle that stops. Has no one ever been curious about this?"

"It is curious," he said. "You suspect some living agency? Wouldn't that have shown in core samples?"

"What would have shown? Alien plant matter . . . or animal? Who could recognize it?" She turned back to the slope. "The water is stopped. Something plugs it. That's my suspicion."

"Perhaps the reason's known," he said. "The Harkonnens sealed off many sources of information about Arrakis. Perhaps there was reason to suppress this."

"What reason?" she asked. "And then there's the atmospheric moisture. Little enough of it, certainly, but there's some. It's the major source of water here, caught in windtraps and precipitators. Where does that come from?"

"The polar caps?"

"Cold air takes up little moisture, Wellington. There are things here behind the Harkonnen veil that bear close investigation, and not all of those things are directly involved with the spice."

"We are indeed behind the Harkonnen veil," he said. "Perhaps we'll. . . ." He broke off, noting the sudden intense way she was looking at him. "Is something wrong?"

"The way you say 'Harkonnen,'" she said. "Even my Duke's voice doesn't carry that weight of venom when he uses the hated name. I didn't know you had personal reasons to hate them, Wellington."

Great Mother! he thought. *I've aroused her suspicions! Now I must use every trick my Wanna taught me. There's only one solution: tell the truth as far as I can.*

He said: "You didn't know that my wife, my Wanna. . . ." He shrugged, unable to speak past a sudden constriction in his throat. Then: "They. . . ." The words would not come out. He felt panic, closed his eyes tightly, experiencing the agony in his chest and little else until a hand touched his arm gently.

"Forgive me," Jessica said. "I did not mean to open an old wound." And she thought: *Those animals! His wife was Bene Gesserit—the signs are all over him. And it's obvious the Harkonnens killed her. Here's another poor victim bound to the Atreides by a cherem of hate.*

"I am sorry," he said. "I'm unable to talk about it." He opened his eyes, giving himself up to the internal awareness of grief. That, at least, was truth.

Jessica studied him, seeing the up-angled cheeks, the dark sequins of almond eyes, the butter complexion, and stringy mustache hanging like a curved frame around purpled lips and narrow chin. The creases of his cheeks and forehead, she saw, were as much lines of sorrow as of age. A deep affection for him came over her.

"Wellington, I'm sorry we brought you into this dangerous place," she said.

"I came willingly," he said. And that, too, was true.

"But this whole planet's a Harkonnen trap. You must know that."

"It will take more than a trap to catch the Duke Leto," he said. And that, too, was true.

"Perhaps I should be more confident of him," she said. "He is a brilliant tactician."

"We've been uprooted," he said. "That's why we're uneasy."

"And how easy it is to kill the uprooted plant," she said. "Especially when you put it down in hostile soil."

"Are we certain the soil's hostile?"

"There were water riots when it was learned how many people the Duke was adding to the population," she said. "They stopped only when the people learned we were installing new windtraps and condensers to take care of the load."

"There is only so much water to support human life here," he said. "The people know if more come to drink a limited amount of water, the price goes up and the very poor die. But the Duke has solved this. It doesn't follow that the riots mean permanent hostility toward him."

"And guards," she said. "Guards everywhere. And shields. You see the blurring of them everywhere you look. We did not live this way on Caladan."

"Give this planet a chance," he said.

But Jessica continued to stare hard-eyed out the window. "I can smell death in this place," she said. "Hawat sent advance agents in here by the battalion. Those guards outside are his men. The cargo handlers are his men. There've been unexplained withdrawals of large sums from the treasury. The amounts mean only one thing: bribes in high places." She shook her head. "Where Thufir Hawat goes, death and deceit follow."

"You malign him."

"Malign? I praise him. Death and deceit are our only hopes now. I just do not fool myself about Thufir's methods."

"You should . . . keep busy," he said. "Give yourself no time for such morbid—"

"Busy! What is it that takes most of my time, Wellington? I am the Duke's secretary—so busy that each day I learn new things to fear . . . things even he doesn't suspect I know." She compressed her lips, spoke thinly: "Sometimes I wonder how much my Bene Gesserit business training figured in his choice of me."

"What do you mean?" He found himself caught by the cynical tone, the bitterness that he had never seen her expose.

"Don't you think, Wellington," she asked, "that a secretary bound to one by love is so much safer?"

"That is not a worthy thought, Jessica."

The rebuke came naturally to his lips. There was no doubt how the Duke felt about his concubine. One had only to watch him as he followed her with his eyes.

She sighed. "You're right. It's not worthy."

Again, she hugged herself, pressing the sheathed crysknife against her flesh and thinking of the unfinished business it represented.

"There'll be much bloodshed soon," she said. "The Harkonnens won't rest until they're dead or my Duke destroyed. The Baron cannot forget that Leto is a cousin of the royal blood—no matter what the distance— while the Harkonnen titles came out of the CHOAM pocketbook. But the poison in him, deep in his mind, is the knowledge that an Atreides had a Harkonnen banished for cowardice after the Battle of Corrin."

"The old feud," Yueh muttered. And for a moment he felt an acid touch of hate. The old feud had trapped him in its web, killed his Wanna or—worse—left her for Harkonnen tortures until her husband did their bidding. The old feud had trapped him and these people were part of that poisonous thing. The irony was that such deadliness should come to flower here on Arrakis, the one source in the universe of melange, the prolonger of life, the giver of health.

"What are you thinking?" she asked.

"I am thinking that the spice brings six hundred and twenty thousand solaris the decagram on the open market right now. That is wealth to buy many things."

"Does greed touch even you, Wellington?"

"Not greed."

"What then?"

He shrugged. "Futility." He glanced at her. "Can you remember your first taste of spice?"

"It tasted like cinnamon."

"But never twice the same," he said. "It's like life—it presents a different face each time you take it. Some hold that the spice produces a learned-flavor reaction. The body, learning a thing is good for it, interprets the flavor as pleasurable—slightly euphoric. And, like life, never to be truly synthesized."

"I think it would've been wiser for us to go renegade, to take ourselves beyond the Imperial reach," she said.

He saw that she hadn't been listening to him, focused on her words, wondering: *Yes—why didn't she make him do this? She could make him do virtually anything.*

He spoke quickly because here was truth and a change of subject: "Would you think it bold of me . . . Jessica, if I asked a personal question?"

She pressed against the window ledge in an unexplainable pang of disquiet. "Of course not. You're . . . my friend."

"Why haven't you made the Duke marry you?"

She whirled, head up, glaring. "Made him marry me? But—"

"I should not have asked," he said.

"No." She shrugged. "There's good political reason—as long as my Duke remains unmarried some of the Great Houses can still hope for alliance. And. . . ." She sighed. ". . . motivating people, forcing them to your will, gives you a cynical attitude toward humanity. It degrades everything it touches. If I made him do . . . this, then it would not be his doing."

"It's a thing my Wanna might have said," he murmured. And this, too, was truth. He put a hand to his mouth, swallowing convulsively. He had never been closer to speaking out, confessing his secret role.

Jessica spoke, shattering the moment. "Besides, Wellington, the Duke is really two men. One of them I love very much. He's charming, witty, considerate . . . tender—everything a woman could desire. But the other man is . . . cold, callous, demanding, selfish—as harsh and cruel as a winter wind. That's the man shaped by the father." Her face contorted. "If only that old man had died when my Duke was born!"

In the silence that came between them, a breeze from a ventilator could be heard fingering the blinds.

Presently, she took a deep breath, said, "Leto's right—these rooms are nicer than the ones in the other sections of the house." She turned, sweeping the room with her gaze. "If you'll excuse me, Wellington, I want another look through this wing before I assign quarters."

He nodded. "Of course." And he thought: *If only there were some way not to do this thing that I must do.*

Jessica dropped her arms, crossed to the hall door and stood there a moment, hesitating, then let herself out. *All the time we talked he was hiding something, holding something back*, she thought. *To save my feelings, no doubt. He's a good man.* Again, she hesitated, almost turned back to confront Yueh and drag the hidden thing from him. *But that would only shame him, frighten him to learn he's so easily read. I should place more trust in my friends.*

Many have remarked the speed with which Muad'Dib learned the necessities of Arrakis. The Bene Gesserit, of course, know the basis of this speed. For the others, we can say that Muad'Dib learned rapidly because his first training was in how to learn. And the first lesson of all was the basic trust that he could learn. It is shocking to find how many people do not believe they can learn, and how many more believe learning to be difficult. Muad'Dib knew that every experience carries its lesson.

—FROM "THE HUMANITY OF MUAD'DIB"
BY THE PRINCESS IRULAN

Paul lay on the bed feigning sleep. It had been easy to palm Dr. Yueh's sleeping tablet, to pretend to swallow it. Paul suppressed a laugh. Even his mother had believed him asleep. He had wanted to jump up and ask her permission to go exploring the house, but had realized she wouldn't approve. Things were too unsettled yet. No. This way was best.

If I slip out without asking I haven't disobeyed orders. And I will stay in the house where it's safe.

He heard his mother and Yueh talking in the other room. Their words were indistinct—something about the spice . . . the Harkonnens. The conversation rose and fell.

Paul's attention went to the carved headboard of his bed—a false headboard attached to the wall and concealing the controls for this room's functions. A leaping fish had been shaped on the wood with thick brown waves beneath it. He knew if he pushed the fish's one visible eye that would turn on the room's suspensor lamps. One of the waves, when twisted, controlled ventilation. Another changed the temperature.

Quietly, Paul sat up in bed. A tall bookcase stood against the wall to his left. It could be swung aside to reveal a closet with drawers along one side. The handle on the door into the hall was patterned on an ornithopter thrust bar.

It was as though the room had been designed to entice him.

The room and this planet.

He thought of the filmbook Yueh had shown him—"Arrakis: His Imperial Majesty's Desert Botanical Testing Station." It was an old filmbook from before discovery of the spice. Names flitted through Paul's mind, each with its picture imprinted by the book's mnemonic pulse: *saguaro, burro bush, date palm, sand verbena, evening primrose, barrel cactus, incense bush, smoke tree, creosote bush . . . kit fox, desert hawk, kangaroo mouse. . . .*

Names and pictures, names and pictures from man's terranic past— and many to be found now nowhere else in the universe except here on Arrakis.

So many new things to learn about—the spice.

And the sandworms.

A door closed in the other room. Paul heard his mother's footsteps retreating down the hall. Dr. Yueh, he knew, would find something to read and remain in the other room.

Now was the moment to go exploring.

Paul slipped out of the bed, headed for the bookcase door that opened into the closet. He stopped at a sound behind him, turned. The carved headboard of the bed was folding down onto the spot where he had been sleeping. Paul froze, and immobility saved his life.

From behind the headboard slipped a tiny hunter-seeker no more than five centimeters long. Paul recognized it at once—a common assassination weapon that every child of royal blood learned about at an early age. It was a ravening sliver of metal guided by some nearby hand and eye. It could burrow into moving flesh and chew its way up nerve channels to the nearest vital organ.

The seeker lifted, swung sideways across the room and back.

Through Paul's mind flashed the related knowledge, the hunter-seeker limitations: Its compressed suspensor field distorted the room to reflect his target, the operator would be relying on motion—anything that moved. A shield could slow a hunter, give time to destroy it, but Paul had put aside his shield on the bed. Lasguns would knock them down, but lasguns were expensive and notoriously cranky of maintenance—and there was always the peril of explosive pyrotechnics if the laser beam intersected a hot shield. The Atreides relied on their body shields and their wits.

Now, Paul held himself in near catatonic immobility, knowing he had only his wits to meet this threat.

The hunter-seeker lifted another half meter. It rippled through the slatted light from the window blinds, back and forth, quartering the room.

I must try to grab it, he thought. *The suspensor field will make it slippery on the bottom. I must grip tightly.*

The thing dropped a half meter, quartered to the left, circled back around the bed. A faint humming could be heard from it.

Who is operating that thing? Paul wondered. *It has to be someone near. I could shout for Yueh, but it would take him the instant the door opened.*

The hall door behind Paul creaked. A rap sounded there. The door opened.

The hunter-seeker arrowed past his head toward the motion.

Paul's right hand shot out and down, gripping the deadly thing. It hummed and twisted in his hand, but his muscles were locked on it in desperation. With a violent turn and thrust, he slammed the thing's nose against the metal doorplate. He felt the crunch of it as the nose eye smashed and the seeker went dead in his hand.

Still, he held it—to be certain.

Paul's eyes came up, met the open stare of total blue from the Shadout Mapes.

"Your father has sent for you," she said. "There are men in the hall to escort you."

Paul nodded, his eyes and awareness focusing on this odd woman in a sacklike dress of bondsman brown. She was looking now at the thing clutched in his hand.

"I've heard of suchlike," she said. "It would've killed me, not so?"

He had to swallow before he could speak. "I . . . was its target."

"But it was coming for me."

"Because you were moving." And he wondered: *Who is this creature?*

"Then you saved my life," she said.

"I saved both our lives."

"Seems like you could've let it have me and made your own escape," she said.

"Who are you?" he asked.

"The Shadout Mapes, housekeeper."

"How did you know where to find me?"

"Your mother told me. I met her at the stairs to the weirding room down the hall." She pointed to her right. "Your father's men are still waiting."

Those will be Hawat's men, he thought. *We must find the operator of this thing.*

"Go to my father's men," he said. "Tell them I've caught a hunter-seeker in the house and they're to spread out and find the operator. Tell them to seal off the house and its grounds immediately. They'll know how to go about it. The operator's sure to be a stranger among us."

And he wondered: *Could it be this creature?* But he knew it wasn't. The seeker had been under control when she entered.

"Before I do your bidding, manling," Mapes said, "I must cleanse the way between us. You've put a water burden on me that I'm not sure I care to support. But we Fremen pay our debts—be they black debts or white debts. And it's known to us that you've a traitor in your midst. Who it is, we cannot say, but we're certain sure of it. Mayhap there's the hand guided that flesh-cutter."

Paul absorbed this in silence: *a traitor.* Before he could speak, the odd woman whirled away and ran back toward the entry.

He thought to call her back, but there was an air about her that told him she would resent it. She'd told him what she knew and now she was going to do his *bidding*. The house would be swarming with Hawat's men in a minute.

His mind went to other parts of that strange conversation: *weirding room*. He looked to his left where she had pointed. *We Fremen.* So that was a Fremen. He paused for the mnemonic blink that would store the pattern of her face in his memory—prune-wrinkled features darkly browned, blue-on-blue eyes without any white in them. He attached the label: *The Shadout Mapes*.

Still gripping the shattered seeker, Paul turned back into his room, scooped up his shield belt from the bed with his left hand, swung it around his waist and buckled it as he ran back out and down the hall to the left.

She'd said his mother was someplace down here—stairs . . . a *weirding room*.

What had the Lady Jessica to sustain her in her time of trial? Think you carefully on this Bene Gesserit proverb and perhaps you will see: "Any road followed precisely to its end leads precisely nowhere. Climb the mountain just a little bit to test that it's a mountain. From the top of the mountain, you cannot see the mountain."

—FROM "MUAD'DIB: FAMILY COMMENTARIES"
BY THE PRINCESS IRULAN

At the end of the south wing, Jessica found a metal stair spiraling up to an oval door. She glanced back down the hall, again up at the door.

Oval? she wondered. *What an odd shape for a door in a house.*

Through the windows beneath the spiral stair she could see the great white sun of Arrakis moving on toward evening. Long shadows stabbed down the hall. She returned her attention to the stairs. Harsh sidelighting picked out bits of dried earth on the open metalwork of the steps.

Jessica put a hand on the rail, began to climb. The rail felt cold under her sliding palm. She stopped at the door, saw it had no handle, but there was a faint depression on the surface of it where a handle should have been.

Surely not a palm lock, she told herself. *A palm lock must be keyed to one individual's hand shape and palm lines.* But it looked like a palm lock. And there were ways to open any palm lock—as she had learned at school.

Jessica glanced back to make certain she was unobserved, placed her palm against the depression in the door. The most gentle of pressures to distort the lines—a turn of the wrist, another turn, a sliding twist of the palm across the surface.

She felt the click.

But there were hurrying footsteps in the hall beneath her. Jessica lifted her hand from the door, turned, saw Mapes come to the foot of the stairs.

"There are men in the Great Hall say they've been sent by the Duke to get young Master Paul," Mapes said. "They've the ducal signet and the guard has identified them." She glanced at the door, back to Jessica.

A cautious one, this Mapes, Jessica thought. *That's a good sign.*

"He's in the fifth room from this end of the hall, the small bedroom," Jessica said. "If you have trouble waking him, call on Dr. Yueh in the next room. Paul may require a wakeshot."

Again, Mapes cast a piercing stare at the oval door, and Jessica thought she detected loathing in the expression. Before Jessica could ask about the door and what it concealed, Mapes had turned away, hurrying back down the hall.

Hawat certified this place, Jessica thought. *There can't be anything too terrible in here.*

She pushed the door. It swung inward onto a small room with another oval door opposite. The other door had a wheel handle.

An airlock! Jessica thought. She glanced down, saw a door prop fallen to the floor of the little room. The prop carried Hawat's personal mark. *The door was left propped open*, she thought. *Someone probably knocked the prop down accidentally, not realizing the outer door would close on a palm lock.*

She stepped over the lip into the little room.

Why an airlock in a house? she asked herself. And she thought suddenly of exotic creatures sealed off in special climates.

Special climate!

That would make sense on Arrakis where even the driest of off-planet growing things had to be irrigated.

The door behind her began swinging closed. She caught it and propped it open securely with the stick Hawat had left. Again, she faced the wheel-locked inner door, seeing now a faint inscription etched in the metal above the handle. She recognized Galach words, read:

"O, Man! Here is a lovely portion of God's Creation; then, stand before it and learn to love the perfection of Thy Supreme Friend."

Jessica put her weight on the wheel. It turned left and the inner door opened. A gentle draft feathered her cheek, stirred her hair. She felt change in the air, a richer taste. She swung the door wide, looked through into massed greenery with yellow sunlight pouring across it.

A yellow sun? she asked herself. Then: *Filter glass!*

She stepped over the sill and the door swung closed behind.

"A wet-planet conservatory," she breathed.

Potted plants and low-pruned trees stood all about. She recognized a mimosa, a flowering quince, a sondagi, green-blossomed pleniscenta, green and white striped akarso . . . roses. . . .

Even roses!

She bent to breathe the fragrance of a giant pink blossom, straightened to peer around the room.

Rhythmic noise invaded her senses.

She parted a jungle overlapping of leaves, looked through to the center of the room. A low fountain stood there, small with fluted lips. The rhythmic noise was a peeling, spooling arc of water falling thud-a-gallop onto the metal bowl.

Jessica sent herself through the quick sense-clearing regimen, began a methodical inspection of the room's perimeter. It appeared to be about ten meters square. From its placement above the end of the hall and from subtle differences in construction, she guessed it had been added onto the roof of this wing long after the original building's completion.

She stopped at the south limits of the room in front of the wide reach of filter glass, stared around. Every available space in the room was crowded with exotic wet-climate plants. Something rustled in the greenery. She tensed, then glimpsed a simple clock-set servok with pipe and hose arms. An arm lifted, sent out a fine spray of dampness that misted her cheeks. The arm retracted and she looked at what it had watered: a fern tree.

Water everywhere in this room—on a planet where water was the most precious juice of life. Water being wasted so conspicuously that it shocked her to inner stillness.

She glanced out at the filter-yellowed sun. It hung low on a jagged horizon above cliffs that formed part of the immense rock uplifting known as the Shield Wall.

Filter glass, she thought. *To turn a white sun into something softer and more familiar. Who could have built such a place? Leto? It would be like him to surprise me with such a gift, but there hasn't been time. And he's been busy with more serious problems.*

She recalled the report that many Arrakeen houses were sealed by airlock doors and windows to conserve and reclaim interior moisture. Leto had said it was a deliberate statement of power and wealth for this house to ignore such precautions, its doors and windows being sealed only against the omnipresent dust.

But this room embodied a statement far more significant than the lack of waterseals on outer doors. She estimated that this pleasure room used water enough to support a thousand persons on Arrakis—possibly more.

Jessica moved along the window, continuing to stare into the room. The move brought into view a metallic surface at table height beside the fountain and she glimpsed a white notepad and stylus there partly concealed by an overhanging fan leaf. She crossed to the table, noted Hawat's daysigns on it, studied a message written on the pad:

"TO THE LADY JESSICA—

May this place give you as much pleasure as it has given me. Please permit the room to convey a lesson we learned from the same teachers: the proximity of a desirable thing tempts one to overindulgence. On that path lies danger.

My kindest wishes,
MARGOT LADY FENRING"

Jessica nodded, remembering that Leto had referred to the Emperor's former proxy here as Count Fenring. But the hidden message of the note demanded immediate attention, couched as it was in a way to inform her the writer was another Bene Gesserit. A bitter thought touched Jessica in passing: *The Count married his Lady.*

Even as this thought flicked through her mind, she was bending to seek out the hidden message. It had to be there. The visible note contained the code phrase every Bene Gesserit not bound by a School Injunction was required to give another Bene Gesserit when conditions demanded it: "On that path lies danger."

Jessica felt the back of the note, rubbed the surface for coded dots. Nothing. The edge of the pad came under her seeking fingers. Nothing. She replaced the pad where she had found it, feeling a sense of urgency.

Something in the position of the pad? she wondered.

But Hawat had been over this room, doubtless had moved the pad. She looked at the leaf above the pad. The leaf! She brushed a finger along the under surface, along the edge, along the stem. It was there! Her fingers detected the subtle coded dots, scanned them in a single passage:

"Your son and the Duke are in immediate danger. A bedroom has been designed to attract your son. The H loaded it with death traps to be discovered, leaving one that may escape detection." Jessica put down the urge to run back to Paul; the full message had to be learned. Her fingers sped over the dots: "I do not know the exact nature of the menace, but it has something to do with a bed. The threat to your Duke involves defection of a trusted companion or lieutenant. The H plan to give you as gift to a minion. To the best of my knowledge, this conservatory is safe. Forgive that I cannot tell more. My sources are few as my Count is not in the pay of the H. In haste, MF."

Jessica thrust the leaf aside, whirled to dash back to Paul. In that instant, the airlock door slammed open. Paul jumped through it, holding something in his right hand, slammed the door behind him. He saw his mother, pushed through the leaves to her, glanced at the fountain, thrust his hand and the thing it clutched under the falling water.

"Paul!" She grabbed his shoulder, staring at the hand. "What is that?"

He spoke casually, but she caught the effort behind the tone: "Hunter-seeker. Caught it in my room and smashed its nose, but I want to be sure. Water should short it out."

"Immerse it!" she commanded.

He obeyed.

Presently, she said: "Withdraw your hand. Leave the thing in the water."

He brought out his hand, shook water from it, staring at the quiescent metal in the fountain. Jessica broke off a plant stem, prodded the deadly sliver.

It was dead.

She dropped the stem into the water, looked at Paul. His eyes studied the room with a searching intensity that she recognized—the B.G. Way.

"This place could conceal anything," he said.

"I've reason to believe it's safe," she said.

"My room was supposed to be safe, too. Hawat said—"

"It was a hunter-seeker," she reminded him. "That means someone inside the house to operate it. Seeker control beams have a limited range. The thing could've been spirited in here after Hawat's investigation."

But she thought of the message of the leaf: "... *defection of a trusted companion or lieutenant.*" *Not Hawat, surely. Oh, surely not Hawat.*

"Hawat's men are searching the house right now," he said. "That seeker almost got the old woman who came to wake me."

"The Shadout Mapes," Jessica said, remembering the encounter at the stairs. "A summons from your father to—"

"That can wait," Paul said. "Why do you think this room's safe?"

She pointed to the note, explained about it.

He relaxed slightly.

But Jessica remained inwardly tense, thinking: *A hunter-seeker! Merciful Mother!* It took all her training to prevent a fit of hysterical trembling.

Paul spoke matter-of-factly: "It's the Harkonnens, of course. We shall have to destroy them."

A rapping sounded at the airlock door—the code knock of one of Hawat's corps.

"Come in," Paul called.

The door swung wide and a tall man in Atreides uniform with a Hawat insignia on his cap leaned into the room. "There you are, sir," he said. "The housekeeper said you'd be here." He glanced around the room. "We found a cairn in the cellar and caught a man in it. He had a seeker console."

"I'll want to take part in the interrogation," Jessica said.

"Sorry, my Lady. We messed him up catching him. He died."

"Nothing to identify him?" she asked.

"We've found nothing yet, my Lady."

"Was he an Arrakeen native?" Paul asked.

Jessica nodded at the astuteness of the question.

"He has the native look," the man said. "Put into that cairn more'n a month ago, by the look, and left there to await our coming. Stone and mortar where he came through into the cellar were untouched when we inspected the place yesterday. I'll stake my reputation on it."

"No one questions your thoroughness," Jessica said.

"I question it, my Lady. We should've used sonic probes down there."

"I presume that's what you're doing now," Paul said.

"Yes, sir."

"Send word to my father that we'll be delayed."

"At once, sir." He glanced at Jessica. "It's Hawat's order that under such circumstances as these the young Master be guarded in a safe place." Again, his eyes swept the room. "What of this place?"

"I've reason to believe it safe," she said. "Both Hawat and I have inspected it."

"Then I'll mount guard outside here, m'Lady, until we've been over the house once more." He bowed, touched his cap to Paul, backed out and swung the door closed behind him.

Paul broke the sudden silence, saying: "Had we better go over the house later ourselves? Your eyes might see things others would miss."

"This wing was the only place I hadn't examined," she said. "I put it off to last because. . . ."

"Because Hawat gave it his personal attention," he said.

She darted a quick look at his face, questioning.

"Do you distrust Hawat?" she asked.

"No, but he's getting old . . . he's overworked. We could take some of the load from him."

"That'd only shame him and impair his efficiency," she said. "A stray insect won't be able to wander into this wing after he hears about this. He'll be shamed that. . . ."

"We must take our own measures," he said.

"Hawat has served three generations of Atreides with honor," she said. "He deserves every respect and trust we can pay him . . . many times over."

Paul said: "When my father is bothered by something you've done he says *'Bene Gesserit!'* like a swear word."

"And what is it about me that bothers your father?"

"When you argue with him."

"You are not your father, Paul."

And Paul thought: *It'll worry her, but I must tell her what that Mapes woman said about a traitor among us.*

"What're you holding back?" Jessica asked. "This isn't like you, Paul."

He shrugged, recounted the exchange with Mapes.

And Jessica thought of the message of the leaf. She came to sudden decision, showed Paul the leaf, told him its message.

"My father must learn of this at once," he said. "I'll radiograph it in code and get it off."

"No," she said. "You will wait until you can see him alone. As few as possible must learn about it."

"Do you mean we should trust no one?"

"There's another possibility," she said. "This message may have been meant to get to us. The people who gave it to us may believe it's true, but it may be that the only purpose was to get this message to us."

Paul's face remained sturdily somber. "To sow distrust and suspicion in our ranks, to weaken us that way," he said.

"You must tell your father privately and caution him about this aspect of it," she said.

"I understand."

She turned to the tall reach of filter glass, stared out to the southwest where the sun of Arrakis was sinking—a yellowed ball above the cliffs.

Paul turned with her, said: "I don't think it's Hawat, either. Is it possible it's Yueh?"

"He's not a lieutenant or companion," she said. "And I can assure you he hates the Harkonnens as bitterly as we do."

Paul directed his attention to the cliffs, thinking: *And it couldn't be Gurney . . . or Duncan. Could it be one of the sub-lieutenants? Impossible. They're all from families that've been loyal to us for generations—for good reason.*

Jessica rubbed her forehead, sensing her own fatigue. *So much peril here!* She looked out at the filter-yellowed landscape, studying it. Beyond the ducal grounds stretched a high-fenced storage yard—lines of spice silos in it with stilt-legged watchtowers standing around it like so many startled spiders. She could see at least twenty storage yards of silos reaching out to the cliffs of the Shield Wall—silos repeated, stuttering across the basin.

Slowly, the filtered sun buried itself beneath the horizon. Stars leaped out. She saw one bright star so low on the horizon that it twinkled with a clear, precise rhythm—a trembling of light: blink-blink-blink-blink-blink . . .

Paul stirred beside her in the dusky room.

But Jessica concentrated on that single bright star, realizing that it was *too* low, that it must come from the Shield Wall cliffs.

Someone signaling!

She tried to read the message, but it was in no code she had ever learned.

Other lights had come on down on the plain beneath the cliffs: little yellows spaced out against blue darkness. And one light off to their left grew brighter, began to wink back at the cliff—very fast: blinksquirt, glimmer, blink!

And it was gone.

The false star in the cliff winked out immediately.

Signals . . . and they filled her with premonition.

Why were lights used to signal across the basin? she asked herself. *Why couldn't they use the communications network?*

The answer was obvious: the communinet was certain to be tapped now by agents of the Duke Leto. Light signals could only mean that messages were being sent between his enemies—between Harkonnen agents.

There came a tapping at the door behind them and the voice of Hawat's man: "All clear, sir . . . m'Lady. Time to be getting the young Master to his father."

It is said that the Duke Leto blinded himself to the perils of Arrakis, that he walked heedlessly into the pit. Would it not be more likely to suggest he had lived so long in the presence of extreme danger he misjudged a change in its intensity? Or is it possible he deliberately sacrificed himself that his son might find a better life? All evidence indicates the Duke was a man not easily hoodwinked.

—FROM "MUAD'DIB: FAMILY COMMENTARIES" BY THE PRINCESS IRULAN

The Duke Leto Atreides leaned against a parapet of the landing control tower outside Arrakeen. The night's first moon, an oblate silver coin, hung well above the southern horizon. Beneath it, the jagged cliffs of the Shield Wall shone like parched icing through a dust haze. To his left, the lights of Arrakeen glowed in the haze—yellow . . . white . . . blue.

He thought of the notices posted now above his signature all through the populous places of the planet: "Our Sublime Padishah Emperor has charged me to take possession of this planet and end all dispute."

The ritualistic formality of it touched him with a feeling of loneliness. *Who was fooled by that fatuous legalism? Not the Fremen, certainly. Nor the Houses Minor who controlled the interior trade of Arrakis . . . and were Harkonnen creatures almost to a man.*

They have tried to take the life of my son!

The rage was difficult to suppress.

He saw lights of a moving vehicle coming toward the landing field from Arrakeen. He hoped it was the guard and troop carrier bringing Paul. The delay was galling even though he knew it was prompted by caution on the part of Hawat's lieutenant.

They have tried to take the life of my son!

He shook his head to drive out the angry thoughts, glanced back at the field where five of his own frigates were posted around the rim like monolithic sentries.

Better a cautious delay than . . .

The lieutenant was a good one, he reminded himself. A man marked for advancement, *completely loyal.*

"Our Sublime Padishah Emperor. . . ."

If the people of this decadent garrison city could only see the Emperor's private note to his "Noble Duke"—the disdainful allusions to veiled men and women: ". . . but what else is one to expect of barbarians whose dearest dream is to live outside the ordered security of the faufreluches?"

The Duke felt in this moment that his own dearest dream was to end all class distinctions and never again think of deadly order. He looked up and out of the dust at the unwinking stars, thought: *Around one of those little lights circles Caladan . . . but I'll never again see my home.* The longing for Caladan was a sudden pain in his breast. He felt that it did not come from within himself, but that it reached out to him from Caladan. He could not bring himself to call this dry wasteland of Arrakis his home, and he doubted he ever would.

I must mask my feelings, he thought. *For the boy's sake. If ever he's to have a home, this must be it. I may think of Arrakis as a hell I've reached before death, but he must find here that which will inspire him. There must be something.*

A wave of self-pity, immediately despised and rejected, swept through him, and for some reason he found himself recalling two lines from a poem Gurney Halleck often repeated—

"My lungs taste the air of Time
Blown past falling sands. . . ."

Well, Gurney would find plenty of falling sands here, the Duke thought. The central wastelands beyond those moon-frosted cliffs were desert—barren rock, dunes, and blowing dust, an uncharted dry wilderness with here and there along its rim and perhaps scattered through it, knots of Fremen. If anything could buy a future for the Atreides line, the Fremen just might do it.

Provided the Harkonnens hadn't managed to infect even the Fremen with their poisonous schemes.

They have tried to take the life of my son!

A scraping metal racket vibrated through the tower, shook the parapet beneath his arms. Blast shutters dropped in front of him, blocking the view.

Shuttle's coming in, he thought. *Time to go down and get to work.* He turned to the stairs behind him, headed down to the big assembly room, trying to remain calm as he descended, to prepare his face for the coming encounter.

They have tried to take the life of my son!

The men were already boiling in from the field when he reached the yellow-domed room. They carried their spacebags over their shoulders, shouting and roistering like students returning from vacation.

"Hey! Feel that under your dogs? That's gravity, man!" "How many G's does this place pull? Feels heavy." "Nine-tenths of a G by the book."

The crossfire of thrown words filled the big room.

"Did you get a good look at this hole on the way down? Where's all the loot this place's supposed to have?" "The Harkonnens took it with 'em!" "Me for a hot shower and a soft bed!" "Haven't you heard, stupid? No showers down here. You scrub your ass with sand!" "Hey! Can it! The Duke!"

The Duke stepped out of the stair entry into a suddenly silent room.

Gurney Halleck strode along at the point of the crowd, bag over one shoulder, the neck of his nine-string baliset clutched in the other hand. They were long-fingered hands with big thumbs, full of tiny movements that drew such delicate music from the baliset.

The Duke watched Halleck, admiring the ugly lump of a man, noting the glass-splinter eyes with their gleam of savage understanding. Here was a man who lived outside the faufreluches while obeying their every precept. What was it Paul had called him? *"Gurney, the valorous."*

Halleck's wispy blond hair trailed across barren spots on his head. His wide mouth was twisted into a pleasant sneer, and the scar of the inkvine whip slashed across his jawline seemed to move with a life of its own. His whole air was of casual, shoulder-set capability. He came up to the Duke, bowed.

"Gurney," Leto said.

"My Lord." He gestured with the baliset toward the men in the room. "This is the last of them. I'd have preferred coming in with the first wave, but. . . ."

"There are still some Harkonnens for you," the Duke said. "Step aside with me, Gurney, where we may talk."

"Yours to command, my Lord."

They moved into an alcove beside a coil-slot water machine while the men stirred restlessly in the big room. Halleck dropped his bag into a corner, kept his grip on the baliset.

"How many men can you let Hawat have?" the Duke asked.

"Is Thufir in trouble, Sire?"

"He's lost only two agents, but his advance men gave us an excellent line on the entire Harkonnen setup here. If we move fast we may gain a measure of security, the breathing space we require. He wants as many men as you can spare—men who won't balk at a little knife work."

"I can let him have three hundred of my best," Halleck said. "Where shall I send them?"

"To the main gate. Hawat has an agent there waiting to take them."

"Shall I get about it at once, Sire?"

"In a moment. We have another problem. The field commandant will hold the shuttle here until dawn on a pretext. The Guild Heighliner that brought us is going on about its business, and the shuttle's supposed to make contact with a cargo ship taking up a load of spice."

"Our spice, m'Lord?"

"Our spice. But the shuttle also will carry some of the spice hunters from the old regime. They've opted to leave with the change of fief and the Judge of the Change is allowing it. These are valuable workers, Gurney, about eight hundred of them. Before the shuttle leaves, you must persuade some of those men to enlist with us."

"How strong a persuasion, Sire?"

"I want their willing cooperation, Gurney. Those men have experience and skills we need. The fact that they're leaving suggests they're not part of the Harkonnen machine. Hawat believes there could be some bad ones planted in the group, but he sees assassins in every shadow."

"Thufir has found some very productive shadows in his time, m'Lord."

"And there are some he hasn't found. But I think planting sleepers in this outgoing crowd would show too much imagination for the Harkonnens."

"Possibly, Sire. Where are these men?"

"Down on the lower level, in a waiting room. I suggest you go down and play a tune or two to soften their minds, then turn on the pressure. You may offer positions of authority to those who qualify. Offer twenty per cent higher wages than they received under the Harkonnens."

"No more than that, Sire? I know the Harkonnen pay scales. And to men with their termination pay in their pockets and the wanderlust on them . . . well, Sire, twenty per cent would hardly seem proper inducement to stay."

Leto spoke impatiently: "Then use your own discretion in particular cases. Just remember that the treasury isn't bottomless. Hold it to twenty per cent whenever you can. We particularly need spice drivers, weather scanners, dune men—any with open sand experience."

"I understand, Sire. 'They shall come all for violence: their faces shall sup up as the east wind, and they shall gather the captivity of the sand.'"

"A very moving quotation," the Duke said. "Turn your crew over to a lieutenant. Have him give a short drill on water discipline, then bed the men down for the night in the barracks adjoining the field. Field personnel will direct them. And don't forget the men for Hawat."

"Three hundred of the best, Sire." He took up his spacebag. "Where shall I report to you when I've completed my chores?"

"I've taken over a council room topside here. We'll hold staff there. I want to arrange a new planetary dispersal order with armored squads going out first."

Halleck stopped in the act of turning away, caught Leto's eye. "Are you anticipating *that* kind of trouble, Sire? I thought there was a Judge of the Change here."

"Both open battle and secret," the Duke said. "There'll be blood aplenty spilled here before we're through."

"'And the water which thou takest out of the river shall become blood upon the dry land,'" Halleck quoted.

The Duke sighed. "Hurry back, Gurney."

"Very good, m'Lord." The whipscar rippled to his grin. "'Behold, as a wild ass in the desert, go I forth to my work.'" He turned, strode to the center of the room, paused to relay his orders, hurried on through the men.

Leto shook his head at the retreating back. Halleck was a continual amazement—a head full of songs, quotations, and flowery phrases . . . and the heart of an assassin when it came to dealing with the Harkonnens.

Presently, Leto took a leisurely diagonal course across to the lift, acknowledging salutes with a casual hand wave. He recognized a propaganda corpsman, stopped to give him a message that could be relayed to the men through channels: those who had brought their women would want to know the women were safe and where they could be found. The others would wish to know that the population here appeared to boast more women than men.

The Duke slapped the propaganda man on the arm, a signal that the message had top priority to be put out immediately, then continued across the room. He nodded to the men, smiled, traded pleasantries with a subaltern.

Command must always look confident, he thought. *All that faith riding on your shoulders while you sit in the critical seat and never show it.*

He breathed a sigh of relief when the lift swallowed him and he could turn and face the impersonal doors.

They have tried to take the life of my son!

Over the exit of the Arrakeen landing field, crudely carved as though with a poor instrument, there was an inscription that Muad'Dib was to repeat many times. He saw it that first night on Arrakis, having been brought to the ducal command post to participate in his father's first full staff conference. The words of the inscription were a plea to those leaving Arrakis, but they fell with dark import on the eyes of a boy who had just escaped a close brush with death. They said: "O you who know what we suffer here, do not forget us in your prayers."

—FROM "MANUAL OF MUAD'DIB"
BY THE PRINCESS IRULAN

"The whole theory of warfare is calculated risk," the Duke said, "but when it comes to risking your own family, the element of *calculation* gets submerged in . . . other things."

He knew he wasn't holding in his anger as well as he should, and he turned, strode down the length of the long table and back.

The Duke and Paul were alone in the conference room at the landing field. It was an empty-sounding room, furnished only with the long table, old-fashioned three-legged chairs around it, and a map board and projector at one end. Paul sat at the table near the map board. He had told his father the experience with the hunter-seeker and given the reports that a traitor threatened him.

The Duke stopped across from Paul, pounded the table: "Hawat told me that house was secure!"

Paul spoke hesitantly: "I was angry, too—at first. And I blamed Hawat. But the threat came from outside the house. It was simple, clever, and direct. And it would've succeeded were it not for the training given me by you and many others—including Hawat."

"Are you defending him?" the Duke demanded.

"Yes."

"He's getting old. That's it. He should be—"

"He's wise with much experience," Paul said. "How many of Hawat's mistakes can you recall?"

"I should be the one defending him," the Duke said. "Not you."

Paul smiled.

Leto sat down at the head of the table, put a hand over his son's. "You've . . . matured lately, Son." He lifted his hand. "It gladdens me." He matched his son's smile. "Hawat will punish himself. He'll direct more anger against himself over this than both of us together could pour on him."

Paul glanced toward the darkened windows beyond the map board, looked at the night's blackness. Room lights reflected from a balcony railing out there. He saw movement and recognized the shape of a guard in Atreides uniform. Paul looked back at the white wall behind his father, then down to the shiny surface of the table, seeing his own hands clenched into fists there.

The door opposite the Duke banged open. Thufir Hawat strode through it looking older and more leathery than ever. He paced down the length of the table, stopped at attention facing Leto.

"My Lord," he said, speaking to a point over Leto's head, "I have just learned how I failed you. It becomes necessary that I tender my resig—"

"Oh, sit down and stop acting the fool," the Duke said. He waved to the chair across from Paul. "If you made a mistake, it was in overestimating the Harkonnens. Their simple minds came up with a simple trick. We didn't count on simple tricks. And my son has been at great pains to point out to me that he came through this largely because of your training. You didn't fail there!" He tapped the back of the empty chair. "Sit down, I say!"

Hawat sank into the chair. "But—"

"I'll hear no more of it," the Duke said. "The incident is past. We have more pressing business. Where are the others?"

"I asked them to wait outside while I—"

"Call them in."

Hawat looked into Leto's eyes. "Sire, I—"

"I know who my true friends are, Thufir," the Duke said. "Call in the men."

Hawat swallowed. "At once, my Lord." He swiveled in the chair, called to the open door: "Gurney, bring them in."

Halleck led the file of men into the room, the staff officers looking grimly serious followed by the younger aides and specialists, an air of eagerness among them. Brief scuffing sounds echoed around the room as the men took seats. A faint smell of rachag stimulant wafted down the table.

"There's coffee for those who want it," the Duke said.

He looked over his men, thinking: *They're a good crew. A man could do far worse for this kind of war.* He waited while coffee was brought in from the adjoining room and served, noting the tiredness in some of the faces.

Presently, he put on his mask of quiet efficiency, stood up and commanded their attention with a knuckle rap against the table.

"Well, gentlemen," he said, "our civilization appears to've fallen so deeply into the habit of invasion that we cannot even obey a simple order of the Imperium without the old ways cropping up."

Dry chuckles sounded around the table, and Paul realized that his father had said the precisely correct thing in precisely the correct tone to lift the mood here. Even the hint of fatigue in his voice was right.

"I think first we'd better learn if Thufir has anything to add to his report on the Fremen," the Duke said. "Thufir?"

Hawat glanced up. "I've some economic matters to go into after my general report, Sire, but I can say now that the Fremen appear more and more to be the allies we need. They're waiting now to see if they can trust us, but they appear to be dealing openly. They've sent us a gift—stillsuits of their own manufacture . . . maps of certain desert areas surrounding strongpoints the Harkonnens left behind. . . ." He glanced down at the table. "Their intelligence reports have proved completely reliable and have helped us considerably in our dealings with the Judge of the Change. They've also sent some incidental things—jewelry for the Lady Jessica, spice liquor, candy, medicinals. My men are processing the lot right now. There appears to be no trickery."

"You like these people, Thufir?" asked a man down the table.

Hawat turned to face his questioner. "Duncan Idaho says they're to be admired."

Paul glanced at his father, back to Hawat, ventured a question: "Have you any new information on how many Fremen there are?"

Hawat looked at Paul. "From food processing and other evidence, Idaho estimates the cave complex he visited consisted of some ten thousand people, all told. Their leader said he ruled a sietch of two thousand hearths. We've reason to believe there are a great many such sietch communities. All seem to give their allegiance to someone called Liet."

"That's something new," Leto said.

"It could be an error on my part, Sire. There are things to suggest this Liet may be a local deity."

Another man down the table cleared his throat, asked: "Is it certain they deal with the smugglers?"

"A smuggler caravan left this sietch while Idaho was there, carrying a heavy load of spice. They used pack beasts and indicated they faced an eighteen-day journey."

"It appears," the Duke said, "that the smugglers have redoubled their operations during this period of unrest. This deserves some careful thought. We shouldn't worry too much about unlicensed frigates working off our planet—it's always done. But to have them completely outside our observation—that's not good."

"You have a plan, Sire," Hawat asked.

The Duke looked at Halleck. "Gurney, I want you to head a delegation, an embassy if you will, to contact these romantic businessmen. Tell them I'll ignore their operations as long as they give me a ducal tithe. Hawat here estimates that graft and extra fighting men heretofore required in their operations have been costing them four times that amount."

"What if the Emperor gets wind of this?" Halleck asked. "He's very jealous of his CHOAM profits, m'Lord."

Leto smiled. "We'll bank the entire tithe openly in the name of Shaddam IV and deduct it legally from our levy support costs. Let the Harkonnens fight that! And we'll be ruining a few more of the locals who grew fat under the Harkonnen system. No more graft!"

A grin twisted Halleck's face. "Ahh, m'Lord, a beautiful low blow. Would that I could see the Baron's face when he learns of this."

The Duke turned to Hawat. "Thufir, did you get those account books you said you could buy?"

"Yes, my Lord. They're being examined in detail even now. I've skimmed them, though, and can give a first approximation."

"Give it, then."

"The Harkonnens took ten billion solaris out of here every three hundred and thirty Standard days."

A muted gasp ran around the table. Even the younger aides, who had been betraying some boredom, sat up straighter and exchanged wide-eyed looks.

Halleck murmured: "'For they shall suck of the abundance of the seas and of the treasure hid in the sand.'"

"You see, gentlemen," Leto said. "Is there anyone here so naive he believes the Harkonnens have quietly packed up and walked away from all this merely because the Emperor ordered it?"

There was a general shaking of heads, murmurous agreement.

"We will have to take it at the point of the sword," Leto said. He turned to Hawat. "This'd be a good point to report on equipment. How many sandcrawlers, harvesters, spice factories, and supporting equipment have they left us?"

"A full complement, as it says in the Imperial inventory audited by the Judge of the Change, my Lord," Hawat said. He gestured for an aide to pass him a folder, opened the folder on the table in front of him. "They neglect to mention that less than half the crawlers are operable, that only about a third have carryalls to fly them to spice sands—that everything the Harkonnens left us is ready to break down and fall apart. We'll be lucky to get half the equipment into operation and luckier yet if a fourth of it's still working six months from now."

"Pretty much as we expected," Leto said. "What's the firm estimate on basic equipment?"

Hawat glanced at his folder. "About nine hundred and thirty harvester factories that can be sent out in a few days. About sixty-two hundred and fifty ornithopters for survey, scouting, and weather observation . . . carryalls, a little under a thousand."

Halleck said: "Wouldn't it be cheaper to reopen negotiations with the Guild for permission to orbit a frigate as a weather satellite?"

The Duke looked at Hawat. "Nothing new there, eh, Thufir?"

"We must pursue other avenues for now," Hawat said. "The Guild agent wasn't really negotiating with us. He was merely making it plain—one Mentat to another—that the price was out of our reach and would remain so no matter how long a reach we develop. Our task is to find out why before we approach him again."

One of Halleck's aides down the table swiveled in his chair, snapped: "There's no justice in this!"

"Justice?" The Duke looked at the man. "Who asks for justice? We make our own justice. We make it here on Arrakis—win or die. Do you regret casting your lot with us, sir?"

The man stared at the Duke, then: "No, Sire. You couldn't turn and I could do nought but follow you. Forgive the outburst, but. . . ." He shrugged. ". . . we must all feel bitter at times."

"Bitterness I understand," the Duke said. "But let us not rail about justice as long as we have arms and the freedom to use them. Do any of the rest of you harbor bitterness? If so, let it out. This is friendly council where any man may speak his mind."

Halleck stirred, said: "I think what rankles, Sire, is that we've had no volunteers from the other Great Houses. They address you as 'Leto the Just' and promise eternal friendship, but only as long as it doesn't cost them anything."

"They don't know yet who's going to win this exchange," the Duke said. "Most of the Houses have grown fat by taking few risks. One cannot truly blame them for this; one can only despise them." He looked at Hawat. "We were discussing equipment. Would you care to project a few examples to familiarize the men with this machinery?"

Hawat nodded, gestured to an aide at the projector.

A solido tri-D projection appeared on the table surface about a third of the way down from the Duke. Some of the men farther along the table stood up to get a better look at it.

Paul leaned forward, staring at the machine.

Scaled against the tiny projected human figures around it, the thing was about one hundred and twenty meters long and about forty meters wide. It was basically a long, buglike body moving on independent sets of wide tracks.

"This is a harvester factory," Hawat said. "We chose one in good repair for this projection. There's one dragline outfit that came in with the first team of Imperial ecologists, though, and it's still running . . . although I don't know how . . . or why."

"If that's the one they call 'Old Maria,' it belongs in a museum," an aide said. "I think the Harkonnens kept it as a punishment job, a threat hanging over their workers' heads. Be good or you'll be assigned to Old Maria."

Chuckles sounded around the table.

Paul held himself apart from the humor, his attention focused on the projection and the question that filled his mind. He pointed to the image on the table, said: "Thufir, are there sandworms big enough to swallow that whole?"

Quick silence settled on the table. The Duke cursed under his breath, then thought: *No—they have to face the realities here.*

"There're worms in the deep desert could take this entire factory in one gulp," Hawat said. "Up here closer to the Shield Wall where most of the spicing's done there are plenty of worms that could cripple this factory and devour it at their leisure."

"Why don't we shield them?" Paul asked.

"According to Idaho's report," Hawat said, "shields are dangerous in the desert. A body-size shield will call every worm for hundreds of meters around. It appears to drive them into a killing frenzy. We've the Fremen word on this and no reason to doubt it. Idaho saw no evidence of shield equipment at the sietch."

"None at all?" Paul asked.

"It'd be pretty hard to conceal that kind of thing among several thousand people," Hawat said. "Idaho had free access to every part of the sietch. He saw no shields or any indication of their use."

"It's a puzzle," the Duke said.

"The Harkonnens certainly used plenty of shields here," Hawat said. "They had repair depots in every garrison village, and their accounts show a heavy expenditure for shield replacements and parts."

"Could the Fremen have a way of nullifying shields?" Paul asked.

"It doesn't seem likely," Hawat said. "It's theoretically possible, of course—a shire-sized static counter charge is supposed to do the trick, but no one's ever been able to put it to the test."

"We'd have heard about it before now," Halleck said. "The smugglers have close contact with the Fremen and would've acquired such a device if it were available. And they'd have had no inhibitions against marketing it off planet."

"I don't like an unanswered question of this importance," Leto said. "Thufir, I want you to give top priority to solution of this problem."

"We're already working on it, my Lord." He cleared his throat. "Ah-h, Idaho did say one thing: he said you couldn't mistake the Fremen attitude toward shields. He said they were mostly amused by them."

The Duke frowned, then: "The subject under discussion is spicing equipment."

Hawat gestured to his aide at the projector.

The solido-image of the harvester factory was replaced by a projection of a winged device that dwarfed the images of human figures around it. "This is a carryall," Hawat said. "It's essentially a large 'thopter, whose sole function is to deliver a factory to spice-rich sands, then to rescue the factory when a sandworm appears. They always appear.

Harvesting the spice is a process of getting in and getting out with as much as possible."

"Admirably suited to Harkonnen morality," the Duke said.

Laughter was abrupt and too loud.

An ornithopter replaced the carryall in the projection focus.

"These 'thopters are fairly conventional," Hawat said. "Major modifications give them extended range. Extra care has been used in sealing essential areas against sand and dust. Only about one in thirty is shielded—possibly discarding the shield generator's weight for greater range."

"I don't like this de-emphasis on shields," the Duke muttered. And he thought: *Is this the Harkonnen secret? Does it mean we won't even be able to escape on shielded frigates if all goes against us?* He shook his head sharply to drive out such thoughts, said: "Let's get to the working estimate. What'll our profit figure be?"

Hawat turned two pages in his notebook. "After assessing the repairs and operable equipment, we've worked out a first estimate on operating costs. It's based naturally on a depreciated figure for a clear safety margin." He closed his eyes in Mentat semitrance, said: "Under the Harkonnens, maintenance and salaries were held to fourteen per cent. We'll be lucky to make it at thirty per cent at first. With reinvestment and growth factors accounted for, including the CHOAM percentage and military costs, our profit margin will be reduced to a very narrow six or seven per cent until we can replace worn-out equipment. We then should be able to boost it up to twelve or fifteen per cent where it belongs." He opened his eyes. "Unless my Lord wishes to adopt Harkonnen methods."

"We're working for a solid and permanent planetary base," the Duke said. "We have to keep a large percentage of the people happy—especially the Fremen."

"Most especially the Fremen," Hawat agreed.

"Our supremacy on Caladan," the Duke said, "depended on sea and air power. Here, we must develop something I choose to call *desert* power. This may include air power, but it's possible it may not. I call your attention to the lack of 'thopter shields." He shook his head. "The Har-konnens relied on turnover from off planet for some of their key person-nel. We don't dare. Each new lot would have its quota of provocateurs."

"Then we'll have to be content with far less profit and a reduced harvest," Hawat said. "Our output the first two seasons should be down a third from the Harkonnen average."

"There it is," the Duke said, "exactly as we expected. We'll have to move fast with the Fremen. I'd like five full battalions of Fremen troops before the first CHOAM audit."

"That's not much time, Sire," Hawat said.

"We don't have much time, as you well know. They'll be here with Sardaukar disguised as Harkonnens at the first opportunity. How many do you think they'll ship in, Thufir?"

"Four or five battalions all told, Sire. No more, Guild troop-transport costs being what they are."

"Then five battalions of Fremen plus our own forces ought to do it. Let us have a few captive Sardaukar to parade in front of the Landsraad Council and matters will be much different—profits or no profits."

"We'll do our best, Sire."

Paul looked at his father, back to Hawat, suddenly conscious of the Mentat's great age, aware that the old man had served three generations of Atreides. *Aged.* It showed in the rheumy shine of the brown eyes, in the cheeks cracked and burned by exotic weathers, in the rounded curve of the shoulders and the thin set of his lips with the cranberry-colored stain of sapho juice.

So much depends on one aged man, Paul thought.

"We're presently in a war of assassins," the Duke said, "but it has not achieved full scale. Thufir, what's the condition of the Harkonnen ma-chine here?"

"We've eliminated two hundred and fifty-nine of their key people, my Lord. No more than three Harkonnen cells remain—perhaps a hun-dred people in all."

"These Harkonnen creatures you eliminated," the Duke said, "were they propertied?"

"Most were well situated, my Lord—in the entrepreneur class."

"I want you to forge certificates of allegiance over the signatures of each of them," the Duke said. "File copies with the Judge of the Change. We'll take the legal position that they stayed under false allegiance. Confiscate their property, take everything, turn out their families, strip them. And make sure the Crown gets its ten per cent. It must be entirely legal."

Thufir smiled, revealing red-stained teeth beneath the carmine lips. "A move worthy of your grandsire, my Lord. It shames me I didn't think of it first."

Halleck frowned across the table, noticing a deep scowl on Paul's face. The others were smiling and nodding.

It's wrong, Paul thought. *This'll only make the others fight all the harder. They've nothing to gain by surrendering.*

He knew the actual no-holds-barred convention that ruled in kanly, but this was the sort of move that could destroy them even as it gave them victory.

"'I have been a stranger in a strange land,'" Halleck quoted.

Paul stared at him, recognizing the quotation from the O.C. Bible, wondering: *Does Gurney, too, wish an end to devious plots?*

The Duke glanced at the darkness out the windows, looked back at Halleck. "Gurney, how many of those sandworkers did you persuade to stay with us?"

"Two hundred eighty-six in all, Sire. I think we should take them and consider ourselves lucky. They're all in useful categories."

"No more?" The Duke pursed his lips, then: "Well, pass the word along to—"

A disturbance at the door interrupted him. Duncan Idaho came through the guard there, hurried down the length of the table and bent over the Duke's ear.

Leto waved him back, said: "Speak out, Duncan. You can see this is strategy staff."

Paul studied Idaho, marking the feline movements, the swiftness of reflex that made him such a difficult weapons teacher to emulate. Idaho's dark round face turned toward Paul, the cave-sitter eyes giving no hint of recognition, but Paul recognized the mask of serenity over excitement.

Idaho looked down the length of the table, said: "We've taken a force of Harkonnen mercenaries disguised as Fremen. The Fremen themselves sent us a courier to warn of the false band. In the attack, however, we found the Harkonnens had waylaid the Fremen courier—badly wounded him. We were bringing him here for treatment by our medics when he died. I'd seen how badly off the man was and stopped to do what I could. I surprised him in the attempt to throw something away." Idaho glanced down at Leto. "A knife, m'Lord, a knife the like of which you've never seen."

"Crysknife?" someone asked.

"No doubt of it," Idaho said. "Milky white and glowing with a light of its own like." He reached into his tunic, brought out a sheath with a black-ridged handle protruding from it.

"Keep that blade in its sheath!"

The voice came from the open door at the end of the room, a vibrant and penetrating voice that brought them all up, staring.

A tall, robed figure stood in the door, barred by the crossed swords of the guard. A light tan robe completely enveloped the man except for a gap in the hood and black veil that exposed eyes of total blue—no white in them at all.

"Let him enter," Idaho whispered.

"Pass that man," the Duke said.

The guards hesitated, then lowered their swords.

The man swept into the room, stood across from the Duke.

"This is Stilgar, chief of the sietch I visited, leader of those who warned us of the false band," Idaho said.

"Welcome, sir," Leto said. "And why shouldn't we unsheath this blade?"

Stilgar glanced at Idaho, said: "You observed the customs of cleanliness and honor among us. I would permit you to see the blade of the man you befriended." His gaze swept the others in the room. "But I do not know these others. Would you have them defile an honorable weapon?"

"I am the Duke Leto," the Duke said. "Would you permit me to see this blade?"

"I'll permit you to earn the right to unsheath it," Stilgar said, and, as a mutter of protest sounded around the table, he raised a thin, darkly veined hand. "I remind you this is the blade of one who befriended you."

In the waiting silence, Paul studied the man, sensing the aura of power that radiated from him. He was a leader—a *Fremen* leader.

A man near the center of the table across from Paul muttered: "Who's he to tell us what rights we have on Arrakis?"

"It is said that the Duke Leto Atreides rules with the consent of the governed," the Fremen said. "Thus I must tell you the way it is with us: a certain responsibility falls on those who have seen a crysknife." He passed a dark glance across Idaho. "They are ours. They may never leave Arrakis without our consent."

Halleck and several of the others started to rise, angry expressions on their faces. Halleck said: "The Duke Leto determines whether—"

"One moment, please," Leto said, and the very mildness of his voice held them. *This must not get out of hand*, he thought. He addressed himself to the Fremen: "Sir, I honor and respect the personal dignity of any man who respects my dignity. I am indeed indebted to you. And I *always* pay my debts. If it is your custom that this knife remain sheathed here, then it is so ordered—by *me*. And if there is any other way we may honor the man who died in our service, you have but to name it."

The Fremen stared at the Duke, then slowly pulled aside his veil, revealing a thin nose and full-lipped mouth in a glistening black beard. Deliberately he bent over the end of the table, spat on its polished surface.

As the men around the table started to surge to their feet, Idaho's voice boomed across the room: "Hold!"

Into the sudden charged stillness, Idaho said: "We thank you, Stilgar, for the gift of your body's moisture. We accept it in the spirit with which it is given." And Idaho spat on the table in front of the Duke.

Aside to the Duke, he said: "Remember how precious water is here, Sire. That was a token of respect."

Leto sank back into his own chair, caught Paul's eye, a rueful grin on his son's face, sensed the slow relaxation of tension around the table as understanding came to his men.

The Fremen looked at Idaho, said: "You measured well in my sietch, Duncan Idaho. Is there a bond on your allegiance to your Duke?"

"He's asking me to enlist with him, Sire," Idaho said.

"Would he accept a dual allegiance?" Leto asked.

"You wish me to go with him, Sire?"

"I wish you to make your own decision in the matter," Leto said, and he could not keep the urgency out of his voice.

Idaho studied the Fremen. "Would you have me under these conditions, Stilgar? There'd be times when I'd have to return to serve my Duke."

"You fight well and you did your best for our friend," Stilgar said. He looked at Leto. "Let it be thus: the man Idaho keeps the crysknife he holds as a mark of his allegiance to us. He must be cleansed, of course, and the rites observed, but this can be done. He will be Fremen and soldier of the Atreides. There is precedent for this: Liet serves two masters."

"Duncan?" Leto asked.

"I understand, Sire," Idaho said.

"It is agreed, then," Leto said.

"Your water is ours, Duncan Idaho," Stilgar said. "The body of our friend remains with your Duke. His water is Atreides water. It is a bond between us."

Leto sighed, glanced at Hawat, catching the old Mentat's eye. Hawat nodded, his expression pleased.

"I will await below," Stilgar said, "while Idaho makes farewell with his friends. Turok was the name of our dead friend. Remember that when it comes time to release his spirit. You are friends of Turok."

Stilgar started to turn away.

"Will you not stay a while?" Leto asked.

The Fremen turned back, whipping his veil into place with a casual gesture, adjusting something beneath it. Paul glimpsed what looked like a thin tube before the veil settled into place.

"Is there reason to stay?" the Fremen asked.

"We would honor you," the Duke said.

"Honor requires that I be elsewhere soon," the Fremen said. He shot another glance at Idaho, whirled, and strode out past the door guards.

"If the other Fremen match him, we'll serve each other well," Leto said.

Idaho spoke in a dry voice: "He's a fair sample, Sire."

"You understand what you're to do, Duncan?"

"I'm your ambassador to the Fremen, Sire."

"Much depends on you, Duncan. We're going to need at least five battalions of those people before the Sardaukar descend on us."

"This is going to take some doing, Sire. The Fremen are a pretty independent bunch." Idaho hesitated, then: "And, Sire, there's one other thing. One of the mercenaries we knocked over was trying to get this blade from our dead Fremen friend. The mercenary says there's a Harkonnen reward of a million solaris for anyone who'll bring in a single crysknife."

Leto's chin came up in a movement of obvious surprise. "Why do they want one of those blades so badly?"

"The knife is ground from a sandworm's tooth; it's the mark of the Fremen, Sire. With it, a blue-eyed man could penetrate any sietch in the land. They'd question me unless I were known. I don't look Fremen. But...."

"Piter de Vries," the Duke said.

"A man of devilish cunning, my Lord," Hawat said.

Idaho slipped the sheathed knife beneath his tunic.

"Guard that knife," the Duke said.

"I understand, m'Lord." He patted the transceiver on his belt kit.

"I'll report soon as possible. Thufir has my call code. Use battle language." He saluted, spun about, and hurried after the Fremen.

They heard his footsteps drumming down the corridor.

A look of understanding passed between Leto and Hawat. They smiled.

"We've much to do, Sire," Halleck said.

"And I keep you from your work," Leto said.

"I have the report on the advance bases," Hawat said. "Shall I give it another time, Sire?"

"Will it take long?"

"Not for a briefing. It's said among the Fremen that there were more than two hundred of these advance bases built here on Arrakis during the Desert Botanical Testing Station period. All supposedly have been abandoned, but there are reports they were sealed off before being abandoned."

"Equipment in them?" the Duke asked.

"According to the reports I have from Duncan."

"Where are they located?" Halleck asked.

"The answer to that question," Hawat said, "is invariably: 'Liet knows.'"

"God knows," Leto muttered.

"Perhaps not, Sire," Hawat said. "You heard this Stilgar use the name. Could he have been referring to a real person?"

"Serving two masters," Halleck said. "It sounds like a religious quotation."

"And you should know," the Duke said. Halleck smiled.

"This Judge of the Change," Leto said, "the Imperial ecologist—Kynes. . . . Wouldn't he know where those bases are?"

"Sire," Hawat cautioned, "this Kynes is an Imperial servant."

"And he's a long way from the Emperor," Leto said. "I want those bases. They'd be loaded with materials we could salvage and use for repair of our working equipment."

"Sire!" Hawat said. "Those bases are still legally His Majesty's fief."

"The weather here's savage enough to destroy anything," the Duke said. "We can always blame the weather. Get this Kynes and at least find out if the bases exist."

"'Twere dangerous to commandeer them," Hawat said. "Duncan was clear on one thing: those bases or the idea of them hold some deep significance for the Fremen. We might alienate the Fremen if we took those bases."

Paul looked at the faces of the men around them, saw the intensity of the way they followed every word. They appeared deeply disturbed by his father's attitude.

"Listen to him, Father," Paul said in a low voice. "He speaks truth."

"Sire," Hawat said, "those bases could give us material to repair every piece of equipment left us, yet be beyond reach for strategic reasons. It'd be rash to move without greater knowledge. This Kynes has arbiter authority from the Imperium. We mustn't forget that. And the Fremen defer to him."

"Do it gently, then," the Duke said. "I wish to know only if those bases exist."

"As you will, Sire." Hawat sat back, lowered his eyes.

"All right, then," the Duke said. "We know what we have ahead of us—work. We've been trained for it. We've some experience in it. We know what the rewards are and the alternatives are clear enough. You all have your assignments." He looked at Halleck. "Gurney, take care of that smuggler situation first."

"'I shall go unto the rebellious that dwell in the dry land,'" Halleck intoned.

"Someday I'll catch that man without a quotation and he'll look undressed," the Duke said.

Chuckles echoed around the table, but Paul heard the effort in them.

The Duke turned to Hawat. "Set up another command post for intelligence and communications on this floor, Thufir. When you have them ready, I'll want to see you."

Hawat arose, glancing around the room as though seeking support.

He turned away, led the procession out of the room. The others moved hurriedly, scraping their chairs on the floor, balling up in little knots of confusion.

It ended up in confusion, Paul thought, staring at the backs of the last men to leave. Always before, Staff had ended on an incisive air. This meeting had just seemed to trickle out, worn down by its own inadequacies, and with an argument to top it off.

For the first time, Paul allowed himself to think about the real possibility of defeat—not thinking about it out of fear or because of warnings such as that of the old Reverend Mother, but facing up to it because of his own assessment of the situation.

My father is desperate, he thought. *Things aren't going well for us at all.*

And Hawat—Paul recalled how the old Mentat had acted during the conference—subtle hesitations, signs of unrest.

Hawat was deeply troubled by something.

"Best you remain here the rest of the night, Son," the Duke said. "It'll be dawn soon, anyway. I'll inform your mother." He got to his feet, slowly, stiffly. "Why don't you pull a few of these chairs together and stretch out on them for some rest."

"I'm not very tired, sir."

"As you will."

The Duke folded his hands behind him, began pacing up and down the length of the table.

Like a caged animal, Paul thought.

"Are you going to discuss the traitor possibility with Hawat?" Paul asked.

The Duke stopped across from his son, spoke to the dark windows. "We've discussed the possibility many times."

"The old woman seemed so sure of herself," Paul said. "And the message Mother—"

"Precautions have been taken," the Duke said. He looked around the room, and Paul marked the hunted wildness in his father's eyes. "Remain here. There are some things about the command posts I want to discuss with Thufir." He turned, strode out of the room, nodding shortly to the door guards.

Paul stared at the place where his father had stood. The space had been empty even before the Duke left the room. And he recalled the old woman's warning: ". . . for the father, nothing."

On that first day when Muad'Dib rode through the streets of Arrakeen with his family, some of the people along the way recalled the legends and the prophecy and they ventured to shout: "Mahdi!" But their shout was more a question than a statement, for as yet they could only hope he was the one foretold as the Lisan al-Gaib, the Voice from the Outer World. Their attention was focused, too, on the mother, because they had heard she was a Bene Gesserit and it was obvious to them that she was like the other Lisan al-Gaib.

—FROM "MANUAL OF MUAD'DIB"
BY THE PRINCESS IRULAN

The Duke found Thufir Hawat alone in the corner room to which a guard directed him. There was the sound of men setting up communications equipment in an adjoining room, but this place was fairly quiet. The Duke glanced around as Hawat arose from a paper-cluttered table. It was a green-walled enclosure with, in addition to the table, three suspensor chairs from which the Harkonnen "H" had been hastily removed, leaving an imperfect color patch.

"The chairs are liberated but quite safe," Hawat said. "Where is Paul, Sire?"

"I left him in the conference room. I'm hoping he'll get some rest without me there to distract him."

Hawat nodded, crossed to the door to the adjoining room, closed it, shutting off the noise of static and electronic sparking.

"Thufir," Leto said, "the Imperial and Harkonnen stockpiles of spice attract my attention."

"M'Lord?"

The Duke pursed his lips. "Storehouses are susceptible to destruction." He raised a hand as Hawat started to speak. "Ignore the Emperor's hoard. He'd secretly enjoy it if the Harkonnens were embarrassed. And can the Baron object if something is destroyed which he cannot openly admit that he has?"

Hawat shook his head. "We've few men to spare, Sire."

"Use some of Idaho's men. And perhaps some of the Fremen would enjoy a trip off planet. A raid on Giedi Prime—there are tactical advantages to such a diversion, Thufir."

"As you say, my Lord." Hawat turned away, and the Duke saw evidence of nervousness in the old man, thought: *Perhaps he suspects I distrust him. He must know I've private reports of traitors. Well—best quiet his fears immediately.*

"Thufir," he said, "since you're one of the few I can trust completely, there's another matter bears discussion. We both know how constant a watch we must keep to prevent traitors from infiltrating our forces . . . but I have two new reports."

Hawat turned, stared at him.

And Leto repeated the stories Paul had brought.

Instead of bringing on the intense Mentat concentration, the reports only increased Hawat's agitation.

Leto studied the old man and, presently, said: "You've been holding something back, old friend. I should've suspected when you were so nervous during Staff. What is it that was too hot to dump in front of the full conference?"

Hawat's sapho-stained lips were pulled into a prim, straight line with tiny wrinkles radiating into them. They maintained their wrinkled stiffness as he said: "My Lord, I don't quite know how to broach this."

"We've suffered many a scar for each other, Thufir," the Duke said. "You know you can broach *any* subject with me."

Hawat continued to stare at him, thinking: *This is how I like him best. This is the man of honor who deserves every bit of my loyalty and service. Why must I hurt him?*

"Well?" Leto demanded.

Hawat shrugged. "It's a scrap of a note. We took it from a Harkonnen courier. The note was intended for an agent named Pardee. We've good reason to believe Pardee was top man in the Harkonnen underground here. The note—it's a thing that could have great consequence or no consequence. It's susceptible to various interpretations."

"What's the delicate content of this note?"

"Scrap of a note, my Lord. Incomplete. It was on minimic film with the usual destruction capsule attached. We stopped the acid action just short of full erasure, leaving only a fragment. The fragment, however, is extremely suggestive."

"Yes?"

Hawat rubbed at his lips. "It says: '. . . eto will never suspect, and when the blow falls on him from a beloved hand, its source alone should be enough to destroy him.' The note was under the Baron's own seal and I've authenticated the seal."

"Your suspicion is obvious," the Duke said and his voice was suddenly cold.

"I'd sooner cut off my arms than hurt you," Hawat said. "My Lord, what if . . ."

"The Lady Jessica," Leto said, and he felt anger consuming him. "Couldn't you wring the facts out of this Pardee?"

"Unfortunately, Pardee no longer was among the living when we intercepted the courier. The courier, I'm certain, did not know what he carried."

"I see."

Leto shook his head, thinking: *What a slimy piece of business. There can't be anything in it. I know my woman.*

"My Lord, if—"

"No!" the Duke barked. "There's a mistake here that—"

"We cannot ignore it, my Lord."

"She's been with me for sixteen years! There've been countless opportunities for— You yourself investigated the school and the woman!"

Hawat spoke bitterly: "Things have been known to escape me."

"It's impossible, I tell you! The Harkonnens want to destroy the Atreides *line*—meaning Paul, too. They've already tried once. Could a woman conspire against her own son?"

"Perhaps she doesn't conspire against her son. And yesterday's attempt could've been a clever sham."

"It couldn't have been a sham."

"Sire, she isn't supposed to know her parentage, but what if she does know? What if she were an orphan, say, orphaned by an Atreides?"

"She'd have moved long before now. Poison in my drink . . . a stiletto at night. Who has had better opportunity?"

"The Harkonnens mean to *destroy* you, my Lord. Their intent is not just to kill. There's a range of fine distinctions in kanly. This could be a work of art among vendettas."

The Duke's shoulders slumped. He closed his eyes, looking old and tired. *It cannot be*, he thought. *The woman has opened her heart to me.*

"What better way to destroy me than to sow suspicion of the woman I love?" he asked.

"An interpretation I've considered," Hawat said. "Still. . . ."

The Duke opened his eyes, stared at Hawat, thinking: *Let him be suspicious. Suspicion is his trade, not mine. Perhaps if I appear to believe this, that will make another man careless.*

"What do you suggest?" the Duke whispered.

"For now, constant surveillance, my Lord. She should be watched at all times. I will see it's done unobtrusively. Idaho would be the ideal choice for the job. Perhaps in a week or so we can bring him back. There's a young man we've been training in Idaho's troop who might be ideal to send to the Fremen as a replacement. He's gifted in diplomacy."

"Don't jeopardize our foothold with the Fremen."

"Of course not, Sire."

"And what about Paul?"

"Perhaps we could alert Dr. Yueh."

Leto turned his back on Hawat. "I leave it in your hands."

"I shall use discretion, my Lord."

At least I can count on that, Leto thought. And he said: "I will take a walk. If you need me, I'll be within the perimeter. The guard can—"

"My Lord, before you go, I've a filmclip you should read. It's a first-approximation analysis on the Fremen religion. You'll recall you asked me to report on it."

The Duke paused, spoke without turning. "Will it not wait?"

"Of course, my Lord. You asked what they were shouting, though. It was 'Mahdi!' They directed the term at the young Master. When they—"

"At Paul?"

"Yes, my Lord. They've a legend here, a prophecy, that a leader will come to them, child of a Bene Gesserit, to lead them to true freedom. It follows the familiar messiah pattern."

"They think Paul is this . . . this. . . ."

"They only hope, my Lord." Hawat extended a filmclip capsule.

The Duke accepted it, thrust it into a pocket. "I'll look at it later."

"Certainly, my Lord."

"Right now, I need time to . . . think."

"Yes, my Lord."

The Duke took a deep sighing breath, strode out the door. He turned to his right down the hall, began walking, hands behind his back, paying little attention to where he was. There were corridors and stairs and balconies and halls . . . people who saluted and stood aside for him.

In time he came back to the conference room, found it dark and Paul asleep on the table with a guard's robe thrown over him and a ditty pack for a pillow. The Duke walked softly down the length of the room and onto the balcony overlooking the landing field. A guard at the corner of the balcony, recognizing the Duke by the dim reflection of lights from the field, snapped to attention.

"At ease," the Duke murmured. He leaned against the cold metal of the balcony rail.

A predawn hush had come over the desert basin. He looked up. Straight overhead, the stars were a sequin shawl flung over blue-black. Low on the southern horizon, the night's second moon peered through a thin dust haze—an unbelieving moon that looked at him with a cynical light.

As the Duke watched, the moon dipped beneath the Shield Wall cliffs, frosting them, and in the sudden intensity of darkness, he experienced a chill. He shivered.

Anger shot through him.

The Harkonnens have hindered and hounded and hunted me for the last time, he thought. *They are dung heaps with village provost minds! Here I make my stand!* And he thought with a touch of sadness: *I must rule with eye and claw—as the hawk among lesser birds.* Unconsciously, his hand brushed the hawk emblem on his tunic.

To the east, the night grew a faggot of luminous gray, then seashell opalescence that dimmed the stars. There came the long, bell-tolling movement of dawn striking across a broken horizon.

It was a scene of such beauty it caught all his attention.

Some things beggar likeness, he thought.

He had never imagined anything here could be as beautiful as that shattered red horizon and the purple and ochre cliffs. Beyond the landing field where the night's faint dew had touched life into the hurried seeds of Arrakis, he saw great puddles of red blooms and, running through them, an articulate tread of violet . . . like giant footsteps.

"It's a beautiful morning, Sire," the guard said.

"Yes, it is."

The Duke nodded, thinking: *Perhaps this planet could grow on one. Perhaps it could become a good home for my son.*

Then he saw the human figures moving into the flower fields, sweeping them with strange scythelike devices—dew gatherers. Water so precious here that even the dew must be collected.

And it could be a hideous place, the Duke thought.

There is probably no more terrible instant of enlightenment than the one in which you discover your father is a man— with human flesh.

—FROM "COLLECTED SAYINGS OF MUAD'DIB" BY THE PRINCESS IRULAN

The Duke said: "Paul, I'm doing a hateful thing, but I must." He stood beside the portable poison snooper that had been brought into the conference room for their breakfast. The thing's sensor arms hung limply over the table, reminding Paul of some weird insect newly dead.

The Duke's attention was directed out the windows at the landing field and its roiling of dust against the morning sky.

Paul had a viewer in front of him containing a short filmclip on Fremen religious practices. The clip had been compiled by one of Hawat's experts and Paul found himself disturbed by the references to himself.

"Mahdi!"

"Lisan al-Gaib!"

He could close his eyes and recall the shouts of the crowds. *So that is what they hope,* he thought. And he remembered what the old Reverend Mother had said: Kwisatz Haderach. The memories touched his feelings of terrible purpose, shading this strange world with sensations of familiarity that he could not understand.

"A hateful thing," the Duke said.

"What do you mean, sir?"

Leto turned, looked down at his son. "Because the Harkonnens think to trick me by making me distrust your mother. They don't know that I'd sooner distrust myself."

"I don't understand, sir."

Again, Leto looked out the windows. The white sun was well up into its morning quadrant. Milky light picked out a boiling of dust clouds that spilled over into the blind canyons interfingering the Shield Wall.

Slowly, speaking in a slow voice to contain his anger, the Duke explained to Paul about the mysterious note.

"You might just as well mistrust me," Paul said.

"They have to think they've succeeded," the Duke said. "They must think me this much of a fool. It must look real. Even your mother may not know the sham."

"But, sir! Why?"

"Your mother's response must not be an act. Oh, she's capable of a supreme act . . . but too much rides on this. I hope to smoke out a traitor. It must seem that I've been completely cozened. She must be hurt this way that she does not suffer greater hurt."

"Why do you tell me, Father? Maybe I'll give it away."

"They'll not watch you in this thing," the Duke said. "You'll keep the secret. You must." He walked to the windows, spoke without turning. "This way, if anything should happen to me, you can tell her the truth—that I never doubted her, not for the smallest instant. I should want her to know this."

Paul recognized the death thoughts in his father's words, spoke quickly: "Nothing's going to happen to you, sir. The—"

"Be silent, Son."

Paul stared at his father's back, seeing the fatigue in the angle of the neck, in the line of the shoulders, in the slow movements.

"You're just tired, Father."

"I *am* tired," the Duke agreed. "I'm morally tired. The melancholy degeneration of the Great Houses has afflicted me at last, perhaps. And we were such strong people once."

Paul spoke in quick anger: "Our House hasn't degenerated!"

"Hasn't it?"

The Duke turned, faced his son, revealing dark circles beneath hard eyes, a cynical twist of mouth. "I should wed your mother, make her my Duchess. Yet . . . my unwedded state gives some Houses hope they may yet ally with me through their marriageable daughters." He shrugged. "So, I. . . ."

"Mother has explained this to me."

"Nothing wins more loyalty for a leader than an air of bravura," the Duke said. "I, therefore, cultivate an air of bravura."

"You lead well," Paul protested. "You govern well. Men follow you willingly and love you."

"My propaganda corps is one of the finest," the Duke said. Again, he turned to stare out at the basin. "There's greater possibility for us here on Arrakis than the Imperium could ever suspect. Yet sometimes I think it'd have been better if we'd run for it, gone renegade. Sometimes I wish we could sink back into anonymity among the people, become less exposed to. . . ."

"Father!"

"Yes, I *am* tired," the Duke said. "Did you know we're using spice residue as raw material and already have our own factory to manufacture filmbase?"

"Sir?"

"We mustn't run short of filmbase," the Duke said. "Else, how could we flood village and city with our information? The people must learn how well I govern them. How would they know if we didn't tell them?"

"You should get some rest," Paul said.

Again, the Duke faced his son. "Arrakis has another advantage I almost forgot to mention. Spice is in everything here. You breathe it and eat it in almost everything. And I find that this imparts a certain natural immunity to some of the most common poisons of the Assassins' Handbook. And the need to watch every drop of water puts all food production—yeast culture, hydroponics, chemavit, everything—under the strictest surveillance. We cannot kill off large segments of our population with poison—and we cannot be attacked this way, either. Arrakis makes us moral and ethical."

Paul started to speak, but the Duke cut him off, saying: "I have to have someone I can say these things to, Son." He sighed, glanced back at the dry landscape where even the flowers were gone now—trampled by the dew gatherers, wilted under the early sun.

"On Caladan, we ruled with sea and air power," the Duke said. "Here, we must scrabble for desert power. This is your inheritance, Paul. What is to become of you if anything happens to me? You'll not be a renegade House, but a guerrilla House—running, hunted."

Paul groped for words, could find nothing to say. He had never seen his father this despondent.

"To hold Arrakis," the Duke said, "one is faced with decisions that may cost one his self-respect." He pointed out the window to the Atreides green and black banner hanging limply from a staff at the edge of the landing field. "That honorable banner could come to mean many evil things."

Paul swallowed in a dry throat. His father's words carried futility, a sense of fatalism that left the boy with an empty feeling in his chest.

The Duke took an antifatigue tablet from a pocket, gulped it dry. "Power and fear," he said. "The tools of statecraft. I must order new emphasis on guerrilla training for you. That filmclip there—they call you 'Mahdi'—'Lisan al-Gaib'—as a last resort, you might capitalize on that."

Paul stared at his father, watching the shoulders straighten as the tablet did its work, but remembering the words of fear and doubt.

"What's keeping that ecologist?" the Duke muttered. "I told Thufir to have him here early."

My father, the Padishah Emperor, took me by the hand one day and I sensed in the ways my mother had taught me that he was disturbed. He led me down the Hall of Portraits to the ego-likeness of the Duke Leto Atreides. I marked the strong resemblance between them—my father and this man in the portrait—both with thin, elegant faces and sharp features dominated by cold eyes. "Princess-daughter," my father said, "I would that you'd been older when it came time for this man to choose a woman." My father was 71 at the time and looking no older than the man in the portrait, and I was but 14, yet I remember deducing in that instant that my father secretly wished the Duke had been his son, and disliked the political necessities that made them enemies.

— FROM "IN MY FATHER'S HOUSE"
BY THE PRINCESS IRULAN

His first encounter with the people he had been ordered to betray left Dr. Kynes shaken. He prided himself on being a scientist to whom legends were merely interesting clues, pointing toward cultural roots. Yet the boy fitted the ancient prophecy so precisely. He had "the questing eyes," and the air of "reserved candor."

Of course, the prophecy left certain latitude as to whether the Mother Goddess would bring the Messiah with her or produce Him on the scene. Still, there was this odd correspondence between prediction and persons.

They met in midmorning outside the Arrakeen landing field's administration building. An unmarked ornithopter squatted nearby, humming softly on standby like a somnolent insect. An Atreides guard stood beside it with bared sword and the faint air-distortion of a shield around him.

Kynes sneered at the shield pattern, thinking: *Arrakis has a surprise for them there!*

The planetologist raised a hand, signaled for his Fremen guard to fall back. He strode on ahead toward the building's entrance—the dark hole in plastic-coated rock. So exposed, that monolithic building, he thought. So much less suitable than a cave.

Movement within the entrance caught his attention. He stopped, taking the moment to adjust his robe and the set of his stillsuit at the left shoulder.

The entrance doors swung wide. Atreides guards emerged swiftly, all of them heavily armed—slow-pellet stunners, swords and shields. Behind them came a tall man, hawk-faced, dark of skin and hair. He wore a jubba cloak with Atreides crest at the breast, and wore it in a way that betrayed his unfamiliarity with the garment. It clung to the legs of his stillsuit on one side. It lacked a free-swinging, striding rhythm.

Beside the man walked a youth with the same dark hair, but rounder in the face. The youth seemed small for the fifteen years Kynes knew him to have. But the young body carried a sense of command, a poised assurance, as though he saw and knew things all around him that were not visible to others. And he wore the same style cloak as his father, yet with casual ease that made one think the boy had always worn such clothing.

"The Mahdi will be aware of things others cannot see," went the prophecy.

Kynes shook his head, telling himself: *They're just people.*

With the two, garbed like them for the desert, came a man Kynes recognized—Gurney Halleck. Kynes took a deep breath to still his resentment against Halleck, who had briefed him on how to *behave* with the Duke and ducal heir.

"You may call the Duke 'my Lord' or 'Sire.' 'Noble Born' also is cor-

*rect, but usually reserved for more formal occasions. The son may be
addressed as 'young Master' or 'my Lord.' The Duke is a man of much
leniency, but brooks little familiarity.*

And Kynes thought as he watched the group approach: *They'll learn
soon enough who's master on Arrakis. Order me questioned half the night
by that Mentat, will they? Expect me to guide them on an inspection of
spice mining, do they?*

The import of Hawat's questions had not escaped Kynes. They
wanted the Imperial bases. And it was obvious they'd learned of the
bases from Idaho.

I will have Stilgar send Idaho's head to this Duke, Kynes told himself.

The ducal party was only a few paces away now, their feet in desert
boots crunching the sand.

Kynes bowed. "My Lord, Duke."

As he had approached the solitary figure standing near the ornithopter, Leto had studied him: tall, thin, dressed for the desert in loose
robe, stillsuit, and low boots. The man's hood was thrown back, its veil
hanging to one side, revealing long sandy hair, a sparse beard. The eyes
were that fathomless blue-within-blue under thick brows. Remains of
dark stains smudged his eye sockets.

"You're the ecologist," the Duke said.

"We prefer the old title here, my Lord," Kynes said. "Planetologist."

"As you wish," the Duke said. He glanced down at Paul. "Son, this
is the Judge of the Change, the arbiter of dispute, the man set here to see
that the forms are obeyed in our assumption of power over this fief." He
glanced at Kynes. "And this is my son."

"My Lord," Kynes said.

"Are you a Fremen?" Paul asked.

Kynes smiled. "I am accepted in both sietch and village, young Master. But I am in His Majesty's service, the Imperial Planetologist."

Paul nodded, impressed by the man's air of strength. Halleck had
pointed Kynes out to Paul from an upper window of the administration
building: "The man standing there with the Fremen escort—the one
moving now toward the ornithopter."

Paul had inspected Kynes briefly with binoculars, noting the prim, straight mouth, the high forehead. Halleck had spoken in Paul's ear: "Odd sort of fellow. Has a precise way of speaking—clipped off, no fuzzy edges—razor-apt."

And the Duke, behind them, had said: "Scientist type."

Now, only a few feet from the man, Paul sensed the power in Kynes, the impact of personality, as though he were blood royal, born to command.

"I understand we have you to thank for our stillsuits and these cloaks," the Duke said.

"I hope they fit well, my Lord," Kynes said. "They're of Fremen make and as near as possible the dimensions given me by your man Halleck here."

"I was concerned that you said you couldn't take us into the desert unless we wore these garments," the Duke said. "We can carry plenty of water. We don't intend to be out long and we'll have air cover—the escort you see overhead right now. It isn't likely we'd be forced down."

Kynes stared at him, seeing the water-fat flesh. He spoke coldly: "You never talk of likelihoods on Arrakis. You speak only of possibilities."

Halleck stiffened. "The Duke is to be addressed as my Lord or Sire!"

Leto gave Halleck their private hand signal to desist, said: "Our ways are new here, Gurney. We must make allowances."

"As you wish, Sire."

"We are indebted to you, Dr. Kynes," Leto said. "These suits and the consideration for our welfare will be remembered."

On impulse, Paul called to mind a quotation from the O.C. Bible, said: "'The gift is the blessing of the giver.'"

The words rang out overloud in the still air. The Fremen escort Kynes had left in the shade of the administration building leaped up from their squatting repose, muttering in open agitation. One cried out: "Lisan al-Gaib!"

Kynes whirled, gave a curt, chopping signal with a hand, waved the guard away. They fell back, grumbling among themselves, trailed away around the building.

"Most interesting," Leto said.

Kynes passed a hard glare over the Duke and Paul, said: "Most of the desert natives here are a superstitious lot. Pay no attention to them. They mean no harm." But he thought of the words of the legend: *"They will greet you with Holy Words and your gifts will be a blessing."*

Leto's assessment of Kynes—based partly on Hawat's brief verbal report (guarded and full of suspicions)—suddenly crystallized: the man was Fremen. Kynes had come with a Fremen escort, which could mean simply that the Fremen were testing their new freedom to enter urban areas—but it had seemed an honor guard. And by his manner, Kynes was a proud man, accustomed to freedom, his tongue and his manner guarded only by his own suspicions. Paul's question had been direct and pertinent.

Kynes had gone native.

"Shouldn't we be going, Sire?" Halleck asked.

The Duke nodded. "I'll fly my own 'thopter. Kynes can sit up front with me to direct me. You and Paul take the rear seats."

"One moment, please," Kynes said. "With your permission, Sire, I must check the security of your suits."

The Duke started to speak, but Kynes pressed on: "I have concern for my own flesh as well as yours . . . my Lord. I'm well aware of whose throat would be slit should harm befall you two while you're in my care."

The Duke frowned, thinking: *How delicate this moment! If I refuse, it may offend him. And this could be a man whose value to me is beyond measure. Yet . . . to let him inside my shield, touching my person when I know so little about him?*

The thoughts flicked through his mind with decision hard on their heels. "We're in your hands," the Duke said. He stepped forward, opening his robe, saw Halleck come up on the balls of his feet, poised and alert, but remaining where he was. "And, if you'd be so kind," the Duke said, "I'd appreciate an explanation of the suit from one who lives so intimately with it."

"Certainly," Kynes said. He felt up under the robe for the shoulder seals, speaking as he examined the suit. "It's basically a micro-sandwich—a high-efficiency filter and heat-exchange system." He adjusted the shoulder seals. "The skin-contact layer's porous. Perspiration passes through it, having cooled the body . . . near-normal evaporation process. The next two layers . . ." Kynes tightened the chest fit. ". . . include heat-exchange filaments and salt precipitators. Salt's reclaimed."

The Duke lifted his arms at a gesture, said: "Most interesting."

"Breathe deeply," Kynes said.

The Duke obeyed.

Kynes studied the underarm seals, adjusted one. "Motions of the body, especially breathing," he said, "and some osmotic action provide the pumping force." He loosened the chest fit slightly. "Reclaimed water circulates to catchpockets from which you draw it through this tube in the clip at your neck."

The Duke twisted his chin in and down to look at the end of the tube. "Efficient and convenient," he said. "Good engineering."

Kynes knelt, examined the leg seals. "Urine and feces are processed in the thigh pads," he said, and stood up, felt the neck fitting, lifted a sectioned flap there. "In the open desert, you wear this filter across your face, this tube in the nostrils with these plugs to insure a tight fit. Breathe in through the mouth filter, out through the nose tube. With a Fremen suit in good working order, you won't lose more than a thimbleful of moisture a day—even if you're caught in the Great Erg."

"A thimbleful a day," the Duke said.

Kynes pressed a finger against the suit's forehead pad, said: "This may rub a little. If it irritates you, please tell me. I could slit-patch it a bit tighter."

"My thanks," the Duke said. He moved his shoulders in the suit as Kynes stepped back, realizing that it did feel better now—tighter and less irritating.

Kynes turned to Paul. "Now, let's have a look at you, lad."

A good man but he'll have to learn to address us properly, the Duke thought.

Paul stood passively as Kynes inspected the suit. It had been an odd sensation putting on the crinkling, slick-surfaced garment. In his fore-consciousness had been the absolute knowledge that he had never before worn a stillsuit. Yet, each motion of adjusting the adhesion tabs under Gurney's inexpert guidance had seemed natural, instinctive. When he had tightened the chest to gain maximum pumping action from the motion of breathing, he had known what he did and why. When he had fitted the neck and forehead tabs tightly, he had known it was to prevent friction blisters.

Kynes straightened, stepped back with a puzzled expression. "You've worn a stillsuit before?" he asked.

"This is the first time."

"Then someone adjusted it for you?"

"No."

"Your desert boots are fitted slip-fashion at the ankles. Who told you to do that?"

"It . . . seemed the right way."

"That it most certainly is."

And Kynes rubbed his cheek, thinking of the legend: *"He shall know your ways as though born to them."*

"We waste time," the Duke said. He gestured to the waiting 'thopter, led the way, accepting the guard's salute with a nod. He climbed in, fastened his safety harness, checked controls and instruments. The craft creaked as the others clambered aboard.

Kynes fastened his harness, focused on the padded comfort of the aircraft—soft luxury of gray-green upholstery, gleaming instruments, the sensation of filtered and washed air in his lungs as doors slammed and vent fans whirred alive.

So soft! he thought.

"All secure, Sire," Halleck said.

Leto fed power to the wings, felt them cup and dip—once, twice. They were airborne in ten meters, wings feathered tightly and afterjets thrusting them upward in a steep, hissing climb.

"Southeast over the Shield Wall," Kynes said. "That's where I told your sandmaster to concentrate his equipment."

"Right."

The Duke banked into his air cover, the other craft taking up their guard positions as they headed southeast.

"The design and manufacture of these stillsuits bespeaks a high degree of sophistication," the Duke said.

"Someday I may show you a sietch factory," Kynes said.

"I would find that interesting," the Duke said. "I note that suits are manufactured also in some of the garrison cities."

"Inferior copies," Kynes said. "Any Dune man who values his skin wears a Fremen suit."

"And it'll hold your water loss to a thimbleful a day?"

"Properly suited, your forehead cap tight, all seals in order, your major water loss is through the palms of your hands," Kynes said. "You can wear suit gloves if you're not using your hands for critical work, but most Fremen in the open desert rub their hands with juice from the leaves of the creosote bush. It inhibits perspiration."

The Duke glanced down to the left at the broken landscape of the Shield Wall—chasms of tortured rock, patches of yellow-brown crossed by black lines of fault shattering. It was as though someone had dropped this ground from space and left it where it smashed.

They crossed a shallow basin with the clear outline of gray sand spreading across it from a canyon opening to the south. The sand fingers ran out into the basin—a dry delta outlined against darker rock.

Kynes sat back, thinking about the water-fat flesh he had felt beneath the stillsuits. They wore shield belts over their robes, slow-pellet stunners at the waist, coin-sized emergency transmitters on cords around their necks. Both the Duke and his son carried knives in wrist sheaths and the sheaths appeared well worn. The people struck Kynes as a strange combination of softness and armed strength. There was a poise to them totally unlike the Harkonnens.

"When you report to the Emperor on the change of government here, will you say we observed the rules?" Leto asked. He glanced at Kynes, back to their course.

"The Harkonnens left; you came," Kynes said.

"And is everything as it should be?" Leto asked.

Momentary tension showed in the tightening of a muscle along Kynes' jaw. "As Planetologist and Judge of the Change, I am a direct subject of the Imperium . . . my Lord."

The Duke smiled grimly. "But we both know the realities."

"I remind you that His Majesty supports my work."

"Indeed? And what is your work?"

In the brief silence, Paul thought: *He's pushing this Kynes too hard.* Paul glanced at Halleck, but the minstrel-warrior was staring out at the barren landscape.

Kynes spoke stiffly: "You, of course, refer to my duties as planetologist."

"Of course."

"It is mostly dry land biology and botany . . . some geological work—core drilling and testing. You never really exhaust the possibilities of an entire planet."

"Do you also investigate the spice?"

Kynes turned, and Paul noted the hard line of the man's cheek. "A curious question, my Lord."

"Bear in mind, Kynes, that this is now my fief. My methods differ from those of the Harkonnens. I don't care if you study the spice as long as I share what you discover." He glanced at the planetologist. "The Harkonnens discouraged investigation of the spice, didn't they?"

Kynes stared back without answering.

"You may speak plainly," the Duke said, "without fear for your skin."

"The Imperial Court is, indeed, a long way off," Kynes muttered.

And he thought: *What does this water-soft invader expect? Does he think me fool enough to enlist with him?*

The Duke chuckled, keeping his attention on their course. "I detect a sour note in your voice, sir. We've waded in here with our mob of tame killers, eh? And we expect you to realize immediately that we're different from the Harkonnens?"

"I've seen the propaganda you've flooded into sietch and village," Kynes said. "'Love the good Duke!' Your corps of—"

"Here now!" Halleck barked. He snapped his attention away from the window, leaned forward.

Paul put a hand on Halleck's arm.

"Gurney!" the Duke said. He glanced back. "This man's been long under the Harkonnens."

Halleck sat back. "Ayah."

"Your man Hawat's subtle," Kynes said, "but his object's plain enough."

"Will you open those bases to us, then?" the Duke asked.

Kynes spoke curtly: "They're His Majesty's property."

"They're not being used."

"They could be used."

"Does His Majesty concur?"

Kynes darted a hard stare at the Duke. "Arrakis could be an Eden if its rulers would look up from grubbing for spice!"

He didn't answer my question, the Duke thought. And he said: "How is a planet to become an Eden without money?"

"What is money," Kynes asked, "if it won't buy the services you need?"

Ah, now! the Duke thought. And he said: "We'll discuss this another time. Right now, I believe we're coming to the edge of the Shield Wall. Do I hold the same course?"

"The same course," Kynes muttered.

Paul looked out his window. Beneath them, the broken ground began to drop away in tumbled creases toward a barren rock plain and a knife-edged shelf. Beyond the shelf, fingernail crescents of dunes marched toward the horizon with here and there in the distance a dull smudge, a darker blotch to tell of something not sand. Rock outcroppings, perhaps. In the heat-addled air, Paul couldn't be sure.

"Are there any plants down there?" Paul asked.

"Some," Kynes said. "This latitude's life-zone has mostly what we call minor water stealers—adapted to raiding each other for moisture, gobbling up the trace-dew. Some parts of the desert teem with life. But all of it has learned how to survive under these rigors. If *you* get caught down there, you imitate that life or you die."

"You mean steal water from each other?" Paul asked. The idea outraged him, and his voice betrayed his emotion.

"It's done," Kynes said, "but that wasn't precisely my meaning. You see, my climate demands a special attitude toward water. You are aware of water at all times. You waste nothing that contains moisture."

And the Duke thought: *". . . my climate!"*

"Come around two degrees more southerly, my Lord," Kynes said. "There's a blow coming up from the west."

The Duke nodded. He had seen the billowing of tan dust there. He banked the 'thopter around, noting the way the escort's wings reflected milky orange from the dust-refracted light as they turned to keep pace with him.

"This should clear the storm's edge," Kynes said.

"That sand must be dangerous if you fly into it," Paul said. "Will it really cut the strongest metals?"

"At this altitude, it's not sand but dust," Kynes said. "The danger is lack of visibility, turbulence, clogged intakes."

"We'll see actual spice mining today?" Paul asked.

"Very likely," Kynes said.

Paul sat back. He had used the questions and hyperawareness to do what his mother called "registering" the person. He had Kynes now—tone of voice, each detail of face and gesture. An unnatural folding of the left sleeve on the man's robe told of a knife in an arm sheath. The waist bulged strangely. It was said that desert men wore a belted sash into which they tucked small necessities. Perhaps the bulges came from such a sash—certainly not from a concealed shield belt. A copper pin engraved with the likeness of a hare clasped the neck of Kynes' robe. Another smaller pin with similar likeness hung at the corner of the hood which was thrown back over his shoulders.

Halleck twisted in the seat beside Paul, reached back into the rear compartment and brought out his baliset. Kynes looked around as Halleck tuned the instrument, then returned his attention to their course.

"What would you like to hear, young Master?" Halleck asked.

"You choose, Gurney," Paul said.

Halleck bent his ear close to the sounding board, strummed a chord and sang softly:

> *"Our fathers ate manna in the desert,*
> *In the burning places where whirlwinds came.*
> *Lord, save us from that horrible land!*
> *Save us . . . oh-h-h-h, save us*
> *From the dry and thirsty land."*

Kynes glanced at the Duke, said: "You *do* travel with a light complement of guards, my Lord. Are all of them such men of many talents?"

"Gurney?" The Duke chuckled. "Gurney's one of a kind. I like him with me for his eyes. His eyes miss very little."

The planetologist frowned.

Without missing a beat in his tune, Halleck interposed:

> *"For I am like an owl of the desert, o!*
> *Aiyah! am like an owl of the des-ert!"*

The Duke reached down, brought up a microphone from the instrument panel, thumbed it to life, said: "Leader to Escort Gemma. Flying object at nine o'clock, Sector B. Do you identify it?"

"It's merely a bird," Kynes said, and added: "You have sharp eyes."

The panel speaker crackled, then: "Escort Gemma. Object examined under full amplification. It's a large bird."

Paul looked in the indicated direction, saw the distant speck: a dot of intermittent motion, and realized how keyed up his father must be. Every sense was at full alert.

"I'd not realized there were birds that large this far into the desert," the Duke said.

"That's likely an eagle," Kynes said. "Many creatures have adapted to this place."

The ornithopter swept over a bare rock plain. Paul looked down from their two thousand meters' altitude, saw the wrinkled shadow of their craft and escort. The land beneath seemed flat, but shadow wrinkles said otherwise.

"Has anyone ever walked out of the desert?" the Duke asked.

Halleck's music stopped. He leaned forward to catch the answer.

"Not from the deep desert," Kynes said. "Men have walked out of the second zone several times. They've survived by crossing the rock areas where worms seldom go."

The timbre of Kynes' voice held Paul's attention. He felt his senses come alert the way they were trained to do.

"Ah-h, the worms," the Duke said. "I must see one sometime."

"You may see one today," Kynes said. "Wherever there is spice, there are worms."

"Always?" Halleck asked.

"Always."

"Is there a relationship between worm and spice?" the Duke asked.

Kynes turned and Paul saw the pursed lips as the man spoke. "They defend spice *sands*. Each worm has a—territory. As to the spice . . . who knows? Worm specimens we've examined lead us to suspect complicated chemical interchanges within them. We find traces of hydrochloric acid in the ducts, more complicated acid forms elsewhere. I'll give you my monograph on the subject."

"And a shield's no defense?" the Duke asked.

"Shields!" Kynes sneered. "Activate a shield within the worm zone and you seal your fate. Worms ignore territory lines, come from far around to attack a shield. No man wearing a shield has ever survived such attack."

"How are worms taken, then?"

"High voltage electrical shock applied separately to each ring segment is the only known way of killing and preserving an entire worm," Kynes said. "They can be stunned and shattered by explosives, but each ring segment has a life of its own. Barring atomics, I know of no explosive powerful enough to destroy a large worm entirely. They're incredibly tough."

"Why hasn't an effort been made to wipe them out?" Paul asked.

"Too expensive," Kynes said. "Too much area to cover."

Paul leaned back in his corner. His truthsense, awareness of tone shadings, told him that Kynes was lying and telling half-truths. And he thought: *If there's a relationship between spice and worms, killing the worms would destroy the spice.*

"No one will have to walk out of the desert soon," the Duke said. "Trip these little transmitters at our necks and rescue is on its way. All our workers will be wearing them before long. We're setting up a special rescue service."

"Very commendable," Kynes said.

"Your tone says you don't agree," the Duke said.

"Agree? Of course I agree, but it won't be much use. Static electricity from sandstorms masks out many signals. Transmitters short out. They've been tried here before, you know. Arrakis is tough on equipment. And if a worm's hunting you there's not much time. Frequently, you have no more than fifteen or twenty minutes."

"What would you advise?" the Duke asked.

"You ask my advice?"

"As planetologist, yes."

"You'd follow my advice?"

"If I found it sensible."

"Very well, my Lord. Never travel alone."

The Duke turned his attention from the controls. "That's all?"

"That's all. Never travel alone."

"What if you're separated by a storm and forced down?" Halleck asked. "Isn't there anything you could do?"

"*Anything* covers much territory," Kynes said.

"What would *you* do?" Paul asked.

Kynes turned a hard stare at the boy, brought his attention back to the Duke. "I'd remember to protect the integrity of my stillsuit. If I were outside the worm zone or in rock, I'd stay with the ship. If I were down in open sand, I'd get away from the ship as fast as I could. About a thousand meters would be far enough. Then I'd hide beneath my robe. A worm would get the ship, but it might miss me."

"Then what?" Halleck asked.

Kynes shrugged. "Wait for the worm to leave."

"That's all?" Paul asked.

"When the worm has gone, one may try to walk out," Kynes said. "You must walk softly, avoid drum sands, tidal dust basins—head for the nearest rock zone. There are many such zones. You might make it."

"Drum sand?" Halleck asked.

"A condition of sand compaction," Kynes said. "The slightest step sets it drumming. Worms always come to that."

"And a tidal dust basin?" the Duke asked.

"Certain depressions in the desert have filled with dust over the centuries. Some are so vast they have currents and tides. All will swallow the unwary who step into them."

Halleck sat back, resumed strumming the baliset. Presently, he sang:

"*Wild beasts of the desert do hunt there,*
Waiting for the innocents to pass.
Oh-h-h, tempt not the gods of the desert,
Lest you seek a lonely epitaph.
The perils of the—"

He broke off, leaned forward. "Dust cloud ahead, Sire."

"I see it, Gurney."

"That's what we seek," Kynes said.

Paul stretched up in the seat to peer ahead, saw a rolling yellow cloud low on the desert surface some thirty kilometers ahead.

"One of your factory crawlers," Kynes said. "It's on the surface and that means it's on spice. The cloud is vented sand being expelled after the spice has been centrifugally removed. There's no other cloud quite like it."

"Aircraft over it," the Duke said.

"I see two . . . three . . . four spotters," Kynes said. "They're watching for wormsign."

"Wormsign?" the Duke asked.

"A sandwave moving toward the crawler. They'll have seismic probes on the surface, too. Worms sometimes travel too deep for the wave to show." Kynes swung his gaze around the sky. "Should be a carryall wing around, but I don't see it."

"The worm always comes, eh?" Halleck asked.

"Always."

Paul leaned forward, touched Kynes' shoulder. "How big an area does each worm stake out?"

Kynes frowned. The child kept asking adult questions.

"That depends on the size of the worm."

"What's the variation?" the Duke asked.

"Big ones may control three or four hundred square kilometers. Small ones—" He broke off as the Duke kicked on the jet brakes. The ship bucked as its tail pods whispered to silence. Stub wings elongated, cupped the air. The craft became a full 'thopter as the Duke banked it, holding the wings to a gentle beat, pointing with his left hand off to the east beyond the factory crawler.

"Is that wormsign?"

Kynes leaned across the Duke to peer into the distance.

Paul and Halleck were crowded together, looking in the same direction, and Paul noted that their escort, caught by the sudden maneuver, had surged ahead, but now was curving back. The factory crawler lay ahead of them, still some three kilometers away.

Where the Duke pointed, crescent dune tracks spread shadow ripples toward the horizon and, running through them as a level line stretching into the distance, came an elongated mount-in-motion—a cresting of sand. It reminded Paul of the way a big fish disturbed the water when swimming just under the surface.

"Worm," Kynes said. "Big one." He leaned back, grabbed the microphone from the panel, punched out a new frequency selection. Glancing at the grid chart on rollers over their heads, he spoke into the microphone: "Calling crawler at Delta Ajax niner. Wormsign warning. Crawler at Delta Ajax niner. Wormsign warning. Acknowledge, please." He waited.

The panel speaker emitted static crackles, then a voice: "Who calls Delta Ajax niner? Over."

"They seem pretty calm about it," Halleck said.

Kynes spoke into the microphone: "Unlisted flight—north and east of you about three kilometers. Wormsign is on intercept course, your position, estimated contact twenty-five minutes."

Another voice rumbled from the speaker: "This is Spotter Control. Sighting confirmed. Stand by for contact fix." There was a pause, then: "Contact in twenty-six minutes minus. That was a sharp estimate. Who's on that unlisted flight? Over."

Halleck had his harness off and surged forward between Kynes and the Duke. "Is this the regular working frequency, Kynes?"

"Yes. Why?"

"Who'd be listening?"

"Just the work crews in this area. Cuts down interference."

Again, the speaker crackled, then: "This is Delta Ajax niner. Who gets bonus credit for that spot? Over."

Halleck glanced at the Duke.

Kynes said: "There's a bonus based on spice load for whoever gives first worm warning. They want to know—"

"Tell them who had first sight of that worm," Halleck said.

The Duke nodded.

Kynes hesitated, then lifted the microphone: "Spotter credit to the Duke Leto Atreides. The Duke Leto Atreides. Over."

The voice from the speaker was flat and partly distorted by a burst of static: "We read and thank you."

"Now, tell them to divide the bonus among themselves," Halleck ordered. "Tell them it's the Duke's wish."

Kynes took a deep breath, then: "It's the Duke's wish that you divide the bonus among your crew. Do you read? Over."

"Acknowledged and thank you," the speaker said.

The Duke said: "I forgot to mention that Gurney is also very talented in public relations."

Kynes turned a puzzled frown on Halleck.

"This lets the men know their Duke is concerned for their safety," Halleck said. "Word will get around. It was on an area working frequency—not likely Harkonnen agents heard." He glanced out at their air cover. "And we're a pretty strong force. It was a good risk."

The Duke banked their craft toward the sandcloud erupting from the factory crawler. "What happens now?"

"There's a carryall wing somewhere close," Kynes said. "It'll come in and lift off the crawler."

"What if the carryall's wrecked?" Halleck asked.

"Some equipment *is* lost," Kynes said. "Get in close over the crawler, my Lord; you'll find this interesting."

The Duke scowled, busied himself with the controls as they came into turbulent air over the crawler.

Paul looked down, saw sand still spewing out of the metal and plastic monster beneath them. It looked like a great tan and blue beetle with many wide tracks extending on arms around it. He saw a giant inverted funnel snout poked into dark sand in front of it.

"Rich spice bed by the color," Kynes said. "They'll continue working until the last minute."

The Duke fed more power to the wings, stiffened them for a steeper descent as he settled lower in a circling glide above the crawler. A glance left and right showed his cover holding altitude and circling overhead.

Paul studied the yellow cloud belching from the crawler's pipe vents, looked out over the desert at the approaching worm track.

"Shouldn't we be hearing them call in the carryall?" Halleck asked.

"They usually have the wing on a different frequency," Kynes said.

"Shouldn't they have two carryalls standing by for every crawler?" the Duke asked. "There should be twenty-six men on that machine down there, not to mention cost of equipment."

Kynes said: "You don't have enough ex—"

He broke off as the speaker erupted with an angry voice: "Any of you see the wing? He isn't answering."

A garble of noise crackled from the speaker, drowned in an abrupt override signal, then silence and the first voice: "Report by the numbers! Over."

"This is Spotter Control. Last I saw, the wing was pretty high and circling off northwest. I don't see him now. Over."

"Spotter one: negative. Over."

"Spotter two: negative. Over."

"Spotter three: negative. Over."

Silence.

The Duke looked down. His own craft's shadow was just passing over the crawler. "Only four spotters, is that right?"

"Correct," Kynes said.

"There are five in our party," the Duke said. "Our ships are larger. We can crowd in three extra each. Their spotters ought to be able to lift off two each."

Paul did the mental arithmetic, said: "That's three short."

"Why don't they have two carryalls to each crawler?" barked the Duke.

"You don't have enough extra equipment," Kynes said.

"All the more reason we should protect what we have!"

"Where could that carryall go?" Halleck asked.

"Could've been forced down somewhere out of sight," Kynes said.

The Duke grabbed the microphone, hesitated with thumb poised over its switch. "How could they lose sight of a carryall?"

"They keep their attention on the ground looking for wormsign," Kynes said.

The Duke thumbed the switch, spoke into the microphone. "This is your Duke. We are coming down to take off Delta Ajax niner's crew. All spotters are ordered to comply. Spotters will land on the east side. We will take the west. Over." He reached down, punched out his own command frequency, repeated the order for his own air cover, handed the microphone back to Kynes.

Kynes returned to the working frequency and a voice blasted from the speaker: ". . . almost a full load of spice! We have almost a full load! We can't leave that for a damned worm! Over."

"Damn the spice!" the Duke barked. He grabbed back the microphone, said: "We can always get more spice. There are seats in our ships for all but three of you. Draw straws or decide any way you like who's to go. But you're going, and that's an order!" He slammed the microphone back into Kynes' hands, muttered: "Sorry," as Kynes shook an injured finger.

"How much time?" Paul asked.

"Nine minutes," Kynes said.

The Duke said: "This ship has more power than the others. If we took off under jet with three-quarter wings, we could crowd in an additional man."

"That sand's soft," Kynes said.

"With four extra men aboard on a jet takeoff, we could snap the wings, Sire," Halleck said.

"Not on this ship," the Duke said. He hauled back on the controls as the 'thopter glided in beside the crawler. The wings tipped up, braked the 'thopter to a skidding stop within twenty meters of the factory.

The crawler was silent now, no sand spouting from its vents. Only a faint mechanical rumble issued from it, becoming more audible as the Duke opened his door.

Immediately, their nostrils were assailed by the odor of cinnamon—heavy and pungent.

With a loud flapping, the spotter aircraft glided down to the sand on the other side of the crawler. The Duke's own escort swooped in to land in line with him.

Paul, looking out at the factory, saw how all the 'thopters were dwarfed by it—gnats beside a warrior beetle.

"Gurney, you and Paul toss out that rear seat," the Duke said. He manually cranked the wings out to three-quarters, set their angle, checked the jet pod controls. "Why the devil aren't they coming out of that machine?"

"They're hoping the carryall will show up," Kynes said. "They still have a few minutes." He glanced off to the east.

All turned to look the same direction, seeing no sign of the worm, but there was a heavy, charged feeling of anxiety in the air.

The Duke took the microphone, punched for his command frequency, said: "Two of you toss out your shield generators. By the numbers. You can carry one more man that way. We're not leaving any men for that monster." He keyed back to the working frequency, barked: "All right, you in Delta Ajax niner! Out! Now! This is a command from your Duke! On the double or I'll cut that crawler apart with a lasgun!"

A hatch snapped open near the front of the factory, another at the rear, another at the top. Men came tumbling out, sliding and scrambling down to the sand. A tall man in a patched working robe was the last to emerge. He jumped down to a track and then to the sand.

The Duke hung the microphone on the panel, swung out onto the wing step, shouted: "Two men each into your spotters."

The man in the patched robe began tolling off pairs of his crew, pushing them toward the craft waiting on the other side.

"Four over here!" the Duke shouted. "Four into that ship back there!" He jabbed a finger at an escort 'thopter directly behind him. The guards were just wrestling the shield generator out of it. "And four into that ship over there!" He pointed to the other escort that had shed its shield generator. "Three each into the others! Run, you sand dogs!"

The tall man finished counting off his crew, came slogging across the sand followed by three of his companions.

"I hear the worm, but I can't see it," Kynes said.

The others heard it then—an abrasive slithering, distant and growing louder.

"Damn sloppy way to operate," the Duke muttered.

Aircraft began flapping off the sand around them. It reminded the Duke of a time in his home planet's jungles, a sudden emergence into a clearing, and carrion birds lifting away from the carcass of a wild ox.

The spice workers slogged up to the side of the 'thopter, started climbing in behind the Duke. Halleck helped, dragging them into the rear.

"In you go, boys!" he snapped. "On the double!"

Paul, crowded into a corner by sweating men, smelled the perspiration of fear, saw that two of the men had poor neck adjustments on their stillsuits. He filed the information in his memory for future action. His father would have to order tighter stillsuit discipline. Men tended to become sloppy if you didn't watch such things.

The last man came gasping into the rear, said, "The worm! It's almost on us! Blast off!"

The Duke slid into his seat, frowning, said: "We still have almost three minutes on the original contact estimate. Is that right, Kynes?" He shut his door, checked it.

"Almost exactly, my Lord," Kynes said, and he thought: *A cool one, this Duke.*

"All secure here, Sire," Halleck said.

The Duke nodded, watched the last of his escort take off. He adjusted the igniter, glanced once more at wings and instruments, punched the jet sequence.

The takeoff pressed the Duke and Kynes deep into their seats, compressed the people in the rear. Kynes watched the way the Duke handled the controls—gently, surely. The 'thopter was fully airborne now, and the Duke studied his instruments, glanced left and right at his wings.

"She's very heavy, Sire," Halleck said.

"Well within the tolerances of this ship," the Duke said. "You didn't really think I'd risk this cargo, did you, Gurney?"

Halleck grinned, said: "Not a bit of it, Sire."

The Duke banked his craft in a long easy curve—climbing over the crawler.

Paul, crushed into a corner beside a window, stared down at the silent machine on the sand. The wormsign had broken off about four hundred meters from the crawler. And now, there appeared to be turbulence in the sand around the factory.

"The worm is now beneath the crawler," Kynes said. "You are about to witness a thing few have seen."

Flecks of dust shadowed the sand around the crawler now. The big machine began to tip down to the right. A gigantic sand whirlpool began forming there to the right of the crawler. It moved faster and faster. Sand and dust filled the air now for hundreds of meters around.

Then they saw it!

A wide hole emerged from the sand. Sunlight flashed from glistening white spokes within it. The hole's diameter was at least twice the length of the crawler, Paul estimated. He watched as the machine slid into that opening in a billow of dust and sand. The hole pulled back.

"Gods, what a monster!" muttered a man beside Paul.

"Got all our floggin' spice!" growled another.

"Someone is going to pay for this," the Duke said. "I promise you that."

By the very flatness of his father's voice, Paul sensed the deep anger. He found that he shared it. This was criminal waste!

In the silence that followed, they heard Kynes.

"Bless the Maker and His water," Kynes murmured. "Bless the coming and going of Him. May His passage cleanse the world. May He keep the world for His people."

"What's that you're saying?" the Duke asked.

But Kynes remained silent.

Paul glanced at the men crowded around him. They were staring fearfully at the back of Kynes' head. One of them whispered: "Liet."

Kynes turned, scowling. The man sank back, abashed.

Another of the rescued men began coughing—dry and rasping. Presently, he gasped: "Curse this hell hole!"

The tall Dune man who had come last out of the crawler said: "Be you still, Coss. You but worsen your cough." He stirred among the men until he could look through them at the back of the Duke's head. "You be the Duke Leto, I warrant," he said. "It's to you we give thanks for our lives. We were ready to end it there until you came along."

"Quiet, man, and let the Duke fly his ship," Halleck muttered.

Paul glanced at Halleck. He, too, had seen the tension wrinkles at the corner of his father's jaw. One walked softly when the Duke was in a rage.

Leto began easing his 'thopter out of its great banking circle, stopped at a new sign of movement on the sand. The worm had withdrawn into the depths and now, near where the crawler had been, two figures could be seen moving north away from the sand depression. They appeared to glide over the surface with hardly a lifting of dust to mark their passage.

"Who's that down there?" the Duke barked.

"Two Johnnies who came along for the ride, Soor," said the tall Dune man.

"Why wasn't something said about them?"

"It was the chance they took, Soor," the Dune man said.

"My Lord," said Kynes, "these men know it's of little use to do anything about men trapped on the desert in worm country."

"We'll send a ship from base for them!" the Duke snapped.

"As you wish, my Lord," Kynes said. "But likely when the ship gets here there'll be no one to rescue."

"We'll send a ship, anyway," the Duke said.

"They were right beside where the worm came up," Paul said. "How'd they escape?"

"The sides of the hole cave in and make the distances deceptive," Kynes said.

"You waste fuel here, Sire," Halleck ventured.

"Aye, Gurney."

The Duke brought his craft around toward the Shield Wall. His escort came down from circling stations, took up positions above and on both sides.

Paul thought about what the Dune man and Kynes had said. He sensed half-truths, outright lies. The men on the sand had glided across the surface so surely, moving in a way obviously calculated to keep from luring the worm back out of its depths.

Fremen! Paul thought. *Who else would be so sure on the sand? Who else might be left out of your worries as a matter of course—because* they are in no danger? They *know how to live here!* They *know how to outwit the worm!*

"What were Fremen doing on that crawler?" Paul asked.

Kynes whirled.

The tall Dune man turned wide eyes on Paul—blue within blue within blue. "Who be this lad?" he asked.

Halleck moved to place himself between the man and Paul, said: "This is Paul Atreides, the ducal heir."

"Why says he there were Fremen on our rumbler?" the man asked.

"They fit the description," Paul said.

Kynes snorted. "You can't tell Fremen just by looking at them!" He looked at the Dune man. "You. Who were those men?"

"Friends of one of the others," the Dune man said. "Just friends from a village who wanted to see the spice sands."

Kynes turned away. "Fremen!"

But he was remembering the words of the legend: "*The Lisan al-Gaib shall see through all subterfuge.*"

"They be dead now, most likely, young Soor," the Dune man said. "We should not speak unkindly on them."

But Paul heard the falsehood in their voices, felt the menace that had brought Halleck instinctively into guarding position.

Paul spoke dryly: "A terrible place for them to die."

Without turning, Kynes said: "When God hath ordained a creature to die in a particular place, He causeth that creature's wants to direct him to that place."

Leto turned a hard stare at Kynes.

And Kynes, returning the stare, found himself troubled by a fact he had observed here: *This Duke was concerned more over the men than he was over the spice. He risked his own life and that of his son to save the men. He passed off the loss of a spice crawler with a gesture. The threat to men's lives had him in a rage. A leader such as that would command fanatic loyalty. He would be difficult to defeat.*

Against his own will and all previous judgments, Kynes admitted to himself: *I like this Duke.*

Greatness is a transitory experience. It is never consistent. It depends in part upon the myth-making imagination of humankind. The person who experiences greatness must have a feeling for the myth he is in. He must reflect what is projected upon him. And he must have a strong sense of the sardonic. This is what uncouples him from belief in his own pretensions. The sardonic is all that permits him to move within himself. Without this quality, even occasional greatness will destroy a man.

—FROM "COLLECTED SAYINGS OF MUAD'DIB"
BY THE PRINCESS IRULAN

In the dining hall of the Arrakeen great house, suspensor lamps had been lighted against the early dark. They cast their yellow glows upward onto the black bull's head with its bloody horns, and onto the darkly glistening oil painting of the Old Duke.

Beneath these talismans, white linen shone around the burnished reflections of the Atreides silver, which had been placed in precise arrangements along the great table—little archipelagos of service waiting beside crystal glasses, each setting squared off before a heavy wooden chair. The classic central chandelier remained unlighted, and its chain twisted upward into shadows where the mechanism of the poison snooper had been concealed.

Pausing in the doorway to inspect the arrangements, the Duke thought about the poison snooper and what it signified in his society.

All of a pattern, he thought. *You can plumb us by our language—the* precise and delicate delineations for ways to administer treacherous death. Will someone try chaumurky tonight—poison in the drink? Or will it be chaumas—poison in the food?

He shook his head.

Beside each plate on the long table stood a flagon of water. There was enough water along the table, the Duke estimated, to keep a poor Arrakeen family for more than a year.

Flanking the doorway in which he stood were broad laving basins of ornate yellow and green tile. Each basin had its rack of towels. It was the custom, the housekeeper had explained, for guests as they entered to dip their hands ceremoniously into a basin, slop several cups of water onto the floor, dry their hands on a towel and fling the towel into the growing puddle at the door. After the dinner, beggars gathered outside to get the water squeezings from the towels.

How typical of a Harkonnen fief, the Duke thought. *Every degradation of the spirit that can be conceived.* He took a deep breath, feeling rage tighten his stomach.

"The custom stops here!" he muttered.

He saw a serving woman—one of the old and gnarled ones the housekeeper had recommended—hovering at the doorway from the kitchen across from him. The Duke signaled with upraised hand. She moved out of the shadows, scurried around the table toward him, and he noted the leathery face, the blue-within-blue eyes.

"My Lord wishes?" She kept her head bowed, eyes shielded.

He gestured. "Have these basins and towels removed."

"But . . . Noble Born. . . ." She looked up, mouth gaping.

"I know the custom!" he barked. "Take these basins to the front door. While we're eating and until we've finished, each beggar who calls may have a full cup of water. Understood?"

Her leathery face displayed a twisting of emotions: dismay, anger. . . .

With sudden insight, Leto realized that she must have planned to sell the water squeezings from the foot-trampled towels, wringing a few coppers from the wretches who came to the door. Perhaps that also was a custom.

His face clouded, and he growled: "I'm posting a guard to see that my orders are carried out to the letter."

He whirled, strode back down the passage to the Great Hall. Memories rolled in his mind like the toothless mutterings of old women. He remembered open water and waves—days of grass instead of sand—dazed summers that had whipped past him like windstorm leaves.

All gone.

I'm getting old, he thought. *I've felt the cold hand of my mortality. And in what? An old woman's greed.*

In the Great Hall, the Lady Jessica was the center of a mixed group standing in front of the fireplace. An open blaze crackled there, casting flickers of orange light onto jewels and laces and costly fabrics. He recognized in the group a stillsuit manufacturer down from Carthag, an electronics equipment importer, a water-shipper whose summer mansion was near his polar-cap factory, a representative of the Guild Bank (lean and remote, that one), a dealer in replacement parts for spice mining equipment, a thin and hard-faced woman whose escort service for off-planet visitors reputedly operated as cover for various smuggling, spying, and blackmail operations.

Most of the women in the hall seemed cast from a specific type—decorative, precisely turned out, an odd mingling of untouchable sensuousness.

Even without her position as hostess, Jessica would have dominated the group, he thought. She wore no jewelry and had chosen warm colors—a long dress almost the shade of the open blaze, and an earth-brown band around her bronzed hair.

He realized she had done this to taunt him subtly, a reproof against his recent pose of coldness. She was well aware that he liked her best in these shades—that he saw her as a rustling of warm colors.

Nearby, more an outflanker than a member of the group, stood Duncan Idaho in glittering dress uniform, flat face unreadable, the curling black hair neatly combed. He had been summoned back from the Fremen and had his orders from Hawat—*"Under pretext of guarding her, you will keep the Lady Jessica under constant surveillance."*

The Duke glanced around the room.

There was Paul in the corner surrounded by a fawning group of the younger Arrakeen richece, and, aloof among them, three officers of the House Troop. The Duke took particular note of the young women. What a catch a ducal heir would make. But Paul was treating all equally with an air of reserved nobility.

He'll wear the title well, the Duke thought, and realized with a sudden chill that this was another death thought.

Paul saw his father in the doorway, avoided his eyes. He looked around at the clusterings of guests, the jeweled hands clutching drinks (and the unobtrusive inspections with tiny remote-cast snoopers). Seeing all the chattering faces, Paul was suddenly repelled by them. They were cheap masks locked on festering thoughts—voices gabbling to drown out the loud silence in every breast.

I'm in a sour mood, he thought, and wondered what Gurney would say to that.

He knew his mood's source. He hadn't wanted to attend this function, but his father had been firm. "You have a place—a position to uphold. You're old enough to do this. You're almost a man."

Paul saw his father emerge from the doorway, inspect the room, then cross to the group around the Lady Jessica.

As Leto approached Jessica's group, the water-shipper was asking: "Is it true the Duke will put in weather control?"

From behind the man, the Duke said: "We haven't gone that far in our thinking, sir."

The man turned, exposing a bland round face, darkly tanned. "Ah-h, the Duke," he said. "We missed you."

Leto glanced at Jessica. "A thing needed doing." He returned his attention to the water-shipper, explained what he had ordered for the laving basins, adding: "As far as I'm concerned, the old custom ends now."

"Is this a ducal order, m'Lord?" the man asked.

"I leave that to your own . . . ah . . . conscience," the Duke said. He turned, noting Kynes come up to the group.

One of the women said: "I think it's a very generous gesture—giving water to the—" Someone shushed her.

The Duke looked at Kynes, noting that the planetologist wore an old-style dark brown uniform with epaulets of the Imperial Civil Servant and a tiny gold teardrop of rank at his collar.

The water-shipper asked in an angry voice: "Does the Duke imply criticism of our custom?"

"This custom has been changed," Leto said. He nodded to Kynes, marked the frown on Jessica's face, thought: *A frown does not become her, but it'll increase rumors of friction between us.*

"With the Duke's permission," the water-shipper said, "I'd like to inquire further about customs."

Leto heard the sudden oily tone in the man's voice, noted the watchful silence in this group, the way heads were beginning to turn toward them around the room.

"Isn't it almost time for dinner?" Jessica asked.

"But our guest has some questions," Leto said. And he looked at the water-shipper, seeing a round-faced man with large eyes and thick lips, recalling Hawat's memorandum: *". . . and this water-shipper is a man to watch—Lingar Bewt, remember the name. The Harkonnens used him but never fully controlled him."*

"Water customs are so interesting," Bewt said, and there was a smile on his face. "I'm curious what you intend about the conservatory attached to this house. Do you intend to continue flaunting it in the people's faces . . . m'Lord?"

Leto held anger in check, staring at the man. Thoughts raced through his mind. It had taken bravery to challenge him in his own ducal castle, especially since they now had Bewt's signature over a contract of allegiance. The action had taken, also, a knowledge of personal power. Water was, indeed, power here. If water facilities were mined, for instance, ready to be destroyed at a signal. . . . The man looked capable of such a thing. Destruction of water facilities might well destroy Arrakis. That could well have been the club this Bewt held over the Harkonnens.

"My Lord, the Duke, and I have other plans for our conservatory," Jessica said. She smiled at Leto. "We intend to keep it, certainly, but only to hold it in trust for the people of Arrakis. It is our dream that someday the climate of Arrakis may be changed sufficiently to grow such plants anywhere in the open."

Bless her! Leto thought. *Let our water-shipper chew on that.*

"Your interest in water and weather control is obvious," the Duke said. "I'd advise you to diversify your holdings. One day, water will not be a precious commodity on Arrakis."

And he thought: *Hawat must redouble his efforts at infiltrating this Bewt's organization. And we must start on standby water facilities at once. No man is going to hold a club over my head!*

Bewt nodded, the smile still on his face. "A commendable dream, my Lord." He withdrew a pace.

Leto's attention was caught by the expression on Kynes' face. The man was staring at Jessica. He appeared transfigured—like a man in love . . . or caught in a religious trance.

Kynes' thoughts were overwhelmed at last by the words of prophecy: *"And they shall share your most precious dream."* He spoke directly to Jessica: "Do you bring the shortening of the way?"

"Ah, Dr. Kynes," the water-shipper said. "You've come in from tramping around with your mobs of Fremen. How gracious of you."

Kynes passed an unreadable glance across Bewt, said: "It is said in the desert that possession of water in great amount can inflict a man with fatal carelessness."

"They have many strange sayings in the desert," Bewt said, but his voice betrayed uneasiness.

Jessica crossed to Leto, slipped her hand under his arm to gain a moment in which to calm herself. Kynes had said: ". . . the shortening of the way." In the old tongue, the phrase translated as "Kwisatz Haderach." The planetologist's odd question seemed to have gone unnoticed by the others, and now Kynes was bending over one of the consort women, listening to a low-voiced coquetry.

Kwisatz Haderach, Jessica thought. *Did our Missionaria Protectiva plant that legend here, too?* The thought fanned her secret hope for Paul. *He could be the Kwisatz Haderach. He could be.*

The Guild Bank representative had fallen into conversation with the water-shipper, and Bewt's voice lifted above the renewed hum of conversations: "Many people have sought to change Arrakis."

The Duke saw how the words seemed to pierce Kynes, jerking the planetologist upright and away from the flirting woman.

Into the sudden silence, a house trooper in uniform of a footman cleared his throat behind Leto, said: "Dinner is served, my Lord."

The Duke directed a questioning glance down at Jessica.

"The custom here is for host and hostess to follow their guests to table," she said, and smiled: "Shall we change that one, too, my Lord?"

He spoke coldly: "That seems a goodly custom. We shall let it stand for now."

The illusion that I suspect her of treachery must be maintained, he thought. He glanced at the guests filing past them. *Who among you believes this lie?*

Jessica, sensing his remoteness, wondered at it as she had done frequently the past week. *He acts like a man struggling with himself*, she thought. *Is it because I moved so swiftly setting up this dinner party? Yet, he knows how important it is that we begin to mix our officers and men with the locals on a social plane. We are father and mother surrogate to them all. Nothing impresses that fact more firmly than this sort of social sharing.*

Leto, watching the guests file past, recalled what Thufir Hawat had said when informed of the affair: *"Sire! I forbid it!"*

A grim smile touched the Duke's mouth. What a scene that had been. And when the Duke had remained adamant about attending the dinner, Hawat had shaken his head. "I have bad feelings about this, my Lord," he'd said. "Things move too swiftly on Arrakis. That's not like the Harkonnens. Not like them at all."

Paul passed his father escorting a young woman half a head taller than himself. He shot a sour glance at his father, nodded at something the young woman said.

"Her father manufactures stillsuits," Jessica said. "I'm told that only a fool would be caught in the deep desert wearing one of the man's suits."

"Who's the man with the scarred face ahead of Paul?" the Duke asked. "I don't place him."

"A late addition to the list," she whispered. "Gurney arranged the invitation. Smuggler."

"Gurney arranged?"

"At my request. It was cleared with Hawat, although I thought Hawat was a little stiff about it. The smuggler's called Tuek, Esmar Tuek. He's a power among his kind. They all know him here. He's dined at many of the houses."

"Why is he here?"

"Everyone here will ask that question," she said. "Tuek will sow doubt and suspicion just by his presence. He'll also serve notice that you're prepared to back up your orders against graft—by enforcement from the smugglers' end as well. This was the point Hawat appeared to like."

"I'm not sure *I* like it." He nodded to a passing couple, saw only a few of their guests remained to precede them. "Why didn't you invite some Fremen?"

"There's Kynes," she said.

"Yes, there's Kynes," he said. "Have you arranged any other little surprises for me?" He led her into step behind the procession.

"All else is most conventional," she said.

And she thought: *My darling, can't you see that this smuggler controls fast ships, that he can be bribed? We must have a way out, a door of escape from Arrakis if all else fails us here.*

As they emerged into the dining hall, she disengaged her arm, allowed Leto to seat her. He strode to his end of the table. A footman held his chair for him. The others settled with a swishing of fabrics, a scraping of chairs, but the Duke remained standing. He gave a hand signal, and the house troopers in footman uniform around the table stepped back, standing at attention.

Uneasy silence settled over the room.

Jessica, looking down the length of the table, saw a faint trembling at the corners of Leto's mouth, noted the dark flush of anger on his cheeks. *What has angered him?* she asked herself. *Surely not my invitation to the smuggler.*

"Some question my changing of the laving basin custom," Leto said. "This is my way of telling you that many things will change."

Embarrassed silence settled over the table.

They think him drunk, Jessica thought.

Leto lifted his water flagon, held it aloft where the suspensor lights shot beams of reflection off it. "As a Chevalier of the Imperium, then," he said, "I give you a toast."

The others grasped their flagons, all eyes focused on the Duke. In the sudden stillness, a suspensor light drifted slightly in an errant breeze from the serving kitchen hallway. Shadows played across the Duke's hawk features.

"Here I am and here I remain!" he barked.

There was an abortive movement of flagons toward mouths—stopped as the Duke remained with arm upraised. "My toast is one of those maxims so dear to our hearts: 'Business makes progress! Fortune passes everywhere!'"

He sipped his water.

The others joined him. Questioning glances passed among them.

"Gurney!" the Duke called.

From an alcove at Leto's end of the room came Halleck's voice. "Here, my Lord."

"Give us a tune, Gurney."

A minor chord from the baliset floated out of the alcove. Servants began putting plates of food on the table at the Duke's gesture releasing them—roast desert hare in sauce cepeda, aplomage sirian, chukka under glass, coffee with melange (a rich cinnamon odor from the spice wafted across the table), a true pot-a-oie served with sparkling Caladan wine.

Still, the Duke remained standing.

As the guests waited, their attention torn between the dishes placed before them and the standing Duke, Leto said: "In olden times, it was the duty of the host to entertain his guests with his own talents." His knuckles turned white, so fiercely did he grip his water flagon. "I cannot sing, but I give you the words of Gurney's song. Consider it another toast—a toast to all who've died bringing us to this station."

An uncomfortable stirring sounded around the table.

Jessica lowered her gaze, glanced at the people seated nearest her— there was the round-faced water-shipper and his woman, the pale and austere Guild Bank representative (he seemed a whistle-faced scarecrow with his eyes fixed on Leto), the rugged and scar-faced Tuek, his blue-within-blue eyes downcast.

"Review, friends—troops long past review," the Duke intoned. "All to fate a weight of pains and dollars. Their spirits wear our silver collars. Review, friends—troops long past review: Each a dot of time without pretense or guile. With them passes the lure of fortune. Review, friends—troops long past review. When our time ends on its rictus smile, we'll pass the lure of fortune."

The Duke allowed his voice to trail off on the last line, took a deep drink from his water flagon, slammed it back onto the table. Water slopped over the brim onto the linen.

The others drank in embarrassed silence.

Again, the Duke lifted his water flagon, and this time emptied its remaining half onto the floor, knowing that the others around the table must do the same.

Jessica was first to follow his example.

There was a frozen moment before the others began emptying their flagons. Jessica saw how Paul, seated near his father, was studying the reactions around him. She found herself also fascinated by what her guests' actions revealed—especially among the women. This was clean, potable water, not something already cast away in a sopping towel. Reluctance to just discard it exposed itself in trembling hands, delayed reactions, nervous laughter . . . and violent obedience to the necessity.

One woman dropped her flagon, looked the other way as her male companion recovered it.

Kynes, though, caught her attention most sharply. The planetologist hesitated, then emptied his flagon into a container beneath his jacket. He smiled at Jessica as he caught her watching him, raised the empty flagon to her in a silent toast. He appeared completely unembarrassed by his action.

Halleck's music still wafted over the room, but it had come out of its minor key, lilting and lively now as though he were trying to lift the mood.

"Let the dinner commence," the Duke said, and sank into his chair.

He's angry and uncertain, Jessica thought. *The loss of that factory crawler hit him more deeply than it should have. It must be something more than that loss. He acts like a desperate man.* She lifted her fork, hoping in the motion to hide her own sudden bitterness. *Why not? He is desperate.*

Slowly at first, then with increasing animation, the dinner got under way. The stillsuit manufacturer complimented Jessica on her chef and wine.

"We brought both from Caladan," she said.

"Superb!" he said, tasting the chukka. "Simply superb! And not a hint of melange in it. One gets so tired of the spice in everything."

The Guild Bank representative looked across at Kynes. "I understand, Doctor Kynes, that another factory crawler has been lost to a worm."

"News travels fast," the Duke said.

"Then it's true?" the banker asked, shifting his attention to Leto.

"Of course, it's true!" the Duke snapped. "The blasted carryall disappeared. It shouldn't be possible for anything that big to disappear!"

"When the worm came, there was nothing to recover the crawler," Kynes said.

"It should *not* be possible!" the Duke repeated.

"No one saw the carryall leave?" the banker asked.

"Spotters customarily keep their eyes on the sand," Kynes said. "They're primarily interested in wormsign. A carryall's complement usually is four men—two pilots and two journeymen attachers. If one— or even two of this crew were in the pay of the Duke's foes—"

"Ah-h-h, I see," the banker said. "And you, as Judge of the Change, do you challenge this?"

"I shall have to consider my position carefully," Kynes said, "and I certainly will not discuss it at table." And he thought: *That pale skeleton of a man! He knows this is the kind of infraction I was instructed to ignore.*

The banker smiled, returned his attention to his food.

Jessica sat remembering a lecture from her Bene Gesserit school days. The subject had been espionage and counter-espionage. A plump, happy-faced Reverend Mother had been the lecturer, her jolly voice contrasting weirdly with the subject matter.

A thing to note about any espionage and/or counter-espionage school is the similar basic reaction pattern of all its graduates. Any enclosed discipline sets its stamp, its pattern, upon its students. That pattern is susceptible to analysis and prediction.

Now, motivational patterns are going to be similar among all espionage agents. That is to say: there will be certain types of motivation that are similar despite differing schools or opposed aims. You will study first how to separate this element for your analysis—in the beginning, through interrogation patterns that betray the inner orientation of the interrogators; secondly, by close observation of language-thought orientation of those under analysis. You will find it fairly simple to determine the root languages of your subjects, of course, both through voice inflection and speech pattern.

Now, sitting at table with her son and her Duke and their guests, hearing that Guild Bank representative, Jessica felt a chill of realization: the man was a Harkonnen agent. He had the Giedi Prime speech pattern—subtly masked, but exposed to her trained awareness as though he had announced himself.

Does this mean the Guild itself has taken sides against House Atre-

ides? she asked herself. The thought shocked her, and she masked her emotion by calling for a new dish, all the while listening for the man to betray his purpose. *He will shift the conversation next to something seemingly innocent, but with ominous overtones,* she told herself. *It's his pattern.*

The banker swallowed, took a sip of wine, smiled at something said to him by the woman on his right. He seemed to listen for a moment to a man down the table who was explaining to the Duke that native Arrakeen plants had no thorns.

"I enjoy watching the flights of birds on Arrakis," the banker said, directing his words at Jessica. "All of our birds, of course, are carrion-eaters, and many exist without water, having become blood-drinkers."

The stillsuit manufacturer's daughter, seated between Paul and his father at the other end of the table, twisted her pretty face into a frown, said: "Oh, Soo-Soo, you say the most disgusting things."

The banker smiled. "They call me Soo-Soo because I'm financial adviser to the Water Peddlers Union." And, as Jessica continued to look at him without comment, he added: "Because of the water-sellers' cry—'Soo-Soo Sook!'" And he imitated the call with such accuracy that many around the table laughed.

Jessica heard the boastful tone of voice, but noted most that the young woman had spoken on cue—a set piece. She had produced the excuse for the banker to say what he had said. She glanced at Lingar Bewt. The water magnate was scowling, concentrating on his dinner. It came to Jessica that the banker had said: *"I, too, control that ultimate source of power on Arrakis—water."*

Paul had marked the falseness in his dinner companion's voice, saw that his mother was following the conversation with Bene Gesserit intensity. On impulse, he decided to play the foil, draw the exchange out. He addressed himself to the banker.

"Do you mean, sir, that these birds are cannibals?"

"That's an odd question, young Master," the banker said. "I merely said the birds drink blood. It doesn't have to be the blood of their own kind, does it?"

"It was *not* an odd question," Paul said, and Jessica noted the brittle riposte quality of her training exposed in his voice. "Most educated people know that the worst potential competition for any young organism can come from its own kind." He deliberately forked a bite of food from his companion's plate, ate it. "They are eating from the same bowl. They have the same basic requirements."

The banker stiffened, scowled at the Duke.

"Do not make the error of considering my son a child," the Duke said. And he smiled.

Jessica glanced around the table, noted that Bewt had brightened, that both Kynes and the smuggler, Tuek, were grinning.

"It's a rule of ecology," Kynes said, "that the young Master appears to understand quite well. The struggle between life elements is the struggle for the free energy of a system. Blood's an efficient energy source."

The banker put down his fork, spoke in an angry voice: "It's said that the Fremen scum drink the blood of their dead."

Kynes shook his head, spoke in a lecturing tone: "Not the blood, sir. But all of a man's water, ultimately, belongs to his people—to his tribe. It's a necessity when you live near the Great Flat. All water's precious there, and the human body is composed of some seventy per cent water by weight. A dead man, surely, no longer requires that water."

The banker put both hands against the table beside his plate, and Jessica thought he was going to push himself back, leave in a rage.

Kynes looked at Jessica. "Forgive me, my Lady, for elaborating on such an ugly subject at table, but you were being told falsehood and it needed clarifying."

"You've associated so long with Fremen that you've lost all sensibilities," the banker rasped.

Kynes looked at him calmly, studied the pale, trembling face. "Are you challenging me, sir?"

The banker froze. He swallowed, spoke stiffly: "Of course not. I'd not so insult our host and hostess."

Jessica heard the fear in the man's voice, saw it in his face, in his breathing, in the pulse of a vein at his temple. The man was terrified of Kynes!

"Our host and hostess are quite capable of deciding for themselves when they've been insulted," Kynes said. "They're brave people who understand defense of honor. We all may attest to their courage by the fact that they are here . . . now . . . on Arrakis."

Jessica saw that Leto was enjoying this. Most of the others were not. People all around the table sat poised for flight, hands out of sight under the table. Two notable exceptions were Bewt, who was openly smiling at the banker's discomfiture, and the smuggler, Tuek, who appeared to be watching Kynes for a cue. Jessica saw that Paul was looking at Kynes in admiration.

"Well?" Kynes said.

"I meant no offense," the banker muttered. "If offense was taken, please accept my apologies."

"Freely given, freely accepted," Kynes said. He smiled at Jessica, resumed eating as though nothing had happened.

Jessica saw that the smuggler, too, had relaxed. She marked this: the man had shown every aspect of an aide ready to leap to Kynes' assistance. There existed an accord of some sort between Kynes and Tuek.

Leto toyed with a fork, looked speculatively at Kynes. The ecologist's manner indicated a change in attitude toward the House of Atreides. Kynes had seemed colder on their trip over the desert.

Jessica signaled for another course of food and drink. Servants appeared with *langues de lapins de garenne*—red wine and a sauce of mushroom-yeast on the side.

Slowly, the dinner conversation resumed, but Jessica heard the agitation in it, the brittle quality, saw that the banker ate in sullen silence. *Kynes would have killed him without hesitating*, she thought. And she realized that there was an offhand attitude toward killing in Kynes' manner. He was a casual killer, and she guessed that this was a Fremen quality.

Jessica turned to the stillsuit manufacturer on her left, said: "I find myself continually amazed by the importance of water on Arrakis."

"Very important," he agreed. "What is this dish? It's delicious."

"Tongues of wild rabbit in a special sauce," she said. "A very old recipe."

"I must have that recipe," the man said.

She nodded. "I'll see that you get it."

Kynes looked at Jessica, said: "The newcomer to Arrakis frequently underestimates the importance of water here. You are dealing, you see, with the Law of the Minimum."

She heard the testing quality in his voice, said, "Growth is limited by that necessity which is present in the least amount. And, naturally, the least favorable condition controls the growth rate."

"It's rare to find members of a Great House aware of planetological problems," Kynes said. "Water is the least favorable condition for life on Arrakis. And remember that *growth* itself can produce unfavorable conditions unless treated with extreme care."

Jessica sensed a hidden message in Kynes' words, but knew she was missing it. "Growth," she said. "Do you mean Arrakis can have an orderly cycle of water to sustain human life under more favorable conditions?"

"Impossible!" the water magnate barked.

Jessica turned her attention to Bewt. "Impossible?"

"Impossible on Arrakis," he said. "Don't listen to this dreamer. All the laboratory evidence is against him."

Kynes looked at Bewt, and Jessica noted that the other conversations around the table had stopped while people concentrated on this new interchange.

"Laboratory evidence tends to blind us to a very simple fact," Kynes said. "That fact is this: we are dealing here with matters that originated and exist out-of-doors where plants and animals carry on their normal existence."

"Normal!" Bewt snorted. "Nothing about Arrakis is normal!"

"Quite the contrary," Kynes said. "Certain harmonies could be set up here along self-sustaining lines. You merely have to understand the limits of the planet and the pressures upon it."

"It'll never be done," Bewt said.

The Duke came to a sudden realization, placing the point where Kynes' attitude had changed—it had been when Jessica had spoken of holding the conservatory plants in trust for Arrakis.

"What would it take to set up the self-sustaining system, Doctor Kynes?" Leto asked.

"If we can get three per cent of the green plant element on Arrakis involved in forming carbon compounds as foodstuffs, we've started the cyclic system," Kynes said.

"Water's the only problem?" the Duke asked. He sensed Kynes' excitement, felt himself caught up in it.

"Water overshadows the other problems," Kynes said. "This planet has much oxygen without its usual concomitants—widespread plant life and large sources of free carbon dioxide from such phenomena as volcanoes. There are unusual chemical interchanges over large surface areas here."

"Do you have pilot projects?" the Duke asked.

"We've had a long time in which to build up the Tansley Effect—small-unit experiments on an amateur basis from which my science may now draw its working facts," Kynes said.

"There isn't enough water," Bewt said. "There just isn't enough water."

"Master Bewt is an expert on water," Kynes said. He smiled, turned back to his dinner.

The Duke gestured sharply down with his right hand, barked: "No! I want an answer! Is there enough water, Doctor Kynes?"

Kynes stared at his plate.

Jessica watched the play of emotion on his face. *He masks himself well*, she thought, but she had him registered now and read that he regretted his words.

"Is there enough water!" the Duke demanded.

"There . . . may be," Kynes said.

He's faking uncertainty! Jessica thought.

With his deeper truthsense, Paul caught the underlying motive, had to use every ounce of his training to mask his excitement. *There is enough water! But Kynes doesn't wish it to be known.*

"Our planetologist has many interesting dreams," Bewt said. "He dreams with the Fremen—of prophecies and messiahs."

Chuckles sounded at odd places around the table. Jessica marked them—the smuggler, the stillsuit manufacturer's daughter, Duncan Idaho, the woman with the mysterious escort service.

Tensions are oddly distributed here tonight, Jessica thought. *There's too much going on of which I'm not aware. I'll have to develop new information sources.*

The Duke passed his gaze from Kynes to Bewt to Jessica. He felt oddly let down, as though something vital had passed him here. "*May*be," he muttered.

Kynes spoke quickly: "Perhaps we should discuss this another time, my Lord. There are so many—"

The planetologist broke off as a uniformed Atreides trooper hurried in through the service door, was passed by the guard and rushed to the Duke's side. The man bent, whispering into Leto's ear.

Jessica recognized the capsign of Hawat's corps, fought down uneasiness. She addressed herself to the stillsuit manufacturer's feminine companion—a tiny, dark-haired woman with a doll face, a touch of epicanthic fold to the eyes.

"You've hardly touched your dinner, my dear," Jessica said. "May I order you something?"

The woman looked at the stillsuit manufacturer before answering, then: "I'm not very hungry."

Abruptly, the Duke stood up beside his trooper, spoke in a harsh tone of command: "Stay seated, everyone. You will have to forgive me, but a matter has arisen that requires my personal attention." He stepped aside. "Paul, take over as host for me, if you please."

Paul stood, wanting to ask why his father had to leave, knowing he had to play this with the grand manner. He moved around to his father's chair, sat down in it.

The Duke turned to the alcove where Halleck sat, said: "Gurney, please take Paul's place at table. We mustn't have an odd number here. When the dinner's over, I may want you to bring Paul to the field C.P. Wait for my call."

Halleck emerged from the alcove in dress uniform, his lumpy ugliness seeming out of place in the glittering finery. He leaned his baliset against the wall, crossed to the chair Paul had occupied, sat down.

"There's no need for alarm," the Duke said, "but I must ask that no one leave until our house guard says it's safe. You will be perfectly secure as long as you remain here, and we'll have this little trouble cleared up very shortly."

Paul caught the code words in his father's message—*guard-safe-secure-shortly.* The problem was security, not violence. He saw that his mother had read the same message. They both relaxed.

The Duke gave a short nod, wheeled and strode through the service door followed by his trooper.

Paul said: "Please go on with your dinner. I believe Doctor Kynes was discussing water."

"May we discuss it another time?" Kynes asked.

"By all means," Paul said.

And Jessica noted with pride her son's dignity, the mature sense of assurance.

The banker picked up his water flagon, gestured with it at Bewt. "None of us here can surpass Master Lingar Bewt in flowery phrases. One might almost assume he aspired to Great House status. Come, Master Bewt, lead us in a toast. Perhaps you've a dollop of wisdom for the boy who must be treated like a man."

Jessica clenched her right hand into a fist beneath the table. She saw a hand signal pass from Halleck to Idaho, saw the house troopers along the walls move into positions of maximum guard.

Bewt cast a venomous glare at the banker.

Paul glanced at Halleck, took in the defensive positions of his guards, looked at the banker until the man lowered the water flagon. He said: "Once, on Caladan, I saw the body of a drowned fisherman recovered. He—"

"Drowned?" It was the stillsuit manufacturer's daughter.

Paul hesitated, then: "Yes. Immersed in water until dead. Drowned."

"What an interesting way to die," she murmured.

Paul's smile became brittle. He returned his attention to the banker. "The interesting thing about this man was the wounds on his shoulders—made by another fisherman's claw-boots. This fisherman was one of several in a boat—a craft for traveling on water—that foundered . . . sank beneath the water. Another fisherman helping recover the body said he'd seen marks like this man's wounds several times. They meant another drowning fisherman had tried to stand on this poor fellow's shoulders in the attempt to reach up to the surface—to reach air."

"Why is this interesting?" the banker asked.

"Because of an observation made by my father at the time. He said the drowning man who climbs on your shoulders to save himself is understandable—except when you see it happen in the drawing room." Paul hesitated just long enough for the banker to see the point coming, then: "And, I should add, except when you see it at the dinner table."

A sudden stillness enfolded the room.

That was rash, Jessica thought. *This banker might have enough rank to call my son out.* She saw that Idaho was poised for instant action. The house troopers were alert. Gurney Halleck had his eyes on the men opposite him.

"Ho-ho-ho-o-o-o!" It was the smuggler, Tuek, head thrown back laughing with complete abandon.

Nervous smiles appeared around the table.

Bewt was grinning.

The banker had pushed his chair back, was glaring at Paul.

Kynes said: "One baits an Atreides at his own risk."

"Is it Atreides custom to insult their guests?" the banker demanded.

Before Paul could answer, Jessica leaned forward, said: "Sir!" And she thought: *We must learn this Harkonnen creature's game. Is he here to try for Paul? Does he have help?*

"My son displays a general garment and you claim it's cut to your fit?" Jessica asked. "What a fascinating revelation." She slid a hand down to her leg to the crysknife she had fastened in a calf-sheath.

The banker turned his glare on Jessica. Eyes shifted away from Paul and she saw him ease himself back from the table, freeing himself for action. He had focused on the code word: *garment. "Prepare for violence."*

Kynes directed a speculative look at Jessica, gave a subtle hand signal to Tuek.

The smuggler lurched to his feet, lifted his flagon. "I'll give you a toast," he said. "To young Paul Atreides, still a lad by his looks, but a man by his actions."

Why do they intrude? Jessica asked herself.

The banker stared now at Kynes, and Jessica saw terror return to the agent's face.

People began responding all around the table.

Where Kynes leads, people follow, Jessica thought. *He has told us he sides with Paul. What's the secret of his power? It can't be because he's Judge of the Change. That's temporary. And certainly not because he's a civil servant.*

She removed her hand from the crysknife hilt, lifted her flagon to Kynes, who responded in kind.

Only Paul and the banker—(*Soo-Soo! What an idiotic nickname!* Jessica thought.)—remained empty-handed. The banker's attention stayed fixed on Kynes. Paul stared at his plate.

I was handling it correctly, Paul thought. *Why do they interfere?* He glanced covertly at the male guests nearest him. Prepare for violence? From whom? Certainly not from that banker fellow.

Halleck stirred, spoke as though to no one in particular, directing his words over the heads of the guests across from him: "In our society, people shouldn't be quick to take offense. It's frequently suicidal." He looked at the stillsuit manufacturer's daughter beside him. "Don't you think so, miss?"

"Oh, yes. Yes. Indeed I do," she said. "There's too much violence. It makes me sick. And lots of times no offense is meant, but people die anyway. It doesn't make sense."

"Indeed it doesn't," Halleck said.

Jessica saw the near perfection of the girl's act, realized: *That empty-headed little female is not an empty-headed little female.* She saw then the pattern of the threat and understood that Halleck, too, had detected it. They had planned to lure Paul with sex. Jessica relaxed. Her son had probably been the first to see it—his training hadn't overlooked that obvious gambit.

Kynes spoke to the banker: "Isn't another apology in order?"

The banker turned a sickly grin toward Jessica, said: "My Lady, I fear I've overindulged in your wines. You serve potent drink at table, and I'm not accustomed to it."

Jessica heard the venom beneath his tone, spoke sweetly: "When strangers meet, great allowance should be made for differences of custom and training."

"Thank you, my Lady," he said.

The dark-haired companion of the stillsuit manufacturer leaned toward Jessica, said: "The Duke spoke of our being secure here. I do hope that doesn't mean more fighting."

She was directed to lead the conversation this way, Jessica thought.

"Likely this will prove unimportant," Jessica said. "But there's so much detail requiring the Duke's personal attention in these times. As long as enmity continues between Atreides and Harkonnen we cannot be too careful. The Duke has sworn kanly. He will leave no Harkonnen agent alive on Arrakis, of course." She glanced at the Guild Bank agent. "And the Conventions, naturally, support him in this." She shifted her attention to Kynes. "Is this not so, Dr. Kynes?"

"Indeed it is," Kynes said.

The stillsuit manufacturer pulled his companion gently back. She looked at him, said: "I do believe I'll eat something now. I'd like some of that bird dish you served earlier."

Jessica signaled a servant, turned to the banker: "And you, sir, were speaking of birds earlier and of their habits. I find so many interesting things about Arrakis. Tell me, where is the spice found? Do the hunters go deep into the desert?"

"Oh, no, my Lady," he said. "Very little's known of the deep desert. And almost nothing of the southern regions."

"There's a tale that a great Mother Lode of spice is to be found in the southern reaches," Kynes said, "but I suspect it was an imaginative invention made solely for purposes of a song. Some daring spice hunters do, on occasion, penetrate into the edge of the central belt, but that's extremely dangerous—navigation is uncertain, storms are frequent. Casualties increase dramatically the farther you operate from Shield Wall bases. It hasn't been found profitable to venture too far south. Perhaps if we had a weather satellite. . . ."

Bewt looked up, spoke around a mouthful of food: "It's said the Fremen travel there, that they go anywhere and have hunted out soaks and sip-wells even in the southern latitudes."

"Soaks and sip-wells?" Jessica asked.

Kynes spoke quickly: "Wild rumors, my Lady. These are known on other planets, not on Arrakis. A soak is a place where water seeps to the surface or near enough to the surface to be found by digging according to certain signs. A sip-well is a form of soak where a person draws water through a straw . . . so it is said."

There's deception in his words, Jessica thought.

Why is he lying? Paul wondered.

"How very interesting," Jessica said. And she thought: *"It is said. . . ." What a curious speech mannerism they have here. If they only knew what it reveals about their dependence on superstitions.*

"I've heard you have a saying," Paul said, "that polish comes from the cities, wisdom from the desert."

"There are many sayings on Arrakis," Kynes said.

Before Jessica could frame a new question, a servant bent over her with a note. She opened it, saw the Duke's handwriting and code signs, scanned it.

"You'll all be delighted to know," she said, "that our Duke sends his reassurances. The matter which called him away has been settled. The missing carryall has been found. A Harkonnen agent in the crew overpowered the others and flew the machine to a smugglers' base, hoping to sell it there. Both man and machine were turned over to our forces." She nodded to Tuek.

The smuggler nodded back.

Jessica refolded the note, tucked it into her sleeve.

"I'm glad it didn't come to open battle," the banker said. "The people have such hopes the Atreides will bring peace and prosperity."

"Especially prosperity," Bewt said.

"Shall we have our dessert now?" Jessica asked. "I've had our chef prepare a Caladan sweet: pongi rice in sauce dolsa."

"It sounds wonderful," the stillsuit manufacturer said. "Would it be possible to get the recipe?"

"Any recipe you desire," Jessica said, *registering* the man for later mention to Hawat. The stillsuit manufacturer was a fearful little climber and could be bought.

Small talk resumed around her: "Such a lovely fabric. . . ." "He is having a setting made to match the jewel. . . ." "We might try for a production increase next quarter. . . ."

Jessica stared down at her plate, thinking of the coded part of Leto's message: *The Harkonnens tried to get in a shipment of lasguns. We captured them. This may mean they've succeeded with other shipments. It certainly means they don't place much store in shields. Take appropriate precautions.*

Jessica focused her mind on lasguns, wondering. The white-hot beams of disruptive light could cut through any known substance, provided that substance was not shielded. The fact that feedback from a shield would explode both lasgun and shield did not bother the Harkonnens. Why? A lasgun-shield explosion was a dangerous variable, could be more powerful than atomics, could kill only the gunner and his shielded target.

The unknowns here filled her with uneasiness.

Paul said: "I never doubted we'd find the carryall. Once my father moves to solve a problem, he solves it. This is a fact the Harkonnens are beginning to discover."

He's boasting, Jessica thought. *He shouldn't boast. No person who'll be sleeping far below ground level this night as a precaution against lasguns has the right to boast.*

There is no escape—we pay for the violence of our ancestors.

—FROM "COLLECTED SAYINGS OF MUAD'DIB"
BY THE PRINCESS IRULAN

Jessica heard the disturbance in the Great Hall, turned on the light beside her bed. The clock there had not been properly adjusted to local time, and she had to subtract twenty-one minutes to determine that it was about 2 A.M.

The disturbance was loud and incoherent.

Is this the Harkonnen attack? she wondered.

She slipped out of bed, checked the screen monitors to see where her family was. The screen showed Paul asleep in the deep cellar room they'd hastily converted to a bedroom for him. The noise obviously wasn't penetrating to his quarters. There was no one in the Duke's room, his bed was unrumpled. Was he still at the field C.P.?

There were no screens yet to the front of the house.

Jessica stood in the middle of her room, listening.

There was one shouting, incoherent voice. She heard someone call for Dr. Yueh. Jessica found a robe, pulled it over her shoulders, pushed her feet into slippers, strapped the crysknife to her leg.

Again, a voice called out for Yueh.

Jessica belted the robe around her, stepped into the hallway. Then the thought struck her: *What if Leto's hurt?*

The hall seemed to stretch out forever under her running feet. She turned through the arch at the end, dashed past the dining hall and down the passage to the Great Hall, finding the place brightly lighted, all the wall suspensors glowing at maximum.

To her right near the front entry, she saw two house guards holding Duncan Idaho between them. His head lolled forward, and there was an abrupt, panting silence to the scene.

One of the house guards spoke accusingly to Idaho: "You see what you did? You woke the Lady Jessica."

The great draperies billowed behind the men, showing that the front door remained open. There was no sign of the Duke or Yueh. Mapes stood to one side staring coldly at Idaho. She wore a long brown robe with serpentine design at the hem. Her feet were pushed into unlaced desert boots.

"So I woke the Lady Jessica," Idaho muttered. He lifted his face toward the ceiling, bellowed: "My sword was firs' blooded on Grumman!"

Great Mother! He's drunk! Jessica thought.

Idaho's dark, round face was drawn into a frown. His hair, curling like the fur of a black goat, was plastered with dirt. A jagged rent in his tunic exposed an expanse of the dress shirt he had worn at the dinner party earlier.

Jessica crossed to him.

One of the guards nodded to her without releasing his hold on Idaho. "We didn't know what to do with him, my Lady. He was creating a disturbance out front, refusing to come inside. We were afraid locals might come along and see him. That wouldn't do at all. Give us a bad name here."

"Where has he been?" Jessica asked.

"He escorted one of the young ladies home from the dinner, my Lady. Hawat's orders."

"Which young lady?"

"One of the escort wenches. You understand, my Lady?" He glanced at Mapes, lowered his voice. "They're always calling on Idaho for special surveillance of the ladies."

And Jessica thought: *So they are. But why is he drunk?*

She frowned, turned to Mapes. "Mapes, bring a stimulant. I'd suggest caffeine. Perhaps there's some of the spice coffee left."

Mapes shrugged, headed for the kitchen. Her unlaced desert boots slap-slapped against the stone floor.

Idaho swung his unsteady head around to peer at an angle toward Jessica. "Killed more'n three hunner' men f'r the Duke," he muttered. "Whadduh wanna know is why'm mere? Can't live unner th' groun' here. Can't live onna groun' here. Wha' kinna place is 'iss, huh?"

A sound from the side hall entry caught Jessica's attention. She turned, saw Yueh crossing to them, his medical kit swinging in his left hand. He was fully dressed, looked pale, exhausted. The diamond tattoo stood out sharply on his forehead.

"Th' good docker!" Idaho shouted. "Whad're you, Doc? Splint 'n' pill man?" He turned blearily toward Jessica. "Makin' uh damn fool uh m'self, huh?"

Jessica frowned, remained silent, wondering: *Why would Idaho get drunk? Was he drugged?*

"Too much spice beer," Idaho said, attempting to straighten.

Mapes returned with a steaming cup in her hands, stopped uncertainly behind Yueh. She looked at Jessica, who shook her head.

Yueh put his kit on the floor, nodded greeting to Jessica, said: "Spice beer, eh?"

"Bes' damn stuff ever tas'ed," Idaho said. He tried to pull himself to attention. "My sword was firs' blooded on Grumman! Killed a Harkon . . . Harkon . . . killed 'im f'r th' Duke."

Yueh turned, looked at the cup in Mapes' hand. "What is that?"

"Caffeine," Jessica said.

Yueh took the cup, held it toward Idaho. "Drink this, lad."

"Don't wan' any more t' drink."

"Drink it, I say!"

Idaho's head wobbled toward Yueh, and he stumbled one step ahead, dragging the guards with him. "I'm almighdy fed up with pleasin' th' 'Mperial Universe, Doc. Jus' once, we're gonna do th' thing my way."

"After you drink this," Yueh said. "It's just caffeine."

"'Sprolly like all res' uh this place! Damn sun 'stoo brighd. Nothin' has uh righd color. Ever'thing's wrong or. . . ."

"Well, it's nighttime now," Yueh said. He spoke reasonably. "Drink this like a good lad. It'll make you feel better."

"Don' wanna feel bedder!"

"We can't argue with him all night," Jessica said. And she thought: *This calls for shock treatment.*

"There's no reason for you to stay, my Lady," Yueh said. "I can take care of this."

Jessica shook her head. She stepped forward, slapped Idaho sharply across the cheek.

He stumbled back with his guards, glaring at her.

"This is no way to act in your Duke's home," she said. She snatched the cup from Yueh's hands, spilling part of it, thrust the cup toward Idaho. "Now drink this! That's an order!"

Idaho jerked himself upright, scowling down at her. He spoke slowly, with careful and precise enunciation: "I do not take orders from a damn Harkonnen spy."

Yueh stiffened, whirled to face Jessica.

Her face had gone pale, but she was nodding. It all became clear to her—the broken stems of meaning she had seen in words and actions around her these past few days could now be translated. She found herself in the grip of anger almost too great to contain. It took the most profound of her Bene Gesserit training to quiet her pulse and smooth her breathing. Even then she could feel the blaze flickering.

They were always calling on Idaho for surveillance of the ladies!

She shot a glance at Yueh. The doctor lowered his eyes.

"You knew this?" she demanded.

"I . . . heard rumors, my Lady. But I didn't want to add to your burdens."

"Hawat!" she snapped. "I want Thufir Hawat brought to me immediately!"

"But, my Lady. . . ."

"Immediately!"

It has to be Hawat, she thought. *Suspicion such as this could come from no other source without being discarded immediately.*

Idaho shook his head, mumbled: "Chuck th' whole damn thing."

Jessica looked down at the cup in her hand, abruptly dashed its contents across Idaho's face. "Lock him in one of the guest rooms of the east wing," she ordered. "Let him *sleep* it off."

The two guards stared at her unhappily. One ventured: "Perhaps we should take him someplace else, m'Lady. We could. . . ."

"He's supposed to be here!" Jessica snapped. "He has a job to do here." Her voice dripped bitterness. "He's so good at watching the ladies."

The guard swallowed.

"Do you know where the Duke is?" she demanded.

"He's at the command post, my Lady."

"Is Hawat with him?"

"Hawat's in the city, my Lady."

"You will bring Hawat to me at once," Jessica said. "I will be in my sitting room when he arrives."

"But, my Lady. . . ."

"If necessary, I will call the Duke," she said. "I hope it will not be necessary. I would not want to disturb him with this."

"Yes, my Lady."

Jessica thrust the empty cup into Mapes' hands, met the questioning stare of the blue-within-blue eyes. "You may return to bed, Mapes."

"You're sure you'll not need me?"

Jessica smiled grimly. "I'm sure."

"Perhaps this could wait until tomorrow," Yueh said. "I could give you a sedative and. . . ."

"You will return to your quarters and leave me to handle this my way," she said. She patted his arm to take the sting out of her command. "This is the only way."

Abruptly, head high, she turned and stalked off through the house to her rooms. Cold walls . . . passages . . . a familiar door. . . . She jerked the door open, strode in, and slammed it behind her. Jessica stood there glaring at the shield-blanked windows of her sitting room. *Hawat! Could he be the one the Harkonnens bought? We shall see.*

Jessica crossed to the deep, old-fashioned armchair with an embroidered cover of schlag skin, moved the chair into position to command the door. She was suddenly very conscious of the crysknife in its sheath on her leg. She removed the sheath and strapped it to her arm, tested the drop of it. Once more, she glanced around the room, placing everything precisely in her mind against any emergency: the chaise near the corner, the straight chairs along the wall, the two low tables, her stand-mounted zither beside the door to her bedroom.

Pale rose light glowed from the suspensor lamps. She dimmed them, sat down in the armchair, patting the upholstery, appreciating the chair's regal heaviness for this occasion.

Now, let him come, she thought. *We shall see what we shall see.* And she prepared herself in the Bene Gesserit fashion for the wait, accumulating patience, saving her strength.

Sooner than she had expected, a rap sounded at the door and Hawat entered at her command.

She watched him without moving from the chair, seeing the crackling sense of drug-induced energy in his movements, seeing the fatigue beneath. Hawat's rheumy old eyes glittered. His leathery skin appeared faintly yellow in the room's light, and there was a wide, wet stain on the sleeve of his knife arm.

She smelled blood there.

Jessica gestured to one of the straight-backed chairs, said: "Bring that chair and sit facing me."

Hawat bowed, obeyed. *That drunken fool of an Idaho!* he thought. He studied Jessica's face, wondering how he could save this situation.

"It's long past time to clear the air between us," Jessica said.

"What troubles my Lady?" He sat down, placed hands on knees.

"Don't play coy with me!" she snapped. "If Yueh didn't tell you why I summoned you, then one of your spies in my household did. Shall we be at least that honest with each other?"

"As you wish, my Lady."

"First, you will answer me one question," she said. "Are you now a Harkonnen agent?"

Hawat surged half out of his chair, his face dark with fury, demanding: "You dare insult me so?"

"Sit down," she said. "You insulted me so."

Slowly, he sank back into the chair.

And Jessica, reading the signs of this face that she knew so well, allowed herself a deep breath. *It isn't Hawat.*

"Now I know you remain loyal to my Duke," she said. "I'm prepared, therefore, to forgive your affront to me."

"Is there something to forgive?"

Jessica scowled, wondering: *Shall I play my trump? Shall I tell him of the Duke's daughter I've carried within me these few weeks? No . . . Leto himself doesn't know. This would only complicate his life, divert him in a time when he must concentrate on our survival. There is yet time to use this.*

"A Truthsayer would solve this," she said, "but we have no Truthsayer qualified by the High Board."

"As you say. We've no Truthsayer."

"Is there a traitor among us?" she asked. "I've studied our people with great care. Who could it be? Not Gurney. Certainly not Duncan. *Their* lieutenants are not strategically enough placed to consider. It's not you, Thufir. It cannot be Paul. I *know* it's not me. Dr. Yueh, then? Shall I call him in and put him to the test?"

"You know that's an empty gesture," Hawat said. "He's conditioned by the High College. *That* I know for certain."

"Not to mention that his wife was a Bene Gesserit slain by the Harkonnens," Jessica said.

"So that's what happened to her," Hawat said.

"Haven't you heard the hate in his voice when he speaks the Harkonnen name?"

"You know I don't have the ear," Hawat said.

"What brought this base suspicion on me?" she asked.

Hawat frowned. "My Lady puts her servant in an impossible position. My first loyalty is to the Duke."

"I'm prepared to forgive much because of that loyalty," she said.

"And again I must ask: Is there something to forgive?"

"Stalemate?" she asked.

He shrugged.

"Let us discuss something else for a minute, then," she said. "Duncan Idaho, the admirable fighting man whose abilities at guarding and surveillance are so esteemed. Tonight, he overindulged in something called spice beer. I hear reports that others among our people have been stupefied by this concoction. Is that true?"

"You have your reports, my Lady."

"So I do. Don't you see this drinking as a symptom, Thufir?"

"My Lady speaks riddles."

"Apply your Mentat abilities to it!" she snapped. "What's the problem with Duncan and the others? I can tell you in four words—they have no home."

He jabbed a finger at the floor. "Arrakis, that's their home."

"Arrakis is an unknown! Caladan was their home, but we've uprooted them. They have no home. And they fear the Duke's failing them."

He stiffened. "Such talk from one of the men would be cause for—"

"Oh, stop that, Thufir. Is it defeatist or treacherous for a doctor to diagnose a disease correctly? My only intention is to cure the disease."

"The Duke gives me charge over such matters."

"But you understand I have a certain natural concern over the progress of this disease," she said. "And perhaps you'll grant I have certain abilities along these lines."

Will I have to shock him severely? she wondered. *He needs shaking up—something to break him from routine.*

"There could be many interpretations for your concern," Hawat said. He shrugged.

"Then you've already convicted me?"

"Of course not, my Lady. But I cannot afford to take *any* chances, the situation being what it is."

"A threat to my son got past you right here in this house," she said. "Who took that chance?"

His face darkened. "I offered my resignation to the Duke."

"Did you offer your resignation to me . . . or to Paul?"

Now he was openly angry, betraying it in quickness of breathing, in dilation of nostrils, a steady stare. She saw a pulse beating at his temple.

"I'm the Duke's man," he said, biting off the words.

"There is no traitor," she said. "The threat's something else. Perhaps it has to do with the lasguns. Perhaps they'll risk secreting a few lasguns with timing mechanisms aimed at house shields. Perhaps they'll. . . ."

"And who could tell after the blast if the explosion wasn't atomic?" he asked. "No, my Lady. They'll not risk anything *that* illegal. Radiation lingers. The evidence is hard to erase. No. They'll observe *most* of the forms. It has to be a traitor."

"You're the Duke's man," she sneered. "Would you destroy him in the effort to save him?"

He took a deep breath, then: "If you're innocent, you'll have my most abject apologies."

"Look at you now, Thufir," she said. "Humans live best when each has his own place, when each knows where he belongs in the scheme of things. Destroy the place and destroy the person. You and I, Thufir, of all those who love the Duke, are most ideally situated to destroy the other's place. Could I not whisper suspicions about you into the Duke's ear at night? When would he be most susceptible to such whispering, Thufir? Must I draw it for you more clearly?"

"You threaten me?" he growled.

"Indeed not. I merely point out to you that someone is attacking us through the basic arrangement of our lives. It's clever, diabolical. I propose to negate this attack by so ordering our lives that there'll be no chinks for such barbs to enter."

"You accuse me of whispering baseless suspicions?"

"Baseless, yes."

"You'd meet this with your own whispers?"

"*Your* life is compounded of whispers, not mine, Thufir."

"Then you question my abilities?"

She sighed. "Thufir, I want you to examine your own emotional involvement in this. The *natural* human's an animal without logic. Your projections of logic onto all affairs is *un*natural, but suffered to continue for its usefulness. You're the embodiment of logic—a Mentat. Yet, your problem solutions are concepts that, in a very real sense, are projected outside yourself, there to be studied and rolled around, examined from all sides."

"You think now to teach me my trade?" he asked, and he did not try to hide the disdain in his voice.

"Anything outside yourself, this you can see and apply your logic to it," she said. "But it's a human trait that when we encounter personal problems, those things most deeply personal are the most difficult to bring out for our logic to scan. We tend to flounder around, blaming everything but the actual, deep-seated thing that's really chewing on us."

"You're deliberately attempting to undermine my faith in my abilities as a Mentat," he rasped. "Were I to find one of our people attempting thus to sabotage any other weapon in our arsenal, I should not hesitate to denounce and destroy him."

"The finest Mentats have a healthy respect for the error factor in their computations," she said.

"I've never said otherwise!"

"Then apply yourself to these symptoms we've both seen: drunkenness among the men, quarrels—they gossip and exchange wild rumors about Arrakis; they ignore the most simple—"

"Idleness, no more," he said. "Don't try to divert my attention by trying to make a simple matter appear mysterious."

She stared at him, thinking of the Duke's men rubbing their woes together in the barracks until you could almost smell the charge there, like burnt insulation. *They're becoming like the men of the pre-Guild legend,* she thought: *Like the men of the lost star-searcher, Ampoliros—sick at their guns—forever seeking, forever prepared and forever unready.*

"Why have you never made full use of my abilities in your service to the Duke?" she asked. "Do you fear a rival for *your* position?"

He glared at her, the old eyes blazing. "I know some of the training they give you Bene Gesserit. . . ." He broke off, scowling.

"Go ahead, say it," she said. "Bene Gesserit *witches*."

"I know something of the *real* training they give you," he said. "I've seen it come out in Paul. I'm not fooled by what your schools tell the public: you exist only to serve."

The shock must be severe and he's almost ready for it, she thought.

"You listen respectfully to me in Council," she said, "yet you seldom heed my advice. Why?"

"I don't trust your Bene Gesserit motives," he said. "You may think you can look through a man; you may *think* you can make a man do exactly what you—"

"You poor *fool*, Thufir!" she raged.

He scowled, pushing himself back in the chair.

"Whatever rumors you've heard about our schools," she said, "the truth is far greater. If I wished to destroy the Duke . . . or you, or any other person within my reach, you could not stop me."

And she thought: *Why do I let pride drive such words out of me? This is not the way I was trained. This is not how I must shock him.*

Hawat slipped a hand beneath his tunic where he kept a tiny projector of poison darts. *She wears no shield*, he thought. *Is this just a brag she makes? I could slay her now . . . but, ah-h-h-h, the consequences if I'm wrong.*

Jessica saw the gesture toward his pocket, said: "Let us pray violence shall never be necessary between us."

"A worthy prayer," he agreed.

"Meanwhile, the sickness spreads among us," she said. "I must ask you again: Isn't it more reasonable to suppose the Harkonnens have planted this suspicion to pit the two of us against each other?"

"We appear to've returned to stalemate," he said.

She sighed, thinking: *He's almost ready for it.*

"The Duke and I are father and mother surrogates to our people," she said. "The position—"

"He hasn't married you," Hawat said.

She forced herself to calmness, thinking: *A good riposte, that.*

"But he'll not marry anyone else," she said. "Not as long as I live. And we are surrogates, as I've said. To break up this natural order in our affairs, to disturb, disrupt, and confuse us—which target offers itself most enticingly to the Harkonnens?"

He sensed the direction she was taking, and his brows drew down in a lowering scowl.

"The Duke?" she asked. "Attractive target, yes, but no one with the possible exception of Paul is better guarded. Me? I tempt them, surely, but they must know the Bene Gesserit make difficult targets. And there's a better target, one whose duties create, necessarily, a monstrous blind spot. One to whom suspicion is as natural as breathing. One who builds his entire life on innuendo and mystery." She darted her right hand toward him. "You!"

Hawat started to leap from his chair.

"I have not dismissed you, Thufir!" she flared.

The old Mentat almost fell back into the chair, so quickly did his muscles betray him.

She smiled without mirth.

"Now you know something of the *real* training they give us," she said.

Hawat tried to swallow in a dry throat. Her command had been regal, peremptory—uttered in a tone and manner he had found completely irresistible. His body had obeyed her before he could think about it. Nothing could have prevented his response—not logic, not passionate anger . . . nothing. To do what she had done spoke of a sensitive, intimate knowledge of the person thus commanded, a depth of control he had not dreamed possible.

"I have said to you before that we should understand each other," she said. "I meant *you* should understand *me*. I already understand you. And I tell you now that your loyalty to the Duke is all that guarantees your safety with me."

He stared at her, wet his lips with his tongue.

"If I desired a puppet, the Duke would marry me," she said. "He might even think he did it of his own free will."

Hawat lowered his head, looked upward through his sparse lashes. Only the most rigid control kept him from calling the guard. Control . . . and the suspicion now that the woman might not permit it. His skin crawled with the memory of how she had controlled him. In the moment of hesitation, she could have drawn a weapon and killed him!

Does every human have this blind spot? he wondered. *Can any of us be ordered into action before he can resist?* The idea staggered him. *Who could stop a person with such power?*

"You've glimpsed the fist within the Bene Gesserit glove," she said. "Few glimpse it and live. And what I did was a relatively simple thing for us. You've not seen my entire arsenal. Think on that."

"Why aren't you out destroying the Duke's enemies?" he asked.

"What would you have me destroy?" she asked. "Would you have me make a weakling of our Duke, have him forever leaning on me?"

"But, with such power. . . ."

"Power's a two-edged sword, Thufir," she said. "You think: 'How easy for her to shape a human tool to thrust into an enemy's vitals.' True, Thufir; even into your vitals. Yet, what would I accomplish? If enough of us Bene Gesserit did this, wouldn't it make all Bene Gesserit suspect? We don't want that, Thufir. We do not wish to destroy ourselves." She nodded. "We truly exist only to serve."

"I cannot answer you," he said. "You know I cannot answer."

"You'll say nothing about what has happened here to anyone," she said. "I know you, Thufir."

"My Lady. . . ." Again the old man tried to swallow in a dry throat. And he thought: *She has great powers, yes. But would these not make her an even more formidable tool for the Harkonnens?*

"The Duke could be destroyed as quickly by his friends as by his enemies," she said. "I trust now you'll get to the bottom of this suspicion and remove it."

"If it proves baseless," he said.

"*If*," she sneered.

"If," he said.

"You *are* tenacious," she said.

"Cautious," he said, "and aware of the error factor."

"Then I'll pose another question for you: What does it mean to you that you stand before another human, that you are bound and helpless and the other human holds a knife at your throat—yet this other human refrains from killing you, frees you from your bonds and gives you the knife to use as you will?"

She lifted herself out of the chair, turned her back on him. "You may go now, Thufir."

The old Mentat arose, hesitated, hand creeping toward the deadly weapon beneath his tunic. He was reminded of the bull ring and of the Duke's father (who'd been brave, no matter what his other failings) and one day of the *corrida* long ago: The fierce black beast had stood there, head bowed, immobilized and confused. The Old Duke had turned his back on the horns, cape thrown flamboyantly over one arm, while cheers rained down from the stands.

I am the bull and she the matador, Hawat thought. He withdrew his hand from the weapon, glanced at the sweat glistening in his empty palm.

And he knew that whatever the facts proved to be in the end, he would never forget this moment nor lose this sense of supreme admiration for the Lady Jessica.

Quietly, he turned and left the room.

Jessica lowered her gaze from the reflection in the windows, turned, and stared at the closed door.

"Now we'll see some proper action," she whispered.

Do you wrestle with dreams?
Do you contend with shadows?
Do you move in a kind of sleep?
Time has slipped away.
Your life is stolen.
You tarried with trifles,
Victim of your folly.

—DIRGE FOR JAMIS ON THE FUNERAL PLAIN,
FROM "SONGS OF MUAD'DIB"
BY THE PRINCESS IRULAN

Leto stood in the foyer of his house, studying a note by the light of a single suspensor lamp. Dawn was yet a few hours away, and he felt his tiredness. A Fremen messenger had brought the note to the outer guard just now as the Duke arrived from his command post.

The note read: "A column of smoke by day, a pillar of fire by night." There was no signature.

What does it mean? he wondered.

The messenger had gone without waiting for an answer and before he could be questioned. He had slipped into the night like some smoky shadow.

Leto pushed the paper into a tunic pocket, thinking to show it to Hawat later. He brushed a lock of hair from his forehead, took a sighing breath. The antifatigue pills were beginning to wear thin. It had been a

long two days since the dinner party and longer than that since he had
slept.

On top of all the military problems, there'd been the disquieting
session with Hawat, the report on his meeting with Jessica.

Should I waken Jessica? he wondered. *There's no reason to play the
secrecy game with her any longer. Or is there?*

Blast and damn that Duncan Idaho!

He shook his head. *No, not Duncan. I was wrong not to take Jessica
into my confidence from the first. I must do it now, before more damage
is done.*

The decision made him feel better, and he hurried from the foyer
through the Great Hall and down the passages toward the family wing.

At the turn where the passages split to the service area, he paused.
A strange mewling came from somewhere down the service passage.
Leto put his left hand to the switch on his shield belt, slipped his kindjal
into his right hand. The knife conveyed a sense of reassurance. That
strange sound had sent a chill through him.

Softly, the Duke moved down the service passage, cursing the inadequate illumination. The smallest of suspensors had been spaced about
eight meters apart along here and tuned to their dimmest level. The
dark stone walls swallowed the light.

A dull blob stretching across the floor appeared out of the gloom
ahead.

Leto hesitated, almost activated his shield, but refrained because
that would limit his movements, his hearing . . . and because the captured shipment of lasguns had left him filled with doubts.

Silently, he moved toward the gray blob, saw that it was a human
figure, a man face down on the stone. Leto turned him over with a foot,
knife poised, bent close in the dim light to see the face. It was the smuggler, Tuek, a wet stain down his chest. The dead eyes stared with empty
darkness. Leto touched the stain—warm.

How could this man be dead here? Leto asked himself. *Who killed
him?*

The mewling sound was louder here. It came from ahead and down the side passage to the central room where they had installed the main shield generator for the house.

Hand on belt switch, kindjal poised, the Duke skirted the body, slipped down the passage and peered around the corner toward the shield generator room.

Another gray blob lay stretched on the floor a few paces away, and he saw at once this was the source of the noise. The shape crawled toward him with painful slowness, gasping, mumbling.

Leto stilled his sudden constriction of fear, darted down the passage, crouched beside the crawling figure. It was Mapes, the Fremen housekeeper, her hair tumbled around her face, clothing disarrayed. A dull shininess of dark stain spread from her back along her side. He touched her shoulder and she lifted herself on her elbows, head tipped up to peer at him, the eyes black-shadowed emptiness.

"S'you," she gasped. "Killed . . . guard . . . sent . . . get . . . Tuek . . . escape . . . m'Lady . . . you . . . you . . . here . . . no. . . ." She flopped forward, her head thumping against the stone.

Leto felt for pulse at the temples. There was none. He looked at the stain: she'd been stabbed in the back. Who? His mind raced. Did she mean someone had killed a guard? And Tuek—had Jessica sent for him? Why?

He started to stand up. A sixth sense warned him. He flashed a hand toward the shield switch—too late. A numbing shock slammed his arm aside. He felt pain there, saw a dart protruding from the sleeve, sensed paralysis spreading from it up his arm. It took an agonizing effort to lift his head and look down the passage.

Yueh stood in the open door of the generator room. His face reflected yellow from the light of a single, brighter suspensor above the door. There was stillness from the room behind him—no sound of generators.

Yueh! Leto thought. *He's sabotaged the house generators! We're wide open!*

Yueh began walking toward him, pocketing a dartgun.

Leto found he could still speak, gasped: "Yueh! How?" Then the paralysis reached his legs and he slid to the floor with his back propped against the stone wall.

Yueh's face carried a look of sadness as he bent over, touched Leto's forehead. The Duke found he could feel the touch, but it was remote . . . dull.

"The drug on the dart is selective," Yueh said. "You can speak, but I'd advise against it." He glanced down the hall, and again bent over Leto, pulled out the dart, tossed it aside. The sound of the dart clattering on the stones was faint and distant to the Duke's ears.

It can't be Yueh, Leto thought. *He's conditioned.*

"How?" Leto whispered.

"I'm sorry, my dear Duke, but there *are* things which will make greater demands than this." He touched the diamond tattoo on his forehead. "I find it very strange, myself—an override on my pyretic conscience—but I wish to kill a man. Yes, I actually wish it. I will stop at nothing to do it."

He looked down at the Duke. "Oh, not you, my dear Duke. The Baron Harkonnen. I wish to kill the Baron."

"Bar . . . on Har. . . ."

"Be quiet, please, my poor Duke. You haven't much time. That peg tooth I put in your mouth after the tumble at Narcal—that tooth must be replaced. In a moment, I'll render you unconscious and replace that tooth." He opened his hand, stared at something in it. "An exact duplicate, its core shaped most exquisitely like a nerve. It'll escape the usual detectors, even a fast scanning. But if you bite down hard on it, the cover crushes. Then, when you expel your breath sharply, you fill the air around you with a poison gas—most deadly."

Leto stared up at Yueh, seeing madness in the man's eyes, the perspiration along brow and chin.

"You were dead anyway, my poor Duke," Yueh said. "But you will get close to the Baron before you die. He'll believe you're stupefied by drugs beyond any dying effort to attack him. And you will be drugged—and tied. But attack can take strange forms. And *you* will remember the tooth. The *tooth*, Duke Leto Atreides. You will remember the tooth."

The old doctor leaned closer and closer until his face and drooping mustache dominated Leto's narrowing vision.

"The tooth," Yueh muttered.

"Why?" Leto whispered.

Yueh lowered himself to one knee beside the Duke. "I made a shaitan's bargain with the Baron. And I must be certain he has fulfilled his half of it. When I see him, I'll know. When I look at the Baron, then I *will* know. But I'll never enter his presence without the price. You're the price, my poor Duke. And I'll know when I see him. My poor Wanna taught me many things, and one is to see certainty of truth when the stress is great. I cannot do it always, but when I see the Baron—then, I *will* know."

Leto tried to look down at the tooth in Yueh's hand. He felt this was happening in a nightmare—it could not be.

Yueh's purple lips turned up in a grimace. "I'll not get close enough to the Baron, or I'd do this myself. No. I'll be detained at a safe distance. But you . . . ah, now! You, my lovely weapon! He'll want you close to him—to gloat over you, to boast a little."

Leto found himself almost hypnotized by a muscle on the left side of Yueh's jaw. The muscle twisted when the man spoke.

Yueh leaned closer. "And you, my good Duke, my precious Duke, you must remember this tooth." He held it up between thumb and forefinger. "It will be all that remains to you."

Leto's mouth moved without sound, then: "Refuse."

"Ah-h, no! You mustn't refuse. Because, in return for this small service, I'm doing a thing for you. I will save your son and your woman. No other can do it. They can be removed to a place where no Harkonnen can reach them."

"How . . . save . . . them?" Leto whispered.

"By making it appear they're dead, by secreting them among people who draw knife at hearing the Harkonnen name, who hate the Harkonnens so much they'll burn a chair in which a Harkonnen has sat, salt the ground over which a Harkonnen has walked." He touched Leto's jaw. "Can you feel anything in your jaw?"

The Duke found that he could not answer. He sensed distant tugging, saw Yueh's hand come up with the ducal signet ring.

"For Paul," Yueh said. "You'll be unconscious presently. Goodbye, my poor Duke. When next we meet we'll have no time for conversation."

Cool remoteness spread upward from Leto's jaw, across his cheeks. The shadowy hall narrowed to a pinpoint with Yueh's purple lips centered in it.

"Remember the tooth!" Yueh hissed. "The tooth!"

There should be a science of discontent. People need hard times and oppression to develop psychic muscles.

—FROM "COLLECTED SAYINGS OF MUAD'DIB"
BY THE PRINCESS IRULAN

Jessica awoke in the dark, feeling premonition in the stillness around her. She could not understand why her mind and body felt so sluggish. Skin raspings of fear ran along her nerves. She thought of sitting up and turning on a light, but something stayed the decision. Her mouth felt . . . strange.

Lump-lump-lump-lump!

It was a dull sound, directionless in the dark. Somewhere.

The waiting moment was packed with time, with rustling needle-stick movements.

She began to feel her body, grew aware of bindings on wrists and ankles, a gag in her mouth. She was on her side, hands tied behind her. She tested the bindings, realized they were krimskell fiber, would only claw tighter as she pulled.

And now, she remembered.

There had been movement in the darkness of her bedroom, something wet and pungent slapped against her face, filling her mouth, hands grasping for her. She had gasped—one indrawn breath—sensing the narcotic in the wetness. Consciousness had receded, sinking her into a black bin of terror.

It has come, she thought. *How simple it was to subdue the Bene Gesserit. All it took was treachery. Hawat was right.*

She forced herself not to pull on her bindings.

This is not my bedroom, she thought. *They've taken me someplace else.*

Slowly, she marshaled the inner calmness.

She grew aware of the smell of her own stale sweat with its chemical infusion of fear.

Where is Paul? she asked herself. *My son—what have they done to him?*

Calmness.

She forced herself to it, using the ancient routines.

But terror remained so near.

Leto? Where are you, Leto?

She sensed a diminishing in the dark. It began with shadows. Dimensions separated, became new thorns of awareness. White. A line under a door.

I'm on the floor.

People walking. She sensed it through the floor.

Jessica squeezed back the memory of terror. *I must remain calm, alert, and prepared. I may get only one chance.* Again, she forced the inner calmness.

The ungainly thumping of her heartbeats evened, shaping out time. She counted back. *I was unconscious about an hour.* She closed her eyes, focused her awareness onto the approaching footsteps.

Four people.

She counted the differences in their steps.

I must pretend I'm still unconscious. She relaxed against the cold floor, testing her body's readiness, heard a door open, sensed increased light through her eyelids.

Feet approached: someone standing over her.

"You are awake," rumbled a basso voice. "Do not pretend."

She opened her eyes.

The Baron Vladimir Harkonnen stood over her. Around them, she recognized the cellar room where Paul had slept, saw his cot at one side—empty. Suspensor lamps were brought in by guards, distributed near the open door. There was a glare of light in the hallway beyond that hurt her eyes.

She looked up at the Baron. He wore a yellow cape that bulged over his portable suspensors. The fat cheeks were two cherubic mounds beneath spider-black eyes.

"The drug was timed," he rumbled. "We knew to the minute when you'd be coming out of it."

How could that be? she wondered. *They'd have to know my exact weight, my metabolism, my. . . . Yueh!*

"Such a pity you must remain gagged," the Baron said. "We could have such an interesting conversation."

Yueh's the only one it could be, she thought. *How?*

The Baron glanced behind him at the door. "Come in, Piter."

She had never before seen the man who entered to stand beside the Baron, but the face was known—and the man: *Piter de Vries, the Mentat-Assassin.* She studied him—hawk features, blue-ink eyes that suggested he was a native of Arrakis, but subtleties of movement and stance told her he was not. And his flesh was too well firmed with water. He was tall, though slender, and something about him suggested effeminacy.

"Such a pity we cannot have our conversation, my dear Lady Jessica," the Baron said. "However, I'm aware of your abilities." He glanced at the Mentat. "Isn't that true, Piter?"

"As you say, Baron," the man said.

The voice was tenor. It touched her spine with a wash of coldness. She had never heard such a chill voice. To one with the Bene Gesserit training, the voice screamed: *Killer!*

"I have a surprise for Piter," the Baron said. "He thinks he has come here to collect his reward—you, Lady Jessica. But I wish to demonstrate a thing: that he does not really want you."

"You play with me, Baron?" Piter asked, and he smiled.

Seeing that smile, Jessica wondered that the Baron did not leap to defend himself from this Piter. Then she corrected herself. The Baron could not read that smile. He did not have the Training.

"In many ways, Piter is quite naive," the Baron said. "He doesn't admit to himself what a deadly creature you are, Lady Jessica. I'd show him, but it'd be a foolish risk." The Baron smiled at Piter, whose face had become a waiting mask. "I know what Piter really wants. Piter wants power."

"You promised I could have *her*," Piter said. The tenor voice had lost some of its cold reserve.

Jessica heard the clue-tones in the man's voice, allowed herself an inward shudder. *How could the Baron have made such an animal out of a Mentat?*

"I give you a choice, Piter," the Baron said.

"What choice?"

The Baron snapped fat fingers. "This woman and exile from the Imperium, or the Duchy of Atreides on Arrakis to rule as you see fit in my name."

Jessica watched the Baron's spider eyes study Piter.

"You could be Duke here in all but name," the Baron said.

Is my Leto dead, then? Jessica asked herself. She felt a silent wail begin somewhere in her mind.

The Baron kept his attention on the Mentat. "Understand yourself, Piter. You want her because she was a Duke's woman, a symbol of his power—beautiful, useful, exquisitely trained for her role. But an entire duchy, Piter! That's more than a symbol; that's the reality. With it you could have many women . . . and more."

"You do not joke with Piter?"

The Baron turned with that dancing lightness the suspensors gave him. "Joke? I? Remember—*I* am giving up the boy. You heard what the traitor said about the lad's training. They are alike, this mother and son—deadly." The Baron smiled. "I must go now. I will send in the guard I've reserved for this moment. He's stone deaf. His orders will be to convey you on the first leg of your journey into exile. He will subdue this woman if he sees her gain control of you. He'll not permit you to untie her gag until you're off Arrakis. If you choose not to leave . . . he has other orders."

"You don't have to leave," Piter said. "I've chosen."

"Ah, hah!" the Baron chortled. "Such quick decision can mean only one thing."

"I will take the duchy," Piter said.

And Jessica thought: *Doesn't Piter know the Baron's lying to him? But—how could he know? He's a twisted Mentat.*

The Baron glanced down at Jessica. "Is it not wonderful that I know Piter so well? I wagered with my Master at Arms that this would be Piter's choice. Hah! Well, I leave now. This is much better. Ah-h, much better. You understand, Lady Jessica? I had no rancor toward you. It's a necessity. Much better this way. Yes. And I've not *actually* ordered you destroyed. When it's asked of me what happened to you, I can shrug it off in all truth."

"You leave it to me then?" Piter asked.

"The guard I send you will take your orders," the Baron said. "Whatever's done I leave to you." He stared at Piter. "Yes. There will be no blood on my hands here. It's your decision. Yes. I know nothing of it. You will wait until I've gone before doing whatever you must do. Yes. Well . . . ah, yes. Yes. Good."

He fears the questioning of a Truthsayer, Jessica thought. *Who? Ah-h-h, the Reverend Mother Gaius Helen, of course! If he knows he must face her questions, then the Emperor is in on this for sure. Ah-h-h-h, my poor Leto.*

With one last glance at Jessica, the Baron turned, went out the door. She followed him with her eyes, thinking: *It's as the Reverend Mother warned—too potent an adversary.*

Two Harkonnen troopers entered. Another, his face a scarred mask, followed and stood in the doorway with drawn lasgun.

The deaf one, Jessica thought, studying the scarred face. *The Baron knows I could use the Voice on any other man.*

Scarface looked at Piter. "We've the boy on a litter outside. What are your orders?"

Piter spoke to Jessica. "I'd thought of binding you by a threat held over your son, but I begin to see that would not have worked. I let emotion cloud reason. Bad policy for a Mentat." He looked at the first pair of troopers, turning so the deaf one could read his lips: "Take them into the desert as the traitor suggested for the boy. His plan is a good one. The worms will destroy all evidence. Their bodies must never be found."

"You don't wish to dispatch them yourself?" Scarface asked.

He reads lips, Jessica thought.

"I follow my Baron's example," Piter said. "Take them where the traitor said."

Jessica heard the harsh Mentat control in Piter's voice, thought: *He, too, fears the Truthsayer.*

Piter shrugged, turned, and went through the doorway. He hesitated there, and Jessica thought he might turn back for a last look at her, but he went out without turning.

"Me, I wouldn't like the thought of facing that Truthsayer after this night's work," Scarface said.

"You ain't likely ever to run into that old witch," one of the other troopers said. He went around to Jessica's head, bent over her. "It ain't getting our work done standing around here chattering. Take her feet and—"

"Why'n't we kill 'em here?" Scarface asked.

"Too messy," the first one said. "Unless you wants to strangle 'em. Me, I likes a nice straightforward job. Drop 'em on the desert like that traitor said, cut 'em once or twice, leave the evidence for the worms. Nothing to clean up afterwards."

"Yeah . . . well, I guess you're right," Scarface said.

Jessica listened to them, watching, registering. But the gag blocked her Voice, and there was the deaf one to consider.

Scarface holstered his lasgun, took her feet. They lifted her like a sack of grain, maneuvered her through the door and dumped her onto a suspensor-buoyed litter with another bound figure. As they turned her, fitting her to the litter, she saw her companion's face—Paul! He was bound, but not gagged. His face was no more than ten centimeters from hers, eyes closed, his breathing even.

Is he drugged? she wondered.

The troopers lifted the litter, and Paul's eyes opened the smallest fraction—dark slits staring at her.

He mustn't try the Voice! she prayed. *The deaf guard!*

Paul's eyes closed.

He had been practicing the awareness-breathing, calming his mind, listening to their captors. The deaf one posed a problem, but Paul contained his despair. The mind-calming Bene Gesserit regimen his mother had taught him kept him poised, ready to expand any opportunity.

Paul allowed himself another slit-eyed inspection of his mother's face. She appeared unharmed. Gagged, though.

He wondered who could've captured her. His own captivity was plain enough—to bed with a capsule prescribed by Yueh, awaking to find himself bound to this litter. Perhaps a similar thing had befallen her. Logic said the traitor was Yueh, but he held final decision in abeyance. There was no understanding it—a Suk doctor a traitor.

The litter tipped slightly as the Harkonnen troopers maneuvered it through a doorway into starlit night. A suspensor-buoy rasped against the doorway. Then they were on sand, feet grating in it. A 'thopter wing loomed overhead, blotting the stars. The litter settled to the ground.

Paul's eyes adjusted to the faint light. He recognized the deaf trooper as the man who opened the 'thopter door, peered inside at the green gloom illuminated by the instrument panel.

"This the 'thopter we're supposed to use?" he asked, and turned to watch his companion's lips.

"It's the one the traitor said was fixed for desert work," the other said.

Scarface nodded. "But—it's one of them little liaison jobs. Ain't room in there for more'n them an' two of us."

"Two's enough," said the litter-bearer, moving up close and presenting his lips for reading. "We can take care of it from here on, Kinet."

"The Baron, he told me to make sure what happened to them two," Scarface said.

"What you so worried about?" asked another trooper from behind the litter-bearer.

"She is a Bene Gesserit witch," the deaf one said. "They have powers."

"Ah-h-h. . . ." The litter-bearer made the sign of the fist at his ear. "One of them, eh? Know whatcha mean."

The trooper behind him grunted. "She'll be worm meat soon enough. Don't suppose even a Bene Gesserit witch has powers over one of them big worms. Eh, Czigo?" He nudged the litter-bearer.

"Yee-up," the litter-bearer said. He returned to the litter, took Jessica's shoulders. "C'mon, Kinet. You can go along if you wants to make sure what happens."

"It is nice of you to invite me, Czigo," Scarface said.

Jessica felt herself lifted, the wing shadow spinning—stars. She was pushed into the rear of the 'thopter, her *krimskell* fiber bindings examined, and she was strapped down. Paul was jammed in beside her, strapped securely, and she noted his bonds were simple rope.

Scarface, the deaf one they called Kinet, took his place in front. The litter-bearer, the one they called Czigo, came around and took the other front seat.

Kinet closed his door, bent to the controls. The 'thopter took off in a wing-tucked surge, headed south over the Shield Wall. Czigo tapped his companion's shoulder, said: "Whyn't you turn around and keep an eye on them two?"

"Sure you know the way to go?" Kinet watched Czigo's lips.

"I listened to the traitor same's you."

Kinet swiveled his seat. Jessica saw the glint of starlight on a lasgun in his hand. The 'thopter's light-walled interior seemed to collect illumination as her eyes adjusted, but the guard's scarred face remained dim. Jessica tested her seat belt, found it loose. She felt roughness in the strap against her left arm, realized the strap had been almost severed, would snap at a sudden jerk.

Has someone been at this 'thopter, preparing it for us? she wondered. *Who?* Slowly, she twisted her bound feet clear of Paul's.

"Sure do seem a shame to waste a good-looking woman like this," Scarface said. "You ever have any highborn types?" He turned to look at the pilot.

"Bene Gesserit ain't all highborn," the pilot said.

"But they all looks heighty."

He can see me plain enough, Jessica thought. She brought her bound legs up onto the seat, curled into a sinuous ball, staring at Scarface.

"Real pretty, she is," Kinet said. He wet his lips with his tongue. "Sure do seem a shame." He looked at Czigo.

"You thinking what I think you're thinking?" the pilot asked.

"Who'd be to know?" the guard asked. "Afterwards. . . ." He shrugged. "I just never had me no highborns. Might never get a chance like this one again."

"You lay a hand on my mother. . . ." Paul grated. He glared at Scarface.

"Hey!" the pilot laughed. "Cub's got a bark. Ain't got no bite, though."

And Jessica thought: *Paul's pitching his voice too high. It may work, though.*

They flew on in silence.

These poor fools, Jessica thought, studying her guards and reviewing the Baron's words. *They'll be killed as soon as they report success on their mission. The Baron wants no witnesses.*

The 'thopter banked over the southern rim of the Shield Wall, and Jessica saw a moonshadowed expanse of sand beneath them.

"This oughta be far enough," the pilot said. "The traitor said to put 'em on the sand anywhere near the Shield Wall." He dipped the craft toward the dunes in a long, falling stoop, brought it up stiffly over the desert surface.

Jessica saw Paul begin taking the rhythmic breaths of the calming exercise. He closed his eyes, opened them. Jessica stared, helpless to aid him. *He hasn't mastered the Voice yet*, she thought, *if he fails.* . . .

The 'thopter touched sand with a soft lurch, and Jessica, looking north back across the Shield Wall, saw a shadow of wings settle out of sight up there.

Someone's following us! she thought. *Who?* Then: *The ones the Baron set to watch this pair. And there'll be watchers for the watchers, too.*

Czigo shut off his wing rotors. Silence flooded in upon them.

Jessica turned her head. She could see out the window beyond Scar-face a dim glow of light from a rising moon, a frosted rim of rock rising from the desert. Sandblast ridges streaked its sides.

Paul cleared his throat.

The pilot said: "Now, Kinet?"

"I dunno, Czigo."

Czigo turned, said: "Ah-h-h, look." He reached out for Jessica's skirt.

"Remove her gag," Paul commanded.

Jessica felt the words rolling in the air. The tone, the timbre excellent—imperative, very sharp. A slightly lower pitch would have been better, but it could still fall within this man's spectrum.

Czigo shifted his hand up to the band around Jessica's mouth, slipped the knot on the gag.

"Stop that!" Kinet ordered.

"Ah, shut your trap," Czigo said. "Her hands're tied." He freed the knot and the binding dropped. His eyes glittered as he studied Jessica.

Kinet put a hand on the pilot's arm. "Look, Czigo, no need to. . . ."

Jessica twisted her neck, spat out the gag. She pitched her voice in low, intimate tones. "Gentlemen! No need to *fight* over me." At the same time, she writhed sinuously for Kinet's benefit.

She saw them grow tense, knowing that in this instant they were convinced of the need to fight over her. Their disagreement required no other reason. In their minds, they *were* fighting over her.

She held her face high in the instrument glow to be sure Kinet would read her lips, said: "You mustn't disagree." They drew farther apart, glanced warily at each other. "Is any woman worth fighting over?" she asked.

By uttering the words, by being there, she made herself infinitely worth their fighting.

Paul clamped his lips tightly closed, forced himself to be silent. There had been the one chance for him to succeed with the Voice. Now—everything depended on his mother whose experience went so far beyond his own.

"Yeah," Scarface said. "No need to fight over. . . ."

His hand flashed toward the pilot's neck. The blow was met by a splash of metal that caught the arm and in the same motion slammed into Kinet's chest.

Scarface groaned, sagged backward against his door.

"Thought I was some dummy didn't know that trick," Czigo said. He brought back his hand, revealing the knife. It glittered in reflected moonlight.

"Now for the cub," he said and leaned toward Paul.

"No need for that," Jessica murmured.

Czigo hesitated.

"Wouldn't you rather have me cooperative?" Jessica asked. "Give the boy a chance." Her lip curled in a sneer. "Little enough chance he'd have out there in that sand. Give him that and. . . ." She smiled. "You could find yourself well rewarded."

Czigo glanced left, right, returned his attention to Jessica. "I've heard me what can happen to a man in this desert," he said. "Boy might find the knife a kindness."

"Is it so much I ask?" Jessica pleaded.

"You're trying to trick me," Czigo muttered.

"I don't want to see my son die," Jessica said. "Is that a trick?"

Czigo moved back, elbowed the door latch. He grabbed Paul, dragged him across the seat, pushed him half out the door and held the knife posed. "What'll y' do, cub, if I cut y'r bonds?"

"He'll leave here immediately and head for those rocks," Jessica said.

"Is that what y'll do, cub?" Czigo asked.

Paul's voice was properly surly. "Yes."

The knife moved down, slashed the bindings of his legs. Paul felt the hand on his back to hurl him down onto the sand, feigned a lurch against the doorframe for purchase, turned as though to catch himself, lashed out with his right foot.

The toe was aimed with a precision that did credit to his long years of training, as though all of that training focused on this instant. Almost every muscle of his body cooperated in the placement of it. The tip struck the soft part of Czigo's abdomen just below the sternum, slammed upward with terrible force over the liver and through the diaphragm to crush the right ventricle of the man's heart.

With one gurgling scream, the guard jerked backward across the seats. Paul, unable to use his hands, continued his tumble onto the sand, landing with a roll that took up the force and brought him back to his feet in one motion. He dove back into the cabin, found the knife and held it in his teeth while his mother sawed her bonds. She took the blade and freed his hands.

"I could've handled him," she said. "He'd have had to cut my bindings. That was a foolish risk."

"I saw the opening and used it," he said.

She heard the harsh control in his voice, said: "Yueh's house sign is scrawled on the ceiling of this cabin."

He looked up, saw the curling symbol.

"Get out and let us study this craft," she said. "There's a bundle under the pilot's seat. I felt it when we got in."

"Bomb?"

"Doubt it. There's something peculiar here."

Paul leaped out to the sand and Jessica followed. She turned, reached under the seat for the strange bundle, seeing Czigo's feet close to her face, feeling dampness on the bundle as she removed it, realizing the dampness was the pilot's blood.

Waste of moisture, she thought, knowing that this was Arrakeen thinking.

Paul stared around them, saw the rock scarp lifting out of the desert like a beach rising from the sea, wind-carved palisades beyond. He turned back as his mother lifted the bundle from the 'thopter, saw her stare across the dunes toward the Shield Wall. He looked to see what drew her attention, saw another 'thopter swooping toward them, realized they'd not have time to clear the bodies out of this 'thopter and escape.

"Run, Paul!" Jessica shouted. "It's Harkonnens!"

Arrakis teaches the attitude of the knife—chopping off what's incomplete and saying: "Now, it's complete because it's ended here."

—FROM "COLLECTED SAYINGS OF MUAD'DIB"
BY THE PRINCESS IRULAN

A man in Harkonnen uniform skidded to a stop at the end of the hall, stared in at Yueh, taking in at a single glance Mapes' body, the sprawled form of the Duke, Yueh standing there. The man held a lasgun in his right hand. There was a casual air of brutality about him, a sense of toughness and poise that sent a shiver through Yueh.

Sardaukar, Yueh thought. *A Bashar by the look of him. Probably one of the Emperor's own sent here to keep an eye on things. No matter what the uniform, there's no disguising them.*

"You're Yueh," the man said. He looked speculatively at the Suk School ring on the Doctor's hair, stared once at the diamond tattoo and then met Yueh's eyes.

"I am Yueh," the Doctor said.

"You can relax, Yueh," the man said. "When you dropped the house shields we came right in. Everything's under control here. Is this the Duke?"

"This is the Duke."

"Dead?"

"Merely unconscious. I suggest you tie him."

"Did you do for these others?" He glanced back down the hall where Mapes' body lay.

"More's the pity," Yueh muttered.

"Pity!" the Sardaukar sneered. He advanced, looked down at Leto. "So that's the great Red Duke."

If I had doubts about what this man is, that would end them, Yueh thought. *Only the Emperor calls the Atreides the Red Dukes.*

The Sardaukar reached down, cut the red hawk insignia from Leto's uniform. "Little souvenir," he said. "Where's the ducal signet ring?"

"He doesn't have it on him," Yueh said.

"I can see that!" the Sardaukar snapped.

Yueh stiffened, swallowed. *If they press me, bring in a Truthsayer, they'll find out about the ring, about the 'thopter I prepared—all will fail.*

"Sometimes the Duke sent the ring with a messenger as surety that an order came directly from him," Yueh said.

"Must be damned trusted messengers," the Sardaukar muttered.

"Aren't you going to tie him?" Yueh ventured.

"How long'll he be unconscious?"

"Two hours or so. I wasn't as precise with his dosage as I was for the woman and boy."

The Sardaukar spurned the Duke with his toe. "This was nothing to fear even when awake. When will the woman and boy awaken?"

"About ten minutes."

"So soon?"

"I was told the Baron would arrive immediately behind his men."

"So he will. You'll wait outside, Yueh." He shot a hard glance at Yueh. "Now!"

Yueh glanced at Leto. "What about. . . ."

"He'll be delivered to the Baron all properly trussed like a roast for the oven." Again, the Sardaukar looked at the diamond tattoo on Yueh's forehead. "You're known; you'll be safe enough in the halls. We've no more time for chit-chat, traitor. I hear the others coming."

Traitor, Yueh thought. He lowered his gaze, pressed past the Sardaukar, knowing this as a foretaste of how history would remember him: *Yueh the traitor.*

He passed more bodies on his way to the front entrance and glanced at them, fearful that one might be Paul or Jessica. All were house troopers or wore Harkonnen uniform.

Harkonnen guards came alert, staring at him as he emerged from the front entrance into flame-lighted night. The palms along the road had been fired to illuminate the house. Black smoke from the flammables used to ignite the trees poured upward through orange flames.

"It's the traitor," someone said.

"The Baron will want to see you soon," another said.

I must get to the 'thopter, Yueh thought. *I must put the ducal signet where Paul will find it.* And fear struck him: *If Idaho suspects me or grows impatient—if he doesn't wait and go exactly where I told him— Jessica and Paul will not be saved from the carnage. I'll be denied even the smallest relief from my act.*

The Harkonnen guard released his arm, said, "Wait over there out of the way."

Abruptly, Yueh saw himself as cast away in this place of destruction, spared nothing, given not the smallest pity. *Idaho must not fail!*

Another guard bumped into him, barked: "Stay out of the way, you!"

Even when they've profited by me they despise me, Yueh thought. He straightened himself as he was pushed aside, regained some of his dignity.

"Wait for the Baron!" a guard officer snarled.

Yueh nodded, walked with controlled casualness along the front of the house, turned the corner into shadows out of sight of the burning palms. Quickly, every step betraying his anxiety, Yueh made for the rear yard beneath the conservatory where the 'thopter waited—the craft they had placed there to carry away Paul and his mother.

A guard stood at the open rear door of the house, his attention focused on the lighted hall and men banging through there, searching from room to room.

How confident they were!

Yueh hugged the shadows, worked his way around the 'thopter, eased open the door on the side away from the guard. He felt under the front seats for the Fremkit he had hidden there, lifted a flap and slipped in the ducal signet. He felt the crinkling of the spice paper there, the note he had written, pressed the ring into the paper. He removed his hand, resealed the pack.

Softly, Yueh closed the 'thopter door, worked his way back to the corner of the house and around toward the flaming trees.

Now, it is done, he thought.

Once more, he emerged into the light of the blazing palms. He pulled his cloak around him, stared at the flames. *Soon I will know. Soon I will see the Baron and I will know. And the Baron—he will encounter a small tooth.*

There is a legend that the instant the Duke Leto Atreides died a meteor streaked across the skies above his ancestral palace on Caladan.

—FROM "INTRODUCTION TO A CHILD'S HISTORY OF MUAD'DIB" BY THE PRINCESS IRULAN

The Baron Vladimir Harkonnen stood at a viewport of the grounded lighter he was using as a command post. Out the port he saw the flame-lighted night of Arrakeen. His attention focused on the distant Shield Wall where his secret weapon was doing its work.

Explosive artillery.

The guns nibbled at the caves where the Duke's fighting men had retreated for a last-ditch stand. Slowly measured bites of orange glare, showers of rock and dust in the brief illumination—and the Duke's men were being sealed off to die by starvation, caught like animals in their burrows.

The Baron could feel the distant chomping—a drumbeat carried to him through the ship's metal: *broomp . . . broomp.* Then: *BROOMP-broomp!*

Who would think of reviving artillery in this day of shields? The thought was a chuckle in his mind. *But it was predictable the Duke's men would run for those caves. And the Emperor will appreciate my cleverness in preserving the lives of our mutual force.*

He adjusted one of the little suspensors that guarded his fat body against the pull of gravity. A smile creased his mouth, pulled at the lines of his jowls.

A pity to waste such fighting men as the Duke's, he thought. He smiled more broadly, laughing at himself. *Pity should be cruel!* He nodded. Failure was, by definition, expendable. The whole universe sat there, open to the man who could make the right decisions. The uncertain rabbits had to be exposed, made to run for their burrows. Else how could you control them and breed them? He pictured his fighting men as bees routing the rabbits. And he thought: *The day hums sweetly when you have enough bees working for you.*

A door opened behind him. The Baron studied the reflection in the night-blackened viewport before turning.

Piter de Vries advanced into the chamber followed by Umman Kudu, the captain of the Baron's personal guard. There was a motion of men just outside the door, the mutton faces of his guard, their expressions carefully sheeplike in his presence.

The Baron turned.

Piter touched finger to forelock in his mocking salute. "Good news, m'Lord. The Sardaukar have brought in the Duke."

"Of course they have," the Baron rumbled.

He studied the somber mask of villainy on Piter's effeminate face. And the eyes: those shaded slits of bluest blue-in-blue.

Soon I must remove him, the Baron thought. *He has almost outlasted his usefulness, almost reached the point of positive danger to my person. First, though, he must make the people of Arrakis hate him. Then—they will welcome my darling Feyd-Rautha as a savior.*

The Baron shifted his attention to the guard captain—Umman Kudu: scissors-line of jaw muscles, chin like a boot toe—a man to be trusted because the captain's vices were known.

"First, where is the traitor who gave me the Duke?" the Baron asked. "I must give the traitor his reward."

Piter turned on one toe, motioned to the guard outside.

A bit of black movement there and Yueh walked through. His motions were stiff and stringy. The mustache drooped beside his purple lips. Only the old eyes seemed alive. Yueh came to a stop three paces into the room, obeying a motion from Piter, and stood there staring across the open space at the Baron.

"Ah-h-h, Dr. Yueh."

"M'Lord Harkonnen."

"You've given us the Duke, I hear."

"My half of the bargain, m'Lord."

The Baron looked at Piter.

Piter nodded.

The Baron looked back at Yueh. "The letter of the bargain, eh? And I. . . ." He spat the words out: "What was I to do in return?"

"You remember quite well, m'Lord Harkonnen."

And Yueh allowed himself to think now, hearing the loud silence of clocks in his mind. He had seen the subtle betrayals in the Baron's manner. Wanna was indeed dead—gone far beyond their reach. Otherwise, there'd still be a hold on the weak doctor. The Baron's manner showed there was no hold; it was ended.

"Do I?" the Baron asked.

"You promised to deliver my Wanna from her agony."

The Baron nodded. "Oh, yes. Now, I remember. So I did. That was my promise. That was how we bent the Imperial Conditioning. You couldn't endure seeing your Bene Gesserit witch grovel in Piter's pain amplifiers. Well, the Baron Vladimir Harkonnen always keeps his promises. I told you I'd free her from the agony and permit you to join her. So be it." He waved a hand at Piter.

Piter's blue eyes took a glazed look. His movement was catlike in its sudden fluidity. The knife in his hand glistened like a claw as it flashed into Yueh's back.

The old man stiffened, never taking his attention from the Baron.

"So join her!" the Baron spat.

Yueh stood, swaying. His lips moved with careful precision, and his voice came in oddly measured cadence: "You . . . think . . . you . . . de . . . feated . . . me. You . . . think . . . I . . . did . . . not . . . know . . . what . . . I . . . bought . . . for . . . my . . . Wanna."

He toppled. No bending or softening. It was like a tree falling.

"So join her," the Baron repeated. But his words were like a weak echo.

Yueh had filled him with a sense of foreboding. He whipped his attention to Piter, watched the man wipe the blade on a scrap of cloth, watched the creamy look of satisfaction in the blue eyes.

So that's how he kills by his own hand, the Baron thought. *It's well to know.*

"He *did* give us the Duke?" the Baron asked.

"Of a certainty, my Lord," Piter said.

"Then get him in here!"

Piter glanced at the guard captain, who whirled to obey.

The Baron looked down at Yueh. From the way the man had fallen, you could suspect oak in him instead of bones.

"I never could bring myself to trust a traitor," the Baron said. "Not even a traitor I created."

He glanced at the night-shrouded viewport. That black bag of stillness out there was his, the Baron knew. There was no more crump of artillery against the Shield Wall caves; the burrow traps were sealed off. Quite suddenly, the Baron's mind could conceive of nothing more beautiful than that utter emptiness of black. Unless it were white on the black. Plated white on the black. Porcelain white.

But there was still the feeling of doubt.

What had the old fool of a doctor meant? Of course, he'd probably known what would happen to him in the end. But that bit about thinking he'd been defeated: *"You think you defeated me."*

What had he meant?

The Duke Leto Atreides came through the door. His arms were bound in chains, the eagle face streaked with dirt. His uniform was torn where someone had ripped off his insignia. There were tatters at his waist where the shield belt had been removed without first freeing the uniform ties. The Duke's eyes held a glazed, insane look.

"Wel-l-l-l," the Baron said. He hesitated, drawing in a deep breath.

He knew he had spoken too loudly. This moment, long-envisioned, had lost some of its savor.

Damn that cursed doctor through all eternity!

"I believe the good Duke is drugged," Piter said. "That's how Yueh caught him for us." Piter turned to the Duke. "Aren't you drugged, my dear Duke?"

The voice was far away. Leto could feel the chains, the ache of muscles, his cracked lips, his burning cheeks, the dry taste of thirst whispering its grit in his mouth. But sounds were dull, hidden by a cottony blanket. And he saw only dim shapes through the blanket.

"What of the woman and the boy, Piter?" the Baron asked. "Any word yet?"

Piter's tongue darted over his lips.

"You've heard something!" the Baron snapped. "What?"

Piter glanced at the guard captain, back to the Baron. "The men who were sent to do the job, m'Lord—they've . . . ah . . . been . . . ah . . . found."

"Well, they report everything satisfactory?"

"They're dead, m'Lord."

"Of course they are! What I want to know is—"

"They were dead when found, m'Lord."

The Baron's face went livid. "And the woman and boy?"

"No sign, m'Lord, but there was a worm. It came while the scene was being investigated. Perhaps it's as we wished—an accident. Possibly—"

"We do not deal in possibilities, Piter. What of the missing 'thopter? Does that suggest anything to my Mentat?"

"One of the Duke's men obviously escaped in it, m'Lord. Killed our pilot and escaped."

"Which of the Duke's men?"

"It was a clean, silent killing, m'Lord. Hawat, perhaps, or that Halleck one. Possibly Idaho. Or any top lieutenant."

"Possibilities," the Baron muttered. He glanced at the swaying, drugged figure of the Duke.

"The situation is in hand, m'Lord," Piter said.

"No, it isn't! Where is that stupid planetologist? Where is this man Kynes?"

"We've word where to find him and he's been sent for, m'Lord."

"I don't like the way the Emperor's servant is helping us," the Baron muttered.

They were words through a cottony blanket, but some of them burned in Leto's mind. *Woman and boy—no sign.* Paul and Jessica had escaped. And the fate of Hawat, Halleck, and Idaho remained an unknown. There was still hope.

"Where is the ducal signet ring?" the Baron demanded. "His finger is bare."

"The Sardaukar say it was not on him when he was taken, my Lord," the guard captain said.

"You killed the doctor too soon," the Baron said. "That was a mistake. You should've warned me, Piter. You moved too precipitately for the good of our enterprise." He scowled. "Possibilities!"

The thought hung like a sine wave in Leto's mind: *Paul and Jessica have escaped!* And there was something else in his memory: a bargain. He could almost remember it.

The tooth!

He remembered part of it now: *a pill of poison gas shaped into a false tooth.*

Someone had told him to remember the tooth. The tooth was in his mouth. He could feel its shape with his tongue. All he had to do was bite sharply on it.

Not yet!

The someone had told him to wait until he was near the Baron. Who had told him? He couldn't remember.

"How long will he remain drugged like this?" the Baron asked.

"Perhaps another hour, m'Lord."

"Perhaps," the Baron muttered. Again, he turned to the night-blackened window. "I am hungry."

That's the Baron, that fuzzy gray shape there, Leto thought. The shape danced back and forth, swaying with the movement of the room. And the room expanded and contracted. It grew brighter and darker. It folded into blackness and faded.

Time became a sequence of layers for the Duke. He drifted up through them. *I must wait.*

There was a table. Leto saw the table quite clearly. And a gross, fat man on the other side of the table, the remains of a meal in front of him. Leto felt himself sitting in a chair across from the fat man, felt the chains, the straps that held his tingling body in the chair. He was aware there had been a passage of time, but its length escaped him.

"I believe he's coming around, Baron."

A silky voice, that one. That was Piter.

"So I see, Piter."

A rumbling basso: the Baron.

Leto sensed increasing definition in his surroundings. The chair beneath him took on firmness, the bindings were sharper.

And he saw the Baron clearly now. Leto watched the movements of the man's hands: compulsive touchings—the edge of a plate, the handle of a spoon, a finger tracing the fold of a jowl.

Leto watched the moving hand, fascinated by it.

"You can hear me, Duke Leto," the Baron said. "I know you can hear me. We want to know from you where to find your concubine and the child you sired on her."

No sign escaped Leto, but the words were a wash of calmness through him. *It's true, then: they don't have Paul and Jessica.*

"This is not a child's game we play," the Baron rumbled. "You must know that." He leaned toward Leto, studying the face. It pained the Baron that this could not be handled privately, just between the two of them. To have others see royalty in such straits—it set a bad precedent.

Leto could feel strength returning. And now, the memory of the false tooth stood out in his mind like a steeple in a flat landscape. The nerve-shaped capsule within that tooth—the poison gas—he remembered who had put the deadly weapon in his mouth.

Yueh.

Drug-fogged memory of seeing a limp corpse dragged past him in this room hung like a vapor in Leto's mind. He knew it had been Yueh.

"Do you hear that noise, Duke Leto?" the Baron asked.

Leto grew conscious of a frog sound, the burred mewling of someone's agony.

"We caught one of your men disguised as a Fremen," the Baron said. "We penetrated the disguise quite easily: the eyes, you know. He insists he was sent among the Fremen to spy on them. I've lived for a time on this planet, cher cousin. One does not spy on those ragged scum of the desert. Tell me, did you buy their help? Did you send your woman and son to them?"

Leto felt fear tighten his chest. *If Yueh sent them to the desert fold . . . the search won't stop until they're found.*

"Come, come," the Baron said. "We don't have much time and pain is quick. Please don't bring it to this, my dear Duke." The Baron looked up at Piter who stood at Leto's shoulder. "Piter doesn't have all his tools here, but I'm sure he could improvise."

"Improvisation is sometimes the best, Baron."

That silky, insinuating voice! Leto heard it at his ear.

"You had an emergency plan," the Baron said. "Where have your woman and the boy been sent?" He looked at Leto's hand. "Your ring is missing. Does the boy have it?"

The Baron looked up, stared into Leto's eyes.

"You don't answer," he said. "Will you force me to do a thing I do not want to do? Piter will use simple, direct methods. I agree they're sometimes the best, but it's not good that *you* should be subjected to such things."

"Hot tallow on the back, perhaps, or on the eyelids," Piter said. "Perhaps on other portions of the body. It's especially effective when the subject doesn't know where the tallow will fall next. It's a good method and there's a sort of beauty in the pattern of pus-white blisters on naked skin, eh, Baron?"

"Exquisite," the Baron said, and his voice sounded sour.

Those touching fingers! Leto watched the fat hands, the glittering jewels on baby-fat hands—their compulsive wandering.

The sounds of agony coming through the door behind him gnawed at the Duke's nerves. *Who is it they caught?* he wondered. *Could it have been Idaho?*

"Believe me, cher cousin," the Baron said. "I do not want it to come to this."

"You think of nerve couriers racing to summon help that cannot come," Piter said. "There's an artistry in this, you know."

"You're a superb artist," the Baron growled. "Now, have the decency to be silent."

Leto suddenly recalled a thing Gurney Halleck had said once, seeing a picture of the Baron: *"And I stood upon the sand of the sea and saw a beast rise up out of the sea . . . and upon his heads the name of blasphemy.'"*

"We waste time, Baron," Piter said.

"Perhaps."

The Baron nodded. "You know, my dear Leto, you'll tell us in the end where they are. There's a level of pain that'll buy you."

He's most likely correct, Leto thought. *Were it not for the tooth . . . and the fact that I truly don't know where they are.*

The Baron picked up a sliver of meat, pressed the morsel into his mouth, chewed slowly, swallowed. *We must try a new tack,* he thought.

"Observe this prize person who denies he's for hire," the Baron said. "Observe him, Piter."

And the Baron thought: *Yes! See him there, this man who believes he cannot be bought. See him detained there by a million shares of himself sold in dribbles every second of his life! If you took him up now and shook him, he'd rattle inside. Emptied! Sold out! What difference how he dies now?*

The frog sounds in the background stopped.

The Baron saw Umman Kudu, the guard captain, appear in the doorway across the room, shake his head. The captive hadn't produced the needed information. Another failure. Time to quit stalling with this fool Duke, this stupid soft fool who didn't realize how much hell there was so near him—only a nerve's thickness away.

This thought calmed the Baron, overcoming his reluctance to have a royal person subject to pain. He saw himself suddenly as a surgeon exercising endless supple scissor dissections—cutting away the masks from fools, exposing the hell beneath.

Rabbits, all of them!

And how they cowered when they saw the carnivore!

Leto stared across the table, wondering why he waited. The tooth would end it all quickly. Still—it had been good, much of this life. He found himself remembering an antenna kite updangling in the shell-blue sky of Caladan, and Paul laughing with joy at the sight of it. And he remembered sunrise here on Arrakis—colored strata of the Shield Wall mellowed by dust haze.

"Too bad," the Baron muttered. He pushed himself back from the table, stood up lightly in his suspensors and hesitated, seeing a change come over the Duke. He saw the man draw in a deep breath, the jawline stiffen, the ripple of a muscle there as the Duke clamped his mouth shut.

How he fears me! the Baron thought.

Shocked by fear that the Baron might escape him, Leto bit sharply on the capsule tooth, felt it break. He opened his mouth, expelled the biting vapor he could taste as it formed on his tongue. The Baron grew smaller, a figure seen in a tightening tunnel. Leto heard a gasp beside his ear—the silky-voiced one: Piter.

It got him, too!

"Piter! What's wrong?"

The rumbling voice was far away.

Leto sensed memories rolling in his mind—the old toothless mutterings of hags. The room, the table, the Baron, a pair of terrified eyes—blue within blue, the eyes—all compressed around him in ruined symmetry.

There was a man with a boot-toe chin, a toy man falling. The toy man had a broken nose slanted to the left: an offbeat metronome caught forever at the start of an upward stroke. Leto heard the crash of crockery—so distant—a roaring in his ears. His mind was a bin without end, catching everything. Everything that had ever been: every shout, every whisper, every . . . silence.

One thought remained to him. Leto saw it in formless light on rays of black: *The day the flesh shapes and the flesh the day shapes.* The thought struck him with a sense of fullness he knew he could never explain.

Silence.

The Baron stood with his back against his private door, his own bolt hole behind the table. He had slammed it on a room full of dead men. His senses took in guards swarming around him. *Did I breathe it?* he asked himself. *Whatever it was in there, did it get me, too?*

Sounds returned to him . . . and reason. He heard someone shouting orders—gas masks . . . keep a door closed . . . get blowers going.

The others fell quickly, he thought. *I'm still standing. I'm still breathing. Merciless hell! That was close!*

He could analyze it now. His shield had been activated, set low but still enough to slow molecular interchange across the field barrier. And he had been pushing himself away from the table . . . that and Piter's shocked gasp which had brought the guard captain darting forward into his own doom.

Chance and the warning in a dying man's gasp—these had saved him.

The Baron felt no gratitude to Piter. The fool had got himself killed. And that stupid guard captain! He'd said he scoped everyone before bringing them into the Baron's presence! How had it been possible for the Duke . . . ? No warning. Not even from the poison snooper over the table—until it was too late. How?

Well, no matter now, the Baron thought, his mind firming. *The next guard captain will begin by finding answers to these questions.*

He grew aware of more activity down the hall—around the corner at the other door to that room of death. The Baron pushed himself away from his own door, studied the lackeys around him. They stood there staring, silent, waiting for the Baron's reaction.

Would the Baron be angry?

And the Baron realized only a few seconds had passed since his flight from that terrible room.

Some of the guards had weapons leveled at the door. Some were directing their ferocity toward the empty hall that stretched away toward the noises around the corner to their right.

A man came striding around that corner, gas mask dangling by its straps at his neck, his eyes intent on the overhead poison snoopers that lined this corridor. He was yellow-haired, flat of face with green eyes. Crisp lines radiated from his thick-lipped mouth. He looked like some water creature misplaced among those who walked the land.

The Baron stared at the approaching man, recalling the name: Nefud. Iakin Nefud. Guard corporal. Nefud was addicted to semuta, the drug-music combination that played itself in the deepest consciousness. A useful item of information, that.

The man stopped in front of the Baron, saluted. "Corridor's clear, m'Lord. I was outside watching and saw that it must be poison gas. Ventilators in your room were pulling air in from these corridors." He glanced up at the snooper over the Baron's head. "None of the stuff escaped. We have the room cleaned out now. What are your orders?"

The Baron recognized the man's voice—the one who'd been shouting orders. *Efficient, this corporal,* he thought.

"They're all dead in there?" the Baron asked.

"Yes, m'Lord."

Well, we must adjust, the Baron thought.

"First," he said, "let me congratulate you, Nefud. You're the new captain of my guard. And I hope you'll take to heart the lesson to be learned from the fate of your predecessor."

The Baron watched the awareness grow in his newly promoted guardsman. Nefud knew he'd never again be without his semuta.

Nefud nodded. "My Lord knows I'll devote myself entirely to his safety."

"Yes. Well, to business. I suspect the Duke had something in his mouth. You will find out what that something was, how it was used, who helped him put it there. You'll take every precaution—"

He broke off, his chain of thought shattered by a disturbance in the corridor behind him—guards at the door to the lift from the lower levels of the frigate trying to hold back a tall colonel bashar who had just emerged from the lift.

The Baron couldn't place the colonel bashar's face: thin with mouth like a slash in leather, twin ink spots for eyes.

"Get your hands off me, you pack of carrion-eaters!" the man roared, and he dashed the guards aside.

Ah-h-h, one of the Sardaukar, the Baron thought.

The colonel bashar came striding toward the Baron, whose eyes went to slits of apprehension. The Sardaukar officers filled him with unease. They all seemed to look like relatives of the Duke . . . the late Duke. And their manners with the Baron!

The colonel bashar planted himself half a pace in front of the Baron, hands on hips. The guard hovered behind him in twitching uncertainty.

The Baron noted the absence of salute, the disdain in the Sardaukar's manner, and his unease grew. There was only the one legion of them locally—ten brigades—reinforcing the Harkonnen legions, but the Baron did not fool himself. That one legion was perfectly capable of turning on the Harkonnens and overcoming them.

"Tell your men they are not to prevent me from seeing you, Baron," the Sardaukar growled. "My men brought you the Atreides Duke before I could discuss his fate with you. We will discuss it now."

I must not lose face before my men, the Baron thought.

"So?" It was a coldly controlled word, and the Baron felt proud of it.

"My Emperor has charged me to make certain his royal cousin dies cleanly without agony," the colonel bashar said.

"Such were the Imperial orders to me," the Baron lied. "Did you think I'd disobey?"

"I'm to report to my Emperor what I see with my own eyes," the Sardaukar said.

"The Duke's already dead," the Baron snapped, and he waved a hand to dismiss the fellow.

The colonel bashar remained planted facing the Baron. Not by flicker of eye or muscle did he acknowledge he had been dismissed. "How?" he growled.

Really! the Baron thought. *This is too much.*

"By his own hand, if you must know," the Baron said. "He took poison."

"I will see the body now," the colonel bashar said.

The Baron raised his gaze to the ceiling in feigned exasperation while his thoughts raced. *Damnation! This sharp-eyed Sardaukar will see the room before a thing's been changed!*

"Now," the Sardaukar growled. "I'll see it with my own eyes."

There was no preventing it, the Baron realized. The Sardaukar would see all. He'd know the Duke had killed Harkonnen men . . . that the Baron most likely had escaped by a narrow margin. There was the evidence of the dinner remnants on the table, and the dead Duke across from it with destruction around him.

No preventing it at all.

"I'll not be put off," the colonel bashar snarled.

"You're not being put off," the Baron said, and he stared into the Sardaukar's obsidian eyes. "I hide nothing from my Emperor." He nodded to Nefud. "The colonel bashar is to see everything, at once. Take him in by the door where you stood, Nefud."

"This way, sir," Nefud said.

Slowly, insolently, the Sardaukar moved around the Baron, shouldered a way through the guardsmen.

Insufferable, the Baron thought. *Now, the Emperor will know how I slipped up. He'll recognize it as a sign of weakness.*

And it was agonizing to realize that the Emperor and his Sardaukar were alike in their disdain for weakness. The Baron chewed at his lower lip, consoling himself that the Emperor, at least, had not learned of the Atreides raid on Giedi Prime, the destruction of the Harkonnen spice stores there.

Damn that slippery Duke!

The Baron watched the retreating backs—the arrogant Sardaukar and the stocky, efficient Nefud.

We must adjust, the Baron thought. *I'll have to put Rabban over this damnable planet once more. Without restraint. I must spend my own Harkonnen blood to put Arrakis into a proper condition for accepting Feyd-Rautha. Damn that Piter! He would get himself killed before I was through with him.*

The Baron sighed.

And I must send at once to Tleielax for a new Mentat. They undoubtedly have the new one ready for me by now.

One of the guardsmen beside him coughed.

The Baron turned toward the man. "I am hungry."

"Yes, m'Lord."

"And I wish to be diverted while you're clearing out that room and studying its secrets for me," the Baron rumbled.

The guardsman lowered his eyes. "What diversion does m'Lord wish?"

"I'll be in my sleeping chambers," the Baron said. "Bring me that young fellow we bought on Gamont, the one with the lovely eyes. Drug him well. I don't feel like wrestling."

"Yes, m'Lord."

The Baron turned away, began moving with his bouncing, suspensor-buoyed pace toward his chambers. *Yes,* he thought. *The one with the lovely eyes, the one who looks so much like the young Paul Atreides.*

O Seas of Caladan,
O people of Duke Leto—
Citadel of Leto fallen,
Fallen forever . . .

—FROM "SONGS OF MUAD'DIB"
BY THE PRINCESS IRULAN

Paul felt that all his past, every experience before this night, had become sand curling in an hourglass. He sat near his mother hugging his knees within a small fabric and plastic hutment—a stilltent—that had come, like the Fremen clothing they now wore, from the pack left in the 'thopter.

There was no doubt in Paul's mind who had put the Fremkit there, who had directed the course of the 'thopter carrying them captive.

Yueh.

The traitor doctor had sent them directly into the hands of Duncan Idaho.

Paul stared out the transparent end of the stilltent at the moon-shadowed rocks that ringed this place where Idaho had hidden them.

Hiding like a child when I'm now the Duke, Paul thought. He felt the thought gall him, but could not deny the wisdom in what they did.

Something had happened to his awareness this night—he saw with sharpened clarity every circumstance and occurrence around him. He felt unable to stop the inflow of data or the cold precision with which each new item was added to his knowledge and the computation was centered in his awareness. It was Mentat power and more.

Paul thought back to the moment of impotent rage as the strange 'thopter dived out of the night onto them, stooping like a giant hawk above the desert with wind screaming through its wings. The thing in Paul's mind had happened then. The 'thopter had skidded and slewed across a sand ridge toward the running figures—his mother and himself. Paul remembered how the smell of burned sulfur from abrasion of 'thopter skids against sand had drifted across them.

His mother, he knew, had turned, expected to meet a lasgun in the hands of Harkonnen mercenaries, and had recognized Duncan Idaho leaning out the 'thopter's open door shouting: "Hurry! There's wormsign south of you!"

But Paul had known as he turned who piloted the 'thopter. An accumulation of minutiae in the way it was flown, the dash of the landing—clues so small even his mother hadn't detected them—had told Paul *precisely* who sat at those controls.

Across the stilltent from Paul, Jessica stirred, said: "There can be only one explanation. The Harkonnens held Yueh's wife. He hated the Harkonnens! I cannot be wrong about that. You read his note. But why has he saved us from the carnage?"

She is only now seeing it and that poorly, Paul thought. The thought was a shock. He had known this fact as a by-the-way thing while reading the note that had accompanied the ducal signet in the pack.

"Do not try to forgive me," Yueh had written. "I do not want your forgiveness. I already have enough burdens. What I have done was done without malice or hope of another's understanding. It is my own tahaddi al-burhan, my ultimate test. I give you the Atreides ducal signet as token that I write truly. By the time you read this, Duke Leto will be dead. Take consolation from my assurance that he did not die alone, that one we hate above all others died with him."

It had not been addressed or signed, but there'd been no mistaking the familiar scrawl—Yueh's.

Remembering the letter, Paul re-experienced the distress of that moment—a thing sharp and strange that seemed to happen outside his new mental alertness. He had read that his father was dead, known the truth of the words, but had felt them as no more than another datum to be entered in his mind and used.

I loved my father, Paul thought, and knew this for truth. *I should mourn him. I should feel something.*

But he felt nothing except: *Here's an important fact.*

It was one with all the other facts.

All the while his mind was adding sense impressions, extrapolating, computing.

Halleck's words came back to Paul: *"Mood's a thing for cattle or for making love. You fight when the necessity arises, no matter your mood."*

Perhaps that's it, Paul thought. *I'll mourn my father later . . . when there's time.*

But he felt no letup in the cold precision of his being. He sensed that his new awareness was only a beginning, that it was growing. The sense of terrible purpose he'd first experienced in his ordeal with the Reverend Mother Gaius Helen Mohiam pervaded him. His right hand—the hand of remembered pain—tingled and throbbed.

Is this what it is to be their Kwisatz Haderach? he wondered.

"For a while, I thought Hawat had failed us again," Jessica said. "I thought perhaps Yueh wasn't a Suk doctor."

"He was everything we thought him . . . and more," Paul said. And he thought: *Why is she so slow seeing these things?* He said, "If Idaho doesn't get through to Kynes, we'll be—"

"He's not our only hope," she said.

"Such was not my suggestion," he said.

She heard the steel in his voice, the sense of command, and stared across the gray darkness of the stilltent at him. Paul was a silhouette against moon-frosted rocks seen through the tent's transparent end.

"Others among your father's men will have escaped," she said. "We must regather them, find—"

"We will depend upon ourselves," he said. "Our immediate concern is our family atomics. We must get them before the Harkonnens can search them out."

"Not likely they'll be found," she said, "the way they were hidden."

"It must not be left to chance."

And she thought: *Blackmail with the family atomics as a threat to the planet and its spice—that's what he has in mind. But all he can hope for then is escape into renegade anonymity.*

His mother's words had provoked another train of thought in Paul—a duke's concern for all the people they'd lost this night. *People are the true strength of a Great House*, Paul thought. And he remembered Hawat's words: *"Parting with people is a sadness; a place is only a place."*

"They're using Sardaukar," Jessica said. "We must wait until the Sardaukar have been withdrawn."

"They think us caught between the desert and the Sardaukar," Paul said. "They intend that there be no Atreides survivors—total extermination. Do not count on any of our people escaping."

"They cannot go on indefinitely risking exposure of the Emperor's part in this."

"Can't they?"

"Some of our people are bound to escape."

"Are they?"

Jessica turned away, frightened of the bitter strength in her son's voice, hearing the precise assessment of chances. She sensed that his mind had leaped ahead of her, that it now saw more in some respects than she did. She had helped train the intelligence which did this, but now she found herself fearful of it. Her thoughts turned, seeking toward the lost sanctuary of her Duke, and tears burned her eyes.

This is the way it had to be, Leto, she thought. *"A time of love and a time of grief."* She rested her hand on her abdomen, awareness focused on the embryo there. *I have the Atreides daughter I was ordered to produce, but the Reverend Mother was wrong: a daughter wouldn't have saved my Leto. This child is only life reaching for the future in the midst of death. I conceived out of instinct and not out of obedience.*

"Try the communinet receiver again," Paul said.

The mind goes on working no matter how we try to hold it back, she thought.

Jessica found the tiny receiver Idaho had left for them, flipped its switch. A green light glowed on the instrument's face. Tinny screeching came from its speaker. She reduced the volume, hunted across the bands. A voice speaking Atreides battle language came into the tent.

". . . back and regroup at the ridge. Fedor reports no survivors in Carthag and the Guild Bank has been sacked."

Carthag! Jessica thought. *That was a Harkonnen hotbed.*

"They're Sardaukar," the voice said. "Watch out for Sardaukar in Atreides uniforms. They're. . . ."

A roaring filled the speaker, then silence.

"Try the other bands," Paul said.

"Do you realize what that means?" Jessica asked.

"I expected it. They want the Guild to blame us for destruction of their bank. With the Guild against us, we're trapped on Arrakis. Try the other bands."

She weighed his words: *I expected it.* What had happened to him? Slowly, Jessica returned to the instrument. As she moved the bandslide, they caught glimpses of violence in the few voices calling out in Atreides battle language: ". . . fall back. . . ." ". . . try to regroup at. . . ." ". . . trapped in a cave at. . . ."

And there was no mistaking the victorious exultation in the Harkonnen gibberish that poured from the other bands. Sharp commands, battle reports. There wasn't enough of it for Jessica to register and break the language, but the tone was obvious.

Harkonnen victory.

Paul shook the pack beside him, hearing the two literjons of water gurgle there. He took a deep breath, looked up through the transparent end of the tent at the rock escarpment outlined against the stars. His left hand felt the sphincter-seal of the tent's entrance. "It'll be dawn soon," he said. "We can wait through the day for Idaho, but not through another night. In the desert, you must travel by night and rest in shade through the day."

Remembered lore insinuated itself into Jessica's mind: *Without a stillsuit, a man sitting in shade on the desert needs five liters of water a day to maintain body weight.* She felt the slick-soft skin of the stillsuit against her body, thinking how their lives depended on these garments.

"If we leave here, Idaho can't find us," she said.

"There are ways to make any man talk," he said. "If Idaho hasn't returned by dawn, we must consider the possibility he has been captured. How long do you think he could hold out?"

The question required no answer, and she sat in silence.

Paul lifted the seal on the pack, pulled out a tiny micromanual with glowtab and magnifier. Green and orange letters leaped up at him from the pages: "literjons, stilltent, energy caps, recaths, sandsnork, binoculars, stillsuit repkit, baradye pistol, sinkchart, filt-plugs, paracompass, maker hooks, thumpers, Fremkit, fire pillar. . . ."

So many things for survival on the desert.

Presently, he put the manual aside on the tent floor.

"Where can we possibly go?" Jessica asked.

"My father spoke of *desert power*," Paul said. "The Harkonnens cannot rule this planet without it. They've never ruled this planet, nor shall they. Not even with ten thousand legions of Sardaukar."

"Paul, you can't think that—"

"We've all the evidence in our hands," he said. "Right here in this tent—the tent itself, this pack and its contents, these stillsuits. We know the Guild wants a prohibitive price for weather satellites. We know that—"

"What've weather satellites to do with it?" she asked. "They couldn't possibly. . . ." She broke off.

Paul sensed the hyperalertness of his mind reading her reactions, computing on minutiae. "You see it now," he said. "Satellites watch the terrain below. There are things in the deep desert that will not bear frequent inspection."

"You're suggesting the Guild itself controls this planet?"

She was so slow.

"No!" he said. "The Fremen! They're paying the Guild for privacy, paying in a coin that's freely available to anyone with desert power—spice. This is more than a second-approximation answer; it's the straight-line computation. Depend on it."

"Paul," Jessica said, "you're not a Mentat yet; you can't know for sure how—"

"I'll never be a Mentat," he said. "I'm something else . . . a freak."

"Paul! How can you say such—"

"Leave me alone!"

He turned away from her, looking out into the night. *Why can't I mourn?* he wondered. He felt that every fiber of his being craved this release, but it would be denied him forever.

Jessica had never heard such distress in her son's voice. She wanted to reach out to him, hold him, comfort him, help him—but she sensed there was nothing she could do. He had to solve this problem by himself.

The glowing tab of the Fremkit manual between them on the tent floor caught her eye. She lifted it, glanced at the flyleaf, reading: "Manual of 'The Friendly Desert,' the place full of life. Here are the ayat and burhan of Life. Believe, and al-Lat shall never burn you."

It reads like the Azhar Book, she thought, recalling her studies of the Great Secrets. *Has a Manipulator of Religions been on Arrakis?*

Paul lifted the paracompass from the pack, returned it, said: "Think of all these special-application Fremen machines. They show unrivaled sophistication. Admit it. The culture that made these things betrays depths no one suspected."

Hesitating, still worried by the harshness in his voice, Jessica returned to the book, studied an illustrated constellation from the Arrakeen sky: "Muad'Dib: The Mouse," and noted that the tail pointed north.

Paul stared into the tent's darkness at the dimly discerned movements of his mother revealed by the manual's glowtab. *Now is the time to carry out my father's wish*, he thought. *I must give her his message now while she has time for grief. Grief would inconvenience us later.* And he found himself shocked by precise logic.

"Mother," he said.

"Yes?"

She heard the change in his voice, felt coldness in her entrails at the sound. Never had she heard such harsh control.

"My father is dead," he said.

She searched within herself for the coupling of fact and fact and fact—the Bene Gesserit way of assessing data—and it came to her: the sensation of terrifying loss.

Jessica nodded, unable to speak.

"My father charged me once," Paul said, "to give you a message if anything happened to him. He feared you might believe he distrusted you."

That useless suspicion, she thought.

"He wanted you to know he never suspected you," Paul said, and explained the deception, adding: "He wanted you to know he always trusted you completely, always loved you and cherished you. He said he would sooner have mistrusted himself and he had but one regret—that he never made you his Duchess."

She brushed the tears coursing down her cheeks, thought: *What a stupid waste of the body's water!* But she knew this thought for what it was—the attempt to retreat from grief into anger. *Leto, my Leto,* she thought. *What terrible things we do to those we love!* With a violent motion, she extinguished the little manual's glowtab.

Sobs shook her.

Paul heard his mother's grief and felt the emptiness within himself. *I have no grief,* he thought. *Why? Why?* He felt the inability to grieve as a terrible flaw.

"A time to get and time to lose," Jessica thought, quoting to herself from the O.C. Bible. *"A time to keep and a time to cast away; a time for love and a time to hate; a time of war and a time of peace."*

Paul's mind had gone on in its chilling precision. He saw the avenues ahead of them on this hostile planet. Without even the safety valve of dreaming, he focused his prescient awareness, seeing it as a computation of most probable futures, but with something more, an edge of mystery—as though his mind dipped into some timeless stratum and sampled the winds of the future.

Abruptly, as though he had found a necessary key, Paul's mind climbed another notch in awareness. He felt himself clinging to this new level, clutching at a precarious hold and peering about. It was as though he existed within a globe with avenues radiating away in all directions . . . yet this only approximated the sensation.

He remembered once seeing a gauze kerchief blowing in the wind and now he sensed the future as though it twisted across some surface as undulant and impermanent as that of the windblown kerchief.

He saw people.

He felt the heat and cold of uncounted probabilities.

He knew names and places, experienced emotions without number, reviewed data of innumerable unexplored crannies. There was time to probe and test and taste, but no time to shape.

The thing was a spectrum of possibilities from the most remote past to the most remote future—from the most probable to the most improbable. He saw his own death in countless ways. He saw new planets, new cultures.

People.

People.

He saw them in such swarms they could not be listed, yet his mind catalogued them.

Even the Guildsmen.

And he thought: *The Guild—there'd be a way for us, my strangeness accepted as a familiar thing of high value, always with an assured supply of the now-necessary spice.*

But the idea of living out his life in the mind-groping-ahead-through-possible-futures that guided hurtling spaceships appalled him. It *was* a way, though. And in meeting the *possible future* that contained Guildsmen he recognized his own strangeness.

I have another kind of sight. I see another kind of terrain: the available paths.

The awareness conveyed both reassurance and alarm—so many places on that other kind of terrain dipped or turned out of his sight.

As swiftly as it had come, the sensation slipped away from him, and he realized the entire experience had taken the space of a heartbeat.

Yet, his own personal awareness had been turned over, illuminated in a terrifying way. He stared around him.

Night still covered the stilltent within its rock-enclosed hideaway. His mother's grief could still be heard.

His own lack of grief could still be felt . . . that hollow place somewhere separated from his mind, which went on in its steady pace—dealing with data, evaluating, computing, submitting answers in something like the Mentat way.

And now he saw that he had a wealth of data few such minds ever before had encompassed. But this made the empty place within him no easier to bear. He felt that something must shatter. It was as though a clockwork control for a bomb had been set to ticking within him. It went on about its business no matter what he wanted. It recorded minuscule shadings of difference around him—a slight change in moisture, a fractional fall in temperature, the progress of an insect across their stilltent roof, the solemn approach of dawn in the starlighted patch of sky he could see out the tent's transparent end.

The emptiness was unbearable. Knowing how the clockwork had been set in motion made no difference. He could look to his own past and see the start of it—the training, the sharpening of talents, the refined pressures of sophisticated disciplines, even exposure to the O.C. Bible at a critical moment . . . and, lastly, the heavy intake of spice. And he could look ahead—the most terrifying direction—to see where it all pointed.

I'm a monster! he thought. *A freak!*

"No," he said. Then: "No. No! NO!"

He found that he was pounding the tent floor with his fists. (The implacable part of him recorded this as an interesting emotional datum and fed it into computation.)

"Paul!"

His mother was beside him, holding his hands, her face a gray blob peering at him. "Paul, what's wrong?"

"You!" he said.

"I'm here, Paul," she said. "It's all right."

"What have you done to me?" he demanded.

In a burst of clarity, she sensed some of the roots in the question, said: "I gave birth to you."

It was, from instinct as much as her own subtle knowledge, the precisely correct answer to calm him. He felt her hands holding him, focused on the dim outline of her face. (Certain gene traces in her facial structure were noted in the new way by his onflowing mind, the clues added to other data, and a final-summation answer put forward.)

"Let go of me," he said.

She heard the iron in his voice, obeyed. "Do you want to tell me what's wrong, Paul?"

"Did you know what you were doing when you trained me?" he asked.

There's no more childhood in his voice, she thought. And she said: "I hoped the thing any parent hopes—that you'd be . . . superior, different."

"Different?"

She heard the bitterness in his tone, said: "Paul, I—"

"You didn't want a son!" he said. "You wanted a Kwisatz Haderach! You wanted a male Bene Gesserit!"

She recoiled from his bitterness. "But Paul. . . ."

"Did you ever consult my father in this?"

She spoke gently out of the freshness of her grief: "Whatever you are, Paul, the heredity is as much your father as me."

"But not the training," he said. "Not the things that . . . awakened . . . the sleeper."

"Sleeper?"

"It's here." He put a hand to his head and then to his breast. "In me. It goes on and on and on and on and—"

"Paul!"

She had heard the hysteria edging his voice.

"Listen to me," he said. "You wanted the Reverend Mother to hear about my dreams: You listen in her place now. I've just had a *waking* dream. Do you know why?"

"You must calm yourself," she said. "If there's—"

"The spice," he said. "It's in everything here—the air, the soil, the food, the *geriatric* spice. It's like the Truthsayer drug. It's a poison!"

She stiffened.

His voice lowered and he repeated: "A poison—so subtle, so insidious . . . so irreversible. It won't even kill you unless you stop taking it. We can't leave Arrakis unless we take part of Arrakis with us."

The terrifying *presence* of his voice brooked no dispute.

"You and the spice," Paul said. "The spice changes anyone who gets this much of it, but thanks to *you*, I could bring the change to consciousness. I don't get to leave it in the unconscious where its disturbance can be blanked out. I can *see* it."

"Paul, you—"

"I *see* it!" he repeated.

She heard madness in his voice, didn't know what to do.

But he spoke again, and she heard the iron control return to him: "We're trapped here."

We're trapped here, she agreed.

And she accepted the truth of his words. No pressure of the Bene Gesserit, no trickery or artifice could pry them completely free from Arrakis: the spice was addictive. Her body had known the fact long before her mind awakened to it.

So here we live out our lives, she thought, *on this hell planet. The place is prepared for us, if we can evade the Harkonnens. And there's no doubt of my course: a broodmare preserving an important bloodline for the Bene Gesserit Plan.*

"I must tell you about my waking dream," Paul said. (Now there was fury in his voice.) "To be sure you accept what I say, I'll tell you first I know you'll bear a daughter, my sister, here on Arrakis."

Jessica placed her hands against the tent floor, pressed back against the curving fabric wall to still a pang of fear. She knew her pregnancy could not show yet. Only her own Bene Gesserit training had allowed her to read the first faint signals of her body, to know of the embryo only a few weeks old.

"Only to serve," Jessica whispered, clinging to the Bene Gesserit motto. "We exist only to serve."

"We'll find a home among the Fremen," Paul said, "where your Missionaria Protectiva has bought us a bolt hole."

They've prepared a way for us in the desert, Jessica told herself. *But how can he know of the Missionaria Protectiva?* She found it increasingly difficult to subdue her terror at the overpowering strangeness in Paul.

He studied the dark shadow of her, seeing her fear and every reaction with his new awareness as though she were outlined in blinding light. A beginning of compassion for her crept over him.

"The things that can happen here, I cannot begin to tell you," he said. "I cannot even begin to tell myself, although I've seen them. This *sense* of the future—I seem to have no control over it. The thing just happens. The immediate future—say, a year—I can see some of that . . . a *road* as broad as our Central Avenue on Caladan. Some places I don't see . . . shadowed places . . . as though it went behind a hill" (and again he thought of the surface of a blowing kerchief) ". . . and there are branchings. . . ."

He fell silent as memory of that *seeing* filled him. No prescient dream, no experience of his life had quite prepared him for the totality with which the veils had been ripped away to reveal naked time.

Recalling the experience, he recognized his own terrible purpose— the pressure of his life spreading outward like an expanding bubble . . . time retreating before it. . . .

Jessica found the tent's glowtab control, activated it.

Dim green light drove back the shadows, easing her fear. She looked at Paul's face, his eyes—the inward stare. And she knew where she had seen such a look before: pictured in records of disasters—on the faces of children who experienced starvation or terrible injury. The eyes were like pits, mouth a straight line, cheeks indrawn.

It's the look of terrible awareness, she thought, *of someone forced to the knowledge of his own mortality.*

He was, indeed, no longer a child.

The underlying import of his words began to take over in her mind, pushing all else aside. Paul could see ahead, a way of escape for them.

"There's a way to evade the Harkonnens," she said.

"The Harkonnens!" he sneered. "Put those twisted humans out of your mind." He stared at his mother, studying the lines of her face in the light of the glowtab. The lines betrayed her.

She said: "You shouldn't refer to people as humans without—"

"Don't be so sure you know where to draw the line," he said. "We carry our past with us. And, mother mine, there's a thing you don't know and should—*we* are Harkonnens."

Her mind did a terrifying thing: it blanked out as though it needed to shut off all sensation. But Paul's voice went on at that implacable pace, dragging her with it.

"When next you find a mirror, study your face—study mine now. The traces are there if you don't blind yourself. Look at my hands, the set of my bones. And if none of this convinces you, then take my word for it. I've walked the future, I've looked at a record, I've seen a place, I have all the data. We're Harkonnens."

"A . . . renegade branch of the family," she said. "That's it, isn't it? Some Harkonnen cousin who—"

"You're the Baron's own daughter," he said, and watched the way she pressed her hands to her mouth. "The Baron sampled many pleasures in his youth, and once permitted himself to be seduced. But it was for the genetic purposes of the Bene Gesserit, by one of *you.*"

The way he said *you* struck her like a slap. But it set her mind to working and she could not deny his words. So many blank ends of meaning in her past reached out now and linked. The daughter the Bene

Gesserit wanted—it wasn't to end the old Atreides-Harkonnen feud, but to fix some genetic factor in their lines. *What?* She groped for an answer.

As though he saw inside her mind, Paul said: "They thought they were reaching for me. But I'm not what they expected, and I've arrived before my time. And *they* don't know it."

Jessica pressed her hands to her mouth.

Great Mother! He's the Kwisatz Haderach!

She felt exposed and naked before him, realizing then that he saw her with eyes from which little could be hidden. And *that*, she knew, was the basis of her fear.

"You're thinking I'm the Kwisatz Haderach," he said. "Put that out of your mind. I'm something unexpected."

I must get word out to one of the schools, she thought. *The mating index may show what has happened.*

"They won't learn about me until it's too late," he said.

She sought to divert him, lowered her hands and said: "We'll find a place among the Fremen?"

"The Fremen have a saying they credit to Shai-hulud, Old Father Eternity," he said. "They say: 'Be prepared to appreciate what you meet.'"

And he thought: *Yes, mother mine—among the Fremen. You'll acquire the blue eyes and a callus beside your lovely nose from the filter tube to your stillsuit . . . and you'll bear my sister: St. Alia of the Knife.*

"If you're not the Kwisatz Haderach," Jessica said, "what—"

"You couldn't possibly know," he said. "You won't believe it until you see it."

And he thought: *I'm a seed.*

He suddenly saw how fertile was the ground into which he had fallen, and with this realization, the terrible purpose filled him, creeping through the empty place within, threatening to choke him with grief.

He had seen two main branchings along the way ahead—in one he confronted an evil old Baron and said: "Hello, Grandfather." The thought of that path and what lay along it sickened him.

The other path held long patches of gray obscurity except for peaks of violence. He had seen a warrior religion there, a fire spreading across the universe with the Atreides green and black banner waving at the head of fanatic legions drunk on spice liquor. Gurney Halleck and a few others of his father's men—a pitiful few—were among them, all marked by the hawk symbol from the shrine of his father's skull.

"I can't go that way," he muttered. "That's what the old witches of your schools really want."

"I don't understand you, Paul," his mother said.

He remained silent, thinking like the seed he was, thinking with the race consciousness he had first experienced as terrible purpose. He found that he no longer could hate the Bene Gesserit or the Emperor or even the Harkonnens. They were all caught up in the need of their race to renew its scattered inheritance, to cross and mingle and infuse their bloodlines in a great new pooling of genes. And the race knew only one sure way for this—the ancient way, the tried and certain way that rolled over everything in its path: jihad.

Surely, I cannot choose that way, he thought.

But he saw again in his mind's eye the shrine of his father's skull and the violence with the green and black banner waving in its midst.

Jessica cleared her throat, worried by his silence. "Then . . . the Fremen will give us sanctuary?"

He looked up, staring across the green-lighted tent at the inbred, patrician lines of her face. "Yes," he said. "That's one of the ways." He nodded. "Yes. They'll call me . . . Muad'Dib, 'The One Who Points the Way.' Yes . . . that's what they'll call me."

And he closed his eyes, thinking: *Now, my father, I can mourn you.* And he felt the tears coursing down his cheeks.

BOOK TWO

MUAD'DIB

When my father, the Padishah Emperor, heard of Duke Leto's death and the manner of it, he went into such a rage as we had never before seen. He blamed my mother and the compact forced on him to place a Bene Gesserit on the throne. He blamed the Guild and the evil old Baron. He blamed everyone in sight, not excepting even me, for he said I was a witch like all the others. And when I sought to comfort him, saying it was done according to an older law of self-preservation to which even the most ancient rulers gave allegiance, he sneered at me and asked if I thought him a weakling. I saw then that he had been aroused to this passion not by concern over the dead Duke but by what that death implied for all royalty. As I look back on it, I think there may have been some prescience in my father, too, for it is certain that his line and Muad'Dib's shared common ancestry.

—FROM "IN MY FATHER'S HOUSE"
BY THE PRINCESS IRULAN

"Now Harkonnen shall kill Harkonnen," Paul whispered.

He had awakened shortly before nightfall, sitting up in the sealed and darkened stilltent. As he spoke, he heard the vague stirrings of his mother where she slept against the tent's opposite wall.

Paul glanced at the proximity detector on the floor, studying the dials illuminated in the blackness by phosphor tubes.

"It should be night soon," his mother said. "Why don't you lift the tent shades?"

Paul realized then that her breathing had been different for some time, that she had lain silent in the darkness until certain he was awake.

"Lifting the shades wouldn't help," he said. "There's been a storm. The tent's covered by sand. I'll dig us out soon."

"No sign of Duncan yet?"

"None."

Paul rubbed absently at the ducal signet on his thumb, and a sudden rage against the very substance of this planet which had helped kill his father set him trembling.

"I heard the storm begin," Jessica said.

The undemanding emptiness of her words helped restore some of his calm. His mind focused on the storm as he had seen it begin through the transparent end of their stilltent—cold dribbles of sand crossing the basin, then runnels and tails furrowing the sky. He had looked up to a rock spire, seen it change shape under the blast, becoming a low, cheddar-colored wedge. Sand funneled into their basin had shadowed the sky with dull curry, then blotted out all light as the tent was covered.

Tent bows had creaked once as they accepted the pressure, then—silence broken only by the dim bellows wheezing of their sand snorkel pumping air from the surface.

"Try the receiver again," Jessica said.

"No use," he said.

He found his stillsuit's watertube in its clip at his neck, drew a warm swallow into his mouth, and he thought that here he truly began an Arrakeen existence—living on reclaimed moisture from his own breath and body. It was flat and tasteless water, but it soothed his throat.

Jessica heard Paul drinking, felt the slickness of her own stillsuit clinging to her body, but she refused to accept her thirst. To accept it would require awakening fully into the terrible necessities of Arrakis where they must guard even fractional traces of moisture, hoarding the few drops in the tent's catchpockets, begrudging a breath wasted on the open air.

So much easier to drift back down into sleep.

But there had been a dream in this day's sleep, and she shivered at the memory of it. She had held dreaming hands beneath sandflow where a name had been written: *Duke Leto Atreides*. The name had blurred with the sand and she had moved to restore it, but the first letter filled before the last was begun.

The sand would not stop.

Her dream became wailing: louder and louder. That ridiculous wailing—part of her mind had realized the sound was her own voice as a tiny child, little more than a baby. A woman not quite visible to memory was going away.

My unknown mother, Jessica thought. *The Bene Gesserit who bore me and gave me to the Sisters because that's what she was commanded to do. Was she glad to rid herself of a Harkonnen child?*

"The place to hit them is in the spice," Paul said.

How can he think of attack at a time like this? she asked herself.

"An entire planet full of spice," she said. "How can you hit them there?"

She heard him stirring, the sound of their pack being dragged across the tent floor.

"It was sea power and air power on Caladan," he said. "Here, it's *desert power.* The Fremen are the key."

His voice came from the vicinity of the tent's sphincter. Her Bene Gesserit training sensed in his tone an unresolved bitterness toward her.

All his life he has been trained to hate Harkonnens, she thought. *Now, he finds he is Harkonnen . . . because of me. How little he knows me! I was my Duke's only woman. I accepted his life and his values even to defying my Bene Gesserit orders.*

The tent's glowtab came alight under Paul's hand, filled the domed area with green radiance. Paul crouched at the sphincter, his stillsuit hood adjusted for the open desert—forehead capped, mouth filter in place, nose plugs adjusted. Only his dark eyes were visible: a narrow band of face that turned once toward her and away.

"Secure yourself for the open," he said, and his voice was blurred behind the filter.

Jessica pulled the filter across her mouth, began adjusting her hood as she watched Paul break the tent seal.

Sand rasped as he opened the sphincter and a burred fizzle of grains ran into the tent before he could immobilize it with a static compaction tool. A hole grew in the sandwall as the tool realigned the grains. He slipped out and her ears followed his progress to the surface.

What will we find out there? she wondered. *Harkonnen troops and the Sardaukar, those are dangers we can expect. But what of the dangers we don't know?*

She thought of the compaction tool and the other strange instruments in the pack. Each of these tools suddenly stood in her mind as a sign of mysterious dangers.

She felt then a hot breeze from surface sand touch her cheeks where they were exposed above the filter.

"Pass up the pack." It was Paul's voice, low and guarded.

She moved to obey, heard the water literjons gurgle as she shoved the pack across the floor. She peered upward, saw Paul framed against stars.

"Here," he said and reached down, pulled the pack to the surface.

Now she saw only the circle of stars. They were like the luminous tips of weapons aimed down at her. A shower of meteors crossed her patch of night. The meteors seemed to her like a warning, like tiger stripes, like luminous grave slats clabbering her blood. And she felt the chill of the price on their heads.

"Hurry up," Paul said. "I want to collapse the tent."

A shower of sand from the surface brushed her left hand. *How much sand will the hand hold?* she asked herself.

"Shall I help you?" Paul asked.

"No."

She swallowed in a dry throat, slipped into the hole, felt static-packed sand rasp under her hands. Paul reached down, took her arm. She stood beside him on a smooth patch of starlit desert, stared around. Sand almost brimmed their basin, leaving only a dim lip of surrounding rock. She probed the farther darkness with her trained senses.

Noise of small animals.

Birds.

A fall of dislodged sand and faint creature sounds within it.

Paul collapsing their tent, recovering it up the hole.

Starlight displaced just enough of the night to charge each shadow with menace. She looked at patches of blackness.

Black is a blind remembering, she thought. *You listen for pack sounds, for the cries of those who hunted your ancestors in a past so ancient only your most primitive cells remember. The ears see. The nostrils see.*

Presently, Paul stood beside her, said: "Duncan told me that if he was captured, he could hold out . . . this long. We must leave here now." He shouldered the pack, crossed to the shallow lip of the basin, climbed to a ledge that looked down on open desert.

Jessica followed automatically, noting how she now lived in her son's orbit.

For now is my grief heavier than the sands of the seas, she thought. *This world has emptied me of all but the oldest purpose: tomorrow's life. I live now for my young Duke and the daughter yet to be.*

She felt the sand drag her feet as she climbed to Paul's side.

He looked north across a line of rocks, studying a distant escarpment.

The faraway rock profile was like an ancient battleship of the seas outlined by stars. The long swish of it lifted on an invisible wave with syllables of boomerang antennae, funnels arcing back, a pi-shaped upthrusting at the stern.

An orange glare burst above the silhouette and a line of brilliant purple cut downward toward the glare.

Another line of purple!

And another upthrusting orange glare!

It was like an ancient naval battle, remembered shellfire, and the sight held them staring.

"Pillars of fire," Paul whispered.

A ring of red eyes lifted over the distant rock. Lines of purple laced the sky.

"Jetflares and lasguns," Jessica said.

The dust-reddened first moon of Arrakis lifted above the horizon to their left and they saw a storm trail there—a ribbon of movement over the desert.

"It must be Harkonnen 'thopters hunting us," Paul said. "The way they're cutting up the desert . . . it's as though they were making certain they stamped out whatever's there . . . the way you'd stamp out a nest of insects."

"Or a nest of Atreides," Jessica said.

"We must seek cover," Paul said. "We'll head south and keep to the rocks. If they caught us in the open. . . ." He turned, adjusting the pack to his shoulders. "They're killing anything that moves."

He took one step along the ledge and, in that instant, heard the low hiss of gliding aircraft, saw the dark shapes of ornithopters above them.

My father once told me that respect for the truth comes close to being the basis for all morality. "Something cannot emerge from nothing," he said. This is profound thinking if you understand how unstable "the truth" can be.

—FROM "CONVERSATIONS WITH MUAD'DIB"
BY THE PRINCESS IRULAN

"I've always prided myself on seeing things the way they truly are," Thufir Hawat said. "That's the curse of being a Mentat. You can't stop analyzing your data."

The leathered old face appeared composed in the predawn dimness as he spoke. His sapho-stained lips were drawn into a straight line with radial creases spreading upward.

A robed man squatted silently on sand across from Hawat, apparently unmoved by the words.

The two crouched beneath a rock overhang that looked down on a wide, shallow sink. Dawn was spreading over the shattered outline of cliffs across the basin, touching everything with pink. It was cold under the overhang, a dry and penetrating chill left over from the night. There had been a warm wind just before dawn, but now it was cold. Hawat could hear teeth chattering behind him among the few troopers remaining in his force.

The man squatting across from Hawat was a Fremen who had come across the sink in the first light of false dawn, skittering over the sand, blending into the dunes, his movements barely discernible.

The Fremen extended a finger to the sand between them, drew a figure there. It looked like a bowl with an arrow spilling out of it. "There are many Harkonnen patrols," he said. He lifted his finger, pointed upward across the cliffs that Hawat and his men had descended.

Hawat nodded.

Many patrols. Yes.

But still he did not know what this Fremen wanted and this rankled. Mentat training was supposed to give a man the power to see motives.

This had been the worst night of Hawat's life. He had been at Tsimpo, a garrison village, buffer outpost for the former capital city, Carthag, when the reports of attack began arriving. At first, he'd thought: *It's a raid. The Harkonnens are testing.*

But report followed report—faster and faster.

Two legions landed at Carthag.

Five legions—fifty brigades!—attacking the Duke's main base at Arrakeen.

A legion at Arsunt.

Two battle groups at Splintered Rock.

Then the reports became more detailed—there were Imperial Sardaukar among the attackers—possibly two legions of them. And it became clear that the invaders knew precisely which weight of arms to send where. Precisely! Superb Intelligence.

Hawat's shocked fury had mounted until it threatened the smooth functioning of his Mentat capabilities. The size of the attack struck his mind like a physical blow.

Now, hiding beneath a bit of desert rock, he nodded to himself, pulled his torn and slashed tunic around him as though warding off the cold shadows.

The size of the attack.

He had always expected their enemy to hire an occasional lighter from the Guild for probing raids. That was an ordinary enough gambit in this kind of House-to-House warfare. Lighters landed and took off on Arrakis regularly to transport the spice for House Atreides. Hawat had taken precautions against random raids by false spice lighters. For a full attack they'd expected no more than ten brigades.

But there were more than two thousand ships down on Arrakis at the last count—not just lighters, but frigates, scouts, monitors, crushers, troop carriers, dump-boxes. . . .

More than a hundred brigades—ten legions!

The entire spice income of Arrakis for fifty years might just cover the cost of such a venture.

It might.

I underestimated what the Baron was willing to spend in attacking us, Hawat thought. *I failed my Duke.*

Then there was the matter of the traitor.

I will live long enough to see her strangled! he thought. *I should've killed that Bene Gesserit witch when I had the chance.* There was no doubt in his mind who had betrayed them—the Lady Jessica. She fitted all the facts available.

"Your man Gurney Halleck and part of his force are safe with our smuggler friends," the Fremen said.

"Good."

So Gurney will get off this hell planet. We're not all gone.

Hawat glanced back at the huddle of his men. He had started the night just past with three hundred of his finest. Of those, an even twenty remained and half of them were wounded. Some of them slept now, standing up, leaning against the rock, sprawled on the sand beneath the rock. Their last 'thopter, the one they'd been using as a ground-effect machine to carry their wounded, had given out just before dawn. They had cut it up with lasguns and hidden the pieces, then worked their way down into this hiding place at the edge of the basin.

Hawat had only a rough idea of their location—some two hundred kilometers southeast of Arrakeen. The main traveled ways between the Shield Wall sietch communities were somewhere south of them.

The Fremen across from Hawat threw back his hood and stillsuit cap to reveal sandy hair and beard. The hair was combed straight back from a high, thin forehead. He had the unreadable total blue eyes of the spice diet. Beard and mustache were stained at one side of the mouth, his hair matted there by pressure of the looping catchtube from his nose plugs.

The man removed his plugs, readjusted them. He rubbed at a scar beside his nose.

"If you cross the sink here this night," the Fremen said, "you must not use shields. There is a break in the wall. . . ." He turned on his heels, pointed south. ". . . there, and it is open sand down to the erg. Shields will attract a. . . ." He hesitated. ". . . worm. They don't often come in here, but a shield will bring one every time."

He said worm, Hawat thought. *He was going to say something else. What? And what does he want of us?*

Hawat sighed.

He could not recall ever before being this tired. It was a muscle weariness that energy pills were unable to ease.

Those damnable Sardaukar!

With a self-accusing bitterness, he faced the thought of the soldier-fanatics and the Imperial treachery they represented. His own Mentat assessment of the data told him how little chance he had ever to present evidence of this treachery before the High Council of the Landsraad where justice might be done.

"Do you wish to go to the smugglers?" the Fremen asked.

"Is it possible?"

"The way is long."

"Fremen don't like to say no," Idaho had told him once.

Hawat said: "You haven't yet told me whether your people can help my wounded."

"They are wounded."

The same damned answer every time!

"We know they're wounded!" Hawat snapped. "That's not the—"

"Peace, friend," the Fremen cautioned. "What do your wounded say? Are there those among them who can see the water need of your tribe?"

"We haven't talked about water," Hawat said. "We—"

"I can understand your reluctance," the Fremen said. "They are your friends, your tribesmen. Do you have water?"

"Not enough."

The Fremen gestured to Hawat's tunic, the skin exposed beneath it. "You were caught in-sietch, without your suits. You must make a water decision, friend."

"Can we hire your help?"

The Fremen shrugged. "You have no water." He glanced at the group behind Hawat. "How many of your wounded would you spend?"

Hawat fell silent, staring at the man. He could see as a Mentat that their communication was out of phase. Word-sounds were not being linked up here in the normal manner.

"I am Thufir Hawat," he said. "I can speak for my Duke. I will make promissory commitment now for your help. I wish a limited form of help, preserving my force long enough only to kill a traitor who thinks herself beyond vengeance."

"You wish our siding in a vendetta?"

"The vendetta I'll handle myself. I wish to be freed of responsibility for my wounded that I may get about it."

The Fremen scowled. "How can you be responsible for your wounded? They are their own responsibility. The water's at issue, Thufir Hawat. Would you have me take that decision away from you?"

The man put a hand to a weapon concealed beneath his robe.

Hawat tensed, wondering: *Is there betrayal here?*

"What do you fear?" the Fremen demanded.

These people and their disconcerting directness! Hawat spoke cautiously. "There's a price on my head."

"Ah-h-h-h." The Fremen removed his hand from his weapon. "You think we have the Byzantine corruption. You don't know us. The Harkonnens have not water enough to buy the smallest child among us."

But they had the price of Guild passage for more than two thousand fighting ships, Hawat thought. And the size of that price still staggered him.

"We both fight Harkonnens," Hawat said. "Should we not share the problems and ways of meeting the battle issue?"

"We are sharing," the Fremen said. "I have seen you fight Harkonnens. You are good. There've been times I'd have appreciated your arm beside me."

"Say where my arm may help you," Hawat said.

"Who knows?" the Fremen asked. "There are Harkonnen forces everywhere. But you still have not made the water decision or put it to your wounded."

I must be cautious, Hawat told himself. *There's a thing here that's not understood.*

He said: "Will you show me your way, the Arrakeen way?"

"Stranger-thinking," the Fremen said, and there was a sneer in his tone. He pointed to the northwest across the clifftop. "We watched you come across the sand last night." He lowered his arm. "You keep your force on the slip-face of the dunes. Bad. You have no stillsuits, no water. You will not last long."

"The ways of Arrakis don't come easily," Hawat said.

"Truth. But we've killed Harkonnens."

"What do you do with your own wounded?" Hawat demanded.

"Does a man not know when he is worth saving?" the Fremen asked. "Your wounded know you have no water." He tilted his head, looking sideways up at Hawat. "This is clearly a time for water decision. Both wounded and unwounded must look to the tribe's future."

The tribe's future, Hawat thought. *The tribe of Atreides. There's sense in that.* He forced himself to the question he had been avoiding.

"Have you word of my Duke or his son?"

Unreadable blue eyes stared upward into Hawat's. "Word?"

"Their fate!" Hawat snapped.

"Fate is the same for everyone," the Fremen said. "Your Duke, it is said, has met his fate. As to the Lisan al-Gaib, his son, that is in Liet's hands. Liet has not said."

I knew the answer without asking, Hawat thought.

He glanced back at his men. They were all awake now. They had heard. They were staring out across the sand, the realization in their expressions: there was no returning to Caladan for them, and now Arrakis was lost.

Hawat turned back to the Fremen. "Have you heard of Duncan Idaho?"

"He was in the great house when the shield went down," the Fremen said. "This I've heard . . . no more."

She dropped the shield and let in the Harkonnens, he thought. *I was the one who sat with my back to a door. How could she do this when it meant turning also against her own son? But . . . who knows how a Bene Gesserit witch thinks . . . if you can call it thinking?*

Hawat tried to swallow in a dry throat. "When will you hear about the boy?"

"We know little of what happens in Arrakeen," the Fremen said. He shrugged. "Who knows?"

"You have ways of finding out?"

"Perhaps." The Fremen rubbed at the scar beside his nose. "Tell me, Thufir Hawat, do you have knowledge of the big weapons the Harkonnens used?"

The artillery, Hawat thought bitterly. *Who could have guessed they'd use artillery in this day of shields?*

"You refer to the artillery they used to trap our people in the caves," he said. "I've . . . theoretical knowledge of such explosive weapons."

"Any man who retreats into a cave which has only one opening deserves to die," the Fremen said.

"Why do you ask about these weapons?"

"Liet wishes it."

Is that what he wants from us? Hawat wondered. He said: "Did you come here seeking information about the big guns?"

"Liet wished to see one of the weapons for himself."

"Then you should just go take one," Hawat sneered.

"Yes," the Fremen said. "We took one. We have it hidden where Stilgar can study it for Liet and where Liet can see it for himself if he wishes. But I doubt he'll want to: the weapon is not a very good one. Poor design for Arrakis."

"You . . . took one?" Hawat asked.

"It was a good fight," the Fremen said. "We lost only two men and spilled the water from more than a hundred of theirs."

There were Sardaukar at every gun, Hawat thought. *This desert madman speaks casually of losing only two men against Sardaukar!*

"We would not have lost the two except for those others fighting beside the Harkonnens," the Fremen said. "Some of those are good fighters."

One of Hawat's men limped forward, looked down at the squatting Fremen. "Are you talking about Sardaukar?"

"He's talking about Sardaukar," Hawat said.

"Sardaukar!" the Fremen said, and there appeared to be glee in his voice. "Ah-h-h, so that's what they are! This was a good night indeed. Sardaukar. Which legion? Do you know?"

"We . . . don't know," Hawat said.

"Sardaukar," the Fremen mused. "Yet they wear Harkonnen clothing. Is that not strange?"

"The Emperor does not wish it known he fights against a Great House," Hawat said.

"But *you* know they are Sardaukar."

"Who am I?" Hawat asked bitterly.

"You are Thufir Hawat," the man said matter-of-factly. "Well, we would have learned it in time. We've sent three of them captive to be questioned by Liet's men."

Hawat's aide spoke slowly, disbelief in every word: "You . . . *captured* Sardaukar?"

"Only three of them," the Fremen said. "They fought well."

If only we'd had the time to link up with these Fremen, Hawat thought. It was a sour lament in his mind. *If only we could've trained them and armed them. Great Mother, what a fighting force we'd have had!*

"Perhaps you delay because of worry over the Lisan al-Gaib," the Fremen said. "If he is truly the Lisan al-Gaib, harm cannot touch him. Do not spend thoughts on a matter which has not been proved."

"I serve the . . . Lisan al-Gaib," Hawat said. "His welfare is my concern. I've pledged myself to this."

"You are pledged to his water?"

Hawat glanced at his aide, who was still staring at the Fremen, returned his attention to the squatting figure. "To his water, yes."

"You wish to return to Arrakeen, to the place of his water?"

"To . . . yes, to the place of his water."

"Why did you not say at first it was a water matter?" The Fremen stood up, seated his nose plugs firmly.

Hawat motioned with his head for his aide to return to the others. With a tired shrug, the man obeyed. Hawat heard a low-voiced conversation arise among the men.

The Fremen said: "There is always a way to water."

Behind Hawat, a man cursed. Hawat's aide called: "Thufir! Arkie just died."

The Fremen put a fist to his ear. "The bond of water! It's a sign!" He stared at Hawat. "We have a place nearby for accepting the water. Shall I call my men?"

The aide returned to Hawat's side, said: "Thufir, a couple of the men left wives in Arrakeen. They're . . . well, you know how it is at a time like this."

The Fremen still held his fist to his ear. "Is it the bond of water, Thufir Hawat?" he demanded.

Hawat's mind was racing. He sensed now the direction of the Fremen's words, but feared the reaction of the tired men under the rock overhang when they understood it.

"The bond of water," Hawat said.

"Let our tribes be joined," the Fremen said, and he lowered his fist.

As though that were the signal, four men slid and dropped down from the rocks above them. They darted back under the overhang, rolled the dead man in a loose robe, lifted him and began running with him along the cliff wall to the right. Spurts of dust lifted around their running feet.

It was over before Hawat's tired men could gather their wits. The group with the body hanging like a sack in its enfolding robe was gone around a turn in the cliff.

One of Hawat's men shouted: "Where they going with Arkie? He was—"

"They're taking him to . . . bury him," Hawat said.

"Fremen don't bury their dead!" the man barked. "Don't you try any tricks on us, Thufir. We know what they do. Arkie was one of—"

"Paradise were sure for a man who died in the service of Lisan al-Gaib," the Fremen said. "If it is the Lisan al-Gaib you serve, as you have said it, why raise mourning cries? The memory of one who died in this fashion will live as long as the memory of man endures."

But Hawat's men advanced, angry looks on their faces. One had captured a lasgun. He started to draw it.

"Stop right where you are!" Hawat barked. He fought down the sick fatigue that gripped his muscles. "These people respect our dead. Customs differ, but the meaning's the same."

"They're going to render Arkie down for his water," the man with the lasgun snarled.

"Is it that your men wish to attend the ceremony?" the Fremen asked.

He doesn't even see the problem, Hawat thought. The naïveté of the Fremen was frightening.

"They're concerned for a respected comrade," Hawat said.

"We will treat your comrade with the same reverence we treat our own," the Fremen said. "This is the bond of water. We know the rites. A man's flesh is his own; the water belongs to the tribe."

Hawat spoke quickly as the man with the lasgun advanced another step. "Will you now help our wounded?"

"One does not question the bond," the Fremen said. "We will do for you what a tribe does for its own. First, we must get all of you suited and see to the necessities."

The man with the lasgun hesitated.

Hawat's aide said: "Are we buying help with Arkie's . . . water?"

"Not buying," Hawat said. "We've joined these people."

"Customs differ," one of his men muttered.

Hawat began to relax.

"And they'll help us get to Arrakeen?"

"We will kill Harkonnens," the Fremen said. He grinned. "And Sardaukar." He stepped backward, cupped his hands beside his ears and tipped his head back, listening. Presently, he lowered his hands, said: "An aircraft comes. Conceal yourselves beneath the rock and remain motionless."

At a gesture from Hawat, his men obeyed.

The Fremen took Hawat's arm, pressed him back with the others. "We will fight in the time of fighting," the man said. He reached beneath his robes, brought out a small cage, lifted a creature from it.

Hawat recognized a tiny bat. The bat turned its head and Hawat saw its blue-within-blue eyes.

The Fremen stroked the bat, soothing it, crooning to it. He bent over the animal's head, allowed a drop of saliva to fall from his tongue into the bat's upturned mouth. The bat stretched its wings, but remained on the Fremen's opened hand. The man took a tiny tube, held it beside the bat's head and chattered into the tube; then, lifting the creature high, he threw it upward.

The bat swooped away beside the cliff and was lost to sight.

The Fremen folded the cage, thrust it beneath his robe. Again, he bent his head, listening. "They quarter the high country," he said. "One wonders who they seek up there."

"It's known that we retreated in this direction," Hawat said.

"One should never presume one is the sole object of a hunt," the Fremen said. "Watch the other side of the basin. You will see a thing."

Time passed.

Some of Hawat's men stirred, whispering.

"Remain silent as frightened animals," the Fremen hissed.

Hawat discerned movement near the opposite cliff—flitting blurs of tan on tan.

"My little friend carried his message," the Fremen said. "He is a good messenger—day or night. I'll be unhappy to lose that one."

The movement across the sink faded away. On the entire four to five kilometer expanse of sand nothing remained but the growing pressure of the day's heat—blurred columns of rising air.

"Be most silent now," the Fremen whispered.

A file of plodding figures emerged from a break in the opposite cliff, headed directly across the sink. To Hawat, they appeared to be Fremen, but a curiously inept band. He counted six men making heavy going of it over the dunes.

A "thwok-thwok" of ornithopter wings sounded high to the right behind Hawat's group. The craft came over the cliff wall above them—an Atreides 'thopter with Harkonnen battle colors splashed on it. The 'thopter swooped toward the men crossing the sink.

The group there stopped on a dune crest, waved.

The 'thopter circled once over them in a tight curve, came back for a dust-shrouded landing in front of the Fremen. Five men swarmed from the 'thopter and Hawat saw the dust-repellent shimmering of shields and, in their motions, the hard competence of Sardaukar.

"Aiihh! They use their stupid shields," the Fremen beside Hawat hissed. He glanced toward the open south wall of the sink.

"They are Sardaukar," Hawat whispered.

"Good."

The Sardaukar approached the waiting group of Fremen in an enclosing half-circle. Sun glinted on blades held ready. The Fremen stood in a compact group, apparently indifferent.

Abruptly, the sand around the two groups sprouted Fremen. They were at the ornithopter, then in it. Where the two groups had met at the dune crest, a dust cloud partly obscured violent motion.

Presently, dust settled. Only Fremen remained standing.

"They left only three men in their 'thopter," the Fremen beside Hawat said. "That was fortunate. I don't believe we had to damage the craft in taking it."

Behind Hawat, one of his men whispered: "Those were Sardaukar!"

"Did you notice how well they fought?" the Fremen asked.

Hawat took a deep breath. He smelled the burned dust around him, felt the heat, the dryness. In a voice to match that dryness, he said: "Yes, they fought well, indeed."

The captured 'thopter took off with a lurching flap of wings, angled upward to the south in a steep, wing-tucked climb.

So these Fremen can handle 'thopters, too, Hawat thought.

On the distant dune, a Fremen waved a square of green cloth: once . . . twice.

"More come!" the Fremen beside Hawat barked. "Be ready. I'd hoped to have us away without more inconvenience."

Inconvenience! Hawat thought.

He saw two more 'thopters swooping from high in the west onto an area of sand suddenly devoid of visible Fremen. Only eight splotches of blue—the bodies of the Sardaukar in Harkonnen uniforms—remained at the scene of violence.

Another 'thopter glided in over the cliff wall above Hawat. He drew in a sharp breath as he saw it—a big troop carrier. It flew with the slow, spread-wing heaviness of a full load—like a giant bird coming to its nest.

In the distance, the purple finger of a lasgun beam flicked from one of the diving 'thopters. It laced across the sand, raising a sharp trail of dust.

"The cowards!" the Fremen beside Hawat rasped.

The troop carrier settled toward the patch of blue-clad bodies. Its wings crept out to full reach, began the cupping action of a quick stop.

Hawat's attention was caught by a flash of sun on metal to the south, a 'thopter plummeting there in a power dive, wings folded flat against its sides, its jets a golden flare against the dark silvered gray of the sky. It plunged like an arrow toward the troop carrier which was unshielded because of the lasgun activity around it. Straight into the carrier the diving 'thopter plunged.

A flaming roar shook the basin. Rocks tumbled from the cliff walls all around. A geyser of red-orange shot skyward from the sand where the carrier and its companion 'thopters had been—everything there caught in the flame.

It was the Fremen who took off in that captured 'thopter, Hawat thought. *He deliberately sacrificed himself to get that carrier. Great Mother! What are these Fremen?*

"*A reasonable exchange,*" said the Fremen beside Hawat. "There must've been three hundred men in that carrier. Now, we must see to their water and make plans to get another aircraft." He started to step out of their rock-shadowed concealment.

A rain of blue uniforms came over the cliff wall in front of him, falling in low-suspensor slowness. In the flashing instant, Hawat had time to see that they were Sardaukar, hard faces set in battle frenzy, that they were unshielded and each carried a knife in one hand, a stunner in the other.

A thrown knife caught Hawat's Fremen companion in the throat, hurling him backward, twisting face down. Hawat had only time to draw his own knife before blackness of a stunner projectile felled him.

Muad'Dib could indeed see the Future, but you must understand the limits of this power. Think of sight. You have eyes, yet cannot see without light. If you are on the floor of a valley, you cannot see beyond your valley. Just so, Muad'Dib could not always choose to look across the mysterious terrain. He tells us that a single obscure decision of prophecy, perhaps the choice of one word over another, could change the entire aspect of the future. He tells us "The vision of time is broad, but when you pass through it, time becomes a narrow door." And always, he fought the temptation to choose a clear, safe course, warning "That path leads ever down into stagnation."

—FROM "ARRAKIS AWAKENING"
BY THE PRINCESS IRULAN

As the ornithopters glided out of the night above them, Paul grabbed his mother's arm, snapped: "Don't move!"

Then he saw the lead craft in the moonlight, the way its wings cupped to brake for landing, the reckless dash of the hands at the controls.

"It's Idaho," he breathed.

The craft and its companions settled into the basin like a covey of birds coming to nest. Idaho was out of his 'thopter and running toward them before the dust settled. Two figures in Fremen robes followed him. Paul recognized one: the tall, sandy-bearded Kynes.

"This way!" Kynes called and he veered left.

Behind Kynes, other Fremen were throwing fabric covers over their ornithopters. The craft became a row of shallow dunes.

Idaho skidded to a stop in front of Paul, saluted. "M'Lord, the Fremen have a temporary hiding place nearby where we—"

"What about that back there?"

Paul pointed to the violence above the distant cliff—the jetflares, the purple beams of lasguns lacing the desert.

A rare smile touched Idaho's round, placid face. "M'Lord . . . Sire, I've left them a little sur—"

Glaring white light filled the desert—bright as a sun, etching their shadows onto the rock floor of the ledge. In one sweeping motion, Idaho had Paul's arm in one hand, Jessica's shoulder in the other, hurling them down off the ledge into the basin. They sprawled together in the sand as the roar of an explosion thundered over them. Its shock wave tumbled chips off the rock ledge they had vacated.

Idaho sat up, brushed sand from himself.

"Not the family atomics!" Jessica said. "I thought—"

"You planted a shield back there," Paul said.

"A big one turned to full force," Idaho said. "A lasgun beam touched it and. . . ." He shrugged.

"Subatomic fusion," Jessica said. "That's a dangerous weapon."

"Not weapon, m'Lady, defense. That scum will think twice before using lasguns another time."

The Fremen from the ornithopters stopped above them. One called in a low voice: "We should get under cover, friends."

Paul got to his feet as Idaho helped Jessica up.

"That blast *will* attract considerable attention, Sire," Idaho said.

Sire, Paul thought.

The word had such a strange sound when directed at him. Sire had always been his father.

He felt himself touched briefly by his powers of prescience, seeing himself infected by the wild race consciousness that was moving the human universe toward chaos. The vision left him shaken, and he allowed Idaho to guide him along the edge of the basin to a rock projection. Fremen there were opening a way down into the sand with their compaction tools.

"May I take your pack, Sire?" Idaho asked.

"It's not heavy, Duncan," Paul said.

"You have no body shield," Idaho said. "Do you wish mine?" He glanced at the distant cliff. "Not likely there'll be any more lasgun activity about."

"Keep your shield, Duncan. Your right arm is shield enough for me."

Jessica saw the way the praise took effect, how Idaho moved closer to Paul, and she thought: *Such a sure hand my son has with his people.*

The Fremen removed a rock plug that opened a passage down into the native basement complex of the desert. A camouflage cover was rigged for the opening.

"This way," one of the Fremen said, and he led them down rock steps into darkness.

Behind them, the cover blotted out the moonlight. A dim green glow came alive ahead, revealing the steps and rock walls, a turn to the left. Robed Fremen were all around them now, pressing downward. They rounded the corner, found another down-slanting passage. It opened into a rough cave chamber.

Kynes stood before them, jubba hood thrown back. The neck of his stillsuit glistening in the green light. His long hair and beard were mussed. The blue eyes without whites were a darkness under heavy brows.

In the moment of encounter, Kynes wondered at himself: *Why am I helping these people? It's the most dangerous thing I've ever done. It could doom me with them.*

Then he looked squarely at Paul, seeing the boy who had taken on the mantle of manhood, masking grief, suppressing all except the position that now must be assumed—the dukedom. And Kynes realized in that moment the dukedom still existed and solely because of this youth—and this was not a thing to be taken lightly.

Jessica glanced once around the chamber, registering it on her senses in the Bene Gesserit way—a laboratory, a civil place full of angles and squares in the ancient manner.

"This is one of the Imperial Ecological Testing Stations my father wanted as advance bases," Paul said.

His father wanted! Kynes thought.

And again Kynes wondered at himself: *Am I foolish to aid these fugitives? Why am I doing it? It'd be so easy to take them now, to buy the Harkonnen trust with them.*

Paul followed his mother's example, gestalting the room, seeing the workbench down one side, the walls of featureless rock. Instruments lined the bench—dials glowing, wire gridex planes with fluting glass emerging from them. An ozone smell permeated the place.

Some of the Fremen moved on around a concealing angle in the chamber and new sounds started there—machine coughs, the whinnies of spinning belts and multidrives.

Paul looked to the end of the room, saw cages with small animals in them stacked against the wall.

"You've recognized this place correctly," Kynes said. "For what would you use such a place, Paul Atreides?"

"To make this planet a fit place for humans," Paul said.

Perhaps that's why I help them, Kynes thought.

The machine sounds abruptly hummed away to silence. Into this void there came a thin animal squeak from the cages. It was cut off abruptly as though in embarrassment.

Paul returned his attention to the cages, saw that the animals were brown-winged bats. An automatic feeder extended from the side wall across the cages.

A Fremen emerged from the hidden area of the chamber, spoke to Kynes: "Liet, the field-generator equipment is not working. I am unable to mask us from proximity detectors."

"Can you repair it?" Kynes asked.

"Not quickly. The parts. . . ." The man shrugged.

"Yes," Kynes said. "Then we'll do without machinery. Get a hand pump for air out to the surface."

"Immediately." The man hurried away.

Kynes turned back to Paul. "You gave a good answer."

Jessica marked the easy rumble of the man's voice. It was a *royal* voice, accustomed to command. And she had not missed the reference to him as Liet. Liet was the Fremen alter ego, the other face of the tame planetologist.

"We're most grateful for your help, Doctor Kynes," she said.

"Mm-m-m, we'll see," Kynes said. He nodded to one of his men. "Spice coffee in my quarters, Shamir."

"At once, Liet," the man said.

Kynes indicated an arched opening in the side wall of the chamber. "If you please?"

Jessica allowed herself a regal nod before accepting. She saw Paul give a hand signal to Idaho, telling him to mount guard here.

The passage, two paces deep, opened through a heavy door into a square office lighted by golden glowglobes. Jessica passed her hand across the door as she entered, was startled to identify plasteel.

Paul stepped three paces into the room, dropped his pack to the floor. He heard the door close behind him, studied the place—about eight meters to a side, walls of natural rock, curry-colored, broken by metal filing cabinets on their right. A low desk with milk glass top shot full of yellow bubbles occupied the room's center. Four suspensor chairs ringed the desk.

Kynes moved around Paul, held a chair for Jessica. She sat down, noting the way her son examined the room.

Paul remained standing for another eyeblink. A faint anomaly in the room's air currents told him there was a secret exit to their right behind the filing cabinets.

"Will you sit down, Paul Atreides?" Kynes asked.

How carefully he avoids my title, Paul thought. But he accepted the chair, remained silent while Kynes sat down.

"You sense that Arrakis could be a paradise," Kynes said. "Yet, as you see, the Imperium sends here only its trained hatchetmen, its seekers after the spice!"

Paul held up his thumb with its ducal signet. "Do you see this ring?"

"Yes."

"Do you know its significance?"

Jessica turned sharply to stare at her son.

"Your father lies dead in the ruins of Arrakeen," Kynes said. "You are technically the Duke."

"I'm a soldier of the Imperium," Paul said, "*technically* a hatchet-man."

Kynes' face darkened. "Even with the Emperor's Sardaukar standing over your father's body?"

"The Sardaukar are one thing, the legal source of my authority is another," Paul said.

"Arrakis has its own way of determining who wears the mantle of authority," Kynes said.

And Jessica, turning back to look at him, thought: *There's steel in this man that no one has taken the temper out of . . . and we've need of steel. Paul's doing a dangerous thing.*

Paul said: "The Sardaukar on Arrakis are a measure of how much our beloved Emperor feared my father. Now, *I* will give the Padishah Emperor reasons to fear the—"

"Lad," Kynes said, "there are things you don't—"

"You will address me as Sire or my Lord," Paul said.

Gently, Jessica thought.

Kynes stared at Paul, and Jessica noted the glint of admiration in the planetologist's face, the touch of humor there.

"Sire," Kynes said.

"I am an embarrassment to the Emperor," Paul said. "I am an embarrassment to all who would divide Arrakis as their spoil. As I live, I shall continue to be such an embarrassment that I stick in their throats and choke them to death!"

"Words," Kynes said.

Paul stared at him. Presently, Paul said: "You have a legend of the Lisan al-Gaib here, the Voice from the Outer World, the one who will lead the Fremen to paradise. Your men have—"

"Superstition!" Kynes said.

"Perhaps," Paul agreed. "Yet perhaps not. Superstitions sometimes have strange roots and stranger branchings."

"You have a plan," Kynes said. "This much is obvious . . . *Sire.*"

"Could your Fremen provide me with proof positive that the Sardaukar are here in Harkonnen uniform?"

"Quite likely."

"The Emperor will put a Harkonnen back in power here," Paul said. "Perhaps even Beast Rabban. Let him. Once he has involved himself beyond escaping his guilt, let the Emperor face the possibility of a Bill of Particulars laid before the Landsraad. Let him answer there where—"

"Paul!" Jessica said.

"Granted that the Landsraad High Council accepts your case," Kynes said, "there could be only one outcome: general warfare between the Imperium and the Great Houses."

"Chaos," Jessica said.

"But I'd present my case to the Emperor," Paul said, "and give him an alternative to chaos."

Jessica spoke in a dry tone: "Blackmail?"

"One of the tools of statecraft, as you've said yourself," Paul said, and Jessica heard the bitterness in his voice. "The Emperor has no sons, only daughters."

"You'd aim for the throne?" Jessica asked.

"The Emperor will not risk having the Imperium shattered by total war," Paul said. "Planets blasted, disorder everywhere—he'll not risk that."

"This is a desperate gamble you propose," Kynes said.

"What do the Great Houses of the Landsraad fear most?" Paul asked. "They fear most what is happening here right now on Arrakis—the Sardaukar picking them off one by one. That's why there *is* a Landsraad. This is the glue of the Great Convention. Only in union do they match the Imperial forces."

"But they're—"

"This is what they fear," Paul said. "Arrakis would become a rallying cry. Each of them would see himself in my father—cut out of the herd and killed."

Kynes spoke to Jessica: "Would his plan work?"

"I'm no Mentat," Jessica said.

"But you are Bene Gesserit."

She shot a probing stare at him, said: "His plan has good points and bad points . . . as any plan would at this stage. A plan depends as much upon execution as it does upon concept."

"'Law is the ultimate science,'" Paul quoted. "Thus it reads above the Emperor's door. I propose to show him law."

"And I'm not sure I could trust the person who conceived this plan," Kynes said. "Arrakis has its own plan that we—"

"From the throne," Paul said, "I could make a paradise of Arrakis with the wave of a hand. This is the coin I offer for your support."

Kynes stiffened. "My loyalty's not for sale, *Sire.*"

Paul stared across the desk at him, meeting the cold glare of those blue-within-blue eyes, studying the bearded face, the commanding appearance. A harsh smile touched Paul's lips and he said: "Well spoken. I apologize."

Kynes met Paul's stare and, presently, said: "No Harkonnen ever admitted error. Perhaps you're not like them, Atreides."

"It could be a fault in their education," Paul said. "You say you're not for sale, but I believe I've the coin you'll accept. For your loyalty I offer *my* loyalty to you . . . totally."

My son has the Atreides sincerity, Jessica thought. *He has that tremendous, almost naive honor—and what a powerful force that truly is.*

She saw that Paul's words had shaken Kynes.

"This is nonsense," Kynes said. "You're just a boy and—"

"I'm the Duke," Paul said. "I'm an Atreides. No Atreides has ever broken such a bond."

Kynes swallowed.

"When I say totally," Paul said, "I mean without reservation. I would give my life for you."

"Sire!" Kynes said, and the word was torn from him, but Jessica saw that he was not now speaking to a boy of fifteen, but to a man, to a superior. Now Kynes meant the word.

In this moment he'd give his life for Paul, she thought. *How do the Atreides accomplish this thing so quickly, so easily?*

"I know you mean this," Kynes said. "Yet the Harkon—"

The door behind Paul slammed open. He whirled to see reeling violence—shouting, the clash of steel, wax-image faces grimacing in the passage.

With his mother beside him, Paul leaped for the door, seeing Idaho blocking the passage, his blood-pitted eyes there visible through a shield blur, claw hands beyond him, arcs of steel chopping futilely at the shield. There was the orange fire-mouth of a stunner repelled by the shield. Idaho's blades were through it all, flick-flicking, red dripping from them.

Then Kynes was beside Paul and they threw their weight against the door.

Paul had one last glimpse of Idaho standing against a swarm of Harkonnen uniforms—his jerking, controlled staggers, the black goat hair with a red blossom of death in it. Then the door was closed and there came a snick as Kynes threw the bolts.

"I appear to've decided," Kynes said.

"Someone detected your machinery before it was shut down," Paul said. He pulled his mother away from the door, met the despair in her eyes.

"I should've suspected trouble when the coffee failed to arrive," Kynes said.

"You've a bolt hole out of here," Paul said. "Shall we use it?"

Kynes took a deep breath, said: "This door should hold for at least twenty minutes against all but a lasgun."

"They'll not use a lasgun for fear we've shields on this side," Paul said.

"Those were Sardaukar in Harkonnen uniform," Jessica whispered.

They could hear pounding on the door now, rhythmic blows.

Kynes indicated the cabinets against the right-hand wall, said: "This way." He crossed to the first cabinet, opened a drawer, manipulated a handle within it. The entire wall of cabinets swung open to expose the black mouth of a tunnel. "This door also is plasteel," Kynes said.

"You were well prepared," Jessica said.

"We lived under the Harkonnens for eighty years," Kynes said. He herded them into the darkness, closed the door.

In the sudden blackness, Jessica saw a luminous arrow on the floor ahead of her.

Kynes' voice came from behind them: "We'll separate here. This wall is tougher. It'll stand for at least an hour. Follow the arrows like that one on the floor. They'll be extinguished by your passage. They lead through a maze to another exit where I've secreted a 'thopter. There's a storm across the desert tonight. Your only hope is to run for that storm, dive into the top of it, ride with it. My people have done this in stealing 'thopters. If you stay high in the storm you'll survive."

"What of you?" Paul asked.

"I'll try to escape another way. If I'm captured . . . well, I'm still Imperial Planetologist. I can say I was your captive."

Running like cowards, Paul thought. *But how else can I live to avenge my father?* He turned to face the door.

Jessica heard him move, said, "Duncan's dead, Paul. You saw the wound. You can do nothing for him."

"I'll take full payment for them all one day," Paul said.

"Not unless you hurry now," Kynes said.

Paul felt the man's hand on his shoulder.

"Where will we meet, Kynes?" Paul asked.

"I'll send Fremen searching for you. The storm's path is known. Hurry now, and the Great Mother give you speed and luck."

They heard him go, a scrambling in the blackness.

Jessica found Paul's hand, pulled him gently. "We must not get separated," she said.

"Yes."

He followed her across the first arrow, seeing it go black as they touched it. Another arrow beckoned ahead.

They crossed it, saw it extinguish itself, saw another arrow ahead.

They were running now.

Plans within plans within plans within plans, Jessica thought. *Have we become part of someone else's plan now?*

The arrows led them around turnings, past side openings only dimly sensed in the faint luminescence. Their way slanted downward for a time, then up, ever up. They came finally to steps, rounded a corner and were brought short by a glowing wall with a dark handle visible in its center.

Paul pressed the handle.

The wall swung away from them. Light flared to reveal a rock-hewn cavern with an ornithopter squatting in its center. A flat gray wall with a doorsign on it loomed beyond the aircraft.

"Where did Kynes go?" Jessica asked.

"He did what any good guerrilla leader would," Paul said. "He separated us into two parties and arranged that he couldn't reveal where we are if he's captured. He won't really know."

Paul drew her into the room, noting how their feet kicked up dust on the floor.

"No one's been here for a long time," he said.

"He seemed confident the Fremen could find us," she said.

"I share that confidence."

Paul released her hand, crossed to the ornithopter's left door, opened it, and secured his pack in the rear. "This ship's proximity masked," he said. "Instrument panel has remote door control, light control. Eighty years under the Harkonnens taught them to be thorough."

Jessica leaned against the craft's other side, catching her breath.

"The Harkonnens will have a covering force over this area," she said. "They're not stupid." She considered her direction sense, pointed right. "The storm we saw is that way."

Paul nodded, fighting an abrupt reluctance to move. He knew its cause, but found no help in the knowledge. Somewhere this night he had passed a decision-nexus into the deep unknown. He knew the time-area surrounding them, but the here-and-now existed as a place of mystery. It was as though he had seen himself from a distance go out of sight down into a valley. Of the countless paths up out of that valley, some might carry a Paul Atreides back into sight, but many would not.

"The longer we wait the better prepared they'll be," Jessica said.

"Get in and strap yourself down," he said.

He joined her in the ornithopter, still wrestling with the thought that this was *blind* ground, unseen in any prescient vision. And he realized with an abrupt sense of shock that he had been giving more and more reliance to prescient memory and it had weakened him for this particular emergency.

"If you rely only on your eyes, your other senses weaken." It was a Bene Gesserit axiom. He took it to himself now, promising never again to fall into that trap . . . if he lived through this.

Paul fastened his safety harness, saw that his mother was secure, checked the aircraft. The wings were at full spread-rest, their delicate metal interleavings extended. He touched the retractor bar, watched the wings shorten for jet-boost takeoff the way Gurney Halleck had taught him. The starter switch moved easily. Dials on the instrument panel came alive as the jetpods were armed. Turbines began their low hissing.

"Ready?" he asked.

"Yes."

He touched the remote control for lights.

Darkness blanketed them.

His hand was a shadow against the luminous dials as he tripped the remote door control. Grating sounded ahead of them. A cascade of sand swished away to silence. A dusty breeze touched Paul's cheeks. He closed his door, feeling the sudden pressure.

A wide patch of dust-blurred stars framed in angular darkness appeared where the door-wall had been. Starlight defined a shelf beyond, a suggestion of sand ripples.

Paul depressed the glowing action-sequence switch on his panel.

The wings snapped back and down, hurling the 'thopter out of its nest. Power surged from the jetpods as the wings locked into lift attitude.

Jessica let her hands ride lightly on the dual controls, feeling the sureness of her son's movements. She was frightened, yet exhilarated. *Now, Paul's training is our only hope,* she thought. *His youth and swiftness.*

Paul fed more power to the jetpods. The 'thopter banked, sinking them into their seats as a dark wall lifted against the stars ahead. He gave the craft more wing, more power. Another burst of lifting wingbeats and they came out over rocks, silver-frosted angles and outcroppings in the starlight. The dust-reddened second moon showed itself above the horizon to their right, defining the ribbon trail of the storm.

Paul's hands danced over the controls. Wings snicked in to beetle stubs. G-force pulled at their flesh as the craft came around in a tight bank.

"Jetflares behind us!" Jessica said.

"I saw them."

He slammed the power arm forward.

Their 'thopter leaped like a frightened animal, surged southwest toward the storm and the great curve of desert. In the near distance, Paul saw scattered shadows telling where the line of rocks ended, the basement complex sinking beneath the dunes. Beyond stretched moonlit fingernail shadows—dunes diminishing one into another.

And above the horizon climbed the flat immensity of the storm like a wall against the stars.

Something jarred the 'thopter.

"Shellburst!" Jessica gasped. "They're using some kind of projectile weapon."

She saw a sudden animal grin on Paul's face. "They seem to be avoiding their lasguns," he said.

"But we've no shields!"

"Do they know that?"

Again the 'thopter shuddered.

Paul twisted to peer back. "Only one of them appears to be fast enough to keep up with us."

He returned his attention to their course, watching the storm wall grow high in front of them. It loomed like a tangible solid.

"Projectile launchers, rockets, all the ancient weaponry—that's one thing we'll give the Fremen," Paul whispered.

"The storm," Jessica said. "Hadn't you better turn?"

"What about the ship behind us?"

"He's pulling up."

"Now!"

Paul stubbed the wings, banked hard left into the deceptively slow boiling of the storm wall, felt his cheeks pull in the G-force.

They appeared to glide into a slow clouding of dust that grew heavier and heavier until it blotted out the desert and the moon. The aircraft became a long, horizontal whisper of darkness lighted only by the green luminosity of the instrument panel.

Through Jessica's mind flashed all the warnings about such storms— that they cut metal like butter, etched flesh to bone and ate away the bones. She felt the buffeting of dust-blanketed wind. It twisted them as Paul fought the controls. She saw him chop the power, felt the ship buck. The metal around them hissed and trembled.

"Sand!" Jessica shouted.

She saw the negative shake of his head in the light from the panel. "Not much sand this high."

But she could feel them sinking deeper into the maelstrom.

Paul sent the wings to their full soaring length, heard them creak with the strain. He kept his eyes fixed on the instruments, gliding by instinct, fighting for altitude.

The sound of their passage diminished.

The 'thopter began rolling off to the left. Paul focused on the glowing globe within the attitude curve, fought his craft back to level flight.

Jessica had the eerie feeling that they were standing still, that all motion was external. A vague tan flowing against the windows, a rumbling hiss reminded her of the powers around them.

Winds to seven or eight hundred kilometers an hour, she thought.

Adrenalin edginess gnawed at her. *I must not fear,* she told herself, mouthing the words of the Bene Gesserit litany. *Fear is the mind-killer.*

Slowly her long years of training prevailed.

Calmness returned.

"We have the tiger by the tail," Paul whispered. "We can't go down, can't land . . . and I don't think I can lift us out of this. We'll have to ride it out."

Calmness drained out of her. Jessica felt her teeth chattering, clamped them together. Then she heard Paul's voice, low and controlled, reciting the litany:

"Fear is the mind-killer. Fear is the little death that brings total obliteration. I will face my fear. I will permit it to pass over me and through me. And when it has gone past me I will turn to see fear's path. Where the fear has gone there will be nothing. Only I will remain."

> What do you despise? By this are you truly known.

—FROM "MANUAL OF MUAD'DIB"
> BY THE PRINCESS IRULAN

"They are dead, Baron," said Iakin Nefud, the guard captain. "Both the woman and the boy are certainly dead."

The Baron Vladimir Harkonnen sat up in the sleep suspensors of his private quarters. Beyond these quarters and enclosing him like a multi-shelled egg stretched the space frigate he had grounded on Arrakis. Here in his quarters, though, the ship's harsh metal was disguised with draperies, with fabric paddings and rare art objects.

"It is a certainty," the guard captain said. "They are dead."

The Baron shifted his gross body in the suspensors, focused his attention on an ebaline statue of a leaping boy in a niche across the room. Sleep faded from him. He straightened the padded suspensor beneath the fat folds of his neck, stared across the single glowglobe of his bed-chamber to the doorway where Captain Nefud stood blocked by the pentashield.

"They're certainly dead, Baron," the man repeated.

The Baron noted the trace of semuta dullness in Nefud's eyes. It was obvious the man had been deep within the drug's rapture when he received this report, and had stopped only to take the antidote before rushing here.

"I have a full report," Nefud said.

Let him sweat a little, the Baron thought. *One must always keep the tools of statecraft sharp and ready. Power and fear—sharp and ready.*

"Have you seen their bodies?" the Baron rumbled.

Nefud hesitated.

"Well?"

"M'Lord . . . they were seen to dive into a sandstorm . . . winds over eight hundred kilometers. Nothing survives such a storm, m'Lord. Nothing! One of our own craft was destroyed in the pursuit."

The Baron stared at Nefud, noting the nervous twitch in the scissors line of the man's jaw muscles, the way the chin moved as Nefud swallowed.

"You have seen the bodies?" the Baron asked.

"M'Lord—"

"For what purpose do you come here rattling your armor?" the Baron roared. "To tell me a thing is certain when it is not? Do you think I'll praise you for such stupidity, give you another promotion?"

Nefud's face went bone pale.

Look at the chicken, the Baron thought. *I am surrounded by such useless clods. If I scattered sand before this creature and told him it was grain, he'd peck at it.*

"The man Idaho led us to them, then?" the Baron asked.

"Yes, m'Lord!"

Look how he blurts out his answer, the Baron thought. He said: "They were attempting to flee to the Fremen, eh?"

"Yes, m'Lord."

"Is there more to this . . . report?"

"The Imperial Planetologist, Kynes, is involved, m'Lord. Idaho joined this Kynes under mysterious circumstances . . . I might even say *suspicious* circumstances."

"So?"

"They . . . ah, fled together to a place in the desert where it's apparent the boy and his mother were hiding. In the excitement of the chase, several of our groups were caught in a lasgun-shield explosion."

"How many did we lose?"

"I'm . . . ah, not sure yet, m'Lord."

He's lying, the Baron thought. *It must've been pretty bad.*

"The Imperial lackey, this Kynes," the Baron said. "He was playing a double game, eh?"

"I'd stake my reputation on it, m'Lord."

His reputation!

"Have the man killed," the Baron said.

"M'Lord! Kynes is the *Imperial* Planetologist, His Majesty's own serv—"

"Make it look like an accident, then!"

"M'Lord, there were Sardaukar with our forces in the subjugation of this Fremen nest. They have Kynes in custody now."

"Get him away from them. Say I wish to question him."

"If they demur?"

"They will not if you handle it correctly."

Nefud swallowed. "Yes, m'Lord."

"The man must die," the Baron rumbled. "He tried to help my enemies."

Nefud shifted from one foot to the other.

"Well?"

"M'Lord, the Sardaukar have . . . two persons in custody who might be of interest to you. They've caught the Duke's Master of Assassins."

"Hawat? Thufir Hawat?"

"I've seen the captive myself, m'Lord. 'Tis Hawat."

"I'd not've believed it possible!"

"They say he was knocked out by a stunner, m'Lord. In the desert where he couldn't use his shield. He's virtually unharmed. If we can get our hands on him, he'll provide great sport."

"This is a Mentat you speak of," the Baron growled. "One doesn't waste a Mentat. Has he spoken? What does he say of his defeat? Could he know the extent of . . . but no."

"He has spoken only enough, m'Lord, to reveal his belief that the Lady Jessica was his betrayer."

"Ah-h-h-h-h."

The Baron sank back, thinking; then: "You're sure? It's the Lady Jessica who attracts his anger?"

"He said it in my presence, m'Lord."

"Let him think she's alive, then."

"But, m'Lord—"

"Be quiet. I wish Hawat treated kindly. He must be told nothing of the late Doctor Yueh, his true betrayer. Let it be said that Doctor Yueh died defending his Duke. In a way, this may even be true. We will, instead, feed his suspicions against the Lady Jessica."

"M'Lord, I don't—"

"The way to control and direct a Mentat, Nefud, is through his information. False information—false results."

"Yes, m'Lord, but . . ."

"Is Hawat hungry? Thirsty?"

"M'Lord, Hawat's still in the hands of the Sardaukar!"

"Yes. Indeed, yes. But the Sardaukar will be as anxious to get information from Hawat as I am. I've noticed a thing about our allies, Nefud. They're not very devious . . . politically. I do believe this is a deliberate thing; the Emperor wants it that way. Yes. I do believe it. You will remind the Sardaukar commander of my renown at obtaining information from reluctant subjects."

Nefud looked unhappy. "Yes, m'Lord."

"You will tell the Sardaukar commander that I wish to question both Hawat and this Kynes at the same time, playing one off against the other. He can understand that much, I think."

"Yes, m'Lord."

"And once we have them in our hands. . . ." The Baron nodded.

"M'Lord, the Sardaukar will want an observer with you during any . . . questioning."

"I'm sure we can produce an emergency to draw off any unwanted observers, Nefud."

"I understand, m'Lord. That's when Kynes can have his accident."

"Both Kynes and Hawat will have accidents then, Nefud. But only Kynes will have a real accident. It's Hawat I want. Yes. Ah, yes."

Nefud blinked, swallowed. He appeared about to ask a question, but remained silent.

"Hawat will be given both food and drink," the Baron said. "Treated with kindness, with sympathy. In his water you will administer the residual poison developed by the late Piter de Vries. *And* you will see that the antidote becomes a regular part of Hawat's diet from this point on . . . unless I say otherwise."

"The antidote, yes." Nefud shook his head. "But—"

"Don't be dense, Nefud. The Duke almost killed me with that poison-capsule tooth. The gas he exhaled into my presence deprived me of my most valuable Mentat, Piter. I need a replacement."

"Hawat?"

"Hawat."

"But—"

"You're going to say Hawat's completely loyal to the Atreides. True, but the Atreides are dead. We will woo him. He must be convinced he's not to blame for the Duke's demise. It was all the doing of that Bene Gesserit witch. He had an inferior master, one whose reason was clouded by emotion. Mentats admire the ability to calculate without emotion, Nefud. We will woo the formidable Thufir Hawat."

"Woo him. Yes, m'Lord."

"Hawat, unfortunately, had a master whose resources were poor, one who could not elevate a Mentat to the sublime peaks of reasoning that are a Mentat's right. Hawat will see a certain element of truth in this. The Duke couldn't afford the most efficient spies to provide his Mentat with the required information." The Baron stared at Nefud. "Let us never deceive ourselves, Nefud. The truth is a powerful weapon. We know how we overwhelmed the Atreides. Hawat knows, too. We did it with wealth."

"With wealth. Yes, m'Lord."

"We will woo Hawat," the Baron said. "We will hide him from the Sardaukar. And we will hold in reserve . . . the withdrawal of the antidote for the poison. There's no way of removing the residual poison. And, Nefud, Hawat need never suspect. The antidote will not betray itself to a poison snooper. Hawat can scan his food as he pleases and detect no trace of poison."

Nefud's eyes opened wide with understanding.

"The absence of a thing," the Baron said, "this can be as deadly as the *presence*. The absence of air, eh? The absence of water? The absence of anything else we're addicted to." The Baron nodded. "You understand me, Nefud?"

Nefud swallowed. "Yes, m'Lord."

"Then get busy. Find the Sardaukar commander and set things in motion."

"At once, m'Lord." Nefud bowed, turned, and hurried away.

Hawat by my side! the Baron thought. *The Sardaukar will give him to me. If they suspect anything at all it's that I wish to destroy the Mentat. And this suspicion I'll confirm! The fools! One of the most formidable Mentats in all history, a Mentat trained to kill, and they'll toss him to me like some silly toy to be broken. I will show them what use can be made of such a toy.*

The Baron reached beneath a drapery beside his suspensor bed, pressed a button to summon his older nephew, Rabban. He sat back, smiling.

And all the Atreides dead!

The stupid guard captain had been right, of course. Certainly, nothing survived in the path of a sandblast storm on Arrakis. Not an ornithopter . . . or its occupants. The woman and the boy were dead. The bribes in the right places, the *unthinkable* expenditure to bring overwhelming military force down onto one planet . . . all the sly reports tailored for the Emperor's ears alone, all the careful scheming were here at last coming to full fruition.

Power and fear—fear and power!

The Baron could see the path ahead of him. One day, a Harkonnen would be Emperor. Not himself, and no spawn of his loins. But a Harkonnen. Not this Rabban he'd summoned, of course. But Rabban's younger brother, young Feyd-Rautha. There was a sharpness to the boy that the Baron enjoyed . . . a ferocity.

A lovely boy, the Baron thought. *A year or two more—say, by the time he's seventeen, I'll know for certain whether he's the tool that House Harkonnen requires to gain the throne.*

"M'Lord Baron."

The man who stood outside the doorfield of the Baron's bedchamber was low built, gross of face and body, with the Harkonnen paternal line's narrow-set eyes and bulge of shoulders. There was yet some rigidity in his fat, but it was obvious to the eye that he'd come one day to the portable suspensors for carrying his excess weight.

A muscle-minded tank-brain, the Baron thought. *No Mentat, my nephew . . . not a Piter de Vries, but perhaps something more precisely devised for the task at hand. If I give him freedom to do it, he'll grind over everything in his path. Oh, how he'll be hated here on Arrakis!*

"My dear Rabban," the Baron said. He released the doorfield, but pointedly kept his body shield at full strength, knowing that the shimmer of it would be visible above the bedside glowglobe.

"You summoned me," Rabban said. He stepped into the room, flicked a glance past the air disturbance of the body shield, searched for a suspensor chair, found none.

"Stand closer where I can see you easily," the Baron said.

Rabban advanced another step, thinking that the damnable old man had deliberately removed all chairs, forcing a visitor to stand.

"The Atreides are dead," the Baron said. "The last of them. That's why I summoned you here to Arrakis. This planet is again yours."

Rabban blinked. "But I thought you were going to advance Piter de Vries to the—"

"Piter, too, is dead."

"Piter?"

"Piter."

The Baron reactivated the doorfield, blanked it against all energy penetration.

"You finally tired of him, eh?" Rabban asked.

His voice fell flat and lifeless in the energy-blanketed room.

"I will say a thing to you just this once," the Baron rumbled. "You insinuate that I obliterated Piter as one obliterates a trifle." He snapped fat fingers. "Just like that, eh? I am not so stupid, Nephew. I will take it unkindly if ever again you suggest by word or action that I am so stupid."

Fear showed in the squinting of Rabban's eyes. He knew within certain limits how far the old Baron would go against family. Seldom to the point of death unless there were outrageous profit or provocation in it. But family punishments could be painful.

"Forgive me, m'Lord Baron," Rabban said. He lowered his eyes as much to hide his own anger as to show subservience.

"You do not fool me, Rabban," the Baron said.

Rabban kept his eyes lowered, swallowed.

"I make a point," the Baron said. "Never obliterate a man unthinkingly, the way an entire fief might do it through some *due process of law.* Always do it for an overriding purpose—and *know your purpose!*"

Anger spoke in Rabban: "But you obliterated the traitor, Yueh! I saw his body being carried out as I arrived last night."

Rabban stared at his uncle, suddenly frightened by the sound of those words.

But the Baron smiled. "I'm very careful about dangerous weapons," he said. "Doctor Yueh was a traitor. He gave me the Duke." Strength poured into the Baron's voice. "*I* suborned a doctor of the Suk School! The *Inner* School! You hear, boy? But that's a wild sort of weapon to leave lying about. I didn't obliterate him casually."

"Does the Emperor know you suborned a Suk doctor?"

This was a penetrating question, the Baron thought. *Have I misjudged this nephew?*

"The Emperor doesn't know it yet," the Baron said. "But his Sardaukar are sure to report it to him. Before that happens, though, I'll have my own report in his hands through CHOAM Company channels. I will explain that I *luckily* discovered a doctor who pretended to the conditioning. A false doctor, you understand? Since everyone *knows* you cannot counter the conditioning of a Suk School, this will be accepted."

"Ah-h-h, I see," Rabban murmured.

And the Baron thought: *Indeed, I hope you do see. I hope you do see how vital it is that this remain secret.* The Baron suddenly wondered at himself. *Why did I do that? Why did I boast to this fool nephew of mine—the nephew I must use and discard?* The Baron felt anger at himself. He felt betrayed.

"It must be kept secret," Rabban said. "I understand."

The Baron sighed. "I give you different instructions about Arrakis this time, Nephew. When last you ruled this place, I held you in strong rein. This time, I have only one requirement."

"M'Lord?"

"Income."

"Income?"

"Have you any idea, Rabban, how much we spent to bring such military force to bear on the Atreides? Do you have even the first inkling of how much the Guild charges for military transport?"

"Expensive, eh?"

"Expensive!"

The Baron shot a fat arm toward Rabban. "If you squeeze Arrakis for every cent it can give us for sixty years, you'll just barely repay us!"

Rabban opened his mouth, closed it without speaking.

"Expensive," the Baron sneered. "The damnable Guild monopoly on space would've ruined us if I hadn't planned for this expense long ago. You should know, Rabban, that *we* bore the entire brunt of it. We even paid for transport of the Sardaukar."

And not for the first time, the Baron wondered if there ever would come a day when the Guild might be circumvented. They were insidious—bleeding off just enough to keep the host from objecting until they had you in their fist where they could force you to pay and pay and pay.

Always, the exorbitant demands rode upon military ventures. "Hazard rates," the oily Guild agents explained. And for every agent you managed to insert as a watchdog in the Guild Bank structure, they put two agents into your system.

Insufferable!

"Income then," Rabban said.

The Baron lowered his arm, made a fist. "You must squeeze."

"And I may do anything I wish as long as I squeeze?"

"Anything."

"The cannons you brought," Rabban said. "Could I—"

"I'm removing them," the Baron said.

"But you—"

"You won't need such toys. They were a special innovation and are now useless. We need the metal. They cannot go against a shield, Rabban. They were merely the unexpected. It was predictable that the Duke's men would retreat into cliff caves on this abominable planet. Our cannon merely sealed them in."

"The Fremen don't use shields."

"You may keep some lasguns if you wish."

"Yes, m'Lord. And I have a free hand."

"As long as you squeeze."

Rabban's smile was gloating. "I understand perfectly, m'Lord."

"You understand nothing perfectly," the Baron growled. "Let us have that clear at the outset. What you *do* understand is how to carry out my orders. Has it occurred to you, Nephew, that there are at least five million persons on this planet?"

"Does m'Lord forget that I was his regent-siridar here before? And if m'Lord will forgive me, his estimate may be low. It's difficult to count a population scattered among sinks and pans the way they are here. And when you consider the Fremen of—"

"The Fremen aren't worth considering!"

"Forgive me, m'Lord, but the Sardaukar believe otherwise."

The Baron hesitated, staring at his nephew. "You know something?"

"M'Lord had retired when I arrived last night. I . . . ah, took the liberty of contacting some of my lieutenants from . . . ah, before. They've been acting as guides to the Sardaukar. They report that a Fremen band ambushed a Sardaukar force somewhere southeast of here and wiped it out."

"Wiped out a Sardaukar force?"

"Yes, m'Lord."

"Impossible!"

Rabban shrugged.

"Fremen defeating Sardaukar," the Baron sneered.

"I repeat only what was reported to me," Rabban said. "It is said this Fremen force already had captured the Duke's redoubtable Thufir Hawat."

"Ah-h-h-h-h-h."

The Baron nodded, smiling.

"I believe the report," Rabban said. "You've no idea what a problem the Fremen were."

"Perhaps, but these weren't Fremen your lieutenants saw. They must've been Atreides men trained by Hawat and disguised as Fremen. It's the only possible answer."

Again, Rabban shrugged. "Well, the Sardaukar think they were Fremen. The Sardaukar already have launched a program to wipe out all Fremen."

"Good!"

"But—"

"It'll keep the Sardaukar occupied. And we'll soon have Hawat. I know it! I can feel it! Ah, this has been a day! The Sardaukar off hunting a few useless desert bands while we get the real prize!"

"M'Lord. . . ." Rabban hesitated, frowning. "I've always felt that we underestimated the Fremen, both in numbers and in—"

"Ignore them, boy! They're rabble. It's the populous towns, cities, and villages that concern us. A great many people there, eh?"

"A great many, m'Lord."

"They worry me, Rabban."

"Worry you?"

"Oh . . . ninety per cent of them are of no concern. But there are always a few . . . Houses Minor and so on, people of ambition who might try a dangerous thing. If one of them should get off Arrakis with an unpleasant story about what happened here, I'd be most displeased. Have you any idea how displeased I'd be?"

Rabban swallowed.

"You must take immediate measures to hold a hostage from each House Minor," the Baron said. "As far as anyone off Arrakis must learn, this was straightforward House-to-House battle. The Sardaukar had no part in it, you understand? The Duke was offered the usual quarter and exile, but he died in an unfortunate accident before he could accept. He was about to accept, though. That is the story. And any rumor that there were Sardaukar here, it must be laughed at."

"As the Emperor wishes it," Rabban said.

"As the Emperor wishes it."

"What about the smugglers?"

"No one believes smugglers, Rabban. They are tolerated, but not believed. At any rate, you'll be spreading some bribes in that quarter . . . and taking other measures which I'm sure you can think of."

"Yes, m'Lord."

"Two things from Arrakis, then, Rabban: income and a merciless fist. You must show no mercy here. Think of these clods as what they are—slaves envious of their masters and awaiting only the opportunity to rebel. Not the slightest vestige of pity or mercy must you show them."

"Can one exterminate an entire planet?" Rabban asked.

"Exterminate?" Surprise showed in the swift turning of the Baron's head. "Who said anything about exterminating?"

"Well, I presumed you were going to bring in new stock and—"

"I said *squeeze*, Nephew, not exterminate. Don't waste the population, merely drive them into utter submission. You must be the carnivore, my boy." He smiled, a baby's expression in the dimple-fat face. "A carnivore never stops. Show no mercy. Never stop. Mercy is a chimera. It can be defeated by the stomach rumbling its hunger, by the throat crying its thirst. You must be always hungry and thirsty." The Baron caressed his bulges beneath the suspensors. "Like me."

"I see, m'Lord."

Rabban swung his gaze left and right.

"It's all clear then, Nephew?"

"Except for one thing, Uncle: the planetologist, Kynes."

"Ah, yes, Kynes."

"He's the Emperor's man, m'Lord. He can come and go as he pleases. And he's very close to the Fremen . . . married one."

"Kynes will be dead by tomorrow's nightfall."

"That's dangerous work, Uncle, killing an Imperial servant."

"How do you think I've come this far this quickly?" the Baron demanded. His voice was low, charged with unspeakable adjectives. "Besides, you need never have feared Kynes would leave Arrakis. You're forgetting that he's addicted to the spice."

"Of course!"

"Those who know will do nothing to endanger their supply," the Baron said. "Kynes certainly must know."

"I forgot," Rabban said.

They stared at each other in silence.

Presently, the Baron said: "Incidentally, you will make my own supply one of your first concerns. I've quite a stockpile of private stuff, but that suicide raid by the Duke's men got most of what we'd stored for sale."

Rabban nodded. "Yes, m'Lord."

The Baron brightened. "Now, tomorrow morning, you will assemble what remains of organization here and you'll say to them: 'Our Sublime Padishah Emperor has charged me to take possession of this planet and end all dispute.'"

"I understand, m'Lord."

"This time, I'm sure you do. We will discuss it in more detail tomorrow. Now, leave me to finish my sleep."

The Baron deactivated his doorfield, watched his nephew out of sight.

A tank-brain, the Baron thought. *Muscle-minded tank-brain. They will be bloody pulp here when he's through with them. Then, when I send in Feyd-Rautha to take the load off them, they'll cheer their rescuer. Beloved Feyd-Rautha, Benign Feyd-Rautha, the compassionate one who saves them from a beast. Feyd-Rautha, a man to follow and die for. The boy will know by that time how to oppress with impunity. I'm sure he's the one we need. He'll learn. And such a lovely body. Really a lovely boy.*

As Paul fought the 'thopter's controls, he grew aware that he was sorting out the interwoven storm forces, his more than Mentat awareness computing on the basis of fractional minutiae. He felt dust fronts, billowings, mixings of turbulence, an occasional vortex.

The cabin interior was an angry box lighted by the green radiance of instrument dials. The tan flow of dust outside appeared featureless, but his inner sense began to *see* through the curtain.

I must find the right vortex, he thought.

For a long time now he had sensed the storm's power diminishing, but still it shook them. He waited out another turbulence.

The vortex began as an abrupt billowing that rattled the entire ship. Paul defied all fear to bank the 'thopter left.

Jessica saw the maneuver on the attitude globe.

"Paul!" she screamed.

The vortex turned them, twisting, tipping. It lifted the 'thopter like a chip on a geyser, spewed them up and out—a winged speck within a core of winding dust lighted by the second moon.

Paul looked down, saw the dust-defined pillar of hot wind that had disgorged them, saw the dying storm trailing away like a dry river into the desert—moon-gray motion growing smaller and smaller below as they rode the updraft.

"We're out of it," Jessica whispered.

Paul turned their craft away from the dust in swooping rhythm while he scanned the night sky.

"We've given them the slip," he said.

Jessica felt her heart pounding. She forced herself to calmness, looked at the diminishing storm. Her time sense said they had ridden within that compounding of elemental forces almost four hours, but part of her mind computed the passage as a lifetime. She felt reborn.

It was like the litany, she thought. *We faced it and did not resist. The storm passed through us and around us. It's gone, but we remain.*

"I don't like the sound of our wing motion," Paul said. "We suffered some damage in there."

He felt the grating, injured flight through his hands on the controls. They were out of the storm, but still not out into the full view of his prescient vision. Yet, they had escaped, and Paul sensed himself trembling on the verge of a revelation.

He shivered.

The sensation was magnetic and terrifying, and he found himself caught on the question of what caused this trembling awareness. Part of it, he felt, was the spice-saturated diet of Arrakis. But he thought part of it could be the litany, as though the words had a power of their own.

"I shall not fear . . ."

Cause and effect: he was alive despite malignant forces, and he felt himself poised on a brink of self-awareness that could not have been without the litany's magic.

Words from the Orange Catholic Bible rang through his memory: *"What senses do we lack that we cannot see or hear another world all around us?"*

"There's rock all around," Jessica said.

Paul focused on the 'thopter's launching, shook his head to clear it. He looked where his mother pointed, saw uplifting rock shapes black on the sand ahead and to the right. He felt wind around his ankles, a stirring of dust in the cabin. There was a hole somewhere, more of the storm's doing.

"Better set us down on sand," Jessica said. "The wings might not take full brake."

He nodded toward a place ahead where sandblasted ridges lifted into moonlight above the dunes. "I'll set us down near those rocks. Check your safety harness."

She obeyed, thinking: *We've water and stillsuits. If we can find food, we can survive a long time on this desert. Fremen live here. What they can do we can do.*

"Run for those rocks the instant we're stopped," Paul said. "I'll take the pack."

"Run for. . . ." She fell silent, nodded. "Worms."

"Our friends, the worms," he corrected her. "They'll get this 'thopter. There'll be no evidence of where we landed."

How direct his thinking, she thought.

They glided lower . . . lower . . .

There came a rushing sense of motion to their passage—blurred shadows of dunes, rocks lifting like islands. The 'thopter touched a dune top with a soft lurch, skipped a sand valley, touched another dune.

He's killing our speed against the sand, Jessica thought, and permitted herself to admire his competence.

"Brace yourself!" Paul warned.

He pulled back on the wing brakes, gently at first, then harder and harder. He felt them cup the air, their aspect ratio dropping faster and faster. Wind screamed through the lapped coverts and primaries of the wings' leaves.

Abruptly, with only the faintest lurch of warning, the left wing, weakened by the storm, twisted upward and in, slamming across the side of the 'thopter. The craft skidded across a dune top, twisting to the left. It tumbled down the opposite face to bury its nose in the next dune amid a cascade of sand. They lay stopped on the broken wing side, the right wing pointing toward the stars.

Paul jerked off his safety harness, hurled himself upward across his mother, wrenching the door open. Sand poured around them into the cabin, bringing a dry smell of burned flint. He grabbed the pack from the rear, saw that his mother was free of her harness. She stepped up onto the side of the right-hand seat and out onto the 'thopter's metal skin. Paul followed, dragging the pack by its straps.

"Run!" he ordered.

He pointed up the dune face and beyond it where they could see a rock tower undercut by sandblast winds.

Jessica leaped off the 'thopter and ran, scrambling and sliding up the dune. She heard Paul's panting progress behind. They came out onto a sand ridge that curved away toward the rocks.

"Follow the ridge," Paul ordered. "It'll be faster."

They slogged toward the rocks, sand gripping their feet.

A new sound began to impress itself on them: a muted whisper, a hissing, an abrasive slithering.

"Worm," Paul said.

It grew louder.

"Faster!" Paul gasped.

The first rock shingle, like a beach slanting from the sand, lay no more than ten meters ahead when they heard metal crunch and shatter behind them.

Paul shifted his pack to his right arm, holding it by the straps. It slapped his side as he ran. He took his mother's arm with his other hand. They scrambled onto the lifting rock, up a pebble-littered surface through a twisted, wind-carved channel. Breath came dry and gasping in their throats.

"I can't run any farther," Jessica panted.

Paul stopped, pressed her into a gut of rock, turned and looked down onto the desert. A mound-in-motion ran parallel to their rock island—moonlit ripples, sand waves, a cresting burrow almost level with Paul's eyes at a distance of about a kilometer. The flattened dunes of its track curved once—a short loop crossing the patch of desert where they had abandoned their wrecked ornithopter.

Where the worm had been there was no sign of the aircraft.

The burrow mound moved outward into the desert, coursed back across its own path, questing.

"It's bigger than a Guild spaceship," Paul whispered. "I was told worms grew large in the deep desert, but I didn't realize . . . how big."

"Nor I," Jessica breathed.

Again, the thing turned out away from the rocks, sped now with a curbing track toward the horizon. They listened until the sound of its passage was lost in gentle sand stirrings around them.

Paul took a deep breath, looked up at the moon-frosted escarpment, and quoted from the Kitab al-Ibar: "Travel by night and rest in black shade through the day." He looked at his mother. "We still have a few hours of night. Can you go on?"

"In a moment."

Paul stepped out onto the rock shingle, shouldered the pack and adjusted its straps. He stood a moment with a paracompass in his hands.

"Whenever you're ready," he said.

She pushed herself away from the rock, feeling her strength return. "Which direction?"

"Where this ridge leads." He pointed.

"Deep into the desert," she said.

"The Fremen desert," Paul whispered.

And he paused, shaken by the remembered high relief imagery of a prescient vision he had experienced on Caladan. He had seen this desert. But the *set* of the vision had been subtly different, like an optical image that had disappeared into his consciousness, been absorbed by memory, and now failed of perfect registry when projected onto the real scene. The vision appeared to have shifted and approached him from a different angle while he remained motionless.

Idaho was with us in the vision, he remembered. *But now Idaho is dead.*

"Do you see a way to go?" Jessica asked, mistaking his hesitation.

"No," he said. "But we'll go anyway."

He settled his shoulders more firmly in the pack, struck out up a sand-carved channel in the rock. The channel opened onto a moonlit floor of rock with benched ledges climbing away to the south.

Paul headed for the first ledge, clambered onto it. Jessica followed.

She noted presently how their passage became a matter of the immediate and particular—the sand pockets between rocks where their steps were slowed, the wind-carved ridge that cut their hands, the obstruction that forced a choice: Go over or go around? The terrain enforced its own rhythms. They spoke only when necessary and then with the hoarse voices of their exertion.

"Careful here—this ledge is slippery with sand."

"Watch you don't hit your head against this overhang."

"Stay below this ridge; the moon's at our backs and it'd show our movement to anyone out there."

Paul stopped in a bight of rock, leaned the pack against a narrow ledge.

Jessica leaned beside him, thankful for the moment of rest. She heard Paul pulling at his stillsuit tube, sipped her own reclaimed water. It tasted brackish, and she remembered the waters of Caladan—a tall fountain enclosing a curve of sky, such a richness of moisture that it hadn't been noticed for itself . . . only for its shape, or its reflection, or its sound as she stopped beside it.

To stop, she thought. *To rest . . . truly rest.*

It occurred to her that mercy was the ability to stop, if only for a moment. There was no mercy where there could be no stopping.

Paul pushed away from the rock ledge, turned, and climbed over a sloping surface. Jessica followed with a sigh.

They slid down onto a wide shelf that led around a sheer rock face. Again, they fell into the disjointed rhythm of movement across this broken land.

Jessica felt that the night was dominated by degrees of smallness in substances beneath their feet and hands—boulders or pea gravel or flaked rock or pea sand or sand itself or grit or dust or gossamer powder.

The powder clogged nose filters and had to be blown out. Pea sand and pea gravel rolled on a hard surface and could spill the unwary. Rock flakes cut.

And the omnipresent sand patches dragged against their feet.

Paul stopped abruptly on a rock shelf, steadied his mother as she stumbled into him.

He was pointing left and she looked along his arm to see that they stood atop a cliff with the desert stretched out like a static ocean some two hundred meters below. It lay there full of moon-silvered waves—shadows of angles that lapsed into curves and, in the distance, lifted to the misted gray blur of another escarpment.

"Open desert," she said.

"A wide place to cross," Paul said, and his voice was muffled by the filter trap across his face.

Jessica glanced left and right—nothing but sand below.

Paul stared straight ahead across the open dunes, watching the movement of shadows in the moon's passage. "About three or four kilometers across," he said.

"Worms," she said.

"Sure to be."

She focused on her weariness, the muscle ache that dulled her senses. "Shall we rest and eat?"

Paul slipped out of the pack, sat down and leaned against it. Jessica supported herself by a hand on his shoulder as she sank to the rock beside him. She felt Paul turn as she settled herself, heard him scrabbling in the pack.

"Here," he said.

His hand felt dry against hers as he pressed two energy capsules into her palm.

She swallowed them with a grudging spit of water from her stillsuit tube.

"Drink all your water," Paul said. "Axiom: the best place to conserve your water is in your body. It keeps your energy up. You're stronger. Trust your stillsuit."

She obeyed, drained her catchpockets, feeling energy return. She thought then how peaceful it was here in this moment of their tiredness, and she recalled once hearing the minstrel-warrior Gurney Halleck say, "Better a dry morsel and quietness therewith than a house full of sacrifice and strife."

Jessica repeated the words to Paul.

"That was Gurney," he said.

She caught the tone of his voice, the way he spoke as of someone dead, thought: *And well poor Gurney might be dead.* The Atreides forces were either dead or captive or lost like themselves in this waterless void.

"Gurney always had the right quotation," Paul said. "I can hear him now: 'And I will make the rivers dry, and sell the land into the hand of the wicked: and I will make the land waste, and all that is therein, by the hand of strangers.'"

Jessica closed her eyes, found herself moved close to tears by the pathos in her son's voice.

Presently, Paul said: "How do you . . . feel?"

She recognized that his question was directed at her pregnancy, said: "Your sister won't be born for many months yet. I still feel . . . physically adequate."

And she thought: *How stiffly formal I speak to my own son!* Then, because it was the Bene Gesserit way to seek within for the answer to such an oddity, she searched and found the source of her formality: *I'm afraid of my son; I fear his strangeness; I fear what he may see ahead of us, what he may tell me.*

Paul pulled his hood down over his eyes, listened to the bug-hustling sounds of the night. His lungs were charged with his own silence. His nose itched. He rubbed it, removed the filter and grew conscious of the rich smell of cinnamon.

"There's melange spice nearby," he said.

An eider wind feathered Paul's cheeks, ruffled the folds of his burnoose. But this wind carried no threat of storm; already he could sense the difference.

"Dawn soon," he said.

Jessica nodded.

"There's a way to get safely across that open sand," Paul said. "The Fremen do it."

"The worms?"

"If we were to plant a thumper from our Fremkit back in the rocks here," Paul said. "It'd keep a worm occupied for a time."

She glanced at the stretch of moonlighted desert between them and the other escarpment. "Four kilometers' worth of time?"

"Perhaps. And if we crossed there making only *natural* sounds, the kind that don't attract the worms...."

Paul studied the open desert, questing in his prescient memory, probing the mysterious allusions to thumpers and maker hooks in the Fremkit manual that had come with their escape pack. He found it odd that all he sensed was pervasive terror at thought of the worms. He knew as though it lay just at the edge of his awareness that the worms were to be respected and not feared ... if ... if....

He shook his head.

"It'd have to be sounds without rhythm," Jessica said.

"What? Oh. Yes. If we broke our steps ... the sand itself must shift down at times. Worms can't investigate every little sound. We should be fully rested before we try it, though."

He looked across at that other rock wall, seeing the passage of time in the vertical moonshadows there. "It'll be dawn within the hour."

"Where'll we spend the day?" she asked.

Paul turned left, pointed. "The cliff curves back north over there. You can see by the way it's wind-cut that's the windward face. There'll be crevasses there, deep ones."

"Had we better get started?" she asked.

He stood, helped her to her feet. "Are you rested enough for a climb down? I want to get as close as possible to the desert floor before we camp."

"Enough." She nodded for him to lead the way.

He hesitated, then lifted the pack, settled it onto his shoulders and turned along the cliff.

If only we had suspensors, Jessica thought. *It'd be such a simple matter to jump down there. But perhaps suspensors are another thing to avoid in the open desert. Maybe they attract the worms the way a shield does.*

They came to a series of shelves dropping down and, beyond them, saw a fissure with its ledge outlined by moonshadow leading along the vestibule.

Paul led the way down, moving cautiously but hurrying because it was obvious the moonlight could not last much longer. They wound down into a world of deeper and deeper shadows. Hints of rock shape climbed to the stars around them. The fissure narrowed to some ten meters' width at the brink of a dim gray sandslope that slanted downward into darkness.

"Can we go down?" Jessica whispered.

"I think so."

He tested the surface with one foot.

"We can slide down," he said. "I'll go first. Wait until you hear me stop."

"Careful," she said.

He stepped onto the slope and slid and slipped down its soft surface onto an almost level floor of packed sand. The place was deep within the rock walls.

There came the sound of sand sliding behind him. He tried to see up the slope in the darkness, was almost knocked over by the cascade. It trailed away to silence.

"Mother?" he said.

There was no answer.

"Mother?"

He dropped the pack, hurled himself up the slope, scrambling, digging, throwing sand like a wild man. "Mother!" he gasped. "Mother, where are you?"

Another cascade of sand swept down on him, burying him to the hips. He wrenched himself out of it.

She's been caught in the sandslide, he thought. *Buried in it. I must be calm and work this out carefully. She won't smother immediately. She'll compose herself in bindu suspension to reduce her oxygen needs. She knows I'll dig for her.*

In the Bene Gesserit way she had taught him, Paul stilled the savage beating of his heart, set his mind as a blank slate upon which the past few moments could write themselves. Every partial shift and twist of the slide replayed itself in his memory, moving with an interior stateliness that contrasted with the fractional second of real time required for the total recall.

Presently, Paul moved slantwise up the slope, probing cautiously until he found the wall of the fissure, an outcurve of rock there. He began to dig, moving the sand with care not to dislodge another slide. A piece of fabric came under his hands. He followed it, found an arm. Gently, he traced the arm, exposed her face.

"Do you hear me?" he whispered.

No answer.

He dug faster, freed her shoulders. She was limp beneath his hands, but he detected a slow heartbeat.

Bindu suspension, he told himself.

He cleared the sand away to her waist, draped her arms over his shoulders and pulled downslope, slowly at first, then dragging her as fast as he could, feeling the sand give way above. Faster and faster he pulled her, gasping with the effort, fighting to keep his balance. He was out on the hard-packed floor of the fissure then, swinging her to his shoulder and breaking into a staggering run as the entire sandslope came down with a loud hiss that echoed and was magnified within the rock walls.

He stopped at the end of the fissure where it looked out on the desert's marching dunes some thirty meters below. Gently, he lowered her to the sand, uttered the word to bring her out of the catalepsis.

She awakened slowly, taking deeper and deeper breaths.

"I knew you'd find me," she whispered.

He looked back up the fissure. "It might have been kinder if I hadn't."

"Paul!"

"I lost the pack," he said. "It's buried under a hundred tons of sand . . . at least."

"Everything?"

"The spare water, the stilltent—everything that counts." He touched a pocket. "I still have the paracompass." He fumbled at the waist sash. "Knife and binoculars. We can get a good look around the place where we'll die."

In that instant, the sun lifted above the horizon somewhere to the left beyond the end of the fissure. Colors blinked in the sand out on the open desert. A chorus of birds held forth their songs from hidden places among the rocks.

But Jessica had eyes only for the despair in Paul's face. She edged her voice with scorn, said: "Is this the way you were taught?"

"Don't you understand?" he asked. "Everything we need to survive in this place is under that sand."

"You found me," she said, and now her voice was soft, reasonable.

Paul squatted back on his heels.

Presently, he looked up the fissure at the new slope, studying it, marking the looseness of the sand.

"If we could immobilize a small area of that slope and the upper face of a hole dug into the sand, we might be able to put down a shaft to the pack. Water might do it, but we don't have enough water for. . . ." He broke off, then: "Foam."

Jessica held herself to stillness lest she disturb the hyperfunctioning of his mind.

Paul looked out at the open dunes, searching with his nostrils as well as his eyes, finding the direction and then centering his attention on a darkened patch of sand below them.

"Spice," he said. "Its essence—highly alkaline. And I have the paracompass. Its power pack is acid-base."

Jessica sat up straight against the rock.

Paul ignored her, leaped to his feet, and was off down the wind-compacted surface that spilled from the end of the fissure to the desert's floor.

She watched the way he walked, breaking his stride—step . . . pause, step-step . . . slide . . . pause . . .

There was no rhythm to it that might tell a marauding worm something not of the desert moved here.

Paul reached the spice patch, shoveled a mound of it into a fold of his robe, returned to the fissure. He spilled the spice onto the sand in front of Jessica, squatted and began dismantling the paracompass, using the point of his knife. The compass face came off. He removed his sash, spread the compass parts on it, lifted out the power pack. The dial mechanism came out next, leaving an empty dished compartment in the instrument.

"You'll need water," Jessica said.

Paul took the catchtube from his neck, sucked up a mouthful, expelled it into the dished compartment.

If this fails, that's water wasted, Jessica thought. *But it won't matter then, anyway.*

With his knife, Paul cut open the power pack, spilled its crystals into the water. They foamed slightly, subsided.

Jessica's eyes caught motion above them. She looked up to see a line of hawks along the rim of the fissure. They perched there staring down at the open water.

Great Mother! she thought. *They can sense water even at that distance!*

Paul had the cover back on the paracompass, leaving off the reset button which gave a small hole into the liquid. Taking the reworked instrument in one hand, a handful of spice in the other, Paul went back up the fissure, studying the lay of the slope. His robe billowed gently without the sash to hold it. He waded part way up the slope, kicking off the sand rivulets, spurts of dust.

Presently, he stopped, pressed a pinch of the spice into the paracompass, shook the instrument case.

Green foam boiled out of the hole where the reset button had been. Paul aimed it at the slope, spread a low dike there, began kicking away the sand beneath it, immobilizing the opened face with more foam.

Jessica moved to a position below him, called out: "May I help?"

"Come up and dig," he said. "We've about three meters to go. It's going to be a near thing." As he spoke, the foam stopped billowing from the instrument.

"Quickly," Paul said. "No telling how long this foam will hold the sand."

Jessica scrambled up beside Paul as he sifted another pinch of spice into the hole, shook the paracompass case. Again, foam boiled from it.

As Paul directed the foam barrier, Jessica dug with her hands, hurling the sand down the slope. "How deep?" she panted.

"About three meters," he said. "And I can only approximate the position. We may have to widen this hole." He moved a step aside, slipping in loose sand. "Slant your digging backward. Don't go straight down."

Jessica obeyed.

Slowly, the hole went down, reaching a level even with the floor of the basin and still no sign of the pack.

Could I have miscalculated? Paul asked himself. *I'm the one that panicked originally and caused this mistake. Has that warped my ability?*

He looked at the paracompass. Less than two ounces of the acid infusion remained.

Jessica straightened in the hole, rubbed a foam-stained hand across her cheek. Her eyes met Paul's.

"The upper face," Paul said. "Gently, now." He added another pinch of spice to the container, sent the foam boiling around Jessica's hands as she began cutting a vertical face in the upper slant of the hole. On the second pass, her hands encountered something hard. Slowly, she worked out a length of strap with a plastic buckle.

"Don't move any more of it," Paul said and his voice was almost a whisper.

"We're out of foam."

Jessica held the strap in one hand, looked up at him.

Paul threw the empty paracompass down onto the floor of the basin, said: "Give me your other hand. Now listen carefully. I'm going to pull you to the side and downhill. Don't let go of that strap. We won't get much more spill from the top. This slope has stabilized itself. All I'm going to aim for is to keep your head free of the sand. Once that hole's filled, we can dig you out and pull up the pack."

"I understand," she said.

"Ready?"

"Ready." She tensed her fingers on the strap.

With one surge, Paul had her half out of the hole, holding her head up as the foam barrier gave way and sand spilled down. When it had subsided, Jessica remained buried to the waist, her left arm and shoulder still under the sand, her chin protected on a fold of Paul's robe. Her shoulder ached from the strain put on it.

"I still have the strap," she said.

Slowly, Paul worked his hand into the sand beside her, found the strap. "Together," he said. "Steady pressure. We mustn't break it."

More sand spilled down as they worked the pack up. When the strap cleared the surface, Paul stopped, freed his mother from the sand. Together then they pulled the pack downslope and out of its trap.

In a few minutes they stood on the floor of the fissure holding the pack between them.

Paul looked at his mother. Foam stained her face, her robe. Sand was caked to her where the foam had dried. She looked as though she had been a target for balls of wet, green sand.

"You look a mess," he said.

"You're not so pretty yourself," she said.

They started to laugh, then sobered.

"That shouldn't have happened," Paul said. "I was careless."

She shrugged, feeling caked sand fall away from her robe.

"I'll put up the tent," he said. "Better slip off that robe and shake it out." He turned away, taking the pack.

Jessica nodded, suddenly too tired to answer.

"There's anchor holes in the rock," Paul said. "Someone's tented here before."

Why not? she thought as she brushed at her robe. This was a likely place—deep in rock walls and facing another cliff some four kilometers away—far enough above the desert to avoid worms but close enough for easy access before a crossing.

She turned, seeing that Paul had the tent up, its rib-domed hemisphere blending with the rock walls of the fissure. Paul stepped past her, lifting his binoculars. He adjusted their internal pressure with a quick twist, focused the oil lenses on the other cliff, lifting golden tan in morning light across open sand.

Jessica watched as he studied that apocalyptic landscape, his eyes probing into sand rivers and canyons.

"There are growing things over there," he said.

Jessica found the spare binoculars in the pack beside the tent, moved up beside Paul.

"There," he said, holding the binoculars with one hand and pointing with the other.

She looked where he pointed.

"Saguaro," she said. "Scrawny stuff."

"There may be people nearby," Paul said.

"That could be the remains of a botanical testing station," she warned.

"This is pretty far south into the desert," he said. He lowered his binoculars, rubbed beneath his filter baffle, feeling how dry and chapped his lips were, sensing the dusty taste of thirst in his mouth. "This has the feeling of a Fremen place," he said.

"Are we certain the Fremen will be friendly?" she asked.

"Kynes promised their help."

But there's desperation in the people of this desert, she thought. *I felt some of it myself today. Desperate people might kill us for our water.*

She closed her eyes and, against this wasteland, conjured in her mind a scene from Caladan. There had been a vacation trip once on Caladan—she and the Duke Leto, before Paul's birth. They'd flown over the southern jungles, above the weed-wild shouting leaves and rice paddies of the deltas. And they had seen the ant lines in the greenery—man-gangs carrying their loads on suspensor-buoyed shoulder poles. And in the sea reaches there'd been the white petals of trimaran dhows.

All of it gone.

Jessica opened her eyes to the desert stillness, to the mounting warmth of the day. Restless heat devils were beginning to set the air aquiver out on the open sand. The other rock face across from them was like a thing seen through cheap glass.

A spill of sand spread its brief curtain across the open end of the fissure. The sand hissed down, loosed by puffs of morning breeze, by the hawks that were beginning to lift away from the clifftop. When the sand-fall was gone, she still heard it hissing. It grew louder, a sound that once heard, was never forgotten.

"Worm," Paul whispered.

It came from their right with an uncaring majesty that could not be ignored. A twisting burrow-mound of sand cut through the dunes within their field of vision. The mound lifted in front, dusting away like a bow wave in water. Then it was gone, coursing off to the left.

The sound diminished, died.

"I've seen space frigates that were smaller," Paul whispered.

She nodded, continuing to stare across the desert. Where the worm had passed there remained that tantalizing gap. It flowed bitterly endless before them, beckoning beneath its horizontal collapse of skyline.

"When we've rested," Jessica said, "we should continue with your lessons."

He suppressed a sudden anger, said: "Mother, don't you think we could do without. . . ."

"Today you panicked," she said. "You know your mind and bindu-nervature perhaps better than I do, but you've much yet to learn about your body's prana-musculature. The body does things of itself some-times, Paul, and I can teach you about this. You must learn to control every muscle, every fiber of your body. You need review of the hands. We'll start with finger muscles, palm tendons, and tip sensitivity." She turned away. "Come, into the tent, now."

He flexed the fingers of his left hand, watching her crawl through the sphincter valve, knowing that he could not deflect her from this determination . . . that he must agree.

Whatever has been done to me, I've been a party to it, he thought.

Review of the hand!

He looked at his hand. How inadequate it appeared when measured against such creatures as that worm.

We came from Caladan—a paradise world for our form of life. There existed no need on Caladan to build a physical paradise or a paradise of the mind—we could see the actuality all around us. And the price we paid was the price men have always paid for achieving a paradise in this life—we went soft, we lost our edge.

—FROM "MUAD'DIB: CONVERSATIONS"
BY THE PRINCESS IRULAN

"So you're the great Gurney Halleck," the man said.

Halleck stood staring across the round cavern office at the smuggler seated behind a metal desk. The man wore Fremen robes and had the half-tint blue eyes that told of off-planet foods in his diet. The office duplicated a space frigate's master control center—communications and viewscreens along a thirty-degree arc of wall, remote arming and firing banks adjoining, and the desk formed as a wall projection—part of the remaining curve.

"I am Staban Tuek, son of Esmar Tuek," the smuggler said.

"Then you're the one I owe thanks for the help we've received," Halleck said.

"Ah-h-h, gratitude," the smuggler said. "Sit down."

A ship-type bucket seat emerged from the wall beside the screens and Halleck sank onto it with a sigh, feeling his weariness. He could see his own reflection now in a dark surface beside the smuggler and scowled at the lines of fatigue in his lumpy face. The inkvine scar along his jaw writhed with the scowl.

Halleck turned from his reflection, stared at Tuek. He saw the family resemblance in the smuggler now—the father's heavy, overhanging eyebrows and rock planes of cheeks and nose.

"Your men tell me your father is dead, killed by the Harkonnens," Halleck said.

"By the Harkonnens or by a traitor among your people," Tuek said.

Anger overcame part of Halleck's fatigue. He straightened, said: "Can you name the traitor?"

"We are not sure."

"Thufir Hawat suspected the Lady Jessica."

"Ah-h-h, the Bene Gesserit witch . . . perhaps. But Hawat is now a Harkonnen captive."

"I heard." Halleck took a deep breath. "It appears we've a deal more killing ahead of us."

"We will do nothing to attract attention to us," Tuek said.

Halleck stiffened. "But—"

"You and those of your men we've saved are welcome to sanctuary among us," Tuek said. "You speak of gratitude. Very well; work off your debt to us. We can always use good men. We'll destroy you out of hand, though, if you make the slightest open move against the Harkonnens."

"But they killed your father, man!"

"Perhaps. And if so, I'll give you my father's answer to those who act without thinking: 'A stone is heavy and the sand is weighty; but a fool's wrath is heavier than them both.'"

"You mean to do nothing about it, then?" Halleck sneered.

"You did not hear me say that. I merely say I will protect our contract with the Guild. The Guild requires that we play a circumspect game. There are other ways of destroying a foe."

"Ah-h-h-h-h."

"Ah, indeed. If you've a mind to seek out the witch, have at it. But I warn you that you're probably too late . . . and we doubt she's the one you want, anyway."

"Hawat made few mistakes."

"He allowed himself to fall into Harkonnen hands."

"You think *he's* the traitor?"

Tuek shrugged. "This is academic. We think the witch is dead. At least the Harkonnens believe it."

"You seem to know a great deal about the Harkonnens."

"Hints and suggestions . . . rumors and hunches."

"We are seventy-four men," Halleck said. "If you seriously wish us to enlist with you, you must believe our Duke is dead."

"His body has been seen."

"And the boy, too—young Master Paul?" Halleck tried to swallow, found a lump in his throat.

"According to the last word we had, he was lost with his mother in a desert storm. Likely not even their bones will ever be found."

"So the witch is dead then . . . all dead."

Tuek nodded. "And Beast Rabban, so they say, will sit once more in the seat of power here on Dune."

"The Count Rabban of Lankiveil?"

"Yes."

It took Halleck a moment to put down the upsurge of rage that threatened to overcome him. He spoke with panting breath: "I've a score of my own against Rabban. I owe him for the lives of my family. . . ." He rubbed at the scar along his jaw. ". . . and for this. . . ."

"One does not risk everything to settle a score prematurely," Tuek said. He frowned, watching the play of muscles along Halleck's jaw, the sudden withdrawal in the man's shed-lidded eyes.

"I know . . . I know." Halleck took a deep breath.

"You and your men can work out your passage off Arrakis by serving with us. There are many places to—"

"I release my men from any bond to me; they can choose for themselves. With Rabban here—I stay."

"In your mood, I'm not sure we want you to stay."

Halleck stared at the smuggler. "You doubt my word?"

"No-o-o. . . ."

"You've saved me from the Harkonnens. I gave loyalty to the Duke Leto for no greater reason. I'll stay on Arrakis—with you . . . or with the Fremen."

"Whether a thought is spoken or not it is a real thing and it has power," Tuek said. "You might find the line between life and death among the Fremen to be too sharp and quick."

Halleck closed his eyes briefly, feeling the weariness surge up in him. "Where is the Lord who led us through the land of deserts and of pits?" he murmured.

"Move slowly and the day of your revenge will come," Tuek said. "Speed is a device of Shaitan. Cool your sorrow—we've the diversions for it; three things there are that ease the heart—water, green grass, and the beauty of woman."

Halleck opened his eyes. "I would prefer the blood of Rabban Harkonnen flowing about my feet." He stared at Tuek. "You think that day will come?"

"I have little to do with how you'll meet tomorrow, Gurney Halleck. I can only help you meet today."

"Then I'll accept that help and stay until the day you tell me to revenge your father and all the others who—"

"Listen to me, *fighting man*," Tuek said. He leaned forward over his desk, his shoulders level with his ears, eyes intent. The smuggler's face was suddenly like weathered stone. "My father's water—I'll buy that back myself, with my own blade."

Halleck stared back at Tuek. In that moment, the smuggler reminded him of Duke Leto: a leader of men, courageous, secure in his own position and his own course. He was like the Duke . . . before Arrakis.

"Do you wish my blade beside you?" Halleck asked.

Tuek sat back, relaxed, studying Halleck silently.

"Do you think of me as *fighting man*?" Halleck pressed.

"You're the only one of the Duke's lieutenants to escape," Tuek said.

"Your enemy was overwhelming, yet you rolled with him. . . . You defeated him the way we defeat Arrakis."

"Eh?"

"We live on sufferance down here, Gurney Halleck," Tuek said. "Arrakis is our enemy."

"One enemy at a time, is that it?"

"That's it."

"Is that the way the Fremen make out?"

"Perhaps."

"You said I might find life with the Fremen too tough. They live in the desert, in the open, is that why?"

"Who knows where the Fremen live? For us, the Central Plateau is a no-man's land. But I wish to talk more about—"

"I'm told that the Guild seldom routes spice lighters in over the desert," Halleck said. "But there are rumors that you can see bits of greenery here and there if you know where to look."

"Rumors!" Tuek sneered. "Do you wish to choose now between me and the Fremen? We have a measure of security, our own sietch carved out of the rock, our own hidden basins. We live the lives of civilized men. The Fremen are a few ragged bands that *we* use as spice-hunters."

"But they can kill Harkonnens."

"And do you wish to know the result? Even now they are being hunted down like animals—with lasguns, because they have no shields. They are being exterminated. Why? Because they killed Harkonnens."

"Was it Harkonnens they killed?" Halleck asked.

"What do you mean?"

"Haven't you heard that there may've been Sardaukar with the Harkonnens?"

"More rumors."

"But a pogrom—that isn't like the Harkonnens. A pogrom is wasteful."

"I believe what I see with my own eyes," Tuek said. "Make your choice, fighting man. Me or the Fremen. I will promise you sanctuary and a chance to draw the blood we both want. Be sure of that. The Fremen will offer you only the life of the hunted."

Halleck hesitated, sensing wisdom and sympathy in Tuek's words, yet troubled for no reason he could explain.

"Trust your own abilities," Tuek said. "Whose decisions brought your force through the battle? Yours. Decide."

"It must be," Halleck said. "The Duke and his son are dead?"

"The Harkonnens believe it. Where such things are concerned, I incline to trust the Harkonnens." A grim smile touched Tuek's mouth. "But it's about the only trust I give them."

"Then it must be," Halleck repeated. He held out his right hand, palm up and thumb folded flat against it in the traditional gesture. "I give you my sword."

"Accepted."

"Do you wish me to persuade my men?"

"You'd let them make their own decision?"

"They've followed me this far, but most are Caladan-born. Arrakis isn't what they thought it'd be. Here, they've lost everything except their lives. I'd prefer they decided for themselves now."

"Now is no time for you to falter," Tuek said. "They've followed you this far."

"You need them, is that it?"

"We can always use experienced fighting men . . . in these times more than ever."

"You've accepted my sword. Do you wish me to persuade them?"

"I think they'll follow you, Gurney Halleck."

"'Tis to be hoped."

"Indeed."

"I may make my own decision in this, then?"

"Your own decision."

Halleck pushed himself up from the bucket seat, feeling how much of his reserve strength even that small effort required. "For now, I'll see to their quarters and well-being," he said.

"Consult my quartermaster," Tuek said. "Drisq is his name. Tell him it's my wish that you receive every courtesy. I'll join you myself presently. I've some off-shipments of spice to see to first."

"Fortune passes everywhere," Halleck said.

"Everywhere," Tuek said. "A time of upset is a rare opportunity for our business."

Halleck nodded, heard the faint sussuration and felt the air shift as a lockport swung open beside him. He turned, ducked through it and out of the office.

He found himself in the assembly hall through which he and his men had been led by Tuek's aides. It was a long, fairly narrow area chewed out of the native rock, its smooth surface betraying the use of cutteray burners for the job. The ceiling stretched away high enough to continue the natural supporting curve of the rock and to permit internal air-convection currents. Weapons racks and lockers lined the walls.

Halleck noted with a touch of pride that those of his men still able to stand were standing—no relaxation in weariness and defeat for them. Smuggler medics were moving among them tending the wounded. Litter cases were assembled in one area down to the left, each wounded man with an Atreides companion.

The Atreides training—*"We care for our own!"*—it held like a core of native rock in them, Halleck noted.

One of his lieutenants stepped forward carrying Halleck's ninestring baliset out of its case. The man snapped a salute, said: "Sir, the medics here say there's no hope for Mattai. They have no bone and organ banks here—only outpost medicine. Mattai can't last, they say, and he has a request of you."

"What is it?"

The lieutenant thrust the baliset forward. "Mattai wants a song to ease his going, sir. He says you'll know the one . . . he's asked it of you often enough." The lieutenant swallowed. "It's the one called 'My Woman,' sir. If you—"

"I know." Halleck took the baliset, flicked the multipick out of its catch on the fingerboard. He drew a soft chord from the instrument, found that someone had already tuned it. There was a burning in his eyes, but he drove that out of his thoughts as he strolled forward, strumming the tune, forcing himself to smile casually.

Several of his men and a smuggler medic were bent over one of the litters. One of the men began singing softly as Halleck approached, catching the counter-beat with the ease of long familiarity:

> "My woman stands at her window,
> Curved lines 'gainst square glass.
> Uprais'd arms ... bent ... downfolded.
> 'Gainst sunset red and golded—
> Come to me ...
> Come to me, warm arms of my lass.
> For me ...
> For me, the warm arms of my lass."

The singer stopped, reached out a bandaged arm and closed the eyelids of the man on the litter.

Halleck drew a final soft chord from the baliset, thinking: *Now we are seventy-three.*

Family life of the Royal Creche is difficult for many people to understand, but I shall try to give you a capsule view of it. My father had only one real friend, I think. That was Count Hasimir Fenring, the genetic-eunuch and one of the deadliest fighters in the Imperium. The Count, a dapper and ugly little man, brought a new slave-concubine to my father one day and I was dispatched by my mother to spy on the proceedings. All of us spied on my father as a matter of self-protection. One of the slave-concubines permitted my father under the Bene Gesserit-Guild agreement could not, of course, bear a Royal Successor, but the intrigues were constant and oppressive in their similarity. We became adept, my mother and sisters and I, at avoiding subtle instruments of death. It may seem a dreadful thing to say, but I'm not at all sure my father was innocent in all these attempts. A Royal Family is not like other families. Here was a new slave-concubine, then, red-haired like my father, willowy and graceful. She had a dancer's muscles, and her training obviously had included neuro-enticement. My father looked at her for a long time as she postured unclothed before him. Finally he said: "She is too beautiful. We will save her as a gift." You have no idea how much consternation this restraint created in the Royal Creche. Subtlety and self-control were, after all, the most deadly threats to us all.

—FROM "IN MY FATHER'S HOUSE"
BY THE PRINCESS IRULAN

Paul stood outside the stilltent in the late afternoon. The crevasse where he had pitched their camp lay in deep shadow. He stared out across the open sand at the distant cliff, wondering if he should waken his mother, who lay asleep in the tent.

Folds upon folds of dunes spread beyond their shelter. Away from the setting sun, the dunes exposed greased shadows so black they were like bits of night.

And the flatness.

His mind searched for something tall in that landscape. But there was no persuading tallness out of heat-addled air and that horizon—no bloom or gently shaken thing to mark the passage of a breeze . . . only dunes and that distant cliff beneath a sky of burnished silver-blue.

What if there isn't one of the abandoned testing stations across there? he wondered. *What if there are no Fremen, either, and the plants we see are only an accident?*

Within the tent, Jessica awakened, turned onto her back and peered sidelong out the transparent end at Paul. He stood with his back to her and something about his stance reminded her of his father. She sensed the well of grief rising within her and turned away.

Presently she adjusted her stillsuit, refreshed herself with water from the tent's catchpocket, and slipped out to stand and stretch the sleep from her muscles.

Paul spoke without turning: "I find myself enjoying the quiet here."

How the mind gears itself for its environment, she thought. And she recalled a Bene Gesserit axiom: *"The mind can go either direction under stress—toward positive or toward negative: on or off. Think of it as a spectrum whose extremes are unconsciousness at the negative end and hyperconsciousness at the positive end. The way the mind will lean under stress is strongly influenced by training."*

"It could be a good life here," Paul said.

She tried to see the desert through his eyes, seeking to encompass all the rigors this planet accepted as commonplace, wondering at the possible futures Paul had glimpsed. *One could be alone out here,* she thought, *without fear of someone behind you, without fear of the hunter.*

She stepped past Paul, lifted her binoculars, adjusted the oil lenses and studied the escarpment across from them. Yes, saguaro in the arroyos and other spiny growth . . . and a matting of low grasses, yellow-green in the shadows.

"I'll strike camp," Paul said.

Jessica nodded, walked to the fissure's mouth where she could get a sweep of the desert, and swung her binoculars to the left. A salt pan glared white there with a blending of dirty tan at its edges—a field of white out here where white was death. But the pan said another thing: *water*. At some time water had flowed across that glaring white. She lowered her binoculars, adjusted her burnoose, listened for a moment to the sound of Paul's movements.

The sun dipped lower. Shadows stretched across the salt pan. Lines of wild color spread over the sunset horizon. Color streamed into a toe of darkness testing the sand. Coal-colored shadows spread, and the thick collapse of night blotted the desert.

Stars!

She stared up at them, sensing Paul's movements as he came up beside her. The desert night focused upward with a feeling of lift toward the stars. The weight of the day receded. There came a brief flurry of breeze across her face.

"The first moon will be up soon," Paul said. "The pack's ready. I've planted the thumper."

We could be lost forever in this hellplace, she thought. *And no one to know.*

The night wind spread sand runnels that grated across her face, bringing the smell of cinnamon: a shower of odors in the dark.

"Smell that," Paul said.

"I can smell it even through the filter," she said. "Riches. But will it buy water?" She pointed across the basin. "There are no artificial lights across there."

"Fremen would be hidden in a sietch behind those rocks," he said.

A sill of silver pushed above the horizon to their right: the first moon. It lifted into view, the hand pattern plain on its face. Jessica studied the white-silver of sand exposed in the light.

"I planted the thumper in the deepest part of the crevasse," Paul said. "Whenever I light its candle it'll give us about thirty minutes."

"Thirty minutes?"

"Before it starts calling . . . a . . . worm."

"Oh. I'm ready to go."

He slipped away from her side and she heard his progress back up their fissure.

The night is a tunnel, she thought, *a hole into tomorrow . . . if we're to have a tomorrow.* She shook her head. *Why must I be so morbid? I was trained better than that!*

Paul returned, took up the pack, led the way down to the first spreading dune where he stopped and listened as his mother came up behind him. He heard her soft progress and the cold single-grain dribbles of sound—the desert's own code spelling out its measure of safety.

"We must walk without rhythm," Paul said and he called up memory of men walking the sand . . . both prescient memory and real memory.

"Watch how I do it," he said. "This is how Fremen walk the sand."

He stepped out onto the windward face of the dune, following the curve of it, moved with a dragging pace.

Jessica studied his progress for ten steps, followed, imitating him. She saw the sense of it: they must sound like the natural shifting of sand . . . like the wind. But muscles protested this unnatural, broken pattern: Step . . . drag . . . drag . . . step . . . step . . . wait . . . drag . . . step. . . .

Time stretched out around them. The rock face ahead seemed to grow no nearer. The one behind still towered high.

"Lump! Lump! Lump! Lump!"

It was a drumming from the cliff behind.

"The thumper," Paul hissed.

Its pounding continued and they found difficulty avoiding the rhythm of it in their stride.

"Lump . . . lump . . . lump . . . lump. . . ."

They moved in a moonlit bowl punctured by that hollowed thumping. Down and up through spilling dunes: step . . . drag . . . wait . . . step. . . . Across pea sand that rolled under their feet: drag . . . wait . . . step. . . .

And all the while their ears searched for a special hissing.

The sound, when it came, started so low that their own dragging passage masked it. But it grew . . . louder and louder . . . out of the west.

"Lump . . . lump . . . lump . . . lump. . . ." drummed the thumper.

The hissing approach spread across the night behind them. They turned their heads as they walked, saw the mound of the coursing worm.

"Keep moving," Paul whispered. "Don't look back."

A grating sound of fury exploded from the rock shadows they had left. It was a flailing avalanche of noise.

"Keep moving," Paul repeated.

He saw that they had reached an unmarked point where the two rock faces—the one ahead and the one behind—appeared equally remote.

And still behind them, that whipping, frenzied tearing of rocks dominated the night.

They moved on and on and on. . . . Muscles reached a stage of mechanical aching that seemed to stretch out indefinitely, but Paul saw that the beckoning escarpment ahead of them had climbed higher.

Jessica moved in a void of concentration, aware that the pressure of her will alone kept her walking. Dryness ached in her mouth, but the sounds behind drove away all hope of stopping for a sip from her stillsuit's catchpockets.

"Lump . . . lump. . . ."

Renewed frenzy erupted from the distant cliff, drowning out the thumper.

Silence!

"Faster," Paul whispered.

She nodded, knowing he did not see the gesture, but needing the action to tell herself that it was necessary to demand even more from muscles that already were being taxed to their limits—the unnatural movement. . . .

The rock face of safety ahead of them climbed into the stars, and Paul saw a plane of flat sand stretching out at the base. He stepped onto it, stumbled in his fatigue, righted himself with an involuntary out-thrusting of a foot.

Resonant booming shook the sand around them.

Paul lurched sideways two steps.

"Boom! Boom!"

"Drum sand!" Jessica hissed.

Paul recovered his balance. A sweeping glance took in the sand around them, the rock escarpment perhaps two hundred meters away.

Behind them, he heard a hissing—like the wind, like a riptide where there was no water.

"Run!" Jessica screamed. "Paul, run!"

They ran.

Drum sound boomed beneath their feet. Then they were out of it and into pea gravel. For a time, the running was a relief to muscles that ached from unfamiliar, rhythmless use. Here was action that could be understood. Here was rhythm. But sand and gravel dragged at their feet. And the hissing approach of the worm was storm sound that grew around them.

Jessica stumbled to her knees. All she could think of was the fatigue and the sound and the terror.

Paul dragged her up.

They ran on, hand in hand.

A thin pole jutted from the sand ahead of them. They passed it, saw another.

Jessica's mind failed to register on the poles until they were past.

There was another—wind-etched surface thrust up from a crack in rock.

Another.

Rock!

She felt it through her feet, the shock of unresisting surface, gained new strength from the firmer footing.

A deep crack stretched its vertical shadow upward into the cliff ahead of them. They sprinted for it, crowded into the narrow hole.

Behind them, the sound of the worm's passage stopped.

Jessica and Paul turned, peered out onto the desert.

Where the dunes began, perhaps fifty meters away at the foot of a rock beach, a silver-gray curve broached from the desert, sending rivers of sand and dust cascading all around. It lifted higher, resolved into a giant, questing mouth. It was a round, black hole with edges glistening in the moonlight.

The mouth snaked toward the narrow crack where Paul and Jessica huddled. Cinnamon yelled in their nostrils. Moonlight flashed from crystal teeth.

Back and forth the great mouth wove.

Paul stilled his breathing.

Jessica crouched staring.

It took intense concentration of her Bene Gesserit training to put down the primal terrors, subduing a race-memory fear that threatened to fill her mind.

Paul felt a kind of elation. In some recent instant, he had crossed a time barrier into more unknown territory. He could sense the darkness ahead, nothing revealed to his inner eye. It was as though some step he had taken had plunged him into a well . . . or into the trough of a wave where the future was invisible. The landscape had undergone a profound shifting.

Instead of frightening him, the sensation of time-darkness forced a hyper-acceleration of his other senses. He found himself registering every available aspect of the thing that lifted from the sand there seeking him. Its mouth was some eighty meters in diameter . . . crystal teeth with the curved shape of crysknives glinting around the rim . . . the bellows breath of cinnamon, subtle aldehydes . . . Acids. . . .

The worm blotted out the moonlight as it brushed the rocks above them. A shower of small stones and sand cascaded into the narrow hiding place.

Paul crowded his mother farther back.

Cinnamon!

The smell of it flooded across him.

What has the worm to do with the spice, melange? he asked himself. And he remembered Liet-Kynes betraying a veiled reference to some association between worm and spice.

"Barrrroooom!"

It was like a peal of dry thunder coming from far off to their right.

Again: "Barrrroooom!"

The worm drew back onto the sand, lay there momentarily, its crystal teeth weaving moonflashes.

"Lump! Lump! Lump! Lump!"

Another thumper! Paul thought.

Again it sounded off to their right.

A shudder passed through the worm. It drew farther away into the sand. Only a mounded upper curve remained like half a bell mouth, the curve of a tunnel rearing above the dunes.

Sand rasped.

The creature sank farther, retreating, turning. It became a mound of cresting sand that curved away through a saddle in the dunes.

Paul stepped out of the crack, watched the sand wave recede across the waste toward the new thumper summons.

Jessica followed, listening: "Lump . . . lump . . . lump . . . lump . . . lump. . . ."

Presently the sound stopped.

Paul found the tube into his stillsuit, sipped at the reclaimed water.

Jessica focused on his action, but her mind felt blank with fatigue and the aftermath of terror. "Has it gone for sure?" she whispered.

"Somebody called it," Paul said. "Fremen."

She felt herself recovering. "It was so big!"

"Not as big as the one that got our 'thopter."

"Are you sure it was Fremen?"

"They used a thumper."

"Why would they help us?"

"Maybe they weren't helping us. Maybe they were just calling a worm."

"Why?"

An answer lay poised at the edge of his awareness, but refused to come. He had a vision in his mind of something to do with the telescoping barbed sticks in their packs—the "maker hooks."

"Why would they call a worm?" Jessica asked.

A breath of fear touched his mind, and he forced himself to turn away from his mother, to look up the cliff. "We'd better find a way up there before daylight." He pointed. "Those poles we passed—there are more of them."

She looked, following the line of his hand, saw the poles—wind-scratched markers—made out the shadow of a narrow ledge that twisted into a crevasse high above them.

"They mark a way up the cliff," Paul said. He settled his shoulders into the pack, crossed to the foot of the ledge and began the climb upward.

Jessica waited a moment, resting, restoring her strength; then she followed.

Up they climbed, following the guide poles until the ledge dwindled to a narrow lip at the mouth of a dark crevasse.

Paul tipped his head to peer into the shadowed place. He could feel the precarious hold his feet had on the slender ledge, but forced himself to slow caution. He saw only darkness within the crevasse. It stretched away upward, open to the stars at the top. His ears searched, found only sounds he could expect—a tiny spill of sand, an insect *brrr*, the patter of a small running creature. He tested the darkness in the crevasse with one foot, found rock beneath a gritting surface. Slowly, he inched around the corner, signaled for his mother to follow. He grasped a loose edge of her robe, helped her around.

They looked upward at starlight framed by two rock lips. Paul saw his mother beside him as a cloudy gray movement. "If we could only risk a light," he whispered.

"We have other senses than eyes," she said.

Paul slid a foot forward, shifted his weight, and probed with the other foot, met an obstruction. He lifted his foot, found a step, pulled himself up onto it. He reached back, felt his mother's arm, tugged at her robe for her to follow.

Another step.

"It goes on up to the top, I think," he whispered.

Shallow and even steps, Jessica thought. *Man-carved beyond a doubt.*

She followed the shadowy movement of Paul's progress, feeling out the steps. Rock walls narrowed until her shoulders almost brushed them. The steps ended in a slitted defile about twenty meters long, its floor level, and this opened onto a shallow, moonlit basin.

Paul stepped out into the rim of the basin, whispered: "What a beautiful place."

Jessica could only stare in silent agreement from her position a step behind him.

In spite of weariness, the irritation of recaths and nose plugs and the confinement of the stillsuit, in spite of fear and the aching desire for rest, this basin's beauty filled her senses, forcing her to stop and admire it.

"Like a fairyland," Paul whispered.

Jessica nodded.

Spreading away in front of her stretched desert growth—bushes, cacti, tiny clumps of leaves—all trembling in the moonlight. The ring-walls were dark to her left, moon-frosted on her right.

"This must be a Fremen place," Paul said.

"There would have to be people for this many plants to survive," she agreed. She uncapped the tube to her stillsuit's catchpockets, sipped at it. Warm, faintly acrid wetness slipped down her throat. She marked how it refreshed her. The tube's cap grated against flakes of sand as she replaced it.

Movement caught Paul's attention—to his right and down on the basin floor curving out beneath them. He stared down through smoke bushes and weeds into a wedged slab sand-surface of moonlight inhabited by an *up-hop, jump, pop-hop* of tiny motion.

"Mice!" he hissed.

Pop-hop-hop! they went, into shadows and out.

Something fell soundlessly past their eyes into the mice. There came a thin screech, a flapping of wings, and a ghostly gray bird lifted away across the basin with a small, dark shadow in its talons.

We needed that reminder, Jessica thought.

Paul continued to stare across the basin. He inhaled, sensed the softly cutting contralto smell of sage climbing the night. The predatory bird—he thought of it as the way of this desert. It had brought a stillness to the basin so unuttered that the blue-milk moonlight could almost be heard flowing across sentinel saguaro and spiked paintbush. There was a low humming of light here more basic in its harmony than any other music in his universe.

"We'd better find a place to pitch the tent," he said. "Tomorrow we can try to find the Fremen who—"

"Most intruders here regret finding the Fremen!"

It was a heavy masculine voice chopping across his words, shattering the moment. The voice came from above them and to their right.

"Please do not run, intruders," the voice said as Paul made to withdraw into the defile. "If you run you'll only waste your body's water."

They want us for the water of our flesh! Jessica thought. Her muscles overrode all fatigue, flowed into maximum readiness without external betrayal. She pinpointed the location of the voice, thinking: *Such stealth! I didn't hear him.* And she realized that the owner of that voice had permitted himself only the small sounds, the natural sounds of the desert.

Another voice called from the basin's rim to their left. "Make it quick, Stil. Get their water and let's be on our way. We've little enough time before dawn."

Paul, less conditioned to emergency response than his mother, felt chagrin that he had stiffened and tried to withdraw, that he had clouded his abilities by a momentary panic. He forced himself now to obey her teachings: relax, then fall into the semblance of relaxation, then into the arrested whipsnap of muscles that can slash in any direction.

Still, he felt the edge of fear within him and knew its source. This was blind time, no future he had seen . . . and they were caught between wild Fremen whose only interest was the water carried in the flesh of two unshielded bodies.

This Fremen religious adaptation, then, is the source of what we now recognize as "The Pillars of the Universe," whose Qizara Tafwid are among us all with signs and proofs and prophecy. They bring us the Arrakeen mystical fusion whose profound beauty is typified by the stirring music built on the old forms, but stamped with the new awakening. Who has not heard and been deeply moved by "The Old Man's Hymn"?

> I drove my feet through a desert
> Whose mirage fluttered like a host.
> Voracious for glory, greedy for danger,
> I roamed the horizons of al-Kulab.
> Watching time level mountains
> In its search and its hunger for me.
> And I saw the sparrows swiftly approach,
> Bolder than the onrushing wolf.
> They spread in the tree of my youth.
> I heard the flock in my branches
> And was caught on their beaks and claws!

—FROM "ARRAKIS AWAKENING"
BY THE PRINCESS IRULAN

The man crawled across a dune top. He was a mote caught in the glare of the noon sun. He was dressed only in torn remnants of a jubba cloak, his skin bare to the heat through the tatters. The hood had been ripped from the cloak, but the man had fashioned a turban from a torn strip of cloth. Wisps of sandy hair protruded from it, matched by a sparse beard and thick brows. Beneath the blue-within-blue eyes, remains of a dark stain spread down to his cheeks. A matted depression across mustache and beard showed where a stillsuit tube had marked out its path from nose to catchpockets.

The man stopped half across the dune crest, arms stretched down the slipface. Blood had clotted on his back and on his arms and legs. Patches of yellow-gray sand clung to the wounds. Slowly, he brought his hands under him, pushed himself to his feet, stood there swaying. And even in this almost-random action there remained a trace of once-precise movement.

"I am Liet-Kynes," he said, addressing himself to the empty horizon, and his voice was a hoarse caricature of the strength it had known. "I am His Imperial Majesty's Planetologist," he whispered, "planetary ecologist for Arrakis. I am steward of this land."

He stumbled, fell sideways along the crusty surface of the windward face. His hands dug feebly into the sand.

I am steward of this sand, he thought.

He realized that he was semidelirious, that he should dig himself into the sand, find the relatively cool underlayer and cover himself with it. But he could still smell the rank, semisweet esthers of a pre-spice pocket somewhere underneath this sand. He knew the peril within this fact more certainly than any other Fremen. If he could smell the pre-spice mass, that meant the gasses deep under the sand were nearing explosive pressure. He had to get away from here.

His hands made weak scrabbling motions along the dune face.

A thought spread across his mind—clear, distinct: *The real wealth of a planet is in its landscape, how we take part in that basic source of civilization—agriculture.*

And he thought how strange it was that the mind, long fixed on a single track, could not get off that track. The Harkonnen troopers had left him here without water or stillsuit, thinking a worm would get him if the desert didn't. They had thought it amusing to leave him alive to die by inches at the impersonal hands of his planet.

The Harkonnens always did find it difficult to kill Fremen, he thought.

We don't die easily. I should be dead now . . . I will be dead soon . . . but I can't stop being an ecologist.

"The highest function of ecology is understanding consequences."

The voice shocked him because he recognized it and knew the owner of it was dead. It was the voice of his father who had been planetologist here before him—his father long dead, killed in the cave-in at Plaster Basin.

"Got yourself into quite a fix here, Son," his father said. "You should've known the consequences of trying to help the child of that Duke."

I'm delirious, Kynes thought.

The voice seemed to come from his right. Kynes scraped his face through sand, turning to look in that direction—nothing except a curving stretch of dune dancing with heat devils in the full glare of the sun.

"The more life there is within a system, the more niches there are for life," his father said. And the voice came now from his left, from behind him.

Why does he keep moving around? Kynes asked himself. *Doesn't he want me to see him?*

"Life improves the capacity of the environment to sustain life," his father said. "Life makes needed nutrients more readily available. It binds more energy into the system through the tremendous chemical interplay from organism to organism."

Why does he keep harping on the same subject? Kynes asked himself. *I knew that before I was ten.*

Desert hawks, carrion-eaters in this land as were most wild creatures, began to circle over him. Kynes saw a shadow pass near his hand, forced his head farther around to look upward. The birds were a blurred patch on silver-blue sky—distant flecks of soot floating above him.

"We are generalists," his father said. "You can't draw neat lines around planet-wide problems. Planetology is a cut-and-fit science."

What's he trying to tell me? Kynes wondered. *Is there some consequence I failed to see?*

His cheek slumped back against the hot sand, and he smelled the burned rock odor beneath the pre-spice gasses. From some corner of logic in his mind, a thought formed: *Those are carrion-eater birds over me. Perhaps some of my Fremen will see them and come to investigate.*

"To the working planetologist, his most important tool is human beings," his father said. "You must cultivate ecological literacy among the people. That's why I've created this entirely new form of ecological notation."

He's repeating things he said to me when I was a child, Kynes thought.

He began to feel cool, but that corner of logic in his mind told him: *The sun is overhead. You have no stillsuit and you're hot; the sun is burning the moisture out of your body.*

His fingers clawed feebly at the sand.

They couldn't even leave me a stillsuit!

"The presence of moisture in the air helps prevent too-rapid evaporation from living bodies," his father said.

Why does he keep repeating the obvious? Kynes wondered.

He tried to think of moisture in the air—grass covering this dune . . . open water somewhere beneath him, a long qanat flowing with water open to the sky except in text illustrations. Open water . . . irrigation water . . . it took five thousand cubic meters of water to irrigate one hectare of land per growing season, he remembered.

"Our first goal on Arrakis," his father said, "is grassland provinces. We will start with these mutated poverty grasses. When we have moisture locked in grasslands, we'll move on to start upland forests, then a few open bodies of water—small at first—and situated along lines of prevailing winds with windtrap moisture precipitators spaced in the lines to recapture what the wind steals. We must create a true sirocco— a moist wind—but we will never get away from the necessity for windtraps."

Always lecturing me, Kynes thought. *Why doesn't he shut up? Can't he see I'm dying?*

"You will die, too," his father said, "if you don't get off the bubble that's forming right now deep underneath you. It's there and you know it. You can smell the pre-spice gasses. You know the little makers are beginning to lose some of their water into the mass."

The thought of that water beneath him was maddening. He imagined it now—sealed off in strata of porous rock by the leathery half-plant, half-animal little makers—and the thin rupture that was pouring a cool stream of clearest, pure, liquid, soothing water into. . . .

A pre-spice mass!

He inhaled, smelling the rank sweetness. The odor was much richer around him than it had been.

Kynes pushed himself to his knees, heard a bird screech, the hurried flapping of wings.

This is spice desert, he thought. *There must be Fremen about even in the day sun. Surely they can see the birds and will investigate.*

"Movement across the landscape is a necessity for animal life," his father said. "Nomad peoples follow the same necessity. Lines of movement adjust to physical needs for water, food, minerals. We must control this movement now, align it for our purposes."

"Shut up, old man," Kynes muttered.

"We must do a thing on Arrakis never before attempted for an entire planet," his father said. "We must use man as a constructive ecological force—inserting adapted terraform life: a plant here, an animal there, a man in that place—to transform the water cycle, to build a new kind of landscape."

"Shut up!" Kynes croaked.

"It was lines of movement that gave us the first clue to the relationship between worms and spice," his father said.

A worm, Kynes thought with a surge of hope. *A maker's sure to come when this bubble bursts. But I have no hooks. How can I mount a big maker without hooks?*

He could feel frustration sapping what little strength remained to him. Water so near—only a hundred meters or so beneath him; a worm sure to come, but no way to trap it on the surface and use it.

Kynes pitched forward onto the sand, returning to the shallow depression his movements had defined. He felt sand hot against his left cheek, but the sensation was remote.

"The Arrakeen environment built itself into the evolutionary pattern of native life forms," his father said. "How strange that so few people ever looked up from the spice long enough to wonder at the near-ideal nitrogen-oxygen-CO_2 balance being maintained here in the absence of large areas of plant cover. The energy sphere of the planet is there to see and understand—a relentless process, but a process nonetheless. There is a gap in it? Then something occupies that gap. Science is made up of so many things that appear obvious after they are explained. I knew the little maker was there, deep in the sand, long before I ever saw it."

"Please stop lecturing me, Father," Kynes whispered.

A hawk landed on the sand near his outstretched hand. Kynes saw it fold its wings, tip its head to stare at him. He summoned the energy to croak at it. The bird hopped away two steps, but continued to stare at him.

"Men and their works have been a disease on the surface of their planets before now," his father said. "Nature tends to compensate for diseases, to remove or encapsulate them, to incorporate them into the system in her own way."

The hawk lowered its head, stretched its wings, refolded them. It transferred its attention to his outstretched hand.

Kynes found that he no longer had the strength to croak at it.

"The historical system of mutual pillage and extortion stops here on Arrakis," his father said. "You cannot go on forever stealing what you need without regard to those who come after. The physical qualities of a planet are written into its economic and political record. We have the record in front of us and our course is obvious."

He never could stop lecturing, Kynes thought. *Lecturing, lecturing, lecturing—always lecturing.*

The hawk hopped one step closer to Kynes' outstretched hand, turned its head first one way and then the other to study the exposed flesh.

"Arrakis is a one-crop planet," his father said. "One crop. It supports a ruling class that lives as ruling classes have lived in all times while, beneath them, a semihuman mass of semislaves exists on the leavings. It's the masses and the leavings that occupy our attention. These are far more valuable than has ever been suspected."

"I'm ignoring you, Father," Kynes whispered. "Go away."

And he thought: *Surely there must be some of my Fremen near. They cannot help but see the birds over me. They will investigate if only to see if there's moisture available.*

"The masses of Arrakis will know that we work to make the land flow with water," his father said. "Most of them, of course, will have only a semimystical understanding of how we intend to do this. Many, not understanding the prohibitive mass-ratio problem, may even think we'll bring water from some other planet rich in it. Let them think anything they wish as long as they believe in us."

In a minute I'll get up and tell him what I think of him, Kynes thought. *Standing there lecturing me when he should be helping me.*

The bird took another hop closer to Kynes' outstretched hand. Two more hawks drifted down to the sand behind it.

"Religion and law among our masses must be one and the same," his father said. "An act of disobedience must be a sin and require religious penalties. This will have the dual benefit of bringing both greater obedience and greater bravery. We must depend not so much on the bravery of individuals, you see, as upon the bravery of a whole population."

Where is my population now when I need it most? Kynes thought. He summoned all his strength, moved his hand a finger's width toward the nearest hawk. It hopped backward among its companions and all stood poised for flight.

"Our timetable will achieve the stature of a natural phenomenon," his father said. "A planet's life is a vast, tightly interwoven fabric. Vegetation and animal changes will be determined at first by the raw physical forces we manipulate. As they establish themselves, though, our changes will become controlling influences in their own right—and we will have to deal with them, too. Keep in mind, though, that we need control only three per cent of the energy surface—only three per cent—to tip the entire structure over into our self-sustaining system."

Why aren't you helping me? Kynes wondered. *Always the same: when I need you most, you fail me.* He wanted to turn his head, to stare in the direction of his father's voice, stare the old man down. Muscles refused to answer his demand.

Kynes saw the hawk move. It approached his hand, a cautious step at a time while its companions waited in mock indifference. The hawk stopped only a hop away from his hand.

A profound clarity filled Kynes' mind. He saw quite suddenly a potential for Arrakis that his father had never seen. The possibilities along that different path flooded through him.

"No more terrible disaster could befall your people than for them to fall into the hands of a Hero," his father said.

Reading my mind! Kynes thought. *Well . . . let him.*

The messages already have been sent to my sietch villages, he thought. *Nothing can stop them. If the Duke's son is alive they'll find him and protect him as I have commanded. They may discard the woman, his mother, but they'll save the boy.*

The hawk took one hop that brought it within slashing distance of his hand. It tipped its head to examine the supine flesh. Abruptly, it straightened, stretched its head upward and with a single screech, leaped into the air and banked away overhead with its companions behind it.

They've come! Kynes thought. *My Fremen have found me!*

Then he heard the sand rumbling.

Every Fremen knew the sound, could distinguish it immediately from the noises of worms or other desert life. Somewhere beneath him, the pre-spice mass had accumulated enough water and organic matter from the little makers, had reached the critical stage of wild growth. A gigantic bubble of carbon dioxide was forming deep in the sand, heaving upward in an enormous "blow" with a dust whirlpool at its center. It would exchange what had been formed deep in the sand for whatever lay on the surface.

The hawks circled overhead screeching their frustration. They knew what was happening. Any desert creature would know.

And I am a desert creature, Kynes thought. *You see me, Father? I am a desert creature.*

He felt the bubble lift him, felt it break and the dust whirlpool engulf him, dragging him down into cool darkness. For a moment, the sensation of coolness and the moisture were blessed relief. Then, as his planet killed him, it occurred to Kynes that his father and all the other scientists were wrong, that the most persistent principles of the universe were accident and error.

Even the hawks could appreciate these facts.

Prophecy and prescience—How can they be put to the test in the face of the unanswered question? Consider: How much is actual prediction of the "wave form" (as Muad'Dib referred to his vision-image) and how much is the prophet shaping the future to fit the prophecy? What of the harmonics inherent in the act of prophecy? Does the prophet see the future or does he see a line of weakness, a fault or cleavage that he may shatter with words or decisions as a diamond-cutter shatters his gem with a blow of a knife?

—FROM "PRIVATE REFLECTIONS ON MUAD'DIB"
BY THE PRINCESS IRULAN

"*Get their water*," the man calling out of the night had said. And Paul fought down his fear, glanced at his mother. His trained eyes saw her readiness for battle, the waiting whipsnap of her muscles.

"It would be regrettable should we have to destroy you out of hand," the voice above them said.

That's the one who spoke to us first, Jessica thought. *There are at least two of them—one to our right and one on our left.*

"Cignoro hrobosa sukares hin mange la pchagavas doi me kamavas na beslas lele pal hrobas!"

It was the man to their right calling out across the basin.

To Paul, the words were gibberish, but out of her Bene Gesserit training, Jessica recognized the speech. It was Chakobsa, one of the ancient hunting languages, and the man above them was saying that perhaps these were the strangers they sought.

In the sudden silence that followed the calling voice, the hoopwheel face of the second moon—faintly ivory blue—rolled over the rocks across the basin, bright and peering.

Scrambling sounds came from the rocks—above and to both sides . . . dark motions in the moonlight. Many figures flowed through the shadows.

A whole troop! Paul thought with a sudden pang.

A tall man in a mottled burnoose stepped in front of Jessica. His mouth baffle was thrown aside for clear speech, revealing a heavy beard in the sidelight of the moon, but face and eyes were hidden in the overhang of his hood.

"What have we here—jinn or human?" he asked.

When Jessica heard the true-banter in his voice, she allowed herself a faint hope. This was the voice of command, the voice that had first shocked them with its intrusion from the night.

"Human, I warrant," the man said.

Jessica sensed rather than saw the knife hidden in a fold of the man's robe. She permitted herself one bitter regret that she and Paul had no shields.

"Do you also speak?" the man asked.

Jessica put all the royal arrogance at her command into her manner and voice. Reply was urgent, but she had not heard enough of this man to be certain she had a register on his culture and weaknesses.

"Who comes on us like criminals out of the night?" she demanded.

The burnoose-hooded head showed tension in a sudden twist, then slow relaxation that revealed much. The man had good control.

Paul shifted away from his mother to separate them as targets and give each of them a clearer arena of action.

The hooded head turned at Paul's movement, opening a wedge of face to moonlight. Jessica saw a sharp nose, one glinting eye—*dark, so dark the eye, without any white in it*—a heavy brown and upturned mustache.

"A likely cub," the man said. "If you're fugitives from the Harkonnens, it may be you're welcome among us. What is it, boy?"

The possibilities flashed through Paul's mind: *A trick? A fact?* Immediate decision was needed.

"Why should you welcome fugitives?" he demanded.

"A child who thinks and speaks like a man," the tall man said. "Well, now, to answer your question, my young wali, I am one who does not pay the fai, the water tribute, to the Harkonnens. That is why I might welcome a fugitive."

He knows who we are, Paul thought. *There's concealment in his voice.*

"I am Stilgar, the Fremen," the tall man said. "Does that speed your tongue, boy?"

It is the same voice, Paul thought. And he remembered the Council with this man seeking the body of a friend slain by the Harkonnens.

"I know you, Stilgar," Paul said. "I was with my father in Council when you came for the water of your friend. You took away with you my father's man, Duncan Idaho—an exchange of friends."

"And Idaho abandoned us to return to his Duke," Stilgar said.

Jessica heard the shading of disgust in his voice, held herself prepared for attack.

The voice from the rocks above them called: "We waste time here, Stil."

"This is the Duke's son," Stilgar barked. "He's certainly the one Liet told us to seek."

"But . . . a child, Stil."

"The Duke was a man and this lad used a thumper," Stilgar said. "That was a brave crossing he made in the path of *shai-hulud.*"

And Jessica heard him excluding her from his thoughts. Had he already passed sentence?

"We haven't time for the test," the voice above them protested.

"Yet he could be the Lisan al-Gaib," Stilgar said.

He's looking for an omen! Jessica thought.

"But the woman," the voice above them said.

Jessica readied herself anew. There had been death in that voice.

"Yes, the woman," Stilgar said. "And her water."

"You know the law," said the voice from the rocks. "Ones who cannot live with the desert—"

"Be quiet," Stilgar said. "Times change."

"Did Liet *command* this?" asked the voice from the rocks.

"You heard the voice of the cielago, Jamis," Stilgar said. "Why do you press me?"

And Jessica thought: *Cielago!* The clue of the tongue opened wide avenues of understanding: this was the language of Ilm and Fiqh, and cielago meant *bat*, a small flying mammal. *Voice of the cielago*: they had received a distrans message to seek Paul and herself.

"I but remind you of your duties, friend Stilgar," said the voice above them.

"My duty is the strength of the tribe," Stilgar said. "That is my only duty. I need no one to remind me of it. This child-man interests me. He is full-fleshed. He has lived on much water. He has lived away from the father sun. He has not the eyes of the Ibad. Yet he does not speak or act like a weakling of the pans. Nor did his father. How can this be?"

"We cannot stay out here all night arguing," said the voice from the rocks. "If a patrol—"

"I will not tell you again, Jamis, to be quiet," Stilgar said.

The man above them remained silent, but Jessica heard him moving, crossing by a leap over a defile and working his way down to the basin floor on their left.

"The voice of the cielago suggested there'd be value to us in saving you two," Stilgar said. "I can see possibility in this strong boy-man: he is young and can learn. But what of yourself, woman?" He stared at Jessica.

I have his voice and pattern registered now, Jessica thought. *I could control him with a word, but he's a strong man . . . worth much more to us unblunted and with full freedom of action. We shall see.*

"I am the mother of this boy," Jessica said. "In part, his strength which you admire is the product of my training."

"The strength of a woman can be boundless," Stilgar said. "Certain it is in a Reverend Mother. Are you a Reverend Mother?"

For the moment, Jessica put aside the implications of the question, answered truthfully, "No."

"Are you trained in the ways of the desert?"

"No, but many consider my training valuable."

"We make our own judgments on value," Stilgar said.

"Every man has the right to his own judgments," she said.

"It is well that you see the reason," Stilgar said. "We cannot dally here to test you, woman. Do you understand? We'd not want your shade to plague us. I will take the boy-man, your son, and he shall have my countenance, sanctuary in my tribe. But for you, woman—you understand there is nothing personal in this? It is the rule, Istislah, in the general interest. Is that not enough?"

Paul took a half-step forward. "What are you talking about?"

Stilgar flicked a glance across Paul, but kept his attention on Jessica. "Unless you've been deep-trained from childhood to live here, you could bring destruction onto an entire tribe. It is the law, and we cannot carry useless. . . ."

Jessica's motion started as a slumping, deceptive faint to the ground. It was the obvious thing for a weak outworlder to do, and the obvious slows an opponent's reactions. It takes an instant to interpret a known thing when that thing is exposed as something unknown. She shifted as she saw his right shoulder drop to bring a weapon within the folds of his robe to bear on her new position. A turn, a slash of her arm, a whirling of mingled robes, and she was against the rocks with the man helpless in front of her.

At his mother's first movement, Paul backed two steps. As she attacked, he dove for shadows. A bearded man rose up in his path, half-crouched, lunging forward with a weapon in one hand. Paul took the man beneath the sternum with a straight-hand jab, sidestepped and chopped the base of his neck, relieving him of the weapon as he fell.

Then Paul was into the shadows, scrambling upward among the rocks, the weapon tucked into his waist sash. He had recognized it in spite of its unfamiliar shape—a projectile weapon, and that said many things about this place, another clue that shields were not used here.

They will concentrate on my mother and that Stilgar fellow. She can handle him. I must get to a safe vantage point where I can threaten them and give her time to escape.

There came a chorus of sharp spring-clicks from the basin. Projectiles whined off the rocks around him. One of them flicked his robe. He squeezed around a corner in the rocks, found himself in a narrow vertical crack, began inching upward—his back against one side, his feet against the other—slowly, as silently as he could.

The roar of Stilgar's voice echoed up to him: "Get back, you worm-headed lice! She'll break my neck if you come near!"

A voice out of the basin said: "The boy got away, Stil. What are we—"

"Of course he got away, you sand-brained . . . Ugh-h-h! Easy, woman!"

"Tell them to stop hunting my son," Jessica said.

"They've stopped, woman. He got away as you intended him to. Great gods below! Why didn't you say you were a weirding woman and a fighter?"

"Tell your men to fall back," Jessica said. "Tell them to go out into the basin where I can see them . . . and you'd better believe that I know how many of them there are."

And she thought: *This is the delicate moment, but if this man is as sharp-minded as I think him, we have a chance.*

Paul inched his way upward, found a narrow ledge on which he could rest and look down into the basin. Stilgar's voice came up to him.

"And if I refuse? How can you . . . ugh-h-h! Leave be, woman! We mean no harm to you, now. Great gods! If you can do this to the strongest of us, you're worth ten times your weight of water."

Now, the test of reason, Jessica thought. She said: "You ask after the Lisan al-Gaib."

"You could be the folk of the legend," he said, "but I'll believe that when it's been tested. All I know now is that you came here with that stupid Duke who. . . . Aiee-e-e! Woman! I care not if you kill me! He was honorable and brave, but it was stupid to put himself in the way of the Harkonnen fist!"

Silence.

Presently, Jessica said: "He had no choice, but we'll not argue it. Now, tell that man of yours behind the bush over there to stop trying to bring his weapon to bear on me, or I'll rid the universe of you and take him next."

"You there!" Stilgar roared. "Do as she says!"

"But, Stil—"

"Do as she says, you wormfaced, crawling, sand-brained piece of lizard turd! Do it or I'll help her dismember you! Can't you see the worth of this woman?"

The man at the bush straightened from his partial concealment, lowered his weapon.

"He has obeyed," Stilgar said.

"Now," Jessica said, "explain clearly to your people what it is you wish of me. I want no young hothead to make a foolish mistake."

"When we slip into the villages and towns we must mask our origin, blend with the pan and graben folk," Stilgar said. "We carry no weapons, for the crysknife is sacred. But you, woman, you have the weirding ability of battle. We'd only heard of it and many doubted, but one cannot doubt what he sees with his own eyes. You mastered an armed Fremen. *This* is a weapon no search could expose."

There was a stirring in the basin as Stilgar's words sank home.

"And if I agree to teach you the . . . weirding way?"

"My countenance for you as well as your son."

"How can we be sure of the truth in your promise?"

Stilgar's voice lost some of its subtle undertone of reasoning, took on an edge of bitterness. "Out here, woman, we carry no paper for contracts. We make no evening promises to be broken at dawn. When a man says a thing, that's the contract. As leader of my people, I've put them in bond to my word. Teach us this weirding way and you have sanctuary with us as long as you wish. Your water shall mingle with our water."

"Can you speak for all Fremen?" Jessica asked.

"In time, that may be. But only my brother, Liet, speaks for all

Fremen. Here, I promise only secrecy. My people will not speak of you to any other sietch. The Harkonnens have returned to Dune in force and your Duke is dead. It is said that you two died in a Mother storm. The hunter does not seek dead game."

There's a safety in that, Jessica thought. *But these people have good communications and a message could be sent.*

"I presume there was a reward offered for us," she said.

Stilgar remained silent, and she could almost see the thoughts turning over in his head, sensing the shifts of his muscles beneath her hands.

Presently, he said: "I will say it once more: I've given the tribe's word-bond. My people know your worth to us now. What could the Harkonnens give us? Our freedom? Hah! No, you are the taqwa, that which buys us more than all the spice in the Harkonnen coffers."

"Then I shall teach you my way of battle," Jessica said, and she sensed the unconscious ritual-intensity of her own words.

"Now, will you release me?"

"So be it," Jessica said. She released her hold on him, stepped aside in full view of the bank in the basin. *This is the test-mashad,* she thought. *But Paul must know about them even if I die for his knowledge.*

In the waiting silence, Paul inched forward to get a better view of where his mother stood. As he moved, he heard heavy breathing, suddenly stilled, above him in the vertical crack of the rock, and sensed a faint shadow there outlined against the stars.

Stilgar's voice came up from the basin: "You, up there! Stop hunting the boy. He'll come down presently."

The voice of a young boy or a girl sounded from the darkness above Paul: "But, Stil, he can't be far from—"

"I said leave him be, Chani! You spawn of a lizard!"

There came a whispered imprecation from above Paul and a low voice: "Call *me* spawn of a lizard!" But the shadow pulled back out of view.

Paul returned his attention to the basin, picking out the gray-shadowed movement of Stilgar beside his mother.

"Come in, all of you," Stilgar called. He turned to Jessica. "And now I'll ask you how *we* may be certain you'll fulfill your half of our bargain? You're the ones lived with papers and empty contracts and such as—"

"We of the Bene Gesserit don't break our vows any more than you do," Jessica said.

There was a protracted silence, then a multiple hissing of voices: "A Bene Gesserit witch!"

Paul brought his captured weapon from his sash, trained it on the dark figure of Stilgar, but the man and his companions remained immobile, staring at Jessica.

"It *is* the legend," someone said.

"It was said that the Shadout Mapes gave this report on you," Stilgar said. "But a thing so important must be tested. If you are the Bene Gesserit of the legend whose son will lead us to paradise. . . ." He shrugged.

Jessica sighed, thinking: *So our Missionaria Protectiva even planted religious safety valves all through this hell hole. Ah, well . . . it'll help, and that's what it was meant to do.*

She said: "The seeress who brought you the legend, she gave it under the binding of karama and ijaz, the miracle and the inimitability of the prophecy—this I know. Do you wish a sign?"

His nostrils flared in the moonlight. "We cannot tarry for the rites," he whispered.

Jessica recalled a chart Kynes had shown her while arranging emergency escape routes. How long ago it seemed. There had been a place called "Sietch Tabr" on the chart and beside it the notation: "Stilgar."

"Perhaps when we get to Sietch Tabr," she said.

The revelation shook him, and Jessica thought: *If only he knew the tricks we use! She must've been good, that Bene Gesserit of the Missionaria Protectiva. These Fremen are beautifully prepared to believe in us.*

Stilgar shifted uneasily. "We must go now."

She nodded, letting him know that they left with her permission.

He looked up at the cliff almost directly at the rock ledge where Paul crouched. "You there, lad: you may come down now." He returned his attention to Jessica, spoke with an apologetic tone: "Your son made an incredible amount of noise climbing. He has much to learn lest he endanger us all, but he's young."

"No doubt we have much to teach each other," Jessica said. "Meanwhile, you'd best see to your companion out there. My noisy son was a bit rough in disarming him."

Stilgar whirled, his hood flapping. "Where?"

"Beyond those bushes." She pointed.

Stilgar touched two of his men. "See to it." He glanced at his companions, identifying them. "Jamis is missing." He turned to Jessica. "Even your cub knows the weirding way."

"And you'll notice that my son hasn't stirred from up there as you ordered," Jessica said.

The two men Stilgar had sent returned supporting a third who stumbled and gasped between them. Stilgar gave them a flicking glance, returned his attention to Jessica. "The son will take only your orders, eh? Good. He knows discipline."

"Paul, you may come down now," Jessica said.

Paul stood up, emerging into moonlight above his concealing cleft, slipped the Fremen weapon back into his sash. As he turned, another figure arose from the rocks to face him.

In the moonlight and reflection off gray stone, Paul saw a small figure in Fremen robes, a shadowed face peering out at him from the hood, and the muzzle of one of the projectile weapons aimed at him from a fold of robe.

"I am Chani, daughter of Liet."

The voice was lilting, half filled with laughter.

"I would not have permitted you to harm my companions," she said.

Paul swallowed. The figure in front of him turned into the moon's path and he saw an elfin face, black pits of eyes. The familiarity of that face, the features out of numberless visions in his earliest prescience, shocked Paul to stillness. He remembered the angry bravado with which he had once described this face-from-a-dream, telling the Reverend Mother Gaius Helen Mohiam: "I will meet her."

And here was the face, but in no meeting he had ever dreamed.

"You were as noisy as shai-hulud in a rage," she said. "And you took the most difficult way up here. Follow me; I'll show you an easier way down."

He scrambled out of the cleft, followed the swirling of her robe across a tumbled landscape. She moved like a gazelle, dancing over the rocks. Paul felt hot blood in his face, was thankful for the darkness.

That girl! She was like a touch of destiny. He felt caught up on a wave, in tune with a motion that lifted all his spirits.

They stood presently amidst the Fremen on the basin floor.

Jessica turned a wry smile on Paul, but spoke to Stilgar: "This will be a good exchange of teachings. I hope you and your people feel no anger at our violence. It seemed . . . necessary. You were about to . . . make a mistake."

"To save one from a mistake is a gift of paradise," Stilgar said. He touched his lips with his left hand, lifted the weapon from Paul's waist with the other, tossed it to a companion. "You will have your own maula pistol, lad, when you've earned it."

Paul started to speak, hesitated, remembering his mother's teaching: *"Beginnings are such delicate times."*

"My son has what weapons he needs," Jessica said. She stared at Stilgar, forcing him to think of how Paul had acquired the pistol.

Stilgar glanced at the man Paul had subdued—Jamis. The man stood at one side, head lowered, breathing heavily. "You are a difficult woman," Stilgar said. He held out his left hand to a companion, snapped his fingers. "Kushti bakka te."

More Chakobsa, Jessica thought.

The companion pressed two squares of gauze into Stilgar's hand. Stilgar ran them through his fingers, fixed one around Jessica's neck beneath her hood, fitted the other around Paul's neck in the same way.

"Now you wear the kerchief of the bakka," he said. "If we become separated, you will be recognized as belonging to Stilgar's sietch. We will talk of weapons another time."

He moved out through his band now, inspecting them, giving Paul's Fremkit pack to one of his men to carry.

Bakka, Jessica thought, recognizing the religious term: *bakka—the weeper*. She sensed how the symbolism of the kerchiefs united this band. *Why should weeping unite them?* she asked herself.

Stilgar came to the young girl who had embarrassed Paul, said: "Chani, take the child-man under your wing. Keep him out of trouble."

Chani touched Paul's arm. "Come along, child-man."

Paul hid the anger in his voice, said: "My name is Paul. It were well you—"

"We'll give you a name, manling," Stilgar said, "in the time of the mihna, at the test of aql."

The test of reason, Jessica translated. The sudden need of Paul's ascendancy overrode all other consideration, and she barked, "My son's been tested with the gom jabbar!"

In the stillness that followed, she knew she had struck to the heart of them.

"There's much we don't know of each other," Stilgar said. "But we tarry overlong. Day-sun mustn't find us in the open." He crossed to the man Paul had struck down, said, "Jamis, can you travel?"

A grunt answered him. "Surprised me, he did. 'Twas an accident. I can travel."

"No accident," Stilgar said. "I'll hold you responsible with Chani for the lad's safety, Jamis. These people have my countenance."

Jessica stared at the man, Jamis. His was the voice that had argued with Stilgar from the rocks. His was the voice with death in it. And Stilgar had seen fit to reinforce his order with this Jamis.

Stilgar flicked a testing glance across the group, motioned two men out. "Larus and Farrukh, you are to hide our tracks. See that we leave no trace. Extra care—we have two with us who've not been trained." He turned, hand upheld and aimed across the basin. "In squad line with flankers—move out. We must be at Cave of the Ridges before dawn."

Jessica fell into step beside Stilgar, counting heads. There were forty

Fremen—she and Paul made it forty-two. And she thought: *They travel as a military company—even the girl, Chani.*

Paul took a place in the line behind Chani. He had put down the black feeling at being caught by the girl. In his mind now was the memory called up by his mother's barked reminder: "My son's been tested with the gom jabbar!" He found that his hand tingled with remembered pain.

"Watch where you go," Chani hissed. "Do not brush against a bush lest you leave a thread to show our passage."

Paul swallowed, nodded.

Jessica listened to the sounds of the troop, hearing her own footsteps and Paul's, marveling at the way the Fremen moved. They were forty people crossing the basin with only the sounds natural to the place—ghostly feluccas, their robes flitting through the shadows. Their destination was Sietch Tabr—Stilgar's sietch.

She turned the word over in her mind: sietch. It was a Chakobsa word, unchanged from the old hunting language out of countless centuries. Sietch: a meeting place in time of danger. The profound implications of the word and the language were just beginning to register with her after the tension of their encounter.

"We move well," Stilgar said. "With Shai-hulud's favor, we'll reach Cave of the Ridges before dawn."

Jessica nodded, conserving her strength, sensing the terrible fatigue she held at bay by force of will . . . and, she admitted it: by the force of elation. Her mind focused on the value of this troop, seeing what was revealed here about the Fremen culture.

All of them, she thought, *an entire culture trained to military order. What a priceless thing is here for an outcast Duke!*

The Fremen were supreme in that quality the ancients called "spannungsbogen"—which is the self-imposed delay between desire for a thing and the act of reaching out to grasp that thing.

—FROM "THE WISDOM OF MUAD'DIB"
BY THE PRINCESS IRULAN

They approached Cave of the Ridges at dawnbreak, moving through a split in the basin wall so narrow they had to turn sideways to negotiate it. Jessica saw Stilgar detach guards in the thin dawnlight, saw them for a moment as they began their scrambling climb up the cliff.

Paul turned his head upward as he walked, seeing the tapestry of this planet cut in cross section where the narrow cleft gaped toward gray-blue sky.

Chani pulled at his robe to hurry him, said: "Quickly. It is already light."

"The men who climbed above us, where are they going?" Paul whispered.

"The first daywatch," she said. "Hurry now!"

A guard left outside, Paul thought. *Wise. But it would've been wiser still for us to approach this place in separate bands. Less chance of losing the whole troop.* He paused in the thought, realizing that this was guerrilla thinking, and he remembered his father's fear that the Atreides might become a guerrilla house.

"Faster," Chani whispered.

Paul sped his steps, hearing the swish of robes behind. And he thought of the words of the sirat from Yueh's tiny O.C. Bible.

"Paradise on my right, Hell on my left, and the Angel of Death behind." He rolled the quotation in his mind.

They rounded a corner where the passage widened. Stilgar stood at one side motioning them into a low hole that opened at right angles.

"Quickly!" he hissed. "We're like rabbits in a cage if a patrol catches us here."

Paul bent for the opening, followed Chani into a cave illuminated by thin gray light from somewhere ahead.

"You can stand up," she said.

He straightened, studied the place: a deep and wide area with domed ceiling that curved away just out of a man's handreach. The troop spread out through shadows. Paul saw his mother come up on one side, saw her examine their companions. And he noted how she failed to blend with the Fremen even though her garb was identical. The way she moved—such a sense of power and grace.

"Find a place to rest and stay out of the way, child-man," Chani said. "Here's food." She pressed two leaf-wrapped morsels into his hand. They reeked of spice.

Stilgar came up behind Jessica, called an order to a group on the left. "Get the doorseal in place and see to moisture security." He turned to another Fremen: "Lemil, get glowglobes." He took Jessica's arm. "I wish to show you something, weirding woman." He led her around a curve of rock toward the light source.

Jessica found herself looking out across the wide lip of another opening to the cave, an opening high in a cliff wall—looking out across another basin about ten or twelve kilometers wide. The basin was shielded by high rock walls. Sparse clumps of plant growth were scattered around it.

As she looked at the dawn-gray basin, the sun lifted over the far escarpment illuminating a biscuit-colored landscape of rocks and sand. And she noted how the sun of Arrakis appeared to leap over the horizon.

It's because we want to hold it back, she thought. *Night is safer than day.* There came over her then a longing for a rainbow in this place that would never see rain. *I must suppress such longings,* she thought. *They're a weakness. I no longer can afford weaknesses.*

Stilgar gripped her arm, pointed across the basin. "There! There you see proper Druses."

She looked where he pointed, saw movement: people on the basin floor scattering at the daylight into the shadows of the opposite cliff-wall. In spite of the distance, their movements were plain in the clear air. She lifted her binoculars from beneath her robe, focused the oil lenses on the distant people. Kerchiefs fluttered like a flight of multicolored butterflies.

"That is home," Stilgar said. "We will be there this night." He stared across the basin, tugging at his mustache. "My people stayed out over-late working. That means there are no patrols about. I'll signal them later and they'll prepare for us."

"Your people show good discipline," Jessica said. She lowered the binoculars, saw that Stilgar was looking at them.

"They obey the preservation of the tribe," he said. "It is the way we choose among us for a leader. The leader is the one who is strongest, the one who brings water and security." He lifted his attention to her face.

She returned his stare, noted the whiteless eyes, the stained eyepits, the dust-rimmed beard and mustache, the line of the catchtube curving down from his nostrils into his stillsuit.

"Have I compromised your leadership by besting you, Stilgar?" she asked.

"You did not call me out," he said.

"It's important that a leader keep the respect of his troop," she said.

"Isn't a one of those sandlice I cannot handle," Stilgar said. "When you bested me, you bested us all. Now, they hope to learn from you . . . the weirding way . . . and some are curious to see if you intend to call me out."

She weighed the implications. "By besting you in formal battle?"

He nodded. "I'd advise you against this because they'd not follow you. You're not of the sand. They saw this in our night's passage."

"Practical people," she said.

"True enough." He glanced at the basin. "We know our needs. But not many are thinking deep thoughts now this close to home. We've been out overlong arranging to deliver our spice quota to the free traders for the cursed Guild . . . may their faces be forever black."

Jessica stopped in the act of turning away from him, looked back up into his face. "The Guild? What has the Guild to do with your spice?"

"It's Liet's command," Stilgar said. "We know the reason, but the taste of it sours us. We bribe the Guild with a monstrous payment in spice to keep our skies clear of satellites and such that none may spy what we do to the face of Arrakis."

She weighed out her words, remembering that Paul had said this must be the reason Arrakeen skies were clear of satellites. "And what is it you do to the face of Arrakis that must not be seen?"

"We change it . . . slowly but with certainty . . . to make it fit for human life. Our generation will not see it, nor our children nor our children's children nor the grandchildren of their children . . . but it will come." He stared with veiled eyes out over the basin. "Open water and tall green plants and people walking freely without stillsuits."

So that's the dream of this Liet-Kynes, she thought. And she said: "Bribes are dangerous; they have a way of growing larger and larger."

"They grow," he said, "but the slow way is the safe way."

Jessica turned, looked out over the basin, trying to see it the way Stilgar was seeing it in his imagination. She saw only the grayed mustard stain of distant rocks and a sudden hazy motion in the sky above the cliffs.

"Ah-h-h-h," Stilgar said.

She thought at first it must be a patrol vehicle, then realized it was a mirage—another landscape hovering over the desert-sand and a distant wavering of greenery and in the middle distance a long worm traveling the surface with what looked like Fremen robes fluttering on its back.

The mirage faded.

"It would be better to ride," Stilgar said, "but we cannot permit a maker into this basin. Thus, we must walk again tonight."

Maker—their word for worm, she thought.

She measured the import of his words, the statement that they could not *permit* a worm into this basin. She knew what she had seen in the mirage—Fremen riding on the back of a giant worm. It took heavy control not to betray her shock at the implications.

"We must be getting back to the others," Stilgar said. "Else my people may suspect I dally with you. Some already are jealous that my hands tasted your loveliness when we struggled last night in Tuono Basin."

"That will be enough of that!" Jessica snapped.

"No offense," Stilgar said, and his voice was mild. "Women among us are not taken against their will . . . and with you. . . ." He shrugged. ". . . even that convention isn't required."

"You will keep in mind that I was a duke's lady," she said, but her voice was calmer.

"As you wish," he said. "It's time to seal off this opening, to permit relaxation of stillsuit discipline. My people need to rest in comfort this day. Their families will give them little rest on the morrow."

Silence fell between them.

Jessica stared out into the sunlight. She had heard what she had heard in Stilgar's voice—the unspoken offer of more than his *countenance.* Did he need a wife? She realized she could step into that place with him. It would be one way to end conflict over tribal leadership— female properly aligned with male.

But what of Paul then? Who could tell yet what rules of parenthood prevailed here? And what of the unborn daughter she had carried these few weeks? What of a dead Duke's daughter? And she permitted herself to face fully the significance of this other child growing within her, to see her own motives in permitting the conception. She knew what it was—she had succumbed to that profound drive shared by all creatures who are faced with death—the drive to seek immortality through progeny. The fertility drive of the species had overpowered them.

Jessica glanced at Stilgar, saw that he was studying her, waiting. *A daughter born here to a woman wed to such a one as this man—what would be the fate of such a daughter?* she asked herself. *Would he try to limit the necessities that a Bene Gesserit must follow?*

Stilgar cleared his throat and revealed then that he understood some of the questions in her mind. "What is important for a leader is that which makes him a leader. It is the needs of his people. If you teach me your powers, there may come a day when one of us must challenge the other. I would prefer some alternative."

"There are several alternatives?" she asked.

"The Sayyadina," he said. "Our Reverend Mother is old."

Their Reverend Mother!

Before she could probe this, he said: "I do not necessarily offer myself as mate. This is nothing personal, for you are beautiful and desirable. But should you become one of my women, that might lead some of my young men to believe that I'm too much concerned with pleasures of the flesh and not enough concerned with the tribe's needs. Even now they listen to us and watch us."

A man who weighs his decisions, who thinks of consequences, she thought.

"There are those among my young men who have reached the age of wild spirits," he said. "They must be eased through this period. I must leave no great reasons around for them to challenge me. Because I would have to maim and kill among them. This is not the proper course for a leader if it can be avoided with honor. A leader, you see, is one of the things that distinguishes a mob from a people. He maintains the level of individuals. Too few individuals, and a people reverts to a mob."

His words, the depth of their awareness, the fact that he spoke as much to her as to those who secretly listened, forced her to reevaluate him.

He has stature, she thought. *Where did he learn such inner balance?*

"The law that demands our form of choosing a leader is a just law," Stilgar said. "But it does not follow that justice is always the thing a people needs. What we truly need now is time to grow and prosper, to spread our force over more land."

What is his ancestry? she wondered. *Whence comes such breeding?* She said: "Stilgar, I underestimated you."

"Such was my suspicion," he said.

"Each of us apparently underestimated the other," she said.

"I should like an end to this," he said. "I should like friendship with you . . . and trust. I should like that respect for each other which grows in the breast without demand for the huddlings of sex."

"I understand," she said.

"Do you trust me?"

"I hear your sincerity."

"Among us," he said, "the Sayyadina, when they are not the formal leaders, hold a special place of honor. They teach. They maintain the strength of God here." He touched his breast.

Now I must probe this Reverend Mother mystery, she thought. And she said: "You spoke of your Reverend Mother . . . and I've heard words of legend and prophecy."

"It is said that a Bene Gesserit and her offspring hold the key to our future," he said.

"Do you believe I am that one?"

She watched his face, thinking: *The young reed dies so easily. Beginnings are times of such great peril.*

"We do not know," he said.

She nodded, thinking: *He's an honorable man. He wants a sign from me, but he'll not tip fate by telling me the sign.*

Jessica turned her head, stared down into the basin at the golden shadows, the purple shadows, the vibrations of dust-mote air across the lip of their cave. Her mind was filled suddenly with feline prudence. She knew the cant of the Missionaria Protectiva, knew how to adapt the techniques of legend and fear and hope to her emergency needs, but she sensed wild changes here . . . as though someone had been in among these Fremen and capitalized on the Missionaria Protectiva's imprint.

Stilgar cleared his throat.

She sensed his impatience, knew that the day moved ahead and men waited to seal off this opening. This was a time for boldness on her part, and she realized what she needed: some dar al-hikman, some school of translation that would give her. . . .

"Adab," she whispered.

Her mind felt as though it had rolled over within her. She recognized the sensation with a quickening of pulse. Nothing in all the Bene Gesserit training carried such a signal of recognition. It could be only the adab, the demanding memory that comes upon you of itself. She gave herself up to it, allowing the words to flow from her.

"Ibn qirtaiba," she said, "as far as the spot where the dust ends." She stretched out an arm from her robe, seeing Stilgar's eyes go wide. She heard a rustling of many robes in the background. "I see a . . . Fremen with the book of examples," she intoned. "He reads to al-Lat, the sun whom he defied and subjugated. He reads to the Sadus of the Trial and this is what he reads:

> *"Mine enemies are like green blades eaten down*
> *That did stand in the path of the tempest.*
> *Hast thou not seen what our Lord did?*
> *He sent the pestilence among them*
> *That did lay schemes against us.*
> *They are like birds scattered by the huntsman.*
> *Their schemes are like pellets of poison*
> *That every mouth rejects."*

A trembling passed through her. She dropped her arm.

Back to her from the inner cave's shadows came a whispered response of many voices: "Their works have been overturned."

"The fire of God mount over thy heart," she said. And she thought: *Now, it goes in the proper channel.*

"The fire of God set alight," came the response.

She nodded. "Thine enemies shall fall," she said.

"Bi-la kaifa," they answered.

In the sudden hush, Stilgar bowed to her. "Sayyadina," he said. "If the Shai-hulud grant, then you may yet pass within to become a Reverend Mother."

Pass within, she thought. *An odd way of putting it. But the rest of it fitted into the cant well enough.* And she felt a cynical bitterness at what she had done. *Our Missionaria Protectiva seldom fails. A place was prepared for us in this wilderness. The prayer of the salat has carved out our hiding place. Now ... I must play the part of Auliya, the Friend of God ... Sayyadina to rogue peoples who've been so heavily imprinted with our Bene Gesserit soothsay they even call their chief priestesses Reverend Mothers.*

Paul stood beside Chani in the shadows of the inner cave. He could still taste the morsel she had fed him—bird flesh and grain bound with spice honey and encased in a leaf. In tasting it he had realized he never before had eaten such a concentration of spice essence and there had been a moment of fear. He knew what this essence could do to him—the *spice change* that pushed his mind into prescient awareness.

"Bi-la kaifa," Chani whispered.

He looked at her, seeing the awe with which the Fremen appeared to accept his mother's words. Only the man called Jamis seemed to stand aloof from the ceremony, holding himself apart with arms folded across his breast.

"Duy yakha hin mange," Chani whispered. "Duy punra hin mange. I have two eyes. I have two feet."

And she stared at Paul with a look of wonder.

Paul took a deep breath, trying to still the tempest within him. His mother's words had locked onto the working of the spice essence, and he had felt her voice rise and fall within him like the shadows of an open fire. Through it all, he had sensed the edge of cynicism in her—he knew her so well!—but nothing could stop this thing that had begun with a morsel of food.

Terrible purpose!

He sensed it, the race consciousness that he could not escape. There was the sharpened clarity, the inflow of data, the cold precision of his

awareness. He sank to the floor, sitting with his back against rock, giving himself up to it. Awareness flowed into that timeless stratum where
he could view time, sensing the available paths, the winds of the future . . . the winds of the past: the one-eyed vision of the past, the one-
eyed vision of the present and the one-eyed vision of the future—all
combined in a trinocular vision that permitted him to see time-
become-space.

There was danger, he felt, of overrunning himself, and he had to
hold onto his awareness of the present, sensing the blurred deflection of
experience, the flowing moment, the continual solidification of that-
which-is into the perpetual-was.

In grasping the present, he felt for the first time the massive steadiness of time's movement everywhere complicated by shifting currents,
waves, surges, and countersurges, like surf against rocky cliffs. It gave
him a new understanding of his prescience, and he saw the source of
blind time, the source of error in it, with an immediate sensation of
fear.

The prescience, he realized, was an illumination that incorporated
the limits of what it revealed—at once a source of accuracy and meaningful error. A kind of Heisenberg indeterminacy intervened: the expenditure of energy that revealed what he saw, changed what he saw.

And what he saw was a time nexus within this cave, a boiling of
possibilities focused here, wherein the most minute action—the wink
of an eye, a careless word, a misplaced grain of sand—moved a gigantic
lever across the known universe. He saw violence with the outcome
subject to so many variables that his slightest movement created vast
shiftings in the pattern.

The vision made him want to freeze into immobility, but this, too,
was action with its consequences.

The countless consequences—lines fanned out from this cave, and
along most of these consequence-lines he saw his own dead body with
blood flowing from a gaping knife wound.

My father, the Padishah Emperor, was 72 yet looked no more than 35 the year he encompassed the death of Duke Leto and gave Arrakis back to the Harkonnens. He seldom appeared in public wearing other than a Sardaukar uniform and a Burseg's black helmet with the Imperial lion in gold upon its crest. The uniform was an open reminder of where his power lay. He was not always that blatant, though. When he wanted, he could radiate charm and sincerity, but I often wonder in these later days if anything about him was as it seemed. I think now he was a man fighting constantly to escape the bars of an invisible cage. You must remember that he was an emperor, father-head of a dynasty that reached back into the dimmest history. But we denied him a legal son. Was this not the most terrible defeat a ruler ever suffered? My mother obeyed her Sister Superiors where the Lady Jessica disobeyed. Which of them was the stronger? History already has answered.

—FROM "IN MY FATHER'S HOUSE"
BY THE PRINCESS IRULAN

Jessica awakened in cave darkness, sensing the stir of Fremen around her, smelling the acrid stillsuit odor. Her inner timesense told her it would soon be night outside, but the cave remained in blackness, shielded from the desert by the plastic hoods that trapped their body moisture within this space.

She realized that she had permitted herself the utterly relaxing sleep of great fatigue, and this suggested something of her own unconscious assessment on personal security within Stilgar's troop. She turned in the hammock that had been fashioned of her robe, slipped her feet to the rock floor and into her desert boots.

I must remember to fasten the boots slip-fashion to help my stillsuit's pumping action, she thought. *There are so many things to remember.*

She could still taste their morning meal—the morsel of bird flesh and grain bound within a leaf with spice honey—and it came to her that the use of time was turned around here: night was the day of activity and day was the time of rest.

Night conceals; night is safest.

She unhooked her robe from its hammock pegs in a rock alcove, fumbled with the fabric in the dark until she found the top, slipped into it.

How to get a message out to the Bene Gesserit? she wondered. *They* would have to be told of the two strays in Arrakeen sanctuary.

Glowglobes came alight farther into the cave. She saw people moving there, Paul among them already dressed and with his hood thrown back to reveal the aquiline Atreides profile.

He had acted so strangely before they retired, she thought. *Withdrawn.* He was like one come back from the dead, not yet fully aware of his return, his eyes half shut and glassy with the inward stare. It made her think of his warning about the spice-impregnated diet: *addictive.*

Are there side effects? she wondered. *He said it had something to do with his prescient faculty, but he has been strangely silent about what he sees.*

Stilgar came from shadows to her right, crossed to the group beneath the glowglobes. She marked how he fingered his beard and the watchful, cat-stalking look of him.

Abrupt fear shot through Jessica as her senses awakened to the tensions visible in the people gathered around Paul—the stiff movements, the ritual positions.

"They have my countenance!" Stilgar rumbled.

Jessica recognized the man Stilgar confronted—Jamis! She saw then the rage in Jamis—the tight set of his shoulders.

Jamis, the man Paul bested! she thought.

"You know the rule, Stilgar," Jamis said.

"Who knows it better?" Stilgar asked, and she heard the tone of placation in his voice, the attempt to smooth something over.

"I choose the combat," Jamis growled.

Jessica sped across the cave, grasped Stilgar's arm. "What is this?" she asked.

"It is the amtal rule," Stilgar said. "Jamis is demanding the right to test your part in the legend."

"She must be championed," Jamis said. "If her champion wins, that's the truth in it. But it's said. . . ." He glanced across the press of people. ". . . that she'd need no champion from the Fremen—which can mean only that she brings her own champion."

He's talking of single combat with Paul! Jessica thought.

She released Stilgar's arm, took a half-step forward. "I'm always my own champion," she said. "The meaning's simple enough for. . . ."

"You'll not tell us our ways!" Jamis snapped. "Not without more proof than I've seen. Stilgar could've told you what to say last morning. He could've filled your mind full of the coddle and you could've bird-talked it to us, hoping to make a false way among us."

I can take him, Jessica thought, *but that might conflict with the way they interpret the legend.* And again she wondered at the way the Missionaria Protectiva's work had been twisted on this planet.

Stilgar looked at Jessica, spoke in a low voice but one designed to carry to the crowd's fringe. "Jamis is one to hold a grudge, Sayyadina. Your son bested him and—"

"It was an accident!" Jamis roared. "There was witch-force at Tuono Basin and I'll prove it now!"

". . . and I've bested him myself," Stilgar continued. "He seeks by this tahaddi challenge to get back at me as well. There's too much of violence in Jamis for him ever to make a good leader—too much ghafla, the distraction. He gives his mouth to the rules and his heart to the sarfa, the turning away. No, he could never make a good leader. I've preserved him this long because he's useful in a fight as such, but when he gets this carving anger on him he's dangerous to his own society."

"Stilgar-r-r-r!" Jamis rumbled.

And Jessica saw what Stilgar was doing, trying to enrage Jamis, to take the challenge away from Paul.

Stilgar faced Jamis, and again Jessica heard the soothing in the rumbling voice. "Jamis, he's but a boy. He's—"

"You named him a man," Jamis said. "His mother *says* he's been through the gom jabbar. He's full-fleshed and with a surfeit of water. The ones who carried their pack say there's literjons of water in it. Literjons! And us sipping our catchpockets the instant they show dewsparkle."

Stilgar glanced at Jessica. "Is this true? Is there water in your pack?"

"Yes."

"Literjons of it?"

"Two literjons."

"What was intended with this wealth?"

Wealth? she thought. She shook her head, feeling the coldness in his voice.

"Where I was born, water fell from the sky and ran over the land in wide rivers," she said. "There were oceans of it so broad you could not see the other shore. I've not been trained to your water discipline. I never before had to think of it this way."

A sighing gasp arose from the people around them: "Water fell from the sky . . . it ran *over* the land."

"Did you know there're those among us who've lost from their catchpockets by accident and will be in sore trouble before we reach Tabr this night?"

"How could I know?" Jessica shook her head. "If they're in need, give them water from our pack."

"Is that what you intended with this wealth?"

"I intended it to save life," she said.

"Then we accept your blessing, Sayyadina."

"You'll not buy us off with water," Jamis growled. "Nor will you anger me against yourself, Stilgar. I see you trying to make me call you out before I've proved my words."

Stilgar faced Jamis. "Are you determined to press this fight against a child, Jamis?" His voice was low, venomous.

"She must be championed."

"Even though she has my countenance?"

"I invoke the amtal rule," Jamis said. "It's my right."

Stilgar nodded. "Then, if the boy does not carve you down, you'll answer to my knife afterward. And this time I'll not hold back the blade as I've done before."

"You cannot do this thing," Jessica said. "Paul's just—"

"You must not interfere, Sayyadina," Stilgar said. "Oh, I know you can take me and, therefore, can take anyone among us, but you cannot best us all united. This must be; it is the amtal rule."

Jessica fell silent, staring at him in the green light of the glowglobes, seeing the demoniacal stiffness that had taken over his expression. She shifted her attention to Jamis, saw the brooding look to his brows and thought: *I should've seen that before. He broods. He's the silent kind, one who works himself up inside. I should've been prepared.*

"If you harm my son," she said, "you'll have me to meet. I call you out now. I'll carve you into a joint of—"

"Mother." Paul stepped forward, touched her sleeve. "Perhaps if I explain to Jamis how—"

"Explain!" Jamis sneered.

Paul fell silent, staring at the man. He felt no fear of him. Jamis appeared clumsy in his movements and he had fallen so easily in their night encounter on the sand. But Paul still felt the nexus-boiling of this cave, still remembered the prescient visions of himself dead under a knife. There had been so few avenues of escape for him in that vision. . . .

Stilgar said: "Sayyadina, you must step back now where—"

"Stop calling her Sayyadina!" Jamis said. "That's yet to be proved. So she knows the prayer! What's that? Every child among us knows it."

He has talked enough, Jessica thought. *I've the key to him. I could immobilize him with a word.* She hesitated. *But I cannot stop them all.*

"You will answer to me then," Jessica said, and she pitched her voice in a twisting tone with a little whine in it and a catch at the end.

Jamis stared at her, fright visible on his face.

"I'll teach you agony," she said in the same tone. "Remember *that* as you fight. You'll have agony such as will make the gom jabbar a happy memory by comparison. You will writhe with your entire—"

"She tries a spell on me!" Jamis gasped. He put his clenched right fist beside his ear. "I invoke the silence on her!"

"So be it then," Stilgar said. He cast a warning glance at Jessica. "If you speak again, Sayyadina, we'll know it's your witchcraft and you'll be forfeit." He nodded for her to step back.

Jessica felt hands pulling her, helping her back, and she sensed they were not unkindly. She saw Paul being separated from the throng, the elfin-faced Chani whispering in his ear as she nodded toward Jamis.

A ring formed within the troop. More glowglobes were brought and all of them tuned to the yellow band.

Jamis stepped into the ring, slipped out of his robe and tossed it to someone in the crowd. He stood there in a cloudy gray slickness of stillsuit that was patched and marked by tucks and gathers. For a moment, he bent with his mouth to his shoulder, drinking from a catch-pocket tube. Presently he straightened, peeled off and detached the suit, handed it carefully into the crowd. He stood waiting, clad in loincloth and some tight fabric over his feet, a crysknife in his right hand.

Jessica saw the girl-child Chani helping Paul, saw her press a crysknife handle into his palm, saw him heft it, testing the weight and balance. And it came to Jessica that Paul had been trained in prana and bindu, the nerve and the fiber—that he had been taught fighting in a deadly school, his teachers men like Duncan Idaho and Gurney Halleck, men who were legends in their own lifetimes. The boy knew the devious ways of the Bene Gesserit and he looked supple and confident.

But he's only fifteen, she thought. *And he has no shield. I must stop this. Somehow, there must be a way to. . . .* She looked up, saw Stilgar watching her.

"You cannot stop it," he said. "You must not speak."

She put a hand over her mouth, thinking: *I've planted fear in Jamis' mind. It'll slow him some . . . perhaps. If I could only pray—truly pray.*

Paul stood alone now just into the ring, clad in the fighting trunks he'd worn under his stillsuit. He held a crysknife in his right hand; his feet were bare against the sand-gritted rock. Idaho had warned him time and again: *"When in doubt of your surface, bare feet are best."* And there were Chani's words of instruction still in the front of his consciousness: *"Jamis turns to the right with his knife after a parry. It's a habit in him we've all seen. And he'll aim for the eyes to catch a blink in which to slash you. And he can fight either hand; look out for a knife shift."*

But strongest in Paul so that he felt it with his entire body was training and the instinctual reaction mechanism that had been hammered into him day after day, hour after hour on the practice floor.

Gurney Halleck's words were there to remember: *"The good knife fighter thinks on point and blade and shearing-guard simultaneously. The point can also cut; the blade can also stab; the shearing-guard can also trap your opponent's blade."*

Paul glanced at the crysknife. There was no shearing-guard; only the slim round ring of the handle with its raised lips to protect the hand. And even so, he realized that he did not know the breaking tension of this blade, did not even know if it *could* be broken.

Jamis began sidling to the right along the edge of the ring opposite Paul.

Paul crouched, realizing then that he had no shield, but was trained to fighting with its subtle field around him, trained to react on defense with utmost speed while his attack would be timed to the controlled slowness necessary for penetrating the enemy's shield. In spite of constant warning from his trainers not to depend on the shield's mindless blunting of attack speed, he knew that shield-awareness was part of him.

Jamis called out in ritual challenge: "May thy knife chip and shatter!"

This knife will break then, Paul thought.

He cautioned himself that Jamis also was without shield, but the man wasn't trained to its use, had no shield-fighter inhibitions.

Paul stared across the ring at Jamis. The man's body looked like knotted whipcord on a dried skeleton. His cryknife shone milky yellow in the light of the glowglobes.

Fear coursed through Paul. He felt suddenly alone and naked standing in dull yellow light within this ring of people. Prescience had fed his knowledge with countless experiences, hinted at the strongest currents of the future and the strings of decision that guided them, but this was the *real-now*. This was death hanging on an infinite number of minuscule mischances.

Anything could tip the future here, he realized. Someone coughing in the troop of watchers, a distraction. A variation in a glowglobe's brilliance, a deceptive shadow.

I'm afraid, Paul told himself.

And he circled warily opposite Jamis, repeating silently to himself the Bene Gesserit litany against fear. *"Fear is the mind-killer. . . ."* It was a cool bath washing over him. He felt muscles untie themselves, become poised and ready.

"I'll sheath my knife in your blood," Jamis snarled. And in the middle of the last word he pounced.

Jessica saw the motion, stifled an outcry.

Where the man struck there was only empty air and Paul stood now behind Jamis with a clear shot at the exposed back.

Now, Paul! Now! Jessica screamed it in her mind.

Paul's motion was slowly timed, beautifully fluid, but so slow it gave Jamis the margin to twist away, backing and turning to the right.

Paul withdrew, crouching low. "First, you must find my blood," he said.

Jessica recognized the shield-fighter timing in her son, and it came over her what a two-edged thing that was. The boy's reactions were those of youth and trained to a peak these people had never seen. But the attack was trained, too, and conditioned by the necessities of penetrating a shield barrier. A shield would repel too fast a blow, admit only the slowly deceptive counter. It needed control and trickery to get through a shield.

Does Paul see it? she asked herself. *He must!*

Again Jamis attacked, ink-dark eyes glaring, his body a yellow blur under the glowglobes.

And again Paul slipped away to return too slowly on the attack.

And again.

And again.

Each time, Paul's counterblow came an instant late.

And Jessica saw a thing she hoped Jamis did not see. Paul's defensive reactions were blindingly fast, but they moved each time at the precisely correct angle they would take if a shield were helping deflect part of Jamis' blow.

"Is your son playing with that poor fool?" Stilgar asked. He waved her to silence before she could respond. "Sorry; you must remain silent."

Now the two figures on the rock floor circled each other: Jamis with knife hand held far forward and tipped up slightly; Paul crouched with knife held low.

Again, Jamis pounced, and this time he twisted to the right where Paul had been dodging.

Instead of faking back and out, Paul met the man's knife hand on the point of his own blade. Then the boy was gone, twisting away to the left and thankful for Chani's warning.

Jamis backed into the center of the circle, rubbing his knife hand. Blood dripped from the injury for a moment, stopped. His eyes were wide and staring—two blue-black holes—studying Paul with a new wariness in the dull light of the glowglobes.

"Ah, that one hurt," Stilgar murmured.

Paul crouched at the ready and, as he had been trained to do after first blood, called out: "Do you yield?"

"Hah!" Jamis cried.

An angry murmur arose from the troop.

"Hold!" Stilgar called out. "The lad doesn't know our rule." Then, to Paul: "There can be no yielding in the tahaddi-challenge. Death is the test of it."

Jessica saw Paul swallow hard. And she thought: *He's never killed a man like this . . . in the hot blood of a knife fight. Can he do it?*

Paul circled slowly right, forced by Jamis' movement. The prescient knowledge of the time-boiling variables in this cave came back to plague him now. His new understanding told him there were too many swiftly compressed decisions in this fight for any clear channel ahead to show itself.

Variable piled on variable—that was why this cave lay as a blurred nexus in his path. It was like a gigantic rock in the flood, creating maelstroms in the current around it.

"Have an end to it, lad," Stilgar muttered. "Don't play with him."

Paul crept farther into the ring, relying on his own edge in speed.

Jamis backed now that the realization swept over him—that this was no soft offworlder in the tahaddi ring, easy prey for a Fremen crysknife.

Jessica saw the shadow of desperation in the man's face. *Now is when he's most dangerous,* she thought. *Now he's desperate and can do anything. He sees that this is not like a child of his own people, but a fighting machine born and trained to it from infancy. Now the fear I planted in him has come to bloom.*

And she found in herself a sense of pity for Jamis—an emotion tempered by awareness of the immediate peril to her son.

Jamis could do anything . . . any unpredictable thing, she told herself. She wondered then if Paul had glimpsed this future, if he were reliving this experience. But she saw the way her son moved, the beads of perspiration on his face and shoulders, the careful wariness visible in the flow of muscles. And for the first time she sensed, without understanding it, the uncertainty factor in Paul's gift.

Paul pressed the fight now, circling but not attacking. He had seen the fear in his opponent. Memory of Duncan Idaho's voice flowed through Paul's awareness: *"When your opponent fears you, then's the moment when you give the fear its own rein, give it the time to work on him. Let it become terror. The terrified man fights himself. Eventually, he attacks in desperation. That is the most dangerous moment, but the ter-*

rified man can be trusted usually to make a fatal mistake. You are being trained here to detect these mistakes and use them."

The crowd in the cavern began to mutter.

They think Paul's toying with Jamis, Jessica thought. *They think Paul's being needlessly cruel.*

But she sensed also the undercurrent of crowd excitement, their enjoyment of the spectacle. And she could see the pressure building up in Jamis. The moment when it became too much for him to contain was as apparent to her as it was to Jamis . . . or to Paul.

Jamis leaped high, feinting and striking down with his right hand, but the hand was empty. The crysknife had been shifted to his left hand.

Jessica gasped.

But Paul had been warned by Chani: *"Jamis fights with either hand."* And the depth of his training had taken in that trick *en passant*. *"Keep the mind on the knife and not on the hand that holds it,"* Gurney Halleck had told him time and again. *"The knife is more dangerous than the hand and the knife can be in either hand."*

And Paul had seen Jamis' mistake: bad footwork so that it took the man a heartbeat longer to recover from his leap, which had been intended to confuse Paul and hide the knife shift.

Except for the low yellow light of the glowglobes and the inky eyes of the staring troop, it was similar to a session on the practice floor. Shields didn't count where the body's own movement could be used against it. Paul shifted his own knife in a blurred motion, slipped sideways and thrust upward where Jamis' chest was descending—then away to watch the man crumble.

Jamis fell like a limp rag, face down, gasped once and turned his face toward Paul, then lay still on the rock floor. His dead eyes stared out like beads of dark glass.

"Killing with the point lacks artistry," Idaho had once told Paul, *"but don't let that hold your hand when the opening presents itself."*

The troop rushed forward, filling the ring, pushing Paul aside. They hid Jamis in a frenzy of huddling activity. Presently a group of them hurried back into the depths of the cavern carrying a burden wrapped in a robe.

And there was no body on the rock floor.

Jessica pressed through toward her son. She felt that she swam in a sea of robed and stinking backs, a throng strangely silent.

Now is the terrible moment, she thought. *He has killed a man in clear superiority of mind and muscle. He must not grow to enjoy such a victory.*

She forced herself through the last of the troop and into a small open space where two bearded Fremen were helping Paul into his stillsuit.

Jessica stared at her son. Paul's eyes were bright. He breathed heavily, permitting the ministrations to his body rather than helping them.

"Him against Jamis and not a mark on him," one of the men muttered.

Chani stood at one side, her eyes focused on Paul. Jessica saw the girl's excitement, the admiration in the elfin face.

It must be done now and swiftly, Jessica thought.

She compressed ultimate scorn into her voice and manner, said: "Well-l-l, now—how does it feel to be a killer?"

Paul stiffened as though he had been struck. He met his mother's cold glare and his face darkened with a rush of blood. Involuntarily he glanced toward the place on the cavern floor where Jamis had lain.

Stilgar pressed through to Jessica's side, returning from the cave depths where the body of Jamis had been taken. He spoke to Paul in a bitter, controlled tone: "When the time comes for you to call me out and try for my burda, do not think you will play with me the way you played with Jamis."

Jessica sensed the way her own words and Stilgar's sank into Paul, doing their harsh work on the boy. The mistake these people made—it served a purpose now. She searched the faces around them as Paul was doing, seeing what he saw. Admiration, yes, and fear . . . and in some— loathing. She looked at Stilgar, saw his fatalism, knew how the fight had seemed to him.

Paul looked at his mother. "You know what it was," he said.

She heard the return to sanity, the remorse in his voice. Jessica swept her glance across the troop, said: "Paul has never before killed a man with a naked blade."

Stilgar faced her, disbelief in his face.

"I wasn't playing with him," Paul said. He pressed in front of his mother, straightening his robe, glanced at the dark place of Jamis' blood on the cavern floor. "I did not want to kill him."

Jessica saw belief come slowly to Stilgar, saw the relief in him as he tugged at his beard with a deeply veined hand. She heard muttering awareness spread through the troop.

"That's why y' asked him to yield," Stilgar said. "I see. Our ways are different, but you'll see the sense in them. I thought we'd admitted a scorpion into our midst." He hesitated, then: "And I shall not call you lad the more."

A voice from the troop called out: "Needs a naming, Stil."

Stilgar nodded, tugging at his beard. "I see strength in you . . . like the strength beneath a pillar." Again he paused, then: "You shall be known among us as Usul, the base of the pillar. This is your secret name, your troop name. We of Sietch Tabr may use it, but none other may so presume . . . Usul."

Murmuring went through the troop: "Good choice, that . . . strong . . . bring us luck." And Jessica sensed the acceptance, knowing she was included in it with her champion. She was indeed Sayyadina.

"Now, what name of manhood do *you* choose for us to call you openly?" Stilgar asked.

Paul glanced at his mother, back to Stilgar. Bits and pieces of this moment registered on his prescient *memory*, but he felt the differences as though they were physical, a pressure forcing him through the narrow door of the present.

"How do you call among you the little mouse, the mouse that jumps?" Paul asked, remembering the *pop-hop* of motion at Tuono Basin. He illustrated with one hand.

A chuckle sounded through the troop.

"We call that one muad'dib," Stilgar said.

Jessica gasped. It was the name Paul had told her, saying that the Fremen would accept them and call him thus. She felt a sudden fear *of* her son and *for* him.

Paul swallowed. He felt that he played a part already played over countless times in his mind ... yet ... there were differences. He could see himself perched on a dizzying summit, having experienced much and possessed of a profound store of knowledge, but all around him was abyss.

And again he remembered the vision of fanatic legions following the green and black banner of the Atreides, pillaging and burning across the universe in the name of their prophet Muad'Dib. *That must not happen,* he told himself.

"Is that the name you wish, Muad'Dib?" Stilgar asked.

"I am an Atreides," Paul whispered, and then louder: "It's not right that I give up entirely the name my father gave me. Could I be known among you as Paul-Muad'Dib?"

"You are Paul-Muad'Dib," Stilgar said.

And Paul thought: *That was in no vision of mine. I did a different thing.*

But he felt that the abyss remained all around him.

Again a murmuring response went through the troop as man turned to man: "Wisdom with strength ... Couldn't ask more ... It's the legend for sure ... Lisan al-Gaib ... Lisan al-Gaib...."

"I will tell you a thing about your new name," Stilgar said. "The choice pleases us. Muad'Dib is wise in the ways of the desert. Muad'Dib creates his own water. Muad'Dib hides from the sun and travels in the cool night. Muad'Dib is fruitful and multiplies over the land. Muad'Dib we call 'instructor-of-boys.' That is a powerful base on which to build your life, Paul-Muad'Dib, who is Usul among us. We welcome you."

Stilgar touched Paul's forehead with one palm, withdrew his hand, embraced Paul and murmured, "Usul."

As Stilgar released him, another member of the troop embraced Paul, repeating his new troop name. And Paul was passed from embrace to embrace through the troop, hearing the voices, the shadings of tone: "Usul . . . Usul . . . Usul." Already, he could place some of them by name. And there was Chani who pressed her cheek against his as she held him and said his name.

Presently Paul stood again before Stilgar, who said: "Now, you are of the Ichwan Bedwine, our brother." His face hardened, and he spoke with command in his voice. "And now, Paul-Muad'Dib, tighten up that stillsuit." He glanced at Chani. "Chani! Paul-Muad'Dib's nose plugs are as poor a fit I've ever seen! I thought I ordered you to see after him!"

"I hadn't the makings, Stil," she said. "There's Jamis', of course, but—"

"Enough of that!"

"Then I'll share one of mine," she said. "I can make do with one until—"

"You will not," Stilgar said. "I know there are spares among us. Where are the spares? Are we a troop together or a band of savages?"

Hands reached out from the troop offering hard, fibrous objects. Stilgar selected four, handed them to Chani. "Fit these to Usul and the Sayyadina."

A voice lifted from the back of the troop: "What of the water, Stil? What of the literjons in their pack?"

"I know your need, Farok," Stilgar said. He glanced at Jessica. She nodded.

"Broach one for those that need it," Stilgar said. "Watermaster . . . where is a watermaster? Ah, Shimoom, care for the measuring of what is needed. The necessity and no more. This water is the dower property of the Sayyadina and will be repaid in the sietch at field rates less pack fees."

"What is the repayment at field rates?" Jessica asked.

"Ten for one," Stilgar said.

"But—"

"It's a wise rule as you'll come to see," Stilgar said.

A rustling of robes marked movement at the back of the troop as men turned to get the water.

Stilgar held up a hand, and there was silence. "As to Jamis," he said, "I order the full ceremony. Jamis was our companion and brother of the Ichwan Bedwine. There shall be no turning away without the respect due one who proved our fortune by his tahaddi-challenge. I invoke the rite . . . at sunset when the dark shall cover him."

Paul, hearing these words, realized that he had plunged once more into the abyss . . . blind time. There was no past occupying the future in his mind . . . except . . . except . . . he could still sense the green and black Atreides banner waving . . . somewhere ahead . . . still see the jihad's bloody swords and fanatic legions.

It will not be, he told himself. *I cannot let it be.*

God created Arrakis to train the faithful.

—FROM "THE WISDOM OF MUAD'DIB"
BY THE PRINCESS IRULAN

In the stillness of the cavern, Jessica heard the scrape of sand on rock as people moved, the distant bird calls that Stilgar had said were the signals of his watchmen.

The great plastic hood-seals had been removed from the cave's opening. She could see the march of evening shadows across the lip of rock in front of her and the open basin beyond. She sensed the daylight leaving them, sensed it in the dry heat as well as the shadows. She knew her trained awareness soon would give her what these Fremen obviously had—the ability to sense even the slightest change in the air's moisture.

How they had scurried to tighten their stillsuits when the cave was opened! Deep within the cave, someone began chanting:

"*Ima trava okolo!*
I korenja okolo!"

Jessica translated silently: *These are ashes! And these are roots!*
The funeral ceremony for Jamis was beginning.
She looked out at the Arrakeen sunset, at the banked decks of color in the sky. Night was beginning to utter its shadows along the distant rocks and the dunes.

Yet the heat persisted.

Heat forced her thoughts onto water and the observed fact that this whole people could be trained to be thirsty only at given times.

Thirst.

She could remember moonlit waves on Caladan throwing white robes over rocks . . . and the wind heavy with dampness. Now the breeze that fingered her robes seared the patches of exposed skin at cheeks and forehead. The new nose plugs irritated her, and she found herself overly conscious of the tube that trailed down across her face into the suit, recovering her breath's moisture.

The suit itself was a sweatbox.

"Your suit will be more comfortable when you've adjusted to a lower water content in your body," Stilgar had said.

She knew he was right, but the knowledge made this moment no more comfortable. The unconscious preoccupation with water here weighed on her mind. *No,* she corrected herself: *it was preoccupation with* moisture.

And that was a more subtle and profound matter.

She heard approaching footsteps, turned to see Paul come out of the cave's depths trailed by the elfin-faced Chani.

There's another thing, Jessica thought. *Paul must be cautioned about their women. One of these desert women would not do as wife to a Duke. As concubine, yes, but not as wife.*

Then she wondered at herself, thinking: *Have I been infected with his schemes?* And she saw how well she had been conditioned. *I can think of the marital needs of royalty without once weighing my own concubinage. Yet . . . I was more than concubine.*

"Mother."

Paul stopped in front of her. Chani stood at his elbow.

"Mother, do you know what they're doing back there?"

Jessica looked at the dark patch of his eyes staring out from the hood. "I think so."

"Chani showed me . . . because I'm supposed to see it and give my . . . permission for the weighing of the water."

Jessica looked at Chani.

"They're recovering Jamis' water," Chani said, and her thin voice came out nasal past the nose plugs. "It's the rule. The flesh belongs to the person, but his water belongs to the tribe . . . except in the combat."

"They say the water's mine," Paul said.

Jessica wondered why this should make her suddenly alert and cautious.

"Combat water belongs to the winner," Chani said. "It's because you have to fight in the open without stillsuits. The winner has to get his water back that he loses while fighting."

"I don't want his water," Paul muttered. He felt that he was a part of many images moving simultaneously in a fragmenting way that was disconcerting to the inner eye. He could not be certain what he would do, but of one thing he was positive: he did not want the water distilled out of Jamis' flesh.

"It's . . . water," Chani said.

Jessica marveled at the way she said it. *"Water."* So much meaning in a simple sound. A Bene Gesserit axiom came to Jessica's mind: *"Survival is the ability to swim in strange water."* And Jessica thought: *Paul and I, we must find the currents and patterns in these strange waters . . . if we're to survive.*

"You will accept the water," Jessica said.

She recognized the tone in her voice. She had used that same tone once with Leto, telling her lost Duke that he would accept a large sum offered for his support in a questionable venture—because money maintained power for the Atreides.

On Arrakis, water was money. She saw that clearly.

Paul remained silent, knowing then that he would do as she ordered—not because she ordered it, but because her tone of voice had forced him to reevaluate. To refuse the water would be to break with accepted Fremen practice.

Presently Paul recalled the words of 467 Kalima in Yueh's O.C. Bible. He said: "From water does all life begin."

Jessica stared at him. *Where did he learn that quotation?* she asked herself. *He hasn't studied the mysteries.*

"Thus it is spoken," Chani said. "Giudichar mantene: It is written in the Shah-Nama that water was the first of all things created."

For no reason she could explain (and *this* bothered her more than the sensation), Jessica suddenly shuddered. She turned away to hide her confusion and was just in time to see the sunset. A violent calamity of color spilled over the sky as the sun dipped beneath the horizon.

"It is time!"

The voice was Stilgar's ringing in the cavern. "Jamis' weapon has been killed. Jamis has been called by Him, by Shai-hulud, who has ordained the phases for the moons that daily wane and—in the end—appear as bent and withered twigs." Stilgar's voice lowered. "Thus it is with Jamis."

Silence fell like a blanket on the cavern.

Jessica saw the gray-shadow movement of Stilgar like a ghost figure within the dark inner reaches. She glanced back at the basin, sensing the coolness.

"The friends of Jamis will approach," Stilgar said.

Men moved behind Jessica, dropping a curtain across the opening. A single glowglobe was lighted overhead far back in the cave. Its yellow glow picked out an inflowing of human figures. Jessica heard the rustling of the robes.

Chani took a step away as though pulled by the light.

Jessica bent close to Paul's ear, speaking in the family code: "Follow their lead; do as they do. It will be a simple ceremony to placate the shade of Jamis."

It will be more than that, Paul thought. And he felt a wrenching sensation within his awareness as though he were trying to grasp some thing in motion and render it motionless.

Chani glided back to Jessica's side, took her hand. "Come, Sayyadina. We must sit apart."

Paul watched them move off into the shadows, leaving him alone. He felt abandoned.

The men who had fixed the curtain came up beside him.

"Come, Usul."

He allowed himself to be guided forward, to be pushed into a circle of people being formed around Stilgar, who stood beneath the glow-globe and beside a bundled, curving, and angular shape gathered beneath a robe on the rock floor.

The troop crouched down at a gesture from Stilgar, their robes hissing with the movement. Paul settled with them, watching Stilgar, noting the way the overhead globe made pits of his eyes and brightened the touch of green fabric at his neck. Paul shifted his attention to the robe-covered mound at Stilgar's feet, recognized the handle of a baliset protruding from the fabric.

"The spirit leaves the body's water when the first moon rises," Stilgar intoned. "Thus it is spoken. When we see the first moon rise this night, whom will it summon?"

"Jamis," the troop responded.

Stilgar turned full circle on one heel, passing his gaze across the ring of faces. "I was a friend of Jamis," he said. "When the hawk plane stooped upon us at Hole-in-the-Rock, it was Jamis pulled me to safety."

He bent over the pile beside him, lifted away the robe. "I take this robe as a friend of Jamis—leader's right." He draped the robe over a shoulder, straightening.

Now, Paul saw the contents of the mound exposed: the pale glistening gray of a stillsuit, a battered literjon, a kerchief with a small book in its center, the bladeless handle of a crysknife, an empty sheath, a folded pack, a paracompass, a distrans, a thumper, a pile of fist-sized metallic hooks, an assortment of what looked like small rocks within a fold of cloth, a clump of bundled feathers . . . and the baliset exposed beside the folded pack.

So Jamis played the baliset, Paul thought. The instrument reminded him of Gurney Halleck and all that was lost. Paul knew with his memory of the future in the past that some chance-lines could produce a meeting with Halleck, but the reunions were few and shadowed. They puzzled him. The uncertainty factor touched him with wonder. *Does it mean that something I will do . . . that I may do, could destroy Gurney . . . or bring him back to life . . . or. . . .*

Paul swallowed, shook his head.

Again, Stilgar bent over the mound.

"For Jamis' woman and for the guards," he said. The small rocks and the book were taken into the folds of his robe.

"Leader's right," the troop intoned.

"The marker for Jamis' coffee service," Stilgar said, and he lifted a flat disc of green metal. "That it shall be given to Usul in suitable ceremony when we return to the sietch."

"Leader's right," the troop intoned.

Lastly, he took the crysknife handle and stood with it. "For the funeral plain," he said.

"For the funeral plain," the troop responded.

At her place in the circle across from Paul, Jessica nodded, recognizing the ancient source of the rite, and she thought: *The meeting between ignorance and knowledge, between brutality and culture—it begins in the dignity with which we treat our dead.* She looked across at Paul, wondering: *Will he see it? Will he know what to do?*

"We are friends of Jamis," Stilgar said. "We are not wailing for our dead like a pack of garvarg."

A gray-bearded man to Paul's left stood up. "I was a friend of Jamis," he said. He crossed to the mound, lifted the distrans. "When our water went below minim at the siege at Two Brids, Jamis shared." The man returned to his place in the circle.

Am I supposed to say I was a friend of Jamis? Paul wondered. *Do they expect me to take something from that pile?* He saw faces turn toward him, turn away. *They do expect it!*

Another man across from Paul arose, went to the pack and removed the paracompass. "I was a friend of Jamis," he said. "When the patrol caught us at Bight-of-the-Cliff and I was wounded, Jamis drew them off so the wounded could be saved." He returned to his place in the circle.

Again, the faces turned toward Paul, and he saw the expectancy in them, lowered his eyes. An elbow nudged him and a voice hissed: "Would you bring the destruction on us?"

How can I say I was his friend? Paul wondered.

Another figure arose from the circle opposite Paul and, as the hooded face came into the light, he recognized his mother. She removed a kerchief from the mount. "I was a friend of Jamis," she said. "When the spirit of spirits within him saw the needs of truth, that spirit withdrew and spared my son." She returned to her place.

And Paul recalled the scorn in his mother's voice as she had confronted him after the fight. *"How does it feel to be a killer?"*

Again, he saw the faces turned toward him, felt the anger and fear in the troop. A passage his mother had once filmbooked for him on "The Cult of the Dead" flickered through Paul's mind. He knew what he had to do.

Slowly, Paul got to his feet.

A sigh passed around the circle.

Paul felt the diminishment of his *self* as he advanced into the center of the circle. It was as though he lost a fragment of himself and sought it here. He bent over the mound of belongings, lifted out the baliset. A string twanged softly as it struck against something in the pile.

"I was a friend of Jamis," Paul whispered.

He felt tears burning his eyes, forced more volume into his voice. "Jamis taught me . . . that . . . when you kill . . . you pay for it. I wish I'd known Jamis better."

Blindly, he groped his way back to his place in the circle, sank to the rock floor.

A voice hissed: "He sheds tears!"

It was taken up around the ring: "Usul gives moisture to the dead!"

He felt fingers touch his damp cheek, heard the awed whispers.

Jessica, hearing the voices, felt the depth of the experience, realized what terrible inhibitions there must be against shedding tears. She focused on the words: *"He gives moisture to the dead."* It was a gift to the shadow world—tears. They would be sacred beyond a doubt.

Nothing on this planet had so forcefully hammered into her the ultimate value of water. Not the water-sellers, not the dried skins of the natives, not stillsuits or the rules of water discipline. Here there was a substance more precious than all others—it was life itself and entwined all around with symbolism and ritual.

Water.

"I touched his cheek," someone whispered. "I felt the gift."

At first, the fingers touching his face frightened Paul. He clutched the cold handle of the baliset, feeling the strings bite his palm. Then he saw the faces beyond the groping hands—the eyes wide and wondering.

Presently, the hands withdrew. The funeral ceremony resumed. But now there was a subtle space around Paul, a drawing back as the troop honored him by a respectful isolation.

The ceremony ended with a low chant:

> *"Full moon calls thee—*
> *Shai-hulud shalt thou see;*
> *Red the night, dusky sky,*
> *Bloody death didst thou die.*
> *We pray to a moon: she is round—*
> *Luck with us will then abound,*
> *What we seek for shall be found*
> *In the land of solid ground."*

A bulging sack remained at Stilgar's feet. He crouched, placed his palms against it. Someone came up beside him, crouched at his elbow, and Paul recognized Chani's face in the hood shadow.

"Jamis carried thirty-three liters and seven and three-thirty-seconds drachms of the tribe's water," Chani said. "I bless it now in the presence of a Sayyadina. Ekkeri-akairi, this is the water, fillissin-follasy of Paul-Muad'Dib! Kivi a-kavi, never the more, nakalas! Nakelas! to be measured and counted, ukair-an! by the heartbeats jan-jan-jan of our friend . . . Jamis."

In an abrupt and profound silence, Chani turned, stared at Paul.

Presently she said: "Where I am flame be thou the coals. Where I am dew be thou the water."

"Bi-lal kaifa," intoned the troop.

"To Paul-Muad'Dib goes this portion," Chani said. "May he guard it for the tribe, preserving it against careless loss. May he be generous with it in time of need. May he pass it on in his time for the good of the tribe."

"Bi-lal kaifa," intoned the troop.

I must accept that water, Paul thought. Slowly, he arose, made his way to Chani's side. Stilgar stepped back to make room for him, took the baliset gently from his hand.

"Kneel," Chani said.

Paul knelt.

She guided his hands to the waterbag, held them against the resilient surface. "With this water the tribe entrusts thee," she said. "Jamis is gone from it. Take it in peace." She stood, pulling Paul up with her.

Stilgar returned the baliset, extended a small pile of metal rings in one palm. Paul looked at them, seeing the different sizes, the way the light of the glowglobe reflected off them.

Chani took the largest ring, held it on a finger. "Thirty liters," she said. One by one, she took the others, showing each to Paul, counting them. "Two liters; one liter; seven watercounters of one drachm each; one watercounter of three-thirty-seconds drachms. In all—thirty-three liters and seven and three-thirty-seconds drachms."

She held them up on her finger for Paul to see.

"Do you accept them?" Stilgar asked.

Paul swallowed, nodded. "Yes."

"Later," Chani said, "I will show you how to tie them in a kerchief so they won't rattle and give you away when you need silence." She extended her hand.

"Will you . . . hold them for me?" Paul asked.

Chani turned a startled glance on Stilgar.

He smiled, said, "Paul-Muad'Dib who is Usul does not yet know our ways, Chani. Hold his watercounters without commitment until it's time to show him the manner of carrying them."

She nodded, whipped a ribbon of cloth from beneath her robe, linked the rings onto it with an intricate over and under weaving, hesitated, then stuffed them into the sash beneath her robe.

I missed something there, Paul thought. He sensed the feeling of humor around him, something bantering in it, and his mind linked up a prescient memory: *watercounters offered to a woman—courtship ritual.*

"Watermasters," Stilgar said.

The troop arose in a hissing of robes. Two men stepped out, lifted the waterbag. Stilgar took down the glowglobe, led the way with it into the depths of the cave.

Paul was pressed in behind Chani, noted the buttery glow of light over rock walls, the way the shadows danced, and he felt the troop's lift of spirits contained in a hushed air of expectancy.

Jessica, pulled into the end of the troop by eager hands, hemmed around by jostling bodies, suppressed a moment of panic. She had recognized fragments of the ritual, identified the shards of Chakobsa and Bhotani Jib in the words, and she knew the wild violence that could explode out of these seemingly simple moments.

Jan-jan-jan, she thought. *Go-go-go.*

It was like a child's game that had lost all inhibition in adult hands.

Stilgar stopped at a yellow rock wall. He pressed an outcropping and the wall swung silently away from him, opening along an irregular crack. He led the way through past a dark honeycomb lattice that directed a cool wash of air across Paul when he passed it.

Paul turned a questioning stare on Chani, tugged her arm. "That air felt damp," he said.

"Sh-h-h-h," she whispered.

But a man behind them said: "Plenty of moisture in the trap tonight. Jamis' way of telling us he's satisfied."

Jessica passed through the secret door, heard it close behind. She saw how the Fremen slowed while passing the honeycomb lattice, felt the dampness of the air as she came opposite it.

Windtrap! she thought. *They've a concealed windtrap somewhere on the surface to funnel air down here into cooler regions and precipitate the moisture from it.*

They passed through another rock door with latticework above it, and the door closed behind them. The draft of air at their backs carried a sensation of moisture clearly perceptible to both Jessica and Paul.

At the head of the troop, the glowglobe in Stilgar's hands dropped below the level of the heads in front of Paul. Presently he felt steps beneath his feet, curving down to the left. Light reflected back up across hooded heads and a winding movement of people spiraling down the steps.

Jessica sensed mounting tension in the people around her, a pressure of silence that rasped her nerves with its urgency.

The steps ended and the troop passed through another low door. The light of the glowglobe was swallowed in a great open space with a high curved ceiling.

Paul felt Chani's hand on his arm, heard a faint dripping sound in the chill air, felt an utter stillness come over the Fremen in the cathedral presence of water.

I have seen this place in a dream, he thought.

The thought was both reassuring and frustrating. Somewhere ahead of him on this path, the fanatic hordes cut their gory path across the universe in his name. The green and black Atreides banner would become a symbol of terror. Wild legions would charge into battle screaming their war cry: "Muad'Dib!"

It must not be, he thought. *I cannot let it happen.*

But he could feel the demanding race consciousness within him, his own terrible purpose, and he knew that no small thing could deflect the juggernaut. It was gathering weight and momentum. If he died this instant, the thing would go on through his mother and his unborn sister. Nothing less than the deaths of all the troop gathered here and now—himself and his mother included—could stop the thing.

Paul stared around him, saw the troop spread out in a line. They pressed him forward against a low barrier carved from native rock. Beyond the barrier in the glow of Stilgar's globe, Paul saw an unruffled dark surface of water. It stretched away into shadows—deep and black—the far wall only faintly visible, perhaps a hundred meters away.

Jessica felt the dry pulling of skin on her cheeks and forehead relaxing in the presence of moisture. The water pool was deep; she could sense its deepness, and resisted a desire to dip her hands into it.

A splashing sounded on her left. She looked down the shadowy line of Fremen, saw Stilgar with Paul standing beside him and the watermasters emptying their load into the pool through a flowmeter. The meter was a round gray eye above the pool's rim. She saw its glowing pointer move as the water flowed through it, saw the pointer stop at thirty-three liters, seven and three-thirty-seconds drachms.

Superb accuracy in water measurement, Jessica thought. And she noted that the walls of the meter trough held no trace of moisture after the water's passage. The water flowed off those walls without binding tension. She saw a profound clue to Fremen technology in the simple fact: they were perfectionists.

Jessica worked her way down the barrier to Stilgar's side. Way was made for her with casual courtesy. She noted the withdrawn look in Paul's eyes, but the mystery of this great pool of water dominated her thoughts.

Stilgar looked at her. "There were those among us in need of water," he said, "yet they would come here and not touch this water. Do you know that?"

"I believe it," she said.

He looked at the pool. "We have more than thirty-eight million decaliters here," he said. "Walled off from the little makers, hidden and preserved."

"A treasure trove," she said.

Stilgar lifted the globe to look into her eyes. "It is greater than treasure. We have thousands of such caches. Only a few of us know them all." He cocked his head to one side. The globe cast a yellow-shadowed glow across face and beard. "Hear that?"

They listened.

The dripping of water precipitated from the windtrap filled the room with its presence. Jessica saw that the entire troop was caught up in a rapture of listening. Only Paul seemed to stand remote from it.

To Paul, the sound was like moments ticking away. He could feel time flowing through him, the instants never to be recaptured. He sensed a need for decision, but felt powerless to move.

"It has been calculated with precision," Stilgar whispered. "We know to within a million decaliters how much we need. When we have it, we shall change the face of Arrakis."

A hushed whisper of response lifted from the troop: "Bi-lal kaifa."

"We will trap the dunes beneath grass plantings," Stilgar said, his voice growing stronger. "We will tie the water into the soil with trees and undergrowth."

"Bi-lal kaifa," intoned the troop.

"Each year the polar ice retreats," Stilgar said.

"Bi-lal kaifa," they chanted.

"We shall make a homeworld of Arrakis—with melting lenses at the poles, with lakes in the temperate zones, and only the deep desert for the maker and his spice."

"Bi-lal kaifa."

"And no man ever again shall want for water. It shall be his for dipping from well or pond or lake or canal. It shall run down through the qanats to feed our plants. It shall be there for any man to take. It shall be his for holding out his hand."

"Bi-lal kaifa."

Jessica felt the religious ritual in the words, noted her own instinctively awed response. *They're in league with the future*, she thought. *They have their mountain to climb. This is the scientist's dream . . . and these simple people, these peasants, are filled with it.*

Her thoughts turned to Liet-Kynes, the Emperor's planetary ecologist, the man who had gone native—and she wondered at him. This was a dream to capture men's souls, and she could sense the hand of the ecologist in it. This was a dream for which men would die willingly. It was another of the essential ingredients that she felt her son needed: people with a goal. Such people would be easy to imbue with fervor and fanaticism. They could be wielded like a sword to win back Paul's place for him.

"We leave now," Stilgar said, "and wait for the first moon's rising. When Jamis is safely on his way, we will go home."

Whispering their reluctance, the troop fell in behind him, turned back along the water barrier and up the stairs.

And Paul, walking behind Chani, felt that a vital moment had passed him, that he had missed an essential decision and was now caught up in his own myth. He knew he had seen this place before, experienced it in a fragment of prescient dream on faraway Caladan, but details of the place were being filled in now that he had not seen. He felt a new sense of wonder at the limits of his gift. It was as though he rode within the wave of time, sometimes in its trough, sometimes on a crest—and all around him the other waves lifted and fell, revealing and then hiding what they bore on their surface.

Through it all, the wild jihad still loomed ahead of him, the violence and the slaughter. It was like a promontory above the surf.

The troop filed through the last door into the main cavern. The door was sealed. Lights were extinguished, hoods removed from the cavern openings, revealing the night and the stars that had come over the desert.

Jessica moved to the dry lip of the cavern's edge, looked up at the stars. They were sharp and near. She felt the stirring of the troop around her, heard the sound of a baliset being tuned somewhere behind her, and Paul's voice humming the pitch. There was a melancholy in his tone that she did not like.

Chani's voice intruded from the deep cave darkness: "Tell me about the waters of your birthworld, Paul-Muad'Dib."

And Paul: "Another time, Chani. I promise."

Such sadness.

"It's a good baliset," Chani said.

"Very good," Paul said. "Do you think Jamis'll mind my using it?"

He speaks of the dead in the present tense, Jessica thought. The implications disturbed her.

A man's voice intruded: "He liked music betimes, Jamis did."

"Then sing me one of your songs," Chani pleaded.

Such feminine allure in that girl-child's voice, Jessica thought. *I must caution Paul about their women . . . and soon.*

"This was a song of a friend of mine," Paul said. "I expect he's dead now, Gurney is. He called it his evensong."

The troop grew still, listening as Paul's voice lifted in a sweet boy tenor with the baliset tinkling and strumming beneath it:

> *"This clear time of seeing embers—*
> *A gold-bright sun's lost in first dusk.*
> *What frenzied senses, desp'rate musk*
> *Are consort of rememb'ring."*

Jessica felt the verbal music in her breast—pagan and charged with sounds that made her suddenly and intensely aware of herself, feeling her own body and its needs. She listened with a tense stillness.

> *"Night's pearl-censered requi-em . . .*
> *'Tis for us!*
> *What joys run, then—*
> *Bright in your eyes—*
> *What flower-spangled amores*
> *Pull at our hearts . . .*
> *What flower-spangled amores*
> *Fill our desires."*

And Jessica heard the after-stillness that hummed in the air with the last note. *Why does my son sing a love song to that girl-child?* she asked herself. She felt an abrupt fear. She could sense life flowing around her and she had no grasp on its reins. *Why did he choose that song?* she wondered. *The instincts are true sometimes. Why did he do this?*

Paul sat silently in the darkness, a single stark thought dominating his awareness: *My mother is my enemy. She does not know it, but she is. She is bringing the jihad. She bore me; she trained me. She is my enemy.*

The concept of progress acts as a protective mechanism to shield us from the terrors of the future.

—FROM "COLLECTED SAYINGS OF MUAD'DIB"
BY THE PRINCESS IRULAN

On his seventeenth birthday, Feyd-Rautha Harkonnen killed his one hundredth slave-gladiator in the family games. Visiting observers from the Imperial Court—a Count and Lady Fenring—were on the Harkonnen homeworld of Giedi Prime for the event, invited to sit that afternoon with the immediate family in the golden box above the triangular arena.

In honor of the na-Baron's nativity and to remind all Harkonnens and subjects that Feyd-Rautha was heir-designate, it was holiday on Giedi Prime. The old Baron had decreed a meridian-to-meridian rest from labors, and effort had been spent in the family city of Harko to create the illusion of gaiety: banners flew from buildings, new paint had been splashed on the walls along Court Way.

But off the main way, Count Fenring and his lady noted the rubbish heaps, the scabrous brown walls reflected in the dark puddles of the streets, and the furtive scurrying of the people.

In the Baron's blue-walled keep, there was fearful perfection, but the Count and his lady saw the price being paid—guards everywhere and weapons with that special sheen that told a trained eye they were in regular use. There were checkpoints for routine passage from area to area even within the keep. The servants revealed their military training in the way they walked, in the set of their shoulders . . . in the way their eyes watched and watched and watched.

"The pressure's on," the Count hummed to his lady in their secret language. "The Baron is just beginning to see the price he really paid to rid himself of the Duke Leto."

"Sometime I must recount for you the legend of the phoenix," she said.

They were in the reception hall of the keep waiting to go to the family games. It was not a large hall—perhaps forty meters long and half that in width—but false pillars along the sides had been shaped with an abrupt taper, and the ceiling had a subtle arch, all giving the illusion of much greater space.

"Ah-h-h, here comes the Baron," the Count said.

The Baron moved down the length of the hall with that peculiar waddling-glide imparted by the necessities of guiding suspensor-hung weight. His jowls bobbed up and down; the suspensors jiggled and shifted beneath his orange robe. Rings glittered on his hands and opafires shone where they had been woven into the robe.

At the Baron's elbow walked Feyd-Rautha. His dark hair was dressed in close ringlets that seemed incongruously gay above sullen eyes. He wore a tight-fitting black tunic and snug trousers with a suggestion of bell at the bottom. Soft-soled slippers covered his small feet.

Lady Fenring, noting the young man's poise and the sure flow of muscles beneath the tunic, thought: *Here's one who won't let himself go to fat.*

The Baron stopped in front of them, took Feyd-Rautha's arm in a possessive grip, said, "My nephew, the na-Baron, Feyd-Rautha Harkonnen." And, turning his baby-fat face toward Feyd-Rautha, he said, "The Count and Lady Fenring of whom I've spoken."

Feyd-Rautha dipped his head with the required courtesy. He stared at the Lady Fenring. She was golden-haired and willowy, her perfection of figure clothed in a flowing gown of ecru—simple fitness of form without ornament. Gray-green eyes stared back at him. She had that Bene Gesserit serene repose about her that the young man found subtly disturbing.

"Um-m-m-m-ah-hm-m-m-m," said the Count. He studied Feyd-Rautha. "The, hm-m-m-m, *precise* young man, ah, my . . . hm-m-m-m . . . dear?" The Count glanced at the Baron. "My dear Baron, you say you've spoken of us to this *precise* young man? What did you say?"

"I told my nephew of the great esteem our Emperor holds for you, Count Fenring," the Baron said. And he thought: *Mark him well, Feyd! A killer with the manners of a rabbit—this is the most dangerous kind.*

"Of course!" said the Count, and he smiled at his lady.

Feyd-Rautha found the man's actions and words almost insulting. They stopped just short of something overt that would require notice. The young man focused his attention on the Count: a small man, weak-looking. The face was weaselish with overlarge dark eyes. There was gray at the temples. And his movements—he moved a hand or turned his head one way, then he spoke another way. It was difficult to follow.

"Um-m-m-m-m-ah-h-h-hm-m-m, you come upon such, mm-m-m, preciseness so rarely," the Count said, addressing the Baron's shoulder. "I . . . ah, congratulate you on the hm-m-m perfection of your ah-h-h heir. In the light of the hm-m-m elder, one might say."

"You are too kind," the Baron said. He bowed, but Feyd-Rautha noted that his uncle's eyes did not agree with the courtesy.

"When you're mm-m-m ironic, that ah-h-h suggests you're hm-mm-m thinking deep thoughts," the Count said.

There he goes again, Feyd-Rautha thought. *It sounds like he's being insulting, but there's nothing you can call out for satisfaction.*

Listening to the man gave Feyd-Rautha the feeling his head was being pushed through mush . . . *um-m-m-ah-h-h-hm-m-m-m!* Feyd-Rautha turned his attention back to the Lady Fenring.

"We're ah-h-h taking up too much of this young man's time," she said. "I understand he's to appear in the arena today."

By the houris of the Imperial hareem, she's a lovely one! Feyd-Rautha thought. He said: "I shall make a kill for you this day, my Lady. I shall make the dedication in the arena, with your permission."

She returned his stare serenely, but her voice carried whiplash as she said: "You do *not* have my permission."

"Feyd!" the Baron said. And he thought: *That imp! Does he want this deadly Count to call him out?*

But the Count only smiled and said: "Hm-m-m-m-um-m-m."

"You really *must* be getting ready for the arena, Feyd," the Baron said. "You must be rested and not take any foolish risks."

Feyd-Rautha bowed, his face dark with resentment. "I'm sure everything will be as you wish, Uncle." He nodded to Count Fenring. "Sir." To the lady: "My Lady." And he turned, strode out of the hall, barely glancing at the knot of Families Minor near the double doors.

"He's so young," the Baron sighed.

"Um-m-m-m-ah indeed hmmm," the Count said.

And the Lady Fenring thought: *Can that be the young man the Reverend Mother meant? Is that a bloodline we must preserve?*

"We've more than an hour before going to the arena," the Baron said. "Perhaps we could have our little talk now, Count Fenring." He tipped his gross head to the right. "There's a considerable amount of progress to be discussed."

And the Baron thought: *Let us see now how the Emperor's errand boy gets across whatever message he carries without ever being so crass as to speak it right out.*

The Count spoke to his lady: "Um-m-m-m-ah-h-h-hm-m-m, you mm-m-m will ah-h-h excuse us, my dear?"

"Each day, some time each hour, brings change," she said. "Mmm-mm." And she smiled sweetly at the Baron before turning away. Her long skirts swished and she walked with a straight-backed regal stride toward the double doors at the end of the hall.

The Baron noted how all conversation among the Houses Minor there stopped at her approach, how the eyes followed her. *Bene Gesserit!* the Baron thought. *The universe would be better rid of them all!*

"There's a cone of silence between two of the pillars over here on our left," the Baron said. "We can talk there without fear of being overheard." He led the way with his waddling gait into the sound-deadening field, feeling the noises of the keep become dull and distant.

The Count moved up beside the Baron, and they turned, facing the wall so their lips could not be read.

"We're not satisfied with the way you ordered the Sardaukar off Arrakis," the Count said.

Straight talk! the Baron thought.

"The Sardaukar could not stay longer without risking that *others* would find out how the Emperor helped me," the Baron said.

"But your nephew Rabban does not appear to be pressing strongly enough toward a solution of the Fremen problem."

"What does the Emperor wish?" the Baron asked. "There cannot be more than a handful of Fremen left on Arrakis. The southern desert is uninhabitable. The northern desert is swept regularly by our patrols."

"Who says the southern desert is uninhabitable?"

"Your own planetologist said it, my dear Count."

"But Doctor Kynes is dead."

"Ah, yes . . . unfortunate, that."

"We've word from an overflight across the southern reaches," the Count said. "There's evidence of plant life."

"Has the Guild then agreed to a watch from space?"

"You know better than that, Baron. The Emperor cannot legally post a watch on Arrakis."

"And *I* cannot afford it," the Baron said. "Who made this overflight?"

"A . . . smuggler."

"Someone has lied to you, Count," the Baron said. "Smugglers cannot navigate the southern reaches any better than can Rabban's men. Storms, sand-static, and all that, you know. Navigation markers are knocked out faster than they can be installed."

"We'll discuss various types of static another time," the Count said.

Ah-h-h-h, the Baron thought. "Have you found some mistake in my accounting then?" he demanded.

"When you imagine mistakes there can be no self-defense," the Count said.

He's deliberately trying to arouse my anger, the Baron thought. He took two deep breaths to calm himself. He could smell his own sweat, and the harness of the suspensors beneath his robe felt suddenly itchy and galling.

"The Emperor cannot be unhappy about the death of the concubine and the boy," the Baron said. "They fled into the desert. There was a storm."

"Yes, there were so many convenient accidents," the Count agreed.

"I do not like your tone, Count," the Baron said.

"Anger is one thing, violence another," the Count said. "Let me caution you: Should an unfortunate accident occur to me here the Great Houses all would learn what you did on Arrakis. They've long suspected how you do business."

"The only recent business I can recall," the Baron said, "was transportation of several legions of Sardaukar to Arrakis."

"You think you could hold that over the Emperor's head?"

"I wouldn't think of it!"

The Count smiled. "Sardaukar commanders could be found who'd confess they acted without orders because they wanted a battle with your Fremen scum."

"Many might doubt such a confession," the Baron said, but the threat staggered him. *Are Sardaukar truly that disciplined?* he wondered.

"The Emperor does wish to audit your books," the Count said.

"Anytime."

"You . . . ah . . . have no objections?"

"None. My CHOAM Company directorship will bear the closest scrutiny." And he thought: *Let him bring a false accusation against me and have it exposed. I shall stand there, promethean, saying: "Behold me, I am wronged." Then let him bring any other accusation against me, even a true one. The Great Houses will not believe a second attack from an accuser once proved wrong.*

"No doubt your books will bear the closest scrutiny," the Count muttered.

"Why is the Emperor so interested in exterminating the Fremen?" the Baron asked.

"You wish the subject to be changed, eh?" The Count shrugged. "It is the Sardaukar who wish it, not the Emperor. They needed practice in killing . . . and they hate to see a task left undone."

Does he think to frighten me by reminding me that he is supported by bloodthirsty killers? the Baron wondered.

"A certain amount of killing has always been an arm of business," the Baron said, "but a line has to be drawn somewhere. Someone must be left to work the spice."

The Count emitted a short, barking laugh. "You think you can harness the Fremen?"

"There never were enough of them for that," the Baron said. "But the killing has made the rest of my population uneasy. It's reaching the point where I'm considering another solution to the Arrakeen problem, my dear Fenring. And I must confess the Emperor deserves credit for the inspiration."

"Ah-h-h?"

"You see, Count, I have the Emperor's prison planet, Salusa Secundus, to inspire me."

The Count stared at him with glittering intensity. "What possible connection is there between Arrakis and Salusa Secundus?"

The Baron felt the alertness in Fenring's eyes, said: "No connection yet."

"Yet?"

"You must admit it'd be a way to develop a substantial work force on Arrakis—use the place as a prison planet."

"You anticipate an increase in prisoners?"

"There has been unrest," the Baron admitted. "I've had to squeeze rather severely, Fenring. After all, you know the price I paid that damnable Guild to transport our mutual force to Arrakis. That money has to come from *somewhere*."

"I suggest you not use Arrakis as a prison planet without the Emperor's permission, Baron."

"Of course not," the Baron said, and he wondered at the sudden chill in Fenring's voice.

"Another matter," the Count said. "We learn that Duke Leto's Mentat, Thufir Hawat, is not dead but in your employ."

"I could not bring myself to waste him," the Baron said.

"You lied to our Sardaukar commander when you said Hawat was dead."

"Only a white lie, my dear Count. I hadn't the stomach for a long argument with the man."

"Was Hawat the real traitor?"

"Oh, goodness, no! It was the false doctor." The Baron wiped at perspiration on his neck. "You must understand, Fenring, I was without a Mentat. You know that. I've never been without a Mentat. It was most unsettling."

"How could you get Hawat to shift allegiance?"

"His Duke was dead." The Baron forced a smile. "There's nothing to fear from Hawat, my dear Count. The Mentat's flesh has been impregnated with a latent poison. We administer an antidote in his meals. Without the antidote, the poison is triggered—he'd die in a few days."

"Withdraw the antidote," the Count said.

"But he's useful!"

"And he knows too many things no living man should know."

"You said the Emperor doesn't fear exposure."

"Don't play games with me, Baron!"

"When I see such an order above the Imperial seal I'll obey it," the Baron said. "But I'll not submit to your whim."

"You think it whim?"

"What else can it be? The Emperor has obligations to me, too, Fenring. I rid him of the troublesome Duke."

"With the help of a few Sardaukar."

"Where else would the Emperor have found a House to provide the disguising uniforms to hide his hand in this matter?"

"He has asked himself the same question, Baron, but with a slightly different emphasis."

The Baron studied Fenring, noting the stiffness of jaw muscles, the careful control. "Ah-h-h, now," the Baron said. "I hope the Emperor doesn't believe he can move against *me* in total secrecy."

"He hopes it won't become necessary."

"The Emperor cannot believe I threaten him!" The Baron permitted anger and grief to edge his voice, thinking: *Let him wrong me in that! I could place myself on the throne while still beating my breast over how I'd been wronged.*

The Count's voice went dry and remote as he said: "The Emperor believes what his senses tell him."

"Dare the Emperor charge me with treason before a full Landsraad Council?" And the Baron held his breath with the hope of it.

"The Emperor need *dare* nothing."

The Baron whirled away in his suspensors to hide his expression. *It could happen in my lifetime!* he thought. *Emperor! Let him wrong me! Then—the bribes and coercion, the rallying of the Great Houses: they'd flock to my banner like peasants running for shelter. The thing they fear above all else is the Emperor's Sardaukar loosed upon them one House at a time.*

"It's the Emperor's sincere hope he'll never have to charge you with treason," the Count said.

The Baron found it difficult to keep irony out of his voice and permit only the expression of hurt, but he managed. "I've been a most loyal subject. These words hurt me beyond my capacity to express."

"Um-m-m-m-ah-hm-m-m," said the Count.

The Baron kept his back to the Count, nodding. Presently he said, "It's time to go to the arena."

"Indeed," said the Count.

They moved out of the cone of silence and, side by side, walked toward the clumps of Houses Minor at the end of the hall. A bell began a slow tolling somewhere in the keep—twenty-minute warning for the arena gathering.

"The Houses Minor wait for you to lead them," the Count said, nodding toward the people they approached.

Double meaning . . . double meaning, the Baron thought.

He looked up at the new talismans flanking the exit to his hall—the mounted bull's head and the oil painting of the Old Duke Atreides, the late Duke Leto's father. They filled the Baron with an odd sense of foreboding, and he wondered what thoughts these talismans had inspired in the Duke Leto as they hung in the halls of Caladan and then on Arrakis—the bravura father and the head of the bull that had killed him.

"Mankind has ah only one mm-m-m science," the Count said as they picked up their parade of followers and emerged from the hall into the waiting room—a narrow space with high windows and floor of patterned white and purple tile.

"And what science is that?" the Baron asked.

"It's the um-m-m-ah-h science of ah-h-h discontent," the Count said.

The Houses Minor behind them, sheep-faced and responsive, laughed with just the right tone of appreciation, but the sound carried a note of discord as it collided with the sudden blast of motors that came to them when pages threw open the outer doors, revealing the line of ground cars, their guidon pennants whipping in a breeze.

The Baron raised his voice to surmount the sudden noise, said, "I hope you'll not be discontented with the performance of my nephew today, Count Fenring."

"I ah-h-h am filled um-m-m only with a hm-m-m sense of anticipation, yes," the Count said. "Always in the ah-h-h proces verbal, one um-m-m ah-h-h must consider the ah-h-h office of origin."

The Baron did his sudden stiffening of surprise by stumbling on the first step down from the exit. *Proces verbal! That was a report of a crime against the Imperium!*

But the Count chuckled to make it seem a joke, and patted the Baron's arm.

All the way to the arena, though, the Baron sat back among the armored cushions of his car, casting covert glances at the Count beside him, wondering why the Emperor's *errand boy* had thought it necessary to make that particular kind of joke in front of the Houses Minor. It was obvious that Fenring seldom did anything he felt to be unnecessary, or used two words where one would do, or held himself to a single meaning in a single phrase.

They were seated in the golden box above the triangular arena—horns blaring, the tiers above and around them jammed with a hubbub of people and waving pennants—when the answer came to the Baron.

"My dear Baron," the Count said, leaning close to his ear, "you know, don't you, that the Emperor has not given official sanction to your choice of heir?"

The Baron felt himself to be within a sudden personal cone of silence produced by his own shock. He stared at Fenring, barely seeing the Count's lady come through the guards beyond to join the party in the golden box.

"That's really why I'm here today," the Count said. "The Emperor wishes me to report on whether you've chosen a worthy successor. There's nothing like the arena to expose the true person from beneath the mask, eh?"

"The Emperor promised me free choice of heir!" the Baron grated.

"We shall see," Fenring said, and turned away to greet his lady. She sat down, smiling at the Baron, then giving her attention to the sand floor beneath them where Feyd-Rautha was emerging in giles and tights—the black glove and the long knife in his right hand, the white glove and the short knife in his left hand.

"White for poison, black for purity," the Lady Fenring said. "A curious custom, isn't it, my love?"

"Um-m-m-m," the Count said.

The greeting cheer lifted from the family galleries, and Feyd-Rautha paused to accept it, looking up and scanning the faces—seeing his cousines and cousins, the demibrothers, the concubines and out-freyn relations. They were so many pink trumpet mouths yammering amidst a flutter of colorful clothing and banners.

It came to Feyd-Rautha then that the packed ranks of faces would look just as avidly at his blood as at that of the slave-gladiator. There was not a doubt of the outcome in this fight, of course. Here was only the form of danger without its substance—yet. . . .

Feyd-Rautha held up his knives to the sun, saluted the three corners of the arena in the ancient manner. The short knife in white-gloved hand (white, the sign of poison) went first into its sheath. Then the long blade in the black-gloved hand—the pure blade that now was unpure, his secret weapon to turn this day into a purely personal victory: poison on the black blade.

The adjustment of his body shield took only a moment, and he paused to sense the skin-tightening at his forehead assuring him he was properly guarded.

This moment carried its own suspense, and Feyd-Rautha dragged it out with the sure hand of a showman, nodding to his handlers and distractors, checking their equipment with a measuring stare—gyves in place with their prickles sharp and glistening, the barbs and hooks waving with their blue streamers.

Feyd-Rautha signaled the musicians.

The slow march began, sonorous with its ancient pomp, and Feyd-Rautha led his troupe across the arena for obeisance at the foot of his uncle's box. He caught the ceremonial key as it was thrown.

The music stopped.

Into the abrupt silence, he stepped back two paces, raised the key and shouted. "I dedicate this truth to. . . ." And he paused, knowing his uncle would think: *The young fool's going to dedicate to Lady Fenring after all and cause a ruckus!*

". . . to my uncle and patron, the Baron Vladimir Harkonnen!" Feyd-Rautha shouted.

And he was delighted to see his uncle sigh.

The music resumed at the quick-march, and Feyd-Rautha led his men scampering back across the arena to the prudence door that admitted only those wearing the proper identification band. Feyd-Rautha prided himself that he never used the pru-door and seldom needed distractors. But it was good to know they were available this day—special plans sometimes involved special dangers.

Again, silence settled over the arena.

Feyd-Rautha turned, faced the big red door across from him through which the gladiator would emerge.

The special gladiator.

The plan Thufir Hawat had devised was admirably simple and direct, Feyd-Rautha thought. The slave would not be drugged—that was the danger. Instead, a key word had been drummed into the man's unconscious to immobilize his muscles at a critical instant. Feyd-Rautha rolled the vital word in his mind, mouthing it without sound: "Scum!" To the audience, it would appear that an undrugged slave had been slipped into the arena to kill the na-Baron. And all the carefully arranged evidence would point to the slavemaster.

A low humming arose from the red door's servo-motors as they were armed for opening.

Feyd-Rautha focused all his awareness on the door. This first moment was the critical one. The appearance of the gladiator as he emerged told the trained eye much it needed to know. All gladiators were supposed to be hyped on elacca drug to come out kill-ready in fighting stance—but you had to watch how they hefted the knife, which way they turned in defense, whether they were actually aware of the audience in the stands. The way a slave cocked his head could give the most vital clue to counter and feint.

The red door slammed open.

Out charged a tall, muscular man with shaved head and darkly pitted eyes. His skin was carrot-colored as it should be from the elacca drug, but Feyd-Rautha knew the color was paint. The slave wore green leotards and the red belt of a semishield—the belt's arrow pointing left to indicate the slave's left side was shielded. He held his knife sword-fashion, cocked slightly outward in the stance of a trained fighter. Slowly, he advanced into the arena, turning his shielded side toward Feyd-Rautha and the group at the pru-door.

"I like not the look of this one," said one of Feyd-Rautha's barbmen. "Are you sure he's drugged, m'Lord?"

"He has the color," Feyd-Rautha said.

"Yet he stands like a fighter," said another helper.

Feyd-Rautha advanced two steps onto the sand, studied this slave.

"What has he done to his arm?" asked one of the distractors.

Feyd-Rautha's attention went to a bloody scratch on the man's left forearm, followed the arm down to the hand as it pointed to a design drawn in blood on the left hip of the green leotards—a wet shape there: the formalized outline of a hawk.

Hawk!

Feyd-Rautha looked up into the darkly pitted eyes, saw them glaring at him with uncommon alertness.

It's one of Duke Leto's fighting men we took on Arrakis! Feyd-Rautha thought. *No simple gladiator this!* A chill ran through him, and he wondered if Hawat had another plan for this arena—a feint within a feint within a feint. And only the slavemaster prepared to take the blame!

Feyd-Rautha's chief handler spoke at his ear: "I like not the look on that one, m'Lord. Let me set a barb or two in his knife arm to try him."

"I'll set my own barbs," Feyd-Rautha said. He took a pair of the long, hooked shafts from the handler, hefted them, testing the balance. These barbs, too, were supposed to be drugged—but not this time, and the chief handler might die because of that. But it was all part of the plan.

"You'll come out of this a hero," Hawat had said. *"Killed your gladiator man to man and in spite of treachery. The slavemaster will be executed and your man will step into his spot."*

Feyd-Rautha advanced another five paces into the arena, playing out the moment, studying the slave. Already, he knew, the experts in the stands above him were aware that something was wrong. The gladiator had the correct skin color for a drugged man, but he stood his ground and did not tremble. The aficionados would be whispering among themselves now: "See how he stands. He should be agitated—attacking or retreating. See how he conserves his strength, how he waits. He should not wait."

Feyd-Rautha felt his own excitement kindle. *Let there be treachery in Hawat's mind,* he thought. *I can handle this slave. And it's my long knife that carries the poison this time, not the short one. Even Hawat doesn't know that.*

"Hai, Harkonnen!" the slave called. "Are you prepared to die?"

Deathly stillness gripped the arena. *Slaves did not issue the challenge!*

Now, Feyd-Rautha had a clear view of the gladiator's eyes, saw the cold ferocity of despair in them. He marked the way the man stood, loose and ready, muscles prepared for victory. The slave grapevine had carried Hawat's message to this one: *"You'll get a true chance to kill the na-Baron."* That much of the scheme was as they'd planned it, then.

A tight smile crossed Feyd-Rautha's mouth. He lifted the barbs, seeing success for his plans in the way the gladiator stood.

"Hai! Hai!" the slave challenged, and crept forward two steps.

No one in the galleries can mistake it now, Feyd-Rautha thought.

This slave should have been partly crippled by drug-induced terror. Every movement should have betrayed his inner knowledge that there was no hope for him—he could not win. He should have been filled with the stories of the poisons the na-Baron chose for the blade in his white-gloved hand. The na-Baron never gave quick death; he delighted in demonstrating rare poisons, could stand in the arena pointing out interesting side effects on a writhing victim. There was fear in the slave, yes—but not terror.

Feyd-Rautha lifted the barbs high, nodded in an almost-greeting.

The gladiator pounced.

His feint and defensive counter were as good as any Feyd-Rautha had ever seen. A timed side blow missed by the barest fraction from severing the tendons of the na-Baron's left leg.

Feyd-Rautha danced away, leaving a barbed shaft in the slave's right forearm, the hooks completely buried in flesh where the man could not withdraw them without ripping tendons.

A concerted gasp lifted from the galleries.

The sound filled Feyd-Rautha with elation.

He knew now what his uncle was experiencing, sitting up there with the Fenrings, the observers from the Imperial Court, beside him. There could be no interference with this fight. The forms must be observed in front of witnesses. And the Baron would interpret the events in the arena only one way—threat to himself.

The slave backed, holding knife in teeth and lashing the barbed shaft to his arm with the pennant. "I do not feel your needle!" he shouted. Again he crept forward, knife ready, left side presented, his body bent backward to give it the greatest surface of protection from the half-shield.

That action, too, didn't escape the galleries. Sharp cries came from the family boxes. Feyd-Rautha's handlers were calling out to ask if he needed them.

He waved them back to the pru-door.

I'll give them a show such as they've never had before, Feyd-Rautha thought. *No tame killing where they can sit back and admire the style. This'll be something to take them by the guts and twist them. When I'm Baron they'll remember this day and won't be a one of them can escape fear of me because of this day.*

Feyd-Rautha gave ground slowly before the gladiator's crablike advance. Arena sand grated underfoot. He heard the slave's panting, smelled his own sweat and a faint odor of blood on the air.

Steadily, the na-Baron moved backward, turning to the right, his second barb ready. The slave danced sideways. Feyd-Rautha appeared to stumble, heard the scream from the galleries.

Again, the slave pounced.

Gods, what a fighting man! Feyd-Rautha thought as he leaped aside. Only youth's quickness saved him, but he left the second barb buried in the deltoid muscle of the slave's right arm.

Shrill cheers rained from the galleries.

They cheer me now, Feyd-Rautha thought. He heard the wildness in the voices just as Hawat had said he would. They'd never cheered a family fighter that way before. And he thought with an edge of grimness on a thing Hawat had told him: *"It's easier to be terrified by an enemy you admire."*

Swiftly, Feyd-Rautha retreated to the center of the arena where all could see clearly. He drew his long blade, crouched and waited for the advancing slave.

The man took only the time to lash the second barb tight to his arm, then sped in pursuit.

Let the family see me do this thing, Feyd-Rautha thought. *I am their enemy: let them think of me as they see me now.*

He drew his short blade.

"I do not fear you, Harkonnen swine," the gladiator said. "Your tortures cannot hurt a dead man. I can be dead on my own blade before a handler lays finger to my flesh. And I'll have you dead beside me!"

Feyd-Rautha grinned, offered now the long blade, the one with the poison. "Try this on," he said, and feinted with the short blade in his other hand.

The slave shifted knife hands, turned inside both parry and feint to grapple the na-Baron's short blade—the one in the white-gloved hand that tradition said should carry the poison.

"You will die, Harkonnen," the gladiator gasped.

They struggled sideways across the sand. Where Feyd-Rautha's shield met the slave's halfshield, a blue glow marked the contact. The air around them filled with ozone from the field.

"Die on your own poison!" the slave grated.

He began forcing the white-gloved hand inward, turning the blade he thought carried the poison.

Let them see this! Feyd-Rautha thought. He brought down the long blade, felt it clang uselessly against the barbed shaft lashed to the slave's arm.

Feyd-Rautha felt a moment of desperation. He had not thought the barbed shafts would be an advantage for the slave. But they gave the man another shield. And the strength of this gladiator! The short blade was being forced inward inexorably, and Feyd-Rautha focused on the fact that a man could also die on an unpoisoned blade.

"Scum!" Feyd-Rautha gasped.

At the key word, the gladiator's muscles obeyed with a momentary slackness. It was enough for Feyd-Rautha. He opened a space between them sufficient for the long blade. Its poisoned tip flicked out, drew a red line down the slave's chest. There was instant agony in the poison. The man disengaged himself, staggered backward.

Now, let my dear family watch, Feyd-Rautha thought. *Let them think on this slave who tried to turn the knife he thought poisoned and use it against me. Let them wonder how a gladiator could come into this arena ready for such an attempt. And let them always be aware they cannot know for sure which of my hands carries the poison.*

Feyd-Rautha stood in silence, watching the slowed motions of the slave. The man moved within a hesitation-awareness. There was an orthographic thing on his face now for every watcher to recognize. The death was written there. The slave knew it had been done to him and he knew how it had been done. The wrong blade had carried the poison.

"You!" the man moaned.

Feyd-Rautha drew back to give death its space. The paralyzing drug in the poison had yet to take full effect, but the man's slowness told of its advance.

The slave staggered forward as though drawn by a string—one dragging step at a time. Each step was the only step in his universe. He still clutched his knife, but its point wavered.

"One day . . . one . . . of us . . . will . . . get . . . you," he gasped.

A sad little moue contorted his mouth. He sat, sagged, then stiffened and rolled away from Feyd-Rautha, face down.

Feyd-Rautha advanced in the silent arena, put a toe under the gladiator and rolled him onto his back to give the galleries a clear view of the face when the poison began its twisting, wrenching work on the muscles. But the gladiator came over with his own knife, protruding from his breast.

In spite of frustration, there was for Feyd-Rautha a measure of admiration for the effort this slave had managed in overcoming the paralysis to do this thing to himself. With the admiration came the realization that here was *truly* a thing to fear.

That which makes a man superhuman is terrifying.

As he focused on this thought, Feyd-Rautha became conscious of the eruption of noise from the stands and galleries around him. They were cheering with utter abandon.

Feyd-Rautha turned, looking up at them.

All were cheering except the Baron, who sat with hand to chin in deep contemplation—and the Count and his lady, both of whom were staring down at him, their faces masked by smiles.

Count Fenring turned to his lady, said: "Ah-h-h-um-m-m, a resourceful um-m-m-m young man. Eh, mm-m-m-ah, my dear?"

"His ah-h-h synaptic responses are very swift," she said.

The Baron looked at her, at the Count, returned his attention to the arena, thinking: *If someone could get that close to one of mine!* Rage began to replace his fear. *I'll have the slavemaster dead over a slow fire this night . . . and if this Count and his lady had a hand in it. . . .*

The conversation in the Baron's box was remote movement to Feyd-Rautha, the voices drowned in the foot-stamping chant that came now from all around:

"Head! Head! Head! Head!"

The Baron scowled, seeing the way Feyd-Rautha turned to him. Languidly, controlling his rage with difficulty, the Baron waved his hand toward the young man standing in the arena beside the sprawled body of the slave. *Give the boy a head. He earned it by exposing the slavemaster.*

Feyd-Rautha saw the signal of agreement, thought: *They think they honor me. Let them see what I think!*

He saw his handlers approaching with a saw-knife to do the honors, waved them back, repeated the gesture as they hesitated. *They think they honor me with just a head!* he thought. He bent and crossed the gladiator's hands around the protruding knife handle, then removed the knife and placed it in the limp hands.

It was done in an instant, and he straightened, beckoned his handlers. "Bury this slave intact with his knife in his hands," he said. "The man earned it."

In the golden box, Count Fenring leaned close to the Baron, said: "A grand gesture, that—true bravura. Your nephew has style as well as courage."

"He insults the crowd by refusing the head," the Baron muttered.

"Not at all," Lady Fenring said. She turned, looking up at the tiers around them.

And the Baron noted the line of her neck—a truly lovely flowing of muscles—like a young boy's.

"They like what your nephew did," she said.

As the import of Feyd-Rautha's gesture penetrated to the most distant seats, as the people saw the handlers carrying off the dead gladiator intact, the Baron watched them and realized she had interpreted the reaction correctly. The people were going wild, beating on each other, screaming and stamping.

The Baron spoke wearily. "I shall have to order a fete. You cannot send people home like this, their energies unspent. They must see that I share their elation." He gave a hand signal to his guard, and a servant above them dipped the Harkonnen orange pennant over the box—once, twice, three times—signal for a fete.

Feyd-Rautha crossed the arena to stand beneath the golden box, his weapons sheathed, arms hanging at his sides. Above the undiminished frenzy of the crowd, he called: "A fete, Uncle?"

The noise began to subside as people saw the conversation and waited.

"In your honor, Feyd!" the Baron called down. And again, he caused the pennant to be dipped in signal.

Across the arena, the pru-barriers had been dropped and young men were leaping down into the arena, racing toward Feyd-Rautha.

"You ordered the pru-shields dropped, Baron?" the Count asked.

"No one will harm the lad," the Baron said. "He's a hero."

The first of the charging mass reached Feyd-Rautha, lifted him on their shoulders, began parading around the arena.

"He could walk unarmed and unshielded through the poorest quarters of Harko tonight," the Baron said. "They'd give him the last of their food and drink just for his company."

The Baron pushed himself from his chair, settled his weight into his suspensors. "You will forgive me, please. There are matters that require my immediate attention. The guard will see you to the keep."

The Count arose, bowed. "Certainly, Baron. We're looking forward to the fete. I've ah-h-h-mm-m-m never seen a Harkonnen fete."

"Yes," the Baron said. "The fete." He turned, was enveloped by guards as he stepped into the private exit from the box.

A guard captain bowed to Count Fenring. "Your orders, my Lord?"

"We will ah-h-h wait for the worst mm-m-m crush to um-m-m pass," the Count said.

"Yes, m'Lord." The man bowed himself back three paces.

Count Fenring faced his lady, spoke again in their personal humming-code tongue: "You saw it, of course?"

In the same humming tongue, she said: "The lad knew the gladiator wouldn't be drugged. There was a moment of fear, yes, but no surprise."

"It was planned," he said. "The entire performance."

"Without a doubt."

"It stinks of Hawat."

"Indeed," she said.

"I demanded earlier that the Baron eliminate Hawat."

"That was an error, my dear."

"I see that now."

"The Harkonnens may have a new Baron ere long."

"If that's Hawat's plan."

"That will bear examination, true," she said.

"The young one will be more amenable to control."

"For us . . . after tonight," she said.

"You don't anticipate difficulty seducing him, my little broodmother?"

"No, my love. You saw how he looked at me."

"Yes, and I can see now why we must have that bloodline."

"Indeed, and it's obvious we must have a hold on him. I'll plant deep in his deepest self the necessary prana-bindu phrases to bend him."

"We'll leave as soon as possible—as soon as you're sure," he said.

She shuddered. "By all means. I should not want to bear a child in this terrible place."

"The things we do in the name of humanity," he said.

"Yours is the easy part," she said.

"There *are* some ancient prejudices I overcome," he said. "They're quite primordial, you know."

"My poor dear," she said, and patted his cheek. "You know this is the only way to be sure of saving that bloodline."

He spoke in a dry voice: "I quite understand what we do."

"We won't fail," she said.

"Guilt starts as a feeling of failure," he reminded.

"There'll be no guilt," she said. "Hypno-ligation of that Feyd-Rautha's psyche and his child in my womb—then we go."

"That uncle," he said. "Have you ever seen such distortion?"

"He's pretty fierce," she said, "but the nephew could well grow to be worse."

"Thanks to that uncle. You know, when you think what this lad could've been with some other upbringing—with the Atreides code to guide him, for example."

"It's sad," she said.

"Would that we could've saved both the Atreides youth and this one. From what I heard of that young Paul—a most admirable lad, good union of breeding and training." He shook his head. "But we shouldn't waste sorrow over the aristocracy of misfortune."

"There's a Bene Gesserit saying," she said.

"You have sayings for everything!" he protested.

"You'll like this one," she said. "It goes: 'Do not count a human dead until you've seen his body. And even then you can make a mistake.'"

Muad'Dib tells us in "A Time of Reflection" that his first collisions with Arrakeen necessities were the true beginnings of
his education. He learned then how to pole the sand for its
weather, learned the language of the wind's needles stinging
his skin, learned how the nose can buzz with sand-itch and
how to gather his body's precious moisture around him to
guard it and preserve it. As his eyes assumed the blue of the
Ibad, he learned the Chakobsa way.

—STILGAR'S PREFACE TO "MUAD'DIB, THE MAN"
BY THE PRINCESS IRULAN

Stilgar's troop returning to the sietch with its two strays from the desert
climbed out of the basin in the waning light of the first moon. The
robed figures hurried with the smell of home in their nostrils. Dawn's
gray line behind them was brightest at the notch in their horizon-
calendar that marked the middle of autumn, the month of Caprock.

Wind-raked dead leaves strewed the cliffbase where the sietch children had been gathering them, but the sounds of the troop's passage
(except for occasional blunderings by Paul and his mother) could not be
distinguished from the natural sounds of the night.

Paul wiped sweat-caked dust from his forehead, felt a tug at his arm,
heard Chani's voice hissing. "Do as I told you: bring the fold of your
hood down over your forehead! Leave only the eyes exposed. You waste
moisture."

A whispered command behind them demanded silence: "The desert hears you!"

A bird chirruped from the rocks high above them.

The troop stopped, and Paul sensed abrupt tension.

There came a faint thumping from the rocks, a sound no louder than mice jumping in the sand.

Again, the bird chirruped.

A stir passed through the troop's ranks. And again, the mouse-thumping pecked its way across the sand.

Once more, the bird chirruped.

The troop resumed its climb up into a crack in the rocks, but there was a stillness of breath about the Fremen now that filled Paul with caution, and he noted covert glances toward Chani, the way she seemed to withdraw, pulling in upon herself.

There was rock underfoot now, a faint gray swishing of robes around them, and Paul sensed a relaxing of discipline, but still that quiet-of-the-person about Chani and the others. He followed a shadow shape—up steps, a turn, more steps, into a tunnel, past two moisture-sealed doors and into a globelighted narrow passage with yellow rock walls and ceiling.

All around him, Paul saw the Fremen throwing back their hoods, removing nose plugs, breathing deeply. Someone sighed. Paul looked for Chani, found that she had left his side. He was hemmed in by a press of robed bodies. Someone jostled him, said, "Excuse me, Usul. What a crush! It's always this way."

On his left, the narrow bearded face of the one called Farok turned toward Paul. The stained eyepits and blue darkness of eyes appeared even darker under the yellow globes. "Throw off your hood, Usul," Farok said. "You're home." And he helped Paul, releasing the hood catch, elbowing a space around them.

Paul slipped out his nose plugs, swung the mouth baffle aside. The odor of the place assailed him: unwashed bodies, distillate esthers of reclaimed wastes, everywhere the sour effluvia of humanity with, over it all, a turbulence of spice and spicelike harmonics.

"Why are we waiting, Farok?" Paul asked.

"For the Reverend Mother, I think. You heard the message—poor Chani."

Poor Chani? Paul asked himself. He looked around, wondering where she was, where his mother had got to in all this crush.

Farok took a deep breath. "The smells of home," he said.

Paul saw that the man was enjoying the stink of this air, that there was no irony in his tone. He heard his mother cough then, and her voice came back to him through the press of the troop: "How rich the odors of your sietch, Stilgar. I see you do much working with the spice . . . you make paper . . . plastics . . . and isn't that chemical explosives?"

"You know this from what you smell?" It was another man's voice.

And Paul realized she was speaking for his benefit that she wanted him to make a quick acceptance of this assault on his nostrils.

There came a buzz of activity at the head of the troop and a prolonged indrawn breath that seemed to pass through the Fremen, and Paul heard hushed voices back down the line: "It's true then—Liet is dead."

Liet, Paul thought. Then: *Chani, daughter of Liet.* The pieces fell together in his mind. Liet was the Fremen name of the planetologist.

Paul looked at Farok, asked: "Is it the Liet known as Kynes?"

"There is only one Liet," Farok said.

Paul turned, stared at the robed back of a Fremen in front of him. *Then Liet-Kynes is dead,* he thought.

"It was Harkonnen treachery," someone hissed. "They made it seem an accident . . . lost in the desert . . . a 'thopter crash. . . ."

Paul felt a burst of anger. The man who had befriended them, helped save them from the Harkonnen hunters, the man who had sent his Fremen cohorts searching for two strays in the desert . . . another victim of the Harkonnens.

"Does Usul hunger yet for revenge?" Farok asked.

Before Paul could answer, there came a low call and the troop swept forward into a wider chamber, carrying Paul with them. He found himself in an open space confronted by Stilgar and a strange woman wearing a flowing wraparound garment of brilliant orange and green. Her arms were bare to the shoulders, and he could see she wore no stillsuit. Her skin was a pale olive. Dark hair swept back from her high forehead, throwing emphasis on sharp cheekbones and aquiline nose between the dense darkness of her eyes.

She turned toward him, and Paul saw golden rings threaded with water tallies dangling from her ears.

"*This* bested my Jamis?" she demanded.

"Be silent, Harah," Stilgar said. "It was Jamis' doing—*he* invoked the tahaddi al-burhan."

"He's not but a boy!" she said. She gave her head a sharp shake from side to side, setting the water tallies to jingling. "My children made fatherless by another child? Surely, 'twas an accident!"

"Usul, how many years have you?" Stilgar asked.

"Fifteen Standard," Paul said.

Stilgar swept his eyes over the troop. "Is there one among you cares to challenge me?"

Silence.

Stilgar looked at the woman. "Until I've learned his weirding ways, I'd not challenge him."

She returned his stare. "But—"

"You saw the stranger woman who went with Chani to the Reverend Mother?" Stilgar asked. "She's an out-freyn Sayyadina, mother to this lad. The mother and son are masters of the weirding ways of battle."

"Lisan al-Gaib," the woman whispered. Her eyes held awe as she turned them back toward Paul.

The legend again, Paul thought.

"Perhaps," Stilgar said. "It hasn't been tested, though." He returned his attention to Paul. "Usul, it's our way that you've now the responsibility for Jamis' woman here and for his two sons. His yali . . . his quarters, are yours. His coffee service is yours . . . and this, his woman."

Paul studied the woman, wondering: *Why isn't she mourning her man? Why does she show no hate for me?* Abruptly, he saw that the Fremen were staring at him, waiting.

Someone whispered: "There's work to do. Say how you accept her."

Stilgar said: "Do you accept Harah as woman or servant?"

Harah lifted her arms, turning slowly on one heel. "I am still young, Usul. It's said I still look as young as when I was with Geoff . . . before Jamis bested him."

Jamis killed another to win her, Paul thought.

Paul said: "If I accept her as servant, may I yet change my mind at a later time?"

"You'd have a year to change your decision," Stilgar said. "After that, she's a free woman to choose as she wishes . . . or you could free her to choose for herself at any time. But she's your responsibility, no matter what, for one year . . . and you'll always share some responsibility for the sons of Jamis."

"I accept her as servant," Paul said.

Harah stamped a foot, shook her shoulders with anger. "But I'm young!"

Stilgar looked at Paul, said: "Caution's a worthy trait in a man who'd lead."

"But I'm young!" Harah repeated.

"Be silent," Stilgar commanded. "If a thing has merit, it'll be. Show Usul to his quarters and see he has fresh clothing and a place to rest."

"Oh-h-h-h!" she said.

Paul had registered enough of her to have a first approximation. He felt the impatience of the troop, knew many things were being delayed here. He wondered if he dared ask the whereabouts of his mother and Chani, saw from Stilgar's nervous stance that it would be a mistake.

He faced Harah, pitched his voice with tone and tremolo to accent her fear and awe, said: "Show me my quarters, Harah! We will discuss your youth another time."

She backed away two steps, cast a frightened glance at Stilgar. "He has the weirding voice," she husked.

"Stilgar," Paul said. "Chani's father put heavy obligation on me. If there's anything. . . ."

"It'll be decided in council," Stilgar said. "You can speak then." He nodded in dismissal, turned away with the rest of the troop following him.

Paul took Harah's arm, noting how cool her flesh seemed, feeling her tremble. "I'll not harm you, Harah," he said. "Show me our quarters." And he smoothed his voice with relaxants.

"You'll not cast me out when the year's gone?" she said. "I know for true I'm not as young as once I was."

"As long as I live you'll have a place with me," he said. He released her arm. "Come now, where are our quarters?"

She turned, led the way down the passage, turning right into a wide cross tunnel lighted by evenly spaced yellow overhead globes. The stone floor was smooth, swept clean of sand.

Paul moved up beside her, studied the aquiline profile as they walked. "You do not hate me, Harah?"

"Why should I hate you?"

She nodded to a cluster of children who stared at them from the raised ledge of a side passage. Paul glimpsed adult shapes behind the children partly hidden by filmy hangings.

"I . . . bested Jamis."

"Stilgar said the ceremony was held and you're a friend of Jamis." She glanced sidelong at him. "Stilgar said you gave moisture to the dead. Is that truth?"

"Yes."

"It's more than I'll do . . . can do."

"Don't you mourn him?"

"In the time of mourning, I'll mourn him."

They passed an arched opening. Paul looked through it at men and women working with stand-mounted machinery in a large, bright chamber. There seemed an extra tempo of urgency to them.

"What're they doing in there?" Paul asked.

She glanced back as they passed beyond the arch, said: "They hurry to finish the quota in the plastics shop before we flee. We need many dew collectors for the planting."

"Flee?"

"Until the butchers stop hunting us or are driven from our land."

Paul caught himself in a stumble, sensing an arrested instant of time, remembering a fragment, a visual projection of prescience—but it was displaced, like a montage in motion. The bits of his prescient memory were not quite as he remembered them.

"The Sardaukar hunt us," he said.

"They'll not find much excepting an empty sietch or two," she said. "And they'll find their share of death in the sand."

"They'll find this place?" he asked.

"Likely."

"Yet we take the time to. . . ." He motioned with his head toward the arch now far behind them. ". . . make . . . dew collectors?"

"The planting goes on."

"What're dew collectors?" he asked.

The glance she turned on him was full of surprise. "Don't they teach you anything in the . . . wherever it is you come from?"

"Not about dew collectors."

"Hai!" she said, and there was a whole conversation in the one word.

"Well, what are they?"

"Each bush, each weed you see out there in the erg," she said, "how do you suppose it lives when we leave it? Each is planted most tenderly in its own little pit. The pits are filled with smooth ovals of chromoplastic. Light turns them white. You can see them glistening in the dawn if you look down from a high place. White reflects. But when Old Father Sun departs, the chromoplastic reverts to transparency in the dark. It cools with extreme rapidity. The surface condenses moisture out of the air. That moisture trickles down to keep our plants alive."

"Dew collectors," he muttered, enchanted by the simple beauty of such a scheme.

"I'll mourn Jamis in the proper time for it," she said, as though her mind had not left his other question. "He was a good man, Jamis, but quick to anger. A good provider, Jamis, and a wonder with the children. He made no separation between Geoff's boy, my firstborn, and his own true son. They were equal in his eyes." She turned a questing stare on Paul. "Would it be that way with you, Usul?"

"We don't have that problem."

"But if—"

"Harah!"

She recoiled at the harsh edge in his voice.

They passed another brightly lighted room visible through an arch on their left. "What's made there?" he asked.

"They repair the weaving machinery," she said. "But it must be dismantled by tonight." She gestured at a tunnel branching to their left. "Through there and beyond, that's food processing and stillsuit maintenance." She looked at Paul. "Your suit looks new. But if it needs work, I'm good with suits. I work in the factory in season."

They began coming on knots of people now and thicker clusterings of openings in the tunnel's sides. A file of men and women passed them carrying packs that gurgled heavily, the smell of spice strong about them.

"They'll not get our water," Harah said. "Or our spice. You can be sure of that."

Paul glanced at the openings in the tunnel walls, seeing the heavy carpets on the raised ledge, glimpses of rooms with bright fabrics on the walls, piled cushions. People in the openings fell silent at their approach, followed Paul with untamed stares.

"The people find it strange you bested Jamis," Harah said. "Likely you'll have some proving to do when we're settled in a new sietch."

"I don't like killing," he said.

"Thus Stilgar tells it," she said, but her voice betrayed her disbelief.

A shrill chanting grew louder ahead of them. They came to another side opening wider than any of the others Paul had seen. He slowed his pace, staring in at a room crowded with children sitting cross-legged on a maroon-carpeted floor.

At a chalkboard against the far wall stood a woman in a yellow wraparound, a projecto-stylus in one hand. The board was filled with designs—circles, wedges and curves, snake tracks and squares, flowing arcs split by parallel lines. The woman pointed to the designs one after the other as fast as she could move the stylus, and the children chanted in rhythm with her moving hand.

Paul listened, hearing the voices grow dimmer behind as he moved deeper into the sietch with Harah.

"Tree," the children chanted. "Tree, grass, dune, wind, mountain, hill, fire, lightning, rock, rocks, dust, sand, heat, shelter, heat, full, winter, cold, empty, erosion, summer, cavern, day, tension, moon, night, caprock, sandtide, slope, planting, binder. . . ."

"You conduct classes at a time like this?" Paul asked.

Her face went somber and grief edged her voice: "What Liet taught us, we cannot pause an instant in that. Liet who is dead must not be forgotten. It's the Chakobsa way."

She crossed the tunnel to the left, stepped up onto a ledge, parted gauzy orange hangings and stood aside: "Your yali is ready for you, Usul."

Paul hesitated before joining her on the ledge. He felt a sudden reluctance to be alone with this woman. It came to him that he was surrounded by a way of life that could only be understood by postulating an ecology of ideas and values. He felt that this Fremen world was fishing for him, trying to snare him in its ways. And he knew what lay in that snare—the wild jihad, the religious war he felt he should avoid at any cost.

"This is your yali," Harah said. "Why do you hesitate?"

Paul nodded, joined her on the ledge. He lifted the hangings across from her, feeling metal fibers in the fabric, followed her into a short entrance way and then into a larger room, square, about six meters to a side—thick blue carpets on the floor, blue and green fabrics hiding the rock walls, glowglobes tuned to yellow overhead bobbing against draped yellow ceiling fabrics.

The effect was that of an ancient tent.

Harah stood in front of him, left hand on hip, her eyes studying his face. "The children are with a friend," she said. "They will present themselves later."

Paul masked his unease beneath a quick scanning of the room. Thin hangings to the right, he saw, partly concealed a larger room with cushions piled around the walls. He felt a soft breeze from an air duct, saw the outlet cunningly hidden in a pattern of hangings directly ahead of him.

"Do you wish me to help you remove your stillsuit?" Harah asked.

"No . . . thank you."

"Shall I bring food?"

"Yes."

"There is a reclamation chamber off the other room." She gestured. "For your comfort and convenience when you're out of your stillsuit."

"You said we have to leave this sietch," Paul said. "Shouldn't we be packing or something?"

"It will be done in its time," she said. "The butchers have yet to penetrate to our region."

Still she hesitated, staring at him.

"What is it?" he demanded.

"You've not the eyes of the Ibad," she said. "It's strange but not entirely unattractive."

"Get the food," he said. "I'm hungry."

She smiled at him—a knowing, woman's smile that he found disquieting. "I am your servant," she said, and whirled away in one lithe motion, ducking behind a heavy wall hanging that revealed another passage before falling back into place.

Feeling angry with himself, Paul brushed through the thin hanging on the right and into the larger room. He stood there a moment caught by uncertainty. And he wondered where Chani was . . . Chani who had just lost her father.

We're alike in that, he thought.

A wailing cry sounded from the outer corridors, its volume muffled by the intervening hangings. It was repeated, a bit more distant. And again. Paul realized someone was calling the time. He focused on the fact that he had seen no clocks.

The faint smell of burning creosote bush came to his nostrils, riding on the omnipresent stink of the sietch. Paul saw that he had already suppressed the odorous assault on his senses.

And he wondered again about his mother, how the moving montage of the future would incorporate her . . . and the daughter she bore. Mutable time-awareness danced around him. He shook his head sharply, focusing his attention on the evidences that spoke of profound depth and breadth in this Fremen culture that had swallowed them.

With its subtle oddities.

He had seen a thing about the caverns and this room, a thing that suggested far greater differences than anything he had yet encountered.

There was no sign of a poison snooper here, no indication of their use anywhere in the cave warren. Yet he could smell poisons in the sietch stench—strong ones, common ones.

He heard a rustle of hangings, thought it was Harah returning with food, and turned to watch her. Instead, from beneath a displaced pattern of hangings, he saw two young boys—perhaps aged nine and ten—staring out at him with greedy eyes. Each wore a small kindjal-type of crysknife, rested a hand on the hilt.

And Paul recalled the stories of the Fremen—that their children fought as ferociously as the adults.

The hands move, the lips move—
Ideas gush from his words,
And his eyes devour!
He is an island of Selfdom.

—DESCRIPTION FROM "A MANUAL OF MUAD'DIB"
BY THE PRINCESS IRULAN

Phosphor tubes in the faraway upper reaches of the cavern cast a dim light onto the thronged interior, hinting at the great size of this rock-enclosed space . . . larger, Jessica saw, than even the Gathering Hall of her Bene Gesserit school. She estimated there were more than five thousand people gathered out there beneath the ledge where she stood with Stilgar.

And more were coming.

The air was murmurous with people.

"Your son has been summoned from his rest, Sayyadina," Stilgar said. "Do you wish him to share in your decision?"

"Could he change my decision?"

"Certainly, the air with which you speak comes from your own lungs, but—"

"The decision stands," she said.

But she felt misgivings, wondering if she should use Paul as an excuse for backing out of a dangerous course. There was an unborn daughter to think of as well. What endangered the flesh of the mother endangered the flesh of the daughter.

Men came with rolled carpets, grunting under the weight of them, stirring up dust as the loads were dropped onto the ledge.

Stilgar took her arm, led her back into the acoustical horn that formed the rear limits of the ledge. He indicated a rock bench within the horn. "The Reverend Mother will sit here, but you may rest yourself until she comes."

"I prefer to stand," Jessica said.

She watched the men unroll the carpets, covering the ledge, looked out at the crowd. There were at least ten thousand people on the rock floor now.

And still they came.

Out on the desert, she knew, it already was red nightfall, but here in the cavern hall was perpetual twilight, a gray vastness thronged with people come to see her risk her life.

A way was opened through the crowd to her right, and she saw Paul approaching flanked by two small boys. There was a swaggering air of self-importance about the children. They kept hands on knives, scowled at the wall of people on either side.

"The sons of Jamis who are now the sons of Usul," Stilgar said. "They take their escort duties seriously." He ventured a smile at Jessica.

Jessica recognized the effort to lighten her mood and was grateful for it, but could not take her mind from the danger that confronted her.

I had no choice but to do this, she thought. *We must move swiftly if we're to secure our place among these Fremen.*

Paul climbed to the ledge, leaving the children below. He stopped in front of his mother, glanced at Stilgar, back to Jessica. "What is happening? I thought I was being summoned to council."

Stilgar raised a hand for silence, gestured to his left where another way had been opened in the throng. Chani came down the lane opened there, her elfin face set in lines of grief. She had removed her stillsuit and wore a graceful blue wraparound that exposed her thin arms. Near the shoulder on her left arm, a green kerchief had been tied.

Green for mourning, Paul thought.

It was one of the customs the two sons of Jamis had explained to him by indirection, telling him they wore no green because they accepted him as guardian-father.

"Are you the Lisan al-Gaib?" they had asked. And Paul had sensed the jihad in their words, shrugged off the question with one of his own—learning then that Kaleff, the elder of the two, was ten, and the natural son of Geoff. Orlop, the younger, was eight, the natural son of Jamis.

It had been a strange day with these two standing guard over him because he asked it, keeping away the curious, allowing him the time to nurse his thoughts and prescient memories, to plan a way to prevent the jihad.

Now, standing beside his mother on the cavern ledge and looking out at the throng, he wondered if any plan could prevent the wild outpouring of fanatic legions.

Chani, nearing the ledge, was followed at a distance by four women carrying another woman in a litter.

Jessica ignored Chani's approach, focusing all her attention on the woman in the litter—a crone, a wrinkled and shriveled ancient thing in a black gown with hood thrown back to reveal the tight knot of gray hair and the stringy neck.

The litter-carriers deposited their burden gently on the ledge from below, and Chani helped the old woman to her feet.

So this is their Reverend Mother, Jessica thought.

The old woman leaned heavily on Chani as she hobbled toward Jessica, looking like a collection of sticks draped in the black robe. She stopped in front of Jessica, peered upward for a long moment before speaking in a husky whisper.

"So you're the one." The old head nodded once precariously on the thin neck. "The Shadout Mapes was right to pity you."

Jessica spoke quickly, scornfully: "I need no one's pity."

"That remains to be seen," husked the old woman. She turned with surprising quickness and faced the throng. "Tell them, Stilgar."

"Must I?" he asked.

"We are the people of Misr," the old woman rasped. "Since our

Sunni ancestors fled from Nilotic al-Ourouba, we have known flight and death. The young go on that our people shall not die."

Stilgar took a deep breath, stepped forward two paces.

Jessica felt the hush come over the crowded cavern—some twenty thousand people now, standing silently, almost without movement. It made her feel suddenly small and filled with caution.

"Tonight we must leave this sietch that has sheltered us for so long and go south into the desert," Stilgar said. His voice boomed out across the uplifted faces, reverberating with the force given it by the acoustical horn behind the ledge.

Still the throng remained silent.

"The Reverend Mother tells me she cannot survive another hajra," Stilgar said. "We have lived before without a Reverend Mother, but it is not good for people to seek a new home in such straits."

Now, the throng stirred, rippling with whispers and currents of disquiet.

"That this may not come to pass," Stilgar said, "our new Sayyadina Jessica of the Weirding, has consented to enter the rite at this time. She will attempt to pass within that we not lose the strength of our Reverend Mother."

Jessica of the Weirding, Jessica thought. She saw Paul staring at her, his eyes filled with questions, but his mouth held silent by all the strangeness around them.

If I die in the attempt, what will become of him? Jessica asked herself. Again she felt the misgivings fill her mind.

Chani led the old Reverend Mother to a rock bench deep in the acoustical horn, returned to stand beside Stilgar.

"That we may not lose all if Jessica of the Weirding should fail," Stilgar said, "Chani, daughter of Liet, will be consecrated in the Sayyadina at this time." He stepped one pace to the side.

From deep in the acoustical horn, the old woman's voice came out to them, an amplified whisper, harsh and penetrating: "Chani has returned from her hajra—Chani has seen the waters."

A sussurant response arose from the crowd: "She has seen the waters."

"I consecrate the daughter of Liet in the Sayyadina," husked the old woman.

"She is accepted," the crowd responded.

Paul barely heard the ceremony, his attention still centered on what had been said of his mother.

If she should fail?

He turned and looked back at the one they called Reverend Mother, studying the dried crone features, the fathomless blue fixation of her eyes. She looked as though a breeze would blow her away, yet there was that about her which suggested she might stand untouched in the path of a coriolis storm. She carried the same aura of power that he remembered from the Reverend Mother Gaius Helen Mohiam who had tested him with agony in the way of the gom jabbar.

"I, the Reverend Mother Ramallo, whose voice speaks as a multitude, say this to you," the old woman said. "It is fitting that Chani enter the Sayyadina."

"It is fitting," the crowd responded.

The old woman nodded, whispered: "I give her the silver skies, the golden desert and its shining rocks, the green fields that will be. I give these to Sayyadina Chani. And lest she forget that she's servant of us all, to her fall the menial tasks in this Ceremony of the Seed. Let it be as Shai-hulud will have it." She lifted a brown-stick arm, dropped it.

Jessica, feeling the ceremony close around her with a current that swept her beyond all turning back, glanced once at Paul's question-filled face, then prepared herself for the ordeal.

"Let the watermasters come forward," Chani said with only the slightest quaver of uncertainty in her girl-child voice.

Now, Jessica felt herself at the focus of danger, knowing its presence in the watchfulness of the throng, in the silence.

A band of men made its way through a serpentine path opened in the crowd, moving up from the back in pairs. Each pair carried a small skin sack, perhaps twice the size of a human head. The sacks sloshed heavily.

The two leaders deposited their load at Chani's feet on the ledge and stepped back.

Jessica looked at the sack, then at the men. They had their hoods thrown back, exposing long hair tied in a roll at the base of the neck. The black pits of their eyes stared back at her without wavering.

A furry redolence of cinnamon arose from the sack, wafted across Jessica. *The spice?* she wondered.

"Is there water?" Chani asked.

The watermaster on the left, a man with a purple scar line across the bridge of his nose, nodded once. "There is water, Sayyadina," he said, "but we cannot drink of it."

"Is there seed?" Chani asked.

"There is seed," the man said.

Chani knelt and put her hands to the sloshing sack. "Blessed is the water and its seed."

There was familiarity to the rite, and Jessica looked back at the Reverend Mother Ramallo. The old woman's eyes were closed and she sat hunched over as though asleep.

"Sayyadina Jessica," Chani said.

Jessica turned to see the girl staring up at her.

"Have you tasted the blessed water?" Chani asked.

Before Jessica could answer, Chani said: "It is not possible that you have tasted the blessed water. You are outworlder and unprivileged."

A sigh passed through the crowd, a sussuration of robes that made the nape hairs creep on Jessica's neck.

"The crop was large and the maker has been destroyed," Chani said. She began unfastening a coiled spout fixed to the top of the sloshing sack.

Now, Jessica felt the sense of danger boiling around her. She glanced at Paul, saw that he was caught up in the mystery of the ritual and had eyes only for Chani.

Has he seen this moment in time? Jessica wondered. She rested a hand on her abdomen, thinking of the unborn daughter there, asking herself: *Do I have the right to risk us both?*

Chani lifted the spout toward Jessica, said: "Here is the Water of Life, the water that is greater than water—Kan, the water that frees the soul. If you be a Reverend Mother, it opens the universe to you. Let Shai-hulud judge now."

Jessica felt herself torn between duty to her unborn child and duty to Paul. For Paul, she knew, she should take that spout and drink of the sack's contents, but as she bent to the proffered spout, her senses told her its peril.

The stuff in the sack had a bitter smell subtly akin to many poisons that she knew, but unlike them, too.

"You must drink it now," Chani said.

There's no turning back, Jessica reminded herself. But nothing in all her Bene Gesserit training came into her mind to help her through this instant.

What is it? Jessica asked herself. *Liquor? A drug?*

She bent over the spout, smelled the esthers of cinnamon, remembering then the drunkenness of Duncan Idaho. *Spice liquor?* she asked herself. She took the siphon tube in her mouth, pulled up only the most minuscule sip. It tasted of the spice, a faint bite acrid on the tongue.

Chani pressed down on the skin bag. A great gulp of the stuff surged into Jessica's mouth and before she could help herself, she swallowed it, fighting to retain her calmness and dignity.

"To accept a little death is worse than death itself," Chani said. She stared at Jessica, waiting.

And Jessica stared back, still holding the spout in her mouth. She tasted the sack's contents in her nostrils, in the roof of her mouth, in her cheeks, in her eyes—a biting sweetness, now.

Cool.

Again, Chani sent the liquid gushing into Jessica's mouth.

Delicate.

Jessica studied Chani's face—elfin features—seeing the traces of Liet-Kynes there as yet unfixed by time.

This is a drug they feed me, Jessica told herself.

But it was unlike any other drug of her experience, and Bene Gesserit training included the taste of many drugs.

Chani's features were so clear, as though outlined in light.

A drug.

Whirling silence settled around Jessica. Every fiber of her body accepted the fact that something profound had happened to it. She felt that she was a conscious mote, smaller than any subatomic particle, yet capable of motion and of sensing her surroundings. Like an abrupt revelation—the curtains whipped away—she realized she had become aware of a psychokinesthetic extension of herself. She was the mote, yet not the mote.

The cavern remained around her—the people. She sensed them: Paul, Chani, Stilgar, the Reverend Mother Ramallo.

Reverend Mother!

At the school there had been rumors that some did not survive the Reverend Mother ordeal, that the drug took them.

Jessica focused her attention on the Reverend Mother Ramallo, aware now that all this was happening in a frozen instant of time—suspended time for her alone.

Why is time suspended? she asked herself. She stared at the frozen expressions around her, seeing a dust mote above Chani's head, stopped there.

Waiting.

The answer to this instant came like an explosion in her consciousness: her personal time was suspended to save her life.

She focused on the psychokinesthetic extension of herself, looking within, and was confronted immediately with a cellular core, a pit of blackness from which she recoiled.

That is the place where we cannot look, she thought. *There is the place the Reverend Mothers are so reluctant to mention—the place where only a Kwisatz Haderach may look.*

This realization returned a small measure of confidence, and again she ventured to focus on the psychokinesthetic extension, becoming a mote-self that searched within her for danger.

She found it within the drug she had swallowed.

The stuff was dancing particles within her, its motions so rapid that even frozen time could not stop them. Dancing particles. She began recognizing familiar structures, atomic linkages: a carbon atom here, helical wavering . . . a glucose molecule. An entire chain of molecules confronted her, and she recognized a protein . . . a methyl-protein configuration.

Ah-h-h!

It was a soundless mental sigh within her as she saw the nature of the poison.

With her psychokinesthetic probing, she moved into it, shifted an oxygen mote, allowed another carbon mote to link, reattached a linkage of oxygen . . . hydrogen.

The change spread . . . faster and faster as the catalyzed reaction opened its surface of contact.

The suspension of time relaxed its hold upon her, and she sensed motion. The tube spout from the sack was touched to her mouth—gently, collecting a drop of moisture.

Chani's taking the catalyst from my body to change the poison in that sack, Jessica thought. *Why?*

Someone eased her to a sitting position. She saw the old Reverend Mother Ramallo being brought to sit beside her on the carpeted ledge. A dry hand touched her neck.

And there was another psychokinesthetic mote within her awareness! Jessica tried to reject it, but the mote swept closer . . . closer.

They touched!

It was like an ultimate *simpatico,* being two people at once: not telepathy, but mutual awareness.

With the old Reverend Mother!

But Jessica saw that the Reverend Mother didn't think of herself as old. An image unfolded before the mutual mind's eye: a young girl with a dancing spirit and tender humor.

Within the mutual awareness, the young girl said, "Yes, that is how I am."

Jessica could only accept the words, not respond to them.

"You'll have it all soon, Jessica," the inward image said.

This is hallucination, Jessica told herself.

"You know better than that," the inward image said. "Swiftly now, do not fight me. There isn't much time. We. . . ." There came a long pause, then: "You should've told us you were pregnant!"

Jessica found the voice that talked within the mutual awareness. "Why?"

"This changes both of you! Holy Mother, what have we done?"

Jessica sensed a forced shift in the mutual awareness, saw another mote-presence with the inward eye. The other mote darted wildly here, there, circling. It radiated pure terror.

"You'll have to be strong," the old Reverend Mother's image-presence said. "Be thankful it's a daughter you carry. This would've killed a male fetus. Now . . . carefully, gently . . . touch your daughter-presence. Be your daughter-presence. Absorb the fear . . . soothe . . . use your courage and your strength . . . gently now . . . gently. . . ."

The other whirling mote swept near, and Jessica compelled herself to touch it.

Terror threatened to overwhelm her.

She fought it the only way she knew: *"I shall not fear. Fear is the mind-killer. . . ."*

The litany brought a semblance of calm. The other mote lay quiescent against her.

Words won't work, Jessica told herself.

She reduced herself to basic emotional reactions, radiated love, comfort, a warm snuggling of protection.

The terror receded.

Again, the presence of the old Reverend Mother asserted itself, but now there was a tripling of mutual awareness—two active and one that lay quietly absorbing.

"Time compels me," the Reverend Mother said within the awareness. "I have much to give you. And I do not know if your daughter can accept all this while remaining sane. But it must be: the needs of the tribe are paramount."

"What—"

"Remain silent and accept!"

Experiences began to unroll before Jessica. It was like a lecture strip in a subliminal training projector at the Bene Gesserit school . . . but faster . . . blindingly faster.

Yet . . . distinct.

She knew each experience as it happened: there was a lover—virile, bearded, with the Fremen eyes, and Jessica saw his strength and tenderness, all of him in one blink-moment, through the Reverend Mother's memory.

There was no time now to think of what this might be doing to the daughter fetus, only time to accept and record. The experiences poured in on Jessica—birth, life, death—important matters and unimportant, an outpouring of single-view time.

Why should a fall of sand from a clifftop stick in the memory? she asked herself.

Too late, Jessica saw what was happening: the old woman was dying and, in dying, pouring her experiences into Jessica's awareness as water is poured into a cup. The other mote faded back into pre-birth awareness as Jessica watched it. And, dying-in-conception, the old Reverend Mother left her life in Jessica's memory with one last sighing blur of words.

"I've been a long time waiting for you," she said. "Here is my life."

There it was, encapsuled, all of it.

Even the moment of death.

I am now a Reverend Mother, Jessica realized.

And she knew with a generalized awareness that she had become, in truth, precisely what was meant by a Bene Gesserit Reverend Mother. The poison drug had transformed her.

This wasn't exactly how they did it at the Bene Gesserit school, she knew. No one had ever introduced her to the mysteries of it, but she knew.

The end result was the same.

Jessica sensed the daughter-mote still touching her inner awareness, probed it without response.

A terrible sense of loneliness crept through Jessica in the realization of what had happened to her. She saw her own life as a pattern that had slowed and all life around her speeded up so that the dancing interplay became clearer.

The sensation of mote-awareness faded slightly, its intensity easing as her body relaxed from the threat of the poison, but still she felt that *other* mote, touching it with a sense of guilt at what she had allowed to happen to it.

I did it, my poor, unformed, dear little daughter, I brought you into this universe and exposed your awareness to all its varieties without any defenses.

A tiny outflowing of love-comfort, like a reflection of what she had poured into it, came from the other mote.

Before Jessica could respond, she felt the adab presence of demanding memory. There was something that needed doing. She groped for it, realizing she was being impeded by a muzziness of the changed drug permeating her senses.

I could change that, she thought. *I could take away the drug action and make it harmless.* But she sensed this would be an error. *I'm within a rite of joining.*

Then she knew what she had to do.

Jessica opened her eyes, gestured to the watersack now being held above her by Chani.

"It has been blessed," Jessica said. "Mingle the waters, let the change come to all, that the people may partake and share in the blessing."

Let the catalyst do its work, she thought. *Let the people drink of it and have their awareness of each other heightened for a while. The drug is safe now . . . now that a Reverend Mother has changed it.*

Still, the demanding memory worked on her, thrusting. There was another thing she had to do, she realized, but the drug made it difficult to focus.

Ah-h-h-h-h . . . the old Reverend Mother.

"I have met the Reverend Mother Ramallo," Jessica said. "She is gone, but she remains. Let her memory be honored in the rite."

Now, where did I get those words? Jessica wondered.

And she realized they came from another memory, the *life* that had been given to her and now was part of herself. Something about that gift felt incomplete, though.

"Let them have their orgy," the other-memory said within her. "They've little enough pleasure out of living. Yes, and you and I need this little time to become acquainted before I recede and pour out through your memories. Already, I feel myself being tied to bits of you. Ah-h-h, you've a mind filled with interesting things. So many things I'd never imagined."

And the memory-mind encapsulated within her opened itself to Jessica, permitting a view down a wide corridor to other Reverend Mothers until there seemed no end to them.

Jessica recoiled, fearing she would become lost in an ocean of oneness. Still, the corridor remained, revealing to Jessica that the Fremen culture was far older than she had suspected.

There had been Fremen on Poritrin, she saw, a people grown soft with an easy planet, fair game for Imperial raiders to harvest and plant human colonies on Bela Tegeuse and Salusa Secundus.

Oh, the wailing Jessica sensed in *that* parting.

Far down the corridor, an image-voice screamed: "They denied us the Hajj!"

Jessica saw the slave cribs on Bela Tegeuse down that inner corridor, saw the weeding out and the selecting that spread men to Rossak and Harmonthep. Scenes of brutal ferocity opened to her like the petals of a terrible flower. And she saw the thread of the past carried by Sayyadina after Sayyadina—first by word of mouth, hidden in the sand chanteys, then refined through their own Reverend Mothers with the discovery of the poison drug on Rossak . . . and now developed to subtle strength on Arrakis in the discovery of the Water of Life.

Far down the inner corridor, another voice screamed: "Never to forgive! Never to forget!"

But Jessica's attention was focused on the revelation of the Water of Life, seeing its source: the liquid exhalation of a dying sandworm, a maker. And as she saw the killing of it in her new memory, she suppressed a gasp.

The creature was drowned!

"Mother, are you all right?"

Paul's voice intruded on her, and Jessica struggled out of the inner awareness to stare up at him, conscious of duty to him, but resenting his presence.

I'm like a person whose hands were kept numb, without sensation from the first moment of awareness—until one day the ability to feel is forced into them.

The thought hung in her mind, an enclosing awareness.

And I say: "Look! I have no hands!" But the people all around me say: "What are hands?"

"Are you all right?" Paul repeated.

"Yes."

"Is this all right for me to drink?" He gestured to the sack in Chani's hands. "They want me to drink it."

She heard the hidden meaning in his words, realized he had detected the poison in the original, unchanged substance, that he was concerned for her. It occurred to Jessica then to wonder about the limits of Paul's prescience. His question revealed much to her.

"You may drink it," she said. "It has been changed." And she looked beyond him to see Stilgar staring down at her, the dark-dark eyes studying.

"Now, we know you cannot be false," he said.

She sensed hidden meaning here, too, but the muzziness of the drug was overpowering her senses. How warm it was and soothing. How beneficent these Fremen to bring her into the fold of such companionship.

Paul saw the drug take hold of his mother.

He searched his memory—the fixed past, the flux-lines of the possible futures. It was like scanning through arrested instants of time, disconcerting to the lens of the inner eye. The fragments were difficult to understand when snatched out of the flux.

This drug—he could assemble knowledge about it, understand what it was doing to his mother, but the knowledge lacked a natural rhythm, lacked a system of mutual reflection.

He realized suddenly that it was one thing to see the past occupying the present, but the true test of prescience was to see the past in the future.

Things persisted in not being what they seemed.

"Drink it," Chani said. She waved the hornspout of a watersack under his nose.

Paul straightened, staring at Chani. He felt carnival excitement in the air. He knew what would happen if he drank this spice drug with its quintessence of the substance that brought the change onto him. He would return to the vision of pure time, of time-become-space. It would perch him on the dizzying summit and defy him to understand.

From behind Chani, Stilgar said: "Drink it, lad. You delay the rite."

Paul listened to the crowd then, hearing the wildness in their voices—"Lisan al-Gaib," they said. "Muad'Dib!" He looked down at his mother. She appeared peacefully asleep in a sitting position—her breathing even and deep. A phrase out of the future that was his lonely past came into his mind: *She sleeps in the Waters of Life.*

Chani tugged at his sleeve.

Paul took the hornspout into his mouth, hearing the people shout. He felt the liquid gush into his throat as Chani pressed the sack, sensed giddiness in the fumes. Chani removed the spout, handed the sack into hands that reached for it from the floor of the cavern. His eyes focused on her arm, the green band of mourning there.

As she straightened, Chani saw the direction of his gaze, said: "I can mourn him even in the happiness of the waters. This was something he gave us." She put her hand into his, pulling him along the ledge. "We are alike in a thing, Usul: We have each lost a father to the Harkonnens."

Paul followed her. He felt that his head had been separated from his

body and restored with odd connections. His legs were remote and rub-
bery.

They entered a narrow side passage, its walls dimly lighted by
spaced-out glowglobes. Paul felt the drug beginning to have its unique
effect on him, opening time like a flower. He found need to steady himself against Chani as they turned through another shadowed tunnel.
The mixture of whipcord and softness he felt beneath her robe stirred
his blood. The sensation mingled with the work of the drug, folding
future and past into the present, leaving him the thinnest margin of
trinocular focus.

"I know you, Chani," he whispered. "We've sat upon a ledge above
the sand while I soothed your fears. We've caressed in the dark of the
sietch. We've. . . ." He found himself losing focus, tried to shake his
head, stumbled.

Chani steadied him, led him through thick hangings into the yellow
warmth of a private apartment—low tables, cushions, a sleeping pad
beneath an orange spread.

Paul grew aware that they had stopped, that Chani stood facing
him, and that her eyes betrayed a look of quiet terror.

"You must tell me," she whispered.

"You are Sihaya," he said, "the desert spring."

"When the tribe shares the Water," she said, "we're together—all of
us. We . . . share. I can . . . sense the others with me, but I'm afraid to
share with you."

"Why?"

He tried to focus on her, but past and future were merging into the
present, blurring her image. He saw her in countless ways and positions
and settings.

"There's something frightening in you," she said. "When I took you
away from the others . . . I did it because I could feel what the others
wanted. You . . . press on people. You . . . make us *see* things!"

He forced himself to speak distinctly: "What do you see?"

She looked down at her hands. "I see a child . . . in my arms. It's our child, yours and mine." She put a hand to her mouth. "How can I know every feature of you?"

They've a little of the talent, his mind told him. *But they suppress it because it terrifies.*

In a moment of clarity, he saw how Chani was trembling.

"What is it you want to say?" he asked.

"Usul," she whispered, and still she trembled.

"You cannot back into the future," he said.

A profound compassion for her swept through him. He pulled her against him, stroked her head. "Chani, Chani, don't fear."

"Usul, help me," she cried.

As she spoke, he felt the drug complete its work within him, ripping away the curtains to let him see the distant gray turmoil of his future.

"You're so quiet," Chani said.

He held himself poised in the awareness, seeing time stretch out in its weird dimension, delicately balanced yet whirling, narrow yet spread like a net gathering countless worlds and forces, a tightwire that he must walk, yet a teeter-totter on which he balanced.

On one side he could see the Imperium, a Harkonnen called Feyd-Rautha who flashed toward him like a deadly blade, the Sardaukar raging off their planet to spread pogrom on Arrakis, the Guild conniving and plotting, the Bene Gesserit with their scheme of selective breeding. They lay massed like a thunderhead on his horizon, held back by no more than the Fremen and their Muad'Dib, the sleeping giant Fremen poised for their wild crusade across the universe.

Paul felt himself at the center, at the pivot where the whole structure turned, walking a thin wire of peace with a measure of happiness, Chani at his side. He could see it stretching ahead of him, a time of relative quiet in a hidden sietch, a moment of peace between periods of violence.

"There's no other place for peace," he said.

"Usul, you're crying," Chani murmured. "Usul, my strength, do you give moisture to the dead? To whose dead?"

"To ones not yet dead," he said.

"Then let them have their time of life," she said.

He sensed through the drug fog how right she was, pulled her against him with savage pressure. "Sihaya!" he said.

She put a palm against his cheek. "I'm no longer afraid, Usul. Look at me. I see what you see when you hold me thus."

"What do you see?" he demanded.

"I see us giving love to each other in a time of quiet between storms. It's what we were meant to do."

The drug had him again and he thought: *So many times you've given me comfort and forgetfulness.* He felt anew the hyperillumination with its high-relief imagery of time, sensed his future becoming memories—the tender indignities of physical love, the sharing and communion of selves, the softness and the violence.

"You're the strong one, Chani," he muttered. "Stay with me."

"Always," she said, and kissed his cheek.

BOOK THREE

THE PROPHET

No woman, no man, no child ever was deeply intimate with my father. The closest anyone ever came to casual camaraderie with the Padishah Emperor was the relationship offered by Count Hasimir Fenring, a companion from childhood. The measure of Count Fenring's friendship may be seen first in a positive thing: he allayed the Landsraad's suspicions after the Arrakis Affair. It cost more than a billion solaris in spice bribes, so my mother said, and there were other gifts as well: slave women, royal honors, and tokens of rank. The second major evidence of the Count's friendship was negative. He refused to kill a man even though it was within his capabilities and my father commanded it. I will relate this presently.

—FROM "COUNT FENRING: A PROFILE"
BY THE PRINCESS IRULAN

The Baron Vladimir Harkonnen raged down the corridor from his private apartments, flitting through patches of late afternoon sunlight that poured down from high windows. He bobbed and twisted in his suspensors with violent movements.

Past the private kitchen he stormed—past the library, past the small reception room and into the servants' antechamber where the evening relaxation already had set in.

The guard captain, Iakin Nefud, squatted on a divan across the chamber, the stupor of semuta dullness in his flat face, the eerie wailing of semuta music around him. His own court sat near to do his bidding.

"Nefud!" the Baron roared.

Men scrambled.

Nefud stood, his face composed by the narcotic but with an overlay of paleness that told of his fear. The semuta music had stopped.

"My Lord Baron," Nefud said. Only the drug kept the trembling out of his voice.

The Baron scanned the faces around him, seeing the looks of frantic quiet in them. He returned his attention to Nefud, and spoke in a silken tone:

"How long have you been my guard captain, Nefud?"

Nefud swallowed. "Since Arrakis, my Lord. Almost two years."

"And have you always anticipated dangers to my person?"

"Such has been my only desire, my Lord."

"Then where is Feyd-Rautha?" the Baron roared.

Nefud recoiled. "M'Lord?"

"You do not consider Feyd-Rautha a danger to my person?" Again, the voice was silken.

Nefud wet his lips with his tongue. Some of the semuta dullness left his eyes. "Feyd-Rautha's in the slave quarters, my Lord."

"With the women again, eh?" The Baron trembled with the effort of suppressing anger.

"Sire, it could be he's—"

"Silence!"

The Baron advanced another step into the antechamber, noting how the men moved back, clearing a subtle space around Nefud, dissociating themselves from the object of wrath.

"Did I not command you to know precisely where the na-Baron was at all times?" the Baron asked. He moved a step closer. "Did I not say to you that you were to know *precisely* what the na-Baron was saying at all times—and to whom?" Another step. "Did I not say to you that you were to tell me whenever he went into the quarters of the slave women?"

Nefud swallowed. Perspiration stood out on his forehead.

The Baron held his voice flat, almost devoid of emphasis: "Did I not say these things to you?"

Nefud nodded.

"And did I not say that you were to check all slave boys sent to me and that you were to do this yourself . . . *personally*?"

Again, Nefud nodded.

"Did you, perchance, not see the blemish on the thigh of the one sent me this evening?" the Baron asked. "Is it possible you—"

"Uncle."

The Baron whirled, stared at Feyd-Rautha standing in the doorway. The presence of his nephew here, now—the look of hurry that the young man could not quite conceal—all revealed much. Feyd-Rautha had his own spy system focused on the Baron.

"There is a body in my chambers that I wish removed," the Baron said, and he kept his hand at the projectile weapon beneath his robes, thankful that his shield was the best.

Feyd-Rautha glanced at two guardsmen against the right wall, nodded. The two detached themselves, scurried out the door and down the hall toward the Baron's apartments.

Those two, eh? the Baron thought. *Ah, this young monster has much to learn yet about conspiracy!*

"I presume you left matters peaceful in the slave quarters, Feyd," the Baron said.

"I've been playing cheops with the slavemaster," Feyd-Rautha said, and he thought: *What has gone wrong? The boy we sent to my uncle has obviously been killed. But he was perfect for the job. Even Hawat couldn't have made a better choice. The boy was perfect!*

"Playing pyramid chess," the Baron said. "How nice. Did you win?"

"I . . . ah, yes, Uncle." And Feyd-Rautha strove to contain his disquiet.

The Baron snapped his fingers. "Nefud, you wish to be restored to my good graces?"

"Sire, what have I done?" Nefud quavered.

"That's unimportant now," the Baron said. "Feyd has beaten the slavemaster at cheops. Did you hear that?"

"Yes . . . Sire."

"I wish you to take three men and go to the slavemaster," the Baron said. "Garrote the slavemaster. Bring his body to me when you've finished that I may see it was done properly. We cannot have such inept chess players in our employ."

Feyd-Rautha went pale, took a step forward. "But, Uncle, I—"

"Later, Feyd," the Baron said, and waved a hand. "Later."

The two guards who had gone to the Baron's quarters for the slave boy's body staggered past the antechamber door with their load sagging between them, arms trailing. The Baron watched until they were out of sight.

Nefud stepped up beside the Baron. "You wish me to kill the slave-master, now, my Lord?"

"Now," the Baron said. "And when you've finished, add those two who just passed to your list. I don't like the way they carried that body. One should do such things neatly. I'll wish to see their carcasses, too."

Nefud said, "My Lord, is it anything that I've—"

"Do as your master has ordered," Feyd-Rautha said. And he thought: *All I can hope for now is to save my own skin.*

Good! the Baron thought. *He yet knows how to cut his losses.* And the Baron smiled inwardly at himself, thinking: *The lad knows, too, what will please me and be most apt to stay my wrath from falling on him. He knows I must preserve him. Who else do I have who could take the reins I must leave someday? I have no other as capable. But he must learn! And I must preserve myself while he's learning.*

Nefud signaled men to assist him, led them out the door.

"Would you accompany me to my chambers, Feyd?" the Baron asked.

"I am yours to command," Feyd-Rautha said. He bowed, thinking: *I'm caught.*

"After you," the Baron said, and he gestured to the door.

Feyd-Rautha indicated his fear by only the barest hesitation. *Have I failed utterly?* he asked himself. *Will he slip a poisoned blade into my back . . . slowly, through the shield? Does he have an alternative successor?*

Let him experience this moment of terror, the Baron thought as he walked along behind his nephew. *He will succeed me, but at a time of my choosing. I'll not have him throwing away what I've built!*

Feyd-Rautha tried not to walk too swiftly. He felt the skin crawling on his back as though his body itself wondered when the blow could come. His muscles alternately tensed and relaxed.

"Have you heard the latest word from Arrakis?" the Baron asked.

"No, Uncle."

Feyd-Rautha forced himself not to look back. He turned down the hall out of the servants' wing.

"They've a new prophet or religious leader of some kind among the Fremen," the Baron said. "They call him Muad'Dib. Very funny, really. It means 'the Mouse.' I've told Rabban to let them have their religion. It'll keep them occupied."

"That's very interesting, Uncle," Feyd-Rautha said. He turned into the private corridor to his uncle's quarters, wondering: *Why does he talk about religion? Is it some subtle hint to me?*

"Yes, isn't it?" the Baron said.

They came into the Baron's apartments through the reception salon to the bedchamber. Subtle signs of a struggle greeted them here—a suspensor lamp displaced, a bedcushion on the floor, a soother-reel spilled open across a bedstand.

"It was a clever plan," the Baron said. He kept his body shield tuned to maximum, stopped, facing his nephew. "But not clever enough. Tell me, Feyd, why didn't you strike me down yourself? You've had opportunity enough."

Feyd-Rautha found a suspensor chair, accomplished a mental shrug as he sat down in it without being asked.

I must be bold now, he thought.

"You taught me that my own hands must remain clean," he said.

"Ah, yes," the Baron said. "When you face the Emperor, you must be able to say truthfully that you did not do the deed. The witch at the Emperor's elbow will hear your words and know their truth or falsehood. Yes. I warned you about that."

"Why haven't you ever bought a Bene Gesserit, Uncle?" Feyd-Rautha asked. "With a Truthsayer at your side—"

"You know my tastes!" the Baron snapped.

Feyd-Rautha studied his uncle, said: "Still, one would be valuable for—"

"I trust them not!" the Baron snarled. "And stop trying to change the subject!"

Feyd-Rautha spoke mildly: "As you wish, Uncle."

"I remember a time in the arena several years ago," the Baron said. "It seemed there that day a slave had been set to kill you. Is that truly how it was?"

"It's been so long ago, Uncle. After all, I—"

"No evasions, please," the Baron said, and the tightness of his voice exposed the rein on his anger.

Feyd-Rautha looked at his uncle, thinking: *He knows, else he wouldn't ask.*

"It was a sham, Uncle. I arranged it to discredit your slavemaster."

"Very clever," the Baron said. "Brave, too. That slave-gladiator almost took you, didn't he?"

"Yes."

"If you had finesse and subtlety to match such courage, you'd be truly formidable." The Baron shook his head from side to side. And as he had done many times since that terrible day on Arrakis, he found himself regretting the loss of Piter, the Mentat. There'd been a man of delicate, devilish subtlety. It hadn't saved him, though. Again, the Baron shook his head. Fate was sometimes inscrutable.

Feyd-Rautha glanced around the bedchamber, studying the signs of the struggle, wondering how his uncle had overcome the slave they'd prepared so carefully.

"How did I best him?" the Baron asked. "Ah-h-h, now, Feyd—let me keep some weapons to preserve me in my old age. It's better we use this time to strike a bargain."

Feyd-Rautha stared at him. *A bargain! He means to keep me as his*

*heir for certain, then. Else why bargain? One bargains with equals or
near equals!*

"What bargain, Uncle?" And Feyd-Rautha felt proud that his voice
remained calm and reasonable, betraying none of the elation that filled
him.

The Baron, too, noted the control. He nodded. "You're good material, Feyd. I don't waste good material. You persist, however, in refusing
to learn my true value to you. You are obstinate. You do not see why I
should be preserved as someone of the utmost value to you. This. . . ."
He gestured at the evidence of the struggle in the bedchamber. "This
was foolishness. I do not reward foolishness."

Get to the point, you old fool! Feyd-Rautha thought.

"You think of me as an old fool," the Baron said. "I must dissuade
you of that."

"You speak of a bargain."

"Ah, the impatience of youth," the Baron said. "Well, this is the substance of it, then: You will cease these foolish attempts on my life. And
I, when you are ready for it, will step aside in your favor. I will retire to
an advisory position, leaving you in the seat of power."

"Retire, Uncle?"

"You still think me the fool," the Baron said, "and this but confirms
it, eh? You think I'm begging you! Step cautiously, Feyd. This old fool
saw through the shielded needle you'd planted in that slave boy's thigh.
Right where I'd put my hand on it, eh? The smallest pressure and—
snick! A poison needle in the old fool's palm! Ah-h-h, Feyd. . . ."

The Baron shook his head, thinking: *It would've worked, too, if Ha-
wat hadn't warned me. Well, let the lad believe I saw the plot on my own.
In a way, I did. I was the one who saved Hawat from the wreckage of
Arrakis. And this lad needs greater respect for my prowess.*

Feyd-Rautha remained silent, struggling with himself. *Is he being
truthful? Does he really mean to retire? Why not? I'm sure to succeed him
one day if I move carefully. He can't live forever. Perhaps it was foolish to
try hurrying the process.*

"You speak of a bargain," Feyd-Rautha said. "What pledge do we give to bind it?"

"How can we trust each other, eh?" the Baron asked. "Well, Feyd, as for you: I'm setting Thufir Hawat to watch over you. I trust Hawat's Mentat capabilities in this. Do you understand me? And as for me, you'll have to take me on faith. But I can't live forever, can I, Feyd? And perhaps you should begin to suspect now that there're things I know which you *should* know."

"I give you my pledge and what do you give me?" Feyd-Rautha asked.

"I let you go on living," the Baron said.

Again, Feyd-Rautha studied his uncle. *He sets Hawat over me! What would he say if I told him Hawat planned the trick with the gladiator that cost him his slavemaster? He'd likely say I was lying in the attempt to discredit Hawat. No, the good Thufir is a Mentat and has anticipated this moment.*

"Well, what do you say?" the Baron asked.

"What can I say? I accept, of course."

And Feyd-Rautha thought: *Hawat! He plays both ends against the middle . . . is that it? Has he moved to my uncle's camp because I didn't counsel with him over the slave boy attempt?*

"You haven't said anything about my setting Hawat to watch you," the Baron said.

Feyd-Rautha betrayed anger by a flaring of nostrils. The name of Hawat had been a danger signal in the Harkonnen family for so many years . . . and now it had a new meaning: still dangerous.

"Hawat's a dangerous toy," Feyd-Rautha said.

"Toy! Don't be stupid. I know what I have in Hawat and how to control it. Hawat has deep emotions, Feyd. The man without emotions is the one to fear. But deep emotions . . . ah, now, those can be bent to your needs."

"Uncle, I don't understand you."

"Yes, that's plain enough."

Only a flicker of eyelids betrayed the passage of resentment through Feyd-Rautha.

"And you do not understand Hawat," the Baron said.

Nor do you! Feyd-Rautha thought.

"Who does Hawat blame for his present circumstances?" the Baron asked. "Me? Certainly. But he was an Atreides tool and bested me for years until the Imperium took a hand. That's how he sees it. His hate for me is a casual thing now. He believes he can best me anytime. Believing this, he is bested. For I direct his attention where I want it—against the Imperium."

Tensions of a new understanding drew tight lines across Feyd-Rautha's forehead, thinned his mouth. "Against the Emperor?"

Let my dear nephew try the taste of that, the Baron thought. *Let him say to himself: "The Emperor Feyd-Rautha Harkonnen!" Let him ask himself how much that's worth. Surely it must be worth the life of one old uncle who could make that dream come to pass!*

Slowly, Feyd-Rautha wet his lips with his tongue. Could it be true what the old fool was saying? There was more here than there seemed to be.

"And what has Hawat to do with this?" Feyd-Rautha asked.

"He thinks he uses us to wreak his revenge upon the Emperor."

"And when that's accomplished?"

"He does not think beyond his revenge. Hawat's a man who must serve others, and doesn't even know this about himself."

"I've learned much from Hawat," Feyd-Rautha agreed, and felt the truth of the words as he spoke them. "But the more I learn, the more I feel we should dispose of him . . . and soon."

"You don't like the idea of his watching you?"

"Hawat watches everybody."

"And he may put you on a throne. Hawat is subtle. He is dangerous, devious. But I'll not yet withhold the antidote from him. A sword is dangerous, too, Feyd. We have the scabbard for this one, though. The poison's in him. When we withdraw the antidote, death will sheathe him."

"In a way, it's like the arena," Feyd-Rautha said. "Feints within feints within feints. You watch to see which way the gladiator leans, which way he looks, how he holds his knife."

He nodded to himself, seeing that these words pleased his uncle, but thinking: *Yes! Like the arena! And the cutting edge is the mind!*

"Now you see how you need me," the Baron said. "I'm yet of use, Feyd."

A sword to be wielded until he's too blunt for use, Feyd-Rautha thought.

"Yes, Uncle," he said.

"And now," the Baron said, "we will go down to the slave quarters, we two. And I will watch while you, with your own hands, kill all the women in the pleasure wing."

"Uncle!"

"There will be other women, Feyd. But I have said that you do not make a mistake casually with me."

Feyd-Rautha's face darkened. "Uncle, you—"

"You will accept your punishment and learn something from it," the Baron said.

Feyd-Rautha met the gloating stare in his uncle's eyes. *And I must remember this night,* he thought. *And remembering it, I must remember other nights.*

"You will not refuse," the Baron said.

What could you do if I refused, old man? Feyd-Rautha asked himself. But he knew there might be some other punishment, perhaps a more subtle one, a more brutal lever to bend him.

"I know you, Feyd," the Baron said. "You will not refuse."

All right, Feyd-Rautha thought. *I need you now. I see that. The bargain's made. But I'll not always need you. And . . . someday . . .*

Deep in the human unconscious is a pervasive need for a logical universe that makes sense. But the real universe is always one step beyond logic.

—FROM "THE SAYINGS OF MUAD'DIB"
BY THE PRINCESS IRULAN

I've sat across from many rulers of Great Houses, but never seen a more gross and dangerous pig than this one, Thufir Hawat told himself.

"You may speak plainly with me, Hawat," the Baron rumbled. He leaned back in his suspensor chair, the eyes in their folds of fat boring into Hawat.

The old Mentat looked down at the table between him and the Baron Vladimir Harkonnen, noting the opulence of its grain. Even this was a factor to consider in assessing the Baron, as were the red walls of this private conference room and the faint sweet herb scent that hung on the air, masking a deeper musk.

"You didn't have me send that warning to Rabban as an idle whim," the Baron said.

Hawat's leathery old face remained impassive, betraying none of the loathing he felt. "I suspect many things, my Lord," he said.

"Yes. Well, I wish to know how Arrakis figures in your suspicions about Salusa Secundus. It is not enough that you say to me the Emperor is in a ferment about some association between Arrakis and his mysterious prison planet. Now, I rushed the warning out to Rabban only because the courier had to leave on that Heighliner. You said there could be no delay. Well and good. But now I will have an explanation."

He babbles too much, Hawat thought. *He's not like Leto who could tell me a thing with the lift of an eyebrow or the wave of a hand. Nor like the Old Duke who could express an entire sentence in the way he accented a single word. This is a clod! Destroying him will be a service to mankind.*

"You will not leave here until I've had a full and complete explanation," the Baron said.

"You speak too casually of Salusa Secundus," Hawat said.

"It's a penal colony," the Baron said. "The worst riff-raff in the galaxy are sent to Salusa Secundus. What else do we need to know?"

"That conditions on the prison planet are more oppressive than anywhere else," Hawat said. "You hear that the mortality rate among new prisoners is higher than sixty per cent. You hear that the Emperor practices every form of oppression there. You hear all this and do not ask questions?"

"The Emperor doesn't permit the Great Houses to inspect his prison," the Baron growled. "But he hasn't seen into my dungeons, either."

"And curiosity about Salusa Secundus is . . . ah. . . ." Hawat put a bony finger to his lips. ". . . discouraged."

"So he's not proud of some of the things he must do there!"

Hawat allowed the faintest of smiles to touch his dark lips. His eyes glinted in the glowtube light as he stared at the Baron. "And you've never wondered where the Emperor gets his Sardaukar?"

The Baron pursed his fat lips. This gave his features the look of a pouting baby, and his voice carried a tone of petulance as he said: "Why . . . he recruits . . . that is to say, there are the levies and he enlists from—"

"Faaa!" Hawat snapped. "The stories you hear about the exploits of the Sardaukar, they're not rumors, are they? Those are first-hand accounts from the limited number of survivors who've fought against the Sardaukar, eh?"

"The Sardaukar are excellent fighting men, no doubt of it," the Baron said. "But I think my own legions—"

"A pack of holiday excursionists by comparison!" Hawat snarled. "You think I don't know why the Emperor turned against House Atreides?"

"This is not a realm open to your speculation," the Baron warned.

Is it possible that even he doesn't know what motivated the Emperor in this? Hawat asked himself.

"Any area is open to my speculation if it does what you've hired me to do," Hawat said. "I am a Mentat. You do not withhold information or computation lines from a Mentat."

For a long minute, the Baron stared at him, then: "Say what you must say, Mentat."

"The Padishah Emperor turned against House Atreides because the Duke's Warmasters Gurney Halleck and Duncan Idaho had trained a fighting force—a *small* fighting force—to within a hair as good as the Sardaukar. Some of them were even better. And the Duke was in a position to enlarge his force, to make it every bit as strong as the Emperor's."

The Baron weighed this disclosure, then: "What has Arrakis to do with this?"

"It provides a pool of recruits already conditioned to the bitterest survival training."

The Baron shook his head. "You cannot mean the Fremen?"

"I mean the Fremen."

"Hah! Then why warn Rabban? There cannot be more than a handful of Fremen left after the Sardaukar pogrom and Rabban's oppression."

Hawat continued to stare at him silently.

"Not more than a handful!" the Baron repeated. "Rabban killed six thousand of them last year alone!"

Still, Hawat stared at him.

"And the year before it was nine thousand," the Baron said. "And before they left, the Sardaukar must've accounted for at least twenty thousand."

"What are Rabban's troop losses for the past two years?" Hawat asked.

The Baron rubbed his jowls. "Well, he has been recruiting rather heavily, to be sure. His agents make rather extravagant promises and—"

"Shall we say thirty thousand in round numbers?" Hawat asked.

"That would seem a little high," the Baron said.

"Quite the contrary," Hawat said. "I can read between the lines of Rabban's reports as well as you can. And you certainly must've understood my reports from our agents."

"Arrakis is a fierce planet," the Baron said. "Storm losses can—"

"We both know the figure for storm accretion," Hawat said.

"What if he has lost thirty thousand?" the Baron demanded, and blood darkened his face.

"By your own count," Hawat said, "he killed fifteen thousand over two years while losing twice that number. You say the Sardaukar accounted for another twenty thousand, possibly a few more. And I've seen the transportation manifests for their return from Arrakis. If they killed twenty thousand, they lost almost five for one. Why won't you face these figures, Baron, and understand what they mean?"

The Baron spoke in a coldly measured cadence: "This is your job, Mentat. What do they mean?"

"I gave you Duncan Idaho's head count on the sietch he visited," Hawat said. "It all fits. If they had just two hundred and fifty such sietch communities, their population would be about five million. My best estimate is that they had at least twice that many communities. You scatter your population on such a planet."

"Ten million?"

The Baron's jowls quivered with amazement.

"At least."

The Baron pursed his fat lips. The beady eyes stared without wavering at Hawat. *Is this true Mentat computation?* he wondered. *How could this be and no one suspect?*

"We haven't even cut heavily into their birth-rate-growth figure," Hawat said. "We've just weeded out some of their less successful specimens, leaving the strong to grow stronger—just like on Salusa Secundus."

"Salusa Secundus!" the Baron barked. "What has this to do with the Emperor's prison planet?"

"A man who survives Salusa Secundus starts out being tougher than most others," Hawat said. "When you add the very best of military training—"

"Nonsense! By your argument, I could recruit from among the Fremen after the way they've been oppressed by my nephew."

Hawat spoke in a mild voice: "Don't you oppress any of your troops?"

"Well . . . I . . . but—"

"Oppression is a relative thing," Hawat said. "Your fighting men are much better off than those around them, heh? They see unpleasant alternative to being soldiers of the Baron, heh?"

The Baron fell silent, eyes unfocused. The possibilities—had Rabban unwittingly given House Harkonnen its ultimate weapon?

Presently he said: "How could you be sure of the loyalty of such recruits?"

"I would take them in small groups, not larger than platoon strength," Hawat said. "I'd remove them from their oppressive situation and isolate them with a training cadre of people who understood their background, preferably people who had preceded them from the same oppressive situation. Then I'd fill them with the mystique that their planet had really been a secret training ground to produce just such superior beings as themselves. And all the while, I'd show them what such superior beings could earn: rich living, beautiful women, fine mansions . . . whatever they desired."

The Baron began to nod. "The way the Sardaukar live at home."

"The recruits come to believe in time that such a place as Salusa Secundus is justified because it produced them—the elite. The commonest Sardaukar trooper lives a life, in many respects, as exalted as that of any member of a Great House."

"Such an idea!" the Baron whispered.

"You begin to share my suspicions," Hawat said.

"Where did such a thing start?" the Baron asked.

"Ah, yes: Where did House Corrino originate? Were there people on Salusa Secundus before the Emperor sent his first contingents of prisoners there? Even the Duke Leto, a cousin on the distaff side, never knew for sure. Such questions are not encouraged."

The Baron's eyes glazed with thought. "Yes, a very carefully kept secret. They'd use every device of—"

"Besides, what's there to conceal?" Hawat asked. "That the Padishah Emperor has a prison planet? Everyone knows this. That he has—"

"Count Fenring!" the Baron blurted.

Hawat broke off, studied the Baron with a puzzled frown. "What of Count Fenring?"

"At my nephew's birthday several years ago," the Baron said. "This Imperial popinjay, Count Fenring, came as official observer and to . . . ah, conclude a business arrangement between the Emperor and myself."

"So?"

"I . . . ah, during one of our conversations, I believe I said something about making a prison planet of Arrakis. Fenring—"

"What did you say exactly?" Hawat asked.

"Exactly? That was quite a while ago and—"

"My Lord Baron, if you wish to make the best use of my services, you must give me adequate information. Wasn't this conversation recorded?"

The Baron's face darkened with anger. "You're as bad as Piter! I don't like these—"

"Piter is no longer with you, my Lord," Hawat said. "As to that, whatever *did* happen to Piter?"

"He became too familiar, too demanding of me," the Baron said.

"You assure me you don't waste a useful man," Hawat said. "Will you waste me by threats and quibbling? We were discussing what you said to Count Fenring."

Slowly, the Baron composed his features. *When the time comes,* he thought, *I'll remember his manner with me. Yes. I will remember.*

"One moment," the Baron said, and he thought back to the meeting in his Great Hall. It helped to visualize the cone of silence in which they had stood. "I said something like this," the Baron said. "'The Emperor knows a certain amount of killing has always been an arm of business.' I was referring to our work force losses. Then I said something about considering another solution to the Arrakeen problem and I said the Emperor's prison planet inspired me to emulate him."

"Witch blood!" Hawat snapped. "What did Fenring say?"

"That's when he began questioning me about you."

Hawat sat back, closed his eyes in thought. "So that's why they started looking into Arrakis," he said. "Well, the thing's done." He opened his eyes. "They must have spies all over Arrakis by now. Two years!"

"But certainly my innocent suggestion that—"

"Nothing is innocent in an Emperor's eyes! What were your instructions to Rabban?"

"Merely that he should teach Arrakis to fear us."

Hawat shook his head. "You now have two alternatives, Baron. You can kill off the natives, wipe them out entirely, or—"

"Waste an entire work force?"

"Would you prefer to have the Emperor and those Great Houses he can still swing behind him come in here and perform a curettement, scrape out Giedi Prime like a hollow gourd?"

The Baron studied his Mentat, then: "He wouldn't dare!"

"Wouldn't he?"

The Baron's lips quivered. "What is your alternative?"

"Abandon your dear nephew, Rabban."

"Aband. . . ." The Baron broke off, stared at Hawat.

"Send him no more troops, no aid of any kind. Don't answer his messages other than to say you've heard of the terrible way he's handled things on Arrakis and you intend to take corrective measures as soon as you're able. I'll arrange to have some of your messages intercepted by Imperial spies."

"But what of the spice, the revenues, the—"

"Demand your baronial profits, but be careful how you make your demands. Require fixed sums of Rabban. We can—"

The Baron turned his hands palms up. "But how can I be certain that my weasel nephew isn't—"

"We still have our spies on Arrakis. Tell Rabban he either meets the spice quotas you set him or he'll be replaced."

"I know my nephew," the Baron said. "This would only make him oppress the population even more."

"Of course he will!" Hawat snapped. "You don't want that stopped now! You merely want your own hands clean. Let Rabban make your Salusa Secundus for you. There's no need even to send him any prisoners. He has all the population required. If Rabban is driving his people to meet your spice quotas, then the Emperor need suspect no other motive. That's reason enough for putting the planet on the rack. And you, Baron, will not show by word or action that there's any other reason for this."

The Baron could not keep the sly tone of admiration out of his voice. "Ah, Hawat, you are a devious one. Now, how do we move into Arrakis and make use of what Rabban prepares?"

"That's the simplest thing of all, Baron. If you set each year's quota a bit higher than the one before, matters will soon reach a head there. Production will drop off. You can remove Rabban and take over yourself . . . to correct the mess."

"It fits," the Baron said. "But I can feel myself tiring of all this. I'm preparing another to take over Arrakis for me."

Hawat studied the fat round face across from him. Slowly the old soldier-spy began to nod his head. "Feyd-Rautha," he said. "So that's the reason for the oppression now. You're very devious yourself, Baron. Perhaps we can incorporate these two schemes. Yes. Your Feyd-Rautha can go to Arrakis as their savior. He can win the populace. Yes."

The Baron smiled. And behind his smile, he asked himself: *Now, how does this fit in with Hawat's personal scheming?*

And Hawat, seeing that he was dismissed, arose and left the red-walled room. As he walked, he could not put down the disturbing unknowns that cropped into every computation about Arrakis. This new religious leader that Gurney Halleck hinted at from his hiding place among the smugglers, this Muad'Dib.

Perhaps I should not have told the Baron to let this religion flourish where it will, even among the folk of pan and graben, he told himself. *But it's well known that repression makes a religion flourish.*

And he thought about Halleck's reports on Fremen battle tactics. The tactics smacked of Halleck himself . . . and Idaho . . . and even of Hawat.

Did Idaho survive? he asked himself.

But this was a futile question. He did not yet ask himself if it was possible that Paul had survived. He knew the Baron was convinced that all Atreides were dead. The Bene Gesserit witch had been his weapon, the Baron admitted. And that could only mean an end to all—even to the woman's own son.

What a poisonous hate she must've had for the Atreides, he thought. *Something like the hate I hold for this Baron. Will my blow be as final and complete as hers?*

There is in all things a pattern that is part of our universe. It has symmetry, elegance, and grace—those qualities you find always in that which the true artist captures. You can find it in the turning of the seasons, in the way sand trails along a ridge, in the branch clusters of the creosote bush or the pattern of its leaves. We try to copy these patterns in our lives and our society, seeking the rhythms, the dances, the forms that comfort. Yet, it is possible to see peril in the finding of ultimate perfection. It is clear that the ultimate pattern contains its own fixity. In such perfection, all things move toward death.

—FROM "COLLECTED SAYINGS OF MUAD'DIB"
BY THE PRINCESS IRULAN

Paul-Muad'Dib remembered that there had been a meal heavy with spice essence. He clung to this memory because it was an anchor point and he could tell himself from this vantage that his immediate experience must be a dream.

I am a theater of processes, he told himself. *I am a prey to the imperfect vision, to the race consciousness and its terrible purpose.*

Yet, he could not escape the fear that he had somehow overrun himself, lost his position in time, so that past and future and present mingled without distinction. It was a kind of visual fatigue and it came, he knew, from the constant necessity of holding the prescient future as a kind of memory that was in itself a thing intrinsically of the past.

Chani prepared the meal for me, he told himself.

Yet Chani was deep in the south—in the cold country where the sun was hot—secreted in one of the new sietch strongholds, safe with their son, Leto II.

Or, was that a thing yet to happen?

No, he reassured himself, for Alia-the-Strange-One, his sister, had gone there with his mother and with Chani—a twenty-thumper trip into the south, riding a Reverend Mother's palanquin fixed to the back of a wild maker.

He shied away from the thought of riding the giant worms, asking himself: *Or is Alia yet to be born?*

I was on razzia, Paul recalled. *We went raiding to recover the water of our dead in Arrakeen. And I found the remains of my father in the funeral pyre. I enshrined the skull of my father in a Fremen rock mound overlooking Harg Pass.*

Or was that a thing yet to be?

My wounds are real, Paul told himself. *My scars are real. The shrine of my father's skull is real.*

Still in the dreamlike state, Paul remembered that Harah, Jamis' wife, had intruded on him once to say there'd been a fight in the sietch corridor. That had been the interim sietch before the women and children had been sent into the deep south. Harah had stood there in the entrance to the inner chamber, the black wings of her hair tied back by water rings on a chain. She had held aside the chamber's hangings and told him that Chani had just killed someone.

This happened, Paul told himself. *This was real, not born out of its time and subject to change.*

Paul remembered he had rushed out to find Chani standing beneath the yellow globes of the corridor, clad in a brilliant blue wraparound robe with hood thrown back, a flush of exertion on her elfin features. She had been sheathing her crysknife. A huddled group had been hurrying away down the corridor with a burden.

And Paul remembered telling himself: You always know when they're carrying a body.

Chani's water rings, worn openly in sietch on a cord around her neck, tinkled as she turned toward him.

"Chani, what is this?" he asked.

"I dispatched one who came to challenge you in single combat, Usul."

"*You* killed him?"

"Yes. But perhaps I should've left him for Harah."

(And Paul recalled how the faces of the people around them had showed appreciation for these words. Even Harah had laughed.)

"But he came to challenge *me!*"

"You trained me yourself in the weirding way, Usul."

"Certainly! But you shouldn't—"

"I was born in the desert, Usul. I know how to use a crysknife."

He suppressed his anger, tried to talk reasonably. "This may all be true, Chani, but—"

"I am no longer a child hunting scorpions in the sietch by the light of a handglobe, Usul. I do not play games."

Paul glared at her, caught by the odd ferocity beneath her casual attitude.

"He was not worthy, Usul," Chani said. "I'd not disturb your meditations with the likes of him." She moved closer, looking at him out of the corners of her eyes, dropping her voice so that only he might hear. "And, beloved, when it's learned that a challenger may face *me* and be brought to shameful death by Muad'Dib's woman, there'll be fewer challengers."

Yes, Paul told himself, *that had certainly happened. It was true-past. And the number of challengers testing the new blade of Muad'Dib did drop dramatically.*

Somewhere, in a world not-of-the-dream, there was a hint of motion, the cry of a nightbird.

I dream, Paul reassured himself. *It's the spice meal.*

Still, there was about him a feeling of abandonment. He wondered if it might be possible that his ruh-spirit had slipped over somehow into the world where the Fremen believed he had his true existence—into the alam al-mithal, the world of similitudes, that metaphysical realm where all physical limitations were removed. And he knew fear at the thought of such a place, because removal of all limitations meant removal of all points of reference. In the landscape of a myth he could not orient himself and say: "I am I because I am here."

His mother had said once: "The people are divided, some of them, in how they think of you."

I must be waking from the dream, Paul told himself. For this had happened—these words from his mother, the Lady Jessica who was now a Reverend Mother of the Fremen, these words had passed through reality.

Jessica was fearful of the religious relationship between himself and the Fremen, Paul knew. She didn't like the fact that people of both sietch and graben referred to Muad'Dib as *Him.* And she went questioning among the tribes, sending out her Sayyadina spies, collecting their answers and brooding on them.

She had quoted a Bene Gesserit proverb to him: "When religion and politics travel in the same cart, the riders believe nothing can stand in their way. Their movement becomes headlong—faster and faster and faster. They put aside all thought of obstacles and forget that a precipice does not show itself to the man in a blind rush until it's too late."

Paul recalled that he had sat there in his mother's quarters, in the inner chamber shrouded by dark hangings with their surfaces covered by woven patterns out of Fremen mythology. He had sat there, hearing her out, noting the way she was always observing—even when her eyes were lowered. Her oval face had new lines in it at the corners of the mouth, but the hair was still like polished bronze. The wide-set green eyes, though, hid beneath their overcasting of spice-imbued blue.

"The Fremen have a simple, practical religion," he said.

"Nothing about religion is simple," she warned.

But Paul, seeing the clouded future that still hung over them, found himself swayed by anger. He could only say: "Religion unifies our forces. It's our mystique."

"You deliberately cultivate this air, this bravura," she charged. "You never cease indoctrinating."

"Thus you yourself taught me," he said.

But she had been full of contentions and arguments that day. It had been the day of the circumcision ceremony for little Leto. Paul had understood some of the reasons for her upset. She had never accepted his liaison—the "marriage of youth"—with Chani. But Chani had produced an Atreides son, and Jessica had found herself unable to reject the child with the mother.

Jessica had stirred finally under his stare, said: "You think me an unnatural mother."

"Of course not."

"I see the way you watch me when I'm with your sister. You don't understand about your sister."

"I know why Alia is different," he said. "She was unborn, part of you, when you changed the Water of Life. She—"

"You know nothing of it!"

And Paul, suddenly unable to express the knowledge gained out of its time, said only: "I don't think you unnatural."

She saw his distress, said: "There is a thing, Son."

"Yes?"

"I do love your Chani. I accept her."

This was real, Paul told himself. This wasn't the imperfect vision to be changed by the twistings out of time's own birth.

The reassurance gave him a new hold on his world. Bits of solid reality began to dip through the dream state into his awareness. He knew suddenly that he was in a hiereg, a desert camp. Chani had planted their stilltent on flour sand for its softness. That could only mean Chani was nearby—Chani, his soul, Chani his sihaya, sweet as the desert spring, Chani up from the palmaries of the deep south.

Now, he remembered her singing a sand chanty to him in the time for sleep.

>   "O my soul,
>   Have no taste for Paradise this night,
>   And I swear by Shai-hulud

You will go there,
Obedient to my love."

And she had sung the walking song lovers shared on the sand, its rhythm like the drag of the dunes against the feet:

"Tell me of thine eyes
And I will tell thee of thy heart.
Tell me of thy feet
And I will tell thee of thy hands.
Tell me of thy sleeping
And I will tell thee of thy waking.
Tell me of thy desires
And I will tell thee of thy need."

He had heard someone strumming a baliset in another tent. And he'd thought then of Gurney Halleck. Reminded by the familiar instrument, he had thought of Gurney whose face he had seen in a smuggler band, but who had not seen him, could not see him or know of him lest that inadvertently lead the Harkonnens to the son of the Duke they had killed.

But the style of the player in the night, the distinctiveness of the fingers on the baliset's strings, brought the real musician back to Paul's memory. It had been Chatt the Leaper, captain of the Fedaykin, leader of the death commandos who guarded Muad'Dib.

We are in the desert, Paul remembered. *We are in the central erg beyond the Harkonnen patrols. I am here to walk the sand, to lure a maker and mount him by my own cunning that I may be a Fremen entire.*

He felt now the maula pistol at his belt, the crysknife. He felt the silence surrounding him.

It was that special pre-morning silence when the nightbirds had gone and the day creatures had not yet signaled their alertness to their enemy, the sun.

"You must ride the sand in the light of day that Shai-hulud shall see and know you have no fear," Stilgar had said. "Thus we turn our time around and set ourselves to sleep this night."

Quietly, Paul sat up, feeling the looseness of a slacked stillsuit around his body, the shadowed stilltent beyond. So softly he moved, yet Chani heard him.

She spoke from the tent's gloom, another shadow there: "It's not yet full light, beloved."

"Sihaya," he said, speaking with half a laugh in his voice.

"You call me your desert spring," she said, "but this day I'm thy goad. I am the Sayyadina who watches that the rites be obeyed."

He began tightening his stillsuit. "You told me once the words of the Kitab al-Ibar," he said. "You told me: 'Woman is thy field; go then to thy field and till it.'"

"I am the mother of thy firstborn," she agreed.

He saw her in the grayness matching him movement for movement, securing her stillsuit for the open desert. "You should get all the rest you can," she said.

He recognized her love for him speaking then and chided her gently: "The Sayyadina of the Watch does not caution or warn the candidate."

She slid across to his side, touched his cheek with her palm. "Today, I am both the watcher and the woman."

"You should've left this duty to another," he said.

"Waiting is bad enough at best," she said. "I'd sooner be at thy side."

He kissed her palm before securing the faceflap of his suit, then turned and cracked the seal of the tent. The air that came in to them held the chill not-quite-dryness that would precipitate trace dew in the dawn. With it came the smell of a pre-spice mass, the mass they had detected off to the northeast, and that told them there would be a maker nearby.

Paul crawled through the sphincter opening, stood on the sand and stretched the sleep from his muscles. A faint green-pearl luminescence etched the eastern horizon. The tents of his troop were small false dunes around him in the gloom. He saw movement off to the left—the guard, and knew they had seen him.

They knew the peril he faced this day. Each Fremen had faced it. They gave him this last few moments of isolation now that he might prepare himself.

It must be done today, he told himself.

He thought of the power he wielded in the face of the pogrom—the old men who sent their sons to him to be trained in the weirding way of battle, the old men who listened to him now in council and followed his plans, the men who returned to pay him that highest Fremen compliment: "Your plan worked, Muad'Dib."

Yet the meanest and smallest of the Fremen warriors could do a thing that he had never done. And Paul knew his leadership suffered from the omnipresent knowledge of this difference between them.

He had not ridden the maker.

Oh, he'd gone up with the others for training trips and raids, but he had not made his own voyage. Until he did, his world was bounded by the abilities of others. No true Fremen could permit this. Until he did this thing himself, even the great southlands—the area some twenty thumpers beyond the erg—were denied him unless he ordered a palanquin and rode like a Reverend Mother or one of the sick and wounded.

Memory returned to him of his wrestling with his inner awareness during the night. He saw a strange parallel here—if he mastered the maker, his rule was strengthened; if he mastered the inward eye, this carried its own measure of command. But beyond them both lay the clouded area, the Great Unrest where all the universe seemed embroiled.

The differences in the ways he comprehended the universe haunted him—accuracy matched with inaccuracy. He saw it in situ. Yet, when it was born, when it came into the pressures of reality, the *now* had its own life and grew with its own subtle differences. Terrible purpose remained. Race consciousness remained. And over all loomed the jihad, bloody and wild.

Chani joined him outside the tent, hugging her elbows, looking up at him from the corners of her eyes the way she did when she studied his mood.

"Tell me again about the waters of thy birthworld, Usul," she said.

He saw that she was trying to distract him, ease his mind of tensions before the deadly test. It was growing lighter, and he noted that some of his Fedaykin were already striking their tents.

"I'd rather you told me about the sietch and about our son," he said. "Does our Leto yet hold my mother in his palm?"

"It's Alia he holds as well," she said. "And he grows rapidly. He'll be a big man."

"What's it like in the south?" he asked.

"When you ride the maker you'll see for yourself," she said.

"But I wish to see it first through your eyes."

"It's powerfully lonely," she said.

He touched the nezhoni scarf at her forehead where it protruded from her stillsuit cap. "Why will you not talk about the sietch?"

"I have talked about it. The sietch is a lonely place without our men. It's a place of work. We labor in the factories and the potting rooms. There are weapons to be made, poles to plant that we may forecast the weather, spice to collect for the bribes. There are dunes to be planted to make them grow and to anchor them. There are fabrics and rugs to make, fuel cells to charge. There are children to train that the tribe's strength may never be lost."

"Is nothing then pleasant in the sietch?" he asked.

"The children are pleasant. We observe the rites. We have sufficient food. Sometimes one of us may come north to be with her man. Life must go on."

"My sister, Alia—is she accepted yet by the people?"

Chani turned toward him in the growing dawnlight. Her eyes bored into him. "It's a thing to be discussed another time, beloved."

"Let us discuss it now."

"You should conserve your energies for the test," she said.

He saw that he had touched something sensitive, hearing the withdrawal in her voice. "The unknown brings its own worries," he said.

Presently she nodded, said, "There is yet . . . misunderstanding because of Alia's strangeness. The women are fearful because a child little more than an infant talks . . . of things that only an adult should know. They do not understand the . . . change in the womb that made Alia . . . different."

"There is trouble?" he asked. And he thought: *I've seen visions of trouble over Alia.*

Chani looked toward the growing line of the sunrise. "Some of the women banded to appeal to the Reverend Mother. They demanded she exorcise the demon in her daughter. They quoted the scripture: 'Suffer not a witch to live among us.'"

"And what did my mother say to them?"

"She recited the law and sent the women away abashed. She said: 'If Alia incites trouble, it is the fault of authority for not foreseeing and preventing the trouble.' And she tried to explain how the change had worked on Alia in the womb. But the women were angry because they had been embarrassed. They went away muttering."

There will be trouble because of Alia, he thought.

A crystal blowing of sand touched the exposed portions of his face, bringing the scent of the pre-spice mass. "El-Sayal, the rain of sand that brings the morning," he said.

He looked out across the gray light of the desert landscape, the landscape beyond pity, the sand that was form absorbed in itself. Dry lightning streaked a dark corner to the south—sign that a storm had built up its static charge there. The roll of thunder boomed long after.

"The voice that beautifies the land," Chani said.

More of his men were stirring out of their tents. Guards were coming in from the rims. Everything around him moved smoothly in the ancient routine that required no orders.

"Give as few orders as possible," his father had told him . . . once . . . long ago. "Once you've given orders on a subject, you must always give orders on that subject."

The Fremen knew this rule instinctively.

The troop's watermaster began the morning chanty, adding to it now the call for the rite to initiate a sandrider.

"The world is a carcass," the man chanted, his voice wailing across the dunes. "Who can turn away the Angel of Death? What Shai-hulud has decreed must be."

Paul listened, recognizing that these were the words that also began the death chant of his Fedaykin, the words the death commandos recited as they hurled themselves into battle.

Will there be a rock shrine here this day to mark the passing of another soul? Paul asked himself. *Will Fremen stop here in the future, each to add another stone and think on Muad'Dib who died in this place?*

He knew this was among the alternatives today, a *fact* along lines of the future radiating from this position in time-space. The imperfect vision plagued him. The more he resisted his terrible purpose and fought against the coming of the jihad, the greater the turmoil that wove through his prescience. His entire future was becoming like a river hurtling toward a chasm—the violent nexus beyond which all was fog and clouds.

"Stilgar approaches," Chani said. "I must stand apart now, beloved. Now, I must be Sayyadina and observe the rite that it may be reported truly in the Chronicles." She looked up at him and, for a moment, her reserve slipped, then she had herself under control. "When this is past, I shall prepare thy breakfast with my own hands," she said. She turned away.

Stilgar moved toward him across the flour sand, stirring up little dust puddles. The dark niches of his eyes remained steady on Paul with their untamed stare. The glimpse of black beard above the stillsuit mask, the lines of craggy cheeks, could have been wind-etched from the native rock for all their movement.

The man carried Paul's banner on its staff—the green and black banner with a water tube in the staff—that already was a legend in the land. Half pridefully, Paul thought: *I cannot do the simplest thing without its becoming a legend. They will mark how I parted from Chani, how I greet Stilgar—every move I make this day. Live or die, it is a legend. I must not die. Then it will be only legend and nothing to stop the jihad.*

Stilgar planted the staff in the sand beside Paul, dropped his hands to his sides. The blue-within-blue eyes remained level and intent. And

Paul thought how his own eyes already were assuming this mask of color from the spice.

"They denied us the Hajj," Stilgar said with ritual solemnity.

As Chani had taught him, Paul responded: "Who can deny a Fremen the right to walk or ride where he wills?"

"I am a Naib," Stilgar said, "never to be taken alive. I am a leg of the death tripod that will destroy our foes."

Silence settled over them.

Paul glanced at the other Fremen scattered over the sand beyond Stilgar, the way they stood without moving for this moment of personal prayer. And he thought of how the Fremen were a people whose living consisted of killing, an entire people who had lived with rage and grief all of their days, never once considering what might take the place of either—except for a dream with which Liet-Kynes had infused them before his death.

"Where is the Lord who led us through the land of desert and of pits?" Stilgar asked.

"He is ever with us," the Fremen chanted.

Stilgar squared his shoulders, stepped closer to Paul and lowered his voice. "Now, remember what I told you. Do it simply and directly—nothing fancy. Among our people, we ride the maker at the age of twelve. You are more than six years beyond that age and not born to this life. You don't have to impress anyone with your courage. We know you are brave. All you must do is call the maker and ride him."

"I will remember," Paul said.

"See that you do. I'll not have you shame my teaching."

Stilgar pulled a plastic rod about a meter long from beneath his robe. The thing was pointed at one end, had a spring-wound clapper at the other end. "I prepared this thumper myself. It's a good one. Take it."

Paul felt the warm smoothness of the plastic as he accepted the thumper.

"Shishakli has your hooks," Stilgar said. "He'll hand them to you as you step out onto that dune over there." He pointed to his right. "Call a big maker, Usul. Show us the way."

Paul marked the tone of Stilgar's voice—half ritual and half that of a worried friend.

In that instant, the sun seemed to bound above the horizon. The sky took on the silvered gray-blue that warned this would be a day of extreme heat and dryness even for Arrakis.

"It is the time of the scalding day," Stilgar said, and now his voice was entirely ritual. "Go, Usul, and ride the maker, travel the sand as a leader of men."

Paul saluted his banner, noting how the green and black flag hung limply now that the dawn wind had died. He turned toward the dune Stilgar had indicated—a dirty tan slope with an S-track crest. Already, most of the troop was moving out in the opposite direction, climbing the other dune that had sheltered their camp.

One robed figure remained in Paul's path: Shishakli, a squad leader of the Fedaykin, only his slope-lidded eyes visible between stillsuit cap and mask.

Shishakli presented two thin, whiplike shafts as Paul approached. The shafts were about a meter and a half long with glistening plasteel hooks at one end, roughened at the other end for a firm grip.

Paul accepted them both in his left hand as required by the ritual.

"They are my own hooks," Shishakli said in a husky voice. "They never have failed."

Paul nodded, maintaining the necessary silence, moved past the man and up the dune slope. At the crest, he glanced back, saw the troop scattering like a flight of insects, their robes fluttering. He stood alone now on the sandy ridge with only the horizon in front of him, the flat and unmoving horizon. This was a good dune Stilgar had chosen, higher than its companions for the viewpoint vantage.

Stooping, Paul planted the thumper deep into the windward face where the sand was compacted and would give maximum transmission to the drumming. Then he hesitated, reviewing the lessons, reviewing the life-and-death necessities that faced him.

When he threw the latch, the thumper would begin its summons. Across the sand, a giant worm—a maker—would hear and come to the drumming. With the whiplike hook-staffs, Paul knew, he could mount the maker's high curving back. For as long as a forward edge of a worm's ring segment was held open by a hook, open to admit abrasive sand into the more sensitive interior, the creature would not retreat beneath the desert. It would, in fact, roll its gigantic body to bring the opened segment as far away from the desert surface as possible.

I am a sandrider, Paul told himself.

He glanced down at the hooks in his left hand, thinking that he had only to shift those hooks down the curve of a maker's immense side to make the creature roll and turn, guiding it where he willed. He had seen it done. He had been helped up the side of a worm for a short ride in training. The captive worm could be ridden until it lay exhausted and quiescent upon the desert surface and a new maker must be summoned.

Once he was past this test, Paul knew, he was qualified to make the twenty-thumper journey into the southland—to rest and restore himself—into the south where the women and the families had been hidden from the pogrom among the new palmaries and sietch warrens.

He lifted his head and looked to the south, reminding himself that the maker summoned wild from the erg was an unknown quantity, and the one who summoned it was equally unknown to this test.

"You must gauge the approaching maker carefully," Stilgar had explained. "You must stand close enough that you can mount it as it passes, yet not so close that it engulfs you."

With abrupt decision, Paul released the thumper's latch. The clapper began revolving and the summons drummed through the sand, a measured "lump . . . lump . . . lump. . . ."

He straightened, scanning the horizon, remembering Stilgar's words: "Judge the line of approach carefully. Remember, a worm seldom makes an unseen approach to a thumper. Listen all the same. You may often hear it before you see it."

And Chani's words of caution, whispered at night when her fear for him overcame her, filled his mind: "When you take your stand along the maker's path, you must remain utterly still. You must think like a patch of sand. Hide beneath your cloak and become a little dune in your very essence."

Slowly, he scanned the horizon, listening, watching for the signs he had been taught.

It came from the southeast, a distant hissing, a sand-whisper. Presently he saw the faraway outline of the creature's track against the dawnlight and realized he had never before seen a maker this large, never heard of one this size. It appeared to be more than half a league long, and the rise of the sandwave at its cresting head was like the approach of a mountain.

This is nothing I have seen by vision or in life, Paul cautioned himself. He hurried across the path of the thing to take his stand, caught up entirely by the rushing needs of this moment.

"Control the coinage and the courts—let the rabble have the rest." Thus the Padishah Emperor advised you. And he tells you: "If you want profits, you must rule." There is truth in these words, but I ask myself: "Who are the rabble and who are the ruled?"

—MUAD'DIB'S SECRET MESSAGE TO THE LANDSRAAD
FROM "ARRAKIS AWAKENING"
BY THE PRINCESS IRULAN

A thought came unbidden to Jessica's mind: *Paul will be undergoing his sandrider test at any moment now. They try to conceal this fact from me, but it's obvious.*

And Chani has gone on some mysterious errand.

Jessica sat in her resting chamber, catching a moment of quiet between the night's classes. It was a pleasant chamber, but not as large as the one she had enjoyed in Sietch Tabr before their flight from the pogrom. Still, this place had thick rugs on the floor, soft cushions, a low coffee table near at hand, multicolored hangings on the walls, and soft yellow glowglobes overhead. The room was permeated with the distinctive acrid furry odor of a Fremen sietch that she had come to associate with a sense of security.

Yet she knew she would never overcome a feeling of being in an alien place. It was the harshness that the rugs and hangings attempted to conceal.

A faint tinkling-drumming-slapping penetrated to the resting chamber. Jessica knew it for a birth celebration, probably Subiay's. Her time was near. And Jessica knew she'd see the baby soon enough—a blue-eyed cherub brought to the Reverend Mother for blessing. She knew also that her daughter, Alia, would be at the celebration and would report on it.

It was not yet time for the nightly prayer of parting. They wouldn't have started a birth celebration near the time of ceremony that mourned the slave raids of Poritrin, Bela Tegeuse, Rossak, and Harmonthep.

Jessica sighed. She knew she was trying to keep her thoughts off her son and the dangers he faced—the pit traps with their poisoned barbs, the Harkonnen raids (although these were growing fewer as the Fremen took their toll of aircraft and raiders with the new weapons Paul had given them), and the natural dangers of the desert—makers and thirst and dust chasms.

She thought of calling for coffee and with the thought came that ever-present awareness of paradox in the Fremen way of life: how well they lived in these sietch caverns compared to the graben pyons; yet, how much more they endured in the open hajr of the desert than anything the Harkonnen bondsmen endured.

A dark hand inserted itself through the hangings beside her, deposited a cup upon the table and withdrew. From the cup arose the aroma of spiced coffee.

An offering from the birth celebration, Jessica thought.

She took the coffee and sipped it, smiling at herself. *In what other society of our universe,* she asked herself, *could a person of my station accept an anonymous drink and quaff that drink without fear? I could alter any poison now before it did me harm, of course, but the donor doesn't realize this.*

She drained the cup, feeling the energy and lift of its contents—hot and delicious.

And she wondered what other society would have such a natural regard for her privacy and comfort that the giver would intrude only enough to deposit the gift and not inflict her with the donor? Respect and love had sent the gift—with only a slight tinge of fear.

Another element of the incident forced itself into her awareness: she had thought of coffee and it had appeared. There was nothing of telepathy here, she knew. It was the tau, the oneness of the sietch community, a compensation from the subtle poison of the spice diet they shared. The great mass of the people could never hope to attain the enlightenment the spice seed brought to her; they had not been trained and prepared for it. Their minds rejected what they could not understand or encompass. Still they felt and reacted sometimes like a single organism.

And the thought of coincidence never entered their minds.

Has Paul passed his test on the sand? Jessica asked herself. *He's capable, but accident can strike down even the most capable.*

The waiting.

It's the dreariness, she thought. *You can wait just so long. Then the dreariness of the waiting overcomes you.*

There was all manner of waiting in their lives.

More than two years we've been here, she thought, *and twice that number at least to go before we can even hope to think of trying to wrest Arrakis from the Harkonnen governor, the Mudir Nahya, the Beast Rabban.*

"Reverend Mother?"

The voice from outside the hangings at her door was that of Harah, the other woman in Paul's menage.

"Yes, Harah."

The hangings parted and Harah seemed to glide through them. She wore sietch sandals, a red-yellow wraparound that exposed her arms almost to the shoulders. Her black hair was parted in the middle and swept back like the wings of an insect, flat and oily against her head. The jutting, predatory features were drawn into an intense frown.

Behind Harah came Alia, a girl-child of about two years.

Seeing her daughter, Jessica was caught as she frequently was by Alia's resemblance to Paul at that age—the same wide-eyed solemnity to her questing look, the dark hair and firmness of mouth. But there were subtle differences, too, and it was in these that most adults found Alia disquieting. The child—little more than a toddler—carried herself with a calmness and awareness beyond her years. Adults were shocked to find her laughing at a subtle play of words between the sexes. Or they'd catch themselves listening to her half-lisping voice, still blurred as it was by an unformed soft palate, and discover in her words sly remarks that could only be based on experiences no two-year-old had ever encountered.

Harah sank to a cushion with an exasperated sigh, frowned at the child.

"Alia." Jessica motioned to her daughter.

The child crossed to a cushion beside her mother, sank to it and clasped her mother's hand. The contact of flesh restored that mutual awareness they had shared since before Alia's birth. It wasn't a matter of shared thoughts—although there were bursts of that if they touched while Jessica was changing the spice poison for a ceremony. It was something larger, an immediate awareness of another living spark, a sharp and poignant thing, a nerve-*simpatico* that made them emotionally one.

In the formal manner that befitted a member of her son's household, Jessica said: "Subakh ul kuhar, Harah. This night finds you well?"

With the same traditional formality, she said: "Subakh un nar. I am well." The words were almost toneless. Again, she sighed.

Jessica sensed amusement from Alia.

"My brother's ghanima is annoyed with me," Alia said in her half-lisp.

Jessica marked the term Alia used to refer to Harah—ghanima. In the subtleties of the Fremen tongue, the word meant "something acquired in battle" and with the added overtone that the something no longer was used for its original purpose. An ornament, a spearhead used as a curtain weight.

Harah scowled at the child. "Don't try to insult me, child. I know my place."

"What have you done this time, Alia?" Jessica asked.

Harah answered: "Not only has she refused to play with the other children today, but she intruded where. . . ."

"I hid behind the hangings and watched Subiay's child being born," Alia said. "It's a boy. He cried and cried. What a set of lungs! When he'd cried long enough—"

"She came out and touched him," Harah said, "and he stopped crying. Everyone knows a Fremen baby must get his crying done at birth, if he's in sietch because he can never cry again lest he betray us on hajr."

"He'd cried enough," Alia said. "I just wanted to feel his spark, his life. That's all. And when he felt me he didn't want to cry anymore."

"It's just made more talk among the people," Harah said.

"Subiay's boy is healthy?" Jessica asked. She saw that something was troubling Harah deeply and wondered at it.

"Healthy as any mother could ask," Harah said. "They know Alia didn't hurt him. They didn't so much mind her touching him. He settled down right away and was happy. I was. . . ." Harah shrugged.

"It's the strangeness of my daughter, is that it?" Jessica asked. "It's the way she speaks of things beyond her years and of things no child her age could know—things of the past."

"How could she know what a child looked like on Bela Tegeuse?" Harah demanded.

"But he does!" Alia said. "Subiay's boy looks just like the son of Mitha born before the parting."

"Alia!" Jessica said. "I warned you."

"But, Mother, I saw it and it was true and. . . ."

Jessica shook her head, seeing the signs of disturbance in Harah's face. *What have I borne?* Jessica asked herself. *A daughter who knew at birth everything that I knew . . . and more: everything revealed to her out of the corridors of the past by the Reverend Mothers within me.*

"It's not just the things she says," Harah said. "It's the exercises, too: the way she sits and stares at a rock, moving only one muscle beside her nose, or a muscle on the back of a finger, or—"

"Those are the Bene Gesserit training," Jessica said. "You know that, Harah. Would you deny my daughter her inheritance?"

"Reverend Mother, you know these things don't matter to me," Harah said. "It's the people and the way they mutter. I feel danger in it.

They say your daughter's a demon, that other children refuse to play with her, that she's—"

"She has so little in common with the other children," Jessica said. "She's no demon. It's just the—"

"Of course she's not!"

Jessica found herself surprised at the vehemence in Harah's tone, glanced down at Alia. The child appeared lost in thought, radiating a sense of . . . waiting. Jessica returned her attention to Harah.

"I respect the fact that you're a member of my son's household," Jessica said. (Alia stirred against her hand.) "You may speak openly with me of whatever's troubling you."

"I will not be a member of your son's household much longer," Harah said. "I've waited this long for the sake of my sons, the special training *they* receive as the children of Usul. It's little enough I could give them since it's known I don't share your son's bed."

Again Alia stirred beside her, half-sleeping, warm.

"You'd have made a good companion for my son, though," Jessica said. And she added to herself because such thoughts were ever with her: *Companion . . . not a wife.* Jessica's thoughts went then straight to the center, to the pang that came from the common talk in the sietch that her son's companionship with Chani had become a permanent thing, the marriage.

I love Chani, Jessica thought, but she reminded herself that love might have to step aside for royal necessity. Royal marriages had other reasons than love.

"You think I don't know what you plan for your son?" Harah asked.

"What do you mean?" Jessica demanded.

"You plan to unite the tribes under *Him,*" Harah said.

"Is that bad?"

"I see danger for him . . . and Alia is part of that danger."

Alia nestled closer to her mother, eyes opened now and studying Harah.

"I've watched you two together," Harah said, "the way you touch. And Alia is like my own flesh because she's sister to one who is like my brother. I've watched over her and guarded her from the time she was a mere baby, from the time of the razzia when we fled here. I've seen many things about her."

Jessica nodded, feeling disquiet begin to grow in Alia beside her.

"You know what I mean," Harah said. "The way she knew from the first what we were saying to her. When has there been another baby who knew the water discipline so young? What other baby's first words to her nurse were: 'I love you, Harah'?"

Harah stared at Alia. "Why do you think I accept her insults? I know there's no malice in them."

Alia looked up at her mother.

"Yes, I have reasoning powers, Reverend Mother," Harah said. "I could have been of the Sayyadina. I have seen what I have seen."

"Harah. . . ." Jessica shrugged. "I don't know what to say." And she felt surprise at herself, because this literally was true.

Alia straightened, squared her shoulders. Jessica felt the sense of waiting ended, an emotion compounded of decision and sadness.

"We made a mistake," Alia said. "Now we need Harah."

"It was the ceremony of the seed," Harah said, "when you changed the Water of Life, Reverend Mother, when Alia was yet unborn within you."

Need Harah? Jessica asked herself.

"Who else can talk among the people and make them begin to understand me?" Alia asked.

"What would you have her do?" Jessica asked.

"She already knows what to do," Alia said.

"I will tell them the truth," Harah said. Her face seemed suddenly old and sad with its olive skin drawn into frown wrinkles, a witchery in the sharp features. "I will tell them that Alia only pretends to be a little girl, that she has never been a little girl."

Alia shook her head. Tears ran down her cheeks, and Jessica felt the wave of sadness from her daughter as though the emotion were her own.

"I know I'm a freak," Alia whispered. The adult summation coming from the child mouth was like a bitter confirmation.

"You're not a freak!" Harah snapped. "Who dared say you're a freak?"

Again, Jessica marveled at the fierce note of protectiveness in Harah's voice. Jessica saw then that Alia had judged correctly—they did need Harah. The tribe would understand Harah—both her words and her emotions—for it was obvious she loved Alia as though this were her own child.

"Who said it?" Harah repeated.

"Nobody."

Alia used a corner of Jessica's aba to wipe the tears from her face. She smoothed the robe where she had dampened and crumpled it.

"Then don't you say it," Harah ordered.

"Yes, Harah."

"Now," Harah said, "you may tell me what it was like so that I may tell the others. Tell me what it is that happened to you."

Alia swallowed, looked up at her mother.

Jessica nodded.

"One day I woke up," Alia said. "It was like waking from sleep except that I could not remember going to sleep. I was in a warm, dark place. And I was frightened."

Listening to the half-lisping voice of her daughter, Jessica remembered that day in the big cavern.

"When I was frightened," Alia said, "I tried to escape, but there was no way to escape. Then I saw a spark . . . but it wasn't exactly like seeing it. The spark was just there with me and I felt the spark's emotions . . . soothing me, comforting me, telling me that way that everything would be all right. That was my mother."

Harah rubbed at her eyes, smiled reassuringly at Alia. Yet there was a look of wildness in the eyes of the Fremen woman, an intensity as though they, too, were trying to hear Alia's words.

And Jessica thought: *What do we really know of how such a one thinks . . . out of her unique experiences and training and ancestry?*

"Just when I felt safe and reassured," Alia said, "there was another spark with us . . . and everything was happening at once. The other spark was the old Reverend Mother. She was . . . trading lives with my mother . . . everything . . . and I was there with them, seeing it all . . . everything. And it was over, and I was them and all the others and myself . . . only it took me a long time to find myself again. There were so many others."

"It was a cruel thing," Jessica said. "No being should wake into consciousness thus. The wonder of it is you could accept all that happened to you."

"I couldn't do anything else!" Alia said. "I didn't know how to reject or hide my consciousness . . . or shut it off . . . everything just happened . . . everything. . . ."

"We didn't know," Harah murmured. "When we gave your mother the Water to change, we didn't know you existed within her."

"Don't be sad about it, Harah," Alia said. "I shouldn't feel sorry for myself. After all, there's cause for happiness here: I'm a Reverend Mother. The tribe has two Rev. . . ."

She broke off, tipping her head to listen.

Harah rocked back on her heels against the sitting cushion, stared at Alia, bringing her attention then up to Jessica's face.

"Didn't you suspect?" Jessica asked.

"Sh-h-h," Alia said.

A distant rhythmic chanting came to them through the hangings that separated them from the sietch corridors. It grew louder, carrying distinct sounds now: "Ya! Ya! Yawm! Ya! Ya! Yawm! Mu zein, wallah! Ya! Ya! Yawm! Mu zein, Wallah!"

The chanters passed the outer entrance, and their voices boomed through to the inner apartments. Slowly the sound receded.

When the sound had dimmed sufficiently, Jessica began the ritual, the sadness in her voice: "It was Ramadhan and April on Bela Tegeuse."

"My family sat in their pool courtyard," Harah said, "in air bathed by the moisture that arose from the spray of a fountain. There was a tree of portyguls, round and deep in color, near at hand. There was a basket with mish-mish and baklawa and mugs of liban—all manner of good things to eat. In our gardens and in our flocks, there was peace . . . peace in all the land."

"Life was full with happiness until the raiders came," Alia said.

"Blood ran cold at the scream of friends," Jessica said. And she felt the memories rushing through her out of all those other pasts she shared.

"La, la, la, the women cried," said Harah.

"The raiders came through the mushtamal, rushing at us with their knives dripping red from the lives of our men," Jessica said.

Silence came over the three of them as it was in all the apartments of the sietch, the silence while they remembered and kept their grief thus fresh.

Presently, Harah uttered the ritual ending to the ceremony, giving the words a harshness that Jessica had never before heard in them.

"We will never forgive and we will never forget," Harah said.

In the thoughtful quiet that followed her words, they heard a muttering of people, the swish of many robes. Jessica sensed someone standing beyond the hangings that shielded her chamber.

"Reverend Mother?"

A woman's voice, and Jessica recognized it: the voice of Tharthar, one of Stilgar's wives.

"What is it, Tharthar?"

"There is trouble, Reverend Mother."

Jessica felt a constriction at her heart, an abrupt fear for Paul. "Paul . . ." she gasped.

Tharthar spread the hangings, stepped into the chamber. Jessica glimpsed a press of people in the outer room before the hangings fell. She looked up at Tharthar—a small, dark woman in a red-figured robe of black, the total blue of her eyes trained fixedly on Jessica, the nostrils of her tiny nose dilated to reveal the plug scars.

"What is it?" Jessica demanded.

"There is word from the sand," Tharthar said. "Usul meets the maker for his test . . . it is today. The young men say he cannot fail, he will be a sandrider by nightfall. The young men are banding for a razzia. They will raid in the north and meet Usul there. They say they will raise the cry then. They say they will force him to call out Stilgar and assume command of the tribes."

Gathering water, planting the dunes, changing their world slowly but surely—these are no longer enough, Jessica thought. *The little raids, the certain raids—these are no longer enough now that Paul and I have trained them. They feel their power. They want to fight.*

Tharthar shifted from one foot to the other, cleared her throat.

We know the need for cautious waiting, Jessica thought, *but there's the core of our frustration. We know also the harm that waiting extended too long can do us. We lose our senses of purpose if the waiting's prolonged.*

"The young men say if Usul does not call out Stilgar, then he must be afraid," Tharthar said.

She lowered her gaze.

"So that's the way of it," Jessica muttered. And she thought: *Well I saw it coming. As did Stilgar.*

Again, Tharthar cleared her throat. "Even my brother, Shoab, says it," she said. "They will leave Usul no choice."

Then it has come, Jessica thought. *And Paul will have to handle it himself. The Reverend Mother dare not become involved in the succession.*

Alia freed her hand from her mother's, said: "I will go with Tharthar and listen to the young men. Perhaps there is a way."

Jessica met Tharthar's gaze, but spoke to Alia: "Go, then. And report to me as soon as you can."

"We do not want this thing to happen, Reverend Mother," Tharthar said.

"We do not want it," Jessica agreed. "The tribe needs *all* its strength." She glanced at Harah. "Will you go with them?"

Harah answered the unspoken part of the question: "Tharthar will allow no harm to befall Alia. She knows we will soon be wives together, she and I, to share the same man. We have talked, Tharthar and I." Harah looked up at Tharthar, back to Jessica. "We have an understanding."

Tharthar held out a hand for Alia, said: "We must hurry. The young men are leaving."

They pressed through the hangings, the child's hand in the small woman's hand, but the child seemed to be leading.

"If Paul-Muad'Dib slays Stilgar, this will not serve the tribe," Harah said. "Always before, it has been the way of succession, but times have changed."

"Times have changed for you, as well," Jessica said.

"You cannot think I doubt the outcome of such a battle," Harah said. "Usul could not but win."

"That was my meaning," Jessica said.

"And you think my personal feelings enter into my judgment," Harah said. She shook her head, her water rings tinkling at her neck. "How wrong you are. Perhaps you think, as well, that I regret not being the chosen of Usul, that I am jealous of Chani?"

"You make your own choice as you are able," Jessica said.

"I pity Chani," Harah said.

Jessica stiffened. "What do you mean?"

"I know what you think of Chani," Harah said. "You think she is not the wife for your son."

Jessica settled back, relaxed on her cushions. She shrugged. "Perhaps."

"You could be right," Harah said. "If you are, you may find a surprising ally—Chani herself. She wants whatever is best for *Him*."

Jessica swallowed past a sudden tightening in her throat. "Chani's very dear to me," she said. "She could be no—"

"Your rugs are very dirty in here," Harah said. She swept her gaze around the floor, avoiding Jessica's eyes. "So many people tramping through here all the time. You really should have them cleaned more often."

You cannot avoid the interplay of politics within an orthodox religion. This power struggle permeates the training, educating and disciplining of the orthodox community. Because of this pressure, the leaders of such a community inevitably must face that ultimate internal question: to succumb to complete opportunism as the price of maintaining their rule, or risk sacrificing themselves for the sake of the orthodox ethic.

—FROM "MUAD'DIB: THE RELIGIOUS ISSUES"
BY THE PRINCESS IRULAN

Paul waited on the sand outside the gigantic maker's line of approach. *I must not wait like a smuggler—impatient and jittering,* he reminded himself. *I must be part of the desert.*

The thing was only minutes away now, filling the morning with the friction-hissing of its passage. Its great teeth within the cavern-circle of its mouth spread like some enormous flower. The spice odor from it dominated the air.

Paul's stillsuit rode easily on his body and he was only distantly aware of his nose plugs, the breathing mask. Stilgar's teaching, the painstaking hours on the sand, overshadowed all else.

"How far outside the maker's radius must you stand in pea sand?" Stilgar had asked him.

And he had answered correctly: "Half a meter for every meter of the maker's diameter."

"Why?"

"To avoid the vortex of its passage and still have time to run in and mount it."

"You've ridden the little ones bred for the seed and the Water of Life," Stilgar had said. "But what you'll summon for your test is a wild maker, an old man of the desert. You must have proper respect for such a one."

Now the thumper's deep drumming blended with the hiss of the approaching worm. Paul breathed deeply, smelling mineral bitterness of sand even through his filters. The wild maker, the old man of the desert, loomed almost on him. Its cresting front segments threw a sand-wave that would sweep across his knees.

Come up, you lovely monster, he thought. *Up. You hear me calling. Come up. Come up.*

The wave lifted his feet. Surface dust swept across him. He steadied himself, his world dominated by the passage of that sand-clouded curving wall, that segmented cliff, the ring lines sharply defined in it.

Paul lifted his hooks, sighted along them, leaned in. He felt them bite and pull. He leaped upward, planting his feet against that wall, leaning out against the clinging barbs. This was the true instant of the testing: if he had planted the hooks correctly at the leading edge of a ring segment, opening the segment, the worm would not roll down and crush him.

The worm slowed. It glided across the thumper, silencing it. Slowly, it began to roll—up, up—bringing those irritant barbs as high as possible, away from the sand that threatened the soft inner lapping of its ring segment.

Paul found himself riding upright atop the worm. He felt exultant, like an emperor surveying his world. He suppressed a sudden urge to cavort there, to turn the worm, to show off his mastery of this creature.

Suddenly he understood why Stilgar had warned him once about brash young men who danced and played with these monsters, doing handstands on their backs, removing both hooks and replanting them before the worm could spill them.

Leaving one hook in place, Paul released the other and planted it lower down the side. When the second hook was firm and tested, he brought down the first one, thus worked his way down the side. The maker rolled, and as it rolled, it turned, coming around the sweep of flour sand where the others waited.

Paul saw them come up, using their hooks to climb, but avoiding the sensitive ring edges until they were on top. They rode at last in a triple line behind him, steadied against their hooks.

Stilgar moved up through the ranks, checked the positioning of Paul's hooks, glanced up at Paul's smiling face.

"You did it, eh?" Stilgar asked, raising his voice above the hiss of their passage. "That's what you think? You did it?" He straightened. "Now I tell you that was a very sloppy job. We have twelve-year-olds who do better. There was drumsand to your left where you waited. You could not retreat there if the worm turned that way."

The smile slipped from Paul's face. "I saw the drumsand."

"Then why did you not signal for one of us to take up position secondary to you? It was a thing you could do even in the test."

Paul swallowed, faced into the wind of their passage.

"You think it bad of me to say this now," Stilgar said. "It is my duty. I think of your worth to the troop. If you had stumbled into that drumsand, the maker would've turned toward you."

In spite of a surge of anger, Paul knew that Stilgar spoke the truth. It took a long minute and the full effort of the training he had received from his mother for Paul to recapture a feeling of calm. "I apologize," he said. "It will not happen again."

"In a tight position, always leave yourself a secondary, someone to take the maker if you cannot," Stilgar said. "Remember that we work together. That way, we're certain. We work together, eh?"

He slapped Paul's shoulder.

"We work together," Paul agreed.

"Now," Stilgar said, and his voice was harsh, "show me you know how to handle a maker. Which side are we on?"

Paul glanced down at the scaled ring surface on which they stood, noted the character and size of the scales, the way they grew larger off to his right, smaller to his left. Every worm, he knew, moved characteristically with one side up more frequently. As it grew older, the characteristic up-side became an almost constant thing. Bottom scales grew larger, heavier, smoother. Top scales could be told by size alone on a big worm.

Shifting his hooks, Paul moved to the left. He motioned flankers down to open segments along the side and keep the worm on a straight course as it rolled. When he had it turned, he motioned two steersmen out of the line and into positions ahead.

"Ach, haiiiii-yoh!" he shouted in the traditional call. The left-side steersman opened a ring segment there.

In a majestic circle, the maker turned to protect its opened segment. Full around it came and when it was headed back to the south, Paul shouted: "Geyrat!"

The steersman released his hook. The maker lined out in a straight course.

Stilgar said, "Very good, Paul-Muad'Dib. With plenty of practice, you may yet become a sandrider."

Paul frowned, thinking: *Was I not first up?*

From behind him there came sudden laughter. The troop began chanting, flinging his name against the sky.

"Muad'Dib! Muad'Dib! Muad'Dib! Muad'Dib!"

And far to the rear along the worm's surface, Paul heard the beat of the goaders pounding the tail segments. The worm began picking up speed. Their robes flapped in the wind. The abrasive sound of their passage increased.

Paul looked back through the troop, found Chani's face among them. He looked at her as he spoke to Stilgar. "Then I am a sandrider, Stil?"

"Hal yawm! You are a sandrider this day."

"Then I may choose our destination?"

"That's the way of it."

"And I am a Fremen born this day here in the Habbanya erg. I have had no life before this day. I was as a child until this day."

"Not quite a child," Stilgar said. He fastened a corner of his hood where the wind was whipping it.

"But there was a cork sealing off my world, and that cork has been pulled."

"There is no cork."

"I would go south, Stilgar—twenty thumpers. I would see this land we make, this land that I've only seen through the eyes of others."

And I would see my son and my family, he thought. *I need time now to consider the future that is a past within my mind. The turmoil comes and if I'm not where I can unravel it, the thing will run wild.*

Stilgar looked at him with a steady, measuring gaze. Paul kept his attention on Chani, seeing the interest quicken in her face, noting also the excitement his words had kindled in the troop.

"The men are eager to raid with you in the Harkonnen sinks," Stilgar said. "The sinks are only a thumper away."

"The Fedaykin have raided with me," Paul said. "They'll raid with me again until no Harkonnen breathes Arrakeen air."

Stilgar studied him as they rode, and Paul realized the man was seeing this moment through the memory of how he had risen to command of the Tabr sietch and to leadership of the Council of Leaders now that Liet-Kynes was dead.

He has heard the reports of unrest among the young Fremen, Paul thought.

"Do you wish a gathering of the leaders?" Stilgar asked.

Eyes blazed among the young men of the troop. They swayed as they rode, and they watched. And Paul saw the look of unrest in Chani's glance, the way she looked from Stilgar, who was her uncle, to Paul-Muad'Dib, who was her mate.

"You cannot guess what I want," Paul said.

And he thought: *I cannot back down. I must hold control over these people.*

"You are mudir of the sandride this day," Stilgar said. Cold formality rang in his voice: "How do you use this power?"

We need time to relax, time for cool reflection, Paul thought.

"We shall go south," Paul said.

"Even if I say we shall turn back to the north when this day is over?"

"We shall go south," Paul repeated.

A sense of inevitable dignity enfolded Stilgar as he pulled his robe tightly around him. "There will be a Gathering," he said. "I will send the messages."

He thinks I will call him out, Paul thought. *And he knows he cannot stand against me.*

Paul faced south, feeling the wind against his exposed cheeks, thinking of the necessities that went into his decisions.

They do not know how it is, he thought.

But he knew he could not let any consideration deflect him. He had to remain on the central line of the time storm he could see in the future. There would come an instant when it could be unraveled, but only if he were where he could cut the central knot of it.

I will not call him out if it can be helped, he thought. *If there's another way to prevent the jihad. . . .*

"We'll camp for the evening meal and prayer at Cave of Birds beneath Habbanya Ridge," Stilgar said. He steadied himself with one hook against the swaying of the maker, gestured ahead at a low rock barrier rising out of the desert.

Paul studied the cliff, the great streaks of rock crossing it like waves. No green, no blossom softened that rigid horizon. Beyond it stretched the way to the southern desert—a course of at least ten days and nights, as fast as they could goad the makers.

Twenty thumpers.

The way led far beyond the Harkonnen patrols. He knew how it would be. The dreams had shown him. One day, as they went, there'd be a faint change of color on the far horizon—such a slight change that he might feel he was imagining it out of his hopes—and there would be the new sietch.

"Does my decision suit Muad'Dib?" Stilgar asked. Only the faintest touch of sarcasm tinged his voice, but Fremen ears around them, alert to every tone in a bird's cry or a cielago's piping message, heard the sarcasm and watched Paul to see what he would do.

"Stilgar heard me swear my loyalty to him when we consecrated the Fedaykin," Paul said. "My death commandos know I spoke with honor. Does Stilgar doubt it?"

Real pain exposed itself in Paul's voice. Stilgar heard it and lowered his gaze.

"Usul, the companion of my sietch, him I would never doubt," Stilgar said. "But you are Paul-Muad'Dib, the Atreides Duke, and you are the Lisan al-Gaib, the Voice from the Outer World. These men I don't even know."

Paul turned away to watch the Habbanya Ridge climb out of the desert. The maker beneath them still felt strong and willing. It could carry them almost twice the distance of any other in Fremen experience. He knew it. There was nothing outside the stories told to children that could match this old man of the desert. It was the stuff of a new legend, Paul realized.

A hand gripped his shoulder.

Paul looked at it, followed the arm to the face beyond it—the dark eyes of Stilgar exposed between filter mask and stillsuit hood.

"The one who led Tabr sietch before me," Stilgar said, "he was my friend. We shared dangers. He owed me his life many a time . . . and I owed him mine."

"I am your friend, Stilgar," Paul said.

"No man doubts it," Stilgar said. He removed his hand, shrugged. "It's the way."

Paul saw that Stilgar was too immersed in the Fremen way to consider the possibility of any other. Here a leader took the reins from the dead hands of his predecessor, or slew among the strongest of his tribe if a leader died in the desert. Stilgar had risen to be a naib in that way.

"We should leave this maker in deep sand," Paul said.

"Yes," Stilgar agreed. "We could walk to the cave from here."

"We've ridden him far enough that he'll bury himself and sulk for a day or so," Paul said.

"You're the mudir of the sandride," Stilgar said. "Say when we . . ." He broke off, stared at the eastern sky.

Paul whirled. The spice-blue overcast on his eyes made the sky appear dark, a richly filtered azure against which a distant rhythmic flashing stood out in sharp contrast.

Ornithopter!

"One small 'thopter," Stilgar said.

"Could be a scout," Paul said. "Do you think they've seen us?"

"At this distance we're just a worm on the surface," Stilgar said. He motioned with his left hand. "Off. Scatter on the sand."

The troop began working down the worm's sides, dropping off, blending with the sand beneath their cloaks. Paul marked where Chani dropped. Presently, only he and Stilgar remained.

"First up, last off," Paul said.

Stilgar nodded, dropped down the side on his hooks, leaped onto the sand. Paul waited until the maker was safely clear of the scatter area, then released his hooks. This was the tricky moment with a worm not completely exhausted.

Freed of its goads and hooks, the big worm began burrowing into the sand. Paul ran lightly back along its broad surface, judged his moment carefully and leaped off. He landed running, lunged against the slipface of a dune the way he had been taught, and hid himself beneath the cascade of sand over his robe.

Now, the waiting. . . .

Paul turned, gently, exposed a crack of sky beneath a crease in his robe. He imagined the others back along their path doing the same.

He heard the beat of the 'thopter's wings before he saw it. There was a whisper of jetpods and it came over his patch of desert, turned in a broad arc toward the ridge.

An unmarked 'thopter, Paul noted.

It flew out of sight beyond Habbanya Ridge.

A bird cry sounded over the desert. Another.

Paul shook himself free of sand, climbed to the dune top. Other figures stood out in a line trailing away from the ridge. He recognized Chani and Stilgar among them.

Stilgar signaled toward the ridge.

They gathered and began the sandwalk, gliding over the surface in a broken rhythm that would disturb no maker. Stilgar paced himself beside Paul along the windpacked crest of a dune.

"It was a smuggler craft," Stilgar said.

"So it seemed," Paul said. "But this is deep into the desert for smugglers."

"They've their difficulties with patrols, too," Stilgar said.

"If they come this deep, they may go deeper," Paul said.

"True."

"It wouldn't be well for them to see what they could see if they ventured too deep into the south. Smugglers sell information, too."

"They were hunting spice, don't you think?" Stilgar asked.

"There will be a wing and a crawler waiting somewhere for that one," Paul said. "We've spice. Let's bait a patch of sand and catch us some smugglers. They should be taught that this is our land and our men need practice with the new weapons."

"Now, Usul speaks," Stilgar said. "Usul thinks Fremen."

But Usul must give way to decisions that match a terrible purpose, Paul thought.

And the storm was gathering.

When law and duty are one, united by religion, you never become fully conscious, fully aware of yourself. You are always a little less than an individual.

—FROM "MUAD'DIB: THE NINETY-NINE
WONDERS OF THE UNIVERSE"
BY THE PRINCESS IRULAN

The smuggler's spice factory with its parent carrier and ring of drone ornithopters came over a lifting of dunes like a swarm of insects following its queen. Ahead of the swarm lay one of the low rock ridges that lifted from the desert floor like small imitations of the Shield Wall. The dry beaches of the ridge were swept clean by a recent storm.

In the con-bubble of the factory, Gurney Halleck leaned forward, adjusted the oil lenses of his binoculars and examined the landscape. Beyond the ridge, he could see a dark patch that might be a spiceblow, and he gave the signal to a hovering ornithopter that sent it to investigate.

The 'thopter waggled its wings to indicate it had the signal. It broke away from the swarm, sped down toward the darkened sand, circled the area with its detectors dangling close to the surface.

Almost immediately, it went through the wing-tucked dip and circle that told the waiting factory that spice had been found.

Gurney sheathed his binoculars, knowing the others had seen the signal. He liked this spot. The ridge offered some shielding and protection. This was deep in the desert, an unlikely place for an ambush . . .

still. . . . Gurney signaled for a crew to hover over the ridge, to scan it, sent reserves to take up station in pattern around the area—not too high because then they could be seen from afar by Harkonnen detectors.

He doubted, though, that Harkonnen patrols would be this far south. This was still Fremen country.

Gurney checked his weapons, damning the fate that made shields useless out here. Anything that summoned a worm had to be avoided at all costs. He rubbed the inkvine scar along his jaw, studying the scene, decided it would be safest to lead a ground party through the ridge. Inspection on foot was still the most certain. You couldn't be too careful when Fremen and Harkonnen were at each other's throats.

It was Fremen that worried him here. They didn't mind trading for all the spice you could afford, but they were devils on the warpath if you stepped foot where they forbade you to go. And they were so devilishly cunning of late.

It annoyed Gurney, the cunning and adroitness in battle of these natives. They displayed a sophistication in warfare as good as anything he had ever encountered, and he had been trained by the best fighters in the universe then seasoned in battles where only the superior few survived.

Again Gurney scanned the landscape, wondering why he felt uneasy. Perhaps it was the worm they had seen . . . but that was on the other side of the ridge.

A head popped up into the con-bubble beside Gurney—the factory commander, a one-eyed old pirate with full beard, the blue eyes and milky teeth of a spice diet.

"Looks like a rich patch, sir," the factory commander said. "Shall I take 'er in?"

"Come down at the edge of that ridge," Gurney ordered. "Let me disembark with my men. You can tractor out to the spice from there. We'll have a look at that rock."

"Aye."

"In case of trouble," Gurney said, "save the factory. We'll lift in the 'thopters."

The factory commander saluted. "Aye, sir." He popped back down through the hatch.

Again Gurney scanned the horizon. He had to respect the possibility that there were Fremen here and he was trespassing. Fremen worried him, their toughness and unpredictability. Many things about this business worried him, but the rewards were great. The fact that he couldn't send spotters high overhead worried him, too. The necessity of radio silence added to his uneasiness.

The factory crawler turned, began to descend. Gently it glided down to the dry beach at the foot of the ridge. Treads touched sand.

Gurney opened the bubble dome, released his safety straps. The instant the factory stopped, he was out, slamming the bubble closed behind him, scrambling out over the tread guards to swing down to the sand beyond the emergency netting. The five men of his personal guard were out with him, emerging from the nose hatch. Others released the factory's carrier wing. It detached, lifted away to fly in a parking circle low overhead.

Immediately the big factory crawler lurched off, swinging away from the ridge toward the dark patch of spice out on the sand.

A 'thopter swooped down nearby, skidded to a stop. Another followed and another. They disgorged Gurney's platoon and lifted to hoverflight.

Gurney tested his muscles in his stillsuit, stretching. He left the filter mask off his face, losing moisture for the sake of a greater need—the carrying power of his voice if he had to shout commands. He began climbing up into the rocks, checking the terrain—pebbles and pea sand underfoot, the smell of spice.

Good site for an emergency base, he thought. Might be sensible to bury a few supplies here.

He glanced back, watching his men spread out as they followed him. Good men, even the new ones he hadn't had time to test. Good men. Didn't have to be told every time what to do. Not a shield glimmer showed on any of them. No cowards in this bunch, carrying shields into the desert where a worm could sense the field and come to rob them of the spice they found.

From this slight elevation in the rocks, Gurney could see the spice patch about half a kilometer away and the crawler just reaching the near edge. He glanced up at the coverflight, noting the altitude—not too high. He nodded to himself, turned to resume his climb up the ridge.

In that instant, the ridge erupted.

Twelve roaring paths of flame streaked upward to the hovering 'thopters and carrier wing. There came a blasting of metal from the factory crawler, and the rocks around Gurney were full of hooded fighting men.

Gurney had time to think: *By the horns of the Great Mother! Rockets! They dare to use rockets!*

Then he was face to face with a hooded figure who crouched low, crysknife at the ready. Two more men stood waiting on the rocks above to left and right. Only the eyes of the fighting man ahead of him were visible to Gurney between hood and veil of a sand-colored burnoose, but the crouch and readiness warned him that here was a trained fighting man. The eyes were the blue-in-blue of the deep-desert Fremen.

Gurney moved one hand toward his own knife, kept his eyes fixed on the other's knife. If they dared use rockets, they'd have other projectile weapons. This moment argued extreme caution. He could tell by sound alone that at least part of his skycover had been knocked out. There were gruntings, too, the noise of several struggles behind him.

The eyes of the fighting man ahead of Gurney followed the motion of hand toward knife, came back to glare into Gurney's eyes.

"Leave the knife in its sheath, Gurney Halleck," the man said.

Gurney hesitated. That voice sounded oddly familiar even through a stillsuit filter.

"You know my name?" he said.

"You've no need of a knife with me, Gurney," the man said. He straightened, slipped his crysknife into its sheath back beneath his robe. "Tell your men to stop their useless resistance."

The man threw his hood back, swung the filter aside.

The shock of what he saw froze Gurney's muscles. He thought at first he was looking at a ghost image of Duke Leto Atreides. Full recognition came slowly.

"Paul," he whispered. Then louder: "Is it truly Paul?"

"Don't you trust your own eyes?" Paul asked.

"They said you were dead," Gurney rasped. He took a half-step forward.

"Tell your men to submit," Paul commanded. He waved toward the lower reaches of the ridge.

Gurney turned, reluctant to take his eyes off Paul. He saw only a few knots of struggle. Hooded desert men seemed to be everywhere around. The factory crawler lay silent with Fremen standing atop it. There were no aircraft overhead.

"Stop the fighting," Gurney bellowed. He took a deep breath, cupped his hands for a megaphone. "This is Gurney Halleck! Stop the fight!"

Slowly, warily, the struggling figures separated. Eyes turned toward him, questioning.

"These are friends," Gurney called.

"Fine friends!" someone shouted back. "Half our people murdered."

"It's a mistake," Gurney said. "Don't add to it."

He turned back to Paul, stared into the youth's blue-blue Fremen eyes.

A smile touched Paul's mouth, but there was a hardness in the expression that reminded Gurney of the Old Duke, Paul's grandfather. Gurney saw then the sinewy harshness in Paul that had never before been seen in an Atreides—a leathery look to the skin, a squint to the eyes and calculation in the glance that seemed to weigh everything in sight.

"They said you were dead," Gurney repeated.

"And it seemed the best protection to let them think so," Paul said.

Gurney realized that was all the apology he'd ever get for having been abandoned to his own resources, left to believe his young Duke . . . his friend, was dead. He wondered then if there were anything left here of the boy he had known and trained in the ways of fighting men.

Paul took a step closer to Gurney, found that his eyes were smarting. "Gurney. . . ."

It seemed to happen of itself, and they were embracing, pounding each other on the back, feeling the reassurance of solid flesh.

"You young pup! You young pup!" Gurney kept saying.

And Paul: "Gurney, man! Gurney, man!"

Presently, they stepped apart, looked at each other. Gurney took a deep breath. "So you're why the Fremen have grown so wise in battle tactics. I might've known. They keep doing things I could've planned myself. If I'd only known. . . ." He shook his head. "If you'd only got word to me, lad. Nothing would've stopped me. I'd have come arunning and. . . ."

A look in Paul's eyes stopped him . . . the hard, weighing stare.

Gurney sighed. "Sure, and there'd have been those who wondered why Gurney Halleck went arunning, and some would've done more than question. They'd have gone hunting for answers."

Paul nodded, glanced to the waiting Fremen around them—the looks of curious appraisal on the faces of the Fedaykin. He turned from the death commandos back to Gurney. Finding his former swordmaster filled him with elation. He saw it as a good omen, a sign that he was on the course of the future where all was well.

With Gurney at my side. . . .

Paul glanced down the ridge past the Fedaykin, studied the smuggler crew who had come with Halleck.

"How do your men stand, Gurney?" he asked.

"They're smugglers all," Gurney said. "They stand where the profit is."

"Little enough profit in our venture," Paul said, and he noted the subtle finger signal flashed to him by Gurney's right hand—the old hand code out of their past. There were men to fear and distrust in the smuggler crew.

Paul pulled at his lip to indicate he understood, looked up at the men standing guard above them on the rocks. He saw Stilgar there. Memory of the unsolved problem with Stilgar cooled some of Paul's elation.

"Stilgar," he said, "this is Gurney Halleck of whom you've heard me speak. My father's master-of-arms, one of the swordmasters who instructed me, an old friend. He can be trusted in any venture."

"I hear," Stilgar said. "You are his Duke."

Paul stared at the dark visage above him, wondering at the reasons which had impelled Stilgar to say just that. *His Duke.* There had been a strange subtle intonation in Stilgar's voice, as though he would rather have said something else. And that wasn't like Stilgar, who was a leader of Fremen, a man who spoke his mind.

My Duke! Gurney thought. He looked anew at Paul. *Yes, with Leto dead, the title fell on Paul's shoulders.*

The pattern of the Fremen war on Arrakis began to take on new shape in Gurney's mind. *My Duke!* A place that had been dead within him began coming alive. Only part of his awareness focused on Paul's ordering the smuggler crew disarmed until they could be questioned.

Gurney's mind returned to the command when he heard some of his men protesting. He shook his head, whirled. "Are you men deaf?" he barked. "This is the rightful Duke of Arrakis. Do as he commands."

Grumbling, the smugglers submitted.

Paul moved up beside Gurney, spoke in a low voice. "I'd not have expected you to walk into this trap, Gurney."

"I'm properly chastened," Gurney said. "I'll wager yon patch of spice is little more than a sand grain's thickness, a bait to lure us."

"That's a wager you'd win," Paul said. He looked down at the men being disarmed. "Are there any more of my father's men among your crew?"

"None. We're spread thin. There're a few among the free traders. Most have spent their profits to leave this place."

"But you stayed."

"I stayed."

"Because Rabban is here," Paul said.

"I thought I had nothing left but revenge," Gurney said.

An oddly chopped cry sounded from the ridgetop. Gurney looked up to see a Fremen waving his kerchief.

"A maker comes," Paul said. He moved out to a point of rock with Gurney following, looked off to the southwest. The burrow mound of a worm could be seen in the middle distance, a dust-crowned track that cut directly through the dunes on a course toward the ridge.

"He's big enough," Paul said.

A clattering sound lifted from the factory crawler below them. It turned on its treads like a giant insect, lumbered toward the rocks.

"Too bad we couldn't have saved the carryall," Paul said.

Gurney glanced at him, looked back to the patches of smoke and debris out on the desert where carryall and ornithopters had been brought down by Fremen rockets. He felt a sudden pang for the men lost there—his men, and he said: "Your father would've been more concerned for the men he couldn't save."

Paul shot a hard stare at him, lowered his gaze. Presently, he said: "They were your friends, Gurney. I understand. To us, though, they were trespassers who might see things they shouldn't see. You must understand that."

"I understand it well enough," Gurney said. "Now, I'm curious to see what I shouldn't."

Paul looked up to see the old and well-remembered wolfish grin on Halleck's face, the ripple of the inkvine scar along the man's jaw.

Gurney nodded toward the desert below them. Fremen were going about their business all over the landscape. It struck him that none of them appeared worried by the approach of the worm.

A thumping sounded from the open dunes beyond the baited patch of spice—a deep drumming that seemed to be heard through their feet. Gurney saw Fremen spread out across the sand there in the path of the worm.

The worm came on like some great sandfish, cresting the surface, its rings rippling and twisting. In a moment, from his vantage point above the desert, Gurney saw the taking of a worm—the daring leap of the first hookman, the turning of the creature, the way an entire band of men went up the scaly, glistening curve of the worm's side.

"There's one of the things you shouldn't have seen," Paul said.

"There's been stories and rumors," Gurney said. "But it's not a thing easy to believe without seeing it." He shook his head. "The creature all men on Arrakis fear, you treat it like a riding animal."

"You heard my father speak of desert power," Paul said. "There it is. The surface of this planet is ours. No storm nor creature nor condition can stop us."

Us, Gurney thought. *He means the Fremen. He speaks of himself as one of them.* Again, Gurney looked at the spice blue in Paul's eyes. His own eyes, he knew, had a touch of the color, but smugglers could get offworld foods and there was a subtle caste implication in the tone of the eyes among them. They spoke of "the touch of the spicebrush" to mean a man had gone too native. And there was always a hint of distrust in the idea.

"There was a time when we did not ride the maker in the light of day in these latitudes," Paul said. "But Rabban has little enough air cover left that he can waste it looking for a few specks in the sand." He looked at Gurney. "Your aircraft were a shock to us here."

To us . . . to us. . . .

Gurney shook his head to drive out such thoughts. "We weren't the shock to you that you were to us," he said.

"What's the talk of Rabban in the sinks and villages?" Paul asked.

"They say they've fortified the graben villages to the point where you cannot harm them. They say they need only sit inside their defenses while you wear yourselves out in futile attack."

"In a word," Paul said, "they're immobilized."

"While you can go where you will," Gurney said.

"It's a tactic I learned from you," Paul said. "They've lost the initiative, which means they've lost the war."

Gurney smiled, a slow, knowing expression.

"Our enemy is exactly where I want him to be," Paul said. He glanced at Gurney. "Well, Gurney, do you enlist with me for the finish of this campaign?"

"Enlist?" Gurney stared at him. "My Lord, I've never left your service. You're the only one left me . . . to think you dead. And I, being cast adrift, made what shrift I could, waiting for the moment I might sell my life for what it's worth—the death of Rabban."

An embarrassed silence settled over Paul.

A woman came climbing up the rocks toward them, her eyes between stillsuit hood and face mask flicking between Paul and his companion. She stopped in front of Paul. Gurney noted the possessive air about her, the way she stood close to Paul.

"Chani," Paul said, "this is Gurney Halleck. You've heard me speak of him."

She looked at Halleck, back to Paul. "I have heard."

"Where did the men go on the maker?" Paul asked.

"They but diverted it to give us time to save the equipment."

"Well then. . . ." Paul broke off, sniffed the air.

"There's wind coming," Chani said.

A voice called out from the ridgetop above them: "Ho, there—the wind!"

Gurney saw a quickening of motion among the Fremen now—a rushing about and sense of hurry. A thing the worm had not ignited was brought about by fear of the wind. The factory crawler lumbered up onto the dry beach below them and a way was opened for it among the rocks . . . and the rocks closed behind it so neatly that the passage escaped his eyes.

"Have you many such hiding places?" Gurney asked.

"Many times many," Paul said. He looked at Chani. "Find Korba. Tell him that Gurney has warned me there are men among this smuggler crew who're not to be trusted."

She looked once at Gurney, back to Paul, nodded, and was off down the rocks, leaping with a gazelle-like agility.

"She is your woman," Gurney said.

"The mother of my firstborn," Paul said. "There's another Leto among the Atreides."

Gurney accepted this with only a widening of the eyes.

Paul watched the action around them with a critical eye. A curry color dominated the southern sky now and there came fitful bursts and gusts of wind that whipped dust around their heads.

"Seal your suit," Paul said. And he fastened the mask and hood about his face.

Gurney obeyed, thankful for the filters.

Paul spoke, his voice muffled by the filter: "Which of your crew don't you trust, Gurney?"

"There're some new recruits," Gurney said. "Offworlders. . . ." He hesitated, wondering at himself suddenly. *Offworlders.* The word had come so easily to his tongue.

"Yes?" Paul said.

"They're not like the usual fortune-hunting lot we get," Gurney said. "They're tougher."

"Harkonnen spies?" Paul asked.

"I think, m'Lord, that they report to no Harkonnen. I suspect they're men of the Imperial service. They have a hint of Salusa Secundus about them."

Paul shot a sharp glance at him. "Sardaukar?"

Gurney shrugged. "They could be, but it's well masked."

Paul nodded, thinking how easily Gurney had fallen back into the pattern of Atreides retainer . . . but with subtle reservations . . . differences. Arrakis had changed him, too.

Two hooded Fremen emerged from the broken rock below them, began climbing upward. One of them carried a large black bundle over one shoulder.

"Where are my crew now?" Gurney asked.

"Secure in the rocks below us," Paul said. "We've a cave here—Cave of Birds. We'll decide what to do with them after the storm."

A voice called from above them: "Muad'Dib!"

Paul turned at the call, saw a Fremen guard motioning them down to the cave. Paul signaled he had heard.

Gurney studied him with a new expression. "You're Muad'Dib?" he asked. "You're the will-o'-the-sand?"

"It's my Fremen name," Paul said.

Gurney turned away, feeling an oppressive sense of foreboding. Half his own crew dead on the sand, the others captive. He did not care about the new recruits, the suspicious ones, but among the others were good men, friends, people for whom he felt responsible. *"We'll decide what to do with them after the storm."* That's what Paul had said, Muad'Dib had said. And Gurney recalled the stories told of Muad'Dib, the Lisan al-Gaib—how he had taken the skin of a Harkonnen officer to make his drumheads, how he was surrounded by death commandos, Fedaykin who leaped into battle with their death chants on their lips.

Him.

The two Fremen climbing up the rocks leaped lightly to a shelf in front of Paul. The dark-faced one said: "All secure, Muad'Dib. We best get below now."

"Right."

Gurney noted the tone of the man's voice—half command and half request. This was the man called Stilgar, another figure of the new Fremen legends.

Paul looked at the bundle the other man carried, said: "Korba, what's in the bundle?"

Stilgar answered: "'Twas in the crawler. It had the initial of your friend here and it contains a baliset. Many times have I heard you speak of the prowess of Gurney Halleck on the baliset."

Gurney studied the speaker, seeing the edge of black beard above the stillsuit mask, the hawk stare, the chiseled nose.

"You've a companion who thinks, m'Lord," Gurney said. "Thank you, Stilgar."

Stilgar signaled for his companion to pass the bundle to Gurney, said: "Thank your Lord Duke. His countenance earns your admittance here."

Gurney accepted the bundle, puzzled by the hard undertones in this conversation. There was an air of challenge about the man, and Gurney wondered if it could be a feeling of jealousy in the Fremen. Here was someone called Gurney Halleck who'd known Paul even in the times before Arrakis, a man who shared a cameraderie that Stilgar could never invade.

"You are two I'd have be friends," Paul said.

"Stilgar, the Fremen, is a name of renown," Gurney said. "Any killer of Harkonnens I'd feel honored to count among my friends."

"Will you touch hands with my friend Gurney Halleck, Stilgar?" Paul asked.

Slowly, Stilgar extended his hand, gripped the heavy calluses of Gurney's swordhand. "There're few who haven't heard the name of Gurney Halleck," he said, and released his grip. He turned to Paul. "The storm comes rushing."

"At once," Paul said.

Stilgar turned away, led them down through the rocks, a twisting and turning path into a shadowed cleft that admitted them to the low entrance of a cave. Men hurried to fasten a doorseal behind them. Glowglobes showed a broad, dome-ceilinged space with a raised ledge on one side and a passage leading off from it.

Paul leaped to the ledge with Gurney right behind him, led the way into the passage. The others headed for another passage opposite the entrance. Paul led the way through an anteroom and into a chamber with dark, wine-colored hangings on its walls.

"We can have some privacy here for a while," Paul said. "The others will respect my—"

An alarm cymbal clanged from the outer chamber, was followed by shouting and clashing of weapons. Paul whirled, ran back through the anteroom and out onto the atrium lip above the outer chamber. Gurney was right behind, weapon drawn.

Beneath them on the floor of the cave swirled a melee of struggling figures. Paul stood an instant assessing the scene, separating the Fremen robes and bourkas from the costumes of those they opposed. Senses that his mother had trained to detect the most subtle clues picked out a significant face—the Fremen fought against men wearing smuggler robes, but the smugglers were crouched in trios, backed into triangles where pressed.

That habit of close fighting was a trademark of the Imperial Sardaukar.

A Fedaykin in the crowd saw Paul, and his battle cry was lifted to echo in the chamber: "Muad'Dib! Muad'Dib! Muad'Dib!"

Another eye had also picked Paul out. A black knife came hurtling toward him. Paul dodged, heard the knife clatter against stone behind him, glanced to see Gurney retrieve it.

The triangular knots were being pressed back now.

Gurney held the knife up in front of Paul's eyes, pointed to the hairline yellow coil of Imperial color, the golden lion crest, multifaceted eyes at the pommel.

Sardaukar for certain.

Paul stepped out to the lip of the ledge. Only three of the Sardaukar remained. Bloody rag mounds of Sardaukar and Fremen lay in a twisted pattern across the chamber.

"Hold!" Paul shouted. "The Duke Paul Atreides commands you to hold!"

The fighting wavered, hesitated.

"You Sardaukar!" Paul called to the remaining group. "By whose orders do you threaten a ruling Duke?" And, quickly, as his men started to press in around the Sardaukar: "Hold, I say!"

One of the cornered trio straightened. "Who says we're Sardaukar?" he demanded.

Paul took the knife from Gurney, held it aloft. "This says you're Sardaukar."

"Then who says you're a ruling Duke?" the man demanded.

Paul gestured to the Fedaykin. "These men say I'm a ruling Duke. Your own emperor bestowed Arrakis on House Atreides. *I* am House Atreides."

The Sardaukar stood silent, fidgeting.

Paul studied the man—tall, flat-featured, with a pale scar across half his left cheek. Anger and confusion were betrayed in his manner, but still there was that pride about him without which a Sardaukar appeared undressed—and with which he could appear fully clothed though naked.

Paul glanced to one of his Fedaykin lieutenants, said: "Korba, how came they to have weapons?"

"They held back knives concealed in cunning pockets within their stillsuits," the lieutenant said.

Paul surveyed the dead and wounded across the chamber, brought his attention back to the lieutenant. There was no need for words. The lieutenant lowered his eyes.

"Where is Chani?" Paul asked and waited, breath held, for the answer.

"Stilgar spirited her aside." He nodded toward the other passage, glanced at the dead and wounded. "I hold myself responsible for this mistake, Muad'Dib."

"How many of these Sardaukar were there, Gurney?" Paul asked.

"Ten."

Paul leaped lightly to the floor of the chamber, strode across to stand within striking distance of the Sardaukar spokesman.

A tense air came over the Fedaykin. They did not like him thus exposed to danger. This was the thing they were pledged to prevent because the Fremen wished to preserve the wisdom of Muad'Dib.

Without turning, Paul spoke to his lieutenant: "How many are our casualties?"

"Four wounded, two dead, Muad'Dib."

Paul saw motion beyond the Sardaukar; Chani and Stilgar were standing in the other passage. He returned his attention to the Sardaukar, staring into the offworld whites of the spokesman's eyes. "You, what is your name?" Paul demanded.

The man stiffened, glanced left and right.

"Don't try it," Paul said. "It's obvious to me that you were ordered to seek out and destroy Muad'Dib. I'll warrant you were the ones suggested seeking spice in the deep desert."

A gasp from Gurney behind him brought a thin smile to Paul's lips. Blood suffused the Sardaukar's face.

"What you see before you is more than Muad'Dib," Paul said. "Seven of you are dead for two of us. Three for one. Pretty good against Sardaukar, eh?"

The man came up on his toes, sank back as the Fedaykin pressed forward.

"I asked your name," Paul said, and he called up the subtleties of Voice: "Tell me your name!"

"Captain Aramsham, Imperial Sardaukar!" the man snapped. His jaw dropped. He stared at Paul in confusion. The manner about him that had dismissed this cavern as a barbarian warren melted away.

"Well, Captain Aramsham," Paul said, "the Harkonnens would pay dearly to learn what you now know. And the Emperor—what he wouldn't give to learn an Atreides still lives despite his treachery."

The captain glanced left and right at the two men remaining to him. Paul could almost see the thoughts turning over in the man's head. Sardaukar did not submit, but the Emperor *had* to learn of this threat.

Still using the Voice, Paul said: "Submit, Captain."

The man at the captain's left leaped without warning toward Paul, met the flashing impact of his own captain's knife in his chest. The attacker hit the floor in a sodden heap with the knife still in him.

The captain faced his sole remaining companion. "I decide what best serves His Majesty," he said. "Understood?"

The other Sardaukar's shoulders slumped.

"Drop your weapon," the captain said.

The Sardaukar obeyed.

The captain returned his attention to Paul. "I have killed a friend for you," he said. "Let us always remember that."

"You're my prisoners," Paul said. "You submitted to me. Whether you live or die is of no importance." He motioned to his guard to take the two Sardaukar, signaled the lieutenant who had searched the prisoners.

The guard moved in, hustled the Sardaukar away.

Paul bent toward his lieutenant.

"Muad'Dib," the man said. "I failed you in. . . ."

"The failure was mine, Korba," Paul said. "I should've warned you what to seek. In the future, when searching Sardaukar, remember this. Remember, too, that each has a false toenail or two that can be combined with other items secreted about their bodies to make an effective transmitter. They'll have more than one false tooth. They carry coils of shigawire in their hair—so fine you can barely detect it, yet strong enough to garrote a man and cut off his head in the process. With Sardaukar, you must scan them, scope them—both reflex and hard ray—cut off every scrap of body hair. And when you're through, be certain you haven't discovered everything."

He looked up at Gurney, who had moved close to listen.

"Then we best kill them," the lieutenant said.

Paul shook his head, still looking at Gurney. "No. I want them to escape."

Gurney stared at him. "Sire. . . ." he breathed.

"Yes?"

"Your man here is right. Kill those prisoners at once. Destroy all evidence of them. You've shamed Imperial Sardaukar! When the Emperor learns that he'll not rest until he has you over a slow fire."

"The Emperor's not likely to have that power over me," Paul said. He spoke slowly, coldly. Something had happened inside him while he faced the Sardaukar. A sum of decisions had accumulated in his awareness. "Gurney," he said, "are there many Guildsmen around Rabban?"

Gurney straightened, eyes narrowed. "Your question makes no. . . ."

"Are there?" Paul barked.

"Arrakis is crawling with Guild agents. They're buying spice as though it were the most precious thing in the universe. Why else do you think we ventured this far into. . . ."

"It is the most precious thing in the universe," Paul said. "To them."

He looked toward Stilgar and Chani who were now crossing the chamber toward him. "And we control it, Gurney."

"The Harkonnens control it!" Gurney protested.

"The people who can destroy a thing, they control it," Paul said. He waved a hand to silence further remarks from Gurney, nodded to Stilgar who stopped in front of Paul, Chani beside him.

Paul took the Sardaukar knife in his left hand, presented it to Stilgar. "You live for the good of the tribe," Paul said. "Could you draw my life's blood with that knife?"

"For the good of the tribe," Stilgar growled.

"Then use that knife," Paul said.

"Are you calling me out?" Stilgar demanded.

"If I do," Paul said, "I shall stand there without weapon and let you slay me."

Stilgar drew in a quick, sharp breath.

Chani said, "Usul!" then glanced at Gurney, back to Paul.

While Stilgar was still weighing his words, Paul said: "You are Stilgar, a fighting man. When the Sardaukar began fighting here, you were not in the front of battle. Your first thought was to protect Chani."

"She's my niece," Stilgar said. "If there'd been any doubt of your Fedaykin handling those scum. . . ."

"Why was your first thought of Chani?" Paul demanded.

"It wasn't!"

"Oh?"

"It was of you," Stilgar admitted.

"Do you think you could lift your hand against me?" Paul asked.

Stilgar began to tremble. "It's the way," he muttered.

"It's the way to kill offworld strangers found in the desert and take their water as a gift from Shai-hulud," Paul said. "Yet you permitted two such to live one night, my mother and myself."

As Stilgar remained silent, trembling, staring at him, Paul said: "Ways change, Stil. You have changed them yourself."

Stilgar looked down at the yellow emblem on the knife he held.

"When I am Duke in Arrakeen with Chani by my side, do you think I'll have time to concern myself with every detail of governing Tabr sietch?" Paul asked. "Do you concern yourself with the internal problems of every family?"

Stilgar continued staring at the knife.

"Do you think I wish to cut off my right arm?" Paul demanded.

Slowly, Stilgar looked up at him.

"You!" Paul said. "Do you think I wish to deprive myself or the tribe of your wisdom and strength?"

In a low voice, Stilgar said: "The young man of my tribe whose name is known to me, this young man I could kill on the challenge floor, Shai-hulud willing. The Lisan al-Gaib, him I could not harm. You knew this when you handed me this knife."

"I knew it," Paul agreed.

Stilgar opened his hand. The knife clattered against the stone of the floor. "Ways change," he said.

"Chani," Paul said, "go to my mother, send her here that her counsel will be available into—"

"But you said we would go to the south!" she protested.

"I was wrong," he said. "The Harkonnens are not there. The war is not there."

She took a deep breath, accepting this as a desert woman accepted all necessities in the midst of a life involved with death.

"You will give my mother a message for her ears alone," Paul said. "Tell her that Stilgar acknowledges me Duke of Arrakis, but a way must be found to make the young men accept this without combat."

Chani glanced at Stilgar.

"Do as he says," Stilgar growled. "We both know he could overcome me . . . and I could not raise my hand against him . . . for the good of the tribe."

"I shall return with your mother," Chani said.

"Send her," Paul said. "Stilgar's instinct was right. I am stronger when you are safe. You will remain in the sietch."

She started to protest, swallowed it.

"Sihaya," Paul said, using his intimate name for her. He whirled away to the right, met Gurney's glaring eyes.

The interchange between Paul and the older Fremen had passed as though in a cloud around Gurney since Paul's reference to his mother.

"Your mother," Gurney said.

"Idaho saved us the night of the raid," Paul said, distracted by the parting with Chani. "Right now we've—"

"What of Duncan Idaho, m'Lord?" Gurney asked.

"He's dead—buying us a bit of time to escape."

The she-witch alive! Gurney thought. *The one I swore vengeance against, alive! And it's obvious Duke Paul doesn't know what manner of creature gave him birth. The evil one: Betrayed his own father to the Harkonnens!*

Paul pressed past him, jumped up to the ledge. He glanced back, noted that the wounded and dead had been removed, and he thought bitterly that here was another chapter in the legend of Paul-Muad'Dib. *I didn't even draw my knife, but it'll be said of this day that I slew twenty Sardaukar by my own hand.*

Gurney followed with Stilgar, stepping on ground that he did not even feel. The cavern with its yellow light of glowglobes was forced out of his thoughts by rage. *The she-witch alive while those she betrayed are bones in lonesome graves. I must contrive it that Paul learns the truth about her before I slay her.*

How often it is that the angry man rages denial of what his inner self is telling him.

—FROM "COLLECTED SAYINGS OF MUAD'DIB"
BY THE PRINCESS IRULAN

The crowd in the cavern assembly chamber radiated that pack feeling Jessica had sensed the day Paul killed Jamis. There was murmuring nervousness in the voices. Little cliques gathered like knots among the robes.

Jessica tucked a message cylinder beneath her robe as she emerged to the ledge from Paul's private quarters. She felt rested after the long journey up from the south, but still rankled that Paul would not yet permit them to use the captured ornithopters.

"We do not have full control of the air," he had said. "And we must not become dependent upon offworld fuel. Both fuel and aircraft must be gathered and saved for the day of maximum effort."

Paul stood with a group of the younger men near the ledge. The pale light of glowglobes gave the scene a tinge of unreality. It was like a tableau, but with the added dimension of warren smells, the whispers, the sounds of shuffling feet.

She studied her son, wondering why he had not yet trotted out his surprise—Gurney Halleck. The thought of Gurney disturbed her with its memories of an easier past—days of love and beauty with Paul's father.

Stilgar waited with a small group of his own at the other end of the ledge. There was a feeling of inevitable dignity about him, the way he stood without talking.

We must not lose that man, Jessica thought. *Paul's plan must work. Anything else would be the highest tragedy.*

She strode down the ledge, passing Stilgar without a glance, stepped down into the crowd. A way was made for her as she headed toward Paul. And silence followed her.

She knew the meaning of the silence—the unspoken questions of the people, awe of the Reverend Mother.

The young men drew back from Paul as she came up to him, and she found herself momentarily dismayed by the new deference they paid him. *"All men beneath your position covet your station,"* went the Bene Gesserit axiom. But she found no covetousness in these faces. They were held at a distance by the religious ferment around Paul's leadership. And she recalled another Bene Gesserit saying: *"Prophets have a way of dying by violence."*

Paul looked at her.

"It's time," she said, and passed the message cylinder to him.

One of Paul's companions, bolder than the others, glanced across at Stilgar, said: "Are you going to call him out, Maud'Dib? Now's the time for sure. They'll think you a coward if you—"

"Who dares call me coward?" Paul demanded. His hand flashed to his crysknife hilt.

Bated silence came over the group, spreading out into the crowd.

"There's work to do," Paul said as the man drew back from him. Paul turned away, shouldered through the crowd to the ledge, leaped lightly up to it and faced the people.

"Do it!" someone shrieked.

Murmurs and whispers arose behind the shriek.

Paul waited for silence. It came slowly amidst scattered shufflings and coughs. When it was quiet in the cavern, Paul lifted his chin, spoke in a voice that carried to the farthest corners.

"You are tired of waiting," Paul said.

Again, he waited while the cries of response died out.

Indeed, they are tired of waiting, Paul thought. He hefted the message cylinder, thinking of what it contained. His mother had showed it to him, explaining how it had been taken from a Harkonnen courier.

The message was explicit: Rabban was being abandoned to his own resources here on Arrakis! He could not call for help or reinforcements!

Again, Paul raised his voice: "You think it's time I called out Stilgar and changed the leadership of the troops!" Before they could respond, Paul hurled his voice at them in anger: "Do you think the Lisan al-Gaib that stupid?"

There was stunned silence.

He's accepting the religious mantle, Jessica thought. *He must not do it!*

"It's the way!" someone shouted.

Paul spoke dryly, probing the emotional undercurrents. "Ways change."

An angry voice lifted from a corner of the cavern: "We'll say what's to change!"

There were scattered shouts of agreement through the throng.

"As you wish," Paul said.

And Jessica heard the subtle intonations as he used the powers of Voice she had taught him.

"You will say," he agreed. "But first you will hear my say."

Stilgar moved along the ledge, his bearded face impassive. "That is the way, too," he said. "The voice of any Fremen may be heard in Council. Paul-Muad'Dib is a Fremen."

"The good of the tribe, that is the most important thing, eh?" Paul asked.

Still with that flat-voiced dignity, Stilgar said: "Thus our steps are guided."

"All right," Paul said. "Then, who rules this troop of our tribe—and who rules all the tribes and troops through the fighting instructors we've trained in the weirding way?"

Paul waited, looking over the heads of the throng. No answer came.

Presently, he said: "Does Stilgar rule all this? He says himself that he does not. Do I rule? Even Stilgar does my bidding on occasion, and the sages, the wisest of the wise, listen to me and honor me in Council."

There was shuffling silence among the crowd.

"So," Paul said. "Does my mother rule?" He pointed down to Jessica in her black robes of office among them. "Stilgar and all the other troop leaders ask her advice in almost every major decision. You know this. But does a Reverend Mother walk the sand or lead a razzia against the Harkonnens?"

Frowns creased the foreheads of those Paul could see, but still there were angry murmurs.

This is a dangerous way to do it, Jessica thought, but she remembered the message cylinder and what it implied. And she saw Paul's intent: Go right to the depth of their uncertainty, dispose of that, and all the rest must follow.

"No man recognizes leadership without the challenge and the combat, eh?" Paul asked.

"That's the way!" someone shouted.

"What's our goal?" Paul asked. "To unseat Rabban, the Harkonnen beast, and remake our world into a place where we may raise our families in happiness amidst an abundance of water—is this our goal?"

"Hard tasks need hard ways," someone shouted.

"Do you smash your knife before a battle?" Paul demanded. "I say this as fact, not meaning it as boast or challenge: there isn't a man here, Stilgar included, who could stand against me in single combat. This is Stilgar's own admission. He knows it, so do you all."

Again, the angry mutters lifted from the crowd.

"Many of you have been with me on the practice floor," Paul said. "You know this isn't idle boast. I say it because it's fact known to us all, and I'd be foolish not to see it for myself. I began training in these ways earlier than you did and my teachers were tougher than any you've ever seen. How else do you think I bested Jamis at an age when your boys are still fighting only mock battles?"

He's using the Voice well, Jessica thought, *but that's not enough with these people. They've good insulation against vocal control. He must catch them also with logic.*

"So," Paul said, "we come to this." He lifted the message cylinder, removed its scrap of tape. "This was taken from a Harkonnen courier. Its authenticity is beyond question. It is addressed to Rabban. It tells him that his request for new troops is denied, that his spice harvest is far below quota, that he must wring more spice from Arrakis with the people he has."

Stilgar moved up beside Paul.

"How many of you see what this means?" Paul asked. "Stilgar saw it immediately."

"They're cut off!" someone shouted.

Paul pushed message and cylinder into his sash. From his neck he took a braided shigawire cord and removed a ring from the cord, holding the ring aloft.

"This was my father's ducal signet," he said. "I swore never to wear it again until I was ready to lead my troops over all of Arrakis and claim it as my rightful fief." He put the ring on his finger, clenched his fist.

Utter stillness gripped the cavern.

"Who rules here?" Paul asked. He raised his fist. "I rule here! I rule on every square inch of Arrakis! This is my ducal fief whether the Emperor says yea or nay! He gave it to my father and it comes to me through my father!"

Paul lifted himself onto his toes, settled back to his heels. He studied the crowd, feeling their temper.

Almost, he thought.

"There are men here who will hold positions of importance on Arrakis when I claim those Imperial rights which are mine," Paul said. "Stilgar is one of those men. Not because I wish to bribe him! Not out of gratitude, though I'm one of many here who owe him life for life. No! But because he's wise and strong. Because he governs this troop by his own intelligence and not just by rules. Do you think me stupid? Do you think I'll cut off my right arm and leave it bloody on the floor of this cavern just to provide you with a circus?"

Paul swept a hard gaze across the throng. "Who is there here to say I'm not the rightful ruler on Arrakis? Must I prove it by leaving every Fremen tribe in the erg without a leader?"

Beside Paul, Stilgar stirred, looked at him questioningly.

"Will I subtract from our strength when we need it most?" Paul asked. "I am your ruler, and I say to you that it is time we stopped killing off our best men and started killing our real enemies—the Harkonnens!"

In one blurred motion, Stilgar had his crysknife out and pointed over the heads of the throng. "Long live Duke Paul-Muad'Dib!" he shouted.

A deafening roar filled the cavern, echoed and re-echoed. They were cheering and chanting: "Ya hya chouhada! Muad'Dib! Muad'Dib! Muad'Dib! Ya hya chouhada!"

Jessica translated it to herself: *"Long live the fighters of Muad'Dib!"* The scene she and Paul and Stilgar had cooked up between them had worked as they'd planned.

The tumult died slowly.

When silence was restored, Paul faced Stilgar, said: "Kneel, Stilgar."

Stilgar dropped to his knees on the ledge.

"Hand me your crysknife," Paul said.

Stilgar obeyed.

This was not as we planned it, Jessica thought.

"Repeat after me, Stilgar," Paul said, and he called up the words of investiture as he had heard his own father use them. "I, Stilgar, take this knife from the hands of my Duke."

"I, Stilgar, take this knife from the hands of my Duke," Stilgar said, and accepted the milky blade from Paul.

"Where my Duke commands, there shall I place this blade," Paul said.

Stilgar repeated the words, speaking slowly and solemnly.

Remembering the source of the rite, Jessica blinked back tears, shook her head. *I know the reasons for this,* she thought. *I shouldn't let it stir me.*

"I dedicate this blade to the cause of my Duke and the death of his enemies for as long as our blood shall flow," Paul said.

Stilgar repeated it after him.

"Kiss the blade," Paul ordered.

Stilgar obeyed, then, in the Fremen manner, kissed Paul's knife arm. At a nod from Paul, he sheathed the blade, got to his feet.

A sighing whisper of awe passed through the crowd, and Jessica heard the words: "The prophecy—A Bene Gesserit shall show the way and a Reverend Mother shall see it." And, from farther away: "She shows us through her son!"

"Stilgar leads this tribe," Paul said. "Let no man mistake that. He commands with my voice. What he tells you, it is as though I told you."

Wise, Jessica thought. *The tribal commander must lose no face among those who should obey him.*

Paul lowered his voice, said: "Stilgar, I want sandwalkers out this night and cielagos sent to summon a Council Gathering. When you've sent them, bring Chatt, Korba and Otheym and two other lieutenants of your own choosing. Bring them to my quarters for battle planning. We must have a victory to show the Council of Leaders when they arrive."

Paul nodded for his mother to accompany him, led the way down off the ledge and through the throng toward the central passage and the living chambers that had been prepared there. As Paul pressed through the crowd, hands reached out to touch him. Voices called out to him.

"My knife goes where Stilgar commands it, Paul-Muad'Dib! Let us fight soon, Paul-Muad'Dib! Let us wet our world with the blood of Harkonnens!"

Feeling the emotions of the throng, Jessica sensed the fighting edge of these people. They could not be more ready. *We are taking them at the crest*, she thought.

In the inner chamber, Paul motioned his mother to be seated, said: "Wait here." And he ducked through the hangings to the side passage.

It was quiet in the chamber after Paul had gone, so quiet behind the hangings that not even the faint soughing of the wind pumps that circulated air in the sietch penetrated to where she sat.

He is going to bring Gurney Halleck here, she thought. And she wondered at the strange mingling of emotions that filled her. Gurney and his music had been a part of so many pleasant times on Caladan before the move to Arrakis. She felt that Caladan had happened to some other person. In the nearly three years since then, she had *become* another person. Having to confront Gurney forced a reassessment of the changes.

Paul's coffee service, the fluted alloy of silver and jasmium that he had inherited from Jamis, rested on a low table to her right. She stared at it, thinking of how many hands had touched that metal. Chani had served Paul from it within the month.

What can his desert woman do for a Duke except serve him coffee? she asked herself. *She brings him no power, no family. Paul has only one major chance—to ally himself with a powerful Great House, perhaps even with the Imperial family. There are marriagable princesses, after all, and every one of them Bene Gesserit-trained.*

Jessica imagined herself leaving the rigors of Arrakis for the life of power and security she could know as mother of a royal consort. She glanced at the thick hangings that obscured the rock of this cavern cell, thinking of how she had come here—riding amidst a host of worms, the palanquins and pack platforms piled high with necessities for the coming campaign.

As long as Chani lives, Paul will not see his duty, Jessica thought. *She has given him a son and that is enough.*

A sudden longing to see her grandson, the child whose likeness carried so much of the grandfather's features—so like Leto, swept through her. Jessica placed her palms against her cheeks, began the ritual breathing that stilled emotion and clarified the mind, then bent forward from the waist in the devotional exercise that prepared the body for the mind's demands.

Paul's choice of this Cave of Birds as his command post could not be questioned, she knew. It was ideal. And to the north lay Wind Pass opening onto a protected village in a cliff-walled sink. It was a key village, home of artisans and technicians, maintenance center for an entire Harkonnen defensive sector.

A cough sounded outside the chamber hangings. Jessica straightened, took a deep breath, exhaled slowly.

"Enter," she said.

Draperies were flung aside and Gurney Halleck bounded into the room. She had only time for a glimpse of his face with its odd grimace, then he was behind her, lifting her to her feet with one brawny arm beneath her chin.

"Gurney, you fool, what are you doing?" she demanded.

Then she felt the touch of the knife tip against her back. Chill awareness spread out from that knife tip. She knew in that instant that Gurney meant to kill her. *Why?* She could think of no reason, for he wasn't the kind to turn traitor. But she felt certain of his intention. Knowing it, her mind churned. Here was no man to be overcome easily. Here was a killer wary of the Voice, wary of every combat stratagem, wary of every trick of death and violence. Here was an instrument she herself had helped train with subtle hints and suggestions.

"You thought you had escaped, eh, witch?" Gurney snarled.

Before she could turn the question over in her mind or try to answer, the curtains parted and Paul entered.

"Here he is, Moth—" Paul broke off, taking in the tensions of the scene.

"You will stand where you are, m'Lord," Gurney said.

"What. . . ." Paul shook his head.

Jessica started to speak, felt the arm tighten against her throat.

"You will speak only when I permit it, witch," Gurney said. "I want only one thing from you for your son to hear it, and I am prepared to send this knife into your heart by reflex at the first sign of a counter against me. Your voice will remain in a monotone. Certain muscles you will not tense or move. You will act with the most extreme caution to gain yourself a few more seconds of life. And I assure you, these are all you have."

Paul took a step forward. "Gurney, man, what is—"

"Stop right where you are!" Gurney snapped. "One more step and she's dead."

Paul's hand slipped to his knife hilt. He spoke in a deadly quiet: "You had best explain yourself, Gurney."

"I swore an oath to slay the betrayer of your father," Gurney said. "Do you think I can forget the man who rescued me from a Harkonnen slave pit, gave me freedom, life, and honor . . . gave me friendship, a thing I prized above all else? I have his betrayer under my knife. No one can stop me from—"

"You couldn't be more wrong, Gurney," Paul said.

And Jessica thought: *So that's it! What irony!*

"Wrong, am I?" Gurney demanded. "Let us hear it from the woman herself. And let her remember that I have bribed and spied and cheated to confirm this charge. I've even pushed semuta on a Harkonnen guard captain to get part of the story."

Jessica felt the arm at her throat ease slightly, but before she could speak, Paul said: "The betrayer was Yueh. I tell you this once, Gurney. The evidence is complete, cannot be controverted. It was Yueh. I do not care how you came by your suspicion—for it can be nothing else—but if you harm my mother. . . ." Paul lifted his crysknife from its scabbard, held the blade in front of him. ". . . I'll have your blood."

"Yueh was a conditioned medic, fit for a royal house," Gurney snarled. "He could not turn traitor!"

"I know a way to remove that conditioning," Paul said.

"Evidence," Gurney insisted.

"The evidence is not here," Paul said. "It's in Tabr sietch, far to the south, but if—"

"This is a trick," Gurney snarled, and his arm tightened on Jessica's throat.

"No trick, Gurney," Paul said, and his voice carried such a note of terrible sadness that the sound tore at Jessica's heart.

"I saw the message captured from the Harkonnen agent," Gurney said. "The note pointed directly at—"

"I saw it, too," Paul said. "My father showed it to me the night he explained why it had to be a Harkonnen trick aimed at making him suspect the woman he loved."

"Ayah!" Gurney said. "You've not—"

"Be quiet," Paul said, and the monotone stillness of his words carried more command than Jessica had ever heard in another voice.

He has the Great Control, she thought.

Gurney's arm trembled against her neck. The point of the knife at her back moved with uncertainty.

"What you have not done," Paul said, "is heard my mother sobbing in the night over her lost Duke. You have not seen her eyes stab flame when she speaks of killing Harkonnens."

So he has listened, she thought. Tears blinded her eyes.

"What you have not done," Paul went on, "is remembered the lessons you learned in a Harkonnen slave pit. You speak of pride in my father's friendship! Didn't you learn the difference between Harkonnen and Atreides so that you could smell a Harkonnen trick by the stink they left on it? Didn't you learn that Atreides loyalty is bought with love while the Harkonnen coin is hate? Couldn't you see through to the very nature of this betrayal?"

"But Yueh?" Gurney muttered.

"The evidence we have is Yueh's own message to us admitting his treachery," Paul said. "I swear this to you by the love I hold for you, a love I will still hold even after I leave you dead on this floor."

Hearing her son, Jessica marveled at the awareness in him, the penetrating insight of his intelligence.

"My father had an instinct for his friends," Paul said. "He gave his love sparingly, but with never an error. His weakness lay in misunderstanding hatred. He thought anyone who hated Harkonnens could not betray him." He glanced at his mother. "She knows this. I've given her my father's message that he never distrusted her."

Jessica felt herself losing control, bit at her lower lip. Seeing the stiff formality in Paul, she realized what these words were costing him. She wanted to run to him, cradle his head against her breast as she never had done. But the arm against her throat had ceased its trembling; the knife point at her back pressed still and sharp.

"One of the most terrible moments in a boy's life," Paul said, "is when he discovers his father and mother are human beings who share a love that he can never quite taste. It's a loss, an awakening to the fact that the world is *there* and *here* and we are in it alone. The moment carries its own truth; you can't evade it. I *heard* my father when he spoke of my mother. She's not the betrayer, Gurney."

Jessica found her voice, said: "Gurney, release me." There was no special command in the words, no trick to play on his weaknesses, but Gurney's hand fell away. She crossed to Paul, stood in front of him, not touching him.

"Paul," she said, "there are other awakenings in this universe. I suddenly see how I've used you and twisted you and manipulated you to set you on a course of my choosing . . . a course I had to choose—if that's any excuse—because of my own training." She swallowed past a lump in her throat, looked up into her son's eyes. "Paul . . . I want you to do something for me: choose the course of happiness. Your desert woman, marry her if that's your wish. Defy everyone and everything to do this. But choose your own course. I. . . ."

She broke off, stopped by the low sound of muttering behind her.

Gurney!

She saw Paul's eyes directed beyond her, turned.

Gurney stood in the same spot, but had sheathed his knife, pulled the robe away from his breast to expose the slick grayness of an issue stillsuit, the type the smugglers traded for among the sietch warrens.

"Put your knife right here in my breast," Gurney muttered. "I say kill me and have done with it. I've besmirched my name. I've betrayed my own Duke! The finest—"

"Be still!" Paul said.

Gurney stared at him.

"Close that robe and stop acting like a fool," Paul said. "I've had enough foolishness for one day."

"Kill me, I say!" Gurney raged.

"You know me better than that," Paul said. "How many kinds of an idiot do you think I am? Must I go through this with every man I need?"

Gurney looked at Jessica, spoke in a forlorn, pleading note so unlike him. "Then you, my Lady, please . . . you kill me."

Jessica crossed to him, put her hands on his shoulders. "Gurney, why do you insist the Atreides must kill those they love?" Gently, she pulled the spread robe out of his fingers, closed and fastened the fabric over his chest.

Gurney spoke brokenly: "But . . . I. . . ."

"You thought you were doing a thing for Leto," she said, "and for this I honor you."

"My Lady," Gurney said. He dropped his chin to his chest, squeezed his eyelids closed against the tears.

"Let us think of this as a misunderstanding among old friends," she said, and Paul heard the soothers, the adjusting tones in her voice. "It's over and we can be thankful we'll never again have that sort of misunderstanding between us."

Gurney opened eyes bright with moisture, looked down at her.

"The Gurney Halleck I knew was a man adept with both blade and baliset," Jessica said. "It was the man of the baliset I most admired. Doesn't that Gurney Halleck remember how I used to enjoy listening by the hour while he played for me? Do you still have a baliset, Gurney?"

"I've a new one," Gurney said. "Brought from Chusuk, a sweet instrument. Plays like a genuine Varota, though there's no signature on it. I think myself it was made by a student of Varota's who. . . ." He broke off. "What can I say to you, my Lady? Here we prattle about—"

"Not prattle, Gurney," Paul said. He crossed to stand beside his mother, eye to eye with Gurney. "Not prattle, but a thing that brings happiness between friends. I'd take it a kindness if you'd play for her now. Battle planning can wait a little while. We'll not be going into the fight till tomorrow at any rate."

"I . . . I'll get my baliset," Gurney said. "It's in the passage." He stepped around them and through the hangings.

Paul put a hand on his mother's arm, found that she was trembling.

"It's over, Mother," he said.

Without turning her head, she looked up at him from the corners of her eyes. "Over?"

"Of course. Gurney's. . . ."

"Gurney? Oh . . . yes." She lowered her gaze.

The hangings rustled as Gurney returned with his baliset. He began tuning it, avoiding their eyes. The hangings on the walls dulled the echoes, making the instrument sound small and intimate.

Paul led his mother to a cushion, seated her there with her back to the thick draperies of the wall. He was suddenly struck by how old she seemed to him with the beginnings of desert-dried lines in her face, the stretching at the corners of her blue-veiled eyes.

She's tired, he thought. *We must find some way to ease her burdens.*

Gurney strummed a chord.

Paul glanced at him, said: "I've . . . things that need my attention. Wait here for me."

Gurney nodded. His mind seemed far away, as though he dwelled for this moment beneath the open skies of Caladan with cloud fleece on the horizon promising rain.

Paul forced himself to turn away, let himself out through the heavy hangings over the side passage. He heard Gurney take up a tune behind him, and paused a moment outside the room to listen to the muted music.

> *"Orchards and vineyards,*
> *And full-breasted houris,*
> *And a cup overflowing before me.*
> *Why do I babble of battles,*
> *And mountains reduced to dust?*
> *Why do I feel these tears?*
>
> *Heavens stand open*
> *And scatter their riches;*
> *My hands need but gather their wealth.*
> *Why do I think of an ambush,*

> *And poison in molten cup?*
> *Why do I feel my years?*
>
> *Love's arms beckon*
> *With their naked delights,*
> *And Eden's promise of ecstasies.*
> *Why do I remember the scars,*
> *Dream of old transgressions . . .*
> *And why do I sleep with fears?"*

A robed Fedaykin courier appeared from a corner of the passage ahead of Paul. The man had hood thrown back and fastenings of his stillsuit hanging loose about his neck, proof that he had come just now from the open desert.

Paul motioned for him to stop, left the hangings of the door and moved down the passage to the courier.

The man bowed, hands clasped in front of him the way he might greet a Reverend Mother or Sayyadina of the rites. He said: "Muad'Dib, leaders are beginning to arrive for the Council."

"So soon?"

"These are the ones Stilgar sent for earlier when it was thought. . . ." He shrugged.

"I see." Paul glanced back toward the faint sound of the baliset, thinking of the old song that his mother favored—an odd stretching of happy tune and sad words. "Stilgar will come here soon with others. Show them where my mother waits."

"I will wait here, Muad'Dib," the courier said.

"Yes . . . yes, do that."

Paul pressed past the man toward the depths of the cavern, headed for the place that each such cavern had—a place near its water-holding basin. There would be a small shai-hulud in this place, a creature no more than nine meters long, kept stunted and trapped by surrounding water ditches. The maker, after emerging from its little maker vector, avoided water for the poison it was. And the drowning of a maker was the greatest Fremen secret because it produced the substance of their union—the Water of Life, the poison that could only be changed by a Reverend Mother.

The decision had come to Paul while he faced the tension of danger to his mother. No line of the future he had ever seen carried that moment of peril from Gurney Halleck. The future—the gray-cloud-future—with its feeling that the entire universe rolled toward a boiling nexus hung around him like a phantom world.

I must see it, he thought.

His body had slowly acquired a certain spice tolerance that made prescient visions fewer and fewer . . . dimmer and dimmer. The solution appeared obvious to him.

I will drown the maker. We will see now whether I'm the Kwisatz Haderach who can survive the test that the Reverend Mothers have survived.

> And it came to pass in the third year of the Desert War that Paul-Muad'Dib lay alone in the Cave of Birds beneath the kiswa hangings of an inner cell. And he lay as one dead, caught up in the revelation of the Water of Life, his being translated beyond the boundaries of time by the poison that gives life. Thus was the prophecy made true that the Lisan al-Gaib might be both dead and alive.
>
> —FROM "COLLECTED LEGENDS OF ARRAKIS"
> BY THE PRINCESS IRULAN

Chani came up out of the Habbanya basin in the predawn darkness, hearing the 'thopter that had brought her from the south go whir-whirring off to a hiding place in the vastness. Around her, the escort kept its distance, fanning out into the rocks of the ridge to probe for dangers—and giving the mate of Muad'Dib, the mother of his firstborn, the thing she had requested: a moment to walk alone.

Why did he summon me? she asked herself. *He told me before that I must remain in the south with little Leto and Alia.*

She gathered her robe and leaped lightly up across a barrier rock and onto the climbing path that only the desert-trained could recognize in the darkness. Pebbles slithered underfoot and she danced across them without considering the nimbleness required.

The climb was exhilarating, easing the fears that had fermented in her because of her escort's silent withdrawal and the fact that a precious 'thopter had been sent for her. She felt the inner leaping at the nearness of reunion with Paul-Muad'Dib, her Usul. His name might be a battle cry over all the land: *"Muad'Dib! Muad'Dib! Muad'Dib!"* But she knew a different man by a different name—the father of her son, the tender lover.

A great figure loomed out of the rocks above her, beckoning for speed. She quickened her pace. Dawn birds already were calling and lifting into the sky. A dim spread of light grew across the eastern horizon.

The figure above was not one of her own escort. *Otheym?* she wondered, marking a familiarity of movement and manner. She came up to him, recognized in the growing light the broad, flat features of the Fedaykin lieutenant, his hood open and mouth filter loosely fastened the way one did sometimes when venturing out on the desert for only a moment.

"Hurry," he hissed, and led her down the secret crevasse into the hidden cave. "It will be light soon," he whispered as he held a doorseal open for her. "The Harkonnens have been making desperation patrols over some of this region. We dare not chance discovery now."

They emerged into the narrow side-passage entrance to the Cave of Birds. Glowglobes came alight. Otheym pressed past her, said: "Follow me. Quickly, now."

They sped down the passage, through another valve door, another passage and through hangings into what had been the Sayyadina's alcove in the days when this was an overday rest cave. Rugs and cushions now covered the floor. Woven hangings with the red figure of a hawk hid the rock walls. A low field desk at one side was strewn with papers from which lifted the aroma of their spice origin.

The Reverend Mother sat alone directly opposite the entrance. She looked up with the inward stare that made the uninitiated tremble.

Otheym pressed palms together, said: "I have brought Chani." He bowed, retreated through the hangings.

And Jessica thought: *How do I tell Chani?*

"How is my grandson?" Jessica asked.

So it's to be the ritual greeting, Chani thought, and her fears returned. *Where is Muad'Dib? Why isn't he here to greet me?*

"He is healthy and happy, my mother," Chani said. "I left him with Alia in the care of Harah."

My mother, Jessica thought. *Yes, she has the right to call me that in the formal greeting. She has given me a grandson.*

"I hear a gift of cloth has been sent from Coanua sietch," Jessica said.

"It is lovely cloth," Chani said.

"Does Alia send a message?"

"No message. But the sietch moves more smoothly now that the people are beginning to accept the miracle of her status."

Why does she drag this out so? Chani wondered. *Something was so urgent that they sent a 'thopter for me. Now, we drag through the formalities!*

"We must have some of the new cloth cut into garments for little Leto," Jessica said.

"Whatever you wish, my mother," Chani said. She lowered her gaze. "Is there news of battles?" She held her face expressionless that Jessica might not see the betrayal—that this was a question about Paul-Muad'Dib.

"New victories," Jessica said. "Rabban has sent cautious overtures about a truce. His messengers have been returned without their water. Rabban has even lightened the burdens of the people in some of the sink villages. But he is too late. The people know he does it out of fear of us."

"Thus it goes as Muad'Dib said," Chani said. She stared at Jessica, trying to keep her fears to herself. *I have spoken his name, but she has not responded. One cannot see emotion in that glazed stone she calls a face . . . but she is too frozen. Why is she so still? What has happened to my Usul?*

"I wish we were in the south," Jessica said. "The oases were so beautiful when we left. Do you not long for the day when the whole land may blossom thus?"

"The land is beautiful, true," Chani said. "But there is much grief in it."

"Grief is the price of victory," Jessica said.

Is she preparing me for grief? Chani asked herself. She said: "There are so many women without men. There was jealousy when it was learned that I'd been summoned north."

"I summoned you," Jessica said.

Chani felt her heart hammering. She wanted to clap her hands to her ears, fearful of what they might hear. Still, she kept her voice even: "The message was signed Muad'Dib."

"I signed it thus in the presence of his lieutenants," Jessica said. "It was a subterfuge of necessity." And Jessica thought: *This is a brave woman, my Paul's. She holds to the niceties even when fear is almost overwhelming her. Yes. She may be the one we need now.*

Only the slightest tone of resignation crept into Chani's voice as she said: "Now you may say the thing that must be said."

"You were needed here to help me revive Paul," Jessica said. And she thought: *There! I said it in the precisely correct way. Revive. Thus she knows Paul is alive and knows there is peril, all in the same word.*

Chani took only a moment to calm herself, then: "What is it I may do?" She wanted to leap at Jessica, shake her and scream: *"Take me to him!"* But she waited silently for the answer.

"I suspect," Jessica said, "that the Harkonnens have managed to send an agent among us to poison Paul. It's the only explanation that seems to fit. A most unusual poison. I've examined his blood in the most subtle ways without detecting it."

Chani thrust herself forward onto her knees. "Poison? Is he in pain? Could I. . . ."

"He is unconscious," Jessica said. "The processes of his life are so low that they can be detected only with the most refined techniques. I shudder to think what could have happened had I not been the one to discover him. He appears dead to the untrained eye."

"You have reasons other than courtesy for summoning me," Chani said. "I know you, Reverend Mother. What is it you think I may do that you cannot do?"

She is brave, lovely and, ah-h-h, so perceptive, Jessica thought. *She'd have made a fine Bene Gesserit.*

"Chani," Jessica said, "you may find this difficult to believe, but I do not know precisely why I sent for you. It was an instinct . . . a basic intuition. The thought came unbidden: 'Send for Chani.'"

For the first time, Chani saw the sadness in Jessica's expression, the unveiled pain modifying the inward stare.

"I've done all I know to do," Jessica said. "That *all* . . . it is so far beyond what is usually supposed as *all* that you would find difficulty imagining it. Yet . . . I failed."

"The old companion, Halleck," Chani asked, "is it possible he's a traitor?"

"Not Gurney," Jessica said.

The two words carried an entire conversation, and Chani saw the searching, the tests . . . the memories of old failures that went into this flat denial.

Chani rocked back onto her feet, stood up, smoothed her desert-stained robe. "Take me to him," she said.

Jessica arose, turned through hangings on the left wall.

Chani followed, found herself in what had been a storeroom, its rock walls concealed now beneath heavy draperies. Paul lay on a field pad against the far wall. A single glowglobe above him illuminated his face. A black robe covered him to the chest, leaving his arms outside it stretched along his sides. He appeared to be unclothed under the robe. The skin exposed looked waxen, rigid. There was no visible movement to him.

Chani suppressed the desire to dash forward, throw herself across him. She found her thoughts, instead, going to her son—Leto. And she realized in this instant that Jessica once had faced such a moment—her man threatened by death, forced in her own mind to consider what might be done to save a young son. The realization formed a sudden bond with the older woman so that Chani reached out and clasped Jessica's hand. The answering grip was painful in its intensity.

"He lives," Jessica said. "I assure you he lives. But the thread of his life is so thin it could easily escape detection. There are some among the leaders already muttering that the mother speaks and not the Reverend

Mother, that my son is truly dead and I do not want to give up his water to the tribe."

"How long has he been this way?" Chani asked. She disengaged her hand from Jessica's, moved farther into the room.

"Three weeks," Jessica said. "I spent almost a week trying to revive him. There were meetings, arguments . . . investigations. Then I sent for you. The Fedaykin obey my orders, else I might not have been able to delay the. . . ." She wet her lips with her tongue, watching Chani cross to Paul.

Chani stood over him now, looking down on the soft beard of youth that framed his face, tracing with her eyes the high browline, the strong nose, the shuttered eyes—the features so peaceful in this rigid repose.

"How does he take nourishment?" Chani asked.

"The demands of his flesh are so slight he does not yet need food," Jessica said.

"How many know of what has happened?" Chani asked.

"Only his closest advisers, a few of the leaders, the Fedaykin and, of course, whoever administered the poison."

"There is no clue to the poisoner?"

"And it's not for want of investigating," Jessica said.

"What do the Fedaykin say?" Chani asked.

"They believe Paul is in a sacred trance, gathering his holy powers before the final battles. This is a thought I've cultivated."

Chani lowered herself to her knees beside the pad, bent close to Paul's face. She sensed an immediate difference in the air about his face . . . but it was only the spice, the ubiquitous spice whose odor permeated everything in Fremen life. Still. . . .

"You were not born to the spice as we were," Chani said. "Have you investigated the possibility that his body has rebelled against too much spice in his diet?"

"Allergy reactions are all negative," Jessica said.

She closed her eyes, as much to blot out this scene as because of sudden realization of fatigue. *How long have I been without sleep?* she asked herself. *Too long.*

"When you change the Water of Life," Chani said, "you do it within yourself by the inward awareness. Have you used this awareness to test his blood?"

"Normal Fremen blood," Jessica said. "Completely adapted to the diet and the life here."

Chani sat back on her heels, submerging her fears in thought as she studied Paul's face. This was a trick she had learned from watching the Reverend Mothers. Time could be made to serve the mind. One concentrated the entire attention.

Presently, Chani said: "Is there a maker here?"

"There are several," Jessica said with a touch of weariness. "We are never without them these days. Each victory requires its blessing. Each ceremony before a raid—"

"But Paul-Muad'Dib has held himself aloof from these ceremonies," Chani said.

Jessica nodded to herself, remembering her son's ambivalent feelings toward the spice drug and the prescient awareness it precipitated.

"How did you know this?" Jessica asked.

"It is spoken."

"Too much is spoken," Jessica said bitterly.

"Get me the raw Water of the maker," Chani said.

Jessica stiffened at the tone of command in Chani's voice, then observed the intense concentration in the younger woman and said: "At once." She went out through the hangings to send a waterman.

Chani sat staring at Paul. *If he has tried to do this*, she thought. *And it's the sort of thing he might try. . . .*

Jessica knelt beside Chani, holding out a plain camp ewer. The charged odor of the poison was sharp in Chani's nostrils. She dipped a finger in the fluid, held the finger close to Paul's nose.

The skin along the bridge of his nose wrinkled slightly. Slowly, the nostrils flared.

Jessica gasped.

Chani touched the dampened finger to Paul's upper lip.

He drew in a long, sobbing breath.

"What is this?" Jessica demanded.

"Be still," Chani said. "You must convert a small amount of the sacred water. Quickly!"

Without questioning, because she recognized the tone of awareness in Chani's voice, Jessica lifted the ewer to her mouth, drew in a small sip.

Paul's eyes flew open. He stared upward at Chani.

"It is not necessary for her to change the Water," he said. His voice was weak, but steady.

Jessica, a sip of the fluid on her tongue, found her body rallying, converting the poison almost automatically. In the light elevation the ceremony always imparted, she sensed the life-glow from Paul—a radiation there registering on her senses.

In that instant, she knew.

"You drank the sacred water!" she blurted.

"One drop of it," Paul said. "So small . . . one drop."

"How could you do such a foolish thing?" she demanded.

"He is your son," Chani said.

Jessica glared at her.

A rare smile, warm and full of understanding, touched Paul's lips. "Hear my beloved," he said. "Listen to her, Mother. She knows."

"A thing that others can do, he must do," Chani said.

"When I had the drop in my mouth, when I felt it and smelled it, when I knew what it was doing to me, then I knew I could do the thing that you have done," he said. "Your Bene Gesserit proctors speak of the Kwisatz Haderach, but they cannot begin to guess the many places I have been. In the few minutes I. . . ." He broke off, looking at Chani with a puzzled frown. "Chani? How did you get here? You're supposed to be. . . . Why are you here?"

He tried to push himself onto his elbows. Chani pressed him back gently.

"Please, my Usul," she said.

"I feel so weak," he said. His gaze darted around the room. "How long have I been here?"

"You've been three weeks in a coma so deep that the spark of life seemed to have fled," Jessica said.

"But it was. . . . I took it just a moment ago and. . . ."

"A moment for you, three weeks of fear for me," Jessica said.

"It was only one drop, but I converted it," Paul said. "I changed the Water of Life." And before Chani or Jessica could stop him, he dipped his hand into the ewer they had placed on the floor beside him, and he brought the dripping hand to his mouth, swallowed the palm-cupped liquid.

"Paul!" Jessica screamed.

He grabbed her hand, faced her with a death's head grin, and he sent his awareness surging over her.

The rapport was not as tender, not as sharing, not as encompassing as it had been with Alia and with the Old Reverend Mother in the cavern . . . but it was a rapport: a sense-sharing of the entire being. It shook her, weakened her, and she cowered in her mind, fearful of him.

Aloud, he said: "You speak of a place where you cannot enter? This place which the Reverend Mother cannot face, show it to me."

She shook her head, terrified by the very thought.

"Show it to me!" he commanded.

"No!"

But she could not escape him. Bludgeoned by the terrible force of him, she closed her eyes and focused inward—the-direction-that-is-dark.

Paul's consciousness flowed through and around her and into the darkness. She glimpsed the place dimly before her mind blanked itself away from the terror. Without knowing why, her whole being trembled at what she had seen—a region where a wind blew and sparks glared, where rings of light expanded and contracted, where rows of tumescent white shapes flowed over and under and around the lights, driven by darkness and a wind out of nowhere.

Presently, she opened her eyes, saw Paul staring up at her. He still held her hand, but the terrible rapport was gone. She quieted her trembling. Paul released her hand. It was as though some crutch had been removed. She staggered up and back, would have fallen had not Chani jumped to support her.

"Reverend Mother!" Chani said. "What is wrong?"

"Tired," Jessica whispered. "So . . . tired."

"Here," Chani said. "Sit here." She helped Jessica to a cushion against the wall.

The strong young arms felt so good to Jessica. She clung to Chani.

"He has, in truth, seen the Water of Life?" Chani asked. She disengaged herself from Jessica's grip.

"He has seen," Jessica whispered. Her mind still rolled and surged from the contact. It was like stepping to solid land after weeks on a heaving sea. She sensed the old Reverend Mother within her . . . and all the others awakened and questioning: *"What was that? What happened? Where was that place?"*

Through it all threaded the realization that her son was the Kwisatz Haderach, the one who could be many places at once. He was the fact out of the Bene Gesserit dream. And the fact gave her no peace.

"What happened?" Chani demanded.

Jessica shook her head.

Paul said: "There is in each of us an ancient force that takes and an ancient force that gives. A man finds little difficulty facing that place within himself where the taking force dwells, but it's almost impossible for him to see into the giving force without changing into something other than man. For a woman, the situation is reversed."

Jessica looked up, found Chani was staring at her while listening to Paul.

"Do you understand me, Mother?" Paul asked.

She could only nod.

"These things are so ancient within us," Paul said, "that they're ground into each separate cell of our bodies. We're shaped by such forces. You can say to yourself, 'Yes, I see how such a thing may be.' But when you look inward and confront the raw force of your own life unshielded, you see your peril. You see that this could overwhelm you. The greatest peril to the Giver is the force that takes. The greatest peril to the Taker is the force that gives. It's as easy to be overwhelmed by giving as by taking."

"And you, my son," Jessica asked, "are you one who gives or one who takes?"

"I'm at the fulcrum," he said. "I cannot give without taking and I cannot take without. . . ." He broke off, looking to the wall at his right.

Chani felt a draft against her cheek, turned to see the hangings close.

"It was Otheym," Paul said. "He was listening."

Accepting the words, Chani was touched by some of the prescience that haunted Paul, and she knew a thing-yet-to-be as though it already had occurred. Otheym would speak of what he had seen and heard. Others would spread the story until it was a fire over the land. Paul-Muad'Dib is not as other men, they would say. There can be no more doubt. He is a man, yet he sees through to the Water of Life in the way of a Reverend Mother. He is indeed the Lisan al-Gaib.

"You have seen the future, Paul," Jessica said. "Will you say what you've seen?"

"Not the future," he said. "I've seen the Now." He forced himself to a sitting position, waved Chani aside as she moved to help him. "The Space above Arrakis is filled with the ships of the Guild."

Jessica trembled at the certainty in his voice.

"The Padishah Emperor himself is there," Paul said. He looked at the rock ceiling of his cell. "With his favorite Truthsayer and five legions of Sardaukar. The old Baron Vladimir Harkonnen is there with Thufir Hawat beside him and seven ships jammed with every conscript he could muster. Every Great House has its raiders above us . . . waiting."

Chani shook her head, unable to look away from Paul. His strangeness, the flat tone of voice, the way he looked through her, filled her with awe.

Jessica tried to swallow in a dry throat, said: "For what are they waiting?"

Paul looked at her. "For the Guild's permission to land. The Guild will strand on Arrakis any force that lands without permission."

"The Guild's protecting us?" Jessica asked.

"Protecting us! The Guild itself caused this by spreading tales about what we do here and by reducing troop transport fares to a point where even the poorest Houses are up there now waiting to loot us."

Jessica noted the lack of bitterness in his tone, wondered at it. She couldn't doubt his words—they had that same intensity she'd seen in him the night he'd revealed the path of the future that'd taken them among the Fremen.

Paul took a deep breath, said: "Mother, you must change a quantity of the Water for us. We need the catalyst. Chani, have a scout force sent out . . . to find a pre-spice mass. If we plant a quantity of the Water of Life above a pre-spice mass, do you know what will happen?"

Jessica weighed his words, suddenly saw through to his meaning. "Paul!" she gasped.

"The Water of Death," he said. "It'd be a chain reaction." He pointed to the floor. "Spreading death among the little makers, killing a vector of the life cycle that includes the spice and the makers. Arrakis will become a true desolation—without spice or maker."

Chani put a hand to her mouth, shocked to numb silence by the blasphemy pouring from Paul's lips.

"He who can destroy a thing has the real control of it," Paul said. "We can destroy the spice."

"What stays the Guild's hand?" Jessica whispered.

"They're searching for me," Paul said. "Think of that! The finest Guild navigators, men who can quest ahead through time to find the safest course for the fastest Heighliners, all of them seeking me . . . and unable to find me. How they tremble! They know I have their secret here!" Paul held out his cupped hand. "Without the spice they're blind!"

Chani found her voice. "You said you see the *now!*"

Paul lay back, searching the spread-out *present*, its limits extended into the future and into the past, holding onto the awareness with difficulty as the spice illumination began to fade.

"Go do as I commanded," he said. "The future's becoming as muddled for the Guild as it is for me. The lines of vision are narrowing. Everything focuses here where the spice is . . . where they've dared not interfere before . . . because to interfere was to lose what they must have. But now they're desperate. All paths lead into darkness."

And that day dawned when Arrakis lay at the hub of the universe with the wheel poised to spin.

—FROM "ARRAKIS AWAKENING"
BY THE PRINCESS IRULAN

"Will you look at that thing!" Stilgar whispered.

Paul lay beside him in a slit of rock high on the Shield Wall rim, eye fixed to the collector of a Fremen telescope. The oil lens was focused on a starship lighter exposed by dawn in the basin below them. The tall eastern face of the ship glistened in the flat light of the sun, but the shadow side still showed yellow portholes from glowglobes of the night. Beyond the ship, the city of Arrakeen lay cold and gleaming in the light of the northern sun.

It wasn't the lighter that excited Stilgar's awe, Paul knew, but the construction for which the lighter was only the centerpost. A single metal hutment, many stories tall, reached out in a thousand-meter circle from the base of the lighter—a tent composed of interlocking metal leaves—the temporary lodging place for five legions of Sardaukar and His Imperial Majesty, the Padishah Emperor Shaddam IV.

From his position squatting at Paul's left, Gurney Halleck said: "I count nine levels to it. Must be quite a few Sardaukar in there."

"Five legions," Paul said.

"It grows light," Stilgar hissed. "We like it not, your exposing yourself, Muad'Dib. Let us go back into the rocks now."

"I'm perfectly safe here," Paul said.

"That ship mounts projectile weapons," Gurney said.

"They believe us protected by shields," Paul said. "They wouldn't waste a shot on an unidentified trio even if they saw us."

Paul swung the telescope to scan the far wall of the basin, seeing the pockmarked cliffs, the slides that marked the tombs of so many of his father's troopers. And he had a momentary sense of the fitness of things that the shades of those men should look down on this moment. The Harkonnen forts and towns across the shielded lands lay in Fremen hands or cut away from their source like stalks severed from a plant and left to wither. Only this basin and its city remained to the enemy.

"They might try a sortie by 'thopter," Stilgar said. "If they see us."

"Let them," Paul said. "We've 'thopters to burn today . . . and we know a storm is coming."

He swung the telescope to the far side of the Arrakeen landing field now, to the Harkonnen frigates lined up there with a CHOAM Company banner waving gently from its staff on the ground beneath them. And he thought of the desperation that had forced the Guild to permit these two groups to land while all the others were held in reserve. The Guild was like a man testing the sand with his toe to gauge its temperature before erecting a tent.

"Is there anything new to see from here?" Gurney asked. "We should be getting under cover. The storm *is* coming."

Paul returned his attention on the giant hutment. "They've even brought their women," he said. "And lackeys and servants. Ah-h-h, my dear Emperor, how confident you are."

"Men are coming up the secret way," Stilgar said. "It may be Otheym and Korba returning."

"All right, Stil," Paul said. "We'll go back."

But he took one final look around through the telescope—studying the plain with its tall ships, the gleaming metal hutment, the silent city, the frigates of the Harkonnen mercenaries. Then he slid backward around a scarp of rock. His place at the telescope was taken by a Fedaykin guardsman.

Paul emerged into a shallow depression in the Shield Wall's surface. It was a place about thirty meters in diameter and some three meters deep, a natural feature of the rock that the Fremen had hidden beneath a translucent camouflage cover. Communications equipment was clustered around a hole in the wall to the right. Fedaykin guards deployed through the depression waited for Muad'Dib's command to attack.

Two men emerged from the hole by the communications equipment, spoke to the guards there.

Paul glanced at Stilgar, nodded in the direction of the two men. "Get their report, Stil."

Stilgar moved to obey.

Paul crouched with his back to the rock, stretching his muscles, straightened. He saw Stilgar sending the two men back into that dark hole in the rock, thought about the long climb down that narrow manmade tunnel to the floor of the basin.

Stilgar crossed to Paul.

"What was so important that they couldn't send a cielago with the message?" Paul asked.

"They're saving their birds for the battle," Stilgar said. He glanced at the communications equipment, back to Paul. "Even with a tight beam, it is wrong to use those things, Muad'Dib. They can find you by taking a bearing on its emission."

"They'll soon be too busy to find me," Paul said. "What did the men report?"

"Our pet Sardaukar have been released near Old Gap low on the rim and are on their way to their master. The rocket launchers and other projectile weapons are in place. The people are deployed as you ordered. It was all routine."

Paul glanced across the shallow bowl, studying his men in the filtered light admitted by the camouflage cover. He felt time creeping like an insect working its way across an exposed rock.

"It'll take our Sardaukar a little time afoot before they can signal a troop carrier," Paul said. "They are being watched?"

"They are being watched," Stilgar said.

Beside Paul, Gurney Halleck cleared his throat. "Hadn't we best be getting to a place of safety?"

"There is no such place," Paul said. "Is the weather report still favorable?"

"A great grandmother of a storm coming," Stilgar said. "Can you not feel it, Muad'Dib?"

"The air does feel chancy," Paul agreed. "But I like the certainty of poling the weather."

"The storm'll be here in the hour," Stilgar said. He nodded toward the gap that looked out on the Emperor's hutment and the Harkonnen frigates. "They know it there, too. Not a 'thopter in the sky. Everything pulled in and tied down. They've had a report on the weather from their friends in space."

"Any more probing sorties?" Paul asked.

"Nothing since the landing last night," Stilgar said. "They know we're here. I think now they wait to choose their own time."

"We choose the time," Paul said.

Gurney glanced upward, growled: "If *they* let us."

"That fleet'll stay in space," Paul said.

Gurney shook his head.

"They have no choice," Paul said. "We can destroy the spice. The Guild dares not risk that."

"Desperate people are the most dangerous," Gurney said.

"Are we not desperate?" Stilgar asked.

Gurney scowled at him.

"You haven't lived with the Fremen dream," Paul cautioned. "Stil is thinking of all the water we've spent on bribes, the years of waiting we've added before Arrakis can bloom. He's not—"

"Arrrgh," Gurney scowled.

"Why's he so gloomy?" Stilgar asked.

"He's always gloomy before a battle," Paul said. "It's the only form of good humor Gurney allows himself."

A slow, wolfish grin spread across Gurney's face, the teeth showing white above the chip cut of his stillsuit. "It glooms me much to think on all the poor Harkonnen souls we'll dispatch unshriven," he said.

Stilgar chuckled. "He talks like a Fedaykin."

"Gurney was born a death commando," Paul said. And he thought: *Yes, let them occupy their minds with small talk before we test ourselves against that force on the plain.* He looked to the gap in the rock wall and back to Gurney, found that the troubadour-warrior had resumed a brooding scowl.

"Worry saps the strength," Paul murmured. "You told me that once, Gurney."

"My Duke," Gurney said, "my chief worry is the atomics. If you use them to blast a hole in the Shield Wall. . . ."

"Those people up there won't use atomics against us," Paul said. "They don't dare . . . and for the same reason that they cannot risk our destroying the source of the spice."

"But the injunction against—"

"The injunction!" Paul barked. "It's fear, not the injunction that keeps the Houses from hurling atomics against each other. The language of the Great Convention is clear enough: 'Use of atomics against humans shall be cause for planetary obliteration.' We're going to blast the Shield Wall, not humans."

"It's too fine a point," Gurney said.

"The hair-splitters up there will welcome any point," Paul said. "Let's talk no more about it."

He turned away, wishing he actually felt that confident. Presently, he said: "What about the city people? Are they in position yet?"

"Yes," Stilgar muttered.

Paul looked at him. "What's eating you?"

"I never knew the city man could be trusted completely," Stilgar said.

"I was a city man myself once," Paul said.

Stilgar stiffened. His face grew dark with blood. "Muad'Dib knows I did not mean—"

"I know what you meant, Stil. But the test of a man isn't what you think he'll do. It's what he actually does. These city people have Fremen blood. It's just that they haven't yet learned how to escape their bondage. We'll teach them."

Stilgar nodded, spoke in a rueful tone: "The habits of a lifetime, Muad'Dib. On the Funeral Plain we learned to despise the men of the communities."

Paul glanced at Gurney, saw him studying Stilgar. "Tell us, Gurney, why were the cityfolk down there driven from their homes by the Sardaukar?"

"An old trick, my Duke. They thought to burden us with refugees."

"It's been so long since guerrillas were effective that the mighty have forgotten how to fight them," Paul said. "The Sardaukar have played into our hands. They grabbed some city women for their sport, decorated their battle standards with the heads of the men who objected. And they've built up a fever of hate among people who otherwise would've looked on the coming battle as no more than a great inconvenience . . . and the possibility of exchanging one set of masters for another. The Sardaukar recruit for us, Stilgar."

"The city people do seem eager," Stilgar said.

"Their hate is fresh and clear," Paul said. "That's why we use them as shock troops."

"The slaughter among them will be fearful," Gurney said. Stilgar nodded agreement.

"They were told the odds," Paul said. "They know every Sardaukar they kill will be one less for us. You see, gentlemen, they have something to die for. They've discovered they're a people. They're awakening."

A muttered exclamation came from the watcher at the telescope. Paul moved to the rock slit, asked: "What is it out there?"

"A great commotion, Muad'Dib," the watcher hissed. "At that monstrous metal tent. A surface car came from Rimwall West and it was like a hawk into a nest of rock partridge."

"Our captive Sardaukar have arrived," Paul said.

"They've a shield around the entire landing field now," the watcher said. "I can see the air dancing even to the edge of the storage yard where they kept the spice."

"Now they know who it is they fight," Gurney said. "Let the Harkonnen beasts tremble and fret themselves that an Atreides yet lives!"

Paul spoke to the Fedaykin at the telescope. "Watch the flagpole atop the Emperor's ship. If my flag is raised there—"

"It will not be," Gurney said.

Paul saw the puzzled frown on Stilgar's face, said: "If the Emperor recognized my claim, he'll signal by restoring the Atreides flag to Arrakis. We'll use the second plan then, move only against the Harkonnens. The Sardaukar will stand aside and let us settle the issue between ourselves."

"I've no experience with these offworld things," Stilgar said. "I've heard of them, but it seems unlikely the—"

"You don't need experience to know what they'll do," Gurney said.

"They're sending a new flag up on the tall ship," the watcher said. "The flag is yellow . . . with a black and red circle in the center."

"There's a subtle piece of business," Paul said. "The CHOAM Company flag."

"It's the same as the flag at the other ships," the Fedaykin guard said.

"I don't understand," Stilgar said.

"A subtle piece of business indeed," Gurney said. "Had he sent up the Atreides banner, he'd have had to live by what that meant. Too many observers about. He could've signaled with the Harkonnen flag on his staff—a flat declaration that'd have been. But, no—he sends up the CHOAM rag. He's telling the people up there. . . ." Gurney pointed toward space. ". . . where the profit is. He's saying he doesn't care if it's an Atreides here or not."

"How long till the storm strikes the Shield Wall?" Paul asked.

Stilgar turned away, consulted one of the Fedaykin in the bowl. Presently, he returned, said: "Very soon, Muad'Dib. Sooner than we expected. It's a great-great grandmother of a storm . . . perhaps even more than you wished."

"It's my storm," Paul said, and saw the silent awe on the faces of the Fedaykin who heard him. "Though it shook the entire world it could not be more than I wished. Will it strike the Shield Wall full on?"

"Close enough to make no difference," Stilgar said.

A courier crossed from the hole that led down into the basin, said: "The Sardaukar and Harkonnen patrols are pulling back, Muad'Dib."

"They expect the storm to spill too much sand into the basin for good visibility," Stilgar said. "They think we'll be in the same fix."

"Tell our gunners to set their sights well before visibility drops," Paul said. "They must knock the nose off every one of those ships as soon as the storm has destroyed the shields." He stepped to the wall of the bowl, pulled back a fold of the camouflage cover and looked up at the sky. The horsetail twistings of blow sand could be seen against the dark of the sky. Paul restored the cover, said: "Start sending our men down, Stil."

"Will you not go with us?" Stilgar asked.

"I'll wait here a bit with the Fedaykin," Paul said.

Stilgar gave a knowing shrug toward Gurney, moved to the hole in the rock wall, was lost in its shadows.

"The trigger that blasts the Shield Wall aside, that I leave in your hands, Gurney," Paul said. "You will do it?"

"I'll do it."

Paul gestured to a Fedaykin lieutenant, said: "Otheym, start moving the check patrols out of the blast area. They must be out of there before the storm strikes."

The man bowed, followed Stilgar.

Gurney leaned in to the rock slit, spoke to the man at the telescope: "Keep your attention on the south wall. It'll be completely undefended until we blow it."

"Dispatch a cielago with a time signal," Paul ordered.

"Some ground cars are moving toward the south wall," the man at the telescope said. "Some are using projectile weapons, testing. Our people are using body shields as you commanded. The ground cars have stopped."

In the abrupt silence, Paul heard the wind devils playing overhead—the front of the storm. Sand began to drift down into their bowl through gaps in the cover. A burst of wind caught the cover, whipped it away.

Paul motioned his Fedaykin to take shelter, crossed to the men at the communications equipment near the tunnel mouth. Gurney stayed beside him. Paul crouched over the signalmen.

One said: "A great-great-*great* grandmother of a storm, Muad'Dib."

Paul glanced up at the darkening sky, said: "Gurney, have the south wall observers pulled out." He had to repeat his order, shouting above the growing noise of the storm.

Gurney turned to obey.

Paul fastened his face filter, tightened the stillsuit hood.

Gurney returned.

Paul touched his shoulder, pointed to the blast trigger set into the tunnel mouth beyond the signalmen. Gurney went into the tunnel, stopped there, one hand at the trigger, his gaze on Paul.

"We are getting no messages," the signalman beside Paul said. "Much static."

Paul nodded, kept his eye on the time-standard dial in front of the signalman. Presently, Paul looked at Gurney, raised a hand, returned his attention to the dial. The time counter crawled around its final circuit.

"Now!" Paul shouted, and dropped his hand.

Gurney depressed the blast trigger.

It seemed that a full second passed before they felt the ground beneath them ripple and shake. A rumbling sound was added to the storm's roar.

The Fedaykin watcher from the telescope appeared beside Paul, the telescope clutched under one arm. "The Shield Wall is breached, Muad'Dib!" he shouted. "The storm is on them and our gunners already are firing."

Paul thought of the storm sweeping across the basin, the static charge within the wall of sand that destroyed every shield barrier in the enemy camp.

"The storm!" someone shouted. "We must get under cover, Muad'Dib!"

Paul came to his senses, feeling the sand needles sting his exposed cheeks. *We are committed,* he thought. He put an arm around the signalman's shoulder, said: "Leave the equipment! There's more in the tunnel." He felt himself being pulled away, Fedaykin pressed around him to protect him. They squeezed into the tunnel mouth, feeling its comparative silence, turned a corner into a small chamber with glowglobes overhead and another tunnel opening beyond.

Another signalman sat there at his equipment.

"Much static," the man said.

A swirl of sand filled the air around them.

"Seal off this tunnel!" Paul shouted. A sudden pressure of stillness showed that his command had been obeyed. "Is the way down to the basin still open?" Paul asked.

A Fedaykin went to look, returned, said: "The explosion caused a little rock to fall, but the engineers say it is still open. They're cleaning up with lasbeams."

"Tell them to use their hands!" Paul barked. "There are shields active down there!"

"They are being careful, Muad'Dib," the man said, but he turned to obey.

The signalmen from outside pressed past them carrying their equipment.

"I told those men to leave their equipment!" Paul said.

"Fremen do not like to abandon equipment, Muad'Dib," one of his Fedaykin chided.

"Men are more important than equipment now," Paul said. "We'll have more equipment than we can use soon or have no need for any equipment."

Gurney Halleck came up beside him, said: "I heard them say the way down is open. We're very close to the surface here, m'Lord, should the Harkonnens try to retaliate in kind."

"They're in no position to retaliate," Paul said. "They're just now finding out that they have no shields and are unable to get off Arrakis."

"The new command post is all prepared, though, m'Lord," Gurney said.

"They've no need of me in the command post yet," Paul said. "The plan would go ahead without me. We must wait for the—"

"I'm getting a message, Muad'Dib," said the signalman at the communications equipment. The man shook his head, pressed a receiver phone against his ear. "Much static!" He began scribbling on a pad in front of him, shaking his head waiting, writing . . . waiting.

Paul crossed to the signalman's side. The Fedaykin stepped back, giving him room. He looked down at what the man had written, read:

"Raid . . . on Sietch Tabr . . . captives . . . Alia (blank) families of (blank) dead are . . . they (blank) son of Muad'Dib. . . ."

Again, the signalman shook his head.

Paul looked up to see Gurney staring at him.

"The message is garbled," Gurney said. "The static. You don't know that. . . ."

"My son is dead," Paul said, and knew as he spoke that it was true. "My son is dead . . . and Alia is a captive . . . hostage." He felt emptied, a shell without emotions. Everything he touched brought death and grief. And it was like a disease that could spread across the universe.

He could feel the old-man wisdom, the accumulation out of the experiences from countless possible lives. Something seemed to chuckle and rub its hands within him.

And Paul thought: *How little the universe knows about the nature of real cruelty!*

And Muad'Dib stood before them, and he said: "Though we deem the captive dead, yet does she live. For her seed is my seed and her voice is my voice. And she sees unto the farthest reaches of possibility. Yea, unto the vale of the unknowable does she see because of me."

—FROM "ARRAKIS AWAKENING"
BY THE PRINCESS IRULAN

The Baron Vladimir Harkonnen stood with eyes downcast in the Imperial audience chamber, the oval selamlik within the Padishah Emperor's hutment. With covert glances, the Baron had studied the metal-walled room and its occupants—the noukkers, the pages, the guards, the troop of House Sardaukar drawn up around the walls, standing at ease there beneath the bloody and tattered captured battle flags that were the room's only decoration.

Voices sounded from the right of the chamber, echoing out of a high passage: "Make way! Make way for the Royal Person!"

The Padishah Emperor Shaddam IV came out of the passage into the audience chamber followed by his suite. He stood waiting while his throne was brought, ignoring the Baron, seemingly ignoring every person in the room.

The Baron found that he could not ignore the Royal Person, and studied the Emperor for a sign, any clue to the purpose of this audience. The Emperor stood poised, waiting—a slim, elegant figure in a gray Sardaukar uniform with silver and gold trim. His thin face and cold eyes reminded the Baron of the Duke Leto long dead. There was that same look of the predatory bird. But the Emperor's hair was red, not black, and most of that hair was concealed by a Burseg's ebon helmet with the Imperial crest in gold upon its crown.

Pages brought the throne. It was a massive chair carved from a single piece of Hagal quartz—blue-green translucency shot through with streaks of yellow fire. They placed it on the dais and the Emperor mounted, seated himself.

An old woman in a black aba robe with hood drawn down over her forehead detached herself from the Emperor's suite, took up station behind the throne, one scrawny hand resting on the quartz back. Her face peered out of the hood like a witch caricature—sunken cheeks and eyes, an overlong nose, skin mottled and with protruding veins.

The Baron stilled his trembling at sight of her. The presence of the Reverend Mother Gaius Helen Mohiam, the Emperor's Truthsayer, betrayed the importance of this audience. The Baron looked away from her, studied the suite for a clue. There were two of the Guild agents, one tall and fat, one short and fat, both with bland gray eyes. And among the lackeys stood one of the Emperor's daughters, the Princess Irulan, a woman they said was being trained in the deepest of the Bene Gesserit ways, destined to be a Reverend Mother. She was tall, blonde, face of chiseled beauty, green eyes that looked past and through him.

"My dear Baron."

The Emperor had deigned to notice him. The voice was baritone and with exquisite control. It managed to dismiss him while greeting him.

The Baron bowed low, advanced to the required position ten paces from the dais. "I came at your summons, Majesty."

"Summons!" the old witch cackled.

"Now, Reverend Mother," the Emperor chided, but he smiled at the Baron's discomfiture, said: "First, you will tell me where you've sent your minion, Thufir Hawat."

The Baron darted his gaze left and right, reviled himself for coming here without his own guards, not that they'd be much use against Sardaukar. Still. . . .

"Well?" the Emperor said.

"He has been gone these five days, Majesty." The Baron shot a glance at the Guild agents, back to the Emperor. "He was to land at a smuggler base and attempt infiltrating the camp of the Fremen fanatic, this Muad'Dib."

"Incredible!" the Emperor said.

One of the witch's clawlike hands tapped the Emperor's shoulder. She leaned forward, whispered in his ear.

The Emperor nodded, said: "Five days, Baron. Tell me, why aren't you worried about his absence?"

"But I *am* worried, Majesty!"

The Emperor continued to stare at him, waiting. The Reverend Mother emitted a cackling laugh.

"What I mean, Majesty," the Baron said, "is that Hawat will be dead within another few hours, anyway." And he explained about the latent poison and need for an antidote.

"How clever of you, Baron," the Emperor said. "And where are your nephews, Rabban and the young Feyd-Rautha?"

"The storm comes, Majesty. I sent them to inspect our perimeter lest the Fremen attack under cover of the sand."

"Perimeter," the Emperor said. The word came out as though it puckered his mouth. "The storm won't be much here in the basin, and that Fremen rabble won't attack while I'm here with five legions of Sardaukar."

"Surely not, Majesty," the Baron said. "But error on the side of caution cannot be censured."

"Ah-h-h-h," the Emperor said. "Censure. Then I'm not to speak of how much time this Arrakis nonsense has taken from me? Nor the CHOAM Company profits pouring down this rat hole? Nor the court functions and affairs of state I've had to delay—even cancel—because of this stupid affair?"

The Baron lowered his gaze, frightened by the Imperial anger. The delicacy of his position here, alone and dependent upon the Convention and the dictum familia of the Great Houses, fretted him. *Does he mean to kill me?* the Baron asked himself. *He couldn't! Not with the other Great Houses waiting up there, aching for any excuse to gain from this upset on Arrakis.*

"Have you taken hostages?" the Emperor asked.

"It's useless, Majesty," the Baron said. "These mad Fremen hold a burial ceremony for every captive and act as though such a one were already dead."

"So?" the Emperor said.

And the Baron waited, glancing left and right at the metal walls of the selamlik, thinking of the monstrous fanmetal tent around him. Such unlimited wealth it represented that even the Baron was awed. *He brings pages,* the Baron thought, *and useless court lackeys, his women and their companions—hair-dressers, designers, everything . . . all the fringe parasites of the Court. All here—fawning, slyly plotting, "roughing it" with the Emperor . . . here to watch him put an end to this affair, to make epigrams over the battles and idolize the wounded.*

"Perhaps you've never sought the right kind of hostages," the Emperor said.

He knows something, the Baron thought. Fear sat like a stone in his stomach until he could hardly bear the thought of eating. Yet, the feeling was like hunger, and he poised himself several times in his suspensors on the point of ordering food brought to him. But there was no one here to obey his summons.

"Do you have any idea who this Muad'Dib could be?" the Emperor asked.

"One of the Umma, surely," the Baron said. "A Fremen fanatic, a religious adventurer. They crop up regularly on the fringes of civilization. Your Majesty knows this."

The Emperor glanced at his Truthsayer, turned back to scowl at the Baron. "And you have no other knowledge of this Muad'Dib?"

"A madman," the Baron said. "But all Fremen are a little mad."

"Mad?"

"His people scream his name as they leap into battle. The women throw their babies at us and hurl themselves onto our knives to open a wedge for their men to attack us. They have no . . . no . . . decency!"

"As bad as that," the Emperor murmured, and his tone of derision did not escape the Baron. "Tell me, my dear Baron, have you investigated the southern polar regions of Arrakis?"

The Baron stared up at the Emperor, shocked by the change of subject. "But . . . well, you know, Your Majesty, the entire region is uninhabitable, open to wind and worm. There's not even any spice in those latitudes."

"You've had no reports from spice lighters that patches of greenery appear there?"

"There've always been such reports. Some were investigated—long ago. A few plants were seen. Many 'thopters were lost. Much too costly, Your Majesty. It's a place where men cannot survive for long."

"So," the Emperor said. He snapped his fingers and a door opened at his left behind the throne. Through the door came two Sardaukar herding a girl-child who appeared to be about four years old. She wore a black aba, the hood thrown back to reveal the attachments of a stillsuit hanging free at her throat. Her eyes were Fremen blue, staring out of a soft, round face. She appeared completely unafraid and there was a look to her stare that made the Baron feel uneasy for no reason he could explain.

Even the old Bene Gesserit Truthsayer drew back as the child passed and made a warding sign in her direction. The old witch obviously was shaken by the child's presence.

The Emperor cleared his throat to speak, but the child spoke first—a thin voice with traces of a soft-palate lisp, but clear nonetheless. "So here he is," she said. She advanced to the edge of the dais. "He doesn't appear much, does he—one frightened old fat man too weak to support his own flesh without the help of suspensors."

It was such a totally unexpected statement from the mouth of a child that the Baron stared at her, speechless in spite of his anger. *Is it a midget?* he asked himself.

"My dear Baron," the Emperor said, "become acquainted with the sister of Muad'Dib."

"The sist. . . ." The Baron shifted his attention to the Emperor. "I do not understand."

"I, too, sometimes err on the side of caution," the Emperor said. "It has been reported to me that your *uninhabited* south polar regions exhibit evidence of human activity."

"But that's impossible!" the Baron protested. "The worms . . . there's sand clear to the. . . ."

"These people seem able to avoid the worms," the Emperor said.

The child sat down on the dais beside the throne, dangled her feet over the edge, kicking them. There was such an air of sureness in the way she appraised her surroundings.

The Baron stared at the kicking feet, the way they moved the black robe, the wink of sandals beneath the fabric.

"Unfortunately," the Emperor said, "I only sent in five troop carriers with a light attack force to pick up prisoners for questioning. We barely got away with three prisoners and one carrier. Mind you, Baron, my Sardaukar were almost overwhelmed by a force composed mostly of women, children, and old men. This child here was in command of one of the attacking groups."

"You see, Your Majesty!" the Baron said. "You see how they are!"

"I allowed myself to be captured," the child said. "I did not want to face my brother and have to tell him that his son had been killed."

"Only a handful of our men got away," the Emperor said. "Got away! You hear that?"

"We'd have had them, too," the child said, "except for the flames."

"My Sardaukar used the attitudinal jets on their carrier as flame-throwers," the Emperor said. "A move of desperation and the only thing that got them away with their three prisoners. Mark that, my dear Baron: Sardaukar forced to retreat in confusion from women and children and old men!"

"We must attack in force," the Baron rasped. "We must destroy every last vestige of—"

"Silence!" the Emperor roared. He pushed himself forward on his throne. "Do not abuse my intelligence any longer. You stand there in your foolish innocence and—"

"Majesty," the old Truthsayer said.

He waved her to silence. "You say you don't know about the activity we found, nor the fighting qualities of these superb people!" The Emperor lifted himself half off his throne. "What do you take me for, Baron?"

The Baron took two backward steps, thinking: *It was Rabban. He has done this to me. Rabban has. . . .*

"And this fake dispute with Duke Leto," the Emperor purred, sinking back into his throne. "How beautifully you maneuvered it."

"Majesty," the Baron pleaded. "What are you—"

"Silence!"

The old Bene Gesserit put a hand on the Emperor's shoulder, leaned close to whisper in his ear.

The child seated on the dais stopped kicking her feet, said: "Make him afraid some more, Shaddam. I shouldn't enjoy this, but I find the pleasure impossible to suppress."

"Quiet, child," the Emperor said. He leaned forward, put a hand on her head, stared at the Baron. "Is it possible, Baron? Could you be as simpleminded as my Truthsayer suggests? Do you not recognize this child, daughter of your ally, Duke Leto?"

"My father was never his ally," the child said. "My father is dead and this old Harkonnen beast has never seen me before."

The Baron was reduced to stupefied glaring. When he found his voice it was only to rasp: "Who?"

"I am Alia, daughter of Duke Leto and the Lady Jessica, sister of Duke Paul-Muad'Dib," the child said. She pushed herself off the dais, dropped to the floor of the audience chamber. "My brother has promised to have your head atop his battle standard and I think he shall."

"Be hush, child," the Emperor said, and he sank back into his throne, hand to chin, studying the Baron.

"I do not take the Emperor's orders," Alia said. She turned, looked up at the old Reverend Mother. "She knows."

The Emperor glanced up at his Truthsayer. "What does she mean?"

"That child is an abomination!" the old woman said. "Her mother deserves a punishment greater than anything in history. Death! It cannot come too quickly for that *child* or for the one who spawned her!" The old woman pointed a finger at Alia. "Get out of my mind!"

"T-P?" the Emperor whispered. He snapped his attention back to Alia. "By the Great Mother!"

"You don't understand, Majesty," the old woman said. "Not telepathy. She's in my mind. She's like the ones before me, the ones who gave me their memories. She stands in my mind! She cannot be there, but she is!"

"What others?" the Emperor demanded. "What's this nonsense?"

The old woman straightened, lowered her pointing hand. "I've said too much, but the fact remains that this *child* who is not a child must be destroyed. Long were we warned against such a one and how to prevent such a birth, but one of our own has betrayed us."

"You babble, old woman," Alia said. "You don't know how it was, yet you rattle on like a purblind fool." Alia closed her eyes, took a deep breath, and held it.

The old Reverend Mother groaned and staggered.

Alia opened her eyes. "That is how it was," she said. "A cosmic accident . . . and you played your part in it."

The Reverend Mother held out both hands, palms pushing the air toward Alia.

"What is happening here?" the Emperor demanded. "Child, can you truly project your thoughts into the mind of another?"

"That's not how it is at all," Alia said. "Unless I'm born as you, I cannot think as you."

"Kill her," the old woman muttered, and clutched the back of the throne for support. "Kill her!" The sunken old eyes glared at Alia.

"Silence," the Emperor said, and he studied Alia. "Child, can you communicate with your brother?"

"My brother knows I'm here," Alia said.

"Can you tell him to surrender as the price of your life?"

Alia smiled up at him with clear innocence. "I shall not do that," she said.

The Baron stumbled forward to stand beside Alia. "Majesty," he pleaded, "I knew nothing of—"

"Interrupt me once more, Baron," the Emperor said, "and you will lose the powers of interruption . . . forever." He kept his attention focused on Alia, studying her through slitted lids. "You will not, eh? Can you read in my mind what I'll do if you disobey me?"

"I've already said I cannot read minds," she said, "but one doesn't need telepathy to read your intentions."

The Emperor scowled. "Child, your cause is hopeless. I have but to rally my forces and reduce this planet to—"

"It's not that simple," Alia said. She looked at the two Guildsmen. "Ask them."

"It is not wise to go against my desires," the Emperor said. "You should not deny me the least thing."

"My brother comes now," Alia said. "Even an Emperor may tremble before Muad'Dib, for he has the strength of righteousness and heaven smiles upon him."

The Emperor surged to his feet. "This play has gone far enough. I will take your brother and this planet and grind them to—"

The room rumbled and shook around them. There came a sudden cascade of sand behind the throne where the hutment was coupled to the Emperor's ship. The abrupt flicker-tightening of skin pressure told of a wide-area shield being activated.

"I told you," Alia said. "My brother comes."

The Emperor stood in front of his throne, right hand pressed to right ear, the servo-receiver there chattering its report on the situation. The Baron moved two steps behind Alia. Sardaukar were leaping to positions at the doors.

"We will fall back into space and re-form," the Emperor said. "Baron, my apologies. These madmen *are* attacking under cover of the storm. We will show them an Emperor's wrath, then." He pointed at Alia. "Give her body to the storm."

As he spoke, Alia fled backward, feigning terror. "Let the storm have what it can take!" she screamed. And she backed into the Baron's arms.

"I have her, Majesty!" the Baron shouted. "Shall I dispatch her now-eeeeeeeeeeeh!" He hurled her to the floor, clutched his left arm.

"I'm sorry, Grandfather," Alia said. "You've met the Atreides gom jabbar." She got to her feet, dropped a dark needle from her hand.

The Baron fell back. His eyes bulged as he stared at a red slash on his left palm. "You . . . you. . . ." He rolled sideways in his suspensors, a sagging mass of flesh supported inches off the floor with head lolling and mouth hanging open.

"These people are insane," the Emperor snarled. "Quick! Into the ship. We'll purge this planet of every. . . ."

Something sparkled to his left. A roll of ball lightning bounced away from the wall there, crackled as it touched the metal floor. The smell of burned insulation swept through the selamlik.

"The shield!" one of the Sardaukar officers shouted. "The outer shield is down! They. . . ."

His words were drowned in a metallic roaring as the shipwall behind the Emperor trembled and rocked.

"They've shot the nose off our ship!" someone called.

Dust boiled through the room. Under its cover, Alia leaped up, ran toward the outer door.

The Emperor whirled, motioned his people into an emergency door that swung open in the ship's side behind the throne. He flashed a hand signal to a Sardaukar officer leaping through the dust haze. "We will make our stand here!" the Emperor ordered.

Another crash shook the hutment. The double doors banged open at the far side of the chamber admitting windblown sand and the sound of shouting. A small, black-robed figure could be seen momentarily against the light—Alia darting out to find a knife and, as befitted her Fremen training, to kill Harkonnen and Sardaukar wounded. House Sardaukar charged through a greened yellow haze toward the opening, weapons ready, forming an arc there to protect the Emperor's retreat.

"Save yourself, Sire!" a Sardaukar officer shouted. "Into the ship!"

But the Emperor stood alone now on his dais pointing toward the doors. A forty-meter section of the hutment had been blasted away there and the selamlik's doors opened now onto drifting sand. A dust cloud hung low over the outside world blowing from pastel distances. Static lightning crackled from the cloud and the spark flashes of shields being shorted out by the storm's charge could be seen through the haze. The plain surged with figures in combat—Sardaukar and leaping gyrating robed men who seemed to come down out of the storm.

All this was as a frame for the target of the Emperor's pointing hand.

Out of the sand haze came an orderly mass of flashing shapes— great rising curves with crystal spokes that resolved into the gaping mouths of sandworms, a massed wall of them, each with troops of Fremen riding to the attack. They came in a hissing wedge, robes whipping in the wind as they cut through the melee on the plain.

Onward toward the Emperor's hutment they came while the House Sardaukar stood awed for the first time in their history by an onslaught their minds found difficult to accept.

But the figures leaping from the worm backs were men, and the blades flashing in that ominous yellow light were a thing the Sardaukar had been trained to face. They threw themselves into combat. And it was man to man on the plain of Arrakeen while a picked Sardaukar bodyguard pressed the Emperor back into the ship, sealed the door on him, and prepared to die at the door as part of his shield.

In the shock of comparative silence within the ship, the Emperor stared at the wide-eyed faces of his suite, seeing his oldest daughter with the flush of exertion on her cheeks, the old Truthsayer standing like a black shadow with her hood pulled about her face, finding at last the faces he sought—the two Guildsmen. They wore the Guild gray, unadorned, and it seemed to fit the calm they maintained despite the high emotions around them.

The taller of the two, though, held a hand to his left eye. As the Emperor watched, someone jostled the Guildsman's arm, the hand moved, and the eye was revealed. The man had lost one of his masking contact lenses, and the eye stared out a total blue so dark as to be almost black.

The smaller of the pair elbowed his way a step nearer the Emperor, said: "We cannot know how it will go." And the taller companion, hand restored to eye, added in a cold voice: "But this Muad'Dib cannot know, either."

The words shocked the Emperor out of his daze. He checked the scorn on his tongue by a visible effort because it did not take a Guild navigator's single-minded focus on the main chance to see the immediate future out on that plain. Were these two so dependent upon their *faculty* that they had lost the use of their eyes and their reason? he wondered.

"Reverend Mother," he said, "we must devise a plan."

She pulled the hood from her face, met his gaze with an unblinking stare. The look that passed between them carried complete understanding. They had one weapon left and both knew it: treachery.

"Summon Count Fenring from his quarters," the Reverend Mother said.

The Padishah Emperor nodded, waved for one of his aides to obey that command.

He was warrior and mystic, ogre and saint, the fox and the innocent, chivalrous, ruthless, less than a god, more than a man. There is no measuring Muad'Dib's motives by ordinary standards. In the moment of his triumph, he saw the death prepared for him, yet he accepted the treachery. Can you say he did this out of a sense of justice? Whose justice, then? Remember, we speak now of the Muad'Dib who ordered battle drums made from his enemies' skins, the Muad'Dib who denied the conventions of his ducal past with a wave of the hand, saying merely: "I am the Kwisatz Haderach. That is reason enough."

—FROM "ARRAKIS AWAKENING"
BY THE PRINCESS IRULAN

It was to the Arrakeen governor's mansion, the old Residency the Atreides had first occupied on Dune, that they escorted Paul-Muad'Dib on the evening of his victory. The building stood as Rabban had restored it, virtually untouched by the fighting although there had been looting by townspeople. Some of the furnishings in the main hall had been overturned or smashed.

Paul strode through the main entrance with Gurney Halleck and Stilgar a pace behind. Their escort fanned out into the Great Hall, straightening the place and clearing an area for Muad'Dib. One squad began investigating that no sly trap had been planted here.

"I remember the day we first came here with your father," Gurney said. He glanced around at the beams and the high, slitted windows. "I didn't like this place then and I like it less now. One of our caves would be safer."

"Spoken like a true Fremen," Stilgar said, and he marked the cold smile that his words brought to Muad'Dib's lips. "Will you reconsider, Muad'Dib?"

"This place is a symbol," Paul said. "Rabban lived here. By occupying this place I seal my victory for all to understand. Send men through the building. Touch nothing. Just be certain no Harkonnen people or toys remain."

"As you command," Stilgar said, and reluctance was heavy in his tone as he turned to obey.

Communications men hurried into the room with their equipment, began setting up near the massive fireplace. The Fremen guard that augmented the surviving Fedaykin took up stations around the room. There was muttering among them, much darting of suspicious glances. This had been too long a place of the enemy for them to accept their presence in it casually.

"Gurney, have an escort bring my mother and Chani," Paul said. "Does Chani know yet about our son?"

"The message was sent, m'Lord."

"Are the makers being taken out of the basin yet?"

"Yes, m'Lord. The storm's almost spent."

"What's the extent of the storm damage?" Paul asked.

"In the direct path—on the landing field and across the spice storage yards of the plain—extensive damage," Gurney said. "As much from battle as from the storm."

"Nothing money won't repair, I presume," Paul said.

"Except for the lives, m'Lord," Gurney said, and there was a tone of reproach in his voice as though to say: "*When did an Atreides worry first about things when people were at stake?*"

But Paul could only focus his attention on the inner eye and the gaps

---

visible to him in the time-wall that still lay across his path. Through each gap the jihad raged away down the corridors of the future.

He sighed, crossed the hall, seeing a chair against the wall. The chair had once stood in the dining hall and might even have held his own father. At the moment, though, it was only an object to rest his weariness and conceal it from the men. He sat down, pulling his robes around his legs, loosening his stillsuit at the neck.

"The Emperor is still holed up in the remains of his ship," Gurney said.

"For now, contain him there," Paul said. "Have they found the Harkonnens yet?"

"They're still examining the dead."

"What reply from the ships up there?" He jerked his chin toward the ceiling.

"No reply yet, m'Lord."

Paul sighed, resting against the back of his chair. Presently, he said: "Bring me a captive Sardaukar. We must send a message to our Emperor. It's time to discuss terms."

"Yes, m'Lord."

Gurney turned away, dropped a hand signal to one of the Fedaykin who took up close-guard position beside Paul.

"Gurney," Paul whispered. "Since we've been rejoined I've yet to hear you produce the proper quotation for the event." He turned, saw Gurney swallow, saw the sudden grim hardening of the man's jaw.

"As you wish, m'Lord," Gurney said. He cleared his throat, rasped: "'And the victory that day was turned into mourning unto all the people: for the people heard say that day how the king was grieved for his son.'"

Paul closed his eyes, forcing grief out of his mind, letting it wait as he had once waited to mourn his father. Now, he gave his thoughts over to this day's accumulated discoveries—the mixed futures and the hidden *presence* of Alia within his awareness.

Of all the uses of time-vision, this was the strangest. "I have breasted the future to place my words where only you can hear them," Alia had said. "Even you cannot do that, my brother. I find it an interesting play. And . . . oh, yes—I've killed our grandfather, the demented old Baron. He had very little pain."

Silence. His time sense had seen her withdrawal.

"Muad'Dib."

Paul opened his eyes to see Stilgar's black-bearded visage above him, the dark eyes glaring with battle light.

"You've found the body of the old Baron," Paul said.

A hush of the person settled over Stilgar. "How could you know?" he whispered. "We just found the body in that great pile of metal the Emperor built."

Paul ignored the question, seeing Gurney return accompanied by two Fremen who supported a captive Sardaukar.

"Here's one of them, m'Lord," Gurney said. He signed to the guard to hold the captive five paces in front of Paul.

The Sardaukar's eyes, Paul noted, carried a glazed expression of shock. A blue bruise stretched from the bridge of his nose to the corner of his mouth. He was of the blond, chisel-featured caste, the look that seemed synonymous with rank among the Sardaukar, yet there were no insignia on his torn uniform except the gold buttons with the Imperial crest and the tattered braid of his trousers.

"I think this one's an officer, m'Lord," Gurney said.

Paul nodded, said: "I am the Duke Paul Atreides. Do you understand that, man?"

The Sardaukar stared at him unmoving.

"Speak up," Paul said, "or your Emperor may die."

The man blinked, swallowed.

"Who am I?" Paul demanded.

"You are the Duke Paul Atreides," the man husked.

He seemed too submissive to Paul, but then the Sardaukar had never been prepared for such happenings as this day. They'd never known anything but victory which, Paul realized, could be a weakness in itself. He put that thought aside for later consideration in his own training program.

"I have a message for you to carry to the Emperor," Paul said. And he couched his words in the ancient formula: "I, a Duke of a Great House, an Imperial Kinsman, give my word of bond under the Convention. If the Emperor and his people lay down their arms and come to me here I will guard their lives with my own." Paul held up his left hand with the ducal signet for the Sardaukar to see. "I swear it by this."

The man wet his lips with his tongue, glanced at Gurney.

"Yes," Paul said. "Who but an Atreides could command the allegiance of Gurney Halleck."

"I will carry the message," the Sardaukar said.

"Take him to our forward command post and send him in," Paul said.

"Yes, m'Lord." Gurney motioned for the guard to obey, led them out. Paul turned back to Stilgar.

"Chani and your mother have arrived," Stilgar said. "Chani has asked time to be alone with her grief. The Reverend Mother sought a moment in the weirding room; I know not why."

"My mother's sick with longing for a planet she may never see," Paul said. "Where water falls from the sky and plants grow so thickly you cannot walk between them."

"Water from the sky," Stilgar whispered.

In that instant, Paul saw how Stilgar had been transformed from the Fremen naib to a *creature* of the Lisan al-Gaib, a receptacle for awe and obedience. It was a lessening of the man, and Paul felt the ghost-wind of the jihad in it.

I have seen a friend become a worshiper, he thought.

In a rush of loneliness, Paul glanced around the room, noting how proper and on-review his guards had become in his presence. He sensed the subtle, prideful competition among them—each hoping for notice from Muad'Dib.

Muad'Dib from whom all blessings flow, he thought, and it was the bitterest thought of his life. *They sense that I must take the throne,* he thought. *But they cannot know I do it to prevent the jihad.*

Stilgar cleared his throat, said: "Rabban, too, is dead."

Paul nodded.

Guards to the right suddenly snapped aside, standing at attention to open an aisle for Jessica. She wore her black aba and walked with a hint of striding across sand, but Paul noted how this house had restored to her something of what she had once been here—concubine to a ruling duke. Her presence carried some of its old assertiveness.

Jessica stopped in front of Paul, looked down at him. She saw his fatigue and how he hid it, but found no compassion for him. It was as though she had been rendered incapable of *any* emotion for her son.

Jessica had entered the Great Hall wondering why the place refused to fit itself snugly in to her memories. It remained a foreign room, as though she had never walked here, never walked here with her beloved Leto, never confronted a drunken Duncan Idaho here—never, never, never. . . .

There should be a word-tension directly opposite to adab, the demanding memory, she thought. *There should be a word for memories that deny themselves.*

"Where is Alia?" she asked.

"Out doing what any good Fremen child should be doing in such times," Paul said. "She's killing enemy wounded and marking their bodies for the water-recovery teams."

"Paul!"

"You must understand that she does this out of kindness," he said. "Isn't it odd how we misunderstand the hidden unity of kindness and cruelty?"

Jessica glared at her son, shocked by the profound change in him. *Was it his child's death did this?* she wondered. And she said: "The men tell strange stories of you, Paul. They say you've all the powers of the legend—nothing can be hidden from you, that you see where others cannot see."

"A Bene Gesserit should ask about legends?" he asked.

"I've had a hand in whatever you are," she admitted, "but you mustn't expect me to—"

"How would you like to live billions upon billions of lives?" Paul asked. "There's a fabric of legends for you! Think of all those experiences, the wisdom they'd bring. But wisdom tempers love, doesn't it? And it puts a new shape on hate. How can you tell what's ruthless unless you've plumbed the depths of both cruelty and kindness? You should fear me, Mother. I am the Kwisatz Haderach."

Jessica tried to swallow in a dry throat. Presently, she said: "Once you denied to me that you were the Kwisatz Haderach."

Paul shook his head. "I can deny nothing anymore." He looked up into her eyes. "The Emperor and his people come now. They will be announced any moment. Stand beside me. I wish a clear view of them. My future bride will be among them."

"Paul!" Jessica snapped. "Don't make the mistake your father made!"

"She's a princess," Paul said. "She's my key to the throne, and that's all she'll ever be. Mistake? You think because I'm what you made me that I cannot feel the need for revenge?"

"Even on the innocent?" she asked, and she thought: *He must not make the mistakes I made.*

"There are no innocent anymore," Paul said.

"Tell that to Chani," Jessica said, and gestured toward the passage from the rear of the Residency.

Chani entered the Great Hall there, walking between the Fremen guards as though unaware of them. Her hood and stillsuit cap were thrown back, face mask fastened aside. She walked with a fragile uncertainty as she crossed the room to stand beside Jessica.

Paul saw the marks of tears on her cheeks—*She gives water to the dead.* He felt a pang of grief strike through him, but it was as though he could only feel this thing through Chani's presence.

"He is dead, beloved," Chani said. "Our son is dead."

Holding himself under stiff control, Paul got to his feet. He reached out, touched Chani's cheek, feeling the dampness of her tears. "He cannot be replaced," Paul said, "but there will be other sons. It is Usul who promises this." Gently, he moved her aside, gestured to Stilgar.

"Muad'Dib," Stilgar said.

"They come from the ship, the Emperor and his people," Paul said. "I will stand here. Assemble the captives in an open space in the center of the room. They will be kept at a distance of ten meters from me unless I command otherwise."

"As you command, Muad'Dib."

As Stilgar turned to obey, Paul heard the awed muttering of Fremen guards: "You see? He knew! No one told him, but he knew!"

The Emperor's entourage could be heard approaching now, his Sardaukar humming one of their marching tunes to keep up their spirits. There came a murmur of voices at the entrance and Gurney Halleck passed through the guard, crossed to confer with Stilgar, then moved to Paul's side, a strange look in his eyes.

Will I lose Gurney, too? Paul wondered. *The way I lost Stilgar—losing a friend to gain a creature?*

"They have no throwing weapons," Gurney said. "I've made sure of that myself." He glanced around the room, seeing Paul's preparations. "Feyd-Rautha Harkonnen is with them. Shall I cut him out?"

"Leave him."

"There're some Guild people, too, demanding special privileges, threatening an embargo against Arrakis. I told them I'd give you their message."

"Let them threaten."

"Paul!" Jessica hissed behind him. "He's talking about the Guild!"

"I'll pull their fangs presently," Paul said.

And he thought then about the Guild—the force that had specialized for so long that it had become a parasite, unable to exist independently of the life upon which it fed. They had never dared grasp the sword . . . and now they could not grasp it. They might have taken Arrakis when they realized the error of specializing on the melange awareness-spectrum narcotic for their navigators. They *could* have done this, lived their glorious day and died. Instead, they'd existed from mo-

ment to moment, hoping the seas in which they swam might produce a
new host when the old one died.

The Guild navigators, gifted with limited prescience, had made the
fatal decision: they'd chosen always the clear, safe course that leads ever
downward into stagnation.

Let them look closely at their new host, Paul thought.

"There's also a Bene Gesserit Reverend Mother who says she's a
friend of your mother," Gurney said.

"My mother has no Bene Gesserit friends."

Again, Gurney glanced around the Great Hall, then bent close to
Paul's ear. "Thufir Hawat's with 'em, m'Lord. I had no chance to see him
alone, but he used our old hand signs to say he's been working with the
Harkonnens, thought you were dead. Says he's to be left among 'em."

"You left Thufir among those—"

"He wanted it . . . and I thought it best. If . . . there's something
wrong, he's where we can control him. If not—we've an ear on the other
side."

Paul thought then of prescient glimpses into the possibilities of this
moment—and one time-line where Thufir carried a poisoned needle
which the Emperor commanded he use against "this upstart Duke."

The entrance guards stepped aside, formed a short corridor of
lances. There came a murmurous swish of garments, feet rasping the
sand that had drifted into the Residency.

The Padishah Emperor Shaddam IV led his people into the hall. His
Burseg helmet had been lost and the red hair stood out in disarray. His
uniform's left sleeve had been ripped along the inner seam. He was belt-
less and without weapons, but his presence moved with him like a
force-shield bubble that kept his immediate area open.

A Fremen lance dropped across his path, stopped him where Paul
had ordered. The others bunched up behind, a montage of color, of
shuffling and of staring faces.

Paul swept his gaze across the group, saw women who hid signs of
weeping, saw the lackeys who had come to enjoy grandstand seats at a

Sardaukar victory and now stood choked to silence by defeat. Paul saw the bird-bright eyes of the Reverend Mother Gaius Helen Mohiam glaring beneath her black hood, and beside her the narrow furtiveness of Feyd-Rautha Harkonnen.

There's a face time betrayed to me, Paul thought.

He looked beyond Feyd-Rautha then, attracted by a movement, seeing there a narrow, weaselish face he'd never before encountered—not in time or out of it. It was a face he felt he should know and the feeling carried with it a marker of fear.

Why should I fear that man? he wondered.

He leaned toward his mother, whispered: "That man to the left of the Reverend Mother, the evil-looking one—who is that?"

Jessica looked, recognizing the face from her Duke's dossiers. "Count Fenring," she said. "The one who was here immediately before us. A genetic-eunuch . . . and a killer."

The Emperor's errand boy, Paul thought. And the thought was a shock crashing across his consciousness because he had seen the Emperor in uncounted associations spread through the possible futures—but never once had Count Fenring appeared within those prescient visions.

It occurred to Paul then that he had seen his own dead body along countless reaches of the time web, but never once had he seen his moment of death.

Have I been denied a glimpse of this man because he is the one who kills me? Paul wondered.

The thought sent a pang of foreboding through him. He forced his attention away from Fenring, looked now at the remnants of Sardaukar men and officers, the bitterness on their faces and the desperation. Here and there among them, faces caught Paul's attention briefly: Sardaukar officers measuring the preparations within this room, planning and scheming yet for a way to turn defeat into victory.

Paul's attention came at last to a tall blonde woman, green-eyed, a face of patrician beauty, classic in its hauteur, untouched by tears, completely undefeated. Without being told it, Paul knew her—Princess Royal, Bene Gesserit-trained, a face that time vision had shown him in many aspects: Irulan.

There's my key, he thought.

Then he saw movement in the clustered people, a face and figure emerged—Thufir Hawat, the seamed old features with darkly stained lips, the hunched shoulders, the look of fragile age about him.

"There's Thufir Hawat," Paul said. "Let him stand free, Gurney."

"M'Lord," Gurney said.

"Let him stand free," Paul repeated.

Gurney nodded.

Hawat shambled forward as a Fremen lance was lifted and replaced behind him. The rheumy eyes peered at Paul, measuring, seeking.

Paul stepped forward one pace, sensed the tense, waiting movement of the Emperor and his people.

Hawat's gaze stabbed past Paul, and the old man said: "Lady Jessica, I but learned this day how I've wronged you in my thoughts. You needn't forgive."

Paul waited, but his mother remained silent.

"Thufir, old friend," Paul said, "as you can see, my back is toward no door."

"The universe is full of doors," Hawat said.

"Am I my father's son?" Paul asked.

"More like your grandfather's," Hawat rasped. "You've his manner and the look of him in your eyes."

"Yet I'm my father's son," Paul said. "For I say to you, Thufir, that in payment for your years of service to my family you may now ask anything you wish of me. Anything at all. Do you need my life now, Thufir? It is yours." Paul stepped forward a pace, hands at his side, seeing the look of awareness grow in Hawat's eyes.

He realizes that I know of the treachery, Paul thought.

Pitching his voice to carry in a half-whisper for Hawat's ears alone, Paul said: "I mean this, Thufir. If you're to strike me, do it now."

"I but wanted to stand before you once more, my Duke," Hawat said. And Paul became aware for the first time of the effort the old man exerted to keep from falling. Paul reached out, supported Hawat by the shoulders, feeling the muscle tremors beneath his hands.

"Is there pain, old friend?" Paul asked.

"There is pain, my Duke," Hawat agreed, "but the pleasure is greater." He half turned in Paul's arms, extended his left hand, palm up, toward the Emperor, exposing the tiny needle cupped against the fingers. "See, Majesty?" he called. "See your traitor's needle? Did you think that I who've given my life to service of the Atreides would give them less now?"

Paul staggered as the old man sagged in his arms, felt the death there, the utter flaccidity. Gently, Paul lowered Hawat to the floor, straightened and signed for guardsmen to carry the body away.

Silence held the hall while his command was obeyed.

A look of deadly waiting held the Emperor's face now. Eyes that had never admitted fear admitted it at last.

"Majesty," Paul said, and noted the jerk of surprised attention in the tall Princess Royal. The words had been uttered with the Bene Gesserit controlled atonals, carrying in it every shade of contempt and scorn that Paul could put there.

Bene Gesserit-trained indeed, Paul thought.

The Emperor cleared his throat, said: "Perhaps my respected kinsman believes he has things all his own way now. Nothing could be more remote from fact. You have violated the Convention, used atomics against—"

"I used atomics against a natural feature of the desert," Paul said. "It was in my way and I was in a hurry to get to you, Majesty, to ask your explanation for some of your strange activities."

"There's a massed armada of the Great Houses in space over Arrakis right now," the Emperor said. "I've but to say the word and they'll—"

"Oh, yes," Paul said, "I almost forgot about them." He searched through the Emperor's suite until he saw the faces of the two Guildsmen, spoke aside to Gurney. "Are those the Guild agents, Gurney, the two fat ones dressed in gray over there?"

"Yes, m'Lord."

"You two," Paul said, pointing. "Get out of there immediately and dispatch messages that will get that fleet on its way home. After this, you'll ask my permission before—"

"The Guild doesn't take your orders!" the taller of the two barked. He and his companion pushed through to the barrier lances, which were raised at a nod from Paul. The two men stepped out and the taller leveled an arm at Paul, said: "You may very well be under embargo for your—"

"If I hear any more nonsense from either of you," Paul said, "I'll give the order that'll destroy all spice production on Arrakis . . . forever."

"Are you mad?" the tall Guildsman demanded. He fell back half a step.

"You grant that I have the power to do this thing, then?" Paul asked.

The Guildsman seemed to stare into space for a moment, then: "Yes, you could do it, but you must not."

"Ah-h-h," Paul said and nodded to himself. "Guild navigators, both of you, eh?"

"Yes!"

The shorter of the pair said: "You would blind yourself, too, and condemn us all to slow death. Have you any idea what it means to be deprived of the spice liquor once you're addicted?"

"The eye that looks ahead to the safe course is closed forever," Paul said. "The Guild is crippled. Humans become little isolated clusters on their isolated planets. You know, I might do this thing out of pure spite . . . or out of ennui."

"Let us talk this over privately," the taller Guildsman said. "I'm sure we can come to some compromise that is—"

"Send the message to your people over Arrakis," Paul said. "I grow tired of this argument. If that fleet over us doesn't leave soon there'll be no need for us to talk." He nodded toward his communications men at the side of the hall. "You may use our equipment."

"First we must discuss this," the tall Guildsman said. "We cannot just—"

"Do it!" Paul barked. "The power to destroy a thing is the absolute control over it. You've agreed I have that power. We are not here to discuss or to negotiate or to compromise. You will obey my orders or suffer the *immediate* consequences!"

"He means it," the shorter Guildsman said. And Paul saw the fear grip them.

Slowly the two crossed to the Fremen communications equipment.

"Will they obey?" Gurney asked.

"They have a narrow vision of time," Paul said. "They can see ahead to a blank wall marking the consequences of disobedience. Every Guild navigator on every ship over us can look ahead to that same wall. They'll obey."

Paul turned back to look at the Emperor, said: "When they permitted you to mount your father's throne, it was only on the assurance that you'd keep the spice flowing. You've failed them, Majesty. Do you know the consequences?"

"Nobody *permitted* me to—"

"Stop playing the fool," Paul barked. "The Guild is like a village beside a river. They need the water, but can only dip out what they require. They cannot dam the river and control it, because that focuses attention on what they take, it brings down eventual destruction. The spice flow, that's their river, and I have built a dam. But my dam is such that you cannot destroy it without destroying the river."

The Emperor brushed a hand through his red hair, glanced at the backs of the two Guildsmen.

"Even your Bene Gesserit Truthsayer is trembling," Paul said. "There are other poisons the Reverend Mothers can use for their tricks, but once they've used the spice liquor, the others no longer work."

The old woman pulled her shapeless black robes around her, pressed forward out of the crowd to stand at the barrier lances.

"Reverend Mother Gaius Helen Mohiam," Paul said. "It has been a long time since Caladan, hasn't it?"

She looked past him at his mother, said: "Well, Jessica, I see that your son is indeed the one. For that you can be forgiven even the abomination of your daughter."

Paul stilled a cold, piercing anger, said: "You've never had the right or cause to forgive my mother anything!"

The old woman locked eyes with him.

"Try your tricks on me, old witch," Paul said. "Where's your gom jabbar? Try looking into that place where you dare not look! You'll find me there staring out at you!"

The old woman dropped her gaze.

"Have you nothing to say?" Paul demanded.

"I welcomed you to the ranks of humans," she muttered. "Don't besmirch that."

Paul raised his voice: "Observe her, comrades! This is a Bene Gesserit Reverend Mother, patient in a patient cause. She could wait with her sisters—ninety generations for the proper combination of genes and environment to produce the one person their schemes required. Observe her! She knows now that the ninety generations have produced that person. Here I stand ... But ... I ... will ... never ... do ... her ... bidding!"

"Jessica!" the old woman screamed. "Silence him!"

"Silence him yourself," Jessica said.

Paul glared at the old woman. "For your part in all this I could gladly have you strangled," he said. "You couldn't prevent it!" he snapped as she stiffened in rage. "But I think it better punishment that you live out your years never able to touch me or bend me to a single thing your scheming desires."

"Jessica, what have you done?" the old woman demanded.

"I'll give you only one thing," Paul said. "You saw part of what the race needs, but how poorly you saw it. You think to control human breeding and intermix a select few according to your master plan! How little you understand of what—"

"You mustn't speak of these things!" the old woman hissed.

"Silence!" Paul roared. The word seemed to take substance as it twisted through the air between them under Paul's control.

The old woman reeled back into the arms of those behind her, face blank with shock at the power with which he had seized her psyche. "Jessica," she whispered. "Jessica."

"I remember your gom jabbar," Paul said. "You remember mine. I can kill you with a word."

The Fremen around the hall glanced knowingly at each other. Did the legend not say: *"And his word shall carry death eternal to those who stand against righteousness."*

Paul turned his attention to the tall Princess Royal standing beside her Emperor father. Keeping his eyes focused on her, he said: "Majesty, we both know the way out of our difficulty."

The Emperor glanced at his daughter, back to Paul. "You dare? You! An adventurer without family, a nobody from—"

"You've already admitted who I am," Paul said. "Royal kinsman, you said. Let's stop this nonsense."

"I am your ruler," the Emperor said.

Paul glanced at the Guildsmen standing now at the communications equipment and facing him. One of them nodded.

"I could force it," Paul said.

"You will not dare!" the Emperor grated.

Paul merely stared at him.

The Princess Royal put a hand on her father's arm. "Father," she said, and her voice was silky soft, soothing.

"Don't try your tricks on me," the Emperor said. He looked at her. "You don't need to do this, Daughter. We've other resources that—"

"But here's a man fit to be your son," she said.

The old Reverend Mother, her composure regained, forced her way to the Emperor's side, leaned close to his ear and whispered.

"She pleads your case," Jessica said.

Paul continued to look at the golden-haired Princess. Aside to his mother, he said: "That's Irulan, the oldest, isn't it?"

"Yes."

Chani moved up on Paul's other side, said: "Do you wish me to leave, Muad'Dib?"

He glanced at her. "Leave? You'll never again leave my side."

"There's nothing binding between us," Chani said.

Paul looked down at her for a silent moment, then: "Speak only truth with me, my Sihaya." As she started to reply, he silenced her with a finger to her lips. "That which binds us cannot be loosed," he said. "Now, watch these matters closely for I wish to see this room later through your wisdom."

The Emperor and his Truthsayer were carrying on a heated, low-voiced argument.

Paul spoke to his mother: "She reminds him that it's part of their agreement to place a Bene Gesserit on the throne, and Irulan is the one they've groomed for it."

"Was that their plan?" Jessica said.

"Isn't it obvious?" Paul asked.

"I see the signs!" Jessica snapped. "My question was meant to remind you that you should not try to teach me those matters in which I instructed you."

Paul glanced at her, caught a cold smile on her lips.

Gurney Halleck leaned between them, said: "I remind you, m'Lord, that there's a Harkonnen in that bunch." He nodded toward the dark-haired Feyd-Rautha pressed against a barrier lance on the left. "The one with the squinting eyes there on the left. As evil a face as I ever say. You promised me once that—"

"Thank you, Gurney," Paul said.

"It's the na-Baron . . . Baron now that the old man's dead," Gurney said. "He'll do for what I've in—"

"Can you take him, Gurney?"

"M'Lord jests!"

"That argument between the Emperor and his witch has gone on long enough, don't you think, Mother?"

She nodded. "Indeed."

Paul raised his voice, called out to the Emperor: "Majesty, is there a Harkonnen among you?"

Royal disdain revealed itself in the way the Emperor turned to look at Paul. "I believe my entourage has been placed under the protection of your ducal word," he said.

"My question was for information only," Paul said. "I wish to know if a Harkonnen is officially a part of your entourage or if a Harkonnen is merely hiding behind a technicality out of cowardice."

The Emperor's smile was calculating. "Anyone accepted into the Imperial company is a member of my entourage."

"You have the word of a Duke," Paul said, "but Muad'Dib is another matter. *He* may not recognize your definition of what constitutes an entourage. My friend Gurney Halleck wishes to kill a Harkonnen. If he—"

"Kanly!" Feyd-Rautha shouted. He pressed against the barrier lance. "Your father named this vendetta, Atreides. You call me coward while you hide among your women and offer to send a lackey against me!"

The old Truthsayer whispered something fiercely into the Emperor's ear, but he pushed her aside, said: "Kanly, is it? There are strict rules for kanly."

"Paul, put a stop to this," Jessica said.

"M'Lord," Gurney said, "you promised me my day against the Harkonnens."

"You've had your day against them," Paul said and he felt a harlequin abandon take over his emotions. He slipped his robe and hood from his shoulders, handed them to his mother with his belt and crysknife, began unstrapping his stillsuit. He sensed now that the universe focused on this moment.

"There's no need for this," Jessica said. "There are easier ways, Paul."

Paul stepped out of his stillsuit, slipped the crysknife from its sheath in his mother's hand. "I know," he said. "Poison, an assassin, all the old familiar ways."

"You promised me a Harkonnen!" Gurney hissed, and Paul marked the rage in the man's face, the way the inkvine scar stood out dark and ridged. "You owe it to me, m'Lord!"

"Have you suffered more from them than I?" Paul asked.

"My sister," Gurney rasped. "My years in the slave pits—"

"My father," Paul said. "My good friends and companions, Thufir Hawat and Duncan Idaho, my years as a fugitive without rank or succor . . . and one more thing: it is now kanly and you know as well as I the rules that must prevail."

Halleck's shoulders sagged. "M'Lord, if that swine . . . he's no more than a beast you'd spurn with your foot and discard the shoe because it'd been contaminated. Call in an executioner, if you must, or let me do it, but don't offer yourself to—"

"Muad'Dib need not do this thing," Chani said.

He glanced at her, saw the fear for him in her eyes. "But the Duke Paul must," he said.

"This is a Harkonnen animal!" Gurney rasped.

Paul hesitated on the point of revealing his own Harkonnen ancestry, stopped at a sharp look from his mother, said merely: "But this being has human shape, Gurney, and deserves human doubt."

Gurney said: "If he so much as—"

"Please stand aside," Paul said. He hefted the crysknife, pushed Gurney gently aside.

"Gurney!" Jessica said. She touched Gurney's arm. "He's like his grandfather in this mood. Don't distract him. It's the only thing you can do for him now." And she thought: *Great Mother! What irony.*

The Emperor was studying Feyd-Rautha, seeing the heavy shoulders, the thick muscles. He turned to look at Paul—a stringy whipcord of a youth, not as desiccated as the Arrakeen natives, but with ribs there to count, and sunken in the flanks so that the ripple and gather of muscles could be followed under the skin.

Jessica leaned close to Paul, pitched her voice for his ears alone: "One thing, Son. Sometimes a dangerous person is prepared by the Bene Gesserit, a word implanted into the deepest recesses by the old pleasure-pain methods. The word-sound most frequently used is Urosh-nor. If this one's been prepared, as I strongly suspect, that word uttered in his ear will render his muscles flaccid and—"

"I want no special advantage for this one," Paul said. "Step back out of my way."

Gurney spoke to her: "Why is he doing this? Does he think to get himself killed and achieve martyrdom? This Fremen religious prattle, is that what clouds his reason?"

Jessica hid her face in her hands, realizing that she did not know fully why Paul took this course. She could feel death in the room and knew that the changed Paul was capable of such a thing as Gurney suggested. Every talent within her focused on the need to protect her son, but there was nothing she could do.

"Is it this religious prattle?" Gurney insisted.

"Be silent," Jessica whispered. "And pray."

The Emperor's face was touched by an abrupt smile. "If Feyd-Rautha Harkonnen . . . of my entourage . . . so wishes," he said, "I relieve him of all restraint and give him freedom to choose his own course in this." The Emperor waved a hand toward Paul's Fedaykin guards. "One of your rabble has my belt and short blade. If Feyd-Rautha wishes it, he may meet you with my blade in his hand."

"I wish it," Feyd-Rautha said, and Paul saw the elation on the man's face.

He's overconfident, Paul thought. *There's a natural advantage I can accept.*

"Get the Emperor's blade," Paul said, and watched as his command was obeyed. "Put it on the floor there." He indicated a place with his foot. "Clear the Imperial rabble back against the wall and let the Har-konnen stand clear."

A flurry of robes, scraping of feet, low-voiced commands and protests accompanied obedience to Paul's command. The Guildsmen remained standing near the communications equipment. They frowned at Paul in obvious indecision.

They're accustomed to seeing the future, Paul thought. *In this place and time they're blind . . . even as I am.* And he sampled the time-winds, sensing the turmoil, the storm nexus that now focused on this moment place. Even the faint gaps were closed now. Here was the unborn jihad, he knew. Here was the race consciousness that he had known once as his own terrible purpose. Here was reason enough for a Kwisatz Haderach or a Lisan al-Gaib or even the halting schemes of the Bene Gesserit. The race of humans had felt its own dormancy, sensed itself grown stale and knew now only the need to experience turmoil in which the genes would mingle and the strong new mixtures survive. All humans were alive as an unconscious single organism in this moment, experiencing a kind of sexual heat that could override any barrier.

And Paul saw how futile were any efforts of his to change any smallest bit of this. He had thought to oppose the jihad within himself, but the jihad would be. His legions would rage out from Arrakis even without him. They needed only the legend he already had become. He had shown them the way, given them mastery even over the Guild which must have the spice to exist.

A sense of failure pervaded him, and he saw through it that Feyd-Rautha Harkonnen had slipped out of the torn uniform, stripped down to a fighting girdle with a mail core.

This is the climax, Paul thought. *From here, the future will open, the clouds part onto a kind of glory. And if I die here, they'll say I sacrificed myself that my spirit might lead them. And if I live, they'll say nothing can oppose Muad'Dib.*

"Is the Atreides ready?" Feyd-Rautha called, using the words of the ancient kanly ritual.

Paul chose to answer him in the Fremen way: "May thy knife chip and shatter!" He pointed to the Emperor's blade on the floor, indicating that Feyd-Rautha should advance and take it.

Keeping his attention on Paul, Feyd-Rautha picked up the knife, balancing it a moment in his hand to get the feel of it. Excitement kindled in him. This was a fight he had dreamed about—man against man, skill against skill with no shields intervening. He could see a way to power opening before him because the Emperor surely would reward whoever killed this troublesome Duke. The reward might even be that haughty daughter and a share of the throne. And this yokel Duke, this back-world adventurer could not possibly be a match for a Harkonnen trained in every device and every treachery by a thousand arena combats. And the yokel had no way of knowing he faced more weapons than a knife here.

Let us see if you're proof against poison! Feyd-Rautha thought. He saluted Paul with the Emperor's blade, said: "Meet your death, fool."

"Shall we fight, cousin?" Paul asked. And he cat-footed forward, eyes on the waiting blade, his body crouched low with his own milk-white crysknife pointing out as though an extension of his arm.

They circled each other, bare feet grating on the floor, watching with eyes intent for the slightest opening.

"How beautifully you dance," Feyd-Rautha said.

He's a talker, Paul thought. *There's another weakness. He grows uneasy in the face of silence.*

"Have you been shriven?" Feyd-Rautha asked.

Still, Paul circled in silence.

And the old Reverend Mother, watching the fight from the press of the Emperor's suite, felt herself trembling. The Atreides youth had called the Harkonnen cousin. It could only mean he knew the ancestry they shared, easy to understand because he was the Kwisatz Haderach. But the words forced her to focus on the only thing that mattered to her here.

This could be a major catastrophe for the Bene Gesserit breeding scheme.

She had seen something of what Paul had seen here, that Feyd-Rautha might kill but not be victorious. Another thought, though, almost overwhelmed her. Two end products of this long and costly program faced each other in a fight to the death that might easily claim both of them. If both died here that would leave only Feyd-Rautha's bastard daughter, still a baby, an unknown, an unmeasured factor, and Alia, the abomination.

"Perhaps you have only pagan rites here," Feyd-Rautha said. "Would you like the Emperor's Truthsayer to prepare your spirit for its journey?"

Paul smiled, circling to the right, alert, his black thoughts suppressed by the needs of the moment.

Feyd-Rautha leaped, feinting with right hand, but with the knife shifted in a blur to his left hand.

Paul dodged easily, noting the shield-conditioned hesitation in Feyd-Rautha's thrust. Still, it was not as great a shield conditioning as some Paul had seen, and he sensed that Feyd-Rautha had fought before against unshielded foes.

"Does an Atreides run or stand and fight?" Feyd-Rautha asked.

Paul resumed his silent circling. Idaho's words came back to him, the words of training from the long-ago practice floor on Caladan: *"Use the first moments in study. You may miss many an opportunity for quick victory this way, but the moments of study are insurance of success. Take your time and be sure."*

"Perhaps you think this dance prolongs your life a few moments," Feyd-Rautha said. "Well and good." He stopped the circling, straightened.

Paul had seen enough for a first approximation. Feyd-Rautha led to the left side, presenting the right hip as though the mailed fighting girdle could protect his entire side. It was the action of a man trained to the shield and with a knife in both hands.

Or . . . And Paul hesitated. . . . the girdle was more than it *seemed*.

The Harkonnen appeared too confident against a man who'd this day led the forces of victory against Sardaukar legions.

Feyd-Rautha noted the hesitation, said: "Why prolong the inevitable? You but keep me from exercising my rights over this ball of dirt."

If it's a flip-dart, Paul thought, *it's a cunning one. The girdle shows no signs of tampering.*

"Why don't you speak?" Feyd-Rautha demanded.

Paul resumed his probing circle, allowing himself a cold smile at the tone of unease in Feyd-Rautha's voice, evidence that the pressure of silence was building.

"You smile, eh?" Feyd-Rautha asked. And he leaped in midsentence.

Expecting the slight hesitation, Paul almost failed to evade the downflash of blade, felt its tip scratch his left arm. He silenced the sudden pain there, his mind flooded with realization that the earlier hesitation had been a trick—an overfeint. Here was more of an opponent than he had expected. There would be tricks within tricks within tricks.

"Your own Thufir Hawat taught me some of my skills," Feyd-Rautha said. "He gave me first blood. Too bad the old fool didn't live to see it."

And Paul recalled that Idaho had once said, *Expect only what happens in the fight. That way you'll never be surprised.*

Again the two circled each other, crouched, cautious.

Paul saw the return of elation to his opponent, wondered at it. Did a scratch signify that much to the man? Unless there were poison on the blade! But how could there be? His own men had handled the weapon, snooped it before passing it. They were too well trained to miss an obvious thing like that.

"That woman you were talking to over there," Feyd-Rautha said. "The little one. Is she something special to you? A pet perhaps? Will she deserve my special attentions?"

Paul remained silent, probing with his inner senses, examining the blood from the wound, finding a trace of soporific from the Emperor's blade. He realigned his own metabolism to match this threat and change the molecules of the soporific, but he felt a thrill of doubt. They'd been prepared with soporific on a blade. A soporific. Nothing to alert a poison snooper, but strong enough to slow the muscles it touched. His enemies had their own plans within plans, their own stacked treacheries.

Again Feyd-Rautha leaped, stabbing.

Paul, the smile frozen on his face, feinted with slowness as though inhibited by the drug and at the last instant dodged to meet the down-flashing arm on the crysknife's point.

Feyd-Rautha ducked sideways and was out and away, his blade shifted to his left hand, and the measure of him that only a slight paleness of jaw betrayed the acid pain where Paul had cut him.

Let him know his own moment of doubt, Paul thought. *Let him suspect poison.*

"Treachery!" Feyd-Rautha shouted. "He's poisoned me! I do feel poison in my arm!"

Paul dropped his cloak of silence, said: "Only a little acid to counter the soporific on the Emperor's blade."

Feyd-Rautha matched Paul's cold smile, lifted blade in left hand for a mock salute. His eyes glared rage behind the knife.

Paul shifted his crysknife to his left hand, matching his opponent. Again, they circled, probing.

Feyd-Rautha began closing the space between them, edging in, knife held high, anger showing itself in squint of eye and set of jaw. He feinted right and under, and they were pressed against each other, knife hands gripped, straining.

Paul, cautious of Feyd-Rautha's right hip where he suspected a poison flip-dart, forced the turn to the right. He almost failed to see the needle point flick out beneath the belt line. A shift and a giving in Feyd-Rautha's motion warned him. The tiny point missed Paul's flesh by the barest fraction.

On the left hip!

Treachery within treachery within treachery, Paul reminded himself. Using Bene Gesserit-trained muscles, he sagged to catch a reflex in Feyd-Rautha, but the necessity of avoiding the tiny point jutting from his opponent's hip threw Paul off just enough that he missed his footing and found himself thrown hard to the floor, Feyd-Rautha on top.

"You see it there on my hip?" Feyd-Rautha whispered. "Your death, fool." And he began twisting himself around, forcing the poisoned needle closer and closer. "It'll stop your muscles and my knife will finish you. There'll be never a trace left to detect!"

Paul strained, hearing the silent screams in his mind, his cell-stamped ancestors demanding that he use the secret word to slow Feyd-Rautha, to save himself.

"I will not say it!" Paul gasped.

Feyd-Rautha gaped at him, caught in the merest fraction of hesitation. It was enough for Paul to find the weakness of balance in one of his opponent's leg muscles, and their positions were reversed. Feyd-Rautha lay partly underneath with right hip high, unable to turn because of the tiny needle point caught against the floor beneath him.

Paul twisted his left hand free, aided by the lubrication of blood from his arm, thrust once hard up underneath Feyd-Rautha's jaw. The point slid home into the brain. Feyd-Rautha jerked and sagged back, still held partly on his side by the needle imbedded in the floor.

Breathing deeply to restore his calm, Paul pushed himself away and got to his feet. He stood over the body, knife in hand, raised his eyes with deliberate slowness to look across the room at the Emperor.

"Majesty," Paul said, "your force is reduced by one more. Shall we now shed sham and pretense? Shall we now discuss what must be? Your daughter wed to me and the way opened for an Atreides to sit on the throne."

The Emperor turned, looked at Count Fenring. The Count met his stare—gray eyes against green. The thought lay there clearly between them, their association so long that understanding could be achieved with a glance.

Kill this upstart for me, the Emperor was saying. *The Atreides is young and resourceful, yes—but he is also tired from long effort and he'd be no match for you, anyway. Call him out now . . . you know the way of it. Kill him.*

Slowly, Fenring moved his head, a prolonged turning until he faced Paul.

"Do it!" the Emperor hissed.

The Count focused on Paul, seeing with eyes his Lady Margot had trained in the Bene Gesserit way, aware of the mystery and hidden grandeur about this Atreides youth.

I could kill him, Fenring thought—and he knew this for a truth.

Something in his own secretive depths stayed the Count then, and he glimpsed briefly, inadequately, the advantage he held over Paul—a way of hiding from the youth, a furtiveness of person and motives that no eye could penetrate.

Paul, aware of some of this from the way the time nexus boiled, understood at last why he had never seen Fenring along the webs of prescience. Fenring was one of the might-have-beens, an almost-Kwisatz Haderach, crippled by a flaw in the genetic pattern—a eunuch, his talent concentrated into furtiveness and inner seclusion. A deep compassion for the Count flowed through Paul, the first sense of brotherhood he'd ever experienced.

Fenring, reading Paul's emotion, said, "Majesty, I must refuse."

Rage overcame Shaddam IV. He took two short steps through the entourage, cuffed Fenring viciously across the jaw.

A dark flush spread up and over the Count's face. He looked directly at the Emperor, spoke with deliberate lack of emphasis: "We have been friends, Majesty. What I do now is out of friendship. I shall forget that you struck me."

Paul cleared his throat, said: "We were speaking of the throne, Majesty."

The Emperor whirled, glared at Paul. "I sit on the throne!" he barked.

"You shall have a throne on Salusa Secundus," Paul said.

"I put down my arms and came here on your word of bond!" the Emperor shouted. "You dare threaten—"

"Your person is safe in my presence," Paul said. "An Atreides promised it. Muad'Dib, however, sentences you to your prison planet. But have no fear, Majesty. I will ease the harshness of the place with all the powers at my disposal. It shall become a garden world, full of gentle things."

As the hidden import of Paul's words grew in the Emperor's mind, he glared across the room at Paul. "Now we see true motives," he sneered.

"Indeed," Paul said.

"And what of Arrakis?" the Emperor asked. "Another garden world full of gentle things?"

"The Fremen have the word of Muad'Dib," Paul said. "There will be flowing water here open to the sky and green oases rich with good things. But we have the spice to think of, too. Thus, there will always be desert on Arrakis . . . and fierce winds, and trials to toughen a man. We Fremen have a saying: 'God created Arrakis to train the faithful.' One cannot go against the word of God."

The old Truthsayer, the Reverend Mother Gaius Helen Mohiam, had her own view of the hidden meaning in Paul's words now. She glimpsed the jihad and said: "You cannot loose these people upon the universe!"

"You will think back to the gentle ways of the Sardaukar!" Paul snapped.

"You cannot," she whispered.

"You're a Truthsayer," Paul said. "Review your words." He glanced at the Princess Royal, back to the Emperor. "Best be done quickly, Majesty."

The Emperor turned a stricken look upon his daughter. She touched his arm, spoke soothingly: "For this I was trained, Father."

He took a deep breath.

"You cannot stay this thing," the old Truthsayer muttered.

The Emperor straightened, standing stiffly with a look of remembered dignity. "Who will negotiate for you, kinsman?" he asked.

Paul turned, saw his mother, her eyes heavy-lidded, standing with Chani in a squad of Fedaykin guards. He crossed to them, stood looking down at Chani.

"I know the reasons," Chani whispered. "If it must be . . . Usul."

Paul, hearing the secret tears in her voice, touched her cheek. "My Sihaya need fear nothing, ever," he whispered. He dropped his arm, faced his mother. "You will negotiate for me, Mother, with Chani by your side. She has wisdom and sharp eyes. And it is wisely said that no one bargains tougher than a Fremen. She will be looking through the eyes of her love for me and with the thought of her sons to be, what they will need. Listen to her."

Jessica sensed the harsh calculation in her son, put down a shudder. "What are your instructions?" she asked.

"The Emperor's entire CHOAM Company holdings as dowry," he said.

"Entire?" She was shocked almost speechless.

"He is to be stripped. I'll want an earldom and CHOAM directorship for Gurney Halleck, and him in the fief of Caladan. There will be titles and attendant power for every surviving Atreides man, not excepting the lowliest trooper."

"What of the Fremen?" Jessica asked.

"The Fremen are mine," Paul said. "What they receive shall be dispensed by Muad'Dib. It'll begin with Stilgar as Governor on Arrakis, but that can wait."

"And for me?" Jessica asked.

"Is there something you wish?"

"Perhaps Caladan," she said, looking at Gurney. "I'm not certain. I've become too much the Fremen . . . and the Reverend Mother. I need a time of peace and stillness in which to think."

"*That* you shall have," Paul said, "and anything else that Gurney or I can give you."

Jessica nodded, feeling suddenly old and tired. She looked at Chani. "And for the royal concubine?"

"No title for me," Chani whispered. "Nothing. I beg of you."

Paul stared down into her eyes, remembering her suddenly as she had stood once with little Leto in her arms, their child now dead in this violence. "I swear to you now," he whispered, "that you'll need no title. That woman over there will be my wife and you but a concubine because this is a political thing and we must weld peace out of this moment, enlist the Great Houses of the Landsraad. We must obey the forms. Yet that princess shall have no more of me than my name. No child of mine nor touch nor softness of glance, nor instant of desire."

"So you say now," Chani said. She glanced across the room at the tall princess.

"Do you know so little of my son?" Jessica whispered. "See that princess standing there, so haughty and confident. They say she has pretensions of a literary nature. Let us hope she finds solace in such things; she'll have little else." A bitter laugh escaped Jessica. "Think on it, Chani: that princess will have the name, yet she'll live as less than a concubine—never to know a moment of tenderness from the man to whom she's bound. While we, Chani, we who carry the name of concubine—history will call us wives."

APPENDIXES

APPENDIX I

THE ECOLOGY OF DUNE

Beyond a critical point within a finite space, freedom diminishes as numbers increase. This is as true of humans in the finite space of a planetary ecosystem as it is of gas molecules in a sealed flask. The human question is not how many can possibly survive within the system, but what kind of existence is possible for those who do survive.

—PARDOT KYNES,
FIRST PLANETOLOGIST OF ARRAKIS

The effect of Arrakis on the mind of the newcomer usually is that of overpowering barren land. The stranger might think nothing could live or grow in the open here, that this was the true wasteland that had never been fertile and never would be.

To Pardot Kynes, the planet was merely an expression of energy, a machine being driven by its sun. What it needed was reshaping to fit it to man's needs. His mind went directly to the free-moving human population, the Fremen. What a challenge! What a tool they could be! Fremen: an ecological and geological force of almost unlimited potential.

A direct and simple man in many ways, Pardot Kynes. One must evade Harkonnen restrictions? Excellent. Then one marries a Fremen woman. When she gives you a Fremen son, you begin with him, with Liet-Kynes, and the other children, teaching them ecological literacy, creating a new language with symbols that arm the mind to manipulate an entire landscape, its climate, seasonal limits, and finally to break through all ideas of force into the dazzling awareness of *order*.

"There's an internally recognized beauty of motion and balance on any man-healthy planet," Kynes said. "You see in this beauty a dynamic stabilizing effect essential to all life. Its aim is simple: to maintain and produce coordinated patterns of greater and greater diversity. Life improves the closed system's capacity to sustain life. Life—all life—is in the service of life. Necessary nutrients are made available to life *by* life in greater and greater richness as the diversity of life increases. The entire landscape comes alive, filled with relationships and relationships within relationships."

This was Pardot Kynes lecturing to a sietch warren class.

Before the lectures, though, he had to convince the Fremen. To understand how this came about, you must first understand the enormous single-mindedness, the innocence with which he approached any problem. He was not naive, he merely permitted himself no distractions.

He was exploring the Arrakis landscape in a one-man ground car one hot afternoon when he stumbled onto a deplorably common scene. Six Harkonnen bravos, shielded and fully armed, had trapped three Fremen youths in the open behind the Shield Wall near the village of Windsack. To Kynes, it was a ding-dong battle, more slapstick than real, until he focused on the fact that the Harkonnens intended to kill the Fremen. By this time, one of the youths was down with a severed artery, two of the bravos were down as well, but it was still four armed men against two striplings.

Kynes wasn't brave; he merely had that single-mindedness and caution. The Harkonnens were killing Fremen. They were destroying the tools with which he intended to remake a planet! He triggered his own shield, waded in and had two of the Harkonnens dead with a slip-tip before they knew anyone was behind them. He dodged a sword thrust from one of the others, slit the man's throat with a neat *entrisseur*, and left the lone remaining bravo to the two Fremen youths, turning his full attention to saving the lad on the ground. And save the lad he did . . . while the sixth Harkonnen was being dispatched.

Now here was a pretty kettle of sandtrout! The Fremen didn't know what to make of Kynes. They knew who he was, of course. No man arrived on Arrakis without a full dossier finding its way into the Fremen strongholds. They knew him: he was an Imperial servant.

But he killed Harkonnens!

Adults might have shrugged and, with some regret, sent his shade to join those of the six dead men on the ground. But these Fremen were inexperienced youths and all they could see was that they owed this Imperial servant a mortal obligation.

Kynes wound up two days later in a sietch that looked down on Wind Pass. To him, it was all very natural. He talked to the Fremen about water, about dunes anchored by grass, about palmaries filled with date palms, about open qanats flowing across the desert. He talked and talked and talked.

All around him raged a debate that Kynes never saw. What to do with this madman? He knew the location of a major sietch. What to do? What of his words, this mad talk about a paradise on Arrakis? Just talk. He knows too much. But he killed Harkonnens! What of the water burden? When did we owe the Imperium anything? He killed Harkonnens. Anyone can kill Harkonnens. I have done it myself.

But what of this talk about the flowering of Arrakis?

Very simple: Where is the water for this?

He says it is here! And he *did* save three of ours.

He saved three fools who had put themselves in the way of the Harkonnen fist! And he has seen crysknives!

The necessary decision was known for hours before it was voiced. The tau of a sietch tells its members what they must do; even the most brutal necessity is known. An experienced fighter was sent with a consecrated knife to do the job. Two watermen followed him to get the water from the body. Brutal necessity.

It's doubtful that Kynes even focused on his would-be executioner. He was talking to a group that spread around him at a cautious distance. He walked as he talked: a short circle, gesturing. Open water, Kynes said. Walk in the open without stillsuits. Water for dipping it out of a pond! Portyguls!

The knifeman confronted him.

"Remove yourself," Kynes said, and went on talking about secret windtraps. He brushed past the man. Kynes' back stood open for the ceremonial blow.

What went on in that would-be executioner's mind cannot be known now. Did he finally listen to Kynes and believe? Who knows? But what he did is a matter of record. Uliet was his name, *Older* Liet. Uliet walked three paces and deliberately fell on his own knife, thus "removing" himself. Suicide? Some say Shai-hulud moved him.

Talk about omens!

From that instant, Kynes had but to point, saying "Go there." Entire Fremen tribes went. Men died, women died, children died. But they went.

Kynes returned to his Imperial chores, directing the Biological Testing Stations. And now, Fremen began to appear among the Station personnel. The Fremen looked at each other. They were infiltrating the "system," a possibility they'd never considered. Station tools began finding their way into the sietch warrens—especially cutterays which were used to dig underground catchbasins and hidden windtraps.

Water began collecting in the basins.

It became apparent to the Fremen that Kynes was not a madman totally, just mad enough to be holy. He was one of the umma, the brotherhood of prophets. The shade of Uliet was advanced to the sadus, the throng of heavenly judges.

Kynes—direct, savagely intent Kynes—knew that highly organized research is guaranteed to produce nothing new. He set up small-unit experiments with regular interchange of data for a swift Tansley effect, let each group find its own path. They must accumulate millions of tiny facts. He organized only isolated and rough run-through tests to put their difficulties into perspective.

Core samplings were made throughout the bled. Charts were developed on the long drifts of weather that are called climate. He found that in the wide belt contained by the 70-degree lines, north and south, temperatures for thousands of years hadn't gone outside the 254–332 degrees (absolute) range, and that this belt had long growing seasons where temperatures ranged from 284 to 302 degrees absolute: the "bonanza" range for terraform life . . . once they solved the water problem.

When will we solve it? the Fremen asked. When will we see Arrakis as a paradise?

In the manner of a teacher answering a child who has asked the sum of 2 plus 2, Kynes told them: "From three hundred to five hundred years."

A lesser folk might have howled in dismay. But the Fremen had learned patience from men with whips. It was a bit longer than they had anticipated, but they all could see that the blessed day was coming. They tightened their sashes and went back to work. Somehow, the disappointment made the prospect of paradise more real.

The concern on Arrakis was not with water, but with moisture. Pets were almost unknown, stock animals rare. Some smugglers employed the domesticated desert ass, the kulon, but the water price was high even when the beasts were fitted with modified stillsuits.

Kynes thought of installing reduction plants to recover water from the hydrogen and oxygen locked in native rock, but the energy-cost factor was far too high. The polar caps (disregarding the false sense of water security they gave the pyons) held far too small an amount for his project . . . and he already suspected where the water had to be. There was that consistent increase of moisture at median altitudes, and in certain winds. There was that primary clue in the air balance—23 per cent oxygen, 75.4 per cent nitrogen and .023 per cent carbon dioxide—with the trace gases taking up the rest.

There was a rare native root plant that grew above the 2,500-meter level in the northern temperate zone. A tuber two meters long yielded half a liter of water. And there were the terraform desert plants: the tougher ones showed signs of thriving if planted in depressions lined with dew precipitators.

Then Kynes saw the salt pan.

His 'thopter, flying between stations far out on the bled, was blown off course by a storm. When the storm passed, there was the pan—a giant oval depression some three hundred kilometers on the long axis—

a glaring white surprise in the open desert. Kynes landed, tasted the pan's storm-cleaned surface.

Salt.

Now, he was certain.

There'd been open water on Arrakis—once. He began reexamining the evidence of the dry wells where trickles of water had appeared and vanished, never to return.

Kynes set his newly trained Fremen limnologist to work: their chief clue, leathery scraps of matter sometimes found with the spice-mass after a blow. This had been ascribed to a fictional "sandtrout" in Fremen folk stories. As facts grew into evidence, a creature emerged to explain these leathery scraps—a sandswimmer that blocked off water into fertile pockets within the porous lower strata below the 280° (absolute) line.

This "water-stealer" died by the millions in each spice-blow. A five-degree change in temperature could kill it. The few survivors entered a semidormant cyst-hibernation to emerge in six years as small (about three meters long) sandworms. Of these, only a few avoided their larger brothers and pre-spice water pockets to emerge into maturity as the giant shai-hulud. (Water is poisonous to shai-hulud as the Fremen had long known from drowning the rare "stunted worm" of the Minor Erg to produce the awareness-spectrum narcotic they call Water of Life. The "stunted worm" is a primitive form of shai-hulud that reaches a length of only about nine meters.)

Now they had the circular relationship: little maker to pre-spice mass; little maker to shai-hulud; shai-hulud to scatter the spice upon which fed microscopic creatures called sand plankton; the sand plankton, food for shai-hulud, growing, burrowing, becoming little makers.

Kynes and his people turned their attention from these great relationships and focused now on micro-ecology. First, the climate: the sand surface often reached temperatures of 344° to 350° (absolute). A foot below ground it might be 55° cooler; a foot above ground, 25° cooler. Leaves or black shade could provide another 18° of cooling. Next, the nutrients: sand of Arrakis is mostly a product of worm digestion; dust (the truly omnipresent problem there) is produced by the constant surface creep, the "saltation" movement of sand. Coarse grains are found on the downwind sides of dunes. The windward side is packed smooth and hard. Old dunes are yellow (oxidized), young dunes are the color of the parent rock—usually gray.

Downwind sides of old dunes provided the first plantation areas. The Fremen aimed first for a cycle of poverty grass with peatlike hair cilia to intertwine, mat and fix the dunes by depriving the wind of its big weapon: movable grains.

Adaptive zones were laid out in the deep south far from Harkonnen watchers. The mutated poverty grasses were planted first along the downwind (slipface) of the chosen dunes that stood across the path of the prevailing westerlies. With the downwind face anchored, the windward face grew higher and higher and the grass was moved to keep pace. Giant sifs (long dunes with sinuous crest) of more than 1,500 meters height were produced this way.

When barrier dunes reached sufficient height, the windward faces were planted with tougher sword grasses. Each structure on a base about six times as thick as its height was anchored—"fixed."

Now, they came in with deeper plantings—ephemerals (chenopods, pigweeds, and amaranth to begin), then scotch broom, low lupine, vine eucalyptus (the type adapted for Caladan's northern reaches), dwarf tamarisk, shore pine—then the true desert growths: candelilla, saguaro, and bis-naga, the barrel cactus. Where it would grow, they introduced camel sage, onion grass, gobi feather grass, wild alfalfa, burrow bush, sand verbena, evening primrose, incense bush, smoke tree, creosote bush.

They turned then to the necessary animal life—burrowing creatures to open the soil and aerate it: kit fox, kangaroo mouse, desert hare, sand terrapin . . . and the predators to keep them in check: desert hawk, dwarf owl, eagle and desert owl; and insects to fill the niches these couldn't reach: scorpion, centipede, trapdoor spider, the biting wasp and the wormfly . . . and the desert bat to keep watch on these.

Now came the crucial test: date palms, cotton, melons, coffee, medicinals—more than 200 selected food plant types to test and adapt.

"The thing the ecologically illiterate don't realize about an ecosystem," Kynes said, "is that it's a system. A system! A system maintains a certain fluid stability that can be destroyed by a misstep in just one niche. A system has order, a flowing from point to point. If something dams that flow, order collapses. The untrained might miss that collapse until it was too late. That's why the highest function of ecology is the understanding of consequences."

Had they achieved a system?

Kynes and his people watched and waited. The Fremen now knew what he meant by an open-end prediction to five hundred years.

A report came up from the palmaries:

At the desert edge of the plantings, the sand plankton is being poisoned through interaction with the new forms of life. The reason: protein incompatibility. Poisonous water was forming there which the Arrakis life would not touch. A barren zone surrounded the plantings and even shai-hulud would not invade it.

Kynes went down to the palmaries himself—a twenty-thumper trip (in a palanquin like a wounded man or Reverend Mother because he never became a sandrider). He tested the barren zone (it stank to heaven) and came up with a bonus, a gift from Arrakis.

The addition of sulfur and fixed nitrogen converted the barren zone to a rich plant bed for terraform life. The plantings could be advanced at will!

"Does this change the timing?" the Fremen asked.

Kynes went back to his planetary formulae. Windtrap figures were fairly secure by then. He was generous with his allowances, knowing he couldn't draw neat lines around ecological problems. A certain amount of plant cover had to be set aside to hold dunes in place; a certain amount for foodstuffs (both human and animal); a certain amount to lock moisture in root systems and to feed water out into surrounding parched areas. They'd mapped the roving cold spots on the open bled by this time. These had to be figured into the formulae. Even shai-hulud had a place in the charts. He must never be destroyed, else spice wealth would end. But his inner digestive "factory," with its enormous concentrations of aldehydes and acids, was a giant source of oxygen. A medium worm (about 200 meters long) discharged into the atmosphere as much oxygen as ten square kilometers of green-growing photosynthesis surface.

He had the Guild to consider. The spice bribe to the Guild for preventing weather satellites and other watchers in the skies of Arrakis already had reached major proportions.

Nor could the Fremen be ignored. Especially the Fremen, with their windtraps and irregular landholdings organized around water supply; the Fremen with their new ecological literacy and their dream of cycling vast areas of Arrakis through a prairie phase into forest cover.

From the charts emerged a figure. Kynes reported it. Three per cent. If they could get three per cent of the green plant element on Arrakis involved in forming carbon compounds, they'd have their self-sustaining cycle.

"But how long?" the Fremen demanded.

"Oh, that: about three hundred and fifty years."

So it was true as this umma had said in the beginning: the thing would not come in the lifetime of any man now living, nor in the lifetime of their grandchildren eight times removed, but it would come.

The work continued: building, planting, digging, training the children.

Then Kynes-the-Umma was killed in the cave-in at Plaster Basin.

By this time his son, Liet-Kynes, was nineteen, a full Fremen and sandrider who had killed more than a hundred Harkonnens. The Imperial appointment for which the elder Kynes already had applied in the name of his son was delivered as a matter of course. The rigid class structure of the faufreluches had its well-ordered purpose here. The son had been trained to follow the father.

The course had been set by this time, the Ecological-Fremen were aimed along their way. Liet-Kynes had only to watch and nudge and spy upon the Harkonnens . . . until the day his planet was afflicted by a Hero.

APPENDIX II

THE RELIGION OF DUNE

Before the coming of Muad'Dib, the Fremen of Arrakis practiced a religion whose roots in the Maometh Saari are there for any scholar to see. Many have traced the extensive borrowings from other religions. The most common example is the Hymn to Water, a direct copy from the Orange Catholic Liturgical Manual, calling for rain clouds which Arrakis had never seen. But there are more profound points of accord between the Kitab al-Ibar of the Fremen and the teachings of Bible, Ilm, and Fiqh.

Any comparison of the religious beliefs dominant in the Imperium up to the time of Muad'Dib must start with the major forces which shaped those beliefs:

1. The followers of the Fourteen Sages, whose Book was the Orange Catholic Bible, and whose views are expressed in the Commentaries and other literature produced by the Commission of Ecumenical Translators. (C.E.T.);

2. The Bene Gesserit, who privately denied they were a religious order, but who operated behind an almost impenetrable screen of ritual mysticism, and whose training, whose symbolism, organization, and internal teaching methods were almost wholly religious;

3. The agnostic ruling class (including the Guild) for whom religion was a kind of puppet show to amuse the populace and keep it docile, and who believed essentially that all phenomena—even religious phenomena—could be reduced to mechanical explanations;

4. The so-called Ancient Teachings—including those preserved by the Zensunni Wanderers from the first, second, and third Islamic movements; the Navachristianity of Chusuk, the Buddislamic Variants

of the types dominant at Lankiveil and Sikun, the Blend Books of the Mahayana Lankavatara, the Zen Hekiganshu of III Delta Pavonis, the Tawrah and Talmudic Zabur surviving on Salusa Secundus, the pervasive Obeah Ritual, the Muadh Quran with its pure Ilm and Fiqh preserved among the pundi rice farmers of Caladan, the Hindu outcroppings found all through the universe in little pockets of insulated pyons, and finally, the Butlerian Jihad.

There *is* a fifth force which shaped religious belief, but its effect is so universal and profound that it deserves to stand alone.

This is, of course, space travel—and in any discussion of religion, it deserves to be written thus:

SPACE TRAVEL!

Mankind's movement through deep space placed a unique stamp on religion during the one hundred and ten centuries that preceded the Butlerian Jihad. To begin with, early space travel, although widespread, was largely unregulated, slow, and uncertain, and, before the Guild monopoly, was accomplished by a hodgepodge of methods. The first space experiences, poorly communicated and subject to extreme distortion, were a wild inducement to mystical speculation.

Immediately, space gave a different flavor and sense to ideas of Creation. That difference is seen even in the highest religious achievements of the period. All through religion, the feeling of the sacred was touched by anarchy from the outer dark.

It was as though Jupiter in all his descendant forms retreated into the maternal darkness to be superseded by a female immanence filled with ambiguity and with a face of many terrors.

The ancient formulae intertwined, tangled together as they were fitted to the needs of new conquests and new heraldic symbols. It was a time of struggle between beast-demons on the one side and the old prayers and invocations on the other.

There was never a clear decision.

During this period, it was said that Genesis was reinterpreted, permitting God to say:

"Increase and multiply, and fill the *universe*, and subdue it, and rule over all manner of strange beasts and living creatures in the infinite airs, on the infinite earths and beneath them."

It was a time of sorceresses whose powers were real. The measure of them is seen in the fact they never boasted how they grasped the firebrand.

Then came the Butlerian Jihad—two generations of chaos. The god of machine-logic was overthrown among the masses and a new concept was raised:

"Man may not be replaced."

Those two generations of violence were a thalamic pause for all humankind. Men looked at their gods and their rituals and saw that both were filled with that most terrible of all equations: fear over ambition.

Hesitantly, the leaders of religions whose followers had spilled the blood of billions began meeting to exchange views. It was a move encouraged by the Spacing Guild, which was beginning to build its monopoly over all interstellar travel, and by the Bene Gesserit who were banding the sorceresses.

Out of those first ecumenical meetings came two major developments:

1. The realization that all religions had at least one common commandment: "Thou shalt not disfigure the soul."

2. The Commission of Ecumenical Translators.

C.E.T. convened on a neutral island of Old Earth, spawning ground of the mother religions. They met "in the common belief that there exists a Divine Essence in the universe." Every faith with more than a million followers was represented, and they reached a surprisingly immediate agreement on the statement of their common goal:

"We are here to remove a primary weapon from the hands of disputant religions. That weapon—the claim to possession of the one and only revelation."

Jubilation at this "sign of profound accord" proved premature. For more than a Standard year, that statement was the only announcement from C.E.T. Men spoke bitterly of the delay. Troubadours composed witty, biting songs about the one hundred and twenty-one "Old Cranks" as the C.E.T. delegates came to be called. (The name arose from a ribald joke which played on the C.E.T. initials and called the delegates "Cranks—Effing-Turners.") One of the songs, "Brown Repose," has undergone periodic revival and is popular even today:

> *"Consider leis.*
> *Brown repose—and*
> *The tragedy*
> *In all of those*
> *Cranks! All those Cranks!*
> *So laze—so laze*
> *Through all your days.*
> *Time has toll'd for*
> *M'Lord Sandwich!"*

Occasional rumors leaked out of the C.E.T. sessions. It was said they were comparing texts and, irresponsibly, the texts were named. Such rumors inevitably provoked anti-ecumenism riots and, of course, inspired new witticisms.

Two years passed . . . three years.

The Commissioners, nine of their original number having died and been replaced, paused to observe formal installation of the replacements and announced they were laboring to produce one book, weeding out "all the pathological symptoms" of the religious past.

"We are producing an instrument of Love to be played in all ways," they said.

Many consider it odd that this statement provoked the worst outbreaks of violence against ecumenism. Twenty delegates were recalled by their congregations. One committed suicide by stealing a space frigate and diving it into the sun.

Historians estimate the riots took eighty million lives. That works out to about six thousand for each world then in the Landsraad League. Considering the unrest of the time, this may not be an excessive estimate, although any pretense to real accuracy in the figure must be just that—pretense. Communication between worlds was at one of its lowest ebbs.

The troubadours, quite naturally, had a field day. A popular musical comedy of the period had one of the C.E.T. delegates sitting on a white sand beach beneath a palm tree singing:

"For God, woman and the splendor of love
We dally here sans fears or cares.
Troubadour! Troubadour, sing another melody
For God, woman and the splendor of love!"

Riots and comedy are but symptoms of the times, profoundly revealing. They betray the psychological tone, the deep uncertainties . . . and the striving for something better, plus the fear that nothing would come of it all.

The major dams against anarchy in these times were the embryo Guild, the Bene Gesserit and the Landsraad, which continued its 2,000-year record of meeting in spite of the severest obstacles. The Guild's part appears clear: they gave free transport for all Landsraad and C.E.T. business. The Bene Gesserit role is more obscure. Certainly, this is the time in which they consolidated their hold upon the sorceresses, explored the subtle narcotics, developed prana-bindu training and conceived the Missionaria Protectiva, that black arm of superstition. But it is also the period that saw the composing of the Litany against Fear and the assembly of the Azhar Book, that bibliographic marvel that preserves the great secrets of the most ancient faiths.

Ingsley's comment is perhaps the only one possible:

"Those were times of deep paradox."

For almost seven years, then, C.E.T. labored. And as their seventh anniversary approached, they prepared the human universe for a momentous announcement. On that seventh anniversary, they unveiled the Orange Catholic Bible.

"Here is a work with dignity and meaning," they said. "Here is a way to make humanity aware of itself as a total creation of God."

The men of C.E.T. were likened to archeologists of ideas, inspired by God in the grandeur of rediscovery. It was said they had brought to light "the vitality of great ideals overlaid by the deposits of centuries," that they had "sharpened the moral imperatives that come out of a religious conscience."

With the O.C. Bible, C.E.T. presented the Liturgical Manual and the Commentaries—in many respects a more remarkable work, not only because of its brevity (less than half the size of the O.C. Bible), but also because of its candor and blend of self-pity and self-righteousness.

The beginning is an obvious appeal to the agnostic rulers.

"Men, finding no answers to the *sunnan* [the ten thousand religious questions from the Shari-ah] now apply their own reasoning. All men seek to be enlightened. Religion is but the most ancient and honorable way in which men have striven to make sense out of God's universe. Scientists seek the lawfulness of events. It is the task of Religion to fit man into this lawfulness."

In their conclusion, though, the Commentaries set a harsh tone that very likely foretold their fate.

"Much that was called religion has carried an unconscious attitude of hostility toward life. True religion must teach that life is filled with joys pleasing to the eye of God, that knowledge without action is empty. All men must see that the teaching of religion by rules and rote is largely a hoax. The proper teaching is recognized with ease. You can know it without fail because it awakens within you that sensation which tells you this is something you've always known."

There was an odd sense of calm as the presses and shigawire imprinters rolled and the O.C. Bible spread out through the worlds. Some interpreted this as a sign from God, an omen of unity.

But even the C.E.T. delegates betrayed the fiction of that calm as they returned to their respective congregations. Eighteen of them were lynched within two months. Fifty-three recanted within the year.

The O.C. Bible was denounced as a work produced by "the hubris of reason." It was said that its pages were filled with a seductive interest in logic. Revisions that catered to popular bigotry began appearing. These revisions leaned on accepted symbolisms (Cross, Crescent, Feather Rattle, the Twelve Saints, the thin Buddha, and the like) and it soon became apparent that the ancient superstitions and beliefs had *not* been absorbed by the new ecumenism.

Halloway's label for C.E.T.'s seven-year effort—"Galactophasic Determinism"—was snapped up by eager billions who interpreted the initials G.D. as "God-Damned."

C.E.T. Chairman Toure Bomoko, a Ulema of the Zensunnis and one of the fourteen delegates who never recanted ("The Fourteen Sages" of popular history), appeared to admit finally the C.E.T. had erred.

"We shouldn't have tried to create new symbols," he said. "We should've realized we weren't supposed to introduce uncertainties into accepted belief, that we weren't supposed to stir up curiosity about God. We are daily confronted by the terrifying instability of all things human, yet we permit our religions to grow more rigid and controlled, more conforming and oppressive. What is this shadow across the highway of Divine Command? It is a warning that institutions endure, that symbols endure when their meaning is lost, that there is no summa of all attainable knowledge."

The bitter double edge in this "admission" did not escape Bomoko's critics and he was forced soon afterward to flee into exile, his life dependent upon the Guild's pledge of secrecy. He reportedly died on Tupile, honored and beloved, his last words: "Religion must remain an outlet for people who say to themselves, 'I am not the kind of person I want to be.' It must never sink into an assemblage of the self-satisfied."

It is pleasant to think that Bomoko understood the prophecy in his words: "Institutions endure." Ninety generations later, the O.C. Bible and the Commentaries permeated the religious universe.

When Paul-Muad'Dib stood with his right hand on the rock shrine enclosing his father's skull (the right hand of the blessed, not the left hand of the damned) he quoted word for word from "Bomoko's Legacy"—

"You who have defeated us say to yourselves that Babylon is fallen and its works have been overturned. I say to you still that man remains on trial, each man in his own dock. Each man is a little war."

The Fremen said of Muad'Dib that he was like Abu Zide whose frigate defied the Guild and rode one day *there* and back. *There* used in this way translates directly from the Fremen mythology as the land of the ruh-spirit, the alam al-mithal where all limitations are removed.

The parallel between this and the Kwisatz Haderach is readily seen. The Kwisatz Haderach that the Sisterhood sought through its breeding program was interpreted as "The shortening of the way" or "The one who can be two places simultaneously."

But both of these interpretations can be shown to stem directly from the Commentaries: "When law and religious duty are one, your selfdom encloses the universe."

Of himself, Muad'Dib said: "I am a net in the sea of time, free to sweep future and past. I am a moving membrane from whom no possibility can escape."

These thoughts are all one and the same and they harken to 22 Kalima in the O.C. Bible where it says: "Whether a thought is spoken or not it is a real thing and has powers of reality."

It is when we get into Muad'Dib's own commentaries in "The Pillars of the Universe" as interpreted by his holy men, the Qizara Tafwid, that we see his real debt to C.E.T. and Fremen-Zensunni.

> Muad'Dib: "Law and duty are one; so be it. But remember these limitations—Thus are you never fully self-conscious. Thus do you remain immersed in the communal tau. Thus are you always less than an individual."
>
> O.C. Bible: Identical wording. (61 Revelations.)

Muad'Dib: "Religion often partakes of the myth of progress that shields us from the terrors of an uncertain future."

C.E.T. Commentaries: Identical wording. (The Azhar Book traces this statement to the first-century religious writer, Neshou; through a paraphrase.)

Muad'Dib: "If a child, an untrained person, an ignorant person, or an insane person incites trouble, it is the fault of authority for not predicting and preventing that trouble."

O.C. Bible: "Any sin can be ascribed, at least in part, to a natural bad tendency that is an extenuating circumstance acceptable to God." (The Azhar Book traces this to the ancient Semitic Tawra.)

Muad'Dib: "Reach forth thy hand and eat what God has provided thee; and when thou are replenished, praise the Lord."

O.C. Bible: a paraphrase with identical meaning. (The Azhar Book traces this in slightly different form to First Islam.)

Muad'Dib: "Kindness is the beginning of cruelty."

Fremen Kitab al-Ibar: "The weight of a kindly God is a fearful thing. Did not God give us the burning sun (Al-Lat)? Did not God give us the Mothers of Moisture (Reverend Mothers)? Did not God give us Shaitan (Iblis, Satan)? From Shaitan did we not get the hurtfulness of speed?"

(This is the source of the Fremen saying: "Speed comes from Shaitan." Consider: for every one hundred calories of heat generated by exercise [speed] the body evaporates about six ounces of perspiration. The Fremen word for perspiration is bakka or tears and, in one pronunciation, translates: "The life essence that Shaitan squeezes from your soul.")

Muad'Dib's arrival is called "religiously timely" by Koneywell, but timing had little to do with it. As Muad'Dib himself said: "I am here; so. . . ."

It is, however, vital to an understanding of Muad'Dib's religious impact that you never lose sight of one fact: the Fremen were a desert people whose entire ancestry was accustomed to hostile landscapes.

Mysticism isn't difficult when you survive each second by surmounting open hostility. "You are there—so. . . ."

With such a tradition, suffering is accepted—perhaps as unconscious punishment, but accepted. And it's well to note that Fremen ritual gives almost complete freedom from guilt feelings. This isn't necessarily because their law and religion were identical, making disobedience a sin. It's likely closer to the mark to say they cleansed themselves of guilt easily because their everyday existence required brutal judgments (often deadly) which in a softer land would burden men with unbearable guilt.

This is likely one of the roots of Fremen emphasis on superstition (disregarding the Missionaria Protectiva's ministrations). What matter that whistling sands are an omen? What matter that you must make the sign of the fist when first you see First Moon? A man's flesh is his own and his water belongs to the tribe—and the mystery of life isn't a problem to solve but a reality to experience. Omens help you remember this. And because you are *here*, because you have *the* religion, victory cannot evade you in the end.

As the Bene Gesserit taught for centuries, long before they ran afoul of the Fremen:

"When religion and politics ride the same cart, when that cart is driven by a living holy man (baraka), nothing can stand in their path."

APPENDIX III

REPORT ON BENE GESSERIT MOTIVES AND PURPOSES

Here follows an excerpt from the Summa prepared by her own agents at the request of the Lady Jessica immediately after the Arrakis Affair. The candor of this report amplifies its value far beyond the ordinary.

Because the Bene Gesserit operated for centuries behind the blind of a semimystic school while carrying on their selective breeding program among humans, we tend to award them with more status than they appear to deserve. Analysis of their "trial of fact" on the Arrakis Affair betrays the school's profound ignorance of its own role.

It may be argued that the Bene Gesserit could examine only such facts as were available to them and had no direct access to the person of the Prophet Muad'Dib. But the school had surmounted greater obstacles and its error here goes deeper.

The Bene Gesserit program had as its target the breeding of a person they labeled "Kwisatz Haderach," a term signifying "one who can be many places at once." In simpler terms, what they sought was a human with mental powers permitting him to understand and use higher order dimensions.

They were breeding for a super-Mentat, a human computer with some of the prescient abilities found in Guild navigators. Now, attend these facts carefully:

Muad'Dib, born Paul Atreides, was the son of the Duke Leto, a man whose bloodline had been watched carefully for more than a thousand years. The Prophet's mother, Lady Jessica, was a natural daughter of the

Baron Vladimir Harkonnen and carried gene-markers whose supreme importance to the breeding program was known for almost two thousand years. She was a Bene Gesserit bred and trained, and *should have been a willing tool of the project.*

The Lady Jessica was ordered to produce an Atreides daughter. The plan was to inbreed this daughter with Feyd-Rautha Harkonnen, a nephew of the Baron Vladimir, with the high probability of a Kwisatz Haderach from that union. Instead, for reasons she confesses have never been completely clear to her, the concubine Lady Jessica defied her orders and bore a son.

This alone should have alerted the Bene Gesserit to the possibility that a wild variable had entered their scheme. But there were other far more important indications that they virtually ignored:

1. As a youth, Paul Atreides showed ability to predict the future. He was known to have had prescient visions that were accurate, penetrating, and defied four-dimensional explanation.

2. The Reverend Mother Gaius Helen Mohiam, Bene Gesserit Proctor who tested Paul's humanity when he was fifteen, deposes that he surmounted more agony in the test than any other human of record. Yet she failed to make special note of this in her report!

3. When Family Atreides moved to the planet Arrakis, the Fremen population there hailed the young Paul as a prophet, "the voice from the outer world." The Bene Gesserit were well aware that the rigors of such a planet as Arrakis with its totality of desert landscape, its absolute lack of open water, its emphasis on the most primitive necessities for survival, inevitably produces a high proportion of sensitives. Yet this Fremen reaction and the obvious element of the Arrakeen diet high in spice were glossed over by Bene Gesserit observers.

4. When the Harkonnens and the soldier-fanatics of the Padishah Emperor reoccupied Arrakis, killing Paul's father and most of the Atreides troops, Paul and his mother disappeared. But almost immediately there were reports of a new religious leader among the Fremen, a man called Muad'Dib, who again was hailed as "the voice from the outer world." The reports stated clearly that he was accompanied by a new

Reverend Mother of the Sayyadina Rite "who is the woman who bore him." Records available to the Bene Gesserit stated in plain terms that the Fremen legends of the Prophet contained these words: "He shall be born of a Bene Gesserit witch."

(It may be argued here that the Bene Gesserit sent their Missionaria Protectiva onto Arrakis centuries earlier to implant something like this legend as safeguard should any members of the school be trapped there and require sanctuary, and that this legend of "the voice from the outer world" was properly to be ignored because it appeared to be the standard Bene Gesserit ruse. But this would be true only if you granted that the Bene Gesserit were correct in ignoring the other clues about Paul-Muad'Dib.)

5. When the Arrakis Affair boiled up, the Spacing Guild made overtures to the Bene Gesserit. The Guild hinted that its navigators, who use the spice drug of Arrakis to produce the limited prescience necessary for guiding spaceships through the void, were "bothered about the future" or saw "problems on the horizon." This could only mean they saw a nexus, a meeting place of countless delicate decisions, beyond which the path was hidden from the prescient eye. This was a clear indication that some agency was interfering with higher order dimensions!

(A few of the Bene Gesserit had long been aware that the Guild could not interfere directly with the vital spice source because Guild navigators already were dealing in their own inept way with higher order dimensions, at least to the point where they recognized that the slightest misstep they made on Arrakis could be catastrophic. It was a known fact that Guild navigators could predict no way to take control of the spice without producing just such a nexus. The obvious conclusion was that someone of higher order powers *was* taking control of the spice source, yet the Bene Gesserit missed this point entirely!)

In the face of these facts, one is led to the inescapable conclusion that the inefficient Bene Gesserit behavior in this affair was a product of an even higher plan of which they were completely unaware!

THE ALMANAK EN-ASHRAF
(Selected Excerpts of the Noble Houses)

SHADDAM IV (10,134–10,202)

The Padishah Emperor, 81st of his line (House Corrino) to occupy the Golden Lion Throne, reigned from 10,156 (date his father, Elrood IX, succumbed to chaumurky) until replaced by the 10,196 Regency set up in the name of his eldest daughter, Irulan. His reign is noted chiefly for the Arrakis Revolt, blamed by many historians on Shaddam IV's dalliance with Court functions and the pomp of office. The ranks of Bursegs were doubled in the first sixteen years of his reign. Appropriations for Sardaukar training went down steadily in the final thirty years before the Arrakis Revolt. He had five daughters (Irulan, Chalice, Wensicia, Josifa, and Rugi) and no legal sons. Four of the daughters accompanied him into retirement. His wife, Anirul, a Bene Gesserit of Hidden Rank, died in 10,176.

LETO ATREIDES (10,140–10,191)

A distaff cousin of the Corrinos, he is frequently referred to as the Red Duke. House Atreides ruled Caladan as a siridar-fief for twenty generations until pressured into the move to Arrakis. He is known chiefly as the father of Duke Paul-Muad'Dib, the Umma Regent. The remains of Duke Leto occupy the "Skull Tomb" on Arrakis. His death is attributed to the treachery of a Suk doctor, and is an act laid to the Siridar-Baron, Vladimir Harkonnen.

LADY JESSICA (HON. ATREIDES) (10,154–10,256)

A natural daughter (Bene Gesserit reference) of the Siridar-Baron Vladimir Harkonnen. Mother of Duke Paul-Muad'Dib. She graduated from the Wallach IX B.G. School.

LADY ALIA ATREIDES (10,191–)

Legal daughter of Duke Leto Atreides and his formal concubine, Lady Jessica. Lady Alia was born on Arrakis about eight months after Duke Leto's death. Prenatal exposure to an awareness-spectrum narcotic is the reason generally given for Bene Gesserit references to her as "Accursed One." She is known in popular history as St. Alia or St. Alia-of-the-Knife. (For a detailed history, see *St. Alia, Huntress of a Billion Worlds* by Pander Oulson.)

VLADIMIR HARKONNEN (10,110–10,193)

Commonly referred to as Baron Harkonnen, his title is officially Siridar (planetary governor) Baron. Vladimir Harkonnen is the direct-line male descendant of the Bashar Abulurd Harkonnen who was banished for cowardice after the Battle of Corrin. The return of House Harkonnen to power generally is ascribed to adroit manipulation of the whale fur market and later consolidation with melange wealth from Arrakis. The Siridar-Baron died on Arrakis during the Revolt. Title passed briefly to the na-Baron, Feyd-Rautha Harkonnen.

COUNT HASIMIR FENRING (10,133–10,225)

A distaff cousin of House Corrino, he was a childhood companion of Shaddam IV. (The frequently discredited *Pirate History of Corrino* related the curious story that Fenring was responsible for the chaumurky which disposed of Elrood IX.) All accounts agree that Fenring was the closest friend Shaddam IV possessed. The Imperial chores carried out by Count Fenring included that of Imperial Agent on Arrakis during the Harkonnen regime there and later Siridar-Absentia of Caladan. He joined Shaddam IV in retirement on Salusa Secundus.

COUNT GLOSSU RABBAN (10,132–10,193)

Glossu Rabban, Count of Lankiveil, was the eldest nephew of Vladimir Harkonnen. Glossu Rabban and Feyd-Rautha Rabban (who took the name Harkonnen when chosen for the Siridar-Baron's household) were

legal sons of the Siridar-Baron's youngest demibrother, Abulurd. Abulurd renounced the Harkonnen name and all rights to the title when
given the subdistrict governorship of Rabban-Lankiveil. Rabban was a
distaff name.

TERMINOLOGY OF THE IMPERIUM

In studying the Imperium, Arrakis, and the whole culture which produced Muad'Dib, many unfamiliar terms occur. To increase understanding is a laudable goal, hence the definitions and explanations given below.

A

ABA: loose robe worn by Fremen women; usually black.

ACH: left turn; a worm steersman's call.

ADAB: the demanding memory that comes upon you of itself.

AKARSO: a plant native to Sikun (of 70 Ophiuchi A) characterized by almost oblong leaves. Its green and white stripes indicate the constant multiple condition of parallel active and dormant chlorophyll regions.

ALAM AL-MITHAL: the mystical world of similitudes where all physical limitations are removed.

AL-LAT: mankind's original sun; by usage: any planet's primary.

AMPOLIROS: the legendary "Flying Dutchman" of space.

AMTAL or **AMTAL RULE:** a common rule on primitive worlds under which something is tested to determine its limits or defects. Commonly: testing to destruction.

AQL: the test of reason. Originally, the "Seven Mystic Questions" beginning: "Who is it that thinks?"

ARRAKEEN: first settlement on Arrakis; long-time seat of planetary government.

ARRAKIS: the planet known as Dune; third planet of Canopus.

ASSASSINS' HANDBOOK: third-century compilation of poisons commonly used in a War of Assassins. Later expanded to include those deadly devices permitted under the Guild Peace and Great Convention.

AULIYA: in the Zensunni Wanderers' religion, the female at the left hand of God; God's handmaiden.

AUMAS: poison administered in food. (Specifically: poison in solid food.) In some dialects: Chaumas.

AYAT: the signs of life. (*See* Burhan.)

B

BAKKA: in Fremen legend, the weeper who mourns for all mankind.

BAKLAWA: a heavy pastry made with date syrup.

BALISET: a nine-stringed musical instrument, lineal descendant of the zithra, tuned to the Chusuk scale and played by strumming. Favorite instrument of Imperial troubadors.

BARADYE PISTOL: a static-charge dust gun developed on Arrakis for laying down a large dye marker area on sand.

BARAKA: a living holy man of magical powers.

BASHAR (often Colonel Bashar): an officer of the Sardaukar a fractional point above Colonel in the standardized military classification. Rank created for military ruler of a planetary subdistrict. (Bashar of the Corps is a title reserved strictly for military use.)

BATTLE LANGUAGE: any special language of restricted etymology developed for clear-speech communication in warfare.

BEDWINE: *see* Ichwan Bedwine.

BELA TEGEUSE: fifth planet of Kuentsing: third stopping place of the Zensunni (Fremen) forced migration.

BENE GESSERIT: the ancient school of mental and physical training established primarily for female students after the Butlerian Jihad destroyed the so-called "thinking machines" and robots.

B.G.: idiomatic for Bene Gesserit except when used with a date. With a date it signifies Before Guild and identifies the Imperial dating system based on the genesis of the Spacing Guild's monopoly.

BHOTANI JIB: *see* Chakobsa.

BI-LA KAIFA: amen. (Literally: "Nothing further need be explained.")

BINDU: relating to the human nervous system, especially to nerve training. Often expressed as Bindu-nervature. (*See* Prana.)

BINDU SUSPENSION: a special form of catalepsis, self-induced.

BLED: flat, open desert.

BOURKA: insulated mantle worn by Fremen in the open desert.

BURHAN: the proofs of life. (Commonly: the ayat and burhan of life. *See* Ayat.)

BURSEG: a commanding general of the Sardaukar.

BUTLERIAN JIHAD: *see* Jihad, Butlerian (*also* Great Revolt).

C

CAID: Sardaukar officer rank given to a military official whose duties call mostly for dealings with civilians; a military governorship over a full planetary district; above the rank of Bashar but not equal to a Burseg.

CALADAN: third planet of Delta Pavonis; birthworld of Paul-Muad'Dib.

CANTO and **RESPONDU:** an invocation rite, part of the panoplia propheticus of the Missionaria Protectiva.

CARRYALL: a flying wing (commonly "wing"), the aerial workhorse of Arrakis, used to transport large spice mining, hunting, and refining equipment.

CATCHPOCKET: any stillsuit pocket where filtered water is caught and stored.

CHAKOBSA: the so-called "magnetic language" derived in part from the ancient Bhotani (Bhotani Jib—jib meaning dialect). A collection of ancient dialects modified by needs of secrecy, but chiefly the hunting language of the Bhotani, the hired assassins of the first War of Assassins.

CHAUMAS: (Aumas in some dialects): poison in solid food as distinguished from poison administered in some other way.

CHAUMURKY (Musky or Murky in some dialects): poison administered in a drink.

CHEOPS: pyramid chess; nine-level chess with the double object of putting your queen at the apex and the opponent's king in check.

CHEREM: a brotherhood of hate (usually for revenge).

CHOAM: acronym for Combine Honnete Ober Advancer Mercantiles—the universal development corporation controlled by the Emperor and Great Houses with the Guild and Bene Gesserit as silent partners.

CHUSUK: fourth planet of Theta Shalish; the so-called "Music Planet" noted for the quality of its musical instruments. (*See* Varota.)

CIELAGO: any modified *Chiroptera* of Arrakis adapted to carry dis-trans messages.

CONE OF SILENCE: the field of a distorter that limits the carrying power of the voice or any other vibrator by damping the vibrations with an image-vibration 180 degrees out of phase.

CORIOLIS STORM: any major sandstorm on Arrakis where winds across the open flatlands are amplified by the planet's own revolutionary motion to reach speeds up to 700 kilometers per hour.

CORRIN, BATTLE OF: the space battle from which the Imperial House Corrino took its name. The battle fought near Sigma Draconis in the year 88 B.G. settled the ascendancy of the ruling House from Salusa Secundus.

COUSINES: blood relations beyond cousins.

CRUSHERS: military space vessels composed of many smaller vessels locked together and designed to fall on an enemy position, crushing it.

CRYSKNIFE: the sacred knife of the Fremen on Arrakis. It is manufactured in two forms from teeth taken from dead sandworms. The two forms are "fixed" and "unfixed." An unfixed knife requires proximity to a human body's electrical field to prevent disintegration. Fixed knives are treated for storage. All are about 20 centimeters long.

CUTTERAY: short-range version of lasgun used mostly as a cutting tool and surgeon's scalpel.

D

DAR AL-HIKMAN: school of religious translation or interpretation.

DARK THINGS: idiomatic for the infectious superstitions taught by the Missionaria Protectiva to susceptible civilizations.

DEATH TRIPOD: originally, the tripod upon which desert executioners hanged their victims. By usage: the three members of a Cherem sworn to the same revenge.

DEMIBROTHERS: sons of concubines in the same household and certified as having the same father.

DERCH: right turn; a worm steersman's call.

DEW COLLECTORS or **DEW PRECIPITATORS:** not to be confused with dew gatherers. Collectors or precipitators are egg-shaped devices about four centimeters on the long axis. They are made of chromoplastic that turns a reflecting white when subjected to light, and reverts to transparency in darkness. The collector forms a markedly cold surface upon which dawn dew will precipitate. They are used by Fremen to line concave planting depressions where they provide a small but reliable source of water.

DEW GATHERERS: workers who reap dew from the plants of Arrakis, using a scythelike dew reaper.

DICTUM FAMILIA: that rule of the Great Convention which prohibits the slaying of a royal person or member of a Great House by informal treachery. The rule sets up the formal outline and limits the means of assassination.

DISTRANS: a device for producing a temporary neural imprint on the nervous system of *Chiroptera* or birds. The creature's normal cry then carries the message imprint which can be sorted from that carrier wave by another distrans.

DOORSEAL: a portable plastic hermetic seal used for moisture security in Fremen overday cave camps.

DRUM SAND: impaction of sand in such a way that any sudden blow against its surface produces a distinct drum sound.

DUMP BOXES: the general term for any cargo container of irregular shape and equipped with ablation surfaces and suspensor damping system. They are used to dump material from space onto a planet's surface.

DUNE MEN: idiomatic for open sand workers, spice hunters and the like on Arrakis. Sandworkers. Spiceworkers.

DUST CHASM: any deep crevasse or depression on the desert of Arrakis that has been filled with dust not apparently different from the surrounding surface; a deadly trap because human or animal will sink in it and smother. (*See* Tidal Dust Basin.)

E

ECAZ: fourth planet of Alpha Centauri B; the sculptors' paradise, so called because it is the home of *fogwood,* the plant growth capable of being shaped in situ solely by the power of human thought.

EGO-LIKENESS: portraiture reproduced through a shigawire projector that is capable of reproducing subtle movements said to convey the ego essence.

ELACCA DRUG: narcotic formed by burning blood-grained elacca wood of Ecas. Its effect is to remove most of the will to self-preservation. Druggee skin shows a characteristic carrot color. Commonly used to prepare slave-gladiators for the ring.

EL-SAYAL: the "rain of sand." A fall of dust which has been carried to medium altitude (around 2,000 meters) by a coriolis storm. El-sayals frequently bring moisture to ground level.

ERG: an extensive dune area, a sea of sand.

F

FAI: the water tribute, chief specie of tax on Arrakis.

FANMETAL: metal formed by the growing of jasmium crystals in duraluminum; noted for extreme tensile strength in relationship to weight. Name derives from its common use in collapsible structures that are opened by "fanning" them out.

FAUFRELUCHES: the rigid rule of class distinction enforced by the Imperium. "A place for every man and every man in his place."

FEDAYKIN: Fremen death commandos; historically: a group formed and pledged to give their lives to right a wrong.

FILMBOOK: any shigawire imprint used in training and carrying a mnemonic pulse.

FILT-PLUG: a nose filter unit worn with a stillsuit to capture moisture from the exhaled breath.

FIQH: knowledge, religious law; one of the half-legendary origins of the Zensunni Wanderers' religion.

FIRE, PILLAR OF: a simple pyrocket for signaling across the open desert.

FIRST MOON: the major satellite of Arrakis, first to rise in the night; notable for a distinct human fist pattern on its surface.

FREE TRADERS: idiomatic for smugglers.

FREMEN: the free tribes of Arrakis, dwellers in the desert, remnants of the Zensunni Wanderers. ("Sand Pirates" according to the Imperial Dictionary.)

FREMKIT: desert survival kit of Fremen manufacture.

FRIGATE: largest spaceship that can be grounded on a planet and taken off in one piece.

G

GALACH: official language of the Imperium. Hybrid Inglo-Slavic with strong traces of cultural-specialization terms adopted during the long chain of human migrations.

GAMONT: third planet of Niushe; noted for its hedonistic culture and exotic sexual practices.

GARE: butte.

GATHERING: distinguished from Council Gathering. It is a formal convocation of Fremen leaders to witness a combat that determines tribal leadership. (A Council Gathering is an assembly to arrive at decisions involving all the tribes.)

GEYRAT: straight ahead; a worm steersman's call.

GHAFLA: giving oneself up to gadfly distractions. Thus: a changeable person, one not to be trusted.

GHANIMA: something acquired in battle or single combat. Commonly, a memento of combat kept only to stir the memory.

GIEDI PRIME: the planet of Ophiuchi B (36), homeworld of House Harkonnen. A median-viable planet with a low active-photosynthesis range.

GINAZ, HOUSE OF: one-time allies of Duke Leto Atreides. They were defeated in the War of Assassins with Grumman.

GIUDICHAR: a holy truth. (Commonly seen in the expression Giudichar mantene: an original and supporting truth.)

GLOWGLOBE: suspensor-buoyed illuminating device, self-powered (usually by organic batteries).

GOM JABBAR: the high-handed enemy; that specific poison needle tipped with meta-cyanide used by Bene Gesserit Proctors in the death-alternative test of human awareness.

GRABEN: a long geological ditch formed when the ground sinks because of movements in the underlying crustal layers.

GREAT CONVENTION: the universal truce enforced under the power balance maintained by the Guild, the Great Houses, and the Imperium. Its chief rule prohibits the use of atomic weapons against human targets. Each rule of the Great Convention begins: "The forms must be obeyed. . . ."

GREAT MOTHER: the horned goddess, the feminine principle of space (commonly: Mother Space), the feminine face of the male-female-neuter trinity accepted as Supreme Being by many religions within the Imperium.

GREAT REVOLT: common term for the Butlerian Jihad. (*See* Jihad, Butlerian.)

GRIDEX PLANE: a differential-charge separator used to remove sand from the melange spice mass; a device of the second stage in spice refining.

GRUMMAN: second planet of Niushe, noted chiefly for the feud of its ruling House (Moritani) with House Ginaz.

GUILD: the Spacing Guild, one leg of the political tripod maintaining the Great Convention. The Guild was the second mental-physical training school (*see* Bene Gesserit) after the Butlerian Jihad. The Guild monopoly on space travel and transport and upon international banking is taken as the beginning point of the Imperial Calendar.

H

HAGAL: the "Jewel Planet" (II Theta Shaowei), mined out in the time of Shaddam I.

HAIIIII-YOH!: command to action; worm steersman's call.

HAJJ: holy journey.

HAJRA: journey of seeking.

HAL YAWM: "Now! At last!" A Fremen exclamation.

HARJ: desert journey, migration.

HARMONTHEP: Ingsley gives this as the planet name for the sixth stop in the Zensunni migration. It is supposed to have been a no longer existent satellite of Delta Pavonis.

HARVESTER or **HARVESTER FACTORY:** a large (often 120 meters by 40 meters) spice mining machine commonly employed on rich, uncontaminated melange blows. (Often called a "crawler" because of buglike body on independent tracks.)

HEIGHLINER: major cargo carrier of the Spacing Guild's transportation system.

HIEREG: temporary Fremen desert camp on open sand.

HIGH COUNCIL: the Landsraad inner circle empowered to act as supreme tribunal in House to House disputes.

HOLTZMAN EFFECT: the negative repelling effect of a shield generator.

HOOKMAN: Fremen with Maker hooks prepared to catch a sandworm.

HOUSE: idiomatic for Ruling Clan of a planet or planetary system.

HOUSES MAJOR: holders of planetary fiefs; interplanetary entrepreneurs. (*See* House *above*.)

HOUSES MINOR: planet-bound entrepreneur class (Galach: "Richece").

HUNTER-SEEKER: a ravening sliver of suspensor-buoyed metal guided as a weapon by a nearby control console; common assassination device.

I

IBAD, EYES OF: characteristic effect of a diet high in melange wherein the whites and pupils of the eyes turn a deep blue (indicative of deep melange addiction).

IBN QIRTAIBA: "Thus go the holy words. . . ." Formal beginning to Fremen religious incantation (derived from panoplia propheticus).

ICHWAN BEDWINE: the brotherhood of all Fremen on Arrakis.

IJAZ: prophecy that by its very nature cannot be denied; immutable prophecy.

IKHUT-EIGH!: cry of the water-seller on Arrakis (etymology uncertain). (*See* Soo-Soo Sook!)

ILM: theology; science of religious tradition; one of the half-legendary origins of the Zensunni Wanderers' faith.

IMPERIAL CONDITIONING: a development of the Suk Medical Schools: the highest conditioning against taking human life. Initiates are marked by a diamond tattoo on the forehead and are permitted to wear their hair long and bound by a silver Suk ring.

INKVINE: a creeping plant native to Giedi Prime and frequently used as a whip in the slave cribs. Victims are marked by beet-colored tattoos that cause residual pain for many years.

ISTISLAH: a rule for the general welfare; usually a preface to brutal necessity.

IX: *see* Richese.

J

JIHAD: a religious crusade; fanatical crusade.

JIHAD, BUTLERIAN: (*see also* Great Revolt)—the crusade against computers, thinking machines, and conscious robots begun in 201 B.G. and concluded in 108 B.G. Its chief commandment remains in the O.C. Bible as "Thou shalt not make a machine in the likeness of a human mind."

JUBBA CLOAK: the all-purpose cloak (it can be set to reflect or admit radiant heat, converts to a hammock or shelter) commonly worn over a stillsuit on Arrakis.

JUDGE OF THE CHANGE: an official appointed by the Landsraad High Council and the Emperor to monitor a change of fief, a kanly negotiation, or formal battle in a War of Assassins. The Judge's arbitral authority may be challenged only before the High Council with the Emperor present.

K

KANLY: formal feud or vendetta under the rules of the Great Convention carried on according to the strictest limitations. (*See* Judge of the Change.) Originally the rules were designed to protect innocent bystanders.

KARAMA: a miracle; an action initiated by the spirit world.

KHALA: traditional invocation to still the angry spirits of a place whose name you mention.

KINDJAL: double-bladed short sword (or long knife) with about 20 centimeters of slightly curved blade.

KISWA: any figure or design from Fremen mythology.

KITAB AL-IBAR: the combined survival handbook-religious manual developed by the Fremen on Arrakis.

KRIMSKELL FIBER or **KRIMSKELL ROPE:** the "claw fiber" woven from strands of the *hufuf* from Ecaz. Knots tied in krimskell will claw tighter and tighter to preset limits when the knot-lines are pulled. (For a more detailed study, see Holjance Vohnbrook's "The Strangler Vines of Ecaz.")

KULL WAHAD!: "I am profoundly stirred!" A sincere exclamation of surprise common in the Imperium. Strict interpretation depends on context. (It is said of Muad'Dib that once he watched a desert hawk chick emerge from its shell and whispered: "Kull wahad!")

KULON: wild ass of Terra's Asiatic steppes adapted for Arrakis.

KWISATZ HADERACH: "Shortening of the Way." This is the label applied by the Bene Gesserit to the *unknown* for which they sought a genetic solution: a male Bene Gesserit whose organic mental powers would bridge space and time.

L

LA, LA, LA: Fremen cry of grief. (La translates as ultimate denial, a "no" from which you cannot appeal.)

LASGUN: continuous-wave laser projector. Its use as a weapon is limited in a field-generator-shield culture because of the explosive pyrotechnics (technically, subatomic fusion) created when its beam intersects a shield.

LEGION, IMPERIAL: ten brigades (about 30,000 men).

LIBAN: Fremen liban is spice water infused with yucca flour. Originally a sour milk drink.

LISAN AL-GAIB: "The Voice from the Outer World." In Fremen messianic legends, an offworld prophet. Sometimes translated as "Giver of Water." (*See* Mahdi.)

LITERJON: a one-liter container for transporting water on Arrakis; made of high-density, shatterproof plastic with positive seal.

LITTLE MAKER: the half-plant-half-animal deep-sand vector of the Arrakis sandworm. The Little Maker's excretions form the pre-spice mass.

M

MAHDI: in the Fremen messianic legend, "The One Who Will Lead Us to Paradise."

MAKER: *see* Shai-hulud.

MAKER HOOKS: the hooks used for capturing, mounting, and steering a sandworm of Arrakis.

MANTENE: underlying wisdom, supporting argument, first principle. (*See* Giudichar.)

MATING INDEX: the Bene Gesserit master record of its human breeding program aimed at producing the Kwisatz Haderach.

MAULA: slave.

MAULA PISTOL: spring-loaded gun for firing poison darts; range about forty meters.

MELANGE: the "spice of spices," the crop for which Arrakis is the unique source. The spice, chiefly noted for its geriatric qualities, is mildly addictive when taken in small quantities, severely addictive when imbibed in quantities above two grams daily per seventy kilos of body weight. (*See* Ibad, Eyes of; Water of Life; *and* Pre-spice

Mass.) Muad'Dib claimed the spice as a key to his prophetic powers. Guild navigators make similar claims. Its price on the Imperial market has ranged as high as 620,000 solaris the decagram.

MENTAT: that class of Imperial citizens trained for supreme accomplishments of logic. "Human computers."

METAGLASS: glass grown as a high-temperature gas infusion in sheets of jasmium quartz. Noted for extreme tensile strength (about 450,000 kilos per square centimeter at two centimeters' thickness) and capacity as a selective radiation filter.

MIHNA: the season for testing Fremen youths who wish admittance to manhood.

MINIMIC FILM: shigawire of one-micron diameter often used to transmit espionage and counterespionage data.

MISH-MISH: apricots.

MISR: the historical Zensunni (Fremen) term for themselves: "The People."

MISSIONARIA PROTECTIVA: the arm of the Bene Gesserit order charged with sowing infectious superstitions on primitive worlds, thus opening those regions to exploitation by the Bene Gesserit. (*See* Panoplia propheticus.)

MONITOR: a ten-section space warcraft mounting heavy armor and shield protection. It is designed to be separated into its component sections for lift-off after planet-fall.

MUAD'DIB: the adapted kangaroo mouse of Arrakis, a creature associated in the Fremen earth-spirit mythology with a design visible on the planet's second moon. This creature is admired by Fremen for its ability to survive in the open desert.

MUDIR NAHYA: the Fremen name for Beast Rabban (Count Rabban of Lankiveil), the Harkonnen cousin who was siridar governor on Arrakis for many years. The name is often translated as "Demon Ruler."

MUSHTAMAL: a small garden annex or garden courtyard.

MUSKY: poison in a drink. (*See* Chaumurky.)

MU ZEIN WALLAH!: Mu zein literally means "nothing good," and wallah is a reflexive terminal exclamation. In this traditional opening for a Fremen curse against an enemy, Wallah turns the emphasis back upon the words Mu zein, producing the meaning: "Nothing good, never good, good for nothing."

N

NA-: a prefix meaning "nominated" or "next in line." Thus: na-Baron means heir apparent to a barony.

NAIB: one who has sworn never to be taken alive by the enemy; traditional oath of a Fremen leader.

NEZHONI SCARF: the scarf-pad worn at the forehead beneath the stillsuit hood by married or "associated" Fremen women after birth of a son.

NOUKKERS: officers of the Imperial bodyguard who are related to the Emperor by blood. Traditional rank for sons of royal concubines.

O

OIL LENS: hufuf oil held in static tension by an enclosing force field within a viewing tube as part of a magnifying or other light-manipulation system. Because each lens element can be adjusted individually one micron at a time, the oil lens is considered the ultimate in accuracy for manipulating visible light.

OPAFIRE: one of the rare opaline jewels of Hagal.

ORANGE CATHOLIC BIBLE: the "Accumulated Book," the religious text produced by the Commission of Ecumenical Translators. It contains elements of most ancient religions, including the Maometh Saari, Mahayana Christianity, Zensunni Catholicism and Buddislamic traditions. Its supreme commandment is considered to be: "Thou shalt not disfigure the soul."

ORNITHOPTER (commonly: 'thopter): any aircraft capable of sustained wing-beat flight in the manner of birds.

OUT-FREYN: Galach for "immediately foreign," that is: not of your immediate community, not of the select.

P

PALM LOCK: any lock or seal which may be opened on contact with the palm of the human hand to which it has been keyed.

PAN: on Arrakis, any low-lying region or depression created by the subsiding of the underlying basement complex. (On planets with sufficient water, a pan indicates a region once covered by open water. Arrakis is believed to have at least one such area, although this remains open to argument.)

PANOPLIA PROPHETICUS: term covering the infectious superstitions used by the Bene Gesserit to exploit primitive regions. (*See* Missionaria Protectiva.)

PARACOMPASS: any compass that determines direction by local magnetic anomaly; used where relevant charts are available and where a planet's total magnetic field is unstable or subject to masking by severe magnetic storms.

PENTASHIELD: a five-layer shield-generator field suitable for small areas such as doorways or passages (large reinforcing shields become increasingly unstable with each successive layer) and virtually impassable to anyone not wearing a dissembler tuned to the shield codes. (*See* Prudence Door.)

PLASTEEL: steel which has been stabilized with stravidium fibers grown into its crystal structure.

PLENISCENTA: an exotic green bloom of Ecaz noted for its sweet aroma.

POLING THE SAND: the art of placing plastic and fiber poles in the open desert wastes of Arrakis and reading the patterns etched on the poles by sandstorms as a clue to weather prediction.

PORITRIN: third planet of Epsilon Alangue, considered by many Zensunni Wanderers as their planet of origin, although clues in their language and mythology show far more ancient planetary roots.

PORTYGULS: oranges.

PRANA (Prana-musculature): the body's muscles when considered as units for ultimate training. (*See* Bindu.)

PRE-SPICE MASS: the stage of fungusoid wild growth achieved when water is flooded into the excretions of Little Makers. At this stage, the spice of Arrakis forms a characteristic "blow," exchanging the material from deep underground for the matter on the surface above it. This mass, after exposure to sun and air, becomes melange. (*See also* Melange *and* Water of Life.)

PROCES VERBAL: a semiformal report alleging a crime against the Imperium. Legally: an action falling between a loose verbal allegation and a formal charge of crime.

PROCTOR SUPERIOR: a Bene Gesserit Reverend Mother who is also regional director of a B.G. school. (Commonly: Bene Gesserit with the Sight.)

PRUDENCE DOOR or **PRUDENCE BARRIER** (idiomatically: pru-door or pru-barrier): any pentashield situated for the escape of selected persons under conditions of pursuit. (*See* Pentashield.)

PUNDI RICE: a mutated rice whose grains, high in natural sugar, achieve lengths up to four centimeters; chief export of Caladan.

PYONS: planet-bound peasants or laborers, one of the base classes under the Faufreluches. Legally: wards of the planet.

PYRETIC CONSCIENCE: so-called "conscience of fire"; that inhibitory level touched by Imperial conditioning. (*See* Imperial conditioning.)

Q

QANAT: an open canal for carrying irrigation water under controlled conditions through a desert.

QIRTAIBA: *see* Ibn Qirtaiba.

QUIZARA TAFWID: Fremen priests (after Muad'Dib).

R

RACHAG: a caffeine-type stimulant from the yellow berries of akarso. (*See* Akarso.)

RAMADHAN: ancient religious period marked by fasting and prayer; traditionally, the ninth month of the solar-lunar calendar. Fremen mark the observance according to the ninth meridian-crossing cycle of the first moon.

RAZZIA: a semipiratical guerrilla raid.

RECATHS: body-function tubes linking the human waste disposal system to the cycling filters of a stillsuit.

REPKIT: repair and replacement essentials for a stillsuit.

RESIDUAL POISON: an innovation attributed to the Mentat Piter de Vries whereby the body is impregnated with a substance for which repeated antidotes must be administered. Withdrawal of the antidote at any time brings death.

REVEREND MOTHER: originally, a proctor of the Bene Gesserit, one who has transformed an "illuminating poison" within her body, raising herself to a higher state of awareness. Title adopted by Fremen for their own religious leaders who accomplished a similar "illumination." (*See also* Bene Gesserit *and* Water of Life.)

RICHESE: fourth planet of Eridani A, classed with Ix as supreme in machine culture. Noted for miniaturization. (For a detailed study on how Richese and Ix escaped the more severe effects of the Butlerian Jihad, see *The Last Jihad* by Sumer and Kautman.)

RIMWALL: second upper step of the protecting bluffs on the Shield Wall of Arrakis. (*See* Shield Wall.)

RUH-SPIRIT: in Fremen belief, that part of the individual which is always rooted in (and capable of sensing) the metaphysical world. (*See* Alam al-Mithal.)

S

SADUS: judges. The Fremen title refers to holy judges, equivalent to saints.

SALUSA SECUNDUS: third planet of Gamma Waiping; designated Imperial Prison Planet after removal of the Royal Court to Kaitain. Salusa Secundus is homeworld of House Corrino, and the second stopping point in migrations of the Wandering Zensunni. Fremen tradition says they were slaves on S.S. for nine generations.

SANDCRAWLER: general term for machinery designed to operate on the Arrakis surface in hunting and collecting melange.

SANDMASTER: general superintendent of spice operations.

SANDRIDER: Fremen term for one who is capable of capturing and riding a sandworm.

SANDSNORK: breathing device for pumping surface air into a sand-covered stilltent.

SANDTIDE: idiomatic for a dust tide: the variation in level within certain dust-filled basins on Arrakis due to gravitational effects of sun and satellites. (*See* Tidal Dust Basin.)

SANDWALKER: any Fremen trained to survive in the open desert.

SANDWORM: *see* Shai-hulud.

SAPHO: high-energy liquid extracted from barrier roots of Ecaz. Commonly used by Mentats who claim it amplifies mental powers. Users develop deep ruby stains on mouth and lips.

SARDAUKAR: the soldier-fanatics of the Padishah Emperor. They were men from an environmental background of such ferocity that it killed six out of thirteen persons before the age of eleven. Their military training emphasized ruthlessness and a near-suicidal disregard for personal safety. They were taught from infancy to use cruelty as a standard weapon, weakening opponents with terror. At the apex of their sway over the affairs of the Universe, their swordsmanship was said to match that of the Ginaz tenth level and their cunning abilities at in-fighting were reputed to approach those of a Bene Gesserit adept. Any one of them was rated a match for any ten ordinary Landsraad military conscripts. By the time of Shaddam IV, while they were still formidable, their strength had been sapped by overconfidence, and the sustaining mystique of their warrior religion had been deeply undermined by cynicism.

SARFA: the act of turning away from God.

SAYYADINA: feminine acolyte in the Fremen religious hierarchy.

SCHLAG: animal native to Tupile once hunted almost to extinction for its thin, tough hide.

SECOND MOON: the smaller of the two satellites of Arrakis, noteworthy for the kangaroo mouse figure in its surface markings.

SELAMLIK: Imperial audience chamber.

SEMUTA: the second narcotic derivative (by crystal extraction) from burned residue of elacca wood. The effect (described as timeless, sustained ecstasy) is elicited by certain atonal vibrations referred to as semuta music.

SERVOK: clock-set mechanism to perform simple tasks; one of the limited "automatic" devices permitted after the Butlerian Jihad.

SHADOUT: well-dipper, a Fremen honorific.

SHAH-NAMA: the half-legendary First Book of the Zensunni Wanderers.

SHAI-HULUD: Sandworm of Arrakis, the "Old Man of the Desert," "Old Father Eternity," and "Grandfather of the Desert." Significantly, this name, when referred to in a certain tone or written with capital letters, designates the earth deity of Fremen hearth superstitions. Sandworms grow to enormous size (specimens longer than 400 meters have been seen in the deep desert) and live to great age unless slain by one of their fellows or drowned in water, which is poisonous to them. Most of the sand on Arrakis is credited to sandworm action. (*See* Little Maker.)

SHAITAN: Satan.

SHARI-A: that part of the panoplia propheticus which sets forth the superstitious ritual. (*See* Missionaria Protectiva.)

SHIELD, DEFENSIVE: the protective field produced by a Holtzman generator. This field derives from Phase One of the suspensor-nullification effect. A shield will permit entry only to objects moving at slow speeds (depending on setting, this speed ranges from six to nine centimeters per second) and can be shorted out only by a shire-sized electric field. (*See* Lasgun.)

SHIELD WALL: a mountainous geographic feature in the northern reaches of Arrakis which protects a small area from the full force of the planet's coriolis storms.

SHIGAWIRE: metallic extrusion of a ground vine *(Narvi narviium)* grown only on Salusa Secundus and III Delta Kaising. It is noted for extreme tensile strength.

SIETCH: Fremen: "Place of assembly in time of danger." Because the Fremen lived so long in peril, the term came by general usage to designate any cave warren inhabited by one of their tribal communities.

SIHAYA: Fremen: the desert springtime with religious overtones implying the time of fruitfulness and "the paradise to come."

SINK: a habitable lowland area on Arrakis surrounded by high ground that protects it from the prevailing storms.

SINKCHART: map of the Arrakis surface laid out with reference to the most reliable paracompass routes between places of refuge. (*See* Paracompass.)

SIRAT: the passage in the O.C. Bible that describes human life as a journey across a narrow bridge (the Sirat) with "Paradise on my right, Hell on my left, and the Angel of Death behind."

SLIP-TIP: any thin, short blade (often poison-tipped) for left-hand use in shield fighting.

SNOOPER, POISON: radiation analyzer within the olfactory spectrum and keyed to detect poisonous substances.

SOLARI: official monetary unit of the Imperium, its purchasing power set at quatricentennial negotiations between the Guild, the Landsraad, and the Emperor.

SOLIDO: the three-dimensional image from a solido projector using 360-degree reference signals imprinted on a shigawire reel. Ixian solido projectors are commonly considered the best.

SONDAGI: the fern tulip of Tupali.

SOO-SOO SOOK!: water-seller's cry on Arrakis. Sook is a market place. (*See* Ikhut-eigh!)

SPACING GUILD: *see* Guild.

SPICE: *see* Melange.

SPICE DRIVER: any Dune man who controls and directs movable machinery on the desert surface of Arrakis.

SPICE FACTORY: *see* Sandcrawler.

SPOTTER CONTROL: the light ornithopter in a spice-hunting group charged with control of watch and protection.

STILLSUIT: body-enclosing garment invented on Arrakis. Its fabric is a micro-sandwich performing functions of heat dissipation and filter for bodily wastes. Reclaimed moisture is made available by tube from catchpockets.

STILLTENT: small, sealable enclosure of micro-sandwich fabric designed to reclaim as potable water the ambient moisture discharged within it by the breath of its occupants.

STUNNER: slow-pellet projectile weapon throwing a poison- or drug-tipped dart. Effectiveness limited by variations in shield settings and relative motion between target and projectile.

SUBAKH UL KUHAR: "Are you well?": a Fremen greeting.

SUBAKH UN NAR: "I am well. And you?": traditional reply.

SUSPENSOR: secondary (low-drain) phase of a Holtzman field generator. It nullifies gravity within certain limits prescribed by relative mass and energy consumption.

T

TAHADDI AL-BURHAN: an ultimate test from which there can be no appeal (usually because it brings death or destruction).

TAHADDI CHALLENGE: Fremen challenge to mortal combat, usually to test some primal issue.

TAQWA: literally: "The price of freedom." Something of great value. That which a deity demands of a mortal (and the fear provoked by the demand).

TAU, THE: in Fremen terminology, that *oneness* of a sietch community enhanced by spice diet and especially the tau orgy of oneness elicited by drinking the Water of Life.

TEST-MASHAD: any test in which honor (defined as spiritual standing) is at stake.

THUMPER: short stake with spring-driven clapper at one end. The purpose: to be driven into the sand and set "thumping" to summon shai-hulud. (*See* Maker hooks.)

TIDAL DUST BASIN: any of the extensive depressions in the surface of Arrakis which have been filled with dust over the centuries and in which actual dust tides (*see* Sandtide) have been measured.

TLEILAX: lone planet of Thalim, noted as renegade training center for Mentats; source of "twisted" Mentats.

T-P: idiomatic for telepathy.

TRAINING: when applied to Bene Gesserit, this otherwise common term assumes special meaning, referring to that conditioning of nerve and muscle (*see* Bindu *and* Prana) which is carried to the last possible notch permitted by natural function.

TROOP CARRIER: any Guild ship designed specifically for transport of troops between planets.

TRUTHSAYER: a Reverend Mother qualified to enter truthtrance and detect insincerity or falsehood.

TRUTHTRANCE: semihypnotic trance induced by one of several "awareness spectrum" narcotics in which the petit betrayals of deliberate falsehood are apparent to the truthtrance observer. (Note: "awareness spectrum" narcotics are frequently fatal except to desensitized individuals capable of transforming the poison-configuration within their own bodies.)

TUPILE: so-called "sanctuary planet" (probably several planets) for defeated Houses of the Imperium. Location(s) known only to the Guild and maintained inviolate under the Guild Peace.

U

ULEMA: a Zensunni doctor of theology.

UMMA: one of the brotherhood of prophets. (A term of scorn in the Imperium, meaning any "wild" person given to fanatical prediction.)

UROSHNOR: one of several sounds empty of general meaning and which Bene Gesserit implant within the psyches of selected victims for purposes of control. The sensitized person, hearing the sound, is temporarily immobilized.

USUL: Fremen: "The base of the pillar."

V

VAROTA: famed maker of balisets; a native of Chusuk.

VERITE: one of the Ecaz will-destroying narcotics. It renders a person incapable of falsehood.

VOICE: that combined training originated by the Bene Gesserit which permits an adept to control others merely by selected tone shadings of the voice.

W

WALI: an untried Fremen youth.

WALLACH IX: ninth planet of Laoujin, site of the Mother School of the Bene Gesserit.

WAR OF ASSASSINS: the limited form of warfare permitted under the Great Convention and the Guild Peace. The aim is to reduce involvement of innocent bystanders. Rules prescribe formal declaration of intent and restrict permissible weapons.

WATER BURDEN: Fremen: a mortal obligation.

WATERCOUNTERS: metal rings of different size, each designating a specific amount of water payable out of Fremen stores. Watercounters have profound significance (far beyond the idea of money) especially in birth, death, and courtship ritual.

WATER DISCIPLINE: that harsh training which fits the inhabitants of Arrakis for existence there without wasting moisture.

WATERMAN: a Fremen consecrated for and charged with the ritual duties surrounding water and the Water of Life.

WATER OF LIFE: an "illuminating" poison (*see* Reverend Mother). Specifically, that liquid exhalation of a sandworm (*see* Shai-hulud) produced at the moment of its death from drowning which is changed within the body of a Reverend Mother to become the narcotic used in the sietch tau orgy. An "awareness spectrum" narcotic.

WATERTUBE: any tube within a stillsuit or stilltent that carries reclaimed water into a catchpocket or from the catchpocket to the wearer.

WAY, BENE GESSERIT: use of the minutiae of observation.

WEATHER SCANNER: a person trained in the special methods of predicting weather on Arrakis, including ability to pole the sand and read the wind patterns.

WEIRDING: idiomatic: that which partakes of the mystical or of witchcraft.

WINDTRAP: a device placed in the path of a prevailing wind and capable of precipitating moisture from the air caught within it, usually by a sharp and distinct drop in temperature within the trap.

Y

YA HYA CHOUHADA: "Long live the fighters!" The Fedaykin battle cry. Ya (now) in this cry is augmented by the hya form (the ever-extended now). Chouhada (fighters) carries this added meaning of fighters *against* injustice. There is a distinction in this word that specifies the fighters are not struggling *for* anything, but are consecrated *against* a specific thing—that alone.

YALI: a Fremen's personal quarters within the sietch.

YA! YA! YAWM!: Fremen chanting cadence used in time of deep ritual significance. Ya carries the root meaning of "Now pay attention!" The yawm form is a modified term calling for urgent immediacy. The chant is usually translated as "Now, hear this!"

Z

ZENSUNNI: followers of a schismatic sect that broke away from the teachings of Maometh (the so-called "Third Muhammed") about 1381 B.G. The Zensunni religion is noted chiefly for its emphasis on the mystical and a reversion to "the ways of the fathers." Most scholars name Ali Ben Ohashi as leader of the original schism but there is some evidence that Ohashi may have been merely the male spokesman for his second wife, Nisai.

CARTOGRAPHIC NOTES

Baseline for altitude determination: the Great Bled.

Basis for latitude: meridian through Observatory Mountain.

Polar Sink: 500 m. below Bled level.

Carthag: about 200 km. northeast of Arrakeen.

Cave of Birds: in Habbanya Ridge.

Funeral Plain: open erg.

Great Bled: open, flat desert, as opposed to the erg-dune area. Open desert runs from about 60° north to 70° south. It is mostly sand and rock, with occasional outcroppings of basement complex.

Great Flat: an open depression of rock blending into erg. It lies about 100 m. above the Bled. Somewhere in the Flat is the salt pan which Pardot Kynes (father of Liet-Kynes) discovered. There are rock outcroppings rising to 200 m. from Sietch Tabr south to the indicated sietch communities.

Harg Pass: the Shrine of Leto's skull overlooks this pass.

Old Gap: a crevasse in the Arrakeen Shield Wall down to 2240 m.; blasted out by Paul-Muad'Dib.

Palmaries of the South: do not appear on this map. They lie at about 40° south latitude.

Red Chasm: 1582 m. below Bled level.

Rimwall West: a high scarp (4600 m.) rising out of the Arrakeen Shield Wall.

Wind Pass: cliff-walled, this opens into the sink villages.

Wormline: indicating farthest north points where worms have been recorded. (Moisture, not cold, is determining factor.)

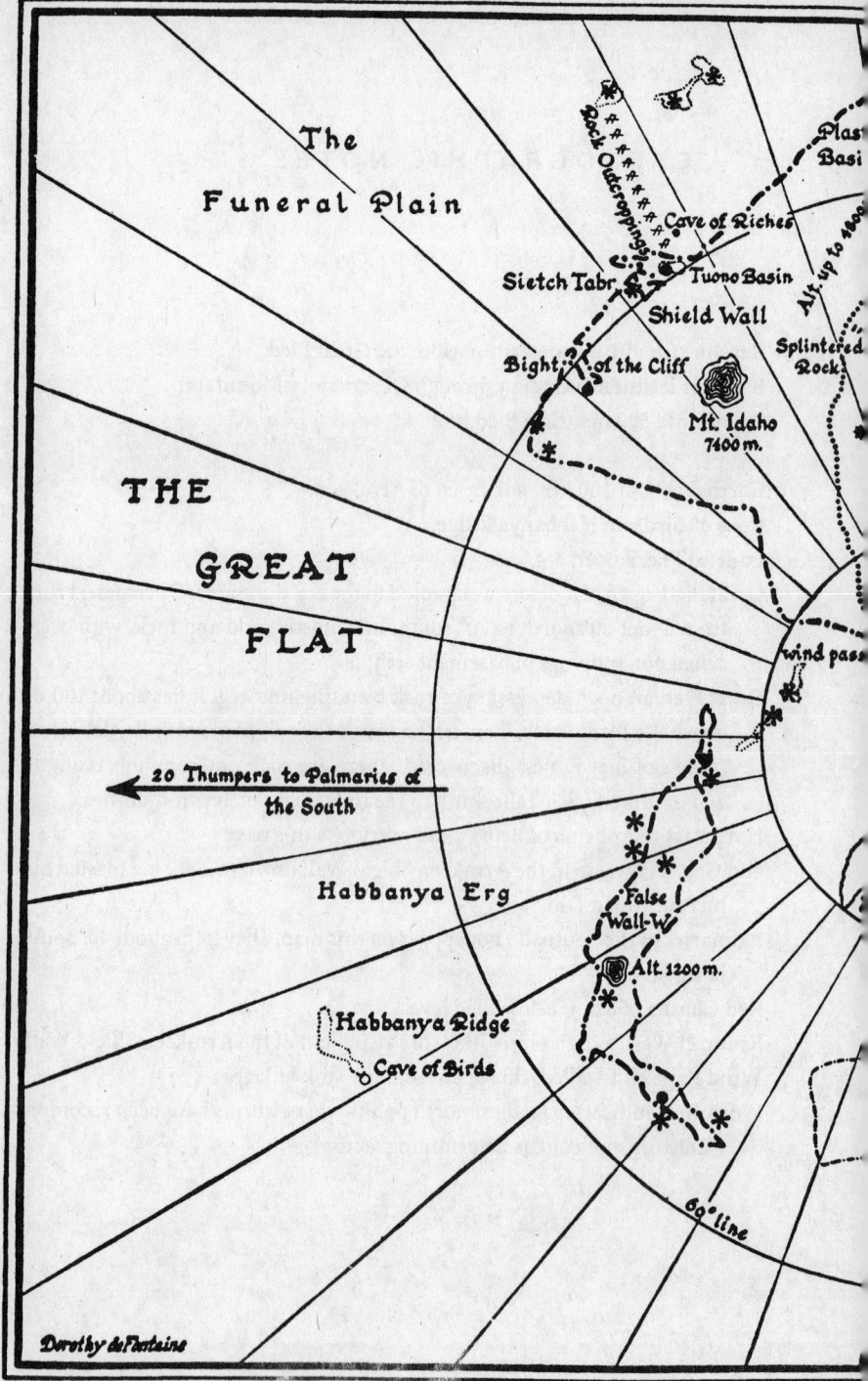

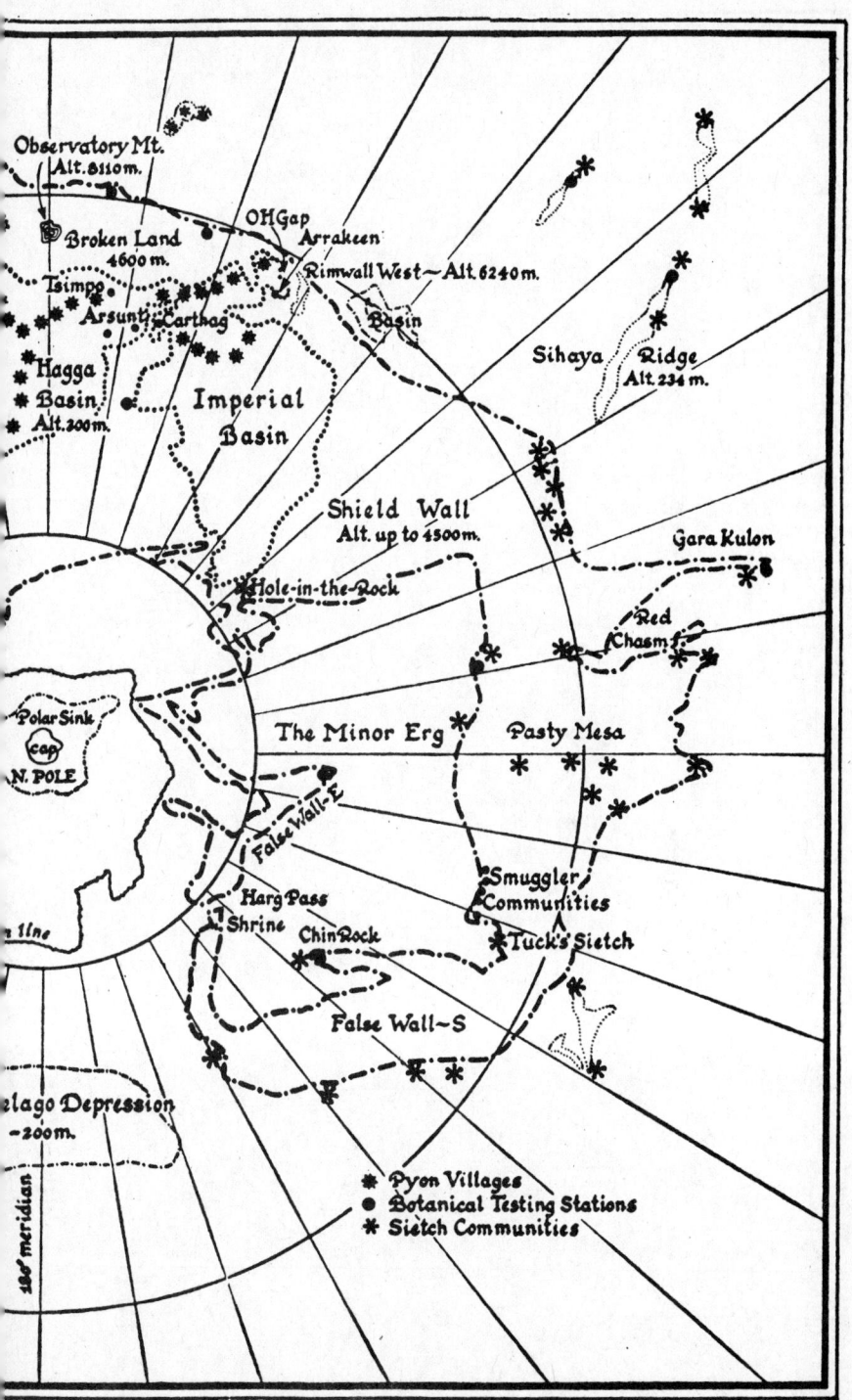

AFTERWORD

by Brian Herbert

I knew Frank Herbert for more than thirty-eight years. He was a magnificent human being, a man of great honor and distinction, and the most interesting person at any gathering, drawing listeners around him like a magnet. To say he was an intellectual giant would be an understatement, since he seemed to contain all of the knowledge of the universe in his marvelous mind. He was my father, and I loved him deeply.

Nonetheless, a son's journey to understand the legendary author was not always a smooth one, as I described in my biography of him, *Dreamer of Dune*. Growing up in Frank Herbert's household, I did not understand his need for absolute silence so that he could concentrate, the intense desire he had to complete his important writing projects, or the confidence he had that one day his writing would be a success, despite the steady stream of rejections that he received. To my young eyes, the characters he created in *Dune* and his other stories were the children of his mind, and they competed with me for his affections. In the years it took him to write his magnum opus, he spent more time with Paul Atreides than he did with me. Dad's study was off-limits to me, to my sister Penny, and to my brother Bruce. In those days, only my mother Beverly really understood Dad's complexities. Ultimately, it was through her love for him, and the love he gave back to her, that I came to see the nurturing, loving side of the man.

By that time I was in my mid-twenties, having rebelled against his exacting ways for years. When I finally saw the soul of my father and began to appreciate him for the care he gave my mother when she was terminally ill, he and I became the best of friends. He helped me with my own writing career by showing me what editors wanted to see in books; he taught me how to construct interesting characters, how to build suspense, how to keep readers turning the pages. After perusing an early draft of *Sidney's Comet* (which would become my first published novel), he marked up several pages and then wrote me this note: "These pages . . . show how editing tightens the story. Go now and do likewise." It was his way of telling me that he could open the door for me and let me peek through, but I would have to complete the immense labors involved with writing myself.

Beverly Herbert was the window into Frank Herbert's soul. He shared that reality with millions of readers when he wrote a loving, three-page tribute to her at the end of *Chapterhouse: Dune*, describing their life together. His writing companion and intellectual equal, she suggested the title for that book, and she died in 1984 while he was writing it. Earlier in *Dune*, Frank Herbert had modeled Lady Jessica Atreides after Beverly Herbert, with her dignified, gentle ways of influence, and even her prescient abilities, which my mother actually possessed. He also wrote of "Lady Jessica's latent (prophetic) abilities," and in this he was describing my mother, thinking of all the amazing paranormal feats she had accomplished in her lifetime. In an endearing tone, he often referred to her as his "white witch," or good witch. Similarly, throughout the Dune series, he described the heroic Bene Gesserit women as "witches."

Dune is the most admired science fiction novel ever written and has sold tens of millions of copies all over the world, in more than twenty languages. It is to science fiction what the Lord of the Rings trilogy is to fantasy, the most highly regarded, respected works in their respective genres. Of course, *Dune* is not just science fiction. It includes strong elements of fantasy and contains so many important layers beneath the story line that it has become a mainstream classic. As one dimension of this, just look at the cover on the book in your hands, the quiet dignity expressed in the artwork.

The novel was first published in hardcover in 1965 by Chilton Books, best known for their immense auto-repair novels. No other publisher would touch the book, in part because of the length of the manuscript. They felt it was far too long at 215,000 words, when most novels of the day were only a quarter to a third that length. *Dune* would require immense printing costs and a high hardcover price for the time, in excess of five dollars. No science fiction novel had ever commanded a retail price that high.

Publishers also expressed concern about the complexity of the novel and all of the new, exotic words that the author introduced in the beginning, which tended to slow the story down. One editor said that he could not get through the first hundred pages without becoming confused and irritated. Another said that he might be making a huge mistake in turning the book down, but he did so anyway.

Initial sales of the book were slow, but Frank Herbert's science fiction–writing peers and readers recognized the genius of the work from the beginning, awarding it the coveted Nebula and Hugo awards for best novel of the year. It was featured in *The Whole Earth Catalog* and began to receive excellent reviews, including one from the *New York Times*. A groundswell of support was building.

In 1969, Frank Herbert published the first sequel, *Dune Messiah*, in which he warned about the dangers of following a charismatic leader and showed the dark side of Paul Atreides. Many fans didn't understand this message, because they didn't want to see their superhero brought down from his pedestal. Still, the book sold well, and so did its predecessor. Looking back at *Dune*, it is clear that Dad laid the seeds of the troublesome direction he intended to take with his hero, but a lot of readers didn't want to see it. John W. Campbell, the editor of *Analog* who made many useful suggestions when *Dune* was being serialized, did not like *Dune Messiah* because of this Paul Atreides issue.

Having studied politics carefully, my father believed that heroes made mistakes . . . mistakes that were amplified by the number of people who followed such leaders slavishly. In a foreshadowing epigraph, Frank Herbert wrote in *Dune*: "Remember, we speak now of the Muad'Dib who ordered battle drums made from his enemies' skins, the Muad'Dib who denied the conventions of his ducal past with a wave of the hand, saying merely: 'I am the Kwisatz Haderach. That is reason enough.'" And in a dramatic scene, as Liet-Kynes lay dying in the desert, he remembered the long-ago words of his own father: "No more terrible disaster could befall your people than for them to fall into the hands of a Hero."

By the early 1970s, sales of *Dune* began to accelerate, largely because the novel was heralded as an environmental handbook, warning about the dangers of destroying the Earth's finite resources. Frank Herbert spoke to more than 30,000 people at the first Earth Day in Philadelphia, and he toured the country, speaking to enthusiastic college audiences. The environmental movement was sweeping the nation, and Dad rode the crest of the wave, a breathtaking trip. When he published *Children of Dune* in 1976, it became a runaway bestseller, hitting every important list in the country.

Children of Dune was the first science fiction novel to become a *New York Times* bestseller in both hardcover and paperback, and sales reached into the millions. After that, other science fiction writers began to have their own bestsellers, but Frank Herbert was the first to obtain such a high level of readership; he brought science fiction out of the ghetto of literature. By 1979, *Dune* itself had sold more than 10 million copies, and sales kept climbing. In early 1985, shortly after David Lynch's movie *Dune* was released, the paperback version of the novel reached #1 on the *New York Times* bestseller list. This was a phenomenal accomplishment, occurring twenty years after its first publication, and sales remain brisk today.

IN 1957, DAD FLEW TO THE OREGON COAST TO WRITE A MAGAZINE article about a U.S. Department of Agriculture project there, in which the government had successfully planted poverty grasses on the crests of sand dunes, to keep them from inundating highways. He intended to call the article "They Stopped the Moving Sands," but soon realized that he had a much bigger story on his hands.

Frank Herbert's life experiences are layered into the pages of the Dune series, combined with an eclectic assortment of fascinating ideas that sprang from his researches. Among other things, the Dune universe is a spiritual melting pot, a far future in which religious beliefs have combined into interesting forms. Discerning readers will recognize Buddhism, Sufi Mysticism and other Islamic belief systems, Catholicism, Protestantism, Judaism, and Hinduism. In the San Francisco Bay Area, my father even knew Zen Master Alan Watts, who lived on an old ferryboat. Dad drew on a variety of religious influences, without adhering to any one of them. Consistent with this, the stated purpose of the Commission of Ecumenical Translators, as described in an appendix to *Dune*, was to eliminate arguments between religions, each of which claimed to have "the one and only revelation."

When he was a boy, eight of Dad's Irish Catholic aunts tried to force Catholicism on him, but he resisted. Instead, this became the genesis of the Bene Gesserit Sisterhood. This fictional organization would claim it did not believe in organized religion, but the sisters were spiritual nonetheless. Both my father and mother were like that as well.

During the 1950s, Frank Herbert was a political speechwriter and publicity writer for U.S. senatorial and congressional candidates. In that decade, he also journeyed twice to Mexico with his family, where he studied desert conditions and crop cycles, and was subjected unwittingly to the effects of a hallucinogenic drug. All of those experiences, and a great deal from his childhood, found their way onto the pages of *Dune*. The novel became as complex and multilayered as Frank Herbert himself.

As I said in *Dreamer of Dune*, the characters in *Dune* fit mythological archetypes. Paul is the hero prince on a quest who weds the daughter of a "king" (he marries Princess Irulan, whose father is the Emperor Shaddam Corrino IV). Reverend Mother Gaius Helen Mohiam is a witch mother archetype, while Paul's sister Alia is a virgin witch, and Pardot Kynes is the wise old man of Dune mythology. Beast Rabban Harkonnen, though evil and aggressive, is essentially a fool.

For the names of heroes, Frank Herbert selected from Greek mythology and other mythological bases. The Greek House Atreus, upon which House Atreides in *Dune* was based, was the ill-fated family of kings Menelaus and Agamemnon. A heroic family, it was beset by tragic flaws and burdened with a curse pronounced against it by Thyestes. This foreshadows the troubles Frank Herbert had in mind for the Atreides family. The evil Harkonnens of *Dune* are related to the Atreides by blood, so when they assassinate Paul's father Duke Leto, it is kinsmen against kinsmen, similar to what occurred in the household of Agamemnon when he was murdered by his wife Clytemnestra.

Dune is a modern-day conglomeration of familiar myths, a tale in which great sandworms guard a precious treasure of melange, the geriatric spice that represents, among other things, the finite resource of oil. The planet Arrakis features immense, ferocious worms that are like dragons of lore, with "great teeth" and a "bellows breath of cinnamon." This resembles the myth described by an unknown English poet in *Beowulf*, the compelling tale of a fearsome fire dragon who guarded a great treasure hoard in a lair under cliffs, at the edge of the sea.

The desert of Frank Herbert's classic novel is a vast ocean of sand, with giant worms diving into the depths, the mysterious and unrevealed domain of Shai-hulud. Dune tops are like the crests of waves, and there are powerful sandstorms out there, creating extreme danger. On Arrakis, life is said to emanate from the Maker (Shai-hulud) in the desert-sea; similarly all life on Earth is believed to have evolved from our oceans. Frank Herbert drew parallels, used spectacular metaphors, and extrapolated present conditions into world systems that seem entirely alien at first blush. But close examination reveals they aren't so different from systems we know . . . and the book characters of his imagination are not so different from people familiar to us.

Paul Atreides (who is the messianic "Muad'Dib" to the Fremen) resembles Lawrence of Arabia (T. E. Lawrence), a British citizen who led Arab forces in a successful desert revolt against the Turks during World War I. Lawrence employed guerrilla tactics to destroy enemy forces and communication lines, and came close to becoming a messiah figure for the Arabs. This historical event led Frank Herbert to consider the possibility of an outsider leading native forces against the morally corrupt occupiers of a desert world, in the process becoming a godlike figure to them.

One time I asked my father if he identified with any of the characters in his stories, and to my surprise he said it was Stilgar, the rugged leader of the Fremen. I had been thinking of Dad more as the dignified, honorable Duke Leto, or the heroic, swashbuckling Paul, or the loyal Duncan Idaho. Mulling this over, I realized Stilgar was the equivalent of a Native American chief in *Dune*—a person who represented and defended time-honored ways that did not harm the ecology of the planet. Frank Herbert was that, and a great deal more. As a child, he had known a Native American who hinted that he had been banished from his tribe, a man named Indian Henry who taught my father some of the ways of his people, including fishing, the identification of edible and medicinal plants in the forest, and how to find red ants and protein-rich grub worms for food.

When he set up the desert planet of Arrakis and the galactic empire encompassing it, Frank Herbert pitted western culture against primitive culture and gave the nod to the latter. In *Dune* he wrote, "Polish comes from the cities; wisdom from the desert." (Later, in his mainstream novel *Soul Catcher*, he would do something similar and would favor old ways over modern ways.) Like the nomadic Bedouins of the Arabian plateau, the Fremen live an admirable, isolated existence, separated from civilization by vast stretches of desert. The Fremen take psychedelic drugs during religious rites, like the Navajo Indians of North America. And like the Jews, the Fremen have been persecuted, driven to hide from authorities and survive away from their homeland. Both Jews and Fremen expect to be led to the promised land by a messiah.

The words and names in *Dune* are from many tongues, including Navajo, Latin, Chakobsa (a language found in the Caucasus), the Nahuatl dialect of the Aztecs, Greek, Persian, East Indian, Russian, Turkish, Finnish, Old English, and, of course, Arabic.

In *Children of Dune*, Leto II allowed sandtrout to attach themselves to his body, and this was based in part upon my father's own experiences as a boy growing up in Washington State, when he rolled up his trousers and waded into a stream or lake, permitting leeches to attach themselves to his legs.

The legendary life of the divine superhero Muad'Dib is based on themes found in a variety of religious faiths. Frank Herbert even used lore and bits of information from the people of the Gobi Desert in Asia, the Kalahari Desert in Southwest Africa, and the aborigines of the Australian Outback. For centuries such people have survived on very small amounts of water, in environments where water is a more precious resource than gold.

The Butlerian Jihad, occurring ten thousand years before the events described in *Dune*, was a war against thinking machines who at one time had cruelly enslaved humans. For this reason, computers were eventually made illegal by humans, as decreed in the Orange Catholic Bible: "Thou shalt not make a machine in the likeness of a human mind." The roots of the jihad went back to individuals my parents knew, to my mother's grandfather Cooper Landis and to our family friend Ralph Slattery, both of whom abhorred machines.

Still, there are computers in the Dune universe, long after the jihad. As the series unfolds, it is revealed that the Bene Gesserits have secret computers to keep track of their breeding records. And the Mentats of *Dune*, capable of supreme logic, are "human computers." In large part these human calculators were based upon my father's paternal grandmother, Mary Stanley, an illiterate Kentucky hill-woman who performed incredible mathematical calculations in her head. Mentats were the precursors of *Star Trek*'s Spock, First Officer of the starship *Enterprise* . . . and Frank Herbert described the dangers of thinking machines back in the 1960s, years before Arnold Schwarzenegger's Terminator movies.

Remarkably, no aliens inhabit the Dune universe. Even the most exotic of creatures, the mutant Guild Navigators, are humans. So are the vile genetic wizards, the Tleilaxu, and the gholas grown in their flesh vats. Among the most unusual humans to spring from Frank Herbert's imagination, the women of the Bene Gesserit Sisterhood have a collective memory—a concept based largely upon the writings and teachings of Carl Gustav Jung, who spoke of a "collective unconscious," that supposedly inborn set of "contents and modes of behavior" possessed by all human beings. These were concepts my father discussed at length with Ralph Slattery's wife Irene, a psychologist who had studied with Jung in Switzerland in the 1930s.

Frank Herbert's life reached a crescendo in the years after 1957, when he focused his unusual experiences and knowledge on creating his great novel. In the massive piles of books he read to research *Dune*, he recalled reading somewhere that ecology was the science of understanding consequences. This was not his original concept, but as he learned from Ezra Pound, he "made it new" and put it in a form that was palatable to millions of people. With a worldview similar to that of an American Indian, Dad saw western man inflicting himself on the environment, not living in harmony with it.

Despite all the work *Dune* required, my father said it was his favorite book to write. He used what he called a "technique of enormous detail," in which he studied and prepared notes over a four-year period, between 1957 and 1961, then wrote and rewrote the book between 1961 and 1965.

As Dad expanded and contracted the manuscript, depending upon which editor was giving him advice, an error found its way into the final manuscript. The age of Emperor Shaddam Corrino IV is slightly inconsistent in the novel, but it is one of the few glitches in the entire Dune series. This is remarkable, considering the fact that Frank Herbert wrote the books on typewriters . . . more than a million words without the use of a computer to keep all of the information straight.

Late in 1961, in the midst of his monumental effort, Dad fired his literary agent Lurton Blassingame, because he didn't feel the agent was supportive enough and because he couldn't bear the thought of sending any more stories into the New York publishing industry, which had been rejecting him for years. A couple of years later, when the new novel was nearly complete, he got back together with Blassingame and went through the ordeal of rejection after rejection—more than twenty of them—until Chilton finally picked up the book and paid an advance of $7,500 for it.

If not for a farsighted editor at Chilton, Sterling Lanier, *Dune* might never have been published, and world literature would be the poorer for it.

WHEN MY FATHER AND I BECAME CLOSE IN MY ADULTHOOD AND WE began to write together, he spoke to me often of the importance of detail, of density of writing. A student of psychology, he understood the subconscious, and liked to say that *Dune* could be read on any of several layers that were nested beneath the adventure story of a messiah on a desert planet. Ecology is the most obvious layer, but alongside that are politics, religion, philosophy, history, human evolution, and even poetry. *Dune* is a marvelous tapestry of words, sounds, and images. Sometimes he wrote passages in poetry first, which he expanded and converted to prose, forming sentences that included elements of the original poems.

Dad told me that you could follow any of the novel's layers as you read it, and then start the book all over again, focusing on an entirely different layer. At the end of the book, he intentionally left loose ends and said he did this to send the readers spinning out of the story with bits and pieces of it still clinging to them, so that they would want to go back and read it again. A neat trick, and he pulled it off perfectly.

As his eldest son, I see familial influences in the story. Earlier, I noted that my mother is memorialized in *Dune* and so is Dad. He must have been thinking of himself when he wrote that Duke Leto's "qualities as a father have long been overlooked." The words have deep significance to me, because at the time he and I were not getting along well at all. I was going through a rebellious teenage phase, reacting to the uncompromising manner in which he ruled the household.

At the beginning of *Dune*, Paul Atreides is fifteen years old, around the same age I was at the time the book was first serialized in *Analog*. I do not see myself much in the characterization of Paul, but I do see Dad in Paul's father, the noble Duke Leto Atreides. In one passage, Frank Herbert wrote: "Yet many facts open the way to this Duke: his abiding love for his Bene Gesserit lady; the dreams he held for his son . . ." Late in his life, Dad responded to interview questions about my own writing career by saying,

"The acorn doesn't fall far from the oak tree." He often complimented me to others, more than he did to me directly. To most of his friends he seemed like an extrovert, but in family matters he was often quite the opposite, preferring to retire to his study. Frequently, his strongest emotions went on the page, so I often feel him speaking to me as I read his stories.

Once, I asked my father if he thought his magnum opus would endure. He said modestly that he didn't know and that the only valid literary critic was time. *Dune* was first published in 1965, and Frank Herbert would be pleased to know that interest in his fantastic novel, and the series it spawned, has never waned. An entire new generation of readers is picking up *Dune* and enjoying it, just as their parents did before them.

Like our own universe, the universe of Dune continues to expand. Frank Herbert wrote six novels in the series, and I have written a number of others in collaboration with Kevin J. Anderson, including the dramatic final chapter in the Dune series. Frank Herbert was working on that project when he died in 1986, and it would have been the third book in a trilogy that he began with *Heretics of Dune* and *Chapterhouse: Dune*. In those novels he set up a great mystery, and now, decades after his death, the solution is the most closely guarded secret in science fiction.

By the time we complete those stories, there will be a wealth of Dune novels, along with the 1984 movie directed by David Lynch and two television miniseries—"Frank Herbert's Dune" and "Frank Herbert's Children of Dune"—both produced by Richard Rubinstein. As of December 2017, there is a new feature film of *Dune* in development with Legendary Entertainment. The Oscar-nominated director Denis Villeneuve is working on the project, along with the Oscar-winning screenwriter Eric Roth. We envision other projects in the future, but all of them must measure up to the lofty standard that my father established with his own novels. When all of the good stories have been told, the series will end. But that will not really be a conclusion, because we can always go back to *Dune* itself and read it again and again.

BRIAN HERBERT
SEATTLE, WASHINGTON

FRANK HERBERT is the bestselling author of the Dune saga. He was born in Tacoma, Washington, and educated at the University of Washington, Seattle. He worked a wide variety of jobs—including TV cameraman, radio commentator, oyster diver, jungle survival instructor, lay analyst, creative writing teacher, reporter, and editor of several West Coast newspapers—before becoming a full-time writer.

In 1952, Herbert began publishing science fiction with "Looking for Something?" in *Startling Stories*. But his emergence as a writer of major stature did not occur until 1965, with the publication of *Dune*. This was followed by *Dune Messiah, Children of Dune, God Emperor of Dune, Heretics of Dune,* and *Chapterhouse: Dune* to complete the bestselling saga. Herbert is also the author of some twenty other books, including *The White Plague, The Dosadi Experiment,* and *Destination: Void*. He died in 1986.

THE DUNE CHRONICLES

BY FRANK HERBERT

AVAILABLE NOW FROM

CHILDREN OF DUNE

"A major event."
—Los Angeles Times

"Ranging from palace intrigue and desert chases to religious speculation and confrontations with the supreme intelligence of the universe,
there is something here for all science fiction fans."
—Publishers Weekly

"Herbert adds enough new twists and turns to the ongoing saga that
familiarity with the recurring elements brings pleasure."
—Challenging Destiny

GOD EMPEROR OF DUNE

"Rich fare. . . . Heady stuff."
—Los Angeles Times

"A fourth visit to distant Arrakis that is every bit as fascinating as the
other three—every bit as timely."
—Time

"Book four of the Dune series has many of the same strengths as the
previous three, and I was indeed kept up late at night."
—Challenging Destiny

HERETICS OF DUNE

"A monumental piece of imaginative architecture . . . indisputably magical." —*Los Angeles Herald Examiner*

"Appealing and gripping. . . . Fascinating detail, yet cloaked in mystery and mysticism." —*The Milwaukee Journal*

"Herbert works wonders with some new speculation and an entirely new batch of characters. He weaves together several fascinating story lines with almost the same mastery as informed *Dune*, and keeps the reader intent on the next revelation or twist." —*Challenging Destiny*

CHAPTERHOUSE: DUNE

"Compelling . . . a worthy addition to this durable and deservedly popular series." —*The New York Times*

"The vast and fascinating Dune saga sweeps on—as exciting and gripping as ever." —*Kirkus Reviews*

THE DUNE CHRONICLES BY FRANK HERBERT

DUNE

DUNE MESSIAH

CHILDREN OF DUNE

GOD EMPEROR OF DUNE

HERETICS OF DUNE

CHAPTERHOUSE: DUNE

OTHER BOOKS BY FRANK HERBERT

THE BOOK OF FRANK HERBERT

DESTINATION: VOID
(revised edition)

DIRECT DESCENT

THE DOSADI EXPERIMENT

EYE

THE EYES OF HEISENBERG

THE GODMAKERS

THE GREEN BRAIN

THE MAKER OF DUNE

THE SANTAROGA BARRIER

SOUL CATCHER

WHIPPING STAR

THE WHITE PLAGUE

THE WORLDS OF FRANK HERBERT

MAN OF TWO WORLDS
(with Brian Herbert)

BOOKS BY FRANK HERBERT AND BILL RANSOM

THE JESUS INCIDENT

THE LAZARUS EFFECT

THE ASCENSION FACTOR

CHAPTERHOUSE:
DUNE

BOOK SIX IN THE DUNE CHRONICLES

FRANK HERBERT

With an Introduction by
BRIAN HERBERT

ACE
NEW YORK

ACE
Published by Berkley
An imprint of Penguin Random House LLC
penguinrandomhouse.com

ISBN: 9780593201770

The Library of Congress has catalogued the hardcover edition
of this book as follows:

Herbert, Frank.
Chapterhouse Dune / Frank Herbert ; with a new introduction
by Brian Herbert.—Ace hardcover ed.
p. cm.—(Dune chronicles ; bk. 6)
ISBN 9780441017218
1. Dune (Imaginary place)—Fiction.   I. Title.
PS3558.E63C48 2009
813'.54—dc22

G. P. Putnam's Sons hardcover edition / April 1985
Berkley trade paperback edition / October 1986
Ace mass-market edition / July 1987
Ace hardcover edition / August 2009
Ace premium edition / June 2019
Ace trade paperback edition / July 2020

Printed in the United States of America
7th Printing

Cover design and illustration by Jim Tierney
Interior art: Desert Cave © masher/Shutterstock Images
Book design by Kristin del Rosario

INTRODUCTION
by Brian Herbert

Chapterhouse: Dune is set thousands of years in mankind's future, when the known universe is ruled by women. It is a fascinating milieu, populated by gholas grown from dead human cells, as well as shape-shifting Face Dancers, half-human Futars, cloned humans, and mutant, conspiratorial Guild Navigators. There are immense Heighliners that fold space to traverse vast distances in the blink of an eye, along with nearly invisible no-ships and no-chambers that contain mysterious machinery.

As the novel opens, the planet Dune has already been destroyed by Honored Matres, powerful, enigmatic women who emerged from the Scattering that the God Emperor set into motion long ago in order to spread humankind across uncounted star systems. On planet Chapterhouse, the Bene Gesserit Sisterhood has a giant sandworm, obtained surreptitiously, that is metamorphosing into sandtrout. Thus the Sisters have initiated a desertification process that could result in a new Dune, and a new source of the priceless spice melange, a finite resource that they need and hope to control . . .

This is the sixth novel in Frank Herbert's classic, wildly popular science fiction series, and the last story in the highly imaginative Dune universe that he wrote. He typed much of the novel at his home in Hawaii, where he tended to the serious medical needs of my mother, Beverly Herbert. A professional writer herself, she helped with the plotting of the book and provided him with the title before she passed away in 1984. My father did not complete the writing task, however, until after her death, when he returned to Washington State.

It is impossible for me to read *Chapterhouse: Dune*, or to even think about it, without experiencing powerful reminders of my mother and the relationship she had with my father for almost four decades. An extraordinary woman, she was the basis of the literary character Lady Jessica in the first three novels of the Dune series, and the source of many of the aphorisms that are so familiar to Dune fans. The strong presence of women later in the epic saga—particularly in the fifth and sixth novels—stemmed from her as well.

As their son, I watched my parents interact and strengthen each other in countless ways. I can honestly say that I never heard them raise their voices to each other, though they did have subtle disagreements that others might not have noticed. The words and signs that passed between them were on a different, barely perceptible level. My parents were symbiotic, highly intelligent human organisms, so closely linked that thoughts seemed to pass between them as if contained within one mind.

Frank Herbert's best friend, Howie Hansen, put it this way: "There are two Frank Herberts—the one I knew prior to Bev and the one that you know who was created by Bev. Frank Herbert the author would not exist had there not been a Beverly [Herbert] to marry him and . . . coalesce him mentally . . ."

After my mother passed away in Hawaii, Dad wrote a long and poignant tribute to her that is published at the end of *Chapterhouse: Dune*, describing their life together and what they meant to each other. For years afterward, I thought that this moving testimonial was the best place to conclude the entire series. After all, they had been a writing team and had embarked on their marriage in 1946 with dreams that both of them would become successful writers. They achieved that, and along the way they shared numerous great adventures together—a remarkable story of love and sacrifice that I described in *Dreamer of Dune* (2003), the biography of Frank Herbert.

Chapterhouse: Dune carries on the suspense-filled account of the destructive Honored Matres that was begun in *Heretics of Dune*. Brutal women who are rumored to be renegade Bene Gesserit, they threaten to obliterate the ancient Sisterhood, and a great deal more. They seem unstoppable. And yet there is something else out there in the universe that is chasing the Honored Matres, but its identity is unrevealed by Frank Herbert. Cleverly, the author sprinkled clues throughout the novel about what it might be, and at the end the reader is left wondering and considering the options.

Back in the 1950s and 1960s, Frank Herbert attempted to sell a number of mystery stories and—encouraged by his friend and fellow author Jack Vance—even joined Mystery Writers of America. In 1964, Dad did sell a short story to *Analog*, "The Mary Celeste Move," which was a well-drawn science fiction mystery about the investigation of a peculiar phenomenon of human behavior. Aside from that, however, his mystery-writing efforts in those days went largely unrewarded. He kept running into problems with story length and genre, and publishers were not interested. So back he went to science fiction, where he enjoyed unparalleled success.

After all of the rejections my father suffered with his mysteries, it is particularly interesting and satisfying that he wrote a widely published mystery story and immersed it into the Dune universe. For more than a decade after his death from an illness in 1986, the solution to this mystery was the most intriguing and widely debated subject in science fiction. How fitting this was for the legacy of a man who was so often rejected by publishers and who might never have reached a wide audience if not for the brave editor Sterling Lanier, who took a chance and accepted *Dune* for hardcover publication after more than twenty other editors had turned it down.

Just before Frank Herbert passed away, he seemed to his family like a much younger man than his sixty-five years, filled with boundless enthusiasm and energy. His passing left us with a feeling that he might have accomplished a great deal more in his already productive life if he had only lived longer . . . that even more remarkable achievements might have flowed from the marvelously inventive mind that created the Dune universe, the acclaimed Native American novel *Soul Catcher*, and other memorable novels.

Sadly, the additional works were taken from him. And from us.

My father left loose ends when he died, many uncompleted dreams.

Like the painter Jean Gericault, at the end of his life Dad spoke of all the things he would do when he was well again. He wanted to spend a year in Paris, wanted to be the oldest man to climb Mount Everest. There were more Dune stories to tell, along with an epic novel about Native Americans, and maybe even a movie to direct. But like Gericault, he never got well.

The fifth and sixth novels in Frank Herbert's Dune series—*Heretics of Dune* and *Chapterhouse: Dune*—were intended to be the first two books in a new trilogy that would complete the epic story chronologically. Using my father's outline and notes, I eventually co-wrote the grand climax with Kevin J. Anderson in two novels—*Hunters of Dune* (2006) and *Sandworms of Dune* (2007).

As you read *Chapterhouse: Dune*, look for intriguing clues that Frank Herbert wove into the story. Then go back and reread his preceding five novels in the series, and you'll discover more clues. He left so many possibilities, so many avenues to stretch the imaginations of his readers. Truly, the Dune saga is a tour de force, unmatched in the annals of literature.

BRIAN HERBERT
SEATTLE, WASHINGTON
FEBRUARY 7, 2009

Those who would repeat the past must control the teaching of history.

—BENE GESSERIT CODA

When the ghola-baby was delivered from the first Bene Gesserit axlotl tank, Mother Superior Darwi Odrade ordered a quiet celebration in her private dining room atop Central. It was barely dawn, and the two other members of her Council—Tamalane and Bellonda—showed impatience at the summons, even though Odrade had ordered breakfast served by her personal chef.

"It isn't every woman who can preside at the birth of her own father," Odrade quipped when the others complained they had too many demands on their time to permit of "time-wasting nonsense."

Only aged Tamalane showed sly amusement.

Bellonda held her over-fleshed features expressionless, often her equivalent of a scowl.

Was it possible, Odrade wondered, that Bell had not exorcised resentment of the relative opulence in Mother Superior's surroundings? Odrade's quarters were a distinct mark of her position but the distinction represented her duties more than any elevation over her Sisters. The small dining room allowed her to consult aides during meals.

Bellonda glanced this way and that, obviously impatient to be gone. Much effort had been expended without success in attempts to break through Bellonda's coldly remote shell.

"It felt very odd to hold that baby in my arms and think: *This is my father*," Odrade said.

"I heard you the first time!" Bellonda spoke from the belly, almost a baritone rumbling as though each word caused her vague indigestion.

She understood Odrade's wry jest, though. The old Bashar Miles Teg had, indeed, been the Mother Superior's father. And Odrade herself had collected cells (as fingernail scrapings) to grow this new ghola, part of a long-time "possibility plan" should they ever succeed in duplicating Tleilaxu tanks. But Bellonda would be drummed out of the Bene Gesserit rather than go along with Odrade's comment on the Sisterhood's vital equipment.

"I find this frivolous at such a time," Bellonda said. "Those mad-women hunting us to exterminate us and you want a celebration!"

Odrade held herself to a mild tone with some effort. "If the Honored Matres find us before we are ready perhaps it will be because we failed to keep up our morale."

Bellonda's silent stare directly into Odrade's eyes carried frustrating accusation: *Those terrible women already have exterminated sixteen of our planets!*

Odrade knew it was wrong to think of those planets as Bene Gesserit possessions. The loosely organized confederation of planetary governments assembled after the Famine Times and the Scattering depended heavily on the Sisterhood for vital services and reliable communications, but old factions persisted—CHOAM, Spacing Guild, Tleilaxu, remnant pockets of the Divided God's priesthood, even Fish Speaker auxiliaries and schismatic assemblages. The Divided God had bequeathed humankind a divided empire—all of whose factions were suddenly moot because of rampaging Honored Matre assaults from the Scattering. The Bene Gesserit—holding to most of their old forms—were the natural prime target for attack.

Bellonda's thoughts never strayed far from this Honored Matre threat. It was a weakness Odrade recognized. Sometimes, Odrade hesitated on the point of replacing Bellonda, but even in the Bene Gesserit there were factions these days and no one could deny that Bell was a supreme organizer. Archives had never been more efficient than under her guidance.

As she frequently did, Bellonda without even speaking the words managed to focus Mother Superior's attention on the hunters who stalked them with savage persistence. It spoiled the mood of quiet success Odrade had hoped to achieve this morning.

She forced herself to think of the new ghola. *Teg!* If his original memories could be restored, the Sisterhood once more would have the finest Bashar ever to serve them. A Mentat Bashar! A military genius whose prowess already was the stuff of myths in the Old Empire.

But would even Teg be of use against these women returned from the Scattering?

By whatever gods may be, the Honored Matres must not find us! Not yet!

Teg represented too many disturbing unknowns and possibilities. Mystery surrounded the period before his death in the destruction of Dune. *He did something on Gammu to ignite the unbridled fury of the Honored Matres. His suicidal stand on Dune should not have been enough to bring this berserk response.* There were rumors, bits and pieces from his days on Gammu before the Dune disaster. *He could move too fast for the human eye to see!* Had he done that? Another outcropping of wild abilities in Atreides genes? Mutation? Or just more of the Teg myth? The Sisterhood had to learn as soon as possible.

An acolyte brought in three breakfasts and the sisters ate quickly, as though this interruption must be put behind them without delay because time wasted was dangerous.

Even after the others had gone, Odrade was left with the aftershock of Bellonda's unspoken fears.

And my fears.

She arose and went to the wide window that looked across lower rooftops to part of the ring of orchards and pastures around Central. Late spring and already fruit beginning to form out there. *Rebirth. A new Teg was born today!* No feeling of elation accompanied the thought. Usually she found the view restorative but not this morning.

What are my real strengths? What are my facts?

The resources at a Mother Superior's command were formidable: profound loyalty in those who served her, a military arm under a Teg-trained Bashar (far away now with a large portion of their troops guarding the school planet, Lampadas), artisans and technicians, spies and agents throughout the Old Empire, countless workers who looked to the Sisterhood to protect them from Honored Matres, and all the Reverend Mothers with Other Memories reaching into the dawn of life.

Odrade knew without false pride that she represented the peak of what was strongest in a Reverend Mother. If her personal memories did not provide needed information, she had others around her to fill the gaps. Machine-stored data as well, although she admitted to a native distrust of it.

Odrade found herself tempted to go digging in those other lives she carried as secondary memory—these subterranean layers of awareness. Perhaps she could find brilliant solutions to their predicament in experiences of Others. Dangerous! You could lose yourself for hours, fascinated by the multiplicity of human variations. Better to leave Other Memories balanced in there, ready on demand or intruding out of necessity. Consciousness, that was the fulcrum and her grip on identity.

Duncan Idaho's odd Mentat metaphor helped.

Self-awareness: facing mirrors that pass through the universe, gathering new images on the way—endlessly reflexive. The infinite seen as finite, the analogue of consciousness carrying the sensed bits of infinity.

She had never heard words come closer to her wordless awareness. "Specialized complexity," Idaho called it. "We gather, assemble, and reflect our systems of order."

Indeed, it was the Bene Gesserit view that humans were life designed by evolution to create order.

And how does that help us against these disorderly women who hunt us? What branch of evolution are they? Is evolution just another name for God?

Her Sisters would sneer at such "bootless speculation."

Still, there *might* be answers in Other Memory.

Ahhhh, how seductive!

How desperately she wanted to project her beleaguered self into past identities and feel what it had been to live then. The immediate peril of this enticement chilled her. She felt Other Memory crowding the edges of awareness. *"It was like this!" "No! It was more like this!"* How greedy they were. You had to pick and choose, discreetly animating the past. And was that not the purpose of consciousness, the very essence of being alive?

Select from the past and match it against the present: Learn consequences.

That was the Bene Gesserit view of history, ancient Santayana's words resonating in their lives: *"Those who cannot remember the past are condemned to repeat it."*

The buildings of Central itself, this most powerful of all Bene Gesserit establishments, reflected that attitude wherever Odrade turned. Usiform, that was the commanding concept. Little about any Bene Gesserit working center was allowed to become non-functional, preserved out of nostalgia. The Sisterhood had no need for archeologists. Reverend Mothers embodied history.

Slowly (much slower than usual) the view out her high window produced its calming effect. What her eyes reported, that was Bene Gesserit order.

But Honored Matres could end that order in the next instant. The Sisterhood's situation was far worse than what they had suffered under the Tyrant. Many of the decisions she was forced to make now were odious. Her workroom was less agreeable because of actions taken here.

Write off our Bene Gesserit Keep on Palma?

That suggestion was in Bellonda's morning report waiting on the worktable. Odrade fixed an affirmative notation to it. *"Yes."*

Write it off because Honored Matre attack is imminent and we cannot defend them or evacuate them.

Eleven hundred Reverend Mothers and the Fates alone knew how many acolytes, postulants, and others dead or worse because of that one word. Not to mention all of the "Ordinary lives" existing in the Bene Gesserit shadow.

The strain of such decisions produced a new kind of weariness in Odrade. Was it a weariness of the soul? Did such a thing as a soul exist? She felt deep fatigue where consciousness could not probe. Weary, weary, weary.

Even Bellonda showed the strain and Bell feasted on violence. Tamalane alone appeared above it but that did not fool Odrade. Tam had entered the age of superior observation that lay ahead of all Sisters if they survived into it. Nothing mattered then except observations and judgments. Most of this was never uttered except in fleeting expressions on wrinkled features. Tamalane spoke few words these days, her comments so sparse as to be almost ludicrous:

"Buy more no-ships."

"Brief Sheeana."

"Review Idaho records."

"Ask Murbella."

Sometimes, only grunts issued from her, as though words might betray her.

And always the hunters roamed out there, sweeping space for any clue to the location of Chapterhouse.

In her most private thoughts, Odrade saw the no-ships of Honored Matres as corsairs on those infinite seas between the stars. They flew no black flags with skull and crossbones, but that flag was there nonetheless. Nothing whatsoever romantic about them. *Kill and pillage! Amass your wealth in the blood of others. Drain that energy and build your killer no-ships on ways lubricated with blood.*

And they did not see they would drown in red lubricant if they kept on this course.

There must be furious people out there in that human Scattering where Honored Matres originated, people who live out their lives with a single fixed idea: Get them!

It was a dangerous universe where such ideas were allowed to float around freely. Good civilizations took care that such ideas did not gain energy, did not even get a chance for birth. When they did occur, by chance or accident, they were to be diverted quickly because they tended to gather mass.

Odrade was astonished that the Honored Matres did not see this or, seeing it, ignored it.

"Full-blown hysterics," Tamalane called them.

"Xenophobia," Bellonda disagreed, always correcting, as though control of Archives gave her a better hold on reality.

Both were right, Odrade thought. The Honored Matres behaved hysterically. All *outsiders* were the enemy. The only people they appeared to trust were the men they sexually enslaved, and those only to a limited degree. Constantly testing, according to Murbella (*our only captive Honored Matre*), to see if their hold was firm.

"Sometimes out of mere pique they may eliminate someone just as an example to others." Murbella's words and they forced the question: *Are they making an example of us? "See! This is what happens to those who dare oppose us!"*

Murbella had said, "You've aroused them. Once aroused, they will not desist until they have destroyed you."

Get the outsiders!

Singularly direct. *A weakness in them if we play it right,* Odrade thought.

Xenophobia carried to a ridiculous extreme?

Quite possibly.

Odrade pounded a fist on her worktable, aware that the action would be seen and recorded by Sisters who kept constant watch on Mother Superior's behavior. She spoke aloud then for the omnipresent comeyes and watchdog Sisters behind them.

"We will not sit and wait in defensive enclaves! We've become as fat as Bellonda (and let her fret over that!) thinking we've created an untouchable society and enduring structures."

Odrade swept her gaze around the familiar room.

"This place is one of our weaknesses!"

She took her seat behind the worktable thinking (of all things!) about architecture and community planning. Well, that was a Mother Superior's right!

Sisterhood communities seldom grew at random. Even when they took over existing structures (as they had with the old Harkonnen Keep on Gammu) they did so with rebuilding plans. They wanted pneumotubes to shunt small packages and messages. Lightlines and hardray projectors to transmit encrypted words. They considered themselves masters at safeguarding communications. Acolyte and Reverend Mother couriers (committed to self-destruction rather than betray their superiors) carried the more important messages.

She could visualize it out there beyond her window and beyond this planet—her web, superbly organized and manned, each Bene Gesserit an extension of the others. Where Sisterhood survival was concerned, there was an untouchable core of loyalty. Backsliders there might be, some spectacular (as the Lady Jessica, grandmother of the Tyrant), but they slid only so far. Most upsets were temporary.

And all of that was a Bene Gesserit pattern. A weakness.

Odrade admitted a deep agreement with Bellonda's fears. *But I'll be damned if I allow such things to depress all joy of living!* That would be giving in to the very thing those rampaging Honored Matres wanted.

"It's our strengths the hunters want," Odrade said, looking up at the ceiling comeyes. *Like ancient savages eating the hearts of enemies. Well . . . we will give them something to eat all right! And they will not know until too late that they cannot digest it!*

Except for preliminary teachings tailored to acolytes and postulants, the Sisterhood did not go in much for admonitory sayings, but Odrade had her own private watchwords: *"Someone has to do the plowing."* She smiled to herself as she bent to her work much refreshed. This room, this Sisterhood, these were her garden and there were weeds to be removed, seeds to plant. *And fertilizer. Mustn't forget the fertilizer.*

When I set out to lead humanity along my Golden Path I promised a lesson their bones would remember. I know a profound pattern humans deny with words even while their actions affirm it. They say they seek security and quiet, conditions they call peace. Even as they speak, they create seeds of turmoil and violence.

—LETO II, THE GOD EMPEROR

So she calls me Spider Queen!

Great Honored Matre leaned back in a heavy chair set high on a dais. Her withered breast shook with silent chuckles. *She knows what will happen when I get her in my web! Suck her dry, that's what I'll do.*

A small woman with unremarkable features and muscles that twitched nervously, she looked down on the skylighted yellow-tile floor of her audience room. A Bene Gesserit Reverend Mother sprawled there in shigawire bindings. The captive made no attempt to struggle. Shigawire was excellent for this purpose. *Cut her arms off, it would!*

The chamber where she sat suited Great Honored Matre as much for its dimensions as for the fact that it had been taken from others. Three hundred meters square, it had been designed for convocations of Guild Navigators here on Junction, each Navigator in a monstrous tank. The captive on that yellow floor was a mote in immensity.

This weakling took too much joy in revealing what her so-called Superior named me!

But it still was a lovely morning, Great Honored Matre thought.

Except that no tortures or mental probes worked on these witches. How could you torture someone who might choose to die at any moment? And did! They had ways of suppressing pain, too. Very wily, these primitives.

She's loaded with shere, too! A body infused with that damnable drug deteriorated beyond the reach of probes before it could be examined adequately.

Great Honored Matre signaled an aide. That one nudged the sprawled Reverend Mother with a foot and, at a further signal, eased the shigawire bindings to allow minimal movement.

"What is your name, child?" Great Honored Matre asked. Her voice rasped hoarsely with age and false bonhomie.

"I am called Sabanda." Clear young voice, still untouched by the pain of probings.

"Would you like to watch us capture a weak male and enslave him?" Great Honored Matre asked.

Sabanda knew the proper response to this. They had been warned. "I will die first." She said it calmly, staring up at that ancient face the color of a dried root left too long in the sun. Those odd orange flecks in the crone's eyes. A sign of anger, Proctors had told her.

A loosely hung red-gold robe with black dragon figures down its open face and red leotards beneath it only emphasized the scrawny figure they covered.

Great Honored Matre did not change expression even with a recurrent thought about these witches: *Damn them!* "What was your task on that dirty little planet where we took you?"

"A teacher of the young."

"I'm afraid we didn't leave any of your young alive." *Now why does she smile? To offend me! That's why!*

"Did you teach your young ones to worship the witch, Sheeana?" Great Honored Matre asked.

"Why should I teach them to worship a Sister? Sheeana would not like that."

"Would not . . . Are you saying she has come back to life and you know her?"

"Is it only the living we know?"

How clear and fearless the voice of this young witch. They had remarkable self-control, but even that could not save them. Odd, though, how this cult of Sheeana persisted. It would have to be rooted out, of course, destroyed the way the witches themselves were being destroyed.

Great Honored Matre lifted the little finger of her right hand. A waiting aide approached the captive with an injection. Perhaps this new drug would free a witch's tongue, perhaps not. No matter.

Sabanda grimaced when the injector touched her neck. In seconds she was dead. Servants carried the body away. It would be fed to captive Futars. Not that Futars were much use. Wouldn't breed in captivity, wouldn't obey the most ordinary commands. Sullen, waiting.

"Where Handlers?" one might ask. Or other useless words would spill from their humanoid mouths. Still, Futars provided some pleasures. Captivity also demonstrated they were vulnerable. Just as these primitive witches were. *We'll find the witches' hiding place. It's only a matter of time.*

The person who takes the banal and ordinary and illumi-
nates it in a new way can terrify. We do not want our ideas
changed. We feel threatened by such demands. "I already
know the important things!" we say. Then Changer comes
and throws our old ideas away.

—THE ZENSUFI MASTER

Miles Teg enjoyed playing in the orchards around Central. Odrade had
first taken him here when he could just toddle. One of his earliest
memories: hardly more than two years old and already aware he was a
ghola, though he did not understand the word's full meaning.

"You are a special child," Odrade said. "We made you from cells
taken from a very old man."

Although he was a precocious child and her words had a vaguely
disturbing sound, he was more interested then in running through tall
summer grass beneath the trees.

Later, he added other orchard days to that first one, accumulating
as well impressions about Odrade and the others who taught him. He
recognized quite early that Odrade enjoyed the excursions as much as
he did.

One afternoon in his fourth year, he told her: "Spring is my favorite
time."

"Mine, too."

When he was seven and already showing the mental brilliance
coupled to holographic memory that had caused the Sisterhood to

place such heavy responsibilities on his previous incarnation, he suddenly saw the orchards as a place touching something deep inside him.

This was his first real awareness that he carried memories he could not recall. Deeply disturbed, he turned to Odrade, who stood outlined in light against the afternoon sun, and said: "There are things I can't remember!"

"One day you will remember," she said.

He could not see her face against the bright light and her words came from a great shadow place, as much within him as from Odrade.

That year he began studying the life of the Bashar Miles Teg, whose cells had started his new life. Odrade had explained some of this to him, holding up her fingernails. "I took tiny scrapings from his neck— cells of his skin and they held all we needed to bring you to life."

There was something intense about the orchards that year, fruit larger and heavier, bees almost frenetic.

"It's because of the desert growing larger down there in the south," Odrade said. She held his hand as they walked through a dew-fresh morning beneath burgeoning apple trees.

Teg stared southward through the trees, momentarily mesmerized by leaf-dappled sunlight. He had studied about the desert, and he thought he could feel the weight of it on this place.

"Trees can sense their end approaching," Odrade said. "Life breeds more intensely when threatened."

"The air is very dry," he said. "That must be the desert."

"Notice how some of the leaves have gone brown and curled at the edges? We've had to irrigate heavily this year."

He liked it that she seldom talked down to him. It was mostly one person to another. He saw curled brown on leaves. The desert did that.

Deep in the orchard, they listened quietly for a time to birds and insects. Bees working the clover of a nearby pasture came to investigate but he was pheromone-marked, as were all who walked freely on Chapterhouse. They buzzed past him, sensed identifiers and went away about their business with blossoms.

Apples. Odrade pointed westward. *Peaches.* His attention went where she directed. And yes, there were the cherries east of them be-yond the pasture. He saw resin ribbing on the limbs.

Seeds and young shoots had been brought here on the original no-ships some fifteen hundred years ago, she said, and had been planted with loving care.

Teg visualized hands grubbing in dirt, gently patting earth around young shoots, careful irrigation, the fencing to confine the cattle to wild pastures around the first Chapterhouse plantations and buildings.

By this time he already had begun learning about the giant sand-worm the Sisterhood had spirited from Rakis. Death of that worm had produced creatures called sandtrout. Sandtrout were why the desert grew. Some of this history touched accounts of his previous incarnation—a man they called "The Bashar." A great soldier who had died when terrible women called Honored Matres destroyed Rakis.

Teg found such studies both fascinating and troubling. He sensed gaps in himself, places where memories ought to be. The gaps called out to him in dreams. And sometimes when he fell into reverie, faces appeared before him. He could almost hear words. Then there were times he knew the names of things before anyone told him. Especially names of weapons.

Momentous things grew in his awareness. This entire planet would become desert, a change started because Honored Matres wanted to kill these Bene Gesserit who raised him.

Reverend Mothers who controlled his life often awed him—black-robed, austere, those blue-in-blue eyes with absolutely no white. The spice did that, they said.

Only Odrade showed him anything he took for real affection and Odrade was someone *very* important. Everyone called her Mother Su-perior and that was what she told him to call her except when they were alone in the orchards. Then he could call her Mother.

On a morning walk near harvest time in his ninth year, just over the third rise in the apple orchards north of Central, they came on a shallow depression free of trees and lush with many different plants. Odrade put a hand on his shoulder and held him where they could admire black stepping-stones in a meander track through massed greenery and tiny flowers. She was in an odd mood. He heard it in her voice.

"Ownership is an interesting question," she said. "Do we own this planet or does it own us?"

"I like the smells here," he said.

She released him and urged him gently ahead of her. "We planted for the nose here, Miles. Aromatic herbs. Study them carefully and look them up when you get back to the library. Oh, do step on them!" when he started to avoid a plant runner in his path.

He placed his right foot firmly on green tendrils and inhaled pungent odors.

"They were made to be walked on and give up their savor," Odrade said. "Proctors have been teaching you how to deal with nostalgia. Have they told you nostalgia often is driven by the sense of smell?"

"Yes, Mother." Turning to look back at where he had stepped, he said: "That's rosemary."

"How do you know?" Very intense.

He shrugged. "I just know."

"That may be an original memory." She sounded pleased.

As they continued their walk in the aromatic hollow, Odrade's voice once more became pensive. "Each planet has its own character where we draw patterns of Old Earth. Sometimes, it's only a faint sketch, but here we have succeeded."

She knelt and pulled a twig from an acid-green plant. Crushing it in her fingers, she held it to his nose. "Sage."

She was right but he could not say how he knew.

"I've smelled that in food. Is that like melange?"

"It improves flavor but won't change consciousness." She stood and looked down at him from her full height. "Mark this place well, Miles. Our ancestral worlds are gone, but here we have recaptured part of our origins."

He sensed she was teaching him something important. He asked Odrade: "Why did you wonder if this planet owned us?"

"My Sisterhood believes we are stewards of the land. Do you know about stewards?"

"Like Roitiro, my friend Yorgi's father. Yorgi says his oldest sister will be steward of their plantation someday."

"Correct. We have a longer residence on some planets than any other people we know of but we are only stewards."

"If you don't own Chapterhouse, who does?"

"Perhaps nobody. My question is: How have we marked each other, my Sisterhood, and this planet?"

He looked up at her face then down at his hands. Was Chapterhouse marking him right now?

"Most of the marks are deep inside us." She took his hand. "Come along." They left the aromatic dell and climbed up into Roitiro's domain, Odrade speaking as they went.

"The Sisterhood seldom creates botanical gardens," she said. "Gardens must support far more than eyes and nose."

"Food?"

"Yes, supportive first of our lives. Gardens produce food. That dell back there is harvested for our kitchens."

He felt her words flow into him, lodging there among the gaps. He sensed planning for centuries ahead: trees to replace building beams, to hold watersheds, plants to keep lake and river banks from crumbling, to hold topsoil safe from rain and wind, to maintain seashores and even in the waters to make places for fish to breed. The Bene Gesserit also thought of trees for shade and shelter, or to cast interesting shadows on lawns.

"Trees and other plants for all of our symbiotic relationships," she said.

"Symbiotic?" It was a new word.

She explained with something she knew he already had encountered—going out with others to harvest mushrooms.

"Fungi won't grow except in the company of friendly roots. Each has a symbiotic relationship with a special plant. Each growing thing takes something it needs from the other."

She went on at length and, bored with learning, he kicked a clump of grass, then saw how she stared at him in that disturbing way. He had done something offensive. Why was it right to step on one growing thing and not on another?

"Miles! Grass keeps the wind from carrying topsoil into difficult places such as the bottoms of rivers."

He knew that tone. Reprimanding. He stared down at the grass he had offended.

"These grasses feed our cattle. Some have seeds we eat in bread and other foods. Some cane grasses are windbreaks."

He knew *that*! Trying to divert her, he said: "Wind-brakes?" spelling it.

She did not smile and he knew he had been wrong to think he could fool her. Resigned to it, he listened as she went on with the lesson.

When the desert came, she told him, grapes, their taproots down several hundred meters, probably would be the last to go. Orchards would die first.

"Why do they have to die?"

"To make room for more important life."

"Sandworms and melange."

He saw he had pleased her by knowing the relationship between sandworms and the spice the Bene Gesserit needed for their existence. He was not sure how that need worked but he imagined a circle: *Sandworms to sandtrout to melange and back again.* And the Bene Gesserit took what they needed from the circle.

He was still tired of all this teaching, and asked: "If all these things are going to die anyway, why do I have to go back to the library and learn their names?"

"Because you're human and humans have this deep desire to classify, to apply labels to everything."

"Why do we have to name things like that?"

"Because that way we lay claim to what we name. We assume an ownership that can be misleading and dangerous."

So she was back on *ownership*.

"My street, my lake, my planet," she said. "My label forever. A label you give to a place or thing may not even last out your lifetime except as a polite sop granted by conquerors . . . or as a sound to remember in fear."

"Dune," he said.

"You are quick!"

"Honored Matres burned Dune."

"They'll do the same to us if they find us."

"Not if I'm your Bashar!" The words were out of him without thought but, once spoken, he felt they might have some truth. Library accounts said the Bashar had made enemies tremble just by appearing on a battlefield.

As though she knew what he was thinking, Odrade said: "The Bashar Teg was just as famous for creating situations where no battle was necessary."

"But he fought your enemies."

"Never forget Dune, Miles. He died there."

"I know."

"Do the Proctors have you studying Caladan yet?"

"Yes. It's called Dan in my histories."

"Labels, Miles. Names are interesting reminders but most people don't make other connections. Boring history, eh? Names—convenient pointers, useful mostly with your own kind?"

"Are you my kind?" It was a question that plagued him but not in those words until this instant.

"We are Atreides, you and I. Remember that when you return to your study of Caladan."

When they went back through the orchards and across a pasture to the vantage knoll with its limb-framed view of Central, Teg saw the administrative complex and its barrier plantations with new sensitivity. He held this close as they went down the fenced lane to the arch into First Street.

"A living jewel," Odrade called Central.

As they passed under it, he looked up at the street name burned into the entrance arch. Galach in an elegant script with flowing lines, Bene Gesserit decorative. All streets and buildings were labeled in that same cursive.

Looking around him at Central, the dancing fountain in the square ahead of them, the elegant details, he sensed a depth of human experience. The Bene Gesserit had made this place supportive in ways he did not quite fathom. Things picked up in studies and orchard excursions, simple things and complex, came to new focus. It was a latent Mentat reponse but he did not know this, only sensing that his unfailing memory had shifted some relationships and reorganized them. He stopped suddenly and looked back the way they had come—the orchard out there framed in the arch of the covered street. It was all related. Central's effluent produced methane and fertilizer. (He had toured the plant with a Proctor.) Methane ran pumps and powered some of the refrigeration.

"What are you looking at, Miles?"

He did not know how to answer. But he remembered an autumn afternoon when Odrade had taken him over Central in a 'thopter to tell him about these relationships and give him "the overview." Only words then but now the words had meaning.

"As near to a closed ecological circle as we can create," Odrade had said in the 'thopter. "Weather Control's orbiters monitor it and order the flow lines."

"Why are you standing there looking at the orchard, Miles?" Her voice was full of imperatives against which he had no defenses.

"In the ornithopter, you said it was beautiful but dangerous."

They had taken only one 'thopter trip together. She caught the reference immediately. *"The ecological circle."*

He turned and looked up at her, waiting.

"Enclosed," she said. "How tempting it is to raise high walls and keep out change. Rot here in our own self-satisfied comfort."

Her words filled him with disquiet. He felt he had heard them before . . . some other place with a different woman holding his hand.

"Enclosures of any kind are a fertile breeding ground for hatred of outsiders," she said. "That produces a bitter harvest."

Not exactly the same words but the same lesson.

He walked slowly beside Odrade, his hand sweaty in hers.

"Why are you so silent, Miles?"

"You're farmers," he said. "That's really what you Bene Gesserit do."

She saw immediately what had happened, Mentat training coming out in him without his knowing. Best not explore that yet. "We are concerned about everything that grows, Miles. It was perceptive of you to see this."

As they parted, she to return to her tower, he to his quarters in the school section, Odrade said: "I will tell your Proctors to place more emphasis on subtle uses of power."

He misunderstood. "I'm already training with lasguns. They say I'm very good."

"So I've heard. But there are weapons you cannot hold in your hands. You can only hold them in your mind."

> Rules build up fortifications behind which small minds create satrapies. A perilous state of affairs in the best of times, disastrous during crises.
>
> —BENE GESSERIT CODA

Stygian blackness in Great Honored Matre's sleeping chamber. Logno, a Grand Dame and senior aide to the High One, entered from the unlighted hallway as she had been summoned to do and, seeing darkness, shuddered. These consultations with no illumination terrified her and she knew Great Honored Matre took pleasure from that. It could not be the only reason for darkness, though. Was Great Honored Matre fearful of attack? Several High Ones had been deposed in bed. No . . . not just that, although it might bear on the choice of setting.

Grunts and moans in the darkness.

Some Honored Matres snickered and said Great Honored Matre dared bed a Futar. Logno thought it possible. This Great Honored Matre dared many things. Had she not salvaged some of The Weapon from the disaster of the Scattering? Futars, though? The Sisters knew Futars could not be bonded by sex. At least not by sex with humans. That might be the way the Enemies of Many Faces did it, though. Who knew?

There was a furry smell in the bedchamber. Logno closed the door behind her and waited. Great Honored Matre did not like to be interrupted in whatever she did there within shielding blackness. *But she permits me to call her Dama.*

Another moan, then: "Sit on the floor, Logno. Yes, there by the door."

Does she really see me or only guess?

Logno did not have the courage to test it. *Poison. I'll get her that way someday. She's cautious but she can be distracted.* Although her Sisters might sneer at it, poison was an accepted tool of succession . . . provided the successor possessed further ways to maintain ascendancy.

"Logno, those Ixians you spoke with today. What do they say of The Weapon?"

"They do not understand its function, Dama. I did not tell them what it was."

"Of course not."

"Will you suggest again that Weapon and Charge be united?"

"Are you sneering at me, Logno?"

"Dama! I would never do such a thing."

"I hope not."

Silence. Logno understood that they both considered the same problem. Only three hundred units of The Weapon survived the disaster. Each could be used only once, provided the Council (which held the Charge) agreed to arm them. Great Honored Matre, controlling The Weapon itself, had only half of that awful power. Weapon without Charge was merely a small black tube that could be held in the hand. With its Charge, it cut a brief swath of bloodless death across the arc of its limited range.

"The Ones of Many Faces," Great Honored Matre muttered.

Logno nodded to the darkness where that muttering originated.

Perhaps she can see me. I do not know what else she salvaged or what the Ixians may have provided her.

And the Ones of Many Faces, curse them through eternity, had caused the disaster. Them and their Futars! The ease with which all but that handful of The Weapon had been confiscated! Awesome powers. *We must arm ourselves well before we return to that battle. Dama is right.*

"That planet—Buzzell," Great Honored Matre said. "Are you sure it's not defended?"

"We detect no defenses. Smugglers say it is not defended."

"But it is so rich in soostones!"

"Here in the Old Empire, people seldom dare attack the witches."

"I do not believe there are only a handful of them on that planet! It's a trap of some kind."

"That is always possible, Dama."

"I do not trust smugglers, Logno. Bond a few more of them and test this thing of Buzzell again. The witches may be weak but I do not think they are stupid."

"Yes, Dama."

"Tell the Ixians they will displease us if they cannot duplicate The Weapon."

"But without the Charge, Dama . . ."

"We will deal with that when we must. Now, leave."

Logno heard a hissing "Yesssssss!" as she let herself out. Even the darkness of the hallway was welcome after the bedchamber and she hurried toward the light.

We tend to become like the worst in those we oppose.

—BENE GESSERIT CODA

The water images again!

We're turning this whole damned planet into a desert and I get water images!

Odrade sat in her workroom, the usual morning clutter around her, and sensed Sea Child floating in the waves, washed by them. The waves were the color of blood. Her Sea Child self anticipated bloody times.

She knew where these images originated: the time before Reverend Mothers ruled her life; childhood in the beautiful home on the Gammu seacoast. Despite immediate worries, she could not prevent a smile. Oysters prepared by Papa. The stew she still preferred.

What she remembered best of childhood was the sea excursions. Something about being afloat spoke to her most basic self. Lift and fall of waves, the sense of unbounded horizons with strange new places just beyond the curved limits of a watery world, that thrilling edge of danger implicit in the very substance that supported her. All of it combined to assure her she was Sea Child.

Papa was calmer there, too. And Mama Sibia happier, face turned into the wind, dark hair blowing. A sense of balance radiated from those times, a reassuring message spoken in a language older than Odrade's oldest Other Memory. *"This is my place, my medium. I am Sea Child."*

Her personal concept of sanity came from those times. *The ability to balance on strange seas. The ability to maintain your deepest self despite unexpected waves.*

Mama Sibia had given Odrade that ability long before the Reverend Mothers came and took away their "hidden Atreides scion." Mama Sibia, *only* a foster mother, had taught Odrade to love herself.

In a Bene Gesserit society where any form of love was suspect, this remained Odrade's ultimate secret.

At root, I am happy with myself. I do not mind being alone. Not that any Reverend Mother was ever truly alone after the Spice Agony flooded her with Other Memories.

But Mama Sibia and, yes, Papa, too, acting in loco parentis for the Bene Gesserit, had impressed a profound strength upon their charge during those hidden years. The Reverend Mothers had been reduced to amplifying that strength.

Proctors had tried to root out Odrade's "deep desire for personal affinities," but failed at last, not quite sure they had failed but always suspicious. They had sent her to Al Dhanab finally, a place deliberately maintained as a mimic of the worst in Salusa Secundus, there to be conditioned on a planet of constant testing. A place worse than Dune in some respects: high cliffs and dry gorges, hot winds and frigid winds, too little moisture and too much. The Sisterhood had thought of it as a proving ground for those destined to survive on Dune. But none of this had touched that secret core within Odrade. Sea Child remained intact.

And it is Sea Child warning me now.

Was it a prescient warning?

She had always possessed this *bit of talent*, this little twitching that told of immediate peril to the Sisterhood. Atreides genes reminding her of their presence. Was it a threat to Chapterhouse? No . . . the ache she could not touch said it was others in danger. Important, though.

Lampadas? Her bit of talent could not say.

The Breeding Mistresses had tried to erase this dangerous prescience from their Atreides line but with limited success. "We dare not risk another Kwisatz Haderach!" They knew of this quirk in their Mother Superior, but Odrade's late predecessor, Taraza, had advised "cautious use of her talent." It had been Taraza's view that Odrade's prescience worked only to warn of dangers to the Bene Gesserit.

Odrade agreed. She experienced unwanted moments when she glimpsed threats. Glimpses. And lately she dreamed.

It was a vividly recurring dream, every sense attuned to the immediacy of this thing occurring in her mind. She walked across a chasm on a tightrope and someone (she dared not turn to see who) was coming from behind with an axe to cut the rope. She could feel the rough twists of fiber beneath bare feet. She felt a cold wind blowing, a smell of burning on that wind. And she *knew* the one with the axe approached!

Each perilous step required all of her energy. Step! Step! The rope swayed and she stretched her arms out straight on each side, struggling for balance.

If I fall, the Sisterhood falls!

The Bene Gesserit would end in the chasm beneath the rope. As with any living thing, the Sisterhood must end sometime. A Reverend Mother dared not deny it.

But not here. Not falling, the rope severed. We must not let the rope be cut! I must get across the chasm before the axe-wielder comes. "I must! I must!"

The dream always ended there, her own voice ringing in her ears as she awoke in her sleeping chamber. Chilled. No perspiration. Even in the throes of nightmare, Bene Gesserit restraints did not permit unnecessary excesses.

Body does not need perspiration? Body does not get perspiration.

As she sat in her workroom remembering the dream, Odrade felt the depth of reality behind that metaphor of a slender rope: *The delicate strand on which I carry the fate of my Sisterhood.* Sea Child sensed the approaching nightmare and intruded with images of bloody waters. This was no trivial warning. Ominous. She wanted to stand and shout: "Scatter into the weeds, my chicks! Run! Run!"

And wouldn't that shock the watchdogs!

The duties of a Mother Superior required her to put a good face on her tremors and act as though nothing mattered except the formal decisions in front of her. Panic must be avoided! Not that any of her immediate decisions were truly trivial in these times. But calm demeanor was required.

Some of her chicks already were running, gone off into the unknown. Shared lives in Other Memory. The rest of her chicks here on Chapterhouse would know when to run. *When we are discovered.* Their behavior would be governed then by the necessities of the moment. All that really mattered was their superb training. That was their most reliable preparation.

Each new Bene Gesserit cell, wherever it finally went, was prepared as was Chapterhouse: total destruction rather than submission. The screaming fire would engorge itself on precious flesh and records. All a captor would find would be useless wreckage: twisted shards peppered with ashes.

Some Chapterhouse Sisters might escape. But flight at the moment of attack—how futile!

Key people shared Other Memory anyway. Preparation. Mother Superior avoided it. *Reasons of morale!*

Where to run and who might escape, who might be captured? Those were the real questions. What if they captured Sheeana down there at the edge of the new desert waiting for sandworms that might never appear? Sheeana plus the sandworms: a potent religious force Honored Matres might know how to exploit. And what if Honored Matres captured ghola-Idaho or ghola-Teg? There might never again be a hiding place if one of those possibilities occurred.

What if? What if?

Angry frustration said: "Should've killed Idaho the minute we got him! We should never have grown ghola-Teg."

Only her Council members, immediate advisors and some among the watchdogs shared her suspicion. They sat on it with reservations. None of them felt really secure about those two gholas, not even after mining the no-ship, making it vulnerable to the screaming fire.

In those last hours before his heroic sacrifice, had Teg been able to *see* the unseeable (including no-ships)? *How did he know where to meet us on that desert of Dune?*

And if Teg could do it, the dangerously talented Duncan Idaho with his uncounted generations of accumulated Atreides (and unknown) genes might also stumble upon the ability.

I might do it myself!

With sudden shocking insight, Odrade realized for the first time that Tamalane and Bellonda watched their Mother Superior with the same fears that Odrade felt in watching the two gholas.

Merely knowing it could be done—that a human could be sensitized to detect no-ships and the other forms of that shielding—would have an unbalancing effect on their universe. It would certainly set the Honored Matres on a runaway track. There were uncounted Idaho offspring loose in the universe. He had always complained he was "no damned stud for the Sisterhood," but he had performed for them many times.

Always thought he was doing it for himself. And maybe he was.

Any mainline Atreides offspring might have this talent the Council suspected had come to flower in Teg.

Where did the months and years go? And the days? Another harvest season and the Sisterhood remained in its terrible limbo. Midmorning already, Odrade realized. The sounds and smells of Central made themselves known to her. People out there in the corridor. Chicken and cabbage cooking in the communal kitchen. Everything normal.

What was normal to someone who dwelt in water images even during these working moments? Sea Child could not forget Gammu, the smells, the breeze-blown substance of ocean weeds, the ozone that made every breath oxygen-rich, and the splendid freedom in those around her so apparent in the way they walked and spoke. Conversation on the sea went deeper in a way she had never plumbed. Even small talk had its subterranean elements there, an oceanic elocution that flowed with the currents beneath them.

Odrade felt compelled to remember her own body afloat in that childhood sea. She needed to recapture the forces she had known there, take in the strengthening qualities she had learned in more innocent times.

Face down in salty water, holding her breath as long as she could, she floated in a sea-washed *now* that cleansed away woes. This was stress management reduced to its essence. A great calmness flooded her.

I float, therefore I am.

Sea Child warned and Sea Child restored. Without ever admitting it, she had needed restoration desperately.

Odrade had looked at her own face mirrored in a workroom window the previous night, shocked by the way age and responsibilities combined with fatigue to suck in her cheeks and turn down the corners of her mouth: the sensual lips thinner, the gentle curves of her face elongated. Only the all-blue eyes blazed with their accustomed intensity and she still was tall and muscular.

On impulse, Odrade punched up the call symbols and stared at a projection above the table: the no-ship sitting on the ground at the Chapterhouse spacefield, a giant bump of mysterious machinery, separated from Time. Over the years of its semi-dormancy, it had depressed a great sunken area into the landing flat, becoming almost wedged there. It was a great lump, its engines ticking away only enough to keep it hidden from prescient searchers, especially from Guild Navigators who would take a special joy in selling out the Bene Gesserit.

Why had she called up this image just now?

Because of the three people confined there—Scytale, the last surviving Tleilaxu Master; Murbella and Duncan Idaho, the sexually bonded pair, held as much by their mutual entrapment as they were by the no-ship.

Not simple, any of it.

There seldom were simple explanations for any major Bene Gesserit undertaking. The no-ship and its mortal contents could only be classified as a major effort. Costly. Very costly in energy even in its standby mode.

The appearance of parsimonious metering to all of that expenditure spoke of energy crisis. One of Bell's concerns. You could hear it in her voice even when she was being her most objective: "Down to the bone and nowhere else to cut!" Every Bene Gesserit knew the watchful eyes of Accounting were on them these days, critical of the Sisterhood's outflowing vitality.

Bellonda strode into the workroom unannounced with a roll of ridulian crystal records under her left arm. She walked as though she hated the floor, stamping on it as if to say "There! Take that! And that!" Beating the floor because it was guilty of being underfoot.

Odrade felt her chest tighten as she saw the look in Bell's eyes. The ridulian records went "Slap!" as Bellonda threw them onto the table.

"Lampadas!" Bellonda said and there was agony in her voice.

Odrade had no need to open the roll. *Sea Child's bloody water has become reality.*

"Survivors?" Her voice sounded strained.

"None." Bellonda slumped into the chairdog she kept on her side of Odrade's table.

Tamalane entered then and sat behind Bellonda. Both looked stricken.

No survivors.

Odrade permitted herself a slow shudder that went from her breast to the soles of her feet. She did not care that the others saw such a revealing reaction. This workroom had seen worse behavior from Sisters.

"Who reported?" Odrade asked.

Bellonda said, "It came through our CHOAM spies and had the special mark on it. The Rabbi supplied the information, no doubt of it."

Odrade did not know how to respond. She glanced at the wide bow window behind her companions, seeing a soft flutter of snowflakes. Yes, this news deservedly went with winter marshaling its forces out there.

The sisters of Chapterhouse were unhappy about the sudden plunge into winter. Necessities had forced Weather Control to let the temperature drop precipitately. No gradual decline into winter, no kindness to growing things that now must pass through the freezing dormancy. This was three and four degrees colder every night. Get the whole thing over in a week or so and plunge them all into the seemingly interminable chill.

Cold to match the news about Lampadas.

One result of this weather shift was fog. She could see it dissipating as the brief snow flurry ended. Very confusing weather. They got the dewpoint next to the air temperature and the fog rolled into the remaining wet spots. It lifted from the ground in tulle mists that wandered through leafless orchards like a poisonous gas.

No survivors at all?

Bellonda shook her head from side to side in answer to Odrade's questioning look.

Lampadas—a jewel in the Sisterhood's network of planets, home of their most prized school, another lifeless ball of ashes and hardened melt. And the Bashar Alef Burzmali with all of his hand-picked defense force. *All dead?*

"All dead," Bellonda said.

Burzmali, favorite student of the old Bashar Teg, gone and nothing gained by it. Lampadas—the marvelous library, the brilliant teachers, the premier students . . . all gone.

"Even Lucilla?" Odrade asked. The Reverend Mother Lucilla, vice chancellor of Lampadas, had been instructed to flee at the first sign of trouble, taking with her as many of the doomed as she could store in Other Memory.

"The spies said all dead," Bellonda insisted.

It was a chilling signal to surviving Bene Gesserit: "You may be next!"

How could any human society be anesthetized to such brutality? Odrade wondered. She visualized the news with breakfast at some Honored Matre base: "We've destroyed another Bene Gesserit planet. Ten billion dead, they say. That makes six planets this month, doesn't it? Pass the cream, will you, dear?"

Almost glassy-eyed with horror, Odrade picked up the report and glanced through it. *From the Rabbi, no doubt of that.* She put it down gently and looked at her Councillors.

Bellonda—old, fat and florid. Mentat-Archivist, wearing lenses to read now, uncaring what that revealed about her. Bellonda showed her blunt teeth in a wide grimace that said more than words. She had seen Odrade's reaction to the report. Bell might argue once more for retaliation in kind. That could be expected from someone valued for her natural viciousness. She needed to be thrown back into Mentat mode where she would be more analytical.

In her own way, Bell is right, Odrade thought. *But she won't like what I have in mind. I must be cautious in what I say now. Too soon to reveal my plan.*

"There are circumstances where viciousness can blunt viciousness," Odrade said. "We must consider it carefully."

There! That would forestall Bell's outburst.

Tamalane shifted slightly in her chair. Odrade looked at the older woman. Tam, composed there behind her mask of critical patience. Snowy hair above that narrow face: the appearance of aged wisdom.

Odrade saw through the mask to Tam's extreme severity, the pose that said she disliked everything she saw and heard.

In contrast to the surface softness of Bell's flesh, there was a bony solidity to Tamalane. She still kept herself in trim, her muscles as well-toned as possible. In her eyes, though, was the thing that belied this: *a sense of withdrawing there, pulling back from life.* Oh, she observed yet, but something had begun the final retreat. Tamalane's famed intelligence had become a kind of shrewdness, relying mostly on past observations and past decisions rather than on what she saw in the immediate present.

We must begin readying a replacement. It will be Sheeana, I think. Sheeana is dangerous to us but shows great promise. And Sheeana was blooded on Dune.

Odrade focused on Tamalane's shaggy eyebrows. They tended to hang over her lids in a concealing disarray. *Yes. Sheeana to replace Tamalane.*

Knowing the complicated problems they must solve, Tam would accept the decision. At the moment of announcement, Odrade knew she would only have to turn Tam's attention to the enormity of their predicament.

I will miss her, dammit!

You cannot know history unless you know how leaders move with its currents. Every leader requires outsiders to perpetuate his leadership. Examine my career: I was leader and outsider. Do not assume I merely created a Church-State. That was my function as leader and I copied historical models. Barbaric arts of my time reveal me as outsider. Favorite poetry: epics. Popular dramatic ideal: heroism. Dancers: wildly abandoned. Stimulants to make people sense what I took from them. What did I take? The right to choose a role in history.

—LETO II (THE TYRANT),
VETHER BEBE TRANSLATION

I am going to die! Lucilla thought.

Please, dear Sisters, don't let it come before I pass along the precious burden I carry in my mind!

Sisters!

The idea of family seldom was expressed among the Bene Gesserit but it was there. In a genetic sense, they *were* related. And because of Other Memory, they often knew where. They had no need for special terms such as "second cousin" or "great-aunt." They saw the relationships as a weaver sees his cloth. They knew how the warp and weft created the *fabric*. A better word than Family, it was the fabric of the Bene Gesserit that formed the Sisterhood but it was the ancient instinct of Family that provided the warp.

Lucilla thought of her sisters only as Family now. The Family needed what she carried.

I was a fool to seek refuge on Gammu!

But her damaged no-ship would limp no farther. How diabolically extravagant Honored Matres had been! The hatred this implied terrified her.

Strewing the escape lanes around Lampadas with deathtraps, the Foldspace perimeter seeded with small no-globes, each containing a field projector and a lasgun to fire on contact. When the laser hit the Holzmann generator in the no-globe, a chain reaction released the nuclear energy. Bzzz into the trap field and a devastating explosion spread silently across you. Costly but efficient! Enough such explosions and even a giant Guildship would become a crippled derelict in the void. Her ship's system of defensive analyses had penetrated the nature of the trap only when it was too late, but she had been lucky, she supposed.

She did not feel lucky as she looked out the second-story window of this isolated Gammu farmhouse. The window was open and an afternoon breeze carried the inevitable smell of oil, something dirty in the smoke of a fire out there. The Harkonnens had left their oily mark on this planet so deep it might never be removed.

Her contact here was a retired Suk doctor but she knew him as much more, something so secret that only a limited number in the Bene Gesserit shared it. The knowledge lay in a special classification: *The secrets of which we do not speak, even among ourselves, for that would harm us. The secrets we do not pass from Sister to Sister in the sharing of lives for there is no open path. The secrets we dare not know until a need arises.* Lucilla had stumbled into it because of a veiled remark by Odrade.

"You know an interesting thing about Gammu? Mmmmm, there's a whole society there that bands itself on the basis that they all eat consecrated foods. A custom brought in by immigrants who have never been assimilated. Keep to themselves, frown on outbreeding, that sort of thing. They ignite the usual mythic detritus, of course:

whispers, rumors. Serves to isolate them even more. Precisely what they want."

Lucilla knew of an ancient society that fitted itself neatly into this description. She was curious. The society she had in mind supposedly had died out shortly after the Second Inter-space Migrations. Judicious browsing in Archives whetted her curiosity even more. Living styles, rumor-fogged descriptions of religious rituals—especially the candelabra—and the keeping of special holy days with a proscription against any work on those days. And they were not just on Gammu!

One morning, taking advantage of an uncommon lull, Lucilla entered the workroom to test her "projective surmise," something not as reliable as a Mentat's equivalent but more than theory.

"You have a new assignment for me, I suspect."

"I see you've been spending time in Archives."

"It seemed a profitable thing to do just now."

"Making connections?"

"A surmise." *That secret society on Gammu—they're Jews, aren't they?*

"You may have need of special information because of where we are about to post you." Extremely casual.

Lucilla sank into Bellonda's chairdog without invitation.

Odrade picked up a stylus, scribbled on a sheet of disposable and passed it to Lucilla in a way that hid it from the comeyes.

Lucilla took the hint and bent over the message, holding it close beneath the shield of her head.

"Your surmise is correct. You must die before revealing it. That is the price of their cooperation, a mark of great trust." Lucilla shredded the message.

Odrade used eye and palm identification to unseal a panel on the wall behind her. She removed a small ridulian crystal and handed it to Lucilla. It was warm but Lucilla felt a chill. What could be so secret? Odrade swung the security hood from beneath her worktable and pivoted it into position.

Lucilla dropped the crystal into its receptacle with a trembling hand and pulled the hood over her head. Immediately, words formed in her mind, an oral sense of extremely old accents clipped for recognition: "The people to whom your attention has been called are the Jews. They made a defensive decision eons ago. The solution to recurrent pogroms was to vanish from public view. Space travel made this not only possible but attractive. They hid on countless planets—their own Scattering—and they probably have planets where only their people live. This does not mean they have abandoned age-old practices in which they excelled out of survival necessity. The old religion is sure to persist even though somewhat altered. It is probable that a rabbi from ancient times would not find himself out of place behind the Sabbath menorah of a Jewish household in your age. But their secrecy is such that you could work a lifetime beside a Jew and never suspect. They call it 'Complete Cover,' although they know its dangers."

Lucilla accepted this without question. That which was so secret would be perceived as dangerous by anyone who even suspected its presence. *"Else why do they keep it secret, eh? Answer me that!"*

The crystal continued to pour its secrets into her awareness: "At the threat of discovery, they have a standard reaction, 'We seek the religion of our roots. It is a revival, bringing back what is best from our past.'"

Lucilla knew this pattern. There were always "nutty revivalists." It was guaranteed to blunt most curiosity. *"Them? Oh, they're another bunch of revivalists."*

"The masking system (the crystal continued) did not succeed with us. We have our own well-recorded Jewish heritage and a fund of Other Memory to tell us reasons for secrecy. We did not disturb the situation until I, Mother Superior during and after the battle of Corrin (*Very old, indeed!*), saw that our Sisterhood had need of a secret society, a group responsive to our requests for assistance."

Lucilla felt a surge of skepticism. *Requests?*

The long-ago Mother Superior had anticipated skepticism. "On occasion, we make demands they cannot avoid. But they make demands on us as well."

Lucilla felt immersed in the mystique of this underground society. It was more than ultra-secret. Her clumsy questions in Archives had elicited mostly rejections. "Jews? What's that? Oh, yes—an ancient sect. Look it up for yourself. We don't have time for idle religious research."

The crystal had more to impart: "Jews are amused and sometimes dismayed at what they interpret as our copying them. Our breeding records dominated by the female line to control the mating pattern are seen as Jewish. You are only a Jew if your mother was a Jew."

The crystal came to its conclusion: "The Diaspora will be remembered. Keeping this secret involves our deepest honor."

Lucilla lifted the hood from her head.

"You are a very good choice for an extremely touchy assignment on Lampadas," Odrade had said, restoring the crystal to its hiding place.

That is the past and likely dead. Look where Odrade's "touchy assignment" has brought me!

From her vantage in the Gammu farmhouse, Lucilla noted a large produce carrier had entered the grounds. There was a bustle of activity below her. Workers came from all sides to meet the big carrier with towbins of vegetables. She smelled the pungent juices from the cut stems of marrows.

Lucilla did not move from the window. Her host had supplied her with local garments—a long gown of drab gray everwear and a bright blue headscarf to confine her sandy hair. It was important to do nothing calling undue attention to herself. She had seen other women pause to watch the farm work. Her presence here could be taken as curiosity.

It was a large carrier, its suspensors laboring under the load of produce already piled in its articulated sections. The operator stood in a transparent house at the front, hands on the steering lever, eyes straight ahead. His legs were spread wide and he leaned into the web of sloping supports, touching the power bar with his left hip. He was a large man, face dark and deeply wrinkled, hair laced with gray. His body was an extension of the machinery—guiding ponderous movement. He flicked his gaze up to Lucilla as he passed, then back to the track into the wide loading area defined by buildings below her.

Built into his machine, she thought. That said something about the way humans were fitted to the things they did. Lucilla sensed a weakening force in this thought. If you fitted yourself too tightly to one thing, other abilities atrophied. *We become what we do.*

She pictured herself suddenly as another operator in some great machine, no different from that man in the carrier.

The big machine trundled past her out of the yard, its operator not sparing her another glance. He had seen her once. Why look twice?

Her hosts had made a wise choice in this hiding place, she thought. A sparsely populated area with trustworthy workers in the immediate vicinity and little curiosity among the people who passed. Hard work dulled curiosity. She had noted the character of the area when she was brought here. Evening then and people already trudging toward their homes. You could measure the urban density of an area by when work stopped. Early to bed and you were in a loosely packed region. Night activity said people remained restless, twitchy with inner awareness of others active and vibrating too near.

What has brought me to this introspective state?

Early in the Sisterhood's first retreat, before the worst onslaughts of the Honored Matres, Lucilla had experienced difficulty coming to grips with belief that "someone out there is hunting us with intent to kill."

Pogrom! That was what the Rabbi had called it before going off that morning "to see what I can do for you."

She knew the Rabbi had chosen his word from long and bitter memory, but not since her first experience of Gammu before this *pogrom* had Lucilla felt such confinement to circumstances she could not control.

I was a fugitive then, too.

The Sisterhood's present situation bore similarities to what they had suffered under the Tyrant, except that the *God Emperor* obviously (in retrospect) never intended to exterminate the Bene Gesserit, only to rule them. And he certainly ruled!

Where is that damned Rabbi?

He was a large, intense man with old-fashioned spectacles. A broad face browned by much sunlight. Few wrinkles despite the age she could read in his voice and movements. The spectacles focused attention on deeply set brown eyes that watched her with peculiar intensity.

"Honored Matres," he had said (right here in this bare-walled upper room) when she explained her predicament. "Oh, my! That is difficult."

Lucilla had expected that response and, what was more, she could see he knew it.

"There is a Guild Navigator on Gammu helping the search for you," he said. "It is one of the Edrics, very powerful, I am told."

"I have Siona blood. He cannot *see* me."

"Nor me nor any of my people and for the same reason. We Jews adjust to many necessities, you know."

"This Edric is a gesture," she said. "He can do little."

"But they have brought him. I'm afraid there is no way we can get you safely off the planet."

"Then what can we do?"

"We will see. My people are not entirely helpless, you understand?"

She recognized sincerity and concern for her. He spoke quietly of resisting the sexual blandishments of Honored Matres, "doing it unobtrusively so as not to arouse them."

"I will go whisper in a few ears," he said.

She felt oddly restored by this. There often was something coldly remote and cruel about falling into the hands of the medical professions. She reassured herself with the knowledge that Suks were conditioned to be alert to your needs, compassionate and supportive. *(All of those things that can fall by the wayside in emergencies.)*

She bent her efforts to restoring calm, focusing on the personal mantra she had gained in *solo death education.*

If I am to die, I must pass along a transcendental lesson. I must leave with serenity.

That helped but still she felt a trembling. The Rabbi had been gone too long. Something was wrong.

Was I right to trust him?

Despite a growing sense of doom, Lucilla forced herself to practice Bene Gesserit naivete as she reviewed her encounter with the Rabbi. Her Proctors had called this "the innocence that goes naturally with inexperience, a condition often confused with ignorance." Into this naivete all things flowed. It was close to Mentat performance. Information entered without prejudgment. "You are a mirror upon which the universe is reflected. That reflection is all you experience. Images bounce from your senses. Hypotheses arise. Important even when wrong. Here is the exceptional case where more than one wrong can produce dependable decisions."

"We are your willing servants," the Rabbi had said.

That was guaranteed to alert a Reverend Mother.

The explanations of Odrade's crystal felt suddenly inadequate. *It's almost always profit.* She accepted this as cynical but from vast experience. Attempts to weed it out of human behavior always broke up on the rocks of application. Socializing and communistic systems only changed the counters that measured profits. Enormous managerial bureaucracies—the counter was power.

Lucilla warned herself that the manifestations were always the same. Look at this Rabbi's extensive farm! Retirement retreat for a Suk? She had seen something of what lay behind the establishment: servants, richer quarters. And there must be more. No matter the system it was always the same: the best foods, beautiful lovers, unrestricted travel, magnificent holiday accommodations.

It gets very tiresome when you've seen it as often as we have.

She knew her mind was jittering but felt powerless to prevent it. *Survival. The very bottom of the demand system is always survival. And I threaten the survival of the Rabbi and his people.*

He had fawned upon her. *Always beware of those who fawn upon*

us, nuzzling up to all of that power we're supposed to have. How flatter-
ing to find great mobs of servants waiting and anxious to do our bid-
ding! How utterly debilitating.

The mistake of Honored Matres.

What is delaying the Rabbi?

Was he seeing how much he could get for the Reverend Mother
Lucilla?

A door slammed below her, shaking the floor under her feet. She
heard hurried footsteps on a stairway. How primitive these people
were. Stairways! Lucilla turned as the door opened. The Rabbi entered
bringing a rich smell of melange. He stood by the door assessing her
mood.

"Forgive my tardiness, dear lady. I was summoned for questioning
by Edric, the Guild Navigator."

That explained the smell of spice. Navigators were forever bathed
in the orange gas of melange, their features often fogged by the vapors.
Lucilla could visualize the Navigator's tiny v of a mouth and the ugly
flap of nose. Mouth and nose appeared small on a Navigator's gigantic
face with its pulsing temples. She knew how threatened the Rabbi must
have felt listening to the singsong ululations of the Navigator's voice
with its simultaneous mechtranslation into impersonal Galach.

"What did he want?"

"You."

"Does he . . ."

"He does not know for sure but I am certain he suspects us. However, he suspects everybody."

"Did they follow you?"

"Not necessary. They can find me any time they want."

"What shall we do?" She knew she spoke too fast, much too loud.

"Dear lady . . ." He came three steps closer and she saw the perspiration on his forehead and nose. Fear. She could smell it.

"Well, what is it?"

"The economic view behind the activities of Honored Matres—we
find them quite interesting."

His words crystallized her fears. *I knew it! He's selling me out!*

"As you Reverend Mothers know very well, there are always gaps in economic systems."

"Yes?" Profoundly wary.

"Incomplete suppression of trade in any commodity always increases the profits of the tradesmen, especially the profits of the senior distributors." His voice was warningly hesitant. "That is the fallacy of thinking you can control unwanted narcotics by stopping them at your borders."

What was he trying to tell her? His words described elementary facts known even to acolytes. Increased profits were always used to buy safe paths past border guards, often by buying the guards themselves.

Has he bought servants of the Honored Matres? Surely, he doesn't believe he can do that safely.

She waited while he composed his thoughts, obviously forming a presentation he believed most likely to gain her acceptance.

Why did he point her attention toward border guards? That certainly was what he had done. Guards always had a ready rationalization for betraying their superiors, of course. "If I don't, someone else will."

She dared to hope.

The Rabbi cleared his throat. It was apparent he had found the words he wanted and had placed them in order.

"I do not believe there is any way to get you off Gammu alive."

She had not expected such a blunt condemnation. "But the . . ."

"The information you carry, that is a different matter," he said.

So that was behind all of the focusing on borders and guards!

"You don't understand, Rabbi. My information is not just a few words and some warnings." She tapped a finger against her forehead. "In here are many precious lives, all of those irreplaceable experiences, learning so vital that—"

"Ahhh, but I do understand, dear lady. Our problem is that *you* do not understand."

Always these references to understanding!

"It is your honor upon which I depend at this moment," he said.

Ahhhh, the legendary honesty and trustworthiness of the Bene Gesserit when we have given our word!

"You know I will die rather than betray you," she said.

He spread his hands wide in a rather helpless gesture. "I am fully confident of that, dear lady. The question is not one of betrayal but of something we have never before revealed to your Sisterhood."

"What are you trying to tell me?" Quite peremptory, almost with Voice (which she had been warned not to try on these Jews).

"I must exact a promise from you. I must have your word that you will not turn against us because of what I am about to reveal. You must promise to accept my solution to our dilemma."

"Sight unseen?"

"Only because I ask it of you and assure you that we honor our commitment to your Sisterhood."

She glared at him, trying to see through this barrier he had erected between them. His surface reactions could be read but not the mysterious thing beneath his unexpected behavior.

The Rabbi waited for this fearsome woman to reach her decision. Reverend Mothers always made him uneasy. He knew what her decision must be and pitied her. He saw that she could read the pity in his expression. They knew so much and so little. Their powers were manifest. And their knowledge of Secret Israel so perilous!

We owe them this debt, though. She is not of the Chosen, but a debt is a debt. Honor is honor. Truth is truth.

The Bene Gesserit had preserved Secret Israel in many hours of need. And a pogrom was something his people knew without lengthy explanations. Pogrom was embedded in the psyche of Secret Israel. And thanks to the *Unspeakable,* the chosen people would never forget. No more than they could forgive.

Memory kept fresh in daily ritual (with periodic emphasis in communal sharings) cast a glowing halo on what the Rabbi knew he must do. And this poor woman! She, too, was trapped by memories and circumstances.

Into the cauldron! Both of us!

"You have my word," Lucilla said.

The Rabbi returned to the room's only door and opened it. An older woman in a long brown gown stood there. She stepped in at the Rabbi's beckoning gesture. Hair the color of old driftwood neatly bound in a bun at the back of her head. Face pinched in and wrinkled, dark as a dried almond. The eyes, though! Total blue! And that steely hardness within them . . .

"This is Rebecca, one of our people," the Rabbi said. "As I am sure you can see, she has done a dangerous thing."

"The Agony," Lucilla whispered.

"She did it long ago and she serves us well. Now, she will serve you."

Lucilla had to be certain. "Can you Share?"

"I have never done it, lady, but I know it." As Rebecca spoke, she approached Lucilla and stopped when they were almost touching.

They leaned toward each other until their foreheads made contact. Their hands went out and gripped the offered shoulders.

As their minds locked, Lucilla forced a projective thought: "This must get to my Sisters!"

"I promise, dear lady."

There could be no deception in this total mixing of minds, this ultimate candor powered by imminent and certain death or the poisonous melange essence that ancient Fremen had rightly called "the little death." Lucilla accepted Rebecca's promise. This wild Reverend Mother of the Jews committed her life to the assurance. Something else! Lucilla gasped as she saw it. The Rabbi intended to sell her to the Honored Matres. The driver of the produce carrier had been one of their agents come to confirm that there was indeed a woman of Lucilla's description at the farmhouse.

Rebecca's candor gave Lucilla no escape: "It is the only way we can save ourselves and maintain our credibility."

So that was why the Rabbi had made her think of guards and power brokers! *Clever, clever. And I accept it as he knew I would.*

You cannot manipulate a marionette with only one string.

—THE ZENSUNNI WHIP

The Reverend Mother Sheeana stood at her sculpting stand, a gray-clawed shaper covering each hand like exotic gloves. The black sensiplaz on the stand had been taking form under her hands for almost an hour. She felt herself close to the creation that sought realization, surging from a wild place within her. The intensity of the creative force made her skin tremble and she wondered that passersby in the hall to her right did not sense it. The north window of her workroom admitted gray light behind her and the western window glowed orange with a desert sunset.

Prester, Sheeana's senior assistant here at the Desert Watch Station, had paused in the doorway a few minutes ago but the entire station complement knew better than to interrupt Sheeana at this work.

Stepping back, Sheeana brushed a strand of sun-streaked brown hair from her forehead with the back of a hand. The black plaz stood in front of her like a challenge, its curves and planes *almost* fitted to the form she sensed within her.

I come here to create when my fears are greatest, she thought.

This thought dampened the creative surge and she redoubled her efforts to complete the sculpture. Her shaper-clad hands dipped and swooped over the plaz and black shape followed each intrusion like a wave driven by an insane wind.

The light from the north window faded and the automatics compensated with a yellow-gray glow from the ceiling edges but it was not the same. It was not the same!

Sheeana stepped back from her work. Close . . . but not close enough. She could almost touch the form within her and feel it striving for birth. But the plaz was not right. One sweeping stroke of her right hand reduced it to a black blob on the stand.

Damn!

She stripped off the shapers and dropped them to the shelf beside the sculpting stand. The horizon out the western window still carried a strip of orange. Fading fast the way she felt the fading of her creative surge.

Striding to the sunset window, she was in time to see the last of the day's search teams return. Their landing lights were firefly darts off to the south where a temporary flat had been established in the path of the advancing dunes. She could see from the slow way the 'thopters came down that they had found no spiceblows or other signs that sandworms were at last developing from the sandtrout planted here.

I am shepherd to worms that may never come.

The window gave back to her a dark reflection of her features. She could see where the Spice Agony had left its marks. The slender, brown-skinned waif of Dune had become a tall, rather austere woman. But her brown hair still insisted on escaping the tight coif at the nape of her neck. And she could see the wildness in her all-blue eyes. Others could see it, too. And that was the problem, source of some of her fears.

There appeared to be no stopping the Missionaria in its preparations for our *Sheeana*.

If the giant sandworms developed—Shai-hulud returned! And the Missionaria Protectiva of the Bene Gesserit was ready to launch her onto an unsuspecting humanity prepared for religious adoration. The myth become real . . . just the way she tried to make that sculpture back there a reality.

Holy Sheeana! The God Emperor is her thrall! See how the sacred sandworms obey her! Leto is returned!

Would it influence the Honored Matres? Probably. They gave at least lip service to the God Emperor in his name of Guldur.

Not likely they would follow "Holy Sheeana's" lead except in the matter of sexual exploits. Sheeana knew her own sexual behavior, outrageous even by Bene Gesserit standards, was a form of protest against this role the Missionaria tried to impose on her. The excuse that she only polished the males trained in sexual bondage by Duncan Idaho was just that . . . an excuse.

Bellonda suspects.

Mentat Bell was a constant danger to Sisters who got out of line. And that was a major reason Bell held her powerful position in the high Council of the Sisterhood.

Sheeana turned away from the window and flung herself onto the orange and umber spread covering her cot. Directly in front of her, a large black and white drawing of a giant worm poised above a tiny human figure.

That's the way they were and may never be again. What was I trying to say with that drawing? If I knew I might be able to complete the plaz sculpture.

It had been perilous to develop a secret hand-talk with Duncan. But there were things the Sisterhood could not know—not yet.

There might be a way of escape for both of us.

But where could they go? It was a universe beset by Honored Matres and other forces. It was a universe of scattered planets peopled mostly by humans who wanted only to live out their lives in peace—accepting Bene Gesserit guidance in some places, squirming under Honored Matre suppression in many regions, mostly hoping to govern themselves as best they could, the perennial dream of democracy, and then there were always the unknowns. And always the lesson of the Honored Matres! Murbella's clues said Fish Speakers and Reverend Mothers in extremis formed the Honored Matres. Fish Speaker democracy become Honored Matre autocracy! The clues were too numerous to ignore. But why had they emphasized unconscious compulsions with their T-probes, cellular induction, and sexual prowess?

Where is the market to accept our fugitive talents?

This universe no longer possessed a single bourse. A species of sub-terranean webworks could be defined. It was extremely loose, based on old compromises and temporary agreements.

Odrade had once said: "It resembles an old garment with frayed edges and patched holes."

CHOAM's tightly bound trading network of the Old Empire was no more. Now, it was fearful bits and pieces held together by the loos-est of ties. People treated this patched thing with contempt, longing always for the good old days.

What kind of a universe would accept us merely as fugitives and not as the Sacred Sheeana with her consort?

Not that Duncan was a consort. That had been the Bene Gesserit's original plan: "Bond Sheeana to Duncan. We control him and he can control her."

Murbella cut that plan short. *And a good thing for both of us. Who needs a sexual obsession?* But Sheeana was forced to admit she harbored oddly confused feelings about Duncan Idaho. The hand-talks, the touching. And what could they say to Odrade when she came prying? Not if, but when.

"We talk about ways for Duncan and Murbella to escape you, Mother Superior. We talk about other ways to restore Teg's memories. We talk about our own private rebellion against the Bene Gesserit. Yes, Darwi Odrade! Your former student has become a rebel against you."

Sheeana admitted to mixed feelings about Murbella as well.

She domesticated Duncan where I might have failed.

The captive Honored Matre was a fascinating study . . . and amus-ing at times. There was her joking doggerel posted on the wall of the ship's Acolyte dining room.

> *Hey, God! I hope you're there.*
> *I want you to hear my prayer.*
> *That graven image on my shelf;*
> *Is it really you or just myself?*

Well, anyway, here it goes:
Please keep me on my toes.
Help me past my worst mistakes,
Doing it for both our sakes,
For an example of perfection
To the Proctors of my section;
Or merely for the Heaven of it,
Like bread, for the leaven of it.
For whatever reason may incline,
Please act for yours and mine.

The subsequent confrontation with Odrade, caught by the comeyes, had been a beautiful thing to watch. Odrade's voice oddly strident: "Murbella? You?"

"I'm afraid so." No contrition in her at all.

"Afraid so?" Still strident.

"Why not?" Quite defiant.

"You joke about the Missionaria! Don't protest. That was your intent."

"They're so damned pretentious!"

Sheeana could only sympathize as she reflected on that confrontation. Rebellious Murbella was a symptom. What ferments until you are forced to notice it?

I fought in just that way against the everlasting discipline, "which will make you strong, child."

What was Murbella like as a child? What pressures shaped her? Life was always a reaction to pressures. Some gave in to easy distractions and were shaped by them: pores bloated and reddened by excesses. Bacchus leering at them. Lust fixing its shape on their features. A Reverend Mother knew it by millennial observation. *We are shaped by pressures whether we resist them or not.* Pressures and shapings— that was life. *And I create new pressures by my secret defiance.*

Given the Sisterhood's present state of alertness to all threats, the hand-talk with Duncan probably was futile.

Sheeana tipped her head and looked at the black blob on the sculpting stand.

But I will persist. I will create my own statement of my life. I will create my own life! Damn the Bene Gesserit!

And I will lose the respect of my Sisters.

There was something antique about the way respectful conformity was forced upon them. They had preserved this thing from their most ancient past, taking it out regularly to polish and make the necessary repairs that time required of all human creations. And here it was today, held in unspoken reverence.

Thus you are a Reverend Mother and by no other judgment shall that be true.

Sheeana knew then she would be forced to test that antique thing to its limits, probably breaking it. And that black plaz form seeking outlet from the wild place within her was only one element of what she knew she had to do. Call it rebellion, call it by any other name, the force she felt in her breast could not be denied.

Confine yourself to observing and you always miss the point of your own life. The object can be stated this way: Live the best life you can. Life is a game whose rules you learn if you leap into it and play it to the hilt. Otherwise, you are caught off balance, continually surprised by the shifting play. Non-players often whine and complain that luck always passes them by. They refuse to see that they can create some of their own luck.

—DARWI ODRADE

"Have you studied the latest comeye record of Idaho?" Bellonda asked.

"Later! Later!" Odrade knew she was feeling peckish and it had come out in the response to Bell's pertinent question.

Pressures confined the Mother Superior more and more these days. She had always tried to face her duties with an attitude of broad interest. The more things to interest her, the wider her scan and that was sure to bring more usable data. Using the senses improved them. Substance, that was what her questing interests desired. Substance. It was like hunting for food to assuage a deep hunger.

But her days were becoming duplicates of this morning. Her liking for personal inspections was well known but these workroom walls held her. She must be where she could be reached. Not only reached, but able to dispatch communications and people on the instant.

Damn! I will make the time. I must!

It was time pressure as much as anything.

Sheeana said: "We trundle along on borrowed days."

Very poetic! Not much help in the face of pragmatic demands. They had to get as many Bene Gesserit cells as possible Scattered before the axe fell. Nothing else had that priority. The Bene Gesserit fabric was being torn apart, sent to destinations no one on Chapterhouse could know. Sometimes, Odrade saw this flow as rags and remnants. They went flapping away in their no-ships, a stock of sandtrout in their holds, Bene Gesserit traditions, learning and memories as guide. But the Sisterhood had done this long ago in the first Scattering and none came back or sent a message. Not one. Not one. Only Honored Matres returned. If they had ever been Bene Gesserit, they now were a terrible distortion, blindly suicidal.

Will we ever be whole again?

Odrade looked down at the work on her table: more selection charts. Who shall go and who shall remain? There was little time to pause and take a deep breath. Other Memory from her late predecessor, Taraza, took on an "I told you so!" character. "See what I had to go through?"

And I once wondered if there was room at the top.

There might be room at the top (as she was fond of telling acolytes) but there was seldom enough time.

When she thought of the largely passive non–Bene Gesserit populace "out there," Odrade sometimes envied them. They were permitted their illusions. What a comfort. You could pretend your life was forever, that tomorrow would be better, that the gods in their heavens watched you with care.

She recoiled from this lapse with disgust at herself. The unclouded eye was better, no matter what it saw.

"I've studied the latest Idaho records," she said, looking across the table at the patient Bellonda.

"He has interesting instincts," Bellonda said.

Odrade thought about that. Comeyes throughout the no-ship missed little. The Council's theory about ghola-Idaho became daily less a theory and more a conviction. How many memories from the serial Idaho lifetimes did this ghola contain?

"Tam is raising doubts about their children," Bellonda said. "Do they have dangerous talents?"

That was to be expected. The three children Murbella had borne Idaho in the no-ship had been removed at birth. All were being observed with care as they developed. Did they have that uncanny reactive speed Honored Matres displayed? Too early to say. It was a thing that developed in puberty, according to Murbella.

Their captive Honored Matre accepted the removal of her children with angry resignation. Idaho, however, showed little reaction. Odd. Did something give him a broader view of procreation? Almost a Bene Gesserit view?

"Another Bene Gesserit breeding program," he sneered.

Odrade let her thoughts flow. Was it really the Bene Gesserit attitude they saw in Idaho? The Sisterhood said emotional attachments were ancient detritus—important for human survival in their day but no longer required in the Bene Gesserit plan.

Instincts.

Things that came with egg and sperm. Often vital and loud: "This is the species talking to you, dolt!"

Loves . . . offspring . . . hungers . . . All of those unconscious motives to compel specific behavior. It was dangerous to meddle in such matters. The Breeding Mistresses knew this even while they did it. The Council debated it periodically and ordered a careful watch on consequences.

"You've studied the records. Is that all the answer I get?" Quite plaintive for Bellonda.

The comeye record of such interest to Bell was of Idaho questioning Murbella about Honored Matre sexual-addiction techniques. *Why?* His parellel abilities came from Tleilaxu conditioning impressed on his cells in the axlotl tank. Idaho's abilities originated as an unconscious pattern akin to instincts but the result was indistinguishable from the Honored Matre effect: ecstasy amplified until it drove out all reason and bound its victims to the source of such rewards.

Murbella went only so far in a verbal exploration of her abilities. Obvious residual fury that Idaho had addicted her with the same techniques she had been taught to use.

"Murbella blocks up when Idaho questions motives," Bellonda said.

Yes, I've seen that.

"I could kill you and you know it!" Murbella had said.

The comeye record showed them in bed in Murbella's no-ship quarters, having just satiated their mutual addiction. Sweat glistened on bare flesh. Murbella lay with a blue towel across her forehead, green eyes staring up at the comeyes. She appeared to be looking directly at the observers. Little orange flecks in her eyes. Anger flecks from her body's residual store of the spice substitute Honored Matres employed. She was on melange now—and no adverse symptoms.

Idaho lay beside her, black hair in disarray around his face, a sharp contrast to the white pillow beneath his head. His eyes were closed but the lids flickered. Thin. He wasn't eating enough despite tempting dishes sent by Odrade's own chef. His high cheekbones were strongly defined. The face had become craggy in the years of his confinement.

Murbella's threat was backed by physical ability, Odrade knew, but it was psychologically false. *Kill her lover? Not likely!*

Bellonda was thinking along these same lines. "What was she doing when she demonstrated her physical speed? We've seen that before."

"She knows we watch."

The comeyes showed Murbella defying post-coital fatigue to leap from bed. Moving with blurred speed (much faster than anything the Bene Gesserit had ever achieved), she kicked out with her right foot, stopping the blow only a hair's breadth from Idaho's head.

At her first movement, Idaho opened his eyes. He watched without fear, without flinching.

That blow! Fatal if it struck. You had only to see such a thing once to fear it. Murbella moved with no resort to her central cortex. Insect-like, an attack triggered by nerves at the point of muscle ignition.

"You see!" Murbella lowered her foot and glared down at him.

Idaho smiled.

Watching it, Odrade reminded herself that the Sisterhood had three of Murbella's children, all female. The Breeding Mistresses were excited. In time, Reverend Mothers born of this line might match that Honored Matre ability.

In time we probably don't have.

But Odrade shared the excitement of the Breeding Mistresses. That speed! Add that to the nerve-muscle training, the great pranabindu resources of the Sisterhood! What that might create lay wordlessly within her.

"She did that for us, not for him," Bellonda said.

Odrade was not sure. Murbella resented the constant watch over her but she had come to an accommodation with it. Many of her actions obviously ignored the people behind the comeyes. This record showed her returning to her place in the bed beside Idaho.

"I have restricted access to that record," Bellonda said. "Some aco-lytes are becoming troubled."

Odrade nodded. *Sexual addiction.* That aspect of Honored Matre abilities created disturbing ripples in the Bene Gesserit, especially among acolytes. Very suggestive. And most of the Sisters on Chapter-house knew the Reverend Mother Sheeana, alone among them, prac-ticed some of these techniques in defiance of a general fear this could weaken them.

"We must not become Honored Matres!" Bell was always saying that. *But Sheeana represents a significant control factor. She teaches us something about Murbella.*

One afternoon, catching Murbella alone in her no-ship quarters and obviously relaxed, Odrade had tried a direct question. "Before Idaho, were none of you ever tempted to, let us say, 'join in the fun'?"

Murbella had recoiled with angry pride. "He caught me by acci-dent!"

The same kind of anger she showed to Idaho's questions. Remembering this, Odrade leaned over her worktable and called up the original record.

"Look at how angry she gets," Bellonda said. "A hypnotrance injunction against answering such questions. I'd stake my reputation on it."

"That'll come out in the Spice Agony," Odrade said.

"If she ever gets to it!"

"Hypnotrance is supposed to be our secret."

Bellonda chewed on the obvious inference. *No Sister we sent out in the original Scattering ever returned.*

It was written large in their minds: "Did renegade Bene Gesserit create the Honored Matres?" Much suggested it. Then why did they resort to sexual enslavement of males? Murbella's historical prattlings did not satisfy. Everything about this went against Bene Gesserit teaching.

"We have to learn," Bellonda insisted. "What little we know is very disturbing."

Odrade recognized the concern. How much of a lure was this ability? Very big, she thought. Acolytes complained that they dreamed about becoming Honored Matres. Bellonda was rightly worried.

Create or arouse such unbridled forces and you built carnal fantasies of enormous complexity. You could lead whole populations around by their desires, by their fantasy projections.

There was the terrible power the Honored Matres dared use. Let it be known that they had the key to blinding ecstasy and they had won half the battle. The simple clue that such a thing existed, that was the beginning of surrender. People at Murbella's level in that other Sisterhood might not understand this but the ones at the top . . . Was it possible they merely used this power without caring or even suspecting its deeper force? *If that were the case, how were our first Scattered Ones lured into this dead end?*

Earlier, Bellonda had offered her hypothesis:

Honored Matre with captive Reverend Mother taken prisoner in that first Scattering. "Welcome, Reverend Mother. We would like you to witness a small demonstration of our powers." Interlude of sexual demonstration followed by a display of Honred Matre physical speed. Then—withdrawal of melange and injection of the adrenaline-based substitute laced with a hypnodrug. In that hypothetical trance, the Reverend Mother was sexually imprinted.

That coupled to the selective agony of melange withdrawal (Bell suggested) might make the victim deny her origins.

Fates help us! Were the original Honored Matres all Reverend Mothers? Do we dare test this hypothesis on ourselves? What can we learn of this from that pair in the no-ship?

Two sources of information lay there under the Sisterhood's watchful eyes but the key had yet to be found.

Woman and man no longer just breeding partners, no longer a comfort and support to each other. Something new has been added. The stakes have been escalated.

In the comeye record playing at the worktable, Murbella said something that caught the Mother Superior's full attention.

"We Honored Matres did this to ourselves! Can't blame anyone else."

"You hear that?" Bellonda demanded.

Odrade shook her head sharply, wanting all of her attention on this exchange.

"You can't say the same about me," Idaho objected.

"That's an empty excuse," Murbella accused. "So you were conditioned by the Tleilaxu to snare the first Imprinter you encountered!"

"And to kill her," Idaho corrected. "That's what they intended."

"But you didn't even try to kill me. Not that you could have."

"That's when . . ." Idaho broke off with an involuntary glance at the recording comeyes.

"What was he about to say there?" Bellonda pounced. "We must find out!"

But Odrade continued her silent observation of the captive pair. Murbella demonstrated a surprising insight. "You think you caught me through some accident in which you were not involved?"

"Exactly."

"But I see something in you that accepted all of it! You didn't just go along with your conditioning. You performed to your limits."

An inward look filmed Idaho's eyes. He tipped his head back, stretching his chest muscles.

"That's a Mentat expression!" Bellonda accused.

All of Odrade's analysts suggested this but they had yet to wrest an admission from Idaho. If he was a Mentat, why withhold that information?

Because of the other things implied by such abilities. He fears us and rightly so.

Murbella spoke with a sneer. "You improvised and improved on what the Tleilaxu did to you. There was something in you that made no complaint whatsoever!"

"That's how she deals with her own guilt feelings," Bellonda said. "She has to believe it's true or Idaho would not have been able to trap her."

Odrade pursed her lips. The projection showed Idaho amused. "Perhaps it was the same for both of us."

"You can't blame the Tleilaxu and I can't blame the Honored Matres."

Tamalane entered the workroom and sank into her chairdog beside Bellonda. "I see it has your interest, too." She gestured at the projected figures.

Odrade shut down the projector.

"I've been inspecting our axlotl tanks," Tamalane said. "That damned Scytale has withheld vital information."

"There's no flaw in our first ghola, is there?" Bellonda demanded.

"Nothing our Suks can find."

Odrade spoke in a mild tone: "Scytale has to keep some bargaining chips."

Both sides shared a fantasy: Scytale was paying the Bene Gesserit for rescue from the Honored Matres and sanctuary on Chapterhouse. But every Reverend Mother who studied him knew something else drove the last Tleilaxu Master.

Clever, clever, the Bene Tleilax. Far more clever than we suspected. And they have dirtied us with their axlotl tanks. The very word "tank"— another of their deceptions. We pictured containers of warmed amniotic fluid, each tank the focus of complex machinery to duplicate (in a subtle, discrete and controllable way) the workings of the womb. The tank is there all right! But look at what it contains.

The Tleilaxu solution was direct: Use the original. Nature already had worked it out over the eons. All the Bene Tleilax need do was add their own control system, their own way of replicating information stored in the cell.

"The Language of God," Scytale called it. *Language of Shaitan was more appropriate.*

Feedback. The cell directed its own womb. That was more or less what a fertilized ovum did anyway. The Tleilaxu merely refined it.

A sigh escaped Odrade, bringing sharp glances from her companions. *Does Mother Superior have new troubles?*

Scytale's revelations trouble me. And what those revelations have done to us. Oh, how we recoiled from the "debasement." Then, rationalizations. And we knew they were rationalizations! "If there is no other way. If this produces the gholas we need so desperately. Volunteers probably can be found." Were found! Volunteers!

"You're woolgathering!" Tamalane grumbled. She glanced at Bellonda, started to say something and thought better of it.

Bellonda's face went soft-bland, a frequent accompaniment to her darker moods. Her voice came out little more than a guttural whisper. "I strongly urge that we eliminate Idaho. And as for that Tleilaxu monster . . ."

"Why do you make such a suggestion with a euphemism?" Tamalane demanded.

"Kill him then! And the Tleilaxu should be subjected to every persuasion we—"

"Stop it, both of you!" Odrade ordered.

She pressed both palms briefly against her forehead and, staring at the bow window, saw icy rain out there. Weather Control was making more mistakes. You couldn't blame them, but there was nothing humans hated more than the unpredictable. *"We want it natural!"* *Whatever that means.*

When such thoughts came over her, Odrade longed for an existence confined to the order that pleased her: an occasional walk in the orchards. She enjoyed them in all seasons. A quiet evening with friends, the give and take of probing conversations with those for whom she felt warmth. *Affection?* Yes. The Mother Superior dared much—even love of companions. And good meals with drinks chosen for their enhancement of flavors. She wanted that, too. How fine it was to play upon the palate. And later . . . yes, later—a warm bed with a gentle companion sensitive to her needs as she was sensitive to his.

Most of this could not be, of course. Responsibilities! What an enormous word. How it burned.

"I'm getting hungry," Odrade said. "Shall I order lunch served here?"

Bellonda and Tamalane stared at her. "It's only half past eleven," Tamalane complained.

"Yes or no?" Odrade insisted.

Bellonda and Tamalane exchanged a private look. "As you wish," Bellonda said.

There was a saying in the Bene Gesserit (Odrade knew) that the Sisterhood ran smoother when Mother Superior's stomach was satisfied. That had just tipped the scales.

Odrade keyed the intercom to her private kitchen. "Lunch for three, Duana. Something special. You choose."

Lunch, when it came, featured a dish Odrade especially enjoyed, a veal casserole. Duana displayed a delicate touch with herbs, a bit of rosemary in the veal, the vegetables not overcooked. Superb.

Odrade savored every bite. The other two plodded through the meal, spoon-to-mouth, spoon-to-mouth.

Is this one of the reasons I am Mother Superior and they are not?

While an acolyte cleared away the remains of lunch, Odrade turned to one of her favorite questions: "What is the gossip in the common rooms and among the acolytes?"

She remembered in her own acolyte days how she had hung on the words of the older women, expecting great truths and getting mostly small talk about Sister So-and-so or the latest problems of Proctor X. Occasionally, though, the barriers came down and important data flowed.

"Too many acolytes talk of wanting to go out in our Scattering," Tamalane rasped. "Sinking ships and rats, I say."

"There's a great interest in Archives lately," Bellonda said. "Sisters who know better come looking for confirmation—whether such-and-so acolyte has a heavy Siona gene-mark."

Odrade found this interesting. Their common Atreides ancestor from the Tyrant's eons, Siona Ibn Fuad al-Seyefa Atreides, had imparted to her descendants this ability that hid them from prescient searchers. Every person walking openly on Chapterhouse shared that ancestral protection.

"A heavy mark?" Odrade asked. "Do they doubt that the ones in question are protected?"

"They want reassurance," Bellonda growled. "And now may I return to Idaho? He has the genetic mark and he does not. It worries me. Why do some of his cells not have the Siona marker? What were the Tleilaxu doing?"

"Duncan knows the danger and he's not suicidal," Odrade said.

"We don't know what he is," Bellonda complained.

"Probably a Mentat, and we all know what that could mean," Tamalane said.

"I understand why we keep Murbella," Bellonda said. "Valuable information. But Idaho and Scytale . . ."

"That's enough!" Odrade snapped. "Watchdogs can bark too long!"

Bellonda accepted this grudgingly. *Watchdogs.* Their Bene Gesserit term for constant monitoring by Sisters to see that you did not fall into shallow ways. Very trying to acolytes but just another part of life to Reverend Mothers.

Odrade had explained it one afternoon to Murbella, the two of them alone in a gray-walled interview chamber of the no-ship. Stand-

ing close together facing each other. Eyes at a level. Quite informal and
intimate. Except for the knowledge of those comeyes all around them.

"Watchdogs," Odrade said, responding to a question from Murbella. "It means we are mutual gadflies. Don't make that more than it
is. We seldom nag. A simple word can be enough."

Murbella, her oval face drawn into a look of distaste, the wide-set
green eyes intent, obviously thought Odrade referred to some common signal, a word or saying the Sisters used in such situations.

"What word?"

"Any word, dammit! Whatever's appropriate. It's like a mutual reflex. We share a common 'tic' that comes not to annoy us. We welcome
it because it keeps us on our toes."

"And you'll watchdog *me* if I become a Reverend Mother?"

"We want our watchdogs. We'd be weaker without them."

"It sounds oppressive."

"We don't find it so."

"I think it's repellent." She looked at the glittering lenses in the
ceiling. "Like those damned comeyes."

"We take care of our own, Murbella. Once you're a Bene Gesserit,
you're assured of lifelong maintenance."

"A comfortable niche." Sneering.

Odrade spoke softly. "Something quite different. You are challenged throughout your life. You repay the Sisterhood right up to the
limits of your abilities."

"Watchdogs!"

"We're always mindful of one another. Some of us in positions of
power can be authoritarian at times, familiar even, but only to a point
carefully measured for the requirements of the moment."

"Never really warm or tender, eh?"

"That's the rule."

"Affection, maybe, but no love?"

"I've told you the rule." And Odrade could see the reaction clearly on
Murbella's face: *There it is! They will demand that I give up Duncan!*

"So there's no love among the Bene Gesserit." How sad her tone. There was hope for Murbella yet.

"Loves occur," Odrade said, "but my Sisters treat them as aberrations."

"So what I feel for Duncan is aberration?"

"And Sisters will try to treat it."

"Treat! Apply correctional therapy to the afflicted!"

"Love is considered a sign of rot in Sisters."

"I see signs of rot in you!"

As though she followed Odrade's thoughts, Bellonda dragged Odrade out of reverie. "That Honored Matre will never commit herself to us!" Bellonda wiped a bit of luncheon gravy from the corner of her mouth. "We're wasting our time trying to teach her our ways."

At least Bell was no longer calling Murbella "whore," Odrade thought. *That was an improvement.*

All governments suffer a recurring problem: Power attracts pathological personalities. It is not that power corrupts but that it is magnetic to the corruptible. Such people have a tendency to become drunk on violence, a condition to which they are quickly addicted.

—MISSIONARIA PROTECTIVA,
TEXT QIV (DECTO)

Rebecca knelt on the yellow tile floor as she had been ordered to do, not daring to look up at Great Honored Matre seated so remotely high, so dangerous. Two hours Rebecca had waited here almost in the center of a giant room while Great Honored Matre and her companions ate a lunch served by obsequious attendants. Rebecca marked the manners of the attendants with care and emulated them.

Her eye sockets still ached from transplants the Rabbi had given her less than a month ago. These eyes showed a blue iris and white sclera, no clue to the Spice Agony in her past. It was a temporary defense. In less than a year, the new eyes would betray her with total blue.

She judged the ache in her eyes to be the least of her problems. An organic implant fed her metered doses of melange, concealing her dependence. The supply was gauged to last about sixty days. If these Honored Matres held her longer than that, withdrawal would plunge her into an agony that would make the original appear mild by comparison. The most immediately dangerous thing was the shere being metered to her with the spice. If these women detected it, they certainly would be suspicious.

You are doing well. Be patient. That was Other Memory from the horde of Lampadas. The voice rang softly in her head. It had the sound of Lucilla but Rebecca could not be sure.

It had become a familiar voice in the months since the Sharing when it had announced itself as "Speaker of your Mohalata." *These whores cannot match our knowledge. Remember that and let it give you courage.*

The presence of Others Within who subtracted none of her attention from what went on around her had filled her with awe. *We call it Simulflow,* Speaker had said. *Simulflow multiplies your awareness.* When she had tried to explain this to the Rabbi, he had reacted in anger.

"You have been tainted by unclean thoughts!"

They had been in the Rabbi's study late at night. "Stealing time from the days alloted us," he called it. The study was an underground room, its walls lined with old books, ridulian crystals, scrolls. The room was protected from probes by the best Ixian devices and they had been modified by his own people to improve them.

She was allowed to sit beside his desk at such times while he leaned back in an old chair. A glowglobe placed low beside him cast an antique yellow light on his bearded face, glinting off the spectacles he wore almost as a badge of office.

Rebecca pretended confusion. "But you said it was required of us to save this treasure from Lampadas. Have the Bene Gesserit not been honorable with us?"

She saw the worry in his eyes. "You heard Levi talking yesterday of the questions being asked here. Why did the Bene Gesserit witch come to us? That is what they ask."

"Our story is consistent and believable," Rebecca protested. "The Sisters have taught us ways that even Truthsay cannot penetrate."

"I don't know . . . I don't know." The Rabbi shook his head sadly. "What is a lie? What is truth? Do we condemn ourselves with our own mouths?"

"It is pogrom that we resist, Rabbi!" That usually stiffened his resolve.

"Cossacks! Yes, you are right, daughter. There have been cossacks in every age and we are not the only ones who have felt their knouts and swords as they rode into the village with murder in their hearts."

It was odd, Rebecca thought, how he managed to give the impression that these events were of recent occurrence and that his eyes had seen them. Never to forgive, never to forget. Lidiche was yesterday. What a powerful thing that was in the memory of Secret Israel. Pogrom! Almost as powerful in its continuity as these Bene Gesserit presences she carried in her awareness. Almost. That was the thing the Rabbi resisted, she told herself.

"I fear that you have been taken from us," the Rabbi said. "What have I done to you? What have I done? And all in the name of honor."

He looked at the instruments on his study wall that reported the nightly power accumulations from the vertical-axis windmills placed around the farmstead. The instruments said the machines were humming away up there, storing energy for the morrow. That was a gift of the Bene Gesserit: freedom from Ix. Independence. What a peculiar word.

Without looking at Rebecca, he said: "I find this thing of Other Memory very difficult and always have. Memory should bring wisdom but it does not. It is how we order the memory and where we apply our knowledge."

He turned and looked at her, his face falling into shadows. "What is it this one inside you says? This one you think of as Lucilla?"

Rebecca could see it pleased him to say Lucilla's name. If Lucilla could speak through a daughter of Secret Israel, then she still lived and had not been betrayed.

Rebecca lowered her gaze as she spoke. "She says we have these inner images, sounds and sensations that come at command or intrude under necessity."

"Necessity, yes! And what is that except reports of senses from flesh that may have been where you should not have been and done offensive things?"

Other bodies, other memories, Rebecca thought. Having experienced this she knew she could never willingly abandon it. *Perhaps I have indeed become Bene Gesserit. That is what he fears, of course.*

"I will tell you a thing," the Rabbi said. "This 'crucial intersection of living awareness,' as they call it, that is nothing unless you know how your own decisions go out from you like threads into the lives of others."

"To see our own actions in the reactions of others, yes, that is how the Sisters view it."

"That is wisdom. What is it the lady says they seek?"

"Influence on the maturing of humankind."

"Mmmmmm. And she finds that events are not beyond her influence, merely beyond her senses. That is almost wise. But maturity . . . ahhh, Rebecca. Do we interfere with a higher plan? Is it the right of humans to set limits on the nature of Yaweh? I think Leto II understood that. This lady in you denies it."

"She says he was a damnable tyrant."

"He was but there have been wise tyrants before him and doubtless will be more after us."

"They call him Shaitan."

"He had Satan's own powers. I share their fear of that. He was not so much prescient as he was a cement. He fixed the shape of what he saw."

"That is what the lady says. But she says it is their grail that he preserved."

"Again, they are almost wise."

A great sigh shook the Rabbi and once more he looked to the instruments on his wall. *Energy for the morrow.*

He returned his attention to Rebecca. She was changed. He could not avoid awareness of it. She had become very like the Bene Gesserit. It was understandable. Her mind was filled with all of those *people* from Lampadas. But they were not Gadarene swine to be driven into the sea and their diabolism with them. *And I am not another Jesus.*

"This thing they tell you about the Mother Superior Odrade—that she often damns her own Archivists and the Archives with them. What a thing! Are not Archives like the books in which we preserve our wisdom?"

"Then am I an Archivist, Rabbi?"

Her question confounded him but it also illuminated the problem. He smiled. "I tell you something, daughter. I admit to a little sympathy with this Odrade. There is always something grumbling about Archivists."

"Is that wisdom, Rabbi?" How shyly she asked it!

"Believe me, daughter, it is. How carefully the Archivist suppresses even the smallest hint of judgment. One word after another. Such arrogance!"

"How do they judge which words to use, Rabbi?"

"Ahhh, a bit of wisdom comes to you, daughter. But these Bene Gesserit have not achieved wisdom and it is their grail that prevents it."

She could see it on his face. *He tries to arm me with doubts about these lives I carry.*

"Let me tell you a thing about the Bene Gesserit," he said. Nothing came into his mind then. No words, no sage advice. This had not happened to him for years. There was only one course open to him: speak from the heart.

"Perhaps they have been too long on the road to Damascus without a blinding flash of illumination, Rebecca. I hear them say they act for the benefit of humankind. Somehow, I cannot see this in them, nor do I believe the Tyrant saw it."

When Rebecca started to reply, he stopped her with an upraised hand. "Mature humanity? That is their grail? Is it not the mature fruit that is plucked and eaten?"

On the floor of Junction's Great Hall, Rebecca remembered these words, seeing the personification of them not in the lives she preserved but in the actions of her captors.

Great Honored Matre had finished eating. She wiped her hands on the gown of an attendant.

"Let her approach," Great Honored Matre said.

Pain lanced Rebecca's left shoulder and she lurched forward on her knees. The one called Logno had come up behind with the stealth of a hunter and had jabbed a shuntgoad into the captive's flesh.

Laughter echoed through the room.

Rebecca staggered to her feet and, staying just ahead of the goad, arrived at the foot of the steps leading up to the Great Honored Matre where the goad stopped her.

"Down!" Logno emphasized the command with another jab.

Rebecca sank to her knees and stared straight ahead at the risers of the steps. The yellow tiles displayed tiny scratches. Somehow, these flaws reassured her.

Great Honored Matre said: "Let her be, Logno. I wish answers, not screams." Then to Rebecca: "Look at me, woman!"

Rebecca raised her eyes and stared up at the face of death. What an unremarkable face it was to have that threat in it. So . . . so evenly featured. Almost plain. Such a small figure. This amplified the peril Rebecca sensed. What powers the small woman must have to rule these terrible people.

"Do you know why you are here?" Great Honored Matre demanded.

In her most obsequious tones, Rebecca said: "I was told, O Great Honored Matre, that you wished me to recount the lore of Truthsay and other matters of Gammu."

"You were mated to a Truthsayer!" It was accusation.

"He is dead, Great Honored Matre."

"No, Logno!" This was directed at the aide who lunged forward with the goad. "This wretch does not know our ways. Now, go stand at the side, Logno, where I will not be annoyed by your impetuosity."

"You will speak to me only in response to questions or when I command it, wretch!" Great Honored Matre shouted.

Rebecca cringed.

Speaker whispered in Rebecca's head: *That was almost Voice. Be warned.*

"Have you ever known any of the ones who call themselves Bene Gesserit?" Great Honored Matre asked.

Really now! "Everyone has encountered the witches, Great Honored Matre."

"What do you know of them?"

So this is why they brought me here.

"Only what I have heard, Great Honored Matre."

"Are they brave?"

"It is said they always try to avoid risks, Great Honored Matre."

You are worthy of us, Rebecca. That is the pattern of these whores. The marble rolls down the incline in its proper channel. They think you dislike us.

"Are these Bene Gesserit rich?" Great Honored Matre asked.

"I think the witches are poor beside you, Honored Matre," Rebecca said.

"Why do you say that? Do not speak just to please me!"

"But Honored Matre, could the witches send a great ship from Gammu to here just to carry me? And where are the witches now? They hide from you."

"Yes, where are they?" Honored Matre demanded.

Rebecca shrugged.

"Were you on Gammu when the one they called Bashar fled us?" Honored Matre asked.

She knows you were. "I was there, Great Honored Matre, and heard the stories. I do not believe them."

"Believe what we tell you to believe, wretch! What are the stories you heard?"

"That he moved with a speed the eye could not see. That he killed many . . . people with only his hands. That he stole a no-ship and fled into the Scattering."

"Believe that he fled, wretch." *See how she fears! She cannot hide the trembling.*

"Speak of the Truthsay," Great Honored Matre commanded.

"Great Honored Matre, I do not understand the Truthsay. I know only the words of my Sholem, my husband. I can repeat his words if you wish."

Great Honored Matre considered this, glancing from side to side at her aides and councillors, who were beginning to show signs of boredom. *Why doesn't she just kill this wretch?*

Rebecca, seeing the violence in eyes that glared orange at her, shrank into herself. She thought of her husband by his love-name, Shoel, now, and his words comforted. He had shown the "proper talent" while still a child. Some called it an instinct but Shoel had never used that word. "Trust your gut feelings. That's what my teachers always said."

It was such a down-to-earth expression that he said it usually threw off the ones who came seeking "the esoteric mystery."

"There is no secret," Shoel had said. "It's training and hard work like anything else. You exercise what they call 'petit perception,' the ability to detect very small variations in human reactions."

Rebecca could see such small reactions in those who stared down at her. *They want me dead. Why?*

Speaker had advice. *The great one likes to show off her power over the others. She does not do what others want but what she thinks they do not want.*

"Great Honored Matre," Rebecca ventured, "you are so rich and powerful. Surely you must have a place of menial employment where I may be of service to you."

"You wish to enter my service?" *What a feral grin!*

"It would make me happy, Great Honored Matre."

"I am not here to make you happy."

Logno took a step forward onto the floor. "Then make us happy, Dama. Let us have some sport with—"

"Silence!" *Ahhh, that was a mistake, calling her by the intimate name here among the others.*

Logno drew back and almost dropped the goad.

Great Honored Matre stared down at Rebecca with an orange glare. "You will go back to your miserable existence on Gammu, wretch. I will not kill you. That would be a mercy. Having seen what we could give you, live your life without it."

"Great Honored Matre!" Logno protested. "We have suspicions about—"

"I have suspicions about you, Logno. Send her back and alive! Hear me? Do you think us incapable of finding her if we ever have need of her?"

"No, Great Honored Matre."

"We are watching you, wretch," Great Honored Matre said.

Bait! She thinks of you as something to capture larger game. How interesting. This one has a head and uses it in spite of her violent nature. So that's how she came to power.

All the way back to Gammu, confined to stinking quarters in a ship that had once served the Guild, Rebecca considered her predicament. Surely, those whores had not expected her to mistake their intent. But . . . perhaps they did. Subservience, cringing. *They revel in such things.*

She knew this came from a bit of her Shoel's Truthsay as much as from the Lampadas advisors.

"You accumulate a lot of small observations, sensed but never brought to consciousness," Shoel had said. "Cumulatively, they say things to you but not in a language anyone speaks. Language isn't necessary."

She had thought this one of the oddest things she had ever heard. But that was before her own Agony. In bed at night, comforted by darkness and the touch of loving flesh, they had acted wordlessly but had shared words, too.

"Language obstructs you," Shoel had said. "What you do is learn to read your own reactions. Sometimes, you can find words to describe this . . . sometimes . . . not."

"No words? Not even for the questions?"

"Words you want, is it? How are these? Trust. Belief. Truth. Honesty."

"Those are good words, Shoel."

"But they miss the mark. Don't depend on them."

"Then what do you depend on?"

"My own internal reactions. I read myself, not the person in front of me. I always know a lie because I want to turn my back on the liar."

"So that's how you do it!" Pounding his bare arm.

"Others do it differently. One person I heard say she knew a lie because she wanted to put her arm through the liar's arm and walk a ways, comforting the liar. You may think that's nonsense, but it works."

"I think it's very wise, Shoel." Love speaking. She did not really know what he meant.

"My precious love," he said, cradling her head on his arm, "Truthsayers have a Truthsense that, once awakened, works all the time. Please don't tell me I'm wise when it's your love speaking."

"I'm sorry, Shoel." She liked the smell of his arm and buried her head in the crook of it, tickling him. "But I want to know everything you know."

He pushed her head into a more comfortable position. "You know what my Third Stage instructor said? 'Know nothing! Learn to be totally naive.'"

She was astonished. "Nothing at all?"

"You approach everything with a clean slate, nothing on you or in you. Whatever comes is written there by itself."

She began to see it. "Nothing to interfere."

"Correct. You are the original ignorant savage, completely unsophisticated to the point where you back right into ultimate sophistication. You find it without looking for it, you might say."

"Now, that is wise, Shoel. I'll bet you were the best student they ever had, the quickest and the—"

"I thought it was interminable nonsense."

"You didn't!"

"Until one day I read a little twitch in me. It wasn't the movement of a muscle or something someone else might detect. Just a . . . a twitch."

"Where was it?"

"Nowhere I could describe. But my Fourth Stage instructor had prepared me for it. 'Grab that thing with gentle hands. Delicately.' One of the students thought he meant your real hands. Oh, how we laughed."

"That was cruel." She touched his cheek and felt the beginning of his dark stubble. It was late but she did not feel sleepy.

"I suppose it was cruel. But when the twitch came, I knew it. I had never felt such a thing before. I was surprised by it, too, because knowing it then, I knew it had been there all along. It was familiar. It was my Truthsense twitching."

She thought she could feel Truthsense stirring within herself. The feeling of wonder in his voice aroused something.

"It was mine then," he said. "It belonged to me and I belonged to it. No separation ever again."

"How wonderful that must be." Awe and envy in her voice.

"No! Some of it I hate. Seeing some people this way is like seeing them eviscerated, their guts hanging out."

"That's disgusting!"

"Yes, but there are compensations, love. These are people you meet, people who are like beautiful flowers extended to you by an innocent child. Innocence. My own innocence responds and my Truthsense is strengthened. That is what you do for me, my love."

The no-ship of the Honored Matres arrived at Gammu and they sent her down to the Landing Flat in the garbage lighter. It disgorged her beside the ship's discards and excrement but she did not mind. *Home! I'm home and Lampadas survives.*

The Rabbi, however, did not share her enthusiasm.

Once more, they sat in his study, but now she felt more familiar with Other Memory, much more confident. He could see this.

"You are even more like them than ever! It's unclean."

"Rabbi, we all have unclean ancestors. I am fortunate in that I know some of mine."

"What is this? What are you saying?"

"All of us are descendants of people who did nasty things, Rabbi. We don't like to think of barbarians in our ancestry but they're there."

"Such talk!"

"Reverend Mothers can recall them all, Rabbi. Remember, it is the victors who breed. You understand?"

"I've never heard you talk so boldly. What has happened to you, daughter?"

"I survived, knowing that victory sometimes is achieved at a moral price."

"What is this? These are evil words."

"Evil? Barbarism is not even the proper word for some of the evil things our ancestors did. The ancestors of all of us, Rabbi."

She saw she had hurt him and felt the cruelty of her own words but could not stop. How could he escape the truth of what she said? He was an honorable man.

She spoke more softly but her words cut him even deeper. "Rabbi, if you shared witness to some of the things Other Memory has forced me to know, you would come back seeking new words for evil. Some things our ancestors have done debase the worst label you could imagine."

"Rebecca . . . Rebecca . . . I know necessities of . . ."

"Don't make excuses about 'necessities of the times'! You, a Rabbi, know better. When are we without a moral sense? It's just that sometimes we don't listen."

He put his hands over his face, rocking back and forth in the old chair. It creaked mournfully.

"Rabbi, you I have always loved and respected. I went through the Agony for you. I shared Lampadas for you. Do not deny what I have learned from this."

He lowered his hands. "I do not deny, daughter. But permit me my pain."

"Out of all these realizations, Rabbi, the thing I must deal with most immediately and without respite is that there are no innocents."

"Rebecca!"

"Guilty may not be the right word, Rabbi, but our ancestors did things for which payment must be made."

"That I understand, Rebecca. It is a balance that—"

"Don't tell me you understand when I know you don't." She stood and glared down at him. "It's not a balance book that you set aright. How far back would you go?"

"Rebecca, I am your Rabbi. You must not talk this way, especially to me."

"The farther back you go, Rabbi, the worse the evil atrocities and higher the price. You cannot go back that far but I am forced to it."

Turning, she left him, ignoring the pleading in his voice, the painful way he said her name. As she closed the door, she heard him say: "What have we done? Israel, help her."

The writing of history is largely a process of diversion. Most historical accounts distract attention from the secret influences behind great events.

—THE BASHAR TEG

When left to his own devices, Idaho often explored his no-ship prison. So much to see and learn about this Ixian artifact. It was a cave of wonders.

He paused on this afternoon's restless walk through his quarters and looked at the tiny comeyes built into the glittering surface of a doorway. They were watching him. He had the odd sensation of seeing himself through those prying eyes. What did the Sisters think when they looked at him? The blocky ghola-child from Gammu's long-dead Keep had become a lanky man: dark skin and hair. The hair was longer than when he had entered this no-ship on the last day of Dune.

Bene Gesserit eyes peered below the skin. He was sure they suspected he was a Mentat and he feared how they might interpret that. How could a Mentat expect to hide the fact from Reverend Mothers indefinitely? Foolishness! He knew they already suspected him of Truthsay.

He waved at the comeyes and said: "I'm restless. I think I'll explore."

Bellonda hated it when he took that jocular attitude toward surveillance. She did not like him to roam the ship. She did not try to hide it from him. He could see the unspoken question in her glowering features whenever she came to confront him: *"Is he looking for a way to escape?"*

Exactly what I'm doing, Bell, but not in the way you suspect.

The no-ship presented him with fixed limits: the exterior forcefield he could not penetrate, certain machinery areas where the drive (so he was told) had been temporarily disabled, guard quarters (he could see into some of them but not enter), the armory, the section reserved to the captive Tleilaxu, Scytale. He occasionally met Scytale at one of the barriers and they peered at each other across the silencing field that held them apart. Then there was the information barrier—sections of Shiprecords that would not respond to his questions, answers his warders would not give.

Within these limits lay a lifetime of things to see and learn, even the lifetime of some three hundred Standard Years he could reasonably expect.

If Honored Matres do not find us.

Idaho saw himself as the game they sought, wanting him even more than they wanted the women of Chapterhouse. He had no illusions about what the hunters would do to him. They knew he was here. The men he trained in sexual bonding and sent out to plague the Honored Matres—those men taunted the hunters.

When the Sisters learned of his Mentat ability they would know immediately that his mind carried the memories of more than one ghola lifetime. *The original did not have that talent.* They would suspect he was a latent Kwisatz Haderach. Look how they rationed his melange. They were clearly terrified of repeating the mistake they had made with Paul Atreides and his Tyrant son. *Thirty-five hundred years of bondage!*

But dealing with Murbella required Mentat awareness. He entered every encounter with her not expecting to achieve answers then or later. It was a typical Mentat approach: concentrate on the questions. Mentats accumulated questions the way others accumulated answers. Questions created their own patterns and systems. This produced the most important *shapes*. You looked at your universe through self-created patterns—all composed of images, words, and labels (everything temporary), all mingled in sensory impulses, that reflected off his internal constructs the way light bounced from bright surfaces.

Idaho's original Mentat instructor had formed the temporary words for that first tentative construct: "Watch for consistent movements against your internal screen."

From that first hesitant dip into Mentat powers, Idaho could trace the growth of a sensitivity to changes in his own observations, always *becoming* Mentat.

Bellonda was his most severe trial. He dreaded her penetrating gaze and slashing questions. Mentat probing Mentat. He met her forays delicately, with reserve and patience. *Now, what are you after?*

As if he didn't know.

He wore patience as a mask. But fear came naturally and there was no harm in showing it. Bellonda did not hide her wish to see him dead.

Idaho accepted the fact that soon the watchers would see only one possible source for the skills he was forced to use.

A Mentat's real skills lay in that mental *construct* they called "the great synthesis." It required a patience that non-Mentats did not even imagine possible. Mentat schools defined it as perseverance. You were a primitive tracker, able to read minuscule signs, tiny disturbances in the environment, and follow where these led. At the same time, you remained open to broad motions all around and within. This produced naivete, the basic Mentat posture, akin to that of Truthsayers but far more sweeping.

"You are open to whatever the universe may do," his first instructor had said. "Your mind is not a computer; it is a response-tool keyed to whatever your senses display."

Idaho always recognized when Bellonda's senses were open. She stood there, gaze slightly withdrawn, and he knew few preconceptions cluttered her mind. His defense lay in her basic flaw: Opening the senses required an idealism that was foreign to Bellonda. She did not ask the best questions and he wondered at this. Would Odrade use a flawed Mentat? It went against her other performances.

I seek the questions that form the best images.

Doing this, you never thought of yourself as clever, that you had *the* formula to provide *the* solution. You remained as responsive to new questions as you did to new patterns. Testing, re-testing, shaping and reshaping. A constant process, never stopping, never satisfied. It was your own private pavane, similar to that of other Mentats but it carried always your own unique posture and steps.

"You are never truly a Mentat. That is why we call it 'The Endless Goal.'" The words of his teachers were burned into his awareness.

As he accumulated observations of Bellonda, he came to appreciate a viewpoint of those great Mentat Masters who had taught him. "Reverend Mothers do not make the best Mentats."

No Bene Gesserit appeared capable of completely removing herself from that binding absolute she achieved in the Spice Agony: loyalty to her Sisterhood.

His teachers had warned against absolutes. They created a serious flaw in a Mentat.

"Everything you do, everything you sense and say is experiment. No deduction final. Nothing stops until dead and perhaps not even then, because each life creates endless ripples. Induction bounces within and you sensitize yourself to it. Deduction conveys illusions of absolutes. Kick the truth and shatter it!"

When Bellonda's questions touched on the relationship between himself and Murbella, he saw vague emotional responses. *Amusement? Jealousy?* He could accept amusement (and even jealousy) about the compelling sexual demands of this mutual addiction. *Is the ecstasy truly that great?*

He wandered through his quarters this afternoon feeling displaced, as though newly here and not yet accepting these rooms as home. *That is emotion talking to me.*

Over the years of his confinement, these quarters had taken on a lived-in appearance. This was his cave, the former supercargo suite: large rooms with slightly curved walls—bedroom, library-workroom, sitting room, a green-tiled bath with dry and wet cleansing systems, and a long practice hall he shared with Murbella for exercise.

The rooms bore a unique collection of artifacts and marks of his presence: that slingchair placed at just the right angle to the console and projector linking him to Shipsystems, those ridulian records on that low side table. And there were stains of occupancy—that dark brown blot on the worktable. Spilled food had left its indelible mark.

He moved restlessly into his sleeping quarters. The light was dimmer. His ability to identify the familiar held true for odors. There was a saliva-like smell to the bed—the residue of last night's sexual collision. *That is the proper word: collision.*

The no-ship's air—filtered, recycled, and sweetened—often bored him. No break in the no-ship maze to the exterior world ever remained open long. He sometimes sat silently sniffing, hoping for a faint trace of air that had not been adjusted to the prison's demands.

There is a way to escape!

He wandered out of his quarters and down the corridor, took the dropchute at the end of the passage and emerged in the ship's lowest level.

What is really happening out there in that world open to the sky?

The bits Odrade told him about events filled him with dread and a trapped feeling. *No place to run! Am I wise to share my fears with Sheeana? Murbella merely laughed. "I will protect you, love. Honored Matres won't hurt me." Another false dream.*

But Sheeana . . . how quickly she had picked up the hand-language and entered the spirit of his conspiracy. Conspiracy? No . . . I doubt that any Reverend Mother will act against her Sisters. Even the Lady Jessica went back to them in the end. But I don't ask Sheeana to act against the Sisterhood, only that she protect us from Murbella's folly.

The enormous powers of the hunters made only the destruction predictable. A Mentat had but to look at their disruptive violence. They brought something else as well, something hinting at matters out there in the Scattering. What were these Futars Odrade mentioned with such casualness? *Part human, part beast?* That had been Lucilla's guess. *And where is Lucilla?*

He found himself presently in the Great Hold, the kilometer-long cargo space where they had carried the last giant sandworm of Dune, bringing it to Chapterhouse. The area still smelled of spice and sand, filling his mind with long-ago and the dead far away. He knew why he came so often to the Great Hold, doing it sometimes without even thinking, as he had just done. It both attracted and repelled. The illusion of unlimited space with traces of dust, sand, and spice carried the nostalgia of lost freedoms. But there was another side. This is where it always happened to him.

Will it happen today?

Without warning, the sense of being in the Great Hold would vanish. Then . . . the net shimmering in a molten sky. He was aware when the vision came that he was not really *seeing* a net. His mind translated what the senses could not define.

A shimmering net undulating like an infinite borealis.

Then the net would part and he would see two people—man and woman. How ordinary they appeared and yet extraordinary. A grandmother and grandfather in antique clothing: bib coveralls for the man and a long dress with headscarf for the woman. Working in a flower garden! He thought it must be more of the illusion. *I am seeing this but it is not really what I see.*

They always noticed him eventually. He heard their voices. "There he is again, Marty," the man would say, calling the woman's attention to Idaho.

"I wonder how it is he can look through?" Marty asked once. "Doesn't seem possible."

"He's spread pretty thin, I think. Wonder if he knows the danger?"

Danger. That was the word that always jerked him out of the vision.

"Not at your console today?"

For just an instant, Idaho thought it was the vision, the voice of that odd woman, then he realized it was Odrade. Her voice came from close behind. He whirled and saw he had failed to close the hatch. She had followed him into the Hold, stalking him quietly, avoiding the scattered patches of sand that might have grated underfoot and betrayed her approach.

She looked tired and impatient. *Why did she think I would be at my console?*

As though answering his unspoken question, she said: "I find you at your console so often lately. For what do you search, Duncan?"

He shook his head without speaking. *Why do I suddenly feel in peril?*

It was a rare feeling in Odrade's company. He could remember other occasions, though. Once when she had stared suspiciously at his hands in the field of his console. *Fear associated with my console. Do I reveal my Mentat hunger for data? Do they guess that I have hidden my private self there?*

"Do I get no privacy at all?" Anger and attack.

She shook her head slowly from side to side as much to say, "You can do better than that."

"This is your second visit today," he accused.

"I must say you're looking well, Duncan." More circumlocution.

"Is that what your watchers say?"

"Don't be petty. I came for a chat with Murbella. She said you'd be down here."

"I suppose you know Murbella's pregnant again." Was that trying to placate her?

"For which we are grateful. I came to tell you that Sheeana wants to visit you again."

Why would Odrade announce that?

Her words filled him with images of the Dune waif who had become a full Reverend Mother (the youngest ever, so they said). Sheeana, his confidante, out there watching over that last great sandworm. Had it finally perpetuated itself? Why should Odrade interest herself in Sheeana's visit?

"Sheeana wants to discuss the Tyrant with you."

She saw the surprise this produced.

"What could I possibly add to Sheeana's knowledge of Leto II?" he demanded. "She's a Reverend Mother."

"You knew the Atreides intimately."

Ahhhhh. She's hunting for the Mentat.

"But you said she wanted to discuss Leto and it's not safe to think of him as Atreides."

"Oh, but he was. Refined into something more elemental than anyone before him, but one of us, nonetheless."

One of us! She reminded him that she, too, was Atreides. Calling in his never-ending debt to the family!

"So you say."

"Shouldn't we stop playing this foolish game?"

Caution gripped him. He knew she saw it. Reverend Mothers were so damnably sensitive. He stared at her, not daring to speak, knowing even this told her too much.

"We believe you remember more than one ghola lifetime." And when he still did not respond, "Come, come, Duncan! Are you a Mentat?"

The way she spoke, as much accusation as question, he knew concealment had ended. It was almost a relief.

"And if I am?"

"The Tleilaxu mixed the cells from more than one Idaho ghola when they grew you."

Idaho-ghola! He refused to think of himself in that abstraction. "Why is Leto suddenly so important to you?" No escaping the admission in that reponse.

"Our worm has become sandtrout."

"Are they growing and propagating?"

"Apparently."

"Unless you contain them or eliminate them, Chapterhouse may become another Dune."

"You figured that out, did you?"

"Leto and I together."

"So you remember many lives. Fascinating. It makes you somewhat like us." How unswerving her stare!

"Very different, I think." *Have to get her off that track!*

"You acquired the memories during your first encounter with Murbella?"

Who guessed it? Lucilla? She was there and might have guessed, confiding her suspicions to her Sisters. He had to bring the deadly issue into the open. "I'm not another Kwisatz Haderach!"

"You're not?" Studied objectivity. She allowed this to reveal itself, a cruelty, he thought.

"You know I'm not!" He was fighting for his life and knew it. Not so much with Odrade as with those others who watched and reviewed the comeye records.

"Tell me about your serial memories." That was a command from the Mother Superior. No escaping it.

"I know those . . . lives. It's like one lifetime."

"That accumulation could be very valuable to us, Duncan. Do you also remember the axlotl tanks?"

Her question sent his thoughts into the misty probings that caused him to imagine strange things about the Tleilaxu—great mounds of human flesh softly visible to the imperfect newborn eyes, blurred and unfocused images, almost-memories of emerging from birth canals. How could that accord with *tanks*?

"Scytale has provided us with the knowledge to make our own axlotl system," Odrade said.

System? Interesting word. "Does that mean you also duplicate Tleilaxu spice production?"

"Scytale bargains for more than we will give. But spice will come in time, one way or another."

Odrade heard herself speak firmly and wondered if he detected uncertainty. *We might not have the time to do it.*

"The Sisters you Scatter are hobbled," he said, giving her a small taste of Mentat awareness. "You're drawing on your spice stockpiles to supply them and those must be finite."

"They have our axlotl knowledge and sandtrout."

He was shocked to silence by the possibility of countless Dunes being reproduced in an infinite universe.

"They will solve the problem of melange supply with tanks or worms or both," she said. This she could say sincerely. It came from statistical expectation. One among those Scattered bands of Reverend Mothers should accomplish it.

"The tanks," he said. "I have strange . . . dreams." He had almost said "musings."

"And well you should." Briefly, she told him how female flesh was incorporated.

"For making the spice, too?"

"We think so."

"Disgusting!"

"That's juvenile," she chided.

In such moments, he disliked her intensely. Once, he had reproached her for the way Reverend Mothers removed themselves from "the common stream of human emotions," and she had given him that identical answer.

Juvenile!

"For which there probably is no remedy," he said. "A disgraceful flaw in my character."

"Were you thinking to debate morality with me?"

He thought he heard anger. "Not even ethics. We work by different rules."

"Rules are often an excuse to ignore compassion."

"Do I hear a faint echo of conscience in a Reverend Mother?"

"Deplorable. My Sisters would exile me if they thought conscience ruled me."

"You can be prodded, but not ruled."

"Very good, Duncan! I like you much better when you're openly Mentat."

"I distrust your liking."

She laughed aloud. "How like Bell!"

He stared at her dumbly, plunged by her laughter into sudden knowledge of the way to escape his warders, remove himself from the constant Bene Gesserit manipulations and live his own life. The way out lay not in machinery but in the Sisterhood's flaws. The absolutes by which they thought they surrounded and held him—there was the way out!

And Sheeana knows! That's the bait she dangles in front of me.

When Idaho did not speak, Odrade said: "Tell me about those other lives."

"Wrong. I think of them as one continuous life."

"No deaths?"

He let a response form silently. Serial memories: the deaths were as informative as the lives. Killed so many times by Leto himself!

"The deaths do not interrupt my memories."

"An odd kind of immortality," she said. "You know, don't you, that Tleilaxu Masters recreated themselves? But you—what did they hope to achieve, mixing different gholas in one flesh?"

"Ask Scytale."

"Bell felt sure you were a Mentat. She will be delighted."

"I think not."

"I will see to it that she is delighted. My! I have so many questions I'm not sure where to begin." She studied him, left hand to her chin.

Questions? Mentat demands flowed through Idaho's mind. He let the questions he had asked himself so many times move of themselves, forming their patterns. *What did the Tleilaxu seek in me?* They could not have included cells from all of his ghola-selves for this incarnation. Yet . . . he had all of the memories. What cosmic linkage accumulated all of those lives in this one self? Was that the clue to the visions that beset him in the Great Hold? Half-memories formed in his mind: his body in warm fluid, fed by tubes, massaged by machines, probed and questioned by Tleilaxu observers. He sensed murmurous responses from semi-dormant selves. The words had no meaning. It was as though he listened to a foreign language coming from his own lips but he knew it was ordinary Galach.

The scope of what he sensed in Tleilaxu actions awed him. They investigated a cosmos no one but the Bene Gesserit had ever dared touch. That the Bene Tleilax did this for selfish reasons did not subtract from it. The endless rebirths of Tleilaxu Masters were a reward worthy of daring.

Face Dancer servants to copy any life, any mind. The scope of the Tleilaxu dream was as awesome as Bene Gesserit achievements.

"Scytale admits to memories of Muad'Dib's times," Odrade said. "You might compare notes with him someday."

"That kind of immortality is a bargaining chip," he warned. "Could he sell it to the Honored Matres?"

"He might. Come. Let's go back to your quarters."

In his workroom, she gestured him to the chair at his console and he wondered if she was still hunting for his secrets. She bent over him to manipulate the controls. The overhead projector produced a scene of desert to a horizon of rolling dunes.

"Chapterhouse?" she said. "A wide band along our equator."

Excitement gripped him. "Sandtrout, you said. But are there any new worms?"

"Sheeana expects them soon."

"They require a large amount of spice as catalyst."

"We've gambled a great deal of melange out there. Leto told you about the catalyst, didn't he? What else do you remember of him?"

"He killed me so many times it's an ache when I think about it."

She had the records of Dar-es-Balat on Dune to confirm this. "Killed you himself, I know. Did he just throw you away when you were used up?"

"I sometimes performed up to expectations and was allowed a natural death."

"Was his Golden Path worth it?"

We don't understand his Golden Path nor the fermentations that produced it. He said this.

"Interesting choice of word. A Mentat thinks of the Tyrant's eons as fermentation."

"That erupted in the Scattering."

"Driven also by the Famine Times."

"You think he didn't anticipate famines?"

She did not reply, held to silence by his Mentat view. *Golden Path: humankind "erupting" into the universe . . . never again confined to any single planet and susceptible to a singular fate. All of our eggs no longer in one basket.*

"Leto thought of all humankind as a single organism," he said.

"But he enlisted us in his dream against our will."

"You Atreides always do that."

You Atreides! "Then you've paid your debt to us?"

"I didn't say that."

"Do you appreciate my present dilemma, Mentat?"

"How long have the sandtrout been at work?"

"More than eight Standard Years."

"How fast is our desert growing?"

Our desert! She gestured at the projection. "That's more than three times larger than it was before the sandtrout."

"So fast!"

"Sheeana expects to see small worms any day."

"They tend not to surface until they reach about two meters."

"So she says."

He spoke in a musing tone. "Each with a pearl of Leto's awareness in his 'endless dream.'"

"So he said and he never lied about such things."

"His lies were more subtle. Like a Reverend Mother's."

"You accuse us of lying?"

"Why does Sheeana want to see me?"

"Mentats! You think your questions are answers." Odrade shook her head in mock dismay. "She must learn as much as possible about the Tyrant as the center of religious adoration."

"Gods below! Why?"

"The cult of Sheeana has spread. It's all over the Old Empire and beyond, carried by surviving priests from Rakis."

"From Dune," he corrected her. "Don't think of it as Arrakis or Rakis. It fogs your mind."

She accepted his correction. He was fully Mentat now and she waited patiently.

"Sheeana talked to the sandworms on Dune," he said. "They responded." He met her questioning stare. "Up to your old tricks with your Missionaria Protectiva, eh?"

"The Tyrant is known as Dur and Guldur in the Scattering," she said, feeding his Mentat naivete.

"You have a dangerous assignment for her. Does she know?"

"She knows and you could make it less dangerous."

"Then open your data systems to me."

"No limits?" She knew what Bell would say to that!

He nodded, unable to allow himself the hope that she might agree. *Does she suspect how desperately I want this?* It was an ache where he held his knowledge of how he might escape. *Unimpeded access to information! She will think I want the illusion of freedom.*

"Will you be my Mentat, Duncan?"

"What choice do I have?"

"I will discuss your request in Council and give you our answer."

Is the escape door opening?

"I must think like an Honored Matre," he said, arguing for the comeyes and the watchdogs who would review his request.

"Who could do it better than the one who lives with Murbella?" she asked.

Corruption wears infinite disguises.

—TLEILAXU THU-ZEN

They do not know what I think nor what I can do, Scytale thought. *Their Truthsayers cannot read me.* That, at least, he had salvaged from disaster—the art of deception learned from his perfected Face Dancers.

He moved softly through his area of the no-ship, observing, cataloguing, measuring. Every look weighed people or place in a mind trained to seek flaws.

Each Tleilaxu Master had known that someday God might set him a task to test his commitment.

Very well! This was such a task. The Bene Gesserit who claimed they shared his Great Belief swore it falsely. They were unclean. He no longer had companions to cleanse him on his return from alien places. He had been cast into the powindah universe, made prisoner by servants of Shaitan, was hunted by whores from the Scattering. But none of those evil ones knew his resources. None suspected how God would help him in this extremity.

I cleanse myself, God!

When the women of Shaitan had plucked him from the hands of the whores, promising sanctuary and "every assistance," he had known them false.

The greater the test, the greater my faith.

Only a few minutes ago, he had watched through a shimmering

barrier as Duncan Idaho took a morning walk down the long corridor. The forcefield that kept them apart prevented the passage of sound, but Scytale saw Idaho's lips move and read the curse. *Curse me, ghola, but we made you and still may use you.*

God had introduced a *Holy Accident* into the Tleilaxu plan for this ghola, but God always had larger designs. It was the task of the faithful to fit themselves into God's plans and not demand that God follow the designs of humans.

Scytale set himself to this test, renewing his holy pledge. It was done without words in the ancient Bene Tleilax way of *s'tori*. "To achieve s'tori no understanding is needed. S'tori exists without words, without even a name."

The magic of his God was his only bridge. Scytale felt this deeply. The youngest Master in the highest kehl, he had known from the beginning he would be chosen for this ultimate task. That knowledge was one of his strengths and he saw it every time he looked in a mirror. *God formed me to deceive the powindah!* His slight, childlike appearance was formed in a gray skin whose metallic pigments blocked scanning probes. His diminutive shape distracted those who saw him and hid the powers he had accumulated in serial ghola incarnations. Only the Bene Gesserit carried older memories, but he knew evil guided them.

Scytale rubbed his breast, reminding himself of what was hidden there with such skill that not even a scar marked the place. Each Master had carried this resource—a nullentropy capsule preserving the seed cells of a multitude: fellow Masters of the central kehl, Face Dancers, technical specialists and *others* he knew would be attractive to the women of Shaitan . . . and to many weakling powindah! Paul Atreides and his beloved Chani were there. (Oh what that had cost in searching garments of the dead for random cells!) The original Duncan Idaho was there with other Atreides minions—the Mentat Thufir Hawat, Gurney Halleck, the Fremen Naib Stilgar . . . enough potential servants and slaves to people a Tleilaxu universe.

The prize of prizes in the nullentropy tube, the ones he longed to bring into existence, made him catch his breath when he thought of them. Perfect Face Dancers! Perfect mimics. Perfect recorders of a victim's persona. Capable of deceiving even the witches of the Bene Gesserit. Not even shere could prevent them from capturing the mind of another.

The tube he thought of as his ultimate bargaining power. No one must know of it. For now, he catalogued flaws.

There were enough gaps in the no-ship's defenses to gratify him. In his serial lifetimes, he had collected skills the way his fellow Masters collected pleasing baubles. They had always considered him too serious but now he had found the place and time for vindication.

Study of the Bene Gesserit had always attracted him. Over the eons, he had acquired a body of knowledge about them. He knew it held myths and misinformation, but faith in the purposes of God assured him the view he held would serve the Great Belief, no matter the rigors of Holy Testing.

Part of his Bene Gesserit catalogue he called "typicals," from the frequent remark: "That's typical of them!"

The *typicals* fascinated him.

It was *typical* for them to tolerate gross but non-threatening behavior in others they would not accept in themselves. "Bene Gesserit standards are higher." Scytale had heard that even from some of his late companions.

"We have the gift of seeing ourselves as others see us," Odrade had once said.

Scytale included this among *typicals*, but her words did not accord with the Great Belief. Only God saw your ultimate self! Odrade's boast had the sound of hubris.

"They tell no casual lies. Truth serves them better."

He often wondered about that. Mother Superior herself quoted it as a rule of the Bene Gesserit. There remained the fact that witches appeared to hold a cynical view of truth. She dared claim it was Zensunni. *"Whose truth? Modified in what way? In what context?"*

They had been seated the previous afternoon in his no-ship quarters. He had asked for "a consultation on mutual problems," his euphemism for bargaining. They were alone except for comeyes and the comings and goings of watchful Sisters.

His quarters were comfortable enough: three plaz-walled rooms in restful green, a soft bed, chairs reduced to fit his diminutive body.

This was an Ixian no-ship and he felt certain his warders did not suspect how much he knew of it. *As much as the Ixians.* Ixian machines all around but never an Ixian to be seen. He doubted there was a single Ixian on Chapterhouse. The witches were notorious for doing their own maintenance.

Odrade moved and spoke slowly, watching him with care. *"They are not impulsive."* You heard that often.

She asked after his comfort and appeared concerned for him.

He glanced around his sitting room. "I see no Ixians."

She pursed her lips with displeasure. "Is this why you asked for consultation?"

Of course not, witch! I merely practice my arts of distraction. You would not expect me to mention things I wished to conceal. Then why would I call your attention to Ixians when I know it is unlikely there are any dangerous intruders walking freely on your accursed planet? Ahhh, the much vaunted Ixian connection we Tleilaxu maintained so long. You know of that! You punished Ix memorably more than once.

The technocrats of Ix might hesitate to irritate the Bene Gesserit, he thought, but they would be extremely careful not to arouse the ire of Honored Matres. Secret trading was indicated by the presence of this no-ship but the price must have been ruinous and the circumlocutions exceptional. Very nasty, those whores from the Scattering. They might need Ix themselves, he guessed. And Ix might secretly defy the whores to make an arrangement with the Bene Gesserit. But the limits were tight and chances of betrayal many.

These thoughts comforted him as he bargained. Odrade, in a brittle mood, unsettled him several times with silences during which she stared at him in that disturbing Bene Gesserit way.

The bargaining chips were large—no less than survival for each of them and always in the pot that tenuous thing: ascendancy, control of the human universe, perpetuation of your own ways as the dominant pattern.

Give me a small opening that I may expand, Scytale thought. *Give me my own Face Dancers. Give me servants who will do only my bidding.*

"It is a small thing to ask," he said. "I seek personal comfort, my own servants."

Odrade continued to stare at him in that weighted way of the Bene Gesserit that always seemed to peel away the masks and see deep into you.

But I have masks you have not penetrated.

He could see that she found him repulsive—the way her gaze fixed sequentially on each of his features. He knew what she was thinking. *An elfin figure with narrow face and puckish eyes. Widow's peak.* Her gaze moved down: *tiny mouth with sharp teeth and pointed canines.*

Scytale knew himself to be a figure out of humankind's most dangerously disturbing mythologies. Odrade would ask herself: *Why did the Bene Tleilax choose this particular physical appearance when their control of genetics could have given them something more impressive?*

For the very reason that it disturbs you, powindah dirt!

He thought immediately of another *typical*: "The Bene Gesserit seldom scatter dirt."

Scytale had seen the dirty aftermath of many Bene Gesserit actions. *Look at what happened to Dune! Burnt to cinders because you women of Shaitan chose that holy ground to challenge the whores. Even the revenants of our Prophet gone to their reward. Everyone dead!*

And he hardly dared contemplate his own losses. No Tleilaxu planet had escaped the fate of Dune. *The Bene Gesserit caused that!* And he must suffer their tolerance—a refugee with only God to support him.

He asked Odrade about *scattered dirt* on Dune.

"You find that only when we are in extremis."

"Is that why you attracted the violence of those whores?"

She refused to discuss it.

One of Scytale's late companions had said: "The Bene Gesserit leave straight tracks. You might think them complex, but when you look closely their way smooths."

That companion and all the others had been butchered by the whores. His only survival lay in cells of a nullentropy capsule. So much for a dead Master's wisdom!

Odrade wanted more technical information about axlotl tanks. Ohhhh, how cleverly she worded her questions!

Bargaining for survival, and each little bit carried a heavy weight. What had he received for his tiny measured pieces of data about the axlotl tanks? Odrade took him out of the ship occasionally now. But the whole planet was as much a prison to him as this ship. Where could he go that the witches would not find him?

What were they doing with their own axlotl tanks? He was not even sure about this. The witches lied with such facility.

Was it wrong to supply them even with limited knowledge? He realized now he had told them far more than the bare biotechnical details to which he had confined himself. They definitely deduced how Masters had created a limited immortality—always a ghola-replacement growing in the tanks. That, too, was lost! He wanted to scream this at her in his frustrated rage.

Questions . . . obvious questions.

He parried her questions with wordy arguments about "my need for Face Dancer servants and my own Shipsystem console."

She was slyly adamant, probing for more knowledge of the tanks. "The information to produce melange from our tanks might induce us to be more liberal with our guest."

Our tanks! Our guest!

These women were like a plasteel wall. No tanks for his personal use. *All of that Tleilaxu power gone.* It was a thought full of mournful self-pity. He restored himself with a reminder: God obviously tested his resourcefulness. *They think they hold me in a trap.* But their restrictions hurt. No Face Dancer servants? Very well. He would seek other servants. Not Face Dancers.

Scytale felt the deepest anguish of his many lives when he thought of his lost Face Dancers—his mutable slaves. *Damn these women and their pretense that they shared the Great Belief! Omnipresent acolytes and Reverend Mothers always snooping around. Spies! And comeyes everywhere. Oppressive.*

On first coming to Chapterhouse, he had sensed a shyness about his jailers, a privacy that became intense when he probed into the workings of their order. Later, he came to see this as a circling up, all facing outward at any threat. *What is ours is ours. You may not enter!*

Scytale recognized a parental posturing in this, a maternal view of humankind: "Behave or we will punish you!" And Bene Gesserit punishments certainly were to be avoided.

As Odrade continued to demand more than he would give, Scytale fastened his attention on a *typical* he felt sure was true: *They cannot love.* But he was forced to agree. Neither love nor hate were purely rational. He thought of such emotions as a dark fountain shadowing the air all around, a primitive gusher that sprayed unsuspecting humans.

How this woman does chatter! He watched her, not really listening. What were their flaws? Was it a weakness that they avoided music? Did they fear the secret play on emotions? The aversion appeared to be heavily conditioned, but the conditioning did not always succeed. In his many lives he had seen witches appear to enjoy music. When he questioned Odrade, she became quite heated, and he suspected a deliberate display to mislead him.

"We cannot let ourselves be distracted!"

"Don't you ever replay great musical performances in memory? I'm told that in ancient times . . ."

"Of what use is music played on instruments no longer known to most people?"

"Oh? What instruments are those?"

"Where would you find a piano?" *Still in that false anger.* "Terrible instruments to tune and even more difficult to play."

How prettily she protests. "I've never heard of this . . . this . . . piano, did you say? Is it like the baliset?"

"Distant cousins. But it could only be tuned to an approximate key. An idiosyncracy of the instrument."

"Why do you single out this . . . this piano?"

"Because I sometimes think it too bad we no longer have it. Producing perfection from imperfection is, after all, the highest of art forms."

Perfection from imperfection! She was trying to distract him with Zensunni words, feeding the illusion that these witches shared his Great Belief. He had been warned many times about this peculiarity of Bene Gesserit bargaining. They approached everything from an oblique angle, revealing only at the last instant what they really sought. But he knew what they bargained for here. She wanted all of his knowledge and sought to pay nothing. Still, how tempting her words were.

Scytale felt a deep wariness. Her words fitted themselves so neatly into her claim that the Bene Gesserit sought only to perfect human society. So she thought she could teach him! Another *typical*: "They see themselves as teachers."

When he expressed doubt of this claim, she said, "Naturally we build up pressures in societies we influence. We do it that we may direct those pressures."

"I find this discordant," he complained.

"Why Master Scytale! It's a very common pattern. Governments often do this to produce violence against chosen targets. You did it yourselves! And see where it got you."

So she dares claim the Tleilaxu brought this calamity on themselves!

"We follow the lesson of the Great Messenger," she said, using the Islamiyat for the Prophet Leto II. The words sounded alien on her lips, but he was taken back. She knew how all Tleilaxu revered the Prophet.

But I have heard these women call Him Tyrant!

Still speaking Islamiyat, she demanded, "Was it not His goal to divert violence, producing a lesson of value to all?"

Does she joke about the Great Belief?

"That is why we accepted Him," she said. "He did not play by our rules but He played for our goal."

She dared say *she* accepted the Prophet!

He did not challenge her, although the provocation was great. A delicate thing, a Reverend Mother's view of herself and her behavior. He suspected they constantly readjusted this view, never bouncing far in any direction. No self-hate, no self-love. Confidence, yes. Maddening self-confidence. But that did not require hate or love. Only a cool head, every judgment ready for correction, just as she claimed. It would seldom require praise. *A job well done? Well, what else did you expect?*

"Bene Gesserit training strengthens the character." That was Folk Wisdom's most popular *typical*.

He tried to start an argument with her on this. "Isn't Honored Matres' conditioning the same as yours? Look at Murbella!"

"Is it generalities you want, Scytale?" *Was that amusement in her tone?*

"A collision between two conditioning systems, isn't that a good way to view this confrontation?" he ventured.

"And the more powerful will emerge victorious, of course." *Definitely sneering!*

"Isn't that how it always works?" His anger not well bridled.

"Must a Bene Gesserit remind a Tleilaxu that subtleties are another kind of weapon? Have you not practiced deception? A feigned weakness to deflect your enemies and lead them into traps? Vulnerabilities can be created."

Of course! She knows about the eons of Tleilaxu deception, creating an image of inept stupidities.

"So that's how you expect to deal with our foes?"

"We intend to punish them, Scytale."

Such implacable determination!

New things he learned about the Bene Gesserit filled him with misgivings.

Odrade, taking him for a well-guarded afternoon stroll in the cold winter outside the ship (burly Proctors just a pace behind), stopped to watch a small procession coming from Central. Five Bene Gesserit women, two of them acolytes by their white-trimmed robes, but the other three in an unrelieved gray not known to him. They wheeled a cart into one of the orchards. A frigid wind blew across them. A few old leaves whipped from the dark branches. The cart bore a long bundle shrouded in white. A body? It was the right shape.

When he asked, Odrade regaled him with an account of Bene Gesserit burial practices.

If there was a body to bury, it was done with the casual dispatch he now witnessed. No Reverend Mother ever had an obituary or wanted time-wasting rituals. Did her memory not live on in her Sisters?

He started to argue that this was irreverent but she cut him off.

"Given the phenomenon of death, all attachments in life are temporary! We modify that somewhat in Other Memory. You did a similar thing, Scytale. And now we incorporate some of your abilities in our bag of tricks. Oh, yes! That's the way we think of such knowledge. It merely modifies the pattern."

"An irreverent practice!"

"Nothing irreverent about it. Into the dirt they go where, at least, they can become fertilizer." And she continued to describe the scene without giving him a chance for further protests.

They had this regular routine he now observed, she said. A large mechanical auger was wheeled into the orchard, where it drilled a suitable hole in the earth. The corpse, bound in that cheap cloth, was buried vertically and an orchard tree planted over it. Orchards were laid out in grid patterns, a cenotaph at one corner where the locations of burials were recorded. He saw the cenotaph when she pointed it out, a square green thing about three meters high.

"I think that body's being buried at about C-21," she said, watching the auger at work while the burial team waited, leaning against the cart. "That one will fertilize an apple tree." She sounded ungodly happy about it!

As they watched the auger withdraw and the cart being tipped, the body sliding into the hole, Odrade began to hum.

Scytale was surprised. "You said the Bene Gesserit avoided music."

"Just an old ditty."

The Bene Gesserit remained a puzzle and, more than ever, he saw the weakness of *typicals*. How could you bargain with people whose patterns did not follow an acceptable path? You might think you understood them and then they shot off in a new direction. They were *untypical*! Trying to understand them disrupted his sense of order. He was certain he had not received anything real in all of this bargaining. A bit more freedom that was actually the illusion of freedom. Nothing he really wanted came from this cold-faced witch! It was tantalizing to try piecing together any substance from what he knew about the Bene Gesserit. There was, for instance, the claim they did without most bureaucratic systems and record keeping. Except for Bellonda's Archives, of course, and every time he mentioned those, Odrade said, "Heaven guard us!" or something equivalent.

Now he asked, "How do you maintain yourselves without officials and records?" He was deeply puzzled.

"A thing needs doing, we do it. Bury a Sister?" She pointed to the scene in the orchard where shovels had been brought into play and dirt was being tamped on the grave.

"That's how it's done and there's always someone around who's responsible. They know who they are."

"Who . . . who takes care of this unwholesome . . . ?"

"It's not unwholesome! It's part of our education. Failed Sisters usually supervise. Acolytes do the work."

"Don't they . . . I mean, isn't this distasteful to them? Failed Sisters, you say. And acolytes. It would seem to be more of a punishment than . . ."

"Punishment! Come, come, Scytale. Have you only one song to sing?" She pointed at the burial party. "After their apprenticeship, all of our people willingly accept their jobs."

"But no . . . ahhh, bureaucratic . . ."

"We're not stupid!"

Again, he did not understand, but she responded to his silent puzzlement.

"Surely you know bureaucracies always become voracious aristocracies after they attain commanding power."

He had difficulty seeing the relevance. Where was she leading him?

When he remained silent, she said: "Honored Matres have all the marks of bureaucracy. Ministers of this, Great Honored Matres of that, a powerful few at the top and many functionaries below. They already are full of adolescent hungers. Like voracious predators, they never consider how they exterminate their prey. A tight relationship: Reduce the numbers of those upon whom you feed and you bring your own structure crashing down."

He found it difficult to believe the witches really saw Honored Matres this way and said so.

"If you survive, Scytale, you will see my words made real. Great cries of rage by those unthinking women at the necessity to retrench. Much new effort to wring the most out of their prey. Capture more of them! Squeeze them harder! It will just mean quicker extermination. Idaho says they're already in the die-back stage."

The ghola says this? So she was using him as a Mentat! "Where do you get such ideas? Surely this does not originate with your ghola." *Continue to believe he's yours!*

"He merely confirmed our assessment. An example in Other Memory alerted us."

"Ohh?" This thing of Other Memory bothered him. Could their claim be true? Memories from his own multiple lives were of enormous value. He asked for confirmation.

"We remembered the relationship between a food animal called a snowshoe rabbit and a predatory cat called a lynx. The cat population always grew to follow the population of the rabbits, and then overfeeding dumped the predators into famine times and severe die-back."

"An interesting term, die-back."

"Descriptive of what we intend for the Honored Matres."

When their meeting ended (without anything gained for him), Scytale found himself more confused than ever. Was that truly their intent? The damnable woman! He could not be sure of anything she said.

When she returned him to his quarters in the ship, Scytale stood for a long time looking through the barrier field at the long corridor where Idaho and Murbella sometimes came on their way to their practice floor. He knew that must be where they went through a wide doorway down there. They always emerged sweating and breathing deeply.

Neither of his fellow prisoners appeared, although he loitered there for more than an hour.

She uses the ghola as a Mentat! That must mean he has access to a Shipsystems console. Surely, she would not deprive her Mentat of his data. Somehow, I must contrive it that Idaho and I meet intimately. There's always the whistling language we impress on every ghola. I must not appear too anxious. A small concession in the bargaining, perhaps. A complaint that my quarters are confining. They see how I chafe at imprisonment.

Education is no substitute for intelligence. That elusive quality is defined only in part by puzzle-solving ability. It is in the creation of new puzzles reflecting what your senses report that you round out the definition.

—MENTAT TEXT ONE (DECTO)

They wheeled Lucilla into Great Honored Matre's presence in a tubular cage—a cage within a cage. Shigawire netting confined her to the center of the thing.

"I am Great Honored Matre," the woman in the heavy black chair greeted her. *Small woman, red-gold leotards.* "The cage is for your protection should you try to use Voice. We are immune. Our immunity takes the form of a reflex. We kill. A number of you have died that way. We know Voice and use it. Remember it when I release you from your cage." She waved away the servants who had brought the cage. "Go! Go!"

Lucilla looked around the room. Windowless. Almost square. Lighted by a few silvery glowglobes. Acid-green walls. Typical interrogation setting. It was somewhere high. They had brought her cage in a nulltube shortly before dawn.

A panel behind Great Honored Matre snapped aside and a smaller cage came sliding into the room on a hidden mechanism. This cage was square and in it stood what she thought at first was a naked man until he turned and looked at her.

Futar! It had a wide face and she saw the canines.

"Want back rub," the Futar said.

"Yes, darling. I'll rub your back later."

"Want eat," the Futar said. It glared at Lucilla.

"Later, darling."

The Futar continued to study Lucilla. "You Handler?" it asked.

"Of course she's not a Handler!"

"Want eat," the Futar insisted.

"Later, I said! For now, you just sit there and purr for me."

The Futar squatted in its cage and a rumbling sound issued from its throat.

"Aren't they sweet when they purr?" Great Honored Matre obviously did not expect an answer.

The presence of the Futar puzzled Lucilla. Those things were supposed to hunt and kill Honored Matres. It was caged, though.

"Where did you capture it?" Lucilla asked.

"On Gammu." She did not see what she had revealed.

And this is Junction, Lucilla thought. She had recognized it from the lighter the evening before.

The Futar stopped purring. "Eat," it grumbled.

Lucilla would have liked something to eat. They had not fed her in three days and she was forced to suppress hunger pangs. Small sips of water from a literjon left in the cage helped but that was almost empty. The servants who had brought her had laughed at her request for food. "Futars like lean meat!"

It was the absence of melange that plagued her most. She had begun to feel the first withdrawal pains that morning.

I shall have to kill myself soon.

The Lampadas horde pleaded for her to endure. *Be brave. What if that wild Reverend Mother fails us?*

Spider Queen. That is what Odrade calls this woman.

Great Honored Matre continued to study her, hand to chin. It was a weak chin. In a face without positive features, the negative attracted the gaze.

"You will lose in the end, you know," Great Honored Matre said.

"Whistling past the graveyard!" Lucilla said and then had to explain the expression.

There was a polite show of interest on Great Honored Matre's face. *How interesting.*

"Any of my aides would have killed you immediately for saying that. This is one of the reasons we are alone. I am curious why you would say such a thing?"

Lucila glanced at the squatting Futar. "Futars did not occur overnight. They were genetically created from wild animal stock for one purpose."

"Careful!" Orange flamed in Great Honored Matre's eyes.

"Generations of development went into the creation of the Futars," Lucilla said.

"We hunt them for our pleasure!"

"And the hunter becomes the hunted."

Great Honored Matre leaped to her feet, eyes completely orange. The Futar became agitated and began whining. This calmed the woman. Slowly, she sank back into her chair. One hand gestured at the caged Futar. "It's all right, darling. You'll eat soon and then I'll rub your back."

The Futar resumed its purring.

"So you think we came back here as refugees," Great Honored Matre said. "Yes! Don't try to deny it."

"Worms often turn," Lucilla said.

"Worms? You mean like those monstrosities we destroyed on Rakis?"

It was tempting to prod this Honored Matre and evoke the dramatic response. Alarm her enough and she would certainly kill.

Please, Sister! the Lampadas horde begged. *Endure.*

You think I can escape from this place? That silenced them, except for one faint protest. *Remember! We are the ancient doll: seven times down, eight times up.* It came with a rocking image of a small red doll, grinning Buddha face and hands clasped over its fat belly.

"You're obviously referring to the revenants of the God Emperor," Lucilla said. "I had something else in mind."

Great Honored Matre took her time considering this. The orange faded from her eyes.

She's playing with me, Lucilla thought. *She intends to kill me and feed me to her pet.*

But think of the tactical information you could provide if we did escape!

We! But there was no avoiding the accuracy of that protest. They had brought her cage from the lighter while it was still daylight. Approaches to the Spider Queen's lair were well planned for difficult access but the planning amused Lucilla. Very ancient, out-of-date planning. Narrow places in the approach lanes with observation turrets projecting from the ground like dull gray mushrooms appearing at the proper places on their mycelium. Sharp turns at critical points. No ordinary ground vehicle could negotiate such turns at speed.

There was mention of this in Teg's critique of Junction, she recalled. Nonsense defenses. One had only to bring in heavy equipment or go over such crude installations another way and the things were isolated. Linked underground, naturally, but that could be disrupted by explosives. Ligate them, cut them off from their source, and they would fall piecemeal. *No more precious energy coming down your tube, idiots!* Visible sense of security and Honored Matres kept it. For reassurance! Their defenders must spend a great deal of energy on useless displays to give these women a false sense of security.

The hallways! Remember the hallways.

Yes, the hallways in this gigantc building were enormous, the better to accommodate giant tanks in which Guild Navigators were forced to live groundside. Ventilation systems low along the halls to take out and reclaim spilled melange gas. She could imagine hatches thumping open and closed with disturbing reverberations. Guildsmen never seemed to mind loud noises. Energy transmission lines for mobile suspensors were thick black snakes winding across passages and into every room she had glimpsed. Wouldn't do to keep a Navigator from snooping any place he desired.

Many of the people she had seen wore guide pulsers. Even Honored Matres. So they got lost here. Everything under the one giant mound of a roof with its phallic towers. The new residents found this attractive. Heavily insulated from the crude outdoors (where none of the important people go anyway except to kill things or watch the slaves at their amusing work and play). Through much of it, she had seen a shabbiness that said minimal expenditure on maintenance. *They are not changing much. Teg's ground plan is still accurate.*

See how valuable your observations could be?

Great Honored Matre stirred from her reverie. "It is just possible that I could permit you to live. Provided you satisfy some of my curiosity."

"How do you know I won't respond to your curiosity with a flow of pure shit?"

Vulgarity amused Great Honored Matre. She almost laughed. Apparently no one had ever warned her to beware of the Bene Gesserit when they resorted to vulgarity. The motivation for it was sure to be something distressing. *No Voice, eh? She thinks that's my only resource?* Great Honored Matre had said enough and reacted enough to give any Reverend Mother a sure handle on her. Body and speech signals always carried more information than was necessary for comprehension. There was inevitable extra information to be sampled.

"Do you find us attractive?" Great Honored Matre asked.

Odd question. "People from the Scattering all possess a certain attraction." *Let her think I've seen many of them, including her enemies.* "You're exotic, meaning strange and new."

"And our sexual prowess?"

"There's an aura to that, naturally. Exciting and magnetic to some."

"But not to you."

Go for the chin! It was a suggestion from the horde. *Why not?*

"I've been studying your chin, Great Honored Matre."

"You have?" Surprised.

"It's obviously your childhood chin and you should be proud of that youthful remembrance."

Not pleased at all but unable to show it. Hit the chin again.

"I'll bet your lovers often kiss your chin," Lucilla said.

Angry now and still unable to vent it. *Threaten me, will you! Warn me not to use Voice!*

"Kiss chin," the Futar said.

"I said later, darling. Now will you shut up!"

Taking it out on her poor pet.

"But you have questions you want to ask me," Lucilla said. Sweetness itself. Another warning signal to the knowledgeable. *I'm one of those who pours sugar syrup over everything. "How nice! Such a pleasant time when we're with you. Isn't that beautiful! Weren't you clever to get it so cheaply! Easily. Quickly." Supply your own adverb.*

Great Honored Matre was a moment composing herself. She sensed that she had been placed at a disadvantage but could not say how. She covered the moment with an enigmatic smile, then: "But I said I would release you." She pressed something on the side of her chair and a section of the tubular cage swung aside, taking the shigawire netting with it. In the same instant, a low chair lifted from a panel in the floor directly in front of her and not a pace away.

Lucilla seated herself in the chair, knees almost touching her inquisitor. *Feet. Remember they kill with their feet.* She flexed her fingers, realizing then that she had been gripping her hands into fists. Damn the tensions!

"You should have some food and drink," Great Honored Matre said. She pushed something else on the side of her chair. A tray came up beside Lucilla—plate, spoon, a glass brimming with red liquid. *Showing off her toys.*

Lucilla picked up the glass.

Poison? Smell it first.

She sampled the drink. Stimtea and melange! *I'm hungry.*

Lucilla returned an empty glass to the tray. The stim on her tongue smelled sharply of melange. *What is she doing? Wooing me?* Lucilla felt a flow of relief from the spice. The plate proved to hold beans in a piquant sauce. She ate it all after sampling the first bite for unwanted additives. Garlic in the sauce. She was hung up for the barest fraction of a second on Memory of this ingredient—adjunct to fine cooking, specific against werewolves, potent treatment for flatulence.

"You find our food pleasant?"

Lucilla wiped her chin. "Very good. You are to be complimented on your chef." *Never compliment the chef in a private establishment. Chefs can be replaced. Hostess is irreplaceable.* "A nice touch with garlic."

"We've been studying some of the library salvaged from Lampadas." Gloating: *See what you lost?* "So little of interest buried in all of that prattle."

Does she want you to be her librarian? Lucilla waited silently.

"Some of my aides think there may be clues to your witches' nest there or, at least, a way to eliminate you quickly. So many languages!"

Does she need a translator? Be blunt!

"What interests you?"

"Very little. Who could possibly need accounts of the Butlerian Jihad?"

"They destroyed libraries, too."

"Don't patronize me!"

She's sharper than we thought. Keep it blunt.

"I thought I was the object of patronage."

"Listen to me, witch! You think you can be ruthless in defense of your nest but you do not understand what it is to be ruthless."

"I don't think you have yet told me how I can satisfy your curiosity."

"It's your science we want, witch!" She pitched her voice lower. "Let us be reasonable. With your help we could achieve utopia."

And conquer all of your enemies and achieve orgasm every time.

"You think science holds the keys to utopia?"

"And better organization for our affairs."

Remember: Bureaucracy elevates conformity . . . make that elevates "fatal stupidity" to the status of religion.

"Paradox, Great Honored Matre. Science must be innovative. It brings change. That's why science and bureaucracy fight a constant war."

Does she know her roots?

"But think of the power! Think of what you could control!" *She doesn't know.*

Honored Matre assumptions about control fascinated Lucilla. You controlled your universe; you did not balance with it. You looked outward, never inward. You did not train yourself to sense your own subtle responses, you produced muscles (forces, powers) to overcome everything you defined as an obstacle. Were these women blind?

When Lucilla did not speak, Honored Matre said: "We found much in the library about the Bene Tleilax."

"You joined them for many projects, witch. Multiple projects: how to nullify a no-ship's invisibility, how to penetrate the secrets of the living cell, your Missionaria Protectiva, and something called 'the Language of God.'"

Lucilla produced a tight smile. Did they fear there might be a real god out there somewhere? *Give her a little taste! Be candid.*

"We joined the Tleilaxu in nothing. Your people misinterpret what they found. You worry about being patronized? How do you think God would feel about it? We plant protective religions to help us. That is the Missionaria's function. The Tleilaxu have only one religion."

"You organize religions?"

"Not quite. The organizational approach to religion is always apologetic. We do not apologize."

"You are beginning to bore me. Why did we find so little about the God Emperor?" *Pouncing!*

"Perhaps your people destroyed it."

"Ahhh, then you do have an interest in him."

And so do you, Madame Spider!

"I would have presumed, Great Honored Matre, that Leto II and his Golden Path were subjects of study at many of your academic centers."

That was cruel!

"We have no academic centers!"

"I find your interest in him surprising."

"Casual interest, no more."

And that Futar sprang from an oak tree struck by lightning!

"We call his Golden Path 'the paper chase.' He blew it into the infinite winds and said: 'See? There is where it goes.' That's the Scattering."

"Some prefer to call it the Seeking."

"Could he really predict our future? Is that what interests you?" *Bullseye!*

Great Honored Matre coughed into her hand.

"We say Muad'Dib created a future. Leto II un-created it."

"But if I could know . . ."

"Please! Great Honored Matre! People who demand that the oracle predict their lives really want to know where the treasure is hidden."

"But of course!"

"Know your entire future and nothing will ever surprise you? Is that it?"

"In so many words."

"You don't want the future, you want now extended forever."

"I could not have said it better."

"And you said I bored you!"

"What?"

Orange in her eyes. Careful.

"Never another surprise? What could be more boring?"

"Ahhhh . . . Oh! But that's not what I mean."

"Then I'm afraid I do not understand what you want, Great Honored Matre."

"No matter. We'll return to it tomorrow."

Reprieve!

Great Honored Matre stood. "Back into your cage."

"Eat?" The Futar sounded plaintive.

"I have some wonderful food for you downstairs, darling. Then I'll rub your back."

Lucilla entered her cage. Great Honored Matre threw a chair cushion in after her. "Use that against the shigawire. See how kind I can be?"

The cage door sealed with a click.

The Futar in its cage slid back into the wall. The panel snapped closed over it.

"They get so restless when they're hungry," Great Honored Matre said. She opened the door to the room and turned to contemplate Lucilla for a moment. "You will not be disturbed here. I am refusing permission for anyone else to enter this room."

Many things we do naturally become difficult only when we try to make them intellectual subjects. It is possible to know so much about a subject that you become totally ignorant.

—MENTAT TEXT TWO (DICTO)

Periodically, Odrade went for dinner with acolytes and their Proctor-Watchers, the most immediate warders in this *mind-prison* from which many would never be released.

What the acolytes thought and did really informed the depths of Mother Superior's consciousness on how well Chapterhouse functioned. Acolytes responded from their moods and forebodings more directly than Reverend Mothers. Full Sisters got very good at not being seen at their worst. They did not try to conceal essentials, but anyone could walk in an orchard or close a door and be out of the view of watchdogs.

Not so the acolytes.

There was little slack time in Central these days. Even the dining halls had their constant streams of occupants no matter the hour. Workshifts were staggered and it was easy for a Reverend Mother to adjust her circadian rhythms to off-beat time. Odrade could not waste energy on such adjustments. At the evening meal, she paused at the door to the Acolyte Hall and heard the sudden hush.

Even the way they conveyed food to their mouths said something. Where did the eyes go as the chopsticks progressed mouthward? Was it a quick stab and a rapid chew before a convulsive swallow? That was a one to watch. She was brewing upsets. And that thoughtful one over there who looked at each mouthful as though wondering how they hid the poison in such slop? A creative mind behind those eyes. Test her for a more sensitive position.

Odrade entered the hall.

The floor had a large checkerboard pattern, black and white plaz, virtually unscratchable. Acolytes said the pattern was for Reverend Mothers to use as a game board: "Place one of us here and another over there and some along that central line. Move them thus—winner take all."

Odrade took a seat near the corner of a table beside the western windows. The acolytes made room for her, their movements quietly unobtrusive.

This hall was part of the oldest construction on Chapterhouse. Built of wood with clear-span beams overhead, enormously thick and heavy things finished in dull black. They were some twenty-five meters long without a joint. Somewhere on Chapterhouse there was a grove of genetically tailored oaks reaching up to sunlight in their carefully tended plantations. Trees going up thirty meters at least without a limb, and more than two meters through the boles. They had been planted when this hall was built, replacements for these beams when age weakened them. Nineteen hundred SY the beams were supposed to endure.

How carefully the acolytes around her watched Mother Superior without ever appearing to look directly at her.

Odrade turned her head to peer out the western windows at the sunset. *Dust again.* The spreading intrusion from the desert inflamed the setting sun and set it glowing like a distant ember that might explode into uncontrollable fire at any instant.

Odrade suppressed a sigh. Thoughts such as these recreated her nightmare: *the chasm . . . the tightrope.* She knew if she closed her eyes she would feel herself swaying on the rope. The hunter with the axe was nearer!

Acolytes eating close by stirred nervously as though they sensed her disquiet. Perhaps they did. Odrade heard the movement of fabrics and this dragged her out of her nightmare. She had become sensitized to a new note in the sounds of Central. There was a grating noise behind the most commonplace movements—that chair being shifted behind her . . . and the opening of that kitchen door. Rasping grit. Cleaning crews complained of sand and "the damnable dust."

Odrade stared out the window at the source of that irritation: wind from the south. A dull haze, something between tan and earth brown, drew a curtain across the horizon. After the wind, dustings of its deposits would be found in building corners and on lee sides of hills. There was a flinty aroma to it, something alkaline that irritated the nostrils.

She looked down at the table as a serving acolyte placed her meal in front of her.

Odrade found herself enjoying this change from quick meals in her workroom and private dining room. When she ate alone up there, acolytes brought food so quietly and cleared away with such silent efficiency that sometimes she was surprised to find everything gone. Here, dining was bustle and conversation. In her quarters, Chef Duana might come in clucking, "You are not eating enough." Odrade generally heeded such admonitions. Watchdogs had their uses.

Tonight's meal was sligpork in a sauce of soy and molasses, minimal melange, a touch of basil and lemon. Fresh green beans cooked al dente with peppers. Dark red grape juice to drink. She took a bite of sligpork with anticipation and found it passable, a bit overcooked for her taste. Acolyte chefs had not missed it by much.

Then why this feeling of too many such meals?

She swallowed and hypersensitivity identified additives. This food was not here just to replenish Mother Superior's energy. Someone in the kitchen had asked for her day's nutrition list and adjusted this plate accordingly.

Food is a trap, she thought. *More addictions.* She did not like the cunning ways Chapterhouse chefs concealed things they put in the food "for the good of the diners." They knew, of course, that a Reverend Mother could identify ingredients and adjust metabolism within her limits. They were watching her right now, wondering how Mother Superior would judge tonight's menu.

As she ate, she listened to the other diners. None intruded on her— not physically or vocally. Sounds returned almost to what they had been before her entrance. Waggling tongues always changed their tone slightly when she entered and resumed at lower volume.

An unspoken question lay in all of those busy minds around her: *Why is she here tonight?*

Odrade sensed quiet awe in some nearby diners, a reaction Mother Superior sometimes employed to her advantage. Awe with an edge on it. Acolytes whispered among themselves (so the Proctors reported), "She has Taraza." They meant Odrade possessed her late predecessor as Primary. The two of them were a historical pair, required study for postulants.

Dar and Tar, already a legend.

Even Bellonda (dear old vicious Bell) came at Odrade obliquely because of this. Few frontal attacks, very little blaring in her accusatory arguments. Taraza was credited with saving the Sisterhood. That silenced much opposition. Taraza had said Honored Matres were essentially barbarians and their violence, although not totally deflectable, could be guided into bloody displays. Events had more or less verified this.

Correct up to a point, Tar. None of us anticipated the extent of their violence.

Taraza's classical veronica (how apt the bullring image) had aimed the Honored Matres into such episodes of carnage that the universe was mordant with potential supporters of their brutalized victims.

How do I defend us?

It was not so much that defensive plans were inadequate. They could become irrelevant.

That, of course, is what I seek. We must be purified and made ready for a supreme effort.

Bellonda had sneered at that idea. "For our demise? Is that why we must be purified?"

Bellonda would be ambivalent when she discovered what Mother Superior planned. Bellonda-vicious would applaud. Bellonda-Mentat would argue for delay "until a more propitious moment."

But I will seek my own peculiar way despite what my Sisters think.

And many Sisters thought Odrade quite the strangest Mother Superior they had ever accepted. Elevated more with the left hand than with the right. *Taraza Primary. I was there when you died, Tar. No one else to gather your persona. Elevation by accident?*

Many disapproved of Odrade. But when opposition arose, back they went to "Taraza Primary—the best Mother Superior in our history."

Amusing! Taraza Within was the quickest to laugh and ask: *Why don't you tell them about my mistakes, Dar? Especially about how I misjudged you.*

Odrade chewed reflectively on a bite of sligpork. *I'm overdue for a visit to Sheeana. South into the desert and that soon. Sheeana must be made ready to replace Tam.*

The changing landscape loomed large in Odrade's thoughts. More than fifteen hundred years of Bene Gesserit occupancy on Chapterhouse. *Signs of us everywhere.* Not just in special groves or vineyards and orchards. What it must be doing to the collective psyche, seeing such changes come over their familiar land.

The acolyte seated beside Odrade made a soft throat-clearing sound. Was she about to address Mother Superior? A rare occurrence. The young woman continued to eat without speaking.

Odrade's thoughts returned to the prospective journey into the desert. Sheeana must have no forewarning. *I must be sure she is the one we need.* There were questions for Sheeana to answer.

Odrade knew what she would find on inspection stops en route. In Sisters, in plant and animal life, in the very foundations of Chapterhouse, she would see changes gross and changes subtle, things to wrench at Mother Superior's vaunted serenity. Even Murbella, never out of the no-ship, sensed these changes.

Only that morning, seated with her back to her console, Murbella had listened with new attentiveness to Odrade standing over her. Edgy alertness in the captive Honored Matre. Her voice betrayed doubts and unbalanced judgments.

"*All* is transient, Mother Superior?"

"That is knowledge impressed on you by Other Memory. No planet, no land or sea, no part of any land or sea is here forever."

"A morbid thought!" Rejection.

"Wherever we stand, we are only stewards."

"A useless viewpoint." Hesitant, questioning why Mother Superior chose this moment to say such things.

"I hear Honored Matres talking through you. They gave you greedy dreams, Murbella."

"So you say!" Deeply resentful.

"Honored Matres think they can buy infinite security: a small planet, you know, with plenty of subservient population."

Murbella produced a grimace.

"More planets!" Odrade snapped. "Always more and more and more! That's why they come swarming back."

"Poor pickings in this Old Empire."

"Excellent, Murbella! You're beginning to think like one of us."

"And that makes me a *nothing*!"

"Neither fish nor fowl, but your own true self? Even there, you're only a steward. Beware, Murbella! If you think you own something, that's like walking on quicksand."

This got a puzzled frown. Something would have to be done about the way Murbella allowed her emotions to play so openly on her face. It was permissible here, but someday . . .

"So nothing is safely owned. So what!" Bitter, bitter.

"You speak some of the right words but I don't think you've yet found a place in yourself where you can endure for your lifetime."

"Until an enemy finds me and slaughters me?"

Honored Matre training clings like glue! But she spoke to Duncan the other night in a way that tells me she is ready. The Van Gogh painting, I do believe, has sensitized her. I heard it in her voice. I must review that record.

"Who would slaughter you, Murbella?"

"You'll never withstand an Honored Matre attack!"

"I've already stated the basic fact that concerns us: No place is eternally safe."

"Another of your useless damned lessons!"

In the Acolyte Hall, Odrade recalled she had not found time to review that comeye record of Duncan and Murbella. A sigh almost escaped her. She covered it with a cough. Never do to let the young women see disturbance in Mother Superior.

To the desert and Sheeana! Inspection tour as soon as I can make time for it. Time!

Again, the acolyte seated beside Odrade made that throat noise. Odrade watched peripherally—blond, short black dress trimmed in white—Intermediate Third Stage. No movement of the head toward Odrade, no sidelong glances.

This is what I will find on my inspection tour: Fears. And in the landscape, those things we always see when we run out of time: trees left uncut because woodcutters have gone—dragooned into our Scattering, gone to their graves, gone to unknown places, perhaps even to peonage. Will I see architectural Fancies becoming attractive because they are incomplete, builders departed? No. We don't go in much for Fancies.

Other Memory held examples she wished she might find: old buildings more beautiful because they were unfinished. The builder bankrupt, an owner angered at his mistress . . . Some things were more interesting because of that: old walls, old ruins. Time sculpture.

What would Bell say if I ordered a Fancy in my favorite orchard?

The acolyte beside Odrade said: "Mother Superior?"

Excellent! They so seldom find the courage.

"Yes?" Faint questioning. *This had better be important.* Would she hear?

She heard. "I intrude, Mother Superior, because of the urgency and because I know your interest in the orchards."

Superb! This acolyte had thick legs but that did not extend to her mind. Odrade stared at her silently.

"I am the one making the map for your bedchamber, Mother Superior."

So this was a reliable adept, a person trusted with work for Mother Superior. Even better.

"Will I have my map soon?"

"Two days, Mother Superior. I am adjusting projection overlays where I will mark the desert's daily growth."

A brief nod. That had been in the original order: an acolyte to keep the map current. Odrade wanted to awaken each morning, her imagination ignited by that changing view, the first thing impressed on awareness at arising.

"I put a report in your workroom this morning, Mother Superior. 'Orchard Management.' Perhaps you did not see it."

Odrade had seen only the label. She had been late coming from exercises, anxious to visit Murbella. So much depended on Murbella!

"The plantations around Central must either be abandoned or action taken to sustain them," the acolyte said. "That's the gist of the report."

"Repeat the report verbatim."

Night fell and the room lights brightened as Odrade listened. Concise. Terse even. The report carried a note of admonishment Odrade recognized as originating with Bellonda. No Archival signature but Weather's warnings went through Archives and this acolyte had lifted some of the original words.

The acolyte fell silent, report concluded.

How do I respond? Orchards, pastures and vineyards were not merely a buffer against alien intrusions, pleasant decorations on the landscape. They supported Chapterhouse morale and tables.

They support my morale.

How quietly this acolyte waited. Curly blond hair and round face. Pleasing countenance, though the mouth was wide. Food remained on her plate but she was not eating. Hands folded in her lap. *I am here to serve you, Mother Superior.*

While Odrade composed her response, memory intruded—an old

incident simulflowing over immediate observations. She remembered her ornithopter training course. *Two acolyte students with instructor at midday high over the wetlands of Lampadas.* She had been paired with as inept an acolyte as could have been accepted by the Sisterhood. Obviously a gene-choice. The Breeding Mistresses wanted her for a characteristic to be passed along to offspring. *It certainly wasn't emotional balance or intelligence!* Odrade remembered the name: Linchine.

Linchine had shouted at their instructor: "I am going to fly this damned 'thopter!"

And all the while a whirling sky and landscape of trees and marshy lakeshore dizzied them. *That was how it seemed: us stationary and the world moving.* Linchine doing the wrong thing every time. Each movement created worse gyrations.

The instructor cut her out of the system by pulling the disconnect only he could reach. He did not speak until they were flying straight and level.

"No way are you ever going to fly this, lady. Not ever! You don't have the right reactions. You have to begin training those into someone like you before puberty."

"I am! I am! I'll fly this damned thing." Hands jerking at the useless controls.

"You're washed out, lady. Grounded!"

Odrade breathed easier, realizing she had known all along that Linchine might kill them.

Whirling toward Odrade in the rear, Linchine screamed: "Tell him! Tell him he must obey a Bene Gesserit!"

Addressing the fact that Odrade, several years ahead of Linchine, already displayed a commanding presence.

Odrade sat in silence, features immobile.

Silence is often the best thing to say, some Bene Gesserit humorist had scrawled on a washroom mirror. Odrade found that good advice then and later.

Recalling herself to the needs of the acolyte in the dining hall, Odrade wondered why that old memory had come of itself. Such things seldom happened without purpose. *Not silence now, certainly. Humor?* Yes! That was the message. Odrade's humor (applied later) had taught Linchine something about herself. *Humor under stress.*

Odrade smiled at the acolyte beside her in the dining hall. "How would you like to be a horse?"

"What?" The word was startled out of her but she responded to Mother Superior's smile. Nothing alarming in that. Warm even. Everyone said Mother Superior permitted affections.

"You don't understand, of course," Odrade said.

"No, Mother Superior." Still smiling and patient.

Odrade allowed her gaze to quest over the young face. Clear blue eyes not yet touched by the engulfing blue of Spice Agony. A mouth almost like Bell's but without the viciousness. Dependable muscles and dependable intelligence. She would be good at anticipating Mother Superior's needs. Witness her map assignment and that report. Sensitive. Went with her superior intelligence. Not likely to rise to the very top but always in key positions where you needed her qualities.

Why did I sit beside this one?

Odrade frequently selected a particular companion at mealtime visits. Acolytes mostly. They could be so revealing. Reports often found their way to Mother Superior's workroom: personal observations from Proctors about one acolyte or another. But sometimes, Odrade chose a seat for no reason she could explain. *As I did tonight. Why this one?*

Conversation rarely occurred unless Mother Superior initiated it. Gentle initiation usually, easing into more intimate matters. Others around them listened avidly.

At such moments, Odrade often produced a manner of almost religious serenity. It soothed nervous ones. Acolytes were . . . well, acolytes, but Mother Superior was the supreme witch of them all. Nervousness was natural.

Someone behind Odrade whispered: "She has Streggi on the coals tonight."

On the coals. Odrade knew the expression. It had been used in her acolyte days. So this one was named Streggi. *Let it be unspoken for now. Names carry magic.*

"Do you enjoy tonight's dinner?" Odrade asked.

"It's acceptable, Mother Superior." One tried not to give false opinions, but Streggi was confused by the shift in conversation.

"They've overcooked it," Odrade said.

"Serving so many, how can they please everyone, Mother Superior?"

She speaks her mind and speaks it well.

"Your left hand is trembling," Odrade said.

"I'm nervous with you, Mother Superior. And I've just come from the practice floor. Very tiring today."

Odrade analyzed the tremors. "They have you doing the long-arm lift."

"Was it painful in your day, Mother Superior?" (In those ancient times?)

"Just as painful as today. Pain teaches, they told me."

That softened things. Shared experiences, the patter of the Proctors.

"I don't understand about horses, Mother Superior." Streggi looked at her plate. "This cannot be horse meat. I'm sure I . . ."

Odrade laughed loudly, attracting startled looks. She put a hand on Streggi's arm and subsided to a gentle smile. "Thank you, my dear. No one has made me laugh that much in years. I hope this is the beginning of a long and joyous association."

"Thank you, Mother Superior, but I—"

"I will explain about the horse, my own little joke and no intent to demean you. I want you to carry a young child on your shoulders, to move him more rapidly than his short legs will carry him."

"As you wish, Mother Superior." No objections, no more questions. Questions were there, but the answers would come in their own time and Streggi knew it.

Magic time.

Withdrawing her hand, Odrade said: "Your name?"

"Streggi, Mother Superior. Aloana Streggi."

"Rest easy, Streggi. I will see to the orchards. We need them for morale as much as for food. You report to Reassignment tonight. Tell them I want you in my workroom at six tomorrow morning."

"I will be there, Mother Superior. Will I continue to mark your map?" As Odrade was rising to leave.

"For now, Streggi. But ask Reassignment for a new acolyte and begin training her. Soon, you will be much too busy for the map."

"Thank you, Mother Superior. The desert is growing very fast."

Streggi's words gave Odrade a certain satisfaction, dispelling gloom that had hampered her most of the day.

The cycle was getting another chance, turning once more as it was impelled to do by those subterranean forces called "life" and "love" and other unnecessary labels.

Thus it turns. Thus it renews. Magic. What witchery could take your attention from this miracle?

In her workroom, she issued an order to Weather, then silenced the tools of her office and went to the bow window. Chapterhouse glowed pale red in the night from reflections of groundlights against low clouds. It gave a romantic appearance to rooftops and walls that Odrade quickly rejected.

Romance? There was nothing romantic about what she had done in the Acolyte Dining Hall.

I have finally done it. I have committed myself. Now, Duncan must restore our Bashar's memories. A delicate assignment.

She continued to stare into the night, suppressing knots in her stomach.

I not only commit myself but I commit what remains of my Sisterhood. So this is how it feels, Tar.

This is how it feels and your plan is tricky.

It was going to rain. Odrade sensed it in the air coming through the ventilators around the window. No need to read a Weather Dispatch. She seldom did that these days, anyway. Why bother? But Streggi's report carried a potent warning.

Rains were becoming rarer here and rather to be welcomed. Sisters would emerge to walk in it despite the cold. There was a touch of sadness in the thought. Each rain she saw brought the same question: *Is this the last one?*

The people of Weather did heroic things to keep an expanding desert dry and the growing areas irrigated. Odrade did not know how they had managed this rain to comply with her order. Before long, they would not be able to obey such commands, even from Mother Superior. *The desert will triumph because that is what we have set in motion.*

She opened the central panes of her window. The wind at this level had stopped. Just the clouds moving overhead. Wind at higher elevations harrying things along. A sense of urgency in the weather. The air was chilly. So they had made temperature adjustments to bring this bit of rain. She closed the window, feeling no desire to go outside. Mother Superior had no time to play the game of *last rain.* One rain at a time. And always out there the desert moving inexorably toward them.

That, we can map and watch. But what of the hunter behind me— the nightmare figure with the axe? What map tells me where she is tonight?

Religion (emulation of adults by the child) encysts past mythologies: guesses, hidden assumptions of trust in the universe, pronouncements made in search of personal power, all mingled with shreds of enlightenment. And always an unspoken commandment: Thou shalt not question! We break that commandment daily in the harnessing of human imagination to our deepest creativity.

—BENE GESSERIT CREDO

Murbella sat cross-legged on the practice floor, alone, shivering after her exertions. Mother Superior had been here less than an hour this afternoon. And, as often happened, Murbella felt she had been abandoned in a fever dream.

Odrade's parting words reverberated in the dream: "The hardest lesson for an acolyte to learn is that she must always go the limit. Your abilities will take you farther than you imagine. Don't imagine, then. Extend yourself!"

What is my response? That I was taught to cheat?

Odrade had done something to call up the patterns of childhood and Honored Matre education. *I learned cheating as an infant. How to simulate a need and gain attention.* Many "how-to's" in the cheating pattern. The older she got, the easier the cheating. She had learned what the *big people* around her were demanding. *I regurgitated on demand. That was called "education."* Why were the Bene Gesserit so remarkably different in their teaching?

"I don't ask you to be honest with me," Odrade had said. "Be honest with yourself."

Murbella despaired of ever rooting out all of the cheating in her past. *Why should I? More cheating!*

"Damn you, Odrade!"

Only after the words were out did she realize she had spoken them aloud. She started to put a hand to her mouth and aborted the movement. Fever said: "What's the difference?"

"Educational bureaucracies dull a child's questing sensitivity." *Odrade explaining.* "The young must be damped down. Never let them know how good they can be. That brings change. Spend lots of committee time talking about how to deal with exceptional students. Don't spend any time dealing with how the conventional teacher feels threatened by emerging talents and squelches them because of a deep-seated desire to feel superior and safe in a safe environment."

She was talking about Honored Matres.

Conventional teachers?

There it was: Behind that façade of wisdom, the Bene Gesserit were unconventional. They often did not think about teaching: they just did it.

Gods! I want to be like them!

The thought shocked her and she leaped to her feet, launching herself into a training routine for wrists and arms.

Realization bit deeper than ever. She did not want to disappoint these teachers. *Candor and honesty.* Every acolyte heard that. "Basic tools of learning," Odrade said.

Distracted by her thoughts, Murbella tumbled hard and stood up, rubbing a bruised shoulder.

She had thought at first that the Bene Gesserit protestation must be a lie. *I am being so candid with you that I must tell you about my unswerving honesty.*

But actions confirmed their claim. Odrade's voice persisted in the fever dream: "That is how you judge."

They had something in the mind, in memory and a balance of intellect no Honored Matre had ever possessed. This thought made her feel small. *Enter corruption.* It was like liver spots in her feverish thoughts.

But I have talent! It required talent to become an Honored Matre.

Do I still think of myself as an Honored Matre?

The Bene Gesserit knew she had not fully committed herself to them. *What skills do I have that they could possibly want? Not the skills of deception.*

"*Do actions agree with words? There's your measure of reliability. Never confine yourself to the words.*"

Murbella put her hands over her ears. *Shut up, Odrade!*

"*How does a Truthsayer separate sincerity from a more fundamental judgment?*"

Murbella dropped her hands to her sides. *Maybe I'm really sick.* She swept her gaze around the long room. No one there to utter these words. Anyway, it was Odrade's voice.

"*If you convince yourself, sincerely, you can speak utter balderdash (marvelous old word; look it up), absolute poppylarky in every word and you will be believed. But not by one of our Truthsayers.*"

Murbella's shoulders sagged. She began to wander aimlessly around the practice floor. Was there no place to escape?

"*Look for the consequences, Murbella. That's how you ferret out things that work. That's what our much-vaulted truths are all about.*"

Pragmatism?

Idaho found her then and responded to the wild look in her eyes. "What's wrong?"

"I think I'm sick. Really sick. I thought it was something Odrade did to me but . . ."

He caught her as she fell.

"Help us!"

For once, he was glad of the comeyes. A Suk was with them in less than a minute. She bent over Murbella where Idaho cradled her on the floor.

The examination was brief. The Suk, a graying older Reverend Mother with the traditional diamond brand on her forehead, straightened and said: "Overstressed. She's not trying to find her limits, she's going beyond them. We'll put her back into the sensitizing class before we let her continue. I'll send the Proctors."

Odrade found Murbella in the Proctor's Ward that evening, propped up in a bed, two Proctors taking turns testing her muscle response. A small gesture and they left Odrade alone with Murbella.

"I tried to avoid complicating things," Murbella said. *Candor and honesty.*

"Trying to avoid complications often creates them." Odrade sank into a chair beside the bed and put a hand on Murbella's arm. Muscles quivered under the hand. "We say 'words are slow, feeling's faster.'" Odrade withdrew. "What decisions have you been making?"

"You let me make decisions?"

"Don't sneer." She lifted a hand to prevent interruption. "I didn't take your previous conditioning into sufficient account. The Honored Matres left you practically incapable of making decisions. Typical of power-hungry societies. Teach their people to diddle around forever. 'Decisions bring bad results!' You teach avoidance."

"What's that have to do with me collapsing?" Resentful.

"Murbella! The worst products of what I'm describing are almost basket cases—can't make decisions about anything, or leave them until the last possible second and then leap at them like desperate animals."

"You told me to go the limit!" Almost wailing.

"Your limits, Murbella. Not mine. Not Bell's or those of anyone else. Yours."

"I've decided I want to be like you." Very faint.

"Marvelous! I don't believe I've ever tried to kill myself. Especially when I was pregnant."

In spite of herself, Murbella grinned.

Odrade stood. "Sleep. You're going into a special class tomorrow where we'll work on your ability to mesh your decisions with sensitivity to your limits. Remember what I told you. We take care of our own."

"Am I yours?" Almost whispered.

"Since you repeated the oath before the Proctors." Odrade turned out the lights as she left. Murbella heard her speak to someone before the door closed. "Stop fussing with her. She needs rest."

Murbella closed her eyes. The fever dream was gone but in its place was her own memory. "I am a Bene Gesserit. I exist only to serve."

She heard herself saying those words to the Proctors but memory gave them an emphasis not in the original.

They knew I was being cynical.

What could you hide from such women?

She felt the remembered hand of the Proctor on her forehead and heard the words that had possessed no meaning until this moment.

"I stand in the sacred human presence. As I do now, so should you stand some day. I pray to your presence that this be so. Let the future remain uncertain for that is the canvas to receive our desires. Thus the human condition faces its perpetual tabula rasa. We possess no more than this moment where we dedicate ourselves continuously to the sacred presence we share and create."

Conventional but unconventional. She realized that she had not been physically or emotionally prepared for this moment. Tears flowed down her cheeks.

> Laws to suppress tend to strengthen what they would pro-
> hibit. This is the fine point on which all the legal professions
> of history have based their job security.
>
> —BENE GESSERIT CODA

On her restless prowlings through Central (infrequent these days but more intense because of that), Odrade looked for signs of slackness and especially for areas of responsibility that were running too smoothly.

The *Senior Watchdog* had her own watch*words*: "Show me a completely smooth operation and I'll show you someone who's covering mistakes. Real boats rock."

She said this often and it became an identifying phrase the Sisters (and even some acolytes) employed to comment on Mother Superior.

"Real boats rock." Soft chuckles.

Bellonda accompanied Odrade on today's early morning inspection, not mentioning that "once a month" had been stretched to "once every two months"—if that. This inspection was a week past the mark. Bell wanted to use this time for warnings about Idaho. And she had dragged Tamalane along although Tam was supposed to be reviewing Proctor performance at this hour.

Two against one? Odrade wondered. She did not think Bell or Tam suspected what Mother Superior intended. Well, it would come out, as had Taraza's plan. *In its own time, eh, Tar?*

Down the corridors they stalked, black robes swishing with urgency, eyes missing little. It was all familiar and yet they looked for things that were new. Odrade carried her Ear-C over her left shoulder like a misplaced diving weight. *Never be out of communication range these days.*

Behind the scenes in any Bene Gesserit center were the support facilities: clinic-hospital, kitchen, morgue, garbage control, reclamation systems (attached to sewage and garbage), transport and communications, kitchen provisioning, training and physical maintenance halls, schools for acolytes and postulants, quarters for all of the denominations, meeting centers, testing facilities and much more. Personnel often changed because of the Scattering and movement of people into new responsibilities, all according to subtle Bene Gesserit awareness. But tasks and places for them remained.

As they strode swiftly from one area to another, Odrade spoke of the Sisterhood Scattering, not trying to hide her dismay at "the atomic family" they had become.

"I find it difficult to contemplate humankind spreading into an unlimited universe," Tam said. "The possibilities . . ."

"Infinite numbers game." Odrade stepped across a broken curb. "That should be repaired. We've been playing the infinity game since we learned to jump Foldspace."

There was no joy in Bellonda. "It's not a game!"

Odrade could appreciate Bellonda's feelings. *We have never seen empty space. Always more galaxies. Tam's right. It's daunting when you focus on that Golden Path.*

Memories of explorations gave the Sisterhood a statistical handle on it but little else. So many habitable planets in a given assemblage and, among those, an expected additional number that could be terraformed.

"What's evolving out there?" Tamalane demanded.

A question they could not answer. Ask what Infinity might produce and the only answer possible was, "Anything."

Any good, any evil; any god, any devil.

"What if Honored Matres are fleeing something?" Odrade asked. "Interesting possibility?"

"These speculations are useless," Bellonda muttered. "We don't even know if Foldspace introduces us to one universe or many . . . or even an infinite number of expanding and collapsing bubbles."

"Did the Tyrant understand this any better than we do?" Tamalane asked.

They paused while Odrade looked into a room where five Advanced acolytes and a Proctor studied a projection of regional melange stores. The crystal holding the information performed an intricate dance in the projector, bouncing on its beam like a ball on a fountain. Odrade saw the summation and turned away before scowling. Tam and Bell did not see Odrade's expression. *We will have to start limiting access to melange data. Too depressing to morale.*

Administration! It all came back to Mother Superior. Delegate heavily to only the same people and you fell into bureaucracy.

Odrade knew she depended too much on her inner sense of administration. A system frequently tested and revised, using automation only where essential. "The machinery" they called it. By the time they became Reverend Mothers, all of them had some sensitivity to "the machinery" and tended to use it without question thereafter. There lay the danger. Odrade pressed for constant improvements (even tiny ones) to introduce change into their activities. Randomness! No absolute patterns that others could find and use against them. One person might not see such shifts in a lifetime but differences over longer periods were sure to be measurable.

Odrade's party came down to ground level and onto the major thoroughfare of Central. "The Way," Sisters called it. An in-joke, referring to the training regimen popularly known as "The Bene Gesserit Way."

The Way reached from the square beside Odrade's tower to the southern outskirts of the urban area—straight as a lasgun beam, almost twelve klicks of tall buildings and low ones. The low ones all had something in common: they had been built strong enough to expand upward.

Odrade flagged an open transporter with empty seats and the three of them crowded into a space where they could continue to talk. Frontage on The Way carried an old-fashioned appeal, Odrade thought. Buildings such as these with their tall rectangular windows of insulating plaz had framed Bene Gesserit "Ways" through much of the Sisterhood's history. Down the center ran a line of elms genetically tailored for height and narrow profile. Birds nested in them and the morning was bright with flitting spots of red and orange—orioles, tanagers.

Is it dangerously patterned for us to prefer this familiar setting?

Odrade led them off the transporter at Tipsy Trail, thinking how Bene Gesserit humor came out in curious names. Waggish in the streets. Tipsy Trail because the foundation of one building had subsided slightly, giving that structure a curiously drunken appearance. The one member of the group stepping out of line.

Like Mother Superior. Only they don't know it yet.

Her Ear-C buzzed as they came to Tower Lane. "Mother Superior?" It was Streggi. Without stopping, Odrade signaled that she was online. "You asked for a report on Murbella. Suk Central says she is fit for assigned classes."

"Then assign her." They continued down Tower Lane: all one-story buildings.

Odrade spared a brief glance for the low buildings on both sides of the street. A two-story addition was being made to one of them. Might be a real Tower Lane here someday and the joke (such as it was) abandoned.

It was argued that naming was just a convenience anyway and they might as well enjoy this venture into what was a delicate subject for the Sisterhood.

Odrade stopped abruptly on a busy walkway and turned to her companions. "What would you say if I suggested we name streets and places after departed Sisters?"

"You're full of nonsense today!" Bellonda accused.

"They are not departed," Tamalane said.

Odrade resumed her prowling walk. She had expected that. Bell's thoughts could almost be heard. *We carry the "departed" around in Other Memory!*

Odrade wanted no argument here in the open but she thought her idea had merit. Some Sisters died without Sharing. Major Memory Lines were duplicated but you lost a thread and its terminated carrier. Schwangyu of the Gammu Keep had gone that way, killed by attacking Honored Matres. Plenty of memories remained to carry her good qualities . . . and complexities. One hesitated to say her mistakes taught more than her successes.

Bellonda increased her pace to walk beside Odrade in a relatively empty stretch. "I must speak of Idaho. A Mentat, yes, but those multiple memories. Supremely dangerous!"

They were passing a morgue, the strong smell of antiseptics even in the street. The arched doorway stood open.

"Who died?" Odrade asked, ignoring Bellonda's anxiety.

"A Proctor from Section Four and an orchard maintenance man," Tamalane said. Tam always knew.

Bellonda was furious at being ignored and made no attempt to hide it. "Will you two stick to the point?"

"What is the point?" Odrade asked. Very mild.

They emerged on the south terrace and stopped at the stone rail to look over the plantations—vineyards and orchards. The morning light had a dusty haze in it not at all like the mists created of moisture.

"You know the point!" Bell would not be deflected.

Odrade stared at the vista, pressing herself against the stones. The railing was frigid. That mist out there was a different color, she thought. Sunlight came through dust with a different reflective spectrum. More bounce and sharpness to the light. Absorbed in a different way. The nimbus was tighter. The blowing dust and sand crept into every crevice the way water did but the grating and rasping betrayed its source. The same with Bell's persistence. No lubrication.

"That's desert light," Odrade said, pointing.

"Stop avoiding me," Bellonda said.

Odrade chose not to answer. The dusty light was a classical thing, but not reassuring in the way of the elder painters and their misty mornings.

Tamalane came up beside Odrade. "Beautiful in its own way." The remote tone said she made Other Memory comparisons similar to Odrade's.

If that's how you were conditioned to look for beauty. But something deep within Odrade said this was not the beauty for which she longed.

In the shallow swales below them, where once there had been greenery, now there was dryness and a sense of the earth being gutted the way ancient Egyptians had prepared their dead—dried to essential matter, preserved for their Eternity. *Desert as deathmaster, swaddling the dirt in nitron, embalming our beautiful planet with all of its jewels concealed.*

Bellonda stood behind them, muttering and shaking her head, refusing to look at what their planet would become.

Odrade almost shuddered in a sudden thrust of simulflow. Memory flooded her: She felt herself searching Sietch Tabr's ruins, finding desert-embalmed bodies of spice pirates left where killers had dropped them.

What is Sietch Tabr now? A molten flow solidified and without anything to mark its proud history. Honored Matres: killers of history.

"If you won't eliminate Idaho, then I must protest your using him as a Mentat."

Bell was such a fussy woman! Odrade noted that she was showing her age more than ever. Reading lenses on her nose even now. They magnified her eyes until she had the look of a great-orbed fish. Use of lenses and not one of the more subtle prostheses said something about her. She flaunted a reverse vanity that announced: "I am greater than the devices my failing senses require."

Bellonda was definitely irritated by Mother Superior. "Why are you staring at me that way?"

Odrade, caught by abrupt awareness of a weakness in her Council, shifted her attention to Tamalane. Cartilage never stopped growing and this had enlarged Tam's ears, nose and chin. Some Reverend Mothers adjusted this by metabolism control or sought regular surgical correction. Tam would not bow to such vanity. *"Here's what I am. Take it or leave it."*

My advisors are too old. And I . . . I should be younger and stronger to have these problems on my shoulders. Oh, damn this for a lapse into self-pity!

Only one supreme danger: action against survival of the Sisterhood.

"Duncan is a superb Mentat!" Odrade spoke with all the force of her position. "But I use none of you beyond your capabilities."

Bellonda remained silent. She knew a Mentat's weaknesses.

Mentats! Odrade thought. They were like walking Archives but when you most needed answers they relapsed into questions.

"I don't need another Mentat," Odrade said. "I need an inventor!"

When Bellonda still did not speak, Odrade said: "I am freeing his mind, not his body."

"I insist on an analysis before you open all data sources to him!"

Considering Bellonda's usual stance, that was mild. But Odrade did not trust it. She detested those sessions—endless rehashing of Archival reports. Bellonda doted on them. Bellonda of Archival minutiae and boring excursions into irrelevant details! Who cared if Reverend Mother X preferred skimmed milk on her porridge?

Odrade turned her back on Bellonda and looked at the southern sky. *Dust! We would sift more dust!* Bellonda would be flanked by assistants. Odrade felt boredom just imagining it.

"No more analysis." Odrade spoke more sharply than she had intended.

"I do have a point of view." Bellonda sounded hurt.

Point of view? Are we no more than sensory windows on our universe, each with only a point of view?

Instincts and memories of all types . . . even Archives—none of these things spoke for themselves except by compelling intrusions. None carried weight until formulated in a living consciousness. But whoever produced the formulation tipped the scales. *All order is arbitrary!* Why this datum rather than some other? Any Reverend Mother knew events occurred in their own flux, their own relative environment. Why couldn't a Mentat Reverend Mother act from that knowledge?

"Do you refuse counsel?" That was Tamalane. Was she siding with Bell?

"When have I ever refused counsel?" Odrade let her outrage show. "I am refusing another of Bell's Archival merry-go-rounds."

Bellonda intruded. "Then, in reality—"

"Bell! Don't talk to me about reality!" Let her simmer in that! *Reverend Mother and Mentat! There is no reality. Only our own order imposed on everything. A basic Bene Gesserit dictum.*

There were times (and this was one of them) when Odrade wished she had been born in an earlier era—a Roman matron in the long pax of the aristocrats, or a much-pampered Victorian. But she was trapped by time and circumstances.

Trapped forever?

Must face that possibility. The Sisterhood might have only a future confined to secret hideaways, always fearing discovery. The future of the hunted. *And here at Central we may be allowed no more than one mistake.*

"I've had enough of this inspection!" Odrade called for private transport and hurried them back to her workroom.

What will we do if the hunters come upon us here?

Each of them had her own scenario, a little playlet full of planned reactions. But every Reverend Mother was sufficiently a realist to know her playlet might be more hindrance than help.

In the workroom, morning light harshly revealing on everything around them, Odrade sank into her chair and waited for Tamalane and Bellonda to take their seats.

No more of those damned analysis sessions. She really needed access to something better than Archives, better than anything they had ever used before. Inspiration. Odrade rubbed her legs, feeling muscles tremble. She had not slept well for days. This inspection left her feeling frustrated.

One mistake could end us and I am about to commit us to a no-return decision.

Am I being too tricky?

Her advisors argued against tricky solutions. They said the Sisterhood must move with steady assurance, the ground ahead known in advance. Everything they did lay counterpoised by the disaster awaiting them at the slightest misstep.

And I am on the tightrope over the chasm.

Did they have room to experiment, to test possible solutions? They all played that game. Bell and Tam screened a constant flow of suggestions but nothing more effective than their atomic Scattering.

"We must be prepared to kill Idaho at the slightest sign he is a Kwisatz Haderach," Bellonda said.

"Don't you have work to do? Get out of here, both of you!"

As they stood, the workroom around Odrade took on an alien feeling. What was wrong? Bellonda stared down at her with that awful look of censure. Tamalane appeared more wise than she could possibly be.

What is it about this room?

The workroom would have been recognized for its function by humans from pre-space history. What felt so alien? A worktable was a worktable and the chairs were in convenient positions. Bell and Tam preferred chairdogs. Those would have seemed odd to the early human in Other Memory she suspected was coloring her view. The ridulian crystals might glisten strangely, the light pulsing in them and blinking. Messages dancing above the table might be surprising. Instruments of her labors could appear strange to an early human sharing her awareness.

But it felt alien to me.

"Are you all right, Dar?" Tam spoke with concern.

Odrade waved her away but neither woman moved.

Things were happening in her mind that could not be blamed on the long hours and insufficient rest. This was not the first time she had felt she worked in alien surroundings. The previous night while eating a snack at this table, the surface littered with assignment orders as it was now, she had found herself just sitting and staring at uncompleted work.

Which Sisters could be spared from what posts for this terrible Scattering? How could they improve survival chances of the few sandtrout the Scattered Sisters took? What was a proper allotment of me-lange? Should they wait before sending more Sisters into the unknown? Wait for the possibility that Scytale could be induced to tell them how axlotl tanks produced the spice?

Odrade recalled that the alien feeling had occurred to her as she chewed on a sandwich. She had looked at it, opening it slightly. *What is this thing I'm eating?* Chicken liver and onions on some of the best Chapterhouse bread.

Questioning her own routines, that was part of this alien sensation.

"You look ill," Bellonda said.

"Just fatigue," Odrade lied. They knew she was lying but would they challenge her? "You both must be equally tired." Affection in her tone.

Bell was not satisfied. "You set a bad example!"

"What? Me?" The jesting was not lost on Bell.

"You know damned well you do!"

"It's your displays of affection," Tamalane said.

"Even for Bell."

"I don't want your damned affection! It's wrong."

"Only if I let it rule my decisions, Bell. Only then."

Bellonda's voice fell to a husky whisper. "Some think you're a dan-gerous romantic, Dar. You know what that could do."

"Ally Sisters with me for other than our survival. Is that what you mean?"

"Sometimes you give me a headache, Dar!"

"It's my duty and right to give you a headache. When your head fails to ache, you become careless. Affections bother you but hates don't."

"I know my flaw."

You couldn't be a Reverend Mother and not know it.

The workroom once more had become a familiar place but now Odrade knew a source of her alien feelings. She was thinking of this place as part of ancient history, viewing it as she might when it was long gone. As it certainly would be if her plan succeeded. She knew what she had to do now. Time to reveal the first step.

Careful.

Yes, Tar, I'm as cautious as you were.

Tam and Bell might be old but their minds were sharp when necessity required it.

Odrade fixed her gaze on Bell. "Patterns, Bell. It is our pattern not to offer violence for violence." Raising a hand to stop Bell's response. "Yes, violence builds more violence and the pendulum swings until the violent ones are shattered."

"What are you thinking?" Tam demanded.

"Perhaps we should consider baiting the bull more strongly."

"We dare not. Not yet."

"But we also dare not sit here witlessly waiting for them to find us. Lampadas and our other disasters tell us what will happen when they come. When, not if."

As she spoke, Odrade sensed the chasm beneath her, the nightmare hunter with the axe ever nearer. She wanted to sink into the nightmare, turning there to identify the one who stalked them, but dared not. That had been the mistake of the Kwisatz Haderach.

You do not see that future, you create it.

Tamalane wanted to know why Odrade raised this issue. "Have you changed your mind, Dar?"

"Our ghola-Teg is ten years old."

"Much too young for us to attempt restoring his original memories," Bellonda said.

"Why have we recreated Teg if not for violent uses?" Odrade asked. "Oh, yes!" As Tam started to object. "Teg did not always solve our problems with violence. The peaceful Bashar could deflect enemies with reasonable words."

Tam spoke musingly. "But Honored Matres may never negotiate."

"Unless we can drive them to extremis."

"I think you are proposing to move too fast," Bellonda said. Trust Bell to reach a Mentat summation.

Odrade drew in a deep breath and looked down at her worktable. It had come at last. On that morning when she had removed the baby ghola from his obscene "tank," she had sensed this moment waiting for her. Even then she had known she would put this ghola into the crucible before his time. Ties of blood notwithstanding.

Reaching beneath her table, Odrade touched a call field. Her two councillors stood silently waiting. They knew she was about to say something important. One thing a Mother Superior could be sure of— her Sisters listened to her with great care, with an intensity that would have gratified someone more ego-bound than a Reverend Mother.

"Politics," Odrade said.

That snapped them to attention! A loaded word. When you entered Bene Gesserit politics, marshaling your powers for the rise to eminence, you became a prisoner of responsibility. You saddled yourself with duties and decisions that bound you to the lives of those who depended on you. This was what really tied the Sisterhood to their Mother Superior. That one word told councillors and the watchdogs the First-Among-Equals had reached a decision.

They all heard the small scuffling sound of someone arriving outside the workroom door. Odrade touched the white plate in the near right corner of her table. The door behind her opened and Streggi stood there awaiting the Mother Superior's orders.

"Bring him," Odrade said.

"Yes, Mother Superior." Almost emotionless. A very promising acolyte, that Streggi.

She stepped out of sight and returned leading Miles Teg by the hand. The boy's hair was quite blond but streaked with darker lines that said the light coloration would go dark when he matured. His face was narrow, nose just beginning to show that hawkish angularity so characteristic of Atreides males. His blue eyes moved alertly taking in room and occupants with expectant curiosity.

"Wait outside, please, Streggi."

Odrade waited for the door to close.

The boy stood looking at Odrade with no sign of impatience.

"Miles Teg, ghola," Odrade said. "You remember Tamalane and Bellonda, of course."

He favored the two women with a short glance but remained silent, apparently unmoved by the intensity of their inspection.

Tamalane frowned. She had disagreed from the first with calling this child a ghola. Gholas were grown from cells of a cadaver. This was a clone, just as Scytale was a clone.

"I am going to send him into the no-ship with Duncan and Murbella," Odrade said. "Who better than Duncan to restore Miles to his original memories?"

"Poetic justice," Bellonda agreed. She did not speak her objections although Odrade knew they would come out when the boy had gone. *Too young!*

"What does she mean, poetic justice?" Teg asked. His voice had a piping quality.

"When the Bashar was on Gammu, he restored Duncan's original memories."

"Is it really painful?"

"Duncan found it so."

Some decisions must be ruthless.

Odrade thought that a great barrier to accepting the fact that you could make your own decisions. Something she would not be required to explain to Murbella.

How do I soften the blow?

There were times when you could not soften it; in fact when it was kinder to rip off the bandages in one swift shot of agony.

"Can this . . . this Duncan Idaho really give me back my memories from . . . before?"

"He can and he will."

"Are we not being too precipitous?" Tamalane asked.

"I've been studying accounts of the Bashar," Teg said. "He was a famous military man and a Mentat."

"And you're proud of that, I suppose?" Bell was taking out her objections on the boy.

"Not especially." He returned her gaze without flinching. "I think of him as someone else. Interesting, though."

"Someone else," Bellonda muttered. She looked at Odrade with ill-concealed disagreement. "You're giving him the deep teaching!"

"As his birth-mother did."

"Will I remember her?" Teg asked.

Odrade gave him a conspiratorial smile, one they had shared often in their orchard walks. "You will."

"Everything?"

"You'll remember all of it—your wife, your children, the battles. Everything."

"Send him away!" Bellonda said.

The boy smiled but looked to Odrade, awaiting her command.

"Very well, Miles," Odrade said. "Tell Streggi to take you to your new quarters in the no-ship. I'll come along later and introduce you to Duncan."

"May I ride on Streggi's shoulders?"

"Ask her."

Impulsively, Teg dashed up to Odrade, lifted himself onto his toes and kissed her cheek. "I hope my real mother was like you."

Odrade patted his shoulder. "Very much like me. Run along now."

When the door closed behind him, Tamalane said: "You haven't told him you're one of his daughters!"

"Not yet."

"Will Idaho tell him?"

"If it's indicated."

Bellonda was not interested in petty details. "What are you planning, Dar?"

Tamalane answered for her. "A punishment force commanded by our Mentat Bashar. It's obvious."

She took the bait!

"Is that it?" Bellonda demanded.

Odrade favored them both with a hard stare. "Teg was the best we ever had. If anyone can punish our enemies . . ."

"We'd better start growing another one," Tamalane said.

"I don't like the influence Murbella may have on him," Bellonda said.

"Will Idaho cooperate?" Tamalane asked.

"He will do what an Atreides asks of him."

Odrade spoke with more confidence than she felt but the words opened her mind to another source of the alien feelings.

I'm seeing us as Murbella sees us! I can think like at least one Honored Matre!

We do not teach history; we recreate the experience. We follow the chain of consequences—the tracks of the beast in its forest. Look behind our words and you see the broad sweep of social behavior that no historian has ever touched.

—BENE GESSERIT PANOPLIA PROPHETICUS

Scytale whistled while he walked down the corridor fronting his quarters, taking his afternoon exercise. Down and back. Whistling.

Get them accustomed to me whistling.

As he whistled, he composed a ditty to go with the sound: "Tleilaxu sperm does not talk." Over and over, the words rolled in his mind. They could not use his cells to bridge the genetic gap and learn his secrets.

They must come to me with gifts.

Odrade had stopped by to see him earlier "on my way to confer with Murbella." She mentioned the captive Honored Matre to him frequently. There was a purpose but he had no idea what it might be. Threat? Always possible. It would be revealed eventually.

"I hope you are not fearful," Odrade had said.

They had been standing at his food slot while he waited for lunch to appear. The menu was never quite to his liking but acceptable. Today, he had asked for seafood. No telling what form it would take.

"Fearful? Of you? Ahhh, dear Mother Superior, I am priceless to you alive. Why should I fear?"

"My Council reserves judgment on your latest requests."

I expected that.

"It's a mistake to hobble me," he said. "Limits your choices. Weakens you."

Those words had taken several days of planning for him to compose. He waited for their effect.

"It depends on how one intends to employ the tool, Master Scytale. Some tools break when you don't use them properly."

Damn you, witch!

He smiled, showing his sharp canines. "Testing to extinction, Mother Superior?"

She made one of her rare sallies into humor. "Do you really expect me to strengthen you? For what do you bargain now, Scytale?"

So I'm no longer Master *Scytale. Strike her with the flat of the blade!*

"You Scatter your Sisters, hoping some will escape destruction. What are the economic consequences of your hysterical reaction?"

Consequences! They always talk about consequences.

"We trade for time, Scytale." Very solemn.

He gave this a silent moment of reflection. The comeyes were watching them. Never forget it! *Economics, witch! Who and what do we buy and sell?* This alcove by the food slot was a strange place for bargaining, he thought. Bad management of the economy. The management hustle, the planning and strategy session, should occur behind closed doors, in high rooms with views that did not distract the occupants from the business at hand.

The serial memories of his many lives would not accept that. *Necessity. Humans conduct their merchant affairs wherever they can—on the decks of sailing ships, in tawdry streets full of bustling clerks, in the spacious halls of a traditional bourse with information flowing above their heads for all to see.*

Planning and strategy might come from those high rooms but the evidence of it was like the common information of the bourse—there for all to see.

So let the comeyes watch.

"What are your intentions toward me, Mother Superior?"

"To keep you alive and strong."

Careful, careful.

"But not give me a free hand."

"Scytale! You speak of economics and then want something free?"

"But my strength is important to you?"

"Believe it!"

"I do not trust you."

The food slot took that moment to disgorge his lunch: a white fish sauteed in a delicate sauce. He smelled herbs. Water in a tall glass, faint aroma of melange. A green salad. *One of their better efforts.* He felt himself salivating.

"Enjoy your lunch, Master Scytale. There is nothing in it to harm you. Is that not a measure of trust?"

When he did not respond, she said: "What does trust have to do with our bargaining?"

What game is she playing now?

"You tell me what you intend for Honored Matres but you do not say what you intend for me." He knew he sounded plaintive. Unavoidable.

"I intend to make the Honored Matres aware of their mortality."

"As you do with me!"

Was that satisfaction in her eyes?

"Scytale." *How soft her voice.* "People thus made aware truly listen. They hear you." She glanced at his tray. "Would you like something special?"

He drew himself up as best he could. "A small stimulant drink. It helps when I must think."

"Of course. I'll see that it's sent down at once." She turned her attention out of the alcove toward the main room of his quarters. He watched where she paused, her gaze shifting from place to place, item to item.

Everything in its place, witch. I am not an animal in its cave. Things must be convenient, where I can find them without thinking. Yes, those are stimpens beside my chair. So I use 'pens. But I avoid alcohol. You notice?

The stimulant, when it came, tasted of a bitter herb he was a moment identifying. Casmine. A genetically modified blood strengthener from the Gammu pharmacopoeia.

Did she intend to remind him of Gammu? They were so devious, these witches!

Poking fun at him over the question of economics. He felt the sting of this as he turned at the end of his corridor and continued his exercise in a brisk walk back to his quarters. What glue had actually held the Old Empire together? Many things, some small and some large, but mostly economic. Lines of connection thought of often as conveniences. And what kept them from blasting one another out of existence? The Great Convention. "You blast anyone and we unite to blast you."

He stopped outside his door, brought up short by a thought.

Was that it? How could punishment be enough to stop the greedy powindah? Did it come down to a glue composed of intangibles? The censure of your peers? But what if your peers balked at no obscenity? You could do anything. And that said something about Honored Matres. It certainly did.

He longed for a sagra chamber in which to bare his soul.

The Yaghist is gone! Am I the last Masheikh?

His chest felt empty. It was an effort to breathe. Perhaps it would be best to bargain more openly with the women of Shaitan.

No! That is Shaitan himself tempting me!

He entered his chambers in a chastened mood.

I must make them pay. Make them pay dearly. Dearly, dearly, dearly. Each *dearly* accompanied a step toward his chair. When he sat, his right hand reached out automatically for a 'pen. Soon, he felt his mind driving at speed, thoughts pouring through in marvelous array.

They do not guess how well I know the Ixian ship. It's here in my head.

He spent the next hour deciding how he would record these moments when it came time to tell his fellows how he had triumphed over the powindah. *With God's help!*

They would be glittering words, filled with drama and the tensions of his testing. History, after all, was always written by the victors.

They say Mother Superior can disregard nothing—a meaningless aphorism until you grasp its other significance: I am
the servant of all my Sisters. They watch their servant with
critical eyes. I cannot spend too much time on generalities
nor on trivia. Mother Superior must display insightful action
else a sense of disquiet penetrates to the farthest corners
of our order.

—DARWI ODRADE

Something of what Odrade called "my servant-self" went with her as
she walked the halls of Central this morning, making this her exercise
rather than take time on a practice floor. *A disgruntled servant!* She did
not like what she saw.

*We are too tightly bound up in our difficulties, almost incapable of
separating petty problems from great ones.*

What had happened to their conscience?

Although some denied it, Odrade knew there was a Bene Gesserit
conscience. But they had twisted and reshaped it into a form not easily
recognized.

She felt loath to meddle with it. Decisions taken in the name of
survival, the Missionaria (their interminable Jesuitical arguments!)—
all diverged from something far more demanding of human judgment.
The Tyrant had known this.

To be human, that was the issue. But before you could be human,
you had to feel it in your guts.

No clinical answers! It came down to a deceptive simplicity whose complex nature appeared when you applied it.

Like me.

You looked inward and found who and what you believed you were. Nothing else would serve.

So what am I?

"Who asks that question?" It was a skewering thrust from Other Memory.

Odrade laughed aloud and a passing Proctor named Praska stared at her in astonishment. Odrade waved to Praska and said: "It's good to be alive. Remember that."

Praska produced a faint smile before going on about her business.

So who asks: What am I?

Dangerous question. Asking it put her in a universe where nothing was quite human. Nothing matched the undefined thing she sought. All around her, clowns, wild animals and puppets reacted to the pull of hidden strings. She sensed the strings that jerked *her* into movement.

Odrade continued along the corridor toward the tube that would take her up to her quarters.

Strings. What came with the egg? *We speak glibly of "the mind at its beginning." But what was I before the pressures of living shaped me?*

It wasn't enough to seek something "natural." No "Noble Savage." She had seen plenty of those in her lifetime. The strings jerking them were quite visible to a Bene Gesserit.

She felt the taskmaster within her. Strong today. It was a force she sometimes disobeyed or avoided. Taskmaster said: "Strengthen your talents. Do not flow gently in the current. Swim! Use it or lose it."

With a gasping sensation of near panic, she realized she had barely retained her humanity, that she had been on the point of losing it.

I've been trying too hard to think like an Honored Matre! Manipulating and maneuvering anyone I could. And all in the name of Bene Gesserit survival!

Bell said there were no limits beyond which the Sisterhood would refuse to go in preserving the Bene Gesserit. A modicum of truth in this boast but it was the truth of all boasting. There were indeed things a Reverend Mother would not do to save the Sisterhood.

We would not block the Tyrant's Golden Path.

Survival of humankind took precedence over survival of the Sisterhood. *Else our grail of human maturity is meaningless.*

But oh, the perils of leadership in a species so anxious to be told what to do. How little they knew of what they created by their demands. Leaders made mistakes. And those mistakes, amplified by the numbers who followed without questioning, moved inevitably toward great disasters.

Lemming behavior.

It was right that her Sisters watched her carefully. All governments needed to remain under suspicion during their time of power including that of the Sisterhood itself. *Trust no government! Not even mine!*

They are watching me this very instant. Very little escapes my Sisters. They will know my plan in time.

It required constant mental cleansing to face up to the fact of her great power over the Sisterhood. *I did not seek this power. It was thrust upon me.* And she thought: *Power attracts the corruptible. Suspect all who seek it.* She knew the chances were great that such people were susceptible to corruption or already lost.

Odrade made a mental note to scribe and transmit a Coda memo to Archives. (Let Bell sweat this one!) "We should grant power over our affairs only to those who are reluctant to hold it and then only under conditions that increase the reluctance."

Perfect description of the Bene Gesserit!

"Are you well, Dar?" It was Bellonda's voice from the tube door beside Odrade. "You look . . . strange."

"I just thought of something to do. You getting off?"

Bellonda stared at her as they exchanged places. The tube-field caught Odrade and whisked her away from that questioning gaze.

Odrade entered the workroom and saw her table piled with things her aides thought only she could resolve.

Politics, she recalled as she sat at her table and prepared to deal with responsibilities. Tam and Bell had heard her clearly the other day but they had only the vaguest idea of what they would be asked to support. They were worried and increasingly watchful. *As they should be.*

Almost any subject had political elements, she thought. As emotions were whipped up, political forces came more and more into the foreground. This put *lie!* to that old nonsense about "separation of church and state." Nothing more susceptible to emotional heat than religion.

No wonder we distrust emotions.

Not all emotions, of course. Only the ones you could not escape in moments of necessity: love, hate. Let in a little anger sometimes but keep it on a short leash. That was the Sisterhood's belief. Utter nonsense!

The Tyrant's Golden Path made their mistake no longer tolerable. The Golden Path left the Bene Gesserit in a perpetual backwater. You could not minister to Infinity!

Bell's recurrent question had no answer. "What did he really want us to do?" *Into what actions was he manipulating us? (As we manipulate others!)*

Why look for meaning where there is none? Would you follow a path you knew led nowhere?

Golden Path! A track laid down in one imagination. *Infinity is nowhere!* And the finite mind balked. Here was where Mentats found mutable *projections*, always producing more questions than answers. It was the empty grail of those who, noses close to an endless circle, looked for "the one answer to all things."

Looking for their own kind of god.

She found it hard to censure them. The mind recoiled in the face of infinity. The Void! Alchemists of any age were like rag pickers bent over their bundles, saying: "There must be order in here somewhere. If I keep on, I'm sure to find it."

And all the time, the only order was the order they themselves created.

Ahhh, Tyrant! You droll fellow. You saw it. You said: "I will create order for you to follow. Here is the path. See it? No! Don't look over there. That is the way of the Emperor-Without-Clothes (a nakedness apparent only to children and the insane). Keep your attention where I direct it. This is my Golden Path. Isn't that a pretty name? It's all there is and all there ever will be."

Tyrant, you were another clown. Pointing us into endless recycling of cells from that lost and lonely ball of dirt in our common past.

You knew the human universe could never be more than communities and weak glue binding us when we Scattered. A common birth tradition so far away in our past that pictures of it carried by descendants are mostly distorted. Reverend Mothers carry the original, but we cannot force it onto unwilling people. You see, Tyrant? We heard you: "Let them come asking for it! Then, and only then . . ."

And that was why you preserved us, you Atreides bastard! That's why I must get to work.

Despite the peril to her sense of humanity, she knew she would continue to insinuate herself into the ways of Honored Matres. *I must think as they think.*

The hunters' problem: predator and prey shared it. Not quite needle-in-the-haystack. More a question of tracking across a terrain littered with the familiar and the unfamiliar. Bene Gesserit deceptions insured that the familiar would cause Honored Matres at least as much difficulty as the unfamiliar.

But what have they done for us?

Interplanetary communication worked for the hunted. Limited by economics for millennia. Not much of it except among Important People and Traders. Important meant what it had always meant: rich, powerful; bankers, officials, couriers. Military. "Important" labeled many categories—negotiators, entertainers, medical personnel, skilled technicians, spies, and other specialists. It was not much different in kind from the days of the Master Masons on Old Terra. Mainly a difference in numbers, quality and sophistication. Boundaries were transparent to some as they had always been.

She felt it important to review this occasionally, looking for flaws.

The great mass of planet-bound humanity spoke of "the silence of space," meaning they could not afford the cost of such travel or communication. Most people knew the news they received across this barrier was managed for special interests. It had always been that way.

On a planet, terrain and avoiding telltale radiation dictated the communications systems used: tubes, messengers, light-lines, nerve riders and many permutations. Secrecy and encryption were important, not only between planets but on them.

Odrade saw it as a system Honored Matres could tap if they found an entry point. Hunters had to begin by deciphering the system, but then: Where did a trail to Chapterhouse originate?

Untrackable no-ships, Ixian machines, and Guild Navigators—all contributed to the blanket of silence between planets except for the privileged few. Give hunters no starting points!

It came as a surprise then when an aging Reverend Mother from a Bene Gesserit punishment planet appeared at Mother Superior's workroom shortly before the lunch break. Archives identified her: *Name: Dortujla. Sent to special perdition years ago for an unforgivable infraction.* Memory said it had been a love affair of some kind. Odrade did not ask for details. Some of them were displayed anyway. (Bellonda interfering again!) Emotional upheaval at the time of Dortujla's banishment, Odrade noted. Futile attempts by the lover to prevent separation.

Odrade recalled gossip about Dortujla's disgrace. "The Jessica crime!" Much valuable information arrived via gossip. Where the devil had Dortujla been posted? Never mind. Not important at the moment. More important: *Why is she here? Why did she dare a trip that might lead the hunters to us?*

Odrade asked Streggi when she announced the arrival. Streggi did not know. "She says what she must reveal is for your ears alone, Mother Superior."

"Alone?" Odrade almost chuckled, considering the constant monitoring (surveillance was a better term) of her every action. "This Dortujla has not said why she is here?"

"The ones who told me to interrupt you, Mother Superior, said they thought you should see her."

Odrade pursed her lips. The fact that the banished Reverend Mother had penetrated this far aroused Odrade's curiosity. A persistent Reverend Mother could cross ordinary barriers but these barriers were not ordinary. Dortujla's reason for coming already had been told. Others had heard and passed her. It was apparent that Dortujla had not relied on Bene Gesserit wiles to persuade her Sisters. That would have brought immediate rejection. No time for such nonsense! So she had observed the chain of command. Her action spoke of careful assessment, a message within whatever message she brought.

"Bring her."

Dortujla had aged smoothly on her backwater planet. She revealed her years mostly in shallow wrinkles around her mouth. The hood of her robe concealed her hair but the eyes peering from beneath it were bright and alert.

"Why are you here?" Odrade's tone said: "This had damned well better be important."

Dortujla's story was straightforward enough. She and three Reverend Mother associates had spoken to a band of Futars from the Scattering. Dortujla's post had been searched out and asked to get a message to Chapterhouse. Dortujla had filtered the request through Truthsense, she said, reminding Mother Superior that even in backwaters there could be *some* talent. Judging the message truthful, her Sisters concurring, Dortujla had acted with speed, not unmindful of caution.

"All due dispatch in our own no-ship," was the way she put it. The ship, she said, was small, a smuggler type.

"One person can operate it."

The heart of the message was fascinating. Futars wished to ally themselves with Reverend Mothers in opposition to Honored Matres. How much of a force these Futars commanded was difficult to assess, Dortujla said.

"They refused to say when I asked."

Odrade had assessed many stories about Futars. Killers of Honored

Matres? There were reasons to believe it but Futar performance was confusing, especially in accounts from Gammu.

"How many in this party?"

"Sixteen Futars and four Handlers. That's what they called themselves: Handlers. And they say Honored Matres have a dangerous weapon they can use only once."

"You only mentioned Futars. Who are these Handlers? And what is this about a secret weapon?"

"I reserved mention of them. They appear to be human within variables noted from the Scattering: three men and a woman. As to the weapon, they would not say more."

"Appear to be human?"

"There you have it, Mother Superior. I had the odd first impression they were Face Dancers. None of the criteria applied. Pheromones negative. Gestures, expressions—everything negative."

"Just that first impression?"

"I cannot explain it."

"What of the Futars?"

"They matched the descriptions. Human in outward appearance but with unmistakable ferocity. Cat family origins, I would judge."

"So others have said."

"They speak but it's an abbreviated Galach. Word bursts, I thought them. 'When eat?' 'You nice lady.' 'Want head scratch.' 'Sit here?' They appeared immediately responsive to the Handlers but not fearful. Between Futars and Handlers I had the impression there was mutual respect and liking."

"Knowing the risks, why did you think this important enough to bring immediately?"

"These are people from the Scattering. Their offer of alliance is an opening into places where Honored Matres originate."

"You asked about them, of course. And about conditions in the Scattering."

"No answers."

The fact, simply stated. One could not sneer at the banished Sister no matter how much of a cloud she carried over her past. More questions were indicated. Odrade asked them, observing closely as answers came, watching the old mouth like a withered fruit opening purple and closing pink.

Something in Dortujla's service, the long years of penitence perhaps, had gentled her but left the core of Bene Gesserit toughness untouched. She spoke with natural hesitancy. Her gestures were softly fluid. She looked at Odrade with kindness. (*There* was the flaw her Sisters condemned: Bene Gesserit cynicism held at bay.)

Dortujla interested Odrade. Sister to Sister, she spoke, a strong and well-composed mind behind her words. A mind toughened by adversity in the years at a punishment post. Doing what she could now to make up for that lapse of her youth. No attempt to appear some time-server not up on current affairs. An account pared to essentials. Let it be known that she had as full as possible an awareness of necessities. Bowed to Mother Superior's decisions and caution about the dangerous visit but still felt that "you should have this information."

"I'm convinced it's not a trap."

Dortujla's demeanor was above reproach. Direct gaze, eyes and face held in proper composure but no attempts at concealment. A Sister could read through this mask for a proper assessment. Dortujla acted from a sense of urgency. She had been a fool once but she no longer was a fool.

What was the name of her punishment planet?

The worktable's projector produced it: Buzzell.

That name brought an alertness to Odrade. Buzzell! Her fingers danced in the console, confirming memories. Buzzell: mostly ocean. Cold. Very cold. Hardscrabble islands, none bigger than a large no-ship. The Bene Gesserit once had considered Buzzell a punishment. Object lesson: "Careful, girl, or you'll be sent to Buzzell." Odrade recalled the other key then: soostones. Buzzell was a place where they had naturalized the monoped sea creature, Cholister, whose abraded carapace produced marvelous tumors, one of the most valued jewels in the universe.

Soostones.

Dortujla was wearing one of the things just visible above the tuck of her neckline. The workroom light turned it an elegant blend of deeply glowing sea-green and mauve. It was larger than a human eyeball, flaunted there like a declaration of wealth. They probably thought little of such decorations on Buzzell. Pick them up on the beaches.

Soostones. That was significant. By Bene Gesserit design, Dortujla had frequent dealings with smugglers. (Witness her possession of that no-ship.) This must be addressed with care. No matter the Sister-to-Sister discussion, it was still Mother Superior and Reverend Mother from a punishment planet.

Smuggling. A major crime to Honored Matres and others who had not faced the fact of unenforceable laws. Foldspace had not changed it for smuggling, just made small intrusions easier if anything. Tiny no-ships. How small could you make one of them? A gap in Odrade's knowledge. Archives corrected it: "Diameter, meters 140."

Small enough, then. Soostones were a cargo with natural attraction. Foldspace was a critical economic barrier: How valuable a cargo compared to size and mass? You could spend many Solars moving massive stuff. Soostones—magnetic to smugglers. They had special interest to Honored Matres as well. Simple economics? Always a big market. As attractive to smugglers as melange now that the Guild was being so free with it. The Guild had always stockpiled with generations of spice in scattered storage and (doubtless) many hidden backups.

They think they can buy immunity from Honored Matres! But that offered something she sensed might be turned to advantage. In their wild anger, Honored Matres had destroyed Dune, only known *natural* source of melange. Still unthinking of consequences (odd, that), they had eliminated the Tleilaxu, whose axlotl tanks had flooded the Old Empire with spice.

And we have creatures capable of recreating Dune. We also may have the only living Tleilaxu Master. Locked in Scytale's mind—the way to turn axlotl tanks into a melange cornucopia. If we can get him to reveal it.

The immediate problem was Dortujla. The woman conveyed her ideas with a conciseness that did her credit. Handlers and their Futars, she said, were disturbed by something they would not reveal. Dortujla had been wise not to attempt Bene Gesserit persuasives. No telling how people from the Scattering might react. But what disturbed them?

"Some threat other than Honored Matres," Dortujla suggested. She would not venture more but the possibility was there and had to be considered.

"The essential thing is that they say they want an alliance," Odrade said.

"Common cause for a common problem," was the way they had put it. Despite Truthsense, Dortujla advised only a cautious exploration of the offer.

Why go to Buzzell at all? Because Honored Matres had missed Buzzell or judged it insignificant in their angry sweeps?

"Not likely," Dortujla said.

Odrade agreed. Dortujla, no matter how grubby her original posting, now commanded a valuable property and, much more important, she was a Reverend Mother with a no-ship to take her to Mother Superior. She knew the location of Chapterhouse. Useless to the hunters, of course. They knew a Reverend Mother would kill herself before betraying that secret.

Problems compounded problems. But first, some Sisterly sharing. Dortujla was sure to make a correct interpretation of Mother Superior's motives. Odrade shifted the conversation into personal matters.

It went well. Dortujla was clearly amused but willing to talk.

Reverend Mothers on lonely posts tended to have what Sisters called "other interests." An earlier age had called them hobbies but attention devoted to interests often was extreme. Odrade thought most *interests* boring but found it significant that Dortujla called hers a hobby. *She collected old coins, did she?*

"What kind?"

"I have two early Greek in silver and a perfect gold obol."

"Authentic?"

"They're real." Meaning she had done a self-scan of Other Memory to authenticate them. Fascinating. She exercised her abilities in a strengthening way, even with her hobby. Inner history and exterior coincided.

"This is all very interesting, Mother Superior," Dortujla said finally. "I appreciate your reassurance that we are still Sisters and find your interest in ancient paintings a parallel hobby. But we both know why I risked coming here."

"The smugglers."

"Of course. Honored Matres cannot have overlooked my presence on Buzzell. Smugglers will sell to the high bidders. We must assume they have profited from their valuable knowledge about Buzzell, the soostones, and a resident Reverend Mother with attendants. And we must not forget that Handlers found me."

Damn! Odrade thought. *Dortujla is the kind of advisor I like to have near me. I wonder how many more such buried treasures are out there, tucked away for mean motives? Why do we so often shunt our talented ones aside? It's an ancient weakness the Sisterhood has not exorcised.*

"I think we have learned something valuable about Honored Matres," Dortujla said.

There was no need to nod agreement. This was the core of what had brought Dortujla to Chapterhouse. The ravening hunters had come swarming into the Old Empire, killing and burning wherever they suspected the presence of Bene Gesserit establishments. But the hunters had not touched Buzzell even though its location must be known.

"Why?" Odrade asked, voicing what was in their minds.

"Never damage your own nest," Dortujla said.

"You think they're already on Buzzell?"

"Not yet."

"But you believe Buzzell is a place they want."

"Prime projection."

Odrade merely stared at her. So Dortujla had another *hobby!* She burrowed into Other Memory, revived and perfected talents stored there. Who could blame her? Time must drag on Buzzell.

"A Mentat summation," Odrade accused.

"Yes, Mother Superior." Very meek. Reverend Mothers were supposed to dig into Other Memory this way only with Chapterhouse permission and then only with guidance and support from companion Sisters. So Dortujla remained a rebel. She followed her own desires the way she had with her forbidden lover. Good! The Bene Gesserit needed such rebels.

"They want Buzzell undamaged," Dortujla said.

"A water world?"

"It would make a suitable home for amphibian servants. Not the Futars or Handlers. I studied them carefully."

The evidence suggested a plan by Honored Matres to bring in enslaved servants, amphibians perhaps, to harvest soostones. Honored Matres could have amphibian slaves. Knowledge that produced Futars might create many forms of sentient life.

"Slaves, dangerous imbalance," Odrade said.

Dortujla showed her first strong emotion, deep revulsion that drew her mouth into a tight line.

It was a pattern the Sisterhood had long recognized: the inevitable failure of slavery and peonage. You created a reservoir of hate. Implacable enemies. If you had no hope of exterminating all of these enemies, you dared not try. Temper your efforts by the sure awareness that oppression will make your enemies strong. The oppressed *will* have their day and heaven help the oppressor when that day comes. It was a two-edged blade. The oppressed always learned from and copied the oppressor. When the tables were turned, the stage was set for another round of revenge and violence—roles reversed. And reversed and reversed ad nauseam.

"Will they never mature?" Odrade asked.

Dortujla had no answer but she did have an immediate suggestion. "I must return to Buzzell."

Odrade considered this. Once more, the banished Reverend Mother was ahead of Mother Superior. As disagreeable as the decision was, they both knew it as their best move. Futars and Handlers would return. More important, with a planet Honored Matres desired, odds were high that visitors from the Scattering had been observed. Honored Matres would have to make a move and that move could reveal much about them.

"Of course, they think Buzzell is bait for a trap," Odrade said.

"I could let it be known that I was banished by my Sisters," Dortujla said. "It can be verified."

"Use yourself as bait?"

"Mother Superior, what if they could be tempted into a parley?"

"With us?" *What a startling idea!*

"I know their history is not one of reasonable negotiations but still . . ."

"It's brilliant! But let us make it even more enticing. Say I am convinced I must come to them with a proposal for submission of the Bene Gesserit."

"Mother Superior!"

"I have no intention of surrendering. But what better way to get them to talk?"

"Buzzell is not a good place for a meeting. Our facilities are very poor."

"They are on Junction in force. If they suggested Junction as a meeting place, could you let yourself be persuaded?"

"It would take careful planning, Mother Superior."

"Oh, *very* careful." Odrade's fingers flickered in her console. "Yes, tonight," she said answering a visible question, and then, speaking to Dortujla across the cluttered worktable: "I want you to meet with my Council and others before you return. We will brief you thoroughly but I give you my personal assurance you will have an open assignment. The important thing is to get them to a meeting on Junction . . . and I hope you know how much I dislike using you as bait."

When Dortujla remained deep in thought and not responding, Odrade said: "They may ignore our overtures and wipe you out. Still, you're the best bait we have."

Dortujla showed she still had her sense of humor. "I don't much like the idea of dangling on a hook myself, Mother Superior. Please keep a firm grip on the line." She stood and, with a worried look at the work on Odrade's table, said: "You have so much to do and I fear I have kept you far past lunch."

"We will dine here together, Sister. For the moment, you are more important than anything else."

All states are abstractions.

—OCTUN POLITICUS,
BG ARCHIVES

Lucilla cautioned herself not to assume too familiar a feeling about this acid-green room and the recurring presence of Great Honored Matre. This was Junction, stronghold of the ones who sought extermination of the Bene Gesserit. This was the enemy. Day seventeen.

The infallible mental clock that had been set ticking during the Spice Agony told her she had adapted to the planet's circadian rhythms. Awake at dawn. No telling when she would be fed. Honored Matre confined her to one meal a day.

And always that Futar in its cage. A reminder: *Both of you in cages. This is how we treat dangerous animals. We may let them out occasionally to stretch their legs and give us pleasure but back to the cage afterward.*

Minimal amounts of melange in the food. Not being parsimonious. Not with their wealth. A small show of "what could be yours if you would only be reasonable."

When will she come today?

Great Honored Matre arrivals had no set time. Random appearances to confuse the captive? Probably. There would be other demands on a commander's time. Fit the dangerous pet into the regular schedule wherever you could.

I may be dangerous, Spider Lady, but I am not your pet.

Lucilla felt the presence of scanning devices, things that did more than provide stimulus for eyes. These looked *into* flesh, probing for concealed weapons, for the functioning of organs. *Does she have strange implants? What about additional organs surgically added to her body?*

None of those, Madame Spider. We rely on things that come with birth.

Lucilla knew her greatest immediate danger—that she would feel inadequate in such a setting. Her captors had her at a terrible disadvantage but they had not destroyed her Bene Gesserit capabilities. She could will herself to die before the shere in her body was depleted to the point of betrayal. She still had her mind . . . and the horde from Lampadas.

The Futar panel opened and it came sliding out in its cage. So Spider Queen was on her way. Displaying threat ahead of her as usual. *Early today. Earlier than ever.*

"Good morning, Futar." Lucilla spoke with a merry lilt.

The Futar looked at her but did not speak.

"You must hate it in that cage," Lucilla said.

"Not like cage."

She had already determined that these creatures possessed a degree of language facility but the extent of it still eluded her.

"I suppose she keeps you hungry, too. Would you like to eat me?"

"Eat." Definite show of interest.

"I wish I were your Handler."

"You Handler?"

"Would you obey me if I were?"

Spider Queen's heavy chair lifted from its concealment under the floor. No sign of her yet but it had to be assumed she listened to these conversations.

The Futar stared at Lucilla with peculiar intensity.

"Do Handlers keep you caged and hungry?"

"Handler?" Clear inflections of a question.

"I want you to kill Great Honored Matre." That would be no surprise to them.

"Kill Dama!"

"And eat her."

"Dama poison." Dejected.

Ooooh. Isn't that an interesting bit of information!

"She's not poison. Her meat is the same as mine."

The Futar approached her to the cage's limits. The left hand peeled down its lower lip. Angry redness of a scar there, appearance of a burn.

"See poison," it said, dropping its hand.

I wonder how she did that? No smell of poison about her. Human flesh plus adrenaline-based drug to produce orange eyes in response to anger . . . and those other responses Murbella revealed. A sense of absolute superiority.

How far did Futar comprehension go? "Was it a bitter poison?"

The Futar grimaced and spat.

Action faster and more powerful than words.

"Do you hate Dama?"

Bared canines.

"Do you fear her?"

Smile.

"Then why don't you kill her?"

"You not Handler."

It requires a kill command from a Handler!

Great Honored Matre entered and sank into her chair.

Lucilla pitched her voice in the merry lilt: "Good morning, Dama."

"I did not give you permission to call me that." Low and with beginning flecks of orange in the eyes.

"Futar and I have been having a conversation."

"I know." More orange in the eyes. "And if you have spoiled him for me . . ."

"But Dama—"

"Don't call me that!" Out of her chair, eyes blazing orange.

"Do sit down," Lucilla said. "This is no way to conduct an interrogation." Sarcasm, a dangerous weapon. "You said yesterday you wanted to continue our discussion of politics."

"How do you know what time it is?" Sinking back in her chair but eyes still flaming.

"All Bene Gesserit have this ability. We can feel the rhythms of any planet after a short time on it."

"A strange talent."

"Anyone can do it. A matter of being sensitized."

"Could I learn this?" Orange fading.

"I said *anyone*. You're still human, aren't you?" *A question not yet fully answered.*

"Why do you say you witches have no government?"

Wants to change the subject. Our abilities worry her. "That's not what I said. We have no *conventional* government."

"Not even a social code?"

"There's no such thing as a social code to meet all necessities. A crime in one society can be a moral requirement in another society."

"People always have government." Orange completely faded. *Why does this interest her so much?*

"People have politics. I told you that yesterday. Politics: the art of appearing candid and completely open while concealing as much as possible."

"So you witches conceal."

"I did not say that. When we say 'politics,' that's a warning to our Sisters."

"I don't believe you. Humans always create some form of . . ."

"Accord?"

"As good a word as any!" *It angers her.*

When Lucilla made no further response, Great Honored Matre leaned forward. "You're concealing!"

"Isn't it my right to hide from you things that might help you defeat us?" *There's a juicy morsel of bait!*

"I thought so!" Leaning back with a look of satisfaction.

"However, why not reveal it? You think the niches of authority are always there for the filling and you don't see what that says about my Sisterhood."

"Oh, please tell me." *Heavy-handed with her sarcasm.*

"You believe all of this conforms to instincts going back to tribal days and beyond. Chiefs and Elders. Mystery Mother and Council. And before that, the Strong Man (or Woman) who saw to it that everyone was fed, that all were guarded by fire at the cave's mouth."

"It makes sense."

Does it really?

"Oh, I agree. Evolution of the forms is quite clearly laid out."

"Evolution, witch! One thing piled on another."

Evolution. See how she snaps at key words?

"It's a force that can be brought under control by turning it upon itself."

Control! Look at the interest you've aroused. She loves that word.

"So you make laws just like anyone else!"

"Regulations, perhaps, but isn't everything temporary?"

Intensely interested. "Of course."

"But your society is administered by bureaucrats who know they cannot apply the slightest imagination to what they do."

"That's important?" *Really puzzled. Look at her scowl.*

"Only to you, Honored Matre."

"Great Honored Matre!" *Isn't she touchy!*

"Why don't you permit me to call you Dama?"

"We're not intimates."

"Is Futar an intimate?"

"Stop changing the subject!"

"Want tooth clean," the Futar said.

"You shut up!" *Really blazing.*

The Futar sank to its haunches but it was not cowed.

Great Honored Matre turned her orange gaze toward Lucilla. "What about bureaucrats?"

"They have no room to maneuver because that's the way their superiors grow fat. If you don't see the difference between regulation and law, both have the force of law."

"I see no difference." *She doesn't know what she reveals.*

"Laws convey the myth of enforced change. A bright new future will come because of this law or that one. Laws enforce the future. Regulations are believed to enforce the past."

"Believed?" *She doesn't like that word, either.*

"In each instance, action is illusory. Like appointing a committee to study a problem. The more people on the committee, the more preconceptions applied to the problem."

Careful! She's really thinking about this, applying it to herself.

Lucilla pitched her voice in its most reasonable tones. "You live by a past-magnified and try to understand some unrecognized future."

"We don't believe in prescience." *Yes, she does! At last. This is why she keeps us alive.*

"Dama, please. There's always something unbalanced about confining yourself to a tight circle of laws."

Be careful! She didn't bridle at your calling her Dama.

Great Honored Matre's chair creaked as she shifted in it. "But laws are necessary!"

"Necessary? That's dangerous."

"How so?"

Softly. She feels threatened.

"Necessary rules and laws keep you from adapting. Inevitably, everything comes crashing down. It's like bankers thinking they buy the future. 'Power in my time! To hell with my descendants!'"

"What are descendants doing for me?"

Don't say it! Look at her. She's reacting out of the common insanity. Give her another small taste.

"Honored Matres originated as terrorists. Bureaucrats first and terror as your chosen weapon."

"When it's in your hands, use it. But we were rebels. Terrorists? That's too chaotic."

She likes that word "chaos." It defines everything on the outside. She doesn't even ask how you know her origins. She accepts our mysterious abilities.

"Isn't it odd, Dama . . ." *No reaction; continue.* ". . . how rebels all too soon fall into old patterns if they are victorious? It's not so much a pitfall in the path of all governments as it is a delusion waiting for anyone who gains power."

"Hah! And I thought you would tell me something new. We know that one: 'Power corrupts. Absolute power corrupts absolutely.'"

"Wrong, Dama. Something more subtle but far more pervasive: Power attracts the corruptible."

"You dare accuse me of being corrupt?"

Watch the eyes!

"I? Accuse you? The only one who can do that is yourself. I merely give you the Bene Gesserit opinion."

"And tell me nothing!"

"Yet we believe there's a morality above any law, which must stand watchdog on all attempts at unchanging regulation."

You used both words in one sentence and she didn't notice.

"Power always works, witch. That's the law."

"And governments that perpetuate themselves long enough under *that* belief always become packed with corruption."

"Morality!"

She's not very good at sarcasm, especially when she's on the defensive.

"I've really tried to help you, Dama. Laws are dangerous to everyone—innocent and guilty alike. No matter whether you believe yourself powerful or helpless. They have no human understanding in and of themselves."

"There's no such thing as human understanding!"

Our question is answered. Not human. Talk to her unconscious side. She's wide open.

"Laws must always be interpreted. The law-bound want no latitude for compassion. No elbow room. "'The law is the law!'"

"It is!" *Very defensive.*

"That's a dangerous idea, especially for the innocent. People know this instinctively and resent such laws. Little things are done, often unconsciously, to hamstring 'the law' and those who deal in that nonsense."

"How dare you call it nonsense?" Half rising from her chair and sinking back.

"Oh, yes. And the law, personified by all whose livelihoods depend on it, becomes resentful hearing words such as mine."

"Rightly so, witch!" *But she doesn't tell you to be silent.*

"'More law!' you say. 'We need more law!' So you make new instruments of non-compassion and, incidentally, new niches of employment for those who feed on the system."

"That's the way it's always been and always will be."

"Wrong again. It's a rondo. It rolls and rolls until it injures the wrong person or the wrong group. Then you get anarchy. Chaos." *See her jump?* "Rebels, terrorists, increasing outbursts of raging violence. A jihad! And all because you created something nonhuman."

Hand on her chin. Watch it!

"How did we wander so far away from politics, witch? Was this your intention?"

"We haven't wandered a fraction of a millimeter!"

"I suppose you're going to tell me you witches practice a form of democracy."

"With an alertness you cannot imagine."

"Try me." *She thinks you'll tell her a secret. Tell her one.*

"Democracy is susceptible to being led astray by having scapegoats paraded in front of the electorate. Get the rich, the greedy, the criminals, the stupid leader and so on ad nauseam."

"You believe as we do." *My! How desperately she wants us to be like her.*

"You said you were bureaucrats who rebelled. You know the flaw. A top-heavy bureaucracy the electorate cannot touch always expands to the system's limits of energy. Steal it from the aged, from the retired, from anyone. Especially from those we once called middle class because that's where most of the energy originates."

"You think of yourselves as . . . as middle class?"

"We don't think of ourselves in any fixed way. But Other Memory tells us the flaws of bureaucracy. I presume you have some form of civil service for the 'lower orders.'"

"We take care of our own." *That's a nasty echo.*

"Then you know how that dilutes the vote. Chief symptom: People don't vote. Instinct tells them it's useless."

"Democracy is a stupid idea anyway!"

"We agree. It's demagogue-prone. That's a disease to which electoral systems are vulnerable. Yet demagogues are easy to identify. They gesture a lot and speak with pulpit rhythms, using words that ring of religious fervor and god-fearing sincerity."

She's chuckling!

"Sincerity with nothing behind it takes so much practice, Dama. The practice can always be detected."

"By Truthsayers?"

See how she leans forward? We have her again.

"By anyone who learns the signs: Repetition. Great attempts to keep your attention on words. You must pay no attention to words. Watch what the person does. That way you learn the motives."

"Then you don't have a democracy." *Tell me more Bene Gesserit secrets.*

"But we do."

"I thought you said . . ."

"We guard it well, watching for the things I've just described. The dangers are great but so are the rewards."

"Do you know what you've told me? That you're a pack of fools!"

"Nice lady!" the Futar said.

"Shut up or I'll send you back to the herd!"

"You not nice, Dama."

"See what you've done, witch? You've ruined him!"

"I suppose there are always others."

Ohhhhh. Look at that smile.

Lucilla matched the smile precisely, pacing her own breaths to those of the Great Honored Matre. *See how alike we are? Of course I tried to injure you. Wouldn't you have done the same in my place?*

"So you know how to make a democracy do whatever you want." A gloating expression.

"The technique is quite subtle but easy. You create a system where most people are dissatisfied, vaguely or deeply."

That's how she sees it. Look at her nod in time to your words.

Lucilla held herself to the rhythm of Great Honored Matre's nodding head. "This builds up widespread feelings of vindictive anger. Then you supply targets for that anger as you need them."

"A diversionary tactic."

"I prefer to think of it as distraction. Don't give them time to question. Bury your mistakes in more laws. You traffic in illusion. Bullring tactics."

"Oh, yes! That's good!" *She's almost gleeful. Give her more bullring.*

"Wave the pretty cape. They'll charge it and be confused when there's no matador behind the thing. That dulls the electorate just as it dulls the bull. Fewer people use their vote intelligently next time."

"And that's why we do it!"

We do it! Does she listen to herself?

"Then you rail against the apathetic electorate. Make them feel guilty. Keep them dull. Feed them. Amuse them. Don't overdo it!"

"Oh, no! Never overdo it."

"Let them know hunger awaits them if they don't fall into line. Give them a look at the boredom imposed on boat rockers." *Thank you, Mother Superior. It's an appropriate image.*

"Don't you let the bull get an occasional matador?"

"Of course. Thump! Got that one! Then you wait for the laughter to subside."

"I knew you didn't allow a democracy!"

"Why won't you believe me?" *You're tempting fate!*

"Because you'd have to permit open voting, juries and judges and . . ."

"We call them Proctors. A sort of Jury of the Whole."

Now you've confused her.

"And no laws . . . regulations, whatever you want to call them?"

"Didn't I say we defined them separately? Regulation—past. Law—future."

"You limit these . . . these Proctors, somehow!"

"They can arrive at any decision they desire, the way a jury should function. The law be damned!"

"That's a very disturbing idea." *She's disturbed all right. Look at how dull her eyes are.*

"The first rule of our democracy: no laws restricting juries. Such laws are stupid. It's astonishing how stupid humans can be when acting in small, self-serving groups."

"You're calling me stupid, aren't you!"

Beware the orange.

"There appears to be a rule of nature that says it's almost impossible for self-serving groups to act enlightened."

"Enlightened! I knew it!"

That's a dangerous smile. Be careful.

"It means flowing with the forces of life, adjusting your actions that life may continue."

"With the greatest amount of happiness for the greatest number, of course."

Quick! We've been too clever! Change the subject!

"That was an element the Tyrant left out of his Golden Path. He didn't consider happiness, only survival of humankind."

We said change the subject! Look at her! She's in a rage!

Great Honored Matre dropped her hand away from her chin. "And I was going to invite you into our order, make you one of us. Release you."

Get her off this! Quick!

"Don't speak," Great Honored Matre said. "Don't even open your mouth."

Now you've done it!

"You'd help Logno or one of the others and she'd be in my seat!!" She glanced at the crouching Futar. "Eat, darling?"

"Not eat nice lady."

"Then I'll throw her carcass to the herd!"

"Great Honored Matre—"

"I told you not to speak! You *dared* call me Dama."

She was out of her chair in a blur. Lucilla's cage door slammed open with a crash against the wall. Lucilla tried to dodge but the shigawire confined her. She did not see the kick that crushed her temple.

As she died, Lucilla's awareness was filled with a scream of rage— the horde of Lampadas venting emotions it had confined for many generations.

Some never participate. Life happens to them. They get by on little more than dumb persistence and resist with anger or violence all things that might lift them out of resentment-filled illusions of security.

Back and forth, back and forth. All day long, back and forth. Odrade shifted from one comeye record to another, searching, undecided, uneasy. First a look a Scytale, then young Teg out there with Duncan and Murbella, then a long stare out a window while she thought about Burzmali's last report from Lampadas.

How soon could they try to restore the Bashar's memories? Would a restored ghola obey?

Why no more word from the Rabbi? Should we begin Extremis Progessiva, Sharing among ourselves as far as possible? The effect on morale would be devastating.

Records were projected above her table while aides and advisors entered and departed. Necessary interruptions. Sign this. Approve that. Decrease melange for this group?

Bellonda was here, seated at the table. She had stopped asking what Odrade sought and merely watched with that unwavering stare. Merciless.

They had argued about whether a new sandworm population in the Scattering might restore the Tyrant's malign influence. That *endless dream* in each revenant of the worm still worried Bell. But population numbers alone said the Tyrant's hold on their destiny was ended.

Tamalane had come in earlier seeking some record from Bellonda. Fresh from a new accumulation of Archives, Bellonda had launched herself into a diatribe about Sisterhood population shifts, the drain on resources.

Odrade stared out the window now as dusk moved across the landscape. It became darker in almost imperceptible shadings. As full dark fell, she became aware of lights far out in the plantation houses. She knew those lights had been turned on much earlier but she had the sensation that night created the lights. Some blanked out occasionally as people moved about in their dwellings. *No people—no lights. Don't waste energy.*

Winking lights held her attention for a moment. A variation on the old question about a tree falling in the forest: Was there sound if no one heard? Odrade voted on the side of those who said vibrations existed no matter whether a sensor recorded them.

Do secret sensors follow our Scattering? What new talents and inventions do the first Scattered Ones use?

Bellonda had allowed long enough silence. "Dar, you're sending worrisome signals through Chapterhouse."

Odrade accepted this without comment.

"Whatever you're doing, it's being interpreted as indecision." *How sad Bell sounds.* "Important groups are discussing whether to replace you. Proctors are voting."

"Only the Proctors?"

"Dar, did you really wave at Praska the other day and tell her it was good to be alive?"

"I did."

"What *have* you been doing?"

"Reassessing. No word yet from Dortujla?"

"You've asked that at least a dozen times today!" Bellonda gestured at the worktable. "You keep going back to Burzmali's last report from Lampadas. Something we've overlooked?"

"Why do our enemies hold fast on Gammu? Tell me, Mentat."

"I've insufficient data and you know it!"

"Burzmali was no Mentat but his picture of events has a persistent force, Bell. I tell myself, well, after all, he was the Bashar's favorite student. It's understandable that Burzmali would show characteristics of his teacher."

"Out with it, Dar. What do you see in Burzmali's report?"

"He fills in an empty picture. Not completely but . . . tantalizing the way he keeps referring to Gammu. Many economic forces have powerful connections there. Why are those threads not cut by our enemies?"

"They're in that same system, obviously."

"What if we mounted an all-out attack on Gammu?"

"No one wants to do business in violent surroundings. That what you're saying?"

"Partly."

"Most parties to that economic system probably would want to move. Another planet, another subservient population."

"Why?"

"They could predict with more reliability. They would increase defenses, of course."

"This alliance we sense there, Bell, they would redouble their efforts to find and obliterate us."

"Certainly."

Bellonda's terse comment forced Odrade's thoughts outward. She lifted her gaze to the distant snow-tonsured mountains glimmering in starlight. Would attackers come from that direction?

The thrust of that thought might have dulled a lesser intellect. But Odrade needed no Litany Against Fear to remain clear-headed. She had a simpler formula.

Face your fears or they will climb over your back.

Her attitude was direct. The most terrifying things in the universe came from human minds. The nightmare (the white horse of Bene Gesserit extinction) possessed both mythic and reality forms. The hunter with the axe could strike mind or flesh. But you could not flee the terrors of the mind.

Face them then!

What did she confront in this darkness? Not that faceless hunter with her axe, not the drop into the unknown chasm (both visible to her *bit of talent*), but the very tangible Honored Matres and whoever supported them.

And I dare not use even my small prescience to guide us. I could lock our future into unchanging form. Muad'Dib and his Tyrant son did that and the Tyrant spent thirty-five hundred years extricating us.

Moving lights in the middle distance caught her attention. Gardeners working late, still pruning the orchards as though those venerable trees would go on forever. Ventilators gave her a faint odor of smoke from fires where orchard trimmings were being burned. Very attentive to such details, the Bene Gesserit gardeners. Never leave deadwood around to attract parasites that might then take the next step into living trees. Clean and neat. Plan ahead. Maintain your habitat. This moment is part of forever.

Never leave deadwood around?

Was Gammu deadwood?

"What is it about orchards that fascinates you so much?" Bellonda wanted to know.

Odrade spoke without turning. "They restore me."

Only two nights ago she had gone walking out there, the weather cold and bracing, a touch of mist close to the ground. Her feet stirred leaves. Faint smell of compost where a sparse rain had settled in warmer low places. A rather attractive, marshy smell. Life in its usual ferment even at that level. Empty limbs above her stood out starkly against starlight. Depressing, really, when compared with springtime or harvest season. But beautiful in its flow. Life once more waiting for its call to action.

"Aren't you worried about the Proctors?" Bellonda asked.

"How will they vote, Bell?"

"It's very close."

"Will others follow them?"

"There's concern about your decisions. Consequences."

Bell was very good at that: a great deal of data in a few words. Most

Bene Gesserit decisions moved through a triple maze: Effectiveness, Consequences, and (most vital) Who Can Carry Out Orders? You matched deed and person with great care, precise attention to details. This had a heavy influence on Effectiveness and that, in turn, ruled Consequences. A good Mother Superior could wend her way through decision mazes in seconds. Liveliness in Central then. Eyes brightened. Word was passed that "She acted without hesitation." That created confidence among acolytes and other students. Reverend Mothers (Proctors especially) waited to assess Consequences.

Odrade spoke to her reflection in the window as much as to Bellonda. "Even Mother Superior must take her own time."

"But what has you in such turmoil?"

"Are you urging speed, Bell?"

Bellonda drew back in her chairdog as though Odrade had pushed her.

"Patience is extremely difficult in these times," Odrade said. "But choosing the right moment influences my choices."

"What do you intend with our new Teg? That's the question you must answer."

"If our enemies removed themselves from Gammu, where would they go, Bell?"

"You would attack them there?"

"Push them a bit."

Bellonda spoke softly. "That's a dangerous fire to feed."

"We need another bargaining chip."

"Honored Matres don't bargain!"

"But their associates do, I think. Would they remove themselves to . . . let us say, Junction?"

"What is so interesting about Junction?"

"Honored Matres are based there in force. And our beloved Bashar kept a memory-dossier of the place in his lovely Mentat mind."

"Ohhhhhhh." It was as much a sigh as a word.

Tamalane entered then and demanded attention by standing silently until Odrade and Bellonda looked at her.

"The Proctors support Mother Superior." Tamalane held up a clawed finger. "By one vote!"

Odrade sighed. "Tell us, Tam, the Proctor I greeted in the hallway, Praska, how did she vote?"

"She voted for you."

Odrade aimed a tight smile at Bellonda. "Send out spies and agents, Bell. We must goad the hunters into meeting us on Junction."

Bell will deduce my plan by morning.

When Bellonda and Tamalane had gone, muttering to each other, worry in the sound of their voices, Odrade went out into the short corridor to her private quarters. The corridor was patrolled by its usual acolytes and Reverend Mother servitors. A few acolytes smiled at her. So word of the Proctors' vote had reached them. Another crisis passed.

Odrade went through her sitting room to her sleeping cell, where she stretched out on her cot fully clothed. One glow-globe bathed the room in pale yellow light. Her gaze went past the desert map to the Van Gogh painting in its protective frame and cover on the wall at the foot of her cot.

Cottages at Cordeville.

A better map than the one marking the growth of the desert, she thought. *Remind me, Vincent, of where I came from and what I yet may do.*

This day had drained her. She had gone beyond fatigue into a place where the mind caught itself in tight circles.

Responsibilities!

They hemmed her in and she knew she could be her most disagreeable self when beset by duties. Forced to expend energy just maintaining a semblance of calm demeanor. *Bell saw this in me.* It was maddening. The Sisterhood was cut off at every passage, made almost ineffectual.

She closed her eyes and tried to construct an image of an Honored Matre commander to address. *Old . . . steeped in power. Sinewy. Strong and with that blinding speed they have.* No face on her but the visualized body stood there in Odrade's mind.

Forming the words silently, Odrade spoke to the faceless Honored Matre.

"It is difficult for us to let you make your own mistakes. Teachers always find this hard. Yes, we consider ourselves teachers. We do not so much teach individuals as the species. We provide lessons for all. If you see the Tyrant in us, you are right."

The image in her mind made no reply.

How could teachers teach when they could not emerge from hiding? Burzmali dead, ghola Teg an unknown quantity. Odrade felt invisible pressures converging on Chapterhouse. No wonder Proctors voted. A web enclosed the Sisterhood. The strands held them tightly. And somewhere on that web, a faceless Honored Matre commander crouched.

Spider Queen.

Her presence was known by actions of her minions. A trap strand of her web trembled and attackers hurled themselves onto entangled victims, insanely violent, uncaring how many of their own died or how many they butchered.

Someone commanded the search: Spider Queen.

Is she sane by our standards? Into what awful perils have I sent Dortujla?

Honored Matres went beyond megalomania. They made the Tyrant appear a ridiculous pirate by comparison. Leto II, at least, had known what the Bene Gesserit knew: how to balance on the point of the sword, aware that you would be mortally cut when you slid from that position. *The price you pay for seizing such power.* Honored Matres ignored this inevitable fate, hewing and slashing around them like a giant in the throes of terrible hysteria.

Nothing ever before had opposed them successfully and they chose to respond now with the killing rage of berserkers. Hysteria by choice. Deliberate.

Because we left our Bashar on Dune to spend his pitiful force in a suicidal defense? No telling how many Honored Matres he killed. And Burzmali at the death of Lampadas. Surely, the hunters felt his sting. Not to mention Idaho-trained males we send out to pass along Honored Matre techniques of sexual enslavement. And to men!

Was that enough to bring such rage? Possibly. But what of the stories from Gammu? Did Teg display a new talent that terrified Honored Matres?

If we restore our Bashar's memories, we must watch him carefully.

Would a no-ship contain him?

What really made Honored Matres so reactive? They wanted blood. Never bring such people bad news. No wonder their minions behaved with frenzy. A powerful person in fright might kill the bearer of bad tidings. Bring no bad tidings. Better to die in battle.

Spider Queen's people went beyond arrogance. Far beyond. No censure possible. You might just as well berate a cow for eating grass. The cow would be justified in looking at you with its moonstruck eyes, inquiring: "Isn't this what I'm supposed to do?"

Knowing probable consequences, why did we ignite them? We aren't like the person who hits out at a round gray object with a stick and finds that the object was a hornet's nest. We knew what we struck. Taraza's plan and none of us questioned.

The Sisterhood faced an enemy whose deliberate policy was hysterical violence. "We will run amok!"

And what would happen if Honored Matres met painful defeat? What would their hysteria become?

I fear it.

Did the Sisterhood dare feed this fire?

We must!

Spider Queen would redouble her efforts to find Chapterhouse. Violence would escalate to an even more repulsive stage. What then? Would Honored Matres suspect everyone and anyone of being sympathetic to the Bene Gesserit? Might they not turn against their own supporters? Did they contemplate being alone in a universe devoid of other sentient life? More likely this did not even enter their minds.

What do you look like, Spider Queen? How do you think?

Murbella said she did not know her supreme commander or even sub-commanders of her Hormu Order. But Murbella provided a suggestive description of a sub-commander's quarters. Informative. What does a person call home? Who does she keep close to share life's little homilies?

Most of us choose our companions and surroundings to reflect ourselves.

Murbella said: "One of her personal servants took me into the private area. Showing off, demonstrating that she had access to the sanctum. The public area was neat and clean but the private rooms were messy—clothing left where it had been dropped, unguent jars open, bed unmade, food drying in dishes on the floor. I asked why they had not cleaned up this mess. She said it was not her job. The one who cleaned was allowed into the quarters just before nightfall."

Secret vulgarities.

Such a one would have a mind to match that private display.

Odrade's eyes snapped open. She focused on the Van Gogh painting. *My choice.* It put tensions on the long span of human history that Other Memory could not. *You sent me a message, Vincent. And because of you, I will not cut off my ear . . . or send useless love messages to ones who do not care. That's the least I can do to honor you.*

The sleeping cell had a familiar odor, peppery pungency of carnation. Odrade's favorite floral perfume. Attendants kept it here as a nasal background.

Once more, she closed her eyes and her thoughts snapped back to Spider Queen. Odrade felt this exercise creating another dimension to that faceless woman.

Murbella said an Honored Matre commander had but to give an order and anything she wanted was brought.

"Anything?"

Murbella described known instances: grossly distorted sexual partners, cloying sweetmeats, emotional orgies ignited by performances of extraordinary violence.

"They're always looking for extremes."

Reports of spies and agents fleshed out Murbella's semi-admiring accounts.

"Everyone says they have a right to rule."

Those women evolved from an autocratic bureaucracy.

Much evidence confirmed it. Murbella spoke of history lessons that said early Honored Matres conducted research to gain sexual dominance over their populations "when taxation became too threatening to those they governed."

A right to rule?

It did not appear to Odrade that these women insisted on such a right. No. They assumed that their rightness must never be questioned. Never! No decisions wrong. Disregard consequences. It never happened.

Odrade sat upright on her cot, knowing she had found the insight she sought.

Mistakes never happen.

That would require an extremely large bag of unconsciousness to contain it. Very tiny consciousness then peering out at a tumultuous universe they themselves created!

Ohhhh, lovely!

Odrade summoned her night attendant, a first-stage acolyte, and asked for melange tea containing a dangerous stimulant, something to help her delay the body's demands for sleep. But at a cost.

The acolyte hesitated before obeying. She returned in a moment with the mug steaming on a small tray.

Odrade had decided long ago that melange tea made with the deep cold water of Chapterhouse had a taste that worked its way into her psyche. The bitter stimulant deprived her of that refreshing taste and gnawed at her conscience. Word would go out from the ones who watched. *Worry, worry, worry.* Would Proctors take another vote?

She sipped slowly, giving the stimulant time to work. *Condemned woman rejects last dinner. Sips tea.*

Presently, she put aside the empty mug and called for warm clothing. "I'm going for a walk in the orchards." The night attendant made no comment. Everyone knew she often went walking there, even at night.

Within minutes she was in the narrow, link-fenced path to her favorite orchard, her way lighted by a miniglobe fixed on a short cord to her right shoulder. A small herd of the Sisterhood's black cattle came up to the fence beside Odrade and gazed at her as she passed. She looked at the wet muzzles, inhaled the rich smell of alfalfa in the steam of their breathing and paused. The cows sniffed and sensed the phero-mone that told them to accept her. They went back to eating forage piled near the fence by herdsmen.

Turning her back on the cattle, Odrade looked at leafless trees across from the pasture. Her miniglobe drew a circle of yellow light that emphasized winter starkness.

Few understood why this place attracted her. It was not enough to say she found troubled thoughts soothed here. Even in winter, with frost crunching underfoot. This orchard was a hard-bought silence between storms. She extinguished her miniglobe and let her feet follow the familiar way in darkness. Occasionally, she glanced up at starlight defined by leafless branches. *Storms.* She felt one approaching that no meteorologist could anticipate. *Storms beget storms. Rage begets rage. Revenge begets revenge. Wars beget wars.*

The old Bashar had been a master at breaking those circles. Would his ghola still have that talent?

What a perilous gamble.

Odrade looked back at the cattle, a dark blob of movement and starlighted steam. They had herded close for warmth and she heard a familiar grinding as they chewed their cuds.

I must go south into the desert. Face to face with Sheeana there. The sandtrout thrive. Why are there no sandworms?

She spoke aloud to the cattle clustered by the fence: "Eat your grass. It's what you're supposed to do."

If a spying watchdog chanced on that remark, Odrade knew she would have serious explaining to do.

But I have seen through to the heart of our enemy this night. And I pity them.

To know a thing well, know its limits. Only when pushed beyond its tolerances will true nature be seen.

—THE AMTAL RULE

Do not depend only on theory if your life is at stake.

—BENE GESSERIT COMMENTARY

Duncan Idaho stood almost in the center of the no-ship's practice floor
and three paces from the ghola-child. Sophisticated training instruments were near at hand, some exhausting, some dangerous.

The child looked admiring and trusting this morning.

*Do I understand him better because I, too, am a ghola? A question-
able assumption. This one has been brought up in a way much different
from the one they designed for me. Designed! The precise term.*

The Sisterhood had copied as much of Teg's original childhood as
possible. Even to an adoring younger companion standing in for the
long-lost brother. And Odrade giving him the deep teaching! As Teg's
birth-mother did.

Idaho remembered the aged Bashar whose cells had produced this
child. A thoughtful man whose comments were to be heeded. With
only a slight effort, Idaho recalled the man's manner and words.

"The true warrior often understands his enemy better than he understands his friends. A dangerous pitfall if you let understanding lead
to sympathy as it will naturally do when left unguided."

Difficult to think of the mind behind those words as latent some-where in this child. The Bashar had been so insightful, teaching about sympathies on that long-ago day in the Gammu Keep.

"Sympathy for the enemy—a weakness of police and armies alike. Most perilous are the unconscious sympathies directing you to preserve your enemy intact because the enemy is your justification for existence."

"Sir?"

How could that piping voice become the commanding tones of the old Bashar?

"What is it?"

"Why are you just standing there looking at me?"

"They called the Bashar 'Old Reliability.' Did you know that?"

"Yes, sir. I've studied the story of his life."

Was it "Young Reliability" now? Why did Odrade want his original memories restored so quickly?

"Because of the Bashar, the entire Sisterhood has been digging into Other Memory, revising their views of history. Did they tell you that?"

"No, sir. Is it important for me to know? Mother Superior said you would train my muscles."

"You liked to drink Danian Marinete, a very fine brandy, I recall."

"I'm too young to drink, sir."

"You were a Mentat. Do you know what that means?"

"I'll know when you restore my memories, won't I?"

No respectful *sir*. Calling the teacher to task for unwanted delays.

Idaho smiled and got a grin in response. An engaging child. Easy to show him natural affection.

"Watch out for him," Odrade had said. "He's a charmer."

Idaho recalled Odrade's briefing before bringing the child.

"Since every individual is accountable ultimately to the self," she said, "the formation of that self demands our utmost care and attention."

"Is that necessary with a ghola?"

They had been in Idaho's sitting room that night, Murbella a fascinated listener.

"He will remember everything you teach him."

"So we do a little editing of the original."

"Careful, Duncan! Give a bad time to an impressionable child,
teach that child not to trust anyone, and you create a suicide—slow or
fast suicide, doesn't make any difference."

"Are you forgetting that I knew the Bashar?"

"Don't you remember, Duncan, how it was before your memories
were restored?"

"I knew the Bashar could do it and I thought of him as my salvation."

"And that's how he sees you. It's a special kind of trust."

"I'll treat him honestly."

"You may think you act from honesty but I advise you to look
deeply into yourself every time you come face to face with his trust."

"And if I make a mistake?"

"We will correct it if possible." She glanced up at the comeyes and
back to him.

"I know you'll be watching us!"

"Don't let it inhibit you. I'm not trying to make you self-conscious.
Just cautious. And remember that my Sisterhood has efficient methods
of healing."

"I'll be cautious."

"You might remember it was the Bashar who said: 'The ferocity we
display to our foes is always tempered by the lesson we hope to teach.'"

"I can't think of him as a foe. The Bashar was one of the finest men
I've ever known."

"Excellent. I place him in your hands."

And here the child was on the practice floor getting more than a
little impatient with his teacher's hesitations.

"Sir, is this part of a lesson, just standing here? I know sometimes—"

"Be still."

Teg came to military attention. No one had taught him that. This was from his original memories. Idaho was suddenly fascinated by this glimpse of the Bashar.

They knew he would catch me this way!

Never underestimate Bene Gesserit persuasiveness. You could find yourself doing things for them without knowing pressures had been applied. Subtle and damnable! There were compensations, of course. You lived in interesting times, as the ancient curse/benison had it. All in all, Idaho decided, he preferred interesting times, even these times.

He took a deep breath. "Restoring your original memories will cause pain—physical and mental. In some ways, the mental pains are worse. I am to prepare you for that."

Still at attention. No comment.

"We will begin without weapons, using an imaginary blade in your right hand. This is a variation on the 'five attitudes.' Each response arises before the need. Drop your arms to your sides and relax."

Moving behind Teg, Idaho grasped the child's right arm below the elbow and demonstrated the first movements.

"Each attacker is a feather floating on an infinite path. As the feather approaches, it is diverted and removed. Your response is like a puff of air blowing the feather away."

Idaho stepped aside and observed as Teg repeated the movements, correcting occasionally with a sharp blow to an offending muscle.

"Let your body do the learning!" When Teg asked why he did that.

In a rest period, Teg wanted to know what Idaho meant by "mental pains."

"You have ghola-imposed walls around your original memories. At the proper moment, some of those memories will come flooding back. Not all memories will be pleasant."

"Mother Superior says the Bashar restored your memories."

"Gods of the deep, child! Why do you keep saying 'the Bashar'? That was you!"

"But I don't know that yet."

"You present a special problem. For a ghola to reawaken, there should be memory of death. But the cells for you do not carry death memory."

"But the . . . Bashar is dead."

"The Bashar! Yes, he's dead. You must feel that where it hurts most and know that *you* are the Bashar."

"Can you really give me back that memory?"

"If you can stand the pain. Do you know what I said to you when *you* restored my memories? I said: 'Atreides! You're all so damned alike!'"

"You hated . . . me?"

"Yes, and you were disgusted with yourself for what you did to me. Does that give you any idea of what I must do?"

"Yes, sir." Very low.

"Mother Superior says I must not betray your trust . . . yet you betrayed my trust."

"But I restored your memories?"

"See how easy it is to think of yourself as Bashar? You were shocked. And yes, you restored my memories."

"That's all I want."

"So you say."

"Mother . . . Superior says you're a Mentat. Will that help . . . that I was a Mentat, too?"

"Logic says 'Yes.' But we Mentats have a saying, that logic moves blindly. And we're aware there's a logic that kicks you out of the nest into chaos."

"I know what chaos means!" Very proud of himself.

"So you think."

"And I trust you!"

"Listen to me! We are servants of the Bene Gesserit. Reverend Mothers did not build their order on trust."

"Shouldn't I trust Mother . . . Superior?"

"Within limits you will learn and appreciate. For now, I warn you the Bene Gesserit work under a system of organized *distrust*. Have they taught you about democracy?"

"Yes, sir. That's where you vote for—"

"That's where you distrust anyone with power over you! The Sisters know it well. Don't trust too much."

"Then I should not trust you, either?"

"The only trust you can place in me is that I will do my best to restore your original memories."

"Then I don't care how much it hurts." He looked up at the com-eyes, knowledge of their purpose in his expression. "Do they mind that you say these things about them?"

"Their feelings don't concern a Mentat except as data."

"Does that mean fact?"

"Facts are fragile. A Mentat can get tangled in them. Too much *reliable* data. It's like diplomacy. You need a few good lies to get at your projections."

"I'm . . . confused." He used the word hesitantly, not sure it was what he meant.

"I said that once to Mother Superior. She said: 'I've been behaving badly.'"

"You're not supposed to . . . confuse me?"

"Unless it teaches." And when Teg still looked puzzled, Idaho said: "Let me tell you a story."

Teg immediately sat on the floor, an action revealing that Odrade often used the same technique. Good. Teg already was receptive.

"In one of my lives I had a dog that hated clams," Idaho said.

"I've had clams. They come from the Great Sea."

"Yes, well, my dog hated clams because one of them had the temerity to spit in his eye. That stings. But even worse, it was an innocent hole in the sand that did the spitting. No clam visible."

"What'd your dog do?" Leaning forward, chin on fist.

"He dug up the offender and brought it to me." Idaho grinned. "Lesson one: Don't let the unknown spit in your eye."

Teg laughed and clapped his hands.

"But look at it from the dog's viewpoint. Go after the spitter! Then—glorious reward: Master is pleased."

"Did your dog dig more clams?"

"Every time we went to the beach. He went growling after spitters and Master took them away never to be seen again except as empty shells with bits of meat still clinging to the insides."

"You ate them."

"See it as the dog did. Spitters get their just punishment. He has a way to rid his world of offensive things and Master is pleased with him."

Teg demonstrated his brightness. "Do the Sisters think of us as dogs?"

"In a way. Never forget it. When you get back to your rooms, look up 'lèse majesté.' It helps place our relationship to our Masters."

Teg looked up at the comeyes and back to Idaho but said nothing.

Idaho lifted his attention to the door behind Teg and said: "That story was for you, too."

Teg jumped to his feet, turning and expecting to see Mother Superior. But it was only Murbella.

She was leaning against the wall near the door.

"Bell won't like you talking about the Sisterhood that way," she said.

"Odrade told me I have a free hand." He looked at Teg. "We've wasted enough time on stories! Let me see if your body has learned anything."

An odd feeling of excitement had come over Murbella as she entered the training area and saw Duncan with the child. She watched for a time, aware that she was seeing him in a new and almost Bene Gesserit light. Mother Superior's briefing came out in Duncan's candor with Teg. Extremely odd sensation, this new awareness, as though she had come a full step away from her former associates. The feeling was poignant with loss.

Murbella found herself missing strange things in her former life. Not the hunting in the streets, seeking new males to captivate and bring under Honored Matre control. The powers that came from creating sexual addicts had lost their savor under Bene Gesserit teaching and her experiences with Duncan. She admitted to missing one element of that power, though: the sense of belonging to a force nothing could stop.

It was both abstract and specific. Not the recurrent conquests but the expectation of inevitable victory that came in part from the drug she shared with Honored Matre Sisters. As the need waned in the shift to melange, she saw the old addiction from a different perspective. Bene Gesserit chemists, tracing the adrenaline substitute from samples of her blood, held it ready if she required it. She knew she did not. Another withdrawal plagued her. Not the captivated males but the flow of them. Something within her said this was gone forever. She would never re-experience it. New knowledge had changed her past.

She had prowled the corridors between her quarters and the practice floor this morning, wanting to watch Duncan with the child, afraid her presence might interfere. This prowling was a thing she often did these days after the more strenuous of her morning lessons with a Reverend Mother teacher. Thoughts of Honored Matres were much with her at these times.

She could not escape this feeling of loss. It was an emptiness such that she wondered if anything could possibly fill it. The sensation was worse than that of growing old. Growing old as an Honored Matre had offered its compensations. Powers gathered in *that* Sisterhood had a tendency to grow rapidly with age. Not that. It was an *absolute* loss.

I have been defeated.

Honored Matres never contemplated defeat. Murbella felt herself forced to it. She knew Honored Matres were sometimes slain by enemies. Those enemies always paid. It was the law: whole planets blackened to get one offender.

Murbella knew Honored Matres hunted for Chapterhouse. As a matter of former loyalties, she was aware she should be assisting those hunters. The poignancy of her personal defeat lay in the fact that she did not want the Bene Gesserit to pay the remembered price.

The Bene Gesserit are too valuable.

They were infinitely valuable to Honored Matres. Murbella doubted that any other Honored Matre even suspected this.

Vanity.

That was the judgment she attached to her former Sisters. *And to myself as I was.* A terrible pride. It had grown out of being subjugated so many generations before they gained their own ascendancy. Murbella had tried to convey this to Odrade, recounting from history taught by Honored Matres.

"The slave makes an awful master," Odrade said.

There was an Honored Matre pattern, Murbella realized. She had accepted it once but now rejected it and could not give all of her reasons for this change.

I have grown out of those things. They would be childish to me now.

Duncan once more had stopped the practice session. Perspiration poured from both teacher and student. They stood panting, regaining breath, an odd exchange of looks between them. *Conspiracy?* The child looked strangely mature.

Murbella recalled Odrade's comment: "Maturity imposes its own behavior. One of our lessons—make those imperatives available to consciousness. Modify instincts."

They have modified me and will do so even more.

She could see the same thing at work in Duncan's behavior with the ghola-child.

"This is an activity that creates many stresses in the societies we influence," Odrade had said. "That forces us to constant adjustments."

But how can they adjust to my former Sisters?

Odrade revealed characteristic sangfroid when braced with this question.

"We face major adjustments because of our past activities. It was the same during the reign of the Tyrant."

Adjustments?

Duncan was talking to the child. Murbella moved closer to listen.

"You've been exposed to the story of Muad'Dib? Good. You're an Atreides and that includes flaws."

"Does that mean mistakes, sir?"

"You're damned right it does! Never choose a course just because it offers the opportunity for a dramatic gesture."

"Is that how I died?"

He had the child thinking of his former self in the first person.

"You be the judge. But it was always an Atreides weakness. Attractive things, gestures. Die on the horns of a great bull as Muad'Dib's grandfather did. A grand spectacle for his people. The stuff of stories for generations! You can even hear bits of it around after all of these eons."

"Mother Superior told me that story."

"Your birth-mother probably told it to you, too."

The child shuddered. "It gives me a funny feeling when you say birth-mother." Awe in his young voice.

"Funny feelings are one thing; this lesson is another. I'm talking about something with a persistent label: *The Desian Gesture.* It used to be *Atreidesian* but that's too cumbersome."

Once more the child touched that core of mature awareness. "Even a dog's life has its price."

Murbella caught her breath, glimpsing how it would be—an adult mind in that child's body. Disconcerting.

"Your birth-mother was Janet Roxbrough of the Lernaeus Roxbroughs," Idaho said. "She was Bene Gesserit. Your father was Loschy Teg, a CHOAM station factor. In a few minutes I'm going to show you the Bashar's favorite picture of his home on Lernaeus. I want you to keep it with you and study it. Think of it as your favorite place."

Teg nodded but the expression on his face said he was afraid.

Was it possible the great Mentat Warrior had known fear? Murbella shook her head. She had an intellectual knowledge of what Duncan was doing but felt gaps in the accounts. This was something she might never experience. What would the feeling be—reawakening to new life with the memories of another lifetime intact? Much different from a Reverend Mother's Other Memory, she suspected.

"Mind at its beginning," Duncan called it. "Awakening of your True Self. I felt I had been plunged into a magic universe. My awareness was a circle and then a globe. Arbitrary forms became transient. The table was not a table. Then I fell into a trance—everything around me had a shimmering quality. Nothing was real. This passed and I felt I had lost the one reality. My table was a table once more."

She had studied the Bene Gesserit manual "On Awakening a Ghola's Original Memories." Duncan was diverging from those instructions. Why?

He left the child and approached Murbella.

"I have to talk to Sheeana," he said as he passed her. "There's got to be a better way."

Ready comprehension is often a knee-jerk response and the most dangerous form of *understanding*. It blinks an opaque screen over your ability to learn. The judgmental precedents of law function that way, littering your path with dead ends. Be warned. Understand nothing. All comprehension is temporary.

—MENTAT FIXE (ADACTO)

Idaho, seated alone at his console, encountered an entry he had stored in Shipsystems during his first days of confinement, and found himself dumped (he applied the word later) into attitudes and sensory awareness of that earlier time. It no longer was afternoon of a frustrating day in the no-ship. He was back *there*, stretched between *then* and *now* the way serial ghola lives linked this incarnation to his original birth.

Immediately, he saw what he had come to call "the net" and the elderly couple defined by criss-crossed lines, bodies visible through a shimmering of jeweled ropes—green, blue, gold, and a silver so brilliant it made his eyes ache.

He sensed godlike stability in these people, but something common about them. The word *ordinary* came to mind. The by-now-familiar garden landscape stretched out behind them: floral bushes (roses, he thought), rolling lawns, tall trees.

The couple stared back at him with an intensity that made Idaho feel naked.

New power in the vision! It no longer was confined to the Great

Hold, an increasingly compulsive magnet drawing him down there so frequently he knew the watchdogs were alerted.

Is he another Kwisatz Haderach?

There was a level of suspicion the Bene Gesserit could achieve that would kill him if it grew. And they were watching him now! Questions, worried speculations. Despite this, he could not turn away from the vision.

Why did that elderly couple look so familiar? Someone from his past? Family?

Mentat riffling of his memories produced nothing to fit the speculation. Round faces. Abbreviated chins. Fat wrinkles at the jowls. Dark eyes. The net obscured their color. The woman wore a long blue and green dress that concealed her feet. A white apron stained with green covered the dress from ample bosom to just below her waist. Garden tools dangled from apron loops. She carried a trowel in her left hand. Her hair was gray. Wisps of it had escaped a confining green scarf and blew around her eyes, emphasizing laughter lines there. She appeared . . . grandmotherly.

The man suited her as though created by the same artist as a perfect match. Bib overalls over a mounded stomach. No hat. Those same dark eyes with reflections twinkling in them. A brush of close-cropped wiry gray hair.

He had the most benign expression Idaho had ever seen. Upcurved smile creases at the corners of his mouth. He held a small shovel in his left hand, and on his extended right palm he balanced what appeared to be a small metal ball. The ball emitted a piercing whistle that made Idaho clap his hands over his ears. This did not stop the sound. It faded away of itself. He lowered his hands.

Reassuring faces. That thought aroused Idaho's suspicions because now he recognized the familiarity. They looked somewhat like Face Dancers, even to the pug noses.

He leaned forward but the vision kept its distance. "Face Dancers," he whispered.

Net and elderly couple vanished.

They were replaced by Murbella in practice-floor leotards of glistening ebony. He had to reach out and touch her before he could believe she really stood there.

"Duncan? What is it? You're all sweaty."

"I . . . think it's something the damned Tleilaxu planted in me. I keep seeing . . . I think they're Face Dancers. They . . . they look at me and just now . . . a whistle. It hurt."

She glanced up at the comeyes but did not appear worried. This was something the Sisters could know without it presenting immediate dangers . . . except possibly to Scytale.

She sank to her haunches beside him and put a hand on his arm. "Something they did to your body in the tanks?"

"No!"

"But you said . . ."

"My body's not just a piece of new baggage for this trip. It has all of the chemistry and substance I ever had. It's my mind that's different."

That worried her. She knew the Bene Gesserit concern over wild talents. "Damn that Scytale!"

"I'll find it," he said.

He closed his eyes and heard Murbella stand. Her hand went away from his arm.

"Maybe you shouldn't do that, Duncan."

She sounded far away.

Memory. Where did they hide the secret thing? Deep in the original cells? Until this moment, he had thought of his memory as a Mentat tool. He could call up his own images from long-ago moments in front of mirrors. Close up, examining an age wrinkle. Looking at a woman behind him—two faces in the mirror and his face full of questions.

Faces. A succession of masks, different views of this person he called *myself.* Slightly imbalanced faces. Hair sometimes gray, sometimes the jet karakul of his current life. Sometimes humorous, sometimes grave and seeking inward for wisdom to meet a new day. Somewhere in all of that lay a consciousness that observed and deliberated. Someone who made choices. The Tleilaxu had tampered with that.

Idaho felt his blood pumping hard and knew danger was present. This was what he was intended to experience . . . but not by the Tleilaxu. He had been born with it.

This is what it means to be alive.

No memory from his other lives, nothing the Tleilaxu had done to him, none of that changed his deepest awareness one whit.

He opened his eyes. Murbella still stood near but her expression was veiled. *So that's how she will look as a Reverend Mother.*

He did not like this change in her.

"What happens if the Bene Gesserit fail?" he asked.

When she did not reply, he nodded. *Yes. That's the worst assumption. The Sisterhood down history's sewerpipe. And you don't want that, my beloved.*

He could see it in her face when she turned and left him.

Looking up at the comeyes, he said: "Dar. I must talk to you, Dar."

No response from any of the mechanisms around him. He had not expected one. Still, he knew he could talk to her and she would have to listen.

"I've been coming at our problem from the other direction," he said. And he imagined the busy whirring of recorders as they spun the sounds of his voice into ridulian crystals. "I've been getting into the minds of Honored Matres. I know I've done it. Murbella resonates."

That would alert them. He had an Honored Matre of his own. But *had* was not the proper word. He did not *have* Murbella. Not even in bed. They had each other. Matched the way those people in his vision appeared to be matched. Was that what he saw there? Two older people sexually trained by Honored Matres?

"I look at another issue now," he said. "How to overcome the Bene Gesserit."

That threw down the gauntlet.

"Episodes," he said. A word Odrade was fond of using.

"That's how we have to see what's happening to us. Little episodes. Even the worst-case assumption has to be screened against that background. The Scattering has a magnitude that dwarfs anything we do."

There! That demonstrated his value to the Sisters. It put Honored Matres in a better perspective. They were back here in the Old Empire. Fellow dwarves. He knew Odrade would see it. Bell would make her see it.

Somewhere out there in the Infinite Universe, a jury had brought in a verdict against Honored Matres. Law and its managers had not prevailed for the hunters. He suspected that his vision had shown him two of the jurors. And if they were Face Dancers, they were not Scytale's Face Dancers. Those two people behind the shimmering net belonged to no one but themselves.

Major flaws in government arise from a fear of making radical internal changes even though a need is clearly seen.

—DARWI ODRADE

For Odrade, the first melange of the morning was always different. Her flesh responded like a starveling who clutched at sweet fruit. Then followed the slow, penetrating and painful restoration.

This was the fearful thing about melange addiction.

She stood at the window of her sleeping chamber waiting for the effect to run its course. Weather Control, she noted, had achieved another morning rain. The landscape was washed clean, everything immersed in a romantic haze, all edges blurred and reduced to essences like old memories. She opened the window. Damp cold air blew across her face, drawing recollections around her the way one put on a familiar garment.

She inhaled deeply. Smells after a rain! She remembered the essentials of life amplified and smoothed by falling water but these rains were different. They left a flinty aftersmell she could taste. Odrade did not like it. The message was not of things washed clean but of life resentful, wanting all rain stopped and locked away. This rain no longer gentled and brought fullness. It carried inescapable awareness of change.

Odrade closed the window. At once, she was back in the familiar odors of her quarters, and that constant smell of shere from the metering implants required of everyone who knew the location of Chapterhouse. She heard Streggi enter, the slip-slip sounds of the desert map being changed.

An efficient sound in Streggi's movements. Weeks of close association had confirmed Odrade's first judgment. Reliable. Not brilliant but supremely sensitive to Mother Superior's needs. Look how quietly she moved. Transfer Streggi's sensitivity to the needs of young Teg and they had his required height and mobility. *A horse? Much more.*

Odrade's melange assimilation reached its peak and subsided. Streggi's reflection in the window showed her waiting for assignment. She knew these moments were given over to the spice. At her stage, she would be looking forward to the day when she entered this mysterious enhancement.

I wish her well of it.

Most Reverend Mothers followed the teaching and seldom thought of their spice as addiction. Odrade knew it every morning for what it was. You took your spice during the day as your body demanded, following a pattern of early training: dosage minimal, just enough to whet the metabolic system and drive it into peak performance. Biological necessities meshed more smoothly with melange. Food tasted better. Barring accident or fatal assault, you lived much longer than you could without it. But you were addicted.

Her body restored, Odrade blinked and considered Streggi. Curiosity about the morning's long ritual was plain in her. Speaking to Streggi's reflection in the window, Odrade said: "Have you learned about melange withdrawal?"

"Yes, Mother Superior."

Despite warnings to keep awareness of addiction low key, it was never more than an eyeblink away from Odrade and she felt the accumulated resentments. Mental preparations as an acolyte (firmly impressed in the Agony) had been eroded by Other Memory and accumulations of time. The admonition: "Withdrawal removes an essential of your life and, if it occurs in late middle age, can kill you." How little that meant now.

"Withdrawal has intense meaning for me," Odrade said. "I am one of those for whom the morning melange is painful. I'm sure they told you this happens."

"I'm sorry, Mother Superior."

Odrade studied the map. It showed a longer finger of desert thrusting northward and a pronounced widening of drylands to the southeast of Central where Sheeana had her station. Presently, Odrade returned her attention to Streggi, who was watching Mother Superior with new interest.

Brought up short by thoughts of the spice's darker side!

"The uniqueness of melange is seldom considered in our age," Odrade said. "All of the old narcotics in which humans have indulged possess a remarkable factor in common—all except the spice. They all brought shorter life and pain."

"We were told, Mother Superior."

"But you probably were not told that a fact of governance could be obscured by our concern with Honored Matres. There's an energy greed in governments (yes, even in ours) that can dump you into a trap. If you serve me, you will feel it in your guts because every morning you will watch me suffer. Let knowledge of it sink into you, this deadly trap. Don't become uncaring pushers, caught in a system that displaces life with careless death as Honored Matres do. Remember: Acceptable narcotics can be taxed to pay salaries or otherwise create jobs for uncaring functionaries."

Streggi was puzzled. "But melange extends our lives, increases health and arouses appetites for—"

She was stopped by Odrade's scowl.

Right out of the Acolyte Manual!

"It has this other side, Streggi, and you see it in me. The Acolyte Manual does not lie. But melange is a narcotic and we are addicted."

"I know it's not gentle with everyone, Mother Superior. But you said Honored Matres don't use it."

"The substitute they employ replaces melange with few benefits except to prevent withdrawal agonies and death. It is parallel addictive."

"And the captive?"

"Murbella used it and now she uses melange. They are interchangeable. Interesting?"

"I . . . suppose we will learn more of this. I notice, Mother Superior, that you never call them whores."

"As acolytes do? Ahh, Streggi, Bellonda has been a bad influence. Oh, I recognize the pressures." As Streggi started to protest. "Acolytes feel the threat. They look at Chapterhouse and think of it as their fortress for the long night of the whores."

"Something like that, Mother Superior." Extremely hesitant.

"Streggi, this planet is only another temporary place. Today we go south and impress that upon you. Find Tamalane, please, and tell her to make the arrangements we discussed for our visit to Sheeana. Speak to no one else about it."

"Yes, Mother Superior. Do you mean I will accompany you?"

"I want you by my side. Tell the one you are training that she now has full charge of my map."

As Streggi left, Odrade thought of Sheeana and Idaho. *She wants to talk to him and he wants to talk to her.*

Comeye analysis noted that these two sometimes conversed by hand-signals while hiding most of the movements with their bodies. It had the look of an old Atreides battle language. Odrade recognized some of it but not enough to determine content. Bellonda wanted an explanation from Sheeana. "Secrets!" Odrade was more cautious. "Let it go a bit. Perhaps something interesting will come of it."

What does Sheeana want?

Whatever Duncan had in mind it concerned Teg. Creating the pain required for Teg to recover his original memories went against Duncan's grain.

Odrade had noted this when she interrupted Duncan at his console yesterday.

"You're late, Dar." Not looking up from whatever it was he did there. *Late? It was early evening.*

He had been calling her Dar frequently for several years, a goad, a reminder that he resented his fishtank existence. The goad irritated Bellonda, who argued against "his damned familiarities." He called Bellonda "Bell," of course. Duncan was generous with his needle.

Remembering this, Odrade paused before entering her workroom. Duncan had slammed a fist into the counter beside his console. "There's got to be a better way for Teg!"

A better way? What does he have in mind?

Movement down the corridor beyond the workroom brought her out of this reflection. Streggi returning from Tamalane. Streggi entered the Acolyte Ready Room. *Giving the word to her replacement on the desert map.*

A stack of Archival records waited on Odrade's table. *Bellonda!* Odrade stared at the pile. No matter how much she tried to delegate there was always this organized residue that her councillors insisted only Mother Superior could handle. Much of this new lot came from Bellonda's demand for "suggestions and analyses."

Odrade touched her console. "Bell!"

The voice of an Archives clerk responded: "Mother Superior?"

"Get Bell up here! I want her in front of me as fast as her fat legs can move!"

It was less than a minute. Bellonda stood in front of the worktable like a chastened acolyte. They all knew that tone in Mother Superior's voice.

Odrade touched the stack on her table and jerked her hand back as though shocked. "What in the name of Shaitan is all of that?"

"We judged it significant."

"You think I have to see everything and anything? Where's the keynoting? This is sloppy work, Bell! I'm not stupid and neither are you. But this . . . in the face of this . . ."

"I delegate as much as—"

"Delegate? Look at this! Which must I see and which may I delegate? Not one keynote!"

"I'll see that it's corrected immediately."

"Indeed you will, Bell. Because Tam and I are going south today, an unannounced inspection tour and a visit with Sheeana. And while I'm gone, you will sit in my chair. See how *you* like this daily deluge!"

"Will you be out of touch?"

"I'll have a lightline and Ear-C at all times."

Bellonda breathed easier.

"I suggest, Bell, that you get back to Archives and put someone in charge who will take responsibility. I'm damned if you're not beginning to act like bureaucrats. Covering your asses!"

"Real boats rock, Dar."

Was that Bell attempting humor? All was not lost!

Odrade waved a hand over her projector and there was Tamalane in the Transport Hall. "Tam?"

"Yes?" Without turning from an assignment list.

"How soon can we leave?"

"About two hours."

"Call me when you're ready. Oh, and Streggi goes with us. Make room for her." Odrade blanked the projection before Tamalane could respond.

There were things she should be doing, Odrade knew. Tam and Bell were not the only sources of Mother Superior's concerns.

Sixteen planets remaining to us . . . and that includes Buzzell, definitely a place in peril. Only sixteen! She pushed that thought aside. No time for it.

Murbella. Should I call her and . . . No. That can wait. The new Board of Proctors? Let Bell deal with that. Community disbandings?

Siphoning personnel into a new Scattering had forced consolidations. *Staying ahead of the desert!* It was depressing and she did not feel she could face it today. *I'm always fidgety before a trip.*

Abruptly, Odrade fled the workroom and went stalking the corridors, looking into how her charges were performing, pausing in doorways, noting what the students read, how they behaved in their everlasting prana-bindu exercises.

"What are you reading there?" demanded of a young second-stage acolyte at a projector in a semi-darkened room.

"The diaries of Tolstoy, Mother Superior."

That knowing look in the acolyte's eyes said: "Do you have his words directly in Other Memory?" The question was right there on the edge of the girl's tongue! They were always trying such petty gambits when they caught her alone.

"Tolstoy was a *family* name!" Odrade snapped. "By your mention of diaries, I presume you refer to Count Leo Nikolayevich."

"Yes, Mother Superior." Abashedly aware of censure.

Softening, Odrade threw a quotation at the girl: "'I am not a river, I am a net.' He spoke those words at Yasnaya Polyana when he was only twelve. You'll not find them in his diaries but they are probably the most significant words he ever uttered."

Odrade turned away before the acolyte could thank her. *Always teaching!*

She wandered down to the main kitchens then and inspected them, tracing inner edges of racked pots for grease, noting the cautious way even the teaching chef observed her progress.

The kitchen was steamy with good smells from lunch preparations. There was a restorative sound of chopping and stirring but the usual banter stopped at her entrance.

She went around the long counter with its busy cooks to the teaching chef's raised platform. He was a great beefy man with prominent cheekbones, his face as florid as the meats over which he ministered. Odrade had no doubts he was one of history's great chefs. His name suited him: Placido Salat. He was assured of a warm place in her thoughts for several reasons, including the fact that he had trained her personal chef. Important visitors in the days before Honored Matres had received a kitchen tour and a taste of specialties.

"May I introduce our senior chef, Placido Salat?"

His beef placido (low case his choice) was the envy of many. Almost raw and served with an herbed and spicy mustard sauce that did not obscure the meat.

Odrade thought the dish too exotic but never judged it aloud.

When she had Salat's full attention (after a slight interruption to correct a sauce) Odrade said: "I'm hungry for something special, Placido."

He recognized the opening. This was how she always began a request for her "special dish."

"Perhaps an oyster stew," he suggested.

It's a dance, Odrade thought. They both knew what she wanted.

"Excellent!" she agreed and went into the required performance. "But it must be treated gently, Placido, the oysters not overcooked. Some of our own powdered dry celery in the broth."

"And perhaps a bit of paprika?"

"I always prefer it that way. Be extremely careful with the melange. A breath of it and no more."

"Of course, Mother Superior!" Eyes rolling in horror at the thought he might use too much melange. "So easy for the spice to dominate."

"Cook the oysters in clam nectar, Placido. I would prefer you watch over them yourself, stirring gently until the edges of the oysters just start to curl."

"Not a second longer, Mother Superior."

"Heat some quite creamy milk on the side. Don't boil it!"

Placido displayed astonishment that she might suspect him of boiling the milk for her oyster stew.

"A small pat of butter in the serving bowl," Odrade said. "Pour the combined broth over it."

"No sherry?"

"How glad I am that you are taking personal charge of my special dish, Placido. I forgot the sherry." (Mother Superior never forgot anything and they all knew it but this was a required step in the dance.)

"Three ounces of sherry in the cooking broth," he said.

"Heat it to get rid of the alcohol."

"Of course! But we must not bruise the flavors. Would you like croutons or saltines?"

"Croutons, please."

Seated at an alcove table, Odrade ate two bowls of oyster stew, remembering how Sea Child had savored it. Papa had introduced her to this dish when she was barely capable of conveying spoon to mouth. He had made the stew himself, his own specialty. Odrade had taught it to Salat.

She complimented Salat on the wine.

"I particularly enjoyed your choice of a chablis for accompaniment."

"A flinty chablis with a sharp edge on it, Mother Superior. One of our better vintages. It sets off the oyster flavors admirably."

Tamalane found her in the alcove. They always knew where to find Mother Superior when they wanted her.

"We are ready." Was that displeasure on Tam's face?

"Where will we stop tonight?"

"Eldio."

Odrade smiled. She liked Eldio.

Tam catering to me because I'm in a critical mood? Perhaps we have the makings of a small diversion.

Following Tamalane to the transport docks, Odrade thought how characteristic it was that the older woman preferred to travel by tube. Surface trips annoyed her. "Who wants to waste time at my age?"

Odrade disliked tubes for personal transport. You were so closed in and helpless! She preferred surface or air and used tubes only when speed was urgent. She had no hesitation about using smaller tubes for chits and notes. *Notes don't care just as long as they get there.*

This thought always made her conscious of the network that adjusted to her movements wherever she went.

Somewhere in the heart of things (there was always a "heart of things") an automated system routed communications and made sure (most of the time) that important missives arrived where addressed.

When Private Dispatch (they all called it PD) was not needed, stat or viz was available along scrambled sorters and lightlines. Off-planet was another matter, especially in these hunted times. Safest to send a Reverend Mother with memorized message or distrans implant. Every messenger took heavier doses of shere these days. T-probes could read even a dead mind not guarded by shere. Every off-planet message was encrypted but an enemy might hit on the one-time cover concealing it. Great risk off-planet. Perhaps that was why the Rabbi remained silent.

Now why am I thinking such things at this moment?

"No word yet from Dortujla?" she asked as Tamalane prepared to enter the Dispatch roundelay where the others in their party waited. So many people. Why so many?

Odrade saw Streggi up ahead at the edge of the dock talking to a Communications acolyte. There were at least six other people from Communications nearby.

Tamalane turned in obvious pique. "Dortujla! We have all said we will notify you the instant we hear!"

"I was just asking, Tam. Just asking."

Meekly, Odrade followed Tamalane into Dispatch. *I should put a monitor on my mind and question everything that rises there.* Mental intrusions always had good reason behind them. That was the Bene Gesserit way, as Bellonda often reminded her.

Odrade felt surprise at herself then, realizing she was more than a little sick of Bene Gesserit ways.

Let Bell worry about such things for a change!

This was a time for floating free, for responding like a will o' the wisp to the currents moving around her.

Sea Child knew about currents.

Time does not count itself. You have only to look at a circle and this is apparent.

—LETO II (THE TYRANT)

"Look! Look what we have come to!" the Rabbi wailed. He sat cross-legged on the cold curved floor with his shawl pulled up over his head and almost concealing his face.

The room around him was gloomy and resonating with small machinery sounds that made him feel weak. If those sounds should stop!

Rebecca stood in front of him, hands on her hips, a look of weary frustration on her face.

"Do not stand there like that!" the Rabbi commanded. He peered up at her from beneath the shawl.

"If you despair, then are we not lost?" she asked.

The sound of her voice angered him and he was a moment putting this unwanted emotion aside.

She dares to instruct me? But was it not said by wiser men that knowledge can come from a weed? A great shuddering sigh shook him and he dropped the shawl to his shoulders. Rebecca helped him stand.

"A no-chamber," the Rabbi muttered. "In here, we hide from . . ." His gaze searched upward at a dark ceiling. "Better left unspoken even here."

"We hide from the unspeakable," Rebecca said.

"The door cannot even be left open at Passover," he said. "How will the Stranger enter?"

"Some strangers we do not want," she said.

"Rebecca." He bowed his head. "You are more than a trial and a problem. This little cell of Secret Israel shares your exile because we understand that—"

"Stop saying that! You understand nothing of what has happened to me. My problem?" She leaned close to him. "It is to remain human while in contact with all of those past lives."

The Rabbi recoiled.

"So you are no longer one of us? Are you a Bene Gesserit then?"

"You will know when I'm Bene Gesserit. You will see me looking at myself as I look at myself."

His brows drew down in a scowl. "What are you saying?"

"What does a mirror look at, Rabbi?"

"Hmmmmph! Riddles now." But a faint smile twitched at his mouth. A look of determination returned to his eyes. He stared around him at the room. There were eight of them here—more than this space should hold. *A no-chamber!* It had been assembled painstakingly with smuggled bits and pieces. So small. Twelve and a half meters long. He had measured it himself. A shape like an ancient barrel laid on its side, oval in cross section and with half-globe closures at the ends. The ceiling was no more than a meter above his head. The widest point here at the center was only five meters and the curve of floor and ceiling made it seem even narrower. Dried food and recycled water. That was what they must live on and for how long? One SY maybe if they were not found. He did not trust the security of this device. Those peculiar sounds in the machinery.

It had been late in the day when they crept into this hole. Darkness up there now for sure. And where were the rest of his people? Fled to whatever sanctuary they could find, drawing on old debts and honorable commitments for past services. Some would survive. Perhaps they would survive better than this remnant in here.

The entrance to the no-chamber lay concealed beneath an ash pit with a free-standing chimney beside it. The reinforcing metal of the chimney contained threads of ridulian crystal to relay exterior scenes into this place. Ashes! The room still smelled of burned things and it already had begun to take on a sewer stink from the small recycling chamber. What a euphemism for a toilet!

Someone came up behind the Rabbi. "The searchers are leaving. Lucky we were warned in time."

It was Joshua, the one who had built this chamber. He was a short, slender man with a sharply triangular face narrowing to a thin chin. Dark hair swept over his broad forehead. He had widely spaced brown eyes that looked out at his world with a brooding inwardness the Rabbi did not trust. *He looks too young to know so much about these things.*

"So they are leaving," the Rabbi said. "They will be back. You will not think us lucky then."

"They will not guess we hid so near the farm," Rebecca said. "The searchers were mostly looting."

"Listen to the Bene Gesserit," the Rabbi said.

"Rabbi." What a chiding sound in Joshua's voice! "Have I not heard you say many times that the blessed ones are they who hide the flaws of others even from themselves?"

"Everybody's a teacher now!" the Rabbi said. "But who can tell us what will happen next?"

He had to admit the truth of Joshua's words, though. *It is the anguish of our flight that troubles me. Our little diaspora. But we do not scatter from Babylon. We hide in a . . . a cyclone cellar!*

This thought restored him. *Cyclones pass.*

"Who is in charge of the food?" he asked. "We must ration ourselves from the start."

Rebecca heaved a sigh of relief. The Rabbi was at his worst in the wide oscillations—too emotional or too intellectual. He had himself in hand once more. He would become intellectual next. That would have to be dampened, too. Bene Gesserit awareness gave her a new view of the people around her. *Our Jewish susceptibility. Look at the intellectuals!*

It was a thought peculiar to the Sisterhood. The drawbacks of anyone placing considerable reliance on intellectual achievements were large. She could not deny all of that evidence from the Lampadas horde. Speaker paraded it for her whenever she wavered.

Rebecca had come almost to enjoy the pursuit of memory fancies, as she thought of them. Knowing earlier times forced her to deny her own earlier times. She had been required to believe so many things she now knew were nonsense. Myths and chimera, impulses of extremely childish behavior.

"Our gods should mature as we mature."

Rebecca suppressed a smile. Speaker did that to her often—a little nudge in the ribs from someone who knew you would appreciate it.

Joshua had gone back to his instruments. She saw that someone was reviewing the catalogue of food stores. The Rabbi watched this with his normal intensity. Others had rolled themselves into blankets and were sleeping on the cots in the darkened end of the chamber. Seeing all of this, Rebecca knew what her function must be. *Keep us from boredom.*

"The games master?"

Unless you have something better to suggest, don't try to tell me about my own people, Speaker.

Whatever else she might say about these inner conversations, there was no doubt that all of the pieces were connected—the past with this room, this room with her projections of consequences. And that was a great gift from the Bene Gesserit. *Do not think of "The Future." Predestination? Then what happens to the freedom you are given at birth?*

Rebecca looked at her own birth in a new light. It had embarked her on movement toward an unknown destiny. Fraught with unseen perils and joys. So they had come around a bend in the river and found attackers. The next bend might reveal a cataract or a stretch of peaceful beauty. And here lay the magical enticement of prescience, the lure to which Muad'Dib and his Tyrant son had succumbed. *The oracle knows what is to come!* The horde of Lampadas had taught her not to seek oracles. The known could beleaguer her more than the unknown. The sweetness of the new lay in its surprises. Could the Rabbi see it?

"Who will tell us what happens next?" he asks.

Is that what you want, Rabbi? You will not like what you hear. I guarantee it. From the moment the oracle speaks your future becomes identical to your past. How you would wail in your boredom. Nothing new, not ever. Everything old in that one instant of revelation.

"But this is not what I wanted!" I can hear you saying it.

No brutality, no savagery, no quiet happiness nor exploding joy can come upon you unexpectedly. Like a runaway tube train in its wormhole, your life will speed through to its final moment of confrontation. Like a moth in the car you will beat your wings against the sides and ask Fate to let you out. "Let the tube undergo a magical change of direction. Let something new happen! Don't let the terrible things I have seen come to pass!"

Abruptly, she saw that this must have been Muad'Dib's travail. To whom had he muttered his prayers?

"Rebecca!" It was the Rabbi calling her.

She went to where he stood beside Joshua now, looking at the dark world outside of their chamber as it was revealed in the small projection above Joshua's instruments.

"There is a storm coming," the Rabbi said. "Joshua thinks it will make a cement of the ash pit."

"That is good," she said. "It is why we built here and left the cover off the pit when we entered."

"But how do we get out?"

"We have tools for that," she said. "And even without tools, there's always our hands."

A major concept guides the Missionaria Protectiva: *Purposeful instruction of the masses.* This is firmly seated in our belief that the aim of argument should be to change the nature of truth. In such matters, we prefer the use of power rather than force.

—THE CODA

To Duncan Idaho, life in the no-ship had taken on the air of a peculiar game since the advent of his vision and insights into Honored Matre behavior. Entry of Teg into the game was a deceptive move, not just the introduction of another player.

He stood beside his console this morning and recognized elements in this game parallel to his own ghola childhood at the Bene Gesserit Keep on Gammu with the aging Bashar as weapons master-guardian.

Education. That had been a primary concern then as it was now. And the guards, mostly unobtrusive in the no-ship but always there as they had been on Gammu. Or their spy devices present, artfully camouflaged and blended into the decor. He had become an adept at evading them on Gammu. Here, with Sheeana's help, he had raised evasion to a fine art.

Activity around him was reduced to low background. Guards carried no weapons. But they were mostly Reverend Mothers with a few senior acolytes. They would not believe they needed weapons.

Some things in the no-ship contributed to an illusion of freedom, chiefly its size and complexity. The ship was large, how large he could not determine but he had access to many floors and to corridors that ran for more than a thousand paces.

Tubes and tunnels, access piping that conveyed him in suspensor pods, dropchutes and lifts, conventional hallways and wide corridors with hatches that hissed open at a touch (or remained sealed: *Forbidden!*)—all of it was a place to lock in memory, becoming there his own turf, private to him in a way far different from what it was to guards.

The energy required to bring the ship down to the planet and maintain it spoke of a major commitment. The Sisterhood could not count the cost in any ordinary way. The comptroller of the Bene Gesserit treasury did not deal merely in monetary counters. Not for them the Solar or comparable currencies. They banked on their people, on food, on payments due sometimes for millennia, payments often in kind—both materials and loyalties.

Pay up, Duncan! We're calling in your note!

This ship was not just a prison. He had considered several Mentat Projections. Prime: it was a laboratory where Reverend Mothers sought a way to nullify a no-ship's ability to confuse human senses.

A no-ship gameboard—puzzle and warren. All to confine three prisoners? No. There had to be other reasons.

The game had secret rules, some he could only guess. But he had found it reassuring when Sheeana entered into the spirit of it. *I knew she would have her own plans. Obvious when she began practicing Honored Matre techniques. Polishing my trainees!*

Sheeana wanted intimate information about Murbella and much more—his memories of people he had known in his many lives, especially memories of the Tyrant.

And I want information about the Bene Gesserit.

The Sisterhood kept him in minimal activity. Frustrating him to increase Mentat abilities. He was not at the heart of that larger problem he sensed outside the ship. Tantalizing fragments came to him when Odrade gave him glimpses of their predicament through her questions.

Enough to offer new premises? Not without access to data that his console refused to display.

It was his problem, too, damn them! He was in a box within their box. All of them trapped.

Odrade had stood beside this console one afternoon a week ago and blandly assured him the Sisterhood's data sources were "opened wide" to him. Right there she had stood, her back to the counter, leaning on it casually, arms folded across her breast. Her resemblance to the adult Miles Teg was uncanny at times. Even to that need (was it a compulsion?) to stand while talking. She disliked chairdogs, too.

He knew he had an extremely loose comprehension of her motives and plans. But he didn't trust them. Not after Gammu.

Decoy and bait. That was how they had used him. He was lucky not to have gone the way of Dune—a dead husk. Used up by the Bene Gesserit.

When he fidgeted this way, Idaho preferred to slump into the chair at his console. Sometimes, he sat here for hours, immobile, his mind trying to encompass complexities of the ship's powerful data resources. The system could identify any human in it. *So it has automatic monitors.* It had to know who was speaking, making demands, assuming temporary command.

Flight circuits defy my attempts to break through the locks. Disconnected? That was what his guards said. But the ship's way of identifying who tapped the circuits—he knew his key lay there.

Would Sheeana help? It was a dangerous gamble to trust her too much. Sometimes when she watched him at his console he was reminded of Odrade. *Sheeana was Odrade's student.* That was a sobering memory.

What was their interest in how he used Shipsystems? As if he needed to ask!

During his third year here he had made the system hide data for him, doing this with his own keys. To thwart the prying comeyes, he hid his actions in plain sight. Obvious insertions for later retrieval but with an encrypted second message. Easy for a Mentat and useful mostly as a trick, exploring the potentials of Shipsystems. He had booby-trapped his data to a random dump without hope of recovery.

Bellonda suspected, but when she questioned him about it, he only smiled.

I hide my history, Bell. My serial lives as a ghola—all of them back to the original non-ghola. Intimate things I remember about those experiences: a dumping ground for poignant memories.

Sitting now at the console, he experienced mixed feelings. Confinement galled him. No matter the size and richness of his prison, it still was a prison. He had known for some time that he very likely could escape but Murbella and his increasing knowledge about their predicament held him. He felt as much a prisoner of his thoughts as of the elaborate system represented by guards and this monstrous device. The no-ship was a device, of course. A tool. A way to move unseen in a dangerous universe. A means of concealing yourself and your intentions even from prescient searchers.

With accumulated skills of many lifetimes, he looked on his surroundings through a screen of sophistication and naivete. Mentats cultivated naivete. Thinking you knew something was a sure way to blind yourself. It was not growing up that slowly applied brakes to learning (Mentats were taught) but an accumulation of "things I know."

New data sources the Sisterhood had opened to him (if he could rely on them) raised questions. How was opposition to Honored Matres organized in the Scattering? Obviously there were groups (he hesitated to call them powers) who hunted Honored Matres the way Honored Matres hunted the Bene Gesserit. Killed them, too, if you accepted Gammu evidence.

Futars and Handlers? He made a Mentat Projection: A Tleilaxu offshoot in the first Scattering had engaged in genetic manipulations. Those two he saw in his vision: were they the ones who created Futars? Could that couple be Face Dancers? Independent of Tleilaxu Masters? All was not singular in the Scattering.

Dammit! He needed access to more data, to potent sources. His present sources were not even remotely adequate. A tool of limited purpose, his console could be adapted to larger requirements but his adaptations limped. He needed to stride out as a Mentat!

I've been hobbled and that's a mistake. Doesn't Odrade trust me? She's an Atreides, damn her! She knows what I owe her family. More than one lifetime and the debt never paid!

He knew he was fidgeting. Abruptly, his mind locked on that. Mentat fidgeting! A signal that he stood poised at the edge of breakthrough. *A Prime Projection!* Something they had *not* told him about Teg?

Questions! There were unasked questions lashing at him.

I need perspective! Not necessarily a matter of distance. You could gain perspective from within if your questions carried few distortions.

He sensed that somewhere in Bene Gesserit experiences (perhaps even in Bell's jealously guarded Archives) lay missing pieces. Bell should appreciate this! A fellow Mentat must know the excitement of this moment. His thoughts were like tesserae, most of the pieces at hand and ready to fit into a mosaic. It was not a matter of solutions.

He could hear his first Mentat teacher, the words rumbling in his mind: *"Assemble your questions in counterpoise and toss your temporary data onto one side of the scales or the other. Solutions unbalance any situation. Imbalances reveal what you seek."*

Yes! Achieving imbalances with sensitized questions was a Mentat's juggling act.

Something Murbella had said the night before—what? They had been in her bed. He recalled seeing the time projected on the ceiling: 9:47. And he had thought: *That projection takes energy.*

He could almost feel the flow of the ship's power, this giant enclosure cut out of Time. Frictionless machinery to create a mimetic presence no instrument could distinguish from natural background. Except for now when it was on standby, shielded not from eyes but from prescience.

Murbella beside him: another kind of power, both aware of the force trying to pull them together. The energy it took to suppress that mutual magnetism! Sexual attraction building and building and building.

Murbella talking. Yes, that was it. Oddly self-analytic. She approached her own life with a new maturity, a Bene Gesserit—heightened awareness and confidence that something of great strength grew in her.

Every time he recognized this Bene Gesserit change, he felt sad. *Nearer the day of our parting.*

But Murbella was talking. "She (Odrade was often 'she') keeps asking me to assess my love for you."

Remembering this, Idaho allowed it to replay.

"She has tried the same approach with me."

"What do you say?"

"Odi et amo. Excrucior."

She lifted herself on one elbow and looked down at him. "What language is that?"

"A very old one Leto had me learn once."

"Translate." Peremptory. Her old Honored Matre self.

"I hate her and I love her. And I am racked."

"Do you really hate me?" Unbelieving.

"What I hate is being tied this way, not the master of my *self.*"

"Would you leave me if you could?"

"I want the decision to recur moment by moment. I want control of it."

"It's a game where one of the pieces can't be moved."

There it was! Her words.

Remembering, Idaho felt no elation but as though his eyes had suddenly been opened after a long sleep. *A game where one of the pieces can't be moved. Game.* His view of the no-ship and what the Sisterhood did here.

There was more to the exchange.

"The ship is our own special school," Murbella said.

He could only agree. The Sisterhood reinforced his Mentat capacities to screen data and display what had not gone through. He sensed where this might lead and felt leaden fear.

"You clear the nerve passages. You block off distractions and useless mind-wanderings."

You redirected your responses into that dangerous mode every Mentat was warned to avoid. "You can lose yourself there."

Students were taken to see human vegetables, "failed Mentats," kept alive to demonstrate the peril.

How tempting, though. You could sense the power in that mode. *Nothing hidden. All things known.*

In the midst of that fear, Murbella turning toward him on the bed, he felt the sexual tensions become almost explosive.

Not yet. Not yet!

One of them had said something else. What? He had been thinking about the limits of logic as a tool to expose the Sisterhood's motives.

"Do you often try to analyze them?" Murbella asked.

Uncanny how she did that, addressing his unspoken thoughts. She denied she read minds. "I just read you, ghola mine. You are mine, you know."

"And vice versa."

"Too true." Almost bantering but it covered something deeper and convoluted.

There was a pitfall in any analysis of human psyches and he said this. "Thinking you know why you behave as you do gives you all sorts of excuses for extraordinary behavior."

Excuses for extraordinary behavior! There was another piece in his mosaic. More of the game but these counters were guilt and blame.

Murbella's voice was almost musing. "I suppose you can rationalize almost anything by laying it on some trauma."

"Rationalize such things as burning entire planets?"

"There's a kind of brutal self-determination in that. *She* says making determined choices firms up the psyche and gives you a sense of identity you can rely on under stress. Do you agree, Mentat mine?"

"The Mentat is not yours." No force in his voice.

Murbella laughed and slumped back onto her pillow. "You know what the Sisters want of us, Mentat mine?"

"They want our children."

"Oh, much more than that. They want our willing participation in their dream."

Another piece of the mosaic!

But who other than a Bene Gesserit knew that dream? The Sisters were actresses, always performing, letting little that was real come through their masks. The real person was walled in and metered out as needed.

"Why does she keep that old painting?" Murbella asked.

Idaho felt his stomach muscles tighten. Odrade had brought him a holorecord of the painting she kept in her sleeping chamber. *Cottages at Cordeville by Vincent Van Gogh.* Awakening him in this bed at some witching hour of the night almost a month ago.

"You asked for my hold on humanity and here it is." Thrusting the holo in front of his sleep-fogged eyes. He sat up and stared at the thing, trying to comprehend. What was wrong with her? Odrade sounded so excited.

She left the holo in his hands while she turned on all of the lights, giving the room a sense of hard and immediate shapes, everything vaguely mechanical the way you would expect it in a no-ship. Where was Murbella? They had gone to sleep together.

He focused on the holo and it touched him in an unaccountable way, as though it linked him to Odrade. *Her hold on her humanity?* The holo felt cold to his hands. She took it from him and propped it on the side table where he stared at it while she found a chair and sat near his head. Sitting? Something compelled her to be near him!

"It was painted by a madman on Old Terra," she said, bringing her cheek close to his while both looked at the copy of the painting. "Look at it! An encapsulated human moment."

In a landscape? Yes, dammit. She was right.

He stared at the holo. *Those marvelous colors!* It was not just the colors. It was the totality.

"Most modern artists would laugh at the way he created that," Odrade said.

Couldn't she be silent while he looked at it?

"That was a human being as ultimate recorder," Odrade said. "The human hand, the human eye, the human essence brought to focus in the awareness of one person who tested the limits."

Tested the limits! More of the mosaic.

"Van Gogh did that with the most primitive materials and equipment." She sounded almost drunk. "Pigments a caveman would have recognized! Painted on a fabric he could have made with his own hands. He might have made the tools himself from fur and wild twigs."

She touched the surface of the holo, her finger placing a shadow across the tall trees. "The cultural level was crude by our standards, but see what he produced?"

Idaho felt he should say something but words would not come. Where was Murbella? Why wasn't she here?

Odrade pulled back and her next words burned themselves into him.

"That painting says you cannot suppress the wild thing, the uniqueness that *will* occur among humans no matter how much we try to avoid it."

Idaho tore his gaze away from the holo and looked at Odrade's lips when she spoke.

"Vincent told us something important about our fellows in the Scattering."

This long-dead painter? About the Scattering?

"They have done things out there and are doing things we cannot imagine. Wild things! The explosive size of that Scattered population insures it."

Murbella entered the room behind Odrade, belting a soft white robe, her feet bare. Her hair was damp from a shower. So that was where she had gone.

"Mother Superior?" Murbella's voice was sleepy.

Odrade spoke over her shoulder without fully turning. "Honored Matres think they can anticipate and control every wildness. What nonsense. They cannot even control it in themselves."

Murbella came around to the foot of the bed and stared questioningly at Idaho. "I seem to have come in on the middle of a conversation."

"Balance, that's the key," Odrade said.

Idaho kept his attention on Mother Superior.

"Humans can balance on strange surfaces," Odrade said. "Even on unpredictable ones. It's called 'getting in tune.' Great musicians know it. Surfers I watched when I was a child on Gammu, they knew it. Some waves throw you but you're prepared for that. You climb back up and go at it once more."

For no reason he could explain, Idaho thought of another thing Odrade had said: "We have no attic storerooms. We recycle everything."

Recycle. Cycle. Pieces of the circle. Pieces of the mosaic.

He was random hunting and knew better. Not the Mentat way. Recycle, though—Other Memory was not an attic storeroom then but something they considered as recycling. It meant they used their past only to change it and renew it.

Getting in tune.

A strange allusion from someone who claimed she avoided music.

Remembering, he sensed his mental mosaic. It had become a jumble. Nothing fitted anywhere. Random pieces that probably did not go together at all.

But they did!

Mother Superior's voice continued in his memory. *So there is more.*

"People who know this go to the heart of it," Odrade said. "They warn that you cannot think about what you're doing. That's a sure way to fail. You just do it!"

Don't think. Do it. He sensed anarchy. Her words threw him back onto resources other than Mentat training.

Bene Gesserit trickery! She did this deliberately, knowing the effect. Where was the affection he sometimes felt radiating from her? Could she have concern for the well-being of someone she treated this way?

When Odrade left them (he barely noticed her departure), Murbella sat on the bed and straightened the robe around her knees.

Humans can balance on strange surfaces. Movement in his mind: the pieces of the mosaic trying to find relationships.

He felt a new surge in the universe. Those two strange people in his vision? They were part of it. He knew this without being able to say why. What was it the Bene Gesserit claimed? "We modify old fashions and old beliefs."

"Look at me!" Murbella said.

Voice? Not quite but now he was sure she tried it on and she had not told him they were training her in this witchery.

He saw the alien look in her green eyes that told him she was thinking about her former associates.

"Never try to be more clever than the Bene Gesserit, Duncan."

Speaking for the comeyes?

He could not be sure. It was the intelligence behind her eyes that gripped him these days. He could feel it growing there, as though her teachers blew into a balloon and Murbella's intellect expanded the way her abdomen expanded with new life.

Voice! What were they doing to her?

That was a stupid question. He knew what they were doing. They were taking her away from him, making a Sister of her. *No longer my lover, my marvelous Murbella.* A Reverend Mother then, remotely calculating in everything she did. *A witch.* Who could love a witch?

I could. And always will.

"They grab you from your blind side to use you for their own purposes," he said.

He could see his words take hold. She had awakened to this trap after the fact. The Bene Gesserit were so damnably clever! They had enticed her into their trap, giving her small glimpses of things as magnetic as the force binding her to him. It could only be an enraging realization to an Honored Matre.

We trap others! They do not trap us!

But this had been done by the Bene Gesserit. They were in a different category. Almost Sisters. Why deny it? And she wanted their abilities. She wanted out of this probation into the full teaching she could sense just beyond the ship's walls. Didn't she know why they still kept her on probation?

They know she still struggles in their trap.

Murbella slipped out of her robe and climbed into the bed beside him. Not touching. But keeping that armed sense of nearness between their bodies.

"They originally intended me to control Sheeana for them," he said.

"As you control me?"

"Do I control you?"

"Sometimes I think you're a comic, Duncan."

"If I can't laugh at myself I'm really lost."

"Laugh at your pretensions to humor, too?"

"Those first." He turned toward her and cupped her left breast in his hand, feeling the nipple harden under his palm. "Did you know I was never weaned?"

"Never in all of those . . ."

"Not once."

"I might have guessed." A smile formed fleetingly on her lips, and abruptly both of them were laughing, clutching each other, helpless with it. Presently, Murbella said, "Damn, damn, damn."

"Damn who?" as his laughter subsided and they pulled apart, forcing the separation.

"Not who, what. Damn fate!"

"I don't think fate cares."

"I love you and I'm not supposed to do that if I'm to be a proper Reverend Mother."

He hated these excursions so close to self-pity. *Joke then!* "You've never been a proper anything." He massaged the pregnant swelling of her abdomen.

"I *am* proper!"

"That's a word they left out when they made you."

She pushed his hand away and sat up to look down at him. "Reverend Mothers are never supposed to love."

"I know that." *Did my anguish reveal itself?*

She was too caught up in her own worries. "When I get to the Spice Agony . . ."

"Love! I don't like the idea of agony associated with you in any way."

"How can I avoid it? I'm already in the chute. Very soon they'll have me up to speed. I'll go very fast then."

He wanted to turn away but her eyes held him.

"Truly, Duncan. I can feel it. In a way, it's like pregnancy. There comes a point when it's too dangerous to abort. You must go through with it."

"So we love each other!" Forcing his thoughts away from one danger into another.

"And they forbid it."

He looked up at the comeyes. "The watchdogs are watching us and they have fangs."

"I *know*. I'm talking to *them* right now. My love for you is not a flaw. Their coldness is the flaw. They're just like Honored Matres!"

A game where one of the pieces can't be moved.

He wanted to shout it but listeners behind the comeyes would hear more than spoken words. Murbella was right. It was dangerous to think you could gull Reverend Mothers.

Something veiled in her eyes as she looked down at him. "How very strange you looked just then." He recognized the Reverend Mother she might become.

Veer away from that thought!

Thinking about the strangeness of his memories sometimes diverted her. She thought his previous incarnations made him somehow similar to a Reverend Mother.

"I've died so many times."

"You remember it?" The same question every time.

He shook his head, not daring to say anything more for the watchdogs to interpret.

Not the deaths and reawakenings.

Those became dulled by repetition. Sometimes he didn't even

bother to put them into his secret data-dump. No . . . it was the unique encounters with other humans, the long collection of recognitions.

That was a thing Sheeana claimed she wanted from him. "Intimate trivia. It's the stuff all artists want."

Sheeana did not know what she asked. All of those living encounters had created new meanings. Patterns within patterns. Minuscule things gained a poignancy he despaired of sharing with anyone . . . even with Murbella.

The touch of a hand on my arm. A child's laughing face. The glitter in an attacker's eyes.

Mundane things without counting. A familiar voice saying: "I just want to put my feet up and collapse tonight. Don't ask me to move."

All had become part of him. They were bound into his character. Living had cemented them inextricably and he could not explain it to anyone.

Murbella spoke without looking at him. "There were many women in those lives of yours."

"I've never counted them."

"Did you love them?"

"They're dead, Murbella. All I can promise is that there are no jealous ghosts in my past."

Murbella extinguished the glowglobes. He closed his eyes and felt darkness close in as she crept into his arms. He held her tightly, knowing she needed it, but his mind rolled of its own volition.

An old memory produced a Mentat teacher's saying: *"The greatest relevancy can become irrelevant in the space of a heartbeat. Mentats should look upon such moments with joy."*

He felt no joy.

All of those serial lives continued within him in defiance of Mentat relevancies. A Mentat came at his universe fresh in each instant. Nothing old, nothing new, nothing set in ancient adhesives, nothing truly *known*. You were the net and you existed only to examine the catch.

What did not go through? How fine a mesh did I use on this lot?

That was the Mentat view. But there was no way the Tleilaxu could have included all of those ghola-Idaho cells to recreate him. There had to be gaps in their serial collection of his cells. He had identified many of those gaps.

But no gaps in my memory. I remember them all.

He was a network linked outside of Time. *That is how I can see the people of that vision . . . the net.* It was the only explanation Mentat awareness could provide and if the Sisterhood guessed, they would be terrified. No matter how many times he denied it, they would say: "Another Kwisatz Haderach! Kill him!"

So work for yourself, Mentat!

He knew he had most of the mosaic pieces but still they did not go together in that *Ahh, hah!* assembly of questions Mentats prized.

A game where one of the pieces can't be moved.

Excuses for extraordinary behavior.

"They want our willing participation in their dream."

Test the limits!

Humans can balance on strange surfaces.

Get in tune. Don't think. Do it.

The best art imitates life in a compelling way. If it imitates a
dream, it must be a dream of life. Otherwise, there is no
place where we can connect. Our plugs don't fit.

—DARWI ODRADE

As they traveled south toward the desert in the early afternoon,
Odrade found the countryside disturbingly changed from her previous inspection three months earlier. She felt vindicated in having chosen ground vehicles. Views framed by the thick plaz protecting them
from the dust revealed more details at this level.

Much drier.

Her immediate party rode in a relatively light car—only fifteen
passengers including the driver. Suspensors and sophisticated jet drive
when they were not on ground-effect. Capable of a smooth three hundred klicks an hour on the glaze. Her escort (too large, thanks to an
overzealous Tamalane) followed in a bus that also carried changes of
clothing, foods and drinks for wayside stops.

Streggi, seated beside Odrade and behind the driver, said: "Could
we not manage a small rain here, Mother Superior?"

Odrade's lips thinned. Silence was the best answer.

They had been late starting. All of them assembled on the loading
dock and were ready to leave when a message came down from Bellonda. Another disaster report requiring Mother Superior's personal
attention at the last minute!

It was one of those times when Odrade felt her only possible role was that of official interpreter. Walk to the edge of the stage and tell them what it meant: "Today, Sisters, we learned that Honored Matres have obliterated four more of our planets. We are that much smaller."

Only twelve planets (including Buzzell) and the faceless hunter with the axe is that much closer.

Odrade felt the chasm yawning beneath her.

Bellonda had been ordered to contain this latest bad news until a more appropriate moment.

Odrade looked out the window beside her. What was an appropriate moment for such news?

They had been driving south a little more than three hours, the burner-glazed roadway like a green river ahead of them. This passage led them through hillsides of cork oaks that stretched out to ridge-enclosed horizons. The oaks had been allowed to grow gnomelike in less regimented plantations than orchards. There were meandering rows up the hills. The original plantation had been laid out on existing contours, semiterraces now obscured by long brown grass.

"We grow truffles in there," Odrade said.

Streggi had more bad news. "I am told the truffles are in trouble, Mother Superior. Not enough rain."

No more truffles? Odrade hesitated on the edge of bringing a Communications acolyte from the rear and asking Weather if this dryness could be corrected.

She glanced back at her attendants. Three rows, four people in each row, specialists to extend her observational powers and carry out orders. And look at that bus following them! One of the larger such vehicles on Chapterhouse. Thirty meters long, at least! Crammed with people! Dust whirled across and around it.

Tamalane rode back there at Odrade's orders. Mother Superior could be peppery when aroused, everyone thought. Tam had brought too many people but Odrade had discovered it too late for changes.

"Not an inspection! A damned invasion!" *Follow my lead, Tam. A little political drama. Make transition easier.*

She returned her attention to the driver, only male in this car.

Clairby, a vinegary little transport expert. Pinched-up face, skin the color of newly turned damp earth. Odrade's favorite driver. Fast, safe, and wary of limits of his machine.

They crested a hill and cork oaks thinned out, replaced ahead by fruit orchards surrounding a community.

Beautiful in this light, Odrade thought. Low buildings of white walls and orange-tiled roofs. An arch-shaded entrance street could be seen far down the slope and, in a line behind it, the tall central structure containing regional overview offices.

The sight reassured Odrade. The community had a glowing look softened by distance and a haze rising from its ring orchards. Branches still bare up here in this winter belt but surely capable of at least one more crop.

The Sisterhood demanded a certain beauty in its surroundings, she reminded herself. A cosseting that provided support for the senses without subtracting from needs of the stomach. Comfort where possible . . . but not too much!

Someone behind Odrade said: "I do believe some of those trees are starting to leaf."

Odrade took a more careful look. Yes! Tiny bits of green on dark boughs. Winter had slipped here. Weather Control, struggling to make seasonal shifts, could not prevent occasional mistakes. The expanding desert was creating higher temperatures too early here: odd warming patches that caused plants to leaf or bloom just in time for an abrupt frost. Die-back of plantations was becoming much too common.

A Field Advisor had dredged up the ancient term "Indian Summer" for a report illustrated by projections of an orchard in full blossom being assaulted by snow. Odrade had felt memory stirring at the advisor's words.

Indian Summer. How appropriate!

Her councillors sharing that little view of their planet's travail recognized the metaphor of a marauding freeze coming on the heels of inappropriate warmth: an unexpected revival of warm weather, a time when raiders could plague their neighbors.

Remembering, Odrade felt the chill of the hunter's axe. *How soon?* She dared not seek the answer. *I'm not a Kwisatz Haderach!*

Without turning, Odrade spoke to Streggi. "This place, Pondrille, have you ever been here?"

"It was not my postulant center, Mother Superior, but I presume it is similar."

Yes, these communities were much alike: mostly low structures set in garden plots and orchards, school centers for specific training. It was a screening system for prospective Sisters, the mesh finer the closer you got to Central.

Some of these communities such as Pondrille concentrated on toughening their charges. They sent women out for long hours every day to manual labor. Hands that grubbed in dirt and became stained with fruit seldom balked at muckier tasks later in life.

Now that they were out of the dust, Clairby opened the windows. Heat poured in! What was Weather doing?

Two buildings at the edge of Pondrille had been joined one story above the street, forming a long tunnel. All it needed, Odrade thought, was a portcullis to duplicate a town gate out of pre-space history. Armored knights would not find the dusky heat of this entry unfamiliar. It was defined in dark plastone, visually identical to stone. Comeye apertures overhead surely were places where guardians lay in wait.

The long, shaded entry to the community was clean, she saw. Nostrils were seldom assailed by rot or other offensive odors in Bene Gesserit communities. No slums. Few cripples hobbling along the walks. Much healthy flesh. Good management took care to keep a healthy population happy.

We have our disabled, though. And not all of them physically disabled.

Clairby parked just within the exit from the shaded street and they emerged. Tamalane's bus pulled to a stop behind them.

Odrade had hoped the entry passage would provide relief from the heat but perversity of nature had made an oven of the place and the temperature actually increased here. She was glad to pass through into the clear light of the central square where sweat burning off her body provided a few seconds of coolness.

The illusion of relief passed abruptly as the sun scorched her head and shoulders. She was forced to call on metabolic control to adjust her body heat.

Water splashed in a reflecting circle at the central square, a careless display that soon would have to end.

Leave it for now. Morale!

She heard her companions following, the usual groans against "sitting too long in one position." A greeting delegation could be seen hurrying from the far side of the square. Odrade recognized Tsimpay, Pondrille's leader, in the van.

Mother Superior's attendants moved onto the blue tiles of the fountain plaza—all except Streggi, who stood at Odrade's shoulder. Tamalane's group, too, was attracted to splashing water. All part and parcel of a human dream so ancient it could never be completely discarded, Odrade thought.

Fertile fields and open water—clear, potable water you can dip your face into for thirst-quenching relief.

Indeed, some of her party were doing just that at the fountain. Their faces glistened with dampness.

The Pondrille delegation came to a stop near Odrade while still on the blue tiles of the fountain plaza. Tsimpay had brought three other Reverend Mothers and five older acolytes.

Near the Agony, all of those acolytes, Odrade observed. Showing their awareness of the trial in directness of gaze.

Tsimpay was someone Odrade saw infrequently at Central where she came sometimes as a teacher. She was looking fit: brown hair so dark it appeared reddish-black in this light. The narrow face was almost bleak in its austerity. Her features centered on all-blue eyes under heavy brows.

"We are glad to see you, Mother Superior." Sounded as though she meant it.

Odrade inclined her head, a minimal gesture. *I hear you. Why are you so glad to see me?*

Tsimpay understood. She gestured to a tall, hollow-cheeked Reverend Mother beside her. "You remember Fali, our Orchard Mistress? Fali has just been to me with a delegation of gardeners. A serious complaint."

Fali's weathered face looked a bit gray. *Overworked?* She had a thin mouth above a sharp chin. Dirt under her fingernails. Odrade noted it with approval. *Not afraid to join in the grubbing.*

Delegation of gardeners. So there was an escalation of complaints. Must have been serious. Not like Tsimpay to dump it on Mother Superior.

"Let's hear it," Odrade said.

With a glance at Tsimpay, Fali went through a detailed recital, even providing qualifications of delegation leaders. All of them good people, of course.

Odrade recognized the pattern. There had been conferences concerning this inevitable consequence. Tsimpay in attendance at some of them. How could you explain to your people that a distant sandworm (perhaps not even in existence yet) required this change? How could you explain to farmers that it was *not* a matter of "just a bit more rain" but went straight to the heart of the planet's total weather. More rain here could mean a diversion of high-altitude winds. That in its turn would change things elsewhere, cause moisture-laden siroccos where they would be not only upsetting but also dangerous. Too easy to bring on great tornadoes if you inserted the wrong conditions. A planet's weather was no simple thing to treat with easy adjustments. *As I have sometimes demanded.* Each time, there was a total equation to be scanned.

"The planet casts the final vote," Odrade said. It was an old reminder in the Sisterhood of human fallibility.

"Does Dune still have a vote?" Fali asked. More bitterness in the question than Odrade had anticipated.

"I feel the heat. We saw the leaves on your orchards as we arrived," Odrade said. *I know what concerns you, Sister.*

"We will lose part of the crop this year," Fali said. Accusation in her words: *This is your fault!*

"What did you tell your delegation?" Odrade asked.

"That the desert must grow and Weather no longer can make every adjustment we need."

Truth. The agreed response. Inadequate, as truth often was, but all they had now. Something would have to give soon. Meanwhile, more delegations and loss of crops.

"Will you take tea with us, Mother Superior?" Tsimpay, the diplomat, intervening. *You see how it is escalating, Mother Superior? Fali will now go back to dealing with fruits and vegetables. Her proper place. Message delivered.*

Streggi cleared her throat.

That damnable gesture will have to be suppressed! But the meaning was clear. Streggi had been put in charge of their schedule. *We must be going.*

"We got a late start," Odrade said. "We stopped only to stretch our legs and see if you have problems you cannot meet on your own."

"We can handle the gardeners, Mother Superior."

Tsimpay's brisk tone said much more and Odrade almost smiled.

Inspect if you wish, Mother Superior. Look anywhere. You will find Pondrille in Bene Gesserit order.

Odrade glanced at Tamalane's bus. Some of the people already were returning to the air-conditioned interior. Tamalane stood by the door, well within earshot.

"I hear good reports of you, Tsimpay," Odrade said. "You can do without our interference. I certainly don't want to intrude on you with an entourage that is far too large." This last loud enough that all would be certain to hear.

"Where will you spend the night, Mother Superior?"

"Eldio."

"I've not been down there for some time but I hear the sea is much smaller."

"Overflights confirm what you've heard. No need to warn them that we're coming, Tsimpay. They already know. We had to prepare them for this invasion."

Orchard Mistress Fali took a small step forward. "Mother Superior, if we could get just . . ."

"Tell your gardeners, Fali, that they have a choice. They can grumble and wait here until Honored Matres arrive to enslave them or they can elect to go Scattering."

Odrade returned to her car and sat, eyes closed, until she heard the doors sealed and they were well on their way. Presently, she opened her eyes. They already were out of Pondrille and onto the glassy lane through the southern ring orchards. There was charged silence behind her. Sisters were looking deeply into questions about Mother Superior's behavior back there. An unsatisfactory encounter. Acolytes naturally picked up the mood. Streggi looked glum.

This weather demanded notice. Words no longer could smooth over the complaints. Good days were measured by lower standards. Everyone knew the reason but changes remained a focal point. Visible. You could not complain about Mother Superior (not without good cause!) but you could grumble about the weather.

"Why did they have to make it so cold today? Why today when I have to be out in it? Quite warm when we came out but look at it now. And me without proper clothing!"

Streggi wanted to talk. *Well, that's why I brought her.* But she had become almost garrulous as enforced intimacy eroded her awe of Mother Superior.

"Mother Superior, I've been searching in my manuals for an explanation of—"

"Beware of manuals!" How many times in her life had she heard or spoken those words? "Manuals create habits."

Streggi had been lectured often about habits. The Bene Gesserit had them—those things the Folk preserved as "Typical of the Witches!" But patterns that allowed others to predict behavior, those must be carefully excised.

"Then why do we have manuals, Mother Superior?"

"We have them mainly to disprove them. The Coda is for novices and others in primary training."

"And the histories?"

"Never ignore the banality of recorded histories. As a Reverend Mother, you will relearn history in each new moment."

"Truth is an empty cup." Very proud of her remembered aphorism. Odrade almost smiled.

Streggi is a jewel.

It was a cautioning thought. Some precious stones could be identified by their impurities. Experts mapped impurities within the stones. A secret fingerprint. People were like that. You often knew them by their defects. The glittering surface told you too little. Good identification required you to look deep inside and see the impurities. *There* was the gem quality of a total being. What would Van Gogh have been without impurities?

"It is comments of perceptive cynics, Streggi, things *they* say *about* history, that should be your guides before the Agony. Afterward, you will be your own cynic and you will discover your own values. For now, the histories reveal dates and tell you something occurred. Reverend Mothers search out the *somethings* and learn the prejudices of historians."

"That's all?" Deeply offended. *Why did they waste my time that way?*

"Many histories are largely worthless because prejudiced, written to please one powerful group or another. Wait for your eyes to be opened, my dear. We are the best historians. We were there."

"And my viewpoint will change daily?" Very introspective.

"That's a lesson the Bashar reminded us to keep fresh in our minds. The past must be reinterpreted by the present."

"I'm not sure I will enjoy that, Mother Superior. So many moral decisions."

Ahhhh, this jewel saw to the heart of it and spoke her mind like a true Bene Gesserit. There were brilliant facets among Streggi's impurities.

Odrade looked sideways at the pensive acolyte. Long ago, the Sisterhood had ruled that each Sister must make her own moral decisions. *Never follow a leader without asking your own questions.* That was why moral conditioning of the young took such high priority.

That is why we like to get our prospective Sisters so young. And it may be why a moral flaw has crept into Sheeana. We got her too late. What do she and Duncan talk about so secretly with their hands?

"Moral decisions are always easy to recognize," Odrade said. "They are where you abandon self-interest."

Streggi looked at Odrade with awe. "The courage it must take!"

"Not courage! Not even desperation. What we do is, in its most basic sense, natural. Things done because there is no other choice."

"Sometimes you make me feel ignorant, Mother Superior."

"Excellent! That's beginning wisdom. There are many kinds of ignorance, Streggi. The basest is to follow your own desires without examining them. Sometimes, we do it unconsciously. Hone your sensitivity. Be aware of what you do unconsciously. Always ask: 'When I did that, what was I trying to gain?'"

They crested the final hill before Eldio and Odrade welcomed a reflexive moment.

Someone behind her murmured, "There's the sea."

"Stop here," Odrade ordered as they neared a wide turnout at a curve overlooking the sea. Clairby knew the place and was prepared for it. Odrade often asked him to stop here. He brought them to a halt where she wanted. The car creaked as it settled. They heard the bus pull up behind, a loud voice back there calling on companions to "Look at that!"

Eldio lay off to Odrade's left far down there: delicate buildings, some raised off the ground on slender pipes, wind passing under and through them. This was far enough south and down off the heights where Central perched that it was much warmer. Small vertical-axis windmills, toys from this distance, whirled at the corners of Eldio's buildings to help power the community. Odrade pointed them out to Streggi.

"We thought of them as independence from bondage to a complex technology controlled by others."

As she spoke, Odrade shifted her attention to the right. *The sea!* It was a dreadfully condensed remnant of its once glorious expanse. Sea Child hated what she saw.

Warm vapor lifted from the sea. The dim purple of dry hills drew a blurred outline of horizon on the far side of the water. She saw that Weather had introduced a wind to disperse saturated air. The result was a choppy froth of waves beating against the shingle below this vantage.

There had been a string of fishing villages here, Odrade recalled. Now that the sea had receded, villages lay farther back up the slope. Once, the villages had been a colorful accent along the shore. Much of their population had been siphoned off in the new Scattering. People who remained had built a tram to get their boats to and from the water.

She approved of this and deplored it. Energy conservation. The whole situation struck her suddenly as grim—like one of those Old Empire geriatric installations where people waited around to die.

How long until these places die?

"The sea is so small!" It was a voice from the rear of the car. Odrade recognized it. An Archives clerk. *One of Bell's damned spies.*

Leaning forward, Odrade tapped Clairby on the shoulder. "Take us down to the near shore, that cove almost directly below us. I wish to swim in our sea, Clairby, while it still exists."

Streggi and two other acolytes joined her in the warm waters of the cove. The others walked along the shore or watched this odd scene from the car and bus.

Mother Superior swimming nude in the sea!

Odrade felt energizing water around her. Swimming was required because of command decisions she must make.

How much of this last great sea could they afford to maintain during these final days of their planet's temperate life? The desert was coming—*total desert* to match that of lost Dune. *If the axe-bearer gives us time.* The threat felt very close and the chasm deep. *Damn this wild talent! Why do I have to know?*

Slowly, Sea Child and wave motions restored her sense of balance. This body of water was a major complication—much more important than scattered small seas and lakes. Moisture lifted from here in significant amounts. Energy to charge unwanted deviations in Weather's barely controlled management. Yet, this sea still fed Chapterhouse. It was a communication and transport route. Sea carriers were cheapest. Energy costs must be balanced against other elements in her decision. But the sea would vanish. That was sure. Whole populations faced new displacements.

Sea Child's memories interfered. Nostalgia. It blocked paths of proper judgment. *How fast must the sea go?* That was the question. All of the inevitable relocations and resettlements waited on that decision.

Best it were done quickly. The pain banished into our past. Let us get on with it!

She swam to the shallows and looked up at the puzzled Tamalane. Tam's robed skirts were dark with splashings from an unexpected wave. Odrade lifted her head clear of the small surges.

"Tam! Eliminate the sea as fast as possible. Get Weather to plot a swift dehydration scheme. Food and Transport will have to be brought into it. I'll approve the final plan after our usual review."

Tamalane turned away without speaking. She beckoned appropriate Sisters to accompany her, glancing only once at Mother Superior as she did this. *See! I was right to bring along the necessary cadre!*

Odrade climbed from the water. Wet sand gritted under her feet. *Soon, it will be dry sand.* She dressed without bothering to towel herself. Clothing gripped her flesh uncomfortably, but she ignored this, walking up the strand away from the others, not looking back at the sea.

Souvenirs of memory must be only that. Things to be taken up and fondled occasionally for evocation of past joys. No joy can be permanent. All is transient. "This, too, shall pass away" applies to all of our living universe.

Where the beach became loamy dirt and a few sparse plants, she turned finally and looked back at the sea she had just condemned.

Only life itself mattered, she told herself. And life could not endure without an ongoing thrust of procreation.

Survival. Our children must survive. The Bene Gesserit must survive!

No single child was more important than the totality. She accepted this, recognizing it as the species talking to her from her deepest self, the self she had first encountered as Sea Child.

Odrade allowed Sea Child one last sniff of salt air as they returned to their vehicles and prepared to drive into Eldio. She felt herself grow calm. That essential balance, once learned, did not require a sea to maintain it.

Uproot your questions from their ground and the dangling roots will be seen. More questions!

—MENTAT ZENSUFI

Dama was in her element.

Spider Queen!

She liked the witches' title for her. This was the heart of her web, this new control center on Junction. The exterior of the building still did not suit her. Too much Guild complacency in its design. Conservative. But the interior had begun to take on a familiarity that soothed her. She could almost imagine she had never left Dur, that there had been no Futars and the harrowing flight back into the Old Empire.

She stood in the open door of the Assembly Room looking out at the Botanical Garden. Logno waited four paces behind. *Not too close behind me, Logno, or I shall have to kill you.*

There was still dew on the lawn beyond the tiles where, when the sun had risen far enough, servants would distribute comfortable chairs and tables. She had ordered a sunny day and Weather had damned well better produce it. Logno's report was interesting. So the old witch had returned to Buzzell. And she was angry, too. Excellent. Obviously, she knew she was being watched and she had visited her supreme witch to ask for removal from Buzzell, for sanctuary. And she had been refused.

They don't care that we destroy their limbs just as long as the central body remains hidden.

Speaking over her shoulder to Logno, Dama said: "Bring that old witch to me. And all of her attendants."

As Logno turned to obey, Dama added: "And begin starving some Futars. I want them hungry."

"Yes, Dama."

Someone else moved into Logno's attendant position. Dama did not turn to identify the replacement. There were always enough aides to carry out necessary orders. One was much like another except in the matter of threat. Logno was a constant threat. *Keeps me alert.*

Dama inhaled deeply of the fresh air. It was going to be a good day precisely because that was what she desired. She gathered in her secret memories then and let them soothe her.

Guldur be blessed! We've found the place to rebuild our strength.

Consolidation of the Old Empire was proceeding as planned. There would not be many witches' nests left out there and, once that damnable Chapterhouse was found, the limbs could be destroyed at leisure.

Ix, now. There was a problem. *Perhaps I should not have killed those two Ixian scientists yesterday.*

But the fools had dared demand "more information" from her. Demanded! And after saying they still had no solution to rearming The Weapon. Of course, they did not know it was a weapon. Did they? She could not be sure. So it had been a good thing to kill those two after all. Teach them a lesson.

Bring us answers, not questions.

She liked the order she and her Sisters were creating in the Old Empire. There had been too much wandering about and too many different cultures, too many unstable religions.

Worship of Guldur will serve them as it serves us.

She felt no mystical affinity to her religion. It was a useful tool of power. The roots were well known: Leto II, the one those witches called "The Tyrant," and his father, Muad'Dib. Consummate power brokers, both of them. Lots of schismatic cells around but those could be weeded out. Keep the essence. It was a well-lubricated machine.

The tyranny of the minority cloaked in the mask of the majority.

That was what the witch Lucilla had recognized. No way to let her live after discovering she knew how to manipulate the masses. The witch nests would have to be found and burned. Lucilla's perceptiveness clearly was not an isolated example. Her actions betrayed the workings of a school. They taught this thing! Fools! You had to manage reality or things really got out of control.

Logno returned. Dama could always tell the sound of her footsteps. Furtive.

"The old witch will be brought from Buzzell," Logno said. "And her attendants."

"Don't forget about the Futars."

"I have given the orders, Dama."

Oily voice! You'd like to feed me to the herd, wouldn't you, Logno?

"And tighten up security on the cages, Logno. Three more of them escaped last night. They were wandering around in the garden when I awoke."

"I was told, Dama. More cage guards have been assigned."

"And don't tell me they're harmless without a Handler."

"I do not believe that, Dama."

And that's truth from her, for once. Futars terrify her. Good.

"I believe we have our power base, Logno." Dama turned, noting that Logno had encroached at least two millimeters into the danger zone. Logno saw it, too, and retreated. *As close as you want in front where I can see you, Logno, but not behind my back.*

Logno saw the orange blaze in Dama's eyes and almost knelt. *Definite bending of the knees.* "It is my eagerness to serve you, Dama!"

Your eagerness to replace me, Logno.

"What of that woman from Gammu? Odd name. What was it?"

"Rebecca, Dama. She and some of her companions have . . . ahhh, temporarily eluded us. We will find them. They cannot get off the planet."

"You think I should have kept her here, don't you?"

"It was wise to think of her as bait, Dama!"

"She's still bait. That witch we found on Gammu did not go to those people by accident."

"Yes, Dama."

Yes, Dama! But the subservient sound in Logno's voice was enjoyable. "Well, get on with it!"

Logno scurried away.

There were always those little cells of potential violence meeting secretly somewhere. Building up their mutual charges of hate, swarming out to disrupt the orderly lives around them. Someone always had to clean up after those disruptions. Dama sighed. Terror tactics were so . . . so temporary!

Success, that was the danger. It had cost them an empire. If you waved your success around like a banner someone always wanted to cut you down. Envy!

We will hold our success more cautiously this time.

She fell into a semi-reverie, still alert to the sounds behind her, but relishing the evidence of new victories that had been displayed to her this morning. She liked to roll the names of captive planets silently on her tongue.

Wallach, Kronin, Reenol, Ecaz, Bela Tegeuse, Gammu, Gamont, Niushe . . .

Humans are born with a susceptibility to that most persistent and debilitating disease of intellect: self-deception. The best of all possible worlds and the worst get their dramatic coloration from it. As nearly as we can determine, there is no natural immunity. Constant alertness is required.

—THE CODA

With Odrade away from Central (and probably only for a short time) Bellonda knew swift action was required. *That damned Mentat-ghola is too dangerous to live!*

Mother Superior's party was barely out of sight into the lowering afternoon before Bellonda was on her way to the no-ship.

Not for Bellonda a thoughtful approach through ring orchards. She ordered space on a tube, windowless, automatic, and fast. Odrade, too, had observers who might send unwanted messages.

En route, Bellonda reviewed her assessment of Idaho's many lives. A record she had kept in Archives ready for quick retrieval. In the original and early gholas, his character had been dominated by impulsiveness. Quick to hate, quick to give loyalty. Later Idaho-gholas tempered this with cynicism but the underlying impulsiveness remained. The Tyrant had called it to action many times. Bellonda recognized a pattern.

He can be goaded by pride.

His long service to the Tyrant fascinated her. Not only had he been a Mentat several times but there was evidence he had been a Truthsayer in more than one incarnation.

Idaho's appearance reflected what she saw in her records. Interesting character lines, a look around the eyes and a set to his mouth that went with complex inner development.

Why would Odrade not accept the danger of this man? Bellonda had felt frequent misgivings when Odrade spoke of Idaho with such flaunting of her emotions.

"He thinks clearly and directly. There's a fastidious cleanliness about his mind. It's restorative. I like him and I know that's a trivial thing to influence my decisions."

She admits his influence!

Bellonda found Idaho alone and seated at his console. His attention was fixed on a linear display she recognized: the no-ship's operational schematics. He washed the projection when he saw her.

"Hello, Bell. Been expecting you."

He touched his console field and a door opened behind him. Young Teg entered and took up a position near Idaho, staring silently at Bellonda.

Idaho did not invite her to sit or find a chair for her, forcing her to bring one from his sleeping chamber and place it facing him. When she was seated, he turned a look of wary amusement to her.

Bellonda remained taken aback by his greeting. *Why did he expect me?*

He answered her unspoken question. "Dar projected earlier, told me she was off to see Sheeana. I knew you'd waste no time getting to me when she was gone."

Simple Mentat Projection or . . . "She warned you!"

"Wrong."

"What secrets do you and Sheeana share?" Demanding.

"She uses me the way you want her to use me."

"The Missionaria!"

"Bell! Two Mentats together. Must we play these stupid games?"

Bellonda took a deep breath and sought Mentat mode. Not easy under these circumstances, that child staring at her, the amusement on Idaho's face. Was Odrade displaying an unsuspected slyness? Working against a Sister with this ghola?

Idaho relaxed when he saw Bene Gesserit intensity become that doubled focus of the Mentat. "I've known for a long time that you want me dead, Bell."

Yes . . . I have been readable in my fears.

It had been very close there, he thought. Bellonda had come to him with death in mind, a little drama to create "the necessity" all prepared. He entertained few illusions about his ability to match her in violence. But Bellonda-Mentat would observe before acting.

"It's disrespectful the way you use our first names," she said, goading.

"Different recognition, Bell. You're no longer Reverend Mother and I'm not 'the ghola.' Two human beings with common problems. Don't tell me you're unaware of this."

She glanced around his workroom. "If you expected me why didn't you have Murbella here?"

"Force her to kill you while protecting me?"

Bellonda assessed this. *The damned Honored Matre probably could kill me, but then . . .* "You sent her away to protect her."

"I've a better protector." He gestured at the child.

Teg? A protector? There were those stories from Gammu about him. Does Idaho know something?

She wanted to ask but did she dare risk diversion? Watchdogs must receive a clear scenario of danger.

"Him?"

"Would he serve the Bene Gesserit if he saw you kill me?"

When she did not answer, he said: "Put yourself in my place, Bell. I'm a Mentat caught not only in your trap but in that of the Honored Matres."

"Is that all you are, a Mentat?"

"No. I'm a Tleilaxu experiment but I don't see the future. I'm not a Kwisatz Haderach. I'm a Mentat with memories of many lives. You, with your Other Memories—think about the leverage that gives me."

While he was speaking, Teg came to lean against the console at Idaho's elbow. The boy's expression was one of curiosity but she saw no fear of her.

Idaho gestured at the projection focus over his head, silver motes dancing there ready to create their images. "A Mentat sees his relays producing discrepancies—winter scenes in summer, sunshine when his visitors have come through rain . . . Didn't you expect me to discount your little playlets?"

She heard Mentat summation. To that extent, they shared common teaching. She said: "You naturally told yourself not to minimize the Tao."

"I asked different questions. Things that happen together can have underground links. What is cause and effect when confronted with simultaneity?"

"You had good teachers."

"And not just in one life."

Teg leaned toward her. "Did you really come here to kill him?"

No sense lying. "I still think he is too dangerous." Let watchdogs argue that!

"But he's going to give me back my memories!"

"Dancers on a common floor, Bell," Idaho said. "Tao. We may not appear to dance together, may not use the same steps or rhythms but we are seen together."

She began to suspect where he might be leading and wondered if there might be another way to destroy him.

"I don't know what you're talking about," Teg said.

"Interesting coincidences," Idaho said.

Teg turned to Bellonda. "Maybe you would explain, please?"

"He's trying to tell me we need each other."

"Then why doesn't he say so?"

"It's more subtle than that, boy." And she thought: *The record must show me warning Idaho.* "The nose of the donkey doesn't cause the tail, Duncan, no matter how often you see the beast pass that thin vertical space limiting your view of it."

Idaho met Bellonda's fixed gaze. "Dar came here once with a sprig of apple blossoms, but my projection showed harvest time."

"It's riddles, isn't it?" Teg said, clapping his hands.

Bellonda recalled the record of that visit. Precise movements by Mother Superior. "You didn't suspect a hothouse?"

"Or that she just wanted to please me?"

"Am I supposed to guess?" Teg asked.

After a long silence, Mentat gaze locked to Mentat gaze, Idaho said: "There's anarchy behind my confinement, Bell. Disagreement in your highest councils."

"There can be deliberation and judgment even in anarchy," she said.

"You're a hypocrite, Bell!"

She drew back as though he had struck her, a purely involuntary movement that shocked her by the forced reaction. *Voice?* No . . . something reaching deeper. She was suddenly terrified of this man.

"I find it marvelous that a Mentat *and a Reverend Mother* could be such a hypocrite," he said.

Teg tugged at Idaho's arm. "Are you fighting?"

Idaho brushed the hand away. "Yes, we're fighting."

Bellonda could not tear her gaze from Idaho's. She wanted to turn and flee. What was he doing? This had gone completely awry!

"Hypocrites and criminals among you?" he asked.

Once more, Bellonda remembered the comeyes. He was playing not only her but the watchers as well! And doing it with exquisite care. She was suddenly filled with admiration for his performance but this did not allay her fear.

"I ask why your Sisters tolerate you?" His lips moved with such delicate precision! "Are you a necessary evil? A source of valuable data and, occasionally, good advice?"

She found her voice. "How dare you?" Guttural and containing all of her vaunted viciousness.

"It could be that you strengthen your Sisters." Voice flat, not changing tone in the slightest. "Weak links create places others must reinforce and that would strengthen those others."

Bellonda realized she was barely keeping her hold on Mentat

mode. Could any of this be true? Was it possible Mother Superior saw her that way?

"You came with criminal disobedience in mind," he said. "All in the name of necessity! A little drama for the comeyes, proving you had no other choice."

She found his words restoring Mentat abilities. Did he do that knowingly? She was fascinated by the need to study his manner as well as his words. Did he really read her that well? The record of this encounter might be far more valuable than her little playlet. And the outcome no different!

"You think Mother Superior's wishes are law?" she asked.

"Do you really think me unobservant?" Waving a hand at Teg, who started to interrupt. "Bell! Be only a Mentat."

"I hear you." *And so do many others!*

"I'm deep into your problem."

"We've given you no problem!"

"But you have. *You* have, Bell. You're misers the way you parcel out the pieces but I see it."

Bellonda abruptly remembered Odrade saying: "I don't need a Mentat! I need an inventor."

"You . . . need . . . me," Idaho said. "Your problem is still in its shell but the meat's there and must be extracted."

"Why would we possibly need you?"

"You need my imagination, my inventiveness, things that kept me alive in the face of Leto's wrath."

"You've said he killed you so many times you lost count." *Eat your own words, Mentat!*

He gave her an exquisitely controlled smile, so precise that neither she nor the comeyes could mistake its intent. "But how can you trust me, Bell?"

He condemns himself!

"Without something new you're doomed," he said. "Only a matter of time and you all know it. Perhaps not this generation. Perhaps not even the next one. But inevitably."

Teg pulled sharply at Idaho's sleeve. "The Bashar could help, couldn't he?"

So the boy really listened. Idaho patted Teg's arm. "The Bashar's not enough." Then to Bellonda: "Underdogs together. Must we growl over the same bone?"

"You've said that before." *And doubtless will say it again.*

"Still Mentat?" he asked. "Then discard drama! Get the romantic haze off our problem."

Dar's the romantic! Not me!

"What's romantic," he asked, "about little pockets of Scattered Bene Gesserit waiting to be slaughtered?"

"You think none will escape?"

"You're seeding the universe with enemies," he said. "You're feeding Honored Matres!"

She was fully (and only) Mentat then, required to match this ghola ability for ability. Drama? Romance? The body got in the way of Mentat performance. Mentats must use the body, not let it interfere.

"No Reverend Mother you've Scattered has ever returned or sent a message," he said. "You try to reassure yourselves by saying only the Scattered ones know where they go. How can you ignore the message they send in this other fact? Why has not one tried to communicate with Chapterhouse?"

He's chiding all of us, damn him! And he's right.

"Have I stated our problem in its most elemental form?"

Mentat questioning!

"Simplest question, simplest projection," she agreed.

"Amplified sexual ecstasy: Bene Gesserit imprint? Are Honored Matres trapping your people out there?"

"Murbella?" A one-word challenge. *Assess this woman you say you love! Does she know things we should know?*

"They're conditioned against raising their own enjoyment to addictive levels but they are vulnerable."

"She denies there are Bene Gesserit sources in Honored Matre history."

"As she was conditioned to do."

"A lust for power instead?"

"At last, you have asked a proper question." And when she did not reply, he said: "Mater Felicissima." Addressing her by the ancient term for Bene Gesserit Council members.

She knew why he did it and felt the word produce the wanted effect. She was firmly balanced now. Mentat Reverend Mother encompassed by the *mohalata* of her own Spice Agony—that union of benign Other Memory protecting her from domination by malignant ancestors.

How did he know to do that? Every observer behind the comeyes would be asking that question. *Of course! The Tyrant trained him thus, time and time again. What do we have here? What is this talent Mother Superior dares employ? Dangerous, yes, but far more valuable than I suspected. By the gods of our own creation! Is he the tool to free us?*

How calm he was. He knew he had caught her.

"In one of my lives, Bell, I visited your Bene Gesserit house on Wallach IX and there talked to one of your ancestors, Tersius Helen Anteac. Let her guide you, Bell. She knows."

Bellonda felt familiar prodding in her mind. *How could he know Anteac was my ancestor?*

"I went to Wallach IX at the Tyrant's command," he said. "Oh, yes! I often thought of him as Tyrant. My orders were to suppress the Mentat school you thought you had hidden there."

Anteac-simulflow intruded: *"I show you now the event of which he speaks."*

"Consider," he said. "I, a Mentat, forced to suppress a school that trained people the way I was trained. I knew why he ordered it, of course, and so do you."

Simulflow poured it through her awareness: *Order of Mentats, founded by Gilbertus Albans; temporary sanctuary with Bene Tleilax who hoped to incorporate them into Tleilaxu hegemony; spread into uncounted "seed schools"; suppressed by Leto II because they formed a nu-*

cleus of independent opposition; spread into the Scattering after the Famine.

"He kept a few of the finest teachers on Dune, but the question Anteac forces you to confront now does not go there. Where have your Sisters gone, Bell?"

"We have no way of knowing yet, do we?" She looked at his console with new awareness. It was wrong to block such a mind. If they were to use him, they must use him fully.

"By the way, Bell," as she stood to leave. "Honored Matres could be a relatively small group."

Small? Didn't he know how the Sisterhood was being overwhelmed by terrifying numbers on planet after planet?

"All numbers are relative. Is there something in the universe truly immovable? Our Old Empire could be a last retreat for them, Bell. A place to hide and try to regroup."

"You suggested that before . . . to Dar."

Not Mother Superior. Not Odrade. Dar. He smiled. "And perhaps we could help with Scytale."

"We?"

"Murbella to gather information, I to assess it."

He did not like the smile this produced.

"Precisely what are you suggesting?"

"Let our imaginations roam and fashion our experiments accordingly. Of what use would even a no-planet be if someone could penetrate the shielding?"

She glanced at the boy. Idaho knew their suspicion that the Bashar had *seen* the no-ships? Naturally! A Mentat of his abilities . . . bits and pieces assembled into a masterful projection.

"It would require the entire output of a G-3 sun to shield any halfway livable planet." Dry and very cool the way she looked down at him.

"Nothing is out of the question in the Scattering."

"But not within our present capabilities. Do you have something less ambitious?"

"Review the genetic markers in the cells of your people. Look for common patterns in Atreides inheritance. There may be talents you have not even guessed."

"Your inventive imagination bounces around."

"G-3 suns to genetics. There may be common factors."

Why these mad suggestions? No-planets and people for whom prescient shields are transparent? What is he doing?

She did not flatter herself that he spoke only for her benefit. There were always the comeyes.

He remained silent, one arm thrown negligently across the boy's shoulders. Both of them watching her! A challenge?

Be a Mentat if you can!

No-planets? As the mass of an object increased, energy to nullify gravitation passed thresholds matched to prime numbers. No-shields met even greater energy barriers. Another magnitude of exponential increase. Was Idaho suggesting that someone in the Scattering might have found a way around the problem? She asked him.

"Ixians have not penetrated Holzmann's unification concept," he said. "They merely use it—a theory that works even when you don't understand it."

Why does he direct my attention to the technocracy of Ix? Ixians had their fingers in too many pies for the Bene Gesserit to trust them.

"Aren't you curious why the Tyrant never suppressed Ix?" he asked. And when she continued to stare at him: "He only bridled them. He was fascinated by the idea of human and machine inextricably bound to each other, each testing the limits of the other."

"Cyborgs?"

"Among other things."

Didn't Idaho know the residue of revulsion left by the Butlerian Jihad even among the Bene Gesserit? Alarming! The convergence of what each—human *and* machine—could do. Considering machine limitations, that was a succinct description of Ixian shortsightedness. Was Idaho saying the Tyrant subscribed to the idea of Machine Intelligence? Foolishness! She turned away from him.

"You're leaving too quickly, Bell. You should be more interested in Sheeana's immunity to sexual bonding. The young men I send for polishing are *not* imprinted and neither is she. Yet no Honored Matre is more of an adept."

Bellonda saw now the value Odrade placed in this ghola. *Priceless! And I might have killed him.* This nearness of that error filled her with dismay.

When she reached the doorway, he stopped her once more. "The Futars I saw on Gammu—why were we told they hunt and kill Honored Matres? Murbella knows nothing of this."

Bellonda left without looking back. Everything she had learned about Idaho today increased his danger . . . but they had to live with it . . . for now.

Idaho took a deep breath and looked at the puzzled Teg. "Thank you for being here and I do appreciate the fact that you remained silent in the face of great provocation."

"She wouldn't really have killed you . . . would she?"

"If you had not gained me those first few seconds, she might have."

"Why?"

"She has the mistaken idea that I might be a Kwisatz Haderach."

"Like Muad'Dib?"

"And his son."

"Well, she won't hurt you now."

Idaho looked at the door where Bellonda had gone. Reprieve. That was all he had achieved. Perhaps he no longer was *just* a cog in the machinations of others. They had achieved a new relationship, one that could keep him alive if carefully exploited. Emotional attachments had never figured in it, not even with Murbella . . . nor with Odrade. Deep down, Murbella resented sexual bondage as much as he did. Odrade might hint at ancient ties of Atreides loyalty but emotions in a Reverend Mother could not be trusted.

Atreides! He looked at Teg, seeing family appearance already beginning to shape the immature face.

And what have I really achieved with Bell? They no longer were likely to provide him with false data. He could place a certain reliance in what a Reverend Mother told him, coloring this by awareness that any human might make mistakes.

I'm not the only one in a special school. The Sisters are in my school now!

"May I go find Murbella?" Teg asked. "She promised to teach me how to fight with my feet. I don't think the Bashar ever learned that."

"*Who* never learned it?"

Head down, abashed. "*I* never learned it."

"Murbella's on the practice floor. Run along. But let me tell her about Bellonda."

Schooling in a Bene Gesserit environment never stopped, Idaho thought as he watched the boy leave. But Murbella was right when she said they were learning things available only from the Sisters.

This thought stirred misgivings. He saw an image in memory: Scytale standing behind the field barrier in a corridor. What was their fellow prisoner learning? Idaho shuddered. Thinking of the Tleilaxu always called up memories of Face Dancers. And that recalled Face Dancer ability to "reprint" the memories of anyone they killed. This in its turn filled him with fears of his visions. Face Dancers?

And I am a Tleilaxu experiment.

This was not something he dared explore with a Reverend Mother or even within the sight or hearing of one.

He went out in the corridors then and into Murbella's quarters, where he settled himself in a chair and examined the residue of a lesson she had studied. Voice. There was the clairtone she used to echo her vocal experiments. The breathing harness to force pranabindu responses lay across a chair, carelessly discarded in a tangle. She had bad habits from Honored Matre days.

Murbella found him there when she returned. She wore skin-tight white leotards blotched with perspiration and was in a hurry to remove this clothing and make herself comfortable. He stopped her on her way to the shower, using one of the tricks he had learned.

"I've discovered some things about the Sisterhood that we didn't know before."

"Tell me!" It was *his* Murbella demanding this, perspiration glistening on her oval face, green eyes admiring. *My Duncan saw through them again!*

"A game where one of the pieces cannot be moved," he reminded her. *Let the comeye watchdogs play with that one!* "They not only expect me to help them create a new religion around Sheeana, *our willing participation in their dream,* I'm supposed to be their gadfly, their conscience, making them question their own excuses for *extraordinary behavior.*"

"Has Odrade been here?"

"Bellonda."

"Duncan! That one is dangerous. You should never see her alone."

"The boy was with me."

"He never said!"

"He obeys orders."

"All right! What happened?"

He gave her a brief account, even to describing Bellonda's facial expressions and other reactions. (And wouldn't the comeye watchers have great sport with that!)

Murbella was enraged. "If she harms you I will never again cooperate with any of them!"

Right on cue, my darling. Consequences! You Bene Gesserit witches should re-examine your behavior with great care.

"I'm still stinking from the practice floor," she said. "That boy. He is a quick one. I've never seen a child that bright."

He stood. "Here, I'll scrub you."

In the shower, he helped her out of the sweaty leotards, his hands cool on her skin. He could see how much she enjoyed his touch.

"So gentle and yet so strong," she whispered.

Gods below! The way she looked at him, as though she could devour him.

For once, Murbella's thoughts of Idaho were free of self-accusation. *I remember no moment when I awakened and said: "I love him!"* No, it had wormed its way into this deeper and deeper addiction until, accomplished fact, it must be accepted in every living moment. Like breathing . . . or heartbeats. *A flaw? The Sisterhood is wrong!*

"Wash my back," she said and laughed when the shower drenched his clothing. She helped him undress and there in the shower it happened once more: this uncontrollable compulsion, this male-female mingling that drove away everything except sensation. Only afterward could she remember and say to herself: *He knows every technique I do.* But it was more than technique. *He wants to please me! Dear Gods of Dur! How was I ever this fortunate?*

She clung to his neck while he carried her out of the shower and dropped her still wet onto her bed. She pulled him down beside her and they lay there quietly, letting their energies rebuild.

Presently, she whispered: "So the Missionaria will use Sheeana."

"Very dangerous."

"Puts the Sisterhood in an exposed position. I thought they always tried to avoid that."

"From my point of view, it's ludicrous."

"Because they intended you to control Sheeana?"

"No one can control her! Perhaps no one should." He looked up at the comeyes. "Hey, Bell! You have more than one tiger by the tail."

Bellonda, returning to Archives, stopped at the door of Comeye-Recording and looked a question at the Watch Mother.

"In the shower again," the Watch Mother said. "It gets boring after a while."

"Participation Mystique!" Bellonda said and strode off to her quarters, her mind roiling with changed perceptions that needed reorganizing. *He's a better Mentat than I am!*

I'm jealous of Sheeana, damn her! And he knows it!

Participation Mystique! The orgy as energizer. Honored Matre sexual knowledge was having an effect on the Bene Gesserit akin to that primitive submersion in shared ecstasy. We take one step toward it and one step away.

Just knowing this thing exists! How repellent, how dangerous . . . and yet, how magnetic.

And Sheeana is immune! Damn her! Why did Idaho have to remind them of that just now?

Give me the judgment of balanced minds in preference to laws every time. Codes and manuals create patterned behavior. All patterned behavior tends to go unquestioned, gathering destructive momentum.

—DARWI ODRADE

Tamalane appeared in Odrade's quarters at Eldio just before dawn, bringing news about the glazeway ahead of them.

"Drifting sand has made the road dangerous or impassable in six places beyond the sea. Very large dunes."

Odrade had just completed her daily regimen: mini-Agony of spice followed by exercise and cold shower. Eldio's guest sleeping cell had only one slingchair (they knew her preferences) and she had seated herself to await Streggi and the morning report.

Tamalane's face appeared sallow in the light of two silvery glowglobes but there was no mistaking her satisfaction. *If you had listened to me in the first place!*

"Get us 'thopters," Odrade said.

Tamalane left, obviously disappointed at Mother Superior's mild reaction.

Odrade summoned Streggi. "Check alternate roads. Find out about passage around the sea's western end."

Streggi hurried away, almost colliding with Tamalane who was returning.

"I regret to inform you that Transport cannot give us enough 'thopters immediately. They are relocating five communities east of us. We probably can have them by noon."

"Isn't there an observation terminal at the edge of that desert spur south of us?" Odrade asked.

"The first obstruction is just beyond it." Tamalane still was too pleased with herself.

"Have the 'thopters meet us there," Odrade said. "We will leave immediately after breakfast."

"But Dar . . ."

"Tell Clairby you are riding with me today. Yes, Streggi?" The acolyte stood in the doorway behind Tamalane.

The set of her shoulders as she left said Tamalane did not take the new seating arrangements as forgiveness. *On the coals!* But Tam's behavior fitted itself to their need.

"We can get to the observation terminal," Streggi said, indicating she had heard. "We'll stir up dust and sand but it's safe."

"Let's hurry breakfast."

The closer they came to the desert, the more barren the country, and Odrade commented on this as they sped south.

Within one hundred klicks of the last reported desert fringe, they saw signs of communities uprooted and removed to colder latitudes. Bare foundations, unsalvageable walls damaged in dismantling and left behind. Pipes cut off at foundation level. Too expensive to dig them out. Sand would cover all of this unsightly mess before long.

They had no Shield Wall here as there had been on Dune, Odrade observed to Streggi. Someday soon, the population of Chapterhouse would remove itself to polar regions and mine the ice for water.

"Is it true, Mother Superior," someone in back with Tamalane asked, "that we're already making spice-harvesting equipment?"

Odrade turned in her seat. The question had come from a Communications clerk, senior acolyte: an older woman with responsibility wrinkles deep in her forehead; dark and squinty from long hours at her equipment.

"We must be ready for the worms," Odrade said.

"If they come," Tamalane said.

"Have you ever walked on the desert, Tam?" Odrade asked.

"I was on Dune." Very short answer.

"But did you go out into open desert?"

"Only to some small drifts near Keen."

"That is not the same." A short answer deserved an equally short rejoinder.

"Other Memory tells me what I need to know." That was for the acolytes.

"It's not the same, Tam. You have to do it yourself. A very curious sensation on Dune, knowing a worm could come at any instant and consume you."

"I've heard about your Dune . . . exploit."

Exploit. Not "experience." Exploit. Very precise with her censure. Quite like Tam. "Too much of Bell has rubbed off on her," some will say.

"Walking on that sort of desert changes you, Tam. Other Memory becomes clearer. It's one thing to tap experiences of a Fremen ancestor. It's quite different walking there as a Fremen yourself, if only for a few hours."

"I did not enjoy it."

So much for Tam's venturesome spirit, and everyone in the car had seen her in a bad light. Word would spread.

On the coals, indeed!

But now the shift to Sheeana on the Council (*if she suits*) would have an easier explanation.

The observation terminal was a fused expanse of silica, green and glassy with heat bubbles through it. Odrade stood at the fused edge and noted how grass below her ended in patches, sand already invading the lower slopes of this once verdant hill. There were new saltbushes (planted by Sheeana's people, one of Odrade's entourage said) forming a random gray screen along the encroaching fingers of desert. A silent war. Chlorophyll-based life fighting a rear-guard action against the sand.

A low dune lifted above the terminal to her right. Waving for the others not to follow, she climbed the sandhill, and just beyond its concealing bulk, there was the desert of memory.

So this is what we are creating.

No signs of habitation. She did not look back at growing things making their last desperate struggle against invading dunes but kept her attention focused outward to the horizon. There was the boundary desert dwellers watched. Anything moving in that dry expanse was potentially dangerous.

When she returned to the others, she kept her gaze for a time on the glazed surface of the terminal.

The older Communications acolyte came up to Odrade with a request from Weather.

Odrade scanned it. Concise and inescapable. Nothing sudden about the changes spelled out in these words. They were asking for more ground equipment. This did not come with the abruptness of an accidental storm but with Mother Superior's decision.

Yesterday? Did I decide to phase out the sea only yesterday?

She returned the report to the Communications acolyte and looked beyond her at the sand-marked glaze.

"Request approved." Then: "It saddens me to see all of those buildings gone back there."

The acolyte shrugged. *She shrugged!* Odrade felt like striking her. (And wouldn't that send upsets rumbling through the Sisterhood!)

Odrade turned her back on the woman.

What could I possibly say to her? We have been on this ground five times the lifetime of our oldest sisters. And this one shrugs.

Yet . . . by some standards, she knew the Sisterhood's installations had barely reached maturity. Plaz and plasteel tended to maintain an orderly relationship between buildings and their settings. *Fixed in land and memory.* Towns and cities did not submit easily to other forces . . . except to human whims.

Another natural force.

The concept of respect for age was an odd one, she decided. Humans carried it inborn. She had seen it in the old Bashar when he spoke of his family holdings on Lernaeus.

"We thought it fitting to keep my mother's decor."

Continuity. Would a revived ghola revive those feelings as well?

This is where my kind have been.

That took on a peculiar patina when "my kind" were blood-related ancestors.

Look how long we Atreides persisted on Caladan, restoring the old castle, polishing deep carvings in ancient wood. Whole teams of retainers just to keep the creaking old place at a level of barely tolerable functionalism.

But those retainers had not thought themselves ill used. There had been a sense of privilege in their labors. Hands that polished the wood almost caressed it.

"Old. Been with the Atreides a long time now."

People and their artifacts. She felt tool sense as a living part of herself.

"I'm better because of this stick in my hand . . . because of this fire-sharpened spear to kill my meat . . . because of this shelter against the cold . . . because of my stone cellar to store our winter food . . . because of this swift sailing vessel . . . this giant ocean liner . . . this ship of metal and ceramics that carries me into space . . ."

Those first human venturers into space—how little they suspected of where the voyage would extend. How isolated they were in those ancient times! Little capsules of livable atmosphere linked to cumbersome data sources by primitive transmission systems. Solitude. Loneliness. Limited opportunity for anything but surviving. Keep the air washed. Be sure of potable water. Exercise to prevent the debilitation of weightlessness. Stay active. Healthy mind in a healthy body. What was a healthy mind, anyway?

"Mother Superior?"

That damned Communications acolyte again!

"Yes?"

"Bellonda says to tell you immediately there has been a messenger from Buzzell. Strangers came and took all of the Reverend Mothers away."

Odrade whirled. "Her entire message?"

"No, Mother Superior. The strangers are described as commanded by a woman. The messenger says she had the look of an Honored Matre but was not wearing one of their robes."

"Nothing from Dortujla or the others?"

"They were not given the opportunity, Mother Superior. The messenger is a First-Stage acolyte. She came in the small no-ship following explicit orders from Dortujla."

"Tell Bell that acolyte must not be allowed to leave. She has dangerous information. I will brief a messenger when I return. It must be a Reverend Mother. Do you have that?"

"Of course, Mother Superior." Hurt at the suggestion of doubt.

It was happening! Odrade contained her excitement with difficulty. *They have taken the bait. Now . . . are they on the hook?*

Dortujla did a dangerous thing depending on an acolyte that way. Knowing Dortujla, that must be an extremely reliable acolyte. Prepared to kill herself if captured. I must see this acolyte. She may be ready for the Agony. And perhaps that's a message Dortujla sends me. It would be like her.

Bell would be incensed, of course. *Foolish to depend on someone from a punishment station!*

Odrade summoned a Communications team. "Set up a link with Bellonda."

The portable projector was not as clear as a fixed installation but Bell and her setting were recognizable.

Sitting at my table as though she owned it. Excellent!

Not giving Bellonda time for one of her outbursts, Odrade said: "Determine if that messenger acolyte is ready for the Agony."

"She is." *Gods below! That was terse for Bell.*

"Then see to it. Perhaps she can be our messenger."

"Already have."

"Is she resourceful?"

"Very."

What in the name of all the devils has happened to Bell? She's acting extremely odd. Not like her usual self at all. Duncan!

"Oh, and Bell, I want Duncan to have an open link with Archives."

"Did that this morning."

Well, well. Contact with Duncan is having its effect.

"I'll talk to you after I've seen Sheeana."

"Tell Tam she was right."

"About what?"

"Just tell her."

"Very well. I must say, Bell, I couldn't be more satisfied with the way you're handling matters."

"After the way you've handled me, how could I fail?"

Bellonda was actually smiling as they broke the connection. Odrade turned to find Tamalane standing behind her.

"Right about what, Tam?"

"That there's more to contacts between Idaho and Sheeana than we've suspected." Tamalane moved close to Odrade and lowered her voice. "Don't put her in my chair without discovering what they keep secret."

"I'm aware you knew my intentions, Tam. But . . . am I that transparent?"

"In some things, Dar."

"I'm fortunate to have you as a friend."

"You have other supporters. When the Proctors voted, it was your creativity that worked for you. 'Inspired' is the way one of your defenders put it."

"Then you know I'll have Sheeana on the coals quite thoroughly before I make one of my *inspired* decisions."

"Of course."

Odrade signaled Communications to remove the projector and went to wait at the edge of the glassy area.

Creative imagination.

She knew the mixed feelings of her associates.

Creativity!

Always dangerous to entrenched power. Always coming up with something new. New things could destroy the grip of authority. Even the Bene Gesserit approached creativity with misgivings. Maintaining an even keel inspired some to shunt boat-rockers aside. That was an element behind Dortujla's posting. The trouble was that creative ones tended to welcome backwaters. They called it *privacy*. It had taken quite a force to bring Dortujla out.

Be well, Dortujla. Be the best bait we ever used.

The 'thopters came then—sixteen of them, pilots showing displeasure at this added assignment after all the trouble they had been through. *Moving whole communities!*

In a fragile mood, Odrade watched the 'thopters settle to the hard-glazed surface, wing fans folding back into pod sleeves—each craft like a sleeping insect.

An insect designed in its own likeness by a mad robot.

When they were airborne, Streggi once more seated beside Odrade, Streggi asked: "Will we see sandworms?"

"Possibly. But there are no reports of them yet."

Streggi sat back, disappointed by the answer but unable to lever it into another question. Truth could be upsetting at times and they had such high expectations invested in this evolutionary gamble, Odrade thought.

Else why destroy everything we loved on Chapterhouse?

Simulflow intruded with an image of a long-ago sign arching over a narrow entry to a pink brick building: HOSPITAL FOR INCURABLE DISEASES.

Was that where the Sisterhood found itself? Or was it that they tolerated too many failures? Intrusive Other Memory had to have its purpose.

Failures?

Odrade searched it out: *If it comes, we must think of Murbella as a Sister.* Not that their captive Honored Matre was an incurable failure. But she was a misfit and undergoing the deep training at a very late age.

How quiet they were all around her, everyone looking out at windswept sand—whaleback dunes giving way at times to dry wavelets. Early afternoon sun had just begun to provide sufficient sidelighting to define near vistas. Dust obscured the horizon ahead.

Odrade curled up in her seat and slept. *I've seen this before. I survived Dune.*

The stir as they came down and circled over Sheeana's Desert Watch Center awakened her.

Desert Watch Center. We're at it again. We haven't really named it . . . no more than we gave a name to this planet. Chapterhouse! What kind of a name is that? Desert Watch Center! Description, not a name. Accent on the temporary.

As they descended, she saw confirmations of her thought. The sense of temporary housing was amplified by spartan abruptness in all junctures. No softness, no rounding of any connection. *This attaches here and that goes over there.* All joined by removable connectors.

It was a bumpy landing, the pilot telling them that way: "Here you are and good riddance."

Odrade went immediately to the room always set aside for her and summoned Sheeana. Temporary quarters: another spartan cubicle with hard cot. Two chairs this time. A window looked westward onto desert. The temporary nature of these rooms grated on her. Anything here could be dismantled in hours and carted away. She washed her face in the adjoining bathroom, getting the most out of movement. She had slept in a cramped position on the 'thopter and her body complained.

Refreshed, she went out to a window, thankful that the erection crew had included this tower: ten floors, and this the ninth. Sheeana occupied the top floor, a vantage for doing what the name of the place described.

While waiting, Odrade made necessary preparations.

Open the mind. Shed preconceptions.

First impressions when Sheeana arrived must be seen with naive eyes. Ears must not be prepared for a particular voice. Nose must not expect remembered odors.

I chose this one. I, her first teacher, am susceptible to mistakes.

Odrade turned at a sound from the doorway. Streggi.

"Sheeana has just returned from the desert and is with her people. She asks Mother Superior to meet her in the upper quarters, which are more comfortable."

Odrade nodded.

Sheeana's quarters on the top floor still had that prefab look at the edges. Quick shelter ahead of the desert. A large room, six or seven times the size of the guest cubicle, but then it was both workroom and sleeping chamber. Windows on two sides—west and north. Odrade was struck by the mixture of functional and non-functional.

Sheeana had managed to make her rooms reflect herself. A standard Bene Gesserit cot had been covered with a bright orange and umber spread. A black-on-white line drawing of a sandworm, head-on with all of its crystal teeth displayed, filled an end wall. Sheeana had drawn it, relying on Other Memory and her Dune childhood to guide her hand.

It said something about Sheeana that she had not attempted a more ambitious rendering—full color, perhaps, and in traditional desert setting. Just the worm and a hint of sand beneath it, a tiny robed human in the foreground.

Herself?

Admirable restraint and a constant reminder of why she was here. A deep impression of nature.

Nature makes no bad art?

It was a statement too glib to accept.

What do we mean by "nature"?

She had seen atrocious *natural* wilderness: brittle trees looking as though they had been dipped in faulty green pigment and left on a tundra's edge to dry into ugly parodies. Repellent. Hard to imagine such trees having any purpose. And blindworms . . . slimy yellow skins. Where was the art in them? Temporary stopping place on evolution's journey elsewhere. Did the intervention of humans always make a difference? Sligs! The Bene Tleilax had produced something disgusting there.

Admiring Sheeana's drawing, Odrade decided certain combinations offended particular human senses. Sligs as food were delectable. Ugly combinations touched early experiences. Experiences judged.

Bad thing!

Much of what we think of as ART caters to desires for reassurance. Don't offend me! I know what I can accept.

How did this drawing reassure Sheeana?

Sandworm: blind power guarding hidden riches. Artistry in mystic beauty.

It was reported that Sheeana joked about her assignment. "I am shepherd to worms that may never exist."

And even if they did appear, it would be years before any achieved the size indicated by her drawing. Was it her voice from the tiny figure in front of the worm?

"This will come in time."

An odor of melange pervaded the room, stronger than usual in a Reverend Mother's quarters. Odrade passed a searching look across the furnishings: chairs, worktable, illumination from anchored glowglobes—everything placed where it would serve to advantage. But what was that oddly shaped mound of black plaz in the corner? More of Sheeana's work?

These rooms fitted Sheeana, Odrade decided. Little other than the drawing to recall her origins but the view out any window might have been from Dar-es-Balat deep in Dune's dry-lands.

A small rustling sound at the doorway alerted Odrade. She turned and there was Sheeana. Almost shy the way she peered around the door before entering Mother Superior's presence.

Motion as words: *"So she did come to my rooms. Good. Someone might have been careless with my invitation."*

Odrade's readied senses tingled with Sheeana's presence. The youngest-ever Reverend Mother. You often thought of *Quiet Little Sheeana*. She was not always quiet nor was she small but the label stuck. She was not even mousy, but frequently quiet like a rodent waiting at the edge of a field for the farmer to leave. Then the mouse would come darting out to glean fallen grains.

Sheeana came fully into the room and stopped less than a pace from Odrade. "We've been too long apart, Mother Superior."

Odrade's first impression was oddly jumbled.

Candor and concealment?

Sheeana stood quietly receptive.

This descendant of Siona Atreides had developed an interesting face under the Bene Gesserit patina. Maturity working on her according to both Sisterhood and Atreides designs. Marks of many decisions firmly taken. The slender, dark-skinned waif with sun-streaked brown hair had become this poised Reverend Mother. Skin still dark from long hours in the open. Hair still sun-streaked. The eyes, though—the steely total blue that said: "I have been through the Agony."

What is it I sense in her?

Sheeana saw the look on Odrade's face (Bene Gesserit naivete!) and knew this was the long-feared confrontation.

There can be no defense except my truth and I hope she stops short of a full confession!

Odrade watched her former student with exquisite care, every sense open.

Fear! What do I sense? Something when she spoke?

The steadiness of Sheeana's voice had been shaped into the powerful instrument Odrade had anticipated at their first meeting. Sheeana's original nature (a Fremen nature if there ever was one!) had been curbed and redirected. That core of vindictiveness smoothed out. Her capacity for love and hatred brought under tight reins.

Why do I get the impression she wants to hug me?

Odrade felt suddenly vulnerable.

This woman has been inside my defenses. No way to exclude her totally ever again.

Tamalane's judgment came to mind: *"She is one of those who keeps herself to herself. Remember Sister Schwangyu? Like that one but better at it. Sheeana knows where she is going. We'll have to watch her carefully. Atreides blood, you know."*

"I'm Atreides, too, Tam."

"Don't think we ever forget it! You think we'd just stand idly by if Mother Superior chose to breed on her own? There are limits to our tolerance, Dar."

"Indeed, this visit is long overdue, Sheeana."

Odrade's tone alerted Sheeana. She stared back suddenly with that look the Sisterhood called "BG placid," than which there probably was nothing more placid in the universe, nothing more completely a mask of what occurred behind it. This was not just a barrier, it was a *nothing*. Anything on this mask would be transgression. This, in itself, was betrayal. Sheeana realized it immediately and responded with laughter.

"I knew you would come probing! The hand-talk with Duncan, right?" *Please, Mother Superior! Accept this.*

"All of it, Sheeana."

"He wants someone to rescue them if Honored Matres attack."

"That's all?" *Does she think me a complete fool?*

"No. He wants information about our intentions . . . and what we're doing to meet the Honored Matre threat."

"What have you told him?"

"Everything I could." *Truth is my only weapon. I must divert her!*

"Are you his friend at court, Sheeana?"

"Yes!"

"So am I."

"But not Tam and Bell?"

"My informants tell me Bell now tolerates him."

"Bell? Tolerant?"

"You misjudge her, Sheeana. It's a flaw in you." *She is hiding something. What have you done, Sheeana?*

"Sheeana, do you think you could work with Bell?"

"Because I tease her?" *Work with Bell? What does she mean? Not Bell to head that damnable Missionaria project!*

A faint twitching lifted the corners of Odrade's mouth. *Another prank? Could that be it?*

Sheeana was a prime gossip subject in Central's dining rooms. Stories of how she teased Breeding Mistresses (especially Bell) and elaborately detailed accounts of seductions fleshed out with Honored Matre comparisons from Murbella spiced more than the food. Odrade had heard snatches of the latest story only two days ago. "She said, 'I used the *Let-him-misbehave* method. Very effective with men who think they're leading you down the garden path.'"

"Tease? Is that what you do, Sheeana?"

"An appropriate word: reshape by going against the natural inclination." The instant the words were out of her mouth, Sheeana knew she had made a mistake.

Odrade felt warning stillness. *Reshape?* Her gaze went to that odd black mound in the corner. She stared at it with a fixity that surprised her. It drank vision. She kept probing for coherence, something that *spoke* to her. Nothing responded, not even when she probed to her limits. *And that's its purpose!*

"It's called 'Void,'" Sheeana said.

"Yours?" *Please, Sheeana. Say someone else did it. The one who did this has gone where I cannot follow.*

"I did it one night about a week ago."

Is black plaz the only thing you reshape? "A fascinating comment on art in general."

"And not on art specific?"

"I have a problem with you, Sheeana. You alarm some Sisters." *And me. There's a wild place in you we have not found. Atreides gene markers Duncan told us to seek are in your cells. What have they given you?*

"Alarm my Sisters?"

"Especially when they recall that you're the youngest ever to survive the Agony."

"Except for Abominations."

"Is that what you are?"

"Mother Superior!" *She has never deliberately hurt me except as a lesson.*

"You went through the Agony as an act of disobedience."

"Wouldn't you say rather that I went against mature advice?" *Humor sometimes distracts her.*

Prester, Sheeana's acolyte aide, came to the door and rapped lightly on the wall beside it until she had their attention. "You said I was to tell you immediately when the search teams returned."

"What do they report?"

Relief in Sheeana's voice?

"Team eight wants you to look at their scans."

"They always want that!"

Sheeana spoke with forced frustration. "Do you want to look at the scans with me, Mother Superior?"

"I'll wait here."

"This won't take long."

When they had gone, Odrade went to the western window: a clear view across rooftops to the new desert. Small dunes here. Almost sunset and that dry heat so reminiscent of Dune.

What is Sheeana hiding?

A young man, hardly more than a boy, had been sunning nude on a neighboring rooftop, face-up on a sea-green mattress with a golden towel across his face. His skin was a sun-warmed gold to match towel and pubic hair. A breeze touched a corner of the towel and lifted it. One languid hand came up and restored the cover.

How can he be idle? Night worker? Probably.

Idleness was not encouraged and this was flaunting it. Odrade smiled to herself. Anyone could be excused for assuming he was a night worker. He might be depending on that specific guess. The trick would be to remain unseen by those who knew otherwise.

I will not ask. Intelligence deserves some rewards. And, after all, he could be a night worker.

She lifted her gaze. A new pattern emerging here: exotic sunsets. Narrow band of orange drawn along the horizon, bulging where the sun had just dipped below the land. Silvery blue above the orange went darker overhead. She had seen this many times on Dune. Meteorological explanations she did not care to explore. Better to let eyes absorb this transient beauty; better to permit ears and skin to feel sudden stillness descend upon this land in the quick darkness after the orange vanished.

Faintly, she saw the young man pick up mattress and towel and vanish behind a ventilator.

A sound of running in the corridor behind her. Sheeana entered almost breathless. "They found a spice mass thirty klicks northeast of us! Small but compact!"

Odrade did not dare hope. "Could it be wind accumulation?"

"Not likely. I've set a round-the-clock watch on it." Sheeana glanced at the window where Odrade stood. *She has seen Trebo. Perhaps . . .*

"I asked you earlier, Sheeana, if you could work with Bell. It was an important question. Tam is getting very old and must be replaced soon. There must be a vote, of course."

"Me?" It was totally unexpected.

"My first choice." *Imperative now. I want you close where I can keep watch on you.*

"But I thought . . . I mean, the Missionaria's plan . . ."

"That can wait. And there must be someone else who can shepherd worms . . . if that spice mass is what we hope."

"Oh? Yes . . . several of our people but no one who . . . Don't you want me to test whether the worms still respond to me?"

"Work on the Council should not interfere with that."

"I . . . you can see I'm surprised."

"I would have said shocked. Tell me, Sheeana, what really interests you these days?"

Still probing. Trebo, serve me now! "Making sure the desert grows well." *Truth!* "And my sex life, of course. You saw the young man on the roof next door? Trebo, a new one Duncan sent me for polishing."

Even after Odrade had gone, Sheeana wondered why those words had aroused such merriment. Mother Superior had been deflected, though.

No need even to waste her fallback position—truth: *"We've been discussing the possibility that I might imprint Teg and restore the Bashar's memories that way."*

Full confession avoided. *Mother Superior did not learn that I have weaseled out the way to reactivate our no-ship prison and defuse the mines Bellonda put in it.*

No sweeteners will cloak some forms of bitterness. If it tastes
bitter, spit it out. That's what our earliest ancestors did.

—THE CODA

Murbella found herself arising in the night to continue a dream although quite awake and aware of her surroundings: Duncan asleep
beside her, faint ticking of machinery, the chronoprojection on the
ceiling. She insisted on Duncan's presence at night lately, fearful when
alone. He blamed the fourth pregnancy.

She sat on the edge of the bed. The room was ghostly in the dim
light of the chrono. Dream images persisted.

Duncan grumbled and rolled toward her. An outflung arm draped
itself across her legs.

She felt that this mental intrusion was not dreamstuff but it had
some of those characteristics. Bene Gesserit teachings did this. Them
and their damned suggestions about Scytale and . . . and everything!
They precipitated motion she could not control.

Tonight, she was lost in an insane world of words. The cause was
clear. Bellonda that morning had learned Murbella spoke nine languages and had aimed the suspicious acolyte down a mental path
called "Linguistic Heritage." But Bell's influence on this nighttime
madness provided no escape.

Nightmare. She was a creature of microscopic size trapped in
an enormous echoing place labeled in giant letters wherever she

turned: "Data Reservoir." Animated words with grimacing jaws and fearsome tentacles surrounded her.

Predatory beasts and she was their prey!

Awake and knowing she sat on the edge of her bed with Duncan's arm on her legs, she still saw the beasts. They herded her backward. She *knew* she was going backward although her body did not move. They pressed her toward a terrible disaster she could not see. Her head would not turn! Not only did she see these creatures (they hid parts of her sleeping chamber) but she heard them in a cacophony of her nine languages.

They will tear me apart!

Although she could not turn, she sensed what lay behind her: more teeth and claws. Threat all around! If they cornered her, they would pounce and she was doomed.

Done for. Dead. Victim. Torture-captive. Fair game.

Despair filled her. Why would Duncan not awaken and save her? His arm was a lead weight, part of the force holding her and allowing these creatures to herd her into their bizarre trap. She trembled. Perspiration poured from her body. Awful words! They united into giant combinations. A creature with knife-fanged mouth came directly toward her and she saw more words in the gaping blackness between its jaws.

See above.

Murbella began to laugh. She had no control of it. *See above. Done for. Dead. Victim . . .*

The laughter awakened Duncan. He sat up, activated a low glowglobe, and stared at her. How tousled he looked after their earlier sexual collision.

His expression hovered between amusement and upset at being awakened. "Why are you laughing?"

Laughter subsided in gasps. Her sides ached. She was afraid his tentative smile would ignite a new spasm. "Oh . . . oh! Duncan! Sexual collision!"

He knew this was their mutual term for the addiction that bound them but why would it make her laugh?

His puzzled expression struck her as ludicrous.

Between gasps, she said: "Two more words." And she had to clamp her mouth closed to prevent another outburst.

"What?"

His voice was the funniest thing she had ever heard. She thrust a hand at him and shook her head. "Ohhh . . . ohhh . . ."

"Murbella, what's wrong with you?"

She could only continue shaking her head.

He tried a tentative smile. It gentled her and she leaned against him. "No!" When his right hand wandered. "I just want to be close."

"Look what time it is." He lifted his chin toward the ceiling projection. "Almost three."

"It was so funny, Duncan."

"So tell me about it."

"When I catch my breath."

He eased her down onto her pillow. "We're like a damned old married couple. Funny stories in the middle of the night."

"No, darling, we're different."

"A question of degree, nothing else."

"Quality," she insisted.

"What was so funny?"

She recounted her nightmare and Bellonda's influence.

"Zensunni. Very ancient technique. The Sisters use it to rid you of trauma connections. Words that ignite unconscious responses."

Fear returned.

"Murbella, why are you trembling?"

"Honored Matre teachers warned us terrible things would happen if we fell into Zensunni hands."

"Bullcrap! I went through the same thing as a Mentat."

His words conjured another dream fragment. A beast with two heads. Both mouths open. Words in there. On the left, "One word," and on the right, "leads to another."

Mirth displaced fear. It subsided without laughter. "Duncan!"

"Mmmmmmm." Mentat distance in the sound.

"Bell said the Bene Gesserit use words as weapons—Voice. 'Tools of control,' she called them."

"A lesson you must learn almost as instinct. They'll never trust you into the deeper training until you learn this."

And I won't trust you afterward.

She rolled away from him and looked at the comeyes glittering in the ceiling around the time projection.

I'm still on probation.

She was aware her teachers discussed her privately. Conversations were choked off when she approached. They stared at her in their special way, as though she were an interesting specimen.

Bellonda's voice cluttered her mind.

Nightmare tendrils. Midmorning then and the sweat of her own exertions a stink in her nostrils. Probationer a dutiful three paces from Reverend Mother. Bell's voice:

"Never be an expert. That locks you up tight."

All of this because I asked if there were no words to guide the Bene Gesserit.

"Duncan, why do they mix mental and physical teaching?"

"Mind and body reinforce each other." Sleepy. *Damn him! He's going back to sleep.*

She shook Duncan's shoulder. "If words are so damned unimportant, why do they talk about disciplines so much?"

"Patterns," he mumbled. "Dirty word."

"What?" She shook him more roughly.

He turned onto his back, moving his lips, then: "Discipline equals pattern equals bad way to go. They say we're all natural pattern creators . . . means 'order' to them, I think."

"Why is that so bad?"

"Gives others handle to destroy us or traps us in . . . in things we won't change."

"You're wrong about mind and body."

"Hmmmmph?"

"It's pressures locking one to the other."

"Isn't that what I said? Hey! Are we going to talk or sleep or what?"

"No more 'or what.' Not tonight."

A deep sigh lifted his chest.

"They're not out to improve my health," she said.

"Nobody said they were."

"That comes later, after the Agony." She knew he hated reminders of that deadly trial but there was no avoiding it. The prospect filled her mind.

"All right!" He sat up, punched his pillow into shape and leaned back against it to study her. "What's up?"

"They're so damned clever with their word-weapons! She brought Teg to you and said you were fully responsible for him."

"You don't believe it?"

"He thinks of you as his father."

"Not really."

"No, but . . . did you think that about the Bashar?"

"When he restored my memories? Yeah."

"You're a pair of intellectual orphans, always looking for parents who aren't there. He hasn't the faintest idea of how much you will hurt him."

"That tends to split up the family."

"So you hate the Bashar in him and you're glad you'll hurt him."

"Didn't say that."

"Why is he so important?"

"The Bashar? Military genius. Always doing the unexpected. Confounds his foes by appearing where they never expect him to be."

"Can't anyone do that?"

"Not the way he does it. He invents tactics and strategies. Just like that!" Snapping his fingers.

"More violence. Just like Honored Matres."

"Not always. Bashar had a reputation for winning without battle."

"I've seen the histories."

"Don't trust them."

"But you just said . . ."

"Histories focus on confrontations. Some truth in that but it hides more persistent things that go on in spite of upheavals."

"Persistent things?"

"What history touches the woman in the rice paddy driving her water buffalo ahead of her plow while her husband is off somewhere, most likely a conscript, carrying a weapon?"

"Why is that persistent and more important than . . ."

"Her babies at home need food. Man's away on this perennial madness? Someone has to do the plowing. She's a true image of human persistence."

"You sound so bitter . . . I find that odd."

"Considering my military *history*?"

"That, yes, the Bene Gesserit emphasis on . . . on their Bashar and elite troops and . . ."

"You think they're just more self-important people going on about their self-important violence? They'll ride right over the woman with her plow?"

"Why not?"

"Because very little escapes them. The violent ones ride *past* the plowing woman and seldom see they have touched basic reality. A Bene Gesserit would never miss such a thing."

"Again, why not?"

"The self-important have limited vision because they ride a death-reality. Woman and plow are life-reality. Without life-reality there'd be no humankind. My Tyrant saw this. The Sisters bless him for it even while they curse him."

"So you're a willing participant in their dream?"

"I guess I am." He sounded surprised.

"And you're being completely honest with Teg?"

"He asks, I give him candid answers. I don't believe in doing violence to curiosity."

"And you have full responsibility for him?"

"That isn't exactly what she said."

"Ahhhhh, my love. Not *exactly* what she said. You call Bell hypocrite and don't include Odrade. Duncan, if you only knew . . ."

"As long as we're ignoring the comeyes, spit it out!"

"Lies, cheating, vicious . . ."

"Hey! The Bene Gesserit?"

"They have that hoary old excuse: Sister A does it so if I do it that's not so bad. Two crimes cancel each other."

"What crimes?"

She hesitated. *Should I tell him? No. But he expects some answer.* "Bell's delighted the roles are reversed between you and Teg! She's looking forward to his pain."

"Maybe we should disappoint her." He knew it was a mistake to say this as soon as it was out. *Too soon.*

"Poetic justice!" Murbella was delighted.

Divert them! "They aren't interested in justice. Fairness, yes. They have this homily: 'Those against whom judgment is passed must accept the fairness of it.'"

"So they condition you to accept their judgment."

"There are loopholes in any system."

"You know, darling, acolytes learn things."

"That's why they're acolytes."

"I mean we talk to one another."

"We? You're an acolyte? You're a proselyte!"

"Whatever I am, I've heard stories. Your Teg may not be what he seems."

"Acolyte gossip."

"There are stories out of Gammu, Duncan."

He stared at her. *Gammu? He could never think of it by any name other than the original: Giedi Prime. Harkonnen hell hole.*

She took his silence as an invitation to continue. "They say Teg moved faster than the eye could see, that he . . ."

"Probably started those stories himself."

"Some Sisters don't discount them. They're taking a wait-and-see attitude. They want precautions."

"Haven't you learned anything about Teg from your precious *histories*? It would be typical of him to start such rumors. Make people cautious."

"But remember I was on Gammu then. Honored Matres were very upset. Enraged. Something went wrong."

"Sure. Teg did the unexpected. Surprised them. Stole one of their no-ships." He patted the wall beside him. "This one."

"The Sisterhood has its forbidden ground, Duncan. They're always telling me to wait for the Agony. All will become clear! Damn them!"

"Sounds like they're preparing you for the Missionaria teaching. Engineer religions for specific purposes and selected populations."

"You don't see anything wrong in that?"

"Morality. I don't argue that with Reverend Mothers."

"Why not?"

"Religions founder on that rock. BGs don't founder."

Duncan, if you only knew their morality! "It annoys them that you know so much about them."

"Bell only wanted to kill me because of it."

"You don't think Odrade is just as bad?"

"What a question!" *Odrade? A terrifying woman if you let yourself dwell on her abilities. Atreides, for all that. I've known Atreides and Atreides. This one is Bene Gesserit first. Teg's the Atreides ideal.*

"Odrade told me she trusts your loyalty to the Atreides."

"I'm loyal to Atreides honor, Murbella." *And I make my own moral decisions—about the Sisterhood, about this child they've thrust into my care, about Sheeana and . . . and about my beloved.*

Murbella bent close to him, breast brushing his arm, and whispered in his ear. "Sometimes, I could kill any of them within my reach!"

Does she think they can't hear? He sat upright, dragging her with him. "What set you off?"

"*She* wants me to work on Scytale."

Work on. Honored Matre euphemism. *Well, why not? She "worked on" plenty of men before she ran afoul of me.* But he had an antique husband's reaction. Not only that . . . Scytale? A damned Tleilaxu?

"Mother Superior?" He had to be sure.

"The one, the only." Almost lighthearted now that she had unburdened herself.

"What's your reaction?"

"She says it was your idea."

"My . . . No way! I suggested we could try to pry information out of him but . . ."

"She says it's an ordinary thing for the Bene Gesserit just as it is with Honored Matres. Go breed with this one. Seduce that one. All in a day's work."

"I asked for *your* reaction."

"Revolted."

"Why?" *Knowing your background . . .*

"It's you I love, Duncan, and . . . and my body is . . . is to give you pleasure . . . just as you . . ."

"We're an old married couple and the witches are trying to pry us apart."

His words ignited in him a clear vision of Lady Jessica, lover of his long-dead Duke and mother of Maud'Dib. *I loved her. She didn't love me but . . .* The look he saw now in Murbella's eyes, he had seen Jessica look at the Duke that way: blind, unswerving love. The thing the Bene Gesserit distrusted. Jessica had been softer than Murbella. Hard to the core, though. And Odrade . . . she was hard at the beginning. Plasteel all the way.

Then what of the times when he had suspected her of sharing human emotions? The way she spoke of the Bashar when they learned the old man was dead on Dune.

"He was my father, you know."

Murbella dragged him out of reverie. "You may share their dream, whatever that is, but . . ."

"Grow up, humans!"

"What?"

"That's their dream. Start acting like adults and not like angry children in a schoolyard."

"Mama knows best?"

"Yes . . . I believe she does."

"Is that how you really see them? Even when you call them witches?"

"It's a good word. Witches do mysterious things."

"You don't believe it's the long and severe training plus the spice and the Agony?"

"What's belief have to do with it? Unknowns create their own mystique."

"But you don't think they trick people into doing what they want?"

"Sure they do!"

"Words as weapons, Voice, Imprinters . . ."

"None as beautiful as you."

"What's beauty, Duncan?"

"There're styles in beauty, sure."

"Exactly what she says. 'Styles based on procreative roots buried so deeply in our racial psyche we dare not remove them.' So they've thought of meddling there, Duncan."

"And they might dare anything?"

"She says, 'We won't distort our progeny into what we judge to be non-human.' They judge, they condemn."

He thought of the alien figures in his vision. Face Dancers. And he asked: "Like the amoral Tleilaxu? Amoral—not human."

"I can almost hear the gears whirling in Odrade's head. She and her Sisters—they watch, they listen, they tailor every response, everything calculated."

Is that what you want, my darling? He felt trapped. She was right and she was wrong. Ends justifying means? How could he justify losing Murbella?

"You think them amoral?" he asked.

It was as though she did not hear. "Always asking themselves what to say next to get the desired response."

"What response?" Couldn't she hear his pain?

"You never know until too late!" She turned and looked at him. "Exactly like Honored Matres. Do you know how Honored Matres trapped me?"

He could not suppress awareness of how avidly the watchdogs would hang on Murbella's next words.

"I was picked off the streets after an Honored Matre sweep. I think the whole sweep was because of me. My mother was a great beauty but she was too old for them."

"A sweep?" *The watchdogs would want me to ask.*

"They go through an area and people disappear. No bodies, nothing. Whole families vanish. It's explained as punishment because people plot against them."

"How old were you?"

"Three . . . maybe four. I was playing with friends in an open place under trees. Suddenly, there was a lot of noise and shouting. We hid in a hole behind some rocks."

He was caught in a vision of this drama.

"The ground shook." Her gaze went inward with the memory. "Explosions. After a while it was quiet and we peeked out. The whole corner where my house had been was a hole."

"You were orphaned?"

"I remember my parents. He was a big, robust fellow. I think my mother was a servant somewhere. They wore uniforms for such jobs and I remember her in uniform."

"How can you be sure your parents were killed?"

"The sweep is all I know for sure but they're always the same. There was screaming and people running about. We were terrified."

"Why do you think the sweep was because of you?"

"They do that sort of thing."

They. What a victory the watchers would count in that one word.

Murbella was still deep in memory. "I think my father refused to succumb to an Honored Matre. That was always considered dangerous. Big, handsome man . . . strong."

"So you hate them?"

"Why?" Really surprised by his question. "Without that, I would never have been an Honored Matre."

Her callousness shocked him. "So it was worth anything!"

"Love, do you resent whatever brought me to your side?"

Touché! "But don't you wish it had happened some other way?"

"It happened."

What utter fatalism. He had never suspected this in her. Was it Honored Matre conditioning or something the Bene Gesserit did?

"You were just a valuable addition to their stables."

"Right. Enticers, they called us. We recruited valuable males."

"And you did."

"I repaid their investment many times over."

"Do you realize how the Sisters will interpret this?"

"Don't make a big thing of it."

"So you're ready to *work on* Scytale?"

"I didn't say that. Honored Matres manipulated me without my consent. The Sisters need me and want to use me the same way. My price may be too high."

He was a moment speaking past a dry throat. "Price?"

She glared at him. "You, you're just part of my price. No working on Scytale. And more of their famous candor about why they need me!"

"Careful, love. They might tell you."

She turned an almost Bene Gesserit stare toward him. "How could you restore Teg's memories without pain?"

Damn! And just when he thought they were free of that slip. No escape. He could see in her eyes that she guessed.

Murbella confirmed this. "Since I would not agree, I'm sure you've discussed it with Sheeana."

He could only nod. His Murbella had gone farther into the Sisterhood than he suspected. And she knew how his multiple ghola memories had been restored by her *imprinting*. He suddenly saw her as a Reverend Mother and wanted to cry out against it.

"How does this make you different from Odrade?" she asked.

"Sheeana was trained as an Imprinter." His words felt empty even as he spoke.

"That's different from my training?" Accusing.

Anger flared in him. "You'd prefer the pain? Like Bell?"

"You'd prefer the defeat of the Bene Gesserit?" Voice milky soft.

He heard the distance in her tone, as though she already had retreated into the cold observational stance of the Sisterhood. They were freezing his lovely Murbella! There was still that vitality in her, though. It tore at him. She gave off an aura of health, especially in pregnancy. Vigor and boundless enjoyment of life. It glowed in her. The Sisters would take that and dampen it.

She became quiet under his watchful stare.

Desperate, he wondered what he could do.

"I had hoped we were being more open with each other lately," she said. Another Bene Gesserit probe.

"I disagree with many of their actions but I don't distrust their motives," he said.

"I'll know their motives if I live through the Agony."

He went very still, caught in realization that she might not survive. Life without Murbella? Yawning emptiness deeper than anything he had ever imagined. Nothing in his many lives compared with it. Without conscious volition, he reached out and caressed her back. Skin so soft and yet resilient.

"I love you too much, Murbella. That's my Agony."

She trembled under his touch.

He found himself wallowing in sentimentality, building an image of grief until he recalled a Mentat teacher's words about "emotional binges."

"The difference between sentiment and sentimentality is easy to see. When you avoid killing somebody's pet on the glazeway, that's sentiment. If you swerve to avoid the pet and that causes you to kill pedestrians, that is sentimentality."

She took his caressing hand and pressed it against her lips.

"Words plus body, more than either," he whispered.

His words plunged her back into nightmare but now she went with a vengeance, aware of words as tools. She was filled with special relish for the experience, willingness to laugh at herself.

As she exorcised the nightmare, it occurred to her that she had never seen an Honored Matre laugh at herself.

Holding his hand, she stared down at Duncan. Mentat flickering of his eyelids. Did he realize what she had just experienced? Freedom! It no longer was a question of how she had been confined and driven into inevitable channels by her past. For the first time since accepting the possiblity that she could become a Reverend Mother, she glimpsed what it might mean. She felt awe and shock.

Nothing more important than the Sisterhood?

They spoke of an oath, something more mysterious than the Proctor's words at the acolyte initiation.

My oath to Honored Matres was only words. An oath to the Bene Gesserit can be no more.

She remembered Bellonda growling that diplomats were chosen for ability to lie. "*Would you be another diplomat, Murbella?*"

It was not that oaths were made to be broken. How childish! Schoolyard threat: "*If you break your word, I'll break mine! Nyaa, nyaa, nyaaaaa!*"

Futile to worry about oaths. Far more important to find that place in herself where freedom lived. It was a place where something always listened.

Cupping Duncan's hand against her lips, she whispered: "They listen. Oh, how they listen."

Enter no conflict against fanatics unless you can defuse them. Oppose a religion with another religion only if your proofs (miracles) are irrefutable or if you can mesh in a way that the fanatics accept you as god-inspired. This has long been the barrier to science assuming a mantle of divine revelation. Science is so obviously man-made. Fanatics (and many are fanatic on one subject or another) must know where you stand, but more important, must recognize who whispers in your ear.

—MISSIONARIA PROTECTIVA,
PRIMARY TEACHING

The flow of time nagged at Odrade as much as did constant awareness of the hunters approaching. Years passed so quickly that days became a blur. Two months of arguments to gain approval of Sheeana as successor to Tam!

Bellonda had taken to standing day watch when Odrade was absent as she had been today, briefing a new Bene Gesserit remnant being sent Scattering. The Council continued this but with reluctance. Idaho's suggestion that it was a futile strategy had sent shock waves through the Sisterhood. Briefings now carried new defensive plans for "what you may encounter."

When Odrade entered the workroom late in the afternoon, Bellonda sat at the table. Her cheeks looked puffy and her eyes had that hard stare they got when she suppressed fatigue. With Bell here, the daily summation would include sharp comments.

"They've approved Sheeana," she said, pushing a small crystal toward Odrade. "Tam's support did it. And Murbella's new one will be born in eight days, so the Suks *claim*."

Bell had little faith in Suk doctors.

New one? She could be so damned impersonal about life! Odrade found her pulses quickening at the prospect.

When Murbella recovers from this birth—the Agony. She is ready.

"Duncan's extremely nervous," Bellonda said, vacating the chair.

Duncan yet! Those two are getting remarkably familiar.

Bell was not finished. "And before you ask, no word from Dortujla."

Odrade took her seat behind the table and balanced the report crystal on her palm. Dortujla's trusted acolyte, now Reverend Mother Fintil, would not risk the no-ship journey or any of the other message devices they had prepared just to stroke a Mother Superior. No news meant the bait was still out there . . . or wasted.

"Have you told Sheeana she's confirmed?" Odrade asked.

"I left that for you. She's late with her daily report again. Not right for someone on the Council."

So Bell still disapproved the appointment.

Sheeana's daily messages had taken on a repetitive note. "*No wormsign. Spice mass intact.*"

Everything upon which they pinned their hopes lay in terrible suspension. And nightmare hunters crept closer. Tensions accumulated. Explosive.

"You've seen that exchange between Duncan and Murbella enough times," Bellonda said. "Is that what Sheeana was hiding and, if so, why?"

"Teg was my father."

"Such delicacy! A Reverend Mother has qualms about imprinting the ghola of Mother Superior's father!"

"She was my personal student, Bell. She has concerns for me you could not feel. Besides, this is not just a ghola, this is a child."

"We must be certain of her!"

Odrade saw the name form on Bellonda's lips but it remained unspoken. "*Jessica.*"

Another flawed Reverend Mother? Bell was right, they must be sure of Sheeana. *My responsibility.* A vision of Sheeana's black sculpture flickered in Odrade's awareness.

"Idaho's plan has some attraction, but . . ." Bellonda hesitated.

Odrade spoke up: "This is a very young child, growth incomplete. Pain of the usual memory restoration could approach the Agony. It might alienate him. But this . . ."

"Control him with an Imprinter, that part I approve. But what if it doesn't restore his memories?"

"We still have the original plan. And it *did* have that effect on Idaho."

"Different for him but the decision can wait. You're late for your meeting with Scytale."

Odrade hefted the crystal. "Daily summation?"

"Nothing you haven't seen too many times already." From Bell, that was almost a note of concern.

"I'll bring him back here. Have Tam waiting and you come in later on some pretext."

Scytale had become almost accustomed to these walks outside the ship and Odrade observed this in his casual manner when they emerged from her transporter south of Central.

It was more than a stroll and they both knew it but she had made these excursions regular, designing repetition to lull him. *Routine. So useful on occasion.*

"Kind of you to take me for these walks," Scytale said, looking up sideways. "The air is drier than I recall it. Where do we go this evening?"

How tiny his eyes when he squinted against the sun.

"To my workroom." She nodded at outbuildings of Central about half a klick north. It was cold under a cloudless spring sky and warm colors of roofs, lights coming on in her tower, beckoned with promise of relief from a chilling wind that accompanied almost every sunset these days.

With peripheral attention, Odrade watched the Tleilaxu beside her carefully. Such tension! She could feel this also in guardian Reverend

Mothers and acolytes close behind them, all charged to special watchfulness by Bellonda.

*We need this little monster and he knows it. And we still don't know
the extent of Tleilaxu abilities! What talents has he accumulated? Why
does he probe with such evident casualness for contact with his fellow
prisoners?*

Tleilaxu made the Idaho-ghola, she reminded herself. Did they
hide secret things in him?

"I am a beggar come to your door, Mother Superior," he said in that
whining elfin voice. "Our planets in ruins, my people slain. Why do
we go to your quarters?"

"To bargain in more pleasant surroundings."

"Yes, it is very confining in the ship. But I do not understand why
we always leave the car so far away from Central. Why do we walk?"

"I find it refreshing."

Scytale glanced around him at the plantings. "Pleasant, but quite
cold, don't you think?"

Odrade glanced to the south. These southern slopes were planted
to grapes, crests and colder northern faces reserved for orchards.
Improved vinifera, these vineyards. Developed by Bene Gesserit gardeners. Old vines, roots "gone down to hell" where (according to
ancient superstition) they stole water from burning souls. The winery
was underground as were storage and aging caves. Nothing to mar a
landscape of tended vines in orderly rows, plantings just far enough
apart for pickers and tilling equipment.

Pleasant to him? She doubted Scytale saw anything pleasing here.
He was properly nervous as she wanted him to be, asking himself: *Why
does she* really *choose to walk me through these rustic surroundings?*

It galled Odrade that they dared not employ more powerful Bene
Gesserit persuasives on this little man. But she agreed with advice that
said if those efforts failed, they would not get a second chance. Tleilaxu had demonstrated they would die rather than give up secret (and
sacred) knowledge.

"Several things puzzle me," Odrade said, picking her way around a pile of vine trimmings as she spoke. "Why do you insist on having your own Face Dancers *before* acceding to our requests? And what is this interest in Duncan Idaho?"

"Dear lady, I have no companions in my loneliness. That answers both questions." He rubbed absently at his breast where the nullentropy capsule lay concealed.

Why does he rub himself there so frequently? It was a gesture she and analysts had puzzled over. *No scar, no skin inflammation. Perhaps merely a carryover from childhood. But that was so long ago! A flaw in this reincarnation?* No one could say. And that gray skin carried a metallic pigmentation that resisted probing instruments. He was sure to have been sensitized to heavier rays and would know those were used. No . . . now, it was all diplomacy. *Damn this little monster!*

Scytale wondered: Did this powindah female have no natural sympathies on which he could play? *Typicals* were ambivalent on that question.

"The Wekht of Jandola is no more," he said. "Billions of us slain by those whores. To the farthest reaches of the Yaghist, we are destroyed and only I remain."

Yaghist, she thought. *Land of the unruled.* It was a revealing word in Islamiyat, the Bene Tleilax language.

In that language, she said: "The magic of our God is our only bridge."

Once more she claimed to share his Great Belief, the Sufi-Zensunni ecumenism that had spawned the Bene Tleilax. She spoke the language flawlessly, knew the proper words, but he saw falsehoods. *She calls God's Messenger "Tyrant" and disobeys the most basic precepts!*

Where did these women meet in kehl to feel the presence of God? If they truly spoke the Language of God, they would already know what they sought from him with crude bargaining.

As they climbed the last slope to the paved landing at Central, Scytale called on God for help. *The Bene Tleilax come to this! Why have You put this trial upon us? We are the last legalists of the Shariat and I, the last Master of my people, must seek answers from you, God, when You no longer can speak to me in kehl.*

Once more in flawless Islamiyat, Odrade said: "You were betrayed by your own people, ones you sent into the Scattering. You have no more Malik brothers, only sisters."

Then where is your sagra chamber, powindah deceiver? Where is a deep and windowless place only brothers may enter?

"This is a new thing for me," he said. "Malik Sisters? Those two words have always been self-negating. Sisters cannot be Malik."

"Waff, your late Mahai and Abdl, had trouble with that. And he led your people almost to extinction."

"Almost? You know of survivors?" He could not keep excitement from his voice.

"No Masters . . . but we hear of a few Domel and all in Honored Matre hands."

She paused where the edge of a building would cut off their view of the setting sun in the next steps and, still in the secret language of the Tleilaxu, said: "The sun is not God."

The dawn and sunset cry of the Mahai!

Scytale felt faith wavering as he followed her into an arched passage between two squat buildings. Her words were proper but only the Mahai and Abdl should utter them. In the shadowy passage, footsteps of their escort close behind, Odrade confounded him by saying: "Why did you not say the proper words? Are you not the last Master? Does that not make you Mahai and Abdl?"

"I was not chosen so by Malik brothers." It sounded weak even to him.

Odrade summoned a liftfield and paused at the tubeslot. In Other Memory detail, she found kehl and its right of ghufran familiar—words whispered in the night by lovers of long-dead women. "And then we . . ." "And so if we speak these sacred words . . ." *Ghufran!* Acceptance and readmission of one who had ventured among powindah, the returned one begging pardon for contact with unimaginable sins of aliens. *The Masheikh have met in kehl and felt the presence of their God!*

The tubeslot opened. Odrade motioned Scytale and two guards ahead. As he passed, she thought: *Something must give soon. We cannot play our little game to the end he desires.*

Tamalane stood at the bow window, her back to the door, when Odrade and Scytale entered the workroom. Sunset light slanted sharply across the rooftops. The brilliance vanished then and left behind it a sense of contrast, the night darker because of that last glow along the horizon.

In the milky gloom, Odrade waved the guards away, noting their reluctance. Bellonda had charged them to stay, obviously, but they would not disobey Mother Superior. She indicated a chairdog across from her and waited for him to sit. He looked back suspiciously at Tamalane before sinking into the 'dog but covered it by saying: "Why are there no lights?"

"This is a relaxing interlude," she said. *And I know darkness worries you!*

She stood a moment behind her table, identifying bright patches in the gloom, a luster of artifacts placed around her to make this her setting: the bust of long-dead Chenoeh in its niche beside the window, and there on the wall at her right, a pastoral landscape from the first human migrations into space, a stack of ridulian crystals on the table and a silvery reflection off her lightscribe concentrating faint illuminations from the windows.

He has roasted long enough.

She touched a plate on her console. Glowglobes set strategically around walls and ceiling came to life. Tamalane turned on cue, her robe swishing deliberately. She stood two paces behind Scytale, the very picture of ominous Bene Gesserit mystery.

Scytale twitched slightly at Tamalane's movement but now he sat quietly. The chairdog was somewhat too large for him and he looked almost childlike there.

Odrade said, "Sisters who rescued you say you commanded a no-ship at Junction preparing for the first foldspace leap when Honored Matres attacked. You were coming to your ship in a one-man skitter, they said, and veered away just before the explosions. You detected the attackers?"

"Yes." Reluctance in his voice.

"And knew they might locate the no-ship from your trajectory. So you fled, leaving your brothers to be destroyed."

He spoke with the utter bitterness of a tragic witness: "Earlier, when we were outbound from Tleilax, we saw that attack begin. Our explosions to destroy everything of value to attackers and the burners from space created the holocaust. We fled then, too."

"But not directly to Junction."

"Everywhere we searched, they had been before us. They had the ashes but I had our secrets." *Remind her that I still have something of value to trade!* He tapped a finger against his head.

"You sought Guild or CHOAM sanctuary at Junction," she said. "How fortunate our spy ship was there to scoop you up before the enemy could react."

"Sister . . ." How difficult that word! ". . . if you truly are my sister in kehl, why will you not provide me with Face Dancer servants?"

"Still too many secrets between us, Scytale. Why, for instance, were you leaving Bandalong when attackers came?"

Bandalong!

Naming the great Tleilax city constricted his chest and he thought he felt the nullentropy capsule pulse, as though it sought release for its precious contents. *Lost Bandalong. Never again to see the city of carnelian skies, never to feel the presence of brothers, of patient Domel and . . .*

"Are you ill?" Odrade asked.

"I am sick with what I have lost!" He heard fabric slither behind him and sensed Tamalane closer. How oppressive it was in this place! "Why is she behind me?"

"I am the servant of my Sisters and she is here to observe us both."

"You've taken some of my cells, haven't you? You're growing a replacement Scytale in your tanks!"

"Of course we are. You don't think Sisters would let the last Master end here, do you?"

"No ghola of me will do anything I would not!" *And it will carry no nullentropy tube!*

"We know." *But what is it we do not know?*

"This is not bargaining," he complained.

"You misjudge me, Scytale. We know when you lie and when you conceal. We employ senses others do not."

It was true! They detected things from odors of his body, from small movements of muscles, expressions he could not suppress.

Sisters? These creatures are powindah! All of them!

"You were on lashkar," Odrade prodded.

Lashkar! How he wished he were *here* on lashkar. Face Dance warriors. Domel assistants—eliminating this abominable evil! But he dared not lie. The one behind him probably was a Truthsayer. Experience in many lives told him Bene Gesserit Truthsayers were the best.

"I commanded a force of khasadars. We sought a herd of Futars for our defense."

Herd? Did Tleilaxu know something of Futars not revealed to the Sisterhood?

"You went prepared for violence. Did Honored Matres learn of your mission and cut you off? I think it likely."

"Why do you call them Honored Matres?" His voice lapsed almost into a screech.

"Because that is what they call themselves." *Very calm now. Let him stew in his own mistakes.*

She is right! We were betrayed. Bitter thought. He held it close, wondering how he should reply. *A small revelation? There is never a small revelation with these women.*

A sigh shook his breast. The nullentropy capsule and its contents. His most important concern. *Anything to get him access to his own axlotl tanks.*

"Descendants of people we sent into the Scattering returned with captive Futars. A mingling of human and cat, as you doubtless know. But they did not reproduce in our tanks. And before we could determine why, the ones brought to us died." *The betrayers brought us only two! We should have suspected.*

"They didn't bring you very many Futars, did they? You should have suspected they were bait."

See? That is what they do with small revelations!

"Why did the Futars not hunt and kill Honored Matres on Gammu?" It was Duncan's question and deserved an answer.

"We were told no orders were given. They do not kill without orders." *She knows this. She is testing me.*

"Face Dancers also kill on order," she said. "They would even kill you if you ordered it. Not so?"

"That order is reserved for keeping our secrets from the hands of enemies."

"Is that why you want your own Face Dancers? Do you consider us enemies?"

Before he could compose a response, Bellonda's projected figure appeared above the table, lifesize and partly translucent, dancing crystals of Archives behind her. "Urgent from Sheeana!" Bellonda said. "The spice blow has occurred. Sandworms!" The figure turned and looked at Scytale, comeyes perfectly coordinating her movements. "So you have lost a bargaining chip, Master Scytale! We have our spice at last!" The projected figure vanished with an audible *click* and a faint smell of ozone.

"You're trying to trick me!" he blurted.

But the door at Odrade's left opened. Sheeana entered towing a small suspensor pod no more than two meters long. Its transparent sides repeated the glowglobes of the workroom in tiny bursts of yellow light. Something squirmed in the pod!

Sheeana stood aside without speaking, giving them a full view of the contents. So small! The worm was less than half the length of its container but perfect in every detail, stretched out there on a shallow bed of golden sand.

Scytale could not contain a gasp of awe. The Prophet!

Odrade's reaction was pragmatic. She bent close to the pod, peering into the miniature mouth. The scorching huff-huff of a great worm's internal fires reduced to this? What a tiny mimicry!

Crystal teeth flashed as it lifted its front segments.

The worm sent its mouth questing left and right. They all saw behind the teeth the miniature fire in its alien chemistry.

"Thousands of them," Sheeana said. "They came to a spice blow as they always do."

Odrade remained silent. *We have done it!* But this was Sheeana's moment of triumph. Let her make the most of it. Scytale had never looked this defeated.

Sheeana opened the pod and lifted the worm from it, cradling it as though it were an infant. It lay quiescent in her arms.

Odrade took a deep, satisfied breath. *She still controls them.*

"Scytale," Odrade said. He could not take his gaze from the worm.

"Do you still serve the Prophet?" Odrade asked. "There he is!"

He did not know how to respond. Truly a revenant of the Prophet? He wanted to deny his first awed response but his eyes would not permit it.

Odrade spoke softly. "While you were out on your foolish mission, your *selfish* mission, we were serving the Prophet! We rescued his last revenant and brought him here. Chapterhouse will become another Dune!"

She sat back and steepled her hands in front of her. Bell was watching through the comeyes, of course. A Mentat's observations would be valuable. Odrade wished Idaho were also watching. But he could look at a holo. It was clear to her that Scytale had seen the Bene Gesserit only as tools for restoration of his precious Tleilaxu civilization. Would this development force him to reveal inner secrets of his tanks? What would he offer?

"I must have time to think." A tremor in his voice.

"About what would you think?"

He did not answer but kept his attention on Sheeana, who was replacing the tiny worm in its pod. She stroked it once before sealing the lid.

"Tell me, Scytale," Odrade insisted. "How can there be anything for you to reconsider? This is our Prophet! You say you serve the Great Belief. Then serve it!"

She could see his dreams dissolving. *His own Face Dancers to print memories of those they killed, copying each victim's shape and manner.* He had never hoped to gull a Reverend Mother . . . but acolytes and simple workers of Chapterhouse . . . all the secrets he had hoped to acquire, gone! Lost as certainly as the charred husks of Tleilaxu planets.

Our *Prophet, she said.* He turned a stricken look toward Odrade but did not focus. *What am I to do? These women no longer need me. But I need them!*

"Scytale." How softly she spoke. "The Great Convention is ended. It's a new universe out there."

He tried to swallow in a dry throat. The whole concept of violence had taken on a new dimension. In the Old Empire, the Convention had guaranteed retaliation against anyone who dared burn a planet by attacking from space.

"Escalated violence, Scytale." Odrade's voice was almost a whisper. "We *Scatter* pods of rage."

He focused on her. *What is she saying?*

"The hatred being stored up against Honored Matres," she said. *You are not the only one with losses, Scytale. Once, when problems arose in our civilization, the cry went out: "Bring a Reverend Mother!" Honored Matres prevent that. And the myths are recomposed. Golden light is cast upon our past. "It was better in the old days when the Bene Gesserit could help us. Where do you go for reliable Truthsayers these days? Arbitration? These Honored Matres have never heard the word! They were always courteous, the Reverend Mothers. You have to say that for them."*

When Scytale did not respond, she said: "Think of what might happen if that rage were loosed in a Jihad!"

When he still did not speak, she said: "You have seen it. Tleilaxu, Bene Gesserit, priests of the Divided God, and who knows how many more—all hunted like wild game."

"They cannot kill us all!" An agonized cry.

"Can't they? Your Scattered ones made common cause with Honored Matres. Is that a sanctuary you would seek in the Scattering?"

And there goes another dream: Little pods of Tleilaxu, persistent as festering sores, awaiting the day of Scytale's Great Revival.

"People grow strong under oppression," he said, but there was no force in his words. "Even the Priests of Rakis are finding holes in which to hide!" Desperate words.

"Who says this? Some of your returned *friends*?"

His silence was all the answer she needed.

"Bene Tleilax have killed Honored Matres and they know it," she said, hammering at him. "They will be satisfied only with your extermination."

"And yours!"

"We are partners by necessity if not by shared belief." She said it in purest Islamiyat and saw hope leap into his eyes. *Kehl and Shariat may yet take on their old meanings among people who compose their thoughts in the Language of God.*

"Partners?" Faint and extremely tentative.

She adopted new bluntness. "In some ways, that's a more reliable basis for common action than any other. Each of us knows what the other wants. An instrinsic design: Screen everything through that and something reliable can occur."

"And what is it you want from me?"

"You already know."

"How to make the finest tanks, yes." He shook his head, obviously unsure. The changes implied by her demands!

Odrade wondered if she dared snap at him in open anger. How dense he was! But he was close to panic. Old values had changed. Honored Matres were not the only source of turmoil. Scytale did not even know the extent of changes that had infected his own Scattered Ones!

"Times are changing," Odrade said.

Change, what a disturbing word, he thought.

"I must have my own Face Dancer attendants! And my own tanks?" Almost begging.

"My Council and I will consider it."

"What is there to consider?" Throwing her own words at her.

"You need only your own approval. I require approval of others." She gave him a grim smile. "So you do get time to think." Odrade nodded to Tamalane, who summoned guards.

"Back to the no-ship?" He spoke from the doorway, such a diminutive figure amidst burly guards.

"But tonight you ride all the way."

He gave a last lingering stare at the worm as he left.

When Scytale and guards were gone, Sheeana said: "You were right not to press him. He was ready to panic."

Bellonda entered. "Perhaps it would be best just to kill him."

"Bell! Get the holo and go through our meeting again. This time as a Mentat!"

That stopped her.

Tamalane chuckled.

"You take too much joy in your Sister's discomfiture, Tam," Sheeana said.

Tamalane shrugged but Odrade was delighted. *No more teasing of Bell?*

"When you spoke of Chapterhouse becoming another Dune, that was when he began to panic," Bellonda said, her voice Mentat distant.

Odrade had seen the reaction but had not yet made the association. This was a Mentat's value: patterns and systems, building blocks. Bell sensed a pattern to Scytale's behavior.

"I ask myself: Is it the thing become real once more?" Bellonda said.

Odrade saw it at once. An odd thing about lost places. As long as Dune had been a known and living planet, there existed a historical firmness about its presence in the Galactic Register. You could point to a projection and say: "That is Dune. Once called Arrakis and, latterly, Rakis. Dune for its total desert character in Muad'Dib's day."

Destroy the place, though, and a mythological patina in-weighed against projected *reality*. In time, such places became totally mythic. *Arthur and his Round Table. Camelot where it only rains at night. Pretty good Weather Control for those days!*

But now, a new Dune had appeared.

"Myth power," Tamalane said.

Ahhhh, yes. Tam, close to her final departure from flesh, would be more sensitive to workings of myths. Mystery and secrecy, tools of the Missionaria, had been used also on Dune by Muad'Dib and the Tyrant. The seeds were planted. Even with priests of the Divided God gone to their own perdition, myths of Dune proliferated.

"Melange," Tamalane said.

The other Sisters in the workroom knew immediately what she meant. New hope could be injected into the Bene Gesserit Scattering.

Bellonda said: "Why do they want us dead and not captives? That has always puzzled me."

Honored Matres might not want *any* Bene Gesserit alive . . . only the spice knowledge, perhaps. But they destroyed Dune. They destroyed the Tleilaxu. It was a cautioning thought to take into any confrontation with the Spider Queen—should Dortujla succeed.

"No useful hostages?" Bellonda asked.

Odrade saw the looks on the faces of her Sisters. They were following a single track as though all of them thought with one mind. Object lessons by Honored Matres, leaving few survivors, only made potential opposition more cautious. It invoked a rule of silence within which bitter memories became bitter myths. Honored Matres were like barbarians in any age: blood instead of hostages. Strike with random viciousness.

"Dar's right," Tamalane said. "We've been seeking allies too close to home."

"Futars did not create themselves," Sheeana said.

"The ones who created them hope to control us," Bellonda said. There was the clear sound of Prime Projection in her voice. "That's the hesitation Dortujla heard in the Handlers."

There it was and they faced it with all of its perils. It came down to people (as it always did). People—contemporaries. You learned valuable things from people living in your own time and from knowledge they carried out of their pasts. Other Memory was not the only conveyance of history.

Odrade felt that she had come home after a long absence. There was a familiarity about the way all four of them were thinking now. It was a familiarity that transcended place. The Sisterhood itself was Home. Not where they lodged in transient housing but the association.

Bellonda voiced it for them. "I fear we have been working at cross purposes."

"Fear does that," Sheeana said.

Odrade dared not smile. It could be misinterpreted and she did not want to explain. *Give us Murbella as a Sister and a restored Bashar! Then we might have our fighting chance!*

Right there with that good feeling in her, the message signal clicked. She glanced at the projection surface, a pure reflex, and recognized crisis. Such a small thing (relatively) to precipitate crisis. Clairby mortally injured in a 'thopter crash. Mortal unless . . . The unless was spelled out for her and it added up to cyborg. Her companions saw the message in reverse but you got good at reading mirrored information in here. They knew.

Where do we draw the line?

Bellonda, with her antique spectacles when she could have had artificial eyes or any of numerous other prosthetics, voted with her body. *This is what it means to be human. Try to hold on to youth and it mocks you while it sprints away. Melange is enough . . . and perhaps too much.*

Odrade recognized what her own emotions were telling her. But what of Bene Gesserit necessity? Bell could lodge her individual vote and everyone recognized it, even respected it. But Mother Superior's vote carried the Sisterhood with her.

First the axlotl tanks and now this.

Necessity said they could not afford to lose specialists of Clairby's caliber. They had few enough as it was. "Spread thin" did not describe it. Gaps were appearing. Cyborg Clairby, though, and that was the opening wedge.

The Suks were prepared. "A precautionary arrangement" should it be required for someone irreplaceable. *Such as Mother Superior?* Odrade knew she had approved that with her usual cautious reservations. Where were those reservations now?

Cyborg was one of those potpourri words, too. Where did mechanical additions to human flesh become dominant? When was the Cyborg no longer human? Temptations intensified—"Just this one little adjustment." And so easy to *adjust* until the potpourri-human became unquestioningly obedient.

But . . . Clairby?

Conditions of extremis said, "Cyborg him!" Was the Sisterhood that desperate? She was forced to answer in the affirmative.

There it was then—decision not entirely out of her hands, but the ready excuse at hand. *Necessity dictates it.*

The Butlerian Jihad had left its indelible mark on humans. Fought and won . . . for then. And here was another battle in that long-ago conflict.

But now, survival of the Sisterhood was in the balance. How many technical specialists remained on Chapterhouse? She knew the answer without looking. Not enough.

Odrade leaned forward and keyed for transmit. "Cyborg him," she said.

Bellonda grunted. *Approval or disapproval?* She would never say. This was Mother Superior's arena and welcome to it!

Who won this battle? Odrade wondered.

We walk a delicate line, perpetuating Atreides (Siona) genes in our population because that hides us from prescience. We carry the Kwisatz Haderach in that bag! Willfulness created Muad'Dib. Prophets make predictions come true! Will we ever again dare ignore our Tao sense and cater to a culture that hates chance and begs for prophecy?

—ARCHIVAL SUMMARY (ADIXTO)

It was just after dawn when Odrade arrived at the no-ship but Murbella was up and working with a training mek when Mother Superior strode onto the practice floor.

Odrade had walked the last klick through ring orchards around the spacefield. Night's limited clouds had thinned at the approach of dawn, then dissipated to reveal a sky thick with stars.

She recognized a delicate weather shift to wrench another crop from this region but decreasing rainfall was barely enough to keep orchards and pastures alive.

As she walked, Odrade was overcome by dreariness. Winter just past had been a hard-bought silence between storms. Life was holocaust. Dusting of pollen by eager insects, fruiting and seeding that followed the flower. These orchards were a secret storm whose power lay hidden in torrential flows of life. But ohhh! the destruction. New life carried change. The Changer was coming, always different. Sandworms would bring the desert purity of ancient Dune.

The desolation of that transforming power invaded her imagination. She could picture this landscape reduced to windswept dunes, habitat for Leto II's descendants.

And the arts of Chapterhouse would undergo mutation—one civilization's myths replaced by another's.

The aura of these thoughts went with Odrade onto the practice floor and colored her mood as she watched Murbella complete a round of flashing exertion, then step back, panting.

A thin scratch reddened the back of Murbella's left hand where she had missed a move by the big mek. The automated trainer stood there in the center of the room like a golden pillar, its weapons flicking in and out—probing mandibles of an angry insect.

Murbella wore tight green leotards and her exposed skin glistened with perspiration. Even with the prominent mounding of her pregnancy, she appeared graceful. Her skin glowed with health. It came from within, Odrade decided, partly the pregnancy but something more fundamental as well. This had impressed itself on Odrade at their first encounter, a thing Lucilla had remarked after capturing Murbella and rescuing Idaho from Gammu. Health lived below the surface in her, there like a lens to focus attention on a deep freshet of vitality.

We must have her!

Murbella saw the visitor but refused to be interrupted.

Not yet, Mother Superior. My baby is due soon but this body's needs will continue.

Odrade saw then that the mek was simulating anger, a programed response brought on by frustration of its circuitry. An extremely dangerous mode!

"Good morning, Mother Superior."

Murbella's voice came out modulated by her exertions as she dodged and twisted with that almost blinding speed she commanded.

The mek slashed and probed for her, its sensors darting and whirring in attempts to follow her movements.

Odrade sniffed. To speak at such a time amplified the peril of the mek. Risk no distractions when you played this dangerous game. *Enough!*

The mek's controls were in a large green wall panel to the right of the doorway. Murbella's changes could be seen in the circuits—dangling wires, beamfields with memory crystals dislocated. Odrade reached up and stilled the mechanism.

Murbella turned to face her.

"Why did you change the circuitry?" Odrade demanded.

"For the anger."

"Is that what Honored Matres do?"

"As the twig is bent?" Murbella massaged her wounded hand. "But what if the twig knows how it is bent and approves?"

Odrade felt sudden excitement. "Approves? Why?"

"Because there's something . . . grand about it."

"You follow your adrenaline high?"

"You know it's not that!" Murbella's breathing returned to normal. She stood glaring at Odrade.

"Then what is it?"

"It's . . . being challenged to do more than you ever thought possible. You never suspected you could be this . . . this good, this expert and accomplished at anything."

Odrade concealed elation.

Mens sana in corpore sano. We have her at last!

Odrade said: "But what a price you pay!"

"Price?" Murbella sounded astonished. "As long as I have the capacity, I'm delighted to pay."

"Take what you want and pay for it?"

"It's your Bene Gesserit magic cornucopia: As I become increasingly accomplished, my ability to pay increases."

"Beware, Murbella. That cornucopia, as you call it, can become Pandora's box."

Murbella knew the allusion. She stood quite still, her attention fixed on Mother Superior. "Oh?" The sound barely escaped.

"Pandora's box releases powerful distractions that waste energies of your life. You speak glibly of being 'in the chute' and becoming a Reverend Mother but you still don't know what that means nor what we want from you."

"Then it was never our sexual abilities you wanted."

Odrade moved eight paces forward, majestically deliberate. Once Murbella got on that subject there would be no stopping her short of the usual resolution—argument cut short by Mother Superior's peremptory command.

"Sheeana easily mastered your abilities," Odrade said.

"So you *will* use her on that child!"

Odrade heard displeasure. It was a cultural residue. When did human sexuality begin? Sheeana, waiting now in the no-ship guard chambers, had been forced to deal with it. *"I hope you recognize the source of my reluctance and why I was so secretive, Mother Superior."*

"I recognize that a Fremen society filled your mind with inhibitions before we took you in hand!"

That had cleared the air between them. But how was this exchange with Murbella to be redirected? *I must let it run while I seek a way out.*

There would be repetition. Unresolved issues would emerge. The fact that almost every word Murbella uttered could be anticipated, that would be a trial.

"Why do you evade this tested way of dominating others now that you say you need it with Teg?" Murbella asked.

"Slaves, is that what you want?" Odrade countered.

Eyes almost closed, Murbella considered this. *Did I consider the men our slaves? Perhaps. I produced in them periods of wildly unthinking abandon, a giving up to heights of ecstasy they had never dreamed possible. I was trained to give them that and, thereby, make them subject to our control.*

Until Duncan did the same to me.

Odrade saw the hooding of Murbella's eyes and recognized there were things in this woman's psyche twisted in a way difficult to uncover. *Wildness running where we have not followed.* It was as though Murbella's original clarity had been stained indelibly and then that mark covered over and even this cover masked. There was a harshness in her that distorted thoughts and actions. Layer upon layer upon layer . . .

"You're afraid of what I can do," Murbella said.

"There's truth in what you say," Odrade agreed.

Honesty and candor—limited tools now to be used with care.

"Duncan." Murbella's voice came out flat with new Bene Gesserit abilities.

"I fear what you share with him. You find it odd, Mother Superior admitting fear?"

"I know about candor and honesty!" She made candor and honesty sound repellent.

"Reverend Mothers are taught never to abandon self. We are trained not to encumber ourselves that way with concerns of others."

"Is that all of it?"

"It goes deeper and has other threads. Being Bene Gesserit marks you in its own ways."

"I know what you're asking: Choose Duncan or the Sisterhood. I know your tricks."

"I think not."

"There are things I won't do!"

"Each of us is constrained by a past. I make my choices, do what I must because my past is different from yours."

"You'll continue to train me despite what I've just said?"

Odrade heard this in the total receptivity these encounters with Murbella demanded, every sense alerted to things not spoken, messages that hovered on edges of words as though they were cilia wavering there, reaching for contact with a dangerous universe.

The Bene Gesserit must change its ways. And here is one who could guide us into change.

Bellonda would be horrified at the prospect. Many Sisters would reject it. But there it was.

When Odrade remained silent, Murbella said: "Trained. Is that the proper word?"

"Conditioned. That's probably more familiar to you."

"What you really want is to conjoin our experiences, make me sufficiently like you that we can create trust between us. That's what all education does."

Don't play erudite games with me, girl!

"We would flow in the same stream, eh, Murbella?"

Any Third-Stage acolyte would have become watchfully cautious hearing that tone from Mother Superior. Murbella appeared unmoved.

"Except that I will not give him up."

"That is for you to decide."

"Did you let the Lady Jessica decide?"

The way out of this cul-de-sac at last.

Duncan had prompted Murbella to study Jessica's life. *Hoping to thwart us!* Holos of his performance had ignited severe analysis of records.

"An interesting person," Odrade said.

"Love! After all of your teaching, your *conditioning!*"

"You did not think her behavior treasonous?"

"Never!"

Delicately now. "But look at consequences: a Kwisatz Haderach . . . and that grandchild, the Tyrant!" *Argument dear to Bellonda's heart.*

"Golden Path," Murbella said. "Survival of humankind."

"Famine Times and the Scattering."

Are you watching this, Bell? No matter. You will watch it.

"Honored Matres!" Murbella said.

"All because of Jessica?" Odrade asked. "But Jessica returned to the fold and lived out her years on Caladan."

"Teacher of acolytes!"

"Example to them, as well. See what happens when you defy us?" *Defy us, Murbella! Do it more adroitly than Jessica.*

"Sometimes you repel me!" Natural honesty forced her to add: "But you know I want what you have."

What we have.

Odrade recalled her own first encounters with Bene Gesserit attractions. Everything of the body done with exquisite precision, senses honed to detect smallest details, muscles trained to perform in marvelous exactitude. These abilities in an Honored Matre could only add a new dimension amplified by bodily speed.

"You're throwing it back on me," Murbella said. "Trying to force my choice when you already know it."

Odrade remained silent. This was a form of argument ancient Jesuits had almost perfected. Simulflow superimposed disputational patterns: Let Murbella do her own convincing. Supply only the most subtle of nudges. Give her small excuses upon which to enlarge.

But hold fast, Murbella, to love for Duncan!

"You're very clever at parading your Sisterhood's advantages past me," Murbella said.

"We are not a cafeteria line!"

An insouciant grin flicked Murbella's mouth. "I'll take one of those and one of these and I think I'd like one of those creamy things over there."

Odrade enjoyed the metaphor but omnipresent watchers had their own appetites. "A diet that might kill you."

"But I see your offerings displayed so attractively. Voice! What a marvelous thing you've cooked up there. I have this wonderful instrument in my throat and you can teach me to play it in that ultimate way."

"Now, you're a concert master."

"I want your ability to influence those around me!"

"To what end, Murbella? For whose goals?"

"If I eat what you eat, will I grow into your kind of toughness: plasteel on the outside and even harder inside?"

"Is that how you see me?"

"The chef at my banquet! And I must eat whatever you bring—for my good and for yours."

She sounded almost manic. An odd person. Sometimes she appeared to be the most wretched of women, pacing her quarters like a caged beast. That mad look in her eyes, orange flecks in the corneas . . . as there were now.

"Do you still refuse to *work on* Scytale?"

"Let Sheeana do it."

"Will you coach her?"

"And she will use my coaching on the child!"

They stared at each other, realizing they shared a similar thought. *This is not confrontation because each of us wants the other.*

"I am committed to you for what you can give me," Murbella said, her voice low. "But you want to know if I may ever act against that commitment?"

"Could you?"

"No more than you could if circumstances demanded it."

"Do you think you will ever regret your decision?"

"Of course I will!" What kind of damnfool question was that? People always had regrets. Murbella said this.

"Just confirming your self-honesty. We like it that you don't fly under false colors."

"You get false ones?"

"Indeed."

"You must have ways of weeding them out."

"The Agony does that for us. Falsehoods don't come through the Spice."

Odrade sensed Murbella's drumbeat flickering faster.

"And you're not going to demand I give up Duncan?" Very spiny.

"That attachment presents difficulties, but they are your difficulties."

"Another way of asking me to give him up?"

"Accept the possibility, that is all."

"I can't."

"You won't?"

"I mean what I say. I'm incapable."

"And if someone showed you how?"

Murbella stared into Odrade's eyes for a long beat, then: "I almost said that would set me free . . . but . . ."

"Yes?"

"I could not be free while he was bound to me."

"Is that renunciation of Honored Matre ways?"

"Renunciation? Wrong word. I've merely grown beyond my former Sisters."

"Former Sisters?"

"Still my Sisters, but they're Sisters of childhood. Some I remember fondly, some I dislike intensely. Playmates in a game that no longer interests me."

"That decision satisfies you?"

"Are you satisfied, Mother Superior?"

Odrade clapped her hands with unrestrained elation. How swiftly Murbella acquired Bene Gesserit riposte!

"Satisfied? What a hellishly deadly word!"

As Odrade spoke, Murbella felt herself move as in a dream to the edge of an abyss, unable to awaken and prevent the plunge. Her stomach ached with secret emptiness and Odrade's next words came from echoing distance.

"The Bene Gesserit is all to a Reverend Mother. You will never be able to forget that."

As quickly as it had come, the dream sensation passed. Mother Superior's next words were cold and immediate.

"Prepare for more advanced training."

Until you meet the Agony—live or die.

Odrade lifted her gaze to the ceiling comeyes. "Send Sheeana in here. She begins at once with her new teacher."

"So you're going to do it! You're going to *work on* that child."

"Think of him as Bashar Teg," Odrade said. "That helps." *And we're not giving you time to reconsider.*

"I didn't resist Duncan and I can't argue with you."

"Don't even argue with yourself, Murbella. Pointless. Teg was my father and still I must do this."

Until that moment, Murbella had not realized the force behind Odrade's earlier statement. *The Bene Gesserit is all to a Reverend Mother. Great Dur protect me! Will I be like that?*

We witness a passing phase of eternity. Important things happen but some people never notice. Accidents intervene. You are not present at episodes. You depend on reports. And people shutter their minds. What good are reports? History in a news account? Preselected at an editorial conference, digested and excreted by prejudice? Accounts you need seldom come from those who make history. Diaries, memoirs and autobiographies are subjective forms of special pleading. Archives are crammed with such suspect stuff.

—DARWI ODRADE

Scytale noticed the excitement of guards and others when he reached the barrier at the end of his corridor. Rapid movement of people, especially this early in the day, had attracted him first and sent him to the barrier. There went that Suk doctor, Jalanto. He recognized her from the time Odrade had sent her "because you are looking ill." *Another Reverend Mother to spy on me!*

Ahhhh, Murbella's baby. That was why this rushing around and the Suk.

But who were all those others? Bene Gesserit robes in an abundance he had never before seen here. Not just acolytes. Reverend Mothers outnumbered the others he saw rushing about down there. They reminded him of great carrion birds. There went an acolyte at last, carrying a child on her shoulders. Very mysterious. *If only I had a link to Shipsystems!*

He leaned against a wall and waited but the people vanished into various hatches and doorways. Some destinations he could place with fair certainty, others remained a mystery.

By the Holy Prophet! There went Mother Superior herself! She went through a wider doorway where most of the others had gone.

Useless to ask Odrade when next he saw her. She had him in her trap now.

The Prophet is here and in powindah hands!

When no more people appeared in the corridor, Scytale returned to his quarters. The Identification monitor at his doorway flickered at his passage but he forced himself not to look at it. *ID is the key.* With his knowledge, this flaw in the Ixian ship's control system beckoned like a siren.

When I move, they will not give me much time.

It would be an act of desperation with ship and contents hostage. Seconds in which to succeed. Who knew what false panels might have been built, what secret hatches where those awful women could leap out at him. He dared not gamble before exhausting all other avenues. Especially now . . . with the Prophet restored.

Tricky witches. What else did they change in this ship? A disquieting thought. *Does my knowledge still apply?*

The presence of Scytale beyond the barrier had not escaped Odrade's notice but she had other matters to concern her. Murbella's accouchement (she liked the ancient term) had come at an opportune moment. Odrade wanted a distracted Idaho with her for Sheeana's attempt at restoring the Bashar's memories. Idaho was often distracted by thoughts of Murbella. And Murbella obviously could not be with him here, not just now.

Odrade maintained prudent watchfulness in his presence. He was, after all, a Mentat.

She had found him at his console again. As she emerged from the dropchute into the access corridor to his quarters, she heard the clicking of relays and that characteristic buzzing of the comfield and knew immediately where to find him.

He revealed an odd mood when she took him into the observation room where they would monitor Sheeana and the child.

Worry about Murbella? Or about what they would presently see?

The observation room was long and narrow. Three rows of chairs faced the seewall common with the secret room where the experiment would occur. The observation area had been left in gray gloom with only two tiny glowglobes at upper corners behind the chairs.

Two Suks were present . . . although Odrade worried that they might be ineffective. Jalanto, the Suk Idaho considered their best, was with Murbella.

Demonstrate our concern. It's real enough.

Slingchairs had been set up along the seewall. An emergency access hatch into the other room was near at hand.

Streggi brought the child down the outer passage where he would not see the watchers and took him into the room. It had been prepared under Murbella's directions: a bedroom, some of his own things brought from his quarters and some things from the rooms shared by Idaho and Murbella.

An animal's cave, Odrade thought. There was a shabbiness about the place that came from the deliberate disarray often found in Idaho's chambers: discarded clothing on a slingchair, sandals in a corner. The sleeping mat was one Idaho and Murbella had used. Inspecting it earlier, Odrade had noted that smell akin to saliva, an intimate sexual odor. That, too, would work unconsciously on Teg.

Here is where the wild things originate, the things we cannot suppress. What daring, to think we can control this. But we must.

As Streggi undressed the boy and left him naked on the mat, Odrade found her pulse quickening. She shifted her chair forward, noticing her Bene Gesserit companions imitate the same hitching motion.

Dear me, she thought. *Are we nothing but voyeurs?*

Such thoughts were necessary at this moment but she felt them demean her. She lost something in that intrusion. Extremely non–Bene Gesserit thinking. But very human!

Duncan had lapsed into a studied air of indifference, an easily recognized pretense. Too much subjectivity in his thoughts for him to function well as a Mentat. And that was precisely how she wanted him now. Participation Mystique. Orgasm as energizer. Bell had recognized it correctly.

To one of three nearby Proctors, all chosen for strength and here ostensibly as observers, Odrade said: "The ghola wants his original memories restored and fears that utterly. That's the major barrier to be sundered."

"Bullcrap!" Idaho said. "You know what we have working for us right now? His mother was one of you and she gave him the deep training. How likely is it she failed to protect him against your Imprinters?"

Odrade turned sharply toward him. *Mentat?* No, he was back in his immediate past, reliving and making comparisons. That reference to Imprinters, though . . . Was that how the first "sexual collision" with Murbella restored memories of other ghola-lifetimes? Deep resistance against imprinting?

The Proctor Odrade had addressed chose to ignore this impertinent interruption. She had read the Archives material when Bellonda briefed her. All three of them knew they might be called on to kill the ghola-child. Did he have powers dangerous to them? The watchers would not know until (or unless) Sheeana succeeded.

To Idaho, Odrade said: "Streggi told him why he is here."

"What did she tell him?" Very peremptory with Mother Superior. The Proctors glared at him.

Odrade held her voice to deliberate mildness. "Streggi told him Sheeana would restore his memories."

"What did he say?"

"Why isn't Duncan Idaho doing it?"

"She answered him honestly?" *Getting some of his own back.*

"Honestly but revealing nothing. Streggi told him Sheeana had a better way. And that you approved."

"Look at him! He isn't even moving. You haven't drugged him, have you?"

Idaho glared back at the Proctors.

"We wouldn't dare. But he is focused inward. You do recall the necessity for that, don't you?"

Idaho sank back into his chair, shoulders slumping. "Murbella keeps saying: 'He's just a child. He's just a child.' You know we had a fight over it."

"I thought your argument pertinent. The Bashar was not a child. It's the Bashar we're awakening."

He raised crossed fingers. "I hope."

She drew back, looking at the crossed fingers. "I didn't know you were superstitious, Duncan."

"I'd pray to Dur if I thought it would help."

He remembers his own re-awakening pains.

"Don't reveal compassion," he muttered. "Turn it back on him. Keep him focused inward. You want his anger."

Those were words from his own practique.

Abruptly, he said: "This may be the stupidest thing I ever suggested. I should go and be with Murbella."

"You're in good company, Duncan. And there's nothing you can do for Murbella right now. Look!" As Teg leaped off the mat and stared up at the ceiling comeyes.

"Isn't someone coming to help me?" Teg demanded. More desperation in his voice than predicted for this stage. "Where's Duncan Idaho?"

Odrade put a hand on Idaho's arm as he hitched forward. "Stay where you are, Duncan. You can't help him, either. Not yet."

"Isn't someone going to tell me what to do?" The young voice had a lonely, piping sound. "What're you going to do?"

Sheeana's cue and she entered the room through a hidden hatch behind Teg. "Here I am." She wore only a gossamer robe of pale blue, almost transparent. It clung to her as she strode around to face the boy.

He gawked. This was a Reverend Mother? He had never seen one robed that way. "You're going to give me back my memories?" Doubt and desperation.

"I will help you give them back to yourself." As she spoke, she slipped out of the robe and tossed it aside. It floated to the floor like a great blue butterfly.

Teg stared at her. "What're you doing?"

"What do you think I'm doing?" She sat down beside him and put a hand on his penis.

His head tipped forward as though pushed from behind and he stared at her hand as an erection formed in it.

"Why're you doing that?"

"Don't you know?"

"No!"

"The Bashar would know."

He looked up at her face so close to his. "You know! Why won't you tell me?"

"I'm not your memory!"

"Why're you humming like that?"

She put her lips against his neck. The humming was clear to the watchers. Murbella called it an intensifier, feedback keyed to the sexual response. It grew louder.

"What're you doing?" Almost a shriek as she sat him astraddle of her. She swayed, massaging the small of his back.

"Answer me, damn you!" A definite shriek.

Where did that "damn you!" come from? Odrade wondered.

Sheeana slipped him into her. "Here's your answer!"

His mouth formed a soundless "Ohhhhhhhhh."

The watchers saw her concentration on Teg's eyes but Sheeana *watched* him with other senses as well.

"Feel the tensing of his thighs, the telltale vagus pulse and especially note the darkening of his nipples. When you have him at that point, sustain it until his pupils dilate."

"Imprinter!" Teg's scream made the watchers jump.

He beat his fists against Sheeana's shoulders. All of them at the seewall observed an inner flickering of his eyes as he twisted back and forth, something new peering out of him.

Odrade was on her feet. "Has something gone wrong?"

Idaho remained in his chair. "What I predicted."

Sheeana thrust Teg away to escape his clawing fingers.

He sprawled to the floor and whirled with a speed that shocked the watchers. Sheeana and Teg confronted each other for several long heartbeats. Slowly, he straightened and only then did he look down at himself. Presently, he lifted his attention to his left arm held in front of him. His gaze went to the ceiling, to each wall in turn. Again, he looked at his body.

"What in the nether hell . . ." Still childish piping but oddly matured.

"Welcome, ghola-Bashar," Sheeana said.

"You were trying to imprint me!" Angry accusation. "You think my mother didn't teach me how to prevent that?" A distant expression came over his face. "Ghola?"

"Some prefer to think of you as a clone."

"Who're . . . Sheeana!" He whirled, looking all around the room. It had been selected for its concealed access, no visible hatches. "Where are we?"

"In the no-ship you took to Dune just before you were killed there." Still according to the rules.

"Killed . . ." Again, he looked at his hands. Watchers could almost see ghola-imposed filters drop from his memories. "I was killed . . . on Dune?" Almost plaintive.

"Heroic to the end," Sheeana said.

"My . . . the men I took from Gammu . . . were they . . ."

"Honored Matres made an example of Dune. It's a lifeless ball, charred to cinders."

Anger touched his features. He sat and crossed his legs, placing a clenched fist on each knee. "Yes . . . I learned that in the history of the . . . of me." Again, he glanced at Sheeana. She remained seated on the mat, quite still. This was such a plunge into memories as only one who had been through the Agony could appreciate. Utter stillness was required now.

Odrade whispered: "Don't interfere, Sheeana. Let it happen. Let him work it out." She made a hand-signal to the three Proctors. They went to the access hatch, watching her instead of the secret room.

"I find it odd to consider myself a subject of history," Teg said. The child's voice but that recurring sense of maturity in it. He closed his eyes and breathed deeply.

In the observation room, Odrade sank back into her chair and asked: "What did you see, Duncan?"

"When Sheeana pushed him away from her, he turned with a swiftness I have never seen except in Murbella."

"Faster even than that."

"Perhaps . . . it's because his body is young and we have given him prana-bindu training."

"Something else. You alerted us, Duncan. An unknown in Atreides marker cells." She glanced at the watchful Proctors and shook her head. *No. Not yet.* "Damn that mother of his! Hypno-induction to block an Imprinter and she hid it from us."

"But look what she gave us," Idaho said. "A more effective way to restore memories."

"We should have seen that on our own!" Odrade felt anger at herself. "Scytale claims Tleilaxu used pain and confrontation. I wonder."

"Ask him."

"It's not that simple. Our Truthsayers are not certain of him."

"He is opaque."

"When have you studied him?"

"Dar! I have access to comeye records."

"I know, but . . ."

"Dammit! Will you keep your eyes on Teg? Look at him! What's happening?"

Odrade snapped her attention to the seated child.

Teg looked at the comeyes, an expression of terrible intensity on his face.

It had been for him like awakening from sleep in the stress of conflict, an aide's hand shaking him. Something needed his attention!

He recalled sitting in the no-ship's command center, Dar standing beside him with a hand on his neck. *Scratching him?* Something urgent to do. What? His body felt wrong. Gammu . . . and now they were on Dune and . . . He remembered different things: childhood on Chapterhouse? Dar as . . . as . . . More memories meshed. *They tried to imprint me!*

Awareness flowed around this thought like a river spreading itself for a rock.

"Dar! Are you there? You're there!"

Odrade sat back and put a hand to her chin. *What now?*

"Mother!" What an accusatory tone!

Odrade touched a transplate beside her chair. "Hello, Miles. Shall we go for a walk in the orchards?"

"No more games, Dar. I know why you need me. I warn you, though: Violence projects the wrong kinds of people into power. As if you didn't know!"

"Still loyal to the Sisterhood, Miles, in spite of what we just tried?"

He glanced at the watchful Sheeana. "Still your obedient dog."

Odrade shot an accusatory look at the smiling Idaho. "You and your damned stories!"

"All right, Miles—no more games but I have to know about Gammu. They say you moved faster than the eye could follow."

"True." Flat, what-the-hell tone.

"And just now . . ."

"This body's too small to carry the load."

"But you . . ."

"I used it up in just one burst and I'm starving."

Odrade glanced at Idaho. He nodded. *Truth.*

She motioned the Proctors back from the hatch. They hesitated before obeying. What had Bell told them?

Teg was not through. "Do I have it right, daughter? Since every individual is accountable ultimately to the self, formation of that self demands the utmost care and attention?"

That damned mother of his taught him everything!

"I apologize, Miles. We did not know how your mother prepared you."

"Whose idea was it?" He looked at Sheeana as he spoke.

"My idea, Miles," Idaho said.

"Oh, you're there, too?" More memory trickled back.

"And I recall the pain you caused me when you restored my memories," Idaho said.

That sobered him. "Point taken, Duncan. No apology needed." He looked at the speakers relaying their voices. "How's the air at the top, Dar? Rarefied enough for you?"

Damned silly idea! she thought. *And he knows it. Not rarefied at all.* The air was thick with the breathing of those around her, including ones wanting to share her dramatic presence, ones with ideas (sometimes the idea they would be better at her job), ones with offering hands and demanding hands. Rarefied, indeed! She sensed that Teg was trying to tell her something. What?

"Sometimes I must be the autocrat!"

She heard herself saying this to him during one of their orchard walks, explaining "autocrat" to him and adding: *"I have the power and must use it. That drags on me terribly."*

You have the power, so use it! That was what this Mentat Bashar was telling her. *Kill me or release me, Dar.*

Still, she stalled for time and knew he would sense it. "Miles, Burzmali's dead, but he kept a reserve force here he trained himself. The best of—"

"Don't bother me with petty details!" What a voice of command! Thin and reedy but all other essentials there.

Without being told, the Proctors returned to the hatch. Odrade waved them away with an angry gesture. Only then did she realize that she had reached a decision.

"Give him back his clothes and bring him out," she said. "Get Streggi in here."

Teg's first words on emerging alarmed Odrade and made her wonder if she had made a mistake.

"What if I will not do battle the way you want?"

"But you said . . ."

"I've said many things in my . . . lives. Battle doesn't reinforce moral sense, Dar."

She (and Taraza) had heard the Bashar on that subject more than once. *"Warfare leaves a residue of 'eat drink and be merry' that often leads inexorably to moral breakdown."*

Correct but she did not know what he had in mind with his reminder. *"For every veteran who returns with a new sense of destiny ('I survived; that must be God's purpose') more come home with barely submerged bitterness, ready to take 'the easy way' because they saw so much of it in the stresses of war."*

They were Teg's words but her belief.

Streggi hurried into the room but before she could speak, Odrade motioned her to stand aside and wait silently.

For once, the acolyte had the courage to disobey Mother Superior. "Duncan should know he has another daughter. Mother and child live and are healthy." She looked at Teg. "Hello, Miles." Only then did Streggi remove herself to the rear wall and stand quietly.

She is better than I hoped, Odrade thought.

Idaho relaxed into his chair, feeling now the tensions of worry that had interfered with his appreciation of what he had observed here.

Teg nodded to Streggi but spoke to Odrade: "Any more words to whisper in God's ear?" It was essential to control their attention and count on Odrade recognizing it. "If not, I'm really famished."

Odrade raised a finger to signal Streggi and heard the acolyte leave.

She sensed where Teg was directing her attention and, sure enough, he said: "Perhaps you've really created a scar this time."

A barb directed at the Sisterhood's boast that "We don't let scars accumulate on our pasts. Scars often conceal more than they reveal."

"Some scars *reveal* more than they conceal," he said. He looked at Idaho. "Right, Duncan?" *One Mentat to another.*

"I believe I've come in on an old argument," Idaho said.

Teg looked at Odrade. "See, daughter? A Mentat knows old argument when he hears it. You pride yourselves on knowing what's required of *you* at every turn, but the monster at this turning is one of your own making!"

"Mother Superior!" That was a Proctor who did not want her addressed thus.

Odrade ignored her. She felt chagrin, harsh and compelling. Taraza Within remembered the dispute: "*We are shaped by Bene Gesserit associations. In peculiar ways, they blunt us. Oh, we cut swift and deep when we must, but that's another kind of blunting.*"

"I'll not take part in blunting you," Teg said. So he remembered.

Streggi returned with a bowl of stew, brown broth with meat floating in it. Teg sat on the floor and spooned it into his mouth with urgent motions.

Odrade remained silent, her thoughts moving where Teg had sent them. There was a hard shell Reverend Mothers put around themselves against which all things from outside (including emotions) played like projections. Murbella was right and the Sisterhood had to relearn emotions. If they were only observers, they were doomed.

She addressed Teg. "You won't be asked to blunt us."

Both Teg and Idaho heard something else in her voice. Teg put aside his empty bowl but Idaho was first to speak. "Cultivated," he said.

Teg agreed. Sisters were seldom impulsive. You got ordered reactions from them even in times of peril. They went beyond what most people thought of as cultivated. They were driven not so much by dreams of power as by their own long view, a thing compounded by immediacy and almost unlimited memory. So Odrade was following a carefully thought out plan. Teg glanced at the watchful Proctors.

"You were prepared to kill me," he said.

No one answered. There was no need. They all recognized Mentat Projection.

Teg turned and looked back into the room where he had regained his memories. Sheeana was gone. More memories whispered at the edge of awareness. They would speak in their own time. This diminutive body. That was difficult. And Streggi . . . He focused on Odrade. "You were more clever than you thought. But my mother . . ."

"I don't think she anticipated this," Odrade said.

"No . . . she was not that much Atreides."

An electrifying word in these circumstances, it charged a special silence in the room. The Proctors moved closer.

That mother of his!

Teg ignored the hovering Proctors. "In answer to the questions you have not asked, I cannot explain what happened to me on Gammu. My physical and mental speed defies explanation. Given the size and energy, in one of your heartbeats I could be clear of this room and well on my way out of the ship. Ohhh . . ." Hand upraised. "I'm still your obedient dog. I'll do what you require, but perhaps not in the way you imagine."

Odrade saw consternation in the faces of her Sisters. *What have I loosed upon us?*

"We can prevent any living thing from leaving this ship," she said. "You may be fast but I doubt you are faster than the fire that would engulf you should you try to leave without our permission."

"I will leave in my own good time and *with* your permission. How many of Burzmali's special troops do you have?"

"Almost two million." Startled out of her.

"So many!"

"He had more than twice that number with him at Lampadas when Honored Matres obliterated them."

"We shall have to be more clever than poor Burzmali. Would you leave me to discuss this with Duncan? That is why you keep us around, isn't it? Our specialty?" He aimed a smiling look at the overhead comeyes. "I'm sure you'll review our discussion thoroughly before approving."

Odrade and her Sisters exchanged glances. They shared an unspoken question: *What else can we do?*

As she stood, Odrade looked at Idaho. "Here's a real job for a Truthsayer-Mentat!"

When the women were gone, Teg pulled himself up onto one of the chairs and looked into the empty room visible beyond the seewall. It had been close there and he still felt his heart pumping hard from the effort. "Quite a show," he said.

"I've seen better." Extremely dry.

"What I'd like right now is a large glass of Marinete, but I doubt this body could take it."

"Bell will be waiting for Dar when she gets back to Central," Idaho said.

"To the nethermost hell with Bell! We have to defuse those Honored Matres before they find us."

"And our Bashar has just the plan."

"Damn that title!"

Idaho inhaled a sharp breath restricted by shock.

"Tell you something, Duncan!" Intense. "Once when I was arriving for an important meeting with potential enemies, I heard an aide announce me. 'The Bashar is here.' I damned near stumbled, caught by the abstraction."

"Mentat blur."

"Of course it was. But I knew the title removed me from something I did not dare lose. Bashar? I was more than that! I was Miles Teg, the name given me by my parents."

"You were on the name-chain!"

"Certainly, and I realized my name stood at a distance from something more primal. Miles Teg? No, I was more basic than that. I could hear my mother saying, 'Oh, what a beautiful baby.' So there I was with another name: 'Beautiful Baby.'"

"Did you go deeper?" Idaho found himself fascinated.

"I was caught. Name leads to name leads to names leads to nameless. When I walked into that important room, I was nameless. Did you ever risk that?"

"Once." A reluctant admission.

"We all do it at least once. But there I was. I'd been briefed. I had a reference for everyone at that table—face, name, title, plus all of the backgrounding."

"But you weren't really there."

"Oh, I could see the expectant faces measuring me, wondering, worrying. But they did not know me!"

"That gave you a feeling of great power?"

"Exactly as we were warned in Mentat school. I asked myself: 'Is this Mind at its beginning?' Don't laugh. It's a tantalizing question."

"So you went deeper?" Caught by Teg's words, Idaho ignored tugs of warning at the edge of his awareness.

"Oh, yes. And I found myself in the famous 'Hall of Mirrors' they described and warned us to flee."

"So you remembered how to get out and . . ."

"Remembered? You've obviously been there. Did memory get you out?"

"It helped."

"Despite the warnings, I lingered, seeing my 'self of selves' and infinite permutations. Reflections of reflections ad infinitum."

"Fascination of the 'ego core.' Damn few ever escape from that depth. You were lucky."

"I'm not sure it should be called luck. I knew there must be a First Awareness, an awakening . . ."

"Which discovers it is not the first."

"But I wanted a self at the root of the self!"

"Didn't the people at this meeting notice anything odd about you?"

"I found out later I sat down with a wooden expression that concealed these mental gymnastics."

"You didn't speak?"

"I was struck dumb. This was interpreted as 'the Bashar's expected reticence.' So much for reputation."

Idaho started to smile and remembered the comeyes. He saw at once how the watchdogs would interpret such revelations. Wild talent in a dangerous descendant of the Atreides! Sisters knew about the mirrors. Anyone who escaped must be suspect. What did the mirrors show him?

As though he heard the dangerous question, Teg said: "I was caught and knew it. I could visualize myself as a bedridden vegetable but I didn't care. The mirrors were everything until, like something floating up out of water, I saw my mother. She looked more or less the way she had just before she died."

Idaho inhaled a trembling breath. Didn't Teg know what he had just said for the comeyes to record?

"The Sisters will now imagine I'm at least a potential Kwisatz Haderach," Teg said. "Another Muad'Dib. Bullcrap! As you're so fond of saying, Duncan. Neither of us would risk that. We know what he created and we're not stupid!"

Idaho could not swallow. Would they accept Teg's words? He spoke the truth but still . . .

"She took my hand," Teg said. "I could feel it! And she led me right out of the Hall. I expected her to be with me when I felt myself seated at the table. My hand still tingled from her touch but she was gone. I knew that. I just brought myself to attention and took over. The Sisterhood had important advantages to gain there and I gained them."

"Something your mother planted in—"

"No! I saw her the same way Reverend Mothers see Other Memory. It was her way of saying: 'Why the hell are you wasting time here when there's work to do?' She has never left me, Duncan. The past never leaves any of us."

Idaho abruptly saw the purpose behind Teg's recital. *Honesty and candor, indeed!*

"You have Other Memory!"

"No! Except what anyone has in emergencies. The Hall of Mirrors was an emergency and it also let me see and feel the source of help. But I'm not going back there!"

Idaho accepted this. Most Mentats risked one dip into Infinity and learned the transient nature of names and titles but Teg's account was much more than a statement about Time as flow and tableau.

"I figured it was time we introduced ourselves fully to the Bene Gesserit," Teg said. "They should know how far they can trust us. There's work to do and we've wasted enough time on stupidities."

Spend energies on those who make you strong. Energy spent on weaklings drags you to doom. (HM rule) Bene Gesserit Commentary: Who judges?

—THE DORTUJLA RECORD

The day of Dortujla's return did not go well for Odrade. A weapons conference with Teg and Idaho ended without decision. She had sensed the hunter's axe all during the meeting and knew this colored her reactions.

Then the afternoon session with Murbella—words, words, words. Murbella was tangled in questions of philosophy. A dead end if Odrade had ever encountered one.

Now she stood in the early evening at the westernmost edge of Central's perimeter paving. It was one of her favorite places, but Bellonda beside her deprived Odrade of the anticipated quiet enjoyment.

Sheeana found them there and asked: "Is it true you have given Murbella the freedom of the ship?"

"There!" This was one of Bellonda's deepest fears.

"Bell," Odrade cut her off and pointed at the ring orchards. "That little rise over there where we've planted no trees. I want you to order a Folly in that place, built to my requirements. A gazebo with lattice framing for the views."

No stopping Bellonda now. Odrade had seldom seen her this incensed. And the more Bellonda ranted, the more adamant Odrade became.

"You want a . . . a Folly? In that orchard? What else will you waste our substance on? Folly! A most appropriate label for another of your . . ."

It was a silly argument. Both of them knew it twenty words into the thing. Mother Superior could not unbend first and Bell seldom unbent for anything. Even when Odrade fell silent, Bellonda charged onward into empty ramparts. At the end, when Bellonda ran out of energy, Odrade said: "You owe me a fine dinner, Bell. See that it's the best you can arrange."

"Owe you . . ." Bellonda started to splutter.

"A peace offering," Odrade said. "I want it served in my gazebo . . . my Fancy Folly."

When Sheeana laughed, Bellonda was forced to join but with an icy edge. She knew when she had been out-faced.

"Everyone will see it and say: 'See how confident Mother Superior is,'" Sheeana said.

"So you want it for morale!" At this point, Bellonda would have accepted almost any justification.

Odrade beamed at Sheeana. *My clever little darling!* Not only had Sheeana ceased teasing Bellonda, she had taken to reinforcing the older woman's self-esteem wherever possible. Bell knew it, of course, and there remained an inevitable Bene Gesserit question: *Why?*

Recognizing the suspicion, Sheeana said: "We're really arguing about Miles and Duncan. And I, for one, am sick of it."

"If I just knew what you were really doing, Dar!" Bellonda said.

"Energy has its own patterns, Bell!"

"What do you mean?" Quite startled.

"They are going to find us, Bell. And I know how."

Bellonda actually gaped.

"We are slaves of our habits," Odrade said. "Slaves of energies we create. Can slaves break free? Bell, you know the problem as well as I do."

For once, Bellonda was nonplussed.

Odrade stared at her.

Pride, that was what Odrade saw when she looked at her Sisters and their places. Dignity was only a mask. No real humility. Instead, there was this visible conformity, a true Bene Gesserit pattern that, in a society aware of the peril in patterns, sounded a warning klaxon.

Sheeana was confused. "Habits?"

"Your habits always come hunting after you. The self you construct will haunt you. A ghost wandering around in search of your body, eager to possess you. We are addicted to the self we construct. Slaves to what we have done. We are addicted to Honored Matres and they to us!"

"More of your damned romanticism!" Bellonda said.

"Yes, I'm a romantic . . . in the same way the Tyrant was. He sensitized himself to the fixed shape of his creation. I am sensitive to his prescient trap."

But oh how close the hunter and oh how deep the pit.

Bellonda was not placated. "You said you know how they will find us."

"They have only to recognize their own habits and they . . . Yes?" This was to an acolyte messenger emerging from a covered passage behind Bellonda.

"Mother Superior, it's Reverend Mother Dortujla. Mother Fintil has brought her to the Landing Flat and they will be here within the hour."

"Bring her to my workroom!" Odrade looked at Bellonda with a stare that was almost wild. "Has she said anything?"

"Mother Dortujla is ill," the acolyte said.

Ill? What an extraordinary thing to say about a Reverend Mother.

"Reserve judgment." It was Bellonda-Mentat speaking, Bellonda foe of romanticism and wild imagination.

"Get Tam up there as an observer," Odrade said.

Dortujla hobbled in on a cane with Fintil and Streggi helping her. There was a firmness to Dortujla's eyes, though, and a sense of measuring behind every look she focused on her surroundings. She had her hood thrown back revealing hair the dark mottled brown of antique ivory and when she spoke her voice conveyed a sense of fatigue.

"I have done as you ordered, Mother Superior." As Fintil and

Streggi left the room, Dortujla sat without being invited, a slingchair beside Bellonda. Brief glances at Sheeana and Tamalane on her left, then a hard stare at Odrade. "They will meet with you on Junction. They think the place is their own idea and your Spider Queen is there!"

"How soon?" Sheeana asked.

"They want one hundred Standard days counting from just about now. I can be more precise if you want."

"Why so long?" Odrade asked.

"My opinion? They will use the time to reinforce their defenses on Junction."

"What guarantees?" That was Tam, terse as usual.

"Dortujla, what has happened to you?" Odrade was shocked by the trembling weakness apparent in the woman.

"They conducted experiments on me. But that is not important. The arrangements are. For what it's worth, they promise you safe passage in and out of Junction. Don't believe it. You are allowed a *small* entourage of servants, no more than five. Assume they will kill everyone who accompanies you, although . . . I may have taught them the error in that."

"They expect me to bring submission of the Bene Gesserit?" Odrade's voice had never been colder. Dortujla's words raised a specter of tragedy.

"That was the inducement."

"The Sisters who went with you?" Sheeana asked.

Dortujla tapped her forehead, a common Sisterhood gesture. "I have them. We agree the Honored Matres should be punished."

"Dead?" Odrade forced the word between tight lips.

"Attempting to force me into their ranks. '*You see? We will kill another one if you don't agree.*' I told them to kill us all and have done with it and to forget about meeting Mother Superior. They did not accept this until they ran out of hostages."

"You Shared them all?" Tamalane asked. Yes, that would be Tam's concern as she neared her own death.

"While pretending to assure myself they were dead. You may as well know the whole thing. These women are grotesque! They possess caged Futars. The bodies of my Sisters were thrown into the cages where the Futars ate them. The Spider Queen—an appropriate name—made me watch this."

"Disgusting!" Bellonda said.

Dortujla sighed. "They did not know, naturally, that I have worse visions in Other Memory."

"They sought to overwhelm your sensibilities," Odrade said. "Foolish. Were they surprised when you didn't react as they wished?"

"Chagrined, I would say. I think they had seen others react as I did. I told them it was as good a way as any to get fertilizer. I believe that angered them."

"Cannibalism," Tamalane muttered.

"Only in appearance," Dortujla said. "Futars definitely are not human. Barely tamed wild animals."

"No Handlers?" Odrade asked.

"I saw none. The Futars did speak. They said, 'Eat!' before they ate and they jibed at Honored Matres around them. 'You hungry?' That sort of thing. More important was what happened after they ate."

Dortujla lapsed into a fit of coughing. "They tried poisons," she said. "Stupid women!"

When she regained her breath, Dortujla said, "A Futar came to the bars of its cage after their . . . banquet? It looked at the Spider Queen and it screamed. I have never heard such a sound. Chilling! Every Honored Matre in that room froze and I swear to you they were terrified."

Sheeana touched Dortujla's arm. "A predator immobilizing its prey?"

"Undoubtedly. It had qualities of Voice. The Futars appeared surprised that it did not freeze me."

"The Honored Matres' reaction?" Bellonda asked. Yes, a Mentat would require that datum.

"A general clamor when they found their voices. Many shouted for

Great Honored Matre to destroy the Futars. She, however, took a calmer view. 'Too valuable alive,' she said."

"A hopeful sign," Tamalane said.

Odrade looked at Bellonda. "I will order Streggi to bring the Bashar here. Objections?"

Bellonda gave a curt nod. They knew the gamble must be taken despite questions about Teg's intentions.

To Dortujla, Odrade said: "I want you in my own guest quarters. We'll bring in Suks. Order what you need and prepare for a full Council meeting. You are a special advisor."

Dortujla spoke while struggling to her feet. "I've not slept in almost fifteen days and I will need a special meal."

"Sheeana, see to that and get the Suks up here. Tam, stay with the Bashar and Streggi. Regular reports. He'll want to go to the cantonment and take personal charge. Get him a comlink with Duncan. Nothing must impede them."

"You want me here with him?" Tamalane asked.

"You are his leech. Streggi takes him nowhere without your knowledge. He wants Duncan as Weapons Master. Make sure he accepts Duncan's confinement in the ship. Bell, any weapons data Duncan requires—priority. Comments?"

There were no comments. Thoughts about consequences, yes, but the decisiveness of Odrade's behavior infected them.

Sitting back, Odrade closed her eyes and waited until silence told her she was alone. The comeyes were still watching, of course.

They know I'm tired. Who wouldn't be under these circumstances? Three more Sisters killed by those monsters! Bashar! They must feel our lash and know the lesson!

When she heard Streggi arrive with Teg, Odrade opened her eyes. Streggi led him in by the hand but there was something about them saying this was not an adult guiding a child. Teg's movements said he gave Streggi permission to treat him this way. She would have to be warned.

Tam followed and went to a chair near the windows directly beneath the bust of Chenoeh. Significant positioning? Tam did strange things lately.

"Do you wish me to stay, Mother Superior?" Streggi released Teg's hand and stood near the door.

"Sit over there beside Tam. Listen and do not interrupt. You must know what will be required of you."

Teg hitched himself onto the chair recently occupied by Dortujla. "I suppose this is a council of war."

That's an adult behind the childish voice.

"I won't ask your plan yet," Odrade said.

"Good. The unexpected takes more time and I may not be able to tell you what I intend until the moment of action."

"We've been observing you with Duncan. Why are you interested in ships from the Scattering?"

"Long-haul ships have a distinctive appearance. I saw them on the flat at Gammu."

Teg sat back and let this sink in, glad of the briskness he sensed in Odrade's manner. Decisions! No long deliberations. That suited his needs. *They must not learn the full extent of my abilities. Not yet.*

"You would disguise an attack force?"

Bellonda came through the door as Odrade was speaking and growled an objection while sitting: "Impossible! They'll have recognition codes and secret signals for—"

"Let me decide that, Bell, or remove me from command."

"This is the Council!" Bellonda said. "You don't—"

"Mentat?" He looked fully at her, the Bashar apparent in his gaze.

When she fell silent, he said: "Don't question my loyalty! If you would weaken me, replace me!"

"Let him have his say." That was Tam. "This isn't the first Council where the Bashar has appeared as our equal."

Bellonda lowered her chin a fractional millimeter.

To Odrade, Teg said, "Avoiding warfare is a matter of intelligence—the gathered variety and intellectual power."

Throwing our own cant at us! She heard Mentat in his voice and

Bellonda obviously heard this as well. Intelligence and intelligence: the doubled view. Without it, warfare often occurred as an accident.

The Bashar sat silently, letting them stew in their own historical observations. The urge to conflict went far deeper than consciousness. The Tyrant had been right. Humankind acted as "one beast." The forces impelling that great collective animal went back to tribal days and beyond, as did so many forces to which humans responded without thinking.

Mix the genes.

Expand Lebensraum for your own breeders.

Gather the energies of others: collect slaves, peons, servants, serfs, markets, workers . . . The terms often were interchangeable.

Odrade saw what he was doing. Knowledge absorbed from the Sisterhood helped make him the incomparable Mentat Bashar. He held these things as instincts. Energy-eating drove war's violence. This was described as "greed, fear (that others will take your hoard), power hunger" and on and on into futile analyses. Odrade had heard these even from Bellonda who obviously was not taking it well that a *subordinate* should remind them of what they already knew.

"The Tyrant knew," Teg said. "Duncan quotes him: 'War is behavior with roots in the single cell of the primeval seas. Eat whatever you touch or it will eat you.'"

"What do you propose?" Bellonda at her most snappish.

"A feint at Gammu, then strike their base on Junction. For that we need first-hand observations." He stared steadily at Odrade.

He knows! The thought flared in Odrade's mind.

"You think your studies of Junction when it was a Guild base are still accurate?" Bellonda demanded.

"They haven't had time to change the place much from what I stored here." He tapped his forehead in an odd parody of the Sisterhood's gesture.

"Englobement," Odrade said.

Bellonda looked at her sharply. "The cost!"

"Losing everything is more costly," Teg said.

"Foldspace sensors don't have to be large," Odrade said. "Duncan would set them to create a Holzmann explosion on contact?"

"The explosions would be visible and would give us a trajectory." He sat back and looked at an indefinite area on Odrade's rear wall. Would they accept it? He dared not frighten them with another display of wild talent. If Bell knew he could *see* the no-ships!

"Do it!" Odrade said. "You have the command. Use it."

There was a distinct sense of chuckling from Taraza in Other Memories. *Give him his head! That's how I got such a great reputation!*

"One thing," Bellonda said. She looked at Odrade. "You're going to be his spy?"

"Who else can get in there and transmit observations?"

"They'll be monitoring every means of transmission!"

"Even the one that tells our waiting no-ship we have not been betrayed?" Odrade asked.

"An encrypted message hidden in the transmission," Teg said. "Duncan has devised an encryption that would take months to break but we doubt they'll detect its presence."

"Madness," Bellonda muttered.

"I met an Honored Matre military commander on Gammu," Teg said. "Slack when it came to necessary details. I think they're overconfident."

Bellonda stared at him and there was the Bashar staring back at her out of a child's innocent eyes. "Abandon all sanity ye who enter here," he said.

"Get out of here, all of you!" Odrade ordered. "You have work to do. And Miles . . ."

He already had slid off the chair but he stood there looking much as he always had when waiting for *Mother* to tell him something important.

"Did you refer to the lunacy of dramatic events that warfare always amplifies?"

"What else? Surely you didn't think I referred to your Sisterhood!"

"Duncan plays this game sometimes."

"I don't want us catching the Honored Matre madness," Teg said. "It is contagious, you know."

"They've tried to control the sex drive," Odrade said. "That always gets away from you."

"Runaway lunacy," he agreed. He leaned against the table, his chin barely above the surface. "Something drove those women back here. Duncan's right. They're looking for something and running away at the same time."

"You have ninety Standard days to get ready," she said. "Not one day more."

Ish yara al-ahdab hadbat-u. (A hunchback does not see his own hunch.—Folk Saying.) Bene Gesserit Commentary: The hunch may be seen with the aid of mirrors but mirrors may show the whole being.

—THE BASHAR TEG

It was a weakness in the Bene Gesserit that Odrade knew the entire Sisterhood soon must recognize. She gained no consolation from having seen it first. *Denying our deepest resource when we need it most!* The Scatterings had gone beyond the ability of humans to assemble the experiences in manageable form. *We can only extract essentials, and that is a matter of judgment.* Vital data would remain dormant in great and small events, accumulations called instinct. So that was it finally— they must fall back on unspoken knowledge.

In this age, the word "refugees" took on the color of its pre-space meaning. Small bands of Reverend Mothers sent out by the Sisterhood held something in common with old scenes of displaced stragglers trudging down forgotten roads, pitiful belongings bound in bits of cloth, wheeled on decrepit prams and toy wagons, or piled atop lopsided vehicles, remnant humanity clinging to the outsides and densely packed within, every face blank with despair or heated by desperation.

So we repeat history and repeat it and repeat it.

As she entered a tubeslot shortly before lunch, Odrade's thoughts clung to her Scattered Sisters: political refugees, economic refugees, pre-battle refugees.

Is this your Golden Path, Tyrant?

Visions of her Scattered ones haunted Odrade as she entered Central's Reserved Dining Room, a place only Reverend Mothers might enter. They served themselves here at cafeteria lines.

It had been twenty days since she had released Teg to the cantonment. Rumors were flying in Central, especially among Proctors, although there still was no sign of another vote. New decisions must be announced today and they would have to be more than naming the ones who would accompany her to Junction.

She glanced around the dining room, an austere place of yellow walls, low ceiling, small square tables that could be latched in rows for larger groups. Windows along one side revealed a garden court under a translucent cover. Dwarf apricots in green fruit, lawn, benches, small tables. Sisters ate outside when sunlight poured into the enclosed yard. No sunlight today.

She ignored a cafeteria line where a place was being made for her. *Later, Sisters.*

At the corner table near the windows reserved for her, she deliberately moved the chairs. Bell's brown chairdog pulsed faintly at this unaccustomed disturbance. Odrade sat with her back to the room, knowing this would be interpreted correctly: *Leave me to my own thoughts.*

While she waited, she stared out at the courtyard. An enclosing hedge of exotic purple-leaved shrubs was in red flower—giant blossoms with delicate stamens of deep yellow.

Bellonda arrived first, dropping into her chairdog with no comment on its new position. Bell frequently appeared untidy, belt loose, robe wrinkled, bits of food on the bosom. Today, she was neat and clean.

Now, why is that?

Bellonda said, "Tam and Sheeana will be late."

Odrade accepted this without stopping her study of this different Bellonda. Was she a bit slimmer? There was no way to insulate a Mother Superior completely from what went on within her sensory area of concerns but sometimes pressures of work distracted her from small changes. These were a Reverend Mother's natural habitat, though, and negative evidence was as illuminating as positive. On reflection, Odrade realized that this new Bellonda had been with them for several weeks.

Something had happened to Bellonda. Any Reverend Mother could exercise reasonable control over weight and figure. A matter of internal chemistry—banking fires or letting them burn high. For years now, rebellious Bellonda had flaunted a gross body.

"You've lost weight," Odrade said.

"Fat was beginning to slow me too much."

That had never been sufficient reason for Bell to change her ways. She had always compensated with speed of mind, with projections and faster transport.

"Duncan really got to you, didn't he?"

"I'm not a hypocrite nor criminal!"

"Time to send you to a punishment Keep, I guess."

This recurrent humorous thrust usually annoyed Bellonda. Today, it did not arouse her. But under pressure of Odrade's stare, she said: "If you must know, it's Sheeana. She has been after me to improve my appearance and broaden my circle of associates. Annoying! I'm doing it to shut her up."

"Why are Tam and Sheeana late?"

"Reviewing your latest meeting with Duncan. I have severely limited who has access to it. No telling what will happen when it becomes general knowledge."

"As it will."

"Inevitable. I only buy us time to prepare."

"I did not want it suppressed, Bell."

"Dar, what *are* you doing?"

"I will announce that at a Convocation."

No words but Bellonda glared her surprise.

"A Convocation is my right," Odrade said.

Bellonda leaned back and stared at Odrade, assessing, questioning . . . all without words. The last Convocation of the Bene Gesserit had been at the Tyrant's death. And before that, at the Tyrant's seizure of power. A Convocation had not been thought possible since Honored Matres attacked. Too much time taken from desperate labors.

Presently, Bellonda asked: "Will you risk bringing Sisters from our surviving Keeps?"

"No. Dortujla will represent them. There is precedent, as you know."

"First, you free Murbella; now it's a Convocation."

"Free? Murbella is tied by chains of gold. Where would she go without her Duncan?"

"But you've given Duncan freedom to leave the ship!"

"Has he?"

Bellonda said, "You think that information from the ship's armory is all he'll take?"

"I know it."

"I am reminded of Jessica turning her back on the Mentat who would have killed her."

"The Mentat was immobilized by his own beliefs."

"Sometimes the bull gores the matador, Dar."

"More often he does not."

"Our survival should not depend on statistics!"

"Agreed. That is why I call Convocation."

"Acolytes included?"

"Everyone."

"Even Murbella? Does she get an acolyte's vote?"

"I think she may be a Reverend Mother by then."

Bellonda gasped, then: "You move too fast, Dar!"

"These times require it."

Bellonda glanced toward the dining room door. "Here's Tam. Later than I expected. I wonder if they took time to consult Murbella?"

Tamalane arrived, breathing hard from hurrying. She dropped into her blue chairdog, noted the new positions and said: "Sheeana will be along presently. She is showing records to Murbella."

Bellonda addressed Tamalane. "She's going to put Murbella through the Agony and call a Convocation."

"I'm not surprised." Tamalane spoke with her old precision. "The position of that Honored Matre must be resolved as soon as possible."

Sheeana joined them then and took the slingchair at Odrade's left, speaking as she sat. "Have you watched Murbella walk?"

Odrade was caught by the way this abrupt question, uttered without preamble, fixed the attention. *Murbella walking in the ship.* Observed just that morning. Beauty in Murbella and the eye could not avoid it. To other Bene Gesserit, Reverend Mothers and acolytes alike, she was something of an exotic. She had arrived full-grown from the dangerous Outside. *One of them.* It was her movements, though, that compelled the eye. Homeostasis in her that went beyond the norms.

Sheeana's question redirected the observer's mind. Something about Murbella's quite acceptable passage required new examination. What was it?

Murbella's motions were always carefully chosen. She excluded anything not required to go from here to there. *Path of least resistance?* It was a view of Murbella that sent a pang through Odrade. Sheeana had seen it, of course. Was Murbella one of those who would choose an easy way every time? Odrade could see that question on the faces of her companions.

"The Agony will sort it out," Tamalane said.

Oldrade looked squarely at Sheeana. "Well?" She had asked the question, after all.

"Perhaps it's only that she does not waste energy. But I agree with Tam: the Agony."

"Are we making a terrible mistake?" Bellonda asked.

Something in the way this question was asked told Odrade that Bell had made a Mentat summation. *She has seen what I intend!*

"If you know a better course reveal it now," Odrade said. *Or hold your peace.*

Silence gripped them. Odrade looked at her companions in succession, lingering on Bell.

Help us, whatever gods there may be! And I, being Bene Gesserit, am too much agnostic to make that plea with anything more than a hope of covering all possibilities. Don't reveal it, Bell. If you know what I will do, you know it must be seen in its own time.

Bellonda brought Odrade out of reverie with a cough. "Are we going to eat or talk? People are staring."

"Should we have another go at Scytale?" Sheeana asked.

Was that an attempt to divert my attention?

Bellonda said: "Give him nothing! He's in reserve. Let him sweat."

Odrade looked carefully at Bellonda. She was fuming over the silence imposed on her by Odrade's secret decision. Avoiding a meeting of eyes with Sheeana. *Jealous! Bell is jealous of Sheeana!*

Tamalane said, "I am only an advisor now but—"

"Stop that, Tam!" Odrade snapped.

"Tam and I have been discussing that ghola," Bellonda said. (Idaho was "that ghola" when Bellonda had something disparaging to say.) "Why did he think he needed to talk secretly to Sheeana?" A hard stare at Sheeana.

Odrade saw shared suspicion. *She does not accept the explanation. Does she reject Duncan's emotional bias?*

Sheeana spoke quickly. "Mother Superior explained that!"

"Emotion," Bellonda sneered.

Odrade raised her voice and was surprised at this reaction. "Suppressing emotions is a weakness!"

Tamalane's shaggy eyebrows lifted.

Sheeana intruded: "If we won't bend, we can break."

Before Bellonda could respond, Odrade said: "Ice can be chipped apart or melted. Ice maidens are vulnerable to a single form of attack."

"I'm hungry," Sheeana said.

Peace-making? Not a role expected of The Mouse.

Tamalane stood. "Bouillabaisse. We must eat the fish before our sea is gone. Not enough nullentropy storage."

In the softest of simulflows, Odrade noted the departure of her companions to the cafeteria line. Tamalane's accusatory words recalled that second day with Sheeana after the decision to phase out the Great Sea. Standing at Sheeana's window in the early morning, Odrade had watched a seabird move against the desert background. It winged its way northward, a creature completely out of place in that setting but beautiful in a profoundly nostalgic way because of it.

White wings glistened in early sunlight. A touch of black beneath and in front of its eyes. Abruptly, it hovered, wings motionless. Then, lifting on an air current, it tucked its wings like a hawk and plummeted out of view behind the farther buildings. Reappearing, it carried something in its beak, a morsel it swallowed on the wing.

A seabird alone and adapting.

We adapt. We do indeed adapt.

It was not a quiet thought. Nothing to induce repose. Shocking rather. Odrade had felt jarred out of a dangerously drifting course. Not only her beloved Chapterhouse but their entire human universe was breaking out of its old shapes and taking on new forms. Perhaps it was right in this new universe that Sheeana continued to conceal things from Mother Superior. *And she is concealing something.*

Once more, Bellonda's acidic tones brought Odrade to full awareness of her surroundings. "If you won't serve yourself, I suppose we must take care of you." Bellonda placed a bowl of aromatic fish stew in front of Odrade, a great chunk of garlic bread beside it.

When each had sampled the bouillabaisse, Bellonda put down her spoon and stared hard at Odrade. "You're not going to suggest we 'love one another' or some such debilitating nonsense?"

"Thank you for bringing my food," Odrade said.

Sheeana swallowed and a wide grin came over her features. "It's delicious."

Bellonda returned to eating. "It's all right." But she had heard the unspoken comment.

Tamalane ate steadily, shifting attention from Sheeana to Bellonda and then to Odrade. Tam appeared to agree with a proposed softening of emotional strictures. At least, she voiced no objections and older Sisters were most likely to object.

The love the Bene Gesserit tried to deny was everywhere, Odrade thought. In small things and big. How many ways there were to prepare delectable, life-sustaining foods, recipes that really were embodiments of loves old and new. This bouillabaisse so smoothly restorative on her tongue; its origins were planted deeply in love: the wife at home using that part of the day's catch her husband could not sell.

The very essence of the Bene Gesserit was concealed in loves. Why else minister to those unspoken needs humanity always carried? Why else work for the perfectibility of humankind?

Bowl empty, Bellonda put down her spoon and wiped up the dregs with the last of her bread. She swallowed, looking pensive. "Love weakens us," she said. No force in her voice.

An acolyte could have said it no differently. Right out of the Coda. Odrade concealed amusement and countered with another Coda stepping-stone. "Beware jargon. It usually hides ignorance and carries little knowledge."

Respectful wariness entered Bellonda's eyes.

Sheeana pushed herself back from the table and wiped her mouth with her napkin. Tamalane did the same. Her chairdog adjusted as she leaned back, eyes bright and amused.

Tam knows! The wily old witch is still wise in my ways. But Sheeana . . . what game is Sheeana playing? I would almost say she hopes to distract me, to keep my attention away from her. She is very good at it, learned it at my knee. Well . . . two can play that game. I press Bellonda, but watch my little Dune waif.

"What price respectability, Bell?" Odrade asked.

Bellonda accepted this thrust in silence. Hidden in Bene Gesserit jargon was a definition of respectability and they all knew it.

"Should we honor the memory of the Lady Jessica for her humanity?" Odrade asked. *Sheeana is surprised!*

"Jessica put the Sisterhood in jeopardy!" *Bellonda accuses.*

"To thine own Sisters be true," Tamalane murmured.

"Our antique definition of respectability helps keep us human," Odrade said. *Hear me well, Sheeana.*

Her voice little more than a whisper, Sheeana said, "If we lose that we lose it all."

Odrade suppressed a sigh. *So that's it!*

Sheeana met her gaze. "You are instructing us, of course."

"Twilight thoughts," Bellonda muttered. "Best we avoid them."

"Taraza called us 'Latter-day Bene Gesserit,'" Sheeana said.

Odrade's mood went self-accusatory.

The bane of our present existence. Sinister imaginings can destroy us.

How easy it was to conjure a future that looked at them from glazing orange eyes of berserk Honored Matres. Fears out of many pasts crouched within Odrade, breathless moments focused on fangs that went with such eyes.

Odrade forced her attention back to the immediate problem. "Who will accompany me to Junction?"

They knew Dortujla's harrowing experience and word of it had spread throughout Chapterhouse.

"*Whoever goes with Mother Superior could well be fed to Futars.*"

"Tam," Odrade said. "You and Dortujla." *And that may be a death sentence. The next step is obvious.* "Sheeana," Odrade said, "you will Share with Tam. Dortujla and I will Share with Bell. And I also will share with *you* before I go."

Bellonda was aghast. "Mother Superior! I am not suited to take your place."

Odrade held her attention on Sheeana. "That is not being suggested. I will merely make you the repository of my lives." Definite fear on Sheeana's face but she dared not refuse a direct order. Odrade nodded to Tamalane. "I will Share later. You and Sheeana will do it now."

Tamalane leaned toward Sheeana. The strictures of great age and imminent death made this a welcome thing for her but Sheeana involuntarily pulled away.

"Now!" Odrade said. *Let Tam judge whatever it is you hide.*

There was no escape. Sheeana bent her head to Tamalane's until they touched. The flash of the exchange was electric and the entire dining room felt it. Conversation stopped, every gaze turned toward the table by the window.

There were tears in Sheeana's eyes when she withdrew.

Tamalane smiled and made a gentle caressing motion with both hands along Sheeana's cheeks. "It's all right, dear. We all have these fears and sometimes do foolish things because of them. But I am pleased to call you Sister."

Tell us, Tam! Now!

Tamalane did not choose to do that. She faced Odrade and said, "We must cling to our humanity at any cost. Your lesson is well received and you have taught Sheeana well."

"When Sheeana Shares with you, Dar," Bellonda began, "could you not reduce the influence she has on Idaho?"

"I will not weaken a possible Mother Superior," Odrade said. "Thank you, Tam. I think we will make our venture to Junction without excess baggage. Now! I want a report by tonight on Teg's progress. His leech has been too long away from him."

"Will he learn that he has two leeches now?" Sheeana asked. *Such joy in her!*

Odrade stood.

If Tam accepts her then I must. Tam would never betray our Sisterhood. And Sheeana—of us all, Sheeana most reveals the natural traits from our human roots. Still . . . I wish she had never created that statue she calls "The Void."

Religion must be accepted as a source of energy. It can be directed for our purposes, but only within limits that experience reveals. Here is the secret meaning of Free Will.

—MISSIONARIA PROTECTIVA,
PRIMARY TEACHING

A thick cloud cover had moved over Central this morning and Odrade's workroom took on a gray silence to which she felt herself responding with inner stillness, as though she dared not move because that disturbed dangerous forces.

Murbella's day of Agony, she thought. *I must not think of omens.*

Weather had issued a peremptory warning about clouds. They were an *accidental displacement.* Corrective measures were being taken but would require time. Meanwhile, expect high winds, and there could be precipitation.

Sheeana and Tamalane stood at the window looking at this poorly controlled weather. Their shoulders touched.

Odrade watched them from her chair behind the table. Those two had become like a single person since yesterday's Sharing, not an unexpected occurrence. Precedents were known, although not many of them. Exchanges, occurring in the presence of poisonous spicy essence or at an actual moment of death, did not often allow further living contact between participants. It was interesting to observe. The two backs were oddly alike in their rigidity.

The force of extremis that made Sharing possible dictated powerful changes in personality and Odrade knew this with an intimacy that compelled tolerance. Whatever it was Sheeana concealed, Tam also concealed. *Something tied to Sheeana's basic humanity.* And Tam could be trusted. Until another Sister Shared with one of them, Tam's judgment must be accepted. Not that watchdogs would cease probing and observing minutiae but they needed no new crisis just now.

"This is Murbella's day," Odrade said.

"The odds are long she won't survive," Bellonda said, hunched forward in her chairdog. "What happens to our precious plan then?"

Our plan!

"Extremis," Odrade said.

In that context, it was a word with several meanings. Bellonda interpreted it as a possibility of acquiring Murbella's persona-memories at the moment of her death. "Then we must not permit Idaho to observe!"

"My order stands," Odrade said. "It's Murbella's wish and I have given my word."

"Mistake . . . mistake . . ." Bellonda muttered.

Odrade knew the source of Bellonda's doubts. Visible to all of them: Somewhere in Murbella lay something extremely painful. It caused her to shy away from certain questions like an animal confronted by a predator. Whatever it was, the thing went deep. Hypnotrance induction might not explain it.

"All right!" Odrade spoke loudly to emphasize it was for all of her listeners. "It's not the way we've ever done it before. But we cannot take Duncan from the ship so we must go to him. He will be present."

Bellonda was still well and truly shocked. No man, *barring the damned Kwisatz Haderach himself and his Tyrant son*, had ever known the particulars of this Bene Gesserit secret. Both of *those monsters* had felt the Agony. Two disasters! No matter that the Tyrant's Agony had worked its way inward a cell at a time to transform him into a sandworm symbiote (no more original worm, no more original human). And Muad'Dib! He dared the Agony and look what came of that!

Sheeana turned from the window and took one step toward the

table, giving Odrade the curious feeling that the two women standing there had become a Janus figure: back to back but only one persona.

"Bell is *confused* by your promise," Sheeana said. How soft her voice.

"He could be the catalyst to pull Murbella through," Odrade said. "You tend to underestimate the power of love."

"No!" Tamalane spoke to the window in front of her. "We fear its power."

"Could be!" Bell still was scornful but that came naturally to her. The expression on her face said she remained implacably stubborn.

"Hubris," Sheeana murmured.

"What?" Bellonda whirled in her chairdog, causing it to squeak with indignation.

"We share a common failing with Scytale," Sheeana said.

"Oh?" Bellonda was gnawing at Sheeana's secret.

"We think we make history," Sheeana said. She returned to her position beside Tamalane, both of them staring out the window.

Bellonda returned her attention to Odrade. "Do you understand that?"

Odrade ignored her. Let the Mentat work it out for herself. The projector on the worktable clicked and a message was displayed. Odrade reported it. "Still not ready at the ship." She looked at those two rigid backs in front of the window.

History?

On Chapterhouse, there had been little of what Odrade liked to think of as history-making before the Honored Matres. Only the steady graduation of Reverend Mothers passing through the Agony.

Like a river.

It flowed and it went somewhere. You could stand on the bank (as Odrade sometimes thought they did here) and you could observe the flow. A map might tell you where the river went but no map could reveal more essential things. A map could never show intimate movements of the river's cargo. Where did they go? Maps had limited value in this age. A printout or projection from Archives; that was not the map they required. There had to be a better one somewhere, one attached to all of those lives. You could carry *that* map in your memory and have it out occasionally for a closer look.

Whatever happened to the Reverend Mother Perinte we sent out last year?

The *map-in-the-mind* would take over and create a "Perinte Scenario." It was really yourself on the river, of course, but this made little difference. It still was the map they needed.

We don't like it that we're caught in someone else's currents, that we don't know what may be revealed at the river's next bend. We always prefer overflight even though any commanding position must remain part of other currents. Every flow contains unpredictable things.

Odrade looked up to see her three companions watching her. Tamalane and Sheeana had turned their backs to the window.

"Honored Matres have forgotten that clinging to any form of conservatism can be dangerous," Odrade said. "Have we forgotten it as well?"

They continued to stare at her but they had heard. Become too conservative and you were unprepared for surprises. That was what Muad'Dib had taught them, and his Tyrant son had made the lesson forever unforgettable.

Bellonda's glum expression did not change.

In the deep recesses of Odrade's consciousness, Taraza whispered: "*Careful, Dar. I was lucky. Quick to grab advantage. Just as you are. But you cannot depend on luck and that is what bothers them. Don't even expect luck. Much better to trust your water images. Let Bell have her say.*"

"Bell," Odrade said, "I thought you accepted Duncan."

"Within limits." Definitely accusatory.

"I think we should go out to the ship." Sheeana spoke with demanding emphasis. "This is not the place to wait. Do we fear what she may become?"

Tam and Sheeana turned toward the door simultaneously as though the same puppet master controlled their strings.

Odrade found the interruption welcome. Sheeana's question alarmed them. *What could Murbella become? A catalyst, my Sisters. A catalyst.*

The wind shook them when they emerged from Central and for once Odrade was thankful for tube transport. Walking could await warmer temperatures without this blustering mini-tempest tugging at their robes.

When they were seated in a private car, Bellonda once more took up her accusatory refrain. "Everything he does could be camouflage."

Once more, Odrade voiced the oft-repeated Bene Gesserit warning to limit their reliance on Mentats. "Logic is blind and often knows only its own past."

Tamalane chimed in with unexpected support. "You are getting paranoid, Bell!"

Sheeana spoke more softly. "I've heard you say, Bell, that logic is good for playing pyramid chess but often too slow for needs of survival."

Bellonda sat in glowering silence, only a faint hissing rumble of their tube passage intruding on the quiet.

Wounds must not be taken into the ship.

Odrade matched her tone to Sheeana's: "Bell, dear Bell. We do not have time to consider all ramifications of our plight. We no longer can say, 'If this happens, then that must surely follow, and in such a case, our moves must be so and so and so . . .'"

Bellonda actually chuckled. "Oh, my! The ordinary mind is such a clutter. And I must not demand what we all need and cannot have—sufficient time for every plan."

It was Bellonda-Mentat speaking, telling them she knew she was flawed by pride in her ordinary mind. What a badly organized, untidy place that was. *Imagine what the non-Mentat puts up with, imposing so little order.* She reached across the aisle and patted Odrade's shoulder.

"It's all right, Dar. I'll behave."

What would an outsider think, seeing that exchange? Odrade wondered. All four of them acting in concert for the needs of one Sister.

For the needs of Murbella's Agony, as well.

People saw only the outside of this Reverend Mother mask they wore.

When we must (which is most of the time these days) we function at astonishing levels of competence. No pride in that; a simple fact. But let us relax and we hear gibberish at the edges as ordinary folk do. Ours merely has more volume. We live our lives in little congeries like anyone else. Rooms of the mind, rooms of the body.

Bellonda had composed herself, hands clasped in her lap. She knew what Odrade planned and kept it to herself. It was a trust that went beyond Mentat Projection into something more basically human. Projection was a marvelously adaptable tool but a tool nonetheless. Ultimately, all tools depended on the ones who used them. Odrade was at a loss how to show her thanks without reducing trust.

I must walk my tightrope in silence.

She sensed the chasm beneath her, the nightmare image conjured by these reflections. The unseen hunter with an axe was closer. Odrade wanted to turn and identify the stalker but resisted. *I will not make Muad'Dib's mistake!* The prescient warning she had first sensed on Dune in the ruins of Sietch Tabr would not be exorcised until she ended or the Sisterhood ended. *Did I create this terrible threat by my fears? Surely not!* Still, she felt she had stared at Time in that ancient Fremen stronghold as though all past and all future were frozen into a tableau that could not be changed. *I must break free of you utterly, Muad'Dib!*

Their arrival at the Landing Flat pulled her from these fearful musings.

Murbella waited in rooms Proctors had prepared. At the center was a small amphitheater about seven meters along its enclosing back wall. Padded benches were stepped upward in a steep arc, seating for no more than twenty observers. Proctors had left her without explanation on the lowest bench staring at a suspensor-buoyed table. Straps hung over the sides to confine whoever lay on it.

Me.

An astonishing series of rooms, she thought. She had never before been permitted into this part of the ship. She felt exposed here, even more so than she had under open sky. The smaller rooms through which they had brought her to this amphitheater were clearly designed for medical emergencies: resuscitation equipment, sanitary odors, antiseptics.

Her removal to this room had been peremptory, none of her questions answered. Proctors had taken her from an advanced acolyte class in prana-bindu exercises. They said only: "Mother Superior's orders."

The quality of her guardian Proctors told her much. *Gentle but firm.* They were here to prevent flight and to make sure she went where ordered. *I won't try to escape!*

Where was Duncan?

Odrade had promised he would be with her for the Agony. Did his absence mean this was not to be her ultimate trial? Or had they concealed him behind some secret wall through which he could see and not be seen?

I want him at my side!

Didn't they know how to rule her? Certainly they did!

Threaten to deprive me of this man. That's all it takes to hold me and satisfy me. Satisfy! What a useless word. Complete me. That's better. I am less when we're apart. He knows it, too, damn him.

Murbella smiled. *How does he know it? Because he is completed in the same way.*

How could this be love? She felt no weakening from the tugs of desire. Bene Gesserit and Honored Matres alike said love weakened. She felt strenghened by Duncan. Even his small attentions were strengthening. When he brought her a steaming cup of stimtea in the morning, it was better coming from his hands. *Perhaps we have something more than love.*

Odrade and companions entered the amphitheater at the uppermost tier and stood a moment looking down at the figure seated below them. Murbella wore the white-trimmed long robe of a senior acolyte. She sat with elbow on knee, chin resting on fist, her attention concentrated on the table.

She knows.

"Where is Duncan?" Odrade asked.

At her words, Murbella stood and turned. The question confirmed what she had suspected.

"I'll find out," Sheeana said and left them.

Murbella waited in silence, matching Odrade stare for stare.

We must have her, Odrade thought. Never had the Bene Gesserit need been greater. What an insignificant figure Murbella was down there to carry so much in her person. The almost oval face with its widening at the brows revealed new Bene Gesserit composure. Widely set green eyes, arched brows—no squinting—no more orange. Small mouth—no more pouting.

She is ready.

Sheeana returned with Duncan at her side.

Odrade spared him a brief glance. *Nervous.* So Sheeana had told him. *Good.* That was an act of friendship. He might need friends here.

"You will sit up here and remain here unless I call you," Odrade said. "Stay with him, Sheeana."

Without being told, Tamalane flanked Duncan, one of them on each side. At a gentle gesture from Sheeana, they sat.

Bellonda beside her, Odrade descended to Murbella's level and went to the table. Oral syringes on the far side were ready to lift into position but remained empty. Odrade gestured at the syringes and nodded to Bellonda, who went out a side door in search of the Suk Reverend Mother in charge of spice essence.

Moving the table away from the back wall, Odrade began laying out straps and adjusting pads. She moved methodically, checking that everything had been provided on the small ledge beneath the table. Mouth pad to keep the Agonized One from biting her tongue. Odrade felt it to be sure it was strong. Murbella had a muscular jaw.

Murbella watched Odrade work, keeping silent, trying to make no disturbing noises.

Bellonda returned with spice essence and proceeded to fill the syringes. The poisonous essence had a pungent odor—bitter cinnamon.

Catching Odrade's attention, Murbella said, "I'm grateful that you're supervising this yourself."

"She's grateful!" Bellonda sneered, not looking up from her work.

"Leave this to me, Bell." Odrade kept her attention on Murbella.

Bellonda did not pause but something withdrawn took over her movements. Bellonda effacing herself? It never ceased to astonish Murbella how acolytes effaced themselves when they entered Mother Superior's presence. There but not there. Murbella had never quite achieved this even when she left probation and entered advanced status. *Bellonda, too?*

Staring hard at Murbella, Odrade said: "I know what reservations you hold in your breast, limits you place on your commitment to us. Well and good. I make no argument about that because, by and large, your reservations are very little different from those held by any of us."

Candor.

"The difference, if you would know it, is in the sense of responsibility. I am responsible for my Sisterhood . . . as much of it as still survives. They are a deep responsibility and one I sometimes look at with a jaundiced eye."

Bellonda sniffed.

Odrade appeared not to notice this as she continued. "The Bene Gesserit Sisterhood has gone somewhat sour since the Tyrant. Our contact with your Honored Matres has not improved matters. Honored Matres have the stench of death and decadence about them, going downhill into the great silence."

"Why do you tell me these things now?" Fear in Murbella's voice.

"Because, somehow, the worst of Honored Matre decadence did not touch you. Your spontaneous nature, perhaps. Although that has been dampened somewhat since Gammu."

"Your doing!"

"We've just taken a little wildness out of you, given you a better balance. You can live longer and healthier because of it."

"If I survive this!" Jerk of her head toward the table behind her.

"Balance is what I want you to remember, Murbella. Homeostasis.

Any group choosing suicide when it has other options does so out of insanity. Homeostasis gone haywire."

When Murbella looked at the floor, Bellonda snapped: "Listen to her, fool! She's doing her best to help you."

"All right, Bell. This is between us."

When Murbella continued to stare at the floor, Odrade said: "This is Mother Superior giving you an order. Look at me!"

Murbella's head snapped up and she stared into Odrade's eyes.

It was a tactic Odrade had used infrequently but with excellent results. Acolytes could be reduced to hysteria by it and then taught how to deal with their excessive response to emotions. Murbella appeared to be more angered than fearful. Excellent! But now was a time for caution.

"You have complained about the slow pacing of your education," Odrade said. "It was done with your needs foremost in our minds. Your key teachers all were chosen for steadiness, none of them impulsive. My instructions were explicit: 'Don't give you too many abilities too rapidly. Don't open a floodgate of powers that might be more than she can handle.'"

"How do you know what I can handle?" Still angry.

Odrade only smiled.

When Odrade continued silent, Murbella appeared flustered. Had she made a fool of herself before Mother Superior, before Duncan and these others? How humiliating.

Odrade reminded herself it was not good to make Murbella too conscious of her vulnerability. A bad tactic just now. No need to provoke her. She had a sharp sense of the germane, fitting herself into needs of the moment. That was the thing they feared might have its source in a motivation always to choose the path of least resistance. *Let it not be that.* Complete honesty now! The ultimate tool of Bene Gesserit education. The classical technique that bound acolyte to teacher.

"I will be at your side throughout your Agony. If you fail, I will grieve."

"Duncan?" Tears in her eyes.

"Any help he can give, he will be permitted to give."

Murbella looked up the rows of seats and, for a brief moment, her gaze locked with Idaho's. He lifted slightly but Tamalane's hand on his shoulder restrained him.

They may kill my beloved! Idaho thought. *Must I sit here and just watch it happen?* But Odrade had said he would be permitted to help. *There is no stopping this now. I must trust Dar. But, gods below! She does not know the depth of my grief, if . . . if . . .* He closed his eyes.

"Bell." Odrade's voice carried a sense of casting off, a knife edge in its brittleness.

Bellonda took Murbella's arm and helped her onto the table. It bounced slightly adjusting to the weight.

This is the real chute, Murbella thought.

She had only the remotest sense of straps being fastened around her, of purposeful movement beside her.

"This is the usual routine," Odrade said.

Routine? Murbella had hated the routines of becoming Bene Gesserit, all of that study, listening and reacting to Proctors. She had particularly loathed the necessity to refine reactions she had believed adequate but there could be no sloughing off under those watchful eyes.

Adequate! What a dangerous word.

This recognition had been precisely what they sought. Precisely the leverage their acolyte required.

If you loathe it, do it better. Use your loathing as guidance; home in on exactly what you need.

The fact that her teachers saw so directly into her behavior, what a marvelous thing! She wanted that ability. Oh, how she wanted it!

I must excel in this.

It was a thing any Honored Matre might envy. She saw herself abruptly with a form of doubled vision: both Bene Gesserit and Honored Matre. A daunting perception.

A hand touched her cheek, moved her head and went away.

Responsibility. I am about to learn what they mean by "a new sense of history."

The Bene Gesserit view of history fascinated her. How did they look at multiple pasts? Was it something immersed in a grander scheme? The temptation to become one of them had been overwhelming.

This is the moment when I learn.

She saw an oral syringe swing into position above her mouth. Bellonda's hand moved it.

"We carry our grail in our heads," Odrade had said. *"Carry this grail gently if it comes into your possession."*

The syringe touched her lips. Murbella closed her eyes but felt fingers open her mouth. Cold metal touched her teeth. Odrade's remembered voice was with her.

Avoid excesses. Overcorrect and you always have a fine mess on your hands, the necessity to make larger and larger corrections. Oscillation. Fanatics are marvelous creators of oscillation.

"Our grail. It has linearity because each Reverend Mother carries the same determination. We will perpetuate this together."

Bitter liquid gushed into her mouth. Murbella swallowed convulsively. She felt fire flow down her throat into her stomach. No pain except the burning. She wondered if this could be the extent of it. Her stomach felt merely warm now.

Slowly, so slowly she was several heartbeats recognizing it, the warmth flowed outward. When it reached the tips of her fingers she felt her body convulse. Her back arched off the padded table. Something soft but firm replaced the syringe in her mouth.

Voices. She heard them and knew people were speaking but could not distinguish words.

As she concentrated on the voices she became aware she had lost touch with her body. Somewhere, flesh writhed and there was pain but she was removed from it.

A hand touched a hand and clasped it firmly. She recognized Duncan's touch, and abruptly there was her body and agony. Her lungs pained when she exhaled. Not when she inhaled. Then they felt flat and never full enough. Her sense of presence in living flesh became a thin thread that wound through many presences. She sensed others all around her, far too many people for the tiny amphitheater.

Another human being floated into view. Murbella felt herself to be in a factory shuttle . . . in space. The shuttle was primitive. Too many manual controls. Too many blinking lights. A woman at the controls, small and untidy with the sweat of her labors. She had long brown hair and it had been bound up in a chignon from which paler strands escaped to hang around her narrow cheeks. She wore a single garment, a short dress of brilliant reds, blues, and greens.

Machinery.

There was awareness of monstrous machinery just beyond this immediate space. The woman's dress contrasted severely with the drab and dragging sense of machinery. She spoke but her lips did not move. "Listen, you! When it comes time for you to take over these controls, don't become a destroyer. I'm here to help you avoid the destroyers. Do you know that?"

Murbella tried to speak but had no voice.

"Don't try so hard, girl!" the woman said. "I hear you."

Murbella tried to shift her attention away from the woman.

Where is this place?

One operator, a giant warehouse . . . factory . . . everything automated . . . webs of feedback lines centered into this tiny space with its complex controls.

Thinking to whisper, Murbella asked: *"Who are you?"* and heard her own voice roar. Agony in her ears!

"Not so loud! I'm your guide of the mohalata, the one who steers you clear of the destroyers."

Dur protect me! Murbella thought. *This is no* place; *it's me!*

On that thought, the control room vanished. She was a migrant in the void, condemned never to be quiet, never to find a moment of sanctuary. Everything but her own fleeting thoughts became immaterial. She had no substance, only a wispy adherence that she recognized as consciousness.

I have constructed myself out of fog.

Other Memory came, bits and pieces of experiences she knew were not her own. Faces leered at her and demanded her attention but the woman at the shuttle controls pulled her away. Murbella recognized necessities but could not put them into coherent form.

"These are lives in your past." It was the woman at the shuttle controls but her voice had a disembodied quality and came from no discernible place.

"We are descendants of people who did nasty things," the woman said. "We don't like to admit there were barbarians in our ancestry. A Reverend Mother must admit it. We have no choice."

Murbella had the knack of only thinking her questions now. *Why must I . . .*

"The victors bred. We are their descendants. Victory often was gained at great moral price. Barbarism is not even an adequate word for some of the things our ancestors did."

Murbella felt a familiar hand on her cheek. *Duncan!* The touch restored agony. *Oh, Duncan! You're hurting me.*

Through the pain, she sensed gaps in the lives being revealed to her. Things withheld.

"Only what you're capable of accepting now," the disembodied voice said. "Others come later when you're stronger . . . if you survive."

Selective filter. Odrade's words. *Necessity opens doors.*

Persistent wailing came from the other presences. Laments: *"See? See what happens when you ignore common sense?"*

Agony increased. She could not escape it. Every nerve was touched with flame. She wanted to cry, to scream threats, to implore for help. Tumbling emotions accompanied the agony but she ignored them. Everything happened along a thin thread of existence. The thread could snap!

I'm dying.

The thread was stretching. It was going to break! Hopeless to resist. Muscles would not obey. There probably were no muscles remaining to her. She did not want them anyway. They were pain. It was hell and would never end . . . not even if the thread snapped. Flames burned along the thread, licking at her awareness.

Hands shook her shoulders. *Duncan . . . don't.* Each movement was pain beyond anything she had imagined possible. This deserved to be called the Agony.

The thread no longer was stretching. It was pulling back, compressing. It became one small thing, a sausage of such exquisite pain that nothing else existed. The sense of *being* became vague, translucent . . . transparent.

"Do you see?" the voice of her mohalata guide came from far away.

I see things.

Not exactly seeing. A distant awareness of others. Other sausages. Other Memory encased in the skins of lost lives. They extended behind her in a train whose length she could not determine. Translucent fog. It ripped apart occasionally and she glimpsed events. No . . . not events themselves. Memory.

"Share witness," her guide said. "You see what our ancestors have done. They debase the worst curse you can invent. Don't make excuses about necessities of the times! Just remember: There are no innocents!"

Ugly! Ugly!

She could hold on to none of it. Everything became reflections and ripping fog. Somewhere there was a glory that she knew she might attain.

Absence of this Agony.

That was it. How glorious that would be!

Where is that glorious condition?

Lips touched her forehead, her mouth. *Duncan!* She reached up. *My hands are free.* Her fingers slipped into remembered hair. *This is real!*

Agony receded. Only then did she realize that she had come through pain more terrible than words could describe. Agony? It seared the psyche and remolded her. One person entered and another emerged.

Duncan! She opened her eyes and there was his face directly above her. *Do I still love him? He is here. He is an anchor to which I clung in the worst moments. But do I love him? Am I still balanced?*

No answer.

Odrade spoke from somewhere out of view. "Strip those clothes off her. Towels. She's drenched. And bring her a proper robe!"

There were scurrying sounds, then Odrade once more: "Murbella, you did that the hard way, I'm glad to say."

Such elation in her voice. Why was she glad?

Where is the sense of responsibility? Where is the grail I'm supposed to feel in my head? Answer me, someone!

But the woman at the shuttle controls was gone.

Only I remain. And I remember atrocities that might make an Honored Matre quail. She glimpsed the grail then and it was not a *thing* but a question: How to set those balances aright?

> Our household god is this thing we carry forward genera-
> tion after generation: our message for humankind if it ma-
> tures. The closest thing we have to a household goddess is
> a failed Reverend Mother—Chenoeh there in her niche.
>
> —DARWI ODRADE

Idaho thought of his Mentat abilities as a retreat now. Murbella stayed
with him as frequently as their duties allowed—he with his weapons
development and she recovering strength while she adjusted to her
new status.

She did not lie to him. She did not try to tell him she felt no difference between them. But he sensed the pulling away, elastic being
stretched to its limits.

"My Sisters have been taught not to divulge secrets of the heart.
There's the danger they perceive in love. Perilous intimacies. The deepest sensitivities blunted. Do not give someone a stick with which to
beat you."

She thought her words reassuring to him but he heard the inner
argument. *Be free! Break entangling bonds!*

He saw her often these days in the throes of Other Memory. Words
escaped her in the night.

"Dependencies . . . group soul . . . intersection of living awareness . . . Fish Speakers . . ."

She had no hesitation about sharing some of this. "The intersection? Anyone can sense nexus points in the natural interruptions of life. Deaths, diversions, incidental pauses between powerful events, births . . ."

"Birth an interruption?"

They were in his bed, even the chrono darkened . . . but that did not hide them from comeyes, of course. Other energies fed the Sisterhood's curiosity.

"You never thought of birth as an interruption? A Reverend Mother finds that amusing."

Amusing! Pulling away . . . pulling away . . .

Fish Speakers, that was the revelation the Bene Gesserit absorbed with fascination. They had suspected, but Murbella gave them confirmation. Fish Speaker democracy became Honored Matre autocracy. No more doubts.

"The tyranny of the minority cloaked in the mask of the majority," Odrade called it, her voice exultant. "Downfall of democracy. Either overthrown by its own excesses or eaten away by bureaucracy."

Idaho could hear the Tyrant in that judgment. If history had any repetitive patterns, here was one. A drumbeat of repetition. First, a Civil Service law masked in the lie that it was the only way to correct demagogic excesses and spoils systems. Then the accumulation of power in places voters could not touch. And finally, aristocracy.

"The Bene Gesserit may be the only ones ever to create the all-powerful jury," Murbella said. "Juries are not popular with legalists. Juries oppose the law. They can ignore judges."

She laughed in the darkness. "Evidence! What is evidence except those things you are allowed to perceive? That's what Law tries to control: carefully managed reality."

Words to divert him, words to demonstrate her new Bene Gesserit powers. Her words of love fell flat.

She speaks them out of memory.

He saw this bothered Odrade almost as much as it dismayed him. Murbella did not notice either reaction.

Odrade had tried to reassure him. "Every new Reverend Mother goes through an adjustment period. Manic at times. Think of the new ground under her, Duncan!"

How can I not think of it?

"First law of bureaucracy," Murbella told the darkness.

You do not divert me, love.

"Grow to the limits of available energy!" Her voice was indeed manic. "Use the lie that taxes solve all problems." She turned toward him in the bed but not for love. "Honored Matres played the whole routine! Even a social security system to quiet the masses, but everything went into their own energy bank."

"Murbella!"

"What?" Surprised at the sharpness of his tone. *Didn't he know he was talking to a Reverend Mother?*

"I know all of this, Murbella. Any Mentat does."

"Are you trying to shut me up?" Angry.

"Our job is to think like our enemy," he said. "We do have a common enemy?"

"You're sneering at me, Duncan."

"Are your eyes orange?"

"Melange doesn't allow that and you know . . . Oh."

"The Bene Gesserit need your knowledge but you must *cultivate* it!" He turned on a glowglobe and found her flaring at him. Not unexpected and not really Bene Gesserit.

Hybrid.

The word leaped into his mind. Was it hybrid vigor? Did the Sisterhood expect this of Murbella? The Bene Gesserit surprised you sometimes. You found them facing you in odd corridors, eyes unwavering, faces masked in that way of theirs and, behind the masks, unusual responses brewing. That was where Teg learned to do the unexpected. But this? Idaho thought he could grow to dislike this new Murbella.

She saw this in him, naturally. He remained open to her as to no other person.

"Don't hate me, Duncan." No pleading but something deeply hurt behind the words.

"I'll never hate you." But he turned off the light.

She nestled against him almost the way she had before the Agony. *Almost.* The difference tore at him.

"Honored Matres see the Bene Gesserit as competitors for power," Murbella said. "It's not so much that men who follow my former Sisters are fanatics, but they're made incapable of self-determination by their addiction."

"Is that the way *we* are?"

"Now, Duncan."

"You mean I could get this commodity at another store?"

She chose to assume he was talking about Honored Matre fears. "Many would abandon them if they could." Turning toward him fiercely, she demanded a sexual response. Her abandon shocked him. As though this might be the last time she could experience such ecstasy.

Afterward, he lay exhausted.

"I hope I'm pregnant again," she whispered. "We still need our babies."

We need. The Bene Gesserit need. No longer "they need."

He fell asleep to dream he was in the ship's armory. It was a dream touched by realities. The ship remained a weapons factory as it actually had become. Odrade was talking to him in the dream armory. "I make decisions of necessity, Duncan. Little likelihood you'll break out and run amok."

"I am too much the Mentat for that!" How self-important his dream voice! *I'm dreaming and I know I dream. Why am I in the armory with Odrade?*

A list of weapons scrolled before his eyes.

Atomics. (He saw big blasters and deadly dusts.)

Lasguns. (No counting the various models.)

Bacteriologicals.

The scroll was interrupted by Odrade's voice. "We can assume smugglers concentrate as usual on small things that bring a big price."

"Soostones, of course." Still self-important. *I'm not that way!*

"Assassination weapons," she said. "Plans and specifications for new devices."

"Theft of trade secrets is a big item with smugglers." *I'm insufferable!*

"There are always medicines and the diseases that require them," she said.

Where is she? I can hear her but I can't see her. "Do Honored Matres know our universe harbors blackguards not above sowing the problem before providing the solution?" *Blackguards? I never use that word.*

"All things relative, Duncan. They burned Lampadas and butchered four million of our finest."

He awoke and sat upright. *Specifications for new devices!* There it was in delicate detail, a way to miniaturize Holzmann generators. Two centimeters, no more. And much cheaper! *How was that smuggled into my mind?*

He slipped out of bed, not awakening Murbella, and groped his way to a robe. He heard her snuffle as he let himself out into the workroom.

Seating himself at his console, he copied the design from his mind and studied it. Perfect! Englobement for sure. He transmitted to Archives with a flag for Odrade and Bellonda.

With a sigh, he sat back and examined his design once more. It vanished in a return to his dream scroll. *Am I still dreaming? No!* He could feel the chair, touch the console, hear the field buzzing. *Dreams do that.*

The scroll produced cutting and stabbing weapons, including some designed to introduce poisons or bacteria into enemy flesh.

Projectiles.

He wondered how to stop the scroll and study details.

"It's all in your head!"

Humans and other animals bred for attack scrolled past his eyes, hiding the console and its projection. *Futars? How did Futars get in there? What do I know about Futars?*

Disruptors replaced the animals. Weapons to cloud mental activity or interfere with life itself. *Disruptors? I've never heard that name before.*

Disruptors were succeeded by null-G "seekers" designed to hunt specific targets. *Those I know.*

Explosives next, including ones to spread poisons and bacteriologicals.

Deceptives, to project false targets. Teg had used those.

Energizers appeared next. He had a private arsenal of those: ways of increasing capacities of your troops.

Abruptly, the shimmering net from his vision replaced scrolling weapons and he saw the elderly couple in their garden. They glared at him. The man's voice became audible. "Stop spying on us!"

Idaho gripped the arms of his chair and jerked himself forward but the vision disappeared before he could study details.

Spying?

He sensed a residue of the scroll in his mind, no longer visible but a musing voice . . . masculine.

"Defenses often must take on characteristics of the attack weapons. Sometimes, however, simple systems can divert the most devastating weapons."

Simple systems! He laughed aloud. "Miles! Where the hell are you, Teg? I have your disguised attack vessels! Inflated decoys! Empty except for a miniature Holzmann generator and lasgun." He added this to his Archives transmissions.

When he was finished, he asked himself once more about the visions. *Influencing my dreams? What have I tapped?*

In every spare minute since becoming Teg's Weapons Master, he had been calling up Archival records. There had to be some clue in all of that massive accumulation!

Resonances and tachyon theory held his attention for a time. Tachyon theory figured in Holzmann's original design. "Techys," Holzmann had called his energy source.

A *wave system* that ignored light speed's limits. Light speed obviously did not limit foldspace ships. Techys?

"It works because it works," Idaho muttered. "Faith. Like any other religion."

Mentats squirreled away much seemingly inconsequential data. He had a storehouse marked "Techys" and proceeded to go through it without satisfaction.

Not even Guild Navigators professed knowledge of how they guided foldspace ships. Ixian scientists made machines to duplicate Navigator abilities but still could not define what they did.

"Holzmann's formulae can be trusted."

No one claimed to understand Holzmann. They merely used his formulae because they worked. It was the "ether" of space travel. You *folded* space. One instant you were here and the next instant you were countless parsecs distant.

Someone "out there" has found another way to use Holzmann's theories! It was a full Mentat Projection. He knew its accuracy from the new questions it produced.

Murbella's Other Memory ramblings haunted him now even though he recognized basic Bene Gesserit teachings in them.

Power attracts the corruptible. Absolute power attracts the absolutely corruptible. This is the danger of entrenched bureaucracy to its subject population. Even spoils systems are preferable because levels of tolerance are lower and the corrupt can be thrown out periodically. Entrenched bureaucracy seldom can be touched short of violence. Beware when Civil Service and Military join hands!

The Honored Matre achievement.

Power for the sake of power . . . an aristocracy bred from unbalanced stock.

Who were those people he saw? Strong enough to drive out Honored Matres. He knew it for a Projection datum.

Idaho found this realization profoundly dislocating. Honored Matres fugitives! Barbaric but ignorant in the way of all such raiders even from before the Vandals. Moved by impulsive greed as much as by any other force. *"Take Roman gold!"* They filtered all distractions out of awareness. It was a stupefying ignorance that faltered only when the more sophisticated culture insinuated itself into the . . .

Abruptly, he saw what Odrade was doing.

Gods below! What a fragile plan!

He pressed his palms against his eyes and forced himself not to cry out in anguish. *Let them think I'm tired.* But seeing Odrade's plan told him also he would lose Murbella . . . one way or another.

When are the witches to be trusted? Never! The dark side of the magic universe belongs to the Bene Gesserit and we must reject them.

—TYLWYTH WAFF,
MASTER OF MASTERS

The great Common Room in the no-ship, with its tiered seating and raised platform at one end, was packed with Bene Gesserit Sisters, more than had ever before been assembled. Chapterhouse was almost at a standstill this afternoon because few wanted to send proxies and important decisions could not be delegated to service cadre. Black-robed Reverend Mothers dominated the assemblage in their aloof clusterings close to the stage but the room swirled with acolytes in white-trimmed robes and there were even the newly enrolled. Groups of white robes marking the youngest acolytes were sprinkled around in tight little groups, flocking for mutual support. All others had been excluded by Convocation Proctors.

The air was heavy with melange-perfumed breaths and it had that dank, overused quality it got when conditioning machinery was overloaded. Odors of the recent lunch, strong with garlic, rode on this atmosphere like an uninvited intruder. This and stories being spread throughout the room heightened tensions.

Most kept their attention on the raised platform and the side door where Mother Superior must enter. Even while talking to companions or moving about, they focused on that place where they knew someone soon would enter and create profound changes in their lives. Mother Superior did not herd them all into a great Common Room with a promise of important announcements unless something to shake the Bene Gesserit foundations was at hand.

Bellonda preceded Odrade into the room, mounting to the platform with that belligerent waddle which made her easily recognizable even at a distance. Odrade followed Bellonda at five paces. Then came senior councillors and aides, blackrobed Murbella (still looking somewhat dazed from her Agony only two weeks past) among them. Dortujla limped close behind Murbella with Tam and Sheeana at her side. At the end of this procession came Streggi carrying Teg on her shoulders. There were excited murmurs when he appeared. Males seldom shared assemblies but everyone on Chapterhouse knew this was the ghola of their Mentat Bashar, living now at the cantonment with all that remained of a Bene Gesserit military.

Seeing the massed ranks of the Sisterhood this way, Odrade experienced an empty feeling. Some ancient had said it all, she thought. "Any damned fool knows one horse can run faster than another." Often at the minor assemblages here in this copy of a sports stadium she had been tempted to quote that bit of advice but she knew the ritual had its better purposes as well. Assembly showed you to one another.

Here we are together. Our kind.

Mother Superior and attendants moved like a peculiar bundle of energy through the throng to the platform, her position of eminence at the edge of the arena.

Mother Superior was never subjected to the mass scrimmage of assemblies. She never had elbows jammed into her ribs or felt the trodding of a neighbor's foot. She was never forced to move as others moved in a kind of inchworm flow composed of bodies pressed together in unwanted proximity.

Thus did Caesar arrive. Thumbs down on the whole damned thing! To Bellonda, she said: "Let it begin."

Afterward, she knew she would wonder why she had not delegated someone to make this ritual appearance and utter portentous words.

Bellonda would love the pre-eminent position and, for that reason, must never have it. But perhaps there was some lower-echelon Sister who would be embarrassed by elevation and would obey only out of loyalty, out of that underlying need to do what Mother Superior commanded.

Gods! If there are any of you around, why do you permit us to be such sheep?

There they were, Bellonda preparing them for her. *The battalions of the Bene Gesserit.* They were not really battalions, but Odrade often imagined ranked Sisters, cataloguing them by function. *That one is a squad leader. That one is a Captain General. This one is a lowly sergeant and here is a messenger.*

The Sisters would be outraged if they knew this quirk in her. She kept it well concealed behind an "ordinary assignment" attitude. You could assign lieutenants without calling them lieutenants. Taraza had done the same thing.

Bell was telling them now that the Sisterhood might have to make a new accommodation with their captive Tleilaxu. Bitter words for Bell: "We have gone through the crucible, Tleilaxu and Bene Gesserit alike, and we have come out changed. In a way, we have changed each other."

Yes, we are like rocks rubbed against each other for so long that each takes on some of the conforming shape required by the other. But the original rock is still there at the core!

The audience was becoming restive. They knew this was preliminary, no matter the hidden message within these hints about Tleilaxu. Preliminary and relative in importance. Odrade stepped to Bellonda's side, signaling her to cut it short.

"Here is Mother Superior."

How hard the old patterns die. Does Bell think they don't recognize me?

Odrade spoke in compelling tones, just short of Voice.

"Actions have been taken that require me to meet on Junction with Honored Matre leadership, a meeting from which I may not emerge alive. I *probably* will not survive. That meeting will be partly distraction. We are about to punish them."

Odrade waited for murmurs to subside, hearing both agreement and disagreement in the sounds. Interesting. The ones who agreed were closer to the stage and farther back among new acolytes. Disagreement from advanced acolytes? Yes. They knew the warning: *We dare not feed that fire.*

She pitched her voice lower, letting remotes carry it to those in the high tiers. "Before leaving, I will Share with more than one Sister. These times require such caution."

"Your plan?" "What will you do?" Questions were shouted at her from many places.

"We will feint at Gammu. That should drive Honored Matre allies to Junction. We then will take Junction and, I hope, capture the Spider Queen."

"The attack will occur while you are on Junction?" This question came from Garimi, a sober-faced Proctor directly below Odrade.

"That is the plan. I will be transmitting my observations to the attackers." Odrade gestured to Teg seated on Streggi's shoulders. "The Bashar will lead the attack in person."

"Who goes with you?" "Yes. Who are you taking?" No mistaking the worry in those cries. So the word has not yet spread through Chapterhouse.

"Tam and Dortujla," Odrade said.

"Who will Share with you?" Garimi again. *Indeed! That is the political question of most interest. Who may succeed Mother Superior?* Odrade heard nervous stirring behind her. *Bellonda excited? Not you, Bell. You already know that.*

"Murbella and Sheeana," Odrade said. "And one other if Proctors care to name a candidate."

Proctors formed little consulting groups, shouting suggestions from group to group, but no names were submitted. Someone had a question though: "Why Murbella?"

"Who knows Honored Matres better?" Odrade asked.

That silenced them.

Garimi moved closer to the stage and looked up at Odrade with a penetrating stare. *Don't try to mislead a Reverend Mother, Darwi Odrade!* "After our feint at Gammu, they will be even more alert and reinforced on Junction. What makes you think we can take them?"

Odrade stepped aside and motioned Streggi forward with Teg.

Teg had been watching Odrade's performance with fascination. He looked down now at Garimi. She was currently Chief Assignment Proctor and no doubt had been chosen to speak for a bloc of Sisters. It occurred to Teg then that this ludicrous position on the shoulders of an acolyte had been planned by Odrade for reasons other than those she voiced.

To put my eyes closer to a level with adults around me . . . but also to remind them of my lesser stature, to reassure them that a Bene Gesserit (if only an acolyte) still controls my movements.

"I will not go into all of the weaponry details at the moment," he said. *Damn this piping voice!* He had their attention, though. "But we are going for mobility, for decoys that will destroy a great deal of the area around them if a lasgun beam hits them . . . and we are going to englobe Junction with devices to reveal the movements of their no-ships."

When they continued to stare at him, he said: "If Mother Superior confirms my previous knowledge of Junction, we will know our enemy's positions intimately. There should not be significant changes. Not enough time has passed."

Surprise and the unexpected. What else did they expect from their Mentat Bashar? He stared back at Garimi, daring her to voice more doubts of his military ability.

She had another question. "Are we to presume that Duncan Idaho advises you on weapons?"

"When you have the best, you would be a fool not to use it," he said.

"But will he accompany you as Weapons Master?"

"He chooses not to leave the ship and you all know why. What is the meaning of that question?"

He had deflected her and silenced her and she did not like it. A man should not be able to maneuver a Reverend Mother that way!

Odrade stepped forward and put a hand on Teg's arm. "Have you all forgotten that this ghola is our loyal friend, Miles Teg?" She stared at particular faces in the throng, choosing ones she was certain watchdogged the comeyes and knew Teg was her father, moving her gaze from face to face with a deliberate slowness that could not be misinterpreted.

Is there one among you who dares cry "nepotism"? Then look once more at his record in our service!

Sounds of the Convocation became once more those in keeping with other graces they expected in assemblies. No more vulgar clash of demanding voices vying for attention. Now, they fitted their speech into a pattern much like plainsong and yet not quite a chant. Voices moved and flowed together. Odrade always found this remarkable. No one directed the harmony. It happened because they were Bene Gesserit. Naturally. This was the only explanation they needed. It happened because they were practiced in adjusting to each other. The dance of their everyday movements continued in their voices. Partners no matter transitory disagreements.

I will miss this.

"It is never enough to make accurate predictions of distressful events," she said. "Who knows this better than we? Is there one among us who has not learned the lesson of the Kwisatz Haderach?"

No need to elaborate. Evil prediction should not alter their course. That kept Bellonda silent. The Bene Gesserit were enlightened. Not dullards who attacked the bearer of bad tidings. Discount the messenger? *(Who could expect anything useful from the likes of that one?)* That was a pattern to be avoided at all costs. *Will we silence disagreeable messengers, thinking the deep silence of death obliterates the message?* The Bene Gesserit knew better than that! *Death makes a prophet's voice louder. Martyrs are truly dangerous.*

Odrade watched reflexive awareness spread through the room, even up to the highest tiers.

We are entering hard times, Sisters, and must accept that. Even Murbella knows it. And she knows now why I was so anxious to make a Sister of her. We all know it one way or another.

Odrade turned and glanced at Bellonda. No disappointment there. Bell knew why she was not among the chosen. *It's our best course, Bell. Infiltrate. Take them before they even suspect what we're doing.*

Shifting her gaze to Murbella, Odrade saw respectful awareness. Murbella was beginning to get her first batches of good advice from Other Memory. The manic stage had passed and she was even regaining a *fondness* for Duncan. In time perhaps . . . Bene Gesserit training assured that she would judge Other Memory on her own. Nothing in Murbella's stance said: "Keep your lousy advice to yourself!" She had historical comparisons and could not evade their obvious message.

Don't march in the streets with others who share your prejudices. Loud shouts are often the easiest to ignore. "I mean, look at them out there shouting their fool heads off! You want to make common cause with them?"

I told you, Murbella: Now judge for yourself. "To create change you find leverage points and move them. Beware blind alleys. Offers of high positions are a common distraction paraded before marchers. Leverage points are not all in high office. They are often at economic or communications centers and unless you know this, high office is useless. Even lieutenants can alter our course. Not by changing reports but by burying unwanted orders. Bell sits on orders until she believes them ineffective. I give her orders sometimes for this purpose: so she can play her delaying game. She knows it and yet she plays her game anyway. Know this, Murbella! And after we Share, study my performance with great care."

Harmony had been achieved but at a cost. Odrade signaled that Convocation was ended, knowing well that all questions had not been answered nor even asked. But the unasked questions would come filtering through Bell where they would get the most appropriate treatment.

Alert ones among the Sisters would not ask. They already saw her plan.

As she left the Great Common Room, Odrade felt herself accept full commitment for choices she had made, recognizing previous hesitancy for the first time. There were regrets, but only Murbella and Sheeana might know them.

Walking behind Bellonda, Odrade thought about *the places I will never go, the things I will never see except as a reflection in the life of another.*

It was a form of nostalgia that centered on the Scatterings and this eased her pain. There was just too much for one person to see out there. Even the Bene Gesserit with its accumulated memories could never hope to catch up with all of it, not with every last interesting detail. It was back to grand designs. The Big Picture, the Mainstream. *The specialties of my Sisterhood.* Here were essentials Mentats employed: patterns, movements of currents and what those currents carried, where they were going. Consequences. Not maps but the flowings.

At least, I have preserved key elements of our jury-monitored democracy in original form. They may thank me for that one day.

> Seek freedom and become captive of your desires. Seek discipline and find your liberty.
>
> —THE CODA

"Who expected the air machinery to break down?"

The Rabbi asked his question of no one in particular. He sat on a low bench, a scroll clutched to his breast. The scroll had been reinforced by modern artifice but it still was old and fragile. He was not sure of the time. Midmorning probably. They had eaten not long ago food that could be described as breakfast.

"*I* expected it."

He appeared to be addressing the scroll. "Passover has come and gone and our door was locked."

Rebecca came to stand over him. "Please, Rabbi. How does this help Joshua at his labors?"

"We have not been abandoned," the Rabbi told his scroll. "It is we who have hidden ourselves away. When we cannot be found by strangers, where would anyone look who might help us?"

He peered up abruptly at Rebecca, owlish behind his glasses. "Have you brought evil to us, Rebecca?"

She knew his meaning. "Outsiders always think there's something nefarious about the Bene Gesserit," she said.

"So now I, your Rabbi, am Outsider!"

"You estrange yourself, Rabbi. I speak from the viewpoint of the

Sisterhood you made me help. What they do is often boring. Repetitious but not evil."

"I *made* you help? Yes, I did that. Forgive me, Rebecca. If evil joins us, I have done it."

"Rabbi! Stop this. They are an extended clan. And still, they keep a touchy individualism. Does an extended clan mean nothing to you? Does my dignity offend you?"

"I tell you, Rebecca, what offends me. By my hand you have learned to follow different books than . . ." He raised the scroll as though it were a bludgeon.

"No books at all, Rabbi. Oh, they have a Coda but it's just a collection of reminders, sometimes useful, sometimes to be discarded. They always adjust their Coda to current requirements."

"There are books that cannot be *adjusted*, Rebecca!"

She stared down at him with ill-concealed dismay. Was this how he saw the Sisterhood? Or was it fear talking?

Joshua came to stand beside her, hands greasy, black smears on forehead and cheeks. "Your suggestion was the right one. It's working again. How long I don't know. The problem is—"

"You do not know the problem," the Rabbi interrupted.

"The mechanical problem, Rabbi," Rebecca said. "This no-chamber's field distorts machinery."

"We could not bring in frictionless machinery," Joshua said. "Too revealing, not to mention the cost."

"Your machinery is not all that has been distorted."

Joshua looked at Rebecca with raised eyebrows. *What's wrong with him?* So Joshua trusted Bene Gesserit insights, too. That offended the Rabbi. His flock sought guidance elsewhere.

The Rabbi surprised her then. "You think I'm jealous, Rebecca?"

She shook her head from side to side.

"You display talents," the Rabbi said, "that others are quick to use. Your suggestion fixed the machinery? These . . . these Others told you how?"

Rebecca shrugged. This was the Rabbi of old, not to be challenged in his own house.

"I should praise you?" the Rabbi asked. "You have power? Now, you will govern us?"

"No one, least of all I, ever suggested that, Rabbi." She was offended and did not mind showing it.

"Forgive me, daughter. That is what you call 'flip.'"

"I don't need your praise, Rabbi. And of course I forgive."

"Your Others have something to say about this?"

"The Bene Gesserit say fear of praise goes back to an ancient prohibition against praising your child because that brings down the wrath of the gods."

He bowed his head. "Sometimes a bit of wisdom."

Joshua appeared embarrassed. "I'm going to try sleeping. I should be rested." He aimed a meaningful glance at the machinery area where a labored rasping could be heard.

He left them for the darkened end of the chamber, stumbling on a child's toy as he went.

The Rabbi patted the bench beside him. "Sit, Rebecca."

She sat.

"I am fearful for you, for us, for all of the things we represent." He caressed the scroll. "We have been true for so many generations." His gaze swept the room. "And we don't even have a minyan here."

Rebecca wiped tears from her eyes. "Rabbi, you misjudge the Sisterhood. They wish only to perfect humans and their governments."

"So they say."

"So I say. Government, to them, is an art form. You find that amusing?"

"You arouse my curiosity. Are these women self-deluded by dreams of their own importance?"

"They think of themselves as watchdogs."

"Dogs?"

"*Watch*dogs, alert to when a lesson may be taught. That is what they seek. Never try to teach someone a lesson he cannot absorb."

"Always these bits of wisdom." He sounded sad. "And they govern themselves *artistically*?"

"They think of themselves as a jury with absolute powers that no law can veto."

He waved the scroll in front of her nose. "I thought so!"

"No *human* law, Rabbi."

"You tell me these women who make religions to suit themselves believe in a . . . in a power greater than themselves."

"Their belief would not accord with ours, Rabbi, but I do not think it evil."

"What is this . . . this belief?"

"They call it the 'leveling drift.' They see it genetically and as instinct. Brilliant parents are likely to have children closer to the average, for example."

"A drift. *This* is a belief?"

"That is why they avoid prominence. They are advisors, even kingmakers on occasion, but they do not want to be in the target foreground."

"This drift . . . do they believe there is a Drift-Maker?"

"They don't assume there is. Only that there is this observable movement."

"So what do they do in this drift?"

"They take precautions."

"In the presence of Satan, I should think so!"

"They don't oppose the current but seem only to move across it, making it work for them, using the back eddies."

"Oyyy!"

"Ancient sailing masters understood this quite well, Rabbi. The Sisterhood has what amounts to current charts telling them places to avoid and where to make their greatest efforts."

Again, he waved the scroll. "This is no current chart."

"You misinterpret, Rabbi. They know the fallacies about overwhelming machines." She glanced at the laboring machinery. "They see us in currents machinery cannot breast."

"These little wisdoms. I do not know, daughter. Meddling in politics, I accept. But in holy matters . . ."

"A leveling drift, Rabbi. Mass influence on brilliant innovators who move out of the pack and produce new things. Even when the new helps us, the drift catches the innovator."

"Who is to say what helps, Rebecca?"

"I merely tell what they believe. They see taxation as evidence of the drift, taking away free energy that might create more new things. A sensitized person detects it, they say."

"And these . . . these Honored Matres?"

"They fit the pattern. Power-closed government intent on making all potential challengers ineffectual. Screen out the bright ones. Blunt intelligence."

A tiny beeping sound came from the machinery area. Joshua was past them before they could stand. He bent over the screen that revealed events on the surface.

"They are back," he said. "See! They dig in the ashes directly above us."

"Have they found us?" The Rabbi sounded almost relieved.

Joshua watched the screen.

Rebecca placed her head beside his, studying the diggers—ten men with that dreaming look in their eyes of those who had been bonded to Honored Matres.

"They only dig at random," Rebecca said, straightening.

"You're sure?" Joshua stood and looked into her face, seeking secret confirmation.

Any Bene Gesserit could see it.

"Look for yourself." She gestured at the screen. "They are leaving. They go to the sligsty now."

"Where they belong," the Rabbi muttered.

Making workable choices occurs in a crucible of informative mistakes. Thus Intelligence accepts fallibility. And when absolute (infallible) choices are not known, Intelligence takes chances with limited data in an arena where mistakes are not only possible but also necessary.

—DARWI ODRADE

Mother Superior did not just board an outgoing lighter and transfer to any convenient no-ship. There were plans, arrangements, strategies—contingencies on contingencies.

It took eight hectic days. Timing with Teg had to be precise. Consultations with Murbella ate up hours. Murbella had to know what she faced.

Discover their Achilles' heel, Murbella, and you have it all. Stay on the observation ship when Teg attacks but watch carefully.

Odrade took detailed advice from all who could help. Then came the vital-signs implant with encrypting to transmit her secret observations. A no-ship and long-range lighter had to be refitted, crew chosen by Teg.

Bellonda muttered and growled until Odrade intervened.

"You are distracting me! Is that your intent? Weaken me?" It was late morning four days before departure and they were temporarily alone in the workroom. Weather clear but unseasonably cold and air an ochre tinge from a dust storm that had blown across Central in the night.

"Convocation was a mistake!" Bellonda needed her parting shot.

Odrade found herself snapping back at Bellonda, who had become a bit too caustic. "Necessary!"

"To you, maybe! Saying goodbye to your *family*. Now, you leave us here taking in each other's laundry."

"Did you just come up here to complain about the Convocation?"

"I don't like your latest comments on Honored Matres! You should have consulted us before spreading—"

"They're parasites, Bell! It's time we made that clear: a known weakness. And what does a body do when afflicted by parasites?" Odrade delivered this with a broad grin.

"Dar, when you assume this . . . this pseudo-humorous pose, I would like to throttle you!"

"Would you smile as you did it, Bell?"

"Damn you, Dar! One of these days . . ."

"We don't have many more days together, Bell, and that's what's eating you. Answer my question."

"Answer it yourself!"

"The body welcomes periodic delousing. Even addicts dream of freedom."

"Ahhhhh." A Mentat peered from Bellonda's eyes. "You think addiction to Honored Matres could be made painful?"

"In spite of your dreadful inability at humor, you still can function."

A cruel smile flexed Bellonda's mouth.

"I've managed to amuse you," Odrade said.

"Let me discuss this with Tam. She has a better head for strategy. Although . . . Sharing softened her."

When Bellonda had gone, Odrade leaned back and laughed quietly. *Softened! "Don't go soft tomorrow, Dar, when you Share." The Mentat stumbles on logic and misses the heart. She sees the process and worries about failure. What do we do if . . . We open windows, Bell, and let in common sense. Even hilarity. Puts more serious matters in perspective. Poor Bell, my flawed Sister. Always something to occupy your nervousness.*

Odrade left Central on departure morning much entangled in her thinking—an introspective mood, worried by what she had learned Sharing with Murbella and Sheeana.

I'm being self-indulgent.

That offered no relief. Her thoughts were framed by Other Memory and almost cynical fatalism.

Queen bees swarming?

That had been suggested of Honored Matres.

But Sheeana? And Tam approves?

This carried more in it than a Scattering.

I cannot follow into your wild place, Sheeana. My task is to produce order. I cannot risk what you have dared. There are different kinds of artistry. Yours repels me.

Absorbing lifetimes of Murbella's Other Memory helped. Murbella's knowledge was a powerful leverage on Honored Matres but full of disturbing nuances.

Not hypnotrance. They use cellular induction, a byproduct of their damned T-probes! Unconscious compulsion! How tempting to use it for ourselves. But this is where Honored Matres are most vulnerable—enormous unconsciousness content locked in by their own decisions. Murbella's key only emphasizes its danger to us.

They arrived at the Landing Flat in the midst of a windstorm that buffeted them when they emerged from their car. Odrade had vetoed a walk through what remained of orchards and vineyards.

Leaving for the last time? The question in Bellonda's eyes as she said goodbye. In Sheeana's worried frown.

Does Mother Superior accept my decision?

Provisionally, Sheeana. Provisionally. But I have not warned Murbella. So . . . perhaps I do share Tam's judgment.

Dortujla, in the van of Odrade's party, was withdrawn.

Understandable. She has been there . . . and watched her Sisters eaten. Courage, Sister! We are not yet defeated.

Only Murbella had appeared to take this in stride but she was thinking ahead to Odrade's encounter with the Spider Queen.

Have I armed Mother Superior sufficiently? Does she know in her guts how very dangerous this will be?

Odrade pushed such thoughts aside. There were things to do on the crossing. None of them more important than gathering her energies. Honored Matres could be analyzed almost out of reality, but the actual confrontation would be played as it came—a jazz performance. She liked the *idea* of jazz although the music distracted her with its antique flavors and the dips into wildness. Jazz spoke about life, though. No two performances ever identical. Players reacted to what was received from the others: jazz.

Feed us with jazz.

Air and space travel did not often concern itself with weather. Bludgeon your way through transitory interferences. Depend on Weather Control to provide launch windows through storms and cloud cover. Desert planets were an exception and that would have to be entered into Chapterhouse equations before long. Many changes, including return to Fremen mortuary practices. Bodies rendered for water and potash.

Odrade spoke of this as they waited for transport up to the ship. That wide cummerbund of hot, dry land expanding around the planet's equator would begin generating dangerous winds before long. One day, there would be coreolis storms: a blast-furnace from the desert interior with speeds in hundreds of kilometers an hour. Dune had seen winds of more than seven hundred kmh. Even space lighters took notice of such force. Air travel would be subject to the constant whims of surface conditions. And frail human flesh must find whatever shelter it could.

As we always have.

The lounge at the Flat was old. Stone inside and out, their first major building material here. Spartan slingchairs and low tables of molded plaz were more recent. Economy could not be ignored even for Mother Superior.

The lighter arrived in a dusty maelstrom. No nonsense about suspensor cushioning. This would be a quick lift with uncomfortable gees but not high enough to damage flesh.

Odrade felt almost disembodied as she said her final farewells and turned Chapterhouse over to a triumvirate of Sheeana, Murbella, and Bellonda. One last word: "Don't interfere with Teg. And I don't want anything nasty happening to Duncan. Hear me, Bell?"

All of the wonderful technological things they could accomplish and they still could not keep a thick sandstorm from almost blinding them as they lifted. Odrade closed her eyes and accepted the fact that she was not to get a last low-level overview of her beloved planet. She awoke to the thump of docking. Buzzcar waiting in a corridor just beyond the lock. A humming traverse to their quarters. Tamalane, Dortujla, and the acolyte servant maintained silence, respecting Mother Superior's desire to be with her own thoughts.

The quarters, at least, were familiar, standard on Bene Gesserit ships: a small sitting-dining room in elemental plaz of uniform light green; smaller sleeping chamber with walls in the same color and a single hard cot. They knew Mother Superior's preferences. Odrade glanced into a usiform bath and toilet. Standard facilities. Adjoining quarters for Tam and Dortujla were similar. Time later to look at the ship's refittings.

All essentials had been provided. Including unobtrusive elements of psychological support: subdued colors, familiar furnishings, a setting to disturb none of her mental processes. She gave orders for departure before returning to her sitting-dining room.

Food was waiting on a low table—blue fruit, sweet and plummy, a savory yellow spread on bread tailored to her energy needs. Very good. She watched the assigned acolyte at her self-effacing work arranging Mother Superior's effects. The name evaded Odrade for a second, then: *Suipol.* A dark little thing with a round, calm face and manners to match. *Not one of our brightest but guaranteed efficient.*

It struck Odrade suddenly that these assignments had an element of callousness in them. *A small entourage, not to offend Honored Matres. And keep our losses to a minimum.*

"Have you unpacked all of my things, Suipol?"

"Yes, Mother Superior." Very proud of having been chosen for this important assignment. It showed in her walk as she left.

There are some things you cannot unpack for me, Suipol. I carry those in my head.

No Bene Gesserit from Chapterhouse ever left the planet without taking along a certain amount of chauvinism. Other places were never quite as beautiful, never quite as serene, never as pleasant a habitat.

But this is the Chapterhouse that was.

It was an aspect of the desert transformation she had never before viewed in quite that way. Chapterhouse was removing itself. Going away, never to return, at least not in the lifetimes of those who knew it now. It was like being abandoned by a beloved parent—disdainfully and with malice.

You are no longer important to me, child.

On the way to becoming a Reverend Mother, they were taught early that travel could provide a peaceful byway for rest. Odrade fully intended to take advantage of this and told her companions immediately after eating, "Spare me details."

Suipol was sent to summon Tamalane. Odrade spoke in Tam's own terse meter. "Inspect the refitting and tell me what I should see. Take Dortujla."

"Good head, that one." High praise from Tam.

"When we're through, isolate me as much as possible."

During part of the crossing, Odrade strapped herself into the webbing of her cot and occupied herself composing what she thought of as a last will and testament.

Who would be executor?

Murbella was her personal choice, especially after the Sharing with Sheeana. Still . . . the Dune waif remained a potent candidate if this venture to Junction failed.

Some assumed any Reverend Mother could serve if responsibility fell on her. But not in these times. Not with this trap set. Honored Matres were unlikely to avoid the pitfall.

If we've judged them correctly. And Murbella's data says we've done our best. The opening is there for Honored Matres to enter, and oh, how inviting it will appear. They won't see the dead end until they're well into it. Too late!

But what if we fail?

Survivors (if any) would hold Odrade in contempt.

I have often felt diminished but never an object of contempt. Yet the decisions I made may never be accepted by my Sisters. At least, I make no excuses . . . not even to the ones with whom I Shared. They know my response comes from the darkness before a human dawn. Any of us may do a futile thing, even a stupid thing. But my plan can give us victory. We will not "just survive." Our grail requires us to persist together. Humans need us! Sometimes, they need religions. Sometimes, they need merely know their beliefs are as empty as their hopes for nobility. We are their source. After the masks are removed, that remains: Our Niche.

She felt then that this ship was taking her into the pit. Closer and closer to awful threat.

I go to the axe; it does not come to me.

No thoughts of exterminating this foe. Not since the Scattering magnified human population had that been possible. A flaw in Honored Matre schemes.

The high-pitched beep and flashing orange light that signaled arrival brought her out of repose. She struggled from her sling straps and, with Tam, Dortujla, and Suipol close behind, followed a guide to the transport lock where a longrange lighter clung to its shiptit. Odrade looked at the lighter visible in bulkhead scanners. Incredibly small!

"It'll only be nineteen hours," Duncan had said. "But that's as close as we dare bring the no-ship. They're sure to have foldspace sensors close around Junction."

Bell, for once, had agreed. *Don't risk the ship. It's there to plot outer defenses and receive your transmissions, not just to deliver Mother Superior.* The lighter was the no-ship's forward sensor, signaling what it encountered.

And I am the foremost sensor, a fragile body with delicate instruments.

There were guide arrows at the lock. Odrade led the way. They went through a small tube in free-fall. She found herself in a surprisingly rich cabin. Suipol, tumbling behind, recognized it and went up a notch in Odrade's estimation.

"This was a smuggler ship."

One person awaited them. Male by his smell but an opaque pilot's hood bristling with connectors concealed his face.

"Everyone strap in."

Male voice within that instrumentation.

Teg chose him. He'll be the best.

Odrade slipped into a seat behind a landing port and found the lumpy protrusions that unreeled into web harness. She heard the others obeying the pilot's command.

"All secure? Stay strapped in unless I say otherwise." His voice came from a floating speaker behind his seat at the drive console.

The umbilicus went "Bap!" Odrade felt gentle motions, but the view in the relay beside her showed the no-ship receding at a remarkable rate. It winked out of existence.

Going about its business before anyone can come out to investigate.

The lighter had surprising speed. Scanners reported planetary stations and transition barriers at eighteen-plus hours but winking dots identifying them were visible only because they had been enhanced. A window in the scanner said the stations would be naked-eye visible in a little more than twelve of those hours.

The sense of motion ceased abruptly and Odrade no longer felt the acceleration her eyes reported. *Suspensor cabin. Ixian technology for a nullfield this small.* Where had Teg acquired it?

Not necessary for me to know. Why tell Mother Superior where every oak plantation is located?

She watched sensor contacts begin within the hour and gave silent thanks for Idaho's astuteness.

We're beginning to know these Honored Matres.

Junction's defensive pattern was apparent even without scanner analysis. Overlapping planes! Just as Teg predicted. With knowledge of how barriers were spaced, Teg's people could weave another globe around the planet.

Surely it's not that simple.

Were Honored Matres so confident of overwhelming power that they ignored elementary precautions?

Planetary Station Four began calling when they were just under three hours out. "Identify yourself!"

Odrade heard an "or else" in that command.

The pilot's response obviously surprised the watchers. "You come in a little smuggler ship?"

So they recognize it. Teg is right once more.

"I'm about to burn the sensor equipment in the drive," the pilot announced. "It will add to our thrust. Make sure you're all securely harnessed."

Station Four noticed. "Why are you increasing velocity?"

Odrade leaned forward. "Repeat the countersign and say our party is fatigued from too long in cramped quarters. Add that I have equipped myself with a precautionary vital-signs transmitter to alert my people should I die."

They won't find the encryption! Clever Duncan. And wasn't Bell surprised to discover what he hid in Shipsystems. "More romantics!"

The pilot relayed her words. Back came the order: "Reduce velocity and lock onto those coordinates for landing. We are taking over your ship control at this point."

The pilot touched a yellow field on his board. "Just the way the Bashar said they would." A gloating sound in his voice. He lifted the hood off his head and turned.

Odrade was shocked.

Cyborg!

The face was a metal mask with two glittering silver balls for eyes.

We enter dangerous ground.

"They didn't tell you?" he asked. "Waste no pity. I was dead and this gave me life. It's Clairby, Mother Superior. And when I die this time, that will buy me life as a ghola."

Damn! We're trading in coin that may be denied us. Too late to change. And that was Teg's plan. But . . . Clairby?

The lighter landed with a smoothness that spoke of superb control by Station Four. Odrade knew the moment because a manicured landscape visible in her scanner no longer moved. The nullfield was turned off and she felt gravity. The hatch directly in front of her opened. Temperature pleasantly warm. Noise out there. Children playing some competitive game?

Luggage floating behind, she stepped onto a short flight of steps and saw that the noise did indeed come from a large group of children in a nearby field. In their high teens and female. They were butting a suspensor float-ball back and forth, shouting and screaming as they played.

Staged for our benefit?

Odrade thought it likely. There probably were two thousand young women on that field.

Look how many recruits we have coming along!

No one to greet her but Odrade saw a familiar structure down a paved lane to her left. Obvious Spacing Guild artifact with a recent tower added. She spoke of the tower as she glanced around her, giving the implaned transmitter data on a change from Teg's groundplan. Nobody who had ever seen a Guild building could mislabel this place, though.

So this was like other Junction planets. Somewhere in Guild records there doubtless was a serial number and code for it. So long under Guild control before Honored Matres that, in these first moments of debarking, getting their "ground legs," everything around them could be seen to have that special Guild flavor. Even the playing field—designed for outdoor meetings of Navigators in their giant containers of melange gas.

The Guild flavor: It was compounded of Ixian technology and Navigator design—buildings wrapped around space in the most energy-conserving way, paths direct; few slide-walks. They were wasteful and only the gravity-bound needed them. No flowery plantings near the Landing Flat. They were susceptible to accidental destruction. And that permanent grayness to all construction—not silver but as dull as Tleilaxu skin.

The structure on her left was a great bulging shape with extrusions, some rounded and some angular. This had been no lavish hostelry. Opulent little nooks, of course, but those were rare, built for VVIPs, mostly inspectors from the Guild.

Once more, Teg is right. Honored Matres kept existing structures, remodeling minimally. A tower!

Odrade reminded herself then: *This is not only another world but also another society with its own social glue.* She had a handle on that from Sharing with Murbella but did not think she had plumbed what held Honored Matres together. Surely not just a lusting after power.

"We'll walk," she said and led the way down the paved lane toward the giant structure.

Goodbye, Clairby. Blow your ship as soon as you can. Let it be our first great surprise for Honored Matres.

The Guild structure loomed higher as they approached.

The most astonishing thing to Odrade whenever she saw one of these functional constructions was that someone had taken a great deal of care in planning it. Intentional detail in everything although you sometimes had to dig for it. Budget dictated reduced quality in many choices, endurance preferred over luxury or eye appeal. Compromise and, like most compromise, satisfying no one. Guild comptrollers undoubtedly had complained at the price, and present occupants still could feel irritated at shortcomings. No matter. The thing was tangible substance. It was here to be used now. Another compromise.

The lobby was smaller than she had expected. Some interior changes. Only about six meters long and perhaps four meters wide. Reception slot was on their right as they entered. Odrade motioned Suipol to register their party and indicated that the rest of them should wait in the open area well within striking distance of one another. Treachery had not been ruled out.

Dortujla obviously expected it. She looked resigned.

Odrade made a careful inspection and commented on their surroundings. Plenty of comeyes but the rest of it . . .

Each time she entered one of these places, she had the sensation of
being in a museum. Other Memory said hostelries of this sort had not
changed significantly in eons. Even in early times she found proto-
types. A glimpse of the past in the chandeliers—gigantic glittering
things imitative of electric devices but furnished with glowglobes. Two
of them dominated the ceiling like imaginary spaceships descending
in splendor from the void.

There were more glimpses of the past that few transients in this age
would notice. The arrangement of the reception area behind grilled
slots, space for waiting with its mixture of seats and inconvenient
lighting, signs directing them to services—restaurants, narcoparlors,
assignation bars, swimming and other exercise facilities, automassage
rooms, and the like. Only language and script had changed from ancient times. Given an understanding of the language, the signs would
be recognizable to pre-space primitives. This was a temporary stopping place.

Plenty of security installations. Some had the look of artifacts from
the Scattering. Ix and Guild had never wasted gold on comeyes and
sensors.

A frenetic dance of roboservants in the reception area—darting
here and there, cleaning, picking up litter, guiding newcomers. A party
of four Ixians had preceded Odrade's group. She gave them close attention. How self-important yet fearful.

To her Bene Gesserit eye, the people of Ix were always recognizable
no matter the disguises. Basic structure of their society colored its
individuals. Ixians displayed a Hogbenesque attitude toward their science: that political and economic requirements determined permissible research. That said the innocent naivete of Ixian social dreams
had become the reality of bureaucratic centralism—a new aristocracy.
So they were headed into a decline that would not be stopped by whatever accommodation this Ixian party made with Honored Matres.

No matter the outcome of our contest, Ix is dying. Witness: no great Ixian innovations in centuries.

Suipol returned. "They ask us to wait for an escort."

Odrade decided to start negotiations immediately with a chat for the benefit of Suipol, the comeyes, and listeners on her no-ship.

"Suipol, did you notice those Ixians ahead of us?"

"Yes, Mother Superior."

"Mark them well. They are products of a dying society. It is naive to expect any bureaucracy to take brilliant innovations and put them to good use. Bureaucracies ask different questions. Do you know what those are?"

"No, Mother Superior." Spoken after a searching look at their surroundings.

She knows! But she sees what I'm doing. What have we here? I've misjudged her.

"These are typical questions, Suipol: Who gets the credit? Who will be blamed if it causes problems? Will it shift the power structure, costing us jobs? Or will it make some subsidiary department more important?"

Suipol nodded on cue but her glance at the comeyes might have been a little obvious. No matter.

"These are political questions," Odrade said. "They demonstrate how motives of bureaucracy are directly opposed to the need for adapting to change. Adaptability is a prime requirement for life to survive."

Time to talk directly to our hosts.

Odrade turned her attention upward, picking a prominent comeye in a chandelier. "Note those Ixians. Their 'mind in a deterministic universe' has given way to 'mind in an unlimited universe' where *anything* may happen. Creative anarchy is the path to survival in this universe."

"Thank you for this lesson, Mother Superior."

Bless you, Suipol.

"After all of their experiences with us," Suipol said, "surely they no longer question our loyalty to one another."

Fates preserve her! This one is ready for the Agony and may never see it.

Odrade could only agree with the acolyte's summation. Compliance with Bene Gesserit *ways* came from within, from those constantly monitored details that kept their own house in order. It was not philosophical but a pragmatic view of free will. Any claim the Sisterhood might have to making its own way in a hostile universe lay in scrupulous adherence to mutual loyalty, an agreement forged in the Agony. Chapterhouse and its few remaining subsidiaries were nurseries of an order founded in sharing and Sharing. Not based on innocence. That had been lost long ago. It was set firmly in political consciousness and a view of history independent of other laws and customs.

"We are not machines," Odrade said, glancing at the automata around them. "We always rely on personal relationships, never knowing where those may lead us."

Tamalane stepped to Odrade's side. "Don't you think they should be sending us a message at the very least?"

"They've already sent us a message, Tam, putting us up in a second-class hostelry. And I have responded."

Ultimately, all things are *known* because you want to believe you know.

—ZENSUNNI KOAN

Teg took a deep breath. Gammu lay directly ahead, precisely where his navigators had said it would be when they emerged from foldspace. He stood beside a watchful Streggi seeing this in displays of his flagship's command bay.

Streggi did not like it that he stood on his own feet instead of riding her shoulders. She felt superfluous amidst military hardware. Her gaze kept going to the multi-projection fields at command bay center. Aides moving efficiently in and out of pods and fields, bodies draped with esoteric hardware, knew what they were doing. She had only the vaguest idea of these functions.

The comboard to relay Teg's orders lay under his palms, riding there on suspensors. Its command field formed a faint blue glow around his hands. The silvery horseshoe linking him to the attack force rested lightly on his shoulders, feeling familiar there in spite of being much larger relative to his small body than comlinks of his previous lifetime.

None of those around him any longer questioned that this was their famous Bashar in a child's body. They took his orders with brisk acceptance.

The target system looked ordinary from this distance: a sun and its captive planets. But Gammu in center focus was not ordinary. Idaho had been born there, his ghola trained there, his original memories restored there.

And I was changed there.

Teg had no explanation for what he had found in himself under the stresses of survival on Gammu. Physical speed that drained his flesh and an ability to *see* no-ships, to locate them in an image field like a block of space reproduced in his mind.

He suspected a wild outcropping in Atreides genes. Marker cells had been identified in him but not their purpose. It was the heritage Bene Gesserit Breeding Mistresses had meddled with for eons. There was little doubt they would view this ability as something potentially dangerous to them. They might use it but he would certainly lose his freedom.

He put these reflections out of his mind.

"Send in the decoys."

Action!

Teg felt himself assume a familiar stance. There was a sense of climbing onto a refreshing eminence when planning ended. Theories had been articulated, alternatives carefully worked out, and subordinates deployed, all thoroughly briefed. His key squad leaders had committed Gammu to memory—where partisan help might be available, every bolt hole, every known strongpoint and which access routes were most vulnerable. He had warned them especially about Futars. The possibility that humanoid beasts might be allies could not be overlooked. Rebels who had helped ghola-Idaho escape from Gammu had insisted Futars were created to hunt and kill Honored Matres. Knowing the accounts of Dortujla and others, you could almost pity Honored Matres if this were true, except that no pity could be spared for those who never showed it to others.

The attack was taking its designed shape—scout ships laying down a decoy barrage and heavy carriers moving into strike position. Teg became now what he thought of as "the instrument of my instruments." It was difficult to determine which commanded and which responded.

Now, the delicate part.

Unknowns were to be feared. A good commander kept that firmly in mind. There were always unknowns.

Decoys were nearing the defensive perimeter. He *saw* enemy no-ships and foldspace sensors—bright dots arrayed through his awareness. Teg superimposed this onto the positions of his force. Every order he gave must appear to originate from a battle-plot they all shared.

He felt thankful Murbella had not joined him. Any Reverend Mother might see through his deception. But no one had questioned Odrade's order that Murbella wait with her party at a safe distance.

"Potential Mother Superior. Guard this one well."

Explosive demolition of decoys began with a random display of brilliant flashes around the planet. He leaned forward, staring at projections.

"There's the pattern!"

There was no such pattern but his words created belief and pulses quickened. No one questioned that the Bashar had seen vulnerability in the defenses. His hands flashed over the comboard, sending his ships forward in a blazing display that littered space behind them with enemy fragments.

"All right! Let's go!"

He fed the flagship's course directly into Navigation, then turned full attention to Fire Control. Silent explosions dotted space around them as the flagship mopped up surviving elements of Gammu's perimeter guardians.

"More decoys!" he ordered.

Globes of white light blinked in the projection fields.

Attention in the command bay concentrated on the fields, not on their Bashar. *The unexpected!* Teg, justly famous for that, was confirming his reputation.

"I find this oddly romantic," Streggi said.

Romantic? No romance in this! The time for romance was past and yet to come. A certain aura might surround *plans* for violence. He accepted that. Historians created their own brand of drama-cum-romance. But now? This was adrenaline time! Romance distracted you from necessities. You had to be cold inside, a clear and unimpaired line between mind and body.

As his hands moved in the comboard's field, Teg realized what had driven Streggi to speak. Something primitive about the death and destruction being created here. This was a moment cut out of normal order. A disturbing return to ancient tribal patterns.

She sensed a tom-tom in her breast and voices chanting: "Kill! Kill! Kill!"

His vision of guardian no-ships showed survivors fleeing in panic.

Good! Panic has a way of spreading and weakening your enemies.

"There's Barony."

Idaho had converted him to the old Harkonnen name for the sprawling city with its giant black centerpiece of plasteel.

"We'll land on the Flat to the north."

He spoke the words but his hands gave the orders.

Quickly now!

For brief moments when they disgorged troops, no-ships were visible and vulnerable. He held elements of the entire force responsive to his comboard and responsibility was heavy.

"This is only a feint. We go in and out after inflicting serious damage. Junction is our real target."

Odrade's parting admonition lay there in memory. "Honored Matres must be taught a lesson such as never before. Attack us and you get hurt badly. Press us and the pain can be enormous. They've heard about Bene Gesserit punishments. We're notorious. No doubt Spider Queen sniggered a bit. You must shove that snigger down her throat!"

"Quit ship!"

This was the vulnerable moment. Space above them remained empty of threat but fire lances arced inward from the east. His gunners could handle those. He concentrated on the possibility that enemy no-ships might return for a suicide attack. Command bay projections showed his hammerships and troop carriers pouring from the holds. The shock force, an armored elite on suspensors, already had the perimeter secured.

There went the portable comeyes to spread his field of observation and relay the intimate details of violence. Communication, the key to responsive command, but it also displayed bloody destruction.

"All clear!"

The signal rang through the bay.

He lifted off the Flat and repositioned in full invisibility. Now, only the comlinks gave defenders a clue to his position and that was masked by decoy relays.

Projection displayed the monstrous rectangle of the ancient Harkonnen center. It had been built as a block of light-absorbing metal to confine slaves. The elite had lived in garden mansions on top. Honored Matres had returned it to its former oppression.

Three of his giant hammerships came into view.

"Clear the top of that thing!" he ordered. "Wipe it clean but do as little damage as possible to the structure."

He knew his words were superfluous but spoke for the release. Everyone in the attack force knew what he wanted.

"Relay reports!" he ordered.

Information began flowing from the horseshoe on his shoulders. He brought it up on secondary. Comeyes showed his troops clearing the perimeter. Battle overhead and on the ground was well in hand for at least fifty klicks out. Going far better than he had expected. So Honored Matres kept their heavy stuff off-planet, not anticipating bold attack. A familiar attitude and he had Idaho to thank for predicting it.

"They're power-blind. They think heavy armor is for space and only light stuff for the ground. Heavy weapons are brought down as needed. No sense keeping them on planet. Takes too much energy. Besides, awareness of all that heavy stuff up there has a quieting effect on captive populations."

Idaho's concepts of weaponry were devastating.

"We tend to fix our minds on what we believe we know. A projectile is a projectile even when miniaturized to contain poisons or biologicals."

Innovations in protective equipment improved mobility. Built into uniforms where possible. And Idaho had brought back the shield with its awesome destruction when struck by a lasgun beam. Shields on suspensors hidden in what appeared to be soldiers (but were actually inflated uniforms) spread out ahead of troops. Lasgun fire at them produced clean atomics to clear large areas.

Will Junction be this easy?

Teg doubted it. Necessity enforced quick adaptation to new methods.

They could have shields on Junction in two days.

And no inhibitions about how to employ them.

Shields had dominated the Old Empire, he knew, because of that oddly important set of words called "Great Convention." Honorable people did not misuse weapons of their feudal society. If you dishonored the Convention, your peers turned against you with united violence. More than that, there had been the intangible, "Face," that some called "Pride."

Face! My position in the pack.

More important to some than life itself.

"This is costing us very little," Streggi said.

She was becoming quite the battle analyst and much too banal for Teg's liking. Streggi meant they were losing few lives but perhaps she spoke truer than she knew.

"It's difficult to think of cheap devices doing the job," Idaho had said. *"But that's a powerful weapon."*

If your weapons cost only a small fraction of the energy your enemy spent, you had a potent lever that could prevail against seemingly overwhelming odds. Prolong the conflict and you wasted enemy substance. Your foe toppled because control of production and workers was lost.

"We can begin to pull out," he said turning away from the projections as his hands repeated the order. "I want casualty reports as soon as—" He broke off and turned at a sudden stir.

Murbella?

Her projection was repeated in all of the bay's fields. Her voice blared from the images: "Why are you disregarding reports from your perimeter?" She overrode his board and the projections displayed a field commander caught in mid-sentence: ". . . orders, I will have to deny their request."

"Repeat," Murbella said.

The field commander's sweaty features turned toward his mobile comeye. The comsystem compensated and he appeared to look directly into Teg's eyes.

"Repeating: I have self-styled refugees here asking for asylum. Their leader says he has an agreement requiring the Sisterhood to honor his request but without orders . . ."

"Who is he?" Teg demanded.

"He calls himself Rabbi."

Teg moved to resume control of his comboard. "I don't know of any—"

"Wait!" Murbella overrode his board.

How does she do that?

Again her voice filled the bay. "Bring him and his party to the flagship. Make it quick." She silenced the perimeter relay.

Teg was outraged but at a disadvantage. He chose one of the multiple images and glared at it. "How dare you interfere?"

"Because you don't have the proper data. The Rabbi is within his rights. Prepare to receive him with honors."

"Explain."

"No! There's no need for you to know. But it was proper for me to make this decision when I saw you were not responding."

"That commander was in a diversionary area! Not important to—"

"But the Rabbi's request has priority."

"You're as bad as Mother Superior!"

"Perhaps worse. Now hear me! Get those refugees into your flagship. And prepare to receive me."

"Absolutely not! You are to stay where you are!"

"Bashar! There's something about this request that demands a Reverend Mother's attention. He says they are in peril because they gave temporary sanctuary to the Reverend Mother Lucilla. Accept this or step down."

"Then let me get my people aboard and pull back first. We'll ren-dezvous when we're clear."

"Agreed. But treat those refugees with courtesy."

"Now, get off my projections. You've blinded me and that was foolish!"

"You have everything well in hand, Bashar. During this hiatus an-other of our ships accepted four Futars. They came asking that we take them to Handlers but I ordered them confined. Treat them with extreme caution."

The bay's projections resumed battle status. Teg once more called in his force. He was seething and it was minutes before he restored a sense of command. Did Murbella know how she undermined his au-thority? Or should he take this as a measure of the importance she attached to the refugees?

When the situation was secure, he turned the bay over to an aide and, riding on Streggi's shoulders, went to see these *important* refu-gees. What was so vital about them that Murbella risked interference?

They were in a troop-carrier hold, a congealed party held apart by a cautious commander.

Who knows what may be concealed among these unknowns?

The Rabbi, identifiable because he was being deferred to by the field commander, stood with a brown-robed woman at the near side of his people. He was a small, bearded man wearing a white skullcap. Cold light made him appear ancient. The woman shielded her eyes with a hand. The Rabbi was speaking and his words became audible as Teg approached.

The woman was under verbal attack!

"The prideful one will be brought low!"

Without removing her hand from its defensive position, the woman said: "I am not proud of what I carry."

"Nor of the powers this knowledge may bring you?"

With knee pressure, Teg ordered Streggi to stop them about ten paces away. His commander glanced at Teg but stayed in position, ready to act defensively if this should prove to be a diversion.

Good man.

The woman bent her head even lower and pressed her hand against her eyes when she spoke. "Are we not offered knowledge that we might use it in holy service?"

"Daughter!" The Rabbi held himself stiffly erect. "Whatever we may learn that we may better serve, it never can be a great thing. All we call knowledge, were it to encompass everything a humble heart could hold, all of that would be no more than one seed in the furrows."

Teg felt reluctant to interfere. *What an archaic way of speaking.* This pair fascinated him. The other refugees listened to the exchange with rapt attention. Only Teg's field commander appeared aloof, keeping his attention on the strangers and giving an occasional hand-signal to aides.

The woman kept her head respectfully lowered and the shielding hand in place but she still defended herself. "Even a seed lost in the furrows may bring forth life."

The Rabbi's lips tightened into a grim line, then: "Without water and care, which is to say, without the blessing and the word, there is no life."

A great sigh shook the woman's shoulders but she held herself in that oddly submissive position when she responded: "Rabbi, I hear and obey. Still, I must honor this knowledge that has been thrust upon me because it contains the very admonition you have just voiced."

The Rabbi placed a hand on her shoulder. "Then convey it to those who want it and may no evil enter where you go."

Silence told Teg the argument had ended. He urged Streggi forward. Before she could move, Murbella strode past and nodded to the Rabbi while keeping her gaze on the woman.

"In the name of the Bene Gesserit and our debt to you, I welcome you and give you sanctuary," Murbella said.

The brown-robed woman lowered her hand and Teg saw contact lenses glittering in the palm. She lifted her head then and there were gasps all around. The woman's eyes were the total blue of spice addiction but they also held that inner force marking one who had survived the Agony.

Murbella made instant identification. *A wild Reverend Mother!* Not since Dune's Fremen days had one of these been known.

The woman curtsied to Murbella. "I am called Rebecca. And I am filled with joy to be with you. The Rabbi thinks I am a silly goose but I have a golden egg for I carry Lampadas: seven million six hundred twenty-two thousand and fourteen Reverend Mothers and they are rightfully yours."

Answers are a perilous grip on the universe. They can appear sensible yet explain nothing.

—THE ZENSUNNI WHIP

As the wait for their promised escort lengthened, Odrade became first angry and then amused. Finally, she began following lobby robos, interfering with their movements. Most were small and none appeared humanoid.

Functional. Hallmark of Ixian servos. Busy, busy, busy little accompaniments to a sojourn at Junction or its equivalent anywhere.

They were so commonplace that few people noticed them. Since they were not capable of dealing with deliberate interference, they subsided into motionless humming.

"Honored Matres have little or no sense of humor." I know, Murbella. I know. But do they get my message?

Dortujla obviously did. She came out of her funk and watched these antics with a wide grin. Tam looked disapproving but tolerant. Suipol was delighted. Odrade had to restrain her from helping to immobilize the devices.

Let me do the antagonizing, child. I know what is in store for me.

When she was sure she had made her point, Odrade took a position under one of the chandeliers.

"Attend me, Tam," she said.

Tamalane obediently placed herself in front of Odrade with an attentive expression.

"Have you noticed, Tam, that modern lobbies tend to be quite small?"

Tamalane spared a glance for her surroundings.

"Lobbies once were large," Odrade said. "To provide a prestigious feeling of space for the powerful, and impressing others with your importance, of course."

Tamalane caught the spirit of Odrade's playlet and said: "These days you're important if you travel at all."

Odrade looked at the immobilized robos scattered across the lobby floor. Some hummed and jittered. Others waited quietly for someone or some thing to restore order.

The autoreceptionist, a phallic tube of black plaz with a single glittering comeye, came out from behind its cage and picked its way through the stalled robos to confront Odrade.

"Much too humid today." It had a soupy feminine voice. "Don't know what Weather is thinking of."

Odrade spoke past it to Tamalane. "Why do they have to program these mechanicals to simulate friendly humans?"

"It's obscene," Tamalane agreed. She forcibly shouldered the autoreceptionist aside and it swiveled to study the source of this intrusion but made no other move.

Odrade was suddenly aware she had touched on the force that had powered the Butlerian Jihad—mob motivation.

My own prejudice!

She studied the mechanical confronting them. Was it waiting for instructions or must she address the thing directly?

Four more robos entered the lobby and Odrade recognized her party's luggage piled on them.

All of our things carefully inspected, I'm sure. Search where you will. We carry no hint of our legions.

The four scurried along the edge of the room and found their passage blocked by the ones rendered motionless. The luggage robos stopped and waited for this unique state of affairs to be sorted out. Odrade smiled at them. "There go the signs of the transient concealing our secret selves."

Concealing and secret.

Words to annoy the watchers.

Come on, Tam! You know the ploy. Confuse that enormous content of unconsciousness, arouse feelings of guilt they will be incapable of recognizing. Give them the jitters the way I did with the robos. Make them wary. What are the real powers of these Bene Gesserit witches?

Tamalane took her cue. *Transients and secret selves.* She explained for the comeyes in tones one used with children. "What do you carry when you leave your nest? Are you one who tries to pack it all? Or do you prune to necessities?"

What would the watchers classify as necessities? Tools of hygiene and washable or replaceable clothing? Weapons? They sought those in our luggage. But Reverend Mothers tend not to carry visible weapons.

"What an ugly place this is," Dortujla said, joining Tamalane in front of Odrade and picking up on the drama. "You would almost think it deliberate."

Ahhh, you nasty watchers. Observe Dortujla. Remember her? Why has she returned when she must know what you might do to her? Food for Futars? See how little that concerns her?

"A transition point, Dortujla," Odrade said. "Most people would never want this as their destination. An inconvenience, and the small discomforts serve only to remind you of that."

"A wayside stop, and it will never be much more unless they completely rebuild," Dortujla said.

Would they hear? Odrade aimed a look of utter composure at the selected comeye.

This is ugliness that betrays intent. It says to us: "We will provide something for the stomach, a bed, a place to evacuate bladder and bowels, a place to conduct the little maintenance rituals flesh requires, but you will be gone quickly because all we really want is the energy you leave behind."

The autoreceptionist backed around Tamalane and Dortujla, once more trying to make contact with Odrade.

"You will send us to our quarters immediately!" Odrade said, glaring into the cyclopean eye.

"Dear me! We've been inconsiderate."

Where had they found that syrupy voice? Repulsive. But Odrade was on her way out of the lobby in less than a minute, luggage on its robos ahead of them, Suipol close behind, Tamalane and Dortujla following.

There was an air of neglect to one wing clearly visible as they passed it. Did that mean Junction's traffic had declined? Interesting. Shutters had been sealed along an entire corridor. Hiding something? In the resulting gloom she detected dust on floor and ledges with only a few tracks of maintenance mechs. Concealment of what lay outside those windows? Unlikely. This had been closed off for some time.

She detected a pattern in what was being maintained. Very little traffic. Honored Matre effect. Who dared move around much when it felt safer to dig in and pray you would not be noticed by dangerous prowlers? Access lanes to elite private quarters were being kept up. Only the best was being maintained at its best.

When Gammu's refugees arrive, there will be room.

In the lobby, a robo had handed Suipol a guide pulser. "To find your way later." Round blue ball with a yellow arrow floating in it to point your chosen way. "Rings a tiny bell when you arrive."

The pulser's tiny bell rang.

And where have we arrived?

Another place where their hosts had provided "every luxury" while keeping it repellent. Rooms with soft yellow floors, pale mauve walls, white ceilings. No chairdogs. Be thankful for that even though the absence spoke of economics rather than care for a guest's preferences. Chairdogs required sustenance and expensive staff. She saw furnishings with permaflox fabrics. And behind the fabrics she felt plastic resilience. Everything done in the other colors of the rooms.

The bed was a small shock. Someone had taken the request for a hard mat too literally. Flat surface of black plaz without cushion. No bedding.

Suipol, seeing this, started to object but Odrade silenced her. Despite Bene Gesserit resources, comfort sometimes fell by the wayside. Get the job done! That was their first order. If Mother Superior had to sleep occasionally on a hard surface without covers, this could be passed off in the name of duty. Besides, the Bene Gesserit had ways of adjusting to such inconsequentials. Odrade steeled herself to discomfort, aware that if she objected she might find another deliberate insult.

Let them add this to all of that unconscious content and worry about it.

Her summons came while she was inspecting the rest of their quarters, displaying minimal concern and open amusement. A voice piped through ceiling vents intruded as Odrade and her companions emerged into the common sitting room: "Return to the lobby where you will meet your escort to Great Honored Matre."

"I will go alone," Odrade said, silencing objections.

A green-robed Honored Matre waited on a fragile chair where the corridor entered the lobby. She had a face built up like a castle wall—stone laid on stone. Mouth a watergate through which she inhaled some liquid via a transparent straw. Flow of purple up the straw. Sugar odor in the liquid. The eyes were weapons peeking over ramparts. Nose: a slope down which eyes dispatched their hatred. Chin: weak. Not necessary, that chin. An afterthought. Something left over from earlier construction. You could see the infant in it. And hair: artificially darkened to muddy brown. Unimportant. Eyes, nose, and mouth, those were important.

The woman stood slowly, insolently, emphasizing what a favor she did merely by noticing Odrade.

"Great Honored Matre agrees to see you."

Heavy, almost masculine voice. Pride walled up so high she exposed it whatever she did. Packed solid with immovable prejudice. She *knew* so many things she was a walking display of ignorance and fears. Odrade saw her as a perfect demonstration of Honored Matre vulnerability.

At the end of many turnings and corridors, all of them bright and clean, they came to a long room—sun pouring in a line of windows, sophisticated military console at one end; space maps and terrain maps projected there. Center of Spider Queen's web? Odrade entertained doubts. Console too obvious. Something of different design from the Scattering but no mistaking its purpose. Fields that humans could manipulate had physical limits, and a hood for mental interface could be nothing else even though it was a towering oval shape and a peculiar dirty yellow.

She swept her gaze over the room. Sparsely furnished. A few sling-chairs and small tables, a large open area where (presumably) people could await orders. No clutter. This was supposed to be an action center.

Impress that upon the witch!

Windows on one long wall revealed flagstones and gardens beyond. This whole thing was a set piece!

Where is Spider Queen? Where does she sleep? What is the appearance of her lair?

Two women came in through an arched doorway from the flagstones. Both wore red robes with glittering arabesques and dragon shapes on them. Soostones shattered for decorations.

Odrade held her silence, exercising caution until after introductions by the escort, who uttered as few words as possible and left hurriedly.

Without Murbella's hints, the tall one standing beside Spider Queen was the one Odrade would have taken for commander. But it was the smaller one. Fascinating.

This one did not just climb to power. She sneaked between the cracks. One day, her Sisters awoke to accomplished fact. There she was, firmly seated at the center. And who could object? Ten minutes after leaving her you would have difficulty remembering the target of your objections.

The two women examined Odrade with equal intensity.

Well and good. That is needed at this moment.

Spider Queen's appearance was more than a surprise. Until this moment, no physical description of her had been achieved by the Bene Gesserit. Only temporary projections, imaginative constructs based on scattered bits of evidence. Here she was, finally. A small woman. Expected stringy muscles visible under red leotards beneath her robe. Face a forgettable oval with bland brown eyes, orange flecks dancing in them.

Fearful and angered by it but cannot place the precise reasons for her fear. All she has is a target—me. What does she think to gain from me?

The aide was something else: in appearance, far more dangerous. Golden hair so carefully coiffed, slight hook to the nose, thin lips, skin stretched tightly over high cheekbones. And that venomous glare.

Odrade passed her gaze once more over Spider Queen's features: a nose that some would have trouble describing a minute after leaving her.

Straight? Well, somewhat.

Eyebrows a match to straw-colored hair. The mouth opened to become pinkly visible and almost vanished when closed. It was a face in which you had difficulty finding a central focus and thus the entire thing became blurred.

"So you lead the Bene Gesserit."

Voice equally low-key. Oddly inflected Galach and no jargon, yet you sensed it just behind her tongue. Linguistic tricks were there. Murbella's knowledge emphasized that.

"They have something close to Voice. Not the equal of what you gave me but there are other things they do, word tricks of a sort."

Word tricks.

"How should I address you?" Odrade asked.

"I hear you call me the Spider Queen." Orange flecks dancing viciously in her eyes.

"Here at the center of your web and considering your vast powers, I'm afraid I must confess to it."

"So that is what you notice—my powers." Vain!

The first thing Odrade actually had marked was the woman's smell. She was bathed in some outrageous perfume.

Covering up pheromones?

Warned about Bene Gesserit ability to judge on the basis of minuscule sense data? Perhaps. Just as probably she preferred this perfume. The odious concoction had about it an underlying hint of exotic flowers. Something from her homeland?

The Spider Queen put a hand to her forgettable chin. "You may call me Dama."

The companion objected. "This is the last enemy in the Million Planets!"

So that's how they think of the Old Empire.

Dama held up a hand for silence. How casual and how revealing. Odrade saw a luster reminiscent of Bellonda in the aide's eyes. Viciousness watchful in there and looking for places to attack.

"Most are required to address me as Great Honored Matre," Dama said. "I have conferred an honor upon you." She gestured toward the arched doorway behind her. "We will walk outside, just the two of us, while we talk."

No invitation; it was a command.

Odrade paused beside the door to look at a map displayed there. Black on white, little lines of paths and irregular outlines with labels in Galach. It was the gardens beyond the flagstones, identification of plantings. Odrade bent close to study it while Dama waited with amused tolerance. Yes, esoteric trees and bushes, very few bearing edible fruits. Pride of possession and this map was here to emphasize it.

On the patio, Odrade said: "I noticed your perfume."

Dama was thrown back into memories and her voice carried subtle undertones when she responded.

Floral identity marker for her own flamebush. Imagine that! But she is both sad and angry when she thinks of this. And she wonders why I bring it to attention.

"Otherwise, the bush would not have accepted me," Dama said.

Interesting choice of verb tense.

The accented Galach was not hard to understand. She obviously adjusted unconsciously for the listener.

Good ear. Spends a few seconds, watching, listening and adjusts to make herself understood. Very old art form that most humans adopt quickly.

Odrade saw the origins as protective coloration.

Don't want to be taken for an alien.

An adjustable characteristic built into the genes. Honored Matres had not lost it but this was a vulnerability. Unconscious tonalities were not completely covered and they revealed much.

Despite her blatant vanity, Dama was intelligent and self-disciplined. It was a pleasure to come to that opinion. Certain circumlocutions were not necessary.

Odrade stopped where Dama stopped at the edge of the patio. They stood almost shoulder to shoulder and Odrade, gazing outward at the garden, was struck by the almost Bene Gesserit appearance.

"Speak your piece," Dama said.

"What value do I have as a hostage?" Odrade asked.

Orange glare!

"You've obviously asked the question," Odrade said.

"Do continue." Orange subsiding.

"The Sisterhood has three replacements for me." Odrade produced her most penetrating stare. "It is possible for us to weaken each other in ways that would destroy us both."

"We could crush you as we would swat an insect!"

Beware the orange!

Odrade was not deflected by warnings from within. "But the hand that *swatted* us would fester, and eventually, sickness would consume you."

It could not be stated plainer without specific details.

"Impossible!" An orange glare.

"Do you think us unaware of how you were driven back here by your enemies?"

My most dangerous gambit.

Odrade watched it take effect. A dark scowl was not Dama's only visible response. Orange vanished, leaving her eyes an oddly bland discrepancy on the glowering face.

Odrade nodded as though Dama had answered. "We could leave you vulnerable to those who assail you, those who drove you into this cul de sac."

"You think we . . ."

"We know."

At least, now I know.

The knowledge produced both elation and fear.

What is out there to subdue these women?

"We merely gather our forces before—"

"Before returning to an arena where you are sure to be crushed . . . where you cannot count on overwhelming numbers."

Dama's voice relapsed into soft Galach that Odrade had difficulty understanding. "So they have been to you . . . and made their offer. What fools you are to trust the . . ."

"I have not said we trust."

"If Logno back there . . ." Nod of head indicating the aide in the room ". . . heard you talking to me this way you would be dead in less time than I take to warn you of it."

"I am fortunate there are only the two of us."

"Don't count on that to carry you much farther."

Odrade glanced over her shoulder at the building. Alterations in Guild design were visible: a long façade of windows, much exotic wood and jeweled stones.

Wealth.

She was dealing with wealth in an extreme it would be hard for some to imagine. Nothing Dama wanted, nothing that could be provided by the society subservient to her, would be denied. Nothing except freedom to go back into the Scattering.

How firmly did Dama cling to the fantasy that her exile might end?

And what was the force that had driven such power back to the Old Empire? Why here? Odrade dared not ask.

"We will continue this in my quarters," Dama said.

Into the Spider Queen's lair at last!

Dama's quarters were a bit of a puzzle. Richly carpeted floors. She kicked off sandals and went barefoot on entering. Odrade followed this lead.

Look at the callused flesh along the outsides of her feet! Dangerous weapons kept well-conditioned.

Not the soft floor but the room itself puzzled Odrade. One small window looking over the carefully manicured botanical garden. No hangings or pictures on the walls. No decorations. An air vent grill drew shadowy stripes above the door they had entered. One other door on the right. Another air vent. Two soft gray couches. Two small side tables in glistening black. Another larger table in tones of gold with a green shimmer above it to indicate a control field. Odrade identified the fine rectangular outline of a projector inset into the golden table.

Ahhhh, this is her workroom. Are we here to work?

A refined concentration about this place. Care had been taken to eliminate distractions. What distractions would Dama accept?

Where are the decorated rooms? She has to live in particular ways with her surroundings. You cannot always be forming mental barriers to reject things around you that sit disagreeably in your psyche. If you want real comfort, your home cannot be set up in a way that attacks you, especially no attacks on the unconscious side. She is aware of unconscious vulnerabilities! This one is truly dangerous but she has the power to say "Yes."

It was an ancient Bene Gesserit insight. You looked for the ones who could say "Yes." Never bother with underlings who can only say "No." You sought the one who could make an agreement, sign a contract, pay off on a promise. Spider Queen did not often say "Yes" but she had that power and knew it.

I should have realized when she took me aside. She sent me the first

*signal when she permitted me to call her Dama. Have I been too
precipitate, setting up Teg's attack in a way I cannot stop? Too late for
second thoughts. I knew it when I unleashed him.*

But what other forces may we attract?

Odrade had Dama's dominance pattern registered. Words and gestures were likely to make Spider Queen recoil, crouching back to intense awareness of her own heartbeats.

The drama must go forward.

Dama was doing something with her hands in the green field atop
the golden table. She concentrated on it, ignoring Odrade in a way that
was both insult and compliment.

*You will not interfere, witch, because that is not in your best interest
and you know it. Besides, you are not important enough to distract me.*

Dama appeared agitated.

*Has the attack on Gammu been successful? Are refugees beginning
to arrive?*

An orange glare focused on Odrade. "Your pilot has just destroyed
himself and your ship rather than submit to our inspection. What did
you bring?"

"Ourselves."

"There is a signal coming from you!"

"Telling my companions whether I am alive or dead. You already
knew that. Some of our ancestors burned their ships before an attack.
No retreat possible."

Odrade spoke with exquisite care, tone and timing adjusted to
Dama's responses. "If I am successful, you will provide my transport.
My pilot was a Cyborg and shere could not protect him from your
probes. His orders were to kill himself rather than fall into your hands."

"Providing us with coordinates to your planet." The orange subsided from Dama's eyes, but she still was disturbed. "I did not think
your people obeyed you to that extent."

*How do you hold them without sexual bonding, witch? Is the answer
not obvious? We have secret powers.*

Careful now, Odrade cautioned herself. *A methodical approach,*

*alert for new demands. Let her think we choose one method of response
and stick to it. How much does she know about us? She does not know
that even Mother Superior may be only a morsel of bait, a lure to gain
vital information. Does that make us superior? If so, can superior training surmount superior speed and numbers?*

Odrade had no answer.

Dama seated herself behind the golden table, leaving Odrade
standing. There was a nesting sense about the movement. She did not
leave this place often. This was the true center of her web. All things
she thought she needed were here. She had brought Odrade to this
room because it was an inconvenience to be elsewhere. She was uncomfortable in other settings, perhaps even felt threatened. Dama did
not court danger. She had done so once but that was long ago, shut off
behind her somewhere. Now, she wanted only to sit here in a safe and
well-organized cocoon where she could manipulate others.

Odrade found these observations a welcome affirmation of Bene
Gesserit deductions. The Sisterhood knew how to exploit this leverage.

"Have you nothing more to say?" Dama asked.

Stall for time.

Odrade ventured a question. "I am extremely curious why you
agreed to this meeting?"

"Why are you curious?"

"It seems so . . . so out of character for you."

"We determine what is in character for us!" Quite testy there.

"But what is it about us interests you?"

"You think we find you interesting?"

"Perhaps you even find us remarkable, because that is certainly
how we look at you."

A pleased expression made its fleeting appearance on Dama's face.
"I knew you would be fascinated by us."

"The exotic interests the exotic," Odrade said.

This brought a knowing smile to Dama's lips, the smile of someone
whose pet has been clever. She stood and went to the one window.
Summoning Odrade to her side, Dama gestured to a stand of trees

beyond the first flowering bushes and spoke in that soft accent so difficult to follow.

Something ticked off an inner alarm. Odrade fell into simulflow, seeking the source. Something in the room or in Spider Queen? There was a lack of spontaneity about the setting matched by much that Dama did. So all of this was designed to create an effect. Carefully schemed.

Is this one really my Spider Queen? Or is there a more powerful one watching us?

Odrade explored this thought, sorting swiftly. It was a process that provided more questions than answers, a mental shorthand akin to that of Mentats. Sort for relevance and bring up the latent (but orderly) backgrounds. Order generally was a product of human activity. Chaos existed as raw material from which to create order. That was the Mentat approach, giving no unalterable truths but a remarkable lever for decision-making: orderly assemblage of data in a non-discrete system.

She arrived at a Projective.

They revel in chaos! Prefer it! Adrenaline addicts!

So Dama was Dama, Great Honored Matre. Forever the patroness, forever the superior.

There is no greater one watching us. But Dama believes this is bargaining. One would think she had never done it before. Precisely!

Dama touched an unmarked place below the window and the wall folded back, revealing that the window was but an artful projection. The way was opened onto a high balcony paved with dark green tiles. It overlooked plantations much different from those in the window projection. Here was chaos preserved, wilderness left to its own devices and made more remarkable by ordered gardens in the distance. Brambles, fallen trees, thick bushes. And beyond: evenly spaced rows of what appeared to be vegetables with automated harvesters passing back and forth, leaving bare ground behind them.

Love of chaos, indeed!

Spider Queen smiled and led the way onto the balcony.

As she emerged, Odrade once more was stopped by what she saw.

A decoration on the parapet to her left. A life-size figure shaped from an almost ethereal substance, all feathery planes and curved surfaces.

When she squinted at the figure, Odrade saw it was intended to represent a human. Male or female? In some positions male, and in some female. Planes and curves responded to vagrant breezes. Thin, almost invisible wires (looked to be shigawire) suspended it from a delicately curving tube anchored in a translucent mound. The lower extremities of the figure almost touched the pebbled surface of the supporting base.

Odrade stared, captivated.

Why does it remind me of Sheeana's "The Void"?

When the wind moved it, the whole creation appeared to dance, relapsing sometimes into a graceful walk, then a slow pirouette and sweeping turns with outstretched leg.

"It is called 'Ballet Master,'" Dama said. "In some winds it will kick its feet high. I have seen it running as gracefully as a marathoner. Sometimes it is just ugly little motions, arms jerking as though they held weapons. Beautiful and ugly—it is all the same. I think the artist misnamed it. 'Being Unknown' would have been better."

Beautiful and ugly—all the same. Being Unknown.

That was a terrible thing about Sheeana's creation. Odrade felt a cold wash of fear. "Who was the artist?"

"I've no idea. One of my predecessors took it from a planet we were destroying. Why does it interest you?"

It's the wild thing no one can govern. But she said: "I presume we're both seeking a basis for understanding, trying to find similarities between us."

This brought the orange glare. "You may try to understand us but we have no need to understand you."

"Both of us come from societies of women."

"It is dangerous to think of us as your offshoots!"

But Murbella's evidence says you are. Formed in the Scattering by Fish Speakers and Reverend Mothers in extremis.

All ingenuous and fooling nobody, Odrade asked: "Why is that dangerous?"

Dama's laugh conveyed no amusement. Vindictive.

Odrade experienced an abrupt new assessment of danger. More than a Bene Gesserit probe-and-review was demanded here. These women were accustomed to killing when angered. A reflex. Dama had said as much when speaking to her aide, and Dama had just signaled there were limits to her tolerance.

Yet, in her own way, she is trying to bargain. She displays her mechanical marvels, her powers, her wealth. No offer of alliance. Be willing servants, witches, our slaves, and we will forgive much. To gain the last of the Million Planets? More than that, certainly, but an interesting number.

With a new caution, Odrade reformed her approach. Reverend Mothers too easily fell into an adaptive pattern. *I am, of course, quite different from you but I will unbend for the sake of accord.* That would not do with Honored Matres. They would accept nothing to suggest they were not in absolute control. It was a statement of Dama's superiority over her Sisters that she allowed Odrade so much latitude.

Once more, Dama spoke in her imperious manner.

Odrade listened. How odd that Spider Queen thought one of the most attractive things the Bene Gesserit could provide was immunity from new diseases.

Was that the form of attack that drove them here?

Her sincerity was naive. None of this tiresome periodic checking to see if you had acquired secret inhabitants in your flesh. Sometimes not so secret. Sometimes disgustingly perilous. But the Bene Gesserit could end all that and would be suitably rewarded.

How pleasant.

Still that vindictive tone in every word. Odrade caught herself in this thought: Vindictive? That did not catch the proper flavor. Something carried at a deeper level.

Unconsciously jealous of what you lost when you broke away from us!

This was another pattern and it had been stylized!

Honored Matres fell back on repetitive mannerisms.

Mannerisms we abandoned long ago.

This was more than refusal to recognize Bene Gesserit origins. This was garbage disposal.

Drop your discards wherever they lose your interest. Underlings take out the garbage. She is more concerned with the next thing she wants to consume than she is with fouling her own nest.

The Honored Matre flaw was larger than suspected. Much more deadly to themselves and all they controlled. And they could not face it because, to them, it was not there.

Never existed.

Dama remained an untouchable paradox. No question of alliance entered her mind. She would seem to dance up to it but only to test her enemy.

I was right after all to unleash Teg.

Logno came out of the workroom with a tray on which stood two spindly glasses almost filled with golden liquid. Dama took one, sniffed it, and sipped with a pleased expression.

What is that vicious glitter in Logno's eyes?

"Try some of this wine," Dama said, gesturing to Odrade. "It's from a planet I'm sure you've never heard of but where we have concentrated the required elements to produce the perfect golden grape for the perfect golden wine."

Odrade was caught by this long association of humans with their precious ancient drink. The god Bacchus. Berries fermented on the bush or in tribal containers.

"It is not poisoned," Dama said as Odrade hesitated. "I assure you. We kill where it suits our needs but we are not crass. We reserve our more blatant deadliness for the masses. I do not mistake you for one of the masses."

Dama chuckled at her own witticism. The labored friendliness was almost gross.

Odrade took the proffered glass and sipped.

"It's a thing someone devised to please us," Dama said, her attention fixed on Odrade.

The one sip was enough. Odrade's senses detected a foreign substance and she was several heartbeats identifying its purpose.

To nullify the shere protecting me from their probes.

She adjusted her metabolism to render the substance harmless, then announced what she had done.

Dama glared at Logno. "So that is why none of these things work with the witches! And you never suspected!" The rage was an almost physical force directed at the hapless aide.

"It is one of the immune systems with which we combat disease," Odrade said.

Dama hurled her glass to the tiles. She was some time regaining composure. Logno retreated slowly, holding the tray almost as a shield.

So Dama did more than sneak into power. Her Sisters consider her deadly. And so must I consider her.

"Someone will pay for this wasted effort," Dama said. Her smile was not pleasant.

Someone.

Someone made the wine. Someone made the dancing figure. Someone will pay. The identity was never important, only the pleasure or the need for retribution. Subservience.

"Do not interrupt my thoughts," Dama said. She went to the parapet and gazed at her Being Unknown, obviously recomposing her *bargaining* stance.

Odrade turned her attention to Logno. What was that continued watchfulness, rapt attention fixed on Dama? No longer simple fear. Logno suddenly appeared supremely dangerous.

Poison!

Odrade knew it as certainly as though the aide had shouted the word.

I am not Logno's target. Not yet. She has taken this opportunity to make her bid for power.

There was no need to look at Dama. The moment of Spider Queen's death was visible on Logno's face. Turning, Odrade confirmed it. Dama lay in a heap under Being Unknown.

"You will call *me* Great Honored Matre," Logno said. "And you will learn to thank me for it. She (pointing at the red heap in the balcony corner) intended to betray you and exterminate your people. I have other plans. I am not one to destroy a useful weapon at the moment of our greatest need."

Battle? There's always a desire for breathing space motivating it somewhere.

Murbella watched the struggle for Junction with a detachment that did not reflect her feelings. She stood with a coterie of Proctors in her no-ship's command center, attention fixed on relay projections from groundside comeyes.

There were battles all around Junction—bursts of light on darkside, gray eruptions on dayside. A major engagement directed by Teg centered on "the Citadel"—a giant mound of Guild design with a new tower near its rim. Although Odrade's vital-signs transmissions had stopped abruptly, her early reports confirmed that Great Honored Matre was in there.

The need to observe from a distance helped Murbella's sense of detachment but she felt the excitement.

Interesting times!

This ship contained precious cargo. The millions from Lampadas were being Shared and prepared for Scattering in a suite ordinarily reserved for Mother Superior. The wild Sister with her cargo of Memory dominated their priorities here.

Golden Egg for sure!

Murbella thought of the lives being risked in that suite. Preparing for the worst. No lack of volunteers and the threat in the Junction conflict minimized need for spice poison to ignite Sharings, reducing danger. Anyone on this ship could sense all-or-nothing in Odrade's gamble. Imminent threat of death was recognized. Sharing necessary!

Transformation of a Reverend Mother into sets of memories passed around at perilous cost among the Sisters no longer carried a mysterious aura for her, but Murbella still was awed by the responsibility. The courage of Rebecca . . . and Lucilla! . . . demanded admiration.

Millions of Memory Lives! All concentrated in what the Sisterhood called Extremis Progressiva, two by two then four by four and sixteen by sixteen, until each held all of them and any survivor could preserve the precious accumulation.

What they were doing in Mother Superior's suite had some of that flavor. The concept no longer terrified Murbella but it was not yet ordinary. Odrade's words comforted.

"Once you have fully accommodated to the bundles of Other Memory, all else falls into a perspective that is utterly familiar, as though you had known it always."

Murbella recognized that Teg was prepared to die in defense of this multiple awareness that was the Sisterhood of the Bene Gesserit.

Can I do less?

Teg, no longer completely an enigma, remained an object of respect. Odrade Within amplified this with reminders of his exploits, then: *"I wonder how I'm doing down there? Ask."*

Comcommand said, "No word. But her transmissions may have been blocked by energy shielding."

They knew who really asked the question. It was on their faces.

She has Odrade!

Murbella again focused on the battle at the Citadel.

Her own reactions surprised Murbella. Everything colored by historical disgust at repetition of war's nonsense, but still this exuberant spirit reveling in newly acquired Bene Gesserit abilities.

Honored Matre forces had good weapons down there, she noted, and Teg's heat-absorption pads were taking punishment but even as she watched, the defensive perimeter collapsed. She could hear howling as a large Idaho-designed disrupter went bouncing down a passage between tall trees, knocking out defenders right and left.

Other Memory gave her a peculiar comparison. It was like a circus. Ships landing, disgorging their human cargoes.

"In the center ring! The Spider Queen! Acts never before seen by the human eye!"

Odrade's persona produced a sense of amusement. *How's this for closeness of sisterhood?*

Are you dead down there, Dar? You must be. Spider Queen will blame you and be enraged.

Trees placed long afternoon shadows across Teg's lane of attack, she saw. Inviting cover. He ordered his people to go around. Ignore inviting avenues. Look for hard ways to approach and use them.

The Citadel lay in a gigantic botanical garden, strange trees and even stranger bushes mingled with prosaic plantings, all scattered around as though thrown there by a dancing child.

Murbella found the circus metaphor attractive. It gave perspective to what she witnessed.

Announcements in her mind.

Over there, dancing animals, defenders of Spider Queen, all bound to obey! And in the first ring, the main event, supervised by our Ringmaster, Miles Teg! His people do mysterious things. Here is the talent!

It had aspects of a staged battle in the Roman Circus. Murbella appreciated the allusion. It made observation richer.

Battle towers filled with armored soldiers approach. They engage. Flames cut the sky. Bodies fall.

But these were real bodies, real pains, real deaths. Bene Gesserit sensitivities forced her to regret the waste.

Is this how it was for my parents caught in the sweep?

Metaphors from Other Memory vanished. She saw Junction then as she knew Teg must see it. Bloody violence, familiar in memory and yet new. She saw attackers advancing, heard them.

Woman's voice, distinct with shock: "That bush screamed at me!"

Another voice, male: "No telling where some of this originated. That sticky stuff burns your skin."

Murbella heard action on the far side of the Citadel but it grew eerily quiet around Teg's position. She saw his troops flitting through shadows, closing in on the tower. There was Teg on Streggi's shoulders. He took a moment to stare up at the façade confronting them about half a klick away. She chose a projection that looked where he looked. Motion behind windows there.

Where were the mysterious last-ditch weapons Honored Matres were supposed to possess?

What will he do now?

Teg had lost his Command Pod to a laser hit outside the main engagement area. The pod lay on its side behind him and he sat astride Streggi's shoulders in a patch of screening bushes, some still smoldering. He had lost his comboard with the pod but retained the silvery horseshoe of his comlink, although it was crippled without the pod's amplifiers. Communications specialists crouched nearby, jittering because they had lost close contact with the action.

The battle beyond the buildings grew louder. He heard hoarse shouts, the high hissing of burners and the lower buzz of large lasguns mingled with tinny zip-zips of hand weapons. Somewhere off there to his left was a thrum-thrum he recognized as heavy armor in trouble. A scraping sound with it, metal agony. Energy system damaged in that one. It was dragging itself over the ground, probably making a mess of the gardens.

Haker, Teg's personal aide, came dodging down the lane behind the Bashar.

Streggi noticed him first and turned without warning, forcing Teg to look at the man. Haker, dark and muscular, with heavy eyebrows (sweat-dampened now) stopped directly in front of Teg and spoke before fully regaining his breath.

"We have the last pockets bottled up, Bashar."

Haker raised his voice to override the battle sounds and a buzzing squawker over his left shoulder producing low conversations, battle urgency in clipped tones.

"The far perimeter?" Teg demanded.

"Mop up in half an hour, no more. You should get out of here, Bashar. Mother Superior warned us to keep you out of needless danger."

Teg gestured at his useless pod. "Why don't I have a Communications backup?"

"A big laze got both backups in the same burn as they were coming in."

"They were together?"

Haker heard the anger. "Sir, they were . . ."

"No important equipment is sent in together. I'll want to know who disobeyed orders." The quiet voice from immature vocal cords carried more menace than a shout.

"Yes, Bashar." Strictly obedient and no sign from Haker that the mistake was his own.

Damn! "How soon will replacements arrive?"

"Five minutes."

"Get my reserve pod in here as fast as you can." Teg touched Streggi's neck with a knee.

Haker spoke before she could turn. "Bashar, they got the reserve, too. I've ordered another."

Teg repressed a sigh. These things happened in battle but he didn't like depending on primitive coms. "We'll set up here. Get more squawkers." They, at least, had the range.

Haker glanced at the greenery around them. "Here?"

"I don't like the look of those buildings up ahead. That tower commands this area. And they must have underground access. I would."

"There's nothing on the . . ."

"My memory layout doesn't include that tower. Get sonics in here to check the ground. I want our plan brought up to the minute with secure information."

Haker's squawker came alive with an override voice: "Bashar! Is the Bashar available?"

Streggi moved him next to Haker without being told. Teg took the squawker, whistling his code as he grabbed it.

"Bashar, it's a mess at the Flat. About a hundred of them tried to lift and ran into our screen. No survivors."

"Any sign of Mother Superior or her Spider Queen?"

"Negative. We can't tell. I mean it's a real mess. Shall I screen a view?"

"Get me a dispatch. And keep looking for Odrade!"

"I tell you nothing survived here, Bashar." There was a click and a low hum, then another voice: "Dispatch."

Teg brought his voice-print coder from beneath his chin and barked quick orders. "Scramble a hammership over the Citadel. Put the scene at the Landing Flat and their other disasters on open relay. All bands. Make sure they can see it. Announce no survivors at the Flat."

The double click of *received-confirmed* broke the link. Haker said: "Do you really think you can terrify them?"

"Educate them." He repeated Odrade's parting words: "Their education has been sadly neglected."

What had happened to Odrade? He felt sure she must be dead, perhaps the first casualty here. She had expected that. Dead but not lost if Murbella could restrain her impetuosity.

Odrade, at that moment, had Teg in direct sight from the tower. Logno had silenced her vital signs transmissions with a countersignal shield and had brought her to the tower shortly after the arrival of the first refugees from Gammu. No one questioned Logno's supremacy. A dead Great Honored Matre and a live one could only be something familiar.

Expecting to be killed at any moment, Odrade still gathered data as she went up in a nulltube with guards. The tube was an artifact from the Scattering, a transparent piston in a transparent cylinder. Few obstructing walls at the floors they passed. Mostly views of living areas and esoteric hardware Odrade surmised had military purposes. Lush evidence of comfort and quiet increased the higher they went.

Power climbs physically as well as psychologically.

Here they were at the top. A section of the tube cylinder swung outward and a guard pushed her roughly onto a thickly carpeted floor.

The workroom Dama showed me down there was another set piece.

Odrade recognized secrecy. Equipment and furnishings here would have been almost unrecognizable were it not for Murbella's knowledge. So other action centers were for show. Potemkin villages built for Reverend Mother.

Logno lied about Dama's intentions. I was expected to leave unharmed . . . carrying no useful information.

What other lies had they paraded in front of her?

Logno and all but one guard went to a console on Odrade's right. Pivoting on one foot, Odrade looked around. This was the real center. She studied it with care. Odd place. An aura of the sanitary. Treated with chemicals to make it clean. No bacterial or viral contaminants. No strangers in the blood. Everything *debugged* like a showcase for rare viands. And Dama showed interest in Bene Gesserit immunity to diseases. There was bacterial warfare in the Scattering.

They want one thing from us!

And just one surviving Reverend Mother would satisfy them if they could wrest information from her.

A full Bene Gesserit cadre would have to examine the strands of this web and see where they led.

If we win.

The operations console where Logno concentrated her attention was smaller than the showcase ones. Fingerfield manipulation. The hood on a low table beside Logno was smaller and transparent, revealing the medusa tangle of probes.

Shigawire for sure.

The hood showed a close affinity to T-probes from the Scattering Teg and others had described. Did these women possess more technological marvels? They must.

A glittering wall behind Logno, windows on her left opening onto a balcony, a far vista of Junction visible out there with movement of troops and armor. She recognized Teg in the distance, a figure on the shoulders of an adult, but gave no sign she saw anything extraordinary. She continued her slow study. Door to a passage with another nulltube partly visible in a separate area to her immediate left. More green tile on the floor there. Different functions in that space.

A sudden burst of noises erupted beyond the wall. Odrade identified some of them. Boots of soldiers made a distinctive sound on tiles. Swish of exotic fabrics. Voices. She distinguished accents of Honored Matres responding to each other in tones of shock.

We're winning!

Shock was to be expected when the invincible were brought low. She studied Logno. Would it be a plunge into despair?

If so, I may survive.

Murbella's role might be changed. Well, that could wait. Sisters had been briefed on what to do in the event of victory. Neither they nor anyone else in the attack force would lay rough hands on an Honored Matre—erotic or otherwise. Duncan had prepared the men, making the perils of sexual entrapment thoroughly known.

Risk no bondage. Raise no new antagonisms.

The new Spider Queen was revealed now as someone even stranger than Odrade had suspected. Logno left her console and came to within a pace of Odrade. "You have won this battle. We are your prisoners."

No orange in her eyes. Odrade swept her gaze around at the women who had been her guards. Blank expressions, clear eyes. Was this how they showed despair? It did not feel right. Logno and the others revealed no expected emotional responses.

Everything under wraps?

Events of the past hours should create emotional crisis. Logno gave no sign of it. Not a twitch of revealing nerve or muscle. Perhaps a casual concern and that was all.

A Bene Gesserit mask!

It had to be unconscious, something automatic ignited by defeat. So they did not really accept defeat.

We are still in there with them. Latent . . . but there! No wonder

Murbella almost died. She was confronting her own genetic past as a supreme prohibition.

"My companions," Odrade said. "The three women who came with me. Where are they?"

"Dead." Logno's voice was as dead as the word.

Odrade suppressed a pang for Suipol. Tam and Dortujla had lived long and useful lives, but Suipol . . . dead and never Shared.

Another good one lost. And isn't that a bitter lesson!

"I will identify the ones responsible if you desire revenge," Logno said.

Lesson two.

"Revenge is for children and the emotionally retarded."

A small return of orange in Logno's eyes.

Human self-delusion took many forms, Odrade reminded herself. Aware that the Scattering would produce the unexpected, she had armed herself accordingly with a protective remoteness that would allow her a space to assess new places, new things and new people. She had known she would be forced to put many things in different categories to serve her or deflect threats. She took Logno's attitude as a threat.

"You do not seem disturbed, Great Honored Matre."

"Others will avenge me." Flat, very self-composed.

The words were even stranger than her composure. She held everything under that close cover, bits and pieces revealed now in flickering movements aroused by Odrade's observation. Deep and intense things, but buried. It was all inside there, masked the way a Reverend Mother would mask it. Logno appeared to have no power at all and yet she spoke as though nothing essential had changed.

"I am your captive but that makes no difference."

Was she truly powerless? *No!* But that was the impression she wished to convey and all of the other Honored Matres around her mirrored this response.

"See us? Powerless except for the loyalty of our Sisters and the followers they have bonded to us."

Were Honored Matres that confident of their vengeful legions? Possible only if they had never before suffered a defeat of this kind. Yet someone had driven them back into the Old Empire. Into the Million Planets.

Teg found Odrade and her *captives* while seeking a place to assess victory. Battle always required its analytical aftermath, especially from a Mentat commander. It was a comparison test this battle demanded of him more than any other in his experience. This conflict would not be lodged in memory until assessed and shared as far as possible among those who depended on him. It was his invariable pattern and he did not care what it revealed about him. Break that link of inter-locking interests and you prepared yourself for defeat.

I need a quiet place to assemble the threads of this battle and make a preliminary summary.

In his estimation, a most difficult problem of battle was to conduct it in a way that did not release human wildness. A Bene Gesserit dic-tum. Battle must be conducted to bring out the best in those who sur-vived. Most difficult and sometimes all but impossible. The more remote the soldier from carnage, the more difficult. It was one reason Teg always tried to move to the battle scene and examine it personally. If you did not see the pain, you could easily cause greater pain without second thoughts. That was the Honored Matre pattern. But their pains had been brought home. What would they make of this?

That question was in his mind as he and aides emerged from the tube to see Odrade confronting a party of Honored Matres.

"Here is our commander, the Bashar Miles Teg," Odrade said, ges-turing.

Honored Matres stared at Teg.

A child riding on the shoulders of an adult? This is their commander?

"Ghola," Logno muttered.

Odrade spoke to Haker. "Take these prisoners somewhere nearby where they can be comfortable."

Haker did not move until Teg nodded, then politely indicated that captives should precede him into the tiled area on their left. Teg's dom-inance was not lost on Honored Matres. They glowered at him as they obeyed Haker's invitation.

Men ordering women about!

With Odrade beside him, Teg touched a knee to Streggi's neck and they went onto the balcony. There was an oddity to the scene that he was a moment identifying. He had viewed many battle scenes from high vantages, most often from a scout 'thopter. This balcony was fixed in space, giving him a sense of immediacy. They stood about one hundred meters above the botanical gardens where much of the fiercest conflict had taken place. Many bodies lay sprawled in final dislodgment—dolls thrown aside by departing children. He recognized uniforms of some of his troops and felt a pang.

Could I have done something to prevent this?

He had known this feeling many times and called it "Command Guilt." But this scene was different, not just in that uniqueness found in any battle but in a way that nagged at him. He decided it was partly the landscaped setting, a place better suited to garden parties, now torn by an ancient pattern of violence.

Small animals and birds were returning, nervously furtive after the upset of all that noisy human intrusion. Little furry creatures with long tails sniffed at casualties and scampered up neighboring trees for no apparent reason. Colorful birds peered from screening foliage or flitted across the scene—lines of blurred pigmentation that became camouflage when they ducked abruptly under leaves. Feathered accents to the scene, trying to restore that non-tranquility human observers mistook for peace in such settings. Teg knew better. In his pre-ghola life, he had grown up surrounded by wilderness: farm life close by but wild animals just beyond cultivation. It was not tranquil out there.

With that observation he recognized what had tugged at his awareness. Considering the fact they had stormed a well-manned defensive emplacement occupied by heavily armed defenders, the number of casualties down there was extremely small. He had seen nothing to explain this since entering the Citadel. Were they caught off-balance? Their losses in space were one thing—his ability to *see* defender ships produced a devastating advantage. But this complex held prepared positions where defenders could have fallen back and made the assault more costly. Collapse of Honored Matre resistance had been abrupt and now it remained unexplained.

I was wrong to assume they responded to display of their disasters.

He glanced at Odrade. "That Great Honored Matre in there, did she give the command for defense to stop?"

"That's my assumption."

Cautious and a typical Bene Gesserit answer. She, too, was subjecting the scene to careful observation.

Was her assumption a reasonable explanation for the abruptness with which defenders threw down their arms?

Why would they do it? To prevent more bloodshed?

Given the callousness Honored Matres usually demonstrated, that was unlikely. The decision had been made for reasons that plagued him.

A trap?

Now that he thought about it, there were other strange things about the battle scene. None of the usual calls from wounded, no scurrying about with cries for stretchers and medics. He could see Suks moving among the bodies. That, at least, was familiar, but every figure they examined was left where it had fallen.

All dead? No wounded?

He experienced gripping fear. Not an unusual fear in battle but he had learned to read it. Something profoundly wrong. Noises, things within his view, the smells took on a new intensity. He felt himself acutely attuned, a predatory animal in the jungle, knowing his terrain but aware of something intrusive that must be identified lest he become hunted instead of hunter. He registered his surroundings at a different level of consciousness, reading himself as well, searching out arousal patterns that had achieved this response. Streggi trembled beneath him. So she felt his distress.

"Something's very wrong here," Odrade said.

He pushed a hand at her, demanding silence. Even in this tower surrounded by victorious troops, he felt exposed to a threat his clamoring senses failed to reveal.

Danger!

He was sure of it. The unknown frustrated him. It required every bit of his training to keep from falling into a nervous fugue.

Nudging Streggi to turn, Teg barked an order to an aide standing in the balcony doorway. The aide listened quietly and ran to obey. They must get casualty figures. How many wounded compared to deaths? Reports on captured weapons. Urgent!

When he returned to his examination of the scene, he saw another disturbing thing, a basic oddity his eyes had tried to report. Very little blood on those fallen figures in Bene Gesserit uniforms. You expected battle casualties to show that ultimate evidence of common humanity—flowing red that darkened on exposure but always left its indelible mark in the memories of those who saw it. Lack of bloody carnage was an unknown and, in warfare, unknown had a history of bringing extreme peril.

He spoke softly to Odrade. "They have a weapon we have not discovered."

Do not be quick to reveal judgment. Hidden judgment often
is more potent. It can guide reactions whose effects are felt
only when too late to divert them.

—BENE GESSERIT ADVICE TO POSTULANTS

Sheeana smelled worms at a distance: cinnamon undertones of melange mingled with bitter flint and brimstone, the crystal-banked inferno of the great Rakian sand-eaters. But she sensed these tiny
descendants only because they existed out there in such numbers.

They are so small.

It had been hot here at Desert Watch today and now in late afternoon she welcomed the artifically cooled interior. There was a tolerable
temperature adjustment in her old quarters although the window on
the west had been left open. Sheeana went to that window and stared
out at glaring sand.

Memory told her what this vantage would be tonight: starlight
bright in dry air, thin illumination on sand waves that reached to a
darkly curved horizon. She remembered Rakian moons and missed
them. Stars alone did not satisfy her Fremen heritage.

She had thought of this as retreat, a place and time to think about
what was happening to her Sisterhood.

Axlotl tanks, Cyborgs, and now this.

Odrade's plan held no mysteries since their Sharing. A gamble?
And if it succeeded?

We will know perhaps tomorrow and then what will we become?

She admitted to a magnet in Desert Watch, more than a place to consider consequences. She had walked in sun-scorched heat today, proving to herself she could still call worms with her dance, emotion expressed as action.

Dance of Propitiation. My language of the worms.

She had gone dervish-whirling on a dune until hunger shattered her memory-trance. And little worms were spread all around in gaping watchfulness, remembered flames within the frames of crystal teeth.

But why so small?

The words of investigators explained but did not satisfy. *"It is the dampness."*

Sheeana recalled giant Shai-hulud of Dune, "the Old Man of the Desert," large enough to swallow spice factories, ring surfaces hard as plastrete. Masters in their own domain. God and devil in the sands. She sensed the potential from her window vantage.

Why did the Tyrant choose symbiotic existence in a worm?

Did those tiny worms carry his endless dream?

Sandtrout inhabited this desert. Accept them as a new skin and she might follow the Tyrant's path.

Metamorphosis. The Divided God.

She knew the lure.

Do I dare?

Memories of her last moments of ignorance came over her—barely eight then, the month of Igat on Dune.

Not Rakis. Dune, as my ancestors named it.

Not difficult to recall herself as she had been: a slender, dark-skinned child, streaked brown hair. Melange hunter (because that was a task for children) running into open desert with childhood companions. How dear it felt in memory.

But memory had its darker side. Focusing attention into the nostrils, a girl detected intense odors—a pre-spice mass!

The Blow!

Melange explosion brought Shaitan. No sandworm could resist a spice blow in its territory.

You ate it all, Tyrant, that miserable collection of shacks and hovels we called "home" and all of my friends and family. Why did you spare me?

What a rage had shaken that slender child. Everything she loved taken by a giant worm that refused her attempts to sacrifice herself in its flames and carried her into the hands of Rakian priests, thence to the Bene Gesserit.

"She talks to the worms and they spare her."

"They who spared me are not spared by me." That was what she had told Odrade.

And now Odrade knows what I must do. You cannot suppress the wild thing, Dar. I dare call you Dar now that you are within me.

No response.

Was there a pearl of Leto II's awareness in each of the new sand-worms? Her Fremen ancestors insisted on it.

Someone handed her a sandwich. Walli, the senior acolyte assistant who had assumed command of Desert Watch.

At my insistence when Odrade elevated me to the Council. But not just because Walli learned my immunity to Honored Matre sexual bonding. And not because she is sensitive to my needs. We speak a secret language, Walli and I.

Walli's large eyes no longer were entrances to her soul. They were filmed barriers giving evidence she already knew how to block probing stares; a light blue pigmentation that soon would be all blue if she survived the Agony. Almost albino and a questionable genetic line for breeding. Walli's skin reinforced this judgment: pale and freckled. A skin you saw as a surface transparency. You did not focus on the skin itself but on what lay beneath: pink, blood-suffused flesh unprotected from a desert sun. Only here in the shade could Walli expose that sensitive surface to questioning eyes.

Why this one in command over us?

Because I trust her best to do what must be done.

Sheeana ate the sandwich absently while she returned her attention to the sandscape. The whole planet thus one day. Another Dune?

No . . . similar but different. How many such places are we creating in an infinite universe? Senseless question.

Desert vagary placed a small black dot in the distance. Sheeana squinted. Ornithopter. It grew slowly larger and then smaller. Quartering the sand. Inspecting.

What are we really creating here?

When she looked at encroaching dunes, she sensed hubris.

Look upon my works, tiny human, and despair.

But we did this, my Sisters and I.

Did you?

"I can feel a new dryness in the heat," Walli said.

Sheeana agreed. No need to speak. She went to the large worktable while she still had daylight to study the topomap spread out there: little flags sticking in it, green thread on pushpins just as she had designed it.

Odrade had asked once: "Is this really preferable to a projection?"

"I need to touch it."

Odrade accepted that.

Projections palled. Too far removed from dirt. You could not draw a finger down a projection and say, "We will go down here." A finger in a projection was a finger in empty air.

Eyes are never enough. The body must feel its world.

Sheeana detected pungency of male perspiration, a musty smell of exertion. She lifted her head and saw a dark young man standing in the doorway, arrogant pose, arrogant look.

"Oh," he said. "I thought you would be alone, Walli. I'll come back later."

One piercing stare at Sheeana and he was gone.

There are many things the body must feel to know them.

"Sheeana, why are you here?" Walli asked.

You who are so busy on the Council, what do you seek? Don't you trust me?

"I came to consider what the Missionaria still thinks I may do.

They see a weapon—the myths of Dune. Billions pray to me: 'The Holy One who spoke to the Divided God.'"

"Billions is not an adequate number," Walli said.

"But it measures the force my Sisters see in me. Those worshipers believe I died with Dune. I've become 'a powerful spirit in the pantheon of the oppressed.'"

"More than a missionary?"

"What might happen, Walli, if I appeared in that waiting universe, a sandworm beside me? The potential of such a thing fills some of my Sisters with hope and misgivings."

"Misgivings I understand."

Indeed. The very kind of religious implant Muad'Dib and his Tyrant son set loose on unsuspecting humankind.

"Why do they even consider it?" Walli insisted.

"With me as fulcrum, what a lever they would have to move the universe!"

"But how could they control such a force?"

"That is the problem. Something so inherently unstable. Religions are never really controllable. But some Sisters think they could *aim* a religion built around me."

"And if their aim is poor?"

"They say the religions of women always flow deeper."

"True?" Questioning a superior source.

Sheeana could only nod. Other Memory confirmed it.

"Why?"

"Because within us, life renews itself."

"That's all of it?" Openly doubting.

"Women often bear the aura of underdog. Humans reserve a special sympathy for ones at the bottom. I am a woman and if Honored Matres want me dead then I must be blessed."

"You sound as though you agree with the Missionaria."

"When you're one of the hunted, you consider any path of escape. I am revered. I cannot ignore the potential."

Nor the danger. So my name has become a shining light in the darkness of Honored Matre oppression. How easy for that light to become a consuming flame!

No . . . the plan she and Duncan had worked out was better. Escape from Chapterhouse. It was a deathtrap not only for its inhabitants but for Bene Gesserit dreams.

"I still don't understand why you're here. We may no longer be hunted."

"May?"

"But why just now?"

I cannot speak it openly because then the watchdogs would know.

"I have this fascination with worms. It's partly because one of my ancestors led the original migration to Dune."

You remember this, Walli. We spoke of it once out there on the sand with only the two of us to hear. And now you know why I have come visiting.

"I remember you saying she was a proper Fremen."

"And a Zensunni Master."

I will lead my own migration, Walli. But I will need worms only you can provide. And it must be done quickly. The reports from Junction urge speed. And the first ships will return soon. Tonight . . . tomorrow. I fear what they bring.

"Are you still interested in taking a few worms back to Central where you can study them closely?"

Oh, yes, Walli! You do remember.

"It might be interesting. I don't have much time for such things but any knowledge we gain may help us."

"It will be too wet for them back there."

"The great Hold of the no-ship on the Flat could be reconverted into a desert lab. Sand, controlled atmosphere. The essentials are there from when we brought the first worm."

Sheeana glanced at the western window. "Sunset. I would like to go down again and walk on the sand."

Will the first ships return tonight?

"Of course, Reverend Mother." Walli stood aside, opening the way to the door.

Sheeana spoke as she was leaving. "Desert Watch will have to be moved before long."

"We are prepared."

The sun was dipping below the horizon when Sheeana emerged from the arched street at the edge of the community. She strode into starlit desert, exploring with her senses as she had done as a child. Ahhh, there was the cinnamon essence. Worms near.

She paused and, turning northeast away from the last sunglow, placed her palms flat above and below her eyes in the old Fremen way, confining view and light. She stared out of a horizontal frame. Whatever fell from heaven must pass this narrow slit.

Tonight? They will come just after dark to delay the moment of explanation. A full night for reflection.

She waited with Bene Gesserit patience.

An arc of fire drew a thin line above the northern horizon. Another. Another. They were positioned right for the Landing Flat.

Sheeana felt her heart beating fast.

They have come!

And what would be their message for the Sisterhood? *Returning warriors triumphant or refugees?* There could be little difference, given the evolution of Odrade's plan.

She would know by morning.

Sheeana lowered her hands and found she was trembling. Deep breath. The Litany.

Presently, she walked the desert, sandwalking in the remembered stride of Dune. She had almost forgotten how the feet dragged. As though they carried extra weight. Seldom-used muscles were called into play but the random walk, once learned, was never forgotten.

Once, I never dreamed I would ever again walk this way.

If watchdogs detected that thought they might wonder about their Sheeana.

It was a failure in herself, she thought. She had grown into the rhythms of Chapterhouse. This planet talked to her at a subterranean level. She felt earth, trees, and flowers, every growing thing as though all were part of her. And now, here was disturbing movement, something in a language from a different planet. She sensed the desert changing and that, too, was an alien tongue. Desert. Not lifeless but living in a way profoundly different from once-verdant Chapterhouse.

Less life but more intense.

She heard the desert: small slitherings, creaking chirps of insects, a dark rustle of hunting wings overhead and the quickest of *ploppings* on the sand—kangaroo mice brought here in anticipation of this day when worms would once more begin their rule.

Walli will remember to send flora and fauna from Dune.

She stopped atop a tall barracan. In front of her, darkness blurring its edges, was an ocean caught in stop motion, a shadow surf beating on a shadow beach of this changing land. It was a limitless desert-sea. It had originated far away and it would go to stranger places than this.

I will take you there if I am able.

A night breeze from drylands to moister places behind her deposited a film of dust on her cheeks and nose, lifting the edges of her hair as it passed. She felt saddened.

What might have been.

That no longer was important.

The things that are—they matter.

She took a deep breath. Cinnamon stronger. Melange. Spice and worms near. Worms aware of her presence. How soon would this air be dry enough for the sandworms to grow great and work their crop as they had on Dune?

The planet and the desert.

She saw them as two halves of the same saga. Just as the Bene Gesserit and the humankind they served. Matched halves. Either without the other was diminished, an emptiness with lost purpose. Not better dead, perhaps, but moving aimlessly. There lay the threat of Honored Matre victory. Aimed by blind violence!

Blind in a hostile universe.

And *there* was why the Tyrant had preserved the Sisterhood.

He knew he only gave us the path without direction. A paper chase laid down by a jokester and left empty at the end.

A poet in his own right, though.

She recalled his "Memory Poem" from Dar-es-Balat, a bit of jetsam the Bene Gesserit preserved.

And for what reason do we preserve it? So I can fill my mind with it now? Forgetting for the moment what I may confront tomorrow?

> *The fair night of the poet,*
> *Fill it with innocent stars.*
> *A pace apart Orion stands.*
> *His glare sees everything,*
> *Marking our genes forever.*
> *Welcome darkness and stare,*
> *Blinded in the afterglow.*
> *There's barren eternity!*

Sheeana felt abruptly that she had won a chance to become the ultimate artist, filled to overflowing and presented with a blank surface where she might create as she wished.

An unrestricted universe!

Odrade's words from those first childhood exposures to Bene Gesserit purpose came back to her. "Why did we fasten onto you, Sheeana? It's really simple. We recognized in you a thing we had long awaited. You arrived and we saw it happen."

"It?" *How naive I was!*

"Something new lifting over the horizon."

My migration will seek the new. But . . . I must find a planet with moons.

Looked at one way, the universe is Brownian movement, nothing predictable at the elemental level. Muad'Dib and his Tyrant son closed the cloud chamber where movement occurred.

—STORIES FROM GAMMU

Murbella entered a time of incongruent experiences. It bothered her at first, seeing her own life with multiple vision. Chaotic events at Junction had ignited this, creating a jumble of immediate necessities that would not leave her, not even when she returned to Chapterhouse.

I warned you, Dar. You can't deny it. I said they could turn victory into defeat. And look at the mess you dumped in my lap! I was lucky to save as many as I did.

This inner protest always immersed her in the events that had elevated her to this awful prominence.

What else could I have done?

Memory displayed Streggi slumping to the floor in bloodless death. The scene had played on the no-ship's relays like a fictional drama. The projection framework in the ship's command bay added to the illusion that this was not really happening. The actors would arise and take their bows. Teg's comeyes, humming away automatically, missed none of it until someone silenced them.

She was left with images, an eerie afterglow: Teg sprawled on the floor of that Honored Matre aerie. Odrade staring in shock.

Loud protests greeted Murbella's declaration that she must rush groundside. The Proctors were adamant until she laid out the details of Odrade's gamble and demanded: "Do you want total disaster?"

Odrade Within won that argument. But you were prepared for it from the first, weren't you, Dar? Your plan!

The Proctors said: "There's still Sheeana." They gave Murbella a one-man lighter and sent her to Junction alone.

Even though she transmitted her Honored Matre identity ahead of her, there were touchy moments at the Landing Flat.

A squad of armed Honored Matres confronted her as she emerged from the lighter beside a smoking pit. The smoke smelled of exotic explosives.

Where Mother Superior's lighter was destroyed.

An ancient Honored Matre led the squad, her red robe stained, some of its decorations gone and a rip down the left shoulder. She was like some dried-up lizard, still poisonous, still with a bite but running on well-used angers, most of her energy gone. Disarrayed hair like the outer skin of a fresh-dug ginger root. There was a demon in her. Murbella saw it peering from orange-flecked eyes.

For all the fact that a full squad backed up the old one, the two of them faced each other as though isolated at the foot of the lighter's drop, wild animals cautiously sniffing, trying to judge the extent of danger.

Murbella watched the old one carefully. This lizard would dart her tongue a bit, testing the air, giving vent to her emotions, but she was sufficiently shocked to listen.

"Murbella is my name. I was taken captive by the Bene Gesserit on Gammu. I am an adept of the Hormu."

"Why are you wearing a witch's robes?" The old one and her squad stood ready to kill.

"I have learned everything they had to teach and have brought that treasure to my Sisters."

The old one studied her a moment. "Yes, I recognize your type. You're a Roc, one we chose for the Gammu project."

The squad behind her relaxed slightly.

"You did not come all the way in that lighter," the old one accused.

"I escaped from one of their no-ships."

"Do you know where their nest is?"

"I do."

A wide smile spread on the old one's lips. "Well! You are a prize! How did you escape?"

"Do you have to ask?"

The old one considered this. Murbella could read the thoughts on her face as though they were spoken: *These ones we brought from Roc—deadly, all of them. They can kill with hands, feet, or any other movable part of their bodies. They all should carry a sign: "Dangerous in any position."*

Murbella moved away from the lighter, displaying the sinewy grace that was a mark of her identity.

Speed and muscle, Sisters. Beware.

Some of the squad pressed forward, curious. Their words were full of Honored Matre comparisons, eager questions Murbella was forced to parry.

"Did you kill many of them? Where is their planet? Is it rich? Have you bonded many males there? You were trained on Gammu?"

"I was on Gammu for the third stage. Under Hakka."

"Hakka! I've met her. Did she have that injured left foot when you knew her?"

Still testing.

"It was the right foot and I was with her when she took the injury!"

"Oh, yes, the right foot. I remember now. How was she injured?"

"Kicking a lout in the rear. He had a sharp knife in his hip pocket. Hakka was so angry she killed him."

Laughter swept through the squad.

"We will go to Great Honored Matre," the old one said.

So I've passed first inspection.

Murbella sensed reservations, though.

Why is this Hormu adept wearing those enemy robes? And she has a strange look to her.

Best face that one at once.

"I took their training and they accepted me."

"The fools! Did they really?"

"You question my word?" How easy it was to revert, adopting touchy Honored Matre ways.

The old one bristled. She did not lose hauteur but she sent a warning look to her squad. All of them took a moment to digest what Murbella had said.

"You became one of them?" someone behind her asked.

"How else could I steal their knowledge? Know this! I was the personal student of their Mother Superior."

"Did she teach you well?" That same challenging voice from behind.

Murbella identified the questioner: middle echelon and ambitious. Anxious for notice and advancement.

This is the end of you, anxious one. And little loss to the universe.

A Bene Gesserit feint drifted the feather that was her foe into range. One Hormu-style kick for them to recognize. The questioner lay dead on the ground.

Marriage of Bene Gesserit and Honored Matre abilities creates a danger you should all recognize and envy.

"She taught me admirably," Murbella said. "Any other questions?"

"Ehhhhh!" the old one said.

"How are you called?" Murbella demanded.

"I am a Senior Dame, Honored Matre of the Hormu. I am called Elpek."

"Thank you, Elpek. You may call me Murbella."

"I am honored, Murbella. It is indeed a treasure you have brought us."

Murbella studied her a moment with Bene Gesserit watchfulness before smiling without humor.

The exchange of names! You in your red robe that marks you as one of the powerful surrounding Great Honored Matre, do you know what you have just accepted into your circle?

The squad remained shocked and looked at Murbella with wariness. She saw this with her new sensitivity. The Old Girl network had never gained a foothold in the Bene Gesserit but it performed for Honored Matres. Simulflow amused her with a parade of confirmation. How subtle the power transfers: right school, right friends, graduation and transfer onto the first rungs of the ladder—all guided by relatives and their connections, mutual back-scratching that managed alliances, including marriages. Simulflow told her it led into the pit but ones on the ladder, the ones in controlling niches, never let that worry them.

Today is sufficient unto today, and that is how Elpek sees me. But she does not see what I have become, only that I am dangerous but potentially useful.

Turning slowly on one foot, Murbella studied Elpek's squad. No bonded males here. This was too sensitive a duty for any but trusted women. Good.

"Now, you will listen to me, all of you. If you have any loyalty to our Sisterhood, which I will judge on future performance, you will honor what I have brought. I intend it as a gift for those who deserve it."

"Great Honored Matre will be pleased," Elpek said.

But Great Honored Matre did not appear pleased when Murbella was presented.

Murbella recognized the tower setting. Almost sunset now but Streggi's body still lay where it had fallen. Some of Teg's specialists had been killed, mostly the comeye crew who doubled as his guard.

No, we Honored Matres do not like others spying on us.

Teg still lived, she saw, but he was swathed in shigawire and shoved disdainfully into a corner. Most surprising of all: Odrade stood unfettered near Great Honored Matre. It was a gesture of contempt.

Murbella felt she had lived through such a scene many times—aftermath of Honored Matre Victory: swaths of their enemies' bodies left where they had been brought down. Honored Matre attack with the bloodless weapon had been swift and deadly, a typical viciousness that killed when killing no longer was required. She suppressed a shudder at the memory of this deadly reversal. There had been no warning, only the troops dropping in wide lines—a domino effect that left the survivors in shock. And Great Honored Matre obviously enjoyed the shock.

Looking at Murbella, Great Honored Matre said, "So this is the bag of insolence you say you trained in your ways."

Odrade almost smiled at the description.

Bag of insolence?

A Bene Gesserit would accept it without rancor. This rheumy-eyed Great Honored Matre faced a quandary and could not call on her weapon that killed without blood. Very delicate balance of power. Agitated conversations among Honored Matres had revealed their problem.

All of their secret weapons had been exhausted and could not be reloaded, something they had lost when driven back here.

"Our weapon of last resort and we wasted it!"

Logno, who thought herself supreme, stood in a different arena now. And she had just learned of the fearful ease with which Murbella could kill one of the elect.

Murbella cast a measuring gaze over Great Honored Matre's entourage, gauging their potentials. They recognized this situation, of course. Familiar. How did they vote?

Neutral?

Some were wary and all were waiting.

Anticipating a diversion. No concern over who triumphed as long as power continued to flow in their direction.

Murbella let her muscles flow into the waiting stance of combat she had learned from Duncan and the Proctors. She felt as cool as though standing on the practice floor, running through responses. Even as she reacted, she knew she moved in ways for which Odrade had prepared her—mentally, physically, and emotionally.

Voice first. Give them a taste of inner chill.

"I see you have assessed the Bene Gesserit quite poorly. The arguments of which you are so proud, these women have heard them so many times your words go beyond boredom."

This was delivered with scathing vocal control, a tone that brought orange to Logno's eyes but held her motionless.

Murbella was not through with her. "You consider yourself powerful and clever. One begets the other, eh? What idiocy! You're a consummate liar and you lie to yourself."

As Logno remained motionless in the face of this attack, those around her began moving away, opening space that said, *She is all yours.*

"Your fluency in these lies does not hide them," Murbella said. She swept a scornful gaze across the ones behind Logno. "Like the ones I know in Other Memory, you are headed for extinction. The problem is that you take so infernally long dying. Inevitable but oh, the boredom meanwhile. You dare call yourself Great Honored Matre!" Returning her attention to Logno. "Everything about you is a cesspool. You have no style."

It was too much. Logno attacked, left foot slashing outward with blinding speed. Murbella grasped the foot as she would catch a windblown leaf and, continuing the flow of it, levered Logno into a threshing club that ended with her head pulped on the floor. Without pausing, Murbella pirouetted, left foot almost decapitating the Honored Matre who had stood at Logno's right, the right hand crushing the throat of the one who had stood at Logno's left. It was over in two heartbeats.

Examining the scene without breathing hard (*to show how easy it was, Sisters*), Murbella experienced a sense of shock and recognition of the inevitable. Odrade lay on the floor in front of Elpek, who obviously had chosen sides without hesitation. The twisted position of Odrade's neck and flaccid appearance of her body said she was dead.

"She tried to interfere," Elpek said.

Having killed a Reverend Mother, Elpek expected Murbella (a Sister, after all!) to applaud. But Murbella did not react as expected. She knelt beside Odrade and put her head against that of the corpse, staying there an interminable time.

The surviving Honored Matres exchanged questioning looks but dared not move.

What is this?

But they were immobilized by Murbella's terrifying abilities.

When she had Odrade's recent past, all of the new added to previous Sharing, Murbella stood.

Elpek saw death in Murbella's eyes and took one backward step before trying to defend herself. Elpek was dangerous but no match for this demon in the black robe. It was over with the same shocking abruptness that had taken Logno and her aides: a kick to the larynx. Elpek sprawled across Odrade.

Once more, Murbella studied the survivors, then stood a moment looking down at Odrade's body.

In a way, that was my doing, Dar. And yours!

She shook her head from side to side, absorbing consequences.

Odrade is dead. Long live Mother Superior! Long live Great Honored Matre! And may the heavens protect us all.

She gave her attention then to what must be done. These deaths had created an enormous debt. Murbella took a deep breath. This was another Gordian knot.

"Release Teg," she said. "Clean up in here as quickly as possible. And somebody get me a proper robe!"

It was Great Honored Matre giving orders but those who leaped to obey sensed the Other in her.

The one who brought her a red robe elaborate with soostone dragons held it deferentially from a distance. Large woman with heavy bones and square face. Cruel eyes.

"Hold it for me," Murbella said and when the woman tried to take advantage of proximity to attack her, Murbella dumped the woman hard. "Try again?"

This time there were no tricks.

"You are the first member of my Council," Murbella said. "Name?"

"Angelika, Great Honored Matre." *See! I was first to call you by your proper title. Reward me.*

"Your reward is that I promote you and let you live."

Proper Honored Matre response. Accepted as such.

When Teg came to her rubbing his arms where the shigawire had bitten deep, some Honored Matres tried to caution Murbella. "Do you know what this one can—"

"He serves me now," Murbella interrupted. Then in Odrade's mocking tones: "Isn't that right, Miles?"

He gave her a rueful smile, an old man on a child's face. "Interesting times, Murbella."

"Dar liked apples," Murbella said. "See to that."

He nodded. Return her to a cemetery orchard. Not that prized Bene Gesserit orchards would endure long in a desert. Still, some traditions were worth perpetuating while you could.

What do Holy Accidents teach? Be resilient. Be strong. Be
ready for change, for the new. Gather many experiences and
judge them by the steadfast nature of our faith.

—TLEILAXU DOCTRINE

Well within Teg's original timetable, Murbella picked her Honored
Matre entourage and returned to Chapterhouse. She expected certain
problems and the messages she sent ahead paved the way for solutions.

"*I bring Futars to attract Handlers. Honored Matres fear a biological weapon from the Scattering that made vegetables of them. Handlers
may be the source.*"

"*Prepare to keep Rabbi and party in no-ship. Honor their secrecy.
And remove the protective mines from the ship!*" (That went in keeping
of a Proctor messenger.)

She was tempted to ask for her children but that was non–Bene
Gesserit. Someday . . . maybe.

Immediately on returning, she had Duncan to accommodate and
this confused Honored Matres. They were as bad as the Bene Gesserit.
"What's so special about one man?"

No longer a reason for him to remain in the ship but he refused to
leave. "I've a mental mosaic to assemble: a piece that cannot be moved,
extraordinary behavior, and willing participation in their dream. I
must find limits to test. That's missing. I know how to find it. Get in
tune. Don't think; do it."

It made no sense. She humored him although he was changed. A stability to this new Duncan that she accepted as a challenge. By what right did he assume a self-satisfied air? No . . . not self-satisfied. It was more being at peace with a decision. He refused to share it!

"I've accepted things. You must do the same."

She had to admit this described what she was doing.

On her first morning back, she arose at dawn and entered the workroom. Wearing the red robe, she sat in Mother Superior's chair and summonded Bellonda.

Bell stood at one end of the worktable. She knew. The design became clear in execution. Odrade had imposed a debt on her as well. Thus, the silence: assessing how she must pay.

Service to this Mother Superior, Bell! That is how you pay. No Archival declension of these events will put them into proper perspective. Action is required.

Bellonda spoke finally. "The only crisis I'd care to compare with this one is the advent of the Tyrant."

Murbella reacted sharply. "Hold your tongue, Bell, unless you've something useful to say!"

Bellonda took the reprimand calmly (uncharacteristic response). "Dar had changes in mind. This what she expected?"

Murbella softened her tone. "We'll rehash ancient history later. This is an opening chapter."

"Bad news." That was the old Bellonda.

Murbella said: "Admit the first group. Be cautious. They are Great Honored Matre's High Council."

Bell left to obey.

She knows I have every right to this position. They all know it. No need for a vote. No room for a vote!

Now was the time for the historical art of politics she had learned from Odrade.

"In all things you must appear important. No minor decisions pass through your hands unless they are quiet acts called 'favors' done for people whose loyalty can be earned."

Every reward came from on high. Not a good policy with the Bene

Gesserit but this group entering the workroom, they were familiar with a Patroness Great Honored Matre; they would accept "new political necessities." Temporarily. It was always temporary, especially with Honored Matres.

Bell and watchdogs knew she would be a long time sorting this out. *Even with amplified Bene Gesserit abilities.*

It would require extremely demanding attention from all of them. And the first thing was the sharply discerning gaze of innocence.

That is what Honored Matres lost, and we must restore it before they can fade into the background where "we" belong.

Bellonda ushered in the Council and retired silently.

Murbella waited until they were seated. A mixed lot: some aspirants to supreme power. Angelika there smiling so prettily. Some waiting (not even daring to hope yet) but gathering what they could.

"Our Sisterhood was acting with stupidity," Murbella accused. She noted the ones who took this angrily. "You would have killed the goose!"

They did not understand. She dredged up the parable. They listened with proper attention, even when she added: "Don't you realize how desperately we need every one of these witches? We outnumber them so greatly that each of them will carry an enormous teaching burden!"

They considered this and, bitter though it was, they were forced to a qualified acceptance because she said it.

Murbella hammered it home. "Not only am I your Great Honored Matre . . . Does anyone question that?"

No one questioned.

". . . but I am Bene Gesserit Mother Superior. They can do little else but confirm me in office."

Two of them started to protest but Murbella cut them short. "No! You would be powerless to enforce your will on them. You would have to kill them all. But they will obey me."

The two continued to babble and she shouted them down: "Compared to me with what I acquired from them, the lot of you are miserable weaklings! Do any of you challenge that?"

No one challenged but orange flecks were there.

"You are children with no knowledge of what you might become," she said. "Would you return defenseless to face the ones of many faces? Would you become vegetables?"

That caught their interest. They were accustomed to this tone from older commanders. The content held them now. It was difficult to accept from one so young . . . still . . . the things she had done. And to Logno and her aides!

Murbella saw them admire the bait.

Fertilization. This group will carry it away with them. Hybrid vigor. We are fertilized to grow stronger. And flower. And go to seed? Best not dwell on that. Honored Matres will not see it until they are almost Reverend Mothers. Then they will look back angrily as I did. How could we have been that stupid?

She saw submission take shape in councillors' eyes. There would be a honeymoon. Honored Matres would be children in a candy store. Only gradually would the inevitable grow plain to them. Then they would be trapped.

As I was trapped. Don't ask the oracle what you can gain. That's the trap. Beware the real fortune teller! Would you like thirty-five hundred years of boredom?

Odrade Within objected.

Give the Tyrant some credit. It couldn't all have been boredom. More like a Guild Navigator picking his passage through foldspace. Golden Path. An Atreides paid for your survival, Murbella.

Murbella felt burdened. The Tyrant's payment dumped on her shoulders. *I didn't ask him to do it for me.*

Odrade could not let that pass. *He did it nonetheless.*

Sorry, Dar. He paid. Now, I must pay.

So you are a Reverend Mother at last!

The councillors had grown restive under her stare.

Angelika elected to speak for them. *After all, I am first chosen.*

Watch that one! A blaze of ambition in her eyes.

"What response are you asking us to take with these witches?"

Alarmed by her own boldness. Was not Great Honored Matre also a witch now?

Murbella spoke softly. "You will tolerate them and offer them no violence whatsoever."

Angelika was emboldened by Murbella's mild tone. "Is that Great Honored Matre's decision or the—"

"Enough! I could bloody the floor of this room with the lot of you! Do you wish to test it?"

They did not wish to test it.

"And what if I say to you that it is Mother Superior speaking? You will ask do I have a policy to meet our problem? I will say: Policy? Ahh, yes. I have a policy for unimportant things such as insect infestations. Unimportant things call for policies. For such of you as do not see the wisdom in my decision, I need no policy. Your kind I dispose of quickly. Dead before you know you've been injured! That is my response to the presence of filth. Is there any filth in this room?"

It was language they recognized: the lash of the Great Honored Matre backed by ability to kill.

"You are my Council," Murbella said. "I expect wisdom from you. The least you can do is pretend you are wise."

Humorous sympathy from Odrade: *If that's the way Honored Matres give and take orders, it won't require much deep analysis by Bell.*

Murbella's thoughts went elsewhere. *I am no longer Honored Matre.*

The step from one to another was so recent she found her Honored Matre performance uncomfortable. Her adjustments were a metaphor of what would happen to her former Sisters. A new role and she did not wear it well. Other Memory simulated long association with herself as this new person. This was no mystical transubstantiation, merely new abilities.

Merely?

The change was profound. Did Duncan realize this? It pained her that he might never see through to this new person.

Is that the residue of my love for him?

Murbella drew back from her questions, not wanting an answer.

She felt repelled by something that went deeper than she cared to burrow.

There will be decisions I must make that love would prevent. Decisions for the Sisterhood and not for myself. That is where my fear is pointing.

Immediate necessities restored her. She sent her councillors away, promising pain and death if they failed to learn this new restraint.

Next, Reverend Mothers must be taught a new diplomacy: getting along with no one—not even with each other. It would grow easier in time. Honored Matres slipping into Bene Gesserit ways. One day, there would be no Honored Matres; only Reverend Mothers with improved reflexes and augmented knowledge of sexuality.

Murbella felt haunted by words she had heard but not accepted until this moment. "The things we will do for Bene Gesserit survival have no limits."

Duncan will see this. I cannot keep it from him. The Mentat will not hold to a fixed idea of what I was before the Agony. He opens his mind as I open a door. He will examine his net. "What have I caught this time?"

Was this what happened to Lady Jessica? Other Memory carried Jessica threaded into the warp and woof of Sharings. Murbella unraveled a bit and paraded elder knowledge.

Heretic Lady Jessica? Malfeasance in office?

Jessica had plunged into love as Odrade had plunged into the sea and the resultant waves had all but engulfed the Sisterhood.

Murbella sensed this taking her where she did not want to go. Pain clutched her chest.

Duncan! Ohhhh, Duncan! She dropped her face into her hands. *Dar, help me. What am I to do?*

Never ask why you're a Reverend Mother.

I must! The progression is clear in my memory and . . .

That's a sequence. Thinking of it as cause and effect beguiles you away from totality.

Tao?

Simpler: You are here.

But Other Memory goes back and back and . . .

Imagine it's pyramids—interlocked.

Those are just words!

Is your body still functioning?

I hurt, Dar. You don't have a body anymore and it's useless to . . .

We occupy different niches. The pains I felt are not your pains. My joys are not yours.

I don't want your sympathy! Ohh, Dar! Why was I born?

Were you born to lose Duncan?

Dar, please!

So you were born and now you know that's never enough. So you became an Honored Matre. What else could you do? Still not enough? Now you're a Reverend Mother. You think that's enough? It's never enough as long as you're alive.

You're telling me I must always reach beyond myself.

Pah! You don't make decisions on that basis. Didn't you hear him? Don't think; do it! Will you choose the easy way? Why should you feel sad because you've encountered the inevitable? If that's all you can see, confine yourself to improving the breed!

Damn you! Why did you do this to me?

Do what?

Make me see myself and my former Sisters this way!

What way?

Damn you! You know what I mean!

Former Sisters, you say?

Oh, you are insidious.

All Reverend Mothers are insidious.

You never stop teaching!

Is that what I do?

How innocent I was! Asking you what you really do.

You know as well as I do. We wait for humankind to mature. The Tyrant only provided them time to grow but now they need care.

What's the Tyrant have to do with my pain?

You foolish woman! Did you fail the Agony?

You know I didn't!

Stop stumbling over the obvious.

Oh, you bitch!

I prefer witch. Either is preferable to whore.

The only difference between Bene Gesserit and Honored Matre is the marketplace. You married our Sisterhood.

Our Sisterhood?

You bred for power! How is that different from . . .

Don't twist it, Murbella! Keep your eyes on survival.

Don't tell me you had no power.

Temporary authority over people intent on survival.

Survival again!

In a Sisterhood that promotes the survival of others. Like the married woman who bears children.

So it comes down to procreation.

That's a decision you make for yourself: family and what binds it. What tickles life and happiness?

Murbella began to laugh. She dropped her hands and opened her eyes to find Bellonda standing there watching.

"That's always a temptation for a new Reverend Mother," Bellonda said. "Chat a bit with Other Memory. Who was it this time? Dar?"

Murbella nodded.

"Don't trust anything they give you. It's lore and you judge it for yourself."

Odrade's words exactly. Look through the eyes of the dead at scenes long gone. What a peep show!

"You can get lost in there for hours," Bellonda said. "Exercise restraint. Be sure of your ground. One hand for yourself and one for the ship."

There it was again! The past applied to the present. How rich Other Memory made everyday life.

"It'll pass," Bellonda said. "It gets to be old hat after a time." She laid a report in front of Murbella.

Old hat! One hand for yourself and one for the ship. So much just in idioms.

Murbella leaned back in the slingchair to scan Bellonda's report, fancying herself suddenly in Odrade's idiom: *Spider Queen in the center of my web.* The web might be a bit frayed just now but it was still there catching things to be digested. Twitch a trigger strand and Bell came running, mandibles flexing in anticipation. The twitch-words were "Archives" and "Analysis."

Seeing Bellonda in this light, Murbella saw the wisdom in the ways Odrade had employed her, flaws as valuable as the strengths. When Murbella finished the report, Bellonda still stood there in characteristic attitude.

Murbella recognized that Bellonda looked on all who summoned her as ones who had not measured up, people who called on Archives for frivolous reasons and had to be set straight. Frivolity: Bellonda's bête noire. Murbella found this amusing.

Murbella kept amusement masked while enjoying Bellonda. The way to deal with her was to be scrupulous. Nothing to subtract from strengths. This report was a model of concise and pertinent argument. She made her points with few embellishments, just enough to reveal her own conclusions.

"Does it amuse you to summon me?" Bellonda asked.

She's sharper than she was! Did I summon her? Not in so many words but she knows when she's needed. She says here our Sisters must be models of meekness. Mother Superior may be anything she needs to be but not so the rest of the Sisterhood.

Murbella touched the report. "A starting point."

"Then we should start before your friends find the comeye center." Bellonda sank into her chairdog with familiar confidence. "Tam's gone but I could send for Sheeana."

"Where is she?"

"At the ship. Studying a collection of worms in the Great Hold, says any of us can be taught to control them."

"Valuable if true. Leave her. What of Scytale?"

"Still in the ship. Your friends haven't found him yet. We're keeping him under wraps."

"Let's continue that. He's a good reserve bargaining chip. And they're not my friends, Bell. How are the Rabbi and his party?"

"Comfortable but worried. They know Honored Matres are here."

"Keep them under wraps."

"It's uncanny. A different voice but I hear Dar."

"An echo in your head."

Bellonda actually laughed.

"Now here's what you must spread among the Sisters. We act with extreme delicacy while showing ourselves as people to admire and emulate. 'You Honored Matres may not choose to live as we live but you can learn our strengths.'"

"Ahhhhhh."

"It comes down to ownership. Honored Matres are owned by things. 'I want that place, that bauble, that person.' Take what you want. Use it until you tire of it."

"While we go along our path admiring what we see."

"And there's our flaw. We don't give ourselves easily. Fear of love and affection! To be self-possessed has its own greed. 'See what I have? You can't have it unless you follow my ways!' Never take that attitude with Honored Matres."

"Are you telling me we have to love them?"

"How else can we make them admire us? That was Jessica's victory. When she gave, she gave it all. So much bottled up by our ways and then that overwhelming wash: everything given. It's irresistible."

"We don't compromise that easily."

"No more do Honored Matres."

"That's the way of their bureaucratic origins!"

"Yet, theirs is a training ground for following the path of least resistance."

"You're confusing me, Da . . . Murbella."

"Have I said we should compromise? Compromise weakens us, and we know there are problems compromise cannot solve, decisions we must make no matter how bitter."

"*Pretend* to love them?"

"That's a beginning."

"It'll be a bloody union, this joining of Bene Gesserit and Honored Matre."

"I suggest we Share as widely as possible. We may lose people while Honored Matres are learning."

"A marriage made on the battlefield."

Murbella stood, thinking of Duncan in the no-ship, remembering the ship as she had seen it last. There it was finally, not hidden to any sense. A lump of strange machinery, oddly grotesque. A wild conglomeration of protrusions and juttings with no apparent purpose. Hard to imagine the thing lifting on its own power, enormous as that was, and vanishing into space.

Vanishing into space!

She saw the shape of Duncan's mental mosaic.

A piece that cannot be moved! Get in tune . . . Don't think; do it!

With an abruptness that chilled her, she knew his decision.

When you think to take determination of your fate into your own hands, that is the moment you can be crushed. Be cautious. Allow for surprises. When we create, there are always other forces at work.

—DARWI ODRADE

"Move with extreme care," Sheeana had warned him.

Idaho did not think he needed warning but appreciated it nonetheless.

Presence of Honored Matres on Chapterhouse eased his task. They made the ship's Proctors and other guards nervous. Murbella's orders kept her former Sisters out of the ship but everyone knew the enemy was here. Scanner relays showed a seemingly endless stream of lighters disgorging Honored Matres on the Flat. Most of the new arrivals appeared curious about that monstrous no-ship sitting there but no one disobeyed Great Honored Matre.

"Not while she's alive," Idaho muttered where Proctors could hear him. "They have a tradition of assassinating their leaders to replace them. How long can Murbella hold out?"

Comeyes did his work for him. He knew his muttering would spread through the ship.

Sheeana came to him in his workroom shortly afterward and made a show of disapproval. "What are you trying to do, Duncan? You're upsetting people."

"Go back to your worms!"

"Duncan!"

"Murbella's playing a dangerous game! She's all that stands between us and disaster."

He already had voiced this worry to Murbella. It was not new to the watchers but reinforcement made everyone who heard him edgy—comeye monitors in Archives, ship guards, everyone.

Except Honored Matres. Murbella was keeping them out of Bellonda's Archives.

"Time for that later," she said.

Sheeana had her cue. "Duncan, either stop feeding our worries or tell us what we should do. You're a Mentat. Function for us."

Ahhh, the Great Mentat performs for all to see.

"What you should do is obvious but it's not up to me. I can't leave Murbella."

But I can be taken away.

Now it was up to Sheeana. She left him and went to spread her own brand of change.

"We have the Scattering for our example."

By evening, she had the Reverend Mothers in the ship neutralized and gave him a hand-signal that they could take the next step.

"They will follow my lead."

Without intending it, the Missionaria had set the stage for Sheeana's ascendancy. Most Sisters knew the power latent in her. Dangerous. But it was *there*.

Unused power was like a marionette with visible strings, nobody holding them. A compelling attraction: *I could make it dance.*

Feeding the deception, he called Murbella.

"When will I see you?"

"Duncan, please." Even in projection, she looked harried. "I'm busy. You know the pressures. I'll be out in a few days."

Projection showed Honored Matres in the background scowling at this odd behavior in their leader. Any Reverend Mother could read their faces.

"Has Great Honored Matre gone soft? That's nothing but a man out there!"

When he broke off, Idaho emphasized what every monitor on the ship had seen. "She's in danger! Doesn't she know it?"

And now, Sheeana, it's up to you.

Sheeana had the key to reinstate the ship's flight controls. The mines were gone. No one could destroy the ship at the last instant with a signal to hidden explosives. There was only the human cargo to consider, Teg especially.

Teg will see my choices. The others—the Rabbi's party and Scytale—will have to take their chances with us.

The Futars in their security cells did not worry him. Interesting animals but not significant at the moment. For that matter, he gave only a passing thought to Scytale. The little Tleilaxu remained under the eyes of guards, who were not relaxing their watch on him no matter their other worries.

He went to bed with a nervousness that had ready explanation for any watchdog in Archives.

His precious Murbella is in peril.

And she was in peril but he could not protect her.

My very presence is a danger to her now.

He was up at dawn, back to the armory dismantling a weapons factory. Sheeana found him there and asked him to join her in the guard section.

A handful of Proctors greeted them. The leader they had chosen did not surprise him. Garimi. He had heard about her performance at the Convocation. Suspicious. Worried. Ready to make her own gamble. She was a sober-faced woman. Some said she seldom smiled.

"We have diverted the comeyes in this room," Garimi said. "They show us having a snack and questioning you about weapons."

Idaho felt a knot in his stomach. Bell's people would spot a simulation quickly. Especially a projected mock-up of himself.

Garimi responded to his frown. "We have allies in Archives."

Sheeana said: "We are here to ask if you wish to leave before we escape in this ship."

His surprise was genuine.

Stay behind?

He had not considered it. Murbella was no longer his. The bond had been broken in her. She did not accept it. Not yet. But she would the first time she was asked to make a decision putting him in danger for Bene Gesserit purposes. Now, she merely stayed away from him more than was necessary.

"You're going to Scatter?" he asked, looking at Garimi.

"We'll save what we can. Voting with our feet, it was called once. Murbella is subverting the Bene Gesserit."

There was the unspoken argument he had trusted to win them. Disagreement over Odrade's gamble.

Idaho took a deep breath. "I will go with you."

"No regrets!" Garimi warned.

"That's stupid!" he said, venting his repressed grief.

Garimi would not have been surprised by that response from a Sister. Idaho shocked her and she was several seconds recovering. Honesty compelled her.

"Of course it's stupid. I'm sorry. You're sure you won't stay? We owe you the chance to make your own decision."

Bene Gesserit fastidiousness with those who served them loyally!

"I'll join you."

The grief they saw on his face was not simulated. He wore it openly when he returned to his console.

My assigned position.

He did not try to hide his actions when he coded for the ship's ID circuits.

Allies in Archives.

The circuits came flashing up on his projections—colored ribbons with a broken link into flight systems. The way around that breakage was visible after only a few moments' study. Mentat observations had been prepared for it.

Multiples through the core!

Idaho sat back and waited.

Lift-off was a skull-rattling moment of blankness that stopped abruptly when they were far enough clear of the surface to engage nullfields and enter foldspace.

Idaho watched his projection. There they were: the old couple in their garden setting! He saw the net shimmering in front of them, the man gesturing at it, smiling in round-faced satisfaction. They moved in a transparent overlay that revealed ship circuits behind them. The net grew larger—not lines but ribbons thicker than the projected circuits.

The man's lips shaped words but there was no sound. *"We expected you."*

Idaho's hands went to his console, fingers splayed in the comfield to grasp required elements of the circuit control. No time for niceties. Gross disruption. He was into the core within a second. From there, it was a simple matter to dump entire segments. Navigation went first. He saw the net begin to thin, the look of surprise on the man's face. Nullfields were next. Idaho felt the ship lurching in foldspace. The net tipped, becoming elongated with the two watchers foreshortened and thinned. Idaho wiped out star-memory circuits, taking his own data with them.

Net and watchers vanished.

How did I know they would be there?

He had no answer except a certainty rooted in the repeated visions.

Sheeana did not look up when he found her at the temporary flight-control board in the guard quarters. She was bent over the board, staring at it in consternation. The projection above her showed they had emerged from foldspace. Idaho recognized none of the visible star patterns but he had expected that.

Sheeana swiveled and looked at Garimi standing over her. "We've lost all data storage!"

Idaho tapped his temple with a forefinger. "No we haven't."

"But it'll take years to recover even the essentials!" Sheeana protested. "What happened?"

"We're an unidentifiable ship in an unidentifiable universe," Idaho said. "Isn't that what we wanted?"

There's no secret to balance. You just have to feel the waves.

—DARWI ODRADE

Murbella felt that an age had passed since she recognized Duncan's decision.

Vanish into space! Leave me!

The unvarying time sense of the Agony told her only seconds had elapsed since awareness of his intentions but she felt she had known this from the first.

He must be stopped!

She was reaching for her comboard when Central began to shudder. The quaking continued for an interminable time and subsided slowly.

Bellonda was on her feet. "What . . ."

"The no-ship at the Flat has just lifted," Murbella said.

Bellonda reached for the comboard but Murbella stopped her.

"It's gone."

She must not see my pain.

"But who . . ." Bellonda fell silent. She had her own assessments of consequences and saw then what Murbella saw.

Murbella sighed. She had all of the curses of history at her disposal and wanted none of them.

"At lunchtime, I will eat in my private dining room with councillors and I want you present," Murbella said. "Tell Duana oyster stew again."

Bellonda started to protest but all that came out was: "Again?"

"You will recall I ate alone downstairs last night?" Murbella resumed her seat.

Mother Superior has duties!

There were maps to change and rivers to follow and Honored Matres to domesticate.

Some waves throw you, Murbella. But you get back up and go on with it. Seven times down, eight times up. You can balance on strange surfaces.

I know, Dar. Willing participation in your dream.

Bellonda stared at her until Murbella said, "I made my councillors sit at a distance from me at dinner last night. It was strange—only the two tables in the whole dining room."

Why do I continue this inane chatter? What excuses do I have for my extraordinary behavior?

"We wondered why none of us were permitted in our own dining room," Bellonda said.

"To save your lives! But you should have seen their interest. I read their lips. Angelika said: 'She's eating some kind of stew. I heard her discussing it with the chef. Isn't this a marvelous world we've acquired? We must sample that stew she ordered.'"

"Samples," Bellonda said. "I see." Then: "You know, don't you, Sheeana took the Van Gogh painting from . . . your sleeping chamber?"

Why does that hurt?

"I noticed it was missing."

"Said she was borrowing it for her room in the ship."

Murbella's lips went thin.

Damn them! Duncan and Sheeana! Teg, Scytale . . . all of them gone and no way to follow. But we still have axlotl tanks and Idaho cells from our children. Not the same . . . but close. He thinks he's escaped!

"Are you all right, Murbella?" Concern in Bell's voice.

You warned me about wild things, Dar, and I didn't listen.

"After we've eaten, I will take my councillors on an inspection tour of Central. Tell my acolyte I'll want cider before retiring."

Bellonda left, muttering. That was more like her.

How do you guide me now, Dar?

You want guidance? A guided tour of your life? Is that why I died?

But they took the Van Gogh, too!

Is that what you'll miss?

Why did they take it, Dar?

Caustic laughter greeted this and Murbella was glad no one else heard.

Can't you see what she intends?

The Missionaria scheme!

Oh, more than that. It's the next phase: Muad'Dib to Tyrant to Honored Matres to us to Sheeana . . . to what? Can't you see it? The thing is right here at the lip of your thoughts. Accept it as you would swallow a bitter drink.

Murbella shuddered.

See it? The bitter medicine of a Sheeana future? We once thought all medicines had to be bitter or they were not effective. No healing power in the sweet.

Must it happen, Dar?

Some will choke on that medicine. But the survivors may create interesting patterns.

Paired opposites define your longings and those longings imprison you.

—THE ZENSUNNI WHIP

"You deliberately let them get away, Daniel!"

The old woman rubbed her hands down the stained front of her garden apron. It was a summer morning around her, flowers blooming, birds calling from nearby trees. There was a misty look to the sky, a yellow radiance near the horizon.

"Now, Marty, it was not deliberate," Daniel said. He took off his porkpie hat and rubbed the bushy stubble of gray hair before replacing the hat. "He surprised me. I knew he saw us but I didn't suspect he saw the net."

"And I had such a nice planet picked out for them," Marty said. "One of the best. A real test of their abilities."

"No use moaning about it," Daniel said. "They're where we can't touch them now. He was spread so thin, though, I expected to catch him easy."

"They had a Tleilaxu Master, too," Marty said. "I saw him when they went under the net. I would have so liked to study another Master."

"Don't see why. Always whistling at us, always making it necessary to stomp them down. I don't like treating Masters that way and you know it! If it weren't for them . . ."

"They're not gods, Daniel."

"Neither are we."

"I still think you let them escape. You're so anxious to prune your roses!"

"What would you have said to the Master, anyway?" Daniel asked.

"I was going to joke when he asked who we were. They always ask that. I was going to say: 'What did you expect, God Himself with a flowing beard?'"

Daniel chuckled. "That would've been funny. They have such a hard time accepting that Face Dancers can be independent of them."

"I don't see why. It's a natural consequence. They gave us the power to absorb the memories and experiences of other people. Gather enough of those and . . ."

"It's personas we take, Marty."

"Whatever. The Masters should've known we would gather enough of them one day to make our own decisions about our own future."

"And theirs?"

"Oh, I'd have apologized to him after putting him in his place. You can do just so much managing of others, isn't that right, Daniel?"

"When you get that look on your face, Marty, I go prune my roses." He went back to a line of bushes with verdant leaves and black blooms as large as his head.

Marty called after him: "Gather up enough people and you get a big ball of knowledge, Daniel! That's what I'd have told him. And those Bene Gesserit in that ship! I'd have told them how many of them I have. Ever notice how alienated they feel when we peek at them?"

Daniel bent to his black roses.

She stared after him, hands on her hips.

"Not to mention Mentats," he said. "There were two of them on that ship—both gholas. You want to play with them?"

"The Masters always try to control them, too," she said.

"That Master is going to have trouble if he tries to mess with that big one," Daniel said, snipping off a ground shoot from the root stock of his roses. "My, this is a pretty one."

"Mentats, too!" Marty called. "I'd have told them. Dime a dozen, they are."

"Dimes? I don't think they'd have understood that, Marty. The Reverend Mothers, yes, but not that big Mentat. He didn't thin out that far back."

"You know what you let get away, Daniel?" she demanded, coming up beside him. "That Master had a nullentropy tube in his chest. Full of ghola cells, too!"

"I saw it."

"That's why you let them get away!"

"Didn't let them." His pruning shears went snick-snick. "Gholas. He's welcome to them."

Here is another book dedicated to Bev, friend, wife, dependable helper and the person who gave this one its title. The dedication is posthumous and the words below, written the morning after she died, should tell you something of her inspiration.

One of the best things I can say about Bev is there was nothing in our life together I need forget, not even the graceful moment of her death. She gave me then the ultimate gift of her love, a peaceful passing she had spoken of without fear or tears, allaying thereby my own fears. What greater gift is there than to demonstrate you need not fear death?

The formal obituary would read: Beverly Ann Stuart Forbes Herbert, born October 20, 1926, Seattle, Washington; died 5:05 P.M. February 7, 1984, at Kawaloa, Maui. I know that is as much formality as she would tolerate. She made me promise there would be no conventional funeral "with a preacher's sermon and my body on display." As she said: "I will not be in that body then but it deserves more dignity than such a display provides."

She insisted I go no further than to have her cremated and scatter her ashes at her beloved Kawaloa "where I have felt so much peace and love." The only ceremony—friends and loved ones to watch the scattering of her ashes during the singing of "Bridge Over Troubled Water."

She knew there would be tears then as there are tears while I write these words but in her last days she often spoke of tears as futile. She recognized tears as part of our animal origins. The dog howls at the loss of its master.

Another part of human awareness dominated her life: Spirit. Not in any mawkish religious sense nor in anything most Spiritualists would associate with the word. To Bev, it was the light shining from awareness onto everything she encountered. Because of this, I can say despite my grief and even within grief that joy fills my spirit because of the love she gave and continues to give me. Nothing in the sadness at her death is too high a price to pay for the love we shared.

Her choice of a song to sing at the scattering of her ashes went to what we often said to each other—that she was my bridge and I was hers. That epitomizes our married life.

We began that sharing with a ceremony before a minister in Seattle on June 20, 1946. Our honeymoon was spent on a firewatch lookout atop Kelley Butte in Snoqualmie National Forest. Our quarters were twelve feet square with a cupola above only six feet square and most of that filled by the firefinder with which we located any smoke we saw.

In cramped quarters with a spring-powered Victrola and two portable typewriters taking up considerable space on the one table, we pretty well set the pattern of our life together: work to support music, writing and the other joys living provides.

None of this is to say we experienced constant euphoria. Far from it. We had moments of boredom, fears, and pains. But there was always time for laughter. Even at the end, Bev still could smile to tell me I had positioned her correctly on her pillows, that I had eased the aching of her back with a gentle massage and the other things necessary because she could no longer do them for herself.

In her final days, she did not want anyone but me to touch her. But our married life had created such a bond of love and trust she often said the things I did for her were as though she did them. Though I had to provide the most intimate care, the care you would give an infant, she did not feel offended nor that her dignity had been assaulted. When I picked her up in my arms to make her more comfortable or bathe her, Bev's arms always went around my shoulders and her face nestled as it often had in the hollow of my neck.

It is difficult to convey the joy of those moments but I assure you it was there. Joy of the spirit. Joy of life even at death. Her hand was in mine when she died and the attending doctor, tears in his eyes, said the thing I and many others had said of her.

"She had grace."

Many of those who saw that grace did not understand. I remember when we entered the hospital in the pre-dawn hours for the birth of our first son. We were laughing. Attendants looked at us with disapproval. Birth is painful and dangerous. Women die giving birth. Why are these people laughing?

We were laughing because the prospect of new life that was part of both of us filled us with such happiness. We were laughing because the birth was about to occur in a hospital built on the site of the hospital where Bev was born. What a marvelous continuity!

Our laughter was infectious and soon others we met on the way to the delivery room were smiling. Disapproval became approval. Laughter was her grace note in moments of stress.

Hers was also the laughter of the constantly new. Everything she encountered had something new in it to excite her senses. There was a naivete about Bev that was, in its own way, a form of sophistication. She wanted to find what was good in everything and everyone. As a result, she brought out that response in others.

"Revenge is for children," she said. "Only people who are basically immature want it."

She was known to call people who had offended her and plead with them to put away destructive feelings. "Let us be friends." The source of none of the condolences that poured in after her death surprised me.

It was typical of her that she wanted me to call the radiologist whose treatment in 1974 was the proximate cause of her death and thank him "for giving me these ten beautiful years. Make sure he understands I know he did his best for me when I was dying of cancer.

He took the state of the art to its limits and I want him to know my appreciation."

Is it any wonder that I look back on our years together with a happiness transcending anything words can describe? Is it any wonder I do not want or need to forget one moment of it? Most others merely touched her life at the periphery. I shared it in the most intimate ways and everything she did strengthened me. It would not have been possible for me to do what necessity demanded of me during the final ten years of her life, strengthening her in return, had she not given of herself in the preceding years, holding back nothing. I consider that to be my great good fortune and most miraculous privilege.

FRANK HERBERT
PORT TOWNSEND, WA
APRIL 6, 1984

FRANK HERBERT is the bestselling author of the Dune saga. He was born in Tacoma, Washington, and educated at the University of Washington, Seattle. He worked a wide variety of jobs—including TV cameraman, radio commentator, oyster diver, jungle survival instructor, lay analyst, creative writing teacher, reporter, and editor of several West Coast newspapers—before becoming a full-time writer.

In 1952, Herbert began publishing science fiction with "Looking for Something?" in *Startling Stories*. But his emergence as a writer of major stature did not occur until 1965, with the publication of *Dune*. This was followed by *Dune Messiah, Children of Dune, God Emperor of Dune, Heretics of Dune*, and *Chapterhouse: Dune* to complete the bestselling saga. Herbert is also the author of some twenty other books, including *The White Plague, The Dosadi Experiment*, and *Destination: Void*. He died in 1986.

THE DUNE CHRONICLES

BY FRANK HERBERT

AVAILABLE NOW FROM